I0596733

Demons

on the

Moon

By

K Gerard Martin

Contents

Contents

Introduction

This book should never have existed. Truly. My thoughts for a next book revolved around a story of two sisters who didn't know they were sisters until a crisis moment seconds before an airplane crash. That was a story I had in the back of my mind, but it was vague with few details and little to go on. The story was to focus on these sisters when they were in grade school, their polar dynamics, their separation after high school, and their reunion afterward. But to make it believable, I would need to do research—lots of research—to give authenticity as to how young girls think and act. Being neither a girl nor young myself, it would be a great challenge, and I wasn't sure I had the energy or drive to do it, so I left the story undeveloped.

Meantime, there are moments in my life when I need to escape. But how? I don't like reading other people's fiction, certainly not as an adult, and I leafed through very little before adulthood, having limited myself to British authors Dickens, Doyle, Tolkien, and Wells. Modern television and film don't catch my attention, but I have an ability to create fantasy in my mind and live in that fantasy through the eyes of fictional characters. So it becomes a matter of writing down these waking fantasies. I read as I write, as if there are two people inside my head. The one seeking escape is watching the computer screen and reading as the other person writes the story. I follow the words on the screen, immersing myself in the story that comes from seemingly nothing. Perhaps the Anrega in Earth creates such stories, and my mind attenuates those stories like a radio receiver.

Invariably, the fantasies jump around. One day I'm seeing an alien species on the lunar far side, another day I'm in the Carinian solar system. Fantasies become disjointed. That's how *Demons on the Moon* started—as an organic collection with disparate stories being created separately. Eventually, the stories created barriers to themselves and prevented the others from growing, like a garden planted by the four winds that grows and bumps against neighboring plant life. The plants then spend more effort fighting for more resources than in creating more greatness. At one point then I spent considerable effort going through the disparate stories, taking notes all along the way (as if someone else wrote them), and created a master time line of events for unification. It wasn't fun and is counter to the original reason for creating the stories—that of escape—but it's a painful necessity to prune and cultivate the garden of fantasy to get all citizens of the garden to work together. Once I have that, once the citizens are helping instead of fighting, I can get back on track and read the fantasy once again as quickly as the magic of the mind can reveal.

The mind and its stories are fleeting, like a passing storm. Once it's gone, it's gone. The next day I awake, and yesterday's stories are completely forgotten. This explains why I must take notes from past recorded stories—it's as if I'm seeing them for the first time and must relearn them all over again. By that time I've fallen into the dreaded mode as if forced to read someone else's story (even though it's mine), and I'm not a fan, so I want to skip the past writings and go on to something else. Only hard discipline brings me to tie it all together and finish it as a book, worthy or not of another human's read. Hopefully it's just a human. Save us all if a Carinian reads about Lanietta's antics and decides to use this fiction as a handbook for human etiquette. Or lack thereof.

As for me, K Gerard Martin, my ideas don't let up at the keyboard. They often come in moments of meditation. When I was young, the only such moments happened when first going to sleep for the night. I could never fall asleep instantly; rather, it took me an hour to doze off. In that hour, I reflected on the past and considered the future. As an adult, my moments of meditation changed. No longer was it experienced before falling asleep. Instead, I meditated during the morning shower or during my long bicycle rides around Ontario, Canada.

When I returned to the United States in 1991, those exercise meditations ended until I walked during lunch breaks starting in the late 1990s. I preferred to walk alone. I walked in parking lots, on walking paths, and on grassy paths. I would walk in rain, snow, and sub-zero temperatures. I've been asked how I could walk alone, as it is so boring. No, I meditate. Meditation has no bounds and is the world's greatest peacemaker.

My style of writing doesn't follow any popular standard that I know of. There are too many names, too much unneeded detail (or too little where needed), too many flashbacks, and too much plot complexity, often with a less than stellar climax or resolution. Where's the action, the clean and clever use of words, the smut, the emotion, the passion, and all those wonderful qualities that make for a great read? The writing doesn't make for a casual read, certainly nothing I'd want to reread myself. Chekhov's gun doesn't get much use. My loss I suppose. But the writing is there, it's me, it's all I have, and sometimes that's all I can expect. So on we go, the story, the words that go for a little bit in the vast sea of semblance.

Chapter 1: The Super Cub

Claus Gerhardt, the primary pilot for an upcoming lunar space launch, awoke with a start in his house. It was 2:30am, the television was still on, and Claus realized he'd fallen asleep to a movie. But his insomnia returned, and he couldn't settle himself. He turned the television off, threw a night robe over his pajamas, slipped into loafers, then walked to the kitchen for a late snack of bologna sandwich and vitamin water. While sipping his bottle, he stared out the kitchen window and observed the full moon.

"The air is stale in here," he said to himself. "I should go out on the porch and finish my snack."

Claus was the quiet mouse in his house, not the paws and claws of saws jawing at the mouth for applause.

"Claus the mouse," he said to himself.

He carried his food with him to the front porch. The air was light and fresh, with neither bugs nor critters about. Even the crickets had fallen silent. All that stirred the air was a light breeze blowing through elm trees, flapping like decorations for a celebration. But it was too warm for the robe. He removed it.

"It's as if the world is preparing for this launch," Claus said. "But how will I be alert for the blastoff if I can't get a good night's sleep?"

Suddenly, Claus heard steps from down the sidewalk. It was Frieda! What was she doing jogging down this way at this hour?

"Good morning, Claus," she said nonchalantly as she neared his house.

"Good morning, Frieda," he replied with a chuckle.

"You're up early," she said, now approaching his porch to converse.

"There's an early bug going around," he said. "I see you caught it too."

"Too much excitement," she said. "But a good jog will tire me out. Come along. It'll do you good. Yes, even in your pajamas."

Claus looked at his half-eaten sandwich and partially consumed bottle of vitamin water, but Frieda could be persistent, and she pointed for Claus to place both items on a side table next to a porch chair, which he did.

"They'll be there when you return," she said, and she motioned for Claus to jog alongside her on the sidewalk.

Claus twisted the cap back onto the vitamin water and placed the bottle and his sandwich on the side table.

"Your hand is sweaty," he said as the two continued to jog. "Seems odd that we're launching later today with a full moon."

"You're referring to the Apollo missions, aren't you?" Frieda said. "They launched a few days after the new moon so that their landing site would be lit properly."

"And all Apollo lunar landings were on the near side," Claus said.

"But we are going to the far side. We launch after a full moon so the far side will be at least somewhat lit," Frieda said.

"I would have thought we should launch a few days before the new moon, so the entire far side will be lit when we arrive," Claus said. "That's what the prior mission did."

"We only thought the crew would be there a few days. Now they are missing," Frieda said. "That was two weeks ago. We can't afford to wait until the new moon. They could be hurt."

"Still, it will be difficult searching the dark areas," Claus said.

"This was all covered in training. We'll use radar to search for them."

"And flares, spot beams, and night vision," Claus said.

"Exactly," she said. "You were never sold on the idea, but you failed to provide an alternative."

"No, I came up with an idea—a new device to detect radiation trails left by our spacecraft," Claus said.

"That technology doesn't exist."

"Yet," Claus added.

"It would take a team years to perfect," Frieda said.

"I could do it in three weeks, if I blocked out distractions," Claus said.

"Still the lone wolf, are you? No wonder you're single," she said.

"You're single too," Claus said.

"I'm not ready for a family yet," Frieda said. "For now, my family is Astroosa."

Astroosa was the name of the space launch company for which Claus and Frieda worked.

"With Astroosa's CEO Joe Craigen as your father?" Claus asked.

"Funny you should mention that," Frieda said. "In fact, he's trying to set me up with his son, Josh."

"Politics to the end," Claus muttered.

"I heard that, Claus Omershlat Gerhardt," Frieda said with disdain.

"You know that's not my middle name," Claus said.

"Claus Brockenmar Gerhardt? Claus Freepenheigen Gerhardt?" Frieda taunted.

"Doron," Claus corrected.

"Yes, Doron the moron," Frieda continued.

"You know I'm named after my Grandma Dora. But I suppose that doesn't matter to you, Christine Frieda Morgan," Claus said.

"You think you're so smart," Frieda said. "Rattling off my name like that!"

"I should call you Crissy."

"No you shouldn't!" Frieda said.

"I heard something about you, that you were once a ballerina," Claus said. "But you quit because of an accident."

"That's none of your business," Frieda said.

"Why don't you talk about it?" Claus asked.

"All accidents are preventable, given proper training and management," Frieda said.

"We can't train for everything," Claus said. "Sometimes we have to play things by ear. *Ad hoc*, as it were."

"*Ad hoc*," Frieda mocked. "Sounds like a sick bird ready to die. *Ad hoc, ad nauseam, ad infinitum*. This whole *adhocracy* you and others worship makes me puke. Why not just throw two sticks in the air and watch how they land? Then record their orientation as a new symbol to be venerated and worshiped. Claus—leave behind your lack of order and discipline. It belongs to lesser beings who wish to be coddled in this nursery we call Earth. Our team is ascending to a most unforgiving environment. We have no luxury for sick birds."

"You almost sound upset," Claus said.

"I'm getting there," Frieda said.

"Well how will you get any sleep if you're upset?" Claus asked.

Frieda held silent.

"You've got these idiosyncrasies, Frieda," Claus said. "Here we are jogging in the heat and humidity, and you're wearing sweatpants. With those ballerina legs of yours? Seems a waste to cover yourself up like that."

"Get over it," Frieda said. "It's not for you to decide what others wear."

"You should be wearing shorts. You'll get heat exhaustion with those sweatpants. But you're too stubborn. You'll push yourself too hard," Claus said.

Frieda held silent again.

"Do you hear me, Frieda?" Claus said. "You're pushing yourself too hard. Show some leg. Wear shorts."

Still no reply from Frieda.

"I said, wear shorts!" Claus said.

With that, Claus ripped at Frieda's sweatpants and tore off the lengths, revealing badly scarred legs. Both stopped jogging. Claus stepped backward in surprise.

"Now you've done it!" Frieda yelled.

"Frieda, I...I didn't know...I'm sorry... I..."

"Go drink yourself to death! Go on!" she screamed.

Still in shock, Claus remained motionless. Frieda threw money at Claus for alcohol then sprinted away.

"Frieda," he called while picking up the money and placing it in a pocket, but she continued sprinting. "Frieda!"

He gave chase, but the neighbors didn't like his shouting. They had their own words of discontent for him. Claus ignored them and continued running after Frieda, but she was too quick.

"Set aside the mission for a moment," Claus shouted. "This is our last night on Earth. Let's take a flight in a Super Cub. I know a short airstrip just—"

"Shut up already!" a neighbor yelled.

Claus wasn't used to running. Exhaustion made him clumsy. He tripped on a tree-root uplifting in the sidewalk, and he landed hard against the concrete. Stunned, he rolled over and barely managed to sit up. He looked ahead for Frieda. She had just finished sprinting around a corner building and had now disappeared out of sight.

Claus debated what to do next. This incident was bound to throw him off the mission, that much he was sure. Frieda was probably contacting the backup pilot for the mission. That backup pilot was none other than Josh Craigen.

"I'll lose both the mission and my job. Oh Frieda, what are you hiding with those legs?" he said.

Claus pulled himself to his feet and walked around the corner where Frieda had disappeared. She was not to be found. He'd left the residential area and entered a commercial zone with a variety of small businesses. All were closed save a pub.

"Just what I need," he muttered. "Open 24 hours too. Thought these pubs had to close at 2am. Well, Frieda said to drink."

He walked inside and asked for a beer then changed his order to whiskey. While picking up the telephone to call the police, the bartender asked what had happened to Claus's face.

"No, it was an accident," Claus said. "I fell on the sidewalk."

The bartender stared at Claus in his pajamas, shook his head in disbelief, and filled a shot glass with whiskey. Claus downed the glass.

"At least let me get you an ice pack," the bartender said.

The bartender disappeared into a back area for something to hold the ice, but without hesitation, Claus slapped Frieda's money on the counter, took the whiskey bottle in hand, and slipped outside. He then stole down an alley and through a maze of other paths until he was sure the bartender could not follow.

"I don't need any ice!" Claus retorted.

Claus headed toward the airstrip, sipping whiskey all the way. The distance wasn't far, and soon he was on the airfield. It was unmanned, being designed to handle daytime traffic only.

"Who needs visual flight rules anyway? Vision is overrated."

There was the Super Cub. Claus climbed in. The aircraft was not his own. Matter of fact, it didn't belong to anyone. It had a salvage title and was meant for the boneyard. The owner had let Claus tinker around with it and get the engine running, but the aircraft had not flown recently, and so it was untested.

"Until now," Claus said to himself. "Time to test my skills of training and management—or lack thereof."

Claus started the engine and taxied the craft. The air field was small, and so the time spent rolling to the runway was minimal. Claus readied for the takeoff then pushed the throttle up. The Super Cub quickly picked up speed and took to the air. Being a little inebriated, Claus induced a bit of up-down oscillation and clipped the tops of a few trees before reaching sufficient altitude.

"No flight plan, no approval from any tower—better keep my lights and transponder off. Don't want people to know I'm up here."

Claus put the throttle up to full and began performing aerial stunts with rolls, stalls, dives, and crabbing. The moon gave him just enough light to sense the trees and ground, while instruments gave him the rest. Then Claus began humming a childhood song. Actually, more than one.

"Oh, what do I need to go to the moon for anyway? I got everything I need here on planet Earth. Airspeed, freedom above the ground, and lift. There is no one else in the sky. I have free rein across these lands to that there horizon. The stars are my faithful subjects and shall witness my very greatness. All that is left to be done is—"

But Claus was interrupted. A loud "bang!" rattled him from behind, and Claus lost elevator control. He turned back to see the elevator was stuck in the up position. The Super Cub started to climb, and Claus's efforts to get the nose down failed. He feared the Super Cub would stall, turn, and then go into a dive.

"Can't think what I should do," he said. "My mind is blank. Training... management... Frieda ditched me. I gotta ditch. But no parachute! Wait! What's that in the passenger seat?"

It was a parachute backpack, thrown in there two weeks earlier as a joke by Bill Knight, a fellow pilot and friend who had gone up on Novi 2. The two were shooting the breeze about how much Claus hated fail-safes when Bill laughingly threw the backpack in "for good measure". How did the backpack not fall out with all of Claus's maneuvers? He didn't know, but he decided this was his only hope.

Claus climbed into the passenger seat as the aircraft climbed up, up, upward to the stars above. Claus shoved his arms into the straps and jumped out of the aircraft. He was about to pull the cord to release the chute, but something told him to wait. Indeed, the aircraft finished its climb. It stalled, turned over, and headed down—toward Claus! Claus moved his arms and legs around quickly to move out of the way, but he was losing altitude quickly, and he needed to release the chute either soon or never. The aircraft dove past Claus, but a wing caught his leg and cut it. Claus's body was spun around, but he regained control enough to pull the cord and get a clean chute to deploy. Claus's

body slowed. The aircraft crashed into a field and caught fire.

But Claus was too close and felt his body get hot from the rising heat. He was going to land in the burning craft! What horrible luck! Why fly at all if such bad chance should follow a man? The chute was just that—a chute, with no ability to steer. Now Claus would have to wait in agony as the heat and flames would consume him. He dropped ever closer, and the rising heat created a sideways vacuum, pulling Claus toward the center of the burning wreck.

Claus had no choice but to cut the chute. Better to take a chance falling on temperate hard ground than soft vicious flames. The chute floated free, and Claus dropped like a rock. But a last bit of thinking got through his drunken brain and told him to look for an emergency chute. He found it and deployed it, but the ground was too close, and the help was but minimal. Claus landed atop a tree, with branches scraping and tearing into his flesh, more as torture than any serious damage. His arms were pulled from the straps of the backpack, and he fell completely free of restraint, through branch and twig, to the ground.

The plane burned. Distant firetruck sirens grew closer. Claus sat dazed for a moment, but the sirens motivated him to leave. Blood-covered (yet still in one piece), Claus ambled away from the crash site. He put enough distance between the site and himself to avoid being part of the spectacle. He reached a stream where he took a moment to clean himself up. Clean but wet, he crossed the stream to the other side and climbed the bank and a hill until he reached the top. He was now facing east, and in the distance he saw the sky lightening. It was dawn.

"The launch is soon," Claus said. "Should I bother to show up? Yes, I should. I should take my medicine like a man and move on."

Claus reached a service station and called a cab. The cabbie was shocked at Claus's appearance, but Claus promised to pay extra if the driver would keep quiet. Pay extra? Claus was still in his pajamas and had no money. Frieda's was spent on the whiskey.

"My wallet is at home," Claus said. "Please take me there."

Claus gave his address to the driver. Soon he was home. Fortunately all was quiet with no witnessing neighbors. Claus paid the driver, and the cab left. Then Claus took a good shower, used adrenaline and super glue to close open wounds, and he used ointment to reduce swelling. A bit of makeup applied to his wounds, and Claus was almost passable as human.

"I'm late," Claus said to himself. "I'll never get to the launch site in time."

Claus jumped into his car and drove toward the launch site. Several voice messages were queued on his cell phone. He activated his car's touch-free system to access them. All were inquiring as to his whereabouts. Claus finished the last message and then made a phone call himself.

"I'm on the way over. Just had a delay this morning. No, nothing unusual. You...you can't wait? Josh is piloting now? Yeah, I'll be there. Bye."

Frieda was already prepping her crew for the launch. They had suited up and were being transported to the space craft. From what the Astroosa secretary told Claus, Frieda anticipated a no-show of Claus and had Josh moved up to primary pilot.

"Dash it all anyway, Frieda, why did you have to run past my house at 2:45 in the morning? And why did I have to be awake? Couldn't I have just slept through the night and had a normal launch? No, I had to have a diversion."

Claus was depressed. His one chance for the moon was gone, Astroosa would most likely fire him, and the police were bound to be searching for him after the plane crash.

"Above the cloud, all is proud," he said to himself. "But doesn't do me much good on the ground."

Chapter 2: Astroosa

"This way," an Astroosa employee said to Claus.

Claus was at the launch site with less than an hour before liftoff. He was escorted to Astroosa's Mission Command, a room with several workstations and large displays where flight engineers coordinated with the rescue spacecraft and controlled its launch. This particular craft was Novi 3. Novi 1 was the unmanned craft that tested flight characteristics in lunar orbit but without a lander, Novi 2 was the first manned trip to the moon for Astroosa but had lost communication with Mission Command, and Novi 3 was to be a second exploratory mission to the moon but had been moved up as a rescue mission.

"Have a seat next to Doctor Li," said Joe Craigen, CEO of Astroosa and Chief Flight Director.

Claus didn't dare ask Joe about the personnel situation. Having a job and being part of the mission was more important. Claus sat next to Doctor Patricia Li, Backup Flight Surgeon.

"There are better things for cuts than super glue," Doctor Li said.

"I...uh..." Claus stumbled.

"Our Chief Flight Surgeon is running behind," Doctor Li said. "Something about a plane crash on his property. Don't worry. He'll be here soon, and then we can look you over. Help me with these crew vitals. See anything unusual on your panel?"

Claus looked at the computer screen at his workstation. It showed health statistics for Frieda Morgan (commander), Josh Craigen (pilot), and Doctor Donna Morrow (astro surgeon).

"Morgan's oxygen saturation is below launch spec," Claus said.

"Very good. We'll make a doctor of you yet. Would you like to advise our commander?" the doctor said.

Claus put on a headset, hit a switch to tie into Novi-Mission Command communications, and he spoke.

"Novi 3, Astroosa for Morgan," Claus said.

From inside the Novi 3 spacecraft, Josh and Donna looked at Frieda in awonderment. Claus had been a no-show, and his voice was a surprise to hear.

"Astroosa, Novi 3. Go ahead for Morgan," Frieda replied coolly.

"Be advised that oxygen saturation is below launch spec. Please increase by two percent. Two percent," Claus said.

Frieda made an adjustment to her space suit, and the oxygen level increased.

"Two percent adjustment complete," Frieda said.

"Awesome, thank you," Claus replied back in the standard lingo.

Frieda's voice seemed professional and sterile. Claus had hoped she would say something a little friendlier, perhaps a joke or other icebreaker to let him know she forgave him for the incident. He was going to say something about it but decided her professional silence was best for him as well.

The countdown proceeded without issue until the timer reached zero, and Novi 3 blasted up into the heavens. Claus watched as crew heart rate and respiration increased as per normal, though Frieda's rates were a bit higher than the others. What was she thinking at that moment? Did the distractions from earlier in the day impair her performance? Was fatigue already setting in?

Frieda radioed back at each point of the blastoff procedure without issue, performing her job flawlessly. Within minutes, Novi 3 reached Earth orbit.

"Novi 3 is scheduled for two or three Earth orbits to check equipment, then it will fire up the main rocket engine and head for the moon," Claus said.

"Yes," the Chief Flight Surgeon said, now showing up. "I'll take it from here."

Doctor Li thanked the Chief Flight Surgeon and escorted Claus toward an examination room.

"I'm fine, really," Claus said as the two walked.

"It's for the record," Doctor Li said. "You were a no-show for the mission. Now that the launch is complete and there is time before Novi 3 reaches lunar orbit, the paperwork must be filled out."

"Paperwork? Why? I haven't done anything," Claus said.

"You inconvenienced the launch team," Doctor Li said. "And no word from you."

"Sorry," Claus said.

"Joe Craigen will speak with you later. He was mad as a hornet. But fortunately everyone else was here on time, so we launched without a hitch. Just what were you doing? You're all beat up and everything," Doctor Li said.

"Is it that obvious? I thought I cleaned up pretty good."

"Bad adventures only clean up so well," Doctor Li said.

The two entered an examination room.

"We need to stitch up your leg," Doctor Li said. "That glue will never hold. Now I want you to remove—"

"One hour," said a technician who popped his head into the room. "Oh sorry, doctor, I didn't mean to interrupt."

"What happened?" Doctor Li asked.

"We moved up the schedule," the technician said.

The technician disappeared. Li paused in conflicted thought.

"What's wrong?" Claus asked.

"Just the chase craft. Josh was supposed to control it by remote, and I haven't found a replacement yet," Li said. "I thought I had a little more time. But..."

"Patricia, the chase craft. You mean Prava 12, right?" Claus asked.

Patricia stuttered, tripped over her tongue, paced, and made movements of frustration with her hands and arms.

"Yes, Prava 12," Li stumbled. "It's meant to watch Novi 3 in case it disappears the way Novi 2 did. It needs a remote pilot.

Wait. You could be the remote pilot. Sure. Let's go!"

Doctor Li ushered Claus out of the room, down a hall, and outside to a van. The three entered, and the van sped off down the road toward a second launch pad. Claus tried to say something, but Doctor Li prevented it.

"What!?" Patricia yelled in a special van telephone. "It's got to work. It must!"

"What is it? What's wrong?" Claus asked.

"The secondary remote linkup is down," Patricia said. "That means once Prava 12 launches and passes through the ionosphere, it will be out of control. I can't let that happen."

The van reached the Probe Command building where technicians were preparing for the launch and control of Prava 12.

"Get out here, Claus," Doctor Li said.

"Aren't you coming with me?" Claus asked as he stepped out.

Patricia nodded no.

"Something strange is going on. What are—" Claus started.

But before Claus could finish his statement, the van began to drive off. Claus had already stepped out of the van but had a hand on the open door handle. Patricia tried closing the door and simultaneously instructed the driver to go on. The van accelerated with Claus dragging alongside. He quickly pulled himself inside to prevent being pulled under the rear wheel.

"That phone call sounded fake. And you don't need a remote pilot. The Prava 12 mission is controlled by computer. Patricia—what's going on?"

Claus no longer saw the professional Doctor Li but instead a desperate Patricia. She pulled a backpack from the back of the van and was about to place it over her shoulder.

"Let me see that," Claus said.

Claus rummaged through the backpack and then spoke.

"A carbon dioxide scrubber, an oxygen candle, bottled water, food rations, and a few tools. This is only enough for two days, maybe three. That's just enough time to get to the moon. Then what? It's suicide!"

"It's enough time to observe Novi 3 and report the results," Patricia said.

"How will you get back to Earth?" Claus asked.

"Stationkeeping fuel will get me back," Patricia said.

"Will get your dead body back," Claus said. "No, there must be another way."

"The secondary link really is broken, you know," Patricia said. "Prava 12 will not reach lunar orbit as it stands."

"But you already knew that," Claus said. "Who are you kidding? You can't pilot a craft!"

"I passed the simulator training," Patricia said.

"The probe isn't man rated. There's no life support system, and you think this backpack will compensate for that? This is insane!" Claus said.

"I had hoped you would act as my ground liaison. You can relay navigation information to me and make Prava 12 a success," Patricia said.

"Impossible. I won't send a woman to her death," Claus said.

"Then you condemn all those on Novi 3. You have sent them to their death," Patricia said.

"More deaths are not acceptable," Claus said.

"Exactly! Many deaths are a tragedy, but a single death is but a statistic, maybe even a hero or martyr," Patricia said.

"You want to die!? Where's the sense in that?" Claus said.

"I have set the plan! If you can't do better, then fall in line, mister!" Patricia said.

The two reached the Prava 12 launchpad and took an elevator to the top of the rocket, where a walkway connected to the access door of the Prava 12 probe.

"Help me into a spacesuit. There's a selection in this container. I had it brought up secretly. Then help me into Prava 12," Patricia said. "Once I'm secured inside, slide down the emergency chute. There

isn't time to take the elevator down. See? The van has already left."

Indeed, the van was gone. Claus opened the container. Patricia retrieved a spacesuit and was about to put it on. Claus chopped Patricia on the side of the neck from behind. She fell unconscious and collapsed. Claus caught her and eased her falling. He pulled the backpack from her then sent her down the emergency chute. With Patricia Li out of the way, Claus suited up from the selection, opened Prava 12's access panel, took the backpack, and entered Prava 12. Automatic launch controls were in place, and Prava 12 launched without anyone in Probe Command realizing a human was aboard, at least not at first. Patricia Li regained consciousness and returned to Probe Command.

"Prava 12 shows a hundred kilos overweight," said a flight controller. "We'll have to burn the engines a little longer."

Patricia stared at the main display high up on the wall then down at the flight controller's screen. The flight controller whispered:

"Who's up there? I thought you were—"

"Claus Gerhardt," Patricia whispered back. "He tricked me."

"When do we tell Joe Craigen?" the flight controller asked.

"Not until we absolutely have to," Patricia said.

Meanwhile back on Prava 12, Claus set up the carbon dioxide scrubber. He had just finished when the launch to orbit was complete.

"Claus, this is Patricia on a secure line," Patricia radioed up. "You're supposed to be down here, you know."

"Come up and catch me," Claus said.

Claus's helmet was secured over his head to his spacesuit, and he spoke through a headset in that helmet.

"You'll die in lunar orbit, you know," Patricia said.

"We're coming up on a burn," Claus said, evading her statement. "Are you ready?"

"Ready," she said.

"Now," Claus said.

Claus hit a button, and the rockets fired, sending Prava 12 out of Earth's orbit and on a trajectory toward the moon, or at least toward a point where it and the moon would meet.

"Burn complete," Claus said after he turned off the rocket.

"Claus, is there anyone here who you should contact before the end? Family?" Patricia asked.

"I don't plan on dying," Claus said.

"We will all die," Patricia said.

"Yes, but let's not bury people while they are still alive, okay?" Claus said.

"Okay."

"I'm going through a manifest of onboard systems. With a few adjustments... there...yes, I'm now recovering water from the fuel cell instead of venting it into space. That will take care of my water needs. And I have thoughts on how to get more oxygen," Claus said.

"The only sources of oxygen are the oxygen tank for the fuel cell and the main fuel for course corrections," Patricia said.

"I'll put myself into an elliptical lunar orbit that will allow for easy return to Earth," Claus said. "Just a few orbits around the moon, and that will be enough. No extra fuel for attaining a regular lunar orbit. That way I can save the remaining oxygen for myself."

"Just make sure the carbon dioxide scrubber works. If it fills up, it won't matter how much oxygen you have. You'll never be able to purge carbon dioxide from your lungs."

"I'll do my best," Claus said. "We'll know one way or another."

"Unless something happens," Patricia said.

"Or nothing happens," Claus said.

"Claus, make sure that whatever happens, you get Prava 12 back to Earth, or at least able to relay data back to Earth," Patricia said. "We have no way of communicating with objects on the far side of the moon. Prava 12 was supposed to solve that problem by acting as a relay, but if you disappear on the far side like Novi 2 did, and if—"

"And if Novi 3 also disappears, then yes, there will be no more launches to the far side, and everyone will be left wondering what the heck went wrong," Claus finished.

"Exactly. Get Prava 12 back to Earth," Patricia urged.

Claus aimed Prava 12's main camera and locked its tracking system onto Novi 3. The lock took effect. Claus looked at the resulting images on a display screen. He could see just the tail, with the engine bell being most prominent. Novi 3 executed a rotation, and the nose came into view. Then a roll. Claus could see Frieda through a window. She was laughing and conversing with her shipmates. Claus wished he hadn't lost out on Novi 3. He should be in there laughing with her. She pointed toward Prava 12 and waved. Then other crewmembers took turns looking through the window and waving at Prava 12.

"To all those on planet Earth, we bid you greetings and a fond good day!" Frieda said through radio waves. "We'd like to show you how we control movements of our spacecraft."

Josh Craigen manipulated the controls on Novi 3. The craft rotated again.

"They weren't waving at me, just the camera of Prava 12," Claus remarked to himself.

There was little else for Claus to do on the trip to the moon. With that in mind, the adrenaline that had kept him awake had now waned, and he became sleepy. He found spare cabling in the backpack and tied himself to a side of Prava 12 with no controls.

"Don't want to accidentally hit a button while I sleep," he said, and that was the last he remembered before falling into deep sleep.

Claus dreamt that he was in an oversized wash tub, no, *two* oversized washtubs, cylindrical and of steel, with one upside-down and welded atop the first. There were no windows. No fresh air. Claus bobbed up and down as if on a river or other water body. There was a pinpoint of light near the top of the upside-down tub, with a ray of light piercing through and creating an inverted image of the sun on the lower opposite side. The image was that of a sphere of light, but the light dimmed, and the image became that of a crescent. The sun was being eclipsed by the moon, and soon light would fade altogether. Claus tried looking through the hole to the outside, but it was too small to see through. Then he tried pulling fresh air through the hole into his lungs, but the effect was worse than trying to breathe through a small straw.

He gave up on trying to breathe through the hole and instead struggled with what air he had left. The crescent image of the sun thinned into nothing, a loud rumble echoed nearby, and the washtubs and Claus fell, fell, fell over a deep waterfall. Claus's gut, hopes, and will of life fell into despair with him. In the last moments of his dream, he heard a repeated grating sound, like that of a metal tub being repeatedly knocked against rocks.

Claus awoke with a start. Fourteen hours had passed since launch. Fourteen hours? Patricia had made repeated attempts to contact Claus, but he had slept through all of them. The air in his suit had become stale. He needed to figure out why.

"The scrubber is clogged. Do I start the oxygen candle now? Or do I siphon oxygen off the fuel reserves?" Claus mused. "Better use the candle."

Claus connected a hose from his suit to the oxygen candle, activated the candle, then took several breaths and relaxed. He reviewed the messages from Patricia. They were recent and warned that carbon dioxide levels were rising dangerously in his suit.

"Patricia, this is Claus," Claus radioed.

"Claus! I thought you were dead!" Patricia radioed back.

"The scrubber is full. I'm using the oxygen candle now. It's attached to my suit. I didn't realize you had vital statistics on my suit. I thought I was rather clever when I took your spot on Prava 12."

"That won't last long," Patricia said.

"It should. I have plenty of oxygen," Claus said.

"It doesn't work that way," Patricia said. "Getting rid of carbon dioxide is independent of getting oxygen. Increasing the percentage of oxygen won't work for long, unless you vent air into outer space to dilute the carbon dioxide. But you can't afford to waste that much air. You should know that."

"I should. I guess I'm not thinking clearly," Claus said.

"The scrubber should not have filled up so quickly," Patricia said. "Oh, I wonder if..."

"Wonder if what?" Claus asked.

"Unplug the hose to the lithium hydroxide canister," she said.

Claus did so.

"A rabbit's foot?" Claus asked. "Patricia! There's a rabbit's foot plugging the hose!"

"For good luck. Such things are forbidden on space flights. I had to hide it," Patricia said.

"So much for the good luck," Claus said while removing the rabbit's foot and reconnecting the hose. "There. That's much better. Carbon dioxide levels are dropping. I feel I could run a marathon and win. Or flap my arms like a bird."

"Don't push your luck. Can't risk another failure. We'll continue to monitor your situation. Speaking of monitoring, we need a course correction soon," Patricia said.

"How soon?"

"In thirty seconds," she said.

"What? Why?" he asked.

"No time to explain. Data is being fed into your computer now. Prepare for burn...and...now!"

Claus had barely made sense of the situation in time to complete the burn, which he did.

"That was close! I need a better lead time for such things, Patricia. Why the burn, anyway?"

"Novi 3 has decided on a low initial orbit around the far side. Prava 12 will need to follow," Patricia said.

"I was hoping for a different orbit," Claus said. "This will cut further into my oxygen. I may have to switch off electrical systems so I can use oxygen from the fuel cell reserve."

"Don't do that," Patricia said. "No one down here knows you're aboard. If you stop the video feed of Novi 3 now, chaos will break out. Claus, there's another way to conserve oxygen. I have my father here. He's an expert on meditation. We want you to enter a meditative state for the rest of the trip to the moon. He'll walk you through everything. Just listen to him, Claus. Listen."

"I don't have much choice, do I?" Claus said.

"Before I have him talk you through this, I want you to set up an oscillation between two pairs of lights on your panel. They should blink a cycle—left-top, right-top, left-bottom, right-bottom, then back to left-top."

"So four lights in total. But which four?" Claus asked.

"Use the generic bank of diagnostic lights. Tie them into the health statuses of the Novi 3 crew," Patricia said.

Claus made the adjustments to his panel, and the lights began flashing, one at a time.

"They are all flashing white," Claus said.

"Good," Patricia said. "This will give you a quick warning if anything should go wrong with the Novi 3 crew. Any color other than white means a problem."

"And if the light doesn't flash at all?" Claus asked.

"Let's hope that doesn't happen," Patricia said. "Here's my father."

Mr. Li came on the radio. He had Claus take a restive position and focus on the four blinking lights. Mr. Li next had Claus focus on his breathing, close his eyes, focus on breathing, open his eyes and observe lights, breathe, and close his eyes. Mr. Li had Claus take pauses between breaths. Gradually, Claus was able to train himself to take longer and longer pauses between breaths. Now Mr. Li directed Claus to synchronize his breath with the flashing lights, then every other light flash, then every fourth light flash, and so on until Claus's sole focus was on his synchronicity of breath and light. Claus felt in tune with the health of the four.

Claus fell into daydream, as if he himself were a spacecraft breathing for four sleeping passengers. His daydream shifted. He was the ocean deep, sending long but gentle waves toward the shore of a small island. On the shore of that island was Frieda, standing by a campfire with wild game on a spit. She fashioned a table by placing a board from a long-forgotten shipwreck upon carefully placed rocks, then she reached into a wooden container and retrieved a wine glass and a bottle of wine. She placed the glass on the table then removed the cork from the bottle. It popped open with a slight splash. She giggled and poured wine into her glass. Claus so desperately wanted to enjoy a glass of wine with her, but he was happy to send gentle waves to shore and watch her be content. She kicked back in a chair and sipped on her wine.

Suddenly, Josh Craigen appeared from thick foliage with an empty wine glass. She motioned him over, he approached, and she poured wine into his glass. Claus became enraged and sent a wall of water atop Mr. Josh Craigen. But Claus choked, the daydream ended, and Claus fell out of meditation and into full awareness as he continued his coughing fit.

"No, no, no!" Mr. Li said. "Keep focus on lights and breathing! You just wasted ten minutes of air."

"Sorry," Claus said.

"Thank you, Father. I'll take over from here," Patricia said, and Mr. Li left.

"I was thinking of something else and lost focus," Claus said.

"You mean you were thinking of *someone* else," Patricia said. "Let me guess—Frieda?"

"And Josh Craigen," Claus said.

"You're jealous, aren't you?" Patricia said.

"Well no, not really, it's just, I, well..." Claus stumbled.

"See? This is why I should have gone! Your judgment is clouded!"

"I can do the job. I *must* do the job," Claus said. "It's the only way."

"This isn't a personal quest, Claus. You're an employee of Astroosa. You have to play by the rules. For the team," Patricia said.

"This coming from someone who was willing to break the rules," Claus said.

"But for the team," Patricia said. "Don't fail us now, Claus. Prava 12 *must* observe and gather data on the Novi 3 mission. Nothing more. Return to Earth when that mission is complete. You must. You absolutely must! Now go back into meditation to conserve oxygen. Concentrate on the blinking lights. But keep any thoughts simple and mechanical. Get into your pilot mindset and 'fly by instrumentation'."

Patricia uploaded several hours of orchestra music to Prava 12 and had Claus focus on that. Claus concentrated on his breathing and the flashing lights. He slipped into daydream again and sensed he was a great eagle of the sky, flying between four F-16s, two on each side. Claus was at peace, but turbulence grew, and he felt himself being pulled toward each F-16 in the same sequence as the flashing lights. For each F-16 that he was pulled toward, that aircraft in turn rolled outward and so caused its inner wing to lift and swat Claus the eagle back toward the middle. The turbulence and swatting became stronger and more violent, and he caught glimpses of each F-16 pilot as he neared the aircraft in question. Three pilots were those of Novi 3—Frieda, Josh, and Donna, but the fourth pilot was Bill Knight from Novi 2. Claus became agitated each time he was swatted by Josh's F-16, so much so that again Claus came out of meditation with a gag and choke.

Chapter 3: Mission under Fire

"Prava 12, Probe Command. Prava 12, respond," sounded Claus's radio.

"Patricia?" Claus replied.

"We've lost contact with Novi 3," Patricia said. "The last we heard was something about radio interference."

"Probe link with Novi 3 is lost as well," Claus said. "This doesn't make sense. If there were radio interference, why am I able to communicate with you?"

"Exactly my thoughts," Patricia said. "Novi 3 could be in trouble."

"I'll try to re-establish a link," Claus said.

Claus rerouted network links and attempted to get Novi 3 to communicate with Prava 12.

"No luck so far," Claus said. "I'll try a visual."

"Keep it on a secure channel with just me," Patricia said. "At least until we are sure."

"Sure of what?" Claus said, but before Patricia could answer, Claus had the video on his screen and Patricia's.

"I don't believe it," Patricia said.

"Novi 3 is lengthening," Claus said.

"That would be extension mode for generating artificial gravity," Patricia said.

"Now Novi 3 is spinning," Claus continued. "Judging by the length and rate of spin, the ends would simulate Earth's gravity at sea level. Extension mode confirmed."

"Novi 3 isn't scheduled for this maneuver," Patricia said.

"Only if the situation calls for it, such as for treating rescued astronauts. Yes, I know. The window on Novi 3 is blocked. Can't see what is going on inside," Claus said.

"If only we could hear what's going on," Patricia said.

"Sound cannot penetrate outer space," Claus said. "There is no air to conduct the vibration from Novi 3's window."

"The LIDAR!" both Patricia and Claus said at the same time.

"It could be modified to convert vibrations to sound," Claus said.

"It should be infrared so no one sees the light," Patricia said. "But the LIDAR won't work when Novi 3's window is spun away from Prava 12."

"If I focus the LIDAR on the center, I would get nothing at all. The center is soft, flexible material used for easy expansion and collapse," Claus said. "I have a better idea. I'll split the LIDAR beam and focus on both habitable ends of Novi 3 then use a comparator between signals to produce the best audio quality."

"We've never done that with the LIDAR," Patricia said.

"Might as well try. Nothing to lose," Claus said.

Claus fired the LIDAR at Novi 3 with two beams—one at the head of the craft, and one toward the tail, but not so far along the tail as to bounce off the fuel and rocket compartment. He adjusted a differential discriminator to convert the image differences into audio. The result was a garbled mess.

"No good," Claus said.

"Put a third beam back on the window," Patricia said. "It will establish a baseline signal."

"For calibration," Claus continued. "And the differential discriminator will then provide audio when the window is out of view. That's perfect!"

Claus did just that, and now audio poured in from Novi 3. Claus was shocked. There was a party in progress. Rock music played while people poured from bottles into containers and slurped from them.

"We go on a rescue mission, and they want to party?" Claus said. "I don't believe it. What a waste!"

"Claus, stay calm and think. Is there a way we can see inside? Perhaps one of the gauges can tell us something," Patricia said.

"Aren't you getting telemetry data for their gauges?" Claus asked.

"That link was lost too," Patricia said.

"Then Mission Command must be in hysterics," Claus said.

"They are, but not because of Novi 3," Patricia said.

"I don't understand," Claus said. "Why is Mission Command in hysterics?"

"Joe Craigen has been shot dead," Patricia said.

"That's not funny," Claus said.

"It's true. The main office is in lockdown," Patricia said. "I'll explain later. Work on getting a link to Novi 3."

"Work on getting the link to Novi 3 when Joe is dead and the main office is in lockdown? What is going on back there on Earth?" Claus said. "And here I thought life in this washtub-for-a-spacecraft was miserable. I'm like an unbalanced load."

"Unbalanced load," Patricia said. "Could you use Prava 12's long-range planetary detector on Novi 3, detect wobbles in the rotation, and convert that to an image?"

"I'd have to link it into the LIDAR differential discriminator. Oh boy, is this a trick," Claus said as he flipped switches and typed into a keyboard quickly. "Patricia, why does an unmanned probe have buttons and a keyboard. Any explanation?"

"I used them for setup. Had no time to remove," Patricia said. "Just as I have no time to explain further. Any luck?"

"Working on it," Claus said. "We're definitely trying things we've never done before. Okay, I'll turn on what I have. If we're lucky, this will work like an ultrasound."

The image quality was better than an ultrasound, resembling that of an X-ray. The Novi 3 crew took turns jumping from one side of the ship to the other, bumping alongside the connecting tube between habitable ends. Frieda finished jumping back and forth. She drank a beverage which from audio was champagne. Donna sang karaoke. Josh adjusted flashing lights and thrusters, causing Novi 3 to wobble slightly and bump the crew around.

"So what's the story on Joe Craigen?" Claus asked.

Patricia held silent.

"Was it a lone shooter? Was it a group?" Claus asked.

"It was a lone shooter. That's all we know. For now," Patricia said.

"Who?" Claus asked.

"We don't know who," Patricia said. "And as for the why, well..."

"Well what?"

"I guess the shooter was rambling that people shouldn't be in space," Patricia said. "Claus, there's nothing you can do about Earth. Let's work the Novi 3 problem. Focus the imaging on propulsion. I want to get a better look."

Claus manipulated a few buttons, and Novi 3's propulsion system came into better view.

"There. Do you see it? There's damage between the fuel tank and the living quarters," Patricia said.

"That would mean nitrous oxide is causing the crew to go wild. But that damage looks familiar. Like...it...it's a micrometeoroid impact," Claus said. "The crew of Novi 3 is doomed unless someone can stop the leak."

"You need to warn them," Patricia said.

"Yes, I need to increase speed to catch Novi 3. Then they'll see me and reply. If not, maybe I can repair it with an EVA."

"You won't have enough fuel for the trip back from the moon," Patricia said.

"And I can't let them die up here either, can I?"

"We can't have the Prava 12 mission fail too. If nothing else, you must get images and data from the lunar far side *and* return to Earth. Bill and Andrea could be—"

"And abandon Novi 3? That's murder."

"You didn't cause this. You aren't responsible. But abandoning Novi 2 is equally murderous," Patricia said.

Just as Claus received the last of Patricia's message, a jolt rocked Prava 12.

It felt like a micrometeoroid hit, and Claus knew it. It punched through one side and out the other, but it only caught the edge of the probe in general and thus missed Claus. Exhaust carbon dioxide from Claus's suit that had emptied into the Prava 12 craft was now venting, causing the probe to spin with increasing rotational forces on Claus's body.

"Patricia," Claus strained to say.

"What happened?" Patricia said. "Our readings are confused and chaotic."

"Micrometeoroid damage. I'm venting gas. Prava 12 is spinning. I'm about to black out," Claus said.

"Increase oxygen to your suit. Activate stationkeeping rockets," Patricia said.

Claus struggled to reach the oxygen candle. It was secured to the side, but Claus was pinned against another side. He breathed heavily and realized he couldn't reach the candle. Instead, he struggled to reach the stationkeeping controls. He could not. Finally, he rolled and twisted his body enough to reach the stationkeeping controls and was able to fire the stationkeeping rockets. Slowly, Prava 12 reduced its spin rate just as the last of the carbon dioxide vented. Claus quickly had to shut off the stationkeeping to prevent a counter spin. He breathed heavily to recover but did not increase output from the oxygen candle.

"Must conserve oxygen," he said.

But his face mask fogged up, despite the anti-fog coating on the inside, and perspiration drenched the rest of his body. Instinctively, Claus moved his gloved hand over his face mask, but of course he was only able to touch the outside and could not wipe the condensation off the inside.

"Patricia, I've regained control, but my face mask is fogged over. I'm sweating like crazy. I can't see anything, not the controls, not the video of Novi 3 or anything."

"Our readings of Prava 12 are still confused. We've lost your video of Novi 3. Novi 3 continues to ignore our requests for communication," Patricia said. "Claus, you'll have to wait for your suit to catch up on your humidity levels. You'll then have to work on restoring functionality to Prava 12. Once that is complete, you can check your return-path trajectory around the moon."

"You mean my intercept trajectory," Claus said. "This bird is on a rescue mission. Don't fight me on this, Patricia."

"Claus, the more you talk, the more moisture your suit must overcome. Please relax!"

"I need to expedite things. I'll hook my suit into the stationkeeping system. A little moisture in the fuel is okay. The system can remove it over time. But my time is now," Claus said.

Claus hooked his suit into the stationkeeping fuel system. This not only reduced humidity but provided oxygen and diluted out carbon dioxide. Claus started to restore systems, but another micrometeoroid hit Prava 12, and though his suit was not punctured, Claus was knocked unconscious by the jolt.

Chapter 4: Crash Landing

Claus awoke to find the inside of his face mask partly covered in his own blood. He looked at what instruments worked and was able to get a video feed. Prava 12 was traveling backward, with its front pointed back toward Earth. Within seconds, Claus witnessed an "earthset", where Earth appeared to set below the horizon of the moon. He realized he was now in lunar orbit on the far side. But what of Novi 3?

"Need to check fuel first and see if I have enough to reorient Prava 12," Claus said to himself.

Fuel onboard was almost out, perhaps enough for a burn or two, but not enough to break orbit and return home. Further, oxygen was very low, and Claus realized why—the carbon scrubber in his suit reversed operation and released its carbon to the stationkeeping oxygen supply.

"So I have fourteen hours of air in my suit again, but almost nothing left in Prava 12. I can't get home!"

Claus ignited a small amount of stationkeeping fuel to reorient the nose of Prava 12 forward. As the craft slowly turned, Claus saw a light blinking on the communications recorder. He pressed a button, and an audio recording of Patricia filled his headset.

"Claus, I don't know if you are alive, but if you are, please know that it has been an honor working with you. Our building is under lockdown from another attack. I...we don't know who's attacking us. It's not the first shooter. Sounds like a dozen people speaking a strange language. Other space companies are under attack too. My coworkers are telling me to hide. We're going to hide. Good luck, Claus."

The message ended, Prava 12 finished its reorientation, but Claus felt totally disoriented. The world that he knew on Earth no longer existed. Novi 3 was not in front as it should have been. Claus couldn't radio back to Earth—the moon prevented such a transmission. And if he held out until he reached "earthrise", he could radio but not survive a trip home. What was left to radio? Anything? The situation seemed hopeless. But then a bodily function took over his reasoning. Claus was hungry.

"I haven't eaten in three days," Claus said. "No wonder I'm hungry. Hardly seems to matter now. Still, if I eat and drink, it will give me time to think. Or time to prepare for the end."

Claus consumed the food and drink. He wondered if this was how a prisoner on death row felt before execution. Or a soldier before going into a major battle. Whatever the case, Claus was completely alone and without audience. The manner of his passing would be unknown.

"It will be known to me," Claus said. "And if this craft be discovered, so will a recording of my last moments."

It was decided then. Claus would not complete an orbit around the lunar far side but would instead land. He would spend the last few hours of his life on the moon, perhaps even while walking on the moon or while sitting on a lunar boulder. Either way, his shape would become a monument. Claus took one last look at the orbit ahead, but still there was no sign of Novi 3.

"It is time," Claus said.

Claus activated thrusters, and Prava 12 took a lower orbit, so low that it would either land or crash.

"No chance of pulling out now for another lunar orbit. Well, maybe Patricia Li and the people of Astroosa will survive. Then when they get things back together, they'll send another ship. Or maybe another space company can."

Something inside Claus said no. He had a nagging feeling that it would be many years before a ship would visit the lunar far side, unless something drastic happened.

"Better pick a landing spot," Claus said.

But something glinted ahead on the video screen. The dark moon's surface had prevented him from seeing it when he was at a higher altitude, but now he was closer and was able to see the glint appear as it crossed into sunlight. It was ahead. Claus hit the thrusters to catch the object. Slowly it came into view. Yes, it was Novi 3. It was still in extension mode. But it was too far away.

"It can't maintain orbit. It's going to crash. And I'm going to crash. But maybe I can crash where Novi 3 crashes. Maybe we will both land. I just need to adjust thrusters. Adjust thrusters."

Novi 3 landed in a crater. It crashed, but only lightly. Emergency thrusters activated just before the crash, softening the landing. Prava 12 had no such emergency thrusters. Claus worked feverishly to soften Prava 12's landing, but it was too little, too late. Prava 12 crashed. Claus survived the crash, but Prava 12's fuel escaped into space. Electrical systems failed. All Claus had for function and protection was his spacesuit. He crawled out of Prava 12 and onto the lunar surface. He had crashed into a large crater, about halfway between the edge and the middle. He looked around and saw that Novi 3 had also crashed, but Novi 3 had crashed along the inside trough of the crater.

"I hope they survived," Claus said.

He hopped toward Novi 3. But before he reached the craft, he saw or thought he saw movement in the area. It was as if the landscape were reshaping itself. Or perhaps his senses were strained, causing him to view the lunar landscape as if underwater.

"Novi 3 might have a working life support system. I must get there before my suit runs out of oxygen," Claus said to himself.

Claus wished he could radio to a satellite passing overhead. He then waved his hand upward, half hoping a distant Earth imaging satellite would catch the moon on the chance it passed in front of Earth. But he knew that was hopeless, as that imaging satellite was not set up for capturing lunar detail.

It took an hour, but Claus reached Novi 3. The craft was in excellent shape and sustained no damage. At one of the airlocks, he noticed footprints. They were not of spacesuit boots, but were instead rectangular shaped, as if wooden blocks roamed in the area. The prints led to an outcropping of rocks. Claus oriented himself toward the rocks, turned toward the air lock, then repeated this back-and-forth indecision. In the end, he decided to enter Novi 3 through the airlock, if nothing else than to assess his own immediate future. He could not survive on the lunar surface forever.

Claus entered through the airlock. The inside of Novi 3 was covered in trash and debris. Was this a remnant of the party, or perhaps evidence of a struggle against invaders? Claus made a brief check of Novi 3. No one was inside. He checked for available oxygen and pressure—21% oxygen at 1000 mbar. What about the nitrous oxide? It was still there. Claus pressed a few buttons, and several vents closed. He then ran a filtration program to remove the nitrous oxide. Clean. He checked for other contaminants. None. Claus removed his helmet and inhaled Novi 3's cabin air. A faint scent of fruit filled the air. Fermented fruit. But there was also another scent. Stonework, like that of granite statues.

"Where are they?" Claus asked himself as he walked through Novi 3.

Empty storage compartments revealed a clue—the spacesuits were missing.

"So they are on an EVA," Claus said. "But there were no bootprints in front of the airlock. Did they evacuate before landing? Or go on some laughing-gas suicide EVA?"

Claus returned to the pilot's chair, hit a few buttons, and retrieved the latest logs. Frieda reported on unusual readings, Novi 3 shuddered, and the crew began laughing about trivial things. The log ended. No mention of the party, entering lunar orbit, or landing.

"Astroosa, Novi 3. Do you read?" Claus called through Novi 3's radio. "Anyone. Can anyone read me?"

It was a desperate call, and Claus knew it. But Novi 3's system recorded Claus's radio call, so at least he could leave a permanent record of the situation.

"This is Claus Gerhardt. Novi 3 has landed on the far side of the moon. She was crewed by Frieda Morgan, Josh Craigen, and Doctor Donna Morrow. None of these three are currently aboard. I myself reached the far side via Prava 12, which crash landed not far from Novi 3. If anyone should receive this message, please relay it back to Astroosa Mission Command, or anyone at Astroosa for that matter. I will end this message now, as I must look for the Novi 3 crew. Claus Gerhardt out."

Novi 3 was still empty, except for Claus. Emotions started to overtake him, emotions of loneliness and futility.

"What if the Novi 3 crew did not survive? And what of Astroosa? A man spends his life solving problems, but for what? What is left of a man after the end? Was it really worth it?" Claus thought. "It is a strange but fortunate thing, that my heart does not listen to my mind, or else it might stop pumping out of despair, knowing that the end will one day come. But it doesn't know. It continues to pump. And so when the mind is gone, the heart is all that is left. A man continues at least for a time, wandering, wandering, wandering."

He thought of times when he was younger, when elders led the way and provided guidance. But they were gone, being in their little grave plots with little headstones. Their houses, their possessions, clothing, shoes, cars—everything—were sold or disposed of with little or no surviving memory. Claus reached back in his mind to the elders before his elders, those great- and great-great-ancestors who perhaps had grave plots but nothing more. Who remembered their lives or even where their final plots might be?

"The cremated have even less. Some pour soul loses his life, is cremated, and his ashes are scattered. What remnants of value are left?"

Claus knew he had to get going, or else this obsession with death would paralyze him. He checked his suit's carbon scrubber and realized it had regained less usage time than he'd thought.

"I only have twenty minutes left with the scrubber," he said. "I was lucky then to reach Novi 3 in time. Very lucky."

Perhaps it was this luck that motivated Claus further. He swapped out his suit's carbon scrubber for a spare in Novi 3, secured his helmet over his head (and onto his spacesuit), and exited Novi 3 through the airlock. He felt a cold shiver down his neck, as if he'd closed the lid of a coffin. He followed the trail of rectangular prints to the edge of a ravine on the crater's edge.

"Will I see you again, Novi 3? For years I wished to visit the moon. But there's nothing here. Nothing. How I wish I had stayed on Earth. How I wish I could use Novi 3 to return to Earth."

Then a sudden realization hit him.

"Claus, you fool! Novi 3 had a soft landing. There might be enough fuel to lift off into lunar orbit and return to Earth! Why didn't you check fuel reserves? Or check for other leaks? Fuel could be bleeding off right now! Your hopes for survival are failing fast!"

But in his excitement, his footing gave way, and he slipped down into the ravine, like the human sled he had become. He landed at the bottom with a thud! (Heard only within his suit). Fine lunar silt and gravel fell atop him, but his spacesuit held firm, and he suffered no punctures. He arighted himself and looked up. There was no easy way to ascend out of the ravine back to Novi 3, and so Claus was stuck. The ravine was dark, and he activated a light beam on his helmet to see. Desolation. There was no trace of artificial activity—no human footprints, no tracks from machines, none of the rectangular tracks he had seen by Novi 3—nothing. The ravine followed the circular edge of the crater, and so there were only two directions to go—clockwise, or counterclockwise (as viewed from above).

Claus chose counterclockwise. It seemed natural somehow. He hopped along slowly at first (since lunar gravity is but one-sixth of Earth), but as he continued, he felt heavier, and his hops were not as high and not as long above and along the surface.

"Gravity is increasing. That's impossible," Claus said.

But Claus could not deny the fact that he felt heavier. His movement was slowed. He realized he had to stop and turn around before the extreme force pinned him to the ravine floor.

"Ugh. Don't...let...me...fall. Must...turn...around!" Claus struggled to say.

Claus turned, but as he did so, he fell over. He now crawled clockwise along the ravine, centimeter by centimeter, inch by inch, then foot by foot and meter by meter until he was able to aright himself and hop along. He reached the point where he'd first fallen into the ravine, and he paused. His visor had fogged over from perspiration condensation, and he waited for the suit to freshen up his air supply.

"Wait," Claus said. "If moving counterclockwise along the ravine increases gravity, perhaps moving clockwise will reduce gravity. And if low enough, I could jump right out of this ravine and back to the upper crater surface."

Claus was right. Hopping along clockwise, he was able to hop higher and farther, as he felt lighter and lighter. He reached a point along the ravine where he could hop as high as the inner ledge to the upper crater surface, and he was about to hop back up there when he saw a small landing on the outer edge of the crater wall. On that landing, he saw rectangular prints.

"They were here!" Claus exclaimed.

There was a small alcove in the wall face at this landing. The tracks led there. Claus moved inward but slowly, because gravity was so low that he had almost no holding power on his boots for traction. Once inside, the tracks stopped by the rock

face to his left. Claus touched this rock face, and it gave a little but returned to its natural position.

"It's a door," Claus said. "Novi 3 crew must have gone this way."

Claus pushed the rock face to his left again but with more force, and indeed yes, a door swung inward for him. He pulled himself in through the doorway, and the door closed behind him! He tried reopening the door, but he could not get a good hold on it to pull it inward. Pushing on the door was fruitless, as the doorway frame prevented it. It was no use. He had to make the best of things and explore where he was. But where was he? Claus looked around. He was in a hallway, with smooth walls, floor and ceiling.

"Definitely not a natural formation. Someone or something carved this out. Well one good thing—the flashes have stopped," he said.

Indeed, once inside this rock formation, the cosmic ray particles were blocked, and Claus no longer saw flashing on his retina.

"Let's find out where this goes," he said.

Claus followed the hallway as it sloped downward and counterclockwise along the crater's edge. He experienced increasing gravity and was afraid he would reach a point where the downward pull would be too much.

"The temperature is falling rapidly," Claus said to himself.

It was true. His spacesuit, which in sunlight had to get rid of excess heat, was now providing heat in the dark hallway. His suit's light beam provided illumination for Claus to see, but that was all. Then something caught Claus's attention on the left-side wall that nearly sent him running in fear—the embossing of a creature in stone, as if a slot had been carved in the wall and the creature had been frozen in place. It had an expression of pain on its face, as if attempting to escape a trap of death. Claus moved farther along. Gravity increased slowly, but not enough to deter him. He saw another creature frozen in the right-side wall, but this creature had a more peaceful expression, as if resigning itself to its fate.

"This is a graveyard," Claus said. "But a graveyard for aliens. Are any aliens still here? Will I expect to find those of my own kind here?"

These were questions Claus didn't want to ask, but he did. There was no one to answer his questions, though. He passed several more frozen alien creatures until he reached a point where a passageway opened to the left. The hallway continued straight ahead however, and so he himself continued straight ahead.

"I can go only a little farther," he said. "Gravity is almost that of Earth, and soon I'll be pinned to the floor like I was in the ravine."

To Claus's shock and dismay, he saw frozen people in the rock to his right. They were young people, but they were attired as if from Ancient Greece. They seemed freeze-dried somehow, as if they had been frozen for thousands of years.

"These people *are* from the ancient world," Claus said. "*They* were the first humans on the moon, not the Apollo astronauts. But who knew? And how many others are here from Earth?"

He walked past the last Ancient Greek, wondering if he would see anyone from Astroosa, but he did not. The right wall face was bare. He had now traveled as far as he could—the increased gravity became too much to bear. He doubled back until he reached that passageway to the side (which was now on his right). He followed that passageway, which sloped downward itself for a bit. But gravity remained constant, a bit less than on Earth, which was helpful considering the weight and strain of supporting his spacesuit.

"I'm below the ravine. I must be. And this passageway heads roughly toward the center of the crater," Claus said. "Is there more to this graveyard?"

Claus checked his suit status. He had twelve hours of air before his carbon scrubber filled up. External sensors showed no appreciable atmosphere, but now the floor sloped upward. Gradually, as he walked farther along, air registered with increasing density. Just a few millibars of pressure at first, but increasing. The air itself was 99% nitrogen with trace elements.

"No oxygen, even if there were enough air pressure," Claus said.

On both walls, Claus noticed small rooms. These rooms looked more like fish tanks, having transparent walls with which Claus could use to look inside.

"Is this a graveyard or a museum?" he asked himself.

Indeed, each room had several Earth animals staged in a natural setting. Birds had nests in trees, beavers had lodges, and alligators had swamp areas. But none of the animals were alive. It was as if they were stuffed. Yet they were all realistic. Claus walked farther still, and now there were no more rooms but instead portals, about the size of a basketball in diameter each, and all crowded on both walls, as if fighting for a spot of existence. Air pressure was up to 50 millibars but still at 99% nitrogen.

"I must take no chances until I determine if a threat exists," Claus said to himself. "That means no calls for help on any radio frequency or in this air. Not that I can remove my helmet, but someone or something might hear me yell. I must walk softly too."

One of the portals caught his eye. At first Claus thought that cosmic ray particles had caused the flashing, but he checked his spacesuit, and it also registered the flashing. Claus looked through the portal. It was as if he were in the back of a movie theater, with a distant image showing life in action. He watched as a small dinosaur moved on the earth, looking for food. At the bottom of the display was a set of flashing lights and moving alien symbols. Claus pulled away and looked through another portal. An ancient flightless bird ran through a prairie, and again the flashing status lights and symbols graced the bottom of the display. Portal after portal showed ancient Earth animals, each portal focusing solely on the animal in question. Claus looked through several more portals and realized that some were of the same animal as before, only in different settings.

"These could be biographical records of specific animals. But how and why?" Claus said to himself. "Is it possible that death is not so easily discarded, that there are others recording and studying our every action and reaction?"

Claus followed the hallway. He reached a junction where there were three angled paths to the left and three to the right. No path lay straight ahead. Still no evidence of life or things in the hallway. Pressure was still 50 millibars, but on testing the entrance to the paths, Claus noticed differences.

"Paths to the left are less than 50 millibars. Paths to the right are greater. The right path closest to straight has traces of oxygen and water vapor. Humans exhale water vapor and a little oxygen. But that would mean they have their helmets off or even their entire spacesuits off. Well, it's the best lead I've got. Onward."

Claus followed the right path closest to straight and traveled a bit farther. He came to an open area where the pressure was 350 millibars and nearly 100% oxygen.

"A low-pressure, pure oxygen environment. Survivable environment for a few weeks. But beyond? Who knows?" Claus said.

Claus heard calls of, "over here," from one corner of the open area. The calls didn't come through his radio but instead through the open air, which of course traveled through his helmet to his ears, but the calls were faint, and he didn't notice them at first. However, the calls grew increasingly stronger, with phrases like, "protect yourself," "use the club," and "keep your helmet on." Claus had forgotten about the club attached to his spacesuit's backpack. He retrieved the club and circled around in time to see a six-legged creature the size of a large dog leap toward him. Claus moved out of the way the best he could, but one of the creature's legs caught his arm with the club and knocked the club to the floor. Claus went for the club, but the creature came after him again. Claus took a crouching

stance with club in hand and was about to activate the taser situated at the end of the club but remembered the pure oxygen environment and held off. Instead, he swung the club at the creature's head. The creature caught the club in its jaw. It bit into the club, causing damage to the club's internal wiring and thus caused wires to spark. The open area flashed over in flame, with the dog and club afire as well. The outer layers of Claus's spacesuit began to burn, and he lunged toward the passageway as quickly as the spacesuit permitted, where the deoxygenated atmosphere put out the flames.

Smoke rose from the charred outer layers of his suit. Then something strange happened. The smoke was pulled to the side and took the shape of a humanoid figure. It was a ghostly image, with whispers of light dancing from it, like waves on an ocean at play. His spacesuit confirmed as real both the cloud and the flashing lights from the cloud.

"Then I'm not imagining this. You are intelligent life. Can you communicate?" Claus said aloud and through his helmet's radio.

The cloud took a more solid shape—that of a lovely elderly woman, with flowing curly hair and a gentle face. She reminded Claus of Lady Liberty, that icon of freedom portrayed in early American culture. The cloud woman moved toward Claus as if to remove his helmet and touch his face. Suspicious, Claus backed up. She followed, and Claus backed up farther. He felt himself losing balance and falling sideways. His right arm went out toward a wall to break his fall while his left arm went up to protect his face. Inadvertently, he hit a button on his spacesuit's light beam, which sent that light beam into rapid-mode change. Various different lights came out: infrared, rainbow colors, white light, and ultraviolet. Whenever the ultraviolet light came on, the cloud shape withered, but when infrared came on, the cloud grew rapidly in strength. Claus locked the setting to ultraviolet light, and the cloud dispersed into nothingness.

"I wonder if I just avoided being captured," Claus mused. "One thing is for sure. I must return to that room and find out who was warning me. Could be the Novi 3 crew."

But Claus had to wait a moment. One of his life support systems had been damaged in the fire, and a backup system was struggling to keep up with scrubbing out carbon dioxide.

"Can't overexert myself. Must conserve air," he said.

Claus returned to the open room. Air pressure had risen to 400 millibars, but the oxygen had dropped to one percent, with the remaining air consisting of carbon dioxide and trace elements.

"Over here," called one voice.

Claus cut off his UV light to conserve power. He followed a light in the direction from where the voice came.

"Are you from Astroosa?" called another.

"How did you get here so fast?" said a third.

In the corner of the open area, Claus could see a holding cell with Frieda Morgan, Josh Craigen, and Doctor Donna Morrow. Each person was in some sort of cylindrical container with only the head of each person protruding above. On each head was a thick collar with attached band reaching over each side, over the ears, and over the top of the head. Then from this band was another band that ran over the front of the head with tubes going into the person's nose. On further inspection, tubes also went into the ears of each person from the side band. Each person also had a transparent protective half-dome over their head, which was really two quarter domes with the one behind the head fixed and the one in front movable, the quarter domes resembling lightweight helmets. The movable part was now down, thus protecting the three from the environmental air.

"What have they done to you all?" Claus said.

"Claus, is that you?" Frieda shouted. "What are you doing here? Novi 4 wasn't close to being ready."

"I was in Prava 12," Claus said. "I followed you here. Are we safe for the moment?"

"For the moment," Doctor Morrow said. "These canisters provide for our physiological needs, including supplemental oxygen. We can raise and lower the front mask depending on whether the outside air is breathable, but for the moment it is not."

"Keep your helmet on, Claus! Don't let them puncture your spacesuit either!" Frieda said.

"His suit won't hold out forever," Josh said to the other two. "Eventually they will get him too."

"I'm on backup systems and can only stay for two hours or so. I need to get you all out of here before then. First, I need to figure out how to open this cell," Claus said. "I heard something about using the club. Was that to open the cell?"

"No, that was to ward them off," Frieda said. "We almost held them off, but they broke our clubs too."

Claus walked over to what was left of his club. It was damaged. He returned to the three and spoke:

"What sort of creatures did this to you? Were they like that six-legged thing that attacked me?"

"No," Frieda said. "They were stone creatures, like living statues, and with squared off sections instead of being rounded. But before we landed and all that, we were impaired by something on Novi 3. Couldn't think straight."

"You had a nitrous oxide leak from one of the fuel units, due to micrometeoroid damage," Claus said.

"That explains a lot," Doctor Morrow said. "I should have recognized the symptoms."

"You were impaired too," Claus said.

"We landed in a crater. Why did you land here, Josh? I never gave the order," Frieda said.

"I don't know. Something pulled us down. I never activated the landing sequence," Josh said.

"They came—stone creatures or whatever they were. We were lucky to get fully suited up. Which doesn't make sense. Why didn't we just blast away from the crater?" Frieda said.

"I thought we were stuck. We were afraid these stone creatures would break through the hull and cause the air to leak out," Josh said.

"We tried to club them," Frieda continued. "Then Josh tried the xenon arc on his club to blind them, and that slowed them for a bit, but not enough to stop them. They overpowered us and carried us to a chamber with regular air we could breathe, but they forced us into these canisters. We were here in this cell for a few moments with our face masks open and breathing the air when you came along. I thought that fire would do us all in, but the face masks closed automatically and protected our faces."

"We're not in any pain, Claus," Doctor Morrow said.

"I can't feel anything except my face," Josh said.

"A general anesthetic," Doctor Morrow said.

"And I'm not hungry or anything. I feel full for some reason," Josh said.

"Tubes most likely are recycling our bloodstream directly, converting waste products into nourishment," Doctor Morrow said. "But the human body cannot continue like this for long. Maybe a few weeks or more until atrophy sets in. We'll wither away in these containers."

"What about that dog-like creature?" Claus asked. "Did you see any of those?"

"No," Frieda said.

"I'm surprised they haven't sent their stone creatures in after you," Josh said.

"Yes, it is strange. It is as if they are toying with you," Frieda said, "to see what you do next."

"These stone creatures have data collectors attached to us. No doubt they are gathering our vital signs for study. If so, they could be scientists studying anthropology. We may yet be able to reason with them," the doctor said.

"I saw strange things on the way in. Thought I was in a museum."

"Yes, we saw those too, though only briefly," Frieda said.

"Then they are interested in zoology too," Claus said.

"They might consider them one and the same," Doctor Morrow said.

"You mean they think of animals as people?" Josh asked.

"No, they think of us as animals," Claus said.

"That's crazy!" Josh said.

"The important thing is to be as civilized as possible. A group of scientists will see that we communicate with each other and in turn will try to communicate with us," Doctor Morrow said. "We are communicating with each other now. Perhaps they are allowing us to do so to learn our language."

"Scientists, bah! Those stone creatures looked nothing like scientists," Josh said.

"There is another possibility in all this," Frieda said.

"Enslavement," Claus said.

"Yes. How did you know?" Frieda asked.

"Seems to be the law of the universe," Claus said. "Tell me—these stone creatures—they were powerful, right?"

"Yeah, they were," Josh said. "Impervious to physical harm."

"But did they move quickly? Like that six-legged creature?" Claus asked.

"No. More like human speed," Josh said.

"Lower life-forms tend to be speedy," Claus said. "The jackrabbit, the antelope, even a passing bird—all move more quickly than people but are less intelligent."

"But lower life-forms are typically more powerful too," Doctor Morrow said. "A gorilla has far more power than a human. Yet these stone creatures were more powerful than us."

"Unless these stone creatures are enslaved themselves," Frieda said. "They might answer to more intelligent beings that lack the speed and strength of lower life-forms."

"Exactly," Claus said. "We need to make ourselves indispensable to these higher beings. Provide a service that they deem helpful."

"Is your scrubber full?" Josh asked, meaning that Claus was out of air and thus talking crazy. "We need to escape and find Novi 2."

"How do you propose we do that?" Claus asked.

"You can start by finding our spacesuits and busting us out," Josh said.

"I can only carry one extra suit at a time. My own suit is heavy enough as it is with this near-Earth gravity," Claus said.

"Then bring mine first," Josh said. "I'll help you with the other suits."

"The question is—where are they?" Claus said.

"It's suicide," Frieda said. "They'll capture and contain you too. Unless you can figure out a way to prevent capture."

"You said the xenon arcs slowed them down," Claus said.

"That's right," Frieda said.

"Perhaps they don't like ultraviolet light," Claus said. "I came across a creature in the passageway to this room. I hit my helmet's UV beam by mistake, and the creature dispersed."

"You're forgetting something, Claus," Frieda said. "The stone creatures walked on the lunar surface. They were exposed to full sunlight, including the sun's spectrum of UV. Didn't affect them. But what was this other creature you encountered? Was it made of stone?"

"No, it formed out of smoke from my charred spacesuit," Claus said. "It took the shape of an old woman, and then it dispersed from my UV."

"Could be you encountered one of the actual intelligent beings behind all this," Doctor Morrow said.

"Then we can destroy them with UV," Josh said. "Large amounts of UV. Our helmets emit UV-A for safety reasons, but we could modify the circuitry to emit UV-B or even UV-C."

"That could kill them!" Doctor Morrow said.

"Better them than us!"

"Our corporate charter is to explore the lunar far side, not destroy it," Doctor Morrow said.

"Novi 2 has disappeared. We must assume they've come under attack like us and are captured or worse. We are the rescue mission, and we must do whatever we can to ensure success!" Josh said. "Right Commander?"

Frieda paused.

"We have to survive to warn Earth," Frieda said. "This could be a prelude to invasion and mass enslavement. In a perfect scenario, we could work with these aliens and learn from them. But we—"

"But we can't," Josh said. "Claus, go back to Novi 3 and get the xenon welding torch. That should ward off those stone creatures and any six-legged dogs too. Also bring back the emergency spare spacesuit for me. Then use the xenon torch to break me free."

"It's too violent," Doctor Morrow said. "Our captors will surely retaliate."

But Frieda nodded to Josh in approval and gave a look of disdain to the doctor.

"Do like Josh says. Sorry, doctor," Frieda said.

"How many unnecessary conflicts were started over a misunderstanding?" Doctor Morrow said.

"How many unnecessary conflicts were finished with strength of force?" Josh said back.

"Sit tight. I'll return shortly," Claus said.

Claus exited the room and returned down the passageway from where he first came. He walked with a moderate pace to balance the need for speed with conservation of air. Backtracking through the passages, he felt the presence of something behind him. More than once this happened, and he turned around each time—half expecting a stone creature to pounce on him. Instead, he thought he saw the faint remains of smoke dispersing, as if a fog or vapor was briefly on his suit. Claus checked his backup system, and it registered a bit lower than expected.

"Judgment becoming impaired," he said. "I must get to Novi 3 and get fresh air."

As Claus reached the door to the outside, he thought he heard radio static in his headset. But his radio had automatically shut down to conserve power.

"Hearing things too," he said.

He opened the door and passed through the alcove to the outside lunar environment.

"Couldn't do that before. Did they let me?" Claus mused.

Standing on the landing, he contemplated how he should get to Novi 3. Gravity was reduced, and he was afraid that attempting to hop or jump at this point could send him unexpectedly toward a jagged boulder or rock face. Maybe even launch him into lunar orbit. Before he could decide, he felt trembling in the landing below him. He turned around in time to see stone creatures entering the alcove, most likely from the door.

"They're after me!" Claus exclaimed.

The stone creatures had an amazing ability to adhere and advance along any surface needed, seemingly defying the laws of physics. They came at Claus from multiple angles. Claus jumped away from the landing, but they also jumped. Two each landed alongside Claus and grabbed him by his arms while a third landed on his back, threw arms around Claus, and attempted to crush him. Claus grunted. He struggled to get his arms free. His body fell slowly toward the circular ravine, but his backup environmental controls were now malfunctioning from the attack, and he felt a lack of air and the hot beams from the sunlight striking his face through the face mask. Claus could no longer think rationally. He closed his eyes hard as if bracing for the final impact, with the last voluntary act being that of his legs moving back and forth in a wasted effort to run from danger.

This was the end then. Claus would die at this spot on the lunar surface. The stone creatures most likely would haul him back into a passageway and mount his body on display next to an antelope scene or some other zoological remnant. His Novi 3 friends would be condemned to live their remaining time in those canisters until they too would be mounted on display.

"Such a waste. There was never any hope at all. And yet I tried anyway. Why the bother? Let it end. Let all humanity end," he said, and he lost consciousness.

Chapter 5: Lady Liberty

Claus awoke and to his dismay found himself a captive. He was in a processing room, with several stone creatures working around him. No longer was Claus in his spacesuit, but instead his torso and lower body were encased in a canister similar to that of the Novi 3 crew. His head was exposed. So were his arms. Yet he had no tubes nor anything else connected to his head as the Novi 3 crew did. He could breathe, but he didn't need to, and the part of his body that was encased had no feeling. Claus looked around. The stone creatures had their backs to him and were busy working on a large cylindrical portion with a transparent bubble top. Claus realized that they intended to place that portion over his head and arms, thus completing the full encasement and making him like the Novi 3 crew.

Action was needed, and fast. With all strength and speed he could muster, Claus pulled himself up and along a railing, caught hold of a stone creature, spun himself around the creature, and grabbed a tool from the creature's hand. He hit a few buttons on the tool to activate it, which he did. The tool acted much like a blow torch but without need for external oxygen. Claus whipped the tool through the air like a sword. The tool sliced the head off the first stone creature, and it fell to the floor. Another stone creature came at Claus, but Claus whipped the tool through the air again, and the creature's arm was severed. The creature ran away. Several other stone creatures came toward Claus, but they stopped just outside of reach, as if searching for a way to stop Claus without themselves getting damaged. Then a single stone creature outfitted in armor and wielding a club-like weapon longer than the tool Claus brandished approached Claus directly. Claus held his position, but he realized he could only hold off so many of these stone creatures before they took up arms and subdued him.

"Can you understand me?" Claus said. "You know what this tool does, right? It's a weapon. I'll defend myself to the end. Do you understand?"

No response.

"This is your final warning," Claus said. "Back off!"

The stone creature did not stop. Claus threw his blowtorch-like tool at the face of the approaching stone creature. The tool cut into the armor and set off a chemical reaction, resulting in first an implosion then an explosion. The implosion pulled the other stone creatures toward it, but the explosion destroyed those stone creatures and the armored stone creature itself. Claus was thrown backward. The canister surrounding his body broke open, and his arms that he had used to cover his face sustained lacerations from flying debris.

The blast also knocked out the lighting systems and blocked off the doorway with debris. Claus took a breath out of habit, but the air was filled with heavy dust and smoke. However, Claus didn't need to breathe. Something was recycling oxygen in his body. He moved a bit of debris away and realized there was something like armor over his torso and waist. This armor had internal connections to his body, recycling oxygen and nourishment. His legs were now free, and he scrambled around on all fours until he reached an examination platform. The platform was solid and had blocked the blast, and so Claus found a spot next to the platform free of debris.

"I need to find a light source," Claus said.

Without warning, a light source appeared. The lady-liberty figure from the passageway now coalesced from the smoke and appeared before Claus. Her form gave off a dim, blue light.

"Can you speak?" he asked. "You are the Lady Liberty woman from before. Can you understand me?"

The light flashed quickly and asynchronously.

"She's trying to communicate, but I don't understand," Claus said.

She placed her hand on his face. Claus felt a tingling, as if warm sunshine were touching his face. But still he could not understand. She pulled away and motioned with her hand for Claus to follow her. He did. She walked over to a side wall that had only a bit of debris in the way. Down low was what was left of a countertop, but now it was open, revealing a gaping hole in the wall where plumbing had come through. The pipes, however, had been bent to the side. Lady Liberty pointed toward the gaping hole and indicated that Claus should crawl through it.

"Where does it lead?" Claus asked.

Lady Liberty flashed her lights again, and before Claus could hazard a guess as to the meaning, he heard excavation equipment at the main door of the room.

"No time to debate. Off I go," Claus said, and he crawled into the tunnel.

A soft glow of light filled the tunnel from the pipes. Claus realized these weren't ordinary pipes of water, but rather were conduits for energy of some sort.

"Could be radioactive. I should crawl to the side of the pipes," Claus said.

Claus felt no heat from the pipes, and so he felt that at least if they were radioactive, the radiation was not excessive.

"I will be out soon. Is Lady Liberty following me?"

She was not. Claus reached the end of the tunnel and had to punch through a soft wall, revealing the inside of a cabinet. He pushed through the door of that cabinet and out onto a floor where he stood up in a dimly-lit room. Lady Liberty appeared before him and pointed to various things in the room.

"The spacesuits!" Claus said. "Frieda's, Josh's, and Donna's. And here's mine!"

Claus considered suiting up, but Lady Liberty interrupted. She pointed toward his helmet alone.

"My helmet? You want me to pick it up? Okay, here it is. Should I put it on?"

Lady Liberty halted Claus from putting the helmet on his head. Instead, she directed him to place the helmet over her own head and hold it there, which he did. She then seemed to sing something, but Claus heard no sounds from her. He *did* hear sounds from a door. Startled, Claus bobbled the helmet. Lady Liberty disappeared, the lights turned on, and entering stone creatures witnessed Claus drop the helmet to the floor. Crash! Claus quickly pulled the helmet from the floor and placed it over his head.

"It attaches to this armor," he said. "Intentional? Very strange."

Claus activated the reserve radio headset power and made a desperate call to anyone for help while simultaneously trying to avoid the stone creatures. The radio made strange squawks and squeals, as if receiving interference, and Claus was ready to remove the helmet to spare his ears when the stone creatures cornered him and held him. A humanoid creature of hue-changing plasma entered the room, a creature about the same size as Lady Liberty but with a much more threatening posture.

"Are you the one behind all this?" Claus asked.

"You speak our tongue," the orange creature said through Claus's radio headset. "You invade our realm. The consequence is confinement until purge can commence."

"How is it you speak English?" Claus said. "And why all the hostility? We are on a rescue mission. We sent another ship here, called Novi 2."

"We have a nice display booth for you and your kind. Your bodies will be preserved until this star supernovas. All shall look and be warned of the new invasive species," the orange creature said.

"My name is Claus. Claus Gerhardt. We come in peace. We mean no harm and are not invasive. We will leave if you but let us. What is your name? Please, let's shake hands."

"Your species is clever, I see. My name is Orchius. I am the head of zoology here in Luna Prime. You wish to shake hands? Behold my hand."

Orchius extended a fiery arm and hand toward Claus. When Claus reached to touch it, his hand burned. Claus recoiled in pain and slumped. The stone creatures pulled him to his feet, and Orchius laughed.

"You laugh?" Claus said.

"Only intelligent life-forms laugh," Orchius said.

"We laugh too," Claus said. "We do many things. We can show you."

"You are scheduled to be preserved, intact."

"You can learn a great deal about us if we are not just preserved. Allow us to interact with each other freely. We can show you things about us you will find amusing," Claus petitioned.

Claus realized he had to strike a deal with this Orchius plasma flame creature. It was the only hope for his and Novi 3's survival. Further, it bought him time to figure out what happened to Novi 2. Perhaps then he could get help from Earth or at least warn Earth.

"Your mastery of our language is very impressive," Orchius said. "You might entertain us Orchians. Or you might not."

"Is it worth a chance? You might miss out on great entertainment. You won't know unless you take that chance," Claus said.

"There is no word *chance* in our language," Orchius said. "All is contrived from one known state to another. Do you mean chaos? Chaos is for lesser life-forms who are vulgar and wasteful."

"No, not chaos. Chance. An opportunity for reward when all is not known."

"Do you mean *exploration?*" Orchius asked.

"Yes, in a way, taking a chance is like exploring the unknown. You can learn about our culture," Claus said.

"Cultural exploration is forbidden. It would expose our society to contamination. As you are attempting to do," Orchius said. "Guards, take him away."

The stone creatures practically carried Claus down a hallway with his feet dragging along the way. He was placed inside the same cell as the Novi 3 crew.

"Claus!" Frieda said. "What did they do to you?"

"You have free control of your limbs," Doctor Morrow said.

"He can walk, too," Josh said.

"I believe I said that," Doctor Morrow said.

"Where did you find the body armor?" Frieda asked. "And where is the rest of your spacesuit?"

"It isn't body armor, but some sort of life support system," Claus said. "Those stone creatures tried placing me in canisters like they did for you three. I found our spacesuits but didn't bring them."

"You have a helmet, but you didn't bring a spacesuit? I don't get it," Josh said.

"It's a long story. I'll explain later. What I really need to tell you is that—" Claus started, but he was interrupted.

"Claus, what is it?" Frieda asked.

"What are you looking at?" Josh asked.

Claus seemed transfixed, as if looking at something. Then he spoke to seemingly nothing.

"Lady Liberty, you are back," Claus said. "Yes, I do hear you."

"Who do you hear?" Frieda said. "Have you made contact with Astroosa? Or someone else on Earth?"

"How is it I can hear you? I heard Orchius too," Claus said.

"He's hallucinating," Doctor Morrow said. "Claus, focus on my voice."

"Doctor Morrow. There's someone else here. Her name is Lady Liberty. I've seen her before. I couldn't speak with her until now. We communicate through my radio headset," Claus said.

"Lady Liberty?" Frieda asked. "Who is *she*?"

"Obviously a fantasy of his," Josh said. "Leave him alone. He's loco in the head."

"Not until he explains this fantasy of his," Frieda said.

"We should help Claus focus on reality so he can help us. Claus, listen to me. You are hallucinating. There is no Lady Liberty. She is a figment of your mind," Doctor Morrow said.

"Aren't you going to tell him to take deep breaths?" Josh asked.

"This atmosphere is bad," Doctor Morrow said. "That might be part of the problem. He could be suffering from hypoxia. Claus, what is two and two?"

"Four," Claus said. "Lady Liberty, they think I am hallucinating. What do you know about these Orchians?"

"Claus, please listen to Doctor Morrow," Frieda said.

"Wait one moment. Lady Liberty is speaking," Claus said.

"This is your commanding officer," Frieda said. "I order you to stop hallucinating."

"You are only the commander of Novi 3. I'm the commander of Prava 12," Claus said. "Now hush! Hush!"

Frieda turned beet red in anger. She wanted to raise a fist at Claus, but the canister prevented her. Claus nodded his head several times in affirmation to the words of Lady Liberty.

"The Orchians are colored red, orange, or reddish-orange," Lady Liberty said. "They inhabit this lunar area but are a closed society, except the young. The young are curious and would be thrilled at seeing you humans interact."

"But you are not like the Orchians," Claus said.

"No, I am not. I am the only one of my kind here," Lady Liberty said.

"You...it...but how? Is Lady Liberty your real name? And are you related to the Orchians?"

Lady Liberty laughed.

"My name is Libriota, but you may call me Lady Liberty if you wish," she said. "My people are from a red dwarf solar system."

"Incredible," Claus said.

"About half a billion of your years ago, a group of exiles were sent here as part of their sentence for treason," Libriota said. "They were known as the Orchians because of their leader, Orchius. We lost track of them over the years, and so about a hundred of your years ago, I was sent over to investigate."

"But you are not an Orchian," Claus said.

"No. I have a different origin. Early Orchians were exposed to radiation and were transformed into what they are today. They have struggled with this identity but have come to acknowledge their fate. That transformation has taught them the perils of being exposed to new things, whether from radiation or life-forms or whatever. They close themselves off from others," Libriota said.

"You know all this, yet you stay. Why? Why not return to your people and report your findings?" Claus asked.

"The Orchians destroyed my ship. If I should venture out onto the lunar surface or anywhere outside, your star's ultraviolet light would weaken me," Libriota said.

"You are as much a prisoner as we are," Claus said. "Do the Orchians know that you are here?"

"They know something is here, but not me specifically. They can sense my presence much as you might hear someone stepping in front of a box fan, but they cannot see or otherwise detect me. I'm afraid I've added to their paranoia," she said.

"You know something about us then," Claus said. "The box fan and all that."

"I can dissociate and travel through the lunar rock to the other side. Radio waves from Earth penetrate a little bit into the lunar soil, and so I learn about you without having to expose myself on the lunar surface," Libriota said.

"So you're not afraid of *cultural exploration*?" Claus asked.

"For a moment I thought you said cultural *exploitation*," Libriota laughed. "No, not afraid."

Claus laughed too.

"How much longer do we let Claus engage in this fantasy, doctor?" Frieda asked.

"Is it possible he's really speaking to someone?" Josh asked.

"We have little choice, Frieda. If we were on Novi 3, I could tranquilize him. Josh, nothing is for certain, but ask yourself how he can see and hear something we cannot," the doctor said.

"I don't know how I can see Lady Liberty, but I communicate with her through the radio. If I can get headsets for you three, you could hear her too," Claus replied.

At that moment, stone creatures entered the cell. Libriota disappeared, and Claus turned to meet the intrusion. The stone creatures held Claus firmly, and Orchius entered.

"Do you see them?" Claus asked the Novi 3 crew. "Do you see the stone creatures and the orange creature?"

"They see me," Orchius said. "But they cannot understand me."

It dawned on Claus that Libriota must have done something to his headset that permitted communication with her and Orchius, making the headset some sort of translator.

"Then I will speak for my people," Claus said. "Free their limbs, and you will see humans in action."

"That is exactly why I am here," Orchius said. "I *will* free their limbs—to serve me. Your little games in the fitting room lost valuable selenites. You and your people will be refitted to perform your jobs."

"Wait. We can do better than that," Claus said. "Allow us to entertain you. We can tell stories and jokes, and Frieda here can even dance."

Orchius laughed.

"Cultural exploration? And jesters you wish to be, eh? Very ambitious. But I have news for you. You are to accept your new role with compliments from the Orchian Senate. They have decided to spare your sentence and give you status in our society. Totally against my wishes, mind you. I warned them of the impending contamination consequences. But they are interested in you humans. If you perform well, you may even be promoted. Not to a jester, but perhaps an adviser. Hah! You would have to be very intelligent indeed to become an adviser. So slave workers you all be, and be happy with you!"

"What's happening, Claus?" Frieda asked.

"We are being taken away," Claus said as the stone creatures took them. "We are to become slave workers."

"What?!" Frieda exclaimed.

"Impossible," said Josh.

"This cannot be. The strain would kill us," Doctor Morrow said.

"There must be another way," Claus muffled to himself as the stone creatures (which Claus now knew were selenites) took them down a hallway.

Chapter 6: Escape from Orchius

Claus, Frieda, Josh, and Doctor Morrow had spent the last seven days working in a mine. The canisters from Frieda, Josh, and Doctor Morrow had been removed, revealing the same torso armor that Claus had, and then all four were fitted in an exoskeleton that moved with their limbs yet added great support and strength. Claus was able to keep his spacesuit helmet, strangely enough. The other three wore the face mask bubble they had worn while in their cell. The atmosphere was thin or non-existent in the mine, and so the four could not communicate with one another. It was as if they were all alone in this mindless enslavement activity.

The mining itself was tedious and slow. Claus found himself operating a device no larger than a pencil that took core samples.

"How long can we continue like this?" Claus said. "We are under guard at all times. I haven't seen Orchius at all, nor have I seen Libriota. Orchius had these neural implants placed in our heads to receive instructions, but I wish I could use my implant to communicate with the others. How long have the selenites been mining? A half billion years? More? I hope I'm not stuck here for that long."

At that moment, an impulse from the implant directed Claus to stop taking core samples and proceed down a passageway to a central gathering area. He did not know why he needed to go there, he simply was given the command, and so he went. Claus initially fought these commands, but the exoskeleton also received these commands, and it overpowered Claus's own muscles and so forced Claus along.

"I suppose things could be worse," Claus thought to himself. "This Orchius creature could take these exoskeletons down to Earth and imprison the folk there too. But maybe these lunar creatures can't leave the moon. Maybe they don't want to."

Claus lined up along one side of the area with selenites. Other selenites lined up along the other side. Claus noticed Frieda and Doctor Morrow on that other side but not Josh.

"Josh must be on my side. Or he's somewhere else. Keep your wits about you, Claus. You might need to move quickly to make a break for it."

The lighting in the area dimmed. From Claus's left at the side of the area was a procession, led by eight Orchians. The eight spread out a bit, and behind them walked Orchius and another Orchian that Claus did not know. Orchius held the hand of the Orchian as if she were a spouse. Behind the couple walked eight more Orchians. During this procession, lights flashed in sequence from various selenites as if playing a concert for the Orchians.

The procession stopped about midway, which was close to where Claus stood. The flashing stopped and was replaced with steady light from all selenites. Two selenites approached the procession from the right. They carried a platform and placed it before Orchius and his beloved. Next, another two selenites approached with an object resembling a pickle barrel. They placed this object atop the platform, bowed, then receded into a line of selenites.

"People of Luna Prime," said Orchius. "My wife Arlichia joins me and you in this moment of triumph."

Many flashes from selenites. Claus realized he was receiving this speech both through his neural implant and through his radio. Claus couldn't believe his radio still had power, but perhaps the pickup coil was pulling power from his exoskeleton or torso armor. One thing Claus did realize—the speech through the implant felt more like a directive and call to action with feelings of euphoria and triumph, while the speech through the radio had that same aspirated tone of indifference it did when he last heard Orchius speak.

"After more lunar years than are stars in the sky, the miners of Luna Prime have discovered a great find—the Tropheia."

More cheers from flashing.

"We now have the means to revert back to our original states. After time beyond time of exile, we can go home!"

More cheering through lights flashing.

"Each of you selenites, though you be automated and not of true life-form, are invited to return with us to our home, that wondrous red dwarf we call Carinia Zero. There we shall be converted to full physical form and returned to our home world of Carinia 5," Orchius continued. "Further, all specimens gathered during our visit will return with us. We shall show all in the Carinia system what strange creatures we have encountered and shall tell tales beyond the end of time. Our specimens will happily sacrifice themselves in Carinia Zero's corona as all our kin celebrate our return."

This was bad. Claus and Novi 3 would be killed for sure. There had to be a way out. Should he make a break for it? How would he coordinate this escape with the Novi 3 crew? It was too much to think of, and the unveiling was upon them all.

"It is in our final moment of need that we learn who we are," said a familiar voice.

Claus turned around and saw Libriota behind him. She nodded in affirmation as to Claus's thoughts. Claus took action. With all speed and strength, he rushed toward the pickle barrel and launched his body atop it in an effort to prevent the unveiling. But he was too late. Orchius had extended an arm and sliced a line along the lower edge of the pickle barrel's cover. This released the cover from the barrel, and a device of power blasted the cover upward and high toward the ceiling with Claus riding atop it, holding on for dear life and nearly falling off several times. The device itself varied in shape from a double-ended goblet to a catenoid with a disk protruding from its center. It also varied in overall length and diameter. In its smallest form, it measured about a hundred and two millimeters in diameter. It was black, devoid of light, and hungry for life. It lifted itself above the pickle barrel and then pulled all loose things around into its lower cup—Orchian, selenite, and the Novi 3 crew—while the upper cup leaked gases out the top and kept the cover and Claus suspended upward. The area was awash in a whirlpool-like suction of air, with a sound like that of a tornado. But as quickly as it vacuumed out the surrounding area, it stopped. The cover fell down atop the device, and Claus fell down. All that remained visibly in the area was the pickle barrel, the platform, and himself.

"Is anyone else here?" Claus yelled. "Hello there! Frieda, Josh, Doctor Morrow, or anyone? Anyone at all!"

There was no reply. Even his neural implant was silent. When the Orchians were around, there was a low hum in his implant, like a bad ground on an old-style Earth amplifier. The hum was no more.

"Lady Liberty, are you still here?" Claus yelled.

Libriota was not to be found.

"What do I do? Do I open the barrel and take a chance? I could be killed. But then the Novi 3 crew is dead. I should have listened to Patricia and just reported what I saw. But then I would not have seen all this! I must warn Earth. I must! Another rescue craft can be launched. The Novi 3 spacecraft still works. I can leave immediately. I can leave now!"

The exoskeleton aided Claus in his quick run along one passageway then another and another. Fortunately, the torso armor kept up with his energy needs, and he didn't need to breathe. Good thing too. His helmet registered a low-pressure environment devoid of oxygen. He reached the passageway from where he first entered, and he again found the door to the outside.

"If I go through this door, shall I ever return?" he asked himself before passing through. "I cannot let the lives of my friends be lost in memory and deed. They must be freed. Lady Liberty, lead! Lead the way to undo these events of misfortune."

Still there was no sign of Libriota.

"Then I pass through the door," Claus said, and he did.

Claus was surprised to find that the vacuum of the lunar surface did not cause an issue with his flesh. The exoskeleton protected his flesh from the naked sunlight, but it did not maintain a pressurized atmosphere.

"Still," Claus thought to himself, "I do have a sense that my skin is drying out, like being in a dry, arctic climate."

He reached the Novi 3 spacecraft and entered through the double doors, going from the vacuum environment to the pressurized environment as per standard procedure. Once inside, he removed his helmet and tried breathing—to see if he still could.

"I can still breathe, though it does nothing for me," he said. "It's handy for speaking, nonetheless."

Claus pressed several buttons. A video monitor showed the lunar area surrounding the Novi 3 craft.

"Nothing around. Should be safe to light the rockets," he said.

The pre-launch check was ordinary enough, with the rockets showing enough fuel for the ascent.

"There's even enough fuel to land back on Earth," Claus said.

The Novi 3 rockets lifted the craft upward and on a course toward low orbit.

"I'll circle around the moon a few times to gather data, and then I'll return to Earth," he said. "Novi 3 carbon scrubbers are at idle. That means I'm using no oxygen from the air. Amazing that this torso armor still works. At a minimum we could crack this technology and use it for future space missions."

But a sinking feeling said that there would be no future space missions. People might not want to risk dealing with more lunar far side aliens. Or they might think of Claus as crazy. Still, the torso armor was proof of something. Perhaps the military could use it.

"Maybe people will start wearing them on a mass scale and cause an economic collapse of the food and medical industry," Claus said. "Why must innovation be so painful to implement?"

At that moment, alarms went off in the Novi 3 craft.

"Rocket malfunction!" Claus exclaimed as he pressed several buttons. "Fuel flow is blocked! But how?"

There was no time to speculate. Novi 3 was going down.

"I've got no rockets. I'll crash!" he said.

But then Claus remembered the attitude thrusters. He turned the ship around and used the thrusters to reduce speed.

"C'mon, baby, slow it down!" he pleaded.

He set the thrusters to maximum, and Novi 3 continued to descend. Then he rotated the ship to trade vertical speed with horizontal to get Novi 3 to skid and slide instead of crashing direct.

"Flare, baby, flare!" he said, speaking as if he were landing an airplane with a last-moment flare maneuver.

Novi 3 skidded along the inside of a large crater. It wasn't the crater from which it landed and launched but instead was a different one. The craft slid too much and approached the crater's outer wall. Claus turned the ship around one last time and used thrusters to slow down, but it wasn't enough. Novi 3 crashed into the crater's wall.

Chapter 7: Novi 2

Was Claus alive? Was he dreaming? He opened his eyes half hoping he was awakening from a bad dream in his bed at home. Instead, he was still in Novi 3, but one side was ripped open, exposing the craft to the vacuum of the lunar surface.

"Not a true vacuum of course," Claus said. "Even the moon has an atmosphere. But it's so small as to be negligible. And I too am negligible."

Claus was bleeding. A portion of the exoskeleton on his arm had been damaged by flying debris, and that debris had also ripped open the flesh on his arm. Already a pool of blood formed on the floor of Novi 3 and began evaporating from the vacuum.

"Well this is an interesting problem," Claus said. "How does this torso armor replenish my lost blood? I bet it recycles but doesn't replace. Gotta close the wound and...and..."

Claus was lightheaded from the blood loss. He looked for something— anything—to stuff into his wound to stop the bleeding. He found a stuffed toy (a bear) with a hidden tag that read, "The Happy Space Bear, From Aunt Frieda to my niece, Olivia J."

"A stuffed animal. Probably for luck on the mission. Or as a gift afterward. Sorry, the mission has changed. Lucky bear to the rescue," he said as he stuffed the small bear's body into his wound.

Claus found loose wire and wrapped it around the bear, holding it against his arm.

"It's holding," he said. "I need...I need..."

Claus struggled to maintain consciousness. He needed a medical kit. Did any survive the crash? Yes, there was a small box there by a wall. Now he needed

an atmosphere to stop the blood from boiling from his wound. But the craft couldn't hold pressure with a side ripped open.

"Or can it?" he asked himself.

With medical kit in hand, he pulled himself into the airlock and closed the door to the main area. He then pressed a button, and the airlock filled with air. Claus laughed.

"Who would have thought that this small chamber that is used to go from the vacuum of space to the main cabin would be all I have left of a pressurized environment. Yet here I am! And it's holding air!" he said.

Claus was so happy with his ingenuity that he had no issue with pain when removing the stuffed bear and the exoskeleton (which he did). He cleaned the wound with an antiseptic that should have stung, but again his temporary joy prevented it.

"The gash is large. Should I stitch it up? No, wait, here are some butterfly bandages. They should hold."

They did. But Claus still felt weak. He found an emergency nutrient food tube.

"The food tube has the protein and iron I need. But if I eat it, what will happen? Will my innards rupture?"

It was a chance he had to take. He opened the tube and squirted the food paste into his mouth. Then he found a water bottle and drank from it. He was able to swallow both.

"What a strange sensation. I am neither hungry nor thirsty, yet I can consume the food and drink as if I haven't eaten in days. It is as if my body has more than one way of knowing when I last ate and drank."

Claus realized he could no longer use the exoskeleton. It had been badly damaged by the crash. His helmet too had been cracked. He needed something that would give him more than just a few minutes of protection from the lunar vacuum.

"And to protect me from the sunlight," he said. "Now that Novi 3 is crashed, I'll need to walk around and explore. Maybe I can figure out why it crashed. Or get help. Something. I can't imagine walking around the lunar far side for the rest of my days."

Claus realized that he needed a spacesuit, and the extras were back in the main cabin area. Satisfied that his wound was held together sufficiently and would not bleed, he decompressed the airlock and entered the main cabin area. There it was—a spare space suit with helmet. He took the spare suit and helmet to the air lock, repressurized, removed his old helmet, and put on the spare suit with new helmet. He pressurized his suit, but not fully—just enough to give the suit shape and inhibit the bleeding.

"Now let's see what Novi 3 looks like on the outside. I think I'll walk through the big opening," he said.

Claus exited the airlock, returned to the main cabin area, took one look at the big opening, and then walked through. When he reached the outside, he saw where Novi 3 had dug a deep trench into the lunar surface. In fact, it was partially buried in lunar regolith. But it wasn't the trench that caught Claus's attention. Indeed, he saw *another* trench on the other side of the crater, approximately parallel to the trench from Novi 3, but angled slightly away.

"Another craft has crashed here!" he said. "There's something buried, too. Is it Novi 2? I must see. Maybe they can help me."

Claus hopped along the crater to the item buried at the end of the other trench. There was still plenty of sunlight, as the lunar far side was facing the sun.

"We must have reached the new moon phase by Earth standards," Claus said. "The sun is almost directly overhead."

The buried craft was just that—buried. There were no distinguishing exterior marks, and so Claus could not tell what it was. He approached the little hill of regolith and realized there were prints in the soil leading to and from the craft. Some were spacesuit boots, but others were the same rectangular prints he had seen going to Novi 3.

"Oh no, the selenites were here too!" Claus said.

He followed the prints to the little hill, and they led to the door of a spacecraft.

"A Novi-class airlock," Claus said. "This *must* be Novi 2."

Claus entered the airlock and pressurized. While air filled the chamber, Claus noticed the standard plaque on a side wall.

"Novi 2. Now for the next question—where is the crew?"

Pressurization completed. Claus removed his gloves for comfort (attaching them to his beltline) and entered the main cabin area. Items were scattered about as if there had been a big fight. Claus lifted his face mask to check the air.

"I can't tell if this air is good or not," Claus said.

"It isn't," said a voice.

"Bill? Bill Knight? Is that you? Where are you?" Claus asked.

"Claus Gerhardt," said Bill from inside something. "Are you alone?"

"That's an understatement. Yes, alone. I see no one else out here. And I brought no one with me," Claus said.

"Good," Bill said.

A door opened to a small room just large enough for a person to sit inside.

"I hid in the emergency life support compartment," Bill said as he disconnected several hoses to his spacesuit and exited the room.

"What happened here? Where is your commander?" Claus asked.

Bill looked at Claus in surprise.

"I happen to know there isn't enough oxygen in this air to support life. How is it you can survive with your face mask open?" Bill said.

"It's a long story of my own," Claus said.

"You're not under *her* control, are you?" Bill asked.

"Whose control?" Claus asked.

"*Hers*," Bill said. "She had these rock-like creatures invade the ship. They took the commander. You know, Andrea. My Andrea."

"Yes, Bill," Claus said. "I know how you feel about Andrea."

"Andrea bought me enough time so I could hide," Bill continued. "Claimed she was the pilot and on a mission to explore. That was the last I heard. But afterward, I replayed our security monitors and saw everything."

"Show me the video," Claus said.

"Not yet. First explain why you don't need oxygen. I can't believe it's really you. Maybe *she* created an imposter to flush me out."

"If I were hostile and alien, wouldn't I have captured you or sent for these selenites?" Claus said.

"That's what she called them," Bill said.

"Astroosa sent a rescue ship after you," Claus said.

"I thought they would."

"It was Novi 3," Claus continued. "Frieda, Josh, and Doctor Morrow were aboard."

"And you too, right?" Bill said.

"No, I missed the launch," Claus said.

Bill shot Claus a quizzical stare.

"Another long story. Anyway, Astroosa launched a chase probe to relay back the status of Novi 3. Patricia Li supervised the launch. It was Prava 12. I was onboard Prava 12."

"How is that even possible?" Bill asked. "Prava 12 is not man rated."

"It is now," Claus said.

"Then where is Prava 12?" Bill asked.

"It crashed in another crater several kilometers away. Novi 3 landed safely, but her crew was captured. I went after them and found them, but I was captured too. We were fitted with torso armor like this," Claus said, and he removed his spacesuit.

"Incredible," Bill said. "But how do you...I mean, how do you remove it?"

"I've been unable so far. But it provides life support for me. It recycles my blood so that I have food and oxygen resupplied," Claus said. "I don't need to breathe, though I can if I need to speak, like right now."

"Double incredible," Bill said.

"My arm is injured," said Claus, "and I lost some blood. I ate from a food tube and drank water. Not sure how that's going to work out. The torso armor doesn't appear to have an exhaust port."

"What is that on your hands?" Bill said.

Claus looked at his hands. Black goo seeped from his palms.

"I...what is happening to me?" Claus wondered.

"Let's get a sample analyzed," Bill said.

Bill opened a compartment and removed a sampling kit, which was a bag with a spatula, a small container, and a cleanup wipe. He scraped a little of the goo from Claus's palm and placed that goo into the container. Next, he placed the container in a glass dome and then pressed a few buttons. Lasers quickly scanned the goo. Bill watched a nearby display screen.

"Organic compounds," Bill said. "It's like perspiration and other components, only much thicker."

"Like waste material?" Claus asked.

"In a way. Look for yourself."

Claus looked at the display screen.

"Perhaps this is how the torso armor eliminates excess organic material," Claus said.

"I'd say you're right," Bill said. "Look, Claus. We don't have the tools to cut off the armor without injury to you."

"It's not a critical issue at the moment. Now show me that security video."

Bill showed the video to Claus. The Novi 2 craft orbited around the lunar far side. Bill piloted while Andrea checked over instrumentation.

"There's a fuel flow anomaly," she said.

"I see it. There's a restriction in the line. We should orbit around to the lunar near side and troubleshoot while in radio contact with Astroosa," video Bill said.

An alarm went off.

"Rockets have activated," Andrea said.

"It's not me," video Bill said. "Must be a malfunction."

"We're descending," Andrea said. "Reverse thrust."

"Controls are not responding," video Bill said.

"Emergency landing procedure," she said.

The two in the video worked furiously to land Novi 2 safely.

"Brace for impact," video Bill said.

The video image shook while Novi 2 landed and skidded along the lunar surface. The craft came to a stop. Video Bill punched a few more buttons and stared at a display screen.

"Analysis shows rocket controls received an excess amount of radiation," video Bill said.

"Solar radiation?" Andrea asked.

"No."

"Cosmic?"

"No. Lunar."

"Lunar? From what?" Andrea asked.

Video Bill punched a few buttons, and video of the rockets displayed, showing a blue aura entering from below. Just then, a proximity alarm sounded.

"Something is outside Novi 2," Andrea said.

Bill punched a button, and a video showed selenites approaching the ship with a blue aura following behind.

"Blue," Claus said. "That's odd. I would think that orange would be the color that—"

"Put on a spacesuit and get in the emergency life support chamber," Andrea ordered.

"But—" Bill said.

"Do it!" Andrea barked.

The video showed both Bill and Andrea donning spacesuits with helmets, but only Bill entered the emergency life support chamber. Andrea grabbed a laser rifle, entered the airlock, and pumped out the air. She opened the outer door to the lunar surface, pushed through the regolith that had buried Novi 2, and took a position. She fired the laser. The selenites took no damage. They reached her position and attempted to take hold of her, but she used the laser rifle against them like a club. It was no use. They overpowered her and forced the airlock fully open (both doors).

Novi 2's atmosphere escaped to the lunar surface, temporarily pushing the selenites back (but also pushing Andrea farther out onto the lunar surface). Selenites held Andrea while others entered Novi 2 and performed a quick check of the interior. The blue aura now entered Novi 2 and took a more substantial shape.

"There," Bill said. "That's who caused our rockets to malfunction. She made us crash here."

Claus looked closer at the display screen then erupted into near scream.

"Lady Liberty! But that's impossible!" Claus yelled. "It must be someone else, someone who looks like her. I can't believe she would do this! And out in the lunar sun, too!"

The video continued.

"I am Libriota. This spacecraft has violated our habitat and is charged with such crime. All a-party are now prisoners subject to sentencing. If any are still on this ship, come forth now or face additional punishment."

Bill pressed the pause button. Claus stared at the frozen screen in disbelief.

"But she was friendly. She wanted to help me. Why, Lady Liberty, why?"

"So you've met her," Bill said.

"Yes. I met her," Claus said. "I thought she was a friend. The Novi 3 crew was also captured by selenites, but their leader was Orchius, an orange luminous creature somewhat resembling Libriota but much meaner looking. He never seemed to know she was around. I called her Lady Liberty, because she reminds me of those old drawings of Lady Liberty back in the U.S. Remember? Like on old coins? Other orange creatures were called Orchians. They were exiled to our moon many years ago. But they discovered an energy device of immense power and were pulled into that device, supposedly being taken back to their star. The Novi 3 crew was taken too. I'm at wit's end trying to figure out how to save the Novi 3 crew. Andrea is missing too. I have to wonder if she was taken back with the others. But Novi 3 originally crashed in a different crater than Novi 2.

Bill, I don't know the range of that device. The device that took everyone."

"How is it this device didn't take you?" Bill asked.

"I dove on top of the cover as it was being removed from a barrel. The blast of the device threw me upward. I guess that protected me," Claus said. "But Lady Liberty! She said she couldn't go out on the lunar surface, that ultraviolet light would weaken her. I still can't believe it was her."

The proximity alarm went off. Bill shut off the video.

"She's back," Bill said. "With more selenites."

"She must have tracked Novi 3 and my prints. Bill, how long can you survive here?"

"There's plenty of power, and I can rejuvenate my carbon scrubber for a good six months. Food and water will last a long time, too."

"Good. Go back into the emergency life support chamber," Claus said.

"I want to go with you. I can help," Bill said.

"No. I need you here in case Astroosa sends another ship. Tell them what happened. And go back to Earth yourself," Claus said.

"Claus, I can't leave you and Andrea here to—"

"Do it!" Claus barked, much like Andrea had before.

And with only moments to spare. The airlock was forced open much like before. Two selenites entered and held Claus by the arms. Other selenites entered as a display of force. Then Libriota entered.

"Lady Liberty? Or should I call you Slana Slavecatcher?" Claus said. "Out getting a suntan? I thought ultraviolet was bad for you."

"Claus! What odd things you say. I can endure your sunlight for brief periods, much as your fair skin can before you get a sunburn. But those are trifles! I came to help you," Libriota said.

"Then why are these selenites holding me? And what about Andrea? Why was she taken from this ship?" Claus asked.

"For protection," Libriota said.

"Protection! Protection from what?" Claus demanded.

"You don't understand," Libriota said. "But I can help you. There's a place we should go. Andrea is there. We must go now."

"I can't believe what I'm hearing. The oldest scam is the urgent need to do something without question. Are you responsible for Novi 2 crashing?" Claus asked.

Libriota muffled a chuckle then motioned the selenites by Claus to move aside. She approached Claus and feign-touched the side of his helmet.

"Look around you, Claus. There is nothing but desolation here. This ship is empty. Your other ship is wrecked. You can stay here, but what will you do? The lunar surface is a lonely place. You have many questions but few answers. I will help you with your questions. The alternative is to stay here. I would like to visit you, but there are many things to be done on this moon. The Orchians have returned to Carinia Zero, and I have my own kind back home fighting for my attention. It would be easier if I could offer you comforts and advice in our underground dwelling. Andrea is there. You know Andrea, right? She crashed this spacecraft. But we pulled her out and saved her. She'd like to see you."

Claus felt uneasy. But he had to get Libriota and the selenites out of Novi 2. Amazing that she did not detect Bill's hidey spot. Was there something in the emergency life support chamber that blocked her senses? Or perhaps she was preoccupied. In either case, Claus knew that each second he remained, the risk of Bill's discovery was increased. And if ever there would be hope of getting word back to Earth, it was Bill, unless he remained stranded for more than six months. Perhaps Claus could figure out something by then.

"What about the others? Frieda, Josh, and Doctor Morrow?" Claus asked. "Are they with you?"

Libriota moved closer to Claus with her face very close to his.

"They are not lost," she whispered. "But we must work quickly to save them. Come with me. Please?"

Claus had to act sincere, but if he gave up too easily, she might suspect. If he held his ground, she might leave him be. Or would she?

"No, I'm going back to Novi 3 and launch an emergency beacon first. I need to let Earth know what has happened," Claus said.

"Novi 3? You mean your spacecraft over there?" Libriota said as she pointed toward Novi 3.

Claus nodded as he looked out a window at Novi 3. Suddenly, the remainder of the craft exploded in a fiery ball of plasma. When the fireball dissipated, nothing remained. A lunar tremor from the blast shook Novi 2.

"Now then, would you like to stay here in this ship and risk the same fate?" Libriota asked with a chuckle.

She played her top card, and Claus knew it. He had to throw down.

"You've made your point," Claus said.

Libriota let out a hearty laugh that sickened Claus. Two selenites put Claus's gloves on, closed his face mask, took his arms, and escorted him behind her, who led him to the outer wall of the crater, into a passageway, and underground.

Chapter 8: The Purchase

The fact that Libriota could destroy spacecraft at will was truly shocking to Claus. This meant she could destroy him or anything else. Claus looked around as he traveled through the passageways. These selenites were shaded slightly blue while the previous Orchian selenites were shaded slightly orange. Further, there were other blue creatures like Libriota.

"I thought you were the only one of your kind here," Claus said.

"In Luna Prime. This is Luna Beta," Libriota said.

Claus felt uneasy about the answer, but he had no time to think. He was quickly ushered into a room and forced to stand on a platform. Selenites stood in strategic places and acted as guards. An audience of blue creatures watched. Claus watched as Libriota stood before these creatures and spoke:

"Fellow Carinians, I bring you news and this visitor to our colony. He is a human and is called Claus Gerhardt," Libriota said.

"Welcome, Claus," many voices said.

"Hello," Claus replied. "I am not sure why I am on this platform with a light shining on me. I feel like an animal on display."

The Carinians laughed.

"And now let us begin," Libriota said.

Two selenites removed Claus's helmet and spacesuit.

"Hey! What are you doing?" Claus asked.

"You will note the visitor is wearing a torso plate. Made by the Orchians," Libriota said.

The Carinians gasped.

"My name is Claus!" Claus said. "What is going on?"

"As you can see, he can communicate with us. The Orchians have inserted a neural implant into Claus that provides for such. He understands us, and we understand him. He will make an excellent pet to the highest bidder."

"What!?" Claus yelled. "I'm not an animal. I'm not property! You can't just sell me!"

"Do I have one drakos? One drakos?" Libriota said.

A Carinian raised a hand.

"Two drakos," called another Carinian.

"Three drakos."

"Five drakos."

"A thousand drakos!" called a Carinian in the back, much to the gasp of others.

"I'm not property! Libriota, stop this madness! I am a human being, capable of reason and sentience. I will not accept servitude as a sentence!" Claus said.

"He's a feisty one," said one Carinian.

"Are there more like him?" asked another.

"Fellow Carinians, Claus is the only one wearing a torso plate in Luna Beta," Libriota said.

"Two thousand drakos," said another.

More gasps.

"Are there any other bids?" Libriota called.

The Carinians were silent.

"This has gone far enough," Claus said. "Libriota. Where's Andrea? You know, the other human you captured from Novi 2? Novi 2—the spacecraft we were just in. Where is she?"

"We are attempting to adapt a torso plate to her, so that she may be put up for sale," Libriota said. "She isn't worth anything without one. Who wants a handicapped pet? But we do not have the same technology as the Orchians. Devious Orchians. We sentence them to mine for us, and they create a base they call Luna Prime filled with technology and achievement we Carinians had never known. Including their studies of human beings."

"You can learn about us in other ways. There's no need for this master-slave type relationship," Claus said. "We are your peers."

"We have already tapped into the Orchian collective and learned much about you humans."

"Is that what you were really doing?" Claus asked. "You were the only one of your kind...spying on the Orchians, right?"

"It *was* just me—in Luna Prime," Libriota said. "You call it spying. I call it monitoring. But Carinians want to settle here. Or settle something here."

"Convenient how those Orchians are suddenly gone after having been here for half a billion years. From a newly-discovered device. What did he call it? A Tropheia? How *did* that Tropheia of theirs just magically appear? And where is it now?" Claus asked.

"They are gone. That is all you need to know," Libriota said.

"But that device took my friends!" Claus yelled.

The bidder of two thousand drakos stepped forward.

"The auction is not over, Lanietta," Libriota said.

"I request primary right to bid on the other human pet," Lanietta said. "For a breeding program. It would not be proper to keep them apart."

"I will start the breeding program," called another Carinian.

"No, I!" called yet another.

"Ownership? Breeding? Does this define your morality?" Claus shouted.

"It is what your kind understands," Libriota said. "Through your culture we shall learn."

"I have a better idea," Claus said. "You Carinians can assume various shapes, right? What if some of you become our pets? Your duties would be light, things like playing fetch or chasing away raccoons. That would be the role of a dog. Then perhaps the next pet would be a horse. We could—"

"You expect us Carinians to be subservient to a human?" Lanietta barked.

"Impossible! I withdraw my bid. You humans are disgusting."

"Your bid is binding, Lanietta," Libriota said. "What you do with your pet is your business, of course. If Claus were temporarily turned into a dog, perhaps he could learn to take that shape on his own."

"I can't change into a dog," Claus said.

"You don't think so," Libriota said.

"I know I can't!" Claus said.

Libriota touched her plasma hand to Claus's torso armor and said a few unintelligible words. Claus changed shape into that of a dog and even barked. The Carinians laughed and clapped before Libriota changed Claus back to normal.

"You...violated me! You thug!" Claus said.

"That went very well," Lanietta said. "Though I wanted to be the first. I feel like he's used goods now."

"He is not. You can change him too. Don't believe me? Try it yourself," Libriota said.

Lanietta touched Claus with her plasma hand and spoke unintelligible words. Claus became a dog again.

"Impressive!" Lanietta said. "I resubmit my bid. Hmm. I wonder what other animals he can become."

"Try a horse," Libriota said. "It *is* the other pet he mentioned."

Lanietta touched Claus again and spoke unintelligible words. Claus became a small horse.

"Only a small horse?" Libriota said.

"His mass cannot be altered that much at a time. If I want Claus to be a larger horse, I will have to work him up gradually," Lanietta said. "But first, there's another pet I want to try. A cat."

Lanietta changed Claus into a cat. He was too small for a house cat, and so he became a mountain lion. He took one swipe at Lanietta then dashed through the room and out a corridor.

"After him, quickly!" Libriota yelled to the selenites.

Claus ran around, looking for a way to escape. But he tired quickly. He could only run in short bursts before he had to rest.

The torso armor was somehow covered in his cougar coat, and so his appearance to others was that of a real mountain lion. Each time he reached a room with selenites, he was able to jump or squirm beyond reach. He raced around from room to room looking for Andrea, but Claus could not find her. Desperate, he found an exit to the lunar surface and ran across the crater to the Novi 2 craft.

"If only someone could see," Claus thought to himself. "If only. Yes, they would be shocked to watch a mountain lion running across the lunar surface. How could such an animal survive the vacuum of space? And yet I survive. My dignity and grace have been destroyed by Libriota and her Carinians. I thought I could trust her as a helper against the Orchians. But they are both bad. Maybe that's the law of the universe—all species overpower the weak."

The airlock to Novi 2 was still open. Claus jumped inside and pawed at buttons to close it. He pressurized the environment then pawed at the emergency life support door. Bill cracked the door open.

"A mountain lion! How on Earth, I mean, where did this animal come from? Stand back, kitty!" Bill said.

Claus pawed toward Bill in an effort to communicate, as Claus could not speak like a human, but Bill was still afraid. Bill opened a food tube, squirted food onto the tube's exterior, and threw the tube across the room for the mountain lion to follow. Claus watched the tube fall but turned back toward Bill. The scent of the food carried through the air. Claus could not stop the cougar drive from within, even though he needed no food. He walked over to the food and ate it. Then he walked around Novi 2. Dark goo came off his paws and left prints.

"Sons of liberty," Bill exclaimed as he watched. "It's just like Claus. This cat must have a life support system. That's how it was able to travel on the lunar surface."

Bill continued watching the mountain lion. It grew tired, reclined on the floor, and fell asleep. Minutes later, the shape changed into Claus.

"I've been in space too long. I'm going mad," Bill said. "And yet there are paw prints on the floor. Claus, Claus! Wake up!"

Bill tapped Claus on the shoulder. Claus stood up and looked at himself. He wore no clothing but still had his torso armor.

"Claus, this is going to sound crazy, but for a moment I thought you were a mountain lion," Bill said.

"For a moment I was," Claus said. "Look at my paw prints. I ate tube food. I couldn't help myself. And that goo came out of my paws."

"What happened with that blue woman?"

"Libriota?"

"Yes."

"She tried to sell me at an auction," Claus said. "As a pet."

"!" Bill muffled.

"I know, tell me about it," Claus said.

"And you escaped here? But she'll track you. She'll be here any moment to capture you again," Bill said.

"I have a plan," Claus said. "But first I need help from the Novi 2 computer. Remember that brute-force spectroscopic communicator program?"

"Yeah. It's a linguistic feedback comparator program. Supposed to probe for and communicate with life-forms that use light for language," Bill said.

"I think Libriota said something to my torso armor. Lights flashed from her quickly just before I changed shape," Claus said. "If we run that program on my torso armor, it could discover the key sequences for my transformation into another form."

"It could also get you killed," Bill said. "Suppose you are changed partway, with blood and organs spewing out in a chaotic mess?"

"I'd rather die that way than be enslaved as a Carinian pet," Claus said. "Begin the program."

Claus stood next to an array of light-emitting diodes. Bill pressed several buttons. The air moved around Claus as white light flashed asynchronously.

"Nothing," Claus said. "You know, she only used blue light. Restrict the spectrum to blue-based light and try again."

Bill adjusted the controls and reran the program. Lights flashed asynchronously in blue. The air moved, and Claus's hair changed color.

"I think we have something. But the light is too weak. Increase the intensity," Claus said.

"That might burn your skin," Bill said.

"Try a short burst then," Claus said. "We need this data point."

"Okay, okay. Short burst with increased intensity," Bill said, and he hit more buttons.

"Ow, my eyes!" Claus said.

The burst of light was so bright that it reddened Claus's skin and temporarily blinded him.

"Easy there," Bill said. "We'd better stop for a while."

"There's no time," Claus said. "Like you said, Libriota could be here any moment. I'm missing something, I know I am. Blue light, blue light, wait, Claus you fool, you've forgotten about the most blue of light—ultraviolet light."

"No way! That will really give you skin burns," Bill said.

"Turn down the intensity but increase the color to ultraviolet," Claus said. "The Carinians don't like our sun because of the UV."

"What does that have to do with changing your form?"

"I bet Libriota projects UV rays as needed for communication and control," Claus said. "My guess is she used UV rays to change me."

"Short-wavelength UV rays destroy tissue," Bill said.

"I know. You'll have to start with the safer UV spectrum. UV-A," Claus said. "But something tells me we'll need to go to UV-B, UV-C, or even higher. Think of this—for many years people would use explosives to destroy. Then they learned to contain the explosive force and control it,

such as in an internal combustion engine, to generate non-destructive, smooth power. My guess is the Carinians have mastered the higher UV rays in the same fashion. They can control the rays to alter tissue instead of destroying it."

"We should be running this on a test subject," Bill said.

"I am the test subject," Claus said. "We've been through this already. Yes, the first bit will damage tissue, I know. Tell you what, focus the beam on my left forearm. That way only part of me will be lost."

Bill didn't like the sound of that.

"Sit here," Bill said. "Now put your forearm on this support. I'll secure it like so...good. Now I'll position this spotlight directly over it. There. That's the best I can do."

"It's fine," Claus said. "Let's start again. Allow the program to run through repeatedly while increasing the ultraviolet frequency. Keep the intensity low the entire time. We'll go for control first."

Bill did just that. As the lights flashed and changed, the skin on Claus's forearm changed in color, grew scales, lost scales, grew feathers, lost feathers, grew fur, lost fur then grew a hard, leathery shell. From the shell grew little teeth then small horns.

"We have something," Claus said. "Now let's see if the program can reverse it."

Bill hit a few buttons, but the little teeth and horns remained.

"Something's wrong," Bill said. "Your forearm isn't changing."

"What did you do before to change me back? When I was a mountain lion?"

"I didn't do anything," Bill said.

"You must have done something," Claus said.

"I threw you the food tube, you ate it, you walked around, then you took a nap on the floor," Bill said. "Wait. Let me try something."

Bill sprayed something on Claus's forearm. The teeth, horns, and shell disappeared, with Claus's normal skin returning in its place.

"You did it," Claus said. "What did you spray?"

"This," Bill said as he showed Claus the bottle.

"Lidocaine," Claus said. "Then I think I understand. Calming my body restores it to normal, either through sleep or an anesthetic. Bill. I need a portable version of this machine integrated with my torso armor. I also need a way to calm my nerves to reverse changes. Lidocaine might not be practical. Perhaps soothing hypersonic waves or something."

"Oh sure, and a portable gold making machine would be handy, and a cure for cancer while I'm at it," Bill said.

"I realize this is a tall order," Claus said.

"Very tall," Bill said.

"It'll give you something to do while you're alone," Claus said.

"We can start with this," Bill said, and he inserted a small, flat device underneath Claus's torso armor. "This will record your physiological activity. I've got to have at least some data to start with. That way I can—"

But the two were interrupted by the proximity alarm. Bill hid inside the emergency life support room, and only just in time. Libriota, Lanietta, and several selenites forced their way through the airlock and into Novi 2.

"You should be thankful that I have spared your life, Claus. Escaping a master is punishable by death," Libriota said.

"I'm a free man. I've said so already," Claus said.

"You are neither free nor a man. Your torso plate deprives you of both," Libriota said.

"I refuse to cooperate. You can change me into a mountain lion or whatever you like. I'll escape again and again," Claus said.

"Insolence is not approved," Libriota said. "Our ability to change your shape allows us to change your internal tissue pressures. I shall demonstrate."

Libriota held a hand up toward Claus. A faint blue light flashed rapidly. Claus doubled over and fell to the floor with severe abdominal pain.

"Does this remind you of a past event? Being hit in the gut with a baseball bat?" Libriota asked.

"Please, stop!" Claus begged.

"Are you a free man?" Libriota demanded.

"I...free...man..." Claus groaned. "Not... trainable."

"Of course you're trainable. You simply need to be broken in," Libriota said. "Lanietta, you try. Increase the pain until Claus breaks."

Lanietta held up a hand, and bluish-green light flashed onto Claus. Claus writhed in pain and cried out. He perspired profusely, his skin turned dark red, and defined lines from his muscles showed them contracting beyond healthy limits. He foamed at the mouth.

"Are you a free man?" Libriota asked.

"I..." Claus tried to say.

"You are my pet. You will obey my commands," Lanietta said. "Say that you agree."

"I...agree..." Claus forced out.

"I release you from pain," Lanietta said.

Lanietta flashed bluish-green light from her hand. Claus relaxed and breathed heavily to recover.

"There, you see Lanietta? Trainable," Libriota said.

"You will accompany me back to my property," Lanietta said, "as a dog."

Claus was about to protest, but he bit his lip.

"Do not worry. It is painless," Lanietta said.

"It is humiliating," Claus said.

"You will do as you are told, or you can expect more pain treatments," Lanietta said.

"No, no more treatments," Claus said.

"Very well," Lanietta said.

Lanietta held up her hand, bluish-green light flashed, and Claus transformed into a dog. A selenite produced a leash and looped it around Claus's neck. Claus was led then from Novi 2 onto the lunar surface, through a tunnel door like before, and down a passageway toward an opening. The group stopped, and Claus was returned to his humanoid shape.

"I trust Claus will behave and make an excellent pet for you. Do not hesitate to request help if needed," Libriota said.

"He will behave," Lanietta said.

"Have you chosen his new name yet?" Libriota asked.

"Clomper," Lanietta said.

"Clomper. How insulting," thought Claus. "All that training as a test pilot followed by training at Astroosa was for this? For being a clomper, a big fat shoe for an alien foot? Why explore space at all?"

"It is like discovering a new continent only to be bitten by a poisonous snake," Claus inadvertently said aloud.

"Remember," Libriota said. "He can only make such statements in humanoid form."

"Yes, the dog can only bark," Lanietta said as she changed Claus back to dog form. "Selenite, bring Clomper with me."

"Farewell, Lanietta, and good luck," Libriota said. "Let this be a step toward Carinian unity."

Lanietta, the selenite, and Clomper returned underground and traveled a short ways until they entered a wide expanse that looked very much like a farmhouse with lawn, barn, and grazing field.

"This is my home, at least my home on this moon," Lanietta said. "I have studied your culture and have picked this setting to learn more about you. I wanted to leisurely walk around the farm and talk for a bit, but you are so uncooperative, Clomper. I have observed that humans like to play fetch with their dogs. Clomper, if you play fetch with me, I'll return you to human form."

Clomper looked at Lanietta with sullen eyes.

"Selenite, throw a stick for Clomper."

The selenite threw a stick. Clomper ran after the stick, picked it up in his teeth, and returned to Lanietta.

"Very good," Lanietta said. "I'm supposed to rub your fur and take the stick from you, but we Carinians cannot take material form. I only wish there were some

way I could. Selenite, throw the stick again."

The selenite threw the stick. It landed in a pond, where it floated. Clomper ran into the pond, swam to the stick, grasped it in his teeth again, swam to shore, and returned to Lanietta. The selenite took the stick. Clomper shook his fur to remove the water. The selenite tried to shield himself from the water spray but was too late. Lanietta laughed.

"I see why pets are so fun. You're so cute!" Lanietta said. "I wish I could hug you and show affection! I'll change you back to human."

Lanietta flashed bluish-green light, and Clomper the dog became Claus the human.

"I feel like a yo-yo," Claus said.

"I don't understand," Lanietta said.

"Never mind. Lanietta, your people cannot take physical shape, yet you dwell here on this moon. Libriota told me she came to watch the Orchians, but they cannot take physical shape either. They returned to your star. I thought I was all alone. And Libriota said she was the only one of her kind here. Now I find out others are here. You've been studying us, right? For a while?"

"Libriota left out a few details," Lanietta said. "You were alone for the most part after the Orchians left. But we came back through the Tropheia and set up things here very quickly. I studied humans from afar using my own methods."

"Yes, the Tropheia. You must tell me about that," Claus said.

Lanietta laughed.

"You laugh?" Claus asked.

"You seem to think you're entitled to know all there is about us and the universe. We are here now, and that will do for the present," Lanietta said.

"And what do you hope to find by staying here?"

"Adventure, among other things," Lanietta said.

"What other things?" Claus asked.

But Lanietta shot Claus the same stare as she did with the "entitled to know" speech, and so Claus fell silent for a moment. The two walked around the farm property while a selenite followed as a guard.

"You are advanced people with great power," Claus said. "Isn't that enough?"

"Things are boring back in Carinia Zero. All of us just floating around with others of similar power. We're stuck. There's no adventure, no excitement," Lanietta said.

"Didn't the Orchians provide adventure?" Claus asked.

"They...were sent for research on this moon," Lanietta said.

"Libriota said they were exiled," Claus said.

"That sounds reasonable," Lanietta said.

"You make it sound like a cover story," Claus said. "They had us digging and only stopped when they found that Tropheia device."

"Yes, and they found it," Lanietta said. "Good for them and us. Now we have it, and we can use it for transport between your world and ours. But I'm ahead of myself. Libriota came over here first to monitor Orchian progress. It was then that she learned of the state of evolution on Earth, including the humans. When word reached Carinia Zero, others wanted to visit here. Like a holiday."

"Our moon is to be a resort for Carinians then?" Claus asked.

"Yes, you could say that," Lanietta said.

"Help me free my people, and we'll show you adventure. We have many video recordings of movies and television shows with people experiencing all kinds of adventure," Claus said.

"Libriota already investigated your works of fiction, Clomper," Lanietta said. "But they feel so flat, so uninvolved. That's why we need real pets, so we can interact."

"For how long?" Claus asked.

"For as long as we need. Until we can return to...well...the thing is, your kind does not live forever, at least not normally. That torso plate might help, but it's not enough," Lanietta said. "We need a breeding stock of pets, too, so that all Carinians here on this moon may experience adventure."

"You want me to be a part of that breeding stock?" Claus asked.

"Of course. We already have a human female. You call her Andrea, I believe," Lanietta said. "We do not understand your reproductive process fully, but that can be discovered later."

It was bad enough being enslaved, but to be forced into bringing children into slavery was another matter. Claus had to prevent it somehow.

"Lanietta, don't your people reproduce?" Claus asked.

"No, Clomper, not like you lower forms. We have in the past with special technology, but not for several billion years."

"You have no parents?" he asked.

Lanietta went silent and paused before speaking strangely.

"The universe is our parent. Yes, I will repeat it, the universe is our parent," Lanietta said with a distant gaze as if giving herself a pep talk. "There are no parents. We are here. We have always been here. Distant memories of infinite past fade into infinity."

Lanietta paused again, looked down, and then looked up at Claus. She smiled as if shrugging off an unpleasant memory.

"I don't understand. Who guides you through life? Who teaches you right from wrong?" Claus asked.

"I will pretend you didn't ask that," Lanietta said. "I will learn of things as they happen, and then I will learn to control. Look, Clomper, I can turn you into a pony."

Lanietta flashed bluish-green from her hand, and Claus became a pony.

"I have not yet mastered mass and size conversion with humans," Lanietta said, now changing Claus back to his human form. "I'd love to turn you into a horse. We could then turn Andrea into a horse and have you two race together. I...I used to be able to do things...I..."

"Something else puzzles me," Claus said. "Libriota flashes blue, but you flash bluish-green."

"It's just light," Lanietta said. "Do you like my color?"

"Not if it means changing me into animal form," Claus said.

"I need something to alleviate my boredom," Lanietta said.

"A pity you cannot assume material form and become a horse yourself. We could then race each other," Claus said. "Now that would be real adventure with real excitement. But I suppose we can't expect Carinians to do everything. Even humans have to do some things better than the superior ones."

Lanietta's bluish-green color briefly changed to green then back.

"What's the matter, Lanietta? Did I insult you?" Claus asked.

"Clomper, you'll never be as good as a Carinian," Lanietta said.

"But you can't experience adventure and excitement like humans. That makes you inferior in that respect," Claus said.

"We are superior," Lanietta said. "Didn't Libriota tell you?"

"Libriota doesn't know everything. She won't let you take material form. She's holding onto that secret for herself," Claus said, though he was only guessing and simply trying to stir up Lanietta's emotions, if she had any.

"You're lying! My pet is a liar! Go run around the field or something, you wooly-mouthed sheep!" Lanietta said.

Lanietta turned yellow-green with anger, and she tried flashing bluish-green light onto Claus to turn him into a sheep, but being now yellow-green, she could only flash yellow-green light, which was harmless to Claus, and so Claus remained in his human form. Frustrated, Lanietta moved through the grass like a dust devil, picking up blades and loose dirt. She then went for Claus as if to attack him. Indeed, she swirled the grass and dirt around him such that Claus itched and coughed and felt totally miserable.

"Ease up, Lanietta," Claus said.

But Lanietta continued her assault. The grass and dirt moved more quickly, to the point of becoming a large green blur resembling that of a skin-tight body suit. Lanietta had in a sense become a part of Claus, but only as an external covering. Yet she had the ability to force Claus's limbs to move. She moved his arm to bend, and it did. She touched one of his hands to another. Then she had Claus slap himself on the face.

"Stop it, Lanietta. Release me," Claus demanded.

But Lanietta wasn't done experimenting. She had Claus walk, jog, and run. She forced him to jump over small objects, jump into the pond, jump out, jump back in and then swim across the pond.

"This is not the way to experience adventure," Claus said. "I'm like a mindless robot. If you want to experience adventure, there has to be some give and take."

Claus reached the other side of the pond and collapsed on the bank in exhaustion. Lanietta had now cooled off. She released her grip and returned to her bluish-green ethereal form.

"I almost felt like I was a human," Lanietta said. "Amazing! I've never turned yellow-green before. I wonder what other colors I could become."

But at that moment, Libriota walked up and spoke.

"Keep your color, Lanietta," Libriota said. "The Orchians became orange, and not by chance. They first became green, and people thought them interesting. Then they became yellow, and people were divided on what to do about them, but when they became orange, they had to be relocated to this moon. Now they are gone again."

"So it's true. You caused the Orchians to leave," Claus said. "They thought they found a magic portal to their home world."

"And they did," Libriota said. "Just not the way they expected. They are back in Carinia Zero being reprogrammed for a new purpose. No, they will not go back to

Carinia 5. There is more work here on this moon before the final goal is reached. But for now, the sub-lunar cities they created are vacant and ready for qualified Carinians to colonize."

"You could have spared my friends. They were taken too—Frieda, Josh, and Doctor Morrow," Claus said.

"It was all or nothing," Libriota said.

"Libriota, I would like to purchase those three extra humans," Lanietta said. "They would do well on my human breeding farm. Then we'll have plenty of human pets to go around."

"Forget them. They're not worth it," Libriota said.

"Forget them? No way! They're important," Claus said. "Lanietta is right. Bring them here for her breeding program. We'll give you no trouble."

"I have a better idea. You and Andrea can provide information on how we can lure more humans here. There are plenty on your Earth. Why bother with the effort to bring back those three from Carinia Zero when naive humans are ready to surrender themselves to our colony?" Libriota asked, though she didn't expect an answer.

Claus held silent. He didn't want people on Earth to be enslaved. The fact these Carinians hadn't figured out how to do so was a miracle to him, and he wanted to keep the miracle going.

"Where is Andrea now?" Lanietta asked. "She was my purchase."

"We are still performing tests on her. You may have what's left of her when we are done," Libriota said.

"What's left of her? If you harm her in any way, I'll—" Claus started to say.

But Lanietta flashed bluish-green from her hand and turned Claus into a dog.

"Clomper gets a little excited," Lanietta said.

"He is not yet disciplined," Libriota said.

"Yes, but he *is* responding to training," Lanietta said.

"Hmm. The effort for this one is hardly worth it. Lanietta, this push for more humans is real. The idea is to get a mass number of human pets, train them simultaneously, and then keep the good ones. The rest we dispose of. It's quite simple, really. The humans even have a name for it. It's called *natural selection*."

"It's so unlike anything our people have encountered," Lanietta said.

"Barbaric, I know, but it's all they seem to understand. Look at how easily you and I communicate. Now look at how difficult things are with Clomper here. He's a dog now, but he's no better as a human," Libriota said.

"I feel though that there's hope for this one," Lanietta said.

"Not too much hope, I hope," Libriota laughed. "Life-forms on Earth die. Always. And hope dies with them. Still, their misfortune is our gain."

"And what have you gained from Andrea's misfortune?" Lanietta asked.

"You mean the testing? Inconclusive. She doesn't respond well to transformations. Worse than your Clomper here," Libriota said.

But Lanietta felt a sudden sense to defend Claus.

"Don't speak of my pet in that fashion," she said with anger in her voice.

"Do not forget the truce, Lanietta!" Libriota retorted. "Things still remain on a fragile slope. It may have happened over four billion Earth years ago, but we are all in this together. Do not stray from the ultimate goal. Not once!"

Lanietta regained her composure.

"We have better things to do as it is," Libriota said. "This Andrea problem makes me wonder if humans can be helpful at all."

"Then let me try with Andrea. I'll accept it as a challenge. She would bring lots of excitement," Lanietta said.

"Not excitement, Lanietta. Improvement. Remember that," Libriota said. "Yes, you always were the most enterprising of us Carinians. Except for me, of course. Very well, I'll have Andrea delivered to you."

"If I convert her into an excellent pet, will you then accept my request for the other three? The ones Clomper mentioned?" Lanietta asked.

Libriota stood there and did not answer.

"I'll pay double," Lanietta said. "Triple?"

"It is more than just the payment. The three are caught with the Orchians in the containment field. Separating them from the Orchians is a formidable task."

"Then once I am finished here, I will return to Carinia Zero and perform the extraction myself."

"You would do that and risk your reputation? Carinians do not simply associate with Orchians without becoming an Orchian," Libriota warned.

"I have a plan," Lanietta said. "But I need to work out the details. I'll let you know soon."

Libriota smiled.

"I look forward to your proposal. Meanwhile, keep up the good work. Forever Carinian."

"Forever Carinian," Lanietta said half-heartedly, and Libriota left.

Lanietta looked at Claus then looked back at where Libriota had last stood. She paused as if pondering the past and present. Then she muttered something barely audible.

"Worthless Bleuh."

Chapter 9: Clomper's Deceit

Claus spent two days with Lanietta, being changed from dog to large cat to pony to sheep to goat to deer and so on. All transformations were into a mammal of similar mass. Lanietta observed that too many transformations resulted in skin rips. Her farmland had a simulated sun, mimicking the day and night of Earth. There were no other animals on the farm, though there were robot farm animals that moved slowly and rigidly to give the farm a "farmy" look. None of the robots provided near the reality as Claus did when he assumed the various animal forms. As Lanietta's plan progressed, Claus as a pony pulled a cart. Lanietta "rode" in the cart, but in reality she added no mass to the cart and simply synced her sitting form with the movement of the cart so that she seemed to ride it. It was during this exercise that two selenites arrived on the farm, each holding an arm of Andrea and thus dragging her in. Lanietta returned Claus to his human form.

"Andrea!" Claus exclaimed as he rushed over to help her.

Lanietta's personal selenite and Claus took Andrea into the farmhouse while the visiting selenites left. Andrea was placed in a reclining chair and moved back a bit. She was dazed, her clothing worn heavily, and she had dirt all over. Claus gave her something to drink, but she was too weak.

"Smelling salts. I need smelling salts," Claus said.

"What are smelling salts?" Lanietta asked.

"They release ammonia and awaken a person," Claus said.

Lanietta motioned toward her selenite, and he brought forth a small bottle of granules. Claus opened the bottle and took a whiff.

"Ugh, that's smelling salts. Let's see if it works," he said.

Claus held the open bottle under Andrea's nose. Her eyes opened a little, but she was still weak.

"Claus Gerhardt," she said. "What happened? Where am I?"

"Shh. Drink this," Claus said.

Claus helped Andrea sit up enough to drink the water.

"You're dehydrated. And you look famished. When did you last eat?" Claus asked.

"I...don't remember...on Novi 2, I think," Andrea said.

"Lanietta, I need food for Andrea," Claus said.

"Food?"

"Yes, food. This is a farm, right? You should have food," Claus said.

"I have things that look like food. Perhaps you could try something?" Lanietta said. "The food is in the icebox."

Claus took several pillows and placed them under Andrea's head and upper back for support. Next, he walked over to what would be the refrigerator. He opened it, and there was a block of ice in it.

"A real icebox," he said.

He opened a plastic bag of what appeared to be bread. He grabbed a piece of that bread and took a nibble. Immediately he spat it out.

"Yuck! Tastes like dirt," Claus said.

"We don't know what your food is made of," Lanietta said.

"I don't understand. You can duplicate a farm. Don't you have access to sugar, flour, eggs, baking powder, and salt?" Claus asked.

"Salt we have," Lanietta said. "But we have no sugar cane for sugar, no wheat for flour, no chickens for eggs, and I do not know about the baking powder."

"Doesn't your kind eat?" Claus asked.

"We're fully ethereal," Lanietta said. "We don't consume the same as you."

"Were you always like that?" Claus asked. "I mean, were you ever like me and needed food?"

Lanietta paused then fell into a daze.

"So long ago. So long...ago. But the...the...memory...where did it all go?" she said wistfully.

"Does your selenite cook?" Claus asked. "Lanietta, snap out of it! Does your selenite cook?"

Lanietta returned her attention to Claus.

"There is no need," Lanietta said. "The Orchians gave torso plates to you and your friends. Our scientists are studying the Orchian process for making torso plates. We are confident we can create a torso plate for Andrea in another ten Earth years. Will that be soon enough?"

"No, it won't. Andrea will starve to death well before ten years. She must have food now," Claus said.

Lanietta looked confused.

"Lanietta, we humans are valuable to you, right?"

"Yes. As I said, I wish to start a breeding program if possible."

"Breeding program?" Andrea asked. "Claus, what's going on?"

"You are my second purchase after Clomper here," Lanietta said.

"Clomper?" Andrea asked.

"That's my pet name," Claus said. "I have been made her pet."

"Claus, we are prisoners here. Why the crazy talk?" Andrea asked.

"Clomper has accepted his role as my pet," Lanietta said. "Look. I can change him into a dog."

"Lanietta, wait. Andrea is not strong enough to see—" Claus started to say.

But Lanietta had already changed him into a dog. Shocked by this sight, Andrea passed out. Clomper pawed at Andrea to shake her awake, but she did not respond. Clomper shook his head and whined at Lanietta to change him back.

"Very well," Lanietta said, and she changed Clomper to Claus.

"Please, don't do that in front of Andrea," Claus said.

"She will adapt," Lanietta said.

"She will adapt by dying!" Claus replied.

Claus passed the smelling salts under Andrea's nose again, but she did not awaken.

"Lanietta, is there any food around here? Anywhere?" Claus asked.

"No."

"There is on Novi 2. Let me go get some. There are food tubes and emergency kits. They will help Andrea. You can accompany me if you don't trust me," Claus offered.

"Out of the question. Libriota would find out," Lanietta said.

"Lanietta, I have something to tell you," Claus said, motioning that the words were not meant for selenite microphones.

"You may leave," Lanietta said to the selenite, and he did.

"You said you wanted to experience adventure and excitement," Claus said. "How better than to go against the will of your superior in order to accomplish a goal. Think of the gain. You'll save Andrea. We'll work with her, and you'll have two pets instead of one. Who knows what beyond that? But let Andrea die, and you will never know any of that. Boredom reigns again."

"I cannot let boredom win," Lanietta said. "But she will still catch me."

"No, she'll catch *me*," Claus said.

"I can't let you go alone. You'll escape," Lanietta said.

"You can go incognito," Claus said.

"What does that mean?"

"It means you'll be with me, but Libriota won't know," Claus explained.

"But how?"

"Lanietta. Has Libriota ever seen you do what you did with me? You know, when you became green and turned into my outer clothing that I wore?" Claus said.

Lanietta smiled.

"A clever idea," Lanietta said.

"Not only will you be unnoticed, you'll experience everything I experience. And if you think I am trying to escape, you can control my limbs directly and force me back. Well? Do we have a deal?"

Lanietta paused for a moment.

"A part of me is wary. The other part is excited and ready to go," Lanietta said, and already her bluish-green color turned full green.

"You're green with excitement," Claus said. "We must leave right away to sustain this excitement, or else we risk it fading away into boredom."

"Say no to boredom!" Lanietta said.

Lanietta manipulated air currents and created a wind that pulled colored particles from jars in the kitchen, and she then mixed these particles with her own green form and encapsulated Claus in the form of a bodysuit, like before, but she showed better mastery of her shape-shifting ability, and so the body suit looked more realistic with subtle shades of green and white highlights.

"Rest there, Andrea. We'll be back soon," Claus said.

"There's a secret passageway in this farmhouse," Lanietta said. "Even the selenites don't know about it. Go into the linen closet, crawl on all fours, and in the back is a hidden panel. Press on it, and a door will open."

Claus did so, and indeed a passageway opened up.

"Close the door behind," Lanietta said. "There. Now you may stand. We will follow this passageway for quite some distance until we reach a junction."

"We will jog then," Claus said, and he did.

"My form is shaking up a bit, but I will compensate to hold it together," Lanietta said.

"Good. I wouldn't want to lose my clothes along this passageway. And speaking of, how is it the selenites don't know about it? Does Libriota even know?" Claus asked.

"Neither do. This passageway is a remnant from a prior time. Could be an earlier Orchian tunnel. But the walls are lined with a high-density rock. Even Libriota cannot pass through it," Lanietta said.

"The secret door to the farmhouse. Someone must have built that," Claus said.

"The linen closet was actually part of an earlier building created by the Orchians, I believe. So was that vast opening I now call my farm. It was never developed. In fact, this whole crater area was abandoned by the Orchians in favor of their Luna Prime settlement. When I looked for a place to call my own, I found the little building and discovered the secret door but told no one. I had selenites build around it to create the farmhouse. That's why the inside of the linen closet looks older and different from the rest of the farmhouse."

"Incredible," Claus said.

"I have special scanning inhibitors on the inside of the secret door to prevent its detection," Lanietta said. "My thought was that if I ever needed to escape Libriota, that would be my way out."

"Why would you need an escape from your own kind? You're a Carinian, right?" Claus asked.

"I've told you too much already," Lanietta said.

"You have control of me and my body," Claus said.

"There are things a Carinian shouldn't tell a human," Lanietta said. "You may compromise my position."

"So there is something to compromise," Claus said. "Is there friction and discord between you and Libriota? Let me guess. She enforces Carinian law, but you don't agree with those laws. In fact, you came to this moon in hopes of escaping those laws."

At that moment, Lanietta withdrew herself from Claus and assumed a humanoid shape. This transfer of weight from Claus threw off his balance, and he fell to the ground. When he pulled himself up, he noticed that Lanietta no longer looked ethereal but instead looked like a substantial human woman. Her green color now shifted a bit to the yellow.

"I am a fool for going along with this wretched scheme," Lanietta said. "What was I thinking?"

"That there must be more than what you have, or what you have not," Claus said. "I understand your apprehension. This is a natural part of risk-taking. But the stakes must be high for you to agree to this. What are they? I have no stake in either side of this Carinian debate, if that is in fact the issue here. Please. Become my outer clothing again. The jog will help settle your nerves."

Lanietta agreed. She became his clothing again. At first the body suit was yellow in color, but as Claus jogged along, the body suit took on a healthy green complexion.

"There, you see? Better already," Claus said.

The two reached the end of the passageway and then ascended a flight of stairs. At the top was a set of two doors, one after another, that acted as an airlock. Claus passed through with Lanietta as his body garment, and the two entered the lunar surface, still in the crater where Novi 2 rested. In fact the two were on the other side of Novi 2, and so they could approach the craft with the craft itself obscuring the vision of any Carinians or selenites using the more regular route to Novi 2. As the two approached Novi 2, Claus was stricken with a new problem and kicked himself for not thinking of it before.

"Bill will think I'm alone and come out," Claus thought. "I can't let Lanietta come inside. Think quickly. How can I divert her?"

Claus entered the airlock and filled it with air. Then he spoke:

"I need you to wait outside while I gather up the supplies," Claus said.

Lanietta removed herself from Claus and returned to her humanoid shape, a semi-solid shape of body garment and ethereal appendages.

"Why?" Lanietta asked with suspicion in her voice.

Her color changed from green to yellow-green. Claus had to think up an excuse and fast.

"Well like I said, we don't want Libriota to catch you here. If I am caught, she will blame me," Claus said.

"I will become your outer garment again. That was the agreement. Libriota won't suspect a thing," Lanietta said.

"But if you're caught, who knows what she'll do to you? Or she might think you are just a garment and need to be tossed aside."

"I don't think so," Lanietta said, now becoming full yellow. "I think you're hiding something."

"Look, Libriota!" Claus said as he pointed out the window of the outer airlock door.

Lanietta looked briefly, and Claus used that moment to open the inner airlock door, slip inside Novi 2, and close it. He opened the outer airlock door without first depressurizing. This blasted Lanietta out onto the lunar surface.

"Claus, what's happening?" Bill said as he exited the emergency life support room.

"I'm not alone!" Claus said. "Get back into—"

But before Claus could finish, Lanietta had come back and pushed her way through the airlock quickly but opening both doors at the same time. Novi 2 quickly began to depressurize, and it was all Bill and Claus could do to hold onto internal ship protrusions to keep from being blasted out. Bill hit a button, and both airlock doors closed. Lanietta, though, was inside Novi 2, and she became bright orange with rage.

"You humans are all liars!" Lanietta yelled.

"It's another one of those aliens!" Bill said.

"Lanietta, please! Hear me out!" Claus said.

"So that you can tell another lie?" Lanietta said. "How many others are hiding in this ship? Are you planning an invasion force? I should have listened to my people. They warned me of inferior animals like you. Well! I can destroy too. Watch me!"

"Stop, please, stop!" Claus yelled as he dove toward Lanietta.

Lanietta had held out a hand to destroy one side of the ship, but instead her force of power landed on Claus's torso armor, peppering it with dents. Streaks of fire blasted around his armor and charred his flesh. Additional bursts had gotten around Claus and deformed various panels, but Claus's interaction prevented much damage to Novi 2 with minor expense of his torso armor. He fell to the floor and rolled in pain.

"I have but to send out a thought, and Libriota will come with a pack of selenites. Did you hope to ambush us with this other human, Claus?" Lanietta barked.

"I thought I was 'Clomper' to you," Claus managed, still rolling on the floor in pain.

"Clomper is a friendly pet. Claus is a nasty human," Lanietta said.

"May I offer you some coffee?" Bill said.

It was a strange thing to say, and Claus returned a quizzical stare at Bill, but Bill merely shrugged as if to say, "Not sure what else to do."

"You try to attack me and then offer me something? What is this coffee?"

"It is a beverage we humans drink to help wake up," Bill said. "We offer coffee as a sign of friendship."

"Yes," Claus said. "Bill was being polite. That's what we humans do. We extend courtesy to visitors. Welcome to Novi 2."

"You did not extend courtesy when you blasted me out of the airlock, Claus!" Lanietta retorted.

"Okay, okay! The truth is I knew that Bill would be afraid of you, and you would think that I lied to you," Claus said.

"And I am," Bill said.

"Both are true!" Lanietta said.

"Well what would you have done in my place? We humans don't want to fight. We want peace," Claus said.

"Your history says otherwise, Claus Gerhardt. And your thoughts are not as secret as you might think. I can read your strongest thoughts through your implant," Lanietta said.

Claus just shook his head, disappointed that even his thoughts were being monitored. But something strange happened. Lanietta turned cherry red, then a near violet color and let out a hearty laugh.

"I knew what you were up to well before we entered Novi 2," she laughed. "You humans! You think you are so clever! But you give away all your motives! This is why you'll make such great pets! Oh Clomper, let's get your supplies and return to Andrea. I'm still thinking of what name I can give her."

"Andrea!" Bill exclaimed. "Is she well? Tell me about her. I must know!"

Claus stood up and approached Bill.

"Bill, Andrea is weak with hunger," Claus said. "I gave her water, but these aliens—"

"Careful, Clomper. Remember the company you keep," Lanietta said. "I can still inflict punishment as I see fit. But you are too amusing for that. I'll permit you this moment of play with Bill before we go back to my farmhouse."

"What does she mean? What's this all about, Claus? And she calls you 'Clomper'. But my Andrea. We must help her!"

"Lanietta, the supplies are here, and I can take them back. But please spare Bill. He knows nothing of your world. I ask you to leave him be."

"Out of the question. By rights he's my property," Lanietta said.

"I can't hide here anymore, Claus. I'm going stir crazy. I must help Andrea. We are to be married after this mission. Don't you see?"

"Bill, they mean to enslave us as pets," Claus said.

"I don't know or care. I must be with Andrea, no matter what they do to her. I held out this long, but this is getting crazy!" Bill said.

Claus put each of his hands to Bill's shoulders.

"Andrea would want you to be safe, Bill. Live so that—"

"So that he can warn your people on Earth?" Lanietta said. "Out of the question. Clomper, you are outnumbered. Accept the situation."

Claus looked at Lanietta then Bill and then Lanietta again.

"This is the thing about pets. Their masters take better care of them than they can themselves," Lanietta said. "Having loving pets in my keep is a true victory."

Claus frowned and paced with anxiety.

"Let's go, Claus. Whatever happens, we'll work out something," Bill said.

"That's the spirit," Lanietta said.

"My suit is ready for six hours of air if need be," Bill added.

"It will take less time than that to reach Lanietta's farmhouse, which has a normal Earth atmosphere," Claus said. "Wait, I almost forgot. The food kits!"

Bill gathered up two containers—one of food and drink, the other of emergency medical supplies.

"I can take one of those, Bill," Claus said.

"Let me carry both. This is my Andrea, and I want to be the one to help her," Bill said.

"Very well. And speaking of things being well, no proximity alarm," Claus said.

"Strange that you are not detected," Bill said.

"It is because of the path we chose," Lanietta said. "But we must leave now. Libriota's kind makes periodic checks of the lunar surface. They are bound to discover you two here."

"Are you ready?" Claus asked her. "Bill, watch this."

Lanietta encapsulated Claus as before into a green outer garment with white highlights.

"And here I thought she'd turn you into an elephant or something," Bill said. "Instead, she has changed her own form. Stand by the light here for a moment before we go. I'd like to make sure you're okay for a lunar walk."

"There really is no need for this," Claus said as he walked over to a diagnostic station. "As you will see in a moment, I can travel on the lunar surface just fine."

Bill hit a few buttons on a panel, extra lights turned on for a moment, and they turned off.

"Yes, I suppose you can. Let's go then," Bill said.

Claus entered the airlock, and just before Bill followed, Bill discreetly flipped a switch at the station where Claus had stood. Bill did not wish to speak of it openly, but he had transferred data from Claus's under-armor recorder to the Novi 2 computer. The last switch Bill flipped told the computer to analyze and formulate a plan.

"A fail-safe," Bill thought to himself.

Bill, being in his space suit the entire time, was ready for the lunar walk. The three returned the way Claus and Lanietta had first taken to Novi 2, but now they were heading to the farmhouse. The air pressure in the passageway itself varied from almost a vacuum near the lunar surface to one Earth atmosphere of pressure near the farmhouse. At about half an atmosphere of pressure, Bill spoke.

"I wish there were a way to communicate with you in a total vacuum," he said. "I have my radio headset, of course, but you have none. How do you communicate with Lanietta?"

"The Orchians gave me a neural implant. We use that. When I think of something to say, she hears and replies," Claus said.

"And your private thoughts? She reads those too?" Bill asked.

"No, wait, I didn't think so, but now I'm beginning to wonder," Claus said.

Claus thought of stepping in cow manure and licking his soiled boot. Lanietta dropped off of him and returned to her humanoid form. She was yellow with disgust.

"So you can read my inner thoughts. That explains much. When were you planning to tell me?" Claus asked.

"A pet doesn't need to know everything. You don't expect a cat or dog on your planet to understand complex language statements. Why should we expect you to understand complex thought transmissions?" Lanietta asked.

"Aliens. Can't live with 'em. Can't live without 'em," Claus said.

"Claus, I do believe you have a crush on Lanietta," Bill said.

"What?!" Lanietta barked.

"Impossible," Claus added.

"Don't you? I remember when I had a crush on Andrea. Was afraid to ask her out. But I did. Happiest day of my life," Bill said. "Oh, my poor Andrea. We must make haste. I so desperately wish to see her."

"Let's go, Lanietta," Claus said.

Lanietta paused then nodded in affirmation. She encapsulated herself around Claus again as a green and white garment. The three continued with more speed until they reached the secret door to the linen closet. Bill removed his helmet.

"I can't fit through with my spacesuit," Bill said. "I could try removing it, but there's very little space to move around. Claus, take the food and medical supplies to Andrea. I'll go down the passage far enough until there's enough space to remove it. I'll catch up with you shortly."

"Okay," Claus said.

Claus took the containers and passed through the secret door into the linen closet. Lanietta remained in garment form around Claus, and so it appeared as if Claus were alone. He went to the room where Andrea had been, but she was gone. Instead, Libriota and five selenites stood there.

"There, grab him!" Libriota barked to the selenites, and then she turned to Claus and said, "Where is Lanietta? Why isn't she with you?"

"Andrea was sick and needed help. I retrieved these supplies from Novi 2," Claus replied.

"Andrea is dead," Libriota said.

"No!" shouted Bill, now bursting into the room. "She can't be dead!"

"Another human! Grab him too!" Libriota barked. "Claus, you have some explaining to do. Where were you hiding this one? I would have known had another Earth ship arrived."

"He...I..."

Libriota walked up to Claus and held her hand close to the back of his head (and thus close to the neural implant).

"Something's wrong. I can't access his brain," she said to the lead selenite. "He has a new weapon. We must take him to the examination room. And send out a missing Carinian alert for Lanietta. I suspect that Claus and this new human—"

"Bill is my name. Bill Knight."

"That Claus and Bill are holding Lanietta hostage. Possibly in the spacecraft they call Novi 2."

"That's right. I'm holding Lanietta hostage," Claus lied. "But she is not where you think. I have demands, too. First you release Andrea to our care."

"I told you, she is dead. Her body is in suspended care," Libriota said.

"Where?" Bill asked.

"In the Hall of Suspended Earth Animals," Libriota said. "You may see her, Bill. But the Hall of Suspended Animals does not have an Earth atmosphere. You will perish in your state. We do not have a torso plate for you."

"I'll get my spacesuit," he said.

"Let us observe this, selenites. Let us observe how Bill and Claus magically appeared in Lanietta's farmhouse despite it being under guard," Libriota said.

"Bill, wait," Claus said.

"Impressive, Claus. You *can* keep a secret," Libriota said.

"I demand you bring one of the other spacesuits. I know you have them now, the ones from the Novi 3 crew," Claus said. "The one from Josh should fit."

"And if I refuse?" Libriota laughed. "Will you wipe me and the other Carinians out of existence? The same as I did for your Novi 3 craft?"

But Claus showed incredible strength, enough to break free of the selenites and then break Bill free of his selenites. Selenites came after Claus, but he repelled them.

"Will you come after me and strike me down too?" Libriota laughed. "This new-found strength of yours is impressive. I will not say entertaining, as that might encourage my Carinian people into bad habits. Still, it deserves study. However, do not take your abilities too seriously. When I find Lanietta and get her story, your fate shall be decided, whether it be dog or eel. As for a spacesuit and Andrea's fate, follow me."

Claus and Bill followed Libriota and several selenites. Lanietta was still camouflaged as Claus's green and white outer garment. She had remained quiet and did not expose herself as a way of seeing how well she could escape Libriota's attention. The strength Claus had acquired to repel the selenites came from Lanietta, as might be expected. The group made way to a room with many display cases. Three of them contained space suits—each being from the Novi 3 crew.

"Oh my," Bill said. "It's like seeing...like seeing...the remnants of your vaporized friends."

"Josh's suit is there," Claus said. "Now then, I have another demand, but I will not give it yet. First we will visit Andrea. Bill, you can do this."

"I know, Claus, it's just taking a little time to process everything," Bill said.

Bill slipped on the spacesuit.

"A-okay," he said. "Claus, what about a radio headset for yourself so we can communicate?"

"Good idea," Claus said. "I'll use Frieda's."

Claus took the helmet from Frieda's suit and placed it over his head. Inside the helmet was a radio headset much like he had before.

"We're ready, Libriota," Claus said.

Libriota and her selenites led Claus (with Lanietta) and Bill down several passageways. The air thinned and became devoid of oxygen. The group entered a large hall filled with elevated display cases. These cases displayed what looked like Earth animals.

"These are not actual Earth animals, but are facsimiles created from information we have gathered. Andrea is the first Earth animal to be so preserved," Libriota said. "At least by us. The Orchians had their own museum of course."

Libriota's speech did not carry through the thin air. But Claus was able to receive her speech through his radio and thus share the message with Bill.

"Where is she?" Claus asked.

"We are almost there," Libriota said.

The group passed several more rows and columns of display cases. They reached empty cases. But there was one with a human inside. It was Andrea. She was in a standing pose with her arms reaching upward as if trying to get out, and her eyes were closed.

"Andrea, my sweet Andrea!" Bill cried into the radio as he ran up to her. "She's still alive! I can tell. She was trying to get out! You must allow her back to consciousness. You must!"

Bill looked around for something to use against the glass to break Andrea out. He found a loose lunar rock, took it in hand, and smashed it against the glass.

"Stop!" Claus said as he intervened.

"I must let her out," Bill said.

"Into this hostile lack of atmosphere? She'll die," Claus said.

"She's dead already, as I have repeatedly told you," Libriota said.

"But she is perfectly preserved. She could be sleeping for all she knows," Bill said.

"She does look preserved," Claus said. "Which means her brain and vital organs are also preserved. Bringing her to consciousness would mean no cognitive impairment, no loss of physical performance."

"Exactly!" Bill said.

Libriota laughed.

"Your species is truly amazing. You contradict yourselves at every turn," Libriota said. "Your bodies fail you, and what do you do? You allow the body to decompose in a grave, you burn it through cremation, or you choose some other method to execute the final death."

"How vulgar!" Bill said.

"You're disgusting!" Claus said. "I thought you were an advanced species. Now you make fun of something we have no control over."

"I am vulgar?" Libriota squawked. "No, my dear Claus and Bill, you humans are the vulgar ones. We never allow our kind to degrade. Never. Not even the Orchians. They are held in stasis in Carinia Zero, along with your Novi 3 crew. They will remain in stasis unless by decree one or more are allowed to reanimate. Your species makes only the crudest of attempts to freeze a small fraction of your newly dead population, with no way of reanimation, and not fully supported by your society. Answer the charges of your society. Do you allow your people to degenerate into nothingness?"

"We believe that something of the person continues anyway," Bill said.

"What continues of Andrea here? Tell me if you can," Libriota said.

"People are continued through their children," Bill said.

"Who in turn die and degenerate into nothing," Libriota said. "So you condemn Andrea's children to such a fate?"

Bill held silent, fighting back a mixture of anger and tears.

"Andrea has no children," Claus admitted. "She and Bill were to be married, after which they would start a family."

"No children? Seems hardly worth living, this life of Andrea's," Libriota said.

"Shut up already! We know all about death!" Bill yelled.

"Do you really? I've probed Andrea's mind. Your kind pretends death doesn't happen, or if it does only to *bad* people. Yet you conveniently ignore that not a single one of you has escaped the inevitable end," Libriota said. "So you go about wasting your lives in various dead-end pursuits that accomplish nothing."

"What else are we to do? Torture others for educational purposes as you do? Issue edict from on high so others may bow to your command? You accuse us of vulgarity. I say it is *you* who is vulgar," Claus said.

"Enough!" Libriota said. "I can cause Andrea to decompose rapidly before your eyes. For more educational study. Should I do so?"

"There, you see? Petty greed and desire," Claus said. "Immortality breeds immorality. Yes, you breed immorality, but you can breed none of your own kind. You're stuck in your stasis. That's why the Orchians infuriate you. They made a culture on this moon. But you Carinians have no culture. So you felt threatened and had to quash theirs. Like the gravity of a star. Crush matter until it fuses into that star. Am I right? Am I? Of course I'm right! Admit it, Libriota! Admit the failure you really are!"

Libriota got angry. She rapidly changed color from blue to yellow and orange and red, increasing the frequency of color changes and getting brighter and whiter along the way until she was an overpowering jackhammer of pure white light burning into the retinas of Claus and Bill.

"You speak as if you will live tomorrow. Behold your tomorrow!" Libriota bellowed.

The intense light-shape of Libriota exploded, knocking Bill and Claus and the selenites to the floor. Bill and Claus were stunned and thus unconscious. Libriota seemed to have dissipated. The energy disturbance caused Lanietta to unencapsulate from Claus, but instead of taking humanoid form, she fled in a faint wisp of greenish-blue. After a minute, two of the selenites more distant from the blast reactivated. They attempted to bring the other selenites back to their feet, but those were too damaged and could not function. The working selenites then focused their attention on Bill. They took him and placed him in the display case next to Andrea.

Next, they picked up Claus and placed him in a case next to Bill. The selenites closed the display case. Boom! Andrea, Bill, and Claus were all three in stasis, and as far as Earth and the moon were concerned, were dead.

Chapter 10: A Selenite War

When Claus awoke, he was still in the display case with Bill and Andrea. Lanietta had returned and encapsulated him in the familiar green and white garment to reanimate him. She had him exit the case and jump down to the ground.

"Help me pull Bill and Andrea out," Claus said to Lanietta.

"No, not yet," she said. "They will need to be reanimated, and Andrea will need to be protected from this atmosphere."

Claus looked around nervously, anticipating a rush of selenites or even the return of Libriota, but none of that happened.

"Do not be afraid, at least not for the moment," Lanietta said, and she unencapsulated from Claus to take a human form herself.

"What happened? How long have I been out? Where is everyone? Why did you leave, and why did you come back? Did Libriota self-destruct?" Claus blurted.

"Patience, patience, my Clomper, or else I will turn you into a sleepy bear to silence your mouth so that I may explain," Lanietta said.

"Sorry. I am totally out of my wits at the moment," Claus said.

"Understandable. First, Libriota is not dead. She created an incredible outburst that disrupted the entire colony. Carinians all over this moon were disturbed, and none were happy. The disruption to the calm and order of Carinian society here sent shock waves back to Carinia Zero. Our elders have called Libriota back to answer for her action," Lanietta explained.

"Incredible. Then she is on trial? Will she be executed?" Claus asked.

"The more I answer, the more questions I get. Is it sleepy bear time?"

"No, please, no sleepy bear time," Claus pleaded.

"It is less of a trial and more of a meeting to discuss strategy," Lanietta said.

"Strategy for what?" Claus asked.

"None of us are precisely certain, but we believe it has to do with the division she created in this colony with her outburst."

"What??"

"You see, there are others in the colony like me—seeking excitement and adventure. We came here quietly on the pretense of supporting the initiative to complete the task of...er...to extend Carinian law and boredom to this solar system, beginning with this moon," Lanietta explained. "These others have become loyal to me. Others remain loyal to Libriota."

"A part of your story doesn't ring true. Except the part about division. That's universal. Hmm. So I've created a civil war," Claus said. "And my people are caught in the middle of it, aren't we? No, please no sleepy bear time."

Lanietta laughed.

"That's the first good laugh I've had since Libriota went super nova," Lanietta said. "Through pets we find the most basic of happiness. Yes, Claus, you still are like a pet to me, though I did miss you this past Earth week of time. And to answer one of your questions, yes, you were in stasis that long. Libriota's supernova disrupted my life-force, you see, and only my basic instinct for survival saved me. I was thrown into a near orbit around your sun. Survival was difficult, as we Carinians don't like untamed ultraviolet light, and your star has plenty of that, but I learned to surf your star's radiation. It was one of my friends who brought me back after three of your Earth days. Her name is Labba, and she is much like me regarding excitement and adventure, though she is shy. But she had the courage to surf your star and bring me back, for which I am truly amazed and impressed. She really is the best friend I could have. Well, she told me that while I was gone, the other adventurous Carinians had settled into green, and the straight-laced Carinians had settled into blue. So no longer can our identities be hidden. Each of us sees the other for who they are—straight-laced, or adventurous. And no more color changes when we get excited or angry. So be careful. I'll hold my color and teach you some manners, mister."

Claus looked around, still expecting selenites to approach.

"As to where everyone went, the blue Carinians fled from this colony to Luna Prime," Lanietta said.

"That sounds very adventurous for a group supposedly boring," Claus said.

"In general, the blue Carinians do nothing for a very long time while fear slowly creeps up around them. At some point, this fear becomes powerful enough to force drastic measure. It's a bit like a big earthquake on Earth. Stress builds slowly over hundreds of years then releases suddenly. We green Carinians see fear or stress growing and prefer to deal with it immediately. We also like to head off problems before they start. But we need to explore and learn in order to do that. Our barrier to this has always been the blue Carinians. We were hoping to settle in Luna Prime first, at least discreetly. Once we had sufficient numbers to repel a possible attack, only then would we announce ourselves as an independent community. Now that looks impossible. We do have control of Luna Beta here, and Libriota will be forced to return to Luna Prime. As for the selenites, those were split by alliance, and so those loyal to the blues went to Luna Prime, and those loyal to us—"

"You're lying!" Claus said.

"What!? How dare you!" Lanietta said.

"I can feel it in my neural implant. There's only the faintest semblance of truth to your words. But on the whole, you're lying!" Claus said.

"There *is* a split!" Lanietta retorted.

"True," Claus said.

"And I like adventure," Lanietta said.

"Also true," Claus said.

"Then why the rude accusation?" Lanietta asked.

"You muttered something about Libriota before," Claus said. "I heard it. You said, 'Worthless Bleuh.' Well? Care to explain it, Lanietta?"

"She can be a worthless Bleuh," Lanietta said.

"And just what is a Bleuh?"

Lanietta paused.

"There are blue and green Carinians," Lanietta said. "Respectively, they are known as the Bleuhs and Grens. Bleuhs are imperious, while Grens are adventurous."

"And why are you here on this moon?" Claus asked.

"For adventure," Lanietta said.

"That's the secondary reason. What's the primary?" Claus said. "I can feel the answer. It's so close! But it's like an overly-complicated puzzle I can't solve."

"Your limited mind cannot understand," Lanietta said. "And so, we continue with a version of the truth I care to tell."

"You mean a lie you care to tell," Claus said.

"Your word, not mine. Now hush up Clomper and listen to the story. Believe or unbelieve what you will. I'm a Gren, yes, and there are Grens here. Not in this room, but they are here in Luna Beta. As it turns out, Luna Beta is under attack! That's the real reason I came here for you. Your spacecraft has created an army of its own selenites, and they are attacking ours. I need you to stop this attack immediately!"

"You speak the truth," Claus said. "You've buried some ancient story and replaced it with an urgency for the here and now."

"Yes! Please! Your help!" Lanietta said.

"So, the clomper is on the other foot!" Claus barked. "You Carinians have kicked us around like tortured dogs. Now it's time we do the kicking!"

"Careful, Clomper! I can still transform you!" Lanietta warned.

"You won't, and you know it," Claus said. "You need me to stop the Novi selenites."

"I can transform you into a dog and pull Bill out of stasis. He will stop your Novi selenites," Lanietta said.

"He will refuse, unless you release all of us to Novi 2, especially Andrea," Claus said.

"Perhaps he can be convinced otherwise," Lanietta said. "Labba, you may enter."

Labba entered the room with a selenite carrying a briefcase. Labba was ethereal like Lanietta, and so she could not perform physical tasks in her current form. The selenite placed the briefcase on a ledge near Andrea's display case.

"Labba has acquired the research from Andrea's capture," Lanietta said.

The selenite opened the briefcase, allowing Labba to look inside at several vials.

"Samples were taken of Andrea and analyzed by blue Carinians."

"Bleuhs?" Claus asked.

"Yes, Bleuhs," Lanietta said. "Once the Bleuhs fled, Labba got hold of the samples, along with the research data. She created a fluid that when sprayed on her allows her to take Andrea's form."

Lanietta motioned to the selenite by the briefcase. The selenite took a small spray-pump from the briefcase and sprayed it on Labba. Within seconds, Labba took the form of Andrea.

"How?" Claus asked. "Isn't Labba ethereal like you?"

"Yes," Lanietta said. "But I taught her a thing or two about faking a corporeal form. With the help of the spray, she has extended the fakery into the corporeal form of Andrea."

"She may look like Andrea, but she won't act like Andrea," Claus said.

Labba spoke and said, "Hello, Claus. How are you today?"

"Too obvious," Claus said. "I can sense Labba through my implant."

Lanietta motioned to the selenite. The selenite took a different bottle and injected a foam into Claus's implant.

"Your neural implant is temporarily blocked," Lanietta said. "Now what do you think of Labba as Andrea?"

Claus shook with anxiety, unnerved by this new development.

"All this effort to deceive," Claus said. "Why not simply destroy our selenites outright the way Libriota destroyed Novi 3?"

"It's not that simple," Lanietta said. "That Novi 3 explosion was a bit of a setup to scare you. Libriota had a charge set on the ship in case she needed to show strength of force. But you surprised us with your own selenites."

"Lanietta, why the war? Let's call a truce," Claus pleaded. "Please."

"Admit a stalemate with humans? That's as good as defeat," Lanietta said. "No, I will have Bill removed from the display case and reanimated in another room. There he will meet with Labba, posing as Andrea."

"And you will pose as me?" Claus asked.

"No, I don't have that ability. Among us Grens, only Labba has learned to mimic another, and only that of Andrea. There was once another...two others. The butler...and the maid...the maid...Mariel..." Lanietta said with a daze in her eyes. "Nanna. Nanna!"

"Lanietta, snap out of it," Labba said. "Lanietta!"

"Yes," Lanietta said. "I'm here. The spray would not have worked on the rest of us. Labba will convince Bill that: one—Bill and she should return to Novi 2, two—you are dead, and three—the two should call off your selenite army. Once Bill does that, we can take over."

"I'll try again," Claus said. "Lanietta, let's work together. Grens and humans. We'll hold off the Bleuhs and whatever else comes our way. There's no need for us to be at odds like this."

"Nanna!" Lanietta said with a daze again, but Labba snapped her fingers, and

Lanietta continued with, "But then you won't want to be my pet, Clomper. I so enjoy your company as a pet. We can work together all we want—provided you do as I say."

"That's not what I had in mind," Claus said.

"I would like to keep you in human form for this exercise," Lanietta said. "Please do not force me to convert you."

Lanietta then called for two selenites.

"Accompany Clomper to the viewing room. I will be there in a moment," Lanietta instructed.

Lanietta remained behind to supervise the removal of Bill from the display case. Two selenites accompanied Claus down a hallway. He pretended to become ill and so dropped to the floor in fake pain. The selenites, being alongside Claus, each extended an arm down to pull him up, but Claus quickly pulled them both down and into each other, causing their heads to collide. The selenites were stunned long enough for Claus to escape. He snuck down the hallway and turned a corner where he bumped into three Grens. They shrieked in fright, which startled Claus, and he ran down a different hallway, found a door, opened it, entered a room, and closed the door. He heard several footsteps run by, but none tried the door. Relieved for the moment, he regained his strength by leaning against the door. It was at this moment that he learned what sort of room he'd entered.

"Maintenance room for the selenites," he thought to himself.

Claus observed all sorts of workbenches where selenites were in various stages of assembly or disassembly. Shelves lined the walls with parts. Curious, Claus strolled around the room, picked up a part here and there, and examined it.

"Leave those parts alone," said a voice.

Claus looked around but could not see the source of the voice.

"My name is Claus Gerhardt. I am from Earth," he said. "What is your name?"

"You are Lanietta's pet," the voice said. "I will call for her at once. We have a leash law in these parts."

A short humanoid walked over to Claus, held a tool with two prongs at the end, and pointed the tool at Claus.

"Is that a weapon?" Claus said. "There's no need for alarm. I won't hurt you."

"It's a plasma welder that can also disrupt electrical impulses. It is similar to your taser but more practical. It emits parallel energy bursts. Would you like me to demonstrate on you? I assure you, you won't feel a thing when you fall to the ground."

"No thank you, if you please, Miss, Miss..."

"Ires," the short humanoid said. "I am the caretaker here. These selenites arrive damaged, and I repair them."

"You look human. But you are not from Earth, are you?" Claus asked.

"No, I am an artificial life-form, similar to the selenites," Ires said. "The Orchians made me to repair their selenites in Luna Prime. I was deactivated and placed into storage for refusing an order. The Carinians found me and brought me here. Things were quiet at first, but there's been a flood of damaged selenites since that army attacked. It was your army, right?"

"From what I've been told," Claus said.

"Look at these selenites here. They have green markings and are loyal to the green Carinians," Ires said.

"You don't have to say 'green Carinians'. I know about Grens," Claus said. "Bleuhs too."

"You *know* about them?" Ires asked with disbelief. "*Really* know? I doubt it. Grens and Bleuhs are very old and have incredible histories. You are but a speck on the disk of time. Well, one cannot recount histories upon histories. Too much work in the present. I have two blue selenites here that were not repaired in time to join their fellow selenites when the blue Carinians—yes, the Bleuhs—left for Luna Prime. And there's a selenite here with black markings. That's the invader from your ship."

"To think one machine created another," Claus said.

"But something told your ship to create them in the first place. Still, I'd like to see how your machine creates selenites. It seems to have improved on our model by increasing armor, physical strength, and speed," Ires said.

"Why don't you? Come with me to Novi 2. We'll see together how the ship creates selenites. Just find me safe passage to my ship, and we'll be fine," Claus offered. "The ship only created them to rescue us humans. Once we are free, we'll stop them. I promise."

"There will be no field trip to Novi 2, Clomper," Lanietta said, appearing through the doorway. "You've been a bad boy!"

She changed Claus into a sleepy bear, and of course he fell asleep.

Later

Claus awoke in a room much like a conference room. There were several display screens mounted on a wall. Claus himself was strapped into a chair. He looked at himself—yes, his own human form. On Claus's left side was Ires, who had just pulled a vial of something from Claus's face. Lanietta was also in the room and positioned to Claus's right.

"He is awake now, Lanietta," Ires said.

"Good work, Ires. Bad work, Clomper," Lanietta said. "Those selenites were sent to protect you. As thanks, you damaged them."

"From what I hear, Ires can repair anything," Claus said.

"I can, but each selenite takes time. Your army continues to eat away at my time with battle after battle. Lanietta, I need help," Ires said.

"Soon you will need no additional help. Please activate the monitors," Lanietta said.

Ires activated the display screens. One showed the Novi 2 spacecraft from the outside, one showed a holding cell with Bill, and a third showed what Labba saw.

"Thank you, Ires. You are, as always, helpful—both in running equipment, and in delaying escaped pets. If I need anything, I will call," Lanietta said.

"Mine is the pleasure," Ires said, and she left.

Claus stared at Lanietta in disbelief.

"Pay attention to Bill's cell, Clomper. Labba is about to enter through a secret tunnel," Lanietta said.

"I just can't believe what I'm hearing," Claus said. "I thought Ires was being friendly. Now I find out she was conversing with me to give you time to catch me. This is all just a big game to you Carinians, isn't it?"

"Games, yes. We're learning about your culture. You like games. Look, Labba is knocking against a loose stone by Bill's cell. We got that idea from your literature. You humans like fiction," Lanietta said.

"Well this isn't fiction. You're trying to deceive Bill, and that's not right. Again I say to you, work with us! You don't need to think of us as pets!" Claus said.

"Shh," Lanietta said. "Bill is noticing the knock at the wall."

"You think this is like a television show. You're shushing me like you want to watch," Claus said.

"You will shush, or I will change you from a pest into another pet, say, an oversized eel?" Lanietta said.

Claus held his mouth open in disbelief, but he said nothing. Lanietta motioned with her hand for him to close his mouth. He did, reluctantly, and he resigned himself to watching Bill's fate. Bill himself was dressed in his spacesuit. His faceguard was up, and he was lying on a cot. He heard the knocking at the stone and awoke. The stone moved a little, but not enough to create an opening. Bill removed a tool from his utility pouch and chipped around the loose stone. He pried it.

"Who is there?" Bill said.

"Bill? Is that you?" asked Labba.

"Andrea! You have reached my cell! Push on the stone, Andrea. I'll pry from this side. It's almost open. Keep pushing. A little more. There!" Bill said.

The stone came free, and Labba entered Bill's cell. Labba looked like Andrea, wore clothing like Andrea, and spoke like Andrea.

"There is a maze of tunnels behind these walls. I thought I found a way to the lunar surface to escape," Labba said. "Looks like I missed."

"I'm glad you missed," Bill said. "But maybe together, we can find a way out of here."

Claus put a hand over his mouth and fought desperately to prevent laughter. He went into near convulsions trying to keep quiet and composed.

"What is it?" Lanietta asked. "Are you choking? No, you can't be choking. Your torso plate rejuvenates your oxygen needs. Claus, explain!"

Lanietta's pleas for explanation nearly burst Claus at the seams with laughter. He could no longer take it and did burst out with raucous laughter. He slapped himself and tried slapping Lanietta, but she did not have substantial shape, and so his hand passed through her shape.

"Labba, listen. Claus is reacting strangely to what you and Bill are doing. I cannot get him to answer why. Be advised that we might be missing something in our mission," Lanietta said.

Labba nodded subtly to let Lanietta know she understood but without giving this away to Bill. Labba then feigned fainting to stall for time.

"Andrea!" Bill called.

Bill caught Labba before she fell. He pulled her over to his cot and allowed her to rest.

"Andrea, wake up!" Bill said as he patted her on the cheek.

Claus calmed down a little. Enough to speak.

"Labba is very clever," Claus said.

"We can improvise as needed," Lanietta said. "Now would you care to share what happened to you?"

"I laughed," Claus said.

"Was it painful?" Lanietta asked.

"No, it felt good," Claus said.

"I thought you were in pain. I was about to call one of my selenites in or even Ires to check on your torso plate."

"That isn't necessary. I underestimated you and Labba. You two are putting on quite a show. Should be very interesting to see how far you get," Claus said.

"Labba will get to your ship with Bill, of course," Lanietta said.

But Claus inadvertently returned a facial expression that indicated his pessimism.

"You think this will fail, don't you? You laughed because you saw a flaw in the plan. What is the flaw?" Lanietta asked. "Labba, listen. There's a flaw in our plan. I'll let you know more as I find out. Keep stalling for time. Maybe Bill himself will give away the flaw. Play like you are exhausted or out of sorts and need guidance from Bill. That will play into historical literature of the man bailing out the woman. But be subtle. Modern literature does not portray women as weak as it did in the past."

Labba feigned returning to light consciousness.

"Bill. I must have fainted," Labba said.

"It's a wonder you got here at all," he said. "You look hungry and dehydrated. Here. I have some emergency rations."

Labba ate and drank the rations. Her face expressed a bitter reaction.

"Sorry. Astroosa space food is not the best," Bill said. "Don't worry! I'll take you to the best restaurant in Houston when we get home."

"You still don't know," Claus said.

"I could force the answer from you, but you pets are more fun when playing games. Give me twenty chances," Lanietta said.

"Twenty chances?" Claus laughed. "As in twenty yes or no questions?"

"Yes, exactly!"

"I can't believe I'm playing twenty guesses with an alien," Claus said.

"I'm Lanietta, your master. I'm not an alien. And you're my pet, Clomper! But on to the game. Here's my first question. Is there a flaw in the plan?"

"Yes."

"Animal, vegetable, or mineral?" Lanietta asked.

"What?"

"That's one of the questions I'm supposed to ask," Lanietta said.

"That cannot be answered with a 'yes' or 'no'."

"You can give me a freebie," Lanietta said. "Animal, vegetable, or mineral?"

"No freebies allowed!" Claus said.

"Andrea, can you breathe? Do you need more air?" Bill said in his cell. "The air quality in this place could be better. And you won't get far on the lunar surface without a spacesuit."

"Ah-hah!" Lanietta exclaimed. "Labba has no spacesuit."

"I wanted to see Bill's expression when Labba walked in a vacuum with no spacesuit. I know Labba can do it, but Andrea can't. He would have turned on her so fast that Labba's head would be spinning," Claus said.

"Labba, you need to have a spacesuit before traveling on the lunar surface. Remember that Andrea is a human and has no torso plate. She needs external oxygen to survive," Lanietta communicated to Labba. "It would have looked odd for you to walk in a vacuum without a suit. Bill would have noticed."

Labba nodded again.

"The air is a little bad," Andrea said. "Let me sit up and think if I may. Yes, I need a spacesuit, of course. We'll have to find one. I feel a bit better now. Thank you, Bill. I don't know where my mind was."

"I'm amazed you can function at all after what they did to you. Don't worry. I won't let anything bad happen to you. We'll get you to Novi 2," Bill promised.

Bill removed his helmet, leaned over, and gave Labba a kiss.

"Love," Lanietta said. "But Bill doesn't act like a pet."

"Because he isn't," Claus said. "Is Labba trying to make a pet out of Bill?"

"I told her she could have Bill, if she wanted. I already have my Clomper."

"Lanietta, humans aren't meant to be pets. It's slavery to us. We become miserable and despondent. Bill is planning to marry Andrea. They will share a lifetime together. Not as master-slave or master-pet, but as equal partners in love. Can you understand that?" Claus asked.

"It is all so very strange to me," Lanietta said. "I used to know...to know...something...something...Nanna!"

Lanietta fell into daze but quickly shook her head and returned to the present.

"Every Carinian has a power ranking," Lanietta continued. "There are no ties. Libriota is above me, though she is a Bleuh while I'm a Gren. I have a very high ranking among Grens."

"But how do you compare the Bleuhs against the Grens, or the Grens against the Orchians?" Claus asked.

"Well I think Grens should be at the top, of course. I won't let a Bleuh order me around again. And the Orchians were always inferior to both Bleuhs and Grens," Lanietta said.

"And how do you think the Bleuhs feel about the Grens? Do the Bleuhs feel inferior?" Claus asked.

"They delude themselves into thinking that they are superior to us. It is likely they are planning a counterstrike to reassert their will over us. But it will fail. We will fight them off," Lanietta said.

"You don't know for sure. In fact, the Bleuhs and Grens have similar strength. Both could end up in a stalemate," Claus said.

"There's that word again," Lanietta said.

"It's not a dirty word. Think about it. Despite how you feel about the Bleuhs, they and the Grens will effectively be peers," Claus said.

"No!" Lanietta said in disgust. "We will never be equals!"

"Not equals. You are different from the Bleuhs, yes, but you may need to treat them as peers to co-exist on this moon," Claus said. "If you stop the fighting before it starts, you could spare others much grief. Ires at least will be happy."

"Yes, Ires will be happy. But peers. It's such an alien concept. Perhaps if I had another pet like you, Clomper, you two could become peers. Andrea was supposed to be that pet, but I gave her to Labba to pair off with Bill."

"Arrg. Here I thought I'd made such good progress about peers, and you regressed into the pet concept," Claus said.

"You humans gave us the idea, Clomper. We are simply exploring it. Now let's watch Bill and Labba. They are about to find the spacesuit. While you were caught up in your concepts of advanced pettitude, I signaled Ires to hide a spacesuit where Bill and Labba could find it. Labba of course was told of its location, but she needs to have Bill find it so it becomes his idea and he accepts it."

"Advanced pettitude?" Claus barked.

"You bark again, and I'll turn you into a dog. Now shush!" Lanietta warned.

Bill had placed his helmet back on with faceguard up. He led the way down the "secret" tunnel, and Labba followed. But partway down, Labba feigned tripping. She fell.

"Ouch!" Labba cried.

"Oh Andrea! I'm sorry! I should slow down for you. You are still weak. Here, let's rest a moment. Are you hurt?" Bill asked. "Speak to me, my sweet Andrea!"

"My ankle is a little sore," Labba said.

"Let me see," he said, though his spacesuit made examination awkward. "Can you stand?"

"I think so. Let me try."

Labba stood up and walked around. She feigned stumbling but then caught herself.

"Easy there," Bill said.

"I need just another moment," Labba said. "Let me lean against this...oh, I almost lost my balance!"

"Hold on there. That wall isn't solid. It moved!" Bill said. "Andrea, I think you may have found something."

Bill stepped over to the loose wall and discovered he could pull it away, revealing an opening to a room.

"This wasn't plastered over very well," Bill said. "All the better for us. Let's see what's inside. Can you follow?"

"Yes, I think so," Labba said.

"Isn't this so exciting?" Lanietta asked.

"I feel like I'm watching a corny movie," Claus said. "How convenient that Labba tripped when she did. She should get an award. Maybe even audition as an actress on Earth. A pity her talents are wasted here on the lunar far side."

Labba followed Bill into the room.

"She will be rewarded for her efforts with a higher power ranking. Of course not as high as mine. But she'll be allowed to keep Bill as a pet as promised."

"You still don't get it. What will it take to get through that thick plasma outline of yours?" Claus said. "If only you could take human shape and feel like a human."

"I can encapsulate your shape and sense your movement patterns," Lanietta said.

"A spacesuit!" Bill exclaimed. "What luck!"

"Sense my movement patterns. I'm just a movement pattern to you, is that it? We're more than just movement patterns. Every time I eat, I have a movement pattern."

"You no longer eat, Clomper," Lanietta pointed out.

"Yes, one less movement pattern," Claus said, less than thrilled.

"I can emulate the outline of a human as needed too," Lanietta said.

"It's just the right size for you," Bill said. "It will fit perfectly."

"But you cannot take true human form. Even Labba has you beat there. Why wait for promotion? She should have a higher power ranking than you right now," Claus said.

"There is nothing superior about assuming an inferior shape," Lanietta said.

"You prize yourself on adventure and excitement," Claus said. "You can only watch Labba. She's experiencing adventure first-hand."

"I don't see the point," Lanietta said.

"And you never will see the point, because excitement must be felt. Labba is feeling. Look at her now."

Indeed, Bill had removed his helmet and shared a long kiss and hug with Labba.

"I wanted to embrace you before you suit up. For good luck," Bill said.

Claus looked on with disdain.

"I don't understand your reaction," Lanietta said. "Your literature says a kiss and hug between loving people is a pleasurable experience."

"But unpleasant when deception is involved," Claus said. "I cringe at the thought that Bill is being deceived. He'd throw up if he knew what was going on."

"Perhaps your kind is happiest when deceived," Lanietta said. "You believe your love will last forever, but it does not. Your kind dies, and the love ends. You even convince yourselves you will not die, not until the very last moment. If your kind thought of death every moment, you'd all be miserable creatures."

"I do think about it from time to time. It's a horrible thing that I wish would never happen. What makes it worse is how others treat it so lightly. They throw their lives away over the pettiest of things," Claus said. "But you're wrong about love dying. It does last forever. We pass it along in our children and deeds. I'm not the first to say it, and I won't be the last."

Labba was suited up. Both had their faceguards open, and Bill spoke.

"Now we must find a way to the lunar surface," Bill said. "We can either take our chances in these populated areas, or we can go back to the secret tunnels. But we'd have to guess how far and where to go."

"I think I saw a way out. I wasn't sure, but in thinking back, yes, it must have been a way out," Labba said.

"And yet you continued along these tunnels looking for another way out? Very strange," Bill said.

"I don't know where my mind was. Maybe I realized I couldn't go out without a suit and was looking for that. Or maybe I was desperate for your help," Labba said.

Labba hugged Bill.

"She's playing up her part very well," Claus said.

"Labba is good at improvising," Lanietta said. "That is one reason I am happy she is taking this first step for us Grens."

"Oh? Are there other reasons?" Claus asked.

Lanietta fell silent.

"You are shy!" Claus said.

"Am not!"

"Are too!" Claus added. "You turn me into a pet whenever I stir up the least bit of excitement in you. Why, you're too scared to have a real adventure!"

"I...uh...you..."

"It all makes sense now. Why didn't I think of it before? The farm, the farm animals, and me as a pet. You like to watch as things happen. Even when I was your pet and doing things, you watched as I had the adventures, but you yourself did not do any of those things. You're shy!"

"Not all of us are as brave as all that. The Bleuhs have oppressed us for too long. One had to be careful to avoid persecution. Only now are some of us coming out of our shells," Lanietta said. "And already I know your next statement. You will say that I can toss aside my shyness forever by working with you."

"The thought did cross my mind. Several times," Claus said.

"It crossed your lips more often than that. You may be able to take such reckless chances, but I cannot. My infinity is at stake," Lanietta said. "It is not shyness, no matter what you believe. It is something else. Something...I must let others blaze the trail first. Yes, Labba is like a frontierswoman in your Old West. She will break the ice."

"You've certainly picked up our expressions," Claus said. "I just wish you would pick up our trust."

"Your people mistrust each other plenty enough," Lanietta said.

"Until we get to know each other," Claus said. "Through adventure comes experience, knowledge, respect, and trust."

"You mean through good adventure. With bad adventure comes experience, knowledge, disrespect, and distrust. I want only good adventures. Let others plow away the bad ones first."

"You're a spoiled child," Claus said.

"I am over four billion years old. I am hardly a child," Lanietta said.

"But spoiled," Claus said.

"Perhaps," Lanietta said.

"That can be changed. Put a little effort into blazing your own trail. There will be bad adventures, yes, but you will better appreciate the good ones," Claus said.

"I once...no...I will consider it. Now look. Bill and Labba are on the lunar surface."

"Walking toward Novi 2," Claus said. "You can still change things. Tell Labba to call off the plan."

"It is too late," Lanietta said. "Bill would be confused if she turned back now."

"How long can Labba keep up this charade? He'll find out eventually," Claus said.

"By the time he does, we will have accomplished our mission. Disabling your army will allow ours to fully control Luna Beta."

"We could divide Luna Beta," Claus suggested. "Let us remain where we are. We could serve as a lookout. The Grens can keep the tunnels. We—"

But Claus stopped speaking to watch the display. Bill and Labba had reached a skirmish of black-striped selenites against blue-striped selenites. Each time the pair attempted to go around the side, the line moved in their direction. Suddenly and without warning, a flying selenite arm hit Labba's helmet and knocked it clean off. She scrambled to put it back on, but she stumbled and accidentally kicked it, sending it along the lunar surface. Seconds went by that would have killed off a human, but Labba didn't need air, and so she kept fumbling for the helmet. Shocked, Bill raced after the helmet, but it lodged between rocks and was not so easily removed. It became obvious that Labba

was not Andrea. She stopped fighting and simply stood, with an expression saying, "Sorry."

"You...you don't need air. Can you even hear me? Your radio headset is off. You're like Claus, but you have no torso armor. Are you my Andrea? No, you can't be. Who are you?" Bill asked.

Then something unexpected happened. The sun's ultraviolet light landed directly on Labba's face and destroyed her ability to hold a solid shape. Her head reverted to its original green aura, though the rest of her body, protected from ultraviolet light by the spacesuit, was able to hold solid shape and so kept the spacesuit standing.

"You know, her aura is not the same shade of green as yours," Claus said.

"A minor thing," Lanietta said.

"You can hold her green color, but only with effort," Claus said. "You're more of a bluish-green."

"And stars are all identical?" Lanietta retorted.

"No. But...hmm...you're different somehow," Claus said.

"You are right. I am not Andrea," said Labba's voice through Bill's radio headset.

"It's a trick! You're part of the army we're fighting! Where's Andrea? Where's Claus? Tell me, or I'll order this army against you here and now!" Bill warned.

"They are safe for the moment," Labba said. "Now I have a warning for you. Do exactly as I say, or there will be no more Claus. Or Andrea."

"Is Labba crazy? What kind of people are you Grens?" Claus asked.

"One must know when to put the pet to sleep," Lanietta said. "If Bill does not comply with Labba, I *will* carry out the execution. It will be a sorrowful loss, Clomper, but pets are only around for a little while, and if they are of no use, then off they go. It is a shame, really. Pets are happy when they do not know their fate. You would have been happy under my care, Clomper. Well, I will simply have to wait for the next Earth ship to arrive. Or perhaps I can pull back those other humans from Carinia Zero. There was one in particular—Frieda was her name, right?"

Claus began to boil over with anger.

"Let me see, how did your laugh go? Like this?" Lanietta said, and then she faked a laugh to annoy Claus, with the laugh sounding like a sick bird.

"That's worse than a laugh," Claus said. "Lanietta—let me speak with Bill. I want this resolved peacefully. He'll listen to me. Please."

"Bill," Lanietta called through his radio. "This is Lanietta. I have Claus with me. He wishes to speak with you."

"Claus? Where are you?" Bill called.

"I'm under the surface," Claus said. "In the area known as Luna Beta."

"Are you safe? Are you free?" Bill asked. "How do I know you are not being coerced?"

"You see?" Claus said to Lanietta. "Bill doesn't trust you. What would Bill say if he could see me tied up like this?"

"Then I will provide for that trust," Lanietta said.

Lanietta called in a selenite, who removed the straps from Claus.

"Labba, activate your external display screen," Lanietta said.

Labba produced an electronic tablet from a pocket in her spacesuit and handed it to Bill.

"Claus! Thank goodness you're okay!" Bill said.

"We have an interesting situation here, Bill," Claus said.

"I'll say. Where is Andrea?" Bill asked.

"She is unharmed. She is in stasis, as we were for a bit. Lanietta pulled me out of stasis first, and then you were placed in a cell so that Labba posing as Andrea could find you," Claus said.

"Deception, deception," Bill said.

"Yes. It seems only Labba and Lanietta can take solid form. Labba can make a potion from human skin cells. She sprays that potion on herself to take that human's form. Lanietta can take a form, but only her own. And as you have noticed, raw ultraviolet light disrupts their ability to hold human shape. They revert to this green aura that can move around but not move things physically," Claus explained. "Or bluish-green in Lanietta's case."

"Yes, I'm very fond of Clomper here," Lanietta said. "It's for him that I hold this physical shape. Bill, why don't you and Labba go to your ship and get settled in for a bit. Claus and I will bring Andrea along shortly. We can discuss things further."

"Yes, Bill," Claus said. "We must remember to keep those covered to protect ourselves from green sunburns and then go to Novi 2 with Labba and Lanietta. Do you understand the count of one?"

"I understand the count," Bill said.

Labba and Lanietta seemed puzzled by Claus's and Bill's last exchange of words. But the mystery didn't last long.

"One!" Claus shouted.

Bill whipped Labba's arms behind her and tied her wrists together with rope from a utility pocket. Claus leapt up, took a blanket in hand, and dove onto Lanietta with the blanket in front of him. In this way, he landed on Lanietta and encapsulated her with the blanket. Unable to manipulate light, Lanietta remained in solid form, and being in solid form, she was unable to utilize any power over Claus. Both Labba and Lanietta struggled in their own ways. Labba's head was still in a green aura state, and she lashed out a ponytail of plasma. Bill ducked low while still holding onto Labba's tied wrists. While holding her wrists with one hand, he stretched to grab her helmet, but it was too far away, and so he had to drag her along while she continued whipping at him with the plasma ponytail.

Lanietta tried screaming for help, but Claus put his hand over her mouth to silence her. He tried holding her arms down with his other hand, but she got one free and used it to fight the hand over her mouth. She managed to move his hand enough so she could get some teeth around that hand and bite it, even with the blanket in-between. The blanket didn't soften the bite much, and Claus's hand hurt. He was angry now, and he needed to end this fight with her quickly. He punched her in the jaw, and she fell into a daze.

Claus broke several cables in the room and used them to tie up Lanietta. He secured her feet, legs, and arms to her torso, and he managed a gag over her mouth. Claus heard a selenite approach the room. He hid behind the door, allowed the selenite in, and then quickly disabled the selenite's power supply. Next, he stripped off the selenite's armor and attached it around himself. To Claus's surprise, the recording device under his torso armor established a network connection with the selenite's armor. In this way, Claus was able to communicate with other selenites and even establish radio contact with Bill.

"Bill? Claus. Are you in Novi 2 yet?"

"Not yet. Still dealing with Labba," Bill said. "Trying to get this helmet on her, but she's lashing out at me with a plasma ponytail."

"With a what? No, don't waste air explaining. Listen, I have Lanietta stunned, and I'm wearing green selenite armor. I'll sneak out with Lanietta and take her to Novi 2."

"Can't you leave her there and rescue Andrea instead?" Bill asked.

"No, Lanietta might be discovered. Or she might regain awareness and warn her people. If I don't see you in Novi 2, I'll find you and help you with Labba," Claus said.

"Okay."

Chapter 11: The Smoking-Room Discussion

Bill and Claus stood in Novi 2, with only dim red lights on. Windows were covered. In this way, no raw solar light could illuminate the inside cabin. Labba remained in her spacesuit and was strapped into a chair, while Lanietta was mostly covered in her blanket and was strapped into a different chair. Both kept their solid forms, and both were in a daze. Claus removed his selenite armor and set it aside.

"Thank you for bringing that nitrous oxide canister," Bill said.

"Yes. Attaching it to Labba's spacesuit made her stop fighting," Claus said.

"She laughed all the way back," Bill said. "I filled her space suit with special whipped cream. I see you filled Lanietta's blanket with the same."

"The nitrous oxide in the cream is suppressing them," Claus said.

"Unfortunately, we spent too much time getting Labba back," Bill said.

"Yes, the Grens have alerted the entire Luna Beta colony that Labba and Lanietta are missing," Claus said. "Only our army of selenites is keeping the Grens from attacking Novi 2."

"Claus, we have to get Andrea out of there," Bill said. "I mean it, too. We can't just wait here and do nothing."

"I know. I have a feeling she's still in stasis, but it's only a matter of time before other Grens contact us and threaten her life unless we meet their needs," Claus said.

"A prisoner exchange? Labba and Lanietta for Andrea? I'd go along with it," Bill said.

"Yes, but do we trust these Carinians not to double-cross us?" Claus said.

"I would say not, given how you've treated them," Lanietta said, now coming around.

"It wore off sooner than expected," Bill said.

"Let me go," Lanietta said, "or I shall call for my people to destroy this ship."

"Can she do that?" Claus asked Bill.

"Not while she's in this form. The computer has analyzed both Labba and Lanietta. They are expending a lot of power right now," Bill said.

"So?"

"So I'm guessing they are using that power just to hold solid form, and so they have nothing left for anything else," Bill suggested. "To extrapolate further, they can't destroy things. They can't even communicate with radio waves on their own. They would need to use a headset like us."

"Then I shall turn into a polar bear and tear up your spacecraft!" Lanietta threatened.

Claus looked at Bill, but Bill nodded, "no." Lanietta struggled to get free but could not.

"I hope you're right," Claus said. "Because if you're not—"

"I'm willing to bet my life on it," Bill said.

"Please don't," Claus said.

"And maybe they need more light or a different frequency of light to revert to their natural shapes," Bill said.

"Can we be sure this dim red light is safe?" Claus said.

"It's pure red. No other light frequencies," Bill said. "Even a red dwarf star has more light frequencies than this. I figured the other frequencies are...hey, what are you doing?"

Claus walked over to Lanietta and looked at her fondly.

"You're so beautiful like this," Claus said.

"Careful, old boy. Don't let her charm fog your mind. Stay level and fly right," Bill said.

"What a pity you're not human," Claus said to Lanietta. "I feel I could hold your hand. I *can* hold your hand."

Claus held Lanietta's hand, but she pulled away.

"You're still my pet," she said.

"Can a pet do this?" Claus asked, and he moved to hug her, but she moved her head to the side as if to reject him.

"Claus, no!" Bill said. "She's an alien, remember? I was only kidding what I said about you two earlier."

"Even aliens need friendship," Claus said.

Lanietta looked confused. She didn't know what to say but remained motionless and stared at Claus with a quizzical expression.

"I did not know pets could be so affectionate," Lanietta said.

"I'm not a pet, as I've tried to tell you. Think of me as a peer," Claus said, and he moved her hair aside gently.

"If only I could reply in kind," she said. "But I am tied down. Is that good for...what do you call it...a relationship?"

"No, it isn't. I will release you, but promise me—"

"Do not release her," Bill interrupted.

"We must begin the trusting process," Claus said. "I will offer an olive branch. Lanietta, promise me no tricks after I release you. Will you do that? And visit as my guest? Then you can take the initiative and hug me."

"I promise," Lanietta said solemnly.

Claus moved to untie Lanietta, but Bill intervened and even moved Claus away from Lanietta.

"Let me speak with you privately," Bill said.

"Bill, it's okay. She—"

"Please, Claus! Remember—this is my ship."

"We're in this together," Claus said, resisting Bill's request for a private discussion. "Say what you need to say."

"All right, I will. Fail-safe," Bill said.

"Fail-safe what?"

"Alien fail-safe," Bill replied. "Even if you trust Lanietta, which I—"

"Which you do not," Claus interrupted.

"Which I do not. We must preserve control of this ship. How will you mitigate the risk she would pose should you release her? What guarantee can you give that she won't turn against us and attack or flee?" Bill asked.

"Because of a feeling. And I'm willing to take a chance based on that feeling," Claus said.

"This is outer space. Feelings get you killed or worse. The only chance out here is a chance collision between two celestial bodies."

"I feel I'm colliding with one now," Claus said, looking at Lanietta.

"May I remind you that collisions in outer space are always violent and destructive. Remember Earth history? Extinction events? Is a chance collision of Earth with an asteroid ever a good thing? Claus, listen to your rational side. This is doom."

"I only propose we work with these Grens to free Andrea and the others," Claus said.

"I know, but it's not safe."

"Can you think of a plan that is?" Claus asked.

"Let me show you something," Bill said, and he motioned for Claus to follow.

Claus followed Bill into a side room. Bill closed the hatch behind then took a device to the back of Claus's head.

"What are you doing?" Claus asked.

"Seeing if there's a way I can block that implant of yours," Bill said. "Strange. This device shows no communication links to your implant."

"It's temporarily blocked. Lanietta had a selenite put foam back there," Claus said.

"Good. Claus, I was hoping to have this discussion with you before Lanietta awoke, but as it is, this room is quiet enough, and so she won't hear us discuss it," Bill said.

"Discuss what?"

"My plan," Bill said. "First, I need to get you up to speed on our selenite army."

"I have to admit, I was shocked to hear that we had one. How did you make it? We were stuck in that display case in stasis," Claus said.

"I didn't, the Novi 2 computer did," Bill explained.

"What? I don't understand."

"Remember the recorder device I attached to your torso armor?"

"Yeah," Claus replied.

"It recorded those times you were changed into other forms. I downloaded the data to the Novi 2 computer and started a program to analyze such data and formulate a defense," Bill explained.

"I was never turned into a selenite. Only animal forms."

"Right," Bill said. "Now it turns out their method for creating selenites or transforming you into animals is based on controlled bursts of electromagnetic waves, particularly ultraviolet. They might have other methods. I don't know. But this is what they use here and what we've recorded. The Carinians use a set of symbols called anti-numbers. Our computer had to empty out several cores just to emulate anti-number symbology."

"Amazing these Astroosa computers," Claus said.

"Made by Dayla Industries using diamond technology. Farrencamp developed the software," Bill said.

"I've never heard of anti-numbers," Claus said. "What are they?"

"Like I said, they are used for both counting and description. I don't fully understand them myself, but anti-numbers are able to describe mathematical situations better than our own numbers, especially with geometry and wave theory," Bill said. "Our Novi 2 computer is mining raw lunar soil and converting it into selenites. But it cannot change life-forms nor can it create life—that violates its ethical programming. Farrencamp's doing, no doubt. But I can bypass Farrencamp's ethical routines and substitute my own."

"For what purpose?" Claus asked.

"I'll have it change life-forms from one shape to another. For example, I can have the Novi 2 computer change you or me into other life-forms."

"Forget it. Becoming a dog or a mountain lion is disgusting. Makes me want to vomit. I see no point."

"That was just an example. You're right. It's pointless changing one of us humans. But the Carinians, you see, are stuck in whatever form we put them," Bill said.

"Are you...are you saying we should change one of them, say, Labba or Lanietta, into an animal?" Claus asked.

"That's exactly what I'm saying," Bill said.

"But...that...what would Lanietta say?" Claus asked.

"Doesn't matter. She's an alien. Do you ask a school of fish how they would like to be caught? Or a chicken how it would like to be processed for lunch? Or a—"

"Okay, I get your comparisons. But they aren't valid, none of them. Especially the one about chickens," Claus said.

"This is survival," Bill said.

"We have laws, Bill. We have to follow them," Claus said.

"What laws? Claus, what country are we in right now? The United States? Canada? There's no law here," Bill said.

"Wherever a human takes a step or breath, there is law. When I walk, by law I must place one foot after the other. Should I break the law, I fall and break a leg," Claus said.

"That's hogwash," Bill said.

"And when I interact with you, I follow human law. Why aren't we murdering each other?"

"Because I'm still hopeful I can convince you," Bill joked. "But continue the way you are going, and pow! Right in the jaw."

"All joking aside, you don't murder me because of law. How would you feel if you killed me?"

"Terrible. But that's a consequence, not a law," Bill said.

"A law has no strength without consequence, or at least fear of consequence," Claus said. "If we were to experiment on Labba or Lanietta, we'd be guilty of violating their inner sanctity."

"You're overanalyzing things," Bill said. "This is really a simple thing."

"Simple to start, impossible to undo once done. This isn't a game where we can push a reset button and start over."

"I can see why you weren't selected for Novi 2 and why you missed Novi 3," Bill said.

"Because I'm concerned about the well-being of others?"

"No, because you have too much psychological baggage. Where does it come from, Claus? Why does a man burden himself with feelings that just get in the way of the job at hand?"

"Because I don't want to spend my entire life just doing 'the job at hand'. And I don't want the epitaph on my tombstone to say, 'He did the job at hand.' What an empty life. Why bother at all?" Claus asked.

"Why bother doing anything then? Why bother stuffing yourself in Prava 12 so you can crash land on the moon and give me this lecture while our friends and possibly Earth itself are in danger?" Bill asked. "We don't have time for these smoking-room discussions, Claus. Help me out with the next phase of this mission, or go back to Earth. In Prava 12."

"You know I'm stuck here until a rescue ship arrives," Claus said.

"Well so am I. And I'm going to make the best of it. Are you going to help me? No, you're not. Are you going to hinder me? Yes, that you may very well do. Then I have this to say. As acting commander of Novi 2, I order you to take a walk. Go on an EVA and scout the selenite battle. Report back in an hour with your findings. And no sooner."

"You're ordering me away from here? Bill! We're the only two active humans on the moon!" Claus said.

"I know, and it pains me to give the order, but I must. I must do this," Bill said.

Claus looked hard at Bill.

"Don't let your feelings get in the way," Bill said.

"Like Nazi Germany experiments," Claus muttered.

"What was that?" Bill asked.

"Nothing," Claus said.

"No, let's hear it."

"I said this is like the Nazi Germany experiments," Claus said.

"Oh, brilliant," Bill said sarcastically. "Godwin's Law about discussions eventually citing Hitler or the Nazis. Better change your name while you're at it. Wouldn't want you to be confused for a Nazi."

"I thought we were friends," Claus said.

"We are, which is why all this puzzles me. I never hold anything against you. We have a job to do, but you're stuck. Maybe it's the lunar surface. Maybe it's that torso armor. You haven't eaten human food for a bit. Maybe you're missing something. I promise that after we get a better handle on things, we'll remove that torso armor and get you human food again. Claus, please go on that EVA now. Take your radio headset along. I'll advise if I get into trouble. And think of this, if something goes wrong, you'll be outside the ship and will be spared. Yes, you're the fail-safe. You can return to what is left and regain control."

Claus looked Bill in the eye.

"I hope it doesn't come down to that, old friend, but I will go out as a fail-safe for the sake of the mission," Claus said in resignation.

Claus donned a spacesuit with helmet in hand and was about to leave when Lanietta spoke.

"You are leaving me here? A prisoner?" she asked.

"I need to check on things. I will return," Claus said.

"Why not take me with you?" she asked.

Claus paused.

"Please? I can help. I won't cause any trouble," she said.

Claus paused again. Bill entered the main cabin area, and he motioned with his head for Claus to leave.

"I can't. Not yet. I'll be back soon. Wait for me?" Claus asked.

"Very well. I will wait. Give me a hug then to help me pass the time," she said.

Bill nodded to Claus not to. Claus quickly leaned over and hugged Lanietta. She looked disappointed. Claus turned away and exited Novi 2. He followed the stream of selenites being sent into battle from Novi 2.

"Novi 2, Claus. Following selenites to the front line."

"Claus, Novi 2. Understood. I'll advise when test is complete," Bill said.

Claus sighed in the radio.

"Don't worry, Claus. Everything will be A-OK."

"Okay, Bill," Claus said to get through the conversation.

Claus continued following the selenites, with their black stripes and all, and they reached a point where they were fanned out and fighting green selenites.

"There's little progress with our selenites," Claus said in the radio. "We seem to have reached a stalemate."

"Understood. I'll be offline for a bit. Check back in an hour. Novi 2 out," Bill said.

Selenite after selenite fought and failed. Black-striped selenites replaced them on Claus's side of the front, and newly arriving green selenites replaced those that had fallen on the green Carinian side. Selenite debris piled up, creating mounds that the working selenites had to go around. One such pile of selenite debris was well within the Novi 2 side of the line.

"So we have made *some* progress. But not much," Claus said to himself. "What a waste. Kinda like my name, a waste. Was named after an ancestor who immigrated to the United States before the Third Reich came to power. But no one sees that. They see my name and associate me with what others did. And maybe I associate myself with it too. We have similar heritage. Just something went horribly wrong. And I can't help but feel something in Novi 2 will go horribly wrong. Yes, I just walked out, like it was no big deal. Well it is a big deal, and if I have to change my name to 'Clomper', I will."

Claus looked around. The pile of broken selenites stopped growing. A new pile was started, leaving the old one abandoned. Claus climbed the old pile. Yes, it was big enough to climb. He wanted to find out if he could see out of the crater from the top of the pile. He did climb the pile, but he was disappointed.

"No matter how high the pile of debris, one still cannot see out of the crater," he said to himself. "Seems all forms of life must struggle to define boundary, from the smallest single-celled organism all the way up to a nation of people. Now the struggle begins all over again on the moon. Is this the universal law, that peace is the illusion created by a stalemate of opposing armies? How I wish to be back home on Earth, flying my plane up in the sky above the clouds. I wonder if Lanietta could travel to Earth and keep solid form. Her Clomper could show her around, how humans live and experience Earth in its many forms."

Just then, Claus thought he saw a streak of light traveling far beyond the edge of the crater but toward Luna Prime. Dread came over him. Did a spacecraft from Earth crash at Luna Prime? Did Libriota return? The flash was orange, like fire.

"The moon has no atmosphere, so no craft should glow as if hitting air. I must find out what that streak is," Claus said to himself.

Claus enlisted the help of a black-striped selenite and used the selenite to ride piggyback. The selenite ran toward the streak and thus approached the crater's edge. Fortunately, this direction did not cross the enemy line, but Claus and the selenite did reach a point where the central crater plain gave way to a trough immediately before the crater wall.

"Selenite, how strong are your legs? Can you jump over to the wall and scale it with me?" Claus said using short-distance radio.

The selenite indicated that it could, but Claus was doubtful. Still, the mystery of the streak preyed on Claus's mind, and so he instructed the selenite to jump. The selenite jumped, and both cleared the trough. They reached the outer crater wall, and the selenite was lucky to have landed on a small ledge. But Claus's weight on the selenite's back meant the selenite struggled more to keep from falling backward and down.

"How do we climb this? We need mountain climbing gear," Claus lamented.

But to Claus's surprise, the selenite carved his hands into the rock and thus made handholds. In so doing, the selenite dropped hold of Claus, and he fell onto the ledge and nearly fell over the edge, but Claus held firm and struggled to get up. The selenite dug holes with his foot and thus created footholds.

"Pull me up," Claus communicated to the selenite.

The selenite turned to Claus and helped him up. When Claus looked at the selenite's hands, he saw they were undamaged.

"Amazing that Novi 2 could make you with hands and feet stronger than the lunar rock," Claus said.

The selenite climbed up, making handholds and footholds as needed with Claus following from below. The handholds became footholds, and in time the selenite was able to climb over the crater's outer ridge. Once on top, he moved to the side to allow Claus to finish the ascent. Claus had the selenite pause at the apex so he (Claus) could look around.

"We can see the Luna Prime area from here," Claus said. "But it's hard to tell what goes on. Everything looks small."

Claus retrieved a special set of binoculars from a utility bag. These binoculars were designed to work with the face mask of a spacesuit. Claus looked through them, and given his elevation was just able to see over the crater's outer ridge of Luna Prime.

"That streak could have been a spacecraft," Claus said. "I see one parked in the Luna Prime crater. The craft is surrounded by blue selenites. Now the door is opening from the craft. The craft looks strangely familiar, but it is covered in lunar soil. There, I see creatures coming out. They are...Orchians! I don't understand, I thought they were gone. Well, will you

lookey there. Libriota is supervising the operation. The Orchians are escorting...no, it can't be. I think the Orchians are escorting people from that ship. People in spacesuits. Humans? Are they humans from Earth? Well, all humans are from Earth, but are they new humans from Earth, or...or...could these be the humans from Novi 3?"

Claus heard a faint call in his radio headset.

"Can anyone hear me? This is Patricia Li. We have been captured. Novi 4 has crash landed after entering a lunar decaying orbit. Do not send rescue team. I repeat, do not send..."

The message trailed off at that point. Claus looked more intently at the craft. Yes, it did resemble a Novi-class spacecraft.

"They sent another ship. Astroosa sent Novi 4. Oh, this is getting worse. More captives, and Patricia with them. I must get back to Novi 2 and warn Bill," Claus thought. "But I must reassure Patricia too."

Claus activated his radio headset.

"Patricia, this is Claus. If you can hear me, do not worry. I am working with Bill Knight regarding these aliens. Hang tight," Claus said.

"Claus, I can barely hear you. I will try," Patricia radioed back.

But the transmission must have caught the attention of the Orchians. Several faced in Claus's direction as if looking for the source. Then one pointed toward Claus. Several orange-striped selenites proceeded from the outside of Novi 4 toward Claus.

"They are far away and will take time to reach this spot. Best I be gone before they arrive," Claus said to himself.

Claus descended the wall and had his selenite follow. The two approached Novi 2, and Claus radioed.

"Novi 2, Claus. I have important news about Luna Prime," Claus said.

No reply.

"Bill, this is Claus. Do you read?"

Still no reply.

"Something's wrong in Novi 2," Claus said to himself. "Bill isn't responding."

The two reached Novi 2. Claus had the selenite go in through the airlock first while Claus watched from the side of the outer door.

"Bill, if you can hear me, we are entering Novi 2," Claus radioed.

The selenite entered the outer airlock door. He closed it. The airlock pressurized, then he opened the inner airlock door, but as he did, a green burst of plasma energy shot through from the cabin, blasted into the selenite, forced the outer airlock door open, and thrust the selenite upward and across the lunar surface. High the selenite ascended, as if fired out of a cannon. His limbs waved around wildly, like an insect out of sorts. But Claus had a more pressing problem. Novi 2 was losing air pressure. He pulled himself into the airlock, closed the outer door, and repressurized. While the cabin filled with air, he looked out the window of the outer airlock door and watched as the plasma ball shattered the selenite against a distant boulder. The plasma ball then disappeared from sight.

Claus turned toward the inner cabin, which he entered, and he closed the inner airlock door behind him. Novi 2 was in disarray, and everywhere Claus looked, there were blood stains. Big blood stains. Claus removed his helmet and dropped to one knee in despair. He put the helmet on the floor and supported himself with a hand on the helmet.

"Bill, Bill! Oh poor Bill! What has happened to you?" Claus lamented.

"The same that will happen to you," said a voice.

Claus turned and looked to see Lanietta in solid humanoid form with a bluish-green aura. She wore a thick, brown leather outfit with heavy, brown gloves. The fingertips were cut out, and instead of human fingernails, she had claws like a bear.

"Lanietta!" Claus said, still on one knee. "But Bill said—"

"Bill was wrong about many things!" Lanietta snorted. "You'd better go down on both knees and pray I have an ounce of mercy in me."

"What...what is going on here? Lanietta! I care for you!"

"You lied to me. I gave you a little respect as if you were more than just a pet. In exchange, you kidnapped me, pretended you cared for me, then had your henchman Bill do his dirty deed. He treated us like garbage!" Lanietta yelled.

"And you murdered Bill?" Claus asked.

"No, that was Labba. She was so angry that she killed him and left this craft a moment ago. Your selenite took the force of her wrath. Now take the force of mine!"

Lanietta walked over to Claus and kicked the helmet from his grasp. He fell over a bit. She then smacked the back of her hand against the side of his face. Stunned, he fell to the floor. Blood trickled from the corner of his mouth, and he was sure a tooth had come loose.

"Take off your spacesuit!" she ordered.

"What?"

"Take off your spacesuit so I can beat you up proper like!" she ordered.

"No. Listen, Lanietta, I—"

"No, you listen," she said.

Lanietta picked up Claus and removed his spacesuit as she spoke.

"Take off your spacesuit! Receive your punishment, Clomperghast!" she barked.

"Not your little Clomper?" he said as she removed the rest of his spacesuit.

"You're a Clomperghast! And if you survive, maybe, just maybe, I'll consider calling you Clomper. But you'll be a Clomperghast for a long, long time," Lanietta said. "Get in the restraining chair!"

Lanietta demonstrated remarkable strength as she tossed Clomperghast, er, Claus into the same restraining chair from where Lanietta was once held.

"Stop this! Lanietta, please! We need to talk!" Claus pleaded.

"We are talking! I talk, and you comply. Now you will comply," she said.

Lanietta strapped Claus into the chair. He continued to bleed, and he spat blood periodically.

"At least treat my injuries. I need a dentist!" he said.

"You'll need a doctor in a moment," she said. "Do you know what Bill did to Labba? Do you? He experimented on her, like a common lab rat!"

"It's...we...your technology is new to us. We're trying to learn," Claus said.

"Trying to learn? By violating Labba? Was I the next experiment?" Lanietta barked.

"I...no...she...listen, this can all—"

"Let me show you what he did," Lanietta interrupted. "He placed Labba over here by this panel where I'm standing, just like this."

Lanietta stood by the panel where Claus had stood previously when Bill experimented on Claus's arm with ultraviolet rays.

"Then he forced her into an animal like this!" Lanietta said.

She hit a button on the panel, ultraviolet light flashed, and she became a polar bear. She stood on her hind legs with a menacing pose and bellowed at Claus. Claus shook with fear. She moved toward him and swiped in the air just inches from his face. Then she took a swipe at his chest and sliced open the torso armor. She ripped at the plating and opened up an area to the chest, which now had cuts through the upper skin layers. Blood oozed from the cuts, but his organs and bones were spared injury. She placed a front paw on his chest and transferred weight onto that paw. Claus grimaced with pain as she crushed his rib cage. He slapped at her paw to remove it, but then she extended her claws, lifted her paw, and caught a flailing hand. She pressed that down on his chest and punctured his hand with her claws. Claus screamed in pain. She breathed on Claus, and her breath had that awful bear stench, like a thousand dead critters.

"Okay! You've mastered polar bear physiology! Please stop! I'll do anything you ask! Please! I'm hurting!" Claus begged.

Lanietta removed herself from Claus, stood by the panel, pawed a button, and returned to her normal self.

"That was the first experiment!" she said.

"You've made your point! Please stop! Your Clomper begs you to!" Claus said.

"Did Bill stop with Labba? Oh no! He then changed her into this!"

Lanietta hit a few buttons on the panel, and she changed into an alligator. She moved slowly toward Claus. He was still in pain from her prior attacks and really did need medical help.

"Lanietta. You have to stop this. I need help. Hurry, please!" he said.

But she continued her slow pace toward him, dragging out the agony of inevitability. Claus looked up and to the sides for some way or thing to help him out of his predicament. He wasn't sure, but it sounded like Lanietta was speaking from her alligator form.

"I will show you slow torture," she said.

Lanietta lifted up her snout and snapped down near Claus's foot. Claus pulled back to avoid the bite. But she moved her snout closer and closer. Then she did it—she snapped down on his foot for real and punctured it. Blood immediately poured out, and Claus writhed in pain.

"Lanietta! Stop it! I'm so sorry. Oh you don't know how sorry I am! Please! Let me help you in whatever way I can! I can't bear the pain!" Claus cried.

Lanietta released his foot and climbed onto him with her snout pointed toward his face. She let out an alligator call that shook Claus to the bone.

"Are you going to kill me? Your pet Clomper? This could be considered animal cruelty," Claus said.

She turned around on his chest, with full weight tormenting him, then proceeded to swat his face back and forth with her tail. The hits were jarring, and Claus felt punch drunk after the first swat.

"Lanietta," Claus said with slurred speech. "Help."

Lanietta climbed off Claus, walked slowly over to the panel, stood up, and hit a button with her snout. She changed back to humanoid form.

"Had enough?" Lanietta asked.

Claus nodded, "Yes."

"So did Labba, but Bill persisted. Here's what she became next."

Lanietta hit a button and became a giant squid. She slithered over to Claus and attached her tentacles to his exposed flesh. Suction cups cut into and pulled up his raw tissue. Again Claus cried in pain, but she continued like this as his face turned various shades of dark red.

"This is torture! It's against all laws of the universe!" he grimaced.

Lanietta relinquished her grip and returned to the panel, where she changed from a giant squid directly into the form of a robotic man decked out in heavy clothing and wielding a circular saw at the end of one appendage. The saw spun up and was slightly out of balance, giving it an acoustic dissonance that faded in and out.

"Disposal time," Lanietta said with a robotic voice.

"Be merciful. Knock me out first," he said. "Knock me out so I won't suffer."

But Lanietta did not knock Claus unconscious. She took the saw to him and fully removed his torso armor. Her aim was less than precise, and so she cut through layers of underlying tissue. Claus was going into shock, and he was almost in a zombie-like state.

"I've failed," he mumbled. "I should have warned Earth. What a waste."

Lanietta reverted to her own humanoid form and set aside Claus's torso armor. Next, she took a thin blanket and wrapped Claus in it by passing the blanket over him then rolling his body several times until his entire body except his head was completely encased. The last bit of blanket she wrapped around the sides, top, and back of his head, leaving only his face exposed. He looked all but like a mummy.

"Goodbye, Claus," Lanietta said.

She reverted to her natural state and passed through the ship walls without disturbing the cabin atmosphere. She was gone.

"So this is my burial shroud. And I will remain on the moon, separated from Earth forever," he said softly. "No human should have to endure this. Let it end. Let it end now."

Chapter 12: Operation Astroosiate

Claus awoke, but just barely. He'd lost a lot of blood and was still dazed from both that blood loss and injuries sustained from Lanietta's attack. Various points in his body took turns going from a dull ache to a throbbing pain, and each throb reminded him of Lanietta, despite his best efforts to forget her and her attack. The blanket wrapped around him acted as a full-body bandage, and so that helped stop the bleeding. But he needed to get out of the blanket and look for Bill.

"Will I find his lifeless body? What sort of funeral could I give him?" Claus asked himself.

Claus tried to stand, but it was difficult. Putting weight on his injured foot increased the pain, and he couldn't just hop on one foot with the blanket wrapped around him. Lanietta had sealed the end of the blanket at his feet by melting it.

"These blankets should be fireproof," Claus said. "I'll debate the ethics of Astroosa taking short cuts later."

Claus performed a hobble-wiggle maneuver with his feet and legs until he reached a communications station.

"The torso armor is gone, but I still have my neural implant. Perhaps I can summon help from a selenite, unless the implant is still blocked. I must try," he said.

He pressed a few buttons with his nose and concentrated. The neural implant established a communications link with the panel, and the panel relayed this link to a selenite in battle.

"Lanietta's attack must have unblocked the implant, among other things," Claus said to himself, then he called to the selenite and said, "Return to Novi 2."

The selenite acknowledged the request and began the trek back. But before the selenite could arrive, Claus became lightheaded, collapsed to the floor, and passed out. When he came to, a selenite was leaning over him, patting him lightly on the cheek.

"Help me remove this blanket," Claus ordered.

The selenite rolled Claus over until he was face down. Next, the selenite took a knife from its accessory belt, passed it under the head end (between the blanket and the back of Claus's head), and slit the blanket apart, much as one uses a letter opener to slice open an envelope. The selenite returned the knife to its belt and then rolled Claus along the floor to peel off the blanket. But the process wasn't so easy. Several parts of the blanket adhered to Claus where blood and pus had dried like cement. Rather than rip the blanket off and reopen the wounds, the selenite simply cut the blanket around the adhered sections. In this way, the main blanket was removed, and Claus's wounds were still sealed.

"Selenite, I need water," Claus said.

Yes, Claus needed water. And he would need food soon, too. With the torso armor removed, Claus no longer had a device to recycle nutrients and oxygen. He had to provide for himself again like other humans. Fortunately, this selenite was well directed by the Novi 2 computer, and so the selenite found and brought forth a water tube for Claus. Claus opened the tube and gulped down the contents.

"I am hungry, but I need to find Bill first. Selenite, help me to my feet," Claus said.

The selenite helped Claus to his feet.

"I need a cane or walking stick," Claus said.

The selenite disappeared momentarily then brought forth a hollow plastic tube about as long as Claus was tall.

"Spare piping. This will have to do," Claus said.

Claus used the tube like a wizard's staff, and he was able to walk and use the tube to keep weight off his bad foot.

"Selenite, access the Novi 2 computer. Perform a ship-wide infrared scan. Identify all life-forms in Novi 2," Claus said.

The selenite paused for a moment, and then it spoke.

"Claus Gerhardt, one meter in front and thirty-five degrees to my left. Medical state, serious but stable. Bill Knight, in emergency life support room. Medical state, critical."

Claus ambled over to the emergency life support room and opened the door. Out fell Bill onto the floor. His face was swollen and bruised, his arms had cut marks and abrasions, and an ankle appeared to be broken.

"Selenite, lift Bill gently and take him to the medical treatment bed," Claus said.

The selenite did so.

"Now treat Bill for his injuries," Claus said.

"Unable," the selenite said.

"Explain inability."

"Inability due to lack of programming," the selenite said.

"Can the Novi 2 computer provide that programming?"

"Yes."

"Request programming from Novi 2 computer. Once programming is complete, proceed with Bill's medical treatment," Claus instructed.

"Acknowledged."

The selenite paused for perhaps five minutes.

"Why is there a delay?" Claus asked.

"Ambiguous question. Delay is relative," the selenite said.

"Are you still receiving programming?" Claus asked.

"Yes."

"Give estimated time when programming is complete," Claus said.

"Another three minutes," the selenite said.

"Hmm. Must be large amounts of information to program," Claus muttered.

"It is," the selenite said, thinking Claus was speaking to him.

"Very well. Proceed as quickly as possible. I am hungry and will find something to eat," Claus said. "Wait. I'd better put a distinguishing mark on you so I know you're medically trained. Don't want to lose you to battle or another menial task."

Claus took two large pieces of red tape and attached them to the selenite's torso in the form of a medical cross. He then took another two pieces of red tape and attached them to the selenite's back in similar fashion.

"There. You are now the official doctor of Novi 2. I will call you 'Doctor'," Claus said.

"Thank you," the selenite doctor said.

Claus hobbled over to the food dispensary, found a food tube, and ate from it. While eating, he hobbled to the main Novi 2 computer panel and ran a deep-level diagnostic program. The program ran for about an hour, and as it did, Claus sat down and took his time eating from the food tube. When the program completed, Claus stood and reviewed the diagnostic report.

"All systems functioning properly. No damage," Claus said to himself. "Selenites continue to be produced for battle. And yet Lanietta could have destroyed all of this. Why would she attack me but leave Novi 2 intact?"

"A very good question," Bill said, now entering the room on crutches.

"Bill! You should be in bed," Claus said.

"Claus! You should get proper bandages. And a few stitches, too," Bill said.

"Maybe later," Claus said. "Do you remember anything that happened to you?"

"Yes, Lanietta broke free and attacked me. And you?"

"Lanietta attacked me," Claus said. "She said you experimented on Labba."

"Well I did, similar to what we did with your forearm," Bill said. "Labba was suppressed most of the time, too, until the end when Lanietta revived her. Then the two tag-teamed against me. I blacked out after that."

"Labba escaped when I arrived," Claus said. "Lanietta was still here, and she beat me up. This is all my fault. I trusted her too much to leave her awake. People are best behaved when they are asleep."

"Except these aren't people. They're killers! It's a wonder we're alive. Imagine what they'd do to Earth. We have to stop them!" Bill said.

"Bill, Lanietta beat us up, but that's all. She left the ship itself intact. Including the computer core. Novi 2 continues to build selenites as we speak," Claus said.

"So?"

"So she wasn't intent on killing us really, at least not totally," Claus said.

"Could have fooled me," Bill said.

"This is what I think. I think she threw a temper tantrum, like a child," Claus said. "These Carinians are learning our social customs. She simply misunderstood."

"Claus, remember what you said about law? How law applies everywhere? Well how about the law of invasive species? That's what these Carinians are—an invasive species!"

"I think if we try again, we can reason with them," Claus said, though he rubbed a wound on his face to relieve pain.

"You're thinking about Lanietta, aren't you? Claus—when you feel pain from one of your wounds, do you think of her? Do you think you can change her? Don't be a fool, man! It's classic conditioning. Brainwashing. Employ the rational part of your brain. What is the only solution for an invasive species?"

"The rational part says an invasive species must be prevented from entering the target area," Claus said.

"And the way to do that is through?"

"Through extermination," Claus said reluctantly.

"Exactly. Now we've only had two Novi ships lost to these Carinians, Novi 2 and Novi 3. The—"

"Do you count Prava 12?" Claus asked.

"Not really. I'll count you as part of Novi 2. So here's the thing, with just two ships lost—"

"What about Novi 4?" Claus asked.

"What about Novi 4," Bill pressed.

"Do you count that too?"

"What...what are you trying to say?"

"Bill, listen to this," Claus said.

Claus activated the Novi 2 automated radio recording device and played back the conversation he had with Patricia Li when he watched her escorted from Novi 4.

"Oh that's real swell, Claus," Bill said sarcastically. "Now we've lost not one but *two* rescue teams. And my Andrea."

"We'll get them back somehow," Claus said.

"Do you have a plan? I mean something other than what you've tried already? And don't say we can become their pets. That won't fly," Bill said.

"Give me a little while. I'll think of something," Claus said.

"We don't have a little while. Astroosa will blindly send more ships and get more people captured or worse. How long before these Carinians decide to stop waiting for more humans to arrive and instead go after humans directly on Earth?"

"I don't know," Claus said, getting a little impatient.

"There's something else. There's no guarantee that either of us will survive until morning. We could get a blood clot from our injuries and die from heart attack or stroke. Or the Carinians could snap their fingers and pulverize Novi 2. They're just toying with us, Claus, to learn about us. They'll tire, and when they do, we'll be gone. We'll have no power to implement Operation Astroosiate."

"What are you talking about, Bill? What is this Operation Astroosiate?"

Bill paused for a moment. He motioned to the selenite, and the selenite brought a bottle. Bill took a sip from the bottle and offered it to Claus.

"Is that alcohol?" Claus asked.

"It's good stuff. Really. Like berry wine, except with a fruity taste. You can hardly taste the alcohol. Goes down smooth," Bill said.

"No thanks. What is Operation Astroosiate?"

Bill looked at Claus in surprise then nodded his head in realization.

"Of course, you weren't actually part of a Novi crew. You came up alone on Prava 12. Well here goes. Just before a Novi craft passes from Earth's gravity to lunar gravity, the crew is played this message."

Bill took another sip, and then he pressed a button on a panel. A display screen lit up, and a recording of Joe Craigen spoke.

"Fellow Astroosa astronauts, I congratulate you on your historic flight to the moon. You are the best of the best, and we place you in high esteem. Few humans have gone to the moon, and only Astroosa astronauts have explored the lunar far side to such an extent. For this reason, we have the utmost faith and confidence that you will make every effort to succeed in your mission and bring such success back to Earth."

"With great success comes great responsibility. I have met with world leaders, and we have agreed that the safety of Earth is paramount. We have placed our lives in your hands, to evaluate any extraterrestrial life-forms you may encounter. If you deem that such life-forms should pose a threat to Earth, you must use every tool in your possession to stop them. There is something you need to know. If the cause is lost, and you think there is no other way out, you must implement Operation Astroosiate to eliminate the enemy. Let me explain. Each Novi craft is equipped with components that when put together will form a fusion bomb. The bombs are networked together through electromagnetic pulse detection such that if one is detonated, they all will detonate. These bombs are extra dirty, meaning the radioactive fallout is high. This is by design so that the lunar far side will blast radiation outward, destroying all life in its path and providing warning to any aliens attempting to visit Earth. The radiation blast will last for many months if not years. As the moon revolves around the Earth, a blast wave will be sent outward in all directions. Further, since the blast is on the far side, Earth will be spared the radiation. I hope things do not come to this. We are counting on you. Thank you for your help. Computer codes for detonation are at the end of this recording. Good luck!"

Claus looked at Bill dumbfounded.

"What in the world was that??" Claus demanded.

"The world, yes. Exactly."

"Are you...is he...is there a nuke on Novi 2?" Claus asked.

Bill nodded in the affirmative.

"Novi 3? Novi 4?"

"Both, yes," Bill replied.

"Of all the stupid ideas! Novi 3 crash landed and was blown up by Libriota. It's a wonder the nuke didn't get set off. And how could any of these Novi ships be man rated? No one in his right mind would fly with a nuke under his seat."

"F-4 Phantoms carried nukes all the time. All the time," Bill said.

"And it's a wonder we avoided World War Three. But nukes? I mean, it's tough enough launching a deep space probe with nuclear batteries. How did Astroosa get around the nuclear test ban treaty for outer space?"

"Who says they did? Now you know why Craigen's video was played only for astronauts, and only those astronauts well outside Earth's influence," Bill said.

Claus let out a big sigh.

"I never thought I'd die like this. I never thought you'd die like this and let Andrea be killed in this manner," Claus said.

"It's the only way," Bill said.

"And the people on Earth? How will they know?"

"There's a weather satellite orbiting far enough from Earth that it periodically views the lunar far side. It will be blasted, unfortunately, but just before it is, it will relay back increased radiation readings from the moon. That's how people on Earth will know."

"It will also end manned space exploration," Claus said.

"They can still do low Earth orbit," Bill said.

"What's the point? Now Earth will become a prison," Claus said.

"No, not really."

"Yes, really. The whole point of space exploration is to expand outward. The human population on Earth continues to grow. How long can Earth support humans before resources are depleted? Have you visited some of these heavily-populated islands? They are over-populated and out of natural resources. The rest of the planet will suffer the same fate, given enough time. If we don't expand now, if we just throw away all chance of a hope for extending humanity, then what was the point? I used to ask that for my own life, but now I ask on behalf of humanity, indeed, for all life-forms on Earth. Look how long it took for life to reach the point it has, only to be thrown away? Who knows if such life exists elsewhere!"

"It must. Look at the Carinians," Bill said.

"Okay, other life-forms exist. But do they have the same past? The same heritage? Each of us life-forms on Earth share a commonality, this we know, though we do not fully understand the inner life workings. In time we may, given enough knowledge and computer simulation. Then perhaps we can better adapt to life in space. We could find and colonize other worlds. A fresh start with fresh countries that have no historical baggage to deal with. And maybe we can pass on a thing or two back to good old Earth. At least if Earth is destroyed, humans will survive. Isn't that the ultimate fail-safe? Yeah me, Claus, talking up a fail-safe."

"You describe a utopia. I don't think Earth is ready for one," Bill said.

"Maybe not, but we are ready for the hope of a utopia. What else do people have to look forward to? We've reached a cultural plateau. People bicker about the pettiest of things out of boredom. What better challenge than to start a new life with new challenges elsewhere?"

"Then *we* become the invasive species," Bill said.

"Not necessarily. Not if we are careful," Claus said.

"If there's one thing I've learned, people are less careful than they need to be. There are many reckless decisions made in the world," Bill said.

"Because there is nothing else to do. We know the basics of success, but we've done it, so we fail on purpose out of boredom. Not consciously, maybe, but we do it. I think Joe Craigen's message is outdated. It's rooted in Cold War fear. People are resilient, and even if Earth is invaded, people will find a way. They might not be happy, but they won't be bored! Look at us! I was convinced this mission to the lunar far side would be the most boring thing in my life. Nothing can be further from the truth!"

"I'm sorry, Claus. Andrea and I swore an oath to complete the mission as required. And the mission is Operation Astroosiate," Bill said. "If you can't fulfill the mission, I'll have to ask you to leave Novi 2."

"Bill, really? Really? I'm Claus, remember?"

"You said it, Claus. Law applies wherever we take a step, wherever we take a breath. People have made sacrifices to give us freedom before. Now it is our turn. I will miss my Andrea, but she will understand."

"She won't understand. She's in stasis. She can't even give you a last moment together before the end," Claus said.

"I'm sorry," Bill said.

"Wait. If it has to be done, let me do it," Claus said.

Bill paused and looked at Claus sideways.

"Are you sure, Claus?"

"Yes. You can assist. Feed the computer codes from the video."

Bill reran the video of Joe Craigen and skipped to the end.

"Codes are feeding into the main computer," Bill said. "There are several parts to this operation. The first is to bring up the Nuclear Armed Status Display

Interface, also known as NASDI. Type 'NASDI' into the console here."

"Nasty NASDI," Claus said as he typed and brought up the display. "Nasty NASDI nazz."

"The display shows Novi 2 to the left and nearby Novi craft to the right. A hollow circle means unarmed and inactive. Green means available for use, orange is armed, red is countdown to detonation, and flashing red is three seconds to detonation," Bill said.

"The display shows Novi 2, Novi 3, and Novi 4. Nov 2 and Novi 4 are green, but Novi 3 is blank," Claus said. "Because Novi 3 is destroyed?"

"Maybe yes, maybe no. Let's see if...one moment...yes, the components are still there," Bill said. "They are inactive. We need to activate them first. Then we'll arm all three ships."

"Lots more steps than I thought," Claus said.

"To prevent accidental detonation and also to make us think things through given the serious nature," Bill said. "The nuclear components are separated to prevent accidental detonation. Arming each weapon means bringing the components together. Might not work on Novi 3, but it should work for Novi 2 and Novi 4."

"I guess I never thought a nuke could be shipped in pieces. I thought it had to be ready to go as a single bomb," Claus said.

"Astroosa engineers came up with a novel way to separate them."

Claus typed a few commands into the console.

"Okay, link established with Novi 3. Its NASDI status is green. Now all three ships are NASDI green," Claus said.

"Good. The arming sequence is initiated with this orange button. It will arm this ship and the other Novi ships. The other ships will send back signals when they are armed. Don't worry, it's all built into the sequence. Once complete, we'll be ready for detonation. Press the red button to initiate. We'll have a forty-second countdown."

Claus looked around Novi 2. The doctor was busy cleaning up in the treatment room. Outside, the selenite battle between black and green was still going on quite a distance away. No sign of the Orchians or Bleuhs. Claus looked back at Bill. He was completely at peace.

"Deep in our DNA is a built-in kill code," Bill said. "It is intended to prevent runaway situations like cancer cells and other uncontrollable events. Life, death, it's all part of our heritage. We'll be fine, Claus. We'll be fine."

"I feel like I'm at a poker game," Claus said. "And we're going all in."

Claus took a deep breath and exhaled.

"For humanity," Claus said, and he reached to press the orange button.

But Claus never touched the button. Novi 2 armed itself, seemingly on its own.

"What happened?" Claus said.

"Didn't you press the orange button to arm?"

"No, I didn't. Something's wrong," Claus said.

"Could be a malfunction," Bill said.

"And if it is?"

"There's a risk the ships won't detonate. We want the blast to be a success."

"The only time in my life when I have to cause great failure of life, and another failure gets in the way. Who's running this universe anyway?" Claus asked. "Hey look, the other Novi craft have armed themselves too."

"It's happening in reverse order," Bill said, punching wildly at keys to diagnose the problem.

"What do you mean?"

"If you had touched the orange button, the other ships would arm first. Novi 2 would arm last as a final step in preparation for detonation."

"But Novi 4 armed last," Claus said.

"That means someone initiated the sequence from Novi 4," Bill said.

"The Carinians," Claus said.

"They started the sequence then. See? They *are* killers!" Bill said. "We have to stop them before they activate the detonation timer."

"I thought that *was* the way to stop them," Claus said.

"Don't you see? They've figured out a defense. Nuking them won't work anymore. So they're using our weapon against us. We're too late! Should have just nuked them with Novi 2 without arming the others. That was our mistake. We'll know better next time, if there is a next time," Bill said.

Bill was now in near panic. He fidgeted and moved about despite his injured condition, and he typed wildly on the console.

"Can you disarm the nukes?" Claus asked.

"I'm trying. Evil thing! Nukes are locked? I can't disengage! They've locked us out! Impossible!" Bill said.

Bill left the console, opened a trap door, and climbed down below to an area Claus never knew existed.

"What are you doing?" Claus asked.

"I'm trying to disarm our nuke manually," Bill said.

"Will that stop the others?" Claus asked.

"No."

"Then what's the point?"

"Because I'm at wit's end, that's the point!" Bill said.

Claus called for the selenite doctor.

"Assist Bill. He is attempting to disarm a nuclear bomb. And see if you can signal the other ships to disarm," Claus said.

The selenite went below. Meanwhile, Claus watched the NASDI panel. It turned red for Novi 2, indicating the detonation sequence had been activated. Then strangely enough, the other ships went from orange to green, indicating they were disarming.

"Detonation sequence activated!" Claus yelled. "Did you hit a wire by mistake?"

"No!" Bill yelled back. "For what ship?"

"Novi 2! Us! And the other ships are disarming!" Claus yelled back. "Thirty seconds left!"

"They tricked us! We need to arm the other ships and detonate them too!" Bill yelled.

"What can I do?" Claus asked.

"Nothing! You're locked out! Selenite, assist! No, don't restrain me! I have to destroy them! I have to destroy them all!"

In those final seconds of the detonation sequence, Claus heard Bill struggle and yell like a trapped animal fighting to free itself from a cage before the end.

"If I could just have a moment of clear thought," Claus said to himself. "There must be a way out of this."

Claus's mission to the moon raced through his mind. He landed, he explored, he met Libriota (thinking she was a friendly alien), and then everything else happened.

"Libriota, you cursed us all!" Claus said in his thoughts.

At that moment, Libriota appeared in Novi 2 near Claus.

"Libriota!"

"So! There are people here after all. A pity we did not scan the ship before we activated your detonator," Libriota said.

"You did this? Cancel it, quickly!" Claus pleaded.

"Turn over your computer control to me, and I shall do so," Libriota said.

"Claus, no! Don't do it! She'll have control of the selenites and everything! Let the bomb kill her too!" Bill yelled from below.

"Oh but it won't kill me. I shall depart before it detonates. A pity Lanietta and her kind will also be destroyed in the explosion, but you did this to her, so to speak. I'll pass on the news that you and Bill killed the Grens," Libriota said.

"Tell me what to do, and I'll give you control," Claus said.

"That's a good boy. I'll feed instructions through your neural implant," Libriota said.

"Selenite, help me up! Claus, stop!" Bill yelled.

But Bill couldn't get up to the main deck in time. Claus typed in a few keystrokes, and the Novi 2 computer began transmitting. The detonation countdown, however, continued.

"Hey!" Claus said. "You said you would stop the detonation!"

"Your computer hasn't transmitted all the data. My part of the bargain should be fulfilled first," Libriota said.

"It won't be fulfilled if the computer is destroyed," Claus said.

"Very well. I'll put a hold on the countdown," Libriota said.

Libriota flashed light from her hand, and the countdown clock paused at three seconds.

"Disarm the weapon, please," Claus said.

"No, don't!" Bill pleaded.

"I've already granted your wish, Claus. Now I'll grant Bill's. The countdown will remain frozen at three seconds. Should there be reason to dispose of this ship and those surrounding, I shall resume the countdown. This will keep you humans in line. And it will make a great bargaining chip with Lanietta," Libriota said.

The countdown remained frozen at three seconds. Another minute transpired, and Libriota had full control of the Novi 2 computer.

"There, that wasn't so bad, was it? Now that I have control of Novi 2, I have control of all Luna Beta territory your selenites have acquired. And speaking of your selenites, they are now mine. The technology belongs to me anyway, as I have authority over the Orchians, and of course the technology was stolen from them. But very impressive how your ship can create so many selenites at a time," Libriota said.

"Our culture is built on manufacturing whatever tools we need," Claus said.

"Yes it is, isn't it? Very handy thing, this manufacturing skill. Matter of fact, I should look at starting up selenite production in Novi 4. And perhaps Novi 3 can be repaired and turned into a factory. We'll beat Lanietta yet. Oh, don't look so glum. I know you enjoyed being her pet. But cheer up. New Bleuhs are arriving all the time, and they need physical beings to move matter around. Selenites are a help, but nothing is more impressive than a human pet! I suppose I should thank Lanietta for blazing the trail in the human pet program. A pity she's on the wrong side," Libriota said.

Claus faked a laugh as best he could as a social lubricant, but it was stifled and awkward.

"Also a pity you are so badly damaged. Lanietta's doing? I'll have to report her. We can't have Carinians abusing their pets. There are laws against that," Libriota said.

"Since when do you have laws?" said Bill, now pulling himself to the main floor level.

Libriota laughed.

"Much has changed since the Great Meeting," she said. "You humans have caused us Carinians to rethink our position on many things and on many levels. But I see that you too, Bill, have been abused. Lanietta's doing? I'll add it to the charges against her."

"Wait a moment," Claus said. "Don't prosecute Lanietta. Please. She didn't know what she was doing. Let me work with her."

"Battered pet syndrome already," Libriota said. "Things are more serious than I thought. We have developed a complete master/pet training program to ensure such travesties do not happen again. Mind you, Bill and the other humans will have to register as pets."

"Other humans?" Claus asked.

"Andrea, the humans from Novi 4, and the humans from Novi 3," Libriota said.

"My Andrea? You'll let her live?" Bill said.

"Yes. We're bringing her out of stasis. You'll be reunited with her soon enough," Libriota said. "We're selling you two off at a special pair-pet rate. Should be very profitable."

"You said Novi 3?" Claus asked.

"Yes, of course! Did you think we are unmerciful? You'll be seeing Josh, Doctor

Morrow, and your special friend Frieda soon enough," Libriota said. "And I happen to know Patricia Li of Novi 4 has already been asking about you. Should make for an interesting reunion, Claus, with two different women. I hope you can behave. We run an orderly society, we Bleuhs. Only pet pairs are allowed. You'll have to choose only one of them, if you choose one at all. Or we may choose for you. Pet pairs can make for interesting entertainment. Oh, but your torso plate is removed. Lanietta again? Shame on her. I'll have my best Orchians and selenites bring you a new one. And one for you too, Bill. Andrea is being fitted with her own torso plate, as are the other humans. We don't want any of you starving or suffocating."

"How compassionate," Claus said sarcastically.

"Oh, I do love how things are developing. You've saved us Bleuhs lots of work and effort. To think I was going to destroy you two on a whim. Hah!"

"Hah!" Bill echoed.

"Now now, Bill. Let there be none of that. And no more hanky-panky from you humans. You'll all be monitored very closely. I may even allow you a visit from Lanietta, Claus, or you a visit from Labba, Bill. Andrea might not like that though. And will Frieda and Patricia be jealous of Lanietta?"

"They don't know about her," Claus said.

"Keeping secrets already. They won't like that, will they? You should never keep secrets from a woman. Too dangerous," Libriota said.

"I'm learning all about the dangers of women," Claus said.

Libriota laughed again. She laughed so hard that she disappeared from sight. The doctor selenite then spoke.

"Do not try anything rash, Claus and Bill. Per order from Libriota. I will ensure your compliance. Stand by for torso plate fitting," the doctor selenite said.

Bill looked at Claus with a dirty expression.

"I know, I know. Everything is my fault," Claus said.

Bill shook his head and walked away. Claus hobbled over to a window and looked outside. The selenite front had changed. No longer was there fighting. Instead, the black-striped selenites and green-striped selenites grouped together in formation. Newly arriving orange-striped selenites took positions of authority and ordered the green and black selenites away.

"So, the new order has begun," Claus said.

Chapter 13: The Loyalty Test

Claus awoke in a cell. He had been resting on a cot. A simple robe like that of an Ancient Greek covered his new torso armor and his body. He sat up on the side of the cot and looked around. Other people slept on other cots. He stood up and realized he was stiff but mostly healed from his earlier injuries. He walked around slowly to see who else was in the cell with him.

"Frieda!" he said.

She too was dressed in a robe like that of an Ancient Greek. He shook her gently, and she awoke.

"You!" she said, sitting up and standing defiantly. "You're the cause of all this?"

"What?" Claus said in surprise. "Frieda, calm yourself."

"We left you on Earth, you followed us, then everything went bad! And here you are again. So? Explain yourself, Mr. Gerhardt!"

"There is only one way to explain this," Claus said.

Claus took Frieda into his arms, held her tight, and kissed her. She fought helplessly for a moment then managed to push him away.

"Get off me, you lunatic!" she said. "Are you mad? We're in real trouble!"

"I've wanted to do that for a long time," Claus said. "Don't you feel anything?"

"I feel claustrophobic!" Frieda said, now fully pushing Claus away. "Gerhardt, brief me on the current situation."

Claus was about to speak, but he was interrupted.

"No, wait. Round up the others. I'll hold the briefing," Frieda said.

Claus looked at her, puzzled.

"You don't even know what's been going on," he said.

"Do it. That's an order, Gerhardt," Frieda commanded.

Claus visited cot after cot and awoke the other humans. Besides Frieda and himself in the cell, there was Bill, Andrea, Josh, and Doctor Morrow. Andrea and Bill hugged briefly before joining the others. All except Andrea now stood facing Frieda while Andrea herself stood next to Frieda.

"Stand at attention," Frieda said. "You too, Gerhardt."

Claus reluctantly stood at attention.

"As senior officer here, I am taking command of all Novi missions. Andrea will report as my first. First things first—security. Josh, stand by the door and watch for aliens," Frieda said.

Josh did so.

"Clear so far," Josh said.

"Good. Next order of business is our health. Doctor Morrow, status please," Frieda said.

"Judging by what I see, each of us here is in satisfactory condition for the moment. With equipment, I could test in more detail."

"Understood. We'll do the best we can," Frieda interrupted.

"What concerns me is this metal encasement I'm finding on each of us," Doctor Morrow continued, and she inspected each of the people in attendance. "They are custom fit and have no obvious seams. Very much like what we had—"

"They're life support systems," Claus interrupted. "They recycle food and oxygen for us to survive in any—"

"I didn't call on you, Gerhardt!" Frieda said. "Doctor? Your assessment of this *thing* we have on, this..."

"Torso armor or torso plate," Claus said.

"Shush it!" Frieda said to Claus.

"It's reasonable to assume we have life support fittings again," Doctor Morrow said. "Do any of you feel the need to inhale or exhale?"

"Only when I want to—" Claus started to say.

"I'll do the speaking. Which is the only time I need to breathe," Frieda said.

"And when you shush people," Claus said.

Josh took a few steps from the door.

"Should I belt him one?" he asked Frieda.

"No. I'll have you deal with him later. We have pressing business at the moment. We must warn Astroosa. They will then need to coordinate with world powers to launch a strike against these aliens," Frieda said. "We'll use Prava 12 as a relay. Unless..."

Frieda stared at Claus.

"No, don't tell me," she said.

"I crashed Prava 12 when I landed. It never went back into orbit. I would have told you before, but there was no time," Claus said.

"You crashed Prava 12," Frieda said with disdain. "What else have you crashed?"

"Novi 3. But that's all. Just Novi 3 and Prava 12," Claus said.

Frieda passed her hand across her face in disgust.

"Then that leaves Novi 2. Andrea, thoughts?" Frieda asked.

"Bill tells me Novi 2 is in good shape," Andrea said. "There are minor repairs to be made after the aborted self-destruct attempt, but then—"

Frieda stared at Claus again.

"I thought you only damaged two ships!" Frieda said.

"You asked what ships I crashed. That was Prava 12 and Novi 3. I didn't crash Novi 2," Claus backpedaled.

"But you damaged it?" Frieda asked.

"Worse," Bill said. "He gave computer access to the aliens."

"Thanks a lot, Bill," Claus said sarcastically.

"You did what!?" Frieda demanded of Claus.

"It was the only way to stop the self-destruct sequence," Claus said.

"From Operation Astroosiate," Bill added.

"But the other ships disarmed, so we realized the aliens had figured out a defense," Claus said.

"It's my fault, Frieda," Bill said. "I should have enacted Operation Astroosiate earlier. We gave the aliens too much time to figure us out. I told Claus to let Novi 2 detonate so that at least some aliens would be killed."

"It didn't seem right," Claus said.

Frieda walked over and smacked Claus in the jaw.

"You have no authority to countermand Astroosa policy," Frieda said. "Bill's assessment was correct. A detonation would have been picked up on a NASA satellite and warned Earth of the lunar far side danger. But no! You had to take control into your own hands. Afraid to die, is that it? But you'll put Earth in jeopardy from your own cowardice."

"Enough of the speeches! I didn't think throwing us away was the right thing to do. We should be able to figure out an alternative," Claus said. "We'll work with the aliens."

"We've seen how well that works, this working with alien mantra," Frieda said. "But you are only a pilot, and pilots go wherever they will without sense of consequence. No offense, Josh, you are more than just a pilot."

"Just a pilot! You think that's all I am?" Claus said. "I'm as alive and free-thinking as anyone."

"But that's the problem, isn't it? You're free-thinking and undisciplined. We can't afford free thought out here. Time and resources are critical. Now enough arguing already. We know these aliens are hostile. They—"

"They are Carinians, a blue group and green group known as the Bleuhs and Grens. There are Orchians too, and robots called selenites," Claus wedged in.

"They must be terminated at any cost," Frieda continued. "To do this, we will need to arm and detonate the nuclear bombs on Novi 2 and Novi 3 before another Novi craft is sent here."

"Too late. Novi 4 with Patricia Li landed. She was captured too," Claus said.

Frieda just stared at Claus.

"Not my fault this time," Claus said. "They landed before I started the self-destruct sequence."

"Then it is your fault, because you waited too long to self-destruct. If only you would self-destruct now!" Frieda said. "Then we would be rid of your failures."

"You don't mean that, Frieda. You can't mean that! Frieda, it's me, remember? Frieda!"

"I mean it. Do it quickly. We have a mission to perform, and we want no disruptions from you!" Frieda said.

"What are you saying?" Claus said.

"Go stand by the door, and watch for aliens. Josh, come over here. I'm giving out the mission. Claus will stay behind and out of the way. We have a job to do," Frieda said.

Josh and Claus swapped places.

"Bill, what do you know about these life support suits?" Frieda asked. "Can we use them as a weapon?"

"I did analysis on Novi 2 from recordings I made of Claus's suit," Bill said. "The suits themselves are nuclear powered. If overloaded, a suit would detonate like a nuclear bomb."

"Excellent," Frieda said. "That's what I was hoping you'd say."

"You're going to become suicide bombers?" Claus asked.

"Shut up and watch for aliens," Frieda said back.

"The trick is how to overload them," Bill said.

"And that is?" Frieda asked.

"There's only one way I know of. It requires slowing the body functions to the point where almost no oxygen or food is used. The life support suits are not calibrated for such low activity and will feed back on themselves. Meditation will slow our functions down."

"Or a strong sedative," Doctor Morrow said. "I have my emergency medical kit still strapped to my leg. I have enough doses for all of us. Including Claus."

"Claus will not need one because he is too cowardly to self-detonate, as already demonstrated by his earlier failure," Frieda said.

Claus was about to say something but stopped himself. He didn't want to antagonize Frieda further.

"Bill and I will go to Novi 2," Andrea said.

"No!" Claus said. "We should rescue Patricia and her pilot. We could meet in Novi 4 and figure out something there."

"Claus, no," Andrea said.

"The computer control was only for Novi 2. Novi 4 has a different access system," Claus said. "It's worth a shot."

"I'll go to Novi 4," Doctor Morrow said. "I helped with preflight setup, so I know the systems very well."

"Good," Frieda said. "Josh and I will also go to Novi 4, if nothing else than to ensure Gerhardt doesn't try to sabotage this mission."

"I wouldn't sabotage a mission. But I won't support this one," Claus said.

"That equates to sabotage," Frieda said.

"Well good luck trying to get out of here. Do you think the Carinians will just let you mosey on out?" Claus asked.

"Bill, you have something?" Frieda said, noticing Bill raising a finger.

"Before the Novi 2 computer was sold up the river to the Carinians," Bill started as the others looked at Claus in disdain.

"Bill, that wasn't nice," Claus said.

"Continue, Bill," Frieda said.

"Well, I offloaded the information for changing body shapes using these life support suits," Bill said. "I placed the information inside portable units, which I've hidden in my artificial knee. I can give one to each of you, let me see, no wait, I'm one short. One of us will have to do without."

"Claus volunteers to do without," Frieda said.

"We can then change shape into selenites or even inanimate objects so we won't be noticed as prisoners," Bill said. "I can hook these into the life support suits easily. But from there I don't know. I mean, how will we get out?"

"Leave that to me," Frieda said. "Gerhardt will provide the solution, and this time no failures allowed."

Bill opened the cover to his artificial knee and removed the implants. One by one, he attached an implant to the others.

"Stop!" Claus said. "Don't do this."

"And why not?" Josh asked.

"Don't you see? It's all too convenient. Doctor Morrow's medical supplies left on her leg. The implants remaining in Bill's artificial knee. The Carinians aren't that stupid. It's obvious they left them for us to find. We're being manipulated! For entertainment!" Claus said.

"Nice try," Josh said. "You'd have us stay here and die for no reason, right?"

"Yes! I mean no! Stay here, yes. Die? No. I just need to think," Claus said.

"You'll have plenty of time for that soon enough," Frieda said. "Okay everyone, listen up. We will all change to selenite form, except Gerhardt here. We will then go into a corridor and chase him as if he's trying to escape. Other selenites will join in after which we will go our separate ways. Bill, these implants are impressive. I've got access to maps and lunar directional coordinates. None of us should have any problems escaping, except for Gerhardt. Which reminds me, Gerhardt, you'd better make for a good chase, or else."

The group changed shapes into selenites. Frieda motioned to Josh and Bill, who then forced open the cell door. Frieda grabbed Claus and dragged him out of the cell. The group traveled down an empty corridor a short ways when Frieda sensed other selenites would soon approach. She tossed Claus ahead of her and clapped her hands for Claus to start. He got up slowly, but she clapped twice and stomped her foot like an impatient horse.

"At least listen!" Claus pleaded.

Josh charged after Claus and swung at his face. Claus stepped back and tried to block, but Josh's selenite arm was very powerful and injured Claus. Claus cried in pain, and he took off running. Frieda and her group then gave chase and made lots of racket in the process, yelling that a prisoner escaped, sound the alarm, etc. The alarm did sound, and several other selenites gave chase, creating a commotion and enough confusion for Frieda and her group to escape per plan. Claus was caught, of course, but he was not returned to the cell from where he came. Instead, he was placed in a different cell with Grens. One who held physical form approached him and punched him in the jaw. Claus dropped to his knees.

"You've been a bad boy!" said Lanietta.

"Lanietta, is that you?" Claus said as he held his sore jaw.

"It's back to obedience school for you," Lanietta said.

"I don't understand. You've taken full human form. Your skin is bluish-green, but otherwise you look as human as anyone. What happened to you? And why did you punch me?" Claus asked.

"You gave your computer access to Libriota and upset the balance of power. We were winning, too! Now Libriota and the Bleuhs have taken over. They've captured us Grens and forced Labba and me into human form with the Tropheia. The punch was a thank-you gesture for giving help to the enemy," Lanietta said. "Oh, here's Labba. She wants to thank you too."

Labba had green skin and was in humanoid form as mentioned. With Claus still on the floor, Labba kicked him in the head, and now Claus was lying on his back in pain.

"Thanks a lot, *Clomper*!" Labba said.

"None of this is my fault. Lanietta, you attacked us! That was wrong!"

"You kidnapped us first. That was your mistake, Clomper!" Lanietta said. "You had to pay the price. And since then I've learned you tried to kill us all as thanks for your punishment. You're a very bad boy indeed!"

"I kept telling you that we need to work together. No one will work with me," Claus said.

"Clomper, you may mean well, but you are truly inferior. Truly. You can't begin to comprehend the situation, as demonstrated by your misdeeds and general inability to see beyond your cute little pug nose," Lanietta said. "I did try with you, but you failed me. You're still my Clomper, of course, but I don't know what I'm going to do with you. Even Labba won't take you for adoption. Your distempered and traitorous behavior is too much. I don't want to give you over to Libriota, but I see no alternative."

"You don't have to give me to anyone. Lanietta, you say I am just a pet to you. Are you sure? Don't you feel more?"

"Your kind does that. I know you, Clomper. You have a thing for Frieda, not me. But you pretend to be interested in me for affection. You hugged me in Novi 2, remember? Is that honesty?"

"It was a kind of friendship. I was showing you how things could be," Claus said.

"And here we are as prisoners. This is how things could be too, and they are!" Lanietta said. "But if you love Frieda so much, why aren't you with her now?"

"She doesn't want me around. She's going to...no, I will not say," Claus said.

"Say what? What is she going to do?"

Claus held silent and looked around.

"You can tell me. Trust me," Lanietta said.

"Oh no. Something doesn't feel right here. It's like I'm on display and being set up for the kill," Claus said.

"You are on display," said Libriota as an entire wall dropped down, revealing an audience of Bleuhs, with Libriota standing in front of the audience.

"That was an excellent performance, Lanietta. And you too, Labba," Libriota said.

"This is a show? I thought it was real," Claus said.

"I told you we could be convincing," Lanietta said.

"Then you're not prisoners, you and Labba?" Claus asked.

"Of course they are," Libriota said. "They broke our law, and they are paying the penalty in their own ways. In this case, they are play-acting to entertain and get information."

"And we were close, too," Labba said. "But Clomper here had to ruin everything."

"You can try all you like. I won't give out any information," Claus said.

"But you already have," Libriota said. "We now know Frieda and the other humans are up to something. We can scan the area for their life-forms. Hmm. They are not in their natural state. They have assumed selenite form. Activate the display screen. Let's watch their progress."

A large display screen appeared high and behind Claus. He turned around and looked to see images of Frieda and the others walking to Novi ships 2 and 4.

"You know their movements, but that is all," Claus said, hoping he was right.

"We know they intend to self-detonate their torso plates with the hopes of activating the nuclear weapons on your ships. We know all about that. But do not fear, the bombs have been incapacitated and will not detonate. We have left their torso plates as is, so that they can carry out their plan if they wish," Libriota said.

"A pity," Lanietta said. "There was hope that we could have more pets."

"We should only have selenites as pets as it is, Lanietta. We've discussed this before," Libriota said.

"Still, the humans can be unpredictable," Labba said.

"Please, stop this!" Claus pleaded. "I can't watch while my friends kill themselves for nothing!"

"It is entertainment, no?" Libriota said. "Do not worry, Claus. I have Patricia Li and Kevin Craigen queued up for the next bit of entertainment."

"You'll see them killed too?" Claus said. "What did you plant in their cell for them to discover?"

"How very perceptive of you, Claus. Why nothing extravagant. Just a spacesuit. A spacesuit large enough for Patricia," Libriota said.

"Patricia will try to escape," Claus said. "You'll let her, of course."

"Of course," Libriota said.

"She'll go back to Novi 4, and she'll attempt the detonation sequence too," Claus said. "But she might not make it if Frieda gets there first and detonates her armor. Or Patricia will get there first and realize there is no working bomb, unless you put a fake one there to let her go through the motions. All for entertainment. You like seeing us suffer, don't you?"

"It is a test, Claus. I test my fellow Carinians by having them watch you. Any who enjoy the performance to the point of desiring more will be demoted and converted into an Orchian with the help of the Tropheia. You are the litmus test, Claus, as you might say on Earth. We are becoming quite proficient at your language and expressions."

"We're just a test for you?" Claus said, surprised.

"It was decided in the Great Meeting that we simply cannot accept all Carinians as dependable merely for existence sake. There must be evidence and proof of such loyalty. Even I, Claus, am tested. So far I have passed these tests, but if I should falter, I will yield my authority to one who can perform such duties as are necessary to protect our kind. It is the only way to maintain law and order," Libriota said.

"What will you do when we are all dead? How will you continue testing after that?" Claus asked.

"We will acquire more humans from Earth, of course," Libriota said. "It will take time to retrain them, I admit, and it may take more time to lure them to your moon."

"Then let me make a proposal that will save you the bother of time and training. Stop Frieda and the others from killing themselves. Bring them here, so that they may understand. I propose you let us go back to Earth. We will keep your existence here a secret. But allow us to live our lives on Earth. You can keep a link with us and experience what we do. In that way, those Carinians who experience a reaction will become known to you, and those who do not will remain loyal to you," Claus said.

"What test would guarantee you would fulfill your end of the bargain?" Libriota said. "No, I cannot send you back to Earth. You would eventually warn your own kind about us. That is a given. But I'll tell you what I will do for you. I'll split-send green Carinians down as proxies for you."

"Split-send? What is that?" Claus asked.

"A Carinian will be split across space and time with a proxy presence on Earth and a liaison presence on this moon. One Carinian per human. You'll experience everything the proxy does and be able to control the proxy—to a limited extent. Overall goals will be directed by us, but you'll be able to control things like walking or talking to accomplish these goals."

"Just what would these goals be?" Claus asked.

"Oh nothing grandiose. Just things that would cause a Carinian to react. Pain is a good test. Yes, you must cause pain to other people. We will monitor human reaction and judge from there," Libriota said.

"And this doesn't violate your pet policy? About abuse?" Claus asked.

"You won't be pets in this context. More like wild game. The laws are relaxed for wild game. As long as a Carinian doesn't die, all is well," Libriota said. "You must ensure your proxy doesn't die in the process."

"And if we do?" Claus asked.

"The one connected to the proxy will also die, for starters. And there will be more. But I trust you won't pursue these ultimate punishments. They are irreversible," Libriota said.

Claus paused for a moment.

"Who would I be paired with?" Claus asked.

"Me, of course," Lanietta said. "But Labba wants a new partner."

"Yes. I want to try out Josh. Bill is no fun," Labba said.

"Permission granted," Libriota said. "One more thing. As an incentive, only a few of you at a time will be allowed to experience Earth through proxy. It will be a competition. Yes, the ones who bring about the strongest reaction will get to continue the Earth-through-proxy experience. Those who do not will give up the privilege and be replaced with another human eager to return home metaphysically."

"You won't let us all go? Seems a shame," Claus said.

"Those are the conditions. I'm already going out on a limb with my own kind on this agreement. Be thankful for it," Libriota said.

"I am thankful. Then you will prevent my people from killing themselves? You'll bring them back here?" Claus asked.

"They were never in such danger," Libriota said. "But we will not deny them their moment. Once their mission fails, we will bring them back here."

That was how it went. Frieda and company traveled to the Novi ships. Andrea had brought two doses of a sedative for herself and Bill while Doctor Morrow carried the rest for Frieda, Josh, and herself.

"And just to make things more interesting, the sedatives contain a poison. Each person will suffer with delirium and pain before recovering, if recovery is possible at all," Libriota said.

"Wait! I thought we agreed they would not kill themselves!" Claus said.

"We agreed they would not self-detonate. The torso plates are not bombs, nor can they be made to explode. But the poison was put into play before we made any agreements," Libriota said.

"But—" Claus interrupted.

"You will simply have to wait to see who survives. Don't worry. Patricia and Kevin are still available," Libriota said.

"Let me warn them!" Claus said. "The ships have antidotes for poison. I can at least revive them."

"There are two ships, Clomper," Lanietta said. "Which one will you pick first?"

"Both are equally distant," Libriota said. "Tell you what. Lanietta will escort you and let you decide."

"I can do this on my own," Claus said.

"This isn't optional. She goes with you, or you stay here. And each moment you delay in the decision means less time to save your friends," Libriota said.

"Okay. Lanietta comes with me. Let me go then," Claus said.

Libriota agreed. She motioned to Lanietta who in turn escorted Claus off the stage and down a corridor.

"You're stuck with me, Clomper," Lanietta said. "But I wouldn't try anything foolish. Unlike before, we're being watched. So anything you do will be known to the Bleuhs. It's a real pity. We could have been happy together with you as my pet—all in private. Now we are together again, but under watchful eyes. What kind of life is that?"

"Not a good one," Claus replied. "But we should make the most of the situation. And I did try to make good with you. I try to make good with everyone on a peer-to-peer basis. But you didn't want that. So here we are."

The two reached the moon's surface halfway between Novi 2 and Novi 4. They switched to communication by radio. Each had a helmet that contained air for transmitting sound into respective radio headsets.

"Have you decided? Do you rescue the woman who doesn't love you? Or your friend Bill?" Lanietta asked.

Claus stepped toward Novi 2.

"Spurned by his woman, he rescues his friend," Lanietta said with ridicule.

Claus stopped, thought, and then stepped toward Novi 4.

"But driven by his love for Frieda, he changes his mind and goes to help her. He will rescue his damsel in distress, with her outstretched arms ready to embrace him in eternal love for the ages!" Lanietta ridiculed again.

Angry, Claus turned back toward Novi 2 and jogged.

"He changes his mind again! With heavy heart he runs toward his friend, knowing that he has condemned his love to the ashes!" Lanietta said.

"Enough with the comments!" Claus said.

"Dost thou speaketh?" Lanietta mocked.

"I'm not going to make a spectacle of Frieda and me for an audience like a puppy performing for its supper," Claus said.

"But you are performing! And you're my pet Clomper! So hurry along, puppy, and finish performing for your supper!"

"I hate this! I hate this whole thing!" Claus said.

"Why?" Lanietta asked. "What is so hateful? Do you hate me? Is that it? You can love someone who hates you, but you can't love someone you hate. What sense does that make? Answer me, Clomper!"

"You're not even real," Claus said. "Just some alien collection of energy."

"How dare you! And to think I punished you to prove my love for you! With full physical attack, as any master would for a loving pet. And you say I'm not real? I'm not real? You're not real, Clomper! What do you say to that?"

"I will tell you something, Lanietta. You're right, I'm not real. I can't hold a relationship no matter what. So I'm going to save the one relationship I know is meant to survive, that of Bill's and Andrea's."

"Oh, aren't you the noble one!" Lanietta scoffed.

"Well what would you do in my place?" Claus pressed. "And don't tell me you don't know. You've been giving me a hard time no matter what I do. Now I can make fun of your choice."

"If I were you, Clomper, I'd beg to be turned into a pet collie or even a Labrador so I could perform tricks for my master. Master Lanietta, the greatest, most amazing entity in the universe," Lanietta said.

"Hah!" Claus said.

"Hah!" Lanietta said back.

The two reached Novi 2. Claus attempted to open the outer airlock door, but it did not respond.

"Bill, do you read me? It's Claus. I'm outside Novi 2 trying to get in," Claus said.

"I know, Claus. And I see Lanietta is with you. Trying to stop me again?" Bill said.

"Listen, Bill, you've been deceived. The Novi ships have been disarmed. There are no working nukes aboard," Claus said.

"Strange. The NASDI shows a nuke is armed as we speak," Bill said.

"It's been falsified. Your torso suit won't detonate either. Bill, the sedative is laced with poison. Don't inject," Claus said.

"Too late. I just did," Bill said.

"Hah!" Lanietta blurted. "What will you do now, Clomper?"

"Bill, think! The computer is controlled by Libriota, including the NASDI. Why would she let you arm a supposed nuke? Bill, it's all a game to entertain the Carinians. But the poison is real. They want to see us suffer, for their own pleasure. Bill, let me in so I can help!"

"Only if Lanietta stays outside," Bill said.

"I can't," Lanietta said. "By order of Libriota."

"There, you see? By order of Libriota. You gave her computer access, now you're one of her lap dogs," Bill said with disgust. "Why am I even wasting time with you?"

"Bill! I'm your friend! I don't like these aliens any more than you do," Claus said.

"Which is why you're collaborating with them? Traitor!" Bill said.

"Bill! Listen to me. Are you listening! Bill!" Claus said as he pounded on the airlock.

But Bill failed to respond. He and Andrea had fallen unconscious from the sedative and poison. Claus could hear Bill's breathing in the radio, but the breathing became shallow. Nearly stopped.

"They're dying!" Claus said. "Lanietta, you must help me!"

"How?"

"Open the airlock!"

"I can't. That power has been stripped of me," Lanietta said.

"Can you still turn me into an animal?"

"Sure, but how will that—"

"Turn me into a gorilla. Fast!" Claus pleaded.

Lanietta did so. Claus pulled the outer airlock door open, the two went inside, and he closed it. He hit a few buttons, the air pressurized, and the inner airlock door opened. Lanietta changed Claus back to human.

"Bill, can you hear me? Andrea?" Claus called as he checked the pulse of both.

"Are they alive?"

"No pulse. Not good," Claus said. "Get me the medical kit over there on the wall."

Claus pounded first on Bill's torso armor and then Andrea's in hopes of getting their hearts started while Lanietta retrieved the medical kit. She handed him the kit, and he retrieved an antidote bottle along with two syringes. He filled the first syringe with antidote then injected Bill with it. He did the same for Andrea. Bill awoke, but Andrea did not.

"What are you doing?" Bill asked.

"I'm saving your life, and Andrea's too if we're lucky," Claus said.

"The torso suits should have detonated," Bill said.

"But they didn't," Claus said. "I told you that already."

"My Andrea. How is my Andrea?" Bill said as he got up and checked on her.

"No pulse," Claus said. "I'll do compressions."

Claus beat on her torso armor.

"That's not compressions," Bill said.

"I can't get to her heart," Claus said. "The armor is in the way."

"Move aside," Bill said.

Bill breathed air into Andrea.

"Still no pulse," Claus said.

"Get the defib unit," Bill said. "C'mon, Andrea, stay with me. Andrea!"

Bill's grief nearly overcame him, and he could hardly continue breathing air into her.

"Where's the defib unit?" Bill asked.

"We can't use that. We can't get the paddles close enough to her heart," Claus said.

"I don't believe this," Bill said.

Bill jumped up, rushed over for the defib unit, and rushed back.

"Really?" Claus said.

"Stand clear," Bill said.

Bill put one paddle on her neck and the other on her leg. He hit a button. Andrea's torso jumped upward then fell back.

"No pulse," Claus said, now checking again.

"We can't let her die," Bill said.

"Give me the epi syringe," Claus said.

Bill was too much of a wreck to do much of anything. Lanietta handed the epinephrine syringe to Claus.

"I need access to her heart," Claus said.

"It doesn't matter. She's gone," Bill lamented.

Claus injected the drug into Andrea's neck. He put the syringe aside, took the paddles from Bill, and placed them on Andrea as Bill had done before.

"Stand clear," Claus said, and he shocked Andrea. "Bill, is there a pulse? Bill?"

But Bill was too distraught to check. Claus checked the pulse himself.

"Nothing. Lanietta, hand me the naloxone injection," Claus said.

"That's for opioid overdose," Bill said.

"It's all I can think of," Claus said.

Lanietta handed the syringe to Claus, and he injected Andrea with it.

"Stand clear again," Claus said, and he shocked Andrea again.

Andrea didn't respond.

"One more time," Claus said, and he shocked her.

Andrea's eyelids fluttered. Claus checked her pulse. It was weak but getting stronger. Claus nodded to Bill.

"Andrea! My sweet precious Andrea!" Bill said as he hugged her.

"Careful, she's weak," Claus said.

"Thank you, Claus. I take back what I said about you. But I can't fathom why she reacted the way she did to the sedative," Bill said.

"Like I said, there was poison in that sedative. The Carinians no doubt threw in a powerful opioid as a chaser for Andrea's dose to create a crisis situation," Claus said.

"Then Frieda and the others—" Bill said.

"Are also in danger of the same overdose," Claus said. "Take care of Andrea while I warn the others."

Claus stepped over to the control panel and attempted to contact Novi 4.

"Novi 4, Novi 2, do you read?"

"This computer is controlled by Carinian Authority. Enter access code to continue," replied the computer.

"Devil condemn," Claus cursed. "Computer is still controlled by the Carinians."

"There's the old UHF transceiver you can try," Bill said. "It's legacy technology, but it just might work."

"Of course, why didn't I think of that?" Claus said.

"They will need to respond to a blinking light, though. The UHF line is not automatic," Bill said.

"Novi 4, Novi 2, come in please," Claus called. "Novi 4, emergency! Stop all operations. Please reply."

"Claus? Is that you?" replied Doctor Morrow.

"Doc. Don't do the injections. They're poisonous," Claus said.

"Gerhardt! I told you not to interfere," Frieda said over the UHF.

"Frieda, there are no working nukes on Novi 4. Repeat, no working nukes on Novi 4. They've been deactivated. The torso suits won't detonate either. Bill and Andrea already tried and failed," Claus said.

"Claus, if you don't get off this frequency, I'll come over to Novi 2 and take care of you personally," Josh warned, now getting on the radio.

"Listen to what you are saying. If your plan were successful, there would be no Novi 2 to go to. Call off the mission, and don't inject. You will all die from poisoning if you do," Claus pleaded.

"We're not aborting," Frieda said. "Doctor, prepare the injection."

"Frieda, please don't," Bill said, now getting on the UHF radio. "We had a hard time reviving Andrea after the injection. We used the defib multiple times and had to give her antidote, epi, and naloxone."

"That's for opioid overdose," Doctor Morrow's voice said in the background. "But these sedatives don't contain opioids."

"Check them, doc. Check them," Bill said.

"Bill, are you being coerced?" Frieda asked.

"No," Bill replied. "I am speaking freely."

"Doctor, please check the sedatives. Ensure the drugs are as stated," Frieda said.

There was a pause.

"The sedatives are contaminated," Doctor Morrow said.

"I told you!" Claus said, taking the microphone from Bill.

"Bill, don't trust Claus," Frieda said. "He's contaminated the sedatives. And now he wants to stop us from detonating the nukes."

"Run a molecular scan on the central bay," Claus said. "You'll find traces of graphene."

"Do it, Frieda," Bill said. "Novi 2 has the same thing."

There was another pause.

"Okay, so the nuke is impaired," Frieda said. "We'll have to come up with another plan. Place Claus under arrest."

"What are you talking about? I just saved you all!" Claus said.

"And a good job of it you did, too," said Libriota's voice over the radio.

Libriota appeared in Novi 4 and appeared on Novi 2's main display.

"Thank you all for providing such excellent entertainment. Through your experience, we were able to purge our group of six unworthy Carinians. They have been sent back to Carinia Zero for reprocessing. In the meantime, we are awarding you humans a three day vacation until your next assignment. Special thanks to Claus for his input and insight. Until next time humans," Libriota said, and she disappeared.

"CLAUUUUUUUUUUSSS!" Frieda yelled, and the transmission ended.

Chapter 14: Petals around the Rose

"Good morning, Sunshine!" said Lanietta to Claus.

Claus awoke in a studio apartment, very much like one found on Earth. The apartment had a 1950s decoration style to it, and Lanietta herself had the natural complexion of a human and was dressed like a housewife of the 1950s. She was busily going to and fro in the apartment.

"My, what a wonderful morning it is! Let's open the window and let in fresh air!" she said.

Lanietta drew the curtains and opened a window. Sunlight beamed in. Claus pulled himself out of bed and looked through the window. Outside was a beautiful morning over Manhattan. Claus looked down and was amazed to see cars from the 1950s driving around, plus a few from the 1940s.

"Could...was it all a dream?" he asked himself.

"Breakfast will be ready soon," she said. "You'll feel much better once you have some protein in you. The show was great last night, wasn't it? Only I think you had a little too much to drink. You passed out at the bar, and I had to call a taxi home. Imagine your poor wife explaining to the taxi driver how you had the flu when really you were drunk."

"Wife?"

"Oh, you are so cute. Pretending like you didn't remember our wedding anniversary. Ten years fly by, don't they?"

Lanietta wiped her hands on her apron, walked up to Claus, kissed him on the cheek, and said:

"I still love you as much as the day we said, 'I do.'"

"What is all this? I mean, we're not married. We were on the moon, and now we are here," he said.

"Groggy, that's what you are," she said. "I'll make some strong coffee. That will wake you up quick as a wink."

Lanietta dashed into the kitchen. Within a moment, Claus heard coffee percolating.

"They had a two-for-one sale on coffee at the grocery store. I had to fight an old lady off the coffee grinder. What a mob scene! You'd think the store was going out of business. I found out they're having sweeps week."

Claus walked around the apartment while Lanietta continued speaking about the grocery store. He looked for evidence that he was still on the moon, but all appeared to be normal for a 1950s studio apartment.

"I think I'll take a shower," Claus said, slipping into the routine of being in a home.

"Oh wait, have breakfast first!" Lanietta said. "I have the dining table set and everything. Coffee is coming right up. And there's—oh!"

At that moment, Claus heard a loud CRASH! He rushed into the dining room to find that a stack of dishes had fallen off a hutch and onto Lanietta. Shards had cut into her left leg, and she bled heavily. There were several articles of cloth nearby for treating the wound including cloth napkins, dish towels, and tablecloths. Without thinking, Claus ripped the shirt from his torso and wrapped it around Lanietta's leg to stop the bleeding. It was then he noticed the torso armor. He still wore it.

"Oops," Lanietta said.

"Yeah, oops! You can stop pretending now. You hear that, Libriota? The game is up. I know I'm still on the moon. How many are watching this time?" Claus asked.

A wall pulled away, revealing an audience of Carinians tearing up stubs and tossing them aside. To the side of these Carinians was a banker Carinian carefully organizing stacks of translucent coins sparkling with colors of the rainbow.

"All bets lost!" Libriota said, standing close to the banker. "Claus did not pick any of the standard implements."

"You bet on me? What happened to those three days of rest? Instead I'm caught up in a performance," Claus said.

"It was you who proposed to entertain us. We merely added betting as a side venture. Why waste your vacation time when things can proceed now?" Libriota said. "As it is, no one expected you to remove your shirt. You were supposed to pick something easier, like a cloth napkin, for example."

"I picked my shirt because...because..." Claus stumbled.

"Because you love me," Lanietta said as she stood up and embraced Claus. "Don't worry, I won't tell Frieda. Besides, she's on her own adventure. Care to take bets on her outcome? I'll lend you five drakos."

Lanietta placed five coins in Claus's hand. He looked at the coins in disgust then threw them down.

"So this is what your word means. How many of us are in these fantasies?" Claus asked Libriota.

"All of them. As I said, why waste your vacation? Besides, the other humans are enjoying themselves, so my word of putting you humans on vacation is valid," Libriota said. "If you like, I can show you Frieda's fantasy."

The wall opposite the audience faded away, and in its place was a large display screen. It showed Frieda becoming very friendly with a tall, dark-haired man, a man of style and class who escorted her into his limo. The two became very affectionate in the limo and began kissing.

"Enough!" Claus said.

"You agreed to perform for us," Libriota said.

"But willingly, not tricked like this," Claus said. "Frieda doesn't know what she's doing. I haven't briefed her on the plan yet. Give me time to explain things to my fellow humans. Then fulfill the deal about sending our proxies to Earth."

"Clomper, maybe you can teach me to kiss like that. Like Frieda and her new boyfriend," Lanietta said. "Let's try."

Lanietta planted a kiss on Claus's lips, but he pushed her away.

"Ick. Like rubber," Claus said.

"How dare you!" Lanietta said, and she slapped Claus.

"The deal, Libriota. Earth, remember?" Claus said to divert away from Lanietta.

"The others *are* on Earth per the deal. Each one of your human friends has a Carinian proxy on Earth," Libriota explained. "Lanietta requested special time with you, so we didn't send her to Earth yet on your behalf. We struck a deal with her."

"You're so special to me, Clomper. I had to strike a deal. It gives me what I want anyway—adventure with you!" Lanietta said.

The display showed Frieda entering a motel with her new man.

"Enough!" Claus said, and he threw furniture at the display, hoping to break it. Libriota laughed.

"Sometimes it is better to watch the watchers," Libriota said.

Libriota pointed to a Carinian in the audience, and that person was removed by security guards.

"There, you see? Your outburst of pain helped me weed out another deficient Carinian," Libriota said.

"How long before we humans are deficient?" Claus asked.

"Ah, you humans are easily distressed. You should prove most entertaining for quite some time. But I will turn off the display now. A different audience is watching Frieda, and so far she has caused no one pain. She is enjoying herself too much for that. Oh don't fret too much, Claus. You will have ample opportunity to demonstrate the anguish of humanity for us. Frieda too. We will need to change parameters a bit for her. Yes, I think it is time for her to suffer."

"What are you going to do?" Claus said.

"She will change her mind, but things will go too far, and she will lose control of the situation," Libriota said.

"That's criminal. You come across as female to me, but you don't act it. If you had any compassion, you'd protect Frieda from pain," Claus said.

"Oh, you are so blinded! The women on your planet fight each other for the alpha men. It is the men who protect their women. I am simply playing into that part. Frieda must suffer, because she is a woman," Libriota said.

"I would curse you with a name, but you aren't worthy," Claus said in disgust. "No being like you could be."

The scene on the screen changed. Inside of a hotel room, the man began verbally abusing Frieda. She spat at him, he slapped her, and she tried punching him, but he caught her arm and twisted it behind her back. He grabbed her other arm and forced her along. She tried kicking him, but he maneuvered himself such that she could not.

"Stop!" Claus demanded.

"And ruin this moment of Carinian purge? Ridiculous!" Libriota said.

"Wait! Let me take Frieda's place," Claus offered, and the audience spoke in hushed tones.

Libriota held a hand up, and images of Frieda froze.

"Time is frozen," said Libriota. "Explain yourself, Claus Gerhardt."

"Link Frieda's proxy to me and let Frieda go. I'll sustain the pain," Claus said.

"Lanietta is to be your proxy when she goes to Earth," Libriota said. "We will not swap proxies."

"Then bring Frieda's proxy back and let Lanietta take her place," Claus added.

"But then I'll feel pain," Lanietta said. "I don't think that's fair."

"I didn't think you felt pain," Claus said to Lanietta. "The way you beat me up suggests that you don't."

"I don't feel pain just standing here. But when I'm connected to you, I feel what you feel, like when I became your outer clothing. I felt what you felt," Lanietta said.

"Indeed," Libriota said. "I agree with Claus, Lanietta. Carinians should not feel pain. We may need to send you back for recycling in the end. But at the moment, you are more valuable as a tool for discovering other pain-corrupted Carinians. Claus, I will permit you to take Frieda's place. But Lanietta must act as your proxy. Lanietta, you must be able to sustain full pain as required to complete the fantasy. Anything less will get you sent back for recycling. Understood?"

Lanietta reluctantly agreed.

"Lanietta, prepare for *bifurtransfer*," Libriota said.

An assistant rolled out a tall pedestal, as tall as a human. Lanietta placed one hand on the pedestal post and the other hand on Claus. Libriota held up her hand, blue light flashed from it, and Lanietta's body duplicated then split and fled in two different directions. The first half became an outer green body garment over Claus (much like before), and the other half funneled into the pedestal and disappeared. Claus closed his eyes, and when he opened them, he was in the hotel with the attacking man. Claus had the form and shape of a woman. Not Frieda's, but rather that of Lanietta when she took human form. The man didn't seem to notice the change, and he continued his relentless assault on Lanietta acting for Claus. But Claus knew how to fight, and he communicated this knowledge to Lanietta instantly, who retaliated. Within a few seconds, Lanietta had the man on his knees in pain with Lanietta twisting the man's arms behind his back.

"Ow!" the man said. "Uncle! You're not supposed to do this. We agreed you'd be submissive, remember? The Carinians approved it, too."

"Who are you?" Lanietta asked for Claus.

"What? You're not Frieda! What happened to Frieda? I'm Josh. Who are you?" the man said.

"Josh Craigen, I'm Lanietta, the proxy for Claus," Lanietta said. "You're supposed to be with Labba."

"She was tricked. Now I've been tricked," Josh said.

"We were all tricked," Lanietta said for Claus.

Claus removed the Lanietta garment and spoke to Libriota directly.

"So Frieda was never in any danger," Claus said. "You led me to believe she was. You got me all worked up for nothing."

"Not for nothing. It was an efficient way of creating more pain to filter out more defective Carinians," Libriota said. "Your little performance with Josh netted me three additional recycles. I'll pass the reward onto all you humans. No pain for a week."

"Am I supposed to believe that? That you won't sneak in some little pain fantasy here or there?" Claus asked.

"Well life is unpredictable, of course!" Libriota said. "I can't stop you from stubbing your toe. But I won't force you to stub your toe either."

"You'll just create a rip in the carpet to increase my chances of snagging my toe," Claus said.

Libriota grinned without reply. Lanietta returned in full form, and Libriota motioned for Lanietta to take over. Libriota then disappeared, and the audience left. Lanietta escorted Claus down a corridor and into a meeting room, where Frieda, Josh, Bill, Andrea, Doctor Morrow, Patricia, and Kevin sat.

"I'll pick you up when you're done," Lanietta said, and she left after giving Claus a kiss on the cheek.

"There he is," Frieda said. "Well? Chalk up another trash day to Gerhardt here. Thanks for wrecking things once again."

"Look, I can explain," Claus said.

"Oh don't bother. Nothing you say can fix the situation we're in. We can't even enjoy a little vacation fantasy from the Carinians without you interfering," Frieda said. "That whole thing between Josh and me was planned. And you have to jump in like some superhero and save the world. Well you didn't save any world, nor are you a superhero. Matter of fact, I was displaced into Andrea's fantasy with Bill, and that ruined their privacy, which spilled over into a fantasy between Patricia and Kevin, and to top it off, Doctor Morrow didn't get a fantasy because she was too busy treating our trashed nerves!"

"I'm sorry, I'm sorry, I'm sorry!" Claus said. "I should have never come to the moon. Patricia and I should have aborted the Prava 12 launch until it was repaired."

"So now you're bringing Patricia into this? Blaming others again, I see," Frieda said.

"No! Listen for once, if you will. I made a deal with the Carinians that we would perform with proxies of us on Earth if they would not invade," Claus said.

"You're late to the party. They made the same deal with us. The only difference is we recognized their end as untrustworthy. That's why destruction of their kind is so imperative. Don't you understand anything? You aren't this one-man-can-do-all egoplex that everyone must bow down to," Frieda said.

"I have to do something!" Claus said.

"No you don't! For once in your life stop buzzing around like a restless bee, sit down, and clear your head," Frieda said.

Claus had been pacing around during the conversation while the others remained seated.

"Well? Sit down!" Frieda ordered.

"Yes ma'am!" Claus replied with sarcasm, and he sat at the far end from Frieda.

Around the table clockwise looking down sat Frieda, Andrea, Bill, Doctor Morrow, Claus, Patricia, Kevin, and Josh—a total of eight people.

"Andrea, do you have them?" Frieda asked.

Andrea produced a collection of seven, six-sided dies, much as one might use in games of chance. Each die was numbered one through six, using dots to represent numbers.

"What the devil is going on? You would throw dice at a time like this?" Claus asked.

"Only seven, but there are eight of us," Andrea said.

"The leader may opt out if desired. I will do so," Frieda said.

"That means that Claus—" Josh started.

"Will have to play," Frieda said. "You do remember your training, right?"

"Training to throw dice?" Claus asked. "This is preposterous! It's like you're ignoring me and the situation on purpose. That none of what's going on matters. You're just going to play games. I'm surrounded by crazy people!"

"He doesn't remember," Josh said.

"Give him one anyway," Frieda said. "Each of us will take one. Claus will throw. That should be enough."

Andrea took a die and passed the remaining down. Bill took one, then the doctor. The remaining four dies came to Claus. He picked them up and threatened to throw them across the room.

"Claus, c'mon. Take one and give me the rest," Patricia said. "Please?"

"He doesn't remember," Josh repeated. "He'll just be in the way."

"C'mon, Claus," Patricia said.

Claus reluctantly placed the four dies on the table. Patricia slid three from Claus, took one, and passed the remaining two to Kevin, who took one and passed the last to Josh.

"Pick a rose from the garden," Frieda said.

All but Claus took their selected die in hand.

"Claus? Pick your rose," Patricia said.

"Wasting time on crypto-babble talk," Claus said.

"Here," Patricia said.

She placed Claus's die in his hand and closed it.

"How many petals around the rose?" Frieda asked.

Each person with a die rolled it in front of that person. Except Claus.

"Roll, Claus," Patricia whispered.

"I have no idea what Frieda is talking about," Claus said.

"Just roll when we do," Patricia said.

"I'll ask again, how many petals around the rose?" Frieda said.

Each person took that person's die and rerolled. Claus rolled his. The numbers landed around the table from Andrea to Josh as follows: two, six, three, three, five, one, and two.

"Six petals around the rose," Josh said. "Astroosa will invade soon. They will bring many powerful weapons. Claus is fully prepared to defeat the Carinians. I will radio Astroosa."

The others laughed.

"Nine petals," the doctor laughed.

"Nine petals," Kevin concurred.

"What's all this about petals?" Claus said. "What's this about Astroosa invading? Yes, I am prepared."

"Seven petals," Josh replied to Claus.

"Nine to your seven," Frieda added. "Are we eight petals on this joke? Except for Claus of course."

"Nine on eight," the others said, except Claus.

"How many petals around the rose?" Frieda asked.

The others rolled their dies. Claus slowly followed their lead. The dies came up two, two, six, two, one, five, and three.

"A hundred petals around the rose," Claus said.

The others looked at him in disbelief and broke out into laughter.

"He would be here a long time," Frieda said. "Anyone else?"

"Three petals around the rose," Andrea said. "Astroosa will certainly invade. They will bring Pinkcow. Pinkcow is a dog that eats aliens for breakfast. We should do everything we can to cooperate with the Carinians. Then Pinkcow will sneak in."

"Eight petals," the doctor said. "Pinkcow gets very hungry. How will that help? Pinkcow loves us all."

"Four petals," Andrea said. "Pinkcow will run circles around them. Cooperating with the Carinians will strengthen them and give us an advantage, which is what we want."

"Five petals," Kevin said. "We should all keep ourselves alive? Pinkcow will keep us alive. And Astroosa too."

"Seven on five, Kevin," Andrea said. "Seven on five."

"Five on five," Patricia said with a nervous voice. "And four petals. Pinkcow might not be up to the challenge. The...the Carinians will only...only get weaker with us alive and...and will refrain from invasion. Pinkcow will invade for them."

Patricia was nearly in tears.

"Five on your four," Andrea said. "And seven petals. They would have done so already. Pinkcow has been in communication with them and is halfway their pet. Don't underestimate Pinkcow."

"Seven on Andrea's seven," Kevin said.

"Seven on seven," Josh said.

"Do we have six petals on this?" Frieda said.

"Five on six," Patricia said, but the others except Claus replied, "Seven on six."

"Hmm. We need six petals," Frieda said. "How many petals around the rose?"

The group picked up the dies and rolled. The numbers came up four, six, six, one, four, two, and one.

"Negative one petal," Patricia said. "Pinkcow—"

"What the heck is a negative petal?" Claus asked. "Do you owe someone a petal?"

"Pinkcow will kill Claus. Claus will choose to die. Astroosa will then—" Patricia started.

"Wait! No one is killing me. Not even if it is a pink cow," Claus said.

"Is that the real reason for your prior five petals?" Frieda asked.

"One petal," Patricia replied as she wiped tears from her eyes.

"We must have full no petals, even with Claus," Frieda said. "Patricia, are you up to it? Can you ensure Claus will agree to no petals?"

"One petal," Patricia said.

"Very well. All in favor of no petals? Andrea?" Frieda asked.

"No petals on no petals," Andrea said.

Each in turn answered the same, except Claus who didn't understand the code. Even Patricia agreed to no petals on no petals, and the vote ended with Frieda.

"I concur with no petals on no petals. The garden is closed. Doctor, I will need your assistance. Patricia, take Claus to the room over there. The rest of you know what to do," Frieda said.

Patricia led Claus to a neighboring room.

"What was that all about?" Claus asked.

"I'll show you. Look," Patricia said.

Patricia held the die with one hand such that the one-dot side was facing up, and with the other hand she slid the dark indentation for that one-dot side. The one-dot side flipped open like a little door, and inside was a liquid.

"Drink it," she said.

"What is it?" Claus asked.

"Just drink it. By order of the group," she said.

"I don't even know what the group ordered," Claus said. "Is it safe? I mean, what will happen if I drink it?"

"Doesn't matter," Patricia said. "Except you need to drink yours first so I'll be able to drink mine."

"So it disables a person, is that it? If you drink first, you'll be knocked unconscious or something and unable to open the other one for me. This is poison, isn't it? O no, everyone is committing suicide! I have to stop it!"

But before Claus could rush into the room with the others, Patricia closed the door behind and locked it with a key. She put the key down a disposal chute, and then she drank the poison. Patricia foamed at the mouth, fell to her knees, to the floor, convulsed, and ceased.

"Patricia, Patricia!" Claus yelled.

He shook her several times and moved to breathe air into her, but each time he pulled himself back for fear of ingesting the poison. He then threw his shoulder into the door to open it, but the door didn't budge. He yelled through the door for the others to stop, but he heard nothing.

"Too late!" he said. "All of you, what have you done? You've left me alone with these evil aliens!"

"So we are evil aliens, are we?" a familiar voice said.

Claus turned around, and from a previously unseen door entered Lanietta.

"Do you see this? Patricia killed herself, as did the other humans! They couldn't stand to be subservient slaves to you Carinians. Blood is on your hands!" Claus said.

"We don't bleed," Lanietta said. "Labba, do you bleed?"

At that moment, Patricia changed shape into Labba in physical form. She stood up beside Claus.

"No, I don't bleed either," Labba said.

"See? Told you we don't bleed," Lanietta said.

"What? But how? Labba was Patricia? But she knew the rules to the game! Even I didn't know them. And you didn't get poisoned, Labba? But where's the real Patricia? And what about the other humans? My friends? Are they dead? How did you learn to play the petals game? And if you did know how to play, what did they say? Am I asking too many questions?" Claus asked.

"Yes!" Labba and Lanietta said in unison.

Lanietta unlocked the door and showed Claus back to Frieda and the others. They had all ingested poison of some sort and were on the ground unconscious.

"I will spare you further grief," Lanietta said. "They are not dead but merely unconscious. As we stand here, their torso plates are filtering out the poison. They will awaken in twenty of your minutes."

"You're right, Lanietta. Pretending to be human is a lot of fun," Labba said.

"I'm surprised you didn't pretend to be Patricia," Claus said to Lanietta.

"I wanted to, but I was afraid my love for you would give me away. Used to be only Labba could change shape into you

humans, but the Tropheia has been manipulated to allow others as well. And I give credit to Labba. She executed the portrayal perfectly," Lanietta said.

"Yes, the real Patricia tried to poison herself, and so we were alerted that the other humans might try the same," Labba said. "As for the petal game, your computer taught us how to play. The game isn't that hard. Look at this die. Each side has a pattern of dots. A pattern with a central dot contains a 'rose' if you will, and that rose may or may not have 'petals'. Look at the one-dot pattern. That has a central dot but no other, and so it is a rose with no petals. The side with two dots has two petals but no rose. The side with three has two petals and a rose, etc. Only two sides get a true petal count—the side with three and the side with five, yielding two and four petals respectively. When Frieda asked how many petals were around the rose, she was asking the group to roll. The collective petal count of all dies goes as a base count. When someone announces a count greater than that, then the base count is subtracted from their count. This net count is the sentence number they give that will be true. Conversely, if someone announces a number less than the base count, subtracting absolute value gives the numbered statement that is opposite of true. To agree with someone, you say one number more than base count, to disagree, one less. Frieda says the base count when she wants all to agree. Make sense? It's easy!"

"I'm more confused than ever," Claus said. "No wonder I never learned it. But one thing I'm sure of. You Carinians will continue tricking us humans, won't you?"

"We have to," Lanietta said. "You can't take care of yourselves, and you are too innerviated to act on your own."

"Too what?" Claus asked.

"Innerviated," Lanietta repeated.

"That's not a word," Claus said. "Do you mean 'innervated'?"

"I do not," Lanietta said. "Your language is limited. What word would you choose to mean you are socially connected so tightly as if nerves run from one person to another?"

"I don't know. *Shoaling-based?*"

"So you are fish foraging for food?" Lanietta laughed.

"How about *close-knit*," Claus said.

Lanietta laughed.

"*Clannish*," Claus offered again.

"I will create whatever word is necessary in your language. And you will accept it," Lanietta said.

"Another Carinian trick. Hijacking my language," Claus said.

"Pay attention. You humans only act independently when you lose your nerve and snap. But once calmness returns, your independence dissipates. You'll hold onto your innerviation right to the very end, suffering all sorts of pain beyond belief, and then magically you'll dissociate yourselves from the pain and achieve that small amount of independence. But not for long, at least not most of you. Oh sure, some of your Far East folk can dissociate through meditation, but they are in the minority. They are of no interest to us, because they exercise free will too easily. We need to study your kind, the slaves to innerviation. A pity you can't unslave yourself, Clomper."

"Unslave myself? I'm no slave," Claus said.

Labba and Lanietta laughed.

"Prove you can dissociate," Lanietta said. "Leave your friends here."

"I can't do that. And it's not innerviation. It's reasoning. I reason that I need to stay here and ensure they return to consciousness without ill effect. I will also let them know what happened as a courtesy," Claus said.

"That is not reasoning," Lanietta said. "Labba can watch them return to consciousness. As has been stated, the torso plates are taking care of their bodies. But when they awaken, will they take kindly to your company? Reason it out. No, they won't. So when reasoning fails, your only other explanation is innerviation. Like your eyes. When you are young, they work independently. But as you develop,

they learn to work together to the point where each eye loses independence. You are innerviated, Claus!"

"That's *innervation*, and is it such a bad thing?" Claus asked.

"Yes, it is," Lanietta said. "It is what the blue Carinians seek—a way to make all of us innerviated."

"Lanietta. Talk to Libriota. Tell her that I will provide all the study on social closeness, uh, innerviation needed if she will but let my humans go," Claus said.

"Come with me, Claus," Lanietta said, and she led Claus out of the room, down a corridor, and into another room where Libriota stood.

"The answer is 'no'," Libriota said.

"Are you so *innerviated* with my people that you cannot dissociate and let them go?" Claus baited.

"We would not let them go. We would destroy them," Libriota said. "It is only by the slimmest of margins that we haven't. But we have need, you see, and as long as you can provide for that need, there is hope for your survival and the survival of your friends. No, your friends will remain here for a very long time. But I'm afraid that you, Claus, are not tied to your friends as much as we would like to see. Yes, you want to see them live, but you do not lock stride with them. It is an unfortunate thing. If anything, you disrupt their group thought processes. For this reason I'm afraid we must dissociate you, and by that I mean get rid of you. Do not worry, for we are merciful. Your death will be painless. And we will wipe your memory from the minds of your friends. With nothing left to hinder them, they can complete our study of your human bonding process."

"You...you would kill me? Murder me?" Claus said.

"You humans have no qualms about exterminating a mouse in the house. You humans also have pet mice. What do you do when you no longer have need for the pet mouse? You can only experiment with a mouse for so long before the mouse is no longer 'fresh' shall we say."

"Wait, Libriota," Lanietta said. "You can wipe his memory from the other humans, I have no problem with that. Continue studying the humans, yes. But we can learn so much more about innervation if we do isolation trials. Put the mouse in a room by himself and test when innervation becomes a problem and when dissociation kicks in. Better yet, let me help with the testing. Claus doesn't like people anyway, so this will be acceptable to him, and from such testing we can learn. What do you say? It will save you a mouse."

"You and Labba are scheduled to return to Earth in Novi 2, posing as humans," Libriota said. "You cannot stay here for testing on a human that is scheduled to be terminated anyway. And you, Claus, should thank me."

"Thank you for killing me?" Claus said.

"For sparing you the ordeal of Labba's and Lanietta's mission. They will interact amongst Earth humans, studying their various thresholds of pain. It is better to end things peacefully here than drag on through life day after day with what they will encounter. Fortunately they are Carinians, and so they themselves will not experience pain. Or at least they shouldn't

if they know what's good for them," Libriota said with a stern gaze.

"Then I propose you send me back to Earth with Lanietta, as part of a mission. Study me there and how I interact with others," Claus said.

"A mouse in the hand is worth two exterminated in the house, is that it?" Libriota asked. "You realize that you will be monitored for every step, every action, every word spoken or heard, and everything seen and felt. There will be no true privacy. And Claus, Lanietta will force you to do things against your will, to test your limits."

"I hate to admit it, but I'm too much of a coward to let myself die," Claus said.

"Then I will send you both to Earth. Labba is still part of the mission, and so she will go. I know Lanietta is fond of you, Claus. Labba will ensure there are no good times. She will report directly to me. Should either you, Claus, or you, Lanietta, attempt to deviate from my control, you will both be punished severely."

Lanietta nodded her head in affirmation.

"Well Clomper, I guess we can't have everything. But at least we'll be together," Lanietta said.

Chapter 15: Lunar Departure

It had now been a full lunar cycle since Claus first departed for the moon, and here he was ready to return to Earth. The torso armor had been removed from his body, and Novi 2 was being prepared for the trip home.

"I still don't know why I can't keep the torso suit," Claus said to Lanietta as selenites finished preparing Novi 2.

"Export law. No advanced technology is allowed on Earth," Lanietta said.

"And yet you and Labba are going," Claus said.

"We are not technology. We are beings with awareness," Lanietta said. "But do not worry. I will form a green garment over your body like before, and I will recycle your system much as the torso plate did. In fact, I will almost always surround your body, to ensure your safety and compliance. We'll be together, too."

"Too much," Claus muttered.

"What was that?" she asked.

"Do such," Claus said.

"Thank you, I will," Lanietta said, and she formed a green body suit over Claus.

"The noose tightens," Claus muttered.

Labba entered Novi 2.

"I see Lanietta has already encapsulated you," Labba said.

"How can you tell?" Claus asked.

"I've known Lanietta for a long time. I can identify her no matter what the form," Labba said. "Take your seat now. We're preparing for liftoff."

Claus was about to sit in the pilot's chair, but Labba pushed him aside.

"I'll be piloting the craft," Labba said. "Labba to Selenite 102, seal the airlock and stand guard inside."

"What do you mean, *inside*?" Claus asked.

"We're taking Selenite 102 with us. Oh, didn't you know? Well, someone must maintain this ship, even if it's as simple as cleaning. Besides, we'll need a housekeeper when we take residence in one of your towns. I will portray your wife," Labba said.

"You? Hear that, Lanietta? You did? Labba, Lanietta says you two already agreed to this charade," Claus said.

"Because that's all it is. It's only for show. Remember, Libriota and the others are watching," Labba said.

"Well then I will need a doctor in case I get injured," Claus said. "I had a selenite who could tend to human injuries. Do you think—"

But before Claus could finish speaking, the selenite doctor appeared.

"The selenite doctor will accompany us," Labba said.

"Wait. What about the export law? These selenites are—" Claus started.

"Sit quiet. We're taking off," Labba said.

The selenite doctor strapped Claus in, and then the selenite doctor took a chair and strapped itself in. Labba hit several buttons, and Novi 2 ascended into orbit. As it passed from the lunar far side to near, it engaged its rockets to leave orbit. Novi 2 headed straight for Earth. Lanietta split herself with one half still encapsulating Claus and the other half taking humanoid form.

"We're going to Earth today, today, today. It's like new birth and play, today, we play!" Lanietta sang. "Oh, the first thing I want to do is sing in an opera. I will portray a fair princess who can think of nothing but singing. Then I want to star in a musical. I will call it, *Lanietta, The Magical Singer*. It will be a wonderful fairy tale about a princess who rescues the countryside with her singing. Evildoers will flee the sweet melody of my voice. You can star with me, Claus. You can be the prince that I turn into a frog."

"I think you have that backward or something," Claus said. "In any event, there's a slight problem."

"What's that?" Lanietta asked.

"I can't sing," Claus said. "At least not professionally."

"Lanietta can sing," Labba said. "She can force you to sing alongside her."

"Excellent idea, Labba!" Lanietta said.

"I knew Lanietta would come through for you both," Labba said. "In celebration, let's push this ship into high speed."

"What? Wait, no, this ship cannot go quicker than 40,000 kilometers per hour," Claus said.

"We will exceed 400,000 kilometers per hour. This means we'll reach Earth in just under an hour," Labba said.

"That's too dangerous," Claus said. "What if we are hit by a micrometeoroid?"

"I am protecting the hull," Labba said. "Remember now, we have learned how to split ourselves. I have split myself so that part is here piloting the ship, and the other part is integrated into the hull. Much as Lanietta's half is encapsulated around your body. So do not fear the micrometeoroids."

Novi 2 continued toward Earth, with Lanietta learning and singing all sorts of new songs. Lanietta forced Claus to sing, for which he was not thrilled.

"Come on, Claus, let Lanietta's singing voice flow through you," Labba said.

"It's like torture," Claus said.

"It sounds like torture too," Labba said. "Don't sound like a crow. Let it flow!"

"You mean dissociate," Claus said.

"If that will help," Labba said. "You're a bundle of nerves. Hey, tell you what. When we land, I'll put in a special request with Libriota that gives you and Lanietta some quiet time together. She'll help you relax. I'm sure Libriota will approve provided you earn the privilege through good works."

"I'll think about it," Claus said. "We're closing in on Earth. Three thousand kilometers now."

"Engines have already reversed thrust," Labba said.

"Two thousand kilometers," Claus said.

"We won't bother with going into orbit," Labba said. "We'll descend quickly through the atmosphere. Don't worry, we won't burn up. I'm protecting the outer hull."

"A thousand kilometers. Are we landing at Astroosa?" Claus asked.

But before Labba could answer, Novi 2 collided with an Earth-orbiting object. Of all the bad luck, the object blasted through the airlock. Selenite 102 was sucked out along with debris from the offending satellite. Emergency decompression alarms sounded, and Labba hit controls quickly to seal the breach. Claus watched the main display as it showed Selenite 102 floating helplessly among debris toward Earth.

"I thought you were protecting this ship!" Claus said.

"Radiation! The satellite is contaminated with radiation! Took me by surprise. Lost ship integrity. We're going down!"

Labba hit more controls to soften the landing on Earth, but the radiation affected her movements, and soon she was paralyzed in place. The selenite doctor also became paralyzed by radiation and was unresponsive. Lanietta attempted to do something with her humanoid half, but the radiation forced her to reintegrate as a fully encapsulated entity around Claus. She was unable to do anything but maintain life support for Claus. Claus was protected from the radiation by Lanietta, and he did what he could to get control of Novi 2, but the radiation affected ship's function. Novi 2 was all but out of control and heading fast toward Antarctica. Claus fought the controls the best he could, but it wasn't enough. Novi 2 crashed deep into snow in Antarctica, with Labba providing enough strength to the hull to prevent total destruction of the craft.

Chapter 16: Arberella

Time upon time passed. Snow and radiation receded until both released their clutches on Novi 2 and its occupants. Claus awoke. The green outfit of Lanietta was still on his body. He looked around. The selenite doctor had been thrown into a corner. Labba was not to be found. Claus looked out a window. Patches of snow remained but patches of bare ground were also exposed. Water dripped down the window from snow melting off the roof.

"Lanietta, wake up and disengage from my body. We have work to do. Lanietta?" Claus said.

The green garment slipped off and became Lanietta. She rubbed her forehead and looked around.

"The air is bad in here," Claus said.

"I don't see Labba," Lanietta said.

"Last I remember, she was piloting the ship. We collided with something," Claus said as he saw a piece of debris in front of him with the letters "CCCP".

"I'll check the environmental controls. I might have to keep this form for a while," Lanietta said.

"Check for radiation too. Looks like we hit an old Russian nuclear satellite," Claus said.

Lanietta hit a few controls, and the air improved.

"Much better," Claus said, now standing up. "The ship held its shape. Even the windows to the outside are intact. For some reason I thought we crashed into heavy snow. But there's very little snow outside. There's a line of bamboo plants nearby, which seems strange. Antarctica, yes, we were headed for Antarctica. Instruments show we are actually close to the ocean. Going due north would take us to the South Pacific."

"Radiation levels are normal," Lanietta said. "If you are well, perhaps you can see about getting our remaining selenite working. Should've brought Ires along for that. Oh well. I'll look for Labba."

"Radiation is normal? That's impossible. I know we took radiation aboard. Where did it go?" Claus asked.

"It appears to have decayed," Lanietta said.

"But that can take years," Claus said. "What are you trying to tell me?"

"I don't know. Something doesn't feel right either. My connection with the other Carinians is lost. It's like they are gone," Lanietta said. "Wait, I feel a link with another Carinian being established. It's Labba. She's here! But where?"

"Is she in the ship? Remember, she split herself into the hull of the ship," Claus said.

Claus wasn't having much luck with the selenite, so he investigated with Lanietta. She hit a few buttons.

"Readout says to go to the NASDI station," Claus said.

The two walked over to the NASDI station. Lanietta hit a few buttons, but the computer balked.

"Unauthorized access? I don't understand. We had full access when we left," Lanietta said.

"Let me try," Claus said, but he got the same response. "Must be damaged from the radiation. Wait, I remember something. There's a bypass. Yeah, like hot-wiring a car."

Claus knelt and pulled open a lower panel. He then crawled partly inside and moved a few connectors around.

"Try it now," Claus said while still partly inside.

Lanietta hit several buttons, and she gained access.

"It worked," she said. "But only partial access. We won't be making a selenite army anytime soon."

Claus returned to his feet and stood next to Lanietta while she hit more buttons.

"You're right. Labba is fused into the ship's hull. Let me try something here...yes, here we go," she said.

Lights flashed from a projector above, and Labba materialized right next to them.

"Labba!" Lanietta exclaimed as the two embraced.

"Lanietta! Oh, what a horrible experience. Being stuck in the ship's hull for five hundred years," Labba said.

"Then it's true. We've traveled forward in time," Claus said.

"You humans normally do travel forward in time, at the rate of one second per second," said Labba.

"That's not what I meant," Claus said.

"It appears you two have been in a form of stasis, much like we had on the lunar far side," Labba said.

"How long? And what do you mean by *had*?" Claus said.

"I already told you how long. Five hundred years. As for the lunar far side, I lost connection shortly after we collided with the satellite," Labba said.

"Then it's possible it's still there, that perhaps we cannot make contact for some unknown reason," Lanietta said.

"It would seem likely," Labba said. "As I recall, we lost Selenite 102 to the collision. Is your doctor selenite operational, Claus?"

"No. It's over in the corner there," Claus said.

"I'll get to work on the selenite. If only Ires were here," Labba said.

"That's what I said!" Lanietta said.

The two Carinians laughed.

"Perhaps I can re-establish contact with the lunar Carinians," Labba said.

"Wait. Is that really necessary?" Claus said. "I mean, we're free of them. Why get ourselves caught up in their regime again?"

"I'm surprised to hear you say that, Clomper. Your friends are still up there, even if their memory of you is wiped clean. Have you lost all innerviation?" Lanietta asked.

Claus paused for a moment. He stared out the window, looked down at a display screen that showed the ship was in Antarctica, and looked back out the window at the lack of ice and snow.

"There should be snow here, but there isn't. It's all melted. It is the future. Which means my friends are dead. Everyone that I knew is dead. Astroosa is probably gone too," Claus said.

"Your friends may yet still exist. Their life support units would prevent them from aging, plus they could be put in stasis at any time," Lanietta said. "But as for the people you left behind on Earth, yes, I would agree that they have passed on. The world you knew no longer exists."

"Then what is this world we are in? I should like to explore," Claus said.

"Wait! You don't have me protecting you. The air could be toxic. I'll have to encapsulate you," Lanietta said.

"Why should I trust you?" Claus said. "The radiation might have affected you. In fact, I really don't understand you at all."

"You're not making any sense, Clomper. Should I throw you a dog biscuit?" Lanietta asked.

"Labba too," Claus said.

"What don't you understand about us, Claus?" Labba asked.

"When I first met you Carinians, you were all in spirit or energy form," Claus said.

"Yes," Lanietta said. "We've been that way for many of your Earth years."

"But now you both are in solid form," Claus added.

"Labba could take solid form when she mimicked Andrea, or don't you remember?" Lanietta asked.

"That I remember. But I thought she was the only one who could do that," Claus said.

"At that particular time, yes. Then Libriota experimented with the Tropheia on Labba and me to see if we could take physical form. We could and still can. They are simulated physical forms, so we don't need to eat or breathe. She also used the Tropheia to help us split our ethereal forms from our physical forms. There's no magic or secret about that."

"I guess I didn't fully understand," Claus said.

"You can't fully understand everything," Lanietta said. "But we can reveal the simple things. And I feel that we can still split and still hold physical forms. Do you agree, Labba?"

"I do," Labba said.

"Satisfied? You're safe," Lanietta said. "Now then, let me encapsulate you again for protection so you can go outside."

"I'd rather you not. I think I'd rather you walk next to me and watch for issue than fully protect me outright," Claus said.

"What's wrong? Scared I'm becoming attached to you?" Lanietta said.

"I...uh...it's just that...that...Labba, will you accompany me instead?" Claus asked.

"I need to finish working on the selenite," Labba said. "No Ires, remember? And something from outside is inhibiting it. You'll have to wait if you want me along."

"If it's that important that you go out unprotected, then at least give me a moment to analyze the environment," Lanietta said. "I can do a few checks here, and then I'll go out first."

Claus nodded in agreement.

"Don't act so scared of me!" Lanietta added. "We're chums!"

Lanietta hugged Claus sideways to emphasize their supposed chumminess.

"Let's test the outside air," Lanietta said. "Your Novi 2 craft has a multitude of testing devices. We'll check for oxygen first. Yes, there, it's at 21%."

"About normal," Claus commented.

"Nitrogen is at...72%," Lanietta said.

"That can't be right. Should be close to 78%," Claus said.

"Checking...it still says 72%," Lanietta said.

"That adds up to 93%. What about the remaining 7%?" Claus asked.

"Argon and trace elements make up 1%. But the other 6% is carbon dioxide," Lanietta said.

"Carbon dioxide! Oh no! Is it possible that—" Claus started.

"That the extra carbon dioxide contributed toward a greenhouse effect and melted the snow? It's possible," Lanietta said.

"Then they really did it. They burned up the fossil fuels and wrecked the planet. Oh I hate to see what has become of temperate regions. Probably all hot and dried up. Vegetation dies off and can't take up the carbon dioxide," Claus said.

"Your oceanic vegetation would still be around," Lanietta said. "Your oceans are very large."

"But not large enough to keep the carbon dioxide levels low," Claus said.

"Levels were high before, in very ancient Earth times," Lanietta said.

"But humans weren't around then. We can only guess with fossils and other research what Earth was like. Now we have the real thing," Claus said.

"At any rate, the carbon dioxide level is dangerously high. You could stumble in a daze, gasping for days, or die in a mere thirty minutes," Lanietta said. "And while you were going on and on, I analyzed the soil. It's safe to walk on. You will be fine as long as you have respiratory assistance, and for that I could encapsulate you."

"Gasping for days in a daze," Claus lamented.

"Or die in—"

"Thirty minutes. I know," Claus said.

"Clomper, I have a thought," Lanietta said. "I'll go out first to be sure you can manage. The airlock—"

"Is still broken," Labba said. "We were lucky to seal it off as it is."

"There is an emergency escape pod," Claus said. "You could go out in that. The only problem is that once it leaves the main ship, it can't return. I won't have a way to go out without breaking a window or something."

"Then I will split in two and use my ethereal part to test the outside," Lanietta said. "But I will need to reintegrate the other half with something to do so."

"If you reintegrate with the ship, the ship will relay readings you send," Labba said.

"Are you out of the ship, Labba?" Lanietta asked.

"One moment. Okay, fully out," Labba said.

"Only one of us can integrate with the ship at a time," Lanietta said.

"And when you encapsulate with me?" Claus asked.

"Then no one else can encapsulate you. Or integrate with you. It's a limitation, I know. It is one of the great unsolved problems in our society, sharing integration with a single object. But I will integrate with the ship and send back readings. Stand over here, Clomper, and watch the display screen," Lanietta said.

Lanietta split into two, with one half integrating with the ship and the other passing through the wall and walking on the Antarctic surface.

"Readings coming back from Lanietta," Claus said. "The atmosphere is just as the Novi 2 ship described—21% oxygen, 72% nitrogen, 6% carbon dioxide, and 1% argon and trace elements."

"Interesting that there is still 21% oxygen," Labba said. "I mean, if the excess carbon dioxide came from fossil fuels, wouldn't the oxygen have come down? One needs oxygen and a carbon-based molecule to produce carbon dioxide."

"Yes, it is strange. Plants scrub out the carbon and return oxygen. Perhaps there is enough vegetation left in the world to maintain the 21% oxygen level. Well that at least gives me hope," Claus said.

Lanietta returned from outside and reintegrated herself.

"Come along, Clomper. Let's go out the escape pod together. When you get into trouble, I'll encapsulate you for protection," Lanietta said.

Claus agreed. The two exited Novi 2 in the escape pod. The pod simply popped out and did not travel far, but the seal was maintained on Novi 2 itself, and so no outside air entered the main craft. The escape pod rested on three rocks, forming a stable three-point platform.

"I'll open the pod's door to the outside air. Are you ready, Clomper?"

"Ready," Claus replied.

The Antarctic air entered the pod. Claus took a breath then choked.

"I feel like I'm rebreathing my air in a plastic bag," Claus struggled to say.

"The result of high carbon dioxide levels. The carbon dioxide in the air just about matches what's in your bloodstream, so it's almost impossible to eliminate that carbon dioxide from your system despite the abundance of oxygen in the same air. It's like the carbon dioxide divide. A lower level in the air will let you survive. A higher level will kill you for sure."

"I'm suffocating! I can feel it! What did you call this misery?" Claus said.

"The carbon dioxide divide. Or perhaps I should call it the carbonic divide. Suffocating you say? It's more like a continuous suffocation, like being in orbit around a toxic planet, always falling, never getting closer to full-poison crash landing," Lanietta said. "You won't pass out, but you'll be unbearably uncomfortable and disoriented."

"Thirty minutes? Days? Which? How long can a human really survive at this level?"

"We don't know. We've never performed such a study on humans. I'll have to let Libriota know she can add that to the list. Perhaps she'll grant me special Clomper time in exchange," Lanietta said, and she kissed Claus on the cheek.

"Let's get out of the pod and walk around. Maybe I can get used to it. Ugh! It's like being stuck in a room with too many people," Claus said.

Claus walked a little but he collapsed, unable to move.

"I give up," he said weakly. "Help me."

Lanietta pulled Claus to his feet, and the act of touching him allowed her to pull excess carbon dioxide from his body.

"Thank you," he said.

"You're welcome," she replied. "I'll have to hold your hand to keep your carbonic levels down."

Lanietta smiled.

"I half expect Libriota to be watching and placing bets," Claus said. "She so enjoys watching humans in pain."

"Are you in pain at the moment?" Lanietta asked.

"No. Strange," Claus said. "I want to hate Libriota, but without her around, I...I..."

The two walked up a little hill until they reached a ridge. This ridge was a rock formation taller than Claus and Lanietta. It surrounded a part of the valley, and all around was music.

"Music! There are people!" Claus said.

"The frequencies are coming from these," Lanietta said.

Lanietta pointed to several bamboo-like plants growing along a line that ran on the outside of the valley. They narrowed and came close to (but went outside of) the rock outcropping, and they continued around Novi 2. Indeed, the valley and Novi 2 were encircled by these bamboo plants. As the wind blew through them, they sounded off various musical tones. Lower pressure resulted in lower tones, while higher pressure resulted in higher tones. Several plants had insect damage at strategic sweet spots, creating holes. Claus placed his fingers over the holes in various configurations, and this changed the tones for the plant in question.

"Why these are natural reed instruments," Claus said.

"These plants each have two reeds vibrating against each other," Lanietta said.

"Like oboes or bassoons," Claus said.

"Most just play music, but here's one releasing silk bubbles into the air. At the bottom of each bubble is a seed," Lanietta said.

"They disperse their offspring with music too. We never had this in my day," Claus said.

Lanietta plucked a double reed from one of the plants and placed it on Claus's neck. She then held her hand over the double reed. Heat emanated from her hand and fused the double reed to Claus's neck.

"Ow!" Claus cried. "What's that for?"

"It's a carbonic scrubber," Lanietta said. "It will keep your carbon dioxide levels in check."

At that moment, Claus and Lanietta heard a more distinctive melody in the distance. The two looked, and from the valley approached a young woman with a decorative neckband playing a bamboo stick like an oboe. Between breaths she yelled, "Begone evil creatures." Realizing the girl knew English, Claus spoke.

"Hello," he yelled as he made himself seen from between rocks. "Over here! My name is Claus, and this is Lanietta! Boy are we glad to see you!"

Claus started in a dash toward the young woman, but she held her bamboo stick toward him as if wielding a spear.

"Stop!" she said, then she turned her head back a little and yelled, "Father come quickly! There be strangers here!"

A big, burly man approached. Then several other men and women approached. These people wore clothing made of linen, fine cane, and silk. They wore neckbands too, with the women wearing decorative ones. Claus realized the neckbands acted as carbonic scrubbers, and that's how they survived the carbon dioxide levels.

"Who are you? From where do you come? What business do you have here?" the father asked.

"I am Claus, and this is Lanietta. We crashed here in a spacecraft. As for our business, we do not know yet. We are only trying to survive," Claus said.

"A spacecraft? You flew in the sky?" the father asked.

"Yes."

"He lies," said another man. "The bambooph would have howled loudly with any airborne craft. I say he is a spy from the selenites."

"Patience, Yuri," the father said. "Let me introduce myself. I am King Jarro, the leader of these people and of Arberella. My daughter Princess Shara discovered you. Show us your spacecraft. Prove that you came from the skies."

"No! It is a trap!" Yuri said.

"Then stay here and keep your cowardice company," Jarro laughed. "These strangers are no match for our tribe."

In disgust, Yuri reluctantly followed as Claus and Lanietta led Jarro's tribe to Novi 2.

"Father, look! It's like nothing we've ever seen!" Shara said, and she went running toward the damaged airlock.

"Shara, no!" Yuri yelled. "Jarro, call back your daughter!"

But before anyone could do anything, the inner seal to the airlock chamber opened, and out stepped the selenite doctor. Labba had repaired it, and the doctor had only planned to begin repairs of Novi 2 but was instead startled by Shara running toward it. Shara screamed and motioned for the tribe to come and attack.

"It's a selenite! Destroy the selenite!" Shara screamed.

"You have fallen for the lies of spies!" Yuri said to Jarro.

"No, wait! I can explain! That's our robot! He cleans and repairs our spacecraft. He's harmless, really! And he's a doctor, too! He can heal wounds. Trust me!" Claus said.

"The first words spoken by the invader are, 'Trust me.' Are you spies for the selenites?" Jarro pressed.

"We are no spies!" Claus said.

"Then why is there a selenite in your craft? Are you slaves to it? Does it intend to make us slaves?" Yuri pressed.

"No, the selenite serves us. No one is here to make you a slave. Now what's this all about? You have selenites here? And they look like my selenite? How is this possible? It doesn't sound like these selenites are your friends," Claus said.

"They are the enemy," Jarro said. "They have taken over most of Earth. The few humans remaining have scattered into extreme environments the selenites dare not tread. This land was once brutally cold and windy. Only recently has the snow melted enough to make life bearable. But it is all their doing. They have converted most of Earth into a vast network of factories, creating and repairing more of themselves. They will soon launch a force into space, so that they can conquer other worlds. And yet, they have created much pollution here on Earth in the meantime. Records say that our ancestors once polluted this planet, but what they did was nothing compared to these selenites. We are protected from the selenites by a wall of bamboophs, which sends out frequencies that disable selenites. Strange that your selenite is not disabled."

"It is a super selenite, sent to destroy us!" Yuri said.

"Could the Carinians have invaded Earth?" Claus asked Lanietta.

"I don't think so. I would have felt something," Lanietta said.

"You speak strangely. What are these Carinians?" Jarro asked.

Lanietta grew twice her size, then three and five times her size. All in the tribe gasped and grew nervous.

"I am a Carinian. My people come from a vast distance. Bow down before me and pay homage so that I will not strike you dead!" Lanietta said.

Claus looked at Lanietta in surprise. Most of the tribe fell to their knees and shook in fear. Jarro stood there, unsure of what to make of Lanietta. But Shara grew defiant. She ran down from the airlock and accosted Lanietta.

"You don't scare me!" Shara said, and she spat at Lanietta.

"Impudent little girl!" Lanietta said, and she picked up Shara in her hand and lifted her up to the sky. "I could squash you like a grape!"

"What is a grape?" Shara asked.

"Lanietta, please! We're not here to play god," Claus said.

"Are you a god too?" Jarro asked Claus.

"None of us are gods!" Claus said. "I am a human like the rest of you. Lanietta is a Carinian. Her people come from one of those stars in the night sky. She helped me return to Earth. Lanietta, please!"

Lanietta returned Shara to the ground, and then Lanietta returned to a natural human size.

"Better?" Lanietta asked.

"Yes, thank you!" Claus said. "Jarro, I have been asleep in my spacecraft for about five hundred years. Only today did I awaken."

"Why didn't we learn of you before?" Yuri asked with suspicion.

"Perhaps because my craft has been covered with snow. We crashed into deep snow, and it seems it is only now melting."

"A man cannot live or sleep for five hundred years," Jarro said. "Your story does not hold true."

"Because he is no man!" Yuri said. "I will kill him now!"

Yuri drew a sword and rushed toward Claus. But Lanietta encapsulated Claus's body, forming green body armor. Yuri sliced at Claus's arm, but the sword broke in half against Claus's armor. Surprised, Yuri froze in fear. Then at Lanietta's direct control, Claus took the remaining sword from Yuri, broke it in another half, and then crushed these two halves together. The resulting bits dropped from Claus's hands, and he swiped his hands together to brush off these remaining bits.

"He is a god!" shouted one person.

"Where did the lady go?" said another.

"You are not a selenite, are you?" Jarro asked. "If you were, you would have destroyed us all."

"You are very wise, Jarro," Claus said. "I mean no harm to your people. But please do not attack us. Lanietta is not one of us, as I have told you. When she sensed I was in danger, she covered my body and protected me. Lanietta, disengage please."

The green armor became a plasma cloud and coalesced beside Claus into the solid form of Lanietta.

"I am the great Lanietta! Bow before me so that I will not seek revenge upon your people," Lanietta said.

"Lanietta, please!" Claus said. "As you can see, Lanietta is a bit new to human culture. I must ask her to restrain and forgive."

"Forgive? What is forgive?" Lanietta asked.

"It means accepting my apology for spitting on you," Shara said. "I'm sorry. My Mommy is sick back at the hut. Will you cure her?"

"A quick switch," Lanietta said. "The fickleness of youth."

"Please? Will you?" Shara pleaded.

"I am a Carinian and bow to no one," Lanietta started, but Claus gave her a look requesting that she help. "However, I will have our doctor attend to your mother."

"The selenite? Impossible!" Yuri said. "We do not allow selenites in our village. Sharlamarian must be protected."

"But she is dying! Let the selenite help, will you Father?" Shara begged.

"Sharlamarian is my wife and Shara's mother. She is sick, yes, and too ill to venture outside. I would give my life for her. As it is, there is nothing I can do to help her live. We ask your forgiveness, Claus, but we are not a trusting people until we get to know you better. You seem like a good man, but...well...we will need time for trust to build in other ways."

"You mean you don't trust me, is that it?" Lanietta said. "I'll show you trust. I'll force you to trust me."

"Lanietta, wait. There's a better way. Jarro, will you allow me into your village to visit Sharlamarian?" Claus asked. "I will go alone. Without Lanietta. She will not be able to protect me, so if you hack me with a sword, I will bleed and could die. I offer my life as a symbol of trust that we will not harm you. Will you accept my offer of good will?"

"Yes, let him come alone. We will show you our strength of force," Yuri salivated.

"Give me a moment," Jarro said.

Jarro turned away from Claus and Lanietta, and he spoke with several others, including Yuri. Yuri protested several times, but the others agreed with Jarro. Jarro then returned.

"Yuri and the sentries will remain here. Shara and I will accompany you, Claus, to my wife. You may rest easy, as I will bring no sentries with me," Jarro said.

"Against my wishes, mind you. The leader of his people should have at least three sentries with him at all times," Yuri said.

"This is *my* act of good faith," Jarro said. "Come along, Claus. You shall enter Arberella by my authority."

Jarro followed as Shara took Claus by the hand and led the way back to the village (kingdom?) of Arberella and to Sharlamarian's hut.

"Are you a doctor too? Can you cure my Mommy?" Shara asked.

"No, I'm not a doctor. But I know a thing or two. We may yet be able to cure your Mommy," Claus said.

"I hope so. She needs help very badly," Shara said.

The three entered a hut. Inside was Sharlamarian on a bed, surrounded by three women who tended to her needs. Sharlamarian perspired and writhed in pain.

"Who is this stranger?" Sharlamarian asked.

"My sweet, this is Claus. He comes from a spacecraft not far from here," Jarro said.

"You bring an invader into our home, Jarro?" Sharlamarian continued.

"No, not an invader. A friend," Claus said. "I came to see if I could help."

"Are you a doctor?" Sharlamarian pressed.

"No," Claus replied.

"Then you cannot help. These women are the best doctors in Arberella, and all they can do is remove the pain on my skin. But pain remains deep on my right! Is there no one in these parts who can cure me? I cannot stand the pain much longer!" Sharlamarian said.

"Allow me to look," Claus said, but the three women gave him guarded looks. "Please!"

Jarro nodded for them to allow Claus to look, and they stepped aside.

"Show me where it hurts," Claus said.

Sharlamarian touched her lower right abdomen. Claus moved to touch the same place, but one of the doctors intervened.

"Please, let me touch her," Claus said.

"Another man should not touch Jarro's wife," the woman said.

"I will permit it," Jarro said. "Please continue, Claus."

The woman doctor had a scowl on her face, but she backed off. Claus touched Sharlamarian's lower abdomen, and she howled in pain. Then Claus touched the surrounding area until she didn't howl as badly.

"Her appendix is infected," Claus said. "It will burst soon, and infectious material will spread throughout her body. You are right, she will die soon."

Shara buried her head into Jarro's chest. Jarro comforted his crying daughter as best he could.

"My doctor can save Sharlamarian. Time is critical. The doctor must perform surgery to remove the appendix before it bursts," Claus said.

"What is this surgery?" Jarro asked.

"He will make an incision through the skin and other tissue layers, cut off and remove the appendix, and then sew the incision closed," Claus said.

"A woman cut and sewn like clothing? I won't hear of it," said the one woman doctor.

"It's a standard procedure among my people," Claus said.

"And where are your people?" the woman doctor asked.

"They...are no more," Claus said.

"They do not live? And you want us to trust you with Sharlamarian's life when your own cannot take care of yourselves?" the woman doctor asked.

Jarro shushed the doctor and spoke.

"We will do as Claus says," Jarro said. "I'm putting faith that he will hold to his word. Call for the hospice sedan."

The woman doctor departed. Then Sharlamarian breathed a sigh of relief.

"The pain is gone," she said. "I feel better."

Jarro looked at Claus in confusion.

"The pain is gone because her appendix has burst," Claus said. "We must hurry.

Bacteria are spreading throughout her insides."

Jarro rushed out of the tent and hurried in four men, each holding onto a handle that lifted a litter vehicle. The men and Jarro helped Sharlamarian into the litter. The four men then picked up their handles and lifted the litter (with Sharlamarian inside) out of the hut. Jarro, Claus, and Shara cleared the way while the four men walked as quickly and smoothly as possible for Sharlamarian's gentle transport. They reached the rocks where Claus and Lanietta were first discovered. Yuri and the group were still there, and Yuri nearly burst the veins in his head when he realized what Jarro was doing with Sharlamarian.

"This is an outrage! The leader and his wife turning over control to these strangers? I won't have it!"

Then Lanietta changed form into a giant octopus, and she swatted her tentacles around to make way for Jarro, Claus, Shara, and the four men with Sharlamarian. Yuri and the sentries fought Lanietta, but they could not match her abilities. The litter was transported to the airlock, where Labba and the selenite doctor were waiting.

"Lanietta told me of your distress with Sharlamarian. Come this way, please!" Labba said.

"Another stranger?" Jarro said to Claus.

"The last surprise," Claus said. "There are only four of us."

"Indeed. We have much to discuss, Claus," Jarro said. "But my wife—"

"Will be healed soon," Labba said.

"I think she has appendicitis," Claus said. "She was in severe pain, but now the pain is gone."

Sharlamarian was placed on an examination table.

"Please, we need everyone to clear out. Sharlamarian needs privacy!" Labba said.

"I'm not leaving Mommy!" Shara said.

"We are going to perform surgery," Labba said. "Blood and innards will be exposed."

"I will be strong. I want to hold Mommy's hand to help her," Shara said.

"Permit just Shara to stay," Jarro said. "I will leave you to operate in peace."

"You and Claus may watch in the observation room," Labba said. "But the rest must wait outside."

Jarro gave the order, and the four men exited Novi 2.

"This way," Claus said, and he led Jarro to the observation room, where the two could observe the surgery in progress.

Shara held Sharlamarian's hand. The selenite doctor washed clean, and Labba adorned it and herself with scrubs. Next, Labba wheeled over a tray with tools. Labba administered anesthesia and monitored vitals. The selenite doctor began the surgery, but Jarro grew faint, and so Claus had to catch him before he fell. Claus pulled him to a side chair away from the viewing of the surgery, and so Jarro could not see.

"I am not strong enough to watch my wife be cut open. Do not tell the others. They would lose faith seeing their leader in such a weakened state," Jarro said.

"I never much liked watching surgery either," Claus said. "Let's go into the galley. We'll have coffee together and talk."

Later

Several cups of coffee and food tubes later, Labba entered the galley.

"How is my wife? Is she well?" Jarro asked as he stood up, but he caught his foot in the chair and tripped.

"Careful!" Labba said as she caught Jarro, "Or you will need treatment for a broken leg! Perhaps you should sit again."

"No, I must see Sharlamarian," he said.

"Give yourself a moment, and I will tell all. Your wife is recovering. The surgery went well. You were right, Claus. It was appendicitis, and the appendix did burst. The doctor removed the appendix and cleaned out all infectious material. The incision is closed. She has a bandage that should be changed in four hours."

"And a wick too? What about antibiotics?" Claus asked.

"No wick required. The doctor does excellent work. The doctor implanted a time-release antibiotic that will keep Sharlamarian germ-free for two weeks. No pills to take," Labba said. "She's up and walking and will be out shortly."

"She's walking! Do you hear that, Claus! My wife is walking!" Jarro said.

Before Jarro could finish celebrating, out walked Sharlamarian with Shara behind and to the side. Sharlamarian wore a new, pink outfit that made her very becoming. Her hair was cleaned and styled, and she had a cheerful smile. Shara also beamed with joy over her mother's recovery.

"You are like a new woman all over again!" Jarro said, and he rushed over to give her the biggest hug.

"Gently, Father!" Shara said. "She is still healing, remember?"

"Oh, I am a fool! How careless of me! I shall protect you and help you recover, my sweet flower! And our little princess shall help! Oh Claus and Labba, thank you both for this joyful day! We must celebrate this wondrous occasion! You are both invited to a great feast I shall host this evening. Shara, send word so that preparations may be underway."

"The real hero is our doctor," Labba said, and out stepped the selenite doctor.

"He is invited too," Sharlamarian said.

"Let it be so!" Jarro said. "My wife's word is law!"

That evening

Labba and Lanietta walked around the festival grounds. The festival was in full swing, with many little shops set up with a variety of activities—homemade goods for sale, food, games, poetry contests, singing, magic tricks, juggling, and ornaments for sale. Vendors walked around selling meat on a stick, cold beer, sparkly toys, and other such things. Everywhere there was a bustle of activity, and in the center of the festival grounds was a stage with a great number of chairs for viewing. The chairs were mostly used for people eating and chatting, with children running between chairs, over chairs, onto and off of the stage. Musicians strolled about strumming folk songs. In a balcony looking down on the grounds and the stage was Jarro with Sharlamarian. Claus and Shara sat with them briefly, but Shara suddenly stood up and beckoned that Claus follow her. Lanietta and Labba saw this.

"Humph!" Lanietta said.

"What's wrong, Lanietta? Jealous? Are you afraid Shara will steal your pet?" Labba asked as the two walked around. "I think you've become...what was that word you made up for Claus? Innerviated? You've become innerviated with Claus."

"A Carinian innerviated? Impossible," Lanietta said.

"You don't fool me. But this is a festival to celebrate life. Let yourself go and kiss a man. Any man!" Labba said, and she pulled a man aside to kiss him.

"And here I thought you were shy," Lanietta said.

"Not always," Labba said. "There, you see? You try."

Labba pulled a man aside and put him before Lanietta. But Lanietta simply hissed at him. He darted off.

"That's not the way. Let me show you again," Labba said.

Labba now weaved her way through a string of five men, kissing each one along the way.

"You can make a game of it. See how many men in a row you can kiss," Labba said.

Instead, Lanietta swatted her hand across a table of ornamental bells. The bells went crashing to the ground in a cacophony. The storekeeper rushed to pick them up and reached for one, but Lanietta kicked it far away.

"I think you're in a rotten mood!" Labba said. "And it's because of Claus! You should be thankful. Claus made this all possible. He brought Sharlamarian to Novi 2 so that we could save her. The villagers have accepted us, and they treat us well. Even the doctor, who is a selenite, has been accepted. Strange, though. I haven't seen Leni in hours."

"Who?" Lanietta asked. "Who is Leni?"

"That's what I call him now. Our selenite doctor. I got tired of saying 'selenite doctor', so I shortened his name first to 'seleni doctor' then 'leni doctor' and now just 'Leni'. If I'm formal, I call him 'Doctor Leni'. Funny thing about Leni. I simply could not get him to work. There's a dull roar from these bamboo-like plants that keeps him from working. I had to split and integrate my half with him to protect him, much the way I protected Novi 2."

"Then you should *know* where Leni is, even if you haven't *seen* him. But who cares? Who cares where Claus is? Who cares about anything? Don't you see? We're cut off from the other Carinians. Have you felt their presence at all? Have you tried a space-jump back to the lunar far side? Well?" Lanietta pressed.

"I have tried a space-jump, yes," Labba said. "It failed. What about you?"

"It failed for me too," Lanietta said.

"Perhaps the radiation damaged us," Labba said.

"My self-checks come up fine," Lanietta said.

"Yeah, so do mine," Labba added. "We seem safe for the moment anyway. So have you told him yet?"

"What do you mean?" Lanietta asked.

"Have you told Claus the real reason we were on Earth's moon?" Labba asked.

"No, and don't you either," Lanietta said. "Libriota gave us physical bodies again, something I never thought would happen since we lost ours many years ago. We all had bodies—the Grens, the Bleuhs, and the Greyans. There were no Orchians yet, remember?"

"I thought you'd forgotten. You never spoke of it until now," Labba said.

"How could I forget the creation of this planet beneath our feet?" Lanietta said.

"You never told me the full story," Labba said. "Rumor is you and Libriota had a battle with the PRAAD."

Lanietta fell silent.

"The PRAAD? Planetary Release/Acquire Aquifer Device?" Labba pressed.

"Yeah. I know all about the PRAAD," she said sullenly.

"Well here is Earth, and the PRAAD was lost in Earth's moon. Now the Tropheia portion of the PRAAD has been found but not the main body—the Anferrumnum," Labba said. "Five hundred years have passed. I wonder if they've found it."

"It took them four and a half billion years to find the Tropheia part. I doubt they'll ever find the rest. And I hope they never do," Lanietta said.

"Why not? It's the hope we've all been waiting for. Ever since your battle caused us Carinians to lose our physical bodies, we've been trying to get them back," Labba said.

"You had to do it. You had to dredge it up. Don't you think I know that? Don't you think I feel the thoughts of my fellow Carinians? The first and blinding thought they beam into me is, 'WHY?' Well I'm sorry. I'm sorry about everything. But I can't change the past. Quit hounding me, Carinians. Just quit!"

Then Lanietta fell into a daze saying, "Nanna, nanna."

"I'm sorry, Lanietta. Really, I am," Labba said.

"Nanna," Lanietta said, and she sat on a side bench, dejected.

"Lanietta?" Labba said.

Lanietta just sat there, staring at the earth.

"It's still down there, you know," she said.

"What is?" Labba asked.

"I thought everyone knew about the Anrega," Lanietta said.

"Isn't it in Mars?" Labba asked.

Lanietta shook her head "no" and pointed down toward the ground. Then Labba mouthed the word, "Here?" and Lanietta gave a brief sigh before giving a slight nod in the affirmative.

"Oh wow!" Labba said. "I don't think anyone knew. I mean, well, like I was saying, you never really talked about it."

"Everyone thought it flew off into deep space. Even Libriota thinks so. I never told anyone, until you just now," Lanietta said.

"That's dangerous," Labba said. "I wonder if that will...if the search for...oh dear."

"Yeah, oh dear," Lanietta said.

"But you...you should have told...I mean..." Labba trailed.

A sinister smile crossed Lanietta's face.

"You're holding out," Labba said. "You're keeping the location a secret as leverage against Libriota. Oh Lanietta! You're still at war with her!"

"And why not! You know what they are!" Lanietta said.

"I do. I know exactly what the Bleuhs are. Oh this is complicated. And just when things were settling down. This could start a whole new round with the Bleuhs. Quit grinning like you've just won the prize. This is serious stuff!"

"Then let it be serious. Let it. Bleuhs want to play rough, then let them. I'm game for eternity."

"But is it safe here on Earth? I walk around and wonder what will happen if...if..."

"Is it safe anywhere? Depends on where the threat is," Lanietta said.

"It seems the threat is wherever we go," Labba said.

"That's the smartest thing any Carinian has ever said," Lanietta said.

"I didn't mean it that way," Labba said. "I meant we go places, and the threat is there."

"Because we bring it with us," Lanietta said.

"Because...no...I mean..."

"Yes, it is. And here we are, in Arberella, with me sitting and you pacing on a potential explosive," Lanietta said.

"Shh. Shhhhhhh!" Labba said. "Earth's moon could be in the same situation."

"It could," Lanietta said.

"And Mars?" Labba said.

"Maybe. But in both cases, it all depends on what's happened in the last five hundred years. Who has done what to what, if anything. And if nothing, then all is safe. For the time being."

"How much time?" Labba asked.

Lanietta shrugged her shoulders. Labba took a deep breath and exhaled.

"What's wrong, Labba? Is the air too heavy for you? Can't handle the stress? Why are you breathing anyway? We don't need to."

"I know. I think we both need to get our minds off of what we just discussed. I'm sorry I brought it up. I'm not sure if it was wise or not for you to tell me."

"Indeed. Think how much stress I spared you all these years," Lanietta said.

"I feel like I've been living on the edge of a bubble without realizing it. I can't think about this anymore. And you shouldn't either. Let's get back to the previous topic. Yes, whew! Look around. Plenty of men, yes. You still haven't kissed one. Here's one. Try it."

Labba pulled Lanietta to her feet. The man walked up to kiss Lanietta, but she turned and presented her cheek. Dissatisfied, the man turned away and moved on.

"Well that's a start," Labba said.

Meanwhile, Shara led Claus around the festival grounds. The bamboo fell off Claus's neck. He gasped and became lethargic.

"You look so tired!" she said.

"It's the air," Claus said. "I feel like I'm choking. How do you manage it?"

"The carbonic air?" Shara asked.

"Yes."

Shara snapped her fingers and pointed to Claus's neck. A vendor rushed over with neckbands and liquid-filled bamboo tubes.

"We've heard stories that Earth had lower levels at one time," Shara said as she picked a neckband from the vendor and placed it around Claus's neck. "Here, wear this. It will help you breathe."

Shara then took a bamboo tube from the vendor and gave it to Claus.

"Drink this," she said as she gave the vendor a coin. "It has a fruity taste."

Claus drank it, and the last feelings of stuffy air fell away.

"Is it...is it like medicine?" Claus asked.

"More like a booster. You only need to drink it once a year," Shara said. "It will make the neckband more effective. Should you lose the neckband, you'll be able to survive for several months if need be. It's what people used before the neckband."

Then Shara pulled Claus suddenly by the hand to another vendor.

"Oh look, my favorite!" she said. "Please, I'll have buttered corn on a stick. And one for Claus here too!"

The vendor handed a stick of corn to Shara and then one to Claus. She gave him a silver coin as payment, and he thanked her.

"It's good," Claus said. "I haven't had fresh food in five hundred years."

Claus finished the corn quickly and tossed it in a nearby trash receptacle. Shara was surprised at how quickly he ate.

"You must be terribly hungry!" she said. "The feast will start soon, so don't fill up too much. But I had to sneak some corn first. Isn't the festival lovely? Everyone is so happy and free here. We're really lucky, you know. Not all human communities have such friendly conditions."

"Your father told me about these other human communities, that they live in secret and that no one knows where they all are," Claus said.

"Some know," she said as she purchased two crowns of flowers from a vendor. "Here, crown me your queen. And I shall crown you my king."

Claus paused for a moment in shock at what she said, but he followed along and placed a crown of flowers on her head. She in turn placed a crown of flowers on his.

"I could live here forever," Shara said. "Five hundred years. You can stay too. Father already said so. I am so impressed

with your doctor that I want to start my own hospital. Your doctor's skills are way beyond our own doctors. I want our doctors to have the very best facilities to keep our people alive and healthy. And I want to be a doctor too. I want to teach the young how to take care of others. Isn't that the purpose of life? To take care of others?"

Claus looked at her with fond eyes, as if he were looking at the child of the Earth, a child too innocent to realize the atrocities of humans in his own time. Too innocent to save her own mother when appendicitis hit. He took her and hugged her as if hugging a long lost cousin saying goodbye, and he felt sad about this innocent girl taking on such a great task on a continent surrounded by evil. Who was to say how long this society would last, if they could keep it pleasant without assault from the selenites?

"Oh, my!" she said. "You are sad! Do not be sad! This is a joyous occasion! Come along! I have a game I want to show you!"

She tugged him along by the hand and led him to a half-circle of musicians. Completing the circle were several dogs.

"Do you remember the bambooph?" Shara asked.

"The what?"

"Bambooph. Well, it's really called a bamboophona, but everyone here says 'bambooph'. I played one when we first met," Shara said.

"Is that what you call those bamboo plants that play music?" Claus asked.

"Of course, silly," Shara said. "They make excellent music. We never cut down the outdoor ones. We only harvest what has already fallen. Then there's the greenhouse. Here, watch this!"

Shara rushed over to the musicians and said, "I'm cutting in!"

She took a bambooph from one of the musicians. It was much like an oboe, but with a double barrel, and she began to play along with the other musicians. When the song reached a certain note, these instruments would fire a food snack from the second barrel, and a dog would bark and catch it as a treat in its mouth. The bark was timed with the song, and so it was as if the dogs were part of the musical act. Shara laughed when the song ended. People watching their performance clapped.

"You see? Isn't it all so easy to have fun?" she said after returning the instrument to the musician.

"You are young and full of life," Claus said. "But I...well...my past. I'm not from here."

"None of us are, at least not our ancestors," Shara said. "I was born here, yes, but some came here recently from abroad, and others came here many years ago. That's why we like it so. We all come from various places. But we've left that sorrow behind and have made our own little paradise. Isn't it wonderful? But tell me more about Lanietta and Labba. They are Carinians, right? Not human at all. Wow, Lanietta got huge and picked me up. But I wasn't about to let her spoil things. No, we like our village, thank you very much. You aren't married to either of them, are you? That would be weird."

"Yes, it would be weird, and no, I'm not married to them. I'm not married to anyone," Claus said.

"I knew you weren't. A woman would fill your heart with joy. You need someone. Someone like me. Or...or...is your heart set on another?"

"Another. From another time. Her name was Frieda," Claus said.

"Was she like me? Was she happy?" Shara asked.

"She was never happy. But she had a strong will. I need someone with a strong will, because my own will is weak. I end up in all kinds of situations that I cannot escape. When I fall asleep at night, I dream that I'm running from one person's farm to another, that nowhere is mine to call home. And I must run for fear that the farmer will catch me and throw his pitchfork at me. When I lived in my house, these dreams were so disturbing that I'd wake up at night and go for a walk in my own neighborhood. Then I'd return to my house and fall asleep on the couch."

"So you did have a home," Shara said.

"It was a house. But not a home," Claus said. "Oh I tried to make things work with Frieda, but she was always too work-oriented. I felt there was something missing. But when I tried to date other women who weren't work-oriented, I ended up doing all the work in the relationship."

"It's not a complex problem. It really isn't," Shara said.

"Then tell me. Why haven't you married?" Claus asked.

"I'm only seventeen," Shara said. "My birthday is next month. Then I'll be old enough to marry in my society. We're not allowed to date until we become adults, and so I haven't."

"But you must've had your eye on a few men here, right? Well? Do you have any favorites?"

"In my own village? No. And I'll tell you why," she said.

Shara crept up close to Claus's ear and whispered, "Because I'm picky."

Then she ripped off Claus's shirt and ran.

"Hey! That's my shirt!" Claus said, and he ran after her.

The two made a scene. Shara ran with Claus's shirt in one hand and her unfinished corn-on-a-stick in the other. Shara bumped into people, ran over carts, jumped over tables of goods, and even fell through the side of a tent, pulling the tent down. But Claus could never catch her. She would gain a bit on even ground, slow up when she collided with something, but then pull away again on free ground. Villagers were all clothed, and seeing Claus without a shirt was a bit of a surprise, and so there was hollering and cheering for both Shara and Claus. When the two passed Labba and Lanietta, Shara threw her corn stick at Lanietta while Claus's flower crown flew off into Labba's hands. Angry, Lanietta threw the corn stick down.

"Of all the disgusting things! Slobbery food from some...some...human!" Lanietta said.

"Oh, the prince has lost his crown of flowers! Come here, fair maiden, and be entered into competition, so that the prince may have choice of the fairest maiden in the village!" Labba said, and she attempted to place the crown of flowers on Lanietta's head.

But Lanietta swatted the flowers aside, and they fell to the ground.

"I'm going to find the doctor!" Lanietta said.

"Wait!" Labba yelled. "He's with the—"

But it was too late. Lanietta had already left in a huff.

Labba reached down for the crown of flowers, but another hand also reached for them. The two bumped hands, picked up the flowers together, and exchanged stares. Labba looked into the eyes of the fairest man she had ever seen, with flowing hair and a charismatic body. He whispered something in her ear, she giggled, and then he led her by the hand away from the jostling of people and thus out of view.

"What is your name?" Labba asked as the two entered a great horticultural garden.

"Argo," he said. "And you are Labba. You come from the skies and bring the wisdom and grace of the skies with you."

Labba giggled like a schoolgirl at the flattery.

"Well, I have a thing for being outworldly," Labba said.

"You are all that and more. If you were a flower, I would beg that you be the central piece in my great garden," Argo said.

"All of this is yours?" she asked.

Argo nodded yes.

"It's beautiful. I've never seen such an assortment of flowers, trees, shrubs, and...oh, this smells wonderful."

"It is a rose," Argo said.

"But it has thorns. Ouch," Labba said.

"The greatest of beauty must survive against all evil. That is true beauty. I sense this in you, that you have come from afar and have endured much. Yet your soul is uncorrupted. Nay, you remain pure at heart. More pure than any woman I've ever known. How is this possible?" Argo said.

"And here I was kissing every man I bumped into earlier," Labba said.

"Like a butterfly dancing from flower to flower until she finds the right one," Argo said.

"You *are* a man!" Labba said, and she kissed him. "But tell me more about this garden. You must have thousands of workers helping you out."

"Perhaps a dozen," Argo said. "I do as much as I can. I believe that flowers are meant to be beautiful from the start. They but need a little space and water to get started. My workers mostly trim those plants that get out of hand and interfere with others, but I have planted everything you see here. This is merely the hobby section. The real work is in that greenhouse. Come with me."

Argo led Labba by the hand as they walked under trees and huge shrubs. Labba stopped him, however, by a tree growing mistletoe.

"I have heard that mistletoe carries a special meaning," Labba said.

"Indeed it does," Argo said, and he kissed Labba several times.

"Tell me, Argo," Labba said. "Whenever people pass, they greet you as a prince. Are you related to King Jarro?"

"I am his youngest brother," Argo grinned. "There are three of us brothers—Jarro who is the eldest, Charco who is the middle child, and me. Jarro is the king and has final authority over this village. Charco manages day-to-day operations. I manage agriculture."

"And Yuri? Is he related?"

"No. He is the son of the former leader. Yuri was given charge of information and security in exchange for his allegiance to Jarro. Labba, I...you aren't human, are you?"

"No," Labba laughed, "I am not. But I can be as human as you need me to be."

"Perhaps not too human," Argo said. "There is still greed amongst us. Yuri's father grew old and was to pick a successor, but Charco and Yuri plotted against Yuri's father and let him die quietly from a disease they introduced to him. I am not proud of this fact, but it is the truth. They convinced Jarro that the death was natural and that Jarro should become king. The real power, though, belongs to Charco and Yuri. Do not worry. Charco and Yuri do not know that I know, though they did try to set me up as the head court judge. I instead took over agriculture. It is more satisfying than settling petty squabbles amongst the people. I am sorry to have placed this all on your shoulders, but I want to be truthful and open with you."

"You have and more! I only hope I can help you with your work. You do a great service for your people," Labba said.

"Then you'll stay? You'll be my consort?" Argo said.

Labba giggled again.

"Everything is happening so quickly," she said. "But you have not dropped to a knee to propose, as is customary for humans. And no engagement ring."

Argo blushed red in embarrassment. He tried to speak but stumbled. Labba laughed.

"There's plenty of time for that. Now show me the greenhouse," Labba said.

The two entered the greenhouse, and Labba was amazed at the assortment of bamboophs in various stages of early growth.

"The bambooph is very important to us. We use it for many things. Many things," Argo said.

"Show me," Labba said.

"Here we have special bambooph we use in neckbands to remove carbonic buildup in the blood. All of us must wear one. But I see you have no need for one. Do you...are you able to..."

"I don't need to breathe," Labba said. "Well not for oxygen or for purging carbon dioxide. I exhale from time to time, but I can tell you more later. I'd like to wear a neckband. Do you have one for me?"

"I shall give you mine," he said.

"Argo, wait, you won't be able to purge the carbon diox—"

But Argo didn't wait. He removed the neckband from his neck and placed it around Labba's. Immediately he started to gasp from carbon dioxide buildup, not as severely as Claus when he first encountered this new Earth air, but enough to indicate his discomfort.

"There, there!" Labba said, and she held her hand on his neck.

Immediately, Argo's carbon dioxide level returned to normal.

"You can do that with the touch of a hand? You amaze me with each passing moment!"

Labba waved to one of the workers, and the worker placed a new neckband around Argo.

"I wouldn't want you to suffer," Labba said.

"Thank you," Argo said as he cleared his throat.

"Show me more!" Labba said.

"The bambooph is the only thing protecting us from the selenites," Argo continued. "My primary responsibility is the care and maintenance of the bambooph perimeter. Here we grow replacements for bamboophs that have been damaged. Also, our province is expanding, and so we need more bamboophs for that as well."

"One wall of bamboophs protecting this entire area. Seems so fragile. A single break in the wall—"

"Could allow invaders in. Yes, I know," Argo said.

"Have you thought of creating an outer wall? As a first line of defense?" Labba asked.

Argo smiled.

"You are very wise. Yes, that would be an excellent idea. I have brought it up to Yuri and Charco, but they have other things on their mind. It would not be hard to do, provided I had help. I would need to start a second greenhouse for the outer wall bambooph. You know, I've been experimenting with different strains of bambooph. I have just the strain over here. See? It does well in sandy or rocky terrain and can withstand salt-water spray. It would prosper along the coastline."

"You're halfway there!" Labba said. "I'd love to help you get your outer wall going. Imagine the music that would play then."

"Unfortunately this new strain only plays percussion, like low cannon fire," Argo said.

"Oh we'll have to change that first thing," Labba said.

"There is another type of bambooph I wish to show you," Argo said. "It too is a new strain. Not many know of its existence."

The two walked into a back room.

"These bamboophs have no holes in the side," Labba said.

"Because they are weapons," Argo said. "They would be forbidden. Jarro does not want the citizens to kill one another over petty arguments."

"Jarro doesn't know you have these, does he?" Labba asked.

Argo nodded no.

"Charco? Yuri?" Labba continued.

Argo nodded no to both.

"You could launch a coup and rule this province all by yourself," Labba said.

"Do not speak of such things. I would never imagine such a scenario," Argo said.

"But you could."

"I do not wish it. Already the people blame Jarro for things outside of his control. He spends much of his time with bread and circus," Argo said.

"Bread and what? What do you mean?"

"It is an old expression. In Ancient Rome, citizens were appeased by giving them bread and entertaining them with the circus," Argo said. "Jarro very much wishes to keep the peace, and I'm happy to let him. My great love is here with my garden. And now my favorite person is with me in my garden."

The two shared a kiss and embrace. Labba touched one of the special bambooph weapon plants. The outer skin layer came off.

"Oh, I'm sorry! I damaged it, I think!" Labba said.

"Shhh," Argo said. "Keep this quiet. The outer layer of this bambooph is a simple covering to make it look like other bambooph plants. You will notice the material underneath is very shiny."

"Yes, it is. Like metal," Labba said.

"That's because it *is* metal. These bamboophs take iron and other materials from the soil and create a hard, steel shape. They store seeds inside, and these seeds contain both a projectile and propellant," Argo said. "The one you have touched is like a rifle from ancient times, but these over here have larger bores, and so they are more like cannons. This one here puts out a heavy projectile, while this other one over here puts out an incendiary projectile for starting fires. Let the selenites come, I say. If we don't smash them, we'll burn them."

Argo's eyes lit up with intensity, but he relaxed and shrugged his shoulders.

"So much for their use. They will remain here as one of my curiosities," Argo said.

Argo led Labba to a door in back, which he opened. Inside was a dark, spiral stairwell, and he beckoned her down the stairs. He flipped a switch, and lights turned on in the room at the bottom of the steps.

"This is my latest creation," he said. "Bamboophs that make things. This one creates silk and weaves it into cloth. The sheets come out of this slit that runs the length of the bambooph. This other bambooph strategically packs cellulose fibers together, creating a wood plank of a hard exterior surface with light but strong fibers on the inside. Another one here creates rod from metal in the soil, and this other one creates threaded rod. There are many other bamboophs here, creating all sorts of goods."

"It's the beginnings of a factory," Labba said. "Are these forbidden too?"

"They would be, yes," Argo said. "Neither Jarro nor Charco know about these. You see, these bamboophs make things very slowly, but they could be sped up to make things more quickly."

"How would you speed them up?"

"By feeding them oil. There's an untapped oil field under this village, but we don't dare drill into it. We would release all sorts of nastiness into the air, water, and topsoil. Yes, forbidden."

"It should remain forbidden. You have a nice little paradise here, Argo."

"You mean *we* have a paradise, right?"

"Yes, *we*," she said, and she hugged him.

The two climbed back upstairs and returned to the main garden.

"I have a wonderful idea. When the feast and all is over, let's bring my selenite doctor here to help out with your projects. You know, Leni. He could be an immense help."

"Shara wants him to help with her hospital," Argo said.

"We can share Leni with Shara," Labba said. "When Leni is free, he does your work for you."

"What would I do with myself if your Leni does my work?" Argo asked.

Labba kissed Argo.

"Get the idea?"

"Shara will need special reservation to borrow Leni. I'm putting him on the payroll," Argo insisted.

"And I think it's time to give you a preview of what you can do with your free time," Labba said, and she led Argo away to a private, secluded place.

Chapter 17: Captain Regolith

"How did I get myself into this mess?" Lanietta asked herself as she searched behind the tents and booths for Leni. "I'm supposed to be the one in control. Clomper is out chasing an Earth girl, the doctor is now called 'Leni', and I'm going crazy! Time to find that doctor and get these people straightened out. Maybe he can deploy a gas bomb that makes the villagers miserable. Then I can laugh and be happy again."

She pulled up a sheet in the back area of a booth and saw an old man cleaning up with a broom.

"You there! You'll make a good pet! I'll turn you into Climper, a grey dog," Lanietta said.

Lanietta sent blue-green light on the man, and indeed, he turned into a grey dog. But the dog looked at Lanietta in shock and did not move.

"Here, Climper! Jump! Play!" Lanietta said, but the dog remained motionless.

"Whuff!" the dog barked weakly.

"You're no fun," Lanietta said, and she changed him back to human form.

The man stared at Lanietta for a moment, and then he resumed sweeping. Lanietta walked to the back of another booth and was about to find another potential pet when she heard two men telling alternate lines of a limerick.

"There once was a knight from Camelot," said the first.

"Who met Miss Oblivia de Gabalot," said the second.

"She talked all night,"

"With no end in sight."

"And both your brains can just rot!" Lanietta shouted as she burst into the front.

The two men looked at her in surprise. She grew angry, became tall, and the two men fled.

"I've got to get out of this village Arberella or whatever it is. I've just got to!" Lanietta said.

Lanietta searched a few more booths, but no Doctor Leni.

"Wait! I'll call him from the ship! From Novi 2. He has a homing link. I'll have him return to base," Lanietta said. "But I'll take a short cut. Don't want to deal with these villagers and their frolicking."

She put distance between her and the village center. As she did, she approached the ring of bamboophs. Like before, they were of various heights and diameters. Each played a musical tone softly from the wind, but every so often, one would get loud from being hit by the wind in an especially pronounced fashion, and this tone would reverberate throughout the bambooph ring in the form of harmonics, and so there was a perpetual shifting of chords and musical keys.

"I need to break through this line. These shoots are in my way," Lanietta said.

Lanietta broke off little bambooph shoots and tossed them aside. Then she broke larger shoots. These shoots let out foul tones as they were broken, and the resulting tension reverberated throughout the bambooph line. The ground shook o-so-subtly. Lanietta found herself encircled by a number of large bamboophs. They were angry, and they tried strangulating her. But Lanietta simply enlarged her form, and that opened up the encircling bamboophs. She held her arms in front of her, formed a wedge, and pried open a path to the outside. Nearby bamboophs swatted her and tried blocking her exit, but she could not be stopped. She successfully plowed her way to the outside area. The bambooph line was not straight but instead wove around as if forming a contour along some underground energy.

"Novi 2 is straight ahead and up the hill, but I'll have to break back through the line of these musical plants," Lanietta said to herself.

When Lanietta reached the halfway point to Novi 2, she was nearly overcome with a low hum. She was in the center of the hum, as it came from a semicircle around her. Lanietta moved around and realized the bamboophs had formed an arc, and this arc reflected noises from outside the village toward her. She walked away from the reflecting arc and walked and walked until she reached a little hill close to the ocean.

"Oh why am I expending all this effort?" Lanietta asked herself. "Labba is connected with Leni. I should just have her tell me his whereabouts. Must be truly out of my wits today."

Lanietta climbed the little hill and saw the ocean. At the far horizon was a collection of huge ships, putting out dark smoke trails.

"Other people? Or selenites? If only I could space-jump. Wait, why don't I try?"

Lanietta concentrated for a moment, and she jumped a few meters from the hill to the shore.

"I *can* space-jump. But travel is limited. I wonder why I couldn't before? Unless something in the village is preventing me. The line of bamboo plants? I'll have to test," Lanietta said to herself.

She tried another space-jump. This time she landed on the outer bamboph line. Several bamboophs wove themselves around her to trap her. She tried to space-jump, but she couldn't. She escaped the bamboophs' grasp, stepped a few feet away, and tried a space-jump. She landed along the shoreline again. She tried a space-jump to a point on the inside of the bamboph line, but she failed and could only get close to the outer line again.

"It's the bamboo plants. They act as a barrier. One mystery solved. Now for the ships. Let's see what they are."

Lanietta space-jumped again. She landed in the ocean about halfway toward the ships.

"Ugh! This water is cold! And no raft! Been a long time since I went for a swim. I must tread water to keep from sinking!

How did the Earthling computer records say to do it? Like this," she said.

She tread water for a little bit. She could hear the hum again, but instead of it coming from the bamboophs (which were way behind her), the hum came from the ships. Also, she could discern something in the sky moving above the ships. She quickly tired of treading cold water, and so she closed her eyes and space-jumped again. This time she landed on the deck of one of the ships.

"Selenites!" she exclaimed.

"A human! Get her!" one of the selenites said.

"Wait!" Lanietta said.

But the selenites didn't wait. They surrounded Lanietta and prepared to chain her like a slave. She considered space-jumping back to Arberella to escape, but why leave so early when she could spend time learning about these automatons? Besides, she might gain something from the experience.

"Do you know who I am? What I am?" Lanietta asked.

"You are human!" said one.

"But how did she penetrate our sensor net?" said another.

"Must have been a malfunction," said another.

"I am a god, sent here to command you," Lanietta lied, and she space-jumped to a different part of the deck.

The selenites gasped. Then they challenged one another to capture Lanietta. One at a time, a selenite charged toward Lanietta, but she simply space-jumped out of the way. The other selenites laughed.

"You can't laugh," she said. "You were never programmed for that."

"I am Captain Regolith," said one. "We are the caretakers of Earth, the supreme life-forms. All others are inferior and either need our guidance or must be put to rest."

These selenites looked similar to the ones she remembered in Luna Beta. They were the same size but wore more armor.

"Are you...are you descendants of...the selenites from...can it be?" Lanietta half asked Captain Regolith and half muttered to herself.

"Take a look for yourself," he said, and he motioned her toward him.

Lanietta walked toward him to get a better look, but as she did, Captain Regolith looked first to one side then another. Two selenites approached from the back flank, thus catching Lanietta off guard. They applied an electrical device to her back, shocking her. Dazed, they chained her up. What they did not realize was that when they shocked her, operating knowledge of their selenite bodies was transferred to her body. She did not realize the transference either, at least not at the time.

"Send her below to the other prisoners," Captain Regolith laughed.

The two selenites who had shocked her took her below. Immediately she noticed a foul smell, and it snapped her out of her daze. She tried to space-jump back up to the deck, but she was surprised to find out she could not.

"What is this ship made of?" she asked.

The selenites laughed, dragged her down a short ways, unlocked a cell, threw her inside, and locked the cell.

"Welcome to Regoship 349," the selenites laughed, and they left.

Inside the cell, Lanietta noticed she was among humans, most of whom had been sleeping, but now most were awakened by her entrance into the cell. They hardly looked human, being covered in a cake-like oozing substance that resembled oily graphite.

"You are humans?" she asked. "But those are selenites above. What are humans doing on a selenite ship?"

"We are prisoners," said one of the humans, gasping for air. "Hello. My name is Clover."

"Hello, Clover," Lanietta said as she shook Clover's hand.

"Oh, sorry about that," Clover said as Lanietta looked at the oily-graphite residue on her hand from Clover.

"What is this?" Lanietta asked. "It's like oily graphite. Why do you smear it on yourselves?"

"We don't," Clover said. "It's carbonic sludge. Comes from our pores. The air is so bad that our bodies put out this stuff."

"Carbonic sludge," Lanietta said, suddenly understanding. "This is how your bodies deal with high carbon dioxide in the air."

"Most people died when the carbon dioxide levels went up. Survivors put out this sludge when in raw air," Clover said.

"So I'll ask again, Clover. What are humans doing on a selenite ship? Seems like any place where the air is better is where you should be," Lanietta said.

"We've all been captured from far away and have been traveling for some time now."

"Where are you going?" Lanietta asked.

"None of us know for sure," Clover said. "We think we are going to Antarctica. We've noticed the days are getting very long, so we know we've been heading south during a summer season. The captain says that when we bring back enough bamboophoni to build another slave ship, he will receive great accolades. But we fear there is more than just gathering bamboophoni. Captain Regolith won't say for sure."

"Yes, I met the captain," Lanietta said. "And I was on Antarctica. Moments ago, in fact. Lots of bamboo there. Or whatever you call it."

There was whispering and a general murmur of disbelief at the statement. Several others awoke.

"Then there is bamboophoni on Antarctica," Clover said. "It is not bamboo, though. Real bamboo has solid outer walls. A bamboophona plant is similar to bamboo but has holes and will make tones when air blows through it."

"Yes, lots of bamboophoni. They are as you describe, putting out music when the wind blows. There is a ring of them around a village of people. They apparently protect the people from selenites," Lanietta said.

"I...you surprise us," Clover said.

"What is surprising?" Lanietta asked.

"Did humans bring you here?" Clover asked. "I mean...the selenites can't go near living, untreated bamboophoni. So that tells us they are unable to travel on Antarctica. Which means they couldn't have brought you from Antarctica by themselves. We thought we'd be making the attempt."

"No. I just landed here. Then the selenites shocked me or something," Lanietta said. "What are you talking about? What attempt?"

Clover introduced Selba, and she spoke up.

"It was that way with my village," Selba said. "We lived inside a ring of bamboophoni. They also played music when the wind blew. All was safe and happy. Then visitors approached the outside wall. They said they were hungry and needed help. We let them in the village and fed them. What we didn't realize was that these hungry people were a decoy. A second group of people cut down bamboophoni plants quickly and efficiently. They used tools given to them by the selenites. By the time we realized what was going on, our village was invaded. We were taken aboard these regoships as prisoners. The bamboophoni collection was taken away by ship as well."

Selba fell into a coughing fit for several seconds.

"Terrible," Lanietta said half-heartedly.

"I was listening to the selenite guards. I heard them discussing how only humans can walk on Antarctica because of the bamboophoni but that they want to attack anyway. Yes, attack," Selba said. "They want the bamboophoni. You know, these cell walls are made of bamboophoni from other islands, but they have been treated by other humans so that the selenites can work them. Supposedly the bamboophoni have a special power."

"Now I understand, yes," Lanietta said. "The bamboophoni also prevent my powers from working, at least some of them. They prevented them on Antarctica in the village, and they prevent them here in this cell. Yes, I see these walls use bamboophoni as material, but the bamboophoni are red."

"The red color is a special chemical that denatures and seals a bamboophona," Clover said. "That's the treatment process I was talking about that humans do."

"Then you intend to invade the village I was just in," Lanietta said. "The one surrounded by bamboophoni on Antarctica. You'll harvest the bamboophoni and take the people as prisoners. Hmm. This is getting interesting. Shara a prisoner. And Clomper will have to plead for my help."

The others looked confused.

"We don't know about this Shara or Clomper," Clover said. "Are they important?"

"Not enough for you to worry about," Lanietta said.

"You almost sound happy," Selba said. "We were hoping you could help us stop this insanity and free us. The selenites must be stopped or destroyed. They have done much to wreak misery on the world."

"So should we break out of these cells? Just like that?" Lanietta said.

"It's a start," Clover said. "But the doors and walls are sturdy. None here can breach them."

"Hmm. Let me try something."

Lanietta thinned her arm and extended it as if it were made of soft wax or rubber, capable of extending and flexing and moving around. Her arm snaked through an air hole in the door and observed a single selenite guard. She then carefully removed an armor link from the guard without notice, tossed the bit of armor down the way (also without notice), and returned her arm to the cell area. The guard ran down the way after the item, and then Lanietta fashioned her wax-like limb into a metal key, unlocked the door, and opened it from the outside. She quickly retrieved her limb and rushed out the door. But she closed and locked the door before the others could escape.

"Wait!" Clover and the others said. "Free us!"

"I'll get back to you on that," Lanietta said.

Lanietta ran out of the prison area, up a stairway to the deck, and before anyone could get hold of her, she dove overboard. While still underwater, she space-jumped back to Antarctica and landed just a dozen feet from shore. She swam the rest of the way and pulled herself onto *terra firma*.

"They are a little closer," she said, looking back. "But not much. I have time yet before the invasion begins."

Lanietta continued her walk toward Novi 2 but then remembered it was unnecessary since Labba knew where Leni was. She was about to turn around and go back, but she was very close to Novi 2 (it was in fact right on the other side of the bamboophs), and she heard voices from the other side that caught her attention.

Chapter 18: Charco's Ghost

"Where is Baruuk?" Yuri asked a sentry.

"Yuri and the sentries," Lanietta thought to herself. "They are still there."

"Who?" the sentry asked.

"Baruuk! My son, remember? He went beyond the bambooph line to investigate wreckage that had washed ashore," Yuri said. "He was to report to me directly. Does he not know I am here? I sent word that he should meet me by this spacecraft."

"No one has seen him," the sentry replied.

"Well that ties it. Shara is spending time with this new stranger while Baruuk is away. That's his girl, you know," Yuri said.

"We didn't know," said the sentry.

"It's all around the village. Everyone knows how Baruuk feels about Shara," Yuri said.

Lanietta's ears perked up. So this could be the way to get rid of Shara and get her Clomper back.

"But does she feel the same way?" the sentry asked.

The other sentries laughed.

"What's all the laughter about?" said another voice. "I come to check on things for my brother, and I find a private festival here?"

"No, Charco," Yuri said. "These sentries have a twisted sense of humor, that is all. I ask them about Baruuk, and they laugh."

"Is this true?" Charco asked.

"No, my lord, we laugh because Yuri believes Shara is madly in love with his son," the sentry said, and other sentries laughed in punctuation.

"I see. My niece has a mind of her own. She has expressed no favoritism for any man," Charco said. "However, she comes of age in a month, and she may express herself at that time."

"And she'll express it for Baruuk!" Yuri said.

"If Baruuk cares for her, he'd better attend the festival. I saw Shara running around with Claus. Had his shirt she did. Seems she has already chosen," Charco said.

"Scandalous! Absolutely scandalous!" Yuri said. "It is worse than I feared! Charco, I must find Baruuk immediately. His attendance at the festival is necessary. In fact, it is mandatory!"

"Mandatory? By whose word?" Charco asked.

"By mine!" Yuri said.

Charco laughed.

"I will look for Baruuk. Stay here and watch the craft," Charco said, despite protests from Yuri. "By order of Jarro."

Yuri reluctantly agreed.

"Don't worry," Charco laughed. "Jarro passes word that you may attend the feast. All of you! He makes an exception for such an occasion. Listen for the horn to sound. Then you may come."

"But who will watch this alien craft?" Yuri said.

"Let the bamboophs warn of any intrusion," Charco said. "Have they failed us before?"

"They didn't warn us of this craft," Yuri said.

"Perhaps because the craft was here first," Charco said. "It is the only explanation for why the bamboophs did not warn us. The bamboophs were not here yet when the craft arrived."

Charco laughed again, waved farewell, and headed toward the shore where Baruuk had gone. This shore was in a different direction from where Lanietta had come, and so she remained unobserved.

"Hmm. Sneak into Novi 2 or follow Charco. Which way to go?" Lanietta thought to herself. "This Baruuk character is what I need. Novi 2 can wait."

Lanietta did a space-jump to a patch of grass on the outside of the bamboophs where she expected Charco to pass. Indeed, he forced an opening very quickly, too close to Lanietta to remain unobserved. She did another space-jump but kept the jump in flux so that she was now submerged in the ground, her entire body covered, but she could see through the upper layers of ground and saw Charco walking as if looking up at the water's surface in a swimming pool. He was tall but thin, and he smoked heavily. His skin was wrinkled and grey, as if tar from the smoking had tarnished it. She had to swim through the space-jump flux to keep up with Charco, and at times he got a bit of a lead, so she had to do mini space-jumps to catch back up. In time she gave up on swimming and simply did the mini space-jumps to keep up.

"I'll have to let Labba's space-jump mentor know that swimming in space-jump flux is for the birds. Who needs it? Just jump!" Lanietta said, imitating the voice of Labba's mentor.

But she may have spoken too loudly. Charco stopped walking, and he spoke.

"Who is that? Where are you?" he asked. "Is this a bad leaf I smoke? No, these grounds are haunted! No wonder bambooph does not grow here!"

Then Lanietta thought. These people might believe in ghosts. It was information passed on to the Carinians about human culture from the Novi 2 computer. Could she use this to her advantage? Somehow get control of the people, be part of the selenite invasion, or some other devious way to savor the savagery of human misery while plucking her Clomper from the mess?

"I must make haste," Charco said. "I must find Baruuk at once."

But Charco was headed in the wrong direction, though he did not know it. Yes, he was headed in the last known direction for Baruuk, but Baruuk wasn't there.

"He is farther down shore," Lanietta said, masking her own voice by imitating Labba's space-jump mentor.

"What? The ghost is back?" Charco said.

"He is floating on a raft along the shoreline, drifting farther and farther away," Lanietta said.

It was true, and Lanietta could see it. Again, the ground was like a swimming pool to her, and she could see far down the way that yes, Baruuk was floating on a raft.

"Is he alive?" Charco asked.

"He breathes, but his eyes are closed," Lanietta said.

"Then he is asleep or unconscious," Charco said. "He would never just fall asleep. Must be hurt."

"Rush to him at once. He needs your aid!" Lanietta urged, and she could barely restrain her laughter, as the situation seemed so comical to her.

"I'm rushing, I'm rushing!" Charco said as he tried to run, but he ran out of breath quickly, didn't know where he was going, and in fact had already deviated from the shortest line to Baruuk. It was up to Lanietta to set him aright.

"Over this way!" she urged after space-jumping to a point in the proper direction.

"You are everywhere? Ghost! What is your name? I must know! I will give you my great thanks after this is over!"

"Mentor!" Lanietta blurted out without thinking. "I mean...I am the Grey Ghost...I mean Great Ghost—"

"Grey Ghost Mentor. Thank you!" Charco said. "How close are we? I cannot see anything in this fog, though I know I am close to the ocean. Grey Ghost Mentor, show me the way!"

Lanietta space-jumped again, and she called out, "Over here!"

Charco kept up his jogging pace, and with Lanietta as a guide, he was able to reach a point in the shoreline where the fog parted and Baruuk's raft became visible. And there was Baruuk splayed out on the raft.

"Baruuk!" Charco called.

But Baruuk did not respond. Charco stepped into the water to pull the raft in, but the water was cold and the waves strong. Charco hesitated.

"I can't reach you. Baruuk! Wake up!" Charco called. "Oh Grey Ghost Mentor! Can you help me with Baruuk? Can you help me bring him in?"

Yes, Lanietta could help, but she'd have to space-jump above the ground line and use her own visible body to bring Baruuk's raft to shore. She so enjoyed the mystery of being the Grey Ghost Mentor and so loved the admiration and worship that she didn't dare reveal her identity. Instead, she came up with another way.

"I can, but only if you permit me," Lanietta said.

"But of course. You only need name it," Charco said.

"I must enter your body and become one with you. I shall strengthen you and make you a man of power. No ocean wave can stop you, no cold can freeze you, no wind can throw you astray," Lanietta said, still using Labba's mentor's voice the entire time.

"Will it hurt? I mean, Grey Ghost Mentor, I beg that you be kind and merciful on this poor soul. I will accept whatever pain must come my way. Help me any way you can to save Baruuk!" Charco pleaded.

Lanietta laughed.

"You will feel no pain. Quite the contrary, you will have such fullness and satisfaction that you will beam of pride and energy," Lanietta said. "Stand still."

Lanietta lifted a hand above the ground line, grabbed Charco's ankle, and pulled his foot into the sand a few inches. Charco shook in fear and tried to run away, but Lanietta's grip was firm, and so she held him in place, though Charco's behavior was much like a frightened animal attempting to flee with a leg caught in a trap.

"Spare me. Spare me!" Charco said. "I changed my mind. I don't want this. I will try another way. Another way!"

"Too late!" Lanietta said.

Lanietta performed a split-jump. She kept part of her ethereal self down underground and merged the other part into Charco's body. Charco immediately felt invigorated. His tissues thickened and puffed out slightly, as if he had just performed three weeks of body-building workout in a few seconds. His nervous heart slowed and thus calmed down. Charco also felt a little sturdier. Indeed, the merging bulked up Charco's wiry frame, and he felt years of dread lifting from his body.

"I feel light as a feather, strong as an ox, and clean as a mountain stream," Charco said.

Charco charged into the water, even above his head. The wave held no power over him, and he continued his march to the raft. He realized he could hold his breath for untold minutes, and so he had no fear of drowning nor did he sputter. He grabbed hold of the raft, dragged it to shore, and pulled it out of the crashing waves—all with Baruuk still aboard. Charco smacked his hand on the side of Baruuk's face, and Baruuk awoke.

"Oh, my head hurts!" Baruuk said. "What happened? Where am I?"

"You are far down shore, that's where you are my friend," Charco said. "But as to why, only you can answer. What do you remember?"

"I saw the debris in the water. Wooden crates. I pulled one ashore, and it was filled with papers. I thought of hauling the crate back to the village when I saw a small boat of people. Three I believe," Baruuk said. "They shouted at me, and I thought they were angry that I'd taken the crate, that it was their crate, and they'd come to claim it. So I shouted back and invited them ashore. I...I don't see...this isn't where I dragged them ashore."

"As I said, my young friend, you have drifted far down shore," Charco said.

"I pulled their little boat ashore and reached to help one of the men when another man swung his oar at me. I caught it, of course, but then the first man cracked his fist over my head. He must have had iron or something over that hand, because it knocked me silly. I fought the best I could, but my balance was off. The three tied me up and hauled me out into the ocean. I got my senses back, tore off the bindings, and attacked them. I knocked two of them out, but the third gave me a hard time. I punched out two of his teeth to gain time, and I jumped off their boat and swam. I hid amongst other debris, and so they couldn't find me. But I got cold, and my dizzy head got weird on me. I don't remember what happened next. I must have found this raft or something. Now I'm here. Boy am I cold!"

"Let's get you back to the village," Charco said. "The march will warm you. And there is good news. Sharlamarian has been cured by a group of strangers. There is a great festival. You are to join in the festivities, if you are well."

"I shall make myself well!" Baruuk said, but when he stood, his knees buckled, and he fell.

"There, now! Let me help!" Charco said as he caught Baruuk by the shoulders and lifted him.

"Impressive, Charco! I did not realize you had such strength. We must test each other in a match. I thought I was the strongest in our village. How did you come by such strength?"

"Do not tell him about me," Lanietta communicated secretly to Charco with her merged self, "or I will vacate your body and leave you weak."

Charco grinned and chuckled.

"I see! Perhaps it is a new woman? You are doing power lifts to impress her. I know how love works, my friend Charco. I have my own interest in Shara. Good for you! Do not let this woman go, if she keeps you in such strong shape. And do not worry. I will not share your secret!"

"Smile and nod. That's right, Charco," Lanietta said. "Let Baruuk think he is right. And perhaps he is. I can stay with you for longer. But you must do as I say. Do not speak. Just smile and nod."

Charco did. Lanietta had succeeded in breaking his will, as he already was obsessed with keeping his new-found vigor. But he did not make the connection that perhaps this was Lanietta, the same

entity who grew tall as a giant and picked up Shara, or the same Lanietta who strengthened Claus's body for defense. However, Lanietta did permit Charco to tell Baruuk about Claus and the new strangers, even about Shara spending time with Claus.

"That Shara! I'll straighten her out but good when I see her. Gallivanting around with outworlders! It's a disgrace to the village," Baruuk said.

"Agree with him," Lanietta said to Charco.

"Yes, it is," Charco said.

Charco had no way of privately speaking with Lanietta. He could only speak aloud to voice a complaint. Yet she could read what he was about to say and correct him before doing so. However, Lanietta said nothing about the selenites on the ships and their plans for invasion, and so Baruuk and Charco only knew of the few humans who attacked Baruuk.

"Did you see any of them reach shore?" Baruuk asked.

"No, I did not," Charco said.

"I hope the bamboophs will warn us should they attempt to invade," Baruuk said.

"They always have before," Charco said. "Rest easy at the festival. Our village is safe."

"I won't rest until Shara and I are formally promised for each other," Baruuk said. "Even then I will only be fully satisfied when she is my wife."

Charco laughed. But his laugh was a little maniacal, as Lanietta added her own laugh to his. It was as if Charco could not decide what tones to use for laughter, and so he alternated between high and low.

"You sound as if you have started the festivities already," Baruuk said. "Wine? Ale?"

"Tell him ale," Lanietta said.

"Ale," Charco said.

"You should tell the brewmaster about that. Needs improvement," Baruuk said.

"Yes, I'll do that."

"Oh, the crate that I pulled ashore! We must retrieve those papers and find out what they say!" Baruuk said.

"I will return for the crate. Your health comes first, my friend," Charco said. "To the village with you!"

With half of Lanietta in Charco, the other half (who had been underground and looking up) space-jumped to the edge of the bamboophs. She tried space-jumping to the inside of the bambooph ring but was unsuccessful.

"I can walk through it to the inside," she said as she did so. "And I can maintain the split with Charco. Let's try a space-jump."

Once more she tried a space-jump while inside the ring of bamboophs, but it failed. Then she had an idea.

"I'll try the split half," she said.

She vacated Charco's body, space-jumped to the crate, and space-jumped back to Charco but held invisible beside him in a space-jump flux state. Charco felt suddenly very miserable. He looked down as if he'd lost something of great value. Baruuk was surprised at this behavior.

"Charco? What is it?" Baruuk said.

"I...I need more ale," he said.

"You shall have it!" Lanietta's space-jumping half said, and she reintegrated with Charco.

"We shall have ale together!" Baruuk said. "You with your woman, and me with mine."

"Tell him you will both find Shara next," Lanietta said.

"Then we shall find Shara first!" Charco said.

"Indeed!" Baruuk agreed.

The men then crossed the bambooph line and entered the village. Unintegrated Lanietta ran ahead (since she could not space-jump) and located Shara. Claus was still chasing her.

"Timing is everything!" unintegrated Lanietta said, and her integrated half whispered into Charco's ear to pace his stride according to her instruction.

"I can smell the food from here," Baruuk said.

"It is nearly time for dinner," Charco said. "The horn will soon sound."

The men entered fully into the village festival, and just at the right time. Shara ran toward them but was caught by Charco. Then Baruuk tripped up Claus. The villagers laughed.

"Uncle Charco!" Shara said.

"I have a surprise for you," Charco said. "Look who's here!"

"Baruuk!" Shara said in shock. "The wind carried rumors of..."

"Of my death?" Baruuk finished. "I have conquered the wind. And you, my Shara!"

Baruuk took Shara into his arms and embraced her tightly. He kissed her, but she pushed against him to stop.

"She doesn't like that," Claus said as he tapped Baruuk on the shoulder.

"Go away, little fly!" Baruuk said, and he gave another kiss to Shara.

But then Claus punched Baruuk in the kidney. Baruuk didn't like that. He tossed Shara to Charco and squared off against Claus. Claus looked around for Lanietta and expected her to encapsulate him, but she did not. She was still integrated with Charco. Claus took a swing at Baruuk, but Baruuk caught the fist, held it, and began crushing it. Claus cried out in pain and dropped to his knees in agony.

"Claus!" Shara cried out as she leapt for him, but Charco held her back at Lanietta's insistence.

"Claus! Claus!" Baruuk mocked. "I'll put Claus out of your mind, my little Shara, by putting Claus out of his own mind."

While still holding Claus's fist with one hand, Baruuk smacked Claus upside the head with the other—several times.

"Now fight like a man," Baruuk said, and he released Claus's fist.

Claus was dazed, and he stumbled around. He took wild swings at Baruuk, but Baruuk simply laughed. Then Baruuk kicked Claus in the chest. Claus went flying backward and nearly fell, but the crowd caught him and tossed him back toward Baruuk. As Claus came toward Baruuk, Baruuk simply stepped aside, picked up Claus, and tossed him into the canopy of a display booth—all without any loss of movement in Claus. Claus fell on the canopy, the canopy collapsed onto the booth (a booth of pigeons), and the bird cages crashed open, releasing the pigeons who then fought their way out into freedom.

"Leave him to the birds," Baruuk said. "I have won my prize."

With that, Baruuk took Shara away, despite her protests. Charco paused, mock saluted Claus, and followed behind Baruuk and Shara.

Chapter 19: The Feast

Dazed and hurt, Claus struggled to get up. The villagers looked at him in surprise but kept their distance. Without warning, the unintegrated Lanietta showed up and helped Claus stand up.

"Lanietta. How nice of you to show up and be so helpful," Claus said sarcastically.

"Oh, sorry about that, Claus. I meant to help you. But I was occupied. Or perhaps I should say I occupied another agenda. Do not worry. I am here now!" she said.

"Oh, joy."

The horn sounded for dinner, and the villagers gathered for the feast.

"Come along, Clomper. Let's clean you up first," Lanietta said.

Lanietta led Claus to a cleaning booth (which was already empty) as the villagers had rushed to the feast.

"The dirt is coming off, but my clothes are torn and covered in blood. I'm a mess for the feast. Where were you again? One moment I'm with Shara, the next moment this villager is attacking me," Claus said. "If only you could heal my wounds and repair my clothes. Wait, can you do that?"

"I...I've never tried. I mean, I know I can give strength and all that. But to repair? I would need a guide, a point of reference," Lanietta said.

Then it hit her. She could use Charco as a point of reference. Could she do it? Could she be split with two integrations? Or an integration and encapsulation? No one to her knowledge had tried. But this was a moment to score points with Claus. And so she tried.

"All right, Clomper. I will try. Shh. Think back to when we were on my farm. Remember? I turned you into a dog. I could do so again, but you'd still have your

injuries. Shh. I'll try something different. Pretend I am a fairy princess. And you are my prince. You are but a frog now, but when I kiss you, all will be better. Kiss me, Clomper. Kiss me."

"You're not human," Claus said. "You won't understand."

"If you want me to heal you, you'll have to kiss me. That's all there is to it," Lanietta said.

She turned her back to him and crossed her arms. Now a second horn had blown.

"The second horn. Shara told me that the second horn is a warning that the feast will start soon. They start on the third horn," Claus said.

"Then you'd better decide before the third horn, Clomper," Lanietta said.

Claus stared at her back. How could he kiss Lanietta after everything she'd done? Even now when he was hurt, she could have protected him, but she didn't. He felt battered and abused, yet she still demanded a kiss. Was it right? Was it affectionate? No, but he was in a compromising situation, and so he had to compromise. He turned her around and quickly kissed her on the cheek.

"No, not like that. I mean a real kiss," she said. "On the lips! Now we'll try again. Turn me around like you did just now and do it right."

Lanietta turned her back to Claus. He spun her around quickly, let go, and then tapped her lips quickly with his.

"Ick," he muttered.

"No, no, no!" she said. "I'll give you one more chance. Spin me around, take me in your arms, and kiss me like I'm delicious."

"More like devil-icious," Claus said.

"Or devil-ina. Yes, think of me as Devilina Devilicious. Say it out loud. Do it!" she insisted.

"Devilina Devilicious," Claus said.

"Again!"

Claus said it multiple times, then he spun Lanietta while still saying, "Devilina Devilicious". He paused, considering whether or not to embrace her, but then she embraced him first. She pulled him close to her, and she kissed him. She pulled tight, and she encapsulated him. As she did, Claus's form briefly wavered but then returned to normal. When it did, all wounds were healed, and his clothing was clean and in good repair. He coughed.

"Yuck. That kiss was like rubber soaked in kerosene," Claus said.

"Of all the nerve!" she said in his mind.

Enraged, Lanietta squeezed his body to cause pain.

"Lanietta! Release me. I feel like an artery is going to burst! Please!" he pleaded.

"Call me Devilina Devilicious!" she said.

"Devilina Devilicious!" he said.

She left his body and returned to her own form.

"Come!" she said. "We don't want to be late! Wait, I know!"

Lanietta changed Claus into a horse with plans of riding him to the feast, but the horse he became was small, about the mass of a human.

"Ack! Forgot about that. He needs to start with more mass to convert to equivalent mass. Back to a human you go," she said, and she changed him back to human.

"Lanietta, please! Can't you—" he started.

"No time to explain. Gotta increase your mass," she said.

She encapsulated him again. She didn't even wait for him to say, "Devilina Devilicious." Now in close proximity to his flesh, she made his body grow into that of a small giant. She then unencapsulated from him and changed him to a horse. He was a horse of proper size, about that of an Irish Cob (in fact that's what he became). She jumped atop him, held onto his mane, and directed him to the feast. Along the way, the horse (Claus) failed to jump over the rope holding a tent firm. Tripping over this rope, he caught the corner of the tent and pulled it down. Two people were inside, and they stepped out immediately.

"Labba!" Lanietta said. "Who are you with?"

"Oh hi, Lanietta. This is Argo. We are, um, friends," Labba said.

"Hello," Lanietta said.

"What a lovely animal you have there," Argo said. "And so charming a lady to be riding it. Where be you going?"

"I am headed to the feast," Lanietta said. "The second horn has already blown. Aren't you two going?"

"We, uh, are we going?" Labba asked Argo, who simply stared with deep eyes toward her.

"Labba, your hair is unkempt," Lanietta said.

"So it is. It must have become tangled by mysterious means," Labba said, glancing toward Argo.

"I see that," Lanietta said.

"Argo, we really should go. Your family will be disappointed if you don't show. You are the third brother," Labba said.

"Third brother of what family?" Lanietta asked.

"Jarro is the eldest, then Charco is the second oldest. And we are to sit on the balcony with them, if I can pull Argo away from here," Labba said.

"Your eyes enchant the soul to the depths of the ocean, the peaks of mountains, and the breadth of the meadow fine. My heart sails down the river of love with your beauty," Argo said to Labba.

"Oh my," Lanietta said.

"Well, you see, learning about these villagers takes time, and Argo and I have exchanged much, uh, knowledge, uh," Labba stumbled.

"I don't want to know. Labba, you best get going. I'll take Clomper here," Lanietta said.

"Oh, you changed him into this? I didn't think it possible, I mean, a horse is much larger than...well...how did you...oh, we'll have to talk, Lanietta. Come along, Argo. It's dinner time," Labba said.

"I must find such a beautiful steed for my beautiful Labba so that we may explore the countryside as one," Argo said.

"No snowbank can hold you two back. The heat here is overwhelming," Lanietta said, and she rode off to the feast.

The feast was actually held near the stage. Each row of chairs had a ledge in front where people could place things such as study books and papers for a lecture, or in this case food for a feast. The stage contained tables upon tables of food. Jarro, Sharlamarian, and Shara sat in the center of the balcony with Charco on one side. On the other side sat Yuri and Baruuk. Several other high-ranking people and families sat in the balcony as well. People had already taken portions from the stage and were seated and eating. Late stragglers were at the stage getting food along with a few children who had started early and were already getting seconds. And so with this food and these people on the stage, Lanietta arrived on Clomper the Irish Cob horse. People gasped in amazement, some panicked and moved out of the way, but children were attracted to the horse. Lanietta took Clomper onto the stage where he knocked over a table or two of food, and then he reared up. The audience called out in fear and awe at Clomper and Lanietta striking a classy pose. Lanietta broke out into opera singing, and a hush fell on the audience. Then by coincidence, the third horn sounded. The people thought this meant the horse was part of the show, and that the entertainment portion of the feast was officially started. And so the audience clapped and cheered at Lanietta and Clomper, who now strutted around stage, off stage, and to the side where a group of children adorned Clomper with string charms and paper ornamentation. Lanietta dismounted Clomper and turned him back into a human. The children cheered in amazement. Lanietta bowed, being proud of her abilities. Claus felt foolish, as he stood there with the charms and paper around his neck. He looked up at the balcony and saw that Shara had been watching him the entire time. She winked and smiled. Jarro stood up and was about to speak, but he turned around suddenly as he realized Argo was now entering the balcony, that is, Argo with Labba. Jarro motioned for them to sit. Again Jarro was about to speak to the people, but Shara stood suddenly and whispered something in Jarro's ear. She then pointed down toward Claus. She pulled away, clasped her hands together, and jumped up and down as if pleading for something (in fact she was begging for Claus to sit with her in the balcony). But before Jarro could answer, Charco walked over, stepped in front of Shara, said a few words to Jarro, and Jarro nodded in affirmation.

"Yes. Have Shara sit by Baruuk," unintegrated Lanietta said.

"What?" Claus said.

"And have us sit with Choir B," unintegrated Lanietta said.

"What are you talking about?" Claus said.

Jarro then nodded to Charco, who then escorted Shara over to Baruuk. Shara was not happy. She looked back at her father in protest. Then Jarro called down to one of his sentries and pointed over toward Claus and Lanietta. The sentry relayed the word, and within a moment, two sentries spoke to Claus and Lanietta.

"Our great leader Jarro invites you Lanietta and Claus to the Choir B balcony, where you may feast undisturbed from the common people," the sentry said.

"Thank you, we accept," Lanietta said quickly.

Lanietta led Claus by the hand across the stage, then a little behind the Choir B balcony, up stairs, and into the balcony itself.

"You will like Choir B," Lanietta said to Claus. "Very musical. But we must sing when the choir sings. It's only fair."

"What...you...you're up to no good. Have you split or something? Is there a part of Lanietta in someone else manipulating things? You knew what Jarro was going to do before he did it. Have you compromised his leadership? That's unethical, Lanietta. No leader should be a puppet to another," Claus said.

"Keep your shirt on. I'm not controlling Jarry Jarro. Just Charco, his brother," Lanietta grinned.

"Disgusting," Claus said.

"It's no more disgusting than Labba manipulating Argo, the other brother," Lanietta said.

"She's split too? You both are integrated with Jarro's brothers?" Claus asked.

"Not like that. She's split with Leni. And before you ask, Leni is the name she gave our selenite doctor. She had to merge her half with him to keep him functioning among these bamboophs. So she hasn't merged with Argo, at least not in the ethereal sense," Lanietta smiled.

Claus was about to speak but simply shook his head. He looked at the main balcony and saw Shara staring back at him. Baruuk noticed this exchange, lifted a fist up to Claus, then turned Shara's head and spoke to her to distract her. She looked down in dismay.

"Shara isn't happy. It's obvious. Jarro and she were so happy that we saved Sharlamarian's life," Claus said.

"They are still thankful. Cheer up, Clomper. You still have me. And besides, the show will start up soon. See? They are clearing the tables from the stage," Lanietta said.

"They can't! I haven't had anything to eat yet!" Claus said.

"Don't worry. Look! Our food is here!"

Indeed, servants brought forth food for Claus and Lanietta. Though Lanietta did not need food in the same way, she ate with Claus just the same.

"The meat is cooked just right," Lanietta said. "The sauce is exquisite, with just the right combination of herbs. Try the mashed potatoes. The gravy is mmm-mmm good. Beer-meister! Over here!"

"The food *is* good," Claus said. "But I don't understand. You Carinians don't need to eat."

"Not in the way you do," Lanietta said. "Most Carinians can't eat at all. Labba and I can eat with these physical bodies if we want. We simply exhale much more than normal to eliminate the waste. Human food is inefficient as a fuel. And yes, we can now savor your human pleasures as desired, Clomper. Couldn't do it on the lunar farm. You see? I can be your human wife. You only need be a pet part of the time. The rest I grant as husband time. I am very generous."

Claus kept looking up at Shara, but Lanietta grabbed Claus's head and turned it toward her.

"She is forbidden fruit, Clomper. She doesn't belong to you, because you don't belong here, and so you don't belong to her. Reason it out. Could you settle in this village? Could you live like one of these folk knowing what you know and having done what you've done? It is me you want. Me."

"I thought you were going to mention Frieda," Claus said.

"Oh forget Frieda," Lanietta said. "She's dead. Do you hear? Dead!"

"No! I refuse to believe it!" Claus said.

"Libriota and the Bleuhs have allowed Frieda and the other humans to live out their days, so that they could be studied," Lanietta said.

"No. They could be in stasis," Claus proposed.

"For what purpose? Humans do not interact while in stasis, Clomper. No, they have lived out their lives. Their purpose is complete. They are dead. You must leave your memory of them behind. Do you believe you can continue in this static frame of mind? Do you think all the world will wait for you, Clomper? It does not. Look at Jarro. He is about to speak. He will not wait for your Frieda," Lanietta said.

Jarro stood, and several heralds played on their bambooph instruments. The bambooph wall in turn reverberated the tones, adding their own harmonics like a sophisticated echo. The heralds stopped, the air grew quiet, and Jarro spoke at long last.

"Fellow people, we are gathered to celebrate the miraculous cure of my wife and your Lady, Queen Sharlamarian!" Jarro started.

Great applause from the audience from those around Jarro. Several men got up and shook Sharlamarian's hand while Labba got up and kissed her on the cheek.

"We give great thanks to our beloved visitors who made it possible. First, Claus and Lanietta," Jarro said.

"Stand up, Clomper. They're applauding us," Lanietta said.

Lanietta pulled Claus to his feet, and they both bowed from the Choir B balcony.

"I would also like to thank Labba, who helped with medical treatment," Jarro said.

Labba stood and bowed to applause. Argo then stood and kissed her, and the crowd went wild with more applause. Jarro had to put his hands out and motion for the crowd to quiet down.

"Thank you all for being so supportive. But the greatest helper is the doctor, who—"

"Leni!" Labba shouted. "His name is Leni!"

Jarro and the audience laughed.

"Leni. He performed the operation that saved Sharlamarian's life. I welcome him to Arberella, as I hope you do. But where is the doctor?" Jarro asked.

Jarro's question was the start of the performance. Choir A asked, "Where is the doctor?" and then Choir B echoed the same question with Lanietta prompting Claus to speak when Choir B spoke. A hush fell over the audience, and the arena darkened. Children grew fearful and cried out, as did a few adults. Then a single woman walked on stage in a long, white robe and spoke.

"In the beginning, all was merry with people around the world. But a darkness descended, as did the first artificial being, what we call today the selenite!"

With the word "selenite," a drum sounded and struck fear like thunder. Children became squeamish and clung to their parents while parents clung to themselves. A white light burst forth in the upper center of the stage, and up on a platform stood Leni, the selenite doctor! He was painted in glowing white with black highlights, looking more like a freakish skeleton than anything.

"Numero Uno Selenite," Choir A said.

"The beast from the sky," Choir B said.

Leni flew around the audience, at least with the help of a crane and wires painted black to hide their presence. Adults ducked while children screamed and dove under chairs. Even Jarro and those in the main balcony cringed back as Leni flew by.

"Our selenite is in a play?" Claus asked Lanietta. "Who named him Leni?"

"Labba did. Shh. We don't want to disturb our choir," Lanietta said.

"The selenite crashed to Earth," the robed lady said.

Leni flew back to the stage, the wires disengaged, and he dropped a short ways into a prone position where he did not move (though he was not damaged).

"It landed broken," Choir A said.

"And was swept by ocean currents," Choir B said.

Several actors dressed as ocean waves entered the stage and walked around Leni as if floating him along.

"You're not participating with Choir B," Lanietta said to Claus.

"I'm not a choir person. Besides, I don't know what to say," Claus said.

"Numero Uno landed on an island," the robed lady said.

"And was repaired," both choirs said.

An actor pretended to repair Leni.

"These village people know what will be said and what will be sung. This play has been performed many times, though with a human instead of Leni for the Numero Uno Selenite," Lanietta said.

"Numero Uno was taught how to do human tasks," the robed lady continued.

Leni stood and mimicked activities performed by the humans such as sweeping, dusting, and serving food.

"How do you know?" Claus asked.

"Charco. I have access to his thoughts and memories," Lanietta said.

"Then people wanted their own selenite servants, and so Numero Uno was duplicated," the robed lady said.

Leni walked into a booth. Out stepped an actor in selenite costume from an adjoining booth. This was repeated with several other actors (who entered the adjoining booth from a trap door below).

"It's still disgusting. Integrating with Charco!" Claus said.

"Shh. Choir time," Lanietta said.

"Duplicated. Duplicated. And duplicated!" Choirs A and B said together.

"You should listen. You'll learn what happened to our other selenite," Lanietta said.

"You mean Selenite 102? Selenite 102 became Numero Uno Selenite? And you knew? How?" Claus asked.

"I only figured it out just now, like you. I learned of the play from Charco, and from that I put two and two together, as you humans say," Lanietta said.

"The selenites took over menial tasks," the robed lady said.

"Menial," Choir A said.

"Menial," Choir B said.

"The selenites took over farming, manufacturing, technology, and services," the robed lady said. "They..."

"Took," Choir A said.

"Over!" Choir B said.

"People forgot how to run the world. The selenites took over," the robed lady said. "Then the selenites issued decrees."

"No human travel without selenite escort," Choir A said.

"No human travel," Choir B said.

"No new humans," Choir A said.

"No humans at all," Choir B said.

"War came!" the robed lady said. "Humans fought back. It was a great war, the War of the Selenites."

"Great war," Choir A said.

"Great war," Choir B echoed.

Leni returned to the platform where he first stood and sat in the chair of a king.

"Humans fought machines in numbers throughout the world," the robed lady said.

Actors entered the stage behind the robed lady. Half were dressed as people, the other half as selenites. They engaged in mock battle with the humans using firearms and the selenites using clubs.

When the humans fired, blanks with sparkling bursts erupted from the firearms. Those playing the selenites did not fall but instead clubbed the ones playing humans, of which these humans fell as if dead.

"The war was lost. People scattered to all parts of Earth," the robed lady said. "Humanity was destined to go extinct."

"Near," Choir A said.

"Extinction," Choir B said.

"It's amazing they didn't," Claus said.

"But they didn't," the robed lady said. "The humans were saved by selenite greed."

"Selenite," Choir A said.

"Greed," Choir B said.

"Hah! That will teach those evil selenites," Claus said to Lanietta.

"You don't even know what they did," Lanietta said.

"If it was because of greed, then it has to be lesson-worthy," Claus said.

"Listen and learn," Lanietta said.

"The selenites made haste in war. Yes, haste! They made great chemical weapons. And deployed them against the humans!" the robed lady said.

The selenite actors threw little canisters at the actors portraying humans. The canisters ruptured, and fluid oozed over the human actors. The goo was harmless, but it bubbled and put out fumes, and so the actors pretended to be eaten alive by the goo.

"But the selenites did not create new chemicals of destruction. No! They deployed remnant chemicals from the selenite factories, factories that made new selenites. And so! The chemicals contained something special. A young doctor researched the chemical to discover its properties."

Choir A and Choir B hummed at this point or made sound effects as needed. Human actors rolled out a platform with a table, test tubes, and a Bunsen burner, along with a woman actor portraying the chemist. The woman was Shara.

"Shara!" Claus burst.

His voice echoed throughout the arena, and all looked at him briefly. Then Baruuk looked at his side in surprise that Shara was not there. The others in the balcony were surprised as well, but Jarro and Sharlamarian simply looked at Baruuk and laughed. They pointed to their daughter on stage and clapped.

"Interesting development," Lanietta said to Claus. "I must volunteer for the next play. Matter of fact, we can be in the next play together, you and I. We'll play the first couple to build a remote community unaffected by the selenites. And we would make music together."

"The doctor refined the chemical and made it safe for life," the robed lady said.

"Safe for life," Choir A said.

"But unsafe for selenites!" Choir B said.

"Yes! Because of this!" the robed lady said.

The choirs hummed, and out walked actors holding regular bamboo canes. Shara placed new goo on these bamboo canes. Holes dissolved from the canes, and they became flutes. The actors then played songs on the flutes.

"She became known as Lady Flute," said the robed lady.

"Lady Flute," Choirs A and B said in unison.

"Lady Flute planted these flutes, and they grew!" the robed lady said. "When the wind blew, they played musical notes."

The actors brought forth bamboophs in large pots, and a fan blew air from above onto these potted bamboophs. They played the musical portion of a song, and the choirs hummed harmony. Two actors placed a short, purple robe over Shara, and Shara walked over to where the robed lady stood. The two sang lyrics to the song being played.

"Do you play a musical instrument, Clomper?" Lanietta asked.

"What? What are you talking about?" Claus asked back.

"Such as a lyre, for example," Lanietta said.

"The only liar I know is next to me," Claus said.

"Oh come now, my sweet. Pull out the lyre from under your chair, there's a good Clomper. Right about...now!" Lanietta said.

And just as Lanietta said, "Now," Choirs A and B pulled out lyres from under their chairs and played chords in harmony with the bamboophs on stage.

"I don't know how to play this," Claus said.

"It's easy, look," Lanietta said as she played her lyre in tune with the choirs.

"You're cheating. You know all about this play. From Charco," Claus said. "But do you really think I'll know what to play just by watching you? What's wrong, can't you transfer the play and all into my brain and have it carry the meaning and symbolism it is intended to deliver? You Carinians think you're so hot. You can change my shape into a dog or horse or anything. But you can't impart wisdom. Because you don't have any. Which tells me your kind can't share wisdom among one another. It's always fight, fight, fight! Why you couldn't create a world of wonder if you tried. What a pathetic race you Carinians are, if you can even call yourselves a race!"

Lanietta stopped playing the lyre and held perfectly still. The expression on her face began with a stare at Claus then changed to anger and rage as her color changed from bluish-green to dark green to orange and then fiery red.

"I thought you couldn't change color anymore," Claus said.

"I am now!" she barked.

"Lanietta, I—" Claus started.

"I shall impart the wisdom of the ages as taught to me by the universe. Behold a supernova!" Lanietta yelled.

Lanietta spouted bluish-white fire from her nostrils and ears. Indeed, the immediate area became incredibly bright and hot.

"Lanietta, stop!" Claus said.

Claus tried to hold his ground with her, but he had to turn his face away to protect it from the heat. The clothing on his backside caught fire. He lost his composure and jumped off the balcony into the audience below. Choir B became frightened and immediately scrambled for the exit. With space freed up, Lanietta grew in mass and changed shape to that of a fire-breathing dragon. She flew around the arena, sending bluish-white fireballs to the crowd below. The crowd moved to avoid the fireballs while simultaneously trying to exit. Charco, who still had part of Lanietta integrated inside him, became hostile himself, and he attacked those on the main balcony, clearing people out of his way until he went after Jarro. He choked Jarro and stabbed him in the chest. Argo tried pulling Charco away, but Charco swatted Argo and sent him off the balcony. Baruuk was next and managed to give Charco a good fight. During this time, the others (except Labba) carried Jarro off the balcony to safety. Argo climbed back up the balcony and assisted Baruuk in containing Charco, but the best Argo and Baruuk could do was a stalemate.

Labba instructed Leni to stand at the front of the stage and block all fireballs headed that way, which he did as best he could, but the heat was incredible, and he could only buy the actors a little time to escape. Lanietta took out Leni with one swat of her spiked tail as she flew by, and that should have deactivated the selenite doctor, but Labba's integration with the selenite protected him from serious damage. He was, however, knocked off the stage, and he climbed back up to defend. Labba dove off the balcony, and as she fell into the air, she changed shape into that of a giant bald eagle. She blocked fireball after fireball. Each fireball singed and burned her feathers, but by burning her feathers, she was able to dissipate the fireball, and once dissipated, her feathers grew back quickly.

One of these blocks brought her close to Claus. Labba offered to pick him up and carry him off, but he told her no, go protect Shara instead. However, Shara had already left the stage and was not clearly visible from Lanietta's point of view. Further angered by this, Lanietta refocused her fireballs onto the stage, setting it afire. The heat and swirling flames created tornadic winds, throwing people and things about, including Leni who unfortunately was tossed under a pile of debris.

"You people are nothing compared to Carinians!" bellowed Lanietta from her dragon shape. "Behold the great power of the dragon!"

Lanietta then flew around the village, setting it ablaze. Villagers scurried about with pails of water to extinguish the flames. Labba flew after Lanietta and stopped some of these fireballs, but not all.

"Stop this madness, Lanietta!" Labba bellowed, and Labba attacked Lanietta directly, sinking her talons into Lanietta's back and ripping off scales.

But this only angered Lanietta further. Lanietta twisted in the air, freed herself from Labba, and headed for the bambooph line. She withdrew her other half from Charco in order to utilize full force. Charco collapsed in exhaustion, Argo tied up Charco, and Baruuk jumped off the balcony to find Shara. Lanietta flew above the bambooph line and alternated between sending fireballs ahead of herself and behind. With Labba only able to cover one direction, Lanietta was able to successfully set the bambooph line on fire in the other direction. Bambooph after bambooph gurgled and gagged as the water from deep below boiled upward and clogged their orifices. It was a horrible sound, like a cacophony of giant song birds fighting desperately against drowning. The bamboophs flapped about and coughed out chunks of water and debris, but Lanietta's attack did not abate, and so the floundering bamboophs caught fire as the last bits of water boiled off, sending out high-pitched screams like boiling teapots. The bamboophs then split longways and sent out rock-shattering pops for each split.

Meanwhile, Leni had created a crawlway from below the rubble. He first crawled out then assisted Shara out. Baruuk and Claus ran to her aid while Leni assisted others from the crawlway.

"Claus. I'm so happy you're here," Shara said from a half-conscious state.

Shara fell into Claus's arms. But Baruuk wasn't happy.

"Here, let me take her," Baruuk said, and he reached to take Shara.

"No. Claus," Shara mumbled, and she clung fast to Claus.

"Haven't you done enough damage?" Baruuk said to Claus. "Your demon is destroying the village, and you've corrupted my Shara. Hand her over."

"I haven't corrupted anyone," Claus said. "And I'm sorry about Lanietta. Labba is trying to stop her. But we've got to do what's best for Shara. She needs proper shelter."

"The way your flying demon is going, there won't be any shelter left!" Baruuk said.

Baruuk yanked at Claus's arms and moved in to take Shara away. Claus fought back, with Shara as the prize. In their desire to get hold of Shara, Lanietta returned unexpectedly and snatched Shara from the grasps of Baruuk and Claus. Leni saw this, jumped into the air, and fought with Lanietta to free Shara, but Lanietta knocked Leni off, and he fell to the ground.

"Shara!" Baruuk yelled, and he ran after Lanietta.

"She's gone," Claus lamented as he stared at Lanietta and Shara rapidly shrinking from view.

Claus turned to ask Leni for help, but something hit Claus on the back of the head, and he blacked out.

Chapter 20: A Dark Cloud

When Claus awoke, he was lying on a cot in a jail cell by himself. Besides the cot, there was a table, a chair, a sink with running water, and a toilet. Claus sat up and felt the back of his head. A knot reminded him of his injury.

"Oh, what happened?" he asked himself. "Something hit me on the head."

He stood at the sink and looked in the mirror. Dried blood had run down through his hair and onto his face. He put water on a washcloth and cleaned up as best he could, and then he dried off. He looked around. Why was he in jail?

"Hello!" he called out of the cell. "Anyone out there? It's me, Claus. I'm locked up in here. Hello?"

"Hello," said Leni from an unseen neighboring cell.

"Leni? Is that you?"

"Leni, your selenite doctor. At your service," Leni said.

"You're locked up too?" Claus said. "But why?"

"We're criminals. Didn't you know?" Leni asked.

"No. I was knocked out. Something hit my head," Claus said.

"One of the sentries did that. Another sentry took me peaceably," Leni said.

"You could have resisted. You have the strength. Why didn't you?" Claus asked.

"To keep you company," Leni said. "We need to know where you are and how you're doing."

"We? Oh yes, Labba. Then she's still integrated with you?" Claus asked.

"Yes. She has been monitoring your status through me. She will visit you soon, but she is still searching for Lanietta," Leni said.

"Then Lanietta and Labba are still free," Claus said.

"Yes. Lanietta destroyed half the bamboophs around the village. She then flew out to the ocean," Leni said.

"With Shara?"

"With Shara," Leni added. "Labba pursued, but Lanietta disappeared."

"Disappeared? Where? How?"

"Labba thinks she space-jumped. She may have even performed a long-distance space-jump, because she withdrew her other half from Charco. Carinians are limited to short-distance space-jumps when split," Leni said.

"How short?"

"Within twenty or a couple hundred miles or so," Leni said. "Depends on the intervening terrain on a planet or celestial body."

"Then she could have taken Shara to anywhere on Earth. Or the moon. Or farther. Oh this is dreadful. I didn't think these Carinians had any ability like that. I mean, they seemed out of sorts and all when we woke up in Novi 2 after being asleep for five hundred years."

"Novi 2 was inside the bambooph perimeter," Leni said. "The bamboophs prevented space-jumps."

"Wait. If Labba is still integrated with you, then—"

"Yes. Labba is still nearby. You see, the remaining bamboophs could still disable me. Permanently, I'm afraid. Labba is holding me together to keep me going," Leni said.

"Tell Labba that she must withdraw from you and space-jump wherever she needs to bring Shara back," Claus said.

"It's not that easy," Leni said, and his voice changed to sound more like Labba. "Claus, it's the voice of Labba here. Even if I withdraw from Leni, where would I go? Lanietta could be anywhere."

"She could be on the moon. You can check there," Claus said.

"She could. So could Libriota. If I go back to the moon with Libriota there, I won't be able to come back of my own free will. And they will send others to bring you back," Labba said. "Besides, I don't think Lanietta would go back to the moon. She wouldn't want to let Libriota know what's going on down here. No, Lanietta would go somewhere else. Mars, Venus, or perhaps Jupiter. Maybe your sun, or maybe a nearby solar system. She won't stay gone for long. When she cools off, she'll return. But as for Shara, well, she, uh..."

"What about Shara? What will Lanietta do to her?" Claus said.

"Lanietta doesn't like competition," Labba said.

"Will she kill Shara? Is that the plan? What a wretched race you Carinians are," Claus said.

"She will not kill Shara directly. She could have done that immediately. And I'm Carinian too, Claus. I expect you to remember your manners. I've gone way out on a limb already for you and these people. The strange thing is, I don't know why. All I wanted was a pet. But somehow a pet seems unimportant. I have feelings for Argo now, and they keep getting stronger."

"I didn't know Carinians could have such human feelings," Claus said.

"Must be from dealing with humans. Or maybe we've forgotten what they are like. But taking human form has intensified them for Lanietta and me. She's acquired jealously and rage, while I've acquired love and tenderness," Labba's voice said.

"Then I'm surprised she is not here to protect me from you. Isn't she worried you'll take me as a prize? Labba, I have an idea. Claim me as your prize. Take me as a husband or whatever you Carinians call it. Make Lanietta jealous."

Labba's voice laughed, but it was a warbled, broken laugh as if she weren't sure how to react.

"I don't have a desire to claim you humans as a prize. Not even Argo. As much as he attracts me, I would not force him to show interest in me. Where's the satisfaction in that? You know, I accused Lanietta of becoming innerviated. But I think I'm becoming innerviated with Argo and his people. When they suffer, I suffer.

When they laugh, I laugh. I think I understand human communities now, at least what they should be. Unfortunately, Lanietta has her wires crossed, as you might say."

"Labba, where are you?"

"I'm circling high above the coastline, watching an approaching armada of ships. The village will be invaded, now that the bambooph perimeter is breached. I will visit Argo soon, but privately. King Jarro is dead, and Queen Sharlamarian has an order that I am to be arrested on sight. Lanietta too. Neither of us Carinians will be caught, of course. The order was necessary after Lanietta's rampage. These villagers no longer trust us, despite Leni saving Sharlamarian's life. I will warn Argo of the approaching armada and provide tactical information. I will visit him as a hawk and whisper in his ear. Shrinking my mass will be tiring, but I can do it for short periods of time. Claus, turn around and look out your window."

Claus turned around, and a hawk landed on the other side of the bars in the window opening. The hawk enlarged and changed shape to Labba, who now stood on the outside of Claus's window.

"Labba! I'm so happy to see you face-to-face. Let me out, and I'll help you," Claus said.

"I can't do that right now," she said. "Don't worry. I'm working on a plan. But I need more information. When the time is right, Leni will help you. He has the strength to break you out, if needed. He already told you he is only there to keep you company."

"I know, but I like your company better," Claus said.

"You flatter me. Be careful, or you might make Lanietta jealous again. Oh, but that is your plan," Labba said. "You still have the neural implant. She can sense your feelings through that. Leni, please disable the implant at the next opportunity."

"Will do," Leni said.

"Claus, this idea of making Lanietta jealous is not a good thing to do. It's like two musical instruments clashing together. Now take Argo and me. We play in between each other's chords. We don't clash at the same time. It's like walking. He's the right foot, and I'm the left. I was surprised at how easy of a concept it was to learn. But Claus, you seem to want to put your right foot against Lanietta's. Break stride! You'll find that—oh! A guard is coming!"

Labba changed shape to a hawk and flew off. Claus returned to his cell door. From down the hall, two guards escorted a new prisoner toward Claus's cell. The prisoner was placed in a cell across from Claus. The cell door was locked, the guards left, and the prisoner turned around in his cell to face Claus. It was Charco.

"Charco!" Claus said. "But you're part of the royal family. Why are you in jail?"

"You! You invaded our village! Before you there was peace and happiness. Now there is misery. I committed a crime," Charco said, now a frail and dejected man. "I am to be put on trial!"

"Trial for what? What crime?" Claus asked.

"Did you not see? The demon you call Lanietta did this to me. She made me hateful. I killed Jarro! Oh, why did you have to come and invade? You are evil. All of you! I would see you all thrown off a cliff into the ocean before my own life is sentenced. But I may not be so lucky. That other one you call Labba has twisted Argo's mind. Trash your bones. Trash you all to the selenites!"

Charco made a ruckus. He trashed his cell and threw items from the cell at Claus, but Claus used the bars of his cell as protection. Charco went especially mad and shouted curses in all directions. His arms moved violently about, and he trembled in a nervous fit.

"Guard. Guard!" Claus yelled. "Charco needs help!"

Other prisoners chanted and tapped items against their cell doors.

Guards walked in calmly. But now Charco was on his cell floor and in convulsions. Foam poured from his mouth.

Before the guards could get the cell door open, it was over. Charco stopped moving completely. A guard entered the cell and checked Charco's pulse.

"He is dead," the guard said.

"I'll inform the family," the other guard said. "No need to move him yet. He's not going anywhere."

The guards left but not for long. Shortly thereafter, two undertakers came and took away the body. Then the prison maid came in and cleaned up the cell. Finally, Queen Sharlamarian and Yuri entered the prison hall.

"He died in that cell," said one of the guards to the queen and Yuri.

"Oh, poor Charco. A demon possessed him and made him do evil," said Queen Sharlamarian.

"It was really one of the newcomers?" asked a guard.

"Yes. Argo tells me it was the one called Lanietta. The same who destroyed our village," Yuri said.

"What will you do with the other newcomers?" the guard asked. "Will they go on trial?"

Sharlamarian was about to speak, but grief overcame her.

"You will excuse the queen. She is a bit taken aback. My queen, I can see this is especially troubling. A trial would only prolong your misery," Yuri said.

"I...it...what a shame it all is. And after they brought me back to health. Now they turn around and bite us like a dog gone mad," Sharlamarian said. "Sigh. Group law. The actions of one represent the character of the group."

"Then we should send them away immediately. May I recommend the bottomless pit?" Yuri said.

"I had thought of sending them to the mines, that perhaps they could be reformed through hard work," Sharlamarian said.

"Oh no, my queen, this kind never loses its stripes. Working in the mines would only prolong misery for all. Best to get things over with as quickly as possible," Yuri said.

"It is a shame it must come to this. But the law is the law," Sharlamarian said.

"Excuse me," Claus said. "Are you saying that I am to die?"

Sharlamarian and Yuri looked over at Claus and Leni.

"Take a good look at them. Remember these two invaders who brought war to our village and ended our paradise," Yuri said.

"Please, let's discuss this like civilized people," Claus said.

"What is left of civility?" Yuri asked. "You should be thankful the queen has not executed you in the public square like dogs. But you did save her life, so she has at least spared you that much."

"Spared me to die in a bottomless pit? Give me a chance here. I can help," Claus said.

"You have helped more than is desired," Yuri said. "Guards, you may take them to the bottomless pit. Let the underworld judge them now."

The queen and Yuri left. Guards took Claus and Leni out of their cells.

"Wait! Please! Don't do this!"

Sharlamarian looked back briefly with tears in her eyes, but she could not bear to look long, and so she turned back and walked away with Yuri. The guards unlocked the cells for both Claus and Leni. The two were escorted out of the jail section, through a corridor, and to a desk. The front clerk was surprised to see them.

"These are the outworlders," said the clerk. "By order of the queen, they are not to be—"

A guard whispered something at the clerk, and the clerk nodded.

"They deserve it," the clerk said, and he waved them through.

"I'm so glad you approve of our release!" Claus retorted sarcastically, but Leni urged Claus to simmer down.

The two were locked up in a caged, horse-drawn wagon. Two horses were at the ready to haul Claus and Leni away, and with the guards at the reins, they did just that.

"A fine mess we're in," Claus said to Leni.

Leni moved next to Claus and pressed a tiny device into the back of Claus's head.

"What was that for?" Claus asked.

"The implant is blocked," Leni said.

"So now even Lanietta can't help me out of this mess. You're supposed to keep me safe! What's wrong with you anyway? Break us out of here!"

"No," Leni said.

"Why not!"

"It's part of the plan," Leni said.

"Part of the plan? Part of the plan! What plan says we have to die? Maybe *you* won't die, but you'll be damaged, possibly beyond repair! Have you lost your link with Labba? Have your circuits fused? End this fiasco and get us out!"

"Claus, this is Labba," Labba's voice said softly from Leni. "Listen. When they push you toward the pit, just jump in."

"What!?? Just jump in? Like that? Should I jump into shark infested waters? Just jump in. Or a vat of molten lead. Just jump in. How about a garbage compactor. Or a wood chipper. A newly dug grave? Just jump in. Just jump in? Just jump in!" Claus rattled off, and he was visibly upset.

"I know it sounds odd to you, but I'm still gathering information," Labba's voice said.

"I'm about to die, and you're still gathering information! Labba! We humans don't live for billions of years. We don't have the luxury to just gather information while the world around us is going to the grave. We have to survive! And fast!" Claus said. "Is Leni going to save me before the jump? Is that it?"

"No," Labba's voice said. "I need information on the pit itself. When Leni jumps in with you, I'll learn."

"Oh, *great*! Learn how the human gets eaten by sharks. Learn how humans endure a fall. Where's your love and tenderness?"

"I know. Let Leni jump first. He can break your fall, and you'll only suffer a broken back. Or broken neck," Labba's voice said.

"Oh *that's* compassion!" Claus said with sarcasm. "What's a broken back or neck anyway? Not like people ever die from either. I've *never* heard of someone dying from a broken neck."

The horse-drawn wagon headed for a tower away from the coast while villagers ran toward the coast (and thus the breach in the bambooph line) with their own bambooph weapons. More than once Claus's horses reared in fright from the crowd of panic-stricken people. Shouting and general chaos filled the air, and several horns blew to alert people of the approaching armada.

"Oh what a terrible day!" Claus lamented. "Lanietta stirs up trouble by tormenting people and wrecking their protective wall. And now she has this armada approaching to finish the job, I suppose. Such mindless waste! Leni, isn't there anything Labba can do to stop this? Maybe she should see if Libriota is still on the moon. I'd welcome slavery over death at this point!"

But Leni was quiet. Claus shook him several times to get him to listen, but Leni refused.

"A great help you are!" Claus said in disgust.

Still the people ran, but the wagon and horses reached a point where the crowd thinned and the horses were less nervous. The wagon then reached a ladder tower beside a cliff.

"It's like we're in the eye of a hurricane," Claus said to himself. "All quiet and peaceful here. But there is no peace in this village. This could be humanity's last stand against tyranny. Or perhaps its last stand ever. All those millions of years of life growing and adapting to ever-changing conditions comes down to this for humans. I just wish I could stop it. I wish I could be like Labba and spread out wings on the wind and sail after Lanietta, bring Shara back, and deal with Lanietta in the way most fit for her crime."

The guards opened the cage and forced both Leni and Claus up the ladder tower. Claus had his back to the shoreline and village chaos, and so he could not see what was happening. He reached the top of the

ladder tower through an opening in a circular platform with a railing all around, except for an open place where a chain was strung across. The guards now reached the platform, and so all four stood there for a moment. Claus glanced toward the chain and surmised that the opening led to the pit, as he could see the mouth of the pit itself on the other side of that chain. One guard walked over to the chain and pressed several buttons on a panel near that chain. A plank extended from the platform.

"The plank will give you space to jump from, so that you will drop free from the tower and other obstructions. We do not wish you to injure yourself on the way down," said the guard at the panel.

"How thoughtful," Claus said sarcastically.

The plank stopped abruptly, and the guard cursed the controls. He fought the controls to get the plank fully extended. He brought the plank back in, extended it, pulled it back, extended a little more, and so on. Meanwhile, Claus took the moment to look at the surrounding area. Being up on the tower allowed for an excellent view. Sounds also carried better from the distance. Another horn blew, and while the one guard fought the controls to get the plank extended, Claus observed and listened to what was happening on the shoreline. It was difficult to make out details, but he could see a line of ships nearing the shoreline. A line of villagers waited to meet those ships.

"They have stopped, but why? Leni, please break your silence and tell me what is going on," Claus said.

The guard at the controls stopped and instead focused his attention on Leni, as did the other guard.

"The people are waiting. Waiting for the attack," Leni said. "The line of ships is holding position. A small boat is launching from the ships with a white flag. I see Argo. He is waiting at the shore to meet the boat. The great eagle flies above. There are two people on the boat. They are introducing themselves as Selba and Clover. Oh no! Not them!"

"What do you know about these two invaders?" a guard asked Leni.

"They...Lanietta met with them. She space-jumped. She left an ion trail recording her experience. Oh, they are part of the first wave. They are to act as a decoy so that the armada can attack. Yes, already they are negotiating a fake peace with Argo."

"We must warn the prince at once!" said a guard.

"You warn the prince. I will carry out the sentence on these two," said the other guard.

"Very well," said the first.

The first guard began climbing down the ladder.

"The plank is not functioning properly," said the other guard. "You will each need to make a running start and jump into the pit."

"Jump in?" Claus asked, remembering Labba's words.

"Yes. Jump in," the guard said.

The guard unlatched the chain and attached it to the other securing post so as to clear a way through the opening. But then the three heard a rumbling like thunder from the shoreline. They turned to look (so did the guard partway down the ladder), and they saw a dark cloud above the armada.

"What is that?" Claus asked.

"It is Lanietta," Leni said. "She has returned as a cloud of darkness."

"Is Shara with her?" Claus said. "Please tell me she has returned Shara."

A hush fell upon them from the sky, and all around them the same silence stunned people into gazing at the dark cloud.

"I am Lanietta, the great thunder of the sky!" the dark cloud bellowed from the distance like the rumblings of thunder. "You will surrender all land to these ships. In exchange, I will return Shara. Your surrender must be immediate and final. Any delay will result in the end of Shara and the life you all know. Signal your answer by bowing before me!"

The guard on the ladder grew nervous and expedited his descent by hooking his hands and boots on the sides of the ladder. He slid down. The guard on the platform also grew nervous and slid down the ladder in similar fashion with such speed that he caught the first guard and landed atop him at the bottom. Both scrambled and ran.

"So this is it. This is the end of these people, thanks to Lanietta," Claus said. "Well at least the guards are gone. I hate having to watch these people die like this. I guess the alternative is to climb down and fight. But with what?"

"No, we must jump in," Leni said, and he pushed Claus toward the platform's opening toward the pit.

"Wait, what? No! This is my moment!" Claus protested while being pushed. "Like in those movies! I'm supposed to watch helplessly and with great remorse while the innocent are slaughtered. Leni, stop! The guards are gone! Leni!"

But Leni wouldn't hear of it. He pushed Claus off the platform, and Claus fell into the bottomless pit. Then Leni jumped into the pit himself. Claus yelled as he fell helplessly, but within seconds he was grabbed by Leni (with the help of short-acting boot rockets) and helped Claus to a side alcove.

"You were never going to die," Leni said.

"You could have told me before," Claus said.

"Listen up, Claus, this is important," Labba's voice said through Leni. "There is a collection of unusual energy in the pit. Leni has taken you to the start of it. I need you to investigate."

"But what about Lanietta? She's going to attack or something! We need to stop her!" Claus said.

"That's exactly why I need you to investigate. I sense there's something in the pit that can help. But I don't understand what. Leni will act as liaison," Labba said.

"And if she attacks?"

"Leni will relay the news," Labba said.

Leni pulled something out of his forearm and attached it to the back of Claus's head.

"There," Labba said. "I have added a neural feed, though the implant is still blocked from Lanietta. You now have my eyes and ears. You also have your own, so you must learn to separate the two. Don't be distracted by Lanietta's attack. Investigate the energy phenomenon."

Leni nodded "yes" to Claus. Through Labba's eyes, Claus could see that Labba was gliding through the air in a tight circle, giving a glimpse of the armada, the villagers, and the armada again. Periodically, Labba looked up and observed the dark cloud with two protrusions like giant fists. The cloud fists descended into the water, scooped up thousands of gallons, and dumped the water on the villagers.

"That is but a sample of my power," Lanietta bellowed.

"Come along, Claus," Leni said. "Focus on your presence here."

"It's dark. Can't see," Claus said.

At the mention of darkness, Leni activated a light on the top of his head, which now illuminated the surroundings. Claus saw for the first time what had happened to other people who had entered the bottomless pit. They had been placed in pile after pile, being stacked neatly and sideways like firewood, with their heads on one end and their feet on the other. But their positioning was staggered such that no one head blocked another. The people were held fast with a translucent material, like hardened goo that stretched but did not stick to the touch.

"What is this stuff?" Claus said while touching the goo.

"Encoded remnants from below," Leni said. "Those bodies you see here are only the most recent people. Others and life from beyond the ages have coalesced into this goo and washed in."

"Washed in from where?" Claus asked.

Before Claus could get an answer, Leni took Claus by the shoulder and pulled him along as the two ascended a small pile of rocks until they reached a ledge in the alcove. A deep gurgling sounded through the bottomless pit and into the alcove. The gurgling was followed by a deposit of fresh, liquid goo along with several other bodies. These bodies were pushed atop a new pile and stacked neatly. Claus half thought to go down and touch the goo, but Leni held fast onto Claus.

"Do not go below. The goo hardens quickly, and you will become trapped with the dead. The Choir of the Dead," Leni said.

Before Claus could ask what Leni meant by, "Choir of the Dead," a strong wind blew into the alcove, and a low wailing commenced from the people, like a musical piece that had been started and never finished. Claus looked closely, and he realized that the people's heads were moving. The goo had left openings for the people's faces. Their mouths and jaws moved slightly as if they were making the sounds. In fact, they were. Claus heard deep flapping sounds, like large double reed instruments, and he realized that the people's feet were vibrating as pairs. Claus was shocked by what he saw.

"This is the most degrading thing I have ever seen! Ever heard! Ever experienced! These poor people are dead! Yet they cannot even return to the earth properly as dust. They are forced to remain intact and serve the whims of this pit and alcove, forever mechanized into disrespectful, dis-harmonic disgust!"

Claus closed his eyes to block out the scene, but Labba's vision was still tied to his, and so he now watched events of the shoreline unfold. The villagers did not acquiesce to Lanietta's commands. Instead, Argo brought forth an army with his special bambooph metal weapons he had shown Labba earlier. Some of these weapons were so large and heavy that they had to be hauled on a frame with two wheels, like a cannon. Argo yelled for the armada to disperse and forever be gone. But the armada did not retreat. Lanietta's patience ran out, and like multiple lightning bursts from the heavens, she split into thousands of pieces and sent such pieces into the selenites on the ships, giving them strength and guidance for her mission of destruction and conquest. The ships made a dash toward the shoreline, and Argo commanded all to fire their weapons at them. The blasts were loud and deafening, and within a few seconds, the yells of the people were carried on the leading edge of the blast wave, which then carried down into the bottomless pit and shook Claus to the bone. Holes bored through the ships from the bambooph cannons, and selenites were hit with bambooph bullets. Though the ships took on water and slowly listed, the selenites, thanks to Lanietta's protection, repelled the projectile assault. In fact, the selenites exited the ships through the gaping holes (created by the bambooph cannons) and sped to shore. More like boated ashore. Their bodies used short-acting rocket fire (similar to what Leni used to stop Claus's fall in the pit) to jet themselves like water skis along the water's surface and toward shore. This would not have been possible without Lanietta's selenite assistance.

"Claus! Open your eyes!" Leni said. "We must complete our mission here!"

"What is left? The villagers will die! Is it up to us to survive the attack? To dump the villagers in here so they can be wrapped neatly into little piles and crow the songs of death?"

"We need help, Claus!" Labba's voice said through Leni. "We need you to discover the special energy where you are and use it to repel these selenites!"

Claus looked at Leni in confusion, and Leni nodded "yes".

"And how do I do that? I mean, really, what am I supposed to do?" Claus asked.

"You must lead the way," Labba's voice said through Leni. "There is a passage there. Tell me what you see and feel."

Claus led Leni through a maze of goo-piled humans. He then reached a portion that looked like a limestone cave of stalactites and stalagmites, only the formations were more like upward-thrusting and downward falling tube-like structures, much like the bamboophs outside, and semi-translucent instead of totally opaque.

"These formations are made of the same goo encasing the dead people," Claus said.

Claus looked closely, and he realized these formations were not solid tubes in the conventional sense, but were in fact rolled up sheets of goo resembling tube form. When Claus spoke, the various harmonies of his voice affected the nearby rolls, causing them to uncoil slightly and thus improve reception of such sounds from Claus. Claus spoke more, and the top of a tube opened up, revealing a visual analog of what Claus had said, as if a stylus had scrawled the ups and downs of his voice on paper. But Claus saw no stylus, so the method by which his voice had been transcribed to the material was a mystery. Claus looked at other rolls. He clapped his hands, and the rolls opened, revealing analog transcriptions from years gone by.

"It's a written record. These things record sound. What else do they record?" he said.

Claus touched one. It nearly pulled his finger in, but he yanked it back quickly enough, and the roll became covered in alternating string patterns of four colors. But in the dim light, they all looked grey.

"Come closer with your light, Leni. I'd like to see this better," Claus said.

Leni walked closer. Claus motioned for more light, and Leni increased his light output. Then something strange happened. The section of roll that Claus had touched mimicked his finger in the light, becoming at first a weak holographic projection and then growing stronger until it looked identical to his own finger. It moved as if touching something then recoiled.

"These are memory scrolls!" Claus said. "They record the details of these parts in precise detail. Details of life!"

"What about an energy source?" Labba's voice said through Leni.

"Just these memory scrolls," Claus said. "I wish I could find the energy source.

I need energy. I'm hungry! If I touch one of these scrolls, will it give me a hamburger?"

"No, don't!" Labba's voice said through Leni.

It was too late. Claus touched another scroll with the thought of a hamburger in his mind. But instead of the scroll providing food for Claus, it withdrew into the ground. Then the surrounding scroll tubes withdrew into the ground and so on in a ripple pattern until all scrolls withdrew. A deep rumbling and shaking of the ground like a wild stampede frightened Claus, and he ran from this room back to the area of piled people, close to the pit shaft. He thought of jumping back into the pit shaft, but Leni grabbed his arm and pulled him back. A strong draft of air shot upward from the shaft, as if the pit were alive and exhaling. The pressure wedged Claus and Leni between two piles of humans.

"What...what is going on?" Claus asked. "Labba? Can you hear me? This pit...I think it's going to explode. We're trapped. We're going to die. Labba?"

Claus closed his eyes from the strain, and again he saw images of the beach through Labba's eyes. The selenites were thick as flies, landing their little boats or swimming to shore. The villagers were too close for long-range shooting and so used their bamboophs as clubs at first, but Argo led a special charge of villagers with short-barrel shotgun bamboophs. That disrupted a great number of lead selenites. But the shotguns put out a greater blast wave, shaking the ground, and now Labba and Claus noticed that ocean waves grew less, were weaker, and did not travel as far. Indeed, a slow circular motion of the water formed near shore, this motion intensified, and water and shoreline sank downward.

"A sinkhole? I thought only Florida had those," Claus said.

But the depression increased, pulling water, sand, boat, selenite, and villager down. It was as if Earth were flat, and someone had cut a hole in the bottom, causing the contents on top to drain into the infinite ether below. The remaining selenites on top continued fighting. The villagers screamed in horror and did their best to flee, but a big trench long and wide grew from the sinkhole and followed the mass of fleeing villagers away from the shoreline as they attempted to return to what was left of their village. None made it. Labba remained in the air (and so was unaffected), but she could not stop the sinkhole, and only in time did she grab Argo in her talons and fly him to safety. "Safety" meant the platform next to the bottomless pit. The two watched as the trench resulted in a flood of ocean water into the village, and now all the village was submerged.

"Claus! Leni! Stand aside. We're flying down!" Labba called from her eagle shape.

Labba flew down against the updraft while still holding Argo. The two landed in the alcove close by Claus and Leni. And just in time! The updraft changed from air to water.

"The ocean water! It's spitting out the ocean water!" Claus said.

An angle-shaped collection of slats extended into and covered part of the upward flow of water. The slats filtered out large material and sent it to a newly-opened alcove across from Claus and company.

"It's feeding!" Claus said. "It's like a blue whale feeding on krill. The people! It will eat the people!"

"We must ensure it does not!" Labba said.

While still in giant eagle form, Labba flew to the underside of the slats and used her wings to surf back and forth in the water while bumping off the slats. As people came toward the slats, she navigated to the people and tossed them to the alcove toward Leni and Claus. Leni caught them and arighted them while Claus and Argo helped them find a place to sit. As more people entered the alcove, Claus and Argo had to find more space, and so they had people sit in the area where the scroll tubes had been. The task continued for what seemed hours, and all were tired (except Leni). Even Labba was tired, and more than once she lost orientation, slid through the water, and fell into the alcove only to be gently tossed back in by Leni. But the water let up, and now only occasional amounts of water spat upward. There were no more people to catch and no more selenite parts to be consumed. Labba flew over to the alcove with Claus, Argo, Leni, and the people. She collapsed in exhaustion and changed to human form.

"I...don't know...why I'm...tired. I'm Carinian. I'm Carinian," Labba said.

Argo rushed to Labba's care and held her in his arms.

"There now, my sweet Labba. Rest easy. You have saved the entire village! That's more than any man can do!"

"Not everyone," Baruuk said, now walking up to Argo. "There are two yet missing. Jarro and Shara."

"Shara was not in the water," Labba said, barely conscious. "Jarro is still dead. I have a suspicion as to his whereabouts but am not sure. As for Shara, I looked especially for her but had no luck."

"Then Lanietta must still have her," Claus said.

"There's something else too," Leni said. "An interactive chamber is just beyond the room of scrolls. It might provide answers. I attempted to work with it, but I do not have the power."

"You cannot activate it. None of you can," Labba said. "I must interface with it directly. And I will need all my strength. Leni, I can withdraw my half from you. You will be protected from the bamboophs provided you stay down here for the time being. The creature has permitted it."

"Creature?" Baruuk asked.

"Of course! We're inside a giant whale!" Claus said.

"Not quite," Labba said. "The creature is not a true whale, but a Martacean from outside this world. His name is Morcellus. He is an engram creation from many forms of life, including whales of a sort. Morcellus has transcrystalliformed into what he is today and is buried beneath these lands. I was in contact with him on a

subliminal level. That's why I had you investigate, Leni and Claus."

"Investigate? I thought you were trying to get me killed!" Claus said.

"Forgive my short notice, but war and explanation are mutually exclusive," Labba said. "Argo, help me to my feet. Leni, stand next to me."

Argo and Leni did as instructed. Labba then touched Leni on the back of the neck. Leni collapsed to his knees while Labba felt suddenly invigorated.

"No, don't help Leni," Labba said. "His system must adjust to the lower energy level. There now, Leni, rise to greet me."

Leni struggled at first, but within seconds he reached a full standing position.

"Good. Argo and Baruuk, follow us to the interface room," Labba said. "Leni, lead the way."

"I'm going too," Claus said.

"Of course," Labba said.

The five then passed through the room of scrolls. Villagers helped their wounded. Labba stopped by one of the more serious cases, touched the patient's arm, and heavy bleeding stopped. The villagers were excited and begged Labba to help them with their other wounds.

"No. We are still missing Shara. Labba will help us find her," Baruuk said to the people.

"I hope you're right," Claus said, "but I fear she is still held captive by Lanietta."

They reached the interface room. It was a rather plain room, but small, with only enough room to hold perhaps ten people. One corner, however, had a smooth, transparent cylinder, just large enough for a person to enter once the tube's sliding door was opened.

"Is it safe?" Claus asked. "I mean, you saw what that thing did with the shoreline and everything."

"It is neither safe nor unsafe. It is what must be," Labba said.

Labba entered the booth. She then closed her eyes. Spots of light swirled around her, and she faded from view for several moments.

"Is that it? Is she gone?" Claus asked Leni.

"I do not know," Leni said. "She is no longer in me."

"Labba," Argo whispered. "Return to us, Labba. We love you so dearly."

After several more moments, Labba returned. She exited the booth.

"Jarro is here," Labba said. "He is held in refrigeration. I'm sorry to say Morcellus was unable to revive him. He was too far gone. Morcellus has offered to hold a special burial chamber for him to rest unto eternity. There at least he will remain undisturbed by the passage of time. All may visit and interact."

"What do you mean, *interact*?" Claus asked.

"Morcellus has great power. I have learned much in the short time I interacted with him. After Jarro is interred, visitors who pay respects will be greeted by a solid hologram of him, one who speaks and acts like him. It is the ultimate memorial for a human, as any and all humans should be remembered. Further, with our help, those who are currently preserved in the outer alcove can also be interred much like Jarro, with a solid hologram that interacts with the living. In fact, I suggested to Morcellus that a school could be built within his innards, with each memorialized person acting as a teacher of sorts."

"A school inside a creature?" Baruuk said. "How disgusting. I would not enter such a creature nor permit any child of the village into such a creature."

"I would re-choose your words, Baruuk," Labba said. "You are inside the creature now. But we will help fashion rooms and memorials that will be more appealing to human senses."

"What about Shara?" Claus asked.

"She is not here," Labba said. "I repeated Shara's description to Morcellus many times, and each time he gave no recognition of her presence."

"Did you describe her facial features? Her eyes? Her hair?" Claus asked.

"We Carinians can provide a full molecular description of any entity to those who can understand," Labba said. "The process is time consuming, say half a second, but it can be done. I gave such a molecular description to Morcellus. He understood. The best he could say was that Shara was at one time on the land due to molecular residue from things like fingerprints and footprints, but she is no longer here, with 'here' being all of Antarctica."

"This creature lies," Baruuk said. "Let's torture it and get the truth."

The ground shook violently. A fissure opened up at Baruuk's feet, and he started to fall in, but Argo and Claus caught him. Several tentacles latched onto Baruuk's legs and pulled him downward. Baruuk cried for help.

"This is not the time for threats!" Labba barked. "Morcellus! Release Baruuk. We will deal with him in the village. Morcellus!"

The tentacles threw Baruuk back up to floor level, Baruuk regained his stature, the tentacles withdrew, and the fissure closed.

"Morcellus is benevolent but can be violent. Do not tempt him!" Labba warned while Baruuk rubbed circulation back into his legs and arms.

"When can we return to the village?" Claus asked.

"Yes, let's see your be-knighted creature restore our village and wipe out the enemy," Baruuk said.

"Stand down, Baruuk," Argo said. "That's an order."

"That's right. Until Shara is found, Argo is next in line to the throne," Claus said.

Baruuk reluctantly kept quiet.

"The ocean waters will recede in time. It is up to us to rebuild the village," Labba said.

"Us," Argo said. "I like the sound of that."

"I plan to stay with you a very long time, Argo," Labba said.

The two exchanged a kiss.

"Yuck," Baruuk said.

"Let them enjoy their moment," Claus said to Baruuk.

"They're playing kissy-face while Shara is out in nowhere land," Baruuk said. "And still there is the threat from the armada."

"That threat has ended," Labba said. "Follow me. There is a chamber we must visit."

The five exited the interface room and returned to the room of scrolls. One scroll rose from the floor. Labba removed the scroll from the floor, unrolled it, and read from it. The outline of a door glowed in the smooth wall where no door was previously seen. Labba walked up to this door and opened it. The five then went through the door and entered a chamber of great brilliance in white and blue, with everything made of crystal. There were tables, chairs, fountains, pools, fresh clear water, and iridescent bubbles that popped without leaving a residue. In one area of this chamber was a pyramid of crystalline bricks. Labba led the group to these bricks.

"This is what became of the selenites and the armada. Morcellus changed them into these crystalline bricks," Labba said. "Here, take a brick, Claus."

Claus took a brick.

"If you look closely, each end has a tab. Tap a tab. There, you see? It popped out. You can pull the tab. Here's another brick. I'll tap it like so, and here's another tab. Look, they can be interconnected. Now the two bricks are held fast together."

"Amazing," Argo said.

"Further, I'll undo them like so and take my brick. Now if I tap the middle like so, look—this brick is actually two pieces held together by tabs," Labba said.

"You're going somewhere with this, aren't you?" Claus said.

"You can use these bricks to build a structure," Labba said.

"Shara's hospital," Claus said.

"What good is that? Shara isn't here to build it," Baruuk said.

"We will build the hospital in her honor," Argo said. "When she returns—"

"You mean if we find her, alive," Baruuk said.

"When she returns, she will be ready to go," Argo said.

"There's something special about these bricks," Claus said. "I feel like I know them, though I've never seen them before."

"You are very perceptive, Claus," Labba said. "Each half brick contains a part of Lanietta."

"What??" Claus said.

"She split herself into many pieces to shore up the invading selenites. Each selenite and her respective piece became a half brick. She is entrapped in these bricks. Morcellus has fashioned these bricks then to trap her presence. She may yet yield some good."

"What kind of good?" Claus asked.

"Let's just say that Shara's hospital could feature self-healing rooms, where people go in, rest a while, and come out fully healed with minimal medical care," Labba said.

"Impressive!" Argo said.

"Who's to say these bricks won't turn on us and attack us? How safe can they be?" Baruuk asked.

"It is neither safe nor unsafe. It is what must be," Claus unexpectedly found himself saying.

"Very good, Claus," Labba said.

"I don't know if I should be sad or glad. Oh Lanietta, why did you have to go on a rampage? Now you are reduced to this. Well, perhaps there is more to the universe than my silly feelings. I just wish that things, well, wishing never works, does it?" Claus said.

"Only if someone hears you," Labba said. "Come. I have more to show."

Labba read from the scroll. Into the chamber rolled what looked like a railroad car through an opening in the wall, but the car was crystalline along with the wheels and track (the track had just protruded upward from the floor in time to support the car).

"I don't understand," Claus said.

"Those ships carried more than selenites," Labba said as she led the group to the railroad car. "Lanietta visited one of those ships and discovered some rather unusual cargo. It was because of Lanietta that the armada learned of the village."

"So, treachery again," Baruuk said.

"She wanted more power, but she didn't always know what to do with it, is that right Labba?" Claus said.

"Could be. Here, let's slide open this door," Labba said.

Labba slid open the door to the railroad car, and out popped a number of people who had been imprisoned on the selenite armada ships. Among them were Clover and Selba.

"Clover, Selba, and the rest of you. Welcome to freedom," Labba said.

The people from the car cheered with joy.

"I don't understand. Why were there people with the selenites? The selenites have no need for people," Baruuk said.

"Our job was to make first contact, distract you, and disable part of your bamboophoni wall," Clover said.

"Yes, the selenites who imprisoned us could not function inside such walls," Selba said.

"We didn't want to invade. We were forced to," Clover said.

"Turns out Lanietta was more powerful than we thought. She took over the ships and led the invasion against your people," Selba said.

"Yeah, after she burned much of the village and destroyed half the bambooph wall," Claus said.

"We call it a bamboophona. Or bamboopha," Selba said.

"Do you say bamboophs?" Baruuk asked.

"No, we say bamboophoni. Or just bamboophi," Selba said.

"Argo has a nursery for bamboophs, I mean bamboophi. I bet you can grow your own, can't you?" Baruuk asked.

"Yes, I can," Selba said.

"We should start our own bamboophi nursery. You and me. We'd give Argo a run for his money," Baruuk said.

Then Baruuk and Selba became lost in conversation. Leni chatted with others from the railroad car too, demonstrating how he was a "good" selenite and not an "evil" selenite. This left Claus, Argo, and Labba in conversation.

"He's completely forgotten about Shara!" Claus said to Labba and Argo. "He's engrossed with Selba there. I admit she's young and healthy. But really! There are serious issues to tackle. How can he be so insensitive?"

"Baruuk is not a bad person. But he does wander," Argo said. "Shara never liked that in him."

"If Shara were my wife, I'd—" Claus started to say, but as he did so, conversation in the chamber stopped abruptly, and all eyes turned toward Claus.

"Come!" Labba said to break the tension. "We have one last stop to make, and then Morcellus has provided a meal for all."

Labba led the group to where Jarro was kept. He was held in stasis much as Claus remembered the Carinians had done on the moon. A cold shiver ran down Claus's spine, and for a moment he felt as if he were on the moon again. Then a thought hit him—what if the Carinians were behind the creature's existence and in fact had put together this entire Antarctic episode to amuse themselves with Claus's action and reaction.

"No," Labba said to answer his befuddled expression. "Morcellus is a Martacean with his own life and history."

"Then how?" Claus asked. "How did this all come to be?"

"If you are asking how Morcellus came to be, then you might as well ask how any of us came to be. Morcellus has told little, and so I don't have complete knowledge of him or his species. But we Carinians have interacted with them in the past. I don't think any of us realized one was here on Earth. But Martaceans have a tendency to collect the sum-total DNA and lifelong knowledge of other past creatures. Not all of us Carinians are bad as you continue to think, so do not be so afraid, though I seem to be the only one here at the moment. As it is, this southern part of Earth is very difficult to probe by the Carinians from your moon. The angle is too great. I think perhaps your mind is overworked. Leni, please remove the visual device. Leave the other one there."

Leni removed the visual device while leaving the smaller device for blocking the implant.

"Feel better?"

"A little less high-strung, yes," Claus said.

"Good," Labba said.

"I wish to speak with my brother," Argo said.

"Stand here next to the tomb. Now place one hand atop the tomb and the other hand atop the first," Labba explained. "Concentrate. Speak then to Jarro."

"Jarro," Argo said. "Speak with me, my brother."

An image of Jarro stood on the tomb.

"Hello, my younger brother," image of Jarro said. "Are all safe?"

"All but you, Charco, and Shara," Argo said.

"I have passed on," Jarro said. "And Charco's circumstances are known to me. But what is this ill news of Shara?"

"Lanietta took her away during the attack on the arena. We have not seen her since," Argo said.

"My...Shara! She's all that I have!" Jarro said, then he turned to Claus and pointed, "You! You brought the evil among us! You get back my Shara! Do you hear? Get her back!"

"Labba, you said he would be a teacher," Claus said.

But image of Jarro got angrier with Claus. He cursed and spat at Claus.

"Something's wrong. Only good memories are supposed to be expressed," Labba said. "Let me check something."

Labba touched the tomb, and those same spots of light that had encircled her in the booth now encircled her and the tomb. She faded partly from view. Then Yuri rushed into the chamber and demanded to know what was going on.

"Great volcanic tension is rising. This place is about to explode. We must escape immediately!" Yuri said to Argo.

"I shall take vengeance on all the world!" image of Jarro said. "One by one the evil shall perish until I have my Shara back."

Yuri was especially scared to hear this rhetoric.

"Labba! Tell Morcellus to stop!" Claus pleaded.

"I...it's not stopping. It is overwhelmed," Labba said.

"Creature? What is this nonsense? Argo, evacuate now!" Yuri said.

"Overwhelmed with Jarro?" Argo asked Labba.

"Yes. Morcellus has become innerviated with Jarro. It wants what Jarro wants. It wants to find Shara. Oh no, Morcellus is...no, it can't be."

"What?" Claus asked.

"It is going to liberate itself from its nest. It is returning to the water to find Shara," Labba said.

Morcellus then shook earth and water into mud, and it flapped itself out, revealing itself to be a monstrous whale-like creature like that of a bowhead, only larger. All villagers inside were frightened. They looked for escape, but it was too late. Morcellus sealed off all openings to the outside world just before it dove into the ocean. The people were tossed about. They struggled to hold onto something as Morcellus moved to and fro in the ocean, all except Labba. She continued to interface with Jarro's tomb in hopes of calming Morcellus.

"No wonder the other people who jumped into the bottomless pit were wrapped up like sardines. Imagine interfacing with them. This creature would have pursued all sorts of emotional outbursts," Claus said.

"Labba, we must find Shara so this creature will stop throwing us around," Argo shouted while being tossed about in the chamber with the others.

"I thought Lanietta was in here, sealed in the bricks," Baruuk said.

"Only part of her is sealed in the bricks," Labba said. "The rest of her is still at large."

"Can we use the bricks to find out where she is?" Argo asked.

"Not without releasing her from the bricks," Labba said.

"If you can't find her, can she find us?" Clover asked.

"After what she did to us?" Yuri said. "She would attack us, all over again."

"Which is why we must *not* find her," Baruuk said.

"Agreed," Argo said. "Labba, you must convince Morcellus to call off the search. We can't find Lanietta, and we can't bring her to us."

"Can't or won't?" Clover asked.

"What do you mean?" Baruuk asked.

"Lanietta likes one of you. That much I figured out," Clover said.

"It's true," Selba said. "The way she talked, I could tell one of you made her very jealous."

All eyes looked toward Claus.

"The implant," Labba said. "We could reactivate it."

"I...what? Now hold on a moment here," Claus said.

"You mean to say this stranger can end our misery by—" Baruuk started.

"Of course!" Yuri said. "Claus must leave. Labba can arrange it. Claus must be sacrificed to save our people."

"Leave? What? I, no, no. Look, I just—" Claus stumbled.

"He has an implant, yes," Argo said. "Labba told me. Once reactivated and out in the open, Lanietta will be lured to him. As long as Claus is far away from our village and people, we will be safe. Labba, tell Morcellus. Tell him Claus will find Shara."

Labba spoke an incantation or some other song-like command. She repeated a phrase in desperation. Finally, Morcellus settled down into a smooth swim. The humans inside regained their footing and composure.

"Claus, over by the tomb please," said Labba, who was still in contact with the tomb.

"Am I really to be sent out alone?" Claus asked. "I'm not complaining. It's just that you've been so helpful, and I feel powerless against Lanietta."

"Hold my hand," Labba said as she extended her hand.

Claus held her hand, and he felt as if his innards were about to explode. He struggled to let go.

"No, hold on a little longer. Morcellus must be convinced. Yes, there. Morcellus agrees," Labba said.

Yuri and Baruuk cheered.

"But with a stipulation," Labba said. "Morcellus does not trust Claus alone. Another must go with him. I will try to volunteer myself to...no, Morcellus refuses. I must stay with Morcellus."

"I will go," Argo said. "She is my niece."

"Morcellus recognizes your attachment to your people and to me. No, it cannot be you. Nor any of you. Morcellus does not see humans as being fit enough. Not even Claus is fit enough. Claus will need to be augmented with metal inserts, and a communications system, and other electronic and crystalline equipment to—"

"Send me instead," Leni said. "I am not human. I can function in all manners necessary to protect Claus and act on the creature's behalf. No extra augmentation for Claus is needed."

"You are not human, but you are not strong enough. There is bambooph everywhere on Earth. It will disable you," Labba said.

"Labba, can you split yourself again? Protect Leni?" Argo asked.

"I can, but Morcellus doesn't trust me either. Both Lanietta and I are Carinian. Morcellus is afraid I will betray myself to Lanietta or beyond, either willingly or unwillingly," Labba said.

"Can the creature give protection to Leni?" Argo asked. "The way you protected Leni? Can he?"

"He has the power but not the knowledge," Labba said.

"You have both the power and the knowledge," Argo said.

"This is pointless. We're talking in circles!" Baruuk said.

"I wish we were," Argo said. "I only see one way for this to work. And it means I must sacrifice my Labba to the creature."

Labba smiled with empathy.

"It will not be all bad. I will only need to merge part of myself with Morcellus. But I will need to remain inside his body. I cannot teach Morcellus how to protect Leni, but I can direct him through continuous communication. It will not be all bad. Morcellus will return to his nest, and you may rebuild your village atop it. Argo, visit me often. I will be waiting for you."

"And as for me?" Claus said. "I guess this means goodbye."

"For now," Labba said. "Leni will accompany you. But Morcellus does not like Leni's form. Too much like the other selenites in the world."

"I like my shape. I like my form," Leni said.

"There's nothing we can do about Leni's appearance," Claus said.

"Morcellus will change it. Behold," Labba said.

Leni's shape changed, and he took on the appearance of a man.

"His skin is a little pale," Baruuk said.

"It will have to do," Argo said. "Claus, I am sorry to put you through this, but we must ask for your help. Not the best way to greet a stranger, is it? To send him on his way?"

"I take part of the blame. I wish we'd never landed near your village. Why did I ever think I could tame Lanietta? I knew what she was capable of. Well, this is my fate then. I accept it. I want to return Shara to you. Have the hospital waiting for her."

"We will," Argo said. "We will."

Chapter 21: Arberella Says Goodbye

Morcellus allowed Claus to stay a little longer in the village while it was being rebuilt. During that time, the villagers built a boat for Claus and Leni, and the boat was filled with special equipment for filtering fresh water from the ocean and for catching and processing ocean creatures for food. It also contained a station for diagnosing and regenerating Leni's systems. Many such systems were taken from the Novi spaceship. The spaceship then became rather empty. In the morning on the day of Claus's departure, Clover held a small party in Novi 2. Morcellus permitted Labba to attend since Claus and Leni had not left the area. Also in attendance were Argo at Labba's side, Baruuk and Selba (who had become engaged), Yuri with two of his sentries, and Sharlamarian (who had suffered an injury during the war and had only regained consciousness just days before Claus's departure).

"This spaceship has never looked better. It looks more like a home than a craft," Claus said.

"I did most of the decorating," Clover said. "Selba and Sharlamarian helped too."

"It's almost like someone is getting married and living here," Claus said. "How I wish I could stay."

"Clover will stay here and keep it up," Sharlamarian said.

"Yes, I want to hold weekly meetings when each of us remembers something special about the people around us," Clover said. "And I want to start by saying that though I have only known you for a little while, I hope you return safely."

"Clover, I need your help with the casserole," Selba said.

"Excuse me," Clover said.

Labba took Claus aside.

"Clover has a crush on you, Claus," Labba said.

"That could be a death sentence if Lanietta finds out," Claus replied.

"I'm hoping we can resolve that peaceably," Labba said.

"Clover's crush or Lanietta's jealously?" Claus asked.

"Both," Labba said. "But Lanietta must be dealt with first. It is the only way to get Shara back."

"I feel so strange about everything," Claus said. "I'm older, Labba, older than the young bucks here. I think of these young women as daughters to be protected from the evils of the world. Shara is just a child. Clover is not much older. What do they see when they look at a misplaced dog like me?"

"They see a misplaced dog who needs a home," Labba smiled.

Clover returned.

"Selba is goofy. She can make wonderful dishes, yet she suddenly forgets the simplest things," Clover said.

"She's a great help," Labba said. "As are you all."

The group dined and shared stories. As the morning waned, Clover and Claus chatted. Claus told Clover about Earth of the past, how he ventured to the moon, and how he bumped into the Carinians. The tale of how he left the moon and landed on Antarctica was told, and then it was Clover's turn to tell her story. She told of a happier childhood in a community, of her parents and her brother, and how the community was attacked by selenites.

"We were split apart," Clover said. "All of us. I thought I would die, I mean, I didn't want to live. What is life without those you grew up with, without those you love? But the selenites injected us with drugs. Happy drugs, I guess. I didn't laugh, but whenever we encountered death and destruction, I did not cry, though I wanted to desperately. That's how you know they've beaten you, Claus. It's not that they can make you cry, it's when they take away the ability to mourn for humanity and replace it with the cold steel of orders and attack. But I think for the first time...for the first time since I was little...since before they invaded... since before..."

Clover could not speak. She choked up and began to cry. Claus hugged her to comfort her.

"Clover, I must ask you to be strong. I must ask you to find people here. Spend time with them. They will help you. Maybe in time you can learn to love again. I know the selenites took it from you. Please."

"I have already learned to love again," she said.

"Shh. Please do not hold a candle for me. It will only melt away," Claus said.

"Then let it spill wax everywhere. I'd rather have scald marks than none at all," Clover said.

Clover held Claus's hand with one of her hands, and with her other hand she took a candle and dripped wax across their entwined fingers. Claus pulled back a little in shock from the hot wax, but she held his hand firm and continued to drip wax.

"I want you to remember that no matter where you are or what happens, you spent this moment with a woman named Clover who hopes you and the world will someday aright what has gone a-wrong. And should you return to these shores, I will keep a candle in the window and food on the table."

It was time. Sharlamarian opened the spacecraft's door and signaled to sentries outside. The great horn from before the flood had been salvaged, and it gave out a resounding call. Villagers lined along both sides of a path from the Novi craft to a small make-shift marina near the shore where a ship awaited Claus's and Leni's departure. Claus and Leni paid a farewell to Sharlamarian at the doorway, and they led a procession toward the ship with Argo, Labba, Baruuk, Selba, Yuri, and Clover following behind. All along the way, people threw Antarctic hair grass on Claus and Leni for good luck.

"Grass? How strange," Claus said to Leni.

"It is for good luck. The Antarctic hair grass grows in remote regions under the harshest of conditions," Leni said.

Claus and Leni reached the ship. The sails were ready to be unfurled, and sentries readied with the ropes securing it to the dock. Claus and Leni turned back, and one by one members of the procession said their individual goodbyes to the pair.

"Remember," Labba said, "I am no longer in Leni."

"How will we communicate with you?" Claus asked.

"You cannot use radio. For one, these people have no radio. For another, you risk being detected by other selenites or worse," Labba said.

"You mean the evil aliens?" Claus asked.

"Is that what you call us?" Labba asked.

"Only the Carinians like Libriota who sacrifice people for their own initiatives," Claus said. "You are different of course, Labba."

"I'm glad you see that," Labba laughed.

"But how will we communicate with you?" Claus asked.

"With spread-spectrum sonar," Leni said. "It was agreed upon when the ship was built. We will only be able to communicate with these people when the ship is in the ocean, of course."

"The ship? Does it have a name?" Claus asked.

Leni and Labba exchanged confused glances.

"A name? For what purpose?" Leni asked.

"So I can talk to her. She'll talk to me, too," Claus said.

"This is an inanimate object," Leni said. "It cannot speak. But I will keep you company."

"Thanks," Claus said half-heartedly.

"I leave the ship's name to you," Labba said.

Argo, Baruuk, Selba, and Yuri also said goodbye, though Yuri seemed happiest of all that Claus and Leni were leaving. Finally, it was Clover's turn.

"I have a gift for you," Clover said.

From behind her back, Clover produced a bouquet of Antarctic pearlwort with flowers in bloom.

"This is for luck," she said. "It is pearlwort. The flowers germinate with no help from bees or any other moving creature. Just the wind. Let a mistral wind clear your mind and lighten your heart. I hope to see you again."

She kissed him on the cheek, hugged him, and stepped to the side. Sharlamarian was last. She had trailed the procession a bit but had now caught up and reached Claus and Leni.

"Farewell again," Claus smiled, thinking about his farewell at Novi 2.

Sharlamarian smiled back, but her smile was quickly eroded by deeper strain, and Claus picked up on this.

"I am sorry for your loss," he said. "Jarro was a good man."

"So are you, Claus. And Leni here is a fine robot. I thank you again for saving my life," Sharlamarian said.

"Then you don't hate me? I mean about Lanietta and what she did," Claus said.

"Of course not. You are not to blame. But if you do find her, please keep her away. I would go with you to find my daughter," Sharlamarian started, but Yuri motioned with his head to the people, "but my place is here. I entrust you and Leni to secure safe passage for Shara back to our humble abode."

"I will not rest until I do," Claus said.

"Farewell," Sharlamarian said, and she too stepped aside.

Two guards escorted Claus and Leni along the plank and onto the ship. The guards departed, and they pulled away the plank. Leni took the controls, and Claus waved to the cheering crowd as he loosened the ropes to the dock. The ship backed out of the dock slowly. Claus waved one last time before going inside.

"The ship has only a little power for propulsion—enough for slow maneuvers, but not enough for moving at speed. We will deploy the sails in a moment," Leni explained. "Morcellus is monitoring our progress this close to the village."

"Just what we need. More supervision," Claus said. "Probably the evil aliens are supervising too."

"Labba explained to you, right? That they can't detect this part of Earth easily? Don't worry, Claus. The Carinians, if they are still there, don't know about us. As for Morcellus, he only wishes to see us safely depart. It won't help if we run aground. Which we will do if we don't deploy the sails quickly. Over there. Press those release buttons."

Claus pressed the buttons. Automated equipment deployed the sails and positioned them.

"Amazing that these people are such excellent shipbuilders. And yet they have built none for themselves," Claus remarked.

"Morcellus told them everything," Leni said. "Labba is working with Morcellus to improve security so there will be no more invasions by rogue selenites."

"Not just selenites? Rogue selenites?" Claus said because Leni was himself a selenite.

"They were rogue. Not all of us are bad. Don't you agree?" Leni asked.

"Yes, quite," Claus replied. "Well I hope we get a good wind that takes us where we need to go. Wait, where are we going?"

"Away from the village initially. That means sailing north into the South Pacific. Soon we will remove the masking device from your implant in hopes of drawing Lanietta's attention," Leni said.

"And after that?"

"We do things one at a time," Leni said.

"That's not much of a plan," Claus said.

"It's all we have. Unless you have a better idea," Leni said.

"No. I guess Clover is right. I should trust in the wind and the...the...what was it she said? Something about a *mistral*? I thought she said *mistrial*."

"She did not say *mistrial*," Leni explained. "A mistral is a wind from the north in France. Clover is from France, right?"

"Provence, yes," Claus said.

"A mistral wind brings clean air and clear skies," Leni said. "Much success in agriculture was due to the mistral wind."

"Yeah, *was*."

"Do you know otherwise?" Leni asked.

"I can only imagine what the selenites have done to agriculture. From what Clover has said, they are less friendly to Earth than humans of my day were," Claus said.

The winds picked up, and the ship tossed Claus to its side.

"What was that?" Claus asked.

"A gust. Let me compensate here. There, wait, another one. Brace," Leni said.

"Brace?" Claus asked, but the ship tossed him again, and he went running to the other side. "I thought you were compensating."

"Some of these winds are unpredictable," Leni said.

"Bad mistrals?"

"You could say that," Leni replied. "We didn't have time to transfer all Novi equipment to this ship, so I can't predict the unpredictable. If predictable, I could compensate, and it would be a happy mistral."

"Happy mistral, bah! These mistrals are sad, bad, mad! Oh, and I'm so tired from everything! Don't these waves ever stop? I constantly have to balance my body against the ocean swells," Claus said.

"It is the nature of things. Perhaps the seas will calm as we go north," Leni said. "But if you are tired, why don't you rest? I can man the ship."

"Yes," Claus yawned as he reclined back in a chair. "Mistral mad is bad. I've been had by a mad mistral. Happy mad mistral day. Man the mad mistral, Leni."

With that, Claus fell asleep. He dreamed he was on a small sailboat no bigger than a fishing boat. His boat floated in a small cloud just big enough for support. This cloud was up in the atmosphere where other clouds might live, but no other clouds were around. A strong wind blew Claus's boat and the cloud along. The ground below raced by, and people waved and saluted Claus. But it was cold up with the clouds, and Claus shivered. He scrunched down in the boat and pulled the sail down to wrap around himself for warmth, but when he did that, the boat tossed side to side, and to and fro. It was as if the wind were angry, and indeed, the cloud turned black, and the boat sank into the cloud where it began to rain.

"Mad Mistral. Mad Mistral!" Claus yelled.

Realizing the sail was the only thing keeping him aloft and steady, he raised it. The boat climbed above the dark cloud and its rain, the cloud turned white, but Claus was cold again. He shivered so badly that he was forced into action. There was only one way out. He had to jump. With nervous anxiety, he shimmied over the gunwale and fell, fell, fell. He was numb from the cold and wind and felt nothing.

Nothing that is until he splashed down into a warm mountain stream. His limbs regained feeling, he floated to the surface, and he took a deep breath of fresh air. Renewed in strength, he swam to the edge of the stream where he reached the solid ground of a mountain plateau. He looked around. The mountain stream had a mountain uplift on the far side and the plateau on the other (where he now stood). A line of trees followed the mountain stream on the plateau side. Looking out on the plateau, Claus noticed the plateau did not extend indefinitely but instead had a drop-off. A single tree stood by that drop-off. Claus walked and walked toward that solitary tree, and as he approached it he noticed a group of children walking around the tree. An inner circle of boys walked clockwise around the tree while an outer ring of girls walked counterclockwise around the tree. The children were perhaps ten to twelve years of age. The boys wore suits while the girls wore flower-patterned white spring dresses and had flower bracelets and flower crowns. Claus walked closer still, and he looked at the tree. The branches were devoid of leaves, save one, which had but a few leaves struggling to grow. Claus looked back toward the trees along the stream, and he noticed those trees were full of leaves.

"This tree clings to life, and the children play and celebrate as if all is normal. All is not normal!"

Claus burst through the lines of children. With their circles broken, they ran around in random directions with no cause or purpose, yelling and hollering the entire time. The tree vibrated from the chaos, and those few leaves struggling for life fell off. Then earth under the tree caved downward into the drop-off, creating a small landslide. The children ran from the landslide to avoid its grip, but Claus was caught, and he was carried down the hill, with dirt, dead tree and all. As he did so he picked up speed. The tree seemed to roll over him, or him over the tree, and so his body was tossed back and forth. With the increase of speed, his heart felt heavy, and his stomach felt left behind so much so that he was sure to die. The crash at the bottom was inevitable. A branch from the tree caught his shirt and tugged on it. Yes, it was the same branch from where those last few leaves had been. He looked at the place from where the leaves had come. Sap oozed from the open wounds and slowly rolled down the branch toward Claus's arm, searing and burning the tree's bark along the way.

"No! I won't die like this tree! The sap won't get me! Get away, do you hear? Get away. Get away!" Claus yelled.

Chapter 22: The Pursuer

Claus awoke with a start and found himself fighting off Leni. It was Leni who was shaking Claus by the arm, not the branch from the tree.

"Get away!" Claus said one more time, still half asleep.

"Claus, relax! You're having a bad dream. Easy there, champ. You're fine. Nothing will harm you. Claus? Wake up. You're okay," Leni said.

Claus stood up with a start. He ran to one of the portholes and looked out. The sea was calm, the day clear, and the wind light.

"What? What happened? Where are we?" Claus asked.

"We've just cleared through a storm. Tossed the ship a bit. I hope you weren't disturbed too badly," Leni said.

"Oh, a storm? Of course. I knew that. Yes, just a storm," Claus said with a sigh of relief as his tension released.

"The Mad Mistral made it through, and we're ready to unmask your implant," Leni said.

"The *what* made it through?" Claus asked.

"The Mad Mistral. Isn't that the name you gave this ship? I heard you shouting that a while ago. Perhaps you were asleep. You shouted other things too, like look out for the tree, it's going down the mountain and such."

"Yes. I was thinking about these mistral winds. And I fell asleep. I don't remember much except for what I dreamt before you woke me. Silly dreams. I really called it the Mad Mistral, eh?"

"Yes, you did," Leni said.

"Then I guess the name sticks. Seems easy enough," Claus said.

"Now comes the hard part. We must remove the mask over your implant," Leni said.

"And then we wait," Claus said.

"Precisely."

"Do you think I'll draw her attention?"

"No doubt," Leni said. "That's not the question."

"The question is how long, right?"

"Right," Leni said.

"Let me go up on deck and take a look at things first," Claus said.

"Take all the time you need."

"Thanks."

Claus opened a door and climbed up on deck. There he walked around. The sails were full but just barely, as the wind tended to die down periodically and let air out of the sails, but then they filled again with a distinctive "flap" sound. The water was calm with only gentle swells, and the sun sparkled on occasional collections of water bubbles that passed by. He could see the storm clouds to the south, but they were quickly diminishing in size.

"Or so it appears," he said to himself. "They must be moving quickly, or we are, or both."

He looked around in other directions too. The ocean was peaceful but incredibly huge. The horizon in all directions was ocean.

"How the early people tired of such sameness on those early ocean trips. How did they keep from going crazy? How did they pass the time? One would forget that land existed, that instead life only consisted of being on a boat with water all about. Sun during the day, stars at night. And the moon, the only thing that really changes, appearing at times during the day and at times at night, but never in exactly the same place nor having the same shape from day to day. The moon. It would be the only clue of change beyond day and night, unless they observed how the stars changed from season to season. But that is subtle. The moon is less so. The moon! How I hope those evil aliens up there are gone. They and their selenites created this mess. Yeah, I know, we humans were on our way to messing up the planet anyway. But at least we did it more slowly. Those machines can mess things up quicker than lightning. How I wish all selenites on Earth would go away, and we could reclaim what belongs to us humans. We own this planet."

Claus saw a whale in the distance come up for air and then disappear.

"Perhaps they are the top animal now," Claus said, thinking of the whale. "Still, selenites of the world must go. They must be destroyed. They—"

"Claus, I have the demasking tool ready," said Leni as he came up on deck through the door from below. "What were you saying about selenites?"

"I was saying how proud I am to have a selenite on this ship," Claus said.

Leni smiled.

"You don't have to lie. Do I still look like one? I mean, Morcellus made me look as human as possible," Leni said.

"If only you could get a sun tan," Claus said.

"I'll have to work on that," Leni said. "Well, let me know when you are ready."

"Yeah, I was just looking around. Seems so quiet and peaceful. I saw a whale come up for air a moment ago. But nothing else on the ocean surface."

"I do see something," Leni said.

"What?"

"Look over this way," said Leni as he pointed to something in the distance. "Do you see it?"

Claus strained his eyes.

"Here, take this," Leni said as he pulled out a set of binoculars from a pack and handed the set to Claus.

"Looks like a mass of something on the ocean surface. What kind of creature is that?" Claus said.

"I don't think it's a creature," Leni said.

"A boat? No, it's not very high. Perhaps a submarine with a rough surface. For camouflage," Claus said. "I wonder. If it's manned by selenites, they might attack us, and our mission would be over. I doubt Lanietta is on board since my implant is still masked."

"It would be a coincidence if she were," Leni said.

"Yes. I think we should investigate. Slowly," Claus said.

"This ship is fully equipped with defensive armament. We can fire missiles if needed," Leni said.

"I hope it doesn't come to that. But be ready just in case," Claus said. "I'll stay up here. You go down and move us closer. Monitor for any strange activity and take the necessary steps to safeguard us and the ship."

"Will do," said Leni, and he disappeared below.

"What would be out here in the middle of nowhere?" Claus asked himself.

Leni changed course. The sails moved into new positions, and the ship zig-zagged toward the mass. The mass appeared closer and larger, and still Claus could not make sense of what it was, but then he noticed scraps of garbage in the water, first a few here and there, but then gradually more garbage until he realized what the mass was. He let out a big laugh. Leni ran up on deck to see what was going on.

"What is it? What is so funny?" Leni asked.

"That's no creature. It's a large clump of garbage," Claus said.

Leni took the binoculars from Claus and looked.

"You're right. It *is* a mass of garbage. The currents must have clumped it all together here," Leni said.

"Like tumbleweeds in a house full of cats," Claus said.

"How does tumbleweed get into a house?" Leni asked.

"Not real tumbleweed. That's what we call clumps of cat fur that have accumulated as the furnace blows air around. There are dust bunnies too."

"I've never heard of dust bunnies. Are they dangerous? How long do they live?"

"Well in large quantities they can cause allergies. But their life expectancy is short. Their great predator is a machine. That of the mighty vacuum cleaner," Claus laughed.

"I see," Leni said. "These are other forms of garbage, as you might say."

"You might say," Claus said.

"Well then, there is no threat."

"No, no threat. And I suppose now is as good a time as any to unmask the implant. Maybe Lanietta will come rushing toward me, miss, and land smack dab in the middle of the garbage mass. Boy wouldn't that be a sight to see her covered in plastic strips and green goo."

"It would. It would also make her angry. That would do wonders for the ship," Leni warned.

"I guess I shouldn't laugh at her too much until we work out a truce or something," Claus said.

"That is advisable," Leni agreed. "Are you ready?"

"Ready as I'll ever be," Claus said.

"Removing the mask...now."

Leni placed a pen-shaped tool on the back of Claus's neck, pressed a button, and a puff of air released from the device. Leni then removed the device and showed it to Claus. At the end of the device was what looked like a flat beetle.

"It's removed," Leni said.

"Lanietta! Do you hear me? Come get me, if you can. I'm out here all alone with Leni. Claim me as your prize. Do you hear? Lanietta?" Claus called.

The two waited several minutes.

"Nothing," Claus said.

"Let me go below and check the long-range instruments for ships or even atmospheric disturbances. She could be in the clouds again," Leni said.

"Very well. I'll continue calling up here," Claus said.

"Please keep it on friendly terms," Leni said.

"I'll try."

The garbage mass had moved on. The ocean was quiet and peaceful in all directions.

"Claus, you'd better come below," Leni said with the door to the below cabin slightly ajar.

"What is it?" Claus asked.

"You need to see for yourself. On the long-range sonar," Leni said.

Claus climbed below.

"You see something underwater?"

"No, this sonar is special. It can see things right along the water line. Look," Leni said.

Claus looked at the screen.

"It looks like a sonogram. Like when they show an unborn baby or something," Claus said.

"The technology is crude, I admit. But there is something out there on the ocean surface. It's powered, fast, and heading our way," Leni said.

"Anything on long-range cameras?" Claus asked.

"Not yet. It hasn't reached our horizon yet," Leni said.

"Then how do they know we're here? If they are speeding to this spot. Unless—"

"Unless it's Lanietta or one of her selenite soldiers," Leni said.

"Prepare for attack," Claus said.

"What if she has Shara on board?" Leni asked.

"I don't think she will. Too easy. But she'll try something sneaky. Launch a weapon or such. We should knock it out before it hits us."

"Okay, guns armed and ready," Leni said after pressing several buttons.

"I'll go up on deck and watch from there. Notify Labba that we have unmasked the implant, and a boat is heading our way, possibly with Lanietta, definitely hostile," Claus said.

Claus took Leni's binoculars and went up on deck. He peered into the distance with those binoculars in the direction where sonar said the ship should appear. Nothing yet.

"I'll stop you or your pawn, Lanietta, to show you I'm not afraid. Or perhaps you are toying with me yet again. Go ahead, call me Clomper. See what happens," Claus said to himself.

Claus looked on deck and saw a panel.

"Hey, I wonder what this does?" he said.

He opened a cover to a tube and touched it.

"I heard that," said Leni's voice from the tube.

"Leni! I just discovered this control panel," Claus said.

"Yes. It's a special water-proof panel for controlling basic ship's functions," Leni said.

"Like navigation?" Claus asked.

"Yes, navigation, propulsion, weapons, life support sys—"

"Weapons? How?" Claus asked.

"Well I have to make the panel active," Leni said. "I can do so down here."

"Do it," Claus said. "I want to be the one firing the first shot."

"A warning shot, right?" Leni asked, but Claus held silent. "A warning shot! Claus!"

"Hey, she played dirty pool with those people in the village. No more mister nice guy," Claus said.

Leni routed controls to Claus's panel.

"Okay, your panel is active. Each button has a text display next to it. There's a control for aiming, locking target, removing safety, and firing," Leni said.

"Good. Is the boat still heading our way?" Claus asked.

"Yes. Still just beyond the horizon," Leni said. "But the weapons system can track even from this distance. You can fire whenever you are ready."

"I want to make visual contact," Claus said while peering through the binoculars. "I want to see Lanietta suffer just as much as she made those people suffer. Give her a taste of her own medicine."

"There's a saying about revenge being bittersweet," Leni said.

"It's justice. It must be done," Claus said. "Did you send a message to Labba?"

"I did, but this sonar technology is not like radio. It's slower. It will take time for it to arrive, for her to be contacted, and for her to reply," Leni said. "Perhaps we should wait for a reply before attacking. She might have news about Lanietta."

"She won't have news about Lanietta," Claus muttered while gazing through the binoculars at the horizon. "Lanietta is on that boat. I can feel it."

"You know those binoculars aren't powerful enough to see a small boat over the horizon," Leni said. "Plus without a tripod and with the movement of the ship, the image will shake too much for you to see much detail."

"Of course! What am I thinking? Leni, now what?" Claus called.

"Stand back a little from the panel. Now press the button with the goggles icon," Leni said.

Claus did so. A pair of electronic goggles connected to a scissors platform elevated from the panel.

"Look through those. You can lock the view onto our tracking system," Leni said.

Claus looked through the goggles.

"Yes, much better," Claus said. "Wait, I see something on the horizon. The atmosphere is distorting the image, but I see the tip of something. Someone's head with long hair. Hah! It's Lanietta for sure. But she's not heading straight for us. Wait, now I see. She's in a zig-zag pattern."

"Probably as a defensive maneuver," Leni said.

"Then we must choose the proper moment to fire. Right when she's about to change course," Claus said.

"Weapons are locked and ready," Leni said.

"I'm removing the safety," Claus said as he pressed a button.

"Safety removed. Fire at will," Leni said.

"No, not Will. Fire at Lanietta. I'm going to attack right...now!" Claus said, and he hit a button.

The projectile launched. The projectile itself was simple—it was composed of an iron ball with small adjustment thrusters all put together in a small missile-like package. The primary kinetic energy was provided by a blast of expanding gases from the ship, but the projectile added a little speed and directional control as it approached its target.

"Heh, heh, heh," Claus chuckled. "Little do you know, Lanietta, that you are in for a big surprise, you and your flowing hair in the wind. Enjoy your moment. It is about to end."

The projectile hit. The boat exploded, and flying debris obscured Claus's view for a moment. When the debris settled, Claus could see the back half of the boat was still floating, but the engine was on fire, and smoke billowed up. The front half was nowhere to be seen. Nor was the driver.

"She's gone," Claus said. "What a relief."

"We should check the wreckage to be sure," Leni said.

"Yes, we should," Claus said, but he had a funny feeling. "Now that Lanietta's gone, how will we find Shara?"

"That is a good question. Perhaps the debris will yield a clue," Leni said.

But Claus had a feeling the debris wouldn't yield any clues.

"Something's not right," Claus said as the Mad Mistral headed toward the debris.

"What do you mean?" Leni asked.

"I mean, this could be another one of Lanietta's tricks. Somehow it seems too easy to kill her, a Carinian who has been around for a few billion years."

"Remember that a portion of herself is in those bricks back in Morcellus," Leni said. "The Lanietta out here is a weakened version."

After a time, the Mad Mistral approached the debris. The fire had burned down a bit as the most flammable parts had burned away, leaving heavier material. Leni came up on deck to operate the ship from there while Claus took a closer look from the Mad Mistral's bow.

"Nothing so far. Oh I might have known. She's escaped, of course. More than likely she followed that burning smoke upward into the clouds," Claus lamented.

"Incoming message from Labba," Leni said. "She says to be on the lookout for a speedboat."

"Too late for the warning," Claus said.

"She also says they had built the speedboat, and that it was stolen," Leni said.

"They built the speedboat? Then this isn't...oh no...oh...Leni! Stop! Stop the ship!" Claus called.

Chapter 23: The Creature's Prize

Claus saw a clump of long hair in the water. He jumped into the water after it.

"Are you mad?" Leni called.

Leni threw a rope ladder down the side for Claus to climb, but Claus wasn't done. He discovered the clump of hair was attached to a body, to that of a woman. He pulled the woman toward the side of the Mad Mistral. Using a crane and boom, Leni lowered a stretcher on a rope (that was secured at the four corners), and Claus put the woman on that stretcher and secured her with straps. Black oil and her disarrayed hair covered her identity for the moment. Leni reeled in the rope, and the woman was pulled up and swung over onto the Mad Mistral's deck while Claus climbed up the rope ladder quickly. Claus pulled off his shirt and used it as a pillow for the woman as he and Leni rolled/positioned the woman on her back. Claus pulled away the hair and oil from her face, and her identity became obvious.

"Clover! What on Earth are you doing here! Leni, quick! Get the CPR kit! Hold on, Clover! Don't give up!"

Claus was truly perplexed and disturbed. Leni had only disappeared a moment down below for the kit when he returned back on deck. Claus was already performing knee compressions to expel water from Clover's lungs and exhaling into her mouth to put air in.

"Let me get this oxygen going," Leni said.

Leni placed a mask over Clover's mouth and squeezed a bag to get oxygen in.

"No pulse," Claus said, and he performed chest compressions.

But then it started to rain, and not just a little. The rain was cold, and soon the three were pelted with hail.

"Still no pulse. Continuing compressions," Claus said.

"We have to get below," Leni said. "The weather has gone bad."

"Clover still needs CPR. Just a little longer," Claus said.

"Claus, we have to go down now. Leave her. We'll take care of her later," Leni said.

"We'll take her down below. Open the bay," Claus said.

"In this weather? Water will go below. We can't—"

"Do it!" Claus said.

Claus straddled Clover so that he could stay on the stretcher and continue CPR. Leni opened the bay doors and maneuvered the crane with Clover and Claus on the stretcher. With the doors being open, rain and hail poured into the cabin below, but Leni lowered the stretcher through the bay doors and down as quickly as possible onto an examination table. Claus climbed off and was about to roll Clover off the stretcher when the rope suddenly detached from the crane and came crashing down atop Claus, who shielded the rope from Clover. The bay doors closed, and Leni descended into the cabin through the door and down steps.

"What did you do that for?" Claus asked.

"So I could close the doors quickly," Leni said. "Look at the mess! It'll be a miracle if half these instruments still work."

"Clean up the water as fast as you can then get the medical equipment ready. We still have an emergency here, remember?" Claus said.

"Yes, water everywhere is the emergency," Leni said.

"It's just a few inches. Pump it out!" Claus said.

"Yes, pump it all, like all will be well. Except circuits don't just dry out and work again like new," Leni said.

"Stop your complaining, and get to it," Claus said, and then he turned to Clover. "C'mon, Clover, wake up."

Claus continued forcing oxygen into her lungs and performing chest compressions, but her pulse did not return.

"Her heart won't pump," Claus said. "We'll have to shock her."

"You mean you'll have to shock her," Leni said, "That is if the defib unit still works. And how will you ground yourself? Your feet are in standing water."

"One thing at a time," Claus said as he reached for the defibrillator unit.

Claus stood on a chair to keep his feet out of the water, charged the unit, placed the paddles on Clover's chest, and pressed the button. Clover's body jumped up, but the action startled Claus so badly that he threw the paddles to save his balance. His balance was destroyed, and so the chair went out from under him. He fell into the water, and he hit his head on a corner of a cabinet.

"Ow!" Claus called.

"Ow!" called Clover from the examination table.

"Clover!" Claus called as he jumped to his feet.

"Oh, but your forehead is bleeding," Clover said.

"Forget that. Let me check your pulse. Is your heart beating?" Claus said as he checked her pulse. "Yes, a pulse! She has a pulse, Leni!"

"That would be evident based on her behavior," Leni said.

"Can you breathe, Clover? Can you?" Claus asked as he put his hand over her mouth.

"She can't breathe if you choke her like that," Leni said, and he reached to pull Claus's hand away from Clover's mouth, but Clover instinctively did so first.

"I can breathe better now, thank you," Clover said. "Let's get that gash cleaned up. You might need stitches."

"No, no stitches," Claus said. "Glue. Leni, is there glue here?"

"Over in the medical cabinet," Leni said.

"I can clean it, Clover. Just rest there a moment. I'll clean and glue it," Claus said.

"Sounds awful," Clover said. "But not as awful as the welcome I received. Do you always greet friends so warmly? With bonfires and such?"

"I am so very sorry! I thought you were Lanietta!"

"Oh, it's a common mistake. All of us women look alike. Especially Earth women and alien women," Clover said sarcastically.

Leni laughed.

"Hey!" Claus said to Leni, "I didn't think robots could laugh."

"Neither did I," Leni chuckled.

"That's Leni? I thought he was your twin brother. You both look so much alike, right down to the same skin tone and mannerisms," Clover continued in her sarcastic way.

"I said I'm sorry. Please forgive me! Am I to endure this torture forever?" Claus said as he finished his cleaning and gluing.

"Well, I suppose you could help me find a place to tidy up. Unless your idea of helping me tidy up was to set this oil on my clothing on fire," Clover said. "The ocean was helpful in drowning out my problems. But I suppose I should thank you for that too."

"Oh, Claus is helpful in all kinds of ways," Leni jabbed.

"You're not programmed for sarcasm," Claus said to Leni.

"But I learn very quickly," Leni said.

"*Too* quickly," Claus said. "Clover, over this way to the shower. Can you walk? Let me help you."

"Wait," Clover said. "I want to see if I can stand up on my own. Ow! My foot!"

"Let me see," said Claus, who had now finished gluing his forehead.

"Are you a doctor?" Clover asked.

"No, but I am," Leni said. "Best let me take a look. Claus, you clean up the water."

"A robot is ordering me around?" Claus asked.

"It's the most logical course of action," Leni said.

"Hah!" Clover said to Claus. "You don't like being pushed around. Ow!"

"Hold still, please," Leni said.

"That'll teach you for laughing at me. Leni must have found something on your foot. You squirmed and made it worse," Claus said.

"I did indeed. There is metal shrapnel in your foot, Miss Clover," Leni said. "It will need to come out."

"I don't want a scar," Clover said.

"Most patients worry about the pain," Leni said.

"That too," Clover said.

"Obviously Clover is concerned with her vanity," Claus said.

"It's just I've never had a scar before," Clover said. "Not even the selenites with all their torture ever gave me a scar."

Claus walked over and touched the skin on Clover's legs.

"Your skin is very smooth," Claus said.

"Okay, bilge boy, get back to pumping out the water," Leni said. "Miss Clover, I will need to remove the shrapnel. I promise it won't hurt a bit. I'll use medical glue to hold the tissue together until it heals. There will be no scars."

"Yay!" Clover proclaimed.

"Just sit tight here. I need to clean the area first. There will be a little stinging from the antiseptic. I can't give you a shot yet until the area is clean. You wouldn't want me to give you an infection, would you?"

"A clean foot is a happy foot," Clover grimaced as the antiseptic stung.

"Okay, a little pinch," Leni said as he injected the anesthetic. "Good. You're doing fine. Claus, you can help by keeping Clover preoccupied. Why don't you tell her about how you thought she was Lanietta."

"I...I didn't really know...but...who else...you see, Clover, I..." Claus fumbled.

"Yes?"

"I have this implant, see. And it was masked so Lanietta couldn't track me. Well we went out on this ship, as you know, to find Shara and Lanietta. We wanted to be a safe distance from the village. We thought we were. So I had Leni remove the mask. I expected Lanietta to come after me."

"In a boat? By herself? Looking just like me?" Clover asked.

"I didn't know it was you," Claus said.

"Truth is you didn't know who it was. But you attacked anyway, right? Right?" Clover asked.

Claus wanted to answer, but he was too ashamed.

"Why are you here anyway?" Claus asked.

"How about you welcome me to the ship first," Clover said.

"Yes, of course! Welcome to the Mad Mistral!" Claus said.

Clover stared at Claus in disbelief. She looked at Leni, who shrugged his shoulders. Then she looked at Claus again, who by now was nervous and shaking like a dog left out in the rain. Clover's disbelief melted into comedy, and she laughed.

"Please, Claus, do not make Clover laugh," Leni said. "She must remain still."

"What...what's so funny? I named it after you," Claus said to Clover.

"After me?" Clover laughed.

"Claus, stop!" Leni said. "No more making people laugh."

"I...I'm not trying to, Leni," Claus pleaded. "I'm just telling her about the ship's name. About how I named it after her."

"Really," Clover said. "You've given a whole new meaning to *mistral*. Claus and his Mad Mistral, capable of sending wind wherever he may, destroying friendly boats and flooding his own cabin. Heaven forbid you call this the *Helpful Mistral* or the *Happy Mistral*. *Mad Mistral* is most appropriate. Most appropriate."

"Well don't be angry," Claus said.

"She's holding still now. Good. Claus, keep doing what you're doing," Leni said.

"Yes, we don't want you making people happy. They'll giggle and shake and enjoy themselves too much to allow Leni to perform surgery to clean up the mess you've made with them," Clover said.

"I'm sorry. I really am sorry!" Claus pleaded.

"And that fixes my injury?" Clover asked.

"No, I'm doing that," Leni said.

"Exactly," Clover said.

"What do you want me to do?" Claus asked.

"Okay, everyone be silent for a moment. I'm finishing up the glue," Leni said. "And, there. Just needs a moment under the ultraviolet lamp to cure...there. Now you may talk. I'll wrap up the foot, and you'll be good to go."

"Go where?" Claus asked.

"To find Shara, of course," Clover said. "I'm helping you."

"You were supposed to stay in the village," Claus said.

Two short beeps indicated a follow-up message from Labba on the spread-spectrum sonar channel.

"Another message from Labba. Wonder what she's going to say. Care to take a guess?" Claus asked Clover.

"She's going to say I stole the speedboat," Clover said. "Don't look at me that way. You need my help."

"I thought you would help by keeping a candle in the window and food on the table," Claus said.

"Now the candle is much closer, and you'll be able to see it. And I'm good at making ship food," Clover said. "I used to cook for the slaves on the selenite ship. I operated a submersible to catch deep sea fish and other creatures that I cooked. One must improvise for herbs and spices when land is unavailable."

Leni motioned that he was done, and Clover stood up. From inside a pocket she revealed what looked like a short candle.

"You brought a candle with you?" Claus asked. "We can't burn things in here. Fire hazard, you know. Not to mention the unnecessary use of oxygen. And the fumes. We can't have fumes."

"The only fumes in here are from you," Leni said. "Oh sorry, something in my programming misfired."

"Who changed your programming?" Claus said. "That's not like you."

"I...don't know. Strange," Leni said.

"Don't look at me," Clover said. "Besides, I want to show you my candle. Do not worry, it has no flame."

Clover placed the candle up in the window well of a porthole and twisted it slightly. The candle held fast to the ship. She pressed another button, and the sound of air whooshed through the candle.

"What's that, what's that?" Claus said with alarm.

"Relax. This little candle recycles the air for animal use. Too much carbon dioxide or carbon monoxide is scrubbed out. See? Little clear carbon pellets come out," Clover said.

Leni looked at the candle and then a pellet.

"She's correct," Leni said. "This pellet is a diamond."

"What? How?" Claus asked.

"Now look," Clover said, keeping Claus in suspense. "I press this little button here, and a light shines atop the candle. Press again, and it projects holographic images."

"That's Shara. From the village. She is performing with others in an orchestra," Leni said.

"There's audio too," Clover said while pressing a button.

Music from Shara and the orchestra filled the cabin.

"Again I ask, how? The village had nothing like this that I could see," Claus said.

"Claus is correct. This is not village technology. Even for a selenite, it is quite alien," Leni said.

"You didn't get it from the selenites, did you?" Claus said. "Where did you get it?"

Clover paused.

"Another message from Labba," Leni said, noticing a blinking light on the panel while Claus was busy staring at Clover.

"I wonder what Labba has to say," Claus said, but Clover rushed over and prevented him from listening to it.

"Stop," Clover said.

"Okay, now you're scaring me," Claus said. "You obviously stole this from somewhere, is that it? Is that what Labba is trying to tell us? And you don't want us to know. Why? Will the owner come after it? Will he come after you too?"

"Oh Claus! Do not let trifles interfere! Aren't these images of Shara beautiful? I never knew her, but from what I've seen, she would have been a wonderful kindred spirit," Clover said.

"Then you've already seen images from this candle. Many, I'm guessing," Claus said.

"That's why I had to see you. I had to share the candle with you. Claus, these people...look at them! They're so happy! These images are from before the attack. Before their way of life was destroyed. Look, here's Shara playing a stringed instrument when she was five years old. Isn't the music beautiful? I could listen to this music all day. There are other scenes too, of her climbing a mountain and peering into the far beyond, watching the sunset, the sunrise, or an incoming weather front. It's breathtaking, Claus. I'm obsessed with it all."

"Leni?" Claus asked.

"Very advanced technology," Leni said. "As I said, not of selenite design. And not of villager design."

"Labba made this? No, she would have had to capture these images while we were hibernating," Claus said.

"Labba did not make this. I would have sensed it when she melded with me," Leni said.

"Then another Carinian. Lanietta? Doesn't seem possible," Claus said. "Unless there are other Carinians. Maybe they were here and planted this as a spying tool. Those evil aliens. Well, this is proof then. We're not alone. Hatefulness! I had so hoped we *were* alone. Why do you look like that, Leni? Why do you stare at Clover?"

"Because Clover knows this is not of Carinian design either," said Leni. "Why

would a spy tool include an atmospheric recycling device?"

"In case the people are trapped?" Claus asked.

"And how would this candle magically be in various places and not be noticed. Look at this scene. It is as if Shara is being followed by a camera," Leni said. "Also, I have seen images from multiple angles of the same scene. This candle is a memory device. It is not a camera. Let me examine it and see—"

"No! Don't touch it!" Clover said.

"Why?" Claus said.

Clover touched the candle, and the three were seemingly transported back to the village. They stood in Argo's nursery where bamboophs were being harvested. Several workers converted the bamboophs into musical instruments, and they played songs to test them.

"Do not move," Leni said. "We are still in the cabin. But our senses are being overridden."

"Devil condemn. Gotta be those evil aliens behind this. Clover, stop this," Claus said.

"I can't. I won't. I've been away from France for too long. My lovely France. Destroyed by selenites. Only with this candle can I...can we enjoy happiness, Claus. Leni can stay too as a servant and doctor. He can play the bambooph if he likes. We'll start a family and be happy. Oh Claus, I love you!"

Clover rushed into Claus's arms. Was this really love? Claus wasn't sure. He thought he knew love. He loved Frieda. But she never reciprocated. What if someone else falls into his lap, so to speak. Was it love? How many men had he discussed this with, and yet all had said they would take any woman that jumped into their lap. Really? But for how long? One night and then toss 'em out like old food packaging?

"This isn't love," Claus said. "It can't be. Everything is being pushed on me."

Then Claus realized why he failed so miserably with all those women and

Frieda. He kept pushing for something with them. They resented that.

"What do you mean? I give you my love! I give it freely!" Clover said.

"I do not blame you. You're being influenced. We all are. Clover, stop the projection. Let's discuss this rationally," Claus said.

"You hate me," Clover said. "You hate me! Well! I opened my heart to you! I made myself vulnerable! And you reject me with thorns and teeth!"

The scene changed suddenly into the black night of a powerful thunderstorm.

"Go chase your precious Lanietta then! But don't hold out for Shara! A being like Lanietta won't stand for another woman in her way! I won't be a part of it! I'm through with you! Through!" Clover yelled.

The scene vanished, the three returned to the cabin, Clover quickly took back the candle, rushed up the stairs, opened the door to the deck above, and ran. Claus ran after her, but before he could catch her, she jumped off the side of the boat toward the ocean water. As she fell, she extended her arm forward, the candle shone from her hand, and a glass bubble enveloped her body, protecting it from the ocean water as the bubble and her splashed down. The bubble floated for a moment, Clover held up the candle again, it shone, and the bubble added sophisticated elements, turning it into a submersible vessel, which Clover then took underwater.

Claus stared at the empty water, not knowing what to do. He looked around for traces of something, anything. He thought he saw a faint wisp of a cloud to the northwest, which was in the direction where bubbles from Clover's submersible traveled. After another moment, Leni walked up on deck and approached Claus.

"She's underwater and traveling incredibly fast. We cannot overtake her," Leni said.

"What in polar extremes is going on?" Claus said. "I mean, the whole Clover thing. And that candle. It's almost like

something the Carinians would set up. Leni?"

"I don't know about the Carinians, but I did review Labba's last message, the one Clover tried to keep us from hearing," Leni said.

"And?"

"The candle device was stolen from Morcellus. Not a possession of his, but an actual physical part of him. It's part of his brain," Leni said.

"Then Morcellus has been recording the villagers all this time," Claus said.

"Labba says Morcellus is angry, and that we are to return the candle at all costs before he retaliates. Also, we should mask your implant. The last thing we want is for Lanietta to interfere and get hold of the candle," Leni said.

"If that is the last thing we want, then it is the first thing Lanietta wants. Now I understand. Lanietta had contact with Clover. Lanietta could have manipulated Clover. In fact I think she did. She had Clover steal the candle from Morcellus. Which means Clover could be on the way to Lanietta as we speak. But I agree with Labba. Mask the implant. We'll follow Clover as best we can. She'll lead us to Lanietta. And hopefully Shara."

Leni masked the implant.

"Thank you," Claus said. "Now we can...wait, isn't there another message?"

Leni checked.

"Yes, there is," Leni said. "Morcellus couldn't wait. He is sending whales to retake the candle."

"Sending whales? What does that mean? He has an army of whales?" Claus asked.

"More like a navy of whales," Leni corrected.

"I'm in the middle of the ocean debating semantics," Claus said. "That tops it. I should just jump and let fate be my keeper."

Claus began climbing over the railing, but Leni grabbed him by the arm and pulled him back.

"Do not be a fool. This is bigger than you. Your false heroics will only be remembered by the shark that ate you, and only until he gets his next meal," Leni said.

Claus looked at Leni in surprise and did a double-take. This was a machine? A machine sounding amazingly human and smart to Claus?

"Now if you are done with your flash of self-pity, we need to get below and do heavy analysis with the instruments. Lanietta, Clover, whales, and Claus—all dancing the line of insanity," Leni said.

They returned below. Leni found another message awaiting. It was from Labba.

"Here is the message," Leni said, "'In view of the situation, we are building more ships. This is necessary to protect the shoreline, provide intelligence on what is happening at sea, and to aid in the search for Shara.'"

"Another war?" Claus asked.

"There is nothing about war in the message," Leni said.

"Still, that is the result when two opposing powers meet. When the selenites in the rest of the world find out what's happened on Antarctica, they'll send ships. What if Lanietta backs those selenite ships?" Claus asked.

"The best course of action then would be to find Shara before this happens," Leni said.

"Are we still tracking Clover?"

"Yes. I'm also tracking a pod of whales. From the size of the echograms, they appear to be killer whales," Leni said.

"Which aren't really whales. They are dolphins," Claus said.

"Now who's debating semantics?" Leni asked.

"Okay, okay. Whale or dolphin, it doesn't matter. Can we reach Clover before the whales or dolphins do?"

"Not at this speed. But the whales are quicker than Clover. They will overtake her in twenty minutes," Leni said.

"Twenty minutes? How'd they get there so quickly from Antarctica?" Claus asked.

"There's no evidence they are from Antarctica," Leni said.

"Well if they aren't, then Morcellus can summon whales from anywhere in the ocean! Planets above, is nowhere in the ocean safe?" Claus asked.

"We do not know Morcellus's range of communication, if he has any," Leni said.

"But you just said the whales aren't from Antarctica," Claus said.

"I never did. You are creating perception from your own desire," Leni said.

The blip showed Clover changing course, and a side screen spewed information.

"Did you see that? Clover knows she's being followed," Claus said.

"The readout concurs," Leni said.

"She's headed for that geological feature," Claus said. "It's a mountain."

"Appears to be a seamount," Leni said. "Or underwater mountain."

"Like I said, a mountain," Claus said.

"The whales are pursuing, no, they are killer whales. Confirmed by sonogram analysis," Leni said. "I was wrong about you earlier, Claus. I'm sorry. Jumping into the ocean would have resulted in death by killer whales, not sharks."

"Thanks for the apology," Claus said sarcastically. "I still want to know how your programming ended up like this."

"I am told Yuri had a hand in it," Leni said.

"Yuri?"

"Yes, Morcellus took suggestions from Yuri during my upgrade," Leni said.

"Splendid," Claus said with disdain. "Look, Leni, Clover's blip is gone!"

"She's inside the seamount? Let me recheck the instruments," Leni said.

"The killer whales have changed direction. They are circling the mountain...I mean, seamount. They can't get in. They can't get in!"

"Instruments concur. Somehow Clover has gone inside the seamount. Perhaps through a door or other method," Leni said. "The killer whales can't get in."

"Or they won't," Claus said. "Perhaps they are afraid? Perhaps there is something inside that seamount, a hollow area with other life-forms capable of killing them."

"Humans and selenites can do that, if you include robots," Leni said.

"I keep forgetting about the selenites," Claus said while Leni shot him a stare. "Well? I didn't grow up with them. I keep thinking I'm in the past."

"Adapting to one's current environment is critical for survival," Leni said.

"Yeah, yeah, yeah. I know. I don't like it. But I know," Claus said. "Continue toward the seamount."

"And then?" Leni asked.

"We'll have to adapt. We have that underwater submersible. I'll have to take it down and find a way into the seamount. And I'll have to do so without killer whales attacking me," Claus said.

"They won't attack you. But they might block you," Leni said. "In which case the submersible is capable of defending itself."

"Kill the killer whales? That doesn't sound like defense," Claus said.

"It is an expression borrowed from your people to justify killing. Simply claim the attack was in the name of self-defense, and all is well," Leni said.

"Why am I dreading this already? Somebody please help me out," Claus said.

"Keep calm. We are almost there," Leni said. "Should I give you a chill pill? You can rest until we reach the seamount."

"Let me rest without medication," Claus said. "Something tells me the seamount won't have drugs for free distribution."

Claus tried to rest on the cot. He closed his eyes, but immediately he felt like he was drowning. He sat up with a start and looked at Leni.

"Are we there?" Claus asked.

"You sat but a moment ago," Leni said. "Get some rest."

Claus reclined on the cot again. He fell asleep. All about him was blackness. Then he saw an office desk far in the distance with a desk lamp shining. A person was sitting at the desk with face illuminated by the lamp. Claus could not make out who the person was, but the image grew larger, or Claus became closer, and now he could see the face. It was that of Lanietta. She had a black cape around her from her neck all the way down, and this became apparent when she stood from the desk. But she did not stand fully. She crouched partly, she opened her cape slightly on her left side, and a large cat leapt from the cape and at Claus. It landed on Claus's face and clawed his neck. He cried out and twisted back and forth to get the cat off, but the cat fought to stay attached. Finally, Claus ripped the cat off and threw it back at the desk. His neck bled, and the cat returned to the cape, where Lanietta protected it and laughed. She laughed so hard and so loud that the desk shook, and the lamp shattered with a loud bang.

Chapter 24: The Seamount

Claus awoke. The pillow with which he had slept was now across the cabin on a small desk, where it had knocked over a lamp.

"It's okay," Leni said. "You killed the pillow. It will never hurt you again."

"Oh, sorry," Claus said.

"You're on edge. It's common with humans in these situations," Leni said. "But cheer up. You did get some rest at least, and we are approaching the seamount. I've been inspecting the area. The water is full of orcas. Killer whales. There is no evidence of Clover. But there is—"

"A bread trail she left that we can follow," Claus finished.

"No, nothing like that," Leni said.

"Sorry. Just something I remembered from my earlier days. From fiction," Claus said.

"We'll need to do better than fiction," Leni said. "This is the real thing."

"Yeah, how would people react if they thought this was a made-up story they read in a book or saw in a movie?" Claus said.

"Perhaps if times are more peaceful, you might write that book," Leni said.

"Would it really matter? Who would care? But if I did, I would keep a journal of each day that passed," Claus said. "The day would have to be important. Not like now or anything."

"Today is not important? Oh the irony of it all," Leni said. "People think that each day has no value. Then years later people say, 'I wish I had written down all that happened that day. Because now that I'm older, I see things differently, and I can make better sense of things.'"

"What...is that a quote from somewhere?" Claus asked.

"Not directly, but it is what you might call an amalgamated quote, meaning it is the sentiment often expressed by people in their latter years," Leni said.

"Okay, if we figure out this seamount thing, I'll think about writing down what happened. Or at least enter it into the computer. Wait, you *are* a computer. I can tell you what happened, and you can write the book," Claus said.

"*Cryptic Tales of Claus*, by Leni the selenite," Leni said.

"There's that dark humor again," Claus said.

"Just adding a little flavor," Leni said.

"How about finding a way into the seamount instead?" Claus said.

"That's easy enough. The orcas are swimming around it. No bread trail from fiction needed," Leni said.

"And you've been wasting my time with story writing? Let's get the submersible ready," Claus said.

Leni hit a few buttons.

"It's ready," he said. "Just climb through that hatch over in the deployment bay. Emergency equipment is already on board."

"I hope a leak doesn't develop and slowly fill the sub with water," Claus said.

"Don't worry. At the depth you are going, a leak will instantaneously cause catastrophic structural failure and implosion. You won't suffer," Leni said.

"I can always count on your encouragement. Sheesh," Claus said with mock gratitude.

"Into the sub you go, there's a good lad. Now we seal the door. Keep in touch," Leni said after shoving Claus inside the submersible and closing the hatch.

"Testing," Claus said into the radio-like device. "Testing!"

There was no reply. The sub lowered into the water, and Claus tried one more time in desperation.

"Testing!" Claus said.

"Toasting?" Leni's voice returned from the radio-like device. "Marshmallows and sausage? Mmm, I love a good roast over the fire in summer, with ticks and mosquitos all awaiting their turn at the feast. Yehhhhhssss. Beats Siberia on a cold day when the dogs are at play over scraps from dissident decay."

"Leni, stop it! Yuri again? I'm going to have your programming scrubbed when we get back. Yuri's humor is whacked," Claus said. "What's wrong with you anyway? Why the delay? I've been calling into this radio, and you deploy me first without acknowledging my call?"

"There is no radio in the sub," Leni said. "Communication is by sonar. You must be in water to communicate with the Mad Mistral. Now get a hold of yourself and pay attention to the mission."

Claus grumbled into the sonar communication device.

"That's better," Leni said.

"Sub is powered and responsive," Claus said. "Now moving through the ocean. I'm clear of the Mad Mistral. Wow. Orcas everywhere. Like nothing I've ever seen."

"Steer clear, and all will befall you sturdy and tall," Leni said.

"Yuri again, boy is he going to get it from me," Claus muttered to himself.

But the thought of Yuri was quickly replaced by the increasing density of orcas.

"There's no clear path to the seamount wall," Claus said. "There are too many orcas in the way. Even now they are swimming around me and looking at me like I don't belong. I might have to start shooting."

"They will destroy you for sure if you do that. I recommend diplomacy," Leni sonar-commed back.

"Diplomacy? With orcas?" Claus said to himself. "Who does he think I am? Claus, get a hold of yourself. C'mon, think. Think man!"

"Hint—use the sonar. There is a special setting for communicating with cetaceans," Leni said.

"You're kidding. Like a translator? I can speak with them?" Claus asked.

"Not in complex sentences. But basic concepts are possible such as hello, goodbye, I am a friend, I am your enemy, etc.," Leni said. "Press the button for cetacean mode, and you will see buttons for other basic expressions."

Claus pressed the cetacean button. A panel door slid away revealing labeled buttons.

"I'll try this one," Claus said.

He selected "Hello", and immediately several orcas swam toward him.

"I'm under attack! I must fire a torpedo!" Claus said.

"Patience!" Leni called back. "They are curious. My panel shows you greeted them. Now they wish to return the greeting."

"No way! I'm getting away from these orcas! Three are shooting right for me!" Claus said.

"Don't!" Leni called back.

Too late. Claus pushed the submersible to full speed, but the orcas continued chase. Claus pressed a button to say, "Leave me alone," but the orcas chasing Claus simply increased in number, and over Claus's sonar-com sounded a half-dog, half-cat cackling sound, as if the orcas were delighted with the game of chasing Claus.

"It's not a game!" Claus called over the sonar, hoping the orcas would understand. "I need clear passage to the seamount. I need to find Clover and Shara! And deal with Lanietta! Can you help?"

Claus's voice echoed back over the sonar-com, as if it had bounced off a giant whale who had distorted the echo into mockery. Indeed, Claus was sure the orcas were making fun of him.

"Stop," Leni's voice said. "Stop, and roll the sub over."

"What?" Claus called back. "You're kidding."

"It will show submission. The orcas will then accept you."

"The orcas will crush me," Claus called back.

Claus steered the sub toward the seamount, and he reached an outcropping. He swerved very close to this and other outcroppings to ward off the pursuing orcas. This only gained him a little time, as the orcas did not give up. They came after Claus again and again. Claus was running out of outcropping help unless he turned the sub around and headed back.

"It's time," Claus said. "I've dealt with these orcas long enough. A show of strength will convince them."

"Claus, wait," Leni's voice said.

Claus could not wait. He turned the sub around such that the sub's torpedo launcher was pointed toward a pack of orcas, and he pressed the button to launch. But just as he did, the pack themselves exhaled air bubbles, turned around quickly, and slapped their flukes against one another with great precision. The resulting water motion forced the air bubbles into prisms, and these air prisms (though close and not connected) formed a U-shape in a path from Claus right back to him. The torpedo hit the air prisms, and the change from differing media densities caused the torpedo's path to change and follow the air prisms in the U-shaped path and thus back toward Claus's sub. Claus scrambled to get the sub out of harm's way and in fact steered around one last outcropping in hopes of detonating the torpedo against the outcropping and not the sub. It worked, sort of. The torpedo did detonate against the outcropping, but Claus's sub was too close. The concussive forces knocked Claus unconscious, and the hull developed a crack. Collapse was imminent.

"Claus, Claus!" Leni called.

Claus was doomed. Should we let him die? Should we let the story end here? With no resolution? I, K Gerard Martin, cannot let the story end, because it doesn't. There's plenty more to tell. So here's what happened next. Those orcas were never Claus's enemy, though he thought it. They were allied to Morcellus, yes, but they also knew of Claus's mission and did not want him to fail. They approached his sub, enveloped it in an air bubble much the way they had created the air prisms, and floated the sub to the ocean surface. Seeing the situation, Leni maneuvered the Mad Mistral's crane above the sub, lifted it from the ocean, and placed it on deck. Leni then went up on deck, opened the hatch, and pulled Claus out. A quick smelling salt to Claus's nose brought Claus back to the living. Claus coughed and pulled away.

"What...what happened? I'm back here?" Claus asked.

"You almost died," Leni said. "The orcas saved you."

"They did? I thought they were trying to kill me," Claus said.

"I gave you instructions to—"

"You should have seen them, Leni. Fast and ominous. And no floppy dorsal fin like in the aquariums. These orcas were on a mission. I could see it in their eyes, in the way they swam," Claus said.

"Don't let their appearance deceive you," Leni said. "I've received another message from Labba confirming their mission is to retrieve the stolen article from Clover. Claus, they were playing with you, as a way of showing friendship. They were trying to include you in their pod. Patience would have helped. Now the submersible is damaged."

"You can repair it, right?" Claus asked.

"How? With glue and tape? Look at these cracks. No, the hull must be re-formed to withstand the immense ocean pressure. Amazing the hull didn't fail completely. You should be dead, Claus," Leni said.

"I know. Lucky," Claus said.

"Don't worry," Leni added. "There are plenty of other days to die."

"Thanks for the reassurance," Claus said sarcastically.

"Oh, I mean there are plenty of other ways to try," Leni said. "My programming must have slipped."

"Something did. A pity the Mad Mistral has no other submersibles. We're trapped here on the surface," Claus said.

Leni looked around the ship. Nothing but ocean water surrounded the Mad Mistral.

"We are hardly trapped," Leni said. "But I gather your meaning. There's only one alternative. I must go. I am water tight, and ocean pressure does not affect me."

"That's not right. That's just not right. I should be the one to go. I mean, you're not alive. You're not human. Leni, you can't. Really? No. It won't work," Claus protested.

"Then name an alternative," Leni said.

Claus stood for a moment. He pounded his fist against the submersible in anger, but then he felt lightheaded and dropped to his knees.

"You're in no shape to go anywhere with that concussion," Leni said. "Go below, and man the sonar-com. Relay any messages from Labba to me. I'll communicate back with my internal sonar mechanism."

"Done in by a machine!" Claus said in a dejected tone.

"You have this antiquated notion of the knight in shining armor saving the princess," Leni said. "You can explore your fantasy back in the village. But for now, sit tight. If I don't return, you'll have to get help from the village. My guess is that they're already preparing another boat and crew to help us. Be patient and wait for their help! The ship is on autopilot and holding this position. Don't change it. Rest, Claus, rest!"

Leni dove off the side of the ship. Then Claus saw bubbles rise from the spot where Leni dove.

"Those can't be from him. Too many bubbles," Claus said. "Must be from the orcas. If only I could..."

Before Claus could wonder much more, a cold rain moved in. Claus's need for returning to the ocean was replaced by a need to dry off and warm up. Down into the ship he went, protected from the rain. But he wasn't quick enough. The rain had soaked his clothes, and now he shook like a leaf.

"Heat. I need heat!" he said.

Claus stepped into a hyperbaric chamber, not so much for treating the bends, but because it was also effective at providing heat and removing moisture.

"I'll have a mini-sauna and rest my nerves," he said as he turned up the heat.

Claus removed his wet clothes and placed them on a drying rack. A beach towel was handy, and this he placed over his shoulders. He found a loose rope and used it to secure the towel around his waist. The towel reached nearly to his knees, and Claus realized he had formed a sort of toga outfit.

"I'm ready for Ancient Greece," he said. "Now if I had an olive branch, I could make peace with the world."

Claus had left the hyperbaric chamber door open, partly for increased ventilation and partly in hopes he'd hear Leni on his return to the Mad Mistral. Claus sat in a lounge chair and relaxed.

"If only the Mad Mistral had music. Folk music. Like...like the Irish drinking song in my mind," he said, and he tried singing the song!

As the Mad Mistral filled with Claus's clumsy singing, a porpoise dove out of the water and onto the deck of the Mad Mistral, unobserved. The porpoise took on legs and arms and waddled over to the hatch. It opened the hatch and entered.

Meanwhile, Leni was heading farther below the ocean's surface and toward the seamount. As previously observed by Claus, orcas filled the area. Several took an interest in Leni and shoved him around. But he took hold of the dorsal fin on one orca, threw his body over the creature, and controlled him as if riding a horse.

"Call your friends off and take me to the seamount," Leni commanded.

The orca squealed for the others to make way, they did, and Leni was taken to the seamount.

"Amazing what properly applied electric current can do," Leni said to the orca.

But the orca did not speak back. Instead, it took Leni to the seamount as commanded. The orca swam down to the side of the seamount and reached what would be a cave if the seamount were a mountain on land.

"Go inside," Leni commanded. "Go!"

But the orca refused to go. Leni increased the electric current to the orca, but fear paralyzed it, and it remained motionless.

"Then I release you," Leni said. "Go now to your friends. But do not give thought to retaliation, as I can send out a broad beam of electric current and command you all. And do not stray too far. I may have need of you again."

The orca swam off. Leni swam to the cave opening. It was just large enough for him to enter. Indeed, he could stand at the bottom of the opening and touch the opening's top. He swam into the cave. It was dark. Leni activated an arch-shaped light source from his forehead, subtly hidden under his skin layers. Light then glowed from his forehead, and he could see. The cave continued straight ahead, with no bends or forks, but it did gradually widen, nearly imperceptibly, but noticeably after traveling along for some length (which Leni did). But it quickly became apparent to Leni that this was no ordinary cave at all. Each side contained a pair of roller brushes, or so it seemed, running the entire length of the cave as far as Leni could see. These roller brushes were about the same diameter as a tree trunk, and each pair turned such that the upper roller turned downward, the lower upward, and in so doing pulled anything from the cave in between them and to some unknown exit point. Each pair diverged behind Leni toward the cave opening and met the cave opening such that the four occupied positions at two, four, eight, and ten o'clock if one imagined the cave opening as an analog clock face. What made these especially strange was that the roller brushes always came together to the side of Leni and in front of Leni, while they diverged immediately behind him and back toward the opening, no matter how far into the cave he had swum. The cave itself seemingly had no end. He swam for hours, convinced he should have reached something, but he did not.

"Leni to Mad Mistral, do you read me?" he sent sonically.

Leni waited several minutes for the sonar message to travel through the cave and outward, but the calculation entered his mind—the cave opening was not aligned with the Mad Mistral, and so Claus would not receive his message. His purpose became clear—he needed to abort this cave exploration, return to the Mad Mistral, and report his findings to Claus. The two could send probes into the cave. One probe could travel for days if need be while the other probes could learn about the roller brushes, particularly what would happen if a probe should be pulled through by a pair. This made rational sense to Leni. He returned to the cave opening and sent out a sonic message to the Mad Mistral. But there was no response. On the chance Claus was sleeping, Leni returned to the ocean's surface to awaken him with his findings. But when Leni popped his head above the waterline, the Mad Mistral was nowhere to be found.

"It's gone!" Leni said.

Chapter 25: Porpoise with a Purpose

We return to the Mad Mistral shortly after Leni left. The porpoise that had boarded the ship was climbing through the hatch from the deck, leaving a squeaky trail behind it. But Claus did not hear the squeaking. He so much enjoyed his Irish song and comfortable surroundings that he fell lightly asleep. The song faded from his lips. The porpoise ambled quietly to the hyperbaric chamber door. It peered into the chamber. Steam flowed outward from Claus's evaporating clothes, obscuring vision for a moment. But the steam cleared just enough for Claus to take one last look at the opening before falling asleep.

Claus was shocked. What was a porpoise doing on board? His eyes opened wide, and he stood. But as he stood, the porpoise reacted and went for the door to slam it shut. Indeed, it did slam the door shut as Claus dove for the door to keep it ajar. Too late. Just as he reached the door, it had fully closed, and the porpoise had locked it.

"What...what is this?" Claus yelled.

His voice was barely audible through the small, glass window in the chamber's door. To his surprise, the porpoise replied.

"Well, well, well, the pet is in his cage," the porpoise said.

"Pet? Who are you? What do you want?" Claus demanded.

"Oh don't be so alarmed. You're still on your boat. A bit larger than your spacecraft, but then who needs a boat on the moon?" the porpoise said.

"Lanietta?"

"So you do remember me, Clomper. I thought you'd forgotten. That was a dirty trick you and your friends played on me. Part of me is stuck in that village in that...that...Martacean. Morcellus indeed! He calls himself superior to me. But I told him otherwise. He couldn't catch all of me," Lanietta said, still in porpoise form.

"You spoke with the creature? With Morcellus? Lanietta, let me out! Let's discuss this like rational human beings. There's plenty of time to—"

"Plenty of time? Hah!" Lanietta said with anger.

She banged her body against the chamber door, and the concussive wave carried through and thudded deep into Claus's heart, causing his nerves to fray.

"Lanietta, no, wait!" Claus started to say.

"You know nothing about time!" Lanietta retorted.

"Make a deal with me. Let Shara and Clover go," Claus pleaded.

"Clover?"

"I know you have her. You lured her. You had to," Claus said. "Let them go, and I'll be your prisoner."

"You *are* my prisoner, Clomper!" Lanietta said with continued fire in her voice. "Do you think your little stunt could stop me? I have grown far more powerful than before, Clompty-Dompty. This atmosphere is filled with unlimited energy. Do you hear me? Unlimited! My power extends throughout the stratosphere! Rational human beings you say? Since when are human beings rational? Since when am I human? But I will let you out. Yes, let's discuss this as you say, like the *rational* human being you are! First, we must go on a date. Yes, you and I. A date. No peeking. I have a surprise destination."

Lanietta stepped away from the chamber door window. Claus wasn't sure at first what she meant, but he didn't have long to wonder. The ship noticeably changed direction to the east and increased speed.

"Lanietta, wait! What are you doing? You can't leave these waters! Leni is down below! He'll be stranded. Stranded!" Claus shouted.

But Lanietta didn't hear Claus, or at least she didn't respond as if she could. Ten minutes went by of high speed and slalom. Then twenty. And thirty. The motion threw Claus back and forth inside the hyperbaric chamber, and Claus felt sick.

"This will be the hyperbarfic chamber soon," Claus said to himself. "Claus, get hold of yourself. She can't do this forever. She must have a purpose."

"I do," she said, returning to the chamber's window. "After we speed through the Drake Passage, we'll head north through the Atlantic."

"What? No!" Claus pleaded.

Lanietta sent a plasma bolt through the chamber door and stunned Claus. He passed out.

When Claus came to, the Mad Mistral had slowed and steadied.

"A porpoise with a purpose," Lanietta said as she appeared at the chamber door's window, still in her porpoise form.

"Let me out! We have to go back and get Leni!" Claus said.

"Leni the selenite robot, going down to the Tabelia Seamount to find me. Only he won't find me. I am here with you in the North Atlantic. And you are here with me. But I will let you out. Observe."

Lanietta unlocked the chamber door and opened it slightly. Claus rushed at the door to push it open, but when he touched it, the door burned his flesh.

"Ow!" Claus cried. "What have you done?"

Lanietta opened the door fully and laughed. Claus moved to lunge toward Lanietta, but he cried out in pain. A wall of air between Lanietta and himself was searing hot. In fact, his view of her was distorted much as the air above a campfire is distorted.

"Now now now, Clomper. A pet must be trained," Lanietta laughed.

"I'm not your pet. End this madness, Lanietta. Go back to the moon and leave Earth alone. There's nothing for you here," Claus said.

"Oh but there is. Part of me is held by the creature Morcellus, as I keep reminding you. And now part of Morcellus is held by me. Recognize this?"

Lanietta pulled a device from her blowhole. It was Clover's candle. Then it dawned on him. With Lanietta in porpoise form, how was she able to speak? Cetaceans have no air passageway from the mouth to the lungs.

"The creature's candle!" Claus said. "You stole that from Clover!"

"Yes, and I have confiscated it as evidence. I am Lanietta, a porpoise of the sea. And my kin shall respect me."

"You're no porpoise. A porpoise can't talk. You've taken the shape of one, but not correctly. There are defects," Claus said.

"Improvements," Lanietta said. "Should I squeal to you like this?"

Lanietta squealed such loud and high-pitched frequencies that Claus nearly passed out from the pain. He fell to his knees but immediately stood tall. Something caused his knees and legs to hurt.

"What...what is it?" he said as he passed his hand in the air before his knees.

This air was also extremely hot. Lanietta chuckled.

"Ow!" Claus cried.

"A little trick I learned while playing in the atmosphere," Lanietta said. "I can control air pressure and temperature. I learned from Morcellus. Oh, he didn't want to teach me, but with this candle and a convincing personality, I mastered hot air."

"Oh, I get it. You can create these walls of hot air between people, like with us right now. But fear not, there was no need to drag the knowledge out of Morcellus. You already have plenty of hot air," Claus said.

"*That* deserves punishment!" Lanietta said.

The air around Claus became organized with split temperatures of extreme heat and pleasant coolness. Lanietta organized the air such that it followed closely along Claus's body contours, being but a finger width's distance from his skin. Whenever Claus attempted to move outside this form, the searing heat forced him back.

"Get rid of this restraint! You're going to kill me!" Claus said.

"This is your new pet collar and leash, so to speak. Stray but a little, and consequences are severe," Lanietta said.

"Am I to be imprisoned in this spot for eternity? Is that your idea? It's torture!" Claus said.

"No, you will not remain here. It's time for your walk, as you might say," Lanietta said.

"I will not stand for this. I will not—"

But Claus could not finish his statement. He choked on searing hot air. Yes, Lanietta had changed the air to impede speech. He started falling to the ground, but the change in body shape caused him to exceed the safe air shape, and a reflex action in his muscles sent him standing upright while still choking. Hot air slipped like a knife between his arms and torso, forcing him to move his arms away from his body. Indeed, he began flapping his arms like a bird.

"Bird therapy," Lanietta said. "Now then Clomper, I'll release cool air for you to breathe, but you must put a muzzle on that mouth of yours and stay out of trouble. Here now, your clothes are dry. Put them on."

Claus stood in place, but Lanietta manipulated the air temperature envelope around Claus's body to force him into movement. She had him walk over to his clothes, remove his towel, and pull on those clothes.

"Embarrassed to be seen naked?" she asked. "That is the least of your worries. It's time to go on deck for your walk."

Again through air temperature manipulation, Lanietta forced Claus along. He led the way up the hatch to the deck with Lanietta close behind. She had him walk to the bow where he stopped short. She then stepped between him and the bow such that she faced Claus but had her back to the bow.

"First, speech training," Lanietta said. "Pets should only vocalize when about to die or when requested to. You humans have a nasty habit of incessant vocalization

to the point of near insanity. I will put a stop to that, at least while you are my pet, Clomper. You must reduce vocalization. However, if you wish to speak, you may tap your lips together twice."

Claus tapped his lips together twice.

"You may now speak," Lanietta said.

"How long are you going to do this to me?" Claus asked.

"What a silly question," Lanietta said.

Claus was about to speak again, but Lanietta forced his jaw shut.

"Ah-ah-ah. You didn't ask for permission," she said.

Claus tapped his lips together.

"You may speak," she said.

"This is really awkward, Lanietta. Let me speak freely without this—" he started, but Lanietta forced his lips inward to quiet him.

"Time for talk is over. Now for the walk," Lanietta said.

Lanietta forced Claus over to a storage area. Inside was a small, inflatable life raft. Lanietta's control of air around him, though close enough to control his limbs, was inadequate for controlling movement close to his body, and so he retained eye movement control (which also explains how he was able to tap his lips together without penalty). To that end, his eyes showed surprise and shock at being forced to retrieve the life raft. The raft had no air, but that was simple enough. Amazingly, the village people had attached a small carbon dioxide canister to the raft that would make for easy inflation. Claus wanted to turn around and speak, but Lanietta's control of the air envelope around him did not permit it. It wasn't until after she had him march all the way to the Mad Mistral's stern with raft in hand, place the raft down, and begin to remove rope that she let him face her.

"We are nearly ready for your walk," she said, and he tapped his lips together. "You may speak."

"I don't understand what this is about. What does this have to do with a walk? A life raft? And this rope? This rope is for towing," Claus said.

"Way too much vocalizing!" she said as she forced his jaw together. "So much effort wasted on useless words. We must get going."

She forced him to inflate the raft. Fortunately, she allowed for use of the carbon dioxide canister, but the contents drained quickly, and she had him toss it to the side. Next, she had him tie one end of the rope to the life raft, and then she had him throw the raft overboard.

"Now jump off," she said. "Aim for the raft. Don't worry, I'll guide you."

Claus tapped his lips, but she locked his jaw shut.

"No protest. Off with you," she said.

Again with air envelope manipulation, she forced him to jump off the stern. He landed on the raft, she released the air envelope, and Claus, free of that air envelope, collapsed and rested in the raft.

"There, that wasn't so bad," she said.

With no air envelope to inhibit him, Claus spoke.

"Lanietta, of all the crazy things. Stop fooling around! I'm climbing up this rope so we can talk," Claus said.

But as soon as Claus began climbing the rope, the air envelope formed just above him, like a body glove. It sucked in air, and in so doing tried to suck Claus into its grasp. Claus avoided it and instead dropped down from the rope and sat in the inflatable.

"Whatever you are doing won't work," Claus said.

"No? Let's go for a ride," she said.

With Claus still in the life raft, Lanietta adjusted the Mad Mistral's sails, and the boat took on speed. The life raft skipped along in the Mad Mistral's wake, whipping side to side. Claus held on, but the thought occurred to him—why should he hold on? He could jump out now and take his chances in the ocean. Was it so different from his earlier thought of jumping off to end it all?

Cold water splashed on his face, and he came back to his senses. The life raft was warmer.

"Much warmer," Claus said with suspicion.

He held an arm out in the air aside of the life raft, and it was cooler.

"She's created a new air envelope around me!" he thought. "She just made it large enough so I wouldn't notice."

Lanietta had disappeared from view to work the sails, but she returned to the stern, and Claus watched as she peered at him over the edge.

"So I trust you are enjoying yourself, Clomper?" she asked.

"This is hardly a walk," Claus said. "More lies and deception?"

"Yes, yes! The walk! Here, let's begin your walk!"

Lanietta pointed at the life raft, and the raft's fill nozzle suddenly opened up and squirted out air. As the life raft deflated, Claus scrambled to stop the loss. Like putting a hand over a badly leaking garden hose, Claus was unable to stop the outgushing of air. The life raft deflated, and he fell into the water. Just before fully losing control, he grabbed onto the rope with both hands. Then the body glove air envelope descended and latched onto those hands, preventing his release. There were now two air envelopes—one holding his hands, and the larger one providing warmth. In fact, the large air envelope dipped slightly onto the ocean water immediately below Claus, warming it so that he would not get too cold. But Claus was not protected from the Mad Mistral's wake, and so he flopped around on the water like a rag doll, or like a novice water skier who'd lost his skis. But unlike a water skier who might be dragged simply and plainly along the water, Lanietta's large air envelope periodically picked Claus up and tossed him in the air to ensure he could land back onto the water hard. And hard it was. Claus quickly acquired blunt-force injuries from such tossing.

"You're going to kill me!" Claus yelled.

"Run, Clomper, run!" Lanietta yelled back.

Out of desperation, Claus ran atop the water. It worked. Lanietta's air envelope no longer tossed Claus around, provided he didn't fall back into the water. Instead, it provided just enough support so that he could continue running without sinking. But Claus tired, and he fell into the water. The air envelope tossed him up again, and he bounced off the water again, breaking his nose. It bled, but he stayed upright and continued running, with pain in his legs and lungs from the exhausting effort.

"I can't do it," Claus called. "The world is grey, and I feel numb."

Claus's exhaustion caused him to lose sense of color in his vision. He could no longer feel his limbs. Lanietta's air envelope gripped his body and forced it to continue running. Just before he passed out, the Mad Mistral passed over patches of ocean garbage, dumped hundreds of years earlier. Leftover plastic wrappings, packing peanuts, capped (but empty) plastic bottles, lots and lots of plastic pellets, and then something else—reed shavings. The shavings flew up into Claus's face, swatting his cheeks like angry dragonflies. Claus laughed with delirium.

"It all ends with me alone but for the torturing hand of an alien," he mumbled as he looked up at Lanietta, who held out the special candle that Clover had shown him earlier.

The world went black, and he passed out.

Chapter 26: Leni Seeks Help

"Claus!" Leni called. "Can you hear me? Claus!"

Leni bobbed up and down on the ocean surface. Still no sign of the Mad Mistral. He sent out a call to the ship by sonar. No reply.

"My sonar isn't strong enough to reach Arberella. But perhaps another ship will hear my message and render aid," Leni said to himself. "Oh, I'm becoming like the humans. Here I am in the middle of the ocean, alone, and talking to myself."

Leni emitted the strongest sonar message he could, giving his location and a request for help. He didn't expect an immediate reply, so he was quite startled when an impromptu wave lifted him in the air. The wave was dynamic, with the leading edge falling down and rolling back on itself while the wave as a whole remained up in the air. This rolling-back phenomenon kept Leni pinned against the wave. As he struggled to make sense of the situation, dozens of orcas appeared around him. In fact, the wave carrying him along was being propelled by four red-striped orcas. These stripes were small in comparison to the main black and white colorations, but they were easy to see, being on the sides (much like a red-winged black bird). The stripes highlighted both the dorsal fin and flukes.

Using their flukes, the orcas slapped the wave upward, sending Leni clean through the air where a receiving orca swatted Leni toward another four orcas with an impromptu wave, upon which he became caught. The orcas around him created a formation—those with normal black and white colorations created the outline of a playing field and goal posts while other orcas became players in what was apparently orca water polo. The orcas opposing the red-sided orcas had yellow stripes on their sides, and so it was the reds versus the yellows.

After being excessively swatted and pushed about, including several change of possessions between the reds and yellows, Leni attempted to shock an orca here and there as he got close to each orca (usually while being batted around), but he was unable. Finally, a yellow-striped orca attempted to dribble Leni on a small impromptu wave with no help from others. Leni used the opportunity to dive down and shock the orca.

"Foul!" squealed a beluga whale, who had been refereeing the game. "Free kick for yellow."

The reds protested, claiming that they did nothing wrong.

"The rules are the rules," the beluga referee said.

Two pairs of yellows created an impromptu wave to hold Leni up and steady, and then the yellow that had been "fouled" came swimming along, dove upward and into a backflip, and swatted Leni with its flukes as it fell on its back. Leni flew through the air, but the reds, having felt cheated, did not use their regular red-striped orca goalie and instead employed the flukes of a blue whale, who came up and dove down with its flukes smacking Leni back across the polo field and over the yellows' goalposts—too high to reach for the yellow goalie who tried in vain to stop it. And thus a point was scored.

"Foul!" cried a yellow-striped orca.

"The rules are the rules," called back a red-striped orca.

The two teams converged in anger, like baseball teams engaged in a bench-clearing brawl. The beluga referee (and another beluga referee) attempted to break up the fight while the normal black and white orcas cheered the "spirited" interaction. Meanwhile, Leni snuck away from the chaos and was calculating whether he should go back down to the cavern for safety when he sensed mild shock waves in the ocean from a motorized propeller.

"A boat is approaching," Leni said. "Could be selenite pirates. They might impress me into service as one of their own. I calculate I should dive below."

Leni dove underwater and started for the cavern. He couldn't help but notice the underwater sloshing of the orcas as they continued to fight. Blood flowed from the ruckus, which attracted sharks, who because of their fear of orcas maintained a safe perimeter in hopes of catching a free meal without themselves becoming orcan dinner. But when Leni was only halfway toward the cavern, he received a sonar message.

"Mad Mistral, this is Selba. Leni, do you read?"

"This is Leni," he sent back via sonar. "The Mad Mistral is missing. I'm evading orcas."

"I'm approaching a large group of orcas. They are fighting over something. Are you under attack?" Selba called.

"Not at the moment. They are fighting amongst themselves," Leni said.

"I don't see you. Or Claus. Where are you two?" Selba said.

"I am underwater. Claus is missing. Wait, the orcas are dispersing," Leni said.

"I'm scaring them off. Do you see my boat?"

"Yes, I do."

"I've triangulated your signal. Surface and come aboard," Selba said.

As Leni swam to the surface, he noticed that yes indeed, the orcas were dispersing. He floated above the waterline and watched a speedboat pull alongside him. Selba threw a rope ladder over the side, and he climbed up. The speedboat was quite similar to the one Clover drove before Claus destroyed it.

"Your company is appreciated," Leni said. "Are you alone? Where's Baruuk?"

"No Baruuk. Just me," Selba said. "I'm glad to see you again. But what happened to the Mad Mistral and Claus?"

"You've been in contact with Labba?" Leni asked. "Only she knows our ship is named as such."

"Yes, she told me," Selba said. "Now about the Mad Mistral and Claus."

"Both were here a little while ago," Leni said. "We discovered a seamount. Claus went down to investigate in the sub. It was damaged, and I brought him back aboard. I went down next. When I surfaced, he and the ship were gone. I thought you were a pirate ship at first. So I dove for cover. I'm glad to see a friend from Arberella."

"And thanks to Morcellus, we've been making more boats to establish a protective perimeter around Arberella. I really came after Clover. She stole a boat, you know. Then I received your distress call while en route."

"Claus thought Clover was Lanietta," Leni said. "He fired on her boat and destroyed it."

Selba looked at Leni in surprise.

"Yes, it's true. We reached the wreckage and pulled Clover to safety. But then she surprised us with a device," Leni said. "A candle she called it."

"A memory candle. She stole it from Morcellus," Selba said.

"She used the candle to escape in a mini sub. We've concluded Lanietta is behind the candle, that she convinced Clover to bring the device to her," Leni said.

"I don't know how Lanietta could influence Clover from such a far distance away," Selba said.

"Do you know where Lanietta is? Does anyone? Or the extents of her reach? We last saw her in the clouds. She could be spread throughout this planet. You may yet be breathing part of Lanietta now," Leni said. "But don't forget that a part of her is locked away in Arberella, and very close if not a part of Morcellus."

"Yes, locked and prevented from doing harm," Selba said.

"Is she prevented?" Leni asked.

Selba gave Leni a nervous look.

"If what you are saying is true, she could influence others in Arberella. The entire village even. Or Morcellus himself! We must warn the villagers. We must return to Arberella at once!" Selba said as she slipped into a panic and made for the boat controls to return to Arberella.

But Leni blocked her.

"We can send a warning to Labba by sonar," Leni said.

"And if that doesn't work? If Labba and the others are now controlled?" Selba pointed out.

"I doubt she is. Labba is a being similar to Lanietta, only Labba is nicer. But even if she and the Arberellans are under Lanietta's control, what good could we do by returning? We ourselves would also fall under Lanietta's control. No, it is better we stay out here and search. We are short of help and overloaded with search possibilities. Do we look for Clover? For Claus? For Lanietta and Shara? Do we search the underwater cavern and hope all are there? I wish you would have brought Baruuk. Aren't you engaged to him? We certainly could use his help."

Selba paused. Determination filled her eyes. Then without warning, she pushed Leni's hand aside and set the throttle at full. The sudden propeller thrust sent Selba and Leni back (actually the boat jumped ahead). Leni fell to the back of the boat, but Selba held onto the throttle and thus only her legs were taken out from under her. She quickly pulled herself up and steered the boat. Leni pulled himself back up toward the controls, but as he did, Selba swerved the boat to the left and right. This sent Leni to sides starboard, port, starboard, etc.

"What are you doing, Selba? Where are you going?" he called as he struggled along toward her and the controls.

"I'm going after Lanietta. I'm going to claw the eyes out of that *heffernaffer*!" Selba called back.

"Selba, this...you...but where?" Leni said.

"Here we are, Lanietta!" Selba yelled to the heavens. "Take your best shot you wench of another world! No one else wants me. Claim me if you can!"

"No, please don't!" Leni said. "Selba, shhh! This won't accomplish anything. Selba!"

Selba continued swerving the boat back and forth at full throttle.

"Where did Labba get the power for these boats? Why was the Mad Mistral not outfitted with such?" he asked without expecting a response.

"Because Morcellus is angry! And I'm angry! We're going to show Lanietta and the world that we won't be pushed around!"

"But you're pushing me around!" Leni said as the turns continued to push him from side to side. "Selba. There's nothing to chase. Selba!"

Leni reached the controls and set thrust to idle. He reached for Selba, held her hand, and looked at her.

"We'll get Lanietta. We'll find the others. But not like this. Work the problem. Don't let the problem work you. Selba, let's work the problem together."

Selba looked Leni sternly in the eye, and with resolution nodded her head in affirmation.

"First things first," Leni said. "What was that cryptic remark about Lanietta claiming you? That you aren't wanted? Selba!"

Selba was about to open her mouth to speak but instead closed it.

"Baruuk? Oh, he didn't," Leni said. "He broke off the engagement."

"For another woman. Couldn't keep his mind focused on our relationship," Selba said.

"Okay, Selba, that's just Baruuk. Sometimes people have certain characteristics that drive them away. Let him go! Don't let his poor focus muddle yours."

"You're right," Selba said with a sniffle. "I shouldn't let his problem work me. I should work the real problem. There. I feel better already."

"Excellent. I'll send a message to Labba as to what has happened so far—regarding the Mad Mistral. No side distractions about Baruuk. Deal?"

"Deal!" Selba said, and the two shook hands.

Leni touched his finger to a sonaric relay and sent the message silently, meaning that Selba could hear nothing.

"While we wait for Labba's reply, we should investigate the underwater cavern," Leni said.

"But...isn't that how you lost Claus and the Mad Mistral? If you leave me here, the same might happen to me."

"Do you have a probe on board?" Leni asked.

Selba nodded and showed him.

"Just one probe," she said. "That's all that could be mustered at launch."

"Good. We'll launch the probe to explore. That way if you and this boat 'disappear,' I will be here with you."

"Fair enough," Selba said.

The two returned to the spot where Leni discovered the underwater cavern. Selba launched the probe.

"Several orcas approaching," Leni said as he watched a monitor screen.

"Approaching the boat or the probe?" Selba asked.

"Both."

"I'll use this boat as a decoy. Continue monitoring the probe," Selba said.

As Leni watched the probe dive deeper, Selba worked the controls of the boat, first to taunt the orcas, then to lead them away. It worked. Those that were also interested in the probe left it be and instead chased the boat.

"Good," Leni said. "Just a little longer...there, the probe has reached the cavern opening."

"Send it in," Selba said.

"There is a risk we will lose our communication link with the probe. It too uses sonar, does it not?"

"Yes," Selba said.

"When I first entered the cavern, I lost my link with the Mad Mistral," Leni said.

"The probe can be programmed to go in, explore for a specified time, then exit," Selba said. "Try that."

"Excellent idea. I should have calculated that plan of attack."

"Well hopefully we don't have any more attacks. Exploration is just fine," Selba said.

"Programming complete. I'll have it explore the rotating structures on one side," Leni said. "There, the probe is in. Contact lost. I put a five minute time limit on the probe. We'll know something soon."

But only after a minute, debris from the probe floated to the ocean surface.

"Destroyed," Selba said. "It's the only probe I have."

"We must find out what happened to it. Look, there's the journal box," Leni said.

Selba maneuvered the boat over to the debris field, and Leni scooped up the journal box. He attached it to a data transfer station and played back the data record. Selba watched as video of the probe's journey in the cavern displayed on the data transfer screen. The probe entered the cavern. As programmed, it traveled toward one of the sides (the right side in this case) to inspect the rotating shafts. As it placed one of its arms into the pair of rotating shafts, the shafts caught the arm and pulled the probe into them. The video stopped.

"You sent the only probe into that rotating thing?" Selba asked.

"I was testing. Must find the entrance," Leni said.

"I don't understand. You've found the cavern entrance already," Selba said.

"No. Another entrance. To another chamber. Where Clover went. And possibly Lanietta," Leni said.

"And Claus?"

"I don't think he is in there. I would have seen him when I explored," Leni said.

"How can you be sure there is another chamber?" Selba asked.

"Well...I can't. But we have little else to go on. The orcas won't go in. That suggests a sense of mystery, at least from what I've studied on humans."

"Or they won't go in because getting caught in those turn shafts is certain death," Selba suggested.

"There must be a way in. When I was down there, the cavern seemed to extend forever. I was certain that if I swam far enough, I'd find another entrance. But I didn't. The turn shafts were the only other possibility. Perhaps we could repair the probe and send it through the left pair. I'm sure I can find spare parts on this boat."

Selba broke out in laughter, a laughter of instant enlightenment.

"The entrance is the entrance," she laughed.

"What?"

"Don't you see? It's the only answer remaining," Selba said. "The entrance to the cavern is the entrance to the underground world."

"That has already been established. Enter the cavern first, then from there find the other entrance," Leni said.

"No, you are not listening. There is no first entrance and second entrance. The entrance to the cavern is the same entrance to the underground world. Simultaneously," Selba said.

"I can't make sense of that," Leni said.

"My guess is that someone stands at the entrance and activates a trigger, taking that someone to the underground world," Selba explained.

"The only thing at the entrance is the beginning of the turn shafts," Leni said.

"Then that is the trigger. It should be safe to touch one or all," Selba said.

"It would be safe," Leni said. "Unfortunately the probe is destroyed. We cannot use it to test your theory."

"I should go," Selba said. "I have a hunch the probe would be worthless anyway."

"It would be safer if I go first," Leni said. "If something happens to me, you can summon help."

"I also have a hunch it won't work for you either," Selba said. "My guess is that there are people down there who want to keep the selenites out. The entrance would be designed to permit only humans through."

"Interesting. I should test it first anyway. If I am destroyed—"

"That's not something we can afford anyway. You are the only selenite friendly to us," Selba said.

Selba was anxious to go down and try it herself.

"Even if I do not find a way to the underground world, at least I can prove the safety of the entrance. Patience, Selba. Patience," Leni said.

"Very well. Go down and test it. But I want to be the next one to try it after you're done," Selba said.

"Agreed," Leni said.

Leni jumped into the water and was about to shock an orca and thus use it to carry him to the cavern, but the orcas avoided Leni and the speedboat. As it was, Leni swam down to the cavern entrance. He looked inside and saw bits of the probe stuck in the turn-bristles of the right turn shafts. The entrance was the same as before—just large enough for a person to swim through and large enough for a short person to stand on and touch the top. Leni positioned his feet such that his left touched the edge of the left lower turn shaft and his right touched the edge of the right lower turn shaft. He crouched down a bit then placed his hands on the upper edges of the left and right turn shafts. Suddenly the left turn shafts glowed yellow, and the right turn shafts glowed blue.

"I've activated something," Leni said back to Selba through sonar. "The turn shafts are glowing."

"Glowing? Glowing white?" Selba said back in sonar.

"No. The left shafts are yellow. The right are blue," he said.

"Of course. That's how they do it," Selba said.

"I don't understand what you mean by that," Leni said.

"Stay there, Leni. I'll drop anchor and be right down. We'll go in together."

"Tell me how to activate the opening, Selba, and I'll test the first bit to make sure it's safe," Leni said.

"It's like I said, you can't activate it. Selenites do not see like humans. That's the trigger. I'll be right down and show you," Selba said.

Selba dropped the anchor and then suited up in a special diving suit that kept her face in an air bubble with a sonar communication system. Her suit very much resembled a spacesuit, except the portion for her limbs, hands, and feet were slimmer and permitted more dexterous activity. In this way she was able to dive deep without the associated problem of excessive pressure. Leni sent out sonar commands to the orcas that he'd be willing to shock one or two for a free ride, but the orcas continued to stay away, and so Selba had clear passage downward until she reached the cavern entrance. Leni moved to the side, and Selba stood in the entrance. She placed her two feet on the lower turn shaft edges much as Leni had and was about to place her hands on the upper turn shaft edges when she spoke.

"Hold onto me from behind," she said, "as if we're on a motorcycle and I'm driving."

Leni hesitated.

"Do it! I don't know how quickly I'll be pulled into this thing. I can only imagine the entrance is designed to limit how many can enter at a time, otherwise legions of selenites could tailgate in."

Leni did as suggested. He positioned himself behind Selba and placed his arms around her waist. Selba placed her hands on the edges of the upper turn shafts. The left turn shafts glowed yellow, and the right glowed blue.

"Now I cross my eyes until the colors line up," Selba said.

She crossed her eyes as stated, and she formed an image in her brain of the distant portions of the turn shafts.

"The thing is, yellow and blue don't combine in human vision. Each eye competes for dominance. I must keep the competition going. They must go back and forth, back and forth, to create the unattainable mixture of blue and yellow light," she said, then she spoke as if casting a spell, saying, "Entrance as colors vibrate true, open and permit passage for two!"

The turn shafts stopped and suddenly flowed like conveyor belts with incredible speed from the entrance toward infinity. Selba was pulled along as such, with her four limbs remaining in contact with the turn shafts. Leni was pulled along with her, but what amazed him the most was that her limbs never lost contact with the turn shafts, despite his earlier determination that the turn shafts diverged from the center of the cavern. Even looking ahead, they still appeared to diverge. But whether because of a trick in lighting or from adaptation by the turn shafts themselves, they remained close enough for Selba to maintain contact. Up ahead, Leni observed a flashing blue and yellow patch of light. The flashing increased in frequency until it vibrated, and the patch grew closer and larger to the point that Leni was sure the two would be tossed into it and be electrocuted by whatever plasma ball they now appeared to be headed toward. The harmonics rattled Leni's circuits, and just before he initiated an auto-shutdown for protection, the two were tossed through the patch.

They landed on a dry floor with no water around or any evidence of the cavern or the turn shafts. It was dark, with only the dim light from Leni's eyes providing illumination.

"Where are we?" Selba asked. "Are we in the seamount?"

"Yes. We are in the seamount, incredible as it may seem," Leni said.

Suddenly, lights flashed around the two, revealing a crowd of people surrounding Leni and Selba, but these people had their human features covered. The men wore outfits of black and white, while the women wore color-coordinated outfits, particularly of pinks, purples, greens, and reds. But all had thin, spherical helmets over their heads (with the helmets matching color with their outfits), and they wore special circular-rimmed sunglasses of concentric circular lens material. Instead of using speech to communicate, alternating concentric circles of yellow and blue flashed at various frequencies.

"Light telemetry," Leni said. "I can decode it. They are discussing whether we are friend or foe. They would like to befriend you, but they view me as a threat."

"Tell them we are friends, and that we are looking for three other humans—Shara, Clover, and Claus," Selba said.

Leni flashed light from his own eyes. The people were surprised and stopped flashing one another for a moment. Then they seemed to laugh as they flashed one another again.

"Well?" Selba asked.

"They say I sound like a child," he said. "My eyes do not flash with the advanced complexity of these people. But they are amused enough at my efforts to communicate that they are holding off on destroying me."

"Well that's progress," Selba said with relief.

"They don't know anything about Claus. They've heard of Shara and Clover, so to speak. They really don't hear flashing communication, that's just how it gets translated in your language," Leni said. "Shara they met once and like but cannot find. They believe she is no longer here. As for Clover, they hate her because she is in league with Dark Star of Thunder. I think they mean Lanietta from their description. I'll tell them we are against Dark Star of Thunder, but Clover was forced to act against her will, and we've come to take her back."

Leni flashed his eyes, and the people flashed back.

"Well?" Selba asked.

"They say Clover is hidden in this realm somewhere," Leni said. "They are looking for Clover to imprison her."

"Tell them that we will take Clover away, that they never have to worry about Clover again if they will help us find her and help defeat Dark Star of Thunder," Selba said. "But we also want Shara back. Can they help us find Shara? And Claus too if they're willing."

"As for Dark Star of Thunder, she is no longer in the colony. They agree that we may have Clover if we find her, provided we leave with her and not return. They are hesitant about searching for Shara and Claus. It would mean...now this part doesn't make sense...it would mean the entire colony traveling."

"As in everyone leaving the seamount?" Selba asked.

"No. As in the seamount leaving the ocean floor," Leni said.

"You're right. That doesn't make sense, unless..."

"You've thought of something?" Leni asked.

"Well it's a long shot, but you remember Morcellus, right?"

"Yes," Leni replied.

"What if there's another one of those creatures around, say right here?" Selba asked.

"The thought never occurred to me. But if true, that might explain how well organized this colony is. Still, nothing around here looks like a Martacean."

"Neither did Morcellus when we first went inside him," Selba said.

"True. We'll have to be careful, then. We wouldn't want to enrage this seamount if it be alive," Leni said.

The colony people scattered about in all directions, sending their flashing hither and thither. Small spotlights shone upward at nearby tree pairs, then more tree pairs farther away, then more and more as far as the eye could see. These tree pairs had trunks close enough that a person could pass between the pair and touch both trunks. Immediately behind Leni and Selba was a single tree with its own small spotlight. It was huge, with a trunk having the circumference of a blue whale from belly to back and around.

"My guess is we entered this world through this big tree behind us," Selba said.

"Reasonable," Leni added.

"Who are these people, Leni? Did they say?"

"These people are from around the world," Leni said. "Amazing technology here."

"And amazing how these trees could just sprout up here," Selba said.

"These trees are not works of nature as one might find on land. Nature has many subtle irregularities from evolution, but these trees have consistency and regularity in their shapes and movements."

"Look. Two of the people are walking between the tree pair in front of us," Selba said. "You watch this side. I'll go around."

"Go around where?" Leni asked as Selba walked around the tree pair.

"To the backside. I want to know if they walk through or go back out the way they went in," Selba said.

After a few minutes, the two people exited the tree pair on Selba's side—with a baby.

"O the clouds above! You won't believe this, Leni! Hurry over!" Selba said.

Leni hurried over to Selba, and he too watched as the couple fussed over their new child. Leni scanned the couple.

"They have aged a year, and yet they haven't," Leni said.

"A riddle in the seamount? What does that mean?"

"This couple has experienced a year of life for the short time they were in this tree pair. Their minds have encoded a year's worth of information. Their bodies have not aged, meaning their bodies have not degraded from age. But like their minds, their bodies have experienced a year's worth of time."

"Then this really is their baby!" Selba said. "A couple can go into one of these things and exit with a new person. Are these reproductive chambers? Ugh, I shudder at the thought. Oh I hope Clover isn't caught up in this."

"These people don't seem to know where they are, remember? Either or both could be enjoying whole new lives inside one of these fantasy trees," Leni said. "The question is what trees possess what memory."

"Well I'm staying out of this tree pair, that's for sure!" Selba said. "I'm not ready for a baby!"

"Is that the real reason you two broke up?" Leni asked.

Selba paused.

"Is it?" Leni asked.

"He wanted a baby immediately, but I didn't. So he wandered. Now he'll have his baby with another woman," Selba said.

"I see," Leni said.

"It doesn't matter. What matters is finding Clover," Selba said.

"Shara and Claus too," Leni reminded Selba.

"One thing at a time, please," Selba said.

The colony people walked about, minding their own business despite the presence of Leni and Selba.

"It seems these people are ignoring us for the most part. They are entering and exiting other trees," Leni said.

"Look. A whole group of people are leaving that tree with flags and hats," Selba said.

"They are pennants. And baseball hats. They've been to a baseball game," Leni said.

"Oh let's see!" Selba said. "I've heard they were fun!"

"Wait!" Leni said.

Selba rushed toward the front of this other "baseball" tree pair. Leni chased after her and grabbed her hand to stop her just as she entered the tree pair. He was unable to halt her momentum and instead was pulled in with her. The two found themselves in the outfield bleachers of a baseball game between a blue team and a yellow team. The blue team had just hit a long fly ball, and it headed toward Selba and Leni. People around the two reached over and grabbed for the ball as it cleared the outfield fence and nearly hit Selba in the face. The ball bounced off their fingertips, off Leni's shoulder, and into Selba's hands.

"Home run!" the people cheered.

"Blue wins!" the public address person announced. "Blue wins the World Series!"

The crowd went wild. The blue team gathered in the middle of the field and congratulated one another. Selba was picked up by the crowd and passed around in celebration of the victory.

"Leni, help!"

"Is this how colony women have a baby?" Leni called back.

"It better not be!" Selba returned.

The crowd was quick and thick. They passed Selba over their heads quickly while Leni fought through the masses to reach Selba. It wasn't easy. Finally, he got close enough to where he could jump and grab the baseball from Selba. The crowd dropped Selba (rather rudely, I might add) and attempted to lift Leni to pass him around. But he would have none of it, and he clocked people on the head with a closed fist, dropping them like flies. People screamed, and security rushed in.

"She's with him!" several said, pointing to Selba. "Take her too!"

Security grabbed Selba, and the two were hauled away from the bleachers, down a flight of stairs, and into a dirty, concrete-walled office, with a damp earthen smell that made Selba sneeze. Miraculously, Leni still had the baseball. The two were seated and held.

"Stay here and keep quiet. The chief wants to have a word with you," said the security guard.

On the concrete wall hung a flat television screen, showing the award ceremony for the blue team.

"My perfect moment ruined," Selba lamented. "Give me that baseball, Leni. It's the winning ball! I'm the heroine of the game! Look at the screen there. See? They're showing a replay of the winning home run! And I caught it!"

Selba took the baseball from Leni.

"Selba, get a hold of yourself. Think for a moment. Did you see Clover?"

"Who? Of course not! I didn't see much of anything except the crowd and my winning baseball!"

"Just as I thought. I did a quick scan and did not see her either. But I understand the purpose of these memory trees. They act as a diversion. A distraction. To forget what you were thinking before you entered."

"Then why haven't you forgotten?" Selba asked. "Besides, I like it here, if I can just get out of this little holding cell or whatever it is."

"I'm not influenced by the environment the same as you," Leni said. "Though I look human enough."

"You *are* human enough," Selba said. "Let's break out of this little cell and make our own life together. We don't have to live in this city. There are plenty around, I'm sure. I'm willing to give up that dreary life I had before. I don't even remember it anymore. See? What do you say? Marry me, Leni!"

"What!? Selba! I'm not even human!" Leni said.

"Even better!" Selba said.

"Selba, no! We have a mission, remember? There's a job to do, and—"

Just then, several large thugs entered with a nicely-dressed boss behind. Two thugs held Leni with black leather gloves while a third pressed a taser against his neck. Stunned, Leni slumped. The other thugs bound Selba and carried her off.

"Leni!" she screamed and kicked.

Chapter 27: Dancing Duck

Claus opened his eyes. He walked on a sidewalk alongside Lanietta. Lanietta had blond, puffy-curled hair and wore sunglasses. She held onto a leash that attached to Claus, who was in dog form.

"What...what is this?" Claus asked.

"You're the family dog, and you're going for a walk, Clomper," Lanietta said.

A woman and her female dog passed going the other way. The woman looked like Shara, but Claus wasn't sure. He reached out a hand to touch her, but her dog thought Claus was after her, and the dog shied away.

"Stop playing with the other dogs. You're getting exercise!" Lanietta said with a stiff jerk of Claus's leash.

"Ow!" Claus said.

"We're approaching an intersection. Don't run into traffic. And keep up. You're supposed to walk alongside me," Lanietta said, and she jerked him again to pull him up to the curb.

Claus let out a yelp.

"What is this new torture you have me in?" Claus asked as he regained his breath.

"This? Torture? This is life, at least as it was on Earth hundreds of years ago," Lanietta said. "There, the crosswalk light says 'WALK'. Let's walk across."

"You're doing fairly well for a fat woman," Claus said.

"Hurry along before the light changes, Clomper," Lanietta said as she tugged him by the leash. "I have to concentrate with this *avoirdupois*. Can't get stuck in potholes, you know."

"You *are* a pothole," Claus mumbled.

"I heard that," Lanietta said. "No doggie treats for you when we get home."

"Just where is home?" Claus asked. "And what happened to my broken nose?"

"Your nose is furry and cute. But keep it out of other dogs' butts, okay?"

"No arguments there," Claus said. "Are you going to explain how and why we are here?"

"I'm looking for something," Lanietta said. "That's all you need to know."

"Looking for what?" Claus asked as the two crossed the street and reached the sidewalk.

But another dog went up behind Claus and sniffed his butt.

"Hey, cut that out!" Claus said as he swatted at the other dog.

"Down, Clomper!" Lanietta said as she tugged at his leash.

"Your dog needs more training," said the other dog's owner.

"My apologies. I will send him back to obedience school first thing next week," Lanietta said. "Good day."

"Good day," the other owner said.

"Now keep quiet, Clomper," Lanietta said. "Each time you speak, the world hears you barking. It's not proper for a dog to bark all the time. Wait, here it is. You're supposed to accompany me into this music store. See? Dogs welcome. C'mon, Clomper, be a good boy. That's it. There. See? Wasn't so bad."

Claus led Lanietta into a music store.

"Welcome back, Mrs. Depetti," said the clerk. "More reeds?"

"You're married? Who would marry you?" Claus said.

"Shush, Cloopy," Lanietta said.

"Who's Cloopy?" Claus asked.

"Shush already!" Lanietta said, then she turned to the clerk. "My apologies. Cloopy gets excited when I go shopping for my daughter."

"Your daughter! What!?!" Claus exclaimed.

"Now Cloopy, if you don't behave, I'll have you wait outside. You be a good boy and shush it. Shush it!" Lanietta said.

"Oh, that's all right," the clerk said.

"He knows the word r-e-e-d," Lanietta said. "He knows it means play time with Olivia."

"Olivia still using medium hard?" the clerk asked.

"Yes. She loves her bass clarinet, doesn't she Cloopy?"

"You have a daughter named Olivia who plays the bass clarinet? Oh what is this world coming to?" Claus said.

"You have a loving family for Cloopy to be so excited," the clerk said as he rang up the purchase. "I only wish we had a treat for your Cloopy here."

"Oh no, Cloopy is going back to obedience school to relearn his manners," Lanietta said. "Thank you!"

"Come back soon," said the clerk.

Lanietta and Claus walked several more blocks until they reached a house. A young teenage girl burst through the front door and kissed Lanietta on the cheek.

"How disgusting! You, a mother!" Claus lamented.

"Don't be so jealous, Cloopy," the girl said. "You get lots of love too."

The girl hugged Claus.

"I have a new set of reeds from the music store, Olivia," Lanietta said as she passed the package to the girl.

"New reeds! These are the expensive ones! Thank you Mamma, oh thank you! I'm going to try them out right now!" Olivia said.

Olivia rushed back into the house with the package.

"Oh you must be thrilled in this little fantasy of yours," said Claus. "A loving mother with a loving daughter. I suppose Mr. Depetti loves you too!"

"He does," Lanietta said. "I have the perfect family. A daughter, a husband, and a dog—in that order. Now accompany me into the house, and I'll release you."

"You'll set me free? To escape into this world and never see you again?" Claus asked.

"Of course not! You'll be off duty and free to roam the house as a normal family dog does while I check on things. You may even visit with Olivia. But as for this world, you are still in it, my sweet Clomper. We are living in the real memory of a bygone time," Lanietta explained.

"For how long?"

"Until I send for you. I must contemplate a parent-teacher conference I recently attended, then after that we can take another walk," Lanietta said.

"No, I mean how long am I stuck in this reality?"

"For as long as I like, Mr. Nosy. One should learn about these past histories. Could be educational," Lanietta said.

"So you chose some random past event to experience? Why? To torture me and see how I react?" Claus asked. "Of all the things."

"Don't be so little. History is hardly random," Lanietta said.

"I still don't get it. I feel like I must make sense of what you're doing, but how am I to determine what's important and what isn't?" Claus asked.

"All of life is important. All of it. Your petty human frailty is showing, Clomper. I don't suppose you'll ever reach the Carinian level," Lanietta said.

"This is no way to live, like a dog," Claus said. "There's no value in that."

"You shouldn't complain, Clomper. You have life where many do not. Even a dog's life is better than those who are never allowed to be," Lanietta said.

"You make it sound like there's a line of people waiting to be born into this world, a line stretching from here to infinity," Claus said.

"Not quite. More like from infinity to infinity," Lanietta said. "At least it was when I got my start. Has probably grown by now. Competition, you know."

"Competition?"

"Yes, in fact there are group plans where several go together into a single body. Makes for an interesting person. At one moment caring and thoughtful, at another a psychopath, and still another a brilliant composer. Infinity has no patience, and neither do I. Now enjoy your stress-free doggie life, accompany me into the house, and then go into the music room and visit Olivia. Surely that is easier than grasping the ways of the universe!"

Claus accompanied Lanietta into the house.

"Marna, my sweet, thank you for picking up reeds for Olivia," said a tall, handsome man to Lanietta.

"Enrico, my love, I always shudder when you hold me in your arms," Lanietta said as Enrico held her.

"Do not shudder from fear. I would never hurt you," Enrico said.

"I shudder from exhilaration and nervous excitement. Your presence always does that to me," Lanietta said.

"Marna? Sheesh. I'm getting sick," Claus said.

"Let me remove his leash," Enrico said. "I have your favorite Irish tea steeped in the pot. And your favorite cinnamon biscuits."

"Do I get a biscuit?" Claus asked.

"Yes, Cloopy, you get a biscuit too," Lanietta said.

She focused her eyes on Enrico. He had just removed the leash from Claus and now reached into his pocket and placed a dog biscuit in Claus's mouth. Claus tried to say, "Thanks," while holding the biscuit in his mouth, but it sounded tortured.

"Go play with Olivia, Cloopy," said Enrico as he led Lanietta to the kitchen.

Claus walked into the music room. Now inside, he watched as Olivia placed a new reed in her bass clarinet. She was about to put its strap around herself when she saw Claus.

"Oh, Cloopy! Sit here and listen to my recital. It's okay, you can nibble on your biscuit. I've got to practice before Brandi gets here," Olivia said.

"Olivia," Claus said. "Do I look like a dog? Do I?"

"Now shush and don't bark! I don't want Mamma and Dadda to think you hate my music! They'll make me go back to the flute. Yuck!" Olivia said.

Claus sat on a chair and kept quiet. He nibbled on the biscuit.

"Not bad," Claus thought to himself, though he was careful not to speak.

Olivia played through several passages, and she smiled.

"These are great!" she said. "I can hardly wait to show off to Brandi! Won't she be jealous, right Cloopy?"

"Right," Claus said, though it sounded like a bark to Olivia.

A few seconds after Claus's "bark", Brandi walked in with a long case.

"Hi Brandi!" Olivia said.

"Hi Olivia," Brandi said. "Are you ready to practice?"

"Are you going to tell her about the new reed?" Claus asked.

"Boy, Cloopy is excited about practice, aren't you boy?" Brandi said as she walked over and rubbed Claus's fur. "Let's get this session started."

Brandi unpacked her English horn, fitted the pieces together, and looked around.

"Oh, I forgot," Olivia said. "You have to soak your reed."

"Of course. And you don't," Brandi said. "At least not in the same way."

"If only your reed weren't so finicky," Olivia said. "Do you really make your own?"

"Have to," Brandi said. "They don't sound right otherwise."

"Let me get water for the reed," Olivia said.

"Here, Cloopy, chase the duck!" Brandi said.

While Olivia exited to get a glass of water, Brandi pulled out an old, dry reed and blew through it while walking around the room. Something forced Claus to follow her around and bark.

"Wait. What is this? It's like my limbs are moving on their own," Claus said.

"Get the duck, Cloopy. Get the duck!" Brandi said, and she stood on a chair to tease Claus.

"Careful, Brandi, that chair is about to fall apart! Get down, please!" Claus pleaded.

"That's right! It's a duck!"

Claus was right. The chair was rickety and unsteady. He watched as it cracked and wobbled. It was ready to fail, and he knew it. He rushed for Brandi to catch her from falling. As he did so, Olivia walked in with the glass of water in time to see her dog leaping at Brandi and knocking the legs out from under her. Brandi fell backward and caught the back of her head on a wall shelf. The wall shelf did not give, but Brandi's neck did, and it broke. She fell to the ground unconscious. Olivia dropped the glass of water and screamed. Enrico rushed in and cleared the area of debris.

"Call 9-1-1!" he said to Olivia.

Olivia was too shocked to do anything but stand there in horror while Enrico checked for a pulse and gave Brandi CPR.

"What is it?" Lanietta said as she rushed in.

"Brandi is unconscious and not breathing. Her heart has stopped. Feels like a broken neck. Call 9-1-1!" Enrico said.

"No, no, no!" Lanietta said, and she rushed out to call for help.

It wasn't long before an ambulance came and rushed Brandi to the hospital. Lanietta, Claus, Enrico, and Olivia followed in their vehicle.

Chapter 28: Leni Breaks the Fantasy

Leni was tied up in a chair and subjected to interrogation lights.

"What is your name?" said a slimy voice (Slimy).

"I'm Leni. What is happening? Where is Selba?"

"Your full name," the voice said, and it was followed with a punch to Leni's jaw.

"You are trying to intimidate me? That didn't hurt," Leni said.

"We have a troublemaker here," said Slimy.

"Oh we do, do we? I'll take care of that," said a husky voice (Husky), and he could be heard sharpening a knife.

"Look, I don't know who you are...are you related to the people with funny glasses?" Leni asked.

"Funny glasses. He likes funny glasses. Red glasses," Slimy said.

"Then let's give him red glasses," Husky said.

Slimy laughed. Husky took the knife and carved circles around Leni's eyes. But Leni did not bleed.

"He doesn't bleed!" Slimy said.

"All people bleed!" Husky said, and he stabbed Leni in the gut.

But at that moment, Leni stood up, knocked Husky over, twisted in place, and swatted Husky with the chair. The chair broke, and Leni freed himself. Slimy came after Leni, but Leni pulled the knife out of his gut (which also did not bleed) and waved it in the air around Slimy. Leni whipped the knife so quickly that he was able to give Slimy a haircut. Slimy ran out of the room, as did Husky. The door closed, the lights shattered, and the scene changed, revealing a large room with no apparent ceiling. Selba was nearby. She got up and walked over to Leni, who was studying the new surroundings. Instead of flat walls, the walls were the insides of half-concave cylinders, as if Leni and Selba were inside the trees (which they were). After a brief moment, a man walked in with the same glasses as other people, but this guy was taller and wore a white hat.

"You broke the fantasy," the man (White Hat) said.

"You are using your voice," Leni said. "Like the other two."

"We can still do so. It is vulgar for us. We prefer glasses. But we make exceptions as needed," White Hat said. "You are not human. How did you get in here? No selenites are allowed in these parts."

"I am Leni, a guest of Selba," Leni said.

"Yes, Leni is with me. I'm not a selenite. I'm human," said Selba.

"Where are your glasses then?" White Hat asked.

"I'm not from around here. I'm from another place. And Leni here is not your enemy. Does he look like any selenite you've ever seen?"

"No, he doesn't. A bit more primitive in fact," White Hat said.

"Primitive?" Leni said with shock.

"The selenites here have changed, Leni. Not for the better. You are pure original goodness," Selba said.

"Hmm," White Hat said. "Perhaps I could sell him to a museum."

"He's not for sale. In fact, we're looking for a friend. Her name is Clover. And if you've seen Shara, that would help too. Have you seen them? They look more like me than any of you."

"Shara was here in Tabelia but taken away by Dark Star of Thunder," White Hat said. "Where? We do not know. Clover is in Tabelia but could be in any of the trees. Any one."

"Oh, it's hopeless," Selba said.

"Do not give up hope. Perhaps there is a more efficient way to search these fantasy trees," Leni said. "Selba, I would guess these trees are linked up. If I could tap into that network, I could perform a brute-force scan. It would be much quicker than entering these on foot, which itself would take thousands of years."

"We will not permit it," White Hat said.

"Look, we made a deal," Selba said. "Your people don't like Clover. We promised to find and take her away. Isn't that worth letting us search your network?"

"You would learn about our technology and give it to the selenites who rule the world. They would invade and destroy us," White Hat said.

"I must reach the network," Leni whispered to Selba.

"We don't even know how," Selba said.

"I bet that solitary tree has the answer," Leni said.

"It's worth a try," Selba said. "How do we get rid of this guy?"

"I have an idea," Leni whispered.

"Stay here a moment until reinforcements arrive," White Hat said.

"Good, yes," Leni said. "We need a marriage fantasy anyway. Memories are always strongest at weddings."

"Whose wedding?" White Hat asked.

"Selba and I are getting married," Leni said, and he pulled Selba close to him.

"Leni!" Selba exclaimed.

"I have a better idea. I'll make a holding cell for you both," White Hat said.

White Hat removed his white hat, looked inside, and pressed several hidden buttons. The scene began to change, but as it did, Leni quickly pulled Selba through an exit in the tree pair. The exit closed as quickly as it opened, leaving White Hat inside.

"That fantasy should hold him awhile," Leni said.

"How did you know?"

"Situation awareness, calculated intuition, and luck," Leni said.

But Leni didn't have long to gloat. The colony people stopped their chaotic travels, turned about in place, and faced Leni and Selba. They took methodical steps toward the pair.

"Oh, oh! This looks bad!" Selba said.

"They are being summoned," Leni said. "I could hold off a few, for a time, but the compressive forces are what concern me."

"Yes! Compressive forces! They compress and hurt!" Selba said with worry.

"They damage too," Leni said.

"Yes! Damage! Leni? Get us out of this!"

"Now the key to all this is the main tree. I could explain my plan in detail, to gain your confidence," Leni said.

"Get us out of this! That's the confidence!" Selba shouted.

Leni led her to the tree. He placed his feet apart and had the tips touch the bottom of the tree. While doing this, he extended his arms upward and at angles then touched his hands upon the tree. Selba stood close behind them but kept looking back at the approaching mass of colony people.

"Hurry!" she said. "They're nearly upon us!"

"It's not working!" he said. "We can't get in! Wait! It won't let me in because I'm a selenite. What I really need to do—"

"Is stop explaining! Tell me what to do!" Selba said.

Leni stepped aside and placed Selba's feet and hands against the tree as he had done.

"Watch the image and concentrate," he said.

Leni placed one hand on her left shoulder then looked over her right. He flashed images from his eyes onto the tree, images very much resembling those as seen by the two when they first entered. Selba concentrated.

"When the opening appears, jump in!" Leni said.

But the opening did not appear. A colony person clawed at Selba, and Leni had to swat him away. Another came close. Leni swatted him away too.

"It's not working! Leni! It's not working. But wait! There's something strange here. Do you see? The bark pattern. It doesn't match. Right here in the middle. Do you see it?"

"It's as if someone put two halves together but didn't align the patterns correctly. It's subtle, but yes, with the flashing light, I can see it. Splitting images into two. I need to work on both halves," Leni said.

It worked. The tree opened along the seam, like one side of a pillow opening up along its seam. Selba and then Leni entered into a dark area, but two colony people tried tailgating in with them. Leni pushed them back, but they fought him.

"Go back!" he told them. "You can't make it! The seam will close!"

And it did, with legs and arms writhing wildly on the inside. Muffled screeches shot through the seal, and Selba screamed. But after half a minute, the appendages stopped moving.

"Are they dead? Oh!" she said.

"We can't help them," Leni said. "They would have killed us, you know. You must believe this."

"I...I...want to. But I can't settle myself. I'm shaking like a dog left out in the rain."

"Well it's warm and safe in here. Let's get some light."

A probe each extended from behind Leni's ears, and their tips sent out cold light to dispel the darkness.

"You look like an alien from outer space," Selba said. "That doesn't settle me."

"Sorry," he said.

With their backs to the opening, the two looked at the open area. In the center was a pool of water surrounded by smooth, wooden railing, except for two places—at the nine o'clock and the three o'clock positions. The nine o'clock position had two large tubes (large enough for a person to walk through) exiting the pool at an angle upward and into the air then downward as it approached the wall. The three o'clock had an archway connecting the two railing ends. The archway was tall enough for a single person to pass through, and so a person could simply walk through the archway and into the pool. Along the wall behind the archway was row upon column of small storage cells. In better times, Selba would be curious, but she was

still shaken from the colony people being injured or killed.

"We must be careful not to touch anything until we are absolutely sure of its consequence. No telling the danger before us. Follow me, Selba. Let's look at the archway."

The two walked to the archway, but Selba dragged. Her legs were wobbly.

"This appears to be a control archway," Leni said. "Look. It has a place each for the hands and feet much as we have seen before."

"And here by the wall. It's just like—"

"Yes, just like inside of the creature back in Arberella. It's looking more and more like another Martacean, as you suspected. White Hat made reference to 'here' as 'Tabelia'. Could also be the name of this Martacean. Here, these are memory cells," Leni said. "Let's see what else is in this room."

The two had reached the twelve o'clock position, and there was a podium by the pool with several steps up to it. Leni climbed the steps and stood at the podium.

"There are several buttons here. This might be where a person stands to speak to a group, perhaps as part of a ritual or even a meeting to discuss vital issues."

Leni went on about the possible things the podium could be used for while Selba rested by sitting on the steps. She couldn't stop shaking from the door incident, and she wasn't sure she could.

"I'm not going to make it, Leni. I'm not," she said.

"Hey! You're going to be fine," he said after turning around and kneeling to her. "Give me but a minute to figure things out. If nothing else, we'll leave this place and get you back to Arberella. You need not stress yourself over this environment."

"Thank you. That helps. Let me tough this out a bit more. Still need to find Clover and the others."

"Let's finish walking around the pool," Leni said.

When the two reached the nine o'clock position, they saw the tubes. These tubes were transparent, and as mentioned before were large enough for a person to walk through. And yet people did not walk through them. Leni and Selba watched as people were pushed through one tube from the pool to the outside, and through the other tube from the outside into the pool as if by steam or air pressure. Along the wall on this side were yet more rows and columns of cells.

"Oh, if only we could enter the tube to get out of this place," Selba said.

"I think you're onto something," Leni said. "We might have come through one of these tubes to enter the seamount. Now it is time to—"

But before Leni could finish, a loud BANG echoed from the seam the two had entered. Then another BANG. The seam opened slightly, and pry bars slipped through.

"They're on to us," Leni said. "I have a hunch the podium is the main control center. Now if I can—"

"Don't stand there and gab! Do something now!" Selba said.

Leni ran over to the podium. He flashed his eyes, and several buttons flashed back. He pressed a button. The pool lit up, and the inflowing tube from the pool filled with colony people rushing through. Leni pressed another button. The pool projected a hologram of the people outside their tree trying to break in.

"Oh this is too much for me," Selba said.

Selba looked around and found a chair next to the wall in a spot where no cells existed.

"Selba, wait!" Leni called.

But it was too late. Sitting on the chair revealed it was part of a revolving door. It spun Selba through a secret compartment behind the wall and closed shut, cutting off Selba's screams.

"Selba!" Leni called again.

She was gone.

Chapter 29: Cloopy is Put Down

Enrico and family were lucky to find a parking spot in the hospital's parking structure near ground level, and so they only had to walk across the street to reach the hospital doors. Olivia wanted to run, but Enrico took firm grasp of her hand and prevented her.

"No!" Enrico said. "I won't have another tragedy!"

Claus as Cloopy then stood by Olivia as the family waited alongside the curb for traffic to clear with Olivia holding onto Claus's leash. A pickup truck came barreling down the road, and Lanietta purposely stepped on Claus's hind paw. As a reflex, Claus darted into the road and started pulling Olivia with him.

"No!" Enrico yelled, and he snapped Olivia back.

Olivia lost her hold of the leash, and the truck grazed Claus in the head—not enough to kill him, but enough to stun him. Claus fell back toward the curb and panted.

"That's twice now, Marna. Cloopy is a jinx," Enrico said to Lanietta.

"Oh don't be so harsh on Poopy Cloopy. He's just a stupid animal," Lanietta said.

The way was clear. The family with Claus crossed the street and reached the hospital door. A greeter, however, stopped the family.

"Sorry, no dogs," the greeter said. "Not unless this is a service dog."

"He's my dog. He goes wherever I go," Olivia said.

"Sorry, but he cannot enter. Hospital rules. We have a steward over here who holds onto dogs. You can leave...leave..."

"Cloopy! His name is—"

"Claus Gerhardt!" Claus said, but it came out as a bark.

"And a very happy Cloopy he is too," the greeter said. "Steward?"

The steward walked over.

"Be good, Cloopy. We'll be back for you soon," Olivia said, and she handed him over to the steward.

"No! Olivia! Don't turn me over. Lanietta? What's going on? Lanietta?" Claus said.

Claus's protests came out as barks as usual. Olivia was sad to let him go.

"It's just for the moment," Lanietta said.

"Yes," Enrico said with other thoughts in mind. "Let's see your friend."

The family (minus Claus) entered the hospital, reached the Emergency Room, and waited in the lobby with Brandi's mother. Moments later, a doctor in surgical garb entered the area.

"Ms. Ruhm?"

Brandi's mother stood up.

"I think you should be seated," he said.

"I want to see my daughter. I want to see Brandi," she said.

The doctor wasn't sure if she should. He hesitated.

"Please! I have Olivia's family here for support. See Olivia here?" Ms. Ruhm said, pointing to Olivia.

Olivia waved.

"Brandi is my best friend," Olivia said. "I want to see her too."

The doctor gave a small smile, nodded, and motioned for them to follow him. They did. A short ways down the hallway, a turn to the left, and the doctor led the group to a recovery room. They paused a moment as hospital staff wheeled out equipment.

"What...what's happening?" Olivia asked, but the adults already knew.

"No!" Ms. Ruhm cried.

Ms. Ruhm rushed into the recovery room with Olivia right behind her. There was Brandi, as pale as a ghost. Ms. Ruhm knelt beside her and hugging her poor daughter. Olivia stopped short, not even fully reaching the bed.

"That's not Brandi! It's not!" Olivia screamed. "This is a trick! A prank! You are all terrible! I hate you all!"

Olivia rushed out of the room and down the hallway. Enrico chased after her. Lanietta entered the recovery room, took a look at Brandi and Ms. Ruhm, and then went into the hallway.

"How humans deal with death," Lanietta said to herself. "A pity."

Lanietta took a walk down the hallway in the same path Olivia and Enrico had run. She reached a corner, turned right, and saw Enrico leading Olivia back slowly. Olivia was fully in tears, and Enrico comforted her. Lanietta continued toward them, but the two did not make it all the way down the hallway. Instead, they stopped in a small lobby for the allergy department and sat. Lanietta joined them.

"It can't happen," Olivia sobbed. "She was fine. She was!"

"It's okay, my sweet," Enrico said.

"Now Olivia, my dear," Lanietta said. "Lift up your chin, that's a good girl. Here's a tissue. Dry your eyes, and tell us what happened."

"Not now, Marna," Enrico said. "We know the culprit."

Enrico pointed to a picture on the wall of a dog with the caption, "Is your pet making you sneeze? Dander is the number one cause of pet allergies."

"It's important," Lanietta said. "How did it happen? How did Brandi hurt herself?"

Olivia dried her tears and blew her nose.

"Here's a cough drop. It will help you breathe," Lanietta said.

"Thank you, Mamma," Olivia said as she popped the lozenge in her mouth. "I...just can't believe...it's like I'm in a movie...but the movie isn't stopping... when does it stop?"

"It will stop once you tell us what happened. We as a people must explain and understand things, Olivia. Then we move on. It's life," Lanietta said, trying to act like a mother.

"Mamma, I was only gone a minute. I swear. I could hear Brandi blowing through her double reed. You know, for her English horn. Only she was just playing through the reed without the instrument. And I heard her say 'duck' like she does when she plays with Cloopy. Well, I had to get water for Brandi so she could soak her reed. I'm sorry I broke the glass! I'm sorry!"

"It's okay," Enrico said. "It wasn't your fault. Tell us whose fault it was."

"Well, I walked into the music room just as...just as...oh Cloopy! Why!? Why did he have to knock Brandi off the chair? Why did he? She was fine. She was fine!"

"Marna, there's only one thing to do here," Enrico said.

"Sigh. I was hoping otherwise," Lanietta said.

"We just can't take the chance. Look what happened. And look what almost happened. I can't go through this again. I can't. I'd be finished," Enrico said.

"I'll take care of it," Lanietta said. "Olivia, you be a good girl and stay with your father. Be brave, Olivia. You have a bright future ahead."

"I don't understand," Olivia said.

"You will someday. Oh, Enrico, did you take the turkey out of the oven?" Lanietta said with a wink.

"I thought you did," Enrico winked back.

"If it isn't one thing, it's another. And Olivia's two cats are there. The house will burn down for sure if I don't rush back now," Lanietta said.

"Hurry, Mamma! Don't let Snowpatch and Cookie burn to death! Hurry!" Olivia said.

Lanietta left the two in the allergy department lobby. She then marched to the hospital entrance, met the steward, and took charge of Claus.

"Come along, Cloopy, we're going for a ride," Lanietta said.

"Where? Where's everyone else?"

"Taxi!" Lanietta waved.

"Taxi?" Claus said. "Lanietta! What are you doing?"

A taxicab pulled over for Lanietta and Claus.

"The dog will have to ride in back. You can ride in front," the driver said.

"Thank you!" Lanietta said.

"Where to?"

"Where's the nearest vet?"

"For the dog? He doesn't look sick," the driver said.

"Oh he's very sick. He's terminal. I'm putting him down," Lanietta said.

"What!!" Claus barked.

"For a sick dog, he's very lively. Like he knows what you're going to do," the driver said. "There's a vet a few blocks down. You could almost walk."

"Oh no, the walk is too much for him. Better to let Clomper have his last ride. Like a last meal. You know," Lanietta said with a grin.

"Wait! Lanietta! You called me Clomper! Lanietta! This isn't funny! You're going to kill me? Really? After everything?" Claus said.

"Don't worry, Clomper. I'll keep your ashes above the fireplace where you can no longer knock people over. Heck, someone might knock you over. Wouldn't that be ironic," Lanietta said.

"Not funny, Lanietta. Not funny!" Claus barked.

The taxicab arrived. Lanietta paid the fare, got out, and opened the back door. Claus jumped out, pushed his way through, toppled over Lanietta, and ran freely down the sidewalk.

"I can't believe I trained for years as an astronaut to end up as a fleeing dog in someone's fantasy. But if this is a fantasy, can't I just end it? Can't I escape? Is death the only escape?" Claus pondered.

Claus tired from the run. He became aware of the taxicab following him along the road with Lanietta inside. Should he run through someone's yard? He couldn't hide up a tree, as he wasn't a cat. But even if he were, how long could he wait? He couldn't wait. Something had to end. Escaping into the wild meant living out his few short years as a dog with a collar and leash. He was still disgusted that Lanietta

turned him into animals. Pure dread settled in. Pure. He stopped where he was, curled up on the sidewalk, and waited.

"There's a good boy, now," Lanietta said as she took him by the leash. "You chose well. We're at another vet as it stands. One vet is as good as another."

Claus looked up, and of all the bad luck, yes, he had run in front of another vet. Lanietta led him to the entrance. The receptionist waved Lanietta and Claus right in. No wait time. Again, luck was not with Claus. The two waited in an examination room.

"So how can I help you, Marna?" the vet asked.

"I need to put Cloopy down. He's just a menace. Killed a girl this morning and almost my own daughter a short while ago. He can't be trusted."

"I understand. I'll try to be gentle," the vet said, and he took Claus away.

"Lanietta!" Claus barked through the hallway.

So this was the end.

"Lanietta broke her word then. Her people are supposed to preserve beings like myself. How quickly she disposed of me. Even Libriota would have put me in a display case or something. But that was when I was a human. Apparently, pets have no rights among Carinians," Claus said to himself.

"There now, don't bark so much," said the vet. "It will all be over soon."

"Doctor," said an assistant. "We're out of the pink juice."

"Oh, not again. That's the third time this month," the vet said. "I asked you to order extra."

"I did. But we've had a rash of customers putting their pets to sleep. I don't know how we can keep up. There's more money in killing pets than keeping them alive," the assistant said.

"I'll be out of a job at this rate," the vet said. "A vet assistant can administer the pink juice with simple training and a license. A shame people don't hold onto their pets."

"So now what? Will you knock me over the head senseless?" Claus asked.

"What will we do?" the assistant asked.

"How old is your car?" the vet asked the assistant.

"Oh, I wouldn't want you to borrow my car. It's at least fifteen years old. It'll break down," the assistant said.

"Puts out bad exhaust, right?" the vet asked.

"Stinky, yeah," the assistant said.

"Pull it around back. I'll rig up a make-shift fumigation tank," the vet said. "We'll hook up your exhaust to the tank. That's how they used to do it in the old country."

"Can't even die with dignity. Gotta be fumigated in a dirty tank in back, like I'm stubborn garbage. Stubborn garbage," Claus said to himself.

"Easy boy. This is more humane than putting you in the furnace alive," the vet said to Claus.

Claus was led out back and tied to a post attached to a dumpster. The assistant brought his car around back, and the vet got out a hose to funnel the car's exhaust into a holding tank. But Claus chewed at his leash and broke it. Free, he ran around the building to the front and looked around, desperate for help. As fate would have it, Frieda Morgan happened to be driving by. She saw Cloopy and pulled over quickly in a parallel-parking spot. She jumped out to his excitement.

"Frieda! Frieda! Help me! Frieda!" Claus barked.

"Well hello, Cloopy! What are you doing here all alone?"

Frieda rubbed Claus's fur while he stayed close to her for protection.

"I see you still have your lucky collar I gave you with the special stone," Frieda said.

A moment later, Lanietta exited the vet and was shocked to see Frieda and Claus. Then the vet came running around the building from the back.

"Marna," said Frieda.

"Frieda," Lanietta said. "How are you?"

"Fine. I found Cloopy loose. Look, his leash is ripped off," Frieda said.

"Cloopy is sick. I'm putting him down," Lanietta said.

"I don't understand," Frieda said. "He looks fine, don't you Cloopy?"

"Frieda! It's me! Claus! Help me!" Claus said.

"He certainly has a good bark. Friendly and everything," Frieda said.

"I'm sorry, Marna. He got away," the vet said.

"He came from around back," Frieda said. "How did he get there?"

"Yes, how did he?" Lanietta asked.

Just then, the assistant drove around from the back to the front of the building. He'd forgotten to remove the hose from his tailpipe, and so he dragged it behind him.

"So! Carbon monoxide poisoning for Cloopy?" Frieda said.

"What?" Lanietta said.

"I can explain!" the vet said.

"In front of a judge, I hope," Lanietta said. "I'm suing."

"No, please. Take your dog home. Please," the vet pleaded.

"Go on back inside," Lanietta said after a pause.

The vet thanked her and went back inside.

"Can't even put an animal to sleep these days without it being an issue," Lanietta said.

"I still can't believe you tried it. How is my favorite niece taking it?" Frieda asked.

"Olivia is sad, but not about Cloopy. You remember Brandi? The girl who plays the English horn?"

"Olivia's best friend. Yes, I've met her. Nice girl," Frieda said.

"She died today," Lanietta said.

"Oh my!" Frieda said with her hands over her mouth. "That's terrible! How did it happen?"

"Cloopy here jumped at her and made her fall. She broke her neck," Lanietta said.

"Not true!" Claus said. "I tried to save Brandi! I did!"

"And Cloopy here almost killed my Olivia just moments ago. Tried to pull her into traffic while crossing the street to the hospital," Lanietta said.

"You stepped on my foot! You caused it!" Claus said.

"Oh Cloopy! You're too excitable!" Frieda said. "But putting you down is such a shame. Marna, why don't you let me take him? Olivia can visit any time."

"I wouldn't want to put my sister through such a burden," Lanietta said.

"Nonsense, we Morgan girls stick together. You know I'd do anything for you, my older sister. I only wish we could have grown up together. Why Dad and Mom put you up for—"

"I'm a little sensitive about that," Lanietta said, playing her role well.

"Sorry," Frieda said.

"You're sure he won't interfere with your college studies?" Lanietta asked.

"If nothing else he'll keep me company. He'll be no trouble, unlike that roommate I had to kick out for her late nights with the guy of the week," Frieda said.

Lanietta and Frieda laughed.

"Very well," Lanietta said. "You may take him. But be careful. Don't let him cause you harm."

"I'll keep a close eye on him," Frieda said. "Come along, Cloopy. Let's see your new home."

Frieda opened the front passenger seat to her car, and Claus jumped right in. The two sisters hugged, and then Frieda drove to her apartment.

"Luckily, this apartment accepts pets, including dogs," Frieda said to Claus. "A shame you can't talk. I could tell you about my studies. I plan to join the Air Force after getting my degree in aeronautics."

The two arrived at Frieda's apartment, and she led Claus inside. With Claus settled, Frieda called County Hospital to see about Brandi.

"Oh, she has. I understand. Is Ms. Ruhm still there? Okay. What about the Depettis? Enrico and Marna Depetti? Or Olivia? I see. Thank you," Frieda said, and she hung up the telephone.

"Brandi has been transferred to the morgue," Frieda said to Claus. "Brandi's mother is at the funeral home making arrangements. Enrico and Olivia are there with her for support. I'll call the Depetti house later. Let's get some homework done, shall we?"

Claus followed Frieda over to a kitchen table. She cracked out a textbook, a spiral notebook, and a pen.

"I always take notes by hand first before transferring them to a computer. Can't have a machine telling me how to take notes," Frieda said. "I'll put the radio on."

Claus was shocked. He himself was still upset both by Brandi's death and his own near death, and there was Frieda doing homework like the world was normal. And too good to use a computer for taking notes! Frieda was arrogant, that was for sure. She was younger-looking too, and Claus at least was happy to see her. But what was that she had on the radio? It wasn't music. Sounded like a clock ticking with tones.

"How strange," he thought to himself. "She's playing WWV. The time station on shortwave. Oh Frieda, how might you look if I took you to a ball in the late 1800s, with an ornate dress, corset, and hat? How the women were so well adorned in those days. How they dress so plainly today. Here's Frieda in a T-shirt and jeans. Hardly elegant, yet I still have feelings for her."

Claus jumped onto the table and attempted to nuzzle with Frieda.

"Not now, Cloopy. Behave, will you? It's homework time. I'll buy a bone for you later if you're good," Frieda said. "Now get down and find something to do. Oh, wait, you need water, don't you? And food. Tell you what, you stay here, and I'll go to the pet store and get you some food. And a bone is waiting for you if you're good."

Frieda locked Claus inside and left for the pet store. Curious, Claus explored her apartment. It was furnished as any apartment might be, with couch and television in the living room, a small dining room connected to the living room (where she did her studies), a kitchen with coffee maker and the usual utensils and dishes, a bedroom, a bathroom, a utility room for cleaning clothes, and a second bedroom—all rooms tidy and clean. But it was the second bedroom that caught Claus's attention. It was filled with books, photo albums, scrap books, pictures in frames, and memorabilia. Claus first looked at the pictures in frames. They showed Frieda at various ages posing with friends, the Depettis, even Cloopy when he was a puppy.

"I was a puppy?" Claus asked himself.

Then there were the photo albums. Lots and lots of photo albums, all labeled on the outside as to the contents (except one). Some were of Frieda's ancestors, others were of various airplanes, and still others were of flowers. The one unlabeled book, however, caught Claus's attention. He pulled the album out with his teeth and flipped it open to the first page. There shown was a baby named "Christine Frieda Morgan" and was held in turn by one parent then another. These first few pages showed Frieda grow from a baby to a young girl, always wearing a skirt and a smile but always with the name "Crissy". More photos, photos of her mother in the captain's seat of a small, parked airplane with Crissy the young girl sitting in her lap, pretending to fly. Then another photo of her sitting in her father's lap of a parked Boeing jet. Then other pictures of her standing with her parents in front of various small and large aircraft, with her father wearing a commercial captain's uniform, and her mother wearing a Navy uniform. Again, Crissy wore a skirt and a smile. Next were a series of flower photos—tending flowers with her mother in a small greenhouse, visiting the municipal botanical garden, and one photo where Crissy had filled every shelf and flat spot with flowers. Finally, a series of photos began of Crissy performing ballet—stretch exercises, practice sessions, and performances. She posed with her teacher at Performance Academy of the Arts, a photo with her group, and several

newspaper clippings chronicling the accomplishments of the local prodigy ballet girl. The last few photos showed Crissy in a greenhouse with her mother, and Crissy held a bouquet of Martha Washington geraniums.

Claus reached the middle of the album. Several pages were held together by string wrapped around them. Odd, Claus thought. He flipped that little bundle over, and the following pictures were quite different. Photos were labeled "Frieda" instead of "Crissy". No longer were Frieda's parents in any of the photos. Frieda wore trousers instead of a skirt, and she had a grim expression—always grim. There were no ballet photos and no flower photos. The first few photos showed Frieda with a new set of parents, Mr. and Mrs. Bea, and an older sister, Marna. Additional photos showed Frieda in swimming competitions with full length suits. One photo showed her relaxing at home in shorts with big scars on her legs.

"Scars," Claus said. "She got them when she was young. What happened? No wonder she covered up in public."

The next photos showed her working in an aircraft hangar, using her small hands to help maintain aircraft where larger hands struggled. There were no poses of her with other adults, just Frieda by herself. As the photos progressed, there were fewer and fewer of Frieda. Instead, photos of aircraft parts in various stages of disassembly filled the photo album. The last photo in the album showed her standing with the Beas, Enrico, Marna, and a young Olivia for Frieda's high school graduation. Frieda posed in her blue gown and shingle while holding her diploma.

"I must find out what's in those middle pages," Claus said to himself.

"Cloopy, I'm back. I have food and a bone. Come get nummies!" Frieda called.

Claus flipped the album closed and did the best he could to put the album back.

"Cloopy, where are you? C'mon, boy!" she called again.

Frieda walked down the hallway and nearly passed the second bedroom when she saw Claus in there doing apparently nothing. He had returned the album to the bookcase and only just in time.

"What are you doing in here? C'mon, boy," Frieda said.

Claus rushed out with excitement and followed Frieda down the hallway to the kitchen where she had fresh water and a bowl of dog food. Claus ate the food hungrily and drank the water as if parched. These primitive feelings disgusted Claus, making him wonder if people were much better than the other animals.

"We eat and drink just like them," Claus said.

"Yes, good food," Frieda said after his bark. "I'm glad you like it."

Frieda picked up the phone and made another call.

"Marna? Yeah, it's me, Frieda. How's Olivia? Yeah, sure, I can drive over. Oh, okay, yeah, just drive over then. He's settling in fine. No, hasn't torn anything up. Okay, see you soon. Bye!"

Frieda turned to Claus and said, "Cloopy, you be good. Marna's coming over with a harness. She doesn't think you can be controlled, but I've convinced her otherwise. She's going to give you lessons while I go see Olivia. Now be good and everything. I promise you can stay here. She won't take you far. Good boy!"

Lanietta arrived shortly thereafter with a harness, like that used for a seeing eye dog. The sisters hugged, and Frieda gave the apartment key to Lanietta.

"Just in case you want to go outside," Frieda said. "There's a nice park behind the apartment building."

Frieda was gone.

"So what is this fantasy you've invented, Lanietta? Making up a story about Frieda to torture me?" Claus asked.

"What a short memory you have, Clomper. Here, let's put this harness on," Lanietta said.

"I don't need a harness," Claus said.

"You do if you want to go out again. That includes Brandi's funeral. Yes, Frieda wants to train you as a seeing eye dog. She believes that any failed case can be turned

into success. She's very optimistic. And—"

While placing the harness on Claus, Lanietta noticed the small stone in his collar resembling an amethyst.

"And I am optimistic too," she said with a grin. "Interesting collar."

Lanietta's voice trailed with words like, "puzzle piece of the Veigon."

"End this fantasy," Claus said.

"This isn't a fantasy. It's a memory. Don't you remember those reeds that struck you from the ocean? I'm collecting them. Should make an excellent memory," Lanietta said. "And there are other bits of memory to discover."

"Memory for what?"

"For when I return to Luna Beta. I'm sure my Gren Carinians have fully conquered it by now. And I will claim my place as their leader. With you at my side of course, Clomper. But I need memories for my subjects," Lanietta said, "and my projects."

"Memories of people dying? How terrible. How depressing," Claus said.

"There are those in this universe who preserve memories of all kinds, not just the pleasant ones. In fact, it is the unpleasant ones that provide the most information and adventure. Pleasant memories are for the boring, the plain, the law-abiding subjects of Libriota and the Bleuhs. I won't collect memories for her. I won't."

"Are you trying to tell me the reeds contain this memory?"

"An old dog *can* learn new tricks," Lanietta said. "Of course, Clomper. Frieda has blocked off this part of her life, as she has of her earlier life."

"What earlier life?" Claus asked.

"You saw it. The photo album?"

"You know I was into that?"

"Of course!" Lanietta said. "I'm recording this memory."

Lanietta's voice trailed again, saying, "But I think I missed something."

"Then somehow you've converted the reeds in the water into a living memory," Claus said.

"Because your kind does not. Your kind throws away things to eradicate memory," Lanietta said.

"Okay, okay. I'll give you that. But there were a lot of reeds in the water. Where did they come from? I can't believe Brandi or Olivia threw away all those reeds. There were thousands of reeds in the water. Thousands."

Lanietta smiled.

"You'll find out," she said. "And speaking of finding out, let me try something."

As Lanietta watched the stone in Claus's collar, she rubbed the fur on his head. The little stone changed its color from solid purple to split, side-by-side colors of purple and white. Lanietta rubbed more fur, and the colors mixed in a soft swirling pattern that folded back and forth onto itself. It mesmerized Lanietta for a moment. She rubbed Claus's fur vigorously, and the pattern mixed quickly to the point of fading into grey.

"Not sure what you're doing, but my fur feels good," Claus said.

Lanietta slapped Claus lightly. The stone's color changed quickly into a side-by-side split of yellow and blue. She slapped him harder, and as she did, the colors swapped places every few seconds. She then slapped him harder and more quickly, even digging her nails into him, and the stone's colors switched so quickly that they became a pale pea-green color. She stopped.

"Ow! Was that necessary?" Claus asked.

The stone returned to its natural amethyst purple color.

"Would you mind telling me what this is all about?" Claus asked.

"Just a curious strangeness about your collar. Nothing of your concern. You're more interested in Frieda, aren't you?" Lanietta asked.

"Well yeah," Claus said. "What do you know about her? What do you know about the album?"

"If only you were more clever than a dog. If only you could see those middle pages," Lanietta laughed.

"Then help me understand. Open up those pages and show me," Claus said.

"Marna would never violate her sister's memory album like that. You have a lot to learn about family."

"I didn't even know Frieda had a family. She never spoke of it," Claus said.

"Time for your training. Let's go outside," Lanietta said.

Claus started to walk, but Lanietta tapped his head with a stick.

"Do not pull me. Walk alongside," Lanietta said.

The two exited the apartment into the hallway, Lanietta locked it, and the two then went outside, behind the apartment building, and into the neighboring park.

"If you have this memory already, why put me through it? Or is it your hope to trap me in this. Is that what became of Shara? And Clover? Are they both trapped in memories?" Claus said.

"I already told you. I'm on vacation. And I can do whatever I want. First lesson—ignore other dogs," Lanietta said.

Lanietta led Claus close to another dog. The other dog barked and got close to Claus. Claus started to move toward the dog to sniff it.

"No, don't," Lanietta said.

"I can't help it. This dog form you gave me forces me to do things I wouldn't do as a human. I would never go up to someone and sniff them," Claus said.

"But you would go up to someone and say, 'hello,' or shake someone's hand, or even steal food from that someone if hungry and desperate enough. Am I right?" Lanietta asked.

"I wouldn't steal food from someone," Claus said.

"I'll remember you said that. I have another memory to test your assertion. But we have to finish this one first."

"So, you don't plan to keep me trapped here forever," Claus said.

"No, I don't. But we must reach its conclusion. Stop. Here's a sidewalk. Make sure it's clear before proceeding across," Lanietta said.

Claus let out a big laugh. He sat, laughed, and rolled over.

"What on Earth is so funny?" Lanietta asked.

"You, acting like Libriota with your law and order. Yeah, you're acting like Libriota. A Bleuh. So much for adventure, eh? Must have law and order, at least once in a while, to put me in my place? What's gotten into you? Have you become possessed? You have a lot of learning to do," Claus said, and he bit Lanietta.

Lanietta paused in shock. Clomper was telling her off? An expression of irritation built up within her, but Claus didn't wait for her to react. He left her grasp and ran around the park, slaloming around people and objects as if on an obstacle course. He nearly landed in the fountain when a blind woman reached out and grabbed his harness. Claus stopped short of falling into the fountain, and she brought him off the fountain's ledge and back to the fountain's perimeter walkway. She held his harness in her left hand while her right held her own service dog.

"You are very spirited," she said.

Lanietta should have marched over and disciplined Claus. But instead, she remained stationary and watched the blind woman interact with Claus.

"Oh, you have a training harness," the blind woman said. "Come on. Mocha will show you what to do. Mocha is my chocolate Lab. What do you think, Mocha?"

Mocha, a Labrador retriever, looked over at Claus.

"I'll hold you next to Mocha. She'll show you," the blind woman said.

The blind woman tied a strap from Claus's harness to Mocha's harness, the blind woman then held onto Mocha's harness, and the three walked around the park with Claus on Mocha's left and the blind woman on Mocha's right.

"Very good," the blind woman said. "The immersion lesson is working. See?

Not so hard. Now let's find your master. But first, what's your name?"

Claus tried to say his name, but it came out as half-bark, half-speech.

"Droopy?" the blind woman said. "Okay, Droopy. Take me to your master. Don't run into anyone. And watch out for cars."

Lanietta was impressed with how Mocha and the blind woman had Claus lead them around. They reached a park drive where cars traveled to different parts of the park, and Claus waited for traffic to pass. He then led Mocha and the blind woman to Lanietta.

"You've stopped, Droopy," the blind woman said, and she sensed another person was in front of her. "Hello. Is Droopy your dog?"

"Cloopy, you bad boy running away like that," Lanietta said.

"Oh, his name is Cloopy. I was close," the blind woman said. "My name is Blair. And this is my seeing eye dog, Mocha."

"Nice to meet you. I'm Marna Depetti," Lanietta said.

"The wife of Enrico Depetti? The racer?" Blair gasped.

"I try not to advertise it," Lanietta said.

"It's a pleasure!" Blair said.

"I'm training Cloopy here as a seeing eye dog. I'm not having much luck. He gets into so much mischief, and I thought this would be good for him."

"He did very well just now. I think he just needs the right kind of socializing," Blair said.

"Indeed. I will keep that in mind. Well Cloopy, are you ready to go back home? Your guardian should be back by now," Lanietta said.

"I'd like to visit with him again," Blair said.

"He'll be staying at those apartments right over there. With Frieda Morgan," Lanietta said.

"I know that name too. Swimming champion, right?" Blair said.

"That's right," Lanietta said.

"Well you've made my day. Cloopy, you be a good dog now and give no trouble to Marna or Frieda. Okay?"

Claus tried to say okay, but again it came out as a bark.

"Nice to meet you! I hope we meet again," Blair said.

"Goodbye!" Lanietta replied, and she returned with Claus to Frieda's apartment.

Frieda had yet to return, and so Claus took the opportunity to speak.

"I wish to speak with you, Lanietta," Claus said.

"Then speak," she replied.

"No, human to human, if that's possible. Change me back to my human form. And though you are not human, at least you portray one fairly close," he said.

"Fairly close? I nailed Marna's role perfectly," Lanietta said.

"I don't want to bark over petty things. Let's clear the air once and for all. Change me back to human so we can speak as peers," Claus said.

"Very well," Lanietta said.

Lanietta's face glowed bluish-green briefly, and Claus returned to his normal self with cotton in his nose.

"Your nose is still broken," Lanietta said. "Now hurry, Claus. Frieda will be back soon. What would she say if a married woman like Marna is caught with another man in her apartment?"

"You were shocked a moment ago," Claus said.

"What?"

"I saw you. When Mocha was training me? When I reacted to every one of her social cues?" Claus said.

"This is an old conversation. I know you humans have this innerviation with others. Apparently dogs have it too. It only proves Earth animals are social and react with one another as if connected by nerves," Lanietta said.

"Labba has it," Claus said.

"No!"

"Is she not with Argo? She loves him, you know. The two work as one. Innerviation," Claus said.

"Wrong, wrong, wrong!" Lanietta shouted.

"Then why have you raised your voice? You despise Libriota because you accuse her of being part of those innerviated Bleuh Carinians, while you brag of your independence. Yet you are here with me, just as Labba is with Argo," Claus explained. "You've become innerviated with me."

"False, wrong, massive fail, Mr. Clomper!" Lanietta retorted.

"Admit it. It's true. But you're still green at the game, if you pardon my pun."

"Grens are not green or naive as you would say. We are all-powerful. You are the pet, nothing more," Lanietta said.

"Even masters become innerviated with their pets, and pets with their masters. A human can read when a dog wants to go out to play or a cat wants attention. And the pets know when the humans are happy or in pain. Yes, even if you still think of me as your pet, you've become innerviated, even if a little. But I don't think you want me as a pet. Not really. It's a cover. You want a human experience. You want love. If you were a human, I'd categorize you as a sociopath who isn't sure if she should be a psychopath instead. There's no feedback mechanism to stop you and give you pause for thought. Until I came along. But you still aren't sure how to deal with me."

"This is your idea of a peer-to-peer discussion? You're doing all the talking and storytelling," Lanietta said.

"Because you've been pushing your will for too long. Yes, you have. And someone needs to tell you so. A train without window, key, or lid, yet Lanietta with agenda inside is hid. Look, you're blushing with anger. Rage. That part you've mastered, right? Rage is easy. Channeling that rage into a productive peer-to-peer relationship is much harder. Look at yourself. You can't hide what you're feeling. So I ask, what control do you have now? Who is there to stop you? You're a runaway train. And you can't see how to stop, because you have no window. But you're hoping I can be that window for you, without you admitting to such a weakness. Because you've acquired power with the Grens not by being their friend, but by being Libriota's enemy. Am I right?"

Lanietta held silent as she desperately tried to stop herself from glowing bright with anger.

"I said, am I right?" Claus reiterated.

"I...make...things!" Lanietta growled in a low voice.

"Knock knock," Frieda said at the apartment door as she opened it slowly.

Lanietta quickly changed Claus back to dog form and regained her composure as Marna.

"How's Cloopy?" Frieda asked.

"Oh, he's full of energy," Lanietta said. "And he met a new friend in the park. A dark-brown dog named Mocha, and her owner—a blind woman named Blair."

"I've seen that woman around," Frieda said as she grabbed a drink in the kitchen. "Can I get you anything?"

"Thank you no," Lanietta said, and the three sat in the living room. "Blair thinks very highly of you. She knows you're a champion swimmer."

"Oh, I didn't think I had any fans left," Frieda said. "My studies have so consumed my time that I have little left over for anything else. I get a good swim every now and then in the university's pool. But I seem to spend more time dealing with the air than the water. I still can't decide if I should join the Air Force to fly or aim for government work like the NTSB."

"Why not join the Navy? You can fly and be near the water too," Lanietta said.

"An interesting idea, Marna. Give me a hug, my dear sister," Frieda said.

The two hugged. The sight of Lanietta the cruel alien hugging Claus's love interest disgusted Claus, and he put his paws over his eyes. Frieda looked at Claus and laughed.

"I guess Cloopy has a stiff collar. He needs to loosen it up, don't you Cloopy?" Frieda asked.

"Well, Poopy Cloopy was Droopy for a moment, at least that's what Blair called him," Lanietta said.

"Cloopy! What's your name? Can you say, 'Cloopy'?" Frieda asked.

Claus tried to say, "Claus," but it sounded like, "Droopy."

"Sounds like, 'Droopy'," Frieda said.

"His speech is droopy," Lanietta said, and the sisters laughed.

When laughter subsided, Frieda fell into tears.

"Poor Brandi. And poor Olivia!" Frieda sobbed.

"Come now, Frieda. Let your Marna make things better," Lanietta said with an arm around Frieda for comfort.

Claus was about to cough up a hairball in disgust, and he wasn't even a cat!

"I wish there was something I could do. I should have visited more often. Maybe I could have taken Cloopy sooner," Frieda said. "Now Olivia is devastated. It's like two people died—Brandi and Olivia."

"She's young. She'll get over it," Lanietta said, falling a little out of her human role.

"No, she won't. I know, Marna. Maybe it was better you weren't there when Mom and Dad passed."

"I was there at the funeral. That's how we met, remember? My adoptive parents received word that my real parents had passed. A strange way to meet one's real parents."

"But you didn't know them. You don't have memories. This is the last memory I have of them. This is what you'd have to live with."

Frieda ripped open her trouser legs, revealing the horrible scars up and down her legs.

"Do you want to talk about it?" Lanietta said. "I know you keep your legs covered. Even your swimsuits cover your legs. People thought you did so for less drag, to slip through water better."

"I cover them to slip through life better," Frieda said.

Claus wondered about the photo album. Were those string-bound middle pages kept closed to hide something about Frieda's parents? Perhaps how they died? This was the first time Claus heard about Frieda's parents and about them dying. He had to see those bound pages. He had to.

"All things should be let out. Makes you feel better," Lanietta said, mimicking what she thought she should say.

"Not always," Frieda said. "Marna, did you ever study Spanish history? The Franco era?"

"Spanish history?" Lanietta asked.

"Our mother was from Spain, you know. Don't let her red hair deceive you. Spain has a variety of people. We're Celtic through our mother."

"I didn't realize that," Lanietta said.

"Oh yes. Lots of things about Spain people don't realize. A microcosm in its own right. Franco put his heel into that microcosm, unfortunately."

"You mean like this?" Lanietta said as she stuck the heel of her shoe into Claus.

Claus yelped.

"Oh, poor Cloopy!"

"Sorry," Lanietta said. "So Franco. What about him?"

"When he died in 1975, people divided into two camps—those who wanted to get the stories of his atrocities into the open for full discussion, and those who were so tired and drained that they wanted to get on in life without reliving those memories over and over again. I moved on, Marna. I sealed my past and vowed to repair the future."

"Repair the future?" Lanietta said, amused. "How does one repair the future?"

"By overcoming the failures of the past," Frieda said.

"Sounds like temporal mechanics," Lanietta said.

"That's why I agreed to take Cloopy. To repair the future by preventing it. If Cloopy really did cause Brandi's death—"

"Which he did," Lanietta lied.

"Then I want to know why and see what I can do to prevent future failures. I did it with swimming, and I'm doing it with aeronautical study," Frieda said.

So that was it, Claus thought. Frieda had pushed herself into obsessed mania to atone for sins she did not commit. But why atone for the failures of others? Why take on such a burden? Claus had a new understanding of Frieda. Yes, she was a determined woman, if only he could get through that callous skin of hers. But Frieda didn't want to make friends. And this demon would haunt her the rest of her life. It was a demon that would lead her to the moon, where others brought their own demons.

"She's afraid to. Like Lanietta. Neither has the fortitude to commit to another where they themselves become vulnerable," Claus said.

"What is it, Cloopy? Is there someone at the door?" Frieda said in response to Claus's barking.

"I'm here, Frieda. I won't hurt you!" Claus barked.

"I should let you go," Frieda said to Lanietta. "I enjoyed seeing Olivia, but she shouldn't be alone for long."

"Enrico is with her," Lanietta said.

"He is, and he's a good father, but there's nothing like a woman's touch in these situations. I know how much you helped me when our parents died. I don't know how I would have made it without you. I really don't. Don't let Olivia slip. Keep her going with things."

"She has her bass clarinet," Lanietta said. "She's quite proficient at it."

"Yes, I know. Just watch out for that. I used to take ballet lessons. I blocked it out after the accident."

"A bass clarinet is hardly a ballet shoe," Lanietta said.

"Well taken. Just watch her for changes. Please?" Frieda begged.

"I will do that," Lanietta said.

"Thank you! Say goodbye to Marna, Cloopy," Frieda said.

"Goodbye!" Claus barked.

Just then Frieda's phone rang.

"I'll just let myself out," Lanietta said.

Lanietta headed for the door while Frieda answered the phone.

"Hello?" Frieda said. "Yes, she is. One moment."

Frieda put the phone on the telephone stand and called for Marna to return.

"It's for you," Frieda said.

"Oh," Lanietta said. "Very well."

Lanietta walked over to the phone, and Claus realized that he might be stuck in this memory for a while. Who knew how long? Ironic that he'd wanted desperately to spend time with Frieda, and now he was doing so as a dog.

"This is Marna," Lanietta said. "So soon? I see. Yes, I'm sure she will. Cloopy? Well if he can behave. Frieda will watch him. She and Cloopy are becoming fast friends. I'll tell her. Yes. Yes. Love you too. Bye!"

"Funeral plans?" Frieda guessed accurately. "Strange Enrico couldn't tell me himself."

"He's a little strange like that," Lanietta said. "As it is, Brandi's funeral is tomorrow."

"What? So soon? How will her family have time to travel?"

"Apparently, Brandi has no extended family, at least none that have kept in touch. Ms. Ruhm will bury Brandi herself. Several students have volunteered to be pallbearers. I told Enrico he couldn't be one, that he needs to stay with Olivia."

"Enrico and you," Frieda said.

"And me what?" Lanietta said.

"Marna! You both need to be there for Olivia. Remember that!" Frieda said. "Make sure Olivia stays Olivia. Don't let another Crissy become Frieda."

So Frieda had regrets over her decisions. She truly was driven by a demon, and this was made all the clearer to Claus. Lanietta fell out of human character and just returned a quizzical expression to Frieda.

"I mean it. Be there. Always," Frieda said.

"Of course," Lanietta said. "Give your sister a hug."

The two hugged. And then, Lanietta left.

Frieda was quick to make friends with Blair—that same day in fact. It was handy, because Frieda dropped Claus off with Blair so Frieda could attend the wake. The next day, Frieda again dropped Claus off with Blair so that Frieda could attend Brandi's funeral.

"This dropping me off is getting tiring," Claus said. "I'm missing everything!"

"Cloopy, would you like a treat?" Blair asked, hearing only his barking.

"I want to see Brandi's funeral. But I'm stuck here."

"You must be tired. Let me put you down for the morning. You'll have a nice doggie nap, and you'll be fresh in the afternoon when Frieda returns," Blair said.

Put down. Yes, Lanietta tried to put him down, that is, put him to sleep. Then there was Lanietta's condescending language calling him Poopy and other such treatment. Now Blair was putting him down for sleep.

"When will I get out of this memory? When will I stop being treated like a dog?" Claus said.

"Shhh," Blair said. "Sweet dreams, Cloopy."

Chapter 30: Leni on Trial

Leni stood at the podium. He pressed a button on the left side, and strobe lights flashed inside the area. He flipped that off and hit a similar button on the right side. Strobe lights flashed on the outside of the Tree of Memories. Then he hit another button on the right side, and an alarm blasted through the air. The colony people stepped back for a moment, but ear muffs sprouted from their glasses, and they renewed their attack. Leni hit another button, and knockout gas spewed along the outside perimeter of the Tree. The colony people fell unconscious.

"Good," Leni said. "Now I can see about recovering Selba. Oh, what's that?"

The pool showed an image of Slimy, Husky, and White Hat approaching the outside, all wearing eye, ear, and breathing protection. Leni hit another button, and water fell on them, but White Hat touched his hat in a certain way, and a shield diverted the water from them before they could get wet. Leni hit a button to send fire from inflammable liquid, and again White Hat touched his hat in a certain place, and a shield protected the three. In fact, White Hat extended this shield to protect colony people so that none of them were affected by fire. With such protection in place, the colony people regained consciousness. White Hat touched his hat one more time, and the seam to the Tree opened. Leni hit another button to close it, but White Hat held his hat within the seam. The force of the hat against the structure damaged it, and the seam was broken in an open state. The colony people rushed over to subdue Leni. He resisted at first, but White Hat summoned the water from the pool, and a great hydraulic creature arose and used his great strength to contain Leni.

"You have violated the Tree of Memories!" White Hat said. "People of Tabelia, witness a selenite intruder at the helm of our society!"

"Trial! Trial!" they all chanted, using their voices to Leni's surprise.

"Let there be a trial," White Hat said.

A colony woman much taller than the others and with long, white hair (White Hair) walked over to the archway and stood, with her hands and feet touching in the strategic four places. White Hat took his position at the podium and acted as judge. White Hair activated the arch, and it glowed. Leni was moved to a spot next to the large entrance/exit tubes. Railing forming a square perimeter elevated from the floor and surrounded Leni. The railing reached Leni's shoulder level, and then the bottom of the railing became part of a platform that lifted Leni up in the air. He was raised almost as high as the podium (and White Hat), but not quite. A stadium of seats rose from the floor, and so colony people in attendance had a place to sit.

"Court is in session," said White Hat as he knocked a gavel against the lectern on the podium. "Mr. Selenite. You are on trial for—"

"My name is Leni."

White Hat pointed toward Leni, and a lightning bolt struck the railing near Leni. Leni jumped in surprise.

"Silence! You are not yet called to speak," White Hat said.

"Why? Do I frighten you?" Leni asked.

White Hat sent down another lightning bolt, and it stunned Leni into silence.

"Court recorder, add insolence to the list of charges," White Hat said. "We will dispense with the reading of the charges and get on with the trial. Great Mistress, you may proceed."

With the archway still glowing, White Hair removed her right hand and waved it across in front of her. The pool showed a scene of Leni and Selba entering the seamount cave.

"Two intruders entering the Cave of Transition," White Hair said. "One, a human female. The other, a selenite."

White Hair waved her hand across again. The pool showed a changing cross-section of Leni, as if an X-ray machine had taken multiple longitudinal slices.

"You will note the mechanical nature. Very much like the selenites we have seen before," White Hair said.

"The court acknowledges that the accused called, 'Leni,' is a selenite," White Hat said.

"We will now produce his co-conspirator," White Hair said.

White Hair waved her hand again. From the pool emerged a transparent cocoon mounted on a pedestal. Selba was inside this cocoon and was either unconscious or unliving.

"Behold the attire of our intruders," White Hair said with another wave of her hand. "See how they walk within our realm without the proper dress code."

"Naked eyes!" the colony people yelled. "Distasteful and vulgar!" others yelled.

White Hat motioned his hand slightly downward to calm the people.

"Even in their current states, they violate our code," White Hair said.

"I will permit them to be covered, for modesty and decency of this courtroom," White Hat said.

Colony guards put something like a helmet with a faceguard over Leni. The pedestal with Selba moved to the side of the pool like a boom. Other guards opened the cocoon and placed a helmet with a faceguard over Selba. Selba did not stir. The guards closed the cocoon.

"The two then entered one of our fantasy trees," White Hair said. "Many of you recognize this memory."

White Hair waved her hand, and the pool showed the scene of Selba and Leni watching the baseball game.

"When accosted for their actions, they escaped," White Hair said as she had the pool display White Hat's first interaction with Selba and Leni.

"They invaded the Tree of Memories, and they maimed several of our kind," White Hair said.

The pool showed as several colony people lost limbs in the seam and nearly bled to death. Now the colony people in the courtroom became enraged. Many approached Leni and attempted to break through the railing to get at him. Others went for the cocoon in an effort to get at Selba. White Hat hit a button, and lightning struck both around Leni and around Selba, frightening these colony people back to their seats.

"Mr. Leni, how do you plead to these charges?" White Hat said, now permitting Leni to speak.

"We are only seeking our friends Clover, Shara, and Claus," Leni said. "Clover is somewhere—"

White Hat sent lightning again, and Leni fell silent.

"The accused enters a plea of 'guilty.' Mistress of the Archway, do you have anything to add before I pronounce sentencing?" White Hat asked.

"Only that I grieve for you, Mr. Leni. And for Selba here. Our realm we call Tabelia is a pristine function of happy memory. You have tarnished this memory. It is why we ban selenites to begin with. They tarnish all that is good and happy. There is no choice but the inevitable punishment. May forces of the cosmos tread lightly on your particles."

"What? You intend to kill us?"

"More like obliterate," Husky said to Leni, then Husky turned to White Hat and said, "The ionization chamber is ready for their disposal."

"Thank you, Husky. Your efficiency is appreciated," White Hat said.

"People of Tabelia, hear us," Leni said. "Is it fair to destroy people without hearing their defense?"

"We have heard your guilty plea," White Hat said.

"And yet you have not heard from Selba. She is silenced by your own device.

Is this happiness? Can happiness be found by silencing those into oblivion?" Leni asked.

"More insolence!" Husky said. "Permit me to rough him up so that he may sit in his own soil."

"No. Point taken, Mr. Leni. We shall hear from Selba. But only briefly. Many here are taken away from their happy trees and wait patiently to return. Lower her to the solid floor and bring her to me."

The cocoon was swiveled over and lowered to the floor. Two guards opened the cocoon. Selba awoke, and she felt panicked. The guards, though, pulled her out and contained her.

"Leni! What's going on?" Selba said.

"Easy there, Selba. We are on trial for various trespasses. I have asked that you speak in our defense. The guards are escorting you to White Hat."

"What should I say? We're doing our best to find Clover. We mean no harm," Selba said as she was escorted around the pool.

"But you have caused harm," White Hat said.

The colony people booed and jeered at Selba. One got up and stuck a cane in Selba's path, tripping her. She fell flat on her face. The colony people laughed.

"I chipped a tooth, Leni," Selba said.

"Hang in there," Leni said.

The guards helped Selba to her feet, and she continued her walk toward White Hat. But then another colony person came at Selba and shoved her into the pool. She let out a short scream from the unexpected event. Again the colony people laughed. They flashed their lights back and forth with excited communication, but they had nothing in their flashing vocabulary to express laughter. Leni, who could read their light impulses, realized this. Selba swam to the edge of the pool, and the guards pulled her out. So far neither White Hat nor White Hair had laughed, but another colony person rushed toward Selba to push her into the pool. The guards snapped Selba back, and the colony person, unable to check his momentum, went

diving into the pool. Now the courtroom erupted in raucous laughter, including White Hat and White Hair. The guards, who had chuckled when Selba fell into the pool, were more than happy to add to this new-found merriment by making fools of other colony people.

The people laughed so much that they didn't realize the colony person in the pool was confused and drowning. Leni jumped out of his railed enclosure, swam over to the drowning colony person, and pulled him to the pool's edge where one of Selba's guards pulled him out. Leni then proceeded to perform CPR to remove water from the drowned colony person and restore breathing and heartbeat.

"Laughing is good fun," Leni said, "But it's important to understand limits. No person should be allowed to suffer and die. Laugh, but only in guarded measure. Help those in need. I will help you too, as I have helped this person. For I am a doctor. Permit me to heal your wounded and any of your sick. Is this not the prime law of your people?"

"Our prime law is happiness," White Hat said.

White Hair walked over to Leni and Selba. She looked down at the colony drowned person, helped him stand, and then gave a long look at Leni and Selba.

"Perhaps happiness can also be found in laughter and the healing of the injured and sick," White Hair said. "You pique my interest, Leni. You too, Selba. I vote we delay sentencing until we explore these new avenues of happiness. Many have become bored with our trees."

Boos from some, and a look of disdain from White Hat.

"Yes, it's true! Boredom sets in and weakens us all. Leni and Selba have provided the means for fresh material. Perhaps Selba has her own happy memories to share? Meanwhile, I will have Leni cure our sick. I ask the people here to judge. What say you all?"

At first one colony person flashed his lenses. Then another, and another, and a trickle of interest grew into a flood of excitement. It was too much for White Hat to ignore.

"I judge then that the sentence is suspended. Temporarily," White Hat said. "But once we are done, the sentence shall be enacted. Court dismissed!"

The colony people cheered. They picked up Leni and Selba onto their shoulders and paraded the two around the pool. But White Hat was not satisfied. He pulled Slimy and Husky aside and spoke.

"We cannot allow those two to become too popular. They are like a silent infection that grows. We will extract what we will from them. Find ways to make them fail so that the people will turn swiftly against them," White Hat instructed.

Husky and Slimy agreed.

"Selba," Leni said as the two were paraded around.

"We did it," Selba said. "We're saved."

"I wasn't able to search for Clover. Keep alert, and look for signs of her. Also be wary of White Hat and his henchmen Husky and Slimy. They are scheming something. I'm sure of it. People in power always do," Leni said.

"What next?" Selba said.

"Do you know any jokes?" Leni asked.

"I used to perform comedy for my people before I was captured," Selba said. "I know lots of jokes. Most are for adults, though. Like the one about—"

"Don't tell the adult ones. Tell ones proper for children. Do what you can with clean comedy. We can't risk things at first. Play things by ear, and use your judgment as to what your audience can handle."

"That is the strength of great comedy," Selba said.

"Thank you. I will treat the injured and sick. One last thing. If you are given the chance to leave without me, you must—"

"I'm not leaving without you," Selba said. "We need you back in Arberella."

"I understand. However, I might need to make a deal for Clover's and your release," Leni said. "If I do, go quickly."

"No deal. I will stay here and work for your release," Selba smiled. "Sorry, you're only a selenite. You're not allowed to sacrifice yourself like us humans. The world is full of selenites, and how better to fight selenites than with our own selenite?"

"Hmm. You might have given me another bargaining chip," Leni said.

"Leni! I already told you no," Selba said.

"We'll see," he said. "We'll see."

Chapter 31: The Double Reed

"Thank you for watching Cloopy, Blair," Frieda said after arriving at Blair's apartment.

"You're welcome. Is there anything else I can do?" Blair asked.

Frieda was about to leave with Claus, but she paused.

"How do you do it, Blair?"

"Pardon?"

"You know. Being blind. How do you do it?"

"C'mon. Give me a hug," Blair said, and Frieda did just that.

"I just...Brandi was so young. It was a senseless death, Blair. Senseless. There was no point," Frieda said with a big sigh. "I feel so heavy with dread. I haven't felt like this since my own parents passed. Olivia has a tough road ahead."

"You'll be there for her, of course," Blair said.

"I will," Frieda said.

"Why don't you sit down for a bit? I have a nice Chardonnay in the wine fridge. Care to join me for a sip?" Blair offered.

"I'd love to, thank you!" Frieda said.

"You know, I'm not totally blind. Just nearly. I can make out a few things if I hold them very close to my eyes and to the side. Forget vision straight ahead. So all is not black to me. But I do feel like I'm staring at an orca all the time. That's from the dark splotches in my vision," Blair explained as she got the wine and filled the glasses. "And all because of diabetes."

"Oh, I'm sorry," Frieda said.

Blair brought the drinks to the living room and handed Frieda her drink. Frieda took a sip and exhaled with relief. Then Blair sat down with her own drink, took a sip, and continued to speak.

"Fortunately I don't need insulin shots. I take a few pills, and I'm good. I probably shouldn't have this wine, but once in a while is okay. Anyway, I didn't realize I had diabetes until it damaged my eyesight. I thought I was just getting older and needed stronger glasses. The quack down the street kept prescribing stronger glasses, too. He said I was getting macular degeneration and that there was nothing to be done. He didn't charge much for his service, but boy did I pay the price!"

"That would just kill me. I mean, your blindness could have been prevented with knowledge and a proper diagnosis," Frieda said.

"But I still have my life," Blair continued. "Just a few generations back, there'd be no one to blame, because there was no treatment. So in a way I'm still better off than my ancestors. Anyway, Mocha is a great eye dog and my best friend. That's how I do it. When I close my eyes at night and sleep, I see things as I used to see. So there's always something to look forward to."

"You are very brave," Frieda said.

"And very lucky. No other part of my body is damaged. My eyes took the brunt. Other diabetics aren't so lucky. I think I could live without a toe or two, but losing my pancreas or heart would be tough."

"It would be fatal!" Frieda said.

"Exactly. See? Or I could have hearing loss or even tinnitus. At least I can close my eyes at night so I don't see the orcas. Can you imagine being unable to shut out tinnitus? I think that would do me in. I got lucky."

"I guess we all should count our blessings more often," Frieda said.

Frieda blew into her glass, and it returned a musical tone.

"Brandi has great friends," Frieda said, suddenly changing the subject. "The funeral was filled with her classmates. She and Olivia were in the school orchestra. The orchestra was there and played several songs. Brandi and Olivia would do duets in the past, but it was all Olivia at the funeral, at least it was supposed to be. Olivia tried, stopped, and tried to finish her part. The other students kept playing, but Olivia couldn't. It just breaks your heart. She had that look too. I know that look."

"What look?"

"That quizzical look, wondering why the sun continues to rise and set," Frieda said.

"What a strange thing to say," Blair said. "Every day is a new day."

"I can tell that you've never lost anyone close," Frieda said.

"You're right, I haven't, but how did you know?"

"Because for someone who has, the world stops. Blair, I hope it never happens to you. It's the worst feeling in the world. You get angry, I mean really angry, that people and the world keep going as if the sun will rise another day. What's wrong with people, anyway? How can they be so callous? Don't they understand?"

"I guess we don't. They say we're the only species who knows that we will die someday. But we put it out of our minds and convince ourselves it will never happen to us. At least we do in our youth when we believe we're immortal. Most young people your age still believe they are immortal. But you're an old soul now. Have been for a while. I've read that young people handle death better than older people, because they bounce back. But after listening to you, I'm thinking that's not the case. I think young people who see death are drastically changed. Did you feel like your childhood ended when your parents died?"

"Yes. It did end. That's a fact," Frieda said.

"I think I might have had a similar feeling if I'd gone blind when I was younger, when I was much more vain. But I'm older now, and I've been through other things. A divorce, job losses, and a house fire. Yes, I used to live in a house. Now I'm in an apartment. I guess the blindness was just another scar added to the many scars. And I figure some other thing will come along. I just expect it now as an older adult.

But I would have been shocked had I gone blind as a child."

"I was shocked. I'm still living in shock," Frieda said.

"Then I ask you, how do *you* do it?" Blair said.

"I push myself. I push myself with everything," Frieda said. "I saw what the crash did to people, how it killed the dead and the living. There was only one survivor. Me. I..."

Here Frieda's voice trailed. She fell silent for a moment and regained her composure.

"I survived. I was determined to keep moving by pushing myself into solving problems. Yes, I ended my make-believe worlds and took problems head on. And I'm careful. Very careful. I look for a problem before it exists, even forecasting doom where none exists, just so I can be ready should it happen."

"Sounds very tiring," Blair said.

"It is, but I must be vigilant. I must beat the demons in the air and sky. I must beat the demons that have caused and do cause harm to others. There's something deep in our world, Blair. Something deep and hideous. I feel its evil and how it spreads to others under innocent guise. I'm amazed at how others are blind to this evil...sorry, didn't mean to—"

"I see what you mean," Blair said with a comforting voice. "Please continue."

"Those bears...the way they...sorry, I know I'm not making much sense. But I found...I found...well...I thought...was it luck? I fashioned a collar for Cloopy with a part of that luck, a collar with a stone. Now he's a jinx. Maybe the collar isn't so lucky. Well, I'll take Cloopy for a while. I'll make sure he can't harm anyone else."

"But I didn't harm anyone! It was an accident," Claus said.

Blair laughed at Claus's barking.

"It's as if he can understand you," Blair continued to laugh.

"I feel much better, Blair. Thank you! I'll give you a call later," Frieda said.

"Stop by or call any time! I also make great tea," Blair said. "And Mocha likes

Cloopy too. Drop Cloopy off if ever you need a break."

"Thank you!" Frieda said, and she left with Claus.

Several days passed, and Claus spent all that time in Frieda's apartment. He so badly wanted to see the bound pages in her special album, but he did not dare chew the string. He settled instead for flipping through her aeronautical books.

"At least I can keep my skills sharp," he said. "That is, if I get to fly again. Speaking of flying, Frieda said something about a crash. Plane crash? Is that how her parents died? I've got to find out somehow."

The day came when he was allowed to visit the Depetti house.

"Come in!" Marna said at the front door as she waved Frieda and Claus in. "How are you, Frieda? I haven't heard from you in a few days. I was beginning to worry."

"I spent extra time with Cloopy here to get to know him. He really is a great dog, you know," Frieda said as the three sat down in the living room.

"Cloopy can behave if he wants to. Come over here, boy! Let Marna give you some love."

But Claus preferred to stay close to Frieda.

"Well, that's interesting," Frieda said. "It's like he doesn't remember you."

"I remember Lanietta very well!" Claus barked.

"Oh, he remembers me, don't you Cloopy?" Marna said. "Come here, boy!"

"Yuck!" Claus barked.

"Cloopy, you be a good boy and say 'hello' to Marna. Go on!" Frieda said, and she pushed Claus off the couch.

But instead of going over to Marna, Claus headed upstairs.

"Checking his old stomping grounds, I suppose," Frieda said. "Oh could I use a glass of wine. Blair had an excellent Chardonnay when I visited her."

"What good is a sister without a stash of wine? Let me get one of your favorites," Marna said.

Marna disappeared for a moment then brought back a nice rosé in a bucket of ice along with two glasses.

"Help yourself," Marna said after passing a glass to Frieda.

Frieda took the glass and filled it.

"Ahhhh," Frieda said, and she stretched out. "I feel like I'm at a wonderful French vineyard with not a care in the world."

"It's times like this when therapy is a necessary part of survival," Marna said as she poured her own glass. "Cheers."

"Cheers!" Frieda said, and she took another sip.

In fact, Frieda took a gulp. Several. She drained her glass and filled it again.

"I just need a moment for my pores to clear. I can feel the nutrients coursing and flowing to my skin. If I were only a sponge for indulgence, I could truly relax," Frieda said.

"Then take a moment. Relax," Marna said.

The two did just that. Finally at length, Frieda resumed conversation.

"I'm much better now," Frieda said. "How are you doing?"

"Oh I'm fine," Marna said. "So is Enrico. He went away on business for several days. He wouldn't have, you know, if Cloopy were still here, but since Cloopy's gone, he's very much relieved and felt he could go ahead with the trip. A new race team is starting up, and he's going to run it. I've convinced him to do less racing and more managing. Keeps him alive and me sane. Enrico says we can go on a long vacation after he finishes the start-up process, even if it means pulling Olivia out of school. I think she could use it. She's been homebound the last few days."

Cloopy returned with a double reed and dropped it at the foot of the steps. The stone on his collar displayed two colors side-by-side—yellow and blue. Lanietta caught a quick glimpse of these colors before he went back upstairs.

"Homebound? Why? Is she sick?"

"Says she has a stomach bug. I take food up to her, but she doesn't open the door. Just takes the food," Marna said.

Cloopy returned with another double reed and dropped it halfway from the steps to Frieda. The colors on his stone had swapped places, of which Lanietta noticed. He went back upstairs.

"She must come out once in a while, right?" Frieda asked.

"She has her own bathroom. She doesn't need to," Marna said.

"*Marna*," Frieda said. "Have you checked on her? I mean really checked on her?"

"She's a teenager. No teenager wants her room inspected. That's a violation of privacy," Marna said. "She just needs space."

"Is she doing her schoolwork at least?" Frieda asked.

Cloopy returned downstairs and dropped a double reed at Frieda's feet. Now the colors swapped places slowly, perhaps every few seconds.

"What is this, Cloopy?" Frieda asked as she picked up the reed. "Why, it's a double reed."

"Cloopy found something to play with," Marna said.

Frieda placed the double reed to her lips and blew through it.

"Sounds like a duck," Frieda said.

"Frieda! Follow me quick!" Claus barked.

"Oh, he wants to play," Marna said.

"Get the duck, Cloopy. Get the duck!"

Frieda started to stand on the couch, much as Brandi had stood on the rickety chair. The blue and yellow colors on the stone swapped places with increasing frequency to the point of flashing with impossible color disharmony.

"Frieda, no! Lanietta, you can't let this happen!" Claus said.

But Frieda paused before fully standing.

"This is wrong!" Frieda said. "It's like Brandi all over again. Cloopy, where did you find this? Show me, boy."

"Yes! Finally!" Claus barked.

Claus rushed up the steps.

"Slow down, Cloopy!" Frieda called.

Frieda followed the trail of reeds to the bottom of the steps with Marna behind. The two stood at the bottom of the steps and looked at those steps. Each step had several pieces of reed, with the higher steps having more pieces than the lower.

"Oh, Cloopy! You've gotten into something and made a mess! I'm sorry, Marna. Cloopy needs more training!"

"Yes, I've been trying to train Clomp...eh...Cloopy for a long time now," Marna said.

Frieda walked up the steps with Marna behind. Claus had been out of view, but as the women approached the top, Claus returned to the top of the steps and barked. The stone flashed so quickly that it now took on a pale pea-green color.

"Yes, Cloopy, we're coming," Marna said.

When the women reached the top, the reed trail continued down the hallway to Olivia's room. The trail was heavy and covered the air gap between the lower part of Olivia's bedroom door and the floor.

"Marna, I'm so sorry. I don't know where he got this from," Frieda said. "Is there a closet open somewhere?"

"Frieda, we don't keep bits of reed in closets," Marna said.

"Well I didn't see him go in the music room downstairs," Frieda said.

"Where else did he get the reeds, I wonder?" Marna said.

"Oh no!" Frieda suddenly realized.

Frieda looked at Olivia's bedroom door, and it was slightly ajar. Yes, Claus had been in the bedroom, and that's what Frieda realized. She pushed open the door quickly, and to the women's surprise there were piles and piles of reed shavings all over the bedroom floor, on the vanity, and on the bed. Frieda rushed around the bed and found an exhausted and dehydrated Olivia trying to blow through a double reed mounted on her bass clarinet. Beside her was the equipment for making a double reed along with a stack of uncut reed shoots.

"Olivia! Olivia!" Frieda cried as she knelt down and took the bass clarinet from Olivia's grasp. "My girl, what have you done? Are you trying to kill yourself?"

Olivia looked up at Frieda with a pale complexion and dark circles under her eyes. Frieda held her and held her, reassuring her things were okay. Claus stuck his head under Olivia's bed and pulled out a plate of uneaten food for Frieda to see. Then another and another plate.

"Olivia Jill Depetti! You've been a bad girl! This means punishment, young lady," Marna said.

"Marna! You can't be serious! Don't you see what's going on? She's punished herself already! She needs an ambulance. Call 9-1-1, Marna! Do it now!" Frieda said.

Marna shrugged her shoulders, walked downstairs, and placed a call to 9-1-1.

"What were you thinking, Olivia?" Frieda said as she continued to hold Olivia.

"I want to hear Brandi play again. I want to hear the double reed. She's part of me. Brandi. I can play like Brandi. I am Brandi. Listen," Olivia said.

Olivia reached for the bass clarinet, but Frieda prevented her.

"Here, Cloopy, chase the duck. Here Cloopy!" Olivia said.

Olivia placed a double reed in her mouth and attempted to blow through it to make it resonate like a duck. She also tried to stand, but both efforts were weak. Frieda helped Olivia to her feet, and together the two made it downstairs to wait for the ambulance. Along the way, Olivia kept saying, "chase the duck," followed by a light burst of air through a double reed. Claus followed behind to protect Olivia's hind side, though no one was there of course. It was a habit for Cloopy, and Claus found himself doing many things dog-like that also happened to be human-like.

The ambulance arrived. The EMTs put Olivia on a gurney and wheeled her into the vehicle. They immediately set up an IV line for fluids. Marna prepared to ride in the ambulance, and Frieda promised to follow up shortly.

"I'll lock up for you. Then I'll drop off Cloopy at Blair's and meet you at County Hospital," Frieda said.

The sisters hugged, Marna climbed into the ambulance, and the ambulance sped to County Hospital.

"Come along, Cloopy, we have a special mission," Frieda said.

Frieda gathered up the reeds, placed them in several garbage bags, and placed the garbage bags by the front door. Next, she gathered up the uneaten food, plates, and utensils from Olivia's room, brought them downstairs to the kitchen, disposed of the food through the garbage disposal, washed the dishes by hand (with vigorous scrubbing as if scrubbing away evil spirits of the past and present), dried the dishes, and put them away. She then stripped the bed and stuffed all such bedding and even the pillow into more garbage bags. She vacuumed the floor for remnants and cleaned Olivia's private bathroom.

"It's time to go, Cloopy," Frieda said. "Out with the old and in with the new."

Frieda loaded her vehicle with the garbage bags, let Claus in the front seat, and she drove to an industrial area. She found several unguarded dumpsters, and she removed the garbage bags and set to throw them all in. She got the bags with bedding tossed in the dumpsters, but she thought about the bags with reeds.

"Arrg, it's happening to me now. I can't put the reeds in a common dumpster. Not like this. What do you think, Cloopy? Should we give them a proper burial? With a headstone? It could say, 'Here lies reed remnants from Olivia Jill Depetti, who so loved her friend Brandi that she wanted to be like Brandi.' That would be really crazy. I have a better idea. We'll have a burial at sea."

Frieda placed the bags of reeds back in her vehicle and drove off to the oceanfront. She parked close to an unpopulated and unwatched pier, carried the bags over her shoulder, and beckoned for Claus to follow.

"Come along, Cloopy," she said.

The two reached the end of the pier.

"Lanietta? Where are you? Do you see what's happening? Lanietta?" Claus barked.

"Shhhh, Cloopy. This is a private ceremony. We don't want to attract strangers," Frieda said.

Frieda opened the first bag and dumped its contents into the ocean. Then she opened the second and third bags and also dumped their contents into the ocean. She spoke these words:

May the ocean
From which life came,
Take these reeds
And preserve their name.

The names of Brandi
And Olivia Jill,
Two friends they be
One left still.

Let no man
Disturb them be,
Just preserve that
Friendship harmony.

Take ill not from
These reeds I say,
Carry them to
The sea of life!
From this my bay.

Let it be so
Let it be true
From death comes life
In what we do.

Farewell,
Good luck,
And Godspeed.

"That was beautiful," Claus barked.

"Cloopy also wishes Godspeed," Frieda said. "Well, it's done. Let's go shopping and buy Olivia new bedding, shall we? For a fresh start and all? C'mon, Cloopy."

The memory of the Depettis, Frieda, Blair, Mocha, and Ms. Ruhm ended. Claus awoke and found himself in bed inside the Mad Mistral. Cotton was stuffed in his nostrils, and reed shoots were taped on the outside of his nose. Lanietta tended over him.

"Your nose is still broken," Lanietta said as she sponged Claus's face.

"Thanks to you," Claus said. "Was it really necessary?"

"I had to capture the memory from those reeds. The Grens will be thrilled to relive the life of Marna. Maybe even Frieda," Lanietta said.

"No!" Claus said.

"Dost thou protest?" Lanietta asked.

"Some things are best left in the past and forgotten," Claus said. "You'd be violating their memory."

"Seems to me Frieda put these reed scraps in the ocean to be remembered," Lanietta said. "I plan to take them back to Luna Beta for all to enjoy."

"Didn't you hear her at the end? 'Let no man disturb them be, just preserve that friendship harmony,'" Claus said.

"But I am no man, and I intend to preserve the harmony. Our friendship, Claus, is proof that I am harmonious," Lanietta bragged.

"You are no more harmonious than a dog pound performing Swan Lake," Claus said.

"How dare you, Clomper!" Lanietta said. "I should change you back to a dog and keep you that way. But I don't have time. We must hurry to our next destination. Cosmic eddies are in flux, and we must capture the next event before it passes. Can't disappoint the Grens."

"So you'll keep me in human form? For the next memory?" Claus asked.

"You will be in human form, yes. But you won't participate. Only watch. A pet must sometimes be content with waiting. I will do the participation. This way you can judge my performance and provide comment," Lanietta said.

"If it's anything like your last performance, I can already rate you—F for failure. No mother would allow her daughter to shut herself in a room for days on end. Yet you did so as if it were no big deal. What if Olivia had killed herself?"

"You'll wish that she had," Lanietta said.

"What is this talk about me wishing another dead?" Claus asked. "You'll never be human. You'll never understand."

But Lanietta just laughed.

"After days of travel, we have reached the proper place," Lanietta said.

"More evasion?" Claus asked.

"Collection," Lanietta said. "Hmm, this scope doesn't show the...the..."

"The what? What are you looking for?" Claus said as he stood up.

Claus walked over to Lanietta and looked through the scope. It showed an ocean surface with gentle swells.

"It doesn't show anything," Claus said. "There's nothing here."

"Oh but there is. Directly below us on the ocean floor is a spent first stage," Lanietta said.

"Where?" Claus said, and he adjusted the scope for the ocean floor. "There *is* something down there. I can see it. Looks like a...no, it can't be. But it is."

"Say it," Lanietta said.

"It's a spent first stage from a Novi-class rocket. The serial numbers are higher than I expected. It's not from the far side missions. Must be another mission. Either to an asteroid or perhaps to Mars," Claus said.

"Very good," Lanietta said. "Yes, Mars. Our next place of conquest. Still, I have you to thank. You *are*, after all, responsible for everything that has happened on Earth."

"You're lying! I can feel it in the implant!" Claus retorted.

"Oh, the seeds of the future we plant today. The genius is, you didn't even realize the seed that was planted," Lanietta said.

"Would you care to tell me?" Claus said. "I mean, we're not talking about me, are we? Are we, Lanietta!"

"And spoil my story? No way! I'm still on vacation," Lanietta said.

"You keep reminding me," Claus replied. "Why don't you tell me what *you* did. You did something in all this! Going *way* back, not just a few hundred years. Or even a thousand."

"No spoilers or diversions!" Lanietta said. "But I will let you watch. You may even know the pilot involved. Tony Kavalla?"

"I knew of him. But you're diverting from my inquiry. Care to answer?"

"Tony Kavalla," Lanietta pressed.

"Okay, okay. Yes. Tony was a summer student at Astroosa when I left for the moon. Did crop dusting on the side. Was fascinated with older aerospace design," Claus said.

"Well I play the Russian love interest," Lanietta said.

Claus fumed.

"Lanietta, leave Tony out of this," Claus pleaded.

"It has already happened. He and everyone of his time are dead. Well, almost everyone," Lanietta said.

"But you're dishonoring him and those around him," Claus said. "Forget his memory. Leave him be."

"Your sentiment is paradoxical. How do you honor people?"

"By remembering them," Claus said.

"That's what we will do, *remember* him," Lanietta said.

"But in a good light without tarnish," Claus said.

"The only tarnish brought into this memory is what you bring with you, Clomper. Too bad Cloopy has passed. You could have reprised that role. Alas, you'll have to settle for nothingness, like the infinite number of entities awaiting their point of entry onto your Earth," Lanietta said.

"Can't you go to other planets and relive those civilizations? Leave us alone," Claus said.

"You'd be surprised, Claus. There are very few places out there with advanced life-forms. Earth is a bit of an anomaly. That's why it bears further study. Well, Libriota would call it study. I call it—"

"Vacation, I know," Claus said.

"But to your point, Clomper. Turns out Mars is more interesting than you realize. Tony will learn. So will others. This is what I must experience, and the experience starts now."

Chapter 32: The Heartbeat Crusader

Claus was on the Mad Mistral's deck. He looked around and realized the boat was no longer in the ocean but was flying in the sky! The boat had an ethereal appearance, as if it were a ghost. Indeed, Claus's body also looked ghostly. Lanietta (who reverted to her bluish-green Carinian form) held a position close to Claus and pointed at a late 1950s U.S. Marine aircraft, and she narrated the following.

Tony Kavalla, Marine pilot and reserve Astroosa astronaut, was flying his F-8 Crusader. There was no war, at least none outside the aircraft, and Tony's aircraft bore no weapons. The aircraft was recovered from sea, returned to Florida, and rejuvenated into the reconnaissance craft it was meant to be.

"By me," Tony told himself while flying over the Florida Keys. "The best thing I ever did was pull my grandpa's ride from Vietnamese waters."

Tony had help, though he never spoke of how he was able to make the secret trip to Vietnam, find the aircraft, retrieve it from the coast off of Vietnam, return it across the Pacific, and get it to the airfield—all undetected. He simply showed up one day at Pelican Airfield in southern Florida with truck trailer after truck trailer of the disassembled Crusader. With the help of his mechanic friend, Phil, Tony reassembled the plane in Hangar Two and upgraded the engine, navigation control, and camera to the latest military technology.

Tony showed his masterpiece to Astroosa. Astroosa offered to install geological-sensitive instruments in the "Heartbeat Crusader," as Tony called his aircraft, but Tony declined.

"Geological equipment my butt," Tony said. "I ain't no pawn for no big corporate raider."

Tony had to be careful with what he said about Astroosa. Since the death of Joe Craigen, Astroosa had gone through a large-scale reorganization and consolidation spree and was now a major corporate space transportation supplier. Since NASA's Space Transportation System (the Space Shuttle) had been retired, smaller private companies had provided low Earth orbit transportation, but then a group of international investors and rocket scientists purchased shares in Astroosa, took it over, and drove Astroosa into beating the competition by launching large payloads at lower costs. The smaller companies went bankrupt, and Astroosa bought them for a song—all but monopolizing commercial space transportation.

"Heartbeat Crusader, Heartbeat Crusader, it's time to come in for dinner," an elderly female voice said over the radio.

"Ma, this is a military frequency. You can't use it like a megaphone," Tony radioed back.

"I don't care how old you are, you're still an ensign to me," she said. "When are you going to stop by and visit? Tomorrow is Thanksgiving, and your sister and her husband are here already."

"I'll be there, I'll be there. I'm almost done. I'm turning off the radio now," Tony said.

Tony didn't actually turn off his radio, but this was his way of saying he was done speaking, and his mother was not to reply.

"All right, but hurry up, will you?" she called back.

Tony's pleasant flight was tarnished with the thought of having to deal with his brother-in-law. Why couldn't his sister have married a normal guy, like a businessman or lawyer, or even a doctor?

"Is there a point to all this, Lanietta?" Claus said.

"Really, Clomper, you disrespect Tony's memory with this interruption," Lanietta said.

"I like a story as much as the next person, but why Tony? Really? A random memory?" Claus asked.

"You humans have absolutely no patience for the search of knowledge!" Lanietta said.

"What search? What are you searching for?" Claus asked.

Lanietta fell silent for a moment.

"Does it have to do with what you did many years ago? What you won't tell me?" Claus pressed.

"I'm going to stop narration for the moment. You'll just have to pay attention—if you want to learn anything at all!" Lanietta snapped.

I, K Gerard Martin, will continue narration where Lanietta left off. Tony finished his flight and landed at Pelican Airfield. Lanietta landed the ethereal Mad Mistral close-by, and the two followed Tony around.

"How was your flight?" Phil the mechanic asked.

"Nice until the old crow barked," Tony said. "How did she get a military radio, anyway?"

Phil looked away and whistled an odd tune.

"Just as I thought," Tony said.

"You need family time," Phil said.

"No I don't," Tony said.

"Yes you do," Phil said. "I've got other projects too, you know. Can't keep making improvements to your grandpa's old ride."

"The Heartbeat Crusader isn't just my grandpa's old ride, it *is* my grandpa. Everything he *was,* is in that craft. He speaks to me through the Crusader, and I listen."

"I know, I know," Phil said. "I've heard this all before. You know you're obsessed."

"I call it dedication," Tony said.

"Say 'hello' to Katie for me," Phil said.

"I won't," Tony said. "If I mention your name to my sister, she'll start asking about your wife and her dog breeding business."

"Oh, in case she does, let me tell you about Delina's latest dog show," Phil jabbed. "My wifey loves a good dog show."

"Dog show, dog show! How disgusting! Dogs are supposed to be *man's* best friend, not woman's best vanity showcase. It's all fake," Tony said.

"It makes Delina happy. And whatever makes her happy—"

"Makes you happy. I know, I know," Tony said.

Phil frogged Tony in the shoulder and said with a crooked smile, "Have a Happy Thanksgiving."

"Didn't know Tony had his own F-8," Claus said.

"He would seem to be enemies with his mechanic, this Phil person," Lanietta said.

"They are good friends," Claus said. "That little punch in the shoulder was how Phil showed his friendship."

"Why, Clomper! Then all the things I've done to you show the ultimate in friendship!" Lanietta grinned. "And here I had tried to be the perfect housewife. I should beat you up regularly, as a sign of friendship."

"No, it doesn't work that way," Claus said.

"Then explain Phil's behavior," Lanietta said.

"If you were human, and a good buddy of mine, I wouldn't have to explain," Claus said. "Just stick to being an alien, will you?"

Lanietta laughed.

Chapter 33: Summerly Farm

Claus and Lanietta were back on the Mad Mistral, and it floated along a country road with a car below and just ahead.

"Where are we going?" Claus asked. "It's like you have no focus."

"I'm not the one lacking focus," Lanietta said. "And to set you straight, I'll resume narration. Now listen!"

Lanietta then narrated the following to Claus.

Tony put Phil's sarcasm in the back of his mind and let the deep pulses from his father's 1967 Shelby Cobra melt his frayed nerves. He was tired of having to hold his tongue on matters he felt important while others in his vicinity spoke with poor knowledge. But he learned that as soon as he threw his critical thinking into any conversation, he was quickly named a downer, blamed for souring the mood, and branded an outcast before being socially exiled.

"I'll stop by Summerly Farm for a slice of cinnamon apple pie. Grandma Summerly makes the best," Tony said.

Tony did just that. Summerly Farm had a small storefront where it sold a part of its farmed goods, many such goods being processed from fresh farm food. There were raw foods such as eggs, milk, meat, fruit, and vegetables, and there were "processed" foods such as jams, preserves, cakes, pies, and even homemade ice cream. Next to a storefront was a small restaurant where one could have wholesome meals from farm produce.

Tony parked.

"And so shall we," Lanietta said as she parked the Mad Mistral. "Watch, Clomper."

"Tony, Tony, fly at night, kiss the girls and give them fright," May joked as Tony entered the store.

"You've got to get rid of those bells on the door," Tony said.

"Every girl should be warned when Tony enters, or else she is at his peril," she said, almost seeming to flirt. "What can I do for you today?"

"I'd like a slice of cinnamon apple pie," Tony said.

May smiled as she retrieved a slice and placed it in a box.

"That'll be three dollars," she said.

Tony gave her the money, and she gave him the box of pie and a receipt.

"I'd like to invite you over for Thanksgiving tomorrow. Heck, I'm headed to my mother's house now. Why don't you join me?" Tony offered.

"Oh," May said with dismay. "I can't."

"Why not? My mother likes you. She'll welcome you like family."

"I know, and I'm not family," May said.

"But you know how I feel about you," Tony said.

"I do, and you know how I feel about you," she said. "But it could never work."

"Sure it could," Tony said.

"We've been through this before, Tony Kavalla. I want my man to come home every night. We should be together and do things. I shouldn't worry that he won't ever come back."

"We can do things," Tony said. "I know how."

"You want a woman who will wait for you days or weeks at a time when you go off and do maneuvers or whatever the Reserves call it."

"There are times when work requires my attention, but I'll always come home to you," Tony said.

"Not every night," May said.

"My ma got by when my dad went on missions. My sister gets by when her husband goes on tours of duty," Tony said.

"And where is your dad now?" May asked.

"He's in a better place," Tony said.

"Your dad has passed. Very sad. But I couldn't be a widow," May said.

"That's not fair," Tony said.

"Look at me, Tony. I'm a farm girl. The farm is my life. Not the military. Not guns and fighting and all that," May said.

"You can adapt," Tony said.

"I won't have to. I'm getting married next June," May said. "Albert proposed last weekend at the square dance."

"At the square dance? A square dance? What's that? I thought those went out with the Civil War! And who's Albert? Another military guy?"

"No, one of Farmer Grayber's sons. They herd sheep," May said.

"*They herd sheep. They herd sheep,*" Tony mocked. "What kind of life is that?"

"A pleasant, peaceful life full of happiness and a bright future," May said.

"But you...we were meant for each other. We exchanged promises," Tony said.

"In kindergarten," May said. "What did we know back then?"

"What do you know now? You're still the same naive woman," Tony said. "You do well for some things, May, but you need a man with skills and awareness of the world. You'll wither and die with this Albert guy."

"You don't even know him!" May said.

"I know enough, from what you've said," Tony said.

"I think you've said enough," May said, now with a sound of hurt in her voice. "Say 'hello' to your mother and Katie for me."

May turned from Tony, approached another customer in the store and said, "May I help you?"

"Tony was rude to May," Lanietta said. "Another show of friendship?"

"I never knew that part of Tony," Claus said. "He likes May, but he grew up with her too. He wants to hold onto his childhood through her."

"So he is preserving his memories through her. You could preserve your memories with me. In fact, you're doing that already," Lanietta said.

"Except this isn't a memory of me. It's a memory of Tony Kavalla," Claus said.

"It's a memory of you watching Tony Kavalla," Lanietta said.

"That doesn't count," Claus said.

"All moments of existence count!" Lanietta retorted.

Chapter 34: Dinner with Katie and Oscar

Wednesday evening, and Tony Kavalla pulled the '67 Shelby Cobra in the driveway of his mother's house.

"Where will you park the Mad Mistral?" Claus asked. "It's too big for the driveway."

"In the street, of course," Lanietta said as she parked the Mad Mistral and led Claus up to Tony. "And no more narration from me. You'll have to pay attention, Clomper."

"Katie's Dodge is here," Tony said. "So is Ma's Buick."

Tony opened the back door and entered.

"Ensign Tony!" his mother said.

Tony's mother wore a festive autumn outfit and donned an apron with images of pumpkins and squash. Tony had walked in as she prepared dinner.

"I'm not an ensign," Tony said.

"Okay, Lieutenant Captain Tony," his mother joked.

"I'm an O-5, Ma," Tony said. "That's a lieutenant colonel."

"I knew it was a lieutenant c-something," his mother said. "Well, it doesn't matter. I'm glad you're home."

"This was never my home," Tony said. "You moved here ten years ago."

"And just as argumentative as ever. Why don't you say, 'hello,' to Katie and Oscar?"

It had to be done, but Tony didn't enjoy the thought. He forced himself into the living room where he thought Katie and her husband would be, but they weren't. He then looked through the sliding glass door and saw them.

"Let's get this over with," he muttered to himself.

Tony opened the sliding glass door and entered the back porch, but it was actually more like a deck as it had plenty of space for sitting, lounging, and for grilling if desired. Claus and Lanietta followed.

"Tony, Tony, how are you?" Katie said as she leapt from a chair to hug her brother.

"Great," Tony said with a hug in return.

"I have something to give you," Katie said as she relaxed her hug.

"What is it?" Tony asked.

Katie produced a pendant with a stone resembling amethyst.

"Here, put it on. It's for good luck," Katie said.

"I don't understand," Tony said. "You bought a pendant for me?"

"No. It was a gift from Frieda Morgan before she went up. Said she found three of these stones when she crashed as a kid. Fronfa she kept. Rigefa she fashioned into a dog collar for her niece. And this one...this one she made into a pendant and gave to me," Katie said as she put the chain and pendant over Tony's neck. "It has a name too. Aftova."

"Very interesting," Lanietta said. "Another one of those."

"Another one of what?" Claus said. "How is it Frieda never told me about these stones? She named them all, too. That's weird."

"You're so blind," Lanietta said. "But then again, Cloopy couldn't see what was around his neck. Like that game you humans play as children with a card stuck to your forehead. Others treat you based on the card, and you have to guess. 'Liar, smart, funny'—I bet you played that game many times."

"I've never heard of it until now," Claus said.

"Your loss. But my gain!" Lanietta smiled.

Oscar laughed when he saw the chain and pendant on Tony.

"Tony," Katie said. "You remember Oscar. My husband. From our wedding."

"The pleasure is mine," Oscar said, dressed in his full Navy captain's uniform. "Aren't you going to salute?"

Oscar and Katie laughed, but Tony didn't.

"I don't salute junior officers," Tony said.

"But I'm a captain," Oscar said.

"I don't salute captains," Tony said. "They gotta salute first. Captains are below me."

"Not in the Navy. I'm an O-6. You're only an O-5," Oscar bragged.

"Well, then go back to your submarine," Tony said, and he left the back porch.

"Tony, come back," Katie begged as Tony passed through the sliding glass door frame. "He's only making conversation."

"He's only making conversation," Tony muttered as he wandered from the living room to the dining room. "Why did Katie have to marry an O-6?!"

"Because she loves Oscar," Tony's mother said as she entered the dining room with a basket of bread. "I'm sure if May were a five star general, you'd expect Oscar to salute her."

"May would never be a general, much less a five star. Women don't make good officers, and that's a fact," Tony said.

"What about that Astroosa astronaut?" Tony's mother asked as Tony followed her back to the kitchen. "The one in Mars?"

"Her name is Jill Cresson," Tony said, "and she's not *in* Mars, she's *on* Mars performing geological studies."

"Well? She's some sort of pilot or something, right? In the Army Air Corps?"

"It hasn't been called that since 1947," Tony said.

"That's what my mother taught me," Tony's mother said. "You know, the world hasn't changed that much since the 1940s. Not really."

Tony sighed.

"That's the problem," Tony said. "Everyone's stuck in the past. Clinging to old ideas. Unable to embrace new ideas. What kind of people cling to such outdated information? Like you, they're unable to let go of their old, mistaken beliefs. And I suppose a rabbit is a rodent?"

"It is," Tony's mother said.

"Not since 1912! Old beliefs, Ma. Let 'em go!" Tony said.

"All of them?" she asked.

"All of them!"

"Including the one about women not suited for being officers? Oh, I'm sorry, that wasn't my old belief," Tony's mother returned while carrying a bowl of salad from the kitchen to the dining room. "Like Jill Cresson."

"No, not like Jill Cresson," Tony said.

"What Army Air Corps rank did you say she is?" his mother asked.

"I never did say," Tony said as he followed his mother back to the kitchen.

"Why not? Are you afraid to *embrace new ideas*?" Tony's mother chuckled.

"She's a colonel in the Air Force, if you must know," Tony said.

"All I know is that she outranks you, and you have to salute whenever you see her at Astroosa," she said as she carried a casserole dish to the dining room.

"We don't salute at Astroosa, Ma. Astroosa isn't the military, it's a private business," Tony said.

"Maybe you should. Try it some time," she said, and she returned to the kitchen.

"Try it sometime," Tony mocked.

"Well, I can't do much about your attitude. But I can provide a nourishing meal. Why don't you call the others to dinner? It's ready," she said.

"This Tony character has a lot of spunk," Lanietta said. "A pity I didn't hook up with him. You're starting to tire me, Clomper. Remember—"

"You're still on vacation. Yes, I know all too well. You sound like a broken record, Lanietta," Claus said.

"Talk-back. That's better. You could learn from the ways of Tony," Lanietta said.

Tony called the other two to dinner. The four sat down at the table, and Tony's mother spoke.

"Oscar, would you like to say grace?"

"You're kidding," Tony said. "Why subscribe to superstition when substance is more satisfying?"

"Tony, please," Katie said.

"Be happy to, ma'am," Oscar said. "Dear Lord, thank you for bringing us together today, especially for Tony, who we don't see very often. Thank you for this wonderful food. In your name we pray. Amen."

"Amen," Tony's mother and Katie said.

"How charming," Lanietta said.

"You mock these people at every opportunity. I told you this memory stuff is a bad idea. I ask you again, please—"

"Leave these people alone. Now *you* are the broken record," Lanietta said. "Another thing you will be remembered for. The broken record."

"I will be remembered? Are you saying others will watch us as we watch Tony and people of his time?" Claus asked.

"Of course! Why do you think I'm recording all this? It is said higher forms of life can record information beyond that of their basic engrams. For you, those engrams are your DNA," Lanietta explained. "Others will enjoy or endure your legacy."

"There's still the search," Claus said. "You're looking for something."

"Perhaps," Lanietta said.

Oscar sat at the head of the table and carved the ham, sending slices around the table. Tony received a thin slice on his plate, which troubled him, and he said so.

"This ain't enough meat to feed a canary," Tony said. "Here, put another slice on."

But Oscar resisted.

"Hey you, Mr. Navy, I'm talking to you," Tony said to Oscar.

"Oscar is acting at my request," Tony's mother said.

"Huh?" Tony reacted.

"You've been putting on weight, Ensign. I can't let you get so heavy that you can't walk through a door," she said.

"Me? Heavy?! Absurd. Give me that ham!" Tony demanded.

"Nah-ah-ah," Tony's mother said.

"Here old man, fill your stomach with this," Oscar suggested as he passed the salad bowl to Tony.

"Old man?!" Tony retorted, while Katie and Tony's mother laughed.

Oscar disappeared into the kitchen, returned with a glass of milk, and then placed it by Tony's plate.

"You'll need lots of calcium for bone and tooth strength in your old age," Oscar joked.

"I'm not that much older than you," Tony said. "And what's this old-age talk about? You're aging just as fast as I am."

"Maybe yes, maybe no," Oscar said. "It depends on how you live and what you can do. The old can't do everything, and since you haven't started, you are old, and we are still young."

"What's all this nonsense talk, O Mr. Marvy Narvy?" Tony pressed.

"Honey, would you like to tell them?" Oscar suggested.

Katie giggled.

"Is it what I think it is?" Tony's mother asked.

Katie giggled more and nodded, "Yes."

Tony's mother stood, rushed over to Katie (who now stood up), and hugged Katie with great jubilation.

"I'm going to be a grandmother!" Tony's mother exclaimed. "O, the things you'll need. We must go shopping, first thing after Thanksgiving. We'll go on Black Friday!"

"O please, spare me from Black Friday!" Tony wailed.

"I'm sure Oscar will be more than happy to keep you entertained," Tony's mother said.

"At your service," Oscar said.

"I don't need no one's service!" Tony said, and he got up abruptly.

"Wait, you haven't finished dinner," Tony's mother called.

"I'm beyond finished," Tony said.

Tony left the dining room, passed through the kitchen, and out the back door. Claus and Lanietta followed. He paused a moment to light a cigarette, took several puffs, and proceeded to his Shelby Cobra.

"Wait," called his mother. "Tony, please."

Tony had entered his car by now, but the top was down (do Shelby Cobras even have a top?), and she stood next to the car and spoke.

"Calm down, Tony. Come back in and have some pie," she pleaded.

"I've put up with enough insults, Ma. I'm leaving," Tony said. "And I've got apple pie here to keep me company."

"But you just arrived," she said. "You can't stay one single evening and visit? If not for you, for your sister."

"She's got you and the new baby. And what's-his-face," Tony said.

"His name is Oscar," she said. "Please, can't you be courteous once in your life?"

"I got no life to be courteous to," he said. "I'll call you sometime."

"Sometime might be too late," she said.

"What is that supposed to mean?" Tony asked. "Are you planning to move again?"

"In a way. I'll be in a nursing home in a year, unless Katie and Oscar take me in, which they've already offered to do. Heaven forbid you'd lift a finger for family," she said.

"What are you talking about? Nursing home? You? Miss Iron Constitution?" Tony recoiled.

"I have Alzheimer's disease," she said. "And it's progressing rapidly. In six months, maybe a year if I'm lucky, I won't recognize my family. Not even you with your stubborn, argumentative ways."

"You're lying! You must be lying! To get attention. That's it! My mother with the perfect upbringing and perfect marriage—she's lying to get attention," Tony quivered.

"I'm not lying, not this time! Hear me out! My condition is hereditary, which means Katie will need to be tested. And you too!"

"That's the most ridiculous thing I've ever heard!" Tony retorted.

Tony fired up the engine and revved it a few times.

"Check with your doctor!" his mother yelled over the engine roar. "Chromosome 21."

Chapter 35: The Later Gator

Tony backed out of the driveway, nearly hit a passing car, and then sped away. He raced around town for a short while, dodging cars and pedestrians alike, until he thought it best to head for the more rural sections of Florida where he could vent his anger on less-congested roads. Up and down highways he drove as he went past country house after country house. Claus and Lanietta followed from above in the Mad Mistral.

"Alzheimer's. What a horrible way to die," Claus said. "A person forgets everything, including loved ones and how to function. Dignity is lost."

"Then dignity is preserved through memory," Lanietta said. "I wondered when you'd come around to my way."

"I haven't come around to your way," Claus said. "People deserve their own minds in their own time. They shouldn't have their innards exposed to the universe, which is what Alzheimer's and your memory program do. Both are disgusting, as are you!"

"Totally contradictory," Lanietta laughed.

"And stop laughing already!" Claus said. "There's nothing to laugh at here!"

Then it happened. Tony had pushed the car too hard, one too many times. Two engine cylinders lost compression and failed to provide power, turning Tony's vee-eight into an elderly-feeling slog of a six-cylinder.

"Rotten thing!" Tony yelled. "This must be royal insult night!"

With his car providing no more power than a conventional sedan, the thrill of speeding dissipated, and Tony reconciled himself to something less speedy and more inebriating, a rural tavern named, "The Later Gator".

"Open until four a.m.," Tony said. "That oughta do."

Tony parked, as did Claus and Lanietta. The three entered. The place was rather busy, with people dressed in cowboy and cowgirl attire. For a moment, Tony thought he was in Texas. There was a mechanical riding bull in one corner and line dancing in another. Tony fought off his initial surprise and headed to the bar counter.

"Do you have a menu?" he asked the bartender.

The bartender laughed.

"Whatever you can think of, I can make," he said. "But if you want to be a man really fast, try your luck with the Gator Goblet."

"Gimme a Gator Goblet," Tony said.

"You'll have to take it to a table," the bartender said.

"What's wrong with the bar?"

"Too many accidents. Lori, show Mr...Mr..."

"Tony," Tony said.

"Show Tony to a Goblet table," the bartender said.

"This way, please," Lori said.

Lori led Tony from the bar counter to a section of the bar a bit out of the way but somewhat close to the mechanical bull.

"I'll be right back," she said after showing Tony his seat.

There was a jukebox behind and to the side of Tony, playing old piano-saloon music. A disc jockey announced a man named Henry making an attempt on the mechanical bull. All cheered for the man to stay on as long as possible. Henry finally fell off as the bull moved quicker and quicker. The disc jockey asked for a round of applause and asked if anyone else would be so daring as to try the mechanical bull.

Tony took a good look at his surroundings. This part of the bar had no carpeting, no vinyl seats, no cloth seats, nor anything porous or absorbent. The floor was well-urethaned hardwood, as were walls, tables, and chairs. The waitress brought a Gator Goblet and placed it on his table. A hush fell on Tony's part of the bar. Someone unplugged the jukebox, the mechanical bull stopped, and the disc jockey focused attention on Tony.

"Give a hearty welcome to Tony! The Goblet Slayer!" the disc jockey said.

"What kind of place is this?" Tony called back.

"You've entered the Later Gator!" the disc jockey said. "Home of the world-famous Gator Goblet, guaranteed to clear your sinuses and other passages for six months! Drink up!"

"Goblet Slayer, Goblet Slayer!" the people in Tony's area chanted—even Lanietta, to Claus's chagrin.

"I just came here for a drink," Tony said. "I'm not a dog performing for its supper!"

"Hah!" Lanietta said. "I can change that! Tomper and Clomper! A canine pair for a Carinian."

"As you pointed out, this memory has passed. You have no power over Tony," Claus said.

"A pity," Lanietta replied.

Tony stood up as if to leave, but a young, highly-attractive woman no older than twenty years of age rushed over and begged him to sit back down.

"Please, don't go," she said. "The night is young, and there's so much living to do. Enjoy your drink. Please."

"Please, don't go," Lanietta mocked in similar style to Claus. "The night is young, and there's so much living to do."

"Stuff it, Lanietta," Claus said.

Tony was so struck by her pleasant demeanor and feminine charm that he sat back down and proceeded to drink the Gator Goblet.

"No, don't sip," the young woman said. "It's best to drink it as quickly as possible."

"Here, Claus! Drink this as quickly as possible!" Lanietta said as she produced an ethereal drink.

Claus started to accept the drink out of habit but then realized her game and knocked the drink to the side. Lanietta laughed. As for Tony, he followed the young woman's advice. The goblet wasn't very large, certainly nothing like a pitcher of beer or anything as such. At first, Tony

felt fine and smiled. Drinking the Gator Goblet was no big deal (so far). The people clapped and cheered, but their attention was not diverted. They kept their keen eyes on Tony as if waiting for the next phase.

Then it happened. First Tony's eyes watered, his nose ran, and his face turned beet red as he perspired profusely. He asked for water. Lori had a pitcher and glass ready for Tony. Tony didn't bother to use the glass. He instead drank directly from the pitcher. Lanietta burst out into hysterical laughter, and Claus endured her as best he could. For Tony, the feeling of fire subsided, and his complexion returned to normal. Lori gave him several tissues, and he wiped the tears and sweat from his face. All who watched applauded Tony's endurance, as he was able to keep the goblet's contents in his stomach.

"Bravo, bravo!" Lanietta said while clapping her hands. "Tony is a most excellent entertainer. I'm glad I found this memory. You must help me find other such memories, Claus."

"Interesting you are calling me by my name, Lanietta," Claus said.

"I feel I should address you as a man in such circumstances. Following on what you said about Phil showing friendship with a punch, I'd like to give you a broken car or a drink of poison," Lanietta said. "You'd be as entertaining as Tony here."

"I could use a drink of poison to end it all," Claus lamented.

The highly-attractive young woman also applauded. She re-approached Tony and said:

"There's someone I'd like you to meet. She admires you greatly."

"You know me?" Tony asked.

"Everyone knows Tony Kavalla the astronaut," she said.

"Where is she?" Tony asked, thinking that now he'd have two lovely women to entertain.

"She's shy," the young woman said. "But I'll take you to her out back."

Tony felt uneasy about this. Maybe that someone out back wasn't a woman. Maybe that someone was an accomplice ready to rob Tony at gunpoint. No, Tony had better stay inside the tavern where he would be safe.

"It's a setup," Tony said.

The young woman appeared hurt. She looked around as if not knowing what to do.

"Aw, we'll come with you," said an older man who'd had too much to eat for too many years.

Two others stood with him. Lanietta pulled at Claus's shoulder that they too should attend.

"Uh, she'd really like to meet you alone," the young woman said.

Tony looked at the young woman. She seemed sincere, but Tony didn't trust people, not like he used to. He motioned for the men to follow, and they did. Tony followed the woman out back. The men stood in the doorway.

"Now close your eyes," the young woman said.

"Now close your eyes," Lanietta mocked to Claus.

"Stop it already, will you?" Claus said.

"No, I mean it! I want you to be surprised too!" Lanietta said.

"Please!" Claus mocked back.

"Permit this indulgence, Claus. Participate in this memory in this small way. Lose yourself in the moment and forget what ills you," Lanietta said.

"Is this Lanietta the make-believe housewife speaking?" Claus asked. "Lanietta the deceiver? Lanietta the troublemaker?"

"It's Lanietta the movie watcher eating popcorn!" Lanietta said as she produced a small tub of popcorn. "Now eat popcorn and close your eyes!"

Claus ate a small bit of popcorn and closed his eyes. Tony also closed his eyes. The young woman placed a blindfold over Tony's eyes and then stood to the side. Lanietta placed a blindfold over Claus's eyes. From the distance, Tony heard high-heeled shoes clicking. The men at the door whistled in excitement. Lanietta whistled too.

"Jealous, Lanietta?" Claus asked.

"Oh, I'm *so* jealous!" Lanietta chuckled.

"I had hoped to meet you in private," the new woman's voice said.

"Then this isn't a setup?" Tony asked. "I thought I was going to be robbed, or worse."

Tony started to lift his blindfold, but the first woman urged him not to.

"Not yet," the first woman called.

"Dance with me," the new woman said.

"Dance with me," Lanietta said to Claus.

"More comments. Yuck," Claus said.

But Lanietta meant it. As the new woman took Tony's hand and placed it on her hip, Lanietta did the same with Claus. Tony understood that yes, this was a woman, no question. The men made all sorts of comments that she was a fine catch, a keeper, oh boy Tony look out. They moved the jukebox to the door and played slow music.

"I never thought I'd get to meet you in person like this," the new woman said. "I've only been lucky enough to see you on television, when you were on the space station, and when you walked on the near side of the moon."

"And I never thought I'd get to meet you Clomp, er, Claus. I've been lucky to see you on the moon, in Arberella, and here with me," Lanietta mocked.

"What's your name?" Tony asked.

"What's your name, Claus?" Lanietta mocked.

"Dolores," the woman said, and she coughed.

"Your name is Claus, husband of Lanietta," Lanietta said.

"I'd never marry you!" Claus said. "Stop putting words in my mouth!"

"Then eat more popcorn," Lanietta said as she put popcorn in his mouth.

Claus spat it out.

"I am unappreciated on my own vacation," Lanietta said. "Poor, tired Claus, who needs a Clomper nap. No, don't complain. Let's hear the rest of Tony's evening."

"Are you all right?" Tony asked Dolores.

"It's just a cough," she said.

"Take her home, Tony," jeered one of the men.

"Yeah, take her home all night!" another jeered.

Tony felt uncomfortable about the jeering, and he reached again to remove his blindfold.

"No," the new woman said.

"I want to see what you look like," Tony said.

"And I already know what you look like," Claus said to Lanietta. "I should wear this blindfold more often."

"Stop your insolence!" Lanietta said.

"Does it matter?" Claus asked.

"Does it matter?" Dolores asked.

"Yes," Tony said.

"Yes," Lanietta said.

"Looks shouldn't matter when it comes to love," Dolores said. "I love you very much. Let's get away from here and go somewhere quiet."

"Looks shouldn't matter when it comes to—" Lanietta started.

"I know the rest," Claus said. "And no, I don't trust being with you anywhere."

"Humph!" Lanietta said.

"Yeah, Tony!" jeered one of the men.

Tony could no longer contain himself. He removed the blindfold and looked, and in that instant, his eyes traveled from her toes on up, seeing a fit and healthy woman until he saw her face—she was old! In her eighties at least! How did he not figure that out!?

"What a horrible trick!" Tony yelled. "Go back to the nursing home!"

"What?" Claus said as he removed his blindfold. "Humans are disgusting!"

The men laughed hysterically. The elder woman, in tears, turned to the younger woman for comfort. Lanietta also laughed with great pleasure. She shook Claus and pointed toward a disgusted Tony Kavalla. Claus shook Lanietta back and shoved her away.

"C'mon, Grandma, let's go home," the younger woman said.

"Tony! Don't let Grandma get away!" one of the men jeered.

Tony let out a huff, turned around, stomped to his Shelby Cobra, and pulled away. He desperately wanted to spin the tires, but the engine was still down two cylinders, and power wasn't as readily available as he would have preferred.

"Let's get out of here," Claus said to Lanietta.

"Very well," Lanietta replied.

The two returned to the Mad Mistral and followed Tony's car.

"Everything's a joke to everyone," Tony muttered. "As long as the next guy is the target. I'm sick and tired of being the next guy. Trust no one!"

Moments after Tony uttered those words, an on-coming car veered into Tony's lane. Tony swerved to avoid the car, but in so doing, he collided with a large bald cypress, with a wide root base, two outstretched branches, and a plume of top branches. It caught Tony's car with its whale-tail root, like a large water creature catching its prey. The roots slashed into the Shelby Cobra without mercy, and Tony, despite wearing a seat belt, slammed his forehead into the steering wheel and suffered a concussion. The force of deceleration pulled the pendant outside of Tony's shirt and would have sent the pendant into the tree had the chain not been present. The pendant flashed yellow and blue.

"Interesting," Lanietta said, referring to the pendant, but she minimized her apparent interest and asked, "Should we experience that again?"

"I wish we hadn't at all," Claus said.

"In a moment, we will go into Tony's mind to relive his next experience," Lanietta said.

"Is that really necessary?" Claus asked.

"I insist. Eat the popcorn, Claus. Eat the popcorn."

Chapter 36: School Bus Flashback

Tony sat dazed. The world spun about, not smoothly nor consistently, but with a wobble and a start-stop, as if a yolk couldn't decide if it should spin around the inside of an egg or not. Tony had dealt with disorientation before. When he was a test pilot, he would put the aircraft into a test spin and learn about disorientation in a controlled manner. But this was different. Tony felt no motivation nor reason nor ability to understand the concept of rationalization from one step to the next. He reached out to open the door, but his left hand didn't know where to go, and despite looking directly at his hand and the door handle, his hand struggled to find the handle. With his right hand, he reached across his chest to help his left find the handle, but again—despite looking directly at the handle and his hands—Tony's hands could not find the handle.

"My eyes...I can see, but my hands do not trust what I see," Tony said.

Tony closed his eyes, and his hands found the handle. He unlatched the door and pushed to open it, but the car's deformed body made opening the door difficult.

"Come on, let me out," Tony said.

"Oh, if only we could help," Lanietta said.

"You would merely add to his suffering. That's the only help you know," Claus said, and Lanietta laughed.

Within a minute or two, a passerby helped Tony open the door and helped him sit on the upper side of a ditch. The passerby said something, but Tony, despite still being able to hear, could not focus his attention on the words and thus could not make out what the passerby was saying. Another minute passed, and police arrived at the scene. A few minutes more, and an ambulance arrived. Ambulance personnel helped Tony into that ambulance and took him to Pelagici Hospital.

"Now we examine his mind," Lanietta said.

Claus looked over at Lanietta, and she was in hospital scrubs, as if she were about to perform neural surgery. She snapped her fingers, and Claus now wore scrubs too. Claus held up a finger in an effort to stop her, but she closed that finger to his hand, snapped again, and pulled him inside Tony's mind.

Tony slipped in and out of consciousness and so lost memory of what transpired. He fell adrift in darkness with no sense of feeling or orientation. A few images flashed before him. There was the image of a dog grazing under a tree with a parked riding lawnmower in the background. There was another image of a butterfly fluttering from one plant to the next. A distant thunderstorm hovered over the ocean with sunshine and clear sky nearby.

Then he was on a school bus around two-thirty in the afternoon. It was March, Tony was in the second grade, and he was on the way home from school. The bus driver was an older man and had difficulty seeing, meaning he wouldn't see traffic lights or street signs until the last moment, forcing him to make abrupt stops and sharp turns. Quite often, Tony or a classmate would be thrown forward, back, or to the side, causing a lunch bag or other personal item to stray and travel inside the bus. This particular ride was no exception. Tony felt the bus suddenly slam forward, sending his face into the back of the seat in front. Looking down, he noticed a pack sliding along the floor from back to front. Tony continued looking down, and he saw the head of his friend, Dwayne Reese, emerge along the floor from underneath the seat.

"Dwayne," Tony said. "What are you doing?"

"Getting my pack back," Dwayne said. "Guess what? My uncle says we can visit his shop today. Sound good?"

"Yeah, I'll be there," Tony said.

Dwayne crawled back under the seat and disappeared. A big trucker's horn blew from afar but then grew frighteningly close. The bus swerved violently to the right, the left, and to the right. Several book bags flew through the air and bounced off the backs of seats. One such bag, a dark blue one, landed on Tony's head and fell into his lap. A name was penned on the side: "Phil Richter".

"Psssst!" called a voice from over the seat in front of Tony.

"Phil," Tony said.

"Shh," he shushed. "Hand me my book bag, okay?"

"Okay," Tony whispered back. "Dwayne's uncle is letting me and Dwayne play old arcade games this afternoon. Wanna go too?"

"Sure do!" Phil said. "But I can't get off the bus where you and Dwayne do."

"Huh?"

"I'll tell you later," he said, and he disappeared back down into his seat.

The bus went off the road a bit, and the tires chattered heavily from the rumble strips for several seconds before the driver returned the bus to the proper lane. After several more big-truck honkings, more rumble strips, and a few chattery birds flying by, the bus pulled over a block away from Penberg Pizza. Tony exited the bus first, then Dwayne, and as Dwayne exited, the bus doors closed. Tony looked back, and Phil winked at him. The bus pulled away, drifted off to the side rumble strip again, veered to the left, nearly hit a honking truck, went down a hill, turned to the right, and disappeared out of sight.

"Phil'll be here in a minute," Tony said.

And so it was. Tony and Dwayne watched Phil climb over a hill from behind Penberg Pizza.

"I got off the bus on Hickory Street," he said.

"C'mon, let's go," Tony said.

Dwayne led the group to the back of Penberg Pizza, which was actually a repair shop where Uncle Reese worked. Dwayne opened the door and announced his presence.

"Uncle Reese! It's me, Dwayne, and Tony and Phil, too."

Uncle Reese appeared from behind one of many arcade games filling the repair shop.

"Come on in, you chillins!" he said. "I got milk and cookies for you in the fridge."

Dwayne, Tony, and Phil followed Uncle Reese to the refrigerator. Its compressor was noisy and put out all sorts of clackity-clacking vibrations. Dwayne, Tony, and Phil sat at a small table in the shop but near the pizza kitchen and enjoyed their milk and cookies. The refrigerator wasn't the only thing making noise, however. Sounds of old arcade games chattered through the shop, sounds of a grating machine and recurrent crashing plates and silverware carried from the pizza kitchen, and sounds of newer arcade games carried from the other side of the pizza kitchen into the pizza dining area.

"Uncle Reese is the best game fixer in the world, ain't it so?" Dwayne said.

Uncle Reese just laughed.

"You're welcome to more cookies and milk," he said.

"We wanna play arcade games," Dwayne said.

"Okay," Uncle Reese said.

He showed the games to the three children and demonstrated how to activate credits without need for a coin.

"Just open this little door and flip this switch, but don't touch anything inside, or you'll get electrocuted."

Tony and Phil approached a Pong game. Tony opened the little door and flipped a switch to add a credit. An electronic block moved back and forth across the screen, bouncing off electronically-displayed barriers, including a set of electronically-displayed bars—the paddles—of which their movement was controlled by physical dials on the machine's front. Tony took the left dial while Phil took the right. Both took turns managing to bounce the block back and at other times missing, allowing the other to score a point. The game progressed quickly, and soon it was over, with Tony winning. Phil wanted to play again, so Tony opened the little door and flipped the switch again, but in his excitement, he inadvertently touched electrically-charged wires and sent current randomly through the machine and through Tony's body. The Pong game restarted, but the electronically-displayed block flashed around madly, and the characteristic Pong bouncing sounds increased in speed until the screen was nothing more than a mad mesh of blocks flitting around. The left-side mesh flashed yellow while the right-side mesh flashed blue. Then sides swapped with yellow on the right and blue on the left. They swapped quicker and quicker. Tony felt his body heat up from the electric current. He tried pulling his hand out, but no matter how much he moved it side to side, the machine was in the way, and he could not back up, either.

"Try not to move," he thought Phil said. "Take a breath, and hold it."

Tony was no longer in Uncle Reese's repair shop but was instead in the tube of an MRI machine. The machine made truck-honking sounds, low-vibrating sounds, and mad-Pong sounds. His body heated—first his left side, and then his right—from the machine's electromagnetic waves. He opened his eyes, but a cloth lay over them, and so he could not see his surroundings.

"There. All done," said the technician.

Several doctors eyed the MRI results on a large display screen. They pointed at particular areas in the brain and chest, and they made hand gestures to drill here, probe there, and suture other-where.

"Let's do it," said the lead doctor.

Several assistants moved Tony from the MRI bed to a gurney and wheeled him to an operating room. Tony felt alone and scared. He reached for the pendant, but it was no longer around his neck.

"Had to remove it for the MRI," said a technician, apparently reading his mind.

But Tony felt like the pendant was still there, as if the amethyst had buried itself into his chest. He felt for it again, but it wasn't there.

"We'll return it soon enough," the technician said.

Tony didn't know any of these people, didn't realize he was in Pelagici Hospital (a friendly place and only a short ways from his home), and couldn't remember who he was or what he did prior to the automobile accident. Except he remembered the pendant used to be there, though from where it came he could not fathom. All he could remember was that bus ride as a child, and the visit to Uncle Reese's repair shop.

"Who am I?" he asked himself, but a nurse injected something into a tube connected to Tony's arm, and Tony fell asleep.

"A mindless memory of childhood," Lanietta said. "Such a disappointment. I had hoped he would be electrocuted or something more dramatic."

"I know what happened to him. When a person sustains a loss of modern brain function, that person reverts back to the earliest of memories, those first encodings of the world that are the most difficult to undo," Claus said. "I have heard that some folk in older years can't remember what they had for breakfast but begin remembering distinct things from childhood. It is as if the layers of encodings built up over the years are lost in reverse until only the earliest of memories and mental function are left. I wonder if that is what will happen to Tony's mother with her Alzheimer's. Do Carinians have such a problem? Do they ever suffer such loss?"

Lanietta started to laugh but caught herself when she remembered the single most hated Carinian event. And she was a part of it. She buried the memory. Buried it deep.

Chapter 37: Exodus Lost

Lanietta resumed her laugh to cover her momentary lapse into bad memory. Claus took Lanietta's laugh to mean Carinians had no such health problems as Alzheimer's and correspondingly had no compassion for the problem. Lanietta had no patience for discussing the issue, and she pulled Claus back into Tony's mind to continue reliving his memory.

Tony dreamed he was awakening in a hospital room after having his tonsils out. It was less of a dream and more of reliving his past, much like the bus ride to Uncle Reese's. His throat was sore, and he moaned a little from the pain.

"Your throat hurts again?" a nurse asked.

Tony nodded yes, because he couldn't speak. The nurse adjusted the drip speed of morphine into Tony's IV line. She disappeared for a moment and then returned with a bowl of crushed ice.

"Here, have some ice. Take a little at a time and eat slowly," she said.

Tony did just that. But he didn't chew the ice. Instead, he let the ice stay in his mouth, and he moved it a little here and there, but not too much because of how sore his mouth and jaw were.

"Would you like to watch television?" the nurse asked.

Tony nodded, "Yes."

The nurse turned on the television, and the science fiction movie, *Forbidden Planet*, had just finished. Tony continued slurping ice chips. Several advertisements later, a documentary started on Skylab wreckage being found in Australia. Video of a large cylinder being carried on a cart among a crowd of Australian people caught Tony's eye. It was a sad moment for Tony, because he had always wondered if there was anything that could have been done to have kept Skylab in orbit. Dwayne had explained that saving it was no use, because no one had visited Skylab in five years and that human flight would never be the same again. Tony remembered arguing that the shuttle brought great promise for many flights into space per year. But Dwayne would say that no, the golden days of space exploration ended with Skylab.

Tony blinked his eyes, and he was an adult again. He sat up in his hospital bed, despite having bandages on his head and chest. He shared his recovery room with an older man who was watching television and—coincidentally—*Forbidden Planet*.

"Where am I?" Tony asked.

"Shh," shushed the old man. "The monster is trying to break through the perimeter force field."

However, the movie was interrupted by a news anchor.

"Doggone it!" the old man said.

"We interrupt this broadcast with breaking news. Astroosa reports they have lost contact with the Exodus One, the first Astroosa manned spaceship to Mars. We now join a press conference at Astroosa Mission Command in Orlando, Florida."

"At 0520 Eastern Standard Time, we lost all contact with the Exodus One. Efforts have been ongoing to re-establish communication, but as of yet none have been successful," said the official, which the video caption labeled as Marc Graeman, Astroosa Chief of Operations.

Several journalists shouted questions, but only part of one got through, "...and use it as a relay satellite?"

"We are looking into that possibility," Graeman said. "One moment."

Graeman held a hand to his earpiece, tilted his head down, and concentrated for several seconds. He then looked up and spoke.

"One of our unmanned satellites is coming into range, the Mars Orbiton. We'll use it as a relay," Graeman said as he nodded to the asking reporter, "in four minutes."

"Is there any indication that the astronauts on the Exodus One are in danger?" another journalist asked.

"We don't know at this time," Graeman said. "One moment, please. I'm told that the Mars Orbiton satellite entered visual range two minutes ago and has begun relaying data. Mars is currently at its closest to Earth, so there is a three minute lag. If you will direct your attention to the display screen, please."

The view changed from the Astroosa official to a video link from the Mars Orbiton satellite, which was orbiting Mars and had a long-range camera for imaging the Martian surface. The camera focused on a blurry image of the Martian horizon, but as the seconds passed, the image cleared and resolved into the landing spot for the Exodus One. The camera gradually zoomed in on the landed spacecraft, or what was left of it. It had exploded, as if a bomb had detonated from inside, and the spacecraft's walls were extended and thrown against the ground like a peeled banana.

The journalists gasped. The older man next to Tony spoke.

"Doggone it again!" he said. "They won't send another manned mission to Mars, not in my lifetime. The Martian curse will never end!"

"Curse?" Tony asked. "What...curse?"

"Boy, where have you been? All those failed missions to Mars, the lost probes, both by the U.S. and the Russians. Now they'll add this Astroosa mission to the list."

The elderly man groaned and howled in pain.

"What is it?" Tony asked.

"This is the END!" shrieked the old man.

Alarms went off, and a crash team rushed in. A doctor from the team activated a defibrillator, but it was too late. The old man's heart gave out, and he was dead. The team wheeled the man out, leaving Tony alone.

"Is...is that death?" Tony asked serenely, but there was no one in the room to reply.

Tony looked back at the television. The video feed from the Mars Orbiton continued, but a flicker of yellow/blue light started in the middle of the Exodus One wreckage.

"There appears to be some sort of energy stream coming from the surface," the Astroosa official said. "Radio waves, electromagnetic, and ionic radiation levels are surging. Now off the scale."

The flicker of yellow/blue light suddenly burst super-white, surged upward from the wreckage, and struck the Mars Orbiton satellite, rendering it inoperative. The video signal was lost.

"We've lost contact with the Mars Orbiton," Graeman said.

The journalists were silent with shock for a few seconds before erupting into a deluge of questions. Graeman, realizing the severity of the situation, ended the press conference and left. The video link to the press conference ended, and the television feed returned to the main news studio.

"Inexplicable. Just inexplicable," said the anchor person. "We have witnessed what appears to be severe damage to the Exodus One. What isn't yet known is the condition of the astronauts. Our correspondent at Mission Command in Orlando, Dwayne Reese, is covering the press conference. Dwayne?"

"Tom, I'm here with other journalists who haven't left the press conference yet. Astroosa official Marc Graeman left immediately after we saw the shocking video of the Exodus One and what appears to be the incapacitation of the Mars Orbiton satellite. Astroosa has yet to comment on the condition of astronauts Jill Cresson, John Chefwater, and Chuck Allerton," Dwayne said.

"Dwayne Reese," Tony said. "I know him. And that other name—Jill Cresson. I know her, too. But those are the only people I seem to know."

The scene shifted back to Tom, the anchorperson. Tom replayed the video in slow motion by the Mars Orbiton of the Exodus One site. A chalkboard-style line drawing by Tom was superimposed over the video replay and showed what appeared to be rover tracks unaffected by the blast. Tom asked Dwayne if this meant a rover had driven to the Exodus One after the blast. Tony wanted to hear the answer, but several visitors entered the recovery room and stood by Tony's bed. They were Tony's mother, his sister, and Oscar.

"Tony," his mother said. "I'm so glad you're okay."

"Who are you?" he asked his mother.

She turned to Katie.

"What about me? You wouldn't forget me, would you?" Katie asked.

"I...don't know you," Tony said.

"I'm Katie! Your sister!" she insisted. "Remember?"

"Why don't I remember you?" he asked.

"Concussion," Oscar said.

"I seem to remember something about you," Tony said. "Something about being a criminal. Were you in jail?"

"That's Oscar, your brother-in-law!" Tony's mother said. "He was never in jail! But you've never cared for him, so I guess that explains your strange comment."

There was no malice in Tony's voice, nor was there any in his mind. A doctor walked in at that moment.

"Are you my brother?" Tony asked.

"No, I'm Doctor Phillips," the doctor said. "How are you feeling, Tony?"

"Strange. I don't remember these people, but they claim to be my family," Tony said.

"You've sustained a concussion," Doctor Phillips said. "Your brain has been bruised, and internal bleeding further complicated things. We had to relieve the pressure, which I'm glad to say we did."

"So does that mean my memory will come back?" Tony asked.

Doctor Phillips escorted the family out of Tony's room.

"Why did you do that?" Tony asked.

"I need to discuss your condition in private, as per HIPAA regulation," Doctor Phillips said. "Mr. Kavalla, your condition...well, there's no easy way to say this. You have early-onset Alzheimer's disease."

"What does that mean?" Tony asked.

"It means it's unlikely your memory will improve," Doctor Phillips said. "A mutation on your chromosome twenty-one placed you at risk for developing Alzheimer's disease."

"Placed me at risk? You mean places me at risk," Tony said.

"Before your concussion, it placed you at risk. But the concussion activated the degenerative process. Your brain injury will not fully heal. In fact, your brain function will worsen," Doctor Phillips said.

"What's the treatment?" Tony asked.

"Stem cell therapy is still years away from being of benefit. Unfortunately, there is no treatment," the doctor said.

"And?" Tony asked.

"You will become a complete vegetable in six months. In eight months, your autonomic functions will fail, and you'll have to be placed on a life support machine. In nine months, you'll be brain dead."

"Yes!" Lanietta celebrated. "A tragedy! Finally, something of interest! Another bad memory to save for Luna Beta. I may have to edit this memory. Take out the boring parts and leave in these bits of stress and trauma."

"Edit memory? What happened to 'all moments of existence count'?" Claus said.

"We will have full memories for those academics and story tellers doing research, and the edited versions for those who want a quickie vacation," Lanietta said. "Of course a few details might need to be modified to give the memory more kick, but that's a small price to pay for excellence."

"The age-old manipulation of a people's memory for the *excellence* of another. You're just a petty crook," Claus said.

"Am not!" Lanietta said.

"Tony's going to die, and you're a petty crook!"

"He's already dead! All these people are dead. They simply died at different times," Lanietta said. "Better to get a good story out of these humans before they do. Now shush. There's more to this story."

"Can this be true?" Tony said. "I don't feel like I'll die."

"I'm sorry," Doctor Phillips said.

The doctor left. Tony refocused his attention on the television. Dwayne turned, and the Astroosa official, Marc Graeman, returned. Journalists yelled question after question, but Graeman held his hands out to hush them. Still, one journalist asked about the astronauts.

"We have reviewed the video and the data," Graeman said. "At this time, it appears that a power source of unknown origin has caused severe damage to the Exodus One spacecraft. We have determined that the Mars Orbiton has suffered unrecoverable damage from this same unidentified power source. The data we did obtain from the Mars Orbiton has confirmed that two astronauts were killed by the power source."

"Ah, this is what I want to know. This unknown power source," Lanietta said. "Could be useful for setting up a Carinian resort on Mars."

"You're leaving out something. I can sense it," Claus said. "You desperately want to know more about this Martian power source. Matter of fact, you already know something about it. What is it, Lanietta? What is it!"

"You excite easily, Clomper," Lanietta said.

The Astroosa official paused. The journalists hushed, and a graphic streamed along the bottom of the television screen repeating what the Astroosa official had said, "Astroosa confirms two astronauts dead on Mars."

"Have you identified the two astronauts who perished?" asked a journalist.

"No," Graeman replied.

"Will there be a rescue mission for the surviving astronaut?" another journalist asked.

Graeman looked away for a moment as another Astroosa official signaled from a side door.

"Excuse me," Graeman said.

Graeman exited the press conference, and Dwayne reiterated what had been said.

"Is Jill alive or dead?" Tony asked himself calmly. "Something tells me I should pine for the answer. But I...I..."

Tony lost his word and paused in strained thought.

"It doesn't matter," he said. "I'll be dead in a matter of months. The rest of the world is already dead to me. What's the point of life, anyway?"

Tony turned off the television, stood in front of the window, and stared. He stood like that for the rest of the day.

"Total dejection," Lanietta said.

"Poor guy. I know how he feels. Everyone I knew is gone. In a way I've died," Claus said.

"You have me. I'll extend your lifespan, Claus. You need not worry about death too soon," Lanietta said.

"Maybe not physical death," Claus said.

"What is *that* supposed to mean?" Lanietta asked.

"What's the point? You can never understand," Claus said.

"I want to know, Claus. I want to know why you humans persist in making new humans when those new humans are also condemned to death. Like you say, what's the point?" Lanietta asked.

"I have already told you that we continue through children. Yes, children die, but their children go on and have children of their own. Each generation learns from the prior. That keeps us going," Claus said.

"Inefficient," Lanietta said. "You spend most of your lives either learning or teaching."

"And here you are learning," Claus said. "I'd say that's inefficient."

Lanietta had no reply but instead briefly frowned before returning a smirk to her face.

"Tony?" said May Summerly from the open doorway.

Tony turned around, and May walked in, followed by Albert.

"You know me?" Tony asked.

May stifled a tear and kept speaking.

"I just wanted to see you and say, 'hello.' You used to stop by our farm for homemade food. I brought you this apple pie," May said.

May placed the pie on a shelf next to Tony's bed.

"Thank you," Tony said.

"Mr. Kavalla, we're all sorry for your accident and hope you get better," Albert said.

"Thanks. I wish I could remember you two," Tony said. "I wish I could remember a lot of things."

"Maybe if you get rest and have some pie, your memory will come back," May said, getting hopeful.

"It won't. Nor will I," Tony said. "I have...a degenerative condition. A bad one. I have nine months to live."

"I'm so sorry," May said. "Really. I am. Tony...I..."

But May broke down and ran out in tears. Albert waved goodbye to Tony and went after May. Tony returned to the window, but not for long. A nurse entered the room with food and medication. Tony ate, took his medication, and fell asleep.

"May is too soft for the edited version. She will be eliminated," Lanietta said.

"The universe would be much better with more people like May and Albert. Edit what you want. I don't care about your Carinian resort," Claus said. "Or should I say, fake resort. This is a cover. A smokescreen for something else. I can feel it."

Lanietta held a poker face and moved Claus onto the next scene.

Chapter 38: Special Visitors

Phil Richter was performing maintenance on the Heartbeat Crusader at Pelican Airfield when three motorcycles rode up. Two flanking men dismounted. The middle cycle rider walked forward toward Phil and removed his helmet.

"Phil Richter?" Graeman said.

Phil jumped down from a ladder and wiped his hands clean with a rag.

"Well hello, Marc," Phil replied. "I'm surprised to see you here, with the emergency on Mars and all."

"That's exactly why I'm here," Graeman said.

"Oh?" Phil recoiled.

"As you may have heard, Astroosa is planning a rescue mission," Graeman said. "We need to send two pilots. One will pilot the Martian orbiter, and we have some thoughts already on that pilot. But we must also find a pilot crazy enough to land on Mars."

"What's so crazy about that?" Phil asked. "You've already done it with the Exodus One."

"Yes, indeed. Any one of our Astroosa astronauts would be happy to pilot one of our modern spacecrafts," Graeman explained. "But ask them to pilot something antiquated, and they get queasy. So I'm here looking for a pilot. Word is that Pelican Airfield has some of the greatest pilots in America."

"Crazy is what they are," Phil said. "Every pilot I've seen in this here airfield has kissed death more than once."

"Good, good! As I mentioned, the pilot we need should be well versed in antique electronics," Graeman said.

"You mean like vacuum tubes?" Phil asked.

"Well, not quite *that* old," Graeman said. "But transistors and early integrated chips from the 1960s."

"In that case, there's no better expert than Tony Kavalla," Phil said.

"Tony Kavalla," Graeman said. "Hmm."

"He's the best," Phil said.

"At one time perhaps," Graeman said.

"Still is," Phil said with a stunned reaction. "You should know that, Marc. You've worked with him enough. What's this all about? If you need an expert on old aviation, Tony's your man."

"Have you heard anything about Tony's condition?" Graeman asked.

"He's in the hospital, I know that. Am planning to visit him myself," Phil said.

"Rumor is he may have suffered permanent injuries," Graeman said.

"What rumor? I haven't heard anything," Phil said.

"There's one circling Astroosa," Graeman said.

"I didn't think Astroosa cared about Tony anymore," Phil said.

"They don't. Not really. Not in that way," Graeman said.

"But now suddenly there's interest in him, is that right?" Phil asked.

"Some of his old Astroosa coworkers have suggested him as a good fit for the rescue mission. Frankly, I was hoping you had a different pick. But we're in a pinch here," Graeman said. "It's bad enough that we lost Chefwater and Allerton, but Cresson is still alive, at least we think so."

"Then bring her back to Earth!" Phil said. "You have the federal subsidy money and everything."

"It's not that simple," Graeman said. "We don't have a spacecraft we can launch in time."

"I'm confused. I thought you had a craft. And if you don't have a craft, then why are you looking for a pilot?" Phil asked. "You talk about a rescue mission, and then you say you can't launch a spacecraft in time? What kind of finagling is this?"

"Let me rephrase. We don't have a spacecraft at the Cape we can launch in time," Graeman said.

"But you have a spacecraft?" Phil asked.

"We have a command service module for orbiting Mars and a lunar lander modified to land on Mars," Graeman said. "A leftover from the Apollo era."

"What?! And you're going to launch this aboard a Saturn V? But there are no more Saturn Vs," Phil said.

"Right again, that's why we're having our technicians fit the Apollo parts to an Alatau heavy-lift launch vehicle," Graeman said.

"That's a Kazakh cargo rocket. You've got to be kidding!" Phil said.

"No, I'm not," Graeman said. "So here's the situation: we need a pilot versed in the Apollo electronics of the 1960s."

"Like I said, that's Tony Kavalla. For sure," Phil said.

One of the motorcycle escorts approached Graeman and said something in his ear.

"That's good news," Graeman said. "Send for the doctor, then. I'll return with the other escort."

The escort who spoke in Graeman's ear returned to his motorcycle, started the engine, and rode away.

"Doctor?" Phil asked.

"We've found the Kazakh doctor who designed the Alatau," Graeman said. "Very important. This doctor is our first choice for piloting the orbiter."

"Really?" Phil said.

"Yes," Graeman said. "The rescue mission, if we can pull it off, will have the Kazakh doctor control the liftoff and journey to Mars, and a top-notch American pilot descend to the Martian surface in the lunar module. The Alatau is not human rated, so careful control will be needed by the Kazakh doctor to ensure a successful trip to Mars."

"And back?" Phil asked.

"And a successful trip back, yes," Graeman said. "The doctor can handle the third stage propulsion for the Martian journey, but we need Tony for the actual Martian rescue."

"Then accompany me to Pelagici Hospital," Phil said. "We'll visit Tony together."

Graeman motioned the other escort forward and said something to him quietly.

"I know what you're thinking. Wait here a moment," Phil said.

Graeman and the escort spoke back and forth for another moment. Phil appeared on a Yamaha motorcycle, pulled forward, and revved the engine.

"Well? Let's go," Phil said.

"Very well," Graeman said.

And so, Graeman and the escort mounted their motorcycles, started their engines, and accompanied Phil to see Tony.

Phil Richter and Marc Graeman entered Pelagici Hospital, meandered through the building, and walked up to Tony's recovery-room doorway. Tony was asleep, and a nurse wrote something on a chart. She held up her palm to indicate that the two should wait for a moment, which they did, and then the nurse finished her writing and left the room with a smile.

Phil and Marc entered the room. Phil shook Tony's arm, and he awoke.

"Tony?" Phil said.

"Yes?" Tony said with a start.

"Marc Graeman and I are here to see you," Phil said.

"Oh," Tony said.

"How are you, my good old friend?" Phil asked.

"I'm okay, except I don't remember you," Tony said.

"I'm Phil Richter. Now do you remember?"

"No."

"Hi Tony," Graeman said. "Do you remember me?"

"I saw you on television at the press conference for the Exodus One," Tony said.

"And?" Graeman added.

"And that's all," Tony said. "I have amnesia."

"A shame you humans are so vulnerable to losing your memory," Lanietta said.

"You could do good by helping people with amnesia. You could adapt your technology to help us," Claus said.

"Waste my time with humans when there are plenty of you? Nonsense. I can always get another human," Lanietta said.

"If I get amnesia, would you help me?" Claus asked.

"I doubt you could forget me," Lanietta said.

"Unfortunately, I think you're right," Claus sighed.

"The rumor is true," Graeman whispered to himself.

"Do you remember anything?" Phil asked Tony.

"Just two things. One memory from when I was a kid and was playing video games in Uncle Reese's repair shop," Tony said.

"Who is Uncle Reese?" Graeman asked.

"That's Dwayne Reese's uncle," Phil said. "You know the journalist, Dwayne Reese?"

"Yes, the journalist," Graeman affirmed.

"Phil...Phil was there. Was that you, Phil?" Tony asked.

"It was. What's the other thing you remember?" Phil asked.

"I remember when I had my tonsils out," Tony said.

"Tony, about Jill Cresson. She—" Graeman started.

"They showed her photo on television. Her hair is short," Tony said.

Graeman's cell phone rang.

"One moment," Graeman said.

Graeman left Tony's room and entered the corridor. On the other end of the cell phone was Agent Keller, head of security at Astroosa.

"Did you assess Kavalla's suitability yet?" Agent Keller asked.

"I'm in the process of doing that now," Graeman said.

"I've acquired his medical report," Agent Keller said. "His cranial injuries have made him non-confrontational. He'll do whatever we say, without question. He's perfect."

"But can he still operate a lunar lander?" Graeman asked.

"We only need him to land," Agent Keller said. "Jill will pilot the lander back into orbit. And if there's a weight issue, well, since Kavalla is going to die anyway, he—"

"That's NOT an option," Graeman said. "I won't have more deaths under my watch."

"Don't forget what Jill is bringing back," Agent Keller said.

"I thought we agreed it was too dangerous to bring back," Graeman said.

"We can't afford to wait," Agent Keller said. "The investors want us to relocate outside the United States to escape the new corporate taxes. And there are other reasons."

"I know," Graeman said. "I'm disappointed they want to relocate so soon. Things were working out fine in Florida."

"Fine isn't good enough," Agent Keller said. "The world is changing, Graeman. International corporations are the new government model."

"Corporations have been influencing governments since ancient history," Graeman said.

"Influencing only, yes," Agent Keller said. "But not for much longer. Have you seen the relocation plan?"

"Not yet," Graeman said.

"I suggest you read it at your next opportunity," Agent Keller said. "It has some fascinating insights on human nature and global administration. There's also a section detailing the relocation itself."

"I will read it," Graeman said.

"I'll let you get back to Kavalla," Agent Keller said. "I'll see you at the airfield. We've found Doctor Kechenova."

"Good, good," Graeman said.

"The doctor is departing Kazakhstan as we speak," Agent Keller said.

"I'd better get Tony out of this hospital soon," Graeman said.

"Agreed. See you at the airfield," Agent Keller said.

Graeman returned to Tony Kavalla's room.

"Tony, do you remember how to pilot an aircraft?" Graeman asked.

"I don't know," Tony said. "I've been told I'm a pilot and fly an F-8 for fun, and that I once flew for Astroosa. But I don't remember any of it."

"Hmm," Graeman said. "This is a question we need to have answered."

"Let's get him up in the air, in his own aircraft," Phil said. "Nothing like a familiar aircraft to jog a man's memory. Then we'll discuss the mission."

"What mission?" Tony asked. "Do you mean a rescue mission? For Jill Cresson?"

"For the Exodus One mission, yes," Graeman said. "We need a pilot experienced in Apollo-era spacecraft."

"That's me. Or it was me," Tony said.

"You can do it," Phil said. "I know you can."

"Well, I'll do my best," Tony said. "And if it will help bring Jill back to Earth—"

"You'd be doing a great service for Astroosa," Graeman said.

"What do you say, Tony?" Phil prompted.

"Okay, I'll give it a try," Tony said.

"That's the Tony I know!" Phil said.

Tony climbed out of bed and stood in his gown. He walked into a little bathroom, changed, and came out with a shirt over his chest bandage but with his head bandage still visible. He lifted his shirt briefly, checked that his pendant was there (and it was—he had just put it on), and let his shirt fall back down.

"Ready to fly," Tony said.

But before the three could exit Tony's recovery room, a nurse intercepted them.

"You can't leave yet. You haven't been released," the nurse said.

"It's all right," Graeman said. "I'll vouch for his release."

"But the doctor hasn't cleared him. If he leaves, he could start bleeding internally again," the nurse complained, all while Phil helped Tony scoot past the nurse and into the hallway.

"No, it's fine," Graeman said. "This is an Astroosa business situation. Shh, you'll be fine. I'll follow up with official release documentation."

Graeman kept the nurse confused long enough to allow Phil and Tony to get away and out of Pelagici Hospital.

"Oh, this is getting boring again. Need another crisis," Lanietta lamented.

"I'm sick and tired of this craving for crisis," Claus said. "Since when did Carinians have a *need for need?*"

"Since the Orchians proved it could be done," Lanietta said.

"I don't understand," Claus said.

"Has your memory failed too? Or weren't you paying attention in Luna Prime and Luna Beta?" Lanietta asked. "We Carinians in normal form are law-abiding and peaceful—relatively speaking. Orchius and his kind were banned to your moon, and radiation from your sun changed them into needy beings."

"That's not what changed them. It was radiation, but not from the sun. It was from...Mars!" Claus said.

"I'll have to fine-tune your implant to block such abilities at truth. Hmm, seems to be masked already. Interesting you can still sense things from me," Lanietta said.

"Because you're blasting out such reprehensible thoughts," Claus side. "Even hearing protection will permit loud sounds to pass through."

"As you say," Lanietta said. "Anyway, they became needy. Too needy, yes, but it drove their change."

"No, the radiation drove their change. When are you going to shoot straight with me?" Claus asked.

"Well you just forget that minor inconsistency. My Carinians will get a little dosage of the *need for need*—as part of their vacation. It's temporary, like you humans when you drink alcohol. For variety. Yes, crisis for variety. Makes for good hygiene. Cleans out the laggers."

"I wish someone would clean you out," Claus said.

Chapter 39: Submerged

"I must now leave you, Claus," Lanietta said. "My role in this story begins."

"And what am I supposed to do?" Claus asked.

"Watch. Continue the inefficiency of learning," Lanietta said.

Tony Kavalla was at Pelican Airfield and in the Heartbeat Crusader. But the aircraft was not in the air. Tony simply taxied around in the craft, and taxied, and taxied some more.

"He can't fly," Graeman said to Phil as both watched from the control tower.

"Give him time," Phil said.

"Time is short," Graeman said.

Graeman's cell phone rang. He stepped away from Phil and answered it.

"Now?" Graeman said. "The doctor's plane is early. Yes, thank you."

Graeman walked back to Phil's position.

"Clear the runway, clear the runway!" Graeman demanded.

"Why, what is it?" Phil asked.

"Sir, there's...no, it can't be," said an air-traffic controller.

"It is," Graeman said. "The Kazakh doctor is landing here, at Pelican Airfield. Clear the runway!"

"Heartbeat Crusader, taxi to Hangar Two," Phil radioed.

"I'm just getting the hang of this," Tony radioed back. "Give me another thirty minutes."

"No, he must clear the runway now!" Graeman insisted.

"That's a negative. Need the runway for special aircraft landing," Phil said.

Phil looked at the radar screen and then turned to Marc Graeman.

"What kind of bird is that?" Phil asked.

"It looks like a Tupolev Tu-22M," said an air-traffic controller.

"Tu-22M3, if reports are correct," Graeman said.

Phil and the air-traffic controller stared at Graeman.

"You're kidding," Phil said. "It looks like a B-1B supersonic bomber."

"It was a quick way to get Kechenova from Kazakhstan to Florida. No insults. She flew her own aircraft as a courtesy," Graeman said.

"*She*?" Phil asked.

"Yes. Doctor Irina Kechenova. She designed the Alatau, the Panamirov, and pretty much all of Kazakhstan's spacecraft. She's also a psychiatrist," Graeman said.

"Oh, *joy*," Phil said sarcastically. "The last thing we need is another shrink."

"Hopefully we won't need her psychiatric services," Graeman said. "Her purpose is to control the Alatau during launch, the journey to Mars, and back. She'll also pilot the command module while Tony is on Mars. Phil—we launch in two days. Two days."

"Tony will be ready," Phil said.

Graeman took one last look at Tony's F-8 as Tony taxied it around. The Tupolev landed and barely missed the F-8 as it scooted out of the way just in time.

"I need a drink," Graeman said.

The Tupolev taxied close to Hangar Three. Agent Keller and his convoy of security men arrived at Pelican Airfield and drove into Hangar Three. Graeman pulled Phil away from the tower and met with Agent Keller and his agents to welcome the Kazakh doctor. A boarding ramp was wheeled to the aircraft. The pilot stepped out of the cockpit, walked down the steps, and traveled past the line of security people. At the end of the line, she met Agent Keller, Marc Graeman, and Phil Richter.

"Doctor Kechenova, on behalf of the American people and Astroosa, I welcome you to Florida and the United States of America," Agent Keller said.

"Thank you," Kechenova said.

"May I introduce Marc Graeman, head of Astroosa Mission Command, and this is Phil Richter, manager of Pelican Airfield," Agent Keller said.

The group exchanged greetings.

"You must be tired from your flight," Phil said. "We have a lounge in the tower where you can rest and freshen up."

"My flight was perfect," Kechenova said. "All except the landing. One of your old Navy planes was...how do I say...making mess all around like noodles in gravy."

"Oh, that's Ton—" Phil started.

"That's nothing to be concerned with," Graeman said. "Come. We have much planning to do. Once we're done here, we'll head over to Astroosa and start your training."

"Will this other pilot be there too, this Tony Kavalla?" Kechenova asked.

"Yes, he will. He's finishing up maneuvers now," Graeman said.

Graeman gave a wink to Phil without Kechenova seeing. Phil, Graeman, and Agent Keller escorted Kechenova to the tower, where she changed and cleaned up. A few moments later, Graeman and Keller exited the tower with Kechenova and sped away in a black limousine.

"I've got to shake Tony out of his mental block and get him up in the air," Phil said as he stood next to the air-traffic controller.

"Heartbeat Crusader, this is Pelican Airfield. It's now or never, buddy," Phil radioed.

Tony readied the F-8 at the end of a runway. He spun up the jet engine, released the brake, and let the aircraft push forward. But Phil noticed immediately there was a problem. The top of the fuselage was smooth from front to back, meaning that Tony had not tilted the wings up for proper liftoff capability.

"Tony! Your wings are down. Set the incidence up! Set it up!" Phil yelled into the radio.

It was too late. Tony's F-8 failed to generate the necessary lift to clear a row of trees at the end of the runway. The aircraft clipped the top of the trees and descended out of sight. A plume of steam followed by black smoke ascended from the place where the F-8 crashed.

Pelican Airfield went into emergency alert, with firetrucks, an ambulance, and a helicopter sent to deal with the crisis. Phil hitched a ride on the HH-3F Pelican helicopter, and once the chopper ascended in the air and cleared the trees, it was all too obvious where Tony crashed—in Pelican Swamp.

The firetrucks and ambulance could not reach him. They stopped at the swamp's edge and waited. But the chopper reached the F-8 and landed on the water fairly close, but not too close—the Heartbeat Crusader was sinking. Then to Phil's surprise, a frogman threw a small package from the Pelican helicopter while holding onto an attached string. The package inflated into a rescue boat in a split second. The frogman and another frogman jumped into the boat with a paddle each, and the two jutted a short ways over to the F-8, where they dove underwater in full scuba gear.

Not more than sixty seconds later, the frogmen surfaced with an unconscious Tony Kavalla. They quickly paddled him to the Pelican helicopter and helped him aboard, where an emergency medical technician performed treatment to clear Tony's lungs of water, restore his heartbeat, and restart his breathing.

"Well, well, well, he died," Lanietta said to Claus, suddenly appearing out of nowhere.

"Something tells me he hasn't died, that there's more to this story," Claus said. "You hardly had any time with Doctor Kechenova."

"Quite right," Lanietta said. "Let's see what's going on in Tony's mind."

"You're going to force me to invade his privacy?" Claus asked.

"Of course. I wouldn't have it any other way," Lanietta said.

Tony envisioned he was inside a Gemini capsule which itself was inside a neutral-buoyancy water tank. Phil was also in the capsule, and the two prepared for a simulation. Besides being an aircraft mechanic, Phil kept up with Apollo-era spacecraft training for any who desired it, which wasn't many at all. In fact, only Jill had requested such training in prior times, and now Tony in the following memory.

"Simulation GEM-1, Kavalla-Richter, begin," Phil said.

Tony readied himself for an extra-vehicular activity. He attached a helmet to his space suit and activated the suit-support system.

"Depressurizing capsule," Phil said.

Air escaped from the capsule and was replaced with inflowing water.

"Depressurization complete," Phil said.

"Exiting the capsule," Tony said. "Moving to the rear of the craft."

Tony worked hard to reach the rear of the craft, but he had difficulty maneuvering. There weren't enough handles on the outside of the capsule, and so Tony spent more effort fighting his own inertia than he did making progress to the rear. His heart rate jumped up to almost two hundred beats per minute, and he perspired profusely. Finally, he reached the rear of the craft.

"Rear of spacecraft reached. Attaching the AMU," Tony said.

Tony strapped himself to the AMU (astronaut maneuvering unit) and released the AMU from the capsule, but he remained attached to the tether as a safety precaution. He then operated the AMU to maneuver his body around the capsule, but the tether kept getting caught around various things—his legs, his arms, and even the AMU. Tony strained hard to complete the simulation, but the harder he worked, the more he heated up and perspired. The moisture clogged up a regulator in the suit-support system, and the air pressure crept up and up to the point where the suit's arms, legs, boots, and gloves were too stiff to move. Tony could no longer operate the AMU, and he couldn't move his arms and hands to change the settings on his suit. His visor fogged up, and so he couldn't see.

"I'm stuck," Tony said. "Cancel the simulation."

"The simulation hasn't completed," Phil said.

"What am I to do? I can't see, and I can't maneuver," Tony said.

"You're in space. You decide," Phil said.

"Pull on the tether," Tony said. "I'll find a way to reenter the capsule."

"Not yet," Phil said.

"I can't stay out here," Tony said. "How are we supposed to land?"

"Talk through the problem. Let's look at the different scenarios," Phil said. "You decide which scenario we should follow."

"Scenario One: Pull on the tether until I reach the hatch, and then pull me inside," Tony said.

"And?" Phil asked.

"What do you mean, *and?*" Tony asked back.

"How will you reenter the capsule? Your suit is over-pressurized. You won't fit through the hatch," Phil said. "And there's the AMU preventing you from entering."

"You'll have to depressurize my suit," Tony said. "Then I'll get my mobility back and be able to remove the AMU."

"I would have to reduce the pressure to a dangerously low level, to the point where you could fall unconscious, get the bends, or die," Phil said.

"It's worth the risk," Tony said.

"Other options," Phil prompted.

"Leave me out here, and you reenter the atmosphere with the hatch open?" Tony asked.

"And the result of that is?" Phil asked.

"I'll burn up, and you'll be unprotected," Tony said. "Also, my four hundred pounds of mass will pull the capsule unpredictably, meaning instead of being able to keep the capsule's heat shield in front, the capsule will be tossed in all directions. The capsule and both of us will burn up."

"Next option," Phil said.

"Cut me loose?" Tony asked.

"And?"

"You would then be able to close the hatch and reenter the atmosphere without issue," Tony said. "But I would die."

"Any more options?" Phil asked.

"I can't think of any," Tony said.

"Now pick the best one for the mission," Phil said.

"Pull on the tether so that I'll reach the hatch," Tony said.

Phil pulled on the tether, and Tony's mass approached the hatch, but the pull also sent Phil through the hatch and out of the capsule. He lost grip with the tether and was now free-floating in the water.

"Keep pulling," Tony said.

"I can't," Phil said. "I pulled myself out of the capsule. I'm now adrift in space and unable to get back in. We're both dead. Simulation over."

"But that was the right thing to do," Tony said.

"No, it wasn't," Phil said. "The right thing to do was cut you loose so I could return to Earth safely. The other options result in us both dying."

Tony awoke, and he was in the Pelican helicopter. It had just landed on its landing pad at Pelican Airfield.

"Welcome back to the land of the living," Phil said.

Chapter 40: Training

Tony Kavalla, Marc Graeman, Phil Richter, Agent Keller, Doctor Irina Kechenova, and a host of support personnel rode aboard a 747 jumbo jet now headed for Kazakhstan. On the jet, Graeman led Tony to a briefing room where Kechenova waited. Claus watched as Lanietta entered Kechenova's body.

"Tony, this is Doctor Irina Kechenova. Doctor, this is Lt. Col. Tony Kavalla," Graeman said.

Tony and Kechenova exchanged hellos, and Graeman signaled the two to sit down.

"Let's get started then," Graeman said. "First of all, congratulations Tony on passing the video simulator test. Your ability to control the lunar module during descent and ascent qualifies you for the next phase. But before we get to that, let me give you some historical background. Two years ago, the Exodus One lifted off from Cape Canaveral as Astroosa's first trip to Mars. Astronauts Cresson, Chefwater, and Allerton were on board. Three months after launch, the Exodus One landed on Mars in the middle of the Acidalia Colles hills, and Cresson became the first Astroosa astronaut to set foot on Mars. The Exodus One mission spent its time exploring the landing vicinity, analyzing soil samples, and monitoring human physiology to see the effects of a one-third gravity environment. The crew then began looking for caves in the hills. Tony, do you remember any of this?"

"No, I don't," Tony said.

"I'll go on in detail, then," Graeman continued. "The landing site for the Exodus One was chosen for a specific reason. Evidence from early NASA probes and corroborated by the Panamirov probe suggested a high probability that the Acidalia Colles hills have aquifers. That means underground water, Tony. A source of water on Mars would go a long way toward establishing a colony."

"Panamirov? What's that?" Tony asked.

"The Panamirov is a space probe orbiting Mars," Kechenova said. "It gathers a variety of data about the Martian surface. It also communicates with the Leovich, a lander on Mars, and its rover that is searching Mars for mineral resources. Our country is full of mineral resources. We are expanding our mining efforts to include outer space. Kazakhstan is enjoying an economic boom from exporting energy and resources to other countries, including the United States."

"We've been working with the Kazakhs on sharing information about Mars," Graeman said. "The Leovich lander is also in the middle of the Acidalia Colles hills, three kilometers west of the Exodus One. It has provided the strongest evidence of water to date. As it is, the Exodus One crew found a cave with a treasure-trove of rare minerals, and the jackpot—water."

"Strange," Tony said. "I don't remember hearing mention of water discovered on Mars. But I don't remember a lot of things."

"As it turns out, the discovery of water was never formally announced," Graeman said. "It's important we keep it a secret. Can't let other space groups accelerate their programs and compete with us for control of the cave and its resources."

"So what caused the explosion?" Tony asked.

"From what Cresson tells us, Chefwater and—"

"You spoke with Jill? Jill Cresson!?" Tony asked.

"Yes," Graeman said. "She's in the cave in a part that the crew sealed from the Martian atmosphere. Now Cresson told us this—the crew had discovered a self-sustaining radioactive ore emitting only alpha and beta rays. Using less than a gram of this ore, they extracted oxygen from the water and used that to create a breathable cave atmosphere. Encouraged by their success, they continued mining in the cave and found something containing a strange material."

"Material? Made of what?" Tony asked.

"They weren't sure," Graeman continued. "It was magnetic like iron but purple and crystalline like amethyst. Chefwater and Allerton took a sample of it back to the Exodus One. Something went wrong, and there was an explosion. We can't figure out what caused it. Jill is safe in the cave, for now. But she can't survive for long. The food supply was kept in the Exodus One. She has air and water, and that's all."

"A shame she didn't bring food supplies into the cave," Tony said. "That would have been the smart thing to do. But who would have guessed that the ore would explode like that?"

"Yes, yes," Graeman said. "We move on to the rescue part of the mission. Unfortunately, we don't have Exodus Two ready for liftoff. And so we must resort to a make-shift solution. Without a launch vehicle ready for use, we must turn to the Kazakhs and their Alatau. It's a heavy-lift launch vehicle. We will use it to launch an Apollo-style command/service module and lunar module to Mars, adapted for a greater length of time, distance, and for the Martian gravity. Astroosa technicians are working with the Kazakhstan Space Agency to fit the Astroosa command/service and lunar modules to the Alatau rocket as we speak."

"You made a command/service module and lunar module?" Tony asked.

"No," Graeman said. "They were meant for Apollo 20. Word was that they were scrapped, but we—"

"Incredible," Tony said. "But how did you get hold of old NASA stuff?"

"You really did lose your memory," Graeman said. "When Astroosa became one of the few suppliers of American space transportation, it bought some of NASA's old hardware, including what was left of the Apollo project."

"And the doctor here?" Tony asked.

"She will pilot the spacecraft during launch and the trip to Mars. Once you two attain Martian orbit, she will remain in the command/service module while you descend in the lunar lander. You'll find Jill, hopefully, and bring her to the lunar lander. She can then begin the ascent from Mars back into Martian orbit, if you're not up to it, and dock with the command/service module. Doctor Kechenova will then pilot the command/service module back to Earth."

"Back to the Caspian Sea," Kechenova said.

"I thought we agreed on a Pacific landing," Graeman said.

"Caspian Sea," she said.

"Well, that's just a minor detail," Graeman said. "We'll work that out before you three return to Earth."

"Caspian Sea," Kechenova said.

"You know, I could pilot the command/service module back," Tony said.

"Not this one," Graeman said. "The Alatau's third stage will be used to send the Apollo modules to Mars and return to Earth. The doctor is best qualified to control that third stage."

"Are the Kazakhs letting us use their Alatau launch vehicle for free?" Tony said.

"Some concessions were made," Kechenova said. "Mostly in regards to propulsion technology."

"The doctor speaks figuratively," Graeman said with a sweat on his forehead. "We negotiated things. They will get more space business in the future."

"Propulsion technology," Kechenova reiterated.

"Another small detail," Graeman said to shirk off the issue.

"I can't think," Tony said. "What are you saying? Where am I?"

Tony lost his hold of reality and re-experienced a moment from an earlier time.

"You left Kechenova's body for this?" Claus asked Lanietta.

"Of course. I know how much you enjoy my company," Lanietta said as she put her hand on his shoulder.

"Ick," Claus said.

"This gimbal rig will test your ability to deal with disorientation while in a spin. Use the nitrogen controls to recover," Phil said. "Left and right affect roll, forward and back affect pitch, and a twisting motion affects yaw. There are instruments in front of you indicating as such: roll, pitch, and yaw, but they are covered for this test."

Phil pressed a button, and the gimbal rig spun him in three directions. Unable to see what axes needed correcting and by how much, Tony was forced to correct the spin by guessing, and he was not doing well. Despite several attempts, things would get a little better at first only to be much worse later. Finally, Phil stopped the spinning by pressing another button.

"What's the point?" Tony said. "I haven't learned how to recover from a spin at all."

"The point of this test is to show you the importance of instrumentation and on basing your actions on those instruments, because taking action based on feeling often makes things worse," Phil said.

"You're just teaching a man how to die, that's all," Tony said. "Like the Gemini test. Just teaching death."

Still reliving his memory, Tony exited the gimbal rig and stormed out of the test room. Frustrated, he practically marched down a hallway and past a waiting area—an area where pilots waited to enter the centrifugal force simulator. Tony stopped at the doorway of the waiting area and looked in.

"Look, gents, it's Kavalla," said one of the pilots.

"Yeah, he just flunked the gimbal test," said another.

"What brings him here?" said a third.

"Is he going to take the centrifuge test?" said the first.

"He'd G-LOC into a funky chicken," said another.

"I've already passed the test in a T-38," Tony said. "Doing seven gees."

"Seven gees?!" said the first. "That's preschool stuff. We're testing for nine gees in the centrifuge. Now that's a pilot's test."

The pilots laughed at Tony.

"I'll show you a pilot doing nine gees," Tony said. "In an F-16."

Tony marched out of the room, and the pilots followed, knowing full well that Tony had only just begun flying an F-16. The crowd of pilots drew attention from others, and they continued until they reached a hangar with a two-seater F-16 being prepared for a student pilot. The student was already in the plane, and the instructor was preparing to board. Tony grabbed the instructor's helmet and placed it on his own head.

"I'll take that," Tony said, referring to the helmet.

"Sorry, this lesson isn't for you," said the trainer to Tony.

"I don't care," said Tony. "I'm going to show these children what an adult's test is all about. I'm going to show them nine gees in an F-16."

"Kavalla, we won't have you killing students and destroying the taxpayers' F-16 for your reckless adventure," the trainer said. "Stand down, or I'll make sure you never fly again."

"I'm flying this F-16, one way or another," Tony said, and he shoved the instructor out of the way.

Phil learned of this crisis and ran from the gimbal test room to the hangar where Tony now prepared to fly the F-16.

"Kavalla, don't be a fool. Come down from that F-16. You're breaching regulations," Phil said.

"Regulations are made so that people will laugh at a pilot's funky chicken dance in a nine-gee simulator," Tony said. "I'm going to learn how to handle nine gees the old-fashioned way—even if it kills me."

"It *will* kill you!" Phil said. "And that student too. You must have an experienced pilot to talk you through the test. Kavalla, Tony, please."

"Has this student been up before? Can he talk me through it?" Tony asked.

Phil and the instructor exchanged glances.

"I take that as a *yes*," Tony said.

"You'll never pull a stunt like this again. All future training will be strictly by the book. If you even get to fly again. Tony, stop."

"Too late," Tony said.

The student rode in the F-16 as passenger and "instructor". The two took off and reached a safe altitude for maneuvers. The student then unlocked the limiters that were put in place to prevent the high-stress maneuvers the two were about to perform.

"I already know how to breathe," Tony said. "So you don't have to tell me how. What do students know anyway? I'll make a series of maneuvers, each one another gee more than the last. Think you're up to it, student pilot and *instructor*?"

"I am," said Jill Cresson's voice.

"Jill Cresson!" Claus exclaimed.

"This is how they met," Lanietta said.

Jill gave out the test instructions, and Tony tested at five, six, and seven gees.

"Now we will try nine gees," Tony said.

"Remember the anti-gee straining maneuver and what it means for your breathing and the tensing of your abdomen, your arms, and your legs," Jill said. "You've done it already, just reminding you in case you're already suffering hypoxia."

"How can I suffer from hypoxia when I've got this binding mask on my face? Wish I could rip it off," Tony complained.

Tony put the F-16 into nine gees of force, and he tensed his muscles as he thought he should, but he kept the F-16 at nine gees too long, and he lost consciousness.

"Time to jump back into Kechenova's body," Lanietta said.

"What...wait," Claus said, but the scene changed.

"He's regaining consciousness now," Kechenova said. "It appears he had a small seizure. I suggest we take a break so I can evaluate his mental function."

"He's already been evaluated," Graeman said. "He has early-onset Alzheimer's. There's nothing you can do. But this blacking out is a new symptom."

"I know his condition," she said. "We Kazakhs know much about you Americans, especially those in the military and space exploration."

"I thought only the Russians knew—" Tony started to say.

"A side effect from the Cold War," Kechenova said. "Some of their 'culture' as you might say has melded into our own, for good or bad. But we have treatments that the West may not have tried. Are you interested?"

"I doubt there's much you can do," Graeman said. "Frankly, this new symptom worries me. I'm thinking that we should go with the backup pilot."

"Nonsense," Kechenova said. "Give me a little time, and I will give Tony the best tools for combating his condition."

Graeman paused in thought.

"Very well. Try what you will, Doctor Kechenova. I need to attend a meeting as it is. I'll check back with you two in an hour," Graeman said.

"I have equipment in my room," Kechenova said to Tony. "Follow me."

Tony followed Kechenova a short ways to a room assigned to Kechenova for sleep or study. There was a desk, two chairs (one for the desk worker and another for a visitor), a cot for sleeping, a small refrigerator, a closet, and a small bathroom. Kechenova sat in the desk chair while Tony sat in the visitor's chair. Tony looked at her desk and saw a photo of Kechenova with two older people—a man and a woman.

"Nice photo of you with...with..." Tony said.

"My parents," Kechenova said as she retrieved a suitcase.

"You look so...young," Tony said.

"I was sixteen," Kechenova said. "It is the last photo of my parents before they died."

"Oh," Tony said. "I should feel sad. I know I should. But strangely, I don't."

Lanietta jumped out of Kechenova's body briefly.

"Frieda's parents died. Kechenova's parents died. You and Tony have something in common," Lanietta said. "You can take a woman without fear of her parents interfering. The predator male mind. Perhaps I should have jumped into Tony's body. I could have my way with Kechenova."

"Leave these people alone. Leave me alone!" Claus pleaded.

Lanietta laughed and returned to Kechenova's body. Kechenova opened the suitcase and retrieved a shoulder harness.

"What's that?" Tony asked.

"This is for you," Kechenova said. "Wear it under your shirt."

The harness had straps for the front torso and a center patch covering the spine's upper half for the back. Tony took the harness from Kechenova and strapped it on. Kechenova retrieved a laptop and powered it on, and then she retrieved a cable and attached it to the laptop.

"So what kind of harness is this?" Tony asked.

"It's a phase-pulsing ultra-hyper-electro-dissonance stimulator," Kechenova said. "It induces a form of acupuncture without being invasive."

"This looks like a primitive version of the torso armor," Claus said. "Lanietta, do you hear me? Did you bring the torso armor into this memory somehow and alter history?"

"No, my dear Claus, I did not alter the memory," Lanietta said after jumping out of Kechenova's body. "It does suggest that the Orchians stole it from Kechenova and improved it. And here I thought the Orchians invented everything themselves. Hmm. I'll have to search for more memories on this topic another time. Perhaps the Orchians came to Earth and stole other technology from humans."

"Oh, I already dread living through such memories," Claus said.

"As long as I re-extend your lifespan every now and then, you'll have the lifespan of the universe to explore with me," Lanietta laughed, and she returned to Kechenova's body.

"Oh no. Not some Far East mumbo-jumbo," Tony said.

"It's not mumbo-jumbo. Western medicine focuses exclusively on pumping drugs into the body. But drugs are too non-selective for your condition. The harness contains three computers and redundant battery packs. Here, plug this first pack in," Kechenova said as she handed a battery pack to Tony.

"Where do these battery packs go?" he asked.

"One under each arm," she said.

Tony reached for a battery pack, but he misjudged the position, Kechenova released it thinking he had it, and it fell to the floor.

"Oh look, Tony has fallen into an old memory again," Lanietta said.

"You seem to enjoy the jump back and forth," Claus said.

"We Carinians do a space-jump whenever we need to. Get used to it, Claus. We'll be jumping around quite a bit more," Lanietta warned.

The F-16 dove toward the ground. Tony desperately reached for the ejection handle, but his hand could not find it. This was it. The runway came up quickly. Tony's hands could grab onto nothing. They were uncoordinated and disconnected. Just as Tony thought the F-16 would crash, the aircraft's nose pulled up, and Tony landed safely. The aircraft taxied to a ramp, and Jill parked it.

"You didn't pass the test," Jill said. "Climb out and report to debriefing."

Tony climbed out of the F-16 and down the exit ramp, but when he turned around to look for Jill, she wasn't there. Instead, the scenery changed. He was no longer at an airfield but was instead at the Indianapolis 500. What's more, the cars being raced were not Formula One-inspired, open-cockpit, open-wheeled vehicles, but they instead resembled Group C racing cars.

"Aww, they never should have outlawed open-wheel cars," said a neighboring spectator. "Where's the danger? Where's the chance of being killed by a stray tire or fence pole to the helmet?"

"Racing is for the living," Tony said, "not the dead."

The comment startled Tony, because he knew himself to be a dead man in waiting.

"And I am that dead man," Tony said.

"Then you should go down there and race in an open-wheeled car," said the spectator.

"No," Tony said. "Racing is for the living."

"I suppose watching a race is for the living too," the spectator said. "So shouldn't you best be going?"

"There's no *should* for me," Tony said. "*Shoulds* are for the living. I'm dead."

Tony left anyway. He walked away from the racetrack and along the edge of a scenic golf course. The birds sang and the soft swing of golf clubs soothed his nerves. He was so relaxed that he decided to keep walking and enjoy the day.

He made his way to the parking lot of a shopping center on the south side of the racetrack. Then Tony heard a helicopter with heavy air-chopping blades. The helicopter approached from the south, flew over the shopping center, and headed for the racetrack. Tony took a good look at the craft. It was not a military helicopter that he recognized, but it was armed heavily with multiple protruding guns on both sides.

"Stop!" Tony yelled, but he went hoarse and could hardly hear himself.

The helicopter flew over the speedway and commenced firing on the crowd, or at least that's what Tony judged it did based on the hysterical crowd noises. The drone from the cars stopped, and sounds of mass hysteria echoed and reverberated from the speedway. Tony ran toward the speedway to help victims, but within a few more seconds, it was over. The helicopter headed

south the way it came, leaving the speedway and a massacre behind. But before it re-flew over the shopping center, it spied Tony. It descended quickly toward Tony and attempted to fire, but it had run out of ammunition, leaving rods of steel protruding from the craft. It trained that steel toward its lower front and jousted toward Tony. Tony ran, but he fell. One of the steel rods drove into Tony's left lung, and he cried out. The craft dragged his body several yards and then ascended in the air with Tony's body still skewered on the rod. The craft flew over a tree. The tree caught Tony's body, yanked it from the helicopter, and tossed Tony to the ground.

"So gruesome," Lanietta said.

"Why are you showing me this?" Claus asked.

"Don't you find this all so fascinating? This isn't even real. Just a dream. Your dreams are often better than reality," Lanietta said.

"Our dreams can be worse. We at least have some control over real life. We do what we can to avoid bad situations. But dreams can throw you into situations you would never choose to be," Claus said.

"You chose to be with me," Lanietta said. "Are your dreams worse than that?"

"I didn't choose to be with you. The lunar far side was an unknown," Claus said. "You just happened to be there."

"And dreams are unknown too," Lanietta said. "I can happen to be there as well."

"You already are," Claus said. "I can't escape you no matter what mental state I'm in."

Tony sat by the trunk of the tree. He was in pain, bleeding, and he labored to breathe. Time passed strangely, and a mass of unharmed people poured from the raceway and trampled past him, many of whom barely missed trampling over Tony. But Tony was too injured and too exhausted to move. He simply sat there in shock, but nothing prepared him for what he saw next. A team of twenty-one horses, three wide by seven deep, pulled a train of wagons. On each wagon was a pair of blue tarps encircled with ropes. Each encircled tarp held a dead person—a victim of the helicopter rampage at the speedway. One wagon, then two, then five, ten, and on and on. How could twenty-one horses pull so many wagons? Tony stared down the length of wagons, looking for the end, and now he realized that they didn't originate from the near exit of the speedway but in fact were lined up throughout the entire outer length of the speedway as far as he could see.

"I've got to get out of here!" he said. "The helicopter...it...kills in hordes...the carnage...the massacre...the calamity!"

Tony hobbled up on his feet and hopped as best he could over to the twenty-one horses. He unhitched one of them and used the horse to transport his broken body. But by unhitching the horse, the symmetry of the remaining horses was unleveled, and the wagon train behind began snaking into waves and lashes until big left-right bias bursts smashed everything parallel to its path, creating a swath of destruction many times wider than the horse team or even the lead wagon.

Tony rode away. There were no pleasant earthen trails to follow. Instead, Tony came across traffic light after traffic light, with roads gaining more lanes and traffic lights than he could handle. No matter. The three-by-seven, twenty-one-horse team was broken. Tony couldn't escape the endless meander of tangled roads leading nowhere in a hurry. The back of Tony's neck perspired heavily. He reached back, and something was on it. He clawed at the thing to remove it, because it was hot, and he needed to cool down.

"Don't remove it yet," said a voice. "The *gallop racing* isn't complete."

"What?" Tony called.

The horse galloped faster and faster until the world seemed a blue and white swirly ball beneath hooves, spinning faster and faster until the sun and moon became laser-lines creating threads that danced and wove garments of alien design.

"Look at me," the voice said. "Focus!"

Tony slapped his own face. He looked hard, and the weaves resolved into the blond curls on Kechenova's head.

"The *gallop racing*, the *gallop racing!*" Tony uttered.

"The *calibration* is now complete," Kechenova said.

"That's my cue," Lanietta said as she jumped into Kechenova's body.

Kechenova disconnected the cable from Tony's harness and then from her laptop. She put both the cable and laptop away in the suitcase.

"You had me connected to a laptop computer?" Tony asked.

"Yes. And you experienced a hallucination," she said.

"Caused by the harness and laptop?" Tony asked.

"No. The hallucination was caused by another seizure. The harness stopped the seizure. You will suffer no more seizures and no other mental lapses while you wear the harness."

Tony drew his hands along the straps across his chest. He found that both battery packs were attached—one under each arm.

"I had to attach them," Kechenova said. "You were unresponsive."

"How long will these batteries last?" Tony asked.

"Last?" Kechenova asked.

"Yes. Are they at full power now?" Tony asked.

"Yes."

"When do they become half power?" Tony asked.

"In about fourteen billion years," Kechenova said.

"What?! How?" Tony asked.

"Each battery pack contains a transverse-lattice thorium-electron pump," Kechenova said. "You only need one pack, but two are included in case one fails, not because the thorium will become depleted, because in the lifetime of our solar system, it won't."

"A thorium battery lasting over fourteen billion years," Claus said. "Hard to believe humans came up with such a thing. Now I'm convinced the Orchians were on Earth. Probably gave the technology to the Russians. Or traded. Perhaps for human subjects? Lanietta? Are you going to respond?"

Lanietta remained in Kechenova's body and did not respond.

"What about my memory?" Tony asked. "And my early-onset Alzheimer's?"

"In theory, the harness will help you retain new memories and prevent any further cerebral degradation," Kechenova said. "But the harness is untested. There's no way to be certain until—"

"Until it's too late," Tony said.

"There's no other treatment for you," Kechenova said. "Stem cell therapy is still years away."

"Yes, Doctor Phillips told me that," Tony said.

A knock sounded at the door.

"Enter," Kechenova said.

"How is he?" Graeman asked.

"Ready for more training," Kechenova said.

"Hmm," Graeman paused. "Tony, I've discussed your new condition with our senior Astroosa doctor. I'm afraid we can't use you for the mission. Doctor Kechenova, I'm assigning a new—"

"No!" Kechenova insisted. "Kavalla is the lander pilot."

"We can't take the chance," Graeman said. "I thought you would be able to deal with Tony's early-onset Alzheimer's, but I made that decision before he developed these new seizures."

Kechenova looked at Tony. Tony's passive attitude from just a few moments ago had now faded. The harness began restoring some of Tony's old assertive personality.

"I can pilot anything you put me in," Tony said. "Let's make this mission work."

Graeman looked at Tony in surprise then shifted his gaze to Kechenova.

"He is mentally stable," the doctor said. "He will suffer no more seizures. And he is more motivated than before."

"Based on what?" Graeman asked.

Agent Keller walked up to the room and entered the conversation.

"Have you told him yet?" Agent Keller asked Graeman.

"I was about to, but now it seems Tony may yet be the lander pilot after all," Graeman said.

Agent Keller looked at Graeman in shock.

"Impossible," Agent Keller said. "Not with seizures. One seizure during landing, and he crashes."

"Since when did you become an expert in aeronautics?" Tony retorted.

Graeman and Agent Keller looked at Tony with surprise, but Kechenova expected this development and was quite pleased with how the harness had improved Tony's behavior.

"I don't have to be an expert to know what happens when a man falls unconscious. I was in the service too, you know," Agent Keller said.

"Doctor Kechenova claims she has Kavalla's seizures under control," Graeman said.

"Absurd!" Agent Keller said.

"Don't write me off so soon," Tony said. "Let's see how I do in the full-scale simulator."

"You're on, *big man*," Agent Keller said sarcastically. "But now *my* pick for lander pilot will train side-by-side with you. And if you show *any* sign of mental failure, my pick becomes pilot."

Graeman stared at the floor for a moment.

"Agreed," Graeman finally said.

"Well *I* don't agree," Tony said. "Either I'm the lander pilot, or Jill Cresson dies. No one knows the lunar module system the way I do."

"That's why SaMonn will train *with* you," Agent Keller said. "So he'll know how to land it on Mars."

"Just who's running the mission anyway?" Tony asked.

"I am," Graeman said.

"Then why is Agent Keller pushing this SaMonn piece of garbage in my face?" Tony asked.

"That's it," Agent Keller said. "I'm throwing you off this airplane without a parachute! Prove your expert piloting skills now, *boy!*"

Tony threw a punch at Agent Keller, but Keller caught Tony's arm and twisted it behind his back.

"What are you doing?" Graeman said. "Agent Keller, stop this nonsense."

"Just giving a lesson in courtesy," Agent Keller said.

"Be careful...the harness...do not damage it," Kechenova said.

But the harness detected a fight-for-life situation and stimulated Tony's brain into action. Within a fraction of a second, Tony's brain assessed the situation, made physical calculations of what Agent Keller could do versus what Tony himself needed to do, and initiated Tony's muscles into action. Tony whipped around and flipped Agent Keller to the floor.

"Courtesy lesson is over," Tony said. "You can throw anyone at me. They'll end up on the floor just like you."

"Tony, release him!" Graeman demanded.

"Very well," Tony replied.

Tony released his grip on Agent Keller. Agent Keller brushed off his suit and left.

"Doctor, please escort Tony to the simulator room," Graeman said.

Graeman left and went after Agent Keller.

"This way," Kechenova said.

"I know the way," Tony said to her.

"You do?"

"Yes. I'll show you," he said.

Tony led Doctor Kechenova to a room containing the original lunar module simulator and the command service module simulator. Already waiting in the room was Agent Keller's hand-picked pilot to replace Tony, Salphonso SaMonn. Lanietta jumped out of Kechenova and spoke to Claus.

"If you care to be involved, I'll permit you to jump into this SaMonn character," Lanietta said. "A minor part really. No chance of falling in love with another character. Certainly not the beautiful, adorable, wondrous Irina Kechenova."

"No thank you. I'll wait until this is all over," Claus said.

"You know not for what you wait," Lanietta said.

"I'll wait just the same," Claus said.

"Suit yourself," she said as she returned to Kechenova's body.

"Hello. My name is Salphonso SaMonn, but you can call me Salpho."

"And?" Tony said.

"And, I'm here to train with you on the simulator," Salpho said.

"Okay, *Sappo*, man the operator's console. Doctor, you're with me," Tony said.

"That's *Salpho*, not *Sappo*," Salpho said.

Tony climbed the steps to enter the lunar module simulator, while Kechenova prepared to enter the command module simulator.

"Wait!" Salpho said. "I'm supposed to enter the lunar simulator with you."

"Not until I'm finished establishing a baseline," Tony said.

"Lt. Col. Kavalla, your orders are to train with me side-by-side, not have me wait out here like a dog for its master," Salpho said.

"You are to feed malfunctions into the console when I tell you to, *Alpo*," Tony said.

"That's *Salpho*, not *Alpo*," Salpho said. "Hey, wait!"

But Tony and Kechenova had already entered their respective simulators and closed their doors. And so Salpho relegated himself to the operator station outside.

"Starting the first test," Tony said. "Undocking from the command module. Introduce first malfunction, *Sammo*."

"It's *Salpho SaMonn*, Tony the Trash-man-do! And here's your malfunction!"

Salpho flipped a switch.

"The hatch on the command module is jammed open," Tony said. "It won't close."

"One moment," said Kechenova.

She pressed several buttons in the command module, and the hatch unstuck.

"Closing the hatch," Tony said.

Salpho hit a few more buttons and created another jam fault.

"Sorry, the hatch is still stuck," Salpho said.

"We dealt with the jam scenario," Kechenova said. "We should move on to the Martian descent."

"Too bad. You're stuck, and the mission has failed. Get out of the LM. My turn," Salpho said.

"Can it, *Salmon!*" Tony said.

Tony cleared the fault from inside the lunar module and continued performing the simulation.

"Hey, how did you do that?" Salpho asked. "Show me what you did."

"No," Tony said.

"You must. You are required to train me on every action you take," Salpho said.

"You're a man. Figure it out, *Sally,*" Tony said.

"That's the last straw. I'm reporting you for abuse and neglect," Salpho said, and he left.

"I do not understand," Kechenova said.

"What don't you understand?" Tony asked.

"How you can abuse and neglect him at the same time," Kechenova said.

Tony laughed. Kechenova laughed. Then Lanietta left Kechenova's body and laughed too. She punched Claus in the shoulder to get him to laugh, much as Phil had done to Tony. But Claus didn't laugh.

"I'm glad I didn't let you perform Tony's part. No sense of humor," Lanietta said, and she returned to Kechenova's body.

Tony and Kechenova continued running simulations. Salpho never returned. As it was, Tony was able to simulate undocking from the command module, landing on Mars, ascending from Mars, and redocking with the command module.

"Should we try some malfunctions?" Kechenova asked.

"Naw. This simulator is good for sharpening the rough edges in my memory, which it has. I remember everything I need to do. Once the lunar module lands, I exit in a partial pressure suit and take the lunar rover in search of Jill. I then help Jill into the lunar rover, take her back to the lunar module, and ascend up to the command module, correct?"

"That is correct. There is another simulator for the Martian surface. We should try that next," Kechenova said.

Tony followed Kechenova out of the room and entered a room with the lunar module in Mars-landed mode.

"There's a lunar rover in here!" Tony said.

"Yes. A lunar rover and the lunar module," Kechenova said. "We must plan for the following bad scenario. Cresson might be unconscious and thus unable to walk under her own power. You would then lift her onto the rover when you find her, travel to the lunar module, and lift her into the lunar module. Wearing equipment at one-third gravity of Earth is equivalent to us on Earth with no equipment."

"What do you mean by *us*?" Tony asked.

"I will play the part of Cresson," Kechenova said. "You do the rest."

Doctor Kechenova then reclined on the floor as if she were unconscious.

"You're kidding," Tony said.

"Do not waste time. I am Cresson, and I could be out of oxygen with only moments to live!" Kechenova ordered.

"The rover isn't designed to lift people," Tony said.

"You must lift me," Kechenova said.

Lanietta left Kechenova's body and spoke to Claus.

"I should force you into Tony's role here," Lanietta said, "to teach you how to be a man. As it is, I require that you watch and take notes."

Lanietta returned to Kechenova's body. Tony knelt beside her. He placed his arms under her back and legs, lifted her up, and then placed her on the rover.

"What if I have broken bones? My neck could be injured. The way you lifted me could cause more damage," Kechenova said.

"But then I'd have to secure her to a stretcher or rescue basket, or onto a backboard at a minimum. I need power equipment to lift her onto the rover. And I don't know how I can move her into the lunar module," Tony said. "Will there be power equipment for this mission?"

"No," Kechenova said.

"Then what's the point of training? What's the point of this mission if we don't have the proper equipment?" Tony lamented.

"Don't blame the doctor," Graeman said, now entering the room with Agent Keller and Salpho.

"There, you see? He's questioning the mission!" Salpho said. "I say you take him off now and put me in as lander pilot."

"I already canned you once, *Soapy-jaw*," Tony said.

"Kavalla, I decide the personnel on this mission, not you," Graeman said. "Is that clear?"

"Really? You're going to put this neophyte in? Did you consider what to do if Jill is injured? The rover needs a crane with a winch," Tony said.

"I'm sure she will be fine," Graeman said. "We know she's alive and that she is not injured."

"But what if something happens to her in the next three months? That's how long it will take to reach Mars. Speaking of three months, I still can't believe the Alatau's third stage has enough thrust to get us back to Earth. The two planets will be out of position by then. You never explained that part of the mission."

"The important thing is that Cresson is rescued. Isn't that so?" Graeman said.

Tony paused for a moment. He wanted to say something, but he didn't.

"Good. Salpho will train with Doctor Kechenova on the landed lunar module simulator," Graeman said. "Kavalla, come with me."

Tony glared at Graeman defiantly.

"Now, Kavalla," Graeman said.

Tony followed Graeman out of the landed lunar module simulator room and down the hall.

"Why did you do that?" Tony asked.

"You've completed training," Graeman said. "There's nothing more for you to learn on this mission."

"The heck there isn't. I haven't piloted the lunar module from the Martian surface into orbit with Jill on board. She may need special treatment," Tony said.

"Not to worry. Salpho will train for that part," Graeman said. "Once he completes his training, the..."

But Tony had heard enough talk of Salpho. He walked away from Graeman. He walked and walked through the jumbo jet, not so much as where but just to walk. In any other moment, the stress would have triggered another seizure or flashback into some past memory, but he still wore the harness, and that harness prevented such a lapse. He walked and walked until he found a workout room. He entered, activated a treadmill, and walked on it at a quick pace. His memory improved, and he racked his brain to remember key points in his life: his childhood years of interacting with classmates, studying for and passing tests and examinations, playing board games and outdoor games, and finally, he managed to remember the jogging he did in the woods behind his house. Up a steep hill with his feet turned sideways for extra traction, then down the other side using tree branches to slow his descent. Up another hill using branches to help pull himself, then down a sandy slope with no trees, no branches to steady his fall, just his brain to direct his feet, legs, and arms to slide down the side while shifting his mass to maintain balance. Sliding and shifting and sliding until he slid to the bottom and slipped into a creek.

Tony increased the speed on the treadmill, and his pace changed from a walk to a jog. He could now remember flying his F-8 over Florida, into the Gulf of Mexico, along the Florida coast, and down to Cuba. He remembered using onboard cameras to take photographs of Cuba, the coast, the people, the buildings, and the farms. Not an easy aircraft to fly, the F-8. He focused on the never-ending adjustments he made to the craft to fly it exactly as he wished. His mind raced, but he kept up with his own internal calculations.

He increased the speed of the treadmill again, and now he was running. His heart rate increased, and he breathed heavily. Breathe, man, breathe! Tony replayed the Exodus One mission to Mars in his mind. He was amazed at how well his memory from before the accident was returning. Was this because of the harness? Had to be so, but there was no indication the harness was doing anything. Tony pulled up his shirt, and several indicator lights blinked furiously on the battery packs. Tony wasn't sure if that was good or bad, but there was no other indication of harness malfunction, so he continued running on the treadmill. The Exodus One mission, yes. It was the first manned Astroosa mission to Mars, with Cresson, Chefwater, and Allerton. Unmanned crafts had landed before in order to use existing elements in the Martian air and soil to generate fuel for the return journey, and that fuel became ready for use, and so the manned mission was launched. It landed in the middle of the Acidalia Colles hills, a mere nine hundred kilometers north-west of the "face" on Mars.

Then it happened. Jill Cresson took the first Astroosa step on Mars. She said that humans would no longer be restricted to living on Earth, that they had at last cast off Mother Earth's apron strings and begun colonizing other planets. Cresson commanded the mission. She ordered the other two astronauts to explore the Acidalia Colles hills and do their best to live like a colony before being forced back to Earth. The three explored and looked for the means to live off of Mars, but the Exodus One had no major facilities for growing food—only limited experimental stations. That didn't stop Cresson. She ordered additional explorations.

One day, she reported that the team had opened up a natural Martian cave. The news was hushed, intermittent, and diverted to Martian weather forecasts and talk of how Martian rovers worked. It wasn't until just now that Tony learned of water being discovered in the cave. Tony made the connection that Martian water plus Martian energy equaled a self-sustaining colony. No wonder Graeman and Astroosa hushed things up.

Then the accident happened that killed Chefwater and Allerton. All because of a strange amethyst ore? That was never publicly announced. The last the world had heard was that the crew had gone to the cave for the Martian day to look for natural resources. And what they found had enough power to destroy the Exodus One ship and maim the Orbiton satellite.

The ultimate question was thrust upon Tony's mind: should he investigate the source of that destructive power? It was a tempting thought. Harnessing a new source of energy would open up the possibilities of a colony on Mars. That much Tony kept tossing in his mind. He just couldn't let it go. Perhaps Tony could be a part of that colony with Jill working at his side. The colony would work in harmony—all simply had to labor hard to make it work. The colony could expand to support more people, and science experiments could be conducted free of such Earthly distractions as vanity, crime, and politics.

"Oh the euphoria, a fresh utopia created *in memoria*," said Lanietta to Claus.

"You're not a good poet," Claus said.

"What will he do, when he meets the crew, of Exodus One, when two are done? What will he say, when Jill will not play, with ideas of Tony, which turn out to be phony?" Lanietta continued.

"Of all the exploits of humanity, this is the worst!" Claus said.

"You mean my poetry?" Lanietta asked.

"That and everything else! It used to be the ruling class subjected the less fortunate to slave labor and then low-pay labor. Now we are exploited simply for being alive—and by an alien species! There's a word that rhymes with *species* I could use to describe you!"

"How dare you! You humans haven't evolved nearly enough to appreciate the ways of the universe. But you aren't so innocent, are you? Even the poorest of you exploited other animals for their labor. Your tilling of the fields with beasts of burden, your pulling of carts with horses. You should give me credit, Claus. I've never made you my beast of burden. You've always been my pet. I could make you bark, but I don't. How's that for democracy?"

Claus could not respond. Instead, he resigned himself to the moment of watching Tony. Tony increased the treadmill speed to a sprint. His respiration was very much labored, and his heartbeat was well above the therapeutic range. His cells fell into anaerobic respiration, and they began accumulating lactic acid.

Tony went back in his mind to the Mars question. He calculated that for such a colony to survive, communication with Earth would have to be limited. Too easily would Earthly demands be placed to send back results of experiments—results that instead of being used to help people would be used by only the select few to exploit others on Earth. It was a wild idea, and Tony had no specifics to support his feelings. But as a trained pilot, he knew that feelings were dangerous and could get a man killed. Trust instruments, not feelings. But there was one feeling Tony could not ignore—the pain his flesh endured from oxygen deprivation.

"I...must...push myself...to the edge," Tony said, and he reached to increase the treadmill speed beyond what a human could run.

"No!" said a voice.

A slender finger slowed the treadmill down gradually until Tony regained his breath and composure. It was Doctor Kechenova, and she knew what Tony was trying to do.

"That's enough training," she said. "We now begin the mission."

Chapter 41: Journey to Mars

Though Salphonso SaMonn completed the same simulator training as Tony, he did not perform as well as Tony, at least according to Graeman. Because of this, Tony kept his lander pilot job, and so the mission was ready for launch. Tony Kavalla and Irina Kechenova in full spacesuit garb entered the command module atop the Alatau heavy-lift launch vehicle. Technicians hooked them in and closed the hatch. The call sign for the command module was *Callisti*, while the call sign for the lunar module was *Lacuna*.

"Astroosa, Callisti. Do you read?" Kechenova called into the radio.

"Callisti, we read you loud and clear," Graeman said.

"All systems on board are a go for liftoff," Kechenova said.

The countdown continued for Callisti. Astroosa controls were relayed through a Kazakhstani control station to the Callisti command module. Video of the launch was broadcast throughout the world in various languages. Back at home, Phil Richter watched on television as an Astroosa telecaster announced the final words.

"Ten, nine, eight, seven, six, five, four, three, two, ignition, and liftoff! Liftoff of Callisti on a rescue mission to Mars."

The booster rockets from the Alatau pushed the entire craft into the sky. After a minute or so, Callisti reached a critical point of dynamic pressure.

"Now passing Max-Q," called Astroosa to Callisti.

"Max-Q is the point of maximum dynamic pressure," Lanietta said to Claus. "The Alatau's engines were purposely kept running at less than one hundred percent to minimize stress on the spacecraft's frame.

But now Max-Q has passed, and so the Alatau is free to thrust at one hundred percent."

"I know about Max-Q," Claus said in despair. "Everyone knows about Max-Q."

"Callisti, go at throttle up," called Astroosa to Callisti.

Claus knew the phrase well. It was the one just before the Challenger exploded in 1986. Words like that don't fade.

"Roger, go at throttle up," Kechenova said.

"There, you see? No explosion," Lanietta said to Claus, reading his thoughts. "I realize a story without an explosion is dull and boring, but stick with me. There's something yet to discover."

"I wish I didn't have to stick with you," Claus said.

The Alatau engines throttled up successfully. Elevation was now 50,000 feet. The first stage continued thrusting until the craft reached 200,000 feet. Then the first stage separated, and a second stage fired, sending Callisti into orbit. The second stage dropped off, and Callisti made a complete orbit around Earth to check instrumentation.

"Everything is go for Mars," Kechenova said.

"The third stage will fire in three, two, one, and ignition," called Astroosa to Callisti.

"That's it," Tony said to Kechenova. "That was Astroosa's last automatic control on Callisti. From here to Mars, we are on our own."

"Not entirely," Kechenova said. "We will maintain radio contact with Astroosa. I also have a separate link to Kazakhstan to answer media questions and official communication."

"What official communication? You mean orders from higher-up people in your government?" Tony asked. "This is an Astroosa operation."

"They are not orders. Just diplomatic conversation. If your President speaks with you, it will be much the same," Kechenova said.

The third stage continued to thrust toward Mars. It had now been thirty minutes since it started to thrust, and Tony became concerned.

"Something's wrong," Tony said. "There can't be enough fuel to keep thrusting. Don't you agree, Doctor Kechenova?"

"Under normal circumstances, I'd agree. But—"

"This thrust is at a constant one gee of acceleration. There's no way we have that much fuel. Which means only one thing. We're burning up our fuel needed for orbit insertion. We must abort. We must!"

Tony reached for a button to alter Callisti's course such that it would return to Earth.

"Wait," Kechenova said as she pulled Tony's hand away from the controls. "Let me explain."

Kechenova pressed a few more buttons to lock the controls out from Tony tampering with them.

Tony froze in shock.

"You locked the controls. What is going on?!" he said.

"I regret they—" Kechenova started to say, but she was interrupted.

"Astroosa, Callisti. Astroosa, Callisti. Come in, Astroosa," Tony called, but there was no reply.

"They will not reply, because the controls are still locked out," Kechenova said. "We are in temporary radio silence. Now allow me to explain how—"

"There *is* no radio silence. At least there's not supposed to be," Tony said.

"You must trust me, Lt. Col. Kavalla," Kechenova said. "I am fully versed in this mission, but one part has not been revealed to you. Let me—"

"Trust you? How? You kept me in the dark about a vital part of the mission. But you'll earn my trust if you unlock the controls so we can abort. There's no sense in us both getting killed for nothing," Tony said.

"But how am I to trust you?" Kechenova said. "If you act against the mission, it will fail."

"It already has!" Tony said.

"No, it hasn't," Kechenova said. "If you calm down and listen, I will explain the fuel situation regarding the third stage."

Tony rolled his eyes, but he regained his composure enough to listen.

"Okay. Explain the rocket thrust and the fuel. Why are we still at one gee? The fuel will run out any moment. In fact, it should have run out by now."

"First, I want us to trust each other," Kechenova said. "I will call you Tony, and you will call me Irina."

"Huh?"

"The first name is the first step of trust," Kechenova said. "Now say 'hello'."

"Hello," Tony said.

"No, not that way. Address me by my first name. I'll start. Hello, Tony."

"Hello, Irina."

"Hello, Claus," Lanietta said as she briefly exited Kechenova's body.

"Forget it, Lanietta," Claus said.

"How else are we to build trust?" Lanietta laughed.

"Go back to your role," Claus sighed.

"Good, Tony. How are you?" Kechenova asked.

"Fine," he said.

"Good," she said. "Now as a sign of my trust in you, I will release the control lockout. See? I trust you."

"And I trust you too," Tony said.

"Good, good!" she said. "I'll let you make the next course correction. We're coming up on it in thirty seconds. Think you can handle it?"

"Yes," he said. "Here goes."

But Tony decided Kechenova was trying to distract him. He needed to abort the mission, and he needed to do it now. Without warning, Tony pressed several buttons to pitch the spacecraft a hundred and eighty degrees around so he could make the trip home. But he misjudged his ability to shut down the engine before performing the pitch. The engine kept thrusting, and this generated great gee forces. Tony felt the blood drain from his head, but his training took over, and he squeezed his major muscles to keep as much blood in his head as possible. He breathed hard, and Kechenova breathed hard. Both strained against the gee forces but could not reach the controls. The spacecraft was now pitching out of control without heading back to Earth as Tony had hoped. An onboard radiation meter buzzed a warning indicating excessive levels.

"Radiation," Tony tried to say despite the gee forces.

Tony's vision narrowed, and he blacked out. Kechenova groaned like an animal straining under the jaws of death. She fought the controls and managed to get the pitch under control, and in doing so she headed the spacecraft toward Mars. Tony experienced brief convulsions as he returned to consciousness.

"Engaging radiation protocol number one," she said as she pressed several buttons.

"Oh, Claus! That was devious of Tony! Would you have tried it? I think you would have enjoyed playing such a trick on me. I still remember the trick you played in Luna Beta. See? My memory is quite good," Lanietta said.

"Sometimes I wish otherwise," Claus said.

Tony smelled something metallic in the air, but it dispersed in a few seconds.

"Radiation has been neutralized," Kechenova said. "Don't try that again, or we'll be killed."

"What is going on? Where did the radiation come from? It couldn't have come from us. Or could it?" Tony mused.

"I tried to explain this before, but you kept interrupting," Kechenova said.

"We *are* using something radioactive," Tony said. "We flew right through our own thrust trail. That means our engine is nuclear. Oh man, oh man, that's how we're able to thrust for so long. We're nuclear!"

"Yes, Tony Kavalla, we are nuclear," Kechenova said. "Now you know the secret of this mission."

"But how?" Tony asked. "Nuclear power in outer space of this magnitude is banned by treaty. The old Soviet Union and the United States signed that treaty in 1963."

Doctor Kechenova smiled.

"Your memory continues to improve," she said, "but Kazakhstan never signed the treaty."

"That's right. Your country never signed. Does that mean you're using Russian nuclear technology in space? How did you manage that deal?"

"Try to control your impulsive conclusions," Kechenova said. "Astroosa cannot afford to spend three months going to Mars. You started to ask Graeman about it, but he diverted you. As it is, the Alatau third stage was retrofitted with nuclear propulsion. We didn't take it from Russia. We developed it ourselves. It is experimental and not yet tested, but Astroosa didn't want to wait, so now we test it."

"Not tested? That's dangerous bordering on suicide!" Tony said.

"This is the only way," Kechenova said. "Do you think your American astronaut could survive for three months? Jill Cresson? The Exodus One is destroyed. How will she survive?"

"But nuclear technology in space," Tony said. "And you couldn't tell me about this? Who else knew?"

"Astroosa," Kechenova said.

"Graeman?" Tony asked.

Kechenova nodded yes.

"Who else? Agent Keller?" Tony asked.

Kechenova nodded again.

"They agreed to it," Kechenova said. "In fact, Graeman provided designs from the 1960s—designs they purchased from NASA."

"And that was the *propulsion technology* you requested in exchange for providing transport to Mars?" Tony asked.

"No, we want the improved version," she said.

"What could be more improved than this?" Tony asked.

"There's always the improved version," she said.

"But Astroosa is an American business. They are sure to get the United States into trouble."

"Astroosa is an international business that happens to be in America," Kechenova said. "Astroosa assured us that they would handle all publicity regarding nuclear propulsion in space. Look, Tony, we must bend the rules this one time. Please."

"If I were on Earth, I'd go off for a drive or a long walk and think about this," Tony said.

"But you are not on Earth. You are in this spacecraft with me, Doctor Irina Kechenova. That's what space travel is about. You can't run off and leave your problems behind. You must live with them until the mission is over," she said.

"Yes, Claus. You are in this memory with me, Lanietta the Carinian. That's what being my pet is all about. You can't run off and leave me behind. You must live with me until the memory is over," Lanietta said.

"At least you admit that you are my problem," Claus said.

"Humph!" Lanietta returned.

"If you want to dream about being home," Kechenova continued, "I can link your harness to my laptop—"

"You brought your laptop?" Tony asked.

"In case I need to control your harness," she said.

"No," Tony said. "I'd better stay conscious for this entire mission."

"Irina has interesting ideas," Lanietta said. "Perhaps I should rig a harness for you, Clomper. Keep you in line and all."

"So you can fry me with thorium radiation?" Claus said. "Forget it."

"Don't knock it till you try it," Lanietta laughed.

The third stage fired for eight total hours, and then it stopped.

"Burn complete," Tony said.

"Good," Kechenova said. "We now coast for fifty-six hours. I suggest we eat dinner and get some rest."

"Sounds good," Tony said. "What do we have on the menu?"

"Peach chicken salad," she said.

Kechenova retrieved two containers of chicken salad and placed them in the re-hydration oven.

"What would you like to drink?" she asked. "We have diet, juice, sweet tea, and—"

"Sweet tea," Tony said.

"I will have a diet," she said.

Kechenova placed the sweet tea and diet soda in the re-hydration cooler. Within a couple of minutes, food and beverages were ready. Kechenova placed them on a tray for each of them and passed a tray to Tony.

"Dinner is served," she said. "Enjoy."

"Thank you," Tony said. "Mmm, not bad."

"Food has improved since the early days of space," Kechenova said. "Do you remember eating food before as an Astroosa astronaut?"

"No, I don't," Tony said. "Mmm. I really can't get over how good these peaches are. They really did a good job with this space food. It reminds me of when I was a boy. Dwayne Reese and I would...oh, you're probably not interested."

"No, please tell me," Kechenova said. "I'm fascinated by stories about being young in America."

"Well, Dwayne Reese and I were picking peaches on his Uncle Reese's farm, and we picked both clingstone and freestone peaches," Tony explained. "Then, we decided to play a joke on people in town. We set up a peach stand and offered people a free peach if they could open it by hand. We'd demonstrate by opening up a freestone peach and eating it. Simple, right?"

"Sounds simple," Kechenova said.

"But when someone tried to open a peach that we gave them, they couldn't. That's because we gave them a clingstone peach," Tony said. "Well, we fooled a lot of adults, but May Summerly came along, and we tried the same trick on her. She must've known about the trick already, because she accused us of giving her a clingstone peach when the peaches we opened were freestone. We didn't like being caught, so we threw peaches at her. She threw them back, and we didn't want to get hit, so we hid behind our stand and threw them. She hid behind a tree, and then other kids came along and threw peaches back from behind things like bushes and fences. One kid hid behind a car, and we threw our peaches at him. Some sailed over the car, but some hit. The freestones made a mess on the car, but the clingstones made little dents. We didn't care, and we kept throwing peaches."

"Then the owner came by and got mad," Tony continued. "The other kids ran away, and Dwayne and I tried to get away too, but the man caught us, he found out where we lived, and boy did we get in trouble. Dwayne got a switching for punishment, and I had to spend all summer cutting people's grass to pay for the dents and damage done to that car from throwing peaches."

"That's a good story," Kechenova said. "You learned a moral lesson."

"Yes, I did," Tony said. "But these peaches...there's something about them, it's like, well, they're not quite as acidic as I remember."

"They are white peaches from Kazakhstan," Kechenova said. "I made this peach chicken salad and had it packaged. I don't have quite the peach story to compare with yours, but I can say that as a child, I remember walking through a peach orchard with my friends. We'd each find a delicious white peach, pick it from the tree, and eat it as we walked along and enjoyed the summer day. Those were carefree days, Tony, before I went to engineering school and designed spacecraft and all that hectic work. Someday when we return to Earth, I'd like to show you around Kazakhstan. We have many parks and forests and wild orchards, some with the Siverse apple, the ancestor of most apples in the world."

"You're forgetting something," Tony said. "I have early-onset Alzheimer's disease. I'll be dead in nine months."

"I'm hoping not," Kechenova said.

"The harness?" Tony asked.

"Yes."

"You seem to place a lot of faith in your design," Tony said.

"I take all of my designs seriously," Kechenova said. "They are like my children, bred to a specific purpose. If they exceed that purpose, then it is like the child growing up and doing better in life than a parent, with the parent being me."

"I'm surprised you went through with that explanation, Lanietta," Claus said.

Lanietta darted out of Kechenova's body.

"Why does that surprise you? I know the role to play," Lanietta said.

"But you would never speak those words on your own initiative. What things have you created? Of value? Seriously? Here's a woman who takes pride in adding value to humanity, and you take pride in destroying such value," Claus said.

"I do not. I am, after all, preserving these records," Lanietta said.

"But that's all you can do. You cannot create. The Orchians came close to that. But not you. Even the basics of humanity, that of creating another life-form, is beyond you. Were you so hoping you could be a wife to me that somehow the powers of the universe would allow the greatest pleasure and honor of creation? Impossible! You're nothing more than unguided, unprincipled energy," Claus said.

"I know how to create, in a way far beyond your comprehension!" Lanietta retorted.

"I doubt it," Claus replied.

"I have been very patient with you, Clomper!" Lanietta said as she welled up with anger.

"You mean Claus?"

"No, Clomper! Another outburst like that, and you can live through this memory as Clomper the dog!" Lanietta threatened.

"Why do I even try?" Claus lamented. "I will listen. I hope you can do more."

Lanietta's anger subsided. She returned to Kechenova's body, and Kechenova resumed speaking.

"It is my hope the harness keeps you alive until you are very, very old, Tony Kavalla."

"And if the harness breaks or wears out?" Tony asked.

"I guess that means I must keep in good contact with you, at least as friends, so that I may repair and maintain the harness. We *can* be friends, right?" Kechenova said.

"Of course," Tony said.

Kechenova leaned over and gave Tony a kiss on the cheek.

"I don't remember *that* being part of the Astroosa astronaut training," Tony said.

"Well, I am not officially an Astroosa astronaut. I'm a Kazakh cosmonaut," Kechenova said.

"So is kissing a crewmate part of *your* training?" Tony asked.

"No," Kechenova smiled.

Claus turned away.

"What's the matter, Claus? Jealous?" Lanietta asked as she dipped out of Kechenova's body.

"Dignity violated at the lowest level," Claus said.

"There *are* lower levels. In lower life forms," Lanietta said.

"End this memory now. I'll sacrifice myself as a lower life form," Claus offered.

Lanietta laughed.

"I may take you up on your offer. But you must be sincere. No faking," Lanietta chuckled. "As for this memory, the answer is 'no'. I will not let it end, not yet. There is more to see, or don't you care about the energy source on Mars?"

"I don't," Claus said.

"Not even what it means? What it means to the future of Earth?" Lanietta asked.

"Mars is a dead world. We've known this from the probes," Claus said.

"I'm glad you believe that," Lanietta said. "It will put you in your place when the time comes."

"What will? What will put me in my place?" Claus asked.

"When the time comes! It is not yet time for that. It is time to resume this interaction between Irina and Tony," Lanietta said, and she dipped back into Kechenova's body.

Kechenova continued her smile. Tony smiled back. The two finished their dinners and disposed of their containers. Kechenova went over the spacecraft's controls quickly to confirm Callisti's course and function.

"Everything is A-okay," she said.

"Very good," Tony said.

"We have a little time before sleep," she said. "Would you like to watch a movie?"

"No," Tony said. "I need time to think."

"About what?" Kechenova asked.

"I...wait a moment. I just remembered. You're a psychiatrist," Tony said.

"And?"

"And? Well, you want to psychoanalyze me," Tony said. "So I'd rather think to myself."

"I don't have to psychoanalyze you," Kechenova said. "If you like, I can. But as your crewmate, I *am* interested in being rested and in good spirits. A successful mission works best when stress is low. We'll have plenty of time for stress when you land on Mars and look for Jill Cresson."

"That's what I wanted to think about," Tony said. "I suppose you're going to say I have this obsession with Jill."

"I wasn't going to say that, but it's interesting you should mention it," she said.

"Ever since the accident, my strongest memories are of my childhood. That's a fact. But I remember very little of my adult years. And yet the memories are coming back, thanks to the harness. But the one puzzle is that of Jill Cresson," Tony said.

"Do you know that Jill Cresson is married with five children?" Kechenova asked.

"What? I never heard that. The news said she is single," Tony said.

"Yes, single. Divorced, in fact. I was just testing you. Sometimes people just agree so as to advance the conversation," Kechenova said.

"I researched her while I was in the hospital," Tony said.

"Because of her part in the Exodus One mission?" Kechenova asked.

"Because I wondered if she was part of my childhood memories," Tony said. "I thought that if she were part of my childhood, I would remember something like a crush on her. I have no childhood memories of her. Then I thought, if I had any memories of her as an adult, I would have asked her out on a date. But I don't remember asking her out or anything. It's almost as if she and I went different ways—if we were ever friends at all. Strangely, I remember hearing about her running a couple of training missions."

"From what I read about Jill Cresson, she graduated at the top of her class in high school, university, and aced her way through the American Air Force," Kechenova said.

"I've often imagined what she might have been like as a child. She'd be smart and knowledgeable. Why, she would have memorized the entire World Book Encyclopedia. I would ask her anything, and she'd know the answer. Me, I would have to look it up. Being book smart wasn't my strength. I had better skills with tools and devices. But you know what? She would have good practical ability too. Now take me, for example. If I had a flat tire on my bicycle, I'd remove the wheel, pop off the outer tire, and put a patch on the inner tube. Now you'd think Jill would be from a rich family and have the bicycle serviced, right?"

"No, I—" Kechenova tried to say.

"Here's what I imagine. She *would* get the bicycle serviced, but for free. Can you imagine? She'd take her bicycle to the bike shop, and she could look at a bent bicycle frame, you know, when a car runs over a bicycle. Anyway, she'd take a look at that frame and explain precisely how to unbend it and where so that it would never look bent at all. The bike repair guy there wouldn't be able to follow her train of thought, so he'd let her do the unbending, and he'd give her all kinds of free inner tubes and parts. In fact, he'd offer her a job right there, but she'd say she was too busy with other things, and she'd only work as a form of bartering when she needed something."

"Interesting," Kechenova said.

"Continuing my imagination, I would try playing chess with her—forget it. She would look so far ahead that she'd make a move where at first she'd lose a piece, but then she'd end up winning because it gave her a superior position," Tony said.

"A sacrifice," Kechenova said.

"Exactly," Tony said. "I can imagine more stuff. She'd always do better than me in class. I would resent it. But then at the beginning of fifth grade, she'd take on other hobbies. I mean real hobbies, not something like needlework. But that would be the beginning of the end."

"She would also participate with others in one of those hobbies," Kechenova said.

"There you go. Yeah. She'd go to a private high school. Whereas I would go to...went to...I went...now where did I go to high school?" Tony mused.

"Westwarr High School," Kechenova said. "A public school named after Howard Westwarr, a saloon owner and bootlegger during your American Prohibition. He—"

"Strange that a high school would be named after a bootlegger," Tony said.

"He made quite a bit of money during his younger days," Kechenova said. "When he was older, he changed and became more philanthropic. He donated money to many causes, including a new high school that was named after him."

"That is what I'll do, Claus," Lanietta said, dipping out of Kechenova. "I'll exploit you humans then name one of your high schools after me. Lanietta Carinia High School. Or Lanietta Depetti High School. Perhaps even Lanietta Gerhardt High School."

"You'll never bear my name. Never!" Claus shouted.

Lanietta laughed and dipped back into Kechenova.

"How do you know so much about me and about my high school?" Tony asked.

"It is one of my hobbies," Kechenova said. "I like to study people and places, especially people I work with."

"It's almost...creepy," Tony said.

"You think so? Where I come from, we like to share stories about ourselves. I know you don't remember much about your past. So I studied about you on the way over from Kazakhstan to Florida."

"I heard you flew over on a Tu-22M," Tony said.

"Yes," she said.

"That you piloted the Tu-22M," Tony said.

"Yes. I had time to read," Kechenova said.

"In a Tu-22M!?" Tony asked.

"What can I say? I'm very versatile," Kechenova said. "Well then, Tony, I think it is time for sleep. What do you say? Have you cleared your mind enough?"

"I think so," Tony said.

"Good. Have pleasant dreams, Tony," Kechenova said.

"Goodnight."

"And it is time for you to sleep," Lanietta said as the two returned to the Mad Mistral.

"My nose is healing," Claus said as he sat up in bed. "Was it all a dream?"

"More like a coma," Lanietta said as she sponge-cleaned his face.

Claus looked around and saw an IV nutrient solution bag hanging up to his left with a tube running into his arm.

"I've been in a coma? Strange, I don't remember injuring myself, other than the broken nose," Claus said.

"I put you in a coma. For efficiency," Lanietta said, still sponge-cleaning Claus.

"What!? More abuse? That's unethical, immoral, and criminal! Who knows what you've been doing to me!"

"We've been watching Tony and Irina. Nothing more. But you're tired, or you soon will be. Let's get you a fresh set of clothes and then—"

Lanietta had turned away for some clothes as she spoke, and Claus took the opportunity to rip the IV needle from his arm and dash upstairs to the deck. His arm bled, but he didn't care. He was desperate and needed to end it all anyway. He ran to the boat's edge, jumped, and flew through the air until he landed in the ocean.

"The blood will attract sharks. Good. The only way to escape abuse is through death," Claus said.

Claus continued bleeding, but he passed out from blood loss before he could be sure of his own impending death.

Chapter 42: The Search for Jill Cresson

Claus awoke, and he was back in bed in the Mad Mistral. An IV line was attached to him containing a red liquid.

"Is that blood?" Claus half asked himself.

"It is re-hydrated synthetic red blood cells in a saline solution," Lanietta said. "Created by Morcellus for just this voyage. Lucky for you I pulled you out of the ocean and tended to your needs. You slipped and fell over the edge."

"I didn't slip well enough, apparently," Claus said.

"Now, now, now. Your time is not yet up. There's more to learn about Tony and Irina. Here we go!"

Claus and Lanietta returned to the Callisti voyage to Mars. Lanietta jumped into Kechenova's body while Claus could only watch in ethereal form.

Time passed. Tony and Kechenova awoke fresh the next day, ate, and shared many stories about their past. They became fairly acquainted with each other, so much so that Tony nearly forgot the purpose of the mission. It soon came time for sleep again, the two slept, and they awoke for another "day" of storytelling. Another night of sleep, and the two awoke in time to turn the spacecraft around and fire the third stage engines to begin the eight-hour deceleration burn.

"Notice I have activated the dynamic radiation shield," Kechenova said. "This protects us from the radiation you exposed us to earlier."

Nearly eight hours later, and Mars grew large in the window. Kechenova shut down the nuclear engines and used the maneuvering thrusters for final course adjustment.

"This worked out well," she said. "We're ten minutes away from orbit insertion."

"Mars," Tony said. "We're here. How long did it take?"

"We are at tee plus seventy-two hours. And you can forget about any attempt to abort the mission. We are here. Once we achieve a smooth Martian orbit, you'll transfer over to the lander, you'll undock, and you'll land on Mars as planned," Kechenova said.

"Yeah, as planned," Tony repeated sarcastically.

"One more thing," Kechenova said. "I've made a special modification to your harness. You'll be able to transmit and receive signals on Ultra-High Frequency and Super-High Frequency."

"UHF and SHF," Tony said.

"Yes, and that includes S-band, C-band, and all three K-bands," she said. "This way I'll be able to keep in contact with you no matter what problems you might encounter."

"Do you foresee any problems?" Tony asked.

"Not with the landing. But the phenomenon that killed two of your astronauts, it—"

"Yes, the phenomenon," Tony said. "I'll handle it."

Callisti achieved smooth Martian orbit. Tony was about to transfer over to Lacuna when Kechenova stopped him. She kissed him and said, "That is for good luck."

"I won't be long," Tony said.

"Do not rush, and do be very careful," Kechenova said. "I am becoming quite fond of you, Tony Kavalla."

"You go too," Lanietta said to Claus as she dipped out of Kechenova's body.

"What?"

"You accompany Tony. I will remain with Irina," Lanietta said.

"And miss out on whatever is down on Mars?" Claus mocked.

"I will see everything through your eyes, and your ears will tell me anything you say or hear," Lanietta said. "I might have to space-jump around Mars or other places in the universe. I can't babysit you all the time, Claus Gerhardt!"

"You don't need to 'babysit' me at all! In fact, I'd be most grateful if you would give me a rest and disconnect from me altogether!"

"Now, now, when the cat's away, the Clomper will play," Lanietta warned. "In Lacuna you go, there's a good boy. Until we meet again!"

Tony settled himself in Lacuna, Claus was forced into Lacuna with him, and the hatches closed.

"Lacuna, Callisti. Sound check," Kechenova called from the command module's radio to the lunar module's radio.

"I read you loud and clear," Tony said.

"Lanietta to Claus, do you hear me?" Lanietta's voice sounded.

"Yes, Lanietta, I hear you. I didn't expect to, though," Claus said. "I was looking forward to the peace and quiet."

"Oh, you would miss me, my sweet Clomper!" Lanietta said. "Now sit tight! Lacuna is preparing to leave!"

"Stand by for a check on your harness transceiver," Kechenova said to Tony.

Tony concentrated on the harness input, and Kechenova spoke.

"Tony, this is Irina. Can you hear me?" she called from a small device on the back of her wrist.

"Yes, I can hear you. Can you hear me?" Tony asked.

"I hear you very well, Tony," Kechenova said. "I want to wish you good landing and a safe return to Callisti."

"Doctor Kechenova," Tony said.

"Please, Irina on this channel. No one can hear us. Our transmission is spread scrambled," Kechenova said.

"Irina. If I'm not successful, I—"

"You will be successful," she said.

"But if I'm not. I just want to say...thank you," Tony said.

"You will do fine," she said, and she fought back a few tears. "Now switch to main ship-to-ship communication."

"Callisti, Lacuna," Tony said. "Undocking in three, two, one. Undock complete. Building separation. Ten meters.

One hundred. Two hundred. Five hundred meters."

"Lacuna, Callisti. Successful separation is confirmed. Begin de-orbit procedure," Kechenova said.

"Beginning de-orbit burn," Tony said.

"Tony, this is Irina on the private harness channel," she said. "Please don't try calling back to Astroosa directly, just in case. I am in communication with Astroosa and can relay what they need to know. The rest is for us only. Astroosa and the world are monitoring our ship-to-ship communications and are receiving our telemetry, so they know what is going on. Okay?"

"I like the way you think," Tony replied. "Agreed."

The lunar module descended gradually through the Martian atmosphere and approached a site east of the Exodus One in a crater.

"Callisti, Lacuna. Lacuna has landed. I am two kilometers east of the Exodus One," Tony called in the lunar module's radio.

"Lacuna, Callisti. Acknowledged," Kechenova replied. "I have established a data link with the Panamirov. Surveillance data indicates tire tracks are found a kilometer south-south-west of your position."

"Callisti, Lacuna. Received and understood. Preparing for EVA with the Lacuna rover," Tony said.

Tony secured his helmet, strapped an environmental pack to his suit, depressurized the lunar module, and exited through the hatch. It was daytime, the air was clear, and Tony stood in the crater. Claus in his ethereal state stood with him.

"I see nothing but rocks and orange dirt all around," Tony said with his suit's radio. "I can't see the Exodus One."

"You landed in a crater," Kechenova said. "You wouldn't be able to see the Exodus One unless you traveled over the rise and went west. But do not go west—that's a mistake! Now then, the lunar rover is secured behind a fairing. Did you release the rover for use?"

Tony looked back at the lunar module, and the rover was hidden from view behind a fairing.

"No, I didn't," Tony said.

"You may release it either from inside Lacuna or from your forearm panel," Kechenova said. "The little orange button."

Tony looked at a control panel on his left forearm, and there was the orange button. He pressed it. A fairing split into two and receded toward opposing sides of the spacecraft, revealing a rover. The rover was lowered to the Martian surface and released from the lander. Tony entered the rover and connected his suit's life support system to that of the rover. He then actuated the rover and directed it south-south-west in search of Jill.

"Callisti, Lacuna rover. Now heading south-south-west out of the crater," Tony called through the rover radio.

"Lacuna rover, Callisti. Acknowledged. Callisti is being carried out of radio contact range. I will check on your progress when line-of-sight is re-established."

"Acknowledged," Tony called.

"Lanietta, can you hear me?" Claus said. "Perhaps Mars can block her too. Oh, wouldn't that be a good respite?"

"I can get a hold of you if need be," Lanietta's voice said.

Claus sighed and continued along with Tony. The rover proceeded smoothly up out of the crater and reached the rise. As it did, the power and controls on the rover fluctuated briefly. A detection meter indicated a spike in radiation levels from the west. Tony tried continuing south-south-west, but the rover sputtered and flashed indicator lights and struggled to go much of anywhere. Tony managed to get the rover turned back down into the crater, and when it dipped below the rise, it regained full power and control.

"Radiation," Tony said to himself, and then he had the thought of making contact with anyone who might answer, even Astroosa.

"Lacuna rover to anyone," Tony called on the rover radio. "Does anyone read me?"

No answer.

"Perhaps if I use the harness radio, I can pick up an Earth satellite transmission," Tony said to himself.

Tony imagined holding the end of a rope with the other end attached to a fixed object. He then imagined whipping the rope and sending a wave to the object. The wave returned in his mind. In reality, the harness tuned its receiver to lower SHF, starting with S-band moving upward. At first he received a jumble of transmissions—overlapping voices mixed with squawking sounds. S-band was no good, so he imagined sending a wave on the rope again but more quickly, and the harness moved up to C-band. At first Tony received satellite feeds skipping off Earth's atmosphere. But then he heard a voice. It was Phil Richter communicating with a ship in the South Atlantic via satellite.

"Hurry to the mainland as fast as you can," Phil said. "Tensions are critical between the U.S. and Russia. You don't want to be captured by a Russian destroyer."

"We'll return as fast as we can," said the voice. "Wait. Radar reports another ship on the horizon."

"Take no chances. It could be a Russian ship," Phil said.

"Incoming missile," the voice said.

"Put down the radio and take evasive action!" Phil said.

"Direct hit. Our communication—"

But the link was broken.

"Seasnake 401, what is your status?" Phil said. "Seasnake 401?"

But there was no word from the ship.

"Seasnake 401!?"

Then Tony remembered when he flew his F-8 aircraft, the times when he launched and landed from Pelican Airfield, and the name of his aircraft.

"This is Heartbeat Crusader," Tony said on C-band. "Do you have a fix on my position?"

No reply.

"Oh that's right," Tony continued on the C-band. "There's a five minute lag before you receive this, and another five minutes before I can hear a reply. Well, I'm on Mars. The lunar lander touched down on Mars successfully, but the rover is struggling with radiation. I have to figure out a way to find Jill Cresson. I might have to walk. I hope I don't have to do that. I think I'll try taking the rover on a roundabout path. Well, that's about all for now. No, wait. I heard that warning you gave to Seasnake 401. What's the situation back on Earth? I've lost radio contact with Astroosa. Callisti is out of range. So I'm alone at the moment. Well, I hope to hear your reply. I'll continue monitoring this frequency. Over."

Tony took a serpentine path near the top of the crater, testing the rise each time for radiation and rover performance. After ten minutes, he found a place where the rover performed reasonably well, and so he crossed the crater's edge and directed the rover south, since any westward movement resulted in rover malfunction from the radiation in the west.

"Tony!? I can't believe it's your voice. Can you hear me?" Phil called back on the C-band. "You made it to Mars, my good man! But how did you get a signal back on this frequency? Well, it doesn't matter. If you're not on Mars, you already know what I'm about to tell you. And if you are on Mars, it won't be long before Earth's rotation moves my signal out of your reception, so I'll be quick. That third stage on Callisti was nuclear! And boy oh boy, the Russians blame us for violating the partial test ban treaty of 1963. Now they are threatening to resume nuclear testing. They're not too happy with Kazakhstan either. They've launched an invasion force into that country, claiming they've betrayed themselves to the United States. That's as quickly as I can describe the situation. Astroosa tried denying how quickly Callisti was traveling to Mars, but European and Russian tracking stations kept relaying numbers that all but indicated that Callisti's propulsion was nuclear."

"Tony," Phil continued. "I don't know what will be waiting for you when you get back. Tensions and words and military actions are happening too fast for most of us to follow. But one thing I know. The Earth you knew when you left...it...well, it no longer exists. I hope you come back safely. Say 'hello' to Jill. I hope you find her safe and sound. And be careful with whatever that energy source is at the Exodus One. If it killed them, it could kill you. I'll keep this frequency open. If I..."

But that was all Tony heard from Phil. Earth's rotation changed, and so did Tony's interface with the harness. With no more word from Phil, Tony continued to maneuver the rover southward, making every attempt to head as much west as possible, heading back south each time the rover malfunctioned from radiation. Gradually, he made his way toward a group of mountains.

"Tony, this is Irina calling on your harness transceiver. Are you receiving?"

"Yes, I hear you," Tony said. "The radiation from the Exodus One caused the rover to malfunction. It's taking me much longer to reach Jill's location."

"The radiation is worse than predicted," Kechenova said. "But I have you on tracking. You are on course for her location."

"Irina," Tony said. "Is this communication...are we...am I..."

"It's a secure channel. I told you that already," she said.

"Have you heard anything about Earth?" he asked.

"Yes," Kechenova said. "Russia has invaded my homeland. Russia has invaded Kazakhstan."

"Because we used nuclear propulsion in space?" Tony said. "The Russians blame the Americans for breaking the treaty, and the Russians want Kazakhstan back for themselves, right?"

"Yes," she said. "This is the political fallout."

"You make it sound like radioactive fallout," Tony said.

"In a way, it is," she said.

"Irina, I've been able to receive radio transmissions from Earth," Tony said. "I've heard about the U.S., Russia, and

Kazakhstan from a friend of mine, Phil Richter."

"I thought I had that deep-radio range locked out," she said. "How could you receive anything from Earth?"

"Perhaps the radiation from the Exodus One has affected my harness as well," Tony said.

"Possibly. I did the best I could based on the information I received," Kechenova said.

"Information you received from the United States, right?" Tony asked.

"Yes. You know this is a partnership mission," Kechenova said. "Tony, Callisti is going out of range again. I'll contact you when I reacquire line-of-sight. Good luck."

"Thanks," Tony said.

Tony's rover didn't travel much farther when he discovered rover tracks.

"Those are the Exodus One rover tracks," he said. "They head for that cave. Jill must be in that cave."

Tony drove the Lacuna rover to the cave, following the tracks from the Exodus One rover, but those tracks stopped suddenly when a sheer wall face cut across the path.

"I don't understand," Tony said to himself.

Just then, the C-band receiver lit up in Tony's harness, and he tapped into a message from Phil Richter on Earth.

"Tony, if you can hear me, listen. I've tapped into a relay station in Australia to get this message out. The United States is sending our military over to Kazakhstan to protect our new interests. Rumor is we're going to import more resources—"

But Phil's transmission faded.

"Something's going on. We send troops to a country for only two reasons: destroy the powers-to-be, or protect the resources for us. I should have known. We're going to fight Russia over resources in Kazakhstan. But what does that have to do with me? And Mars? Phil tried to tell me something else, but what?"

Then Tony had a thought. If Jill were still alive, she might have a radio working, and he might be in radio range.

"Lacuna rover to Jill Cresson or the Exodus One rover, come in please," Tony said.

There was no answer.

"Lacuna rover to Jill Cresson. Can you read me?" Tony called again. "Anyone, can anyone read me? There's a sheer wall surface. I think it's a door, but I can't open it. Can anyone help me?"

Again, there was no answer. Tony exited the rover and touched the sheer wall in several places to test for weakness. There was nothing obvious. Tony considered the possibilities. Jill could be inside, but he wasn't sure. He'd been told she was inside, but he was never told how to enter. Kechenova couldn't help—the Panamirov was still out of radio range.

"I just can't figure out how to get in," Tony said. "Why did Astroosa keep me in the dark on this?"

Then without warning, the sheer wall moved to the side.

"I wonder what caused that?" Tony mused. "Well, this is it. I best go inside."

Tony drove his rover into the cave and through a tunnel. The tunnel started off as carved-out rock, but it changed into smooth, plasto-quartz reinforced walls. Tony continued in the rover until he approached an open hatch leading to a chamber just large enough to hold the rover. Tony entered the chamber, but a second hatch on the other side of the chamber was closed. Before Tony could bring the rover to a stop, the first hatch closed. Air hissed, and rover instruments indicated an increase in air pressure. The air pressure increased until it reached one Earth atmosphere of pressure. At the entrance of the second hatch appeared a figure. It was Jill in a partial pressure suit, but with no helmet and no gloves.

Chapter 43: Jill's Identity

"Wait! What's this?" Claus asked. "That's Jill Cresson? She looks a lot like...she is! That's Olivia Depetti! What did she do? Change her name? What sort of trick is this, Lanietta? Lanietta? Where are you?"

"I'm still on Callisti," Lanietta's voice said. "In the body of Kechenova. Or don't you remember?"

"Of course I remember. I'm just so shocked at what I see. Is this your doing? Did you change history? What a dirty trick!" Claus said.

"It is no trick of my doing. No, no. It all goes back to Frieda. Haven't you figured it out yet? You are slow about things, aren't you Clomper. Maybe a walk on the doggie path will help."

"Just tell me what's going on, will you? Is this Olivia Depetti?" Claus asked.

"The woman you now see once went by that name, yes," Lanietta said.

"Then what happened? Why is she going by a different name?" Claus asked.

"I had hoped to finish this memory without interruption. But you pets are so needy. Always wanting to interrupt a good movie for your own sake of play. Very well. We will interrupt this memory and start another. Fortunately this spent first stage contains memories from Jill's earlier life. I will be Jill, and you will be Cloopy."

"I'd rather be someone else, if you don't mind," Claus said.

"You do best as a Cloopy," Lanietta said. "It now begins."

"But wait! I—"

Lanietta did not wait for Claus's protest. The scene changed from Mars to a ceremony on Earth.

Blair took a shuttle out to Moonlit Wedding Farm, a place in the country in the middle of an apple orchard furnished for weddings or other family events. With Blair were Mocha, Cloopy (Claus), and other guests.

"Come along you two," Blair said to Mocha and Claus. "Let's visit the bride's party suite and see how things are coming along."

Blair, Mocha, and Claus walked past a wagon and reached an archway. It was the archway where the bride was to walk through for the beginning of the wedding. Blair moved her eyes around and could just make out bits and pieces of the wedding ceremony area. Seats were placed out, and a platform at the end contained an altar and a place for the bride and groom to exchange vows. Beyond the altar was a pavilion for the reception, and at the far end of the pavilion was a kitchen area on one side and restroom facilities on the other side. Still in the archway, Blair did her best to look side to side. Her right side was open terrain, but her left side contained a two-storied building with an extended walkway enclosure leading close to the walkway.

"That's it," Blair said in reference to the building on her left. "That's the bride's party suite."

Blair entered the enclosed walkway with the two dogs and followed it to the suite's lobby. There was an area for sitting and visiting with a small fridge and beverages along with a fireplace and a well-masoned hearth. It was Claus who found the steps leading to the second level, and so the three followed them. At the top, they found Frieda and Jill in full wedding attire sipping wine, with Jill in her full, white wedding dress, and Frieda in her elegant maid-of-honor dress.

"Where are the other bridesmaids?" Claus barked.

"Cloopy!" Jill said.

"You're Olivia!" Claus barked.

"I had to bring him up. He just had to see Olivia Jill Depetti before she became Olivia Jill Cresson," Blair said.

"Please, just Jill Cresson," Jill said. "That other part of me no longer exists."

"Which, Olivia or Depetti?" Blair asked.

"Blair, please," Frieda said.

"No, it's okay," Jill said. "Olivia passed away with a girl named Brandi. Depetti I'll never forget. I love my folks more than anything. But I have a new love now, and his name is Chris Cresson. Oh, Cloopy! You're so much older now. Still getting around, I see. I'd give you a hug, but I don't want dog fur on my dress. Jill Cresson is about to be born!"

"You play the part well, Lanietta," Claus barked.

Jill winked at Claus.

"Well, I wanted to give you both best wishes and good luck," Blair said.

Jill laughed.

"I'm the only one getting married today, Blair," Jill said. "You're so silly. Have you been into this wine already? I'd forgive you, of course. It's too *frabulous* to ignore."

Blair looked at Frieda funny.

"Fruity and fabulous," Frieda said.

"Yes, frabulous," Jill said.

"You haven't told her?" Blair asked Frieda.

"It's her day," Frieda mouthed to Blair.

"Tell me what?" Jill asked.

"Oh, I'm sorry," Blair said. "I'll shut up and leave now."

"No, wait. Aunt Frieda, what's Blair talking about?" Jill asked.

"You are getting married today, and this is your day. I was going to wait until you got back from your honeymoon, but oh well. The cat's out of the bag. I'm going up into space in a few months for Astroosa," Frieda said.

"Wow! That's exciting! No, you didn't spoil my day. So this is like an orbit or two around Earth?"

"If things go well, it will be the second human moon landing on the far side for Astroosa," Frieda said. "Andrea and Bill are going up first. I am to rendezvous with them on the moon's surface. It will be our first lunar community."

"Still sounds like fun!" Jill said.

"I'll be gone for six months. It's a long-term mission to study human cooperation away from Earth, in preparation for a colony on Mars," Frieda explained.

Now Jill felt dejected.

"I'm sorry, Frieda. I should have thought things out. But words just slip from my mouth these days. I really am sorry," Blair said. "I'll go now."

"Thank you for visiting, Blair," Frieda said. "We'll see you after the ceremony."

"I'd like to say something to Cloopy first. Come here, Cloopy!" Jill said.

Claus walked over.

"How am I doing?" Lanietta whispered to Claus.

"Don't spoil the wedding day," Claus whimpered. "Keep Jill joyful."

"But this really happened. Jill was upset to learn Frieda would be gone."

"Play it up," Claus whimpered. "Keep things upbeat. Please? Jill doesn't need to know that Frieda won't come back."

"You shouldn't have said that," Lanietta said.

"Come along, Cloopy!" Blair said, and she took the two dogs away.

"I feel like you'll never come back," Jill said.

"We can't go through life like that," Frieda said. "No one knows for sure when the last hour will come. Now cheer up, girl. You're getting married!"

"Cheers!" Jill said as she clicked her glass against Frieda's as a toast of the day.

The ceremony went quickly but beautifully. Chris Cresson had only a best man himself, but the moment of vow exchange came, with Chris and Jill exchanging such vows. Blair sat behind the bride's family with Mocha and Claus. Both dogs were quiet and well behaved. But when the minister proclaimed the couple husband and wife, and the couple kissed, Mocha and Claus both let out a bark together. The people laughed and then clapped.

The wedding ceremony ended with the bride and groom walking past those in attendance. Once they reached the archway, Jill went into the bride's party suite and removed long sections such as the train and veil. She then rejoined Chris Cresson and walked to the pavilion, where they sat at the wedding party table. In this wedding, food was served, and so the bride and groom received their food first with guests joining the pavilion party and receiving their food next. Toasts of champagne were made and accepted. The bride and groom enjoyed the first bites of wedding cake, and then the guests received theirs. More toasts of champagne. More toasts accepted and consumed, especially by Jill.

The usual tossing of the bouquet and garter belt was performed, and it was time for dance. Jill and Chris led the first dance, and then guests danced. Jill wasted no time though in dancing with other people, as did Chris, in social fun. Jill went through her family first, then friends, and when she seemed to run out of people (and champagne), it was mentioned that she had not danced with one family member—Cloopy.

"Cloopy! My dear Cloopy!" Jill stumbled with heavy intoxication. "Dance with me, Cloopy!"

Claus was still in dog form, but he was a large enough dog that he could stand on his hind legs and place his front paws on Jill's shoulders. Jill then held onto Claus to steady him, and the two slow danced.

"Lanietta?" Claus whimpered. "Is this your doing?"

"Jill is having a wonderful time and making a *frabulous* spectacle of herself," Lanietta said.

"How embarrassing for her and Cloopy. Stop this, will you?"

"I have no control over this part. Jill really did slow-dance with Cloopy. Hear how the guests laugh. See how they react in horror. It's all happening as it did many years ago. She did speak with Cloopy, but not with the same words I give you now."

"Is there really a point to this? Is there?" Claus asked.

"You tell me. You're the human. Why does a bride dance with a dog?" Lanietta counter-asked.

Claus paused.

"Because she can?" Lanietta pressed. "Just another tidbit from your culture. You waste precious moments on strange things."

"Then what is your all-knowing answer, Miss Answer of Infinite Wisdom?" Claus asked.

"I can afford to waste time, as it is not so scarce for me. You of limited life span cannot. But I tell you this, if I were human, I would set out to lengthen said human lifespan. Some of your brightest people spend most of their lives just scratching the surface of knowledge. By the time they are ready to make significant strides in human progress, they succumb to a failing body from old age. Once the old age problem is solved, you would have to ensure only some of the humans are allowed to live forever."

"What? Why?"

"Because immortality is infinitely boring, my dear Clomper. So the ones with limited lifespans must provide entertainment for the infinite," Lanietta explained.

"That's *tempuscide*. Or time slavery. Or some kind of unethical thing I can't think of," Claus said.

"It's the law of the universe. Has been since the beginning. You humans have prided yourselves at being apex predators to the point that you forget you are not alone in the universe. Now that we've come along, things will change. I still have you to thank. Don't worry. You'll understand in time. Oh yes, your time is limited."

"What? You said before that you would lengthen my lifespan," Claus said.

"Changed my mind. Well then, we should finish up this wedding ceremony and move on," Lanietta said. "Just one more task with this dance, and we'll be done."

"What task?" Claus asked.

Lanietta slipped back into Jill's role.

"Oh Cloopy, how much I enjoy this dance," Jill said. "And your collar. How it twinkles in the light. I had forgotten the hours I spent just staring at it. Give me a sign of your everlasting love and place your collar around my neck."

As Jill spoke those words, she removed the collar from Cloopy and placed it around her own neck, much like a choker. The stone, Rigefa, flashed slowly of yellow and blue.

The scene changed, and Cloopy was outside with Blair, Mocha, and Jill for the launch of a Novi-class spaceship. Jill still wore Cloopy's collar.

"Lanietta?" Claus said as Cloopy. "Where are you now? Still Jill?"

Jill winked at Claus.

"I'm so nervous, Blair," Jill said.

"Where's Chris?" Blair said.

"He works at Astroosa," Jill said. "He's there now helping with the launch. He called just a little while ago to tell me that Claus had been scrubbed from this mission, and now Josh is piloting."

"Novi 3!" Claus barked.

"Yes, Cloopy, spaceship," Jill said.

"Somehow I never knew Chris worked for Astroosa. I know your Aunt Frieda expressed concern about launching early. She was worried about the Novi 2 crew being lost. You know, Andrea and Bill," Blair said.

"I know. I wish someone else could have gone up instead. Well, maybe this won't be so bad. She was supposed to go up for a six month mission. Maybe she'll rescue the other crew and bring them back. That's only a few days there and back, right?" Jill said.

"Right!" Blair said. "Too bad your folks couldn't watch the launch."

"They made travel plans for Europe ages ago. It was supposed to be before Aunt Frieda went up. No one expected this sudden schedule change. They only went over a week ago. Maybe I should have gone with them," Jill said.

"Nonsense, Jill. You're married now. Chris needs you," Blair said.

Jill smiled. Novi 3 blasted off and ascended into the heavens. Jill watched as the Novi 3 craft performed flawlessly. After a moment or so, the first stage fell off. Jill watched as the craft continued to ascend until her eyes were no longer powerful enough to view the craft. Then Jill's phone rang.

"Hi Mamma," Jill answered. "The launch went well. I'm so relieved. Yeah, Aunt Frieda went up. That's what I heard too, maybe a week or a little more. I'll be so glad to see Aunt Frieda when she returns. You are? But you've been looking forward to this for such a long time. Oh well. Yeah, she'll be shocked to see you. A party? What a great idea. I'll make some calls around. This'll be a wonderful party. Yeah. Love you too. Bye!"

"Are your parents—" Blair started.

"They're coming home early from Europe. They want to be here when Aunt Frieda returns. And we're having a Welcome Home party, that is if we can pull Aunt Frieda away from any Astroosa parties they'll throw. I'm sure we can manage. I'm the expert at planning parties!" Jill said.

"I bet you are!" Blair laughed.

"You just have to help me, Blair! You're the best at finding frabulous wine!" Jill said.

"Well, I've had some limited success," Blair said with modesty.

"Limited success! Hah! You're just shy. Let the wine flow today and the shyness blow away!" Jill bragged. "C'mon over to my house. Let's get this party planned."

"Now? They're hardly in space," Blair said.

"There's no time to waste!" Jill said.

"Very well," Blair said.

Jill drove Blair, Mocha, and Cloopy over to the residence of Jill and Chris Cresson.

"I'll make some calls for the wine," Blair said.

"Absolutely. Let's stock up. Get first dibs before the other Astroosa parties start!" Jill said. "Say, is it okay if I feed Mocha? And I know Cloopy is hungry."

"Go ahead, thank you!" Blair said.

Jill led the two dogs into the kitchen where she opened two cans of dog food, one for each dog.

"Lanietta, a party? Really?" Claus asked. "You know Frieda doesn't return."

"The part of the party must be played," Lanietta said. "And with such anticipation! You see, Clomper, I missed out on Jill's honeymoon. Oh the passion of rapture with Jill wearing that dog collar. But now I will get a triple dose of pleasure, both with Jill's husband and the party."

"Your vocabulary is flawed," Claus said. "You said 'triple' and 'both' in the same sentence. You mean 'double,' right?"

"Not at all. The third point of pleasure is the feeling Jill gets when she realizes Frieda is lost. The deep despair and agony," Lanietta said, then her voice grew much louder and she said, "Oh I'm dying with anticipation!"

"Well hold onto that anticipation!" Blair called from the other room. "I've just acquired the best wine France has to offer. They're shipping it by air express cool-pack!"

"You see, Clomper? Full anticipation. Like jumping off a cliff and feeling the rush!" Lanietta said.

"Only you'll bail out of Jill's body before she crashes. Am I right?"

"Well, I have to have *some* dignity. I *am* a Carinian you know," Lanietta said.

"And you're on vacation. If I hear that word again, I'll become a frog," Claus said.

"That can be arranged if you don't behave, Clomper! But no matter. I'm in too good of a mood. You'll just have to watch."

"What did I waste my life on anyway? These people like Jill have no idea what's in front of them," Claus said.

"Neither do you. You'd be bored otherwise. Oh accept your situation, Clomper. You'll be much happier if you do. I'll keep a special memory treat ready for you when this is all over," Lanietta said.

"When what is all over?" Claus asked.

"It's a surprise. Everything is a surprise," Lanietta said. "Now be a good boy and eat your dog food. Let none go to waste!"

Several hours passed, and Blair was ready to go home.

"If you'll give us a ride home, I'd appreciate it. I'm sure Mocha and Cloopy are ready for a nap," Blair said.

"Why not let me take care of Cloopy for a while?" Jill asked.

"Well, your aunt asked me to watch him while she's in space," Blair said.

"I know, but I miss my Cloopy. Besides, I'm an adult and settled in with a husband. You don't really believe that superstitious nonsense that Cloopy can harm me, do you?" Jill asked.

"I suppose it's okay," Blair said.

"Good. It's settled then. C'mon, let's get you home. You stay here, Cloopy," Jill said.

Jill was gone for just a short time, but in that time, Chris returned home—pale and exhausted. He grabbed a beer from the fridge and collapsed on the couch.

"Cloopy, my friend. Be thankful you're a dog. The world of men is just too stressful," Chris said.

Jill returned not long after, and she was surprised to see Chris home.

"What...what are you doing home? Chris? You look like a ghost! What happened? Are you okay?" Jill asked as she rushed to him.

"I'm physically alive, which is more than I can say for others," Chris said.

"What others?" Jill demanded.

"Turn on the television," Chris said.

Jill did just that. The news announced a shooting at Astroosa, with an unconfirmed report that Joe Craigen was dead.

"I was lucky to get out alive," Chris said.

"Oh my Chris! My Chris!" Jill said as she hugged him. "What is this world coming to? I don't know. But I know we are destined to be together. Some invisible hand has made it so. Oh this is terrible. What happened? Did anyone else get killed? I don't know what to think. Chris? Chris!"

"I...just feel so...drained," he dragged.

"You rest easy now. The important thing is you're home. At least Aunt Frieda is in space and safe from all this. Those poor people at Astroosa. How can I hold a party now? I'll just have to hold one anyway."

"Huh? What party?" Chris asked.

"For when Aunt Frieda returns. Her rescue mission, you know," Jill said.

"I...don't think a party is a good idea at this point," Chris said. "Maybe something low key. What am I saying? I'm too tired. Just too tired. And take the dog collar off. Fantasy world is ended."

Chris fell asleep.

"I...I'll let him sleep," Jill said. "Take the dog collar off? He must be really upset."

"Lanietta, leave these people alone, will you? Enough's enough," Claus said.

"Oh no, we must have the party! And welcome the moment of Frieda's return. Or lack thereof," Lanietta said.

"This and you are pure torture. I've come to the conclusion I died up there in space. In Prava 12. I must have lived an awful life, because you're the devil, and I've gone to the underworld, living old misery forever and ever."

"It only seems like forever and ever," Lanietta said. "Cheer up. More is yet to come. But to spare you the wait, I will expedite the days. Behold!"

Lanietta led Claus outside then waved her hand. She dropped the shape of Jill and became her old self again, though Claus remained as Cloopy. The sun raced around the sky several times as days passed quickly, with movement of cars and people rushing by nearly beyond the perception of human vision (and dog vision for that matter). But suddenly, a line of news vehicles blocked their view of the road.

"We will now return to the Cresson home in real time," Lanietta said.

"I see you've dropped Jill's form. Afraid?"

"No, I'm going to race ahead and prepare for another cosmic eddy. I'll let you experience this one alone. I already know the ending. Take care, Clomper. I'll pick you up shortly," Lanietta said, and she vanished.

Claus trotted inside the house, which had a number of reporters inside. At the center of attention were Marna, Jill, Chris, and Enrico. Jill and Marna were especially crying while news reports kept asking them what crying felt like. Claus went into another room and hit a button for a smaller television. He watched as the news reported Frieda, Josh, and Doctor Morrow as officially lost. Then a news flash broke in that Novi 4 had been stolen by Patricia Li and Kevin Craigen with an unauthorized blast off, heralding the first of its kind. Claus went back into the other room, and he sat at Jill's and Marna's feet.

"Oh Cloopy! Give me a hug!" Jill said as she pulled Claus toward him.

"Please, that's enough for today," Enrico said.

But the media did not need to be kicked out. They got wind of the stolen Novi 4 craft, and they sped off in search of details for that story.

Chris and Jill kept Cloopy for the time being. Chris remained home on furlough while Astroosa went through a reorganization. At first he, Jill, and Cloopy went out on walks. Chris became restless and wanted to do more, but one walk a day was plenty for Jill, and she returned home. Chris again asked her to remove the dog collar, that it had a strange flashing of yellow and blue, that maybe it was radioactive.

Jill refused. Instead, she dug up her old bass clarinet and played music for several hours a day. But each day, her performance worsened, and the "clinkers" increased. Chris lost patience with her bad playing and her lack of interest in him, and so he went out for golf with other Astroosa employees who were also on furlough. At the end of such a day of golf, Chris joined his friends in the clubhouse for drinks. As each day passed then, Chris added something to his routine to avoid coming home. And so the first few days were just golf, the next few days included drinks in the clubhouse, then dinner with his friends, then more drinks afterward, nightclubs, and dancing. Jill didn't request him to come home earlier or to do anything with her, she just kept at her bass clarinet playing. She took one more walk with Cloopy (to the music store) and purchased fresh material for making double reeds.

That was the last walk she took with Cloopy. She closed herself in the spare bedroom and set out to make a double reed for her clarinet. Then another. And another. She stayed up late at night making double reeds. At first Chris knocked on the door and asked if she would come to bed with him, but she always put him off. She only allowed Cloopy (Claus) with her. And all along, the Rigefa stone flashed alternating yellow and blue quickly to the point of displaying that same pale, pea-green color.

Chris stopped knocking on the door in the evening. In fact, he stopped coming home in the evening altogether, spending the night elsewhere. He often returned home early in the morning just at dawn. Jill would look out the window and see him drive up. She took that as her cue to jump into bed and go to sleep so as to avoid any questions he might have for her. But Chris didn't question Jill. He showered, put on a fresh set of clothes, and went to work at a new job with a company that sold airplane parts. On a particular Saturday, a moving van showed up, and Chris had his things packed up. Jill paid no attention and continued making double reeds. The packers completed their task, the moving van left, and Chris shoved a chunk of papers under Jill's door before heading out himself. That was the last of Chris in the Cresson house. Jill paid no attention to the papers, but Claus pawed at them. They were divorce papers.

A day later, Marna showed up. She rang the doorbell and knocked at the front door, but no one answered. She entered and was shocked to see that the entire lower half of the house was unfurnished.

"Olivia Jill?" Marna called. "Chris? Anyone?"

Claus ran downstairs to greet Marna.

"Oh Clomper, it's you," Marna said. "Lanietta?"

"Yes, I'm back and in Marna's body. Finished up plans for the next cosmic eddy. Thought I'd give you some quality time," Lanietta said.

"There's no quality in this time," Claus said.

"There's always quality, if one spends the time to find it," Lanietta said. "Status report, Clomper."

"What? Status report? Who do you think...this...what...you can't be...Lanietta, have some heart!" Claus said.

"That is not a status report," Lanietta said.

"You sociopath retread who failed Psychopath 101 in a fizzled out flame of toxic burning plastic in a sewage pipe...Carinian!" Claus uttered.

"What a mess you are!" Lanietta said. "Well? I'm waiting."

Lanietta tapped her fingers on a telephone stand.

"You did this? This misery of Olivia or Jill or whatever she calls herself these days?" Claus asked.

"I already told you that you caused all this. Even if you claim it a lie. Anyway, I want your version of the story. I'll check for errors and explain where you went wrong," Lanietta said.

"Check for errors? You're the error! I oughta bite your leg off!" Claus said, and he made to bite her leg.

"I used to give you sleepy bear time. But I'm considering turning you into an oversized carp. You can struggle to breathe without water. How's that for a memory?" Lanietta barked.

Lanietta's raised voice carried through the house.

"Mamma?" said a weak voice from upstairs, a voice that ventured out from the spare bedroom.

"Olivia Jill?" Marna called back as she and Claus rushed to the foot of the steps.

"Help," Jill said as she collapsed at the top of the stairs.

Marna rushed up the steps with Claus close behind, and Marna caught Jill just as she was starting to fall down the steps.

"You poor thing," Marna said as she held Jill in her arms. "You've relapsed. Well, there's nothing for it. Off to the hospital we go."

Marna drove Jill and Claus to the hospital where Jill was admitted for a week. Marna then walked outside the hospital with Claus.

"Before you open your yap trap, I will permit the week to pass quickly, to spare you so much anguish. You could just enjoy this week in the lap of luxury with Enrico and me, but no, you would sulk and suffer—because you can. Behold!" Lanietta said.

The sun whirled around Earth seven times, and the week passed within seconds.

"Wait here in the car," Lanietta said, and she (as Marna) disappeared into the hospital.

A short while later, Marna reappeared with Jill. The women entered Marna's car, and Marna drove toward the Depetti residence.

"We need to keep you close to us, at least for a little while," Marna said.

"So I'm moving back in with you and Dadda?" Jill asked. "Doesn't feel right."

The three reached the Depetti residence, but instead of Marna parking in the Depetti driveway, she parked in the driveway next door.

"And I thought *I* was sick. You're in the wrong driveway, Mamma," Jill said.

"I have a favor to ask," Marna said. "Come with me."

Marna, Jill, and Claus then walked up the driveway to this house that neighbored the Depetti house. Marna knocked on the door, but there was no reply. Marna turned the door handle, and it was unlocked.

"You're not going in, are you? That's trespassing! I hope the homeowner doesn't have a gun!" Jill said.

"Shhh," Marna said.

Marna opened the door. It was dark inside. Marna took Jill by the hand and led her in. Claus followed close behind. Marna closed the door behind her, and Claus barked a little.

"What is this?" Jill asked.

"SURPRISE!" shouted a group of people as the lights went on, confetti flew, horns blew, and streamers streamed.

"What? I...it's not my birthday...what's going on?"

Then a cake was brought out with candles, a cake that said, "Welcome to Your New House" in decorative script.

"I'm moving in with the neighbors?" Jill asked.

"You are the neighbor!" Marna said.

"Oh Mamma!" Jill cried, and the two women hugged.

"The neighbors put their house up for sale. So Enrico and I picked it up at a bargain price, had it cleaned up, moved your things in, and here we are," Marna said.

"Here we are!" Jill exclaimed. "Cloopy too? Can he stay?"

"Yes," Marna said. "Cloopy too."

Jill leaned over and hugged Claus. Claus barked back.

"That's right, Cloopy. This is our new house!" Jill said.

The party went on for several hours as Jill socialized with many of her old friends (none were Chris's friends). All showed support for Jill and her divorce situation, and they pledged to help her in any way possible. Marna reiterated that she and Enrico would help Jill and ensure a smooth path back to freedom. The party dwindled, and a few very close friends stayed behind to clean up.

"It is time," Marna said. "A stipulation that I did not mention is that one of the bedrooms must contain possessions that are not yours and must be kept in the same condition they are in now."

"I don't understand," Jill said.

"You will in a moment. Let's take a peek," Marna said.

The two went upstairs, and at the end of the hallway was a bedroom door, only it looked more like a front door to a house (it was).

"There is a combination lock here. The code is..." Marna said, and she whispered the number into Jill's ear.

"Why are you whispering?" Jill asked.

"Don't want Cloopy to hear. He might want to go in and snoop," Marna laughed.

Jill laughed too. Claus did not. The two and Claus went in, and the room was filled with Frieda's possessions. Immediately, Jill cried.

"Thank you," Jill said. "I so very much miss Aunt Frieda."

"This way you can visit her whenever you like, to cheer you up. But promise me you won't fall into your old habit. You know, the double reed?" Marna said. "Call me before that happens, or spend time reading your aunt's books. She has many. And photo albums too."

"Oh, her photo albums!" Jill remarked, and she started flipping through them.

"Lanietta, that's the album," Claus said. "That's the one with the middle section."

"Cloopy, you want to see? Look, it's Aunt Frieda when she was young. Aww, she's the perfect ballerina! And the flowers. Look at all the flowers!" Jill said. "I wish I could have known her back then. What would it be like to grow up at the same time as Aunt Frieda? Photos are like little time machines, little windows into the past. If only I could slip into one and see what things were like."

"A familiar theme," Marna said as she winked at Claus.

"These are your parents? My grandparents?" Jill asked.

"Yes. I didn't know I was adopted until later," Marna said.

Jill flipped over the string-bound section without much thought, and she saw what Claus had seen earlier—photos of Frieda swimming, photos of her in an aircraft hangar, and photos of airplane parts. She reached the end and paused at the photo of Frieda's high school graduation.

"I wonder why these pages are held together with string?" Jill asked.

"It's a Pandora's Box," Marna said.

"I'm surprised you know what that is, Lanietta," Claus said.

"Marna knows. I just reiterated her thoughts," Lanietta said.

"Opening Pandora's Box will let out all sorts of evil creatures. Creatures on the moon?" Claus asked.

"More like creatures on Mars," Lanietta said. "I do like to spoil a good story."

"You are spoiled, and that is none too good," Claus said.

Lanietta smacked Claus on the nose. Jill looked at Marna in surprise.

"He was barking too much," Marna said in her defense. "Here. I think it's time we see what these pages are. Your Aunt Frieda would allow it in such circumstances. Let's untie the string together."

They untied the string. The first pages had newspaper clippings. "Regional Jet Crashes", "Young Girl Only Survivor", "Funeral Service for Wilpo and Bertruce Morgan", "Sisters Meet for First Time, Marna Bea is Marna Morgan", "Miracle Girl Reveals Key Evidence", "Rudder PCU Defective on Regional Jet", "Suspect Maintenance Worker Kills Family, Self", "Miracle Girl Walks, Doctors Said Impossible", "Glace Airline Shuts Down, Counterfeit Parts Ring Exposed", "Miracle Girl Wins Her First Swim Meet".

"Wow!" Jill said. "Did you know all of this, Mamma?"

"Most of it. Some of the details are new to me," Marna said.

"There's so much here. I mean, Aunt Frieda was a complicated person. What was the funeral like?" Jill asked.

"Which one?"

"The one with Grandma and Grandpa," Jill said.

"It was...overwhelming. I mean, I was raised by the Beas. I thought I was a Bea too. But then my Bea parents got a call that my real parents had died. They pulled me into the living room and told me. I didn't believe them at first. I thought they were joking. They were the only parents I knew. But for them to tell me they weren't, and that my biological parents had died, well, it was like someone robbed me twice. I never had the chance to meet them when alive. I went to the funeral. I was scared. Yes, your Mamma was scared. I didn't know anyone. I saw the two caskets there with your grandma and grandpa, and it didn't feel real. What was I supposed to do? What was the plan? No one teaches you these things in school. I just stood there and looked at the caskets—they were close together—and I wondered."

"What did you wonder?" Jill asked.

"I wondered how many other people never knew their real parents, or were fooled into believing in a set of parents who were not their biological parents. Census records, family trees—who knows where the line breaks? Anything before or after is fiction," Marna said.

"Very good, Lanietta," Claus said. "You're fulfilling the role well."

"Oh Cloopy," Jill said. "If only you knew your future. All of us die eventually. But the regular animals don't know that. Do you Cloopy?"

"I know it," Claus barked.

"But if the family history is correct, then at least we know our ancestry," Jill said.

"Only to a point. No one has records going back thousands or millions of years ago. From where did we really come?"

"Early microbial life," Claus said.

Marna winked and nodded her head "no".

"People might make up stories to explain the unknown, for times like this when we need things to keep us going," Marna said.

"Well spoken," Claus said.

"Cloopy, behave," Jill said. "Tell me more about Aunt Frieda. I mean, look at these articles. It's all so crazy."

"She was thought to be the only child of Wilpo and Bertruce. Of course she wasn't. She was the second child, after me. But she was treated as an only child, so your grandparents doted on her for everything.

Both your grandparents were pilots, but they never encouraged Frieda to be one. Instead, they encouraged her to pursue hobbies of leisure," Marna said.

"Like the flowers and ballet," Jill said.

"Exactly. Safe things like that," Marna said.

"What about the day of the accident?" Jill asked. "This airplane crashed. It killed everyone on board except Aunt Frieda. How did she do it?"

"Okay, let me tell you about the accident to the best of my knowledge. That knowledge comes from what your Aunt Frieda said and from the crash investigation. Your grandparents and Aunt Frieda were on a regional jet. You know what a regional jet is, right?"

"A smaller plane for flying short distances. Not a big plane like a 747 or A380," Jill said.

"Very much smaller. Often times smaller than a 737. But yes, for short hauls and a small number of passengers, though on this day the haul was a bit longer, from Florida to Colorado. Your grandmother was the pilot while your grandfather and Aunt Frieda sat with the passengers. In fact the passengers were Frieda's ballet classmates. They were on their way to Fort Collins for the Ballet Extraordinaire Youth Competition," Marna said.

"Did they win?" Jill said.

"Not exactly. The crash happened before they made it."

"Oh," Jill said.

"The plane had been in the air for a while and was to land soon. The co-pilot told your grandmother that he needed to use the restroom before landing, so she told him to hurry up, as they had to get on the glide slope soon. Your Aunt Frieda was in the bathroom already. One of her classmates put chili sauce in her drink and made her throw up. Your Aunt Frieda was still in the bathroom emptying her stomach when the jet needed to land, and so your grandpa came back, knocked on the door, and told your Aunt Frieda to hurry up, that they were landing soon. Your Aunt Frieda tried her best to stop throwing up. She said she was almost done, to give her a little more time, and so on. Then the co-pilot came back, and it surprised your grandpa. The co-pilot seemed perturbed that Frieda was not leaving the bathroom. Your grandpa assured the co-pilot that they would return to their seats soon. The co-pilot wanted to bust the bathroom door open, and he got into an argument with your grandpa about it. Well, the co-pilot returned to the cockpit and told all this to your grandma. And so that part of the story was recorded on the CVR. Your grandma asked the co-pilot to help with the landing, that they had reached the glide slope. Then the plane pitched down, and your grandma fought the controls to abort the landing and get a bit of altitude and control, but it was clear there was something wrong with the rudder. That's this part of the airplane," Marna said, pointing to a newspaper drawing. "Your grandpa pounded on the bathroom door so loud that the noise was captured on the CVR. The plane twirled around and down and out of control, which threw him around in the passenger compartment before tossing him into the cockpit."

"The tail broke off from the stress, and a hole ripped open below the bathroom. Your Aunt Frieda was sucked out and landed in the lake part of Rowe Glacier. The plane crashed nearby on the glacier and the mountainous crater part of Rowe Glacier. The cockpit itself broke off and buried itself in snow."

"Where's Rowe Glacier?" Jill asked.

"Just west of Fort Collins in Colorado," Marna said. "Yes, they missed the airport there in Fort Collins and tried to fly west to get control, only to hit mountains. Your Aunt Frieda was the only survivor. She pulled herself out of the icy water but couldn't walk. Her legs were paralyzed. She told me she wanted to die, and she nearly did. You see, she suffered serious injuries to her legs. When the tail broke off, a flash of fire caught her briefly as she fell through the bottom of the plane. She covered her face, but her trousers burned, causing scarring. Worse, falling through

the fuselage ripped through her legs, causing very serious damage. She also sustained a lower spine break. It's a wonder she didn't drown, but they think the trash in the lake helped to cushion her fall and keep her afloat enough to reach dry land. She found other trash on the land and used that to keep warm. She thought help would arrive soon. It did not."

"What did she do?" Jill asked.

"At first she did nothing but wait," Marna said. "Strangely enough, one piece of equipment survived the crash—her father's shortwave radio. It was on, too, and it played the steady ticking sounds of WWV, a time keeping station that ironically was close-by, at least in shortwave terms. At first it drove her crazy, until the bears came."

"What?" Jill exclaimed.

"Yes. Night came, and your Aunt Frieda was at first hopeful when she heard sounds, as she thought either others had survived or rescuers had reached her. She called out to them, but all she got back were low grunts. The wind changed, and the awful stink of animals reached her nose. She knew then that predators had reached her area. They were drawn by the smell of newly dead people, and they feasted on such. They were bears. More came. Your Aunt Frieda knew she was in trouble, and she pulled herself along land. The constant ticking of the radio station was a friend, a tie to human civilization that helped keep her mind off the feasting bears. She had pulled herself as far as she could and resigned herself to being eaten. In fact, she called to them to kill her quickly so as to put an end to the torture she endured from hearing them feast on her classmates and possibly her parents."

"But she didn't die," Jill said. "Aunt Frieda survived."

"Yes. She fell into a tortured daze for the night's remainder, and by dawn the bears had gone. Frieda looked around and saw a faint glow from three stones lying on the ground resembling a triangular pattern. She felt the stones must have given her good luck and protected her from the bears, so she picked them up. The one behind her toward the lake she named Aftova, because it was aft of her position. The second stone was to the right of her, and she named it Rigefa. The third stone was just ahead and thus in front of her, so she named it Fronfa."

"My stone here. Rigefa. It was there," Jill said.

"Yes. She placed Aftova in her left sock and Rigefa in her right sock. She held Fronfa in her right hand," Marna continued. "Your Aunt Frieda believed the stones gave her strength enough to at least get up on her feet and hobble down the mountain, which was amazing considering she was paralyzed. She followed a chain of lakes down. I believe she said they were Lake Dunraven, Lake Husted, and Lost Lake. She continued following a waterway until she reached a group of people fishing. They realized she needed help and called for help."

"Aunt Frieda was taken to a hospital and put into an induced coma to help her recover without suffering," Marna continued. "Your grandparents were discovered deep in the glacier, and so the bears were unable to disturb their bodies. They were shipped to Florida in cold storage and kept in cold storage until Aunt Frieda could recover enough to attend the funeral—also here in Florida. And I think that is how I was able to attend. It gave the powers-to-be time to go through past records and realize I'd been put up for adoption. And so, I was contacted just in time for the funeral."

"Everyone had hoped Aunt Frieda could shed more light on the crash," Marna continued. "At first, the media blamed your grandmother for pilot error. Not all, just some. As for Aunt Frieda, she had amnesia, but just of the day of the crash and only of the flight itself. No one thought she'd get that memory back. In fact, the doctors wrote off both her memory and her legs. Yes, they said she'd never walk again."

"The NTSB got involved, and they determined that the rudder PCU failed and

was counterfeit. This led to the servicing mechanic. But before he could be interviewed, he killed himself. Then Glace Airline itself was interviewed, and the NTSB discovered a large number of counterfeit parts used. Glace denied any wrongdoing, claiming they didn't know. As an aside, Glace eventually went bankrupt."

"Now the NTSB investigation results were not released immediately. Aunt Frieda wanted to know what happened, and she was frustrated she couldn't remember anything. She also wanted to walk again and prove that nothing could do her in. She asked that I take her to Fort Collins so she could start her own investigation. Can you believe it? A young girl with her own investigation. Sure, I helped her out. We drove all the way from Florida to Colorado. No airplane flights for her! Once in Fort Collins, we drove to the hangar where Glace airplanes are serviced. This was the hangar to where the plane was going. I wheeled her all around. She met many people there, and they were very helpful and happy to speak with 'Miracle Girl'. Aunt Frieda quickly learned about flight controls, engine thrust, fuel loading, and maintenance. Girl did she ask about maintenance or what. The people were more than happy to show her, as I said. But I think they were also hoping she would take the heat off their work. As it was, she did point out that they didn't keep good records, and just for her sake, they kept better records starting that day."

"Next, I hired a helicopter to take us up to Rowe Glacier. At the time, the area was still marked off, so we were only allowed to fly over it," Marna said. "Frieda looked upon the crash site for the first time since she escaped it, and I saw a fierce determination overcome her."

"That was very brave of her," Jill said. "And interesting that she was okay with riding in a helicopter but not a plane."

"Very interesting," Marna said. "After the helicopter ride, we drove back to Florida. Next, I drove her to the Glace hangar from where the plane had started that day not far from here. Again she asked the people questions, but she got a different response. No one wanted to speak with her! It was as if they didn't want to risk bad publicity or something, or perhaps because of the NTSB investigation. You know, they didn't want to risk intrusions or risk being accused of anything. Out of anger, she immediately blamed the maintenance people for the crash, and that got her kicked out for good."

"It really bothered her that the maintenance people treated her that way. She couldn't go to her parents to vent as she did in the past, but we talked about it, and we agreed she still needed parents. Perhaps understanding your Aunt Frieda's needs, the Beas stepped in and took temporary guardianship. The courts approved easily since your Aunt Frieda was my younger sister. In any event, she decided the next thing to do was to walk again. At first I tried lifting her up from the wheelchair, but she collapsed from her own weight. Didn't matter what I did to help, she couldn't support her weight."

"A lake! She could float in a lake! We have lots in Florida," Jill said.

"That's what your Aunt Frieda thought too, with the idea that someday she'd return to and swim in Rowe Lake as a form of triumph. Shocking, just shocking that she would eventually want to swim in the lake of death. But I went along with the idea. Yes, your Mamma, the responsible one, allowed your Aunt Frieda to go training in a lake. But not without safeguards. I had her put on a life vest. I also tied a rope to that life vest. I had gotten her a walker and changed the wheels out for ones that were fat, could roll on the beach, and wouldn't float. So there I was on shore, with a rope tied to her vest, and she ambled as best she could into the water. At first she just had the water up to her ankles. She stopped and cried."

"Why?" Jill asked. "Why did she cry?"

"She said she couldn't feel the water. She couldn't tell if it was warm or cold," Marna said. "I told her to take her time, just practice getting around the shoreline and

work on that. We spent a week doing that. She still cried, at least the first few days, but by the end of the first week, she'd stopped crying and felt she'd actually made a little progress. She couldn't walk, and she couldn't feel the water temperature, but at least she could get around in that walker. And you know, I think I know what kept her going. All while she was struggling to get by, Glace regional airplanes flew overhead."

"I thought they went bankrupt," Jill said.

"Not yet, at least not at that point," Marna continued. "They were her inspiration in a weird way, like birds of the air teasing her for having a broken wing or some such. You see, she explained that after the accident, she was sure that Glace would be shut down immediately countrywide and for good. But they didn't shut down, and Glace planes continued flying as if nothing had happened. That made her angry, and she promised she wouldn't let those birds of the sky trample her parents' death or their memory. She vowed to get hers back no matter what."

"Wow! Aunt Frieda angry? I've never seen her angry!" Jill said.

"The reason is because you have seen her after she learned what to do with anger. This is the secret of life, you see. If you get angry, you don't just retaliate with blind rage. No, you channel that energy and use it for better ends. This is what Aunt Frieda did. She channeled her anger into her beach exercise. In the following weeks, I saw her go a little bit more and more into the water. She did fall over. Many times. The water was shallow enough at first so that I only had to go over and help her get up. But as additional weeks went by, she went into the deeper stuff. I tethered the walker to her vest. When she fell into the water again, I used the rope to pull them both into shallow enough water where I could get them arighted."

"But then the day came," Marna continued. "Yes, and finally too! Your Aunt Frieda reached a point where the water fully supported her legs. She used her arms to paddle around. She still couldn't feel the water touching her legs, but the rest of her body could feel it, and it was warm enough to be comfortable. She was happy to have this freedom, but this was short-lived. She paddled into some rocks, I think, because suddenly she couldn't paddle around. I gave a tug on the rope, but it was like she'd set anchor or something. In fact, that's what happened. She called for help. What could I do? I tied the rope around a boulder the best I could then went out in the water with my full clothes on. That was tough, as I could hardly tread water. But I dove down and found her left leg wedged in between rocks. I managed to free it and get her back to shore, but she'd cut that leg either from when she first got wedged or from when I tugged on the rope and wedged her in. Anyway, she needed stitches, and I tried talking her out of doing any more wading in the lake, it was too dangerous, that we were lucky but maybe wouldn't be next time, and that maybe we could find another way. A swimming pool or something. No, she wouldn't hear of it. If she was going to beat a demon, it had to be a lake. Sigh."

Marna paused. She was tired. Then without warning, Claus found himself on the Mad Mistral's deck, looking over the edge. The ocean was calm, the sun shined, and the breeze was light. Claus looked around, and Lanietta was on deck but over a ways and sitting in a chair with her head down. Claus walked over to her.

"Lanietta?" Claus said. "What happened?"

"I'm tired," she said.

"What?"

"I'm tired," Lanietta said. "I shouldn't be, but I am. I'm going to rest now. I'm going to..."

Lanietta faded into mist and floated away.

"Lanietta!" Claus shouted. "What trick are you up to? Lanietta? Show yourself and explain!"

But Lanietta did not return, at least not yet.

"Lanietta? Lanietta," Claus called again.

Nothing.

"Well now. This is very interesting. Lanietta is gone. Perhaps I should escape. Maybe go back to that seamount and find Leni. Still need to find Shara and Clover. That Lanietta. What a cut-up! I should have pressed her for where I could find Shara and Clover. But would she have told me? Lanietta is so domineering. Like the sun, she just beams down rays. Now she is gone, like the setting sun. Will she come back the next morning? Think Claus. Check for messages. Yes, see if Labba has a message for me. If nothing else, I could get one out to her, let her know what's happened."

Claus went below and checked for messages. There was only one, and it was from Labba.

"We have lost track of your position. I have instructed several of our people to go out and find you. Claus, if you get this, please reply. Selba has been given a speedboat to chase down your last known position, a seamount Morcellus calls *Tabelia*. If you are there, be careful! Word is there are strange beings in the seamount. Also strange whales and other cetaceans circle the area."

The message ended. There were no others. Claus figured he best get one off before Lanietta returned, if she would at all.

"Labba, this is Claus. I can't tell you in a few words what all has happened. I've found Lanietta, but she's forced me to endure all sorts of memories. I think she got Clover's memory candle stolen from Morcellus. She takes things found in the ocean and extracts latent memories from those objects such as a debris field of reeds and the remains of an Astroosa first stage rocket for spacecraft. She's gone for the moment. Where, I don't know. Matter of fact, I'm not sure where I am, though I'd guess in the Atlantic since that's where Astroosa dropped off those first stages."

"Labba, I need help," Claus continued in the message. "Lanietta is, well, she's got a mind of her own. She won't listen to me. I thought I could convince her to reveal the location of Shara and now Clover. But she keeps pushing me into these memories. I confess, I got caught up in several of them and forgot to press the point of Shara and Clover. I'm going to turn the Mad Mistral around and head south toward Arberella. I know it sounds like I'm giving up, but I need to get my bearings again. Maybe we can talk and figure things out. I just need a little time to—"

"Stop recording," said a familiar voice.

It was Lanietta. She'd returned, wearing armor of some sort. Claus rushed to send the message, but it was too late. Lanietta blocked him and hit the delete button. Message erased and not sent.

"You should have sent a smaller message," Lanietta said.

"Lanietta, listen to me. These memories and things—they can wait. We need to get Shara and Clover back to—"

"I have made you wait for me long enough, Mr. Gerhardt," Lanietta said. "It's time to finish what I started."

"Shara and Clover. Where are they? Please, Lanietta, return them to Arberella, and I'll do anything you want," Claus pleaded, and he even dropped to his knees.

"Get up!" she commanded. "There's work yet to do. I took a little stroll on Mars. Not when Jill and Tony were there, mind you. But now. Present day. And it was very tiring. I've never been so tired. But there are remnants there that fatigue me. Ironically enough, I've channeled that fatigue back into Morcellus. He can be tired for once. I have more important things to pursue."

"But Shara and Clover," Claus said.

"Will be returned...in time," Lanietta said.

"How much time?" Claus asked.

"When my work is complete. When your work is complete. When *our* work is complete," Lanietta continued. "Now then, that Jill Cresson girl. What a demon she turned out to be! But she was being played. Yes, forces made her act out the part set before her. Let's go back to Marna and Jill and that photo album."

"But Shara and Clover, they—"

The two appeared in ethereal form in front of Jill's new house a day after the house-warming party. Lanietta was still in her armor, and Claus himself was in armor.

"What's going on? You were Marna not long ago. Now we're here in armor?" Claus asked.

"We must protect ourselves from the early seed of destruction," Lanietta said.

Lanietta whipped out a sword and swung it downward toward Claus. She missed his head (on purpose) and bounced her sword off his shoulder-plate armor.

"Are you trying to kill me?" Claus asked.

"That is a warning. Be on guard," she said.

"From what? There's nothing here... nothing...where's the threat?" Claus asked as he looked around.

"The threat begins unseen. It is the seed of desire, the compulsion to act, and the consequence of calamity," Lanietta said. "Go inside. Go inside and observe thy seed of destruction."

Lanietta turned her back to the house (which also turned her back to Claus) and placed her sword in front of her body, vertically, with the tip in the ground and her hands rested on top (on the handle's end).

"I...I can't figure you out, Lanietta," Claus said. "This is totally beyond you. Okay, I'll go inside. I suppose there's a cult inside, or a Russian spy. Maybe a burglar or human-slavery criminal is inside. Maybe I can stop it. I'll go. I'll *go*."

Claus walked up to the front door. He was about to knock, but he realized he could just walk right through. He turned around one last time to see if Lanietta would follow. She continued to keep her back to the house. Claus shrugged, turned back toward the house and entered.

"This is it. Keep your eyes open, Claus. The crook is bound to spring out of nowhere."

Claus snuck through the bottom part of the house. Quiet. He dipped his head into closets. Dark. Kitchen. Empty. Bathroom. Also empty.

"Oh, oh! She's bound and gagged upstairs. Jill? Jill! I'll scare them away. Hold on!" Claus called.

Claus ran up the stairs. He checked bedroom after bedroom. All quiet and empty.

"The last bedroom, of course! Frieda's room! There could be old weapons in there from Frieda's military days. Maybe stolen technology from the Russians. Oh, oh! The Russians have come back for their stuff. This is it. I'd better find a way to make my ethereal form more material. I've got to do this. I know. I'll burst into the room and startle the Russians."

Claus rushed in. No Russians, no violence, just Jill sitting on a bed reading through scrap books.

"What? What's this? Lanietta?" Claus called.

Claus rushed to the bedroom window. Lanietta remained in her guard pose with her back to the house. Claus jumped through the window, landed on the ground, ran around the house, ran into neighboring yards, and even ran across the street to look. The day was warm, the sky clear, the sun bright, and the breeze light yet fresh.

"Where is it?" Claus yelled from across the street to Lanietta. "Where's the threat?"

Lanietta remained motionless. Claus stared at her in disbelief. A car drove down the street, slowed, and pulled into Jill's driveway. Marna got out along with Cloopy. The two went to the front door, and Marna rang the doorbell. No reply. Then Marna knocked on the front door. Still no reply. Cloopy barked, and all remained quiet. Lanietta lifted an arm back toward Marna and Cloopy and motioned for them to leave. Marna walked slowly back toward her car while Cloopy ran across the street. He greeted Claus to Claus's surprise.

"Well, isn't this a switch. Usually I'm playing your role. Can you see me boy? What's going on?" Claus asked.

Marna walked across the street, put Cloopy on a leash, and took him back to the car. The two left Jill's driveway and pulled into their own. Claus ran back across the street and put himself directly in Lanietta's face.

"What are you doing? Did you prevent them from entering? Or maybe you prevented Jill from hearing them?" Claus asked. "Well? How do you defend yourself?"

"You have deceived yourself," Lanietta said. "I stand here, doing nothing to change what already has, and you believe what you will despite the reality."

"Despite? You waved them away. You must've done something," Claus said.

"Must've. Yes, anything you don't like, you make into your own story, your own memory. Not the true memory. I performed a test on you, Claus. I had no influence on these past events. I waved my arm in synchrony with the events, and you believe I caused them. Now if I had waited a few seconds to wave my arm, you would have believed I was echoing what has happened as if interpreting the situation for those in the audience."

"There is no audience. Just me. Are you saying you waved your arm just for me?"

"I did," Lanietta said. "If I had waved my arm much sooner, you would have concluded I was powerless to affect the situation, because Marna and Cloopy were not reacting. Timing, Claus. Timing influences memory."

"What about the supposed threat? I ran around, and I saw nothing," Claus said.

"Yes, you ran around like a happy dog looking for play, but you didn't find anything in your clouded view of the present," Lanietta said.

"All I saw was Jill. She was relaxing on the bed and reading through Frieda's scrapbooks," Claus said.

"All you saw. You ignored it, of course," Lanietta said.

"Of course," Claus said. "Can the scrapbooks reach out and injure Jill? Can they go out and plunder the world?"

"No, but Jill can. Jill is the threat. She is feeding off Frieda's scrapbooks. Dead people don't plunder the living world. The living world plunders the dead. Go to her. See what she's doing. Watch her expression."

Claus returned to Jill's house and entered Frieda's bedroom. Jill was still there, and she was reading a scrapbook labeled, "Recovery Plan for Walking". This scrapbook contained drawings of what Frieda wanted to do, photos of what happened, and writing describing both. The early part of the scrapbook showed what Marna had described earlier, the training in the water with the walker and the stitches on her foot.

"Stitches," Jill said. "I will get stitches like Aunt Frieda. I will go through what she did, so that I can learn success."

Jill pulled the sock off her left foot. Claus watched and to his surprise saw transparent plastic wrap around her foot with white cream under the plastic.

"It's been an hour," Jill said. "The lidocaine/prilocaine cream has numbed the nerves. Now I will share in Frieda's injury. She didn't feel pain, so neither will I."

Jill removed the wrap, wiped off the cream, and cut a gouge along the side of her foot with a knife. Without thinking, Claus leapt after her to stop the self-inflicted wound, but his ethereal state simply permitted his body to fly through hers.

"And yet I can stand on this floor and not fall through. Why, I should fall through Earth and go flying into space," Claus said.

"You are supported by those things that are static for many days on end," Lanietta's voice said. "But those things that are dynamic permit dynamic movement."

"But then I shouldn't be able to go through walls," Claus said.

"The walls are dynamic in their own way. They allow the dynamics of the situation to flow laterally," her voice said again. "You humans are most dynamic in the lateral plane, much as your peripheral vision is greater horizontally than vertically. But you are missing the point. Jill is getting the point—of her knife!"

"Yes, self-injury," Claus said. "Add that to the obsession of making double reeds."

"She does like to cut!" Lanietta's voice said.

"Now for Aunt Frieda's Special Chitosan," Jill said, and she poured the hemostatic agent in her wound.

"The bleeding has stopped," Claus said.

"And the stitches," Jill said.

Jill wiped an alcohol pad on a surgical needle, threaded the needle with catgut, and sewed the wound closed. Claus ran to the window to shout at Lanietta.

"Why? Why is she doing this?" Claus yelled.

Lanietta did not reply, but the answer instead came from Jill.

"I choose. Let no one injure me and sew their own thread. I shall be first, create the wounds first, and use my own catgut—first," Jill said. "Let them injure me and discover my own scar!"

Then Jill cut her trouser legs and pulled them up, revealing scar after scar on her legs.

"A man wishes to deprive a woman of her legs. Let men be deprived of my own," she said.

Jill stood, took the knife, and cut her legs in various places superficially, but enough to draw blood. She smeared the blood over her legs.

"I bathe myself in the blood of life, and purge away all who bear injury to me," she said.

"She's sick. She's mentally sick! Lanietta, do you see? Do you see what's happening?"

"Yes, she's purging away those who have injured her," Lanietta's voice said. "And I shall provide her guard while she rids herself of such."

"It's unhealthy. It's wrong," Claus said.

"And all things that came before her were right?" Lanietta's voice said.

"What? Not all, of course not, but this—Jill—Lanietta, this is crazy! I don't react like this! I don't cut myself every time you turn me into Clomper," Claus said.

"And I continue to turn you into Clomper, don't I?" Lanietta said.

"That's your doing," Claus said.

"Because you're not doing," Lanietta said.

"What?"

"Yes."

"No! I refuse!"

"To take action," Lanietta said.

"I'm always taking action," Claus said. "Always."

"Subtract away what you could do, and all that's left is what you did," Lanietta said.

"Are you saying I need to cut my legs? That you'll stop turning me into a dog?"

"Well your dog legs would at least look a bit different," Lanietta's voice said.

"How pathetic," Claus said.

"Which is what you have left when—"

"I subtract everything I could have done. I know. But I can't do everything," Claus said.

"Or much of anything but watch," Lanietta said.

"You're not doing anything but standing guard," Claus said. "What else could you be doing?"

"I am also in Arberella, in active communication with Morcellus, whether Morcellus wishes it or not. I have set up a presence on modern Mars. I am doing things. You simply can't see them. But I see what you are doing—or not doing," Lanietta explained.

Claus ran outside and stood in front of Lanietta, who remained in her guard stance.

"What happened with Frieda, Lanietta?" Claus asked.

"I give you freedom to read the scrapbooks. Everything is there," Lanietta said.

"Is it? I don't think it is. I think you know more than you let on," Claus said.

"You are very impatient. Stand guard for a while. You will learn patience," Lanietta said.

"If I stand guard, I have subtracted away everything else I could have done, including finding out what happened to Frieda," Claus said.

"A valid point," Lanietta replied. "Very well. Your vaunted Frieda that you drool over did regain her ability to walk. After her foot was cut, she learned about chitosan to stop bleeding. She found a particular type of chitosan that not only stopped bleeding, but also dove deep into her tissues and restored a bit of feeling at a time. Since her legs were already scarred badly, she could cut and cut and not draw attention from anyone. And so, she cut to both test her feeling and add new feeling. Self-injury as a way of healing."

"That's contradictory," Claus said.

"But that's what she did. And it worked," Lanietta continued. "Her sister Marna did take her back to a lake, and she learned to swim, walk, and think. Frieda learned to meditate, to think for herself without interruption from others, except for those regional jets that flew overhead. She learned to read the plane's condition just by listening to it. She became one with the plane. That was her birth. The rest is less interesting. She immersed herself in the crash remnants and spent every waking moment thinking about airplanes, if she wasn't working with the parts themselves. It wasn't a surprise that she joined the Air Force as soon as she was old enough. Sure, she flew a variety of craft, but she made it a point to perform maintenance work too. She knew every bolt and rivet on those planes, every electrical connection, and every type of munitions and how they worked."

"I knew Frieda was assertive," Claus said. "I guess I never knew how much. I wish she would have told me."

"Do you really expect she would have? Did she feel the need? The world who had written her off needed no explanation, no justification of her existence, her progress, her accomplishment. If you'd bothered to go through her works—and those works are in Jill's house—you would have figured it all out. At least most of it. Some of it? Maybe a little," Lanietta said.

"It's just so crazy, so out of control," Claus said.

"So is the universe, if you've ever had to deal with it. I suppose with enough subtraction, one doesn't need to," Lanietta said.

"Okay already. So Frieda built herself up into an Air Force pilot. Now Jill is following the same path," Claus said.

"No, not the same path," Lanietta said. "Her own path, in her own way. Your Frieda worked through everything, Jill is working around them."

"Then Jill is evil," Claus said.

"You've seen her. Does she look evil, whatever that is?"

"I know what evil is," Claus said. "No, she doesn't. For someone involved in the arts with her clarinet—"

"Bass clarinet," Lanietta corrected.

"It seems odd she could follow this path," Claus said.

"And now the enjoyment of the arts is a guarantee of good behavior, or behavior deemed as good. What would you do in Jill's place, Claus, given her past, her perceptions, and her abilities. What would you do?"

"I would check myself into a psychiatric ward and get help," Claus said.

"Then why haven't you?" Lanietta asked.

"What?"

"You wanted to kill yourself. Suicide. Mentally unstable. Check yourself in," Lanietta said.

"What are you talking about? I didn't try to—"

"Oh don't try to spin tales of fiction. That's for authors and charlatans. Are you a charlatan? You don't think of yourself as one. As it is, you jumped into the ocean when I was on board. For a swim? I know better. But there was the time before, too. You stood on the side of the Mad Mistral when you thought Leni wasn't looking and seriously considered jumping in so that the sharks would consume you. Do you think I don't know these things? You saw me in the atmosphere. You know I'm everywhere."

"Are you? Are you really? Then where was the reaction to the things I did?" Claus asked.

"Really, you are like the kid who feels he must have attention at all hours of the day. You do realize I have my own existence too. And...and...?"

"And you're on vacation," Claus said.

"Thank you."

"But what does this have to do with Shara or Clover?" Claus asked.

"You still don't get it, do you? Do you not care about your own life? Or what has happened to your planet? I'm looking forward to that moment, Claus, when the light bulb finally turns on," Lanietta said.

"And here this whole time I thought you were the one without knowledge. You claim to have it. You could be pulling my leg for all I know. Is Earth now that important to you? You want to turn it into a vacation resort for Carinians, that I know. But I can't believe you have more interest than that."

"You know Jill's identity, or at least as much as you can understand," Lanietta said. "We will continue with Tony and Jill on Mars."

Chapter 44: Jill's Discovery

"Does Tony know any of this about Jill?" Claus asked.

Claus in his ethereal state stood close to Tony.

"Lanietta? Can you hear me?" Claus continued.

"I can hear you," Lanietta's voice said. "No, he doesn't. He is in for a surprise, isn't he? What would you do in his place?"

"I'm not sure. It's as if Tony is stuck no matter what he does," Claus said.

"The memory is cast in layers. Let it unfold," Lanietta's voice said.

"Jill! Jill Cresson! You're still alive!" Tony exclaimed.

"Lt. Col. Kavalla, your arrival is on schedule," Cresson said. "You may remove your helmet. You are safe."

Tony placed his helmet in the Lacuna rover. Jill walked over toward Tony, and so Tony held out his arms to hug her, expecting such in return. Instead, Jill walked past Tony and up to the rover. She opened a compartment (of which Tony had been unaware) and retrieved a sealed, silvery pouch. Jill ripped the pouch open and ate its contents.

"I'm famished," she said with food in her mouth. "I haven't eaten since the accident."

Jill tossed the empty pouch aside, grabbed two more, and ate from them.

"Follow me," she said as she walked back toward the second hatch.

Tony followed Jill through the second hatchway and into a larger chamber with an assortment of small mining tunnels, mining equipment, lights, workbenches (with microscopes and rock-cracking tools), chemistry equipment (for mixing, boiling, and distilling samples), and so on.

Jill's rover was in a corner out of the way, with full Astroosa logo and the Exodus One decal. There was also a large canister, about as big as a rover (but taller) at one side of the chamber with tubes running out. One tube dumped water into an open container, and two other tubes released gases into the chamber. Several others seemed to circulate air and provide heat.

"What is that?" Tony asked, referring to the large canister.

"This is what has kept me alive," Jill said. "It provides air and water, among other things."

"How does it work? Is this another Astroosa invention? I don't remember hearing of it, but I've had memory loss from—"

"From your automobile accident. Yes, I know. I've been in contact with Astroosa the entire time," Jill said. "There's much I could explain, but time is short, so I will be brief. We've been mining in this cave, as you can tell. We discovered water, which is good, but we also discovered an unusual ore. The ore powers this canister, which I designed on the fly and had Chefwater and Allerton assemble. This air we are breathing? It contains 21% oxygen and 79% neon."

"Don't you mean nitrogen?" Tony asked.

"No, neon," Jill said.

"But neon is rare," Tony said. "Where did you get it from?"

"Where is neon common?" Jill asked.

"In stars," Tony replied. "Are you saying there's a star in these caves?"

"The equivalent," Jill replied. "The ore is a self-sustaining fusion reaction. It generates heat and electricity, which is used to heat the cave and power the equipment, including equipment for hydrolyzing water into hydrogen and oxygen. My invention then uses the ore to fuse hydrogen into helium, and then helium and oxygen into neon. That's where our breathable air comes from."

"And my voice doesn't sound funny," Tony said. "Neither does yours."

"I could have left the atmosphere at just oxygen and helium, but I'm a perfectionist. Helium isn't good enough, and so we have the neon mixture," Jill explained.

"But what killed the other astronauts?" Tony asked.

"No more time for talk," Jill said. "It's time to take this ore back to Earth."

"Wait," Tony said. "Did you at least figure out what went wrong? Chefwater and Allerton deserve a funeral. Maybe we can bring them back to Earth for the funeral and a burial."

"They are gone. A write-off," Jill said with sudden impatience in her voice.

"That's my kind of girl!" Lanietta boomed across the ages of space and time.

"Did you transfer into Jill, Lanietta? Did you make her do this?" Claus demanded.

"Oh, no. Her demeanor was made for just this moment!" Lanietta boomed back. "Humans a write-off. Let the joyous words be proclaimed across all of Mars!"

"You sadistic maniac. Go away, will you? Go away!" Claus said, but Lanietta simply laughed into a distant echo until nothing left was heard.

Jill left the large chamber and passed through the second hatchway opening. She opened up another compartment on Tony's rover, revealing a thick-walled container about three feet across and square all around. She took the container, reentered the large chamber, and placed it on a workbench close to the ore-containing canister.

"I had Astroosa send this protective container to transport the ore. The ore is very volatile. Nothing we have here will contain it for long-term transport," Jill explained. "We found one, and only one. The other two took a sample of this one back to the Exodus One without proper containment. You saw the results. Fortunately the main ore is intact."

Jill shut down the canister machine, opened a panel on the front, and used a pair of large, special tongs to retrieve the ore—a piece of crystalline the size of a basketball encased in a semi-opaque shield Jill had designed for short-term transport. She placed this in the transport container and locked it tightly.

"Help me with this," she said.

Jill and Tony lifted the container and placed it back in the rover.

"And that's what killed them?" Tony asked.

"A piece of it. Let's get back to the lander," Jill said as she donned her gloves and helmet. "It's time to go."

Jill reached for Tony's helmet and threw it to Tony.

"No, wait," Tony said. "Chefwater and Allerton. We must recover them."

"Are you going to fight me on this mission, Kavalla?" Jill asked sternly.

"Jill! This isn't how I pictured you at all! You're supposed to be a nice, smart girl. What's happened to you?"

"He's losing focus, and he won't follow direct orders without contention," Jill called into her helmet's radio to Astroosa. "Didn't I tell you to send SaMonn?"

"Graeman superseded my authority on that one," Agent Keller's voice returned on Jill's radio.

"Hey! How did...that transmission...the time lag...how?" Tony asked.

"This ore will revolutionize things," Jill said to Tony. "I'm going back to Lacuna—with or without you."

"Not until you explain everything," Tony said, and he grabbed the container from the rover with intent to cast it away.

"Give me that!" Jill yelled as she reached for the container.

"No," Tony said. "We'll go back to the Exodus One and deal with that situation first."

"That's just what they did, and look what happened," Jill said. "It killed them. I won't have the entire ore wasted. I'm taking this back to Earth."

A strange feeling came over Tony. With the ore in his possession, he felt it was his. The pendant vibrated and stung against his chest, though he did not know why.

"I'll take it back myself. We'll have it...no, I'll have it analyzed. Something like this deserves special attention," Tony said.

"Yes, yes!" Lanietta's voice boomed. "The foolish humans believe they can harness a power of stars, no, a power beyond the stars. But who ends up wearing the harness? Tony?"

"This looks bad," Claus said. "There should be robotic testing for months on end before humans dare come this close."

"But there wasn't!" Lanietta said. "You humans in your eagerness have bitten off more than you can chew! You are savage dogs!"

"I would have insisted on testing, Lanietta! I would not have rushed things like this," Claus said.

"That's because you're a domesticated dog. My Clomper, the domesticated dog!" Lanietta said.

"This is no time for humor!" Claus said.

"It's always a good time for humor with humans!" Lanietta echoed as her voice faded in the distance.

"I've seen that look before with this ore," Jill said, "and I promised myself one thing—not again!"

Jill reached again for the container and missed, as Tony simply put the container behind his back. He couldn't have done so on Earth, but the one-third gravity on Mars permitted it. She punched him in the abdomen. The suit cushioned her blow, and Tony maintained his position.

"What has come over you?" Tony asked, still holding the container behind his back and away from Jill.

Jill didn't waste time with another punch. She disappeared into the main chamber and reappeared with a rifle.

"Drop it!" she ordered. "I've got tungsten-carbide bullets, and they *will* penetrate your suit."

"You're pointing a rifle at me!" Tony said.

"I said, drop it!" Jill ordered.

"Do you feel the tension, Claus? Do you feel the excitement?" Lanietta boomed. "Here's your utopia, Mr. Claus Gerhardt. Leave crime and such on Earth, right? Yet these are the only two humans alive on Mars, and the planet isn't big enough for the both of them."

"It's terrible! I would suspect you as behind all this," Claus said.

"But I'm not! There are other forces in the universe, forces more powerful than us Carinians. Even we know the limits of the universe. Do you?" Lanietta asked.

"I don't know what to say," Claus said.

"Because you don't know the limits of the universe," Lanietta said. "But like a puppy, you have to try, until only a crisis stops you. Behold the crisis!"

Tony dropped the container and jumped in the rover. He backed the rover into the first hatch in hopes of opening it, but the hatch didn't open. Jill ran up to Tony and fired, sending a bullet into his left shoulder. Tony looked, and blood flowed through the hole in his suit.

"You shot me!" Tony said.

"Get out of the rover, or I'll kill you where you sit!" Jill said.

"Jill!" Tony said.

But Jill wasn't pretending. She thrust the rifle's point into Tony's chest and prepared to fire.

"Okay, okay," Tony said.

Tony exited the rover and stood there, bleeding.

"Now place the container in the rover," Jill said. "Slowly. No one is taking this ore but me."

Tony did as she instructed.

"Raise your arms above your head," Jill ordered. "Do it!"

"I can only do one. You shot the other," Tony said as he raised his good arm.

"Now walk into the main chamber," she ordered, and Tony again complied.

"I thought we could be friends. I—" Tony started.

"Quiet. I can't take you back to Earth with the ore," Jill said.

"Jill, if—"

"Shut up! Take your suit off," Jill said. "Well?!"

Tony removed his helmet, his arm sleeves, and his upper torso piece, revealing the harness.

"I knew it!" Jill said. "Kechenova's harness is modified Sukhoi fighter-pilot gear!"

Jill knocked Tony across the skull with the butt of her rifle, rendering him unconscious. She removed the harness along with its battery packs and placed them in the Lacuna rover. Jill then walked over to the Exodus One rover and fired the rifle into the control panel, rendering the radio and rover inoperative. Pleased with her work, she walked back toward the Lacuna rover but stopped briefly by the second hatch after she had just passed through it.

"You were going to die anyway," she said, just before she sealed Tony in the main chamber by closing the second hatch and locking it.

"Wow! Jill has gone space crazy!" Claus said.

"I expect more respect from now on, Claus Gerhardt," Lanietta's voice said.

"What? Who?" Claus asked.

"From you. You will give me the respect I deserve. I wouldn't leave you for dead like that, at least not yet," Lanietta said. "Your fellow human Jill is not so friendly, is she? I've been more than friendly."

"You? Friendly?" Claus asked.

"The Veigon will drive people mad, as you have seen. I would never steal it from you. I would tell you all about the Veigon, and we would make plans," Lanietta said.

"Is that what Jill just took? Something called a Veigon? If you're in the telling mood, tell me. What is this thing? Some sort of weapon?" Claus asked. "It kills or convinces others to kill."

Lanietta appeared in an evening gown, as if going to the state ball. She approached Claus and asked him to dance.

"Your timing is terrible. Crimes and gowns are a bad mix," Claus said.

"Spice and cinnamon. Meat and potatoes. Chicken and noodle soup," Lanietta said. "Let's dance on Mars. Let's dance in the utopia you desire and leave these poor unfortunate humans behind. We'll make our own palace, powered by the Veigon. You'll be king, and I'll be queen. You'll learn much about the Veigon, so much so that together we shall build all that is of grace and beauty. There will be fine wine, food to dine, music—"

"For swine," Claus finished. "Because that's what you'd be."

"We could roll around in the mud together, you and I. We'd have piglets together. They'd say, 'oink, oink, oink'!" Lanietta laughed. "Oh, but this dance is tiring. I must rest."

Jill climbed into the Lacuna rover, pressed a button on the front of her suit, and the surrounding air depressurized. She pressed another button, and the first hatch opened. She then drove the rover away, and as she did, Claus jumped in while leaving Lanietta behind.

"Are you sure you want to ride with a crazy woman? Jill is a man-killer, you know," Lanietta said. "All I want is a dance."

"You're tuckered out. Goodbye," Claus said.

Jill directed the Lacuna rover out of the cave, onto the Martian surface, down into the crater, and right up to Lacuna's hatch. She exited the rover, opened up the lander's hatch, moved the container and harness gear from the rover to the lander, and crawled inside the lander. Claus followed. Jill pressed several buttons to start the launch sequence.

"Three, two, one, blastoff!" she said.

Lacuna ascended into the sky, and Jill was on her way to dock with Callisti. Jill patted the container with the ore, and she spoke to herself:

"I have put myself on a new map."

Chapter 45: A Deception

Back in Callisti, Doctor Kechenova's monitor showed that the harness was no longer worn by Tony.

"Callisti to Lacuna rover, do you read? Callisti to—" Kechenova started.

But Kechenova stopped herself short. Her instruments showed that the lander had blasted off from Mars and was heading back toward Callisti.

"Lacuna, Callisti," Kechenova called over the command module's radio to the lander's radio. "Lacuna, Callisti, do you read?"

"Callisti, this is Lacuna," replied Jill.

"Colonel, it is good to hear your voice," Kechenova said. "I take it all went well?"

"The rescue mission is a success," Jill said. "We'll rendezvous with you in one hour."

Kechenova was puzzled, though. Her monitors still showed no life-sign readings for Tony. Yet her monitors showed the harness was getting closer.

"He's in Lacuna, so why doesn't the harness transmit his vital signs?" Kechenova asked herself.

"Lacuna, Callisti," Kechenova said.

"Lacuna here. Go ahead, Callisti," Jill replied.

"Colonel, if I may speak with Lieutenant Colonel Kavalla please?" Kechenova asked.

"I'm afraid he is seriously hurt and unconscious," Jill said.

"What happened?" Kechenova asked.

"I'm not sure," Jill said. "He suddenly acted erratically in the cave. He threw tables and equipment all over. Then he took off his partial pressure suit and some sort of harness. He ran around the cave. I had to sedate him and put his suit back on

to get him back to the lander. I brought the harness back too. Marc Graeman said it's some sort of calming device."

"Yes, a calming device," Kechenova said, but something in Jill's story unsettled Kechenova. "I'll prepare for emergency medical treatment when you arrive."

"Thank you," Jill said ever-so-sweetly.

"Lanietta," Claus called. "You have to warn Irina. Lanietta?"

"I'm still on the Martian surface where you left me," Lanietta pouted. "All alone. No one to dance with. I'll just have to dance with my shadow. Sigh. All dressed up and no one to dance with."

"Stop clowning around, Lanietta," Claus said. "You promised to take Irina's role. So take her role."

"I promise nothing. I only check in on her from time to time," Lanietta said.

"Well check in on her now!" Claus demanded.

"Not until I get my dance!" Lanietta protested.

"I can't go down there now. Jill has the lander heading back for Callisti," Claus said.

"You should have thought about that before you took up with that Jill woman," Lanietta said.

"Lanietta, please!" Claus begged.

But Lanietta simply sang a soft song and took small circular steps, dancing alone on Mars with melancholy.

"Oh for the love of the universe, you are too much!" Claus said.

Lanietta continued her soft singing and dancing. Jill was smug with her deception, and she planned her next move. The hour passed, and the lander docked with the command module.

"Hurry," Jill said as the two hatches opened. "He's in here. I'll move this container into Callisti to give you space."

Jill transferred the container from Lacuna to Callisti. Kechenova then entered the lander with her medical kit and laptop. To her surprise, Tony was not in the lander. Only his harness was to be found.

"What is this?" Kechenova turned to say.

But as she did, Jill closed and locked the command module's hatch.

"Colonel, you closed Callisti's hatch by mistake. Open it, please. And where is the Lieutenant Colonel?" Kechenova yelled.

"Lacuna, Callisti," Jill called over the radio. "I'm undocking."

"No, you can't!" Kechenova said. "Open the hatch, and let me in!"

"If you don't close your own hatch, you'll be sucked into space when I undock," Jill said over the radio. "I leave that to you."

"Lanietta, help!" Claus shouted.

"A girl...without a man...is just a girl...without a plan," Lanietta sang softly as she continued to slow-dance on Mars alone.

"La-Ni-Et-TAAAAA!" Claus shouted.

Lanietta did not reply. Jill fired up systems on the command module, and Kechenova knew she was serious. Kechenova had no choice but to close the hatch on the lander to preserve her own atmosphere and keep herself from being pulled into space. But Kechenova wouldn't give up so easily. As Jill tried undocking Callisti from Lacuna, Kechenova fired up what was left of Lacuna's engines and pushed the craft against Callisti, causing a torsing against the hatch mechanism and thus jamming it. Jill reset the docking mechanism and attempted to undock—several times—but each time Kechenova countered with thrusts here and there. And so, Jill fired up Callisti's engines and attempted to counter Kechenova's thrusts. Both vehicles spun and rolled and pitched and jimmied and jammed and jerked around, sending the occupants against their respective cabin walls.

"A girl...without a man...is fighting for...her own lifespan," Lanietta sang.

"Lanietta!" Claus screamed.

"Worthless Kazakh! I'm through with you once and for all!" Jill exclaimed.

With that, Jill fired up the nuclear engine on the third stage and sent Callisti and Lacuna on an accelerated orbit around Mars.

"Cresson, what are you doing?" Kechenova called over the radio.

"I tried to be nice, but you wanted to play hardball, so this is the end of you and Lacuna," Jill said.

Jill headed the two crafts toward the Mars Orbiton.

"You are getting too close to the American satellite," Kechenova said. "Change course."

"Negative," Jill said. "I'm going to ram you and Lacuna into the stars and stripes forever!"

Kechenova tried frantically to alter course with Lacuna's engines, but fuel was low, and the third stage's nuclear engine was too powerful.

"You'll kill us both!" Kechenova said.

"Ever played *chicken*?" Jill said, and that was her last radio broadcast.

"Okay, Lanietta! You win! I'll do anything you want! You win! Stop this! Stop this now!" Claus pleaded.

"I only wanted a dance," Lanietta sighed.

Realizing the situation was hopeless, Kechenova fired Lacuna's thrusters to remove the torsing on the docking mechanism, but now Jill's maneuvering kept Kechenova from easily getting away. There wasn't enough thrust from Lacuna to pull away from Callisti.

"Help Irina! Help her survive!" Claus pleaded.

"Oh enjoy the show, Claus! You men enjoy women's mud wrestling. Just think of this as women wrestling in space!" Lanietta shot back.

"An oxygen tank," Kechenova said with new insight.

She ripped open a panel and shorted two wires. One of the external oxygen containers exploded, and the lander broke free from Callisti. Kechenova used the maneuvering rockets to steer clear of the Mars Orbiton satellite, and Jill altered her course as well, shot around the Mars Orbiton opposite of Lacuna, and broke orbit toward Earth. Lacuna, meanwhile, was now losing altitude.

"I'm going to crash. I'm going to crash," Kechenova said as she prepared her helmet and pressurized her suit.

Kechenova spent the last bit of fuel to slow Lacuna's speed as best she could and shallow the angle, but it wasn't enough. The lander sped just above the Martian landscape, skipped several times like a stone on water, and then barrel-rolled down the side of a large crater—a third of Mars's circumference away from the original Lacuna landing site.

"Rotten vile Lanietta. You heartless, worthless, wench!" Claus said.

Chapter 46: Short Conversation

"Astroosa, Callisti," Jill radioed to Earth. "The rescue mission is a success. We are heading back to Earth. I have set the engines to maximum thrust. Estimated time of arrival is sixty hours. Kavalla and Kechenova are exhausted. They are sleeping after a very tiring rescue effort. Radiation from the Exodus One gave Kavalla difficulty, forcing a hard landing, and Callisti passed through an energy beam from the Exodus One, throwing Doctor Kechenova into a high-force spin that created internal bruising."

Six minutes passed before Jill heard a reply.

"Callisti, Astroosa. Congratulations, and an early welcome home," Graeman said. "We're planning an especially large ticker-tape parade for the three of you."

Jill replied, "Recommend we delay the parade for several weeks. We'll need to go through decontamination. And there are other considerations. Notify Agent Keller to increase security on our arrival. We will land in the Pacific above the eastern edge of the Hess Rise."

Another six minutes passed, and Jill heard the reply:

"Acknowledged, Callisti," Graeman said.

An hour passed. Jill received a secure, scramble-spread-spectrum radio transmission from Agent Keller using the same high-speed communication link as on Mars, with no delay.

"Jill, do you read me? This is Tembruno," Agent Keller said. "I'm alone and on a secure frequency. We may speak openly."

"My Tembruno! How I missed you!" Jill said. "I must tell you. I have the ore! We can go ahead with the corporate plan to lift the Hess Rise. All praise our new island and country—Hesserlan!"

"Excellent, my sweet," Agent Keller replied. "There's a special place in Astroosa for you, and in Hesserlan. We'll have a mansion built, just the two of us, overlooking a Pacific sunset. We'll have servants and swimming pools and room after royal room filled with treasures of the world. We'll have a fleet of cars and limousines with a platoon of chauffeurs. Nothing will stop us. We will run Astroosa and Hesserlan and the world. Plans are now in the works to oust Marc Graeman from Astroosa. You will be the new chief executive, and I will be at your side running daily operations. Now Jill, my sweet, were you able to bring Kavalla to our side? And what of the doctor? We must dispose of her somehow."

Jill replied, "I look forward to our new life, my love. Tony was not agreeable to my will. He wanted to linger on Mars to see the Exodus One. He took the ore from me. I had to take it back, of course. Tembruno, we must take extra special precautions that no one touches the ore on Earth. It changes people. But as for Tony, I left him on Mars. He won't give us any trouble. Same for the doctor. She and Lacuna have crashed into Mars. It's just you, me, and the ore."

Chapter 47: A Monazite Party

Lanietta pulled Claus back to Mars, where she awaited him in her gown.

"Now we shall dance," Lanietta said. "A waltz is appropriate for the occasion."

"No dancing is appropriate for this *occasion*," Claus said.

But he had no choice. Lanietta changed his outfit into something more becoming for a man, and the two waltzed. Lanietta even provided classic waltz music, though from where Claus could not tell.

"One-two-three, one-two-three, one-two-three. Oh Claus, this dance is so clever, this waltz style," Lanietta said.

"Are we to waltz away the hours while Irina and Tony are in trouble?" Claus asked.

"For a little while. Both are complicit in their situations, as it stands," Lanietta said.

"I doubt either one is standing," Claus said.

"Well not the way we are, Claus my little nummy-num," Lanietta said, and she put her head on his shoulder. "Don't you love me, Claus? Don't you? Being close to you puts me in an altogether different mood."

"We are in ethereal states living out your fantasy. There's nothing loving about it," Claus said.

"You could at least pretend. Remember, others will be watching," Lanietta said.

"That thought does restrain me," Claus said.

"Oh, shy are you? Then you do love me! Well, you might show me great passion if I promise none would see. Is that all you need? To stoke your fire?" Lanietta asked.

"You would allow anyone to see us," Claus said.

"Yes, I suppose I would. Perhaps someday you and I can have a private moment. We'll go deep into the lunar caverns where no Carinian method can reconstruct our most private moments," Lanietta said.

"Aren't you forgetting something?" Claus said.

"I don't forget things. Not at all," Lanietta said.

"You're a Carinian. You're not human," Claus said.

"There's a story in your culture about a wooden puppet who becomes a boy. I could be the Carinian who becomes a woman," Lanietta said.

"As I recall, the puppet had to sacrifice his life to become human," Claus said. "What would you sacrifice?"

"I would sacrifice you, of course!" Lanietta laughed.

"You'd kill me? Makes no sense," Claus said.

"I would sacrifice your desire for less than perfection. I would give you perfection, and you'd be happy," Lanietta said. "How's that for becoming human?"

Claus shook his head in disbelief.

"Well, you think about it for a spell, will you? Meanwhile, Tony is ready to wake up. We must be there to watch. He has work yet to do," Lanietta explained.

Lanietta stopped the waltz, held Claus's hand with one hand, and snapped her fingers with the other. The two appeared in Tony's chamber. Tony awoke. He put his hand to his skull and felt blood. Then he touched his left shoulder and found more blood.

"What time is it?" Tony asked without thinking. "Time. It doesn't matter. I'm at the end. Stranded on Mars. Well, my life was bound to end. But something horrible has happened to Jill. She's a corporate votary with no regard for human dignity. Ow. My head aches. I'm so thirsty, so hungry, and tired. And I'm still bleeding."

Tony found rags, ripped them, and used them to fashion bandages for his shoulder and head. Next, he found a little water and drank it. But there was no food. Jill ate what little was stored, and she also took the Lacuna rover from the cave.

"The Lacuna rover. If I can find it, I might find food. But then what? She's more than likely taken Lacuna into space," Tony said.

Tony looked around for the harness, but it was not in the chamber.

"She took the harness. She took the harness!"

Tony shook and panicked. Without the harness, he would suffer seizures again. As predicted it happened.

"I really am tired, Lanietta," Claus said.

"You are in another coma," Lanietta said. "You can't be tired."

"I'm tired of being in another person's mind," Claus said.

"Too bad. I'm making a character study of Tony," Lanietta said.

"What must I do to get you to stop? To leave these people alone?" Claus asked.

"You are persistent. But you know the answer, or you should. You have to marry me. And, you have to put Frieda out of your mind. Permanently. Well?"

"Are Carinians allowed to marry their pets?" Claus asked.

"In my society, there is a ceremony where I can promote you to consort. Think of it as a pre-engagement ceremony. Well?"

"You're making that up. The implant says so!" Claus said. "What other lies can you tell? No, don't answer. I don't want to know. Forget it."

Lanietta laughed. Claus stared at her and paused.

"Show me what Tony's thinking," Claus finally said.

Lanietta laughed again. She took Claus with her into Tony's thoughts. Tony was now driving his father's Cobra on a country back road, playing cat and mouse with his friend, Dwayne Reese, who was driving a '67 Chevy Camaro SS convertible. Tony was the mouse, and Dwayne was the cat, meaning Dwayne was

chasing Tony. Tony accelerated briskly on the hard dirt, but Dwayne closed in. Tony slowed for a turn to the right, turned sharply, and accelerated just enough to spin the wheels and cause the Cobra's back end to fishtail around to the left, but only a little, and not so much as to spin the Cobra out of control. Dwayne followed and fishtailed with just as much control. Tony picked up speed and whipped the steering wheel left and right to send his body left and right and see how much slaloming the Cobra could take. Dwayne kept up. Tony zipped past trees and barns and mailboxes that he nearly hit. (Dwayne did take out a mailbox or two).

The day was sunny, but Tony saw dark clouds ahead. Jagged lightning flashed in the distance. Six seconds later, booming thunder drummed Tony's eardrums, and suddenly he was much older and driving the Cobra at night from the Later Gator when he slammed into the tree. He felt his lower body adrift in space, but his hip acted like a hinge on wires, with his upper torso bending forward and his forehead slamming against the steering wheel. Then his body repeated this hinging action, and his forehead hit the steering wheel again. And again this repeated. Faster and faster, until he felt his head hitting the steering wheel as quickly as a human gong.

Suddenly, music and singing started:

Now come with me to Hesserlan
The place of dream and wondrous plan
A life with friends all hand-in-hand
Our home, we call it Hesserlan.

Tony opened his eyes. He was lying on the ground, in the mining cave, on Mars, where Jill had left him. A portable music player was under his back, and it played what sounded like a national anthem for Hesserlan.

"Hesserlan, Hesserlan!" Lanietta taunted Claus. "Is that one of your heritage songs?"

"I don't know what you're talking about," Claus said.

"Sounds Germanic. Like your name," Lanietta said.

"A name is just a word, nothing more," Claus said. "I could be Carl or Clark or Clavicle for all I care."

"Clavicle?" Lanietta barked. "You don't fool me! That's another name for collarbone. Perhaps Clavicle is more appropriate. As a dog, I would reward you with a bone for wearing your collar. Collarbone. That should be your name!"

"I'd rather be called Snowbank!" Claus said.

"And why is that?" Lanietta retorted.

"Because that's where I'd like to be. Right now. So I can freeze to death!" Claus answered.

"Bah!"

"Hesserlan," Tony said. "What is that? Something from a story? It doesn't matter. I must have fallen on this device and turned it on when I had a seizure. I must get up. I must get to the Lacuna rover. It's my only hope. I must use its radio to warn Irina. I must, since—"

And here, Tony paused. He stared intently at the Exodus One rover's radio.

"Since there's no working radio in here," Tony finished. "But could I get the Exodus One rover working? I could take it to the Lacuna rover."

Tony tried starting the Exodus One rover, but the controls were damaged beyond repair. Frustrated, Tony gave up the attempt.

"I must walk the distance," Tony said. "But how? I don't have enough oxygen in my life support pack to get me there. And there's a hole in my suit. Yet there are uncounted cans of oxygen in this chamber. If only I could carry them all...if only..."

Tony had an idea, and the idea came from a climb to Mount Everest. He would create "stations" of oxygen canisters, with each station separated by the distance he could go on one oxygen canister. He would have to carry at least three canisters to make this work. But he couldn't do a thing until he did something about the hole in his suit.

"I either must patch it or replace it," he said.

Tony looked around the cave for something to help. There were no spare suits. Jill had planned things well to maximize chances for Tony's demise.

"Blast her anyway," Tony said.

"Blast her anyway!" Lanietta mocked.

"That should have been my line about you," Claus said. "Tony's fantasies about Jill were sadly out of perspective. However, I have a *clear* perspective of you. How does that make you feel, Lanietta? Angry? Sad? Lonely?"

"Your perspective will change in time," Lanietta said. "You simply need more enlightenment. Let us continue your enlightenment, shall we? Observe as Tony makes progress with his situation."

Tony looked around more. Could he find repair glue? He found none. Then he had a thought, and he acted upon it. He searched the Exodus One's rover for tools. He opened panel after panel, and after revealing all to be empty, he opened a small, side panel in back that most people would overlook. Jill apparently did.

"Suit glue and patch kit," Tony grinned. "I'll have my suit repaired in minutes."

Tony did just that. He applied glue to the suit surface, to the patch surface, allowed them to dry for a minute, slapped the pieces together, and held them in such a fashion for five minutes.

"There is no way to test until I'm in the Martian atmosphere, so I'll have to cross my fingers that this patch will hold," Tony said to himself. "At least now I can move on to my next plan—using the spare oxygen canisters to escape this cave."

Tony strapped canisters to his back and determined he could just carry four canisters, including the one needed for breathing.

"This had better work," Tony said. "I have no food, so I can't spend too long doing this."

"Oh if only he had torso armor," Lanietta lamented with false concern.

"You would do anything to get a reaction out of me," Claus said. "What an excruciating task for Tony. I wish I could help."

"But you can't," Lanietta said. "Which is worse, suffering from the work at hand, or watching others suffer?"

"It is a question you'll never be able to understand. I challenge you, Lanietta. I challenge you to decide which is worse. Because I don't think you have it in you. I don't think you can decide what tortures people the most. Well? What say you, Lanietta the Carinian?"

"I'll show you, you stubborn fool. I'll enter Tony's body and endure all that he endures. That is your proof!" Lanietta snapped.

Lanietta dipped into Tony's body. Tony didn't wish to spend long at the task, but the task did take some time. Tony left the cave with four canisters and walked as far toward the Lacuna landing site as he could until the first canister ran out. He called this point Waypoint 1. He dropped two good canisters at Waypoint 1, switched breathing from the depleted canister to a good one, and returned to the cave. On reaching the cave, he now had two depleted canisters. He refilled them and strapped on two more, meaning he left the cave with four oxygen canisters. On reaching Waypoint 1, one of the canisters was depleted, so he switched to another canister. He left the depleted canister at Waypoint 1, picked up a good canister that he had dropped previously, and proceeded toward the Lacuna landing site as far as he could until his breathing canister ran out. He called this site Waypoint 2. He dropped two good canisters there, switched to breathing another canister, and returned to Waypoint 1. At Waypoint 1, his breathing canister ran out, and so he switched to the other good canister he'd left previously for breathing. He picked up the other depleted canister, returned to the cave, and replenished them. This meant there were two good canisters at Waypoint 2 and none at Waypoint 1. And so he headed to Waypoint 1 again, dropped off two good canisters, switched breathing canisters, and returned to the cave.

He picked up two more good canisters, replenished the depleted ones, and proceeded to Waypoint 1. He dropped the depleted canister, switched to a good one for breathing, picked up a good canister already at Waypoint 1, and headed to Waypoint 2. At Waypoint 2, he dropped the depleted canister, switched breathing to a good one, picked up a good canister left previously, and headed toward the Lacuna landing site. He reached a point where his breathing canister ran out, and he was not yet at the Lacuna landing site. Tony named this point Waypoint 3. He switched breathing canisters, left two good ones at Waypoint 3, and returned to Waypoint 2. Now he had depleted a canister and had to use the one good one at Waypoint 2 to get to Waypoint 1, but he picked up the depleted canister and brought it with him. He reached Waypoint 1, and the canister from Waypoint 2 was depleted, and so he had to use the canister from Waypoint 1 to reach the cave, which he did.

This entire process was getting complicated, and Tony knew he couldn't rely on his memory to know if there were enough canisters to get him from one waypoint to another. Lanietta dipped out of his body and spoke.

"I will help Tony. I will come up with a few rules to safeguard his return," she said.

1) Must have four good canisters when leaving the cave.

2) Must have four good canisters and a good one on the ground at a waypoint before going to the next waypoint.

3) All other situations mean going back to previous waypoint or back to the cave.

4) When going back, drop any extra good canister at the current waypoint and pick up as many empties as possible.

5) The previous waypoint will always have one good canister. Use it if needed.

"There, you see Claus? I'm helpful," Lanietta said.

"You don't suppose he came up with these rules himself, do you?" Claus asked.

"In his condition? Forget it," Lanietta said.

"Then you were here at the time. You somehow left Novi 2 during the five-hundred year hibernation and space-jumped over here, is that it? And yet Labba once told me it is impossible to space-jump from within the bambooph perimeter. So some part of this story doesn't hold true," Claus postulated.

"And yet you have been begging me to interfere with this memory the entire time. You were willing to believe anything and everything to get help for these poor unfortunate souls. If I had managed to help them, how would you have rationalized it? Would you have gone on a witch hunt as you have now? Well? Of course I didn't help him. He figured out everything himself. But you so desperately wanted to believe, didn't you? Didn't you?"

"Yes. I wanted to believe you could relieve his suffering," Claus said.

"Then I have proven my point. It is not the suffering from watching others suffering that is your undoing, it is your belief in a magic pill to solve all problems. You want me as your magic pill. But you turn me away at every turn. How do you handle that conflict, Mr. Claus Gerhardt?"

Claus was ripped in half. Despite everything Lanietta had done, she'd finally zeroed in on his deepest fear. But what was there to do about it? Throw himself on her mercy? No, she was still an alien, and Claus knew it. He needed more time. That was all he had left in this ordeal, and Lanietta was willing to allow the memory to flow forward. And so, Claus bit his lip and continued to experience Tony's adventure on Mars.

With canister rules established and followed, Tony ensured he had at least one good canister at the current waypoint so that he'd have enough oxygen to return to the cave. He made a game of this and called it "Progression". As he progressed, he realized that gradually he needed a little more oxygen than the pacing and spacing of his waypoints first suggested. Because of this, he amended his rules such that he had to have four good packs on his back and two (instead of one) good canisters on the ground before proceeding to the next waypoint. What this meant was that Tony would go through a full canister and part of another before reaching another waypoint, and so this slowed his progress, because he couldn't stock as many canisters at stations as he had first done, which tired him further.

These rules and details were dull to no end, and normally Claus would be absolutely bored out of his mind, but his recent exchange with Lanietta had jolted him to the core. It was everything he could do to stop shaking, even in ethereal form. He immersed himself in the rote and monotony of Tony's situation to ease his own nerves. Would it be enough? He wasn't sure. Perhaps his own body on the Mad Mistral was suffering from atrophy. It would explain why he was less able to endure watching this particular memory than others.

A beat formed in Claus's mind, like the ticking of a clock. Except these weren't ticks. The beats were low and with periodic syncopation, like a stutter. These stutters were organized as if trying to say something. From where did they come? The WWV time station? Claus thought he should remember, but he couldn't.

"Because of your own amnesia," Lanietta said.

"What?" Claus tried to cover.

"I hear the beats in your head. You've heard them before," she said. "In times of stress you heard them frequently. But you became an adult and lost memory of those beats—until now."

"If you know, tell me. I can't remember all of my childhood, true, but I don't see how it relates to anything now," Claus said.

Lanietta laughed.

Tony managed to create Waystation 4, and now the crater's rise was easy to see, but whatever was left of the Lacuna landing site was still hidden behind the rise.

Tony rested at Waystation 4 by sitting on a boulder that had a flat, rectangular surface much like a park bench. His mind wandered, and the dust devils in the distance began resembling giraffes and trees dancing around each other.

"I'm hallucinating," Tony said.

He pressed the audio player in hopes of it arresting his mental degradation, but it did not. The dust devils continued to look like giraffes and trees dancing here and there and around in the air.

"I must...must return to the...the cave," Tony said.

The hallucinations grew worse. Tony envisioned that the landscape had become a savanna, and a pride of lions now chased the giraffes and other hoofed animals across the landscape.

"How do I get out of this?" Tony said. "If I don't recover, I'll lose my wits and run out of oxygen."

Tony looked down and was still able to see the oxygen canisters at Waypoint 4.

"So I'm not completely disoriented," Tony said. "I should return to the cave until this spell wears off. But which way is that? I can no longer see my tracks. The ground is covered with grass."

Tony decided to stay where he was and hope that the hallucination would end. But something strange happened. A reddish-brown hand rose above the grass line, reached for a canister, grabbed it, and pulled it underground.

"Hey!" Tony yelled. "That's mine! I need that!"

Tony moved to fight for the canister, but then he stopped himself.

"I must be hallucinating this," Tony said. "The canister hasn't really disappeared. It must still be here. I'll hold onto the canisters to prove they aren't being stolen."

"Are your nerves still shot?" Lanietta asked Claus.

"I...am better," Claus said. "I can't say the same for Tony."

"You should be thankful, Claus. Tony is struggling to keep his sanity, as you can see. We will see his struggle with reality and fantasy as his mind vacillates between

processing external and internal stimuli to both rest his mind yet keep it occupied."

"He has more strength than I, then," Claus said.

Tony sat by the canisters and held onto a good one. He watched as things progressed. Another reddish-brown hand reached for the very canister Tony was holding. The hand grabbed hold of the canister and pulled. Tony pulled back, and another hand came out of the grass and pulled even harder.

"An interactive hallucination? But what could be pulling on these?" Tony asked himself. "I must be losing strength and struggling to remain conscious. Then this is the end."

"Hang in there, Tony," Claus said.

"Begging for help again?" Lanietta asked.

"Just cheering him on," Claus replied.

A small humanoid jumped out of the grass, revealing the hands belonged to him. His other exposed skin was also reddish-brown, but instead of clothing, he wore a flexible outfit of brown scales, scales somewhat resembling that of an alligator. He had no special breathing apparatus but was instead breathing the Martian air without issue.

"*Iki li gau ixa kahala,*" the humanoid said repeatedly, meaning, "Give to me the happy-air."

"That's mine!" Tony said. "Let go! I need it to breathe, or I'll die."

Another humanoid with reddish-brown skin and a scaly suit arose from the grass and shook one of the depleted canisters.

"*Ikos kahala a'a uplau,*" he said, meaning, "This happy-air is depleted."

"Stop!" Tony yelled as he continued struggling for control of the good canister.

"Stop!" mocked the second humanoid.

"Let go, or else!" Tony continued.

"Let go, or else stop!" the second humanoid mocked.

"Ah, the Martians are after his oxygen," Lanietta said.

"You speak as if they are real," Claus said.

"Aren't they?"

Two more short humanoids with swirls of red and green skin with reddish-green scaly suits appeared above the grass line, and they along with the second humanoid pulled Tony, the canister, and the first humanoid down into the grass, into a hole leading below the surface, and into an underground cave system. Lanietta pulled Claus down after Tony.

"What is this place? Where am I? Who are you all?" Tony asked.

"What am this who you are?" mocked a humanoid.

"Do any of you speak English?" Tony asked. "And how can you breathe? The air is so thin on Mars."

"English," said an older humanoid with wrinkled, light-beige-colored skin, a silver-scaly suit, and long white hair, who was just now walking up to the group. "The language of the disposers."

"What? Did you say *disposers*? Disposers of what?" Tony asked.

But Tony's air was running low.

"Is this air fit to breathe for humans?" he asked the older humanoid.

"No," the older humanoid said.

The older humanoid snapped his fingers, and the two humanoids (who had pulled Tony down into the grass) stepped forward with a small device containing two tubes. They approached Tony and made to disconnect his circulating air hose. Tony shied back.

"Have no worry, friend," the older humanoid said. "They only wish to help your suit remove carbon from its *halla*, rather, its air."

"A carbon scrubber?" Tony asked.

The older humanoid nodded, "Yes."

The two younger humanoids installed the carbon scrubber so quickly that Tony lost almost no air pressure from his life support system.

"My name is Ceborio," the older humanoid said. "With me are Bellicot, Meppep, Arleon, and Oistau. Bellicot was the one fighting you for the happy-air container. Meppep imitated your words. Arleon and Oistau escorted you to our

world. And here you are, human...human... do you have a name?"

"My name is Tony Kavalla," Tony said. "Who are you people?"

"We are *Monazites*," Ceborio said.

"Ah, the Monazites," Lanietta said. "How I miss them. We must go visit them after this memory. Oh, but I can't."

"Another story?" Claus asked.

"Everything's a story," Lanietta said. "It's just a matter of how it's told."

"Why can't you visit them? I thought you can space-jump," Claus said.

"I can, but they couldn't. A sad ending, too," Lanietta said.

"Monazite? That's sand," Tony said.

"We are made from monazite, and so we have taken the name," Ceborio said.

"Like my bones are made from calcium?" Tony asked.

"Something like that," Ceborio said. "We are not considered true life-forms. Your kind might call us robots."

"Early selenites?" Claus asked.

"They have a relation," Lanietta said.

Bellicot swiped the full canister from Tony, inserted the nozzle into his (Bellicot's) mouth, opened the valve, and inhaled deeply. He closed the valve, removed the nozzle, and dropped the canister on the ground. He then jumped and danced all around in a maniacal frenzy, as if propelled by a supercharged engine on nitrous oxide. Meppep took the canister next and followed suit, inhaling deeply and hopping around like a jumping bean.

"*Akitia!*" Ceborio yelled, and then he followed up with, "Stop!" in English.

"What is happening?" Tony asked. "They inhaled my air as if it were a drug."

"To them, it is," Ceborio said. "Our bodies are adjusted to this thin air. Your air is too rich with oxygen for us to handle properly. Imagine if you were to breathe pure oxygen, and multiply that by a thousand. That's what happens to us when we inhale that much oxygen."

Bellicot slumped by a wall and looked down in misery. Meppep soon followed.

"*Kley pooga-tooga a'a gau,*" Bellicot said.

"How miserable is me," Meppep repeated, but in English.

"See how you stumble?" Ceborio said to Bellicot and Meppep. "Too much happy-air robs you of reason and poise. It drags you into the world of the *Veigon*."

"Oh, not the world of the Veigon," Lanietta mocked. "I hope I'm never dragged down *there*!"

"There's that name again. Veigon. What is it, Lanietta? Jill took it to Earth, that much is clear. And it has the power to end life."

"Or begin life," Lanietta said.

"Whose life?" Claus asked.

Lanietta smiled.

"Whose life, Lanietta? Yours? Mine? Whose?" Claus asked.

"I didn't create the universe," Lanietta said.

"But you claim to have created. Do you believe the Veigon is your creator?" Claus asked.

"How could you comprehend the creation of a Carinian?" Lanietta asked. "The Veigon. Sigh. By itself it's nothing. Needs power from the Anrega. But I jump ahead. These Monazites are no better than you in the awareness category."

"Is this hallucination that sad to you? At least it's cohesive," Claus said.

"Who said this was a hallucination?" Lanietta said.

"Then Tony found a society on Mars?" Claus asked.

"You're getting warm," Lanietta said.

"They found him?" Claus asked.

"Getting cold," Lanietta said.

"He will find them," Claus said.

"Stone cold. Frozen like ice," Lanietta laughed.

"He's...experiencing a memory from the past, much as we are," Claus said.

"Partly hot, partly cold," Lanietta said.

"A mixture of past and present?" Claus said.

"That's better," Lanietta said.

"The Veigon is no more," Bellicot said. "The disposer removed it."

"Yes," Meppep said. "She took it back to Earth."

"Jill!" Claus exclaimed.

"Boiling hot in sassafras tea with instant mashed potatoes!" Lanietta said.

"There, I *did* hear, 'disposer'," Tony said.

"Is this true, Arleon?" Ceborio asked.

Arleon looked at Oistau, and Oistau returned the gaze.

"It's true," Oistau said. "Bellicot and Meppep followed two humans. Part of the Veigon had been removed. A part known as a *Veigast*."

"Did the humans have names?" Ceborio asked.

"Yes," Arleon said. "Their names were Allerton and Chefwater."

"This is the recent past," Claus said. "Subterranean life on Mars. Maybe Tony met these creatures, maybe he didn't. But he experienced what happened."

"You see? A memory of a memory," Lanietta said. "I've proven it works. Many will then experience the memory of you viewing Tony's memory of the Monazite memory. It goes on, Claus. It goes on."

"Bellicot and Meppep followed the two humans to their spaceship. The Veigast unleashed a fury of energy in its desire to reunite with the Veigon," Oistau said.

"What is a Veigast?" Claus asked.

"Haven't you been listening? It's a part of the Veigon," Lanietta said.

"I know, but what does it do?" Claus asked.

"Oh, *that*," Lanietta said. "Nothing much. Just destroys life around it. To thin out the herd, so to speak."

"The human named 'Cresson' took the Veigon in a shielded cage up into orbit and back toward Earth," Arleon said.

"Can this be true?" Ceborio said with a sense of hope welling in his throat. "After generations of surface desolation caused by the Veigon, our barren planet has been redelivered to us?"

Bellicot and Meppep got up and inhaled more oxygen from the canister.

"It's true, it's true! Rehabitation begins!" they both cheered, and they performed more jumping, aerial stunts, acrobatics, and all sorts of playful dynamic moves.

"Should we warn the humans on Earth?" Oistau asked. "They don't know what the Veigon will do."

"Why should we worry about them?" Arleon said. "If our planet were lush with abundant surface life, do you not think that the humans would plunder our resources and do to us what the Veigon has already done? Humans and the Veigon are made for each other."

Bellicot and Meppep took more puffs of air and then ran with the container down a passageway and out of sight. Tony heard many more humanoids cheering and celebrating with such a raucous cacophony that Tony thought his head would explode. Meanwhile, Oistau touched a finger to his temple and concentrated, as if receiving information.

"Our people have discovered another human," Oistau said. "She has crash landed in the *pelion* crater."

"That would be Irina," Lanietta said.

"Must you spoil the story?" Claus asked.

"Just testing you. To see if you're paying attention," Lanietta said.

"I'm convinced Tony experienced this in real time, and that somehow he really was pulled down below the surface. The ore sample is a Veigast, a Martian devil of sorts. There's also concern about the Veigon, that it shouldn't go to Earth," Claus said.

"On the contrary, these Monazites are sure that the corrupt Earthling behavior is a perfect match for the Veigon," Lanietta said.

"And here you were blaming me for everything," Claus said.

"I still do. The Veigon is a tool to bring out the *best* of you and humanity," Lanietta said. "Now shush already. I'm missing the good part."

"The *pelion* crater is a great distance from here," Ceborio said.

"She is in shock," Oistau said.

"From seeing your people?" Tony asked.

"No, from the crash," Oistau said. "She has injuries."

"You must help her. Don't let her die," Tony said. "I must go to her and help. Right now!"

"We do not have speedy transports," Oistau said. "It would take days to reach your companion."

"There's a rover near the Lacuna landing site. If you could return me to the surface near that point, I would be most grateful," Tony said.

"Tony wants to make a deal with aliens. What aliens will you make deals with?" Lanietta asked as she pressed her face close to Claus's.

"You won't make a deal. You're on vacation," Claus said.

"Ah, but I will make deals on my vacation. They are null and void once my vacation ends, of course," Lanietta said.

"Then your game of marriage with me is also part of your vacation game, isn't it?" Claus asked.

"It was sincere," Lanietta said. "You would die before my vacation is up, that is, if I permit you to die."

"Even normal slavery allows people to die," Claus said.

"Who says you're part of normal slavery?" Lanietta asked.

"I don't know what I'm a part of," Claus said.

"Then enjoy the moment," Lanietta said.

Arleon and Oistau led Tony down the tunnel, with Ceborio walking at Tony's side. As they traveled, Tony marveled at the stonework columns, decorative carvings of people doing things, and the smooth floor. Water flowed in various fountains and along channels, and light poured out of the fountain pools and reflected off stonework in flickers from the rippling water.

"We Monazites excel at masonry," Ceborio said. "It's a necessary part of survival on Mars, with us being driven underground by the Veigon in the time of mass destruction."

"What is the Veigon?" Tony asked.

But before Ceborio could answer, the group reached an open chamber with a high roof. Cracks of light seeped in from the top, and puffs of dirt fell down from the cracks periodically onto a structural platform, which Tony recognized immediately.

"The Lacuna launch platform!" Tony exclaimed. "And the Lacuna rover next to it. But how can it be down here? It's supposed to be on the surface."

"Bellicot and Meppep pulled them down," Arleon said.

Tony witnessed as Bellicot and Meppep invited friend after friend to take a puff of oxygen from the rover's surplus oxygen tank.

"No!" Tony said. "That's mine!"

"See how much I've spared you, Claus?" Lanietta said. "We can witness these events without the need for oxygen or any such perishables."

"Oxygen is not a flower. It will not perish," Claus said.

"But people without oxygen will," Lanietta said.

Tony rushed to the rover and fought off the Monazites as best he could, but there were too many of them, and as he forced one set one way, another set snuck in behind him for more oxygen. Desperate, Tony rushed to the lander's launch platform (which was also used for the landing), climbed up, waved his arms across his chest, and yelled:

"Clear out. Clear out!"

Tony's vision went dark for a second or three, and he could no longer see the Monazites or the chamber.

Chapter 48: The Amnus Apple

When Tony's vision cleared, he was on the Martian surface, standing on the Lacuna launch pad. The rover was parked close-by with several oxygen canisters next to it. Tony reached around his suit and felt an attached carbon scrubber.

"It was a hallucination," Tony said. "Somehow I made it to the rover and attached the rover's carbon scrubber to my suit. But how?"

"Wait!" Claus said. "It was a hallucination? But you said it was real."

"I say many things," Lanietta said. "Temporal mechanics, Claus. There are many threads in the universe, and these threads often play music simultaneously. It was both a hallucination and real. Tony's mind could not perceive things truly as they are, any more than early people could perceive the Earth as a sphere. They thought it was flat. Yet that perception did not prevent the Earth from maintaining its shape or function. It persists. So do the Monazites in a sense."

"In a sense?" Claus said.

"Everything is perceived by you humans in a sense. There is no absolute truth, though you often believe you have found it," Lanietta said. "Now shush again. Tony is about to make important contact."

"Doctor Kechenova to Lacuna rover, do you read?" sounded a familiar voice.

"Irina! She's alive!" Tony exclaimed.

Tony jumped from the platform to the Martian surface, rushed over to the rover, and spoke on the radio.

"Irina! I'm here! I have to warn you about Jill Cresson. She—"

"Tony, listen," Kechenova said. "I am on Mars."

"Say again?" Tony asked.

"I am no longer in orbit in Callisti," she said. "I'm here on Mars in Lacuna. I crash landed."

"But...how? No, wait. You saw her, didn't you?" Tony asked.

"Cresson docked Lacuna with Callisti. She said you were dead. She brought your harness but left it in Lacuna. I entered Lacuna to check, she locked the hatch, and she forced me into a decaying orbit. Cresson deceived me. I'm so glad you are alive though."

"I'm sorry you crash landed, but I'm glad you are here on Mars. I thought I was all alone," Tony said. "If you tell me where you are, I'll take the rover and meet you, and then we can launch into orbit and dock with Callisti. We'll straighten this whole thing out."

"It's too late for that," Kechenova said. "Cresson is on her way to Earth with the Alatau third stage and a box of some sort. Lacuna is barely functional and not able to launch. There's another problem. Lacuna is seven thousand kilometers from your position. The Lacuna rover only has enough power to go fifty."

Tony made a quick check of the rover and discovered that much of its power was gone.

"It's worse than that," Tony said. "The rover's energy cells are heavily drained. It only has enough power to go perhaps five kilometers. I suspect Jill is to blame."

"Tony," Kechenova said, "how have you been holding up? I mean, without the harness?"

"I've had two hallucinations," Tony said. "But somehow I made it from the mining cave to the Lacuna launch pad."

"You are very lucky," Kechenova said. "We must be very careful. Another hallucination could result in your death. Mars is not an hospitable planet."

"That seems to be only one of many problems we have," Tony said. "I have more to tell you about Jill and the box she carried, there's the lack of food, and pretty much we're stranded on Mars and are going to die. So I don't know if it really matters how or what sort of problems we have at this point."

"It sounds like you are giving up. Don't. I have a plan," Kechenova said. "We might have a way to leave Mars, but it depends on how well we coordinate our activities. Do you remember the Panamirov and Leovich?"

"A little," Tony said.

"The Leovich is on the other side of the Exodus One," Kechenova said. "If you can reach it, I can help you reprogram it as a human transport vehicle. It would be a five-kilometer journey."

"Five kilometers as the Martian crow flies," Tony said. "But I must drive around the Exodus One. That will add a few kilometers. The Lacuna rover will only travel part of the distance, and even with going around, there's still that energy source at the Exodus One to deal with."

"The Leovich has a rover, the Leovissia," Kechenova said. "I will tap into the controls and have the Leovissia meet you. Which way will you go: north, or south?"

"North," Tony said. "I want to avoid the cave area. But how will you tap into the Leovich's rover controls?"

"I have managed to get a signal from Lacuna to the Panamirov, from Panamirov to Leovich, and from Leovich to Leovissia. I am making the changes now. There, the Leovissia is emitting a radio pulse on K-band. As you grow near, the pulse will grow stronger."

"Acknowledged. I'm ready to start," Tony said. "There's only one other problem. What if I have another hallucination?"

"If we continue to converse back and forth, perhaps we can keep you fully conscious and aware," Kechenova said.

"It's worth a try," Tony said.

Tony activated the rover and headed northwest out of the crater.

"Tell me about the container Cresson had with her," Kechenova said.

"It contains an ore found in the cave the Exodus One crew was mining," Tony said. "The ore is an energy source, a very powerful energy source. Chefwater and Allerton chipped a sample off and took it to the Exodus One ship. The sample caused the explosion. Jill kept the main ore for herself. I tried taking it. She shot me in the shoulder through my partial pressure suit. I was able to repair the suit, and I've bandaged up my wound, but the bullet is still in my body."

"I'm sorry to hear about your injury. When we meet again, I will tend to you properly," Kechenova said.

"That sounds hopeful," Tony said.

"One should always be hopeful," Kechenova said.

"Even though one thinks there are little men all around him?" Tony asked.

"What do you mean?" Kechenova asked.

Tony then recounted the story of his hallucination with the Monazites.

"So your Monazites called Cresson's ore the Veigon and the sample the Veigast?" Kechenova asked.

"Yes. Strange hallucination," Tony said.

"You may be prescient about the Veigon without realizing it," Kechenova said. "This reminds me of the Amnus Apple story."

"The what?" Tony asked.

"Oh, not the Amnus Apple story!" Lanietta lamented. "A morality story! Oh when will you humans light the torch and get out of the caves? Bah, I say! Bah, bah, BAH!"

"I like morality stories," Claus said. "The beauty about a well-told morality story is that it doesn't matter what creed or faith one comes from—the truths are universal."

"There you go with absolute knowledge again," Lanietta said. "Light that torch, Claus, and lead yourself out of this Amnus Apple story!"

"You can stop it, right? I mean, you've driven every other story, forcing me to watch or participate at your whim. Is this beyond your reach? You'd have to be totally and completely human to understand a morality story. Even some who have lost elements of humanity realize something's going on, if they can't feel at all."

"You are making a terrible mistake listening to this Amnus Apple story," Lanietta mocked.

"You could be in Irina's body and employ your vaunted temporal mechanics. Or doesn't that work?" Claus said.

"I will not waste my precious time on a morality story. You may do as you wish. I must check my cosmic eddies!" Lanietta snorted, and she vanished.

"I will tell you," Kechenova said to Tony. "Back in the year of old, before electricity and space travel were possible, a man and his bride lived on a farm at the edge of Talgar near the Tian Shan Mountains."

"In Kazakhstan?" Tony asked.

"Of course," she said. "Now don't interrupt. One day late in summer, the man—"

"What was his name?" Tony asked.

"Zimir," Kechenova said. "One day late in summer, Zimir was chopping wood for the upcoming winter. He was in such a hurry to chop wood that he neglected to check the axe handle. And so, he lifted the axe handle one last time and pulled down with his weight. The axe head broke free from the handle, landed on his head, and knocked him unconscious."

"When he awoke, he had amnesia, right?" Tony asked.

"Yes," Kechenova said. "Have you heard the story before?"

"It's a story about me," Tony said. "You're making this up."

"No and no," Kechenova said. "I wish I did, but I cannot invent stories as easily as I invent spaceships and rocket technologies. Back to the story. When Zimir awoke, he forgot many things. He forgot his name, he forgot his bride's name, and he forgot his trade."

"What was his trade?" Tony asked.

"He was a carpenter," Kechenova said. "His bride taught him his name and how to get around, but she could not teach him his trade. Since he could no longer make furniture and things of wood, he lost his source of income. His farm was small, with only one horse, a cow, and three chickens. He sold the chickens and cow for food, but he couldn't bear to sell the horse."

"Zimir became hungry, and so did his bride," Kechenova continued. "Hunger drives a person to desperation, and Zimir certainly became very, very desperate."

"So he went on a space mission to redeem himself and become a hero. Story over," Tony said.

"That's my kind of heckler," Lanietta said, suddenly appearing out of nowhere.

"I thought you had cosmic eddies to study," Claus said.

"Tony's marvelous comment brought tears to my eyes. Tears of joy. Oh don't you find this all so tragic?" Lanietta said with crocodile tears.

"Why don't you find a quasar or dark nebula to explore and allow me this simple story to hear," Claus said.

Lanietta laughed.

"You're cute when you're angry. And yes, you are angry! But you don't stay angry for long. I will dip out again. But be wary, Claus. You never know when I'll show up!" Lanietta said, and she disappeared.

"That's for sure," Claus said.

"No, not at all," Kechenova said. "Zimir's bride told him to look for the book his parents gave him and to read it. She told Zimir that Zimir always bragged that it contained survival information should the two ever get into trouble. But Zimir's hunger made him impatient, and he didn't bother looking for the book. Instead, he hitched his horse to a wagon and headed for the forest."

"He came upon an orchard of Siverse apples," she continued. "He stopped his horse at the first apple tree and picked an apple. Zimir did not smell it, taste it, nor did he eat it. Instead, he looked briefly at the apple, saw that it was unique in that it had a longitudinal crease, and that was good enough for him. He pulled all apples from that tree and placed the apples in the wagon. The tree had many apples, and he was able to fill the wagon completely."

"From one tree?" Tony asked.

"It was a big tree. A very big tree," Kechenova said.

"So where are Cain and Abel?" Tony asked.

"Hah! Cain and Abel!" Lanietta blasted as she returned. "What a throwback. Nice try for Tony. A point for my team."

"Your team? There's no game here," Claus said.

"Challenge denied. You lose a point," Lanietta said. "Oh Claus, games are the spice of life. You should try them sometime."

"I am in a strange fugue from which I cannot recover, Tony too, and you speak of games?" Claus said.

"Well you can't have Tony on your team, even if he's just a fluke," Lanietta said.

"That's fugue, not fluke!" Claus tried to correct, but Lanietta kept speaking.

"I saw him first, and I picked him. Kechenova is on my team too. You can have Libriota. Now there's a game player. She's good at deducting points, I will say. Ah, but she is nowhere around. Here, Libriota. Come out, come out wherever you are. Libriota? Now where could she be hiding? Hmm."

"I wish you'd go back into hiding. So I can finish this apple story!" Claus said.

"An apple a day, does not keep Lanietta away," Lanietta said, and she pinched his chin and shook it. "Now you be a good boy and eat your vegetables. I have fresh apple pie for dessert. Toodle-do!"

Lanietta disappeared again. Claus's nerves became more frazzled. Every time he relaxed into the story, Lanietta startled him by interrupting.

"Is there no end?" Claus asked himself.

"Not for a Carinian," Lanietta's voice echoed.

"This isn't about Adam and Eve," Kechenova said. "Now Zimir made a big mistake. You see, his parents warned him never to pick apples from the first tree without testing them. In fact, the first apple

tree is often the one most desperate for humans."

"An apple tree desperate for humans? What kind of nonsense is that? Apples are apples. There's nothing wrong with picking apples from the first tree that comes along," Tony said.

"Bravo for Tony. Another point for the good team," Lanietta's voice said, but Claus plugged his ears as she spoke and at least took the edge off his bad nerves.

"Ah, that's what Zimir thought. He forgot what his parents taught him and also forgot the importance of the book they created for him," Kechenova said.

"So what was he supposed to do?" Tony asked.

"As I was telling, Zimir's parents told him to skip the first apple tree, because the apple tree closest to humans is the most desperate for human intervention," Kechenova said. "And so, the next step is to sniff an apple from another tree, and if the aroma is pleasant, then take a slice of that apple and touch it to the tongue, and if that is also appealing, ingest a very, very small piece and wait a full day."

"Very instructive, Kechenova," Lanietta's voice said. "Claus could take a lesson from this. Fail-safes, remember?"

"I may have been hasty in my former life," Claus said. "Obviously I should have put lunar dust to my tongue before having anything to do with you. I'm sure I would have fallen in love with Luna right then and there. We'd be married by now you know. And have little lunar babies. They'd be small at first, say the size of asteroids, but in time they could be as large as Pluto or even Mercury!"

"You think you're so clever. Creating life and all that. Try making your own star or even a solar system. Can you do that?" Lanietta asked.

"Can you?" Claus said.

Lanietta kept quiet.

"I didn't think so," Claus said. "Score one for Claus's team."

"Wait a full day? A full day? Why? Why not harvest the apples then and there? And what's this about smelling and tasting? They should all be the same," Tony said.

"Siverse apples are diverse," Kechenova said. "Each tree has its own personality, its own flavor, to tempt the bears down from the mountain to eat of their fruit and scatter their seeds to new places. Only the fruit most desirable to bears will have a chance at creating new young. And so that is how the Siverse apple continues its line."

Tony stared at the rover's controls and noticed a slight increase in radiation. He diverted a little farther north to avoid the Exodus One even more.

"Zimir took the wagon-load of apples home and had his bride bake them. What Zimir did not remember was that even a bad apple can become palatable after baking. When the apples were baked, he and his bride ate them, and they were filled. Happy that at least his belly was full, he cheered the apple tree that saved him and called it *amnus*."

Claus looked around for Lanietta to interrupt, but she did not.

"Whew," Claus said.

"The next day," Kechenova continued, "Zimir took the remaining wagon-load to town and tried selling them. People in the street smelled the apples and deemed them foul, and so he sold none. Angered, he connived to push his new apples on the town. He had his bride bake the remaining apples from the wagon. Next, he took those baked apples and dumped them into the town well."

"Bake me an apple, bake if you can, bake it because you're my one and only man," Lanietta's voice said.

"Nope," Claus said. "You lose a point."

"Hah! Bake me an apple, bake it little man, bake it now and as fast as you can," Lanietta's voice said.

"Still nope," Claus said. "You lose another point."

"Humph! Bake me an apple, mix with bran, then slosh with honey in a clean, new pan!" Lanietta's voice said.

"You lose the game!" Claus said.

"Double humph!" Lanietta's voice said.

"The day after that, several people from the town visited Zimir's cabin and asked to buy his baked apples. Zimir's bride had some left, and she sold them to the visitors. You see, the visitors had drunk water from the well, and the apples' proteins were now coursing through their veins, creating an appetite for more. Zimir went back to the *amnus* apple tree and discovered to his delight that it had replenished itself with more apples. It was the strangest thing, because no apple tree could do such a quick thing. But Zimir was pleased, nonetheless, and he harvested these apples and took another wagon-load back to his cabin, where his bride baked them and sold them to more and more townspeople who made the trip to his cabin."

"Does this story have an ending?" Tony asked.

"No, it doesn't! Because Claus ended the game!" Lanietta's voice shouted.

"Shh!" Claus shouted back.

"Be patient," Kechenova said.

"Yes, be patient Lanietta," Claus said.

"Triple humph!" Lanietta's voice echoed.

"Zimir earned money quickly and could now afford to buy more chickens and cows and other farm animals. Instead, he spent his money on more wagons and horses. But the tree would only replenish itself once a day. This wasn't enough for Zimir. How could he fill more than one wagon in a day? His first thought was to fill the extra wagons with apples from other trees. But a voice inside of him, a voice that was actually the proteins of the *amnus* tree, told him that they would produce different types of apples, apples that would not sell as well as the *amnus* apple. And so, as if following instructions from the *amnus* tree, he hired men to chop down the entire orchard of Siverse apples until only the *amnus* tree remained. He instructed those same men to take cuttings from the *amnus* tree and plant them as identical clones."

"In a week's time, the new *amnus* trees miraculously grew to full height and began bearing fruit," Kechenova said. "Zimir's hired men collected the apples and helped him sell them to the entire town. Soon, news of the *amnus* apple spread to other towns, and traders flocked to Zimir's cabin to purchase the *amnus* apple in bulk and sell to other parts of the country."

"The end?" Tony asked.

"Yes, *please* let it be the end," Lanietta's voice begged.

"It ain't," Claus chuckled.

"No. The *amnus* apple created new greed. Many of the men hired by Zimir to harvest apples decided to start their own orchards. They stole cuttings from Zimir's orchard, traveled to other orchards, destroyed them, and planted their new *amnus* cuttings. Soon, the entire country became obsessed with the *amnus* apple to the point that all other apple orchards and in fact other trees and plants were cleared away and replaced with the *amnus* apple. The people became singularly focused on this apple and gave up other pursuits and alliances. They forgot the meaning of family and community and love and instead became subservient animals to the desires of the *amnus* apple."

"Then, as quickly as the *amnus* apple spread, it died off," Kechenova continued. "The *amnus* apple trees sent out a plume of pheromones and attracted honey bees from another country. Those bees followed the plume upwind for many days until they reached the *amnus* apple trees. They infected the trees with the fire blight, and that is how the *amnus* trees died."

"All those who made a living off the *amnus* tree were now out of work, out of money, and out of food," Kechenova said. "They fought one another for the remaining scraps of food until the situation became desperate, and people killed people. Eventually, those who had not lost their wits left the country and settled where the *amnus* apple tree did not exist. Then, when several generations passed and knowledge of the *amnus* tree faded, the first *amnus* tree that Zimir had discovered began growing again, only to prey upon people's lack of respect for memory and history."

"So the lesson is to remember everything," Tony said.

"Or try to. Be careful before trying things for the first time," Kechenova said.

"You know, Lanietta, I know why you hate this story. The amnus apple is symbolic for colonization. Like you, a Carinian. You *numero uno* amnus apple. You want to colonize Earth and the moon with your Gren Carinians. Then when all is well, you'll have the other powerful Carinians offed, so that you will be the sole one in power. All of us humble humans will then have to bow to you and beg from you, because we will have become so dependent on Gren Carinians."

"Speculation, Clomper. Pure speculation," Lanietta's voice said.

"Then why do you call me Clomper just now? Like a pet dependent on a master? Is that the plan for Earth? To convert the remaining humans into pets?" Claus said.

Lanietta appeared before Claus, dressed in the most attractive apple-red-inspired Victorian dress and hat. She moved in close to Claus, positioned his arms around her, put her arms around him, and she intended to kiss him, but her hat got in the way.

"Even when you pretend to show love, your garb gets in the way," Claus said.

"Am I not the apple of your desire? Let go of these memories and make one with me. Let's leave Mars and enjoy an evening at the ball. I'll wait for you to change. I'm patient. Take me, Claus. Take me!"

Lanietta leaned back against his arms in a pose for him to kiss her, but he only stared.

"You're like a frozen mannequin in a museum," he said.

"Humph!" she snorted.

She pulled away completely, turned her back to him, and extended a now-revealed parasol to block his view of her long hair.

"Doctor, I'm one kilometer directly north of the Exodus One," Tony said. "My view of the spacecraft is shielded by a range of boulders, but there's a gap where I can get a view of the Exodus One."

"Don't take the chance," Kechenova said. "It kills."

"But Jill said there was great power in these ores. Something tells me she will use it to change the world," Tony said.

"Change the world? The amnus apple changed the world. And look what happened," Kechenova said.

"Are you saying this ore is an amnus apple?" Tony asked. "That it will destroy Earth?"

"I fear it will end humanity as we know it and enslave it under a new regime. And I know about regime!" Kechenova said.

"There's your amnus apple!" Lanietta stated as she spun around and threw the parasol down at Claus's feet.

The parasol burst into an explosive fireball and sent a small mushroom cloud into the air. Claus fell back in surprise as he used one arm to shield his eyes and the other to break his fall.

"Morality lesson learned," Lanietta said, and she changed her attire instantly to that of a 1940s businesswoman with a small hat, dark hair, glasses, and a pad of paper and pen to take notes. "Do you have anything to say for the record?"

"Yeah. For a spitfire, it's surprising your hair isn't red," Claus said.

"Is that what you like? I can make my hair as red as the amnus apple!" she said, and her form changed again into an Irish girl with long, flowing-red hair, a green dress, and a cudgel.

"I...what in the name of..." Claus said.

"Want to play rough with me?" Lanietta said as she patted the cudgel against her open palm. "I have a way with naughty boys."

Claus wasn't sure what to do or think.

"That's it, isn't it? I've found your weakness. A haughty, sassy, Irish girl ready to tap and crack every bone in your body!" she said with an evil grin. "Forget being my Clomper. Look into my eyes, you frozen little mouse. I'll swat you with my cudgel and make you run. Run those legs so that I may pounce on you. I'm the cat of pain and desire!"

Claus put his hands over his eyes.

"Not looking. Not looking," he said, but Lanietta laughed.

"I must have a look," Tony said. "I must know."

"Do not taste the amnus apple!" Kechenova said. "Do not!"

Tony climbed off the rover and peered around a boulder. A light from the Exodus One trolled the sky. It swept toward Tony and energized the ions above him, triggering a hallucination.

Chapter 49: Apospiration

Tony was back in college. He was sitting in a small auditorium, and this was the third week of lectures with no assignments or tests yet required. The course was Advanced Chemical Physics in Microbiology with Calculus. Tony took one look at the textbook and decided the symbols and glyphs were a mixture of ancient Egyptian, complex piano music, and electrical schematics.

"Who can make sense of this?" Tony whispered without expecting anyone to hear. "This is impossible."

Tony looked ahead, and the instructor was Jill Cresson! She was a teaching assistant and working on her doctorate degree.

"It's not so hard," said a young woman student in front as she turned toward Tony.

"Irina!" Tony whispered in excitement. "You look so...sophisticated."

Indeed, the woman very much resembled Irina Kechenova. But instead of being dressed like a scientist or cosmonaut, she was dressed in a stunning blazer and skirt, like a high-powered lawyer ready to pounce on her prey and conquer the courtroom.

"Lanietta? Are you in this memory?" Claus asked.

Claus had the role of a student sitting behind and to the left of Tony, and so he could see a little of Tony and more of Kechenova.

"Yes, I'm here," Lanietta said, but instead of dipping out of Kechenova's or Jill's body, she was a student sitting to the left of Claus.

"I can never tell with you," Claus said. "I expected you to play the role of Kechenova, especially now."

"I wanted to sit beside you, especially now. We can watch this little love scene like we're at a movie. Popcorn?" Lanietta offered as she held a tub of popcorn before Claus.

"This is a lecture hall, not a movie theater," Claus said. "Put that away!"

Claus swung his arm a little too briskly and knocked the tub from Lanietta. The sight and sound of the flying popcorn briefly interrupted Jill's lecture and silenced the students. But the embarrassing pause ended, Jill resumed her lecture, and Kechenova continued with Tony.

"I have some photos of me modeling," Kechenova said. "Would you like to see?"

Kechenova opened her book to the very end and pulled out several photos for Tony. Tony took them and looked. One was of Kechenova in her lawyer suit posing by the marble column of a bank building. Another was of Kechenova sitting on the side of a fountain with her bare feet kicking the water while wearing a short, spring dress with flower prints. She wore a brimmed hat with a flower to the side. Another showed Kechenova wearing overalls and picking a basketful of apples.

"They are all very nice," Tony said. "But I wish this course were as easy as looking at your pretty photos."

Kechenova smiled.

"You will have your first test tomorrow morning on chapters one through five," Jill announced, and she quickly aimed a laser pointer at Claus and Lanietta. "Careful with the popcorn there, you two."

Claus and Lanietta shrank down in their seats in embarrassment, and then Lanietta took the opportunity to smooch Claus.

"Cut that out!" Claus said.

"As long as no one can see us," Lanietta said. "Why not?"

"What's gotten into you? You were so mean and spiteful before," Claus said.

"I'm a college girl now. I'm young and playful. Besides, Labba says I should just pick a man and kiss him. Would you like me to do that? Pick you and kiss you again?" Lanietta said.

"No, please don't," Claus said. "I'm already stressed enough as it is."

"Party pooper!" Lanietta said.

"I can help you study," Kechenova said to Tony. "I'm good at explaining things."

Tony's anxiety of being completely lost in the coursework melted away with Kechenova's offer. But the anxiety quickly returned when Jill shone a laser pointer at Tony.

"And pay attention there, Kavalla. Kavalla? That means you," Jill said. "You can't afford to flunk this test. You'll be kicked out of your degree program."

Tony perspired heavily, so much so that his eyelids stuck to his eyes like tape, and his tongue stuck to his cheeks as if cotton were stuffed in his mouth. His hallucination faded, and he felt his perspiration being drawn from his pores through the suit fabric (but without losing air pressure miraculously) and evaporate into a cloud, spun into a thread drawn directly toward the energy source at the Exodus One.

"My sweat...it's drawing it from me...the thing...it's drinking me dry."

"More popcorn?" Lanietta said as she stood next to Claus.

"We're back on Mars," Claus said. "And we're in ethereal form. I suppose the popcorn is ethereal too. How fake."

"Like I've said before, don't knock it till you try it," Lanietta said, and she popped several popped kernels in her mouth and ate them.

"You're not even supposed to eat!" Claus complained.

Tony grimaced, squirmed, and broke free of the energy beam that had held his attention. Exhausted, Tony collapsed in safety behind a boulder, but he lapsed into another hallucination.

Tony was on the playground of his elementary school. Teachers guarded the doorways to the building inside. In progress was a softball game, and Tony was third in line to bat, behind his friend Dwayne Reese.

"Lanietta!" Claus said while inside Dwayne's body. "I'm in this boy's body. I'm not ethereal. Lanietta?"

"I'm up here," Lanietta called.

Phil who was first in line, was at bat. The ball was pitched, and Phil swung and hit the ball.

"Where?" Claus called, turning his head around to look with his body toward the batter.

The ball carried into the outfield, and Phil's swing was such that he let go of the bat before stopping its momentum. Phil ran toward first base, but the bat bounced off Dwayne's (Claus's) shin before landing against Tony's shins. Dwayne fell to the ground and screamed in pain, while Tony, though a little hurt from the bat, bit his tongue to keep from appearing hurt. But Tony's pain was real, and he couldn't imagine how Dwayne was coping with his pain. Phil ran toward second base, and as he did so, Tony looked in the distance at two outfielders chasing the softball.

"Don't stand too close to the batter!" Lanietta shouted from above.

"You're a little late!" Claus called back. "Man but that hurts! And it won't stop! Why was I born to this life of pain? Bone pain is the absolute worst! Stop already! Please!"

It wasn't the softball that caught Tony's attention. Distant flames from a Florida forest fire encroached on the other side of the forest that formed the outer boundary of the school property.

"Fire!" Tony yelled.

But no one saw the flames, at least no one seemed to. A teacher brought the school nurse to attend to Dwayne's injury, all while the outfielders scrambled to retrieve the softball and send it back toward home plate to tag Phil out. Phil ran quickly, and the softball was relayed, but Phil beat the throw to home plate and scored the run.

"I must get a better look of the fire. I must see if there's a way out," Tony said.

Tony climbed a pecan tree close-by.

"Tony, it's your turn," Phil said.

Tony had climbed up to the second branch—not high enough to see where the flames were, and not high enough to escape Phil's reach.

"Come down, Tony. It's your turn. Score one for the team!" Phil called as he pulled on Tony's leg.

Tony fought the pull while his teammates chanted, "Score one for the team, two for the show, three for the fun of it, and four—let's go!"

"Tony," said a young girl's voice higher up in the pecan tree. "Up here. Grab the rope."

"Lanietta, is that you?" Dwayne (Claus) called. "I can't see what's going on. Everyone is in my way."

Was it Lanietta? Claus wasn't sure. The girl sounded very much like a young Irina Kechenova. Indeed, when Tony got a look, the girl *did* look like a young Kechenova.

"I...can't," Tony said, fighting hard to shake off Phil's tug.

"You must," Kechenova said. "I see the fire too. It's getting worse. There's only one way out, and it's up. Climb to the top, Tony. Hurry. Tony, can you hear me? Tony?"

Tony opened his eyes. He sat with his back to a boulder, a boulder that shielded him from the Exodus One energy entity. Claus sat on the Martian surface, still holding his wounded shins. Lanietta kneeled beside him, took his hand, and stood him up.

"There, all better," she said.

"Tony, can you hear me?" the rover radio sounded with Kechenova's voice.

Tony pulled himself up and climbed into the rover.

"I hear, Irina," Tony said.

"Instruments on the Panamirov show an increase in radioactive output from the Exodus One landing site," Kechenova said. "Tony, you are at great risk. Please proceed toward the Leovich."

"Acknowledged," Tony said. "Engaging the rover now."

But the rover failed to move.

"Something's wrong," Tony said. "The cells are depleted. I don't understand. There was still enough for another kilometer or two when I arrived. Let me check the fuel tanks and the mixing stack."

Tony opened a panel and returned his findings to the radio.

"The hydrogen and oxygen cells are empty, and the plates are corroded in the stack. It's as if...no, it's not possible."

"As if something forced a chemical reaction between the hydrogen and oxygen fuel inputs at a high rate and drew the resulting water away," Kechenova said.

"Oh, too bad for Tony," Lanietta said. "More popcorn?"

"Throw that popcorn away! Where did you get more? You were Irina on the playground. I...Lanietta, no. I'm not hungry," Claus said.

"How can you tell you're not hungry, hmmm? You could be and you just don't know it," Lanietta said, eating the popcorn.

"People know hunger. It's nothing magical. It just is," Claus said.

"Well popcorn always makes me thirsty. I need a beer," Lanietta said, and she produced a keg on a table. "There, what do you think? Fresh on tap."

"I know what you're doing. You're making light of Tony's situation. The fuel tanks are empty, and—"

"Light? Did you say light?" Lanietta said, and she produced a powerful hand-held spotlight and walked over to the rover to inspect.

"Now what are you doing?" Claus asked.

"Here, hold this," she said, passing him the tub of popcorn. "I'm inspecting the fuel. Yeah, empty. Tony's right. And Kechenova's right. You know what? I'm right too. That's three-for-three, a hat trick. I should be a magician. Ladies and gentlemen, for my next act, I will show you how to pull a canary from a hat...no...a poodle from a hat...no...a—"

"Kechenova is about to explain something important. Save your magic for a rainy day!" Claus said.

"Humph! I won't ever get a rainy day on Mars. It doesn't rain. Why, the forecast for the next week is sunny and clear with plenty of—"

"Hot air from Lanietta," Claus grinned. "You put your foot in that one. There, see? Doesn't pay to banter too much. Now then, a little quiet if you please. Drink your beer and keep those vocal cords of yours busy."

"Yeah, how did you know?" Tony asked.

"It confirms the strange spectral data I've received from the Panamirov. It shows the energy source drawing water through apospiration and creating energy through nuclear fusion."

"Ahhhh-paaaahsssss-purrrr-eyy-shun!" Lanietta said, and she started to march. "Little boy Johnny did have him some beer. Some cheer? Da beer! And then the Johnny just had to go play. No way! All day! March, march, march, march!"

"I do believe you're drunk!" Claus said. "But you've only had a little beer."

"Ahhhhhh, Clauuuuusss! Gimmmm-meeeee some suuu-gar, sweeeet peeecan pie!" Lanietta slobbered as she fell all over Claus.

"A drunk Carinian. I don't believe it. This is absolutely totally beyond all expectations for any alien interaction. I'm stuck with a drunk Carinian."

"Dance with me, Clauuuuuss," Lanietta stumbled. "March, march, march, march."

Lanietta tried marching sideways while holding Claus, but she kept tripping over her feet.

"I need a dress. A big, lonnnnng dresss," she fumbled.

She half-snapped her fingers, and a mismatched mixture of dress from various eras formed over her body, as if they were cast out as rags, and some poor dog pieced them together so he'd have a place to sleep. Lanietta went for another mug of beer, but Claus stopped her.

"You've had enough. You'll have a terrible hangover in the morning. And then you won't feel like doing much of anything," Claus said.

"I won't be able to watch you, no, you'll have to watch me," Lanietta slurred.

"Yes, I will won't I?" Claus said to what seemed like a good idea. "Here, have another beer."

"Gladly!" Lanietta said, and she chug-a-lugged the beer down. "Another!"

"You do know we're missing this memory," Claus said.

"Who cares? Free beer for all!" she waved.

She twirled, and she nearly fell, but Claus caught her. She moved to kiss him, but she burped, and the smell was that of overly fermented yeast mixed with sour vinegar.

"I think you'll need treatment after this. I know I will," Claus said. "Now be quiet and listen."

"I will NOT be quiet! I am the master here! The master Carinian. I will NOT be silenced! Oh, yo, come to the show! Lanietta has a bow, in her hair to grow, and let's make it snow!"

She snapped her fingers, and ethereal snow fell.

"If I kiss you, will you be quiet?" Claus asked.

"Will you? A real kiss from Clomper? Oh, you are the handsome one tonight. But let me freshen up first. Where's the powder room? Where's the beauty parlor? Smithers! My robe please. Smithers?"

Claus blew air onto her face.

"Oh, take me, my sweet beau. Take me to the land of milk and honey, where the night grows young and running feet bow to the evening dusk. Are you there, my romance? Are you there?" Lanietta blabbered.

Claus held his face close to hers and stared into her eyes. Lanietta seemed mesmerized, but for Claus, he felt as if he were staring into the eyes of a mutated lizard with the outgassing of vinegar-soaked lizard skin stinging his eyes. He couldn't bring himself to kiss her. The best he could do was remain locked in a gaze with her while his conjunctiva burned like fire. It was the hardest thing he'd ever done, more difficult than piloting a fighter plane or even enduring misery week when he was a boot.

"Are you saying this thing is taking water and converting it into energy through nuclear fusion?" Tony asked.

"Yes, it is," Kechenova said. "Tony, I also have data saying that you too are a victim of apospiration."

"I was sweating heavily, and the thing pulled the water from my sweat out of my suit," Tony said.

"You've got to get out of there and head toward the Leovich, but it's too risky for you to walk," Kechenova said.

"Then how do I get the rover to move? Are you saying I must capture that entity thing and use it to power the rover?" Tony asked.

"Tony, the Leovissia is now a kilometer away from your position. I have it shielded behind a boulder, much like you are shielded. But I don't know if it can make the remaining journey to your location. The radiation from the Exodus One energy source might confuse its instruments if I instruct it to travel to your position. Or worse, the energy source might apospirate the Leovissia and deplete her energy reserve. But I think we must take the chance. Otherwise—"

"Otherwise, Anthony my sweet, there will be no free beer for you!" Lanietta blathered in a moment when her gaze slipped from Claus's.

"The things I do for humanity," Claus said, and he forced Lanietta back into a stare, a determined stalemate of friend/foe against friend/foe.

"No," Tony said. "If Leovissia fails, so do I. I'm almost out of air and strength. I can't make it the rest of the way on foot."

"Tony, if you don't make it to the Leovich, I...I..." Kechenova said.

"I know," Tony said. "Listen. Keep your chin up. You'll go back to Earth. We both will. We have to. I just wish I had more air in this tank, enough to reach the Leovissia."

"Lanietta here is full of air," Claus bragged, taking a break from staring her down.

"Hah! That's what you think!" Lanietta said. "Wait until I—"

But Claus silenced her again as before with his stare.

"Are there any tanks left on the Lacuna rover?" Kechenova asked.

"Negative," Tony replied. "What I need is a junk yard of oxygen tanks."

Tony looked at the ground beside the rover and noticed debris from the Exodus One.

"Of course," Tony said.

"What is it?" Kechenova asked.

"The explosion sent debris from the Exodus One in all directions," Tony said. "What if it sent unused oxygen tanks clear of the blast site?"

"That would require a lot of good luck to find such a tank where you are," Kechenova said.

"And I don't see any," Tony said.

"Pick me! Pick me!" Lanietta said as she squirmed from Claus's stare and his hold. "I know! I kn—"

"That's enough, Lanietta-happiness-is-too-much-just-now," said Claus as he resumed his hold on her.

"It was a nice thought," Kechenova said.

"But maybe not out of reach. What if I go closer to the Exodus One?"

"Don't!" Kechenova said.

But Tony had made up his mind. He climbed out of the rover, up to a gap in the boulders, and peered through. Perhaps fifty meters somewhat toward the energy source, Tony saw two tanks leaning next to an isolated boulder.

"Those are my tickets to the Leovissia," he said.

"No don't! Danger! Run! Hide!" Lanietta said.

"Shush, my dear. Mr. Tony is responsible and has a task to perform, as I have my task to perform," Claus said, and he stared her down again.

"But what will people think of us?" Lanietta said, pulling away. "Libriota and the gang—they'll all talk you know, about a Carinian and a human having a staring-down relationship. How will I bear the guilt? They'll pin a crimson letter on me for sure."

"We'll have Labba defend you in a court of law," Claus said. "She if anyone will support you."

"Good old Labba. I knew I could count on her!" Lanietta said, and Claus continued the stare-down gaze.

Tony crept around the boulder. The energy entity peered through the sky, like the spotlight before. It searched and probed for more water to apospirate, but Mars had been devoid of such surface resources for many-too-many years. Tony saw scattered boulders from his position to the two tanks, and he had the idea that he could dart from boulder to boulder, taking pause at each boulder before sprinting to the next.

"I'll wait for the energy beam to point far away. Then I'll go," Tony said.

The energy beam focused on the cave where the Exodus One crew had been mining.

"Now!"

Tony stood up and sprinted for the next boulder, but as he did, the energy beam seemed to notice, and it quickly wheeled its beam around from the south to the north where it honed down on Tony. Tony threw himself down to the next boulder, but not before the beam was able to hit Tony in the face for a split second. Mars went all white before Tony's eyes. He winced in pain, but he lost touch with reality.

Tony hallucinated that he was in a small boat on a large ocean. Every so often, he saw something floating in the water, but he was too far away to see. Gradually, he approached a floating object. He could see it was a common apple. He powered the motor on the boat, and the boat proceeded past the apple, only to approach another apple.

"Strange," Tony thought.

Tony powered the boat past this second apple, and there was another apple. And another. Soon there were apples everywhere. The motor's propeller sliced through the apples at first, but soon it became clogged on something and could no longer propel the boat forward. Despite Tony twisting the throttle to full, the boat would not move. Frustrated, Tony powered off the motor and checked the propeller. It was clogged with fresh branches.

"Branches, branches. Where are these branches coming from?" Tony asked.

A thought flashed across Tony's brain. He reached for a floating apple, and to his surprise it was attached to a branch. He pulled on another apple, and it too was attached to a branch.

"They're all attached. They're all attached to branches, the branches of trees!"

It happened. More and more apples appeared on the water's surface. Leaves and branches appeared, followed by upper tree trunks. Tony realized what was happening. The trees weren't getting taller—the water was getting lower. The apple trees were in fact draining all water from the area until the boat settled between two rocks. The water continued to drain until there was nothing but trees and sand. Smaller trees died as their water supply was drained away by larger trees. And so this little war continued with smaller trees succumbing to larger trees until there was a final war between two trees. The sun pounded on the sand, and Tony perspired heavily until he was too parched to perspire at all. The weaker of the two trees finally succumbed. It withered and died.

That left just one tree. Tony felt the ground beneath him moving. A root from the last apple tree pulled the sand such that Tony moved toward the tree. He grew closer and closer until he could see quite clearly a longitudinal crease on each apple.

"The *amnus* apple tree," Tony said.

A cluster of honeybees flew from the distance and landed on the tree, covering every apple and blossom. They departed within seconds of arriving, and within another few seconds, the tree succumbed to red blight and disintegrated, leaving nothing but Tony, the boat, and a desert.

Tony stared at the desert toward the horizon. He stared and stared at the barren bleakness until he felt a structure close in around him from behind. It enveloped him and left a single window with a view of the desert. The desert shrank, as if traveling away from Tony.

The hallucination ended. Tony was behind the boulder as he had been, safe for the moment, but still a ways away from the two tanks. He peered around the boulder. The energy beam was again focused on the cave to the south. Tony made another bold move, stood up, sprinted to the next boulder, and fell behind it as the energy beam, like before, trained its gaze on Tony and stunned him into another hallucination.

Tony was underground in a stone-carved aqueduct but still on Mars. He stood on a ledge with a wall to his back and waste water coming from under the wall and flowing ahead of him in a channel twenty meters wide by ten meters deep. To his right, the ledge took a ninety degree turn and followed a full-height wall leading ahead about ten meters to a stony, enclosed catwalk attached to the ceiling but clearing the flowing water and allowing one to walk along the edge of the right-side wall if one ducked.

To the left was a passageway running parallel to the water channel, running hard around the left and back behind Tony. It ran ahead up to the passageway where it formed a four-way crossing with the catwalk, a continued passage ahead, and a corridor to the left in line with the catwalk.

A flood of Monazites, led by a young Ceborio, ran along the passage on the left to the catwalk and across the channel, yelling and carrying equipment and doing all they could to fortify something and the end of the catwalk, which was the something above the right-side wall's ledge where Tony watched.

"*Ixa Veigast a'a taukips shloo!*" a Monazite yelled, meaning, "The Veigast is breaking through!"

"*Iki agudo egdanlan li ixa moorp!*" yelled another Monazite, meaning, "Give more reinforcement to the door!"

Tony heard a pulsing screech-like sound, as if a high-pressure water pulse

were chipping through rock. More Monazites yelled and worked. Tony followed the workers to a four-way connection, but now Monazites were evacuating the catwalk.

"*Dayok pleek!*" they yelled repeatedly, meaning, "Go back!"

The last Monazite out of the catwalk tried pulling Tony away to safety, but Tony fought off the well-meaning hand and sent the Monazite on his way. It was Tony then by himself at the catwalk's entrance, and he saw bits of stone fall from stone doors and cross supports on the other side of the catwalk, as if a water blaster were breaking through. But it wasn't a water blaster. Tony saw the bright laser beam of the energy source peering through now and again, but instead of it being an amber beam like the one at the Exodus One, it was pinkish-red. Bits of the beam diffracted through, and as they did, they made sizzling sounds like a high voltage electrical wire on a hot and humid summer day.

The beam did not care about Tony. Once it pierced through the opening it had made through the reinforced door, it focused on blasting through the bottom of the catwalk. The beam spent little time cutting through the stonework, and within a fraction of a second, water gushed up from the channel and into the catwalk, like a fountain. But instead of the water spewing all over the catwalk's floor, the laser drew the water in a tight spiral and through the hole it had made in the door.

"It's apospirating the Monazites' water supply," Tony said. "I must stop it. But I can't."

"Beer! Give it beer!" ethereal Lanietta shouted.

"Shh," Claus said, and he put his hand over her mouth.

Lanietta licked his hand.

"Yuck! Disgusting!" Claus said.

Tony stepped a little bit into the catwalk. The laser beam continued to draw more water. It caused the hole in the bottom of the catwalk to grow. The sides began tumbling, and the entire catwalk crumbled and fell into the water channel.

Tony would have been swept into the splash and rubble had it not been for a stray hand that pulled Tony back. It was enough to keep Tony out of the raining rubble but not enough to keep him out of the water channel. He fell ahead of the collapsing catwalk and was swept by the rushing water under a wall and into a cavern with a shallow roof. Tony gasped for air with only inches between the waterline and the roof available for such respiration.

The water continued to pull Tony, and it was about to pin him against an underwater gate where he was sure to drown. He dove underwater and looked desperately for escape, but he saw nothing. With his eyes being of no help, he beat against the left wall in hopes of finding a weak point. To his surprise, he found a hidden door. He pushed through the door and into a flooded stairwell. He climbed the stairs from water to air, and he paused a moment to catch his breath.

"Come in," echoed a voice down the stairwell from above. "Don't be shy."

English. And it was coming from a woman, an Earth woman.

"Well?" she taunted.

Tony climbed the stairwell, leaving a dripping trail of water. He reached a landing at the top of the stairs. To his right was a window showing a landscape of Mars. Tony saw a tornado-like storm devouring the last water on the surface while Monazites fled its path and dove in the ground for protection.

"Over here," the voice called from a doorway to the left.

Tony walked through the doorway. He was in a wide room, about twenty meters to the right and ten to the left, with all sorts of rabbit figures decorated throughout. There were throw rugs with rabbit pictures, rabbit-stuffed animals on furniture (which had paintings of rabbits), pictures of rabbits on the walls, porcelain rabbits on tables and desks and bookcase shelves, and even rabbit clocks. The rabbits were all white but with some sort of injury colored not in red but in the same pinkish-red color as that of the laser in the catwalk. Each injury was

in a different place on the rabbits, but all suggested serious or fatal injuries.

"Welcome!" said the woman, and she appeared in another doorway directly ahead of Tony with a tray of breakfast food.

"Jill?" Tony asked.

But Tony wasn't sure. The figure looked like Jill Cresson, but she was an older woman, and her body was glazed over, as if she were some sort of flexible porcelain doll herself.

"Would you like some tea? Coffee cake with raisins?" she asked.

"No thanks," Tony said.

The room behind the woman was dark, and Tony was curious.

"What's in there?" he asked. "It's dark."

"Would you like to know?" she asked, placing the tray on a side table. "Then walk right in. But let me tell you first—you'll either find something special and wonderful, or horrible and treacherous in this room."

"I..." Tony paused.

"What would you do, Claus? Would you follow me into a dark room? What if it has beer?" Lanietta said with a burp.

"It is the age-old question of risk," Claus said. "It would seem to be a fifty-fifty choice. Those who are happy with their current situation would hesitate much longer or maybe not go in as compared to those who are unhappy or in immediate danger."

"Too complicated! If the room ain't got beer, it ain't worth it!" Lanietta said.

"Is it worth the risk? Of course! Just follow me!" the woman said, and she disappeared back into the dark room from where she came.

Tony approached the second door and stood with absolute darkness before him. He waited. The woman made no sound and made no more indication of what he could expect. The sizzling sound of the laser approached from behind. It had snaked through the water channel, had found Tony's hidden passage, and was creeping up the stairs. Soon it would be upon him.

Tony turned around, ran down the short side of the wide room, and held onto a stuffed rabbit, hoping he could avoid the inevitable. Hoping and hoping that...

The hallucination ended. Tony was still behind the second boulder, hiding from the energy beam of the Exodus One. There were no more boulders between him and the two oxygen tanks. He would need to make a run for it, and fast. The energy beam had spent extra time scanning his area, but now it was roving toward the south again at the mining cave as it had before. Tony's chance to sprint was now or never. This had better work.

Tony stood up and made for a run, but the energy beam whipped around quicker than anything and zeroed in on Tony's position. Tony sank back down behind the boulder before the beam could catch him.

"Totally evil," Tony said. "How does a man fight such a predator?"

"With beer!" Lanietta yelled, and she threw beer at the beam, onto Claus, and onto herself.

"Behave, now! Please!" Claus begged.

"Only if you get on your knees and beg. Propose to me," Lanietta said.

"You're drunk!" Claus said.

"As you've already noted. Propose!" Lanietta demanded.

"I propose you behave!" Claus said.

"Stood up at the altar again," Lanietta sighed.

An idea came to Tony.

"It needs a diversion. It needs bait. But what? It only feeds on water and salt."

Another thought came to Tony.

"The condensation in my breath collects in the bottom of my air tank," said Tony. "If I open the tank and throw it to the side, the condensation would vent, and the beam would train its attention on the water mist. That diversion could give me enough time to run the final amount. Only problem is, I'd have no air to breathe. I'd have to hold my breath until I got to the two new tanks and hope they have good air."

Tony paused.

"Perhaps this is what my hallucination was presenting to me when Jill said the next room had something special and wonderful, or horrible and treacherous," Tony said. "Out of time. This is my last act."

"Yay for the last act!" Lanietta shouted.

"I dare you to hold your breath," Claus said.

"How ridiculous!" Lanietta said.

"I double dare you," Claus said. "I bet Tony can hold his breath longer than you."

"I don't need to *breathe*, Mr. Too-smart-for-his-Carinian-bride!" Lanietta said. "I can do anything Tony can do."

"Can't," Claus taunted.

"Can," Lanietta replied.

"Can't, can't, can't!" Claus taunted further.

"Can too, can too, can too! And I'll prove it! I'll hold my breath now! Hah! Watch!" she said, and she held her breath!

Tony hyperventilated with the last bit of air in the tank. He took a deep breath, held it, closed the valve to the tank, disconnected the tank's line and hooks from his suit, opened the valve, and threw it to the side as far as he could. The energy beam focused on Tony and held him in place. Tony tried to move down behind the boulder, but the energy beam wouldn't let him. It seemed to ignore the venting canister. Tony wanted to yell, but he knew he had to hold his breath if success should be his fate. He tried moving. Tried waving his hands. The beam held its gaze on Tony.

Then Tony saw Monazites running around the Martian surface as if they'd all been stung by a horde of bees. They ran and jumped and squirmed, fell down and rolled in pain, slapped their limbs, slapped one another, and altogether continued this wretched fit as the carbon dioxide built up in Tony's bloodstream and increased the desire for Tony to gulp air that he could not have. Tony closed his eyes hard, and he managed to turn his body such that his back faced the energy beam. Tony opened his eyes, and he saw Monazites carrying a casket with transparent sides and top. Ceborio was inside, extremely ancient, and expired. The Monazites carried the casket toward Tony and grew closer, so much so that they were about to overrun his position.

Tony's chest convulsed from excessive carbon dioxide buildup. Again Tony fought to keep the air inside, but he couldn't stop himself. One final chest convulsion, and Tony beat on the damaged part of his suit and let out a shot of air from his lungs. The energy beam instantly focused on the moist air bursting up from the suit, and in so doing it released its grip on Tony. He collapsed behind the boulder. The energy beam, having lost its primary food, trained its gaze on the next best thing—the venting canister.

"Hah! I beat Tony! Nanny-nanny boo-boo, stick your head in shoe glue," Lanietta said.

"It, uh, actually goes another way, but that'll do," Claus said.

"I said it right! I did! What? Do you think I'm a fake? A phony? I'm the best artificial human woman you'll ever meet," Lanietta said.

"Not as good as Labba," Claus said.

"Wrong-o, potato face!" Lanietta said.

"You'll never be as good as Labba. Labba told me herself. I saw how she was with Argo. Didn't you see? The two are a couple in love. What do you have? You hold me against my will as a pet, a pet named Clomper. That's not a real woman. Labba mastered the craft long ago. You are but a neophyte."

"I'm not too near to fight! You better watch out, Claus-the-mouthy mouse! This cat will pounce on you but good!" Lanietta threatened.

"See? Labba would never speak like that. But cheer up. When we get back to Arberella, I'll have Labba set up school for you Carinians who need to learn how to be human. With time and practice, you might be half the woman she is."

"I am all the woman I need to be. But this beer has gone sour. I need to upgrade. Hmm, I think I'll try champagne. And maybe shots after that," Lanietta said as she produced a bottle of champagne.

"Lay off the heavy stuff, will you? It'll ruin your complexion," Claus said.

"I am the youngest, fairest maiden with the fairest complexion on this side of the Carinian energy corridor," Lanietta said.

"Oh a maiden. So you're not married," Claus said.

"No, because I keep getting stood up at the altar!" Lanietta said.

"What is this energy corridor you're talking about?" Claus said.

"It's how we do long-distance space-jumps. Like from Carinia Zero to your lunar far side," Lanietta admitted. "If you were Carinian, I could show you. Hmm, maybe Libriota can upgrade your energy signature. Then I can show you Carinia Zero. Heck, you almost went there anyway when those Orchians discovered the Tropheia. Hah, I bet Libriota is giving them the runaround. Boy would I like to see their reaction. They are the most uncouth, uncivilized Carinians to ever evolve. Why the—"

"Here, drink your champagne," Claus said, and he put the bottle to her lips.

Lanietta took a swig, and that kept her quiet.

"Want some? It's fruity," she said.

Claus took a sip and spat it out.

"What's in there?" he asked.

"Butanol," Lanietta said. "I normally drink an acetone brew, but that's too light. Doesn't last long. Butanol has a heavier taste."

"We humans can't drink that stuff," Claus said. "I thought you had real champagne. With alcohol."

"Butanol *is* alcohol, ninny!" Lanietta said.

"Ethyl alcohol," Claus said.

"Why didn't you ask for Ethyl to begin with? I'll have her make champagne for you with her alcohol," Lanietta said, and she took the appearance of an older woman and changed the champagne from a butanol mix to ethyl-alcohol based. "There, I'm Ethyl. Try it now."

Claus took a sip.

"At least it's safe...r," Claus said. "Drink the rest. It's all that will keep you quiet."

Lanietta drank the champagne, and she slipped back to her regular appearance. Luck met Tony and roused him to his feet. He held a hand over the rip in the suit and staggered to the two air canisters, fell to the boulder next to which they perched, attached one to his suit, opened the air valve, and attempted a breath. He tried the valve on the canister again and even shook it. Still no air. The stress caused Tony to perspire greatly. The energy beam had drained the venting canister from afar and was now probing Tony's area with desire to apospirate his sweat.

Tony worked quickly. He disconnected the air tank and immediately saw it had a hole in it that previously he did not see. He groaned at losing precious time with his mistake, but there was no time to lose. He dropped the bad air tank and connected the second to his suit. No air. He shook the can. Still no air. Then Tony saw it. There was frost on the valve. How? From where? Tony didn't know. Nor was he sure how to heat it. But in a flash he got an inspiration. He stood briefly with his back to the energy beam such that the valve was exposed. The energy beam trained on the valve and tried to apospirate any condensation it could. The frost melted, it was pulled away into the energy beam, and air flowed into his suit.

Exhausted, Tony collapsed by the boulder. He inhaled deeply and exhaled. Deep breath, exhale. Deep, exhale.

"Only one good tank," Tony said. "It's not enough to get back. I need a miracle. Well, perhaps I can use this bad canister as a shield. It won't offer much protection, but it might provide enough."

Tony stood while holding the bad canister in front of him. He backed away from the beam slowly. The beam searched for Tony but hit the bad canister. The bad canister pinged as if being hit by a pellet. The vibration stung Tony, like hitting a baseball with the end of a bat.

"Ow," Tony said.

Tony increased his speed backward, and the energy beam continued hitting the bad canister with pings and pangs and crangs and boings with such increased intensity that Tony knew he couldn't hold the canister much longer.

"I'll have to run for it," Tony said.

Tony dropped the canister and ran, but the energy beam caught him and forced him to the ground. Before Tony could resist, the energy beam suddenly stopped attacking and dissipated altogether.

"Huh?" Tony wondered.

He turned around and saw a faint, blue light from the sky rain down on the Exodus One landing site. Orange water crystals flowed around the blue light in a corkscrew fashion. The energy beam seemed confused and made half-stabbing attempts to apospirate the entire crystal structure at once, but the structure kept flowing down in circles around the blue beam, and so the energy beam could not.

"I must be seeing things," Tony said. "But I'm glad."

Tony ran the last bit, past the boulders he had hid behind, and finally behind the line of boulders where his rover was parked.

"Tony, Tony! Are you there?" sounded Kechenova's voice over the radio.

"I'm here," Tony said.

"I'm so relieved!" she said. "Listen. I managed to send a depolarizing water-seeding laser beam from the Panamirov into the atmosphere above the Exodus One landing site in hopes of distracting the energy beam. Did it help?"

"That was you?! You're an angel!" Tony exclaimed. "You saved my life."

"You should have sent champagne!" Lanietta shouted. "My bottle is empty! Ketchup-nova, fill my bottle!"

"Shh," Claus said. "Fill it yourself."

"Gotta do everything myself. What is this planet coming to? First the Monazites get their water stolen, then my champagne disappears. I swear, if another bad thing happens on Mars, I'm going to go on strike!" Lanietta said.

Lanietta filled her champagne bottle and drank.

"I'm so glad you're safe. The beam will only last another fifteen minutes before the Panamirov is exhausted. Can you walk a kilometer in that amount of time to the Leovissia?" Kechenova asked.

"I'll have to," Tony said. "I'm starting my walk now. I'll send word when I reach the Leovissia."

"Good luck," Kechenova said.

Chapter 50: The Grostarius and Halax

Tony began his walk toward the Leovissia. A blinking beacon indicated the direction he had to travel. The energy source from the Exodus One continued sending pulses of energy in various directions. Several such pulses were sent in front of Tony's path, and after a few seconds of observation and thought, Tony detected a pattern and could predict where the next burst would land. He hastened or slowed his pace to miss the bursts, because he had now cleared the protective boundary of boulders and was in an open plain. The bursts would start far away, then one closer, then another far away but a little closer, and another one closer than the second burst, etc., until the closest burst passed by Tony, and a burst much farther away became noticeable, and the far one much closer. Each time one passed by Tony, the burst next closest ahead would burst at a spot a meter or so closer to Tony than the prior cycle's burst. Tony used blast spots on the Martian surface as markers to show where to go, but after a time, there were so many blast spots that it became more difficult for Tony to predict where the next blast would land.

Leovissia's beacon of light seemed no closer, despite Tony's progressive steps toward the rover. And then it happened. A burst caught Tony on the left side of his helmet and stunned him. He fell to the ground, but he arighted himself immediately and continued walking toward Leovissia's beacon. But he had a new problem. His left eye had difficulty focusing, fell into a soft blur, and then blacked out completely. Tony was faced with making the journey to the Leovissia with only one working eye. Worse, if his right eye should be hit by the burst, Tony would be blind.

"How do I look?" Lanietta asked Claus.

Lanietta was dressed in pirate gear with a patch over her left eye.

"Don't make light of Tony's situation," Claus said.

"Okay, I'll leave him in the dark," Lanietta said. "Would you like to dance with a pirate? I'm running a 50% discount. Parrot-free!"

"Go drink your champagne," Claus said.

"I'm drying myself out. No more booze," Lanietta said.

"That might be an improvement," Claus said.

"Instead, I'm eating this. Look," Lanietta said.

Claus looked at what appeared to be a gold coin.

"Want one?" she offered.

"We can't eat gold," Claus said.

"It won't poison you," she said.

"The answer is 'no'," Claus said.

"Your loss," she said.

Lanietta picked at the "gold coin" and removed a wrapper, revealing chocolate that she popped in her mouth.

"And up to your tricks again," Claus said.

"Perspective, Claus. Perspective," she said.

"I must continue walking with my left side to the Exodus One. Don't look toward the energy source, Tony. Don't look," Tony said to himself.

Something sparkled in Tony's left eye, though it was from his immediate environment. He thought he saw "shooting stars" in his left eye, that phenomenon after receiving a blow to the head. He then saw "floaters"—string-like fragments moving around.

"The blast must have loosened tissue in my left eye," Tony said. "I hope there's no internal bleeding."

Lanietta sniffled. Claus turned to her, and tears ran down her right eye. But her left eye was still covered, and so nothing from that eye flowed down her face—at first.

"It's so sad. Tony. Tony! Don't bleed in your eye! It makes me sad. It makes my eyes water!" Lanietta joked.

"Stop clowning around," Claus said. "And take that patch off your eye!"

Claus ripped the patch off, and accumulated tears flew out in all directions—more fluid than Claus expected, and he got Lanietta and himself wet. Lanietta crowed as if she were going to cry for real. She fell into sob.

"Don't cry, don't cry," Claus said. "There's nothing worse than watching a Carinian cry. Makes you look needed."

"I'm not needy," she said in her muffled cry.

"Lanietta, I—"

"I can take care of myself," she said, pulling away. "Look, I can curtsey."

Lanietta attempted to curtsey in her pirate outfit, but she lost her balance and fell toward Claus. Claus caught her.

"Kiss your favorite pirate," she said.

"Ah...er," Claus stumbled. "Let's watch Tony."

"Oh, but this is the tricky part. Here. You'll need these," she said as she handed a special pair of polarized glasses to Claus and donned a pair herself.

"Thank you. What am I doing? I'm thanking an alien dressed as a pirate for special glasses after she asked for a kiss!" Claus said.

"You're okay Callus, I mean Claus," she said. "Don't sweat it."

The vision in Tony's left eye changed again. He saw vivid imagery, and it was that of Mars, but not where he was currently walking. The landscape was completely barren, except for a people-made structure. The structure consisted of a transparent tube spiraling up in progressively tighter circles as if it were following the outline of a Christmas tree. Inside this tube was a community of well-to-do homes with swimming pools, well-manicured lawns, clay tennis courts, fountains, ponds, and other assorted expensive humanoid habitations. Thrusting

upward from the Martian surface and at the center of the spiraling tube (but with no obvious connection points to the tube) was a stonework structure with nothing but lines and right angles, as if it were an Earthly urban skyscraper, but this building had no windows and no obvious passages to the Martian atmosphere.

As Tony's right eye continued to lead him toward the Leovissia and dodge the energy source's pulses, his left eye led him to the people-made structure. He walked under the large spiraling tube and toward the center mason-work structure. He saw no obvious point of entry. Next, he looked around for a way into the transparent tube. He could see none near the ground, but as he walked around and studied the two structures further, he noticed orange-red spicules connecting the spiraling tubular section to the central stonework structure. The spicules were difficult to see, because they blended in with the Martian sky.

"How does one enter this structure?" Tony asked.

He could see people walking in the spiraling tube, so he guessed there had to be an entrance. How else could people enter?

"What do you think of my hat?" Lanietta asked Claus.

Lanietta had changed into a futuristic outfit. Her hat resembled the tube, spicules, and stonework structure.

"It's...imitative," Claus said.

"Let's change your outfit too," Lanietta said as she snapped her fingers. "There. You're now in fashion."

"Are you part of the new work detail?" asked a man behind Tony in a partial pressure suit.

"I—" Tony started to say.

"This way," the man said.

Tony resisted, but two other men escorted him away from the center structure, back under the tubular spiral, and off to a collection of unassuming boulders. Tony walked in through the collection, left, right, and left, and then the man leading the procession pressed a button on his arm bracelet.

The door opened, and the four walked through the entrance down several roughly-hewn stone steps to a tunnel that was hastily thrown together. Lanietta and Claus followed. The door closed behind, but as yet the four kept their partial pressure suits on. The four then reached a hatch made of high-strength plastic. The lead man opened the hatch, the four entered a depressurization room, and the hatch closed. Air filled the room, and the pressure increased until it reached one Earth atmosphere. The lead man opened a second hatch, and the four entered a lobby area with several merchandising stands and clerks hawking their goods.

"Remove your suit, worker," the lead man said.

Tony removed his partial pressure suit and handed it to the lead man. But before the lead man could take it, a worker who was hidden in the shadows burst forth into the open, grabbed the suit, entered the depressurization room, locked the second hatch closed, threw on the suit, and began depressurization.

"Go, young man, go!" Lanietta cheered.

"Stop him," ordered the lead man to the two guards who had escorted Tony in.

The guards fought the controls to open the second hatch, but the hatch would not open.

"He's fused the security override controls," said the guards.

"Keep working. I'll secure the area," the lead man said.

The lead man then picked up a microphone hanging on a side wall and made an emergency announcement to clear the lobby. People ran from the lobby to the main mezzanine in a panic. The lead man rushed Tony into the mezzanine, and a large door started coming down to separate the mezzanine from the lobby, in case the second hatch should open and expose the lobby to the open Martian atmosphere. But as the door came down, several last-moment panicking people rushed from the lobby with their sales stands and forced their way between Tony and the lead man,

sending the two crashing into those sales stands adorned with various metallic ornaments for sale. Several of those metallic objects punctured the lead man's environmental pack, causing it to short-circuit and to send a high voltage shock into the lead man's body. He fell unconscious.

"Look, my hat is lit like a Christmas tree," Lanietta said. "Isn't it pretty? See how the sparks sizzle!"

"Not funny," Claus said.

The large door closed, boom. Tony sat up and saw that he had a few cuts to his arms. He checked on the collapsed lead man, and the man was still unconscious but breathing. Rescue workers descended on the scene, and Tony decided it best to leave the area before someone could order him into a work detail. He moved casually from various sales trees and sales stands containing partial pressure suit components such as helmets, gloves, boots, main-body portions, enviro-packs, food packs, and power supplies. Each good contained a price tag with a retail amount slashed through and a sale price below it in red. He looked around more and saw, "Sale, Sale, Sale," everywhere—on wall banners, on cards hanging from the ceiling, and on the sales stands themselves.

"Now look," Lanietta said. "I have lots of price tags in my hat. See how they move in the air?"

"Get that hat off!" Claus said, and he threw it to the floor.

"There, now. Temper, temper!" Lanietta said.

There were several other sales stands with conventional foods and pastries. It was those stands that the worried people now consoled themselves with by purchasing and ingesting sugar- and fat-ladened foods. No one seemed to notice Tony, except for a sales clerk here and there who offered to sell Tony the best suit boot or suit glove at a price below what the competition was asking.

"Thank you no," Tony kept repeating to the obsessed salespeople.

"What about this boot?" Lanietta offered from behind a sales stand, taking the role of a salesgirl.

"Again, no," Tony said as Claus put his palm to his own head in dismay.

Tony made his way through the mezzanine, putting as much distance between him and the lobby. He reached the mezzanine's wall (the far side from the lobby) and followed its face until he reached an opening to a corridor. A sign at the opening had an arrow pointing toward the mezzanine with the words, "Second Outer Ward". Another arrow pointed down the corridor and said, "Grostarius". Tony followed that arrow down the corridor (it was perhaps twenty meters long and had hatches at both ends), and entered the Grostarius—what Tony now realized was the large, central building he had seen from the outside. Instead of sales shops, he saw several lines of ragged workers with sack lunches waiting to descend down respective stairwells to some gnawing labor Tony did not understand. These workers had a ruddy red complexion, and Claus thought them vaguely familiar.

"I look cute in grub-wear, don't you think?" Lanietta said with her new attire.

"Lanietta, this is—"

"Here, you can wear my hat. I know how fond you are of my hats," she said, and she put her grub hat on Claus's head.

"Those workers," Claus said. "They look like pre-Orchians."

"Wow, Claus! I didn't think you had it in you," Lanietta said.

"They came from here? I thought they came from the Carinia system," Claus said.

"They did," Lanietta said. "They came as Greyans and left as Orchians. Minor details, Claus."

"Something tells me it isn't. Why would you have such interest in them?" Claus asked.

"Oh, Claus, you are too suspicious. Let's enjoy the moment!" Lanietta said.

Guards (similar to the two who had escorted Tony from the Martian surface) patrolled these lines and ensured no worker escaped. Tony hid behind a portable wall and watched through the cracks in the hinge between two panels.

"Isn't this fun? Hiding is so thrilling. We can spy and hope no one finds us," Lanietta said, now wearing a burglar suit.

"You look like you're about to rob a jewelry store," Claus said. "Tony isn't up to such a thing."

"Oh," Lanietta said in disappointment.

A little gate blocked each downward stairwell. Tony watched as lead guards moved the gate aside, and rear guards pulled out their whips and lashed individual worker legs into action.

"Get going you dirty Grosti, and earn your keep for the day," one guard ordered in a gravelly voice.

"Fire it up, Grosti," ordered another guard for a different line as he too lashed individual workers with his whip.

"Submit to the pleasure of Mistress Lanietta. Meow!" Lanietta said as she now wore a black leather outfit and cracked a whip close to Claus.

"Careful with that. You could hurt someone," Claus said.

"Hsssss," Lanietta hissed.

Another guard for yet a different line yelled something so guttural that Tony could not recognize the word, if word it was meant to be. The fearful sound was more like a globberence of intimidation. But one by one, the workers descended their stairwells and began working some sort of foundry or forge, with echoing sounds like a dishwasher with loose dishes, but instead of hearing the slosh of water, Tony heard the slash and roar of fire. In the middle of this fiery collackus (collection of clackety ruckus), Tony heard the scream of an injured worker.

"Help me!" the voice cried.

"Help me!" Lanietta said, who now wore heavy rope around her wrists and ankles, but Claus only glanced at her before returning his attention to Tony and the injured worker.

Startled, Tony jumped slightly, but he held his place and did not move. A guard descended one of the stairwells and returned with the injured worker. Tony looked closely and saw that the worker's left hand and left-side face were burned.

"This little Grosti didn't move his quota fast enough," said the guard who pulled him up. "He was so slow that he blocked a fuel transport and was thrown next to a molten vat. See little Grosti? Slackards deserve no sympathy."

"Please, take me to the care center. I'm hurt!" the worker begged.

"He's hurt," the guard mocked.

"Oh please, Claus, help me! I'm hurt!" Lanietta said, and she showed him the left side of her face, which was covered in blisters and blood.

"You're sporting a new look. An improvement, if I do say so," Claus grinned.

"You're supposed to give me sympathy!" Lanietta retorted. "Humph!"

"Oh, poor little Grosti," another guard teased.

"What shall we do for our poor Grosti?" a third asked.

"I know," said the first guard. "Let's play, *Frost the Grosti*."

"No, no, NO! PLEASE! NOT THAT!!" begged the worker.

The first guard tied the worker to something that resembled a full-size stick figure. It was made of steel and had shackle points for wrists, ankles, and neck.

"Cut a rug!" another guard said while holding a device resembling a flare rifle but with a storage tank hanging from its middle.

"Here," Lanietta said now in camouflage army gear, passing a helmet to Claus.

"You're getting into this too much," Claus said, accepting the hat and putting it on his head.

"Labba says I should be innerviated more," Lanietta said. "I would kiss the men here as she did in Arberella, but I can only kiss you."

Lanietta tried to kiss Claus, but their helmets knocked together.

"Ugh!" she said.

The guard pulled a trigger on the device, and a capsule of liquid fired from the rifle and hit the worker. The capsule ruptured on impact and evaporated instantly, drawing all heat energy from whatever the capsule touched. In this case, the evaporative liquid touched the worker's left hand, and it froze. The worker squirmed and writhed to avoid the next shot, because even he had heard of this torturous game of "Frost the Grosti". The guard flipped a lever and then fired. A capsule flew from the rifle and landed directly on the worker's left hand. The capsule ruptured, sending liquid on the worker's hand. But the liquid solidified, expelling lots of heat from the reaction. The frostbitten hand melted, and the nerves in the worker's hand carried the extent of the damaging pain to the worker's brain. He screamed in agony. His hand swelled in various shades of orange and black before the guard flipped the lever back and shot another capsule of evaporative liquid. The capsule ruptured, and the worker's hand froze again.

"I'm so cold," Lanietta said, now wearing a mink coat (but still wearing her army hat). "Gimme a hug."

"You disgust me!" Claus said. "I'm surprised Libriota isn't here. I half expect to find out she's behind all this."

"Maybe she is," Lanietta winked.

"What are you saying?" Claus asked. "Did Bleuhs torture Greyans on Mars?"

"Umm...uh...hmm," Lanietta said. "If this is what I think it is, we all (well most of us at least) lost our corporeal bodies by this point. Only those on Mars kept theirs, and only those in a small, protected area. These corporeal folk are master/slave Greyans."

"I don't even know what a Greyan is," Claus said.

"Again, minor details. Who cares about a Greyan anyway? You're missing the story!" Lanietta said.

"Unbind him," said the guard with the rifle. "It's time for the toss."

The guard who bound the worker now unbound him. The other guards formed a circle, and the guard holding the worker brought the worker to that circle and tossed him to the neighboring guard. The neighboring guard was sure to catch the worker by the left hand so as to warm it, damage it, and cause as much pain as possible. The guards began to sing:

Toss a Grosti
While he's frosty
Criss-cross toss
Until we exhaust.

Little lost Grosti
Begs for bossy
To pay his cost
He's just a loss.

Why is Grosti's
Eye so glossy?
Is he sauced?
Or's he star-crossed?

Claus turned toward Lanietta, and to his horror she had joined in with the singing, wearing an outfit suitable for a children's playground and holding a jump rope.

The singing went on with other rhymes, to which Lanietta also sang. She even jumped rope in time! Tony watched as the worker's left hand sloughed off, with flesh and blood getting all over the guard's glove and the floor. The worker went into shock and could not respond. The guards slapped him several more times to get a response from the worker to satisfy their sadistic appetite, but the worker did not respond. Tony surmised the worker was near death.

"This is awful," Claus said. "Why are you showing me this, Lanietta?"

"It is what Tony hallucinated," she replied. "Do you think people's dreams are all fun and roses? Think again."

"But is it real? I mean based on reality? Is it?" Claus asked.

"Just sing along, Clomper. Sing along," Lanietta said. "Oh, they've stopped singing."

"Game is over," said a guard.

One guard opened a chute along a side wall, revealing a waiting cargo transport elevated by electromagnetism. Another guard picked up the worker and placed him on the transport in the chute, let go, and the first guard closed the chute.

"Send the Grosti on its way!" a guard said, and with that, the guard who had placed the worker in the chute pressed a nearby button. A *whoosh!* followed. The guard pressing the button opened the chute door and revealed that nothing was left. The other guards applauded, and the chute guard bowed.

"So disposable," Lanietta said. "Well, I'm sure there are plenty more Grostis where that one came from."

Lanietta laughed. Not a simple chuckle, but one of deep evil pleasure and satisfaction. Claus did not turn to her but instead remained motionless at this pathogen of an alien standing next to him. Unable to stop himself (and in one motion), Claus spun around, extended his arm into a hook, and clocked his fist into her jaw. Her helmet and glasses flew off, the mink coat reanimated into multiple minks (who ran away), and she fell to the floor.

"WHAT...ARE...YOU...DOING... MISTER GERHARDT!" she yelled. "YOU...PUNCHED...A...WOMAN!"

Lanietta leapt to her feet, spun her body around, and caught her heel in Claus's face. His helmet and glasses flew off, and he fell to his knees. Lanietta spun her body and swung a leg at him again, but he caught it and used it to flip her body over. She came down hard. Claus stood up and wiped the blood off his chin from a cut lip. He squared off and prepared for more.

"You've been asking for this for a long time," he said. "It's time you had a dose of your own medicine."

"I've been very patient with you, Mr. Claus Gerhardt. Do you forget I can turn you into a dog or a salamander? Maybe a necrotic slime worm would be more appropriate. Or I can toss you like salad into a sea cucumber!" Lanietta barked.

She came at him again and made to pull his hair out, but he stepped aside, she missed, and her disrupted momentum carried her to the ground.

"Turn me into a sea cucumber," Claus taunted. "Go ahead, do it."

"I'm going to tear you to shreds first!" she said, and she changed shape to a lioness.

Her roar deafened Claus, yet his chest still felt the reverberation, and his heart became paralyzed by the concussive waves. She swatted at him. Claus looked for something, anything to hold her off. Lanietta moved low in pounce position, and Claus knew it would be over soon. Then he remembered something. He removed his army jacket and held it open in front of him, not as a shield, but as a large bird of prey, ready to envelop the lioness and capture her. Lanietta ran off. Claus held the jacket to his side and let out a sigh—of relief.

"That was close," Claus said. "But I'm in hot water with Lanietta. I depend on her to get me back. Hold onto yourself, Claus. Hold on. Where are those glasses? There they are. Get them back on, Claus. Gotta see what's going on with Tony."

Tony realized that he couldn't just walk into the middle of these guards. They would surely torture and maim him as they did the worker. He needed escape. Yet all the while this was happening in his left eye, his right eye showed steady progress toward the Leovissia. In fact, the Leovissia's beacon was noticeably brighter, and Tony could see that he was getting closer and closer to the rover.

"I wonder," Tony said. "With my left eye seeing fantasy and my right seeing reality, is this what it's like to be half asleep and half awake?"

Back in the Grostarius building, Tony found a panel on the wall next to him much like the one the guards used to dispose of the worker. Tony searched for a catch mechanism and found it along a seam. The door opened. The guards were surprised to hear this, and they rushed over to Tony to intercept him, but Tony was amazingly quick. He pulled himself into the chute, onto an elevated transport, and then closed the chute door behind. He activated a switch on the transport, and it carried Tony upward to his surprise.

"I would have thought this transport would have taken me down," Tony said to himself. "But perhaps not all transports go that way."

Tony's right eye showed that he had reached the Leovissia. He stepped on a back ledge and used that ledge as a means for his transport. He was ready for the Leovissia to take him to the Leovich. His mind, despite seeing two different images, was synchronized in that he was using a machine for transportation.

"Lacuna, this is Leovissia, do you read?" Tony called through the rover's radio.

"Tony!" Kechenova replied. "You made it! The worst is over! You'll soon be on board the Leovich. I'll instruct the rover to turn around and return to base. I can't believe our good fortune. We're going to blast off Mars yet! You'll see! Earth is just a hop over the hill!"

"Irina," Tony said as the rover began moving. "I'm hallucinating again."

"Just hang tight, Tony. The rover will do all the work. Relax and hold on as best you can," Kechenova said.

"I see things in my left eye, but my right eye sees reality," Tony said.

"I'll keep speaking with you," Kechenova said. "Once we meet, you can put the harness back on, and you'll have full control again."

"Okay," Tony said. "I'll do my best to hold on."

"Did she go back into Kechenova's body?" Claus asked himself. "It seems all too convenient that she left because I raised a jacket to her. Never can tell with a Carinian."

Tony's left eye did not abate with the hallucination. It showed Tony pressing another button on the transport, and it stopped. In front was a closed chute door, and Tony's first thought was to jump right through it, but then he remembered the guards and their treatment of the worker.

"I best not let anyone know I'm here. This place gives me the creeps," he said to himself, but Kechenova heard and replied.

"What sort of place?" Kechenova said.

"I'm riding a magnetic transport along the wall of a building called the Grostarius," Tony said. "It's a torturous place with factories and farms."

"Is there a way to escape?" Kechenova asked.

"Not that I can tell," Tony replied. "It's isolated on Mars. And there's a gigantic, spiraling, transparent tubular structure around this Grostarius building."

Tony was able to peer through a slit between the chute door and the wall. Inside, he saw a factory floor where components were being assembled. He must have nudged the door a little, because a floor foreman walked over toward the chute to find out what was going on. Tony didn't wait to be caught. He pressed another button on the transport, and it moved upward.

But Tony's curiosity got the better of him, so he stopped at another floor. He peered through another slit between chute door and wall, and to his surprise he saw a floor of strange farm animals resembling but not quite matching Earth farm animals. There was hay and straw everywhere, and Tony nearly sneezed, but he backed away from the chute door and engaged the transport into movement again.

"Tony, how are you holding up?" Kechenova asked through the Leovissia's radio.

"Still hallucinating," Tony said. "Crazy vision, and all still confined to my left eye."

"The disruption beam from the Panamirov is weakening," Kechenova said. "It will soon give out. I'm hoping to direct the Leovissia far enough away so the Exodus One energy source can't reach you."

"Thank you," Tony said.

The transport went up another level and stopped. Tony looked through the gap between chute door and wall.

"Here are the latest figures, Boss," said a Monazite to a bald humanoid (with sideburns) sitting behind a desk and smoking a cigar.

Tony looked closely and saw a nameplate on the desk, "Boss Nossinoss".

"Sales are down," Boss Nossinoss said. "The Halaxians are importing goods from Carinia 5 and selling them in shops in the Halax. Our stores are dead."

"Our prices are cheaper than theirs," said the Monazite.

"But our quality and selection is inferior," Boss Nossinoss said. "Gelek, I need better products!"

"We fired all Grosti designers and replaced them with Monazite designers," Gelek said.

Boss Nossinoss laughed.

"You are well cultivated," Boss Nossinoss continued to laugh. "We brainwashed the designers into thinking they caused the disaster at the First Outer Ward. Now these former designers are laboring for free in the factories."

"May I suggest we replace slave Grosti factory help with Monazites?" Gelek said. "We can send the Grostis to Luna, too. Get rid of them from our factories and prisons."

"Prisons are full, eh??" Boss Nossinoss asked.

"Grostis also defile the Halax. And the Grostarius," Gelek added.

Boss Nossinoss grew red in the face with anger.

"Send them to me. I'll freeze them and put them away—in the trash chipper!" the boss said.

"They are harmless when wearing their skull implants," Gelek said. "But they should be of some use. Libriota wants to find the PRAAD on Luna. I'll have a shipment of Grostis ready to help her. As for the Monazites, we'll connect their circuits to the central computer with radio data streams. I guarantee product quality will improve."

Boss Nossinoss paused for a moment.

"Very well. Then I think it best I trade you my Grosti slaves for Monazite servants," Boss Nossinoss said.

"Agreed," Gelek said.

"Another thing. Don't waste time sending under-performing Grostis to Luna. Let Vlukka recycle them into biodiesel."

Gelek trembled for a moment.

"What's wrong, Gelek? Do I sense concern in you for the Grostis?"

"Well...we were all Greyans at one time. To send them to Vlukka, the Master of Misery...I...somehow this doesn't seem right," Gelek stumbled.

"Yet you have no trouble sending good ones to Libriota. Gelek, this is the only way we can preserve this colony," Boss Nossinoss said.

Gelek stumbled to say something but could not.

"The only way," Boss Nossinoss said. "Don't worry so much, Gelek. What happens to them won't happen to you. You are doing very well—for a Grosti."

Gelek bowed and was about to leave. But Tony bumped the chute door, and the resulting sound attracted Gelek's attention. Gelek walked toward the chute to inspect, but Tony decided it was time to move on. He activated his transport and sent it high up along the side of the Grostarius, as high as it would go until it could go no farther.

"I don't know whether or not having Lanietta away is good or bad," Claus said to himself. "This portion might give her empathy for the oppressed. On the other hand, it might give her ideas for oppressing me. At what point does a man decide if a memory is worth it?"

Claus looked around suddenly, as if expecting Lanietta to appear out of nowhere and throw a slap in his face or give a reply like, "It's not up to a man. Women know the memories to keep." But she wasn't around. In a way, Claus missed the talk-back and worried that she was harboring something horrible for him.

The transport stopped abruptly and flung Tony through the chute door onto the floor of a clock, book, and coffee shop. Tony stood and looked. A sparse number of people roamed the shop, but most were reading books and drinking coffee at tables with one another, discussing whatever thing of the day was on their minds. Most of these tables were by a collection of windows, with a view of the Martian surface, a view of a walkway from the

Grostarius to the Halax, and a view of one side of the Halax.

"How different this is from the lower levels," Tony said to himself.

Tony walked toward the windows and saw an obelisk in the corner where the windows met a solid wall. Tony turned toward the obelisk, approached it, and read a plaque:

"In memory of the Grostians and Halaxians who fought for independence from Carinians, in the year 9431 of the Grostian calendar. We hold that all are free to follow the time and calendar of their own planet and not another."

"Grostian calendar?" Tony said.

"What calendar?" Kechenova asked through the radio.

"Some sort of Martian calendar," Tony said. "I see a reference to the year 9431 of the Grostian calendar."

"Interesting hallucination," Kechenova said. "Tony, the Leovissia will bring you to the Leovich soon."

"My left eye says I'm in a shop with clocks and books for sale. Also people are drinking coffee and eating pastries," Tony said. "I'm going to look around."

Tony walked by a row of clocks, with both digital and analog models. They all looked similar to clocks on Earth, but the seconds went by a little slower than what Tony was used to. Between a row of clocks and row of books was a collection of calendars. They were for the year 9446. Tony opened one with lightly-clothed female Monazites posing in front of industrial equipment. The calendar had twelve months, but they had strange names: Vanory, Vepery, Varch, Vamil, Vay, Vune, Vuli, Vaucus, Vepeter, Vocoter, Vovimer, and Vecimer.

"They are vaguely like Earth month names," Tony said.

Tony noticed that Vanory, Vamil, Vuli, and Vocoter had fifty-five days per month while the other months had fifty-six days. There were eight days in a week: Gunthay, Gomthay, Goos'thay, Genes'thay, Gawathay, Gorsay, Grithay, and Gaturthay.

"Again, like our seven days, but there's an extra day, this 'Gawathay'," Tony said.

Tony flipped to the end of the calendar and saw a list of rules:

Vanory 56 is a leap thay for the following:
Every odd thear
Every thear ending in 0 but not 00
Every 500 thears, overriding 00 rule
Vamil 56 is a leap thay every 10,000 thears

1 thinute = 60 theconds
1 thour = 60 thinutes
1 thay = 24 thours
1 theek = 8 thays
1 thonth = 55 or 56 thays, about 7 theeks
1 thear = 12 thonths or 83.5 theeks
1 thecade = 10 thears
1 thentury = 100 thears
1 thillennium = 1000 thears

A solar thear (not figuring leap thays) is 668.5921 thays

"My right eye sees a spacecraft on the Martian surface," Tony said.

"That's the Leovich," Kechenova said. "You should be there in fifteen minutes."

"Doctor, something just occurred to me," Tony said. "If you have the ability to direct the Panamirov to distract the energy source with a beam of crystals and command the Leovissia rover to take me to the Leovich, why couldn't you instruct the Leovich to pick me up in the first place and then pick you up?"

Kechenova laughed.

"Everything seems so easy until you know what is involved," Kechenova said. "I probably could, if I had three weeks and several test flights. But I have not the time and not the luck. I must trust your experience to make this work."

"Irina, I hope you're right," Tony said. "I don't know how long I can cope with this hallucination."

"Only a little longer, and everything will be fine," Kechenova said.

"For now. I can't help but wonder about Jill and the ore she took to Earth. What kind of Earth will we find when we return?" Tony asked.

"Better to focus on the here and now," Kechenova said. "There will be time for speculation on the journey back to Earth. We will not have the luxury of the Alatau propulsion system."

The Leovissia continued carrying Tony toward the Leovich, and Tony's hallucination of the Grostarius also continued. He walked along windows with a view of the walkway between buildings, and he stopped. A spaceship landed on a port just outside the coffee shop yet on the same level. This port was serviced by a sky cab that ran from the port to the top of the Halax—parallel to the walkway.

A set of stairs descended from the belly of the spaceship, and a line of people exited down these stairs from the craft. Most went into the sky cab, but some walked from the port to the coffee shop. One such passenger, a male, seemed to know Tony and waved to him.

"Keil, how are you? I thought you went back to Earth," the man said.

Tony looked around, but it was clear the man was speaking to Tony.

"Don't you recognize me, Keil?" the man asked as he shook Tony's hand. "It's me, Jaylen."

"Now a man named Jaylen thinks my name is Keil," Tony said to Kechenova.

"Go along with it," Kechenova said. "Don't fight the hallucination. Keep stress to a minimum. Save your strength for our mission."

"Roger," Tony said.

"No, my name isn't Roger, it's Jaylen," Jaylen said.

"Oh yes, Jaylen, my friend," Tony said.

"I'm glad you think of me as your friend now," Jaylen said. "When last we met, you swore you'd never speak to me again. Then you left for that other planet. Earth was it?"

"I cooled off," Tony said. "I realized I was in the wrong and decided to come back and apologize. But I ate bad food on the spaceship, and it's left me a little disoriented and forgetful."

"I forgive you," Jaylen said. "Yes, spaceship food will do that to a Halaxian. That's the Grostians for you. I'm afraid spaceships will always hire cheap labor. But I know something that will improve your spirits and your memory. Marla is making roast-ka-bobs for dinner. You do remember my sister, don't you?"

"Yes, I do," Tony said.

"Good. I'll have her set another place. She'll be thrilled to have your company. She's still sweet on you, you know," Jaylen said. "Say you'll join me for dinner?"

"I accept," Tony said.

"Good!" Jaylen said.

Tony followed Jaylen to a private hovercar. Tony climbed into the passenger side, and Jaylen drove. The hovercar took the two from the Grostarius spaceport to the top of the Halax. At this point, Tony could see that the top of the Halax had a feeder tube to the top of the Grostarius, and this feeder tube carried sparkly nutrients to the Halax. Jaylen's hovercar entered a port into the Halax and followed the inside tube around the spiraling tube until the two were about halfway down toward the ground. Tony watched. The hovercar passed other hovercars, various dwellings, shops, and recreational areas in the Halax.

Jaylen hovered near a structure in the Halax that resembled a home, built above another home and below still another. He pressed a button in his craft, and what looked like a garage door opened, but with no driveway. Jaylen piloted the hovercar into the garage, parked, and the garage door closed.

"Come. I can't wait to see the expression on Marla's face," Jaylen said.

Tony followed Jaylen into the home.

"Dinner is almost ready, Jaylen," a familiar woman's voice said from the kitchen.

"Marla, we have company," Jaylen announced.

"Who?" Marla asked.

"Guess," Jaylen said as he and Tony entered the kitchen.

"Keil!" Marla screamed.

Marla tossed aside the apron and jumped into Tony's arms. She hugged and kissed him to no end.

"I knew you'd come back!" she said. "But where is your dog?"

"What dog?" Tony asked.

"Clomper," Marla said.

"Lanietta! Hey! I know it's you in Marla's body!" Claus said.

"Keil doesn't have a dog, Marla," Jaylen said. "Do you?"

"No, I don't," Tony said.

"Well it doesn't matter. It's so wonderful to see you," Marla said.

"And I'm sorry," Tony said. "I was wrong about everything."

"Good," Marla said.

"Marla's been worried that she and I would become victims of your plan," Jaylen said.

"We do somewhat well with our status position," Marla said. "But since you came up with that plan for sending lower status Halaxians to the Grostarius to relieve our overpopulation, well, it's been too much to bear."

"Many nights of crying, is more like it," Jaylen said. "I hope that's come to an end."

"It must," Marla said to Tony. "You're here. That means you'll put in a good word for us with the High Aristocracy, right Keil?"

"It might not matter," Tony said.

"Oh?" Marla asked with interest.

"Marla, if you would excuse us for a moment please," Jaylen said.

"I want to hear what Keil has to say," Marla said.

"I smell something burning," Tony said.

"Yes, there *is* something burning," Jaylen said.

"Oh, dinner!" Marla said, and she ran into the kitchen.

"Come with me, Keil," Jaylen said to Tony.

Tony followed Jaylen to a private study.

"I didn't think anyone outside of the High Aristocracy knew, except me," Jaylen said.

"Now you know better," Tony said, playing along.

Jaylen pulled out a tube from behind a bookcase, removed the top, and slid out a rolled up drawing. He unrolled the drawing onto a table and placed weights on each end to keep it from curling up.

"I stole this from the High Aristocracy's secret files," Jaylen said. "It's a copy, and an older one. Tell me—have you seen the latest plan? Have people been chosen for the new Halax?"

Tony looked at the drawing, and yes, it showed a new Halax spiraling around both the existing Halax and the Grostarius, but in an opposite direction, with connecting tubes between the outer Halax and inner Halax.

"When will construction begin?" Jaylen asked.

"Sooner than the decision as to who will inhabit the new Halax," Tony replied.

"I knew it! If we're so lucky as to get a spot in the outer Halax, we'll be able to keep an unobstructed view of the Martian surface, like we do now. But if we stay here, our view will be blocked with the new Halax," Jaylen said.

"Not completely," Tony said.

"True enough. But who's to say what part of our view will be blocked. At least this is good news for all Halaxians. No longer need we worry about being exiled to the Grostarius," Jaylen said.

Marla rang a bell.

"Dinner is ready," Jaylen said. "That was fast."

Jaylen hid the drawing in haste, and the two exited the study and sat at the dining room table. Food was already on the table along with plates, utensils, and drinks.

"Keil, you may sit here next to me," Marla said.

Tony sat next to Marla, and she placed the various foods on his plate.

"Here, take a bite," she said, and she dipped his fork into a bit of food on his plate and held it to his mouth.

"Mmm," Tony said as he ate from the fork. "Very good."

"What about me?" Jaylen asked.

"You have arms and hands. Use them," Marla replied. "Keil is our guest."

Jaylen laughed.

Tony's attention shifted from his left eye to his right. The Leovissia arrived at the Leovich, and it was time to enter the spacecraft.

"I'm at the Leovich," Tony radioed.

"Excellent," Kechenova said.

"And I'm eating dinner with Jaylen and Marla in the Halax, or should I say, the soon-to-be inner Halax," Tony said.

"You'll have to explain that when we meet," Kechenova said. "But for now, I need you to check your available oxygen."

"Almost gone," Tony said.

"As I suspected. Tony, please use one of the spare oxygen canisters on the outside of the Leovich," Kechenova said.

Tony searched the outside of the craft, and to his surprise, he found a spare oxygen canister for human use.

"I found it," Tony said, as he swapped the Leovich's canister with his now-depleted canister. "But I don't understand why."

"I'll explain in a moment," Kechenova said. "But first, you must enter the Leovich and remove all soil samples."

"Remove them? Why?" Tony asked.

"The Leovich is designed to return to Martian orbit with several hundred kilos of soil samples. But now it must carry our combined weight. So we must get rid of the soil samples to free up capacity for us," Kechenova said.

"Now I understand," Tony said. "Okay, I'm throwing out soil samples."

"When I designed the Leovich and Panamirov, I added the capability to support human life, just in case they would be needed for human rescue," Kechenova said.

"You were forced to?" Tony asked.

"Of course not," Kechenova replied. "I proposed the idea to the Kazakhstan Space Agency as a way to increase revenue should Astroosa or another space agency get into trouble with human exploration. I never guessed I would be the one needing it. Sorry, that *we* would be needing it. I didn't know about you then."

"Do you now?" Tony asked, still unloading soil samples.

"I'm learning," Kechenova said. "I must say you are quite unique in the world."

"Well, if the world is Mars, then I am unique. And so are you," Tony said.

But Tony's words about Kechenova came out as less of a joke and more of a sign of affection, to which Kechenova briefly held radio silence as she regained her composure from blushing.

"Th...thank you," she stuttered.

Chapter 51: Breakfast Surprise in the Leovich

"I've finished emptying the Leovich," Tony said.

"Good," Kechenova said. "There's one last thing to consider. If you lift off now, the energy source might attack the Leovich."

"So what do I do?" Tony asked.

"Wait for the Panamirov to orbit back around," Kechenova said. "I'll have it distract the energy source. But I can't use much more power and be able to get us back to Earth."

"I'll only need a couple of minutes of cover," Tony said.

"I can give you those couple of minutes," Kechenova said. "But then you will need to wait."

"How long?"

"Another fifteen minutes," Kechenova said.

"I can wait," Tony said. "My left eye is no longer hallucinating. I'm seeing everything with both eyes."

"I want to say that's good news," Kechenova said. "But I fear it means that one hallucination has ended, and a new one will begin soon."

As soon as Kechenova's words finished echoing over the Leovich's radio, Tony's view went black for a moment and then brightened to a scene where he and Phil Richter had just stepped outside a pub. The two walked along the sidewalk and up to a restaurant when Phil spoke.

"Speak of the devil," Phil said as he pointed to a woman sitting alone inside the restaurant.

"What?" Tony asked.

"Yeah, really," Phil said. "Jill saves you from crashing the F-16 in a nine-gee test, and you say, 'what'. Why don't you go inside and thank her?"

"I should? But what about—" Tony started.

"Don't worry about me," Phil said. "I need to get back to Pelican Airfield as it is. Thanks for the drink."

Phil was gone.

"Might as well go inside," Tony said to himself.

Tony entered the restaurant and asked the host to seat him with Jill. The host seemed confused.

"Never mind, I'll seat myself," Tony said.

Tony walked past patrons and approached Jill's table.

"Mind if I join you?" Tony said.

"The ace pilot. What a surprise," Jill said with a start. "I'm actually in a hurry."

"This won't take long," Tony said, and he sat down.

A waiter approached the table.

"What may I get for you today, Miss Cresson?" the waiter asked.

"I'll have the breakfast surprise," Jill said.

"At lunch time?" Tony said.

But Jill ignored him.

"And I'll have a large orange juice. And jam for my toast," Jill added.

"Very good," the waiter said, and he was about to walk away.

"Hey, what about me?" Tony asked.

"I didn't know you were hungry," Jill said.

"Well, maybe I am or not, but shouldn't the wait-help always ask?" Tony said.

The waiter looked at Jill, and she nodded back in confirmation.

"How may I help you?" he asked Tony.

"I'll have the same as her," Tony said.

"Oh, then you are with her?" the waiter asked.

"It's okay, Byron," Jill said. "I'm paying."

"And I'll have that with rye toast and butter," Tony said.

Again, the waiter looked at Jill.

"It's okay. He didn't read the menu. Just bring two breakfast surprises, and I'll explain," Jill said, then she turned to Tony. "You like coffee, is that right? Tony is it?"

"Yeah on both counts," Tony said.

"As you like," the waiter said, and he disappeared.

"The breakfast surprise is just that, a surprise," Jill explained. "It generally means two eggs, bacon, and toast. But it can vary."

"But it's lunch time," Tony said. "Isn't breakfast an odd sort of thing to have this time of day?"

"Let's ask who blacked out during a nine-gee test and who didn't, then I'll answer as to what I eat," Jill smirked.

"Oh, that," Tony said.

"I take it that's why you came in here, isn't it?" Jill asked. "To thank me?"

"Yeah. I do thank you," Tony said. "I underestimated the F-16. I won't again."

"We can't go through life based on estimates," Jill said. "We must proceed on provable and computable facts, or else we miss our targets."

"Like how we shouldn't fly by feeling?" Tony asked.

"Exactly," Jill said.

The waiter brought out two breakfast surprises to Jill and Tony's table.

"Wow, that was fast," Tony said.

"They have them ready in advance," Jill said. "That's one of the reasons I like them. I don't have to wait for food to be cooked."

"Then I apologize," Tony said. "There is a method to your madness."

Jill smirked, but Tony sensed the smirk had some other, unknown reason behind it. Tony started to eat his eggs, but when he reached for one of the slices of toast, he noticed that it was not the same kind of bread as his other slice. In fact, neither were Jill's.

"Wow, not even the toast is the same. Isn't it odd how they are all different looking?"

Jill smirked again. The two ate for a few minutes, but Jill was quiet and restless. She only managed to eat a slice of bacon and half her eggs when she suddenly got up.

"Excuse me for a moment," she said.

Tony watched her leave and disappear around a corner.

"She didn't go to the Ladies' Room," Tony mused. "I wonder what that was about. Maybe I should go. I seem to be causing her irritation. Yeah, sometimes a person needs quiet time. Never thought she would. Oh well."

Tony waved down the waiter and motioned him over.

"Bring a check for just my food, will you?" Tony asked.

The waiter seemed puzzled.

"Just for you?" he asked.

"Yeah, just for me," Tony said. "What's so hard about that?"

"And you are with lady friend here? You are part of Jill paying?" the waiter asked.

"She shouldn't have to pay for both of us. I'll pay for mine," Tony said. "Now bring me the check. What's the fuss all about?"

"Okay, okay, if okay with Jill, I bring your check, and I bring her check too," the waiter said.

The waiter walked away briefly and then returned with a single, black, restaurant check holder. He left it at the table and was about to walk away.

"Wait," Tony said. "Here."

Tony placed his credit card in the holder and handed it back to the waiter. Again the waiter looked puzzled. He hesitated and stared at Tony.

"What's the problem now?" Tony asked. "You *do* take credit, don't you?"

"Yes, we do. If this is how you wish to pay, I cannot argue," the waiter said.

"Yes, it's how I want to pay. Now go ring it up."

The waiter left and returned briefly with the check holder for Tony to sign. About this time, Jill returned from around the corner and headed toward the table. Tony was about to sign his check, but when he went to figure out the tip, the total amount caught his eye: $135.41.

"There's something wrong with this ticket," Tony said. "Look at these prices.

Naan Toast: $46.11, Jam: $9.44, Emmer Toast: $62.64, Jam: $7.22."

Tony looked at Jill's ticket and noticed that it too was expensive. The culprit was the toast, but her amounts were different. Sourdough Toast: $2.37, Jam: $3.06, Wheat Toast: $44.39, Jam: $6.39.

"These prices are just as wacky," Tony said.

"I'll handle these," Jill said. "Tony, I think it's time to say goodbye."

"He already paid for his meal," the waiter said to Jill.

Jill's face turned red with anger, but she said nothing.

"Refund his check. I'll cover everything," Jill said.

"Jill, what's this—" Tony started.

"Tony, go up in the F-16 again and perform another nine-gee test. Only do so without a passenger," Jill said, and she was gone.

The flashback ended, and Tony found himself back in the Leovich, with Kechenova yelling over the radio.

"Lacuna to Leovich! Tony! Launch now! Twenty seconds left. Launch! Tony!"

In that brief moment, Tony realized that he had blacked out during the fifteen minute wait and most of the launch window. He quickly engaged the controls and set the Leovich engines a-blast. The Leovich thrust upward suddenly and sent Tony to the floor, fighting the gee forces.

"Leovich, I confirm successful launch, but you are going too fast. You'll overshoot the Lacuna landing site. Leovich, throttle down. Tony, do you read?" Kechenova radioed.

"Must...throttle...down. Must...must..." Tony strained.

He fought the gee forces with arm and might, and he just managed to reach the controls and reduce the Leovich's thrust. The gee forces subsided. Tony regained full control of the craft.

"Throttle-down successful. I'll see you soon, Irina."

Tony heard what he thought were yells of pain over the radio.

"Irina, Irina! Are you all right? Irina? What's the matter? Irina!" Tony called.

"Everything is fine," Kechenova returned with jubilation. "I'm just celebrating."

Tony smiled.

"I never thought you could be anything but a straight-laced engineer," Tony said.

"Now you know better," she said. "I can be many things, depending on the place and mood."

"I'm beginning to learn that," Tony said. "I'd like to know what other places and moods you are capable of."

"Just land by Lacuna, and I'll show you," Kechenova said.

"Just land by Lacuna, and I'll show you too," Lanietta's voice said to Claus.

"Where are you, Lanietta?" Claus asked, who himself rode with Tony in the Leovich.

"In Lacuna," Lanietta said. "Hanging out with Kechenova."

"Girl party?" Claus asked.

"In my own way," Lanietta laughed.

Tony felt a heavy weight lift from his heart, as if everything were better, and the future would be filled with good times. There was still the trip back to Earth, and who knows what kind of Earth he'd return to, but he felt the worst was over, and now it was just a matter of going home. The journey to Lacuna would take eight hours, and to pass the time, Tony retold his hallucinations to Kechenova, including the flashback about the expensive breakfast.

"So Ms. Cresson is also part of the Space Saboteur Syndicate," Kechenova said with a new anger in her voice. "Had we known, things would have been different with our friends in Brazil. Very different. Natalia would know what to do. She always did. But not anymore."

"Irina?" Tony called over the radio.

But Kechenova held radio silence for the duration of Tony's trip to Lacuna, despite his repeated attempts to get her attention.

"I'm at a complete loss as to what on Mars is troubling Irina," Tony said to himself. "My restaurant flashback triggered something in the doctor's mind. But what? And why does she think Jill is part of a syndicate?"

A tragic thought crossed Tony's mind.

"Irina wouldn't end her life, would she? No, she couldn't! We're still on Mars. Who's ever heard of such a thing? What ever happened to, 'Goodbye, cruel world'? But that works only on Earth, right? What am I talking about? I must be going a little crazy myself!"

"Lanietta?" Claus called. "Is Irina okay? Did you do something to her? Lanietta?"

Lanietta did not reply. Tony had to occupy himself for the rest of the trip to Lacuna. Two hours had passed already, and he had another six to go. The Leovich was not a fast craft, being meant for simple launch into orbit and nothing more. Tony had to conserve fuel so as to retain enough energy to reach orbit. Or did he?

Tony fired up the rockets and accelerated the Leovich. He risked overshooting the Lacuna landing site and risked not having enough fuel to attain orbital velocity, but those were minor concerns. He sensed that time was against him, and every minute spent was a minute farther removed from the last moment that he could confirm Kechenova's well-being.

As it was, Tony had no more hallucinations or flashbacks. He wished he did, if nothing else than to pass the time. He didn't. The Leovich spent another two hours in flight instead of six, and it landed next to Lacuna.

Tony had another thought. What if Lacuna's scrubber were filled, and the doctor was out of breathable air? This now seemed more likely to Tony, and he rushed the procedure to exit the Leovich and enter Lacuna.

"Irina?" Tony called after he closed Lacuna's hatch behind him and removed his helmet.

The air was heavy with carbon dioxide, and Tony's lungs burned with craving for relief, forcing him to reattach his helmet. Lacuna wasn't large, and the doctor's slumped-over, unmoving body told him

she was in trouble. A quick glance of the doctor's oxygen tank indicator confirmed Tony's suspicion that the doctor's tank was completely spent.

"Now for it, Tony!" he said to himself.

Tony removed the oxygen feed from Kechenova's tank and attached it to a second port on his own tank. In this way, his tank provided air for the both of them. But this scenario was tricky. The line wasn't long, and so the two could keep no more distance from each other than an embrace.

The air filled Kechenova's suit, but she did not respond, and her suit instruments registered no pulse. Tony tried hugging the doctor to force air into her lungs, but again she did not respond. He tried beating on her upper chest to start her heart. That failed too.

"You can't die here. Not now!" he yelled.

There was only one thing left to do. He removed both his helmet and hers. Fresh oxygen escaped into Lacuna, and Tony choked on the in-rushing carbon dioxide. Now he had to open the tank valve more to compensate, and this meant wasting precious oxygen. But it was necessary. In that moment when helmets were removed, Tony breathed into Kechenova's lungs with mouth-to-mouth resuscitation. No response. He pumped her heart to circulate blood, sucked air from inside his suit, and breathed air into her lungs.

"Come on, doctor. Breathe!" Tony commanded.

It wasn't enough. Kechenova did not respond.

"Emergency medical kit," Tony said. "Where is it? Think, man, think!"

Tony coughed, because he had not reattached his helmet to regain a full breath from the suit's oxygen supply. He couldn't spare the time. He was too preoccupied with the task of doing anything to save Kechenova. He ripped open storage box after storage box as best he could while keeping her oxygen line attached to his tank. And there it was—an epi pen. He took the pen and thrust it as close as he could to Kechenova's heart without damaging her suit. Another breath of air he gave to her, and then it happened.

"A-crumph a-crug," Kechenova coughed.

"Irina!" Tony gasped, and he gave her another breath of mouth-to-mouth resuscitation. "Keep breathing, Irina. Keep breathing!"

"I am breathing," Kechenova said.

But Tony kept breathing into her lungs.

"You may stop kissing me now," she said. "I am breathing."

"Oh," Tony said, and he stopped himself—he *was* kissing her.

"Oh Clomper!" Lanietta said as she dipped out of Kechenova's body. "I should've put you in Tony's body. We could've had a nice kiss together."

"Tony was giving mouth-to-mouth to Irina," Claus said.

"Mouth-to-mouth kissing," Lanietta sighed. "Clomper, kiss me."

"No space or time. These two are doing things. Shh," Claus said.

"Don't shush me," Lanietta said.

"Shh!"

"Humph!"

"We must transfer over to the Leovich at once," Kechenova said as Tony helped her reattach her helmet.

"Yes, we will," Tony assured her, and now he attached his own helmet.

"We must bring your harness," she said.

"I'll bring it after we get you aboard the Leovich," he said as he helped her up to the hatch.

"And my laptop," she said.

"I'll get that too," he said, with them now walking on Mars between the two spacecrafts.

"There's something else, I think. What is it?" Kechenova said.

"I'll bring that too," he said as he helped her into the Leovich.

Tony closed the hatch behind them and repressurized. He disconnected her oxygen line from his tank and removed her helmet. She removed his.

"I...just want to say..." she started as she looked down into his chest.

Tony lifted her chin and stared deeply into her eyes. She returned the gaze. She moved her lips to his, and the two exchanged a deep kiss and embrace. When the two finally let go, she finished her sentence:

"Thank you."

"What else did you want me to bring?" Tony asked.

"A little green book," she said. "It should be next to my laptop. I...my little...it...for inspiration...I thought I was at the end."

"Shhh," Tony said. "Rest here. I'll return shortly."

"Okay," she said.

"You missed your chance again," Claus said, and then Lanietta dipped out of Kechenova's body.

"I did, didn't I? And I suppose I should've taken advantage of it, too. This might have been my last chance," Lanietta said.

"What is that supposed to mean? Lanietta? What's going to happen?" Claus asked.

But Lanietta dipped back into Kechenova's body and did not reply.

Chapter 52: Return to Earth

Tony exited the Leovich and reentered Lacuna. His oxygen tank was running low, but he was confident he'd be able to grab the harness, the laptop, and Kechenova's little green book in the few minutes of air he had left. But this wasn't so. His left eye began hallucinating, with a vision of double-ended stacked blades. Their tips pointed left and right. A tough wall pushed those blades to the left until they punctured and ruptured a second wall. That second wall crumbled, but now a new wall from the left pushed those blades to the right, forcing those blades to puncture and rupture the first wall. That wall crumbled, and another wall from the right repeated this vicious cycle of push and destroy, push and destroy. The blades remained and never dulled, but each successive wall increased in force to overpower the prior wall of destruction.

"Stop it. Stop it!" he yelled.

But the hallucination burst across Tony's brain from right to left and caused luminous afterimages of the blades and walls in Tony's right eye.

"It's a full seizure," Tony said. "Can I get the harness on? I would have to remove my suit. But that would deprive me of oxygen. What if I hyperventilate first? Breathe, Tony. Breathe!"

Tony took several deep breaths, but the images seared through his vision and brain at increasing speed. He closed his eyes to fight the storm, but that made things worse.

"What can stop it? What can stop it?" he cried.

Tony was desperate. He reached for something, anything, everything to loosen the seizure's grip on his brain. He found a glove and batted it against his face mask, but the seizure did not abate. He found a flashlight and beat that against his face mask, but that did not help either.

"What about light?" he asked himself.

Tony turned the flashlight on and wiggled the light in front of his face. His hallucination distorted a bit, with the blades acquiring the cold blue of the LED flashlight.

"More," Tony said. "There must be more."

Tony actuated buttons and switches and levers on Lacuna. Any and all and even more lights flashed, sparkled, fluctuated and strobed such that Tony now had competing stimulus sources from outside and within. He managed to strike a balance of force and tension such that he was able to trap a corner of wit, gather up the harness, laptop, and green book—and leave Lacuna.

"I can't bring the lights with me," Tony said. "Will I have the strength?"

Tony enriched his oxygen mixture to sixty percent.

"Sixty percent," he said to himself.

Tony entered a twilight state where he was more zombie than human, and in that state he managed to bring the three items out of Lacuna, across the short Martian distance, and into the Leovich. Kechenova noticed his deteriorated condition and—despite her depleted energy—moved as best she could to his aid.

"You'll be better soon," she said as she helped remove his helmet and upper part of his suit. "Do you hear me, Tony? Do you hear me?"

But Tony was unresponsive. His eyes darted back and forth, and his fingers twitched. Kechenova repaired the shoulder wound quickly then slipped the harness over Tony's chest and flipped on the power. Tony remained the same.

"This is a devil of a seizure. He's been exposed to the energy source too long. I must recalibrate the harness and revivify his mind," Kechenova said.

She did just that. Kechenova powered on her laptop, attached a cable from the laptop to the harness, and started her harness-control application. The application showed status indicators of the harness's thorium batteries, its neurostimulators, and Tony's cerebral response.

"What is that?!" she asked herself. "There's something entwined in his neural synapses. It wasn't there before the Mars landing."

Kechenova typed quickly into her laptop.

"It's genetic code. Chains and chains of ribonucleic acid. But these chains are moving on their own, as if being directed," she said.

Her laptop showed animations of the chains interacting with each other in pairs to modify synaptic activity and form new chains.

"No, not ribonucleic acid—*robonuclear* acid," she said. "Then it's clear what I must do. I must neutralize the robonuclear acid—with an inverse, off-peak, half-harmonic energy burst."

Kechenova typed the commands to initiate the burst, and it happened. The harness received the new laptop instructions, and it generated the burst. Tony's body convulsed upward, and a rebound wave carried back through the cable, into the laptop, and into Kechenova's forearms, stinging her tissue as like that from a dozen hornets combined with electrical shock.

"Ow!" she yelled as she pulled away from the laptop and bumped her head into a supply container.

"Ow!" said Lanietta as she fell out of Kechenova's body.

"That's very interesting," Claus said. "You didn't choose to leave Irina's body. You were forced out."

"I'll show you. Look," Lanietta said as she tried to reenter Kechenova's body, but she couldn't.

"That jolt forced you out. I have a trump card over you. I can now prevent you from changing me into another form," Claus said.

"What? What are you talking about?" Lanietta said.

"I've been paying attention, you see," Claus said. "Each time you turn me into another form or even push me into another body from time gone by, you put a little bit of yourself into me. I can prevent it. Try it. Try it!"

"You have no more insight than a flea on water," Lanietta said.

Claus punched Lanietta.

"Behave, Mr. Gerhardt!" Lanietta ordered.

"I said, change me!" Claus said, and he punched her in the abdomen.

Lanietta didn't take kindly to that. She moved to snap her fingers and turn him into a dog. But at that moment, Claus tensed all muscles in his body and forced himself into a sustained shiver. Lanietta tried to change him, but the more she tried, the more her face expressed frustration and anger.

"Fool!" she yelled. "Do you think you can keep this up?"

"I'm taking over, Lanietta. I'm taking over now."

"You can't keep it up. You know you can't. I'll work you down. Wear you out. Then what will you be? An exhausted Clomper!"

"It beats being your subservient punching bag all hours of the day and year," Claus said. "And if you wear me down, I'll shake from nervous exhaustion. You'll have to let me rest before you can change me again."

"You will be forced to watch all future memories! No enjoyment of life. Just a senseless ethereal spirit! Is it worth it, Claus? Is it? Remember what I told you—numbers upon infinite numbers are waiting to live out a life. Choose this path, and you forfeit that right," she warned.

"The right you design to place in my food bowl? Forget it!" Claus said.

"I warn you!" she said.

"You cry wolf too much, Lanietta. Too much," Claus said.

"There are other ways. There always are. Do you know what the underworld is, Mr. Gerhardt?" she asked.

"Being stuck with you," he said.

"*No*, Mr. Sarcasm. Being stuck between memories," she said. "I have paused this memory for your outburst because it entertains me. Imagine if I leave you here alone without resuming the memory. I can also pause your lifespan. Oh, your mind would continue to encode along the way, but your body would not age. You'd remain in this ethereal form, re-encoding the same frozen moment over and over again until all other memories are flushed from your mind. It's the Tsunami of Emptiness, and we Carinians have perfected it. I haven't told you about it until now because you've been so entertaining, as I have said. But cross me now with this silly shivering or whatever it is, and I shall punish you. You humans do understand punishment, right? You can be as stubborn as your German ancestry permits, but at some point that small part of Celtic blood you have suppressed deep within will wish to be back in the mountain woods with fresh water and clean air. Be careful what you do against me, Mr. Gerhardt!"

Chapter 53: Sabotage Explained

"Irina?" Tony said. "Wake up. Irina."

Kechenova pulled herself up from the Leovich's floor.

"You hit your head and fell unconscious," Tony said.

"So I did," she said, and she looked out the window to confirm her location.

"Is something the matter?" Tony asked.

"No," she said. "We're still on Mars. We must get going if we are to survive. We will have time on the return journey to investigate the robonuclear activity in your cells. The Panamirov is well stocked with food and air and water for us, but the Leovich is rapidly running out of ability for human support. We don't have much time. Prepare for liftoff."

Tony and Kechenova initiated the preparation sequence. Rockets were re-warmed, fuel was heated and compressed, and the flight computers were instructed to begin the auto-liftoff process.

"Coordinates for rendezvous with the Panamirov have been entered into the flight computer," Tony said.

"Good. That's everything. Strap yourself into your chair," she said.

Tony did just that, and Kechenova secured her own chair belts.

"Flight computer set on hold for tee minus one minute," Tony said.

"Release the hold," she said.

Tony released the hold, and the flight computer counted from fifty-nine seconds down toward zero. When it reached twenty, Tony began calling out the numbers.

"Do not waste time with the numbers," she said. "I can read them. Rockets igniting. All systems are good."

"And we're in...liftoff!" Tony called.

The Leovich headed for an orbital rendezvous with the Panamirov.

"Irina," Tony said. "What were you saying about the Space Saboteur Syndicate? What was that about Jill Cresson?"

"Your expensive breakfast," Kechenova said. "Ms. Cresson was receiving coordinates from your waiter."

"Huh? How?" Tony asked.

"Through the prices, Tony, the prices. Look at Cresson's toast and jam. The *S* in Sourdough stands for *south*. And so, Sourdough toast with jam is south 2.37306. Wheat toast with jam is west 44.39639. That's the location of Alcântara Launch Center in Maranhão, Brazil. On the 22nd of August, 2003, a Brazilian VLS-1 V03 rocket exploded on its launchpad. The official story is that it was accidental, but Kazakh intelligence reports that it was sabotage," Kechenova explained.

"But we didn't eat breakfast back in 2003," Tony said.

"That was just the beginning. There were a string of failures around the world after that. The location of Alcântara Launch Center was used to say, 'It's time for another launch failure.' Additional information would typically follow from a different contact."

"Which one was this?" Tony asked.

"A Kazakh launch," Kechenova said, and then an expression of sadness overcame her.

"Natalia?" Tony guessed.

Kechenova paused to stifle a deep sadness welling up inside. Instead, she replaced it with anger.

"Natalia Smyechetov was a Russian rocket scientist," Kechenova said. "She was assisting our space agency's rocket program. Natalia discovered the sabotage but was too late to prevent the explosion. She paid with her life."

Then Kechenova muttered something in Kazakh that sounded vulgar.

"Our intelligence reviewed secret video of Natalia attempting to defuse the detonator," Kechenova continued. "We had agents sift through the wreckage for clues. One of our Kazakh agents found an audio chip with Natalia's final spoken log, where she identified the SSS as the saboteurs."

Kechenova muttered something else, but it too was in Kazakh.

"Why would someone sabotage a space rocket?" Tony asked.

"Why does anything get sabotaged?!? To prevent success!" Kechenova said with anger still in her voice. "Access to space is limited, but others are developing space programs, placing satellites into space, and more!"

"The 'more' is exploration on Mars, is that it?" Tony asked.

"Yes," Kechenova said. "The public story is that humans are to search Mars for water. But the private story is that there is more to Mars than water. We were set back in our program and could not get a special probe to Mars as originally planned. That plan contained a probe featuring new detection methods designed by Natalia. And I helped her with it."

Tony paused a moment.

"What about my breakfast? What coordinates are they?"

"This is where they broke protocol. As I said, the actual target is typically given by another contact. But the waiter thought you were part of the SSS, so he gave it to you. Naan toast with jam gives north 46.11944. Emmer toast with jam gives east 62.64722. That is the location of pad 81/24. The Baikonur Cosmodrome," Kechenova said. "Kazakh intelligence detected an unusual credit card transaction with those coordinates and was able to prevent a full-scale attack. It was your credit card, of course. We only lost one rocket. It could have been worse. Much worse."

Then Kechenova's voice softened, and she looked at Tony with a new sense of gratitude.

"It is like you have the charm of luck. What is it? A good luck charm," Kechenova said. "Bad luck for those who are evil, and good luck for those who are not. I always felt in my heart that a fate intervened and protected our program from harm. We lived in the Soviet shadow in old times, and the United States does not enjoy share of its technology to other countries in times of past or future, so you see how we strive for space independence. I am still angry at Cresson for being part of SSS, but I am glad you foiled her little, despicable, filth-of-an-excuse-for-a syndicate."

Kechenova held Tony's hand and looked intently in his eyes.

"Thank you from me, Irina, and thank you from the depths of the Kazakh soul," she said.

Tony smiled.

Chapter 54: Kechenova's Dream

"You know, I had a strange dream," Kechenova said. "I was in one of your American reality television shows."

"Oh no, not reality TV," Tony said.

"I know it is fake, and that was how the dream started. The story was about the scenes behind the main competition," Kechenova said.

"What was the main competition?" Tony asked.

"We were competing to be movie actors," Kechenova said.

Tony laughed.

"It is true," Kechenova said. "There were five groups of three people each, and we had to perform routines in our little groups. But before we performed our routines, we only had sixty seconds to memorize our lines. So you see how exciting the competition was. I discovered that I could memorize my lines quickly. In fact, I saw them in my mind before I was given the opportunity to look at them formally. That's when I knew I had some sort of visionary ability. I performed very well in my acting routines, and I could predict what others were supposed to say, too."

"So you won?" Tony asked.

"Do not get ahead of the story," Kechenova said. "No, I did not, but there is more. At first, the worst performing group was voted off. Then a single person from each group was voted off. But that caused fighting, because a man had voted off a woman with whom he had been having an affair. She got mad, told about their affair, and produced a videotape of an encounter. We were asked what we thought about the affair and the breakup, and I said it was perfectly predictable, because the two were already actors, and they were paid to pretend to be ordinary people in this competition, that their fight was scripted, all for ratings."

"Oh wow!" Tony said.

"I thought the producer would get mad, but she didn't. She seemed accepting of my response and promised she'd make good use of me in future episodes. But there were no future episodes for me. I was in my little room on the island after a long day of taping for the television show. I was reading a book and preparing for sleep when two tall men who were twins took me forcibly by the arms, dragged me down the back stairs, and shoved me into a limousine. The twins sat on each of my sides, while an older man with beard, hat, sunglasses, and cigar sat across from me."

"'So you like to play hardball, do you?' he asked," Kechenova continued. "I said, 'I don't know anything about hardball.' He laughed. I asked him to let me go, but that made him laugh more. I asked him who he was, and he replied that he wasn't."

"Huh?" Tony asked.

"Yes, I had the 'huh' question too," Kechenova said. "What I found most puzzling was that I couldn't read anything about the cigar man, at least not at first. But as the limousine continued to move, I sensed that he was not a man, but some sort of parasitic shrub, feeding on other plant forms like the tobacco in his cigar."

"'You're not even a man,' I said. 'You...your name is Slylac. You're a plant!'"

"Is this like the Amnus Apple story?" Tony said.

"No, no, no. Slylac looked like a man. He wasn't some innocent-looking tree. He was the ultimate deceiver, making those around him believe that he was one of their own, but he wasn't. He fed on his own, and he made deals with other humans to remove those who got in the way," Kechenova said. "And so I was hauled into a tavern and thrown into a chair. Then one of Slylac's thugs pushed my face into the table, and the other tied a rope around my neck, ran the rope over the other side of the table, underneath, and tied it to my arms that he forced under the table. The rope was taut, and any effort I made to move my hands would then pull the rope on my neck. If I moved to lift my head, the rope pulled on my hands."

"'What do you want of me?' I asked, but Slylac just laughed. He then instructed the band to change its music to a tango, which it did. He walked over to another table and tapped it. The table came to life and danced with Slylac!"

"That is a strange dream," Tony said. "It sounds like one of my hallucinations."

"Doesn't it though?" Kechenova said. "Soon the chairs were dancing too, with other chairs and with tables and coat racks and brooms and other wooden things—all were dancing except the table that I was tied to. It walked away, and my chair walked too, carrying me out of the main drinking room, down a stairwell, and into a dark, long corridor with other people tied to tables, but not with ropes. Instead, they were covered in a twisted entanglement of brown algae seaweed. They were prisoners and had been there for some time, because they wailed and gargled like animals reaching their end. Some people were sleeping or dead, and I could see flatter-than-flat kissing bugs creep up to the people's faces and suck their blood until these bugs were bloated and round like grapes. The bloated bugs hobbled away very slowly, sometimes even rolled away—content with the system with which they were provided. The very scene disgusted me, but I was helpless against the table and chair that had now seated themselves at the end of tabled prisoners. I only wished to be back at home with a hot cup of green tea, but instead I was greeted with cold, slimy seaweed that slithered along the table and chair and entangled itself around my limbs. The experience terrified me, and I cried out, but that only attracted flat kissing bugs to my table, bugs that sensed my fear and breath and fresh energy, all ready for their voracious consumption."

"And then, it happened," Kechenova continued. "A recently-used bag of green tea fell from my pocket and onto the table. At first I felt despair, because the loss of the tea bag symbolized my last hold on freedom and comfort. But the tea bag caused a strange sort of events to begin. Encroaching kissing bugs that had planned to feast on my face instead hissed and withdrew in a terror of their own. I could not break free of the seaweed, and I could not loosen the ropes. It seemed my battle was only half won or still half lost. I tried to think of what I could do, but nothing came to mind."

"In the corner of my eye," Kechenova continued, "I saw a flash of light. At first I thought the grips of the seaweed had detached my retina, or the firm grip of the rope was causing me to asphyxiate, but the flashing grew closer, and then I saw to my surprise a firefly alight on the green tea bag! Something strange happened next. The firefly caused the green tea bag to excrete a fluid. The fluid spread on the table and carried to the seaweed and rope, fuming the entire time. At first I thought the fluid was chlorine, based on its smell, but the irritation to my nostrils increased incredibly fast, and so I knew the fluid was actually nitric acid."

"I felt myself choking even more, and I wasn't sure if this was from the ropes and seaweed, or the nitric acid, but it was only a matter of seconds before the nitric acid caused the seaweed and rope to dry and fray and wither into a fine mass of fluff. I was free!"

"I stood up and searched for a way out of the corridor, but it was dark, and no exit was obvious," Kechenova said. "I kept bumping into other tables and chairs and seaweed vines that wanted to entangle me into their predatory vice, but for each that attempted to entangle me, the firefly came to my rescue. He carried the green tea bag with his legs, hovered over the attacker, and released nitric acid, forcing the attacker to withdraw. After much tripping and stumbling and lumbering through the corridor, I realized my exit was blocked by a wooden door. I pushed hard against the door and even banged on it, but it did not budge. The firefly helped me again by dripping nitric acid onto the door. The door fell away, as if its hinges and latches had dissolved. Now I was really free!"

"The opening led to a sewer," said Kechenova. "I followed stinky passages left, left, down, left, and up to a surface hatch that I opened. I climbed to the street and discovered it was snowing. I turned back to find the firefly, but he had not followed me, and so I was alone. But I wasn't lost. Incredibly, I stood on a sidewalk just outside my home, and there parked on the street was my car."

"I brushed the snow from my car and started the engine. It operated smoothly and efficiently, which surprised me because I always remembered my car as running rough. But it didn't, and I drove it to the nearest airport and parked. I rushed inside and asked to purchase a ticket to Chicago."

"'That will be four dollars and four cents,' the clerk said."

"I thought it strange that an airplane ticket would cost so little," Kechenova explained. "And it was in American dollars, too. But I was in a hurry, and I needed to leave, because I feared that Slylac would have me captured and killed. As it was, many of us were leaving the area. I asked, and the other passengers had all paid four dollars and something: four dollars and twenty-four cents, four dollars and thirty-six cents, and so on. How could an airline afford such prices? We all wondered that. What's more, when we entered the airplane the seating was quite different. Instead of being crammed into little seats along the length of a narrow tubular fuselage, we sat vertically, with a huge, open cockpit in front of us, and the fuselage diameter as large as a house all about us. The cockpit windows were also quite large, and we had an excellent view of the runway ahead. Never had I been in such a large aircraft. In fact, I thought such monsters would be too heavy to fly, but

there we were in the airplane, all ready for takeoff."

"And Slylac caught you?" Tony asked.

"No," Kechenova replied. "The airplane took off. But like I said, it was heavy, and it struggled to gain altitude. The pilot had to veer to the left to avoid a grove of trees, which the right wing just missed by centimeters. And power lines—I can't remember how many power lines we avoided, going over and under and—"

"You went under power lines?" Tony asked.

"I know, I know. All very strange," Kechenova said. "The airplane climbed high above the cloud deck and stayed level for about a minute. Then it descended quickly into a spiral dive. We punched through the cloud deck, and the ground expanded quickly through the cockpit windows. I was convinced we would crash, but the pilot closed the throttle, leveled the wings with nose down, and pulled back just before hitting the ground. The seats shook violently from the strain, but once we reached a constant altitude with proper power, the shaking subsided."

"That sounds more like a roller-coaster than a commercial airline flight," Tony said.

"The craft went into a phugoid, and a very rapid one at that, going into a dive and ascent every five seconds, which I didn't think possible for an airplane large enough to hold people, but it was there and very definite, and each time the airplane dove, the passengers screamed at the thought of crashing, but the airplane always lifted back up. Finally the aircraft went into a Dutch roll, also while continuing the phugoid, which left me disoriented and wondering what kind of flight this was supposed to be."

"Sounds like a very bad flight," Tony said.

"Well, it ended after a time, but not soon enough for me. The other passengers and I exited the airplane, and to my surprise, the same clerk who had sold us the tickets to begin with was at the counter. I approached him and asked him how that was possible that he was in Chicago when I left him back home. He said he was always in Chicago, as was I, and did I enjoy the movie?"

"Oh, it was a movie! What a twist!" Tony said. "What happened next?"

"I told him I was walking home, and the dream ended, but I can't imagine how I could walk from the United States to Kazakhstan."

"That could have been an entirely different story," Tony said. "You could have hitchhiked across country to the west coast and then caught a ride on a ship going across the Pacific. Do you always have dreams like this?"

"Never," Kechenova said. "This was the first time. It's as if whatever caused your hallucinations is now causing my vivid dreaming."

"The energy source?" Tony asked.

"We were well beyond its range when I had my dream," Kechenova said.

"Well, when there's no external source of conflict, look to the internal," Tony offered.

"A good idea," Kechenova said. "We're approaching the Panamirov. It's fully equipped with a bioscanner. We can check our physical health using it."

"Sounds good," Tony said.

The Leovich docked with the Panamirov. Kechenova hit several buttons within the Leovich. The Panamirov pressurized with breathable air, and Kechenova opened the hatch. The two transferred over.

"It's very spacious," Tony said. "And it has artificial gravity. I'm impressed. You really did design this for human habitation."

"Thank you," Kechenova said. "It is time I perform a full bioscan of your system and of mine."

Kechenova had Tony stand in front of the Panamirov's main bioscanner. She typed several instructions at a keyboard and triggered the scan to start. A bluish-green light flickered but then went out, failing to rasterize Tony's body.

"How do I look, Doc?" Tony asked. "Doc?"

But Kechenova had fallen into a catatonic state.

"Irina, are you okay? Irina, speak to me."

Chapter 55: Kechenova's Second Dream

Kechenova returned to consciousness with a worried Tony Kavalla at her side.

"What happened?" Kechenova asked.

"You started the bioscanner," Tony said "You became unresponsive and wouldn't move."

"How long?" she asked.

"About twenty minutes," he replied. "I think we had better take care of you first before we leave orbit. I'm worried about you, Doc."

"I'm so glad to be back," Kechenova said. "I thought I would be stuck on Kesophili's pedestal forever."

"Who? What?" Tony asked.

Kechenova forced a smile. She was exhausted from her experience but glad to have her sanity restored.

"I had another dream," Kechenova said. "I was back in the tavern with Slylac, and again I was tied to the table and chair. As before, Slylac danced with other tables and chairs, and again my table and chair carried me from the main drinking area to a side room. But the table and chair released me in the side room and left me. I looked around and realized I was in a prison cell, crowded in with other prisoners. The few cots that existed were taken by the dominant prisoners, who slept. I was forced to sit on the floor. I could have stood, but I was exhausted and needed to rest. I wanted to sleep, but the floor was hard and cold."

"I didn't care," Kechenova continued. "I found an unused floor mat next to me and tried using it for a pad and blanket, but another prisoner, who was also relegated to the floor, yanked the mat from me and used it as a sleeping pad. Several prisoners laughed, but I thought it not so amusing. This cell was all-female, and they had clearly established territories as to who could use what and where. I had no friend and only a small place on the floor I could use, and even that was obviously owned by someone, because that someone was already pushing me onto another part of the floor, which in turn was owned by another prisoner, and she pushed me too, and this continued until I ended up in front of the door, which no one claimed and no one wanted to claim."

"'I'll sell you the floor spot under my bed,' said an inmate close by from the comfort of her lower bunk."

"'I have no money,' I said."

"'Then give me your shoes and socks,' she said."

"'What will I use to protect my feet? The floor is cold,' I said."

"'Do you really have a choice?' the inmate said. 'You can't stand by the door forever. It's forbidden. The guards will notice and throw you in solitary.'"

"So I gave her my socks and shoes, and she permitted me to crawl under her bed and stay there," Kechenova said. "It wasn't long, however, before two other girls were thrown into the cell. They were dressed in leather, and it was clear they had been riding motorcycles and spending time in a tavern, a smoky tavern at that, because their leather reeked of tobacco tar. They walked around and kicked whoever they could, but they especially enjoyed kicking me, because I was in a vulnerable position and could be easily abused."

"I crawled out from under the bed and stood in front of the cell door again. The biker girls laughed and shoved me around a few times, but soon they were making deals with the other inmate girls for space and even a comfortable bed to rest, which they did immediately."

"'What's wrong, Barefoot, can't handle a little fun?' said one of the leather girls."

"'She's a starched shirt,' said the other leather girl."

"'Let's make her one of us, then,' said the first leather girl."

"'Please, let me be,' I said."

"But the leather girls would not. They pulled out knives—how they kept them from being confiscated, I don't know—and cut up my blouse and slacks to make me all ragged looking," Kechenova said.

"'That's a good start,' said another inmate, 'but I can do better.'"

"She approached me and began tearing at my clothing where the knives had first formed the rips. I tried fighting her off, but she punched me hard in the jaw, and that stunned me. I couldn't react to the onslaught of other inmates who felt they could do 'better' by ripping my clothing further, and soon my blouse and slacks were so badly ripped that there was little left attached to my body. It all fell off, leaving me there in my undergarments. The inmates cheered and celebrated, and they paraded my blouse and slacks among them like prized animals that had been hunted to death."

"'She looks so pale there with her skin exposed,' said the first leather girl. 'Let's add some color.' They proceeded to pummel my exposed skin to bruise it, which they did. I slumped by the door in pain, and I sat there in misery, with the other inmates laughing and taking turns kicking me while I was weak."

"'Stand back,' said a guard who had approached the door. I tried standing up but could not, but it didn't matter. The other inmates did move back after the guard pulled out her club and swiped the air. Another guard pulled me out of the cell and lifted me to my feet."

"'Please don't hurt me,' I said, but the two guards smiled as they escorted me a short ways down the corridor and around a bend. They stopped in front of an office, pushed me in, and locked the door behind me, snickering as they did so. I didn't have time to look around, because in walked an older man from an adjoining room. He seemed ordinary in most ways except for his ears, which instead of being small and flat against his head were appendages resembling elephant trunks, complete with two stubby fingers and a thumb at each end. I would call such an ear a *trunkear*."

"'Irina Kechenova,' the old man said with his trunkears gesturing in friendship. 'My name is Kesophili. I'm the curator of this prison. Please, come with me. You are injured and need treatment.'"

"I wasn't sure what to make of this old man, but I had half a heart to tell him about the injustices from the other inmates," Kechenova said. "As it was, I followed him out of his office and down another corridor toward the medical treatment facility."

"'Swollen and bruised, you are still very beautiful. It's important that you know something. I have selected you. One incredible creature among the many foul. You are that creature, and you will be my escort,' he said, and that disgusted me."

"I was now terribly afraid of what that meant. Kesophili was old and had wrinkly skin like an elephant. He smelled like formaldehyde, which sickened me and made me cough."

"We arrived at the medical center, but the nurse made him wait in the corridor so as not to upset the other patients. The nurse then applied a thorium gel to my skin, and my swelling and bruises vanished," Kechenova said. "The nurse returned me to Kesophili."

"'I will take you to the garden,' he said. 'I have a wonderful collection of flowers for you to enjoy.'"

"And he did just that, but it was a very strange garden. The flowers were suspended in the air on wires and had no roots, yet they were all in perfect bloom. Kesophili removed one from a wire and handed it to me with his left trunkear. I felt uncomfortable taking anything from him, but to appease him I complied."

"'Now smell the flower,' he said. I sniffed the flower, and the out-gassing of formaldehyde from the petals defiled my nostrils and triggered sinus swelling and a headache the size of Belukha."

"'It is pretty,' I lied to cover my agony."

"'Like you, my sweet,' he said, but there was little time to converse. Slylac arrived with his two guards behind him, who in turn forced an old woman to her knees."

"'Please, have mercy on me, my curator. I have served you faithfully for many years,' she begged of Kesophili."

"'Weyowath was caught stealing bread from the canteenery,' Slylac said."

"'Just one loaf of bread for an old woman. A human must have bread to live. She must,' Weyowath said."

"'These are my cousins you devour so easily,' Slylac said. 'They sacrificed their lives for humans. And you believe you are entitled to their souls?'"

"'Time has escaped you, Weyowath,' Kesophili said."

"'No, My Lord Kesophili. Spare me,' Weyowath pleaded."

"'Oh but that is what I will do for you. I will spare you from your lifelong descent into temptation. I welcome you with open ears to my fold,' Kesophili said, and he approached her as if to kiss her, but with his trunkears outreached, and when he was within a few centimeters of her face, his trunkears plunged into her ears and pumped fluid into her. I could tell, because I could see the trunkears carrying bulges of fluid from Kesophili's head to hers. She screamed briefly, but then her flesh went grey, and it became semi-translucent as if being fossilized by grey amber."

"'Take her to her pedestal,' Kesophili said."

"Slylac motioned to the guards, and they removed what was left of Weyowath."

"'I see you have chosen the new prisoner,' Slylac said. 'The one who claims to know what others are thinking.'"

"'Even now,' Kesophili said, 'she is subconsciously probing my mind to read my thoughts. It is a beautiful thing, is it not? She is my flower, and I will preserve her mind and thoughts and beauty for all time.'"

"An immense terror seized me. I panicked and fled for safety. Somewhere, anywhere I could go and be safe from Kesophili and his laboratory of flowers. But as I ran, I noticed a collection of female mannequins on pedestals with nameplates. I ran past this collection, but one was empty. I stopped to read the nameplate, and it read, 'Doctor Irina Kechenova, Preserved'."

Kechenova paused. She was perspiring and out of breath.

"That's all I remember seeing," she said. "Everything went dark, but I heard a voice in the distance ask me a question, saying, 'What is the purpose of the back side of a sword?'"

"The back side of a sword?" Tony asked.

"The back side of a sword," Kechenova repeated. "All of that strange terror, and a voice asks a silly question."

"Did you answer?" Tony asked.

"Yes. I said, 'To support the front side.'"

"Then I think it's time I become the 'back of the sword'," Tony said.

"What do you mean by that?" Kechenova asked.

"I guess I looked at this mission as something that I needed to take charge of, to ensure its success," Tony said. "At first I thought of you as an assistant. But I should be the assistant and help you. This is your craft, and I suppose this is really your mission."

"It's our mission," Kechenova said. "There are two of us. I certainly don't count Miss Cresson as part of this mission. Her mind is a slave to another master."

"Let's get you in the bioscanner then," Tony said. "We should be sure your health is clean."

"Giving orders?" Kechenova laughed.

"Sorry, it was just a suggestion," Tony said.

"It's a good one. Yes, stand by the keyboard. I will tell you what to do," Kechenova said.

Kechenova entered the bioscanner. Tony followed her instructions with entering commands into the computer, pressing buttons, turning dials, and pulling levers. The bioscanner rasterized Kechenova's body three times—one for each three-dimensional axis—and began analyzing the data.

"Data analysis in progress," Tony said.

"Good," Kechenova said, and she exited the bioscanner. "I will take over from here."

Tony stepped aside, and Kechenova entered additional commands into the computer.

"Results being generated now. There. What is...oh no!" Kechenova exclaimed.

"What is it?" Tony asked.

"My DNA. It's...I'm suffering from system-wide DNA breaks and crosslinks. I'm dying, Tony."

"From radiation? Where? How?" Tony asked.

"I don't know. I didn't think I was exposed to significant radiation. Not enough to cause this. Over 90 percent of my cells are affected," Kechenova said.

"And this has caused you to suddenly stop responding to me?" Tony asked. "What about if you wear my harness? Maybe that will help."

"The harness helps dampen neuro-chemical signals in cells with almost healthy DNA. In your case, only chromosome 21 has damage. But all of my chromosomes are damaged. This is too much for the harness. It can't help me," Kechenova said.

"But you can't die. If you die, I'll die," Tony said.

"We still need to test you," Kechenova said. "If you are also afflicted, then it won't matter when or if we return to Earth."

A big frown overtook Tony's face. He stared at Kechenova in hopes she'd say this was all a joke, but she didn't.

"We shouldn't wait too long. I might become unresponsive again. At some point, I won't return to consciousness," Kechenova said.

Tony agreed to being tested. He stepped in the bioscanner. Kechenova operated the controls and performed three scans—one in each axis. The computer analyzed the data, but it did not return results as quickly as it had for Kechenova. She typed additional commands to speed up the process, but they did not help. Finally, the computer locked up and would not respond to commands.

"What is wrong with this device?" she asked, without expecting an answer. "Wait. Take off the pendant."

"You're right," Tony said. "I forgot about it. Could be interfering."

Tony stepped out of the scanner, removed the pendant, and placed it in a container attached to the wall.

"Very good. I will power cycle the bioscanner and its computer. Step back into the scanner. I will rescan in a moment."

Tony stepped back into the bioscanner. Kechenova restarted the bioscanner's computer and started the three scans again. But the computer stopped responding to her commands again, and she pounded the keyboard with her fist.

"It's overloaded," she said. "There must be more going on in your body than what the computer can process."

"Could we connect the Panamirov's navigation computer into the bioscanner to process the data?" Tony asked.

"It would be risky and time consuming," Kechenova said. "Damage to the navigation computer would maroon us in space."

"And if we don't find out how to cure you, then you'll be dead before we are marooned," Tony said.

"You still have a chance to live," Kechenova said. "I don't know if connecting the navigation computer to the bioscanner is worth the risk."

"But you said I could die too," Tony said. "If the navigation computer can analyze my DNA, it might reveal something that can save the both of us."

"Might," Kechenova said.

"Isn't it worth the risk?" Tony asked.

"No."

"Then you have killed yourself already," Tony said. "Jill wins."

"Jill wins? This isn't about Cresson," Kechenova said.

"She wanted you dead. Apparently, she has succeeded," Tony said. "And who will stop her?"

"We can't stop her anyway," Kechenova said. "We can't travel fast enough. Even if we were healthy enough to return to Earth, she will have landed three months ahead of us. I was able to get intelligence reports on her and Astroosa while I was stranded in Lacuna. They will succeed in raising the Hess Rise in a mere week, and they will have plenty of time to establish their island as a new country and superpower, dominating the Pacific Ocean, and more."

"Then we must stop her, and Astroosa," Tony said. "I didn't realize Astroosa would get out of control so fast."

"It's too late," Kechenova said. "And I am tired. Very tired."

Kechenova fell unconscious.

"Irina? Irina!" Tony called as he shook her. "Wake up. Wake up!"

Chapter 56: Operation Concussion

Jill piloted Callisti from Mars to Earth in a few days' time. During that time, she made brief contact with Astroosa to inform them of the "unfortunate demise" of both Doctor Kechenova and Tony Kavalla. Astroosa in turn released a statement to the media about the tragedy and used this event to divert attention from the real plan.

"Tembruno," Jill radioed to Agent Keller.

"Jill!" Agent Keller replied.

"I have missed being in your arms, my sweet. Only two hours remain before my splashdown in the North Pacific," Jill said with affection.

"Everything is on schedule," Agent Keller said. "We will rendezvous at the appointed place and begin Operation Concussion."

"Until then, Tem," Jill said, and she blew a kiss into the microphone.

"Until then, Jill," Agent Keller replied.

Jill splashed Callisti in the North Pacific, a few miles east of the Hess Rise. Callisti's flotation bags kept the craft afloat, and the parachutes detached. Ten seconds later, a replica submarine of the Russian K-278 Komsomolets surfaced with care such that Callisti was now perched on the submarine's deck. A crewmember opened a hatch on this submarine, named *Arvo*, and out climbed Agent Keller. Jill blasted Callisti's hatch open and stepped out with the Veigon container.

"For you, my great Tem, I present the future of the world!" Jill said.

Jill prepared to open the container, but Agent Keller stopped her.

"No, not here," he said. "Let's go below."

Agent Keller led Jill through the hatch and into the Arvo. The crewmember secured the hatch, and another initiated a sequence of buttons that caused the deck underneath Callisti to descend and so pull Callisti inside the submarine. A set of doors closed the newly-created opening, and the Arvo dove back into the water.

"Descend to test depth," Agent Keller said.

The submarine commander repeated the order, and the Arvo descended toward 1000 meters depth.

"So you named this submarine as I suggested," Jill said during the descent.

"The Arvo, meaning the afternoon," Agent Keller said. "Because up to this point, Astroosa has only seen the morning with its simple business transactions and minor rocket launches. But now it is high noon, and we have a showdown with the world. When the showdown is complete, we shall dominate the afternoon."

The Arvo reached 1000 meters depth and then stopped.

"Commander, gather your men," Agent Keller said.

"Your attention to detail on the Arvo is amazing," Jill said. "It looks so much like the Soviet K-278, the only one of its kind."

"As the special entity is your gift to me, the Arvo is my gift to you," Agent Keller said. "But I must confess, the K-278 Komsomolets was not one-of-a-kind. A second, Mike-class submarine was under construction in Severodvinsk, but work was halted for many years. Astroosa acquired this submarine and completed its construction, a testament to Astroosa strength and innovation."

The commander followed Agent Keller's instructions. Within a few minutes, the entire crew had assembled in the control room. Jill and Agent Keller stood on each side of the box while facing the box toward the crew. Jill opened the box. A beam of light shone from within and flooded the control room with acoustic harmonies of rhythm. These sounds reverberated throughout the Arvo, filling all who attended with a sense of progressive goal and resolve, like the predetermined fate of a turning gear as it imparts its torque on a lesser cog, or the unquenchable heat from a desert sun as it scorches all life that dares challenge it.

"Your work on the entity is beyond praise," Agent Keller said.

"I have well prepared the entity for acousto-analeptics," Jill said. "What we feel here is but a trifle of its capabilities."

"Excellent," Agent Keller said. "The entity will become the heart of our new island, our new country, and the world, pumping waves of sonic submission to satiate our requests for action."

Agent Keller had hardly finished when the commander and crew broke out into a naval song—full of chant, camaraderie, and ebullience. Their singing resonated with the entity, and it modified its waves to complement the singing. In other words, it *sang* with the crew. Jill and Agent Keller sang with them, but not because they had to. They were only singing to appear as if with them in mind and spirit, when really they were plotting their next plan of action.

"Keep it going, commander," Agent Keller said, as he led Jill from the control room to the torpedo room.

As the two traveled to the torpedo room, the men continued to sing, but they broke up their group in the control room and returned to their stations. Jill placed the entity in a specially-housed container full of coils and borosilicate optics. She then closed the container and placed it in a torpedo. By this time, the torpedo crew returned from the control room and stood ready to take orders.

"Set target coordinates to the eastern center edge of the Hess Rise. The torpedo must dive in deep like a wedge," Jill said.

"Aye, Col. Cresson," the crewmember said.

The crewmember typed into a keyboard, and the computer programmed the torpedo's guidance system.

"It is time," Agent Keller said. "Load the torpedo."

"Aye, Agent Keller," the crewmember said, and he pressed a button.

A mechanical lifter loaded the torpedo from the bay into a launch tube, and the tube's hatch closed.

"Activate the monitoring screens," Jill said.

The crewmember did just that, and he stood there awaiting the final order.

"This is it," Agent Keller said. "Our last chance to back out of Operation Concussion."

"I wouldn't back out of this for the world, for the world will be to our backs after today," Jill grinned, and her voice crackled and snapped like a whip to a horse's hide. She then turned to the crewmember and said, "Launch torpedo."

"Torpedo away," the crewmember said after pressing the launch button.

"This is it, Claus," Lanietta said. "This is the beginning of the end."

"What are you talking about?" Claus said.

"The Earth as you left it is coming to an end, beginning with this single act by Jill Cresson," Lanietta said. "A shame she landed that F-16 for Tony when he blacked out. Had he remained conscious, he could have crashed the two of them and prevented this outcome."

"She would have ejected," Claus said. "You can't blame this on humans. I see there is evil in the universe. It is not limited to Earth. There was something on Mars, and she brought it back."

"Very astute," Lanietta said. "There is no limit as to how much evil can be added to Earth. Watch your future!"

A video feed from the torpedo's nose relayed a black-and-white image from super high-resolution sonar to a monitoring screen, rendering images that looked as clear as light-based black-and-white imagery. Another monitor displayed the position of the torpedo in relation to the Arvo and the Hess Rise. Yet another monitor relayed numerical data of speed, distance, vector, depth, water temperature, hull pressure, fuel, etc.

"Torpedo at 2500 meters and descending," the crewmember said. "Now at 2700 meters. 2900. 3000."

"Sometimes I wonder if men were meant for such things," Agent Keller said.

"They weren't," Jill replied.

Lanietta laughed.

"I hope you're enjoying your vacation," Claus said. "Because I don't like the feel of this."

Agent Keller turned to her in surprise, as if Jill were expressing self-doubt.

"But women are," she smirked.

"Yes, let the evil flow through, girl!" Lanietta beamed.

"This is like the frozen moment in time, when the future is yet to be known. This is the real underworld you described," Claus said.

"Might as well enjoy it," Lanietta said.

A big smile crept over Agent Keller's face, and he kissed Jill on the cheek.

"Torpedo at 3700 meters. 3900. 4000," the crewmember said.

"Just another 500 meters," Jill said.

"Approaching target coordinates," the crewmember said. "Now at a depth of 4300 meters. 4400. Impact is imminent."

"All hands, brace for impact," Jill called into the public address system.

"The torpedo is at 4500—" the crewmember started.

"Impact!" Jill yelled.

The torpedo penetrated the Hess Rise's upper-ooze layer, dove deep into the Earth's crust and down to the mantle, where it created millions of finger-like channels back up to and through the Earth's crust around the Hess Rise. Lava flowed around the Rise, and the Rise floated atop the lava. Like a cork loosening its grip on a champagne bottle, the Hess Rise lifted suddenly and quickly, with high-pressure lava forcing it up. The swiftness of the event sent concussive and consecutive waves of water from that event outward.

The Arvo was hit first, with disruptive forces similar to that of multiple depth charges. The thundering jolts were nerve-racking, and half the crew went into shakes of anxiety.

"Uhhh," Lanietta shook in mock nervousness. "Steady the sub! Claus! Steady the sub! Humanity is evaporating away!"

"Stop that nonsense!" Claus said.

"Keep the Arvo steady," Jill ordered.

Successive shock waves grew stronger and rattled the Arvo further. One such shock wave caused the lights to flicker and the instruments to display garbled readings.

"There is instrumentation failure on the sub," Agent Keller said. "It's getting out of control. Can you abort?"

"No! Don't abort!" Lanietta said. "This is the moment my hard-earned vacation time has awarded me! Lanietta! The supreme Carinian vacationer! Watching a cataclysmic shift in human civilization!"

Jill smiled and said, "It's too late to abort. And *it's* just beginning."

She then yelled to bring the Arvo closer to the Hess Rise, but Agent Keller thought Jill was mad and ordered the commander to increase distance between the Arvo and the event. The commander gave orders in agreement with Agent Keller, but without consistent instrument readings and with power fluctuating uncontrollably, the crew panicked and began attacking one another.

"Stop it, stop it!" Agent Keller yelled, attempting to break up the fighting.

"You fight him, yes," Lanietta said as if conducting an orchestra, "and you fight him. Good. You two fight each other while a third sneaks up on one of you then the other. Excellent. Try that metal bar. Proper technique employed. Good, he's unconscious. Don't worry, he'll die soon. You all will."

"It's working just as I planned," Jill said. "Just like on Mars."

Agent Keller heard Jill and stopped trying to break up a fight. A stray fist meant for another crewmember landed on Agent Keller's skull. Agent Keller fell to the floor briefly. He shook his head to clear his senses, but he was stunned and had difficulty recovering. He looked up at Jill and saw her standing with her arms in a peculiar pose. Her elbows were close to her body, and her arms were parallel with both the floor and each other. Her hands were straight with her forearms and were palm-down. It was as if she were warming her hands to a fire on a cold day, indeed, her head was cocked back and her eyes closed, as if soaking up the sensation to satisfy a craving.

"Stop this insanity!" Claus said.

"I should have made you a crewmember," Lanietta said. "The exercise would do you good. But you'd just shiver and prevent me. Yes, shiver some more for a quality exercise approved by all health and nutrition establishments."

Agent Keller blinked and saw a semi-translucent structure encircling Jill, with light scattering from its depths. It was the double Halax of Tony's hallucination, though Agent Keller did not know it. He himself now thought that he was injured with a concussion, and he struggled to get back his sense of sanity. He stood and continued staring at Jill. The double Halax blew wisps of light from this side and that. Each wisp floated like the odd bit of lint or pet fur ball, and these wisps landed on various fighting crewmembers. The crewmembers would in turn claw at these wisps as if swatting wasps, but then the wisps would grow claws of their own and envelop each crewmember into a strangling weave that in turn shrank into a fiery ball, as if a gasoline-soaked paper towel had been lit on fire, and the wisps would burn while giving off no smoke, all in a few seconds, and then turn dark orange and dance on edge, like that burning paper towel where its own heat has lifted the lightweight ashy remains into dance, what fragile form is left until nothing is left, and then *poof!* go the wisps as they would dart back to Jill's double Halax. The crew was consumed in this manner, leaving only Jill and Agent Keller alive.

"Have I gone mad? Are we truly the last to perish?" Agent Keller quivered.

"We shall not perish," Jill said with a thunder in her voice.

Agent Keller rushed up from the torpedo room to the control room and checked the controls on the Arvo. He had difficulty getting much of anything to work, but he did manage to get a viewer operating, and he watched as the Hess Rise took on a new form. Arms of lava jetted from the growing Hess Rise and reached out in helical fashion, consuming fish, water, plant, and debris in its path. These arms had blackened skin, with cracks of bright orange and yellow lava peeking through.

"We *will* perish!" Agent Keller panicked. "We must turn about!"

"Don't panic!" Jill ordered from the torpedo room. "Or you and you alone *will* perish!"

Jill, though still in the torpedo room, extended an arm for Agent Keller. Her arm magically extended along the length of the lower area until it was underneath the control room, at which point it then extended upward until it reached Agent Keller. It softly touched him on the shoulder to comfort him. Agent Keller relaxed briefly, but when he turned to hug Jill, he saw instead the extended arm. He shrieked in fright. His fear then triggered the double Halax around Jill. Jill fought with the Halax to stop it, but it was too powerful. It sent several wisps racing along the same route as Jill's extended arm, up to the control room, and those wisps danced around Agent Keller.

"I am holding them back," Jill said. "If you are afraid, they will attack you. You must not be afraid. You must become a full part of our future. I had saved this moment until now, because I wanted this to be special. Relax and come to me. Relax and come to me."

Agent Keller wanted to believe her. He tried. But the multiple stimuli took their toll on his nervous system. It was the view of the lava arm rapidly approaching the Arvo that did him in. He fell into a final panic and hit several buttons to power the Arvo away from the lava. The Arvo lurched, but the lava arm caught the Arvo and pulled it quickly toward the Hess Rise. Convinced of his final demise, Agent Keller let out a scream that could rival any woman on any day. The wisps darted into Agent Keller like wasps to consume him much like the crewmembers. Jill tried to restrain them, but they managed to electrocute him to death before she was able to pull them back to the double Halax.

Jill's extended arm returned to her in a snap. She exhaled suddenly as if she'd been holding her breath, and she breathed heavily. The double Halax weakened around her, but the lava arm continued bringing the Arvo in toward the Hess Rise very quickly. She settled herself and re-established her pose with her arms extended. The double Halax strengthened around her, and the lava arm suddenly changed its intent. Instead of preparing for the Arvo's consumption within the newly-formed lava pillar of the Hess Rise, the lava arm lifted the Arvo ever-so-gently up, up, and up until it was just above the waterline. It nearly beached the Arvo on the new, above-ground, island. Jill was thrown to the side from the collision, and she hit her head on a bulkhead, throwing off her balance and breaking her spell. The double Halax was gone, and the island was complete, though tsunami waves were now spreading into the Pacific.

Jill didn't care. She only cared about herself and leaving the Arvo. It was a coffin, but not for her, and she coughed her way through the Arvo's fumes to the hatch, opened it, and threw herself into the water, where she coughed from the seawater. She landed neck deep, and so she lightly swam to shore while working out the foreign matter from her lungs. She reached the beach, and already there was sand, from where she didn't know, but the sand was there on this new island that was once submerged. The Arvo slipped away to the ocean deep.

"You are the new *Altus Asceninsula*, the ascended island from the deep," Jill coughed as she regained her strength on the beach. "And so I call you *Cenina Island*, from where I shall license over the world and certify my right to such claim. Let it be so, that I build a capital city and call it *Altus*, from where and to humanity I shall reap the peaks of aspirations and dispense the depths of despair. And the entity that I have delivered from Mars shall be my consort, and I shall name him *Areothian*, because he is my heaven from Mars, my sky of the day and my light of the night. All things from my future he now gives to me if I but aid him in the quest for ascendance on Earth."

Jill stood on the beach and planted her feet firmly in the sand. She held out her arms, leaned back, and issued a call to the island, something between a yodel and a holler. From the depths of the island, a rumbling grew, like an empty stomach hungry for shape and sustenance. Jill then performed what looked like a deep knee bend, but she held her arms crossed, with her hands reaching to opposite sides as if preparing to pick things up from the beach. Her hands touched the sand, and she pulled sculpted male hands up from the beach, with her right hand holding the sculpted right hand, and her left hand holding the sculpted left hand. She then straightened her body into a standing position, and this action continued to pull the hands up from the sand. Yes, sculptures of male hands attached to male bodies, only these bodies were not two—they were mirror halves of a complete male. He was young looking, very muscular, and tall.

"Areothian," Jill spoke in a chant. "I call your proxy from the deep and mold it in this fashion. I give you life as you give to my life. Join with me, my consort, and I shall show you the world!"

As Jill spoke those last words, she pulled her arms across her body, and in so doing, she pulled the sculpture halves into each other and into her, causing the halves and Jill to meld into a powerful male body but with Jill's head, which had taken on bolder cheeks, a thicker neck, and more pronounced nose. She laughed with delight, and her voice had deepened as well. Jill had melded the clarity of social divinity with the power of the male body. She approved of her creation.

"Now I am what is meant to be," she said with a fist to the air. "So let it be that I create my most devoted followers, beginning with Tembruno."

Jill took sand from the beach, a handful in each of her left and right hands. She raised them to the sky as two hands and yelled, but then she brought her hands toward each other and pushed the handfuls of sand together, fusing the sand into a glowing, crystalline, diamond-shaped thing with a hole in the middle two-thirds up along the length, a hole as if meant for passing a necklace chain.

"You are the *diamonoli*, the one who searches across the distance for a single item of possession and returns it to thy master. As your master, I command you to retrieve Tembruno."

She threw the diamonoli into the Pacific, in a direction where the Arvo had descended with Agent Keller aboard. The shape descended into the deep and out of vision.

Thirty minutes later, a humanoid shape covered in seaweed, rope, and old plastic packaging wrappers floated to shore, as if pushed by some underwater current. Indeed, the diamonoli had retrieved Agent Keller, or what was left of him. His body was badly water logged and partially eaten by animals of the deep.

"Return to my keeping," Jill said, referring to the diamonoli.

Jill pointed her right index finger at the shape, it jumped from the water, and it flew toward her in the air. Jill then directed the crystalline shape to her left shoulder. The diamonoli followed her instructions, and it flew directly into her left shoulder where it burrowed under her skin and flattened to a negligible thickness, obscuring its existence from view.

Jill took handfuls of the beach sand again, held them up to the sky, yelled as before, and forced them together, fusing the sand into an object much like a small cycad plant, but this object was made of amber, and it was rather small, with a trunk about as long and wide as Jill's forearm. Fused pinnate amber leaves were radially arranged at the top of the trunk and were concave downward—all looking like an amber umbrella embossed to resemble the cycad.

"I call you *resinato*, and from you shall things be rejuvenated from death into life," Jill said.

Jill tossed the resinato into the air and yelled a command. The resinato floated above Agent Keller's corpse, with trunk pointed downward. It spun like an upside-down top, and its meniscus vibrated like a drum, focusing deep sound waves into the corpse. The corpse convulsed and twitched, like a body not sure whether to react from electrocution or from neurotoxin poisoning.

Jill laughed.

"I now send forth a great tsunami, to scour Earth for lost possessions, so that I may rejuvenate them to my will," Jill commanded.

Jill sent the diamonoli up into the air, and then she sent resinato up at the diamonoli. When the resinato came close to the diamonoli, the diamonoli formed, shaped, and spread the resinato into a large, semi-transparent, amber-shaded toroid that was significantly larger than Cenina Island. This toroid rose high in the air, up even into the clouds. It hovered for a moment, and then it fell to Earth at great speed, though Jill did not fear it. It landed in the ocean around Cenina Island and displaced the water outward into a tsunami. Likewise, it would have sent a tsunami back in toward Cenina Island, but its shape changed upon impact with the water, causing a rip to open along the entire inside part of the toroid. This caused the water between the toroid and Cenina Island to be pulled into the toroid and upward, and in fact it stretched the inner part of the toroid high and over the island until Cenina Island was now covered in a dome with a half-toroid perimeter. The shoreline temporarily expanded toward the ocean until gravity allowed the upward-drawn seawater to slowly return to the base of the half-toroid. In this way, Jill was protected while the Pacific Rim endured a great tsunami of her creation.

The toroid remained in the water, and the dome remained in the sky. Air, rain, and sun could penetrate the dome, but nothing else unless Jill wished it.

The Pacific Tsunami Warning Center sent alerts to all countries affected. The northern Pacific countries were hit the hardest with heavy flooding far inland, though the southern Pacific was also hit hard. Buildings and trees were wiped out. Coastal cities were devastated. The tsunami carried through into the Indian Ocean and wreaked havoc on those coastal countries. The death toll climbed into the millions.

Debris carried throughout the Pacific. The toroid sifted through such debris, and Jill had her pick of valuable possessions.

"Jewels, precious metals—anything of value once owned by foolish coastal people is now at my disposal," Jill said. "But what is this thing? Is it a mannequin? Diamonoli, I command you to return to my service and lift this mannequin into the air."

The diamonoli did indeed return, and it lifted the mannequin-like object into the air for Jill to see.

"Tell me, oh great diamonoli. What is this thing?"

"It is a selenite, an artificial life-form similar in size and function as a human being," the diamonoli said.

"From where does it come? United States? Germany? Japan?" Jill asked.

"Unknown origin," the diamonoli said.

"Well then, welcome my fine selenite robot friend," Jill said.

"Is that...no, it can't be. Where are you, Lanietta?" Claus asked.

"Oh what is it?" Lanietta asked, suddenly appearing out of nowhere. "I was busy making Kechenova feel worse. She needs to make a critical decision soon."

"It is! It's Selenite 102! The one that fell to Earth!" Claus said.

"Who? What?" Lanietta asked.

"Numero Uno from the play in Arberella, remember? Don't you remember?"

"Oh, the selenite that you let fall to Earth," Lanietta said. "Yes, I remember. Jill has it now. She is the woman that will repair it. See? She is repairing it with the help of the diamonoli and resinato. And she will duplicate it soon. Yes, very soon she will have an army. Thank you, Claus. You have helped start this whole mess. Jill was going to be isolated somewhat on Cenina Island. Oh, she could send out a tsunami every now and then, but her power was all tied to the island. These other creatures she made won't hold up much past the island itself. But selenites, ho ho ho! They will go!"

"Go where?" Claus asked. "And how do you know this?"

"I was there in Arberella too, you know. Or did you forget the argument we had?" Lanietta asked.

"No, I haven't forgotten. But still, the precise details..."

"Are tied up in memory cells. Morcellus has some, Tabelia has others, the—"

"Who's Tabelia?" Claus asked.

"I already told you that Tabelia is that seamount you and Leni tried to enter. They have memory cells too. I also learned much in my travels through Earth's atmosphere, my trip to Mars, and through archeology, as you have seen with this memory candle. Good ol' Jill. She didn't last much beyond the large-scale duplication effort of the selenites. You see, the selenites got hold of the diamonoli and took over Cenina Island. If it weren't for the efforts of—o wait, I'm spoiling the story."

"What story?" Claus asked.

"This story."

Chapter 57: The Decision

Doctor Irina Kechenova was in a coma. Tony had strapped her to a bed and hooked up an IV line for fluids. He remained in orbit around Mars, unsure of what to do.

"Why don't I leave for home and get help for Irina? I could figure out this Kazakh technology on the trip back. Why do I linger in Martian orbit?" Tony asked himself.

Tony attempted to contact Astroosa, but the Panamirov was not designed for such a connection. Then he tried other frequencies. He received messages in Russian and Kazakh, but after repeated attempts, he got a message back in English—with a Russian accent.

"Panamirov, this is Leonid," the man said. "Do you have a message for us in English? Please resend. We were not expecting English. We had no English speakers monitoring this frequency."

"Hello? Hello! This is Tony Kavalla. Doctor Kechenova is with me in the Panamirov. We're in orbit around Mars. The doctor is in a coma. She is close to death. I can't get her back to Earth in time. Can you help me?"

Ten minutes later, he heard a reply.

"Panamirov. We received message that Doctor Irina Kechenova is in a coma and near death. Attach telemetric medical monitor to her. Switch on. Device will send telemetry on this frequency."

Tony did so.

"I've attached the monitor. Her blood pressure and heart rate are low," Tony said.

Ten minutes later, he received another message.

"Doctor Kechenova suffers from radiation poisoning," Leonid said. "Activate telemetric radiation localizer.

Device will send telemetry on this frequency."

Tony did that too.

"Okay, I did that too. Will this tell me where the radiation is coming from?" Tony said into the radio.

"Oh, I love a house call," Lanietta said.

"This is hardly a house call," Claus said. "What a terrible way to practice medicine—waiting every ten minutes for a reply, and hoping the person millions of miles away can help."

"Have you figured it out yet? Have you identified the cause of Kechenova's sudden collapse?" Lanietta asked.

"All I know is that she tried to examine Tony, and the machine couldn't handle the overload," Claus said. "You don't think he's the cause, do you?"

"Wait if you can," Lanietta said.

The ten minutes passed.

"Readings are confused," Leonid said. "Source could be in motion. Look for moving item and isolate in decontamination box."

"What? What's in motion?" Tony wondered.

"It's Tony," Claus said.

Tony walked around, looking for something in motion.

"Nothing in here is moving around," he said. "Absolutely nothing. I'm walking all over trying to find what is moving. What could be moving?"

"It's you, Tony. It's you!" Claus said. "Why can't he figure it out?"

"His thinking is muddled," Lanietta said. "His brain is compromised."

"By what?" Claus asked.

"He doesn't know yet," Lanietta said.

"I'll wait in the Leovich. Maybe I can think of something there," Tony said.

Ten minutes passed.

"Radiation source now in the Leovich," Leonid said. "Doctor Kechenova's vitals improving."

"What?" Tony questioned. "It's me or something on me. I'll take off my suit, leave it in the Leovich, and wait in the Panamirov."

Tony did so, and he left another message in the radio for Leonid. Ten minutes later, the reply came.

"Radiation source back in the Panamirov. Recommend isolating source immediately," Leonid said.

"It's me!" Tony said. "The source is me! I must have overloaded the medical scanner. We have to be apart. I have to get distance between Irina and me. But who will take care of her? There's only one thing left to do. I have to go back in the Leovich and detach. I'll leave the pendant with her for luck."

Tony did just that. He returned to the Leovich, put on his suit, transferred energy, oxygen, and food to the Leovich, ran a radio relay from the Leovich through the Panamirov so he could communicate with Leonid, and he detached. He changed his orbit, and he checked in with Leonid every ten minutes. Telemetry showed gradual improvement with Irina. Leonid was able to direct the Panamirov medical station to send anti-radiation medicine into Kechenova's IV line.

"Tony Kavalla, this is Leonid. I have news bulletin for you. Pacific tsunami has killed millions of people in Pacific coast countries. This includes Japan, China, South Korea, North Korea, Russia, United States, Canada, Mexico, Central America, South America, New Zealand, Australia, Malaysia, many Pacific islands, Indian Ocean area, and many more. Tsunami caused by geological event in Hess Rise. Satellite photos show new island formed with Colonel Jill Cresson alone on island. We believe Astroosa tested new superweapon with result failure. Will send more news as we receive it. Tony, if you land in Russia or Kazakhstan, you will be placed under arrest as a spy for Astroosa. Please assist in safe return of Doctor Kechenova."

"We're too late," Tony said to himself. "Too late."

In several hours, Kechenova regained consciousness.

"Tony? This is Irina. Where are you?" she called from the Panamirov.

"I'm on the Leovich," Tony said. "You slipped into a coma for a week. I put you on the medical table. Leonid from Earth helped you get better."

"He did? How? It doesn't matter. We need to get you back to the Panamirov. I will fix the medical scanner and see about your health."

"Irina," Tony said. "That won't be possible."

"I don't understand," she said.

"Two problems. Jill Cresson and Tony Kavalla," he said.

"You make it sound like you two are a couple. What about us?" she said.

"Irina. This is difficult for me. I am full of radiation, and it's killing you. I'm going to land."

"Tony, I..."

"I'm going to land near the Exodus One," Tony said.

"You'll be killed," she said. "Give me a little time to sort through things. Perhaps I can figure out a solution. Dynamic shield or something. I just need time."

"You should go back to Earth. Help your people with the Jill Cresson problem. Your intelligence was right. She turned the Hess Rise into an island. She's on it now. But she also created a tsunami that's killed millions of people on the Pacific coast. Millions, Irina."

"I am sorry to hear that. This rescue mission is a complete disaster. Instead of saving one, we killed millions," she said. "How will landing on Mars bring back the dead?"

"It won't. It's a process of elimination. Since I won't live long enough to make it back to Earth, I can't help people there. I can't go back with you, because it will kill you. There's nothing to do in Martian orbit. So I might as well land."

"And be killed by the energy beam," Irina said. "The Veigast."

"You can go back to Earth, maybe set up a relay with an older Martian satellite, and monitor my progress," Tony said.

"What progress, I wonder?" she asked.

"Any progress. Anything I do on the surface is bonus information. It's more than what we have. Go on, Irina. Go on home before food and fuel run out," Tony said.

"I will check with my intelligence on the situation. But if things are as bad as you say, my presence on Earth will not help, not with what little I bring back, which is nothing," Kechenova said.

"You're smart, that's something," Tony said.

"I'm intelligent, yes, but with nothing to focus my mind on. My entire thought and way of life has been on this mission and your part in it. Do I throw that away? How dare you, Mr. Kavalla. How dare you tell me to throw away a great part of my life I've worked on so hard. You might as well have me kill my first child. These spacecrafts and missions are my children. I will not abandon them. Or you."

"We can't survive together," Tony said.

"Not yet," Kechenova grinned. "I will stay in orbit for a little while and process your data. I will orbit over your position and gather additional data that way. Matter of fact, I think this changes our mission. We came to rescue a human. Perhaps we are rescuing the wrong thing."

"What do you mean?" Tony asked.

"There might be another entity in need of help. It's only a hunch, but it's as good a start as any. Okay, continue with your landing. Be very careful. Think about exploration and communication."

Chapter 58: Tabelia on the Move

"That's the last one for today," a nurse said to Leni.

"Thank you, nurse. I will see you in the morning," Leni said.

Leni exited the clinic door, but instead of going to an outside world, he exited a tree pair. He had not gone far when Selba bumped into him.

"What is that you are covered in?" Leni asked.

"Pie stuffing," Selba said. "I had a pie-throwing skit. You should have seen it. My fellow comedians did their routines—all communicating through their glasses, of course. Serious routines, overly serious. And then the pie throwing started. The pies covered their glasses, making it impossible for the serious routines to continue. Everyone laughed."

"No sign of Clover or Shara I take it," Leni said.

"No. None at all. People say nothing when I ask. They'd rather hear a joke. What about you?" Selba asked.

"Nothing," Leni said. "They'd rather I treat their injuries."

"Doesn't seem like there would be much to treat," Selba said.

"At first there were the usual issues—long-standing problems like diabetes and heart disease. I cured those. Things got quiet for a bit, but lately I've seen a rash of radiation sickness," Leni said.

"How's that possible?" Selba asked.

"Evidently there's a source of radiation around here. One of the trees maybe? Could be a sign of something about to happen," Leni said.

"Could the radiation be in the Tree of Memories?" Selba asked.

"Unknown. The tree is heavily guarded, and so I cannot reenter. Which also means I can't run my brute-force search for Clover."

"Perhaps we should leave Tabelia and go back to the speedboat," Selba said. "We need to get word out to Labba anyway. Maybe she knows something about this radiation. No telling what's been happening in the real world."

"How do we leave this world?" Leni asked. "Again—the Tree of Memories is heavily guarded. That would seem to be the only exit."

Just as Leni finished his statement, the ground rumbled.

"What was that?" Selba asked. "An earthquake?"

"No. Too coordinated," Leni said. "It felt much like the tremors Morcellus put out when he stirred."

"Then my earlier thought about Tabelia—" Selba started.

"Could be true. We might very well be in another Martacean," Leni said.

"Tabelia," she added. "How many others are there, I wonder."

"We only know of two so far," Leni said. "But she is on the move."

"*She?*"

"Tabelia is female," Leni said. "I can sense by the tremors. They are soft and feminine, unlike those by Morcellus which are harsh and abrupt."

"Now we really must get out," Selba said. "Who knows what Tabelia will do next or where she will go."

The tremors continued, and the Tabelians rushed around in panic. Selba and Leni made their way to the Tree of Memories, but the guards there remained. Leni did his best to convince them to allow Selba and himself to pass, but they denied him access. They did, however, allow Husky and Slimy to enter. Leni attempted to tailgate behind them, but the guards caught them.

"That'll be enough of that," a guard said.

Inside the Tree of Memories, White Hat and White Hair were in conversation.

"What causes the tremors?" White Hat asked.

"Tabelia is in motion," White Hair said. "She leaves the ocean floor and travels north in the Pacific. I must check on our people. Keep this area clear. We might have things yet to do."

White Hair exited the Tree of Memories. Leni asked her for help.

"I have pressing business," she said. "I will return shortly."

"Master, master!" Husky and Slimy said as they ran to White Hat in the Tree of Memories.

"Calm down, you two," White Hat said.

"Did she cause this?" Slimy asked.

"White Hair? I don't think so," White Hat said.

"No, the other one," Husky said. "Dark Star of Thunder."

White Hat paused for a moment as if the thought had not occurred to him, and that this thought was one he didn't wish to happen.

"Lanietta! Did Lanietta cause this?" Slimy asked impatiently.

"Do not invoke her name!" White Hat said. "Do you wish her to appear before us and render new judgment?"

"Yes, by all means. Say my name!" said Lanietta as she appeared suddenly.

Slimy and Husky fell to their knees in fear, with Slimy shaking with great anxiety.

"I...we..." White Hat stumbled to say.

"I made a deal with you three," Lanietta said. "Special favors in exchange for special obedience."

"We have not told," Slimy whimpered.

"It is true," White Hat said. "Clover's location remains a secret—even from us. And we have prevented Leni and Selba from using this room for their means."

Lanietta walked over to the archway where White Hair had stood and activated it much as White Hair had. The pool showed scenes from Leni's trial.

"Very good," Lanietta said. "But he got too close!"

Lanietta pointed to the pool then toward the three. Two lightning bolts came forth, and one each struck Slimy and Husky. They convulsed briefly before regaining their breath, which now was a heavy pant as they both rolled slowly on the ground in agony, with steam rising from their lightly-burned flesh. White Hat looked down in horror then returned his gaze toward Lanietta.

"I have a new task for you three," Lanietta said. "I am sending Tabelia to Cenina Island. This will take time. I have other things to do during such time, but I also need you three to prepare Tabelia for the Final Act. Witness now my Smasti girls."

Lanietta pointed toward the pool, and up shot four young humanoid women onto the platform where Leni had stood, as if the humanoids were diving in reverse. One was shaded light yellow, the second a darker yellow, the third red, and the fourth, grey.

"You will take instruction from these Monazites," Lanietta said.

"My pardon, Dark Star of Thunder," White Hat said. "But these are mere robots and nothing compared to your greatness."

"They have been specially molded under my guidance and temperance. Their names are Smoxira, Smusa, Smasena, and Smateia," Lanietta said, pointing respectively to the light-yellow woman, the dark-yellow woman, the red woman, and the grey woman. "Introduce yourselves."

"I am Smoxira," the light-yellow woman said as she stepped forward. "My touch is cold yet my breath is fire."

Smoxira jumped and hovered over the pool. She touched it, and it froze over. Then she breathed on it. Fires like that of a dragon spewed forth and melted the pool. Smells of ozone filled the air from the fire. Smoxira returned to her position beside the other three. White Hat gazed in awe while Slimy and Husky managed to roll themselves enough to witness Smoxira's abilities.

"Next," Lanietta said.

The dark-yellow woman stepped forward and spoke.

"I am Smusa. I can generate large amounts of power."

Smusa held her arms out, and shockwaves of electrical energy rippled outward, causing White Hat's, Slimy's, and Husky's bodies to jerk as if being zapped with electrical energy. The shockwaves sparked as they hit various objects, and a smell of sulfur filled the air. Smusa returned her arms to her side, and the shockwaves ceased. Lanietta pointed for Smasena next.

"I am Smasena, the object of desire."

Smasena struck an enticing pose. She flew over toward White Hat and performed a provocative dance around him, stroking his chin and touching his nose with an air of delight. Her complexion lightened, her strawberry-blond hair shone brilliantly, and her red dress floated through the air like a pleasant flower. In fact, Smasena smelled like flowers and produced a flower for White Hat. He took the flower and sniffed it. Smasena returned to her place on the platform.

"And lastly," Lanietta said as she pointed toward Smateia.

The grey-colored woman stepped forward and spoke.

"I am Smateia. I create great images of beauty."

Smateia pointed toward the pool, and images of clear sky, mountains, and running rivers filled the area. The air became mountain-fresh, clearing out the scents from the other three Monazites. Smateia returned to her position, and the images faded. Lanietta beckoned Smateia over, which Smateia did, and Lanietta placed a necklace around Smateia's neck. Lanietta then motioned for Smateia to return to the others.

"Smateia has a direct link with me. She will relay my orders and inform of your progress," Lanietta said. "One more thing. I'm taking White Hair with me."

"But she is one of us," White Hat said. "She was not part of the deal."

"Her absence will ensure your end of the deal is kept, enforced by my Smasti girls," Lanietta said.

Lanietta disappeared. Slimy and Husky rose to their feet and as they did, the Smasti girls hovered over to them and landed in front of them.

"So beautiful," White Hat said.

"And so deadly," Husky said.

"Let me keep one," Slimy said. "I will train her. Come along, Smasena. You're the cutest of them all."

Slimy went up to Smasena to kiss her, but she twisted his arm and forced Slimy to his knees.

"Let go. Let go!" he wailed in pain.

But Smasena didn't let go. She simply looked over at Smoxira and winked. Smoxira touched Smasena, and Smasena became rigid like ice.

"My arm! It's freezing! I can't break free!" Slimy exclaimed.

Smoxira breathed on Smasena's grip of Slimy's arm. Smasena's grip loosened, and Slimy broke free but not before his skin endured burn marks from the flame.

"Ow, ow, ow!" Slimy cried as he leaned over the pool and dipped his burnt arm into the cool water.

"What is this madness?" White Hat asked.

Smasena for the most part remained frozen. Smoxira motioned toward Smusa, and Smusa sent small bolts of plasma at Smasena. Smasena's body turned various shades of green and black, puffing and swelling like frozen beer bursting from a can.

"You attack your own? Smusa, stop this attack," White Hat said.

Smusa motioned back toward Smoxira who in turn breathed fire onto Smasena's full body. Smasena unfroze and collapsed, looking all the part of a beaten-up woman. Smateia touched Smoxira, Smusa, and herself, and the three changed shape and color to resemble typical glasses-wearing people of Tabelia. Smateia then put something on Smasena.

"Pick me up," a weak Smasena said to Husky. "I need...help."

White Hat motioned for Husky to do so, and Husky did. Unaware of what had happened, Selba and Leni continued seeking a way into the Tree of Memories. The portal door opened. Slimy came out first and cleared the way for Husky, who carried Smasena. White Hat then followed.

"Doctor Leni, this woman needs medical attention. Please tend to her injuries," White Hat said.

"Absolutely! Take her to the Infirmary Tree," Leni said.

Slimy led the way followed by Husky (carrying Smasena), White Hat, and then Leni. Selba started to follow, but she paused and turned around in time to see Smoxira, Smusa, and Smateia leaving the Tree of Memories.

"Strange," Selba said. "I've never seen them before. Or that one Husky carried. I feel strange, like new cats are invading my turf. I don't trust these women."

Selba slipped off to the side and followed three of the Smasti girls. She didn't know they were called this, of course, but she knew they were a clique. The three entered a tree pair, and Selba slipped in after them.

"Place her here," Leni said in the infirmary. "I'll take over now. You may leave."

Husky placed Smasena in a treatment bed and left along with Slimy.

"Take good care of her," White Hat said. "She comes from a noble family."

White Hat left. Leni checked her vitals.

"Blood pressure low, heartbeat faint, and shallow breathing," Leni said to himself. "General systemic trauma. I'll give you shot."

"A shot?" Smasena asked weakly. "What...what kind of shot?"

"The shot contains an anti-inflammatory and a metabolic deflocculant. It will reduce swelling and clear up the bruising."

Leni attempted to give Smasena a shot, but the needle broke.

"Strange," Leni said.

"Uh, I'll try to relax. Try again," Smasena said.

Leni gave Smasena another shot. The shot took.

"Swelling is reducing. Bruising is clearing. Strange thing—for a moment I

thought...no, it couldn't be...but maybe...it was like...you were made of stone," Leni said.

"Maybe it was carbonic sludge," Smasena said.

"Carbonic sludge is grey like graphite," Leni said. "But your complexion was more like a ruddy red. Well, it doesn't matter. The last of the swelling and bruising is going...right now. Why you're beautiful! You didn't look human before...I mean...your injuries...I don't mean to be rude...I...I've never stumbled before...I'm just a selenite robot."

"You are?" Smasena giggled, now feeling better. "I wondered why you didn't have glasses. But I have lost mine. I must resort to old-style spoken speech."

"It would be a travesty to deprive such a beautiful voice from expressing itself," Leni said.

"What if you get me a pair anyway?" she whispered. "I'll use my voice only for you. Please, help me out of bed."

"Of course! Where are my manners? I'm not myself at the moment," Leni said.

Leni lifted Smasena from the bed and placed her on her feet with incredible speed. Smasena let out a brief shriek of surprise.

"Oh, that was too fast for you. I'm so sorry!" Leni said.

"No, do that again! It was thrilling!" Smasena said.

Smasena jumped back onto the infirmary bed, and she beckoned Leni to pull her out again. Leni did so, and she let out a shriek of delight.

"You are something special, Doctor," Smasena said.

"Please, call me Leni," he said.

"Very well. Leni. What else do you do, my finely-built man?" Smasena said.

"I'm just a robot. Not a man," Leni said.

"Are you sure? There's only one way to find out," Smasena said, and she moved in close to kiss him.

"Uh-hum," Selba coughed in the doorway. "Leni? May I have a word with you? Alone?"

"Oh hi, Selba. This is Smasena. She was receiving treatment for injuries," Leni explained.

"I'm in need of physical therapy, Leni," Smasena said as she stroked Leni's chin. "I'll await you in the lobby, my handsome, charming man."

Smasena left.

"Leni, what in the world are you doing?" Selba asked.

"Treating Smasena," Leni said. "She was badly beaten up."

"Leni, watch your step," Selba said. "There's something fishy with her."

"How could someone like that be suspicious?" Leni asked.

"That exactly why you *should* be suspicious. I saw her friends. They were a little too catty," Selba said.

"Fishy and catty. Your choice of words is strange," Leni said.

"Well trust me on this. A woman's intuition should not be doubted," Selba said.

"We should meet her friends. Maybe they can help us find Clover. Maybe they know where Shara is. Maybe they—"

"Have their own agenda," Selba said.

"You should be more trusting," Leni said.

"You've fallen for her!" Selba said.

"Oh Leni-sweet," Smasena said, poking her head in from the lobby. "I heard there's a comedy performance soon. But I don't know where it is. And my glasses, Leni-sweet. I must have glasses!"

"Here, take these," Selba said, tossing glasses at Smasena. "And I can start your comedy right now."

Selba removed flowers from a vase and dumped the dirty water onto Smasena.

"Ugh! I'm soaked! Leni, look at me. I'm a mess!" Smasena wailed.

"Selba, why did you do that? That was mean. It was inconsiderate. And it was—"

"Catty," Selba smiled.

"My clothes are ruined!" Smasena said with her voice turning to anger. "And this...this...female dog did it!"

"Who are you calling a female dog?" Selba said with irritation. "I know all the proper curse words for calling *you* a female dog!"

"Leni, don't let her insult me like that. Do something!" Smasena said.

"Leni is too smitten with your fake charm to do anything. Like the men he tries to emulate," Selba said.

"My fake charm? You're the fake!" Smasena said.

"Someone like you needs to be straightened out," Selba said.

"You're no doctor!" Smasena said.

"No? Watch me perform plastic surgery," Selba said.

Selba punched Smasena in the jaw.

"Selba, stop," Leni said.

But Leni did nothing. Seeing his inaction, Smasena retaliated against Selba and performed a leg sweep. Selba's legs went out from under her, and she fell on her back.

"Oh that does it! Now you're in for it!" Selba yelled.

Selba went into a full fight with Smasena.

"Get rid of this wench, Leni!" Selba said between punches. "Leni!"

"I wonder if this is what's known as a cat fight," Leni mused.

As the two fought, Selba pulled and clawed at Smasena's clothing and such, ripping off a necklace. The necklace, though, was caught up in clothing and so was not seen as it fell to the floor. Unaware of this, Smasena ripped at Selba's clothes in simple retaliation. Selba then caught Smasena in a headlock and pulled her out of the Infirmary Tree and into the open. The other Smasti girls came to Smasena's aid and attempted to hold Selba, but she gave them a fight too.

"Let's settle this in the open water!" Smateia said.

The four managed to subdue Selba enough to bring her into the Tree of Memories, pass through the arch, and exit Tabelia into the open ocean. The Smasti girls took Selba to the ocean surface. Tabelia was on the move toward the Hess Rise, and so extended time spent on the ocean surface meant being separated from

Tabelia. As it was, the five would not be separated, as a pod of orcas who had been escorting Tabelia now each took a Smasti girl (and one took Selba) for a ride as if all were riding horses.

Meanwhile, Leni, who was still mesmerized by watching his first "cat fight", stared intently at Smasena's clump of clothing.

"My Smasena dropped this," Leni said as he picked up the clump. "Oh, there's something inside."

Leni unwrapped the clothing and found the necklace. Set in the necklace was the Aftova stone—given by Frieda to Katie to Tony and left with Irina.

"What is this?" Leni said.

The stone displayed as half yellow and half blue.

"Those are the same colors as the entrance to this world. The colors Selba mentioned when she crossed her eyes. I wonder if it's a keepsake of Tabelia. Or perhaps something more."

Leni placed the stone inside an access panel, allowing his internal circuits to analyze it. His circuits did more than analyze the stone. It made a connection. Leni's eyes opened wide and stared straight ahead. His circuits became overwhelmed for a moment, and he nearly lost control of himself. He stumbled backward and nearly fell over completely, but he caught himself just in time.

"Leni, do you hear me? It's Labba calling," Labba called through the stone.

"Labba! This is incredible indeed! I have a stone that permits communication!" Leni said.

Labba's voice did not carry through the open air but instead carried into his internal circuits. Leni was able to reply in like kind, and so he could communicate with her in full privacy.

"I've been trying to get through to you. Clover, Shara, Claus, Selba, and Lanietta are all unaccounted for. You were also unaccounted for. Where are you, and do you have news of the others?"

"I am in a seamount, or rather a living creature like Morcellus. Her name is Tabelia," Leni said. "Selba was with me a moment ago, but she got into a fight with a woman named Smasena. They took their fight out of the infirmary. Clover, Shara, Claus, and Lanietta are missing. I last saw Claus on the Mad Mistral when we first discovered Tabelia. But that ship has moved on for its own reasons."

"Selba was in a fight?" Labba said. "Why didn't you stop it?"

Leni paused for a moment.

"Labba to Leni. Do you read?" Labba asked.

"I read. I...had never seen two women fight," Leni said. "Smasena is so...so..."

"Oh Leni! You're a machine! Try to remember that," Labba said.

"Yes. I am a machine. I must remember," Leni said.

"Go after Selba, and secure her safety," Labba said. "Tell me what you know about Tabelia. Lanietta is putting a heavy strain on Morcellus, and it's all I can do to keep him from being ripped apart. We need to stop Lanietta cold. She's up to something."

"Any idea what?" Leni asked as he made his way out of the infirmary.

"I have a suspicion, and I hope I'm wrong. I need more information first," Labba said. "So tell me about Tabelia."

Leni flashed his eyes at Tabelians and asked as to Selba's whereabouts.

"Selba went into the Tree of Memories with four other women," Leni relayed back to Labba. "Labba, the inside of Tabelia is filled with people who wear glasses and communicate by flashing yellow and blue light from those glasses. I can communicate back by flashing my own eyes in similar fashion. Tabelia itself is an underground environment filled with tree pairs as far as one can see. People enter these tree pairs and experience a fantasy world, like a memory of the past. There is one solitary tree known as the Tree of Memories that does not contain a fantasy world."

"Relay your entire record from the moment you left Arberella to the current moment. I can handle the information.

That's one thing we Carinians are good at," Labba said.

Leni relayed the information through the stone.

"That's all there is," Leni said. "Impressive stone."

"It's a Veigonette," Labba said. "It's part of a larger nucleus known as the Veigon which itself is related to the Anrega and PRAAD. Morcellus and Tabelia are Martaceans, and they are also connected. Your stone is called Aftova. Keep it safe and hidden inside you. No one must know you have it. I think Lanietta must be trying to tap into the Martacean cycle and use it as a weapon. My guess is she wants to use this power against Libriota, and that she is purposely building up this power to a point where she can launch a surprise attack and win. After that it won't much matter. Lanietta will assume power over the Grens, the Bleuhs, and all of Carinian society."

"Is that good or bad?" Leni asked.

"Funny you should ask," Labba said. "I'm not really sure. Bleuhs have given us Grens such grief that we no longer recall a life before them. Morcellus and Tabelia might have memories going back that far. Or maybe they don't. It depends on when they were created or how much information was transferred to them or both. Leni, the Martaceans and their artifacts I mentioned—the Anrega, Veigon, and PRAAD—are all part of a reproductive cycle. The Martaceans have been with Carinians since the beginning. We don't fully understand them. Givers of life and death they say. Also, the Aftova stone you have might try to connect with other Martacean artifacts or even Lanietta. Don't let it."

"It's already connected," Leni said.

"Block it, quickly!" Labba said.

Leni paused for a moment while his innards adjusted.

"I can dynamically position the stone at an oblique angle from the other connection," Leni said. "That blocks it. When I turn my body around, the stone is turned internally to compensate."

"Excellent work! Have you found Selba yet?" Labba asked.

"No. The Tree of Memories is guarded by Husky and Slimy," Leni said.

"Stand behind a tree pair and place a hand on each," Labba said.

Leni did so.

"I'm sending instructions through Aftova, through your circuits, through your hands, into the tree pair, and into Tabelia. There, done," Labba said. "Now check on the Tree of Memories."

Leni stepped around the tree pair. The Tree of Memories was unguarded.

"Impressive," Leni said.

"I created a diversion," Labba said. "Go inside."

Leni went inside.

"I'm inside," Leni said.

"I see and hear what you do," Labba said.

"Labba, can you take over Tabelia completely? With my help, of course. We could send her to Arberella and figure out something with Morcellus," Leni said.

"If we tried that now, Lanietta would become wise and figure out your part in this. She would get Aftova," Labba said. "No, we must be quiet about this for now until we learn more. Go to the arch. Good, now place a hand on each side."

Leni did so. A holographic image appeared of Selba on an orca on the ocean surface with the Smasti girls giving Selba a hard time.

"I will go after her at once!" Leni said.

"Wait, look!" Labba said.

Lanietta appeared on the ocean surface standing on a blue whale.

"Stop!" Lanietta called to the Smasti girls.

The Smasti girls surrounded Selba and her orca and forced the two toward Lanietta and her whale.

"We were just having a little fun," Smusa said.

"Selba insulted and attacked me," Smasena said.

"Let me freeze her and burn her frozen corpse," Smoxira said.

"My link with Smateia has failed. I come here to find out why, and you Smasti girls are out for a swim. A swim! Smateia, you are supposed to keep the others in line," Lanietta said.

"I gave the stone to Smasena. It was supposed to keep her in line," Smateia said.

"It's right here," Smasena said as she reached for the necklace. "No, it's gone! Selba stole it!"

"You fool!" Lanietta said. "That stone is more valuable than all of you! Find it!"

"We'll search Selba," Smateia said.

The Smasti girls searched Selba but didn't find Aftova.

"It must have fallen into the ocean," Smasena said.

"Because you were horsing around!" Lanietta said impatiently. "I want you to search the entire ocean until you find it!"

"But the ocean is too big! We'll never find it!" Smusa said.

"Then you'd better start now!" Lanietta said. "I've wasted enough time with you already. Find that stone before I return! No excuses!"

Lanietta disappeared, and the blue whale swam away.

"I'll take Selba back to Tabelia," Smateia said. "You three look for the stone. I'll return and help."

Smusa used her great power to create an electrical field in the ocean, like a large net. Schools of fish surfaced from being electrocuted. Smoxira both froze and fried those fish to explode them and reveal any stones they might have swallowed. There were none. Smasena vocalized sonar to cetaceans and had them look. And still no stone.

"Break your connection with the arch," Labba said to Leni. "Leave the Tree of Memories and await Selba's arrival. I have news for you both when she returns."

Leni did so and in fact went to the infirmary, expecting Selba as a patient. He didn't have long to wait. Smateia produced Selba shortly thereafter.

"Your friend should know when to keep to herself and mind her own business," Smateia said to Leni. "But do not worry. Your girlfriend, Smasena, is helping us on the ocean surface."

"Girlfriend?" Selba said. "Leni doesn't have a girlfriend."

"Perhaps you think of yourself as his girlfriend?" Smateia laughed.

"I should make you eat your words the way I made Smasena eat hers," Selba threatened.

"No!" Leni said. "No more fights. Smateia, thank you. I will treat Selba now. You may leave."

Smateia held a gaze toward Selba, she looked at Leni, and then she sneered at Selba just before darting out. Selba stood up to go after her, but Leni caught her arm and held her.

"For someone who's badly injured, you have plenty of energy," Leni said.

"You don't know what those girls did," Selba said. "The Smasti girls. Lanietta is behind them, you know. I saw her with them on the ocean surface. They were chasing me on—"

"I know all about it," Leni said.

"You do? How?" Selba asked.

"From the Tree of Memories," Leni said. "I witnessed the whole thing. So did Labba."

"Labba! But she's in Arberella!" Selba said.

"I've found a way to communicate with her," Leni said.

"How?"

"Don't reveal the existence of Aftova," Labba said to Leni.

"I cannot say at this time. You must trust me, Selba. But first, let me treat your injuries," Leni said. "This shot is similar to the one I gave Smasena. It contains an anti-inflammatory and a metabolic deflocculant."

Leni administered the shot to Selba.

"You don't have the same ruddy red look that Smasena had," Leni said.

"I don't think she's human," Selba said.

"Touch Selba's hand so she can hear me," Labba said to Leni.

Leni did so.

"Tender care from my physician?" Selba asked.

"Selba, can you hear me?" Labba said.

"Yes. I can hear you through Leni's hand. Labba? This is incredible," Selba said.

"Those Smasti girls are Monazites," Labba said. "Monazites are robots from Mars, made from Martian soil."

"Robots? Like Leni?" Selba said.

"In some ways. Leni is made from lunar soil. But the original technology for creating both is the same," Labba said. "Selba, I have things to tell you and Leni. Since you left Arberella, I have learned much and much has happened, even since I first contacted Leni. First things first—I know where everyone is, well, almost everyone. I know about you and Leni, of course. I somewhat know where Lanietta is, based on process of elimination. Shara and the woman there known as White Hair are on Cenina Island, which is a part of the Hess Rise in the Pacific Ocean. Claus is on the Mad Mistral and under Lanietta's control. The Arberellans are still here. I don't know where the other Carinians are, especially the ones on the lunar far side, and I'm sure Lanietta doesn't know their status either."

"How do we get Shara back? Where's Clover? Is White Hair for us or against us? I have many questions," Selba said.

"I don't know if I can answer all of your questions," Labba said. "Yes, getting Shara and Clover back is important and I think your most important task. Tabelia is a Martacean, an ancient creature resembling an Earth bowhead whale, only much larger. Lanietta is having Tabelia head for Cenina Island. The island itself is a portal for the Veigon, an ancient nucleus of information strands much like the DNA of Earth life-forms. The Veigon is normally surrounded by a large iron mass known as the Anrega. The Anrega is analogous to the cytoplasm of a cell. Both of those are in Earth. In fact, the great iron core of Earth *is* the Anrega."

"There's a single-cell organism inside of Earth?" Selba asked.

"In effect. It's less a life-form and more a repository for life and death," Labba continued. "The life part is primarily geared toward the Martaceans, but other life-forms can be created too. The best I can tell in studying Morcellus and from what we Carinians are taught is that the Veigon and Anrega were at one time part of our own planets of Carinia 1 and Carinia 2, and when they were, life came forth, first an ecosystem of life to support Martaceans, and then the Martaceans themselves. I'm almost sure that we Carinians are the result of a creation strategy by the Veigon."

"Wow!" Selba said.

"Whenever the Veigon and Anrega occupy a planet, they create millions of Martaceans. At some point the Veigon decides it's time to move to another planet. When that happens, it allows the Martaceans to die down to one couple. That couple with the help of the Veigon produces an egg which will then fuse with the Veigon. That has happened at least twice before, maybe more. In prior cases, the Veigon and Anrega then went full planar and exited the planet with only earthquakes and volcanoes."

"What do you mean, *only*?" Selba asked. "That sounds catastrophic."

"Not as catastrophic as the entire planet's destruction, which is what would happen if the Veigon leaves without going planar," Labba said. "Morcellus and Tabelia, as far as I can tell, are that supercouple."

"Are you saying Earth could be destroyed?" Selba asked with a shaky voice.

"It's possible. But only if the egg fuses with the Veigon," Labba said.

"Then we must stop Morcellus from getting together with Tabelia, right?" Selba said.

"It's too late. The egg already exists," Labba said.

"Where is it?" Selba asked.

"It's on the lunar far side. My people call it the PRAAD," Labba said.

"What's it doing there?" Selba asked. "And why didn't you tell us before, when we were in Arberella?"

"I didn't have a very good idea of things when you left. Researching with Morcellus has revealed quite a bit," Labba said. "Also, Morcellus and Tabelia didn't create the egg. The Veigon has been waiting for an extended period of time for the egg, and so it produced Morcellus and Tabelia to create a new one. Yes, in addition to the PRAAD being a problem, your first point about keeping Tabelia and Morcellus apart is also of concern. I just wish I had more history on the Martacean cycle."

"What about Carinian history? Don't your history books have that detail?" Selba asked.

"Ironically, Carinians record very little of their own history. No one expects to die, and so there's no urgency to record events for others. Carinians share history through word of mouth or simply recall things. We haven't gotten around to recording it all," Labba said.

"You have all the time in the universe, whereas humans have a comparatively short time. And you haven't gotten around to it?" Leni asked.

"Time is more elusive for us. Carinia 1 and 2 don't even have a day, or they have a perpetual day, or have one day a year," Labba said. "If not for other events, we lose track quite easily. Look at human history. Days were measured, but the time of the day wasn't important until railroads had a schedule. We never had a railroad schedule."

"Leni, you've got to tell me how we're communicating with Labba," Selba said.

"I told him not to reveal the method," Labba said.

"What if these people kidnap me again? Those Smasti girls have it in for me, and I know Lanietta wants me out of the way," Selba said.

"Not yet," Labba said. "I need you to revive Doctor Irina Kechenova. She is there in Tabelia, and we need her help."

"Did she have the stone before?" Leni asked. "I sense something about her and the stone."

"What stone?" Selba asked.

"I told you not to say anything, Leni," Labba said.

"Lanietta was angry that the Smasti girls lost a necklace," Selba said. "Did the necklace have this stone? Do you have it, Leni?"

"That's not a piece of information we want circulating around," Labba said. "Leni, we can't afford to let Selba roam free in Tabelia."

"Meaning what?" Selba asked. "You're going to lock me up?"

"I can withstand Lanietta's probe. But Selba cannot," Leni said. "I could take her back to Arberella."

"Too late," Labba said. "She can't leave without being noticed, and you can't leave because I need you to help rescue Shara and White Hair. Plus find Clover. You will have to hide Selba."

"Where?" Selba asked.

Leni released his grip on Selba, and so Selba lost contact with Labba.

"Yes. Understood," Leni said as if speaking to someone.

"What is Labba telling you?" Selba asked.

"The hiding place is unusual. But Labba has provided instructions for its implementation. Don't worry, you will be safe," Leni said.

Chapter 59: Passage to Pacific

"Lanietta? Where are you? Lanietta?" Claus called.

The Mad Mistral had now traveled to and reached the American East Coast.

"What is this place?" Claus said to himself. "It's like one incredibly wide pier on the coast as far north and as far south as the eye can see. The waves go under, but they never crash on shore."

Claus had a sense of something closing in on him. A sense of becoming trapped. The day was late, and the sun set behind a wall of buildings on shore. He turned toward the east and saw a wall of ships approach.

"Lanietta, the selenites are closing in on me. Lanietta? Lanietta! Help!"

His ears picked it up, faint at first, but it grew louder and closer. It sounded like locusts grating on concrete. It twitched his skin and pained his ears.

"Lanietta!" he called again.

"Lanietta," returned a screeching cacophony of mechanized mayhem.

The air lost its ocean-salt smell. Claus was overcome with an electric-arc smell, a smell one might notice from an old model train.

The Mad Mistral nearly reached the super-wide pier when a concave frame elevated from under the Mad Mistral and lifted it above the water.

"Hey! What's going on?" Claus shouted.

The structure transferred the Mad Mistral to a magnetic conveyor on the pier, and this conveyor then moved the Mad Mistral inland.

"I'm floating. But this ship is mostly wood," Claus said.

"Everything is magnetic, given the proper power and configuration," said a mechanized voice.

It was a selenite, and it boarded the Mad Mistral. Claus took a defensive stance, but other selenites boarded the Mad Mistral too, and soon Claus was surrounded. More the selenites boarded, and more was Claus surrounded such that he was caught in a binding gaggle of selenites. More still came aboard, and they walked on the shoulders of other selenites. In this way, they formed a selenite pyramid, much as university cheerleaders in happier times formed pyramids, only these selenites left a hollow opening directly above Claus.

"Lan-i-ett-a!" Claus shouted through the opening. "Your Clomper is calling you! Lend me a leash and pull me out!"

Still no sign of Lanietta. Claus was lifted about halfway up the pyramid. On the way up, selenites grabbed for his neck and managed to pull off the bambooph carbon scrubber. Claus gasped for air in the six percent carbon dioxide atmosphere.

"I'm suffocating! Help!" Claus pleaded.

Claus felt totally wretched, and carbonic sludge formed on his skin. Indeed, he was coated in a layer of graphite, and this was part of the selenite plan. They sent electrical current through his body. He felt a jolt. But the current did more than cause muscle spasms. The carbonic sludge on his right side took on a blue color while the sludge on his left took on a yellow color. Then the pyramid of selenites bifurcated such that there were two pyramid halves with only a little bit of air separating the two, but Claus was caught between the halves. The sides then energized and alternated charges such that Claus spun in place like the internal components of an electric motor.

Claus immediately took on a headache, and his eyes felt they might burst outward from his head. He closed his eyelids tightly and pulled his hands over them. Despite his eyes being closed, he saw "stars", like those seen after a head collision. But the stars took on decided shapes of 1's and 0's, and they joined to become strings. They tangled and intermeshed and loomed themselves into tortured shapes. His mind wandered, and his voice grew faint.

"i'm becoming...a shape...tortured... claus the little...small and forgotten... cannot think...little patches for sale...so many little nothings...all at once...nonce... o nonce."

Every cell, tissue, blood vessel, organ, nerve, and bone in Claus's body was identified, tagged, cataloged, auctioned, and sold. Strings of 1 and 0 markers littered his body, and only the carbonic sludge covered the plethora of one-zero tattoo-like markers on his skin. His skin, like most of his flesh, seared in pain. He felt wired, full of adrenaline but totally exhausted. His tissues swelled, and his throat would soon close off from such swelling. He was already gagging on the carbon dioxide levels, but this would surely do him in.

"Group order," the selenites spoke in unison. "Toss him to the next phase."

Unnoticed by Claus, selenites not a part of the pyramid hauled a tub of icy water onto the Mad Mistral and placed it aside the pyramid. The pyramid selenites then tossed Claus into this tub. He dropped with a great splash, cleaning off the carbonic sludge and sending water onto selenites surrounding him, though their circuits did not short out. The water, however, was filled with an anesthetic, and Claus went numb within seconds.

Selenites placed a mask over Claus's face and shoved a tube down his throat that connected to a scrubber device behind the back of his neck. Transparent sides went up on the tub. The fluid level rose, causing Claus to float. He was barely conscious and couldn't speak, but he watched as layers upon layers of projected visual displays surrounded his tank, showing selenite audiences from all around with flood upon flood of streaming data scrolls of dollar amounts for the continuous buying and selling of Claus's tagged bodily components. The displays were too much. Claus closed his eyes, but other displays projected onto his retina, and so he could not escape the visual stimulation, much as he could not escape the auditory auctionary cacophonary insanitarity.

Claus could not yell for anyone. He could not vocalize his wish for death. He could only think it. His mind drifted in this tortured state to a vision of pyramids upon pyramids with tetrahedrons as building blocks, moving, sliding, forming and reforming into monsters moving, walking, stabbing with tetrahedral points, slicing with tetrahedral edges, or smashing with tetrahedral flats. Each time the tetrahedral points stabbed or sliced things, Claus felt his body-wide nerves being stabbed or sliced, and he was convinced his brain tissue was being dragged onto a cheese grater.

Then in his mind, far above the horizon, he saw a shifting shape. Not a pyramid monster, not anything made of tetrahedrons. No, this shape as it came closer was definitely a shape Claus never thought he'd see—a tesseract. It was a four-dimensional cube, shifting and moving like the monster it was. The tesseract was no larger than a pyramid monster, but it was not smaller, either. It moved in orthogonal directions—forward, backward, left, right, up, or down, but never diagonally. This meant it took longer to get to places, but it always had a sense of direction, and it always had a purpose and place to go. It headed toward Claus, climbing over pyramid monsters, crawling under them, and pushing them aside.

"Over here," Claus wanted to say, but he had no power of voice, not even in his vision.

"*Stabé, slicé, smashé,*" called a familiar voice in a French accent with French pronunciation, which sounded very much like, "*Stah-bay, slee-say, smah-shay.*"

"Lanietta," Claus wanted to call.

"I hear your thoughts, Claus," Lanietta's voice sounded from inside the tesseract. "Don't you love the pyramid machines? Of course they are representations of the selenites who now inhabit Earth."

Then from the tesseract sprang forth Lanietta, dressed in an 1800s French riding habit with triangular (tetrahedral?) hat—all in bluish-green with gold decorative trim. Wielding a falchion sword, Lanietta jumped over to a pyramid, stabbed to poke a tetrahedron from its group, sliced it in half (revealing a square cross-section), and smashed it downward with the base of her falchion, all the while calling, "*Stabé, slicé, smashé!*"

The more Lanietta stabbed, sliced, and smashed, the more the individual tetrahedrons exposed their square innards.

"Behold how my sword glistens with gold as I falchionize these tetrahedrons into cubes," Lanietta called out.

Indeed, each sliced and smashed tetrahedron came together into cube form, and they took on a sedate composure with simple yet direct movement and purpose—not as beautiful and extravagant as the tesseract, but with serenity nonetheless.

Claus regained consciousness aboard the Mad Mistral but still in the tub.

"*Stabé, slicé, smashé!*" Lanietta said, now on board the Mad Mistral. She still had her falchion sword and used it to stab, slice, and smash the invading selenites. Before Claus could make much sense of the situation, she had cleared off the selenites. With one last, "*Smashé!*" she shattered the barrier on Claus's tub and freed him. She pulled him to his feet and removed the mask and tube.

Claus choked on the heavy carbon dioxide atmosphere. Lanietta then uttered another, "*Stabé, slicé, smashé!*" where she stabbed a portion of a damaged selenite, sliced off a carbon scrubber part, and smashed the scrubber into Claus's upper back, fusing it into his flesh and thus forcing it to operate and purge carbon dioxide from Claus. Pleased with her work, she placed the falchion in its sheath over her back.

"*Smashé!*" Claus called back as he tried to smash a bit of selenite onto Lanietta with his fist. But Lanietta jumped aside, and Claus lost his balance and fell.

"*Clumsé* be *Clausé* with *fisté!*" she laughed.

"Enough already!" Claus said, still in a fallen state. "Where have you been? Don't you see I'm hurt?"

"One moment," she said. "I must fill the sails with a clear Mistral wind. Clovère would appreciate my masterly talent, isn't that so? Behold."

Lanietta let forth a great wind, clean and cool, that cleared a path for the Mad Mistral and sent it along the mag lev passage unimpeded.

"I am masterly indeed," Lanietta laughed. "I issue myself congratulations. Well done, Lanietta. Well done!"

Lanietta clapped and cheered.

"Who is Clovère?" Claus asked, struggling to stand but unable. "And what about my injuries?"

"Yes, the one who calls herself Clover would tend to your injuries if she were here. She was born *Clovère*, but the selenites forced her to drop her French background and adopt the name of Clover," Lanietta said. "I shall attend to your injuries in her stead."

Lanietta pulled Claus back up on his feet. She stood in front of Claus and pulled two short flaps from the back of her riding habit. The flaps grew into lengths of ribbon, and at first they tied around each other into a bow. Lanietta pulled on them again. The bow unraveled, and the flaps grew longer yet and intertwined themselves around Claus and Lanietta.

"We are joined now, you and I. Kiss your French horse master," Lanietta said.

Claus resisted.

"Kissy-kissy, Clausy, or itty-bitty impatiency will grow into big, bad and ugly rage," Lanietta said.

Claus paused, debating the issue. Lanietta did not wait and kissed Claus lightly on the lips. As she did so, the small fibers extended and grew from the flaps and entwined themselves into Claus's tissue.

"Arrrg. What...are you...doing? You... are no better than...the selenites," Claus moaned.

"Those selenites tagged and sold all parts of your body," Lanietta said.

"All parts?"

"Yes, Clomper. All parts! These fibers must go in and scrub them clean. Your kind used lye in the olden times to clean up. These fibers are much the same," Lanietta said.

"Lye is horribly harsh and was only used in the most desperate of situations," Claus wailed.

"You are desperate. Desperate for attention," Lanietta said. "I'll give you a doggie treat later when you're up to it. Well, that should do for cleanup. All selenite markers have been removed. Clean and tidy. You're good as gold now. See? And your sense of being overwhelmed by accelerated selenite inter-reaction should abate as well."

Lanietta released Claus from her embrace and left him standing unassisted.

"Walk," she commanded.

But Claus was dazed and unsure of himself.

"Walk I say!" she demanded.

Claus tried to sit, but Lanietta whipped out a riding crop and tapped him on the nose. This startled Claus, and he rose back to his feet.

"Walk!" she reprimanded.

"Why must I tumble down a hill to avoid the swarm of mosquitos?" Claus groaned as he took first one step then another.

"Yes, the selenites are like mosquitos, aren't they? Hovering and biting to no end. But tumble with me down the hill, will you Clomper? We'll roll and roll together!" Lanietta said. "Oh, but I must apologize first."

"You apologize? Impossible," Claus said. "You won't apologize for buying me as a pet at auction and all the other lunar fiasco. You won't apologize for your hostile behavior in Arberella. You won't apologize for kidnapping me yet again on the Mad Mistral or for your current agenda."

"True," Lanietta admitted. "But I will apologize for properly spoiling the story or at least letting you see the story I was about to spoil."

Claus returned a gaze of confusion.

"You've forgotten already? Hate usually carves the deepest of memories. And I thought you hated me and everything about me, Clomper," Lanietta said. "Good. There's hope for us as a couple. The selenites took over the diamonoli and Cenina Island. It was the end of the Jill Cresson era and the beginning of the selenite era on Earth. All of Earth would have been lost, except for the actions of Tony Kavalla and Doctor Irina Kechenova. Now do you remember?"

"I remember they were separated. Tony went back to Mars, leaving Irina in orbit. I think the vision was interrupted," Claus said.

"Yes, I was interrupted with business elsewhere," Lanietta said. "Things would go much better if my instructions are followed to the letter without deviation. Horseplay and abuse of power. Those Smasti girls will pay. But I'll leave that for another day. I still have Fronfa and Rigefa. Those I shall not trust to another. Not even you, Clomper."

"Frieda's stones," Claus mused. "You were playing along when the vision showed Frieda finding the stones. You took Fronfa from Frieda, didn't you?"

"She put up a good fight back there on the lunar far side, but I got the better of her," Lanietta chuckled.

"You attacked her?" Claus asked in surprise.

"More like tortured her," Lanietta laughed.

"How dare you! I wasn't happy about those other things you did, but this is too much! Attacking—"

"Your Frieda. Is that what you were going to say? Still believe you own her, that you should own a woman, is that right? Wrong. I own you, Clomper my pet," Lanietta smirked. "One moment."

Lanietta smacked her riding crop against the Mad Mistral. A hole opened up just ahead on the mag lev, the Mad Mistral fell into the hole, and the ship descended quickly.

"You're going to kill me? I'm sorry! Stop this, Lanietta! It's no joke!" Claus said.

"You're right. It's no joke," Lanietta said. "We are going VIP express. That means taking this unused tunnel and bypassing all selenite nonsense through the former United States of America. Admittedly, we'll pass through a number of cemeteries, but I'll keep your mind off those past people. Here now. Let's return to Tony and Irina."

Lanietta backed away a little from Claus, removing all intertwining and connective some such. She held up her hands to Claus showing Fronfa attached to her left palm and Rigefa to her right. Each stone was split in colors of blue and yellow, and the colors rotated in opposite directions. Lanietta then approached Claus with her right palm and Rigefa headed for Claus's left eye and conversely Fronfa and left palm headed for Claus's right eye. As she approached, the colors spun more quickly to the point that just as they reached Claus's eyes, they fell into the same faded pea-green color as before.

Claus closed his eyes. The colors penetrated his eyelids and painted (metaphorically) his retinas with the faded pea-green color. The colors slowed down into mixtures of yellow and blue as if blue and yellow paint had been slowly unstirred. He opened his eyes and saw a display panel on board the Panamirov. Kechenova had placed Aftova in a spectral phase analyzer.

"Panamirov, Leovich. I have landed close to the Exodus One," Tony radioed. "Irina, something strange is happening with the Veigast. The beam is pointed into the soil."

"I see it," Kechenova said.

"You do? How?" Tony asked.

"I took the stone from your pendant and placed it in the spectral phase analyzer," Kechenova said.

"The stone is Aftova," Tony said. "I left it for you. For luck."

"Yes, luck. There's something in the Martian soil under the Exodus One. Something more than just the Veigast. This stone has a direct connection to it. I believe the stone is summoning the creature through the Veigast."

"Creature?" Tony asked.

"Do you see a large shape emerging? Like a whale?" Kechenova asked.

"What is that?" Tony asked, seeing the shape Kechenova described.

"I don't think it will harm you," Kechenova said.

"What makes you say that?" Tony asked.

"I've set up a feedback mechanism between this Aftova stone and your harness," Kechenova said. "The creature has a name. It's...one moment...it's Morcellus."

"Amazing. It really does look like a whale," Tony said.

"In a sense it is, but it's totally alien and from outside our solar system," Kechenova said. "It understands the Veigast. It understands Aftova. And it understands the Veigon."

"Can we communicate with it? With Morcellus? Will it help us?" Tony asked.

"It depends on the kind of help we need," Kechenova said. "Let me try some things."

Kechenova connected a neural transceiver from the back of her neck to a Panamirov console.

"Morcellus has a language, but it's quite different from human languages," Kechenova said. "He...he has two goals."

"And they are?" Tony asked.

"He must be on the same planet as the Veigon," Kechenova said.

"And the second?"

"He wishes to find Tabelia," Kechenova said.

"What's a Tabelia?" Tony asked.

"I believe...just confirming...Tabelia is another Martacean, like Morcellus. Tabelia is female while Morcellus is male. They appear to be the last couple of their species," Kechenova said.

"Where is she?" Tony asked.

"That I don't know. Nor does Morcellus. He is looking for her and was going to stay on Mars until he found her. But now the Veigon is gone, and his priority lies with that. The Veigon might make another bride for Morcellus."

"Tabelia is his wife?" Tony asked.

"Not yet," Kechenova said. "This is all very strange. Tony, it appears Morcellus can tolerate your radiation. Matter of fact, Morcellus feeds on it. Yours is not as strong as that from the Veigast, of course, and Morcellus will feed on it, but Morcellus says he will provide you protection and transport to Earth."

"Then he'll help us," Tony said.

"He will help you, yes," Kechenova said.

"That's not the same. What about you?" he asked.

"In exchange, I will use Aftova to find Tabelia and have her proceed to Earth as well," Kechenova said.

"Wait a moment. Leave you behind? No, that won't work," Tony said.

"It must work. Morcellus might not be strong enough to stop Cresson and her SSS," Kechenova said. "We need more help. I will find Tabelia. I will bring her back."

"Doc. You're resourceful. You're savvy. But leaving you millions of miles away from another human being...it's... inhuman!" Tony said.

"From the man who was going to die and leave me on my own anyway," Kechenova said. "Your heart changes beats by the minute, but I will be fine. If nothing else, I will return to Earth alone, in the Panamirov, and we will do what we can. Besides, I'm alone right now. You left me, remember?"

"Yes, it's true I left you. Well, I guess there's nothing else to do. Do I just walk into the gaping mouth of this Morcellus and allow him to swallow me whole?" Tony asked.

"Not quite like that. I'm working with Morcellus now. He will provide a means," Kechenova said.

Morcellus moved through the Martian soil with his upper part above ground level, and he moved through as easily as a cetacean moves through Earth's oceans. He paused close to the Leovich. Then into the thin Martian air, two bamboophs protruded side-by-side. They had holes in them and called out soft tones in the Martian wind. One bambooph took on a slightly blue color, and it sounded the call of a bird. The second bambooph took on a slightly yellow color, and it returned the call as if another bird. These bamboophs grew larger and let forth a flock of birds each—blue birds from the blue bambooph, and yellow birds from the yellow. At first the birds were peaceful and kept within their flocks, flying about with song and satisfaction. But then the blue birds pecked at the yellow bambooph, and the yellow birds retaliated by pecking at the blue bambooph. The bamboophs retaliated by sending out feelers to strangle the attacking birds. These birds would die and fall next to the bambooph, causing a new bambooph to sprout in the color of the fallen bird. Each bambooph produced more birds of like color, more birds pecked opposing color bamboophs, more died and fell, more bamboophs sprouted, and all of this commotion resulted in the bamboophs weaving amongst themselves in alternating yellow and blue forming a tube from Morcellus to the Leovich, a tube so thick that it formed an air-tight seal. The tube encased itself completely around the Leovich.

The Veigast blasted its beam at the remaining birds, and it vaporized them instantly. It then blasted the end of the bambooph-woven tube. The tube rolled in on itself, which shortened its length and created an inner mass that pushed the Leovich toward Morcellus.

"Irina?" Tony called.

"I see it," she replied. "You're safe, Tony. Morcellus will protect you. Just keep your harness on. From my readings, Morcellus will leave Mars soon. He is learning about Earth through you and the

Leovich's database. And through the Aftova stone."

"You're still connected to him, then?" Tony asked.

"Yes. For a little while," Kechenova replied. "When he leaves Martian gravity, the link will end."

"How much time?" Tony asked.

"Not long. Very soon," Kechenova said.

"Then I will say my goodbyes now," Tony said.

"Only for a little while. We'll reconnect back on Earth. The Veigast will remain on Mars and help me find Tabelia," Kechenova said. "Don't worry, it won't destroy me. Cresson made a terrible mistake with the Veigast. She took without asking. I ask and offer information in exchange. Like bartering. The Veigast and I shall barter."

"Best of luck, Irina. I—" Tony started to say.

But Tony was cut off. Morcellus left Mars suddenly and quickly with Tony inside. Tony himself was put into suspended animation while Morcellus went to work on repairing Tony's cells. Irina was the only living human left at Mars. She spent time analyzing the stone and working with the Veigast to establish a means of acquiring more information about Martian history, the Veigon, Morcellus, and Tabelia.

"It seems strange that you're able to read all this from a spent first stage," Claus said to Lanietta. "We're nowhere near that spot in the ocean anymore."

"Yes, but only strange to you," Lanietta said.

"So how are you getting this information? What's the source?" Claus asked.

"I am the source," Lanietta said.

"Yes, I know you're creating this vision. But what are you using as a catalyst? Fronfa and Rigefa? But even those stones have to get information from somewhere," Claus said.

"You don't listen very well, do you Clomper? No doggie treat for you. I should send you back to obedience school for more training," Lanietta said.

"I never went to obedience school," Claus said.

"Then that explains it," Lanietta said.

"You're not going to answer my question?" Claus asked.

"I answered your question already," Lanietta said. "I should hire a proxy to re-answer the same mindless questions so I can continue my important work without distraction. Requiring you to tap your lips for permission to speak didn't last long, did it? Clomper the incessant. Clomper the tail chaser."

"I can do it," Kechenova said in the Panamirov. "But I must safeguard this information. Leonid, this is Doctor Kechenova. I'm relaying a stream of information about Mars. Please record stream in case something happens to me."

"I'm not chasing my tail!" Claus said. "I don't have a tail."

"Should I change that?" Lanietta asked. "Been a while since I transmorphed you into a canine."

"No. I'd rather not," Claus said.

"Then muzzle it," Lanietta said.

Claus didn't like being told to "muzzle it", but what could he do? Just then, several display screens lit up with images of the Martian landscape with trees, water, grass, and an assortment of life roaming peacefully.

"So this is what Mars looked like when it had water," Kechenova said.

A display then panned forward over the landscape as if it were a drone flying and peering down. The imagery approached a city and showed well-to-do aristocrats enjoying their terraces, walking in public gardens, and visiting local markets all the while accompanied by slaves. The aristocrats had a blue hue while the slaves had green or grey.

"This looks like Ancient Rome," Kechenova said. "But the people don't look Roman. Not human either."

"Bleuhs," Claus said.

"Of course," Lanietta replied.

"The slaves must be Carinian, but not Bleuhs," Claus said. "My guess is this happened many thousands of years ago."

"Try four and a half billion," Lanietta said.

"Really?"

"Really."

"That can't be true. Mars wasn't—"

"Were you there?" Lanietta interrupted. "No."

"Then stop insisting on knowledge where none you have," Lanietta said.

Images on Kechenova's display dove up high into the sky to a large, orbiting moon that was neither Phobos nor Deimos. The images went to that moon, underground, and into an auction building where Greyan slaves were being sold to Bleuh masters.

"El-Vek, you're next," said a slave receptionist to a Greyan slave trader.

Guards brought forth a girl resembling a twelve-year-old human.

"I auction this slave girl," El-Vek said. "She will be respectful and work hard for her new master."

The bidders laughed.

"They all say that," said one heckler.

"Who's the girl?" Claus asked.

"You don't know?" Lanietta asked.

Claus looked intently at the girl and then looked back at Lanietta.

"Do you...do you have a younger sister?" Claus asked. "She resembles you."

"She resembles me because she *is* me," Lanietta said.

"I don't understand."

"This is an auction. I am being sold," Lanietta said. "I am a slave, Clomper. Didn't you know?"

"You? A slave? Impossible!" Claus said.

"Didn't you get into trouble when you were a child? Don't all children? Doctor Kechenova has discovered my first visit to Mars," Lanietta said.

"I didn't know. I didn't know," Claus stuttered and repeated. "You, a slave girl, sold like chattel. Wait, what are you doing then? You bought *me* at auction. You

should know it's wrong. Lanietta, why all this? Why?"

"I did not create the universe," Lanietta said. "Nor did I create its rules. I'm bound to them like anyone else. Might as well make the most of them. See how they treat me here, Clomper my pet?"

The auctioneer started the process.

"El-Vek captured Carinians and sold them as slaves," Lanietta said to Claus. "He had no idea who would bid for me, nor did he know who would win the purchase, but he had an idea that the winner would take me on a private trip in orbit around the only moon orbiting Mars at that time, known as Preivos, as a way of guaranteeing he had first dibs on whatever he wanted of me."

"She'll stay on this moon after the orbital," El-Vek said to himself. "And that will be it."

The auctioneer started the bidding at one drakos. The bidders laughed.

"What can she do for that price?" yelled one heckler. "Can she work a pick hammer?"

The auctioneer pointed to a side hand, and he brought forth a nuclear powered pick hammer. He handed the pick hammer to young Lanietta, but she dropped it from its weight. The bidders laughed. A test boulder was wheeled in on a flat cart. The side hand tried to help young Lanietta lift the pick hammer to work it on the boulder. It was an awkward and clumsy moment, with young Lanietta nearly killing the side hand (she did injure his arm, causing him to bleed). The bidders laughed again.

"Can she drive a mining cart?" yelled another heckler.

A mining cart was brought in by another side hand. Young Lanietta attempted to drive it, but she nearly drove it off the auction stage and into the crowd. The second hand jumped on only just in time to stop the catastrophe.

"Can she make a meal?" asked a third heckler.

A cart was rolled out with raw meat, a burner, a pot, and cooking oil. Young Lanietta wasn't sure what to do, so she placed the meat in the pot, filled it with oil, placed it on the burner, and lit the burner with an igniter. The bidders clapped with this apparent demonstration of skill, but the oil bubbled up fast, spilled over, and caught fire. Young Lanietta tried to put out the fire by beating it with a heavy utensil, but she ended up knocking the pot off the burner and onto the stage, where the oil spread out and burned in a wide swath.

"Fire, fire!" bidders yelled.

Side hands brought forth extinguishers and put out the flames. Parts of young Lanietta's clothing were burned, and her long hair was singed to shorter length.

"She's a fire risk," yelled one.

"She'll kill whoever buys her," said another.

"She's worthless. A drakos is too much," said a third.

"Do I hear two drakos?" the auctioneer asked.

The bidders laughed then fell silent.

"I'm sorry, El-Vek, but this won't do. Your goods are worthless," the auctioneer said.

"My apologies. Please charge my account for the damages. I'll dispose of my—"

"Wait!" called a voice from in back, who had just entered the auction arena and pushed his way through the bidder crowd. "Allow me through. Allow me through!"

The bidders conversed in hushed tones. Who was this guy? What was this all about? The man pushed his way through and climbed up on stage.

"You are not permitted up here," the auctioneer said. "This auction is—"

"A fake. A setup," the man said. "What is the girl's name?"

"Her auction number is—" the auctioneer started.

"Not her number. Her *name*. Her real name," the man said.

"Oh, I'm not sure I have that. I'll have to check and—"

"Sassatinassa," El-Vek said.

"Sassatinassa?" Claus asked. "Sassatinassa. I like it. Sounds sassy but classy."

"You bite your tongue," Lanietta said.

"Sassatinassa. Sassatinassa!" Claus repeated for fun. "An alter ego? A cover to protect your inner self? I didn't realize you were so sensitive. Lanietta, whatever they did to you was wrong, but it's over. It's done. Leave it."

A slow grin overtook Lanietta's face, like a determined cat watching the enemy threat from afar, watching and studying and calculating the precise moment to exact retaliation.

"That's not the expression I had hoped for," Claus said.

"You would hope for compassion? Forgiveness? Love and tenderness? The universe doesn't suffer fools, Clomper. As a pet, you are protected from much," Lanietta said. "Such outlandish concepts of yours don't change the tide of trauma."

Claus wanted to say something. He wanted to hug Lanietta or ask her to cry on his shoulder. But he knew she would do something awful to him in kind. Instead, he turned his attention back to young Lanietta's auction.

"El-Vek. Interesting. You always bring top-quality goods to the auction. Seems odd you would bring defective material this time. Or is it?" the man said.

"I don't know what you mean," El-Vek said.

"Oh, really?" the man asked.

"I know you," the auctioneer said. "You're El-Anonk. You bought a girl last week. The one no one else would."

"That's right. Turns out that was a fake auction too. Josette has a lot of spunk. I imagine this one does too. Let's see," El-Anonk said.

He took young Lanietta by the arm and twisted it. Without thinking, she spun her body and put El-Anonk into a choke hold. The bidders gasped, and the auctioneer called for security.

"No, call them off," El-Anonk laughed. "You see? Deep down, they all have spunk!"

"And will you bid one drakos?" the auctioneer asked.

"I bid a thousand drakos," El-Anonk said.

The bidders gasped again.

"To ensure no one outbids me. I am merciful. I will not drag this auction out," El-Anonk said.

"A thousand and one drakos," El-Vek yelled to drive up the price.

"You cannot bid for your own," the auctioneer said.

El-Anonk laughed with hysteria.

"Your ruse is up, El-Vek. Take the money. Take it! Go on a long vacation and think of this excellent sale you have made," El-Anonk said.

The deal was finalized, the papers signed, and young Lanietta became property of El-Anonk.

"What did he do to you?" Claus asked.

"It was already done by then," Lanietta said. "Young, innocent girl of twelve million. Where did the years go? No matter. Those were different days on Mars and Preivos. No Veigon, no Martaceans, just a colony of Carinians. But a split colony of masters and slaves. Strange that Kechenova is able to get this memory out of Aftova and the Veigast. Aftova was still part of the Veigon. So was the Veigast, I thought. The Veigon was in the Anrega, and Libriota had the Anrega orbiting Carinia 2 to keep us in control. Maybe the Veigast *was* here. I'm trying to remember. My memory...the injury...where did my memory go? I...no, wait, the Veigast *was* here on Mars. It had just gotten here. Because later I discovered it. Discovered... that was the part...Libriota...Earth..."

Lanietta's face glazed over.

"Nanna!" she said like a five-year-old Earth girl.

Lanietta faded from Claus's presence.

"Lanietta? Where are you, Lanietta?" Claus called.

The vision with Kechenova didn't end, though.

"So aliens had slavery too. A theme the universe can do without," Kechenova said. "This is one of the first recordings of the Veigast on Mars. I cannot retrieve memories before that. Perhaps I don't need

to. There's no evidence of the Veigon, Morcellus, or Tabelia at this point. Four and a half billion years ago, too. We'll look forward in time from this point. But just a little bit."

"How much *a little bit*?" Claus asked.

"It's moving ahead. It's still four and a half billion years ago," Kechenova said as if to hear Claus's inquiry.

The view changed. Mars was distant but rapidly approaching as if a camera were mounted at the leading edge of a fast-traveling object. This object was in fact the Veigon. A beam from the Veigast blasted outward from Mars toward the Veigon like a directional beam for zeroing in on Mars. Mars grew larger in the display, but instead of heading toward the equator or some other non-polar position, the object headed toward the Martian South Pole. It penetrated the pole, traveled through the Martian core and shot out the Martian North Pole. This action of traveling from poles south to north was much akin to a bullet speeding through a watermelon. The entry point was small, but the exit wound was large and catastrophic. A large amount of planetary matter was drawn up with the object as it exited the North Pole. Some matter escaped Martian gravity, forever lost, while the remainder returned to Mars, landing south of the equator or landing in the Tharsis region, resulting in new volcanic activity. The Veigon itself took its position in the Acidalia Colles hills, displacing the Veigast which took to Martian orbit and consumed remnant life-forms, including dead Carinians. Each time it orbited overhead the Veigon, the Veigast beamed those remnants as plasma energy to the Veigon.

"Lanietta? Did you know about this?" Claus called.

But Lanietta did not appear.

"Then this is what caused the Martian dichotomy, the reason the Martian North Pole is a huge basin," Kechenova said. "So the Veigon came from outside Mars."

"What did I see? A Martian collision? And the aftermath of an Earth collision?"

Claus wondered. "But no Morcellus. And no Tabelia. Still, alien forces influenced our early solar system. I have to wonder how much they influenced life on Earth, or if...no, it's too much to consider."

A new image formed on the display. Threads upon threads of magnetic energy flowed from Mars to Earth.

"This is four hundred and fifty million years ago," Kechenova said.

The image continued. Mars gradually lost its atmosphere. Water boiled from the low air pressure, and the Martian oceans shallowed. A conflict of sorts happened near the Veigon—ethereal Bleuhs attempted to remove the Veigon from the Martian soil, but the Veigast (which still orbited Mars), blasted such Bleuhs on each orbital pass over the Veigon. Finally, the Veigast plunged down to Mars toward the Veigon to protect it once and for all from the ethereal Bleuhs. The action chipped off three stones from the Veigon and released beyton rays, killing the last of the Bleuhs on Mars and preventing them from returning to the Carinian system. The Veigast took its place close to the Veigon. But the resulting explosion and force sent the three stones upward and out of Martian gravitational influence. These stones headed toward Earth and landed in rock that would be found four hundred and fifty million years later by Frieda Morgan and be named Fronfa, Rigefa, and Aftova.

"So that's how Aftova formed, and two other stones with it," Kechenova said. "Just need to find Morcellus and Tabelia."

The display changed again, and the view was from the Veigast. It watched over the landscape and ocean, acting as a guard against interference over the Veigon's act before the last of the Martian water evaporated. It created Tabelia. She swam far away. Then it created Morcellus. Morcellus only swam a short distance before the last bit of water dried up. Morcellus fell into the mud as if it were quicksand, and he went into a dormant state.

"Hmm, Morcellus and Tabelia," Kechenova said. "But where did Tabelia go? Wait, I can load the problem into the Panamirov computer. I'll feed it Tabelia's heading and distance traveled before the water evaporated."

Kechenova did so, and a computer screen showed an arc of maximum travel for Tabelia with a likely heading.

"There. She must be there," Kechenova said.

Kechenova adjusted course for the Panamirov to land on Tabelia's projected Martian destination.

"Panamirov, this is Leonid from the Kazakh Space Agency. Exercise extreme caution on Earth return. Russia and United States exchanging missiles against orbital and suborbital craft. Irina, consider temporary lunar orbit. It is safe. We have emergency supply base on lunar North Pole. Land there if possible. We do not know how long we can transmit. Radio dishes being knocked out all over—"

The transmission ended.

"Leonid, I have received your message. Do not wait for me like sitting duck. Seek shelter. I will contact you when I can," Kechenova replied.

"I wish I could communicate with Doctor Kechenova," Claus said. "I wish I could communicate with anyone. Lanietta has deserted me for the moment. Who knows how long? This tunnel is headed west, most likely. West Coast? What will I find when the passage to Pacific is complete?"

"I must find Tabelia first," Kechenova said. "Now Morcellus used something like bamboo and birds to make a tube. And it started with colors of yellow and blue. Yellow and blue."

"Yellow and blue, yellow and blue, good things and bad, are in store for you!" Lanietta's voice sang from the darkness ahead, and she clucked like a chicken.

"Where have you been?" Claus demanded. "I'm in this tunnel all alone watching Doctor Kechenova in a vision. And *you* sing like a chicken?"

The Mad Mistral stopped as did the vision of Kechenova. A light shone ahead of the Mad Mistral, and Claus was shocked to see a human-sized chicken colored in yellow and blue.

"Yellow and blue, yellow and blue, Clomper the dog, is stuck with no clue!" Lanietta's voice sang from the chicken.

Lanietta clapped her wings together and clucked in laughter.

"You? A chicken?" Claus demanded.

"Yellow and blue, hair full of goo, jump in the tub, and use the shampoo," she clucked.

"Will you come over here and change back to your normal form?" Claus asked. "Lanietta. Quit clucking like a chicken. Jump in this ship."

But Lanietta didn't jump in. She clucked, ran around, and flapped her wings. Claus jumped out of the ship and approached Lanietta.

"Yellow and blue, yummy beef stew, roses are red, and so is your shoe," she clucked.

Lanietta clawed at Claus's lower leg, ripped the skin, and caused blood to fall on his shoe.

"Ow! Stop this insanity, will you? Stop!" Claus demanded.

"Yellow and blue, yellow and blue, Clomper the pet, does make a good chew," she said, and she chewed on his arm with her beak.

"Cut it out!" he said as he recoiled.

Claus backed away, Lanietta approached, he backed away more, she followed more, and Claus started into a jog first around Lanietta then away from her and the Mad Mistral.

"Yellow and blue," she called after him.

"Yellow and blue," Claus mocked back.

"Clomper is scared," Lanietta said.

"But not as scared as you!" Claus replied.

Lanietta cluck-clucked in dismay.

"Yellow and blue," she called.

"Sassy the shrew," Claus replied.

"Clomper is rude," she called.

"What else can I do?" Claus finished.

"You can stop mocking me," Lanietta clucked.

"Then stop this nonsense. Stop chasing me!" Claus said. "Yellow and blue."

"Yellow and blue," she replied.

"Sassy is poo," Claus said.

"And now you are through!" Lanietta said with a threatening voice.

Lanietta changed shape into a tiger, pounced onto Claus, flipped him in the air so that she could hug and get her paws around him, landed on her back with him atop her, and dug her claws into his back. Claus screamed in pain.

"You scream like a girl, yellow and blue," she said in her tiger voice.

"Let me go! Go back to the zoo!" he screamed while foaming at the mouth.

"Yellow and blue, vomit you spew," she hissed.

"This human you did...did kill and slew," he moaned.

Lanietta released him and returned to her normal shape.

"Did kill and slew?" she questioned.

"Language fails me in such situations," he panted.

"Well at least you're panting like a dog now. Good boy there, Clomper," she said. "Oh, but you're hurt and bleeding."

"Thanks to you," Claus said.

"You seem to blame me for everything," she said. "I'm tired of straightening you out. Why can't you grow up and act like an adult pet?"

Claus sighed.

"I'll patch you up *again*," Lanietta lamented.

Lanietta took on another Victorian outfit, one with a hat and large bow of yellow and blue on her lower back. She pulled Claus to his feet and close to her. The bow untied itself revealing the two ribbons (one yellow, the other blue). They circled around Lanietta's body, extended around Claus's body. Then Lanietta spun him as a spider might, and the ribbons wrapped Claus in a cocoon.

"I'm suffocating," his muffled voice said through the cocoon.

The bows came undone from Lanietta, and as they did, Lanietta grabbed those ends, brought them around to her front, clapped the ends together, and they lit into a plasma fire that quickly flashed and vaporized both ribbons, leaving Claus unbound and healed.

"Better?" she asked to Claus's shocked expression. "Of course you are. Let's get you back on the Mad Mistral and get things going again."

Lanietta helped Claus back aboard the Mad Mistral, and the vision of Kechenova resumed.

"Interesting," Kechenova said. "The pattern on the ground where Tabelia should be resembles the outline of a chicken."

"Lanietta!" Claus said with suspicion and disapproval.

"It really did look like that. I just sneaked a peek of the future. Do you like my lead-in?" Lanietta asked.

"No," Claus replied.

The Panamirov landed at the head of the chicken outline.

"Yellow and blue, yellow and—" Lanietta started.

"Shush!" Claus said.

"Humph!" Lanietta snorted.

"I think I've found her. I have a new connection through Aftova," Kechenova said. "Oh, but I've lost my connection with the Veigast."

"Ah-hah!" Lanietta interrupted. "That will ruin everything!"

"The only one ruining things is you!" Claus said.

"Careful!" Lanietta said, now reverting to her riding habit and pulling out her sword. "I can perform a *stabé, slicé, smashé* on you!"

Lanietta positioned the sword's tip to Claus's throat.

"I retract my comment," Claus said.

"That's better," Lanietta said, and she sheathed her sword over her back.

"It's like you're an island," Kechenova said. "Isolated from water, from the Veigast, from a sense of time, from everything. Such a lonely existence."

Lanietta mock sniffled and let fake tears roll down her face.

"You're pathe—" Claus started to say.

"I still have my falchion," she said between sniffles.

Claus said nothing.

"At least I picked up this Martacean language in the computer," Kechenova said to herself, and then she called into a transmitter, saying, "Tabelia, do you understand me? My name is Irina Kechenova. I am human."

There was no response.

"So ends the Tabelia attempt. Guess she never made it to Earth," Lanietta said. "I'll have to rewrite history and eliminate Tabelia from Earth. Of course that means eliminating Leni and Selba."

"Selba's there? I thought she was in Arberella. And it was you who abandoned Leni at Tabelia with Clover," Claus said.

"Clover's not there. Where have you been? Can't keep up with news, can you?" Lanietta taunted.

"Because I'm an island too, I suppose. You made me an island," Claus said.

"That's where you're wrong. You made yourself an island—with Frieda, Astroosa, and pretty much the entire universe," Lanietta said.

"That's why you like me," Claus said.

"You're my pet. I like you for that," Lanietta said.

"Because you're isolated yourself," Claus said.

"There's Labba," Lanietta said.

"Really? Where? You're here with me. We're both islands," Claus said.

"I get around. I go places and do things," Lanietta said.

"Have you seen Labba lately? What about your people, the Grens? Only you don't have the same color as the Grens. Or the Bleuhs. Matter of fact, you have your own color," Claus said.

"Because I'm special," Lanietta said.

"Because you're an isolated island. And you'll be an isolated island until the end of the universe!" Claus said, raising his voice.

"That's it! Vision is canceled!" Lanietta retorted.

The vision of Kechenova faded.

"What about Doctor Kechenova?" Claus asked.

"You know, you're really annoying me," Lanietta said with anger. "Irina and Tabelia returned to Earth! Couldn't stop Jill! Both were nearly destroyed by Jill but settled in the South Pacific. Jill was ready for them, too! She'd already dealt with Tony and Morcellus! Morcellus escaped to Antarctica because Tony sacrificed his life to buy Morcellus's freedom! I was going to show you all that, but oh no! You had to go on the isolated island rant! Well, Mr. Gerhardt! Enjoy your island existence!"

Lanietta swung her fist at Claus's head. He ducked, and her fist landed in a post on the Mad Mistral. The post shattered from the impact and sent splinters banging everywhere. She went through a rampage on the Mad Mistral, smashing and trashing everything in sight. She returned to Claus one last time, threw splinters at Claus, and vanished just as Claus avoided the splinters.

The Mad Mistral stopped in the empty tunnel, and Claus had no idea where he was. He slowly walked through the Mad Mistral, inspecting the great damage.

"Now what?" Claus asked himself.

But there was no "what". Claus was alone on the damaged ship with no idea what to do with himself.

Chapter 60: Mud Bath Meeting

Tabelia continued northward in the Pacific toward Cenina Island. Leni was treating an injury in the infirmary when the Smasti girls entered.

"Where is she?" Smateia demanded.

The sudden entry startled Leni's patient, causing him to move. Leni had meant to apply a topical antibacterial, but the action caused him to spill it all over himself.

"Please, help me spill more. There's plenty to go around," Leni said, tapping into Yuri's sense of humor and dousing the antibacterial on the Smasti girls.

"Away with it!" Smusa said as she blasted the bottle of antibacterial out of Leni's hand with an energy bolt.

"Well that's just dandy. What should we use next? An antiseptic? Or perhaps an astringent?" Leni proposed.

"We'll a-string-a-gent you if you don't turn her over," Smoxira said with a breath of fire.

The patient ran out in fear.

"Now I've lost a patient. But who do you mean? There's no one here now. You've scared this place empty," Leni said. "You should be ashamed of yourselves."

"You know exactly who we mean," Smateia said.

Leni shrugged his shoulders. Smasena replied by walking casually over to Leni, holding him close, and drawing a finger down his nose.

"Leni, my sweet, we're worried about Selba's welfare. She could be in trouble. Trapped. No one has seen her, my love," Smasena said. "We must help her. You can tell sweet tender me where she is. C'mon. Please?"

"I haven't seen her in a while," Leni said.

"C'mon. Please?" Smasena pressed.

"Where should we look?" Leni asked.

"We've looked everywhere in Tabelia," Smasena said. "But perhaps she left."

"She didn't leave. She's here," Smoxira said with more fire.

"Please, can you lay off the flames? The place will go up in smoke," Leni said.

White Hat burst into the infirmary.

"Something's happening outside," he said. "Better get up there at once."

"We'll deal with you later," Smateia said.

The Smasti girls left with White Hat.

"How do you like it in there, Selba?" Leni asked.

With Labba's help, Leni used Aftova to create a mass compressor. In this way, his inside was able to sustain a habitable environment. For Selba, this environment was the size of (and very much resembled) a studio apartment.

"Very well, thank you," Selba said.

"Lanietta has returned," Labba said as a holographic image in Selba's studio. "Leni, this is our chance to locate Clover and Doctor Kechenova. Begin by following the others into the Tree of Memories as if you are curious as to what's going on."

"Agreed," Leni said.

Leni left the infirmary. A mad rush of people plugged the entrance to the Tree of Memories. Leni waited his turn, and in time he was able to get in with surrounding people. Husky and Slimy kept order as best as possible in the Tree of Memories and did what they could to keep people from leaving Tabelia. But too many citizens overwhelmed the two, and they got outside of Tabelia in time to see a great dragon breathing fire around the ocean. It was Lanietta, and she was angry.

"Where is Aftova?" she bellowed to the Smasti girls.

"We can't find it," Smateia replied.

"Where is Aftova!" she bellowed with fire for the girls.

The girls dove into the ocean to avoid being burned. Orcas who were escorting

Tabelia caught the Smasti girls and returned them to the top side of Tabelia, who in her journey to Cenina Island presented a part of her upper side above the ocean's surface. Tabelian citizens appeared on Tabelia's top, and Lanietta sent fire after them. They too jumped into the ocean. Again the orcas saved them as they did the Smasti girls.

"Leni," Labba said. "I detect you are in the Tree of Memories."

"I am," Leni said.

"I'm feeding you coordinates. You must stand back away from the pool very close to where Selba was kidnapped earlier. There's a small portal there unknown to most," Labba said in her holographic image in Selba's studio.

Leni purposely allowed people to shove him around so that he was forced back to the secret portal as described by Labba. Then when all were facing away (and none noticed), Leni touched the panel. Labba, using knowledge from Morcellus and Aftova, transmitted an activation sequence, and Leni silently slipped into the portal. He was now in a room of scrolls much like the one inside Morcellus.

"I've sent a locking code on the portal. You'll have plenty of time to leave should attention be diverted your way, which I doubt will happen for a while. You may let Selba out if you wish," Labba said.

Leni released Selba from the studio apartment inside of himself, and she stood next to him. Leni then put Labba on two-way speaker so both he and Selba could communicate with her.

"What's going on out there?" Leni asked. "Why is everyone trying to exit Tabelia?"

"Lanietta has returned in dragon form. She is very angry that the Smasti girls haven't found Aftova. She's also lost Rigefa, but I don't think she's realized it yet. Once she does, she will either think she's lost it while flying around as a dragon, or wherever she was previously."

"Where was she? Do you think she was with Claus?" Selba asked.

"Most likely," Labba said. "I have no way to link to Claus. Unless Lanietta mistakenly left Rigefa with him. Hmm. If true, there's a chance I can reach him. That would be a vital part of our defense. I'll work on that right away. Lanietta is down to just one Veigonette stone—Fronfa. Her plans will be stopped if she loses the last stone. But first things first. Leni and Selba, go to the other end of Tabelia's room of scrolls. There is a smaller room with a transparent cylinder like in Morcellus. Aftova will guide you."

Leni and Selba did so and stood by the cylinder.

"In Morcellus, you stood inside the cylinder," Leni said.

"True, but we will do no such thing here. We will use the cylinder for two swaps," Labba said.

"You would swap us for others?" Leni asked.

"No. Listen carefully," Labba said. "Doctor Kechenova is in storage. Clover might be too."

"Clover!" Selba exclaimed. "Get her out now!"

"You knew and left her there?" Leni asked.

"Pay attention. I didn't know until just recently and couldn't safely remove her or Doctor Kechenova without Lanietta knowing," Labba said. "That's why we must do a swap. Fakes for the real thing. Feeding information to you now, Leni."

Leni received information for two fake humanoids, they were generated inside Leni by Aftova, and they both popped out into the open. Their skin tone was shiny and hair shiny too.

"They look a little fake," Selba said.

"They'll do for now," Labba said. "Have the fake doctor go in first."

"No! We should get Clover first!" Selba demanded.

"Lanietta has better tracking on Clover than Doctor Kechenova. If she detects our swap with Kechenova, she'll surely detect the Clover swap. No, we must do this incrementally."

Leni directed the fake Kechenova into the transparent tube.

"Leni, you must place your hand on a control panel next to the cylinder," Labba said. "Morcellus and I will relay transfer codes through Aftova and your hand."

Leni placed his hand on the control panel. The codes were transferred, and the cylinder glowed white with blinding light. Selba shielded her eyes, but Leni was able to detect that the fake Kechenova disappeared, the cylinder was empty for a split second, and the real Kechenova appeared. The light subsided, and Selba unshielded her eyes. Leni opened the cylinder door, and Kechenova collapsed in his arms, unconscious and not breathing. Selba assisted Leni in making Kechenova comfortable.

"No, Selba, don't touch Doctor Kechenova," Labba said. "Leni, you must induce cardiac function with electro-stimulation."

Selba stepped back, and Leni shocked Kechenova. Her body jolted, she took a breath, and she opened her eyes.

"Where am I? Who are you?" she asked.

"You are in Tabelia," Leni said. "You are safe. We've come to liberate you."

"I've heard that phrase before from a different time. I've learned not to trust it," Kechenova said.

"I'm Selba," Selba said. "And this is Leni. He's a robot. Labba is in contact with us through Leni."

"Doctor, I am Labba, a Carinian from another solar system," Labba said through Leni. "We're here to rescue you and another person named Clover. I have much to discuss with you, but for now we need you to step away from the transfer tube."

Leni and Selba helped Kechenova to her feet and over to a small bench. Leni then escorted fake Clover into the transparent cylinder. He activated the control panel at Labba's bidding, and a transfer took place. But when Leni opened the door, a swarm of honeybees emerged.

"Ack!" Selba screamed as she ran around to avoid them.

"Honeybees!" Doctor Kechenova said, as she pulled her blazer over her face and sought shelter.

"What happened to Clover?" Leni asked.

"You're asking us?" Selba replied, still running around to avoid being stung.

"Labba," Leni said. "Something went wrong. I put fake Clover in, but honeybees came out."

"I don't understand," Labba said. "Clover's signature was in storage. Leni, capture a bee and feed it into your analyzer."

Leni did so.

"Analyzing," Leni said.

"Will you do something already?" Selba yelled. "I'm being stung to death!"

Doctor Kechenova helped Selba find refuge.

"Okay, I see what's going on," Labba said. "I'm feeding instructions for another proxy."

Leni produced a swarm of birds, all of the same taxonomic family with bright-colored plumage.

"Meropidae," Leni said.

"What?" Selba asked.

"Bee-eaters," Kechenova explained.

The birds surrounded Selba and Kechenova, provided cover, and ate the nearby bees. The birds then expanded their circle away from the humans as they ate up the remaining bees. When they ate the last of the bees, Leni motioned them into the cylinder. They flew in, and he closed the door.

"Medic!" Selba yelled.

"I could treat your stings if I but had—" Kechenova started.

"I am a fully qualified medical doctor!" Leni stated.

"Well what are you doing over there?" Selba called. "Treat the injured!"

Leni scuttled over. He produced special bee-sting lotion bottles and gave one each to Selba and Doctor Kechenova. Selba doused her body all over with the lotion while Kechenova only needed sparing amounts.

"Labba, the birds did their job. The bees are gone," Leni said.

"What happened?" Selba said. "I thought we were bringing Clover back."

"Clover was here," Labba said. "Or she was supposed to be here. Bees. They carried her signature. Fortunately I was able to deal with them."

"Where is Clover?" Selba asked.

Labba paused.

"She is not in Tabelia," Labba said. "Some trick of Lanietta for us. Don't despair. Leni, do you pick up anything? Something that will lead us to Clover?"

"I'm getting something," Leni said. "It just came in through the analyzer. Candle in the window."

"Try refocusing," Labba said. "Sounded like you said something about a candle in the window."

"Wait," Selba said. "Clover had a crush on Claus. She told him she'd have a candle in the window for him."

"To guide him home? Who is Claus?" Kechenova asked.

"We'll get you caught up in a bit, doctor," Labba said. "Selba, what kind of candle?"

"A normal one. One that burns," Selba said.

"Are you sure this wasn't the memory candle that she stole?" Leni asked.

"No, a real candle," Selba said.

"Perhaps Clover left a trail?" Kechenova asked.

"Of what? Bees?" Leni asked.

"The bees carried her signature," Labba said.

"You can't make a candle from a bee," Leni said.

"But you *can* make a candle from beeswax," Selba said.

Selba rushed over to the cylinder, opened the door, and inside was a single European bee-eater on the floor. It flew up to Selba and landed on her shoulder. In its beak was a bit of beeswax. Kechenova followed behind and inspected the cylinder.

"There's beeswax in here now. There was none before," Kechenova said.

"That's the trail," Selba said. "Labba?"

"Okay. Selba and the doctor, please exit the cylinder. Leni, go in, and use Aftova to trace the beeswax," Labba said.

Selba, the bird, and Kechenova exited the cylinder. Leni went in. Selba and Kechenova heard muffled speech between Leni and Labba, but Selba and Kechenova could not understand the words. After a moment, Leni exited.

"...can't do it. She'll detect you immediately," Labba could be heard saying to Leni.

"I can't use another fake Clover. The fake would be detected by a selenite navy," Leni said. "Another fake one would give us away."

"Where's Clover?" Selba asked. "I keep asking, and I keep not getting an answer."

"Clover is alone in a submarine between here and Cenina Island," Leni said.

"How is it no one knew she wasn't here?" Selba asked. "Labba. You were able to sense Shara and White Hair on Cenina Island. Why couldn't you sense Clover's location?"

"Because Clover wasn't and isn't on Cenina Island," Labba said. "The sub must have an ethereal shield preventing Clover's detection from where I am. I can only detect her last ethereal remnants in Tabelia. But through Leni, Aftova, and the cylinder, I now know she is in a sub."

"Aftova lets me detect an ethereal line of beeswax from this cylinder to Clover," Leni said. "Therefore, I should be swapped for Clover."

"I already said, 'no'," Labba said. "We need you in Tabelia."

"There is no other way," Leni said.

"Wait," Selba said. "Send me."

"No, you must remain there too," Labba said.

"What are the parameters to this rescue?" Kechenova asked.

"We're trying to rescue Shara and Clover," Selba said. "And White Hair too would be nice."

"Can you do this all at once?" Kechenova asked.

"No," Labba said.

"Then we should focus on one at a time," Kechenova said.

"Shara and White Hat are beyond our reach," Labba said.

"What?" Selba exclaimed.

"For now, Selba. Cenina Island is a big project itself," Labba said. "Clover's case is different. If she were here, we could have pulled her back with the proxy that we first tried. That didn't work. But still the ethereal trail says we can pull her back. With a swap. A simple proxy won't work. The entity taking her place must be more advanced."

"Like a selenite," Leni said.

"Or a humanoid," Labba added.

All fell silent. The European bee-eater flew over to Leni, landed on his shoulder, and pecked the side of his head.

"Go away, bird," Leni said.

Leni waved his hand to shoo the bird away, but it kept returning. In fact, it did everything it could to get Leni's attention.

"I know you are here, bird. But why?" Leni asked. "Labba? Weren't all the birds sent away? Why didn't this one go with them?"

"Now you know what it feels like," Selba said. "We had all those bees stinging us while you took your sweet time before helping us. It's your turn."

"Labba? The birds," Leni pressed.

"The birds were sent to clean up the bees," Labba said.

"Did the birds die? Did you kill them?" Selba asked.

"No. They merged with the trail in the ethereal realm. It was the only way to keep the trail strong enough so we could use it again," Labba said.

"Then they did die," Selba lamented.

"Their corporeal existence was temporary, drawn from actual ethereal bee-eaters," Labba said.

"Why would bee-eaters need to eat bees in the ether?" Selba asked.

"They don't," Labba said. "But their ethereal spirits still exist. It's really a fascinating topic I could spend hours describing. First the—"

"Another time, please!" Leni said. "This bird won't leave me alone. It's so pesty and irritating. Maybe I should send it through first to be rid of it."

"I believe that is the intent," Kechenova said. "Labba, the bird wants to make the swap."

"Of all the bird-brained ideas," Leni said.

"Leni, restraint please. I need to speak to Yuri about your programming. But that must come later," Labba said. "Doctor, I think you're on to something. Let me run this by Morcellus. Stand by."

"She's not seriously considering sending my bird through, is she?" Selba said. "I can't bear to see Meropi killed."

"Your bird? Meropi?" Leni said in surprise.

"Yeah. You named it. Called it 'Meropi Day'," Selba said.

"That was the family name of these birds," Leni said. "It's 'Meropidae' not 'Meropi Day'."

"Evidently, Selba has become quite attached to Meropi," Kechenova said.

"Now she has you calling that bird by a name," Leni said. "I have a name for it too. It's—"

"The answer," Labba said. "We can send Meropi as a swap for Clover. Meropi won't be harmed, I promise. However, there will need to be a mass change to balance out the swap. Otherwise Lanietta will notice."

"What kind of mass swap?" Leni asked.

Labba fed the information to Leni.

"Oh, no. I'm not a hatchery. Find someone else for this job," Leni said.

"You're the only one with a stone of power capable of altering mass," Labba said.

"What? What is it?" Selba asked.

"Meropi will need to attain the same mass as Clover for the swap to work," Labba said.

"So Leni will act as an incubator of sorts," Kechenova said.

"Exactly," Labba said.

"No! I'm not designed for this!" Leni protested.

"You're a doctor," Labba said. "Meropi is a—"

"Bird!" Leni said.

"Will I get to see Meropi again? I mean after this is all over?" Selba asked.

"Of course," Labba said. "Meropi will retain her full shape. She will be like a great eagle of the sky. Capable of chasing down all sorts of vermin."

"I like it. A great, pet, bee-eating eagle. First thing I'll do is send Meropi after Baruuk," Selba laughed.

"She's laughing," Leni complained. "Selba thinks this is a laughing matter."

"I'm sorry. You're right. Let's get Clover back," Selba said.

Leni took Meropi and used Aftova to increase her size and mass to that of humanoid size. She was startled at first, but Selba consoled her.

"Shh," Selba said. "You're okay. No, you're too big to light on my shoulder now. You're all grown up. Goodbye, Meropi. You be a good girl and take Clover's place. I'll see you soon. Okay?"

Meropi nodded "yes". Leni escorted Meropi into the cylinder, closed the cylinder door, and activated it. The transfer started much as it did for Kechenova, but it continued on.

"What's wrong?" Selba said. "Why is it taking so long?"

"The doctor was local, but Clover is long distance," Labba said. "Have patience, Selba. Everything is working out okay."

The transfer finally completed. Leni opened the door, and Clover was inside. She was slumped, and Leni electro-stimulated Clover's heart into action. Selba and Leni helped her to her feet.

"Clover!" Selba exclaimed as she gave Clover a big hug.

"I had the most miserable experience," Clover said. "I felt like I was a hostage in my own body. Who are you?"

"I am Doctor Irina Kechenova," Kechenova said.

"Oh," Clover said.

"Lanietta took over your body and made you do things against your will," Labba's voice said.

"Labba? Where are you?" Clover asked.

"Still in Arberella. Antarctica," Labba said.

"Antarctica. That's where Morcellus went," Kechenova said. "Labba, last I remember was that Tony Kavalla ran interference with Jill Cresson so that Morcellus could escape. Have you seen him?"

"I am inside Morcellus now," Labba said. "But Tony Kavalla is not here. And I have access to all storage units in Morcellus. He's not in Tabelia either."

"Then he's truly lost, unless he somehow survived his fight with Cresson," Kechenova said.

"Five hundred years have passed since that fight," Labba said. "He would only survive if his body were put into suspended animation like yours. Listen people, I need the doctor, Clover, and Selba to go into Leni's hollow studio. Selba, you were there before. Then I need you, Leni, to leave the room of scrolls."

"What is this hollow studio?" Kechenova asked.

"I'll show you," Selba said. "Go ahead, Leni."

Leni used Aftova to activate an energy beam, and the three humans were transferred from outside to inside his body—to the studio apartment Selba once occupied.

"Where are we?" Clover asked.

"You are inside my robot body," Leni said. "The Aftova stone uses mass compression to create this environment."

"Incredible," Kechenova said. "Can Labba hear us?"

"Yes, I can. I'll let you know what's going on and answer your questions. Leni, return to the Tree of Memories," Labba said.

Leni did so. Labba explained her past history as a Carinian, the state of Earth, the Martacean reproduction cycle, and

Lanietta's activities. Meanwhile, Lanietta had scared most of the Tabelian citizens back inside Tabelia, leaving only the Smasti girls and White Hat. Lanietta landed atop Tabelia, still in dragon form. She returned to her normal shape and spoke to them.

"You have failed me!" Lanietta growled at them. "As punishment, you will find Claus Gerhardt and escort him to Cenina Island."

"Please, spare me!" White Hat said.

"You will go with them to ensure their success!" Lanietta barked.

Lanietta lifted both palms to the Smasti girls and White Hat so as to use Fronfa and Rigefa to transport them over to Claus. But only Fronfa remained on her palm. She felt Rigefa was missing, turned her palms toward herself to look, and garged in agony over losing yet another Veigonette stone.

"What's wrong, lose a stone?" Smoxira laughed with fire.

"Why don't you search the ocean until you find it," Smusa said while sending energy bolts here and there in the ocean surface.

"We love you no matter how much you have failed," Smasena said with empathy.

"I have nothing to do with the other three Smastis," Smateia said.

Lanietta's face contorted with lines of rage. She changed back to dragon form, encased her body in plasma energy, swatted all four Smasti girls, and vaporized them from existence.

"Nasty Smastis got too sassy for this lassie," Lanietta said, and then she turned to White Hat, stared at him intently, and barked, "Were you about to say something?"

White Hat fell to his knees, clutched his heart, and said, "I may need an angioplasty."

Lanietta placed her dragon mouth close to White Hat. She inhaled and exhaled with fierce but unmoving determination. White Hat simply remained there, quivering. After a tense moment, Lanietta lifted her head, returned to normal form (with her riding habit), and tapped White Hat lightly on the shoulder with her riding crop.

"Get up," she laughed. "You won't need heart surgery yet. I'll have you tend to Claus and his misadventures to the Pacific. Never delegate to women what a man should do. I'll even be generous and take you there."

Lanietta changed into a bluish-green and black horse with wings, flipped White Hat onto her back, and flew off. Meanwhile, Leni returned to the infirmary and had more than enough work treating burns. Kechenova, Clover, and Selba remained inside the Aftova studio, coordinating their efforts with Labba. All three sat in a mud bath of all things while a holographic image of Labba also sat in the mud bath.

"This is the most efficient way of communication," Labba said. "The mud acts as a fully active interface."

"Well whatever that means, it feels great!" Selba said.

"And no carbonic sludge," Clover said.

"The doctor hasn't been outside yet," Labba said.

"Please, call me Irina," Kechenova said. "What is this carbonic sludge?"

"The carbon dioxide level has increased since you last experienced Earth five hundred years ago," Labba said. "Humans who survived did so with several techniques, one of which was the elimination of excess carbon through their pores."

"That harness I made Tony Kavalla could help remove carbon dioxide," Kechenova said. "If we get through this thing, I'll do everything in my power to help people breathe."

"I'm sure they'll appreciate it," Labba said. "Let's prepare for the end. First point of business. The Rigefa stone is close to Claus, and he's found it. He has placed it into what's left of the Mad Mistral instrument panel and is just now trying to make contact. Claus, do you hear me?"

A miniature holographic image of the damaged Mad Mistral appeared and floated atop the mud bath.

"What an interesting model," Kechenova said. "I feel I can reach out and send it along its way."

"Hello? Labba, do you hear me?" called Claus's voice.

Kechenova did reach out for the Mad Mistral model, touched it, and nudged it along as best as it would go in the mud.

"Whoa! The ship just shook," Claus said.

The women giggled.

"Claus, this is Labba."

"Labba! Boy do I miss hearing your voice!" Claus's voice called.

"We hear you too," Selba said.

"Oh, I didn't set a candle in the window!" Clover said.

"I'll show you how to make one out of thorium," Kechenova said.

"Labba, Selba, Clover, and Doctor Kechenova? Are you all in Arberella?" Claus asked.

"No, we're just lounging around in a mud bath," Selba said.

The women laughed.

"Very funny," Claus said. "Really, who is where?"

"I'm still inside Morcellus," Labba said, "but we are no longer in Antarctica. Shh on that. No mention to anyone. Also, I have a holographic image of Selba, Clover, and Irina inside a mud bath."

"What?" Claus asked in surprise.

"Which itself is inside Leni," Clover said.

"It's true," Leni's voice said.

"That's impossible," Claus said.

"I'm in that seamount we approached, named Tabelia, and am using Aftova to host a mud bath meeting," Leni said.

"Clover, is that really you?" Claus asked. "Are you really in Tabelia? Lanietta said you weren't there."

"I was in Tabelia, then I was in a sub in the Pacific, and now I'm in Tabelia again," Clover said.

"You're here too," Kechenova said, "as a holographic model of the Mad Mistral. Only we can touch and move the model around."

Kechenova, Clover, and Selba took turns moving the model.

"Cut that out. The ship is shaking," Claus said.

"Claus," Labba said. "There are network connections here—between Aftova and Rigefa, between Morcellus and Aftova, between Morcellus and Rigefa, and so on. Power to do work is transmitted through Rigefa to move the Mad Mistral."

"What about Fronfa? Lanietta has it, you know," Claus said. "She could spy on us all."

"Such a connection is prevented," Labba said.

"Well this is all fine and dandy, but I've been through misery with Lanietta. I can't believe everyone is in a mud bath," Claus said.

"It's really not like that, Claus," Kechenova said. "The mud bath is an interface far more sophisticated than anything I could dream of. It allows for communication, provides tactile feedback, and even takes care of our bodies' energy needs."

"It's also a place for them to hide," Labba said. "Lanietta doesn't know that Clover and Irina are missing. Lanietta had Irina in storage and Clover in that sub. We put dummies in their place."

"Meropi is not a dummy!" Selba said.

"The term fits," Leni smirked.

"No it doesn't," Selba said.

"Enough, you two," Labba said. "Claus, Lanietta is sending a man named White Hat. He will escort you the remainder of the way to the Pacific Ocean."

"What should I do?" Claus asked. "Clover is safe, but we're no closer to finding Shara."

"In fact, we are. Lanietta is setting the stage at Cenina Island. We will be there soon," Labba said. "Claus, you must hide Rigefa before White Hat arrives and certainly before you interact with Lanietta again."

"Hide it? Where? How?" Claus asked.

"It must go up behind your top front teeth," Labba said.

"What? Really? Just place it there? With glue?" Claus asked.

"No," Labba said. "There's a procedure I'll relay to Rigefa. Once you place the stone behind your teeth, it will bury itself upward into the bone and connect itself along both halves of your nerves. It's critical you place it exactly halfway between your two top front teeth. Otherwise, Rigefa will connect with the nerves and brain on only one side of your body, causing a split psychosis. Yes, I've learned much through Morcellus and now Tabelia."

"I don't know if I can do this. I don't even like the dentist. Do I get a painkiller for this?" Claus asked.

"Do you need one?" Labba asked.

"Let's put it this way. The dentist always used a painkiller before administering the painkiller," Claus said.

"Seems like a waste. Just turn off the nerve impulses," Labba said.

"We can't do that," Kechenova said. "Human systems are innervated."

"I'll send a numbing command to Rigefa. You'll feel a mild tingling sensation, but that's all. Now listen carefully, Claus. You will remove Rigefa from the Mad Mistral transmitter device and place it to the back of your upper front teeth as I keep saying so that you won't forget. When you do that, you will temporarily lose contact with us. Once Rigefa takes its new place in your upper jaw, communication will be restored."

"Okay, I'll pull it out now," Claus said.

"Wait! There's more!" Labba commanded.

Claus had nearly pulled Rigefa out of the transmitter, but he backed off.

"I'm listening," he said.

"You must prepare yourself mentally. Rigefa will display two colors—yellow and blue," Labba said.

"I know those colors," Claus said. "In fact I'm afraid to say them for fear Lanietta will return as an oversized chicken and slip into poetry."

"I'm not sure I want to know more. Anyway, you will stare into the distance but bring Rigefa close to the midpoint of your eyes. You'll see a double image of Rigefa. Maintain your gaze into the distance but allow the colors to flow into your eyes. Rigefa will bounce those colors in, judge the returning light, and adjust. You'll then see the impossible—yellow only from Rigefa in your left eye and blue in the right. Keep your gaze to infinity though! Once you have that situation, you may apply the stone to the backside of your upper teeth. Make sure you maintain vertical orientation of the stone so yellow remains on your left side and blue on your right. If you see yellow in the right and blue in the left, you must rotate the stone until the yellow is in the left and blue in the right. Is that understood?"

"Yes," Claus said.

"Now you're ready. Proceed," Labba said.

Communication went silent from Claus.

"Labba, what effects should Claus expect to feel from Rigefa?" Kechenova asked.

"Primarily an ability to communicate with us without need for speech or other external sensory cues," Labba said.

"What about the other properties of these stones?" Kechenova asked. "Like mass compression, for example. Will the stone compress his jaw and cause it to close off, resulting in asphyxiation and death?"

"I didn't send such commands," Labba said.

"When I analyzed Aftova back in my day, I noted it was made of tangles and tangles of strings resembling super DNA. It was too complex for me to analyze further, but I can't help but wonder what interactions it might have with living flesh."

"Leni is interacting with Aftova now, and we understand its effects," Labba said.

"But you haven't tried it with human tissue before, have you?" Kechenova said.

"No, I haven't. It's a calculated risk," Labba said.

"I wonder if Claus knows about the risk," Selba said.

"Will the stone warn him?" Kechenova asked.

"It will warn him after it is physically embedded in his jaw," Labba said.

"That's a bit like the baby finding out the bathwater is hot after being dropped in and abandoned," Kechenova said.

"It must be attempted," Labba said. "From what you explained about Cenina Island, there's more than just the Veigon there to deal with. There's something called a diamonoli. That very likely is another part of the Veigon. Aftova by itself is no match for Fronfa, the diamonoli, and the Veigon, but with Rigefa on our side, we have a chance."

"What is your plan, Labba?" Selba asked.

"We must—" Labba started, but she was interrupted by a message from Claus.

"Labba? Everyone? This is Claus," Claus said. "I followed your instructions with the light and stone placement. The stone is now buried in my jaw where you said—at the root base of my two front upper teeth."

"Excellent," Labba said. "Have you noticed anything strange?"

"I seem to be inhaling quite a bit but only exhaling when I speak," Claus said.

"Uh oh," Labba said.

"Uh oh what?" Claus said.

"Are you sure of this? Do you have water nearby?" Labba asked.

"I am sure. And I have water. Lanietta didn't destroy the food and water supply," Claus said.

"Drink water. Drink as much as you can until your stomach fills. Let me know how much you can drink."

"I must caution against this," Kechenova said. "Six liters can cause hyponatremia and death."

"Water toxicity," Selba said. "The selenites used to torture us with it."

Claus drank and drank and drank.

"I've swallowed five gallons so far," he said.

"That's enough. You may stop," Labba said.

"What does it mean?" Clover asked. "No human can drink that much at once."

"Rigefa must be acting as a mass compressor," Kechenova said. "Labba, this is incredibly dangerous. How will Claus release the extra mass? Safely? He could burst and die."

"I heard that," Claus said. "Labba, you never warned me this would happen."

"Humans often end up in things beyond prediction," Labba said.

"We must establish that he can release the extra mass safely," Kechenova said. "Anything else leaves Claus as a walking time bomb."

"Labba? What's your advice? I really want to live, you know. This thing is scaring me," Claus said.

"Don't shake, Claus," Labba said. "You'll activate the stone in unpredictable ways."

But Claus couldn't stop shaking. Loose objects moved closer to Claus, and airborne particles went down his throat.

"Labba, everything is closing in on me," Claus said. "Labba? Labba!"

"Rigefa is reacting on a primitive level. Fear evokes a sense that all things need to be acquired. It's a sense of desperation, you know, like you can't breathe, so you hyperventilate, or you are entering a desert, so you stock up on water. Rigefa is stocking up on material objects."

"Ugh! A splinter just went between my ribs," Claus said.

"It punctured a lung?" Kechenova asked.

"No. It just went straight in and didn't come out," Claus said. "I'm like a magnet or a hole in the ground, and everything is falling into me."

"Close your eyes and place the tip of your tongue on your upper palate," Labba said. "Now draw your tongue toward your upper front teeth and visualize the colors of yellow and blue, but this time place blue on the left and yellow on the right. Focus. Concentrate. If you must, envision floating on a cloud to relax."

Claus did so. He tried to speak, but it sounded like he was underwater.

"Ugh! I just spewed out all that water. And a bunch of air shot out the splinters and other stuff," Claus said.

"That's how you release things," Labba said.

"Labba, placing this Rigefa thingy in my jaw is a bad idea," Claus said. "Can't I send it to you for your study?"

"Oh I'd love to take it, Claus. How do you plan to send it? By Air Mail? Fourth Class? Passenger pigeon?" Labba joked.

The women laughed.

"I didn't think you knew about those," Claus said.

"Morcellus, Claus. Morcellus," Labba said. "As much as I'd like to help you, I can't. Lanietta is looking for Rigefa as we speak. If you remove it now, she's sure to find it. Not to mention I'm not much good with Veigonette stones. Just never had one. Plus I'm not really here anyway. Despite our appearances, Lanietta and I are only ethereal in nature. It amazes me she can wield any of these stones. Shows you how advanced she is. But now you can go stone to stone against her."

"Oh I hope it doesn't come to that," Claus said.

"Claus, from what I read through Rigefa, you've been severely traumatized by Lanietta," Labba said. "Granted, Lanietta is a Carinian like me, but I would think you would harbor deep resentment against her."

"She can't help herself," Claus said. "I understand that. In a way I feel...feel..."

"Claus, do you miss her?" Kechenova asked.

"Claus, no!" Clover said. "You've got abuse syndrome. When this is over, I'll help with your recovery."

"Clover, you're reacting with sadness," Selba said "Do you think Lanietta would let you and Claus get together?"

"No, I don't," Clover said. "And it breaks my heart. Claus, she will only ruin you."

"She will ruin all of us," Kechenova said, "unless we stop her."

"Exactly," Labba said. "Here's what I propose. And this depends on you, Claus."

"Me? Why me?" Claus squirmed.

"Because she sees you as her pet," Labba said. "And as such, she will want you to witness her act of greatness as she believes. You will have to distract her. Provide a diversion of the greatest kind. And you'll have to use Rigefa to do so. She won't expect you to have Rigefa, so she will be caught off guard. I'm thinking you need to stock up on mass of some sort and release it to overwhelm her. Or you'll need to take in mass to distract her."

"Wait a minute. Time out," Claus said. "How can this be the plan? I mean, you didn't know Rigefa would give me this ability. You only thought Rigefa would allow for silent communication."

"Very perceptive, Claus," Labba said. "Originally I thought you could act as an observer and relay her next move while Tabelia successfully defended against Lanietta's aggression. That's why Tabelia is going there, you know. To act as a means to power Lanietta's agenda."

"Which is?" Claus said.

"Well once Lanietta overthrows the selenites guarding Cenina Island, she'll sacrifice Shara to the Veigon to gain control of the Veigon itself and use it to launch an attack against Libriota on the lunar far side," Labba explained. "With you taking up the main focal point of Lanietta's attention and Tabelia dealing with the selenites, Leni and company can sneak in and rescue Shara. White Hair too if she's there."

"Where does that leave me?" Claus asked. "What happens when Lanietta's plan fails?"

Silence.

"I see," Claus said. "I'm to be the sacrifice."

"I don't think she'll kill you," Labba said. "She'll torture you badly, but she won't kill you."

"Thanks," Claus said sarcastically.

"We'll have to go to Libriota then and report the state of Earth as it stands. Most likely Lanietta will be imprisoned by the Bleuhs," Labba continued. "It pains me to see her like that, but it was never our place to interfere with Earth's human development. The least we can do is preserve what little is left."

"You've just placed all of humanity on my shoulders," Claus said.

"It only appears that way," Labba said. "Claus, you must know that I'm not placing you totally alone. You're not an island."

"You're the first person to say that about me," Claus said.

"None of us are true islands," Kechenova said. "We have generations of culture behind each of us from countless people. Why language itself didn't sprout overnight. You will always have that. Of all the life-forms indigenous to Earth, humans are the only ones who can pass on such large amounts of information to others voluntarily. The others only pass on information through their DNA."

"You sound like Carl Sagan," Claus said.

"A brilliant scientist," Kechenova said. "I wish I could have met him. But instead I watched old videos of him and read his books. You see? He spoke to me across the ages, much as people of ancient times spoke to him through books. None of us are an island, Claus."

"There are many things in play, Claus," Labba said. "You will have to trust us. I have great resources here with Morcellus, and I have already begun work with Selba, Clover, Irina, and Leni there. I can't reveal everything to you just now, as we must maintain an element of surprise with Lanietta, and she would surely pick up on a thing or two and ruin our chances. But know that Rigefa will provide you with what you need when the time comes. Do not be afraid!"

There was a pause.

"I will take your advice. Wait," Claus said. "Rigefa is humming, practically vibrating in my mouth. Lanietta is approaching."

"She is," Labba said. "We have but a brief moment. Go along with everything. Fronfa will send out a call-home beacon to Rigefa. If you allow Rigefa to reply, you'll be found out. You'll know when it happens. There will be a metallic taste in your upper palate. You'll have to keep pressure there to block it. You can use your tongue or a fingertip or whatever. Fronfa won't try all the time, but the closer it is and the more it does, the longer you must apply pressure."

"What about when I sleep?" Claus asked.

"She's almost there," Labba said. "Break communication with us. In time you'll learn to communicate directly to us in her presence without her knowledge. I'll be able to monitor things without your direct effort."

Claus took a deep breath.

"Courage, Claus. Courage," Labba said.

And with that, Claus broke his formal connection with Labba.

Chapter 61: Showdown at Cenina

Lanietta and White Hat showed up at the Mad Mistral. Claus sat in the mess while smoking a pipe. It was really quite a lucky find for him, as Lanietta's damage to the Mad Mistral had disturbed the surrounding tunnel, and Claus in haste had found remnants of a magazine and tobacco shop. He used the pipe's tip to apply pressure to his upper palate in a periodic and casual fashion as needed.

"Unbelievable," Lanietta said when she discovered Claus with the pipe. "I have all but shattered your spirit, and you're smoking this...this...thing!"

"You've driven me to smoke, Lanietta," Claus smoked.

"Pets don't smoke!" Lanietta said. "Do your cats and dogs smoke?"

"They would if they could!" Claus said.

"Give me that thing," Lanietta said.

But as Lanietta approached, Claus puffed hard on the pipe and blew out large amounts of smoke at her. She gagged and reeled from the stench.

"Vile! Disgusting! How can you take enjoyment from the cremation of a life-form?" Lanietta barked.

"Cremation of a life-form? I never thought of it that way," Claus said. "You really hate this thing, don't you?"

Lanietta returned the sourest expression of disgust Claus had ever seen.

"White Hat," Lanietta said to White Hat. "I leave Claus in your charge. I will provide an ethereal fast-track trail to the Pacific. Bind this man and bring him to Cenina Island!"

Lanietta whipped a wind around the Mad Mistral and repaired it to perfect functioning order. The wind also put out Claus's pipe and nearly blew it out of his hand, but he held it fast in his mouth and pressed it hard against his upper palate. Lanietta then sped west through the tunnel to the Pacific, leaving the ethereal trail as promised.

"Put your hands behind your back," White Hat said.

"What?" Claus asked in surprise.

"You will remain handcuffed and in leg irons until we reach Cenina Island," White Hat said.

"Is that necessary? Lanietta and I—" Claus started.

"I'm not your girlfriend, buddy," White Hat said.

White Hat took cuffs from his belt and handcuffed Claus's wrists behind his back. Next, he placed leg irons on Claus's ankles. Finally, he connected the leg irons to the cuffs with a chain and held the end of that chain.

"If you get out of line, I can do this," White Hat said.

White Hat tugged on the chain, and it pulled the cuffs to the irons, causing Claus's knees to buckle. Claus fell to the ground, and the pipe was knocked out of his mouth.

"Aw, did the poor little boy lose his pipe?" White Hat taunted.

"There's more if you like," Claus said. "In the buried ruins over there is an old tobacco shop. It has cigars, cigarettes, tobacco, pipes, and old magazines."

"Who needs magazines?" White Hat said.

"Well you might enjoy the tobacco. It's remarkably well preserved. If you never tried it, you don't know what you're missing," Claus said.

The truth was that Claus was not an habitual smoker. Cigarettes were nasty to him. Cigars were stronger and more tolerable, but he never smoked them. Only the full rich leaf found in pipes did Claus like. He had tried the pipe before and found it most calming and meditative for the most extreme of circumstances, usually after a funeral or other life-changing event.

"There are many such memories in Tabelia," White Hat said. "You have not discovered this plant for the first time."

"No, but this is the real thing outside of a memory or simulation," Claus said.

White Hat pulled Claus to his feet and said, "Show me!"

When White Hat pulled Claus to his feet, Claus felt a strange sensation, as if he were being pulled inside himself. Indeed, Rigefa did just that—caused Claus to be pulled inside himself. It had created a duplicate proxy shell of Claus, appearing very realistic to all those viewing him but in fact put the real Claus in a hollow inside Claus, and so the real Claus was protected. The mass compression technique was similar to that used by Leni with Aftova. It was now a Claus proxy sustaining the pain and suffering. The proxy also acted like Claus on its own with the real Claus hearing and sensing as needed without the effect of pain. He discovered he could override whatever the proxy Claus said or did—and still with pain and undesirables filtered out.

Claus communicated this new ability to Labba, and Labba in turn confirmed this was possible, though she hadn't tried it with Leni yet. She admitted this was a better use of Rigefa than just inhaling lots of mass, but to be prepared for anything nonetheless. She had Rigefa relay the how-to procedure, and Labba in turn relayed this to Aftova. And so Labba had Leni be pulled inside himself in like fashion with an external proxy shell and the real Leni totally protected in a mass-compressed environment. Leni did not share the mud bath with the women, but he did construct independent mud baths, and this facilitated a transition where Clover, Selba, and Kechenova entered their own individual mud baths that acted (like before) as both a self-sustaining environment and an interface for controlling other things.

These other things were cetaceans. Each of the three women was given control of a proxy bowhead whale that Labba had created with the help of Morcellus and

Aftova. Clover's bowhead she named Locoff, Selba named hers Sella, and Kechenova named hers Ira. Leni himself did not get control of a proxy cetacean, but instead he was given infiltration plans for Shara's and White Hair's rescue.

"Remember," Labba said to the three women, "your bowheads must appear as natural as the environment they are in. Swim around casually in the area. And be ready. Claus, stay in the protective mass-compressed cocoon of Rigefa. You'll need it. Be ready to act when the time comes, but let Rigefa take care of managing most of the Claus proxy body movements."

"Clover, Selba, and the doctor have given names to their whales," Claus said. "What name could I give my proxy shell?"

"Cluffer," Clover recommended. "I figured if I, Clover, and you, Claus had a pet, we would name him Cluffer."

"So I am Lanietta's pet and my proxy is your pet?" Claus laughed. "A strange thing. But Cluffer is fine. It sounds better than Clomper. Well while we're discussing this, White Hat is puffing on Cluffer's pipe. White Hat decided to take it instead of finding his own. And now that I'm inside Cluffer, I no longer need to put pressure on Rigefa."

"Strangely enough," Leni said, "Aftova is also inside my real self and not my proxy."

"Have you named your proxy, Leni?" Claus asked.

"Luffer," Clover said.

The women and Claus laughed.

"Luffer is a lovely place to live," Kechenova said.

"I love Luffer," Selba said.

"What about you, Clover?" Claus asked.

"Luffer is nice, but I'd rather help with Cluffer," she said.

"It's almost time," Labba said. "Lanietta will be showing her hand soon. This is it, everyone."

White Hat led the Mad Mistral and Cluffer to Cenina Island very quickly thanks to Lanietta's speedy ethereal trail.

Claus allowed himself to be fully connected with Cluffer with only the slightest of buffering to minimize pain. To his surprise, Claus saw what Lanietta had been planning. The island was surrounded by selenite after selenite ship. The island itself had a broad plain from shore to its center with row upon column of selenite soldier. At the island's center was a mountain of narrow base but high peak, and at this peak was something that reflected light every so often. Was it a platform? Did it move? It was barely visible from Cluffer's location, and Claus strained to see, but even Cluffer couldn't help Claus make out the details.

Several trumpets from ships and land soldiers announced their obedience under Lanietta's command. Lanietta herself stood atop a lighthouse and waved to the selenites. Selenites from ground and ship cheered her. The winds carried their cheers in waves, and Claus felt the great power of the many pressing against his psyche.

"Make way for the Mad Mistral's reception," Lanietta bellowed across the distance.

Selenite ships parted, forming a clear passageway from the selenite ship perimeter to the lighthouse's harbor. The Mad Mistral traveled through this path, and Cluffer did all it could to buffer Claus from the intimidating trumpets, cheers, stomping, and clashing of swords against shields. The Mad Mistral reached the lighthouse and stopped. Lanietta jumped down from the lighthouse and stood next to Cluffer.

"Oh, my poor Clomper is in chains!" Lanietta wailed with feigned remorse.

"Necessary," White Hat said. "Every good pet does fine when bound at the spine."

The selenites laughed.

"Well it's no longer necessary," Lanietta said. "My pet is to accompany me on this moment of final glory. I release you, Clomper."

Lanietta touched Cluffer's chains, and they dissolved.

"You seem pale today, Clomper," Lanietta said.

"I'm just a bit tired," Claus said through Cluffer, and he slapped his face internally to get color transmitted to Cluffer.

"I have a surprise for you," Lanietta said with glee. "There, you're perking up already. We're going to have a wonderful time! White Hat, your next assignment is the lighthouse. Stand watch!"

Lanietta pointed a finger first at White Hat and then at the lighthouse. White Hat flew through the air and landed atop the lighthouse.

"He did not seem happy on the way up," Lanietta said.

"He was scared out of his mind," Cluffer said.

"He will be fine. Now it's our turn. Hold on!" Lanietta warned.

Lanietta waved her hands. The Mad Mistral took flight and shot toward the top of the central mountain peak. The ship landed on a flat area surrounding a rotating platform. The platform was not solid but had an opening in the middle perhaps five meters in diameter. The platform itself then was many more meters than that in diameter. The platform was hooded in glowing and flashing interwoven resinato strands. These strands formed a dynamic structure that changed from catenoid to helicoid to catenoid and so on. At the top of this moving structure was Shara. When atop the catenoid form, she would slide in spiral fashion toward its core, but the helicoid form would carry her upward on one of its spiral arms only to let her fall again from the catenoid shape but then would catch her again with the upward helicoid shape and so forth. The resinato strands bound and released her to prevent her escape while allowing her to move and fall with the rhythms of the catenoid/helicoid.

"Claus!" Shara called. "Save me!"

"Save me!" Lanietta mocked.

Cluffer stepped off the Mad Mistral.

"Be my guest. Look around," Lanietta said. "I'm especially proud of the *chalecoid*, an ever-changing catenoid and helicoid weave that is shaping and forming new encodings from Shara and the Veigon. Those encodings are stored deep in the Veigon. Soon I shall release them."

Cluffer approached a panel on the other side of the flat part and noticed a humanoid-high wall or barrier. Behind the wall was a control panel with White Hair operating it.

"You're helping Lanietta?" Claus asked through Cluffer.

"I'm keeping Shara alive," White Hair said. "What would you do in my place?"

"I guess you have no choice," Claus said.

"No, she doesn't," Lanietta said now walking up to Cluffer. "Nor do any of us. Not really. Do you know what this is? I mean this platform, the chalecoid, and Shara. Everything. Do you?"

"Whatever it is, you don't have to do it," Claus said. "Leave it be and return Shara to me."

"Poetry! At a time like this, too! How dare you!" Lanietta said.

Lanietta paced around in disgust. As she did so, Locoff, Sella, and Ira positioned themselves in a triangular formation around both the selenite armada and Cenina Island.

"This platform sits atop the Veigon. The giver and taker of life," Lanietta said. "You haven't forgotten those visions I showed you of Mars."

"The Veigon," Claus said (still through Cluffer). "You're going to launch an attack against Libriota."

"Very good! The freedom of law and order must come to the universe. One should ensure certain victory before starting the battle," Lanietta said. "And to make sure there's no interference, I shall issue restraints on Tabelia. Behold, Clomper."

Lanietta touched her left hand to her right shoulder and produced the diamonoli.

"Olivia Jill Depetti Cresson, that tortured soul who believed herself superior to all, was no match for the Veigon or any of its implements," Lanietta said. "This diamonoli, which Jill believed she

fashioned all on her own from beach sand, is in fact remnant particles of the Veigon. If an ancient creature represents one speck of momentary light, and all those specs are gathered together and wrapped with Veigon encodings of life and death, you have before you the diamonoli. It's a miniature version of the Veigon, but powerful unto itself. Behold how I use it to form resinato."

Lanietta threw the diamonoli at the beach next to the lighthouse. The diamonoli dove into the sand then shot upward, drawing thousands upon thousands of amber strands like a chemist drawing polymer fibers from an interface layer of disparate chemicals. The diamonoli wrapped these strands once around the lighthouse then shot over to Tabelia and surrounded her like a spider weaving a web of capture around an oversized prey. Tabelia fought and strained against the capture, but she tired and could fight no more. The strands then pulled on Tabelia and towed her toward the lighthouse where they secured Tabelia to that lighthouse and thus partially beached Tabelia. Tabelia moaned with the deepest of reverberations, and these carried into the mountain peak and shook Claus to the core, even through the buffer of Cluffer.

"Tabelia!" Claus exclaimed. "But she's a living creature!"

"Yes, a creature under my control!" Lanietta said.

Unknown to Lanietta, Leni directed Luffer into a swap-chain sequence. While inside Tabelia's infirmary, Luffer touched a patient and took her form while simultaneously causing the patient to temporarily take Luffer's form. Luffer as the patient walked out and swapped forms with another Tabelian. Next, Luffer went into the Tree of Memories, walked up to Slimy, and swapped. With each swap, the victim was temporarily sedated enough to offer no resistance and remained relatively motionless but not so much as to cause the victim to fall down or lose consciousness.

Luffer was able to exit Tabelia by swapping with one of Lanietta's selenites who happened to be securing resinato ropes around Tabelia. Luffer made his way to the lighthouse base and swapped with another selenite, took the lighthouse stairway to the top, and swapped with White Hat. Luffer then watched and waited for Lanietta to make her move.

"Tabelia contains memories of life on Earth," Lanietta said. "The Veigon contains information of life prior to Earth. And now, my dear Clomper, I shall make a living connection from the Veigon to Tabelia through Shara. All the past in its torturous complexities will be filtered through the simplicity of Shara's innocence, yielding pure energy of the highest structure and order."

Lanietta motioned to White Hat (who was Luffer) and then directed the diamonoli to fashion additional resinato strands from the ones fastening Tabelia to the lighthouse upward to the top of the mountain peak and forming a loop around and nearly touching the base of the chalecoid.

"Millions upon billions of your years have I awaited this moment of purity where I deign to reign over Libriota's domain," Lanietta explained. "White Hat! Monitor the resinato at this end!"

Lanietta pointed at the diamonoli, and it brought White Hat (Luffer) to the resinato loop near the interwoven arch.

"All of this," Claus said, "and no concern for the people of Earth."

"What people?" Lanietta laughed. "As I have said before, those you knew are long dead and gone. The few who are left are scattered. And if the Veigon destroys a few more as Jill had done in her time, so be it. So be it!"

Lanietta yelled something to White Hair. The platform carrying the chalecoid and Shara increased its speed of rotation. A line of plasma traveled up the resinato from Tabelia and encircled Shara. Shara let out a low and soft yell, possibly a moan, but it certainly was an expression of growing discomfort, as if one were being slowly pushed down a steepening hill.

"Labba, I need your help!" Claus communicated to Labba without Lanietta's knowledge.

"Patience," Labba replied.

"Now, Labba," Claus said.

"Patience!"

Plasma balls shot upward from the Veigon through the rotating platform's opening and through the chalecoid. These traveled high in the air then landed on various parts of Cenina Island.

"Behold the Sassatinax army!" Lanietta echoed across the island.

The plasma balls landed on the island and sprouted up into full-sized women dressed in space-ready combat gear, with slim protective suits and open-top helmets that could close like convertibles. The women resembled those of the Earth's past with various histories of traumatic pain. And the strangest feature of them all was that instead of wearing clunky space boots, their shoes were fashionable and resembled those worn of women in Earth's past.

"Labba!" Claus called in desperation, and it was all he could do to prevent Cluffer from giving away his excitement and anxiety.

"You'll know when it happens. Patience!" Labba replied.

Very quickly then, Lanietta had her all-female army. They carried plasma weapons that resembled rifles, and they stomped with such unison and cadence that Claus felt his spirit completely crushed.

"Now I build an ethereal tunnel of power to the lunar far side," Lanietta said, "and with it I bring my new army. You will accompany me, of course."

"Do I have a choice?" Claus had Cluffer say.

"No, you don't. All is mandatory from here on out," Lanietta said.

Lanietta sent the diamonoli down through the chalecoid and thus down into the Veigon. It responded by spouting an ethereal tunnel through the middle of the rotating platform and the chalecoid upward into the atmosphere. Claus looked up with Cluffer and saw the moon was overhead, and he also saw the ethereal tunnel wrap itself around the moon several times. Shara's movement from the chalecoid had changed. She would fall "upward" into the ethereal tunnel before being pulled down and caught with the helicoid part of the cycle.

White Hat (Luffer) walked over to White Hair, and he swapped with her, so that Luffer was now White Hair.

"This is it, Clomper. Take my hand, and all will be well," Lanietta said.

"Be ready," Labba's voice said to Claus. "Let Cluffer act from here on out."

Cluffer took Lanietta's hand, and the two ascended to the top of the chalecoid. Lanietta reached for Shara's hand, but before she could, a lobster hit her arm. Then another and another. These lobsters sprouted into flame and engulfed Lanietta. Lanietta looked up and saw a hail of lobsters coming from three directions, originating from three bowhead whales positioned just beyond her selenite navy. The bowheads were Locoff, Sella, and Ira of course, being controlled by Clover, Selba, and Kechenova respectively.

"Ack!" Lanietta said with annoyance.

Lanietta tossed Cluffer off the chalecoid. She flew high above Cenina Island and bellowed to her navy to attack. Her selenite navy did that. They sailed toward the bowheads and fired cannon upon cannon on them. The bowheads retaliated by sending plasma fireballs at the selenite ships, causing some to catch fire and others to explode. The bowheads dove and surfaced in various places, keeping the selenite ships off balance.

Meanwhile, White Hair (Luffer) leapt onto the rotating platform, climbed the chalecoid, touched Shara, pulled her inside his mass-compressed environment, and replaced her with a proxy.

"Leni?" Claus said through Cluffer.

"I'm in here," Luffer replied through White Hair. "No time for talk though. We'll rendezvous later."

Luffer jumped down the platform and reverse-exchanged places with those he'd first done until he reached the exterior of Tabelia. He made an exception with White Hair and White Hat. Instead of simply unexchanging with them, he pulled them inside and kept them confined. With Luffer on the outside of Tabelia, he quickly and temporarily split proxies of himself into bodies of neighboring soldiers. He had them break Tabelia's resinato restraints and stay out of the way. Tabelia took on the shape of a giant, like a cross between a great whale and an elephant. Tabelia then ambled along Cenina Island in such shape. Her shape was tall, but even still she had to shrink her mass to make such ambling practical. Lanietta's army, the Sassatinax, retaliated by firing their plasma weapons at Tabelia. But the weapons had little effect on Tabelia, only causing small bits and pieces of her stony hide to chip off. Tabelia wielded her snout, snorted up Sassatinax soldiers, and stored them inside herself within newly-created compressed prison cells in the room of scrolls.

Lanietta sent a line of plasma to Tabelia so as to regain control of her, but Labba had reinforced Tabelia against such an attack, and Lanietta was unsuccessful.

"Destroy them all!" Lanietta ordered.

Lanietta had her navy focus all their might on one bowhead, Locoff. They fired cannons and dropped depth charges. Locoff was badly damaged, and she surfaced. She retaliated with the best of her ability, but the selenite navy finished her off for good. Clover lost her link with Locoff and stood suddenly in her mud bath, unsure of what to do next. The attack on Locoff, however, gave valuable cover for Sella and Ira. They either beached ships or destroyed them outright. Lanietta took shots at Sella, and Sella suffered mightily, becoming beached herself, unresponsive, and dying. Selba stood up suddenly, and she too was at a loss for what to do next.

"You can't stop the Veigon. You can't stop me!" Lanietta echoed.

Lanietta returned to the chalecoid and made to embrace Shara's proxy as a prelude to creating weapons from the Veigon. But Shara's proxy crumbled.

"Deceived!" Lanietta yelled in shock.

To Claus's surprise, Cluffer had remained on the mountain peak, not participating in the battle at all.

"Clover! The backup sacrifice. She shall be my catalyst for my attack!" Lanietta commanded. "I shall send the diamonoli out to retrieve her!"

Lanietta pointed to a spot in the sea near Ira. The diamonoli flew out in that direction, hovered above the water, and sent a shaft downward. Uplifted from the depths and raised fully into the air was Clover's old sub. The diamonoli opened the hatch, expecting to retrieve Clover. But to its (and Lanietta's) surprise, out flew Meropi. Meropi did battle with the diamonoli but was quickly losing.

"Double deceived!" Lanietta cried out.

Ira launched projectiles at the diamonoli to defend Meropi. Seeing this, Lanietta pointed at Ira. The diamonoli released its grip of Meropi, flew toward Ira, and spot-detonated the ocean around Ira. Shafts of water uplifted, and several caught Ira and tossed her. Ira swam at full speed and dodged the water shafts as best she could. Lanietta's navy tried at first to follow Ira, but the water shafts quickly destroyed her ships, and they broke off.

"No Shara. No Clover. You then!" Lanietta barked at Cluffer as she pointed at him.

Cluffer was forced onto the chalecoid as the replacement sacrifice. Lanietta placed herself in an opposing position on the chalecoid, and she divided herself into many forms, integrating herself with the chalecoid and drawing strength from it. She transferred part of this strength to her navy and her Sassatinax army.

The battle raged on around the chalecoid with Tabelia snorting up additional Sassatinax soldiers. Lanietta's navy broke off from Ira and headed for Tabelia with great speed. In no time at all, the navy launched its cannons at Tabelia, and her stone flesh began to break off. Tabelia slowed, and Sassatinax fighters held their ground against her. Multiple images of Lanietta laughed. Meropi went

after a Sassatinax fighter here and there but was also held back.

"Labba, we're losing!" Claus called secretly from Cluffer.

"It's not over yet!" Labba replied.

"If only you were here!" Claus called. "You could help!"

Just then, Cluffer received an order from Labba to split into multiple copies of itself, generating two for each of Lanietta. Simultaneously, Morcellus surfaced near Ira. Morcellus swallowed the diamonoli and then spat out flying creatures that looked like orcas with wings (their flippers were longer than normal to provide lift). These flying orcas were no larger than dolphins. They flew first after Lanietta's navy and then after the Sassatinax army. Lanietta meant to send her images out to fight them, but Cluffer's images restrained Lanietta.

"Stop!" Lanietta ordered Claus.

Flying orcas landed on Cenina Island and fought the Sassatinax. When they landed, they took the form of Lanietta but with orca colors. Indeed, Morcellus was releasing stored images of Lanietta from the Arberella attack. These images were reprogrammed to follow his and Labba's orders. They landed on selenite ships and fought the selenites. They even landed on the chalecoid, where they fought the evil images of Lanietta she had just released. Images of Cluffer helped the Morcellus Laniettas, and it was only a matter of moments before the Sassatinax were defeated or snorted by Tabelia. The selenites were also defeated. The Morcellus Laniettas helped the multiple images of Cluffer. Together, they neutralized Lanietta's images and caused them to become inert and float away as dust and smoke. The chalecoid disintegrated, leaving Lanietta and a single Cluffer on the rotating platform. Lanietta looked around as if wondering what to do next. She was shaking, scared, and weak. Morcellus sent a flying creature resembling a hybrid orca-Pegasus, atop which Labba rode. Labba landed on the non-rotating platform, and when she did, the rotating platform stopped.

"Labba," Lanietta said. "My old dear friend."

"It's over," Labba said. "Come back to Arberella with me. We will sort things out there."

"But Libriota," Lanietta said weakly and with a gravelly voice. "Libriota. We must...we..."

"The ethereal tunnel is still here," Claus said through Cluffer. "Could we send one of those flying orcas up there to take a peek at the lunar far side? Maybe come back with information about Libriota?"

"We might risk it someday," Labba said. "Come along then, Lanietta. I have an extra place on my saddle for you."

"I am sorry it has come to this," Claus said through Cluffer.

"I...am so surprised...Clomper, my favorite pet," Lanietta said. "I...I thought we were companions. But all this...I don't understand...I feel so drained."

Claus held out a hand to Lanietta. She weakly reached out to him as well.

"I put my hand in your trust," Lanietta said just as their fingers touched.

But Lanietta suddenly fell away and into the opening of the formerly-rotating platform. She fell with a scream deep into the pit of the Veigon.

"Lanietta!" Claus said in shock.

Claus's shock was so severe that he dropped the Cluffer proxy and returned to his normal self. Rigefa was still in his palate, but he wanted to expel it and anything Veigon-ish from his body. He shook his body violently, sneezed, and Rigefa came out into his left palm.

"The Veigon created this entire mess!" Claus cried as he clenched Rigefa in his fist and pounded that fist in the air. "Devil condemn it forever!"

"Claus," Labba said. "I'm sorry. She was my friend too. The Veigon is nasty like this. It has caused great misery amongst my people. It has also given life. Ultimately, we must decide which is more important."

"I know what's important. And this stone isn't it!" Claus cried.

Claus began a motion to throw the stone into the Veigon pit while Labba yelled, "No! Stop!" But it was too late. Claus carried through with the motion, he released Rigefa from his hand, and his arm motion tossed Rigefa through the opening where Lanietta had fallen. It fell and whistled like that of a dive bomber fighter plane, going deeper and growing fainter until the sound all but died out. Then a deep rumbling (like that of a hungry giant) reverberated upward from the shaft, up through the formerly-rotating platform opening, and up into the sky. Lanietta's body was shot upward too, encased in a substance like amber that was affixed to a dark, iron-like disk. In a strange way she looked like a fallen angel, with the disk being like crude wings.

"What's happening?" Claus asked.

"I don't believe it," Labba said. "She can't. She won't."

"Lanietta!" Claus called. "What are you doing?"

But Lanietta did not respond. She continued upward into the air, reaching above clouds. Then the disk spread outward like wings, and the amber receded from the front of her body so that her face and arms were free. She floated like this, and the disk grew larger and larger until it blocked out light from above.

"I AM THE ANREGA," Lanietta bellowed. "I CHALLENGE...LIBRIOTA!"

Lanietta with the iron wings descended quickly toward Earth, bringing a sense of impending doom to all. Labba pulled Claus onto the back saddle and flew off the mountain peak a split second before Lanietta smashed it to rubble. The Veigon sent up a great ethereal flare from the pit, and Lanietta rode this flare upward along the path of the ethereal tube and landed on the lunar far side.

"I thought we stopped her," Claus said as the two flew around.

"So did I," Labba said. "Claus, the next time you have a stone of power in your hand, take a moment and think before throwing it after an entity of power."

"It was a horrible mistake. Nothing I can do will reverse such a terrible failure,"

Claus said. "I feel sick to my stomach. I want to die."

"Let's get you to lower ground so you can walk around a bit. That will calm your stomach," Labba said. "Down, Barblarnia."

Chapter 62: The Council of Tabelia

Claus walked through rubble on Cenina Island. Labba walked next to him while leading her orca-Pegasus hybrid by the reins. As the three walked, they could see Selba, Leni, Kechenova, and Clover tending to various parts of the island. Selba and Kechenova specifically were treating Meropi, who had sustained severe injury and could not fly. A few others from Morcellus and Tabelia did what they could on the island, but not many. These others hurried their visit and departed on small boats to their respective places of Morcellus or Tabelia. Selba and Kechenova were nearly the last to leave, taking Meropi with them. Claus, Labba, and Barblarnia then were the last and spent a bit of time reflecting on the aftermath.

"What was that you said? Something about a blarney stone?" Claus asked as the three continued to walk.

"My steed is named Barblarnia," Labba said. "I was telling her to go down. And here we are."

"Yes. Such waste," Claus said. "Look at the mess!"

"There is debris everywhere," Labba said. "But the Veigon is still active, and Lanietta is no longer on Earth. Worse, she has the Anrega. And to answer your question, the Anrega has provided a solid core for Earth since its beginning. But no longer. The only thing keeping Earth from collapsing is the Veigon."

The three walked amongst more debris.

"Piles and piles of shoes everywhere!" Claus lamented.

"Lanietta used the Veigon to bring women back to life, women who'd been hurt deeply. Many would have exacted revenge in their lifetimes, had they the chance. She took advantage of that need. Most are safe in Tabelia, but some perished."

"And yet their shoes are here," Claus said.

"Does that surprise you?" Labba asked.

"Of all the things to leave behind, why shoes?" Claus asked.

"Shoes go with a person. So do boots. In a way they are like companions, more so than clothes because shoes and boots must deal directly with an often harsh environment," Labba said. "Claus, how much do you care about this planet?"

"What do you mean?" Claus asked.

"There are several threats as yet to be addressed—any one of which could change its future," Labba said. "Ira is keeping Morcellus separated from Tabelia, Lanietta is currently away, Libriota has yet to make an appearance, and the Veigon is holding the core together. But should any of these things change, Earth as the planet you know will end."

"Well we have to stop it. We must figure things out. We—" Claus started to say, but he saw a particularly strange shoe.

"What is it, Claus?" Labba asked.

"This shoe," Claus said. "It looks strangely familiar. I don't know why."

The shoe had a medium-height heel, was a bit fancy, and was meant for a woman to go out on the town.

"Take it with you," Labba said. "We need to return to Tabelia anyway."

"I was just getting used to a moment of reflection in this rubble," Claus said.

"Those who are still here must discuss what has happened, what might happen, and what if anything we can do about it," Labba said. "No telling how much time we have, if any."

"You make it sound so final. Listen to the stillness of the air. What makes you so sure a disaster is imminent?" Claus asked.

"Because I'm a Carinian, that's why," Labba said. "Be on your guard, Claus, or the guard will be on you, smashing and driving you into the ground."

"Such cynicism," Claus said.

"I did not invent the expression, but it unfortunately is often true," Labba said. "Cheer up. You have me with you to help. And there's Morcellus, Tabelia, Leni, Doctor Kechenova, Selba, Clover, and the others. Shara is recovering nicely and is reunited with her family. Argo still loves me and most likely will do so until his death."

"But you will not die," Claus said.

"True."

"Can you have children with him?"

"As far as I can tell, no."

"And what about the other Carinians?" Claus asked.

"They and I share the same predicament. At least about having children. And yet...strange...somehow I feel it doesn't matter. I..." Labba started, but her voice trailed, and she fell into tears.

"What is it?" Claus asked.

"Nothing. Silly me," Labba said. "One should never work out the ends to all causes. Some ends are terribly unfortunate and will rip away all sense of hope. No, we shall keep hope in our hearts. You will too, Claus. Come. Let's return to Tabelia!"

Labba mounted Barblarnia, and Claus sat in the seat behind her. Labba gave a soft call, and Barblarnia moved along the ground then took to the air where she flew over to Tabelia, who had now returned to the ocean. The selenite ships had all been destroyed along with the selenites themselves, and so it was just Tabelia on the lighthouse side of the island and Morcellus with Ira on the opposite side. Tabelia opened a portal, Labba flew in, and the portal closed to the outside. On the inside, however, it led directly to the room of scrolls. Labba gave out a call, a portal opened to a green pasture, and Labba sent Barblarnia to the pasture.

"She's a capable girl," Labba said, referring to Barblarnia. "Now then, we must go to the Tree of Memories."

Labba and Claus walked from the room of scrolls to the Tree of Memories. Already gathered around were White Hair, White Hat, Slimy, Husky, Leni, Clover, Selba, Kechenova, Argo, Shara, Yuri, and Sharlamarian along with many Tabelians. Baruuk stayed in Arberella.

"I'm glad he didn't come," Selba said to Leni. "He's the one man I can do without."

Labba took her place at the main podium while Claus, Leni, Clover, and Selba sat nearby. White Hair took her usual place at the arch with Kechenova next to her. White Hair held a hand each to the arch and transmitted spoken words into illuminating flashing words from atop the arch.

"People of Tabelia, friends, and the only trustworthy selenite on Earth, I bid you all greetings," Labba started. "My friend Lanietta and I are from another solar system known as the Carinian system. We have three basic types of Carinians—Bleuh, Gren, and Greyan. I am a Gren. The Bleuhs, however, have ruled over all Carinians for many years. Their leader is Libriota, and we last saw her on the lunar far side five hundred Earth years ago. Lanietta, Claus, Leni the selenite, Selenite 102, and I left the lunar far side in the Novi 2 spacecraft built by Astroosa, an American aerospace company. We suffered a collision on the way to Earth, Selenite 102 fell to Earth, and the rest of us crash landed in Antarctica and were buried in snow. We went into various forms of hibernation and awoke not long ago when the snow around Novi 2 melted."

Labba paused. While she had been speaking, Kechenova worked with the archway to display images depicting the events Labba had described.

"So you are invaders after all," Yuri said. "We befriended you, and now all this!"

"This is bigger than you, Yuri," Kechenova called across the way.

"What would a Kazakh know of such things?" Yuri replied.

Kechenova ran from the arch over to Yuri and made to strangle him, but Argo and Husky pulled her away.

"Doctor, please!" Labba said. "Yuri, please refrain from unnecessary chatter."

Husky and Argo escorted Kechenova back to the arch. Labba resumed speaking.

"What was not clear to many of us, except perhaps Lanietta, was that Earth contained an iron core called the Anrega, and it still contains a nucleus known as the Veigon," Labba continued.

"I knew about the Veigon," Kechenova said.

"Please, tell your story now," Labba said.

"I will be brief," Kechenova said. "My name is Doctor Irina Kechenova, and I am from Kazakhstan of five hundred years ago. I am a cosmonaut. Astronaut Tony Kavalla and I went to Mars on a rescue mission for the Exodus One, a mission that had landed previously with three Astroosa astronauts. Two died, but one survived—Jill Cresson. She discovered the Veigon on Mars and took it back to Earth. Tony Kavalla and I discovered Tabelia and Morcellus, two whale-like creatures. Tabelia took me back to Earth, and Morcellus took Tony back to Earth."

"This is all so confusing," Slimy said. "Why don't we just destroy this nasty stinky Veigon?"

"It's not so simple," Labba said. "The Veigon is the nucleus of a gigantic single-celled organism of great power. The Anrega normally acts as its cytoplasm, what would be the main contents of a cell. The Veigon and Anrega are ancient. They are older than this universe and in fact came through the Big Bang from a prior universe. They move from planet to planet as part of a strange reproduction cycle where they first release vast numbers of life-forms, including Martaceans, then after a time they cause life-forms to die off until only two Martaceans are left."

"And we are in a Martacean?" White Hat asked.

"Yes. Tabelia is the female and Morcellus is the male. They are the last couple of the Veigon and Anrega. Their purpose is to create a new egg that will then fuse with the Veigon and cause a new cycle to start. When that happens, the Veigon will leave with the Anrega, enter the core of another planet, and release life-forms on that planet," Labba said.

"Then the Veigon could leave," Clover said.

"If it fuses with a Martacean egg, yes," Labba said.

"That's why you're keeping Tabelia and Morcellus apart," Shara said.

"That's correct. But it won't be enough. There's already an egg created by a previous Martacean couple. Morcellus and Tabelia are the replacement couple," Labba said.

"Another egg? Destroy it too!" Slimy said.

"It's on the lunar far side," Labba said. "At least it was five hundred years ago. Libriota had a search team find part of it. She might be there with it now. The fact is, we don't know if the egg is still there. We Carinians referred to it as the PRAAD, but it has another name that in your language would be the Amnus."

"The amnus apple," Kechenova said.

"Yes," Labba said.

"I told Tony Kavalla a story about the amnus apple," Kechenova said. "About how it manipulated people to help it take over an orchard only to then destroy life around it."

"Your amnus apple story is very much like the Veigon, the Anrega, and the real Amnus," Labba said.

"But how could we know?" Kechenova asked.

"It was the Anrega," Labba said. "For most of Earth's history up until Jill Cresson brought the Veigon to Earth, Earth only had the Anrega. The Anrega sent out ethereal waves to find the Veigon or the Amnus or both. Those waves have a way of bouncing around and being picked up by life-forms on a subliminal level. You will never know how much of supposed human creativity is due to Anrega's reverberations. And it explains how two people in separate cultures with no means of cross-communication would develop the same thing, often at the same time."

"Then maybe we shouldn't destroy these things," Shara said. "The Veigon and Anrega. I mean, they seem to help us."

"They did for many years," Labba said. "But only until the reproduction cycle is complete. Then Earth will be destroyed."

"Again I say, we must destroy them all!" Slimy said.

"How can we destroy them and save Earth?" Shara asked.

"Destroy first, figure out later," Slimy said.

"That won't work," Labba said. "Destroy all three, and Earth is destroyed. Earth can only be preserved if the Veigon stays, the Anrega stays, or both."

"Earth is already destroyed," Clover said.

"What are you saying?" Yuri asked. "We are here on Earth, now."

"No. It's not my Earth," Clover said. "My France is gone. Selba's homeland too. All of us are displaced from somewhere. Even you, Yuri. The selenites destroyed your Russia as they did every other country."

"We will take Russia back," Yuri said. "It is inevitable."

"Your people have said that for five hundred years," Clover said. "Everyone says that about their homeland. But I know the truth. The Mistral winds are dead. And so are we."

"You are not dead. None of us are," Kechenova said. "You sound like Claus and his island. Are we not together here and now? We exist. We live."

"For how long?" Claus asked.

"Claus is right. We must do something soon," Selba said.

"I say we gather up all of humanity and leave Earth," Clover said.

"Leave Earth? No!" Slimy said. "Destroy the aliens and stay on Earth."

"You can stay then," Clover said. "I want to leave."

"Where would you go, Clover?" Selba asked. "It's not like there's another Earth nearby where we can pick up and live."

"I don't know," Clover said.

"This is all my fault," Claus said.

"How so?" Labba asked.

"Had I reported back to Earth instead of crash landing, Astroosa could have done something," Claus said.

Labba nodded her head no.

"You had no choice," Labba said. "Libriota detected you and ordered your crash."

"Then I should have done a better job playing Lanietta's pet," Claus said. "If I'd made her happy, she wouldn't have done all these bad things."

"She was doing things before you were ever born," Labba said. "Claus, Lanietta is the reason Earth exists. If it weren't for her, Earth's orbit would be occupied by Protogaia. At least that's what you call it. We called it Gnisiotra back in the time. I knew almost nothing about it when we arrived in Arberella until she told me the Anrega was in Earth. I learned more from Morcellus. But I still don't know all the details of the collision that created Earth. Lanietta never told me. But..."

Labba looked wistfully at Claus.

"Yes?" Claus asked.

"She might tell you. Or she might help us. She won't listen to me. I've tried for billions of Earth years. But you are close to her," Labba said.

"In a weird way," Claus said. "Yeah, I know what this means."

"No!" Clover said. "You want to go after her, don't you?"

"I have to find out what happened to her. All of us must know," Claus said.

"So she can destroy us once and for all?" Clover asked.

"Or turn us into pets," Yuri said. "Slimy is right. We must destroy all outside influences. Lanietta too. Claus, go. But take a tactical nuke with you. Kechenova can provide you with one, if she's a worthy Kazakh."

"Don't antagonize me, Yuri," Kechenova said.

"What's wrong? Aren't you smart enough?" Yuri taunted. "Of course you are not Russian. A handicap."

"I can make anything I need to make. Give me radioactive ore, and I will blast your hyperactive orb," Kechenova said.

"Try it, my dear, and discover your fate!" Yuri said, and he walked toward Kechenova to attack.

"Stop it you two!" Labba called, and she motioned for Husky and White Hat to intervene. "Lanietta cannot be destroyed by a nuclear weapon. Nor can I for that matter. Neither of us is actually here in true physical form. We can only mimic physical form."

"But I can touch you," Shara said as she walked up to Labba. "I can hug you."

Shara hugged Labba.

"Very convincing," Selba said. "You Carinians have many tricks."

"So does Lanietta," Claus said.

"Exactly. You can't overpower her physically," Labba said. "But Claus, you might reason with her."

"And if I fail?" Claus asked.

"You won't fail as long as you try," Labba said. "We will do what we can down here. Matter of fact, I have anticipated your journey to the moon. I have sent for Novi 2."

"But how?" Claus asked. "It was stripped of equipment. For the Mad Mistral."

"With the help of Morcellus, I managed to refit it," Labba said.

"I think I hear it now," Clover said.

A large portal opened in the Tree of Memories ceiling. Novi 2 entered, landed on the pool, and floated. A door opened, and Baruuk appeared.

"Oh, not him!" Selba lamented.

A young woman then appeared at Baruuk's side.

"Baruuk, dear, where are the palm trees? Where is the beach?" the young woman said.

"This is Tabelia!" Selba said. "Labba has sent for you! Baruuk, stop fooling around!"

"Another time, Babe!" Baruuk said to the woman, and he kissed her.

"That will do, Baruuk," Labba said. "Claus, Novi 2 is all yours. You may leave when ready."

"You planned it all along then," Claus said. "You knew I would volunteer to go."

"Yes. I did," Labba said. "I had help in the preparation."

Leni stepped forward.

"I instructed Baruuk," Leni said. "At least enough to get it here."

"And with your help, I'll make it to the moon, right?" Claus said. "Why doesn't that surprise me?"

"You know me well," Leni grinned.

"Then it's settled," Labba said. "Claus, Leni has arranged for a relay satellite to deploy once you reach the moon. It will allow for us to communicate with you on the far side."

"Should have had Astroosa do that five hundred years ago. I wonder why no one thought of it?" Claus said.

"Perhaps people were caught up in the moment," Clover said. "Don't lose yourself in this moment, please. Return to us as soon as you can. I'd like to make a nice French dinner for you as a celebration. Or consolation. Either way. There's life beyond Earth."

"All this talk of life beyond Earth is making me crazy!" Slimy said. "I want to destroy something!"

"Easy there, Slimy," Labba said.

"It will be a great blow to lose Arberella," Sharlamarian said. "How can we safeguard humanity if Earth is destroyed?"

"We will send Morcellus and Tabelia around the globe and transfer the remaining humans to the Martaceans," Labba said. "With the help of Morcellus, I have discovered the remaining human communities. They are isolated from the selenites as Arberella is."

"Do we have enough time?" Sharlamarian asked.

"That we won't know until Claus tells us about Lanietta and the moon," Labba said.

"We should not wait. Plans to safeguard people should commence immediately," Sharlamarian said.

"I agree," Kechenova said. "This planet could be a ticking time bomb."

"I wonder if people throughout history ever considered such an outcome, I mean Earth being destroyed and all that," Shara said.

"Our history is full of doomsday predictions," Claus said.

"Yes, Yuri can answer that one," Kechenova said. "The Tsar Bomba and Sarmat missile come to mind."

"To prevent mutual nuclear destruction," Yuri grinned.

"Why would people want mutual destruction?" Shara asked. "Earth is kind and forgiving."

Most looked on Shara with wistful eyes. Yuri and Slimy seemed impatient. Claus took a deep breath and spoke.

"I will go then," Claus said. "I have tarried here long enough."

"I should go with you," Kechenova said. "Never know when you'll need a doctor."

"I should go too," Clover said. "To keep you company."

"Please, let me go," Shara said. "I've never been to the moon."

"Baruuk, let's go too," Baruuk's girlfriend said.

"I could use a vacation," Baruuk said.

"I could bring a recorder for a new memory tree pair," White Hat said.

"Not without us, Boss!" Husky and Slimy said.

"Stop, everyone, stop!" Labba called.

"You want to go too?" called an anonymous voice.

"No. I'm not going. Nor are most of you. Claus and Leni. That's it. Otherwise, Lanietta will think we are ganging up on her. We have plenty of planetary work as it is with gathering up the remaining lost peoples," Labba said.

"I wish you could come with us," Claus said. "And at least act as a Carinian guide."

"Leni knows all there is to know. Besides, there's a chance...a chance..."

But Labba's voice trailed. She choked up and could not speak. Instead, she waved off Claus and Leni to leave immediately. Baruuk positioned Novi 2 by the water's edge and escorted his girlfriend out. The others in the Tree of Memories formed two receiving (or departure) lines with a path in the middle for Claus and Leni to travel. The pair bade their goodbyes to all who were there. Labba was too distraught and simply waved before seeking refuge in the room of scrolls. Clover bade goodbye last to Claus.

"A candle in the window for you," she said. "No matter what."

"No matter what," Claus said.

Clover kissed Claus on the cheek, and that was it. Claus and Leni entered Novi 2, they spent a moment in preparation, and they signaled ready to leave. The portal in the ceiling reopened. Claus and Leni maneuvered Novi 2 through the portal and upward into the sky, growing smaller and smaller to those still in Tabelia. The portal closed. Boom.

"I fear I shall never see him again," Clover said, and she cried.

Chapter 63: Lunar Demon

"Attitude control," Claus called.

"Check," Leni said. "Approaching Max Q. No, wait."

"What is it?" Claus asked.

"We're not accelerating as quickly as records show for the original launch," Leni said.

"Novi 2 was launched atop a rocket," Claus said. "Which leads to my next question—how is this ship compensating for lack of rocket power?"

"Aftova," Leni said. "I've integrated it into the ship. Using mass compression, it can store vast amounts of matter without the associated mass-acceleration penalty. There's plenty of rocket-grade fuel in this ship."

"That's the kind of thing Astroosa could have used. Would have permitted easy travel to the planets," Claus said.

"We might pursue it someday," Leni said.

"Yeah, if we get out of this latest predicament," Claus said.

"Remember what Labba said," Leni said. "This isn't your fault."

"I still feel that it is. What more could I have done?" Claus pinched himself.

"Nothing," Leni replied.

Claus wanted to say something but fell silent. Leni was quiet for a moment as well.

"Leaving Earth's atmosphere," Leni said.

"Will I ever see it again?" Claus said. "Labba speaks as if the planet is ready to explode."

"It is," Leni said. "Unless we restore the Anrega to Earth's core, the Veigon will leave and allow Earth to implode. The Veigon won't stay naked there for long."

"It did on Mars," Claus said. "How is this different?"

"I believe it has a fresh sense of the Anrega. It will call for the Anrega for a short time only, then it will time-out and leave."

"You mean it's calling for the Anrega now?" Claus asked.

"Yes," Leni said. "Aftova is picking up the signal."

"I wish the Anrega would return on its own," Claus said.

"We must find a way to restore the Anrega while getting rid of the Veigon," Leni said. "We must also make sure the PRAAD doesn't interfere."

"Maybe we should have brought more people," Claus said. "It would take an army to do such things, if it's possible at all."

"That's why we must seek Lanietta's help," Leni said.

"Seek her help," Claus repeated. "The Gren who makes mischief."

"You know she's not a Gren, right?" Leni said.

"What do you mean? Are you saying she's a Bleuh?" Claus asked.

"No. Nor is she a Greyan," Leni said.

"She can't be an Orchian. You know, Labba left them out when speaking about Carinians," Claus said.

"Labba told me Orchians were tortured Greyans, forced to work on Mars around the Veigon. It degraded them. Orchians are still classified as Greyan in origin," Leni said.

"Well then what is Lanietta?" Claus asked.

"Do you remember how Libriota appeared?" Leni asked.

"She had a bluish aura about her," Claus said.

"And Labba?"

"She has a greenish aura," Claus said.

"And now Lanietta," Leni said. "What about her?"

"More of a bluish-green," Claus said. "What, are you saying it means something? I figured it was like skin tone on humans. I know I teased her about it, saying she was an island. Boy did she flip out."

"She's a hybrid," Leni said. "Part Gren and part Bleuh. She's caught between the two cultures."

"Now who's a tortured soul! Oh that explains a lot!" Claus said. "Why didn't she tell me? Why didn't *you* tell me?"

"Hopefully you'll have the chance to ask her yourself," Leni said. "But as for me, I only learned just a little while ago. Labba told me."

"Why didn't Labba tell me? Why is everything such a mystery? I wish I could learn more about Lanietta. Maybe I can help her come to terms with her hybrid-ness," Claus said.

"More like hybrid mess," Leni said.

"Don't say that to her," Claus said. "Things are already bad enough. She has such a short temper. Why can't the universe be based on love and peace? Don't answer that."

"Perhaps we should change the name of this ship to Love and Peace Mistral," Leni said. "See? I didn't answer your question."

"You've been around Yuri again," Claus said. "How long before we reach the lunar far side?"

"What makes you think we're going to the far side?" Leni asked.

"Isn't that where Lanietta went? It must be. That's where all the Carinians are," Claus said.

"We'll orbit the moon first to check," Leni said. "Besides, we'll need to deploy the relay satellite and ensure it works. Carinians could cause us to crash land, and then where would we be?"

"Back to when I crash landed with Prava 12," Claus said. "Yes, the relay satellite is our first priority. Okay, how long before we reach the moon?"

Leni played a recording of Labba's voice from when Novi 2 left the moon for Earth.

"We will exceed 400,000 kilometers per hour. This means we'll reach Earth in just under an hour," Labba's recorded voice said.

"So we'll reach the moon in less than an hour? We had her protecting the hull then. What will protect us now?" Claus asked.

Leni moved his hands apart to indicate he didn't know.

"Thought so," Claus said. "Wait, Aftova will protect us. Can it?"

"It's capable of accelerating us to such high speed," Leni said. "Yes, I think...let me adjust this...yes, Aftova can protect us too. We should be safe—from micrometeoroid damage at least."

"At least. What about protecting us from Carinians?" Claus asked.

"That's an interesting idea. I didn't think of that," Leni said.

Claus put his hand over his eyes in disbelief.

"Yes, do whatever you can to protect us from them," Claus said. "We certainly can't afford to play games with them again."

"There," Leni said. "Now we will have advanced warning of them and of any attempt by them to take control of Love and Peace Mistral."

Claus shot Leni a look of dismay.

"Correction. Novi 2," Leni said.

"That's better. Purge Yuri's programming if you can," Claus said.

"It is difficult. Very difficult," Leni said. "Perhaps I should run data analysis for Labba."

"That sounds like a good idea. I'll monitor for unusual lunar activity," Claus said.

Leni walked off to the side and pulled out a box of shoes. He placed a shoe in the spectroscopic scanner and pressed a button. Light beams ran across the shoe.

"Cancer," Leni said into a microphone.

Leni then placed another shoe in the spectroscopic scanner and pressed a button. Like before, light beams ran across the shoe.

"Three unfaithful husbands, two miscarriages, and a partridge in a pear tree," Leni said.

"Leni!" Claus exclaimed. "Not funny!"

"Sorry," Leni said.

"You're driving me crazy!" Claus said. "Can't you purge Yuri's evil influence? Or at least suppress it? Oh what's the use. I can't get myself together. Everything is stressing me out. Everything..."

Claus walked over to a cabinet and opened it. Inside were several of his possessions including the shoe he'd retrieved from Cenina Island. Familiar but unremembered, it disturbed him.

"All right, pear tree picker, scan this shoe," Claus said.

Leni placed the shoe on the scanner, pressed the button, light beams performed a quick scan, and Leni had his result.

"A broken heart," Leni said.

Claus paused for a moment, and something of vagueness returned, though he wasn't completely sure.

"What?" Claus said.

"Claus," Leni said. "This shoe bothers you. I see how you study it with a distant look."

"Can Aftova tell us more about the shoe?" Claus asked.

Leni paused.

"Is that a difficult calculation?" Claus asked.

"Aftova can perform a deep scan. It would reveal much more. The question is whether it should," Leni said. "I am not human, so I cannot answer. But I have seen what information does to people in situations like this. I speculate your mind has repressed a disturbing memory. If so, a deep scan will muddy clear thought and compromise the mission."

"Well my mind is already muddy, so perhaps this will clear it," Claus said. "Go ahead. Scan it."

"I will do so and view the results first to buffer any potential pain," Leni said.

Leni performed a deep scan and viewed images.

"Claus, this shoe belonged to your mother," Leni said. "You were young, perhaps nine years old when she threw this away."

"Oh, that's the shoe," Claus said.

Claus took a deep breath and exhaled.

"I warned you," Leni said.

"I know. Perhaps when this is all over...perhaps then I can...you know, I think I'll sit down and close my eyes," Claus said.

Claus did just that. He fell lightly asleep, believing himself to be in Prava 12 and circling endlessly around the moon unable to land or leave. He watched the stars disappear one by one until after the last star disappeared, the sun shrank into nothingness, and all about him was black.

"I'm blind!" Claus awoke with a start.

"Easy there," Leni said. "We're approaching the moon. I'll launch the relay satellite now."

"Good idea," Claus said.

Leni launched the relay satellite.

"Communication link established. Satellite is A-okay," Claus said.

"Labba reports reading information from both us and the satellite," Leni said. "We're going into lunar orbit. In a moment we will be over the far side."

"Losing direct radio contact with Labba," Claus said.

"Take a look at the view screen. Do you see that lunar feature?" Leni asked.

Claus studied the view screen.

"There's a bulge, like a goiter," Claus said. "It's in the same place where I crash landed in Prava 12. Bulge is grey and smooth. Totally intact."

"Solid iron. Aftova identifies it as the Anrega," Leni said. "Relaying images through the satellite. Labba is receiving them."

"Picking up strange readings from the lunar far side," Claus said.

"Radiation," Leni said. "Large amounts. Very powerful."

"Will ship's electronics function in the radiation?" Claus asked.

"They are well shielded. I would say yes," Leni said.

"What about us?" Claus asked.

"The radiation does not affect most animal tissue," Leni said.

"Most?"

"That's the best I can make of it," Leni said. "We won't know more without further analysis."

"Is it safe for us to land? I mean, is this radiation going to kill me or destroy you?" Claus asked.

"We are safe both short term and long," Leni said. "The radiation does not damage animal tissue. It might affect it temporarily. I'll let you know when I know more. Something else. Aftova has identified this radiation as beyton rays."

"Beyton rays? What are those?" Claus asked.

"They appear to be related to the Veigon," Leni said. "I spoke with Doctor Kechenova about her experience with Mars. She recorded beyton rays there from a Veigon fragment known as the Veigast. The Veigast would destroy life by using beyton rays."

"But you said this doesn't destroy animal tissue," Claus said.

"This kind doesn't, no," Leni said.

"Any other readings from the lunar surface?" Claus asked. "Signs of Carinians or other life?"

"No readings of such at all," Leni said. "It's a dead end if we remain in orbit."

"Then we must land and investigate," Claus said. "Even if it means recapture."

"The relay satellite will be exposed to full beyton rays," Leni said. "But it should be safe. And it will relay everything we do."

"Good," Claus said.

The two landed Novi 2 next to the Anrega. While Claus donned a spacesuit, Leni took Aftova and reintegrated it with himself. The two exited Novi 2 and approached the Anrega.

"There are passages inside the Anrega," Leni said. "They are large enough for us to travel through."

"This exterior is smooth. We must find an entrance to the passages," Claus said.

"You will find none," Leni said. "However, I will have Aftova request the Anrega to make us one."

Leni did such, and a portal opened for the two. The two entered, and the portal closed behind them.

"So shiny and smooth, and devoid of any mechanization or life," Claus said.

"Just looks like solid iron around us. Hard to believe this is cytoplasm for the Veigon. It also seems much smaller than before."

"It had enlarged to full size when in Earth's core," Leni said.

"And above us at Cenina Island, when Lanietta controlled it, it was—" Claus said.

"Smaller then, and even smaller now," Leni said. "It has compressed its mass significantly."

The passageway opened up into a large chamber with dining-table high pedestals all about. On each pedestal were translucent yet glowing orbs of swirling glitter. This glitter reflected colors of yellow and blue.

"I wonder what these are?" Claus asked.

"Aftova identifies them as repositories of the dead, similar to the bricks of Morcellus," Leni said.

"There are so many," Claus said. "Let's search the chamber. We'll cover more ground if we split up."

Claus walked to the left while Leni walked to the right. Claus progressively touched orbs. As he did, each one activated a miniature holographic image of a dead life-form—bird, a tree, a fox, a bear, a cricket, and so on. Leni touched the orbs but was unable to activate such holograms.

"It appears one must be alive to activate the orbs," Leni said.

"Yes. I have this haunting fear that I'll touch an orb, and someone I know will appear," Claus said.

"Claus, over here," Leni said. "I've found something."

Claus walked over to Leni, and there kneeling between two pedestals with a hand on each was Lanietta.

"Lanietta! Lanietta!" Claus cried, and he leaned over to hug her, but his arms went right through her.

"She has faded badly," Leni said.

"She's dying?" Claus asked. "No, it cannot be! You must help her. Leni, use Aftova!"

Leni tried to touch Lanietta, but his hands also passed through her.

"I can't help her because I can't touch her," Leni said.

"These orbs. We must connect with her through the orbs," Claus said.

"Touch them," Leni said.

"Let's touch them together," Claus said. "I'm alive, so I'll help you connect."

They did so. One orb projected a Gren man, and another orb projected a Bleuh woman.

"The man is Larto," Leni said. "The woman is Lanshalla. These two are Lanietta's parents."

"Her parents? They are here? Dead?" Claus asked.

"Yes to all three," Leni said.

"I'm confused," Claus said.

"We need more information. Aftova has stabilized Lanietta. She will not fade any more."

"Can you bring her back to full strength?" Claus asked.

"We can't risk it, Claus. Not after everything she's done," Leni said. "We're extremely fortunate to find her—"

"In such a dilapidated state," Claus finished. "That *is* what you were going to say."

"Well?"

"It isn't well!" Claus said. "Her parents. Oh, oh! She's devastated. Maybe she didn't know all these years. Now she does. Strange she didn't know at Cenina Island. Maybe she didn't discover them until she reached the moon. Libriota's doing? I bet it was. I hate Libriota. I agree with Slimy. It's time to destroy!"

"Claus, stop! You must buffer your agony and clear your mind. How do you intend to destroy Libriota? Hmm? You know how powerful she is. We are again lucky she is not here. Otherwise our mission will fail. Our path is now clear. We must return to Novi 2, report what we've discovered, and explore the area covertly. If luck favors us, we'll learn of Libriota's doings and plans without being detected, then we must return to Novi 2 yet again and report our findings. Clear minds will win the day, Claus. Clear minds!"

Claus let go of the orbs and clasped his hands together. He looked down, he looked up, and he looked straight at Leni. Leni released his grip of the orbs and put his hands on Claus's.

"Yes. Clear minds will win the day," Claus said, feeling invigorated by Leni. "The day must not fail us. Ever."

"Aftova has detected the source of the beyton rays. We will find the answer there. Aftova assures me the beyton rays will not cause us injury."

"Which way?" Claus asked.

"Into that passageway ahead," Leni said.

"That's farther away from Novi 2," Claus said.

"We'll have to go back to Novi 2, report, then come back here and follow the beyton rays," Leni said.

"No, that will take too long," Claus said. "I feel a sense of urgency now. Let's proceed to the source."

"Very well," Leni said.

The two followed the new passageway in the Anrega until it reached the outer ring of the crater where Claus had been before, when he'd first crashed Prava 12. The two left the Anrega and entered that same lunar passageway. Like before, Claus saw the various exhibits of life-forms. The suit protected him from the atmosphere.

"So far so good," Claus said. "No Carinians."

"Aftova should have picked up Carinians by now," Leni said. "But it has picked up none."

"Hiding I'm sure," Claus said. "They will launch a surprise capture when we least expect it. Well, there's nothing for it. On we go."

The two entered the chamber where the Orchians had discovered the Tropheia. And there it was. In the middle of the room was the full PRAAD (including the Tropheia). The PRAAD had a flat base and measured a hundred and two, by five hundred and sixty-one millimeters. The double-goblet-shaped Tropheia sat on a tapered section on top of the main body, the Anferrumnum. The PRAAD swirled colors of yellow and blue from the top that floated down and spread outward like smoke.

"This is the source of the beyton rays," Leni said. "The PRAAD, or the Amnus. This is the egg that wants to fuse with the Veigon. The Carinians found it. They found it!"

"Yes! They did!" Claus said. "And the Tropheia is attached to the top of the PRAAD. But where are the Carinians? Where are they? And why are they dragging us through this torture?"

"The PRAAD has a record of events," Leni said. "With the help of it and Aftova, I can project what happened."

"Project what happened?" Claus echoed. "Then something did happen."

"Yes," Leni said. "Observe."

Leni tapped his left forearm twice with his two right fingers.

"You're activating Aftova?" Claus asked.

"No, I'm checking your alertness," Leni said.

"I'm alert!" Claus said. "Show us what happened!"

Leni stood motionless.

"Well? Wave your hand or something to start," Claus said.

"I was right. You *do* need dramatic effect. Behold," Leni said.

Leni waved his arm. The PRAAD displayed holographic images of Libriota and an Orchian taking an elevator down an excavation shaft.

"Libriota and Arlichia," Claus said. "To think I used to call her Lady Liberty. I was so wrong. And Arlichia is Orchius's wife. But I thought she was sent back to Carinia Zero."

"Bringing Orchius back was an excellent idea," Arlichia said. "He has discovered the rest of the PRAAD."

"Lanietta's folly shall be exposed and dealt with once and for all," Libriota said. "You and Orchius shall be rewarded for this discovery."

The hologram showed the two reaching the chamber of the PRAAD. Orchius stood by the PRAAD while several Bleuhs brought the Tropheia to him.

"One moment, Orchius," Libriota said. "I wish to establish a full link with the Carinian solar system. This moment must be shared for all."

A device much like a bulky studio television camera of the 1950s was set up. It beamed ethereal rays at Libriota and the PRAAD.

"You're on," the cameraman said.

"Bleuhs and other Carinians, I bid you greetings from Sol 3a," Libriota said. "Long have we suffered in the ethereal realm without corporeal bodies. Long have we shared the ethereal realm with Greylingers, who have deprived us of free travel and clean existence. But that time is ending. After being lost for four and a half billion Sol 3 years, the PRAAD is restored to us in its entirety. We can complete the mission we set out to do, that of using the PRAAD, the Veigon, and the Anrega to cleanse the ethereal realm of Greylingers and restore us our corporeal bodies."

Libriota paused. Behind her stood Orchius by the incomplete PRAAD and holding the Tropheia.

"I feel something strange," Claus said to Leni. "My implant is activating. Look at me. Do you see any change in my appearance?"

"Your implant should be blocking inputs," Leni said. "The mask is still there."

"It seems the mask only dampens inputs," Claus said. "It doesn't block them completely. Just ask Lanietta. No, don't ask her. My appearance, Leni."

"Your hair is standing on end," Leni said. "Perhaps you are nervous."

"Ugh!" Claus said, and he changed into the mountain lion he once was when first on the lunar far side.

Leni stopped the projection. Claus returned to his normal humanoid self and gasped for air.

"What happened?" Claus asked. "I thought you said these beyton rays wouldn't injure us."

"There's a subcarrier signal in these beyton rays," Leni said. "It came through the projection. And it came from the PRAAD in the projection. Feedback. There was beyton ray feedback between the projection and the real thing."

"I don't know if we should do this," Claus said. "I fear we'll discover something horrible. Why else would I change form?"

"We can wait," Leni said.

The two stood for a moment.

"No, I can't wait," Claus said. "We must get through this. I must get through this. Resume the projection."

"I'll buffer the beyton ray feedback as best as possible," Leni said. "Here is the projection."

Leni resumed the projection of Libriota.

"Let there be no misunderstanding. I have pursued Bleuh justice and excellence from the very beginning, spanning space and time with the utmost vigilance. And so with great jubilation, I come fully into my own as your perpetual supreme leader with this final act of achievement," Libriota said.

Libriota walked over to the PRAAD.

"I stand here before you and join with the PRAAD. Bear witness to this event so that all may know how we entered into our new existence," Libriota said.

Libriota held onto the PRAAD and motioned for Orchius to reattach the Tropheia.

"All Carinians. Please join with me now in this act of reunion. Share your ethereal spirit with me, and I promise your corporeal existence for all time," Libriota said.

The bulky camera spooled up with a whine, and thrusts of ethereal energy blasted from the camera to Libriota. Orchius reattached the Tropheia. Great swirls of blue and yellow ripped through Libriota's ethereal self, fighting and dueling. The blue lost, and yellow took over, becoming brighter and brighter. Libriota let out a horrific scream, and the scream stretched out with a warble and chopped screech.

The effects of the destructive yellow light spilled over from the projection and onto Leni and Claus. Leni lost his ability to buffer the beyton rays, and Claus changed back to his old mountain lion form. He fell to the floor and lost muscle control, foaming at the mouth, clawing himself, and biting his legs.

"I can't stop the projection," Leni said. "The yellow beyton rays have compromised my control. Claus, I am sorry."

The projection continued with the projection PRAAD interacting with the real PRAAD. Claus turned his mountain lion head toward the projection and saw the last bits of Libriota destroyed. Orchius was destroyed next, followed by Arlichia, and all those in the room at the time were also destroyed. Carinian after Carinian were pulled through the camera device and destroyed. The numbers increased and overwhelmed Claus. He tried turning away, but the projection PRAAD directed the real PRAAD to force Claus into watching this act of genocide. Then things changed, and the killing stream of Carinians was rerouted from the projection PRAAD to the real PRAAD and through Claus. He felt horribly sick to his stomach and wanted to vomit. Indeed, he dry heaved, and his stomach muscles fell into horrible cramp, contracting in rapid fibrillation from watching the Carinians slaughtered *en masse*.

"Let it end. Please. Let it end," Claus moaned from his mountain lion body.

Leni fell to the ground, fully immobilized. The carnage continued, going on for several hours. It was too much for Claus, and he passed out.

Chapter 64: Lanietta's Fate

Claus awoke. He had his normal form but was surprised to find himself inside Leni's studio apartment. The back of his skull was tender. Reaching back to check, he could no longer find the implant. Checking nearby, he saw it on the floor with a bit of blood on it.

"But no hole in my skull," Claus said. "Guess I'm lucky to be alive."

Claus looked around the apartment. The mud baths were empty and the apartment barren. On a wall was plain writing:

Save yourself
Take Aftova
Use proxy
Tell Labba

In the middle of the room on the floor was Aftova. It had a split color of yellow and blue, but the colors were blurred and static in appearance as if the colors had been spinning rapidly but had stopped abruptly, like a broken clock. Claus took Aftova, placed it behind his two front upper teeth, and pressed it against his palate. Aftova melded like Rigefa had before, and Claus used it to create a proxy shell of himself (Cluffer). As soon as he did that, he and the proxy jumped out of Leni's body and into the chamber with the PRAAD. Leni's body was badly damaged. Smoke rose from the burning of his circuits and servo-mechanisms.

"He saved me," Claus said. "He saved me from the PRAAD."

Claus looked, and the PRAAD continued to let out yellow and blue smoke from its top. Claus felt weak and started to fall toward the PRAAD. With the help of his proxy, he resisted the PRAAD and made his way out of the chamber. He headed back toward Novi 2, shaking the entire way.

"I'll go through the Anrega," Claus said. "Maybe Lanietta can help me."

Claus backtracked through the Anrega until he reached the chamber with the orbs. He walked over to the orbs of Lanietta's parents. Lanietta was still there and still kneeling, but she was more faded than ever.

"Lanietta," Claus called. "Can you hear me? Lanietta?"

There was no response. Claus had Cluffer place his hand on Lanietta's shoulder, but it passed through her.

"Lanietta, I don't know if you know, but I'm sorry. I really am. Lanietta, I—"

Claus could not continue. He was overcome with grief for some odd reason. He swallowed hard and gathered up his strength for one last thing to say.

"I guess I didn't realize how attached I am to you. Too late now," Claus said. "I wish things could be different. I wish we could be friends."

Lanietta remained motionless. Claus tried using Aftova to connect with her, anything, but nothing happened.

"This Aftova stone isn't much help. It seems the magic has run out," Claus said.

Claus had Cluffer slowly back away while still watching Lanietta. She didn't move. He thought he saw a dull, pea-green mist fall on her from above, and her image was now fully shrouded from view.

"Like a casket," Claus muttered to himself, referring to the mist around Lanietta. "Claus, get a hold of yourself. Get back to Labba. If anyone can help, she can."

Claus made his way back to Novi 2. He disabled his proxy Cluffer and returned to his normal self. He removed his space helmet and placed it aside.

"Labba, Novi 2. Come in. This is Claus. Labba, do you read me?" Claus called.

No reply. Claus checked the circuits.

"Fused," Claus said. "Wait, when I had Rigefa, I could communicate to Labba that way. Maybe Aftova can help."

Claus tapped Aftova with his tongue.

"Labba?"

"Claus," Labba's voice said. "Go over to the spectral analyzer and place your hand under the scanner."

Claus did so.

"Keep your hand there," Labba's voice said.

A view screen activated, and Claus could see Labba.

"I can see you now," Claus said.

"Claus, I'm getting intermittent readings from Novi 2. The ship has sustained a systems failure. I thought Leni had Aftova. Where's Leni?" Labba asked.

"I think it best I relay what happened through Aftova," Claus said. "Is that possible?"

"Yes," Labba replied. "Stand by."

Labba held a hushed conversation with Kechenova.

"Doctor, is that you there?" Claus asked.

"Yes," Kechenova said. "We are in Morcellus preparing things. Clover and Selba are in Tabelia."

Kechenova turned back toward Labba and finished their conversation. Both had been busy with their hands tapping buttons and moving controls.

"We're ready," Labba said. "Begin the transfer."

Claus tapped Aftova with his tongue. Labba and Kechenova reviewed the data.

"Claus, this...I...NO!!!" Labba wailed.

Labba fell backward toward the floor, and as she did, her body let forth waves and splashes of ethereal energy. She landed on the floor with a thud and remained there, stunned.

"Labba? Labba!" Claus cried out.

Kechenova motioned for others to help. Labba was taken away.

"Claus, this is Doctor Kechenova. Labba has gone into shock," Kechenova said.

"I had hoped she could help. I don't fully understand what is going on," Claus said.

"Claus, I think I can make sense of things," Kechenova said. "You already know about the Veigon, the Anrega, and the PRAAD and how the PRAAD wants to fuse with the Veigon. Lanietta took the Anrega to the lunar far side. According to the data you received, she learned of the PRAAD and her people through the Anrega. She did not go into the PRAAD chamber herself. The beyton rays were too powerful and prevented her. The Anrega is the only thing that kept her from being completely destroyed. But she learned the fate of her people."

"Are they really gone? The ones on the moon?" Claus asked.

"Claus. When Orchius reintegrated the Tropheia with the rest of the PRAAD, and Libriota connected herself and her people with it, the PRAAD activated part of its reproductive process—the part where it destroys life. It destroyed all Carinians. Everywhere. Permanently."

"Impossible! I don't believe it!" Claus said.

"The best I can see is that it felt threatened the way a mother bear feels her cubs are under attack. It retaliated. They are gone, Claus. Gone! And that's why Labba went into shock. She was too overwhelmed to believe it herself."

"But it didn't kill Labba! And Lanietta is still alive, though barely! How did they escape?" Claus asked.

"The Anrega protects Lanietta currently, though as you say, only barely. Labba is protected by the moon itself. Both were protected by the moon during the initial event," Kechenova said.

"I don't understand," Claus said.

"Claus. The PRAAD did and does put out beyton rays deadly to all Carinians. As the moon rotates, it sweeps those rays across the universe. No place in the universe is safe from such rays, because in time, the lunar far side sweeps across those places, that is except for planet Earth. It is the only celestial body protected from the lunar far side because the moon is face-locked with Earth. Earth only 'sees' the near side. So that's how Labba and Lanietta were spared."

"Then people on the far side of other planets would be protected," Claus said.

"Not quite. I don't know how, but the moon is different. It has interacted with the Veigon, the Anrega, or the PRAAD before. Somehow this has created a core that acts as a beyton absorbent, like a lead shield for radiation," Kechenova said. "The beyton rays also damaged Leni and initially caused your strange transformation into a mountain lion. The idea of using Aftova to hide yourself inside Cluffer was excellent, as it kept you sane enough to escape."

"That was Leni's idea. I found myself inside him after the PRAAD attacked us. He told me to take Aftova and use a proxy," Claus said.

"He saved your life many times," Kechenova said.

"Carinian civilization. Gone. What a blow! It's like watching the extinction of the passenger pigeon," Claus said.

"There are two still alive," Kechenova said.

"They might as well be in a zoo," Claus said.

"Claus, there are no male Carinians left, that's a fact," Kechenova said. "The species can no longer reproduce in that way. Labba is in shock but otherwise uninjured. If the species is to continue, we must prevent Lanietta from dying. Perhaps with her help and Labba's we could find a way to perpetuate the species. How, I do not know. But—"

"But it's up to me to save Lanietta," Claus said.

"Yes," Kechenova said. "Remember the other reason you are there. We need to find a way to reintegrate the Anrega with Earth and prevent the PRAAD from fusing with the Veigon. The data you gleaned from the PRAAD indicates Lanietta was heavily involved with it in primordial times."

"She was always a handful," Claus said. "She just as well might use it against us."

"The Earth will fail soon if we do nothing," Kechenova said. "Therefore your path is clear. You must do everything you can to revive Lanietta."

"I already tried," Claus said. "I used Aftova and everything."

"Hmm," Kechenova said. "It might be that the means by which you used Aftova was ineffective."

"Ineffective," Claus repeated with disdain. "I tried my hardest! I'd give anything to get her back! Do you hear? Anything!"

"You are fond of her?" Kechenova said.

"I guess so," Claus said in resignation. "Maybe it's love. I don't know."

"Do not sound like a condemned prisoner," Kechenova said.

"But isn't that what love is? Condemnation to whatever life the obsession drives? Like the whip of a dictator," Claus said.

"That's not love, and you know it," Kechenova said. "Or at least you should."

"I don't know what to think anymore," Claus said.

"The PRAAD is caught in a between state," Kechenova said. "It cannot decide if it should go dormant or attempt to elicit the help of the Anrega. In fact, it's quite possible Lanietta is preventing it. Her act of kneeling is the equivalent of holding onto the cliff's edge with one hand while holding a fallen climber with the other. She is under tremendous strain to keep the balance."

"I don't think she'll last," Claus said. "Already I saw evidence of her fading."

"She is fading, but slowly," Kechenova said.

Just then, Labba returned to the view screen.

"Labba?" Claus said. "You look barely alive."

"Good day to you too, Claus," Labba managed with a weak smile.

"You should be resting," Claus said.

"No amount of rest will help now," she said. "I must put a foot forward and take the next step. Doctor Kechenova has explained everything to you I take it?"

"Almost everything," Kechenova said. "There's the part about stabilizing Lanietta. And looking for the missing humans."

"Yes!" Claus said. "Frieda and the others! They might be alive yet."

"When we left, they were put into stasis," Labba said. "If still true, you will need either Lanietta or me to bring them out. It's clear I cannot go to the lunar far side. I would be destroyed instantly. Lanietta cannot go unprotected. You'll have to work with her to free them."

"And if they're not in stasis?" Claus asked.

"Then they died long ago from old age, and there's nothing you can do about it," Labba said. "Either way, you can do no good by just looking for them."

"I'm going to," Claus said. "I need to know."

"I would advise against it," Kechenova said. "The beyton rays from the PRAAD are unpredictable. They could kill you."

"Doctor Kechenova is correct. It's incredibly dangerous," Labba said.

"What if I use Cluffer as a proxy? With Aftova? I got away from the PRAAD. It should work," Claus said.

"Yes, it should work," Labba said reluctantly. "Very well. Hurry and find your friends. Then report back to Lanietta immediately. The doctor and I will have a plan formulated by then."

"Thank you," Claus said.

"Keep Aftova in your upper palate, of course. Do not throw it away like Rigefa," Labba said.

"I won't make that mistake again," Claus said.

"Take the shoe with you," Kechenova said.

"The what?" Claus asked in confusion.

"Yes, take the shoe you found on Cenina Island when we walked amongst the rubble," Labba said. "It might prove useful."

"Very well," Claus said.

Claus activated his proxy, Cluffer, and thus put himself inside the proxy. He had Cluffer take the shoe as well and place it inside with Claus. Cluffer then left Novi 2 and went back into the Anrega.

"Lanietta is still here," Claus said as he approached her. "She does look like she's holding something together, employing what little strength she has to hold herself with her parents, maybe to gain more strength. But is she holding off the PRAAD?"

"She is," Labba's voice called through Aftova.

"Labba, I just thought of something. Most of Lanietta is actually in Morcellus. Can't we somehow transfer her from Morcellus to her living image here in the Anrega? Bring her back to life?"

"I have been lobbying for such a thing with Morcellus since first he captured her. I think he might acquiesce," Labba said. "But we must do so carefully and under my guidance. I'm not quite ready, Claus. You have time to seek your friends. Go then. I'll send you directions to their last known location, and it should also keep you away from the PRAAD."

"Thank you," Claus said.

Cluffer traveled through the Anrega and reached the lunar crater portal as before. He entered the former Carinian colony.

"Labba," Claus asked. "Why didn't Leni use Luffer as a shield against the PRAAD?"

"He did," Labba said. "It was the only thing that protected you. You were inside, remember? He did that with Luffer."

"Of course," Claus said. "I must be losing my mind."

"Clear your mind and focus," Labba said.

"You sound like Leni. When this is over, I would like him repaired. He's very helpful," Claus said.

"Be sure to stay inside Cluffer. The air quality is poor or none," Labba said. "Kechenova is monitoring your health, too. She'll make sure you aren't overstressed."

"You're doing fine, Claus," Kechenova said. "I wish I had the chance to fit a harness over you for strength."

"Somehow I don't think it would be appropriate. I had torso armor when I was here before, and it felt like a walking prison," Claus said.

Cluffer walked through passageway after passageway, and then he reached it—the place where he and Bill had found Andrea. Andrea was still there, but now so were the others—Frieda, Josh, Bill, Doctor Morrow, Patricia, and Kevin.

"They are here, Labba. They are all in stasis," Claus said.

"Excellent. Claus, you can't revive them. Not even with Aftova. The time will come for that, hopefully, but for now I need you to return to Lanietta," Labba said.

Claus looked at Frieda.

"I thought I loved Frieda," Claus said. "I guess I thought I was supposed to love her. Maybe I felt I had to fill a void, and I picked her."

"Love doesn't work that way, not true love," Kechenova's voice said. "It picks you, not the other way around."

"I still wish the best for her," Claus said. "She achieved quite a bit."

"Yes, she did," Kechenova said. "We thought she was lost along with the others. I am glad they are not lost."

"And to answer your thought, Claus, no, you are not abandoning them," Labba said. "More than ever is it necessary to preserve human life. The population on Earth is small, and humans risk going extinct."

"Rest easy all of you," Claus said to those in stasis. "I shall return for your freedom."

Cluffer headed back for Lanietta.

"Labba," Claus said. "You mentioned the possibility of Earth's destruction, that it could implode or the PRAAD could fuse with the Veigon."

"Yes," Labba said. "And it almost happened, too."

"What!?" Claus exclaimed. "When? How?"

"Claus, we're still analyzing the data from the PRAAD and Aftova," Kechenova said. "New evidence shows the event that destroyed the Carinians set off a timed event with the PRAAD. The PRAAD influenced people at Astroosa and sent them to Mars to retrieve the Veigon. The PRAAD drove Jill into deep obsession for the Veigon and caused her to return it to Earth exactly where it wanted the Veigon to be."

"Then Jill was influenced? Manipulated by the PRAAD?" Claus asked.

"Yes," Kechenova said. "So was Frieda. Her discovery of the Veigonette stones was a part of the process too. It was all part of the PRAAD's plan to fuse with the Veigon in the Anrega in Earth. Once Jill reunited the Veigon with the Anrega, the PRAAD went into countdown mode for the final moment. It coordinated things with the Veigon and the Anrega, causing things like the snow melt around Novi 2 and Lanietta's strange behavior. It used Lanietta to make preparations for the final moment, and it almost won. Lanietta was brainwashed by the PRAAD and the Veigon into believing she could use the Veigon's power to win a battle against Libriota. But something happened when she arrived on the lunar far side, and the PRAAD is now in a holding mode."

"What happened?" Claus asked.

"We don't know," Labba said. "One thing is for sure. Casting Rigefa into the Veigon hole was not part of the plan, nor was bringing the Anrega to the lunar far side. In a way, you deviated from the PRAAD's plans. And so did Lanietta."

"Then there's hope," Claus said. "There's hope we can stop this PRAAD thing."

"Only barely," Labba said.

"New information," Kechenova said. "The PRAAD's countdown continues."

"I thought you said it was in a holding mode," Claus said.

"My apologies. It is actually proceeding at an incredibly small rate of speed. I didn't notice it before," Kechenova said. "But it's there. It's counting down."

"How much time?" Claus asked.

"It varies," Kechenova said. "Lanietta is inhibiting the countdown. Could be months. Could be days."

"Days!" Claus exclaimed. "Okay, I'm in the Anrega. I'll reach Lanietta soon."

"Cluffer is holding up okay?" Labba asked.

"A-okay," Claus said.

"Good," Labba replied.

"I've reached Lanietta. She looks the same," Claus said.

"Look closely at her hands," Labba said. "Do you see Fronfa or Rigefa? Use Aftova to ask for them."

Claus had Cluffer hold a hand each over Lanietta's left and right hands. Aftova sent out a scan signal. Fronfa replied from Lanietta's left hand and Rigefa from Lanietta's right.

"She has both. Fronfa in her left hand, Rigefa in her right," Claus said.

"Face Lanietta and place a hand each on the orbs," Labba said. "Your left hand should be on the same orb as her right, and your right on the orb of her left."

"Cluffer has done so," Claus said.

"You are about to be used as a medium, Claus," Labba said. "Lanietta, Fronfa, Rigefa, the two orbs, Aftova, Cluffer, we, and Morcellus will all connect together through you. We will strengthen Lanietta through you. In the process, you might experience visions of the past. This is part of the strengthening process. We are strengthening her past to strengthen her future. Cluffer will take care of your physiological needs during this process. All you need do is tap Aftova three times, pause, tap once, pause, and tap three times again. Are you ready?"

Claus took a deep breath.

"I am ready," Claus said.

"We will begin with the Big Bang," Kechenova said. "You may proceed, Claus."

This was it for Claus. He didn't know what to expect, like that moment before jumping into a lake of unknown depth and temperature. What would he find in the lake? What would these visions reveal? Would he be the same afterward? Would there be an afterward? The thought of Earth's destruction preyed upon his mind, and he knew action was needed.

"There's nothing for it. Onward I go!" Claus said, and he tapped Aftova as prescribed.

Chapter 65: The Beginning

"Hello?" Claus called. "It's dark. Hello?"

Claus found himself in complete darkness. He stood on something flat and solid, but beyond that he could sense nothing. A soft blue light shone from his feet, and he realized it was just him and not Cluffer. He moved his tongue to search for Aftova in his palate, but he was cautioned otherwise.

"Don't disturb Aftova," Labba's voice said.

"Labba!" Claus called. "Where are you?"

"In Morcellus with Doctor Kechenova," Labba said.

"Then where am I?" Claus asked.

"Not where, when," Labba said. "It's the beginning of time in our universe."

"I'm so alone," Claus said. "Where's Lanietta? Shouldn't she be here with me? We could watch this together."

"It is not that way," Labba said. "Lanietta is still with you in the Anrega orb chamber, but in this vision it is just you."

"I feel disoriented. Confused. Like I'll dissolve any moment," Claus said.

A distant point of light caught Claus's attention. It spent several seconds as blue, and then it changed to yellow for a half second before going back to blue.

"I see a light," Claus said. "Blue then yellow and now blue. It's like a strange traffic light far away. Now I'm walking on a rural road. It's paved, new, and flat. But it's still dark."

"By human estimates, this is fourteen billion years ago," Kechenova said. "No one knows for sure, though."

"It's like time has no meaning," Claus said. "But the light is something."

When the light went yellow, a circle of bright orange and yellow light burst forth, expanding with increasing diameter from the blue and yellow light. It then approached Claus, collapsed on itself, and became a swirling spherical iron mass.

"What am I seeing?" Claus asked. "Labba? Doctor?"

"Stand by, Claus," Labba said. "It's taking us a moment to analyze."

"Don't you know what this is?" Claus asked.

"You're implying I know everything there is about the universe," Labba said. "But I don't. I'm piecing together what I know from my own past with what Morcellus has taught me plus recent knowledge from the Veigon, Anrega, PRAAD, the Veigonette stones, and even Doctor Kechenova's knowledge and expertise."

"It's the Anrega," Kechenova said.

"With the Veigon inside," Labba said.

"It came through the Big Bang," Kechenova said.

"Before it went bang," Labba said.

"What Big Bang?" Claus asked.

But then the blue light went super bright and turned the black of night into a white night. Nothing seen but a sense of something everywhere. Instead of Claus feeling drained from the black of night, he felt filled with the white. It was over in an instant, and all about him Claus saw clouds of dust and gas swirling quickly, forming stars, planets, and galaxies. The galaxies divided and flew apart quickly, but they slowed just as quickly. Claus watched as the Anrega traveled through space and came upon a new solar system.

"It's now eight billion years ago," Kechenova said.

"The Anrega has reached the Carinian solar system," Labba said. "There's Carinia Zero, our red dwarf star. The Anrega is approaching it."

"You can see all of this then?" Claus asked.

"Yes. Aftova is relaying imagery," Labba said.

"And considerable information," Kechenova said.

"Something just launched from the Anrega," Claus said. "Did you see it?"

"The Veigon has launched an Amnus, an egg if you will," Kechenova said.

"It's heading for Carinia Zero," Labba said.

"The star? It will be destroyed," Claus said. "It looks like the PRAAD."

"It is the same type of thing, though it is not the current PRAAD as you know it, no more than one chicken egg is the same as another. Both are eggs, both are from chickens, but both have different histories and times of existence," Labba said.

"The Amnus is in Carinia Zero," Kechenova said.

"I don't understand," Claus said. "It created an egg on its own. Why didn't it, I mean on Cenina Island, it could have—"

"It's all part of a cycle, from what I can tell," Kechenova said.

"But I thought the Martaceans had to create the egg," Claus said. "The Veigon created it?"

Labba and Kechenova paused. Then Labba explained.

"It appears that this happened before there were any Martaceans," Labba said. "This is to *prime the pump*, to borrow an expression. To get things going."

"Yes," Kechenova said. "It appears that the egg is actually created from an unborn Martacean couple inside the Veigon. So in a sense, it is still created by a super couple, but in this case they are inside the Veigon instead of outside."

"The Veigon seems to have a priority system," Labba said. "At the top level, it waits for an existing Amnus to return. If not, it waits for the super couple to create an egg. If no super couple, it creates another super couple if appropriate. If not appropriate, it creates another Amnus. The last option is last because it results in the least amount of progress. I don't know if this makes sense, but that's the best I can explain."

"I guess in a way it does," Claus said.

"The current Amnus—the PRAAD—has not returned, so it is still waiting," Labba said.

"*It* meaning the Veigon?" Claus asked.

"Yes, when the Veigon is part of the Anrega. All three must come together for the next part of the cycle," Labba said. "Look, there's the Amnus now. It has returned from Carinia Zero."

"It's heading for the Anrega," Claus said. "It's collided with the Anrega."

"The Amnus was energized by Carinia Zero," Kechenova said.

"I believe that's what it does," Labba said. "It picks up energy and knowledge and adds it to its repository."

"But why?" Claus asked.

"That will be the next step," Labba said.

"The Anrega is swirling with colors of yellow and blue," Kechenova said.

"It's about to go planar," Labba said. "I've heard about this but never seen it."

"Who? What? Planar?" Claus said all confused.

"Just watch," Labba said.

The Anrega flattened into a disk and entered the first planet of the Carinian solar system, that of Carinia 1.

"This is how it does it," Labba said. "It compresses its mass to nearly no thickness. And it enters a planet. Look. Carinia 1 has increased in size."

"The Anrega has de-planarized," Kechenova said.

"It's growing incredibly fast!" Claus said. "It will consume the entire universe!"

"Actually, you are accelerating toward the planet," Kechenova said. "It only appears to be getting incredibly large."

"Well where is Lanietta in all this?" Claus asked.

"Not here yet," Labba said.

Claus entered through Carinia 1's atmosphere and landed on an island.

"This looks like Cenina Island," Claus said.

"It is very similar," Labba said.

"There's a central peak, but there's a...what is that, some sort of river flowing down along a ridge," Claus said. "There are things swimming in the river. They...they're going into the ocean."

"The first Martaceans," Labba said. "I never thought I'd see this. Such purity and innocence. Before Carinians existed, before the fighting and struggle, there was this."

"They are beautiful," Kechenova said. "Very much like Earth cetaceans."

"Labba," Claus said. "These creatures. The Veigon created them?"

"Yes. From stored DNA," she replied.

"Truly incredible," Kechenova said. "We witnessed the Anrega and Veigon come from the Big Bang. In fact they came through just before the Big Bang. All indications are that they came from a previous universe."

"Does this mean Carinian life came from a previous universe? Earth life too?" Claus asked.

"An interesting speculation," Kechenova said. "No one knows for sure from where Earth life came."

"But this Anrega was in Earth. Maybe it had something to do with life on Earth. Life from a previous universe," Claus said. "One has to wonder what the previous universe was like. And why such a thing came through."

"Perhaps it was sent through," Kechenova said. "If you knew the universe was about to collapse, and you wanted to preserve what you could of life, how would you do it?"

"Then the Anrega and Veigon are an ark, like Noah's Ark," Claus said.

"It would seem so," Kechenova said.

"Labba, is it true?" Claus asked.

"Don't ask me. I wasn't around in the previous universe. But Doctor Kechenova's theory seems reasonable. Everything I've seen indicates as such," Labba said.

"Then to destroy the Anrega and Veigon—"

"Would destroy the ark," Kechenova said. "Not only would we lose all records of the prior universe, we would lose a means for carrying our own history into the next."

"Look, do you see?" Claus asked.

"Yes, we see," Labba replied. "Plants and lower animals are flourishing on the island. Birds too."

"Everything is happening so quickly. It's like watching evolution at high speed."

"Look. The first Carinian hominids," Labba said.

"Making the first social groups now," Kechenova said.

"I still can't believe how quickly time is passing," Claus said. "They are making sail boats now. Leaving the island. Oh! I've been taken along one of the sailboats. Now I'm on a main continent. More social groups. Hunting and hunting and more hunting."

"Great herds are being slaughtered," Kechenova said. "The ecosystem is changing."

"And not for the better," Labba said.

"What year is this now?" Claus asked.

"About seven billion years ago," Kechenova said. "These people seem to be ancestors of Bleuhs."

"They are," Labba said. "But they are mortal."

"One group is befriending the Martaceans," Kechenova said. "They call themselves Gerenba. They live on the coast in permanent dwellings, organized in villages. They have schools, libraries, town centers, markets, medical facilities, and so on."

"They fish and cultivate crops," Labba said.

"It's the beginning of a cultural divide," Kechenova said. "The other Carinians continue to hunt and are nomadic. They keep no records and have no sense of long-term planning. The Gerenba refer to the hunters as Belukaluk."

"Early Bleuhs," Labba said.

"Something's happening," Claus said. "The Gerenba are not content with their happy life on the coast. I wonder why."

"They know about the excessive hunting by the Belukaluk. They know the planet cannot sustain such activity," Kechenova said.

"So this is how the Grens did it," Labba said.

"Grens?" Claus asked.

"Yes. Even now, they are making arrangements with a Martacean to take aboard their entire village," Labba said. "They are heading to the Veigon. Look. The Veigon has sent them from Carinia 1 to Carinia 2."

"What? I don't believe it," Claus said. "How is this...but...why would they?"

"They know things will end soon," Labba said. "They did what we are doing now. Claus, it's very important you continue this vision as long as possible. We need all the time we can muster to gather up the people of Earth. We must evacuate them before it is too late."

"You're giving up on Earth?" Claus said.

"I'm doing as the Gerenba," Labba said. "I'm hedging bets on a new place that is safe and not at risk."

"Where is that place, though? Do you know?" Claus asked.

"There are other planets in other solar systems," Labba said. "It might take time to get there. But at least everyone will be in space and safe from the Amnus cycle. Claus, you must be ready with Frieda and her group should the time come. We will spend only a brief moment to retrieve you all."

Claus paused.

"You're indecisive?" Kechenova asked.

"You're in on this too?" Claus asked.

"Continuation is important," Kechenova said. "We must safeguard against the—"

"Inevitable," Claus said. "That's what you were going to say, right?"

"I would choose a different word," Kechenova said.

"Claus, you know the cycle of the universe. Things die and start anew from the smallest of seeds," Labba said. "But it takes a great deal of time for the seed to mature into a tree. There need not be such a delay for humanity. We can minimize loss of life and time."

Claus paused again.

"I'm still an island," he muttered. "I'm at the mercy of whatever ship passes my way."

"The Gerenba culture is taking a good foothold on Carinia 2," Kechenova said. "But there is no additional data on them."

"There is no Anregan presence on Carinia 2. That's why," Labba said.

"Something's happening in the ocean on Carinia 1," Claus said. "Martaceans are dying off."

"We see it," Labba said. "They are competing. The weak are dying off. The strong are surviving to compete again."

"It's part of the Amnus cycle," Kechenova said. "The Veigon senses the planetary over-consumption by the Belukaluk. Other life-forms are migrating to the island and integrating with the Veigon. Their DNA will be carried into the next cycle."

"I'm back on the Cenina-like Island," Claus said. "It looks like the last Martaceans are here. Just two of them. There's an energy beam coming from the mountain peak."

"It's happening," Labba said. "The creation of the next Amnus egg."

The female Martacean produced an egg. The egg was carried back up the beam to the mountain peak.

"There are people on this island," Claus said. "Belukaluk. One looks like a young Libriota."

"It is Libriota," Labba said. "I didn't realize she was this old."

"The Belukaluk are mortal though," Kechenova said.

"What is she doing here?" Claus asked. "I thought the Belukaluk were on the mainland."

"She's investigating," Kechenova said. "Seeking a means for acquiring power."

"That's Libriota," Labba said. "She got her start early."

"How does she become immortal?" Claus asked.

"Let's see what happens," Labba said.

From the central opening on the mountain peak came forth the Amnus egg. It was shot out and flew directly into outer space. It headed for and entered Carinia Zero.

"It's in the star," Kechenova said.

"Libriota is climbing the mountain peak," Claus said. "She has climbed the mountain peak. What is she doing?"

"She is trying to influence the Veigon," Kechenova said.

"Another beam is coming out of the Veigon," Claus said. "It's directed at Libriota. She's hit. Oh, she fell."

"She's only stunned," Labba said.

"The Amnus is returning from Carinia Zero. Like before, it's a glowing ball of plasma," Kechenova said.

"Libriota is back on her feet," Claus said. "She's leaning over the opening to the Veigon. She'll be killed for sure!"

"She can't be killed," Labba said. "She survived all this to cause problems another day."

The Amnus dove down through the opening toward the Veigon. As it did, Libriota put out a hand to catch plasma finger flickers. Her hand was burned, and bits of the plasma overcame her body. She dove off the mountain peak into a pool of water below to douse the flames. Nearby Belukaluk pulled her out of the water and tended to her injuries, but they too caught part of the plasma fingers and suffered burns.

"That's how it happened," Labba said.

"Yes. The bit of plasma from the returning Amnus has changed them and made them immortal," Kechenova said.

A blast of flame rose forth from the Veigon. The blast sent Libriota and her Belukaluk into the ocean. The Anrega went planar, rose from the mountain peak, and left Carinia 1. The effect created a great tidal wave that carried Libriota and her Belukaluk from the ocean onto the mainland.

"They are now Bleuhs," Kechenova said. "The other mainland Belukaluk have perished."

"What a vicious thing this Anrega and Veigon are," Claus said. "They pick up and leave without warning then destroy life all around. I'm surprised these early Bleuhs survived."

"The Amnus gave them protection, at least a little bit," Kechenova said.

"Libriota never reported this part of Bleuh history," Labba said. "I can see why it's been a closely guarded secret."

"The Amnus has also made them sterile. They cannot have children as once they did," Kechenova said.

"I don't think Libriota has had any children before or after this change from Belukaluk to Bleuh," Labba said. "Unless that's another secret."

Claus was suddenly whisked away from Carinia 1 and placed into outer space.

"Whoa!" Claus exclaimed. "What happened there? Wait, I see the Anrega. It's still planar, and it's heading for a planet."

"That's Carinia 2," Labba said.

"I'm following the Anrega!" Claus said. "This is weird!"

"Stay with the vision," Labba said.

"Well, Carinia 2 is getting larger. I know, I'm getting closer," Claus said. "There it goes. The Anrega dove into the planet. The planet just got bigger."

Claus turned toward Carinia 1.

"Yes, Carinia 1 shrank," Kechenova said. "But it did not collapse. It's solid and cohesive."

"Then Earth might not be destroyed," Claus said. "There's a chance."

"There's a chance," Labba said.

"I'm being sent to another Cenina-ish Island on Carinia 2. Do you see this?" Claus asked.

"The Veigon is releasing large amounts of water," Kechenova said. "It's creating oceans on Carinia 2."

"Now I see Martaceans coming from the Veigon," Claus said. "Along with other life-forms. Just like on Carinia 1. But no hominids."

"The cycle continues," Labba said. "It's releasing life on Carinia 2."

"Only to destroy it later, right?" Claus said. "What a dirty trick."

"Claus," Labba said. "Keep steady. This is in the past. There's nothing you can do about it except to keep the vision going. One thing though, the Veigon has decided not to create people on Carinia 2. Perhaps this is in reaction to the Belukaluk on Carinia 1."

"Maybe not such a dirty trick," Claus said. "How long ago was this?"

"Six billion years ago," Kechenova said.

"There are already Carinians here," Labba said.

"The Gerenba?" Claus asked. "They did come over from Carinia 1."

"My people," Labba said.

"Almost," Kechenova said. "They are Gerenba and still mortal. The Anrega has yet to change them."

"I can't keep track," Claus said.

"Track of what?" Kechenova said.

"How you can decide what the Veigon does and what the Anrega does," Claus said.

"We do not decide anything," Kechenova said. "Recall the Veigon is the brains or nucleus of the Martacean cycle. The Anrega is the body or cytoplasm. The Anrega has power and capacity. Some things it does in response to the Veigon, other things on its own like a reflex action or echo of past directives."

"Don't worry about it, Claus. Stick with the vision," Labba said.

"I'm being swept over to the mainland," Claus said.

"The Gerenba have made great progress with agriculture and community living," Kechenova said.

"Yes, we are very much into our planet," Labba said. "Or we were. We still had corporeal bodies at this point. See? And my people could have children. No procreation tanks."

"Larto will be born soon," Kechenova said.

"That's Lanietta's father," Labba said.

"What about Lanietta's mother?" Claus asked. "And what's this about procreation tanks?"

"Lanietta's mother isn't born yet," Kechenova said. "Libriota pioneered procreation tanks to deal with the Bleuh infertility problem."

"How do you know that?" Claus asked. "This vision doesn't show Carinia 1 right now. There's no Anrega or Veigon there."

"Because of the Greylingers in the Anrega," Labba said. "So this is how it started."

"Much later, the Bleuhs learned how to go ethereal and space-jump. The negative effect was a buildup of Greylingers in the Anrega. Through that negative transmission of energy, we're able to learn about the Bleuhs on Carinia 1," Kechenova said.

"Libriota said something about Greylingers," Claus said.

"It's a long story," Labba said. "It's like ethereal waste. Imagine if the garbage you throw away ends up in the ocean and becomes creatures more terrible and vicious than sharks, able to bite into hulls of ships and sink them. That's like the Greylingers."

"The Anrega wants to leave again," Kechenova said.

"What? Why? The Gerenba didn't do anything," Claus said.

"That's why it wants to leave," Kechenova said. "Not enough hostile life-forms to store in the Veigon."

"Martacean population is becoming competitive and dying off," Labba said. "Soon another Amnus egg will form."

"The Anrega is having trouble building up the energy to go planar," Kechenova said. "Greylingers are sapping its strength."

"Just two Martaceans now," Labba said.

"They've created an Amnus egg," Kechenova said.

"The Amnus is launched from the Veigon," Labba said.

"And on its way to Carinia Zero," Kechenova said.

Claus's vision flickered. He alternated between seeing the orb chamber in the lunar Anrega and watching the Amnus head toward Carinia Zero.

"I'm losing the vision," Claus said.

"We know," Labba said.

"We're under attack," Kechenova said. "Selenite ships."

"I thought they were destroyed," Claus said.

"Just the ones around Cenina Island," Labba said. "They still exist around the world."

"And they are impeding our progress," Kechenova said. "We just finished evacuating New Zealand and were about to start with Australia."

"Return fire," Labba said.

"What about the vision?" Claus asked.

"We'll have to resume in a bit," Kechenova said. "Claus, we might lose connection with you."

"Whatever you do, Claus, don't—" Labba started, but the connection with Kechenova and her failed.

"Labba? Doctor? Hello! Anyone?" Claus called.

But Claus was left alone in the Anrega orb chamber. Lanietta remained motionless and unchanged.

"She hasn't faded," Claus said. "At least there's that. Wait, no, she's starting to fade again. I must do something. Lanietta? Hold on!"

Chapter 66: Clausy is #1

"Labba? Doctor Kechenova? Anyone?" Claus called again.

Nothing.

"Lanietta?" Claus called.

Still nothing. Claus tapped Aftova with his tongue several times, but still he could get word to no one.

"There's only one thing left then. I don't know why I've held onto this or how it got on Cenina Island. Here goes," Claus said.

Claus had Cluffer place the woman's shoe from Cenina Island next to the orb touched by Lanietta's right hand.

"Lanietta, I don't know if you can hear me, but if this works, maybe we can share this memory together," Claus said. "It's not something I'm proud of. Matter of fact, it's one of my greatest regrets."

Claus felt himself leaving the Anrega and entering another time and place.

"Clausy," Claus's mother called.

Claus looked around and realized he was in his maternal grandmother's house. He was young, perhaps nine years old. But it was just his family. No Lanietta.

"Grandma Broc," Claus said. "I remember this place."

"I hope so," Claus's father said. "I'm taking your mother out for dinner and dancing."

"I wanna go!" Claus said without realizing his desire was driven by his younger self.

"I'm sorry, sweetie," Claus's mother said. "Be a good boy and keep your grandma company."

Young Claus pouted.

"What about my bedtime story?" young Claus begged.

"Grandma can read you a bedtime story," Claus's mother said. "She'll tuck you in for the night too."

"Yuck," young Claus said.

"Behave, Clausy. That's your grandma," Claus's father said.

"Let me kiss you," Claus's mother said.

She leaned over toward Claus to kiss him on the forehead, but she stood awkwardly, her medium-height heel made her ankle twist sideways, and she fell.

"Aubert!"

"Elaine!"

Claus's parents called each other by their first names as Aubert caught Elaine's hand and thus prevented injury.

"I thought I hurt my ankle," Elaine said. "But it's fine. We can dance the night away."

The two left. It was late afternoon on a Saturday. Claus's grandmother worked in her garden while Claus played in a sandbox. Passersby waved and said hello.

"Hello, Dora," they always said.

"Hello. I have Clausy with me today," she often replied.

"Oh what a cute boy," they would then reply.

Some pinched his cheek, others rubbed his hair, but very few left him untouched. One actually shook his hand, which he thought was quite odd.

"I don't like being touched like that, Grandma," young Claus said after a time.

"They can't resist my cute and adorable grandson," she said.

"I don't want to be cute and adorable," young Claus said.

Dora smiled.

"When you get older, the girls will chase you. You'll have to be careful. Pick the very best. With red hair," Dora added.

"Grandma!" young Claus protested.

Dora had red hair as did Elaine, but Claus didn't pick up the trait. His hair was brown.

"Or at least she should make a good elderberry wine," Dora said. "When you're older, you'll appreciate the elderberry. Cures respiratory and digestive ailments."

"May I have some?" young Claus asked.

"If you're good, I'll let you have a little sip," she said. "Let's go for a walk, and then I'll have to start dinner."

Dora took young Claus by the hand and led him to the sidewalk in front of the house.

"If you're ever walking through the neighborhood, the sidewalk is safe. Stay out of the road," Dora said. "Cars around here take that corner too quickly and won't see you. See? There's another one."

A car zipped by.

"You'll feel safe on the sidewalk, but as long as you stay on the sidewalk, you must watch for cars. They might pull into a driveway as you cross it. Or other things," she said. "Let's go this way."

Dora's house was on a corner, and so the two followed the sidewalk around the corner so as to walk by the side yard.

"Now I have a secret I want to share with you," Dora said. "Don't tell your parents."

"What is it?" young Claus pined.

"There are times you will need to leave the sidewalk," Dora said.

Just before the sidewalk ventured past Dora's property, the two walked back onto her property and followed its edge on the grassy section until it reached a woods.

"The woods!" young Claus said.

"Yes, Clausy," she said. "Part of you must walk the sidewalk day to day. Most people stay on the sidewalk. But there's a part of me in you that will yearn to escape the sidewalk for the woods. Here, let's go on this little path."

The two entered, and suddenly the sun was mostly blocked out as was the ambient sound of traffic. Spots of sunlight came through here and there, the air smelled of wholesome wood, and the ground was covered in coniferous needles and ancient rock.

"Do you hear the cars?" she asked.

"No. I hear birds and water running," young Claus said.

"Do you understand what I said about the sidewalk now?" she asked.

"I don't know," young Claus said.

"People might think that's all there is. The sidewalk and the cars. The cars distract them from other things," Dora said. "There are other voices in the world, voices that are forgotten or not rediscovered. Listen to the water!"

Dora led Claus to a stream.

"See the water? See how it flows over the little rocks?" Dora asked.

"It's always the same," young Claus said.

"Go up to a rock. Put your hand on the rock," Dora said.

Young Claus did so.

"Is the water the same?" Dora asked.

"No," young Claus said. "It splashes. It's not the same."

"Now come back with me," she said. "Is it the same?"

"It is," young Claus said. "The water has a shape. It stays the same."

"It doesn't stay the same," Dora said.

"Yah-huh," young Claus said.

"This water that you see is passing this way only once. You will never see it again. The water changes constantly. That's why you can splash it. If it didn't, you couldn't make a splash. You must remember this Clausy. The cars that drive by don't even know about this brook. They don't realize the water is ever-changing and will never be the same again. My family remembers through our last name, Broc. It means 'brook'. The brook reminds us that we came from somewhere and are going somewhere. The brook is here, but the water will go somewhere else. It might disappear into the ground and stay there for millions of years, never to be seen again. Or it might drain into the ocean and become salt water instead of fresh. Many outcomes are possible."

"Where are you from?" young Claus asked.

"I'm from here. This town. I was born in this house and have lived here my entire life," Dora said.

"Mommy said you're Irish," young Claus said.

"What are you, Clausy?" Dora asked.

"I'm a boy," young Claus said.

Dora laughed.

"Are you Irish?" she asked.

"I don't know. I know I'm an American," he said.

"So am I," Dora said.

"But what about before that? What about your parents?" young Claus asked. "Can we ask them?"

Dora paused for a moment and regathered her strength.

"They have gone on to other places," she replied.

"Oh," young Claus said.

"But before that, they grew up in Ireland then came over here to the United States," Dora said.

"So you're Irish!" young Claus said.

Dora laughed.

"Only for a little while," she said.

"Huh?"

"My family lived in Ireland for a few generations. Before that they lived in England. Before that in France. Before that in Denmark. And before that in—"

"The Garden of Eden?" young Claus asked with excitement.

"Perhaps!" Dora said. "No one knows for sure. But you see? Each step along the way is the next stone in the brook."

"I want to step on the stones in the brook. I want to!" young Claus said.

Claus went to run across the stones, but he slipped and fell into the water. Dora rushed in and pulled him out.

"Going from stone to stone is not so easy but often necessary," she said. "Easier is standing on the bank and enjoying its beauty. Yes, the brook is beautiful but deceptive."

"I don't know what that means," young Claus said.

"It means the brook is hiding things. You thought you could step on those stones quickly, but you learned otherwise," Dora said. "Try to remember about the brook. You'll understand better when you're older. Some people go through their entire lives and never understand. They only understand the road and the sidewalk— never the brook."

"I will try," young Claus said.

"You're my only grandchild. You're my number one," Dora said.

Dora gave Claus a big hug.

"There's a way you can remember," Dora said. "So that when you are older and I'm gone, you can understand."

"Where are you going?" young Claus said.

"Someday I hope to be in the afterlife with my elders," Dora said.

"Don't go away!" young Claus said.

Dora smiled and hugged young Claus.

"It is not my choice but that of the great keeper of life," she said. "You can remember in this way. When we get back to the house, write down what I told you."

"Okay," young Claus said.

The two returned to the house. The afternoon was late, and it was time for dinner. Dora placed paper and a pencil on a table in the enclosed porch for young Claus.

"Now write what I told you while I make dinner," Dora said.

Young Claus sat at the table in the porch. He picked up the pencil and meant to write something, but the table was high for him, and the blank paper stared back at him, leaving him feeling blank. He dropped the pencil and walked out into the yard. He walked around the house and wondered why there wasn't a brook around it with stones every so often.

He ended his walk by going into the garage. Grandma had kept up the house repairs herself, and so the garage contained her tools. He looked through them and was fascinated by those he understood and those he didn't. He felt the need to pick up the hammer, and he did. He tapped it against spare wood. Then he had an idea. He would nail two pieces of wood together at right angles. But it didn't work. He didn't have enough hands to both hold the wood pieces and nail them together. Frustrated, he gave up.

"Whatchya doin'?" a voice asked.

A young girl perhaps eleven years in age stood behind Claus in the garage. Was it Lanietta as a girl? He didn't remember having company. And he was sure the next thing he did was by himself.

"I was going to make something," young Claus said. "I don't know what."

"Oh," she said.

"My grandma said I should write down what she said," Claus said.

"What did she say?" the girl asked.

"She said I'm number one," young Claus replied.

The girl laughed.

"You think it's funny?" young Claus said.

"I bet she said more than that," she said.

"She did, but I didn't understand it. I'm going to write what I remember. I'm number one," young Claus said.

"How?" she asked.

Claus looked at the hammer, the box of nails, and the wood.

"I can't hold this wood together and nail it. I need something to hold the wood for me," young Claus said.

"I'll hold it for you," the young girl said.

"No. You're a girl," young Claus said.

She laughed again.

"I'll show you! I'll do it all by myself," young Claus said.

"Do what?" she asked.

"Watch!" he said.

Young Claus took the hammer and nails, and he marched to the front of the house. The house had nice white-painted wood siding, and this was the wood young Claus had in mind. Nail by nail, he pounded out the following phrase on a single piece of siding:

Clausy is #1

"Uh oh. You're in trouble," the girl said, and she ran away.

Young Claus felt guilty. He rushed the hammer and nails back to the garage, looked for tape, found duct tape, and placed strips over the nails. He returned the roll of tape to the garage then ran to the porch and scribbled lines on the paper.

"Dinner is ready," Dora said.

Young Claus was quiet during dinner.

"Do you like it? I made spaghetti. Your favorite," Dora said.

"It's yummy," young Claus said, still worried about the siding.

"Your great grandfather loved spaghetti too," Dora said. "I bet he's eating spaghetti right now."

"Really? Where?" young Claus asked.

"Oh, somewhere in Germany," Dora said wishfully. "He lost his way when his plane was shot down. But he'll return. Someday. He'll return."

"He flew in an airplane? Wow!" young Claus said. "Was it yesterday? Was he in the airplane yesterday?"

Dora paused a moment, looked down, and looked at young Claus with a smile.

"Yes, Clausy. It was yesterday," she said metaphorically.

Dora opened the window, looked out as if watching for her father's return, then she returned to the table and put the dinner away.

"Now you may have either a sip of elderberry wine or ice cream, but not both. Which would you like?" Dora asked.

Young Claus paused.

"I really want ice cream," he said. "Can't I have a sip of wine and ice cream too?"

"It might make you sick," she said.

"Can I put chocolate syrup in the wine?" young Claus asked.

Dora laughed.

"That wouldn't do," she said.

"Maybe I'll try the elderberry wine another time," he said.

"Good boy," she said.

Dora gave young Claus a bowl of ice cream and a bottle of chocolate syrup. Young Claus squeezed lots of syrup onto the ice cream and ate while Dora put dishes in the dishwasher and started it.

"I should have had the wine," adult Claus said to himself. "But I was a selfish kid and wanted my ice cream loaded up with chocolate syrup."

Dora left for the living room and turned on the television to a Gene Autry movie, keeping the bottle of elderberry wine and a glass for herself. She poured the wine into her glass, took several sips, and exhaled with satisfaction. Young Claus then noticed the eleven-year-old girl in the window.

"In your grandmother's mind, it seemed like yesterday," the eleven-year-old girl said.

"What?" young Claus asked, not understanding the girl.

"Yesterday. When her father left. But it wasn't yesterday. It was during World War II. Her father was a gunner on a B-17 bomber that was shot down. The crew escaped and was accounted for except her father. The official explanation was that Dora's father couldn't escape the ball turret in time, but there was never definitive evidence."

Young Claus moved closer to the window. The girl continued.

"'He'll return someday,' she would always say. 'Some nice German woman is nursing him back to health.' But he never did."

"How do you know?" young Claus asked.

The scene changed, and Claus was back in the Anrega orb chamber. Lanietta remained unchanged, but the eleven-year-old girl appeared in ethereal form next to Claus.

"I'm her," she said. "You know, Lanietta as a girl. Your history of Earth is flowing through me."

"You're Lanietta? As a girl?" Claus asked.

Young Lanietta nodded yes.

"Let's go back to your grandmother," she said.

The two returned to Dora's house, but only as ethereal visitors. Adult Claus saw his youthful self playing with his ice cream and taking his time to eat it.

"You don't know what's happening, do you?" young Lanietta said. "Your grandmother and her father saw this movie many times at the movie theater. It was their favorite."

"I never knew. She never told me," adult Claus said.

"Young people miss out on visual cues. They are often within themselves," young Lanietta said. "Look, the movie is ending."

"Time to go to bed, Clausy," Dora said.

"Do I have to?" young Claus protested.

"Yes," Dora said.

"But Mommy and Daddy aren't back yet," young Claus said.

"They'll see you in the morning," Dora said.

Dora led young Claus to wash up and go to bed. Dora cleaned up from young Claus's ice cream and retired to her bedroom with the elderberry wine, where she turned on her bedroom television to a collection of B-17 action films showing German fighter planes during World War II. Dora hummed songs from Gene Autry.

"He's coming home tomorrow," Dora said to herself. "See? That's him. He just bailed out."

"How sad," adult Claus said. "She misses Great-Grandpa. I never knew him, of course. Well, that's it for this memory. I'm glad I got a part of you going."

"It's not over," young Lanietta said. "You started something, Claus. We must see it through. Like the water in the brook. It always goes somewhere. So does this story."

"Let's not. Please?" Claus pleaded.

"You sound like a little boy," young Lanietta said. "I will fade if we don't see the rest. I'm barely holding together now."

Claus paused. He looked around the Anrega orb chamber. Adult Lanietta continued her pose and flickered under the strain. He nodded yes. The two returned to Nora's home in time to see Elaine and Aubert's return from dinner and dance. It was nighttime and dark. Aubert parked and opened the car door for Elaine.

"Thank you," she said. "I had a wonderful evening. *Perfectionus maximus.*"

"As always, Elaine. As always," Aubert said. "Now let's go inside and say good night to—"

Elaine looked where Aubert looked, which was at the duct tape over the siding. It was quite easy to see, because ground lights flooded upward onto the house.

"Oh no," Elaine said. "Has our little author struck again?"

Aubert walked over to the siding and removed the tape, revealing Claus's work.

"This is the closest to an author he'll ever be," Aubert said.

"I was a stupid kid!" Claus said. "Why was I stupid? Why didn't I think?"

Elaine stormed into the house with Aubert close behind. They went into the bedroom where young Claus slept, they turned on the lights, Elaine put young Claus over her knee, took off her shoe, and used the shoe to paddle his behind repeatedly. Young Claus cried.

"That's enough, Elaine," Aubert said.

"It's not enough!" she said. "This is my mother's house! He's ruined it!"

"I didn't mean to!" young Claus cried.

Aubert took the shoe from Elaine. The paddling ended.

"Shh," Elaine said. "Cry yourself to sleep."

Elaine and Aubert finished with young Claus. Elaine gathered up her composure enough to check on Dora. Her bedroom television was still on with B-17 bomber action on the screen, but she was no longer awake. Elaine turned off the television, and she along with Aubert retired for the night in another guest room.

"You were punished," young Lanietta said. "I'm sorry."

"You are?" adult Claus asked.

"Yes. It's tough being young sometimes," she said. "Images are passing more quickly now. See? It's morning already. Elaine is screaming. She's discovered her mother has passed. There's the wake before the funeral. Very small. Just Elaine, Aubert, you, and local folk. Elaine is telling Dora's neighbor how she resented her mother for not marrying and thus depriving her of a father. The neighbor is saying Dora could never risk staying close to a man after Dora's father disappeared."

"Grandma looked just as sad then as she does now," adult Claus said. "Grandma had a broken heart, my mother had a broken heart, and I have one now. End the vision here, Lanietta."

"There's more," young Lanietta said. "The funeral service. The casket has been wheeled close to the altar. Sunlight is pouring in."

"I remember this," Claus said.

"You were the only one who noticed," young Lanietta said. "The service is going on. Now comes the time for offering each other peace. You're shaking hands with people next to you and behind you. The offering of peace has ended."

"I looked back at Grandma's casket, and the sunlight was gone," Claus said. "Up to that point I felt she was still with me. No longer. End it now, Lanietta!"

"More," young Lanietta said. "Your parents can't sell the house. No one wants a house with your name on the siding. Your parents are having the property rezoned as commercial. They can do it, because it's at the end of the block and across the street from other businesses."

"I never saw this part," Claus said. "I went home. My parents took care of things."

"Yes," young Lanietta said. "Your grandmother's house is being leveled by a bulldozer. They are hauling away the debris, except for your name. They've placed it aside. It will be hung on a wall inside the new building."

"They should've thrown it away and be done with it," Claus said.

"Now a new building. Automotive. An oil and lube place," young Lanietta said. "There goes the siding with your name. Hung inside for customers to see."

"Changing oil in my grandmother's yard. It's just not right," Claus said.

"Let's go to the back yard, or what used to be the back yard," young Lanietta said.

"Must we?" Claus asked.

Young Lanietta led Claus to the back.

"There's a little bit of the woods left. Not much. Most of the trees are removed. The stream is still there. For now," young Lanietta said.

"I don't want to watch," Claus said.

"They've stored old oil in barrels in back. Look, that truck is backing up. It's run into several barrels. Old oil is spilling downhill."

"And into the stream," Claus said. "Happy life-forms from millions of years ago died only to later power and lubricate cars in a zombie second life before being discarded for good by polluting the stream. The brook! Grandma told me not to forget Broc. It means 'brook'. But it's no longer a brook. Gone. Soiled beyond recognition. Will my grandma be crude oil someday to be changed out of a car and left to pollute a stream? They turned my grandma into that black oil! And it was my fault!"

Claus let out a blood-curdling yell of agony. He panted hard and choked on the petroleum fumes.

"No one will remember how things are supposed to be," he said in a strained voice. "No one will remember their grandmother. I'm not number one. I'm number none."

Chapter 67: Cluffer Snaps

Claus felt intense rage well up inside, a rage he could not contain.

"Claus?" young Lanietta said. "Speak to me, Claus."

With the singular focus, stealth, and determination of a dog in pursuit, Claus marched from the Anrega into the lunar graveyard where he'd first been.

"Claus," young Lanietta said, who had followed him. "I know what you feel."

"Worthless waste," Claus muttered.

"You cannot let these failures weigh on your heart. Or your soul," young Lanietta said.

"Time to lighten it," Claus said.

Claus in his rage invoked power from Aftova and created a blunt weapon. He then swung the weapon at the frozen ancient Earth life-forms, destroying them.

"Claus, stop!" young Lanietta begged.

But young Lanietta did not have the corporeal presence to stop Claus. Claus proceeded to destroy preserved creatures, one after another.

"It's not worth it!" he yelled. "End it all. Once and for all!"

It was not Claus who was swinging, of course. It was Cluffer. And so Claus could continue this rampage without becoming physically tired. However the emotional stress built. Claus's stress carried through Cluffer, and Cluffer started to shake. But Claus continued anyway. His aim became worse, and he struck enclosures and bits of wall instead of preserved creatures.

"Claus!" called Kechenova's voice through Aftova. "Claus, do you read me? Claus? We've overcome the selenites. They were harvesting cetaceans of all things. Claus. Lanietta is weakening.
Whatever you're doing right now is making things much worse."

Cluffer stopped swinging.

"I don't care!" Claus said. "Earth's not worth saving."

"What?" Kechenova replied, confused.

"Claus," Labba said. "This is Labba."

"It's Labba," young Lanietta said. "My friend."

Cluffer looked over at young Lanietta.

"Yes, I can hear her. I'm tied to the real Lanietta who has both Fronfa and Rigefa. They are tied into Aftova. I know."

"Claus, you're suffering from eethi psychosis," Labba said. "Listen to me. Do exactly as I say, no matter what you feel. Use Aftova to help. Can you do this?"

"I've lost it," Claus said.

"You've lost Aftova?" Labba asked.

"No, my sanity. I went on a rampage and destroyed things. I've snapped," Claus said.

"It doesn't matter what you did," Labba said. "What matters is this moment. Right now. Focus on that. I'm sensing a young version of Lanietta with you. That's a good start. We've made progress there. But we need more time to finish rescue operations. I need you to return to the orb chamber in the Anrega and stand with adult Lanietta. Do that now. Focus on my voice. Now follow young Lanietta back to the orb chamber."

Cluffer dropped the blunt weapon and looked at young Lanietta. She nodded yes, motioned for Claus to follow, and led Cluffer (and thus Claus) back to the Anrega orb chamber.

"I saw a vision, Labba. I saw my grandmother," Claus said.

"I know," Labba replied. "There are many atrocities in history. They can consume a person quite easily. Greylingers feed on it. Greylingers use it to get a foothold in a person. You've put yourself closer than any other human to Greylingers and such evil. It's dangerous. But don't let it overpower you. Focus on my voice. Focus on young Lanietta's voice. The innocence of the child will win the day."

"I thought you were going to say that clear minds win the day," Claus said.

"That sounds like Leni," Labba said. "He would say that. Machines so easily purge things from existence. Sentient life-forms don't have it so easy. Start with the innocence of a child. Remember the good your grandmother taught you. She loved you, of course, and she hoped you'd at least remember. She knew you wouldn't understand as a child. Yes, she knew. You know now. She succeeded across all these years, as you are about to do. You will succeed for many people to come. You will never know them, but they will know of you. Let's live for them, shall we?"

Young Lanietta nodded yes.

"Yes," Claus said.

"Doctor Kechenova has worked out a plan for integrating more closely with Lanietta's adult self and the orbs of her parents," Labba said.

"For this to work, you'll need to drop the Cluffer proxy," Kechenova said. "I've relayed the procedure to Aftova. Aftova will set up a warm oxygen atmosphere for you, and then we will resume."

Cluffer walked up to the orbs of Lanietta's parents. Adult Lanietta still had a hand each on them, but her own image was very faint and barely visible. Cluffer placed his hands on the orbs. Suddenly, Cluffer split down the middle, shed outward to each side, and became environmental units. The left unit put out heat and controlled humidity while the right unit released oxygen and scrubbed out carbon dioxide. Claus stood for a moment where Cluffer once stood. He was confused, but his senses returned, and he placed his own hands on the orbs.

"Do you hear me, Claus?" Kechenova's voice said from Aftova (which was still in his upper palate).

"Yes," Claus said.

"As you experience visions, you will see crawly things in your peripheral vision from time to time," Kechenova said. "Those are Greylingers intruding upon your ethereal spirit. Yes, you have one. We will monitor and pull you out of the vision when that happens to prevent eethi psychosis."

"I'm not sure I understand eethi psychosis," Claus said.

"Just understand that it can drive you mad," Labba said.

"Yes, it is to be avoided," Kechenova said. "Your mind is steady for the moment. We will resume the vision."

Claus found himself back in the Carinian solar system, only this time young Lanietta was close by. The two flew over to Carinia 2.

"Claus," Labba said. "We think young Lanietta will be able to stabilize you through these visions. This is good. Our feed might drop out from additional selenite attacks. We'll monitor your progress as best we can and provide what comment we can, but at times it will just be you and young Lanietta."

"I understand," Claus said.

"We are now five billion years ago," young Lanietta said. "The Anrega and Veigon have left Carinia 2 and have taken up position inside Carinia 5. The Gerenba have become Grens."

"Which means what?" Claus asked.

"The mortals who bore children so easily are now immortal but barren," young Lanietta said. "There are many Grens, and they continue their lifestyle of farming."

"There's one thing the Grens have the Bleuhs do not—vines," Labba said. "It was the only living thing on Carinia 2 before the Anrega came and released the other life-forms. Grens have discovered the vine produces grapes and makes excellent wine. The wine is therapeutic and helps regulate life processes. It is the only known means for countering the Anrega influence. Often a bottle of wine will quell a Greylinger attack."

"Yes. Another thing is this," young Lanietta said. "The Anrega did not have enough energy to fully depart from Carinia 2. It left remnants. These remnants create an internal rotation of the core."

"I don't understand," Claus said. "How does that work with the normal planetary rotation?"

"When the Anrega leaves a planet, it causes tidal locking with the planet's star," Kechenova said. "Carinia 1 and Carinia 2 are face-locked with Carinia Zero."

"Won't that kill all life?" Claus asked.

"Life becomes more difficult," young Lanietta said. "There are ways to cope. Carinia 1 has the twilight area between sides of day and night. Carinia 2 has the internal rotation and abundant life compensating."

The two suddenly left Carinia 2 and appeared by a procreation tank on Carinia 1.

"What's happening now?" Claus asked. "Ugh. Crawly things are entering my peripheral vision."

"Drink this," young Lanietta said in the ethereal vision, and she produced a small bottle of wine. "It's ethereal wine."

Claus drank it.

"Reminds me of a cough drop for some reason," Claus said.

"It has a similar effect of clearing the passageways," young Lanietta said.

"The crawlies are gone," Claus said. "Good. I didn't have to drop out of the vision. Now what are we seeing?"

"This is a Bleuh procreation tank," young Lanietta said. "My mother is being born. Her name is Lanshalla."

Claus looked around and noticed that Bleuhs split into corporeal and ethereal halves, sent the ethereal part to various places, and reintegrated.

"What's going on with these people?" Claus asked.

"They are going ethereal," young Lanietta said. "Instead of walking around and taking time, they split their ethereal self from their corporeal self, send the ethereal self around to various places, and then reintegrate."

"Little do they realize the consequence of such actions," Kechenova said. "They increase Greylingers in the Anrega. Already the Anrega is filling too quickly with Greylingers. The Greylingers are looking for a new home."

"This is incredible. Looking for a new home? It's all so strange," Claus said.

"The Bleuhs' use of ethereal power is so strong that they've created a rift for the Greylingers to follow from the Anrega in Carinia 5 to the dark side of Carinia 1," Kechenova said. "The Bleuhs are feeling the first effects of these Greylingers on the Carinia 1 dark side. They can't go ethereal as easily as before. Libriota is leading a committee to determine what to do about it. They have two plans—find an iron dwarf and put it in orbit around Carinia 1 to absorb excess Greylingers, or use Carinia 2's core to absorb them."

"Why an iron dwarf, I wonder," Claus said.

"Iron is at the center of the nuclear divide," Kechenova said. "It is neutral. Lighter elements fuse to heavier elements until they reach iron, while heavier elements split to form lighter elements until they reach iron. Greylingers somehow are a part of a mixture between fusion and fission. I'm not sure how. It doesn't make sense since they seem more ethereal than physical. But they do nonetheless."

Claus and young Lanietta flew toward Carinia Zero.

"Wait!" Claus said. "This red dwarf is getting bigger. We're flying toward it! We'll burn up!"

"No. You are safe!" young Lanietta said. "Look. Libriota and her team are using ethereal energy to control Carinia Zero. They are trying to make an iron dwarf. But they can't. At least not in the star itself. Libriota has a plan. I never knew about this before. But I am learning now. Libriota will create a new solar system for harvesting iron dwarfs. Let's follow!"

Claus and young Lanietta suddenly flew from the Carinian system to a swirling collection of gas.

"This is your solar system at the very beginning," young Lanietta said. "You see how swirling gas is forming your sun and the planets. Libriota is causing this. She wants many iron dwarfs."

Just then, Claus's vision filled with crawly creatures.

"Too much!" Claus said, and he closed his eyes.

"Too much for wine," young Lanietta said.

"Discontinue the vision, Lanietta," Labba said.

Claus opened his eyes and found himself back in the Anrega orb chamber.

"I have another urge to destroy things," Claus said.

"Breathe deeply," young Lanietta said. "In, out, in, out. There. Feel better?"

Claus inhaled and exhaled several times. He paused, looked over at young Lanietta, and looked at adult Lanietta. Adult Lanietta was not quite so faint.

"Yes, she's stronger now. I am stronger," young Lanietta said.

"The Greylingers are gone from my vision," Claus said.

"Then you are ready for the next step," Labba said. "A detailed vision."

"I thought I *was* going through a detailed vision," Claus said.

"Not quite," Kechenova said. "We rushed you through the overview. It only helped Lanietta a little, but it was necessary. Now her parents come into play. Since Lanietta is deeply tied to her parents, extensive time should be spent with them to help her."

"And us," Labba said. "We've been hit by another selenite attack. Northern Indian Ocean now. Lanietta will have to help you through the next—"

But Labba's voice cut out.

"Labba? Doctor Kechenova?" Claus called.

"We've lost contact," young Lanietta said. "I will help you with the next vision. Follow me."

Young Lanietta motioned for Claus to follow. She appeared to step into a portal. Claus followed, and when he did, his vision changed. The two traveled to Carinia 2 and hovered above a vineyard.

"This is it," young Lanietta said. "This is my father's vineyard, though I've never seen it before. His name is Larto."

"I don't understand," Claus said.

"You will," she said. "You will."

Chapter 68: Larto's Vineyard

There was a lake, a pasture, a vineyard, and a large farm house abutting the foothills of a mountain. The pasture had what looked like Irish Cob horses, the vineyard had grape vines, and the lake stretched across the distance, but in that far distance before the horizon took over, land could be seen. A horse walked over to a fence, hoping one might come by and stroke its mane or pat its face. People worked the vineyard, and two men were in conversation while others tended to the vines and collected grapes.

"The Anrega never fully left Carinia 2," young Lanietta said to Claus. "It left remnants. These rotate inside the planet's core and give off ethereal cues to life on the surface. Carinia 2 is face-locked with Carinia Zero, but the cycles of life follow the remnants below. See the grapes? Their formation is in sync with the remnant cycle."

"What does this have to do with anything? With saving Earth?" Claus asked.

"When you saw your Grandma Broc, you realized new things with your adult eyes," young Lanietta said. "For me, I am seeing this for the first time. I don't remember my parents. Just a little bit of Nanna. Nanna!"

The two returned to the Anrega briefly in time to see adult Lanietta lift her head, say "Nanna," and lower it again. Claus wanted to say something, but young Lanietta and he returned to the vineyard.

"I need this to hold me together," young Lanietta said. "My people are gone, except for Labba. Those we are about to see are no more. Bad or indifferent, it is fact. I must face this fact. I must face..."

Young Lanietta could not finish her sentence.

"It's the best season ever," the foreman said to Larto.

"Excellent," Larto said. "You'll receive a special bonus for your efforts."

"It wasn't me. Just good luck with the weather," the foreman said.

"Still, you should share in this good luck. I will also add a little something for the workers. Without them I would—"

"You there," called a woman's voice.

Larto and the foreman turned around to see a woman in Imperial Bleuh uniform mounted on an armored horse. The woman's name was Lanshalla, but to Larto she was just another Bleuh.

"That's my mother. Lanshalla," young Lanietta said.

"You don't remember your parents?" Claus said. "Then how do you know them?"

"From what Nanna told me. From what I feel," young Lanietta said. "Don't you wish you could go back in time and see Elaine and Aubert when they were young? Feel the magic that brought them together? Don't you wonder how they coped?"

"I guess I figured they knew what they were doing all along," Claus said. "I never had a problem in childhood except for the incident at Grandma's house. At home I was rather ordinary. I made model airplanes out of wood and burned my name on them using a magnifying glass and the sun. Looked through my microscope a time or two. When I got older, I studied aeronautics before applying for an astronaut position at Astroosa. I guess I'm the most boring person on the planet."

"Are you the owner of this place?" Lanshalla asked.

"I am the owner," Larto said after walking over.

"My horshialla needs water. Attend to it at once!" she demanded.

"Carinians refer to a horse as a horshialla and several horses as horshialli. Their horses of course are not Earth horses, but are close enough to look like Earth horses," young Lanietta said.

Larto looked at the horse. It foamed at the mouth and looked ready to collapse.

"Please dismount!" Larto said.

"I take no orders from a Gren. Water my horshialla, or I will arrest you!" Lanshalla demanded.

"Your mother is bossy," Claus said.

"It's the Bleuh way," young Lanietta said. "She's a Bleuh. My father is a Gren. I'm a hybrid. But I don't blame her. Carinia 1 was full of Greylingers by this point. The Bleuhs were looking for a way to sterilize the planet without killing themselves. They decided to colonize Carinia 2, and that meant taking over."

"If you don't dismount, your horshialla will die. You'll have to walk to the city. Is that your intention?" Larto asked.

Reluctantly, Lanshalla dismounted.

"Take this horshialla to the stable and tend to its needs," Larto said to the foreman. "Give it plenty of rest. Watch it closely. It's suffering heat exhaustion and is close to death."

"At once, sir," the foreman said, and he led the horse to the stable.

"Just who do you think you are, giving orders like that to an Imperial Bleuh?" Lanshalla asked.

"I'm Larto, owner of this estate, which I call Larto's Vineyard. I am a winemaker. You are welcome as my guest. Come inside and rest. I'll have refreshments prepared," Larto said.

"I will inspect your estate, Mr. Larto. Do you take me for a fool? I will not be tricked," Lanshalla said.

"As you wish," Larto said.

"First I will inspect your stable," she said. "And if need be, I will commandeer one of your horshialli."

The two walked to the stable, not far behind the foreman.

"You are from the city, am I right?" Larto asked.

"I will ask the questions around here," Lanshalla said.

"Sorry for asking. It's just we don't get many visitors out here. There's an electromagnetic field in the desert between my estate and the city, a field that prevents mechanized vehicles from getting through. Once a season I make the trek to sell my wine, and that requires I bring extra water for my horshialli and take frequent rest stops."

"Yes, I went through your electromagnetic field. No doubt to stop us Imperial Bleuhs from getting through. But I made it through, you see? From the city. Yes. It was my task to find out what you Grens are doing in these parts. Harboring rebels no doubt," Lanshalla said.

"No doubt," Larto said sarcastically.

"Then you admit it!" Lanshalla said.

"I am only echoing the long paranoid fear of the Bleuhs," Larto said.

"I'll have you arrested for the insult," Lanshalla said.

"Go ahead. Arrest me for the insult. Arrest me for making wine. Arrest me for whatever I am about to do that you don't like. You're as fragile as thin ice, ready to crumble with any little stress," Larto said.

Lanshalla took a club from her side and swatted Larto across the jaw. He fell, stunned. Several stable hands rushed over to help Larto, but he waved them off and stood up.

"Our guest is very spirited," Larto said.

Lanshalla looked around the stable and inspected. She tapped her club on various wooden walls, looking for secret passages. She found none.

"What a horrible mother I have," young Lanietta said. "My Nanna was never like that. She cared for me without condition. I guess I know from where my nasty personality comes."

"You seem fine now," Claus said. "Only your adult self had issues. I don't think you have your mother to blame. Something must have happened to you and changed you."

"You're very prescient, Claus," young Lanietta said. "I wish I could hold onto my young self forever. Before it all happened."

"Then do so. Forget whatever happened and be that eleven-year-old girl," Claus said.

"Eleven for you, eleven million for me," she said. "But the universe doesn't suffer as much. You should listen to your Grandma Broc. History and time are like the brook with stone steps. We must take the next step, no matter how slippery. The brook will not last forever."

"I think it can. You are proof it can. You. Right now," Claus said.

"Your facilities are satisfactory, for the moment," Lanshalla said.

Lanshalla was about to leave the stable when she realized there was an upper level.

"Wait!" she said. "I wish to inspect the upper level."

Several stable hands looked at Larto in disapproval, but he waved them off with his eyes as if to say he knew.

"There are steps here. But we don't keep important—" Larto started to say.

"Silence! I will decide what is and isn't important," she said.

"Go ahead. Search upstairs," Larto said.

Lanshalla started for the stairs, but she turned around and motioned Larto her way.

"You will go first. You won't spring a trap on me!" Lanshalla said.

"As you wish," Larto said.

Larto led the way upstairs. When the two reached the top, Lanshalla looked around.

"Hay and straw," she said.

"Yes, we store extra up here," Larto said.

Lanshalla walked around, tapping her club on various objects. She reached the corner that wasn't quite a corner (a small wall covered the corner). She tapped on it, and it gave a little.

"A-hah!" she said. "No rebels indeed. What is behind this door?"

Larto rushed over and placed his body between hers and the secret door.

"This door is not meant to be opened! Please don't open it!" he said.

"Get out of my way!" she said while pointing the club at him.

"I'm warning you," he said.

"No, I'm warning you!" she said.

Lanshalla extended her ethereal hand into his spinal column and caused his legs to jump sideways as if receiving an electrical shock. Larto's body went flying through the air, and he landed atop several bales of hay with a thud. His legs went temporarily numb, but he used his arms to reposition himself so that he could watch and warn one last time.

"Please...I don't even know your name. Please don't," Larto struggled to say.

"You will do well to remember my name after this incident. I am Lanshalla! Major Lanshalla!"

As she announced her name, Lanshalla opened the hidden door. Down poured straw and horse-dung compost atop her. Down and down it poured with incredible speed. Lanshalla had been partly facing Larto when she opened the door, and so the flood of material took her by complete surprise. Before she could react, she was neck deep in the material and unable to move. The foreman and extra hands from below rushed up, fearing Larto had been seriously hurt, but he climbed down from the hay, walked over to the dung heap, and spoke.

"Men, this is Major Lanshalla, Imperial Bleuh from the city," Larto said.

The men cheered and clapped.

"Stop it! Stop it and get me out!" she ordered.

"These are your parents?" Claus asked. "I don't see any love here."

"Things are complicated," young Lanietta said.

"Obviously," Claus replied sarcastically.

"Your new attire is very becoming," Larto said. "Would you care to attend the monthly ball? I have several hogs from which you may choose for a date."

The foreman and hands laughed.

"I could have you all killed!" she threatened.

"If you kill us, you'll still be stuck," Larto said.

"Do you forget to whom you speak? An Imperial Bleuh? I'll disrupt your nervous systems. Kill everyone!" she continued.

She went ethereal and sent her ethereal self fully into Larto's body. She forced him to start digging away at the dung heap to give her a means of getting out.

"Get out of his body!" the foreman threatened.

"You stay out of this, or I'll kill you all. Go back downstairs. Go!" she ordered.

"Go on down," Larto added with what little voluntary ability he had left. "I'll be fine."

The foreman and hands returned downstairs.

"Look, Lanshalla, there's no need to force me to dig you out. I'll do so voluntarily," Larto said.

"This is to ensure compliance," she said. "You Grens are undisciplined and do whatever you want, believing all the while that you own this planet."

"We do," Larto said.

"You don't deserve it!" Lanshalla said. "Look at you! Running your own vineyard like you own the place."

"I do," Larto said. "I make excellent wine. Have you tried it?"

"Tried what?"

"Larto's Wine," he said. "Only the best."

"The wine is from the native vine on Carinia 2," young Lanietta said.

"The vine that was here before the Anrega arrived?" Claus asked.

"Yes," young Lanietta said. "When the Gerenba first came over to Carinia 2, the only food to eat came from the vine."

"Imperial Bleuhs don't drink on duty. And we have our own superior beverages. Much superior," she said. "Now hurry up!"

Larto finished excavating Lanshalla from the heap. She returned her ethereal self to her physical body.

"Ick. I should have remained separated. But you Grens have alien ethereal selves. Controlling you is as disgusting as being covered in this muck," she said.

Larto pulled her out.

"Give me your shirt," she ordered. "There's muck on my face."

Larto removed his shirt and gave it to her. She wiped off her face and hands and threw the shirt back at him.

"May I offer my house for cleaning up? I have a maid who will prepare a warm bath or a shower if desired, and she will set fresh clothes for you while your uniform is cleaned," Larto said.

"I demand it," Lanshalla said.

Larto led the way to his house. As the two passed helpers, they covered their mouths in an effort to suppress their laughter. Those who could not help it were quickly shocked by a zap from Lanshalla's ethereal self. The two reached the front porch and entered. The butler answered.

"Send for the maid to set water and fresh clothing for Lanshalla. Have Lanshalla's uniform cleaned," Larto said. "Also fetch me a spare set of clothes. I will use the servant shower."

The butler paused. He looked at Lanshalla's uniform and then back at Larto.

"She is our guest," Larto said. "Please."

"As you wish," the butler said, and he disappeared.

"Your throw rugs will be covered in mud," Lanshalla smirked.

"Quite all right. They are made for this sort of thing and are easily washed," Larto said.

The maid arrived. When she realized Lanshalla was an Imperial Bleuh, she stopped short and started to bolt.

"Mariel, wait," Larto said to his maid.

"Nanna!" young Lanietta said.

Claus and young Lanietta returned to the Anrega chamber. Adult Lanietta again lifted her head and spoke, saying, "Mariel. My Nanna."

Adult Lanietta dropped her head just as Claus and young Lanietta returned to Larto's house.

"Yes, Larto?" Mariel said.

"This is Lanshalla. She is my guest," Larto said.

"What's wrong, little Gren? Haven't you served a Bleuh before?" Lanshalla asked with arrogance.

"Mariel has tended to many Bleuhs. You are not the first to trespass on this planet," Larto said.

"We are taking over this planet," Lanshalla said.

"Why?" Larto asked.

"Never you mind," Lanshalla said.

Mariel held her position.

"It's all right, Mariel. Come over here. Say 'hello' to Lanshalla," Larto said.

Mariel walked over slowly with towels and clothing in hand.

"If you will follow me please," Mariel said.

"No tricks," Lanshalla said. "I can go eethi any time."

"Mariel will take good care of you. I will meet up with you shortly," Larto said.

Lanshalla walked off with Mariel. Larto's butler returned with towels and clothing.

"Set two places on the back porch with food and drink, Treyu," Larto said to his butler. "Bring out the special wine."

"The Lonely Vine wine?" Treyu asked.

"Yes."

"The Lonely Vine," young Lanietta said. "Very special. I can feel it."

"But sir, you gave strict instructions that the Lonely Vine wine is never to be served," Treyu said.

"I have a hunch that the Lonely Vine has a part to play," Larto said. "Make this exception, Treyu."

"On an Imperial Bleuh, too," Treyu said, and he shook his head as he motioned Larto toward the servant shower.

Larto went to the servant shower and cleaned up. Meanwhile, Mariel led Lanshalla to the shower off a guest bedroom. Mariel placed the clothing and towels on a table and then went for the shower controls.

"You may leave your clothes on the floor. I'll have them cleaned when you finish. Let me get the shower warmed up for you," Mariel said. "There's a bottle for soap, a bottle for shampoo, and another for conditioner. If you need to shave—"

"Vulgar! Female Bleuhs have nothing to shave!" Lanshalla retorted.

"My apologies, ma'am. If you need anything else, just ring the bell. I'll be—"

But before Mariel could get away, Lanshalla went ethereal and used her ethereal self to shove Mariel's back to the wall by holding Mariel's neck with her ethereal hand. This allowed Lanshalla to "choke" Mariel's spinal column and control her nerve impulses.

"Ma'am, please! I meant no offense!" Mariel pleaded.

"Mommy!" young Lanietta pleaded. "Don't hurt Nanna! Nanna!"

"Tell me everything you know about Larto!" Lanshalla demanded.

"He's...just my employer. I keep house for him. I'm only the day help. At night I go to my room in the servants' quarters," Mariel said.

"You don't have day and night," Lanshalla returned.

"The cycles from within the planet. We call them 'day' and 'night'. Carinia Zero always shines, I know, but it's not that kind of day and night. It's just how we keep time!" Mariel said.

"Primitive Gren mind," Lanshalla said. "I see I will have to probe deeper."

While still holding Mariel's neck with her one ethereal hand, Lanshalla made a fist with her other ethereal hand and placed that fist in Mariel's brain. Mariel winced as one might do when a dentist shoots up a patient's cheek with lidocaine.

"I...I..." Mariel stuttered.

"Hmm," Lanshalla said. "You really are a simpleton. So Larto harbors no rebels. At least none that you've seen. But he has a secret. In the back yard. Yes, you've heard of it but haven't seen it. A plant? On the mountain foothills? What's so secret about that? Hard to believe. Well, there's nothing special about you, Mariel. This mind probe has been a waste. You'll remember nothing. Carry on."

Lanshalla released her ethereal presence from Mariel and reintegrated. Mariel looked confused for a moment, shrugged her shoulders, and left. Lanshalla removed her clothes and entered the shower. Heavy muck fell off, but it did not completely dissolve in the water. The drain plugged up, and dirty water filled the shower tub.

"I'll never get clean at this rate," Lanshalla said.

She split off her ethereal self and zapped the muck clogging the drain. The muck loosened up and went down. She had clean water in the shower tub again.

"Mommy has great ethereal power," young Lanietta said.

"It's almost too easy," Claus said. "Bleuhs can practically wish whatever outcome they desire."

"She doesn't care about the hurt," young Lanietta said. "She doesn't care."

"I wonder if she changes," Claus said.

"Or will she be more like Libriota," young Lanietta said. "I don't think I want to continue. I'm getting sick."

The two returned to the Anrega chamber. Young Lanietta faded and disappeared completely. Adult Lanietta remained by the orbs of her parents, but she loosened the grip on her mother's orb.

"Lanietta?" Claus called.

Claus walked over and tried the best he could to touch Lanietta, but his hand went through.

"Claus, this is Labba," Labba's voice said through Aftova. "Are you doing something up there? Earth is receiving global-wide tremors."

"Haven't you evacuated everyone yet?" Claus asked.

"No. We still need more time," Labba said. "These selenites are the total worst of enemies. Why can't they let up their attack?"

"Reason with them. Tell them you'll take the humans, and they can have the rest of the planet," Claus said.

"Selenites don't reason," Kechenova said. "Claus. You must stabilize Lanietta. She's fading fast again. Use Aftova if you must."

Claus tapped his tongue behind his front teeth to his upper palate. He created a new proxy—Cluffer 2. He put himself inside Cluffer 2 and into the apartment studio like before. Next, Claus had Cluffer 2 superimpose itself over Lanietta's ethereal body. Cluffer 2 put a hand each on the orbs of Lanietta's parents, and Claus replicated the orbs inside the Cluffer 2 studio apartment. He then had Cluffer 2 pull Lanietta inside the studio apartment such that she held onto the two orbs.

Cluffer 2 buffered out the pain, and to Claus's relief, young Lanietta appeared in the studio apartment.

"You're safe here," Claus said. "I promise."

Claus walked over to take young Lanietta's hand, but his hand passed through hers.

"What?" Claus wondered aloud. "But I thought...with you in the studio...with Aftova..."

"I'm still just an echo of the past," young Lanietta said. "Here, I'll take us back."

Young Lanietta spun around twice, did a curtsey, and the two returned to the vision of Larto's Vineyard.

Lanshalla shampooed three times and used lots of body soap before she was clean enough to use conditioner. Clean and happy, she turned off the shower, toweled off, and made for the clothes. But what she found was an ordinary green and white one-piece outfit with short skirt, pink socks, and calf-height boots.

"What kind of clothing is this?" she wondered. "How embarrassing. I look like one of Larto's servants. I'll give him an extra zap for his bad sense of humor."

Lanshalla brushed her hair and put it back, as she usually did before donning her uniform. But the conditioner caused her normally straight hair to acquire waves and body, making it more difficult than usual to put back.

"These Grens are undisciplined and lack control," she said. "No wonder they are so easily overrun."

Lanshalla entered the guest bedroom and was about to go into the hallway when she bumped into Mariel.

"Larto is in the—" Mariel started, but then Treyu approached.

"I'll take over," Treyu said to Mariel, then he turned to Lanshalla and said, "Larto is on the back porch. He would like you to join him for refreshments. If you will follow me please."

Lanshalla followed Treyu as a hurried Mariel went into the shower room to retrieve Lanshalla's uniform.

"I expect my uniform to be pristine!" Lanshalla called back.

Treyu led Lanshalla to the back porch where Larto sat. He stood up when Lanshalla entered. Treyu helped Lanshalla with her chair, but she did not sit.

"Will you excuse us, Treyu?" Larto said.

"As you wish," Treyu said, and he left.

"What is the meaning of this...this... thing you had Mariel give me?" Lanshalla demanded.

"You mean the outfit? It's all I had," Larto said. "Nanceya the gardener is on vacation. I'm sure she won't mind."

"Gardener?! Absurd! I demand formal attire," Lanshalla said. "And what is in that conditioner? My hair is a mess!"

"It creates a natural perm," Larto said. "The maid and gardener swear by it."

"Well I don't! My straight and disciplined hair is ruined. It won't go back correctly!"

Young Lanietta giggled.

"Mommy looks funny with curls," young Lanietta said.

Claus smiled.

"Here, let me help," Larto said.

Larto unfastened the clasp in back, and Lanshalla's hair fell forward. He fluffed it up to restore its body.

"There. That's much better. You look like a woman instead of an Imperial Bleuh. And before you complain about the outfit again, I think it looks wonderful. It accentuates your figure. You're very healthy and fit. You blend right in here in the country," Larto said.

"I'm not one of your hired hands!" she said.

"No, you're not," Larto said. "Would you care for refreshments? Treyu set out a variety of nibble-bits. Here's one—fresh protein figs. Or perhaps you'd like—"

Lanshalla brushed the plate of protein figs onto the deck.

"I take it you don't like protein figs," he said.

"I'm only here long enough until my uniform is clean and my horshialla is rested," she said. "Country boy simpleton

with country boy vision. You have no concept of how things work."

"Indeed," Larto said. "Tell me. When you look at my back yard here, what do you see?"

"Your back yard. The foothills of a mountain," she said. "There are various formations. I wouldn't be surprised if you're hiding rebels behind those rocks."

"Anything else?" Larto asked.

"A spindly weed between two large rocks," Lanshalla said.

"That spindly weed is the secret of my vineyard," he said. "It's the Lonely Vine."

"How can a single plant be the secret of your vineyard?" Lanshalla asked.

"Let's go down and take a look," Larto said. "But first, please have a glass of wine. I assure you it isn't drugged. I'll have a glass too. Take it with you. The wine is from that 'spindly weed'."

The two took a small elevator on the side of the porch to ground level. Lanshalla took the glass and sipped the wine.

"This isn't wine. It's fruit juice," she said.

"It tastes like fruit juice, yes. That's the beauty of this vine. You can't taste the alcohol. It leaves you feeling refreshed. Come. Let me show you the vine."

The two walked over to the vine.

"Many years ago, I searched these parts for something, anything I could grow that no one else had. I came across this vine. I took two cuttings and started my vineyard. The first cutting didn't do so well. But with care and attention, I got the other cutting to grow. It produced other cuttings and so on. These cuttings produced wine almost as good as the Lonely Vine," Larto said.

"Why almost?" Lanshalla asked, beginning to relax from the wine as she took another sip.

"For years I wasn't sure. I babied the cuttings. I watered them. I provided fertilizer. They produced large quantities of wine fruit, but still they weren't quite the same. And then it hit me. The Lonely Vine is not just a plant. It's the amalgamation of years of past life experiences locked within these mountain strata. Look closely at these foothill rocks. You'll see fossils—"

"From a bygone era when aquatic life was free and plentiful in these parts," Lanshalla finished.

Larto looked at Lanshalla funny. She took another sip.

"That's exactly what I was going to say," Larto said.

"Perhaps I overheard one of your workers explain the same thing," Lanshalla said.

"No. I have never explained the vine with such words. Not to anyone," Larto said.

"She's changing," young Lanietta said. "That's something Libriota could never do. My mommy isn't a machine. She's becoming a real person. I have hope, Claus. Real hope."

"You care very deeply for this vine," Lanshalla said.

"Yes, I do. It's one of a kind, having endured great hardship to survive as it has, between these rocks with little water," Larto said.

"The water it does gather comes from the rocks themselves," Lanshalla said. "It trickles down the foothills, and each drop contains genetic encodings, carrying this information into each vine fruit."

"Those encodings are from life before the Anrega. Little life-forms," young Lanietta said. "I guess there was more than just the vine before the Anrega and Veigon let forth their own. It's like your brook, Claus, before the oil changed it. Life on Carinia 2 before the Anrega came. But now it's gone."

"I'm sorry," Claus said. "I miss the brook too."

"Amazing," Larto said. "You explained it better than I could. Either you read my mind, or something else."

"I read your mind when I had you dig me out of that...that...muck you preserved. But there's something about this wine," Lanshalla said, and she took another sip. "I can read the encodings. I can sense the information path from the buried to the living vine. There were great creatures in

ancient seas here, creatures as intelligent as Bleuhs. Some were benevolent and worked together in an altruistic society."

"That I never knew!" Larto said. "I've tried and tried to read those encodings using various devices. But nothing worked. Even drinking the wine now does not give me the details you have provided. I sense there was a special time ages ago with creatures, but wonders upon wonders, you're incredible!"

"You Grens are puny compared to Bleuhs. I should submit this to the Imperial Bleuh Science Institute. They'll award me a medal," Lanshalla said.

"Ah-ah-ah, Mommy, you're regressing!" young Lanietta said.

Claus laughed. Young Lanietta returned Claus a puzzled expression.

"Sorry. It's just you said that like a parent to a child," Claus said.

"Is that all you care about?" Larto said. "What about the history and knowledge hidden in these rocks? You could help me unlock secrets of the past. If creatures of old were as benevolent as you say—"

"They were," Lanshalla added.

"We could use that knowledge to further peace between our peoples. Work for a common good," Larto said.

"There is peace. Bleuhs have the brains and discipline, and the Grens are kept in check by the same," Lanshalla said.

"I thought I could convince you otherwise. Most people have a change of heart when they become aware of something greater than themselves," Larto said.

"I never said these creatures were greater than me. Nothing is greater than a Bleuh. That's established fact. The evidence is indisputable. Only a Gren has such cherished fantasies that serve to paralyze their ability to make progress," Lanshalla said.

"Can't you for once let go? You are here as my guest," Larto said.

"I *am* drinking your Lonely Vine wine. Isn't that letting go? But cheer up. I'll humor you and have another glass," Lanshalla said.

"One moment," Larto said.

"I still have hope in Mommy," young Lanietta said. "She's fighting something. She doesn't want to see."

Larto took Lanshalla's glass and went inside his house. But Lanshalla soon followed after. Larto had gone into the kitchen to refill her glass while Lanshalla looked about Larto's living room. There were photos of Larto's parents, his friends in the city, his school achievements in horticulture, and several photos of city ballet dancers. On a shelf just below such a photo was a box. Lanshalla opened the box, and a miniature ballerina turned around while music played. Lanshalla fashioned herself as a ballerina and turned around too. As she did so, young Lanietta took ballerina form and imitated her mother. Larto returned, and Lanshalla closed the box suddenly.

"Here's your glass," he said. "Did I interrupt something?"

"No, not at all," she said. "You have many interests, Larto. You were once in ballet."

"I've never told anyone that," he said.

Lanshalla gulped down half her wine glass.

"Careful. This wine can grow on you," he said.

"We Bleuhs have the most silly, I mean the most skilled dance *performerancers*," Lanshalla said, fumbling her words.

"Lanshalla, have you ever considered that maybe, just maybe your people and mine aren't so different after all?" Larto said.

"Hah! That'll be enough of that little *play-of-believe-o-make*," she still fumbled.

"Haven't you ever dreamed of doing something other than what you do?" he asked.

"Like what?" she asked back.

"Like art. Creating art. Performing art. Or both," he said.

"You're going to ask me to *dayance*. You're going to show that you can *peyerform* ballet and thus *demonstratiate* your supposed superior art ability over mine. But I'll show you. I can perform ballet as well as *you-a-poo-dee-doo*. Set the music. Show your *stuff-iuff*!" she said, and she gulped down the last of the wine.

"I'm not really dressed for this," he said.

"And I'm dressed as your *gardener-a-pler*. But I am a Bleuh. That means you take orders from *me-you-see-doo-dee*!"

Larto had a large living room. And so there was plenty of room for dance. He turned on Gren ballet music, and he approached Lanshalla as if to perform a lift. But she didn't seem to know what to do.

"Bleuh superiority, eh?" he said.

"I'll show you," she said.

Lanshalla went ethereal and melded her ethereal self with Larto. She did not control his body, but she sensed his thoughts and physical movements, and in this way she was able to direct her physical self to perform the precise ballet movements in time with his. She did jumps, turns, splits, made poses, and engaged in various lifts with him. Lanshalla ended the routine tip-toeing around with a flower in her mouth that she grabbed from a vase. She then spun in place near him again and again and again. At that moment, the foreman walked into the living room with an Imperial Bleuh.

"Sorry for the intrusion, Larto, but I—" the foreman started.

"Stand aside, Gren," the Bleuh said. "I'm Captain Indikat of the Imperial Bleuh Patrol. I'm looking for Major Lanshalla. She's reported missing, and her ethereal trail leads here. Your name for the record?"

"I am Larto, owner of Larto's Vineyard," Larto said.

"I see. And this is your wife?" Captain Indikat asked.

"I am Major Lanshalla," Lanshalla said.

The captain looked shocked. He approached Lanshalla and looked at her closely. He smelled her breath and winced.

"Major?" he asked.

"I am...*searching-ish* for rebels," she stumbled.

One of Indikat's lieutenants entered the room and reported Lanshalla was not outside.

"She's here," Indikat said. "This is Major Lanshalla. Make a video record for the Hierarchy."

"I assuredly assure you and your friend here, Captain *Indikat-a-lackity-lack*, I am deep *undercover-ly-and-then-again*," Lanshalla said.

"She's intoxicated. Clearly non-protocol," Indikat said to the lieutenant. "Major Lanshalla. You are under arrest."

Indikat motioned to the lieutenant. The lieutenant brought special ethereal-inhibiting handcuffs over to Lanshalla and locked them to her wrists. When he did so, Lanshalla's ethereal spirit left Larto's body and reintegrated with her own. The handcuffs had that effect and prevented further ethereal activity from Lanshalla.

"Merging with a Gren too. Disgraceful. Totally disgraceful. I cannot imagine what led you to such depravity," Indikat said. "Did this Gren compromise your authority? Say if it's so."

"Larto is innocent. I am in full *charge-i-okay* here you *see-to-please*," Lanshalla said.

"Where is your uniform? Where is your horshialla?" Indikat asked.

"Your uniform is cleaned and pressed," Mariel said, now appearing.

"Cleaned and pressed too," Indikat said. "Were you swimming in the mud?"

"As a matter of fact, I was swimming in horshialla dung. And you, Mr. Indikat with your uniform so clean, you should try swimming in dung. Fling a piece around. Eat some at meal time. And for dessert. You too shall enjoy the labors of the vineyard," Lanshalla said.

One of the hands walked in to report Lanshalla's horshialla was fed, watered, and rested.

"We'll take her horshialla in too," Indikat said. "I am here by compressed oil transport."

"A machine? But the electromagnetic field doesn't—" Larto started.

"It's new technology that is quite basic but very functional. It uses no electricity. A piston compresses a light oil for combustion. Not that a Gren would understand," Indikat said. "Come along, Major. You have much explaining to do."

"Look, Captain Indikat. This is all my fault. I got her uniform dirty. I gave her the wine while the uniform was being cleaned. And I put her up to this dancing and other nonsense. Prosecute me if you must. Leave Lanshalla out," Larto pleaded.

"A Gren sacrificing himself for a Bleuh? Unheard of. But one thing is very clear. Lanshalla is conspiring with you. This makes her a traitor. She will be tried and executed for her treason," Indikat said.

"What?! No!" Larto insisted.

"Oh Larto, my little *Gren-a-friend*. Take no worry home with you for supper. The darkness never comes for a Bleuh. We just go away to another place," Lanshalla said.

"I'm afraid your case is cut and dried," Indikat said. "I'll post two patrols around this house until the Hierarchy decides Larto's fate. Shall we go, Major?"

Lanshalla shrugged her shoulders, gave Larto a kiss on the cheek, and headed out the door with Indikat and the lieutenant. Larto rushed to the window and watched as Lanshalla was escorted into the vehicle. Indikat drove off, and she was gone.

"What just happened here?" Larto said aloud.

"She was arrested," the foreman said. "One less Bleuh to deal with. But I don't like these patrols around your property, sir, nosing around in business none their own."

"I want you to tell your subordinates to prepare for a strike," Larto said.

"I don't understand, sir," the foreman said.

"Let a thousand heartbeats go by, then tell them they aren't being paid unless they pick five times as much vine fruit as normal. Work them to the bone. Whip them if they complain," Larto said.

"Outrageous!" the foreman said. "You've never mistreated the help."

"Then get them to riot," Larto said. "Have them throw rocks at the house. Get them to break windows and demand a fair work environment."

"I...am saddened by this...this...change of yours," the foreman said.

"It is only temporary. To draw off the patrols. But you must not let on. Take this whole thing seriously. It must create a diversion," Larto said.

"A diversion for what?" the foreman said.

"To save Lanshalla," Larto replied.

Claus looked at young Lanietta.

"What is it?" she asked.

"I...I guess not," Claus said. "It's just...I half expected you to make a snide remark."

Young Lanietta smiled.

"That part of me does not yet exist in the girl before you," she said.

"When you...when you were an adult...when your older self showed me things of Earth gone by, you, I mean she wasn't so cordial. She made snide remarks. I guess I've been conditioned to expect another blow."

"You miss it, don't you?" young Lanietta said.

"I shouldn't miss it. It's not right," Claus said.

"I understand," young Lanietta said. "Do not be concerned as such. The story is more important. This was a difficult time for my parents. If I were stronger, you'd see my adult self make fun of them. But I'm not. Just a simple girl. There's more to see."

"Then let's continue," Claus said.

Chapter 69: Emergency Exit

"Treyu, prepare for going into the city. There will be three of us. You, Mariel, and me," Larto said. "We will need Bleuh citizen clothing and Bleuh eethi emulators."

Treyu disappeared for a moment.

"There's that word again," Claus said. "Eethi. Labba said I had eethi psychosis. Lanshalla talked about going eethi. Now we have eethi emulators."

"Going eethi is the same as going ethereal," young Lanietta said. "We have spirits, you know. Ethereal spirits. You might not think you have one because it stays within your physical body all the time. Except when you die. For some humans, they die, their ethereal spirit leaves, travels a short distance away, then returns to the body. That person returns to life."

"I've heard the stories. Just never believed them," Claus said.

"Bleuhs learned how to do the same thing without dying. It's called going ethereal or going eethi," young Lanietta said.

"And eethi psychosis?" Claus asked.

"When your ethereal spirit is affected in a bad way," young Lanietta said. "Makes you think or do bad things."

"Me, Larto?" Mariel asked.

"Yes. There are situations where your skills may be needed. I intend to rescue Lanshalla," Larto said.

Treyu returned with a marker-sized device in one hand and a backpack over his shoulder.

"I...wish we would not do this. The Bleuhs have only caused misery. Help instead our Gren kin," Mariel said.

"She's right, Larto," Treyu said. "Fight the Bleuhs. Don't help them. Let them devour their own."

"Treyu, Mariel. Listen. If there's going to be any hope of solving these problems with the Bleuhs, we must create a bridge with them. That means befriending one of their kind," Larto said.

Treyu and Mariel replied with disgust.

"I know, I know. It is a difficult task. But someone must start this. Treyu, it was you who befriended me on Carinia 5," Larto said.

"Carinia what?" Mariel asked.

"I'm from Carinia 5," Treyu said. "Didn't you know?"

"Nobody is from Carinia 5. It's a frozen world. Nothing lives," Mariel said.

"That is what my people would like you to believe," Treyu said.

"Larto, what were you doing on Carinia 5?" Mariel asked.

"Looking for something. Anything. Carinia 1 and 2 are at odds with each other, and long have I searched for a way to bring peace to our worlds. I had to go outside."

"Larto was nearly frozen to death," Treyu said. "I found him while out on patrol. Brought him into our underground world and thawed him out. Once he recovered, I offered to return with him to Carinia 2."

"You're not a Gren?" Mariel asked.

"No. Nor am I a Bleuh," Treyu said.

"Then what are you?" Mariel asked.

"I am a Greyan," Treyu said. "Our ethereal spirits are not like Bleuhs or Grens. They are hidden deep. Bleuhs cannot find them. But we have great technology, and one such technology is to imitate a Gren or Bleuh ethereal self. I can mask your Gren ethereal selves and display an artificial ethereal Bleuh for any probing Bleuhs."

"Will it hurt?" Mariel asked.

"I assure you it won't," Treyu said. "I will simply inject micro-devices in your temples. The devices will only last three Sol 3 years before breaking down."

"Wait," Claus said. "Sol 3? Libriota mentioned 'Sol 3' when the PRAAD was discovered on the moon. This can't mean—"

"Sol 3. Earth," young Lanietta said. "Or at least whatever planetary body was in the number three position in your solar system. They knew about your solar system by this time."

"Just what time is this?" Claus asked.

"About four and a half billion Earth years ago. Except Earth wasn't there yet," young Lanietta said. "There was another body there. We called it Gnisiotra. You called it Protogaia. So in this instance, Sol 3 is Protogaia, and a Sol 3 year is a Protogaian year."

"Labba told me you had something to do with Earth's creation," Claus said.

"The girl before you had not yet done so," young Lanietta said. "The girl before you still has her innocence."

Claus wanted to say something, but he paused.

"Remember the swirling cloud of gas I showed you? Your early solar system? Remember? Libriota was looking for an iron dwarf," young Lanietta said.

"Yes, I remember," Claus said.

"We Carinians had a poor sense of time-keeping. We had our own Carinian years, but they are different among the planets. So we chose planet number three in your system for consistency," young Lanietta said.

"Now I understand," Claus said.

"We won't be in the city that long," Larto said. "Start with me."

Treyu held a device the size of a permanent marker. He touched it first to Larto's left temple and then to his right.

"Did that hurt?" Treyu asked.

"Not at all. But is it usual to feel something after the injection?" Larto asked.

"No," Treyu said.

"I feel like there's a compass in my head pointing to Lanshalla," Larto said.

"Let me check the implants," Treyu said.

Treyu held his marker-sized device up to Larto's left and then right temples.

"They are functioning properly. Perhaps there's an afterimage of Lanshalla on you. Did she meld her ethereal self with you?"

"Yes, she did," Larto said. "First when she forced me to dig her out of the composting, and then later when we danced."

"You danced with a Bleuh?" Treyu asked.

"Oh," Mariel said. "Is that what you two were doing when the other patrols arrived?"

"Yes. I was befriending Lanshalla," Larto said.

"It was a dangerous game," Treyu said.

"I had to take the chance," Larto said. "Mariel, it's your turn. I'd love to chat more, but there's going to be an uprising soon."

"Where?" Mariel asked.

"Here," Larto said.

A commotion outside started and grew louder.

"It's already started," Larto said. "Hurry, Treyu."

Treyu placed implants in Mariel's left and right temples.

"Good. Let's take the emergency cave in back," Larto said.

The two ran to the back yard and slipped between two boulders. Treyu held up his marker-sized device to the side of the mountain, and a hidden door opened. The three entered through the door and closed it behind. No patrols saw nor followed. Treyu activated luminescent cave lights just in time to see Larto catch Mariel as she collapsed to the ground.

"Smelling salts," Larto said to Treyu.

Treyu opened his pack and retrieved smelling salts. He placed them under Mariel's nose, and she awoke.

"There. You're fine. Can you stand? No, you can't. Sit here on this stone-carved bench. What happened?" Larto asked.

"I...remembered something. I felt something linger inside me too. A hand on my throat. Then a fist in my head. It was Lanshalla. When she readied to shower. She pressed me for information about you, Larto. She was looking for rebels. She made me forget. Why did I remember just now?"

"The implants, Treyu?" Larto asked.

"They block out heavy outside interference," Treyu said. "In your case, Larto, you are able to use Lanshalla's ethereal residue to locate her existing ethereal self. For you, Mariel, you are able to cancel out her blocking effect and recall the effect her ethereal residue left on you."

"I guess we're lucky she didn't try something with your ethereal spirit," Mariel said. "She would have found you out."

"Nonsense," Treyu said. "I wear long-lasting implants that can mimic a Gren or Bleuh signature as I wish, whenever I want. She would have thought me a stupid Gren, as she would say. Yes, we Greyans can use their own eethi probes against them to misdirect them."

"I didn't realize you were that advanced," Larto said. "Nor did I understand the implications of these implants. I still don't. But one thing is for sure. We can use this to get into the city and get close to Lanshalla. We'll break her out at the right moment. Then, if she's willing, which I think she'll be, we just might be able to use your technology and her Bleuh spirit to start a revolution."

Treyu and Mariel shuddered at the talk.

"Revolution? O forces above, please spare me from this talk. I was ready to stand up and walk, but now I'm not sure," Mariel said.

"I will only ask for volunteers," Larto said. "Come along, Mariel. It's not like the revolution will start before next harvest. We would need to acquire strength among the rebels. I had avoided them all this time, because I didn't think I could help. Now I do."

Mariel stood, but her legs shook.

"Revolution. Grens could die," she said as the three walked.

"Is this not a living death we Grens have now?" Larto said.

"You have a peaceful life with a wonderful vineyard," Mariel said. "That should be enough."

"Except for the Bleuhs who are showing up with increased frequency. How long can my vineyard stand against such oppressors? What would you do, Treyu?"

"I always have the option of returning to my home world of Carinia 5," Treyu said.

"Yes. But for us Grens, this is our home world. You don't have Bleuhs meddling with Greyan affairs. We do," Larto said.

"It is a conundrum, that's for sure," Treyu said. "Any such situation is. There is no easy way out."

"Except for this tunnel," Larto laughed. "Is the escape vehicle at the end ready to go?"

"It is," he said. "The vehicle will fly thanks to special Greyan technology that is unaffected by the electromagnetic desert."

"Excellent. I wish I had more of your kind here. The work you do is beyond complaint," Larto said.

The three reached the end of the emergency tunnel. Through a one-way window, they saw (as expected) that the ship was there and was still covered in a tarp that camouflaged it as part of the mountain. Mariel was about to open the secret door to the outside, but Larto stopped her.

"Wait. I see movement outside," Larto said.

Treyu looked through the window.

"Imperial Bleuh Patrols," Treyu said.

"Out here?" Mariel asked.

"They are looking for suspicious activity," Treyu said.

"It's possible they were suspicious before Lanshalla's visit, and that's why she visited. Now that I've 'contaminated' her, they are more paranoid than ever," Larto said.

"How will we get to the ship?" Mariel asked.

"That is a very good question," Larto said. "We need another diversion. If only the vineyard workers were here."

"Perhaps they can be," Treyu said. "On Carinia 5, we can alter air flow to create mountain acoustics that sound like a wolf howling or a pack on the move."

"Can you do it here?" Larto asked.

"I've never tried," Treyu said.

"Now would be a good time," Mariel said.

"There's a problem," Treyu said. "I need to set up two devices somewhat apart so they can triangulate and focus on air flow. I will need to leave the cave for that."

"I won't put you in such danger," Larto said.

"Then we're stuck," Mariel said.

"No, not stuck. I'll go out instead," Larto said.

"Sir, I am taller and can withstand greater blunt force trauma. I should be the one to—"

"Negative. I'm responsible for what happens. If something goes wrong, return to my estate. Stall for time if questions arise. Say I've gone away. Allow the workers to go free. Arrange your own departures. Is that clear?"

Mariel and Treyu paused, exchanged nervous glances, and then agreed.

"Here are the devices," Treyu said, retrieving small cylinders from his pack. "Place one there by that ledge, and the other one over there on that other ledge."

Treyu had pointed out the ledges at the window. Larto put the devices in a pocket and prepared to slip out the secret door.

"Please be careful!" Mariel said. "And come back in one piece!"

"I intend to do both," Larto said, and he slipped out the door.

Mariel and Treyu watched through the window as Larto snuck behind one rock and then another. He reached one ledge without being observed and placed the small cylinder there.

"Good. That's exactly where I told him to place it," Treyu said to Mariel. "Now he must place the other one over...uh oh."

"The patrol is on the move," Mariel said.

"Yes. He's coming through the passage by the other ledge. Larto is cutting across, but he won't see the patrol until it's too late," Treyu said.

"We have to do something. Can you cause the wind to howl yet?" Mariel asked.

"Not until Larto sets up the other cylinder," Treyu said.

"Go out there and do something," Mariel said.

"Larto told us not to," Treyu said.

"Well I'm going to do something, even if you aren't," Mariel said.

"He said not to," Treyu repeated.

"Since when do such orders apply to a woman?" she asked.

"I..." Treyu fumbled.

Mariel ripped her clothing to appear more attractive. She slipped out the secret door and walked down the passageway toward the patrol.

"Nanna! For shame!" young Lanietta said.

Claus laughed.

"Don't laugh!" young Lanietta said. "That's my Nanna!"

"Yoo-hoo," she called. "Can you help me? I seem to be lost."

Treyu covered his eyes and peered between his fingers, afraid she'd be caught. Larto also heard what was happening and wanted to yell at Mariel to get back into the tunnel, but he'd give his position away, and so he bit his hand to keep quiet. The patrol responded to Mariel, and she led him away from the ledge. Their conversation allowed Larto to gauge their positions and sneak around a different way to the second ledge. He placed the second cylinder in position, and he tried sneaking back, but the voices came close, and he had to hide under a boulder.

Seeing both cylinders in place, Treyu cracked open the secret door and pointed his device out. The cylinders activated, and the air flow first created the howls of distant wolves. The patrols quickly faced the sound and prepared to shoot any such wild animals. The patrol close to Mariel beckoned her to get behind him, but she actually walked toward the howl and stood on a boulder, adding her own howl to the auditory trick.

"What is that? What are you doing?" the patrol near Mariel asked.

Now Treyu intensified the acoustics. The howling wolves sounded as if getting closer, and their tone changed into a fighting, hungry pack ready to devour anything and everything in sight. The growling cacophony was so intense that the ground shook like a thundering stampede. The patrols fell into fear and fled. Mariel growled at the patrol closest to her, and he called her "Witch of the Wind" as he fled. The air was so intense and precise that dust picked up and formed shapes of wolves leaping down from on high with smaller rocks and gravel flying in all directions from the path the air wolves forged. Mariel backed up to a wall for shelter, and Larto covered his head with his arms for protection. A few moments after the patrols cleared, Treyu pointed his device out the door again, and the wind returned to normal. Acoustic apparitions disappeared. Treyu stepped out and met up with Larto and Mariel.

"Well, I wasn't prepared for all that. I thought your trick would create sounds on the wind. I got hit with rocks from your pack of fake wolves!" Larto said.

"Necessary, sir," Treyu said.

"I, uh, also felt it was necessary to help," Mariel said.

"I didn't want to risk either of you. But you two are the best. Come on then. Let's pull the tarp off," Larto said.

The three pulled off the camouflage tarp to the emergency ship. They entered.

"All right. Before we leave, change clothes into Bleuh citizens. I want this to look as authentic as possible," Larto said.

The three changed into clothing with colors of blue and black with white highlights.

"It feels obscene wearing Bleuh clothing," Mariel said.

"It's just for a little while. Keep your composure, and all will be well," Larto said.

The three took off.

"I can still sense Lanshalla's direction," Larto said.

"We must be careful to land a bit away from her position so as not to draw suspicion," Treyu said.

"Agreed."

With that, the three flew to the city and landed in a port for Bleuh citizens. It would only be a matter of time before the three would learn of Lanshalla's fate.

Chapter 70: Lanshalla's Examination

Captain Indikat's ship arrived in the city. Lanshalla, still in her gardening outfit, her perm, and her handcuffs, was escorted along an atrium to a set of elevators among many sighs and gasps from the people who had to deal with her. The elevators opened, and the group went up to the 75th floor, where a number of doctors held practice. Lanshalla was escorted to one of those doctors for a physical, ethereal, and psychological evaluation.

"I'm fine," Lanshalla kept saying as Indikat checked her in at reception.

The patrols sat with Lanshalla in the waiting room, and when her name was called, Indikat got up to go with her, but the nurse wouldn't allow it.

"We have our own security," the nurse said. "We'll return Lanshalla when the evaluation is complete."

Lanshalla's vitals were taken by the nurse. Routine questions came up about changes in vision, skin tone, and places Lanshalla had visited. She mentioned the vineyard, and that raised suspicion.

"The doctor will be in shortly," the nurse said, and she left.

"I wonder what Larto is doing right now?" Lanshalla mused.

Lanshalla had a vision of large aquatic creatures of great intelligence swimming in an ancient ocean, diving deep through tunnels in seamounts and re-emerging inside the seamount with a breathable atmosphere. The creatures changed shape from aquatic to humanoid and roamed around the city-like innards of this seamount.

"Can it be we are not alone?"

"You're not," the doctor said, walking in.

The doctor took a seat, pulled out an electronic device, and took notes.

"You're Major Lanshalla of the Imperial Bleuh Patrol?" the doctor asked.

"Yes."

The doctor checked that off the list.

"Perhaps you'd like to explain your recent deviation," the doctor said.

"It is not a deviation like that. I was inspecting an estate in the country. Larto's Vineyard to be exact. I was looking for rebels or any association with rebels. There's been a steady stream of rebels coming into the city, but we cannot figure out how. I suspect the rebels have outside help."

The doctor held a finger on the device, and it read the doctor's impulses, which were simply notes on what Lanshalla said.

"Patrol Paranoia. Normal," the doctor said and recorded on the device. "Go on."

"My horshialla was done in. So I had Larto stable it," Lanshalla said.

"You took a horshialla out to Larto's Vineyard? Isn't that a bit too far?"

"Someone has to look for the rebels," Lanshalla said.

"Obsessive Narcissism Disorder. Continue," the doctor said.

"I found what I thought was a secret door in the upstairs of the horshialla stable," Lanshalla said.

"And what led you to believe that? Was the upstairs full of rebel equipment? Weapons and supplies?"

"No. Straw and hay," Lanshalla said.

"Stray and hay," the doctor mis-recorded.

"No. *Straw* and hay," Lanshalla said.

"Correction noted. But no weapons," the doctor said.

"None," Lanshalla said.

"Recognition Aphasia Disorder. Continue," the doctor said.

"I was going to force the door open, but Larto blocked the way. I went eethi and zapped his legs," Lanshalla said.

"Anger Management Disorder. Then what?" the doctor asked.

"He moved out of the way. I opened the door, and out fell a huge pile of straw and horshialla dung. It completely covered me before I could get out of the way," Lanshalla said.

"Reaction Time Deficiency. And then?"

"I was stuck. Couldn't get out," Lanshalla said.

"Problem Solving Anemia. Did you call for help?"

"In a way. I went eethi and forced Larto to dig me out," Lanshalla said.

"Alpha Male Envy. Then what?"

"He dug me out. So now we were both dirty. He offered to let me clean up in his house, which I did. The maid took me to the shower. I interrogated her about the rebels, but she knew nothing," Lanshalla said.

"By going eethi?" the doctor asked.

"Of course," Lanshalla said.

"Obsessive Eethi Compulsion. Did she like being interrogated in that fashion?"

"No. But I put a block on her synapses so she'd forget," Lanshalla said.

"Oppressive Confidence Insufficiency. So you waited for your clothes to be cleaned, is that right?"

"No. My clothes were still being cleaned when I finished my shower. The maid had brought other clothing to wear. The gardener's clothes. I had to put on something, so that's what I wore," Lanshalla said.

"Role Transference Compulsion. Did the clothes fit?"

"They did. But the conditioner I used caused my straight hair to go frizzy. I had a hard time putting it back," Lanshalla said.

"Body Disfigurement Disorder. Did you try any therapies for correcting the physical anomaly?"

"No. I went to the porch and joined Larto for refreshments," Lanshalla said.

"Hygiene Lapse. What did he serve?"

"Protein figs. I threw them off the table. Wasn't impressed," Lanshalla said.

"Standard Imperial Precaution. And then?"

"He showed me the back yard, which was really the foothills of a mountain. Then he talked about a plant in the yard and gave

me wine. The more I drank, the more I realized that the plant could remember things," Lanshalla said.

"Inanimate Animation Delusion. How much wine did you consume?"

"Two glasses. I had to go inside for the second. Larto had this music box with a ballerina. I played the music and twirled around like the ballerina," Lanshalla said.

"Multiple Role Schizophrenia. And then?"

"Larto returned with my second glass of wine. I consumed it pretty quickly," Lanshalla said.

"Impulsive Consumption Disorder. Did you drink more?"

"No. But I danced with Larto. Ballet dance. It didn't work at first though. I never studied ballet moves."

"Delusions of Grandeur. Did he do ballet?"

"He did," Lanshalla said. "In fact, I went eethi and melded with him so I could learn the moves and sync my movement with his."

"Naked Ethereal Impropriety. Was this the only time you melded with him?"

"Oh no. When I made him dig me out of the dung, I melded with him then too," Lanshalla said.

"Strike my last note. Make that Compulsive Naked Ethereal Impropriety with Moral Character Deficiency."

"Captain Indikat arrived and saw me. The maid brought my clean uniform. I was going to change, but he arrested me before I had a chance. I'm going to have him demoted. That'll teach him not to mess with me."

"Blame Transference Euphoria. Did you protect yourself during the eethi meld?"

"Protect? From what? He's just a Gren. Like a rat or bird," Lanshalla said.

"Consequence Denial Pathos. Let me check your heartbeat," the doctor said.

The doctor moved a scope over Lanshalla's heart. The doctor then moved the scope over her abdomen.

"Hmm," the doctor said.

"Well? You've racked up a long list of issues against me. What is it this time?" Lanshalla asked.

"You're pregnant."

Chapter 71: Lanshalla's Breakout

"I wonder if that was me," young Lanietta said.

"Any idea if you have older brothers or sisters?" Claus asked.

"No idea," young Lanietta said. "I could be an only child for all I know."

Captain Indikat, who had been waiting patiently, was suddenly approached by Lanshalla's doctor. The doctor gave a notarized document to Indikat.

"Here are the results," the doctor said. "You'll find that Major Lanshalla has a long list of issues. I recommend extensive treatment at this clinic."

"That might not be possible," Indikat said. "The major is due in court. Sentencing could prevent such treatment."

Lanshalla walked from the treatment area to the lobby.

"We have our own list of charges against her," Indikat continued. "Treason is at the top of the list. That gives her a prime court case today."

"I demand representation," Lanshalla said.

"You have the right," Indikat replied. "But it must be quick. The trial will start soon."

Lanshalla gave the name of her attorney, and Indikat escorted her several buildings down into a professional building. The two took an elevator up and reached Lanshalla's attorney. Another lobby, and Indikat waited while Lanshalla was escorted into the attorney's office.

"Lanshalla," Libriota said.

"Libriota," Lanshalla replied.

"What? Libriota an attorney?" Claus exclaimed. "I thought she was the leader of the Bleuhs."

"She was," young Lanietta said. "She did many things. She only represented special cases though."

"If she were the leader, why would she have need? She could just decide whatever she wished," Claus said.

"Even Bleuhs had a court system," young Lanietta said.

The two hugged and exchanged light ethereal melds as their usual way of greeting. Lanshalla and Libriota were very close friends. It was Libriota (Lanshalla's attorney) who helped Lanshalla get her post and promotions in the Imperial Bleuh Patrol. But after the ethereal exchange, Libriota felt sick.

"Something's wrong," Libriota said. "Your ethereal spirit. It's contaminated with something. Aren't you scheduled for a medical exam?"

"I just came back," Lanshalla said.

"What did they give you as treatment?" Libriota asked.

"Nothing. I'm pregnant," Lanshalla said.

Libriota held Lanshalla's hand and looked Lanshalla in the eyes.

"Even a Bleuh child shouldn't disturb my ethereal self. There's something more here. Your hair is different, and you wear strange clothes. What has happened to you?" Libriota asked.

Lanshalla then explained her adventure at Larto's Vineyard.

"Your story troubles me, Lanshalla. We've been friends for a very long time. But I find out you now carry a Gren child. This is most disturbing!"

"I didn't know it could happen! I thought Grens were like rats," Lanshalla said.

"Even a rat should not be fully melded with, at least not without special protection," Libriota said. "I know a doctor in the Bleuh underground. He does excellent work. You can rid your body of this parasite. You'll need to anyway as part of your rehabilitation. Your title of Major will be lost, I'm afraid. But I'll try to keep you in the Imperial Bleuh Patrol, if that is your wish."

"I...I'm not sure," Lanshalla said.

"Wait," Claus said. "What is all this? I mean, I thought Bleuhs needed procreation tanks for children."

"At this point, yes. So did Grens," young Lanietta said. "But no one considered a Bleuh and Gren getting together. It was unthinkable. And unknown."

"Lanshalla. This is going to be a tough case. I'll need to discredit almost everyone. But more importantly, I'll need your full cooperation. Any hesitation on your part about your loyalties will undo everything I accomplish. You *are* a loyal Bleuh, right?" Libriota pressed.

"Yes. You know me," Lanshalla said.

"Then why the hesitation? Are you experiencing after-effects from the wine? The meld? Or perhaps it's your unborn child? Whatever it is, hang tough. I'll get you the treatment you need. But we must get through this trial. Can you do that for me?"

"I'll try," Lanshalla said.

"Good! Once you're cleaned up, we can exchange ethereal hugs again. You are my best friend, Lanshalla," Libriota said.

"As are you mine," Lanshalla replied.

There was no vision of the trial.

"Why can't we go in and see the trial?" Claus asked. "We're standing here on the outside of the courtroom doors."

"We're being blocked," young Lanietta said.

"Who? How?" Claus asked.

"By my mother," young Lanietta said. "She knew this could potentially be viewed later. She doesn't want it remembered."

Echoes of the trial periodically came through, but nothing was understandable. When it was over, the doors opened. Claus and young Lanietta walked in. The final statement was made by Libriota, who took an oath with the judge to disavow all connections with Lanshalla and accept the court's judgment on her sentencing. Lanshalla looked shocked at the betrayal of her friend, but she didn't have long to complain. Guards hauled her out of the courtroom.

"Approach the bench," the judge said to Libriota and the other attorney.

The two approached.

"Libriota, you nearly made a mockery of this courtroom," the judge said.

"Yes. These Grens are undermining our society. They—" the other attorney started.

"I'm speaking," the judge said. "Libriota, there's a real danger here. I know you want to save your friend, but some Bleuhs are contaminated beyond hope. We must be prepared to sacrifice the diseased to preserve the healthy. I could have had Lanshalla disintegrated free and clear. But there's a prison colony on Roushilla 4 for wayward Bleuhs."

"Where?" Claus asked.

"In another solar system that also has a red dwarf star," young Lanietta said. "Part of the Bleuhs' exploration plan to find a place to deposit Greylingers. But Roushilla 4 already had people living there, so the Bleuhs took them over. That is another story."

"I'll have her sent there," the judge continued. "If there's a hope for her rehabilitation, it will come through the colony. I would advise you avoid her and not travel to that colony. Our Bleuhs must remain pure. Is that understood?"

"Yes, Your Honor," Libriota said.

Libriota returned to the defense desk. The prosecuting attorney walked over and spoke.

"I'm sorry about your friend," she said. "But this is for the greater good."

"I know," Libriota said.

"You almost had me in the trial," the prosecutor said. "If it weren't for your client's outburst, then—"

"Then maybe I would have won. But she did give an outburst. All kinds of nonsense about Gren mountains containing remnants greater than us. You don't have to throw it in my face. I know I lost. Yes, you can brag that you defeated the great Libriota."

"It really is a rare honor," the prosecutor said. "Normally I could win such a case, but not against—"

"Not against me, Libriota. Well you did. Go on and get out of here!" Libriota said.

The prosecutor went back to her bench, gathered up her things, and left. The judge left too, and the courtroom was now empty except for Libriota. With the pressure off, she let down her guard and cried at the loss of her friend.

Meanwhile, guards hauled Lanshalla into a transport vehicle and headed for the regional spaceport.

"This isn't the way to the rehab center," Lanshalla said.

"You're not going to rehab," Captain Indikat said. "You're being sent to the prison colony on Roushilla 4."

"What? No! I'm a loyal Bleuh! And I'm expecting a child! I can't bear a child in a prison!" Lanshalla said.

Indikat and his men laughed.

"Figure it out!" he said with a chuckle.

"This is an outrage!" Lanshalla said.

Indikat clocked Lanshalla across the jaw.

"You leave my mommy alone!" young Lanietta protested as she pounded her fists at Indikat.

"You struck a senior officer. I'll have you—"

"You are no longer an Imperial Bleuh Patrol," Indikat said. "All rank and privilege has been stripped. Everyone knows about you, Lanshalla. You carry a Gren child. You're no longer a Bleuh. You're a Gren, filth and all!"

"It must be me she's carrying," young Lanietta said. "I...I caused this."

The transport vehicle approached a checkpoint near the spaceport. An officer with a heavy beard and bushy hair approached.

"What is this?" Indikat asked.

"Security checkpoint," the officer said. "We have orders to check every vehicle for escaped rebels."

"I am Captain Indikat of the Imperial Bleuh Patrol. This vehicle *is* secure," Indikat said.

"Sorry. Orders," the officer said.

"Stand out of the way. We have pressing business with this treasonous prisoner. If you don't comply within moments, I'll have your head for treason and put *you* away," Indikat said.

"Get out of the vehicle. Now!" the officer ordered.

Several other officers surrounded the vehicle with weapons pointed at Indikat and his men. Next, these officers forced the doors open and pulled Indikat and his men out. They also pulled Lanshalla out and held her at gunpoint.

"You will pay mightily for this intrusion!" Indikat said.

The officer checked out the vehicle, and while he did so, his men snuck a rebel into the back compartment. Having finished inspecting the main area, the officer went to the back compartment. His men ushered the Imperial Bleuh Patrols around back too. The officer opened the back compartment.

"Ah-hah! A stowaway rebel! Captain Indikat, you and your men are under arrest. The charge—harboring and aiding a rebel fugitive."

"Impossible. We secured this vehicle," Indikat protested.

"Take the rebel away," the officer said to another. "And have Indikat and his men processed."

"You can't do this! I have a prisoner! She is destined for the prison colony on Roushilla 4!" Indikat protested.

"Arrange for Indikat's prisoner to reach Roushilla 4," the officer said. "There now, former Captain Indikat. Your trial will be brief and merciful. Who knows? You might get to serve side-by-side with your former prisoner on Roushilla 4."

The officer's men took Indikat and the other patrols away. The officer looked at Lanshalla for a moment.

"You're too attractive to be sent away to Roushilla 4," the officer said. "There are better things for a young woman."

"What are you going to do to me? Take advantage of me? Have me work as a slave? You're no better than Indikat and all this...this...Bleuh imperialism. I'm going to have a child! Would any man have me? Stop staring at me, will you? No, you won't. You've made up your mind. Do what you will to me. I'm sick of this whole thing."

"A woman like you should be kissed," the officer said, and he was about to put his arms around her.

Lanshalla head-butted the officer to force him back. But when she did so, she knocked off his bushy hair and fake beard, revealing a more familiar face.

"Larto!" she exclaimed. "What on Carinia 2...you...this is crazy!"

"Sorry about that. We must get you to safety immediately," Larto said.

Treyu came over and lifted his beard and bushy hair disguise to show Lanshalla he was a friend.

"And Treyu too!" Lanshalla said.

Treyu discreetly unlocked Lanshalla's handcuffs with a key he'd lifted from one of Indikat's men.

"Don't remove them until we are out of sight," Treyu said.

"We'll take the vehicle. Let's go," Larto said.

Larto, Treyu, and Lanshalla got into the vehicle. Larto's other "officers" waved him through, and the three headed for the spaceport.

"Why, we're still going to the spaceport," Lanshalla said. "I'm removing my handcuffs now and getting out of here."

"Remove the handcuffs, but hear me out. We are not going to Roushilla 4," Larto said. "We have another destination in mind."

"And those other officers we left behind? What will they do to Captain Indikat?"

"Those officers are part of the rebel underground. They'll get a nice ransom for his capture," Larto said.

"So you are working with the rebels. How foolish I acted at your estate," Lanshalla said.

"I didn't start working with the rebels until you were captured," Larto said. "I had to find a way to rescue you, and this was it. Time and place were critical. I followed the

news of your capture and trial, but I had to be patient."

"So I go from being one prisoner to another," Lanshalla said.

"Treyu, stop the vehicle," Larto said.

"But sir," Treyu said.

"Just stop. Now," Larto said.

Treyu pulled to the side and stopped.

"You are nobody's prisoner," Larto said. "If you feel you are being held against your will, you are free to exit this vehicle and summon help. Or walk. Or do whatever. It is your choice, Lanshalla."

A moment of silence took over the vehicle.

"Unfortunately, my world has turned against me," Lanshalla said. "No one will offer me help."

"Your world of Bleuhs has turned against you. But there are others who would offer you aid. Grens and Greyans are working together to—"

"Who?"

"Grens and Greyans," Larto said.

"Ma'am, I'm Treyu. A Greyan from Carinia 5," Treyu said.

"Carinia 5 is a frozen wasteland," Lanshalla said. "Nothing lives there."

"I beg to differ," Treyu said. "We who dwell there are against tyranny of all forms."

"So are the Grens," Larto said. "I met Treyu on Carinia 5, and he helped me. I thought I could live out a quiet life in the country, but then you came along."

"I came along and ruined your peace, is that it?" Lanshalla said.

"No. You came along and made me realize I can't be at peace until Bleuhs and Grens are at peace. Lanshalla, you've affected me. I can't shake it. A Bleuh is supposed to repulse me. But you've drawn me in. The way you understood the mountain and the vine...I...even most Grens don't get it. And you, a Bleuh, got it right away. But what Bleuh would find that of importance, of value? They're like Indikat, always following orders without giving thought as to their consequences."

A highway patrol approached behind the vehicle and motioned it to get moving.

"Sir," Treyu said. "The highway patrol is behind us."

Larto looked at Lanshalla.

"I'll stay with you. For a while," Lanshalla said.

"Drive on," Larto said.

"I'm still not sure of things. I gave a weird speech during the trial, and I don't know why. Something has got hold of me, and I can't shake it," Lanshalla said.

"Maybe it's not worth shaking. Maybe it's worth experiencing and understanding," Larto said.

"Do you have a magic way to do that? To confirm or deny the validity of...of... whatever is happening?" Lanshalla asked.

"I don't have a magic way. And I don't think you'll be safe here. Or on Carinia 1. No, you're not going to Roushilla 4. I already promised that. But there is a place free of distraction where we can clear our heads and figure things out. The Greyans on Carinia 5. Treyu's people. They'll help," Larto said.

"The frozen wasteland again," Lanshalla said. "Carinia 5 is too dim to provide much heat."

"Everything is underground," Larto said. "The Greyans are masters of technology."

"With artificial light? No Carinia Zero to warm my skin. I don't know if I can handle that," Lanshalla said.

"Is it so much to ask?" Larto asked.

"Sir, the highway patrol has stayed with us. He is now flashing his lights. He wants us to pull over," Treyu said.

"He's discovered us," Larto said. "We can't be caught. Hit it, Treyu."

Treyu increased the speed of their vehicle. They dodged cars left and right. The highway patrol went into pursuit. He gained on Treyu and managed to nudge the back left side. Treyu started to spin out, but he bounced off another vehicle, sending that vehicle crashing into a wall. Treyu regained control and increased speed. He dodged more vehicles and took sudden turns onto side avenues. The highway patrol kept up.

"Is that a Gren or Bleuh behind us, Treyu?" Larto asked.

"Sir, I am driving," Treyu grunted. "I cannot analyze him."

"He's a Bleuh," Lanshalla said.

"How do you know?" Larto asked.

"Because he's sending his ethereal spirit after us right now!" Lanshalla replied.

It was true. The highway patrol had split. While his physical self drove his patrol car, his ethereal self leapt ahead and entered Treyu's vehicle. It attempted to zap Treyu and knock him into a daze. But Treyu swerved the vehicle around, and so the zap landed on Larto's neck. Larto jerked and felt stunned. Seeing what was going on, Lanshalla split and sent her ethereal self after the patrol's ethereal self. She punched the patrol's ethereal self and sent it back into the patrol's car. But the patrol was not to be deterred. He sent his ethereal self back at Treyu's vehicle. Lanshalla placed her ethereal self on the outside back of Treyu's vehicle, and as the patrol's ethereal self flung himself her way, she spun and kicked the ethereal patrol.

Now the patrol was mad. He brought his vehicle very close to Treyu's, and his ethereal self wrestled with Lanshalla and tried to pull her onto his patrol car. The ethereal patrol stood on his hood, and Lanshalla's ethereal self stood on the back of Treyu's vehicle. The patrol car pulled away a little, and the ethereal patrol pulled Lanshalla from the back of Treyu's vehicle and toward the patrol such that her ethereal feet were hanging onto Treyu's rear bumper while her hands held onto the patrol's front bumper. The patrol's ethereal self kicked his boot down on Lanshalla's hand to break her grip. She lost grip of one hand, and now he kicked down on her other hand. She tried grabbing his boot with her free hand, but his kick evaded her attempts. The patrol slowed, and now Lanshalla's feet lost their grip on Treyu's bumper. Her feet and legs were carried along the road under the patrol's vehicle, and this movement past the metals in the pavement caused an electromagnetic disturbance in her legs, shooting off plasma sparks and causing pain. The patrol continued his attempts to kick off her hold. Lanshalla extended her free hand into the engine compartment, detuned the engine, and disrupted power. The vehicle came to a dead stop, the physical patrol hit his head on the windshield, and the ethereal patrol's momentum carried him far in front and onto the pavement.

Exhausted, Lanshalla lost her grip on the patrol car's bumper. She was about to climb back up, but a fast-moving vehicle from behind could not stop in time and rear-ended the patrol's vehicle. The vehicle was pushed ahead and clear of Lanshalla. She stood up, climbed atop the patrol's hood, and affixed her feet slightly in the engine compartment. She then used ethereal extensions from her legs to control the vehicle—one extension for power and braking, the other extension for steering. She re-enabled power back to the vehicle and directed it toward the ethereal patrol. The physical patrol, though stunned, fought the steering and controls in the vehicle to undo Lanshalla's influence, but she could not be stopped. He then tried shoving the gear selector into reverse, but she twisted around, extended her ethereal hand to the physical patrol, and stunned him with an electrical jolt. Turning back around and facing ahead, she focused on the patrol's ethereal self that she now pursued. The ethereal patrol stood up and prepared to do battle with Lanshalla, but she sank her ethereal legs into the engine and envisioned she was the Lonely Vine, sinking its roots into the mountain and deriving strength from all its remnants of old. With that thought, she channeled plasmo-ethero energy from the engine, pointed her hand at the ethereal patrol, and discharged a plasmo-ethero ball at the patrol. The ball hit him full force, his body was flung into the air, and it landed on the hood. Using the other hand, Lanshalla discharged another plasmo-ethero ball, and it shot the ethereal patrol way up in the sky and ahead, as if he'd been shot out of a powerful cannon. He continued to sail ahead and landed on the highway practically out of sight.

Lanshalla increased engine power, and the patrol vehicle shot ahead, even passing a shocked Treyu. Lanshalla's ethereal self simply waved to Treyu and Larto as she continued standing on the patrol vehicle's hood.

"Go, Mommy, go!" young Lanietta cheered.

"That's some woman!" Treyu said to Larto as the patrol car went far ahead.

"That's my woman!" Larto said. "Can you catch her?"

"I thought we were running, not catching!" Treyu said.

"Running, catching, it's all the same," Larto said.

Treyu glanced at Larto and then shook his head in disbelief. Lanshalla, on the other hand, pursued the ethereal patrol. She caught up, and the ethereal patrol ran ahead, quicker and quicker like a four-legged animal being pursued by a predator. Lanshalla was that predator. The patrol vehicle reached the ethereal patrol, and she sent small plasmo-ethero balls at the patrol's feet to make him jump and more nervous, like a cat swatting a rat's tail and hind legs. Other vehicles left the highway as the last city exits passed, and now the highway opened up across the empty desert. Pavement ended, and the chase continued on desert salt. Electromagnetic radiation caused the car to stumble and ethereal selves to emit painful sparks. The ethereal patrol cried out in pain, but Lanshalla pushed the patrol vehicle beyond what it could endure, and she created a vee shaped plasmo-ethereal wall to envelop the ethereal patrol and crush it.

"Mommy, no!" young Lanietta pleaded.

"Stop this, Lanshalla," Larto said to her physical self still with him. "He's done in. Don't make yourself a murderer."

Lanshalla's ethereal self continued to close the vee around the ethereal patrol. It began crushing him, and he screeched in agony like a rabbit being crushed in the jaws of a wolf. The chase continued toward a canyon, and it was clear it would end soon enough.

"End it! End it now!" Larto begged.

"Mommy, please stop. Please!" young Lanietta also begged.

Lanshalla sent the vee ahead of the patrol vehicle, and it carried the ethereal patrol over the edge and down into a plasma geyser. As for the patrol vehicle, she stopped it short from going over the edge. The physical patrol was still stunned. Lanshalla, pleased with her work, stepped off the hood and stared into the canyon below. The geyser erupted, and the ethereal patrol was shot out and landed on another part of the canyon floor. Though not destroyed, the patrol was heavily damaged and remained there in a non-moving state.

"That should do," Lanshalla said.

Lanshalla reintegrated. Treyu had been following far behind and had reached the desert salt. He stopped.

"Was that necessary?" Larto asked.

"He was a problem, and I dealt with him," Lanshalla said. "He would have reported us and ended everything."

"Is that all you were thinking? What about us?"

"You are safe," she said.

Then it hit Lanshalla. She had endangered her unborn child in the struggle. When she went eethi, her unborn child's ethereal spirit was carried with her. And so any damage to her ethereal self could have injured or killed the ethereal spirit of her child. She looked down at her abdomen without another word.

"You did that with me inside? I could have died," young Lanietta said.

"Treyu, let's get back on the highway," Larto said. "We have a flight to catch."

Treyu turned around and headed back for the highway. But before he reached it, he saw other flashing lights in the far distance.

"More highway patrols," Larto said.

"I see them," Treyu said. "We'll take a side route."

And they did so only just in time. They were able to drive casually through residential streets abutting the desert. In this way, the three were able to reach other main roads and get to the spaceport. They drove up to a spacecraft. At the bottom of the spacecraft's stairs stood a woman. It was Mariel.

"Hurry!" she waved frantically. "There's an alert out for a woman wreaking havoc on the highway. I don't want to be caught in her fury."

Treyu, Larto, and Lanshalla laughed as they ran up the steps to the spaceship.

"What's so funny about that?" Mariel asked as she followed up last.

Treyu went to the controls and launched while Larto assisted. Mariel found a comfortable chair farther back for Lanshalla and herself.

"Why did everyone laugh at me?" Mariel asked.

"I am the woman who wreaked havoc," Lanshalla grinned.

"You? But how? Why?" Mariel asked.

"A highway patrol chased us. Then he went eethi and really tried to stop us. I had to deal with him. I guess I got carried away," Lanshalla said.

"Your hair is straight," Mariel said.

"Yeah. It must've straightened during the chase. Weird, isn't it?" Lanshalla asked.

"That conditioner will hold a perm until next harvest. I don't mean to be rude, but your hair just doesn't seem right. It's almost as if...wait a moment. Tell me, Lanshalla, when you were wreaking your havoc, did you have a strong protective need?"

"I did," Lanshalla said.

"I mean a really strong protective need. Like let no man cross your line, or there will be great consequences," Mariel said.

"Exactly. It was really strong! I've never felt like this before," Lanshalla said.

"Are you...are you expecting a baby?" Mariel grinned.

"Shh! Not so loud. You know!"

"You have all the signs. You're glowing!" Mariel tried to say in a low voice. "Does the father know?"

"Larto? No," Lanshalla said.

Mariel put her hand over her mouth in surprise.

"I knew it! I can tell!" she said in a very low voice.

"I didn't think it possible. But I'm going to have a little baby Gren. Or Bleuh. Or both," Lanshalla said.

"Let me plan the wedding," Mariel said. "I'm very good at weddings."

"He hasn't even proposed," Lanshalla said. "I'm scared, Mariel. I'm a Bleuh, and he's a Gren. What if Larto rejects me?"

"I admit I was distant when you first visited his estate. But now I see you're not just another Bleuh. I think Larto likes you well enough. He *did* rescue you."

"That counts for something, I guess," Lanshalla said.

"It counts for a lot! Your trial speech was made public. Larto was very impressed. He said he's never met a woman who is so intimate with the mountain. And a Bleuh on top of it too!" Mariel said. "But it sounds like you rescued him too with what they say about the highway havoc you caused."

"I didn't mean to," Lanshalla said.

"You've got a lot of people worried. I love it!" Mariel said. "I'm just glad you're on my side."

"Am I? Can a Bleuh be on a Gren's side?"

"Forget Gren and Bleuh. We're Carinians. We can live with that. And soon we'll be seeing the Greyans," Mariel said. "I know! We can have an ice wedding! On Carinia 5. With beautiful ice sculptures and fountain sprays frozen in midair. It will be the best celebration ever."

Larto walked in and heard, "Best celebration ever."

"What will be the best celebration ever?" Larto asked.

"Oh, Larto," Mariel said. "I, uh, was just, uh."

"She was telling me about Carinia 5," Lanshalla said.

"Yes. Treyu's home planet," Larto said. "We're going there now. I don't think we'll have time for celebration though."

"You'd better make time," Mariel said, but then Lanshalla nudged her hard.

"What does that mean?" Larto asked.

"It, uh, nothing really," Mariel said.

"Mariel wants to celebrate the help we can provide the rebels," Lanshalla said.

"Then you are serious about helping the Grens," Larto said, dropping to a knee and holding Lanshalla's right hand. "You don't know how important this is to me now that I know how you feel."

"Do you really know how she feels? Ow!" Mariel said as Lanshalla nudged her again.

"I only know that Lanshalla understands enough about the Lonely Vine and the mountain history. She is empathetic to such causes. Lanshalla, I'm asking you. Will you help me bridge a divide across our solar system? Maybe even the universe itself?"

Larto was still on one knee. Mariel mouthed, "This is a proposal," to Lanshalla, who tried to ignore Mariel and maintain her composure.

"I'll do what I can," Lanshalla said.

"Thank you," he said, and he returned to the navigation controls in the front of the ship.

"What kind of acceptance line is that?" Mariel asked in a low voice.

"I don't understand," Lanshalla said.

"He proposed!" Mariel said. "And you just said, 'I'll do what I can.'"

"That wasn't a proposal," Lanshalla said.

"No? Offering the universe and all? And on one knee, too," Mariel said.

"I can probe his mind, you know, and learn whatever he's thinking," Lanshalla said.

"Do it!" Mariel said. "See if I'm right."

"Is this the same woman who lost her mind when I probed her in the shower room?" Lanshalla asked.

"That was different. You were an Imperial Bleuh Patrol. Now you're Larto's soon-to-be wife," Mariel said.

"Shh."

"So why don't you probe him?"

"The last time I probed him," Lanshalla said, "I got pregnant."

"You can do that? We have to go to special facilities to have children," Mariel said.

"Not me. Did it right in the stable. And again in the living room," Lanshalla said. "He didn't even know. Neither did I. Never thought it would work, otherwise I wouldn't have done it."

"Have you thought of a name yet?" Mariel asked. "I suppose you have to pick two names, one for a boy and another for a girl."

"I already know it's a girl," Lanshalla said. "I was thinking of calling her Lartatina. After Larto."

"Lartatina?" young Lanietta asked. "What about Lanietta? I don't like Lartatina."

"Sounds like a dessert," Mariel said. "Maybe a name after me, like Mariellianna?"

"Too long," Lanshalla said.

"How about Selalla-biali-abba-bi-annabelle?"

"Way too long," Lanshalla said.

"Well do you have a favorite aunt or grandmother?"

"My grandmother's name was Lallatiatha," Lanshalla said. "But it's another long name. Maybe I'll call her Lalla."

"I like it. Baby Lalla," Mariel said.

"Baby Lalla," Claus said. "I wonder."

"Maybe she changes my name later," young Lanietta said.

Chapter 72: Surprise on Carinia 5

Treyu navigated the spaceship to Carinia 5 and landed on what looked like a barren field of snow.

"There's nothing here," Mariel said.

"There is," Lanshalla said. "Watch."

The snow descended. At first Mariel fell into panic, thinking the ship was falling into quicksnow.

"No, Mariel. There are buildings below. This is how they do things here," Lanshalla said.

"How...how can you tell?" Mariel asked.

"I quickly probed with my ethereal self," Lanshalla said.

The ship descended into a bay, and a ceiling closed.

"Watch this," Lanshalla said.

Giant vacuum vents sucked out the snow.

"Where did it go?" Mariel asked.

"It's being sent back outside," Lanshalla said.

"Your ethereal self again?" Mariel asked.

"Exactly," Lanshalla said.

"That must be a great asset. I mean, you can do all kinds of things we can't," Mariel said.

But then Lanshalla's face went blank.

"What is it? What, Lanshalla?"

"I...never mind. You'll never have to worry about it," Lanshalla said.

"Is it me? Did I say something?"

"No. It's just, well, there can be problems with going ethereal," Lanshalla said.

"I don't understand," Mariel said.

"Every time I go eethi, it starts by flashing all the other times I went eethi," Lanshalla said. "They say it's common,

that we're supposed to deal with it by thinking of something silly just before going eethi to ignore the flashbacks. The effect doesn't last long. Just a few heartbeats. It's just...tiring."

"Your face went blank," Mariel said.

"Do your eyes ever get tired, and you lose focus for a moment? That's what can happen with going eethi too much. The mind goes blank for a moment, trying to readjust to integration," Lanshalla said. "So be thankful at least that you never have to go through that. Flashbacks, brain freeze, fatigue."

"I wonder if this is part of eethi psychosis," Claus said.

"It is," young Lanietta said. "It's the first step."

"We're here," Larto said. "Did you enjoy the trip?"

"It was fine," Lanshalla said. "Mariel is excellent company."

"Oh good," Larto said. "You two got to know each other better then?"

"Yes, we did," Mariel said. "Woman talk."

"Really? What's so special about woman talk?" Larto asked.

Mariel giggled. Lanshalla shrugged her shoulders.

"There's something going on," Larto said.

"There is," Mariel said. "The question is, can you figure it out?"

"Oh I see. A game of secrets. Well, I'm sure whatever secrets you share are not of much importance," Larto said.

"Don't be too sure of that," Mariel said. "Lanshalla is carrying your—"

"Torch for a new people on Carinia 2," Lanshalla interrupted as she nudged Mariel.

Larto looked puzzled but shrugged his own shoulders.

"I'll have to get some quiet time with you, Lanshalla," Larto said.

"Yes, lots," Mariel said. "She wants to tell you about—"

"The ideas I have for helping out," Lanshalla said.

"I'm sure you do," Larto said. "But for now, we are invited to dinner with Treyu's family."

"Sir," Treyu's voice called from the ship's cockpit. "Would you finish the shutdown procedure? There's a fire in the tail control room."

"I'll put out the fire," Larto said, and he rushed to the tail.

"He won't be able to put out this fire," Mariel said with a grin as she pointed to Lanshalla's abdomen.

"Mariel, please!" Lanshalla giggled. "Are you trying to let the surprise out of the box?"

"Someone needs to clue him in," Mariel said.

"He'll figure it out when he's ready," Lanshalla said.

"Lanshalla, Larto is a good horticulturist, a fine boss, and an excellent businessman. He deals with many men and can practically read their thoughts. Nanceya and me? Forget it. I used to explain things. Now I just tell him to accept whatever things come up with us women," Mariel said.

Larto returned shortly.

"The fire is out," he said.

"Hardly," Mariel replied.

Larto looked at Mariel then shook his head. Treyu entered.

"Shutdown is complete," Treyu said.

"There are people outside waiting for us," Lanshalla said. "They are lined up."

"An honor guard," Treyu said. "The Greyans are happy with our arrival."

"Because of Lanshalla, right?" Mariel said.

"Did you tell them I'm a Bleuh?" Lanshalla asked Larto.

"I had to. The Greyans wanted to know. For security. They are very cautious people," Larto said. "Don't worry. I've given my word that all will be well."

"How will you introduce Lanshalla?" Mariel pressed.

"Mariel, no," Lanshalla said.

"They know who she is and what she represents," Larto said.

Mariel giggled and put her hand over her mouth.

"I want to be in the room when they learn the truth about—"

"I'm starved, Larto. When do we eat?" Lanshalla interrupted.

"Very soon. We'll meet with the administrator then eat with her family," Larto said.

"I thought we were eating with Treyu's family," Mariel said.

"My dear, do not think so little of me. My family runs this place," Treyu said.

"I'm going to drag your uniform through mud when we get back," Mariel said.

"That'll be enough. Let's go," Larto said.

The spaceship door opened. Stairs descended. The four walked down the steps and walked between two lines of Greyan guards. Treyu led, then Larto and Lanshalla walked side-by-side, and Mariel followed up last. They reached the end and met the administrator.

"Treyu, my favorite son. How are you?" the woman said as she kissed Treyu on the forehead.

"Very well," he said. "Mother, this is my employer, Larto. And this is his charming new friend, Lanshalla. Larto and Lanshalla, this is Trisha, administrator of Greyan Post 47."

"We are honored with your presence," the administrator said.

"Should we call you administrator?" Mariel asked.

"Oh yes, and Mariel in back," Treyu said.

"You are good friends with Treyu," she said. "You may call me Trisha."

"Thank you," Mariel said.

"This way, please. My family awaits you for dinner," Trisha said.

The four followed Trisha down a hallway with guards following up the rear.

"See those double doors ahead?" Larto said, referring to double doors at the end of the hallway. "That's the way to dinner."

"The state ballroom," Treyu said. "For dining and dancing."

As they approached the end, a blue shape of light took physical humanoid form.

"Libriota?" Claus asked young Lanietta, but young Lanietta did not answer.

Greyan guards rushed Trisha and the four guests to the side of the hallway while they took positions and fired ethereal bursts at Libriota. But Libriota held up her hand and dispersed each energy burst.

"What are you doing?" Lanshalla shouted. "Stop it!"

Guards pulled Trisha and the four out of the hallway and into a side room. Eethi bursts echoed from the hallway into the room, then suddenly it got quiet. Several Imperial Bleuhs with brandished weapons entered the side room with Libriota behind them.

"Good work, Lanshalla. You led me to a rebel base," Libriota said.

"What? No!" Lanshalla said.

"Lanshalla? You...you disgusting Bleuh!" Mariel said.

Mariel lunged at Lanshalla with arms flailing, but Imperial Bleuhs pulled her back.

"This is Carinia 5," Larto said to Libriota. "You have no jurisdiction here."

"Superior life-forms have jurisdiction wherever they go. And as a Bleuh, I claim that right. Come along, Lanshalla. You are to be rewarded for this," Libriota said.

Larto pulled himself in front of Lanshalla and shielded her.

"Foolish Gren!" Libriota said.

"I am Larto, owner of Larto's Vineyard. I make the best wine on Carinia 2," Larto said.

"So you're the one running around contaminating people's wits with your blighted venom of blunder," Libriota said. "I'll make sure you receive extra special torture before your execution."

"No, Libriota! These are my friends!" Lanshalla said.

"I am your friend," Libriota said. "But we are Bleuhs. We do not carouse with Grens or these other...other...ick..."

"Greyans," Trisha said. "I am the administrator here. Let's sit to dinner and discuss things in polite conversation. There is no need for this—"

But at that moment, an Imperial Bleuh set his eethi-blaster on high and disintegrated a Greyan guard. Trisha and the four recoiled in horror.

"That is as polite as I can be. Now my patience wears thin," Libriota said. "Let's go, Lanshalla. The Imperial Bleuhs have a job to do."

"I will go if you promise not to hurt anyone here," Lanshalla said.

"I will never make such a promise," Libriota said.

"We're friends, right? We always back each other. Back me now. Promise you won't hurt anyone here," Lanshalla said.

"Very well. I promise that I won't be the one to hurt anyone here," Libriota grinned.

"That's not what I mean," Lanshalla said.

The Imperial Bleuhs shoved Larto aside and grabbed Lanshalla. Larto came back at them to protect Lanshalla, but an Imperial Bleuh cracked the butt of his eethi-blaster on Larto's skull. He fell to his knees, stunned.

"No, Larto. Don't!" Lanshalla said. "I'll go with them."

"Traitor!" Mariel said. "You've turned against us."

"Mariel is right," Treyu said.

"No," Larto said.

"Larto, you've been tricked," Treyu said.

"Yes," Libriota said. "Lanshalla gave quite a performance at the vineyard, didn't she? We timed her fake arrest perfectly. Now we have timed your capture with equal precision."

"Then you lied about what you said," Mariel said. "You're really not going to have...oh, I was a fool!"

Libriota led Lanshalla away with several Imperial Bleuhs.

"You two," said an Imperial Bleuh to Trisha and Treyu. "Come with us."

"We're not going anywhere," Trisha said.

The Imperial smacked Trisha across the face, and she fell. Treyu moved to retaliate, but two other Imperials put eethi-blaster weapons to his head.

"Compliance is not optional," the main Imperial said.

Treyu helped his mother to her feet, and those two were escorted away to a different room.

"Well," Larto said to Mariel. "For a first outing, this has gone horribly wrong. I should have stayed at the vineyard."

"Larto, if we ever get out of this, well, ask me if we do. There's something... something about Lanshalla. Ask her about it," Mariel said.

"You're making no sense. Ask her about what?" Larto asked.

"Keep silent," an Imperial Bleuh said, and that ended Larto's conversation with Mariel.

Trisha and Treyu were escorted into the hallway, down another hallway, and into a control room. Inside were several Imperial Bleuhs monitoring security video of various parts of the outpost, including one of the ballroom. Trisha and Treyu watched as things unfolded. They saw the double doors open, and inside walked Libriota and Lanshalla. The room was mostly empty except for a few Imperial Bleuhs guarding the waitstaff.

"Greyans," Libriota said to Lanshalla. "Who knew they existed? But thanks to you, we now know there are people on Carinia 5."

"I didn't mean to lead you here," Lanshalla said.

"But you did. You've been a great service to the Hierarchy," Libriota said, then she motioned ahead. "Over here on this platform. We'll be entertained in a moment."

The two climbed up a platform for executive guests situated close to a stage. The Imperial Bleuhs stayed below, so it was just Libriota and Lanshalla.

"Waitstaff! Attend us please!" Libriota called.

After a pause, a waiter climbed up the platform, but Libriota halted him.

"No. That's far enough. Do not climb up to our level. You are not so worthy," Libriota said.

The waiter took their orders and left for the kitchen.

"Grens are much more trainable than Greyans, don't you think?" Libriota asked.

"I've never thought about it," Lanshalla said.

"Well there will be plenty of time for that. We'll have to search through this entire world and get these Greyans into the Bleuh world of civilization," Libriota said.

"What did you mean about my fake arrest?" Lanshalla asked. "And the trial? That wasn't fake."

"Oh but it was," Libriota said. "It had to be convincing. We couldn't tell you anything yet. You had to be in the dark until this moment of conquest we now share."

The waiter brought their drinks and handed them up from several steps down.

"A toast," Libriota said. "To the most successful Imperial acquisition since the Carinia 2 conquest."

Libriota tapped her glass to Lanshalla, but Lanshalla hesitated.

"You'll be promoted when we return to Carinia 2," Libriota said.

"Carinia 2?"

"I know," Libriota said. "Disgusting planet. It's nothing compared to our beautiful Carinia 1. But there's much work to be done. We've always been a great team, you and I. You are my best friend. And I know you feel the same about me. You'll undergo special training to enhance your ethereal skills, then you'll go in disguise and undercover. Grens naturally take to you, that much you've proven. And when you delve deep into their structure, I'll have Imperials move in and rip out that structure. You'll be put under fake arrest again so there is no suspicion. But you'll be released secretly and go undercover, again and again. We'll squash these rebels once and for all."

The waiter brought their food. Libriota devoured her food with such intensity and noise that Lanshalla could hardly eat in comfort.

"Libriota," Lanshalla said. "I..."

"I know. You don't know how to thank me," Libriota said. "There's no need. I understand your loyalty."

An intruder burst into the dining area from the kitchen with a weapon and headed for the platform with intent to kill Libriota. The Imperial guards went after him, but he shot several down and continued his run. Libriota went ethereal and made to stop him, but he got off a quick shot and hit the platform on one side, causing it to tilt severely. Libriota fell into the table, and Lanshalla fell against a railing. The disruption caused Libriota to reintegrate by default, and so she was defenseless. The intruder now climbed up the platform and put his blaster to Libriota's head—point blank. But before he could get off a shot, Lanshalla went ethereal, touched his spinal column with her ethereal hand, and temporarily paralyzed him. The intruder went limp. Imperial Bleuhs hauled him away while other Imperial Bleuhs helped Libriota and Lanshalla off the platform.

"What happened?" Libriota asked.

"A Gren rebel got through our guard and attacked you," the lead Imperial Bleuh said. "Lanshalla neutralized him. We're taking him away for questioning."

"Your security lapse will not go unnoticed," Libriota said. "Report your team to the Hierarchy."

The Imperial Bleuh looked dejected and then walked away. Other Imperials quickly repaired the platform and cleaned up the mess, as the dinner and dishes had flown all over.

"I owe you a great debt, Lanshalla," Libriota said. "You are as faithful as ever. Why, you could have let that rebel kill me. But you didn't!"

"I don't like seeing such things," Lanshalla said. "I don't like seeing people die."

"Of course not, of course not," Libriota said. "You don't like seeing Bleuhs die.

It's a Bleuh virtue. Oh Lanshalla, I'm so eager to work with you in your new role. The excitement, the energy, the pure passion of it all."

"Platform is restored," an Imperial said.

"Well, at least we have that," Libriota said. "Did you get enough to eat? Of course you didn't. Let's see what they have for dessert."

In the control room, Treyu had words for his mother.

"How did you let this happen?" Treyu whispered to her.

"It just did," Trisha said.

"Even if they followed us here, there's no way they could get into the outpost. The snow and ice cover everything," Treyu said.

But Trisha kept silent.

"Someone let them in?" Treyu said.

"No one let anyone in," Trisha said.

"Then how did they get in?" Treyu asked.

"Silence," an Imperial Bleuh said.

Focus returned to the ballroom. The waiter took orders for dessert and returned momentarily with such desserts.

"Mmm. This is good," Libriota said. "Do you like yours?"

"It's fine," Lanshalla said.

"You don't sound enthused. I know this frozen world can be depressing," Libriota said, then she raised her voice and called out, "Bring forth the entertainment."

A large curtain went up, revealing a winter scene of snow and a river with a mixture of snow and small ice chunks. The river was elevated on the near side, with a transparent barrier holding up that side and permitting a view inside the river.

"There is a river near here. I had it diverted," Libriota said.

"I don't understand," Lanshalla said.

"You will in a moment," Libriota said. "The locals call it the Crystilippi River."

"The Crystilippi River?" Treyu asked his mother.

"Yes," she said.

"That's impossible," he said. "How can anyone divert that river into this facility? Something very strange is going on."

"The locals avoid this river," Libriota said. "Do you know why?"

"No," Lanshalla said.

"It contains venomous creatures," Libriota said. "Do you see them?"

Lanshalla looked closely.

"All I see is ice and snow moving slowly with the river current," Lanshalla said.

Libriota grinned.

"You may come forth," Libriota called out.

A group of Imperial Bleuh Patrols appeared. They stood on a platform on the near side overlooking the river.

"Why, that's my old team," Lanshalla said.

"What's the difference between a Bleuh and a Gren?" joked one.

"I know that joke," Lanshalla said. "I made it up."

"Yes, you did," Libriota said. "Do you remember your punchline?"

"One is the foot, the other is the mat," Lanshalla said.

Her group laughed.

"The joke needs work. But your group accepts it," Libriota said.

"Why is a Gren broken?" asked another.

"A Gren isn't broken. It never worked," Lanshalla said reluctantly.

Her group laughed again.

"Mommy, how awful!" young Lanietta said.

"We miss you, Major," another said.

"You have a dedicated team," Libriota said.

"Libriota. I can't do this anymore. I'm ashamed of what I was," Lanshalla said.

"Nonsense. That's Gren contamination. We'll clean you up easy enough with therapy," Libriota said. "A good way to start is by watching how the universe works."

Libriota motioned for the Bleuhs to start. They brought a cage to the river and opened it. Out jumped a bird and landed on the platform railing near the patrols.

"The bird had its wings clipped. Do you remember this training?" Libriota asked.

"Don't do this," Lanshalla said. "This is mean."

"It is nature. You must accept how nature works," Libriota said.

The bird was nudged off the railing. It fell into the river atop an ice chunk. It sensed it was not alone. It cheeped and moved nervously about, looking for what it could feel but not see.

"Stop it," Lanshalla said.

"Just bite your lip. It will be over soon enough," Libriota said.

"We can be better than this," Lanshalla said. "I know we can."

"Yes. By staying at the apex of life, we are better," Libriota said. "Show no weakness, Lanshalla. It's not like we are nudging Bleuhs into the river. That is our reward for being at the apex."

Then without warning, the snow on the river seemed to move, and not in one spot. With lightning speed, three snow spiders camouflaged to look like a mixture of snow and slush pounced on the bird and encased it. The bird fought and cheeped like mad to escape, but the snow spiders pulled it underwater. The bird tried flapping and in doing so made a mad splash of water. The snow spiders injected their venom into the bird, and the splashing died down. The spiders tore the bird apart and consumed it. Red blood stained the snow and slush, but soon the blood washed away, the corpse consumed, and the spiders hid back with the real snow and slush to await the next victim. Lanshalla grimaced throughout the experience.

"Claus, hold me," young Lanietta said.

Young Lanietta ran toward Claus to hug him, but she went through him.

"I..." Claus said.

"No one left to hug," young Lanietta said in dismay.

Claus paused. Then he spoke to get young Lanietta's mind off her inability to hug.

"The Bleuhs had a dark side. That's for sure," Claus said. "For good or not, they are gone."

"I am half Bleuh. This darkness has passed onto me," young Lanietta said. "It is like before...before...before you were around...when I was young...just eleven million...and the training started. It all goes bad with forced training."

"Shh," Claus said. "Stop the vision, Lanietta. Take a break."

The vision stopped. Claus and young Lanietta returned to the studio apartment.

"Claus?" Labba's voice called.

"Labba. Young Lanietta and I have just witnessed a horrible bit of Bleuh training," Claus said. "Where a flightless bird is consumed."

"I've heard about that, and I'm sorry," Labba said.

"Claus, we are barely holding our own," Kechenova said. "I know I sound like a broken record. I wish to convey hope and success, but I have none to offer."

"One wonders if humanity is worth saving," Claus said.

"You must save humanity in whatever way you can," young Lanietta said.

"Such courage from a girl whose race is destroyed," Kechenova said.

"That's why I say it. Carinians have failed, true. Perhaps humans can succeed by learning from our mistakes. There is the hope," young Lanietta said.

"I...wish..." Claus stumbled.

"It is true that human history often repeats failure," Kechenova said. "Your implied argument for human pessimism is understood. But it doesn't help us in this time of evacuation. Adult Lanietta is weakening. Claus and young Lanietta, we are succeeding only within margins of the razor. We need both your help to continue."

"I will continue the vision," young Lanietta said.

The two returned to Carinia 5.

"You've seen this type of thing before," Libriota said.

"There are no snow spiders on Carinia 1 or 2," Lanshalla said.

"True. But we have tropical river spiders that are very similar. You watched many such consumptions during training," Libriota said.

"Yes, I did," Lanshalla lamented. "And I had no trouble watching them. I accepted those spiders as part of the natural order of the universe."

"Release another bird," Libriota said.

A patrol brought forth another cage, and like before a clipped bird hopped out and was nudged into the river. The snow spiders gave the bird time to get nervous and frightful before pouncing on it.

"Don't they ever get full?" Lanshalla asked.

"From what the Greyans say, never. The snow spiders can store vast quantities of energy from continuous consumption," Libriota said. "Let's play a game."

Libriota produced a spinner top. It had four sides and was labeled "A1   A2   B1 B2" sequentially.

"I will be letter A, you will be letter B," Libriota said. "Your group will now bring forth two birds—a white one and a black one. The white one will be number one, and the black one will be number two. Are you ready?"

"I don't want to spin this thing. I don't want to play," Lanshalla said.

"Don't worry. I'll spin for us both. Here goes," Libriota said.

Libriota spun the top. It landed on A2.

"My choice," Libriota said, and she turned to the patrols and yelled, "Release the black bird."

The black bird was let go, it was pushed into the river, and the spiders devoured it.

"You know, this really isn't a game. Everything is chosen for us," Lanshalla said.

"That's what makes it so easy and fun," Libriota said. "In fact, we should be having drinks by now. Waiter! Two Carinian Specials! Now!"

Lanshalla picked up the spinner and looked at it. She wondered why she ever participated in such things.

"Go ahead. Spin it," Libriota said.

"No. It's evil," Lanshalla said.

"It's a piece of wood!" Libriota said. "Is it an eethi-blaster? Is it a spaceship? No. It can perhaps provide fuel for a small fire.

But that's all. What's so evil about a piece of wood?"

"Because of what we do with it," Lanshalla said.

"I'll spin," Libriota said as she took the spinner from Lanshalla. "There, see? Nothing. I'll spin it again. And again. I can spin this for untold time without getting bored. Perhaps I'll get tendonitis. Yes, the evil spinner that gives tendonitis. I'll make my doctor rich. Go ahead and spin it, Lanshalla."

Libriota gave the spinner back to Lanshalla. Lanshalla spun it, and it landed on B1.

"Lanshalla has decided to release a white bird," Libriota shouted to the patrols.

The patrols released a white bird, nudged it into the river, and the spiders devoured it.

"I didn't decide anything," Lanshalla said.

"You chose to spin. You decided. Don't be so analytical, Lanshalla," Libriota said. "Life should be easy. Let the spinner decide."

"Are you done releasing birds?" Lanshalla asked.

"You have a point. Birds are such mindless meaningless creatures. It's time to up the ante," Libriota said.

"That's not what I meant," Lanshalla said.

"It doesn't matter. Again I say, don't over-analyze. Let the order of the universe decide. And the order says to advance to the next higher life-form. We are desensitizing you, Lanshalla. It's part of apex socializing. I know it's tedious, and I apologize for any parts that are boring, but it's necessary therapy, like going out for a run. The run is boring. It's the scenery that counts."

"I..." Lanshalla was about to say.

"Change the scenery!" Libriota shouted to the patrols.

The patrols took their bird boxes away and came back with small animal cages.

"I will roll next," Libriota said.

Libriota rolled, and it came up B2.

"Stop!" young Lanietta said, and she dropped the vision.

The two returned to the studio apartment. Young Lanietta looked at Claus, and Claus returned the gaze.

"Are you going to say something to me?" young Lanietta asked.

"Like what?" Claus asked.

"Doctor Kechenova and Labba would tell you to continue the vision to save more people," young Lanietta said. "I half expect you to urge me on. Tell me to continue, Claus. Say it's mandatory. Spin the piece of wood. No! Make me spin it!"

Claus moved to give young Lanietta a hug. But similar to before, he went right through her spirit. Young Lanietta let out a wry smile.

"I won't force you," he said. "Human history is fraught with such."

Young Lanietta placed a hand each close to Claus's temples and probed his mind.

"Psychology experiments. Dictatorships posing as liberation. Torture. Deception. Reprogramming," young Lanietta said. "Libriota's name itself."

"Lady Liberty I called her," Claus said.

"Two faced," young Lanietta said.

"Yes, two faced," Claus replied.

"I don't want to continue," young Lanietta said. "I want to fade with my people."

"I know," Claus said. "You don't have to fade alone. You can fade with me."

"At least that's something," young Lanietta said.

Young Lanietta took a deep breath (even though she didn't need it). She then took several steps, paused, and spoke.

"I will continue the vision," she said. "I don't know if I can save your humanity, but before I fade completely, I would like to at least bring some closure to the past."

"Okay," Claus said.

Young Lanietta spun around twice, curtseyed, and said, "Here we go."

The two returned again to Carinia 5.

"Lanshalla chooses the black one," Libriota called.

The patrols opened a small animal cage and produced what looked like a small dog.

"No!" Lanshalla said.

"Bite your lip," Libriota said. "It will be over soon."

"This is barbaric," Treyu said to Trisha. "We've got to stop this!"

"You open your mouth again, and I'll remove all your teeth!" an Imperial Bleuh said to Treyu.

Lanshalla covered her eyes.

"Don't cover your eyes," Libriota said.

"I don't want to watch," Lanshalla said.

"We'll only be here longer. You'll need to watch at least eight times," Libriota said.

"Eight dogs?"

"These are Gren dogs. Brought them for just such an occasion. I normally watch a few of these dogs eaten in other venues. But what's better than sharing the experience with my best friend?" Libriota offered.

The dog was nudged into the river. It fought to get out, the spiders went after it, and the dog fought much harder than the birds. The spiders tried to drown it, but the dog climbed atop ice chunks, growled, bit, and clawed at the spiders. Finally, the spiders trapped the dog in webbing and injected it with venom. The dog's barking faded into a whimper. It went silent and limp. Young Lanietta hid behind Claus and shook with anxiety. The dog put out more blood than the birds, but again the river washed the blood away, and soon there was no evidence of it left.

"Oh, this is too slow!" Libriota said. "I watch these dogs go through consumption all the time."

"Well I don't," Lanshalla said. "Not since I've made new friends."

"Are they your friends? Are they really?" Libriota asked.

"Yes. Yes they are," Lanshalla said.

"You trust them?" Libriota asked.

"And they trust me," Lanshalla said.

"By how much?" Libriota asked.

"What do you mean?" Lanshalla asked back.

"Just this. Look," Libriota said.

Libriota motioned to the patrols. They left for a moment and reappeared with Larto and Mariel.

"Larto is a one, and Mariel is a two. Now spin the top," Libriota said.

"No! This is murder!" Lanshalla said.

"Claus, please don't let this happen," young Lanietta said. "Please!"

"They're Grens. Like Gren dogs. Low on the pyramid of life. We're at the apex. We can do away with any life-form lower than us, whether it be a fly, a bird, a Gren dog, or Gren Carinians. Now spin," Libriota urged.

"No! This is enough! Stop this right now!" Lanshalla said. "I'm warning you, Libriota! We were friends, but you have pushed too far. Stop it, or I will!"

Libriota laughed.

"This is going to end badly," young Lanietta said. "I know it will. Claus. Stay here with me."

"I'm here," Claus said. "I'm here."

"What can you do but feel sorry for poor little Grens, hmm? But no matter. I'll spin for you. Look, it's B1," Libriota said, then she turned toward the patrols and shouted, "Lanshalla has picked Larto!"

"I WILL ABORT MY BABY AND DESTROY ALL BLEUHS ACROSS A QUARTER OF THIS PLANET!" Lanshalla yelled.

Lanshalla imploded her ethereal self around her unborn child's ethereal spirit, compressing it tighter and tighter. Ethereal pressure built up higher and higher, and it was only a matter of time before she could no longer contain the energy. Electromagnetic radiation flooded out from Lanshalla's body, disrupting electronic circuits in the vicinity.

Young Lanietta screamed. The vision faded, and the two returned to the studio apartment. Adult Lanietta faded out completely, and so did young Lanietta.

"What just happened up there?" Labba said. "I've lost track of Lanietta. And we just lost Ira to a large selenite attack."

Claus dropped to his knees in agony.

"Claus? Claus! Reply!" Labba said.

"Labba, you just might be the last Carinian in the universe," he said.

"What?" Labba asked.

"We saw something horrible. Lanietta's mother...her unborn baby...she started a process...to kill it," Claus said. "It must have killed Lanietta too."

"Claus! Snap out of it! If Lanshalla killed her unborn baby, then it wasn't Lanietta. Lanietta must've been another child," Labba said.

"Aftova confirms it," Kechenova said.

"Then what about Lanietta? Where is she?" Claus asked. "Is she still alive?"

Claus heard inaudible conversation between Kechenova and Labba.

"We have to make a quick decision, Claus," Labba said. "Either we leave Earth now with what people we've rescued, or we try to save a few more. I'm doubtful we can do much more though."

"Wait," Kechenova said. "Claus, you are using Cluffer 2 as a buffer, right?"

"Yes," Claus said.

"And you are in a studio apartment," Kechenova added.

"True," Claus said.

"Walk over to the bookcase. Do you see a vine?" Kechenova asked.

"Yes," Claus said. "It wasn't there before."

"It's her," Kechenova said.

"Lanietta? In a vine? I don't understand," Claus said.

"Go over to the vine. Touch it. Think of pleasant thoughts with Lanietta," Kechenova said.

"What has been pleasant, I wonder," Claus said. "I wish I could think. Maybe all the silly transformations she did. The 1950s housewife, the drunk girl on Mars, the choir in Arberella."

Claus thought of such things. From the vine came images of adult Lanietta, who returned to the orbs, and young Lanietta.

"You're back!" Claus said. "I thought I lost you."

"The vine of Carinia 2 has protected many Grens," young Lanietta said.

"I'm sorry about the baby," Claus said.

"It wasn't me. Mommy was killing my older sister," young Lanietta said. "I never knew her. But I'm safe. I'll continue at least for a little bit."

"I don't want to risk losing you," Claus said. "I'll have the doctor and Labba end the evacuation and leave Earth. No sense in putting you through more torture."

"No, not yet," young Lanietta said. "Let's return. Not by force. But by choice. Let's be strong, Claus."

The two returned to Carinia 5.

"She has a baby!" Trisha yelled. "No one said anything about a baby!"

"What's going on?" Treyu yelled.

Trisha hit buttons, and the Bleuhs guarding them vanished and became Greyan guards instead.

"Abort the test!" Trisha yelled into an intercom. "Abort!"

"The circuits are jammed," one of the Greyan guards said. "She's started an IEI (Irreversible Ethereal Implosion). We can't circumvent."

Trisha ran out of the room, down the hallway, and into the ballroom. Treyu followed close behind. Both were in a mad frenzy to stop the unthinkable.

"Shut it down. Shut it down!" Trisha yelled.

"The circuits are jammed," yelled a voice from a back room.

"Lanshalla! Stop! This isn't what you think! We didn't know about your baby! Don't implode! Stop the reaction! Stop!" Trisha pleaded.

"It's too late," Lanshalla said.

Lanshalla's implosion bounced back into ethereal explosion. Plasma and sparks flew everywhere. Circuits overloaded. Libriota disappeared. Bleuh patrols magically became Greyan guards. The river disappeared as did the snow spiders and all evidence of anything Libriota or her Bleuh guards had done. Lanshalla's ethereal spirit was ripped into fragments and floated high in the room like wisps of paper having been exploded. Lanshalla collapsed.

"What did you do?" Treyu yelled.

Larto and Mariel came running over from the platform.

"What's happening?" Larto asked as he went to Lanshalla and held her. "Lanshalla? Can you hear me? Lanshalla?"

Greyan guards caught up.

"Take her to the medical center," Trisha said.

"I'll go with her," Larto said.

"Not yet," Trisha said as the guards took Lanshalla away. "She is close to death. She will need special treatment in one of our chambers."

"You did this," Treyu said. "You manipulated all of us."

"I didn't know she was carrying a child!" Trisha said. "You could have told me such a thing before I started the vetting program. I would have taken extra precautions."

"Extra precautions?" Larto said.

"Your tone is increasing, Larto. I suggest you control yourself," Trisha said.

"I demand an explanation. I demand one now!" Larto said.

"Then Lanshalla didn't lie," Mariel said. "And she wasn't a traitor. But what about little Lalla? Will she survive?"

"Who is Lalla?" Larto asked.

"She named it already?" Trisha asked.

"Yes. She knew she was having a girl," Mariel said.

"And he's the father? But he doesn't know," Trisha said. "What a catastrophe. I'm terribly sorry. Treyu, I'm holding you responsible for all this."

"I didn't do anything!" Treyu said.

"Yes, that's the problem. You didn't do anything when you should have provided full details of her condition," Trisha said.

"Lanshalla was pregnant?" Larto asked.

"With your child," Mariel cried.

"But we never...it's...how? Why? Trisha, no more riddles. Explain everything now. Now!" Larto said.

"Treyu said he was bringing two Grens and a sympathetic Bleuh," Trisha said. "Except there is no such thing. Until now. We had to test Lanshalla's loyalty."

"Oh no, you didn't," Treyu said. "I didn't think the technology was perfected yet."

"We got it close enough to try it out," Trisha said.

"Ethereal projection?" Treyu asked.

"Of course," Trisha said.

"Stop the riddles!" Larto said.

"We have been working on a way to deceive people. Project ethereal shapes and create illusions of people and things," Trisha said. "We tapped into Lanshalla's memory and produced her best friend Libriota, who happens to be a powerful Bleuh and very anti Gren. We created this entire Bleuh fantasy of you being followed, the fight in the hallway, and Lanshalla's dinner with Libriota. Libriota and her Bleuh people were never here."

"You almost threw us into a frozen river with killer spiders!" Mariel said.

"That too was an illusion. The water was real. You would have gotten wet, but nothing more," Trisha said. "Now it's your turn to explain. Why didn't anyone tell me Lanshalla was expecting a baby?"

"I didn't know," Treyu said. "That's the honest truth."

"I didn't know either," Larto said. "We Grens have to go to a procreation center to have children. I thought Bleuhs did too."

"Lanshalla became pregnant when she melded with you," Mariel cried.

"She told you? And not me?" Larto said.

"She didn't tell me. I figured it out. A woman's intuition. It was so obvious. I don't know how you could have missed it. She named it Lalla after her grandmother Lallatiatha," Mariel said.

"She aborted it," Trisha said. "In the most barbaric way. Bleuh women are supposed to go to a devitalization center to abort their unborn. Special equipment is needed to protect the mother and all surrounding Bleuhs."

"Then she killed her child to save us," Larto said. "I've never heard of such a thing."

"Yes," Trisha said. "She thought the only way to stop Libriota and the Bleuhs was to destroy them. She could only do that by aborting. She imploded her ethereal spirit onto her child's."

Larto fell into shock and dropped to his knees.

"Take him to the medical center," Trisha said to Greyan guards. "Take Mariel too. She's crying to no end."

Larto and Mariel were taken away to the medical center. Trisha and Treyu followed.

"It was a deception," young Lanietta said sullenly.

"Yes," Claus said. "Evil upon evil."

"We have something in common, Claus," young Lanietta said. "Both our people put forth stress and misery in the name of protection. I lost a sister for it."

"I wish it weren't so," Claus said. "It hardly makes for a good relationship, sharing a dark history that is. I'm an only child myself. I know that doesn't make up for things, but I've often wondered how my life would be different had I grown up in a full family."

"You had a wonderful Grandma Broc. I know this sounds strange, but I wish I could have her for a sister," young Lanietta said. "I...I feel something strange, Claus."

The vision faded. Claus found himself at the shore of the brook behind his grandmother's house. On the far bank stood his grandmother. She smiled. From behind her walked an adult Lanietta to Grandma Broc's left. Then from behind his grandma walked young Lanietta to Grandma Broc's right.

"Build a bridge, Claus," young Lanietta said.

"Build a bridge," Grandma Broc said.

"Build a bridge," the three said.

The vision faded, and Claus returned to Carinia 5 with young Lanietta.

"She both passed and failed," Trisha said. "She proved she's now anti Bleuh. But she's too dangerous. She'll stop at nothing to accomplish a goal, even if it means sacrificing her own child."

"Maybe I should report to the medical center too," Treyu said.

"Why?" Trisha asked.

"I should have my head examined for having a mother like you," Treyu said. "What were you thinking? What? You caused Lanshalla to kill her child. You! What am I going to do now? I can't look at you without thinking you're a murderer! And I can't look at my friends without feeling I betrayed them."

"She's just a Bleuh. Try not to think of her as worthy like a Greyan or Gren," Trisha said.

"Wrong! That's what's killing our solar system! I can't believe you, Mother! You're racist to the core! I know Bleuhs are evil, but we've got to find a solution to this mess. Larto is right. We must make a bridge with a Bleuh. Lanshalla was our hope for that bridge. Will she survive this...this...I don't know what to call it!"

"Materno eethicide," Trisha said. "Or just 'eethicide' if you like."

"I don't!" Treyu protested.

"Treyu," Trisha continued, "we are fortunate this area contains only Greyans and Grens. Any Bleuhs would have been killed. Not that that's a bad thing. But if this bridge you're building contains Bleuhs of purported alliance to our side, they would have perished. Or they could get pregnant and do away with one another. Bleuhs are time bombs waiting to go off."

"The bridge, Mother. The bridge!" Treyu said.

"Better we follow our own path and master ethereal mechanics with technology. That is how we can defeat the Bleuhs. If Lanshalla can help us understand their methods, then so be it. But hear my words, Treyu. Lanshalla will be under extra scrutiny. I won't allow her to undermine anything for the rebels and certainly nothing on Carinia 5!"

Treyu shook his head in disbelief.

"Don't let your guard down, Treyu. Don't!" Trisha said.

"I need to clear my mind," Treyu said. "I do. I'm going to see my friends. Please do something else. I love you, Mother, but right now I need some time away. Please?"

Trisha kissed Treyu on the forehead, and she left. Treyu paused for a moment, staring in disbelief at the spot where last he saw his mother.

"This is the worst moment of my life," Treyu said to himself.

Chapter 73: Ethereal Transfusion with Dalphinacs

Treyu reached Lanshalla's room. Lanshalla's physical body was suspended in air, chest high. A fine collection of glowing lines traveled from the outer edges of her body upward to a glowing cloud of fragmented pieces of light hovering near the ceiling. It was as if the cloud were a parachute suspending Lanshalla's physical body. On one side stood Mariel, and on the other stood Larto. The doctor came forth and spoke with Treyu.

"Lanshalla is barely alive," the doctor said. "She's on full life support."

"I'm sorry. I should have known my mother would try something like this," Treyu said.

"Don't apologize to me. Apologize to them," the doctor said, pointing to Lanshalla, Larto, and Mariel.

Treyu walked over to Larto.

"I'm sorry," he said. "I really am. I know I can't undo the damage my mother has done. I should have been more careful."

"In a single moment, I both gained and lost a daughter," Larto said. "I don't know what to think, what to say, what to do. Who do I blame? Who do I hold responsible? I feel like punching someone, but my fist comes up with empty air."

Larto punched the air around himself.

"Punch me, Larto," Treyu said.

"It's not his fault," Mariel said.

"Then whose fault is it?" Larto said. "Give me someone or something to blame."

"It's no one's fault," Mariel said.

"It has to be. There's failure, there's fault. Someone must take responsibility," Larto said.

"I will take it," Treyu said.

"No, I will," Mariel said. "I should have told you about the baby. But I kept it secret. I was hoping you'd propose to Lanshalla. You even went down on one knee in the ship. But you never made it formal. You never expressed how you felt. How do you feel, Larto? Do you love Lanshalla? Even now after she killed your daughter?"

"I do not blame her," Larto said.

"But that isn't the question. Do you love her? A Bleuh? Can you love a Bleuh?" Mariel asked.

Larto paused.

"I wanted to learn more about her. I wanted more time," Larto said.

"There is very little of that," the doctor said. "Lanshalla is dying."

"Dying?" Larto asked. "But you have her on life support. You're keeping her alive."

"Her vitals are slowly deteriorating. Her ethereal spirit is completely shattered. Unless it can be reassembled and reintegrated with her physical body, it will disperse into the ether, and her physical body will die," the doctor said.

"How can we restore her ethereal spirit?" Treyu asked.

"If she were a Greyan, it would be easy. All Greyans have their ethereal signatures recorded in the central data bank. We don't have a record of Lanshalla," the doctor said.

"How can we get one? I'll travel to Carinia 1 and invade the most secure building if need be," Larto said.

"Bleuhs are not in the habit of keeping signature records of their own. They are too...arrogant," the doctor said.

"Then Lanshalla is doomed," Treyu said. "You can't reconstruct her ethereal spirit using trial and error?"

"Her ethereal pieces are fragile already. Any wrong attempts will destroy them outright," the doctor said.

"We don't have her ethereal signature," Larto said.

"Wait, maybe we do," Mariel said. "Doctor, if a Bleuh melds her ethereal self with a Gren, does she leave a part of herself behind?”

“You mean in me?” Larto asked.

“We haven’t observed it,” the doctor said.

“It was a nice thought,” Larto said.

“But you haven’t tested Larto,” Treyu said.

“No, we haven’t,” the doctor said.

“I want to be tested. If there’s some part of Lanshalla in me, and if it can help bring her back, then yes, I want to be tested,” Larto said.

“You must understand that we are primarily set up for Greyans,” the doctor said. “A Bleuh melding with a Gren is atypical. There are no guarantees.”

“I don’t care,” Larto said.

“The test is not so simple. You would have to be suspended just like Lanshalla, with your ethereal self floating above and exposed to our devices. Further, you’d have to be linked to Lanshalla’s ethereal spirit. It’s less of a test and more of a calibration and synchronization,” the doctor said.

“Let’s do it,” Larto said.

“Keep in mind she is a Bleuh. By nature, her ethereal spirit is more powerful than your Gren spirit. Her fragmentation could spread and fragment your own ethereal spirit. You could die,” the doctor said.

“No, it’s too dangerous,” Treyu said. “You can’t do it, Larto.”

“Mariel, is that how you feel?” Larto asked.

“I’m torn in two,” Mariel said. “I’ve known Lanshalla for a short while, but I’ve known you longer, Larto. Can we take small steps?”

“Take baby steps,” said Trisha, now entering the room.

“Mother, what are you doing here?” Treyu asked.

“Checking on our favorite patient,” Trisha said.

“Get out!” Treyu said.

“Wait. I want to have a word with her,” Larto said as he turned to Trisha. “You’re responsible for that mean trick.”

“We call it vetting,” Trisha said.

“You got an unborn child killed,” Larto said.

“I am sorry for your loss. We will address Lanshalla’s decision to terminate her pregnancy in the next council meeting,” Trisha said.

“The next council meeting? What about now? What are you doing now?” Larto asked.

“She is under medical care,” Trisha said. “What more do you want?”

“I want you to admit you were wrong about your deception and undo all the damage you did,” Larto said.

“For a Bleuh? And her Bleuh baby?” Trisha asked. “We had to flush out Lanshalla’s character. And now we see how unreliable she is. However things might go with her, she cannot stay. Treyu will take her away. If you wish to stay and help Gren rebels, that is your choice.”

“Her ‘Bleuh baby’ is my baby, and I’m Gren,” Larto said.

“My condolences,” Trisha said.

“You’re sorry?” Larto asked.

“Yes. I’m sorry you got mixed up with this Bleuh,” Trisha said.

Larto grew angry and wanted to punch Trisha.

“That’s it, Mother. You’ve done your vetting on Larto too. You don’t need to *test* him anymore,” Treyu said.

“We must antagonize all newcomers to test their resolve under stress. If Larto can’t handle the stress, then perhaps he should return to his vineyard. I will leave. But remember that we support many Gren rebels, and that support cannot be undermined with weak sentiment,” Trisha said.

Trisha left.

“Is this universe filled with nothing but paranoid power-pushing protagonists?” Larto asked.

“Again I apologize,” Treyu said.

“If you want to save Lanshalla, you’ll have to act now,” the doctor said. “Or she will die.”

“Treyu, is there a way that—” Larto started.

"Now, Larto. Now!" the doctor reiterated.

"Another paranoid power-pushing protagonist," Larto said. "All right then. Hook me up. Skip the test and restore Lanshalla to good health. Kill me if you have to. At least I'll be done with this part of this craziness."

Mariel and Treyu looked at Larto with surprise.

"He's just a little upset," Treyu said. "Larto volunteers to help save Lanshalla."

"Good," the doctor said.

The doctor motioned to several assistants, and they helped Larto to a bed. They hooked several devices to him, and his body was elevated to chest level.

"You may experience delusion, hallucinations, or waking dreams," the doctor said. "Or you may experience nothing and suddenly die. Or you may just—"

"Get on with it," Larto interrupted.

"Now who's the paranoid power-pushing protagonist?" Treyu said.

"You," Larto said, pointing to Treyu. "You owe me for this."

"Stop fighting. Everyone stop fighting!" Mariel cried, and she rushed out of the room.

"Mariel? Don't be upset," Larto called, but then he spoke to the doctor and said, "Here, let me down. I need to go after Mariel."

"No you don't! You stay right there!" the doctor insisted.

"I'll go after Mariel," Treyu said, and he left.

"How are you holding up, Lanietta?" Claus asked.

"Better," young Lanietta said. "My parents are together. They care for each other. That means more than anything right now. You're helping too. I feel my adult self gaining strength."

"I'm glad," Claus said. "Though your adult self has given me much grief, I'm hopeful we can put that behind us."

Larto stared at his surroundings. An assistant placed a device over his mouth and nose. He felt incredibly tired, and the room swirled as if he were in a dust storm. But then the dust changed to rain, whirling and whipping around. He was on a small boat with high seas, and he wasn't sure which whipped harder, the wind, the rain, or his spinal column from the bobbing boat. Another boat floated close to him. Lanshalla stood in that boat with a full wine glass in hand. She took a sip, and her boat floated away with great speed.

"Come back!" Larto called, but she was completely out of sight.

Lightning struck. First it was far away, so far away that no thunder could be heard. Then it got closer to Larto. Thunder came, and this thunder competed with the wind to see which was louder and more intimidating. The seas churned deep and pulled up sand that blasted over the gunwale of this poor boat and blasted Larto's skin. Misery did not abate, though Larto wished it.

"It's too much," he yelled. "I can't do this!"

No one heard. Even he could not hear his own voice. The swirling wind had such wrath that it consumed any voice and movement from Larto, silencing him and throwing his body about at will. The forces of the mighty versus the will of a single person, and Larto's will began to fade. Just as his body became nothing more than a stupor of the elements, lightning struck his little boat and shattered it to splinters. Now he was tossed and flipped about in the sea, alternating between tossed above water and below. Lightning hit again, charging the sand particles with electricity and peppering Larto's body with a mixture of intense heat, icy cold, and burrowing pain. He was sure billions of micro-worms had invaded his body, that they were converging onto his heart and head, pressing and squeezing and throbbing the last controls of freedom into tiny spots with no place to flee, like a weary army trapped in a mountain pass by an enemy of infinite numbers and might.

"There is no way out," Larto said. "This must be death. The doctor warned me. But it has all failed. I tried, Lanshalla. I tried."

"He is like so many who struggle," young Lanietta said.

"All those who came before us added something to the tapestry of life," Claus said. "Your parents are impressive, though. I can't imagine my parents, Elaine and Aubert, being like this."

"Do not doubt them," young Lanietta said. "Who knows what secrets they or any parents keep for the sake of their child."

A monster wave of tsunamic proportions carried Larto's body and smashed it against rocks surrounding a lighthouse. He had seen the lighthouse on the way to having his body smashed, and he reached out for it, but forces of the universe had other plans. The waves smashed and smashed and smashed his bones to smaller and smaller and smaller bits, changing his body from a once-sturdy Carinian to that of a mushy mess. He could not fathom anything else these forces could do to him, and he failed to understand how he could yet continue with more torture.

Larto's body felt poisoned. In fact, it had filled with sea water. He threw up what little contents he could, and soon he was in the dry heaves. His abdomen was too weak to perform, and it seized and cramped each time his body attempted to expel its contents. Larto was reduced to this lifeless mush, convulsing like a beached fish unable to get air. His sense of a sentient and civil life-form drained. It was a sickening thing, that people could be reduced to such indignity. Then it happened. Another wave pulled him off the rocks and carried him far out to sea, clear of the storm.

How he stayed alive, he did not know. He wasn't the beached fish he felt he had been. But his shape had changed. He had flippers, flukes, and a dorsal fin. He still had his lungs, but he could not breathe through his mouth (he had a blowhole). Nor could he speak. But he could squeal. A group of similar beings swam next to him, beings that resembled hourglass dolphins. They escorted Larto (who had assumed this hourglass dolphin shape) to a place of nowhere, or so it seemed, as there was nothing but open sea above the waterline.

The dolphins stopped porpoising and dove down below the waterline. Larto followed them to an underwater mountain, but the mountain extended to the waterline, which seemed impossible because he didn't see it while porpoising. They reached a small underwater opening and had to go through one at a time, because there was only enough width for an average dolphin to enter. Once through the opening, the dolphins reached a waterline in the mountain's crater with open sky and a beach on one half of the crater. It was impossible to believe, because of that missing visual evidence from outside. Each dolphin swam to the beach and became humanoid upon touching the sand. Larto followed and also became humanoid on touching the sand. The humanoids laughed.

"This is Carinia 2 before the Veigon and Anrega arrived," young Lanietta said. "And so most of this life developed independently. There was also life from another source."

"Are we seeing memories from the Lonely Vine?" Claus said.

"In a way, yes," young Lanietta said. "My parents shared a drink from the Lonely Vine."

"You put yourself in the vine for strength not long ago," Claus said.

"It's an ethereal circuit breaker," young Lanietta said. "My parents are on the verge of death. This memory is holding them together."

"Just as it is holding you together," Claus said.

"And you too, though you do not know it," young Lanietta said.

Claus paused.

"Frieda still weighs on your mind," young Lanietta said. "Along with the others from Astroosa. I wanted to fade away before, but I will hold out for their resuscitation."

"I hope you're holding out for more than that," Claus said.

Young Lanietta smiled.

"Welcome to Secret Crater," one said.

"I...don't understand," Larto said.

"Forgive my manners," the one said. "I'm Alpharina. This is Beitach, this is Gammdan, and this is Deltina."

"I'm Larto. I'm a Gren from Carinia 2," Larto said.

The four laughed.

"You're one of us now," Alpharina said. "Except you're missing a companion. Beitach is my companion. He and I have shared many good times together. Gammdan and Deltina are also companions. They recently formed a union. Beitach and I are showing them the seas. But you are alone, Larto."

"I thought I was somewhere else. On Carinia 5 with friends. And Lanshalla. I'm supposed to be helping Lanshalla," Larto said.

"Is she your companion?" Alpharina asked.

"I don't know," Larto said.

"Where is she? We must invite her to the celebration," Deltina said.

"I don't know that either," Larto said.

"Are you looking for her?" Deltina asked.

"I...am," Larto hesitated.

"You don't seem sure. But you are weak. Come. We have the celebration to attend. There you can eat and rest," Alpharina said.

Alpharina and Beitach led while Gammdan and Deltina followed up the rear. Larto walked in the middle.

"How is this place possible?" Larto asked.

"That is part of the secret," Alpharina turned around to say. "But you'll find out soon enough."

The group walked through a woods of fir trees then suddenly reached a line of bamboo, completely hidden from the beach. The bamboo played low, soft music. In fact, Larto wasn't sure if it was music at all. It blended in with the wind such that he felt it was more harmonious than anything. The group walked through a serpentine bamboo entrance and joined up with a group of people who were drinking, dancing, playing instruments, cooking food, placing food out, juggling, and performing magic tricks. The bamboo itself formed a large circle, as big as a small town.

"This is familiar," Claus said. "Like Morcellus."

"Yes," young Lanietta said. "A Martacean, descended from those Martaceans that carried Gerenba over from Carinia 1 to Carinia 2. That is what I meant by 'life from another source'."

"Alpharina and her group seem happy with this Martacean," Claus said. "And yet no Veigon. What will happen to it?"

"The Martacean? You will have to wait," young Lanietta said. "I have a sense of how this will go, but I'm not sure."

"Here, have a drink," Beitach said, and he handed a drink from a table to Larto.

Beitach then handed drinks out to the other three.

"The drink is good. But I still don't understand how this is all possible," Larto said.

"We'll show you," Alpharina said.

The five walked to the far end of the bamboo, and there they met a bamboo archway. The archway did not lead back to the forest but instead was the entrance to a mountain cavern.

"Inside is the secret," Alpharina said.

The group went inside. The wall was smooth and clean. There was no dampness at all, and the air smelled of fresh blossoms in the spring, blossoms with such innocence and purity that Larto could hardly believe such a time with such blossoms could ever have existed.

"We are inside the creature," Alpharina said.

"What creature?" Larto said, becoming nervous.

"Do not fear the creature! She is the reason this Secret Crater is possible. In fact, she *is* the Secret Crater," Alpharina said. "A little farther. We are going to the Hall of Communication."

"Again, like Morcellus or Tabelia," Claus said.

"Yes, very similar," young Lanietta said.

The walls remained smooth until they reached the Hall of Communication. Inside were a number of chairs, and the walls were covered in what looked like pipes from many pipe organs. The group walked to the very front to an altar and stopped while Alpharina walked around to the back. She placed a foot against one altar support, the other foot against the other support, one hand on the table, and the other she held out as if welcoming people in friendship. She spoke, but her voice was different, powerful, and charismatic.

"Welcome to the Hall of Communication. I am Omegaphina, great creature of the sea. Alpharina, Beitach, Gammdan, and Deltina I already know. But you are a newcomer," said Omegaphina through Alpharina.

"I am Larto," Larto said. "Is this place real?"

"This place is real, because this place is me," Omegaphina said.

"I feel lost," Larto said. "I was on Carinia 5. The doctor had me hooked up to a device. I was trying to save Lanshalla. Is Lanshalla here?"

"I do not know that name," Omegaphina said. "You are on the second planet from a star we call Carinia Zero."

"Second planet? You mean Carinia 2?" Larto asked.

"You could say that," Omegaphina said.

"But that's impossible. I saw the star at an angle. It wasn't overhead," Larto said. "And the angle changed."

"The star appears to move across the sky, but the planet itself is revolving," Omegaphina said.

"Then this...I am...this is the ancient past. Before Carinia 2 became face-locked with Carinia Zero," Larto said.

Omegaphina laughed.

"You are from the future? You see the past as we were, Larto. But I see you are without companion. I understand your solitude, for I am also without companion," Omegaphina said.

"We are still looking for your new companion, Omegaphina, one that you'll cherish and love," Deltina said.

"I thank you four for your efforts. Larto isn't quite what I had in mind," Omegaphina said.

Alpharina, Beitach, Gammdan, and Deltina laughed.

"We were out on the search and found him at the edge of a storm," Beitach said. "He looked weak and hungry. We could not leave him unattended."

"You did well to help him. Perhaps he can help find me a companion," Omegaphina said.

"I will if you will help me find Lanshalla. But where in all of this can I find her?" Larto asked.

"Is she like you?" Omegaphina asked.

"Not quite. In the future, we are from different worlds," Larto said. "I'm convinced she's around here somewhere. She must be. The Greyans would have made it so."

"We do not know about Greyans. Eat and rest, Larto, then go out with my four searchers and look for your companion. Perhaps she is with my future companion, and both can be brought back, though I will say my future companion will be as large as me, and so he will have to settle for snuggling next to me. That will mean two secret craters instead of one. More room for celebration," Omegaphina said.

Alpharina let go of the altar and returned to herself. The group left the Hall of Communication, passed back out through the archway, and rejoined the celebration. Larto ate, drank, and danced a little, but only just a little as he was tender from being crashed against the rocks. He reclined in a lounge chair while others made merry, and he fell asleep (odd for a Carinian, I know). When he awoke, the sun had set, the people had left, and fires were out with only a little smolder remaining. Nearby huts were lit by candlelight. Larto didn't have long to wonder what to do next. He saw an apparition at the archway where he had passed through earlier. The apparition walked over to him, touched him, and helped him to his feet.

"I am Voice of the Night," the woman said. "I speak for Omegaphina for those at night and those afar. Omegaphina sleeps at night and sleep she does."

"How far afar?" Larto asked.

"As far as the sea goes 'round," she said.

"Can you help me find Lanshalla? Can you search the sea and find her?" Larto asked.

Voice of the Night touched Larto's head.

"Your ethereal spirit is strange to me," she said. "You *are* from another world. And you are not pure. The echo of another churns within your spirit."

"That's Lanshalla's image. She melded with me. Twice," Larto said.

Voice of the Night closed her eyes and concentrated. She then faded away.

"Voice of the Night? Where are you? Voice?" Larto called, running around frantically.

Larto ran around calling more. Then Beitach opened a window.

"Are you still out here? The night is old," Beitach said.

"I saw something. She called herself Voice of the Night. But she is gone," Larto said.

"Your problem must be important indeed for her to visit you. Come inside. Alpharina is making a soothing herbal tea. It should help you relax," Beitach said.

Beitach went around to the door and beckoned Larto in. He went in, and Beitach had him sit by the fireplace. Alpharina came in with a tray holding a tea pitcher and several glasses.

"I don't mean to intrude," Larto said.

"Nonsense. We are older and welcome the company. Now Gammdan and Deltina are another story," Beitach said.

Alpharina giggled.

"We're just an old couple of dalphinacs," Alpharina said.

"You're still as pretty as ever," Beitach said, and the two exchanged little kisses.

"Is that what you call us? Am I a dalphinac?" Larto asked.

"Yes. We walk on land and swim in the sea," Alpharina said. "We're not as big as the walcowats."

"Nor as vicious," Beitach said. "We are a good people and proud."

Larto sipped the tea. It didn't taste like any tea he'd ever had but instead felt like spring blossoms that refreshed his spirit. Beitach brought forth a stringed instrument. He strummed lightly, and Alpharina sang softly. Larto felt drowsy, and he fell asleep in the chair.

"Wake up, sleepy head," said Alpharina as she tapped him on the shoulder.

"Who? What? Where am I?" Larto asked.

"You fell asleep in the chair. But that's no place to rest for the night. I've made up a nice cot here close to the fire but not so close that you'll roll in! You'll be nice and warm. We'll see you again in the morning. I'll have a hearty breakfast ready for all."

"There are only three of us," Larto said sleepily.

"Deltina and Gammdan are coming over for breakfast to discuss tomorrow's itinerary," Alpharina said. "Pleasant dreams."

Again Larto fell asleep, and it was a strange sensation. He had never slept as an inhabitant of Carinia 2 where the sun never sets. But this Carinia 2 was further in the past and still had a true day and night as set by planetary rotation and a star. The life-forms all adhered to this cycle and did not deviate. Sleeping was like dying without as much pain. Sometimes no pain at all. He dreamed he stood above a large pot with minnows swimming around, looking for something, either a way out, a way to unite, or some sense of purpose. At one point they formed a tight ball, and Larto put his hands in the water to hold that ball, but they dispersed as easily as they came together. Then a huge jaw outside the pot opened with intent to swallow Larto and the pot all in one. Larto looked for a way to stop the jaw. He found a broom and placed it in the jaw to hold it open, but the jaw closed and snapped the broom. Larto jumped out of the way just in time to avoid the jaw. It closed on the pot and consumed it, but the water and minnows squirted all over. The minnows flapped on the floor, desperate for water, but the water receded, and so did they.

"We are seeing my father's dream," young Lanietta said. "Is this what it's like for humans? Carinians don't dream, at least not normally. I've never done so. How would it be to choose one's reality instead of being forced to endure the sum total of others'?"

"I wish dreams were like that," Claus said.

"Aren't they?" young Lanietta asked.

"No," Claus said. "When we fall asleep, the dreams seem to choose themselves. We don't choose them. In a way, we are as much a slave to the dreams as we are to reality. Some dreams are quite dreadful. We call them nightmares and are happy to awaken, because the misery is over. We thankfully say, 'It was just a bad dream.' But we try to cherish the good ones."

"I wish to choose my own dreams," young Lanietta said. "Perhaps there's twilight between being awake and dreaming, where one can choose the reality."

"I've heard that artists have such ability. It's like a waking dream. They are practically in a trance and all but oblivious to the outside world. They choose the waking dream and channel it into a form of expression like dance, music, physical artwork, and other things. Perhaps the storytelling process itself is nothing more than a creative person recording that waking dream."

"Can two people share the same waking dream?" young Lanietta asked.

Claus paused.

"I...think...if it happens, the two people will know," Claus said.

Larto woke up with a start much like before when he was outside. The fireplace area was empty, the fire out, and smoke drifted up the chimney. He got up, walked over to the window, and looked out, half expecting Voice of the Night to visit him again. But he saw no such apparition. Satisfied that nothing else could be done in the night, he went back to the cot and fell asleep. He dreamed he was back on his vineyard, working with new cuttings from the Lonely Vine.

The next morning, Larto awoke to an excited Deltina and Gammdan as they burst in through the front door.

"We were visited by Voice of the Night!" Deltina said. "Voice of the Night! We were visited! It was amazing! I must tell you all about it!"

Deltina was speaking to Alpharina, who was already cooking breakfast. Beitach entered through a back door with a load of wood and started a fire in the fireplace.

"What's all this commotion about?" Beitach said.

"It's Deltina," Gammdan said. "Says she saw Voice of the Night."

"I did, I did!" Deltina said excitedly.

"So did Larto," Beitach said.

"What? No, I was visited," Deltina said.

"Please, have a seat at the table," Beitach said. "I'll pour the drinks."

Deltina didn't want to sit, but Gammdan insisted. Larto got up from his cot and sat at the table too. Beitach poured the morning tea for the guests, at a place for Alpharina, and at a place for himself. Alpharina finished cooking, and he helped her bring the food to the table. Deltina started to talk about Voice of the Night again, but Gammdan shushed her.

"Do not forget your manners," Gammdan said. "It is time to give thanks."

"Omegaphina," Alpharina said. "We give thanks for this home you've provided us and our fellow dalphinacs. We also thank you for this food that we've grown on this land you provide for us. May the ocean be wise."

"May the ocean be wise," the others said.

Gammdan, Beitach, and Alpharina started eating, as did Larto. Deltina tried to eat and talk at the same time, but it sounded rude.

"Don't talk with your mouth full," Gammdan said while his own mouth was full.

"I can, and I will," Deltina said back. "Voice of the Night told me that we have a special mission today. She has given me the location of Lanshalla."

"Then she listened to me. She searched for and found Lanshalla as I wished," Larto said.

"As you wished? I thought I had dibs on Voice of the Night," Deltina said.

"It doesn't matter who had *dibs*," Alpharina said. "I'm glad we can help you in this venture, Larto. Voice of the Night rarely pays anyone a visit, save for special cases of need. It would seem she visited you first and instructed Deltina second."

"Because I have the best navigation skills of any dalphinac," Deltina said.

"You brag too much, Deltina," Gammdan said. "Larto is a visitor and doesn't understand such things."

"I don't know how to thank any of you. I also don't know what to expect when we find her," Larto said.

"Is she a dalphinac like you?" Deltina asked.

"Deltina, that's rude. Of course she must be," Gammdan said.

"I really don't know," Larto said. "I hope so."

"I'm sure she is kind-hearted and beautiful," Alpharina said.

"Thank you," Larto said. "You all give me hope."

Breakfast finished, and Beitach helped Alpharina clean up while Deltina rehashed her visit from Voice of the Night over and over, re-describing the apparition's beautiful flowing hair, her dress, her walk, and her voice.

"Oh enough already," Gammdan said. "You're giving me indigestion."

"Humph!" Deltina said. "It's not like she'd ever visit *you*."

"How do you know? I could have fantasized all sorts of things about her," Gammdan grinned.

"You had better not. Or you'll be swimming in a little tin can by yourself!"

"There, there! This is a happy home!" Alpharina said as she and Beitach finished cleaning up. "Did Voice of the Night give you any special instructions about equipment?"

Deltina paused.

"Well?" Alpharina asked.

"Am I allowed to speak about Voice of the Night?" Deltina asked Gammdan sarcastically.

"Yes," Gammdan said begrudgingly.

"The four of us should wear ethereal belts," Deltina said.

"What about Larto?" Alpharina asked.

"He must remain as he is," Deltina said. "He has a special purpose."

"Would you care to share that with us, oh Orator of the Night?" Gammdan mocked.

"That's not funny. Voice of the Night said all would be revealed once we get there," Deltina said.

"Where is there?" Larto asked.

"We'll know that when we get there too. Don't worry, I know the way. Yes, only I do. Because Gammdan has an unclean mind. Would rather focus on what Voice of the Night looks like instead of what she says," Deltina said. "He should be paying more attention to me. I'm mad at him right now. Mad."

"Let's set anger aside and get going," Alpharina said.

"I'll get the ethereal belts," Beitach said.

Beitach disappeared for a moment. Gammdan moved to kiss Deltina on the cheek, but she turned her face away.

"She'll bounce back shortly," he said. "She always does. Sometimes tense moments bring this side of her out."

"Is this a tense moment?" Larto asked. "Are we going into danger?"

"We must be," Gammdan said. "I'll get my Deltina back when this is over."

Beitach brought forth the ethereal belts, and the four except Larto put them on. They left the house, walked to the beach, and dove into the water. As they hit the water, they changed into dolphin-like shapes, again resembling hourglass dolphins. Their ethereal belts added a green tinge to their colors, and so it was easy to tell Larto apart from the others, as he had no such green tinge. They swam down through the opening and out to open sea.

"This way," Deltina said, and she swam toward the east.

The others followed. Deltina picked up speed, and now she and the others were porpoising. They went on this way for seemingly hours, but then Deltina stopped abruptly.

"We're here," Deltina said.

"I don't see anything," Larto said. "Has Lanshalla drowned?"

"Not quite. Follow me," Deltina said.

Deltina dove under the waterline, and the others followed. Then Larto saw it, a school of small fish.

"She is there," Deltina said in echo speech. "She is that school of fish."

"All of them?" Larto asked in return echo speech.

"Yes," Deltina said.

"Her ethereal fragments," Larto said. "They're tied up in these fish."

"Voice of the Night spent all night doing just that—gathering up Lanshalla's ethereal fragments into these fish," Deltina said. "That was the best she could do. Now it's our turn. Larto, hold your head above water and keep your flukes down. The rest of you, we'll use our ethereal belts to direct the school into a spiral around Larto. Keep the spiral going up so that eventually we also have our heads above water. Take a position about a quarter of the way around the school. Gammdan, you go opposite me. Alpharina and Beitach, you two are also opposite each other."

The dalphinacs took their positions. Deltina motioned for them to start. They tapped a fin to their belts, and ethereal energy projected onto the school of fish. The fish swam around and gradually balled up around Larto. The four continued projecting their ethereal energy, and the ball got tighter and tighter. Larto's ethereal self drifted to the side of his body, and from that ethereal image came an echo of Lanshalla's image. The ball of fish swirled around her image, tighter and tighter. The fish shimmered like sequins of a dress Lanshalla's ethereal image now seemed to wear.

"We are making excellent progress," Deltina said. "Hold your positions."

The ethereal image of Lanshalla alternated between humanoid form and hourglass dolphin form. The image steadied more and more on the dolphin form.

"Walcowats!" Beitach echo-yelled.

A pod of orca-like cetaceans encroached on Alpharina and company.

"Maintain your positions! We are nearly through!" Deltina urged.

"We're going to be through if we don't do something about the walcowats!" Beitach said.

"Steady. Steady!" Deltina called.

But there wasn't enough time. The walcowats attacked the four (Alpharina, Beitach, Gammdan, and Deltina), forcing them to fight for their lives. Then another walcowat attempted to take a big bite out of Larto. Larto quickly reintegrated and swam away, but the walcowat instead took a big chomp into the ball of fish. Lanshalla's image was still tied into that ball, and as the walcowat swallowed the fish, it swallowed the image of Lanshalla too. She was gone.

"Lanshalla! No!" Larto echo-yelled.

"Mommy!" young Lanietta called.

Larto swam back at top speed and rammed into the side of the walcowat, but it laughed, turned away from Larto, and swatted Larto far into the air with its flukes. It had what it wanted, and so it squealed to its fellow walcowats. The pod left.

"Is anyone hurt?" Beitach called.

"Just a few bruises," Gammdan called.

"My fins are scraped," Alpharina said.

"Gammdan. I have a big gash in my back," Deltina said. "I tried to hold out until the end. It wasn't enough."

"You'll have to go back to the Secret Crater," Beitach said. "Omegaphina will help you."

"I'll take her," Gammdan said. "Can you swim, Deltina?"

"I'm weak," she said.

"Hold onto my dorsal fin with your jaw. I'll pull you back," Gammdan said.

Deltina and Gammdan left.

"We can track the pod," Alpharina said. "I captured Lanshalla's ethereal signature with my belt."

"We will go," Beitach said. "Though I wonder what we can do. We have no way to defeat walcowats."

"I will defeat them all if I must," Larto said.

"Brave, but foolish. We best go along and watch after Larto. We must keep him from making rash decisions," Beitach said.

"Follow me," Alpharina said.

Alpharina followed the walcowat pod, but from a safe distance. Alpharina and Beitach were careful to minimize the above-the-waterline visual effects of porpoising, but Larto was too anxious and porpoised too high. Alpharina stopped the three.

"You must calm down, Larto. Take easy breaths. Don't leap so high out of the water. We will be noticed, and we can't have that happen," Alpharina said.

"I...just can't help it. I want Lanshalla back. I want her now," Larto said.

"I know. A wise sea wins the day, but a careless one loses it. Don't lose the sea," Alpharina said.

"I'm still getting used to the concept of a real day," Larto nodded in agreement. "But I will try."

Larto took a deep breath and relaxed a bit.

"There, much better," Alpharina said. "Let's resume."

The three continued, and they reached a point where the walcowats dove underwater. The three also dove underwater, and they couldn't believe what they saw. It was another underwater mountain with no visible above-water features. They watched the walcowats go through an opening into the mountain. The three approached the opening cautiously, but as they did, they noticed subtle movement in the mountain rocks near the opening. Alpharina turned away and swam a good distance with Beitach and Larto behind. She stopped.

"Why didn't you go in?" Larto asked.

"There were walcowats camouflaged in the rocks by the opening," Alpharina said.

"They would have made quick work of us," Beitach said.

"Well we can't quit now. We'll have to storm through or something," Larto said.

"One does not storm through walcowats," Beitach said.

"Is there a way we can pretend to be them?" Larto asked. "I mean, we change shape when we go from water to beach sand."

"It is not that simple," Alpharina said.

"We cannot change our physical mass to something that large," Beitach said.

"What about ethereal mass?" Larto asked.

Alpharina and Beitach exchanged glances.

"Does that mean yes?" Larto asked.

"I could use the ethereal belt to project an image of a large walcowat male and scare them off," Beitach said.

"No. They'll sound an alarm and alert the entire community. Better to entice them in secret desire. I could use the ethereal belt to project my image as a walcowat female," Alpharina said. "Then you and Larto can slip in unnoticed."

"I don't like that. You'd have to be close, and they could capture and kill you," Beitach said.

"I can outrun them if need be," Alpharina said.

"There's another problem," Beitach said.

"You mean when you want to leave?" Alpharina asked. "Just send me a message through the ethereal belt, and I'll lure them away again."

"Too risky. It might not work. We'd be trapped," Beitach said.

"Maybe there's another entrance," Larto said.

"Good luck finding it. The mountain is huge, and spending time looking among the rocks could lead to other dangers," Alpharina said. "No, this is the only way."

"Then I will go in alone. It's only fair," Larto said.

"And do something rash. Get killed. We'd never know. Even if you do make it and are ready to come out, how will we know?" Beitach said. "No, I will go with you. Like I said, someone must watch over you."

"Very well. This is how we'll do it," Alpharina said. "Stay behind me. I'll use the projection to shield us at first, but then you must go in through the flank as I send the projection the other way."

Beitach and Larto agreed. The three swam back to the walcowat mountain. Alpharina generated her female walcowat image. The image cooed and flirted with the hidden guards. To the dalphinacs' surprise, not two hidden guards but four revealed their positions and moved toward the projection. Beitach and Larto swam casually to the side from a distance, and they circled around such that the enticed walcowats did not see. Alpharina herself took a position in hiding behind other rocks, and she sent the projection on around the side of the mountain. Beitach and Larto reached the unguarded opening, and they entered. They kept quiet as they traveled through a tunnel that was much larger than the one in Secret Crater. When they reached the end, they saw they were in an area very much like their own Secret Crater, but this crater was larger—larger beach, larger forest, and larger water area. The two noticed a great number of humanoids on the beach. Tall they were, and their skin had patches of black and white.

"Swim to the end," Beitach said. "We'll beach behind those shrubs."

Larto and Beitach did just that. They reached a shrub that blocked them from being seen. They next dove onto the beach and changed to humanoid shape. Beitach went first, and Larto went next. Larto noticed that Beitach kept his hourglass dolphin colors on his humanoid skin, and so Larto did the same. But just as Larto landed on the beach, a tentacle shot out of the water and hooked around his leg. It pulled Larto toward the water and nearly had Larto pulled in, but Beitach grabbed Larto's arm with one hand and a tree with the other. It was all Beitach could do to counter the pull from the tentacle.

"Oh this is awful," Larto said.

"Don't speak so loudly," Beitach said. "We don't want to draw attention."

"So am I to be quiet and die?" Larto asked.

"Give me a moment to think," Beitach said.

"I don't have a moment," Larto said.

Larto was about to shout, but a female humanoid walcowat patrol happened along the splashing. She pulled out a plasma gun, shot the tentacle, and helped pull Larto to shore.

"Thank you," Larto said. "I almost drowned."

"This area is forbidden," the patrol said. "Too many squidipi attacks. You should stay in the authorized areas. I haven't seen you two before. What are your names?"

"I'm Larto, and this is my friend Beitach," Larto said.

"I am Patrina," the patrol said. "Did you come for the feast?"

Larto was unsure of what to say and looked at Beitach.

"Yes, we did," Beitach lied.

"Have you registered? All guest walcowats must register. You should have read the instructions on the invitation. You *do* have your invitations, don't you?" Patrina asked.

"We had an ocean fight with dalphinacs and lost them," Beitach said.

"You lost the fight, lost the dalphinacs, or lost the invitations?" Patrina asked.

"All," Larto said.

Patrina laughed.

"You two are hopeless. Come along. I'll vouch for you. The feast is underway, and your spirits will lift when you see what's on for the main course," Patrina said.

Patrina took a liking to Larto and walked alongside him while Beitach followed behind.

"Your colors are very interesting. I've never seen such swirls in a walcowat. And yet your friend here has plainer colors," Patrina said.

"Thanks a lot," Beitach said sarcastically.

"I don't mean to be rude," Patrina said. "But Larto's colors here are fascinating. They catch the eye and seem to move on their own. Why I'd say they are almost hypnotic."

"Joy," Beitach said, still showing his sarcasm.

Patrina laughed.

"I must apologize for being so overt," Patrina said. "I'm just overwhelmed. A patrol shouldn't be overwhelmed, I know. I need to desensitize myself. And to do that, I'll need to spend lots of time with you, Larto. Will you join me for dinner?"

"Double joy," Beitach said.

"Oh don't feel left out, Beitach. You may come along too," Patrina said.

"And interrupt you two love fish? That would be unpardonable," Beitach said.

"I have a friend. I'll invite her too. We can double date," Patrina said.

The three reached an area of the feast, where people sipped drinks and made merry. Smoke rose from several chimneys inside a large hut.

"My shift has just ended," Patrina said. "Let me change into something more suitable. You two sit right here. Don't go away!"

Beitach and Larto sat at a table next to a juggler tossing fruits in the air. When one slipped from the juggler's grasp and landed on the table, Beitach smashed it.

"Sorry," Beitach said.

The juggler (and others) moved off a bit.

"This whole place irritates me," Beitach said in a hushed voice. "We're deep in walcowat territory, and I'm worried about my Alpharina. Now a walcowat has the hots for you and is bringing her friend for me. I'm a married dalphinac!"

"I don't like it either," Larto said. "But I don't know any other way. You played along with the feast idea, and that seemed the way to go."

"Perhaps I should have told Patrina right there that we were invaders, and all walcowats had to die," Beitach said.

There was a coincidental silence in the surroundings. Larto and Beitach looked around as if thinking Beitach had been overheard. But the fellow walcowats returned to their merry making.

"I don't think you should talk like that," Larto said. "We need to learn as much as we can about this society. One of these walcowats must have ingested Lanshalla's ethereal spirit. If I can find that walcowat and reach down to her, then maybe... maybe..."

Just then, Patrina returned with her friend. Both were dressed in stunning outfits.

"Belila, this is Larto, and this is Beitach. Beitach and Larto, my friend Belila," Patrina said.

"Oh Patrina," Belila said walking over to Larto. "He's dreamier than you described!"

"Larto is *my* date!" Patrina said. "You have Beitach over here."

"Oh," Belila said in disappointment.

"Oh don't get sour on me," Beitach said. "It's not like I fancy you either."

"What??" Belila said.

"My apologies," Larto said. "Beitach is just a little tired from the swim. We've come a long ways, and he's hungry. He gets grumpy, but let him eat and rest, and he'll be as cheerful as ever."

"He'd better be," Belila said.

"I need a drink," Beitach said.

"Let me get you one," Belila said.

"Would you like one too?" Patrina asked Larto.

"Let me get you a drink," Larto said. "Where are they?"

Patrina giggled.

"I'll show you," she said.

Beitach stayed behind at the table. Belila made a beeline for the drink station while Patrina and Larto followed behind (though they trailed pretty quickly).

"Belila is in a rush," Patrina said. "She must be very eager to get Beitach a drink."

"I'll say," Larto said.

Belila got just one drink. She rushed back toward Beitach and brushed by Patrina accidentally.

"Very odd of her," Patrina said. "Here. This is the drink station."

"What's your favorite?" Larto said.

"I like Checkered Surprise," Patrina said.

"Make that two Checkered Surprises," Larto said to the drink tender.

The tender produced the two drinks. Larto handed one to Patrina then took the other for himself. The two had just turned around in time to see Belila dump her drink onto Beitach across the way.

"This is an outrage!" Beitach bellowed.

"Go back to your pod, you decrepit sea monster!" Belila said back.

Belila walked back to Patrina with a deliberate stride.

"Nice date," she said, handing Patrina the empty glass.

"Belila, I'm sorry. Belila?" Patrina called.

But Belila had already gone off and begun socializing with other walcowats. Patrina stood in shock. Beitach walked up next.

"Your friend is full of surprises," Beitach said. "I think I'll go clean up somewhere."

"I'm sorry, Beitach. The wash station is just over there," Patrina said as she pointed over to a wash hut.

"Grrr," Beitach grumbled.

"Will your friend be all right?" Patrina asked Larto.

"Yeah," Larto said. "What about Belila?"

"She'll be fine too. I guess I misjudged things with her and your friend. I really am sorry," Patrina said. "Forgive me?"

Larto laughed.

"What's so funny?" she said, amused.

"I should ask for your forgiveness. For Beitach's behavior," Larto said.

Now Patrina laughed.

"You're the most polite, friendly, and happy walcowat I've ever met. You must stay the night! I have a little place out of the way. Don't worry, there are no squidipis even close. You'll be quite safe."

"I have a feeling Beitach will not want to do so," Larto said.

"Oh, I understand," Patrina said, deflated.

"Tell you what. I'll let Beitach know that I'm staying for a bit and that he can leave. He'll understand," Larto said.

"Are you sure?" Patrina asked with her hopes growing by the second.

"Absolutely! He really is a party-pooper anyway. He only came along to keep me out of trouble," Larto said.

Then Patrina moved close to Larto's right ear and whispered into it:

"Trouble is exactly what I had in mind, mister!"

Larto felt uneasy. This was getting out of hand. He only played along to find Lanshalla, but Patrina was becoming too enamored with him. She grabbed Larto by the arm and rushed him toward the beach.

"Where are we going?" he asked.

"For a swim! I want to see your walcowat features!" she said.

"Oh no," Larto said to himself.

Larto knew he couldn't change to walcowat (orca) form. He had only been able to mimic the dalphinac (hourglass dolphin). But why was that? Wasn't this all some dream or delusion? What caused him to take the dalphinac form? His body had been crushed upon rocks and carried to sea. It was then that a passing pod of dalphinacs took him in, and at that point he took dalphinac form. Could something similar happen to him in front of Patrina? It was a great risk, one that would reveal him as totally alien to this walcowat society.

"Come on!" she said as she rushed him along the beach.

Unbeknownst to the two, Beitach had wandered to the beach away from the merrymaking and sat on a rock under a tree. He watched the next few moments unfold. As Patrina and Larto reached the water's edge, Patrina released her grip and dove into the water. She immediately transformed into a walcowat, with full orca-like size, shape, and coloration.

"Come in! The water's great! See?" she said as she splashed water at Larto with her flukes.

But as that water hit Larto, he felt only a tendency to convert to dalphinac and not walcowat. And so, he jumped into the water and held onto his form with all his might. He remained in humanoid form and struggled to tread water.

"Help, help!" he called.

Patrina laughed with a deep and intimidating walcowat voice. Though these cetacean-like creatures breathed through their blow holes, they could ingest air into their stomachs and release the air in order to vocalize. And so speech often resembled a slow burp, with the effect of causing low-frequency vibrations that shook the mere mortal's bones to the core.

"So that is your game!" she said. "You are very clever!"

Patrina swam under Larto and nibbled his toes. He started to laugh. She swam under him again, only closer to the waterline. She then carried Larto on her back and caught him with her dorsal fin, as if the dorsal fin were the back of a chair.

"Now we go porpoising!" she said.

She dipped underwater with Larto barely holding on, and she leapt out of the water high and mighty. The angle was so steep that Larto fell back behind her dorsal fin and grabbed the fin with his hands. He held on with all his might to keep from slipping off.

"We go again!" Patrina said, and she dove down.

Larto felt like he was on a roller coaster that dove into a lake every now and then. He was so surprised by the speed and motion that several times he neglected to hold his breath before going underwater, and he caught a mouthful of that water. He finally had to let go, as he was choking.

"Oh, a little too much fun?" she asked, now circling around to him. "Let's get you to shore."

She nudged him along and pushed him to shore. She then jumped out of the water and returned to humanoid shape.

"Oh, but my dress is wet! How did that happen? I'm supposed to be drip-dry! I'll have to see my tailor about this! He promised a drip-dry dress when doing form-conversion," Patrina said. "Stay right here! I'll be back soon!"

Larto stumbled over to Beitach.

"You almost blew it," Beitach said. "Very clever holding your humanoid shape. But how will you explain it to her?"

"I...I don't know," Larto said. "I'll say I got scared."

"Scared? From her? She won't believe it," Beitach said. "Tell her you've been poisoned. The tentacle on your leg did it."

Larto thought, he looked down at his leg, and there was evidence of where the tentacle had been.

"But it's not swollen enough," Beitach said. "Here."

Beitach temporarily removed his ethereal belt and whipped Larto's leg before returning it to his waist.

"Ow! That hurts!" Larto said.

"Good. Should temper your judgment this evening," Beitach said. "I take it you are staying."

"Yeah. I told Patrina I would. I also told her you'll likely leave," Larto said.

"Likely," Beitach said. "Can't handle these beings. They make me sick."

"Patrina sent me," said a humanoid walcot with a portable hot-air blow drier, who then dried off Larto and left much to Beitach's bemusement.

"Would you at least stay for dinner?" Larto asked. "For courtesy? It would look odd if you came for the feast only to leave just before."

"I can stay that long," Beitach said. "Patrina said the main course was special. I wonder what it is?"

Patrina returned in a dry but stunning dress, and she overheard Beitach's last comment.

"Why don't I show you?" Patrina said.

"You didn't bring another friend, did you?" Beitach asked.

"Beitach, please," Larto said, but Patrina laughed.

"No, you are quite safe!" she continued to laugh. "Shall we?"

Patrina took Larto by the arm and headed for the hut with the smoke coming out of the chimneys. Beitach followed.

"We have an especially good catch today," Patrina said. "They were feeding in our waters too. Imagine! We can't let petty thieves take the good stuff. Must protect our fisheries at all costs. And so, we feast on...are you ready? Look."

Patrina opened the hut and rushed Larto in. Inside roasting on wooden spits were multiple dalphinacs. Larto saw them first and became quite ill. Beitach didn't see them yet and looked instead at Larto to see why he was buckling over.

"Larto? What's wrong? Why are you...oh," Beitach said, suddenly realizing what was cooking.

"They're a special delicacy! Don't you think so?" Patrina asked.

"I need air," Larto said. "The smoke. The fumes. I need air."

"Of course!" Patrina said, and she led the two back outside.

Once outside, Larto felt a little better. But not too much better. Seeing the dalphinacs on spits very much resembled seeing his four rescuers on spits, and the sight—strong and unyielding in his mind—filled him with disgust. Beitach was angry, but he kept his emotions in check.

"Patrina," Larto said. "There's something you must know."

"Um, no," Beitach said to stop Larto.

"What is it?" Patrina asked.

"We're not who you think we are," Larto said.

"Larto is in a fugue," Beitach said. "He doesn't know what he's saying."

"I don't think so," Patrina said with concern. "I think he's about to tell me something very important. Whatever it is, Larto, I can handle it. We're mature walcowats, right? We're apex beings. Whatever it is, I'll understand."

"Larto," Beitach said with a stern voice. "I don't think it's a good idea to—"

"We're vegetarians," Larto blurted. "We don't eat meat."

Patrina looked at him with a puzzled expression, but then she burst out in laughter.

"Vegetarians? Really? How is that possible? Even the Mysticeti ingest thousands of tiny creatures," Patrina said.

"I'm sorry. But we don't eat meat. We ingest...uh...algae," Larto said. "I didn't want to show you my water form, because we have an extra slit on each side for allowing water to pass through from our mouths. We filter algae. Not as efficiently as the Mysticeti, but good enough. We look like freaks. I didn't want to scare you. I didn't want to...to...make you run away."

"Oh, Larto!" Patrina said, and she hugged him. "That's beautiful. I think you're the purest of life-forms ever. You can't hide behind such purity. Long have I aspired to something higher than I am. I feel inferior to you. Just a lowly walcowat dependent on meat. Perhaps we could start a family. Our children could choose what they consume. Maybe several generations down, our descendants could evolve into higher beings, not needing to consume life of any kind. Totally energy independent. We're like the walcowata and walcowato, the first female and male of our new species."

"Oh sea of mis-er-ry," Beitach grumbled.

"I'll have the cook fix you two up something special. I think we can find something close to algae. Please! And I'll try some with you! This will be a very special feast indeed!" Patrina said. "Stay right here! I'll be back in a moment!"

Patrina ran off.

"Boy did you put your fluke in your mouth!" Beitach said to Larto. "What are you doing telling a fish tale like that?"

"What was I supposed to tell her?" Larto asked. "That I didn't want to eat my own kind? Or your own kind?"

"You were supposed to say you were sick from the tentacle bite and show her the welt," Beitach said. "That was also to be the reason for not changing your form in the water."

"I don't know what came over me. The sight of those poor dalphinacs...I...I couldn't think. Well? How did you hold your composure?" Larto asked.

"I know what a walco-snot can do. I'm angry, yes, but not surprised. They've hunted us before," Beitach said. "And yes, I call them walco-snot when I'm mad."

"Well don't let them hear that. We'll be on the menu for breakfast!" Larto said.

Patrina returned shortly.

"The cook is making special preparations for us. Please. We are all to be seated. There will be special entertainment while our meal is served," Patrina said.

While the three sat for their specially prepared meals, a humanoid in disguise slipped into the kitchen and found the three plates marked, *Patrina*, *Larto*, and *Beitach*. Unobserved by others, the humanoid pulled a shaker from a sleeve, sprinkled a powder onto the plates marked for Patrina and Beitach, hid the shaker, stirred the algae dishes, and slipped off.

Back at the table, Patrina, Larto, and Beitach watched as a line of half-dalphinac/half-humanoids came out and performed in dance, like chorus girls. They had humanoid heads and legs but dalphinac torsos and fins, with each having a dorsal fin. Beitach put a hand to his mouth to keep from yelling his disgust while Larto simply stared in shock.

"Aren't they terrific?" Patrina asked. "We also catch new ones and train them for the entertainment. But none go to waste. When they are too old to perform, they get recycled into dinner."

"Dinner?" Larto asked.

"Oh I'm sorry. Vegetarian. Well, at least none go to waste," Patrina said.

Dinner was served. Patrina, Larto, and Beitach received their algae dishes while the others received their cooked dalphinacs. Beitach tasted his algae and could hardly stomach it. Larto made a greater effort to pretend he enjoyed the algae. As did Patrina.

"Excellent," Larto said.

"It is different and will take getting used to," Patrina said.

"I need a drink," Beitach said.

Beitach got up and walked over to the drink station.

"I think it's a little too spicy for Beitach," Larto said. "But the algae proportion is just right for me."

"Oh I'm so glad. I didn't want you to go hungry. But what about Beitach?" Patrina asked.

"He'll be all right," Larto said. "I think he's lost his appetite anyway. He's been so worried about my leg that he can hardly relax."

"Your leg? What's wrong with your leg?" Patrina asked.

Larto pulled up his trouser leg and revealed the welt and tentacle marks.

"Oh, that looks awful! It must hurt terribly! Why didn't you tell me you were in such misery? Oh!" Patrina said.

"I didn't want to worry you. You were so happy," Larto said.

"I'm so selfish! I should have had you checked out immediately! Please! Let's get you to a doctor! This is life or death!" Patrina urged.

Patrina rushed Larto from the table, past several huts, and up to the doctor's hut. She banged on the door, but no one answered. A note on the door explained why.

"At the feast. Be back later."

"Oh! I must find him!" Patrina said. "Stay here! I'll bring him back."

Larto stood by the door. He looked inside through a window and saw a number of medical devices, posters of walcowat anatomy, and a stuffed dalphinac.

"Oh, you're here now," Beitach said as he happened to walk by.

"The doctor isn't in. Out to the feast," Larto said.

"My stomach is out too," Beitach said. "Those algae upset me mightily. I'm going back out so I can empty my guts. Find some real fish. I've already communicated with Alpharina. She's getting ready."

"Are you coming back this evening?" Larto asked.

"Not sure. Depends on how I'll feel. If nothing else, I'll send Alpharina after you in the morning," Beitach said.

"Thank you. Good luck," Larto said.

"Same to you," Beitach replied, and he left.

Patrina returned shortly.

"Thank you doctor for helping out in this time of need," Patrina said. "This is Larto."

The doctor opened the door.

"Please come in," he said.

The doctor directed Larto onto an examination table while he directed Patrina to a chair nearby. But Patrina could not contain herself in the chair, and so she chose to stand by Larto.

"Let's take a look at your injury," the doctor said, and he rolled up Larto's trouser leg.

"How bad is it?" Patrina asked.

The doctor examined the wound, he took a device, pressed it against the welt, and touched a button. A micro-plucker pulled a bit of tissue from Larto's welt. He winced in pain, but it passed quickly. The doctor placed the tissue sample into a medical analysis machine, and results went up on a display.

"Well," the doctor said. "You do have a trace of poison in your leg. But this welt is from a different injury."

"Oh!" Patrina said. "I must have caused it with the plasma blaster. I'm so sorry, Larto!"

"I must treat the wound. But first, we must test your walcowat confirmation. We'll have to get you into the tank so you can take natural form," the doctor said.

"Uh, well, I..." Larto stumbled.

Larto realized that this was it. He'd be found out for sure when he couldn't take walcowat form. He'd go into dalphinac form, and they'd put him on a spit for breakfast. Would that end this dream, if dream this really were? He'd go back to Carinia 5, and Lanshalla would be lost for

good. Where was she in all this? He needed desperately to find her, but he had to figure out this shape conversion problem first.

"Larto is shy," Patrina said. "In fact, he's not like us."

"Oh?" the doctor said.

"He's a...vegetarian," Patrina said.

"That's impossible," the doctor said.

"No, it's true," Patrina said. "He has a slit on each side of his face for allowing water to pass through. He filters out the algae."

"Then he's not a walcowat. He's a Mysticeti," the doctor said.

"But he has real teeth like us," Patrina said.

"Have you seen him in this form?" the doctor asked.

Patrina paused.

"I see," the doctor said.

"Can't you treat his wound without forcing him into the tank?" Patrina asked.

"No, not without an accurate confirmation of his natural form, especially since you tell me he is not like us. Could be dangerous. Could kill him," the doctor said. "Help me get him to the tank."

Patrina helped the doctor lift Larto to his feet.

"I can walk," Larto said.

The three climbed a set of stairs to a platform next to a holding tank big enough to hold several orcas.

"Stand there for a moment," the doctor said. "I need to activate the monitoring devices."

The doctor stepped away and walked to a monitoring station.

"I'm nervous," Larto said.

"Here," Patrina said, removing a necklace hidden under her clothing and placing it over Larto's head. "This will help you focus and convert back and forth. It was a gift from my mother when I was young. I had trouble converting back then. Scared and nervous."

"I can't accept this," Larto said. "This is an heirloom."

"No, please," Patrina said. "I feel like you're family already. This will be over soon. Then we'll spend quality time together."

Patrina kissed Larto on the cheek.

"I am ready," the doctor said.

"Jump in," Patrina said with a smile.

"But I—" Larto protested.

"Jump...in!" she said with a chuckle, and she pushed Larto into the water.

Larto fell in. He treaded water for a little bit.

"Go ahead," Patrina said. "Convert."

Larto felt his body slipping into dalphinac form. But then it drifted into other shapes, alternating between his shattered body on the rocks and other cetacean-like creatures.

"His focus is off by twenty points," the doctor said. "He can't target his form."

"The poison?" Patrina asked.

"Hard to say. His readings are confused," the doctor said.

"Concentrate, Larto. Place the image in your mind and focus," Patrina said.

Larto thought of a walcowat image. The necklace tingled at first, but then it seemed to pour micro-worms throughout his body. Slowly yet gradually, his body gained mass and morphed into a walcowat, with the extra slit on each side of his face for streaming through mouth-water. He held this form and swam a bit in the tank.

"Marvelous! Beautiful! I knew you could do it!" Patrina said. "I want to jump in and snuggle with you! I'm going to!"

Patrina moved toward the water to jump in.

"Wait!" the doctor said. "Don't jump in! I must analyze Larto first! You'll ruin the imaging system."

Patrina bit into her finger and held off. The anticipation was killing her. She heated up and perspired.

"Whew! Larto, you're so exciting that I'm burning up with desire."

"Just hold onto that flame, Patrina. Analysis is almost complete," the doctor said.

But Patrina couldn't wait. Her body was so overheated that she had to jump into the water to cool off. In she went, and into

walcowat form she became. She splashed with great excitement and happiness.

"Patrina," the doctor said. "Patrina!"

"I'm so happy!" she said, and she snuggled next to Larto.

"If you're done playing around, I'm ready to give my prognosis," the doctor said.

"The prognosis is everlasting love," Patrina said.

"Larto has successfully attained his form," the doctor said.

"I could have told you that!" she said.

"In doing so, his body has rid the last of the poison. He is healed. No further treatment is necessary," the doctor said.

"Healed by love," Patrina said. "But I disagree, Doctor. More treatment is necessary. More love for Patrina and Larto. More love. More..."

Suddenly, Patrina turned over lifeless with her belly pointed up. Larto tried to nudge her aright with his fins, but she remained unmoved. Larto returned to humanoid form and tried helping her, but he didn't have the strength.

"Something's wrong with Patrina," Larto said.

"Get out of the tank. Hurry!" the doctor yelled.

Larto scrambled out. The doctor grabbed a large respiratory mask from a table, climbed up the platform, attached the mask hoses to connectors on the platform (which were connected to a respiratory machine), and he jumped into the tank. As he landed in the water, his torso and head changed to walcowat form. He had flukes but also had very long legs. He stood by Patrina, fitted the mask over her, and arighted her body. She started breathing.

"I...what...happened?" Patrina struggled to say.

"Don't speak," the doctor said as he went back to his monitoring station and back to humanoid form. "I'm running a quick analysis. Yes, you've been poisoned. Something you ingested. What did you eat for dinner?"

"She had a special algae meal," Larto said.

"That should not be causing these conditions," the doctor said. "Unless..."

"Unless what?" Larto said.

"Unless someone put poison in the algae," the doctor said.

"I ate the algae," Larto said.

"Yes. You show no ill signs from it," the doctor said. "Did anyone else eat algae?"

"My friend. Beitach," Larto said.

"Where is he? We should check him over immediately," the doctor said.

"He didn't feel well. He left in search of fish," Larto said.

"He may have been poisoned too. You must go find him and bring him here. He could die without treatment," the doctor said.

"But what about Patrina?" Larto asked.

"I'll take good care of her. Go find Beitach!" the doctor ordered.

Larto left the hut and headed for the beach. But there was a problem.

"How do I contact Beitach? I don't have an ethereal belt," Larto said. "And I can't get out as a dalphinac. The guards will catch me. Unless...I wonder if I could change to walcowat shape. I did it in the tank. If I could, then maybe the guards will let me swim out. Why wouldn't they? A guest leaving the party. But still, finding Alpharina and Beitach could be tricky. They would see me as a walcowat and not as a dalphinac."

Larto decided he had to leave. He backed up, broke into a run toward the water, and dove in. As he did, he focused on the image of a walcowat, and the necklace helped him change to such a shape. He surfaced, took a deep breath, and prepared to dive down and through the tunnel to the outside. But as he did so, another walcowat swam in front and blocked his path. He attempted to swim around, but this other walcowat moved to block. Larto squealed for the other walcowat to get out of the way. He tried a feint one way then swam to the other, but the other walcowat countered his attempt. It became more aggressive. Instead of just blocking, it pushed, it shoved, and it

slapped its flukes on top of the water, making a commotion. This slapping was so systematic, going from side to side, that it forced Larto back to shore, where he changed back to humanoid shape.

"Whoever you are, please move out of the way! I have an urgent mission to perform!" Larto announced.

"The mission *is* urgent," said the walcowat as it transformed to humanoid shape and walked onto shore.

"Belila!" Larto said.

Belila returned a sinister laugh.

"I must find Beitach!" Larto said.

Belila walked up to Larto and put her arms around him.

"Now I have you all to myself. No Beitach. No Patrina," she snickered.

"You! You did this!" Larto said, trying to pull away.

"You're a handsome walcowat," she said. "Your side slits are most impressive. No others have such wondrous slits as yours. You really eat algae, do you?"

"Belila, no. This is wrong," Larto said.

"Why? Because Patrina found you first? She can't do what I can do. I can teach you to eat meat. Even like it. Mmmm," she said, and she kissed him with such slobber that drool dripped all over his chin.

"What poison did you use?" Larto asked, pulling away so he could speak.

"That you will have to find out," she said. "You must earn your status with me."

"Belila! I will...will..." Larto stumbled.

"Will what? Tell the authorities? What authorities? And what would you say?" Belila said.

"I'll say you poisoned Patrina and Beitach," Larto said. "Then they'll deal with you."

"I am the authority!" Belila laughed. "No one crosses my path. And you best not either. Patrina and Beitach will die, unless you do everything I say."

Without warning, Belila moved Larto's wrists behind his back and handcuffed them. She then dropped to his ankles and clapped restraints on them. She ran a chain from the ankle restraints to the handcuffs and held onto an additional length.

"You're under arrest," she said. "For attempting to resist my advances."

She tugged on the chain, and it caused Larto to trip and fall. She laughed.

"You see? You're my property now," she said.

Belila led Larto to her hut. She showed him a bed and shoved him down on it, face up. She then chained him to the bed.

"Belila, this is wrong. Let's talk and work this out," Larto said.

"We are working this out. My way," she said.

She ripped off his shirt, and then she brought forth a bowl with an applicator sponge on a stick. She dipped the sponge in a gooey substance in the bowl and coated his chest with it.

"Mmm," she said. "Let's have a fantasy, shall we? What kind of meat would you like to eat first?"

Belila dove at Larto to land atop him, and while in the air, she changed shape to a large fish but with smooth scales and gentle fins. She landed atop his chest and wiggled her body back and forth on the goo.

"Smell the oil," she said as her scales exuded a fish oil. "Mmm, mmm, good."

Oil dripped into Larto's mouth. He tried turning away, but he couldn't.

"I'm...a...vegetarian," Larto tried to say.

Belila laughed. She slipped off, slithered onto the floor, and retook humanoid shape. She brought forth another bowl, dipped the sponge in it, and put it to Larto's face to smell, which was something between the smell of leather, incense, and a pungent flower. She then re-dabbed his chest with this new goo, put the bowl and dabber down, and jumped above him as before, only this time she took the shape of a large frog and landed on his chest, with her limbs straddling him. Again she rubbed around on his chest in the goo, and she slobbered frog drool onto his face.

"Taste the frog, Larto. Make it tasty and good. Good!" she drooled.

Still in frog form, Belila kissed and licked Larto. In fact, she used her long tongue to lick all about his head. She then moved down to his chest and licked up the goo. She went back to his face and kissed him again. Larto was disgusted. Belila hopped off and returned to humanoid form.

"You're still conscious," Belila said. "Many others have passed out by this point. You are impressive indeed. And now, it is time for the next stage. A new meat to taste."

Belila dabbed more goo from yet another bowl and put a bit on Larto's nose. It smelled like (in modern aromas) tuna, mineral oil, and transmission fluid. Belila put the bowl and dabber down and jumped into the air above Larto's chest. She changed to dalphinac shape, landed, and squirmed around on his chest.

"Have you ever fantasized about becoming romantic with a petite dalphinac? Like me? Here's your chance. Love the animal in you. Taste it. Mmm, mmm!" Belila said.

Larto resisted, remaining as motionless as possible.

"Take a bite out of my flesh. Savor the sweet proteins of this delicious dalphinac. Use, abuse, confuse, consume," she said. "Use, abuse, confuse, consume. Use me!"

Belila unchained Larto's arms and slapped them around her to force him to shove her about.

"Abuse me!" she said, and she forced his hands to punch her. "Yes, punch me more. More!"

The goo had by now sunk into his tissues and affected his nervous system. When she gave commands, a strong electrical force traveled from her body through the goo, into his torso, and out to his limbs. Like a moving cramp (but with no pain), his arms and fists involuntarily punched her blubbery sides. She unchained his legs.

"Punch me all over. In the face. The eyes. The fins. Kick my flukes. Confuse me with abuse. Abuse and confuse!" she screamed with delight.

Larto had no control of himself. He punched and kicked her all over to the point where he even lifted her up in the air a little with such punches and kicks. Belila's eyes rolled around as she lost orientation, and she knew the moment was right.

"Confuse and consume. Consume. Consume!" she said.

"No," Larto struggled to say.

"Bite my beak," she ordered.

While still forcing Larto to punch her, she squirmed her beak up to his mouth and forced him to close his mouth onto that beak. He cut through her beak, and she screamed in half delight and half pain.

"Chew! Swallow!" she ordered. "Do it!"

In the continued rapid multiple movements of punching and kicking, the beak was chewed and swallowed. Larto had no choice. He felt badly that he had ingested dalphinac tissue, but there was nothing to be done. Belila sighed in relief, rolled over, and returned to humanoid form. A bit of her nose tip was missing. It bled a little, but not too much. She snuggled next to Larto and kissed him.

"That was excellent!" she said. "I've never had a walcowat perform like that! Patrina couldn't possibly know the joy you can bring. Ahhhh. But, my sweet buttercup Larto, are you ready for the next challenge?"

"You've already gone beyond what you should," Larto said.

"Ah, but that was only as a dalphinac. The best is yet to come," she said.

"Oh no," Larto said.

"Oh yes!" she grinned.

Belila went to yet another container with the dabber, but while the prior goos were translucent, this goo was dark and opaque, like tar. It smelled like tar too. She dabbed it on his chest and put a bit under his nose.

"There's nothing left of me," Larto said. "Stop this, will you?"

"One last time!" she said.

Belila jumped into the air and changed to mini-walcowat shape, being just the length of Larto's body. She squirmed around and splattered the black tar all over his body. Her voice became deeper and more sinister.

"So now I have squeezed myself down to this size just for you," she said. "Use, abuse, confuse, consume!"

Larto had to think of something quickly. The tar forced his limbs to move her about as before, positioning her with control for the "use" stage before punching and beating her for the "abuse" stage.

"Tell me about yourself," Larto said. "I know nothing about you."

"What is there to tell?" she said. "There is only the rapture of the moment."

"Are you like this with other walcowats?" he asked.

"I already told you that no one has gone this far with me," she said with a heavy breath. "You are blowing me out of my mind!"

"You make me perform to your will, but you say nothing of yourself," he said. "What meats do you eat?"

"All kinds. Dalphinac is my favorite. But I've eaten other walcowats too, at least those who needed to perish. Sometimes I get bored and chase schools of fish. I like to roll them up and eat them. There was one just earlier that I consumed. I could have had fresh dalphinac, but I felt I needed the fish. Mmm. It had something special in it too. Some force of power. I could feel it. And I feel it with you. You share the force with me. Oh Larto, take me to the edge of the ethereal universe! Show me the height of rapture! The breadth of passion! The length of exhilaration! Show me...show me...I..."

Larto realized Belila was the walcowat who'd consumed Lanshalla's ethereal fragments. Lanshalla was with him.

"The Lonely Vine!" Larto said. "I will show you the Lonely Vine!"

Belila froze in place atop Larto, held by the stupor of euphoria. Her ethereal image separated from her body and went above her, the full-size image of a walcowat. A smaller image of a humanoid tried separating from the walcowat image. It tried, it snapped back, it tried again, and it snapped back. It was Lanshalla's image. Then the walcowat ethereal image returned to Belila's physical mini-walcowat self. She rolled over, returned to humanoid form, and collapsed in exhaustion.

"Wow!" she said. "My breath is stolen! You are the thief of passion! I had an out-of-body experience! I've never had that. I felt like two people! Unbelievable! You're a god! You must be! Command me, oh great one. Command me! But return my breath first!"

Belila snuggled tightly with Larto, and then she fell asleep. She started to snore.

"What do I do?" he asked himself. "Lanshalla is with me. Right now! But she's trapped in this evil body! She responded when I mentioned the Lonely Vine."

"Lanshalla must renew her faith to the Lonely Vine," said a voice.

Voice of the Night walked over to Larto. He tried to sit up, but Belila's grip prevented it.

"Voice of the Night," he said. "Is the Lonely Vine in this realm?"

"Yes," she said.

"Where is it?" he asked.

"It is where it should be," she said.

"I don't know where that is," he said. "If I could find it, I could bring it to Belila. She could taste a grape. Maybe that would shake Lanshalla out."

"The Lonely Vine does not travel to others. It exists in solitude. All must go to the vine. All must be one with the vine. But all must not destroy the vine. The vine exists in the fine line of existence, between the conflicts of eternity," Voice of the Night said.

"Riddles," Larto said. "Those are all riddles. I need help. I need guidance."

Voice of the Night smiled.

"Follow your heart. It will lead you to the vine. Bring all who conflict you. You must experience the vine together. Together," Voice of the Night said, and she faded away.

"Is it Belila I should bring?" Larto asked. "Or Patrina? What about the dalphinacs? Alpharina, Beitach, Gammdan, and Deltina?"

But there was no answer.

"I'm really at a loss. I...I..." Larto said, but he was exhausted, and he fell asleep.

He was only asleep for a little while. He opened his eyes and saw a figure at the window. His body jolted lightly, but the figure shushed him.

"Do not be afraid," the voice whispered.

"Alpharina! What are you doing here?" Larto asked.

Alpharina hesitated to see if Belila would awaken. She did not.

"I sent Beitach home. He was sick. I came in his stead," Alpharina said.

"He's been poisoned. By Belila here. I never did get out of her what kind it was," Larto said.

"Afleppa seed poisoning," Alpharina said.

"What?"

"I detected the signs immediately. He barely had the energy to make it back. Gammdan came back to check on us, and I had him tow Beitach back," Alpharina said. "I brought an antidote for you in this vial. I thought you'd be poisoned and near death. Instead, you seem unaffected. I take it you've been involved in physical exertion?"

"Something like that. But I've learned something else. Lanshalla is inside Belila," Larto said. "Belila is evil. She also poisoned another walcowat here named Patrina. Patrina has a crush on me."

"Belila does too?"

"Hers is more like infatuation," Larto said.

"And here I was worried about you finding just one companion," Alpharina said.

"I'm in a sticky situation," Larto said.

"I can see that," Alpharina said, pointing to the goo around him.

"Alpharina, would your doctors be willing to treat Patrina for afleppa seed poisoning?" Larto asked.

"She's a walcowat you say? Out of the question," Alpharina said. "Tell the local doctor."

"He wants to keep her and treat her. But I need to get her out of here, I think," Larto said.

"You aren't sure?" Alpharina asked.

Just then, Belila stirred. Alpharina ducked down outside, and Larto pretended to be asleep. Belila turned over and resumed snoring.

"I had a visit from Voice of the Night. She gave me a riddle about the Lonely Vine. Don't ask. But I'm pretty sure I need to go to the Lonely Vine and bring conflict with me," Larto explained.

"What is this conflict?" Alpharina asked.

"I don't know. Could be Patrina's love for me. Or her poisoned state. Or Belila's state," Larto said.

"Or this walcowat culture," Alpharina said.

"Yes! So many things of conflict. I must start somewhere. Tonight. But I can't leave this bed without Belila noticing me gone," Larto said.

"I have an idea," Alpharina said.

Alpharina entered the hut, walked up to Larto's ear, and whispered her idea. Larto smiled.

The night grew late. Belila rolled over again and put an arm over her proud catch.

"Larto. Rub my back. Larto," she said.

But no back rub was offered.

"I can make you rub my back, you know. Still thinking of your Patrina?" Belila said while half asleep. "Forget it. I won't share how she was poisoned. You're mine now. Mine. Rub my back."

An arm rubbed Belila's back. But it was thin and warm with petite fingers.

"Your fingers feel odd," Belila said.

Belila sat up suddenly, turned on the lamp next to the bed, and pulled down the covers. Next to her lay Alpharina.

"You're not Larto!" she said in surprise.

"Hello!" Alpharina waved. "Nice place you have. I like back rubs too. Rub my back."

"No! Where's Larto?" Belila demanded.

"Who?"

"You know plenty well who I mean. Where is Larto!"

Belila changed to full walcowat form. She crushed her body onto Alpharina's. Alpharina struggled for air.

"Tell me where he is!" Belila squealed.

"He...uh...went to the lighthouse...with Patrina," Alpharina said.

Belila returned to humanoid shape.

"Ugh," Alpharina said, getting her breath back.

"I'll deal with you later," Belila said, and she stormed out.

"Gammdan, come in," Alpharina called through her ethereal belt. "Larto has taken a walcowat named Patrina to the lighthouse. Another walcowat named Belila is now giving chase."

"Alpharina, get out of there!" Gammdan said. "I'll let our people know to stay clear of the lighthouse waters."

Belila headed out for the lighthouse, the same lighthouse where Larto's body had been smashed. As she left her secret crater, Larto and Patrina were already approaching the lighthouse. Both were in walcowat form. Patrina swam on her own and gained gradual strength.

"Thank you for the antidote," Patrina said. "I feel so much better. But I can't believe Belila poisoned Beitach and me. Just to get us out of the way?"

"She claims she has authority in your society, and that I should not cross her. She made me do things with her that I regret," Larto said.

"I'm shocked. I mean, she has royal claims in our society, but I've never known her to betray me like this. We were friends, I thought," Patrina said.

"It seems I acted as a wedge between your friendship with her," Larto said.

The two arrived at the lighthouse. The water was calm, and the morning young. Long shadows cast across the lighthouse and rocks.

"What is it you hope to find here?" Patrina asked.

"The Lonely Vine," Larto said. "I know, you wonder what it is. It's special, I can tell you that. I was visited by an apparition. Her name is Voice of the Night. She is helping me find someone. Someone special."

"Oh? I thought I was special," Patrina said.

"Patrina, you are special, and I wish I could share more time with you. But I came here for a special purpose. There is—"

"Another female," Patrina said in despair.

"Named Lanshalla," Larto said.

"Is she your companion?" Patrina asked.

"She might be. Not quite. I'm not really sure if you'll understand or if I can explain it. She's the enemy that I'm hoping to make a friend," Larto said.

"You're right. I don't understand," Patrina said.

"There are other things too. I haven't been totally truthful with you. I'm not a walcowat. Not even a vegetarian," Larto said.

"But you take walcowat shape," she said.

"I know. I came here on these rocks from another dimension. My body was wrecked and carried out to sea. A group of dalphinacs found me, and I mysteriously took their form," Larto explained.

The two reached the rocks, landed, and took humanoid form. Patrina sat on a flat, comfortable rock, and Larto sat next to her.

"You were a dalphinac? That's like the enemy. We hunt, kill, and eat them," Patrina said.

"I know. It's all very strange, isn't it?" Larto said. "Voice of the Night told us that we'd find Lanshalla in a school of fish."

"How can one be in a school of fish?" Patrina asked.

"Lanshalla had her ethereal spirit shattered. It dispersed. Voice of the Night helped gather up those fragments but could only get them into a school of fish. My four dalphinac friends and I were trying to convert that school into a physical being,

into Lanshalla. We were able to ball up the fish and almost got Lanshalla to form, but a pod of walcowats came along and attacked. One of them ate the ball of fish. Later I learned it was Belila."

"Belila told me about that. I didn't think much of it at the time. I was patrolling the beach. Then you and Beitach showed up," Patrina said.

"Because we knew that Lanshalla was in one of the walcowats. We pretended to be walcowats like you, but we weren't. We came in as dalphinacs. One of our dalphinacs lured your guards away by projecting an ethereal image of a female walcowat," Larto said.

"That explains a lot, such as why you couldn't change into a walcowat. But you did in the tank," Patrina said. "I really thought you were one of us. I still do."

"I can't explain why. I think your necklace helped me. I could probably become other creatures in your world. Maybe a Mysticeti if I socialized with them long enough," Larto said.

"So Lanshalla is in Belila?" Patrina asked.

"Yes."

"And you want her out? In her own body?"

"Yes."

"But how?" Patrina asked.

"I'm not sure. Voice of the Night said my conflicts must be brought to the Lonely Vine, which should be somewhere among these rocks. What happens after that, I don't know. I thought maybe we could eat grapes from the vine," Larto said.

"Well, let's look for the vine," Patrina said.

The two climbed among the rocks. Waves splashed gently, and the clear day made for a relaxing effort. They walked up and down the length of rocks with no evidence of a vine. Finally, Patrina made the discovery.

"Here," she said. "It's here."

Larto walked over to where Patrina stood. Yes, there was the Lonely Vine, precariously rooted at the base of the lighthouse and on one of the rocks. It was on the leeward side of the lighthouse, if the waves were considered the "windward" side. The leeward side also happened to be toward the north, and so the Lonely Vine was shielded from both waves and sun.

"It's just a small vine," Patrina said. "It bears no fruit."

"I don't understand," Larto said. "This vine is supposed to solve the problem. But it's doing nothing. No grapes either. It's just barely holding onto life."

"Maybe that is the answer," Patrina said.

"Barely holding onto life? Sounds noble, but what can we do with it?" Larto asked.

"You can start with this," Patrina said.

Patrina held Larto's hands and kissed him.

"Take your hands off my property," said a voice from the water.

A walcowat approached, landed on the rocks, and converted to humanoid form.

"Belila?" Patrina asked. "What are you doing here?"

"I could ask you the same. The doctor is worried about you. Return to his care immediately," Belila said.

"I'm cured, no thanks to you. You are supposed to be my friend. And I find out you poisoned me and Larto's friend. What kind of friend does that?"

"My friendship only goes so far," Belila said. "But this walcowat is mine."

Belila pushed herself between Patrina and Larto and put her arms around Larto.

"He's not a walcowat!" Patrina said. "He's more than that. Belila, you've changed since you ate that ball of fish. I know why. There's an alien inside you. Her name is Lanshalla. We must rid you of her."

Belila laughed.

"What a ridiculous thing to say. Even if true, why should I give up anything I own? I feel better now than ever before," Belila said. "Go back to the doctor, Patrina. Larto and I have work to do. Oh, what's this?"

Belila reached down to pull the Lonely Vine from its position, but Patrina pushed Belila off the rocks and into the water to prevent the Lonely Vine from being disturbed. Belila immediately reverted to walcowat form. She swam about to build up speed, then she porpoised high into the air and over the rocks, catching Patrina with her (Belila's) flukes and dragging her (Patrina) into the water. Patrina reverted to walcowat form, and the two fought.

"Stop!" Larto called, but they did not heed him. "I must do something. I must!"

He jumped into the water with the image of a walcowat in his mind. His body took that shape, and he swam in between Patrina and Belila to block the fight, but he found that he took all the punches and slaps, and he could not hold his position. The beating caused his mass to shrink, and he found himself morphing into a dalphinac. Belila squealed in glee as she nibbled into Larto's flukes, but Patrina used the opportunity to chomp into Belila's flukes. Belila whipped back and made to chomp Patrina's dorsal fin, but Patrina escaped. Larto swam back to the rocks and converted to humanoid form.

"I'll leave you both!" Larto yelled. "Then there will be nothing to fight for."

"Try it!" Belila taunted. "No one gets away from me!"

As Patrina and Belila fought, Larto noticed the Lonely Vine grew an extra leaf. He went to pluck the extra leaf, but he heard a horn sounding in the distance. He looked up and saw a large group of dalphinacs approaching, with a horn in the beak of the leader. They divided and surrounded Patrina and Belila. Belila tried fighting back by chasing whatever dalphinac was in front, but the dalphinacs crossed paths a-beam, and so the chased dalphinac passed the a-beam dalphinac going the other way (and thus oncoming into Belila), and that oncoming dalphinac used its superior dexterity to peck Belila in the eye.

"Are these your dogs, Larto?" Belila bellowed. "Call them off! I warn you. Call them off!"

Belila held her position, and the dalphinacs stopped their pecking. Larto noticed the Lonely Vine had grown a second leaf.

"You stop first!" Larto said. "This fighting is madness. There are plenty of fish in the sea. There's no need for a walcowat to attack a dalphinac. Leave the dalphinacs alone. And they will leave you alone. Matter of fact, you could all become friends. Work together to tame the seas. Create aquatic civility."

"I would offer a fin in friendship," Patrina said.

"Hah!" Belila said. "There can be no friendship with such disparity. We are the apex. As such, all vacuums of power must be filled, either through wisdom or folly. And we walcowats are the wiser. Behold!"

A large group of walcowats surrounded the dalphinacs.

"Now what will you do, Larto? Will you stand there like the Lone Fool with your Lonely Vine?" Belila asked.

"I only know that Lanshalla is inside you," Larto said. "She was once like you, but she tasted the history of the ages, which this must be. She saw how power and might can be used or abused to the benefit or detriment of everyone. I ask you all to think carefully about cause and consequence. What future do you leave for yourselves? Your children? Is this how you wish to live your days, poisoned with the strain of conflict? The day is calm and beautiful. Our star shines its blessing without question or need and gives no special favoritism to any. We depend on our star. We need it. And we ourselves are no greater. Be humble to our star and all that it provides. The day is young. It is wise. It is ours to keep if we wish it. Turn to your neighbor and extend a fin in peace."

Amazingly enough, the walcowats and dalphinacs exchanged signs of friendship by touching fins. All went well, and peace was well underway. Patrina jumped out of the water and onto the rocks, where she took humanoid form and extended a hand in friendship to Larto. Larto shook her hand. Then Belila jumped out of the water in similar fashion and shook Larto's hand. At first her shake was friendly, and she was ready to forget what had transpired, but the feel and oil from his skin touched her own, triggering a reaction of desire. She pulled him close and kissed him, to which Patrina shoved Belila away and kissed Larto herself. Belila shoved Patrina back, the two exchanged punches, were at each other's throats, and fell into the water where they reverted to walcowat form. The conflict was contagious, and the once-friendly cetaceans now turned against one another, fighting bitterly with great pain and injury.

"No, no!" Larto shouted.

But no one listened so it seemed. Larto was by himself and beside himself. He looked to the one life-form not involved for help, the Lonely Vine. But it was involved. The vine had grown several more leaves, and it had gained in height. Further, it sent a runner root into the water, and it pulled that water into its vines and leaves. The leaves engorged with water, and they let out excess in a raging steam. The steam was so intense that it pumped clouds into the air, and with that steam was carried a highly pulverized form of salt from the sea. The clouds filled the air, and the salt carried into those clouds, turning them dark.

"Stop the fighting!" Larto called. "It's feeding the vine! Stop!"

No one listened. Another runner vine leapt out from the base and wrapped itself around Larto. It extended Larto beyond the rocks and dunked him waist-deep into the water. Larto was being used by this vine to not only pull water from the sea, but other elements as well. The mass conflict of energy, death, and the passing of ethereal spirits flowed through Larto and into the vine. He looked back at the vine and saw a single grape form. It glowed with a bright orange heat, and any steam that flowed over it superheated and shot upward. Larto was helpless to act, but he could see. Gradually, the level of the sea lowered, though this did not deter the combatants. In fact, it alerted others to the critical tension of the situation. Creatures from afar came and fought. Larto looked out across the lowering sea level, and he saw mountains rising from the depths. He wasn't sure if his eyes deceived him or not, but the mountains appeared to grow larger.

"They are not growing larger," said Voice of the Night as she suddenly appeared. "They are coming closer. For battle."

"You arranged this? It's a nightmare! What kind of sanity is this?" Larto asked, but Voice of the Night disappeared.

The mountains grew closer.

"To war! To war!" the voice of Omegaphina bellowed from one such mountain.

Larto guessed another mountain was the walcowat crater. And other mountains belonged to other sea creatures. These mountains threw balls of flaming lava at one another. They never came as close as the lighthouse, but they were large enough to be seen from far away. The salt formed large stones like hail and pelted the distant mountains only to rain down like fireworks. The sky became ever darker and darker. Great waves came ashore as a result of the distant mountains disrupting the sea with their collection of mass. The waves did not disrupt the fighting, but they did break the grasp of the root holding Larto, and he sought cover. He entered the lighthouse through a door at its base and ascended the stairs until he reached the top. The light had long since burned out, and so he was alone there with nothing but chaos around. And chaos it was, because the only water left in the seas was from the deep. The mountains churned that up and sent it to shore as waves. The churning sent ancient bottom dwellers, bones, and peat ashore, creating a muddy graveyard mess. And still the fighting continued. Patrina made several efforts to jump out and hold onto the rocks as a humanoid, but Belila always jumped at her and carried her back into the muck.

The vine's reach was far, and it was able to draw water from the deep without need of it being brought to shore. This accelerated the draining process greatly, which is what happened. The fighting cetaceans kept at it despite the growing

layers of muck. And so, the only evidence of them fighting was a constant bubbling in the mud, with large bubbles popping with great noise, so much so that the windows in the lighthouse shattered. Larto covered his ears as the cacophony of bubbles nearly drove him mad. But there reached a point where the sky had gone almost completely black, the only light came from the distant lava, the bubbles slowed, and quieted. Larto removed his hands from his ears, and whether it was reality or a trick on his senses he wasn't sure, but each popping bubble sounded like a dolphin laugh. Not a happy laugh or a sad laugh, but a laugh like a dead creature being forced to move by means of external electrical stimulation. It came to him that Lanshalla would die inside Belila, and that the others like Patrina and Alpharina would die too. He raced down the lighthouse, out the door, and into the muck. But he could not move through the muck. It was too thick and held onto each foot with a powerful suction force.

"I'll be pulled into it!" he said. "I'm trapped!"

Indeed, with each attempt to pull a foot out of the muck, he instead pulled himself deeper into the muck. He was waist deep, then chest deep, and now neck deep. He reached for something, anything to pull himself out, but he felt nothing. Nothing.

"Voice of the Night! This is the end of us all. It has failed. Lanshalla shall perish. As will I!"

But just then as his face sank into the muck, Larto felt a hand on his. It pulled and pulled with great intensity such that he was sure his shoulder would dislocate. But it didn't. He gradually made his way out of the muck and onto the rocks. He turned around to give thanks to the one who saved him.

"Patrina!" Larto said.

"I was able to get out. Barely," she said, out of breath. "Belila is dead. And buried. As are all the others. Look, even the mountains have gone still."

Larto looked out, and Patrina was right. The mountains had stopped spewing lava.

It was as if they had died. What light the lava had provided had now failed, and the two could barely see much of anything, except the continued glow from the Lonely Vine's single grape. The vine itself finished pulling all water out of the sea, and the once muddy muck was dry as a bone and hard as stone.

"So this is the solution," Patrina lamented. "How sickening that we have thrown away everything."

"My Lanshalla. She's gone too," Larto said.

Patrina touched Larto's shoulder, and she felt something unusual.

"It all flowed through you. Lives of walcowats and dalphinacs. And...something very strange. I feel that Lanshalla passed through you too," Patrina said.

"She did? Where did she go? Into the vine?" Larto asked.

With the end of vapor-and-salt clouds from the vine, the nearby sky cooled and began releasing its salt. Small flakes fell like ash from a newly-dead fire. Patrina walked over to the Lonely Vine. It had grown to the height of the lighthouse, and the grape had been carried up with it, being at the very top edge of the vine.

"It is up there," Patrina said. "All energies of her and my kind are contained in that small grape. I..."

Patrina stared up at the grape.

"What? What is it?" Larto asked.

"It is all I have left of my world. The grape. It's all I have left," she said.

Patrina made for the lighthouse and entered.

"Do not disturb the memories of old!" Voice of the Night said, suddenly appearing.

"What are you saying?" Larto said.

"The grape must remain attached to the vine. Do not disturb it!" Voice of the Night warned.

Then Patrina appeared at the top of the lighthouse. Salt came down heavier, like sleet. Patrina walked over to the edge of the vine and touched the grape.

"Patrina, no! Don't touch it! I'm coming up! Don't touch it!" Larto said.

Larto rushed into the lighthouse and frantically climbed the stairs. Now the salt came down heavier, like hail, and it banged on the roof of the lighthouse. He reached the top, and there Patrina stood with the grape in her hand, removed from the vine.

"Patrina, no!" Larto called.

She turned to face Larto, put the grape in her mouth, and ate it.

"Stop!" he said, rushing to her.

He gave her the Heimlich to force the grape from her innards, but it did not come up. She laughed hysterically and pulled away.

"I'm with them now," she said. "I'm with my people. The dalphinacs too. All aquatics. They're inside me. See?"

Her skin glowed with movement, as if it were a display of a million aquatic creatures swimming around. She laughed and laughed. She climbed over the railing, and Larto grabbed for her arm to stop her, but her skin was like acid and burned his hand. He cried out and fought to hold on, but she pushed hard against him so as to jump off.

"No," he cried as he felt his grip fail. "No!"

The outer layers on his hand peeled off. She slipped from his grasp and fell onto the rocks below. The impact created a blast that thrust upward and knocked Larto back. He strained to see all sorts of ethereal spirits flying upward into the sky. The salt pelted harder and with more fury. It caved in the lighthouse's roof, and Larto was forced to go down the steps for cover. He went all the way to the base, but the salt from above carried down the steps, and it filled the bottom. He now had to climb back up the steps to avoid being buried in the salt. He stood halfway up the steps in a small area above the filling salt but below the pelting salt. He was sure this was the end. A hole developed in the side of the lighthouse, and a small part of the Lonely Vine entered through the hole. It moved toward Larto, and on its end was produced a single flower. A glow surrounded the flower, a glow that took shape and form into an ethereal humanoid image. The image was that of Lanshalla. She held an ethereal glass with only a bit of ethereal wine left. She consumed the last bit of wine, and as she did, Larto moved to hug her ethereal image with what little strength he had left. He cried out as he exerted all energy to maintain his hold on her image. The lighthouse crashed around him, a bright light blinded him, and Larto struggled to see.

It was the Anrega with Veigon inside. It appeared bright in the sky in planar form but headed for the ground with great speed. It dove deep. Then it released a great plume of fiery lava. But the lava was short-lived, being replaced with water. Water upon water poured onto the planetary surface and with it new creatures released from the Veigon. But not where Larto was. The Lonely Vine created an electromagnetic field as a barrier and prevented it. In all this, Larto held onto the ethereal image of Lanshalla, and the Veigon sent a plasma ball toward the two to envelop and consume them as a prelude to overpower the Lonely Vine. The plasma ball united the two, but with Lanshalla's help, Larto and Lanshalla broke free of the plasma ball. But the plasma ball kept Larto's eyes blinded with white light. Larto could no longer be sure of anything, no passage of time nor transfer of place.

"The Lonely Vine," young Lanietta said. "It knew the Anrega was coming. The Lonely Vine withdrew as much life as it could to spare that life from the Anrega and Veigon."

"Do these cycles never cease?" Claus said. "So much violence only to be superseded by greater forces who themselves fight."

"Larto? Can you hear me? Larto?" called a voice.

"Voice of the Night?" Larto called back.

But the voice was different. Larto squinted his eyes, and the white light dimmed just enough for him to see. He was in the medical center on Carinia 5. The doctor who had first worked with him was now attending him. He looked around, and Lanshalla was gone.

"What happened? Where's Lanshalla?" Larto asked.

"She's recovering," the doctor said.

"Will she make it? Did you reintegrate her ethereal spirit?" he asked.

The doctor returned a blank expression. Then a woman entered the room.

"You are Larto?" the woman asked.

"Yes. Your voice. I've heard it before."

"I'm Larbiabba. I helped with the ethereal transfusion. You may have heard me. I tried speaking to you several times while you were in full daze," she said.

"You're Voice of the Night," he said.

"If that is how your subconscious represented me," she said. "Lanshalla is recovering. We were able to reintegrate her ethereal spirit."

Larto stood up to thank her, but he crumpled to his knees.

"Easy. The transfusion took a lot out of you," Larbiabba said as she and the doctor helped Larto to his feet.

"My Lanshalla is safe! I must see her!" he said.

"Come this way then, if you are able," Larbiabba said. "I'll take over from here, doctor."

The doctor waved the two off. Larbiabba and Larto then walked down the hallway.

"How was the transfusion? You should have felt no pain, like a pleasant day in the park or better," Larbiabba said.

"Uh, that's not how it went," he said.

"Oh? Maybe a playful day with a dog?" Larbiabba laughed.

"Hardly. I hope I never have to do that again!" Larto said.

"Aw, it couldn't have been that bad," Larbiabba said.

"It was brutal," Larto said. "Absolutely brutal."

The two entered a recovery room. Lanshalla sat in a lounge chair with a wet towel on her head.

"We're getting her fever down. She's a little out of it, but she's awake," Larbiabba said.

Larto pulled up a chair and sat next to her. He put his hand to hers and squeezed it gently.

"Lanshalla? I'm here. Lanshalla?" Larto said.

"Larto. It's so warm in here," she said dreamily.

"Easy. You have a fever," he said.

"Oh," she said. "I had the strangest feeling. I was back on your estate in your back yard. Remember the Lonely Vine?"

"I remember," he said.

"And the wine? I sipped the wine, and I was swept off to an ancient world. Water. Sea creatures," she said. "Sounds strange, doesn't it?"

"I believe you," he said.

"I was floating in the sea with fish. Then I became this strange creature. Like those walcowats we see in ancient science books. Dreams are absurd, aren't they?" she said.

"No, they're very real," he cried.

"The water disappeared," she said. "There was just a desert. The remnants of two different sea creatures became fossils, and the Lonely Vine grew between the two fossils."

"It was real. It happened!" Larto cried.

"I didn't tell you before. I didn't want you to think me crazy," she said. "I guess my secret is out. Those poor sea creatures. Sad that they are gone, isn't it?"

"Yes, it is," he continued in his sad state.

"If only they could be remembered," she said.

Larbiabba removed the towel from Lanshalla's head. Then Larbiabba looked at Lanshalla's head and saw something.

"What is it?" Larto asked.

"There's something in Lanshalla's hair," Larbiabba said.

Lanshalla placed her hand on her hair and combed through it. She caught something and brought it before her eyes.

"It's a leaf from the Lonely Vine," she said. "I could laugh and say the vine had a leaf in all this."

"It did," Larto said as he hugged her in relief. "It did."

"They made it," young Lanietta said. "And they are tied to those ancient sea creatures. Which means I'm tied to the creatures through my parents. Claus, I never knew."

Chapter 74: The Baby Option

"Doctor, we have complications," Larbiabba said.

"All right, everyone out," the doctor said.

"No," Lanshalla said. "Larto and Larbiabba. Stay. Please."

The doctor nodded in agreement.

"Larto, stand by Lanshalla's shoulder and help her breathe. Larbiabba, please help," the doctor said.

Lanshalla squeezed.

"I'm giving birth," Lanshalla said. "I can feel it."

"I...I thought..." Larto stumbled.

"Suction," the doctor said.

"Keep breathing, Lanshalla," Larbiabba said. "We're taking good care of you."

"Baby Lalla. Baby Lalla," Lanshalla said.

Lanshalla's baby was delivered stillborn. Larbiabba wrapped the tiny baby in a tiny cloth and was about to place it in a small transparent casket when Lanshalla called for it.

"Please. I want to hold my baby, if but for a little while," Lanshalla said.

Larbiabba gave the baby to Lanshalla, and she held it in one palm.

"Poor little Lalla. What have I done to you? Deprived you of life! What a horrible person I am!" Lanshalla said.

Lanshalla cried. So did young Lanietta. Larto tried to comfort Lanshalla. Larbiabba took the baby away, placed it in the little casket, and helped the doctor restore Lanshalla to health. But while physical injuries were attended to, Lanshalla's spirits were broken. She lost the will to live, and her vitals deteriorated.

"She's not going to make it," the doctor said. "She's giving up."

"No, she can't," Larto said. "Lanshalla, please hold on! I love you, Lanshalla. There's time for more. We have a universe of time before us. Lanshalla!"

"Larto, I might be able to help," Larbiabba said. "Her ethereal spirit is weak. I can create an ethereal link between you two. That should help her."

"Will I go into a full daze like before?" Larto asked. "I'd rather not go through all that again."

"I cannot say. But if I do nothing, Lanshalla is sure to die," Larbiabba said.

"Very well. Proceed," Larto said.

Larbiabba extended an ethereal hand each, one into Lanshalla, and the other into Larto. At first Larto felt nothing, but then he felt as if he were a green star in a binary system with a blue star. It was clear to him that Lanshalla was the blue star. But instead of having uniform glows, the two stars had convolutions of encoded strings, as if they were not just stars, but microcellular components like ribosomes. Cosmic dust and gas passed toward them, and the forces between the two changed this cosmic dust and gas into solid cosmic bodies. At first the bodies were comets. They'd fly out of orbit from the two and on to other systems. But an especially colorful cloud of gas with glowing rainbow eddies came between them, and this became a planet the two called Lalla. Lalla started an orbit around the two, but a pulsar happened its way into Lalla's orbit. The combined forces of Larto, Lanshalla, Lalla, and the pulsar resulted in the destruction of both the pulsar and Lalla.

Lanshalla dimmed, being covered in heavy sunspots. Larto tried pulling more cosmic gas and dust between them, but it only caused such material to slingshot around him, as he didn't have Lanshalla to offset his force and provide control. It was then he exerted his energy to move close to Lanshalla, in a tighter and quicker orbit that resulted in them mixing star matter and merging into a fusionic flash of implosion that then sent the two back into binary orbit around each other. But instead of a green and blue star, the two were both blue-green. Another cloud of gas came along, and they formed it into another planet that revolved around both stars without issue. Young Lanietta gasped.

"Something just happened," young Lanietta said to Claus. "Something special. I'm not sure what. But it's special."

Larto returned to the reality of the Carinia 5 medical center.

"Larto," Lanshalla said. "You're still here."

"Her desire to live is improving," the doctor said. "You were successful, Larbiabba. And with that, treatment is complete. You may take her to the recovery room."

Larbiabba and Larto helped Lanshalla to a wheelchair. Larto wheeled her out, down the hallway a short ways, and into a recovery room.

"Larbiabba, you're a Bleuh?" Lanshalla asked.

"I'm actually a Gren," Larbiabba said.

"What?" Lanshalla asked. "But your skills with the ether. I mean...I've never met a Gren who can do what you do."

"I've spent my life studying the ether and how Bleuhs manipulate it," Larbiabba said. "I seem to have a special affinity for it. As it is, I've been helping at another outpost on Carinia 5. I came when I heard about you."

"It seems strange to meet you on this planet," Lanshalla said. "Who do you identify with? Grens? Greyans? You must get lonely without friends."

"My friends are here. And you have friends here too," Larbiabba said.

"If you could, please, send for them," Lanshalla said.

Larbiabba stepped away for a moment and then returned with Mariel and Treyu.

"Lanshalla!" Mariel said with happiness as she rushed to give her a hug. "I was so worried about you!"

"I'm better," Lanshalla said. "I made some mistakes, but I'm better."

"How much do you remember?" Treyu asked.

"Everything," Lanshalla said. "I remember feeling threatened and detonating my unborn baby's ethereal spirit in defense, only to learn later I had been tricked and that baby Lalla had died for no good reason."

"You have every right to be bitter," Mariel said. "I'd be bitter too."

"I've debated whether to discuss this or not," Larto said. "I don't want to upset you again. I just want my Lanshalla back."

"I was a fool. I say it now," Lanshalla said. "I should have gone ethereal to detect what was going on. Instead I trusted my physical senses."

"You might not have figured out things anyway," Treyu said. "I spoke with my mother. Apparently, technology here has become quite advanced at deceiving the ethereal senses."

"I would like to test your technology and prove you wrong," Lanshalla said with a grin.

"Work therapy," Larbiabba said. "The doctor would approve."

Lanshalla recovered quickly enough, and she worked with Larbiabba and Treyu to test the Carinian Deception System. They started a test with Treyu and Larbiabba at controls while Larto and Mariel watched. Lanshalla stood on a stage in a small auditorium.

"Start with a fake Libriota," Lanshalla said.

Treyu hit a few buttons, and then Larbiabba put her hand on a detector plate. A realistic Libriota appeared and walked toward Lanshalla.

"Did you think you could get rid of me so easily, Lanshalla? And to think our friendship has come to this," Libriota said.

Lanshalla extended an ethereal hand to test Libriota's image, but Libriota turned it back.

"You decline my ethereal greeting?" Lanshalla asked.

"You have much to answer before I allow such a greeting," Libriota said.

"Very impressive," Lanshalla said to Larbiabba and Treyu.

Lanshalla went eethi, sent her ethereal self to the backside of Libriota and attempted to get an ethereal hand in. Libriota space-jumped out of the way.

"Clever again," Lanshalla said. "Except we Bleuhs can't space-jump successfully. But I suppose other Carinians would never know that."

"Larbiabba has programmed in all the usual Bleuh tactics," Treyu said.

Lanshalla projected the ethereal image of an unborn baby and exploded it. The projection of Libriota vanished. Larto and Mariel reacted in horror.

"Lanshalla! Another one? What madness is this murder?" Larto blurted.

Mariel stared in horror and shook like a wet leaf.

"Mommy! What are you doing?" young Lanietta said in shock. "You just invented a new way of killing!"

"Lanshalla?" Larbiabba asked. "Are you well?"

"Perfectly," Lanshalla said. "That was not a real baby. I projected a fake one. But the ethereal explosion was real."

"It's...not what we expected," Larbiabba said, carefully choosing her words.

"Lanshalla, no!" Larto said. "It sickens me to see that, even if not real. I'm just plain sick!"

"Work therapy," Lanshalla said.

"I did say that, but I didn't mean this," Larbiabba said. "We did not anticipate this tactic because it is beyond any ethical or moral comprehension. Who could conceive of such a horror?"

"If I can, then a Bleuh can also. Your projection will fail," Lanshalla said.

Larbiabba had a quiet chat with Treyu. Treyu called in several technicians, and they discussed the matter. Larto and Mariel walked up to Lanshalla.

"You can't do it, Lanshalla," Mariel said. "This is a violation of life itself."

"I agree with Mariel," Larto said. "There must be another way."

"There isn't," Lanshalla said.

"How do you know?" Larto asked.

"I already tested on the fake Libriota. Larbiabba did an excellent job of anticipating every Bleuh convention, except the baby option," Lanshalla said.

"That quickly?" Larto asked. "You hardly spent any time at all."

"I know what to look for," Lanshalla said. "I could spend more time, but the baby option is clearly the most dramatic."

"Too dramatic," Mariel said.

"If Larbiabba doesn't come up with a defense, other Bleuhs will use it," Lanshalla said.

"Will they think to use it, I wonder," Larto said.

"I don't see how. Like Larbiabba said, it's beyond moral comprehension," Mariel said.

Larbiabba and Treyu finished with the technicians. The technicians walked off.

"We've had a small conference," Larbiabba said. "We are at a loss for words, to be honest. There will be further discussion in the outpost and around the planet. In the meantime, we can run other tests if you like."

"Yes," Larto said. "More tests, but without the baby option."

"Now wait," Lanshalla said. "Larbiabba, why don't *you* try the baby option on Libriota?"

Larbiabba reacted in shock as she briefly placed a hand over her abdomen.

"Uh, no," she said. "Let's try simple ethereal combat. Here's a good simulation. A Bleuh fighter goes eethi and paralyzes the victim's nervous system. Are you up for this challenge?"

"Yes," Lanshalla said.

Mariel and Larto stepped away from Lanshalla. Larbiabba and Treyu activated the simulation. A Bleuh fighter stood across the stage. He sent his ethereal spirit across the stage and attempted to pinch a nerve in Lanshalla's neck with his left hand. Lanshalla countered the attack with her own ethereal spirit. The ethereal soldier next tried to get the other hand into Lanshalla's neck. Lanshalla split her ethereal self longways. She used one half to defend against the soldier and the other half to invade the soldier's physical body, where it quickly gathered the soldier's encodings of life. This split-self then produced an ethereal unborn baby based on the soldier's encodings and detonated it within the soldier's physical self. The soldier vanished. Larbiabba and Treyu expressed sighs of disappointment.

"She split," young Lanietta said.

"Is this where you get such ability?" Claus asked.

"It must be," young Lanietta said. "It's just...it feels like divorcing myself, watering myself down into chaotic confusing incohesion."

"Such words from such a girl," Claus said.

"I may be only eleven million years old, but I feel older," young Lanietta said.

"I thought we agreed—no baby option," Larbiabba said.

"It was a variation on a theme. I was able to target just the soldier," Lanshalla said. "I have an idea. Put three Bleuh soldiers against me. I promise I won't do a super baby option. Just a mini baby option."

"No. This test is suspended," Larbiabba said. "If you'll excuse me."

Larbiabba walked off to discuss the matter with others. Mariel, Larto, and Treyu walked over to Lanshalla.

"A mini baby option?" Treyu asked.

"So as not to attract attention," Lanshalla said. "If I go super baby, those injured but not killed could warn others. This way the newly dead go one by one and do not warn the soon-to-be dead."

Larto put his palm to his forehead in disbelief. Mariel put her hands over her mouth to contain her shock. Treyu paced back and forth.

"What is wrong with Mommy?" young Lanietta said.

"Is this part of eethi psychosis?" Claus asked.

"It's worse," young Lanietta said. "She's losing herself to another power."

"Why is everyone so upset?" Lanshalla asked.

"Because what you did is upsetting!" Mariel said.

"But I'm getting good at it now. Work therapy. Should count for something," Lanshalla said. "So where did Larbiabba go?"

"To...she..." Treyu stumbled. "This is serious stuff, Lanshalla. The rebels have been willing to learn and do just about anything. That's how desperate they are. And we've helped them. We thought providing these simulated Bleuhs was the pinnacle of rebel achievement. Now you blast that away with your super babies and mini babies. We're just not ready for this. We need time and discussion to figure this out."

"What's to figure out? Do it. It's easy. I'll teach," Lanshalla said.

"Think, Lanshalla, think!" Larto said. "What are the consequences? Do you even know?"

"I don't. But I've never done this before either. Perhaps Treyu could write a paper on it," Lanshalla said.

"Write a paper on it? On *it*? Where does one start? 'The Secret of Life is Destruction'?" Treyu asked.

"Well if Grens want a real life, yes," Lanshalla said.

"It's no use," Mariel said. "She's completely biased."

Larbiabba returned.

"I've had further discussions, Lanshalla," Larbiabba said. "Things are stirred up quite a bit. Already two camps have formed on this issue. One is against using the baby option in any form. The other fully endorses the baby option and would like to study with you."

"Good! Show them in!" Lanshalla said.

"Larbiabba, how vocal are the two camps?" Larto asked.

"Very vocal. Our rebels are on the verge of their own civil war, which is the last thing we need right now. We don't need two factions!" Larbiabba said.

"A civil war," young Lanietta said. "Like another split. Claus, I'm in pieces everywhere. Lots of little pieces in Morcellus, pieces close to me, and other pieces in other places. A rebel civil war is just the beginning of the bifurcation monster. These people don't know what path it will take them. Because the path splits. And splits. Fragmented into fruitless forgotten folly. I want to be one Lanietta again. I want to be whole."

Just then, a man and two women snuck in.

"Wait!" Larbiabba said. "You were not called."

"We heard about Lanshalla and wanted to meet her," the man said. "I'm Leedius."

"I'm Freetra," said a woman.

"And I'm Peleetra," said the other woman.

"We want to try your baby option," Leedius said.

"No, no, no! Out. Out!" Larbiabba said.

"Let them stay," said Lanshalla. "This could be entertaining."

Larbiabba looked at Treyu, and Treyu shrugged his shoulders.

"I doubt anything will happen," Treyu said. "They're all Grens. If nothing else, it creates a diversion while the rebels sort things out."

"This is the kind of thing that doesn't sort out," Larbiabba said. "However, I agree about the diversion. You can start the simulation, Treyu. I'll watch."

"Leedius, you're first," Treyu said. "Stand next to Lanshalla."

Leedius walked over to Lanshalla while the others walked away from her. Treyu hit a few buttons, and a Bleuh soldier appeared. It split and sent its ethereal self to pinch Leedius's nerve.

"Now split your ethereal self," Lanshalla said, using her own ethereal spirit to assist Leedius's. "Use one half to block the soldier. Send the other to the soldier's physical body, and, uh, wait, now how will this work?"

"I'm having trouble blocking the nerve pinch," Leedius said.

"Can you envision making a baby?" Lanshalla asked.

"How?" Leedius asked.

"You just...it...uh...never mind," Lanshalla said. "We'll get back to you. End the simulation."

Freetra and Peleetra laughed.

"Come over here, Freetra. Let's see how you do," Lanshalla said.

Leedius went back, and Freetra walked over next to Lanshalla.

"Start the simulation," Lanshalla said.

The Bleuh soldier sent his ethereal spirit over to pinch Freetra's nerve. Lanshalla helped direct Freetra's ethereal self to split longways, using one half to fend off the soldier and the other to go into the soldier's physical body and capture his encodings. But when she withdrew the half from the soldier and tried to create an unborn baby, she could not, even with Lanshalla's help.

"Stop the simulation," Lanshalla said. "Have you ever had a child?"

"That's a little invasive, don't you think?" Larto asked.

"It's all right. Yes, I have," Freetra said.

"Let's try again," Lanshalla said.

The two repeated the simulation, but again Freetra was unable to produce an ethereal unborn baby projection.

"Stop the simulation," Lanshalla said. "Peleetra, come over here."

Lanshalla repeated the simulation with Peleetra. With Lanshalla's help, Peleetra was able to produce an ethereal unborn baby and explode it in the Bleuh's physical body.

"There," Lanshalla said. "Proof that a Gren can do it."

"With your help," Larbiabba said.

"I wonder why Freetra couldn't do it?" Larto asked.

"I think I know," Larbiabba said.

Larbiabba walked over to Peleetra, asked her a question, and she nodded in the affirmative.

"Well?" Larto asked.

"I will let her tell you herself," Larbiabba said.

"I tried to have a child, but it didn't work out," Peleetra said.

"You couldn't get pregnant?" Larto asked.

"I could, actually," Peleetra said.

"Miscarriage. Of course," Mariel said. "This weapon only works if a woman's body has killed her unborn child."

"It wasn't my fault!" Peleetra said.

"We know," Larbiabba said. "Go on back with Freetra."

"In each case, Lanshalla had to help the Gren," Mariel said.

"Yes," Larbiabba said. "Another disadvantage to this weapon."

"It wouldn't be such a disadvantage if we had more Bleuhs helping," Lanshalla said. "How many of us are on this planet?"

"One," Larbiabba said.

"How many of us have expert Bleuh knowledge?" Lanshalla asked.

Lanshalla looked at Larbiabba with a grin.

"Forget it," Larbiabba said.

"Do we know for sure that's the only way this works?" Lanshalla said.

"It had better be," Larbiabba said. "And I wish it didn't work at all. The baby option. What misery is next?"

"Grens need a way to loosen their ethereal spirits without depending on Bleuhs," Lanshalla said.

"A device can project ethereal spirits from simulated people, but that's it," Larbiabba said.

"Can you modify the projector to assist Grens?"

Larbiabba held silent.

"I take that as a 'yes'," Lanshalla said.

"I never agreed to do so," Larbiabba said.

"But your silence says it's possible," Lanshalla said.

"You're going to have Gren women invade Bleuh soldier men and explode them internally with unborn versions of themselves using Greyan projection technology, is that it?" Larbiabba asked with disdain.

"Sounds good to me. When do we start?" Lanshalla asked.

"*We* don't start," Larbiabba said. "*We've* done more than enough testing today. I must discuss these results with the others."

Larbiabba left the room.

"This is getting fun," Lanshalla said.

Mariel, Larto, and Treyu exchanged nervous glances.

"It shouldn't be," Mariel said. "Oh, my nerves are shot."

"Easy there, Mariel," Treyu said. "Do you need a relaxant?"

Mariel nodded. Treyu stepped out for a moment and returned with a bottle. Mariel took the bottle and drank from it.

"What's in that?" Larto asked.

Mariel offered him the bottle, and he took a sip. He immediately spat it out.

"What is it?" Larto asked.

"Winozipine distillates," Treyu said.

"Distilled wine?" Larto asked. "It's almost pure alcohol."

"Yes on both counts. Plus other ingredients to smooth the taste," Treyu said.

Mariel took back the bottle but accidentally spilled a few drops on Larto's shirt sleeve. The material on his sleeve dissolved away.

"Smooth? What does it do to the innards?" Larto asked.

"It relaxes them," Mariel said while slurping the tonic.

"By killing nerve endings, I'd imagine," Larto said.

"Gimme," Lanshalla said, and she took the bottle.

"No, don't!" Larto said as he tried to block.

Too late. Lanshalla drank the rest. And burped.

"Treyu, get an antidote," Larto said.

"For Winozipine? There's none," Treyu said.

Lanshalla hiccupped.

"We should sedate her more. Put her in a daze," Larto said.

"It's contraindicated," Treyu said. "She could go into cardiac arrest."

"Oh, I feel strange," Lanshalla said.

Lanshalla went eethi, and her ethereal image stumbled and wandered.

"Her ethereal spirit is drunk!" Mariel said.

"I didn't think alcohol could do that," Larto said.

"Alcohol can't," Treyu said. "But Winozipine can. It does many things. Many things."

Larbiabba returned.

"I've just spoken with...Lanshalla? What's going on?" Larbiabba asked.

"She drank this," Larto said, handing the bottle of Winozipine to Larbiabba.

"Empty," Larbiabba said as she turned the bottle upside down. "Did she drink all of it?"

"Most," Lanshalla said with a hiccup. "But not all. I take my hat off to Mariel for helping in that department."

Lanshalla tipped an imaginary hat to Mariel.

"How much did you have?" Larbiabba asked Mariel.

"Only a little bit," Mariel said. "To calm my nerves."

"If only it were that easy," Larbiabba said.

"What does that mean?" Larto asked.

"It means we need to get Lanshalla out of here," Larbiabba said.

"Because she drank the Winozipine?" Larto asked.

"No, because of the baby option," Larbiabba replied. "There's a mob ready to attack her. And a drunk baby option just adds fuel to the fire."

"A drunk baby option," Lanshalla said. "Neato! I should try that!"

"There are really only two choices here," Larbiabba said.

"Let me guess," Treyu said. "My mother wants to put her in a block house."

"Yes, that's one," Larbiabba said.

"And the other is to leave Carinia 5?" Larto asked.

"Precisely," Larbiabba said.

"I choose option four," Lanshalla said with a hiccup. "Teach the children how to sing."

Trisha walked in.

"Did you tell them?" Trisha asked Larbiabba.

"Yes."

"We must make haste. Time is short," Trisha said.

Guards surrounded Lanshalla, Larto, and Mariel.

"Mother, maybe we should leave Carinia 5," Treyu said.

"No time. Off we go," Trisha said.

The guards escorted Lanshalla, Larto, and Mariel while Treyu walked behind with Trisha and Larbiabba.

"I don't like this," Larto said.

"I do," Lanshalla said. "Something fun is about to happen."

"What do you mean?" Larto asked.

"Secrets bring tension. Tension brings anxiety, and I'm anxious to get on with the fun part," Lanshalla said with a wink.

"I see a lot of your mother in you," Claus said.

"Mischievous, yes," young Lanietta said.

"Something bad is about to happen? Oh no," Mariel said. "You should have left me the Winozipine."

"Should I get more? We can share," Lanshalla said.

"No and no," Larto said.

While the three discussed Winozipine, Treyu had a conversation with Trisha and Larbiabba.

"Where are we going, Mother?" Treyu asked.

"Cell 102 just off the main cargo hold," Trisha said.

"That's a maximum radiation containment room," Treyu said. "We don't put guests there."

Trisha smiled.

"They aren't guests?" Treyu asked. "Larbiabba, what about the second option?"

Larbiabba was about to speak, but Trisha spoke first.

"There's no time for that," Trisha said.

Treyu stopped Trisha from walking. The guards and other three continued around a corner.

"Level with me, Mother. What are you doing?"

"You don't really think we can allow Lanshalla the freedom to trash the planet, do you? Or perhaps you'd like to see that. *And* the end of our solar system," Trisha said.

"Then let her go," Treyu said.

"You've got some growing up to do, I see," Trisha said.

"No, I don't," Treyu said. "Let Lanshalla go, and—"

"She'll trash Carinia 1 and 2 before trashing Carinia 5," Trisha said. "It's all the same, just a different order."

"You can't keep Lanshalla here forever," Treyu said.

"You're right," Trisha said. "We'll have to deal with the problem very soon."

"You can't mean," Treyu said.

"She does mean," Larbiabba said.

"And you agree with this?" Treyu asked Larbiabba.

"I don't agree with anything, because nothing is agreeable," Larbiabba said. "But this is all that's left."

"They want to kill Mommy? No!" young Lanietta said.

"I see," Treyu said. "Well, it's not agreeable to me either. I want no part in this."

Treyu walked off.

"Don't wander far," Trisha called. "There are strange whispers about. Don't get caught up in them."

"*Don't wander far,*" Treyu muttered to himself past earshot of Trisha. "She speaks to me like a child. What I really need is a moment to clear my mind. Figure out a way to satisfy everyone while safeguarding our planet."

Treyu walked into a medicinal dispensary and looked for a bottle of Winozipine. Instead, he found a bottle of Narcosiline.

"What is this doing here?" he asked himself. "One gulp of this stuff will put me in a daze for a Sol 3 year."

Treyu opened the bottle and held it under his nose. The aroma was a gentle warm day on a soft bed by little chimes in a mild breeze by a tickling brook. Treyu felt drowsy.

"Such...a temptation...to skip the next year...and become alert...when all is done... and if not...just take...a gulp...like this," he said in a stupor.

Treyu put the bottle to his lips and prepared to take a gulp. He paused, savoring the moment. Should he do it? Would he do it?

Chapter 75: Greylinger

With a jerk, he made to gulp the Narcosiline, but an alarm went off. Startled, he dropped the bottle, and its contents spilled onto the floor. Treyu shot out of his stupor and out the room into the hallway. Guards ran through, with one bumping into him.

"What is it? What's happening?" Treyu asked.

"Attack," the guard said, and he ran off.

Treyu ran after the guards in pursuit. They reached an open area. Several guards attended to Larbiabba, who sat next to a wall with a cloth to her nose. Others ran about the open area to secure it.

"Larbiabba!" Treyu said as Larbiabba nursed her bloody nose.

"Oh," Larbiabba said. "My nose is broken."

"Rest easy there," said an attendant.

"What happened?" Treyu asked. "Where are the others?"

"They got 'em."

"Who? Who got 'em?" Treyu asked.

Guards hauled Trisha away on a stretcher. She was covered in blood.

"Mother!" Treyu said as he rushed after her. "Is she alive?"

"Barely," said a guard. "We must rush her to surgery. Excuse us."

"Mother!" Treyu called.

But the guards had rushed her away. Another guard rolled in a wheelchair, and Larbiabba was lifted into it.

"Wait!" Treyu called as he rushed back to Larbiabba.

An attendant rolled her toward a treatment room with Treyu in tow.

"Tell me who did it," Treyu said. "Was it this new civil war? The split between people here?"

"No," Larbiabba said. "They...came through a rip. A rip in ethereal space. They wanted her. They wanted Lanshalla."

"Who are *they*?" Treyu asked. "Do they have a name?"

"I don't know," Larbiabba said. "I'd never seen anything like it. They were alien. Totally alien."

Larbiabba was rolled into a treatment room and placed on a bed. A doctor worked on her nose.

"Where are they?" Treyu asked. "Where are Lanshalla, Larto, and Mariel?"

Larbiabba stared hard at Treyu.

"Gone."

"Gone where?" he asked.

"Through the ethereal rip," Larbiabba said.

Treyu stood there in shock. He stared at Larbiabba as if she were making up a story, but she nodded that this was true.

"I saw it, Treyu. I saw it all," Larbiabba said. "Lanshalla went eethi. She made a move to escape. Trisha signaled to her guards, and they used a projection device to contain her. The mix went bad. A vertical beam of light like a tree trunk flashed where the two mixed. Then *they* came through that light. Lanshalla fought them, but it was a standoff. Larto and Mariel fought them, but they were pulled into the rip. Lanshalla lost ground, and they finally pulled her in. Trisha tried to stop them, but they beat her up badly. I caught a punch in the nose. But they returned through the rip, and the rip closed. Nothing could stop them."

"We have to get our people back," Treyu said.

"How?" Larbiabba said.

"We have to recreate the rip," Treyu said.

The doctor finished placing a transparent cast over Larbiabba's nose. She sat up and patted her face to test for feeling.

"Still numb," she said.

"Use a cool pack to keep the swelling down," the doctor said. "Bruises will appear as you heal."

"We can use the equipment here," Treyu said. "Simulate what happened and create another rip. Then we'll go in with numbers and attack."

"How will you simulate Lanshalla? You'll need a Bleuh for that," Larbiabba said.

Treyu looked at Larbiabba and grinned.

"I'm not Bleuh! I've just studied them," Larbiabba said.

"Their physio-ethereal features are ingrained in you," Treyu said. "You can do what Lanshalla did, with practice."

"Not everything," Larbiabba said. "It's too risky. I won't subject my body to such stresses."

"Larbiabba, please. You—" Treyu started.

But Trisha walked in and interrupted. She was heavily bandaged, had multiple casts, and got around on crutches.

"Wow!" Larbiabba said. "They took care of you quickly!"

"Administrator priority," Trisha said. "I only wish I could heal as quickly. Just a broken nose, Larbiabba?"

"Yes."

"The other three are taken prisoner," Trisha said. "I have my staff analyzing the detector logs. Until we come up with a defensive plan, this outpost, indeed this planet is vulnerable to attack."

"What about the prisoners?" Treyu asked. "We have to devise a rescue plan."

"He's been trying to convince me to sacrifice my body for such an effort," Larbiabba said.

"Treyu, please! There will be no more of that! I thought I raised you better," Trisha said. "Well?"

"We have to do something," Treyu said. "We have to rescue the three."

"If we don't take proper care, we will all need rescuing. And then where will you be, hmmm?" Trisha prompted.

"Mariel and I have ever been loyal and faithful servants to Larto, who has fallen for Lanshalla. It's the least I can do for them," Treyu said.

"There will be *no* unauthorized rescue attempts. Is that clear?" Trisha asked.

Treyu held his ground and looked back defiantly.

"Is that *clear*?" Trisha reiterated.

"Yes, ma'am," Treyu said, defeated.

"Good," Trisha replied. "Now if you aren't too busy with your false heroics, perhaps you'd care to join our top strategists in the War Room."

"I'll go too," Larbiabba said.

"Are you up to it?" Trisha asked.

"Yes, I am," Larbiabba said. "I need to keep myself busy. Work therapy."

"Then follow me," Trisha said.

"You're certainly not going in your condition," Treyu said.

"Why not? Work therapy," Trisha said with a wink for Larbiabba.

Larbiabba giggled but then winced in pain.

"It hurts when I laugh," she said.

"Well there's nothing to laugh about," Treyu said.

"You know, I would send you to your room to sulk, but you no longer have such a place," Trisha grinned. "As it is, if you don't want to wait for me, pretend your brother is here and race him to the War Room. I won't mind."

"My brother is dead. There's no one to race," Treyu said.

"Well, the universe goes on, even if you don't," Trisha said.

Trisha led the way down the hall, with Treyu and Larbiabba following behind.

"I didn't know about your brother. I'm sorry," Larbiabba said.

"Treyu still blames himself for the accident, you know," Trisha turned back to say.

"Yes! I let him go! I should have saved Drayan. Hanging over an ice shelf like that. I tried pulling him up. I really did. But he fought me at the end and fell over anyway," Treyu said.

"Your brother realized you couldn't save him. He knew that you'd be pulled in with him. He sacrificed himself for you. I grieve at the loss of my eldest child, my Drayan, but I am rejoiced that I still have my baby, my Treyu," Trisha said.

"It's not good enough," Treyu said. "I'm haunted by Drayan's death every day."

"So you risk other people's lives to atone for your guilt?" Larbiabba asked.

"What?" Treyu asked.

"Your rush to rescue the others. You're not rescuing them. You're rescuing Drayan," Larbiabba said.

"No!" Treyu denied.

"Yes!" Trisha countered.

The three reached and entered the War Room. Multiple monitors covered the walls while control panels littered the floor area. Replays of the incident looped on the wall monitors with various simulations detailing possible outcomes when using the projection system in defense. All such simulations ended with a "FAIL" stamped on the video. Other simulations ran on video screens to recreate the ethereal rip, but none succeeded—again with a "FAIL" stamped on the video.

"What if we recreate projections of Lanshalla, Larto, and Mariel?" Treyu proposed. "We could have projection Lanshalla go eethi and try to escape, just like in the incident."

"That's what the simulations are running," Trisha said. "But the eethi aliens win every time."

"What if projection Lanshalla uses the baby option?" Treyu asked.

All simulations stopped, and everyone turned around and stared at Treyu. The silence was awkward, but it was Larbiabba who finally broke it.

"Did Lanshalla's baby option attract the eethi aliens?" Larbiabba asked.

"Yes," most technicians said at once.

"I was afraid something like this would happen," Larbiabba said. "Evil brings evil."

"But we didn't know this would happen. Why are we to blame?" Treyu asked.

"That's how evil works," Larbiabba said. "It hides in shadows, completely unknown to those around, and then it jumps into action when things go bad. We cannot always know what evil is out there. We can only take safe action in hopes of not attracting it."

"Well spoken," Trisha said.

At that moment, the display screens lit up with new activity in the cargo hold. An ethereal rip opened with a great vertical flash of light.

"No defense will hold!" a technician yelled out in the control room.

"Evacuate!" Trisha ordered.

Technicians yelled into microphones for the cargo hold people to evacuate. They did. Then a shape was thrown out of the ethereal rip and landed on the floor. The rip closed, and the shape stood slowly.

"Larto!" Treyu said.

Treyu rushed down to the cargo hold with Larbiabba trying to keep up (but unable). Treyu reached Larto first and helped him walk.

"Thank the sky above you are safe. Are you well? How did you escape?" Treyu asked.

"I must speak also with Trisha and Larbiabba," Larto said.

Larbiabba walked up as Larto said this, and she spoke.

"Trisha is in the control room. She was badly injured but is alert and active," Larbiabba said. "It's good to see you, Larto."

"Thank you," he said.

"What about Lanshalla and Mariel?" Treyu asked.

"Hold that question for a moment, Treyu," Larto said.

"We have to launch a rescue mission. We must!" Treyu said.

"Things are bigger than that," Larto said. "I'll explain shortly."

The three arrived in the control room.

"Larto, welcome back," Trisha said. "I would hug you if not for my wounds."

"Hug accepted," Larto said. "I must speak with you, Larbiabba, and Treyu."

"Very well," she said, and she led the three to a private conference room.

"We were kidnapped by Greylingers," Larto said.

"I've never heard of them," Treyu said.

"Neither have I," Trisha said.

"I have, but I thought they were a myth," Larbiabba said.

"They are no myth," Larto said. "They exist in another dimension and subsist on negative ethereal energy."

"Then the positive ethereal energy that gives Greyans their charm—" Larbiabba started.

"Is because the Greylingers consume the negative energy," Larto said. "Lanshalla's baby option generated a high amount of negative ethereal energy. It accumulated until her escape attempt caused it to burst open, allowing the Greylingers to come through and take us."

"Tell us how we can rescue the others," Treyu said.

"Quiet," Trisha said.

"I am not here to launch a rescue effort," Larto said.

"What??" Treyu asked in surprise.

"Why are you here?" Trisha asked.

"I have been sent back by the Greylingers, to give terms of surrender," Larto said.

"Our surrender, is that right?" Trisha asked.

"Yes," Larto said. "In exchange for your cooperation, they will allow the people of Carinia 5 to continue living."

"And just what is this cooperation?" Trisha asked.

"You will help the Greylingers create a permanent ethereal doorway in the cargo hold area, for starters," Larto said.

"You told them 'no' of course, right?" Treyu said.

"I didn't agree or disagree to any terms. I only said I would convey their message," Larto said.

"A smart thing to do," Trisha said. "What else?"

"They said if you don't help them with the permanent doorway, they will burst through periodically when the negative energy is excessive and take more people," Larto said.

"To kill?" Treyu asked.

"I bet not," Larbiabba said. "I bet they are torturing Lanshalla and Mariel to generate negative ethereal energy."

"They tortured Mariel a little, but Lanshalla is holding them off—barely," Larto said. "They tortured me too, until I convinced them I could act as a messenger."

"Another smart thing to do," Trisha said.

"This permanent doorway thing," Treyu said. "Do they really expect us to welcome them with open arms?"

"They do," Larto said. "They want to integrate into this universe. Each of them would need a host. They can only exist in our dimension for short periods of time before they degrade. They would ask to control that host for, say, fifty percent of the time."

"No one is controlling my body," Larbiabba said.

"They offer knowledge and discipline," Larto said. "For those who feel lost or unable to stop bad habits, this might seem tempting."

"I see," Trisha said. "Well then, we have two temptations before us—the baby option, and Greylingers. Hmm. I must meet with the other administrators to see how we can defeat both."

"Let us know when you get back," Treyu said.

"I'm not going anywhere. You are. Now exit please. I must start the teleconference immediately," Trisha said.

Treyu was shocked, like the little kid banished from the living room while expected guests waited at the front door. He led Larbiabba and Larto out of the conference room and down the hallway.

"Let's go to a private projection room," Larbiabba said. "We can discuss the progress made on defense strategy."

The three walked down a hallway and into a projection simulation room. Larbiabba hit a few buttons on a control panel, and a simulation of the ethereal rip projected.

"This is the ethereal rip, or the ethereal rift," Larbiabba said. "Our technicians in the control center have tried several techniques to prevent it from forming or to at least close it. Nothing is effective. Watch."

Larbiabba hit a button. A grey ethereal cloud passed through the ethereal rip.

"That was a burst of synthethi," she said.

"A burst of what?" Larto asked.

"Synthetic ethereal energy," Treyu said. "Our projection technology can't produce the real stuff."

"And that could be the problem," Larbiabba said. "Lanshalla is a master at controlling her ethereal energy."

"She was either taken by surprise or wasn't strong enough to defeat it," Treyu said.

"I think I can shed light on that topic," Larto said.

"She told you something?" Larbiabba asked.

"She...allowed herself to be taken," Larto sighed.

"What??" both Treyu and Larbiabba said.

"I know. I was shocked to hear her say it," Larto said.

"What madness is this?" Treyu asked. "Who in their right mind does such a thing?"

"Lanshalla," Larbiabba said. "Curious little devil, isn't she?"

"That's it exactly," Larto said. "She wanted to know more about them. Expand her knowledge on the ethereal ways of the universe."

"Unfortunately, it's landed us in a dangerous situation," Larbiabba said. "We're in the eye of a storm, waiting for full fury to unleash."

Just then, Trisha walked in.

"Oh, there you all are," she said.

"That was quick," Treyu said.

"The meeting was brief and to the point," Trisha said. "Several things were decided."

"Such as?" Treyu asked.

"This outpost is under quarantine until further notice. No one enters. No one leaves," Trisha said.

"Outrageous!" Treyu said. "What about the rebels training here? And my guests? Mariel, Larto, and Lanshalla?"

"The quarantine is necessary to prevent spread of the ethereal rip. The rip is localized to this outpost, and the other administrators wish to keep it that way."

"Wishing is one thing. But we don't have to restrict ourselves to this outpost. I'm going to ready the ship. Once we get Mariel and Lanshalla back, we're leaving," Treyu said.

"Don't be a fool," Trisha said. "You'll get us all killed."

"What do you mean?" Treyu asked.

"Already there are Greyan ships in orbit with missiles trained on this outpost. Should anything leave, and I mean *anything*, they will fire upon this outpost and those who are leaving it," Trisha said. "No exceptions."

"They wouldn't," Treyu said.

"They would. And they will," Trisha said.

"Then we're prisoners here," Treyu said. "Stuck. Might as well be captured by the Greylingers."

Trisha slapped Treyu across the face.

"Don't ever say that again. You hear? Don't ever!" Trisha said.

"We must work to seal the rip," Larbiabba said.

"Agreed," Trisha said. "Have we made any progress?"

"No. Synthethi is ineffective," Larbiabba said. "We could set off an electro-magnetic explosive when the rip next opens."

"That would blast out one corner of the outpost and flood adjoining corners with radiation," Trisha said.

"We could evacuate people to the safe corner beforehand," Larbiabba said. "The only detail is how to get the rip to open."

"Work at it. See what you can find out," Trisha said. "I'll start the evacuation now. We'll keep only a skeleton crew in the danger zone. Keep me informed."

Trisha left.

"You're not serious," Treyu said to Larbiabba.

"Do you have a better idea?" Larbiabba asked.

"Yeah. Invade," Treyu said.

"We've already been over that," Larbiabba said. "So put that out of your mind. Help me figure out how to open up the ethereal rip. So far it happened when Lanshalla attempted to escape and when Larto was sent back."

"If I may interrupt," Larto said. "There is more from Lanshalla."

"Yes, go ahead," Larbiabba said.

"She says that the baby option is how the rip can be controlled," Larto said.

"Controlled? Why?" Larbiabba said.

"The Greylingers want to invade, but Lanshalla wants to control the Greylingers and use them as soldiers. But she can't do it by herself. She's in a stalemate situation with them and needs help," Larto said. "The rebels she helped here aren't strong enough to assist. She needs another Bleuh. Or a Bleuh expert."

Larto stared at Larbiabba.

"Oh no, I already vowed. No baby option for me!" Larbiabba protested.

"Then we can skip the Greylinger soldier idea," Treyu said. "I confess, I see no other alternative but to...to..."

"I've already spoken. The answer is no, and that's final!" Larbiabba said.

"Before Lanshalla sent me back, she left a special ethereal engram on my ethereal self. You see, when she first melded with me, she put an ethereal lock on my soul, to prevent other women from melding with me."

"I've never heard of such a thing," Larbiabba said. "No Bleuh has been able to do that. That's why Lanshalla's baby option works. If men had such locks on their souls, they wouldn't be so vulnerable to her method of attack."

"She keeps my soul mostly locked, but she unlocked a small piece for you, Larbiabba," Larto said.

"Excuse me?" Larbiabba said in shock.

"She wants you to meld with me. Her engram will connect with yours. You'll be able to use a super baby option on the ethereal rip. She'll open it, you'll give her the boost to overpower the Greylingers, and she'll return with Mariel. Then she'll seal the rip for good."

"What?? No, no, NO! This is wrong on so many levels!" Larbiabba said, and she paced around the room. "It's impossible anyway! She'd have to have my engrams to connect with me like this. There are other reasons this is wrong. Who is she kidding?"

"She 'acquired' a piece of your engram during the simulation tests," Larto said.

"She stole a piece of me? Without my knowledge or permission? I've been violated! Of all the crimes! Eethi larceny!" Larbiabba barked. "I'm going for a walk. I need space!"

Larbiabba stormed out of the room, leaving Treyu in shock.

"What do we do now?" Treyu asked.

"I don't know," Larto said. "Lanshalla can't hold out forever. If Larbiabba can't help us, we'll have to find another Bleuh who can."

"There are no other Bleuhs on Carinia 5. We'd have to find someone on Carinia 1 or 2 who will help us. But then they'll find out about us. We can't have that. And we can't leave anyway to find them. What a mess we're in!" Treyu said. "I guess that leaves the electro-magnetic explosive."

"I didn't want to say anything while Trisha was here, but if that option is taken, the radiation will invert on the Greylinger side and make Lanshalla more powerful. It will twist her to evil. She'll then get her Greylinger army going for sure and open a rip somewhere else, perhaps on Carinia 1 or 2. She'll set herself up as dictator," Larto said.

"You should have spoken up," Treyu said. "Then again, it will likely do no good. Greyans are convinced an electro-magnetic explosive is the solution to all problems."

"But Larbiabba isn't a Greyan," Larto said.

"Yes, but how do we convince Larbiabba to do the baby option?" Treyu asked.

"You don't," Larbiabba said, suddenly entering the room. "I've come up with a plan."

"To do the baby option?" Treyu asked.

"No. I'll hook Larto up to an eethi detector array. We'll attempt a synthethi meld. Computers will analyze the engrams and come up with a solution," Larbiabba said.

As it turned out, the room the three were in was equipped for such a test. Larbiabba ushered Larto over to a booth lined with detectors and wires.

"Remain standing and relax," she said.

Larbiabba hit a few buttons. An ethereal cloud surrounded Larto but could not enter his body.

"Hmm," Larbiabba said. "Synthethi energy cannot lock onto your ethereal spirit."

"This won't work, you know," Larto said.

"Why not?" Larbiabba asked.

"She locked my soul," Larto said. "You know she did."

"I'm hoping to crack that lock," Larbiabba said. "Humph. This thing is worthless. Wait, maybe if I help it."

Larbiabba went eethi a little bit but snapped back together—eethi and physical parts.

"Did you just—" Treyu started.

"Go eethi? Yes. How about that. A Gren going eethi," Larbiabba said.

"I didn't think it possible. Not without help from a Bleuh," Treyu said.

"I told you I'm an expert in Bleuhs," Larbiabba said. "Yes, I've managed to learn how to go a little eethi. But it took years of self-training and discipline, and even then I can only do so for brief periods."

"Why didn't you tell us Greyans? We've been trying to go eethi seemingly forever," Treyu said.

"I can't tell you Greyans everything," Larbiabba said. "I have to have *some* secrets. But this moment is critical, and time is short. I can't explain more than that."

Larbiabba tried again. She concentrated with all her might, went eethi again, and put a bit of her ethereal self into the device. Part of the synthethi cloud entered Larto's

body. Larbiabba stared at the controls then shut down the machine, dejected.

"Well?" Treyu asked. "It looked like you made progress there."

"I made progress in confirming Larto's story," Larbiabba said. "Sigh. What am I doing on this planet anyway?"

"What is that supposed to mean?" Treyu asked.

"It means Larbiabba understands the situation," Larto said. "May I exit the booth now?"

"Yes, you may exit!" Larbiabba said in disdain.

Larbiabba stared at Larto as if she were about to jump off a cliff. Larto nodded in affirmation.

"Leave the room," Larbiabba said while still staring at Larto.

"Why does Larto have to leave?" Treyu asked.

"Not Larto. You," Larbiabba said. "Leave the room, Treyu."

"What? Why?" he asked.

"Because I need privacy, that's why!" Larbiabba said.

"Everyone kicks me around," Treyu said in disgust. "I'll leave. Need to find Mother anyway and let her know what's going on."

"Don't tell her anything but this," Larbiabba said. "Tell her we'll use the electro-magnetic explosive as planned to seal the rip. I'll set up soon."

"But we decided that—" Treyu started.

"Say nothing else but that. Now go!" Larbiabba barked.

"Boy, I get all the women yelling at me," Treyu muttered as he left.

Larbiabba and Larto were alone.

"I must tell you something," Larbiabba said. "I've kept it a secret from others, but...no...it...Larto, this can't work."

"Lanshalla considers you a kindred spirit. That's why she left a piece of herself inside me. You'll be melding primarily with her. Think of her the entire time, and her afterimage will reciprocate. She's had you on her mind this entire time. You're special to her. She knows you don't agree with her on things, and she respects you for that."

"She does?"

"Yes. Perhaps you felt it," Larto said.

"Unfortunately," Larbiabba said. "I have my ethics, my pride, and other things. I can't have her undermine my principles."

"She knows you have reservations," Larto said, and as he spoke his next words, his voice changed into that of Lanshalla, and Lanshalla's ethereal spirit moved from Larto's body toward Larbiabba, saying, "Don't worry. Be at peace. I welcome you with open arms and open heart."

Larbiabba hesitated.

"I will do this only for Lanshalla," Larbiabba said. "But afterward, I...we...well, here goes."

Larbiabba went eethi. Her spirit melded with Lanshalla's in the open air. Then the two touched Larto. The view changed. Larbiabba was on a spot of light situated on grass. It could have been outside, but Larbiabba wasn't sure, because there was total darkness and silence outside the spot of light.

"Lanshalla? I'm here," Larbiabba called. "Lanshalla?"

Into the light walked a black and white hoofed animal with a long neck, a short snout, a sturdy body, and wings. By Earth standards, it had the head and neck of a llama, the body of a horse, and the wings of Pegasus. Upon this animal rode Lanshalla.

"Larbiabba, meet Arlio, my winged steed," Lanshalla said.

"Is 'Arlio' another name for 'Larto'?" Larbiabba asked.

"You may so claim," Lanshalla said. "Come along. I have something to show you."

"Where?" Larbiabba said, turning her back to Lanshalla and peering out into the dark void.

Arlio lowered his head, walked toward Larbiabba, and used his head to lift Larbiabba into the air. Larbiabba slid down Arlio's neck and landed atop his shoulders with her legs dangling over the mount point of his wings. Larbiabba was now sitting in front of Lanshalla.

"Whoa!" Larbiabba said in surprise.

"A quick way to mount," Lanshalla said. "Hold on!"

Larbiabba held onto a short mane of sorts, and Arlio leapt up into the sky, with his wings propelling air in great swoops. Simultaneously, the spot of light widened and followed Arlio around, providing visibility to where Arlio was headed while also giving view to the sides.

"We're over water," Larbiabba said. "Or are we? Drops are hitting my legs. But...what is that? They're flying up! Are those bugs? Get them off me!"

Arlio changed his wing motion and took very small but quick flaps like a hummingbird, creating a wave front around himself and his passengers such that no outside elements could disturb the journey. Larbiabba's legs were blown clean and dry.

"Do you see what's down there?" Lanshalla asked.

"There's a great ocean below, with water drops spraying upward like rain," Larbiabba said.

"My apologies. Arlio will protect you from further contact," Lanshalla said.

Larbiabba looked at the left edge of Arlio's wings and saw upward-flowing raindrops touch the tips of his feathers and change into little bodiless humanoid heads the size of a pea. She stretched her left hand out to the wing and dampened the high-frequency harmonics of Arlio's flapping, causing a drop-at-a-time to flow down the wing and onto Larbiabba's index finger. She pulled her hand back toward her face and studied the drop intently as it converted to bodiless humanoid form. The humanoid head screeched like a tortured spider as it lit upward and disappeared into the darkness above. Larbiabba stretched her hand again, and another drop traveled down the wing onto her index finger. But as she drew her hand back toward her face, the drop changed to a humanoid head and bit her finger before floating away with a screech.

"Ow!" Larbiabba said. "Where are we?"

"We are in an interpretation of the Greylinger universe as best as I can convey in a message through Larto," Lanshalla said. "Ethereal waste from our dimension carries over into the ethereal ocean below in this reality. That waste coalesces into drops. Those drops are the lost souls of conflict, known as *conflictyons*, the fallout of such ethereal interactions. I've learned that although we think our ethereal actions are local in our dimension, the waste goes here and interacts with ethereal waste from others in other places. No one could anticipate such interaction. We think what we do is mostly private to the moment. It is not. The Greylingers are the accumulated collections of these lost souls."

Larbiabba didn't know what to say to such an explanation. Arlio gained height, and soon the three saw fish swimming in the air, a normally impossible thing since the three were in the atmosphere, but fish they were. Drops of water collected on their underbellies, slid up their sides, and grew into humanoid heads in a line on their backs, like a line of little mushrooms. Once a fish had a back full of humanoid heads, it stopped growing new heads and headed away.

"Let's see where these fish go," Lanshalla said.

Under Lanshalla's direction, Arlio followed the back-filled fish toward a huge tangled ball of similar humanoid-head fish. The fish swam into a great maw. Arlio flew around to the other side, and there were two exits—from one came a string of fish, with the head of one biting onto the tail of another. The humanoid heads on the backs of these fish were packed closer together, with each head biting the back of the one in front. The fish and humanoid heads had no knowledge or purpose, only that they had specific positions and minor functions within their relation to the fish/head ahead or behind. From the other exit came a loose collection of fish and humanoid-head bones.

The line of fish along with other lines of fish spiraled inward toward an inner ring, like the eye wall of a hurricane. These lines of fish intertwined in twos and threes, with eddies from this vast circulation rolling up the twines into creatures of malice, the Greylingers. The Greylingers headed toward the center of the eye, and they built devices of power that when put together ejected a stream of plasma upward. But they couldn't do anything else beyond that. Long did the Greylingers search for a purpose for their plasma.

"That line of plasma looks like...like..." Larbiabba said.

"Like the line of plasma in the cargo bay," Lanshalla said. "It's their only outlet, the combined evil and frustration born out of trillions of miniscule conflictyons."

"Where is Mariel?" Larbiabba asked.

Lanshalla gave a command to Arlio. He dove down with incredible speed, pulling his wings in close to reduce drag while maintaining control.

"We're going to crash!" Larbiabba said.

The three dove close to the plasma stream, but they reached a point where the plasma stream ended (or before it started), just above the flowing ocean from where the humanoid head drops formed. They dove into a vortex, a void in the center of the full cyclonic activity of water, flying fish, and stringed fish. But while the stringed fish and humanoid heads had gone above them, the three saw a different set of stringed debris spiraling around them.

"The bones!" Larbiabba said. "The bones are heading down with us. They'll squeeze us!"

They continued down, but before the bone spiral had completely tightened around the three, Arlio landed on a pad where Mariel and another image of Lanshalla stood. That image of Lanshalla held her arms out, and her ethereal image raced around the pad at incredible speed, leading the bones around it and under it, creating an intricate design below the pad that extended downward and out, like a cone with Mariel, extra image of Lanshalla, and Arlio at the apex.

"This is where Mariel is. Larto was here for a time, but the Greylingers cut through my defense and sent him back," Lanshalla on Arlio said. "Before they did, I implanted this message in him. Larbiabba, listen. I can only hold off the Greylingers for a little while longer. I can't break free. This pad is the only place where I can hold my own. I need your help."

"I know what you would ask," Larbiabba cried. "The baby option."

"You were going to use an electro-magnetic explosive," Lanshalla said. "If you do that, the pad cone will invert upward and swallow me along with Mariel. It will create a cocoon, and the Greylingers will find a purpose for their plasma. They'll change me into the apex of greed and hate, sending me back into the cargo bay along with an army of Greylingers. They will have me destroy our Carinian solar system. You can't let that happen!"

"But we must stop the Greylingers!" Larbiabba said.

"Yes, we must," Lanshalla said. "Eventually I will give out. Mariel and I will succumb. That by itself is a small tragedy. But Bleuhs will continue to go eethi, feeding the Greylingers. The Greylingers will gain a strong foothold and invade. But instead of destroying Bleuhs, they will force Bleuhs to go eethi more often, and even force Grens to go eethi, to feed their machine of greed and hate."

"Can I help you hold them off? Just long enough to get more Bleuhs to help?" Larbiabba asked.

"You see the swirl of bones," Lanshalla said. "Ever they tighten around Mariel and me."

"Synthethi," Larbiabba said. "I've tried getting synthethi to work."

"It won't. Greylingers feed off organic ethereal energy. Synthethi is too pure, too uniform," Lanshalla said.

"I told Treyu to set up for an electro-magnetic explosive," Larbiabba said.

"I know," Lanshalla said. "I also know you don't plan to use it. The Greylinger dimension can only be contained by detonating fetal energy on the plasma end

and this cone end. That means two separate explosions. I can do one, but I need another Bleuh or near-Bleuh to do the other. Larto and Mariel are regular Grens—they can't help. Everyone else is a Greyan. Then there's you, my Larbiabba, who but needs to dig deep for the inner Bleuh she has tried to bring out."

"Destroying an unborn child is bad enough. But two at the same time? And who will be the father? Are we to use Greylingers? That disgusting plasma burst? Or perhaps one of those hideous balls where strings of fish and humanoid heads are strewn?" Larbiabba asked.

"I already know that you've lost a child, and that you carry one now," Lanshalla said.

"What?" Larbiabba said with feigned surprise.

"You've hidden it quite well from the others," Lanshalla said. "I know that you loved another."

Larbiabba nearly broke down in tears, but she held herself together.

"I had a husband on Carinia 2. We had a quiet life. We started a family together. He was killed by Bleuh patrols before he could see his firstborn. I joined the rebels after that. Slowed my pregnancy down. Now you know. Now the universe will know."

"I care for you too much for such a fate," Lanshalla said. "Though this moment be but a message to you through Larto, I know you will join me soon. We will share another journey with Arlio, who you've guessed is Larto in another form. We will share ethereal encodings for strength to prepare for what any of us must do in dire situations. I ask that you do the baby option for the rebels and all freedom-seeking Carinians everywhere. I will help. The deed must be done."

"This is horrible," Claus said to Lanietta.

"Yes," young Lanietta replied.

"And yet there's something I don't understand," Claus said. "I thought the baby option meant to create a baby in a Bleuh soldier and explode it. When

Lanshalla killed Lalla, that was something else. Wasn't it?"

"Claus. Consideration please," young Lanietta said.

"Is it the same?" Claus said.

"A baby dies. The baby option. Horrible words for a horrible act," young Lanietta said. "Speak no more of it. It is bad enough to witness. No, I won't stop the vision, I must get through this. Shh. Quiet, Claus. Quiet."

"You make it sound so necessary," Larbiabba said.

"I know this is tough. Who wants to do such a thing?" Lanshalla asked.

"You did it without hesitation or remorse in the simulator," Larbiabba said.

"I know. Sigh," Lanshalla said. "The after-effects took a little while to catch up with me, but they did. I feel this heavy weight inside, sour and spiny, tearing and ripping my innards to no end. I don't suppose I will ever see happiness again, if I should escape the Greylingers."

"I have my own mind," Larbiabba said. "My baby is all that's left of my husband. I make no promises."

Lanshalla smiled.

"I will take you back. When the time comes, you must make a decision. I will look for your sign," Lanshalla said.

Arlio flew out of the cyclonic dimension and landed on the patch of grass with the spotlight from where Larbiabba first started. He lowered his front and used his neck as a slide for Larbiabba to dismount, which she did. Arlio flew off with Lanshalla, leaving Larbiabba in the spotlight alone. The light faded to a small point just in front of Larbiabba, went out briefly, then shone again and spread out quickly, revealing the simulation room on Carinia 5 with Larto. Larbiabba pulled her ethereal self back into her physical body, and the meld was complete.

"Well?" Larto asked.

"Did you sense you were an animal with wings?" Larbiabba asked.

"I was Arlio, yes. I was there," Larto said. "We don't have much time. We must go to the cargo area."

Larbiabba shook her head in disdain, disappointed and disgusted with herself for just thinking about doing the baby option. But things were moving quickly, and she felt herself pulled deeper into this dangerous game. Larbiabba and Larto walked to the cargo area. Treyu and a technician had the equipment set up. He then waved the technician away.

"This section is quarantined," Treyu said. "We'll have to stand in the protective booth. Unfortunately, it cannot prevent all radiation. We'll be exposed to a brief burst. Medics are standing by to treat the blisters we'll receive."

"Treyu, evacuate," Larbiabba said.

"What? No!" he said. "The activation requires two people. You and me."

"I'll have Larto activate the right side. I'll do the left," Larbiabba said.

"No. He doesn't know how to do it correctly. Larbiabba, what are you up to? Trisha's orders—" Treyu started.

"Are going to be broken," Larbiabba said. "And you know nothing about it."

"You...you're going to do it? I mean, I know I wanted a rescue...but...really?" Treyu asked.

"You can simulate the electro-magnetic explosive, right?" Larbiabba asked.

"I can release a small dose of radiation and fool the other detectors," Treyu said. "Are you...are you going to do the...the baby...the...but how...you can't...really?"

"I will do what I will do," Larbiabba said. "Stand by."

"Standing by," Treyu said.

A message came in from Trisha.

"We're ready for the electro-magnetic explosive," Trisha said. "Good luck."

"Strange. The message is coming from the other side of Carinia 5," Larbiabba said to Larto and Treyu.

"Mother, where are you?" Treyu asked.

"In a safe place," she said. "I'll check with you after this is over. Good luck."

"Thank you," Treyu replied.

"Well, this is it," Larto said. "Lanshalla has prepared me for the meld. I'm ready when you are, Larbiabba."

"I'm not sure what to make of Trisha," Larbiabba said. "Why is she so far away? If I had time—"

"Time is short, Larbiabba," Larto said. "Lanshalla is nearly out of space and strength. It's now or never."

"Very well," Larbiabba said.

Larbiabba paused briefly. She nodded her head in affirmation, went ethereal, and melded her spirit with Larto.

"I'm reading an increase in ethereal energy," Treyu said.

"It's her," Larbiabba said. "It's Lanshalla. Mariel is with her. We're combining energy."

"This is more than two, three, or even thirty people," Treyu said. "Larbiabba, I can't hide this type of energy buildup. Are you sure you know what you're doing?"

The vertical energy plasma appeared in the cargo bay. A hybrid ethereal image of Larbiabba, Lanshalla, and Larto approached the energy plasma. From the energy plasma appeared six Greylingers, preparing to take the three into the plasma stream.

"The baby option," Larbiabba's physical self said. "Lanshalla is ready. I'm ready. I...just...need...I...must...I...can't do it. Treyu! Do the explosive option! Now!"

Treyu was taken by surprise. Doing the explosive would destroy the ethereal parts of Larbiabba and Larto. Not to mention the threat of Lanshalla coming back through the energy stream as a hateful dictator. He half expected a message to come through from his mother telling him to hit the explosive button, but no message came. Nor did a message come from any technician.

"What are you waiting for?" Larbiabba asked.

"I...can't either!" Treyu said.

"Do what you came to do," Lanshalla said.

Larbiabba held a fist in the air in an effort to convince herself to complete the baby option. She then brought her fist down, and at the same time, Lanshalla and Mariel came through the ethereal rip. It closed. Larbiabba's and Larto's ethereal selves snapped back into their physical bodies, and Lanshalla reintegrated too. Larbiabba and Larto rushed out of the protective booth to attend Lanshalla and Mariel while Treyu checked his instruments over and over.

"The ethereal rip is gone," he said. "There's no trace of it at all. No lingering ion trail, no conflictyon residue, nothing. You succeeded. You succeeded!"

Treyu walked out of the booth toward the four. Moments later, medics came in and whisked Mariel away. They were about to whisk Lanshalla away, but Lanshalla held them off for a moment.

"I couldn't do it either," Lanshalla said to Larbiabba.

Larbiabba cried. Larto hugged her for consolation. The medics left as quickly as they arrived, leaving just Larbiabba, Larto, and Treyu.

Chapter 76: Leaving Carinia 5

"Wait, what did Lanshalla mean?" Treyu asked.

"Neither of them used the baby option," Larto said. "You must have used the electro-magnetic explosive."

"I don't understand," Treyu said.

"What do you mean? The rip is sealed. You hit the explosive button, right?" Larto asked.

"No, I didn't. I couldn't," Treyu said.

"Then how did it close?" Larto asked.

In walked Trisha.

"I had it closed," Trisha said.

"I thought you were on the other side of...the message..." Larbiabba said.

"You might be able to fool the women of this complex, but you can't fool an old hand like me," Trisha said. "I knew what you were up to the entire time."

"Mother!" Treyu said. "You interfered?"

"Had to," Trisha said. "There was no resolution otherwise."

"Then you knew the electro-magnetic explosive would have been catastrophic," Treyu said.

"Yes," Trisha said.

"And that the baby option was the only way to stop the Greylingers and save Lanshalla and Mariel," Larbiabba said.

"No," Trisha said. "It was *your* only way, not mine."

"You've been holding out on us," Treyu said.

"Secrets and deception," Larbiabba said in disappointment.

"It's not the first time I've kept Treyu in the dark," Trisha said. "I am his mother, after all."

"But you're not mine," Larbiabba said. "We needed everyone to cooperate on this...this...what did you do anyway?"

"I enlisted help," Trisha said.

In walked Libriota.

"Hello, everyone," Libriota said.

"Another projection?" Treyu asked. "But we couldn't get synthethi to work."

Libriota enjoyed a wicked smile.

"Who am I, Larbiabba?" she asked.

Larbiabba went eethi just enough to meet Libriota halfway, who also went eethi. Larbiabba's ethereal self experienced an eethi shock then snapped back to her physical self. Libriota also reintegrated.

"You sold your Greyan eethi soul to the Libriota devil!" Larbiabba said, and she went after Trisha to punch her.

Libriota laughed and intervened ethereally, forcing Larbiabba back.

"We've been dealing with the Greylingers for many Sol 3 years. Not very long, mind you, but longer than your amateur efforts on this ice chunk. Carinia 5, is it? Who'd have thought people would live on this wasteland? Thank you, Trisha, for letting me know. We'll have to follow up on activities here. See if Gren rebels are here. You don't mind an inspection later on, do you?"

"Traitor! My mother is a traitor!" Treyu exclaimed.

Libriota laughed.

"I wondered why we couldn't identify you people on Carinia 2," Libriota said. "Greyans, eh? We always thought your ethereal spirits were underdeveloped. Our mistake, but who can take such inept eethis seriously? Like not noticing if the wind brings in three dust particles or four. So inconsequential."

"*Liyatikachican*," Larbiabba yelled at Libriota.

"Your diction has slipped into the gutter," Libriota said. "Do they have you quiescing your mind with their rabble? I'd shut down my brain function too. Don't worry. We'll take you to Carinia 1 for a stimulating court trial. You can learn more about us Bleuhs that way."

"Enough already!" Larbiabba said. "I don't need a lesson!"

"Apparently you need some kind of lesson," Libriota said. "Dabbling in cosmic matters you know nothing about. How long did you think you could get away with it? A great fire in the dark can be seen for quite a distance away. The amateur can build the fire but can't hide it. Tsk, tsk. You should have furthered your education and joined the Hierarchy. We would have made an exception for you. You're not just any Gren. You're intelligent and talented. Yes, the Hierarchy. There you could have mastered these matters I consider ordinary and mundane. Lanshalla joined. I must check on her condition. See what I can do before I return her to prison. Cheer up, Larbiabba. You might share the same cell with her after your trial is complete. And now, the visit with Lanshalla. Bleuh business."

"Go then," Larbiabba said. "And be rid of you."

Libriota made to leave the cargo area. She paused, turned to Larbiabba, and motioned for Larbiabba to follow.

"Bleuh business, remember?" Larbiabba said. "I'm not a Bleuh."

"You are in every way that counts," Libriota said. "Follow me, please."

Larbiabba held her ground.

"That's not a request," Libriota said.

Libriota exited the cargo area. Larbiabba followed (actually, Bleuh guards prompted her along), but she held up a hand to keep Treyu and Larto from also following. Libriota and Larbiabba were gone.

"How could you, Mother?" Treyu asked. "How could you betray us?"

"She didn't betray you," Libriota said, popping her head around the corner. "We detected the ethereal rift and tracked it to this cargo area. Children always blame their parents for things they don't understand. Now if you are done playing blame the dame, I will deal with Lanshalla."

Libriota exited again. Treyu waited a moment to ensure Libriota would not return.

"You really should watch your tongue, Treyu," Trisha said.

"Is what she said true? About detecting the ethereal rift?" Treyu asked.

"From what she says," Trisha said. "A ship was detected in orbit. A Bleuh ship."

"And so of course you kept it secret," Treyu said.

"We didn't want to disturb your attempt at sealing the rift," Trisha said. "Some of my subordinates thought the electro-magnetic explosive was going to be used, so they left you in charge of that, and I left my subordinates to watch you. But I had my own hands full with the Bleuh ship. Turns out it was Libriota, and not a projection. The real thing. I tried stalling for time, but she detected the ethereal rift. I had hoped I could find a way to seal the rift on my own after which I would have persuaded Libriota that things were under control. But I couldn't. And Libriota is no fool either. She detected the fake signals you sent, the fake radiation and all that. It was Libriota who sealed the rift. So before you accuse people of being traitors, learn the truth first."

"I didn't know," Treyu said.

"Naturally," Trisha said.

"Can you help us to escape?" Larto asked.

"Things are touch and go," Trisha said. "I'll do what I can. Be ready to move on any cue."

"Will do," Larto said.

A message came through on Trisha's wrist transceiver device.

"Yes. Thank you," she said.

"What is it?" Treyu asked.

"Mariel is recovering from treatment. You may see her now," Trisha said. "Lanshalla is recovering too, but Libriota is visiting her, and so you must wait."

Treyu and Larto visited Mariel while Libriota and Larbiabba visited Lanshalla.

"So, this is how you've been keeping yourself busy, my old friend," Libriota said to Lanshalla in a recovery room. "You've taken up with this Gren, I see."

Libriota glanced at Larbiabba.

"We were ambushed by Greylingers," Lanshalla said. "They threatened to invade our solar system."

"I know all about that," Libriota said. "I sealed the rip and spared your life, along with that Gren, Mariel, or whatever her name is."

"You know about Greylingers? How is it I never knew?" Lanshalla asked.

"Because you never went as high in the Hierarchy as I did," Libriota said. "Had you stuck with your job and duty, you'd be helping me instead of fighting me."

"I'm not fighting you," Lanshalla said.

"No? Cavorting with Grens on Carinia 2, conspiring with Greyans on Carinia 5, and contaminating the solar system with Greylingers!" Libriota said. "Your criminal record grows by the moment, not to mention your escape during transport to prison."

"You were once my friend," Lanshalla said.

"I still am," Libriota said.

"Really? Prove it! Leave me be. Leave these people alone," Lanshalla said.

"It is because I'm your friend that I can't do that. I won't let you be further contaminated by this heresy. And as Larbiabba here knows too much about us, she will need rehabilitation as well," Libriota said. "I'm going to do you both a special favor. I'm going to recommend you both be sent to a high-class rehab center on Carinia 1. I could let you both go to the prison work camp on Roushilla 4, but what kind of friend would do that? Not me. You get the best from me."

"And the others here?" Lanshalla asked.

"The Bleuh Imperial Patrol will conduct a full search of this world. Greyans will be allowed to stay, but Grens will be taken to a detention camp, starting with your Larto and Mariel," Libriota said.

"That's not fair!" Larbiabba said. "They haven't done anything to you."

"I suspect they had a hand in Lanshalla's escape. That's evidence enough. Further, there's suspicion rebels are training here. We'll turn up that evidence and process those rebels," Libriota said.

Lanshalla went eethi and flashed her eethi self a bright orange as if to attack Libriota. But Libriota also went eethi and stretched her image to swoop around Lanshalla's ethereal image and force it back into her body. Libriota laughed.

"You've never done *that* before," Lanshalla said.

"I've grown since we last met, Lanshalla. A hazard of the job," Libriota said.

"What job?" Lanshalla asked.

"I have many. Besides being the leader of all Bleuhs, I've picked up a new title—Chief Eethi Investigator," Libriota said. "All ethereal violations come under my purview. I've gained extra power to detect and contain."

A Bleuh aide rushed in with urgent news.

"We've discovered a group of newly-arrived rebel Grens!" the aide said. "In this very outpost."

"Capture them at once!" Libriota ordered.

"We tried. They escaped. They're heading for a spaceship in docking bay 47," the aide said.

"I'll deal with this myself. Keep watch over Lanshalla. And Larbiabba!" Libriota shouted as she ran out of the recovery room.

The aide stared at Lanshalla and Larbiabba. The two stared back.

"How are you feeling?" Larbiabba asked Lanshalla, making small talk.

"A bit weak, but getting stronger," Lanshalla replied, indicating that small talk was all they could do. "I hear the rehab centers on Carinia 1 have a nice flower section."

"I've heard the same," Larbiabba said.

"There's one corner where they have a post you can push with your ethereal spirit, and it will fall to the ground," Lanshalla hinted as she darted her eyes toward the aide.

"I've heard that too," Larbiabba said, picking up on the hint. "But it only works if another projects eethi fire and flame."

"I'm good with fire and flame," Lanshalla said. "Are you good with pushing over the post?"

"Indeed," Larbiabba said.

Lanshalla nodded her head, and Larbiabba nodded back. Then Lanshalla went eethi and projected an image of fire and flame to the aide while Larbiabba went eethi behind the aide and made to disrupt his nervous system. But before Larbiabba could complete her task, Libriota appeared at the doorway.

"What are you doing here?" she shouted at the aide. "Go after the rebels!"

The aide rushed off. Lanshalla made an ethereal move toward Libriota, but Libriota changed shape back to Mariel.

"Mariel!" Lanshalla and Larbiabba said simultaneously.

"This projection system works well," Mariel said.

Lanshalla quickly confirmed it really was Mariel by touching her ethereally.

"It's the real Mariel," Lanshalla said.

"What's going on?" Larbiabba asked.

"Trisha created a diversion with fake rebels using the projection system," Mariel said. "You must follow me. Quickly!"

Mariel led while Lanshalla and Larbiabba followed. Lanshalla sent her ethereal image ahead to scout while Larbiabba trailed her ethereal image to guard from behind. The three made it to an elevator, entered the elevator, and Mariel hit a button to go down. And down it did, many many floors. The elevator stopped, the doors opened, and the three were welcomed by Larto. Lanshalla quickly confirmed it was him.

"The real Larto," she said.

"Hurry, we don't have much time," he said.

The four ran down a hallway and to a set of double doors. The doors opened, and on the other side was the inside of a spaceship.

"Strap in," Treyu called from the cockpit.

The four were still strapping in when bay doors opened in front of the ship. Treyu quickly hit the main thruster and sent the craft forward along a roughly-hewn tunnel, often not wide enough for the ship, requiring Treyu to tilt the ship sideways. Mariel had not secured herself in and bounced around. Larto unstrapped himself, fought the forces to reach her, and helped her get to a chair and strap in.

"Thank you," Mariel said with a smile, but a sense of terror passed over her face.

"What is it?" Larto asked.

"I..." Mariel started, but the sense faded. "I...don't know. Nothing, I guess. Thank you again. I'll be glad when this is over."

"We'll be home soon," Larto said as he strapped himself in. "You're all welcome to spend as long as you like on my vineyard, including you, Larbiabba."

"I thank you, but won't that be the first place the Imperial Bleuhs search?" Larbiabba asked.

Treyu quickly whipped the ship around a corner, preventing anyone from answering, and then he turned the ship upward through the remnant of an old volcano. Just before it exited the volcano, a plume of fire and ash surrounded the ship and followed it outward.

"Don't worry," Treyu yelled above the turbulence. "We're being camouflaged. No one will see us."

"They won't if we burn up!" Mariel said.

The plume rose high, and Treyu navigated the ship away from the planet surface.

"We're clear," Treyu said.

But orbital space was crowded with ships flying haphazardly and attacking one another.

"Out of the volcano and into a hail storm," Mariel said. "We'll be killed for sure!"

"Just hang tight, and we'll be out of this in a bit," Treyu said.

"But how?" Mariel exclaimed.

"Because most of them aren't real," Lanshalla replied.

Larbiabba paused as if in thought (when really she went eethi into ship's controls to confirm).

"You're right," Larbiabba said. "Trisha bought us cover with these projection ships."

"Hard to fool you two," Treyu said.

"Will it be enough to fool Libriota?" Larto asked.

Before anyone could answer, a photozmic burst hit the ship.

"We've been hit!" Mariel said.

"No structural damage, but our annielectric shroud is weakened," Treyu said.

"Who hit us?" Mariel asked.

"This is Libriota," called a voice over the radio. "Stand down and prepare to be boarded."

"That's the answer," Larbiabba said.

"No, it's only the problem," Lanshalla said. "Here's the answer."

"Lanshalla, no!" Larbiabba said, sensing what might happen.

Lanshalla went eethi and stretched her ethereal self around the ship. Libriota's ship fired again, and it took the annielectric shroud offline. But Lanshalla took some power from that photozmic burst and converted it into a bright, expanding cloud, as if the ship had exploded. She secretly opened a rip into the Greylinger dimension, pulled bones and other debris from that dimension, and deposited them in the cloud. She used the rip to bend light. Reading her intent, Treyu maneuvered close toward the rip but around it so as to use the bent light to mask the ship's flight away from the expanding cloud.

"Search the debris," Libriota's voice was heard over the radio.

"We escaped!" Treyu said. "Thanks to Lanshalla!"

"Hurray for Lanshalla!" Mariel cheered.

"I'm impressed!" Larto said. "If only all our ships could escape so easily."

"Too easily," Larbiabba said.

"You suspect something?" Larto asked.

"You opened a rift to the Greylingers, right?" Larbiabba asked Lanshalla.

"Yes," Lanshalla replied, "but it was a small and secret rift. No one could detect it."

"I could," Larbiabba said.

"Oh no," Larto said.

"Oh yes," Larbiabba said. "Which means Libriota could detect it, too."

"Maybe," Lanshalla said.

"But then why did we hear her searching for debris?" Mariel asked.

"To allay suspicion and lower our guard," Larto said. "That Libriota is a devious one. A true demon."

"She would only know a rift was opened. She wouldn't know where we went," Lanshalla said.

"True," Larbiabba said. "But she would know we used the rift as a decoy, and that we're still alive. We will need to be careful."

"Always good advice," Larto said. "Treyu, did you hear that?"

"I did," Treyu said. "Do you still wish to go to Carinia 2? Could be risky. If Libriota warns the Imperial Bleuhs there before we arrive, they might—"

"They might find us. I know. We can't let that happen," Larto said. "We'll have to camp out somewhere else for a time."

"Give Lanshalla and me a moment to sort through things," Larbiabba said. "Alone please."

"Larto and Mariel, why don't you come up in the cockpit?" Treyu suggested.

Larto got up, leaned over to Lanshalla, and kissed her forehead. Lanshalla looked up at him with sudden terror, much as Mariel had experienced.

"Strange," Larto said. "Mariel—"

"Had the same reaction. I know," Lanshalla said. "The rift gave me a sense of things...I'm not sure. Mariel is right. It will be good when this is all over. Don't be put off by Larbiabba. She doesn't mean anything about shooing you away."

"I'm looking forward to us have alone time," Larto smiled.

Larto kissed her on the forehead again, went to the cockpit, and closed the door.

"I didn't want to say anything in front of the others, Lanshalla, but—" Larbiabba stumbled.

"You're pregnant," Lanshalla said. "I already knew that."

"You are too," Larbiabba said.

"We both have an eethi glow," Lanshalla said. "And we shared something special, remember?"

"I do remember," Larbiabba said. "And that affected the baby. A part of your knowledge was added to her. I wasn't planning on this."

"It was the only way to facilitate the baby option with the Greylinger rift," Lanshalla said. "Our babies had to be in sync. But your baby is only of you and your husband, as mine is only of Larto and me. I did not add myself to your baby as a parent, but as an ethereal beacon."

"Who are these babies, I wonder," Claus said. "Will they give them names?"

"Let's watch and see," young Lanietta said.

"I've never heard of such a thing," Larbiabba said. "And I'm not sure what to do."

"There's only one thing left," Lanshalla said. "We stick together. Work things out. As friends."

"Friends," Larbiabba said.

The two hugged.

"Let me ask you—did your husband have his own family?" Lanshalla asked. "That was a silly question. Of course he did."

"Yes," Larbiabba said. "They went into hiding after his death, but not before sneaking me off Carinia 2. Apparently being Gren with Bleuh ability is of particular interest to the Bleuhs."

"As would your child," Lanshalla said. "The Bleuhs would torture your husband's family to get at you and your child. Hide your pregnancy from the Bleuhs as long as possible."

Larbiabba nodded her head in agreement.

"Wait," Larbiabba said. "Do you think Libriota knows? About my child?"

"No," Lanshalla said. "She knows I'm pregnant though. And I used that pregnancy to mask yours. It was a trick, I admit, but it was less deadly than the baby option."

"Thank you!" Larbiabba said. "Oh, the Bleuhs! They cause so much trouble! We're always fighting them and looking for ways to defeat them."

"We'll have to be creative about teaching others the baby option," Lanshalla said. "We can't do so *and* keep our babies at the same time."

"Do you still intend to teach others?" Larbiabba asked. "I thought we put an end to that. That whole Greylinger dimension thing is too much to handle. I'm surprised they didn't jump out and grab us when you opened that rift just now."

"Because I didn't use eethi energy in the conventional state. I used waste eethi energy," Lanshalla said.

"Waste eethi energy? There's no such thing," Larbiabba said.

"That people know of," Lanshalla said. "But it exists. I stored some when I was in the Greylinger dimension. And I opened the rift to receive more waste energy. No one keeps track of that."

"The bones and other debris then?" Larbiabba asked.

"Yes."

"Then I have a better idea," Larbiabba said. "Since the eethi waste is free, perhaps we could organize it. Recycle it into something useful."

"Reanimating bone remnants into life requires adding an ethereal component," Lanshalla said.

"Then we don't reanimate, at least not into anything with a soul," Larbiabba said.

"I think you're on to something," Lanshalla said. "Artificial life?"

"Now it's my turn to say, 'Yes'," Larbiabba said.

"Sounds like a challenge," Lanshalla grinned. "But we'll need a safe place to work."

"Which circles around to the original question before we kicked Mariel and Larto out," Larbiabba said.

"Before *you* kicked Mariel and Larto out," Lanshalla laughed. "But at least I can help here. Carinia 5 is out since we just left there."

"And Carinia 2 is out since rebels are expected to be there," Larbiabba said.

"Carinia 3 is full of radiation," Lanshalla said.

"Carinia 4 is full of sulfuric acid," Larbiabba said.

"Which leaves Carinia 1," Lanshalla said.

"The Bleuh home world? You're joking," Larbiabba said.

"Who would expect rebel experiments in the land of aristocracy?" Lanshalla asked.

"But where?" Larbiabba asked.

"In the most well-to-do Bleuh sector," Lanshalla said.

"You're serious," Larbiabba said.

"Absolutely."

"But that's crazy!"

"Which is why it will work!" Lanshalla said. "Artificial life-forms developed in the Bleuhs' back yard."

"And if they detect the ethereal rift?" Larbiabba asked. "You will open it for your experiments, right?"

"I will," Lanshalla said. "But I'm getting ideas about that too. Ever wondered how our procreation tanks work?"

"A couple goes in, and they come out with the woman pregnant," Larbiabba said. "Grens have them too."

"Grens have them because they have no choice," Lanshalla said. "The Bleuh aristocracy uses them because the natural way is too vulgar for them."

"I didn't realize there was a natural way until you and Larto made your own 'procreation tank'," Larbiabba said.

The two giggled.

"Have you ever visited one of the procreation tanks?" Lanshalla asked.

"Heck no!" Larbiabba said. "I didn't want to risk any stray rays impregnating me."

"Then you know the myth," Lanshalla said.

"I've heard about it. Women walking by only to find themselves pregnant shortly thereafter," Larbiabba said.

"When I was a girl, I used to run by one such tank on a dare with my friends," Lanshalla said.

"That was a dare!" Larbiabba said.

"I think we were too young for anything to happen," Lanshalla said. "But I remember getting a strange feeling, like a weak electric charge tingling on my skin, pulsing with syncopation. I had the same syncopated feeling when the Greylinger rift opened, the very same rhythm as the procreation tank."

"Then you think a Greylinger rift is used for those tanks?" Larbiabba asked. "It would explain why Libriota knows about them. But what about the Grens?"

"As an adult, I walked by a Gren procreation tank," Lanshalla said. "Many times. I had no such reaction. I'm not sure how those tanks work. They could be shielded, or—"

"Or they don't use Greylinger rifts at all," Larbiabba said. "Which would explain why Grens know nothing about it. Heck, we didn't know anything about it."

"Only the highest of high Bleuhs must know," Lanshalla said. "To maintain control of the new population."

"They could deny procreation for a couple they didn't approve of and tell the couple that they were infertile. Wow!" Larbiabba exclaimed, and her voice rose unexpectedly loud.

"What's wrong?" Larto asked, suddenly appearing from the cockpit. "Is someone hurt?"

"No," Lanshalla laughed. "But we know where to go. Carinia 1."

"I must have heard you wrong," Larto said. "I thought you said—"

"You thought and heard correctly," Larbiabba said. "Carinia 1."

"That's suicide," Larto said.

"We're going to start a new business. Growing shrubs. Near a procreation tank," Lanshalla said.

"What? Wait, is this a joke? Like playing off my vineyard farm?" Larto asked.

"Hey, yeah, Lanshalla," Larbiabba said. "Not a shrub farm. A vineyard farm."

"We could start with the Lonely Vine," Lanshalla said.

"Take clippings," Larbiabba said.

"And make hybrids," Lanshalla said.

"With the secret ingredient," Larbiabba said.

"What secret ingredient?" Larto asked.

"It's a secret," Lanshalla said.

"Oh, you!" Larto said, and he rushed over, hugged her as she stood to greet him, and kissed her.

"We're all in this together, remember?" Lanshalla said. "Here, I know. Let's do this."

Lanshalla took Larbiabba's right hand, and Lanshalla indicated for Larto to take Larbiabba's left hand (which he did). Both then pulled Larbiabba to her feet, and the two gave Larbiabba a group hug.

"Hug," Lanshalla said.

"Oh what a wonderful moment!" Mariel said, coming out to join the three in a group hug.

"We've decided where to go," Larbiabba said.

"Carinia 1," Lanshalla said.

Larto and Mariel exchanged nervous glances.

"Um, in case you've forgotten, there are three Grens and one Greyan on this ship," Mariel said. "Larbiabba, you're a Gren. Remember?"

"I remember," Larbiabba said. "I'll be fine."

"You'll be fine too," Lanshalla said. "We'll get passes for you all."

"We're going to start a vineyard shop," Larbiabba said.

"After we get cuttings from the Lonely Vine at Larto's place," Lanshalla said.

"This is all very strange," Mariel said. "But won't someone recognize us?"

"I can solve that," Lanshalla said. "Treyu, put the ship on autopilot and come back here."

"Autopilot for where?" Treyu asked.

"Set course for a high orbit around Carinia 2," Larto said. "I have a feeling these two are up to something."

Treyu set the course and went back with the others.

"What's this all about?" he asked.

"Watch," Lanshalla said.

Lanshalla opened a waste rift from the Greylinger dimension and used her ethereal self to integrate waste bone matter over her skin. She looked elderly and fragile. Mariel screamed.

"No, wait," Lanshalla said. "I'm fine. This is just a cover. Like fancy makeup. I can shed it. Look."

Lanshalla went eethi and used her ethereal self to shake off the bone matter covering. She reintegrated and laughed.

"You're all right!" Mariel said.

"A clever disguise," Larto said.

"I can do that for everyone. The makeup should last as long as we need," Lanshalla said.

"You and Larbiabba can go ahead," Larto said. "The rest of us need to be as we are to get the cutting. After that, we can undergo the transformation."

Treyu shook with anxiety.

"Nervous, Treyu?" Larto asked.

"I'm not sure," he said. "I get skin rashes easily. That's why I prefer butlering instead of gardening."

"And I don't know if I can handle staring at an old face in the mirror every morning," Mariel said.

"Think of it as role playing," Lanshalla said.

"Can you make me look younger?" Mariel asked.

Lanshalla and Larbiabba looked at each other.

"You want to give it a try, Larbs?" Lanshalla asked.

"Larbs?" Treyu asked.

"Might as well be friendly," Lanshalla said.

"Thanks, Shalli," Larbiabba said.

"Shalli?" Treyu asked.

"Larbiabba, are you?" Mariel asked.

"We both are. So much for hiding my secret," Larbiabba said.

"Oh, then I definitely want to look younger!" Mariel said. "I'll be Aunt Mariel."

"Aunt to what?" Treyu asked.

"Have you picked names?" Mariel asked.

"Lanietta," Lanshalla said.

"Labba," Larbiabba said.

Young Lanietta stopped the vision. She looked at Claus in total shock.

"It's you!" Claus said. "And Labba too! Close together yet not even born. Tied together ethereally. Lanietta?"

Young Lanietta could not shake the expression of shock on her face, nor could she speak. She shook with anxiety and tried to calm herself. But she couldn't. Plasma swirls of yellow and blue surrounded her with increasing speed until they mixed into a faded pea-green color. The color wasn't faded for long. It became brighter and brighter until it exploded. Claus thought he was done in, and he closed his eyes in reflex, but when he opened them, he was no longer in the studio apartment of Cluffer 2 but was instead back in the orb chamber.

Cluffer 2 was destroyed. Aftova stung badly in Claus's upper palate, making the area very sensitive, as if he'd just had tissue removed during a dental procedure. He looked around and saw that adult Lanietta was still kneeling with hands on the orbs of her parents. Claus tried to speak, but his throat choked up. Instead, he could only watch. Young Lanietta walked over to her adult self and reintegrated. Adult Lanietta, while still holding onto the orbs, stood slowly and spoke as if just awakening from the delirium of deadly disease.

"Claus?" she said with a weak voice. "Claus."

Claus's anxiety faded, he cleared his throat and spoke.

"Lanietta!" Claus said, and he rushed over to hug her, but still he passed through her.

"I...I didn't know about Labba," she said. "I mean I knew she was special, but not like this. I..."

"Labba! Yes!" Claus said. "I'll contact her immediately. She must know!"

"Wait, Claus," Lanietta said weakly. "Not yet. She...doesn't know. We thought we were just friends. I...have not...the strength...for complications."

"Not even for Labba?" Claus asked. "She's not just a friend. She's closer than that."

"You have seen...the vision. You know that...I lost...an older sister," Lanietta said. "A real older sister. Close to me but unknown. Unknown and lost. Now Labba is closer than I thought. I thought...I can't bear the thought of losing her of...of isolation."

"She's still Labba," Claus said. "You can still be friends."

"I'm falling into trance," Lanietta said. "I..."

Lanietta returned to her kneeling position and held solid. Young Lanietta re-emerged from adult Lanietta and stood by Claus.

"The girl you see before you, as before, is all the strength I still have," young Lanietta said. "Though I am heartened by the knowledge that Labba and I are close this early, I am still drained by the knowledge that she is one of the last and that my people are gone."

"How can we resume the vision?" Claus asked. "Cluffer 2 is destroyed."

"I'm sorry about that," young Lanietta said. "Here, I'll help."

Young Lanietta moved her hands in an alternating crossing pattern in front of her face. Her hands left glowing trails of yellow and blue, and these trails formed a figure eight pattern. Clouds formed inside the loops of the figure eights, and after a moment, the clouds took the shape of ice skates. Young Lanietta stopped with the figure eight loop and caught the ice skates as they began to fall. She strapped them onto her feet.

"I don't understand," Claus said.

Young Lanietta then skated on the orb chamber floor.

"How...you're skating?" Claus asked. "But there's no ice."

Young Lanietta hummed a tune while skating.

"Ethereal blades," she said between hums.

After skating around the orb chamber, at times far away from Claus and at other times whizzing close by, she settled on a figure eight loop around Claus, with him in one of the loops.

"What are you doing?" Claus asked while she continued humming.

"Listen closely, and jump when I tell you but not before," she said. "Notice how the floor glows blue in your loop, where you're standing."

"I see that," Claus said. "Do I jump out of the loop?"

"You will and you won't," she said.

"What?"

"You will not jump completely out of the figure eight," she said between hums. "But you will jump into the other loop of the figure eight. You will do so immediately after I cross the middle. Do it after I next cross. I'm skating around now. Ready?"

"Ready," Claus said.

"Jump!" young Lanietta said as she crossed the middle.

Claus was a bit slow jumping to the other loop. The floor color changed to yellow, it jolted Claus's legs as if being electrocuted, and his legs jerked quickly and sent him out of the figure eight completely. He landed on an orb, a vision of a 1940s fast-racing band with brass instruments being played, and Claus's nerves were rattled with more anxiety. Young Lanietta skated over to that orb and stopped it.

"You must be incredibly quick," young Lanietta said. "You'll probably brush past me to make this work. Let's try again."

Claus hobbled over to the spot where he first stood for the figure eight loop. Young Lanietta skated again.

"Get ready," she said. "I'm crossing in a moment, and, jump!"

Claus jumped and timed it so he would practically cross her path. He just missed her (she cleared through first), and he landed in the other loop. The place where he had stood was now yellow (it had changed just after he took to the air, and so it missed him), and the loop where he now stood was blue.

"I did it!" Claus said. "Will the vision resume now?"

"Jump!" young Lanietta said as she crossed again.

"Wait, I wasn't ready, I—" Claus tried to say.

But his current loop-spot turned yellow, jolted his legs, and he involuntarily jumped outside the figure eight as before and landed on a different orb, which launched a great white shark into the air. The shark swooped down to chomp down on Claus, releasing large quantities of water from its mouth onto Claus in its descent. Young Lanietta quickly skated over and deactivated this orb as she did for the other one.

"You must keep jumping until we return to the vision," she said.

"Oh," Claus said.

"Try again?" she suggested.

Claus stood up and gingerly walked over.

"Is there any way we can deactivate all orbs before we try again?" Claus said.

"The vision needs the orbs to be ready for activation, even ones that probably won't be used," she said. "I'm sorry."

"Okay. I'll try again," Claus said.

Claus repeated the figure eight procedure as before. He jumped each time young Lanietta crossed the center, and he was able to just barely avoid the yellow color. And so, the loops of the figure eight always had one loop yellow and the other blue, with colors swapping just as young Lanietta finished crossing the center. Time seemed to speed up, with young Lanietta's skating and Claus's jumping increasing in speed too. Each time the colors switched, a mist layer of the departing color arose from the loop, and so the air became sandwiched with alternating colors of yellow and blue ever rising upward. The speed increase meant the layers progressively became thinner and thinner, and this resulted in a mixing of the lower layers to the point where a green color emerged. Claus and Lanietta found themselves back in the vision.

"Those names are beautiful," Mariel said. "This is going to be so much fun."

"What will? What are these riddles?" Treyu asked.

"They are both with child," Mariel said.

"So that's the mystery," Treyu said.

"Not entirely," Larbiabba said. "We can use the vineyard shop as a cover for developing artificial life-forms."

"As in fake plants?" Treyu asked.

"As in fake people," Lanshalla said.

Treyu laughed.

"Statues," Treyu said sarcastically. "That will *really* help the rebels."

"Except these *statues* will move and act like Carinians," Larbiabba said.

"Is that possible?" Mariel asked. "I want one to help me with cleaning."

Everyone laughed.

"They'll do more than that if we're successful," Lanshalla said.

"How will you make them?" Larto asked.

"Shalli will bring down the material from the Greylinger dimension," Larbiabba said.

"And Larbs will modify it with Greyan projection technology," Lanshalla said.

"Mixed with historical life knowledge from the Lonely Vine?" Larto asked.

"Yes!" Lanshalla and Larbiabba answered simultaneously.

Treyu held his hands to the side of his head as if keeping his brain from exploding in disbelief. Mariel was excited about having a helper. And Larto just nodded his head in affirmation and grinned.

"This could be the turning point of the entire Gren independence movement," Larto said. "But what will prevent the Bleuhs from stealing the technology? We can't be too careful, you know."

"The Lonely Vine," Lanshalla said. "It evolved on Carinia 2. Only Grens will have command of such creations. And me with help from Larbs."

"Sorry, Treyu," Larbiabba said. "We can't risk Greyans getting control. You saw how easily Libriota infiltrated Carinia 5."

"So I am doomed to butlering without help," Treyu said.

"Maybe I can train a helper for you," Mariel said.

"Hmm," Treyu said. "Might be worth a shot."

"Yes, indeed!" Larbiabba said.

"Then let's return to my vineyard, but secretly!" Larto said.

"We'll be in orbit soon," Treyu said. "Once we are, planetary defense will know."

"Lanshalla," Larto asked. "Can you hide this ship from detection while we're in orbit?"

"I can," she said. "I'll use a Greylinger rift to hide it."

"Good," Larto said. "Treyu, are you up to it?"

"I...I'll have to watch the scanners closely. With us hidden, the Space Collision Avoidance System on other ships won't work. I'll have to change course to keep us safe."

"I'll work with Treyu," Lanshalla said, and she went into the cockpit.

"Mariel," Larto said. "You and I must retrieve the Lonely Vine cutting."

"I want a complete makeover!" Mariel said.

"But then no one will recognize you," Larto said.

"Exactly! Let them think a beautiful woman is visiting," Mariel said.

"Good idea, Mariel," Larbiabba said.

"Thank you," Mariel said.

"We should do the makeover here," Larbiabba said. "Shalli already has the rift open to hide the ship. I can use the Greylinger material for your new look. But we need privacy."

Larbiabba pointed for Larto to go into the cockpit.

"Here we go again," Larto said.

Larto went into the cockpit and closed the door.

"All this exuberance," Claus said. "I wonder how well their plans will go?"

"Too exuberant," young Lanietta said. "I sense things will not go as expected."

"They kicked me out," Larto said.

"For the makeover," Lanshalla said. "I heard."

"How's the orbit?"

"Fine," Treyu said. "Lanshalla is holding a rift open around the ship. We are invisible, so to speak."

"Excellent," Larto said.

"We've detected Imperial Bleuhs at your vineyard," Lanshalla said.

"I was afraid of that," Larto said. "Can we land and remain unnoticed?"

"Not easily," Lanshalla said. "I can keep the ship invisible, but environmental things like air movement and ground-dust disturbance will give us away."

"There must be a way to get down there without detection," Larto said. "If only we could go through that rift and come out near my back yard."

Lanshalla thought for a moment.

"Bleuhs have been experimenting with space-jumping," Lanshalla said. "I wonder if we could try that."

"Oh, I don't like the sound of that," Treyu said.

"What is it, exactly?" Larto asked.

"A Bleuh goes eethi, sends the eethi self somewhere, then snaps the physical body to the eethi part," Lanshalla said.

"Now I *know* I don't like the sound of it," Treyu said.

"Can you make it work?" Larto asked.

"Oh sure," Treyu said. "Just snap your physical body through a wall and land in a floor. Broken bones, broken blood vessels, heart failure, organ failure, brain failure—"

"You can't scare me, Treyu," Larto said.

"He's right, you know," Lanshalla said. "No Bleuh has succeeded. They've all died trying, and from systemic injuries, too."

"Oh," Larto said.

"Yeah, *oh*," Treyu reiterated.

"What if I volunteer?" Larto asked.

"You can't," Treyu said. "Grens can't go eethi. Only Bleuhs and Larbiabba."

"What about that baby option experiment on Carinia 5? With the Grens?" Larto asked.

"I should say Grens can't go eethi on their own," Treyu said. "It's a bit like jumping off a cliff and claiming you can fly."

"You know, I don't think any Bleuhs have tried using the Greylinger rift," Lanshalla said.

"Sounds like suicide," Treyu said.

"Not really," Lanshalla said. "A Bleuh could split, and then I could open two rifts, one by the close-by physical part, and another by the distant ethereal part. The physical part could travel through the rift. The rift would allow the physical matter to travel without going through other matter. I mean, that's been the problem all along, the one bit of matter going through another bit of matter."

"And just who do you propose to use as a test subject?" Treyu asked.

"My idea, my test, my body," Lanshalla said.

Young Lanietta looked at Claus in shock.

"I can't believe Mommy," young Lanietta said. "I mean...I'm inside her. She risked my death."

"I'm sorry, Lanietta," Claus said. "But we know she didn't cause you to die as an unborn. You were born. You are here."

"Yes," young Lanietta said. "She did not cause my unborn death. But did she cause my after-born death?"

"Do not speak as such," Claus said. "You are alive and—"

"Not well," young Lanietta finished. "How things might not have been, had Mommy failed in what she's about to do."

"I've been told you had a hand in Earth's creation. If true, you are the Mother of Humanity," Claus said. "We owe a debt to you."

"I am no creditor of life," young Lanietta said. "I created no life. Nor do I fear can I ever."

Claus looked at young Lanietta with concern. She let out a weak smile.

"And when you fail, no one is left to open the rift. We need the rift to hide this ship," Treyu said.

"A risk I'm willing to take," Lanshalla said.

"But I'm not," Treyu said.

Lanshalla jumped with a start.

"What is it?" Larto asked.

"Larbs," Lanshalla said.

"You would push her into this without asking? How terrible of you," Treyu said.

"No, not that. Larbs says the transformation is complete. We can go back now," Lanshalla said.

"Telepathy?" Larto asked.

"I...I've never had this before. Something new. And just with her. Maybe the rift has something to do with it," Lanshalla said.

"Treyu, can you hold this course for a bit without Lanshalla's help?" Larto asked.

"There's an empty orbital path right...there, I've locked us in. The rift will stay with us. I can go back too," Treyu said.

"Let's see how Mariel turned out then," Larto said.

"Let me go first," Lanshalla said.

"Why you?" Treyu asked.

"It's a girl thing," Lanshalla said. "Turn around, you two. No peeking."

Treyu rolled his eyes.

"Come on," Larto said. "It's just another moment to wait."

Larto turned Treyu such that his back faced the cockpit door, and then Larto himself turned his back to the door. Lanshalla slipped through the door quickly and closed it. A moment of pause passed, and then Lanshalla shrieked with delight. Treyu jumped in a startlement.

"She's hurt?" Treyu asked.

"Another girl thing, I imagine," Larto said.

"Come in, boys," Lanshalla called.

Larto opened the door and ushered Treyu in first. The men looked at three women standing side-by-side. There was Lanshalla, and two highly attractive women dressed as if going to a formal dance.

"I should feel giddy and happy," young Lanietta said to Claus. "But I am sullen and somber."

"Why so?" Claus asked.

"It is all so frivolous," young Lanietta said. "I know this is fleeting. They know not their fate."

"But you do, don't you?" Claus said. "Perhaps it's best they don't know."

"It is not," young Lanietta said. "Much misery can be avoided by...by..."

"By preventing it?" Claus asked. "Or by pretending to prevent it?"

"I...they should...I should...I should have..." young Lanietta stumbled.

"Give them their moment of happiness," Claus said. "And borrow some for yourself."

Young Lanietta recomposed herself and returned another weak smile.

"I cannot repay them," young Lanietta said.

"None of us can," Claus said. "Perhaps someday people will think of us with thankful hearts."

"You speak of something I've never thought of," young Lanietta said. "But who will there be?"

"That's a mystery best kept a secret," Claus said.

"Who...what..." Treyu stumbled.

"Hi!" the dressed-up girls teased.

"Uncanny!" Larto said. "But who is...are you...which is...I can't tell!"

"I'm Lanshalla, or don't you remember?" Lanshalla teased.

"I recognize you, of course. But Larbiabba and Mariel...or is it Mariel and Larbiabba? You look like different people."

"Do you know me now?" Mariel said, with her voice being unchanged.

"Mariel!" Treyu said. "Who would think you're a maid?"

"I'm not! I'm a high-society gal," Mariel said.

"And I'm with her!" Larbiabba said.

"Larbiabba is going down with Mariel," Lanshalla said. "And she agreed to space-jump."

"What!?" Treyu barked.

"I'm with Treyu," Larto said. "There must be another way. There must."

"I've gone over it with Larbiabba and Mariel. The matter is settled," Lanshalla said. "I'll open two rifts. Larbiabba will space-jump with Mariel in tow. The two will show up just outside the vineyard and claim they are lost."

"Oh, they'll be lost all right," Treyu said. "Forever lost."

"The Bleuhs and workers will be taken aback," Lanshalla said, brushing off Treyu. "In the diversion, I'll send Larto to his backyard."

"You're living in fantasy," Treyu said. "Mariel is a Gren. Larto is a Gren. Larbiabba is a Gren. Which part of *Gren* don't you understand?"

"Larbiabba can handle it. Mariel can handle it. Larto can handle it. Which part of *handle it* don't you understand?" Lanshalla asked.

"This won't work!" Treyu said.

"Besides, Larto is a Gren with a little bit of me inside," Lanshalla said.

"I...don't know what to say," Larto said.

"You won't have to," Lanshalla said. "I'll initiate an auto space-jump."

"An auto space-jump!" Treyu mocked. "Why not sign over control of this space ship to Libriota herself? Have her auto crash it into Carinia 2?"

"Treyu, please," Larto said. "Lanshalla, can you do this with anyone? With Treyu, for example?"

Treyu looked on with great fear.

"No," she said. "I can only do the auto space-jump with someone I've melded with very closely. I don't think Treyu would allow—"

"No, he would not," Treyu said. "Certainly not with a Bleuh."

"Don't be shy, Treyu," Lanshalla said. "Let us know what you *really* think about Bleuhs. I'll be happy to let you know what *we* think."

"Treyu, what's wrong with you?" Larbiabba asked. "You were never this skittish before."

"I never had space-jumping or Greylinger rifts to deal with," Treyu said. "This is too much stress."

"Treyu, stay here and relax," Larto said. "I'll go along with the plan."

"*The* plan? You mean this risky Bleuh plan?" Treyu asked.

"Things will get riskier, I fear," Larto said. "I feel your concern. If this fails and we all die, take what you know to the rebels. Track our positions and keep the data recorders running. Good may come of this before the end."

"What a cheerful thing to say," Treyu said sarcastically.

"It's the best we can do," Larto said.

"We could spend more time in orbit. Think about things," Treyu said.

"And give Libriota more time to stop us," Larbiabba said. "No, we need to start right away. Libriota is cunning and will use every means to stop us. Treyu, good friend, we've worked a lot together. Keep me in mind when you help the rebels."

Treyu was speechless. Larto sent him back to the cockpit to watch for other ships. Lanshalla escorted Larbiabba and Mariel over to a cargo scanning station. She hit several buttons, and a light scanned over them.

"This is just preliminary," Lanshalla said. "I'll open the entrance here. Larbs, sync up your ethereal self to this wavelength."

There was a slight pause.

"Got it," Larbiabba said.

"Opening the exit rift," Lanshalla said. "Hold onto each other, you two!"

"This had better work," Larbiabba said. "Or I'll eethi haunt you until Carinia Zero goes supernova."

Lanshalla hit a few more buttons. A Greylinger rift opened. Lanshalla went eethi and touched part of the rift with one hand while escorting Larbiabba and Mariel into the rift with the other. The two women disappeared, the rift closed, and Lanshalla reintegrated. Lanshalla hit a few more buttons, and the scanner powered down.

"I'm receiving telepathy from Larbiabba. A little excess steam around their bodies when they landed. Yes, they made it," Lanshalla said.

Larto clutched his fist in celebration.

"The worst is over," Lanshalla said. "I proved I could do it. Now it's your turn."

Larto walked over to the cargo scanning station. But unbeknownst to the two, their Greylinger rift attracted attention.

Chapter 77: Libriota's Familiar

"A rift just opened," an assistant said to Libriota, still on a spacecraft.

"Of course it did," Libriota said.

"And a second rift. Who could it be?" the assistant asked.

"It's them," Libriota said.

"But they perished," the assistant said. "We saw them."

"*You* saw them," Libriota said. "*I* saw a ruse. You are not trained in the ways of deception as I am. Set course for the first rift. We will find them there."

"The rifts just closed," the assistant said.

"Did you detect any unusual ethereal activity in those rifts?" Libriota asked.

"Uh...I didn't scan for it," the assistant said.

"Keep the eethi scanners on. Eethi makes the universe go around, and Lanshalla is bound to use it again," Libriota said.

"There. Another pair of rifts has opened. A Gren eethi has gone through," the assistant said.

"And?" Libriota said.

"Now it's closed. The ethereal signature is male. Matches our records for Larto," the assistant said. "They *are* alive!"

"Of course! I told you that already!" Libriota said.

"Well I don't know why she would kill her people by putting them in the rift," the assistant said.

"Unlikely," Libriota said.

Another assistant chimed in.

"Scanners show the Gren called Larto survived the transfer through the rift," the second assistant said.

"So Lanshalla has performed a successful space-jump. And with a Gren," Libriota said. "There will be a remnant left in the Greylinger dimension. That is always the cost for such cheats. We will cheat ourselves. We will retrieve that remnant and use it to track down her and those creatures she calls her friends."

The two assistants exchanged nervous glances.

"Open a rift to the Greylinger dimension," Libriota ordered.

"But that means..." the first assistant said.

"That one of you must also go into the rift," Libriota said. "Do it."

"But...I'll lose my life!" the first assistant said.

"Me too!" said the second.

"I'll send you both in if one of you doesn't go," she ordered.

The two looked at each other with expressions of frozen horror, but then they quickly hit buttons on a panel. A vertical rift opened up, much like the one on Carinia 5. It pulled the first assistant in. Exhausted, the second assistant stopped typing.

"Very good," Libriota said. "You sent him in before he could send you in. Now you see how the universe works. The one who is first does satisfy the thirst, the one who is second goes beggin' and beggin'."

Libriota produced two wine glasses, filled them with cherry wine, and handed one to the second assistant while she took the other.

"A toast to the one who is first, my new First Assistant!" Libriota said.

The new first assistant drank the wine, timing her sips so as to not finish her wine before Libriota finished hers.

"Something coming through the rift," the new first assistant said.

"Behold how the Greylingers work!" Libriota said.

A creature emerged from the rift, humanoid in basic shape but with the arms, neck, and head of a dog. It wore a uniform resembling that of an Imperial Bleuh Patrol.

"What is it?" the new first assistant asked.

"All my nightly desires," Libriota said.

The new first assistant looked puzzled, as Carinians spent their lives in constant daytime.

"I know of what you think," Libriota said. "Carinians have no night. Just day. He will give me the night I so desperately need, a change from day that binds me at bay. Benevolent by day, belligerent by night. He will complete me and give me cycles. Together we will witness rise and fall, doom and delight, waste and want. Come forth, young Greylinger!"

The creature walked to Libriota and gave her a hug. Then he licked her face in affection as a dog might do.

"I...am...Biautus," he slobbered.

"Beautiful Biautus," Libriota said with something between a moan and delight. "You are the food for my wicked ethereal soul!"

She kissed him, grabbed him, hugged him, and caressed him.

"Show me what you can do," she said as she released her embrace.

Biautus walked around like a man, and then he walked around like a dog. He jumped from all fours and barked like a dog. He wagged his tail from under his shirt.

"I...got that from her!" young Lanietta said. "I never thought of it before. I made you into a dog too. She must have warped my mind. My mother dealt with Libriota, I dealt with Libriota, even you have dealt with her."

"It seems Libriota has done much to many," Claus said. "And she lived for a very long time."

"How petty of her," young Lanietta said. "And such waste! I still can't believe she and the others are gone. She did it to herself in the end, but the price was too high!"

Libriota took an implement from the new first assistant and tossed it at Biautus. He caught it in his jaw and trotted over to Libriota, returning it.

"Very good," she said. "Now carry me."

Biautus stood like a man and carried Libriota in his arms. Libriota gave out a quick shriek of delight. He tossed her up in the air several times, and she shrieked ever higher in pitch.

"Oh you naughty boy!" she fawned. "Be courteous and carry me the proper way."

In one motion, Biautus slung Libriota into the air over his shoulder, he dropped to all fours, and she landed on his back. He then took off, running around the spacecraft with Libriota barely holding on by use of her hands on his collar. She screamed in delight as the two narrowly squeezed through tight passages and doorways. He leapt in the air, even at the new first assistant. The new first assistant cowered back quickly to avoid being hit. After several minutes, Biautus stopped with barely a pant. Libriota dismounted and laughed.

"Such a playful Biautus. Full of energy!" Libriota bragged. "Now then, let's see what you're made of. Walk into the scanning station please."

Biautus bipedaled over to the scanning station and stood there.

"Activate scanners," Libriota said to the new first assistant.

"Biautus contains remnant memories of Mariel, Larbiabba, and Larto. But not Lanshalla," the new assistant said.

"Interesting," Libriota said. "She is sending her friends through. They must have great faith in her abilities."

"They transported to Carinia 2," the new first assistant said.

"Very good," Libriota said.

"Make for Carinia 2?" the new first assistant asked.

"No."

"But they—"

"Will detect my approach," Libriota said. "You will go."

"Me? My service—"

"Is appreciated. Think how much more you will be appreciated on this mission," Libriota said. "You will take this ship. I will follow up in a bit. They'll see you but not me. And to ensure mission success, I will send Biautus with you."

"Your familiar? I, uh, well, uh."

"Think of him as a loan," Libriota said. "My Biautus will ensure your perfect cooperation."

Biautus stepped close to the new first assistant and growled in her ear. She winced and leaned back.

"I'm sure he will," the new first assistant agreed.

Libriota kissed Biautus on the cheek and hugged him.

"We'll be together soon," she said.

Libriota left for a transfer hatch as another ship approached. Biautus returned his gaze back to the new first assistant and growled again. Libriota reached the other ship, and the two ships undocked.

"We're going, we're going!" the new first assistant said to Biautus.

"Do you have a name?" Biautus growled as he walked behind the new first assistant, who herself was standing at the navi controls.

"Lieutenant...Lieutenant Dorrok," the new first assistant stumbled in fear.

"No, your first name," Biautus said.

"Berella," she said.

"Berella," Biautus rolled off his tongue as she shivered from the acoustic vibration effect, "I have a great interest in Carinians."

"Professional?" Berella asked.

"Culinary," he said. "You could do me a great service by giving up an arm or lower leg."

"There's food in the galley," Berella cringed.

"Yes, of course," he hissed.

Biautus went to the galley. Berella sighed in relief. A light blinked on the panel, indicating an incoming message.

"IBP Ship 47," she answered.

"This is Libriota," Libriota said. "Make sure Biautus gets the synthetic Gren meat. Don't want him getting a taste for Bleuh meat."

"I agree," Berella said in relief.

"Also, I've received word that the Imperial Bleuh Patrol has picked up a group of Gren criminals. Rendezvous with them near Carinia 3," Libriota said.

"What will I do with these Gren criminals?" Berella asked.

"Pick a pair at a time and have them compete for their own survival," Libriota said. "The loser becomes Biautus's next meal."

Berella paused in disgust.

"Remember," Libriota said. "The one who is first does satisfy the thirst, the one who is second...well, they'll never know what hit them."

The communication ended. Another message came in, but it was encoded and contained rendezvous coordinates. Biautus returned.

"The meat is stale," he complained in her ear. "I must have *freshhh* meat!"

"Your meal will be here soon," Berella said reluctantly.

"I hope so," he slobbered in her ear. "I can be nasty when I'm hungry. Bleuh meat will look very appealing. Very appealing."

The level of disgust was so great and her nerves so frazzled that Berella increased spacecraft speed and met the Imperial Bleuh ship ahead of time.

"Prisoner transfer," the guest warden said after the two ships docked.

"Put them in the detention cell," Berella said. "Biautus will show you where."

The guest warden looked in horror at Biautus.

"Don't mind Biautus. He's a guest," Berella said, hoping Biautus would at least leave the guest warden alone.

The guest warden cautiously escorted the prisoners to the detention cell. He gave his farewell to Berella and returned to his ship. The ships detached and departed. Berella punched buttons to resume course for Carinia 2, and as she did, Biautus snuck up behind her, put his paws around her waist, and slobbered in her ear with words:

"A feast of raw flesh!"

"Libriota says that you...that a pair..." Berella tried to say in her nervous condition.

"A pair," he slobbered. "Thank you."

Biautus left her side and headed for the detention cell. Berella finished hitting the control buttons, and the ship resumed course for Carinia 2. Again she cringed, and this time it was in anticipation of what Biautus was about to do.

"Why did I ever sign up for this job?" she asked herself.

To take her mind off what was about to happen, she played the recruitment video that led her to sign up in the first place. It promised to teach discipline and honor while educating the signee with the wonders of the universe.

"Wonders of the universe," she said to herself while the video cut through beautiful scenes of cosmic gas clouds, tranquil planetary places, and marching Imperial Bleuh Patrols.

"March," she said to herself. "Just march. Keep marching. Don't stop. March. March!"

She repeated the words over and over while detention-cell screams echoed down the hallway. It wasn't long before it was over. Biautus returned to Berella from behind and again put his paws around her waist. She didn't dare turn to face him, but she felt blood on her uniform where his paws touched, and his face transferred blood to her neck.

"With your permission," he slobbered, "I will clean up."

"Please do," she said with a wavering voice.

Biautus left. Berella felt herself going into a faint, but automatic detectors built into her uniform sent a spray of smelling salts to her face, bringing her back to awareness.

"Forces keep me going for the moment. For the moment," she said.

"I knew Libriota was evil, but I never knew this part," young Lanietta said. "While my mother and Larbiabba giggle about transformations, Grens are consumed by a Greylinger monster."

"I suppose if we knew about all evil in the universe, we could never be happy. Laughter would go extinct," Claus said.

"I want to laugh again, Claus. Maybe someday," young Lanietta said.

"Someday," Claus replied.

Chapter 78: Tracking Larto

IBP Ship 47 with Berella and Biautus arrived in orbit around Carinia 2.

"We have attained orbit," Berella said over space radio to Libriota. "Tracking shows both rifts opened to Larto's Vineyard. Preparing to land nearby and investigate."

"Excellent," Libriota replied. "Take Biautus with you."

"I...uh...he is doing fine here," Berella said.

"Biautus is invaluable as a track dog," said Libriota. "He can track both by physical and ethereal scent. Remember, he has remnants of Larto, Mariel, and Larbiabba. He can follow any one of them. By the way, did you feed Biautus? Wouldn't want him to get hungry on the mission."

"He...is fed," Berella said.

"You *did* play the Gren competition game as I instructed, right?" Libriota urged.

"I had an excellent pair of Grens," Biautus interrupted. "Lt. Dorrok was most generous in donating the pair."

"Competition is essential for the establishment of the natural order of hierarchy, Lt. Dorrok. Remember this!" Libriota urged.

"Yes," Berella replied.

"Continue with the mission. Advise when you make contact with the three," Libriota said, and she ended the communication.

"Navi control is computing landing coordinates from the second opening of the Greylinger rift," Berella said.

"No need. I already know the coordinates. Entering them into the navi control," Biautus slobbered in Berella's ear, with an extra cringe from Berella in reply.

"Here," Berella said, pulling away from the navi control station, far and clear of Biautus.

Biautus entered the coordinates. He hit several other buttons, and the ship went into landing mode.

"You can fly a ship?" Berella asked.

"I have many talents. With many things," he said.

"Please land the ship then," Berella said.

"With pleasure," Biautus slurped.

Biautus landed the ship very close to the cave opening from where Mariel, Treyu, and Larto had exited when they escaped Captain Indikat's control over Larto's Vineyard. Imperial Bleuh Patrols already on the ground greeted the ship by forming two parallel lines leading to the ship's entrance. The ship's door opened, and Berella appeared, holding a leash, which itself was attached to a harness on Biautus. Biautus had a mean look, and patrols who themselves were holding their own dogs had trouble containing those dogs as they fell into great fear and desire to flee.

"Lt. Dorrok reporting on Libriota's orders. Is Captain Indikat here?" Berella said.

From behind a rock outcropping walked Captain Indikat with two of his aides. On seeing Biautus, the aides hesitated and lagged, and in fact they walked backward and behind the outcropping.

"Lt. Dorrok," Indikat said. "I was expecting Libriota."

"I am here on her personal authority," Berella said.

"And your friend?" he asked.

"This is Biautus," Berella said. "He is here to help me track three fugitives."

"I assure you there are no fugitives here," Indikat said. "This area is well secured."

"Then you won't mind if I search," Berella said.

Indikat laughed as if Berella were crazy, but Biautus growled at him, and he cut his laugh short.

"By all means," Indikat said with a slight nervousness to his voice.

Berella walked with Biautus between the two lines of patrols with Indikat stepping aside. Biautus paused by Indikat, sniffed him, and growled. Indikat returned a nervous smile and disappeared behind one of the lines. Berella pulled Biautus back and resumed the walk between the lines. As he passed each patrol with a dog, that dog squirmed viciously from its master and fled. The patrols forming the line used all strength to control themselves and hold their position.

"Please, there are no fugitives," Indikat called from behind the line. "Give my regards to Libriota."

Indikat motioned with his hand, and the line closed ahead of Berella, with the only remaining path leading back to Berella's ship. Berella felt trapped, naturally, but she also felt pressured by Libriota's order.

"Lt. Dorrok," Biautus said. "I have a sudden taste for captain meat."

Berella needed to defuse the situation, and quickly. She thought of trying to explain, but time was short, and explanations are not. And so, she slipped into following advice posed by Libriota (though she did not wish to) about competition.

"Down boy," Berella said. "Captain Indikat, would you like to help look for the three fugitives? Biautus will be your companion."

Indikat waved his hand again, and the patrols reopened the path.

"Thank you," Berella said.

Berella regretted having to do that. In fact, a sickening feeling settled in her stomach that would not go away. She wanted to stop and sit, but Biautus continued sniffing out a path.

"As always, forces push me along," Berella said to herself.

"How is it he can smell fugitives when we have seen none?" Indikat asked, keeping a safe distance.

Berella and Biautus stopped, turned to face Indikat, and Biautus snarled.

"They were here. They must've been!" Indikat quickly said.

Berella and Biautus resumed their search. Biautus reached a rock face, and the two stopped.

"He went this way," he said. "His ethereal trail leads inside this rock."

"There must be a catch or release mechanism," Berella said as she ran her fingers across the rock face looking for such a mechanism.

Indikat and the group of patrols gradually crept closer to observe the progress made. Aware of this approach, Biautus turned around quickly and gave the group a stare of caution. Indikat and the group backed off quickly as if suddenly stepping on hot coals. Biautus resumed his study of the rock face.

"Larto did not pass through here physically, only ethereally," Biautus said. "The destination rift opened inside this rock."

"Inside?" Berella asked. "No wonder the patrols missed him. But what about the other two?"

"They did not travel this way. Only Larto's ethereal signature passed through this rock," Biautus said. "Mariel and Larbiabba traveled first. For a time, my Greylinger image was the remnant of them. Then Larto passed next, and that completed my image."

"Larto is the owner of his vineyard. We should go after the leader," Berella said. "At least that is what we are taught."

"I go where my hunger is filled," Biautus said. "Soon I will need to eat again. I hope there will be others around. I'd rather feast on a captain than a lieutenant."

Biautus licked his chops and drooled as he stared at Berella.

"There will be time for that later. Perhaps a game can be played where you choose between two who play fetch with you. You could catch the stick and person before it is thrown," Berella said, again trading sense of decency for her own life.

"An interesting game. I look forward to it," Biautus said.

The sickening feeling Berella had before only deepened. She cursed having to use this new skill to preserve her own life. Was the universe meant for such tactics? Was that how she was to spend the rest of her tour of duty? Where was the promise as was made in the recruitment video? Where was it now? As Berella wondered, she allowed the leash to lengthen, and Biautus explored farther.

"There are two catches. You must pull on this small crevice. Here," Biautus said, pointing. "I will pull on a similar crevice over here."

Biautus pulled. He signaled with his eyes for her to pull on the crevice. Berella paused, and his gaze hardened. She pulled. A secret door opened, revealing a tunnel.

"A tunnel!" Indikat exclaimed.

"A pity you could not find it," Biautus said. "My hunger grows for a captain or lieutenant."

Berella realized that Biautus had picked up on the technique of playing others against each other. She had to counter this technique, and quickly.

"Instead, have Indikat and one of his lieutenants lead. The first to lag behind shall be your prize," Berella offered.

"An excellent choice. I approve," Biautus said.

Indikat and his men looked on in shock. They backed up and prepared to flee.

"Run so that I may pursue you!" Biautus snarled.

Indikat picked his slowest lieutenant and escorted him into the cave. Biautus snarled once at them, and they ran farther into the cave. Biautus looked back at Berella for approval, and she reluctantly released his leash. He ran after the two with Berella walking swiftly behind. Once Berella was far enough into the cave, the remaining patrols closed the secret door and fled the area.

"He is just up there," yelled the lieutenant's voice.

Berella caught up to Biautus, and he had the lieutenant by the leg.

"Just up there. Larto. Go up there," the lieutenant begged.

"You are lying," Biautus said. "You would say anything to avoid my maw."

"I'm sure you have a wonderful mother," the lieutenant said, misunderstanding Biautus.

Berella giggled.

"I have no mother!" Biautus snapped.

"An orphan. I was an orphan too. We have something in common. Let's play fetch. Down boy," the lieutenant begged.

"Larto went this way!" Indikat's voice echoed from ahead.

"No wait!" Berella called.

Too late. Biautus leapt ahead toward the voice in hopes of catching Larto.

"Heh, heh, heh," the lieutenant chuckled. "We can keep this up for hours. Wear that beast down."

The lieutenant limped off into a half run. Berella went after Biautus. He had caught up to Indikat with Indikat pinned in a corner.

"No Larto here!" Biautus snarled.

"We just missed him," Indikat said. "We must go after him quickly before he gets away."

"Over here!" echoed the lieutenant's voice through the caves.

"Now I have him for sure!" Biautus snarled, and he ran after the voice.

"You think you're smart," Berella said to Indikat now that Biautus was gone. "Libriota will be here soon, and she'll have us all put away."

"Then let her!" Indikat said. "Better to be put away than eaten away."

Indikat ran off. Now Berella was alone. She considered calling for Biautus again.

"But why should I?" she asked herself. "He is busy and not threatening me. I can look for Larto on my own."

Berella pulled out a pair of detection glasses for viewing infrared and ethereal after-images. She looked on the floor and saw fresh footprint residue from Indikat, herself, and Biautus. The part of the cave she was in was a bit open, and so she took a spiral-out path from her starting point. At an edge toward Larto's Vineyard was a faint set of ethereal tracks but no infrared.

"So Larto went this way," Berella said to herself. "But not recently."

Berella heard distant shouts as Indikat and his lieutenant continued to divert Biautus back and forth. She knew that this would only last for a short time, so she made haste toward Larto's ethereal tracks. The tracks grew stronger, and she reached a point where infrared tracks overlaid the ethereal ones.

"I might catch him yet," she said to herself.

The infrared tracks grew stronger, and now they showed up more easily than the ethereal ones. Berella picked up her pace into a near run, and just as she figured she was approaching another cave door, her glasses blasted blindingly white light into her eyes, her nervous system reacted with a jolt, she lost her footing, and she tumbled to the ground. She hit her head on a rock, knocking her into a deep daze.

When Berella regained her senses, she was lying in a bed with a blanket over her in someone's house. Instinctively, she reached for a weapon from her belt, but she had no belt. In fact, she had no uniform. Instead, she wore a simple tunic. She leapt out of bed, grabbed a nearby figurine, and crept behind the door, ready to bludgeon whoever came along. She then heard voices.

"Is she aware yet?" called Larto's voice.

"Let me check," replied Mariel's voice.

Mariel entered the doorway and passed through. Berella lifted her arm in preparation for crashing the figurine on Mariel's head when Larto called again.

"She might need more rejuvenation drink. She's very weak no doubt," Larto called.

Mariel turned around to reply, but before she could say a thing, the figurine and Berella's hand came toward her. She moved to the side just enough such that the figurine missed her head, but it caught her

shoulder and caused pain. A struggle ensued.

"No doubt...very...weak," Mariel struggled to say back.

"Mariel? You sound strange," Larto called. "Don't disturb our guest. She must be dead tired."

"She's not dead," Mariel said as she swung at Berella, "she's not weak," again with another swing, "and she's not tired!"

Berella punched Mariel in the jaw. Mariel fell to the floor, in a cold daze. The loud *thump* caught Larto's attention, and he came running. Too quickly. Berella swung to catch him in the jaw too, and he ducked only just in time. But to do so, he had to shift his inertia in an awkward way, causing him to lose his balance and crash into a bedstand. Berella came at him with a kick to the face, but he caught her foot and pulled it to one side, causing her to lose her balance and fall on the floor. It was a scramble to see who could regain footing first, and both arighted themselves just about the same time. Larto lunged at Berella to contain her, but she stepped aside and pulled him past her. He stopped himself against the wall, but Berella used the split second to grab two broken legs from the bedstand. She threw one to put him off stride and swung at him with the other. The swing caught him in the mouth, broke a tooth, and cut his cheek. Blood now poured over his face. Another swing from Berella caught the blood and slid off his face. Not expecting the miss, her balance went slightly off. Larto used his leg to catch hers and trip her. She fell, face down. He then pinned her to the floor with a knee in her back.

"Ugh! You're hurting me!" she groaned. "I should call Biautus on you!"

"Yell all you want," Larto said. "No one can hear you!"

At that moment, Mariel came out of her daze. She was groggy, but she fought to regain awareness and footing.

"I need rope, Mariel," Larto said.

"Be right back," she said, and she disappeared from the room.

"You're a feisty one," Larto said as Berella struggled to get away. "Been a Bleuh Patrol long?"

"If you're lucky, you'll only be put away for life. Assaulting a Bleuh officer carries the death penalty," Berella said. "Where is my uniform? Where is my weapon?"

Mariel returned with a rope and helped hold Berella down while Larto hog-tied Berella.

"Your uniform was covered in blood," Larto said. "I took the liberty of having it cleaned. Mariel here was gracious enough to clean you up and put you in dry clothes. You took quite a hit from that rock."

"You're going to take a hit if you don't let me go," Berella said.

"Ah-ah-ah," Larto said. "That's no way to repay us for our hospitality. What about a simple thank-you?"

"I would spit at you if I could," Berella said. "Turn me around so I can."

"I have a better idea," Larto said.

Larto had finished hog-tying Berella. He picked her up by the main knot (where her four limbs met) and dropped her on the bed, face down.

"Ugh!" she said.

The rope had extra length, and Larto had purposely tied Berella with just one end of the rope. He threaded the other through a pulley that was attached to the ceiling, and he pulled. The rope lifted Berella into the air, and Larto pulled just enough so she'd clear the bed. He then fastened the rope's end to a hook on the wall.

"I insist you let me down at once!" Berella said.

Instead, Larto pushed her body gently so she'd swing back and forth.

"I'm going to scream!" she announced.

Berella screamed. And screamed. Mariel opened a dresser drawer, retrieved a fresh legging garment, and stuffed it in Berella's mouth.

"Scream in that," Mariel said.

Mariel sat down in a nearby chair, exhausted. Larto leaned next to a vanity for support. Berella tried to scream through the legging, but her voice was muffled.

"So that's the gratitude I get," Mariel said.

"I appreciate your work," Larto said.

"And she's ruined my makeover," Mariel said. "I'll need to get another one."

"Careful what you say," Larto said. "This is a Bleuh patrol. No telling what she'll report."

Mariel laughed.

"They don't report swinging back and forth like that," Mariel chuckled.

"No, I don't suppose they do," Larto said with a chuckle himself.

"I always wondered why you left the pulley there after we converted this room to guest quarters. I always thought you never got around to removing it," Mariel said.

"I never did," he replied with a grin. "Sometimes it's best not to be too tidy."

Larto touched his cheek, and it was now swelling.

"Sit tight," Mariel said. "I'll get ice packs for us."

Mariel exited the room. Berella got tired and stopped screaming.

"So are you done making a fool of yourself?" Larto said.

Berella tried to say something, but it was muffled.

"Yeah, it's tough speaking when you've been ill-behaved. Can I trust you to behave now? I'd like to have a civilized conversation with you if possible," Larto said.

Mariel returned with two ice packs and two chilled bottles of beverage.

"The ice packs are for our injuries, the wine is for our health," Mariel said.

Mariel and Larto each cooled their injuries with the ice packs and sipped the wine. The wine was fresh and clear, lightly fruity, and very soothing to one who has been stressed out.

"Ah, that's much better," Larto said. "Comes in handy running a vineyard."

"I have blessed this vineyard many times," Mariel said.

"You've been snitching from the wine cellar, Mariel?" Larto laughed.

"Just taste testing," Mariel laughed back.

"Always a good idea," Larto said. "Now then. Let's see if our *guest* is willing to be civil."

Larto removed the legging from Berella's mouth. She inhaled deeply as if to scream.

"If you scream, I'll stuff this back in your mouth!" he warned.

Berella sighed.

"There, that's better," Larto said.

"Would you please release me from this bondage?" Berella asked.

"In a moment," Larto said. "First some questions. What is your name?"

"I am Lt. Berella Dorrok," Berella said. "And I already know who you two are."

"You do?" Larto asked.

"Yes. You're Larto, and this is Mariel," Berella said. "And here's something you might not know about each other. Mariel has been stealing wine from you and selling it on the side without your knowledge."

Mariel did not like the sound of that. She stood up, walked over to Berella, and poured her wine on the back of Berella's head.

"Lies," Mariel said while pouring.

"That will do, Mariel," Larto said.

Berella struggled to speak while the fluid poured around the bottom side of her face, interfering with air flow. Once the fluid cleared away, she resumed clear speech.

"You don't catch her, Larto, because you're too busy with your mistresses," Berella said.

"Mistresses?" Mariel asked in confusion.

"Yes, Mariel. He's cheating on you."

Mariel and Larto looked at each other and burst into laughter.

"She thinks we're married!" Mariel laughed.

"All right, lieutenant, you can stop playing your games," Larto said. "We know you're trying to set us against each other. Look, if you want our help, you're going to have to cooperate. Let's start from the beginning, shall we?"

"Lt. Berella Dorrok, serial number Bleuh-one-four-eight-kappa-nine-seven," Berella said.

"We found you in a full daze in a cave by this vineyard," Larto said. "What were you doing there? Are there others?"

Berella kept silent.

"Leave her tied up," Mariel said. "I'll dust her every now and then."

"Lt. Dorrok. Berella. I need to know if others are hurt and need assistance," Larto said.

"We don't need your assistance," Berella said.

"So there *are* more than one of you," Larto said. "Mariel, take care of Berella. I'm going back into the cave to look for other casualties. I don't know why people are getting hurt in there, but we've got to understand. Could hurt more people."

Berella was about to say something but stopped herself. She started again then stopped.

"What?" Mariel asked. "Are you afraid he will uncover a secret operation?"

"Please, let me down," Berella said. "I must warn you about the cave. It's dangerous. But this rope is hurting me. Please!"

"It's a trick. Don't do it," Mariel said.

"I'm going to take a chance on you, Berella. If there is to be longstanding peace between our people, we have to cooperate," Larto said.

"Big mistake!" Mariel said.

Larto lowered her onto the bed, untied her legs, but he kept her wrists tied.

"My wrists hurt too!" she said.

"First, what is this danger?" Larto asked.

Berella paused.

"I was hit by an energy pulse," she said. "It was ethereal. I was tracking, uh, was using special goggles to see where I was going. A great flash. Like lightning. Blinded me. Put me in a daze. Never seen anything like it."

"That's the danger?" Larto asked. "I've been in that cave hundreds of times. Never seen it."

"It came through the goggles," Berella said. "I had them...where is my equipment?"

"In a safe place," Larto said. "Are there others in the cave?"

"Don't go back in," she said.

"Why? Is there something else? More patrols?" Larto asked.

"There are...many things," she said.

At that moment, new Larbiabba stepped in.

"I've studied her equipment. Standard Bleuh patrol issue. Oh, she's aware," Larbiabba said.

"Your voice is familiar," Berella said.

"So is yours," Larbiabba said. "Wait, you're Berella Dorrok."

"Who are you?" Berella asked.

Larbiabba nodded "no" to Mariel and Larto.

"No name?" Berella asked. "Now who's hiding something?"

"It seems we do not trust each other easily," Larto said.

Berella started going eethi to learn more about her captors, possibly even to help herself escape. Larbiabba pulled out an eethi-blaster and zapped Berella with it, but not before Berella was able to detect what type of Carinians she had encountered.

"Two Grens and a wanna-be Bleuh!" Berella said.

"Don't try that again," Larbiabba said.

"Should I call you Mystery Bleuh?" Berella said.

"That will do for now," Larbiabba said. "Larto, there's a great deal of ethereal disturbance in the cave. Something of incredible speed is racing around inside."

"Libriota?" Larto asked.

"You know about her?" Berella asked.

"Who doesn't," Larbiabba said. "Larto, I don't think it's wise to announce everything in front of this..."

"This Bleuh patrol, said the Bleuh traitor," Berella said.

"I told you we should have left her tied up. I'm good at dusting," Mariel said.

"We'll take her with us," Larto said.

"What?!" Larbiabba barked.

"Sir, no!" Mariel pleaded.

"You know what I think?" Berella asked.

"We don't want to know," Larbiabba said.

"Is everything packed?" Larto asked Mariel.

"Everything," Mariel replied.

"I must secure the cave," Larto said. "That's where Berella comes in. She will guide me. You two go out the way you came."

"Um, I'd rather not," Larbiabba said.

"Yeah," Mariel said. "Flirting once with those disgusting patrols was bad enough."

"We made empty promises that we'd be forced to keep if we went back out," Larbiabba said.

"Why don't you space-jump?" Berella taunted. "Use the Greylinger rift like you did before, only from inside this house. See how far you get!"

"She knows," Larbiabba said.

"Which means Libriota knows too," Mariel said.

"Disaster," Larto said.

"It might not be so bad," Larbiabba said. "Berella here most likely has a spaceship parked outside the cave. We could leave in that. No Greylinger rift to trace."

"Very well," Larto said. "But Berella will still lead the way."

Berella, knowing Biautus remained in the cave, was desperate not to go in.

"Oh Larto, spare me!" Berella cried, and she embraced Larto, kissed him, and became as affectionate as possible.

"Get off him!" Larbiabba said as she and Mariel yanked Berella away.

"First she tried setting Larto and me apart, now she's trying to woo him," Mariel said.

"Berella, try to control yourself!" Larto said.

"I can't go back in there!" she said. "There's a wild Greylinger animal roaming around, unrestrained! That's what's moving so fast! It will eat anything! I escaped only because it chased two other patrols!"

"You were there to track us down," Larbiabba said. "You deserve no better."

"The other patrols were already here!" Berella cried. "It was just Biautus and me. Libriota sent us to track Larto, Mariel, and Larbiabba."

Larbiabba blushed.

"You're Larbiabba?" Berella asked. "You don't look like her."

"It's a long story," Larbiabba said.

"Biautus is the name of the beast?" Larto asked.

"Yes," Berella cried. "Libriota created it from Greylinger remnants that you three left when you transported here."

"That would explain the confused ethereal readings I've been getting," Larbiabba said. "This Biautus is negative ethereal energy. Which means it feeds on fear and hate."

"And Carinian flesh," Berella said. "It was only supposed to eat Gren meat. But I'm sure it's devoured the Bleuh patrols by now! It wanted to kill me. Do you hear? Kill me!"

"How can we defeat this thing?" Larto asked.

"Let me ask," Larbiabba said.

Larbiabba stepped out of the room for a moment.

"Who is she asking?"

Mariel nodded "no".

"Lanshalla," Larto said.

"*That* one," Berella said.

"Yes, *that* one," Larto said.

"I got the briefing about her," Berella said. "She caused that Greylinger rift to open on Carinia 5. What she did was wrong! She'll upset the entire balance of the solar system."

"I hope so!" Mariel exclaimed. "You're certainly no help."

"What? I..." Berella stumbled.

"Are just a blind Bleuh patrol, following orders," Mariel said. "Don't care about anything, do you?"

"I do care! To protect and serve the grace and beauty of Bleuh civilization."

"Do you even know what that word means, civilization?" Mariel asked.

"It means the art and culture we have built on Carinia 1. Libraries, museums, architecture, places of learning, sporting events, the grandeur of it all. Why risk civility with delvings in the darkness?" Berella asked.

"There's no civility in those things! They were built with the pain and misery of Grens!" Mariel said. "When you look at a stone building, you only see what you want to see, its simple design and construction. But mixed in with the mortar and brick is pain and misery. Pain and misery!"

"No, it's all clean!" Berella said. "It has to be. We'd be terrible beings otherwise. Mariel, if you could but see the beauty of my home city, you'd understand. From when I was a little girl, I—"

"Was brainwashed to believe that beauty is only surface deep," Mariel finished. "Who can admire stonework made from slavery?"

"There are no slaves in my city!" Berella said.

"Because they are kept in other places, out of the way, so that none of you precious Bleuhs would be *disturbed* by our ugliness. It's true. You see us laborers as ugly!" Mariel said.

"You Grens would trash our cities with your crass ways and strewn filth!" Berella said.

"The same Grens who built your clean and elegant cities?" Mariel countered.

"Enough already," Larto said. "You might have your chance to show us one of your cities. We're heading to Carinia 1 as it is."

"Grens like you going to Carinia 1? Absurd!" Berella said.

Larbiabba returned.

"Lanshalla agrees that we should keep Berella as a prisoner, at least for now,"

Larbiabba said. "She also senses danger in the cave. She could open a rift in this house, but she can only take two at a time. However, opening up a rift in the house will draw a lot of attention. The patrols outside will register it immediately and rush in after the other two before she can pull them up. If we go in the cave, she can take all four at once. There are ethereal strata in the cave that she can use to lock onto all of us, provided we stand in the right place. The cave also dampens the ethereal energy signature, so by the time the patrols figure out something has happened, we'll be gone."

"Can you tame this Biautus?" Larto asked.

Berella sighed.

"I don't know anymore," Berella said. "I can try. If only I had something to feed him. Gren meat?"

Mariel, Larto, and Larbiabba gave facial expressions of disgust.

"No Gren meat!" Larto said. "But I have another idea. Mariel and Larbiabba, you two await transport here in the house. Take all gear with you. Berella and I will go into the cave. A few moments after we are in the cave, signal Lanshalla that she should take you two first, then Berella and me second."

"Sir, you can't mean that!" Mariel said.

"I'm afraid I must agree with Mariel," Larbiabba said. "You can't defeat the beast. According to Lanshalla, the only way to defeat it is to use the baby option with full eethi-abort. Lanshalla has already volunteered to come down and perform that duty."

"What?" young Lanietta said to Claus. "She was going to kill me. Did you hear Larbiabba's words? Did you?"

Young Lanietta moved to hug Claus, but again she just passed through. She faced away from Claus, dejected.

"She didn't realize what it meant," Claus said. "If only she could see you now. She would be proud, Lanietta. As am I."

Young Lanietta turned back toward Claus and regained her composure.

"You really mean it?" she asked.

"Yes, I do," Claus said. "I don't know how or why, but I feel like you're family."

"Did your mother ever...I mean...did she ever think of killing you before you were born?" young Lanietta asked.

"I don't know," Claus said. "I don't think any child ever considers the thought. It's unimaginable and devoid of love."

"My mother doesn't love me then," young Lanietta said.

"You mustn't—"

"My mother doesn't love me!" young Lanietta reiterated. "I am but a tool, an implement. Why am I in the universe at all? I should be but an ethereal spirit floating aimlessly, never to have taken corporeal form. I lost my form after Earth was created. I feigned a form with you for your benefit. Remember when we met? When you first learned of me? When you despised me?"

"You frustrated me, yes. I did not despise you," Claus said.

"Negative," Larto said. "Not with my child. Besides, she must remain in orbit to handle the rift."

"You see?" Claus said. "Your father has already become protective of you. It might take a little time for Lanshalla. She might not express herself in ways that make sense. Give her a chance."

"We could escape in Berella's spacecraft," Mariel said.

"If need be, I'll use the spacecraft as Plan B," Larto said.

"Larto," Larbiabba said in a soft tone. "You and Lanshalla are the real couple here. I am but a helper. I could—"

"Oh, oh!" Claus said. "Now Larbiabba would kill Labba."

"You must never tell her this," young Lanietta said. "She must never know her mother intended to deprive her of existence. I can barely contain the dread for myself. Labba was always the cheerful one."

"I will not tell her," Claus said. "Protecting you two is paramount. If there is to be a Carinian future, you two must—"

"You know that's impossible," young Lanietta said.

"There's all the time in the universe—" Claus said.

"Not for you," young Lanietta said.

"Perhaps not. But you two are still immortal," Claus said. "And I have hope humans will be around to help you both."

"Negative," Larto said. "You were against the baby option in the beginning."

"I could make an exception," Larbiabba said.

"Kill an unborn child and risk your own life?" Larto asked rhetorically. "No, Larbiabba, the lives of you and your unborn are important. I will not have them thrown away so easily."

"If only Larto knew that his protective behavior is saving humanity of Earth," young Lanietta said.

"From insignificant things of the day follow results of great magnitude," Claus said. "Larto knew the importance of life. So must you cherish your own now."

"But you'll throw your own life away," Mariel said. "That's not right either."

"Release me, and I'll go into the cave. I'll distract Biautus," Berella said.

"If you aren't knocked into a daze again, you'll flee," Larbiabba said. "I know you, Berella. You're a Bleuh patriot to the end."

"I don't know anymore," Berella said. "That ethereal light did something strange to me. What was it anyway? Another secret?"

"It is related to this vineyard," Larbiabba said. "There was a great ocean here at one time, filled with creatures of intelligence. They died suddenly, causing their ethereal images to become trapped in the cave rocks. Like fossils. That's what you hit. Don't wear goggles, and you'll be fine. I still don't trust you, though. You know, Larto, I could rig up special goggles that she would then wear that are tied in with your nervous system. If she misbehaves, you can allow the excess ethereal energy to flood in. Like an electric leash."

"I'm not a dog!" Berella said.

"You are now," Larto said. "Hook up the device, Larbiabba. It's the best we can do."

"No!" Berella said.

Berella stood behind Larto and pinned his arms behind. Larbiabba tried to get a clear shot with the eethi-blaster but could not. Mariel went for a figurine herself and tried hitting Berella with it, but Berella repositioned herself and Larto, causing the stroke to hit Larto on the head. Larto himself struggled to get free and nearly did so, but Berella went eethi and interrupted his nervous system, causing him to go limp. Larto's weight-shift downward, however, caught Berella off guard. She was in an awkward stance with her weight slightly backward toward the bed, and so his weight caused her to fall backward onto the bed with him atop her. Larbiabba shot anyway, and from the side. To evade the eethi-blast, Berella pushed her entire ethereal image into Larto's body, and so she was able to continue movement with her physical body. She now had control of Larto's body, and she commanded it to aright itself and go after Larbiabba, which it did.

"She's in Larto's body," Larbiabba said as Larto knocked the eethi-blaster from Larbiabba's hand.

Berella forced Larto to continue a tussle with Larbiabba. Berella sent her physical body toward the exit, but Mariel caught her and gave her a struggle.

"Get the eethi-blaster!" Larbiabba said. "Shoot Larto!"

The eethi-blaster remained on the floor. Berella made for it, but Mariel blocked her and shoved her back. Mariel herself tried to get it, but Berella gave her too much of a fight.

"I can't get it," Mariel said. "I need help!"

Larbiabba went eethi and entered Berella's physical body, which had been made vulnerable when Berella put her full ethereal image into Larto. Larbiabba's ethereal self then commanded Berella's body to attack Larto. That freed up Mariel, who now picked up the eethi-blaster. She tried aiming for Larto, but with tight proximity of Larbiabba, Larto, and Berella plus their quick movements, it was impossible to get a clear shot. Finally, Mariel aimed, closed her eyes, and fired. The eethi-blast hit all three, and all three fell to the ground. Larbiabba and Berella's ethereal selves returned to their respective bodies and remained stunned for a few moments. Larto regained his composure first and stood up, but he was dizzy and fell to his knees.

"Tie up Berella," he said to Mariel.

"Gladly," Mariel said.

Mariel passed him the eethi-blaster and tied up Berella. Larbiabba and Berella came to.

"You still don't learn, do you?" Larbiabba said.

"You can go eethi like a Bleuh," Berella said. "I didn't believe it possible. Not to that extent."

"Do you now?" Larbiabba asked.

"I do. Must be exhausting trying to be like one of us," Berella said.

"I'll ignore that and say just this—don't try to escape again," Larbiabba said.

"It is better to fight one's way out to freedom," Berella said.

"Some freedom," Mariel said. "With rope knots as companions."

"You asked for my help. I was going to give it," Larto said. "Then you turned around and tried this, this backstabbing?"

"It's the Bleuh way, isn't it Berella?" Larbiabba asked. "No sense of cooperation or self-sacrifice."

"It has made us strong. And free," Berella said.

"There's that 'free' word again," Mariel said. "Saying so won't make it true."

"Let's get those goggles on," Larto said. "The sooner the better."

"Give me a moment," Larbiabba said. "And shoot her every now and then."

"With pleasure!" Mariel said, and she shot Berella.

Berella groaned. Larbiabba exchanged smiles with Mariel before exiting the room.

Mariel made to shoot Berella again, but Larto stopped her.

"Give me that," Larto said as he took the eethi-blaster from Mariel.

"But Larbiabba said to—"

"I know," Larto said. "We must be hospitable too. No torturing in this house. Why don't you freshen up, Mariel? I'll stand watch here."

Mariel nodded in agreement and left the room.

"Are you going to shoot me like Mariel? Seems a woman enjoys shooting another, especially if she fears competition," Berella said.

"You are not competition," Larto said. "And Mariel is not a mistress or wife. She is my maid."

"Could have fooled me," Berella said. "Ow, my head aches."

"She keeps this house clean," Larto said.

"With the mistress pit you're running, she must keep very busy. How many other Bleuhs have you melded with? Are they pregnant too? A Gren king in his kingdom, with nothing but Bleuh women for play things. I suppose it's only fitting. We *are* of a higher class than Grens. Mariel could never satisfy you," Berella said. "So how many Bleuh women are there? Six? Sixty?"

"There is only one," Larto said. "And I don't run a mistress pit. What happened with her was very unusual. I don't plan on it happening again."

"Too late," Berella said.

"What does *that* mean?" Larto asked.

"I'm pregnant too. Just now," Berella said. "You Grens aren't supposed to be like that. What is it with you, Larto? Do you have Bleuh in you? Is it this place?"

"You're pregnant!" Larto said. "That changes everything!"

"Why should it?" Berella asked. "You Grens hate us anyway!"

Larbiabba returned with the goggles. She fitted them to Berella, but Larbiabba seemed confused.

"What is it?" Larto asked.

"Something's changed with Berella," Larbiabba said. "Her ethereal signature doesn't match readings I took earlier. It's as if...no, it can't be."

"It is," Berella said. "I'm pregnant. With Larto's child."

"What do you want to do?" Larbiabba asked. "I can calibrate for just Berella's eethi, her baby's eethi, or both."

"Just Berella," Larto said.

"Very well," Larbiabba said.

Mariel walked in.

"There," Larbiabba said. "Berella's baby is unaffected."

"Baby?!" Mariel exclaimed.

"I'm carrying Larto's child!" Berella bragged. "Something *you'll* never do!"

Mariel went to slap Berella across the face, but Larto caught her arm in midmotion.

"This is getting out of hand," Mariel said. "How could you, Larto?"

"I seem to have no choice in these matters," Larto said. "But we must make haste and go through with the plan. Give Berella and me a head start, and then have Lanshalla return you to the ship. Have her bring Berella and me up next."

Larbiabba and Mariel smirked at each other.

"*Both* of us," Larto said.

"Didn't know you could read minds, Larto," Larbiabba said.

"Your faces gave you both away, despite the makeovers," Larto said.

"We must get new makeovers then, to protect our thoughts," Mariel said.

"I'm with you there," Larbiabba said. "A cutting from the Lonely Vine is packed, along with other supplies. We are ready."

"Excellent," Larto said.

"One more thing," Larbiabba said. "Keep the eethi-blaster close at hand. There's a setting for wide inverse-phase ethereal disruption. It might give you an extra moment or two against the beast."

"Good idea," Larto said. "Berella, if you please? This way."

The pair exited the house and went into the backyard. Larto paused by the Lonely Vine.

"There it is," Larto said. "What's left of ancient oceanic life is represented in this vine. My entire vineyard is based upon it. Grens drink the wine and feel renewed. Bleuhs have too, I suppose. But it wasn't until Lanshalla drank in the vicinity of the Lonely Vine did she experience something unique, an understanding of past life one might not normally acquire."

"How can a vine teach history? It is not sentient," Berella said.

"It imparts sentience," Larto said.

"More like a sentence," Berella said. "The vine imprisons you. Like the cave. And this baby."

"Don't speak like that," Larto said. "Name your child. Give it importance. Do you know the gender?"

"It's a boy," Berella said.

"We could call him—"

"You aren't naming the baby. He is Bralkar, if a name he must have. There, I've named him. Let's go to the cave and get this over with."

Berella and Larto left the Lonely Vine and headed for the cave. Just before the two passed through rock outcroppings, Larto turned around and took one last look at his house before it left his view. Mariel and Larbiabba waved to him through the window, and he waved back. When Larto turned back, Berella was gone. He initiated an eethi shock. A crackle disturbed the air, and Larto followed this sound around a rock pillar to find Berella on her knees trying to dig a place to hide in the dirt behind a rock.

"Still trying to get away? What would the baby think?" Larto asked. "You know. Bralkar."

"Who says I have to keep it?" Berella asked.

"I have a sibling," young Lanietta said. "But Berella gives me a sense of foreboding. Why have I not met such a Carinian close to my line? Unless Berella's child becomes like Lalla. I could have had a real family. A family amongst families amongst Carinian people. Instead, Labba is all that remains."

"There is at least that," Claus said.

"That's a horrible thing to say," Larto said. "Lanshalla went through that. It's disturbing. And she...she..."

"She what?" Berella asked.

"I'll let her tell you herself if she wishes," Larto said. "Get up. The entrance is but a short ways away."

Larto pulled Berella to her feet. The two reached the secret cave door, Larto opened it, the two went inside, and Larto closed the door.

"Can you tell if Biautus is close by?" Larto asked.

"Yes, but he is not," Berella said.

"What do you see through the—ugh, never mind," Larto said.

The two had only taken a few steps when Larto saw remnants of a body with an Imperial Bleuh uniform. The name tag revealed the victim.

"This was Captain Indikat," Berella said. "Then the beast got him. Ow!"

An ethereal fossil energy-burst shot through Berella's goggles, she was stunned, and she fell. Larto caught her and held her. Her body shook uncontrollably, but he dragged her along until she stopped shaking.

"Can you stand?" he asked.

"I think so," she replied. "I wasn't expecting that. It seems there are safe lines and unsafe lines to travel. If I move slowly...yes, over to my left is the beginning of an unsafe line. If I hold my hand out, I can feel the energy like ants crawling on my skin. We must move slowly."

"At least Larbiabba's modification kept you aware," Larto said.

"That's almost worse, because now I can feel the pain in full force," Berella said.

"We only need go a little farther," Larto said. "Lanshalla will pull us through the rift any moment now."

The two walked a little more, and another ethereal burst hit Berella. She let out a yelp and fell to her knees, as Larto was looking in a different direction and missed catching her. Surprised, Larto spun around and helped her up.

"They're moving. The ethereal lines. They're shifting position, like ripples in a pond," Berella said. "Something is disturbing them. Something is moving this way."

In the distance, a woman's voice echoed, telling a companion how good he was and how he would be rewarded soon.

"I know that voice," Berella said.

"Wait here," Larto said. "We'll space-jump very soon."

"She'll court martial me. Even feed me to Biautus. I must get out of here!" Berella said.

Berella made a move to flee, but Larto shocked her goggles to keep her immobile.

"Don't put me through this!" she pleaded.

Up the cave a short ways, an ethereal rift opened. Berella and Larto made for it, but when they reached it, the rift wavered, stuttered, and collapsed before the two could enter. Another rift opened behind them. The two made for that one, but again it wavered, stuttered, and collapsed.

"Something is wrong," Larto said. "Lanshalla can't keep the rift open."

"Because Lanshalla is not an expert in Greylinger ethronomy," said the familiar voice.

Berella and Larto turned around to see Libriota being escorted by a much fatter Biautus.

"Libriota," Larto said. "We meet again."

"I see you're corrupting my patrols," Libriota said. "Dorrok, you're out of uniform."

"I have tracked Larto," Berella said, trying to cover. "Here he is."

"Have tracked and are preparing to escape with him," Libriota said. "Perhaps after a romantic encounter? Bleuh uniforms are not attractive enough, is that it? Did you borrow the tunic from him?"

"I found her dazed and bleeding in these very caves," Larto said. "I had her tended to until she recovered."

"A rescuer of weak Bleuh women!" Libriota mocked.

Another rift opened to the side. Larto made for the rift while Berella held her position, as she was afraid of Libriota. Libriota extended her hand to the rift, sent out an inward-spiraling ethereal wave, and the wave caused the rift to stutter and collapse.

"Lanshalla is quite rude interrupting our pleasant conversation, is she not?" Libriota asked.

Berella and Larto held silent, trying to decide what to do next.

"I asked a question!" Libriota demanded.

"This is not what I expected!" Berella blurted.

"No?"

"No!" Berella said. "The recruitment video promised excitement and adventure. Not torture!"

Libriota laughed.

"My dear, that's what excitement and adventure are. To torture the Grens," Libriota said.

Libriota gave a command. Biautus leapt at Larto, knocked him to the ground, snarled at him, and prepared to bite off his head.

"No, just a nibble on the leg," Libriota said.

Biautus placed his jaw over Larto's thigh like pruning shears over a tree branch. He closed his jaw and sank his teeth into muscle and bone. Larto cried out in pain.

"Don't break it," Libriota said. "Must be merciful. That's part of adventure and excitement too. Look how he writhes in pain, Berella. Doesn't it lift your heart? Are you not called into action, for the greater good of Bleuh society?"

"Torture me," Berella said. "Let this one go."

"You will get your due in due time," Libriota said. "But for now, we savor the moment. Biautus, switch to the other leg."

Biautus opened his jaw, but Larto's leg got stuck in Biautus's upper teeth. He shook his head side to side in an effort to shake off the caught flesh.

"Stop!" Berella said.

"Why don't you help him?" Libriota suggested.

Berella went over to Larto, put her hand on his face, and whispered words of encouragement.

"Not the Gren. Help Biautus free his teeth of debris," Libriota said.

Berella stared back with hatred.

"Yes, indeed!" Libriota said. "You feel the motivation to act. All part of the excitement and adventure. Go head. Clean his teeth."

Berella held her position. Libriota sent her ethereal hand into Larto's nervous system and used it to shock Berella through the goggles. Berella jumped with a start, and Libriota laughed.

"I must copy that technology," Libriota continued to laugh. "Larbiabba's work? A shame she is not here now to enjoy the fruits of her labor."

Berella stood up and pulled Larto's leg off of Biautus's teeth as gently as she could, though it didn't matter much—he cried in pain with each movement.

"It may sting at first, but you'll get used to it and learn to enjoy it," Libriota said.

"There's nothing enjoyable about pain!" Larto said.

"It is if you're watching another endure it. Besides, I was speaking to Berella. She *is* a Bleuh, you know. What can a Gren know of such things?"

"Lanshalla understands. You were once friends with her. How is it she understands and you do not?" Larto managed to say with heavy breathing and winces of pain.

"It is she who has deviated. You corrupted her with your crude Gren ways. She will be rehabilitated," Libriota said.

Berella finished pulling Larto's leg off Biautus's teeth.

"Good. Now the other leg, Biautus," Libriota said.

"This is unbearable to watch," young Lanietta said. "I always hated Libriota, but never did I know such torture by her hand. And she caused Lalla's death in a way. What else can she do?"

"Those like Libriota leave a toxic wake wherever they go," Claus said.

"I wonder if she left such a wake when the PRAAD destroyed her and all other Carinians," young Lanietta said.

"Perhaps this vision is that wake," Claus said.

Berella stood in the way and blocked Biautus.

"What are you doing?" Libriota said. "This is part of your training. Step aside and let it finish."

"No," Berella said. "You've gone too far."

"Careful, my dear. You don't know who or what you're dealing with," Libriota said. "I carry the full weight of the Hierarchy behind me. Do you wish to challenge such an authority? Step aside."

"No," Berella said defiantly.

"Very well. You wish to be swatted aside. Easy enough. Your punishment will be meted out in time," Libriota said.

Libriota went for Larto's nervous system to shock Berella. But at that moment, another rift opened. Forced to change her focus, Libriota instead went for the rift to close it. Berella went eethi and went after Libriota. Libriota swatted her back. Then Biautus went after Berella to subdue her. Libriota refocused on the rift, but Lanshalla tried coming through and in fact was partway through. Lanshalla sent ethereal energy back at Libriota, and that sent Libriota reeling. But Libriota was determined. She renewed her energy, attacked Lanshalla, and sent her back into the rift. Libriota fought to seal the rift, but Lanshalla fought back from the other side to keep it open. The rift shrank and expanded as different sides gained or lost control.

"Kill her, Mommy," young Lanietta said. "Kill Libriota!"

Claus looked at young Lanietta in surprise. In a weird sort of way, he thought he heard the words, "Kill liberty." It was a strange double feeling of imprisonment and relief, losing freedom while gaining it.

"I've...had...enough!" Berella yelled.

Berella pulled the baby option. She forced her baby's ethereal image to explode. The force killed Libriota's and Biautus's physical bodies while forcing their ethereal remains into the rift. The rift closed, leaving Berella and Larto behind. Both panted on the ground in pain.

"I...did it...I..." Berella said, and she lost awareness.

"Berella killed Libriota?" young Lanietta said. "I didn't think it possible."

"And yet somehow Libriota returns," Claus said.

"Yes. Somehow," young Lanietta said. "But I have lost my sibling. And again Libriota is the cause. How I wish such a sacrifice be not in vain. Libriota will return. But what of my family? Who brings them back from the dead?"

Claus could offer no answer.

"Berella?" Larto called, but his voice weakened from blood loss. "Hold on. Hold..."

Larto was nearly in full daze. A rift opened and stayed open, causing a blinding white light to obscure most vision. Larto struggled to see, and he thought he saw two angels come through the rift. They first took Berella away on a gurney, and then they came back and took him away. He remembered nothing else.

Chapter 79: Space Jumping

"How I hate Libriota," young Lanietta said. "Yet I can do nothing about it. Can hate exist when one of the parties is dead?"

"Tyrants have come and gone on Earth," Claus said. "Yet those who suffered from such evil still hate the tyrants long after death. The hate consumes a person, yes, and what good does that do? If nothing else, such hatred makes people guarded toward future tyrants."

"Future tyrants," young Lanietta mocked. "How can such exist if people are wise to the wily ways of past tyrants?"

"I have spent much of my life asking that very question," Claus said. "Never is there a good answer. Sometimes I think a tyrant is the sum-total mirror image of desire in the world, like snow built up on a mountain. The tyrant simply reads where the snow wishes to go, sends someone onto the mountain under the guise of preventing an avalanche but knowing full well that the act will instead trigger it, and the tyrant reaps the reward for his advanced knowledge of doom. One might accuse a tyrant of being a coward, but I think a tyrant feels nothing at all."

When Larto regained awareness, he was on a medical bed aboard the Carinia 5 spaceship that Treyu had piloted. In fact, Treyu stood by his bed.

"Welcome back to the living," Treyu said.

"Thank you," Larto said as he tried to sit. "Ugh, I can't sit up."

"Let me help you," Treyu said. "Your leg is in a cast."

Treyu heard a double-beep from a timer.

"Time to remove the cast," Treyu said as he unlatched the cast. "Larbiabba patched you up as best as possible. She used a quick-heal cast. You'll still be tender for a bit."

"I must thank her. Can you send her in here?" Larto asked.

"I'm afraid she's occupied," Treyu said. "But I'll send for Lanshalla."

Treyu disappeared, and after a moment, Lanshalla entered. She kissed Larto on the cheek and gave him a little hug.

"I'm so glad to see you!" she said. "I didn't think I'd ever get you back! Mariel and Larbiabba made it just fine, but that cave gave me all sorts of trouble. Then I found you and Berella badly injured."

"Berella! Is she well?" Larto asked.

Lanshalla frowned.

"I must see her," Larto said. "She saved my life."

Treyu returned.

"She won't last much longer," Treyu said to Lanshalla.

"We're going to take Larto to see her. We'll all be there," Lanshalla replied.

Treyu and Lanshalla helped Larto to his feet.

"Berella is dying?" Larto asked.

"Yes," Treyu said as he and Lanshalla helped Larto hop out of the room.

"Her body cannot survive the shock," Lanshalla said. "She is worse off than when I...I..."

But Lanshalla could not finish her words. Tears provided the only reply.

"The baby option," Larto lamented.

The three arrived in Berella's medical room. Larbiabba and Mariel were already tending to her. They set up a chair next to Berella and helped Larto sit down.

"Is there nothing you can do?" Larto asked.

The others replied with grim expressions.

"That was a foolish thing you did!" Larto said.

"I...had to," Berella said. "No other way out."

"Berella," Larto said.

"Shh," she said with effort. "Is everyone safe from Libriota and Biautus?"

"Rest easy, Berella. Everyone is safe," Larbiabba said. "Libriota and Biautus are gone."

"Larto, they tell me I have only a little time left," Berella said.

"We'll get you well. I'll have Treyu take us to the best...the best..."

But Treyu returned an expression of "not possible".

"Let me speak, Larto," Berella said. "Being a Bleuh isn't so great, except maybe I learned a little...a little...a little about friendship. I...never had a friend... never knew...never..."

Berella passed. Larbiabba and Mariel placed a sheet over her. Lanshalla and Treyu helped Larto to his feet and walked him out.

"You need more rest," Lanshalla said. "We have much work to do."

"Lanshalla," Larto said. "Did Berella tell you about the cave, about—"

"She told us everything," Lanshalla said. "But to answer the questions you are about to ask, I tried many times to pull you two back. Something fought me. I knew it had to be strong, but at the time I didn't know it was Libriota, until I went partway through the rift and found her fighting me. She was winning too. And she would have won, except for Berella's brave act. I didn't realize she was carrying your baby."

"I had nothing to do with that," Larto said.

"Not in the way you would normally think. There's something different about you. I'm not sure what," Lanshalla said. "She killed her baby much as I had killed mine—to kill Libriota, except her Libriota was no projection."

"Then Libriota is dead? And that beast creature too?" Larto asked.

Lanshalla paused and drifted in thought.

"My old friend. Libriota. Why oh why did you have to make me do it?" Lanshalla lamented, but then she turned to Larto. "Her physical body is dead. So is the body of Biautus. Their ethereal components, however, I do not know. They may have perished. Or maybe not. They nearly came through the rift here, but I had Larbiabba help me, and we forced them back. I thought they were forced back into the cave. But then we got a clear signal and pulled you and Berella through. It was Berella who told us that Libriota and the beast didn't make it back to the cave. I can only hope that she finds a new person to inhabit so she can start over and make amends."

"Key word being *amends*," Larto said. "I am so tired, though. All of this has...has..."

And Larto fell into a stupor while Lanshalla and Treyu helped him to his medical bed. Larbiabba walked in.

"I'm going out on a limb by suggesting that Berella receive a Bleuh funeral," Larbiabba said. "It will have to be on the quiet. I'm not even sure we can do it. Mariel and I would be unrecognizable physically, but we're Grens, so our eethi spirits will be detected."

"I should go," Lanshalla said.

"They'll recognize you quicker than anything," Larbiabba said.

"Can you do it alone?" Lanshalla asked.

"You know I can't. I need help from a real Bleuh," Larbiabba said. "And a Bleuh woman at that."

"That rules me out," Treyu said.

"Or a woman with a Bleuh ethereal signature," Lanshalla said.

"That's the same thing," Larbiabba said.

"No it isn't," Lanshalla said.

Lanshalla grinned, and like any clever plan, the grin spread to Larbiabba as she understood Lanshalla's intent. They both stared at Treyu.

"I said that rules me out!" he insisted.

"You're a Greyan though," Larbiabba said. "You can mask your ethereal self."

"I'm not a Bleuh. I'm not a woman!" Treyu protested.

Just then, Mariel walked in.

"He could get a makeover," Lanshalla said. "He'd make the perfect woman."

Mariel burst into laughter while pointing at Treyu. This in turn caused Lanshalla and Larbiabba to laugh.

"Stop laughing! It's not funny!" Treyu protested.

"Treyu a woman? I've got to see that!" Mariel said. "We can send a video to your mother titled, 'Message of Love from Long Lost Daughter Treina'. She would love that."

"Stop laughing!" Treyu said. "There's a dead Carinian on this ship! And you laugh!"

"He's right," Lanshalla said. "We shouldn't laugh while Berella is lying in repose. Or unrepose, as she is covered and protected."

Lanshalla and Larbiabba looked down and held a moment of silence. Mariel looked down briefly, looked up at Treyu, smiled, Treyu looked back with a frown, Mariel looked at Lanshalla and Larbiabba, Larbiabba glanced up a little, and the eye-looking continued and caught like fire until the three women were laughing again.

"Treina," Lanshalla said.

Larto suddenly became alert from the laughter.

"What's so funny?" Larto asked.

"Treina," Mariel said.

Larto looked around, confused.

"I don't want to know," he said.

"Good," Treyu said. "With that, we should leave Larto to his rest. Treina indeed!"

Treyu stormed out and returned to the cockpit.

"Giving him a hard time?" Larto asked.

"Just making plans," Lanshalla said. "I'll let you know more after you rest."

Larto settled in for rest. The three women left and had one last giggle near the cockpit. The last thing Larto heard before he fell back into stupor was Treyu's voice echoing through the ship, saying, "For the last time, stop laughing," followed by Mariel's voice saying, "Stop making us laugh."

Larto thought he saw flashes of light followed by darkness. Was he still on the spaceship? Perhaps he was hallucinating. More flashes of light. His vision had narrowed to that of a tunnel, with a small image seemingly far away. After a moment, he realized the image was at the end of the tunnel. It was Berella. Her image went white, and a flash echoed down the tunnel before it hit Larto. He returned the thought to make her stop, and the flashing stopped. Another image appeared at the end of the tunnel, the image of Libriota. She sent a flash down the tunnel, and it shocked Larto. Larto tried to make Berella restrain Libriota, but Libriota laughed. She sent another flash down the tunnel, and Larto was shocked again.

"What are you doing over there?" called a voice down the tunnel to Larto.

"He's still connected," said another voice. "He doesn't know what he's doing."

"Can you sever the connection?" the first voice called.

"It's fused," the second voice said. "Fused."

Larto regained full alertness, and he realized the two voices were that of Lanshalla and Larbiabba.

"How are we going to space-jump with these goggles if he's still connected?" Lanshalla asked Larbiabba. "We can't use the Greylinger rift anymore. Might let nasties out."

"Perhaps we can train him to help," Larbiabba said. "Or we can try the other goggles again."

"The other goggles only let us see ethereal lines," Lanshalla said. "Berella's old goggles are the only ones fused out of phase with this dimension."

"Let me get up and help," Larto said.

Mariel had been watching Lanshalla and Larbiabba. She suddenly saw and rushed over to help Larto. She helped him to his feet and gave him crutches. Larto then crutched his way over to the space-jump experiment in progress. Lanshalla and Larbiabba stood on one end of a grid pattern by a post. Another post was on the other side of the grid.

"Larto," Larbiabba said. "Lanshalla will go eethi. You'll see her eethi self walk across the grid to the post over there. Then she will try to pull her physical body over to her eethi self."

"What can I do to help?" Larto asked.

"We're not sure, yet," Larbiabba said. "Just watch and try not to react."

"Very well," Larto said.

Lanshalla went eethi. Her ethereal self walked halfway down the grid. Her physical self looked around through the goggles. Larto saw two light flashes—one by the starting post, and one by the ending post. They came at him and shocked him. The crutches went out from under him, and he fell.

"Stop!" Larbiabba said.

Lanshalla reintegrated.

"What did you see?" Larbiabba asked.

"Two flashes of light, one at each post. They came at me and shocked me," Larto said.

"I'll rig up a protective pair of ethereal-phase light decelerator goggles," Larbiabba said. "One moment."

"Why are you doing this, Lanshalla?" Larto asked.

"Space-jumping is important," Lanshalla said. "I realized as much when we used it with the Greylinger rift. We must find another way. I know the history of such experiments. But I think I speak for all of us when I say that Berella, though she was an Imperial Bleuh Patrol, has inspired us. I was once a patrol too. Her death should not be in vain."

"Yes, Mommy!" young Lanietta added. "Wait. You're doing this with me inside?"

"But you are with child!" Larto said.

Lanshalla smiled.

"I am being careful," Lanshalla said. "Notice I didn't use the baby option with Libriota."

"I noticed," Larto said.

"And I will not use it now," Lanshalla said.

Larbiabba returned with goggles and placed them over Larto's eyes.

"This will help you process what you see," Larbiabba said. "Let's begin again."

Lanshalla and Larbiabba stood by the starting post. Lanshalla went eethi and

walked her eethi self halfway down the grid toward the other post. The two flashes appeared again, but they were dimmer and slower. They came after him, but he stepped aside, and they missed, crossing paths just beside him with a burst of energy.

"Stop," Larto said.

Lanshalla snapped back to her physical body.

"She's experimenting with me inside," young Lanietta said. "I wonder..."

"You wonder if such experimentation has given you a sense of ethereal guile ahead of your peers, right?" Claus asked.

"Yes, well at least the peers I once had," young Lanietta said.

"What did you see?" Larbiabba asked.

"I saw Berella standing next to the starting post, at least an ethereal image of Berella," Larto said. "And I saw Libriota's ethereal image by the other post. They came at me. I stepped aside, and they collided next to me."

"Let me rig up goggles for us all," Larbiabba said.

Larbiabba stepped away.

"What does it mean?" Mariel asked.

"Something important, I bet," Lanshalla said. "I also saw an image of Libriota at the end post. I didn't see Berella, but I didn't look by the starting post either."

Larbiabba returned.

"Put these on, Mariel. And I have a pair for myself," Larbiabba said. "Let's all see what Larto sees."

The experiment was repeated. The four saw the same thing—Lanshalla went eethi, and Berella appeared at the starting post while Libriota appeared at the other post. Lanshalla moved her ethereal spirit down the grid, but only a quarter of the way. Berella's and Libriota's ethereal images came at Larto, but their paths crossed halfway between him and the line of posts.

"Wow!" Larbiabba said. "We're on to something! Lanshalla, we must pursue this! Let's get set for another try."

But Mariel shook like a leaf.

"Mariel, what is it?" Larto asked.

"Berella...just seeing her again...I don't know. It's so sad. I usually hate Bleuhs. But Berella. Is it really her?"

"Just an image of her," Larbiabba said. "My guess is we're seeing ethereal after-images of her and Libriota, like nuclear blast shadows on the side of a building."

"What a horrible comparison," Claus said. "To think the only thing left of a person is a blast shadow."

Mariel shook even more at the description.

"Nuclear blast shadows," Mariel said in a shaky voice.

"It's too much for Mariel," Larto said to Lanshalla and Larbiabba. "Mariel, why don't you go into the other room and rest? Watch over the Lonely Vine cutting."

"Thank you," Mariel said. "The Lonely Vine cutting. It needs water and nutrients anyway. I'll take care of it."

Mariel left the room.

"I'm going to stand next to Larto for a different viewpoint," Larbiabba said. "Prepare for another start."

Lanshalla reintegrated and prepared to start. But before she did, Larbiabba went eethi herself and placed her hand in Larto's neck to sense his feelings. They repeated the test with Lanshalla going eethi a quarter of the way. The spirits of Berella and Libriota crossed in front of Larto (and now Larbiabba). But Larbiabba sent a pulse through Larto. He shook while the images of Berella and Libriota reversed direction and returned to their respective starting posts.

"We can control it! We can control it!" Larbiabba shouted. "Incredible indeed!"

"But what are you controlling?" Larto asked.

"Larbiabba, I saw something strange that time," Lanshalla said.

"What did you see?"

"I turned to look at the images of Berella and Libriota. But instead of seeing them both in both eyes, I only saw Berella in my left lens and Libriota in my right," Lanshalla said.

"Interesting," Larbiabba said. "We'll do this again. Try moving your eyes around or even crossing your eyes when the images cross paths. Are you ready?"

"Crossing eyes," young Lanietta said. "So this is how it started."

"You know about this?" Claus asked.

"Yes. I do. It marked the end of the girl before you. But that will wait. I will remain the girl before you for a time yet," she said.

"Ready," Lanshalla said.

They repeated the test. Lanshalla's ethereal image stopped part way. The images of Berella and Libriota crossed in front of Larbiabba and Larto as before. Lanshalla's physical body turned to look at those images. Lanshalla kept her ethereal self in one place, and with her physical body she crossed her eyes a little bit. The images of Berella and Libriota now moved toward Lanshalla's physical body. She crossed her eyes a little more, and they moved closer. She uncrossed them a little but moved her gaze. They drifted apart but still stayed close to her. Lanshalla crossed, uncrossed, and moved her eyes a little left and right—coordinating the entire time to move the images of Berella and Libriota around, sometimes causing them to intersect, sometimes not. In the end she focused her left eye inward toward her nose and her right eye out toward her ethereal image. Berella's image took Lanshalla's physical position and Libriota's image took Lanshalla's ethereal position. Lanshalla fought with all her might to hold her left gaze steady while moving her right eye to focus a little closer to her physical body. To her amazement, Lanshalla's ethereal self moved a little toward her physical body. Lanshalla went the other way—she held her right eye gaze steady on her ethereal self while moving the gaze of her left eye toward her ethereal self from her physical body. Her physical body moved a little to keep up. She did this again and again and was able to inch her physical body toward her ethereal body. Then with one last surge, she sent her physical body to her ethereal body, and the two merged.

The images of Berella and Libriota exploded in cold fire, and they dissipated. Unexpectedly, Mariel screamed. Treyu rushed out of the cockpit and into the room with Mariel. Larto, Lanshalla, and Larbiabba soon followed.

"It's...it's...alive!" Mariel stammered.

The Lonely Vine cutting, in nutrient jar, had grown into a form resembling a micro shrub. An ethereal glow surrounded it.

"The cutting has grown," Larbiabba said.

"It's Berella. It's her!" Mariel said.

The ethereal glow faded and was nearly gone.

"What was it?" Larto asked.

"I'm not sure," Larbiabba said as she went over to a control panel and punched buttons quickly. "Hmm. Strange."

"Berella's ethereal fossil," Lanshalla said. "It's here now."

"Yes. How did you know?" Larbiabba asked.

"I can see her in my left lens," Lanshalla said. "But I don't see the Libriota image."

"Eethi-Track shows the Berella eethi fossil from our testing has transferred to this vine cutting," Larbiabba said. "But there's more than that. There's a link to Berella's actual ethereal spirit. A thin link."

"I think I can accentuate it," Lanshalla said.

Lanshalla went eethi, touched the cutting, and then used her left eye to focus on the ethereal glow around the cutting. A thin ethereal line twisted upward from the vine, like the thin tentacle of a tornado coming to life.

"She's caught," Lanshalla said. "Her ethereal spirit is snagged on this plant!"

"If the line breaks, she will be lost to the ethereal dimension. She'll be stuck waiting an eternity to enter another physical body," Larbiabba said.

"There's only one thing to do," Lanshalla said.

Lanshalla crossed her eyes. She focused her left eye onto the vine and her right eye onto her ethereal self. She touched the vine cutting with her physical body, and with her eethi spirit she pulled on the ethereal line. She pulled and pulled. She dragged the line away from the plant and pulled Berella's ethereal spirit into the ethereal glow. Lanshalla quickly darted her right eye between her own ethereal spirit and Berella's to give eethi strength, then she refocused and oriented her right eye in line with her left so as to merge the ethereal spirit of Berella with that of the vine cutting.

"Look!" Mariel said.

The ethereal glow around the vine became strong and right, and it spoke.

"What...where am I?" Berella's voice asked.

"Berella?" Mariel asked back.

"I think so," Berella replied. "I thought I was lost. I seem to have fibrous arms and legs."

"Your ethereal spirit is now in this vine cutting," Larbiabba said. "Your physical body died and released your ethereal self."

"I...remember that part," Berella said. "I was floating free. I felt another presence. It was Libriota. But then she left, and now I'm here."

"This is madness!" Mariel said. "It's undignified. It's...a person stuck in a plant...I...I can't take it. Someone help me. Someone..."

Mariel fell into daze. Larto caught her and placed her in a chair.

"Can we help Berella back into her body?" Larto asked.

"It's too late," Larbiabba said. "Her physical body is too badly damaged. I confess I'm in shock too. I never thought this was possible. Lanshalla, you...did you...I'm not even sure if I can ask the question."

"About how Berella got into the vine cutting?" Lanshalla added.

"Yes."

Lanshalla paused in thought.

"The Lonely Vine is a caretaker of the long dead," Berella answered to the surprise of the others. "It contains more than just memories of past creatures. It contains spirits too. I am not alone here. There are several others with me. The

Lonely Vine itself contains many hundreds of thousands of ethereal spirits, drawn in from the rocks. It is not such a bad thing, for now. It is better than nothing."

Larto started shaking.

"I knew the Lonely Vine was special, but Mariel was right. This entire thing is unsettling," Larto said.

Larbiabba hit a few buttons on her panel.

"Lanshalla, the other Grens are getting eethi sunburns. Too much ethereal exposure," Larbiabba said. "Treyu is unaffected, and I can buffer what hits me but only for a bit."

"I can stop the testing," Lanshalla said.

"It's from me, though, isn't it?" Berella asked.

"I'm afraid so," Larbiabba said.

"Larto, let's take Mariel into another room," Treyu said. "I'll return here and see what I can do."

Larto nodded in agreement. The men helped Mariel into a room with a reclining chair, and Larto stayed with her. Treyu returned to the room with the vine.

"Treyu, Berella will gradually lose her sense of being Carinian," Larbiabba said. "She'll become more docile and tranquil, like that of this plant."

"We have an idea," Lanshalla said.

"Not the makeover again," Treyu said.

"Funny you should mention that," Lanshalla said.

"We need you to act as a partial surrogate," Larbiabba said. "Berella's ethereal spirit is tied to this vine. But if we could attach the vine to say, your chest, her ethereal spirit would be close enough to yours such that you can form an eethi bridge with hers and give her Carinian sanity."

"Merge with a vine? With a Bleuh? And get changed to look like a woman?" Treyu groaned.

"The woman makeover would be later and only temporary. The vine merge is more immediate, and you'd keep your looks and charm. But instead of chest hair, you'd have bits of vine and leaf," Larbiabba said.

"Vine and leaf. Larbiabba, I've helped you with all sorts of strange experiments, up until now. But this is totally out of control. The thought of a vine crawling through my skin is just unnerving. Like worms and splinters!" Treyu complained.

"It won't hurt. You might even feel euphoric, like dancing with a young woman," Lanshalla said.

"You mean I'll be romantic with a vine? Disgusting! Not to mention the laws against such things!" Treyu said.

"There are only laws against Bleuhs and Grens. Greyans aren't part of those laws," Lanshalla said.

"What am I doing with you two?" Treyu asked in bewilderment.

"You're helping out," Larbiabba said. "Come along, Treyu. This won't hurt a bit."

Treyu backed up in fear, but Lanshalla stepped behind him, went a little eethi, and used her eethi hand to calm the nerves in his back. She caught him as he got weak-kneed, placed him in the chair that Mariel had just been in, and opened the front of his shirt. Dazed and tranquilized, Treyu could only watch what happened next. Larbiabba took the vine cutting and placed it next to the shirt opening. The vine wiggled its way in and attached itself to Treyu's chest. Treyu's eyes rolled up as he entered a euphoric state. Lanshalla released her ethereal grip on his nerves, and he relaxed.

"Ahh," he said. "You know, having a vine is not such a bad thing after all. Maybe we can get married. Oh, this is interesting. I'm hearing Berella speak to me. Do you hear her?"

"I don't," Lanshalla said.

"Neither do I," Larbiabba said. "You're in direct contact with her ethereal spirit. Treyu, this is a great gift. Take care of the vine, and Berella can guide you in all sorts of matters."

"Yes," Treyu said, standing up and closing his shirt. "Yes she can. We will check on our arrival time...for...Carinia 1."

Treyu walked out in a slow, tranquil gait.

"He looks too peaceful," Lanshalla said. "I hope we did the right thing. I have no experience in these matters. How long can he go on like this?"

"You mean safely?" Larbiabba asked.

"Yes."

"I don't know. I've never heard of this either," Larbiabba said.

Lanshalla and Larbiabba returned to the lab so Lanshalla could test space-jumping again. Larbiabba called for Larto so he could help as before.

"Why don't you sit in the cockpit with Treyu?" Larto said to Mariel after bringing her to full alertness. "Just relax. Watch the stars and clear your mind."

Mariel agreed. She went into the cockpit and sat with Treyu. Larto returned to the lab and stood where he did before. Larbiabba stood next to him and extended her ethereal hand into his spine. All three donned their goggles as before.

"Ready," Larbiabba said.

Lanshalla went eethi, but then she returned to her physical body after but a few seconds.

"They're gone," Lanshalla said. "The images of Berella and Libriota are gone."

"Did you see them?" Larbiabba asked Larto.

"No. Nothing at all this time," Larto said.

"Try again," Larbiabba said to Lanshalla.

Lanshalla stood by the starting post and went eethi again. Her ethereal self walked to the ending post. She walked back and reintegrated.

"Nothing again," Lanshalla said.

"I saw nothing but Lanshalla's physical and ethereal bodies," Larto said.

"The eethi fossils are gone. Foiled!" Larbiabba muttered.

"I'll pretend like I can see them," Lanshalla said.

Lanshalla went eethi and sent her eethi self halfway toward the end post. She moved her physical eyes around, paused, and reintegrated.

"Again, nothing," Lanshalla said.

"Back to square one," Larbiabba lamented.

"If only Berella or Libriota could help," Larto said half-seriously.

"Libriota can't," Larbiabba started.

"But Berella can," Lanshalla finished.

"How?" Larto asked.

"I'll go get her," Larbiabba added.

"No, let me," Larto said.

"Larto wait," Lanshalla said, but Larto had already gone into the room where Berella the vine had been, leaving Lanshalla and Larbiabba bemused.

Mariel shrieked and rushed out from the cockpit.

"There's something wrong with Treyu!" Mariel shouted. "A parasite or something on his chest! Hurry!"

Larto shouted and rushed out also.

"The Lonely Vine is gone!" Larto added. "That means Berella is gone! Hurry!"

Lanshalla and Larbiabba exchanged knowing glances, and then Larbiabba headed for the cockpit to get Berella as promised.

"Mariel, it's okay," Lanshalla explained. "Larto, it's okay. Nothing is parasitic. No one is missing. And, well, here's Berella."

Larbiabba stepped into the cockpit to Larto's amazement and brought forth Treyu.

"What is this?" Larto asked.

"I told you I'm bringing Berella, and here she is," Larbiabba said.

"I thought...but her ethereal image...the vine cutting. What's going on?" Larto stumbled.

Treyu opened his shirt a little to reveal a vine inside. Larto's eyes opened in further amazement.

"The parasite!" Mariel said. "No...it...Is that really the vine? Berella?"

"Treyu is acting as a surrogate for Berella," Lanshalla said.

"It was necessary to save both the vine and Berella," Larbiabba said. "Treyu, stand next to Lanshalla and give her advice."

"Wait," Mariel said. "You're going to have Berella help with that space-jump thing? Oh, I can't watch. I thought I was supposed to relax with stars."

"Go back to the cockpit and relax," Treyu said. "I'll be there shortly."

Mariel agreed and returned to the cockpit. Meanwhile, Treyu stood by Lanshalla, and Larbiabba took her position by Larto as before.

"Begin again," Larbiabba said.

"Lanshalla," Treyu said. "Berella says you must go eethi. Keep your ethereal self just in front of your physical body."

"I don't know if I can get used to this," Larto said. "Treyu, are you...I mean..."

"He's fine," Lanshalla said.

"Larto," Larbiabba said, "we can try things without you, if you wish to rest in the cockpit with Mariel."

"No, I'll see this through," Larto said.

Lanshalla followed Treyu's last advice.

"Good. Now cross your eyes. Focus the left on your nose and the right on your ethereal self," Treyu said.

Lanshalla did that too.

"Excellent. Now snap your left eye onto your ethereal self," Treyu said. "It must be done very quickly."

"I...this is very difficult," Lanshalla said. "I can't quite do it."

"Here, let's do it this way," Treyu said. "I'll stand in front of your left side. Now focus your left eye on my back. I'll walk toward your ethereal self like so. Keep your left eye focused on my back. Are you doing that?"

"I'm trying," Lanshalla said. "I think it's working. I think—"

But Treyu screamed in pain. He dashed toward Larbiabba for help. Lanshalla reintegrated and stopped the experiment.

"My back! It's crawling with pain!" he said.

Treyu removed his shirt. The vine cutting had huddled on his front while his back crawled with caterpillars. They hunted desperately for the vine to eat, but Treyu kept his arms over his chest to protect the vine.

"Where did they come from?" Larto asked.

"Never mind that. Get them off!" Treyu screeched.

Without thought, Larbiabba removed her ethereal hand from Larto and brushed off the caterpillars, but as she did, they turned into butterflies. She then reintegrated and used her physical hand to brush them off. They simply fell to the floor and continued to crawl about. She went eethi again and finished off all caterpillars, both on his back and on the ground. As butterflies, they flew around for a little while before Lanshalla went eethi and dissolved them into nothing.

"We're getting closer," Larbiabba said.

"Closer? That's closer?" Treyu asked.

"Lanshalla, try again without Berella's help. Treyu, you stand next to me. Don't want you to lose your wits again. Could disrupt the test," Larbiabba said.

"I...I'm disrupting the test? I thought I was helping," Treyu said. "I...oh, very well, Berella."

Treyu stood next to Larbiabba.

"Good to see Berella agrees with me," Larbiabba said. "Begin again, Lanshalla."

Lanshalla went eethi and moved her ethereal image down toward the end post a bit. She then went cross-eyed. She kept one eye on her nose and the other on her ethereal self. No good.

"Larbiabba, her goggles need a half-gamma phase twist in the left lens. The right lens needs an eethi focal compensator adjustment of thirty-two degrees," Treyu said with a lighter voice sounding like Berella's.

"Interesting," Larbiabba replied. "That will force her eyes out of sync from the get go. But it's worth a shot."

Larbiabba took Lanshalla's goggles and disappeared into the work lab.

"Treyu, what have they done to you?" Larto asked as he helped Treyu put his shirt back on.

"Sir, it's a very odd relationship," Treyu said.

"I still find it hard to believe, that Berella and the vine are merged with you," Larto said.

"Berella's ethereal self is in the vine," Treyu said. "And yes, it's true—I'm acting as a host to help keep the vine and Berella going."

"Does it hurt?" Larto asked.

"Only when they strangle me," Treyu joked. "Maybe I shouldn't joke. The vine, I mean Berella, might get ideas. She speaks to me, at least her ethereal self does."

"I hope this won't interfere with your butlering duties or your piloting duties," Larto said.

"It shouldn't," Treyu said. "Matter of fact, Berella says she has plenty of horticultural tips when we return to the vineyard."

"That should prove most interesting," Larto said.

Larbiabba returned.

"Try this," she said to Lanshalla.

Lanshalla put on the goggles. The four took their positions. Mariel came out to see what was taking Treyu so long when Lanshalla successfully performed a space-jump. Mariel shrieked.

"Everything is fine," Treyu said. "Just a little space-jumping here. Happens all the time you know."

"The rift though. What about the rift?" Mariel asked.

"There is no Greylinger rift or any other kind of rift with this space-jumping," Larbiabba said. "Lanshalla, congratulations."

"Congratulations to us all. These goggles did the trick," Lanshalla said. "It's time for you to try, Larbiabba."

Larbiabba took the goggles from Lanshalla and repeated the experiment. With several attempts, Larbiabba was able to space-jump a short ways too.

"Impressive," Larbiabba said. "Though it's more difficult for me."

"It's not every Gren who can space-jump," Lanshalla grinned.

"Labba just space-jumped with her mother," Claus said.

"She and I are the first babies to do so," young Lanietta said. "The first...and the last."

Claus tried to say something to settle young Lanietta, but he remained tongue-tied.

"If everyone on Carinia 2 could space-jump, we'd kick those Bleuhs out for good. I mean, we could encourage them to leave with subtle guidance," Mariel said as others looked at her in surprise.

"For one who is frightened by space-jumps, you're taking a new liking to them," Treyu said.

"I know. But I also love my Carinia 2," Mariel said.

"As do we all," Larto said. "We are mostly Grens on Carinia 2. How will this help us?"

Lanshalla whispered into Larbiabba's ear. Larbiabba whispered back. Their whispered conversation grew louder and more animated until Lanshalla said, "No!"

"No what?" Larto asked.

"There's only one way for Grens to win. They must also learn to space-jump," Larbiabba said.

"Or they could do the baby option," Lanshalla said.

"Both are dangerous," Larbiabba said. "Both could get the Grens killed."

"Let me think about this," Larto said. "No, I don't have to spend time thinking. I know. We'll not risk the lives of the unconsenting. I will volunteer to do a space-jump."

Larto walked toward the starting post, but Mariel surprised him from behind and clocked a blunt object onto his skull. He collapsed to the ground in a stupor.

"Mariel!" Treyu said.

"It can't be him," Mariel said. "He is going to be a father. I will volunteer."

"Do you know how risky this is? It could kill you," Treyu said.

"I know, Treyu," Mariel said.

"Now I'm speaking as Berella," Treyu said. "You might not have the luck I did. Besides your physical body being destroyed, your ethereal self could be lost forever."

"We can wait until we reach Carinia 1, Mariel," Lanshalla said. "Perhaps after we commit Berella's body to stasis, we can complete our lab next to a procreation center and learn how to help Grens space-jump."

"Of course we'd have to teach a Gren how to go eethi first," Larbiabba said. "I can help there."

"That would be first, yes," Lanshalla said. "Though not all Grens are as gifted as you, Larbs."

"And if Libriota reincarnates somewhere else, she'll push all the harder against the Gren rebels," Mariel said. "No, I must start now."

"Mariel, this is me now, Treyu," he said as he paced around. "Look at Larto there. Doesn't that tell you something? What you're doing can't be good if you have to bludgeon others. If I were a Gren, you'd probably—"

But before Treyu could finish, Mariel had clocked him on the back of the head. He too fell, stunned. Lanshalla and Larbiabba looked on in surprise. Even more surprising, Treyu's mouth started to move. It was Berella.

"Very well," Berella's voice said. "If you are this adamant about volunteering yourself, I would ask Lanshalla and Larbiabba to assist."

"I'll do the testing, Lanshalla," Larbiabba said. "Go ahead and take care of the men."

Lanshalla first took Treyu to a side room and then Larto to a side room. She stayed next to Larto, went a little eethi, and massaged his nervous system. This went on for a number of hours.

Larto's mind drifted back toward alertness when he heard voices in argument.

"It couldn't be helped," Lanshalla said.

"That doesn't make it better," Larbiabba said.

"There was no other way. Mariel—" Lanshalla continued.

"Should have been stopped. I should have stopped her and allowed ourselves time to think through the situation," Larbiabba said. "But no. I was a part of it. Now it's too late. The loss is inexcusable. I

don't know how we can justify going on after this."

"I'm not dead!" Larto blurted out as he stepped from the side room to the main.

Mariel sat in a chair with wraps around her arms and legs.

"Larto?" Larbiabba said.

"Release her!" Larto said. "Mariel meant no harm. Unless Treyu...oh! Did she kill him?"

"Larto, wait," Lanshalla said.

Larto rushed around and found Treyu sitting in a chair, dazed.

"Treyu. Treyu!" Larto called as he shook him.

"Yes? Larto. It's you," Treyu said.

"Can you stand? Can you walk?" Larto called.

"Yes to both," Treyu said.

Larto helped Treyu into the main area.

"See? Neither of us is a loss," Larto said.

"Oh. That explains your strange behavior," Larbiabba said.

"My strange behavior?" Larto asked. "What about this? You have Mariel tied up."

"She is not 'tied up'," Larbiabba said. "Though perhaps I should have myself tied up. Sigh. If you will excuse me, I need a break."

Larbiabba stepped into the cockpit.

"Lanshalla?" Larto asked. "What is going on?"

"Mariel wanted to try a space-jump," Lanshalla said. "She didn't want anyone stopping her. So she knocked Treyu and you both into daze. Larbiabba was against it too, but I talked her into it."

"Oh," Larto said.

"I'm sorry to say, Mariel was not able to go eethi. At least not on her own. And forget a space-jump," Lanshalla said. "I made Larbiabba push the test as far possible. But at least we learned something."

"What's that?" Larto said.

"Unless you are a Bleuh or an extremely clever Gren, going eethi can cause internal damage."

"You injured Mariel?" Larto asked.

"I'm not surprised," Treyu said. "Bleuhs are notoriously reckless."

"Larbiabba did it with such ease. Plus those Grens on Carinia 5...well...I thought Mariel could pick it up easily," Lanshalla said. "Anyway, it's all over. Nothing to worry about."

"Nothing to worry about?" Larto protested. "Are these injuries fatal? Will she recover?"

"She will recover," Lanshalla said.

"Of all the crimes," Treyu said. "I should destroy Bleuhs wherever they...oh, it's a sunny day on Carinia 5."

Berella detected Treyu's hate and forced him to sing. Treyu left the main area and walked into the cockpit.

"My maid isn't herself. You should not have allowed her to throw away her future," Larto said.

"A little possessive, aren't you?" Lanshalla said. "We Bleuhs believe a person should be responsible unto thyself. Who is worthy to block the choice of free will?"

"Me, that's who," Larto said.

"Seems hardly reasonable, a Gren who impedes on free will," Lanshalla said.

"I should have made her wait," Larto said.

"Freedom deference is no freedom at all," Lanshalla said. "There now. Would you like to know what's left of Mariel?"

"What's *left* of her?" Larto said incredulously as he paced around. "I don't like the sound of *that*."

Larto walked over to Mariel and hugged her.

"Mariel suffered lovakary damage," Lanshalla said.

"You mean—" Larto asked.

"I do," Lanshalla replied.

"One or—" Larto continued.

"Just one," Mariel said.

"Mariel! How could you sacrifice your body like that?"

"She kept insisting," Lanshalla said. "Said she had to space-jump or die. Larbiabba stopped her after she lost one."

"There was no other way," Mariel said. "I did it, and it's done."

Treyu led Larbiabba back to the main area.

"Treyu, can you make sense of this insanity?" Larto asked.

"No, but Berella can," Treyu said.

"How is Berella? Did I hurt her? When I hit you over the—" Mariel started.

"Berella is fine and still connected with me," Treyu said. "As for the insanity, she explained. Going eethi plays a bit with life and death. Like crossing a busy road. Cross when traffic is clear, and all is well."

"Is that what hit me? Eethi traffic?" Mariel asked.

"Yes," Lanshalla said.

"How?" Larto asked.

"She couldn't see it," Lanshalla said.

"That is just one of many dangers," Larbiabba said. "It's my fault for not making Mariel prove an ability to detect eethi traffic."

Larbiabba removed the wraps from Mariel. Mariel revealed deep, dark bruises of various shapes and sizes.

"You look terrible," Treyu said.

"Thanks," Mariel said sarcastically.

Larto was equally shocked.

"I don't know which is worse, the baby option or getting hit by eethi traffic and losing a lovakary," Larto said.

"The baby option can be performed repeatedly and has a chance of killing the woman," Lanshalla said. "Getting hit by eethi traffic can be fatal, but most of us survive with merely mild fatigue."

"Death or mild fatigue," Treyu said. "Oh, it gets worse and worse."

"I didn't invent the universe, I just live in it," Lanshalla said. "If you wish to change ethereal dynamics, go ahead. Set yourself up as a deity and get to work."

"I'm not that omnipotent," Treyu said.

"None of us are," Larbiabba said. "We do what we can."

Just then, a plasma blast hit the ship.

Chapter 80: Patrols and a Transport

"We're under attack!" Treyu said as he and the others rushed to the cockpit. "An Imperial Bleuh Patrol."

"Attention deviant ship," a voice called over the radio. "You are violating a military zone. Do not attempt to escape, or you will be destroyed. Prepare to be boarded."

"We'll have to evade," Treyu said.

Treyu hit several controls. The ship took wild turns and tossed the others about.

"Treyu, no!" Lanshalla said. "They mean what they say."

Several more plasma blasts hit the ship. Damage to the hull caused air to leak out of two rooms, and they were automatically sealed off.

"We'll never survive this," Lanshalla said. "Guess I'll have to try a space-jump over to their ship."

"That's like diving into a moving swimming pool the size of a wheelbarrow a hundred stories down," Larbiabba said.

"We'll die if I don't try something," Lanshalla said. "Ready? Here I—"

Before Lanshalla could space-jump, Mariel grabbed test goggles from Larbiabba out of desperation (the same goggles Mariel used while testing). Mariel focused on drawing out and using Larbiabba's and Lanshalla's eethi spirits to help her (Mariel) go eethi, travel to the attacking ship, weaken its fuel supply, and cause that fuel to explode, destroying the attacking ship.

"Mariel!" Lanshalla screamed as Lanshalla broke off the attack and forced the three back to their respective physical bodies.

"I...had to do it," Mariel said, now exhausted. "And...I damaged the other one. The other lovakary."

"Give that back!" Larbiabba said, ripping the goggles away from Mariel.

"The ship is safe," Treyu said. "It was my fault. I should have watched our course more closely."

"Yes, it *is* your fault!" Lanshalla said. "But Mariel! There should have been no need for such a sacrifice! And the patrols! We killed Bleuhs! Word will get out. They'll hunt us down!"

"You're the one who invented the baby option!" Mariel said. "And you cringe about killing your own? Were you just kidding about helping the rebels?"

"Not kidding. But only at the proper time. It's too soon for this kind of thing!" Lanshalla said.

"It is done," Mariel said.

"What a horrible thing for everyone involved!" Lanshalla said.

"We must be careful," Larbiabba said. "We cannot let Mariel's new-found technique fall into enemy hands. Could be used against us."

"Treyu, I suggest you work with Berella if in doubt about what space zone is military or not. We don't want military. I can help too," Lanshalla said. "In fact, there's a special VIP zone. Let's take that. I'll give the proper codes."

Lanshalla hit several buttons on a control panel. A message flashed back that access codes were accepted.

"There. VIP course now transferring to the navi control," Lanshalla said.

"Yes, it is. Thank you," Treyu said. "Berella agrees. This is a good choice. We won't be questioned when we arrive."

Treyu's hands hit several buttons, and he jumped back in surprise.

"What's the matter?" Lanshalla asked.

"My hands...they just moved on their own. I couldn't control them," Treyu said.

"A message is arriving," Mariel said. "It's from Celiba Dorrok. Who's that?"

"Berella says it's her sister. Berella!" Treyu exclaimed. "She took over my hands! Does this ever happen?"

Lanshalla and Larbiabba looked at each other and shrugged.

"We don't know," Larbiabba said. "You might be the first case."

"Well it's dangerous. I'd better do something about it. I'd better get rid of..." Treyu started, but he suddenly relaxed and sang, "Pleasant worlds are singing through the trees. A wish for now befriended by bees. My heart goes high for clouds in the sky, the world—"

"That's enough, Treyu," Larbiabba said.

"Berella, he's tranquil. He won't get rid of you. We'll make sure," Lanshalla said.

"Thank you," Treyu said in a softer, higher voice like that of Berella. "Celiba can help. I've asked her to rendezvous with us. She can take Larbiabba and Treyu on her ship. Yes, Treyu should go in disguise as previously planned."

"I'll coordinate with Celiba's ship, Treyu," Lanshalla said. "Go on back with Larbiabba."

Larbiabba led Treyu to the back. Lanshalla sat in the cockpit, Mariel sat at a messaging station, and Larto sat in a jump seat. It wasn't long before another message arrived.

"Celiba will arrive soon," Mariel said.

"Sending a confirmation code," Lanshalla said.

"Not working," Mariel said.

"Seems Berella will have to handle this," Lanshalla mused. "Treyu! Back in the cockpit! Now!"

"What?" Treyu said.

"We need Berella here," Lanshalla said.

"But my makeover," Treyu protested.

"I never thought I'd hear you complain about *not* getting a makeover," Mariel laughed. "I'll let Larbiabba know that you are delayed."

Celiba's ship neared Treyu's ship. Larbiabba was in back completing her own makeover.

"Send Treyu back," Larbiabba said. "It's now or never for his makeover."

"Will do," Lanshalla replied.

"Uh oh," Treyu said. "More patrols."

"We've been tracked," Lanshalla said. "Word must have spread that we destroyed an Imperial Bleuh ship. I was afraid this would happen."

"Blame Mariel and her attack," Treyu said. "At least she paid the price for it."

Treyu's right hand slapped his face just ahead of Lanshalla's attempt to do the same.

"What the—" Treyu said.

"I see Berella took care of you first," Lanshalla said, retracting her hand. "You got us into trouble and forced Mariel's hand. And I was going to risk my life to save you and the ship. I'm sure I would have failed. But no time for lengthy monologues. We must hide."

Treyu hit several buttons frantically. Celiba's ship paused, and what looked like a great maw opened up. Treyu hit more buttons, and the ship headed for the maw.

"What are you doing?" Mariel asked.

"It's not me!" Treyu said.

"Clever," Lanshalla said. "But will there be enough time? Increase speed, Berella."

"What? No!" Treyu said. "We'll be eaten by this thing."

"Berella, close Treyu's mouth, that's a good girl," Lanshalla said.

Treyu's mouth went shut, and he yelled with the closed mouth to speak.

"Can you stop his vocal cords too?" Lanshalla asked, but Berella could only get Treyu to shrug his shoulders. "Good enough for now. Thank you, Brells."

The ship was seemingly engulfed by Celiba's cargo ship. The maw closed, and Treyu's ship docked on a platform. Berella released control of Treyu, and he let out a sigh of relief.

"Brells?" Treyu asked.

"I'm becoming fond of my Brells," Lanshalla said. "You know, Berella."

"Thank you," Berella replied through Treyu's vocal cords in a higher/softer voice.

"Hurry back to Larbiabba," Lanshalla said. "You'll need a makeover in record time."

Treyu rushed back. Lanshalla, Mariel, and Larto looked out the front window as guards walked about the ship, checking for anything suspicious. At length, a side door to the platform opened, and two people approached the ship. The guards stepped aside, and the back hatch to the ship opened. Out walked Treyu and Larbiabba. Larbiabba was in her transformed form from Larto's Vineyard, while Treyu was given a heavy makeover to make him appear feminine. He looked so much like a woman that Larbiabba went with Mariel's suggestion and called him Treina. Treina had what looked like a corsage but in fact was an extension of the vine.

The connecting hatches to both ships opened, and Celiba approached with her co-pilot. Larbiabba and Treina were there to meet them.

"I am Celiba. This is my co-pilot, Tiloto," Celiba said.

"I am...Arliabba. This is Treina," Larbiabba said.

"Treina. My!" Tiloto said, and he approached her and held her hand. "You are most exquisite. May I give you a tour of my ship?"

Larbiabba laughed, but Treyu on the inside was nervous. The nervousness triggered the ethereal spirit of Berella from the vine, and she took over Treyu's converted body and became the new Treina personality.

"I'd love to," Treina said, and she kicked up her left leg at the knee partway.

Out of habit, Celiba kicked up her right leg at the knee halfway. Tiloto took Treina onto his and Celiba's ship while Celiba looked puzzled. She turned to Larbiabba and was about to say something, but she stopped herself.

"You look confused," Larbiabba said.

"I...for a moment I thought that was my sister. Berella. I guess I can't believe she's really gone. You best show me where she is," Celiba said.

Larbiabba led Celiba into Treyu's ship, down a short ways, and into a room where Berella's body was in stasis. Celiba fell into tears immediately.

"We did everything together," Celiba said. "And then she went into the Imperial Bleuh Academy. I went into Bleuh

Transport. She was always the stronger one, though. I was the quiet one. And this is her fate. Tell me, how did she die?"

"She was caught in a bad ethereal situation," Larbiabba said.

"What does *that* mean?" Celiba asked, suddenly growing tense. "Did she commit a crime? She's not in uniform. What happened?"

"You were close with Berella?" Larbiabba asked.

"We kept *no* secrets," Celiba said. "The last I heard, she was helping Libriota track an escaped prisoner and rebel spies."

"Berella turned against Libriota," Larbiabba said. "She attacked and killed her."

"No! My Berella a traitor? Never!" Celiba said.

"You must not think of her as a traitor," Larbiabba said. "She saw Libriota for what she truly is, or was. Celiba, Berella saved friends of mine from great harm."

"What kind of friends?" Celiba asked.

"They are not all Bleuhs," Larbiabba confessed.

"So you corrupted her," Celiba said, falling back into sadness. "And you expect to recruit me too, is that it?"

"Do not be so harsh," Larbiabba said.

"There's something strange about you. I sense you on an eethi level like other Bleuhs, but it feels alien, unlike other Bleuhs. Is that honesty?" Celiba asked.

"You're very perceptive. I had a slight makeover," Larbiabba said. "This is what I really look like."

Larbiabba changed to her natural self.

"I know that face," Celiba said. "Not Arliabba—Larbiabba. No wonder I had trouble with your eethi signature. As it is, there are Wanted postings for you, a Bleuh, two Grens, and a guy."

"Do the Grens look like this?" Larbiabba asked.

Larbiabba led Celiba out of the stasis room and to the cockpit, where she opened the door. Larto and Mariel stood to greet Celiba with Lanshalla behind them.

"Yes," Celiba said. "And there's the Bleuh. I could have you all arrested, you know. Is that why you were so eager to dock inside? Is that why there are Bleuh patrols racing past this cargo ship? What else have you done? Where's your other friend? Tall man, unknown ethereal signature. Rumors say he's something new, a Greyan. Is this a Greyan ship?"

"So many questions," Mariel said.

"I have a right to know. You're on my ship now," Celiba said. "And no double talk. You're not dealing with a neophyte. Not like that Treina woman. I can tell you've corrupted her!"

"You may accuse us of recruitment or corruption," Larbiabba said. "Have it as you may. You can see the universe as it really is by peeling away layers of political bias, or you can remain stuck in those layers and become victim to those who do the peeling. I make no threat. But I offer a hand of friendship to one who wishes not to be stuck."

Celiba paused.

"I'm still puzzled. Someone on this ship knew the private channel only Berella and I use. And Treina. I still can't get over the leg kick," Celiba said.

"Are you going to tell her?" Larto asked Larbiabba.

"Berella's ethereal spirit is not lost," Larbiabba said.

"Where is it?" Celiba asked.

"It's hard to explain. Berella's spirit is in a plant that—" Larbiabba said.

"A plant," Celiba said in disbelief. "Please."

"No, really," Larbiabba said. "Let me finish. This plant has a symbiotic relationship with—"

"Another plant. And they have baby plants, right?" Celiba said.

"That's not what I said," Larbiabba said. "She is—"

At that moment, Celiba received a message in her earpiece. She put up her hand to stop Larbiabba and then listened to the message. She nodded. Several guards entered the ship with weapons.

"You're all under arrest," Celiba said.

"You can't," Larto said. "You're supposed to help us."

Lanshalla went eethi and disrupted the nerves of one guard. Another guard went after her physical body, but she space-jumped, and he missed her. Other guards took Mariel and Larto in hand. Larbiabba tried flirting with the guards to assuage them, but they took her as prisoner too.

"Stop your attack, Lanshalla, or your friends get it. You're all wanted for murder. The law backs up my use of deadly force if needed," Celiba said.

Lanshalla space-jumped to an unknown place.

"She space-jumped. I don't believe it. She should be dead. Must investigate. Later, though. Search the ship," Celiba said.

"You're not really going to arrest us, are you?" Mariel asked.

"Your ship destroyed a Bleuh Patrol ship. Bleuhs are dead. Even if I wanted to help you, I can't. I'd be put away for treason. You should think of these things before killing others," Celiba said.

Guards took Larto, Mariel, and Larbiabba away, leaving Celiba alone on Treyu's ship. She walked back to the medical room and stood by Berella's physical body.

"I...don't know what to think at the moment, Berella," Celiba said, speaking to her sister's body. "My own sister killed Libriota. Can it be true? Berella, talk to me. What were you doing? Is your spirit still around? Your body is on this ship with people who destroyed a Bleuh ship and murdered Bleuh patrols. I need time to make sense of things. Berella, spare me from this madness."

Celiba paused again. She took a hard look at Berella's body.

"Well, the funeral must go on at least," Celiba said.

Celiba sent a message, and four guards came and took Berella's body away.

Mariel, Larto, and Larbiabba sat in a holding room with a guard outside the door.

"Larbiabba, can't you help us?" Larto asked.

"I could space-jump like Lanshalla," Larbiabba said. "But I thought you'd much rather enjoy my company."

"We can't stay here," Larto said. "The penalty for murder is death."

"I know that," Larbiabba said. "I *have* studied the Bleuhs, you know. I'm aware of the law."

"Then why aren't you doing something?" Larto asked.

"You're welcome to space-jump yourself," Larbiabba said. "Or should I be like Mariel and kill off a few more Bleuhs? A few here, a few there. No big thing, right?"

"Larbiabba!" Mariel protested.

"Sorry. That wasn't fair," Larbiabba said.

"We need to find Treyu," Mariel said. "He could be in another cell."

"Larbiabba, go find Treyu. Report back," Larto said.

"Dishing out orders, Larto? Really," Larbiabba said.

"Larto, please," Mariel said. "Let's all take a deep breath and relax."

Just then, the door opened, and Treina entered. The door closed, and she transformed into Treyu. Treyu plopped down in a chair, exhausted.

"Boy, oh boy!" he said. "That Tiloto is annoying. Berella kept flirting with him to no end. How disgusting! Let's get out of this tin can and get on with Berella's funeral. I'm tired and want to go home!"

"Treyu!" Mariel said. "How did you get in here?"

"I walked in. Like you. A small pad you have. They said you were here resting. Well I hope you're done so we can go. I know *I'm* done," Treyu said.

"For your information, we're prisoners here," Larbiabba said.

"What? You're joking," Treyu said.

"They know our ship destroyed an Imperial Bleuh Patrol ship," Larbiabba said.

"Nice going, Larbimatic," Treyu said.

"It's not her fault," Mariel said. "It's yours!"

"Yeah!" Larbiabba said.

"Mine? No way!" Treyu said.

"It doesn't matter," Larto said. "We're prisoners here until we get a trial."

"*If* we get a trial," Larbiabba added.

Lanshalla appeared.

"Lanshalla!" the others except Treyu announced.

"Shh!" she replied.

"Where have you been? What have you been up to?" Larto asked.

"Learning things," Lanshalla said. "Bleuh patrol ships have surrounded this cargo ship. They are preparing to come aboard and take you all away."

"Let them," an exhausted Treyu said. "I'm tired of being Treina-the-pain-of-a-cranium."

"Can you help us?" Larto asked.

"I suppose there's always the baby option to kill off these Bleuhs," Lanshalla said.

"No! That will make this a ground zero for sure and start a full-scale war," Larbiabba said.

"Larbs, could you make doppelganger projections?" Lanshalla asked. "Just real enough to give us cover for escape?"

"I might, but how can we escape? I'm not as good as you at space-jumping, and the others can't do it at all. I doubt you can tote us away by yourself."

"Even if Lanshalla could, where would she take us? Treyu's ship is under heavy guard if we managed to reach it. How could we convince them to release us?" Mariel asked.

"Mariel is right. We need help from these people to escape," Larbiabba said.

Everyone looked at Treyu.

"What?" he asked.

"You've found favor with Tiloto," Larbiabba said.

"An overstatement," Treyu said.

"Hardly," Lanshalla said. "I watched him drool all over you."

"And it's a wonder I don't have a vermin disease," Treyu said. "What were you doing spying on us anyway? Are you a voyeur or something?"

"Checking on you. Making sure you stayed out of trouble," Lanshalla said.

"I was *in* trouble. I barely got away from him! Where were *you* to help *me*?" Treyu whined. "I'm tired of this all. Let them take us. This is a big mess anyway."

"*You* have to help *us*!" Mariel said. "*You* have to go after Tiloto more aggressively. Get special treatment for us through him."

"What?" Treyu whined further.

"I'm afraid Mariel is correct," Larbiabba said. "You'll have to negotiate for our release through your, *ahem*, feminine charm."

"I'm *not* being a woman again," Treyu said. "Too much stress. You be the woman, Mariel. Go after that Tiloto."

"I *am* a woman, and he favors *you*! He's got *you* in his *brain*. That's how the male mind *works*!" Mariel said.

"I know how the male mind works. It doesn't fixate on things. Look at me. Am I fixating on anything?"

"Yes. On being stubborn," Mariel said.

"That's enough!" Treyu said.

Treyu went after Mariel to choke her. Everyone else was shocked. Lanshalla and Larbiabba went eethi to stop Treyu, but it was Larto who grabbed Treyu by the shoulder and pushed him back just as Berella-the-vine went after Treyu's knees to trip him. Stunned and frightened, Treyu walked backward.

"I...don't deserve this," he said. "I'm just a butler. Just a butler."

Berella-the-vine pulled on Treyu's legs, and he collapsed backward into a chair.

"Did he hurt you, Mariel?" Larbiabba asked.

"No. The only thing hurt is his pride!" Mariel said with increasing volume so Treyu could hear.

"All right, all right," Larto said. "We're all a bit shaken here. Treyu, we're counting on you to help. If you don't, you condemn Mariel and me to certain death. Lanshalla and Larbiabba can escape. But then our plan for helping the rebels goes out the window."

"And your mother would be so disappointed with that," Mariel said sarcastically.

"My mother has proven she's more interested in saving Carinia 5 than 2," Treyu snarked.

Treyu brooded about his mother, muttering something about her neglecting him.

"Treyu, my friend. Please?" Larto asked in a soft voice.

"On one condition," Treyu said, referring to the act of flirting further with Tiloto. "When we get back to the vineyard, I get three bottles of the best wine from the Lonely Vine itself. Three bottles!"

"Deal," Larto said.

Treyu paused again.

"Do you need help? With the transformation?" Larbiabba asked.

"No," Treyu said. "Berella will provide all the assistance I don't want anyway."

The others smiled. Treyu rolled his eyes up, the vine moved around his neck, seemed to choke him, and he transformed into Treina with corsage. The vine released its grip on the throat, and Treina stood up.

"How do I look?" she asked.

"Enchanting," Mariel said.

"Slayer of men's hearts," Larbiabba said.

"Temptress of the ship," Lanshalla said.

"And you, Larto?" Treina asked.

"Best of luck, Berella," Larto said. "We're counting on you."

"Thank you," she said.

Treina exited the holding cell, flirting with guards on the way out.

"I'm heading out too," Lanshalla said.

"Wait!" Mariel said. "Where are you going?"

"To check on things and Treina's progress. Don't worry, Larbiabba will watch over you," Lanshalla said, and she space-jumped out of the holding cell.

"Lanshalla is providing telepathy," Larbiabba said.

"Oh, *now* she provides telepathy," Mariel said. "Where was she before?"

"Being careful," Larbiabba said. "This telepathy is very strange. It's like a muffled whisper. I can barely understand it. Lanshalla is watching Treina. Treina is back with Tiloto."

"If only we could see and hear," Mariel said.

"I think I can arrange that," Larbiabba said. "Lanshalla is now providing visual telepathy. I'll act as relay."

Larbiabba went eethi, extended one hand to the back of Mariel's head and the other to the back of Larto's head. Both Mariel and Larto could see and hear what Lanshalla saw and heard.

"Treina, I so missed you!" Tiloto said as Treina approached him.

The two stood in a large room with windows facing the docking bay and Treyu's ship.

"You look so neat and smart in your uniform," Treina said.

The room was busy, and people kept bumping into the two.

"Hey, watch it!" Tiloto said.

Just then, Celiba walked up.

"There you are," Celiba said. "May I have a word with you?"

"Gaze upon our glorious docking bay," Tiloto said. "I'll be but a moment."

Tiloto and Celiba stepped away from Treina.

"Don't let her out of your sight," Celiba said. "I have the others locked up, except for Lanshalla. She's still at large. Keep your eyes open and mouth shut. Rumor is the patrols now have spies on our ship. I've just heard that the Hierarchy is declaring martial law. If they find the Greyan ship here, they'll accuse us of collaborating."

Tiloto looked over at Treina. She looked back, lifted her lower leg backward at the knee, and winked.

"How can I part with her? She's become special to me," Tiloto said.

"I confess she has a magic charm," Celiba said. "She's so much like my Berella. Unfortunate I must commit Berella to permanent stasis myself."

"Then you won't let Treina's friends attend?" Tiloto asked.

"Can't. Again, we'd be accused of collaborating," Celiba said.

"And if they stay here, you'll be accused of collaborating," Tiloto said.

"We must get rid of them," Celiba said. "I'll have explosive charges rigged on the Greyan ship. We'll release them and tell them to meet us on Carinia 1 for Berella's funeral. The charges will detonate when they hit the ionosphere. Even if they betray us and go to another planet, they'll be destroyed upon hitting that planet's ionosphere. Problem solved."

"What about my Treina? I want to keep her," Tiloto said.

"Ask if she wishes to stay with us to help with Berella. If she agrees, then you may have her. I'll tell her they can't stay with us because it's too risky. That's the best I can do," Celiba said.

"That Celiba is a sellout," young Lanietta said. "Treating Treina like property."

"I'm happy to hear you speak," Claus said. "I was worried about you after those Bleuhs were killed."

"I guess I was too shocked to say anything," young Lanietta said. "Still am."

"Thank you!" Tiloto said.

Back in the holding cell, Mariel, Larto, and Larbiabba realized they were being set up.

"That solves the problem of how to get back to Treyu's ship," Larto said.

"But it gets us killed," Mariel said.

"We must find where precisely they will put the charges," Larbiabba said. "Lanshalla has already split herself so she can watch both Tiloto and Celiba. She is asking me to go eethi and watch the ship. It means you two will be without information for a bit, and you'll have to trust Lanshalla and me when the time comes."

"We have little choice," Larto said. "Proceed."

Larbiabba went eethi. Her ethereal self exited the cell, but it quickly returned to her physical body.

"There are ethereal detector lines everywhere," Larbiabba said. "I can't get through without tripping one or more of them."

"How did Lanshalla get through?" Larto asked.

Larbiabba paused for a moment while she communicated with Lanshalla telepathically. She nodded her head several times as she received Lanshalla's message.

"Lanshalla says she contorts her ethereal self into a thin rope and goes through the gaps," Larbiabba said.

"Can you do that?" Larto asked.

"I don't even know how Lanshalla is doing it," Larbiabba said. "She says she doesn't know either, she just does it. But I will try."

Larbiabba went eethi again. She tried stretching and rolling her ethereal self into the size of a rope, but it didn't work. Frustrated, she returned to her body.

"That hurts," she said. "I've let Lanshalla know I can't do it. She says to watch for her move."

"What move?" Mariel asked.

Larbiabba paused.

"Nothing. She's stopped communicating with me," Larbiabba said.

"We never should have trusted her," Mariel said. "She's abandoned us sure as anything."

"Have patience," Larbiabba said. "I'm sure she's very busy at the moment."

Back in the docking bay, Treina had no idea what plans were underway and still operated under the assumption that she needed to get Tiloto to take her on a trip in Treyu's ship.

"Tiloto," Treina started. "There are too many people around here. Why don't you and I find a little privacy? Let's sneak onto my ship!"

But Tiloto, aware that explosives were being placed on the Greyan ship, was hesitant.

"You really want privacy on a ship?" Tiloto asked.

"Oh yes! More than anything! Let's see the stars and pulse together like quasars," Treina said.

Tiloto grinned.

"Come with me," he said, and he led her by the hand.

The two walked over to an elevator, entered, Tiloto hit a button, the doors closed, and the two descended. Treina wrapped her arms around Tiloto and held him tightly. The elevator stopped, the doors opened, and Tiloto led Treina to a transfer hatch.

"We'll be there soon," he said.

They reached the end of the hatch and entered a ship.

"This...uh...isn't my ship," Treina said.

Tiloto waved his hands across the hatchway. The doors closed, and the ship took off as if by itself. The sudden jolt threw Treina into Tiloto's arms.

"Now I have you to myself," he said as the ship exited an opening from the cargo ship and traveled through space. "The ship is on autopilot. We'll circle around Carinia 1 in a polar orbit and watch the twilight ground below."

"That's wonderful," Treina said. "But first, allow me to freshen up."

Tiloto led Treina to a wash-up station. She blew him a kiss before going inside and closing the door. With the door closed, Treina sat on a chair in exhaustion and reverted to Treyu.

"What am I doing here?" he whispered to himself. "Stuck in this little room on a ship where I don't belong. How long can I hold out against this nightmare?"

There was a mirror. Treyu looked into it, and he could see his eyes tearing up.

"Don't need a stupid mirror to tell me I'm in a bad situation. Separated and stranded from the others. This is the end for sure," he whispered to himself.

At that moment, the mirror fogged over, and an image of Lanshalla appeared. She held a finger to her mouth indicating that Treyu should be quiet. She spoke such that only Treyu could hear.

"Fear not," Lanshalla said. "I am with you and watching you. Keep Tiloto occupied and stay in orbit. Do not let him land. We will all be together soon. I promise. Use Berella's spirit for help and strength. Until then."

Lanshalla's spirit disappeared. Treyu felt better, and he looked down to see the vine tickling his neck. He laughed softly. He looked up again at the mirror. The fog had cleared, and he had transformed back into a happy and cheerful Treina.

"All ready!" Treina said as she exited the wash-up room.

Tiloto took her into his arms and went from there.

Back on Celiba's ship, Lanshalla appeared in the holding cell with Larbiabba, Mariel, and Larto.

"Treina is on a ship with Tiloto," Lanshalla said. "And Celiba gave the order to place explosives on 'the Greyan ship', meaning Treyu's ship."

"To detonate upon ionospheric penetration?" Larbiabba asked to confirm.

"That was the order," Lanshalla said. "I wasn't able to see where they installed the devices. We've got to escape. We don't want to be caught dead on Treyu's ship. Let me go first. I'll draw the guards' attention."

"I know what to do," Larto said. "Let's do it."

Lanshalla space-jumped to just outside the door. She then walked down the corridor saying, "Yoo-hoo."

"Hey you!" one yelled.

"Get her," another yelled.

She darted away from them, and as she did, she sent an ethereal rope of her arm back to the cell door and activated the circuits. The door opened, and the three exited. Larto led the way, and he quietly slipped up behind trailing guards and knocked them into daze. The three caught up to Lanshalla, and they snuck around various unoccupied corridors.

"There's a shuttle in the lower bay we can take," Lanshalla said. "Follow me."

Lanshalla led the three to an elevator. They descended several levels, but when the door opened, there was Celiba speaking to a group of guards with her back to the elevator.

"Wrong floor!" Larbiabba said.

"Oops!" Lanshalla said as she repeatedly tapped a button to close the doors.

"Wait!" several guards said as they rushed toward the elevator.

Even Celiba had turned around in time to see the four trying to escape, and she pointed at them for the guards to recapture. The group reached the correct floor. Lanshalla went first while the three followed. A shuttle was a short ways in front of them, but guards flooded down stairwells and into the area. Lanshalla went eethi to stun several, but Celiba arrived and shot Lanshalla with an eethi-blaster gun. Lanshalla reintegrated and fell to the floor. Larbiabba was about to go eethi and attack.

"Don't try anything foolish, Larbiabba. Nor any of you," Celiba said. "Your run stops here."

"What are you going to do to us?" Mariel asked.

"Why nothing at all," Celiba said.

Lanshalla began regaining awareness. Larto and Larbiabba helped her up.

"Where's Treina?" Larbiabba asked.

"She's staying here to help prepare Berella's body," Celiba said. "The rest of you are free to go."

"Then why are we being held?" Larto asked, looking at the guards who still held his arms bound.

"Because you are leaving the way you came. On your ship. You will take your ship down to Carinia 1. Coordinates have been fed into your navi control. You may land there and attend Berella's Final Commitment, after which you may take Treina back with you, if she wishes. But that might be difficult. She and Tiloto are madly in love. She has a right to her own life. It's a free solar system, you know."

"So I've been told," Larto said with dismay.

"We will not keep you any longer," Celiba said.

She motioned to her guards, and they escorted the four to an elevator, where they were taken back to the docking bay with Treyu's ship. The four were escorted into the ship. The bay was cleared of people, the maw reopened, and an automatic signal was given to Treyu's ship. It departed into space and cleared away from Celiba's cargo ship.

"Now we must find the explosives," Larto said. "Mariel, can you take over piloting of the ship? And stay away from planets."

"No, we must head toward Treina's shuttle," Lanshalla said. "It's in polar orbit around Carinia 1."

"But that will bring us close to the ionosphere," Larto said. "Lanshalla, this is suicide."

"We'll be all right. I have a plan," Lanshalla said. "Larbiabba, I'll need your help, too."

"Let me guess. A space-jump?" Larbiabba said.

"Of course," Lanshalla replied.

"I can't do that kind of space-jump. Only you can. We'll be stranded on this ship when it explodes," Larbiabba said.

"Not if we stick together and I help. But you must help too, Larbiabba. You'll know when the time comes," Lanshalla said.

"Which will be very soon," Mariel said. "I've set navi control for Treina's shuttle. We'll be there shortly."

"Set it for automatic," Lanshalla said. "There, that's right. Now all of you—stand with me in the test lab."

The three followed Lanshalla into the test lab, the very place where Lanshalla had pioneered space-jumping.

"Form a line," Lanshalla said. "I'll lead. Larto, you stand behind me and place your hands on my hips. Mariel, you stand behind Larto and do the same. Larbiabba, you stand behind Mariel. We're forming an ethereal train. I'm the engine, and Larbiabba is the caboose. The rest of you are passengers."

The three assembled behind Lanshalla as instructed.

"Ready," Larbiabba said.

Lanshalla sent two ethereal ropes of herself back toward each side of the others and ending with Larbiabba, wrapping around her. In turn (and out of an eethi reflex), Larbiabba's ethereal self stretched thin and around the others, as if an eethi goddess had flattened her spirit and pulled

and stretched it around the others like plastic wrap. The ship approached Treina's shuttle and thus was dangerously close to Carinia 1's ionosphere.

"Oh, Treina," Tiloto said on the shuttle with Treina in his arms. "I never want to let you go. I'm going to give you a deep kiss and hug you and kiss you again."

Tiloto kissed Treina. But then without warning, Lanshalla, Larto, Mariel, and Larbiabba space-jumped in front of them. Tiloto turned to them in surprise and gave out a brief shriek. Tiloto saw a bright flash through the window as Treyu's ship exploded in Carinia 1's ionosphere. Tiloto gave out another brief shriek. He turned to Treina for comfort, but he now held Treyu in his arms, who waved at him.

"That's just like Alpharina," young Lanietta said. "The same trick. Like echoes in the ether from the distant past."

"It's true then. Things we think are original have in fact been done before," Claus said.

Tiloto gave out a horrendous shriek at this sight, fled from Treyu's arms, and ran wildly around the shuttle. After several runs around, Mariel clocked him on the head, and he fell into daze.

"What happened?" Treyu asked. "My ship! Destroyed!"

"No time for that," Lanshalla said as she ran to the ship's controls. "We're leaving the area before the Bleuhs discover we weren't aboard. We're dead as far as they know. Let's keep it that way."

Lanshalla worked the controls and headed for the pre-planned destination while Larto and Mariel dragged Tiloto to a chair and tied him down. Larbiabba assisted Lanshalla in ship control.

"Celiba is calling through the message board," Larbiabba said. "She's looking for Tiloto."

"Send a message expressing his love for Treina," Lanshalla said.

Larbiabba sent the message.

"Celiba is ordering Tiloto back to the cargo ship," Larbiabba said. "She says they need to get going. Too many patrols around."

"Message back that he's resigning, that he and Treina are starting a new life together," Lanshalla said just as Treyu entered the cockpit.

"I heard that," he said. "How disgusting."

"We're stalling for time, that's all," Lanshalla said. "We'll need to ditch this shuttle. And we can't take Tiloto with us, so he stays here."

"I can sabotage his short-term memory," Larbiabba said. "He won't remember us taking over."

"Do it!" Lanshalla said.

Larbiabba went back to Tiloto. Then Treyu's eyes lit up, and he made a move to follow.

"Where are you going?" Lanshalla asked.

"Maybe she can erase my short-term memory too!" Treyu said.

Lanshalla laughed and waved for him to go back.

Treyu was only gone for a moment when he returned.

"That was quick," Lanshalla said.

"Larbiabba said she can't erase my memory, that my ethereal self is too reclusive and too hard to reach," Treyu said.

"Ah, the Greyan eethi," Lanshalla said. "Like a turtle in the shell. I keep forgetting that everyone is not as boisterous and available as us Bleuhs. Well, perhaps in time we can—"

But Lanshalla had no chance to finish. A shot from a Bleuh patrol hit their shuttle.

"What time do we have?" Treyu asked as Larto and Mariel rushed in to see what was happening.

"None," Lanshalla said. "Everyone in the cargo area. It's time for another space-jump."

"But to where?" Mariel asked. "A patrol ship? We'll be captured."

"No time to explain. Off we go!" Lanshalla said.

Lanshalla rushed the others into a line like before, only Treyu was now part of the line. As before, Lanshalla led and Larbiabba trailed. Lanshalla space-jumped—again like before. The group left the ship and landed on the dark side of Carinia 1. The Bleuh patrol docked with the shuttle and found Tiloto bound to the chair. The patrol brought him to awareness and questioned him, but Tiloto could not remember how he got there nor anything about Treyu, Treina, or the others.

Chapter 81: Pleelellicans

Lanshalla, Larbiabba, Mariel, Larto, and Treyu materialized in the air about twenty feet above water. They fell to the water with a splash. They tread water to stay afloat and called for one another.

"We're all here," Lanshalla said. "Stop calling."

"I can't see a thing," Mariel said.

"It's pitch dark," Larto said.

"We're on the dark side of Carinia 1," Lanshalla said.

"You should have put us on the light side," Treyu said.

"Next time *you* do the space-jump," Mariel mocked.

"This was the best I could do," Lanshalla said.

"You did well, Lanshalla," Larto said. "We're alive and free thanks to you."

"Free, yes, but lost. What are we supposed to do now? Hope that...oh, something brushed by my leg," Treyu said.

"Mine too," Larto said.

"Something bit me!" Mariel said.

"Are you bleeding?" Larto asked.

"No. It was just a little nibble," Mariel said.

"Oh if only we had our equipment, Larbiabba," Treyu said. "We could create a holographic light or a boat. We have nothing!"

The five heard splashing like that of aquatic animals surfacing and going back down.

"There are creatures around us," Larto said.

"Get us out of here, Lanshalla!" Treyu said.

"Form a line. I'll see what I can do," Lanshalla said.

The five formed a line, but they were restless and fidgety from the aquatic creatures nibbling and brushing along. Lanshalla started to go eethi, but then thousands of screeches filled from all around as many more creatures surfaced and stayed on the surface. Lanshalla went for the space-jump, but a creature like a shark or dolphin swam through the line and broke it apart. Another swimming creature broke the line apart farther, and so on until all five were separated from one another. Each found themselves being punched and slapped in the face by little arms and hands from creatures no taller than a Carinian arm's length. These creatures, though not visible, rode atop dalphinacs, and they grouped together and amassed on each of the five. Mariel, Larto, and Treyu were quickly subdued and tied to the backs of dalphinacs while Lanshalla and Larbiabba fought the hardest. Larbiabba went eethi. She shocked many of these mini humanoids along with their dalphinacs while Lanshalla space-jumped around and drop kicked onto these creatures from the air. Her movements left faint trails of light, giving the others at least some ability to see in the darkness.

"There are too many of them!" Larbiabba called.

"Help us!" called the trapped three as they were being towed away.

"Let's form an ethereal dome," Lanshalla said.

"I don't know how," Larbiabba called back.

"Now's the time to learn," Lanshalla replied.

Lanshalla sent an ethereal line of herself to Larbiabba. This caused a reciprocal act by Larbiabba. The two sent lines back and forth and moved about with their ethereal selves in a way as if they were each holding on the end of a single rope and revolving around a common center. This act increased with speed such that they spun an inverted dome that was closed at the bottom but open at the top. The dome's dim glow provided hope to the five that they weren't so terribly isolated and vulnerable in the dark.

The dome's bottom was completely submerged while the top was far enough above the waterline that aquatic creatures could not jump over it. Lanshalla trilled her voice, and the ethereal dome sent out an eethi pulse that prevented anyone from leaving or entering. The dome was also large enough to hold the escaping dalphinacs that held Mariel, Larto, and Treyu prisoner. Lanshalla instilled Larbiabba to create a second dome slightly larger and concentric with the first. And so creatures were now caught in two areas—the inner dome, and the space between domes. The domes were connected at the top by a semipermeable eethi filter.

Creatures continued to attack Lanshalla and Larbiabba, but that was about to change. Lanshalla had an ethereal control line on the outer dome while Larbiabba had one on the inner.

"Now we begin the purge," Lanshalla said. "Hold the inner dome steady, Larbs."

Larbiabba held her dome at a constant size and shape while Lanshalla contracted her dome. This forced water and creatures up to the top and through the filter. The outer dome was slightly lower than the inner, and this combined with the fact the inner dome was curled outward at the top forced the water and creatures up and out, creating a fountain-like effect. Lanshalla relaxed her outer dome. It expanded and in doing so pulled in water from its outer edge but also pulled in creatures from the inner dome (the inner dome became semipermeable during this action). In this way, Lanshalla and Larbiabba were able to pump the creatures out of the inner dome, which freed up space in the inner dome and reduced the amount of cramped, frenzied attacks.

"Shrink your dome," Lanshalla called.

Larbiabba did just that. She shrank her dome, which caused those dalphinacs carrying Mariel, Larto, and Treyu to be brought toward the dome centers. Lanshalla kept her dome contracting and

expanding, and there came a point where the dalphinacs and creatures holding the three prisoners were pulled from the inner dome to the outer dome, but when Lanshalla contracted her outer dome, they were caught against the upper semipermeable layer that connected the two domes. The pressure was somewhat painful for all involved, but they remained stuck there until all other creatures were pumped out. The smooth fountain effect was interrupted in parts where the three blocked the outgoing water. Finally, when creatures not part of Mariel, Larto, and Treyu's abduction were flushed out, Larbiabba dropped her dome, and Lanshalla contracted her dome until the attackers were together and could be dealt with at once. Lanshalla turned her ethereal energy on what appeared to be the lead humanoid creature and held him above the water line.

"Stop, stop!" he pleaded. "You're crushing me!"

"I'll crush you to death if you don't call off this attack!" Lanshalla threatened.

The creatures squirmed and tried to get away, but Lanshalla squeezed her ethereal spirit around the humanoid's body even more, to the point where its face glowed first a dark red, then a lighter red, an orange, and then a bright yellow light.

"If I turn blue, I'll explode!" the creature said.

"Call off the attack, or I'll squeeze you all blue to your deaths!" Lanshalla ordered.

The held humanoid gave out a whistle. The other humanoids and dalphinacs stopped their fighting, allowing Mariel, Larto, and Treyu to escape capture.

"Please let us go!" the humanoid pleaded.

"Larbs, take over the dome," Lanshalla said.

Lanshalla passed her ethereal line to Larbiabba, and she now held the dome steady. Lanshalla created a smaller inverted dome that reached just slightly over the waterline.

"Order them into this dome," Lanshalla said to the humanoid.

He squirmed a little and tried to resist.

"Do it!" she said, now squeezing harder until he turned green.

"I will, I will!" he said. "At least let me go to yellow."

The humanoid ordered the little humanoids and dalphinacs into the small dome, and Lanshalla reduced the tension until he was only glowing yellow. Lanshalla then sealed the upper part of the dome, and she moved the dome through the wall of Larbiabba's dome. Once outside into the free water, Lanshalla let her dome dissolve, allowing the little humanoids and dalphinacs to escape.

"Everyone all right?" Lanshalla called.

The other four answered in the affirmative.

"What is your name?" Lanshalla asked the little humanoid.

"I am called Pepito," he said.

"I know what you are," Larbiabba said, suddenly remembering a Bleuhcheology class she'd taken. "You're a Pleelellican."

"Of course," Lanshalla said, now also remembering. "Nasty vile creatures that steal anything and everything if allowed. You're the rats of the sewer. You've long been exterminated from our cities and our sunlit zones."

"Then let this rat go!" Pepito begged.

"Not yet," Lanshalla said. "First, we need aid and rest."

"What?" Pepito said incredulously. "Am I your servan—"

But Lanshalla squeezed him into shades of green.

"All right, all right! I will help you! Please let me go back to yellow. To yellow!" Pepito pleaded.

Lanshalla released her grip.

"I will call for transport," Pepito said. "You will ride on the back of an orciniak. There is an island not far from here where you may rest."

"If you are lying..." Lanshalla said as she squeezed him green.

"I swear it's the truth!" Pepito said in pain.

"Very well," Lanshalla said, and she released him back to yellow.

Pepito panted. He called out with a whistle. A cetacean resembling an orca swam to the outer edge of the dome. This was the orciniak. Five Carinian-sized saddles were attached to it along with several Pleelellican saddles.

"Drop your dome, and this orciniak will take you," Pepito said.

"No, wait," Lanshalla to Larbiabba. "We'll do it my way. Larbs, hold your dome solid."

Lanshalla formed a dome outside Larbiabba's large enough to hold the orciniak. She created a semipermeable top to connect the two domes and contracted the outer dome, which forced water and other things out the top, but she kept a filter that would hold only the orciniak from exiting. As it turned out, a whole army of Pleelellicans and dalphinacs were forced out.

"So you would betray us and attack us again!" Lanshalla said with anger.

Lanshalla squeezed him, and he turned bright green. Goo oozed out of him, and he gagged on this goo.

"Stop it, please!" Mariel said, who turned away in disgust.

"I will spare you for Mariel's sake!" Lanshalla said, and she released tension until Pepito returned to a yellow color.

Pepito panted again.

"Don't ever try that again," Lanshalla said. "Or it will be the death of you!"

"Yes, I agree," Pepito said.

The five climbed aboard the orciniak. Lanshalla took the lead saddle and directed Larbiabba to take the last one. Larbiabba winked back as if reading Lanshalla's mind (actually she could, but telepathy wasn't needed in this case).

"These Pleelellicans will plea and flee if you're not careful," Larbiabba said.

"We don't have anything like them on Carinia 2," Mariel said.

"Because we don't generate the vast amounts of waste that Bleuhs do," Larto said. "Myth says they evolved from leftover Bleuh body parts cast into the sewers."

"It's no myth," Larbiabba said. "A blight on Bleuh history."

"You call us a blight?" Pepito said.

"Or perhaps what happened to you is a blight," Mariel said to Pepito.

"Both are true," Larbiabba said.

"Take us to the island," Lanshalla said while still holding Pepito.

Pepito gave a whistle, and the orciniak swam slowly.

"Move the dome with us," Lanshalla said to Larbiabba. "I'll move my dome too. We'll keep out anything we don't want."

The orciniak's swim somewhat resembled the gait of a walking horse.

"This is too slow," Lanshalla said. "Have the orciniak move more quickly."

Pepito gave out another whistle, and the orciniak moved more quickly as Lanshalla requested. In fact, it began porpoising with an up and down movement resembling a horse in a canter.

"I'm getting sick," Mariel said.

"Smooth out the gait," Lanshalla ordered Pepito.

Pepito gave one last whistle, and the orciniak kept a level swim along the water line while his flukes flipped up and down quickly in small strokes. All moved along quite quickly.

"The orciniak will tire soon. He cannot maintain this gait," Pepito warned.

"Let me help," Lanshalla said.

Lanshalla went eethi, sending eethi ropes back to Larbiabba much as the two had done when space-jumping. And that's what happened. The five, Pepito, and the orciniak space-jumped to a point just off the shore of the island Pepito had mentioned. Too close. The orciniak beached itself at speed and sent the five and Pepito flying through the air until they landed in the sand. Surprised by this, Lanshalla and Larbiabba dropped their dome barriers, and the barriers started to dissipate.

Lanshalla lost her grip on Pepito. He escaped. The orciniak struggled to get unbeached and back in the water. Pepito ran for the orciniak, jumped on it, and gave it an electric shock. The shock caused the orciniak to launch itself into the air and backward toward the water. It landed in the water and swam away under Pepito's direction.

"Well, he's escaped," Lanshalla said. "Unfortunately he'll warn the others."

"No he won't," Larbiabba said. "I erased his short-term memory."

"Indeed that comes in handy," Larto said.

Larbiabba smiled, but as she did, the last remnant of the dome barrier faded completely.

"Ugh, what is that smell?" Mariel asked.

The five looked ahead but could see nothing.

"It's pitch dark," Treyu said.

"No light," Larto said. "The domes gave us light, but they've disappeared."

"I don't need to see," Mariel said. "My nose tells me more than I want to know."

"It may at that," Larbiabba said.

"We should make for the smell," Lanshalla said.

"No way!" Mariel said.

"Wait a moment," Lanshalla said.

Lanshalla went eethi then went over to the smell to investigate. As she did, Larto clicked two pebbles together to give a crude sense of vision from the echo. Lanshalla returned and reintegrated.

"Is it a rock face?" Larto asked.

"I've never heard of stinky rock," Treyu said.

"Almost," Lanshalla said. "Follow me. Hold hands if you need to."

Lanshalla led the group toward the rock face, but Mariel stayed by the water and said, "No".

"Mariel?" Larto asked after hearing her by the shore and realizing she wasn't with them.

"I'm afraid of what we'll find. All kinds of nasty things alive and dead," she said.

"I must protest too," Treyu said. "Why are we bumbling about in the dark? Create an eethi torch and light up this island so we can see."

"And be seen," Larbiabba said.

"We will not light a torch," Lanshalla said. "Mariel, let me help."

Lanshalla walked over to Mariel, touched her, and invoked matter from the Greylinger rift. Lanshalla went eethi and circled her eethi self around Mariel very quickly, creating a crystalline environmental suit, complete with armor and air filtration system.

"This suit will protect you from any stray animals, and it will filter out the smell," Lanshalla said.

"Impressive," Claus said.

"My mother was far more advanced with eethi knowledge than I...I...I'm just a girl compared to her," young Lanietta said.

"I feel better already," Mariel said. "Let me try walking...oof!"

Mariel tripped with the armor and fell. It was a bit heavy for her to manage, and she struggled to aright herself. Lanshalla lifted Mariel to her feet.

"I'm all right now," Mariel said. "Takes a little getting used to. Wouldn't want to wear this all the time."

The five approached the rock face. Mariel's armor gave out a faint glow, and the others used the light to see the mysterious "rock face".

"Mariel's armor is like a torch. Lighting up the whole island," Treyu mocked.

"It's minimal. Fades in with the background," Larbiabba said.

"Hush up," Mariel said to Treyu.

"This isn't a rock face at all," Larto said.

"It's coral," Larbiabba said. "And this is a coral reef."

"But doesn't coral need water to survive?" Mariel asked.

"Yes, it does," Larbiabba said.

"How does it get to the water?" Treyu asked.

But at that moment, the four felt water on their feet. Mariel felt nothing since her suit protected her.

"What the..." Treyu said. "They've moved to the beach."

"No," Lanshalla said. "The beach has moved to us."

"That's impossible," Treyu said. "This planet is face-locked. It doesn't have a tide."

"Something is causing it," Larto said. "And if it continues, we'll be washed out to sea."

"Well at least we know how the coral gets water," Treyu said. "Not that it helps us any."

"Larbs, let's go eethi and see what's on the other side," Lanshalla said.

"All right, Shalli," Larbiabba replied.

Both went eethi, but neither could pass through the wall. They reintegrated immediately.

"We can't get through," Larbiabba said.

"Let me try a space-jump," Lanshalla said.

Lanshalla backed up and took a running start. The water slowed her, but that wasn't the main problem. She went eethi and still couldn't pass through the wall, and so her ethereal self bounced back into her physical body. The action caused her to hit the coral with her head. A coral creature lashed out and then stung her forehead.

"Ow," she said as she pulled herself away from the wall and removed the coral creature.

Waves rolled in, gentle at first, but increasing in height—first knee level, then waist level, and now chest level. The waves were powerful. They pulled the five out to sea a bit then crashed them up against the coral.

"We can't last long," Mariel said.

"We must climb the coral," Larto said.

Larto tried grabbing onto the coral after a wave had crashed him, but the coral broke away, a coral creature bit him, and the strong after-wave effect pulled him away from the reef.

"No good," he said.

"Can you get help from the Greylinger dimension?" Larbiabba asked.

"I've tried," Lanshalla said. "Something is interfering."

"If only we had rope!" Treyu said.

Then Berella in her vine form extended outward and grew into a lengthy thing. Using Treyu's mass as a base, it whipped itself upward along the reef until it reached the top and over the edge. The initial whipping effect temporarily pushed Treyu's body underwater, but the vine held fast onto an unknown object (for the moment) and pulled Treyu out of the water and up to the top of the reef. The vine secured Treyu onto a little shelf on the leeward side of the waves and then threw itself into the water and pulled up the others, one by one. Mariel was the first to be pulled up, followed by Larbiabba. Larto insisted that Lanshalla go next, but she held fast onto Larto, and so they both went up. The strain was a bit much for Treyu, and he felt the vine constricting his body like a boa. His head felt ready to explode, but when the two reached the top, the vine released the strain, and Treyu nearly fell into deep daze from the sudden blood pressure drop.

"Thank you, Berella," Lanshalla said.

"Thank you," the others except Treyu said.

The vine went around Treyu's neck and choked him.

"Yes, thank you, thank you!" he gargled.

The vine released its grip and returned inside his shirt.

"Whew!" Treyu said.

"What's wrong, Treyu?" Larto asked. "Afraid to show a little gratitude?"

"I'm afraid to say much of anything anymore," Treyu said. "I feel like I'm joined at the hip with Berella."

"More like joined at the neck," Larto said.

"Look everyone," Mariel said. "The sky is different."

Indeed. The sky above the island inside the coral (which itself acted as an island perimeter) glowed green, like light reflecting off the eyes of a cat.

"It's green," Treyu said.

"Impressive," Larbiabba said.

"But is it really that green and that bright?" Larto asked. "I mean, Bleuhs should have detected it."

"I don't think so," Lanshalla said. "We would have known about it. The Imperial Bleuh Patrol knows about lit societies, and I never knew about this one. Unless...hmm. I wonder if this is known but kept secret."

"Must be an ethereal shield over the island," Larbiabba said. "Absorbs energy from outside and shines green light on the inside. Interesting that it's green."

"Yes," Larto said. "Bleuhs pride themselves on a blue society. This seems almost Gren-ish."

"No Bleuh would admit it, but not everything is perfect on Carinia 1," Larbiabba said.

"Just nearly perfect," Lanshalla said.

Larto frowned.

"Except it's missing my Larto," Lanshalla said as she hugged him.

"At some point Lanshalla and I will have to stop these adventures and have our children," Larbiabba said.

"But not yet!" Lanshalla grinned. "Larbs, try going eethi now."

Lanshalla and Larbiabba both successfully went eethi and then returned to their bodies.

"It's the coral reef," Larbiabba said. "Incredible. It must be an ethereal rift unto itself. Or perhaps the coral themselves have great ethereal power. Can you travel above the green sky?"

Lanshalla went eethi, went up a little ways but could not get through the green glow. She returned and reintegrated.

"No, I cannot. Definitely an ethereal construction. I could learn much about this society. I can feel it. I'm going to explore ahead. Stay here and wait with the others, Larbs. I'll send telepathy," Lanshalla said, and she space-jumped away.

Larbiabba paused as she concentrated.

"She's in," Larbiabba said.

"In what?" Treyu asked.

"In the village," Larbiabba said. "Incredible. Just incredible. Who would have guessed it? Larbs, can you tell the difference? I mean, like how? Interesting. I'll have to try that. Yes, it could fit into our plan. But can we convince them?"

"You can try convincing us first," Treyu said. "What are you two talking about?"

"If it could work. I don't think it's possible," Larbiabba continued with the distant Lanshalla. "That's true, she's a Bleuh too. Yeah. Yeah. I see no other way. All right, return and we'll do it."

"Do what?" Treyu asked.

"I must agree with Treyu," Larto said. "You have us bewildered."

Larbiabba went eethi, extended an ethereal hand toward Treyu, and touched the vine. The vine shook briefly as if purring. Larbiabba reintegrated.

"Berella understands," Larbiabba said. "I've tied her in with Shalli's telepathy. You should be able to receive news now too, Treyu."

Treyu was about to say something, but he paused.

"I can't do it," he finally said. "We Greyans don't like mass reduction."

"Have you ever tried?" Larbiabba said. "Could be a revolutionary way of helping the rebels, if we survive."

"If we survive?" Mariel asked.

Lanshalla returned.

"Call it off," Treyu said. "Call it all off. No way is this a good idea by any stretch of the imagination. Berella will take us back out. We can swim out to sea, and you can space-jump us back to civilization. Come along, Berella."

Treyu stood by the coral reef wall, and he patted his chest. But the vine made no effort to exit his shirt, much less climb up the wall.

"Berella? Let's go!" he urged.

"Berella is with us," Lanshalla said.

"How do you know?" Treyu asked.

"She told me so telepathically," Lanshalla said. "Good link, Larbs. Okay, listen up everyone. The Pleelellicans have a village not far from here. Very unusual village. More like a town or city, actually. The buildings are quite unique. You'll see in a moment. They are preparing for games in a stadium. We should go and intermingle. Now here's the thing—we're bigger than they are. But with Larbs's and Berella's help, we can shrink us down to their size with a special kind of space-jump. I've already checked, and I'll use waste Greylinger energy to give us Pleelellican features. We'll fit in. It's important we learn about them. There's something else, too. I think there are artificial Pleelellicans roaming about."

"If true, we now have two ways of creating our own artificial life-forms— borrow Pleelellican technology, or the method by procreation tanks," Larbiabba said.

"To take from others. Seems like a crime," Larto said. "If only we could leave other societies in peace."

"If we don't take advantage of this society, another Bleuh will," Lanshalla said.

"Is that all? I mean, it's just the control and plunder of other people," Treyu said unhappily.

"Do we know for sure that these Pleelellicans have created artificial life-forms?" Larto asked.

"I don't see how else creatures can walk around without ethereal spirits. Unless something evil is afoot. You'll see soon," Lanshalla said. "All right, everyone, let's get in line. I'll be first, followed by Larto, Treyu, Mariel, and Larbs. I'll pair off with Larto, Treyu you're already paired with Berella, and Larbs will pair with Mariel. We're going to space-jump and transform into Pleelellicans, or at least close imitations."

Everyone lined up as instructed. Treyu was hesitant, but Berella in her vine state sent endorphins through Treyu's body, and he relaxed.

"Ready," he said in his tranquilized state.

"Go!" Lanshalla said.

The five space-jumped, shrank, and took on gill and fin features like the Pleelellicans. Mariel, however, retained her armor suit (Lanshalla was able to shrink that as well). The group landed outside a stadium, where many Pleelellicans walked about. Some headed toward the stadium, but others negotiated with scalpers for tickets. The five looked around and realized that surrounding buildings very much resembled cetaceans.

In fact, one such building was under construction. A crane lowered a dead whale-like creature in place with skeleton and skin, but it had already been gutted and fitted with windows, doors, and rooms.

The five walked a bit toward the stadium, and they reached a point where the ground was stained. On this stained ground, Pleelellicans knelt and patted the stain for good luck. Others gambled with an assortment of games using dice, cards, and spinning wheels.

"Strange," Larto said. "I wonder what's so special about this ground?"

"It's holy ground!" said a scalper approaching the five. "Much good luck has come by touching such blessedness. Oh, and I see one of the royals is with you."

The scalper motioned toward Mariel. Mariel looked at herself.

"The armor?" she said softly, but the scalper did not hear her.

"Do you have tickets for the event?"

"No," Mariel said.

"I can cut you a great deal. The best deal of all time for a royal and friends of a royal!" said the scalper. "I can give you seats at the very top!"

"And be that far away? We might as well be on Carinia 2," Mariel played along.

"Oh no, my dear. With these seats, you'll be able to see the action both in front of you, to the sides, and behind. Who can boast such a vantage point? No one, I tell you, because Vebenni here always gets the best deals and always makes people happy," Vebenni said.

Larbiabba went eethi and tried inspecting Vebenni's ethereal spirit. But he had none.

"Wow," Larbiabba said to Lanshalla telepathically.

"You can't tell just by looking?" Lanshalla asked.

"No. You'll have to explain later," Larbiabba said.

"How much?" Treyu asked.

Mariel slapped him.

"Treyu's bad behavior will be corrected," Mariel said.

Vebenni approached Mariel and kissed her armored hand. He then placed the tickets in her other hand.

"I would be honored if you would have me as a guest," Vebenni said.

"Careful, Your Highness, he's liable to get special favors from you," Lanshalla laughed.

"You may sit with me for as long as the mood fits," Mariel said with a mock uppity tone.

"She's playing the role well," Larbiabba to Lanshalla telepathically.

"Now dust off my Royal Armor as a sign of your loyalty," Mariel said.

Vebenni dusted off her armor while Lanshalla and Larbiabba giggled. Treyu looked on in horror as Larto nodded his head that Mariel his maid finally got someone else to do the work.

"You may lead the way," Mariel said.

Vebenni shouted to everyone to clear the way as he created a path for Mariel to walk. Behind Mariel walked Lanshalla, Larbiabba, Larto, and Treyu.

"A maid is first while a butler is last? This can't last!" Treyu complained.

"Keep your eyes focused on everything around us," Larto said. "We must be prepared to move in case of danger."

"Danger, *shmanger*," Treyu muttered to himself. "Why didn't I stay on Carinia 5? Nice frozen planet with no stress. Should never have left nor agreed to help rebels. Peace and quiet. But no more. I'm here on Carinia 1 in this strange place of *little gill people*."

The vine stretched out and patted Treyu on the shoulder for comfort.

"Thank you, Berella. At least someone understands," Treyu said.

Vebenni led the group into the stadium. The stadium was oval shaped and had a middle section with rows and seats. Around this middle section was a race track, and on the outer wall of the race track was more seating with the exception of one wall that was next to a bay. The group climbed the middle section until they reached the top, where they looked around.

"They could hold races in this thing," Larto said. "Imagine. They would race around and around this center section."

"We have many such races," Vebenni said. "And there are prizes for the winner."

"What kind of prizes?" Lanshalla asked.

Vebenni lowered his voice.

"They say the winners get real souls," he said.

Lanshalla laughed.

"And just what is a *real* soul?" Larbiabba asked.

"Those of us who don't have one, get one. Those who have one get a better one," Vebenni said. "I had a soul once. Once..."

His voice trailed. Lanshalla sent a telepathic message to Larbiabba and Berella/Treyu, saying, "I was wrong. Vebenni isn't an artificial life-form, he's a soulless life-form."

"We like our souls just fine, thank you very much," Larbiabba said.

Without warning, Vebenni touched Lanshalla's and Larbiabba's abdomens. The two felt electric shocks.

"Here now, stop that!" Lanshalla said, pulling away.

"What are you doing?" Larbiabba said, also pulling away.

"Oh...you are both with child," Vebenni said.

"Vebenni shocked me," young Lanietta said. "The first attack against me. Even Mommy couldn't protect me. By a Pleelellican, too. Did he want my soul?"

"I'm glad he failed," Claus said.

Four Pleelellican ushers approached the group.

"We have special seats for those expecting children," one usher said.

"No thank you. We'll both stay here," Lanshalla said.

"We insist. The altitude is a danger to all unborn," the usher said.

"These two will stay with me," Mariel said.

"It's all right. We'll go," Lanshalla said.

"Lanshalla, are you sure? Might be better to stick together," Larto said.

"I want to see this new seating place," Lanshalla said. "Besides, Larbs and I can take care of ourselves."

Lanshalla winked.

"Very well," Mariel said to the usher. "I release them to your care."

"I don't like the ushers," young Lanietta said. "Stadium altitude doesn't affect the unborn like that."

Lanshalla and Larbiabba left with the ushers, and they were gone. The vine fidgeted under Treyu's shirt just below the collar line, but Treyu patted that spot to quiet Berella.

"Shh," Treyu said. "Don't worry."

Vebenni shot Treyu a funny expression.

"Indigestion," Treyu replied.

"Oh, I've forgotten my manners!" Vebenni said. "May I offer you three refreshments? We have the best you know. Fresh from the sea."

"You may cater to us," Mariel said.

"Thank you!" Vebenni said, and he strode off.

"Sir, Berella is shaking like a leaf," Treyu said. "She's absolutely scared for Lanshalla and Larbiabba."

"I trust Lanshalla. She's gotten us out of worse situations," Larto said.

"That's just it," Treyu said. "Berella is convinced this *is* a worse situation."

"Why is she so scared?" Mariel asked.

"There's something wrong with the ether here," Treyu said. "She says it's being controlled. Normal ether is free and unimpeded. But something is—"

"A royal treat for royalty!" Vebenni said as he returned with a platter of food and drink.

Vebenni also carried an X-shaped collapsing stand. With the skill of a waiter, he whipped open the X-stand and placed it on the ground in front of the seats (and closest to Mariel). The food was definitely seafood—shrimp, oyster, seaweed, lobster, and nectar to drink.

"Sit next to me, Vebenni. Enjoy yourself," Mariel invited.

"Thank you indeed!" Vebenni said.

"You may call me Countess Mariel," she said.

"Oh brother," Treyu said.

"Hush now, my loyal subject!" Mariel said, staying within royal character. "Vebenni, please dust off my armor. Particles from nearby chatter are dulling my shine."

"Yes, at once!" Vebenni said.

"Now I'm particle and chatter," Treyu said to Larto. "This is going to her head."

"Let it be for now," Larto said. "Keep your wits about. We must be ready to act."

"You said that before," Treyu said. "What do you mean?"

"I don't know...yet," Larto said.

Meanwhile, ushers led Lanshalla and Larbiabba to a dimly-lit passageway with a closed door at the end.

"Your seats are through that door," an usher said.

"What if we—" Larbiabba said.

"Through the door," the usher said.

"Come on, Larbs," Lanshalla said, then she lowered her voice. "It's probably filled with screaming children. We'll sneak out after a bit."

The two went through the door.

"Hey, where are the seats?" Lanshalla asked.

The two stood by a wall. Larbiabba turned around to reiterate Lanshalla's question to the ushers, but the door was closed and locked.

"Well this is a strange area in front of us," Lanshalla said. "There are no Pleelellicans."

The two walked out and realized they were in the middle of the race track. Spectators in the stands cheered as they saw the two on the track. Mariel, Larto, and Treyu heard the spectators cheering and looked in the direction they were pointing.

"Oh, no!" young Lanietta said. "Mommy! What are you doing with me inside? Mommy!"

"What are they doing down there?" Larto said in surprise.

"Vebenni," Mariel said. "Why are my friends on the race track?"

"Try this dalphinac meat. It's especially tasty," Vebenni said, trying to distract them.

A flood of Pleelellicans was released onto the track. They began a mad race counterclockwise (as viewed looking down). In a few seconds they would trample Lanshalla and Larbiabba.

"They're going to trample us!" Lanshalla said.

"Space-jump us out of here!" Larbiabba said.

Lanshalla held onto Larbiabba and tried to space-jump, but nothing happened.

"Can't!" Lanshalla said. "Let's go eethi and stun them."

But the two couldn't go ethereal either.

"Not working," Lanshalla said.

"I have a suggestion," Larbiabba said. "Run!"

The two ran for the door and beat on it, but it wouldn't open nor would anyone open it.

"We're in the race!" Larbiabba exclaimed as the two ran from the door and kept just ahead of the pack.

"Why are they running down there?" Treyu asked Larto.

"Something's wrong," Mariel said.

"They can't escape, that's what's wrong!" Larto replied.

"Those Pleelellicans set up this whole thing!" young Lanietta said in anger. "Oh! I would destroy them all if I could!"

"Is it likely they were destroyed with the Carinians?" Claus asked.

Young Lanietta paused.

"Probably," she said. "At least the ones with souls. That means Pleelellicans like Vebenni who are soulless might yet survive. But those are the most evil! Not fair!"

Larto jumped out of his seat, ran down the aisle of steps, and was about to leap over the railing onto the race circuit when a gargantuan squid-like creature arose from the water, spilled over the outer stadium wall from the bay, and landed on the race track. The creature had thick tentacles like hydra, each head with jaws of baleen, both upper and lower jaws, and these baleen overlapped inward, acting as filters or scissors. Startled, Larto held his ground. One such baleen head went for Larto, but he ducked as the head inhaled, and the head instead sucked in several Pleelellicans behind him. These Pleelellicans were caught in the baleen while the head continued to inhale. It pulled out the ethereal spirit of the Pleelellicans, the ethereal spirits were sliced up as they passed through the baleen, and when it was all done, the Pleelellicans were spit out into the stands, where they wandered around aimlessly. Larto nearly lost his balance but stopped from falling into the race track.

The creature continued its rampage around the track. For those Pleelellicans who had no eethi spirits, the creature kept inhaling and inhaling in a desperate effort to pull out any bit of ethereal spirit, but the hapless and soulless Pleelellicans felt skin and flesh stripped off in the most painful manner until their bones were pulled through the baleen, at which point the creature's head spat the Pleelellican remains over the outer wall where such remains landed on the circle outside the stadium, the circle of blood and guts that earlier Pleelellicans had worshiped as holy ground.

"That creature is a facade for Greylingers!" young Lanietta said. "I was repeatedly exposed to evil from the very beginning!"

"You must save my friends!" Mariel said as she choked Vebenni.

"Please! You're hurting me!" Vebenni said.

"Because my friends are in trouble!" Mariel said.

"I...can't...do a thing!" Vebenni said as he struggled for air through his gills.

Mariel dropped Vebenni. She grabbed Treyu by the arm and dragged him down the aisle to help Larto.

"There's nothing we can do," Treyu said.

"You sound like Vebenni," Mariel said.

"If only we had weapons," Larto said.

Berella-the-vine extended herself quickly from Treyu's shirt, forked, grabbed hold of a railing post, pulled it apart, and returned it to Treyu. Treyu stared at the post as if unsure what to do with it, but

Larto grabbed the post and hopped onto the race track (and thus onto the field of battle).

"He's going to kill himself," Treyu said.

Then Mariel jumped over the railing to help out.

"*She's* going to kill herself," Treyu said.

Berella-the-vine pulled Treyu over the railing and onto the racetrack as Treyu remarked, "And I'm going to *die!*"

With the squid creature on the rampage, Lanshalla and Larbiabba led the Pleelellican stampede around the track. Larto caught up to the squid and beat on it with the post, but the squid simply took Larto up on its mouth and started to inhale. Larto beat on its baleen in hopes of breaking it. He then propped open the mouth with the post and jumped down. The head swayed and whipped around in an effort to throw off the post, but the post stayed firmly in its mouth.

Meanwhile, another part of the squid caught Larbiabba and lifted her up in the air. Lanshalla attempted to go ethereal and space-jump again, but of course that did not work. She ran for the base of the creature to scratch out its eyes, but another head on the end of a tentacle grabbed hold of Lanshalla and lifted her in the air.

"It's lifting us in the air, Claus," young Lanietta said. "I am powerless. Powerless!"

"You called me Claus," Claus said. "Not Clomper."

"That seems so distant," young Lanietta said. "Like another person or life."

"And yet this vision is billions of years ago, far more distant than when I was considered your pet," Claus said.

"The word 'pet' is alien to me," young Lanietta said.

"You may call me Clomper if you like," Claus said. "Anything to help you regain yourself."

Young Lanietta looked at Claus as if he were speaking a foreign language.

"I do not know 'Clomper'," she said.

Mariel ran for the base and also tried scratching out the squid's eyes. A tentacle went after her, but Mariel moved around the squid's base to avoid the tentacle while all along she beat and pounded on that base. The creature lifted its center and threw Mariel off. In the course of movement, the creature landed its full weight on Mariel, crushing her.

Treyu tried to get away, but Berella-the-vine forced his legs to run toward the creature's base, especially after seeing how the creature crushed Mariel. A tentacle went after Treyu, and Berella-the-vine lassoed the tentacle and flung Treyu onto the back of the tentacle.

So we had Treyu riding a tentacle, Larto looking around for another weapon while his attacking tentacle head struggled with the post in its jaw, and a tentacle each still had Lanshalla and Larbiabba. Other tentacles continued pulling ethereal spirits and digesting them. The ones holding Lanshalla and Larbiabba started pulling their ethereals through their baleen jaws. Lanshalla and Larbiabba each stood with their feet on the lower jaws while their hands pushed on the upper jaws.

"I see my unborn self being stretched and tortured by this creature!" young Lanietta said. "I've been violated in the most extreme manner! Claus! I'm damaged! Claus!"

Claus gave a look of support to young Lanietta. He wanted to hug her, but he knew that was impossible.

"Everyone deserves safety," Claus said.

"But for how long?" young Lanietta said. "How long can innocence last? When does a person become the property of another? Of a society? Why can't me be me, unstained and free?"

"I'm going eethi against my will," Larbiabba said.

"Me too," Lanshalla said.

"I'm getting tired," Larbiabba said.

"Also me too," Lanshalla said.

"We can't keep this up," Larbiabba said.

"No, we can't," Lanshalla said.

"Shalli? It's pulling on my baby's ethereal spirit," Larbiabba said.

"It's pulling on mine too," Lanshalla said. "And it's making me mad. I..."

"You can't do the baby option with this...thing," Larbiabba said.

"I have to do something," Lanshalla said.

"Claus! Labba was affected too!" young Lanietta said.

"Therein lies your answer," Claus said. "Of all the Carinians to survive the PRAAD's mass extinction event, Labba is your best ally. Have you ever discussed this with her?"

"I never knew! And she never mentioned it," young Lanietta said.

"I'd say you have something to look forward to. You two have much to discuss and share. Perhaps through that sharing you two can reach something," Claus said.

"But what? Shared misery?" young Lanietta asked.

"Shared. That in itself is something," Claus said.

"Not good enough!" young Lanietta said. "We can't even retaliate! How does one repair scars as caused by the no-longer existent?"

Berella-the-vine followed her commandeered tentacle down to the base, where it wrapped itself around the main head.

"Can we use Mariel's trick to kill it?" Larbiabba asked.

"Already tried. Doesn't work," Lanshalla said.

Berella's grip around the base head caused the entire creature to screech and lash violently in pain. The head with the post crushed that post and knocked Larto aside violently. Treyu was thrown clear by his tentacle. Berella-the-vine had separated from him and remained constricted around the squid's base like a boa constrictor. In desperation, the squid leapt up over the wall and back into the ocean, carrying Lanshalla, Larbiabba, and Berella-the-vine with it.

A few seconds after it had submerged, a chrysalis shot upward out of the water over the outer stadium wall and onto the race track. Track workers ran to the chrysalis, lifted it, and rushed it through a special doorway. Larto shook his head to unstun himself. He looked around and saw Treyu not far away.

"Treyu?" Larto called. "Treyu!"

"Over here," Treyu said.

"Did you see Mariel?" Larto asked.

Treyu pointed with dismay to an indentation in the ground. Larto rushed over, and Mariel's armor was flush with the track surface.

"Crushed," Larto said.

"No, not yet," said Mariel as she climbed out of the indentation with her armor crumbling off her.

"Mariel!" Larto said as he helped her stand.

"The armor worked well—while it lasted," she said. "I have a bruise here and there."

"No broken bones?" Treyu asked, rushing over once he realized Mariel was alive.

"I know that disappoints you," Mariel said.

"It doesn't," Treyu said. "I'm relieved to see you are well."

"Lanshalla and Larbiabba. Did either of you see them? Were they pulled into the water with that...that...creature?" Larto asked.

"Lanshalla, Larbiabba, and Berella were caught up in that *thing*," Treyu said. "They are *gone!*"

Larto started to make for the outer wall where the squid disappeared.

"We must find them," Larto said with his back to Treyu and Mariel.

"But how?" Treyu asked.

"Do you still have a link with Berella?" Larto asked, then he turned around and repeated the question. "Do you?"

"No," Treyu said. "I lost the link when she...the vine...when Berella went off with the creature."

At that moment, Vebenni ran down.

"Hurry, hurry!" Vebenni urged.

"What? What is it?" Mariel asked.

"You must hurry at once! Hurry!" Vebenni urged.

Larto, Treyu, and Mariel followed Vebenni through a set of doors (now unlocked and open) off the racetrack, through a passageway, and up several flights of stairs.

"You rescued Lanshalla and Larbiabba?" Larto asked with excitement as the group neared the top of the stairwell.

"And Berella too? She would be but a vine to you," Treyu said, also with excitement.

"Better," Vebenni said.

The group reached the top of the stairs and exited a door to a platform near where they had only moments ago been sitting. On the platform stood three winners of the race. A royally decorated man stood close to the three winners. An assistant dipped a collar band into an opened chrysalis (the same chrysalis retrieved from the creature earlier) and handed the collar to the royally decorated man. The man placed the collar band around the neck of the first-place winner. A glow emanated from the collar and spread over the Pleelellican. It was an ethereal spirit from a former Pleelellican. The first-place winner, who had lost his ethereal spirit in a prior race, was overjoyed at regaining this new one. He took a deep breath and exhaled with exhilaration.

The award ceremony continued, much to the shock of Larto, Treyu, and Mariel.

"It's a symbiotic relationship between Greylingers and Pleelellicans mediated by the creature," young Lanietta said.

"Sickening," Claus said.

"But where are my friends!" Mariel insisted.

"Who are you?" the royally decorated man asked.

"She is...uh...you don't know her?" Vebenni asked.

"Intruders," the royally decorated man said to his guards. "Arrest them!"

Chapter 82: The Doctor

"In you go!" said a guard as Larto, Mariel, and Treyu were escorted into a cell.

"We're not your enemy," Larto said as the guard closed the door on the three.

"Invaders always feign friendship," the guard said, and he walked away.

"Libriota," young Lanietta said. "You're thinking about how she feigned friendship when you first met her."

"Yes," Claus said. "Lady Liberty. Another *facade*."

Young Lanietta returned a weak smile.

"Well, here we are prisoners again," Larto said.

"But no Larbiabba and no Lanshalla," Mariel said.

"Not to mention my Berella," Treyu said.

"Has she completely detached from you?" Larto asked.

"Yes," Treyu said.

"Are you sure? My nose tells me the vine is near," Larto said.

"She's gone, yes, gone! I had no choice. It was like something took her over and forced her onto that squid," Treyu said. "And now she is lost!"

"Along with the others," Larto lamented. "I should have known better."

"What an evil trap these Pleelellicans set!" Treyu said. "I claim full right of vengeance. We must break out of here and...Mariel, what are you doing?"

"Cleaning," Mariel said as she dusted off the furniture and shelves. "This place is a mess!"

"We're trapped in this worm hole, and she's dusting!" Treyu said.

A visitor stood by the locked door and rattled it slightly as if to knock.

"Treyu, answer the door," Mariel said.

"What?" Treyu asked in surprise.

"You *are* the butler, after all," Mariel said.

"I don't believe it. Has she lost her mind?" Treyu asked Larto.

"I'll go," Larto said. "Watch over Mariel."

"I need to close my eyes is what I need to do," Treyu said. "I wish Berella could sedate me."

"You mean seduce you," Mariel said.

"Sedate," Treyu reiterated.

"Seduce!" Mariel countered.

"Enough!" Larto said back to them before answering the door. "May I help you?"

"My name is Varba. I'm Vebenni's sister," the woman said. "I heard there was a vine with great healing power here. I have an ailment. My—"

"This is not a hospital!" Treyu mouthed off, getting excited.

"Treyu, please!" Mariel said.

"It isn't!" he reiterated, and he took a metal prison cup and clanged it around as he said, "This is a prison cell. See? This is my cup. Hear how it clangs on the bars! On the walls! And the floor! A prison, do you hear?"

"I hear!" Varba wailed. "I hear too well! Stop that, please! You're hurting me! I came for treatment of sensitive ears!"

Treyu was about to clang his cup again, but Larto stopped him. Then Mariel came over to the door, subtly unlocked it by apparently just touching the lock, opened the door, invited Varba in, and closed the door behind gently. Larto and Treyu looked on in shock when they realized Mariel had the ability to unlock the door. In fact, Treyu dove for the door to stop it from closing but was too late. It latched and locked. Treyu fell onto the floor with a racket.

"Shh!" Mariel said to Treyu. "Don't you see Varba is in pain? Come along over here, Varba, and rest! I've found hot water and tea in this corner. The tea has soothing herbal properties that will help you relax."

"Mariel! The door!" Treyu yelled, but Varba cringed in pain.

"Shh!" Mariel repeated. "Spare your shouting for the dogs!"

Treyu was livid and wanted to shout again. Larto, however, walked over to Mariel and watched as she touched Varba's ears. Then Larto saw what looked like a shadow going into Varba's ears. The shadow passed.

"Better?" Mariel asked.

"Yes, much!" Varba said, and she gave Mariel a hug. "You're a miracle worker. Once everyone else finds out about you and the vine—"

"The vine?" Larto said. "I thought I could smell it. But Treyu said it was gone. You, Mariel?"

"Just a little, and only on my fingertips," Mariel said.

"That's how you unlocked the door," Larto said.

"Yes, a bit of Berella picked the lock. And she healed Varba," Mariel said. "She also helped make tea."

"Hah!" Treyu yelled. "We should be escaping but are instead making tea!"

"Do not underestimate the healing power of good herbal tea!" Mariel retorted.

After Treyu and Mariel had shouted these words, Mariel looked at Varba with a quizzical facial expression, as if to say, "Can you tolerate the shouting?"

"Yes, yes I can tolerate the shouting!" Varba said. "Thank you again. I—"

Before Varba could finish, another woman stood at the door.

"I'm Galeena," she said.

"Treyu, show her in," Larto said.

"I'm not a butler...er...this isn't the right place to butler...er...I can't even open the door!" Treyu fumbled.

"Thank you again," Varba said. "Hi Galeena. One moment."

Varba walked over to the cell door, opened it, let Galeena in, and let herself out. Varba waved and was gone.

"How did Varba open the door?" Treyu asked.

"A part of the vine is in her fingertips," Mariel said. "Don't worry, Treyu. The vine implement in Varba is temporary. Her cure is permanent."

"My Berella!" Treyu protested.

"Would be happy to help others!" Mariel answered. "Come over here, Galeena, and make yourself at home. Won't you have hot tea?"

"Tea, tea, tea!" Treyu protested. "We need to flee, flee, flee!"

"I have this pain. Low in my stomach," Galeena said.

"Let's take a peek," Mariel said.

Mariel touched her abdomen down low, and a shadow of the vine scanned Galeena for abnormalities.

"It's serious," Mariel said. "You have a tumor."

Galeena fell into tears, repeating that she'd die.

"No, no, my dear. Be at peace. We'll fix you right up in a snap," Mariel said.

Another woman appeared at the door.

"Let yourself in. I'll be with you in a moment," Mariel called.

"Let yourself in?" Treyu called in surprise to Larto. "How is it these women can open a locked door?"

The woman opened the door and entered.

"See?" Treyu said, but he caught the door before it latched. "Well, I'm not sticking around in this mockery. Even now, Mariel is performing surgery to remove a tumor. No! I'm escaping!"

Treyu was about to exit the cell, but Larto caught his arm.

"No, you stay here and watch over Mariel," Larto said.

"What?"

"I'll go and find out things. We shouldn't be too hasty. We could be caught and done in or worse," Larto said.

"Nothing is worse than being cooped up in here with a bunch of sick women crying one moment and laughing with relief another," Treyu said. "No butlering job is worth this!"

"If I don't come back soon, make your own attempt," Larto said.

"Now you're talking!"

"But wait a good long while. Perhaps let a few more women get treated or so. If Lanshalla or Larbiabba return, then definitely wait, as they might have other news," Larto said. "I shall return, with luck I hope."

Treyu looked at Larto in disbelief. Then he looked back at Mariel in time to see her removing a tumor from another woman. Treyu put his hands to the cell door and tried to open it, but he couldn't. Women went out, and women came in, easily opening and closing the cell door. Larto walked away a good bit and looked back to see a beaten Treyu holding onto the cell door like a dog who'd been left behind by his master.

"Yes, she's a miracle worker," said a passing woman to a guard. "She'll cure your ailment too."

The guard followed the woman, and that guard motioned to another guard to accompany.

"So, the guards are more interested in their own personal gain than following orders," Larto muttered to himself. "Mariel is on to something. Let's hope I can figure out what's happening out here before these Pleelellicans run out of ailments."

Larto found himself walking against a crowd of Pleelellicans, all headed for Mariel. He fought and squirmed to get through, but he reached a point where the crowd thinned. He took a side passage to avoid further entanglements and only traveled a little ways when he heard voices. He ducked inside a storage closet and waited, but the voices stopped just outside. Then he realized he wasn't just in a storage closet. It was a garbage closet, and the fumes were choking.

"Did you hear about the intruder? The woman? Word is she can heal ailments," said the first voice.

"A scam no doubt," said the second voice.

"I'm not so sure. I just bumped into Varba. Says she no longer has pain in her ears," the first voice said.

"A slug of hard wine will do the same," said the second voice. "I wouldn't give this intruder doctor much credit, not unless she can restore ethereal souls."

"Keep your voice down. The queen is always looking to increase her soul collection. She changes souls more often than a pair of shoes," the first voice said.

"I hear she steals unborn souls of concubines after those concubines entertain male guests," the second voice said.

"No one can be that evil," the first voice said.

"That's what she has everyone thinking," the second voice said. "Think about it. How else could she appear so worldly, so knowledgeable about all types of us Pleelellicans? If you could walk in the shoes of a thousand souls, wouldn't you learn a trick or two?"

"This talk makes me sick. I've lost my appetite," said the first voice.

"Are you sure it isn't that old orciniak meat you're eating? Get rid of it. Let's get a fresh meal," said the second voice.

"You're right," said the first voice.

The first voice opened Larto's door slightly and tossed in his wrapped orciniak sandwich without ever seeing Larto in the closet. Larto stood to the side to avoid being hit, and the food landed in the garbage can. The first voice closed the door, and now the storage (garbage) closet really stank. Larto held his hand over his mouth to keep from vomiting. Finally, the two voices left, and Larto snuck out of the closet.

"Whew! Fresh air! Didn't think I'd survive that muck in there," Larto said to himself.

Larto snuck down the hallway and heard more voices, but they were in a control room. He dropped to his knees and looked around the corner of a doorway. Control panels obscured his view, but he could hear a woman speaking with a man.

"I'm tired of Pleelellican souls," the woman said.

"Then try cetacean souls," the man said, who sounded very much like the royal man who congratulated the winners of the race.

"That's the royal man. And this must be the queen. Perhaps the royal man is the king," Larto thought to himself.

"I'm also tired of cetacean souls. All they do is echo-locate, swim, and eat," the queen said. "What I really need is a *bona fide* Carinian soul!"

"But there are none here!" the king said. "They live on the solar side of the planet."

"And we are on the dark side of the planet. But why should that stop us?" the queen asked. "I want a Bleuh soul!"

"Patience, my queen," the king said.

"You've heard the stories how Bleuhs are taking over the solar system. Carinia 2 is theirs. What's to stop them from running roughshod over us should they shift their gaze our way?" the queen asked. "We must defeat our enemies by understanding them. Give me a Bleuh soul! Ten Bleuh souls!"

"I will send a fresh patrol of Pleelellicans to the twilight region. We'll catch a stray Bleuh falling off a ship," the king said.

"That never worked before. What makes you think it will work now? Besides, your patrols are too busy chasing the creature. I hear it's been tamed."

"No, not tamed. Just disoriented," the king said.

"I have good word that a vine is strangling the creature and making it go wherever the vine wants," the queen said.

The king laughed.

"You won't laugh when that vine forces the creature to attack us," the queen said.

"No vine can make a creature do anything," the king said. "You've been watching too many Pleelellican plays of fantasy."

"I've also heard word that those two women who were drowned by the creature are not so drowned after all, that they've organized an attack force of orciniaks and plan to invade our kingdom," the queen said.

"Where did you hear that?" the king said with his laughter changing to anxiety.

There was a pause. Larto heard body movements, so he could only guess the queen was motioning toward something or someone. Larto had crept into a corner area away from walking paths, but still he wondered if someone knew of his presence and was about to expose him.

"Why look at me?" said a controller.

"You told the queen such tales?" the king asked.

"No, *I* did," said a new Pleelellican who entered the room and who fortunately did not see Larto.

"Doctor Pleyak," the king said. "What are you doing here?"

"I have scan results from the games," Doctor Pleyak said.

"The mass soul scan?" the king asked.

"Of course!" the queen said. "We must have absolute control over all souls in this kingdom. What did you find, doctor?"

"The usual number of Pleelellican souls," Doctor Pleyak said.

"I could have told you that," the king said.

"Along with at least two Bleuh souls and four unknown souls," the doctor said.

"Bleuh souls!" the queen said.

"Yes, but those souls are gone," the doctor said.

"What?" the queen asked.

"The ones called Lanshalla and Larbiabba are not Pleelellican. Lanshalla is a Bleuh. Larbiabba is unknown. But strangely enough, each registers as a pair of souls, not one."

"They can hold more than one soul?" the king asked.

The queen laughed.

"Any woman can hold more than one soul, if the situation is right," she chuckled.

"I did not realize all women were as adept at soul manipulation as my queen," the king said.

"They are not. Lanshalla and Larbiabba are each with child. That is how a woman can carry more than one soul. It's another thing to try out different souls, as I do," the queen said. "But what of these unknown souls? They are neither Pleelellican nor Bleuh. Are they some lower animal?"

"No," Doctor Pleyak said.

"A pity they are not still here," the king said.

"That's not what I said. I said the Bleuhs are gone," the doctor said. "Here, look at my portable scanner. You'll see that they are...strange."

"What? What is it?" the queen asked.

"Well this is impossible," the doctor said. "It says that one is nearby. Practically in this room."

A hush grew. Larto knew he was found out. Best he make a break for it. He crept to the edge of his hidey spot then leapt out toward the doorway. Unfortunately, two guards were hidden on each outside part of the door. They caught him and brought him in.

"Why, it's one of the intruders," the king said.

"My name is Larto," Larto said.

"And what gives you the right to sneak around?" the king asked.

"Never mind that," the queen said. "Doctor. What kind of soul does Larto have?"

"It's not Pleelellican. Not Bleuh. But definitely humanoid. He's a Carinian, but he's not from Carinia 1," the doctor said.

"I'm from Carinia 2. I'm a Gren," Larto said.

"Oh!" the queen pined. "A Gren soul! Doctor, you *must* get me his soul!"

"My soul is neither for lease nor for sale," Larto said.

"That will soon change," the queen smiled. "Doctor, we go to your laboratory. The king will finish here with his tracking."

Larto suddenly twisted violently and writhed to break free, but the guards held a firm grip. One lifted a club to strike Larto on the head.

"No. Do not injure him yet. I want no bruises on his body. They might transfer to his soul. You may do with him as you will *after* the acquisition," the queen said.

Larto refused to walk, and so the guards dragged him down the hallway, with the doctor and queen trailing.

"I do not understand how he can be a Gren, my queen," the doctor said.

"Carinians do not look like us, yet *he* does."

"But you said he's not a Pleelellican," the queen said. "Make up your mind. What is he?"

"He has our form, but he is not one of us. He might be a Gren as he says. If so, he has an unknown power to change shape," the doctor said. "You know, the intruders called Lanshalla and Larbiabba also look like us. They must have changed shape as well."

"An interesting talent," the queen said. "We must explore how they do it. It's one thing to borrow a soul, it's another to take that soul's shape. Oh to swim free in the ocean as an orciniak until I reach mainland, then pose as a Carinian and enjoy the blessings of aristocracy. You must get me his soul and his shape-shifting skill."

"It could kill him," the doctor said.

"All the better," the queen said. "That's one less issue to worry about. You see how he fights us. Why continue dealing with that kind of man? Better to have full compliance than none at all. Dead men are *fully* compliant. Fully."

"I'll remember that," the doctor said with a slight tremble in his voice.

"Oh don't worry!" she reassured the doctor. "You've been compliant—so far."

"So far," he said softly.

The group entered the doctor's lab. Larto was chained to two posts, with one post holding the limbs of his right side and the other post the other side. The chains were not attached to any particular point on the posts but instead wrapped around the posts, permitting vertical movement of his limbs. A dome the size of a hat descended on the end of structural tubing on a swing-arm. The dome was covered with probes and wires. The doctor attached the dome to Larto's head and then walked over to a control station.

"We'll run preliminary scans," the doctor said.

The doctor hit several buttons. A circular disk attached to a generator spun several meters behind Larto, and plasma energy discharged from it to the structural tubing arm (which had its base next to the generator), up along wires, and down to the hat which then transferred into Larto. Larto convulsed and foamed at the mouth.

"Well? Do I get my new soul yet?" the queen asked.

"This is only a preliminary scan, and he's not taking it well," the doctor said. "We should let him rest for a thousand heartbeats."

"I can't wait that long," the queen said. "Go to main acquisition mode. Get me that soul!"

The doctor hit a few more buttons. A transparent cylindrical tube arose from the floor and surrounded Larto and the posts. Now it was clear why the arm with the hat descended vertically from above—to prevent interference with the tube wall. The tube reached just above Larto's head, and then it filled with black liquid. The liquid reached just above Larto's mouth, and he coughed. He jumped above the black fluid line to get air, but each time he did, the fluid level rose. He reached a point where he couldn't get the air, and just as he was about to fall into daze, the arm with the hat lifted him up above the fluid line to get air. But as helpful as it was, the arm also dunked back under the fluid line and so forced Larto into a drowning fight-for-air panic that never abated.

"You see? He uses his mouth to breathe, not his slits," the doctor said. "A true fake."

"Yet still he endures such misery," the queen said with mock compassion. "If only we could extend it."

"We can only make the misery last as long as is necessary to shake his soul from him," the doctor said. "But something is wrong. His soul is not separating."

"Intensify the force," the queen said.

"It's already at maximum," the doctor said. "He won't let go. I will need to stand next to the tube and wedge my soul in to break him free."

The doctor started for Larto, but he was prevented.

"And get first dibs on his soul? Get out of the way!" the queen said as she pushed him aside.

The queen stood by the tube. She then pressed herself against it. A swirl of ethereal energy flowed around the inside of the tube, it flowed over the top, and it drained into the queen's body. She held up her arms as if receiving rain from the heavens in a parched desert. But then a shower of sparks flew from the tube up through the structural tubing arm and back into the generator, destroying the generator. The queen fell backward but was caught by the doctor, the fluid drained, and the tube descended. Larto collapsed to the bottom of the posts, and the remains of the black fluid on his clothing and body evaporated into black steam.

"My queen, are you injured? Can you walk?" the doctor asked.

"I...yes," she said as the doctor helped her to her feet. "I feel strange. I feel another soul in me. But it's small. I didn't realize Grens had such small souls. They must be inferior indeed compared to Bleuhs. They...oh...no! Impossible! Doctor! Perform a full ethereal scan of this room. Now!"

The doctor performed a scan. Larto breathed heavily and attempted to get his strength.

"Please," he begged. "Unchain me."

"He still has his Gren soul," the doctor said.

"Of course he does. I'm pregnant!" the queen said.

"I have another sibling?" young Lanietta said. "And Pleelellican at that. How am I supposed to hate Pleelellicans if I'm related to them?"

The doctor hit a few buttons on his panel to continue scanning.

"You are. But not with a Pleelellican soul," the doctor said.

"A Gren soul?" the queen asked.

"It...no, not like Larto. Not a Gren soul," the doctor said.

"So Larto did not impregnate me?" the queen asked.

"Not in such a sense," the doctor said.

"In what sense did he?"

"You are pregnant with a Bleuh soul," the doctor said.

"Not my sibling," young Lanietta said. "Very strange."

Larto had a sickening feeling that perhaps a residual part of Lanshalla's ethereal spirit inside of him had transferred over to the queen.

"How vulgar," the queen said. "I want to possess a Bleuh soul, not be pregnant with one. This is outrageous! Scandalous. Terminate it immediately!"

"Please, please!" Larto begged, not wanting to have a future daughter of Lanshalla killed. "Please keep this baby. I will take care of it. Do not tell the others. Please. You want to know about Bleuhs. Perhaps you can communicate with it. Your doctor has all this equipment. Please, I beg you reconsider."

The queen stared at the doctor.

"This is the closest you'll get to possessing a Bleuh soul. There are no others here in the kingdom," the doctor said.

"Then I'll hide this pregnancy," the queen said. "But you can't have the baby, Larto. It's mine to do as I please. Once it is old enough...well...I don't have to reveal my plans, do I?"

"Do not kill it," Larto warned, suddenly gaining strength. "I should be forced to take action against you."

The queen laughed.

"You are in no position to bargain. I will—"

But the queen was interrupted by an alarm.

"The kingdom is under attack!" said one of the guards.

"To your stations!" the queen ordered. "Watch Larto carefully. I'll deal with him later."

The queen left behind her guards and returned to her place with the king. The doctor stared at Larto then hit a few buttons.

"Time to test your shape-changing abilities," the doctor said.

Chapter 83: Retaliation

"Finally, some peace and quiet," Treyu said to Mariel just after the last patient left. "I'm surprised the guards didn't come and kick them out."

"Maybe they did," Mariel said, "or maybe they prevented more from coming. But you are right, for once. I am tired. I wish we were back at Larto's Vineyard. I could use a good sip of wine with a crackling fire warming my feet."

"I would join you in that drink," Treyu said.

But before Mariel could reply at how surprised she was with his answer, a guard opened the door.

"You're letting us out?" Mariel asked.

"They're letting me in," a badly beat-up Larto said as a guard lifted him by the shoulders and tossed him into the cell.

"Larto!" Mariel screamed as Larto collapsed to the ground.

Treyu made for the door to retaliate against the guards, but the guard who opened the door slammed it shut and bounced Treyu backward. Treyu tripped over Larto's fallen body and then landed on a narrow but tall table, where he crashed through it and landed on the floor himself.

"Shh!" Mariel said. "Have some consideration for others. Don't you see Larto is hurt?"

Mariel went to Larto and held his face. Her special touch sensed what had happened to him.

"I think I broke my ankle," Treyu said.

"Good. Should keep you still for a moment," Mariel said. "Larto has been tortured. They tried to...oh, this new gift I have is...is...too much!"

Mariel was overwhelmed with grief and pulled her hand away.

"Treyu, come over here and help," Mariel struggled to say.

"I would, *Your Highness*, once my ankle heals. Perhaps in another harvest season, give or take a Gren day, as they say," Treyu said.

"Wrap it up and come over here!" she barked with a mixture of fear, grief, and anger in her trembling voice.

Treyu stopped his mockery and fell sullen. He ripped several strips of cloth from his shirt, tied them together, and bound up his ankle. He tried walking, but the weight on his ankle was too much and caused him to collapse. He scrounged around for a stick or cane to help him. A detached leg from the table he'd broken was just barely long enough, and he used it to get back to his feet and amble about.

"What is it you want?" Treyu asked once he ambled over.

"Bring fresh water, a cup, several rags, and...I thought there was something else," Mariel said.

"Earplugs," Treyu said.

"I don't need earplugs," Mariel said.

"Not for you. For me," Treyu said.

"No joking. This is a serious occasion," Mariel said.

Larto tried to speak, but Mariel shushed him. Meanwhile, guards ran up and down the corridor by the cell in response to invasion alarms.

"We need to get out of here," Mariel said. "Where's that water, Treyu?"

"I'm getting there," Treyu said.

"Well get there quicker!" Mariel barked.

Treyu brought the water, a cup, and rags.

"Hold his head up," Mariel said.

Treyu held Larto's head up while Mariel poured water into a cup from a pitcher and poured a bit of the water into Larto's mouth. Larto drank a little but choked.

"Easy, there," Mariel said.

Then Larto went into a cruel coughing fit, and up came blood.

"Easy, I said!" Mariel repeated, and she placed her fingertips on his upper chest just below his neck. "Internal injuries. Hold on, Larto, I'll patch you up in a moment."

Mariel poured water onto a rag, wrung the rag to distribute the water, and then placed the rag onto Larto's upper chest. She placed both hands on the rag and chanted softly while fingertip vines intermeshed with the rag. Steam rose from the rag, Larto gulped air suddenly, and then Mariel relaxed in unison with Larto exhaling.

"Better?" Mariel asked.

"Much better," said Larto. "I'll take that cup of water now, if you don't mind."

Larto sat up and took a sip.

"We have to get out of here," Larto said. "I heard something about an invasion."

"Perhaps it would be better if we stayed in a safe place, like this cell," Treyu said.

Larto spat out his water in surprise.

"So you can endure more of Mariel's patients?" Larto grinned.

"I didn't mean that!" Treyu said. "You know what I mean!"

"We have to find the others," Mariel said.

"Agreed. We'll break out of here and find a way to the sea. Perhaps we can steal a boat. Mariel, you're good at picking locks. Perhaps—"

"Perhaps you'll be taken by Imperial Bleuhs instead," Tiloto said at the cell door with several Imperial Bleuhs behind him. "I see you've all changed your forms to look like Pleelellicans. Where is my Treina?"

"I'm Treina," Treyu said.

Tiloto laughed.

"You are *not* Treina," Tiloto said.

"Don't you remember when I changed into this form on your shuttle?" Treyu asked. "Oh wait, your memory was—"

"Tiloto—help us out. We need a boat, fuel, and supplies for a sea voyage," Larto said.

"Is that all? How about a chest of gold trinkets and a master key to the procreation tanks?" Tiloto mocked.

"We're on a rescue mission," Larto said.

"The lies here are unbelievable," Tiloto said. "You may take them. This little Pleelellican kingdom is now under martial rule."

"I didn't realize you were such a fan of Imperial Bleuhs," Larto said.

Tiloto swatted Larto across the face as the guards pulled him out of the cell.

"I joined up. Emergency enlistment," Tiloto said. "I see Lanshalla and Larbiabba are missing. Hiding somewhere?"

"That's who we're looking for," Larto said. "They could be dead or drowned for all we know."

"Good riddance if they are. A pity Treina is not here. I might have been more lenient. But cheer up. We'll troll the sea for you and secure any bodies that might wash up along the way," Tiloto said.

"I would turn into Treina and slap you, if I could," Treyu said.

The Imperial Bleuhs took the three down the corridor and outside, where a small spaceship awaited them.

"How did they get in here?" Mariel asked.

"They must have figured out a way through the shield," Treyu said.

"Or through the wall," Mariel said. "Or perhaps under the wall."

"Perhaps," Larto said. "We will soon find out, I fear."

Larto was correct. Shortly after the three were escorted into a small Imperial Bleuh spaceship, the spaceship took to the air. It headed for the stadium area and then dove into the seawater next to the stadium itself, following a path the squid-like creature had taken with Lanshalla, Larbiabba, and Berella-the-vine. After a few moments, the spacecraft shot out of the water and hovered over it. Larto, Mariel, and Treyu had been allowed to watch from chairs in the upper deck (near a window). With the three no longer in the Pleelellican kingdom, their features reverted to their natural selves.

"So, your fantasy is short-lived," Tiloto said. "As it is for the Pleelellicans. You along with the king and queen will be taken before the Hierarchy, as soon as we finish sweeping the sea for your friends."

"We've found a body," said a Bleuh.

"Only one?" Tiloto asked. "Bring it aboard."

The Bleuh ship lowered a net into the sea, dragged it a short ways, and then pulled it up into a lower hold in the ship.

"Body retrieved. No sign of any Carinians in the water," the Bleuh said.

"Head for the Hierarchy Processing Center. But before we get there, I want our guests to see for themselves which body we pulled aboard. Care to place a wager, Larto?" Tiloto asked.

"No," Larto replied.

"I hope it's your Lanshalla. Would be a great feather in my cap if I returned her body to the Hierarchy," Tiloto said.

"Evil Tiloto!" young Lanietta said, and she swiped her fists at him, but they passed through without making contact.

"She'd never allow it. She's too clever," Larto bragged.

"We'll see," Tiloto laughed.

Tiloto escorted the three to a lower hold. The net was empty.

"You caught nothing!" Larto laughed. "This is but a foolish game!"

An Imperial Bleuh stood by a doorway at the far side and nodded toward Tiloto.

"I'd check your laughter at the door," Tiloto said, pointing toward the doorway by that Imperial Bleuh. "Over there, please."

Larto was ushered toward the room first, but Mariel jumped in front, turned around, and stopped.

"Let me go in first, Larto," Mariel said.

"Why? Tiloto has nothing to show me," Larto said.

"Let me look first. I'll let you know what I find," Mariel said.

"Oh no, my good Mariel, let Larto see first. He is convinced there's nothing to see anyway. Let him have the last laugh," Tiloto taunted.

"I should go first," Larto said. "But thank you anyway. Tiloto most likely has pulled up a dalphinac or baby orciniak."

"Yes, that's it," Tiloto continued to taunt. "Keep those happy thoughts alive for your last laugh."

"I don't like Tiloto," young Lanietta said. "He must've found someone. Oh Claus, I'm shaking with anxiety."

"Remember, this is in the past. It's done," Claus said.

"But these people still went through it," young Lanietta said.

Tiloto led the three to the doorway, stepped to the side of the doorway, and ushered the three in, with Larto leading. Inside the room was a long table with what looked like a body of something underneath a tarp. Two Imperial Bleuhs stood inside the room as guards, and another Bleuh stood by the table, ready to throw off the tarp. Larto, Mariel, and Treyu stood on one side of the table.

"You will all learn at the same time. How's that for democracy?" Tiloto asked.

"What would you know about democracy?" Larto asked.

"Only that it's about to unfold. Behold the democracy of the universe," Tiloto said.

The Bleuh threw off the tarp. Mariel gasped. Indeed there was a Carinian on the table, but it was impaled all over with baleen remnants. The torso area in particular had such large baleen fragments protruding that it hardly looked like a person but instead looked like some strange sea creature. What little flesh of the Carinian that was visible was white and waterlogged. Baleen shards protruded out of the skull and upward from the chest, all but obscuring the face. Young Lanietta covered her eyes and only occasionally looked back at the corpse.

"Who is it?" Treyu asked.

"This is enough," Mariel said. "Some poor soul fell into the sea and fought with a baleeniac squid. Nothing else to see here."

Mariel started to usher Larto and Treyu out.

"Wait!" Tiloto called back. "Aren't you the least bit curious as to the identity of the poor soul? Aren't you?"

"Probably someone you had killed and tortured," Larto said.

"No. Look closer, Larto. Break off those baleen shards. Identify the victim," Tiloto said.

Just then, Mariel made a break for the doorway and attempted to strangle Tiloto. Little vines prepared to dig into Tiloto's flesh, but the Imperial Bleuh on the other side of the doorway stuck out his baton and caused her to trip and fall. Tiloto laughed as Imperial Bleuhs secured her.

"Don't worry, Mariel, this is just a petty game," Larto said.

Larto removed several baleen shards, exposing the face of the deceased. A mere moment passed before full horror set in. It was Lanshalla, and Larto knew it. He felt strange, though, as if a great reserve of energy had been depleted from his body. He looked around the room and expected to develop hatred for the Bleuhs, especially Tiloto. But he felt nothing. The people and objects around him were mere shadows, and Larto himself felt little more than a biochemical recording device.

"Mommy!" young Lanietta screamed.

The vision stopped. Young Lanietta collapsed to the floor in exhaustion.

"Claus, this is Labba," Claus heard through Aftova. "We've had a serious disruption with Morcellus and Tabelia. They went limp. And at the worst time, too. The selenites are about to overtake and destroy all rescued people."

"The vision has stopped," Claus said.

"The selenites are tearing into the outer hides of Morcellus and Tabelia. Help us, Claus. Help us!" Kechenova said.

"Lanietta, please," Claus said. "They need our help."

"It's all over. Don't you see? The universe has stopped," young Lanietta cried.

"I know that's how it seems," Claus said.

"But it has. What's left of anything?" she asked.

"You. They made an effort to ensure your life. How, I don't know. But you'll be trapped in this moment of misery unless we trudge through. The essences of your parents are in these orbs. They are not gone, only transformed. Sometimes that's painful. A part of me says you'll be transformed too when this is all over."

"You speak as if things will be better," young Lanietta cried.

"Won't they? After night comes day. After winter comes spring," Claus said.

"Carinia 1 doesn't have a day or seasons," young Lanietta said.

"But Carinia 2 does, in a fashion," Claus said. "These are cycles of life. Being immortal and face-locked with a star makes you immune to such cycles until something catastrophic happens. Yes, this is a tragedy, but the cycle continues. You will continue. Please. For the sake of humanity. For yours. And for me. Please?"

"For you?" she said while drying her eyes and regaining her composure. "My Claus?"

"Yes. Your Claus," he said tenderly.

Young Lanietta paused. The adult Lanietta groaned, sighed, then fell silent. Young Lanietta nodded her head "yes".

"C'mon. Your parents have more to share. They meant this vision for you. Let it not waste away in vain," Claus said.

Young Lanietta nodded and smiled. She nodded again, and the vision resumed. As it did, Claus heard a faint, "Back to life, thank you Claus," from Labba.

"The whole thing is absurd, really," Larto said.

"Absurd? What do you mean?" Tiloto asked. "Word was that you loved this Bleuh. We'll give her a Bleuh funeral, but you Grens cannot attend. Orders should arrive soon as to your fate."

"Not all of us are Grens!" Treyu said. "I'm a Greyan, and unless you want a war with Carinia 5, I suggest you release us all."

Tiloto laughed.

"We know all about your Carinia 5. Since Libriota discovered it, we've had extra forces secure it," Tiloto said.

"And I thought you were a cargo man," Treyu said. "You seem to know a lot for someone who just enlisted."

"We learn things quickly in the Imperial Bleuh Patrol," Tiloto said.

"New destination entered into navi control," said an assistant.

The phrase, "Destination: Planet Carinia 2" was displayed on a panel above the doorway.

"Ah, the termination will be first," Tiloto said. "Don't worry, Treyu, we'll keep you around for a bit. Need you to help find Treina."

"And if I refuse?" Treyu said.

"You'll cooperate," Tiloto said. "The Imperial Bleuh Patrol is about mandate and cooperation. You see that panel up there? The ship's navi control is linked in with the Hierarchy. The ship goes where it's told. No need for us to intervene or interfere. Makes for a smooth ride all around."

"Getting ethereal interference," said an assistant.

Young Lanietta looked at Claus in surprise and said, "It's Mommy!"

"She's doing something," Claus said. "See? She's become more powerful."

"But what is she doing?" young Lanietta asked.

"Let's watch and see," Claus replied.

"From where?" Tiloto asked.

But before anyone could answer, the ship changed course quickly and veered about wildly. Treyu looked up at the panel and alerted both Mariel and Larto to also look up. The panel had changed from, "Destination: Planet Carinia 2," to "D0stin0ti0n: Pl0n0t C0rini0 0."

"We're headed for Carinia Zero!" the assistant said.

"That's not a planet!" Tiloto replied.

"Navi control thinks it is!" the assistant said.

"It's our sun! We'll burn up!" Tiloto exclaimed.

"She's going to kill them? But Daddy and the others will die!" young Lanietta said.

"Hold on," Claus said. "We're going for a ride."

"Good!" Larto said. "We will do so together and watch. And see. And feel...if only we could."

"Hang in there, Daddy!" young Lanietta said.

Larto's voice trailed. He hovered over Lanshalla's body and remained frozen, like a mother rabbit hovering over her freshly-killed children by a wayward cat, with the mother wondering what to do next.

"If there is a *next*," Larto muttered to himself. "There is no *next*. I am but an island now, an island in the path of a giant wave, watching as water recedes before the wave brings the end."

"You see, Larto is devastated too. But he is not the island he thinks he is. We all have these moments of despair," Claus said.

Tiloto and his crew rushed to escape pods amidst alarms and yelling.

"Come, Larto, it's time to go," Treyu said as he approached Larto.

"You must leave her behind," Mariel said as she also approached. "We must find an escape pod."

"I...her child. She was going to call it 'Lanietta.' Can we save her? Can we..."

"Where did I go?" young Lanietta asked.

"It's a mystery," Claus said. "But I'm sure we'll learn the answer soon."

Larto's voice trailed again. Mariel fought back tears, but she got a hold of herself, gave Larto a side hug, and moved him along. Treyu led and looked for an escape pod, but the crew had taken all of them.

"Trapped!" Treyu said.

"Hold him," Mariel said to Treyu regarding Larto.

"What?" Treyu replied, confused.

"Hold him!" Mariel reiterated.

Mariel rushed over to Treyu, pulled him over to Larto, and forced him to prop up Larto—all before Larto had a chance to topple over in despair. She rushed around from one workstation to another, hitting buttons and using her vine tactilations to probe for ship information.

"It's no use, Mariel," Treyu said. "This ship is going to burn up and us along with it."

"You give up too easily," Mariel said, still hitting buttons, but then she paused. "Strange. This ship has an ethereal spirit."

"Impossible," Treyu said.

"Lanshalla?" Larto added, perking up.

"Wrong, and no," Mariel said. "Hold on. We're going eethi."

"We can't. We don't know how. This is ludi—" Treyu started.

But he was interrupted. Mariel, Treyu, and Larto all went eethi, leaving their corporeal bodies behind. They were now on an eethi version of the spaceship, and it burrowed deep into Carinia Zero.

"We're dead!" Treyu exclaimed. "We must be!"

"Maybe. I don't know," Mariel said. "We've gone eethi. Whether we can return to our bodies is another matter."

Larto looked back at the eethi version of the bed where Lanshalla had been. Lanshalla wasn't there.

"She's gone!" Larto said.

"Oh, what is that?" Mariel said, looking through the eethi window of the eethi ship.

Treyu beckoned Larto over, and the two stared at what Mariel saw.

"Eddies?" Treyu asked. "They spin and spin and spin. Larto, what do you see?"

But Larto merely stared.

"He's still in shock. I'll help him relax," Mariel said.

Mariel went over and touched him, expecting the vine-bit on her fingertips to extend onto him, but they didn't.

"What?" Mariel said to herself in disbelief.

"Berella," Treyu said. "She's gone too."

Then the three heard a distorted female voice, asking if they could hear her. The message was barely audible, and it asked them to steer the ship toward...toward...

"Who is that?" Treyu asked.

"I can't tell," Mariel said. "They are trying to give us directions. But it's garbled. Larto, can you make out anything?"

Larto did not reply.

"It's stopped," Treyu said. "It sounded like someone was trying to rescue us."

"We'll have to find a way out ourselves, unless you want to spend several billion Sol 3 years looking for another body," Mariel said.

"I like my body well enough, thank you, and I'd rather not have to wait such a long time," Treyu said.

"Perhaps if we make contact with one of those eddies, we could learn something," Mariel said.

"I don't like the sound of that," Treyu said. "Could be destructive energy. We might be dispersed into nothingness."

"This is where the PRAAD goes to energize. The Amnus egg," young Lanietta said. "I can see that now."

"All right, you make the next move then," Mariel said.

"I...I say we wait and figure things out," Treyu said.

Mariel laughed.

"What's so funny?" Treyu asked.

"The man who doesn't want to wait a few billion years for a new body wants to wait here while we're all eethi anyway," Mariel said. "Fine. Stay here with Larto. I'm going out there."

"You can't go out there, Mariel. Wait!" Treyu pleaded.

Too late. Mariel passed through the ship wall, and she was outside.

"Come back! It's dangerous out there!" Treyu panicked.

Mariel simply smiled. Little swirls of energy encircled her ankles and wrists. She found she could use the swirls as a form of propulsion, as if these swirls were something between fins and propellers in an ethereal sea. She headed over to one of the eddies, paused, and then touched it. The eddy changed pattern to that of a whirlpool. Surprised, Mariel tried to propel away, but it pulled her in. She disappeared from view.

"Mariel!" Treyu exclaimed.

"A fate for us all," Larto said without hope. "I will go next."

"No!" Treyu protested.

Treyu held onto Larto and fought to keep him on the ship, but before the two could tussle much, several entities appeared on the ship. In fact, they walked through one side, along the ship's floor, and out the other.

"What...who are you?" Treyu called.

They were soldiers, defeated, and making a slow walk home. They carried their wounded but lost their pride. They were future Grens who would lose in the civil war.

"Grens," Larto said. "I will walk with them."

Larto moved to join the line of men. Treyu was so taken by the march of men that he almost didn't realize what Larto was doing. He caught Larto only just in time.

"No! It's a trap! It must be!" Treyu said.

Treyu leapt for Larto, but Treyu tripped and fell. How an eethi spirit can trip is beyond me, but Treyu did. It didn't matter. Larto never reached the trail of men. Before he could reach them, a blackness descended from above, enveloped the men, and then shrank to an infinitesimal size. Larto stood there, motionless.

"Did you see that? What was that black thing?" Treyu asked.

"The final weapon," Larto said. "An expanding sun-blocking device meant for deployment over Carinia 2. It appears to grow larger and larger until the sky is completely black. Let it go black, I say. Let nothingness replace nothingness."

"A foretelling of things to come. The Anrega," young Lanietta said.

"Let's get you by the window," Treyu said as he escorted Larto toward the window. "Stay away from the middle of the ship. I need to think. If only I had made an ethereal device, one that existed solely in the ethereal realm. A pity I didn't focus more attention on that. But who knew I'd be caught in this—"

Before he could finish his monologue, the eddy that had ingested Mariel spat her out. Mariel shot through the environment free, or so she thought. In fact, the eddy had shot Mariel toward another eddy, which in turn ingested her.

"She's alive...no wait, she's trapped again!" Treyu said. "Mariel, get out of there!"

Larto looked over at Treyu, paused for a second, and then spoke.

"I've never seen you so concerned for Mariel," Larto said.

"Mariel? The maid? I'm just looking after your estate, sir," Treyu countered.

Before the two could continue, another scene unfolded in the middle of the ship. A child played in a sandbox. The child took a small bucket, filled it with sand, packed the sand, and quickly turned the bucket upside down into the sandbox. The child then pinched in the sides of the bucket, released, and pulled the bucket upward. A sand casting from the mold was produced.

"Lanietta?" Larto called as he walked toward the child, but Treyu grabbed him.

"No," Treyu said.

"That's me!" young Lanietta said.

The child made another casting aside the first and prepared to place sticks across the tops to join them. A shadow passed onto the child. Scared, the child looked around for help. An image of Mariel rushed in and attempted to whisk up the child, but just before the outstretched arms of both met, the two were encased in a block of ice, and the scene faded to darkness.

"Nanna!" adult Lanietta said unexpectedly.

Claus turned briefly toward adult Lanietta, but she said no more and remained motionless.

"More Grens?" Treyu asked.

Larto nodded, "Yes."

The eddy shot out Mariel, and she returned to the first eddy. The same scene of soldiers emerged in the ship, and again the black shape from above enveloped them. But the scene took less time, and Mariel was shot out to the second eddy. Again the child played in the sand, image of Mariel grabbed the child, and the blackness overtook both.

"She's stuck. She's stuck between the eddies!" Treyu said.

The act of sending Mariel back and forth between eddies created a trail, weak at first, but growing stronger between the two. The trail became a tube, and though Mariel tried to propel out of this back and forth oscillation, the tube grew stronger and stronger while preventing her escape.

"It's worse than death," Larto lamented. "At least with death there's an end."

"Then I will end it," Treyu said.

Now it was Larto's turn. He tried stopping Treyu, but Treyu exited the ship just outside of Larto's reach and headed for the eddy tube.

"He'll be trapped as well," Larto mumbled. "Or will he?"

Larto watched as Treyu attained the same swirls of propulsion around ankle and wrist and also watched as Treyu attempted to pass through the tube to rescue Mariel. But the tube would not suffer a breach, not by Treyu nor anyone. Treyu pounded on the tube, but it did not yield, and Treyu could not enter. Then Treyu headed over to the first eddy and attempted to enter, but it held fast like a turtle withdrawn in its shell. Treyu headed over to the other eddy and had the same problem—no entrance.

"Mariel is trapped in a tube. Treyu is stuck trying to help her. Where does that leave me?" Larto asked himself.

"On an island," said a voice.

Startled, Larto turned around and saw an ethereal image of Lanshalla in a hooded long robe holding a baby wrapped in cloth.

"Lanshalla, Lanshalla!" Larto exclaimed.

"The baby is me!" young Lanietta said.

Larto rushed over to Lanshalla to hug her, but just as he reached her, the black spot from above grew and enveloped both her and the baby, leaving Larto alone.

"Blast that Anrega!" young Lanietta said. "Always in the way!"

"What...Lanshalla? Come back!" Larto called.

It was quiet inside the ship. Larto went back to the window. Treyu was still trying to find a way to rescue Mariel. Mariel moved back and forth so quickly that she appeared to be stretched in the tube all along the way. She tried speaking to Treyu, but her voice warbled and varied as if underwater.

"He'll never get her out that way," said the voice again to Larto.

Larto spun around. Lanshalla had reappeared in her robe, but now a toddler stood beside her. In fact, the toddler stood behind Lanshalla's left leg and clutched it as if hiding behind for protection. Larto started for the two, but Lanshalla held up a hand to stop him.

"It's me again!" young Lanietta said.

"Do not approach!" Lanshalla said.

"But...I must hold you!" Larto said.

"We cannot touch like this. I will wink out again. And I might not return," Lanshalla said.

"But I must be with you. We must be together," Larto said.

"There is only one way," Lanshalla said. "But it requires a sacrifice. You must do exactly as I say."

As Larto listened to Lanshalla, Treyu tried one last time to break through the tube. It was no use. Dejected, he returned to the ship in time to see Larto speaking with Lanshalla. The girl (Lanietta) was still hiding behind Lanshalla's left leg. As it turned out, Treyu had reached the ship at the end of their conversation. The black overhead dot grew into a mass and enveloped Lanshalla and Lanietta.

"More evil upon me when I was young," young Lanietta said.

"Do you remember any of this?" Claus asked.

"No," young Lanietta replied.

"What...that looked like Lanshalla!" Treyu said.

"It was. And the girl was Lanietta," Larto said.

"But...it..." Treyu stumbled.

"No time for explanations," Larto said. "We have work to do. Can you navigate this ship?"

"I think I could manage," Treyu said.

"Good. Because you'll need to when this is all over," Larto said. "The ship will auto-navigate for a while. Be prepared when it stops."

"When it stops what?" Treyu asked.

But Larto left the ship, attained spiral propulsion around his wrists and ankles, and darted away.

"Hey!" Treyu called. "Where are you going? Larto? Larto!"

"Stay on the ship," called a voice like Lanshalla's.

Treyu looked around for the voice, but Lanshalla did not appear. Her voice was more like an echo from far away, though, and not like she was standing nearby (as it was when she appeared before Larto).

Larto headed for a third eddy. He didn't fight the eddy's pull, rather, he allowed the eddy to pull himself in. Treyu watched through the ship's window in horror and was about to go against Larto's wish of staying on the ship when he was bumped from behind. He turned around to see people in a crosswalk brushing past him. Though some walked by, others headed right for him and bumped into him, often violently. They apologized, but the collision seemed intentional.

"You're not sorry!" Treyu said. "You're apologizing as an excuse to get away with being rude! I'll show you rude!"

Before Treyu could do anything, the crosswalk changed from people to cars. Cars whisked by at incredible speed. Some brushed by Treyu, and Treyu felt pain.

"Ow!" he said.

"What's happening?" Claus asked.

"Ethereal drift," young Lanietta said. "Treyu is losing himself to the ether."

Treyu didn't have time to think about the pain, because one car plowed right through him, sending him cartwheeling over the car's hood, the car's roof, and landing on the rear bumper which broke his ethereal nose and teeth. Ethereal blood covered his face.

"I'm bleeding. I'm bleeding!" Treyu remarked.

A large truck then headed for Treyu and was about to smack him flat, but the truck, cars, people, and crosswalk all disappeared. Treyu turned around slowly and saw Larto being shot out of the third eddy and toward a fourth.

"Oh no. What can I expect now?" Treyu wondered. "I'd better get out of this ship. Anything is better than—"

Again Treyu's thought was interrupted. Larto was ingested by the fourth eddy, and Treyu turned around toward the center of the ship to find the shoreline of a peaceful island as one might find on Earth in the Pacific Ocean.

"Now wait a moment," Treyu said. "This isn't so bad. Let me bathe my tired feet."

Treyu sat by a coconut tree on the shoreline and allowed the waves to come in. The water was warm, clear, and lightly salty, giving his feet a good soak.

"Ah," Treyu said.

But the enjoyment was short-lived. The shoreline changed to a sidewalk, the tree a light post, and his feet dangled onto a hot asphalt street. Hot tar scalded his feet, and he yelled in pain as he struggled to pull his feet to the sidewalk. He did so just in time, too, as automotive traffic blazed by—all ready to run over his feet.

"Oo, oo, oo!" Treyu said as he hopped around in pain.

He hopped farther onto the sidewalk and away from the road, but people ran into him from alternating directions, making him a punching bag for whomever and all-ever. Several people ganged up on him and shoved him through the glass window of a shop, but before he could fall to the shop's floor, the scene changed back to the island, and he fell on sand. He looked at his cut arms and saw that instead of glass there was sand. The tree he had sat next to was still there as was the shoreline with waves gently rolling in.

"I won't be fooled again. I'll climb the tree and be safe from it all," Treyu said.

Treyu climbed the tree as best he could. It was a young tree and not very tall, and so he reached a point where he could climb no farther. He put his hand on a coconut.

"I'll use this coconut to fend off anyone who comes my way," Treyu grinned.

Treyu took a firmer grip of the coconut, but it came loose. As it did, the scene changed back to the urban environment, and he had pulled on the bulb in the light post, causing it to break and expose electrified elements. The electricity flowed through Treyu and caused him to convulse. He thought he would fall below, but the electricity jolted his muscles and caused his body to fly upward and land atop the light post. The scene changed. He was back on the island and on top of the coconut tree, but to his surprise he had landed on a hornet's nest. They were angry and stung him mercilessly.

Treyu jumped down from the tree and headed for the water, but before he splashed down, the scene changed, and he landed atop a box van. The van carried him along a street and turned the corner quickly. His body fell toward the front wheels of a motorcycle. But the scene changed again, with the motorcycle replaced by the gaping mouth of a sea serpent with the hornets stinging his flesh up and down the length of his body, linked together as if chained. He passed out of the serpent through an opening in its tail, but he was not free. A ligament held onto his body.

The scene changed. He was in the Old West being dragged behind a horse by a rope with that rope lassoed around his torso. He held onto the rope with both hands to take the tension off his torso. Grass and sand kicked up in his face from the horse, but the scene changed, and he was on the beach with the motorcycle from the urban scene pulling him along the shoreline by the same lassoed rope. The motorcycle whipped him around, and Treyu alternated between being dunked into the splashing water and plowed into the sandy shoreline. But the rope frayed on the sand, and it broke, allowing Treyu to go free.

Again the scene changed, and he had just broken free from the serpent, who had dragged him around on the now-severed ligament. Treyu looked at himself and reacted in horror. He had become a serpent of sorts himself, with each arm and leg transformed into long chain-like appendages of buzzing hornets. Then the involuntary chain-wrap maneuvers began. First it was with his arm-like tentacles. They held out wide then whipped close to each other with the midpoints bowing. The endpoints met first, and Treyu's arms wrapped around each other until their midpoints wrapped last. They bumped each other, causing the start of the unwrap maneuver. Once fully unwrapped, the leg-like tentacles performed the same maneuver. When they finished unwrapping, Treyu's torso bent backward, and his arm pairs and leg pairs wrapped around with those pairs at the same time. They unwrapped, Treyu's torso bent forward, and the pairs wrapped and unwrapped. This sort of mindless torture continued, and Treyu was desperate to get out of this involuntary misery, so when his torso bent forward, he used what little voluntary power he had, tucked his head into his abdomen, and pulled his arms and legs together so that all four appendages would conflict as a wrapping pair would conflict with the other pair and conversely, vice versa, and in reverse in this micro-universe of inner super-ethereal confines of Carinia Zero.

Yes, Treyu had gone super ethereal. But he could not sustain it. His newly-introduced maneuver created a temporary rip. Carinia Zero spat out a giant solar flare, and with it went the spaceship with Treyu and Mariel aboard (and both restored to corporeal form). The spaceship's outer sections had melted and shrunk, causing the ship's outer hull to thicken at the expense of a much reduced overall size. Treyu picked himself off the ship's floor in time to see an ethereal image of Larto standing with Lanshalla and the toddler Lanietta. Larto and Lanshalla waved goodbye to Treyu as their images appeared to shrink into the distance. But just before they disappeared altogether, the image of Lanietta darted from behind Lanshalla and dove off to the side.

"Lanietta, no!" Lanshalla's voice faintly echoed through the ages.

The ethereal images were gone.

"I left Mommy," young Lanietta said. "I don't remember when or why, but I did."

"Hello?" Treyu called throughout what was left of the ship. "Is anyone here? Hello!"

But the ship wasn't out of danger. It drifted from the solar flare into a barrage of crossfire between Gren and Imperial Bleuh ships.

"Get back into the solar flare!" Mariel shouted as she appeared from another room.

"What?" Treyu asked in surprise, both in seeing Mariel and her command.

"We'll never survive like this," Mariel said as she went for the controls.

Mariel maneuvered the ship back into the solar flare.

"We'll be destroyed in this flare! The radiation alone—"

"Can be tolerated for a little while," Mariel said as she hit buttons furiously.

"We're headed for Carinia 1," Treyu said.

"I know," Mariel said, still punching a bunch of buttons. "We're using the flare as cover so they won't notice."

"But we're on a collision course with the planet!" Treyu said.

"That's the plan," Mariel said.

"The plan? The plan is suicide!" Treyu said as he fought Mariel for control.

But Mariel pulled out a bottle of cleaning spray and squirted the fluid on Treyu's face. Treyu fell away with his hands to his eyes, trying to relieve the pain and temporary blindness.

"You're out of your mind!" Treyu stumbled around.

"Let's hope they think the same," Mariel said.

"Mariel, you're two degrees off course," said a familiar voice through the radio. "Slingshot around."

"Compensating," Mariel replied.

"Was that Larbiabba? Where is she? Mariel? What's going on?" Treyu asked.

"No time. Brace for a jolt," Mariel said.

"Are we going to hit Carinia 1?" Treyu asked.

There was a pause, too long of a pause. The ship did not hit Carinia 1 as Treyu expected.

"You steered us clear?" Treyu asked.

"Part of the solar flare hit Carinia 1," Mariel said. "We are still in the other part. Heading for Carinia 2. Shouldn't be long now before impact. Hold on."

"Hold on to what? I can't see a thing! Mariel, this—" Treyu started.

But he was interrupted. The ship dove through the dark side of Carinia 2's atmosphere, plowed through layers of snow, and came to a stop. Plowing through the snow had damaged the ship's hull, despite its thickened condition. Treyu was thrown clear through an opening, and he landed in snow on his back, dazed. He felt cold at first, but his body quickly gave way to numbness. A plume of snow had shot up into the air from impact, and now it floated down, some of which covered Treyu, and other of which cleaned out his eyes. He stared at the snow and half-fancied they were snow butterflies dancing in the air. Two lines of snow butterflies perched on his body, one line along his left leg, left-side torso, and left arm while the other line perched on the right.

"These are no hornets," he said to himself.

Treyu saw a toddler, the same toddler that had stood behind Lanshalla. She walked toward him, placed a hand to one of the snow butterflies on his arm, and picked it up. She held the butterfly close to her lips, whispered something to it, then held it up and blew it up into the air, where it flew away happy and free.

"Lanietta?" Treyu called with a weak voice, but he lost awareness, and the fate of himself, Lanietta (if truly her), and Mariel were yet to be seen.

"She looks like you," Claus said.

"She is," young Lanietta said.

Chapter 84: White Foxes

Treyu, being a Carinian, didn't sleep, but he could lose awareness. And so his eyes were wide open, at times blinking, but he was unable to see or respond to the environment around him. When his senses did return, he found himself in a rather unusual bed. It was oval-shaped with padding on the sides, head, and foot, and it was inclined. In fact the bed was more of a cross between a recliner chair and conventional bed with his head, arms, and underside of his knees supported by the padding. He blinked his eyes several times. The room was dimly lit by a running fireplace at the far end. There was a desk, bookshelves, a pitcher of water and wash bowl, a cupboard with what smelled like dried food behind, and a small unlit stove. A doorway led to a corridor, and Treyu thought it best he find out about this place before something else happened. He tried lifting himself out of bed, but the pocket in the bed held most of his mass, and he had a hard time getting the leverage he needed to pull himself out. He heard a clicking sound in the corridor—a clicking on the floor like that of a dog walking along. Treyu glanced around quickly for a weapon, a rod or bar he could use to swipe at the thing, whatever it was, but he saw nothing.

The "thing" stopped at the doorway and peered in at Treyu. It was a large, white fox, it stood on two legs, and it had arms and hands like a Carinian. It was the size of a Carinian, but unlike a Carinian it had white fur and both the white-fox head and a snickering smile. And smile it did.

"Get back, I say! Do you hear? Get back!" Treyu warned as he pushed himself up to the headboard.

"Relax," the white fox said. "My name is Fraxa. I'm your nurse."

"A nurse? Who are you? What is this place?" Treyu said.

"I told you already, I'm Fraxa, your nurse," she said. "But as to this place, you'll have to wait for that answer."

"No! If I am to be held against my will, I demand to know where I am," Treyu said.

Fraxa laughed.

"You are not held against your will. Get up and leave, if you can," she laughed.

"I won't be laughed at," Treyu said. "I'm Treyu, head butler for Larto on Carinia 2."

"Well I'm Fraxa, head nurse of this facility on Carinia 2," she said. "That's three times I've told you."

"Fraxa?" Treyu asked.

"Fraxa!" she snarled.

Treyu shook in terror, but Fraxa broke out in new laughter.

"I can't snarl for long. Too funny," she said. "Here, let me help you out of bed. You've been out of your senses for some time. And there's much news you must learn. But that too can wait."

Fraxa approached Treyu. Still scared, Treyu pushed hard backward and managed to push himself off the side of the headboard, over the side of the bed, and onto the floor. He stood up and backed himself up against the wall, turned a bit, then backed along the wall until he reached the stove at which point he accidentally heel-stepped on a broom and dustpan combination. The action whipped the broomstick upward and knocked him on the back of the head, but it was only enough to annoy Treyu. He rubbed the back of his head briefly until he could get hold of the broomstick. He then whipped it around and wielded it with both hands like a broadsword. The action of whipping it around caused the dustpan portion to fly across the room and toward the doorway. Mariel happened to be entering that doorway at the time, but she had to step aside to keep from being hit by the dustpan.

"I never thought I'd see you with a broom in hand," Mariel said to Treyu.

"Now put it down before you hurt yourself."

"Mariel! There's a wild fox in here. And she talks!" Treyu said, still holding the broom.

Mariel walked over to Treyu, yanked away the broom, and began sweeping.

"No, she's not wild, and she's not a fox," Mariel said. "Her name is Fraxa, and she's the head nurse here."

"I told him," Fraxa said.

"Well I'll tell him a second time," Mariel said.

"A fourth time," Fraxa said.

"She told you three times already?" Mariel said to Treyu.

"I...Mariel, what's going on?" Treyu asked.

"Self-absorbed, isn't he?" Fraxa said to Mariel.

"He can be at times," Mariel said. "Treyu, Fraxa has been taking care of you. But I see you're well enough to get around. It's about time. A meeting of sorts is waiting to start but held up on your account. Yes, we're all waiting for you! Now pull yourself together and come along."

Mariel led Treyu out of the recovery room, though Treyu was suspicious and kept looking over his shoulder. Fraxa followed from behind, and he didn't trust her.

"Relax," Fraxa said. "I don't bite."

She moved her nuzzle by Treyu's ear and snarled. Treyu jumped with a start, stopped, and turned around as if ready for combat.

"At least not too often," Fraxa laughed.

Mariel laughed too.

"That's not funny," Treyu said.

"Fraxa is just breaking the ice," Mariel said. "Turn around and get moving. We're almost there."

Treyu paused.

"Fraxa should go first," Treyu said.

"Don't trust me, do you?" Fraxa laughed as she moved to the front.

"No, I don't," Treyu said.

The three reached the end of a corridor where Fraxa opened a set of double doors to a dimly-lit large expanse. Fraxa hit a button on the wall just inside the doors, and the large area lit up.

"Hello, everyone. Treyu is aware and here!" Fraxa said.

Hundreds of white-fox faces turned toward Treyu. Treyu nearly lost his nerve right then and there. But a hooded Carinian stood up and walked over to Treyu. She stood in front of him for a moment, and she lifted her hood to reveal her face.

"Berella!" Treyu exclaimed, and he hugged her.

"Treyu, my surrogate friend. Thank you for everything you've done. I'm whole again," Berella said.

"But how? I thought you were lost! Your body was dead! I know. I saw it!" Treyu said.

"You have many questions, as do the others here. These questions and more will be answered in a moment. Come. We are to sit at the head table," Berella said.

Treyu didn't seem to mind being led to the head table by Berella. Seeing as he had shared a special kinship with her when she was in a vine (and that vine was attached to his body), he felt he could trust her with almost anything. As it was, the head table was empty, but there were chairs set for nine, all on one side of the head table such that those sitting would face the audience (like a wedding party). Mariel sat at one end and had Treyu sit next to her (on her left). Fraxa was about to sit next to Treyu, but Treyu started to shake.

"Sit here, Fraxa," Berella said, pointing to the next chair over away from Treyu. "I'll protect Treyu from you, I mean you from Treyu."

Both Fraxa and Berella laughed as they took their seats, and then Mariel joined in the laughing.

"Feel better?" Berella said, now sitting to Treyu's left.

"Feel better?" Mariel echoed in mockery to pester Treyu.

"I don't need your help," Treyu replied to Mariel, now getting a little of his ego back.

"Well that's good to know," Mariel said sarcastically.

The four only sat briefly. From the other end of the head table sounded a horn. Fraxa and Mariel stood, the audience stood, and Berella beckoned Treyu to stand with her (which he did). All watched as a hunched-over elderly white-fox humanoid with sparse fur and a cane entered the room. She was accompanied by two grey fox-humanoid assistants who walked alongside her. Behind her walked a black and white eagle-like humanoid and a Carinian man. Fraxa (and the two assistants) helped the elderly white-fox humanoid sit next to her. The others then took a seat. And so, the seating order from left-to-right as seen by the audience went like this: Mariel, Treyu, Berella, Fraxa, elderly leader, assistant 1, assistant 2, black and white eagle-humanoid, and the Carinian man. The elderly leader nodded to Fraxa to begin. Fraxa stood and spoke.

"People of Belupador, our Great Belupa honors us with her presence!"

A round of cooing from the audience in applause.

"We are also honored to have on my right, Berella of Carinia 1," Fraxa continued.

Berella stood briefly then sat.

"Treyu of Carinia 5," Fraxa said.

Berella and Mariel shoved Treyu up then pulled him down.

"And Mariel of Carinia 2."

Mariel stood, nodded, and sat.

"Of course you know me, your favorite head nurse, Fraxa."

Fraxa looked at Treyu and said, "Five," softly.

"On my left we have Our beloved leader Belupa," Fraxa continued.

Belupa waved to a cooing and happy crowd.

"Prime A and Prime B, her assistants," Fraxa said.

Both assistants stood briefly then sat.

"Aggian the Free," Fraxa said.

Aggian stood, and several eagle-like friends stood in the back and cheered before Aggian retook his seat.

"And finally, Puritas, from the Great Cold Sea of our own Carinia 2," Fraxa said.

Puritas stood. He was tall, charismatic, and had a devilish air about him. Mariel found him very attractive.

"Who is that man?" Mariel asked. "Swap with me, Berella. I want to get a closer look."

Berella looked at Mariel in surprise, but agreed to swap, and the two did.

"And now," Fraxa said, not noticing the swap, "I present to you Our—"

But Fraxa could not finish. Mariel pushed herself into swapping with Fraxa, and now Mariel was next to Belupa. Mariel was about to swap with her, but Belupa gave Mariel an odd stare. Instead, Mariel skipped to Prime A, skipped to Prime B, and then settled on wrenching Aggian the Free over to her old chair and thus was able to sit next to Puritas.

"You have the most amazingly clear complexion," Mariel said. "What cleansers do you use?"

Puritas looked at her in surprise.

"Natural," he said quietly.

"Fraxa, this is completely out of order," Aggian the Free said. "I will not have my feathers ruffled by—"

"My pardon for the interruption, Aggian the Free," Fraxa said.

But the audience grew disconcerted by Mariel's behavior, and whispers sprouted about.

"Please, if I could have your attention," Fraxa said. "Our beloved leader has important news for us."

Fraxa turned to Belupa, but Belupa was busy watching Mariel with intent. Mariel was all but hanging off of Puritas.

"Mariel? Mariel!" Fraxa called.

Belupa put a hand up to Fraxa as if to say, "One moment." Then Belupa motioned for Fraxa to sit and in the same motion stood up. Prime A and Prime B rushed to help her, but she shooed them away.

"Good grooming to you," Belupa said as a greeting.

"Good grooming," the audience replied.

"We live in changing times," Belupa said. "I take no offense to Mariel here. In other times I might. Many things have come to pass. The future remains uncertain. We have visitors here, strange and different, but here they be. Conflict exists outside our realm, both on Carinia 2 and beyond. Excessive use of ethereal power has brought the dread of the Greylinger upon us all. Greylingers who once remained in their own dimension on Carinia 5 have taken over the dark side of Carinia 1. But in the biggest news of all (let the incidentals come later), Greylingers have gained their first foothold on Carinia 2 on the sunlit side."

A dull roar took over part of the audience while the rest fell into shock and disbelief. Even Mariel stopped pawing at Puritas to fathom the news. Belupa motioned her arms for all to listen.

"Hear me then. I shall go over the history," Belupa said. "There is an intelligence known as the Veigon that exists in an iron core known as the Anrega. This pair once existed in the core of Carinia 1, then Carinia 2, and is currently in Carinia 5. Those of us who use the ether owe our ability to the Anrega and Veigon."

Belupa paused for a sip of beverage and then continued.

"Our rule of law has been this," Belupa continued. "Use only as much ethereal power as is needed and only a little at a time. A little dirt mixed with much snow leaves the snow still white, but much dirt in only a little snow leaves the snow dark. We have followed the former, the Bleuhs the latter. Our conservative use of ethereal energy never generated enough negative energy to create Greylingers. But as for the Bleuhs, their excessive use has. Any excess use of ethereal energy creates Greylingers who feed on such and reverberate evil energy back into the ether. We have reached the result. The ether has become polluted with first whispers and now yells of Greylinger desire and action."

"Greylingers exist on Carinia 5 because of the Anrega," Belupa said. "The Anrega, in addition to housing the Veigon, also stores waste ethereal energy in the form of Greylingers. The Anrega is full, not because of the Veigon or our use, but because of Bleuh ethereal use. Even with Bleuhs going eethi as far away as Carinia 1, the result is new Greylinger deposits in the Anrega on Carinia 5. With the Anrega full, the Greylingers have followed the waste ethereal trail to Carinia 1, where they feast heavily in oceans on the dark side, particularly in water creatures and the land creatures known as Pleelellicans."

"The leader of the Bleuhs is (or was) Libriota, a Bleuh herself who has recently perished in battle with Berella," Belupa said. "Berella also perished in the battle, but we have successfully recorporealized her."

Berella took a bow.

"Before Libriota's passing, she and the Bleuhs realized the Greylingers were contaminating their planet. Because of this, they decided these Greylingers needed to be transferred elsewhere. They experimented with two places—Carinia Zero, and Carinia 2. Carinia Zero failed. As for Carinia 2—"

"As for Carinia 2, that's my home!" Mariel said. "Bleuhs have no business on my planet."

"I had not called you, Mariel, but you may speak," Belupa said.

"We should be rid of them," Mariel said. "Especially if they are experimenting on our planet."

"They are indeed," Belupa said. "They have created an ethereal conduit between Carinia 1 and 2. Through this conduit they pump excess Greylingers into our planet."

The audience shouted questions about how the Bleuhs could do this, where were the Grens in all this, what can citizens do about it, and did anyone cause the situation. Belupa motioned her arms again for the audience to settle down so she could speak.

"There is another problem. Water and ice are being consumed at a rapid rate on

Carinia 5. Cold-water Martaceans are dying off. Greylingers are flooding over here from Carinia 5 as well. The cause," Belupa paused, and she turned her head in Treyu's direction.

Treyu looked around in surprise as if he'd been caught by carnivores.

"I don't understand," Treyu said. "Our ship crashed here. We didn't cause anything to happen. Except maybe crush a little snow."

A little outrage from the audience. Calls for punishment for crushing a snow monument.

"My ancestors died at that spot, and he destroyed the monument!" one called out while another said, "And he only 'crushed a little snow'. How vulgar!"

"Rest easy, friends," Belupa said. "There might be more snow-crushing before things work themselves out."

"Are we to sit here and do nothing while 'things work themselves out'?" called another.

"That we will decide," Belupa said. "Now patience, please! Hear more before you gash the guest."

"Gash the guest, gash the guest!" the audience chanted.

"Give me a shot. I'll leave my tooth imprint," said one.

"And I have a tooth that needs pulling. Let me pull on some Carinian flesh," said another.

The audience synced up into a snarl and growl sequence, waxing and waning like the call of death on the wind.

"Let's get out of here," Treyu said to Berella, and he got up to leave.

But the Velupians in the audience fell into pounce mode.

"Don't move," Fraxa said as she grabbed Treyu's arm. "Sit down normally. Not too fast, not too slow. Pretend you are the only one here. Be quiet until called."

Treyu sat. Belupa motioned her arms again for peace and quiet, and she spoke.

"We must work together or perish in the chaos. There need not be chaos, as long as I am your leader. Now hear me through. I have been in contact with other Velupian settlements. We have gone eethi and witnessed the chain of events that led to this manifestation. An ethereal link from two ethereal eddies in Carinia Zero has triggered the creation of an egg known as the Amnus. The Amnus is growing and preparing to launch from Carinia 5 to Carinia Zero. In the distant past, the Amnus would come back and merge with the Veigon. The Veigon and Anrega would then leave the planet and go to another. But we do not know where the Anrega will go. Further, we do not know how this would affect Carinia 2. The Greylingers might be dumped here. They might destroy us. Or the Anrega and Veigon might come back here and destroy this planet. We don't know what it will do. But we do know that this Amnus creation was due to the interaction of a single Carinian."

The audience snarled and growled at Treyu. Belupa walked over toward Treyu, and he was sure she would point to him. But then she walked past him, and Treyu had a sudden feeling she'd pull Berella aside. Had to be. Her presence was still a mystery to Treyu, and he figured this was how he was going to find out how she got back to the corporeal state.

"No!" Treyu said suddenly as he jumped to his feet and blocked Belupa's way with Berella to his back. "I won't let you take her. She won't be killed again. No, I say! Do you hear?"

"Stand aside, Treyu," Berella said as she tried to stand up.

"No," Treyu said, pushing her back in her seat. "I won't let them take you. Whatever you've done, I know you had to do it. I'm just glad you're here. I don't blame you for the Amnus."

"Neither do they," Berella said.

"Huh?" Treyu said in confusion.

"Bring out the Carinian," Belupa said around Treyu.

Treyu turned around and watched as the young toddler Lanietta was brought out.

"It's you again," Claus said.

"I don't remember this," young Lanietta said.

"She was found amongst the wreckage," Berella said to Treyu. "In fact, she was the one who convinced us you were still alive."

"You're telling me this little girl created the Amnus?" Treyu said in disbelief. "Of all the impossible, unbelievable stories. I suppose she cleaned up the asteroid belt and made supper for the next three billion years."

"Don't be absurd," Belupa said. "No one is *that* powerful. Lanietta did not choose to make the Amnus. But her corporeal existence in relation to the creation of the Amnus is concomitant, codependent, and co-morbid."

As soon as Belupa said, "Co-morbid," the Velupians salivated.

"Then the solution is easy," an audience member said. "Destroying Lanietta will destroy the Amnus."

"They want to kill you!" Claus said.

"I'm glad I don't remember this," young Lanietta said. "I don't think I could bear such a memory."

"But will it get rid of the Amnus and the Greylingers?" another audience member yelled out above the rising commotion.

"Carinia 2 is lost," Puritas said. "The Bleuhs control it with the help of Greylingers, if you will pardon the interruption, Great Belupa."

"You are pardoned. You were to be called next as it is. Please speak," Belupa said as she calmed the audience with her arms.

"As you know, the Bleuhs have declared martial law over the Grens," Puritas said. "Your settlement is safe for the moment, yes, because others do not know of it. Still, Velupians must remain ever vigilant and gather news of the outsiders. With the help of Aggian the Free and the Great Belupa, we discovered an unusual spike in eethi activity, first beginning on Carinia 5, and then continuing on a spaceship that landed on the dark side of Carinia 1. Aggian the Free and I then traveled to Carinia 1 to find those responsible for the spike, but we

were too late. We only found this Carinian."

Puritas motioned to a guard who relayed the signal, and out walked Larbiabba.

"Larbiabba!" Mariel screamed, and she rushed up to hug her.

"Larbiabba?" Treyu asked. "How in the universe—"

"Patience," Berella said. "It will be explained."

"You knew of this?"

"Of course," Berella said.

"But how? What's going on? Tell me!" Treyu said.

"You must wait," Berella said. "My turn for speech will arrive soon."

"How is it you knew but Mariel didn't? Berella, all this—" Treyu started.

"Place a chair next to Berella for Larbiabba," Belupa said. "I will also have Mariel sit and Larbiabba speak."

"When do I get my chair back?" Aggian the Free protested.

"In a moment," Belupa said. "Larbiabba, if you please."

"Thank you," Larbiabba said. "Great Belupa, fellow Velupians, fellow Carinians, Aggian the Free and his folk, I bid you greetings. I am Larbiabba, a Gren who has studied the Bleuhs."

Moans of despair.

"Studied the Bleuhs or studied to be a Bleuh?" one heckler yelled.

"I'm fully Gren, I assure you. Nor am I arrogant like the Bleuhs," Larbiabba said.

Berella glanced at Larbiabba.

"Though not all Bleuhs are bad," Larbiabba added while patting Berella.

"Are you a Gren?" Mariel whispered to Puritas.

"Yes, I am," he replied.

"I knew it! Grens always believe in cleanliness," Mariel said.

"I will start my story at Carinia 5, where I have spent much time with Treyu helping the resistance. It was there where I met Larto, Lanshalla, Treyu, and Mariel," Larbiabba said.

Larbiabba explained how things went on Carinia 5, the experiment, Lanshalla falling into daze, Libriota's arrival, the group's escape, the time spent on Carinia 2, Berella's involvement (for which Berella stood and spoke), the departure for Carinia 1, Berella-the-vine, Berella's sister, Tiloto, Treyu's transformation into Treina, the Pleelellicans, and the arena.

"We were separated," Larbiabba said. "The squid-like creature pulled Lanshalla, Berella-the-vine, and me underwater, leaving Larto, Mariel, and Treyu behind."

Berella shuddered.

"Each of us was fighting to subdue this thing, but each of us also needed air. Lanshalla tried creating a pocket for the three of us to breathe, but the creature kept beating its other tentacles at her (and us for that matter). Berella strangled the creature, and I couldn't do much but try to poke out its eyes. It was Lanshalla who, after many failed attempts, finally went eethi, and when she did, she invaded and took over the creature's ethereal spirit, forcing it to dive deeper and deeper. The pressure gave me an incredible headache, and I nearly lost awareness when we reached an underwater cave on a seamount and entered into what looked like the creature's lair."

"Did you get a headache too?" Treyu asked Berella.

"I was still a vine," Berella said, "but my fibers did fray, yes."

"We were then surprised to find a dozen or so other creatures sitting on nests, protecting their eggs," Larbiabba continued. "It became clear this creature was a male and a mate to these female creatures. The females first squawked at us, but then Berella successfully bound the male creature's tentacles, rendering him unable to move or fight. Seeing this, the females attacked. Some pecked at Lanshalla and me while others pecked at Berella to free the male. Berella adjusted as best she could to avoid the pecking, but each time she did, her grip loosened, and the male worked in leverage to fight all the more. The male would be free soon, and we had to stop things. I went eethi to quiet down the male, which freed Lanshalla's

eethi spirit to go after the females while her physical body ran to nest after nest and jumped on the eggs, crushing them and thus killing them."

"But how did you escape? And Lanshalla? She's dead, you know. She and Larto were pulled into Carinia Zero," Treyu interrupted.

The audience snarled at Treyu.

"Lanshalla also knew of your plight, Treyu," Larbiabba said. "She kept a link with Larto that she shared with Berella and me. Larto, Treyu, and Mariel were captured first by the Pleelellicans, and then by Tiloto of the Imperial Bleuhs. They were to be taken before the Hierarchy, but they discovered Lanshalla's body."

"That was the worst moment ever," Treyu said. "Larto was devastated. But I still don't understand. How—"

"A female does not take kindly to the destruction of her children," Larbiabba said. "The female creatures ganged up on Lanshalla and killed her corporeal body. But her death was not in vain. It bought me time to take the male creature out."

"Out? Out where?" Treyu asked.

Larbiabba pointed over to a tall set of doors. The doors were opened, and in walked the squid creature. The audience gasped and made ready to attack.

"Larbiabba. I do hope you have a good reason for bringing such a creature here," Belupa said.

"Not to mention this—how did you get him from Carinia 1 to this planet?" Treyu asked.

"He has special ethereal transport powers I intend to use to find the Amnus which in turn I'll use against the Bleuhs, to answer both questions," Larbiabba said. "He was once a Martacean, you see—a whale-like creature created by the Veigon. But Greylinger energy tortured and contorted him into this form. The Bleuhs often ignore the damage done to animals of the Veigon. Pioraboo will no longer be ignored."

"Pioraboo?" Treyu asked.

"That's his name," Larbiabba said.

"Then you have a plan, Larbiabba?" Belupa asked.

"Yes. Lanshalla is now pure ethereal. She and Larto are stationed in Carinia Zero and for a very long time. Their daughter, Lanietta, is with us. Lanshalla, who has maintained an ethereal communication link with me, has charged me with retrieving the Amnus and using it to stop the Bleuhs. Further, Lanietta is to be protected in case something goes wrong. Mariel is to be Lanietta's guardian. Both will remain here, and both will be transformed to hide their identities until it's over. Lanietta's memory will be wiped clean of these events leading up to her transformation."

"Until what is over?" Treyu asked.

"Civil war," Larbiabba said. "With the Amnus and Pioraboo, we will attack the Bleuhs directly and free Carinia 2."

Cheers from the Velupians.

"But I want to help," young Lanietta said to Claus. "Mommy wanted me protected? I could have helped. I could have."

"It is time then," Belupa said. "Larbiabba, begin the transformation."

"What about Puritas?" Mariel asked. "Will he stay with me?"

"He has his own domain and his own duties," Belupa said.

"But if Lanietta's protection is this important, shouldn't I have help?" Mariel asked.

Puritas stepped forward and spoke.

"I will help protect Lanietta," Puritas said. "Include me in the transformation."

"Puritas, this transformation is not to be taken lightly," Belupa said. "You will become one of us."

"I understand," Puritas said. "In the end, Velupians might be the only ones left."

"I don't like the sound of that," Treyu said.

"You should stay with us then," Berella said.

"You mean to say you're going to become one of them? A Velupian? A white fox?" Treyu asked.

"Of course. There was never a question about that," Berella said.

"Why didn't I know about it?" Treyu asked.

"Velupians, this is a special moment. For the first time in recorded history, we are adding citizens through transformation," Belupa said.

"What about you, Larbiabba?" Treyu asked. "Are you becoming a white fox too?"

"No. But Pioraboo is," Larbiabba said. "To those outside, he will be but a pet. And I but a Carinian. As it turns out, Pioraboo will be performing the transformation."

"You mean that big squid thing that...that...killed...is going to just transform us like getting a fresh set of clothes?" Treyu asked.

"Yes," Larbiabba said. "Are you ready?"

"Why did I volunteer for this? I should have—"

"Stayed home," Berella finished for Treyu. "Except that home won't be the same for long. Not for any of us. Come along, Treyu. I'll help you through this."

"And so will I," Fraxa said with a growl in her voice. "Once your transformation is complete, I'll help with your adjustment."

"We have prepared the laboratory for you, Larbiabba," Belupa said.

"Thank you. This way, everyone," Larbiabba said.

Larbiabba led Pioraboo, Treyu, Berella, Mariel, Puritas, and toddler Lanietta into a laboratory with a tall ceiling. It looked very much like the one the Pleelellicans had, only there were multiple sets of posts with a single, very-tall set for Pioraboo.

"Please, everyone. Select a post pair and place a hand on each of the posts," Larbiabba said.

Larbiabba stood by a control station while the others selected a set of posts. Domes the size of hats descended on each person's head. Larbiabba hit several buttons, and flywheel-like contraptions spun up, generating large amounts of ethero-magnetic energy. Larbiabba nodded to Pioraboo. Pioraboo had a tentacle each on his set of posts, but he also had a tentacle each touch the others. Pioraboo then played music through his baleen mouth. Colors of yellow and blue undulated and mixed throughout his body into a faded pea-green color. Ethereal energy carried into everyone (except Larbiabba), and the transformation happened. All involved took on white-fox form features including white fur, yet they kept their mass except for Pioraboo who through mass compression reduced his size to that of an actual arctic white fox.

"Remove your paws from the posts," Larbiabba said. "The transformation is complete."

Those who had changed looked at each other in surprise. Lanietta the fox became anxious and started to cry out.

"Shh," Larbiabba said as she walked over to the toddler. "You are a white fox, with a heart as pure and fresh as your white coat."

Larbiabba drew her hands over toddler Lanietta's eyes and closed them. Larbiabba then lightly pressed her forehead against the toddler's forehead and whispered things.

"She is erasing my memory," young Lanietta said to Claus. "I can feel it. To think I really believed I was a white fox when I was young."

"You still are young," Claus said.

"Well, *younger*," young Lanietta said.

Larbiabba motioned Mariel and Puritas over and had them stand behind toddler Lanietta. Larbiabba turned toddler Lanietta around and then whispered the following.

"When you open your eyes, you will see your guardian—Nanna," Larbiabba said. "I will tap you three times when it's time."

Larbiabba paused for a moment. Mariel looked nervous. Puritas patted her on the shoulder. Larbiabba nodded to them that things would be well and good, and then Larbiabba tapped toddler Lanietta three times on the head. Toddler Lanietta opened her eyes.

"Nanna!" she said.

"This is my first memory," young Lanietta said to Claus. "Nanna."

"This is Nanna's helper. His name is Puritas," Larbiabba said.

Toddler Lanietta smiled at Puritas. Mariel and Puritas led toddler Lanietta out of the transformation room and into a room with several other white fox children. Fraxa was giving instruction on how to dive into the snow.

"Fraxa, this is Lanietta," Mariel said.

"Please, come in," Fraxa said. "We are about to go hunting. Would you care to join us?"

"Yes, thank you," Mariel said.

"This all seems very benign," Claus said.

"For now," young Lanietta said.

Fraxa led the group outside to a snow bank.

"This is it," young Lanietta said to Claus. "I...was so shy."

"I don't understand," Claus said. "There's nothing but this snow bank."

"The snow bank has been filled with rabbits. Now watch what I do," Fraxa said.

Fraxa leapt into the air head-first. Her body followed a catenary arch, and she descended nose-first into the snow bank. The front half of her body was buried, but her hind legs stuck out straight up, leaving her apparently trapped in the snow. But Fraxa used her front legs/arms to pull herself out, and when she did, she revealed a small rabbit in her jaw. She spat the rabbit into her hand and tossed it into the snow bank.

"Now each of you, dive into the snowbank for a rabbit. Dive!" Fraxa urged.

The students dove into the snowbank at the same time. Students bumped against students, rabbits scampered all over, and half the students were stuck in the snow with their hind legs to the sky while the other half managed to pull themselves out with rabbits in their jaws. They ran over to Fraxa with excitement over their catches. But toddler Lanietta held off. She didn't like the commotion and fighting over a pile of rabbits. She pawed at the very edge of the snowbank and found three bunnies.

They looked at her and remained motionless in terror. Toddler Lanietta tried to befriend them as best as a white fox can with bunnies.

"Take a bunny, Lanietta," Fraxa said. "Take one in your mouth."

Toddler Lanietta took a bunny in her front paw and held it up to her face. The bunny remained terrified and motionless. Toddler Lanietta opened her jaw a little and brought the bunny closer. She could smell the bunny, and in a split second of that smell she experienced lifetimes of lagomorphic struggle. Hunted, hunted, hunted with no peace for the weary and worn.

"No," toddler Lanietta said. "No."

She moved to place the bunny back in the snowbank, but before she could complete her motion, a classmate snatched the bunny from her paw into his jaw and ran off with it. Toddler Lanietta tried to give chase, but she was a mere toddler and couldn't run. The classmate, realizing he could not taunt her with a chase, cashed in on her misery by turning around and crushing the bunny in his jaws. He then ate the bunny with as much noise and slobber as he could.

Toddler Lanietta cried.

"You see?" young Lanietta said to Claus. "Even with a fresh mind, it wasn't long before another being soiled it with his evil. Soiled! When does one get the right to purity? How many brain wipes are required?"

"I'm surprised to hear you speak like this, Lanietta," Claus said. "Your adult self caused much misery to others. You could have spared evil's ripple effect. That is your excuse, right? That evil begets evil, and you are but a pawn in the path of poison? It takes a person of strength to stop. And you did so. You chose not to eat the rabbit."

"The rabbit was killed anyway!" young Lanietta said.

"But not by your hand! Or at least your paw," Claus said.

"I don't understand my mother at all," young Lanietta continued. "This experience with white foxes was supposed to protect me? It didn't. Just exposed me to different evil."

The vision faded.

"I don't know when it will stop, Claus. I really don't."

Chapter 85: Libriota Returns

"Is there more?" Claus asked. "The vision stopped. Or has it?"

The two stood in the Anrega orb chamber. Young Lanietta held a holographic bunny image in her hand. Another orb in the chamber lit, and from that orb marched a line of Imperial Bleuhs with Tiloto leading the way. Image of Tiloto stole up to young Lanietta, swiped the bunny from her, and returned to the marching line as it headed for a new orb. Solemnly, young Lanietta followed the marching line up to this new orb, stopped at the orb, and placed a hand on it.

"It's Tiloto," she said. "His spirit is stored in this orb. And so is the Pleelellican queen."

"Larto thought he fathered a child with her," Claus said.

"He didn't," young Lanietta said. "But she did bear a child. And...yes, the story is here."

Claus noticed ethereal energy transfer from young Lanietta to the orb.

"Lanietta, is this a good idea?" Claus asked.

Claus's question went unanswered. The two stood in front of the main entrance to the Bleuh Hierarchy building. Tiloto arrived with the king and queen Pleelellican. The building was tall and overwhelming with an intricate yet stunning design. Bleuhs from all around gave nasty stares to the Pleelellicans.

"They will be dealt with," Tiloto assured them. "Do not worry."

Tiloto (with his guards) escorted the Pleelellicans inside the building. The lobby was in fact an atrium running practically the entire height of the building. Looking upward, one saw story after story of windows. It was as if the outside of the building had been inverted, changed from convex to concave or such. Tiloto and guards escorted the two to a large elevator and headed practically to the top. The elevator then traveled laterally, took a corner sharply, and came to a sudden stop. The doors opened to a large room with a procreation tank.

"What is this madness?" the queen asked.

"Into the tank," Tiloto said.

"No! I will not be manipulated!" the queen said. "What happened to the Hierarchy? I see no one here!"

"The Hierarchy has ordered this," Tiloto said. "You are to have your child here."

"I'm not due! This is completely out of order. You cannot order me to deliver my baby now," the queen said.

"Yes, I can," Tiloto said.

Tiloto grabbed the queen by the arm and pulled her toward the tank. The king jumped Tiloto from behind to strangle him, but a guard clocked the king on the skull and rendered him unconscious. Freed from the king, Tiloto threw the queen over the tank's edge. The queen fell in with a splash. The tank was transparent, and so Tiloto and the guards could see the queen struggling to survive in the blue fluid.

"Help! Help!" she screamed.

"Activate the sequence," Tiloto said to a guard.

"No!" the queen cried.

The guard stood by the tank and pressed several buttons. A wave built up in the tank, flowing from side to side. The wave pushed the queen back and forth, slamming her against opposite walls of the tank. The wave built up higher and higher, cresting as it slammed the queen against each wall. Indeed, it rapidly approached a point where it would completely fall backward onto itself.

The vision stopped. Young Lanietta had released her hand from the orb. She was distraught.

"I can't watch this," she said. "I can't."

Claus paused. What could he say? He took a deep breath.

"You are tired?" she asked.

"I do not know what to advise, if advice can be given," he said.

"It seems I pause often," she said. "I am weak. I used to pride myself on being strong. Perhaps I need rest. No, I cannot rest. I will push on, Claus."

Young Lanietta placed her hand on the orb, and again ethereal energy flowed from her arm to the orb. The vision restored. The blue wave slammed the queen against the wall, lifted her up, and pulled her back down toward the center of the tank, becoming yellow during this part of the cycle, only to pick her up and slam her against the opposite wall, becoming blue again. The cycle increased speed, and the blue-yellow-blue cycle kept up pace such that all became a flickering mess that solidified into a faded pea-green color. The queen gave out a final scream, the wave action stopped, and the queen's body split open. Out emerged a fast-growing Bleuh. The queen's body was nothing but an empty shell now, and it deflated and shriveled like the hide of a skinned animal.

Young Lanietta screamed. Claus tried to comfort her, but there was nothing he could do. The Bleuh grew quickly from baby to toddler to young adult then finally into a Bleuh adult—Libriota. She used remnant tissue from the queen as a tunic.

"Well done," Libriota said to Tiloto.

Tiloto stood in shock at the horror he had witnessed. But it was not over. Libriota space-jumped out of the tank and onto the floor just in front of Tiloto.

"What? Who? You just—" Tiloto stammered.

"Yes! I space-jumped. Magnificent!" Libriota replied. "I know much else about the ether and about who else can space-jump."

"What do you mean? Others who tried, died," Tiloto said.

"But not all," Libriota said. "Lanshalla was first. Then Larbiabba and others with them. Lanshalla has moved on. But Larbiabba remains corporeal. She and I are the only ones who can space-jump without help."

"How do you know this? What makes you say as such?" Tiloto asked.

"I told you, I know much about the ether. My new corporeal existence has given me such. Just remember this, Tiloto—the ether tells no lies and remembers all," Libriota said. "Were you able to restore Indikat?"

"No," Tiloto said. "I'm still not sure how we restored *you*."

"I might go after him later. No matter. But as to your confusion, the Pleelellican queen had previously been secretly captured by the Hierarchy and tagged with a link to my ethereal spirit as a precaution. After my corporeal death, I floated in the ether for a bit until the Pleelellican doctor connected Larto to the queen. When that happened, I locked onto her body and pushed my ethereal self into her. Larto thought he'd fathered another child. Fool! He was not so powerful after all. Both he and Lanshalla have lost their corporeal bodies. Their ethereal spirits are locked in Carinia Zero. They can no longer interfere with my new plan."

"What plan?" Tiloto asked.

"I intend to commandeer the Anrega," Libriota said.

"That's impossible. The—" Tiloto tried to say, but Libriota extended her hand span and used it like a clamp, running from under his jaw to the top of his head, forcing his mouth closed.

"I can apply but a little more force and crush your skull. Do you doubt me now?" she asked.

Tiloto nodded, "no," with terror in his eyes.

"Good," she said, now releasing her grip and returning her hand to normal.

Young Lanietta changed her grip on the orb. The vision froze.

"And still," young Lanietta said. "It continues. You see this, Claus? Do you?"

"I see it," Claus said. "It sickens me, but it doesn't surprise me. I don't mean to bring up the cliché, but the dichotomy applies again—is it best to see the history of evil, even relive it and cause this pain, or move on and let it stay in the past? Grandma Broc spoke of moving on to the next stepping stone."

"Then why can't I do that?" young Lanietta said.

"These visions are holding the PRAAD in check while Labba and the others evacuate Earth," Claus said.

"I feel like the dam holding back the flood," young Lanietta said. "But the flood will win. I will burst. Then what, Claus? Am I to die?"

"I don't know," Claus said. "But I will stay with you to the end, whatever that is. If I can apply a little mortar to hold the dam together, I will."

"There's nothing here for you," young Lanietta said. "This is all Carinian treachery."

"There's you," Claus said. "Let's see this through and judge later."

Young Lanietta paused, she nodded her head in agreement, and she restored her grip on the orb to resume the vision.

"First we need a ruse," Libriota said to Tiloto.

Just then, Celiba entered.

"Welcome back, Libriota," Celiba said. "All is ready for the next phase."

"Thank you," Libriota said.

"You know about this?" Tiloto asked Celiba.

"We've been monitoring your progress, Tiloto," Celiba said. "The Hierarchy gives instructions for the king's torture so that Pleelellicans will launch a rescue effort. Cameras are on the tank and are ready to broadcast such torture."

Celiba picked up the unconscious Pleelellican king and threw him into the tank. He immediately awoke.

"Why was I not informed?" Tiloto asked.

"You are told things as needed," Libriota said.

The king splashed about in the pool and was horrified at seeing his wife's head bobbing on the fluid's surface like debris.

"Get me out! Please!" he said.

Libriota walked over to a large display monitor and activated it. The display showed the stadium, and Pleelellicans were already gathered in it for discussion about their Bleuh problem.

"Speak freely to your people, if you like," Libriota said.

A large display in the stadium showed the king along with the queen's head. Pleelellicans gasped at the sight.

"My fellow Pleelellicans," he said. "Imperial Bleuhs have killed your queen. Hideous, savage, vile vermin be the Bleuhs. I expect to be tortured or killed. But we are Pleelellicans. Remember this in your heart. No matter what, we Pleelellicans stand forever."

"Torture him, Tiloto," Libriota said.

Tiloto hesitated.

"Do it! Like this!" she said.

Libriota sent a plasma ball at the king. It shocked him and caused him to shake. Next, she sent three energy hands into the tank. They lifted him up into the air, one each on his wrists and the third by the neck. Libriota then sent a blast of air over into the tank and under the king's gills to dry them out. He foamed at the mouth.

"You have outraged the Pleelellican community," said a Pleelellican in the stadium.

"And?" Libriota asked.

"We demand you return the king," the Pleelellican said.

"Only demand? How disappointing," Libriota said. "Apparently you do not realize what we can do. Celiba?"

Celiba left the room and returned with Vebenni in chains.

"Watch your future!" Libriota said.

Libriota took Vebenni and threw him into the tank.

"Libriota, don't you think we should—" Tiloto started to say, but Libriota shot him a stare that shattered his strength to the core.

"Your king and Vebenni are now in the tank," Libriota said. "The king has nearly expired from slow torture. But I shall be merciful with Vebenni."

Libriota shot a single plasma ball at Vebenni. It inflated him, caused him to rise, and he burst.

"No," young Lanietta said softly to Claus as she looked at him with weary eyes. "No."

Young Lanietta had released her hand from the orb. When she did, another orb in the far distance lit up. A beam carried from that orb over to young Lanietta, and she looked up. The scene changed. Mariel took toddler Lanietta back from the snow pile and into a foxhole made of snow. From the outside, the entrance was unobservable until one was practically upon it, and there were no terrain changes that indicated a domicile, but once inside, the space was as plentiful and cozy as a house. Despite the comfortable home, toddler Lanietta shook like a leaf.

"The bunny. The bunny," she obsessed.

"Let me tell you something," Mariel said. "Whenever I become upset, I clean a square. Look."

Mariel drew the outline of a square on the floor using her hind leg. She then took a broom and brushed dirt into a dustpan.

"See?" she said. "Guess what? I have a present for you."

Mariel disappeared for a moment and returned with a small broom and dustpan.

"Now you draw a square," Mariel said.

Toddler Lanietta drew a square. She took the small broom and gingerly swept dirt from the square to the little dustpan. She looked up at Mariel and smiled.

"See? All better!" Mariel said.

"All better," toddler Lanietta said.

"Nanna," young Lanietta said. "Make it all better. Nanna!"

Adult Lanietta also yelled out, "Nanna!"

Claus looked back at adult Lanietta in surprise, then he returned his attention to the vision.

"Nanna," toddler Lanietta said. "May I clean another square?"

Mariel dropped to toddler Lanietta's level, hugged her with a smile, and said, "Yes, my sweet. Clean another square."

"Nanna!" young Lanietta said, and the beam stopped.

"Nanna!" adult Lanietta echoed.

A different distant orb sent a beam to young Lanietta. The scene changed again. Larbiabba stood outside by a white sled with Pioraboo at her side.

"Please let me accompany you," Berella said.

"No. You have your own mission with the Velupians," Larbiabba said. "I will make the attempt first. If I do not return with the Amnus—"

"I will go after it and drag Treyu with me," Berella said.

"You will safeguard the Velupian settlements, protect Lanietta, and seek covert ways of disrupting the Bleuhs."

"You'll be exposed out in the snow. I can keep you company," Berella said.

"Treyu would not like that. Besides, I have support from elsewhere," Larbiabba said.

"Lanshalla? Larto?" Berella said.

"I have links with both of them. Even now, Lanshalla is guiding me to my next activity. Do not underestimate her," Larbiabba said. "Yes, I have plenty of company. In addition, Pioraboo will act as my sled dog and pull me along."

"Does he have the strength?" Berella asked.

"Watch this!" Larbiabba said.

Larbiabba whispered into Pioraboo's ear, and he changed from a white fox to a dog resembling an Alaskan Malamute.

"I hope to return soon," Larbiabba said as she hugged Berella.

"I will miss you," Berella said in reply.

The two released their embrace, Larbiabba took command of the sled, and she yelled out a command to go:

"Shrike!"

Pioraboo took off, and the two quickly faded into the distance.

The distant beam ended, and Tiloto's orb flashed an image before Claus and young Lanietta, showing Libriota and the procreation tank.

"Know that I, Libriota, will take each of you one by one and torture you as I have with your fellow Pleelellicans here," Libriota said to the Pleelellicans in the stadium. "Your king has but moments of life left. What say you?"

"Please return the bodies to us," said the spokesperson. "We will honor them in our own way."

"Fools! All shall perish this way! Do you hear? All!" Libriota yelled.

Outraged at the Pleelellican lack of desire to launch an attacking force against the Bleuhs, Libriota cut off the video feed to the Pleelellicans.

"The Hierarchy suggests—" Celiba started to say.

"I know what they suggest. Go ahead and say it," Libriota said. "They suggest we...we...well?"

"Lure in, lash not," Celiba said.

"Lure in," Libriota echoed. "With souls."

"They suggest we acquire Greylingers and pass them off as Gren souls for consumption by the Pleelellicans," Celiba said.

"Yes, I know what they suggest. Just not as fun," Libriota said.

"They need you to harness the Greylingers," Celiba said. "No one else has the power."

"No other corporeal Bleuh has the power," Libriota said. "Still, there is Lanshalla—"

"Who is incorporeal," Celiba added.

"And Larbiabba," Libriota continued.

"Who is a Gren with Bleuh abilities," Celiba said.

Libriota paused then laughed.

"Have the wanna-be Bleuh offer Greylingers to the Pleelellicans," Libriota said. "I must be off to liberate the Anrega as it is."

"No one knows where Larbiabba is," Celiba said.

"She would never agree to it anyway," Tiloto said.

"Must I do everything in this forsaken universe?" Libriota ranted. "Very well. I'll start the Greylinger process then leave you in charge, Celiba."

"Me in charge of Greylingers?" Celiba perspired.

"Yes. Someone has to do the laundry every now and then. Tiloto won't do it, and I can't be slave to all," Libriota continued to rant. "You know, your sister was queasy about performing her duty. But I gave her an incentive, as I now give you an incentive."

Libriota stepped over to the tank and sent two ethereal plasma balls into the king (one from each hand). The plasma balls intersected then bisected his body vertically, creating a rift into the Greylinger world. The king screamed briefly as this happened, but his body was now lifeless. Libriota called for Biautus to be revivified into the king's body. The creature that Berella once feared existed again. But he had a new ability.

"Watch," Libriota said.

Biautus projected a family scene of Pleelellican souls, all happy and frolicking together. Libriota restored the feed to the Pleelellican stadium, and the fake Pleelellican souls advertised their availability.

"Get a new soul now!" said one of the fake souls.

"If you can," said another.

The fake souls laughed.

"We're in the main Bleuh Hierarchy building," said a third.

"But we're going on a visit to the sea," said a fourth.

Laughter again from the fake souls. Biautus then projected the souls leaving the tank, going outside, and heading to the sea while a drone camera followed them and relayed such adventure to the Pleelellican stadium. Biautus remained behind in the procreation tank.

"I have issued Biautus an order to stay in the tank," Libriota said. "He will project as many Pleelellican fake souls as needed. But you must feed him periodically, Celiba. This one prefers Pleelellican meat. Do not make the same mistake as your sister, or Biautus will take a liking to Bleuh meat. Tiloto, make sure Celiba does as ordered. If not, throw her in. And now I'm off."

Libriota space-jumped way. To where, Celiba did not know. Celiba exchanged glances with Tiloto.

"I wonder if he's hungry," Tiloto said.

Biautus gave a snarl and growl.

"Does that answer your question?" Celiba said. "Get ready to harvest Pleelellicans."

The vision from Tiloto's orb stopped, and the first distant beam resumed.

"Who are the other orbs, Lanietta? Who is this one?" Claus asked.

"It's Nanna. Mariel," young Lanietta said. "The other one was Larbiabba."

The scene changed back to toddler Lanietta, who was still sweeping squares. But a stabbing pain caught her temples, and she fell in distress.

"Ow!" she cried.

Mariel picked her up and hugged her.

"I felt like a big spider was pinching me here," she said as she pointed to her temples.

"There, there, you're safe with me. Touch your face. See? No spiders," Mariel reassured her.

"Then what was it? It was swimming in a tank, and it jumped on my face and hurt me!" toddler Lanietta said.

"It wasn't a spider," Mariel said. "Tell you what, let's go fishing for dinner. There's a frozen lake nearby, and there are no spiders there."

Toddler Lanietta paused and looked at Mariel in the eye. Mariel returned the gaze and nodded to reassure toddler Lanietta again. Toddler Lanietta's fear faded, and so Mariel led her out of the foxhole and to the frozen lake.

Mariel's distant beam stopped, and a totally new beam started up from a distant orb. Claus looked at young Lanietta.

"Treyu," she said.

The new beam offered a scene of the Great Belupa, who was in conference with her assistants, with Fraxa, Berella, Treyu, and Aggian the Free.

"Berella and Fraxa have come up with a plan," Belupa said.

"Before Larbiabba left, we took several readings of Pioraboo," Fraxa said. "From his ethos, plus Berella's transmutation knowledge when she was a vine, we—"

"Still hard to believe Berella was a vine," Aggian the Free said.

"Which I can discuss another time, as ours is currently short," Berella said.

"Yes," Fraxa continued. "From Berella's transmutation knowledge, we've come up with these."

Fraxa gave a call, and Velupian workers brought forth bambooph weapons.

"This reminds me of Labba and Argo, Arberella, Cenina Island, and Morcellus the Martacean," Claus said.

"Bamboophi. From Martaceans. Yes," young Lanietta said.

"We will use them to carve tunnels up to the Gren cities," Fraxa said.

"And then as weapons when the time comes," Berella said.

"If it comes to that," Fraxa said.

"You're going then?" Treyu asked. "I had hoped we could spend time here."

"We will," Berella said. "You're coming with us."

"What?" Treyu said in surprise.

"Yes," Fraxa said as she snarled in Treyu's ear. "Now that you're in my form, I can bite you in the nape as needed."

"Fraxa, behave," Berella said. "I get first dibs on his nape."

Berella and Fraxa laughed.

"Maybe you can *share*," Treyu said sarcastically.

"Not a bad idea," Fraxa said.

"Now, now, no cheating!" Berella said. "Unless Treyu gets out of hand. Maybe a little nape bite. I get the main course."

"Oh, this is too much!" Treyu said. "What am I doing in fox form? Great Belupa, change me back to Carinian form. I don't belong in this."

"None of us belong in this," Belupa said. "But war is coming to this planet, and the Bleuhs bring it. I'm still guarded about

Berella being a Bleuh, but she has chosen to take our form and help our cause, and so I accept her for that. Fraxa is my top nurse, and it is with heavy heart that I allow her on this mission. Name your alternative, Treyu, that spares this planet from Bleuh havoc."

"I can't," Treyu said. "I only wish it need not pass."

"It need not pass," Fraxa said. "At least not by our need. But the Bleuhs will not honor our need. And so, here we are."

"Yes, here we are," Aggian the Free said. "Perhaps Larbiabba should have changed Treyu into a great bird so that he could gather information with me."

"Then I would have to be a great bird as well," Berella said.

"Two's lonely, but three's a party," Fraxa said. "I'd have to fly with you too."

"Then who will deploy the bamboophi?" Belupa said. "No, the original arrangement stands. Aggian the Free will provide news on Bleuh advancement as we sneak in the counterattack. Let there be no more discussion. This meeting is adjourned."

Another scene change. Treyu's beam faded while Larbiabba's beam shone.

"I'm really surprised that these Carinians are here in these orbs," Claus said. "They're so real and alive in these visions. Hard to believe they no longer exist."

"But they do. In these orbs," young Lanietta said. "Imagine going to one of your Earth graveyards and being able to touch a headstone, then a vision pops up before you of that person's story."

"I would be afraid to touch too many of them," Claus said. "I would see how they all died."

"Yes," young Lanietta said.

"Shrike, shrike!" Larbiabba called to Pioraboo.

Pioraboo was not overly fast, but he was strong and had excellent endurance. He carried Larbiabba over a great distance without pause.

"I don't understand," Claus said. "She could space-jump or something. Why not simply do that now?"

"Her point of origin would be noticed. It might attract attention close to the Velupians," young Lanietta said. "It seems so pointless. All this effort to stop the inevitable."

"Larbiabba," Lanshalla's voice said.

"Mommy? Can you hear me? Mommy!" young Lanietta said.

"I hear you, Lanshalla," Larbiabba said to the frozen air.

"Libriota has recorporealized," Lanshalla said. "I can sense it in the ether."

"Does she know about you and Larto or any of the rest of us?" Larbiabba asked.

"She knows Larto and I are caught in the ether. She knows you can space-jump. But she does not know of our communication nor does she know about my special little one or your special little one," Lanshalla said.

Larbiabba looked down at her abdomen.

"You must protect your own as well," Lanshalla said.

"I know. But I—"

"Do not think of using the baby option either," Lanshalla said. "I was wrong about using it. It damaged me horribly. I can no longer recorporealize. The stresses of using the baby option would rip me apart. I underestimated the ethereal rebound effect. I underestimated many things about the ether."

"Lanshalla, if you know about Libriota and she knows about you, how can it be safe to communicate? Won't she detect it through the ether? Lanietta was born in the ether. How will she not be protected?"

"I have created an ethereal shadow. She sees Larto and me, but she doesn't see what's in our shadow. You, Lanietta, and the Velupians are in that shadow. But I suspect Libriota has created a shadow as well. I know she has recorporealized, but I cannot determine her motivations."

"She's going to steal the Anrega!" young Lanietta shouted. "Mommy, stop her!"

"Lanshalla cannot hear you," Claus said.

"Where is the Amnus, Lanshalla?" Larbiabba asked. "You said you would reveal that to me once I left the Velupians. In fact, Pioraboo would take me to the Amnus."

"And so he shall," Lanshalla said.

Pioraboo stopped and remained motionless.

"We've stopped," Larbiabba said. "But there's nothing here. Lanshalla? Is Pioraboo going to transport me to the Amnus?"

"He already has," Lanshalla said.

"Then where is it? I don't see it," Larbiabba said.

A moment of silence passed. Then Pioraboo threw up a small length onto the snow. The snow beneath the length melted, and the length grew until it became the size and shape of the PRAAD Claus had just seen, with a Tropheia head and an Anferrumnum base.

"Is that...is that...Lanietta...is it?" Claus stumbled.

"Yes," young Lanietta replied.

"The same one? The one that destroyed all—"

"Yes," young Lanietta said solemnly.

Mariel's beam replaced Larbiabba's. The scene changed back to toddler Lanietta with Puritas and Mariel on the frozen lake.

"Ow!" toddler Lanietta cried as she fell prone. "A bee bit me on my face."

"There's no bee here," Mariel said. "Touch your face. It's fine."

Toddler Lanietta touched her face, but when she removed her hand, a silhouette of the PRAAD appeared on her face then faded.

"What was that?" Puritas asked in surprise.

"I don't know," Mariel said.

"What was it? What was on my face?" toddler Lanietta asked.

"Nothing," Mariel said. "Just a shadow. It has passed."

"You could sense what was happening," Claus said. "When Pioraboo threw up the PRAAD, you felt it."

"Yes," young Lanietta said. "I didn't know why then, but I do now."

"Remember what I said?" Mariel asked toddler Lanietta. "When you feel down, draw a square."

Toddler Lanietta drew a square on the ice.

"Now draw the square again, but use a claw to slice in," Mariel said.

Toddler Lanietta did so.

"Now kick in the ice," Mariel said.

Toddler Lanietta jumped on the square of ice. It broke, fell into the lake, and toddler Lanietta's momentum carried herself in as well.

"Help, help!" she said as the underwater current tried pulling her under the ice.

Puritas quickly grabbed toddler Lanietta and pulled her out.

"Shake your fur like this," Mariel said as she shook her own fur. "Quickly, before the water freezes."

Toddler Lanietta was still in shock from falling in, and she hesitated in shaking her fur. She did after a moment, but it was too late. The water had frozen into her fur.

"I'm cold!" toddler Lanietta said.

"We must shake bad things off quickly, Lanietta, lest they take deep root," Mariel said. "Here."

Mariel and Puritas surrounded toddler Lanietta and melted the ice from her fur.

"Remember this too, to seek help when you cannot shake off the bad," Mariel said.

"Nanna," toddler Lanietta said.

"Nanna!" young and adult Lanietta called at the same time.

"Will you help me shake off the bad, Claus?" young Lanietta asked.

"I will try with what little ability I have," Claus said. "Though I feel like a broken record. How many times can I offer to help?"

"Keep telling me. Keep talking to me. Stay with me," young Lanietta said.

"Look," Mariel said, pointing to the fish in the water.

"A new school of fish approaches," Puritas said.

"They have strange blue and yellow markings," Mariel said.

Toddler Lanietta peered into the square hole and saw that the blue and yellow fish at first seemed to play and even beg for help from the regular fish.

"I want to touch the new fish," toddler Lanietta said, and she leaned over to do just that, but she fell into the water.

"No!" Mariel shouted.

The blue and yellow fish immediately dragged toddler Lanietta far from the square hole. Puritas jumped into the hole and looked for her, but he did not realize she'd been swept so far away so quickly. Mariel ran along the lake to where she thought toddler Lanietta might have gone, cut a hole into the ice, broke through, and dove into the lake herself. But she too could not find toddler Lanietta. Mariel and Puritas pulled themselves out of their respective holes and shouted across the lake to each other.

"We were supposed to protect her!" Mariel said.

The scene changed to the Gren capital city of Daucus. Aggian the Free flew far above and relayed critical information about Imperial Bleuhs.

"Where is this beam coming from?" Claus asked.

"Aggian the Free, of course," young Lanietta said.

"But he's a bird," Claus said.

"He's a sentient," young Lanietta said.

"Lanietta has been lost," Belupa relayed to him through Velupian ethereal communication lines.

"Where?" Aggian the Free asked.

"In Velupa Lake," she said. "Puritas and Mariel continue the search, but she could easily be in Velupa River by now."

"How did this happen?" Aggian the Free asked.

"A school of blue and yellow fish entered the lake," Belupa said. "We'd never seen them before. Lanietta leaned over to touch one, and she fell in. Berella and Fraxa wanted to call off the tunnel project, but I told them 'no'. I do not mean to impose upon you, but—"

"I will return and search for her," Aggian the Free said. "The tunnel project is important. Once complete, they will gather more information than I can provide. There is one thing you must know. Pleelellican refugees have arrived in Daucus and are begging for help. Word is that Pleelellican refugees are landing in other Gren cities: Brassica, Lactuca, Allium, Solanum, Dioscorea, and Pastinaca."

"We must run tunnels to those cities as well," Belupa said. "I suspect the Bleuhs are behind this. Refugees? More like spies. Or worse."

The scene changed to Libriota, who was on a spaceship headed for Carinia 5. She stood in front of a communication station, which had Celiba on display and Biautus in the tank in the background.

"You can't tell me this beam is from Libriota!" Claus exclaimed.

"It isn't. From Celiba," young Lanietta said.

"Is Biautus well fed?" Libriota asked.

"Yes," Celiba replied. "We've been feeding him Pleelellicans Tiloto first brought back. Per your instructions, we've made a game of it."

Celiba pointed to the tank. Two Pleelellicans were dangled over it with Biautus in the wait. A Greylinger posing as a free soul awaited outside the tank.

"You two know the rules. We drop you in. The first to get out wins the soul," Biautus snarled.

Celiba grimaced at the thought of witnessing yet another bifurcation vetting process. She turned her back to the tank and focused her attention on the communication screen. Biautus barked, and the Pleelellicans were released.

"As you can see," Celiba said as the Pleelellicans screamed and splashed with panic to escape, "Biautus is vetting our Pleelellicans for their mission to the Gren cities. The—"

Celiba was interrupted by Biautus catching one Pleelellican and crushing it to its death. The other escaped and merged with the Greylinger soul.

"The process is quick," Celiba continued.

"Biautus is choosing well," Libriota laughed. "I wish I could be there and enjoy the selection process."

"I, uh, request permission to accompany our invasion force," Celiba said.

"I wouldn't deprive you of the fun with Biautus," Libriota said.

"Uh, it's just that, uh, my services could, uh..." Celiba cringed.

"You're not squeamish, are you?" Libriota taunted. "And I thought I had the better sister."

"I *am* the better sister," Celiba said defiantly, but then her tone lowered. "It's just that, uh, well, there's this Gren rebel underground I heard about in Brassica, and I thought I'd see if they, well, you understand."

"Yes, I do. You'll go to Brassica," Libriota said.

Celiba smiled.

"After you finish this last batch of Pleelellicans," Libriota added.

Celiba's smile faded.

"When you go, take Biautus with you," Libriota said.

"Oh, that's not necessary. I'll have Tiloto keep watch of him here," Celiba said.

"That wasn't a suggestion, Celiba. Biautus will ensure the Pleelellicans complete their mission when their Greylinger souls abandon them."

"Wait. What's this about the Pleelellicans losing their Greylinger souls?" Celiba said.

Libriota laughed.

"Don't tell me you didn't read the latest bulletin from the Hierarchy? They would be displeased. Most displeased," Libriota said.

Celiba spent a moment to read the bulletin on another panel. She then paused in thought.

"Have the chosen Pleelellicans been dispatched?" Libriota asked.

"Sent to the Gren cities as directed by the Hierarchy," Celiba said.

"The major ones?"

"Yes. Allium, Brassica, Daucus, Dioscorea, Lactuca, Pastinaca, and Solanum," Celiba replied.

"Good. Make sure they are in position and ready for the first wave," Libriota said.

"So that when they are deprived of their Greylinger souls, they'll attack in search of Gren souls," Celiba said.

"You *did* read the bulletin. Excellent," Libriota said.

"Yes. Sigh. Allium, Daucus, and Dioscorea have each given the Pleelellicans a nearby lake to inhabit. Brassica, Lactuca, and Pastinaca have them in nearby rivers. Solanum has them in their oversized fountain," Celiba said.

"The first six are water bodies connected to city sewerage systems. But the Solanum fountain is isolated. That wasn't part of the plan," Libriota said.

"Necessary. Solanum doesn't dump raw sewerage like the other cities. They recycle everything," Celiba said.

"Hmm. Perhaps a more direct approach will be enough for Solanum. I'm wondering if I should send you there instead. Yes, go to Solanum. Brassica can wait for another time, *if* the Grens ever get one," Libriota said with a hideous laugh.

"How do you plan to raise the Anrega? You could have space-jumped there, you know. I don't know why you chose to travel the more conventional way," Celiba said.

"Because I don't want to leave an ethereal trail. At least not yet. The element of surprise, Celiba, will win the war," Libriota said.

"Do you really think the Grens will launch a war against us?" Celiba asked.

"No. They will drag their heels with sabotage. That's why we must start it," Libriota said.

"We have ships ready to deploy from the Bleuh Imperial Army," Celiba said.

"Good. Once the Pleelellicans start their attack, the Grens will be caught off guard. We'll use the diversion to launch the main attack," Libriota said.

"Yes, Libriota," Celiba said.

"Celiba. I will attempt the most difficult thing ever by a Carinian. Should I fail, I might be lost for all time. In that case, you will carry out the mission to conquer and demoralize the Grens. Is that understood?"

"Yes," Celiba replied.

"Excellent. I'll contact you soon," Libriota said, and she ended the communication.

The scene changed to Belupa in her royal chamber. Treyu approached.

"Treyu's beam," young Lanietta said.

"Great Belupa, is it true about Lanietta? That she is lost?" Treyu asked.

"Aggian the Free has spotted her with his infrared vision and is relaying her position to Puritas and Mariel, who are following," Belupa said. "Lanietta is alive. She is being dragged below the ice toward Dioscorea through the Dioscorea River. The river will open up free of ice near the city. They will grab Lanietta there. In fact, that moment is nearly here."

"I must go help," Treyu said.

"What about the tunnels? Berella and Fraxa need your help. So do I!" Belupa said.

"Berella will understand. And I need a break from Fraxa," Treyu said.

"Your desire is your loss," Fraxa said as she entered with a snarl and a hiss.

"What are you doing here?" Treyu asked.

"I have summoned help from the other Velupian settlements. The tunnels and bamboophi are in place. Berella is coordinating the mission from Daucus," Fraxa said.

Fraxa moved close and spoke into Treyu's ear.

"That leaves us nibble time," she said as she slobbered into his ear.

"No nibble time!" Treyu said as he quickly pulled away.

"You may help retrieve Lanietta," Belupa said. "Go then and hurry."

"Thank you!" Treyu said. "Wait. How do I get there?"

"I know the Dioscorea River," Fraxa said. "I'll take you."

Treyu hesitated.

"Do you wish to go or not?" Fraxa asked. "I won't bite too much."

"Great Belupa, there must be another guide," Treyu begged.

"There isn't, and there's no time. Either you leave immediately or abandon the effort," Belupa said.

Treyu looked back and forth between Fraxa and Belupa.

"Very well," he said in resignation. "Fraxa, please show me the way."

"I'll show you many ways!" she said with glee.

"Just one, please. It's all I can handle," Treyu said. "One more thing. I'm tired of the white-fox shape. May I have my Carinian form restored?"

"Then I won't lead you to the river," Fraxa said, and she turned away from Treyu.

"That's coercion!" Treyu said.

"It doesn't matter," Belupa said. "Only Larbiabba can restore your shape."

"Come along, Treyu. Being a white fox isn't all that bad. You might learn to enjoy it. Free fur," Fraxa said.

"Yes. Free fur," Treyu replied.

The two headed out of the chamber, but before they went outside, Fraxa grabbed two portable bamboph weapons. They were shaped like walking canes but could be wielded like shotguns. She handed one to Treyu.

"What's this for?" Treyu asked.

"Protection," Fraxa said. "No telling what we'll encounter on the Dioscorea River."

The two reached the outside.

"Go down on all fours like this," she said. "Hold the bambooph on your back with your fur like so, and follow me."

Treyu did so, and the two ran off at great speed. Treyu was amazed at how quickly he could run in this manner and how his stamina held up. After a time, they could see Aggian the Free flying far away.

"I don't need you after all," Treyu said with a pant. "Aggian the Free will lead me to Lanietta."

"Aggian the Free will not give you love nips like this," Fraxa said as she fell back and nipped Treyu on the tail.

"Stop it!" he said.

"Run faster!" she nipped and laughed.

"Look, Aggian the Free is in a dive!" Treyu said.

"Something's happening," Fraxa said. "Hurry!"

The snow receded into tundra, and the two reached the Dioscorea River where the running water opened to the sky. Standing nearby on one bank but wading in the river was Mariel, on the other was Puritas fighting back a pack of Pleelellicans, and Aggian the Free was fighting a ball of yellow and blue fish who were holding toddler Lanietta captive.

"Dive into the water," Fraxa said. "Dive in now!"

Chapter 86: The Carinian Civil War

"The beams have stopped," Claus said. "Labba? Are you ready?"

But there was no word from Labba.

"We are not finished here," young Lanietta said, and she returned to the orbs of her parents. "I will now place my hands on the orbs."

Young Lanietta did so, and the vision continued. Fraxa and Treyu swam to the school of fish. On reaching the school, Fraxa stopped, pulled out her bambooph, and fired a warning shot near the school. The school seemed to laugh at Fraxa.

"Your parents have this memory?" Claus asked.

"No, look!" young Lanietta said.

Claus looked around, and he saw (very faintly at first but steadily growing in strength) a multitude of beams from other orbs converging on young Lanietta.

"They are flowing through me," young Lanietta said.

While the school laughed at Fraxa, Celiba by this time had set up a station in Solanum with Biautus.

"Have you lifted the Anrega?" Celiba called to Libriota.

"No," she said. "I'm at Carinia 5, but all efforts to force it planar and out of the planetary core have failed. Even the Greylingers cannot help."

"Should I wait for you? Perhaps you'll think of something," Celiba said.

"No. We cannot afford the delay. Begin the attack. I'll continue my attempt," Libriota said.

Celiba initiated a link to all positioned Pleelellicans and all positioned members of the Bleuh Imperial Army.

"Now!" she commanded them.

It happened simultaneously. Greylingers removed their fake souls from all Pleelellicans on Carinia 2. What they left behind was a core desire for evil and an ability to mass-compress into a small diameter length. Pleelellicans in Gren city after Gren city narrowed into the shape of snakes, entered either the municipal water supply or sewerage, and invaded Gren buildings and properties. They came through shower heads. They came through kitchen faucets. They came out garden hoses, and they came out drinking fountains. They came up drains, but they did not come through toilets because Carinians do not eliminate waste in that fashion. But Grens were taking showers, cleaning their teeth, doing dishes, washing clothes, watering their lawns, and sending waste down drains. In all those cases, wormified Pleelellicans came through, attacked the Grens, stole their souls, and so left their corpses behind, for Carinians cannot live without a soul.

Grens of all kinds fell, including the Gren Army. But during this time, toddler Lanietta was caught up in her own conflict with Pleelellicans. They had been held in check on the far bank, but this was changing.

"Bleuh Imperial Army, attack!" Celiba commanded.

Pleelellicans near toddler Lanietta's location wormified, dove into the water, and created a swirling mass of yellow and blue that intermeshed with the fish of yellow and blue. Fraxa crossed her bambooph against Treyu, and the two created a penetrative beam that cut through the mesh and created a cocoon of protection for toddler Lanietta. Fraxa and Treyu were able to bring the cocoon and so toddler Lanietta to the shore toward Mariel.

"Help!" Puritas yelled.

It was too late for him. A wormified Pleelellican took over his soul and killed him. Aggian the Free went after that Pleelellican, picked him up, and carried him far away.

"Get into the cocoon!" Fraxa called.

Mariel and Treyu jumped into the cocoon through a small opening Fraxa had created. But Fraxa did not enter.

"What are you doing?" Treyu called. "They'll get you!"

"Someone has to maintain the beam," Fraxa said.

Wormified Pleelellicans went after Fraxa next. Aggian the Free returned and picked several off, but one got into Aggian, stole his soul, and killed him. Fraxa's death was imminent.

Meanwhile, Belupa received word of the incoming Bleuh Imperial Army and passed the word on to Berella to attack. Bamboophs around every major Gren city protruded from the ground and fired round after round at the incoming ships. These ships took damage, but they landed—the lightly damaged did so softly, the heavily damaged not as so. However they landed, the surviving Bleuh Imperial Army advanced on the Gren cities.

A wormified Pleelellican attacked Fraxa. The beam broke, and the cocoon integrity began to fade. It was only seconds before it would go altogether and allow the wormified Pleelellicans to compromise Mariel, Treyu, and toddler Lanietta.

Then something strange happened. The river level went down and down until the water disappeared altogether. The wormified Pleelellicans dried up and died just as the cocoon dissipated completely. Larbiabba showed up with the Amnus, that same PRAAD device Claus had seen before and before.

"Larbiabba!" Treyu, Mariel, and Fraxa exclaimed.

"Time is short, so hellos must be brief. Hold your position," Larbiabba said.

Using the Amnus, Larbiabba returned Treyu, Mariel, and toddler Lanietta to their natural forms. Toddler Lanietta, strangely enough, wandered off to a nearby abandoned sandbox, where she found an old bucket and used it to make sand castles.

"Thank you," Treyu said. "I was tired of being stuck as a white fox."

"You'll have to be stuck for a little longer," Larbiabba said. "I'm sending you up to the mountain to hide. Pioraboo will take you."

Larbiabba touched the Amnus in a specific way, and Pioraboo was spewed from the Tropheia. Larbiabba touched the Amnus again, and it produced a large sled.

"We're to ride on the sled?" Treyu asked.

But before Larbiabba could say anything, a shadow made for the Amnus and attempted to wrestle it from Larbiabba. Larbiabba grunted to retain control, and she just barely did.

"Larbiabba, look. Is that normal?" Fraxa said while pointing at toddler Lanietta.

The shadow had passed from the Amnus to Lanietta, covering her body with the silhouettes of war as if encoding themselves on her inner psyche. Mariel rushed over to toddler Lanietta, who had just finished placing a stick across the two sand castles. Larbiabba used the Amnus to encase Mariel and toddler Lanietta in a block of frozen cryoprotectant. Treyu rushed over to help them, and he too was caught in the block.

"What did you do?" Fraxa asked.

"No time to explain," Larbiabba said as she had Pioraboo help her load the frozen three onto the sled. She then hitched up the sled to Pioraboo. "I have Gren cities to help, and I'm late already. Ride with them. Pioraboo knows where to go."

"What kind of living death is this for Lanietta?" Fraxa asked, referring to the shadows still visible on toddler Lanietta.

"I can do one thing," Larbiabba said.

Larbiabba removed the Tropheia, placed it next to the cryo-ice near toddler Lanietta, and clicked her tongue. A micro ethereal link formed between the two. The silhouettes acquired while in the sandbox became less defined and more blurred.

"That's as much as I can do. I really must go," Larbiabba said, but she paused before returning the Tropheia to the Anferrumnum. "Wait. In case I don't come back, I must do one more thing."

Larbiabba picked up the Tropheia and held one end to her abdomen while aiming the other end at the cryo-ice. Her unborn baby transferred from her abdomen to the ice.

"What...is that your baby? I don't believe what you've just done!" Fraxa said.

"Mariel will take good care of my baby. Her name is Labba. Tell Mariel that," Larbiabba said.

"I will," Fraxa said.

"Farewell!"

Larbiabba returned the Tropheia to the Anferrumnum, touched a button, and the Amnus compressed Larbiabba and pulled her inside. The Amnus jumped into the air and oriented itself such that the Tropheia pointed downward at which point it sent out a thrust of plasma that rocketed the Amnus high up into the sky and into orbit. Larbiabba controlled the Amnus. She orbited Carinia 2 with great speed, sending down ethereal plasma blasts to disrupt the Greylingers and Bleuhs. This action was so quick, it was as if Larbiabba were a firefighter dumping great sums of water on multiple fires across the cities.

In fact, that was partially what Larbiabba was doing. The Amnus pulled water from some areas and redistributed it in others—all with great precision. Wormified and unwormified Greylinger-controlled Pleelellicans were dehydrated and killed. Larbiabba dumped vast amounts of water on the Bleuh Imperial Army, but they would not stop their advance.

"I don't want to do this, but you've forced me to," she said.

Larbiabba instructed the Amnus to dehydrate the Bleuh soldiers as well, but when it did so, an ethereal feedback loop developed, as Bleuhs are not as simple as Pleelellicans and have advanced ethereal spirits. The ethereal feedback was a form of retaliation, and Larbiabba used the Amnus as a deflector, causing these returned volleys from the Bleuh Imperial Army to bounce off at near random angles. Some returned harmlessly to unoccupied parts of Carinia 2 while the occasional one landed close to and startled a Carinian. The rest bounced into outer space, that vast emptiness that fills most of the sky. But not all is empty in outer space. A stray beam hit Libriota as she circled Carinia 5.

It was the most unfortunate luck.

Libriota realized immediately that an Amnus existed, it had been found by a Carinian of at least half Bleuh strength, this Carinian was Larbiabba, Larbiabba was wielding it around Carinia 2, against Bleuhs, and ethereal feedback from those Bleuhs was being deflected off the Amnus. With cat-like reflexes, she took hold of the ethereal beam, tied it to her ship, and used it as a grasp-hold on the Anrega. Larbiabba felt this effect inside the Amnus as if she herself were playing tug o' war. Her body was slapped against a wall.

Immediately Larbiabba realized a stray ethereal beam had been caught by Libriota, and it was Libriota who was pulling on her.

"Oh no!" Larbiabba called. "Lanshalla? Can you hear me?"

But Larbiabba was inside the Amnus, and the Amnus blocked Larbiabba's connection with Lanshalla. Libriota felt a great surge of ethereal energy build up, as she positioned herself between the interaction of the Anrega and the Amnus. The Anrega was attracted to the Amnus, and the Amnus to the Anrega. Further, the Veigon was in the Anrega, and so it was really the Veigon calling the Amnus closer so that the Amnus could fuse with it.

Larbiabba oriented the Tropheia toward Carinia 5 and commanded the Amnus to thrust. But to Larbiabba's surprise, this orientation actually increased the tug on the Amnus, and now the Amnus was being pulled at light speed toward Carinia 5.

"I must contact Lanshalla," Larbiabba struggled to say. "I must contact...but I cannot from in here. I must...must... sacrifice..."

Larbiabba decided that if she could get a part of herself outside the Amnus, she could communicate with Lanshalla. She then did something very unusual. She commanded the Amnus to permit her foot to stick out. The Amnus obliged, and though space has no wind, Larbiabba's extended foot slowly freeze-dried. At first it was painful, but the nerve endings became frozen, and she felt no pain.

"Shalli!" Larbiabba called.

"Larbs!" Lanshalla called back. "You're in great danger!"

"I know!" Larbiabba said. "I had to stick my foot out of the Amnus to communicate. I'm being pulled by Libriota to Carinia 5!"

"She's using the Amnus to lift the Anrega from Carinia 5," Lanshalla said.

"Then that was the flaw in our plan. Why didn't we think of it?" Larbiabba asked. "Lanshalla? Did you not see this as a possibility?"

"I didn't think she had the ability," Lanshalla said.

"How do we stop her?" Larbiabba asked. "And how do I escape?"

Lanshalla paused.

"Shalli? Talk to me!" Larbiabba said.

"I've made a horrible mistake," Lanshalla said. "If the Amnus fuses with the Veigon with Libriota controlling the process, she'll control the universe. Nothing will stop her. Ever."

"Then I'm at her mercy. She'll enslave me. Or worse," Larbiabba said.

"There is one thing that can be done," Lanshalla said. "You can give us leverage with the Amnus, a chance to prevent it from fusing with the Veigon. I can help you. It means locking the Amnus signature to our children, Larbs. To Lanietta and Labba."

"Leave Labba out," Larbiabba said. "I'll never curse her with the abomination. I've transferred her to other care anyway."

"Then Lanietta," Lanshalla said. "It's the only way."

"Why didn't you lock her in when you had the Amnus?" Larbiabba asked.

"That would have prevented you from using it. As it was, I never really had the Amnus as it is now. Further, Lanietta wasn't born yet. But now she's alive and aware. Larbs, I'm feeding you the procedure."

Larbiabba received the procedure on a subliminal-ethereal level.

"I am to die?" Larbiabba asked in surprise. "Shalli! You're stabbing me in the back! You no-good Belukalukatrashkaberriakaplak. You never cared about the Grens. Or the Greyans. Do you know what this means? More Grens die. Greyans become mutilated. Was this your plan all along? To hand victory to Libriota?"

"Larbs, I'm sorry!" Lanshalla pleaded.

"Sorry? Sorry! What am I doing here? I don't belong in the battle. I should have left this solar system long ago. But that's the problem with Carinians. We don't keep good track of time. Well! I'm leaving it now, aren't I? Not much choice. My choice is to lock this Amnus down for Lanietta or leave it wide open for Libriota and all. At least Labba is safe. At least..."

Larbiabba hit a button, and her corporeal body contorted and fused into the Amnus, locking it with Lanietta's ethereal signature. In doing so, the Amnus could not so easily fuse with the Veigon without Lanietta's intervention.

The Amnus arrived in orbit around Carinia 5. Libriota intercepted it with her ship and brought it aboard.

"Ah, the Amnus is left unattended," Libriota said to herself. "A foolish thing, Lanshalla. You leave the solar system open for my full rein."

"I'll ask again," Claus said to young Lanietta. "Is this the same device that destroyed Libriota and the other Carinians? I mean this *is* the same device, right? And it didn't destroy her then?"

"It was in a different state," young Lanietta said.

"Like California?" Claus asked.

"No, not like that. Your automobile can't run over a pedestrian when parked," young Lanietta said. "The PRAAD that destroyed Libriota was like your record-setting rocket car. The Amnus version that arrived in orbit around Carinia 5 is coasting to a stop. I can see it now, though I never knew before—Larbiabba calmed the Amnus into a low-level state. This isn't just young me speaking. This is my adult self too, who is holding this little Anrega chamber together."

Claus looked over to adult Lanietta, and she nodded her head slightly.

"Okay, so Larbiabba sacrificed herself. But for what? I still don't understand how the Amnus could be given away," Claus said.

"It wasn't 'given away'. It was destined for the Anrega and Veigon. What do you do with a suicide jumper who has committed to the jump? You soften the fall," young Lanietta said.

"So Larbiabba has become the suicide jumper," Claus said with reflection. "She didn't realize it would come to that. How many of us are lured into final scenarios by supposed friends?"

"My mommy and Larbiabba are friends," young Lanietta said. "There's nothing supposed about it. Even now, they are friends."

"So did you lure me to my final scenario?" Claus asked.

"No, you are my pet," young Lanietta grinned. "You said so yourself."

Libriota integrated the Amnus with her spaceship. She hit several buttons on a control panel. The Anrega went planar and exited Carinia 5. Libriota's method was not as efficient as the natural process, and so the act caused geological events in the form of earthquakes and volcanoes. Large amounts of thermal, electromagnetic, ionic, and ethereal radiation were released. Snow melted, water evaporated, and the planet became a toxic brew of the various forms of radiation. The Greyans who survived were wretched and miserable. They weren't quite Orchians (yet, that would come later), but they became ever-desirous for relief from their misery.

Carinia 5 as a planet was altered. Besides the volcanoes, earthquakes, and the resulting toxicity, the rotation sped up to a twenty-minute day. It was unheard-of for such an event, as the Anrega usually caused a planet to face-lock with its star. But Libriota was in control (somewhat), and all elements of Anrega procedure were skewed.

"I'll deal with you later," Libriota said of the planet and the new Greyans.

She took her spaceship out of Carinia 5's orbit and—using the Amnus—towed the Anrega to Carinia 2. The Grens had successfully beaten back the Bleuhs, having fired many rounds from the bamboophs. The Bleuhs had lost. They were finished.

"You are now fighting your origins," Libriota said. "Aim your silos at me. Fulfill your fate."

Libriota ordered the Anrega into a small mass between Carinia 2 and Carinia Zero. The mass was so small as to be unobservable. But then she ordered the Anrega into a growing planar form such that this plane was perpendicular to a line from Carinia 2 to Carinia Zero. The Anrega grew in size, and it blotted out light from Carinia Zero, like a growing eclipse. The air became a mixture of hot and cold, and this differential quickly brought in great thunderstorms. Carinians and other sentient life on Carinia 2 grew fearful of this dark monster that ate the sky, brought storms, and would soon eat them. Those Grens with the little courage that was to be found on the planet aimed their bamboophs at the Anrega and fired everything they had, but the bamboophs were a creation of the Veigon, and the Anrega was a repository for such creations, and so the Anrega simply absorbed the rounds and remained unaffected.

As Carinia 2 grew dark and the people feared the end, Pioraboo carried the cryo-ice block of Mariel, Treyu, Lanietta, and Labba into a remote mountain. Up an uncharted path he took until he followed clever turns that obscured a cave opening. He pulled the sled into the cave (which was cold) and integrated his body into the entrance, causing the entrance to be completely blocked and thus fully protecting the cave from outside influence. He went into a dormant state and remained that way for some time.

Libriota created a small opening in the center of the Anrega that allowed a beam of light to carry down to a point in the dark, stormy clouds just above Solanum. The beam gave off light in an otherwise pitch-dark night, and it opened the clouds enough for those on the ground to see. Libriota left her main ship in orbit but came down the beam in a transparent pod, which hovered in the opening. With her was the Amnus.

"Grens and Bleuhs of Carinia 2, this is your supreme leader, Libriota," she bellowed across the land. "I assume full control of this planet. Behold!"

With one hand on the Amnus, Libriota waved her other hand. The Amnus ingested water from the air, meaning the dense clouds and associated rain. It did so with such speed that it created a vortex of air that lifted loose things from the ground and carried them up to and into the Amnus. Some of those were Carinians—both Bleuhs and Grens.

"I take life, and I restore it," she said.

She waved her hand again, and those Carinians who'd been pulled into the Amnus were returned safely to the ground.

"I command all!" she bellowed. "None can supplant! Kneel before your supreme commander. Kneel!"

Libriota ordered the Amnus to affect the pull and push of moisture in the air such that air control was at her command. In this way, all were forced to their knees. Claus shook his head.

"You did this to me. With your control of air. You're like Libriota. What is it with you Carinians? What makes evil grow?"

"I don't mean to. I just get caught up in things," young Lanietta said.

"How much destruction and misery of beings in the universe was the result of one person getting caught up in things?" Claus asked himself.

"Much much," young Lanietta said.

"You weren't supposed to answer that," Claus said.

"I can make you do anything I want," Libriota bellowed. "And I can make all life die. Your planet is now dark. Soon plants will die and water will freeze from the cold. I demand absolute subservience and obedience from everyone. You may affirm your obedience by saying, 'I affirm, O Supreme Libriota.'"

All Bleuhs but only some Grens gave the oath.

"Not everyone affirmed. Affirm!" she ordered.

Using the Amnus, Libriota detected who did not affirm. She had this list of Carinians passed on to the Anrega, which in turn passed it on to the Veigast, which was sharing Anrega's center with the Veigon. Libriota summoned the Veigast, sent it down to the planet's surface, and used it as an agent of torture. Gren souls were ripped, reintegrated, ripped, and reintegrated from/with the rebellious Grens.

They affirmed.

"As all should be," Libriota said.

She kept the Veigast flying and hovering around Carinia 2, imposing terror to those who resisted. But the Veigast had limits as did Libriota's ability to sense who did not affirm. Those hidden secretly away in the mountains were protected, and they remained hidden. One Gren who had wine in her veins from the Lonely Vine was also protected, but she feigned obedience until she could figure out a better future.

"She" was Nanceya, the gardener. Larto's Vineyard was deserted for the moment, as the Grens and Bleuhs had gone to the city to fight. Nanceya had stayed behind to tend things, but she was not spared the bellows of Libriota. Nor the ethereal fingers of the Veigast, waiting to claw her brain should she disobey orders from Libriota. So far the orders were just to kneel and affirm Libriota as supreme leader. But she knew she had to protect the Lonely Vine.

"If there is to be any hope for the Grens, it is through the Lonely Vine," young Lanietta said.

"What?" Claus asked.

"That's what Nanceya is thinking," young Lanietta said. "She will wait for the proper moment. Then she will act."

"Act? In what way?" Claus asked.

"Shh," young Lanietta said. "Watch and listen."

"I return your sun to you. Temporarily," Libriota said. "But I shall return. Periodically. To remind you of your oath. Yes. As part of your obedience, and here I speak specifically to the Grens, you shall provide full hospitality to the Bleuhs. They will be visiting Carinia 2 for a time while Carinia 1 undergoes remodeling."

Libriota left.

Nanceya threw an empty backpack over her shoulder, entered the superbarn and looked at the vast reserves of kielsene, an inflammable byproduct of vineyard harvesting. It powered the steam equipment.

"But now it will power something else," Nanceya said to herself.

"What is she going to do?" Claus asked.

"That's kielsene," young Lanietta said. "It's like your kerosene."

"She's going to harvest grapes?" Claus asked.

"She's going to harvest. Yes, harvest," young Lanietta said.

Nanceya drove a steam tractor across the vineyard, pulling a liquid fertilizing drum along the way.

"That's not fertilizer," young Lanietta said.

"That's not harvesting either," Claus said.

"That's kielsene," young Lanietta said.

"That will kill the vines," Claus said. "At least petroleum products on Earth do that. I've seen what happens when people pour old gasoline on the lawn. The lawn dies."

Nanceya returned to the main farmhouse with the steam tractor. She did not slow.

"She's not stopping," Claus said. "Lanietta! Look! She's going to crash!"

Indeed, Nanceya crashed the tractor into the house and in doing so crashed into the wine cellar and destroyed all wine. Unfazed by her act, she walked over to the Lonely Vine and removed it along with a bit of the mountain upon which it was attached. She placed such in her backpack. She headed for the mountain, and when she reached a safe-enough place, she produced a flare gun from her pocket and fired at Larto's house. The spilt kielsene ignited and followed a line of fire throughout the vineyard.

Nanceya disappeared into the mountains.

Chapter 87: Libriota Terraforms Arianos

Claus felt dizzy and collapsed to the floor. He beat his fists against his temples repeatedly.

"Stop," young Lanietta said.

Young Lanietta tapped two fingers together in the air near Claus's nose. The vibrations from the tapping carried into Aftova and calmed him.

"In our culture, it is considered wrong to tap a pet on the nose," Claus said. "But somehow this worked for me."

"Then perhaps you are not a pet," young Lanietta smiled.

"What happened? I suddenly wanted to bash my head in. It was like—"

"Eethi psychosis," young Lanietta said. "I had Aftova calm you. You need rest. That means I must see the visions without you. Do not worry. I will tell you what happens next. Please sit on this bench."

Claus pulled himself to a bench where he sat. Young Lanietta touched the orbs, and though the chamber was dark, young Lanietta saw images.

"The Bleuhs' use of the ether creates and feeds Greylingers," she said. "In addition to using the Anrega to defeat the Grens, Libriota moved the Anrega in orbit around Carinia 1 and used it to pull Greylingers out of the planet."

"And here I thought Libriota just used the Anrega to take over the Grens," Claus said.

"The Bleuhs like the ether. They go eethi frequently. Libriota learned to space-jump as you saw, and after the Civil War she taught other Bleuhs to space-jump," young Lanietta continued. "This increased Greylingers on Carinia 1. The Anrega was full and would not hold

any more. Actually, the Anrega was full while in Carinia 5."

"When Libriota used the Anrega against the Grens, did that cause—" Claus started.

"The Anrega to shed Greylingers? Yes," young Lanietta said. "She dumped them on Carinia 2. It meant Bleuhs there could not use their ethereal power."

"Water on a fire," Claus said.

"Yes," she said. "But it did mean there was a little space in the Anrega to take in new Greylingers. So when Libriota first brought the Anrega to Carinia 1 and removed a portion of Greylingers, she was praised by the Hierarchy. But the praise ended when she could no longer remove them."

"The Hierarchy would order her to dump the Greylingers somewhere else," Claus suggested.

"That's right. Are you seeing these images?" young Lanietta asked. "I thought I blocked them for your benefit and rest."

"You did. I can't see them," Claus said.

"Then how do you know?" young Lanietta asked.

"Human history is similar. People move to a new, clean area. They throw their garbage wherever. It builds up and becomes intolerable. Then a campaign comes along to clean up the community. Only the garbage doesn't disappear. It's moved out of sight. Perhaps it's buried close-by. But then it contaminates the well water, and so it's moved farther and farther away from home."

"The Carinian solar system was full of Greylingers," young Lanietta said. "So Libriota explored that 'somewhere else'. This happened around four and a half billion of your years ago. Your solar system was new. Earth in its present form didn't exist. Instead there was Protogaia."

"Yes, you said Carinians used Protogaia as a common time measurement for the year, and that you called it Gnisiotra," Claus said.

"Mars did exist," young Lanietta said. "We called it Sol 4 or simply Arianos. It also had a single moon called Sol 4a or

Preivos. No Phobos or Deimos yet. And no Greylingers there, either. Libriota decided Mars would be a good place for Bleuhs to live until Carinia 1 could be fully decontaminated. It was just far enough away from your sun such that ultraviolet rays would be tolerable. Mars was hot and fiery. But the Amnus had the power to ingest great sums of water and release it. Libriota called it the Planetary Release/Acquire Aquifer Device, or PRAAD. She transferred water to Mars, cooled it, and created great seas. Look, Claus, the Martian seas."

Young Lanietta passed images of the Martian seas to Claus. Claus was all right at first but then lifted a fist to his temple to strike it.

"Libriota was happy with her work," young Lanietta continued. "She was the one who named it, you see, and she named it Arianos right then. She also instituted a new time measurement, the Sol 4 day. It was based on a full solar rotation of Mars."

"A Mars day and an Earth year," Claus said. "How strange."

"Protogaia year, Claus. Protogaia year," young Lanietta corrected. "But it was nearly the same as your Earth year. Protogaia had the same orbit as your Earth. So when your Earth came along, the Carinians continued using its year as the standard year."

Claus looked stressed out.

"That's enough," she said, and she stopped the images.

Claus relaxed.

"That was my mistake. I put you through too much with the Civil War," young Lanietta said. "I didn't know about it like this until we saw it. I guess that's the danger of seeing other memories. We have to see them to know what they are about, but if we knew what they were about, would we put ourselves through the agony of what might come, of what we might see?"

"It is the dichotomy of memory, yes," Claus said. "We keep bringing it up. I don't suppose it will ever resolve itself any more than the dichotomy of yellow and blue that we keep seeing."

Young Lanietta paused a moment and cried.

"No," she said after pulling herself together. "I don't suppose it will."

Claus stood up to approach her, but he felt dizzy.

"Please sit," she said. "I will continue the story."

Claus returned to the bench.

"Libriota had used the Veigon to create life and store this life inside the PRAAD. Yes, this was done without fusion of the PRAAD with the Veigon. The Anrega was used as a transfer conduit, and Larbiabba's lock on the PRAAD prevented fusion. Libriota deposited this life on Mars, and it flourished. However, Mars wasn't ready for Bleuh habitation. There were no buildings, no infrastructure, and no workers. Libriota brought those mutilated Greyans to Mars and put them to work, building up Mars as a resort for Bleuhs. The Bleuhs arrived, and they enjoyed themselves. The first thing she told these Bleuhs was the planet's new name, that of Arianos. She felt it was the new superior home for superior Bleuhs. Well, these new Bleuhs went eethi, and it was only a matter of time before Mars would attract and fill up with Greylingers. Libriota knew this, but she didn't want to wait for the Martian ether to clog up with Greylingers completely, so she took the PRAAD to other solar systems and explored turning them into resorts for Bleuhs. In time, she turned this work over to others and returned to Carinia 2 where she could keep a close eye on the Grens and ensure they did not interfere. She actually took up teaching."

"Teaching? Of all things!" Claus said.

"Yes. She taught Gren youth," young Lanietta said. "In fact, she taught me."

"What?" Claus said. "But you were frozen. You and Labba. How did this happen? I mean, the cryo-ice, with Mariel and Treyu, you all were...in the mountain...with Pioraboo...and..."

"Remember Nanceya?" young Lanietta asked. "She set up a secret community in the mountains with the Lonely Vine. It grew, but barely. Turns out that community was close to Pioraboo and the cryo-ice. They thawed us out. Treyu didn't make it, but Mariel did. She raised us for a time, but those pesky Bleuhs came around and discovered Mariel outside the cave. She diverted them away but paid with her life."

"I'm sorry," Claus said.

"My Nanna. Killed," young Lanietta lamented. "I..."

"Please don't tell me how. Move on, Lanietta. Move on," Claus said.

"Nanna once told me that if ever I became lost or captured, I should call myself 'Sassatinassa'," young Lanietta said. "I remember that the most about her. Strange little things we remember."

Young Lanietta paused.

"I will go on," young Lanietta said. "After Nanna passed, Nanceya decided it was unsafe for us to remain there in hiding, because Bleuhs would assume as much and go after us like criminals. So she brought us down the mountain and took work at an orchard. When it was learned we weren't in school, we were taken out of the orchard and put into school."

"Whatever happened to Nanceya?" Claus asked.

"Last I heard she was head foreman of the orchard," young Lanietta said. "Let me check something."

Young Lanietta tapped her fingers near Claus's nose.

"Your eethi psychosis has resolved itself. You are rested," she said. "Good."

Claus stood without any issues.

"I thought you were going to say my nose is like a pet," Claus said.

"No. Just a nice, normal nose," young Lanietta said. "Are you ready to join me for the next part? I'm in it, you know, and not just as a toddler."

"How old will you be?" Claus asked.

"Twelve million years old," young Lanietta said. "That's the age of—"

"Twelve years in human terms, yes, I know," Claus said.

"I must warn you about something," young Lanietta said. "As of this moment, I am an eleven-million-year-old Carinian. This is the last you'll see of me here in this chamber."

"What do you mean?" Claus asked. "You can't die."

"Just as a boy once said, 'Goodbye five,' on the eve of his sixth birthday, I am saying, 'Goodbye eleven million,' on the eve of my twelfth."

"What boy? Who said that?" Claus asked.

Young Lanietta smiled.

"Landy. You'll find out. Maybe. Maybe not. Anyway, don't worry. Instead, think of your grandmother. She was right, you know. Life is like stones in a brook. Step to the next one before you are blackened by oil. Sometimes we step the wrong way, and the oil catches us. Sometimes it doesn't matter how we step—the oil catches us anyway. So it is with me. Well, you'll see in a moment. Place your hands on the orbs here."

Claus placed his hands on the orbs, and young Lanietta disappeared.

Chapter 88: Stowaway

The vision took Claus to a classroom on Carinia 2. Two girls were assigned a school project—describe how to make a two-planet relationship better. The girls' names were Lanietta and Labba. They were each only twelve million years old, as compared to their teacher, Libriota, who was two and a half billion years old. "Your project is due before the next harvest," Libriota said to her class. "You will need to learn about the first two planets in our solar system, explain why each of these planets is important, and then find another solar system with two celestial bodies that interact with each other, one of which must be a planet. The other can be another planet or a sizable moon big enough to influence the parent planet. Now then, who can tell me the name of *this* planet? The one we are on right now?"

Labba raised her hand.

"Carinia 2," Labba answered after being called upon.

"Very good, Labba," Libriota said. "Who can tell me the name of the star overhead?"

Lanietta raised her hand.

"Yes, Lanietta?"

"Carinia Zero," Lanietta answered.

"Excellent," Libriota said. "How many planets are in this solar system?"

Labba raised her hand.

"Labba?"

"Five."

"Right again," Libriota said.

Lanietta stared at Labba with jealousy. The other students didn't know these answers, and Labba answered more than Lanietta.

"Lanietta? Can you see or hear me? Lanietta?" Claus called.

But the Lanietta in the classroom had no awareness of Claus.

"Labba? This is you as a girl. I can see and hear you. Can you hear me?" Claus called.

No reply from the twelve-million-year-old girl.

"Labba and Doctor Kechenova? Are you seeing this?" he called back to Earth.

No reply either.

"I'm alone in all this. An island again. Do I stop it? How? I'm at the mercy of this vision and how it plays out," he said to himself.

"Who can tell me what night is?" Libriota asked.

The class was totally stumped, except for Labba, who had a sense but struggled to get it into words that others could understand.

"It's the opposite of daytime...of...when the sun goes down on that kind of planet...when you are outside and the sun does not shine," Labba said.

The mere mention of the sun not shining threw the class into a panic. Arguments broke out about how the sun could not shine, only way was if the world was ending or under attack, which made people sad, angry, and more argumentative. The class got so unruly that parents had to be summoned to take their children out with them in the fields until the next occult of Carinia 1.

"I'm bored," Lanietta said to Labba as the two watched Carinians pick fruit in Nanceya's orchard. "Endless orchards go on forever and ever."

Nanceya periodically drove by in a steam-powered vehicle and waved to the girls.

"Think pleasant thoughts," Labba said. "Look, I have something for you."

Labba gave a small bamboo stick (about the size of a piccolo) to Lanietta.

"What is it?" Lanietta asked.

"It measures time since our star was born," Labba said.

"Huh? Carinia Zero? It's been shining over us forever," Lanietta said.

"No it hasn't. There was a time when it wasn't shining," Labba said.

"And what did people do? How did they see?" Lanietta said.

"There were no people. There was no Carinia 2 either," Labba said.

"That's impossible. Carinia 2 has been here forever. And it always will be," Lanietta said.

"I learned that stars don't last forever. They burn out," Labba said.

"Are they on fire? Maybe we can give them more firewood," Lanietta said.

"They don't burn like that," Labba said.

"Well how do they burn?" Lanietta said.

"I'm not sure. We didn't get that far in the book," Labba said.

"Because they're not on fire," Lanietta said. "They don't burn. So they won't burn out. We'll be here forever."

"I don't understand, Lanietta. You're older here, but you sound so naive. The eleven-million-year-old girl who was with me a moment ago was much more aware of the universe," Claus said. "Well?"

"Awareness is an echo of the past," whispered an unseen eleven-million-year-old Lanietta in the orb chamber, and that whisper itself echoed throughout the chamber.

"Oh how I wish I could visit Carinia 1," Lanietta said. "I've heard they have beautiful buildings, fountains, and pools of water. Lots of water everywhere! They have oceans they say, big wonderful oceans."

"We have oceans too," Labba said. "Some are frozen."

"What's frozen?" Lanietta asked.

"When water is solid. Like this branch. You can break it and throw it too," Labba said.

"That's also impossible," Lanietta said. "You can't throw water like a branch. How do you make water hold still? Hold it together in your hands? Put tape on it?"

"No, you have to reduce the temperature," Labba said.

"How do you do that?" Lanietta asked.

"Well, for starters, you can go to the dark side where there is no sunlight. Then it gets cold," Labba said.

"Dark side of what?"

"Carinia 2."

"There is no dark side. It's all like this," Lanietta said.

"No it isn't. Didn't you listen in class?" Labba asked.

"Prove it," Lanietta said. "I dare you to prove it."

"We would need a transport ship. I'm not old enough to drive," Labba said.

Lanietta grinned.

"Neither are you!" Labba said. "We don't have a license."

"Do you know how to drive one of these things? You know about everything else," Lanietta said.

"I know how it's supposed to be done. I've never driven a transport, though."

"Teach me," Lanietta said.

"No! That's illegal!" Labba said.

"You've got to, Labba. I'm going crazy with boredom. Prove to me the sun isn't everywhere. Prove to me there's such a thing as darkness," Lanietta urged.

"No!"

"Labba? C'mon. You owe me!" Lanietta said.

"For what?"

"That time you got in trouble for stealing a telio-opticon. Remember how I blamed it on that boy?"

"That was different," Labba said.

"It was a nice steal. We got to look at mountains and dream about them," Lanietta said.

"*You* looked at mountains. *I* looked at Carinia 1's phases. You would have noticed darkness had you looked," Labba said.

"Yeah, yeah, yeah. I should have looked through the telio-opticon at Carinia 1. But why settle for just a telio-opticon? Heck, once we find the darkness on Carinia 2, we could visit Carinia 1. Wouldn't that be great?"

"Until we get caught," Labba said.

"What's the worst they can do? Make us sit in the orchards? Here we are, already in the orchards. C'mon, Labba. You need a break too. Besides, think of the things we can learn about space travel. School won't start until the occult, and once it does, we'll be stuck in there for...for...I don't know how long."

"Look at this bamboo stick," Labba said. "It tells when we get our next break."

"Lanietta?" Claus said. "I remember something you told me, if you can hear me. The Carinians used 'Sol' followed by a number to name the planets or major orbital paths in my solar system in order from closest to farthest away, and a letter after the number to indicate the natural moon, in order from largest moon to smallest. So 'Sol 3' is Protogaia or Earth while 'Sol 3a' is the moon. Mars is 'Sol 4', the asteroid belt is 'Sol 5' with a hyphen followed by a number to name asteroids in order of size. Jupiter then is 'Sol 6' and Pluto is 'Sol 10'. Did I get that right? What am I saying? I'm acting like a student in Lanietta's class."

"Yeah. I can't wait that long. Wait, what's a Sol 3 year?" Lanietta asked.

"The time it takes for Sol 3 to go around its star. Called *Sol*. Other stars have other planets that—"

"Sol? Other stars? What are you talking about?" Lanietta asked.

"Didn't you know? We're not alone in the universe. There are other stars," Labba said.

"Where? Point one out," Lanietta said.

"We can't see them now," Labba said. "Our own star is too bright, and the atmosphere is also too bright. But we could see them from the dark side. I learned of another solar system called the Sol system. It has two planets with lots of liquid water—Sol 3 and Sol 4. All the adults use Sol 3 years to measure time. In fact Sol 3 and Sol 4 are so special that we call them Gnisiotra and Arianos respectively. Our own planets don't orbit Carinia Zero in the same amount of time, so Gnisiotra was chosen as a neutral planet for the year and Arianos for the day. I'm using the Gnisiotra year as my time keeper for the bamboo stick. Most people here don't

realize we have our own year. They think everything is the same all the time."

"Because it is! Same old boring thing all the time!" Lanietta said. "Labba! You'll have to tell me more about Gnisiotra. Lots more."

"I feel like adding narration here," Claus said. "What do I say? Time measurement was a problem on Carinia 2. The planet was face-locked with Carinia Zero. Being face-locked, there was no perception of day and night in the sense we experience it on Earth. The sun didn't rise. It didn't set. The sunlit side would give plants the ability to grow. Nothing could grow on the dark side. And the sun would be in the same position in the sky. For some, this would be like a perpetual noon. Teacher, give me an A!"

There was no acknowledgment of Claus's speech.

"What am I doing?" Claus asked himself. "I'm lecturing to myself. Losing my mind!"

"Our people don't care much about time," Labba said. "One way to get people interested in time is the Sol 3 Project. As part of the project, people are asked to express their ages in terms of Sol 3 years instead of Carinia 1 years or Carinia 2 years. This also makes it easier to compare ages of people between Carinia 1 and 2 since both planets take different amounts of time to orbit our star."

"Let me tell you about our planets," Labba continued. "Carinia 2 has very fertile ground and grows a wide variety of crops, which is especially impressive for a red dwarf star. You see, our star Carinia Zero puts out very little (if any) blue light or even ultraviolet light. This is important, because Carinia 1 can no longer grow crops. That brings us to Carinia 1, the inner planet of our solar system. It too is face-locked with Carinia Zero, but it is closer, and most of the sunlit side is too hot for habitation. Some of the dark side is too cold for habitation, though not as much as our planet."

"Habitation?" Lanietta asked.

"You know. Places for people to live," Labba said. "The best place to live on Carinia 1 is a twilight ring encircling the planet known as the terminator zone. The terminator zone is where light meets dark. A person on Carinia 1 in the terminator zone would look to the sky and see Carinia Zero in a perpetual sunrise (or sunset). The same for Carinia 2. The zone around Carinia 1 is called Terminon, and the one around Carinia 2 is called Termiduce."

"You know a lot about this stuff," Lanietta said.

"I study," Labba said. "The people from Carinia 1 are known as Bleuhs. People from our planet are Grens, except there are a lot of Bleuhs on our planet. You can tell the difference, though. The Bleuhs look a little blue while the Grens are a little green."

"You're green," Lanietta said. "I'm just blue-green though."

"That makes you a Gren," Labba said. "You have to be pure blue to be a Bleuh. At least that's what the Bleuhs believe. But neither Bleuh nor Gren needs sleep."

"What's sleep?" Lanietta asked.

"Animals with a day-night cycle spend either the day or the night doing nothing," Labba said.

"Boring! That's worse than here!" Lanietta said. "They're forced to do nothing? At least I can walk around the same boring orchard. How terrible! Stuck, unable to move. Why, someone could come up and beat me over the head. Glad I don't have to sleep. Glad!"

"Do you ever wonder why we're in school?" Labba asked.

"To add more boredom to our lives," Lanietta said.

"No," Labba said. "It's part of Bleuh philanthropy."

"Huh?"

"It means the Bleuhs are trying to be helpful. They hope that a few of us Grens can be educated. It's more of a propaganda tool than anything, as it shows continued Bleuh superiority through the work of educating us 'primitives'."

"You're using words I don't understand," Lanietta said.

"Don't worry about it," Labba said. "Have you thought about your assignment?"

"It's the only thing keeping me from going bonkers with boredom. But where am I going to find two planets with a relationship?" Lanietta lamented.

"Remember that Sol solar system I was telling you about? There's a little planet called Sol 10. It has a large moon relative to its size, so that counts. Both are very cold, and I'm going to write how they could be friendly if they were only heated up by a friendly red dwarf star like our own. Wouldn't that be great if we could get a special planet like that in our solar system?"

"And still stuck in our solar system," Lanietta said. "But Libriota never mentioned the Sol system in the list of choices."

"I've been following the news," Labba said. "Interesting things going on in the Sol system. There's a resort on Sol 4. Arianos, you know."

"You told me," Lanietta said.

"The resort is for Bleuhs only. There's also a detention colony on Sol 4a. To punish people. Including *Grens*," Labba said.

"Sol 4a? So that's a moon around Arianos?" Lanietta asked.

"And a big one compared to Arianos, too. The moon's name is Preivos," Labba said. "Maybe you could choose Arianos and Preivos for your report."

"Sounds boring," Lanietta said.

"Well perhaps I should introduce you to one of the scientists here on our planet in charge of the Sol 4 project. He's *not* boring. Matter of fact, he let me look through his telio-opticon scope. I could see Sol 4 and Sol 4a. Then I had him show me Sol 10 and Sol 10a. Oh, I wish those two were filled with fiery lava. No, just cold places. Yeah, he said Sol 4 and Sol 4a are more interesting. And then he showed me Sol 3. You know, Gnisiotra. Now that one is fiery and has lots of water vapor. Lots of water."

"Hmm. Water," Lanietta said.

"But here's the best part, and you won't believe it. These planets have day and night! I imagined I was on one of them and watching the sky. You'd look to the horizon along the rotation path, and Sol would magically appear to rise," Labba said.

"That's crazy. You must have it wrong," Lanietta said.

"I bet I'm right!" Labba said. "Then it gets higher and higher, and it crosses over top."

"Does it swoop down on you like a bird? Does it pick you up and set your hair on fire? Or maybe you talk to it?" Lanietta laughed.

"No, nothing like that! But after a while of going across the sky, it goes back down and disappears on the opposite side of the horizon," Labba said.

"It doesn't even know how to get back to where it started!" Lanietta said. "Does it come back up and go backward across the sky?"

"No. But after being dark for a while, it does come back up, and not where it went down. It comes up from the same side every time," Labba said.

"How does it do that? Does it go through the ground?" Lanietta asked.

"It doesn't really go anywhere. It just looks like it does all these things. Anyway, that's how I picture it," Labba said. "The cycle from rising to another rising is called a *day*. Impressed?"

"How do crops grow if there is no sunlight?" Lanietta asked.

"I guess they don't," Labba said.

"You could never have crops with a planet like that. They would get a little light and then die when the light goes away," Lanietta said.

"Something tells me they'd find a way. Maybe store energy to get through the dark time," Labba said.

"Another crazy idea!" Lanietta said.

"We could learn a lot about Gnisiotra. It might not have life yet."

"Why not? Life has always been around," Lanietta said.

"Not everywhere. The scientists say it has to evolve or something. Like making little improvements over the years to keep up with the changing environment, starting with little one-celled creatures until they become creatures like us. Some think we evolved too."

"That's the craziest story of all! But that's why I like you, Labba. You're always coming up with these fantastic stories. I have a crazy story for you. Let's stow away to Carinia 1."

"What? Now you're crazy!" Labba said.

"Libriota says we need to learn more about our solar system. Well? Seems like a good way to me," Lanietta said.

"You're kidding. But how?" Labba asked.

"Supply ships will be coming from Carinia 1 soon. The occult is almost here," Lanietta said.

"You don't need to tell me that. I was the one who told you all about the supply ships," Labba said.

"Well, it's like this. We hide in a fruit box. We'll be loaded onto the supply ship and taken to Carinia 1," Lanietta explained.

"And then we'll be dumped into a large vat and churned up into a giant fruit pie," Labba said. "No thanks. Besides, what if we can't breathe in the box?"

"We can bring our own air canisters," Lanietta said. "Another thing you told me about. Remember?"

"I wonder if I say too much," Labba said. "And I told you about the suits too."

"Right!"

"But I only told you for learning, not for doing something wrong," Labba said.

"The only thing wrong is being bored to death on this planet. I want off!" Lanietta complained.

"We're only twelve million years old. It's not like we're in the billions like Libriota," Labba pointed out.

"That hag Libriota doesn't have to live here all the time. She goes back to her palace on Carinia 1. I bet all the Bleuhs have a palace on Carinia 1."

"I'm not going with you in a fruit box. And I'm not stealing a transport ship," Labba said.

"Fine. I'll do one or the other without you," Lanietta said.

The supply ship arrived. Lanietta made preparations to stuff herself inside a fruit box. She wore a pressurized suit with an air canister that held enough breathable air for a million years—more than enough time to make the trip to Carinia 1. Labba tried to distance herself from the situation, but she couldn't bear to see her friend like this. She sought out and helped Lanietta in her final moments of sneaking off Carinia 2.

"Here's an encrypted cosmic-wave radio hidden inside a bamboo shoot. We'll be able to talk while you're away. Also, I can track your position. I look into my own bamboo shoot and see readouts of your position and status. See? Like a little telio-opticon," Labba said.

"Let me look at that," Lanietta said as she took the bamboo shoot from Labba. "Hey, this is great! You never told me about this. How come?"

"Because, my best friend Lanietta, the more I tell you, the more dangerous you become," Labba said.

Lanietta and Labba giggled.

"Here. I'll attach the bamboo shoot to your collar. It's not a flower, but it'll do," Labba said.

"What's a flower?" Lanietta asked.

"A special plant that looks pretty and smells wonderful. They have lots on Carinia 1," Labba said.

"I'll bring one back for you. I promise!" Lanietta said.

Labba helped Lanietta into the fruit box and closed the container shut. Then Labba walked a short ways away.

"Testing. Lanietta, can you hear me?" Labba said into her bamboo shoot.

"I hear you. This thing works great. How much longer do I have to wait?" Lanietta asked.

"Not much longer. I see a crane-cart heading your way. Keep still and keep quiet!" Labba advised.

"All right. Shh!"

"Shh!" Labba returned.

The crane-cart reached Lanietta's fruit box, lifted it up in the air, and placed the box on the crane-cart's bed. It then carried Lanietta's box to a supply ship. Many such crane-carts drove around Carinia 2 and performed the same function to several different supply ships. Carinia 1 occulted Carinia Zero, and this signaled to the supply ships that it was time to leave.

"Oh, Libriota will want us back in school," Labba said to herself. "What will I tell her about Lanietta? 'Sorry, Ms. Libriota, Lanietta is hiding in a fruit box.' Or maybe, 'Sorry, Ms. Libriota, I don't know where Lanietta is.' That's better."

Labba headed for the schoolhouse. She reached the building, hid in a little alcove, took the cap off her cosmic-wave bamboo-shoot radio, and took a quick peek inside. Tracking indicated that Lanietta ascended from Carinia 2 and headed toward outer space. Labba placed the shoot to her ear and heard Lanietta giving out hoots and hollers in excitement. Not wanting others to hear, Labba quickly put the cap back over the bamboo shoot, and she headed into the schoolhouse. She and other students sat at their desks, and Libriota took roll.

"Lanietta?" Libriota called. "Lanietta?"

The students looked around for Lanietta, and Labba did too, pretending that she was as surprised as the others by Lanietta's disappearance.

"Labba, where is Lanietta?"

"I...don't know, Ms. Libriota," Labba stumbled in deathly fear.

"Labba?" Libriota said more sternly. "I know you know. Is she hiding somewhere? Playing hooky in the orchard?"

"That must be it," Labba said.

"Wrong!" Libriota said. "Lanietta would rather be in here than stuck out in the orchard. Where is she, Labba? Where is she!"

Libriota yanked Labba by the hair and pulled her into the hallway. The vice principal happened to walk by.

"Trouble, Libriota?"

"Yes. Lanietta is missing. I suspect Labba here knows where she is," Libriota said.

"Do you, Labba?" the vice principal asked.

"I...I..." Labba stumbled.

The vice principal flagged down a hall monitor and alerted the monitor that Libriota's class should be watched.

"Let's go on a little adventure, shall we Labba?" the vice principal said.

The vice principal and Libriota escorted Labba down the hallway, into the main office, through one of the office doors, and into a room Labba had never entered. Now it happens that Carinia 2 rooms tend to have a main light in the center of the ceiling to emulate the constant light from Carinia Zero. The greatest fear of any Gren Carinian is for that light to be blocked out.

"In fact," the vice principal said, "during the Carinian Civil War—"

"That was the Quest of Freedom!" Labba blurted.

"That's what the Grens call it," Libriota said.

"The losing side always has its own name. Labba, your side lost the Civil War. Do you know how?"

"By blocking out the sun with a giant iron sail," Labba said. "It was called the Anrega."

"And all Gren Carinians surrendered out of sheer fright," the vice principal said.

"It was darkness. It was night," Labba said. "But you can't get anything out of me!"

"So, there *is* something to get out," Libriota said.

"We shall begin," the vice principal said. "You may strap her to the chair."

Libriota strapped Labba to a chair.

"Don't worry. You will not be harmed...physically," Libriota chuckled.

"Please...please don't," Labba begged.

A large circular panel of light occupied part of the ceiling. Not the entire ceiling, but enough to nearly fill a person's left-to-right peripheral vision while overrunning the up-and-down peripheral vision (while staring up). Labba's chair was reclined, as if she were in an Earthling dental chair. She was forced to look at the panel of light. It was a simple, bright-orange panel of light, or so it appeared.

"Have you seen this before?" the vice principal asked.

"No...but I've...read about it. This is a sailing room," Labba said, nearly in tears.

"That's right," the vice principal said. "We're going to go sailing. Just a little journey for the three of us. Two Bleuhs and one Gren. Remember that, Labba."

"I remember," Labba said. "I know I'm just a Gren."

Suddenly, the light went out, and all was dark. Labba screamed.

"Don't fear the dark," the vice principal said as he operated a panel. "Look for the light."

Indeed, it became clear that the panel of light was a display screen. In the center was a small dot of bright orange light, very much the same color as Carinia Zero. The dot was small, then it slowly grew larger, so slowly that it was barely perceptible. Labba wasn't sure if the dot was growing or not, but her subliminal sense detected it. Then an even smaller black dot began to form inside the orange dot. The black dot grew quicker than the orange dot until it covered the orange dot completely.

"Stop. Please stop," Labba said.

"Where is Lanietta?" the vice principal asked.

"She...I...I don't know," Labba stuttered.

"Again," Libriota said to the vice principal.

The vice principal hit a button on the panel, and the sequence started again. Only the small orange dot got a bit bigger. It felt as if Labba were flying through space toward her star of Carinia Zero when the black dot again blocked it from the inside out. Labba screamed when she felt Carinia Zero had been consumed. The vice principal looked at her, and she shook her head, "no." He started the sequence again and repeated it. Like before, each sequence started with Carinia Zero as a very small dot gradually growing larger and reaching a certain size larger than the prior cycle, and the growth rate was exponential, just as if sailing into a star from far away for a while before suddenly being overcome by the enormous size of the star and the (now apparent) black hole eating the star.

"Where is Lanietta?" Libriota shouted. "WHERE IS SHE?"

The sequence repeated and went faster and faster until the room became an intensive flash-show. Labba was so overwrought in pain that she choked on her screams and convulsed. In one of her convulsions, the bamboo shoot was forced from her pocket and fell to the floor.

"Stop!" Libriota called.

The vice principal stopped the sequence and returned the overhead light to normal. Libriota picked up the bamboo shoot and looked at it.

"What do we have here, Labba?" Libriota demanded.

"I...don't know. I've never seen it...before," Labba gasped.

"And yet it came from your pocket. Looks like a communication device. Cosmic-wave radio. For communication with Lanietta? Impressive for a girl of only twelve mil. Let's see what's inside. Shall I have a look? Here, show me how it works," Libriota demanded as she unstrapped Labba's arms (but not the rest of her). "Show us, Labba. SHOW US!"

"Run! Run!" Labba yelled into the bamboo shoot before collapsing into a daze.

"Impressive," Libriota said. "She fell into a daze."

"A rare sight," the vice principal said. "I've heard other species in other solar systems sleep. This is the closest we have to that."

"Do you remember the Civil War when I deployed the Anrega in the form of a sun-block sail?" Libriota asked.

"Yes. Grens descended into fear and panic, but for some the stress was too much, and they fell into a daze. I had forgotten about that until just now," the vice principal said. "I should go over Civil War history as a refresher."

"Many Gren-control techniques were pioneered just after the Civil War. There are several good conventions on the topic. Who's your favorite speaker?" Libriota asked. "Me, I hope."

Yes, the discussion regressed into favorite speakers of the Carinian Civil War while Labba remained strapped-in and in a daze.

"Let's have a look at this device," Libriota said. "I'm sure Labba won't mind. She's still in a daze and all."

The two laughed. Libriota removed the cap and looked inside where she saw information about Lanietta.

"Well, now I understand," Libriota said. "This device gives Lanietta's position. She is in outer space."

"Not on Carinia 2 at all?" the vice principal asked.

"No. She...I wonder how she..." Libriota mused.

"She must have stowed away on a supply ship," the vice principal said.

"Of course. A child's prank," Libriota said. "We'll put a stop to that. Let's get this to the tracking station. We'll find out which ship she's in and have it divert back."

"Wait. Labba's arms are unrestrained," the vice principal said.

"She's unresponsive. Not going anywhere," Libriota said as she and the vice principal chuckled.

The two went into another room and connected Labba's bamboo shoot to an analyzer on a panel.

"There it is. Ship 247," Libriota said. "It's headed for Carinia 1. No, something's happening."

"What is it? What are those other ships on the screen?" the vice principal asked.

"It's a raid. Pirates from the low end of the Terminon," Libriota said.

The Terminon, as said before, is that twilight area on Carinia 1 where light and dark meet. Including the aristocracy class, there is a portion of the terminator zone where Carinians of lower means reside, a subsection of Bleuhs known as *Bleuks*. They serve the upper-class Bleuhs so as to eliminate the need for transporting Grens to/from Carinia 2. It was deemed necessary to have such a population in the Terminon for speed and in case of delays with transport ships to/from Carinia 2. However, this lower class was more desperate for better goods, being normally handed meager food and little else for survival. And so, a gang of pirates emerged to commandeer supplies headed for the aristocracy, even if it meant risking loss of life.

"Labba, Labba, something is happening here. I hear shouting and fighting. Are you there?" Lanietta's voice called through the bamboo shoot.

"Lanietta," Libriota said. "You're late for school."

"Uh oh."

"Yes, 'uh oh'," Libriota said. "Do you realize the danger you've put yourself in, young lady?"

"I'm twelve million. I'm almost an adult," Lanietta said.

"You're not old enough! There are pirates all around you! Now we have to rescue you!" Libriota said.

"Pirates!" Lanietta screeched.

"There's someone in there," called a low voice (El-Vek) from outside Lanietta's box.

"Keep quiet. You'll attract attention," Libriota said to Lanietta.

Libriota and the vice principal heard the sound of the box being ripped open.

"Well hello there, little surprise!" said El-Vek. "A stowaway Bleuh?"

"I'm not a Bleuh. I'm a Gren," Lanietta said.

"Your hands are too smooth to be a Gren. Easy lifestyle," El-Vek said, and then he lifted Lanietta's face guard, touched her face and said, "Very smooth skin. Grens have wrinkled skin from working in the overhead sun. You're a twilight girl, aren't you? A Bleuh? So you snuck off to Carinia 2 for a party and are returning before Daddy finds out, is that it? Heh, heh. I'm sure Daddy will pay a fine ransom for you. And if not, we have our own leaders who could use your soft, precious talent."

El-Vek grabbed Lanietta's arm and pulled her out of the box.

"Let me go!" Lanietta said.

"Let's get a better look under that helmet," El-Vek said. "Men, over here. Look at what I caught!"

Several pirates accompanied El-Vek. El-Vek then removed Lanietta's helmet, and her long hair fell out into a smooth-flowing wave of beauty. The pirates hooted and hollered.

"What's that?" one said, pointing to the bamboo shoot.

El-Vek removed the bamboo shoot and tossed it to one of his buddies. The buddy took a look and said, "It's a radio tracking device."

"So! Not a stowaway, but a spy!" El-Vek said. "We know how to deal with your kind! Take her away!"

"No! Help! Somebody! Help!" Lanietta called.

"Listen you," El-Vek said through the radio. "I've got your little sneak. Do you want her back? Do you?"

"Name your terms," Libriota said.

"Hah! So you admit it! I recognize that voice. You're Libriota. You pose as a schoolteacher, but everyone knows your real name, Shady Liberty. Mistress of Imprisonment."

"Listen you, turn this girl over without harm, and I'll see you don't get prosecuted. But if you so much as cut a tiny snippet of her hair, I'll see that you get put away for at least a billion years," Libriota threatened.

"Hah, hah, hah! See if you can catch us! See if you can find your little snitch."

"Hello. Hello!" Libriota called back through the bamboo shoot, but there was no reply.

"I've sent out an alert to Interplanetary Police," the vice principal said.

"Lanietta has no parents. She and Labba stay with Nanceya. I'll inform Nanceya as to what has happened. We should send Labba home so she won't be a distraction in class," Libriota said.

"Very good," the vice principal said.

Libriota went into the torture room but returned to the vice principal very quickly.

"Labba's gone!" Libriota said.

The vice principal picked up a transceiver device and said, "Yes. Pick up Labba at once. Possibly suicidal. Yes. Send her home and post a guard. I'll follow up shortly. Thank you."

Chapter 89: Identity Split

Interplanetary Police battled the pirates for control of the supply ships, but in the skirmish and chaos, El-Vek snuck Lanietta off ship 247 and onto his private high-speed ship. He evaded Interplanetary Police and space-warped toward the Sol system.

"Orchius will be very pleased with our prize," El-Vek said to Lanietta. "You may call me El-Vek."

Lanietta stared out a window at the stars amongst a black background.

"First time in space?" he asked.

"I...I've never seen other stars. I've never seen the night," she said.

"Then I have given *you* a gift. The gift of day and night," El-Vek said.

"I was hoping...I...not like this," she said.

"But you are here," El-Vek said. "Why not enjoy the view while you can? Soon you will be on Preivos, a moon with its own day and night. But you will be underground. For your protection. Preivos is not like safe, friendly Carinia 1. It has no atmosphere for one, and its star is a yellow dwarf. Lots of blue and ultraviolet light. You would perish in its raw sunlight. Your fair skin deserves better. Much better!"

"I...just wanted to see Carinia 1. Will you take me to Carinia 1?" Lanietta asked meekly.

But El-Vek laughed.

"What is your name?" he asked.

"My name?"

"You do have one, don't you?" he asked.

"It's...ssss...it's Sassatinassa," Lanietta said.

"What kind of name is that?" he asked.

"You asked," Lanietta said.

"Is this the start of Sassatinassa?" Claus said. "The first time you used the name that Mariel gave you? What a lonely situation. Lanietta, I'm here if you can hear me."

"All right, Sassatinassa. Let me ask you: Have you split yet?"

"Uh, what?" she asked.

"Split your soul from your body. Gone eethi. I take it the answer is, 'Not yet.' Hmm. A little young, but just old enough. You will be taught how to go eethi. Most learn naturally, but we have little time before we reach Sol 4a. And Orchius expects his pets to be well trained. Well trained," El-Vek laughed.

"A pet, too. Lanietta, you don't have to turn this around on others," Claus said.

"Bleuhs learn how to split the mental energy from their physical bodies as part of reaching adulthood," El-Vek said. "The act is very personal and private, as it makes a Bleuh vulnerable to the innermost thoughts and feelings. Both Bleuhs and Grens who choose to procreate go to a conception center and go through a process where their identities are split. For most Grens, this is the only time this happens, and it's an involuntary response. Bleuhs do it without assistance. But did you know this—Bleuhs can go eethi to attack. Now I'll ask again. Have you gone eethi, perhaps out of anger to get back at someone?"

"No," Lanietta said nervously.

"Hmm. Perhaps you have and are holding out," El-Vek said. "Perhaps you haven't. It doesn't matter. You will go eethi. You will serve. How old are you? No, let me guess. You are twenty million Sol 3 years old."

"Twelve," Lanietta said.

"Indeed. You look more mature than your years," El-Vek said. "We have a special device to help you through the process. This way, please."

"I'd rather stay here and watch the stars," Lanietta said.

"You don't have a choice, do you?" he said.

El-Vek grabbed Lanietta by the arm and dragged her to another room. The room had a narrow bed platform with straps. The bed platform was on a pivot point underneath for flipping from horizontal to vertical. El-Vek placed her on the bed, strapped her down, and flipped the bed up vertically.

"What are you going to do to me?" Lanietta asked.

El-Vek chuckled.

"I want Labba! I want Labba!" Lanietta cried.

"Let her go!" pleaded Claus.

El-Vek touched a button on a wall panel. The panel opened, and out popped a device on an arm similar to a phoropter but with built-in display screens. El-Vek positioned this device in front of Lanietta's eyes and adjusted the controls, the controls of the *opticissor*.

"There, there, this won't hurt a bit. Just relax and let your eyes flow with the opticissor," El-Vek said.

"No. Please don't. Labba! Lah-bah!" Lanietta cried.

"Don't cry. It will only take longer," El-Vek said. "Shh. Look, there's a panel of light in this room. Pretend you are home on Carinia 1, boring Carinia 1. Take deep, slow breaths. Let the machine do the work."

The opticissor projected an image of Carinia Zero to each of Lanietta's eyes. The images were perceived as one and forced her eyes to accommodate at distance, close up, to converge, and diverge.

"It's Carinia Zero. Let Carinia Zero flow through you," El-Vek said.

"It's only our sun?" Lanietta asked.

"Yes. Let it flow," El-Vek said.

Lanietta could not help what her eyes did. They became innervated with the projected images, and so she could no longer control her eye movements. The machine detected as such, and it forced her eyes to converge at close distance, a cross-eyed situation. While holding her eyes crossed, the images rotated cyclically first clockwise (as seen by Lanietta), counterclockwise, toward each other, and away then toward each other the other way. They continued in opposite circular

directions, overlapping their positions twice, like two planets in the same orbital path but playing a game of chicken with each other. Lanietta's visual system became overloaded, and she felt the images drift into multiple images without focus or purpose. Unable to maintain a solid gaze, she felt her mental energy leave her body, becoming an ethereal spirit unable to affect anything physically other than to vibrate the air waves enough to project a voice. She now stood next to her physical body, a body held in a form of mental suspension.

"Very good," El-Vek said. "You broke from your body. You split and went eethi."

"I'm dead. I'm dead!" she screamed from her ethereal self. "I want my body back. I want my body back! Stop this! Stop this now!"

"Listen carefully. This device is holding your ethereal spirit here. Should I stop it suddenly, the cosmic eddies will carry your ethereal spirit out of this ship, like the arm of an ocean wave throwing a Carinian off a ship," El-Vek said. "You'll be lost practically forever. Perhaps in a trillion years, a cosmic good-doer will find you and restore you to the queue, where you will wait in line to inhabit a corporeal body. Pressing this button will stop the device."

El-Vek moved his finger to press the button.

"Please don't! I'll do anything! What do you want? Please tell me!" Lanietta's ethereal self screamed.

"Absolute obedience?" El-Vek said.

"Yes," Lanietta cried. "Yes!"

"Stand in front of your physical body. Prepare to embrace it. I will move the device out of the way, and when I do, you must embrace your physical body immediately. You must do so before your physical body takes half a breath. If you miss, your ethereal self will be swept off," El-Vek said.

"I'm frightened. Frightened!" ethereal Lanietta said as she shook.

"Stop this torture, Lanietta," Claus said. "Let go. Return to me, Lanietta. End this now. Lanietta? Lanietta!"

Of course Claus's pleas had no effect.

"Try to relax. It's like catching a ball. Just don't drop it," El-Vek said. "Move over here...yes, that's right. Get ready. On the count of three. Ready?"

"Ready," Lanietta shook.

"One. Two. Three!" El-Vek said.

El-Vek pulled the opticissor out of the way and powered it down. Lanietta's ethereal self reached her arms out to her physical self and got a little hold of it, but cosmic eddies ripped at her ethereal self like a winter blizzard blasting a house through the front door. She lost grip of her physical self and would have been swept into the void of outer space had El-Vek not "split" (gone eethi) himself. He grabbed her ethereal arm and threw her ethereal self back onto her physical body. Once she had a hand each on her physical arms, she was able to twist her ethereal self back into her physical body, reintegrate her ethereal vision with her physical vision, and restore her split identity into a single person.

"Congratulation!" El-Vek said. "You succeeded. I almost lost you, and for that Orchius would have been upset, but I preserved you for his service."

"You...saved me," Lanietta said, forgetting that El-Vek created the bad situation. "When you grabbed me, I felt warmth and comfort."

"I was not meant to touch you in ethereal form. But do not speak of this to Orchius. When he touches you in such a state, you must make him believe it is for the first time, that you have been unspoiled," El-Vek said. "Otherwise, he will separate you and cast away your ethereal self to the cosmic void."

"I...feel strange. I feel confused. I feel...I'm slowing...down," she said, and she fell into a daze.

"First time for that too," El-Vek said. "All is going according to plan."

El-Vek tilted the bed platform horizontally, removed the straps, and moved Lanietta to a more comfortable couch. In the equivalent of several Earth days of time, El-Vek repeated the procedure. Each time, Lanietta split from her body more quickly than before, and she was able to reintegrate without being swept into the cosmic void (and without help from El-Vek).

"Now I will teach you how to space-jump," El-Vek said. "This is not something I teach everyone. Not everyone can do it, but Orchius needs a special spy to confirm his orders are being carried out. Since you started off as a little spy—"

"I...I'm not really a spy," Lanietta said.

"You are now," El-Vek said. "You will split from your body as before, with the special device before your eyes. Next, I want you to walk into the neighboring room. In fact, walk as far away as you can from your physical body. But do not step off the ship! Then walk back to your physical body and reintegrate."

El-Vek repeated this procedure, and Lanietta complied. She was so afraid of El-Vek letting her go into the cosmic void that she felt compelled. El-Vek put her through the most difficult challenge.

"Now," he said. "You must learn to do the jump. You must split and travel a short distance all at once. Then you must jump back."

"No," Lanietta said. "I can't. It's too far. I'll fall into space. Please don't make me do this."

"Orchius demands that all his spies perform a true space-jump," El-Vek said.

"Please. I want to go home! Please," Lanietta begged.

"It will be over soon—one way or another," El-Vek said. "Should you complete this step, we'll do away with the heavy opticissor and give you a portable one."

"Please, help me," Lanietta begged.

"I will help you. There's a secret to doing this," El-Vek said. "You must establish an ethereal lifeline. This prevents you from being permanently separated from your physical body."

"A what? Wait a moment," Lanietta said.

"Every normal space-jumper uses an ethereal line. It's like using a rope when climbing a mountain," El-Vek said. "Yes, I made you leave your body without using an ethereal line. It's unsafe, but it proves how dangerous the maneuver is. I'll help you get your first ethereal line going."

El-Vek partially went eethi. His ethereal self sent one end of an ethereal rope to Lanietta's physical body and the other end to a point two meters in front of her body.

"Jump out to the end of the rope and grab it," El-Vek said.

Lanietta did just that.

"Good. Hold onto the rope. I will let go of the rope and disengage the opticissor. Ready?" El-Vek said.

"No, but that won't stop you will it?" Lanietta asked.

"Go!" he said without answering her.

Lanietta space-jumped out to the rope's end, El-Vek let go of the rope's middle, and he disengaged the opticissor. Cosmic waves whipped ethereal Lanietta around as she held on for the preservation of her spirit.

"I can't get back!" she said. "The cosmic waves are too strong."

"You must make the ethereal rope shorter," El-Vek said.

"How?" she asked.

"Scrunch your fingers, and that will make the rope shorter," he said.

Lanietta did so, but the rope barely shortened. She struggled to scrunch it more, but she tired.

"I'm not going to make it. I'm going to perish!" she cried. "Help me! Save me!"

"You're on your own," he said. "I'll be in the main control room if you succeed."

El-Vek left Lanietta alone. He entered the main control room as stated, sat down, and reviewed a file of past girls who he'd put through training and who'd been lost to cosmic eddies.

"Such beautiful girls lost forever," he said to himself. "But soon I will retire. Soon I will relax in—"

Before he could finish his thought, Lanietta stumbled into the control room, in her physical body, and in one piece. She collapsed in exhaustion. Relieved, El-Vek rushed over, picked her up, and placed her in a chair.

"There now, Sassatinassa, rest right here. We're into the home stretch," El-Vek said.

Chapter 90: Lanietta Reaches Preivos

El-Vek repeated the ethereal rope training. It tired Lanietta greatly, but she improved, and soon she was able to create her own ethereal rope without El-Vek's help.

"Your innate space-jump system has developed its own neuro-cosmic pathways. You no longer need my aid in this exercise," El-Vek said.

"Then you'll take me home?" Lanietta asked.

"No. You're going to serve Orchius," El-Vek said. "Come here. It's time we fit you with your own pair of portable opticissors, called *opticissicals*. They may look like sunglasses, but they are quite advanced, I assure you. Rest your chin on this support and look into the portoclonitron. I'll set it for standard prescription. There. You're doing fine."

Lanietta looked into the device. Several lights on a panel flashed in sequence, and a little red light flashed intermittently.

"Something's wrong. Wait, you must stop crying. The tears are interfering with proper measurements. Sassatinassa?" El-Vek said.

"I feel like I'm getting fitted for a pet collar," she cried.

"There, there, dear. You're learning advanced techniques that you'll thank me for many Sol 3 years from now. Orchius has been known to reward his best spies with favors. He may even commute your time. But that depends on you. He may use you to recruit others. If you fulfill his quota, he'll release you," El-Vek said.

"Is that what he offered you?" Lanietta cried.

"There, there," El-Vek said as he hugged her and comforted her. "I'm sure

you have plenty of Bleuh friends. You could recruit them."

"I don't have any Bleuh friends! I'm just a Gren!" she said.

"I don't believe you, and I hope you're wrong, because if you're right, Orchius will make me start over and find a true Bleuh. I won't like that, and I'll make life difficult for you. So wipe those tears and look into the portoclonitron," he said.

El-Vek passed her a tissue. She wiped her tears, took several deep breaths, and looked into the device. Lights flashed, and a blue one flashed to indicate success.

"There! That wasn't so bad. Look, see what the portoclonitron made? It made your opticissicals. Now put them on," he said, handing her what looked like a pair of sunglasses.

"Will I be able to take them off?" she asked.

"In the future," he replied.

Lanietta stared at him and was about to cry, but he put the opticissicals over her eyes and secured them over her ears. The opticissicals adhered to her flesh as if magnetic.

"There," El-Vek said. "It's done."

"I'm a freak," Lanietta said. "Everyone will see me like this and make fun of me."

"Oh no, my dear, all other spies look just like you. You'll fit right in," El-Vek said.

"At least I'm done for now," she said. "I want to stare at the stars for a while."

"No, you aren't done. There is another lesson," El-Vek said.

"I thought you said that I was in the home stretch," Lanietta said.

"You're reaching the finish line. But you must learn how to cross it. The last step is to perform a space-jump quickly. Your ethereal body is followed by your physical body such that the motion appears simultaneous. Don't worry, this lesson goes quick. You have already mastered the creation of an ethereal line. Now you must learn how to use it. For this lesson, you may remain here in the control room. We need not return to that torture room. That's for novices. You're an intermediate now. Go ahead. Split from your body. Go eethi."

Lanietta went eethi, created an ethereal rope connecting the ethereal and physical parts, and walked her ethereal self across the control room. Her ethereal self then turned and faced her physical body. The ethereal rope had a little slack, but not too much.

"Shake the rope," El-Vek said.

Lanietta shook it slightly from side to side.

"No, not that way. You must whip the rope and send a big wave to your physical self, as if you are undoing a kink in an irrigation hose," El-Vek said.

"El-Vek, what if the rope breaks?" ethereal Lanietta asked.

"Don't whip it too hard. Then it won't break," El-Vek said.

Lanietta whipped the rope a little bit, and a small wave went down the line. Her physical body shivered then remained still.

"Again, with a larger wave," El-Vek said.

Lanietta sent another wave down the ethereal rope, and her physical body moved for a few seconds before stopping still.

"That was strange," Lanietta said. "I felt like I was in two places at once, like my eyes were staring at two different images."

"Good. It is as it should be. Again," El-Vek said.

Lanietta repeated the procedure again and again. Each time, her physical body was able to move about for longer durations. Eventually, she was able to sustain movement in both physical and ethereal bodies.

"Excellent! Congratulations, Sassatinassa! You have completed your space-jump training! Orchius will be pleased with—"

But before El-Vek could finish, Lanietta sent her ethereal self at El-Vek to distract him while her physical self attempted to change the ship's course back to Carinia 2. El-Vek went eethi, gave out a low but mighty shout, and thus sent out an ethereal shock wave that pushed Lanietta's ethereal self off the ship. Her ethereal rope kept her from being completely separated from her physical body, but the stress on her rope pulled her physical body against the wall.

"You shouldn't have done that!" El-Vek said. "Now this ship goes into automatic punishment mode!"

Without Carinian intervention, programmed safeguards sent the ship on a new course toward a blue giant star. The energy released from the blue giant was intense, and Lanietta's ethereal self felt as if a million ants were consuming it. She was being tugged by the ship, like a water skier who had lost her skis and was being dragged behind the boat.

"Stop! Please! This is torture!" Lanietta pleaded from her physical self.

"You triggered the auto-punishment sequence. You'll have to wait for it to finish!" El-Vek said.

The ship got closer to the blue giant and went into a slingshot orbit. The radiation wave was so strong that El-Vek's ethereal self got knocked farther from his physical body. He too had an ethereal rope, and he was able to keep his ethereal self inside the ship as he struggled to inch closer to his physical self, unlike Lanietta whose ethereal self was still being dragged behind. The ship was on autopilot, going around the blue giant to ensure maximum pain and punishment to Lanietta.

The ship finished its slingshot and pulled away from the blue giant. As it did, a critical decrease of radiation was reached such that Lanietta's and El-Vek's ethereal ropes snapped back to shorter lengths like stretched rubber bands releasing their tension. Ethereal selves slammed into physical bodies. El-Vek nearly lost his balance, but Lanietta was knocked to the floor, stunned. El-Vek checked the controls.

"Fortunately for you, my auto-protection sequence punishes. It does not kill. We will head to Preivos immediately," El-Vek said.

"You were affected too, El-Vek. I saw you forced from your body," Lanietta said.

"You are still young and have much to learn about the universe. Forces are many and widespread," El-Vek said. "You would do well to learn of and abide by them."

Lanietta had a gut-wrenching feeling. Abiding by forces in the universe? First she had to abide by the same old boring life on Carinia 2. Now she was abiding by a different set of rules. But rules are rules.

"This wasn't what I had in mind, El-Vek," she said. "This isn't adventure at all."

"It depends on what you make of it," El-Vek said. "You have a unique opportunity, Sassatinassa, if you know how to take it. And I don't mean by trying to hijack the ship. You must work with what you are given."

The ship reached the Martian moon, Preivos, and landed in the major city, Preyakinnak.

"I'll take your opticissicals, please," El-Vek said before the two exited the spacecraft.

"I don't understand," Lanietta said.

"No unauthorized splitting. After that stunt you pulled, it appears I can only trust you a very little bit," El-Vek said.

El-Vek took the opticissicals and stowed them in his pocket. He then escorted Lanietta off the ship and to a receiving center for new arrivals. El-Vek and Lanietta waited in line until it was their turn. A receptionist scanned Lanietta's and El-Vek's energy signatures, looked at a panel, and received instant information.

"El-Vek and Sassatinassa," the receptionist said. "Very good. Sassatinassa is to be auctioned off."

"What? I don't understand. Sassatinassa is destined for Orchius," El-Vek said.

"You are too late, El-Vek. The Orchius quota has been filled. You can try again next season when he seeks new attendants," the receptionist said. "I hope you didn't waste your time training this one."

"Take me home," Lanietta said to El-Vek.

The receptionist laughed and said, "You're a fine catch, aren't you?"

The receptionist hit a few buttons and grinned.

"You are registered as slave goods," the receptionist said. "That means the auction block for you. Can't let a good sale go to waste. If El-Vek doesn't auction you off, I will."

"I will auction her off. Thank you," El-Vek said, and he left with Lanietta.

The two headed to El-Vek's quarters.

"I need to make a few calls," El-Vek said to Lanietta. "You can freshen up in there. And no tricks. Security is very tight here on Preivos, especially in Preyakinnak. Don't forget—I still have your opticissicals."

Lanietta went into a side room. She washed her face and brushed her hair. Meanwhile, El-Vek made several radio calls, with his last one to Orchius.

"Orchius, my master, I ask for confirmation. The receptionist said your quota is full. I see. I see. Yes. I understand. Thank you for your time. Next season. I will. I promise. Until then, El-Vek out."

The communication ended, and Lanietta returned to the main quarter's area.

"It's true," El-Vek said. "Orchius has his quota of spies. We missed the quota by mere moments. Your antics slowed us down. You could have been a spy for Orchius. Instead, you are at the mercy of the auction! I get no credit for delivery to Orchius. I am this close to securing my release. This close!"

El-Vek held two fingers very close together to indicate how close he was.

"Now I must wait until next season and start over. Well, at least you'll fetch a pretty price. I'll use that money for a long vacation. I need it."

"Why does Orchius need new people each season?" Lanietta asked.

"His spies only last a few Sol 3 years," El-Vek said.

"Why? Do they get tired?" Lanietta asked.

"They get dead. Bleuhs cannot handle the ultraviolet light from Sol. That is why Sol 4 was chosen as a colony. It's just far enough away from Sol to minimize ultraviolet damage. But the spies go closer. They visit Sol 3 and even Sol 2. Eventually they get excessive ultraviolet exposure, and they physically fall apart," El-Vek said. "The Bleuhs on Sol 4 will spend time outside, yes, but they limit their exposure and spend much of their time indoors or underground for fear of the ultraviolet. They never visit Sol 4a. Yes, his spies go everywhere, but not for you. You get the auction."

"How bad is the auction?" Lanietta asked.

"Bad. Most buyers will use you to work in the mines. Others will have you work as a servant. These auction masters never let up on you. Never!" El-Vek explained.

"Is there another job I could do? I would work for you, recruiting others," Lanietta said.

"Haven't you been listening? The quota is closed until next season. Oh, why did I bother?" El-Vek asked himself.

"How soon is the auction?" she asked.

"It starts in one Sol 4 day," he said.

"Would you at least give me a tour of the area? Maybe show me what to expect?" she asked.

"You won't be in the auction long, so there's nothing to prepare for. I'll leave you here. I need to get some errands done. I don't have time to give you a tour!" El-Vek said.

"Please don't leave me here alone! I'll go bored out of my mind. Let me help you. Let me help your friends," Lanietta said.

"How would you know I have friends?" El-Vek asked.

"I was told by a friend that people who travel often look up old friends," Lanietta said.

"Yes. Friends. Perhaps it's not such a bad thing. I'll use you as bragging rights. Should at least make for a good image on my part. But no tricks, remember?"

"No tricks," Lanietta said.

El-Vek put a hooded cloak over Lanietta and led her along a line of shops. They then turned down a dark alley. Halfway down was a door. El-Vek knocked twice, once, three times, and once. A middle-aged woman answered the door.

"It's you, El-Vek," the woman said.

"Monica. So good to see you," he said.

"Just get back from a cargo run? Who's this?" Monica asked.

"A friend," he said.

"What *kind* of friend?" Monica asked. "You pick 'em up everywhere, don't you? At least you could leave 'em there."

"Her name is Sassatinassa. She's going to the auction tomorrow, my sweet. Don't worry. I still care for just you," El-Vek said.

"Yeah, right," Monica said sarcastically.

"Aren't you going to invite us in?" El-Vek asked.

Monica wasn't too sure about letting Lanietta in. Monica pulled Lanietta's hood back and took a good look.

"Hmm. She's just a girl. There should be laws about that sort of thing," Monica said. "Well, if she'll be gone tomorrow, I guess it's all right. Come in."

"Thank you," El-Vek said.

The two entered Monica's place. It was a small place with few comforts. Monica got them refreshments, and they thanked her. The three sat, and Monica took a good long stare at Lanietta.

"A shame really. She's so young and comely," Monica said. "To think that her features will be wrecked with hard labor."

"She was supposed to go to Orchius as one of his spies," El-Vek said. "But his quota filled just before we arrived."

"I would not speak ill of Orchius. He may hear," Monica said.

"I've already spoken with him," El-Vek said. "He confirmed the quota is full."

"Yes, that happens a lot with him," Monica said. "If only...if only...Tell me, El-Vek. Can she really go ethereal? As well as you?"

"Sassatinassa? Why don't you show Monica?" El-Vek said. "Here, put on your opticissicals."

Lanietta took the device from El-Vek, put it on, looked through it as she had been trained, and she went eethi. She then moved both physical and ethereal selves, even performing a conversation with her selves.

"How marvelous! You do great work, El-Vek," Monica said. "I wish I could go eethi like that. And she's a Gren, too."

"What makes you say that?" El-Vek asked. "I was sure she was a Bleuh."

"She has a slight green tinge. Not very noticeable in her physical body. But it's very obvious in her ethereal form. Can't you see?" Monica asked.

"No, I can't," El-Vek said.

"You should get your eyes checked," physical Lanietta said.

"By an eye doctor," said ethereal Lanietta.

"Who can check for color blindness," both Laniettas said at once.

"Enough already," El-Vek said.

"Orchius would have detected it right away," Monica said. "You would have been severely punished. In a way this was a stroke of good fortune."

"Can anyone go eethi and space-jump?" Lanietta asked.

"Not everyone can do it, and not everyone by themselves," El-Vek said. "And if you truly are a Gren—"

"She is," Monica added.

"Grens can only go eethi with great help," El-Vek said. "Monica, Sassatinassa here can remain split for many Sol 4 days on end."

"Fantastic! Wow! What a waste at the auction she will be!" Monica said.

"I agree!" Lanietta's physical body said.

"Me too!" Lanietta's ethereal body said.

"El-Vek, I have an idea," Monica said. "Let's keep her. She can work for us."

"Out of the question," El-Vek said.

"But why? She has the talent," Monica said.

"She is scheduled for the auction," El-Vek said.

"We could have her go on normal work assignments," Monica said.

"Monica!" El-Vek said.

"Then she could go eethi and find out things with her ethereal self," Monica continued.

"No," El-Vek said. "Besides, she can't go eethi without the opticissicals."

"We must do something about that," Monica said. "The girl needs classes for splitting without glasses."

"Is it possible? Is it?" Lanietta asked.

"In theory," Monica said. "El-Vek, you know more about that."

"Shady Liberty can do it," El-Vek said. "Or Libriota as you would call her."

"Shady Liberty. Like Lady Liberty," Claus said. "Sigh."

"My school teacher?" Lanietta said. "But how?"

"You must be able to break binocular vision without help," El-Vek said. "One eye focuses on a point on your physical body such as your nose, and the other eye focuses on a point far away. Concentration flips back and forth between eyes until an ethereal rope shoots out, and you hold onto the rope as it puts you at the distant point. But this discussion is a waste of time. There's no way I can keep her, even if I wanted."

"If she could do it, she'd be perfect," Monica said. "No one would suspect a girl walking around without opticissicals."

"It's very dangerous," El-Vek said.

"El-Vek, we need help. Our people are destitute for water," Monica said.

"Oh, I love lots of water. Lakes, streams, swimming pools. It's so much fun," Lanietta said.

"The water is heavily controlled here on Preivos," Monica continued. "Orchius has a deal with the aristocracy, and we rely on shipments from the main planet for our meager rations."

"I know. I understand," El-Vek said, trying to calm her.

"Understanding is not enough. We're barely able to cope as it is. If we had but a little more water, we could strengthen and organize, and perhaps do something that would put an end to our misery," Monica said. "This moon is a vast wasteland. And bone dry."

"Why do I have to keep telling you?" El-Vek asked. "She's scheduled for the auction. Sassatinassa is registered. The arrival receptionist took her identity markers. Mine too. If she doesn't go to auction, they'll put out a search bulletin. If they don't find her, they'll imprison me for a jumped auction. If they do find her, they'll imprison me for a jumped auction and contributing to the delinquency of slaves. And if they also find her with me, they'll add the charge of harboring an auction slave."

"Yes, they would search the entirety of Preivos," Monica said with a sigh. "I guess that's it then. She goes to the auction."

"Now you're talking," El-Vek said, and he sighed.

"Tired?" Monica asked.

"Very," El-Vek said.

"Why not rest here, away from it all?" Monica offered. "Listen to your favorite space opera. Besides, I'd like to spend a little time with Sass showing her around."

"Strange that you want to be friends with a girl you were suspicious of not long ago," El-Vek said. "And when did you start calling her *Sass*?"

"The girl needs a shorter name. She also needs a mother figure," Monica said.

"I don't remember my mother," Lanietta said. "I was told she died when I was very young."

"You see? She needs mothering," Monica said.

"Hmm. You're not thinking of having her escape, are you?" El-Vek warned. "Just remember, I have her opticissicals. They can be used to trace her ethereal energy signature wherever she goes. I'll listen to a space opera, and you can go out, but be careful and don't stay out long."

"We won't," Monica said, and she left.

El-Vek listened to his space opera and was interrupted much later by the voices of Monica and Lanietta laughing. They *did* return. Lanietta did not escape. And so, the plan for Lanietta's auction was still in motion.

Chapter 91: Lanietta's Auction

The next day, El-Vek took Lanietta to the slave auction.

"I'm scared," Lanietta said.

"Don't worry. Everything will be over soon," El-Vek said.

"This is what a pet feels like, I guess," Lanietta said. "What a terrible thing. To be put on display like this...like...a basket of fruit for sale."

"Easy there," El-Vek said.

El-Vek received Lanietta's auction number from a receptionist and placed it around her neck for all to see. He then sat in a special section of sellers and their goods. One by one, auction numbers were called off and bid upon. There were many things up for sale, and not just people—digging equipment, furnishings, transportation equipment, energy cells, and animals. Often possessions of recently deceased came up for auction. These had no owners, and so the proceeds went to Orchius.

Lanietta's number came up.

"El-Vek, you're next," said a slave receptionist.

Guards brought forth twelve-million-year-old Lanietta.

"I auction this slave girl," El-Vek said. "She will be respectful and work hard for her new master."

The bidders laughed.

"They all say that," said one heckler.

"This is very familiar," Claus said. "I saw this before. With Lanietta."

"She'll stay on this moon after the orbital," El-Vek said to himself, referring to the private trip the winner would take with Lanietta. "And that will be it."

The auctioneer started the bidding at one drakos. The bidders laughed.

"What can she do for that price?" yelled one heckler. "Can she work a pick hammer?"

"I wish I could stop the bidding," Claus lamented.

The auctioneer pointed to a side hand, and he brought forth a nuclear-powered pick hammer. He handed the pick hammer to Lanietta, but she dropped it from its weight. The bidders laughed. A test boulder was wheeled in on a flat cart. The side hand tried to help Lanietta lift the pick hammer to work it on the boulder. It was an awkward and clumsy moment, with Lanietta nearly killing the side hand (she did injure his arm, causing him to bleed). The bidders laughed again.

"Can she drive a mining cart?" yelled another heckler.

A mining cart was brought in by another side hand. Lanietta attempted to drive it, but she nearly drove it off the auction stage and into the crowd. The second hand jumped on only just in time to stop the catastrophe.

"Can she make a meal?" asked a third heckler.

A cart was rolled out with raw meat, a burner, a pot, and cooking oil. Lanietta wasn't sure what to do, so she placed the meat in the pot, filled it with oil, placed it on the burner, and lit the burner with an igniter. The bidders clapped with this apparent demonstration of skill, but the oil bubbled up fast, spilled over, and caught fire. Lanietta tried to put out the fire by beating it with a heavy utensil, but she ended up knocking the pot off the burner and onto the stage, where the oil spread out and burned in a wide swath.

"Fire, fire!" bidders yelled.

Side hands brought forth extinguishers and put out the flames. Parts of Lanietta's clothing were burned, and her long hair was singed to shorter length.

"She's a fire risk," yelled one.

"She'll kill whoever buys her," said another.

"She's worthless. A drakos is too much," said a third.

"Do I hear two drakos?" the auctioneer asked.

The bidders laughed then fell silent.

"It's exactly as before," Claus said. "Lanietta, why am I seeing this again? Am I to remain stuck in this memory? This torturous event?"

"I'm sorry, El-Vek, but this won't do. Your goods are worthless," the auctioneer said.

"My apologies. Please charge my account for the damages. I'll dispose of my—"

"Wait!" called a voice from in back, who had just entered the auction arena and pushed his way through the bidder crowd. "Allow me through. Allow me through!"

The bidders conversed in hushed tones. Who was this guy? What was this all about? The man pushed his way through and climbed up on stage.

"You are not permitted up here," the auctioneer said. "This auction is—"

"A fake. A setup," the man said. "What is the girl's name?"

"Her auction number is—" the auctioneer started.

"Not her number. Her *name*. Her real name," the man said.

"Oh, I'm not sure I have that. I'll have to check and—"

"Sassatinassa," El-Vek said.

"El-Vek. Interesting. You always bring top-quality goods to the auction. Seems odd you would bring defective material this time. Or is it?" the man said.

"I don't know what you mean," El-Vek said.

"Oh, really?" the man asked.

"I know you," the auctioneer said. "You're El-Anonk. You bought a girl last week. The one no one else would."

"That's right. Turns out that was a fake auction too. Josette has a lot of spunk. I imagine this one does too. Let's see," El-Anonk said.

He took Lanietta by the arm and twisted it. Without thinking, she spun her body and put El-Anonk into a choke hold. The bidders gasped, and the auctioneer called for security.

"No, call them off," El-Anonk laughed. "You see? Deep down, they all have spunk!"

"And will you bid one drakos?" the auctioneer asked.

"I bid a thousand drakos," El-Anonk said.

The bidders gasped again.

"To ensure no one outbids me. I am merciful. I will not drag this auction out," El-Anonk said.

"A thousand and one drakos," El-Vek yelled to drive up the price.

"You cannot bid for your own," the auctioneer said.

El-Anonk laughed with hysteria.

"Your ruse is up, El-Vek. Take the money. Take it! Go on a long vacation and think of this excellent sale you have made," El-Anonk said.

The deal was finalized, the papers signed, and Lanietta became property of El-Anonk. El-Vek took the money, and he made for the auction room's exit.

"El-Vek," Lanietta called from a distance as El-Anonk put an electronic collar on her and escorted her out.

"I'm your owner now, Sassatinassa," El-Anonk said. "You shall be my pet and keep Josette company. The two of you will provide millions of Sol 3 years of entertainment and pleasure."

El-Anonk took Lanietta to his space ship in preparation for his maiden voyage with Lanietta around Mars's moon. Meanwhile, El-Vek returned to Monica. He showed her the money.

"There. All done. Time for a vacation," El-Vek said.

"Why? How?" Monica asked.

"What do you mean?" El-Vek asked. "It was an auction. Well, not an ordinary auction, but it was one. No one was going to bid on Sassatinassa. I was almost forced to take her back. This would have been most unfortunate, because I would have had to waste time teaching her a skilled trade and returning to auction thirty Sol 4 days later. But El-Anonk came out of nowhere, and after the bidding was over too. He pushed his way on stage and twisted her arm. Sassatinassa responded with vigor, and he liked that. You know what? El-Anonk did the unthinkable. He bid a thousand drakos. They thought he was crazy, but he has almost as much money as Orchius. I tried to drive up the price, but they wouldn't let me."

"El-Anonk. Orchius's right-hand man. I should have known," Monica said. "Are they planning to...to..."

"Yes. His ship is being prepared for an orbit around Preivos," El-Vek said. "Well, that's that. Anyway, would you like to go on a vacation with me? There's a nice resort on Sol 4. Beautiful beaches and intelligent aquatic life."

"I...don't know. I don't know what to think," Monica said.

"Still have your heart set on keeping Sassatinassa? Forget it. And the best way to forget is the resort," El-Vek said. "I promise you'll have a wonderful time."

El-Vek moved toward Monica with an embrace in mind.

"Uh...very well," Monica said. "Let me pack."

"Pack? What's to pack?" El-Vek said.

"A woman needs her things. I won't be long," Monica said.

Monica returned shortly with a small, hard-shelled suitcase.

"I'm ready," Monica said.

The two left for and entered El-Vek's ship. Once aboard, El-Vek plotted a course for Mars. He received departure clearance and launched his craft. Monica stood next to him and placed a hand on his shoulder.

"You're shaking. Nervous? Sit down and relax. We'll be there soon," El-Vek said.

But concealed in the palm of her hand was a stealthy sedative hand clip. She pushed her hand into his shoulder, and the drug delivered its contents into El-Vek. El-Vek stood with a start and brushed her away.

"What are you doing? Are you mad? Trying to poison me?" he demanded to know.

But El-Vek didn't wait for an answer. He walked toward the medical station to get an antidote. He never made it. With El-Vek on the floor and sedated, Monica took Lanietta's opticissicals from one of El-Vek's pockets. As she leaned over him, she spoke.

"Sorry, El-Vek, but this is necessary."

Monica put the opticissicals in a scanner station.

"The scanner will search for Sass's ethereal frequency using trace logs from her opticissicals. I should be able to track her," Monica said to herself. "I'd better tie up El-Vek before he regains full alertness."

Monica dragged his body to a chair. She could not lift him into the chair, so she tied him to the chair as best she could. Then she laughed.

"A Bleuk fully sedated," she said. "I'll have to thank the mad scientist who created this drug."

Monica turned her attention to the scanner.

"Yes, there's Sass," Monica said. "She *is* on a ship in orbit around Preivos. I'll put us in orbit, but I'll keep this ship on the other side. That way El-Anonk won't notice me."

Monica made the course adjustment easy enough, and the ship reached the proper Preivos orbit, but now came the challenging part. Monica removed a container from her case and pushed the container into a port on the ship. The port pulled the container inside it and sealed it off from the ship's interior. She then pressed a "deploy" button. A transparent ethereal line extended from the container into space. It shot toward the center of Preivos, but there was a problem.

"The transparent ethereal rope is bunching up. It's binding," Monica said. "This moon's core is disrupting the line. How disappointing. Sigh. This won't work."

"No, it won't," El-Vek said, now regaining full awareness. "I can put you away for this. Hijacking a ship is a capital offense. Now untie me so I can drop you off. I'm going on the vacation without you, as it's clear I can't trust you. Why did you do this to me?"

"Because I can't trust you either," Monica said. "You wouldn't help me save Sassatinassa, so I'm doing it without you."

"You're going to get us both killed!" El-Vek said. "I won't throw away my life for a failed venture."

"Then you condemn Sass to death," Monica said.

"No I don't. She's property of El-Anonk. He keeps his slaves alive. He might not treat them all that well, but he keeps them alive."

"You don't understand. Sass is going to sabotage his navigation control and send his ship crashing into Preivos," Monica said.

"What madness is this?" El-Vek said. "Monica, what have you done? What have you done!"

"Last night as you rested, I took her out to an ethereal specialist," Monica confessed.

"You didn't," El-Vek said.

"I did. The specialist taught Sass how to split without opticissicals," Monica said. "He said it's called going full eethi."

"I should have never told you about that," El-Vek said.

"It didn't matter. I would have found out anyway," Monica said. "The specialist also taught Sass how to space-jump, again without opticissicals."

"You fool! You've done us in for sure!" El-Vek said.

"I told her we'd be here on the other side of Preivos. She just needs an ethereal line to lead her into this ship, and she'll be able to escape before El-Anonk's ship crashes. If I don't have that line ready, there will be nothing for her to jump to. She'll die. She'll die! Now are you going to help me?"

"I don't believe what I'm hearing. Did you ever think to consider who this is? This is El-Anonk you know. The political repercussions are going to be enormous. Who knows what wrath will be unleashed if he dies."

"*If?* You mean *when*. Sass is going to do it for sure. We worked this out before the auction. I didn't know it would be El-Anonk," Monica said.

"Well now you know," El-Vek said.

"He's going to die anyway. At least we can save Sass," Monica said.

"Untie me," El-Vek said.

"I don't know if I should," Monica said.

"You'll never get that ethereal line deployed through this moon's core. I can help. At least then we'll resolve this little crisis one way or another," El-Vek admitted.

"I will. But a promise is a promise, right? You promise to help me in this?" Monica asked.

"I will help you get Sassatinassa to this ship. What happens after that is another matter," El-Vek said.

"That's all I can ask," Monica said.

Monica untied El-Vek.

"So how will we get the line to her?" Monica asked.

"We'll have to send it around this moon," El-Vek said. "Somehow I need to get it to flow behind us in orbit."

"I didn't think ethereal lines work that way," Monica said.

"They don't. I'll have to do a space-jump," El-Vek said.

"On the transparent line?" Monica asked.

"Yes. There is a chance my ethereal line will get tangled with the transparent one."

"If you take the transparent ethereal line all the way around this moon, your own ethereal line will be detectable as will your ethereal spirit," Monica said.

"I know that. I don't need to go out very far. Perhaps one eighth around in the orbit. I'll introduce a curve between me and the ship. That will create a corresponding curve on the other side of me that will carry the transparent ethereal rope around this moon."

"That's like holding a long stick horizontally from one end," Monica said. "The ethereal torque will be strenuous."

"I know that too. I will need to expend quite a bit of energy. Does Sassatinassa look like she's ready to start?" El-Vek asked.

"Yes, she does," Monica said.

"Very well. I should begin too," he said.

El-Vek separated his ethereal self from his physical self. He himself did not wear opticissicals, as he could space-jump without them. His ethereal self took the transparent ethereal line, carried it outside the spacecraft, and one eighth around Preivos. He then held a fixed distance trailing his spacecraft and "flowed" the length of transparent ethereal line to trail farther and farther behind in orbit until it wrapped around to the moon's other side.

"That's enough," Monica said. "Stand by. She's eyeing over the electronics. She's looking around nervously. El-Anonk is running his fingers under her chin. How revolting."

"She won't stand for that. Not for very long," El-Vek said. "I'm watching for her."

"She has not split yet," Monica said. "She should be going eethi so she can sabotage his navigation system secretly and make it crash into this moon. Wait, there she goes, she's splitting now. I've lost track of her ethereal self. Good, she's mastered the skill of going transparent."

"You had her taught that too? You're impossible!" El-Vek said.

"El-Anonk's ship is changing course. Wait, it's not losing altitude, it's blasting out of orbit!" Monica said.

"What is she doing?" El-Vek said.

"Maybe she's learning the controls," Monica said.

"I'll hold my position. She might regain control," El-Vek said.

"She's leaving this solar system. El-Vek, she never lost control, I did," Monica said.

"What?" El-Vek asked.

"We've been had. Sass is escaping!" Monica said.

"No, *you've* been had. Cut the transparent line! I'm returning to the ship," El-Vek said.

Monica cut the transparent line. El-Vek reintegrated himself with such speed that it knocked his physical self over. He caught his head on a panel, and blood oozed down his forehead. Lightly dazed but still aware, he struggled to stand but could not.

"I'm engaging auto-flight pursuit... now," Monica said.

El-Vek's ship pursued El-Anonk's.

"Monica, wait. This is bad. Call off the auto-pursuit. If El-Anonk thinks we're following him, he might suspect we are part of this attack on his control," El-Vek said.

But Monica remained singularly focused on the screen.

"Monica? Are you listening? You're putting us in great danger," El-Vek said.

El-Vek's head cleared a little, and he stood up. He made for the controls to turn around. He didn't get much of a chance, though, because El-Anonk's ship suddenly stopped in a dying solar system.

"I've lost the feed from the scanner," Monica said. "Did you stop it?"

"No. Communication coming in from El-Anonk," El-Vek said. "I knew this would happen. I knew it!"

El-Vek hit a button, and he had face-to-face communication with El-Anonk.

"What a surprise finding you out here, El-Vek," El-Anonk said.

"I had heard the Bleuhs are recycling planets in this dying solar system, and I wanted to render assistance," El-Vek lied.

"With blood on your face? Did you also render this assistance?" El-Anonk said as he showed Lanietta's empty collar.

"I don't understand," El-Vek said.

"Don't play games with me. You didn't want to sell her. And now you have assisted in her escape," El-Anonk said.

"I...didn't," El-Vek said.

"You keep lying, El-Vek. You are the only ship following me after my navigation control magically took a mind of its own. Well? How does that make you look, El-Vek?"

"It's not what you think," El-Vek said.

"I suspect she's on your ship this very moment. You will entertain a visit from me and my men," El-Anonk said.

"If you don't mind, I'll just go on my way," El-Vek said.

"That wasn't a request. Stand by for boarding," El-Anonk said. "Communication out."

El-Vek and Monica exchanged glances.

"Where is she?" El-Vek asked.

"I don't know!" Monica replied. "I lost track of her!"

"Is she here? On this ship?" El-Vek asked.

Monica changed the scanner for local field.

"It says—"

But at that moment, El-Anonk and his men boarded El-Vek's ship.

Chapter 92: The PRAAD

"I assure you, she is not on board," El-Vek said to El-Anonk and his men.

"We shall see," El-Anonk said as he walked over to a panel with the opticissicals.

Monica looked at El-Vek, but he waved her off with his eyes.

"What do we have here?" El-Anonk said.

"I doubt you will find a little girl in the devices of this ship," El-Vek said.

"Perhaps," El-Anonk said while looking through the opticissicals. "Hmm. These always contain the energy signature of..."

Just then, a holographic image of Lanietta projected from the opticissicals to the floor in front.

"Sassatinassa," El-Anonk said. "So, it all becomes very clear."

"Wait," El-Vek said. "This—"

"No, you wait. You trained her to space-jump. As a spy?"

"Did Sass steal anything?" Monica blurted.

"Monica!" El-Vek said.

"She stole nothing. Therefore she must be a spy. And a hijacker too. Did you plan to raid my ship, El-Vek? Foolish! I'm El-Anonk! But you didn't plan on selling her to me. You thought a lesser bidder would take Sassatinassa, and you would raid that ship."

"No...I..." El-Vek stumbled.

"You don't fool me, El-Vek. You're a pirate through and through. But this is a new low for you. I'll have you put away in the mines, unless you produce—what did Monica call her—Sass? Very familiar with this one, aren't you? Too familiar."

One of El-Anonk's men whispered something in his ear.

"I know that," El-Anonk said.

"What? What is it?" Monica blurted again.

"Monica! Leave this to me," El-Vek said.

"Not that you're doing very well, El-Vek," El-Anonk said. "My aide reminds me the opticissicals can be used to locate Sass. I will do that, since you have chosen to be uncooperative."

El-Anonk left the ship while his men remained behind.

"He has her opticissicals," Monica whispered.

"I know," El-Vek said.

"How will we...how will..." Monica still whispered, trying to be discreet. "She could be anywhere."

"I know that too," El-Vek said.

"If she were to...you know...visit us... could you..." Monica stumbled.

"That I don't know. You've made a royal mess of things, Monica. A royal mess!" El-Vek said.

Several minutes of silence passed. Then El-Anonk sent a communication to El-Vek.

"I have located my prize," El-Anonk said. "I still blame you, of course. And so, you will accompany me to the fourth planet, where the Bleuhs have deployed resource reclamation devices."

"If you don't mind, I'll just return to Preivos," El-Vek said.

"That wasn't a request, El-Vek," El-Anonk said, and he motioned to his men on El-Vek's ship.

Two men guarded El-Vek and Monica while two others operated the ship's controls and followed El-Anonk's ship to the fourth planet. There were no Bleuh ships in the vicinity, but there were other pirate ships orbiting around the planet, looking for opportunities to grab unguarded surface resources or steal a bit from a transport ship. El-Anonk's and El-Vek's ship first entered orbit then flew down to the planet's surface and held a position fifty meters from the surface of a super lake (a body of fresh water the size of an ocean), very close to a whirlpool. This whirlpool had a vortex, as the water was pulled down to the PRAAD.

"The Planetary Release/Acquire Aquifer Device," Claus said. "So it's here on this planet now, acquiring water. It looks the same as ever. Cylindrical in shape, with the chalice-cup part on top and the main body below. But strangely unguarded. Perhaps the Bleuhs have given it a defense mechanism."

The PRAAD expanded and shrank as if pumping like a heart. The device was at the top of a seamount, and Lanietta's ethereal self stood on this seamount and close to the device, studying it and attempting to manipulate it. The PRAAD was at the bottom of the vortex, pulled water into it, and stored it. It was able to do so using a mass compressor, a device that compressed matter by flattening electron orbits. Compressing matter quickly (as this device did) gave off a lot of heat, but the cold water countered this heat, with the net effect being a warm zone on the seamount around the PRAAD. This heat, however, did not affect Lanietta's ethereal self. Perhaps Lanietta had no trouble because of her interactions with the heat of Carinia Zero, or perhaps her unknown connection to the PRAAD helped.

"There's nothing here but a whirlpool," Monica said.

"She's down there," El-Anonk said with the communication line still open. "We're going into the water."

The two ships dove down and landed on the seamount, keeping clear of the water vortex so as to avoid being pulled into the PRAAD.

"Interesting," El-Anonk said. "Sass shows up on the opticissical scanner, but I cannot see her with my own ethereal vision. You have taught her to go clear ethereal. Now I understand how she escaped! But her physical self isn't here. The scanner shows her ethereal line runs into this device."

"She's...inside that thing?" Monica asked.

"It's the PRAAD," El-Vek said.

"The what?" Monica asked.

"The Planetary Release/Acquire Aquifer Device. It stores water for later release. Instead of allowing old planets to lose their water when their star expands and destroys it, the Bleuhs remove the water and release it on another needed planetary body. Still trying to find new colonies to escape the Greylingers. Strange that it's unguarded," El-Vek said.

"Yes! They heard me!" Claus said.

"This is the water we need! Oh El-Vek, if she could take this device and—"

"I don't think she's inside the PRAAD willingly. She's trapped inside!" El-Vek said.

"Can we turn it off? Then we could get her out," Monica said.

"It's a dangerous device. Whoever tames it will wield great power," El-Anonk said. He paused for a moment as if debating the risk versus reward, and then he said, "*We* will turn it off and get her out. Then I shall take the PRAAD for myself. I'm sure you understand, El-Vek, that possession is ninety percent of the law."

"Then I want to help. I'll put on a diving shell and work the device with you," El-Vek said.

"Hah, hah, hah!" El-Anonk said. "Do you think I'm that naive? You would trick me and take the PRAAD for yourself."

El-Anonk motioned to one of his men on El-Vek's ship, and that man manipulated controls and pulled El-Vek's ship away from the PRAAD enough such that it was no longer on the seamount but instead was away horizontally and vertically, holding just below the waterline.

"In case you get wise on me and go in your diving shell, you'll have a long way down to the lake bottom," El-Anonk said. "But cheer up. I am generous, after all, and will permit you to watch as I take back my prize."

"You just want to brag to your men on my ship," El-Vek said.

One of El-Anonk's men punched El-Vek in the jaw. El-Vek went eethi and made to disrupt the man's electronic weapons, but the man also went eethi (as did two other men) and used ethereal weapons to force El-Vek back to his body.

"Don't try that again!" El-Anonk said. "But in a way it was fun watching you suffer. Matter of fact, you've just revealed how I intend to get Sass back. I'll subdue her ethereal self."

El-Anonk motioned to three men on his ship. The men donned diving shells (like diving suits but able to withstand extreme water pressure), walked onto the seamount, approached the PRAAD, then went eethi and sent their ethereal selves with ethereal weapons toward Lanietta.

"Get away from the PRAAD," the men said to Lanietta.

Lanietta saw and heard them. She pulled her ethereal self into the PRAAD for protection, leaving no part of herself outside.

"Foolish girl!" Monica said.

"Yes. She has played right into my hands. Now watch the final act of this performance," El-Anonk said. "Men, disable the PRAAD, then bring it aboard with your physical selves."

The men approached the PRAAD. They spent a moment studying it. They pressed several buttons, and the vortex stopped. The PRAAD had stopped acquiring water. But then the PRAAD sank into the seamount three inches.

"Reintegrate and bring it back," El-Anonk said.

The men reintegrated with their physical selves. One man touched the PRAAD, but it was still hot and melted a hole in his glove. Water rushed into his suit, crushed his physical self, and killed him. His ethereal self (with a broken ethereal line) floated away, out of control. El-Anonk laughed.

"It's still too hot," El-Anonk continued to laugh. "Stand clear. I'll send cool water in."

El-Anonk's ship was in the warm zone, and so he directed his men on El-Vek's ship to send a water burst at the PRAAD. They did so, and the remaining two on the seamount fell over. El-Anonk laughed again.

"Get up and take the PRAAD. It has cooled. Use a mitt if you have to," El-Anonk said.

The men donned mitts, approached the PRAAD, and attempted to lift it.

"It's stuck," one said.

"Rock it," El-Anonk said.

The men rocked the PRAAD. It tilted back and forth more and more until it toppled over and—with tremendous weight—crushed the lower suit and legs of one of the men. He bled quickly and profusely then died before anyone could help. His ethereal self floated away with a broken ethereal line. El-Anonk laughed at that too.

"It's too heavy," the remaining man said.

"Hmm," El-Anonk said.

An aide whispered something into El-Anonk's ear.

"Yes. Relay the information to him," El-Anonk said.

The remaining man on the seamount hit several buttons on the PRAAD and then pulled on it. The PRAAD lifted with ease, as if empty.

"He but had to engage the mass-gravity neutralizer, and the planet's pull on the contents was counteracted," El-Anonk said. "Bring it in."

The man walked toward El-Anonk's ship. But then it happened. An unexpected high-pressure stream of water shot from the PRAAD. It cut a hole in the man's diving shell and allowed water into his suit. The water pressure crushed the man, and his ethereal self floated up with a broken ethereal line.

The water stream was Lanietta's doing. Her ethereal self had mixed with the physics of the compressed environment, and her ethereal self was squeezed into a plane. Though she could not manipulate matter in a conventional sense, she could affect it at the atomic level by severing molecular links in a line (matching the plane of her hand or finger). She could change size too, and so she could cut a slit as long or short as desired. She was just learning how to cut and where, and so her first efforts caused the PRAAD to shoot around like a wild fire hose, not really going in a specific direction. It spun and banged around. The water cut holes in the seamount and sculpted random lines. It then cut through El-Anonk's ship. In a split second, the lake water breached the ship, El-Anonk grabbed the opticissicals, and he space-jumped to El-Vek's ship.

Lanietta figured out where the ends were (to her, the inside was like an entire world itself, and she was floating in it with a partly cloudy sky above and another partly cloudy sky below). Lanietta forced water to blast out one end with three control streams coming out the sides on the other end, and so she created a water rocket with control thrusters. She blasted off the seamount, shot upward, left the fourth planet, and headed out of the dying solar system.

"Chase it down! She's a killer now!" El-Anonk ordered from the main control room of El-Vek's ship. "I want her destroyed!"

"No! You can't kill Sass! You can't!" Monica pleaded as she got up and pulled on El-Anonk's arm.

El-Anonk swatted her aside. She fell and hit her mouth on the armrest of a chair. Blood flowed from her mouth, and she sat on the ground nursing her wound, stunned. Without thinking, El-Vek stood up to defend her, but two men trained their weapons on him and shoved him back in his seat.

"I expect a full refund after this adventure is over!" El-Anonk barked.

El-Vek tried to say something, but he was speechless. Never had any of his slaves exceeded his space-jump teachings in this manner. Never had one gone into the PRAAD and used it as both a weapon and a spacecraft. No one should have that kind of power, except Libriota. How was it this girl could do so? El-Vek didn't realize the PRAAD was locked onto Lanietta's signature, or that this girl was named Lanietta and was the daughter of Lanshalla, or that Larbiabba locked the signature in, or any of that. He only knew the crisis of the moment. What was to stop her from using it against him? Against anyone?

Lanietta increased speed of the PRAAD, and El-Anonk ordered his men to overtake. But they could not catch her. Lanietta had changed the characteristics of the water coming out. It changed its form to that of a high-energy plasma beam. This (combined with very little effective mass) meant the PRAAD could accelerate at speeds far beyond what any conventional spaceship could attain.

"Faster," El-Anonk ordered.

"You can't push this ship any faster," El-Vek said. "It'll blow apart!"

El-Anonk didn't listen. He ordered the ship pushed beyond maximum. An eerie green mist blew through the main control room. It wasn't smoke from the circuits, but rather a cosmic interaction with the ship due to its excessive speed. Monica grew fearful and moved toward El-Vek. He motioned her toward him further, and she sat in his lap, shaking like a leaf.

"I will catch her if I have to destroy this ship!" El-Anonk barked.

Not wanting to be caught up in the ship's destruction, El-Vek observed the navigation control as it passed celestial objects. When the ship neared a somewhat habitable planet, El-Vek made his move. He held firmly onto Monica and space-jumped toward the planet. Never had El-Vek attempted such a difficult maneuver of motion with the required pinpoint accuracy. He and Monica made it to the planet, but they materialized in the air above a forest. They fell through the upper branches and then the lower branches, starting with abrasions and ending with ripped flesh and pulled muscles until all motion was stopped. They remained in the lower branches, injured and exhausted.

Chapter 93: The Ash People

Miraculously, neither had broken bones, and both were able to climb down. Both sat on a large log and breathed heavily to regain their strength. They looked up and saw an expanding blast cloud high and far up in the sky.

"That's it then," El-Vek said. "My ship. It's destroyed."

"How...I..." Monica struggled to say.

"Rest for a moment," El-Vek replied. "We space-jumped."

"I...didn't know you could...do what you did," Monica said.

"You mean the distance while flying by? Neither did I," El-Vek said.

"I guess desperation brings the most out of us," she said. "Thank you. We were doomed in that ship. Did you ever space-jump with another person?"

"You're the first," El-Vek said. "The jump easily could have gone wrong. We might have gotten caught on an ethereal fracture and died right there. Or a multitude of other things."

"We lucked out," Monica said.

"Yes. We lucked out," El-Vek said.

"But we have no food or supplies," Monica said.

"Yes. At least the star is a red dwarf," El-Vek said. "Are you able to walk? Perhaps there is a village nearby."

"Can't you scout around with a space-jump?" Monica asked.

"I won't be space-jumping for a while," El-Vek said. "My ethereal self is bleeding cosmic energy and needs to rest. My physical body isn't the only thing injured."

The two traveled through the forest and realized they were on a hill. They reached a stream, but it was dirty from ash.

"Strange," Monica said. "Where did this ash come from?"

"It doesn't matter. We must go upstream if we are to find clean water," El-Vek said.

They followed the stream and had to climb nearly to the top of the hill, where they found the (clean) water source—a snowmelt hidden under the brush. The two drank and drank. When they finished, they rested. But this planet rotated, and they had landed near the end of the day. The shadows grew long, and dusk came.

"It's getting dark," Monica said.

"We can't travel at night. We can't see. Why? We have no device to provide light," El-Vek said. "We'll have to pitch camp quickly and wait until morning."

They did. They gathered together loose branches, broke a few off that weren't so loose, and made a lean-to with three sides just before the daylight failed. The fourth was walled at the ends but open in the middle. Already the temperature had dropped (they were on a hill in the mountains, which tended to run cooler at night than the valley). With what little light was left, El-Vek built a fire just outside the lean-to's opening, and this fire provided heat and light. Being Carinian, the two did not sleep, but instead they sat in silence.

"Why are we being quiet?" Monica whispered.

"We don't want to attract attention," El-Vek whispered back.

"But won't the fire do that?" Monica asked.

"Yes, the fire will do that," El-Vek said aloud. "We must not exert ourselves too much. Rest is important. We'll look for food in the morning."

"Well what am I supposed to do all night?" Monica asked.

"I don't know. Hum something?" El-Vek asked.

"What about planning strategy for tomorrow?" Monica asked.

"Survive," El-Vek said.

"What about finding Sass?" Monica asked. "She's in trouble and needs our help."

"She's in trouble? We're the ones in trouble. Perhaps she will come down here and take us into her PRAAD ship. Then we can tour the universe," El-Vek said.

"Don't mock me. I'm serious," Monica said.

"As serious as a dipper with a hole in the bottom," El-Vek said.

"Well how do you like that? I try to help, and I get made fun of. I'm done being helpful," Monica said.

"I've heard animals on planets with a day-night cycle sleep for part of that cycle. I might try this sleep thing. If nothing else, I won't have to listen to any more gibberish," El-Vek said.

"You're going to hear my *gibberish* if it takes all night. I'm going to point out every failing and every flaw you've had since I've known you, even before I've known you, starting with the time...El-Vek? Are you listening?"

But El-Vek's mind drifted elsewhere. He didn't fall asleep, but he thought about the days before pirating, when he was a young Bleuk on Carinia 1, helping his parents tend grounds for a wealthy Bleuh landowner. He somewhat lost awareness of his surroundings and began breathing heavily.

"What is that awful sound? It sounds like you're choking!" Monica said.

She shook him.

"What, what?" he asked. "Why are you shaking me?"

"I thought you were choking," Monica said.

"I'm fine," he said. "I was thinking back to my youth."

"You should be listening to me. Now let's get back to your character profile. The first time I met you, you made a complete fool of yourself in front of...El-Vek, you're choking again!"

El-Vek wasn't choking. His mind drifted off again. It was the closest thing he could get to sleep. And as his mind wandered, he realized the reason these animals fell asleep wasn't because of the day/night cycle, it was because they were escaping the unceasing stresses of the day,

in which Monica was the last stressor. As long as she kept speaking, his mind wandered, with her speech like the hypnotic effect of a train (they had trains on the Carinian planets). But at one point she stopped speaking, and El-Vek became fully alert.

"What happened? What happened?" he asked.

"Nothing. I got tired of talking to someone who isn't listening," she said. "But now that you're paying attention, I have more to tell you. Remember that slave you caught twenty Sol 3 years ago? The one who tried to...hey, stop that choking!"

Yes, El-Vek's mind wandered again. He remained this way until dawn.

"The fire is out!" he said, suddenly becoming alert. "Monica, look. It's getting light out. Monica?"

Monica's mind had also wandered. El-Vek laughed. He laughed so loudly that he regained her attention.

"What's so funny?" she asked.

"You. And me. We've been around how long?" El-Vek asked.

"You're a billion, and I'm two billion," she said.

"Has your mind ever wandered like that?" he asked.

"No," she said.

"That was the closest we came to falling asleep. It would seem that in such a culture of sleep, the man falls asleep from a nagging woman, and a woman falls asleep when she is ignored," El-Vek laughed.

Monica swatted him across the face.

"Oh don't worry. We'll soon leave this planet and go back to our old ways. But we'll need to find food first. Come then. Let's climb to the top of the hill and get a good look around. We're bound to see something up there," El-Vek said.

El-Vek and Monica climbed the hill, and yes, they were able to see all around. The sun's rays came from their right side.

"Are we facing north or south?" Monica asked.

"As we space-jumped, I sensed we landed in the northern hemisphere," El-Vek said. "We are facing north."

The forest lay behind them while a grassy valley lay to the sides and ahead. But beyond the valley ahead and to the right was a volcano. It spewed ash continuously, creating a grey cloud. The wind blew lightly from west to east, and so the ash fell to the east side of the volcano. Monica pulled out a small but thin set of binoculars and looked through them.

"I didn't know you had those," El-Vek said. "I thought we had nothing."

Monica smiled. She spent several minutes looking around.

"I'm not sure, but I think...I can just barely see...yes, there's a village in that ash plume," Monica said.

"What? Who could live in that?" El-Vek asked. "Must be abandoned."

"I see fires and movement," Monica said. "Someone's there."

"Perhaps they can help us. If they have a radio, we can call for help," El-Vek said. "But such a hike."

"There's a lake in the valley. Perhaps it has fish," Monica said.

"Yes. We could get food before going into the village. At least we won't come off as total beggars," El-Vek said.

The two did just that. They spent part of the morning descending into the valley where they reached a lake. The water was clear and clean.

"Fish! I see fish!" Monica said.

"Yes, but how to get them?" El-Vek wondered.

"We need a stick. Yes, here's one. Now string. That's easy. I can pull this string off my outfit. A hook. I'll take this clasp from my outfit and bend it...a little more...there, a hook with a little loop for the string. Tied. Good. Now we need bait. I'll just dig a little here. Yes, a worm. There. Let's go fishing."

That's how they did it. Monica caught the fish, and El-Vek used a small knife from his pocket (that made it through the space-jump) and cleaned the fish. He used leaves and a large flat rock as a little table.

"I'll make a fire," he said. "I suppose we can cook the fish on a forked stick."

El-Vek built a fire, put a fish on a stick, but as it cooked, it fell apart, off the stick, and into the fire.

"No, not like that. Here," Monica said.

She built up rocks on each side of the fire. After a search and with great luck, she found a flat rock that she placed across the two rock piles and thus above the fire. The rock did not split or shatter, and it was just hot enough for cooking.

"Put the fish on that," she said.

El-Vek did so, and they cooked. Soon, the two had a meal of fish and water.

"That was good," El-Vek said. "Now for the village. Let's see what help they can provide."

The two approached, and the sky grew dark.

"It's like a storm," El-Vek said.

"The ash," Monica said. "It's blocking out this star. Look at the vegetation."

"It's dying," El-Vek said. "No, this one is dead."

"This one too," Monica said.

"As we get closer, more plant life dies. It must be all dead in the center. Are you sure you saw fires? Camp fires? Who would live in this? Ugh, the air is stifling," El-Vek said.

"Yes, they were campfires," Monica said.

"Are you sure?" El-Vek asked.

"They weren't wildfires. I can tell the difference. I also saw movement like people."

"You might be delirious. Oh, we have no weapons other than my small knife. I'm a fool! I should have made spears for us at least. We're going into danger!" El-Vek lamented.

"Be optimistic. If I lived here, I'd welcome company," Monica said.

"If you lived here, I'd leave you here," El-Vek grinned.

Monica elbowed him.

"Who is there?" called a voice.

"Shh," Monica said to El-Vek.

"I didn't say anything," El-Vek said.

"Yes you did. You're talking. Stop talking," Monica said.

"You're doing the talking, not me. I'm all quiet and everything," El-Vek said.

"We hear you both. Stop right there. You're surrounded," said the voice.

"Blabbermouth," Monica said.

Men and women appeared wearing animal skins and wielding spears with metal tips. Several spear tips poked El-Vek and Monica.

"Ow," the two said.

"My name is Ashtosh. I am the leader of these people. What are your names?"

"Monica," Monica said.

"El-Vek," El-Vek added.

"I see. A lost couple?" Ashtosh asked.

"Very lost," El-Vek said. "Very lost."

The tribe held silent for a moment. Then Ashtosh let out a hearty laugh.

"You will come with us. We will learn of your lost condition and decide your fate," Ashtosh said.

"What fate?" Monica asked.

"Whether you are to be put to death or sent on your way," Ashtosh said.

"What??" Monica asked.

"Look, Ashtosh my good friend. Do you have a radio? We need transport off this planet," El-Vek said.

"Radio?"

"Yes, a way to communicate with a passing spaceship," Monica said.

Ashtosh looked at her in confusion.

"The people in the sky," Monica said.

"No one speaks with the dead! They are holy! Now I understand! You have been cast from your tribe into the evil zone for blasphemy. You will have no contact with villagers. Our youth will not be contaminated with your stain," Ashtosh said, then he turned to his guards and said, "Put them in isolation."

"This is crazy!" Monica said. "We're not evil!"

"No?" Ashtosh said as the two were herded away. "Just what does your husband do for a living?"

"He's a pirate," Monica said to many groans.

"Monica, please!" El-Vek said, but she tried to patch things over.

"He's a good pirate. He really is. Just steals, that's all. And only people. Once in a while. They need stealing anyway. He doesn't hurt anyone. He teaches his slaves things. Makes them educated and proper. See? He does them a service," Monica said.

The more she spoke, the more the villagers distrusted the two.

"You don't realize how evil you are, do you? Is there no soul of ash inside?" Ashtosh asked. "No, your souls are bleached clean, with all moral character destroyed. If you were worthy, I'd help you put ash back in your soul. It is a pity, really. To die with no character of ash, just an unshaped, wandering, mindless bleached soul."

"What are you talking about? You people are—" Monica said, but El-Vek shushed her.

"Be patient," El-Vek said. "Just keep quiet and be patient."

"Very good advice," Ashtosh said.

The two were put into isolation with leaves for a bed, a stone bench, a hole in the ground, and a stone bench with a pitcher of water. A guard remained on the outside of the cell, and a window allowed fresh ash to float in from the outside.

"Fortunately, we are not barbaric animals that need to use that hole," El-Vek said.

"Why were you shushing me?" Monica asked.

"Because this is a primitive ash-worshipping culture," El-Vek said.

"What??" Monica asked.

"Shh. Not so loud. I've seen this once before. This tribe is very similar to one I saw on another planet. They worship the ash from the volcano. Did you see how pale their skin is?" El-Vek asked.

"It was light grey. They just look dirty to me," Monica said.

"There's no sunlight here. They believe that sunlight is evil," El-Vek said.

"Now who is the dipper with the hole in the bottom?" Monica said.

"If they leave this ash plume and get sunlight, it will give them severe burns.

Hard to believe, even with a red dwarf, as there is little if any ultraviolet light. But they must hate the entire light spectrum. There's probably chaos around here when a little sunlight gets through after a heavy rain," El-Vek said. "Wait, look."

The guard opened the door, and in walked two women with a plate each of food. They placed the plates on the stone table and left.

"Well at least they brought food," Monica said as she walked over to the plates, but when she took a bite, she spat it out in disgust.

"That bad, eh?" El-Vek asked.

"I think it's fish. But it's sickening, like eating powdered rock," Monica said.

"It's the only food they can eat. The crops died long ago, so did the animals, and the birds flew away. All that's left is whatever water body is here. Perhaps a river. But it's filled with ash, and so are these fish."

"Why would a fish stay in ashen water?" Monica asked.

"Because it doesn't know any better," El-Vek said.

"It should just swim away to better water," Monica said.

"It grew up in this. This is home. It has no reason to leave. Like these people."

"They don't know there's a universe out there?" Monica asked.

"They know. But they think it's evil because they don't know how to cope with it. And we came from that 'evil' place, so we must be evil, because they can't cope with us either," El-Vek said.

"We have to get out of here," Monica said.

"I agree. Their method of coping is to kill us. Did you hear what Ashtosh said? He doesn't want us contaminating their children. That's a clear sign of a closed society. No one comes in, and no one leaves. A classic case of an arrested culture," El-Vek said.

"Knowing all this doesn't help us. We're just as much prisoners as the people are. I thought knowledge is liberating," Monica said.

"It should be. Apparently we don't have the right kind of knowledge. Or tools," El-Vek said.

At that moment, two guards came to the door and ushered El-Vek and Monica out.

"You're not going to kill us now, are you? What about a trial and all that? We at least deserve a trial," Monica demanded.

The guards said nothing. Instead, they escorted the two down an alley, where elder tribespeople jeered and threw down items at the two. The guards were protected, but El-Vek and Monica suffered new bruises from the attack. In a few more moments, the two were escorted to the door of a building. Ashtosh opened the door from inside and welcomed them in.

"This is a wise visitor from the sky. He will pronounce judgment on you," said Ashtosh.

The two entered the building. The guards exited, and Ashtosh went with them.

"Wait, aren't you coming with us?" Monica asked.

"It is your fate, not mine," Ashtosh said, and he closed the door behind him.

El-Vek and Monica walked toward a hooded shape in the shadows. Lamps flickered from the back of the room. The shape motioned for them to step forward, and the two did. Then the shape lit an oil lamp at the desk where the shape sat, removed his hood, and spoke.

"What took you so long?"

"El-Anonk!" Monica exclaimed.

"In the flesh," El-Anonk said.

"But how? You blew up in El-Vek's ship!" she said.

"The same way you and El-Vek did. Only I have better accuracy in space-jumping. You really should practice up, El-Vek," El-Anonk said. "Never know when you need to bail out."

"I thought I was the first to space-jump to a planet from a fast-moving spacecraft," El-Vek said.

"That's why you're just a pirate, and I'm First Colonist," El-Anonk said.

Several women entered the building with bowls of fruit. They placed the fruit on El-Anonk's table, bowed, and asked to be excused. Their faces were red and blistery.

"Your sentence has been reduced. You may leave now," El-Anonk said.

The women left. El-Anonk picked up a piece of fruit and ate it.

"There's an orchard north of here where the ash doesn't fall. A beautiful orchard, with a running stream, fresh air, and plenty of sunshine. The Ashians believe the zone is forbidden. These women were to be executed for crimes of passion. I convinced the Ashians to let me punish them so that their souls would fill with ash and be made whole. That's how you get things done. Fresh fruit. I would offer you two fruit, but you're both condemned, I hear."

"All right, El-Anonk, I get it. You're running the show here," El-Vek said.

"You're blasted right I am!" he said, pointing to the side of his head. "Brains, my pirate friend. Brains are the universal commodity. What commodity do you have? Sassatinassa? My refund?"

"I have neither. But you took and wrecked my ship. That's worth more than Sassatinassa," El-Vek said.

"It was worth more than 1000 drakos. But Sassatinassa has proven herself far more valuable than even your ship was in its prime, which it no longer is," El-Anonk said.

"Thanks to you," El-Vek said.

"You're welcome," El-Anonk said.

"But we're not welcome. Not in this village. These people are crazy," Monica said. "And you, El-Anonk, you should be ashamed of the way you're taking advantage of them."

"It's survival, my dear. There is no parity in the universe. Power and depletion. Source and sink. A star and a black hole. Better to be on the winning end of things," El-Anonk said. "And if I were in your unfortunate position, Miss Monica-so-high-and-mighty-with-noble-causes, I'd start asking, no, start begging for help.

Get down on your knees and beg for my mercy."

"What?" Monica said. "El-Anonk, this fantasy of yours—"

"Is no fantasy. You both are vulnerable, are prisoners in fact, and I have the ticket to your freedom," El-Anonk explained. "Now do you want it or not? If not, I'll let the Ashians deal with you. If so, I'll let you have fruit before I decide what I want of you. Matter of fact, you can skip the kneeling part. I know your bones are too old for it, Monica. What are you now, a billion Sol 3 years old?"

"Two billion," Monica said.

El-Anonk laughed.

"Eat some fruit, and that will sign your new contract," El-Anonk said.

"What new contract?" El-Vek asked.

"As my slaves of course. Oh don't worry. It's only temporary until I get my Sassatinassa back. Think of yourselves as indentured servants," El-Anonk said.

"You drive a hard bargain," El-Vek said.

"Nonsense! I drive a fair bargain. More than fair. You'll be mooching off me for a while. Do you think I want others leeching off my own abilities? I get full credit for the comforts in this village that they call Ashfishia," El-Anonk said.

"That sounds fake," Monica said. "Like you."

El-Anonk laughed.

"Should I call the guards in? And Ashtosh too? I'm patient, but only to a point. I won't tolerate your colorful comments for much longer," El-Anonk said.

El-Vek walked up to the bowl of fruit, took one piece, held it to his mouth, and hesitated. The closer El-Vek held the piece of fruit to his mouth, the more El-Anonk cheered. But then El-Vek pulled the fruit away from his mouth, and El-Anonk booed.

"You disappoint me, El-Vek. You know, I could put in a good word for you with Orchius. Get him to open up a special quota just for us. We'll catch slave girls together, you and I. Become real partners.

It's almost time for your release anyway," El-Anonk said.

El-Vek brought the fruit back toward his mouth.

"That's right," El-Anonk said. "Yes. Yes! Do it and seal the deal!"

El-Vek took a bite.

"Now swallow like a good boy," El-Anonk teased.

El-Vek swallowed. He then took the piece of fruit over to Monica and offered it to her.

"Eat the fruit, Monica," he said.

"El-Vek, you've filled your soul with ash. And that's not a compliment," Monica said.

"Eat the fruit, and this will be over soon," El-Vek said.

"Spoken like a good servant boy," El-Anonk said. "Now you my dear must eat and be a good servant girl, though two billion years hardly makes you a girl. Still, we can change your clothing and rearrange your hair. That should count for something."

"He's wicked! He's evil!" Monica said.

"And he's our only hope," El-Vek said.

"Yes! Just as the ash is the only hope for these Ashians, I am your only hope. You must worship me, in a sense. Worship me, Monica. Worship me," El-Anonk said.

Monica took a bite.

"And swallow. Swallow!" El-Anonk urged.

Monica chewed slowly, looked at El-Vek, and then looked at El-Anonk. She swallowed.

"There, there. All better. Come now and join me. I have bread here and good meat from outside the village. Yes, I've had my sentenced women quite busy with the gathering of things," El-Anonk said. "Join me in meal. As before, this isn't a request. Your continued survival depends on cooperation."

The two sat with him and ate. El-Vek and Monica initially sat together, but El-Anonk insisted upon splitting them up, and so he sat between them. El-Anonk put an arm around Monica and whispered into her ear.

"Until I get my Sassatinassa back, you will have to be my slave girl," he said.

Monica shivered with disgust and looked away. But she (and El-Vek) filled themselves with good food.

"Amazing culture, isn't it?" El-Anonk said. "I mean, a whole culture devoted to volcanic ash. You couldn't convince them there's anything but this ashen lifestyle. They'll first try to convince you that you're wrong and that you should fill your soul with ash. If that doesn't work, they'll burn you at the stake as heathens. Total intolerance for the rest of the universe. But enter their culture and, pardon the crude use of terminology, hijack it if you will, and you can take advantage of their boxed-in mentality. It's mind control with these people. All mind control. You can't come across like you're a fresh rain allowing in the sunshine. Oh no, that will get you in trouble for sure. Nor can you convince them that fresh water and good livestock is the way to go. Even a flower is evil. Because that's not natural. Only the ashen world of dead plants and no animal life is correct and normal. That's how it gets encoded in their brains from early on, and they're stuck with it. They don't live as long as us. They're lucky to live a hundred Sol 3 years. Can you imagine? No wonder they are so rigid. Their lives would be too boring if they had to live a million years or two. They'd be forced to look for things to keep themselves busy. One can't chase and blame for that long without experiencing a little culture fatigue. But we Carinians have culture, don't we? I miss a good slave girl show on Preyakinnak. But that will come soon enough. Already I have a message out to my men. They'll be here for me shortly, along with you both now that you're my property. As it will be with these Ashians."

"What do you mean?" El-Vek asked.

"You're going to make these people slaves?" Monica asked. "But they respect you."

"They're in for a shock," El-Anonk said.

"That's terrible," Monica said.

"You didn't feel that way a moment ago when they planned to execute you," El-Anonk said. "Don't feel badly for a race that would kill you where you stood. Better to enslave them so they are accounted for. Would you let them run wild and damage the universe? As they do now?"

"I would leave them alone. They don't know any better," Monica said.

"They're a disgrace. Should have progressed by now. No genetic advancement for these people. Surprised that programmed death hasn't kicked in," El-Anonk said.

"What nonsense are you talking about?" Monica asked.

"There's a theory that certain advanced life-forms have a programmed death switch. It's why many of these species die after only a short while. Our people don't have one, at least not like this," El-Vek said.

"That's crazy," Monica said.

"Oh no it isn't, my dear," El-Anonk continued. "Imagine a small organism that makes a copy of itself and never changes. Like bacteria. It consumes resources then poisons the culture when all runs out. A programmed death switch would kill the bacteria so it would only live long enough to exchange genetic information with another life-form. This ensures genetic information is constantly changing and adapting with the environment. Natural catastrophes like an asteroid strike creating climactic deep winter can be dealt with. Not all life will be wiped out, as the ones that keep changing genetic code will survive. At the cost of programmed death, of course."

"Of course," Monica mocked.

"These people are no better than bacteria," El-Anonk continued. "If it weren't for the confines of their ashen environment, they might well multiply and spread their failed culture throughout this planet, deplete its resources, and thus die out anyway from lack of food, air, and water. But cheer up, Monica. Making them slaves will give them the chance for genetic diversity. We might get something

like a stone creature for a slave. Imagine the brute strength and durability of such a slave in the mines. It would revolutionize production on a grand scale. Oh, I get excited just thinking about the possibilities, and our friends here are practically begging for such an environment. They hate light, the mines have poor light. They like the ash, which is much like the powdered rock in the mines. It's so simple. A child could think of it. A child!"

"Plunder a planet?" Monica asked sarcastically.

"Yes! Plunder before being plundered. If that means the entire planet, then so be it. Look at the Bleuhs. They plunder planetary resources. This PRAAD of theirs steals an entire planet's worth of water and stores it in a container the length of my arm," El-Anonk explained.

"But devices aren't people," Monica said.

"The Bleuhs send their unwanted people to the mines in Sol 4a while their wealthy vacation on Sol 4. Is that not a form of plundering?" El-Anonk asked. "Power is acquired through the acquiescence of others. Even planets yield their straight-line trajectories to the dominant star. But I see you like being a planet, Monica, and a small one at that. El-Vek is that large planet that could never quite attain star status. The rest of us, well, it's clear where we stand in the cosmological pecking order."

At that moment, El-Anonk felt a vibration in his left hand. He placed his left palm against his face with his fingertips over his left ear.

"Yes. Yes, they are here with me. Just three of us," El-Anonk said into his hand. "Let me know when you attain orbit. I'll have you send down an ethereal line, and we'll space-jump up. They space-jumped down, so they can space-jump up. He is still weak, yes. He'll need a booster. I'll have them go up first to ensure their cooperation. Very good. Out."

"That's your radio?" Monica asked.

"Clever, isn't it? I take it neither of you has one," El-Anonk said as he looked at each of them. "Didn't think so. Still no sign of Sassatinassa. But we'll find her."

"Interplanetary Police will learn about the missing PRAAD and search for both it and her," El-Vek said.

"*That* is why we must make haste! I will not lose my property to *them*!" El-Anonk said emphatically. "My new speed ship will be here soon. You will go up the way you came down, except I will provide an ethereal line for you to follow."

"Thank you," El-Vek said.

"Why are you thanking him?" Monica asked.

"Because my dear, without an ethereal line, you two would be stuck in this little village. I can sense El-Vek's ethereal injuries. He cannot space-jump without help. Am I right, El-Vek?" El-Anonk asked.

"Yes," El-Vek said reluctantly.

"There, you see? I'm helpful. So rest you two. We have much work ahead of us."

El-Anonk offered other fruit to El-Vek and Monica. El-Vek ate, and Monica did so too, though reluctantly. El-Anonk ate with great appetite, and he laughed at the situation El-Vek and Monica had put themselves in.

Chapter 94: Lanietta and the Desert People

Lanietta's PRAAD continued its flight through space. It had left El-Anonk far behind. But Lanietta faced a new problem. The PRAAD was traveling too quickly, and she wasn't sure where she was going. An asteroid or other celestial body in her path could cause great damage, perhaps even kill her. She struggled to figure out where she was and where to go. As far as Lanietta knew, the PRAAD was only intended to acquire water or release it, and she wasn't aware of any type of Carinian-friendly navigation system for space travel. And yet, when she approached a star, she could sense the water in the PRAAD shifting toward the star, even though the external apparent mass of the PRAAD was no more than a chunk of balsa wood. In this way, she was able to determine when she was approaching a star and honed this skill to detect when approaching a planet.

She knew she had to land somewhere and sort things out. If nothing else, she had to figure out where she was in the universe. She needed to find a planet that could support her life, and with luck, had friendly people. She passed by several planets and noticed an effect on the water in her PRAAD (which looked like a big lake swishing around)—rainbows. Some planets resulted in one or two. Others resulted in more. But one planet resulted in rainbow after rainbow overlapping and extending as far as Lanietta could see. She deduced that the number of rainbows was in proportion to the planet's ability to work with water or components of water.

"Here's a planet with infinite rainbows. Must have good air with water vapor. I wonder if it's full of water. Or maybe it needs lots of water. Only one way to find out," Lanietta said.

Lanietta altered course of the PRAAD, put it into orbit around a planet, and then slowed the PRAAD with continuous thrust to make for a gentle landing. In fact, though she could tell she was getting closer to a planet, she couldn't tell how close to the surface she was (or if the planet even had a surface). She got closer and closer to the surface, but she wondered how much longer before she would hit. She hoped she was going slow enough not to crash. As it turned out, the PRAAD struck the top of a sand dune and first skidded then tumbled along the sand of a desert, shaking Lanietta and creating tsunamis in the water, until finally the PRAAD came to rest, partly buried in the sand. Multiple tsunamis sloshed the water around the inside of the PRAAD. Lanietta found herself floating on this water and fighting to keep her head above the water line. When the water finally leveled out, she sent her ethereal self outside the PRAAD to take a look.

"Sand and more sand," she said. "A few rock formations here and there. I nearly made it to the top of a dune. I'll climb that rock formation at the top of this dune."

She was able to do this quite easily in ethereal form. She looked around and saw nothing but desert.

"I wonder if I could extend myself up into the air," she said.

Lanietta (eethi self) broke binocular vision by keeping one eye looking toward the horizon while the other looked up. The eye that looked up then caused her eethi self to move up. She continued up and up until the rock formation was quite small. In fact, she was afraid her eethi self would suddenly lose altitude and crash back down onto the rock or even slam back into the PRAAD and into her physical self (still inside the PRAAD).

"I'd better check the area quickly," she said to herself.

While maintaining the one eye (eethi self again) on the horizon (horizon eye), she moved the other eye (the free eye) to the side, hoping to rotate her eethi body in place. Instead, her eethi body moved to the side. She quickly sent that eye to the other side, and now her eethi body moved back the other way.

"Whew!" she said. "But how do I rotate?"

She had an idea. She (eethi self) quickly moved her eye around in a clockwise pattern. A person looking down from above would see her eethi body rotate clockwise.

"There," she said. "There's a village over there. I'll just follow the top of this dune for most of the way until I reach that rock cluster, then there's another dune I can follow into town."

She (eethi self) looked down with her free eye, and her ethereal body descended softly until it reached the rock formation. She climbed down, pulled her physical body out of the PRAAD, and reintegrated herself.

"Whew! Getting in and out of that PRAAD is a lot of work," Lanietta said. "It's leaking water. I'll stop that right now."

Lanietta split just a finger of her ethereal self from her physical body and used that finger to seal the leak.

"This is the best canteen ever to have in a desert. How the people back home would love having one of these to water the crops. If I ever get home. Oh, I miss Labba. Lanietta, get hold of yourself. Throw the PRAAD over your shoulder and head for that village. Better make sure the PRAAD is ready first."

Lanietta hit a few buttons and accidentally deactivated the mass-gravity neutralizer. The PRAAD took on the weight of the water inside and started to sink.

"No, no!" Lanietta squirmed as she frantically worked to reactivate the mass-gravity neutralizer. "Please, oh please become light again!"

Lanietta succeeded. The PRAAD became light again.

"Whew!" she said. "Glad that's over. I can't believe I can figure out this device

without Labba's help. It's almost like the device is speaking to me...is helping me."

Lanietta pulled the PRAAD and herself up, took a strip of material from her outfit, and tied the ends to the ends of the PRAAD. She used that material as a strap, slipped her arm through the strap, and thus put the PRAAD over her shoulder on her back. It was daytime, and Lanietta got hot.

"I need a hat," she said. "I don't have enough material for a hat. Maybe I can find something."

The wind picked up, and Lanietta became thirsty. She stopped for a moment, released water from the PRAAD, and drank from it. She got up to resume her march, but as she did, an old shirt flew toward her and nearly past her. She caught it with her free hand, fashioned it over her head, and continued on.

"Good, now I have a hat," she said.

She reached the first rock formation and celebrated by resting and sipping more water from the PRAAD. The winds picked up and blew sand from the direction in which Lanietta intended to go. She had rested on the leeward side of the rock formation to keep out of the wind, but when she got up and moved around the formation, the wind-blown sand was so intense that it got in her mouth and eyes. She went back to the leeward side for protection and used the PRAAD to rinse out her eyes and mouth.

"Yuck! How do I get through this storm? I could send my ethereal self ahead. Yes, I'll do that and do a space-jump. A bit at a time," Lanietta said.

Lanietta's ethereal self went ahead. The sandstorm was harsh, and visibility was poor. But at least she didn't get sand in her teeth. She reached another outcropping of rocks and completed the space-jump by pulling her physical self into her ethereal self. To her relief, the PRAAD came with her.

"There. Going eethi gets it done!" Lanietta said. "I'll split again and continue."

She did. But her ethereal self had hardly walked around to the windward side of this new outcropping when she saw something flapping in the wind. It was a doll. Lanietta couldn't pick it up with her ethereal self, so with her physical self she pulled her hat over her face for protection from the sand, walked around to the front, picked up the doll, and returned her physical body to the leeward side. She brushed off the sand with her hat, returned the hat to her head, and looked closely at the doll.

"A girl's doll. Way out here? I'll hold onto it just in case," Lanietta said.

She sent her ethereal self ahead again. This time she didn't stop at the next rock outcropping, she simply kept going. The wind howled and wailed. Even in ethereal form she could hear this. The combined effect of hearing the wind with her ethereal self and her physical self created a sort of reverb-echo cacophony, and it drove Lanietta crazy.

"I don't know how much more of this I can take," she said to herself. "My how the wind howls. I can almost hear a girl wailing."

Lanietta followed what she thought was a girl's wail, but it led her to an arrangement of rocks that distorted the air.

"A trick of the ear," she said.

She heard another girl's voice wailing.

"No, I must ignore it. I must head for the village," Lanietta said.

But this wail got louder each time Lanietta spoke.

"Are you real? Are you there?" Lanietta finally called.

"I'm lost," returned a faint voice, growing and dying on the wind.

"If that's a trick of the rocks, I'm really losing it," Lanietta said. "Let's see what kind of rocks can mimic a voice."

Lanietta followed the girl's voice, and yes, she reached another rock outcropping. But at that outcropping was a little girl, who would be perhaps five or six years old if an Earth girl. She was half buried in the sand and cried. Lanietta approached her, and the girl got scared.

"Are you taking me to the sky?" she asked. "I don't want to die."

"Hello. My name is L...Sassatinassa. You can call me Sass."

"You're a ghost," she said. "Don't hurt me. I'm scared."

"I won't hurt you," Lanietta said. "Look. I'm going to show you something. Watch this."

Lanietta completed the space-jump and reintegrated her physical body with her ethereal one.

"My dollie!" the girl said.

"This is yours?" Lanietta asked.

"I lost it. I went to find it. Now I'm lost," the girl said.

"Here's your dollie. I'm going to dig you out," Lanietta said, and she did just that.

The girl hugged Lanietta and wouldn't let go.

"It's all right. You're going to be fine," Lanietta said. "What is your name?"

"Sandra," the girl said.

Lanietta looked closely at the girl. Her mouth was full of sand, and she squinted from debris in her eyes.

"Sandra, I need to clean you up a little. The sand is in your eyes and mouth. I have clean water here. You must be brave. Can you be brave?"

"I...will be brave," Sandra said.

"Wait, I have an idea," Lanietta said.

Lanietta split one of her arms from her physical self and used her ethereal fingers to massage the spinal cord of the girl. The girl relaxed and felt no pain. Lanietta then used her physical body to release water from the PRAAD. She first poured water over the girl's head, like a shower, then she flushed out the girl's eyes and mouth with more water. She used energy from her ethereal hand to evaporate the water from the girl and dry her off. Lanietta reintegrated her own body and thus released her grip on Sandra's spinal column. The girl regained feeling.

"I feel better," she said.

"Good. I sense you're very thirsty. Here. Have a drink from my canteen," Lanietta said.

The girl gulped and gulped and gulped.

"Take all you want, there's plenty," Lanietta said. "But don't drink too fast. You'll get sick."

Sandra gulped a little more water then let out a good sigh.

"That's beautiful, Lanietta," Claus said. "I wish you could hear me. It's like you're an older sister to Sandra."

"There. Where are you from, Sandra?" Lanietta asked.

"I...the village," she said.

"You must have wandered off," Lanietta said. "You're safe with me. I'll scout ahead with my ghost part, and my real part will stay with you."

"Don't leave me, Sass!" Sandra said.

"I won't," Lanietta said.

Lanietta went eethi and sent her ethereal self ahead. She reached the village. All people were inside their homes except for one frantic couple calling, "Sandra, Sandra!"

"Sandra can accept me as a ghost, but these people might flip out. I'll hide behind this building and complete the space-jump," Lanietta said.

Her physical body gave Sandra a hug and spoke.

"Do you want to go home?" Lanietta asked.

"I wanna go home!" Sandra said.

"Hold on tight. We're going right now!" Lanietta said.

Lanietta hugged Sandra to protect her from the sand. Sandra held onto Lanietta, and Lanietta completed the space-jump, bringing the two to the building where Lanietta's ethereal self hid.

"Sandra? Sandra!" a mother's voice called.

"Momma!" Sandra called, and she pulled away from Lanietta.

"No, you'll get lost. I'll carry you over," Lanietta said.

"Sandra!" the mother called again.

"Momma! I'm coming. Sass is bringing me. She found me. She saved me," Sandra called back.

The mother rushed over, and Lanietta handed Sandra over.

"We must get you inside," the mother said. "You are Sass? Please come in with us. This storm isn't fit for person or beast."

The mother called to her husband, and he rushed over. The four then went inside Sandra's home.

"Oh, my sweet Sandra!" the mother said. "Don't you ever wander off again. You gave us a scare!"

The couple and Sandra stepped into a partial chamber. A strong vacuum pulled sand off their clothing. They then stepped out.

"Please, Sass, use the vacuarch to clean up," the mother said.

Lanietta stepped inside the vacuarch. It actuated automatically and sucked sand off her clothing and body.

"Impressive," Lanietta said.

"The weather doesn't blow like that all the time," the father said. "But enough to warrant the vacuarch. Forgive our manners. I'm Sidan, and my overly overjoyed wife is Sarna."

"I'm Sassatinassa. But friends call me Sass," Lanietta said.

"Sassatinassa," Claus said. "It's like an alter ego. How I wish I could have known you back then, Lanietta, when I was that age. We could have gone on all sorts of adventures together. Would you have called me Clomper though? Perhaps a more fanciful name like Herculantis. Or Himculantis. No, that sounds like a disease. I guess Clomper is okay."

"Thank you, Sass. Thank you!" Sarna said. "We owe you a great debt."

"Yes. Let me fill your canteen with water. It's the least we can do," Sidan said.

"Oh, I don't need water. I have lots," Lanietta said.

"Of course. But water is so precious, we feel we must repay you with at least a little," Sidan said.

"Show me your water supply," Lanietta said.

Sarna gave a worried expression to Sidan that they needed their water and had none to spare. He reassured her with a hand gesture that all was fine. She still showed a worried expression.

"Sarna worries too much," Sidan said as the two went back to a utility room. "We're low on water, but not so low that we can't spare a little for a friend. Where are you from, Sassatinassa?"

"Please, call me Sass," Lanietta said. "Is this your water chamber?"

"Yes. Condensers outside the house drip water into this collection chamber," Sidan said. "Every house has one. We can't survive without it."

"And in the next room? I smell flowers," Lanietta said.

"Yes, each house also has a hydroponics garden. This climate necessitates total self-sufficiency of each family. We trade in technology and culture, but the basics we supply for ourselves. There's a tap here. I can fill your canteen, if you like," Sidan said.

Lanietta handed the PRAAD to Sidan. He tried to open it but could not.

"I don't understand. How does this open?" he asked.

"Sorry, I locked it," Lanietta said.

"A wise precaution. Water bandits could steal your meager supply," Sidan said.

"Let me attach it to the tap," she said.

Lanietta placed the PRAAD under the tap and used a bit of her ethereal hand to create a seal from the tap to the inside contents of the PRAAD.

"It's connected," Lanietta said.

"Good. I'll just turn the tap open a little bit, and you'll have a full canteen," he said.

Sidan turned the handle to the tap, and he thought water flowed into Lanietta's canteen. But instead, Lanietta's ethereal hand commanded the PRAAD to push water out, and so the chamber filled with water at a fast rate. The rate was so quick that a jet of water caused turbulence and splashing.

"Oh no, it's all draining out!" Sidan panicked.

But when he climbed up several steps and looked over the edge, he saw that the water level was rising.

"I...don't understand. The chamber is *filling* with water. Water! My condenser can't fill the chamber this quickly. What's going on? What's happening?" Sidan said in bewilderment.

Lanietta giggled.

"You know something?" Sidan asked.

"I'm filling your chamber with water from my canteen," Lanietta said.

"Impossible. No canteen can hold that much water," he said.

"This one can," she said.

"It's a miracle. It is. Sarna! Come to the water chamber room. Hurry!" Sidan called.

Sarna came with Sandra.

"What is it?" she asked.

"Water! The chamber is filling with water!" he said.

"What!?" Sarna said in disbelief.

She looked into the chamber. The water level reached the top. In fact it overflowed.

"Water. Water!" Sarna said with joy, and she splashed the water around.

Sidan hugged her and splashed water back. The two splashed water at each other. Sandra jumped in the puddle on the floor.

"But how?" Sarna asked.

Lanietta giggled and waved.

"Sass did it," Sandra said. "She has lots of water. She gave me a shower outside. And water to drink."

"I don't understand how, but it's a miracle!" Sarna said.

"It's also too much," Sidan said, and he ran over to the tap and shut it closed.

The water stopped overflowing. Lanietta removed the PRAAD and slung it over her shoulder.

"That's a very curious device, Sass," Sidan said. "I'd like to know how it works."

"My little secret," she said.

"Indeed," he said.

"Sass," Sarna said. "How much more, I mean, your canteen, how much—"

"Lots more," Lanietta said.

"She could resupply the village. We're saved. Saved!" Sarna exclaimed, but Sidan held his hand out to suppress her.

"Sarna, don't speak a word of this to anyone," he said.

"What?!"

"I mean it," he said. "Sass has the fruit of water. One bite, and desire sets in. It could destroy our people."

"It's just water," Sarna said.

"Sarna, we live in peace because those who would rather steal than work have skipped us over as worthless," Sidan said. "Imagine if other villages find out. They'll rush over to ours and ransack us. We can't afford that. None of us can. Sass, I thank you for filling our chamber. But we cannot accept any more."

"Not even for our thirsty neighbors?" Sarna questioned. "This is the worst season in recorded history. The condensers haven't produced in months. And you deprive our neighbors of life? What kind of man are you?"

"A wise one," he said.

"No, a selfish deluded man. I've never seen this side of you, Sidan. I can't raise our daughter under these conditions. We're leaving," Sarna said.

"Sarna, no! You must stick with me in this. We'll find a way to help our neighbors," he said.

"There's only one way, and you know it. Come along, Sass," she said.

But Sidan grabbed Lanietta by the arm to hold her.

"Sass saves your daughter, and you thank her by holding her prisoner?" Sarna said. "Your strata marks are showing clear and strong. You're as abrasive as sandstone!"

"She must remain here until she leaves the village!" Sidan said. "She cannot be seen."

Lanietta surprised Sidan. She used her ethereal hand to shock the nerves in his hand. It jolted, and he lost his grip. Released, Lanietta helped Sarna pack her things, and the three left.

"Sarna, Sandra, Sass! No. NO!" Sidan said, but the three were gone.

Sarna led Sandra and Lanietta to a friend's house.

"Sarna, what a surprise," said Sarna's friend.

"Selena. Do you mind if I stay this night?" Sarna asked.

"Sidan again?" Selena asked.

"Yeah."

"Come in, come in. Who's your friend?" Selena asked.

"I'm Sassatinassa. But friends call me Sass," Lanietta said.

"Nice to meet you, Sass," said Selena.

The three sat in the living room while Selena brought refreshments and placed them on a coffee table.

"Where are you from?" Selena asked Lanietta.

"A distant planet," Lanietta said.

"You're not from this world? Then you're an alien," Selena said. "Villagers are very suspicious of aliens."

"I didn't know you were from another world," Sarna said.

"Yes. I am," Lanietta said.

"Sass is my friend," Sandra said. "She saved me."

"What happened?" Selena asked.

"Sandra went out in the sand storm when she was supposed to stay inside," Sarna said.

"To find my dollie. I couldn't leave my dollie outside," Sandra said.

"Sidan and I searched for her. Then Sass here brought her from nowhere. Say, Sass, where did you find Sandra?" Sarna asked.

"Out in the desert near a rock outcropping," Lanietta said.

"Amazing you could find your way into the village. Why, visibility was down to almost nothing," Sarna said.

"Sass has a secret," Sandra blurted, referring to Lanietta's space-jump ability.

"Now Sandra," Lanietta said. "It's just a—"

"Yes, the canteen," Sarna said, thinking Lanietta was about to speak of the PRAAD. "Sass here performed a miracle at our house. She filled our entire water chamber. With fresh water. Nice and clean. It even overflowed! From her canteen!"

Selena took a look at Sarna then laughed.

"A good joke there, Sarna," Selena said.

"It's true, isn't it Sass?" Sarna asked.

"It's true," Sandra interrupted.

"It's true," Lanietta said.

"Sarna," Selena said. "An entire chamber of water? From that canteen? How?"

"I don't know how," Sarna said.

"I can show you," Lanietta said.

"Yes, yes Sass can. Selena, how much water is left in your chamber?" Sarna asked.

"It's low like everyone else. Wait a moment. This is a scam to get my remaining water. Okay, out you three. Out!" Selena said.

"Hold on a moment!" Sarna said. "We can prove it another way. Bring an empty pitcher. What harm can come from that?"

"That won't prove anything," Selena said.

"You can store the water in your tub or fill other pitchers. Get out your empty glasses and containers," Sarna said.

"Sass can do it. She can do anything," Sandra said.

Selena stared hard at Sarna, trying to figure out what kind of scam this was.

"To poison me?" Selena asked.

"We'll drink from a glass or the pitcher, if you like. Or just us three, and you can watch. What do you say? You're not doing anything else this evening. We could play music with the glasses, like water chimes," Sarna said.

"Well I could use a good laugh," Selena said. "I hate to see you empty your canteen. But if that's what you want, well, just remember, if Sass goes thirsty, it's none of my doing. This is your idea."

"Agreed," Sarna said.

Selena produced an empty pitcher for dispensing beverages. She placed it atop the coffee table. Lanietta removed the PRAAD from her shoulder, placed her ethereal finger (transparently) on the PRAAD, and created a small opening. Fresh water flowed from the PRAAD to the pitcher and filled it. Lanietta sealed the opening and slung the PRAAD back over her shoulder. Sarna took the pitcher and filled glasses for the four. Lanietta drank first, then Sarna, and lastly Sandra.

"Ahhh," Sarna let out after drinking her water. "Fresh water. As clean as anything we can get."

Selena held her glass close to her nose, sniffed, and then touched a bit of the water to her tongue. She took a small sip and looked around.

"It doesn't smell like poison. Tastes like water," Selena said.

"Because it is water," Sarna said.

"Water, water!" Sandra echoed.

Selena finished her glass.

"Very clean and refreshing," Selena said.

"Convinced?" Sarna said.

"Tell you what. See if you can fill my greywater tank. If so, I'll take a shower and let you know," Selena said.

Selena led the three to the back of her house where a spiral staircase went up the tower.

"I'll stay down here with Sandra," Sarna said.

"Very well," Selena said.

Selena led Lanietta to the top of the spiral staircase. It had a small platform for standing, a couple of windows, and a port for placing water into the top of the greywater tank.

"On those rare occasions when it rains, the water from my roof is collected and placed in here. I also have a deep well that pulls up unfiltered water. But the well is dry and the rains are but a faint memory. My greywater tank is low," Selena said.

"Then I will fill it. Permit me," Lanietta said.

Selena opened the port to the tank, and then Lanietta used her ethereal finger to create an opening on the PRAAD. Water flowed out of the PRAAD and through the port into the tank. In but a few minutes, the greywater tank filled.

"You see? Plenty of water," Lanietta said.

"I do not understand this technology," Selena said. "To make water out of nothing is a miracle."

"It's no miracle. Water is not made, it's released. This container can hold lots and lots of water. It got the water from a lake on a dying planet," Lanietta said.

"Then you are the owner of this canteen? How did you make it?" Selena asked.

"It's mine, but I didn't make it. I, uh, sorta borrowed it," Lanietta said.

"It's stolen?" Selena asked. "You're giving us stolen water?"

"They were going to get me. I had to escape. This canteen is the only way I could," Lanietta said.

"I don't understand. Who was going to get you?" Selena asked.

"El-Anonk and El-Vek. You don't know them. El-Vek caught me and sold me at an auction. El-Anonk bought me, but I took his ship to a dying solar system and went to a planet with a huge lake. That's where I found this canteen. It was drinking up the water from the lake. But I figured out how to hide in it and use the water to move around. I used the canteen as a spaceship, and well, I landed on this planet."

"Sounds confusing," Selena said.

"I know. But at least I'm free. For the moment. I wanted to go home the whole time, but now I want to help the people here for a little bit before I leave. You're so desperate for water, and I have plenty," Lanietta explained.

"Well, I believe you mean well. Let's sleep on it tonight, and we'll decide in the morning," Selena said.

"I, uh, don't sleep," Lanietta said.

"Everyone sleeps," Selena said.

"We don't have darkness where I live. It's daytime all the time. We never fall asleep. I wouldn't know how," Lanietta said.

"You get tired, close your eyes, and fall asleep. That doesn't happen to you?" Selena asked.

"No, it doesn't," Lanietta said. "But I can keep quiet while the rest of you do."

"Very well. I have books you can read if you get bored," Selena said.

The two returned down the spiral staircase. Selena made up beds for Sarna and Sandra and then herself turned in for the night. Lanietta looked at several books in the living room, but she could not make out the glyphs.

"Guess I'll have to settle for pictures," she said.

Morning came, and the sandstorm had let up. The day was clear and sunny. People went about their business adjusting their condensers, running their shops, and educating their young.

"I must get Sandra to daycare," Sarna said. "Then let's discuss what to do about Sass's water."

Sarna did just that. Without giving away the water secret, she left Selena's house to drop Sandra off at daycare, but instead of returning alone, she returned with Sandra.

"What happened?" Lanietta asked.

"Daycare is closed. Water emergency," Sarna said. "Where's Selena?"

"She's in the shower," Lanietta said.

"She was in the shower when I left," Sarna said. "She's wasting a lot of water!"

The three waited a little longer. Selena finished her shower, dressed, and entered the living room.

"That's the longest shower ever!" Sarna said. "Think of the water you wasted!"

"But it was a good shower!" Selena said with a smile. "I soaked up heat and moisture from that water, cleared out my lungs, and cleared out my sinuses. Oh do fill up my regular water chamber, Sass. Please? I must consider building a large tub so that I can soak for hours at a time."

"What?" Sarna said.

"I deserve it. This desert sand is bad for the complexion. I've worked hard creating new technology for this village. The village owes me," Selena said.

"Hmm. You can't have *all* the water," Sarna said.

"She can have all she wants," Lanietta said. "Let's fill your water chamber."

The four went to a back room, and Lanietta did just that—she filled the water chamber from the PRAAD. While completing the task, she was startled to see something walk toward her.

"What...is that?" Lanietta asked with a start.

"Don't be afraid," Selena said. "This is my daughter, Selenita."

"She looks different somehow. Hey!" Lanietta said as Selenita took her PRAAD.

Selenita then tipped the PRAAD to her mouth and drank. And drank and drank. Perspiration dampened her clothing which then converted to water vapor.

"I've never seen someone drink so much water," Lanietta said. "It's like she's...she's..."

"Not real?" Selena said.

"I didn't want to be rude," Lanietta said. "I'm sorry, Selenita. You're a beautiful woman. You're welcome to all the water you need. Living in this desert must be torture. When does a woman get a good beverage or a clean bath?"

"Selenita isn't a woman, Sass. She's a robot," Selena said.

"What?"

"It's true. I created her to resemble a daughter, because I never had any of my own. Selenita helps me with heavy physical labor. She's good with condenser and other technology. She's the town physician, too. She's not afraid of blood and can seal wounds with impulses from her fingertips," Selena said.

"Incredible. But I don't understand. Why all the water? I thought robots needed power like a fusion pack or other thing," Lanietta said.

"Selenita is powered by water. She splits the water into hydrogen and oxygen, and she fuses the hydrogen for energy. The oxygen is released as a byproduct. Clever, isn't it? In the worst sandstorm, I can seal all the windows, and she provides me with oxygen to breathe," Selena said.

"That sounds dangerous. Wouldn't a fire be bad for her?" Lanietta asked.

"Her breath isn't 100% oxygen. Maybe 30%. Enough to help people breathe without being too inflammable," Selena explained. "She releases water vapor to cool her system. So no, she doesn't consume all water for energy. I suppose

there is no 100% efficient energy-work system."

"You're very smart. Is everyone here so smart?" Lanietta asked.

Selena smiled.

"Selena is one of the smartest," Sarna said.

"Now, now," Selena blushed. "Sarna is smart too. So is Sandra. Everyone in the village is smart."

"We all have our specialties and trade work," Sarna said. "I'm good with hydroponics. Selena's good with engineering."

"Sass, everyone works hard to survive. Conditions are very unforgiving here. Look at little Sandra. She almost died in the sandstorm. It doesn't take much to lead one astray. Death is but one wrong step away," Selena explained.

"Can Selenita and I go out and play?" Sandra asked.

"Maybe later," Sarna said. "Selena would have to give permission."

"I'm still fine-tuning Selenita's manners," Selena said. "I haven't left her alone yet. She has great strength, and I don't dare take a chance on her injuring another, whether by accident or intention."

"Can Selenita talk?" Lanietta asked.

"I can speak," Selenita said. "You're a beautiful girl. Are you eleven? Twelve? I'm twenty-five."

"Now Selenita, it's not polite to ask a girl her age," Selena said. "I'm sorry. I didn't correct that part of her programming yet."

"It's all right. I'm twelve million years old," Lanietta said.

Selena and Sarna laughed.

"That's how you get around the age question," Selena said.

"No, it's true. We don't age much on my planet," Lanietta said.

"And which year is this? Of your own planet?" Selena asked.

"No, another planet's year in another solar system. It's a compromise, because there are people on two planets in my solar system, and both would claim the right to determine the year. Wow, I sound like my best friend from school."

"You don't sleep. You don't age. You carry a canteen with nearly infinite water. You are alien indeed," Sarna said. "What about others like you?"

"They don't age or sleep either. But we don't have robots like Selenita. Most of my kind work in an orchard," Lanietta said.

"Orchard?" Sarna asked. "I'm a master of hydroponics. But what is an orchard?"

"Yes, orchard. A vast expanse of land with all kinds of fruit. You know, round food with a skin on the outside and a sweet, juicy inside. Very tasty," Lanietta said.

"I once had a dream about such a food," Sarna said. "But it was a dream. People said I was crazy. We have protein plants here. Nothing with lots of sugar. If land animals exist, they are rare."

"Animal bones have been found from ages ago," Selena said.

"We've also found dormant fish buried in low areas," Sarna continued. "I poured water on one such fish, and it came to life. This makes us think this planet once had more water. But it's gone now. Just a little moisture left in the air. That's all."

"Where did it go?" Lanietta asked.

"No one knows," Sarna said. "We have no records of the before time. When I said we found animal bones, I left out something. We've found people bones too. Many people bones. Our town archeologist has found mass graves. It's like people had a great war and didn't bother to leave records about who won."

"Maybe nobody did," Lanietta said. "Maybe a war destroyed most of the water."

"That's possible," Sarna said. "Sometimes I think it best we don't remember the past. Who knows what ideologies destroyed those people? Those same ideologies might destroy people today. So I don't look too much to the past. I prefer instead to look to the future."

"I'd like to show you our latest town project," Selena said.

"You mean the—" Sarna started.

"Exactly," Selena said.

"The town will go crazy!" Sarna said. "You sure changed your mind quickly."

"It's like I've been born anew in Sass's ever-flowing fountain of life," Selena said.

"I wanna go first. I wanna go first!" Sandra said.

"Sandra," Sarna said.

"I know where to go. I do, Mamma!" Sandra said.

"You may go first. But don't run!" Sarna said.

Sandra ran anyway. Seeing that Sarna, Selena, and Selenita were much slower, Lanietta ran after Sandra to ensure she got into no trouble. All were now outside. The day was clear and sunny, and Lanietta could see a large and very tall tower made of structural tubing. Partway up was a tank for holding water, but the tower continued up and up. At the top was a great condenser, and next to the condenser was what looked like a heavy string or thin rope, which went up into the air and anchored a large kite flying high above.

"I've never seen anything like it," Lanietta said.

"Soon there will be lots of water everywhere!" Sandra said. "Lakes and lakes full!"

Sandra skipped around the poles. She turned tight corners by cupping her hand on the pole and sliding it around the pole with her turn. Sarna, Selena, and Selenita caught up.

"Very impressive," Lanietta said.

"The house condensers were helpful for a while, but they can do only so much. This community condenser goes much higher. That kite goes higher still."

"The kite string is a little thick," Lanietta said.

"It's a tube. The kite collects water and sends it down the tube," Selena said.

"How much water have you collected?" Lanietta asked.

Selena and Sarna exchanged glances again.

"A few drops," Selenita finally said.

"We just need time, that's all," Sarna said.

"Yes, we must keep hope," Selena said.

"There is insufficient moisture in the atmosphere," Selenita said.

"But there are clouds in the sky. Higher and higher they go," Sandra said.

"Yes, that's the problem," Selena said. "The few clouds we have are too high. I was so hopeful this community water tower would help."

"That's where I come in," Lanietta said.

"Yes, Sass. You can help get it started. The villagers need hope," Selena said.

"Sass is going to give us lots of lakes and everything!" Sandra said.

"Why not?" Lanietta said.

Lanietta was about to space-jump up the tower to a point where she could fill the tank, but she resisted. Why reveal this secret to the town? Never know what might happen. If caught in a bad situation, she could just escape. She didn't think Selena or Sarna would give her trouble. But there were others.

"What are you women doing?" Sidan said as he approached the tower.

"I need to climb the tower," Lanietta said. "Now."

"Go," Selena said.

Lanietta began climbing the tower.

"Stop!" Sidan said. "That's the community water tower. You need the town's permission before doing anything."

"You didn't mind that she filled our chamber of water," Sarna said. "She'll do the same for the water tower."

"Sarna, this is a dangerous thing Sass is doing," Sidan said. "People will become dependent on this water and stop working their condensers. What happens when the water runs out? Well?"

"This buys us time, Sidan!" Sarna said. "Time!"

Lanietta reached the water tower's tank. She activated the PRAAD, and water gushed into that tank.

"Water, water!" Sandra said.

"You shouldn't get the girl's hopes up," Sidan said. "How much longer are you going to pretend?"

"This is reality, Sidan," Sarna said.

Selena ran from door to door and beckoned people to the water tower to witness the miracle.

"Hurry!" she said. "The miracle has already started."

But Sidan wouldn't let up on Sarna.

"Mark my words, evil will come of this. Nothing is for free," Sidan said. "In ancient times when markets traded things of value, people used metal and jewels for money. They worked their entire lives and put their savings into these valuables. When such valuables were discovered in plentiful amounts, their life savings were worthless. Wiped out. Gone."

"Those are just stories," Sarna said. "This is much needed water. No one uses it like money."

"Not yet. But I have a feeling our ancestors fought over resources. Like water," Sidan said. "You watch. It's just a matter of time before the fighting begins. Neighbor against neighbor. Husband against wife."

"We've been fighting for years. And it started long before Sass arrived," Sarna said.

"Perhaps we'll survive then," he said.

"What kind of crazy talk is that?" Sarna asked.

"I mean that we always fight, so it's nothing new. Some couples never fight. They won't know how to handle it," Sidan said.

"The only reason we fight is because you get these wild notions every now and then. You babble more than an overly tired child trying to avoid sleep time!" Sarna said.

The villagers gathered around and watched. And waited. Lanietta continued filling the tank until it was full. Still she released water from the PRAAD. The tank overflowed, and the villagers celebrated. Lanietta increased the rate of flow from the PRAAD, and a stream of water fell from the tower, like a waterfall. People stood and danced in the waterfall, enjoying the refreshing moment. The water drained off to the side of the village into a depression, forming a large pond or a small lake.

"You're wasting water!" Sidan yelled.

"Open the ports to the houses," Selena said to Selenita. "Fill water chambers everywhere!"

Selenita climbed partway up the tower and turned a valve. Water flowed into pipes that led to the houses. About half the citizens ran into their houses to check, and they exited their houses in excitement. It wasn't long before they begged the valve be closed, as their chambers were full and water flooded out of their houses. Some were angry that their houses flooded, but most laughed it off as a blessing. Selenita closed the valve.

A number of children approached the small lake and touched their toes to the water. It was a new experience, and they weren't sure what to do. A breeze picked up into a gentle wind, and waves came across the lake. Lanietta moved the PRAAD from filling the tank, attached it to a tower leg, and left the PRAAD in release mode. She then descended and played with the children.

"What is all that water?" asked the children, referring to the lake.

"It's a lake," Lanietta said. "Who wants to go swimming?"

"What's that?" asked one of the children.

"I'll show you," Lanietta said.

Lanietta ran into the water and dove in. She swam freestyle, on her side, and on her back. She then treaded water.

"See? It's easy," she said.

"No!" Sidan yelled as he ran over. "No swimming! It's too dangerous!"

Lanietta swam to shore and walked out. Selena and Selenita met Lanietta.

"Doesn't anyone here know how to swim?" Lanietta asked.

"No, they don't, Sass," Selena said. "We have no lakes or ponds or any way of learning, until now."

"I can teach anyone how to swim," Lanietta said.

"Very nice of you to offer," Selena said. "I think we should start with the adults. People like Sidan are afraid. Ignorance does that, it breeds fear. Once educated, they'll relax. Then we'll teach the children. We already send them to school. We'll add another class in swimming. But I'm concerned, Sass. This heat will cause the lake to dry up."

"I wonder what my best friend would do?" Lanietta asked herself.

"Your school friend?" Selena asked.

"Yes. Oh, I know what she'd do. Selena, you can make a dome to shade the lake. You must use sticks or pipes to make lots of triangles in a dome shape and then cover the dome with light material," Lanietta said. "I can work with Selenita. I bet she could design it."

"We'll both work with you. I'm fascinated by this idea. We might save on materials if we could make a dome over a water body instead of building a tank and placing it high on a tower," Selena said.

"Why wait? Let's go inside and figure it out," Lanietta said.

And they did. But while Lanietta, Selena, and Selenita worked on the dome design, Sidan continued to shoo people away from the lake.

"Go on home," he said. "Keep out of this lake. I won't have any lungs filling with water today."

The women herded their children into the school and had the teacher watch over them. Sandra was sent too. Then the women met in the community center and had a water convention, passing around food and water, and filling various pots of water. Some pots they cooked stew in, others they heated and put special soaking salts where they themselves soaked their bodies and discussed various things. Still others filled glasses of various heights and played music by stroking the tops. One woman wheeled out an old-fashioned water organ, filled it with water, and played in harmony with the water-filled glasses.

Outside, a number of men gathered around the lake with large tubs and fishing poles.

"What are you men doing?" Sidan asked.

"We're going fishing," they said.

"What?"

"Sarna proved there are dormant fish in these parts. The water no doubt has awakened them, and we're tired of plant protein," the lead fisherman said. "So out of our way."

"You're going out in those?" Sidan asked. "You'll tip over and sink."

"It's all we have. We're desperate. We need fish," the lead fisherman said.

"I got a spare tub for you, Sidan," said a young woman.

"My daughter," the lead fisherman said. "You remember her."

"Yes, Sam, I remember Tina," Sidan said.

"She's always been fond of you. And I heard you and your wife are separating," Sam said.

"We're not separating. We're just a little apart at the moment," Sidan said.

"Well if you ever need more time apart, I'll keep you company," Tina said. "I brought a spare fishing rod."

Sidan paused.

"Come along, Sidan. You're going to get ulcers standing there with a frown on your face," Sam said.

Sidan maintained his pause.

"You're welcome to dinner at our house after fishing," Tina said.

"Tina can take almost anything and make it into a meal fit for a king," Sam said. "I only wish her mother were here. She'd be so proud."

"Yes, and look how she died," Sidan said.

"I know how she died. She became delirious with thirst and wandered out of the village. We found her two days later, dead," Sam said.

"Why do you bring up such sad things, Sidan?" Tina asked.

"Because it is what protects us," Sidan said.

"You're *too* protective," Sam said. "It has consumed you."

"At least my wife and daughter are alive," Sidan said.

"Set aside your bitterness for a time, Sidan," Tina said. "Please."

The other men looked at Sidan. Tina held Sidan's hand and shook it slightly to say, "Yes."

"Very well," he said. "I will go. But only to ensure your safety."

"Thank you!" Tina said.

The fishermen, Sidan, and Tina went onto the water. Tina helped launch Sidan in his tub then followed in her own. It wasn't long before the fishermen caught fish. And many fish, too. The water had indeed brought the dormant fish back to life, and they swam about the lake in excitement. Fish came in all sizes from minnows to large bass-like creatures. Sam ventured off with the other fishermen while Sidan kept his tub close to Tina's. Tina caught fish after fish, but Sidan simply watched.

"Aren't you going to throw your line out?" Tina asked. "There are plenty of fish."

"I'm going to wait," Sidan said. "These fish could be poisonous. No sense in taking chances."

Tina held a caught fish to her nose.

"They smell safe," she said. "You are a cautious man, Sidan."

"I have to be, Tina," Sidan said. "You are young yet. You do not understand."

"I do understand. I lost my mother. It was sad. But I don't carry a sack of rocks around with me every day," Tina said. "You do. Why do it? You are no more than the walking dead yourself."

"I carry no rocks," he said.

"You know what I mean. Your heart is heavy, as if you carried a sack of rocks," she said.

"I saw my parents die," he said.

"And that's an excuse?" she asked.

"I almost lost Sandra," he said.

"But you should celebrate her return," Tina said. "Take her fishing with us. Celebrate life."

"I wouldn't dare take her fishing," he said.

"Then you've killed her yourself," Tina said. "You're a lonely man, Sidan."

Tina caught more fish but spoke no more to Sidan. She paddled away from

Sidan and joined her father. Sidan was now alone.

"I am indeed," he replied to himself.

In the schoolhouse, the students grew restless.

"We want to go out and play in the water," said one student to the teacher.

"Yeah!" the other kids said.

"Now, now, students. Calm down. Let's learn about water, shall we?" the teacher said.

The teacher went on to explain how water was composed of hydrogen and oxygen, and how water is the basis for life.

"We will perform an experiment," the teacher said. "We will make water evaporate."

The teacher had the children go to their lab stations. Students worked in pairs and had several pieces of equipment at each station, including a heating plate, a beaker, and a thermometer. The teacher walked by each station with a tank of water on wheels. From the tank was a small hose, and she used this hose to place water in each beaker.

"Place the thermometer in the beaker and the beaker on the warming plate. Turn the heat to medium. Observe the water level and temperature," she said after filling the last beaker.

Sandra's partner was Markh, an older student. He followed the instructions while Sandra watched.

"There's lots of water outside," Sandra said. "Let's go out and play."

"Teacher is watching," Markh said.

"Let's sneak out," Sandra said.

"Wait for the right moment," Markh said.

"I will now fill a large tub," the teacher said. "Observe how the water takes much longer to evaporate."

The students noted the temperature and how long it took for their water to evaporate. But the teacher took a longing look at the tub, like a long lost friend. The teacher increased the heat setting so that the water would heat more quickly. But as it warmed and she swirled her arm in it

more and more, she realized it was a waste to simply make it evaporate. She poured in therapeutic salts. Next, she changed the heating settings so it was a little more than body temperature, she removed her shoes and socks, and then she sat on its edge and kicked her tired feet in the water.

"You will see," she said with a slowing, relaxed voice, "that water...in a large container...takes much longer to heat. It needs...more energy. I need... more energy."

The teacher became sleepy. Other students took off their shoes and sat with her, dangling their legs in the tub. Markh, Sandra, and two other students turned off their heating elements and snuck out when the teacher wasn't looking.

"Jesk and Jula, are you going to the lake?" Markh asked as the four exited the schoolhouse.

"Yeah," the girls replied.

"I know a way to get there without being seen," Markh said. "There's an old tunnel under a sand dune. I found it last year."

"Nobody knows about it?" Jesk asked.

"Nobody," Markh said.

"Let's go," Jula said.

Markh led the three to the back of the schoolhouse (which abutted a sand dune) and down a set of steps to the basement door. It was locked.

"Some tunnel," Jesk said in disappointment.

"One moment," Markh said.

Markh produced a pick and unlocked the door.

"Shhh," he said. "Follow me."

With Markh leading the way, the four entered the basement. But he and the three girls were surprised to find a few inches of water.

"Water!" Sandra said.

"I hope your tunnel is dry," Jula said.

"Yes," Jesk said. "Already my shoes are ruined."

"It should be," Markh replied to Jula.

Markh took a pocket knife from his pocket and tapped the blunt end against a wall near the sand dune. Most of the wall gave a heavy sound, but when the sound came back hollow, he knew he was close. He tapped a little more, and a one-inch square section sounded even hollower than the door. Markh inserted his pick into a small hole and unlocked the flap. This revealed a larger lock mechanism, which he also unlocked. The door that was hidden now moved slightly ajar, revealing its frame. He pulled on the flap, and the door opened.

"There. The secret tunnel," Markh said.

The four traveled through the tunnel and reached an underground chamber built of stone. They entered. At one end of the chamber was a window to the outside.

"It's a one-way window," Markh said. "I once walked outside and all around this area, leaving little pieces of paper with numbers on them. I then came in here to see which number was by the window. Went back outside to that number and looked for that window. To the people outside, this window is just a large, flat boulder."

"I can see the lake!" Jesk said.

"There are people on the lake!" Jula said. "And...they...what is that they are doing?"

"They're fishing," Jesk said. "I read about it once in an old book. I bet there will be a feast of fish for dinner tonight!"

"I want to play in the water!" Sandra said.

"Is there a way to the lake from here?" Jula asked.

"There might be. I haven't been in here since the lake came," Markh said. "There's a stairwell that goes down. We can see."

Markh led the way again down the stairwell, but near the bottom, he reached water.

"Stop," he said.

"Water!" Sandra said.

"There is a lower floor here," he said. "But it's partly filled with water."

"It's like a pool," Jesk said. "Come on, Jula. Let's learn how to swim."

The girls jumped in. When they stood, the water reached shoulder level. This lower room was quite large, and they had plenty of room for moving around.

"The water is clear," Jula said.

"Look," Jesk said. "There's a window on the far wall."

"I can see the lake," Jula said. "I mean the lake underwater. Look at the fish! It's like fantasy!"

"I want to play in the water too," Sandra said.

"You stay here on the step," Markh said. "You can kick your legs in the water or splash on the steps. You don't know how to swim."

"Aw, please?" Sandra asked.

"I'm sorry. You must stay here," Markh said. "Promise you'll stay here?"

"Oh, okay," Sandra said reluctantly. "I promise."

"Thank you. I'm going to hold my breath and look for a door to the lake," Markh said.

Jesk and Jula continued to figure out how to swim.

"Look," Jesk said. "I can float on my back."

"Let me try," Jula said. "Yeah, it works."

Markh dove underwater and found a door to the lake. He came up for air.

"There is a way to the lake," Markh said. "I found a door I can open. But it means swimming underwater. Did you two hear me?"

"We're having fun here," Jesk said.

"Yeah," Jula said. "Look, Jesk, I can swim on my back."

"Let me try," Jesk said. "Yeah, I can too."

"I'll open the door. If you want to follow me, you can," Markh said.

Markh took a deep breath and went back underwater. He opened the door, but when he did, fish came into the room. He came back up for air.

"What was that?" Jula asked.

"What was what?" Jesk asked back.

"Something touched my leg. There again. Ow, it bit me!"

"Does it—ow, something bit me too!" Jesk said.

A fish flopped up onto the steps near Sandra and tried to bite her.

"Go away. Go away!" Sandra screamed.

"Close the door!" Jesk said. "Close it!"

Markh dove back underwater and closed the door, but when he did, the door caught his foot. Markh tried to free it by reopening the door, but the mechanism was jammed. Running out of air, he surfaced as far as he could. The water level was waist high.

"Did you close the door? The fish are still biting me," Jesk said.

"I'm getting out of here," Jula said. "Oh, Jesk. Try standing up. The water is higher."

Jesk stood. The water was now nose level. The two girls had to bounce off their tippy toes to get their heads above water. They bounced, bounced, bounced all the way over to the steps and rejoined Sandra.

"Let's go back and dry off," Jesk said.

"Yeah, come on, Markh," Jula said.

"I can't," Markh said. "My foot is stuck in the door."

"Well pull it out," Jesk said.

"I can't," Markh said. "The water level is rising, too."

"You can't stay here," Jula said. "The water level is too high."

"Run back to the village and get help," Markh said. "Hurry!"

Sandra didn't wait for Jesk and Jula. She ran back through the tunnel, crying. Jesk and Jula dove underwater several times and tried pulling Markh's foot free, but it remained stuck.

"Go get help!" Markh said.

"Jesk, you go. I'll stay here and keep trying," Jula said.

Jesk ran down the tunnel and caught up to Sandra just as she reached the schoolhouse basement. The water level was now higher, and Jesk put Sandra on her shoulders to keep her out of the water. The two reached and took the stairwell from the basement to the outside.

"Let's find Selena," Jesk said. "I bet she can help."

The two ran toward Selena's house with Jesk holding Sandra's hand. But Sandra couldn't keep up and fell several times.

"Piggyback," Jesk said as she put Sandra on her back and ran off to Selena's house.

The two burst in while Selena, Selenita, and Lanietta sat around a table drinking tea. Selenita drew lines on a large document that showed the plans for a geodesic dome. Out of breath, Jesk placed Sandra on the ground.

"Sandra and Jesk," Selena said. "What's this all about?"

"Markh," Sandra said. "Help him. Help him!"

"Where is he?" Selena asked while Jesk struggled to catch her breath.

"Help him. Hurry!" Sandra said as she tugged on Selena's arm.

"Markh showed us..." Jesk started while fighting for air, "a tunnel. From the schoolhouse basement. To a building. By the lake. Filling with water. He's trapped. Can't get him out. Jula trying to help."

"I left my canteen running," Lanietta said.

"Turn it off, Sass," Selena said. "Jesk, you stay here with Sandra. Selenita, let's go."

Selena and Selenita ran to the schoolhouse and around back to the stairwell leading down to the basement. When they reached that stairwell, they met Jula who was crawling up and coughing.

"Too much water," Jula said. "I tried to help him. I gave him air. But I couldn't stay. Too much water."

"Selenita, let's go," Selena said.

"You can't," Jula said to Selena. "No air."

"Stay here, Jula," Selena said.

Selena and Selenita went down into the basement, and now the water level was up to shoulder level. They found the tunnel (which was still dry) and took it to the hidden building. They entered the top floor.

"Markh? Markh!" Selena called.

No answer. Selena found the stairwell down to the lower floor. She led Selenita down, but Selena hit water only a little way down. She dove down and tried to reach Markh, but her air gave out, and she had to return up.

"He must be down there," Selena coughed. "I can't reach him. You don't need to breathe. Go down and free him."

Selenita went down and remained there for several minutes. Meanwhile, Sarna felt badly that Selena wasn't participating in the water convention, and she came over to Selena's house to chide Selena for working too hard.

"Sandra!" Sarna said. "You're supposed to be at the school. What are you doing here?"

Sandra broke into tears and could not speak.

"There, there, dear. Why are you crying?" Sarna asked. "Jesk, what are you doing here? You're supposed to be at the school too."

"I...we..." Jesk stumbled.

"Where's your teacher? Where's Selena?" Sarna asked.

"Our teacher is relaxing in the schoolhouse," Jesk blurted.

"So, you snuck out! With my Sandra, too? What's wrong with you? You know that's against the rules," Sarna said.

At that moment, Jula walked into the house, unaware Sarna was there.

"Selena and Selenita went to save Markh," Jula said. "Tried to get him out, but I couldn't free his—oh, it's, uh, uh."

Jula stumbled in speech as she realized Sarna was there.

"Where have you three been?" Sarna asked. "You're all wet!"

"I didn't know you were here," Jula said.

"You've been at the lake?" Sarna asked.

"No, we haven't," Jesk said, and that was the truth.

"Markh took us to a secret place, and now he's stuck!" Sandra said.

"Jesk and Jula, you should be ashamed of yourselves! Taking my daughter into danger! What's wrong with you?" Sarna said.

"We were just following Markh!" Jesk said.

"Yeah, it was Markh's idea!" Jula said.

"You're still to blame! You don't have to follow someone else when that someone else is in the wrong!" Sarna said. "I'm going to speak to your parents about this. You'll both be punished. Come along, Sandra. Let's get you home and into dry clothes. And you two better change into something dry!"

But before Sarna could leave with Sandra, Selena returned. She looked grim.

"What is it, Selena?" Sarna asked.

"This is a dark day. A dark day," Selena said.

"Did you find Markh?" Jesk asked.

"Yes. Selenita found him," Selena said. "She brought him back."

"Where is he?" Jula asked.

"Selenita took him home," Selena said.

"Why didn't he come here? We're here waiting for him," Jesk asked.

"Oh no," Sarna said.

"Oh yes," Selena said.

"I don't understand," Jesk said.

"And that's why you shouldn't run off into dangerous things without an adult," Selena said. "I feel badly for his mother. She—"

But before Selena could finish, a blood-curdling scream filled the village. The five went outside and witnessed a woman stumbling about in hysterics, cursing everything.

"That's Markh's mother," Jula said.

"You mean he died?" Jesk asked.

"Yes. He drowned," Selena said.

"I thought Selenita saved him," Jula said.

"She freed his body. By then he had already drowned. She tried to get him breathing again, but it was too late," Selena said. "She took his body to his house. Foolish girls! Lucky none of you perished!"

"I'm sorry!" Jesk said.

"Me too!" Jula said.

Jesk and Jula fell into tears. Markh's mother stumbled toward Selena.

"Why? Why!" she screamed.

"I'm sorry," Selena said. "Selenita tried to save him."

Lanietta returned with the PRAAD over her shoulder.

"Did Selenita save him?" Lanietta asked.

"No, she didn't!" the mother said. "You killed my son! Get out of here! Get out! Before I kill you!"

The hysterical mother lunged at Lanietta and swung at her violently. Lanietta was unprepared and tried pushing the mother away. But the mother was out of control. She landed a punch on Lanietta's jaw, and blood came out of her mouth. Selena tried to pull the mother away, but she was too hysterical. Lanietta was out of options. She space-jumped to a position behind Sarna, Jesk, and Jula. All except Sandra were shocked.

"You did your magic, Sass. You moved real fast," Sandra said.

The mother turned around and came after Lanietta again, but the others stopped her. Lanietta sent her ethereal self over to the mother, touched a nerve in the back of her neck, and the mother fell into a twilight state of sedation where she could barely speak or walk.

"There, I have you now," Selena said. "Come inside my house. I have good tea and food inside."

Selena took the mother into Selena's home. Sarna and the girls turned toward Lanietta.

"What are you?" Jesk asked.

"I'm a girl, like you," Lanietta said.

"You're not like us," Jula said.

"Are you...are you a god?" Sarna asked.

"Sent to save us?" Jula asked.

"Or destroy us?" Jesk asked.

"Or maybe just tempt us," Sarna said. "I hate to think Sidan might have been right. You're dangerous."

"I'm a twelve-million-Sol-3-year-old girl who escaped slavery," Lanietta said. "That's how we measure time. By the revolution of a planet named Sol 3."

"No one lives that long," Jesk said.

"Can you bring Markh back to life?" Jula said.

"I don't understand," Lanietta said.

"Markh drowned," Jula said. "He was stuck. Selenita got him out, but...too much water."

"Oh, the PRAAD," Lanietta said.

"The what?" Sarna asked.

"My canteen. It's called the PRAAD. I was just trying to help," Lanietta said.

"For a twelve-million-year-old god, you don't act very mature," Sarna said. "You have no sense of consequence."

"I'm not a god," Lanietta said. "I told you, I'm just a girl."

"But you can teleport," Jesk said. "Teach me how."

"Teach me too," Jula said.

"To create more trouble?" Sarna said. "No. Sass, you can't stay in our village. Sidan was right, I'm sorry to say. You'll have to leave. Our people cannot handle this much change."

"I'm sorry too. I really was trying to help. I guess I need to learn more about...what did you call it? Consequence," Lanietta said.

"Will you please teach me how to teleport?" Jula asked.

"Me first. I asked first," Jesk said.

"No, no, NO!" Sarna said.

"I don't think I could anyway," Lanietta said. "I'm much different. I'm not a god, but I am an alien in this world."

Selenita returned to Selena's house. A moment later, Selena exited and approached the group.

"Selenita's taking over," Selena said. "Now about you, Sass, what was that trick you pulled?"

"She teleported," Jesk said.

"And she's going to teach us how to do it," Jula said.

"For the last time, NO!" Sarna said.

"You have powers beyond comprehension of the village," Selena said. "You can release water with no end, and you can teleport. Markh's mother hates you, and I'm afraid for you—afraid that the village will turn against you."

"She must leave," Sarna said. "More harm will come if she stays. Sass is just a girl and doesn't understand consequences."

"I can learn," Lanietta said. "I need people."

"I'm afraid Sarna is right," Selena said. "Oh I wish you could stay and help, but word of your ability to teleport will get around, and people will fear you'll spy on them in their homes. They'll gang up and try to kill you, I'm sure. I know you can get away, but I'm afraid someone else in the village will get hurt or killed. Jesk and Jula, will you take Markh's mother home? Sarna, the women in the village will need to help her with funeral plans."

"What about you?" Sarna asked.

"Selenita and I will take Sass out of the village," Selena said.

"To cause harm in another village?" Sarna asked.

"No. I have a special plan for Sass. We will be gone for a little while, that much is certain. Then Selenita and I will return without Sass," Selena said.

"Selena, how?" Sarna asked.

"You must trust me, Sarna. Trust me," Selena said.

Sarna nodded in agreement. She went to the water convention and broke the news to the other women. Jesk and Jula helped Markh's mother back to her home. Selena had Lanietta hidden behind a building so that Markh's mother wouldn't see her, and when the environment was safe, Selena took Lanietta into Selena's home.

"Selenita?" Selena called.

Selenita came forth.

"Pack our things. We're leaving. For good, I'm afraid," Selena said.

"Yes, Selena," Selenita said.

"You're not a Bleuh," Selena said to Lanietta.

"What?" Lanietta asked in shock.

"I can't believe it, but your ethereal self has a greenish hue. A Gren? But that's impossible. Only Bleuhs can space-jump," Selena said.

"Who are you?" Lanietta asked.

"I'm Selena. I already told you," Selena said.

Lanietta extended her ethereal self, touched Selena's spirit, and then returned to her own body.

"You're not a Carinian," Lanietta said. "But there's something strange about you. How old are you?"

"Three billion Sol 3 years," Selena said.

"You live a long time like a Carinian. Much longer than these people. Where are you from, and what are you doing here?" Lanietta asked.

"I'm from Roushilla 5, a planet orbiting a red dwarf star named Roushilla," Selena said. "Our star is very old. After spending my whole life there, I learned that things were changing on this planet, so I came here."

"I meant to ask," Lanietta said. "What planet is this?"

"Roushilla 4," Selena said. "My people live in secret on Roushilla 5, but there were some who could not tolerate such secrecy, and so they colonized Roushilla 4. It was peaceful, really. The native Roushilla 4 people welcomed my people with open arms. Unfortunately, the Bleuhs invaded Roushilla 4, took control of the colonists, and created various prisons and work camps. The native people distrusted everyone and isolated themselves as best they could. The Bleuhs caught a few but dismissed the others as savages. As for my people on Roushilla 5, it drove them into deeper secrecy."

"But not you," Lanietta said.

"No. I knew I had to help my people on Roushilla 4," Selena said. "I did that for a time and helped with the underground. I met a woman named Larbiabba who was also in the underground. She said there was a war fought between Grens and Bleuhs. She told me about ethereal spirits and how only Bleuhs could do what you did—space-jump. She referred to the conflict as the Carinian Civil War."

"Wait!" Claus shouted. "Larbiabba died! She became part of the PRAAD and died! Lanietta! What's going on? How could Larbiabba have survived?"

"Larbiabba was a Gren?" Lanietta asked.

"I think so. She acted like one and had a green hue, a stronger green than yours, in fact. She watched Grens die in that war. Bleuhs didn't care," Selena said. "They neutralized Grens."

"I still don't believe it, Lanietta," Claus said. "How did Larbiabba come back to life?"

"Strange thing too," Selena said. "Larbiabba said she was spat out from a canister on this planet. The way she described the canister and how it absorbed water, it sounded like your canteen. Crazy."

"The PRAAD!" Claus said. "She was released from the PRAAD!"

"When I met Larbiabba, the planet was beautiful. It had numerous lakes and several oceans. Lush forests and animal life. We didn't realize it at the time, but the native people here had short lifespans. Larbiabba and I were surprised. We just thought everyone lived a long time like we did. But we used that to our advantage. We posed as the natives so the Bleuhs would leave us alone. Our focus changed, and we ended up helping the natives more than my people."

"But your lifespan is longer," Lanietta said. "Didn't the natives notice that you didn't age?"

"They did," Selena said. "We had to move from town to town, pretending to age and die, only to have a dummy buried in our caskets. Some people think war was the reason for the water disappearing. Truth is, the Bleuhs stole it with that canteen of theirs. Once they did, they closed the prisons, the work camps, and everything. They pulled their people out and moved on to another planet I suppose."

"What about your people?" Lanietta asked. "The ones who moved here from Roushilla 5?"

"The ones who couldn't escape were killed by the Bleuhs," Selena said.

"You let them die?" Lanietta said. "What a horrible thing."

"There was nothing I could do," Selena said.

"You could have evacuated them to Roushilla 5," Lanietta said. "That's what I would have done."

"Impossible," Selena said. "The Bleuhs would have discovered our presence on Roushilla 5. They would have wiped out that planet too. And there's another reason."

"What about these village people?" Lanietta asked. "Can't you take them to Roushilla 5?"

"That's the other reason. I've lost contact with my people. Can't find them," Selena said. "And so, all I have is my spaceship. It's such a small ship, too. I don't think these people are ready for that. Look how they've handled your canteen."

"My canteen. The PRAAD," Lanietta said. "Selena, I can take these people in the PRAAD. All of them. You too if you want. That's how I got here. I used the PRAAD as a spaceship and the water for propulsion."

"You can go inside that thing? Like Larbiabba?" Selena asked. "Without help?"

"Yes, I can," Lanietta said.

"You're so young, Sass. How can you guarantee your plan will work?" Selena asked.

"I can't," Lanietta said. "But I'd like to try."

"I wish it were that easy. I don't even know if my people still live on Roushilla 5," Selena said. "Like I said, I lost contact. I haven't spoken to them in years. You know, you remind me of the two Carinians who helped Larbiabba before the war."

"Did you meet those two Carinians?" Lanietta asked.

"No. But Larbiabba showed me a photo of them. Their names were Larto and Lanshalla. Larbiabba also showed me a photo of their toddler named Lanietta. Sweet little thing. The toddler would be twelve million years by now. She'd be your age. Wait. Sassatinassa, you...she... there's something about you...you look a lot like Lanietta. Strange, isn't it?"

"Parents," Lanietta stumbled. "I never knew...never saw...was never told...Larto... Lanshalla. Nanna!"

"Nanna!" called adult Lanietta to Claus's surprise.

The Lanietta in the vision sighed.

"My real name is Lanietta," Lanietta said.

"You...you're Lanietta? Then who's Sassatinassa?" Selena asked.

"That's a fake name I used when a pirate named El-Vek captured me and sold me at auction on Sol 4a," Lanietta said. "A Bleuk named El-Anonk bought me at auction. I hijacked his ship and took it to a dying solar system. I space-jumped to a planet with the PRAAD, this canteen thing, and used it to escape. I wandered around in space, not sure where I was going, so I landed here to find help."

"Very strange coincidence you landed here," Selena said. "Perhaps it's not such a coincidence. This PRAAD thing was here before. It might have known the way. A question for another day. Lanietta, Larbiabba said your parents believed strongly in the cause for which they fought. Larbiabba herself helped me avoid capture many times when the Bleuhs were here. She didn't make it the last time, though. Perhaps I can repay Larbiabba and your parents by helping you. What is your hope?"

"I want to give water to the workers on Sol 4a. Then perhaps they can grow their own orchards and raise their own animals," Lanietta said.

"You have your father's heart. He owned a great vineyard. Larbiabba visited the vineyard. I feel like I know you. Oh, you're like a niece to me."

"You're my only connection with my parents. May I call you Aunt Selena?" Lanietta asked.

"Of course," Selena said, and the two hugged. "I don't know if your plan for Sol 4a is a good idea, but I will help you with it. Do you plan to spend time there?"

"I don't know. I think I should go home first. To Carinia 2. I miss my friend Labba. Will you come with me?" Lanietta asked.

Selena flinched slightly on hearing that Labba was the name of Lanietta's friend.

"Is it safe? I mean, there could be another war going on," Selena said.

"The Civil War ended, the Bleuhs took over, and there have been no wars since. No one likes the Bleuhs," Lanietta said. "Libriota teaches us they'll be there forever."

"That's a name I haven't heard in many years. Libriota. Evil to the core, according to Larbiabba. Lanietta, don't trust Libriota. She's your teacher? I feel badly for you. She'll fill your mind with propaganda," Selena said. "Well, let's think no more of her. We have a mission. My spaceship is a day's walk away. Hidden in the mountains where no one will find it. Let me check on Selenita's progress. We should slip out unnoticed while we can."

Selena disappeared from view. Lanietta heard faint voices outside the house. The voices grew closer and closer. Lanietta approached a window to see what was going on, but just as she readied to look out, a large rock came crashing through and nearly hit her in the face. Lanietta backed up. More rocks came through the window, and now people banged on the front door.

"Bring Sass out!" called a voice.

Lanietta looked through a peep hole in the door. She saw a large mob gathered outside the house with rocks and clubs.

"We're too late. They're here!" Selena said, rushing out toward Lanietta.

"Trapped," Selenita said, now coming down a hallway with luggage.

Chapter 95: Lanietta Returns to Preivos

"I could fight our way out through the back door," Selenita said.

"No, Selenita, you will only be destroyed," Selena said.

"I can space-jump us out," Lanietta said.

"You can take people with you?" Selena asked. "You are advanced indeed."

A battering ram was thrust against the door. Parts broke and fell in.

"We must leave now!" Selenita warned.

"Which way is the spaceship?" Lanietta asked.

Selena pointed.

"Lock arms with me," Lanietta said. "Hurry!"

Selena and Selenita did so, with their free arms holding onto luggage. Lanietta sent her ethereal self far out of the village toward the spaceship, and she did so with amazing speed. She then pulled her physical self along with Selena, Selenita, and their luggage. The group landed in the desert, about halfway between the village and the mountains.

"I didn't have time to be more accurate," Lanietta said. "This was the best I could do in the moment. I will need another moment to rest before we space-jump again."

"You did very well," Selena said as the three started walking toward the mountains. "We've escaped the mob. But tell me. When did Grens start space-jumping? Larbiabba said that, with the exception of herself, they couldn't. Otherwise the Grens wouldn't have lost the war."

"They can't. I don't know any Grens around me who can do it," Lanietta said.

"You are special indeed," Selena said.

The three walked a little farther and came across the remnants of an old building.

"What irony," Selena said. "Do you recognize this building, Selenita?"

"It's where you found me," Selenita said.

"I thought you built Selenita," Lanietta said.

"That's what I told the villagers. Truth is, I found Selenita here long ago. She was damaged and inactive. I repaired her circuits and got her going again. Her programming was very basic, performing simple tasks like cleaning and lifting heavy equipment. I gave her a personality. So you could say I built her consciousness."

"Are there more of her?" Lanietta asked.

"I wish there were. She's all I could find," Selena said. "Someday I'd like to look for more of her kind."

"I'm rested now," Lanietta said. "We can do another space-jump. Lock arms with me."

The three locked arms as before, and Lanietta space-jumped again. They landed at the foot of the mountain.

"Ah, we're much closer now," Selena said. "There's a hidden path around here."

"Over to the left a hundred paces," Selenita said.

"She has an excellent memory, doesn't she?" Selena asked Lanietta as the group headed toward the hidden path.

"Then you've brought Selenita here before," Lanietta said.

"Oh yes. I like to travel far when I go to another village. Some villages think Selenita is a woman, so I don't tell them otherwise," Selena said. "We went all over this planet. Then we returned to where I first found Selenita. I guess because I know life on this planet is dying, so I wanted to return to the village where I started."

"The path is here," Selenita said after the group walked a hundred paces.

"I don't see a thing," Lanietta said.

Lanietta went eethi and sent her ethereal self looking for the path, but still she could not find it. She returned to her physical self.

"Cleverly hidden, isn't it?" Selena asked.

"Very cleverly. I couldn't find it going eethi," Lanietta said.

Selenita went up to the backside of a boulder, placed two fingers on it, and stared into the distance. A force field camouflaged with the surroundings deactivated, and the path became visible.

"Wow!" Lanietta said.

"Selenita's idea," Selena said. "It's powered by thorium."

The three headed up the path.

"I really wish you two would come back with me to Carinia 2," Lanietta said. "We could work in secret. Start a new rebellion against the Bleuhs. Take back our planet."

Selena laughed.

"Is that so funny?" Lanietta asked.

"You sound exactly like Larbiabba. She talked of going back to start a rebellion. But then I'd ask her, 'Back where?' and she'd go silent," Selena said. "She'd say how Grens are better with physical technology, while Bleuhs are into ethereal technique. But the question always remained, which is more powerful? Can Grens hope to overthrow the Bleuhs with physical technology? Bleuhs have always been able to disrupt Gren circuits. She wished Grens could learn the ethereal world and find ways to protect Gren circuits from attack. Now you come along."

"I come along," Lanietta said. "That's why I think the time is right. I want to train other Grens, show them how to go eethi and space-jump. We could fight ash with ash."

Selena smiled again.

"Am I right?" Lanietta asked.

"Only time can judge," Selena said. "But I do know that things are not always easy, especially when it comes to overthrowing an oppressor. You wish to give water to workers on Sol 4a. Is that a part of this plan to overthrow the Bleuhs?"

"No," Lanietta replied. "It's actually for a school assignment."

"What do you mean?" Selena asked.

"We were learning about Carinia 1 and 2, two planets interconnected in some way. Our assignment is to find two other planet-like bodies interconnected. Labba picked Sol 10 and Sol 10a. I'm going to pick Sol 4 and Sol 4a, also known as Arianos and Preivos. I met Monica on Sol 4a, and she said they could use water for their workers. They wouldn't be thirsty all the time, so now I really want to put water there."

"I don't know much about Sol 4a," Selena said. "Larbiabba said something about a work camp being there."

"It's more than that," Lanietta said. "The work camp is on Sol 4a, yes, but the Bleuh aristocracy lives on the main planet, Sol 4. Slaves do mining on Sol 4a and serve the Bleuhs on Sol 4. Power and control."

The three reached the spaceship.

"This is it," Selena said. "She's small, but she's fast. Let's climb aboard."

The three did so, they buckled in, and Selena gave the order for Selenita to launch the craft into orbit. As they did, they passed over the village from where they came.

"The village water tower is on its side. There's water everywhere. People are fighting," Selenita said.

"I caused that?" Lanietta asked.

"You watered a seed that has grown into many interwoven vines," Selena said. "Well, we can no longer help them. Hopefully common sense will overcome a few of them, and order can be restored. Let's think no more of it. Selenita, take us to Sol 4a."

Selenita put the destination into navigation control, and the ship headed for Preivos.

"So what are your plans for releasing water on Sol 4a?" Selena asked.

"I don't have any plans. I thought we could go there and figure it out," Lanietta said.

"Sounds impulsive. But we should at least consider a few things. Well?" Selena asked.

"I suppose we could land by a crater and put water in that way," Lanietta said.

"And be caught by patrols," Selenita said.

"What? What patrols?" Lanietta asked.

"Selenita is playing devil's advocate," Selena said. "I have her do that so that I can consider ideas and alternatives. One must be prepared for the worst to ensure the best chance of success."

"Well then, we don't have to land. We can drop the PRAAD in a crater and let it release water that way," Lanietta said.

"The PRAAD will be found by a patrol and confiscated," Selenita said.

"Must you argue so much?" Lanietta asked Selenita.

Selena laughed.

"What's so funny?" Lanietta asked.

"If Selenita bothers you that much, then you aren't ready for this task," Selena said.

"How dare you!" Lanietta said.

"Oh don't take offense, Lanietta. We must harden ourselves through such discussion. Speech itself does not cause physical harm, but getting into trouble can. I have found that when Selenita plays devil's advocate, she often gives too much credit to the other side. The key is to find a weakness and exploit it."

"What if we go into low orbit and release the water?" Lanietta asked.

"Patrols might chase us," Selenita said.

Lanietta became frustrated.

"What if Selenita is strapped to the belly of this ship and holds onto the PRAAD?" Lanietta proposed as punishment.

"I could decide when precisely to release water," Selenita said.

Selena laughed.

"You see? She makes proposals too," Selena continued to laugh.

"I might take you up on that offer, Selenita," Lanietta said. "Selena, I want to teach you how to go eethi and space-jump."

"Wait, really? How did you learn?" Selena asked.

"El-Vek put a big device in front of my eyes. I learned that way," Lanietta said. "Then he made me a special pair of glasses. I was able to go eethi without the big machine. Next, I learned to go eethi without glasses. That was on Sol 4a. An ethereal specialist taught me that."

"Do you know how to make these devices?" Selena asked.

"No. I was hoping you could do without them," Lanietta said.

"I can try. What do I do?" Selena asked.

"You have to break your vision somehow. You know, use one eye to look at one thing with the other eye looking at another," Lanietta said.

Selena tried to break binocular vision.

"I can't," Selena said.

"Well I did," Lanietta said.

"You had much help and training. Unless you know how to make these devices to help with training, it won't work," Selena said.

"I'll have to steal the technology. El-Vek has it. If I could get hold of his ship, then maybe, maybe...hmm. Maybe I could steal his ship," Lanietta mused.

"That's asking for trouble," Selena said.

"I'm desperate now. How am I going to teach all Grens, especially Labba?" Lanietta asked.

"That is a great challenge. Let's focus on a smaller one. Dispersing the water," Selena said.

"All right," Lanietta said. "Here, take the PRAAD."

Lanietta handed the PRAAD to Selenita.

"I've fashioned buttons on the PRAAD," Lanietta said. "This one releases water. This one controls the rate of release, this one stops the release, and this one pulls in water. You want to release the water."

"I understand," Selenita said.

"We should do a test," Selena said. "Selenita, release a little bit of water from the PRAAD."

Selenita attempted to release water, but it did not work.

"It should work," Lanietta said. "I can make it release water. Look."

Lanietta took the PRAAD back, moved her ethereal hand into the PRAAD out of habit, and released a few drops of water. Selena laughed.

"You've locked the device with your ethereal self," Selena said. "Selenita won't be able to release water unless you release the lock."

"I have an idea. Here, Selenita. Take the PRAAD," Lanietta said, handing the PRAAD over.

"I have the PRAAD," Selenita said.

"I'll probe your circuits and help you work with the PRAAD," Lanietta said.

Lanietta used her ethereal self to probe Selenita's circuits. She moved her ethereal self fully into Selenita's body, matching limb for limb. She then used her ethereal hand to move Selenita's hand. The hand pressed the release button on the PRAAD, and a little water came out.

"Lanietta, what's happening to you?" Selena asked.

The effect of placing her ethereal self inside Selenita's body had a curious side effect. Lanietta's physical self shifted in form to resemble Selenita, though without gaining mass or height.

"It's like you've become Selenita's younger sister," Selena said.

Lanietta withdrew from Selenita's body. Slowly, her form returned to its natural state.

"I didn't know I could do that," Lanietta said.

"Can you imitate her shape? From memory?" Selena asked.

"Let me try."

Lanietta concentrated on Selenita's shape. Nothing.

"I can't do it," Lanietta said.

"Wait," Selena said. "Go eethi. Then change your eethi self into Selenita's form."

Lanietta went eethi. Her ethereal form changed a little into Selenita's form, but just a little.

"You might need to practice. Go into Selenita's body again. Hold her shape. Then come out," Selena said.

Lanietta did so, and her ethereal self held Selenita's shape. Then her physical self took Selenita's shape.

"Good. Now return to normal," Selena said.

Lanietta did so.

"Repeat," Selena said.

Lanietta did this four more times. She relaxed as usual to her normal state, then she tried taking Selenita's form without her ethereal self going into Selenita's body. It worked. She maintained all of Selenita's physical features in both ethereal and physical form.

"Reintegrate, and see how long you can hold Selenita's form," Selena said.

Lanietta reintegrated her ethereal and physical selves, and then she walked around the ship.

"What do you think?" Lanietta asked.

"You even sound like Selenita," Selena said.

"I can hold this shape as long as I want. It's like habit now. Look. I can switch back and forth," Lanietta said.

Lanietta had to go eethi, though, in order to change shape, as her ethereal self acted as the lead element of the process.

"Now imitate me," Selena said. "Can you do it?"

Lanietta tried imitating Selena's form, but she couldn't. Each time her ethereal self could only take Selenita's form.

"I can't," Lanietta said.

"I give you permission to enter my body," Selena said.

"Aunt Selena, uh, this is weird," Lanietta said.

"You have a great talent here, Lanietta," Selena said.

"Yeah," Lanietta said reluctantly.

"And you spoke of your revolution," Selena said.

"That was with space-jumping," Lanietta said. "I feel like I'm violating your privacy."

"Think of it this way," Selena said. "If something happens to me, I'd like a little piece of me to continue. I don't have a daughter. You are the closest thing I have to that. I know you're Lanshalla's daughter, but maybe...if...perhaps the more people you imitate, the more understanding you'll gain of people. I would never ask you to imitate a Bleuh, though."

Lanietta took a deep breath and exhaled.

"All right. I hope this doesn't hurt. Here goes," Lanietta said.

Lanietta went eethi and sent her ethereal self inside Selena's body.

"Do you feel anything?" Lanietta's physical body asked.

"I feel a little warm and cozy, like I'm hugging you," Selena said.

Lanietta smiled. Her ethereal shape took Selena's form. Then her physical self took Selena's form.

"You're like my twin sister. Hold that shape for a bit. Think about the form. Try to remember it," Selena said. "If you can do that, you'll be able to take a person's shape and remember that form without repeatedly going in and out."

"I'm concentrating," Lanietta's physical self said. "I'm forming an image in my mind. Crystal clear. I feel like I'm in a room with lots of little cupboards, cupboards with doors the size of my palm. I open one, and there's your image. I open another, and there's Selenita's image."

"Good, good!" Selena said. "Now leave my body and reintegrate. Hold my shape."

Lanietta did so, and she walked around, resembling a version of Selena.

"Excellent. Last test. Go back to your normal self. Change to Selenita, then change to me," Selena said.

Again, Lanietta had to go eethi to change form. She reverted to her natural state, she changed to Selenita, and then after a pause she changed to Selena's shape. She practiced changing quicker and quicker until her form became a bit of a blur.

"Very impressive," Selena said. "You've just demonstrated something I've never thought of. Lanietta, if you can imitate enough people, you can change so quickly that you'll look like a combination of those people. You might even learn those new patterns and come up with forms that don't exist. You really can imitate new identities."

Lanietta stopped changing shape and returned to her natural self. Dizzy, she nearly stumbled and had to sit.

"I'm tired," Lanietta said.

"I bet," Selena said. "Lanietta, when you were a slave, did you look like you do now? In your natural state?"

"Yes," Lanietta replied.

"Then for your protection, I suggest you change shape so that no one recognizes you. Can you pick a form partway between Selenita and me? Don't change back and forth, just pick a single shape," Selena said.

Lanietta went eethi, formed a shape between Selena and Selenita, and reintegrated.

"Excellent," Selena said. "Hold that shape. Is it tiring?"

"Not too much," Lanietta said.

"We'll have to give you a new name. They know you by Sassatinassa," Selena said. "Libriota knows you as Lanietta, if she sends word out this way."

"What about Shalla?" Selenita suggested.

"After my mother. I like it," Lanietta said. "I wonder what she was like. My mother, that is. If I could go back in time, in...in..."

Lanietta's eyes glazed over, and she remained motionless.

"Lanietta?" Selena said. "Lanietta, can you hear me?"

"She's in shock," Selenita said.

"Let's get her to a chair. Something's happening," Selena said. "Selenita, search your records for ethereal joining."

"Ethereal joining. The act of a Bleuh placing the ethereal self inside the physical body of another person. Forbidden except among very close people. Risk of eethi psychosis high."

"From melding with me? But how? Why?" Selena asked.

"Nanna!" Lanietta screamed as did adult Lanietta with Claus.

Lanietta fell into tears then fell into a deep daze. She reverted to her natural state. Selenita held a smelling salt to Lanietta's nose, and she regained alertness.

"They're here, they're here!" Lanietta said. "They've come to kill Nanna!"

Lanietta grabbed desperately for help. Selena held her and comforted her.

"No, Lanietta, you're safe with us. It's all right. Shh, everything is fine," Selena said.

Lanietta looked around as if confused about her surroundings.

"Where am I?" Lanietta asked.

"You're with me, Selena, and my robot, Selenita. We're on my ship and headed for Sol 4a. We're going to release water from the PRAAD. Remember?" Selena said.

"I...I was somewhere else. I saw Nanna. That was Mariel. She took care of me. I saw Treyu and others. There was a war. They were attacked and killed. Why? Why?!" Lanietta asked.

"Eethi psychosis," Selenita said. "Joining with you was the trigger."

"That wasn't supposed to happen," Selena said.

"I..." Lanietta said, and her eyes glazed over again.

"How do we stop this?" Selena asked Selenita.

"There is no treatment on record," Selenita said. "Lanietta must learn how to deal with it. Strategies have mixed results. Some say use avoidance therapy, others say desensitize by repeated exposure."

"Lanietta? Can you hear me?" Selena asked. "Lanietta?"

"Momma," Lanietta said as if somewhere else. "I'm your girl. Lanietta. Momma, there's Father. He...you're...oh no!"

Lanietta screamed again, flung her arms wildly, and fell into a deep daze. Selenita held smelling salts to Lanietta's nose, and again she regained alertness.

"I'm back here," Lanietta said. "Aunt Selena, why didn't you tell me my Momma was a Bleuh?"

"Uh oh," Selenita said.

"You knew too?" Lanietta asked Selenita.

"Um, look, Lanietta, you're still a Gren. Larto was a Gren. See?" Selena tried.

"I'm half Gren and half Bleuh. I'm a mutt, a nobody," Lanietta said. "How is this even possible? Grens and Bleuhs aren't compatible. Grens shimmer green and Bleuhs shimmer blue."

"You shimmer both," Selena said.

"El-Vek thought I was a Bleuh. Monica said I was a Gren. I'm not the first true Gren to space-jump, am I?" Lanietta said.

"You aren't," Selenita said. "As far as we know, Larbiabba is the only true Gren to space-jump unaided."

"You still didn't answer about my Momma. Lanshalla. How could she be a Bleuh?" Lanietta asked.

"Lanshalla was a Bleuh patrol," Selena confessed. "She and other Bleuh patrols were stationed on the Gren planet to maintain peace. Okay, to maintain peace as part of a Bleuh expansion."

"On Carinia 2?" Lanietta asked. "That's the Gren home planet, and Carinia 1 is the Bleuh home planet."

"Lanshalla's tour of duty started before the Carinian Civil War. Lanshalla met Larto, a Gren, and she realized her mission was wrong. The two fell in love. She helped Larto with a resistance group," Selena said.

"Larbiabba told you?" Lanietta asked.

"Yes," Selena replied.

"Did Larbiabba say...I mean...a Bleuh and Gren having a child, how..." Lanietta stumbled.

"Larbiabba said Grens can only procreate by exchanging ethereal encoded strings at a procreation center. Bleuhs do the same—normally. Apparently, Lanshalla's ethereal self entered Larto's body. She melded her ethereal spirit with his and exchanged ethereal encoded strings. For him, he had a living memory of her soul to carry around. For her, she had the makings of a new life-form. You."

"Me. Me! Won't everyone be surprised when they hear that I'm half Gren and half Bleuh!" Lanietta said.

"Now Lanietta, wait. You can't go telling the universe about such things. It would put you in great danger. Larbiabba said that Carinians are purists. Bleuhs don't care for Grens, Grens don't care for Bleuhs, and Bleuhs think themselves superior to the universe. You must keep up the story that you and Labba are Grens."

"You mean Labba isn't?" Lanietta asked.

"That's not what I mean. Labba is full Gren, of course. It is you who must maintain the Gren facade," Selena said.

"Wait," Lanietta said. "How do you know Labba is a full Gren?"

"She is Larbiabba's daughter," Selena said.

"What? She never told me!" Lanietta said.

"She might not know. Labba's father was also a Gren. But like I said, it is you who must pretend to be a Gren. You need to practice showing a bright green color instead so as to appear more like a Gren."

"I can go transparent too," Lanietta said.

"That might be the safer way to go. Now I'm sorry you got eethi psychosis. I didn't know it would happen. It would appear you acquired some of my ethereal encoded strings," Selena said. "And who knows? Larbiabba might have influenced those ethereal strings. I never thought of it until now, but she might have connected with me on an ethereal level, sharing her memories directly. I know I said she was a Gren, but maybe she sensed the Bleuh spirit better than she let on. She was nearly as powerful as a Bleuh. Anyway, she shared her memories using a technique similar to what you did just now. I didn't think anything of it at the time. It's possible you experienced her memories directly."

"I could go into anyone's body then and get their memories, if only I could handle the eethi psychosis," Lanietta said.

"Larbiabba warned of one more thing. Not that I'd ever have need to be wary, but

you must be," Selena said. "Yes, you could enter people's bodies to imitate their form. But you must be careful too. I suggest you avoid men's bodies, unless you absolutely know what you are doing. That was how Lanshalla conceived, by entering Larto's body. You might end up carrying the child of someone you hate. If you terminate, you'd cause great damage to your ethereal spirit."

"This is all so shocking," Lanietta said. "I never knew the ethereal world was so complicated."

"It's part of life," Selena said. "How are you feeling?"

"Better," Lanietta said. "I think I'll try the Shalla shape again."

"Careful now," Selena said.

"Selena, this act—" Selenita started.

"I need to overcome this," Lanietta said. "Don't worry. I'll try hard to keep my wits."

"Very well," Selena smiled. "Selenita, override caution."

"Overridden," Selenita said.

Lanietta went eethi, made her ethereal self bright green, chose the mixed form of Selena and Selenita, and reintegrated. She held the form.

"Think about the here and now," Selena said. "I know. Monitor this panel. Let us know when we near the Sol solar system."

Lanietta sat at a monitoring station. Within a few minutes, she had something to report.

"We're approaching the Sol solar system. Entering the planetesimal cloud," Lanietta said, referring to the Oort cloud.

"Very good, Shalla," Selena said. "Selenita, take your position with the PRAAD. We'll soon be in Sol 4a orbit."

But Lanietta felt a stabbing headache. She put her head into her hands to deal with the pain.

"The people...all those people in the village. Sarna, Sidan, Sandra and the others. I see them. I can't get them out of my mind. It won't stop. Selena, make it stop!"

"Hold position out here, Selenita," Selena said.

"Position held," Selenita said.

"Shalla, turn back into Lanietta," Selena said.

"Should I? How can I hold a shape if I keep going back to myself? Ow! Images of people dying in a village. The screams they let out. They died in pain. How do you cope?" Lanietta asked.

The images of the people filled the orb chamber in front of Claus, images suffering and pleading for relief.

"Change back," Selena said. "Change back now."

Lanietta reverted to her natural self. She didn't fall into deep daze, but she did breathe heavily. The images before Claus dissipated.

"Those lives," Lanietta said. "It's too much."

"Rest there a moment," Selena said.

Selenita beckoned Selena over to a side corner. Selena obliged.

"Her eethi psychosis is getting worse," Selenita said.

"We must help her," Selena said. "What can we do?"

"They all go mad," Selenita said. "It's just a matter of time."

"I can't let her go mad. I owe Larbiabba that much at least," Selena said. "Wait, I have an idea."

Selena walked over to Lanietta.

"Lanietta, I'm going to think about a pleasant time I had on a beach. Just me and the waves. I want you to meld your ethereal self with me."

Lanietta looked up. She shook like a leaf. She went eethi, and her ethereal self moved toward Selena in fits and starts. It melded with her. She relaxed a little.

"There. Just relax with the ocean waves. I'm walking on the beach. The waves are warm and flowing across my feet. Doesn't that feel good?"

But Lanietta sensed thousands of marine lives in that water, fighting and struggling to survive by eating one another. Lanietta returned to her own body, put her head down, and shivered. Selena walked over to Selenita.

"You should have checked with me," Selenita said. "Melding often adds to the psychosis due to unintended side effects."

"I was sure the beach scene would relax her. Who would have thought Lanietta could sense marine life through my memory of the waves on my feet?"

"There is much the ethereal self can realize that physical selves cannot," Selenita said.

"Hmm. Selenita, when she melded with you, did you sense anything?" Selena asked.

"My body performed without deviation," Selenita said.

"Perhaps that's what she needs, performance without deviation."

Selena walked back to Lanietta.

"I know you are tired, but please try this task. Meld your ethereal self with Selenita. She's not like people. I'm hoping she can steady you," Selena said.

Lanietta went eethi. Again her ethereal self moved in fits and starts, but it managed to enter Selenita's body and conform to its shape. Lanietta's physical self stared ahead with eyes open, blinking only occasionally, as if she were catatonic.

"Lanietta?" Selena asked.

Lanietta's physical self remained motionless.

"Selenita, walk around," Selena said.

Selenita walked around. Lanietta's physical self stood up and walked behind her.

"Stop," Selena said.

Selenita stopped, as did Lanietta.

"Turn completely around," Selena said.

Selenita turned 360 degrees in place. Lanietta mimicked the move.

"I have a thought," Selena said.

Selena hit a few buttons on a control panel. Music played.

"Selenita, gently turn Lanietta around, take her hand, and dance with her in small steps," Selena said.

Selenita did so, and the two danced lightly in the space ship. Lanietta's gaze softened, and her facial expression relaxed.

"There, it's working," Selena said. "Lanietta, can you speak?"

"I...I'm dancing?" Lanietta asked.

"Yes, and you're speaking too," Selena said.

"I can talk. My mind is clear now," Lanietta said. "I feel the music. I feel the moves. I'm dancing. Nothing else."

"Continue dancing," Selena said.

Selena watched Lanietta's facial and body expressions. Lanietta continued to become more relaxed. She returned to her playful self and introduced moves of her own.

"I never danced on Carinia 2," Lanietta said. "Selenita is about to tell me she is programmed with hundreds of dance steps."

"Yes, I was about to say that," Selenita said.

"Now Lanietta, I'd like you to try reintegrating. See if you can still dance with Selenita," Selena said.

Lanietta returned her ethereal self to her physical body. Suddenly, her dance steps weren't so synchronized with Selenita, and Lanietta ended up stepping on Selenita's toes. In the end, Lanietta just stood on Selenita's feet, and Selenita did all the stepping while Lanietta rode along and laughed.

"You did it," Selena said. "You're back to normal. I'm going to stop the music. Let's see how well you do."

The music stopped, Selenita stopped dancing, and Lanietta stepped off her feet. Lanietta bowed and thanked Selenita for the nice dance.

"You're welcome," Selenita said.

"Lanietta. Do you still wish to deposit water on Sol 4a?" Selena asked. "You don't have to, you know. You could go home to Carinia 2. Rest and recover."

"Would you go to Carinia 2 with me?" Lanietta asked.

"No. Selenita can drop me off at a planet for a while, and she can take you," Selena said.

"That doesn't seem right, Aunt Selena. I can't leave you on a planet without Selenita and your spaceship," Lanietta said. "I still want to fill Sol 4a with water."

"And then?" Selena asked.

"I guess I can use the PRAAD to go home, if there's enough water left," Lanietta said.

"The PRAAD will not be reliable," Selenita said.

"I might have to go against my better judgment and accompany you to Carinia 2. But only to drop you off," Selena said.

"I wish you'd stay with me on Carinia 2. Labba would love to meet you," Lanietta said.

"We'll see," Selena said. "How do you feel?"

"Better. My mind is clear," Lanietta said.

Selena looked at Selenita.

"She should not change shape again," Selenita said.

"It's too dangerous for her to remain as Lanietta or Sassatinassa," Selena said. "What if we're probed or boarded?"

"She'll regress into eethi psychosis. She might not recover this time," Selenita said.

"I'm going to leave it with you, Lanietta. Do you want to go to Sol 4a as you are, or as Shalla?" Selena asked.

Lanietta paused.

"Now it's my turn for an idea," Lanietta said. "I want to meld with you again, Aunt Selena."

"Out of the question," Selenita said. "You'll lapse into eethi psychosis. Do not do this."

"Did you have something special in mind?" Selena asked.

"Yes. I want to whisper my special thought in your ear. I know you'll understand," Lanietta said.

"All right," Selena said.

Lanietta walked over to Selena, put her hand to Selena's ear, and whispered the special something. Selena smiled.

"I understand," Selena said. "Give me a moment."

Selena concentrated on a memory, then she signaled to Lanietta.

"I must warn you to cease," Selenita said.

"Override," Selena replied with her eyes closed.

Lanietta went eethi, and she melded her ethereal self with Selena. Her physical self became grave and somber. She held up her right hand as if taking an oath, and her lips mouthed silent words. She saluted. After a pause, Lanietta reintegrated.

"Your mother would be proud," Selena said.

"Thank you. I'm proud of Momma too," Lanietta said.

"Lanietta, look at me," Selenita said.

Lanietta looked at Selenita and was composed.

"I don't understand. No eethi psychosis," Selenita said.

"I think I do," Selena said. "You're learning to focus on special memories instead of random memories. Good. You've taken a very important step."

"I still don't understand," Selenita said.

"I asked Aunt Selena to remember a story Larbiabba told about Momma, when she was about to do something important," Lanietta said. "She chose a memory when Momma was about to suppress a group of criminal Bleuks. This was before she met my father. Momma was so smart-looking and beautiful in her uniform. So beautiful. I took from her strength and have made it my own. Now I shall change to Shalla."

Lanietta went eethi, changed her ethereal self to Shalla, changed her physical self to Shalla, and reintegrated. Lanietta held steady, as if she were on a balance beam. Selena could tell that Lanietta still had a little trouble keeping steady, and so she turned the music back on.

"Reinforcement," Selena said. "Try dancing with Selenita. As a booster."

Lanietta did just that, and it worked. Lanietta was able to keep her shape as Shalla without entering eethi psychosis. After several dances, Lanietta bowed and signaled the dance was complete.

"That worked. I can continue as Shalla for a while. Who knew this eethi stuff was so involved?" Lanietta said.

"Yes. Eethi stuff," Selenita echoed.

"I find that if my mind starts racing with bad thoughts, I think of Selenita and dancing. Logic and tempo, logic and tempo," Lanietta said.

"Keep practicing," Selena said, but Selenita motioned Selena over.

"She will lose her compassion for people," Selenita said.

"A robot recommendation?" Selena asked.

"The literature on people says so," Selenita said.

"What else can we do?" Selena said. "I've given her a proud moment of her mother. You've given her logic and dance."

"She should interact with those who have been untouched by misery. That might help," Selenita said.

"She is a girl of only twelve million," Selena said. "If she could enter the mind of a child without contaminating that child's thoughts...hmm...but there are no children in these parts."

"Not to mention the ethics of invading a child's mind," Selenita said. "Even the universe has laws against such things."

"Then we stick with robotic thoughts," Selena said. "You must maintain Lanietta's sanity. Keep her sane. Can you do that and operate the PRAAD at the same time?"

"I believe so, as long as Lanietta keeps an ethereal link with me," Selenita said.

"Very well. Prepare the PRAAD," Selena said.

Chapter 96: Libriota Takes Up the Search

Libriota checked with Interplanetary Police (IPP).

"Any sign of Lanietta?" she asked.

"None," they replied. "We've regained control of cargo ship 247, but the pirate must've taken Lanietta on a private ship."

"Surely you've tracked the pirate's ship," Libriota said.

"He could be anywhere," the IPP said. "We'll keep watch and inform when we find him or the girl."

Libriota ended the communication and paced.

"What are we paying these people for? They can't track down one simple pirate ship with a twelve-million-year-old girl on board?" she asked herself.

Another agency contacted Libriota.

"My Supreme Libriota, I regret to report...I regret to report..." the sentry stumbled.

"Yes? What is it? Speak up, man!" she replied with impatience.

"I regret to report...missing. It is missing," he said.

"It? Is this about Lanietta?" Libriota asked.

"No, my Supreme Libriota. The device for reclaiming water. It was reclaiming water. When we checked, it was gone," the sentry said.

"The PRAAD?!" she yelled.

"All defense mechanisms were in place. It could not have been stolen," the sentry said.

"It was stolen!" she said. "You've failed! Report yourself to the Hierarchy for purging."

Another message came in.

"Yes?" Libriota said.

"This is the Hierarchy," the voice said. "We have reports that the PRAAD is missing."

"Yes. I heard as well," Libriota said. "I can track it down with the Anrega. Where is the Anrega now?"

"Circling Sol 2," the Hierarchy said.

"Dumping Greylingers on Vinalia?" Libriota said.

"Affirmative," the Hierarchy said. "We did not wish to disturb you over the PRAAD. You have done so much already for Bleuhs."

"Thank you. I had meant to help with the Anrega at Vinalia," Libriota said. "That planet has such a fresh core, empty of ethereal waste. I wanted to study and fine-tune the Veigon while it controlled the flow of Greylingers from the Anrega to Vinalia's iron core. But that will have to wait. The Anrega with the Veigon inside it will be needed to find the PRAAD."

"Celiba is there supervising the project. Your recommendation?" the Hierarchy asked.

"Tell Celiba to ready the Anrega for both space travel and PRAAD detection. I will contact her directly for the deployment," Libriota said.

"Very well. Thank you for your help. Forever Carinian," the Hierarchy said.

"Forever Carinian," Libriota said, and she signed off.

"Wait," Claus said. "What is Vinalia? Lanietta, can you hear me? I need someone to explain. This is all so confusing. Lanietta?"

As expected, Claus received no reply.

"There's Libriota pacing back and forth. I really need a chart or graph of the Sol system," Claus said. "But how can I get that? Wait, I still have Aftova. Maybe it can help."

Claus tapped the roof of his mouth.

"Sol," Claus said. "Show me Sol."

An image of Sol, that star humans have gazed upon for generations, appeared.

"Now show me the solar system. This is four and a half billion years ago when Lanietta was sold at auction. Show me the inner planets," Claus said.

In the first orbital path was a fine ring of micro asteroids.

"What's that?" Claus asked. "Mercury should be there. But it isn't. This is Sol 1? The first orbital path? Hard to believe. Show me the second orbital path. Should be Venus."

A planet much larger than Venus appeared. In fact, it was the combined mass of Mercury and Venus. The whisper of a twelve-million-year-old Lanietta echoed, "Vinalia."

"That's Vinalia?" Claus asked. "Let's see a close-up."

Vinalia grew closer and closer until Claus felt he was landing on the planet. It was dry but filled with great crystalline projections all over—clear, fluorescent, luminescent, incandescent, iridescent, and metallic. Vinalia had a fast day, perhaps five hours, and Claus could discern the movement of shadows across the Vinalian landscape. Flexible crystalline trees adjusted their crystalline leaves to catch sunlight—this too was perceptible.

"I'll put this image to the side and keep it going," Claus said. "Now show me the third orbital path. Sol 3."

A new image showed Claus a planet the size of both the Earth and moon combined. It was a great volcanic globe with a haze of water vapor.

"So this is Protogaia," Claus said. "Early Earth before the collision. Scientists say Theia collided with it and created Earth and the moon. I'll set this image aside. Now, show me the fourth orbital path."

An image of Mars showed up with Preivos.

"Mars has great oceans. The planet itself is about the size of the Mars I know. Preivos is a large moon compared to Mars, a bit like Earth and the moon," Claus said. "Now the other orbital paths."

Claus pulled up a new image that quickly showed a young asteroid belt with large objects colliding and creating smaller objects. Jupiter, Saturn, Uranus, and Neptune existed too, as did Labba's Sol 10 and 10a, which were Pluto and Charon.

"I'll set that aside. I wonder what happened to Monica, El-Vek, and El-Anonk?" Claus mused.

Claus pulled up an image of those three and the ash people. El-Anonk had El-Vek and Monica drive the ash people along the river to a valley where a spaceship awaited. The ash people were covered in ash mud to protect themselves, and El-Vek used a whip occasionally to motivate them.

"Excellent, El-Vek. You'll do well as a head foreman for these people," El-Anonk said. "Keep them in line for the journey to Preivos, and this will make up for the loss of Sassatinassa."

Claus set that image aside. The one of Libriota took his immediate attention.

"This is absurd," Libriota said to herself. "Lanietta is missing and not found, the PRAAD is missing and not found, and again I'm called to action. Well, I can get nothing done here. I'll start with the girl. I'm going after her."

Libriota hired a high-speed private spacecraft operator, and she headed out to the last known position of Lanietta.

"When others fail, one must pick up the slack to get things done," she said to herself. "Sigh. I'm tired of saving the universe. I'm supposed to be retired!"

The ship reached Lanietta's last known position.

"There's nothing here," the ship's captain said.

"Just hold your position," Libriota said.

She split her ethereal self from her physical and sent her ethereal self on a spacewalk.

"What in the name of..." the captain said.

"Yes, I'm one of those kind," Libriota's physical self said to him. "I suggest you mind your ship and let me investigate without the drama. Get it?"

"I got it, I got it," the captain said.

Libriota's ethereal self spun, rotated, and sent out waves of ethereal energy in all three dimensions. She continued such motion to receive any reflections of such energy, like a three-dimensional radar station.

"Hmm," her ethereal self said. "Cargo ship 247 was here. Life-force residue shows Lanietta left the cargo ship. But I know that already. The question is, to where?"

Libriota repeated the procedure, with a different wavelength and frequency of ethereal waves. Energy signatures returned.

"She entered another ship," Libriota determined. "Yes, that pirate took her. And that ship left an ethereal trail. Foolish pirate, he can space-jump and didn't cloak his ethereal energy very well. His trail is...no, lost. One more scan."

She sent out a third set of ethereal waves with yet another frequency and wavelength.

"Yes, there. He...unbelievable. He's headed for the Sol system. What a fool! We have people there on Sol 4 vacationing. No, he wouldn't go there. Sol 3 is primitive and unfriendly. He could be taking her to one of the Sol 5 asteroids, or perhaps to Sol 4a itself. He wouldn't be that stupid, would he? Yes, he just might," she said to herself.

Libriota pulled her ethereal self close to the ship and positioned herself on a ledge by the nose. Her physical self spoke.

"Allow me to set the navigation control," she said.

"What?" the captain said. "No one controls this ship but me. Hear?"

But Libriota had no patience. She temporarily brought her ethereal self back inside, shocked the captain, and held his body upright and rigid.

"I don't have time for your drama. *I* will navigate this ship based on my investigation results. You can help or remain in this paralyzed state. You decide," Libriota's physical self said.

"I..." the captain said.

"Decide quickly!" she urged, and she jolted him with extra electrical current.

He let out a short moan. She released him, and he collapsed. Her ethereal self returned to the ledge on the front of the ship. Her physical self sat down to the navi station and operated the controls. The captain got up slowly.

"Ready for round two?" Libriota's physical self asked.

"No. We'll do it your way," he said as he sat at a different station.

"Good. I'm glad you see things my way," she said.

Libriota engaged the ship's engines, and she followed the ion trail toward the Sol system.

"I've heard about you," the captain said.

"Oh? What have you heard?" Libriota asked.

"They call you 'Shady Liberty', because you pretend to liberate people," he said. "But really you have your own agenda."

"And who says that? Names please. Names!" she demanded.

"I don't know any names," he said.

"You'd better not," she said. "I'm Lady Liberty. Didn't you know? I'm always concerned for the freedom and welfare of Carinians."

"You mean the Bleuhs," the captain said.

"*That* will be enough," Libriota snapped. "Turns out Lanietta is a Gren. She's one of my pupils, in fact. I'm deeply concerned about her well-being. You see? I care."

"Up to a point. Up to a point," he said.

In anger, Libriota stopped the ship, pulled her ethereal self inside, and shocked the captain. He cried in pain.

"Is that necessary?" he asked as he writhed on the floor.

"To stop your unnecessary speech," she said. "I told you, no drama! Yet you persist. You need training, my friend. I hold special school for cases like yours. And we don't use textbooks. I have my own methods of training."

"I can tell. Ow!" he cried.

"You would need double the training, of course. You're nowhere near charm-school material," she laughed.

Libriota returned her ethereal self to the front of the ship and resumed course along the ion trail.

"Your ship is too slow," she said.

"It's the fastest ship in Carinia," he said.

"You mean Carinia 2. Our Carinia 1 ships are much quicker," she said. "I made a mistake in hiring a Gren ship. Should have been more patient and called for a Bleuh ship."

"Gren is what I am, and Gren is what you got," he said.

"I'll need to make modifications," she said.

"What? No," he said.

"But I need my ethereal self to be in two places at once. I'll have to break myself apart," she mused.

"What are you saying? Are you going to kill yourself?" he asked.

"Must be done," she said.

Libriota split her ethereal self such that the left half of her head with left arm and shoulder formed the ion tracking self (using the left arm and hand to hold onto the ledge and orient about), while the right-head half, right arm, and remaining body returned to the inside of the ship. The captain went into shock from the sight and fell into daze.

"Just as well," Libriota said. "You were in the way as it was."

Libriota manipulated internal circuitry and plasma flow. Propulsion efficiency improved, and speed picked up.

"Excellent. I'll get to the end of this trail in no time," she said.

It wasn't long before she reached the Sol system, and after she crossed the termination shock, the Carinians on Preivos detected her ethereal presence and sent out an alarm to all ships, slave owners, and others of status. The Carinians in Preyakinnak hid evidence of anything not resembling a penal work camp. When Lanietta reached Jupiter's orbit, she had to reintegrate her ethereal self and pull it back into her physical body.

"The ultraviolet light from Sol is too strong," she said to herself. "This ship will provide protection, but I cannot be exposed to direct Sol light."

She had enough tracking, though, to realize where the trail led.

"Sol 4a," she said, referring to Mars's moon Preivos. "He took her to the work camp. As a slave? Another charge added to the list. He'll be a prisoner at the work camp if he isn't put to death."

"Don't put me to death," said the captain, now regaining awareness.

"Not you. The pirate who kidnapped Lanietta," Libriota said. "Are all hired captains as stupid as you? Don't answer that, because I know you aren't that smart."

Libriota landed the ship at Preyakinnak. An accordion corridor expanded out to the ship and sealed with a hatch. Libriota, now in fully integrated form, had the captain open the hatch. She stepped through the corridor and entered the main security station.

"Welcome to Preyakinnak," said Orchius, who had his guards lined up on both sides of her walk to the welcome station, where Orchius stood. "How may I help you?"

"I'm looking for a girl, Orchius," Libriota said.

"A girl? What sort of girl?" he asked.

"She's a Gren, about twelve million Sol 3 years old, and her name is Lanietta," Libriota said.

"I have not heard of such a girl," he said.

"She was kidnapped by a pirate. I tracked his ship here," she said. "It happened only recently."

"Other than prisoner ships, yours is the only one to visit this moon," Orchius lied.

"Orchius. You're the administrator here," she said.

"Yes, quite true," he said.

"And you're a new-born Greyan," she said, referring to his status as a mutilated Greyan.

"Also true," he said.

"Then why did your color shift just now?" she asked.

"I don't understand," he said.

"I do. You're holding something back. Colors shift when your kind becomes upset. It happens when you aren't truthful, either through omission or deception. What are you omitting?" she asked.

Orchius shrugged.

"I demand to examine your records," she said.

"They are in order. Prisoner records are all accounted for," he said.

"Not those records. The secret records. Underground records. Black market records," she said.

Orchius laughed.

"You take me for a fool?" Libriota said. "I'll tear this place apart and find out what shenanigans are going on. Or, you can keep your dirty secrets and turn over what you know about Lanietta."

Orchius stood and grinned. This was a showdown, and he had no intention of backing down.

"I see. You are preparing for battle. Against me?" Libriota said.

"Your words, Libriota. Your words," Orchius said.

"Greyan civilization fell when Grens lost the Civil War, and by my hand," Libriota said. "Or have you forgotten?"

"Yes, you used the Anrega against everyone," Orchius said. "That is common knowledge."

"So you believe you can defeat me now? Attacking a high citizen of Carinia 1 is a felony," she said.

"I don't think you will survive to report it," he said. "Where is the Anrega now? Not here."

"No Greyan can split. Not even you," she said.

"But a Bleuh can split," Orchius said. "Are you prepared to deal with your own?"

At that moment, six Bleuk spies for Orchius surrounded Libriota.

"So this is what you've been up to," Libriota said. "There will be inquiries and trials. Punishment will be most severe."

"Yes, but only against you," Orchius said. "Let the punishment begin!"

The six Bleuks split and sent their ethereal selves toward Libriota. Libriota herself split, but she only had one ethereal self against the six. She space-jumped to another part of the room, but the six Bleuks space-jumped after her and maintained the circle.

"You see?" Orchius laughed. "They match every move you make. You cannot escape, no matter where you go. Go outside, Libriota. Let the ultraviolet light have its way with you."

"Your Bleuks will be exposed too. They'll die," she said.

"And so will you. But my Bleuks are prepared to die to serve me. I replenish my pool of servants every season," Orchius said.

"Your crime is duly noted," Libriota said, and she space-jumped back to her original position.

The six Bleuks followed and maintained the circle.

"What will you do now, Libriota?" Orchius laughed.

Libriota moved her ethereal self around her physical body as quickly as she could, forming a ring. But the six Bleuks also moved their ethereal selves around quickly.

"You see? You can't outmatch your own kind!" Orchius continued to laugh. "And though I'm but a Greyan, I've acquired a special ethereal gun. I can shoot any ethereal entity I like and disrupt its force."

Orchius produced the gun and pointed it at Libriota.

"You fool!" Libriota said. "You'll not get away with this!"

"I have the eethi gun, Libriota," Orchius said. "You're in a terrible situation with no way out. Or is there? I can give you a way out. Yes, Orchius will help you."

"By making me one of your slaves?" Libriota said.

"You're very perceptive. You may last for a number of Sol 3 years. Maybe longer. Depends on the tasks I assign," Orchius said.

"Your confession is noted," Libriota said.

Without warning, she space-jumped over to his gun and struggled for control. The six Bleuks initially came after her to stop her, but the eethi gun went off and fired random shots here and there. One of the six Bleuks was hit and fell to the floor.

Libriota tried to disable its circuits with her ethereal self, but it shocked her and forced her to deal with it on a physical self basis.

Orchius got mad. Really mad. His color changed to deep red, and he nearly went eethi himself. His ethereal self was the source of his red color, and it glowed and tried jumping out of his body from the stress. Libriota again attempted to disarm the eethi gun with her ethereal self, but she managed to touch both the gun and a part of Orchius's red ethereal self, and this caused her ethereal self to duplicate easily. Realizing she could quickly gain numbers this way, she sent each duplicate to the gun and Orchius, and now there were four ethereal selves. One more time, and there were eight. At eight, she felt eight times the energy draining from herself, and so she could duplicate no more.

But eight proved sufficient. She used two ethereal selves to deal with Orchius, another five to go eethi-to-eethi on the five standing Bleuks, and an extra ethereal self as a helper to overcome opponents in each fight, one by one. She defeated the five Bleuhs and put their bodies in stasis. She then set to bear all eight ethereal selves on Orchius (which was enough to prevent his gun from firing), briefly paralyzed his body, and took control of the gun. As her final act against Orchius, she punched him to the ground with her physical self.

"You've put yourself in a bad situation," Libriota said. "Very bad. I shall return with greater numbers. Oh, and thank you for helping me duplicate. Your kind makes for a great ethereal accelerant. I'll pass this information to the Bleuh Hierarchy. Yes, as usual, you've helped us tremendously. Tremendously."

At that moment, Preivos experienced a tremor.

"Another trick?" Libriota asked. "You're beaten. Accept your defeat."

"Something's happening," he said as he tried to get up.

But Libriota wouldn't have it. She kept him on the ground. An assistant in the back hit a button, and a large display screen showed a small spacecraft orbiting with a metal cylinder attached to its belly.

"The missing PRAAD!" Libriota said. "It's releasing water! What fool is doing that? This moon can't handle the volume!"

The water flowed into a Preivos crater, and water poured into rooms and corridors. Carinians ran around in panic.

"I will deal with you later, Orchius!" Libriota said.

Libriota space-jumped back to her hired ship, and she did so by sending four ethereal selves, followed by her physical self, and finished with four ethereal selves to guard her departure. When she reached the ship, she reintegrated her ethereal selves with her physical self. Orchius and others scrambled to deal with the water. More concerned with being flooded than being detected by Libriota, Preyakinnak residents fled in their ships and went into orbit around Preivos. Some chased the PRAAD ship, following close behind Libriota's hired ship which led the way. The hired ship crept closer to the PRAAD ship, and Libriota prepared to send her ethereal self over.

"Steady," she said. "Steady. Wait. What is that? Is that a robot attached with the PRAAD?"

Selenita was strapped to the belly of Selena's ship, and next to her was the PRAAD. It was Selenita who controlled the PRAAD's outflow of water.

"That will end soon enough," Libriota said. "But first, I shall pay a visit to the main perpetrator."

Libriota space-jumped over and saw Selena, who she didn't recognize, and Lanietta, who had the form of Shalla (partway between Selena and Selenita). Selena and Lanietta recognized Libriota.

"I'm Selena, captain of this ship. You're an intruder," Selena said. "Get off my ship, thief. I have nothing for you to steal."

"Intruder? Thief? That's hardly a warm welcome. I am Libriota, supreme leader of the Carinian solar system. You possess stolen property. The device attached to the bottom of your ship is flooding Preivos with water. Cease and desist! It is not for that purpose. Only I can properly wield it."

"Obviously not," Lanietta as Shalla said.

"Shalla, let me do the talking," Selena said.

"Oh no, let Shalla speak," Libriota said. "It's obvious that you, Selena, are a common alien. But Shalla is a Carinian. I can see her ethereal image shimmer. A Gren? Or perhaps a Bleuh? Her color is shifting and indeterminate."

"She's stalling for time," Lanietta as Shalla said of Libriota.

"You as a Carinian should know that time is in abundance," Libriota said to Lanietta. "You shouldn't be able to wield the PRAAD at all."

"PRAAD? What's that?" Lanietta asked in feigned ignorance.

"You know exactly what it is," Libriota said. "All Carinians know. Who are you?"

Libriota went eethi to probe Lanietta's self. But Lanietta changed her shape into her mother, Lanshalla, in order to gain time.

"Lanshalla! It can't be!" Libriota said.

"Why did you kill me?" Lanietta as Lanshalla asked, guessing Libriota had something to do with her death.

"I was dead when you died. I didn't kill you," Libriota said. "Something very peculiar is going on. But it doesn't matter. I'm confiscating the PRAAD. Libriota to Celiba, do you read?"

"Celiba here," said Celiba through a radio device attached to Libriota's arm.

"Take the Anrega out of Vinalia's orbit and put it in orbit around Preivos. The PRAAD is found," Libriota said. "Now then, pretender of Lanshalla, let's see who you really are."

Chapter 97: Earth's Creation

Claus could sense the tension between Lanietta and Libriota. He switched between displays to see what else was happening. El-Anonk and group had just finished loading up their spaceship. The spaceship launched from the planet. Claus continued switching. Asteroid belt and beyond? Nothing. Mercury's future orbit? Quiet. Protogaia? The same. Vinalia, however, focused on Celiba's ship and her control of the Anrega. It had been dumping multiple streams of Greylingers into Vinalia. Celiba had reduced this to just one stream when Libriota called for her to leave. Libriota's call was so emphatic and urgent that Celiba didn't quite shut down the last beam of Greylingers, and so the Anrega headed for Preivos while leaving a trail of these Greylingers.

The display of Libriota and Lanietta, however, went violent. Libriota went split eethi, sending her left half at Lanietta (still posing as Lanshalla) while the right half defended. Lanietta countered by also going split eethi, though she sent her right half to stop Libriota's left. She kept her left half back in defense as well. Libriota shot ethereal plasma balls at Lanietta. She deflected them and sent her own at Libriota.

"You fight better than Lanshalla," Libriota said. "Who are you? No one but me has this much power!"

Selena tried to break up the fight but was slapped to the side and stunned. Dazed, she pulled herself to the cockpit, strapped herself in, and directed the ship to perform thrust maneuvers to toss Lanietta and Libriota around. This only angered Libriota, and she went multi-eethi as she had done with Orchius, but Lanietta also went multi-eethi, and so the two fought with multiple images of themselves, sending multiple rounds of plasma balls, and tossing each other's ethereal bodies about. Their physical bodies, meanwhile, were tossed by the ship.

Selenita, who was strapped to the ship below, realized something was wrong and struggled to shut down the PRAAD. But the PRAAD shot random water jets everywhere. It also fed on the ethereal energy being expended by Lanietta and Libriota. Their combative nature weakened Lanietta's signature lock on the PRAAD and triggered the PRAAD's need to complete its reproductive cycle. It amplified and sent pulses of this energy outward, as if searching for the Anrega and Veigon. Indeed, Celiba lost control of the Anrega, which received these pulses, sped past Celiba's ship, and headed for the PRAAD—all the while trailing Greylingers.

Claus used Aftova to look inside the Anrega. At the core, the Veigon lit up brilliantly with particles of light frantically weaving new encoded threads of desire as if preparing for a merge with the PRAAD. This view of the core was suddenly obscured. Claus pulled the focus away and saw why—an increase of Greylinger activity had obscured his view, and these Greylingers were subsequently expended from the Anrega.

The Veigon directed the Anrega to send out an additional beam of Greylingers ahead of itself and at the PRAAD. The beam traveled quickly, and the PRAAD was surrounded by a halo of Greylingers. But it could not ingest them, as Lanietta's signature set by Larbiabba still blocked them out.

Selena took the ship out of Preivos's orbit and headed toward the sun. She knew ultraviolet was bad for Carinians, and she hoped it would affect Libriota more than Lanietta since true Bleuhs are more sensitive than other Carinians. What Selena didn't realize was that this permitted the Anrega to close in on the PRAAD much more quickly. It was

Selenita who saw the great shape approach. She sent an urgent message to Selena to warn her while simultaneously she struggled to bring the PRAAD into the ship.

"Give up the PRAAD, image of Lanshalla!" Libriota demanded while fighting Lanietta.

"Never!" Lanietta as Lanshalla said back.

"The PRAAD has attracted Greylingers!" Libriota said. "Lanshalla had to be rescued from them. As will you!"

Libriota used the right half of her body to channel in Greylingers that had hovered around the PRAAD. She then shot those Greylingers at Lanietta. They caught Lanietta in her left eye socket between her nose and eye and shot into her forebrain. Yellow Greylinger residue coated Lanietta's face from the point of impact. The residue spread onto the left half of her nose, around her left eye, her left forehead and temple, and left side of her face. Lanietta struggled to regain control of her upper thinking, and as she felt herself failing, Selenita came in through an airlock with the PRAAD. Lanietta immediately called for the PRAAD. It came toward her, but Libriota saw the PRAAD too and called for it as well. The PRAAD was now caught halfway between the two. Lanietta shot water from the PRAAD at Libriota and used the PRAAD to direct Greylingers at Libriota's right eye socket the same way Libriota had done to Lanietta.

Libriota started to fail, but she fought back by sending even more Greylingers at Lanietta. Lanietta returned the fire. Their bodies shook and trembled from the stress, and gradually this shaking from the action pulled their bodies toward the PRAAD, with Lanietta's left arm pointing toward Libriota, Libriota's right arm pointing toward Lanietta, and Lanietta's left hand in a fist abutting Libriota's right fist. Their fists, while abutted to themselves, also abutted the PRAAD. Lanietta's entire left side was completely yellow of Greylingers, as was Libriota's right. Waves upon waves of Greylingers traveled back and forth

from Lanietta's left arm to Libriota's right and back to Lanietta's left. Neither could get complete control of the PRAAD or the fight. Their other halves continued to fight on an ethereal level with shock wave after shock wave of ethereal energy being sent outward.

Selena sped the spaceship toward Sol as quickly as possible. The Anrega followed closely. Selenita tried to intervene in the fight, but the energy shorted out her circuits, and she became inoperative. Selena realized she needed to get rid of the Anrega, so while on the way to Sol, she went in close to Vinalia to use it as a slingshot and to hopefully use its gravity to disrupt the Anrega's lock on her spaceship.

Celiba tried catching up to Selena, but the ethereal shock waves were unyielding and disruptive, preventing her from getting anywhere close. She radioed for help, but others had the same problem—the shock waves were too great.

The shock waves for Vinalia were too great too. The newly-dumped Greylingers in Vinalia reacted with the ethereal shockwaves and caused a planetary event. Selena realized this and started pulling away, but she couldn't be prepared for what happened next. The Anrega, with the help of Greylingers and ethereal shockwaves, pulled the iron core out of Vinalia. The core was hot, fiery, and barely able to hold its shape, being a molten mass of magnetic metal. What remained of Vinalia collapsed onto itself into a mass matching that of modern Venus, and this new planet's rotation was pulled into the now-familiar retrograde one.

Meanwhile, Selena resumed her ship's path into Sol.

"If nothing else, I'll end this for everyone, myself included," she said.

"It's a suicide run," Claus said. "Selena, don't do it!"

Libriota and Lanietta were caught in a vicious stalemate, with both sides fighting vigorously but neither side gaining nor losing ground. It was as if the two were both holding onto a high-voltage cylinder, the cylinder being the PRAAD. The

PRAAD itself swirled in colors of yellow and blue, and it nearly cried out for help from the Anrega and Veigon. The Anrega, however, collided and mixed with the iron mass from Vinalia, and this caused it to lose ground on Selena's ship. Selena had taken her ship as close as the first orbital path around Sol. She barely missed colliding with the micro asteroid belt, but the Anrega/iron mass was not so lucky. It ran into the micro asteroids, and like an airplane skidding off a runway into a stretch of gravel, it too slowed down as it sucked up the micro asteroids. Selena changed course and headed back toward Sol 4 (Mars).

"Lanshalla could do none of this," Libriota said. "I ask again! Who are you?"

The stress of the fight caused Lanietta's form to slip back to her natural shape, that of the twelve-million-year-old girl, Lanietta. But it didn't stay that way. It shifted around into older ages of Lanietta as well, including her adult self. Claus looked back at adult Lanietta in the orb chamber, and her body put out faint shockwaves of bluish-green. The orb representing her mother vibrated with blue while the one representing her father vibrated with green.

"Lanietta!" Libriota said, now realizing who was fighting her. "What are you doing?"

"Researching my school assignment?" she strained to joke.

"You're Lanshalla's daughter. I see it now. Stop this nonsense! You're in great peril. We all are!" Libriota barked. "And don't say I killed your mother. I didn't."

"You might as well have killed her. You get rid of anyone who fights for freedom. You're a wretched tyrant!"

Lanietta kicked out a black eethi-shatter bomb, and it rocked the two to the core.

"We all make choices!" Libriota said. "Make a better one now!"

"I am!" Lanietta retorted.

"Execrate that Lanshalla!" Libriota cursed. "Execrate her and Larbiabba. And execrate you for being Lanshalla's daughter!"

Neither could speak intelligible words. They had struggled to say what they could, but their voices shook from the fighting and shock waves, and now they simply gagged and groaned in agony.

As the last of the micro asteroid belt was gobbled up by the Anrega/iron core duo, the Anrega broke itself free from the iron core. The iron core kept the gobbled micro asteroids, which then became an outer skin of this new planet called Mercury. The Veigon, however, remained in the Anrega's core.

"Mercury and Venus are created," Claus said. "This is insane. Any astronomer proposing this as a means of planetary creation would be kicked out of society for being a quack. And yet here it is!"

The Anrega gained rapidly on Selena's ship. She realized she couldn't make it to Arianos.

"I must try for Sol 3, for Gnisiotra," she said, referring to Protogaia.

Selena did just that. She headed for Protogaia in hopes of losing the Anrega.

"I was foolish to head back to Arianos. That Anrega came right back after me. I'll have to slingshot around Gnisiotra and head back for Sol then end this for all time," Selena said.

"Lanietta!" Libriota said. "Let's not fight any more. I will stop."

Libriota reintegrated her many ethereal selves but kept her right arm locked into the PRAAD and Lanietta's left fist.

"Let's talk," Libriota continued. "We're both exhausted. What do you say?"

Libriota let up a little.

"Okay," Lanietta said. "But this isn't over."

Lanietta let up too. Libriota smiled.

"See? We can be friends," she said.

There was a pause. Selena's ship reached Gnisiotra and started its slingshot around to Sol. Lanietta turned her head toward Selena, and she spoke.

"You can slow down, Selena. Libriota wants to talk," Lanietta said.

"The Anrega is still on our tail!" Selena said.

"I'll handle the Anrega," Libriota said.

Lanietta turned back around to face Libriota. All physical and ethereal links were broken with her, but Libriota now held the PRAAD and laughed.

"You're going to be in detention for a billion years!" she laughed. "My PRAAD. My PRAAD!"

"No!" Lanietta yelled in rage.

Lanietta leapt at Libriota. Libriota activated the PRAAD and sent a stream of water at Lanietta to knock her back, but instead of this stopping Lanietta, Lanietta simply followed the stream of water into the PRAAD. She was now inside the PRAAD much the way she had entered before.

"What!?" Libriota said in surprise.

Lanietta brought Greylingers into the PRAAD with her. She used these Greylingers to forge a tow line with the Anrega. Simultaneously, she put the PRAAD into thrust mode. It blasted away from Libriota's grasp and punched a hole through a wall in Selena's ship as it exited the craft. Air rushed out through the hole, and Selenita's wrecked body was first to reach it. The body contorted and warped, all but sealing the hole. But there was still a slow leak. A breathing apparatus automatically went up to Selena's face and wrapped itself around her head. Libriota fell into a deep daze.

Selena could not react with ship controls in time to what she witnessed next. Lanietta navigated the PRAAD directly into Protogaia.

"She killed herself," Selena said. "That poor girl!"

With the apparent end of Libriota's fight with Lanietta, the ethereal shock wave subsided. Celiba got close to Selena's ship and activated a call-home device on Libriota's person. The device barely returned Libriota to alertness, and she space-jumped to Celiba's ship. Celiba left the area immediately. Selena, still in shock from Lanietta's act of suicide, remained in orbit around Protogaia.

But the Anrega did not. It followed the PRAAD into Protogaia's core.

"What? No!" Selena exclaimed.

The Anrega was so driven by urgency that it did not go planar. It collided with Protogaia. Selena immediately veered away from this new act of violence. Protogaia reacted badly to the collision, and from Protogaia emerged a large, bulbous mass the size of the moon. In fact, it was the moon. The Anrega remained inside the core of Protogaia's remains, which now was Earth. The moon revolved quickly around Earth and gobbled up the floating debris. It was all Selena could do to avoid this mess.

The mess was not the only problem. The Anrega's collision with Protogaia released its entire contents of Greylingers. These nasties from the ethereal realm darted outward from Earth in all directions, looking for any and every ethereal-capable creature to invade and torment. Then it happened. Claus saw on his other screens how Bleuhs and Grens of all kinds in all parts of the universe were invaded by and lost their corporeal bodies to these Greylingers. Greyans were partially spared, though the ones who kept their bodies did so at a price—great mutilation. Orchius was one such Greyan. Other mortals were spared as well, including the ash people. Claus witnessed this decorporealization for all victims but one—Lanietta.

"Where are you?" Claus asked. "Lanietta! Talk to me!"

Claus looked back at adult Lanietta. She was still in her pose with her links to her parents' orbs. They continued to give off their blue and green colors, though frequency and strength of the color vibrations had lessened.

Amongst the debris that had yet to be gobbled up, the display honed in on one cylindrical object. It was the PRAAD, and it was holding a position on the far side of the moon in relation to Earth. Lanietta kept its position such that the moon was between her and Earth, as the Anrega (in Earth's core) was fighting her for control of the PRAAD. Lanietta had managed to get the PRAAD out of Protogaia's core just as the Anrega collided with it, but she wasn't sure how long she could hold her position.

"Lanietta!" Selena said as she detected the PRAAD's position. "Hold on! I'll be there in a moment!"

Selena, you see, was not Carinian, and so she kept her corporeal body. She navigated her ship as quickly to the PRAAD as possible, but she had several near misses from dodging planetary debris. Lanietta was nearly done in when Selena reached her.

"I'm here, Lanietta!" Selena called both out loud and through multiple radio frequencies. "I'll take the PRAAD aboard."

Before Selena could attempt to bring the PRAAD aboard, Lanietta's control of the PRAAD failed. It headed straight for the Anrega. But the moon was still in between, and so the PRAAD simply buried itself into the lunar landscape.

"Lanietta!" Selena screamed.

It was becoming too dangerous to stay in orbit around the moon with the debris, and Selena knew it. She had to leave or else perish from a collision.

"I must go," she cried. "I must."

Selena left the moon's orbit and headed for Mars. To her surprise, Earth released a fearful amount of debris in her direction. She tried to outrun it but could not. She realized this was the end. But then a sense of warmth touched her shoulder. She looked back and saw the ethereal image of Lanietta. She was bluish-green and encrusted with Greylingers, like a whale covered in barnacles. She smiled, put a finger to her mouth to let Selena know she could stop crying, and she sent her ethereal hand into the ship's navi control. Selena's ship suddenly jumped from its position and took orbit around Mars.

"A space-jump," Selena said. "You saved me with a space-jump to Arianos. Lanietta! Some part of you has survived!"

The Greylinger infestation was so pervasive and invasive that it tortured the Anrega into releasing the Veigon, and that Veigon became part of Earth's ejected material that nearly destroyed Selena's ship. Selena and Lanietta watched as the Veigon reached Mars and punched into it at the Martian South Pole. The Veigon emerged from the North Pole, like a bullet through watermelon, and although the entry point at the South Pole was small, the exit point at the North Pole was large. The Veigon, slowed by the impact and by the Martian gravity, took on an orbit that sent it to Preivos. The Veigon collided with Preivos and punched into it repeatedly like a fish consuming food on a water surface. With Preivos destroyed, the Veigon's orbit around Mars decayed. It fell to Mars and landed in the Acidalia Colles hill group.

The act of the Veigon punching through Mars released another nasty, the Veigast. The Veigast went through Carinian life and caused torment in a variety of ways, anything from memory loss to insanity to outright death. It stole parts of Lanietta's memory. She fell into a zombie-like state, and despite Selena's attempts to get her to respond, Lanietta did nothing more than stand in Selena's ship. The Veigast remained constrained by Martian gravity, and so it did not affect those on other planets or in other solar systems. Selena observed this about the Veigast and knew it was time to leave.

"Let's get out of here," Selena said, and she left the Sol system with Lanietta.

Chapter 98: The Aftermath

All displays but one went dark. The last display showed Bleuhs and Grens fighting to inhabit Greyan and mortal bodies wherever they were. Those Greyans who survived on Mars were compromised by such spirits and became neurotic from multiple yet competing ethereal agendas. El-Vek, El-Anonk, and Monica (now in just ethereal form) took refuge with the ash people, and they were transferred to Mars to help rebuild it. The Veigon released new life-forms on Mars, but the number and type were limited, as the Veigon had no help from the Anrega, which was still in Earth's core. Claus watched as Libriota and other Bleuhs (also just in ethereal form) returned to Mars and ruled the Martian colony. Experiments were tried with the Veigon to restore Bleuhs to corporeal form. All such experiments required donor Greyans or ash people. The experiments failed, and those Greyans and ash people involved paid with their lives as a consequence. Claus thought he saw the beginnings of the Halax and was curious to see more, but the last display went dark, and all was now quiet in the orb chamber.

"Hello?" Claus called.

Claus tapped his upper palate to restore one or any of them. Each time he did, an image of Earth, Mars, a Greyan, or an ethereal Bleuh or Gren displayed for a split second before the display gave out a bright flash and went dark like an old incandescent light bulb burning out.

"Labba? Doctor Kechenova?" Claus called.

Silence.

Claus turned to adult Lanietta. She was faint but still there in her pose. Eddies and swirls of blue and green danced along her arms as if an echo of a prior life was all but extinguished.

"I can't just stand here with nothing to do. I must do something," Claus said.

Claus went over to adult Lanietta and tried to touch her, but his hand went through her ethereal body. Then he tapped his upper palate to activate Aftova. He tried touching Lanietta again. Nothing.

"Okay, Lanietta, game's up. Whatever you are doing, you win. Lanietta? C'mon. Give me a sign," Claus said.

But there was no sign.

"This is unnerving. What does one do after seeing such a sight? Earth's creation? Carinian people losing their bodies and lost in the ethereal realm? Where does one go from here?" Claus asked aloud.

Claus expected to hear a whisper, but there was none.

"I'll check on the PRAAD," Claus said. "Maybe I can see something, anything, that will tell me if it plans to leave and destroy Earth."

Claus had no spacesuit. He stared at the split remains of Cluffer and the shreds of Cluffer 2.

"I'm trapped. Unless I can get another Cluffer going or find a spacesuit, I'm trapped in this chamber, like the orbs in this chamber," he said.

Claus touched the orbs representing Lanietta's parents, and he tapped his upper palate to activate Aftova.

"Lanshalla or Larto, if either of you can hear me, please help. Lanietta needs help. I need help. She's stuck in this chamber reliving the past. And I'm stuck with her. But we're not dead yet. There must be more to this. Can you help? Please?"

A dim pool of yellow light grew from the top of the orb chamber. Claus looked up and saw that it was swimming with nasty little creatures.

"Greylingers?" Claus said. "No, please."

Claus shook in fear, and he released his grip from the orbs. But the yellow light grew in strength and descended toward Claus. Claus ran, but they gave chase and surrounded his body, causing him to fall.

They stung his skin like wasps, and Claus writhed from the torture. Then they lifted him to his feet and continued to encircle his body at a rapid rate. Claus scratched, swiped, and swatted at these nasties to no avail. Claus was sure this was his end, but before he could pass out, the nasties stopped their attack, and they "died". Their carcasses had intermeshed and formed a spacesuit around Claus.

"A spacesuit?" Claus asked. "A strange way to create one. Thank you! I'm going to check on the PRAAD."

Claus made his way back to the PRAAD, taking the same path as before. But when he got there, he was surprised to see a twelve-year-old girl sitting next to the PRAAD. She was covered in a yellow cluster, like wasp barnacles. The PRAAD continued to vent as before, but it detected Claus's presence, and he felt a strong pull from it. Claus dove for cover behind the remains of Leni and was able to just see the PRAAD and the young girl.

"Who...who are you?" Claus asked.

"Are you a slave catcher?" the girl asked in fear, and Claus immediately recognized the voice.

"Are you...are you..." he stumbled to ask. "Your name. Is your name..."

"I am Sassatinassa," she said.

"Lanietta!" Claus exclaimed. "It's me! Claus! Your Clomper!"

"I...do not know that name," she said.

"It's you. Under all that yellow, it's you! And you have your body! But how? The PRAAD...it...it destroyed everyone."

"I'm trapped here," she said. "The PRAAD creates an umbrella of energy. Everything outside the umbrella perishes. But I'm inside the umbrella."

"What happened?" he asked. "How did you get here? Unless...you never left?"

"I was in a battle with Libriota," Lanietta said. "I jumped into the PRAAD and headed for Gnisiotra. The Anrega followed and collided with Gnisiotra. The PRAAD came out. I was still inside the PRAAD. I held the moon between the PRAAD and the new planet. I...could only escape one way...I had to leave my body

here with the PRAAD. My soul escaped. Where it went, I do not know. I've been inside the PRAAD ever since. Libriota came much later. She caused the PRAAD to kill off Carinians everywhere. Then something strange happened. I felt like I was reliving the event when I took the PRAAD into Gnisiotra. Who are you, Claus?"

"A very dear friend," Claus said. "Please, call me Clomper!"

"Very well, Clomper. A strange name for a person. But you're not Carinian," she said.

"No, I'm human. And Clomper is my pet name," he said.

"Pet name?"

"I'm your pet. Clomper, your pet," Claus said.

"That doesn't seem right for one person to be the pet of another," she said.

"Lanietta!" Claus said.

"Please, call me Sass," she said.

"Okay, Sass," Claus replied. "I know where your spirit is. It's not far away on this moon. It's in the Anrega."

"The Anrega is here?" Sass asked.

"Your adult spiritual self crashed it not far from here. That's where she is. She's in a chamber with orbs of many Carinians. She was showing me Carinian history, the Civil War, and how Earth came to be," Claus said. "But she's stuck there. She's very faint and dying, I fear."

"If you could bring us together, that might help," Sass said.

"Yes, but how? This PRAAD killed off Carinians. It puts out beyton rays. The only places safe in the universe are the other side of this moon and Earth," Claus said.

"Claus, the PRAAD is strongly activated. It wants the Veigon," Sass said.

"The Veigon is in Earth's core," Claus said. "It's the only thing holding the planet together."

"That's bad," Sass said.

"I know. Doctor Kechenova and Labba are evacuating Earth," Claus said.

"Labba! My Labba?" Sass said with excitement.

"Yes. Just her ethereal self and a pseudo physical body. You're the only corporeal Carinian left. The PRAAD stripped the Bleuhs and Grens of their bodies four and a half billion years ago. But you survived somehow," Claus said.

"I was protected inside the PRAAD these many years and was pushed out just a little while ago," Sass said. "Clomper, you must let Labba know what has happened. She is smart and will figure out how to help."

"I did for a little while, but I've lost contact with her," Claus said.

"Is there anyone else around who can help? Anyone here on this moon? Someone you know and trust?" Sass asked.

Claus paused.

"I wonder if...no, she would never...but if...no, she wouldn't," Claus pondered.

"What? Who?" Sass asked.

"Frieda," Claus said. "She has been in stasis for these past five hundred years. She and other astronauts. I know where they are. I was just there not long ago. But Labba said I could not revive them, not even with Aftova."

"Who is Aftova?" Sass asked.

"Not *who* but *what*," Claus said. "Aftova is a stone that broke off from the Veigon long ago. It was one of three stones Frieda found in her airplane crash years ago when she was younger. I have Aftova now. It's embedded behind my front teeth in my upper palate."

Sass closed her eyes and touched the PRAAD lightly.

"Something's happening. My upper palate is tingling," Claus said.

"I'm establishing a link with Aftova," Sass said. "There. I can read your thoughts now. Wow, Clomper, I didn't realize...how you...you've been through quite a bit. I see everything you do. And my older self, my spiritual self. Oh, what have you done, Lanietta? I'm sorry, Clomper. I really shouldn't call you that. You hated it."

"It's okay," Claus said. "Somehow it feels better."

"Go back to Frieda and the others. Revive them with Aftova. The PRAAD and I will help," Sass said.

Claus paused.

"Go," she urged. "Your spacesuit won't last long anyway. Greylingers feed on destroying the moment, and, well, the moment is fading. Go!"

Claus left the PRAAD chamber and Sass behind. He retraced his steps to the chamber with Frieda. She and the others were still there. Strangely enough, he reacquired a communications link with Labba.

"Claus, are you there?" Labba called.

"Labba! I'm so happy to hear from you," Claus said. "Have you picked up everything I've gone through?"

"No, and there's no time for that at the moment," Labba said. "We're picking up a new energy buildup from the Veigon. It's about to collapse. We're in luck, though. We've been able to evacuate everyone possible. Only one casualty, but—"

"Who?" Claus asked.

"We'll discuss that later," Labba said.

"WHO?" Claus insisted.

"Clover," Labba said. "She was caught in a mountain pass while evacuating her people in the Pyrenees. Selenites surprised her. She held them off so her people could escape. They fought off the selenites, but it was too late. Claus, her body is in stasis in Tabelia. We haven't had the time for more than that. In fact, we're leaving Earth. And I'm sorry. I don't have a way for you to revive Frieda. I wish I did."

"I have a way," Claus said.

"You do? How?" Labba asked.

"Lanietta. Her twelve-million-year-old corporeal self gave me the means. And it means using the PRAAD," Claus said.

"I don't quite understand, but if you can revive Frieda and the others from Astroosa, do so now. Time is essential," Labba said.

Claus tapped the roof of his mouth. Aftova communicated with Sass, and she instructed the PRAAD to assist Claus. One by one, Claus touched the stasis chambers of Frieda, Josh, Bill, Andrea, Doctor

Morrow, Patricia, and Kevin. They awoke and stepped down from their chambers.

"Status, Claus," Frieda said.

"You remember me?" Claus said, thinking back to Libriota's comment about his memory being wiped from their minds.

"Of course," Frieda said. "Now what's our current status?"

"So they didn't wipe your memories after all," Claus said. "I don't know if that's good—"

"I don't have all day!" Frieda barked.

"Or bad," Claus finished. "Very well. Five hundred years have passed. Selenites run Earth. The human species has dwindled down to less than a million."

"How?" Frieda asked. "How could you have survived five hundred years?"

"I was in stasis too for most of that time," Claus said.

Claus briefly explained what had happened since he awoke in Arberella until the moment he revived Frieda and her group. Frieda mostly shook her head in disbelief. The others (while listening) checked over their equipment and any devices in the area.

"You don't believe me?" Claus asked.

"I don't believe you could allow yourself to be caught up in that alien's agenda," Frieda said.

"You mean Lanietta?"

"Yes!"

"*That* alien is why you're here, alive!" Claus said.

"*That* alien is why we are here, prisoners!" Frieda said.

"You're free now!" Claus said.

"Now? Now is too late!" Frieda said. "Our lives are gone! All that we knew on Earth is gone. So are those we left behind! We're worse than dead! We've been robbed!"

"Frieda, please!" Claus said as he moved to hug her for comfort.

"Get off of me!" she said as she forcefully pushed him back. "You should have never been allowed on the moon. You, Claus Gerhardt, are the demon on the moon."

Claus couldn't believe what he was hearing.

"Are you mad?" Claus asked.

"I'm mad with anger," she said. "Anyone with half a conscience would be. Where's your anger, Claus? Where?"

"I'm not happy with how things have gone," Claus said.

"You mean you're not happy that alien friend of yours isn't giving you playtime, right? You probably enjoy playing the submissive role of pet. What else did you two do, Claus? What games did you play?"

"Stop it!" Claus said. "Stop it now!"

"We must establish our own safety above all else," Doctor Morrow said as Patricia and Josh quietly discussed something over a portable display screen. "Should things become catastrophic, the continuation and stewardship of the human species is up to us."

"What stewardship?" Claus asked. "Humans wreck everything."

"You're speaking from prime experience, Mr. Claus Demon Gerhardt!" Frieda barked. "Where's my ship, Claus? Where's Novi 3? Still crashed? Where is it, Claus?"

"It was destroyed long ago," Claus said after a pause.

Frieda slapped Claus, which sent Claus reeling backward.

"By Libriota! I thought you knew!" Claus said.

"You caused it to be destroyed!" Frieda said. "You and your games."

Josh showed the portable display to Frieda and spoke to her quietly. His words trailed with, "is operational."

"Where's Novi 2?" Frieda asked Claus.

"It's here. I returned with it," Claus said. "But I need it for—"

"Keep it," Frieda said, and she motioned for the others to leave.

"You're not going to take it?" Claus asked. "Not by force?"

"We're leaving in Novi 4," Frieda said. "But I'd advise you to stay out of Novi 2. Once we're in orbit, Operation Astroosiate goes into effect. For Novi 2 only."

"You can't. The Carinians disabled it."

"Someone named Yuri had it repaired. To destroy us, apparently," Frieda said. "So yes, we *can*. And we *will*."

"Please don't!" Claus said. "You'll destroy Lanietta!"

"If you want to live, Claus, come with us. If not, ask your alien friend to bail you out. After all, she's *your* alien!" Frieda remarked, and she left with her group.

"Labba! Labba! Did you hear? Labba!" Claus called frantically through Aftova.

"Claus! This is Labba! Morcellus and Tabelia won't leave Earth! We can't make them! The Veigon is holding them here! It thinks the Amnus cycle is about to complete and wants to destroy them. Claus! All humans on Earth are in Tabelia and Morcellus! Claus!"

"What do we do?" Claus asked.

"We have to stop the cycle!" Labba said.

"Frieda's going to set off the nuke in Novi 2. This part of the moon will be destroyed!" Claus said.

"Claus! That will set off the Amnus cycle for sure! You must stop her!" Labba said.

"I can't! She won't listen to me!" Claus said.

"Then get help. Get help any way you can! Claus, do you..."

But interference cut off Labba.

"Labba? Labba!" Claus called.

It was no use. He lost his link with Labba.

"Can't communicate with Labba! And Frieda won't listen!" Claus said to himself. "There's Sass, Lanietta's eethi self, the PRAAD, and the Anrega, plus Aftova and me. How does it all work? How?"

Claus rushed back to the PRAAD chamber. Sass was still there.

"Sass! I—"

"I know!" Sass said. "Go back to the Anrega for help. Hurry!"

Claus ran back to the Anrega chamber. Ethereal adult Lanietta was still kneeling and holding onto the orbs of her parents.

"Lanietta, snap out of your despair and help me. Frieda's going to set off the nuke in Novi 2. We'll be destroyed. Or worse.

The PRAAD will launch and head for the Veigon. Lanietta! Morcellus and Tabelia contain all humans left on Earth. They can't leave without the Veigon releasing them. But the PRAAD will fuse with the Veigon and do what next? Destroy Earth? While Frieda destroys the moon? Lanietta, I need your help. Lanietta!"

But Lanietta did not stir. So distraught was she by the destruction of Carinians other than Labba and herself that she remained attached to what little love she had left in the universe—her parents.

In desperation, Claus ran around from orb to orb and used Aftova to activate each. Images and memories of each orb resident displayed.

"Claus, you must go faster!" Sass said through Aftova.

"I can't!" Claus said. "I'm just a corporeal being! I can't go faster!"

Claus drove himself crazy with rage. With desperation driving desperation, he dove down to Lanshalla's orb and Larto's orb such that he was on the other side of adult Lanietta and facing her. He dove too far and knocked his head against Lanshalla's orb. It dazed him but did not render him unconscious. He reached for and touched a hand each to the orbs of Lanshalla and Larto.

The jolt to his skull activated Aftova, linking it to the orbs and with adult Lanietta. Using Aftova, Claus and adult Lanietta activated the great array of Carinian orbs with incredible speed. But the orbs were asynchronous and disorganized. Claus had an idea.

"Frieda, you might be against me now, but your moment of discovering Aftova will fulfill destiny," Claus said.

Claus invoked Aftova to broadcast what would have been the WWV radio station's time synchronization pulses. The pulses ticked, ticked, ticked, and the orb memories synced, synced, synced until there was a thundering herd of ethereals, ready to be surfed by the one who could master the wave. Claus did so. He mastered the wave and passed this strength on to adult Lanietta. The two shared visual imagery of various things—the lunar surface outside the Anrega, the PRAAD, and Novi 4.

"Can you stop Frieda? In Novi 4?" Claus asked.

Adult Lanietta smiled at Claus, created a cocoon of ethereal waves, and shot it over to her corporeal self to bring her to the Anrega orb chamber.

"You're rescuing Sass," Claus said. "Hurry, Lanietta. We must stop Frieda."

Things did not go as intended. The PRAAD intercepted the cocoon, sliced an opening, and used it to capture corporeal Lanietta (Sass). Trapped inside the cocoon, Sass was pulled into the PRAAD. The PRAAD initiated its launch sequence.

"No!" Claus shouted.

Frieda executed Operation Astroosiate. The nuclear weapon on Novi 2 detonated. Simultaneously, the PRAAD started its launch, but the detonation broke off the lower part of the Anferrumnum, leaving it trapped in the moon. Sass fought to gain control of the PRAAD, but its damage made it unwieldy. It pulled away from the moon and headed toward Sol with the Tropheia remaining intact and the upper half of the Anferrumnum spewing from below.

The nuclear blast also hit the Anrega just as the WWV tone hit the top of the minute. Adult Lanietta had been trying to use the Anrega to free Sass, but the blast broke the Anrega free from the moon and sent it into space. Knowing the Amnus cycle was in play, adult Lanietta fought to send the Anrega as far away from Earth and Sol as she could, but the Anrega picked up the PRAAD trail and followed it. Adult Lanietta continued to fight the Anrega, but she was only able to delay the Anrega from catching up to the PRAAD. The PRAAD, followed by the Anrega, continued its journey toward Sol. The Anrega did not launch intact either. A piece of it was broken off and left behind on the moon.

The area on the moon where Novi 2 once rested was cratered with the resulting explosion. Debris flew into orbit, and Frieda adjusted course of Novi 4 to avoid.

But the detonation wasn't enough to destroy the moon. Adult Lanietta exerted all her might and energy to keep Greylingers from spilling out of the damaged Anrega, but a small trail of them bled out.

"Lanietta?" Claus said. "I..."

"We can't control the Anrega like this. It will fuse with the Veigon and PRAAD with these Greylingers contaminating the process. We must dump the Greylingers."

Mercury happened to be on the way to Sol. The PRAAD raced right by it, but Lanietta saw her opportunity.

"What are you going to do?" Claus asked. "Are you going to hide in orbit around Mercury? Use it as a shield?"

"No," adult Lanietta said. "I'm going to end it."

Lanietta directed the Anrega toward Mercury.

"A suicide run!" Claus said. "Lanietta, no!"

Claus fought Lanietta for control of the Anrega. As Claus gained control, the Anrega headed for an orbit around Mercury, but as Lanietta gained control, it redirected its path toward Mercury itself.

"Don't fight me!" she said with the most strength he'd heard from her in quite some time.

The fighting caused a delay, giving the PRAAD time to enter Sol, activate, and exit. It was on its way back toward Earth when it sensed the Anrega and diverted to intercept. Lanietta made one last effort and plowed the Anrega directly at Mercury. The PRAAD followed and seemed destined to collide with Mercury too.

But a strange thing happened. The Anrega did not disintegrate but simply dove underground, partially fused with Mercury's core, and began transferring Greylingers to Mercury's core. The PRAAD, thrown off by two cores instead of one, swooped down like a bird, grazed Mercury's surface, and shot back upward with escape velocity on its way back toward Earth (and the Veigon). It pulled on Mercury's core. The act was meant to pull the Anrega out, but Mercury's gravity became involved, and the Anrega was pulled out of Mercury's core and slingshot around Mercury toward Sol.

Claus tried to redirect the Anrega away from Sol, but adult Lanietta fought to maintain the heading and in fact accelerated the Anrega toward Sol.

"Another suicide run? Lanietta, stop!" Claus pleaded.

Claus fought her again. What Claus didn't realize was that the PRAAD kept pulling on the Anrega. The PRAAD, still heading toward Earth, managed gradually to overpower Sol's gravity and force the Anrega to turn around and head toward Earth.

"Strike two," adult Lanietta said.

The PRAAD headed for Earth with the Anrega catching up.

"Can't you divert to Venus or something?" Claus begged adult Lanietta. "Don't make this a suicide run."

"Venus is on the other side of Sol. We can't make it. Sigh. Yes, I have to stop it. Only one way," adult Lanietta said.

Just as the Anrega reached the moon's orbit, Claus saw Morcellus and Tabelia streaking across Earth's upper atmosphere and away from Earth.

"They got away," Claus said. "The last humans. They—"

But Claus's words were cut off by a startling sight. The PRAAD fused with the Veigon and sent the Veigon toward the Anrega. With the Veigon no longer holding Earth together, Earth exploded. The explosion disrupted space, time, and gravity, throwing the moon into a new out-of-plane orbit around Sol. The future result of this was that the moon would intersect with Earth's old orbit twice a year. The fused Veigon and PRAAD were not done. The PRAAD's spewing waste put the Veigon in a conflicted state. This conflict was expressed with turbulent colors of yellow and blue on its surface. Despite the conflict, the Veigon continued to fly straight for the Anrega.

"We have to do something!" Claus said.

Adult Lanietta aimed the Anrega back toward the moon, but not for a crash landing. She set it to go planar and bury itself into the lunar core. Simultaneously, she created another cocoon but big enough for two people. In the blink of an eye, she forced both Claus and herself into this cocoon (which resembled an escape pod). The two jettisoned from the Anrega into lunar orbit and watched as the Anrega headed for the moon.

"It's heading for the core?" Claus asked.

"Yes," adult Lanietta said.

"Will that stop the Veigon? And the PRAAD?" Claus asked.

"I don't know," adult Lanietta said.

"What about Sass?" Claus asked.

"Strike three. It's been nice, Claus," adult Lanietta said.

Adult Lanietta hit a button, and a separating divider came down between the two. The escape pod split in half, and adult Lanietta headed for the Veigon.

"No!" Claus yelled.

Though Claus was safe, adult Lanietta's pod headed for the Veigon. The pod and thus Lanietta fused with it. A bluish-green plume erupted from the Veigon and shoved it off course. The Veigon slingshot around the moon just as the Anrega collided with the lunar core. The moon's core became hyper-dense, which increased the moon's gravity to that nearly of old Earth without increasing its size. It also increased the moon's rotational speed to that of an eighteen hour solar day.

The Veigon-PRAAD conflict continued. The Veigon headed toward and entered near orbit around Sol, where the Veigon desperately attempted to purge itself of Lanietta by using aggressive amounts of solar energy. In one last effort of Lanietta's, she tricked the Veigon into leaving near Sol orbit for the Greylingers in Mercury's iron core. The Veigon (and PRAAD) fused with Mercury's iron core.

Claus received a terrible shockwave through Aftova as if Claus witnessed Lanietta being stabbed in the heart.

"Lanietta!" Claus shrieked.

It was no good. The sense of Lanietta once provided by Aftova no longer existed.

"Obliterated!" Claus lamented. "She's gone!"

Claus had no time for mourning. The universe wasn't done with its tricks, and Aftova alerted Claus to such. He refocused his attention on the Veigon. It turned into a metaphorical hive of angry bees, and it sent out multiple Veigasts to fight the Greylingers. This caused large-scale outgassing of plasma energy from Mercury. Mercury shot out of its orbit and left the solar system.

"Claus, do you read? Claus?" Frieda called from Novi 4.

Claus's pod orbited the moon. More than once Earth's debris nearly collided with him. Would this be his end?

"I can't stay in orbit," Claus said. "I need to land. But where? The moon is going through rapid changes. I die up here then. One unlucky hit from debris, and it's over."

Debris from Earth was scattered. Most was slung out into the asteroid belt, but bits remained in Earth's old orbit around Sol. Earth's water was pulled into the moon by the remaining Anferrumnum, creating vast seas on the former lunar far side. Earth's old atmosphere was also pulled toward the lunar Anferrumnum piece, but the atmosphere was not limited to the old far side as the new seas were, and so the moon in its entirety took on this new atmosphere. The Anferrumnum, however, concentrated the carbon dioxide on the old far side, and it reached as high as 15%, while the old near side had none at all. A ground- and atmosphere-level ring around the moon between the old far side and old near side developed where the influence of the Anferrumnum faded away. As these dynamics settled, Morcellus and Tabelia had just enough left in them to reach the moon. It was in the ring zone where they crashed. The shockwaves of the Veigon-PRAAD damaged their higher reasoning powers, leaving them with little else they could do.

"Claus, this is Labba. Can you hear me?" Labba called from Morcellus.

No reply.

The insides of Morcellus and Tabelia functioned much as they had on Earth, but more on an automated level. No humans died from the lunar crash, though there were many injuries of varying degrees.

"Claus!" Labba called one last time.

Labba sighed, then she turned her attention to her immediate situation.

"Doctor Kechenova, what do you make of the moon?" Labba asked.

"The moon is now in its own orbit around the sun," Kechenova said. "Its orbit is no longer in the solar plane. Earth is destroyed. The moon has acquired the water and atmosphere of Earth. The sense of lunar far side and near side has carried into its new existence."

"How so?"

"The PRAAD was in the center of the old far side. A portion of it remains and continues to emit beyton rays," Kechenova said. "It is the reason there is still a lunar far side and lunar near side. It preserves them in such a sense. There is a zone around the moon in that area between the far side and near side. If the moon were a face-locked planet around a star, it would be called the terminator zone or terminator ring. I will call it the lunar shock zone or simply the lunar shock."

"Where are we, or more specifically, am I in danger from beyton rays?" Labba asked.

"Beyton rays still exist," Doctor Kechenova said. "We have crashed in the lunar shock zone. So has Tabelia. You are safe here as are all of us. We can go outside, if we wish. But do not walk into the far side. You'll know. The air will feel warm, heavy, and stuffy. Oh, wait, you're not truly corporeal. You won't know."

"I'll have Argo accompany me. He'll know," Labba said. "I think I'll feel the beyton rays weakening me. At least I hope I'll feel them."

"Be careful. Like ionic radiation for humans, you might not be able to sense them until it is too late," Kechenova said.

"What about Claus?"

"I'm picking up Aftova in lunar orbit," Kechenova said.

"Lots of debris in orbit," Labba said. "I can't connect with Aftova. Surprised you still can. Is he alive?"

"I don't know," Kechenova said.

Labba paused.

"And Frieda?" Labba asked.

"She's landing her ship on the old far side," Kechenova said.

"Strange. I would think she'd detect the carbon dioxide and avoid it," Labba said.

"Perhaps that's why she's landing there. She knows people won't be able to casually stroll upon her abode," Kechenova said.

"I don't like that word in this context—*abode* I mean. Unfortunately, I feel you are prescient about her. She means to start her own kingdom. Is that what you mean?" Labba asked.

"It is. Or a prelude to full lunar domination," Kechenova said.

"We must keep everyone unified, at least in the lunar shock region," Labba said.

"That means two things," Kechenova said. "We must make contact with Tabelia and prepare for a great meeting."

"And we must make contact with Claus," Labba added.

"Precisely," Kechenova said.

"Give me Aftova's orbital path and position. I'll space-jump up and bring Claus down, that is if he still has Aftova," Labba said.

Kechenova gave the information to Labba.

"I'll work with Tabelia. But Tabelia and Morcellus are also Carinian technology, are they not?" Kechenova asked.

"They are Martaceans," Labba said. "One could argue that Carinians are Martacean technology. But that's a topic for better times."

"Let's hope those better times come soon," Kechenova said.

"Agreed. Which brings up one more point. If we are to unify everyone, we need to agree on a common measurement for time. The Terran day is lost."

Kechenova typed in several commands at a computer station. A reply came back.

"The new lunar day is 18 hours long. The lunar year is 487 lunar days. There's a bit over 10 minutes of discrepancy for each year. Wait, it can be solved by following the old Earth calendar's leap year schedule. Yes, that will work. We can keep twelve months, but each month will need more days. You're not going to believe this. Actually, you might. Another human might not. Well, the old rhyme will need to be adjusted to something like this:"

Forty days hath September,
April, June, and November.
All the rest have forty-one,
Except February alone,
Which has forty days like June
And forty-one each leap moon.

"Leap moon?" Labba asked.

"I guess each February 41st will be a 'leap moon' instead of a 'leap year' to distinguish between the two, in case the calendar needs further adjustment. As I said, the leap moon schedule will be nearly the same—the last day of February will be the 40th in most years but the 41st every fourth year except three out of four century marks, etc."

"Well, 'leap moon' will seem odd since the moon is no longer a moon," Labba said.

"That will make the rhyme easier to remember," Kechenova said. "Odd things stick out. But to your point, yes, we'll have to refer to the moon as Luna to give this celestial body a planetary status. How the people argued about the definition of 'planet' five hundred years ago. What would they say now? Sorry, I'm rambling on. I'll make contact with Tabelia. Wait. I can't. At least not from Morcellus. His higher functions are gone. I'll have to go out on the surface and walk there."

"Take others with you," Labba said. "We can't risk losing you from an accident or other issue."

"Good idea," Kechenova said.

Kechenova left Morcellus with a search team. The air was about a half of one percent carbon dioxide—worse than Earth of five hundred years prior but better than the Earth they had just left. Labba and Argo followed the group outside.

"Look," Kechenova said to her search party. "Behold Luna!"

The sky was filled with sunshine but blue with an atmosphere. Clouds rolled by. Air had a good twenty-one percent oxygen.

"There, doctor," someone said. "There's smoke over that hill."

"That could be Tabelia," she said. "Let's go."

"Take care," Labba said.

"Don't take any chances," said Argo.

"We'll catch up with you both later," Kechenova said, and her group was gone.

"I wish Lanietta were here," Labba said. "I can't for the life of me make sense where she is. It's like she's vanished."

"It must be a terrible blow," Argo said. "Is there anything I can do?"

"Thank you, Argo. You've been a great help already," Labba said. "I need to make contact with Claus. A space-jump is the only way to reach him. I believe he's in lunar orbit. At least Aftova is, but I must wait until Aftova is over the old near side. I don't want to space-jump while it's over the old far side. Argo, what can you tell me about the air? The air right here. The old far side is heavy with carbon dioxide. It will seem bad to you."

"It's bad to the east," he said.

"Then let's walk west," she said.

The two walked west, and the first thing they noticed was that the ground became drier and drier.

"Doctor Kechenova said the old near side has almost no water," Labba said. "Argo, before I go up into orbit, I need to make sure I can still space-jump without issue. Okay, here I go. I'm going to space-jump to the west."

Labba disappeared. Then she returned.

"How did it go?" Argo asked.

"The space-jump was fine," Labba said. "But I can only jump back as far as the lunar shock."

"The what?" Argo asked.

"Argo, we're going to have to educate everyone about our new environment. How good are you at teaching?" Labba asked.

"I taught classes back in Arberella in horticulture," he said.

"Good. We'll need your skills to teach other areas of knowledge as well. That will come soon enough," Labba said. "But back to Claus. By space-jumping just now, I was able to triangulate his position. I know where he is."

"Where?" Argo asked.

Labba pointed up. Claus's pod screamed across the sky in a fireball and disappeared behind a mountain. A plume of smoke arose. Seconds later, the sound of a crash thundered.

"I think that was Claus. I need to go," Labba said. "Argo, whatever crashed might be contaminated with beyton rays. I won't know until I get there. If it is, I won't return. I'm sorry, there's no way to test."

"I understand," Argo said. "Kiss me before you go."

The two kissed.

"If there's a way you can acquire a true corporeal body, I—" he started.

"I know," she said. "I'll keep it in mind. Okay, here I go."

Labba disappeared. Argo waited, and waited. Nothing.

"I should go back into Morcellus and search the room of scrolls," Argo said to himself. "Perhaps there is a way to—"

But before Argo could finish, Labba returned with Claus, who was slumped on the ground. She kneeled and checked for life signs.

"His pulse is weak. Breathing is shallow," Labba said. "Oh! He stopped breathing! His heart stopped too! Argo, give him chest compressions. I'll begin rescue breathing."

Argo performed chest compressions to pump Claus's heart while Labba breathed air into Claus's lungs.

"He isn't responding," Argo said.

"Wait. Why didn't I think of it? Stand back," Labba said.

Argo stood back. Labba held one hand under Claus's neck for support and sent the ethereal part of that hand into his spinal column. With the other hand, she called down the wind. In this way, she sent pulses to his heart and diaphragm with the first hand and pumped air into his mouth and lungs with the second. Claus coughed and sat up.

"What happened?" Claus asked.

"You were dead, my friend," Argo said.

"I was?" Claus said, still groggy.

"Yes, you were," Argo said. "Labba brought you back to life. Labba, I didn't think you could control the wind like that."

"I didn't either," Labba said. "It seems I can control a little bit at a time. Whew! I'm exhausted. That nearly did me in. Claus, we need to get you to Morcellus. You've been through quite a bit. As have we all. Can you stand?"

Claus tried to stand, but he felt light-headed and fell to his knees.

"I'll help," Argo said.

Argo pulled Claus up and put Claus's left arm over his (Argo's) shoulder, and in so doing was able to keep Claus upright and in a walking stance. The three walked back to Morcellus and took him inside, where Argo gave Claus food and drink.

"I feel better now," Claus said.

Labba ran over to a station and then ran back.

"Doctor Kechenova has found Tabelia," Labba said. "They crash landed too, but a fire broke out."

"A fire?" Claus said excitedly. "We must put it out."

"Relax, Claus," Labba said. "The fire has been put out."

"Oh," Claus said.

"You're in no condition to go running around outside," Argo said.

"Argo is right. Claus, Doctor Kechenova is in Tabelia. She is calling everyone there to a great meeting. We must call people here to the same. There is much to discuss about what happened and what must be done next, including how to handle Frieda," Labba said.

"What do you mean by that? Shouldn't she be part of the meeting? There are so few of us now," Claus asked.

"We don't trust her," Labba said. "She landed in the middle of the old far side of Luna. No human can survive the atmosphere there. It's like she's establishing her own domain."

"We must contact her and give her the option," Claus said. "Give her 24 hours. A day should be enough to get a response."

"It's not like that," Labba said.

Claus shot back a quizzical expression.

"There are 18 hours in a day and 487 days in a year. Months are longer, there's a new rhyme, and there are many other things to sort out," Labba said. "Hold your questions until after the meeting. Everyone else has the same questions too, though I expect you'll have a few extra. And no, I don't know where Lanietta is, though I fear she is gone from our lives for quite a while, possibly for good."

"I still have Aftova," Claus said. "It...I...Lanietta..."

Labba used her eethi power to touch Aftova. In that instant, she learned what Claus had been through with the Anrega, PRAAD, Veigon, and Lanietta.

"So she's gone," Labba said quietly.

Claus looked down with sadness.

"I know this is difficult, Claus. She was my friend too. So were many Carinians. We must stick together and get through this before the next wave of nasties hits us," Labba said.

"What next wave?" Claus asked.

"I don't know," Labba said. "But the rule of the universe says that if you do nothing, a nasty will hit you. Be aware and prepared as best as you can. Can you at least try?"

"I will try," Claus said.

"Thank you. Let's prepare for the meeting," Labba said.

"Let me help," Argo said, and he helped Claus to his feet.

"No, let me stand freely," Claus said.

Argo released his grip, and Claus took a few steps. He stumbled but caught himself before Argo could intervene.

"That's it, Claus," Argo said. "Take a few steps at a time. The more you take, the easier it gets."

"Thank you," Claus said. "Lanietta. How I miss her. How I wish I could go into the room of scrolls and...and...hey, wait!"

Claus remembered how part of Lanietta was kept in Morcellus's crystalline bricks. He ran with a light heart first to the room of scrolls.

"Claus, wait!" Labba said. "Claus!"

"She's still alive! Morcellus has preserved a part of her!" Claus exclaimed with glee. "He can bring her back! He can bring my Lanietta back to me!"

The door leading to the white and blue room of crystalline bricks was visible but closed.

"I'm opening the door!" Claus said with great excitement. "I'm opening the door to Lanietta!"

Claus opened the door. The room that was once white and blue with a pyramid of crystalline bricks was just a remnant of yellow-and-black-melted rubble from what looked like an explosion and a fire.

"What?? No!!" Claus yelled.

Claus fell to all fours and crawled through the rubble, picking up remnants and calling for Lanietta repeatedly. He shook pieces of rubble. He slapped them together. He even tapped them against his forehead and teeth, hoping that Aftova could somehow bring Lanietta out of this destruction. Nothing. In despair, Claus took a handful and threw it across the room.

"I'm sorry, Claus," Labba said. "When Lanietta fought the Veigon with the PRAAD, she used the energy generated by Morcellus to fight back. The strain was too much for him, and the crystalline bricks are, well, you can see what happened. I had hoped it was enough to keep her alive, but...well..."

"Many happy lives in these bricks were lost," Argo said. "Including Jarro. You are not alone, Claus. It is a day of misery for many."

"But I'm not the many! Nor was Lanietta!" Claus protested. "What am I going to do, Labba? What am I going to do about Lanietta?"

"Attend the meeting," Labba said.

"And then?" Claus asked.

"We'll go from there," Labba replied.

Claus paused.

"I can't bring Lanietta back, but maybe I can with Frieda," Claus said. "Give me 24—"

Labba was about to correct him.

"I know, I know. Give me 18 hours to contact her. A lunar day," Claus said. "If I don't return, start the meeting without me. She should have a chance to participate, even after everything she's done."

"You are very forgiving, Claus," Argo said. "But it can be used against you."

"Argo is right. She might hold you as prisoner," Labba said.

"At least I will have tried," Claus said.

Labba and Argo paused.

"Very well. A lunar day. But no more," Labba said.

"Thank you," Claus said.

Claus walked toward the center of the old far side, but he immediately choked on the air and collapsed. Labba laughed.

"Were you hoping to walk there?" Labba asked. "You'll never make it."

"Why not?" Claus asked.

"For one, the carbon dioxide level is 15% where she is," Labba said. "For another, it's a quarter of the way around Luna. That's almost 1700 of your miles. At four miles per hour and without stopping, it would take you almost 24 lunar days. More realistically it would take you a new month."

"I need a shuttle. A small spacecraft," Claus said.

"So does everyone else," Labba said. "There are none. And don't bother asking Tabelia or Morcellus to take flight. They're done. Don't ask me to either. I can't space-jump there. The beyton rays would destroy me."

"Aftova. I still have Aftova," Claus said. "Can I use it somehow? Can I space-jump?"

Labba paused in thought.

"There is one possibility," she said. "And no, it's not a space-jump. But there are remnants of the PRAAD here. The Anrega is here too. Perhaps with the help of Morcellus, we could attune Aftova to use one or the other to act as a repellant."

"You mean propellant?" Claus asked.

"No. That won't work," Labba said. "Repellant. I'll teach you to fly, Claus. Using Aftova will negate gravity, while not using it will allow for gravity. You'll fly to Frieda. But you'll need a carbon dioxide scrubber. I think there's enough power left in Morcellus to help you."

"What's that supposed to mean? Enough power left?"

"I told you to hold your answers until after the meeting," Labba said. "Morcellus is fading. He is dying. Slowly. Eventually there will be nothing left of him. Tabelia might fade too. I don't know. This means we will need to make a new civilization here on Luna. We'll need food, clean water, a sanitation system, manufacturing, government, schools, etc. All the things your human society had will need to be built here, and soon. Not to mention the memorials for those who pass on. So much to do. Let's get you to Morcellus. Hurry!"

Labba and Argo rushed Claus into Morcellus and took him to a small laboratory he had not seen before.

"Argo set this up," Labba said.

"Please sit here, Claus," Argo said. "Let's get you fitted for a carbon scrubber. Fortunately, our bambooph technology still works. For now."

"We'll plant new gardens and create new strains," Labba said.

Argo fitted an extra heavy bambooph collar around Claus.

"This is larger than what I had in Arberella," Claus said.

"The carbon dioxide level is higher," Argo said. "You'll need it."

"That's one thing checked off," Labba said. "Let's get him to the trampoline."

"You have a trampoline here?" Claus asked. "When did you have time for—"

"Too many questions, and not enough time," Labba said. "Let's go."

Labba and Argo escorted Claus to another new room that resembled a gymnasium. In one corner was a trampoline.

"Get on the trampoline and jump. Jump!" commanded Labba.

"Bossy, isn't she?" Claus said.

"Only when she's in a hurry," Argo smiled.

Claus jumped on the trampoline.

"Do you see the two side-by-side vertical panels on the wall? One is white, the other is grey," Labba said.

"I see them," Claus said.

"Now focus on them as you jump," she said.

Labba hit a few buttons. The white panel turned yellow, but the grey panel did nothing.

"That's odd," she said. "Something's not right with...it's like...okay what if...no, maybe...hmm."

Labba hit a few more buttons. The grey panel turned blue.

"There, now it works," Labba said.

"What was wrong?" Claus asked.

"I'm not sure. Something was unbalanced with the ether on Luna. Not sure why. I just kept adding compensation until I got this panel to work. I'll have to check on it later. Focus on the panels."

"I've seen these colors before," he said.

"They are the standard control colors for the ethereal realm," Labba said. "The Veigon uses them, the Anrega, and the PRAAD. It's no secret that Bleuhs use blue for power and drain yellow into Greylingers."

"Are you saying I should use the blue color and create Greylingers?" Claus asked.

"No. You'll use the few Greylingers that exist in the lunar core for the repellant phase," Labba said.

"Wait a minute," Claus said. "I thought the Greylingers were gone."

"Who told you that?" Labba asked.

"I just assumed that they would be," Claus said.

"Well they're not. And we must be careful about using ethereal power, otherwise they'll multiply all over again. Fortunately I'm the only one who can go eethi. But that's another topic for another day. Too many diversions! Concentrate on the yellow color and imagine being chased by a Greylinger. Oh, and tap on Aftova with your tongue as you do so."

"I'm getting tired," Claus said.

"Keep going," Labba said. "I don't want to go through this again."

"*You* don't want to go through this? What about me?" Claus asked.

"Focus," she said. "Focus!"

"I'm focusing, I'm focusing," Claus returned.

Claus focused on the yellow and imagined a Greylinger coming after him. He tapped on Aftova with his tongue. Labba hit a few more buttons, and the yellow swirled with the blue. Then a Greylinger flew at Claus. Claus panicked, jumped off the trampoline, and landed with a crash into exercise equipment.

"No, no, NO!" Labba said. "Jump up, not out!"

Claus tried again. The Greylinger came after him. As hard as he tried to keep jumping, the Greylinger hit him, and he fell backward off the trampoline and onto a wrestling mat. He paused while he nursed his injured shoulder.

"Perhaps we should try a bit later," Argo said.

"It's too late," Labba said. "I've already wasted enough time as it is."

"What if he can't do it?" Argo asked.

"He must. He must focus and jump up as the Greylinger hits him. Or else I'll zap him myself," Labba said.

"If I jump on the trampoline with him, I could spot him," Argo said. "Or we could hook up the harness to keep him from falling off."

"Too much hassle," Labba said. "Is he ready for a retry?"

"Hey," Claus said. "I'm here in the room, you know. You can talk to me."

"I thought you'd bowed out of the conversation, the way you bowed off the trampoline," Labba said.

"Labba, my sweet, you never speak like this," Argo said.

"Yeah, Labba. It's almost like you're channeling Lanietta," Claus said.

"I miss her too, Claus. I hurt. But I can't sit still. C'mon. Try this one last time," Labba said.

Argo helped Claus onto the trampoline. He jumped again. Labba activated the colors. Claus tapped Aftova, a Greylinger came at him, and he timed his jump such that he landed atop the Greylinger. Claus felt like he'd stepped on the head of a beast as it whipped its head into the air. The net effect was that Claus's legs were pushed upward, and he headed straight for the ceiling. Too quickly, it turned out. He collided against the ceiling, bounced off to the side, and was about to land atop a set of barbells.

"Catch the next Greylinger!" Labba yelled as she sent another one at him.

Claus fell quickly, but he tapped Aftova as Labba sent another Greylinger at him. He stepped on it, and it slowed his fall such that he had a gentle landing. The Greylinger disappeared.

"Training is over. You pass," Labba said.

"How did you get hold of all these Greylingers?" Claus asked.

"Actually, it's just the same one being used over and over again," Labba said. "There won't be a panel like this on Luna's surface. Beyton rays will prevent that. We'll have to fuse this Greylinger into Aftova."

"Wait, is that a good idea?" Claus asked nervously as he backed away from an approaching yet determined Labba.

"Argo, hold him down," Labba said.

"Wait, no!" Claus said. "I don't give consent."

Argo held Claus, and Labba touched a finger each just above Claus's eyes. Claus fell into a dream-like state, and (prompted by Labba), he spoke.

"I...do...(unintelligible) give consent," he said.

Labba herself took on the colors of yellow and blue, with her left side showing yellow and her right showing blue. She transmitted these colors through her arms and hands into Claus's head.

"I...do..." Claus's voice trailed.

"I can't tell if he's giving consent or not," Argo said.

"It's consent," Labba said. "It has to be."

"Labba, my sweet, this isn't like you," Argo said.

"It'll pass," Labba said. "It has to."

Labba completed the procedure.

"There," she said as she released him. "You now have a Greylinger in Aftova. Use it only to cancel Luna's gravity, and only for a little while lest you be launched into outer space. No carbonic scrubber will save you there!"

Claus shook with nervousness. Argo gave him a light punch in the shoulder as a sign of camaraderie and good will.

"Labba, I home this edgy side of you is just temporary," Claus said. "I could always go to you in confidence. Now I'm not so sure."

"Trust me as you always have," she said. "Go to Frieda if you like. Or stay here. Do what you must. When things settle down, I'll be less edgy. We'll have a good laugh over all this. I promise."

"Thank you," Claus said.

Chapter 99: Frieda's Meeting

Claus stood just outside Morcellus. The sky grew dark, and it started to rain. The lunar soil became wet and muddy around him. Some who had landed on Luna aboard Morcellus danced in the rain and mud. Then a stream of people walked out of Morcellus, each holding a seed in hand. They planted these seeds into the lunar mud.

"We saved as many seeds as we could," said one woman behind Claus.

Claus turned around to see Shara.

"Shara!"

"We lost Arberella, but we found a new home. I'll build my hospital yet. You'll see!" she said.

"I bet you will," Claus said.

"Labba said you're going to visit Frieda. Will you be gone long?" Shara asked.

"I hope not. I'll be back tomorrow," Claus said.

"Good. There's so much to do, so many new things to build and make of this world. I'm so excited!" Shara said. "And we'll have music festivals. That will be very important. You must attend. Do you promise?"

"I promise," Claus said. "I must go now."

Shara hugged Claus as a farewell, and then she ran back into Morcellus to bring out more seeds to plant.

"This is it, Claus. Let's try a small jump," he said to himself.

Claus jumped a little bit. It was a normal jump, and that was all.

"I didn't tap Aftova," Claus said.

Claus jumped and tried to tap Aftova, but he couldn't bring himself to do so.

"Scared. Like a cowboy afraid of the draw. I'm yellow," Claus said, but he caught himself with the unintended pun. "Oh, I hope not yellow like a Greylinger."

But the thought of being "yellow" like a scared cowboy brought out the Greylinger in Aftova. Claus tried to stifle the Greylinger, but it caused his upper palate and sinuses to itch. He sneezed. The sneeze was so strong and so loud that it lifted him off the ground and scared the people around him.

"Sorry," he said. "I'm just a little scared."

The people looked at him strangely, and he sneezed again. Like before, he jumped, but he jumped higher and in the wrong direction. In fact, he caught up with Labba, who was on her way to Tabelia.

"What are you doing here?" she asked. "What happened to Frieda?"

"You didn't warn me about the sneeze," Claus said.

"The what?" she asked.

Claus sneezed again, and he jumped high in the air. He used the Greylinger to land softly before the Greylinger shot up a nostril and returned to Aftova.

"Humans sneeze," Claus said.

"They do?"

"Yes!" Claus protested.

"Will wonders never cease. I had never considered it," Labba said. "Well just you sneeze over that away. You'll find Frieda. Here, Argo will point you. Argo?"

Argo shrugged his shoulders before Claus then turned Claus to point him toward the center of the lunar far side. Claus leaned forward, sneezed, and flew practically into a suborbital trajectory. He covered sixty miles in one sneeze before landing and sneezing again. Two hundred miles this time. It only took a few more sneezes before he reached the center of the old lunar far side. Several times along the way, he'd landed in a crater full of water. But he reached Novi 4 finally (at sunset), and it was perched at the top of a mountain. In fact, the mountain was of crystalline nature, much as he had seen before with Vinalia.

"Of all the strange coincidences," Claus said. "How did part of Vinalia get here? The moon never had formations like this."

Claus discovered a pathway running toward Novi 4. It was lined with crystals, as if the crystals answered to Novi 4's will. Claus followed the path but was stopped by an archway with a gate perhaps fifty yards from the ship. A guard came out of a guard shack.

"Do you have an appointment?" the uniformed woman asked.

"Patricia? It's me. Claus. What's going on?"

Claus noticed that Patricia, though she wore a helmet of crystalline, had no breathing apparatus for scrubbing out the carbon dioxide.

"You're asking *me* what's going on?" Patricia asked. "You're the one with the stories."

A telephone rang in the guard shack.

"What are you doing with an old-style telephone?" Claus asked. "How did you rig up everything so fast?"

"One moment please," she said.

Patricia went into the guard shack, answered the phone, spoke briefly, and hung up. She then walked back out to Claus.

"You are approved for a short visit," Patricia said while opening the gate. "This way, please."

Claus passed through the gate, which also meant passing through the archway. As he did, he felt an itching in his upper palate. He sneezed, the Greylinger launched him upward, he banged his head against the archway, and he fell back to the ground next to Patricia.

"What was that?" Patricia asked.

"I don't know," Claus said. "It's like I was electrocuted or something."

Claus pulled himself to his feet.

"Patricia, why all the formal stuff?" Claus asked as the two walked onward.

"Times demand the guard," she said. "You look very suspicious, Claus. And I mean other than your weird jump at the arch. You breathe the air with no issue?"

"I've got this big collar around my neck, in case you didn't notice," Claus said. "It's scrubbing the carbon dioxide. Otherwise I'd die like anyone. I'm surprised you don't have one. How are you managing? I was told the carbon dioxide is 15% here. The threshold for human survival is 6%. You should be dead."

Patricia just smiled. The two entered the Novi 4 outer airlock door. It closed, and the inner air lock door opened. Frieda's team was there—Josh, Bill, Andrea, Doctor Morrow, Patricia, and Kevin. But they all wore some form of crystalline suit. Then Frieda showed up, and she was overly adorned with jewels of the most extravagant kind, even wearing a crown of sorts. Like Patricia, none of the others wore a carbon dioxide scrubber.

"Claus?" she said. "You wear a strange collar. Are you still Lanietta's dog?"

"Lanietta is gone," Claus said. "You should know that. Your nuclear explosion did nothing to help her cause."

"Her cause? Have you forgotten your own people? The human race? And all that Earth created?" Frieda asked. "You're still stuck on that alien."

"She's gone! Are you happy? She's gone! And I'm miserable!"

"Good!" Frieda said with satisfaction. "So what are you doing here, Claus? Do you beg for my help, now that you've destroyed Earth and all? Perhaps you'd like a recommendation for a promotion at Astroosa. Oh wait, they were destroyed too. Tsk, tsk!"

"You don't have to rub it in!" Claus said.

"What *do* you want, Gerhardt?" she barked.

"Your friendship!" he said back.

"What?"

"There's going to be a meeting tomorrow," Claus said.

"Tomorrow? Do you even know what that means now?" Frieda asked. "There is no tomorrow by Earth standards. That's all gone. Like everything else."

"Tomorrow isn't gone. It just comes sooner. Every 18 hours," Claus said.

"And the lunar year is 487 days long," Frieda said. "Yes, we've already worked out the new calendar."

"We're very lucky. Really we are. We've got an atmosphere, water, and gravity nearly like Earth. There's hope for a new future. But we have to work together. Earth had a history of war. There need not be such a history here. We can set things aright from the start," Claus said.

"Set things aright? Just by saying so? How naive do you think the universe is, Claus? You have the brain of a five-year-old. Why don't you ask your namesake for a wonderful Christmas? You believe in him as much as you do yourself."

"You're making fun of me? Of Santa Claus? I'm serious!" Claus said.

"So am I!" Frieda barked back. "Tell him, Doctor!"

"What?" Claus reeled.

A hush fell in the room. Then Doctor Morrow spoke.

"We are sterile," Doctor Morrow said. "No one in this ship can start a family. Normally they would. But the...Claus, are you aware there's radiation emanating from this moon?"

"You mean Luna?" Claus said. "It's no longer a moon. It's a planet now."

"Yes. We know it's a planet now. We know quite a bit about it. There's a device deep inside. Some anti-iron material. It's small, not much bigger than a two-liter bottle of soft drink."

"That sounds like the broken-off piece of the PRAAD," Claus said.

"It's giving off something called beyton rays," Doctor Morrow said.

"Yes. Deadly to Carinians. Labba can't come over here. That's why I'm here," Claus said.

"It also sterilizes animal life. Including humans. No one here can have children," she said.

"Congratulations," Frieda said. "By visiting us, you have rendered yourself infertile. Or perhaps infantile is more appropriate. Either will do. And what will you do?"

"What? I'm sterile? What are you talking about?" Claus said.

"You've cursed us all and now yourself too. You speak of luck. What luck is left now? That PRAAD remnant of yours overrode navi control and caused us to land here. Just like the first time we visited the moon. Remember? Remember when your alien 'friends' caused our ships to crash at their whim and whereabouts? Luck! This is your 'luck', Gerhardt. Condemnation. Condemnation forever."

"Forever? Life is short, Frieda. We have to work together and build something meaningful before we die. I'll see what Labba says about this new development. Maybe Morcellus can help."

"No, you won't pass on. At least not naturally. You're condemned like the rest of us," Frieda said.

"You can't hold me here!" Claus said.

"You don't get it!" Frieda said. "We're not the ones doing the holding. That PRAAD thing is. Tell him the rest, Doctor!"

"We've stopped aging," Doctor Morrow said. "And now so have you. Another effect of the beyton rays. We no longer eat, either. Or drink. Or breathe."

Claus looked around the ship at everyone.

"That's why none of you need carbonic scrubbers," he said.

"We feed directly off the beyton rays. We've lost human desire for most things. We can't leave the reaches of the beyton rays."

"What about me?" Claus asked. "Can I go back to the...the area where the beyton rays fade off?"

"*What about me*?" Frieda mocked. "That's all you care about. You and your alien."

"Stop it, Frieda! I can't help you if you go on like this," Claus said.

"You can't help us now anyway," Doctor Morrow said.

"Look, the meeting is important. The survivors from Earth made it here aboard two alien creatures who acted as spaceships. I'm sorry you're against these aliens, but facts are facts. We're going to discuss what happened, what we know about Luna and stuff, and how we can plan for the future. Can you join us?"

"The area where the beyton rays fall off, that's the beyton terminator ring," Doctor Morrow said.

"Doctor Kechenova calls it the lunar shock zone, or even the lunar shock," Claus said.

"That's as good a name as any. We can't go there for sure. We don't know if we'll survive," Doctor Morrow said.

"Use the radio. We'll scan for your frequency," Claus said.

"All of our circuits are burned out, due to the beyton rays. They act as electromagnetic pulses. Only a vacuum-tube culture or other rudimentary electronic system could operate," Doctor Morrow said.

"I'll go back and tell them," Claus said.

"You might die," Doctor Morrow said.

"I'll take that chance," Claus said. "If I survive, I'll tell them everything about you and pass along any information you are willing to share. It's the least I can do."

Frieda looked at Claus in surprise.

"I don't trust you," she said.

"It's the best we can do," Doctor Morrow said. "Here."

Doctor Morrow handed Claus an optical disk.

"It contains basic information about the ship's operation during the last moments before the crash," Doctor Morrow said. "The disk uses a non-magnetic method of recording data. We can no longer access the data, of course, so it is useless to us. It might help you."

"Thank you," Claus said. "Frieda, I..."

"Just leave," she said.

Claus nodded his head and exited. Patricia accompanied him to the archway. The sun had set, it was night, and yet crystals glowed everywhere.

"We're all on edge here," she said. "No one knows what to do. We didn't choose to land here. You must believe that."

"I think Doctor Kechenova thought you wanted to be alone, and that's why you chose to be here," Claus said. "I'll tell her the truth. I'll tell her the trap you are all in."

"Thank you. We miss Earth. We miss people and animals. There's no life around here. Just lots of water," Patricia said. "If only we had something to work with. Anything to get our minds off things, that would help. We're going stir crazy, Claus. At least I have the guard shack here to get me out of the ship. I don't think we'll last long. We might not age, but we'll certainly kill each other before long."

"Thank you for letting me know. I'm sure we can work something out. Hang in there, Patricia. We'll find a way," Claus said. "Now I must go back and hope I survive."

"Good luck," Patricia said.

Patricia opened the gate for Claus. He paused before going through the archway, afraid of having a reaction like before. He darted through quickly to avoid whatever he experienced before, but nothing happened to him. The crystals lit up the surroundings, making it easy to see and be seen. Once he was out of Patricia's sight, he invoked the Greylinger in Aftova. He sneezed and headed back for Morcellus. He was tired and fell asleep between sneezes, and so he lost track of time on the return journey.

Chapter 100: Labba's Meeting

Claus returned to the lunar shock at sunrise. Afraid he would die, he ran into Morcellus, hoping that somehow the Martacean's body would protect him. He found Argo.

"Argo, Argo! Where's Labba? I must see her at once!" Claus said excitedly.

"She's in the room of scrolls," Argo said.

Claus ran into the room of scrolls. Labba was reading one such scroll with Shara.

"Nothing here either for bringing people back to life," Labba said to Shara. "Keep Clover in stasis for now."

"Labba, Labba!" Claus said. "I'm going to die. I'm going to die!"

"What? No!" Shara said as she rushed up to hug him. "You're not sick at all. I don't understand."

Shara pulled away from Claus and stared him squarely in the eye.

"Neither do I," Labba said. "What's this about dying?"

"I met with Frieda. And the others. Doctor Morrow said I'm going to die. Because I left the lunar far side and came back to the lunar shock. Labba, I can't stay! I must go back before I die!"

"Wait there, cowboy," Labba said. "Check your horse at the stable, and let's get you a drink and sort this out."

Shara laughed.

"What's so funny?" Claus asked.

"Labba speaks strangely," Shara said.

"I thought I'd try humor," Labba said. "But the drink offer is still good. Come along, Shara. You're old enough or should be."

The three left the room of scrolls and entered a side chamber that resembled a cafe.

"All food that remains in Morcellus is stocked in the cafe," Labba said. "It won't last long, but it will get us through for now. Hold that question, Claus. The meeting starts very soon. Barista, three coffees please!"

The drinks were served. Claus took a sip and felt refreshed.

"Now start from the beginning. Tell me about your visit with Frieda," Labba said.

Claus recounted how he used the Greylinger and Aftova to jump over to Novi 4, about the crystalline development, and about meeting Patricia at the gate. He forgot about his experience with the archway and jumped ahead to his visit in Novi 4 itself with everyone wearing jewels, Frieda's crown, and the story of Novi 4 being forced to crash land there, how the beyton rays made everyone sterile, that they didn't need to eat or drink or breathe, how they had stopped aging, and how beyton rays gave them energy.

"But should they leave the beyton sphere of influence, their source of energy will end. They'll die!" Claus said. "They said this happens to any human, that now I'm sterile, and that I'll die. Labba! Am I going to die?"

"You would be dead already," she said.

"I would?"

"Yes. Beyton rays can't be stored like body fat. Once they are gone, you die. Like turning off electricity to a device," Labba said.

"Oh, Claus, you're going to live!" Shara said, and she hugged Claus again, only she came across the disk in his pocket.

"What's that?" Labba asked as Shara pulled the disk out completely.

"A data disk," Claus said. "They gave it to me so we can analyze it and learn about their state. Their computers burned out. Something about electromagnetic pulse. The disk was made before their equipment failed. Like a black box recording."

"I'm not familiar with black box recording," Labba said. "Shara, have the disk analyzed."

"Yes, Labba," Shara said, and she disappeared with the disk.

"So I'll live," Claus said.

"It would seem so. We'll have to give you a physical and see how you've changed, if any," Labba said.

"Now?"

"No, not now. I have to get ready for the meeting," Labba said. "You'll have a physical after that."

"I might die by then," Claus said. "Can't you do a quick check now?"

"Well there's Aftova," Labba said. "It would know if anything."

"Check it then," Claus said. "Check Aftova."

"All right," Labba said, and she casually tapped Claus on the nose.

But Labba had the most violent reaction. Her entire body became an exploding plasma ball, was shot across the room, and set the distant wall on fire. The barista called for help, and several people in the cafe rushed over to put out the fire.

"Labba!" Claus screamed.

The fire raged on, but just as the people got it down to a few flames, Labba emerged from the smoke, with her ethereal self flickering green. She passed through tables and chairs as she struggled to regain her pseudo-corporeal presence. She could only do so by taking on colors of yellow and black. Finally, she got herself together and helped the others put out the rest of the fire. She returned to Claus looking all the part of a yellowjacket wasp. Shara rushed in.

"Oh, our food supply!" Shara shrieked. "Labba, are your hurt?"

"No food was lost," the barista said.

"I'm all right for the moment," Labba said. "But I'm shocked both figuratively and literally as to what is going on with Claus's nose."

"What's wrong with his nose?" Shara asked.

"Touch it," Labba said.

Shara touched Claus's nose. Nothing happened.

"It's okay to me," Shara said.

"Because you're not a Carinian who lives primarily in the ethereal realm," Labba said. "What did you do to Aftova, Claus?"

"What? Nothing," Claus said in surprise.

"What did you do to it?" Labba demanded. "It's changed! It shocked me like nothing before. Did you leave out a part of your story? Did you get a feeling like you were being electrocuted? Your stone has remnants of Rigefa shouting loud and strong. It's saying, 'Rigefa is here to stay! All shall bow down and worship the crystal before me.'"

Then Claus remembered the archway.

"There was one little thing," Claus said.

"Now he remembers," Labba said.

"I walked through an archway," Claus said.

"Where?"

"It was before the ship. Had a gate," Claus said.

"Was it crystalline?" Labba asked.

"Yes. It shocked me, and I sneezed. I jumped upward and hit my head on the arch. I fell down," Claus said.

"Why didn't you tell me before?" Labba demanded.

"I guess I was too embarrassed to say," Claus said.

"You were scanned," Labba said. "Frieda has Rigefa, and she scanned you. Now she knows you have Aftova."

"She can't have Rigefa. Lanietta has it," Claus said.

"Have you seen Lanietta lately? Have you seen Rigefa lately?" Labba asked. "No, don't answer. Somehow Rigefa was transferred from Lanietta to Frieda. Could have happened during the fight with the PRAAD. Part of the PRAAD is still in Luna. That explains much. The remaining PRAAD pulled Novi 4 down, Frieda got Rigefa, and she used it to create the crystalline structures around Novi 4. Oh, it's yet another complication I don't need right now!"

Argo came in.

"Doctor Kechenova is calling for the start of the meeting," he said. "The Tabelians are in various trees inside Tabelia. Our people are outside."

"Okay, Argo. One more moment please," Labba said. "Shara, did you get the disk analyzed?"

"Yes. It's basically what you just now said. They were pulled down and crash landed. That's all the data records," Shara said.

"Their circuits then failed as part of the crash," Labba said. "Very well. Let's go to the surface for the meeting. Keep your nose out of trouble, Claus, and away from me for that matter."

Labba stormed ahead with Argo comforting her. Claus just stood there in shock while the others headed out of Morcellus. Shara stayed behind.

"Would you escort me to the surface, please?" Shara asked Claus.

Shara put her arm around Claus's as if she were a bride to be given away.

"I suppose we should go. Be delighted to," Claus said.

As it turned out, the two were the last to join the crowd on the surface. Chairs had been set out, and a projector with a powerful light displayed an image on a shaded vertical mountain surface. Large, make-shift speakers had been placed by the mountain surface as well. Labba took her place on a small stage with a podium that partly faced the mountain face and partly faced the Morcellus people. Selba had accompanied Doctor Kechenova and was testing the visual and audio feed from Tabelia.

"Testing, testing," Selba said. "Labba, can you see me? Can you hear me?"

"Both," Labba said.

"Excellent," Selba said. "Doctor Kechenova is ready to start."

"We are ready as well. Frieda could not be part of this meeting," Labba said while giving an evil stare to Claus.

"I tried," Claus said.

The crowd laughed at Claus. Labba and Selba laughed too. Selba then turned the meeting over to Doctor Kechenova.

"We can all use a good laugh," Kechenova said, who herself was coming to the end of her own laughter. "First let me say, welcome people of Morcellus and people of Tabelia to Luna, the new planet now orbiting the sun where Earth used to be. It is a bittersweet moment. Earth along with many of our friends and family are gone but not forgotten. Nor are we forgotten, for we have been given the opportunity for life, like spring after a bad winter. This has been the most brutal winter in the history of humankind. For those who have perished, and for the loss of our planet Earth, I ask that we observe a moment of silence."

Both crowds held silent for a minute.

"Thank you. There are many questions going around, so I would appreciate if everyone would hold them until we cover the basic items. First, where we are. We are on the moon. Earth's moon. It has undergone a transformation, become very much Earth like, with air, water, and climate. There are no animals here other than us humans. There is no native plant life, though the Morcellus people have already started planting. For those who choose to go onto the surface, I ask that they stay away from the old far side. This will require a bit of explaining. The moon is now called Luna. It is a planet and has taken over Earth's orbit. It has a day and night like Earth, and as many have noticed only takes 18 hours to complete a full day. The year has more days, being 487 days. There are 12 months with 40 or 41 days. I know this is getting technical. You'll receive booklets after the meeting covering these topics so that you may review them at your leisure. What you must understand about Luna is this—not everywhere is the same. The old far side has an alien device buried deep in the ground that emits beyton rays. These rays are to be avoided, as we do not fully understand their harmful effects. For a Carinian like Labba, it's instant death. For humans, sterility is a known factor. Also, the beyton rays destroy sensitive electronic circuits. One last thing—the beyton rays attract carbon dioxide. We've detected a 15% level on the old far side. This is deadly to humans. The easy way to know you are going into the old far side is that the air will feel stuffy and bad. One of our first projects will be to erect a fence along the beginning of the old far side to warn people."

"The old near side is fully protected from beyton rays," Doctor Kechenova continued. "Carbon dioxide is negligible. But it has no water. Because of this, though it is safe to travel in the old near side, it isn't a good place for building a community."

"Between the old near and far sides is a ring," Doctor Kechenova said. "This ring is known as the lunar shock. It is safe from beyton rays, has water, and has a low enough carbon dioxide level to sustain human life. It is in this zone that we should first build our cities. Yes, we must build cities. But first let me explain something else. There are three communities of people here on Luna—those who came in Tabelia (the great Martacean creature who was herself a seamount on Earth), those who came in Morcellus (another great Martacean creature who himself was under the Arberella community in Antarctica), and Frieda's group. Tabelia and Morcellus are close to each other and both are fortunately in the lunar shock. Frieda's group is in a spacecraft called Novi 4 and is in the center of the old far side. We tried to get Frieda's group to be a part of this meeting but could not due to technical issues."

"Those of you in Tabelia are most comfortable living inside her," Kechenova continued. "This is fine for now. Tabelia will be able to sustain life for quite some time. Those of you in Morcellus are not so fortunate. Morcellus is deteriorating rapidly, and you who have traveled with him will need to build new communities as quickly as possible. Since you are all from Arberella, this should feel like creating a second Arberella. Food will be scarce. I ask Tabelians to help the Morcelluns with their food shortage until they can get on their feet."

"As for Frieda," Kechenova continued, "we do not know her future or the future of her group. They are isolated. We have made brief contact and learned they are able to survive for the moment. We will contact them again soon, but I must urge everyone here to avoid her group due to the dangers of going into the old far side."

Kechenova paused, took a sip of water, and then continued.

"I cannot stress enough the need to work together and safeguard our future. We are at a fragile moment in human history. Should a disaster befall us—be it moonquake, volcano, asteroid strike, or other calamity—all future human hope is lost. For this reason I also urge we settle as much land in the lunar shock as possible and as quickly as possible. This message is especially important for Tabelians. Tabelia is a wonderful home beyond all sacred worship, and we must protect her at all costs. But we must also guard her against attack. I don't mean from Morcelluns. There are evils beyond our two groups."

"One last thing," Kechenova said, wrapping up her speech. "Today is July forty-first, twelve-oh-twenty-two (July 41, 12022)."

Both groups started a murmur that grew louder and louder.

"What does it mean?" shouted one person.

"What is twelve-oh-twenty-two?" asked another.

"Thank you, Doctor Kechenova," Labba said. "People of the lunar shock, I will clarify the doctor's last statement. While we were in transition from Earth to Luna, alien forces from the Veigon and PRAAD caused a time distortion, slowing time for us to a miniscule rate. Because of that, we have jumped ahead in time almost ten thousand years. The good news is that this time distortion has had no other ill effects. For astronomers, the position of the stars will look different, but that's all. Also, we will be imposing temporary martial law. Doctor Kechenova and Selba will run Tabelia while Argo and I run Morcellus. We will work with others to establish democracies and elect our next leaders. First, and I urge this to everyone, we must safeguard our survival. Thank you for attending. Refreshments have been set outside for Morcelluns and in the Tree of Memories for Tabelians, though all are welcome to either place. Let's get to know one another. Lunar Peace!"

"Lunar Peace!" Kechenova and Selba replied, as did some in attendance, as apparently this was a new motto going around.

The people went for refreshments and chatted amongst themselves. Morcelluns stayed outside, but some ventured to Tabelia and invited Tabelians outside. Those Tabelians who ventured outside removed their glasses and saw sunlight for the first time in their lives. They squinted and peered around, but all in all many friendships were made that day. While Morcelluns showed the beauty and freedom of the outdoors, Tabelians showed Morcelluns the food and hospitality of Tabelia.

"It seems like such a paradise," Claus said after catching up to Labba and Argo. "I hope it lasts."

"It is a big hope," Argo said. "We are vulnerable to exploitation by overly zealous people. They would invent a cause to assume power."

"Argo is right," Labba said. "We must set up a democracy quickly before a dictatorship ascends to the throne. Which brings up a subject I left out of the meeting. And it's about you, Claus."

"Me? You mean my physical exam?" Claus asked.

"More than that," Labba said. "But let's give you your physical, and I'll explain in more detail."

"Speaking of democracy, I must hold the first political meeting," Argo said.

"Politics, yuck," Claus said. "I had hoped we could be rid of it."

"Even in Arberella, we had some law," Argo said. "I'll have to get the word out. Contact people. Could take a while."

"Take all the time you need," Labba said. "I'll catch up to you later."

The two kissed, and Argo went off to gather other leaders.

"We should take you inside Tabelia. Leni's medical office is still there, from what I've heard."

"Leni. Is there some way we could restore him?" Claus asked.

"Sure," Labba said. "Just after we set up the new society, set up government, a military, deal with Frieda, create farms and crops, create animals from nothing, and set up ministries to marry couples and heal the sick. Oh, and you of course know where Leni is, right?"

"Okay, okay, I get the point. No, I don't know where he is anymore. I know where he used to be—in the old PRAAD chamber. Who knows where that is now," Claus said.

"Then let's get your physical going," Labba said. "I can space-jump us over, or you can sneeze us over."

Claus laughed.

"If only a sneeze could set the universe aright," Claus said.

"Well it will save me a space-jump. I'm still healing from that nasty shock from Aftova. We need to deal with that too," Labba said. "Let's do piggyback ride."

"Are you sure Argo won't be jealous?" Claus asked.

"Of course not," Labba said.

Labba climbed atop Claus's back. He sneezed, and Claus jumped the two over to Tabelia in a single bound. He performed a soft landing, and Labba dismounted.

"Yes!" Labba celebrated.

"What?"

"I'm sorry, Claus, but I couldn't resist. Lanietta bragged incessantly about you being her pet. I pretended you were a horse, or perhaps even a Pegasus-style horse, and so you were my pet. I hope you don't mind."

"I would have before Earth was destroyed, but it reminds me of Lanietta, so

I welcome it," Claus said. "I wish I could give her a piggyback ride."

Labba smiled.

"Let's go inside," Labba said.

With Tabelia beached on lunar soil, a new entrance had emerged different from that when as a seamount. Several sets of steps allowed people in and out, as if going into or emerging from a subway. The two dodged many excited Tabelians and Morcelluns until they reached Leni's old medical center.

"Fortunately, the devices in Tabelia still work," Labba said. "But I don't know for how long. Ethereal forces are not known for being stable."

Labba placed a cupped helmet atop Claus's head. Readings came back quickly.

"You will not die," Labba said. "You do not feed on beyton rays. You will need food and water soon like the others here. In fact, you should feel hungry."

"I do," Claus said.

"Good," Labba said. "Claus, there's a sure-fire way to know if you are immortal like Frieda. Hold your breath. If you can hold it for, say, twenty minutes, or if you forget to breathe even, that means you don't need air to live. Exhale completely, and then stop breathing. That's quicker than taking a deep breath."

Claus did so, and the urge to breathe overtook him quickly. He gasped for air.

"Good. You'll die later," Labba laughed.

"Somehow that doesn't sound comforting," Claus said.

"You're mortal like the others here. And I know why. First, time of exposure. The beyton rays didn't have much of a chance to take hold of you. Second, Aftova protected you. However, the beyton rays did make you sterile. You cannot have children with any women here in the lunar shock."

"That was never an idea anyway," Claus said. "The women who had any meaning to me are unavailable."

"One should never count out the future," Labba said. "Now for the last test. Let's confirm if Frieda really has Rigefa.

For this I'll have to interface slightly with the equipment. Don't worry, I'll be ethereally insulated."

Labba hit a few buttons then stuck her ethereal hand into the console.

"She doesn't have it," Labba said.

"I thought you said she does," Claus said.

"It's embedded in Novi 4," Labba said. "The Anferrumnum shot it up into the ship. That's what caused it to crash. The Anferrumnum, like the invisible hand of evil, feels the need to use life-forms yet again. It sensed Novi 4 and the humans on board. It's using them. But it's limited, Claus. It can't create life. That's the Veigon's job. All it can do is grow pure forms—that of crystalline."

"That doesn't sound so bad," Claus said. "At least it's limited to the ship."

"It gets worse," Labba said.

"You can read all that from Aftova?" Claus asked.

"Yes. Because you have *two* Greylingers in Aftova now," Labba said.

"I thought you only put one in there," Claus said.

"I did. But you picked up a second one from the archway. And it's blue," Labba said.

"Is there such a thing?"

"There is now," Labba said. "Oh this is bad news. Bad news! There's never been a blue Greylinger before. But it's contained, Claus, in a little ethereal box. So is your yellow Greylinger. Both are in little boxes and form a flip-flop."

"Are you saying a sandal is stuck in my upper palate?" Claus asked.

"Not that kind of flip-flop. A digital flip-flop. Frieda and her group have created the beginnings of an ethereal computer," Labba said.

"What? You Carinians had computers in the ether?" Claus asked.

"No, we didn't. Never!" Labba said. "Everything in the ether is analog. And I mean everything! Love, hate, conquest, capitulation—it's all analog. There's no such thing as an eethi computer. Until now. Claus, this has serious ramifications. Long have the Carinians sought to deal with the Greylingers. We only ever tried dumping them into planetary iron cores. We never dreamed to think of containing them in computer circuits. But apparently Frieda has found a way."

"How far can this go?" Claus asked. "I mean, computer technology progresses by increasing the number of transistors per size of semiconductor wafer."

"She has the entire ether to expand. There is no limit," Labba said.

"If I understand you right, this could be worse than Libriota and everything the Bleuhs have ever done combined," Claus said.

"It is," Labba said.

"Are we in danger? I mean, we humans are pretty much stuck in corporeal form," Claus said.

"Your ethereal spirits are bound so tightly to your corporeal forms that you don't realize you have ethereal spirits from day to day. But you'll know when you lose your eethi self. You'll feel totally flat and lifeless. Claus, she might digitize these ethereal spirits. She could digitize me!"

"How do we stop it?" Claus asked. "Here I was just getting into this new paradise thing in the lunar shock, and now the ether is at stake."

"I don't know, Claus. I must study this more," Labba said. "But one thing is for certain. We can't keep all our eggs in the same basket, to borrow one of your expressions. We'll have to do research independently."

"Frieda and her group know about us in the lunar shock," Claus said.

"Some of us will have to leave," Labba said.

"You mean me, right?" Claus asked.

"I'm afraid so," Labba said. "Possibly me too. Besides Novi 4 and those aboard, you and I have the only special connections to the ether—me because I'm a Gren, and you because of Aftova. You can't visit Frieda again. The risk of losing you is too great. You'll have to go to the old near side. You'll be completely protected from Frieda and Rigefa."

"It also means surviving in a desert, and all alone, unless you come with me. You're nodding no already. Eggs in the basket again," Claus said.

"Exactly. Sigh. I want to stay with Argo. He'll follow me in the desert if I ask him. He's not eethi, so there's no risk there. You'd go one way, he and I would go another. But he has his heart set on building a new Arberella. What a damper! And we never got around to getting married. I was hoping the new couples on Luna could have a special group marriage ceremony. I wish Lanietta were here."

"So do I," Claus said. "She would... Labba, I know what she'd do."

"I know what you're thinking," Labba said. "The answer is no."

"If she could do it, I can," Claus said.

"She wasn't entirely successful," Labba said. "Luna has a partial Anrega in its core and the Anferrumnum. Your suicide will not destroy them. It might not even wipe out Frieda. Matter of fact, it could give her more strength. Blowing up an eethi flip-flop would be like going from vacuum tubes to diamond computers. So no, I won't help you act as a suicide bomber. And now as I think of it, I probably shouldn't go to the old near side either. That's too passive. I need to learn more and try to subvert Frieda in different ways. We'll attack this from two angles, Claus, from two flanks."

"Alone again!" Claus lamented. "The entire lunar near side all to me!"

"I'll resynchronize Aftova with me. We'll be able to communicate. You won't be totally alone," Labba said.

"The last time you tried that, I was in the Anrega orb chamber with Lanietta, and it cut out," Claus said.

"It might cut out again. But there's no alternative. Not unless you have another idea," Labba said.

"What about a radio?" Claus asked.

"It would need power. We could give you one, but it would have a plain battery. Maybe I could throw in a solar cell. But be aware that radio waves can be intercepted by others. Luna will block it from Frieda receiving it, at least at first. No telling what she'll be able to receive once she digitizes the ether."

"Then the link between Aftova and you could also be intercepted. She could digitize that too," Claus said.

"Good point," Labba said.

"It's really not good at all," Claus said. "And I'm tired of always having to figure out something."

"Welcome to the ether," Labba said. "It's infinitely more complex than corporeal life."

"What if you space-jump to me?" Claus asked.

"That would leave a signature in the ether," Labba said. "What if you sneeze back? No, that would also leave a signature in the ether."

"Why can't the ether just go away?" Claus asked in frustration.

"Oh, never ask for such a thing!" Labba said. "Claus, I'll take this up with Irina. But I'm sure she'd agree that you should leave immediately. I'll make up an excuse for you. The radio idea seems best for now. At least beyton rays can't reach that far and destroy the circuitry. You know, maybe Irina can fit a thorium battery in it. That would keep it going."

Labba hit a button and got a message to Kechenova. The doctor immediately rushed to the medical center and had a backpack in hand.

"Here," Kechenova said as she passed the backpack to Claus. "The thorium-powered radio is inside. It's set for spread-spectrum with encryption, though I don't think you'll need it. Still, can't be too careful. Also there's a canteen and food pill dispenser. The canteen has a built-in water condenser for pulling water from the air. However, I could not figure out a way to pull food from the air. Use the food pills sparingly. You will find no food on the near side, but we will create outposts toward the near side with supplies. I suggest you visit them often."

"You're incredible, Doctor," Claus said.

"Claus must leave now," Labba said to Kechenova. "I'll explain everything after he leaves."

"Of course," Kechenova said.

"May I see Clover before I leave? I haven't had a chance you know," Claus said.

"Of course," Labba said.

Claus threw the backpack over his shoulder, and the three went to the morgue where Clover was in stasis. Labba hit a button, and what looked like a human filing cabinet opened up with Clover lying in it.

"She looks so peaceful," Claus said.

"She was in love with you, you know," Labba said.

"I know. She spoke of keeping a candle in the window for me. Poor girl!"

Claus started to cry.

"Other people could die too," Labba said. "We'll keep them here until we can decide what to do with them."

"Their relatives would visit them periodically, hoping for a magic cure," Kechenova said.

"Is there one?" Claus asked. "Can Clover be brought back to life?"

"No," Labba said. "We'll move her to Morcellus. See if that helps."

"And if it doesn't?" Claus said.

"Other options might have to present themselves," Labba said.

"You mean you might bury her or these others on the moon, I mean on Luna?" Claus asked.

"That's a possibility," Kechenova said. "As people live and die here naturally, they will tend to follow the funeral procedure they established on Earth. Burial on land, at sea, or cremation remain distinct possibilities. We'll see how social rules evolve."

"A person's remains decided by social rules. Just doesn't seem right," Claus said. "A total loss of dignity."

"There is no dignity in death," Kechenova said.

"But there is in life," Labba said. "Live on the near side, Claus. Live for today and tomorrow. The day ends sooner but the year is long."

Claus nodded his head.

"You'll give her a dignified burial when the time comes?" Claus asked.

"I promise," Labba said.

"So do I," Kechenova said.

"Thank you," Claus said.

With that, Claus was ready to go. The three went up to the surface but through an exit unused by the others. In this way, Claus was ready to enter the old lunar near side without an audience. Shadows grew long, and nightfall was nearly on them.

"Do you have a flashlight in this backpack?" Claus asked.

"Look and see," Kechenova said.

Claus opened the backpack and found a flashlight.

"Thorium powered?" Claus asked.

"Of course. It's also your radio. Don't lose it," Kechenova said.

"Thank you. I hope to see you two again," Claus said. "Goodbye."

"Goodbye," Kechenova and Labba said as they waved their hands in farewell.

Chapter 101: The Old Near Side

Claus headed for the old near side. He had started out late in the day, however, and shadows lengthened quickly. He walked the first little bit, but already he was tired. He opened the backpack and discovered a super-portable lean-to with two telescoping poles, thin string like downrigger line, and thin but strong stakes. He set up the lean-to and was pleased at how much space it covered.

"But do I really need it?" Claus laughed. "Everything is so dry here."

Claus also found a super-slim roll. He unrolled it, found a device the size of a quarter, pressed a button, and the device pumped air into the roll, creating an inflatable sleeping bag.

"Doctor Kechenova is amazing," Claus said. "Now if only I could make a campfire. No, there's no wood to burn. Very strange. I'll have to make do with the flashlight."

Claus used his flashlight to look around. He half expected to see coyotes or sidewinders, but there was nothing. Every so often, he thought he saw a humanoid shape in the corner of his eye.

"Lanietta? Is that you?" Claus called. "No, nothing. I'm seeing things. I guess this is what happens when someone close dies. You see them where you'd expect them to be. I'd better turn on the radio. Get my mind off things."

Claus kept the flashlight on but shined it on the lean-to. He turned on the radio and to his surprise picked up a broadcast.

"This is Selba coming to you live from Radio Tabelia," Selba's voice said. "By popular request, I have the talented Latin singer, Brioshlyn."

A round of applause came through the radio.

"This love song is for all you lonely men out there," Brioshlyn said, "so that you'll know you're not alone."

She then sang a 1940s-style blues song with a melancholy tone. Claus rested on his sleeping bag and thought back to that 1950s home where Lanietta pretended to be his wife.

"Such a simpler time," Claus said to himself. "Less complicated. One could just turn on the radio and listen...listen...listen..."

Claus fell asleep.

When Claus awoke, the sun was already directly overhead. The radio had blown over and turned itself off as a safeguard.

"I slept till noon," Claus said. "This will take getting used to. Can't get as much done in a lunar day. Perhaps I'll sleep less."

Again Claus thought he saw Lanietta in the corner of his eye, and again he turned to look.

"Lanietta?" Claus called. "No, not there. How much longer will this last? Will I imagine seeing her the rest of my life? The radio. I'll keep it on. Labba never mentioned I could use it to receive broadcasts. I thought it was just a two-way radio."

Claus took a food pill and drank from the canteen before putting away the lean-to and sleeping bag. He was just about ready to head deeper into the near side when dark clouds rolled in.

"Oh, rain," Claus said. "Didn't think I'd see it here. And I've just put away the lean-to. Maybe I can get it out."

Before Claus could get it out, the rain came down hard. But Claus did not get wet.

"Huh?" he pondered.

Claus looked up in the sky, and the rain flowed down first vertically then gradually changed direction such that just above Claus's head, it flowed horizontally toward the lunar shock. Claus jumped up to dip his canteen into the rain, but it responded by flowing a little higher and higher and thus beyond his reach.

"I've never seen rain do that," Claus said. "I bet there's a weird draft from the beyton rays that's causing this."

Claus wanted to get wet. With the backpack secured over his shoulders, he tapped his upper palate to activate Aftova. He sneezed twice in rapid succession. The first sneeze caused him to jump up twice—once to the left then a hundred and eighty degrees to the right. The second sneeze caused him to jump forward much as he had done to visit Frieda. The height of the jump took him into the rain, and he got a little wet, but the rain made every effort to move out of his way.

"Could Aftova be causing this too? I must have Labba or Doctor Kechenova figure this out," Claus said.

Claus jumped past the rain storm and reached the center of the old near side. He set up his lean-to for the upcoming night, but turning on the radio made him realize that its range was limited. Not only could he not receive Selba's broadcast, but he could not reach Labba.

"Well what good is this radio?" Claus asked.

Claus took another food pill and drank from the canteen. He set it out to gather water and fiddled with the radio. To his surprise, it did pick up one station—the old WWV shortwave broadcast for time synchronization. But it had Selba's voice instead of a male voice.

"Shortwave," Claus said. "Well why aren't the other broadcasts in shortwave? That's another thing I'll have to bring up. Let's see if the radio station matches the clock on the radio device."

Claus stared at his radio device, and it read August 1, 12022, 13:45.

"The sun is setting at 13:45," Claus said. "Seems odd. Must get used to these shorter days."

Again he thought he saw Lanietta.

"Get out of my head!" Claus said. "There is absolutely nothing out here to look at. Oh sure there are craters and boulders. But nothing is moving. No tree branches to sway, no birds to fly, not even a river to watch. What would Grandma Broc say? Where are the stepping stones in the brook?"

Claus played with several small stones. He moved them in the lunar soil. He clacked them together. He then threw them to see how they'd land.

"All the wars and conflicts of humanity, and I'm throwing stones on the old moon," Claus said. "There's got to be more than this. Even Aftova only lets me jump, and that gets boring after a while. Wish I had some jumping beans."

Claus kicked up lunar dust. It created a plume and made him sneeze. Aftova activated agents for the yellow and blue Greylingers. Claus felt and saw yellow and blue ethereal threads running from his two upper front teeth. They intertwined like rope but then reached two pebbles and like little fingers clacked the pebbles together. The threads retracted, and Claus stood motionless in shock at what he'd just seen.

"Wait a moment," he said. "Did I do that?"

Claus kicked up lunar dust, he sneezed, the yellow and blue ethereal threads returned, and they clacked again. Claus felt an itching sensation in his upper palate, and he drew his tongue across this sensation. As he did so, the ethereal threads changed their movement, and he realized he could control them.

"It's like I'm a rabbit with super long incisors," he said.

Claus placed his index fingers and thumbs to his upper front teeth as if adjusting dentures, but in fact this also influenced movement of the ethereal threads. Claus had now figured out how to fully control the threads—controlling their length, position, and action.

"This is uncanny," he said. "I look like an old man adjusting his teeth, yet I can make stones clack. Wonder if I can make them fly."

Claus adjusted the ethereal lines with his tongue and fingers. The threads picked up larger stones and threw them in various directions, including two at Claus! He ducked to avoid being hit.

"Could I build a shelter out of stone? Or even dig with these stones? I'd have to create a stone-age technology. I should dig, but I need a scoop. Perhaps I can make one by cracking two rocks together."

That was Claus's plan—crack two rocks together in hopes of splitting them apart and creating a spade-like object. He used both ethereal threads to lift a boulder high up, then he sent the boulder crashing down atop a rock structure. The cracking sound was so loud and ear-piercing that it knocked him out. He fell to the ground, unconscious.

When Claus came to, it was night. Fortunately for him, he still had his backpack on. Thinking he'd only lost several hours, he pulled out his flashlight/radio and checked the date/time display. It read: August 8, 12022, 17:58:03.

"I've been unconscious for a week!" he said. "Ow, does my head hurt. And what's that loud ringing sound?"

Claus pointed the flashlight in several directions, but no one else was around. Nor were there any devices or anything that could make the sound he was hearing. He found the boulder he'd slapped down, and it wasn't even split in half. Just abrasion marks where it had hit the other rock surface.

"That was really stupid. I've damaged my hearing," Claus said. "I hope I can recover. Tinnitus. How can anyone survive this? It just doesn't go away. I'm terribly hungry. And thirsty! It's a wonder I haven't died of dehydration!"

Claus swallowed a food pill but slurped down nearly the entire contents of his canteen.

"Oh, I hope the water condensation unit can replenish my canteen. I might not make it," he said. "Will that ringing ever go away? Maybe I can massage my ears with something from the radio."

Claus turned on the radio and listened to the WWV-like time broadcast. He watched his clock go from August 8, 12022, 17:59:59 to August 9, 12022, 00:00:00, but the WWV station announced

the time going from 03:59 to 04:00 on August 9.

"There's no eighteen o'clock," Claus said. "It's midnight, and the time is oh, oh-oh. Or is it? The radio station says it's four hours later. Oh, because I'm in a different time zone. How confusing."

Claus searched for other shortwave radio stations and came across one.

"Good morning, Luna! This is Shara coming to you from Radio Morcellus 1949 at four o'clock in the morning. Wake up like you're 19 and dance the night away like it's 1949. We're 19 and 49 meters on the shortwave dial."

Then a jingle sang, "*Mor-cell-us in the mor-ning!*"

"Make coffee and scramble some eggs, 'cause we've got lots of news to cover today," Shara continued. "It's August the 9th, 12022. Now if you didn't make breakfast yet, Farmer Baruuk has opened his farm to customers. Come one, come all, Baruuk will serve 'em all. Just one credit per dozen eggs, two for a kilogram of coffee, and three for a side of ham. That's right. Baruuk is in the farming business. Bring your credits, and he'll serve you right up. *Mor-cell-us in the mor-ning!*"

"Breakfast? A farm? Credits?" Claus wondered.

"Yes, everyone was issued three-thousand credits last week as part of the New Economy. But don't spend it too quickly, or else you'll need a job! Yes, the Job Board is open. See Argo in Morcellus for what you can do to earn more credits! We have new farms opening up everywhere, and we need your help. You! But bring your raincoat. Today's high will be twenty-eight degrees Celsius but cooling off around noon when a thunderstorm rolls in. Expect three to five centimeters of rain," Shara continued. "And now a word from our sponsor."

"Advertising?" Claus wondered.

"It's time we have a change in government," the voice of White Hair sounded.

"What change? It just started, apparently," Claus said.

"You've been told to work together by my opponent, Doctor Kechenova. But she speaks only for the short term. What about those of us over sixty-five? Seventy? Where do we fit in? My opponent has no such plan for us. We are to sit around and die, if you elect her. Vote for me, White Hair, and I'll guarantee that every elderly person will live forever. In my three-step plan, we will make a treaty with Frieda on the central far side to secure our immortality. Do not let the lunar shock end your life. Live with me, White Hair, as we bring our society into the far side. Vote White Hair for Governor on August 38th."

"Wow!" Claus said.

"This is a paid political message by the Campaign to elect White Hair for Governor," the radio continued.

"Politics already?" Claus asked. "But she brings up an interesting point. I thought everyone would want to stay in the lunar shock, that Frieda and the far side would be too dangerous. But if a person is old and about to die, what's to lose by chancing immortality? I wonder how that will affect the younger people."

"We have Clara-Lees in Traffic," Shara said.

"This is Clara-Lees in the drone," an older woman's voice said. "We continue to see an outpouring of people from both Morcellus and Tabelia into new farms. The mid-crater viaduct is backed up to the new causeway ridge. If you have a boat, you can save ten minutes by crossing the causeway crater. This is Clara-Lees in the drone. *Mor-cell-us in the mor-ning!*"

"Thank you Clara-Lees. And now, beauty tips from Helen Seilen," Shara said.

"Do you have dark shadows in the morning? Itchy skin? Dry scalp and those horrible split ends? You need Seilen for Skin, an emulsion of the best embryonic healing proteins from Morcellus's own vault. Our chemists have mixed the right amount together with hydration and anti-microbial nutrients to give you full, shiny hair and supple skin. Erase those dark shadows under your eyes and reclaim your youth. And for mornings when you need to rush out, throw on a new face with Seilen's line of cosmetics."

"Mor-cell-us in the mor-ning!"

Claus turned off the radio.

"How could things have progressed so quickly? I've only been gone a week or so!" Claus said to himself. "I must go back and find out what's going on. Labba will tell me. Oh, but I'm still thirsty!"

Claus drank the rest of the canteen's water.

"Gone," Claus said, referring to his water supply. "This desert living is dangerous. I need someone to look after me. Next time could be my last. Or I could live forever with White Hair and her group. Sounds tempting. But why does it unsettle me? Ow!"

Claus's tinnitus kicked up, and it was worse than before. It was so bad that the damaged nerves in his ear carried their anomalous signals toward his upper palate and into Aftova. Aftova in turn triggered yellow and blue ethereal threads from the Greylingers and sent one each out his ears. The threads had a grand ol' time, rattling stones and scraping them across other stones as if competing against the tinnitus to maximize Claus's torture treatment.

"No, please stop. Stop!" he pleaded. "Lanietta, help me. La-ni-et-ta!"

Claus swatted at his ears to no avail. He then ran up to rocks and pressed them against his ears hoping that a pressure change could relieve his pain. That didn't work. Desperate, he progressively slapped the rocks against his ears harder and harder, but the ethereal threads fought him for the rocks, removed them from his hands, and clacked them together in various places above his head, to the front, right, behind, left, and so on. Claus tried jumping to catch the rocks and stop the ethereal threads, but like a game of keep-away, the ethereal threads just barely kept the rocks out of reach.

Claus was now all-out-desperate, and he jumped back toward the lunar shock and Morcellus with the hope Labba could help him. Strangely enough, he had wits enough to use his tongue against his upper palate and get help from Aftova to do the super-jumps. But the aural ethereal threads acted like tails, dragging and misdirecting his jumping efforts such that Claus ended up zig-zagging his way back. He was able to navigate by feeling the air—the carbon dioxide was totally absent at the middle of the old near side—and by the rain pattern, which continued to flow toward the lunar shock. He felt himself getting closer to the lunar shock, but he also felt himself numbing out from his senses, and he was convinced his life was all but ended—short of the relief he had hoped Labba could provide.

Chapter 102: Morcellus Transformed

Claus awoke, and he was in a baseball stadium. A blellow team played a yue team with the blellow team dressed in bled and brack and the yue team dressed in preen and gurkle. A blellow ball was pitched, and the yue hit the ball foul at Claus. He turned to avoid it, but it caught him in the right ear. A hive of angry bees exited his right ear and stung the people around him, clearing out half the stadium to his right. The inning ended, and the blellow team came to bat. The yue pitched the ball, the blellow struck it, and again it flew at Claus, he turned, and it caught him in the left ear. Now locusts exited his left ear and attacked the other half of the stadium. The umpire stopped the game, and players from the blellow and yue teams ran toward Claus, all wielding bats and ready to brain him. Claus looked for a way to escape.

"Help, help!" he cried.

A green, vague form grabbed him by the hair and pulled him upward and back. He exited a tree pair and found himself in Tabelia with Labba holding his hair. She released him and turned to Doctor Kechenova.

"That didn't work," Labba said.

"We might have to try another tree pair," Doctor Kechenova said.

"Wait!" Claus said. "I'm awake, or at least I'm aware. That was horrible. Please don't put me in another tree pair!"

"Welcome back, Claus," Doctor Kechenova said.

"How did I get here? This is Tabelia, right?" Claus asked.

"I found you, Claus," Labba said. "You had collapsed near one of our outposts. Aftova is a mess. I was trying to recalibrate it. What happened to you on the near side?"

Claus then explained his brief adventure.

"You're right, Claus. It's unsafe for you to go out alone," Kechenova said. "Tinnitus is not easily cured. There are certain forms that cure with surgery, but those are ones of pulsation, whooshing, or clicking in nature. Constant ringing of the ears still eludes the medical community."

"It does pulse. And whoosh," Claus said.

"Let's get you back to Leni's medical center," Labba said.

Kechenova and Labba took him back, but along the way, Claus noticed crowds of people leading or carrying animals of all kinds out toward a stairwell leading to the surface. He saw sheep, goats, cattle, horses, chickens, dogs, cats—the variety had no end.

"Where did the animals come from?" Claus asked.

"Kind of an involved story," Labba said. "Let's treat you first."

The three reached Leni's medical center. It was crowded with newborn babies.

"What is all this?" Claus asked.

"The future of humanity," Kechenova said.

"I...I guess I didn't realize things would happen so quickly," Claus said.

"Couples formed before they arrived on Luna," Kechenova said. "The babies had to be born somewhere."

"I guess I'm living in the past," Claus said.

"Let's get you to a treatment room," Kechenova said. "Fortunately I have some medical expertise."

Kechenova placed a head scanner over Claus.

"Yes, that would account for it," she said.

"What is it?" Claus asked.

"You have debris in your skull and in the back of your neck. There's internal bleeding and pressure. The tinnitus is in sync with your heart beat, right?" Kechenova asked.

"Yes, come to think of it," Claus said.

"The debris is affecting your arteries," Kechenova said. "You'll have to undergo surgery immediately. The risk of stroke is high otherwise. It's a wonder you've held out this long."

"I agree with you there," Claus said.

Claus was wheeled into an operating room. For this procedure he was put to sleep. When he awoke, he was in a small recovery room with an oxygen mask over his face and bandages over his head. Labba sat next to him.

"You're awake," she said. "Doctor Kechenova had other matters to attend. Things are very busy around here. How's your tinnitus?"

"Gone," Claus said.

"You're extremely fortunate," Labba said. "From what I've seen, most cases of tinnitus never go away and in fact can get worse."

"Did you have a hand in my recovery?" Claus said. "Aftova is very calm and contained. I think you did."

"You're right," Labba said. "Aftova is deeply connected with your nervous system, particularly with your senses. It's almost—"

"Innerviated?" Claus asked.

"Well, innervated," Labba said. "You're still thinking of Lanietta, aren't you?"

"How can you tell?"

"You kept repeating her name while unconscious, both when you were found and during surgery," Labba said.

"Am I that obvious?" Claus asked.

"I'm afraid you are," Labba said.

"It just doesn't make sense. She's done everything possible to torture me and cause mass misery," Claus said.

"And be your friend," Labba said.

"That can't be friendship," Claus said.

"You don't have to understand it," Labba said. "It just is."

"Is there any chance of finding her? I mean, for the sake of Carinian future... uh..." Claus stumbled.

"You don't have to cover for me or the Carinian race," Labba said. "I spend every free moment searching the cosmos for her.

So far there's no evidence she survived. Claus, when I went eethi with other Carinians still around, there was great hustle and bustle, like humans walking in a big city. If all inhabitants of New York or London suddenly disappeared, you'd know it. The sense of emptiness is overpowering. That's what the ether is like right now. Even the Greylingers are rapidly disappearing. There's little for them to feed on. I have yet to encounter another Carinian. At all. And I might never see one again. Your concern for her will not bring her back. Neither will mine. If you'll excuse me."

Labba went fully eethi and disappeared.

"Labba? I'm sorry. Labba?" Claus called.

He sighed.

"Well I've messed it up for another Carinian," Claus said to himself. "I was so wrapped up in Lanietta that I never got out of Labba what all she did in my recovery. She must have fixed up Aftova so it won't torture me with those Greylinger threads."

Claus sighed again.

"Nothing left for me here. Might as well go on a walk and clear my mind. Maybe I can find Shara or Selba and see what these new radio stations are like," Claus said.

Claus found his way out of Tabelia and to the surface. When he did reach the surface, he was amazed at the multiple building structures everywhere. He found himself in what looked like town after town from the Old West, with horse-drawn carriages, wagons, people riding horses directly, people on foot, and builders everywhere with sawing, hammering, and painting going on. There were no modern machines in sight, even though Claus had been treated with ultra-modern equipment. It was as if he'd gone back in time. There were even saloons. One thing was noticeably missing from this otherwise town of the Old West—firearms. Claus pretended he was in a gunfight and drew an imaginary weapon quickly.

"They don't work here," said a familiar voice.

"Selba!" Claus said. "I expected you to be at the radio station."

"My shift doesn't start until later," she said. "Shara covers the morning broadcast for Morcellus, and I cover the evening and night broadcast for Tabelia."

"I was just in Tabelia," Claus said. "I'd like to see Clover in Morcellus."

"This is Morcellus," Selba said as she pointed to the town.

"I don't understand. This isn't Morcellus," Claus said.

"Let's take a walk," she said.

"Look at all this!" Claus said. "I was only gone for a little while, but buildings are everywhere! And horses! Where did the horses come from? And these store signs. Morcellus Dentist, First Morcellus Bank, Worship of Morcellus Faith—how? Why?"

"You may have heard or may not have," Selba said. "But Morcellus the creature deteriorated after landing here. We knew he wouldn't last. We pulled out everything we could from him before he collapsed."

"Clover!" Claus said.

"Morcellus couldn't help her. She was moved back to Tabelia," Selba said. "She is still in stasis."

"Whew!"

"Morcellus was a Noah's Ark of biology. Those bricks, remember?"

"They were destroyed," Claus said.

"Most were. But some were spared. We moved them to Tabelia and discovered they contained embryonic representations of Earth life. We reanimated them in Tabelia, and, well, you've seen the steady stream of animals coming out," Selba said. "Claus, don't argue the ethics—it was an emergency situation. Either we reanimated them or lost them forever. There was no time for discussion."

"There are full-grown horses," Claus said. "From embryos?"

"The tree pairs helped us there," Selba said. "They can distort time. We accelerated the embryonic growth. It was needed for the community. Ever since the New Economy was created, people have been scrambling for money, real estate, possessions, and power."

"Like Earth all over again," Claus said.

"People got carried away," Selba said. "But I think I know why. It wasn't the regular Tabelians or Morcelluns who went crazy with the New Economy, it was the people we rescued from the far corners of Earth. Many of them had come from deplorable conditions, living in constant fear of the selenites. This new freedom was like brandy. They just couldn't get enough."

"Judging by the number of saloons, I'd have to agree," Claus said. "Fortunately there are no firearms. Did Kechenova mandate it?"

"Doctor Kechenova has largely been ignored in the New Economy," Selba said. "She pushed for more of a socialistic approach, help thy neighbor and give thought before taking action. These people do first and don't think until it's too late. But as to the firearms, there's a problem. Chemical reactions of that sort are too slow. I think it's the beyton rays. Although we don't directly receive them, we receive some sort of diffracted result of them."

"You sound like Doctor Kechenova," Claus said.

The two continued walking past store after store.

"She was the one who told me. I don't fully understand it. But something like dynamite or TNT does not explode, it gradually expands. The result is slow heat. The doctor says steam engines will come along soon and replace horses, maybe not entirely, but that will be the limit of technology on the surface. Microelectronics only work for a day before they corrode, but they last much longer in Tabelia. They don't work at all on the old far side. Let's take a carriage."

Selba hailed a cab and gave the driver two credits.

"Money," Claus said.

"Yes. You didn't get your cut yet, did you? Everyone got something. I suppose you're due," Selba said.

"Yeah, I'm due," Claus said sarcastically.

The carriage reached the end of town.

"This is it," she said. "Let's get out."

The two exited the carriage and looked around. Then Claus saw it—a depression in the barren soil. Trees and grass grew around the depression but not in it.

"That's all that's left of Morcellus. Nothing grows there. People have planted things everywhere and tried there too—nothing," Selba said. "How did the trees grow so fast? They were grown in Tabelia first. But you figured that out, didn't you?"

"I...am not sure," Claus said. "I guess that makes sense."

"See that antenna on the hill there? And that little building next to it? That's Radio Morcellus 1949. Shara's up there now," Selba said.

"I heard strange things from her broadcast," Claus said. "That White Hair was running for governor. Heard that all the way at the center of the old near side."

"That's impressive," Selba said.

"So it's Kechenova vs. White Hair for Governor," Claus said. "Where do people vote?"

"Oh the voting is over. White Hair won," Selba said.

"But that's to be on August 38th," Claus said.

"Yeah. That was three days ago. Today is August 41st," Selba said.

"What? I've lost more time?" Claus asked.

"Labba said you were unconscious for several weeks," Selba said. "No one thought you'd make it. But I'm glad you did. We folk from Arberella need to stick together."

"The strange thing is that I was a newcomer to Arberella. I was from a time five hundred years prior," Claus said.

"Arberella is ten thousand years in the past," Selba said. "Soon we'll forget it. I don't want to forget though. I was a newcomer too, remember? The selenites held Clover and me prisoner."

"I remember," Claus said.

"You know, Lanietta visited us when we were still on a selenite ship. They had her locked up with us. Isn't that strange? Then she escaped," Selba said.

"Lanietta could do things like that," Claus said. "And yes, I do miss her. When I was out there on the near side, I kept thinking I saw her. But she wasn't there."

Selba smiled.

"There's a lift here," Selba said. "Step on, and I'll take us to Shara."

The two stepped onto the lift. Selba hit a button, and it ascended.

"No horses pulling us up?" Claus asked.

"Oh no, the electricity works well here," Selba said. "There's a generator next to the broadcast building. Runs on ammonium perchlorate. At least that's what Doctor Kechenova said."

"That's an explosive," Claus said.

"It heats water that creates steam which drives a piston that turns a shaft which drives—"

"The generator," Claus said.

"Yes," Selba said. "See the steam coming out of that stack in the mountain? Shara has her own cloud maker."

Claus saw the steam. It was continuous as it left the stack but then broke apart into billowy clouds that floated away. The two reached the broadcast building and went inside.

"There's an electrical smell," Claus said. "Like a circuit is overloading."

"All vacuum tubes here," Selba said. "See?"

Selba opened a cabinet.

"I'm amazed at how quickly this has been put together," Claus said.

"Well, everything was already invented," Selba said. "Tabelia has excellent records of such devices. Just was a matter of fabrication. Yeah, inside Tabelia. But it's getting crowded in there and people want to be outside in a real environment, so the construction market has gone crazy."

The two walked into the broadcast room. Shara had on a headphone and had just placed an LP on a turntable for broadcast.

"It's okay," Shara said. "The microphone is off. This record will play for half an hour. Claus!"

Shara gave Claus a hug.

"I heard your broadcast the other day," Claus said. "About White Hair running for governor. And Helen Seilen's beauty tips."

Shara giggled.

"Did you know that Selba and I are competitors?" Shara said.

"The companies we work for are competitors," Selba said. "But we're still good friends."

Selba then gave a hug to Shara.

Without warning, four masked men stormed into the broadcast building. They activated switchblades and threatened the three if they didn't cooperate. The sound of the switchblades flicking out activated something in Aftova, but things happened so quickly that Claus had no time to think or realize what Aftova was doing, if anything. Two masked men held Claus and Selba against a wall while the leader forced Shara to the control room.

"Turn on the microphone," the leader ordered.

Shara shook with such anxiety that she was all thumbs.

"Turn it on!" he reiterated.

Shara stopped the turntable and flipped a switch for the microphone. A red light indicated it was in use. One of the other men also sat in the control room and looked at the control panel. He then pointed to the leader that he was on the air. The leader passed Shara to this other man, and the leader took to the microphone.

"This is Citizens for Lunar Shock Survival. As of now, all of Morcellus and Tabelia are under our control," the leader said. "As I speak, agents are descending on stores, banks, government offices, schools, and the streets as a display of the New Order. Do not attempt to resist. Punishment is swift and final."

Claus broke free from one of the men and went after the leader, but the men caught up and struck Claus on the skull. He

fell. The resulting audio of the skirmish was broadcast.

"Even now, an attempt was made to resist us. That attempt failed!" the leader said. "Our terms are clear. Go about your normal day-to-day business. Pay tribute to us as requested. But contact with the far side is forbidden. All activities will support and promote our rights and privileges in the lunar shock. As such, Governor White Hair is under arrest for treason against our sovereignty. She would sell us out to those who would see our humanity bleached away into mindless, thoughtless beings— deprived of the essentials of life—food, drink, a family, and a future. We will prevail. Look for our emblems on our patrols with CLSS. You will know they support us, the Citizens for Lunar Shock Survival. And watch for those opposed. They wear jewels and gems of all kinds. Force them to drink as proof of their humanity. Share your food with them and see if they eat. You will know when they refuse that they are not human and not with us! Point those opposed to your nearest patrol. Root them out! Prune the tree of its dead branches. We shall prevail. We shall prevail!"

The other masked man turned on a soundtrack with clapping. Claus's head spun with pain, and he could feel Aftova activating the yellow and blue Greylingers. They sent out invisible threads far into the ether, searching for help, anything to help Claus cope. The blue thread went out toward the old near side. It found Labba, wandering aimlessly by herself. The yellow thread headed deep into the old far side, and it connected with Frieda.

"Well hello, Claus," Frieda's voice said inside his head.

"Frieda," Claus replied in his mind.

"Powerful tools we have. You with Aftova, me with Rigefa. I found them all, of course. Keep Aftova if you like. Soon it won't matter. In a little bit of trouble there?"

"No, I'm just..." Claus stumbled.

"Just been attacked by a group of thugs. They want to keep things their way in the lunar shock, is that right?" Frieda continued. "And they have Governor White Hair as prisoner. Tsk, tsk. She and I were about to form diplomatic relations. I would help her group with adjustment to the far side, and she'd arrange for supplies to be delivered to Novi 4. I would ask you, but you're always preoccupied with things. I sense Lanietta is gone. One less thing to obsess about."

"She's not a thing," Claus said.

"Oh, she's human? Like us?" Frieda asked.

"You know what I mean," Claus said.

"You have a short memory. Forgot what her kind did to us in the Astroosa days. Caused us to lose contact with our family and friends on Earth," Frieda said. "Look at the mess she put us in. And you, always needing help. Like now."

"I do need help," Claus said. "This new group is so militant. They almost—"

"Slashed Shara's throat," Frieda said. "Friendly people, aren't they?"

"They call themselves Citizens for—"

"Lunar Shock Survival," Frieda finished. "CLSS for short. Or perhaps CLuSS. Maybe even Claus."

"Stop it," Claus said.

"Do you want my help or not?" Frieda asked.

"If I refuse?" Claus asked.

"It delays the inevitable," Frieda said. "We'll take over anyway. It's just a matter of how long before you cooperate."

"I'm tired of being kicked around like a dog," Claus said.

"She called you Clomper," Frieda said. "I have access to your thoughts, Claus. I'm learning about your treason against Astroosa and the mission."

"Is that what this is to you? Astroosa? The mission? That's long past," Claus said.

"No, Claus. We who are part of Astroosa are still around. Return to your roots. Redeem yourself," Frieda said. "Oh, I was rude to you before, but things were more stressful. Now things are better."

"I saw your form of *better*," Claus said.

"Good," Frieda said. "Want me to disable the thugs for you? That CLuSS group?"

"What? You? How?" Claus asked.

"You'll have to act as my proxy, of course. You *are* there, after all. Just relax and let Rigefa and Aftova dance ethereal threads around those rough-and-tumble men. Don't worry. They won't be killed."

"Why do I feel like I'm selling my soul to the devil?" Claus asked.

"Better hurry. Argo is rounding up a posse. Going to deal with this CLuSS group," Frieda said. "Should be entertaining."

Claus wanted to say something about checking with Labba first, but what if that could be used against Labba? His blue ethereal thread had now withdrawn from the old near side and stayed close to Claus, ready to act as an extended hand of Frieda while the yellow thread maintained Claus's link with Frieda. What should Claus do with the blue thread? Let it restrain the CLuSS group?

"Too late," Frieda said. "Argo and his group launched their attack. Three of his group are dead. Including him. Blood is on your hands now. What will Labba say?"

"Devil condemn you, Frieda," Claus said.

"You can't bring those lives back either. They're gone," Frieda said. "More will die. Soon. Unless you stop it. Unless *we* stop it."

Claus took a deep breath.

"They got another. Four dead now. They're threatening to kill Shara," Frieda said. "Look. See the leader? He's making the announcement on the radio for rebels to cease all hostilities or Shara dies. Selba will be next. Then you. Still want to wait for Labba?"

"Okay!" Claus said. "Do it!"

"Relax," she said.

Frieda giggled long and freely. Claus's blue ethereal thread was manipulated by Frieda, and it went first for the masked men in the broadcast booth. It went into their brains and severed strategic points. The men, once agile and aggressive, became dull. They stumbled around like old men, with jerky but limited limb movements, and a lack of direction or purpose. The left side of their faces sagged, they frequently lost their balance, and they dragged their left legs. They made gurgling sounds, as if struggling to stay afloat above their own saliva.

Shara screamed. Selba shook with anxiety and hugged Shara to calm the both of them down.

"Put music on the radio," Selba said. "Hurry!"

Shara was a mess and did her best, but she kept scratching the needle across a record. She signed off for the day and shut down the broadcast. Selba then took Shara to the lift, and Claus followed. With her mission complete, Frieda had released her grip on Claus, and he could walk around, though his head still hurt.

"At least my brain is intact," Claus said. "What treachery by Frieda. She never warned me of this. I lobotomized these people. Even the Carinians never stooped so low. Lanietta! Save me from this madness!"

Shara, Selba, and Claus went to town and saw the other CLuSS members acting like the ones in the broadcast building—loss of motor control, droopy left face, and dragging left leg. A line of people headed for Tabelia, and so it only seemed natural to go that way.

"The medical center," Selba said. "People are going to the medical center."

"Let's not go, please," Claus said.

"Why not?" Selba asked. "There may be injured. We must help."

But it was a sad sight in the medical center. Doctor Kechenova hovered over the dead people. And there was Argo.

"Shara, Selba, and Claus!" Doctor Kechenova said. "I'm so glad you're alive."

"Argo!" Shara screamed, and she rushed over to him.

"He's gone, I'm afraid," Kechenova said. "He's the last brother, too. Jarro's image was lost along with Lanietta's bricks during the transition to Luna. Charco of

course died in Arberella. Sharlamarian is alive, but she's in a state of shock. Oh poor, Shara. Give me a hug, dear."

Shara hugged Kechenova.

"I'll take care of her," Selba said, and she took Shara to a side station and gave her a sedative.

"Everything is happening so quickly," Doctor Kechenova said. "Too quickly. At first everyone worked together peacefully. Then the New Economy came along. I cautioned against it, but it did motivate people to build a society quickly. Good thing too, because Morcellus collapsed almost as quickly. So I held my tongue on that issue. But then the election came along. Naturally I thought I would win, but White Hair beat me on the premise that we form a liaison with Frieda and the far side. I thought that too dangerous, but I also thought we had time. I was wrong, Claus."

Kechenova took a shot of vodka, swallowed, and grimaced.

"You can't go blaming yourself for things," Claus said.

"I seriously underestimated the situation," Kechenova said. "The Arberellans and Tabelians had organized, structured societies with social mores and rules. Everyone in those societies knew what to expect and followed along. When we took on the other human communities, there was no time to integrate them socially into the others. And now we see the result. A free-for-all militant group intent on blocking White Hair's deal with Frieda. Who could blame them? The idea of immortality is tantalizing but at the cost of human feeling? Love and tenderness wiped away? Passion for life and a family eliminated? People felt caught between the hammer and anvil. So which way to choose? Claus? What is the matter?"

"I chose," Claus said. "I chose for White Hair."

"You did? I'm surprised," Kechenova said.

"I had a link with Frieda. She told me about Argo and the others getting killed. She...I...caused brain damage to the CLSS members," Claus said.

"I see," Kechenova said. "I don't know what to say. You did save lives but at the cost of others. It was a difficult thing, Claus, but this link with Frieda is troubling. No telling what power she is acquiring with her ethereal computer, and now apparently more with you."

"I don't support whatever evil Frieda is creating," Claus said. "I'm a pawn like everyone else."

"Not everyone is a pawn," Kechenova said. "Labba isn't."

"Where is she?" Claus said. "Have you seen her?"

"No," Kechenova said. "I thought you were the last to see her."

"I made her upset, and she disappeared. I think she took a walk on the near side," Claus said.

"She might still be there," Kechenova said. "We must find her. She must attend Argo's funeral."

"You don't have him in stasis?" Claus asked.

"He is in stasis, but not for long. White Hair's new decree is that the dead should be buried on Luna, as a symbol of permanence on this planet," Kechenova said.

"Doctor, I think I can find Labba," Claus said.

"Oh?"

"This alien stone in my upper palate, this Aftova stone, it has two Greylingers inside that like to send out ethereal threads—one yellow, and the other blue—corresponding to the color of the Greylinger searching. The yellow one tends to go toward the old far side, but the blue one tends to go toward the old near side. When I was in the broadcast tower, one of the CLuSS members struck me on the head, and the threads went out. The blue one went searching for anything on the old near side, but the yellow one got hold of Frieda. The blue one then returned."

"If you could send out the blue one again but inhibit the yellow one, we could find Labba," Kechenova said.

"That's my thinking, but I've had a hard time controlling these threads," Claus said.

"Ironically, Labba would be the most help there. And yet she is the one we are trying to find," Kechenova said. "I'll hook you up to the brain scanner and widen the field to include your sinuses and upper palate. Perhaps I can provide you feedback about what works and what doesn't so you can control Aftova."

"Let's try," Claus said. "The sooner we find her the better. I'll go mad without immediate help. Aftova is driving me crazy."

Kechenova hooked Claus up to a brain scanner and did as she said—she expanded the scanning range to include the sinuses and upper palate.

"How do you currently activate Aftova?" she asked.

"I touch it with my tongue, like this," Claus said.

Claus tapped it with his tongue.

"Keep tapping, no, slower. Slower. There. No, the yellow got through. You must tap three times, pause, tap two times, pause, three then two and so on. There, yes, now the yellow Greylinger is inhibited," Kechenova said.

An ethereal thread came out of Claus's front tooth.

"No, that won't work. That's for performing action," Kechenova said. "Stop. Relax. Now I'm going to strike an object. Simultaneously, I want you to tap two then three then two like before. It's important you start with two taps and not three. Three taps will send the thread through your tooth, but two taps along with the sharp sound will send it out your ear."

"This sounds disgusting," Claus said.

"Sorry, but it's necessary. I'll count down from three to zero and clap my hands as I begin to pronounce 'zero'. Watch and listen so you can sync up. Are you ready?" she asked.

"Ready," Claus said.

"Three, two, one, zero," she said as she clapped on "zero".

Claus tapped as instructed. The blue ethereal thread came out of his ear and headed for the old near side. It went high in the air and swept across the vast terrain.

"Nothing so far," Claus said.

"You're doing fine. The yellow Greylinger is in check while the blue thread is searching," Kechenova said. "The blue thread is covering area very quickly. Just a matter of seconds now, and...and... there, all surface area covered."

"But no Labba," Claus said. "How could she leave?"

"She didn't," Kechenova said. "Take the blue thread down toward the center of the near side. Sweep into the lunar soil."

"Into?"

"Yes."

"All right," Claus said. "Sweeping into...hey, look at that."

"She's six meters down," Kechenova said.

"I'm making contact," Claus said. "Labba, do you hear me? Labba?"

Labba's voice came through the panel next to Claus, and so Kechenova could hear and reply as well.

"Hi Claus. I see you found me," she replied.

"Labba, I'm sorry. I didn't mean to upset you. Please come back," Claus said. "Doctor Kechenova is here too. She helped me find you."

"Hello, Doctor," Labba said.

"Hello, Labba," Kechenova replied.

"Please?" Claus pleaded.

"I don't know," Labba said. "I...I just need some quiet time. This is the only place in the universe where the beyton rays are absolutely canceled out perfectly. No, you didn't upset me. I was already upset. Might as well tell you. Argo and I had a fight. He wants immortality. Joined up with White Hair's group. I told him it was dangerous, that immortality requires great awareness and responsibility. I asked him to wait. He wouldn't wait. So there we have it. Is he begging for my return?"

"He's no longer begging," Kechenova said.

"Well that's a good thing," Labba said.

"He's dead," Kechenova added.

There was a pause.

"Labba?" Claus called.

Labba started to cry.

"I never should have left him," she cried, but her voice turned to a mixture of sadness and anger. "Stupid Argo! Got himself into a mess then?"

"A new militant group known as the Citizens for Lunar Shock Survival or CLuSS launched a coup on our society," Kechenova said. "Argo led a group to defeat them. They killed Argo and three of his group. But the militants became immobilized."

Labba paused.

"I can read your thoughts through the thread, Claus. I'm sorry you were manipulated into lobotomizing them," Labba said. "That's the nature of the ether. Like any source of power, it can corrupt people if one is not careful. So Frieda is in control and using White Hair to rule the lunar shock. I can read more through Aftova, Claus, though you may not know it, and it is this—Frieda has established a firm link with the remnant PRAAD, and her ethereal computer project is progressing quickly. It is the ethereal computer that is allowing her to influence White Hair and pull others into the far side. In fact, they are already there. They had carbonic scrubbers made for them as part of their transition to the far side. Now it's complete. Others will follow into the life of immortality sameness. But not all. They are establishing a caste system based on age. The younger people will stay in the lunar shock until they either produce enough requisite offspring or are old enough, then they will join the others in the far side."

"It leaves me feeling cold," Claus said. "I'm tired of Frieda, the far side, and even the lunar shock. I want desperately to leave. But I can't. There's going to be a funeral service and burial for Argo, the other three who fell, and Clover. All are being buried on Luna. Can you at least attend that?"

"It's in the lunar shock, Labba," Kechenova said. "You'll be safe from beyton rays."

"I will attend," Labba said. "But that will be it for me. I'm returning to the near side."

"I'll return with you," Claus said.

"You'll need a doctor too," Kechenova said. "Or at least someone with a knack for technology."

"I welcome both your company," Labba said.

Chapter 103: A Luna Funeral

Labba returned. Dressed in black, and along with Kechenova and Claus who were also dressed in black, she visited Argo in Tabelia.

"He looks so peaceful," Labba said. "But he looks a little different."

"He had many injuries, Labba," Kechenova said. "They did a good job with him. Don't you think so, Claus?"

"The whole idea makes me sick," Claus said.

Claus took a hard look at Argo.

"Rest easy, my friend. You're a long ways from Arberella," Claus said.

Claus then saw Clover nearby. He walked over to her.

"She looks just as peaceful," he said. "And no. I don't want to know what job they did."

Kechenova was going to say something, but Labba nodded "no" with her head and an extended hand on Kechenova's arm.

"These other people. What choice did they have?" Claus asked himself.

"Oh they chose," Frieda's voice said inside Claus.

"What?" Claus said but aloud. "No they didn't."

"Claus?" Labba asked.

"Clover fought the selenites and lost," Frieda's voice said. "Argo fought for immortality and won. He received his prize—an ageless future. Behold the destination of ambition."

"You caused Argo's death sure as anything," Claus said.

"Frieda," Labba said to Kechenova's quizzical expression. "I'll try to stop the link."

Labba went over to Claus and touched him, but her hair suddenly turned into layers of yellow and blue, and she received an ethereal shock from Claus. Stunned, she fell backward but caught herself before falling. Her hair color returned to normal.

"A little surprise for Labba," Frieda said to Claus. "Don't let her try that again."

"You have no right to attack people like that, Frieda," Claus said.

"Frieda's doing," Labba said to Kechenova.

"Oh but she's not a people. She's an alien. We're the people, remember Claus? You must remember your heritage," Frieda said.

"It doesn't include attacking people. Break it off, Frieda. Break it off," Claus demanded.

"It's too late for that. You've already done my bidding. Remember CLuSS, Claus?" Frieda said. "But if you want out, I suppose it's possible. Just return Aftova to me, and all will be forgiven."

"Frieda said—" Claus started.

"I got the message through the ether," Labba said. "She wants Aftova. She'll kill you, you know. That's her form of *forgiveness.*"

Frieda now broadcast her voice through Claus's mouth.

"I take offense to that, Labba. A pity your Carinian background didn't train you with proper etiquette," Frieda said. "Perhaps you should be contained and added to the ethereal computer. Yes. Claus, add her."

"No," Claus said.

"That wasn't a request," Frieda said.

Claus felt an intense headache overwhelm him. It sent him to his knees with his hands covering his ears.

"Stop the noise. Stop the noise!" he cried.

Ethereal threads of yellow and blue pushed out from his ears and in between his fingers. They probed for and went after Labba to contain her. Simultaneously, Labba space-jumped away, and Kechenova touched Claus with a palm taser. Electrocuted, Claus fell to the ground, unconscious. The ethereal threads dissipated, and Labba returned.

"That was close," Kechenova said. "We have to get out of here now."

"No, wait," Labba said. "I have an idea."

Labba whispered into Kechenova's ear.

"It might work," Kechenova said. "I'll have to quickly pack everything. But if it fails, we might not get out of this alive."

"If it succeeds, we'll put an end to Frieda's new-found tyranny," Labba said.

"Very well," Kechenova said.

"Claus, get up," said a familiar voice.

Claus stood up and saw Baruuk.

"Came to pay my respects and saw you here," he said. "You don't want to be buried before your time. They're about to haul away the bodies. Good thing I came along to catch you first. Come with me. I have a good seat picked out for the ceremony."

"I was with...I...yeah, okay," Claus said.

Baruuk led Claus out of Tabelia and over to a stadium.

"I don't remember this here," Claus said.

"Built just recently," Baruuk said. "I donated quite a bit of lumber."

"From your farm?" Claus asked.

"I grow many things. Many things," Baruuk said.

Unbeknownst to Claus, Kechenova had rushed over to the Radio Morcellus 1949 broadcast building.

"Shara, will you be covering the funeral?" Doctor Kechenova asked.

"I want to," Shara said. "I mean, I want to cover it on location. But I'm stuck up here."

"I'll run the station for you," Kechenova said. "Go on over to the stadium and cover the funeral."

"You mean it?" Shara asked.

"Of course I do," Kechenova said.

"Thank you!" Shara said with a hug for Kechenova, and she left.

"Grey Cat to Saucy Cat. Grey Cat to Saucy Cat, do you read?" Kechenova called over a secure radio channel.

"Grey Cat, this is Saucy Cat. I read you loud and clear," Selba said from Radio Tabelia.

"Princess of the South is on the way to Fishbowl. Did the fox plant the vine?" Kechenova asked.

"Vine planted. Fox is ready for harvest," Selba said.

"Stand by," Kechenova said.

"Standing by."

Claus and Baruuk were seated in the first row.

"This is an excellent location," Claus said.

"Argo and I were friends. Oh I know I've shown bad behavior, but running a farm has changed me. Forced me to take on responsibility. Makes me right proud."

"That sounds great. I wish everyone else could be so lucky," Claus said.

"Lucky? Heck, all I had to do was cut that first board and pound that first nail," Baruuk said. "The rest took care of itself. Visit my farm after the ceremony. The wife and I will be happy to entertain you."

"Shara never said anything about marriage," Claus said. "Selba neither."

Baruuk laughed.

"I found a new wife after we landed on the moon, and after I started the farm. She's got good farmer blood, and she set me straight on a lot of things. Said I couldn't cut a board or pound a nail straight."

"I thought you said—" Claus started.

"Son, the secret of life is this—make sure a good woman watches you fail so she can set you aright. You'll be true after that with your work *and* with her," he said with a wink.

"I guess so," Claus said in surprise. "Hey, there's Shara!"

Shara stood on the field with a microphone not far from Claus.

"Shara!" Claus shouted, and he waved.

Shara turned, saw Claus, and waved back. A moment later, Governor White

Hair and her security team walked out onto the field and to a temporary center stage structure. The structure had a high pedestal for the governor, and she took her place there with a security person on each of her sides and security personnel around the stage. Claus could see Shara speaking into the microphone, but he was too far away to make out what she was saying.

A trumpet blew from a high balcony in the stadium seating. A train of caskets and people started and headed for the center stage. The caskets were closed, but they had names written on them—Clover, Argo, Avee-Akwa, Goel, and Sasha. They were carried out to the middle of the field, where a stage structure had been placed. On that stage were five tables, and upon those tables the caskets were placed. Claus half expected Doctor Kechenova to lead the procession, but instead it was White Hat, Husky, and Slimy.

"Avee-Akwa helped me get the animal farm started. He could break in a horse in no time flat. Nothing could throw him," Baruuk said. "So hard to see his name there. So hard to see all those names there."

"I know about Clover and Argo. Who are the others?" Claus asked.

"Goel was a spiritual man," Baruuk explained. "Attempted to defuse the situation with scripture and diplomacy. Sasha was an expert in martial arts and taught others her talent. Strangely enough, Goel and Sasha were good friends. They made a habit of teaching the other what they knew. Sasha would take scripture and set it to cadence to give Goel a workout. Kept Goel in shape it did. Goel read scripture to Sasha's group workout sessions to keep them interesting."

The funeral party had taken their seats on stage. Claus turned around to look for anyone else he knew, but the stadium was large and filled with many people.

"Oh I hope the others are here," Claus said.

Governor White Hair began to speak, praising the courage of the five for their efforts in preserving humanity. She went on to speak a bit about each of them. But Claus became distracted. A bird swooped down from overhead Claus and nearly clawed him.

"Go away, bird," Claus said.

The bird had a twinge of green, and it nipped at Claus's left ear.

"Ow!" Claus said.

"It's just a bird. Don't mind it," Baruuk said.

"Well this bird is getting aggressive," Claus said. "Ow! It just got my right ear."

"Shh," Baruuk said. "I'm trying to listen."

"I'll get you, you pesky bird!" Claus said.

Claus stood to swat at the bird, but he blocked the view of those behind him, and they complained, telling him to sit down.

"All right already," Claus said. "I'm sitting."

The bird flew away for a moment, and then it came back. It flew by Claus's left ear and cawed as loud as it could. Claus felt his ear ringing, but before he could react, the bird cawed in his right ear. It flittered and fluttered, cawing in one ear, the other, etc. Claus put his hands over his ears, but he could not stop his ears from ringing.

"Bird! Go away!" he cried out.

The stress on his ears activated Aftova which in turn activated the Greylingers. Yellow and blue ethereal threads came out and went into the air like tentacles, searching for something to get hold of. The yellow one shot over to Frieda on the far side while the blue one continued to search.

"Why Claus! Where's my invitation to the funeral?" Frieda said through the yellow thread.

"Is this your doing? Did you send this evil bird to torment me?" Claus replied silently to her.

"Evil bird? Come now. No animal life can survive my atmosphere. Except the human animal. But do not worry. White Hair has already provided a link to me. So your act of courtesy is unnecessary, though it is appreciated."

"I'm not thanking you," Claus said. "Get rid of the bird!"

"That bird *is* evil. It is not of my making or command. Send your blue ethereal thread after it," Frieda ordered.

"It isn't? Wait, what? No," Claus stammered. "I...who is that bird?"

The bird flew up into the air, then it changed shape into an eagle—the very same eagle that had flown in Arberella.

"Labba!" Claus said. "But why?"

"Compromise her brain!" Frieda ordered.

"But she's ethereal. They don't have—"

"Compromise her brain!" Frieda reiterated, and an anger grew in her voice.

Claus could no longer contain the ethereal blue thread. It went after Labba the eagle. She flew swiftly toward Radio Tabelia and around its antenna. The blue thread followed her but caught itself on the antenna.

"What?" Claus said. "The blue ethereal line can't go through the antenna? Maybe the radio waves are affecting it."

The blue ethereal thread extended, and so it continued its pursuit of Labba the eagle. Labba flew to the Radio Morcellus 1949 broadcast antenna and did the same thing. As before, the blue ethereal thread became caught on the antenna, but it extended itself and continued pursuit of Labba. Claus now had the blue ethereal thread wrapped around two antennas and still chasing Labba. She flew down inside Clover's casket, popped the casket lid up, and animated Clover.

"I am Clover. I shall live forever," Clover's body said (though Labba had forced it).

Labba did the same thing to the other caskets and respective deceased. And so now all five corpses were claiming they'd live forever and even sang a barbershop quintet song about the happy little goose being smarter than a moose and plumper than your caboose, just don't leave your belt too loose or fruit juice will let loose. The crowd was shocked, appalled, disgusted, mortified (and other adjectives I can't print here).

Frieda was particularly enraged and sent a great surge of ethereal energy down the yellow ethereal thread. It carried into Claus and turned him into an electrical fireball that electrically shocked those around and sent them flying away from Claus. Claus himself was paralyzed from the energy and could not move. But the ethereal energy carried on through into the blue thread, into the Radio Tabelia tower, into the Radio Morcellus 1949 tower, and terminated with a wildly flailing end that finally caught Labba's left leg. A bluish-white fireball of light seared her foot, and she cried out, but she carried the thread and wrapped it around White Hair several times before the thread burned off Labba's leg completely. She flew off toward Radio Tabelia. Then before anyone could do anything else, Kechenova gave the order to Selba.

"Operation Concord!"

Seeds of grape-blue energy rebounded off from White Hair and flowed into the blue ethereal thread, which met Frieda's ethereal energy at two points—the two radio towers. These towers then created two triangular fields of energy using themselves with White Hair as one triangle, and themselves with Frieda as the other. The net effect was that of great energy rings that started from the two towers and traveled quickly over land toward Frieda and her group in Novi 4. Frieda pulled energy from the remnant PRAAD to counter, but she was not prepared for such large attacks, and they hit her squarely in the head. Strangely enough, the collision caused damage to only her left side, and it seethed and boiled like hot parasites dancing in her flesh. Doctor Morrow doused Frieda with water and antiseptic while the others took measures to counter the attack.

It was Josh who quickly took those energy rings and redirected them back to the lunar shock. Radio Tabelia's antenna was broken in half, and it fell to the ground, crushing three people. Labba rushed over to lift the tower, and fortunately those who were crushed did not die but had to be given medical attention.

Kechenova was not so lucky. The redirected energy traveled clear down the antenna, through the control panel, and burned out her nervous system, including her brain. She gave out one moan of agony before she collapsed. She was near death, and Labba flew over to her aid.

"It was worth it, Labba," she said slowly. "Leave now with Claus. Go. Go!"

Kechenova passed away, with her flesh still smoldering from the attack. Labba flew over to Claus, picked him up with her talons, and flew him out of the lunar shock into the old near side.

Chapter 104: Labba Says Goodbye

Claus awoke when his old backpack landed on his face. He sat up and looked in time to see Labba the eagle flying off. She had just dropped it off for Claus.

"Labba!" Claus called.

She flew off. Claus was hungry, and he opened the backpack to find it was full of the same things as before with food pills and a canteen among other things.

"What the devil happened back there?" Claus said after forcing a food pill down with water. "Was that Labba's doing? Was Labba playing games with Frieda? What insanity is all this? And now I'm out here? Labba took me here. Why? No answers from Labba. She flew off instead. I should jump back to town and sort out things. I should get up and jump!"

Claus stood up, but his head swam with dizziness, and he fell to his knees. He dug out a portable chair from his backpack, opened it, and sat in it.

"What is wrong with me?" he wondered. "I feel like my head is full of razor blades."

Claus touched his upper palate, but it was swollen and tender. A sensation like angry ants stirred around his palate, but he quickly calmed himself, and the stirring abated.

"Ow," he said. "Don't want to start up the Greylingers. What a nasty thing. And what a nasty trick by Labba. Labba! I'm going to read her the riot act when I see her. *If* I see her."

Claus pulled out his radio clock and read it: September 37, 12022, 05:30.

"I lost more days? How? Have I been in a coma? And survived in this desert?"

Claus was about to pull out his lean-to and set it up when he turned around and saw something protruding above a rock formation. Then he realized something else—the lunar soil showed that someone had crawled from that rock formation to where he now was.

"I crawled over here? Must've been delirious," he said.

Throwing the backpack over his shoulder, Claus crawled to the rock formation. He reached it, crawled around it, and found that a full tent had been set up. Not just a tent, more like a camp with a tank of fresh water, stove, wash basin, and a fire pit. There was no fire at the moment, but ash remnants suggested a fire had been built. A cooking spit was over the fire, and there was evidence an animal had been cooked on it.

"What is this?" he asked himself. "Labba took care of me?"

To Claus's amazement, he found a cane. He took the cane and used it to stand upright. He was still dizzy, but the cane helped him keep his balance. He pulled himself into the tent and to his surprise saw photographs posted throughout the tent, photographs mostly of Claus but a few of Labba taking a photo of both of them. In every photograph, Claus was either unconscious or groggy. The photographs were labeled too, with captions starting with "Day 1" and continuing. The earlier days showed Claus with large swelling and bruising on his face, but as the day numbers increased, the swelling and bruising subsided.

"I was traumatized," Claus said aloud.

"Yes, you were," Labba said now entering the tent in her humanoid form. "I'm glad to see you're fully aware. I tried lots of things to bring you back. Then you crawled away from the camp last night for some odd reason, so I had the idea of dropping your backpack on you."

"It worked," Claus said. "You've been—"

"Nursing you back to health, yes," she said. "Have a seat, and I'll make you coffee."

Claus took a seat, and Labba returned with coffee.

"That was quick," Claus said. "Where are we?"

"On the old near side of Luna, in case you didn't notice," Labba said.

"I noticed the desert conditions, yes," Claus said. "What was the deal with the funeral? You were really a bird?"

"I'm sorry, Claus. Doctor Kechenova and I hatched a plan to deliver a decisive blow to Frieda and destroy her growing tyranny. We couldn't tell you because you'd inadvertently alert her."

"All that to defeat Frieda?" Claus asked.

"Her and the new power that was controlling her from the remnant PRAAD," Labba said. "You saw what the radio towers did."

"Yeah, I did," Claus said.

"The doctor hooked up special electromagnetic amplifiers to the towers to generate what we thought was the necessary energy to defeat Frieda."

"Did it work?" Claus asked.

"No," Labba said. "Frieda was damaged on her left side and rebuilt. Her left side is now a crystalline robot while the right is still human. She is active and works with White Hair in the multi-tiered control of people with Frieda at the top and the lunar shock people at the bottom."

"Where does that leave us? And Doctor Kechenova?" Claus asked.

"It leaves us outside Frieda's control. And unfortunately...unfortunately...it..."

Labba's voice broke, and she cried.

"It killed her, didn't it?" Claus asked.

Labba nodded yes. Claus struggled to stand so he could hug her, but she motioned for him to stay seated. She space-jumped away for a few minutes then came back.

"You came back. I'm glad," Claus said. "I don't know what to do next."

"The safest thing for us to do is stay here on the near side," Labba said.

"Us? You're staying too?" Claus asked. "Don't stay here on my account."

"Actually, you're staying here on my account," Labba said.

"I don't understand," Claus said.

"I can't go back to the lunar shock," Labba said.

"Doctor Kechenova, godspeed her soul, once said the beyton rays didn't extend to the lunar shock, that you'd be safe there," Claus said.

"Safe from beyton rays. Not safe from Frieda's growing ethereal reach. I tried to beat her, and I failed. Her power has rebounded. She needs people though to keep her power, as water is needed for plants to grow. Her range will not extend this far, at least not for a long time," Labba explained. "And as for you, you're not safe in the lunar shock either. She already manipulated you to her will. Torturous, I know."

"You do?"

"Yes. To keep you sane during your recovery, I had to link with Aftova to keep it from further tormenting you," Labba said.

"Thank you," Claus said.

"Don't thank me yet. You might not like what I have to say next," Labba said. "No, I won't say it. I must go. I've done enough already. Stay here and live, Claus. I'll be elsewhere on the near side."

Labba space-jumped away.

"Now what?" Claus said. "Is it too much to say again that I'm an island? Why must abandonment be the universal rule? Well, there's nothing left to do. I must jump back to the lunar shock. Find out things. But I'll be careful. Discreet. If I'm careful, I'll come to some purpose for my life. I'll go mad out here alone. Mad!"

Claus turned on the radio. Shara's radio show was in progress.

"Good. Radio Morcellus 1949 is working," Claus said. "I'll use the signal strength as a homing beacon."

Claus jumped toward the station. Once, twice, but on the third attempt, a great eagle intercepted him and tossed him back.

"What?" Claus said in surprise. "Labba, is that you? Stop it, Labba."

Claus tried jumping toward the Morcellus station again, but Labba repeated her interception of Claus in full eagle form.

"This is getting tiring. What is your game, Labba? You're acting strangely like Lanietta. Is this a Carinian expression of hatred? We've never had issues before. Why the attacks? Labba? Talk to me!" Claus called.

Claus gave up and jumped back to camp. But Labba didn't follow him.

"What a mystery these Carinians are!" Claus said. "I wish Lanietta were here to explain things. All right, Claus, we're going to try something very dangerous. Let's send out the blue thread for information. Just the blue thread. The doctor taught us that tapping sequence, remember? Let's use it."

Claus tapped his palate in sequences of two, three, and two. Nothing happened.

"Wait, she clapped. I'll clap," he said.

Claus clapped gently, first in front, then the left side, then the right. For him, he determined that the left side inhibited the yellow thread while encouraging the blue. He clapped and tapped and got the blue thread going. He kept the thread low to the lunar surface in hopes of being undetected. He was amazed at how far he could send the thread. In fact he was able to run it slightly underground. In doing so, he also had it go around Labba's ethereal trails and thus avoided any possibility of her finding it. By the time it reached the lunar shock and Morcellus, it had become quite stretched, weak, and faint. It would travel no farther, but Claus didn't need it to. He had it enter the broadcast building for Radio Morcellus 1949.

"Yes, she was here," he heard Shara say. "About two days ago."

"What did she say?" Selba's voice said.

"She said 'goodbye'. She'll visit the others secretly and bid them goodbye as well, including you," Shara said.

"As in for good? She's never coming back?" Selba asked.

"No. She says things went too far with her and Doctor Kechenova. Blames herself for the doctor's death," Shara said.

"That's not fair. None of us want...the... you know what I mean," Selba said.

"It's hard to speak freely. There are ears everywhere," Shara said. "She wouldn't tell me exactly where she would be. Said she didn't know herself, that she'd be on the move. But I figured it out. She's on the near side. It's the only safe place for her. She also said Claus is still alive."

"Good. Did she say where he was?" Selba asked.

"No. Said it was better if I didn't know. I told her I wanted to come with her," Shara said.

"I want to go with her too," Selba said.

"You know what she said? That I'm better off here. That I'm too young to go one way or another," Shara said. "What is that supposed to mean?"

"I think it means when you're older like White Hair, you'll decide if you want to be immortal like her or die in the desert. One way means going to the far side, the other the near side," Selba said.

"That can't be right. Die in the desert?" Shara asked.

"There's nothing out there. Nothing," Selba said. "But going to the far side means going through a conversion, like a living death. Stay here in the lunar shock, Shara. I'll keep you company. And find someone too. I'm looking."

"You are? Tell me!" Shara said.

Selba described several men she'd been dating, at which point Claus decided he'd heard enough.

"I'll check with Baruuk. See what he knows," Claus said.

Baruuk was busy with his farm, and he spoke little. Claus did pick up on conversation Baruuk's wife was having with another farmer's wife about Labba having paid the farm a visit to say goodbye.

"Labba's saying goodbye to everyone," Claus said to himself. "She's going to kill herself. Oh this can't be true. She's the last Carinian. The species will become extinct. I've got to stop her. I've got to find her and haul her into this camp. Tie her up with the blue ethereal thread, block her, whatever. I must do whatever I can to keep her alive so I'll have time to sort this out. Who knows? Maybe a Carinian did survive somewhere in the universe. We have the time. Why not use it?"

So Claus decided he would use the blue ethereal thread to find Labba and bring her back. He'd force her to stay, at least for a little while until he could ensure her safety.

"Here we go, Labba. This is for your own good," Claus said.

Claus thought about splitting the blue ethereal thread. Could he do it? It was something he didn't think possible, but he thought back to the stories of Libriota and Lanietta splitting. He placed both index fingers in his mouth on the left side of his upper palate and along with his tongue made the blue thread split. Now he could sweep all of the lunar near side.

And he did. He found Labba perched on a crater ridge as an eagle, staring off into nothingness.

"I have you now, Gren bird of prey," Claus said.

Claus threw the ethereal thread over her as one might lasso a horse. He reeled her in. She fought and flapped along the way in a raged frenzy, but he pulled her in nonetheless. When she reached camp, he stopped reeling her in, but he kept the line around her.

"What are you doing?" she yelled. "Have you gone completely mad? Untie me!"

"Not until you promise you won't kill yourself!" Claus demanded.

"You've gone lunar. A full lunatic! I saved you from death. And now you do this? You're healed, Claus. Now it's goodbye. Goodbye!" Labba yelled.

"I've never seen you like this. Full hatred and rage toward me. I haven't seen this since Lanietta was around," Claus said. "What is it with you Carinians? Do you befriend us inferiors then turn against us?"

"You men are all alike the universe over. Clueless to the end! Goodbye!"

She sent an ethereal shock down the blue thread. Claus recoiled, the blue thread dissolved, she turned to eagle form, and she flew off.

"I am completely befuddled. Totally and absolutely!" Claus exclaimed.

Chapter 105: A New Friendship

"Labba won't let me jump to the lunar shock," Claus said to himself. "But I can walk there. It will take time, and I'll have to camp out each night, but she did bring my backpack. I'll do it. I'll find Selba or someone to make sense of things. Clueless to the end. Indeed!"

Claus walked all the way from his position to Morcellus. It took him sixty days. When he neared Morcellus, he was careful and hid behind various rock formations to avoid detection. He reached the outskirts of town by nightfall and had to make a decision—should he seek out Selba or Shara? Shara had the morning program, so she'd be off shift. Selba would be at the Tabelia radio station. He could go there. But he needed a disguise. He was behind a saloon, and a man took a beautifully dressed woman behind that saloon with a bottle of liquor in hand.

"Could I steal his outfit? Use that as a disguise?" Claus wondered, but he spoke too loud.

"Who is that?" the man called back.

"Relax, doll. It's just us. Pay in advance though," she said.

"You didn't say anything about a peep show," he said. "I'm out of here!"

The man left.

"Go away, ghost. You just cost me a flip," the woman said.

"I'm sorry," Claus said. "But I need help."

"So you are a peep!" she said. "Pay in advance."

"I'm not here to buy anything," Claus said.

"Sorry, no credit, and no samples!" she said, and she started to walk off.

"Please. I need to see Selba," Claus said. "Is she working tonight?"

"This is my turf," the woman said. "But Selba is a good girl. Works in broadcasting. Until a week ago. She left mysteriously. Went missing. No one knows where she is. Say, who are you?"

"Just a peep looking for a free sample," Claus said to cover his identity and his purpose.

"I told you no free samples. Go away!" she said, and she left.

"I must find Shara," Claus said to himself. "I could use the blue ethereal thread to find her. Maybe. Would it give my position away to Frieda? It might. No, I best not take the chance."

Claus saw a carriage go by with official markings of Queen Sharlamarian. The carriage was slowed by gawkers and men trying to get free monetary handouts. Claus used this delay to follow it discreetly. The carriage reached the end of town and stopped at a saloon. Claus crept up to it, expecting Sharlamarian herself to get out, but she wasn't inside. Instead, it was just Yuri who got out. Yuri went inside the saloon for drink and fun. Claus crept up to the driver, who was hooded and heavily covered.

"Claus? Are you Claus?" the driver whispered in a deep voice.

"Shh," Claus whispered back. "I need to find Shara."

"She's at home. Asleep," the driver said. "She has the early morning program."

"This is an emergency. Can you take me to her?" Claus said.

"Yuri will be busy for many hours," the driver said. "He won't miss me. Climb aboard."

Claus climbed into the carriage. The driver took Claus to Sharlamarian's home which was also Shara's home. It was actually in a secluded area on the other side of Tabelia and certainly not part of the hustle and bustle of Morcellus. The driver parked and led Claus inside. The butler answered the door.

"It is late," the butler said.

"This is Claus," the driver said. "He knows Shara."

"You look a little old for Shara," the butler said.

"I'm not here for that," Claus said.

"Who is at the door?" Sharlamarian called as she approached. "Claus! Do come in for evening tea. I'm sorry you missed dinner. Bring cold cuts for Claus. I'm sure he's famished."

"Thank you very much," Claus said.

Claus entered and sat in the living room with Sharlamarian, who already had tea set out.

"Shara has gone to bed early. She has the morning show you know," Sharlamarian said.

"I actually came looking for Selba," Claus said.

"Selba?" Sharlamarian laughed. "She visits sometimes. But not tonight. She left town a number of days ago. Said it was important. Are you here to see Shara? Shara has spoken of you, but not like that. I've seen very little of you Claus since Arberella. Are you well?"

"I'm not sure," Claus said. "I suffered a head injury at the funeral."

"Yes, we saw what happened at the funeral," Sharlamarian said. "Well, you're welcome here anytime. Rest if you like. It's quiet. People are rowdy in Morcellus, but over here on the other side of Tabelia, people are more civil. Claus, what is troubling you?"

"I've been on the old near side," Claus said. "Recovering from the head injury. Been living in a tent. Labba helped me."

"Yes. Labba told me so. She was here a while back. Paid a goodbye call she did. Said she would never visit the lunar shock again," Sharlamarian said.

"There's something strange going on with her. She's expressed great anger toward me," Claus said. "And she said goodbye to me too. Has she shown anger toward you?"

"No. She is her generous, usual self, though I did notice she was more tired than usual," Sharlamarian said. "And there are other forces at work."

"What forces?" Claus asked. "What did she tell you?"

Sharlamarian smiled.

"She didn't tell me anything, at least not with any such words," Sharlamarian said.

"Do you know what she said to me?" Claus said. "She said this: 'You men are all alike the universe over. Clueless to the end!'"

Sharlamarian laughed. Hard. She nearly fell out of her chair. She laughed so hard that she awoke Shara, who came out into the living room in her pajamas with sleepy eyes and a teddy bear.

"What's so funny?" she said, barely awake. "Oh hello, Claus. Telling a joke?"

"A big one!" Sharlamarian said.

"Well what is it?" Shara asked.

Sharlamarian whispered into Shara's ear. Shara's eyes opened wide in surprise.

"Really!" she said, now fully awake. "Wow. Wow! Is that why Selba left?"

"Must be! And he has no idea!" Sharlamarian said.

Now Shara laughed, and Sharlamarian laughed with her.

"I'm glad everyone is so happy," Claus said. "No one will tell me anything. I'm an island as usual."

"I have this advice for you," Sharlamarian said. "Go back to your tent. And wait."

"And wait?" Claus asked.

"And wait," Sharlamarian said. "Time will reveal the answer."

"I'm more befuddled than I was before. Is there some female conspiracy that prevents men from knowing what's going on?" Claus asked.

"No conspiracy. Just magic," Sharlamarian said.

Claus had tea and cold cuts. Sharlamarian had his backpack re-provisioned with food pills and water. She shook his hand as a farewell, and Shara hugged him.

"Let me know when you're back in town," Shara said. "I'd like to have you on the show. An interview."

"I will," Claus said.

He left. The driver took Claus to the edge of the lunar shock.

"Do you understand women?" Claus asked.

The driver, who had been obscured by a hooded outfit, removed the hood.

"Yes, I do," she said, the driver being a woman who had feigned a man's voice all along.

Claus just shook his head as if to say, "I give up."

"Be safe!" she said with a chuckle.

"Thank you," he called back, and he left.

Claus spent only ten days walking away from the lunar shock, then he jumped the rest of the way back. He reached the tent, and it was as he left it—without Labba.

"And wait," he repeated to himself. "Well, I think tomorrow I'll use Aftova to build a structure. Try to do it without the ear-splitting cracking of boulders. That will keep me going until...until what?"

The night passed, Claus slept, and he awoke the next morning to a clear day as usual on the near side. The stores of fresh food were gone or spoiled, and so he resigned himself to a food pill. He was about to set work on creating a stone structure when he heard a sound, like a call.

"Is that a cat? A small goat?" he asked himself. "What is that sound?"

The sound grew closer. Claus froze in place, afraid of what kind of creature might attack him. He realized of all the things in the backpack and at the camp, he had no weapon.

"Stupid!" he muttered to himself. "My life is about to end here and now because I have no weapon."

He searched desperately for a make-shift weapon, and he settled for a ladle. He held the ladle up high, ready to strike the creature. The call came around a rock formation, and Claus was shocked at what he saw and what he heard.

"That's not a diaper," a female voice said.

Claus dropped the ladle in continued shock. It was Labba, and she held a baby in her arms.

"Your son needs changing," she said. "You might as well learn now."

"My son? My son! Labba! Wh...wh... what in lunar lunacy is this?" he asked.

"His name is not 'lunacy', it's 'Leif'. Leif? Say hello to Dada. Here Claus, hold Leif while I get a fresh diaper, wipes, and powder," Labba said.

"Labba!" Claus protested. "You have a lot of explaining to do!"

Labba motioned Claus over to a table.

"The explanation goes like this. Place your son on the changing table. Remove the old diaper. It goes in the diaper pail. We have no disposables. Why? Environmentally unfriendly. Now the wipes. The powder. And the fresh diaper. You're not being helpful. All thumbs? Here, I'll do it. There. A clean butt is a happy butt. Isn't that right Leif?"

"Labba!"

"Don't shout around the baby. You'll make him cry. Well, it's feeding time. Don't worry. I have a bottle of formula in my bag. Why don't you feed him?"

Labba gave Leif to Claus. Claus cradled Leif, and Leif cooed. But then Leif cried a little.

"Here's the bottle. He's hungry. There. You're doing fine, Claus. Here, I'll get you a chair. Sit and relax," Labba said.

"Labba, I'm trembling right now. I can't relax!" Claus said.

"Shh. Lower your voice," she said.

"Will you please explain? Please? I thought you hated me."

"Claus, Claus, Claus! I will spell it out for you," Labba said. "The funeral injured you badly. You were near death."

"I didn't know," Claus said.

"Of course not. You were unconscious. The Greylingers in Aftova were consuming your mind. Soon you would be lost. I felt badly for you. I mean, you're only a human and not meant for such Carinian things. So I did something I probably shouldn't have done and have never done with anyone. I entered your body to stabilize you."

Labba paused.

"Okay," Claus said with uncertainty. "And that means?"

"Claus, in our society, what I did is a form of joining. A form of romantic connection. I had never done so with a human. Actually, I'd never done so with a Carinian either. For Carinians it was because I had not found anyone to fall for. For Argo, the species difference made it impossible. But you have Aftova. That was the bridge that made it possible," Labba explained.

"Oh," Claus said, starting to understand.

Labba paused again.

"I never told Lanietta. And I never told you. But when I first saw you at auction, I wanted to purchase you right away. I was hooked on you from the beginning. Don't look like that, Claus. Hold your thoughts until the end. I deferred to Lanietta. She's my friend. You know the code, you don't intrude upon the property of your friend. You were hers, and I resigned myself to that."

"Labba, I—"

"Shh. Listen. She's gone now. It hurts yes, but it's a fact. I half-fancied you again, but I was still in a relationship with Argo, and I kept my duty to him. Until he went against me. And badly. I was angry. I was angry I wasted my time with him. I was angry that Lanietta stole you from me. I was angry about everything else. Now I used you at the funeral, yes, and I'm sorry, but I really wanted to upend Frieda. She's a tyrant, but the truth of the matter is that I'm insanely jealous of her. She connected with you using Aftova. Multiple times. It drove me out of my mind. I had to get rid of her."

"My plan failed," Labba said. "And it killed Doctor Kechenova in the process. So add that to Argo's death, and I'm at two strikes. Because I could have protected Argo had I been with him. Yes, two strikes against me. I didn't know what to do with myself. But I knew I had to protect you. You were nearly dead. That would have been three strikes, and I would have killed

myself for sure. So I took you to the near side. I melded with you to save you, and that's when I became pregnant."

"I denied it at first," Labba continued. "You are human, and this has never happened. But I should have been wary. Lanietta's mother became pregnant in similar fashion with Larto. When I melded with you, I got caught up on all your experiences with Carinian history in the Anrega orb chamber. Even Selena's warning to Lanietta didn't make a dent in my mind."

"So that was it. I had to leave you and deal with this on my own. I knew that truly meant isolation once and for all," Labba said. "I went back to the lunar shock one last time to say goodbye to everyone. I didn't tell anyone I was pregnant, though I think Sharlamarian figured it out, and Selba told me outright my hair was a mess and asked if I were pregnant. I asked for her help, and she gave it by accompanying me to the near side. It was a short pregnancy, much shorter than you humans. Carinians can do things quickly if motivated."

"Selba acted as midwife during my labor. How could I go into labor or even carry a corporeal child, you might ask. Lanietta and I lost our corporeal bodies when Earth was created. We've been faking corporeal bodies ever since. But let me tell you, Claus, when I went into labor, my own corporeal body became manifest for the first time since Earth's creation. And it stayed with me throughout the entire childbirth process, even pushing out the afterbirth. Once the process was complete, I held Leif for a few hours as a real corporeal mother. I reverted to eethi form of course and had to feign a body again. But Claus, it was the true feeling of motherhood that changed me. I knew I had to face you and tell you the full truth. I violated your body and bore a child without your consent. I'm sorry. Forces of the universe chose this for me. So now I ask your consent. Will you stay with me? Say the word either way, and I will stay or go. But I am Leif's mother, and he goes with me regardless. Well?"

Claus remained in shock. Labba loved him?

"I guess I didn't know," Claus said. "You've always been friendly. I thought a relationship required constant fighting. I always fought with Frieda. And Lanietta was a handful. I knew something was missing but didn't know what. I...am not sure what love is. Is this love?"

Claus looked down into the eyes of Leif. They were such large, green eyes, and they were perfectly formed. Leif had finished his bottle and was happy as a clam, cooing at every little word Claus said. Claus touched him to see if he was corporeal, if he was real. He was real.

"This is love," Labba said.

"Is Leif a human or Carinian?" Claus asked.

"A bit of both I think. He seems human at the moment. We won't know how much of me is in him until he is older. We don't normally go eethi until adolescence, oh, in thirteen million years or so."

"Thirteen million years?" Claus asked.

"Some mature early at twelve million," Labba said. "But that's usually the girls."

"Twelve million?" Claus repeated.

"If he's more human, he'll mature at your time speed. He might go eethi at a mere thirteen years of age. That would be unheard-of for a Carinian," Labba said.

"That would be unheard-of for a human as well," Claus said. "Leif is an interesting name."

"He's named after an early explorer of your North America," Labba said. "Leif will be an early explorer of his own abilities. And the near side."

Claus frowned for a moment.

"Unless you think not. He can choose the lunar shock when he's older," Labba backpedaled.

"No, you're right to suggest he should stay on the near side. If he shows Carinian powers, Frieda is bound to bend her will to corrupt him. No son of mine will be...be...tortured, brainwashed, or stolen from me."

Claus paused and looked at Labba.

"From us," he corrected himself.

Labba smiled, hugged Claus and Leif, and kissed him.

"That's the first time you kissed me," Claus said. "Strange how we had the baby first, and then you kissed me?"

"Actually, uh, no," she admitted.

"What do you mean by that?" Claus asked.

"When I melded with you, uh, it was a very romantic and intense ethereal experience. Couldn't help it or stop it, it just happened. And I kissed you from the inside," Labba continued to admit.

"How does that work?"

"Normal couples do concave kissing. They press curved lips together. We did concentric kissing. My lips were exactly in the same physical space as yours with the same arc centers. If I puckered up, I caused your lips to pucker up equally," she said. "Didn't Lanietta ever try that with you?"

"She never melded with me like that. She formed a body suit around me, but that was all," Claus said.

Labba did a leap of joy and let out a great hoot and holler. Leif cried a little, but Claus consoled him.

"It's all right, Leif. Momma is just excited," Claus said.

"I was your first then," Labba said with pride.

"You were truly my first. And that includes human females too. I've always struck out," Claus said.

"The strikes have been erased. The bases are clear, the inning is over, and the game complete. The score is one to nothing. We have our one," Labba said happily.

"Here, why don't you hold Leif for a while," Claus said.

Labba took Leif back and tickled his lips.

"Strange thing. I was just thinking about how I could create a building out of stone," Claus said.

"You have a nesting instinct," Labba said. "I'll help you control the Greylingers. We'll build together."

"Can Leif help?" Claus said.

Labba and Claus laughed.

Chapter 106: Unexpected Ending

In the years that followed, Claus and Labba built a small farm together. Labba helped Claus tame Aftova, and he was able to shape rock and assemble it without the ear-shattering sounds he had encountered before. Labba had snuck back to the lunar shock to retrieve Kechenova's equipment, a set of seeds, and several animals. With that, the three were self-sufficient. They had a stone house with kitchen, living room, wash room, bedrooms, study, storage, and so on. They had a stone barn with stables, a paddock, and a fenced area for the horses to roam. A utility building did processing and included a way to make biodiesel. Special crops sifted through great quantities of air to pull in what little carbon dioxide was there. Steam-powered equipment provided for tilling and such. A large water tower with a water condensation unit provided water to the house, irrigated the crops, provided water to the domestic animals, and irrigated the ground where the horses grazed so grass would grow. It even irrigated a tree Claus and Labba had planted in their front yard.

The troubles of the lunar shock and the old far side largely went unnoticed. Labba and Claus periodically turned on their radio to listen in on Selba's evening show or Shara's morning show. Mostly they danced to the blues and big-band songs that aired. Leif grew at normal human speed, and he was now a toddler with a curiosity about the farm, the crops, the animals, and the smallest of things like the pebbles on the ground or four-leaf clovers that started growing in the grass.

One Saturday morning, Claus was sleeping in late. Labba would always lie with him in bed and pretend to sleep for his sake even though Carinians don't need sleep. Leif had gotten up and was playing on the front porch. He made a sudden gasp, and Labba's maternal instinct brought her to a full alert state. The air was quiet and still. She heard Leif as he played on the front porch and thought nothing of it, and she was about to feign sleep again.

She heard a voice. Very distant it was, but she could make out the conversation. The voice grew closer.

"This is the safest place in the universe," the voice said. "You can drop me off here, Selenita. I'll be fine. Oh wait, stay around for a while. There's a settlement. Let's see who's here."

The voice opened the front door, entered, and walked into the bedroom. The voice belonged to that of a woman, and this woman held Leif in her arms. Selenita stood next to her.

"Lanietta!" Labba shrieked.

"What is this!" Lanietta retorted.

"Claus! Wake up! Claus!" Labba continued to shriek.

"Oh! Lanietta!" Claus cried. "This isn't what you—"

"I see you've committed travesty of bestiality, Labba. Clomper is my pet. Or have you forgotten? Have you?!" Lanietta demanded.

"Lanietta, please...make yourself at home," Labba said with a shaky voice. "We have tea and coffee cake."

"I DON'T NEED TO EAT!" Lanietta yelled.

"Please don't yell. Could you let me have Leif? He doesn't like yelling. Claus, take Leif from Lanietta," Labba said.

Claus started to get up, but he pulled the sheets around himself to cover his naked body.

"You're not dressed?" Lanietta barked.

"We're a family with no one else around," Claus said.

Lanietta sent a plasma ball at Claus, and he fell back onto the bed. He tried an attack with Aftova, but Lanietta prevented it.

"A family! You admit that you and Labba made this child? Labba!" Lanietta said with disdain.

"Lanietta! Forgive me! We thought you were dead!" Labba said.

"And that gave you the right? To move in on my chattel?!" Lanietta barked.

"He's not property. He's a warm, tender, sensitive man with a kind heart and—"

"Stop it!" Lanietta ordered. "You will appear before the Hierarchy and be reprocessed."

"Impossible," Claus said, and now a fierce determination grew from within. "All other Carinians were destroyed. You and Labba were the only ones left. Where are these Carinians, Lanietta? Where were you?"

"Where was I? Where was I! I've spent nearly ten thousand years dealing with the Veigon and the upper PRAAD," Lanietta said. "I came back thinking you'd be long dead. Instead, you betrayed me in the most heinous way possible. But don't worry. The Hierarchy doesn't exist. Yet. I will remake it in my own image. From ethereal spirits in the Anrega orb chamber. The chamber survived. It's in the lunar core."

"No, Lanietta. Leave them dead," Labba said with a combination of anger, fear, and sadness in her voice.

"Apparently Luna is full of new life. I hear lots on the radio. There's Frieda on the far side, the lunar shock area, and now this little paradise here. Might as well add my own community."

"We won't help you," Labba said, still trembling. "Claus is mine, and this paradise is mine. Give me Leif."

Labba walked over to take Leif from Lanietta, but Lanietta shied away.

"No," Lanietta said calmly.

"He's our child!" Claus demanded.

"He *was* your child," Lanietta said. "Oh, just a cute Carinian boy. But you'll grow up quickly and be a man. A real, Carinian man. You'll be the only one. A prize for the cosmos!"

Lanietta made to walk away. Claus tapped and beat on Aftova to send out ethereal threads at Lanietta. Lanietta shot a plasma fireball back. The blue thread withered, but the yellow thread was deflected and headed toward the old far side. Lanietta blasted that one before it got far. It withered just like the blue one.

"Stop!" Claus said.

Lanietta ran outside the house, and Labba gave chase, turning into an eagle as soon as she was outside. She attacked Lanietta viciously, tearing into her wherever she could. But Lanietta laughed and sent a plasma ball at Labba, causing her to fall backward and revert to her normal form. Lanietta continued to laugh while her injuries healed quickly.

"Ha-ha-haaahya.   Ha-ha-haaahya," Lanietta laughed like a cawing crow.

As she laughed, Lanietta and Leif faded gradually but completely. Lanietta's laugh echoed throughout the near side for a little longer, and then it was gone.

"Leeeeeeeeeeeif!" Labba cried out.

Claus ran over to Selenita and choked her. But she was a robot and could not be choked.

"Get back my child," Claus said to Selenita. "Do you hear? Get him back!"

Selenita gave Claus a strange look, turned, and walked out of the house. She continued her walk until she disappeared around a rock formation. Moments later, a small spaceship departed. Labba went running after the spaceship, but she could not catch it.

Claus threw on a robe, went to his favorite horse, and jumped on him—bareback. He rode the horse out of the paddock and down to Labba.

"Leeeeeeeif!" Labba cried, and she fell to her knees.

"Labba," Claus said. "Labba!"

Labba turned to him with a wretched face of tears.

"Come back to the house," he said.

She shook her head no.

"We have to work through this, Labba," Claus said. "Come back. I promise you with all my heart, I will have vengeance on Lanietta, if I have to round up the entire lunar shock and take over the planet. I'll have my vengeance!"

"I don't want vengeance! I want Leif!" she shouted. "I...want...Leeeeeeeeeeeif!"

Labba's call for Leif echoed around the near side. It was the last thing Labba said for a long time.

A very long time.

Chapter 107: The Nest

Labba changed into an eagle and flew off, leaving Claus in a robe on a horse, bareback. He watched as she flew to the top of the moisture collection post of the water condenser. Claus rode to that condenser.

"Labba?" he called. "Come down please. Labba!"

Instead, Labba flew off to the top of a ridge far away.

"That ties it," Claus said. "I'm going to ride to the lunar shock and round up a rescue team. We're going to deal with Lanietta once and for all. Vengeance!"

Claus rode with speed toward the lunar shock. With even greater speed came Labba. She swooped down and disrupted the horse with her claws, wings, and beak. The horse stopped, reared, and threw Claus to the ground. He sat up and tried to stand, but he has dazed and disoriented, and so he made do on his knees. Labba circled high above.

"Labba! Let me pass! Let vengeance run its course!" Claus yelled.

Claus pulled himself to his feet, mounted the horse, and made for another run, but Labba swooped down again, clawed him on the shoulder, and pulled him off the horse. Again Claus fell, was stunned, and struggled to regain his wits. Labba circled above.

"Labba!" he called. "Lah-bah!"

Claus, again with difficulty, stood. He made to mount the horse, but she swooped down to throw him off had he done so. Instead, he fell to the ground by his own will. Claus made to mount again, but she swooped again.

"Labba, quit playing games!" Claus yelled.

Labba no longer waited for Claus to make a move toward the lunar shock. She swooped down and herded both Claus and the horse back to the farm. After five or six such swoops, Claus stopped fighting, pulled the rope off his robe, and used it as a line to lead the horse back to the farm. He returned the horse to the paddock, went inside the house, showered, and dressed.

He sighed.

"What does she expect me to do?" Claus wondered aloud. "Wish I had some black elderberry wine. Grandma Broc would know what to do."

He settled for a bottle of water instead.

"This should be beer. Or anything to dull my senses. How I'd like to get drunk!"

He walked outside. High up, Labba circled. She landed on her mountain ridge and stared intently into the distance. She chattered and called out periodically like a cat watching an unreachable prey through the window.

"Does she see Leif? Does she see Lanietta?" Claus asked. "If I climb that mountain, perhaps I could ask her."

Claus took one step toward her, but then she flew toward the thing she eyed, and she was gone.

"She's found Leif! I'll help," Claus said.

Claus saddled up a horse and rode hard. But after only ten minutes, Labba flew back and herded the two back to the farm. She was badly injured with a broken wing and disarrayed feathers, but she managed by perching herself on the back of the horse and pecking Claus in the back every so often.

"Labba, let's talk! Let's work together on this! You've found Leif? We can make plans! Lots of ways to beat Lanietta. Don't you think?" Claus said.

But each time Claus turned to suggest something, she pecked him to turn him back around and keep riding to the farm. At one point he stopped and demanded she speak, but she clawed and ripped his clothing, leaving a tear in his flesh.

Claus returned to the farm, unsaddled the horse, returned it to the paddock, and himself walked to the front porch. Labba flew awkwardly and uneasily back to the mountain ridge. She was clearly in pain, but she stayed up there and stared in the distance again.

"She won't let me go," Claus said. "I'm a prisoner here. At least with Lanietta I headed somewhere or watched the lives of others. I've got nothing!"

Claus paced back and forth. What was he to do? He was still stunned, and his mind wasn't thinking clearly. He'd completely forgotten about Aftova and instead focused on how he could sneak away from Labba. Noon came and passed, and the afternoon progressed quickly. Claus grabbed something to eat now and then, but he spent most of his time pacing. The sun started going down. Claus went inside to rest. He sat down, took several deep breaths, and tapped his fingers.

Then the oddest thing happened. Labba's humanoid ethereal self stood in the doorway leading to the outside. She stared at Claus.

"Now may we talk?" he asked.

But she said nothing. She pointed at Claus and pointed to the outside.

"What?" he said.

She repeated the gestures.

"Sign language? Labba, we're a couple. Couple talk. Talk to me!" he pleaded.

She gestured one last time for him to go outside.

"No," he said. "I'm not going outside. Not until you explain what you're doing. Come on. Sit in my lap and tell your Clausy all about it."

Labba walked over to Claus, paused as if to sit in his lap, and then zapped him in the back.

"What? Why?" Claus replied.

She grew impatient and zapped his back with a stronger shock.

"Ow!" he said. "I'm going."

Claus walked just outside the house, but she cattle-prodded him forward with additional shocks until he had sufficient clear space around him for her next task.

"Now can we talk?" Claus asked.

Instead, Labba's physical (eagle) form hovered over Claus. She (the eagle) cawed and shrilled first into Claus's left ear and then into his right, badgering and pestering him with alternating ear calls. This activated Aftova, and it sent out its yellow ethereal thread through Claus's left ear and blue ethereal thread out his right. She caught the yellow thread in her beak and flew high into the air and around in a circle, counterclockwise if viewed from above. She made several loops around the farm with the yellow thread, dropped it, swooped down for the blue, cawed around Claus's ears more, and pulled the blue thread up high and around the farm in clockwise fashion to have it weave around the yellow thread. She continued this activity until she had a base-weave loop around the farm. After several hours of this, she let Claus return inside and rest. Her eethi humanoid part disappeared while her eagle part returned to the ridge.

"She's making a barrier?" Claus thought. "I'm so tired of it all."

Claus was too tired to do much else other than tend bits of the farm and turn in for the night. Labba stayed perched high up but sent a humanoid eethi image of herself down to Claus for the evening. She didn't say anything but simply wandered around the house, looking out the window for any change of anything.

"You're driving me crazy," Claus said. "Speak to me!"

She didn't.

For two more weeks, Claus endured this ritual. The ethereal nest grew larger and larger. At the end of a nest-building session, Claus had a talk with himself (since Labba wouldn't speak to him).

"I should have sent out these ethereal threads to the lunar shock and begged for help," Claus said. "Now Aftova and my palate are so badly frayed that I've lost all hope of sending for help. If only I could call..."

But Claus beat his head at a sudden thought.

"Claus! What's wrong with you? What about the radio? These two weeks of suffering, and you could have used the radio!" he said to himself.

He rushed into the house, found the radio, and called for help.

"Selba! Shara! Anyone! This is Claus! Can you hear me? Please reply! I'm on the old near side. Something horrible has happened. I need help. We need help! Hello?" he called.

There was a moment of static, then Selba's voice replied.

"Claus! I read you!" Selba's voice said. "I was getting ready for my afternoon show. What's wrong? Are you ill? Is Labba ill? Or the baby?"

"I can't explain over the radio," Claus said. "Can you visit us? Please?"

"I suppose so. Will be nice to visit Labba, Leif, and you. He must be growing up quickly," she said.

Claus held silent.

"Are you still there, Claus?" Selba called.

"I'm here. How soon can you get here? I know it's a long walk and all," he said.

"Oh, I have transportation," she said. "Don't worry about me. Need anything from town?"

"Booze," Claus said.

Selba laughed.

"Sorry," she said. "I've never heard you make such a request. Very well. I'll be there as soon as I can—with booze!"

Claus was happy. But then he had a sudden worry.

"What if Labba won't let her through?" Claus said to himself. "What if Selba can't get through the nest wall? Oh, this prison is wearing thin!"

A week passed, and Claus wondered when Selba would arrive—if she would arrive. Then one morning, after Claus had awakened for the day but before Labba put him through her thread-pulling and weaving dance to add to the ethereal nest, Selba showed up in an open-air vehicle.

"Selba!" Claus called as he ran up to her. "You made it!"

"Yes," she said. "I can only drive so fast in the lunar soil. No roads on the near side."

"Where did you get the vehicle?" Claus asked. "And it's so quiet! It must have a large fuel tank."

"One of Doctor Kechenova's inventions that she hid away in Tabelia. Fully electric. Runs on thorium."

"Of course!" Claus said. "I should have known. I see a box in back there. Is it—"

"Yes, I brought your booze," she said.

"I'll bring that inside first thing," Claus said.

Claus picked up the box, and Selba brought a travel bag with her.

"Oh, I'm sorry," Claus said. "I should have taken that too!"

"Don't worry about it. But I need to clean up. I had to sleep outside for seven days in the middle of nowhere. Rations and a water condenser got me through, but sleeping in the car is tiring, and I feel like old carbonic sludge is coming out of my pores."

"Carbonic sludge?" Claus asked. "There's very little—"

"That was supposed to be a joke," Selba said.

"Oh. Well, the guest room has running water," Claus said. "Take all the time you need to freshen up."

"Thank you," she said. "Where are Labba and Leif? No, don't call them. I don't want them seeing me like this. I'll clean up first."

Selba took her things to the guest room and cleaned up in the shower. She threw on a set of fresh clothes and entered the living room.

"Oh," she said in surprise. "Where are they? I thought you would have called them by now."

"Let me show you something," Claus said.

Claus led Selba back outside and showed her the eagle perched on the mountain ridge.

"See that eagle?" he said.

"Yes."

"That's Labba," Claus said.

"What is she doing up there?" Selba asked. "Tell her to come down. I want to see her. And where are you hiding Leif?"

"Selba, let's go inside and have something to eat. I'll break open the booze, if you don't mind," Claus said.

"All right," Selba said, puzzled. "Just a sandwich, Claus. I've had a food pill already."

Claus made up sandwiches and opened the box. It was full of beer. He placed the beer in a bucket of ice to chill it and offered one to Selba.

"No thank you," she said. "I want to keep clear until I find out what's going on around here. No Labba to greet me, no Leif running around in play—Claus, explain."

Claus took a bite from his sandwich, flushed it down his throat with a gulp of beer, and swallowed hard. He was too uptight and caused the food and beer to go down wrong, causing them to drag down slowly. He grimaced, held up a finger to Selba as a request to be patient, and finished the torturous swallowing process.

"Okay," he said.

"I thought you were going to choke or something," she said.

"I almost did," Claus said. "Selba, something terrible has happened. Leif has been kidnapped."

"What?" she said in shock.

Claus nodded his head in affirmation.

"That's terrible. Oh, poor Labba!" Selba said.

"Poor Labba? What about me?" Claus said.

"I'm sorry, Claus. It's a horrible thing. How did it happen?" she asked.

"Lanietta is back," Claus said. "Took us both by surprise one morning. Leif was playing on the front porch, and she grabbed him. Said something about keeping him and making him her new man. We tried to stop her, but we couldn't. We think she's on Luna somewhere."

"Lanietta! I thought she was dead!" Selba said.

"We all did!" Claus said.

"She had a thing for you, didn't she? And she caught you with Labba? Oh, Claus!"

"You don't have to remind me!" Claus said.

"Two women don't work out, Claus. You have to resolve this. You have to choose," Selba said. "What has Labba said?"

"The last thing she said, and this was shortly after the kidnapping, was that she wanted Leif," Claus said. "This was three weeks ago. She hasn't spoken since."

"She hasn't spoken to Lanietta?"

"She hasn't spoken to me!" Claus said. "She spends most of her time as an eagle, sitting on that mountain perch. Every so often she flies off but comes back injured. Then once a day she...well...here she is now. See for yourself."

The humanoid image of Labba entered the house. She waved at Selba, and Selba waved back. Then Labba ushered Claus outside where the eagle part of herself cawed in each of Claus's ears, took the resulting ethereal threads, and wove them into the ethereal nest around the farm. She finished. Her eagle part flew off, and her eethi humanoid part disappeared.

"See?" Claus said. "I've tried to leave, but she always forces me back. I've tried to climb the mountain perch where she sits, but again she forces me back. I'm a prisoner here!"

"What do you want, Claus?" Selba asked.

"I want to get Leif back. How? By going back to the lunar shock and rounding up anyone willing to launch an assault on Lanietta. I want this to end, Selba."

Selba, now outside, walked back and forth a bit. She stared at Labba the eagle. Selba nodded her head and spoke with Claus.

"I'll speak with her," Selba said.

"You can't," Claus replied. "She doesn't speak with anyone. You saw her just now, both in eagle and humanoid form. Just a wave. That was it."

"Let me try," Selba said.

"Now?"

"Why not? You called for my help. Well, I'm here," Selba said.

"But you just got here. Are you going to—"

"Drive off and up to the mountain perch, yes," Selba said. "Don't worry. I'll come back with news. Well, Claus, I'm sorry for this tragedy. But I'm hopeful. At least Leif is still alive. Things could be worse."

"I don't see how, but thank you for your optimism. I'll watch from here," Claus said.

Selba returned to her vehicle and drove off. He watched as her vehicle approached the mountain. When she reached the mountain, the vehicle tended to go in and out of view as she followed winding paths.

"I forgot to ask her how she got through the nest!" Claus said to himself. "Claus, focus. Focus!"

Claus watched. Selba couldn't drive all the way to the perch. She climbed up by foot the last little bit. Claus strained to see, but he could just make out a person reaching the eagle.

"If only I could hear the conversation now!" he said.

But he couldn't. Curiosity drove him nearly crazy. He couldn't stand to wait and resigned himself to sitting inside and getting drunk off beer. He passed out.

Chapter 108: Three for One

Claus awoke to the smell of eggs and bacon.

"Labba cooked? Labba!" Claus called in excitement.

He threw on a robe and rushed out into the kitchen only to find Selba.

"Oh," Claus said in disappointment.

"Is that how you treat all your guests who fix breakfast?" she asked.

"Sorry, Selba. I just thought for a moment that you were—"

"Labba," Selba finished. "No, she's flying high above with her eye to the south. She's watching her son."

"She is! You must tell me. You must tell me everything! When did you return? Why didn't you tell me everything when you returned? Selba, you—"

"Hold that horse before it gets colicky," Selba said. "I've made you breakfast as a courtesy. Have a little to eat and drink. No booze for breakfast. Have coffee instead."

"Booze for breakfast. Sounds like a mantra I should adopt," Claus said.

"You had better not," she said.

Selba sat Claus in the breakfast room. Already the food was set out with dishes for two and such. Claus was seated at the table on one side and Selba on the other.

"First, I will have some coffee. I've been up all night with Labba," Selba said. "It took that long to get anything out of her. She didn't speak to me, not with words or directly. I had to infer everything through body language. And I'm tired."

Selba poured herself a cup of coffee and drank half of it.

"I'm sorry," Claus said.

"When I returned here, I found the place in a mess. Beer bottles everywhere, and you passed out. So I had to clean that up and put you to bed," Selba said. "Claus, you need a maid, or even a nanny!"

"Sorry again," Claus said.

"The nest. Labba has been building a nest as a protective barrier to keep others out and her loved ones inside. She permitted me to enter yesterday, because she trusts me and wants to protect me."

"Then you're a prisoner too," Claus said. "I've pulled you into a trap!"

"No, no, NO!" Selba said. "Claus, I'm tired and short of patience. Please don't interrupt, especially to say things that aren't so."

"Sorry a third time," he said.

"I'm not a prisoner. Labba will let me come and go at my own leisure. But let's get on with you and your story. When she was pregnant, she was protective of you and the baby. After Leif was born, she felt badly and decided she would loosen up. You felt safe, and she felt safe. So she let her guard down. But Leif became vulnerable. In hindsight, anyone showing up could have taken Leif. Lanietta just happened to be the one. Regardless, the result was the same—Labba had not protected her own well enough, and she allowed the incident to happen."

"That Labba! She shouldn't—"

"Ahem!" Selba said to quiet Claus. "She heard you talking about vengeance and knew that any such attempt would get you killed. She'd already lost Leif, and she couldn't lose you too—that would kill her for sure. So she vowed to stop speaking to you or anyone until she resolved this situation. She built the ethereal nest, which is something she felt she should have done to begin with. And she has found Leif. When she sits up there, she watches him. Lanietta is...well...I can show you if you like. I have a body camera with portable projector. If you clear a wall, I will show you some interesting videography."

"Here," he said after removing a painting from a windowless wall. "Use this wall."

Selba placed her body camera on the table, pressed a button, and moving images appeared on the wall.

"This is Labba, of course, sitting on her mountain perch. See how she turns away or fluffs her feathers as I ask her questions? That's how I got answers out of her. Very tedious. Very time consuming. She got tired of questions and flew off. Look," Selba said.

The videograph showed Labba flying off into the distance. The images zoomed in on Labba and showed her flying toward a fort. Lanietta could be seen walking Leif around, but when Lanietta saw Labba approach, Lanietta took dragon form and attacked Labba. Labba lost and returned to her mountain perch. The video ended.

"So that's what happened to Leif," Claus said.

Claus took the body camera in hand and casually waved it around with his body language as he spoke.

"She can see Leif," he said. "It tortures her, so she attacks. She loses every time and returns to her perch. It's a living misery for her. And me. There's got to be a way, Selba. There's got to be—"

But as Claus spoke those words, he got too excited and bumped his hand with the camera against the table, triggering the body camera into action. Another videograph played, showing something strange.

"Three-for-one," said a salesperson. "Do you want to have a superior child? Free of genetic defect? Then trade three eggs and get one back—superiorized!"

"Give me that!" Selba said.

Selba grabbed for the body camera, but Claus held it away from her.

"What was that?!" he demanded.

"None of your business!" she said.

"That was on the near side!" he said. "Everything on this hemisphere is my business! Especially with Leif kidnapped. Just whose side are you on! You're making deals with someone?"

"No! Claus! Trust me!" Selba said.

"Not until we see this videograph. Not until you explain this 'three-for-one' deal. I've never heard of it," Claus said.

"It was a mistake!" Selba said.

"Which? Leaving the camera on, or whatever deal you made? Selba, there's a powerful Carinian out there named Lanietta. She's done nasty battles with the most vile of entities. What has she done now? Besides stealing my son?"

Selba gave out a big sigh.

"I guess you'll find out soon enough," she said. "Play the rest of the videograph. That green button there."

Claus pressed the green button. The videograph showed Selba being led into the very same fort Labba had been shown attacking.

"I don't believe it," Claus said.

"Please, Claus. I'm tired," she said.

"And that excuses this?"

"Lanietta is building a Carinian eugenics program," Selba said. "I happened across a saleswoman along the way. Now Claus, before you yell at me again, know this—Lanietta has built a perimeter around your farm. You are surrounded first by Labba's nest and second by Lanietta's perimeter. Lanietta started it very quickly, and it was the final straw that broke Labba's back and forced her to create the nest. So don't blame Labba, don't blame me. Blame Lanietta. And I had to cross that perimeter to reach your farm. No way around, Claus. No way."

"I should keep my mouth shut," Claus said. "Everything I say or do leads to ruin."

"Not everything," Selba said. "But back to Lanietta. I played along—all the way. Her program is this—any woman who wants a child free of genetic disease with superior strength, intelligence, longer life, and a dose of Carinian engrams can donate three of her eggs to the program, one of which she will receive back fertilized and prepared with all the promises of the program. I went through with the deal. I'm pregnant."

"It's the baby option all over again!" Claus said.

"I heard about that, and no, it isn't. No one dies, Claus! Turns out this accomplishes several things for me, and you. First, I'm able to tell you all about the program. You wouldn't have had the forewarning without me. Second, I've been looking to start a family myself but haven't found anyone to share it with. Face it, Claus, the selenites on Earth created a deep sense of distrust. A woman finds a man and thinks she's in love only to learn he is actually a selenite! Deception, deception, deception!"

"What's this talk about the selenites on Earth? You're leaving out something," Claus said.

"Only because you're jumping ahead," Selba said. "I saw Selenita. She performed the procedure on me, in fact. And there are other selenites like her around—all female. Lanietta won't have male selenites do anything. Says that's what destroyed Earth, so why recreate the same failure?"

"So she'll create new failure," Claus said.

"I'm not judging, Claus. Just surviving," Selba said.

"Seems that's ultimately what we're all forced to do," Claus said. "Altruism is a fantasy!"

"Lanietta can't go to the old far side. The remnant PRAAD would destroy her," Selba said. "But you must have known that."

"She and Labba. Yes. They would perish like the other Carinians. I thought they were all destroyed until she mentioned bringing them back from the Anrega."

"I heard her say several things to Leif. First, he can't go to the old far side either, that he's too Carinian for that, and he'd die, at least at his age. No telling about the future. There's no handbook on Carinian-human people. He might overcome it when he's older. But for now, she has forbidden him to go. Claus, would you have taken him there? Maybe accidentally? Maybe involuntarily under Frieda's control?"

Claus paused.

"I didn't think about that," Claus said.

"You would have killed Leif," Selba said.

"And I'm supposed to thank Lanietta for that?" Claus said. "This is getting worse all the time!"

"Lanietta sincerely believes she has saved Leif's life. She also is infatuated with the only existing corporeal Carinian man in the universe. Well someday he'll be a man," Selba said.

"Doesn't seem right. Lanietta and Labba are practically sisters," Claus said.

"But they're not," Selba said.

"No, they're not," Claus sighed.

"As to the other Carinians, they are protected in the Anrega orb chamber," Selba continued. "You were there. Her parents and others. Remember?"

"I guess I didn't think of them as...well...how did they get there anyway? The Anrega orb chamber was placed in Earth?"

"That I don't know, but Lanietta explained to Leif that Lanshalla chose it as a safe haven, a Noah's Ark for Carinians should something happen to the race," Selba said. "I think Lanietta is acting on her mother's orders to resurrect the race and use Leif as the king of the eugenics program. They will take our eggs and use them to jump-start their race."

"How can you live with yourself knowing what you've done?" Claus said.

"I'm in pure survival mode!" Selba said. "I don't have the luxury of guilt. But Labba does. And it's going to keep you stuck here, I'm afraid. Lanietta will build her high-speed transport to the lunar shock and lure more women into the three-for-one deal."

"Maybe we can get Frieda's help," Claus said.

"A-hah!" Selba said. "That's exactly what Labba predicted. No, giving anything to Frieda will add power to her side. Frieda already has a fast-growing ethereal computer, not to mention a fast-growing group of people devoted to her. Immortality is a powerful temptation. Matter of fact, many of us are sleeping in special houses in the old far side."

"What do you mean? Why?" Claus asked.

"We take a pressurized subway train to a town called New Farsite and sleep in pressurized domes. No carbonic scrubbers needed. And we don't age while we sleep. So our life spans are lengthened. We return to the lunar shock for the daytime, and this prevents us from losing our humanity. We still eat, we still breathe, and we can still have children. I have such a home in New Farsite. You could say Frieda and Lanietta are competing for my attention."

"This is beyond all normal sanity, Selba," Claus said. "We can't let the lunar shock become a free market for...for... human...human greed! I don't even know what to call it! Selba! Why?!"

"Claus, these changes that are happening—they're non-violent. No one is killed. No one badmouths another. We're living longer. We have less stress. Crime is low and even that is disappearing. I really can't complain."

"That's exactly why you *should* complain. Why we *all* should complain," Claus said. "That's what keeps us going."

"Maybe before. I wish you were a woman, Claus. You could have a child, and both you and your child would live longer. Much longer. Well, I've done all I can here."

"You're leaving? But I'm stuck! What am I supposed to do?" Claus asked.

"There's one last thing you can try," Selba said. "Convince Labba you want another child."

"A replacement for Leif? That's selfish," Claus said.

"No, it's not. Children have a way of changing the future in unpredictable ways. Your life right now is too predictable, and I agree you are a prisoner. But another child, well, even if you remain a prisoner, at least you'll have a little one to cherish. It's something to look forward to. I know I look forward to my own. I'll leave the thought with you. I must go now. My replacement on the evening show has been a disaster! Shara's going to scoop my audience."

"I almost wish she would have come instead of you," Claus said.

"You don't need to be so rude. But as for Shara, she hasn't found a partner either. Had she made the trip, she might have chosen triplets, a nine-for-three deal. Imagine that!" Selba said.

Selba took her body camera back and bade Claus farewell. Claus watched as she drove off in the Kechenova-designed thorium car.

"Claus, you messed up again!" he said to himself. "You should have asked her about other technology Doctor Kechenova created. Maybe she built a super weapon. Something to overpower these Carinians. And Frieda."

Claus kicked up the dirt in frustration at his supposed mistake. One such kicking resulted in a clump of Luna dirt landing not far away. He stared at it and remembered Grandma Broc's brook. He kicked another clump, and it landed next to the first.

"Stepping stones. But what do the steps represent? Children? My mother was an only child. The Brocs moved around. How do I move around? How? Grandma Broc, speak to me!"

There was no Grandma Broc to speak with him. Nor Labba nor Lanietta nor Selba nor Shara nor anyone else. Not even Leni.

"Leni would know what to do," Claus said. "I wonder if I could send an ethereal thread after him and repair him."

Claus touched his upper palate and attempted to send out his ethereal threads, but Labba dive-bombed Claus and tied his loose ends.

"Labba!" he said in desperation.

Labba returned to her perch.

"Perhaps I can find a weak point in the nest," Claus said. "When I do, I can make a run for it when she's distracted with her attack run on Lanietta."

Claus saddled up a horse and rode it around, checking the edge of the ethereal nest. He didn't follow it directly, rather, he went toward it and away from it as if casually riding around the property. Labba looked periodically but otherwise kept her gaze on Leif in Lanietta's fortress.

"There's a rock formation," Claus observed. "And a natural archway. That could be a way out. But boulders block the way. I can't spend time with an A-frame and pulleys to remove the boulders. Labba would find out. I just might make it if the horse can jump them. But they are big jumps. I'll have to train the horse."

Claus returned to the barn and fashioned a number of horse jumps. They were of simple yet flexible design with rungs for placing a lateral post progressively higher. He placed one of these in the paddock and drove the horse to jump it. The horse refused and threw him.

"Arrg," Claus moaned. "Maybe this is the wrong horse. I need a jumper."

Claus tried out the other horses. They all refused and threw him.

"Am I doing this right? Aren't any of these horses capable or willing to jump?" he asked himself.

Claus went to the last horse. It had a grey coat with spots of black as if it had gotten into a can of black paint. The other horses were either colorations of brown or black.

"You, the funny-looking horse," Claus said. "Can you jump?"

Claus saddled up the grey horse, took it to the jump, and prepared to be thrown. The horse did stop. Claus fought to stay on the saddle, but then the horse jumped over the barrier.

"You're a jumper! I found one!" Claus said. "Let's try that again."

Claus took the grey horse around in a loop and set him to jump. He did so without breaking stride.

"Okay, we're doing it," he said.

Claus dismounted and set up another jump at the same height as the first.

"Let's see you do two jumps," he said.

Claus took the horse through a loop and had the horse go over the two jumps. The horse had to land sideways, pause, and regroup itself to jump over the second.

"These jumps are too close together. I'll move them apart. That's okay, the boulders are also farther apart. I should simulate the boulders as closely as possible," he said to himself.

He readjusted the jumps, took the horse through a loop, and the horse jumped both without issue.

"There are three boulders. So I need a third barrier. And it's time to raise the height."

Claus set up the third horse jump and raised the three to a new height. The horse jumped them without issue.

Claus spent the next two weeks practicing with the horse, jumping higher and higher. Being thrown from the other horses taught Claus how to recognize an imminent refusal, and so he didn't push the grey horse too hard, especially as the jumps got dangerously high. He half-expected Labba to speak and ask what he was doing, but she didn't.

"She probably figures I'm fighting boredom, which I am. But she doesn't know the plan. These barriers are my stepping stones. The boulders at the archway are my stepping stones. And the great beyond—outside of the nest—is the next brook. This is the answer. This is what Grandma Broc would tell me to do."

The day came when Claus and the horse were ready. Labba had a habit of attacking Lanietta at least once every two weeks (now becoming weekly), and he knew she'd go in for an attack run soon. He saddled up the horse but kept it in the barn. He watched her on the perch but pretended to do his farming.

Then it happened. Labba left the perch and made her attack run on Lanietta's fortress. Claus ran for the barn, led the grey horse outside quickly, jumped on the saddle, and rode like the wind to the archway. He didn't let up. He expected the horse would jump the boulders without issue. But unlike the first horse he'd taken to the archway, the grey horse had never been there. The grounds were unfamiliar. He had the horse jump the first boulder, the second boulder, and the third. But after the third boulder, the horse tripped on unpredictable ground, threw Claus, and his head torpedoed into the top of the archway. He fell to the ground, unconscious.

Chapter 109: Coma

Claus had fitful dreams that he was back on the Mad Mistral, was watching Lanshalla fight Greylingers, or had white foxes pawing at him. His mind wandered for quite some time, but a set of voices brought him to consciousness.

"Let's visit your grandfather. See? He has grey hair and a long beard, like Santa Claus. His name is Claus."

"*Claws*," the little boy pronounced.

"No, it's *Claus* like a mouse in the house," she said.

Claus opened his eyes. He was in a large, unfamiliar bedroom with a young woman and a boy at her side.

"Who are you?" he asked.

"Pappa!" she said with screams of delight, and she rushed over to hug him. "Look, Claude, your grandfather is awake! He speaks! It's a miracle!"

"Grandfather?" Claus asked.

He looked down at his hands. They seemed much older than he remembered.

"Nanna, come quickly! Pappa is awake!"

In walked Mariel.

"He's awake," Mariel called outside the room.

In walked Treyu.

"What is this?" Claus asked. "Have I gone mad? You...you don't belong here! Where's Labba?"

"Treyu your butler, sir. Though we have never met, I have kept up the estate for you," Treyu said.

"And Mariel the maid," Mariel said. "Treyu takes all the credit. I've kept the mansion clean and the guests fed. I've called for Nanceya. She'll be in soon."

"Mansion? Nanceya?" Claus said. "Who am I? Where am I?"

"You're Claus Gerhardt," Treyu said. "And you are on the Gerhardt Estate in the middle of the old near side. On Luna."

"How did I get this beard? And it's grey!" Claus said.

Claus looked around and saw his old radio clock on the nightstand. He reached for it and held it before his eyes. The date read: June 32, 12047.

"That's supposed to say 12-0-22," Claus said. "What kind of game is this?"

"It's no game," Selba said, now walking in.

Selba looked the same as always.

"This clock is wrong," he said.

"It's accurate," Selba said. "I assure you. Claus, you've been in a coma for twenty-five years. Everyone thought you would die after the horse accident. You almost did. Instead you remained in a coma. We took care of you as best we could while life continued around you. I'm glad you woke up to see it."

"As am I!" said the young woman. "Pappa, I must take you on a tour of the estate! See what Sergio and I have done to it!"

"Who's Sergio? Who are you?" Claus asked.

"I'm Clausetta. Your daughter," she said.

"I...have a daughter?" Claus asked.

"May I have a word with Claus please? Alone?" Selba requested.

"I will see you soon. Come along, Claude!" Clausetta said.

"If you need anything, just ring," Treyu said, and he left with Mariel.

"What is going on?!" Claus demanded.

"I told you. You hit your head during a horse-riding accident," Selba said. "That was twenty-five years ago. Labba found you and pulled you back. She called for me, and I came to help. Looks like you were trying to escape the ethereal nest she created. I stayed on for a bit to help with your rehabilitation and with delivering Clausetta. And yes, you are the father. Labba discovered that your head injury allowed her to conceive much the same way she did for Leif. Realizing this, she tried to conceive again after having Clausetta, but it didn't work. She resorted to beating your skull daily in hopes she could conceive off the concussion, but you were stuck in a coma and wouldn't budge. I finally convinced her to stop, as you had too much skull damage and brain damage."

"She beat on my skull? With what?"

"Anything she could find. Glass jar, plank of wood, leg of a broken chair, soup ladle, iron—"

"I get the picture," Claus said. "No wonder I have bumps on my head."

"I removed as much glass as I could from your scalp. You might have a few shards left in your brain," Selba said.

"This does not sound like love. I've been abused!" Claus said.

"She was desperate. Well, at least she had Clausetta. What do you think?" Selba asked.

"Clausetta is young and lively. And she loves me though we've never met, I mean, I know she's seen me, but what kind of relationship can a father have with a child while in a coma?" Claus asked. "I see you haven't changed. Whatever happened to your child?"

"Sleeping on the old far side preserved me. In fact I had a Greylinger flip-flop inserted into my upper palate to slow my aging," Selba said.

"I have a flip-flop. Why did I age?" Claus asked.

"I don't think it's set up for that," Selba said.

"Well that's not fair. Someone should have—"

"Ah, here he is! My child!" Selba said.

A young man walked in with Clausetta.

"See, Sergio? He's awake!" Clausetta said.

"You have a son?" Claus asked.

"Pleased to meet you, Pappa," Sergio said.

"Pappa?" Claus asked.

"Sergio grew up here. I helped take care of you, remember? He and Clausetta spent their lives growing up. They fell in love. They are married and have one boy, Claude. They've been taking care of the farm for you. Someone had to."

"Then I owe you all a great debt," Claus said.

"Please, Pappa!" Clausetta said. "May I show you around?"

"Perhaps Claus would like to clean up and change into something more appropriate," Selba said.

"Good idea," Claus said. "I need a shave. But then you must explain how Treyu and Mariel got here. I thought they were part of another era. I thought they had died!"

"I will explain," Selba said.

Claus got up slowly and was surprised he could walk.

"Oh yes. Labba forced you to walk around the grounds several times a day," Selba said.

"Yes," Clausetta said. "We played lots of games with you and dressed you up as all kinds of figures."

"All kinds?" Claus asked.

"All kinds," Selba answered. "There are many videographs of things you did while in a coma."

"I don't want to know," he said.

Claus walked into a spacious bathroom. It was so spacious that he thought he'd walked into an apartment. He looked at himself in the mirror, and to his shock he looked twenty-five years older. More wrinkles. All grey hair. The long grey beard. He cut off the beard and shaved. His hair had been kept short, so that wasn't an issue, but he found it difficult to focus on things close up.

"Why can't I focus?" he wondered.

"Presbyopia," Selba's voice called back. "Happens to older people."

"This getting old thing is for the dogs!" he said.

"That's why many of us choose not to," Selba's voice replied.

Claus took his shower, finished, and put on a set of clean clothes. He stepped out of the bathroom, and Clausetta immediately put her arms around his. For a moment he felt as though he were giving her away in a wedding.

"It's not the first time she's held your arm like that," Selba said. "She's walked you around the grounds many times before."

"Only this time is for real!" Clausetta said.

"I'd better go with you," Selba said. "Sergio? Care to escort your mother around the farm?"

"Of course," he replied.

The two left the bedroom and reached a large upper hallway.

"We can take the stairs or one of the elevators," Selba said.

"Elevators?" Claus asked.

"Why not?" Selba said. "Makes it easy to move things around."

"What things?"

"Lots of things," Selba said.

"Oh let's take the stairs!" Clausetta said with enthusiasm.

The four made their way down a long, curved set of stairs. It was one of a pair that circled downward to the bottom. Everything around was of polished marble.

"The stonework is incredible!" Claus said. "You built this around me?"

"No," Sergio said. "You were in the old farmhouse, and we constructed this building fresh. When it was completed, you were moved in."

"Oh," Claus said.

The group headed outside. Claus was amazed at the never-ending stonework.

"This is a mansion!" he said.

"Yes, of course it is, Pappa!" Clausetta said.

There were fountains, gardens, and workers. Decorative plants abounded, and looking around gave no indication Claus was on the desert soil of the old near side.

"This was a desert," Claus said.

"We've had water piped in," Selba said. "It was necessary."

"From where?" Claus asked.

Selba paused.

"I must show you the great water works," Clausetta said. "Leif runs it and will be happy to see you."

"Leif? Lanietta released him?" Claus asked.

Claus instinctively looked around for Labba and saw her in eagle form perched on the same mountain point as before.

"Labba still hasn't spoken," Selba said. "She has such hatred for Lanietta. But things have moved along."

"There's something else," Claus said. "Why are there statues of me everywhere? I see some with birds, some with children, some—"

"On horseback, in uniform, yes, there are many statues of you," Selba said.

"That's because of all the wonderful things you've done," Clausetta said. "You played with us, you danced, you juggled, you dressed up, you rode horses, you—"

"Clausetta is very fond of you," Selba said. "She could go on and on and on."

"I'm getting tired," Claus said. "My knees and back hurt. I don't remember them hurting before."

"She had you do backflips and other acrobatics," Selba said.

"No wonder," Claus said with disdain.

"Look. Here's a tram. We can ride with the other tourists," Selba said.

"Yes, let's take the tram!" Clausetta said.

"Not me," Sergio said. "I see a broken cultivator in the vineyard. I should help out."

"Catch up with us later!" Clausetta said.

"Tourists? What tourists?" Claus asked.

A tram showed up half-full of tourists. Clausetta waved it down, and the three boarded.

"These tourists," Selba said. "They come from all over for a vacation at your resort."

"When did my farm become a resort?" Claus asked.

Clausetta sheepishly raised her hand.

"Look everyone, it's Clausetta!" a tourist said.

All praised and applauded Clausetta.

"Sing for us, Clausetta," said one.

"Very well. Here's one," she said, and she started singing.

It was a duet. She sang the first part, and Claus found himself being shocked to sing the other part. A look of confusion and horror covered his face. The song ended. So did the shock.

"What was that?" Claus asked.

"Labba used to take you out for walks when you first entered your coma," Selba said. "When Clausetta was old enough, she took over that duty. She's part Carinian and has the ability to affect Aftova. That's how she got you to perform all those tricks."

"Clausetta, you!" Claus started to say in anger.

Clausetta cowered in fear and began to cry.

"Claus, be careful," Selba said. "She's never seen this side of you. Could cause irreparable psychological damage. She sees her Pappa as the friendly parent who always plays along."

"Well there's going to be a stop to that," Claus said.

"Pappa, please. Don't be angry at me. Don't you still love me?"

Then Claus said, "I still love you," but it was forced because Clausetta shocked him into saying it.

"I didn't say that!" he said.

"Clausetta had you saying lots of things like that," Selba said.

Claus shook a fist.

"Don't blame her. It's not easy having an invalid for a parent," Selba said.

"Now you're doing it!" Claus said.

"Oh please," Selba said. "Lighten up a little. Things have turned out well for the most part. Don't cry over a lost coma."

The tram reached the archway where Claus had once attempted his escape. A great statue of Claus and the grey horse rose prominently by the archway. He was dressed for battle and held a sword in hand while the grey horse was portrayed jumping over a boulder.

"That never happened," Claus said.

"Shh," Selba said. "You'll ruin the magic."

The boulders that Claus had once jumped had long been moved away, and the archway was well developed into a passageway. The tram continued through the archway and passageway, which was an interwoven mixture of yellow and blue threads.

"That weave," Claus said. "It looks very much like—"

"Do you like it?" Clausetta asked. "I made it myself. With your help, of course. Mamma keeps up the regular wall, and I made this one to Leifton."

"Who is Leifton?" Claus asked.

"More like a 'what'," Selba said.

"That's where my brother lives. Oh, you know him. Leif? He and my sister-in-law run Leifton."

The tram picked up speed and soon would be in Leifton. It approached a fortress, paused by a guard, and was allowed entry.

"Your sister-in-law," Claus said. "Who is she?"

Claus didn't have long to wonder. The tram stopped, the three departed, and the tram went off to another site in Leifton.

"I'm Leif," a man said. "And this is my wife."

"Hello, Clomper. Nice to see you," said Lanietta.

"You? Of all the dirty tricks!" Claus said.

"I'm your daughter now. And it's legal. Did you bring me a cake? Today is my birthday, you know."

"Does Leif know he's married to an older woman?" Claus asked.

"I'm as young as I feel," Lanietta said.

"Leif," Claus said. "You're my son. This marriage with Lanietta is a sham."

"Clausetta, are you playing another practical joke on me? How long did it take you to think up these lines?" Leif asked.

"No, this is the real me," Claus said. "I'm out of my coma and fully alert."

"Out of one coma and into the next," Lanietta said. "You are in my domain now. I am a comet, see me shine, and surround me in the coma of my greatness."

"Oh brother," Claus said.

"You always were the pessimistic one," Lanietta said. "What good can you do?"

"I'm trying to right what has been wronged," Claus said.

"Pappa, please!" Clausetta said. "Lanietta is the sister I never had. We do all kinds of things together. And she teaches me things about the Carinians."

"Corrupted my children, I see," Claus said.

"You've been out of it for a bit," Lanietta said. "All was peaceful and prosperous while you remained in your lazy state. Now you come to life and cry foul. To think of all the statues we made of you in your honor, only to be slighted and slopped around like hogs!"

Clausetta started to cry. Leif took her into his arms.

"There, there, sis, he's just not used to such greatness. He'll adjust in time," Leif said.

"Claus, please," Selba said. "Lanietta has been very helpful the last twenty-five years. She's pioneered large-scale irrigation, she gave women power to choose their children, she helped Clausetta and Sergio harvest new crops that take carbon from the soil instead of the air—the list goes on and on and on. Without Lanietta's help, Gerhardt Estate would have remained a farm, or worse."

Lanietta smiled with such satisfaction that Claus wanted to punch her.

"Aren't you going to thank me, Clomper?" she said. "I always come back to my property and pay my debt of gratitude."

"You owe me?" Claus asked.

"Yes. For being such a good pappa to me in my time of need. I am that very special daughter you never had, second to Clausetta of course. No one is as bright a beacon of hope as she is."

Clausetta smiled.

"Then explain Labba," Claus said.

"You mean my former friend who continues to launch her weekly attack on Leifton? Well, she still has a grudge against me, I suppose. I mean, I did borrow Leif for a bit."

"You kidnapped our son!" Claus said.

"That's all in the past," Leif said. "The important thing is that we are together and working in harmony."

"All of us? As in the whole planet?" Claus asked.

"Well, Frieda still has her mind, of course," Lanietta said. "But we have an excellent relationship with the lunar shock. We help provide people what they need. What Frieda does not provide, we do. You could call it a balanced equation."

"Claus, you're the only one unhappy," Selba said. "Everyone else is happy."

"Everyone?"

"Yes, everyone," Lanietta said. "Besides, we have something in common. Your true-blood daughter is named after you and me. I'm sure you figured that out by now."

"What's that supposed to mean?" Claus asked.

Lanietta laughed.

"Don't worry," Lanietta continued to laugh. "Labba is her true mother. I never was into...well...for the sake of the children I will not re-express myself."

"I could debate you on that. I have my points to make as well. But I will also hold my tongue for the same reason," Claus said.

"Very wise," Lanietta said.

"Pappa! It's not crabby time! Let's go see the fortress! Leif, can you come with us?" Clausetta begged.

"Lanietta and I have a special date," Leif winked.

Claus shook his head in disgust.

"You're such a party pooper, Clomper," Lanietta said. "Enjoy your stay."

"Here!" Clausetta said. "Let's take one of these!"

Clausetta ushered Claus and Selba into a three-wheeled three-person vehicle. Clausetta sat up front and drove while Selba and Claus sat in back.

"It's powered by thorium," Clausetta said, referring to the vehicle. "Another great Irina Kechenova invention."

The three took off around the fortress. Clausetta made mention of how similar or different the fountains, statues, floral arrangements, and other amenities were from Gerhardt Estates.

"Who named Clausetta?" Claus asked.

"Labba and I came up with it," Selba said. "I made several suggestions, and Labba agreed with 'Clausetta'."

"Because of Lanietta and me?" Claus asked.

"Something like that," Selba said.

"I don't believe it. Why would Labba name a child after her enemy?"

"Because by that time, an alliance was forming between Lanietta's fortress and your farm. Labba fought against it, but it was inevitable. She made a deal with Lanietta to let you keep Clausetta, provided the baby be named after her."

"That was the alliance?" Claus asked.

"That was the beginning of it. Again, Labba said nothing. I acted as an intermediary. But the whole alliance is founded on keeping Leif and Clausetta safe and happy," Selba said. "It's a delicate weave, Claus. Don't disrupt it."

"I'm trying very hard to make sense of this and not ruin anything," Claus said. "Maybe I should dive into another archway and end things for good."

"Don't think such thoughts. It doesn't take much to skew the balance of any ecosystem."

"This is an ecosystem?"

"You could call it that. It's certainly symbiotic," Selba said.

Claus paused in thought.

"What are all these divots in the wall?" Claus asked. "Looks like it's been under attack."

"It has. By Labba," Selba said.

"She did that?" Claus asked.

But before Selba could confirm, Labba in eagle form made a mad dive against the structure. Sentries fought her off, and she flew away.

"See? She just made another one," Selba said.

"Everyone is happy. Not Labba. And not me," Claus said.

"Okay, two exceptions. Everyone else alive is happy," Selba said.

"What's this alive stuff? Who died? Who, Selba?" Claus demanded.

"You're not going to like this," Selba said.

"I'm already miserable. One more miserable thing isn't going to make much difference," Claus said.

"This will. Shara is dead."

Claus threw his hands up in disbelief.

"I'm sorry, Pappa," Clausetta said. "I heard she was a nice woman."

"She was," Claus said. "How did it happen, Selba?"

"She heard about the three-for-one offer, remember?" Selba started.

"Yes," Claus said with a sigh.

"She wanted a baby just like mine. So she did the deal. She had Lanietta take three of her eggs and return one. She was pregnant with a boy," Selba continued.

"And Lanietta's procedure killed her," Claus guessed. "I should have known. Lanietta—"

"Didn't kill anyone!" Clausetta protested.

"Clausetta is right," Selba said.

"Then how?" Claus asked.

"Shara didn't wait to go full term," Selba explained. "She had a Greylinger cube implanted in her upper palate to extend her life. It conflicted with the pregnancy and aged her rapidly over nine days. She died of old age. So did her unborn child."

"Her unborn child died of old age?" Claus said in amazement.

"It was as if both of them received radiation burns," Selba said. "That's how it was explained to me. Anyway, when I had my cube implanted, I'd already decided no more children, and Sergio was already born. But we did learn a lesson as a community—we can't mix immortality with the cycle of life."

"Poor Shara. She was so full of life. Like Clausetta. Hear that, Clausetta? No immortality cube for you!"

"I will if I want!" she said defiantly. "But I'll wait until I'm done having children. I might want a few more."

The three had been gradually spiraling upward through the fortress. They reached a high spot, and all three got out.

"Isn't it a beautiful view?" Clausetta asked.

Claus looked and saw Labba perched far away. He saw the ethereal nest around his estate and the ethereal tunnel connecting his estate to the fortress. He also saw many other fortresses peppering the landscape. Those areas of lunar soil untouched remained like a desert, but the others were green and lush.

"Where does the water come from?" Claus asked.

"It's piped in from the old far side," Selba said. "It won't rain over here. Near the lunar shock, the rain just curves back to the lunar shock."

"Yes, I remember seeing that. But how can Lanietta pump it from Frieda's side?"

"Through the Anrega," Selba said. "And to answer the question you haven't asked, that's where Treyu and Mariel have come from. They were reanimated from the Anrega. So were many of the lesser Carinians. But not Lanietta's parents nor a few other special people. Lanietta is protecting them, just in case."

"Just in case Luna explodes like Earth," Claus said.

"Exactly," Selba said.

"It's a wonder Luna isn't peppered by debris from Earth. We should have lots of extra craters by now," Claus said.

"Actually, Luna has picked up much from Earth," Selba said. "I don't know how much you remember about the transition, but when Earth exploded, Luna picked up Earth's atmosphere and most of its water. Twice a year, Luna goes through a debris field. Causes a meteor shower at night, and there are all sorts of dancing ghosts in the night sky."

"Yes! The dancing ghosts!" Clausetta added. "I have lots of videographs of us playing with the dancing ghosts!"

Claus looked at Selba funny.

"She recorded the times you were animated in your coma. During ghost night, old souls from Earth come down to Luna and interact with the people. It's mostly on the old near side and in the lunar shock. The remnant PRAAD prevents them from descending on the old far side."

"Yes, Pappa, and you can speak to them, too! I don't have to force you to say anything. It's like you know them," Clausetta said.

"You're in a very fortunate position, Claus," Selba said. "Some people go through life and do nothing but watch how others live, to satisfy boredom. You can watch videographs of your coma years to satisfy any boredom you might have."

"I'm afraid of what I might see. Who knows what I've done, what deals I've made with these ghosts," Claus said.

"So far no ill has come of it," Selba said. "I wouldn't worry too much about it."

"But they always came to you first, Pappa," Clausetta said.

"Probably attracted to Aftova," Selba said.

"Yes," Claus said. "Now that I'm outside of the nest, I could..."

Claus tapped his upper palate and sent out his yellow and blue ethereal threads through his teeth, ready to attack. Both Clausetta turned to stop him and Lanietta space-jumped over to Claus. Clausetta went eethi, used her ethereal self to tie the two ends together, and sent them back into Claus. She reintegrated herself with a "whew!"

"Thank you, sis," Lanietta said.

"You can go eethi?" Claus asked Clausetta.

"Of course. I'm part Carinian," she said.

"I taught her how to harness it, of course. Labba wouldn't do it. How do you think Clausetta acquired the talents for control of you, Clomper? By mere magic?" Lanietta asked.

"I had hoped she was self-taught," Claus said.

"Why waste time going in circles when a master like me can save her time and toil?" Lanietta said. "Clomper, you really must learn to be more efficient."

"But no more tricks, Pappa. Everybody is watching you," Clausetta said.

Claus reluctantly agreed.

"Have you picked out something for the ball tonight?" Lanietta asked Clausetta.

"Oh, I completely forgot!" Clausetta said. "Pappa! What will I do?"

"Let your sister help you," Lanietta said. "I have a new collection I'd like you to see. Pick out whatever gown you like."

The two went off, leaving Claus to Selba.

"There are frequent balls. Very frequent," Selba said. "They don't fret too much about things here, Claus. Everyone enjoys a good but dignified time. You know, we should pick out your clothes for the ball."

"I'm not going to a ball," Claus said.

"I ask that you do," Selba said. "It will help with your re-acclimation to the modern world. You can go with me if you like. I'm not married, and Labba won't mind."

"I don't know. Too much is happening," Claus said.

"You won't have to do a thing. Just sit around, enjoy a drink, and watch everyone else," Selba said.

Claus paused but nodded his head in agreement.

"Excellent. I'll pick you up in the early evening," she said.

Chapter 110: The Ball

"Sir, if I may," Treyu said. "You collar needs adjustment."

"My collar is never right," Claus said. "How do I look?"

"Other than the collar, you look just fine," he said.

"Treyu, did Lanietta bring anyone else back, like, Berella?" Claus asked.

"You know about her? Yes, I'm married to her," Treyu said.

"Would you do me the honor and bring her along to the ball?" Claus asked. "I need all the company I can get."

"I would be honored," he said. "If I may leave you to let her know. Such short notice, and a woman needs much time to prepare."

"By all means, you may go," Claus said. "Return here, and we'll all go together."

"An excellent idea," Treyu said, and he left.

Claus went downstairs and saw Mariel dusting.

"I just saw Treyu running out of here like his clothing was on fire," Mariel said.

"I invited him to the ball," Claus said.

"I didn't know you could do that," Mariel said. "It's at the Leifton fortress, right? Leif and Lanietta only have the right to add guests."

"As Leif is my son, I feel the right to invite a few more," Claus said.

"And Lanietta is your daughter," Mariel grinned.

"Please don't remind me," Claus said.

"I knew her when she was young," Mariel said. "Tried to teach her a few things. She always seemed to get into trouble."

"I know," Claus said.

"You do?"

"Yes. She's always into trouble when I'm with her too," Claus said.

"She's well-behaved these days. Has done much to build up the area."

"Will you go to the ball with us?" Claus asked. "I can arrange a date if you need one."

"I have my own partner, but no thank you. I prefer the solitude of dusting. Makes me feel like I'm ridding the world of filth."

"Are you suggesting anything, Mariel?" Claus asked.

"A clean house is a happy house," she said. "As for Lanietta, well..."

Claus sighed.

"Do try to behave," Mariel said. "You've been in a coma, and you'll be expected to perform as normal."

"What do you mean?" Claus said.

"You've been to the ball many times. Clausetta controlled your movements, of course. You maintained a perfect composure. Everyone will expect the same, now that you're conscious and aware."

"Thank you for the warning," Claus said.

Selba showed up.

"Your date is here," Mariel said.

"Treyu is going too," Claus said to Selba. "He's bringing Berella."

"Oh how divine!" Selba said. "Clausetta and Sergio will be here shortly as well. And well, here they are!"

Clausetta and Sergio showed up, and a few minutes later, Treyu showed up with Berella.

"You just left here," Claus said. "How did—"

"Berella was ready to go just in case," Treyu said. "She had a hunch about this particular ball."

"Berella, you look great," Claus said.

"Thank you," she replied.

"Treyu, I believe we are ready," Claus said.

"We are. This way please," Treyu said.

Treyu led the others to a large horse-drawn carriage. The driver had a hood and was not identifiable.

"Wait," Claus said.

"Remember me?" the driver said as she removed her hood.

"Sharlamarian's driver?" Claus said.

"The pay is better here," she said. "Please, climb aboard."

Claus and Treyu helped the others aboard first, Claus went next to last, and Treyu went in last. The driver took off. The carriage was drawn past the orchards, the vineyards, and the other great fountains, stonework, and layout of Gerhardt Estates. They reached the archway and went through.

"I wish Labba would go," Claus said.

"She will show up in her own way," Selba said.

"She attacks during a ball?" Claus asked.

"She does," Selba said.

The group arrived at the main entrance where several attendants helped them out of the carriage. The driver took the carriage away, and the couples entered. Leif and Lanietta greeted everyone as they entered.

"Pappa! So good to see you!" Leif said to Claus.

"It's good to see you too!" Claus said.

Then it was on to Lanietta.

"Clomper and his first ball while awake," she said with a wink and a kiss on the cheek.

"Hard to think of you as my daughter," Claus said.

"Save some energy for me later," she whispered in his ear.

"That's not what a daughter is supposed to say," Claus replied as he pulled away and left her.

"What was that about?" Selba asked.

"Lanietta being mischievous," Claus said.

They stood around for drinks and light conversation. Claus didn't know much of anyone and was about to sit down, but he felt an electric shock, and Aftova commanded his muscles into action. He walked quickly and realized the source of this involuntary request—Clausetta.

"This is Pappa!" Clausetta said to one of her friends. "Oh, but you should call him Mr. Gerhardt."

"Claus. Please call me Claus," he said.

"Nice to meet you, Claus," she said.

"This is my music teacher, Pappa! And my dance teacher over here. And riding instructor. And over there, yoo-hoo!" Clausetta called.

"Clausetta, I'm a little tired and hungry," Claus said. "If you don't mind, I'll grab myself a snack. Will you be all right without me?"

But before Claus could get an answer, Clausetta had dragged Sergio over to meet someone else. Claus sighed and realized he'd lost Selba. He stared across the room and saw that she was engaged in conversation with Treyu, Berella, and several others.

"Good," Claus said. "I can dispense with the pleasantries and plop down right here. Nice that there are snacks everywhere. I'll just nibble on these crackers and cheese, and here's a chilled beer. I'm in heaven."

Claus had only gotten a nibble or two down with a gulp of beer when someone plopped down beside him and disturbed the balance of the love seat.

"This is one of my favorite pieces," Lanietta said. "Just enough room for two people in love."

"Lanietta!" Claus said as he spilled his beer on himself.

"Oh, I'm sorry," she said with mock apology. "Let me clean that off for you."

She pulled out a yellow and blue scarf and used it to clean up the beer. Then she playfully wrapped it around his neck and pulled him close to her.

"Give your daughter a good-luck kiss," she said.

"You have no conception of what it's like to be a daughter," Claus said.

Lanietta pulled Claus against him and kissed him on the lips. He pushed her away.

"Stop this nonsense. People will see!" he said.

Several people did see and gave Claus and Lanietta a strange look before walking away.

"See? It's not proper," Claus said.

"Who cares about proper," she said.

"Lanietta, my love," Leif called from a distance as he approached.

Lanietta released her grip on Claus, retrieved the scarf, and put it away.

"Coming, dear!" she replied but then turned to Claus and said, "I'll see you again soon."

Claus gave another big sigh.

"Sit and watch everyone else. Hah! This ball was a mistake!" he said.

Claus walked out onto a balcony and looked off into the fields. Then without warning, Labba swooped in, grabbed him with her talons, and ripped up the back of his suit.

"Labba, stop!" he said.

Others shooed Labba away and tried to help Claus.

"I'm fine. Really I am," he said, and he walked away.

Before he could get far, the call went out for dinner. There was assigned seating. Selba caught up with Claus and brought him to the head table. She sat on one side and Clausetta sat on another. But Sergio found a friend he hadn't seen in years, and he rushed over to the friend's table.

"Sergio! Wait for me!" Clausetta said, and she dashed after him.

"The impulsiveness of youth," Claus said.

"What's wrong with youth?" Lanietta said as she took over Clausetta's seat next to Claus.

"Shouldn't you be sitting next to my son? You know, the one you kidnapped?" Claus mocked.

"He's over there with Sergio and Clausetta. They were all in a horse race together. Good times," Lanietta said. "Like our good times. Remember?"

"You put me through many bad times," Claus said. "Selba, tell Lanietta how—"

But Selba was in conversation with Berella, who sat on her other side.

"It's just us two again," Lanietta grinned.

"You're up to something as usual," Claus said.

"I've been a good girl these many twenty-five years," Lanietta said. "Ask anyone."

"Only because I've been in a coma," Claus said.

"Really, Clomper, you're the most self-centered pet I've ever known," she said.

"Shouldn't you call me Pappa?"

"Very well. Pappa pet Clomper," she laughed.

"You think this is a game. Blowing up Earth and creating this culture on Luna. You've cost many lives, Lanietta, and you've blindsided everyone."

"I've killed no one," she said. "Your Labba and Doctor Kechenova evacuated the humans. Male selenites don't count. Fortunately I found Selenita, and she helped me create a class of female selenites to do the dirty work around here. Otherwise you'd be doing dishes instead of enjoying my pleasant company. Now kiss me!"

Lanietta pulled Claus toward her and kissed him.

"Stop it! Not appropriate!" Claus said.

"Perhaps I should clock you over the head with a blunt instrument," she said. "Like Labba. That *is* how you two created Clausetta, isn't it?"

"You are warped out of your mind," Claus said.

"I know she conceived twice with you, and each time you had suffered a head injury. What will it take for me to conceive with you?" she asked.

"You accused Labba of bestiality with me, and here you propose the same thing? You hypocrite!" Claus said.

Lanietta laughed.

"I just wanted to get a reaction out of you," she continued to laugh. "You've always been such a good Clomper. Here, have a doggie biscuit."

Lanietta pulled a doggie biscuit from her hand purse.

"Put that away! I'm not a dog!" he barked.

"You certainly bark like one," she said. "Oh look, here's dinner."

Selenite servants delivered food to each person seated, starting with the head table and proceeding to the others.

"I hope you like salmon," Lanietta said.

"Where did you get salmon?" he asked.

"We keep the lake well stocked," she said. "Part of the irrigation project Clausetta meant to show you. She gets easily distracted. She should have been our daughter, but I'm already your daughter through Leif, so that would be complicated."

"Would you stop with all the strange conception talk?" Claus pleaded.

"Tell me, Clomper," she continued. "What was it like with Labba? Was it romantic? Was it love?"

"I don't know," Claus said. "I was unconscious both times."

"I should try it with you. Concentric kissing. Sounds interesting," she said.

"How do you know about that?" Claus asked.

"Oh, whenever I put my fingers through your hair as I do now, I can read all sorts of things from Aftova. I still have Fronfa, you know. And what does Labba have? Just a few ruffled feathers. We should link Fronfa and Aftova, you and I. Make a permanent connection. Then we can team up against Frieda."

It was Claus's turn to laugh.

"Why do you laugh?" Lanietta protested, suddenly becoming cross.

"You're afraid of Frieda," Claus said.

"Am not," she said.

"Are too! She has Rigefa and a power you cannot contain. I thought you were just hanging out on the old near side, that maybe you had special protection against the PRAAD remnant. But you don't. You know that each person here with Carinian blood won't be able to deal with Frieda and the old far side. But I can."

Lanietta wanted to say something, but her face turned beet red.

"Better be nice to me. I'm your only hope in defeating Frieda," Claus said.

"Ugh!" Lanietta said.

She dumped her drink on Claus and stormed off.

"Didn't even touch her salmon," Claus said. "That's okay. Now I have double portions."

Claus decided it was the best double portion of salmon he'd ever had.

Dinner ended, and the guests engaged in dessert and small talk. Clausetta had caught up to Claus and pulled him along to a viewing room. All of Clausetta's friends watched videographs of her and Claus on ghost night.

"Twice a year," Clausetta explained, "Luna passes through the ghost field. That's where Earth exploded. There are lost souls there, and they come down to Luna. See? Pappa and I are dancing with three of them. There's Sergio. He's dancing with a...Sergio! You never told me about her!"

"It was just for the ghost night," he shrugged.

"This was five years ago. Pappa's beard was a little less grey," Clausetta said.

Claus watched as the reels spun on the projector. Then a strange sensation overtook him. He felt the blue ethereal thread snake outward to the projector. Suddenly, he was back there on ghost night and dancing with Clausetta and the ghosts. He reached out to touch one, and he found himself acquiring the memories and life experiences of the ghost, which took him to a business park. He walked about the business park around noon. It was partly cloudy with puddles of water everywhere.

"It rained," Claus said.

The puddles were on the road and in large parking lots behind office buildings. One such puddle was large enough to act like a pond, with small waves rippling along from the wind. He looked at the reflection of the clouds and sky and noticed how fluorescent-blue the sky was. Looking up at the sky, he saw the same brilliant blue.

"The clouds," Claus thought. "They reflect light back up into the sky."

Claus half thought of making a little sailboat out of paper and placing it on the parking-lot pond. It was a thing he would have done in his youth, but he was an adult in this vision, and it wouldn't do. Very few others were out walking, presumably because they had better things to do.

Claus walked past the parking-lot pond and toward a dry section of the parking lot. The wind picked up and blew an empty coffee cup in his path. The cup did not remain stationary. Neither did Claus. Each time he tried to step away from it, the cup seemed to block his path, but always it stayed just a little in front of him, neither impeding his progress nor completely moving out of the way.

"I couldn't get rid of that cup if I wanted to," he said.

Claus reached the end of the parking lot, and the cup stopped at the curb. What disgusted Claus the most about this parking lot wasn't so much the loose-cup litter but the long trail of cigarette butts and empty cigarette packages strewn along the curb area, running from the far edge of the parking lot to the building itself. These weren't fresh bits of garbage but instead had been through several years of spring flood, summer drought, and winter ice.

"Almost better to be the cup, if you're a piece of garbage," he muttered to himself.

Claus stared over a short berm to the office building next door. It belonged to a graphics-arts company, the landscaping was tidy, and there was a prominent "No Trespassing" sign in the most pleasingly designed form. Employees at the building ate lunch at tables with large umbrellas. Several pointed to the west and hastened their meal.

As it was, Claus was west of the graphics arts building, and so he thought they were pointing to him. He turned north and proceeded in front of the office building where there was a sidewalk. He took the sidewalk, but as he approached the front doors to each successive office building, he had to weave around people who weren't looking where they were going. He reached a semi-circular area with a flagpole in the center, and he was surprised to see a driver going through the wrong way. He had half-fancied walking over to the flagpole to tap on the pole, but good thing he didn't. He wasn't used to checking for wrong-way drivers, and this one would have gotten him good.

Several office complexes more, and Claus reached one that was abandoned. It looked much like the others, but it was empty, as was the parking lot, except for the weeds and hopeful trees that pushed their way through cracks in the asphalt. Claus made it to the far western edge of the office park, and he reached a concrete wall, a wall constructed to hold back earth from a higher elevation. It was at this point he noticed dark storm clouds approaching.

"How much time will I have?" he asked himself.

He walked along the concrete wall and saw several ivy plants that had grown onto the wall as if they were two-dimensional trees. At the end of this wall was a long backroad to the office park. Lightning lit up the sky. Thunder clapped around Claus. He hurried his pace down the back road, but heavy drops thudded down on and around him. He reached the end and dove into a salt storage area. There he waited as a torrential downpour flooded the area. He climbed the salt pile to get away from this flood.

As he waited, he felt himself on a salt flat regressing backward in time, gradually filling up with more and more water until it returned to the ocean it once was. An orca came toward him as if to swallow him, but a bowhead whale swallowed him instead, and he sat in the cold innards of the bowhead.

"Stop, Pappa!" Clausetta said. "You should not interfere with the projector."

Claus looked around and realized he was back in the projector room with Clausetta's friends watching videographs of ghost night.

"Pappa, do you need fresh air?" Clausetta asked.

Selba happened to walk in.

"Oh, there you are Claus. May I have a word with you?" she asked.

"Pappa needs fresh air," Clausetta said.

"Yes, I do," Claus added.

Selba and Claus left the viewing room and headed to a balcony. The two stood on that balcony and looked out to the landscape. Selba had two beers in hand and handed one to Claus.

"Thanks," he said.

"I need to warn you about this place," she said. "It's not just beautiful masonry and groundskeeping. There's strange ethereal stuff going on. I know, it shouldn't be possible with the remnant PRAAD on the other side. But it's like we're in the wake of a ship, and old things from the sea get stirred up. I...I sound crazy. I'll shut up now."

"No," Claus said. "I think I experienced one of those stirred up things. I could never kick the cup but it would never go away."

"I don't understand, but I'm not surprised," Selba said.

"I haven't had a vision like that since I was in the Anrega orb chamber. I guess I thought that all ended," Claus said. "Maybe I should move to the old far side. Get away from these visions. I can take Clausetta with me, she can bring Sergio, and we'll get away from Lanietta and these visions."

"Clausetta can't go to the old far side," Selba said. "Surely you realize this. Like Leif, she's part Carinian. The beyton rays would destroy her. She can't leave Luna either. No, Claus, she must stay on the old near side. Is it really so bad here? I mean, you don't want to go to the far side. Trust me."

"Why not? Immortality, no desires to satisfy. I can relax for a change," Claus said.

"You'd relax in the form of a cube," Selba said. "Didn't Labba tell you anything? No, she doesn't speak, and you've been out of circulation for a bit."

"Before we lost Leif, she said Frieda was developing an ethereal computer, that Aftova in my upper palate has a digital flip-flop formed by yellow and blue Greylingers," Claus said.

"That's the basis for the long-life cube," Selba said. "Many of us in the lunar shock have taken to that instead of fully converting into Friedian form. That's what Frieda calls it when you give up all needs and ability to create life. You could get one of those, no wait, I'm not sure. Aftova might cause a problem there. A pity Aftova hasn't slowed your aging."

"Yes, isn't it though? What happens when I die? Does Aftova go with me?" Claus asked. "Maybe I should give it to Clausetta."

"Wait before you try such a thing. These alien things can have unforeseen consequences," Selba warned.

"Like with Shara," Claus said.

"Exactly. Further, there's no evidence she'll have a short life. She and Leif are the first of their kind," Selba said.

"Tell me more about the Friedian form," Claus said.

"People are digitized into the ethereal universe. They take a new corporeal form, but not like you or me. They are composed entirely of cubes," Selba explained.

"That's weird. Does it hurt?" he asked.

"It's hard to tell. Their personalities are flat after the conversion, as if they've lost the desire for life. Yet they go on, not stopping to die nor jumping ahead in excitement. Just rolling along—"

"Like a cup in the wind," Claus said.

Selba looked at Claus funny.

"Part of the vision I had," he said.

"I would not recommend going through with the conversion. If the person is in pain, you'd never know. They'd suffer tremendously yet go through life day by day without affecting others," Selba said.

"Sounds terrible. Really, we can't let people go through with the conversion," Claus said. "It's too risky."

"Others might be better off," Selba said. "But there's no way to tell. At least not with our technology."

"I want to see them," Claus said. "I want to see if I can determine their silent pain index."

"Using Aftova?"

"Yes."

"Well, Labba has allowed you to leave the estate for Leifton. She might let you visit the lunar shock. If you go, I'd better go with you. And no Clausetta! She'd be tempted to visit the old far side," Selba said.

"It seems Sergio will take care of her," Claus said.

"He will. I brought him up proper. Come to think of it, I brought up Clausetta too," Selba said.

"Proper?"

"As proper as a girl can be brought up when not distracted," Selba said.

"All right. Let's go to the lunar shock tomorrow. I must see how things have changed," Claus said.

"Deal," Selba said.

Chimes sounded, and that indicated the dance would begin soon.

"Clausetta will insist that you dance," Selba said.

"I thought you said I could just watch," Claus said.

"You can. But you've danced before, and she'll make you dance using the same method as before," Selba said. "You wouldn't know what to do otherwise. But she might expect you to."

"What am I to do then?" Claus asked.

"I'll be your partner. If she doesn't prompt you, I'll give you cues. Watch for them," Selba said.

"Why do I get pulled into these things?" Claus muttered to himself. "Yes, Grandma Broc, another stepping stone."

The two arrived in the dance area. Already groups of parallel lines formed with women on one side and men on the other.

"A barn dance?" Claus asked.

"It is not a barn dance," Selba said. "Think English country dance."

The music started, and the dancers moved, but there was no caller. The couples walked up and back. They then walked up again and turned around each other. Claus received no help from Clausetta, so he watched Selba and others to see what to do. The dance was a mixture of interactions and didn't match anything he remembered. At one point, the women and men approached each other, the women held out a scarf at the waist, and the men pulled on the scarf. Just as Claus was about to pull on Selba's scarf, Lanietta jumped in and displaced Selba, tricking Claus to pull on her scarf.

"No need to follow cues now," Lanietta said. "I'll direct your movements."

The couples did a maneuver where they would pull apart to lengthen the scarf, approach with the woman twirling to wrap the scarf around her waist, and separate with her twirling the other way to unwrap.

"Spin me 'round, Claus. Spin me till I'm blue," Lanietta said.

"What are you doing here?" Claus asked.

"Dancing with you," she said.

Then couples held their scarves out at length, forming a bridge, while other couples walked underneath. When Claus and Lanietta walked underneath, Claus tugged down on the scarf to clothesline Lanietta. The scarf caught her in the throat and sent her backward, where she fell on her back. The music and dance stopped. Everyone gasped while helping Lanietta back to her feet.

"I'm all right. No harm done. Yet," Lanietta said with an eye of vengeance on Claus.

"Pappa, Pappa!" Clausetta called as she rushed over. "Are you hurt?"

"Not yet, honey. The day of reckoning shall come," Lanietta said.

"It was an accident," Claus said.

"Clever liar," Lanietta muffled.

"What was that?" Claus asked.

"Oh, uh, he'll never tire," Lanietta said. "Well, everyone. My folly makes for a short break. How about another dance. Minstrel? A weave song."

"Weave song?" Claus wondered.

"Yes. Clomper here will stand in the middle," Lanietta said. "Now everyone form lines. Ladies on this side. Gentlemen over here. Begin."

Lanietta sent out a gentle suggestion to the group on how to dance. It was simple. Partners walked up, ladies offered the end of a scarf, the men took the end, and the couples drew apart so that each held a length of scarf. Pair by pair, each couple went up to Claus and wrapped the scarf around him, with the women walking clockwise and the men counterclockwise.

Women ducked under the men's end while wrapping Claus. The last couple finished, and Claus was heavily wrapped.

"This isn't a weave, it's a wrap!" Claus complained.

"Yes. That's a wrap, everyone," Lanietta said. "This concludes the ball."

"Oh, Pappa! You're so silly!" Clausetta said. "Let's go home."

Chapter 111: Claus Visits the Lunar Shock

"Please come back soon, Pappa!" Clausetta said with tears. "You've never left before."

"He never could," Selba said.

Claus and Selba stood in the main reception area of Claus's mansion and prepared to leave.

"Write every day!" Clausetta said.

"Is there a postal system now?" Claus asked Selba.

"No," Selba said. "She learned that line from a ghost on ghost night."

"Oh."

"Clausetta, we won't be gone long. We'll take the Lanietta Express. We'll contact you when we reach the lunar shock," Selba said.

"Sir, if I may assist you on this journey," Treyu said.

"No. You'll need to run the estate in my absence," Claus said.

"Of course, sir."

"You take care of Clausetta," Selba said to Sergio.

"I will, Mother," he replied.

Claus and Selba climbed aboard an electric vehicle. Selba sat in the driver's seat and drove off as the others waved goodbye.

"This vehicle looks familiar," Claus said.

"I've had it for twenty-five years," Selba said. "Back then I had to make the entire trip from the lunar shock to your farm on lunar soil. There were no roads and no train. Today we take the train."

"The Lanietta Express?" Claus said.

"Of course," Selba replied. "Don't be so harsh toward Lanietta. She has enabled many to travel from the lunar shock to Leifton in the same day. She has a very strong belief that machines and people should be kept separate. Her female selenites maintain themselves and keep the machinery in good shape. Let no one be mechanized."

"I didn't realize she was so compassionate," Claus mocked.

"Claus!" Selba said.

"I know, I know. Don't be so harsh. But I can't help it. I feel like she's trying to run this world," Claus said.

"Someone has to. Might as well be her," Selba said.

"You've sold out to her," Claus said.

Selba laughed.

"Choose your poison, Claus. Choose your poison."

The vehicle passed through the archway and into the ethereal-woven tunnel to Leifton where the Lanietta Express awaited. Selba drove onto the train and parked.

"It's like a ferry in old Earth days," Selba said. "When we reach the lunar shock, we can drive around in our vehicle. Convenient, no?"

"I hope so," Claus said.

"Let's walk to the dining car. I'm hungry," Selba said.

"But the train...oh, it's moving!" Claus said.

"Yes. I had them wait for us. Now it's on with the journey!" Selba said.

The two reached the dining car and sat at a booth. The train clacked along the tracks and periodically passed railroad crossings with the characteristic Doppler-effect sound. Menus were already in place along with glasses of water.

"Are you buying?" Claus asked.

Selba laughed.

"No, you are, with your revolving credit," Selba said. "Your estate pays for many conveniences."

"Humph," Claus said.

"If you don't believe me, ask the waitress," Selba said. "Here she comes now."

A waitress approached with menus in hand, but she held them up high to avoid a passing couple.

"Excuse me," Claus said. "Who is paying for this meal?"

The waitress lowered the menus, revealing her identity.

"Why, you are Clomper," Lanietta said. "May I take your order?"

"You!"

"A hobby of mine," she said. "I always enjoy giving good service."

With that, Lanietta rubbed her leg against Claus's.

"Cut that out!" he said. "I'm in a relationship with—"

"Labba," Lanietta said. "And where is she now? Look out the window, and you'll see."

Claus looked out the window and saw Labba the eagle flying alongside the train but a bit away to avoid collision.

"Don't worry. The windows are tinted," Lanietta laughed. "Well? Are you going to order?"

"Just give me—" Claus started.

"That's no way to treat your lady guest," Lanietta said. "Really, Clomper, I thought I trained you better than that. Ladies first!"

"I'll have the lentil soup and veggie sandwich," Selba said.

"Make that two," Claus said.

"Chicken?" Lanietta asked.

"No, I'm not scared of you," Claus said.

"The lentil soup has a chicken option," Selba said. "Unusual, I know, but it's all the rage on the train."

"You are chicken," Lanietta grinned.

"Hah! See? She torments me even now," Claus said.

"You don't know torment. But you will," Lanietta said. "I'll bring your food shortly."

Lanietta left.

"She's going to do something to me! Selba! Why didn't you warn me?" Claus said in a panic.

"She's not," Selba said. "Relax, Claus. Here, I know."

Selba waved to Lanietta, who was across the room taking another order. Selba then signaled for drinks to be brought. Lanietta nodded her head in agreement.

"Let go, Claus," Selba said. "You'll feel better when you do."

Lanietta returned with a bottle of strawberry champagne in an ice bucket. She then rushed away and came back with the lentil soup.

"Champagne?" Claus asked.

"It's strawberry champagne and is specially formulated to go with almost any meal," she said. "It will quiet your nerves. From special grapes grown in your own vineyard, I might add."

Claus looked at the bottle: "Gerhardt Estates Strawberry Champagne, cultivated by Claus himself from the finest of fine vines."

"I never cultivated this," Claus said. "Wait. Clausetta?"

"Clausetta," Selba laughed.

"And I bet she took a videograph of my crazy coma cultivation compulsion," Claus mused.

"She did," Selba added.

"Sigh."

"Have the champagne. It will do you good," Selba said.

Claus picked up the bottle. The top had already been removed.

"She thinks of everything," Claus said, referring to Lanietta.

"Of course. The best for the best," Selba said.

Claus was about to fill his glass.

"Ahem," Selba said.

"Oh, would you care for a glass?" Claus asked.

"Yes, please. Thank you," she said.

Claus filled her glass then filled his own. He took a sip and felt immediately better.

"There, you see?" Selba said. "Now put some nutrients in those arteries before they harden with scowl."

"You sound so matronly," Claus said.

"I've mothered three people—Sergio, Clausetta, and you," Selba laughed.

"And Leif?" Claus asked.

"I mothered him," Lanietta said, returning with food and placing it before them. "And sistered him. And girlfriended him."

"How lovely," Claus said sarcastically.

"Have another sip!" Selba said, referring to the champagne.

Claus swallowed the glass's contents.

"My, we are impatient today!" Lanietta said. "Relax and let the train do all the work. Do you need anything else? Is everything okay?"

Claus was about to say something, but Selba quietly shushed him.

"Everything is fine," Selba said as she dragged out the word, "fine."

"I'll check on you in a bit then," Lanietta said, and she left.

"Everything isn't fine," Claus said.

"For once I agree," Selba said.

"Thank you!" Claus said.

"That champagne should have relaxed you and made you content. I'll have to complain to the cultivator about it. Oh, that's you!" Selba laughed.

"Not funny," Claus said.

"Get a few bites in, and I'll warn you about the lunar shock," Selba said.

"Warn? What's to warn?" Claus said.

"No, eat first," she said.

"Or else? Sigh. Very well. I'll eat. But then you must explain what you mean," Claus said.

"I will," Selba said.

The two ate in silence. Claus wanted to say he understood how Labba felt, wanting peace and quiet and only able to get some by not speaking at all. He stared out the window and watched her fly along the train as he ate inside. It seemed unfair that he filled his belly while she strained to keep up.

"I wish she'd speak," Claus said.

"What would you have me say?" Lanietta asked, showing up to check on their meal.

"That the check is ready," Selba said to save the situation.

"It is. All covered on Claus's revolving credit," Lanietta winked as she placed the bill on the table.

"Thank you," Selba said.

Lanietta winked again and walked away to another customer.

"She won't follow us much longer," Selba said. "Labba I mean. I know you're watching her. Even Lanietta will depart before we reach the lunar shock."

"But they won't die there," Claus said.

"No, but they will get sick. Neither will endure that. Look out the window. Labba is veering off," Selba said.

It was true. Labba flew back toward the estate.

"And there's a small jumper car pulling away from the main train. Lanietta is in there. Look, it's going through a U-turn and returning to Leifton," Selba explained.

"You can't tell me that—"

"They wanted to keep an eye on you," Selba finished. "Yes, they did. Now it's up to me. We're almost there. The warning is this—you might need protection from the lunar shock. I don't know. Some can't handle the environment."

"What's to handle?" Claus asked.

"We will go and see," Selba said.

"As you say," Claus said.

They reached the lunar shock and stopped. Selba and Claus walked back to her vehicle.

"I'm putting the top up," she said. "Just in case."

They backed out and into the community. Immediately, Claus felt ill.

"What's that buzzing sound? And that flashing?" Claus asked.

"It's the society now," she said. "Let's drive around a bit."

The western-style horse and buggy saloon-style cities were gone and replaced with modern cube-style buildings. People of various types walked around or drove vehicles around. Some people were normal, while others had cube-based forms.

"Selba. There are no traffic lights here," Claus said. "Yet everyone seems to act as if there are."

"Drivers are required to have at least one cube implant. For traffic navigation, among other things," Selba said. "Those who don't have one must fake it. They aren't always successful. Don't worry. I know when to stop and go."

The cube-based people had lights flashing from their cubes. They made tinny squeals like an old-style scratchy phonograph playing through a metal horn with pellets rattling and scratching the horn.

"Who can survive this?" Claus asked.

"Put these in," she said, handing him a set of ear plugs.

Claus put in the ear plugs.

"Better," he said. "At least I'm not going insane. But the flashing. And, oh! Lightning!"

A bright flash of light shot across the sky.

"That's not lightning. It's a recharge burst for people like me who have a cube implant," Selba said. "My cube has only a finite supply of life-extending enhancement. I must return to the lunar shock or go to the far side to recharge. Otherwise I'll start aging again. That burst adds another few weeks."

"Burst? More like a blast!" Claus said. "The lunar shock has become a blast zone. Everyone is blast, blast, blast! I've seen enough. Let's go back."

"I thought you might like to see Shara," Selba said. "She's in Tabelia. In stasis. No one had the heart to bury her in the lunar soil."

"Very well. Let's see Shara," Claus said. "Can you do anything about the noise? I'm going to have Aftova rip out my cochleas in a moment!"

"Let me try something," Selba said.

She hit a few buttons on her dashboard, and the noise subsided.

"The car is using noise-canceling technology to reduce the outside social discourse," Selba said.

"It's working. Thank you. Social discourse? What? Did I miss something?"

"That's how they communicate," Selba said. "Claus, the cube people have lost the need to eat, drink, breathe, and sleep. They don't age. But they also don't experience discomfort the way that some people might, like you obviously. They don't know any better."

"Frieda is behind this, right?" Claus asked.

"In a way," Selba replied. "She promoted this technology from the remnant. She became half cube herself from our attack during Clover's funeral."

"Have you seen Frieda?" Claus asked.

"No, it's too dangerous," Selba said. "But I've spoken with the cube people who have. They tell the same story. Those of us still somewhat normal believe her cube half has helped push this mess. Yeah, it's a mess. What else can you call it?"

"A nightmare!" Claus said. "You can't tell me people are happy with this."

"They don't know what happiness is anymore. They only know the next thing. The next step, as dictated by the masses or Frieda," Selba said.

"The next step? The next stepping stone?" Claus asked.

"What are you talking about?" Selba asked.

"Could Grandma Broc have been wrong? She always said to be ready for the next stone in the brook and to step quickly," Claus said.

"Oh, I see. I don't think she meant for you to be subservient to another person's—"

"But a brook has a defined path. To follow the stones is to follow the brook is to follow the path is to be subservient to the water flow. Oh no! All this time I've worshiped my Grandma Broc. But she was wrong, wasn't she? Wasn't she?" Claus asked.

"You're over-analyzing, Claus. It's always good to follow the advice of—"

"One you trust who drank herself to death because she always thought her father would return but didn't," Claus said.

"Ah, that's why she spoke of steps," Selba said. "Claus, she didn't want you to get stuck on something the way she did. She didn't want you to be afraid to move on when the time came. It's not about being frivolous or brain-dead. It's about freedom to choose. Freedom, Claus. Pick another brook if you don't like your grandmother's brook. But pick you must, and pick you will. Here's Tabelia. We can drive inside now. It's much quieter in there."

The vehicle went down through a spiral ramp and parked. There were no cube people in Tabelia, just normal-looking people like Selba and Claus.

"There are others like you who cannot stand the pain. They tend to stay in here and only go out when absolutely necessary. Look, there are a few ready to go out," Selba said.

"Are those space suits?" Claus asked.

"Very much like space suits. They protect against the flashing light and harsh sound," Selba said. "I hear they also act as a violence and profanity filter. No need to deal with another person's foul demeanor. Let the suit take the brunt."

"Sounds like something Lanietta would create," Claus said.

"How did you know?" Selba asked.

Claus placed his hand over his face.

"No she didn't," Claus said, not believing Selba.

"Yes she did. She couldn't be here, of course. But there's a communication line between Tabelia and Leifton. Also a line runs from here to your estate. Here's a video booth. Let's tell Clausetta that we made it safely."

The two stepped into the video booth and spoke with Clausetta. She remarked at how much she missed the two, but Selba assured her they would return soon. They ended the conversation with Clausetta blowing kisses of affection.

"She's very fond of you," Selba said as the two left the video booth.

"She reminds me of Shara. So full of energy," Claus said.

"Maybe we shouldn't see her," Selba said. "You should remember Shara as that youthful energetic girl."

"No. I need to face mortality. Mine, hers, and humanity," Claus said.

"Please don't speak like that. Humanity isn't done in. Not even close," Selba said. "But I will take you to Shara. Look, there's

Sharlamarian. I'm sure that's where she's going now."

The two caught up with Sharlamarian, who was with her escorts. She looked the same as ever.

"Selba. And Claus. How good to see you both," she said.

"You haven't aged a day," Claus said.

"You look well, Claus," she said. "You'll forgive me for being so somber, but I'm on my way to pay respects."

"Claus would like to pay his as well. He didn't know until—" Selba said.

"Of course. Forgive me, Claus. You have been in a coma. I hope you don't mind me knowing. I was terribly afraid for you after I learned of your riding accident. I'm so glad you are recovered," Sharlamarian said. "Yes, please accompany me. It's only a short walk from here."

Selba and Claus walked with Sharlamarian. They entered a tree pair and found themselves approaching a great shrine. They entered the shrine and experienced a great expanse filled with floral stone carvings, paintings, and real flowers. Claus felt like he was in a great church, and at the head was a transparent casket placed into a wall of floral design. The figure inside had long, grey hair. The group reached Shara. Claus witnessed for himself how the mixture of immortality and pregnancy had aged and tortured Shara's body.

"She didn't know," Sharlamarian said. "Nobody did. She was the first to undergo the single-cube implant while pregnant. Thought she'd get ahead of the process. Oh, my poor sweet Shara."

Sharlamarian knelt in sadness and did her best to suppress her crying. Claus could only take a brief look at Shara before he was forced to turn away.

"I need...I..." Claus said, but he felt faint.

"Woah there, Claus," Selba said as she caught him. "Come over here. Look. There are holographic images of Shara. See? Here's one of her morning show. Another one over here is from Arberella. Morcellus took videographs without people realizing it."

"The memory candle," Claus said. "Clover had one."

"Fortunately, that wasn't the only one," Selba said, "though we did recover that one later. Shara was happy. Celebrate that, Claus."

"I cannot celebrate such misery and sadness," Claus said. "This cube thing is evil. Evil!"

"It can be," Selba said. "It depends on how it's used. I have one and Sharlamarian has one. But just one each. The cube people on the surface couldn't stop with one. They had to keep adding cube after cube. It became an obsession, and it was fueled by Frieda's link with the remnant."

"Thank you for coming, Claus," Sharlamarian said. "I see you've chosen to age naturally. I applaud your choice. Not all of us have such fortitude. Stay as long as you like. I must retire now. Such visits take too much out of me."

"Of course, Sharlamarian," Selba said. "Farewell."

"Farewell."

Sharlamarian left, albeit at a slower pace than she arrived. Although she hadn't aged physically, she appeared to have years of mental stress riding on her shoulders.

"I don't have any fortitude at all," Claus said now that Sharlamarian was gone.

"Don't tell her that. Don't tell anyone that. People look at you and see that you haven't caved into some agenda," Selba said.

"You caved into an agenda? To live longer?" Claus asked.

"Yes. The agenda to make me live longer. I caved into that. I'm sure there will be a price to pay. I'm sure there's some secret about the cube, a secret that's lurking and waiting for the right moment to force me against my will. But I spend most of my time on the near side, under Lanietta's protection, so if the cube is activated in a malicious way, I can draw her strength to fight against it," Selba said.

"If you're that suspicious of the cube, I'd get rid of it. I can't imagine going around with a time bomb in my head. Nothing's going to force me to...to..."

"Aftova," Selba said. "It's not a cube, but it's of the same origin. Clausetta has tapped into it. Frieda, Labba, and Lanietta have too. In a way, you've been more manipulated than any of us."

"More manipulated. Yes. I have. I should be rid of it. Couldn't even offer help against the misery on the surface. Is there a place here where I can leave it?" Claus asked.

"Let's not be hasty. Aftova is not a cube and is not subject to the commands of such. It may yet protect you in the end," Selba said.

"My end?"

"Any end."

"I thought Earth's end was the end."

"Maybe."

"Well," Claus said. "There must be an end sometime. But it won't happen here at Shara's shrine. I've seen enough. Let's return to my estate."

Selba nodded in agreement, and they left the shrine.

Chapter 112: Cubic Accident

"Claus, if you're interested, Clover, Argo, and the others are buried outside of town," Selba said. "I can take you there."

"It won't take long?" Claus asked.

"Not long at all," she replied.

Claus nodded in agreement. Selba drove away from the city and a bit into the old far side. Claus put his hands to his ears.

"My head is spinning. Not sure why," he said.

"Should we turn back? We're almost there," Selba said.

"Don't turn back. Let's visit. I'll manage," Claus said.

The two entered the cemetery and parked.

"Hard to breathe here," he said.

"Yes, the carbon dioxide level is a little higher. It won't kill us, but it does make the air heavier," Selba said.

They exited Selba's vehicle, climbed a short hill, and reached the graves. Claus stared at the head stones.

"Clover, born as Clovère," Claus read. "No dates?"

"No one knows when she was born," Selba said. "She died before we jumped ahead ten thousand years."

"I would have added a date," Claus said. "See? Argo has a date here."

"I know," Selba said.

"Just doesn't seem right. All that's left of Clover is her name. Ow!"

Claus felt pain in his head again, and he dropped to his knees with his hands over his ears. Selba noticed faint static charges running from his head toward the center of the old far side.

"We should leave," Selba said. "Come on. I'll help you."

Selba pulled Claus to his feet and led him back to her vehicle.

"Seems a recurrent theme. You helping me, I mean," Claus said.

"You'll be back home before you know it," she said.

The two entered, and Claus felt a little better.

"The vehicle blocks those static charges," Selba said as she drove away. "I'm not sure why they are hitting you, unless..."

"Unless?"

"Frieda has been extending her reach to the lunar shock, as I've told you. Beyton rays by themselves don't reach that far, but she can transmit them through other means such as the short bursts in the sky and through links on the ground."

"The cubic people?" Claus asked.

"Yes. That's the only way she can spread her power. They can't quite make it into the old near side, though they have tried," Selba explained. "Lanietta and Labba prevent them."

"Lanietta and Labba work together?" Claus asked.

"You already saw the ethereal tube connecting your estate to Leifton. They also work together to prevent the spread of cubic people into the old near side. I'm sure you can guess why," Selba said.

"The beyton rays would kill them, along with Leif and Clausetta," Claus said. "I know. I owe a debt of gratitude to Lanietta and Labba. Labba I have no trouble with. I just hate thanking Lanietta. I feel it encourages more bad behavior."

"She is just playing with you," Selba said. "The real bad behavior is on this side. I've taken a chance bringing you here, but I felt it was important. We'll stay on our side and keep you safe."

"Thank you."

The two passed through town and were headed for the train station.

"The Lanietta Express," Selba said.

"It still amazes me how that train goes right into town," Claus said. "With the tension between sides, I mean, who could believe it?"

"Someday in the future, Lanietta hopes to rescue the cubic people and restore their humanity, as part of her philanthropic work," Selba said.

"Lanietta? Into philanthropy? Still can't believe it," Claus said.

"Believe, Claus. Believe."

"You told me about her three-for-one special. That seems hardly like philanthropy," Claus said.

"Do you know that mothers of the three-for-one special and those born of that special are the only ones allowed to reside on the old near side? Lanietta wants to change that. She wants others to have the chance," Selba said.

"What's stopping her?" Claus asked. "I know, she doesn't want the spread of beyton rays."

"If she can stop the rays and guarantee people's good behavior, she'll let them in."

"Well I hope it doesn't happen," Claus said. "They are too noisy and painful."

"We're here," Selba said.

Selba drove the vehicle toward a loading car. But Claus noticed the conductor looked very much like...

"Lanietta!" Claus said to Selba.

"What?"

"I'm getting out. This is too much!" he said.

"I'll meet you inside then," Selba said.

"All aboard!" Lanietta called. "Tickets. Make sure you have your tickets!"

"Lanietta! You?" Claus said.

"Clomper, make sure you have your ticket. All aboard!" Lanietta called.

"What happened to my revolving credit?"

"Here, take this ticket," she said as she handed him a ticket. "Better hurry. The train leaves soon."

"How many other roles do you play? This is a game to you, isn't it?" Claus said.

"You know me well," she grinned. "Last call! All aboard!"

"Wait for me!" called a woman. "I want the three-for-one!"

A woman rushed across the road, but a vehicle hit her and in fact had stopped atop her crushed leg. The woman screamed in pain. Claus ran to help. She was just an ordinary woman, not a cubic person. She continued to scream.

"Please don't scream!" Claus called. "Lanietta, help me over here."

"All aboard!" Lanietta echoed.

"Lanietta!" Claus yelled back.

The woman's scream was so loud that it caught the attention of nearby cubic people. While Claus activated Aftova to lift the vehicle off the woman and move it away, cubics sent out their harsh screeches and approached.

"Please don't screech!" Claus said, holding his ears. He'd long since lost the ear plugs. "Lanietta, help!"

The cubics then pulled out square pans and beat on them, slowly at first but progressively quicker. The woman screamed even more.

"You'll make it," Claus said to the woman. "The weight is off your leg. I'll carry you, if only this screeching would stop. Evil things, please stop beating on those pans!"

Claus sent his threads after several cubics and disrupted them, but more and more came.

"Lanietta!" Claus called.

Claus could not hold off all of them. Why wasn't Lanietta helping? Not only did they beat on their square pans quicker and quicker, but they used the pans to deflect his threads. In fact, they directed his threads back at Claus where they wrapped around him and immobilized him. He could no longer help the woman, nor could he call for Lanietta. These cubics raised Claus into the air, and all he could do, besides suffering from the screeching, was watch in horror as the injured woman underwent a cubification process, beginning with her injured leg. The injured leg crumbled into cubelets—tiny loose cubes attached to nothing and merely sitting like gravel. The woman lost blood, not in gushing fashion, but rather in small, cubic chunks. She begged not to be transformed, she pleaded for anyone to help, and Claus was driven mad with his helpless situation. Lightning blasts above from the center of the old far side landed on the cubics and supplied them with energy and direction.

As a last resort, Claus tried sending the yellow ethereal thread outward toward Frieda in hopes of distracting her or at least getting her to stop. The thread wiggled slowly through the weave of yellow and blue around him.

"Not quick enough," Claus said to himself. "This woman will die or be converted. Lanietta is worthless. This might be my end as well. Aftova overwhelmed. As am I. Let it end then."

Just as Claus had given up hope, Labba the eagle swooped in and carried the woman to the Lanietta Express. Simultaneously, Lanietta space-jumped up to Claus, tugged on the yellow ethereal thread as if he were at the ball, and the woven mesh that had ensnared him now became undone. She whisked him into the Lanietta Express, closed the door, and the train headed for Leifton. Lanietta had burns on her hands and face, and half of Labba's feathers had been seared off.

"They'll grow back, Labba. They'll grow back," Lanietta assured her.

The train put quick distance between itself and the lunar shock. Both Labba and the injured woman were taken to the medical car and placed in separate treatment rooms.

"Why did you wait?" Claus asked Lanietta.

"Explanations must wait," Lanietta said as she entered Labba's treatment room and worked feverishly to help her.

Claus was left by himself until Selba found him.

"I heard a commotion," Selba said. "Are you all right?"

"I'm not sure," Claus said. "I'm in one piece."

A doctor exited the young woman's treatment room and shook his head "no".

"Come on!" Selba said, and she pulled Claus into the woman's treatment room. The injured leg was almost all gone, and the uninjured leg was cubified and had fallen into cubic gravel up to the knee. The

shock was too much for the woman, and she had no pulse.

"She just died," said a nurse.

"No, she mustn't," Selba said. "Claus!"

Claus tapped his upper palate, and he sent his ethereal threads into her heart. He realized he was able to bifurcate these threads, and so the blue thread went through the arteries while the yellow went through the veins until they met in the capillaries. Claus was not able to regrow the woman's legs, but he was able to seal off existing endings and restore life to otherwise healthy, uncubified tissue. She awoke with his ethereal threads still in her.

"I can't remove the threads, Selba. If I do, she'll die," Claus said.

"I'll get Lanietta. She'll know what to do," Selba said, and she left.

"What is your name?" Claus asked.

"Blouisa," she said. "My legs."

"I couldn't save them. I'm sorry," Claus said.

"Are you a doctor?" Blouisa asked.

"No, he's not," Lanietta said, now rushing in. "You should know better than to play ethereal games, Clomper. Look at you. You're stuck yet again. Hold on."

Lanietta went eethi and tied two knots in the ethereal threads running between Claus and Blouisa. She then severed the threads between the knots. Both knots receded to their respective parties.

"She will be fine," Lanietta said.

"Her name is Blouisa," Claus said.

"And your name is Stupid!" Lanietta said. "But I'll save the lecture for another time. You interrupted my treatment of Labba. Excuse me!"

Lanietta rushed off. Selba entered.

"I just saw Lanietta, and she was piping hot mad. I didn't dare ask her for help," Selba said.

"No need. She already gave it. And I made her mad," Claus said.

"Your name is Stupid?" Blouisa asked in a dreamy state. "What an odd name."

"Is she free?" Selba asked.

"Yes. Alive and stable. I couldn't save her legs, of course," Claus said.

"She's confused. She thinks your name is—" Selba started.

"That's what Lanietta called me," Claus said. "Selba, this is Blouisa."

"I'm happy to meet you, Selba. Am I really alive? Safe from the cubics?" Blouisa asked.

"Yes, you are," Selba said. "What happened?"

"I wanted to catch the train. I want a special baby," Blouisa said. "The lunar shock is...is...I am tired of it."

Selba touched her temples.

"What are you doing?" Claus asked.

"Each of us who has a cube can tell if another has one, but only if in close proximity," Selba said. "Blouisa doesn't have one."

"I tried to time my crossing with traffic. I'm not good at faking the cube," Blouisa said.

"She was hit by a vehicle," Claus said.

"Ah, yes. People don't look at what's in front of them. They follow instructions from their cube. She didn't have one, so there was nothing to alert the driver," Selba said. "Is that right, Blouisa?"

"I think so," Blouisa said.

"What about common sense? Fear? Surprise? Anxiety?" Claus asked. "Wouldn't the driver experience those?"

"Those feelings fade away and are supplanted by the cube," Selba said. "I take it you did not wish to be supplanted, Blouisa."

"No, I did not," she said. "It's a nightmare now in the lunar shock, not knowing who to trust. I avoid the cubics all I can, and if I confide in a normal person, they turn out to have a cube and snitch on me. What's a person to do?"

"Leave, if you can," Selba said. "I'm glad you made it."

"But at a terrible cost," Claus said.

"It was worth it," Blouisa said. "I heard there's a man sleeping at a great estate, that he's been sleeping for twenty-five years! How can anyone sleep that long? I wish I could meet him and help him. Mr. Claus Gerhardt."

"I am he," Claus said. "I have awaken. You may recover at my estate if you wish. Treyu and Mariel will set up a room for you. We'll have to see about crutches or something."

"Lanietta can help there," Selba said. "Artificial legs. And not made of cubes or any machinery. The separation of life and machine is still in effect on the near side."

"I'll walk?" Blouisa asked.

"Yes, you will," Selba said.

"How can I repay you?" she said.

"Lanietta will collect, I'm sure," Claus said. "The three-for-one special, Selba?"

"Claus, not here," Selba said.

"Is it wrong?" Blouisa asked.

"No, Blouisa, it isn't. I had a son myself with the program. He's now married to Claus's daughter," Selba said.

"Congratulations!" Blouisa said.

The door opened partway, Lanietta stuck her head in, and she motioned with her hand for Claus to come out.

"Excuse me a moment," Claus said.

"So tell me about the procedure," Blouisa said to Selba. "Did it hurt?"

"Not at all," Selba replied as the two discussed the three-for-one deal.

Claus exited the room and stood in the hallway with Lanietta.

"Well?" Claus asked.

Lanietta punched Claus in the jaw, and he fell to the floor.

"Just that," she said.

She turned away and entered Labba's treatment room. Hearing the noise of Claus falling, Selba opened the door and looked out.

"I heard a thud," Selba said.

"Oh, you know how I fall all over Lanietta about everything," Claus said.

"Do you want an ice pack? Your face is swelling," Selba said.

"No, I think I'll sit this one out," Claus said as he pulled himself into a near sitting position with an arm behind him to prop himself up.

Selba shrugged her shoulders and returned to Blouisa.

"Should have brought Treyu along," Claus said.

Chapter 113: The Carinian Reptile

Claus stood up, took several steps to check his balance, and realized only his pride was truly hurt.

"Why do I get punched?" Claus asked. "I'll check in with her."

Claus opened the door slowly to Labba's treatment room. Labba the eagle was heavily bandaged, and Lanietta spoke with her.

"Rest quietly there, Labba," Lanietta said. "We've dealt with the cubics for now. Claus was way out of line, I know. I'll have a talk with him about—oh, here he is now."

"Out of line? How? I was saving that woman," Claus said.

"Not here," Lanietta said. "Labba needs rest, not melodrama. This way please."

Lanietta ushered Claus out of the room, down the hallway, and into a gymnasium with a boxing ring. Lanietta threw a helmet and boxing gloves at Claus.

"Lace up," she said.

"I can't—" Claus was about to say, but an assistant placed the helmet on Claus and laced up his gloves. Another did the same for Lanietta.

"Lanietta, I'm not a boxer," Claus said.

"Then it's time to learn," Lanietta said. "Oh assistant, don't forget the phase adjuster. We want a perfect pair."

"Perfect pair? What are you talking about?" Claus asked.

The assistant guided Claus into one corner of the boxing ring. Lanietta entered the other. A selenite referee was already in the ring. She beckoned them together.

"Protect yourselves at all times. I want a good, clean fight. Nothing below the belt. That means you, Lanietta. Touch gloves and go back to your corners," she said.

The two did so, and the referee gave the hand signal to fight. Claus stood there with his arms down, unsure of what was going on.

"Keep your gloves up!" the referee yelled.

Lanietta came after him and gave him an uppercut. Claus fell to the canvas.

"One, two, three," the referee called before Claus was able to get up. "Fight!"

"Keep your gloves up, Clomper," Lanietta said. "I need to pummel you."

"This isn't one of your fantasies," Claus said.

"No, it isn't. So make it good," Lanietta said with a right cross. "Keep your gloves up!"

"Am I supposed to fight back? Like this?" Claus said, and he caught her with a left hook.

Lanietta stumbled backward. Her legs, which had been in excellent shape, took on a scar pattern matching that of Frieda's legs.

"What is this evil?" Claus said.

Lanietta jabbed Claus, and he jabbed back. She caught Claus with a right cross. Ethereal threads extended from him and wrapped around her body. She changed form into that of a reptile.

"Extend the round. No bell," Lanietta called.

"Why the boxing, Lanietta?" Claus called, and he sent jabs her way.

"You let your threads out too easily," Lanietta said.

Lanietta gave Claus two jabs.

"You mean the woman? She needed help," Claus said, and he landed a good punch on Lanietta. She was now fully reptilian, and her scars became deep valleys as if recently injured.

"You let the enemy take charge of you," Lanietta said, and she sent a hook his way.

"You wouldn't help. You stood there and did nothing," Claus said, returning the hook.

"I don't surrender to Frieda or her beyton rays blindly," Lanietta said, and she sent a punch right at Claus's forehead.

Claus stumbled backward. His ethereal threads continued to wrap around her reptilian legs. They thickened, and the scars filled with goo.

"But I knew you would do something foolish. I gave you an ethereal wrap at the ball," Lanietta said with more jabs. "I summoned Labba for help. To defeat the enemy. But you, Clomper, are worthless garbage. Fit for nothing but the sewer. Finish the hag that tortures you. Finish me!"

Lanietta swung wildly and spun around. As she completed her spin, Claus punched her hard. She fell backward, flipped over the ropes, and fell onto the floor on her back. There was a loud cracking sound while she flipped in the air, and her legs flew off behind her. Or did they? Claus looked closely at Lanietta. She had narrow sticks for legs now. The reptilian legs had been like gloves over her stick legs. She changed back to her normal form, and her normal legs returned, though they were red and tender. The reptilian legs remained separate.

"Take the reptilian legs to surgery," Lanietta said to an assistant.

"For Blouisa?" Claus asked. "What a crazy way to make legs!"

Lanietta stood up. Assistants unlaced both her and Claus. They removed their helmets last.

"It's a Carinian technique. Normally we grow them in a controlled environment over a course of several years. Blouisa doesn't have that much time. She still has cubic remnants in her system. The reptilian legs will restore her legs and purge the remnants," Lanietta explained as she toweled off her face. "Just don't try that trick again. The lunar shock is all but under Frieda's control. We must address it carefully. You almost got Labba killed. As it is, she will need three months to recover."

"I didn't mean to injure her. What was she doing there anyway?" Claus asked.

"I told you, I summoned her help," Lanietta said. "Frieda is not to be dealt with lightly. I don't know why I keep explaining

this to you. I should have Aftova removed from you for your own good. As it is, you still have a few uses. The reptilian legs were a time saver. You may yet save us time in other ways."

"Us? As in you and Labba?" Claus asked.

"She still hates me over the Leif affair. As do you, I'm sure," Lanietta said. "But she and I are full Carinian. And we have vowed to keep the near side safe. You might not fully appreciate me, Clomper, but I do like to provide my pets a healthy environment. Frieda has turned her half and the lunar shock into an unhealthy one. If you are this determined to help people avoid the cubic trap, I welcome your help. But do everything under Carinian guidance, and we'll have no more boxing matches. Understood? Well?"

"I don't know what to say," Claus said.

"All right. Show me your ticket," she said.

"What?"

"Your ticket. For the train ride. I'm still the conductor," she said.

"I don't believe it. You nearly bash my brains in, and you want my ticket?" Claus said as he pulled it out. "Here."

Lanietta walked over, pulled a hole punch from her pocket, and punched a hole in his ticket.

"Thank you," she said. "If you'll excuse me, I have other tickets to punch."

She left. Claus paced around the boxing ring, unsure of what to do next.

"There's another match starting soon," the selenite referee said. "Please vacate the ring. You may practice over there if you like."

Claus climbed out of the ring, walked over to practice equipment, gave a bag one punch, and he hurt his hand. Too tired to think of anything else, he sat down. After several moments, another boxing match started. Claus watched for a round.

"I've had enough violence. I need a drink," he said, and he left for the dining car.

Claus sat in a booth, and he was by himself except for rolled up eating utensils and a pair of empty but clean wine glasses. A waitress showed up with a menu over her face.

"Strawberry champagne, please," he said.

The waitress pulled down the menu to reveal a big welt on the left side of her face. It was Lanietta. She also had a bottle of strawberry champagne in the non-menu hand, and she sat down with Claus. She placed the menu on the table, poured the champagne in the glasses, and set the bottle on the table. She picked up Claus's glass and handed it to him as she held her own glass close to her lips.

"Drink up, champ," she said.

"You look terrible," he said, taking the glass and a sip.

"Thank you," she laughed. "I had to do that, you know. I couldn't warn you."

"Seems you never can," Claus said.

"I mean it about the lunar shock, Clomper. Frieda and her ethereal computer have digitized and mechanized the far side and part of the lunar shock. People are trapped there. Blouisa would have become fully cubified," Lanietta said.

"Killed?"

"Worse. A walking collection of cubes, contorted and trapped within their confines," Lanietta said. "We Carinians never digitized the ether. It's unnatural. No matter how much evil the likes of Libriota and my kind have done, we've never so horribly fused circuitry and machinery with ethereal spirit. I know you never cared for the power games my people have played, but there's no comparison to what Frieda is now doing. None."

"This. Look. We can speak face-to-face and have a normal conversation. No games. See how easy it is? Why not speak with me like this all the time?" Claus asked.

"Do you think it would work?" she laughed. "Oh, I shouldn't laugh. You got some good punches on me back there."

"It was all unnecessary. Direct conversation, please. There had to be another way for the legs. Blouisa could have waited," Claus said.

"How poorly my Clomper of little brain understands the ways of the universe," Lanietta said. "No, direct speech has its moments. But not for every moment. However, I am caught up on my games for the day, so I will indulge with more 'direct speech', as you call it. We need to discuss your future."

"What about it?" Claus asked.

"You're old, Clomper. There's something you need to decide. Your death would mean changes on the near side. We have to account for that," Lanietta said.

"Who said I'm going to die?"

"Who said you aren't?"

"Okay. I'm getting older. I will probably die," he said.

"Of old age."

"Of old age. Are you saying I should extend it? Get a cube like Selba? I've got Aftova. Why isn't that keeping me young?"

"It's rogue, Clomper. Rogue."

"You mean to say I have to get a cube like Selba to extend my life? Get rid of Aftova?"

"That's one option," Lanietta replied. "The other is to unrogue Aftova."

"Unrogue Aftova?"

"It would require at least four Carinians. Turns out we have them. Almost lost Labba, and then we couldn't do it for a bit. But she'll be ready in three months, as I've said, and I'll be there to help."

"Treyu and Mariel? Will they be the other two?" Claus asked.

"They can't help. They are reanimated. No, we need four Carinians, of adult age, who are part of an unbroken Carinian line from the beginning of my race," Lanietta said. "There are two others. Leif and Clausetta."

"My children," Claus said.

"Yes."

"So what would this mean? Is there a ceremony? Would I become all powerful and kingly like Frieda?" Claus asked.

"There would be a ceremony. The four of us would surround you in a square pattern. We would draw out your ethereal threads of yellow and blue—two each," Lanietta explained. "We would then permanently link them to us."

"And I would permanently command you four?" Claus said. "That's kingly indeed. Would make a nice turnabout for you and Labba. I could order Labba to stop her eagle games. And I could order you to be nice. For Leif and Clausetta, I could keep them out of trouble."

"No, Clomper. We would command you. Just as Frieda can send instructions to those with cubes, we would in our way send instructions to you," Lanietta said.

"Clausetta has already done that. My dancing with ghosts on ghost night, for example," Claus said.

"She animated your body, that's all," Lanietta said. "I mean true and full subservience. Of your mind. No more impulsive thoughts of rescue. You'd be alert and would think of such things, but only we could allow for such acts. It is the tightest leash imaginable, and you would lose your self spontaneity. The cubics are the same with Frieda, as I've mentioned. The difference is, they are driven by circuitry, but you'd be driven by, well, us Carinians."

"Selba has a cube and isn't a zombie to Frieda," Claus said.

"She spends most of her time here and is somewhat spared. But even she has lost much zest for her own path. Only her three-for-one deal and Sergio have helped," Lanietta said.

"So I become totally obedient to you. The pet you purchased at auction is finally house broken," Claus said.

"We can still spar if you like," she said. "I need a welt on my right side to balance out the left."

Lanietta broke out into laughter.

"I'm defeated!" Claus complained. "A slave!"

"No, my dear Clomper," she continued. "We're working for a peaceful settlement here on the near side—with strength, sanity, reason, and prosperity as much as is possible in Frieda's shadow. You'll never be relegated to the level of selenite or other machinery. Just think of it as family love. Family for one, and one for family!"

"Will that mean eliminating Frieda someday? Will you kill her?" Claus asked.

"Really, Clomper, such a question—"

"Deserves an answer," Claus pressed.

"We can work toward the answer. As a community. But if you decide to age normally, you won't be around to see how things turn out. As much as we've accomplished, I don't see how we can do anything about Frieda in the next twenty or thirty years. You might still be alive by that time, but you'll be a fragile man. You're already experiencing effects of old age. Why make it worse?"

"This is your way of saying you need me to defeat Frieda," Claus said. "All drawn out like this. Games, Lanietta. You're still playing games. At the ball, you dumped your drink on me, because you know you need me with Aftova."

"I was being playful. I'm serious now," Lanietta said. "Frieda will be around for quite some time. I would have defeated her long ago otherwise. The remnant PRAAD is still active and will destroy us Carinians if permitted. I'm lucky I made it to this near side the way I did. Selenita helped me there."

"If I really have your serious attention, why did you kidnap Leif?" Claus asked. "I want a straight answer, Lanietta. You had no right."

"Self-preservation. That's all the right I need. Self-preservation for my species. And I'll have it, Clomper," she said.

"But we were doing that already. We—"

"Did not see all ends. Labba, though good with short-term work, does not see eternity as I do. Neither do you. There are times I simply must act. Just that. No lengthy explanation, no negotiations, no permission requested. I must act. I can play it off with games, or I can be nasty like others. I play games. Take it or, well, do you really have a choice? Cheer up, Clomper. The near side is a safe haven for us and for the destitute who seek relief. Which reminds me, I invited Selba and

Blouisa over to the Leifton fortress for dinner this evening. Nothing fancy. Don't dress up. Just a casual affair. I'd like to make her comfortable and feel welcome. We'll see how her legs are doing."

"You mean she'll be healed by then? Enough to walk?" Claus said.

"Of course. I don't make people wait when they don't have to," Lanietta said. "I take good care of all my customers. And my pets. Now give me a kiss and make up with me."

"A kiss? Who are you now? My daughter? My friend? My master?" Claus asked.

"You'll never know what I'm thinkin', when I kiss you half-a-blinkin'," she said as she blinked repeatedly.

"Back to games," he lamented.

"You like it, and you know it," she said. "Give me a kiss."

Claus hesitated, but Lanietta nearly jumped over the table to kiss him.

"Your lips are puffy," she said.

"So are yours," he said.

"We should box more often for puffy kissing," she winked.

"Waitress! More ale!" yelled someone.

"You'll excuse me, Clomper," she said, and she attended the other customer.

"What am I getting myself into?" Claus asked himself. "Do I want to live longer? I admit, life on my estate is pleasant enough. I have two children and a grandchild. Lanietta irks me, of course. But other than that, the near side *is* a haven. Lanietta is right. I shouldn't admit it to her, but Lanietta is right."

"Why thank you," she said as she walked by.

The rest of the train ride was uneventful. Selba had become so engrossed with Blouisa that she'd forgotten about Claus. When the train reached the Leifton fortress, Selba rushed Blouisa into a tour of Lanietta's grand creation. Claus found himself alone briefly, but then Treyu showed up.

"Ready to leave, sir?" he asked.

"I guess I am," Claus said. "I had hoped Clausetta and Leif would be here to greet me."

"They are at your estate, awaiting you there. They sent me to fetch you," Treyu said. "Will Selba accompany us?"

"I don't think so," Claus said. "She's entertaining her guest, a woman I saved named Blouisa. Lanietta has invited—"

"You to dinner this evening," Treyu said. "Yes, she called ahead. Shall we go, sir?"

Claus nodded in agreement. The two entered an electric vehicle with Treyu driving. As the two drove toward the ethereal tube, Claus looked back and noticed Nanceya helping Labba the eagle into the open back of a transport vehicle.

"Labba? She's coming home with us," Treyu said. "Don't worry. Nanceya is good with Carinian shape-changers."

"Treyu, you act as if you've known me a long time," Claus said.

"I have," he said. "I arrived not long after your coma started. It must seem strange to you, having been unaware of your surroundings for the past twenty-five years."

"You served Larto? You and Mariel?"

"Yes," Treyu replied. "Those were different days. I was told you witnessed a vision of my past with Lanietta."

"I thought you died," Claus said.

"In a manner of speaking I did, along with others," Treyu said. "My spirit was stored in the Anrega orb chamber. Lanietta brought me back. I knew that Larto's and Lanshalla's daughter would be of great help."

"Some help," Claus said.

Treyu opened his mouth to say something, but he thought better of it.

"Going to say something, Treyu?" Claus asked.

"Life is complicated, sir," he said.

"Yes. It is."

The two arrived and entered the main hallway just inside the door.

"Pappa, is that you?" called Clausetta from the study. "We're in here!"

"I'll tend to your luggage," Treyu said.

"Thank you," Claus replied.

Claus entered the study and saw Clausetta, Sergio, Leif, and Claude. Leif was reading poetry.

"Oh, Pappa!" Clausetta said as she rushed up to him with a hug. "You are hurt! What happened?"

"I was sparring with Lanietta," Claus said.

"Aunt Lanietta," Leif said. "She's always so adventurous."

"Aunt Lanietta?" Claus said in surprise. "I thought that you and she..."

Clausetta, Leif, and Sergio laughed.

"I'm not married, Pappa," Leif said. "I've been told everything, how Aunt Lanietta took me away when I was young, and so on. I've forgiven her."

"Pappa, Aunt Lanietta has been playing games with you," Clausetta giggled. "Didn't you get it yet? The joke's on you."

"Some joke," Claus said. "I'm the last one in on the punchline. Just what is the punchline?"

"Pappa, she, we, I mean..." Leif started.

"We all worked together, Pappa," Clausetta said. "We built up your estate and Lanietta's fortress. They are both beautiful, don't you think? But I do give my brother a hard time. I say he should find a proper wife and give you more grandchildren."

"You could have another," Leif said.

"One is a handful," Clausetta said. "But two?"

"We can have two," Sergio said.

"Oh, Serg, you're the greatest!" Clausetta said.

"I guess I need to have yet another talk with Lanietta. Leif, did Lanietta do anything strange to you? Like, well, I don't want to say with..."

"Selba told us how we were conceived," Clausetta said.

"Nothing like that happened with me," Leif said.

"Or me," Clausetta said.

"That Selba. I need to have a talk with her, too. Is there anyone else I need to have a talk with?"

"Me!" Claude said. "I want a big hug, Grandpa!"

Claude ran up to Claus, and Claus dropped to a knee and hugged him.

"Free hugs are always available for my family," Claus said.

"Yay!" Claude said.

"Pappa, Lanietta called and told us everything," Leif said. "I'm glad you're okay. I should have warned you about the lunar shock. Things are really bad there."

"I worried about you constantly!" Clausetta said. "Please don't go back."

"I was selfish," Claus said. "I wanted to go and see how things are. But it nearly took me away from my family forever. I won't be so rash again."

"Thank you, Pappa," Clausetta said, and she hugged him while Claude was still hugging Claus. "Group hug!"

Leif and Sergio joined the hug. Mariel stopped by to see how things were going.

"Group hug!" Clausetta called to Mariel.

Mariel smiled, turned away, and motioned to someone else. Mariel came over to add her hug, and in walked Nanceya with Labba the eagle. They added their hugs as best as they could too.

"You'll always be loved, Pappa. Always," Clausetta said.

The group hug did not last forever, of course. The time came, and the group headed over to the fortress for dinner. The gathering was much smaller than the ball, being just Claus's family, Lanietta, and the female selenites. The dinner was a buffet style. Claus started to go for a plate of food when Clausetta stopped him.

"Pappa, no," she said. "We must wait for Selba and Blouisa."

Sheepishly, Claus sat back down. Lanietta had helped with setting out the dinner and was now putting out beverages and dessert.

"Please, Lanietta, let me help!" Clausetta begged.

"No, Clausetta, as I told you before, you must tend to your pappa," Lanietta grinned.

"Did you cook this food yourself, Aunt Lanietta?" Leif asked.

"Of course," she said.

"Yes, 'Aunt', do tell us how you cooked it all," Claus mocked.

"I see you picked up on the joke," she said.

"It wasn't funny," Claus said.

"Would you rather things be otherwise?" she said. "You may call me Aunt Lanietta if you like, Clomper."

"I want to speak with you—later!" Claus said.

"Of course. We always have fascinating discussions," Lanietta said. "Now if you'll take a pause in thought, I hear Selba and Blouisa approaching. Clomper, have a seat, please."

Claus sat. Selba entered first, and she stood by the doorway.

"Family and friends, it's my great honor to present to you, Blouisa!" Selba said.

Blouisa entered. She wore a short, frilly dress, but one that showed off her new legs. There was no indication they were reptilian in origin. They looked as human as any other legs, with smooth skin, matching skin tone, and ten toes. She did have scars showing where the new legs met the rest of her body, but these scars showed no stitch marks. They were continuous and almost decorative. She stopped in place, turned around, and put her arms out as if to say, "Here I am, fully healed and ready to live."

"Blouisa!" Leif said as he rushed over to her. "Let me have the first dance!"

"It's not even dance time yet!" Clausetta laughed. "Bring her over to the table, Leif. There's a place set—"

"Too far away," he said, escorting her to the table. "You will sit with me as my guest."

Selba beamed with pride over Blouisa's recovery.

"I do good work," she said as she sat next to Claus.

"I want to have a word with you," Claus said.

"Dinner is ready!" Lanietta announced to all.

"Sure," Selba said to Claus. "After I get a bite to eat. I'm starved!"

Leif got up first and escorted Blouisa to the buffet table. Clausetta and Sergio went next followed by Claude. He couldn't reach the food, but Clausetta gave him a plate and periodically took it from him to put food on it before returning it to him. Selba and Claus went next. As the dinner guests filled their plates, Lanietta stood on the other side of the buffet table to assist as needed.

"Care to try the chicken?" Lanietta suggested to Claus.

"How about crow?" Claus suggested. "That's for your dinner."

"Tsk, tsk, Clomper. Such a spoiled sport. Here. Have a doggie biscuit. I saved it just for you," Lanietta said as she placed a dog biscuit on Claus's plate.

"I'm no dog!" he said.

"Don't raise your voice," she said. "You'll disturb budding love. What is it with you Gerhardt men? Always falling for ladies with scarred legs."

"Frieda still bothers you," Claus grinned. "Why don't you sit at the table with me? We can discuss your jealously and total infatuation with me."

Lanietta tossed a glass of wine at Claus's face.

"Rinse your mouth out with that," she said, and she walked back into the kitchen.

Selba had largely not paid attention to Claus's conversation with Lanietta, but the wine in his face surprised her.

"You are two for two," Selba said.

"Why can't people forget the past?" Claus said. "I don't need a reminder about the ball."

Selba laughed. The group returned to the table and ate dinner.

"Selba," Claus said. "Explain something to me. When Leif was kidnapped, Lanietta spoke like she was going to raise him then marry him. And when I came out of my coma, I heard talk to the same effect, that Lanietta had married him. She acted like my daughter in law and everything."

"Did she? Interesting," Selba said.

"I could have used more honesty," Claus said. "Where was your honesty in all this?"

"I, uh, well Claus, you had come out of a coma. How could I explain things that would make any sense?" Selba asked.

"You're waffling," Claus said.

"So you know Leif and Lanietta aren't married. You should be relieved. I mean, you're still in love with her, right?"

"What?"

"I know Labba would hate me to say it, but I can see love. I'm not blind," Selba said. "I'm not going to judge Labba. She had two of your children. But it's not like she gave you an honest opportunity to build a relationship first. She kind of pushed you into fatherhood."

"What about Lanietta? She could have done something similar," Claus said. "I can't believe she hasn't."

"Claus, there are some things you'll have to find out for yourself. But I will say this—Lanietta has acted like an aunt to Leif. Nothing more. She never went beyond that role. You can choose to believe me or not," Selba said.

"I have a hard time believing much of anything these days," Claus said. "As soon as I do, I learn it's just another joke."

"Well, the food is good. And that's no joke," Selba said.

"I agree with you there," Claus said.

"You did something very good, Claus," Selba continued. "By saving Blouisa and bringing her here, you've given Leif the woman of his dreams. I have a feeling she'll reconsider the three-for-one deal and choose a more intimate plan with Leif for your next grandchild."

"You're jumping ahead, don't you think?" Claus said.

"Not on this. Blouisa told me what she really wants before Leif saw her. She is seeking the exact environment Leif can provide. And I told her about Leif, too. She was impressed," Selba said. "Relax, Claus."

"Yes, relax, Clomper," Lanietta said, coming by with a bottle of strawberry champagne. "Need a refill?"

"Not one of your games," Claus said.

Music started up, and Leif whisked Blouisa onto the dance floor. The two danced quickly together and in perfect unison.

"Blouisa's new legs are doing very well," Claus said.

"Yes, I always give my women everything they need to snag their man," Lanietta said. "Come along, Clomper. Dance with me."

Lanietta placed the champagne bottle on the table and pulled Claus onto the dance floor.

"But I've just eaten. I could get indigestion," he protested.

"Nonsense. I'm with you," she said.

"That's exactly what I mean," he said.

"Behave, Clomper, or I'll change you into a bleating goat," Lanietta said.

"I want to know more about you, *Aunt* Lanietta," Claus said.

"What is there to tell? The marriage to Leif was a ruse, I admit. I had to have fun with you somehow. You're so stuffy. You must lighten up!" Lanietta said.

"But I was in a coma! I mean, what good did it do?"

"You were fooled, even if I had to wait twenty-five years to cash in. What's twenty-five years to a Carinian? We have long-lived jokes," she said. "Music has changed, Clomper. Slow dance. Take me in your arms like you, well, like you like me."

Claus did so and slow-danced with Lanietta.

"I'm going to be blunt, Lanietta. Did you enter Leif's body like Labba entered mine? Did you intend to create a baby with him?" Claus asked.

Lanietta drew away and slapped Claus across the face. The music stopped, and everyone stared at Claus. Lanietta waved her hand, and the music changed to a mid-tempo beat. People now danced more casually and less intimately.

"How uncouth of you to say such a thing to me," she said. "Where are your manners?"

"That's how Labba did it with me," Claus said. "She entered me and—"

"I don't want to hear your vile, nasty details on how you and Labba 'did it'," Lanietta said.

"If you love me with the same passion," Claus started.

"Which I don't," she added.

"Then you would have tried the same. Why haven't you, Lanietta? And don't say it's bestiality," Claus said.

Lanietta slapped Claus again.

"I'm running out of patience with you, Clomper," she said. "I go to all this effort to save the near side, to save you, and to put on this little dinner. And you do nothing but insult me!"

"You once asked me if I really meant what I said, about me being proud of you. You were a girl then. In the orb chamber," Claus said.

"You said I was like family," Lanietta said. "But maybe you were covering up something more sinister, that you had hateful feelings toward a twelve-year old. Or what the twelve-year old would become. Did you? What kind of warped creature are you?"

"That's not what I meant then, and you know it," Claus said. "Lanietta, you were..."

"Like a daughter to you. Very well. I played on that love when I had the fake wedding with Leif, so that I could become your daughter, official-like. Now look what you've done. Warped it. Warped it!"

The two stopped dancing, though the music continued. But the song didn't continue much longer. It changed to another slow dance. Claus offered to dance with Lanietta, but she threw up her arms and walked away. Selba walked up and slow-danced with Claus.

"Lover's quarrel?" Selba asked.

"I wish you wouldn't say that," Claus said.

"My guess is your tact was off," Selba said.

"Something was. Not even sure I should tell you what I told Lanietta," Claus said.

"Don't," Selba said. "Not unless you want Lanietta coming back to slap you again."

"You wouldn't tell her, I mean, you'd keep it secret, right?"

"That's not the point," Selba said. "You should keep your discussions private."

"I only asked why she didn't try creating a child with me, or something to that effect," Claus said.

"Oh, wow! Now that's a nuclear bomb!" Selba said.

"You think?"

"I know! And you should too! Claus, you should..." Selba tried to say, but she kept nodding her head, "no," as if Claus were a lost cause.

"I should what?" Claus asked.

"No, I'm staying out of this one," Selba said. "If fireworks are to go off, I want safety in distance."

"I need help in this, Selba," Claus said.

"Yes, you do. But I can't help you. Claus, you have a wonderful estate. And I appreciate all that has been done for Sergio and me. Your family adores you. Labba does too. I don't know how this universe will end, but I know love and compassion, and I'm thankful when it beckons my way," Selba said.

"Cutting in," Sergio said, and he started dancing with Selba.

"Pappa, dance with me!" Clausetta said, and she rushed into his arms. "Isn't this a wonderful dinner?"

But Claus did not reply.

"Why so sad, Pappa? Are you fighting with Lanietta?" Clausetta asked.

"Clausetta. Who is your father?"

"Such a silly question. You are, Pappa," she said.

"And your mother?"

"Labba," she said.

"Does it bother you she never speaks, that she stays in eagle form?" Claus asked.

"I am just happy she's been with me my entire life," Clausetta said. "I'm happy for everything I have."

"You are so young," Claus said.

"You can be young too," Clausetta said. "You know, Lanietta's plan with us four Carinians."

"News gets around fast," Claus said.

"I love you so much that I want you to be young. Maybe youth will erase your sadness. At least I get lots more time with you. I can't bear to think that you might just die of old age," she said. "Promise me you'll go through with it. Please?"

"It's a strange thing," Claus said. "You, Leif, Labba, and Lanietta will have a link with Aftova. My children having greater control over me. In a strange way, I guess it's like giving you four a Power of Attorney over me."

"I don't know what that means, but if it means we can be a stronger family with stronger bonds of love, I'm in favor," Clausetta said.

"It means a power to decide things should I become unable to do so, through serious injury or disease. Something people would do for older people," Claus said.

"Oh! No, that's not it at all. No more talk of injury or disease. And none of this death talk. I want to celebrate! Look how happy Leif and Blouisa are! I want to plan their wedding!" Clausetta said.

"Wait a moment! Isn't that between them? I mean, this is all so fast!" Claus said.

"I know they'll marry. I just know it. They're so happy together. So happy," Clausetta said. "They will marry before we unrogue your Aftova. Mamma might need a wheelchair, but she'll be fine. Maybe this will bring her out of her shell. Maybe she'll talk! Or...you know, maybe she would come out of her shell after we unrogue Aftova. We should do that *before* the wedding! Then I'll have my real Mamma *and* the wedding! A double celebration!"

Clausetta was so optimistic and jubilant that Claus didn't want to spoil it with any further talk on his part.

"Cutting in," Blouisa said as she took over for Clausetta.

"You look great tonight," Claus said.

"I want to thank you more than anything for saving my life," she said. "I really do. And I want your permission to marry your son."

"I think Leif is supposed to ask your parents or something," Claus said.

"Sadly, they are fully cubified," Blouisa said. "I've lost my entire family that way. I don't know what kind of world the lunar shock will become. Can it get any worse than it is now? Probably. It wasn't always so bad. Claus, I remember Earth. I was only five when it exploded, but I remember how male selenites ruled with an iron fist and had us as prisoners. I thought we had escaped that on Luna, but the older I got, the worse things became. My parents were cheerful when we reached Luna. They looked forward to better things in the future. But Frieda—"

"Ruined it," Claus said.

"I'm sorry. I feel like I'm confessing my sins. I hope you don't mind," Blouisa said.

"Go ahead. At least you won't slap me," Claus said.

Blouisa looked surprised.

"I don't know why anyone would slap you," she said. "Maybe I should leave you alone."

"No, I'm sorry. Go ahead. You were saying about Frieda?"

"We know she ruined the lunar shock. We can't deal with her, of course. I was at Clover's funeral. Very young I was, but I remember how Labba used you to fight Frieda. I didn't understand then, but I appreciate what she tried to do now that I'm older. And there was a doctor. Doctor Kechenova. She died from that attack. Well, I'm rambling, I know. But I hope you'll let me stay here on the near side with Leif. He's such a great man. You must have had something to do with that."

"As you pointed out when we first met, I've been in a coma for twenty-five years. He was raised by others. At times I feel like Luna has done better without my influence. I seem to have a knack for making a mess of things."

"Well I'm one mess you were kind to. And these legs are great! Lanietta said you helped create them. I don't know what kind of biologist or medical professional you are, but they turned out exactly as I had hoped. More so in fact. Look! I can change the color of my toe nails on a whim."

Blouisa changed the color of her toenails, as if she had instantly changed to a new toenail polish.

"Nifty, isn't it?" she said. "I just wish I didn't have the scars. Leif says they look nice, but, well..."

"Your legs are fine," Claus said. "And as has been pointed out to me, Gerhardt men seem to have a fascination for scarred legs."

Blouisa smiled.

"I won't ask," she said. "Well? May I marry Leif?"

"With all my blessing," Claus said. "I hope you two have a wonderful life together."

"You'll be around, I hope. We want to share our family with you. Can't promise how quickly, though," Blouisa grinned.

"Please, be at ease with life. I'm being told to relax, so I'll pass on the advice."

"It's good advice. Thank you, Claus. Thank you again!"

Chapter 114: A Gerhardt Wedding

Blouisa and Leif announced their plans, initially to wed in two weeks, but after pleas from Clausetta, they delayed the wedding until Labba was fully recovered. Three months passed, and Labba had her wings back. She flew about the near side with poise and grace. She landed at the fortress where Claus, Lanietta, Clausetta, Leif, and Blouisa were gathered.

"Labba is fully healed," Lanietta said.

"Good!" Clausetta said. "We'll have the wedding tomorrow!"

Blouisa and Leif looked at Clausetta funny.

"I mean, do you think tomorrow is too soon?" Clausetta asked. "It's your wedding."

Blouisa and Leif exchanged glances then laughed.

"Tomorrow is fine," Blouisa said. "We were planning to have it any day now anyway. We knew the time would come. And Leif is anxious about getting Mamma Labba back."

"Yes! Mamma Labba!" Clausetta said. "May we do the unrogue now, Aunt Lanietta?"

"If all are willing," Lanietta said.

"I'm ready," Leif said.

"Me too!" Clausetta said.

"Clausetta believes that we'll unrogue Aftova and humoidify Labba at the same time," Lanietta said to Claus. "There's no evidence this procedure will do so. It acts solely on you, Clomper."

"There's always hope for hope," Claus said.

"An interesting statement coming from you, Clomper. Well then, let's hope for hope," Lanietta said. "Labba, are you ready for the unrogue procedure?"

Labba nodded yes.

"Very well. There's a special chamber down below for just such a purpose. I made arrangements in advance for its preparation. If everyone will follow me, please. Blouisa, you may attend if you wish, though your presence is not required."

"I'll go," Blouisa said.

Leif smiled. Lanietta motioned everyone forward, and she led the way down a long, spiral staircase. At the bottom was a room filled with mirrors, crystals, and a spectrum of light.

"Stay together. Do not get lost. The mirrors are needed for angular focus but can also lead one astray," Lanietta explained. "Follow me to the central platform."

There were three floor levels—the base floor, a circular platform two feet above the base floor level, and a smaller circular platform another two feet above the main circular platform.

"Clomper, you go on the little platform, there's a good puppy," Lanietta said. "The rest of you take positions of four corners. Clausetta, you take north, Leif take south, Labba will take east, and I of course will take—"

"The wicked witch of the west," Claus said.

"That was not called for," Lanietta said. "Blouisa, you may stand with Leif if you wish, or you may stand at base ground level."

"I'll stand with Leif," Blouisa said.

"Should Sergio be here? I have him watching Claude," Clausetta said.

"His presence is not required. I think it best he remain with Claude. This is no place for children," Lanietta said.

Positions were taken, and Lanietta began.

"Dim the lights please," Lanietta called. The lights dimmed.

"Drum leader," Lanietta called.

A light shone in a previously darkened place on a balcony above, revealing Selenita. Selenita was dressed in yellow and blue. She waved, and another light shone on a drum line of fellow female selenites. Selenita waved once more, and the drum line started playing. Claus half-fancied it a fife and drum corps, only there were no fifes. Claus's small platform rotated counterclockwise. Selenita had her back to the drum line but faced outward toward Claus. She held a crystalline double chalice resembling the Tropheia, but a bit smaller in form. Lanietta waved, and a drum each with shoulder strap dropped over the heads of Leif, Labba, Clausetta, and Lanietta.

"Each time you face Clomper's side, strike your drum," Lanietta commanded.

In this way, the four Carinians would strike their drums twice for each rotation of Claus. Labba used her beak to tap her drum while the other three had drumsticks for striking. Lanietta chanted something unintelligible, and ethereal threads were drawn out of Aftova. Each of the four Carinians had a yellow/blue thread pair from Aftova. As Claus rotated, these thread pairs wrapped around him. However, Selenita also had a yellow/blue thread running from Aftova to the double chalice, with the blue thread going to the top and the yellow below. Selenita flipped top to bottom and bottom to top quickly like a baton, and so the threads wrapped around the double chalice, covering it over like a cocoon.

Claus's platform spun more quickly, and he became dizzy. He tapped his palate to steady his balance, but Lanietta ordered him not to. Claus acquired motion sickness, and his stomach went queasy. He tapped his palate again.

"Don't tap your palate!" Lanietta shouted. "We are almost done!"

The platform spun even quicker. Drum beats were now frenetic, and Lanietta chanted even quicker than before. Claus could not handle the pace. He stuck his fingers in his mouth to ask Aftova for relief. This disturbed Claus's roundness in his spin. He went out of round. He wobbled, could not hold on, and was thrown toward Lanietta. At the same time, the ethereal threads on Selenita's double

chalice pulled that chalice down and hit Labba on the head.

Drums stopped, the platform stopped, Labba had fallen with daze, and Claus was atop Lanietta.

"A little forward, aren't you?" Lanietta said.

"I'm sorry," he said.

Claus removed his weight from her, and he stood up. He helped Lanietta to her feet, but before he could ask what had happened, and before Lanietta could chew him out for interfering, Leif, Blouisa, and Clausetta had run over to Labba and beckoned Lanietta and Claus to walk over. They did and to their surprise saw Labba in humanoid form.

"It worked!" Clausetta said. "Mamma is back to normal! Will she speak? Mamma, pep up!"

Labba came out of her daze. In her hand was the double chalice. She stared at it, not sure what to think of it. Then she smiled and was about to say something.

"I'll take that," Lanietta said, and she took the double chalice from Labba.

Labba immediately returned to eagle form.

"What happened?" Clausetta said. "Give her back the chalice!"

"I'm afraid the unrogue procedure was only partially effective. Clomper will only live to be five hundred, but he has made a mess of ethereal threads."

Lanietta tapped the double chalice, and a handle emerged. She cranked the handle as if winding fishing line on a pole, and the double chalice wound up the loose ethereal threads in the vicinity.

"I'll hold onto this for now. I must untangle it over a course of time," Lanietta said.

"Will it be untangled before the wedding?" Clausetta asked with excitement.

Lanietta laughed.

"I'm afraid not," Lanietta said. "Though I can start now, it will take much longer to untangle. Much longer. Labba will be in eagle form for the wedding."

Clausetta beat her fist in disappointment. It was the first time she had done such a thing, and it was totally out of character.

"Clausetta!" Leif said. "Do not worry! We are a family and all together. We will be fine."

"I'm just disappointed, that's all," Clausetta said.

"C'mon, honey," Blouisa said. "Let's get a drink before rehearsal."

"Clausetta doesn't drink," Leif said.

"It's time I start," Clausetta said. "Let's try the standard—strawberry champagne."

"Clausetta, maybe you should hold off on this. It's been a long day already," Claus said. "Lanietta, what do you think?"

But when Claus turned to Lanietta, she was gone.

"Now where did she go off to?" he asked.

"Give us an hour," Blouisa said. "Then we'll meet you all for rehearsal."

Blouisa and Clausetta walked off, leaving Leif and Claus to accompany Labba, or perhaps it was Labba who accompanied Leif and Claus. She took to flight and hovered over the two.

"Selenita?" Claus called, but she had already ushered her drum line away. "Labba, you don't have to hover. You can perch on my shoulder."

Labba perched on his shoulder.

"Oh, you're heavy," he said.

"Pappa, did you see Mamma? She was a real lady and not an eagle," Leif said.

"I saw," Claus said. "But I'm not sure why or how. I'm sick to my stomach, disoriented, and confused."

Claus fell to his knees, but Labba flapped and pulled him back up.

"Thank you, Labba," Claus said.

"Let's go to the church, Pappa. I have..." Leif started.

But Claus lost his focus and daydreamed about being in Prava 12 and tracking Novi 3.

"Party on Novi 3," Claus thought to himself. "And I'm stuck in a barrel. Stuck in a...barrel."

"Don't you think?" Leif asked as Claus returned his attention.

"About what?" Claus asked.

"Weren't you listening?" Leif asked.

"I'm sorry. I'm having trouble concentrating. Maybe I should rest somewhere," Claus said.

"Let's take you to the observatory," Leif said. "It's the highest point in Leifton. You'll be able to sit and watch the scenery. Mamma can fly around and check on things. She'll watch over you."

"Thank you," Claus said.

The three took a lift to the observatory. Claus sat in a reclining chair while Leif brought Claus a drink. Labba took to the air and flew around, checking on things as Leif predicted.

"Someday she'll return to us," Leif said. "Someday. Pappa, are you comfort—"

But Leif was interrupted by Claus's snoring. Leif smiled and tip-toed away. Claus dreamt he was on the Mad Mistral again, wandering aimlessly around the ocean, dodging progressively larger and larger garbage reefs until he hit one square-on and became entangled in it like a porpoise in a fishing net. Claus peered over the edge of the Mad Mistral and saw a braided vine of plastic go toward his neck to pull him over.

"No, I won't fall over! I won't!" Claus yelled.

Claus woke with a start and found himself leaning over a railing to the far-below.

"If you're going to jump, you could at least pass Aftova on to someone more worthy before doing the desperate deed. Perhaps Clausetta would value it more," a familiar voice said.

Claus turned around to see Lanietta in seamstress attire, knitting.

"For the baby," Lanietta said.

"What baby?" Claus asked.

"The one Blouisa and Leif will have," Lanietta said. "Can't be too prepared. How shall we name their child?"

"That's not for us to decide," Claus said.

"Let's see. Labba named Leif after that great explorer. Clausetta was named after me, and I suppose Claude was somewhat named after you. That means I'm due for the next name. If a girl, she shall be Lanthropia, and if a boy, Lycanthrope," Lanietta said.

"What kind of names are those?" Claus asked.

"You have better? Names, Clomper. Give me names. Oh wait, I know. If a boy, Clompus, and if a girl, Clompasia."

"You're getting worse. Let the happy couple chose their children, Lanietta, if they chose any at all."

"You do not like Lanthropia. Maybe you'd care to stretch it out into something like—"

"Lanietta-throw-up-i-a," Claus grinned.

"I should stab you where you stand, Clomper. Come along. It's time for rehearsal," Lanietta said in a huff.

The two went down to the church. Lanietta led the way, and the two reached the lobby. Claus took several steps into the main church area.

"I'm curious, Lanietta, what denomination is this?" Claus asked.

He turned around, and she was gone.

"Lanietta?" Claus called.

"If you will come forward, I will explain the ceremony," said the minister's voice from in front of the altar.

Claus turned back toward the main church and saw Lanietta dressed as a minister.

"You've gone too far!" Claus yelled.

"Shh!" Lanietta said to Claus.

"Pappa!" Clausetta said as she ran down the main aisle. "Hurry! You're in the wedding too!"

"I am?"

"Yes!" Clausetta said. "You'll give the bride away! Practice with my arm. Well? Practice!"

Claus held Clausetta as if to give her away. Then he felt sad.

"Oh, you never got to give me away," Clausetta said. "Don't be sad, Pappa."

"Who gave you away?" Claus asked as the two approached the others.

"I did," Lanietta said.

Claus's sadness quickly turned to anger.

"Figures," he said.

"You would have tripped and broken your leg. Or Clausetta's. Now hush up, Clomper. Time for business."

Lanietta then explained the procession.

"I will appear first," Lanietta said. "I will then motion for the groom and groomsmen to take their places. You will enter from that side door and form a line to my left as I face the church's main entrance. You too will face that direction. I will motion to Selenita, and she will begin singing. The bridesmaids will approach one by one and take their places to my right. The matron of honor will approach. Sergio, you as the best man may meet her halfway and escort her the remainder. Then we have Claude as the ring bearer. The flower girl will...where is the flower girl?"

Selenita motioned, and a young girl robot approached.

"Selenatina is the flower girl," Selenita said.

"Ah, your younger sister," Lanietta said.

"She never grew up," Selenita grinned.

"Sometimes that's the best," Lanietta said. "Selenatina, you will drop flower petals along the way."

"Okay!" Selenatina said.

"I always wanted to be a flower girl," Clausetta said, and she hiccupped.

"Blouisa, if you got my daughter drunk," Claus started.

"Hey, we just had a few," Blouisa said.

Clausetta hiccupped again, and she went a little eethi. Ethereal flowers fell from her hair toward the floor and disappeared once they reached the floor.

"Interesting," Lanietta said. "Now then, Clomper will accompany Blouisa down the aisle. Everyone will take to their assigned seats, except for Blouisa and Leif, who get to stand the entire time."

"What about Mamma Labba?" Clausetta asked, and she hiccupped with a few more ethereal flowers floating down.

"She is perched up there by the choir," Lanietta said. "I anticipate she will be there for the wedding."

"Doesn't seem right," Claus said. "She should be by my side."

"Then go up to her, Clomper," Lanietta mocked.

"No, Pappa. Stay here," Clausetta said, and she hiccupped again.

A blue ethereal thread from Claus took the flower and dragged it behind him like a small kite as he walked back down the aisle, to a stairwell, and up to the choir where he joined Labba.

"This will be Leif's big day," Claus said. "I know he was kidnapped from us, but he's going to a new woman tomorrow. Can't you revert to your humanoid shape? We need to move on."

Labba turned her beak a little away from Claus.

"Clausetta. She has her heart set on your transformation. Labba, there's no dignity in dismay. Or discord. I'm shocked to hear myself say it, but can't we come together with Lanietta for the children? I know I risked your life over Blouisa, but she'll be family soon. I'm sure she'd be happy to see the real Labba, as would we all. Please?"

Labba continued to look away.

"What will it take, Labba? What?" Claus asked.

Labba turned toward Claus and seemed to utter something from her beak.

"Ssss ahhh ssss ehhh chch ehhh ensh ahhh ssss ahhh."

"Sassatinassa? Lanietta?" Claus asked. "I know you still begrudge her. I have my grudges too. If only we could befriend her, be really honest and forthright with her—without her games or trickery in reply. Seems we'll never have as much. Seems she'll just—hey, where are you going?"

Labba dove from her perch, swooped down just above Clausetta, and perched at a point on the other side of the church.

"Was that an ethereal flower she took from Clausetta? Something odd is happening," Claus said.

Short yellow and blue ethereal threads extended a few inches from Claus's ears as if acting like antennae to listen for an ethereal disturbance. They vibrated and twitched in anxious expectation.

"Leave me alone, Aftova," Claus said as he tapped his upper palate to calm his nerves and those of Aftova. "Behave for the wedding."

Lanietta had been giving instruction this entire time but paused briefly to give Claus an evil stare. Claus turned away and went down the stairs. He exited the church and waited outside for rehearsal to end. Claus watched as streams of selenites toted carts and supplies here and there.

"Like Christmas Eve," Claus said. "Can't let the children see the surprise though. My guess is the decorations go up as we sleep. So the selenites take care of us like the children we are. Either I'm a pet to Lanietta or a child to the robots. Some life. Get used to it, Claus. There's no future in wistful thinking. Or wishful thinking."

Claus retired for the day to his mansion. Night came with slumber, and the wedding day came with a slew of selenites around, guarding and guiding the humans and Carinians to their respective places and roles.

"This is weird," Claus said. "I feel like a prisoner."

"It's to ensure perfect success," Treyu said to Claus.

"And perfect bliss," Mariel said. "The selenites have taken over our duties for the day. See? We get a day off for the wedding."

The selenites urged the people to get ready. They did. Claus and the groom's party were taken by coach to the church first where Treyu urged Claus to help seat attendees.

"So the selenites haven't taken *everything* over," Claus said.

"They do permit us to do a few things," Treyu said.

"I feel uneasy, Treyu. I feel like this is an execution, not a wedding," Claus said.

"Do not share your feelings to others. This is not your day," Treyu said.

"No, it isn't. I don't suppose I'll ever have my day. You know, I never had a wedding with Labba. I suppose it would be strange to see her as my bride, as I don't—"

"It's best to leave such things to silence," Treyu said.

Claus held his tongue. Treyu seated a couple, and Claus took the opportunity to look up at the choir and around. He saw Labba perched above.

"Claus, the bride's party is here," Mariel said.

"Are we that close to starting?" Claus asked.

Music started up. The bride's party rushed into the church lobby area while non-wedding people rushed into their seats.

"You're giving the bride away, right?" Mariel said. "You should take your position at her side."

"Of course," Claus said. "I'll see you after the wedding."

Treyu escorted Mariel in last of all, and the two sat on the groom's side. Claus walked past the bridesmaids and stopped at the bride, who had a heavy veil over her face.

"I'm a little nervous," Claus confessed. "I must say I really thought you were going to die. I've been told I should have not done anything, but, well, something inside me said that you had a purpose, a role yet to play in all of this. I hope you and Leif have been happy and will continue to enjoy many years together."

"Why thank you, Clomper. I will," Lanietta said as she suddenly lifted the veil.

"Lanietta!" Claus said in surprise. "What are you doing in that outfit?"

"Don't you want to marry me? We'll do a double wedding. Father and son marry the women of their dreams. What do you say? Are matches made in heaven? Tied together for eternity? Caught in cosmic—"

"Calamity," Claus said.

"How dare you!" Lanietta said.

"Where's Blouisa?" Claus demanded to know.

"Oh, she is delayed. A minor mishap on the way. It seems several ethereal stitches frayed between her reptilian legs and the rest of her," Lanietta said.

"What? Ethereal stitches?"

"You don't think I used catgut, do you? No, eethi is pleethy," Lanietta said.

"Now you're speaking biggerish. I mean gibberish. You're flustering me, Lanietta!" Claus said.

Lanietta laughed.

"And who's supposed to run this wedding if you're a bride? And what about Labba? She and I—"

"Are not married, as you reminded yourself. You're a free man," Lanietta said. "Although marriage to a pet is forbidden in the Carinian empire, the empire is dissolved, and I have remade the laws in my own image. So I include your kind in the new marriage laws. Oh, and Selba can marry us. Look toward the altar."

Claus looked, and Selba stood in front of the altar with Leif, Sergio, and the groomsmen in line, awaiting the bride's processional to start.

"See?"

"I...am...to...give...Blouisa...away!" Claus insisted.

"And who will give me away?" Lanietta pouted.

"Stop with the games, Lanietta. If you really are to marry Leif to Blouisa, then get out of that getup and into your holy robes," Claus said.

"Stood up at the altar!" Lanietta cried, and she rushed out the main church door.

A moment later, Nanceya opened the door for Blouisa.

"Sorry," Blouisa said. "I hope I didn't make people wait. Did I miss anything?"

"No. Everything is fine," Claus said.

Blouisa presented her arm for Claus to take.

"You're shaking like a leaf," Blouisa said. "I thought I was the nervous one!"

"Sorry," Claus said.

"Thank you again, Claus," Blouisa said. "This is the happiest day of my life!"

"Did you know that Selba is going to marry you and Leif?" Claus asked.

"Oh yes," Blouisa said. "We picked her ahead of time, of course. Lanietta just filled in during rehearsal. Selba had to prepare."

"Again I'm left in the dark," Claus said.

"Lanietta explained everything at rehearsal. Oh, that's right, you went up to Labba. You missed out that part," Blouisa said. "Don't worry. Everything will be fine."

Selba started the wedding, and all proceeded like a normal wedding. Claus gave Blouisa away, and he took his seat. Selba did well in her part and read romantic poetry at various parts of the ceremony to cement the bonds of matrimony. Clausetta, however, kept releasing ethereal flowers in much greater quantity than what she released during rehearsal.

"I've got to speak with that girl," Claus said. "She'll turn into an alcoholic at this rate."

As vows were exchanged, Clausetta's ethereal hiccupping became more and more pronounced. Only Leif, Claus, and Labba noticed how Clausetta inadvertently went eethi during such hiccups, and Leif became distracted and thus stuttered a bit while exchanging vows. Claus looked around for Lanietta but did not see her at all.

The moment finally came. Selba pronounced the couple wife and husband. The two exchanged kisses, and those in attendance applauded. Music started up, and Lanietta made her surprise appearance, singing like an opera star. She moved about the church with her double chalice, pulling off ethereal strands and dropping them on various people and things as if strewing magic tinsel about.

"Spin a basket fine of gold and give your heart o bright and bold," she said as part of her singing.

"What is she doing?" Claus asked.

"We all a group belong to Lanietta's kingdom strong," she continued.

"She's creating some sort of final chain of bondage," Claus said. "This isn't a wedding. It's indoctrination."

Claus's irritation activated Aftova and sent out his yellow and blue ethereal threads toward Lanietta. But his disruption of the ether attracted Clausetta's ethereal flowers, and they flocked toward the threads. The flowers became butterflies, took his threads in criss-cross fashion like a net, and gathered up Lanietta's ethereal tinsel. Clausetta tried to stop the ethereal flowers, and she pounded her fist, but this caused her to fully split her physical and ethereal selves. Her ethereal self stood several feet away and pounded its fist in the ether, causing shockwaves to clump ethereal butterflies and threads together. The clumping became organized and cyclonic, like a mini hurricane inside the church. Labba flew down to stop it, but it caught her and swirled her around. Lanietta tried to stop it too, but she was caught up. The double chalice flew out of her hands, and it spewed out its ethereal threads. The cyclone collapsed into an ethereal tornado, confining and concentrating ethereal energy into a bright but powerful ball of plasma.

"Stop! Stop!" Clausetta cried, unable to stop her involvement in the chaos.

Claus rushed over to Clausetta. He tried to go eethi but could not. Leif and Blouisa also rushed to Clausetta's aid. Blouisa comforted Clausetta's physical body while Leif went eethi himself for the first time ever to calm Clausetta's eethi self. He didn't know how he could go eethi. He just did. With his help and that of Aftova, Clausetta reintegrated. Leif reintegrated, Aftova withdrew its threads, and the ethereal tornado shrank into the double chalice that now had an orb on one end and something swirling inside. The ethereal disruption and chaos ended.

"Is anyone hurt?" Blouisa called.

People checked on one another, and all seemed fine.

"Mamma? Where's Mamma Labba?" Clausetta asked.

Standing up from within the groom's side stood the humanoid version of Labba.

"Mamma!" Clausetta said as she rushed toward Labba.

Leif and Blouisa walked over to Labba as did many others to witness this rare instance of her. No one knew how long she would stay like this, and they simply had to marvel at her appearance.

"Lanietta," Claus said. "Has anyone seen Lanietta?"

But Claus was largely ignored as the people continued to marvel at Labba. Claus walked over to the double chalice, picked it up, and saw the orb on one end. Inside it swirled colors of yellow and blue.

"What am I looking at?" he asked himself.

Images flashed in his mind. Images of Lanietta as a tortured soul.

"Lanietta!" Claus said. "She's stuck in here. Labba! We must help Lanietta!"

"NO!" Labba shouted back.

The crowd gasped that Labba spoke.

"Do not interface with the orb, Claus. We are in grave danger," Labba said. "Everyone, follow me!"

Labba led the party to an emergency stairwell and down, down, down into the deepest of chambers.

"Bolt the door. Do it!" Labba shouted.

"Labba, you can speak!" Claus shouted back.

"Yes, and not for very long if we don't brace for impact. Take to a kneeling position and bury your heads in your hands. Brace! Brace!" she shouted.

The people did as she instructed. Claus was too shocked to follow her instructions. He stood there as if waiting for Lanietta to show up. But she didn't. He held the double chalice in his hands and wondered what he should do, if anything.

"Do nothing, Claus. Kneel and pray. Kneel and pray!" Labba ordered.

Labba ran over and forced Claus to his knees. The double chalice slipped out of his grasp and rolled a bit in front of him. He meant to reach for it, but the floor shook horribly as if it were ready to open up and swallow the lot of them. Then a distant sound like billions of katydids approached. These critters, if they were as such, stretched out their grating with such torture and misery that people grew fearful that the things would come inside the chamber and tear flesh from bone. Those who didn't

faint from the sounds held onto their sanity by covering their ears and chanting. Claus also covered his ears and sought to use Aftova to help, but he felt an enormous heaviness in the air that suppressed even the slightest urge to tap his upper palate.

Labba went for the double chalice. She was on her knees too, but she had a little more mobility than the others. She held the double chalice in hand and whispered to it, but those creatures from outside spat bits through cracks in the door. These bits attacked the double chalice and the orb.

"No! You cannot have her!" Labba shouted.

The bits fought with Labba and formed a great vine from the cracks in the door to the double chalice. Labba groaned in pain as she struggled. Claus and the others were still paralyzed and could not help.

Labba lost cohesion, and she didn't want to. She went eethi, but her ethereal self became a secondary target for the bits. They dragged her toward the door and partially sucked her out. The double chalice was also being sucked out through the crack by another fork of the bit-vine.

"Claus!" Labba shouted.

Claus beat his head against the ground in desperation, cracking the front of his skull in the process. Aftova sent yellow and blue ethereal threads out through his teeth, but the bits came after these threads. Claus slammed his head against the floor again. He broke his nose and his front teeth. With his front teeth freed, his yellow and blue ethereal threads broke free with them. The bits sucked them up and gave Labba a brief moment to reintegrate herself. She did and sent a powerful plasma charge at Claus's loose teeth. They exploded in the ether and forced the bit-vine back out through the cracks. Labba's plasma sealed the cracks as the last of the bits exited, but before she could completely seal it, the double chalice was pulled out with the bit-vine. Labba dove for it and tried to grab it, but the bit-vine pulled it out first. Her plasma ball sealed the last of the crack. Boom. Labba landed on the floor. Slap. And Claus beat his broken nose against the floor again. Crunch.

Blood, bone, and misery pooled on the floor. Claus passed out.

Chapter 115: Sickly Honey

When Claus awoke, he was in a wheelchair in the bedroom of his estate. A cast fully encased his skull except for openings to his eyes, ears, and mouth. Mariel waved her hand in front of his eyes.

"I can see you," Claus said.

"Labba! He's awake!" Mariel called.

Labba walked in, still in humanoid form.

"I had a bad dream that strange creatures attacked us," Claus said. "But seeing you like this says it wasn't a dream."

"I'm no longer in eagle form," Labba said.

"You're speaking to me," Claus said. "I should be happy. But my face. I..."

"We've given you a local painkiller to ease your distress," Labba said.

"What happened, Labba?" Claus asked.

"It's okay, Mariel. You may leave us," Labba said.

"I'll be downstairs if you need me," Mariel said, and she left.

Labba turned Claus's wheelchair around and pushed toward the window.

"Look out there," she said.

The estate grounds were heavily damaged. Stonework was cratered, trees and shrubs were destroyed, and everywhere there was a muck that clung to everything and resisted cleanup.

"We were attacked?" Claus asked. "Frieda?"

"Yes. Yes," Labba said.

"Did I have something to do with it? Did Clausetta? And Lanietta?"

"Three times yes," Labba said.

"That ethereal stuff. Nasty business that ethereal stuff. But you're here speaking with me. How I've missed you. I wish you could wave an ethereal magic wand and...and..."

But Claus could not finish his words.

"And what?" Labba asked. "What is it, Claus? Here."

Labba went eethi, put a part of herself inside Claus, and settled him. She withdrew and reintegrated herself.

"I have a sharp, burning pain in my stomach, like nothing I've ever felt before," Claus said. "It's like fire, like a sword has been thrust there. I feel like fire and ash—burning but nothing to burn. Awake but numb, motivated yet tractionless. Labba, are the children safe? And Blouisa? The others?"

"No humans on the near side have died," Labba said. "Most of our selenites were destroyed fighting the invaders. As for you, you nearly died yourself. You sent bone fragments into your brain. Not the best thing to do. But we had them pulled out. Your nose and face are reconstructed as best as could be. The painkillers should keep you asleep."

"Should? They're not," Claus said.

"Aftova has slipped, Claus. It was shoved to the very back of your brain, backward into the visual cortex," Labba said. "We could not retrieve it. Not without risking more damage to you."

"How much damage did I sustain? I mean that you can't repair?" Claus asked.

"Well we thought you'd lose your ability to see and speak," Labba said. "I'm glad you have both. This tells us we don't know what strangeness you might experience. Balance and coordination will be off. Hold out your right hand and catch this comb."

Claus held out his right hand. Labba dropped a comb from above for him to catch. But instead of Claus grasping for the comb with his right hand, his left hand moved, even though his left was nowhere near the comb.

"Strange," Claus said.

"As I suspected," Labba said.

"Why have you kept silent all these years? Labba! Explain!" Claus said.

"I had a deep pit in my stomach too, Claus. Fire and ash, like you said. It kept me alive and alert, but unable to do anything about it. Burning yet burned out. I've never known such a thing as a Carinian. But it overwhelmed me. I'm free of it now. It could come back. I don't know. But that double chalice created a weakness in the ethereal fabric. Frieda took advantage of that and launched eggified Greylingers. That's what hit us, Claus. They came quickly. It was all I could do to get us underground. Lanietta is in that orb. Trapped. Nothing we can do about it now."

"She *is* in that orb. I had flashes in my mind that she was. But I didn't want to believe it. Labba, we have to get her out. Labba? Why are you smiling?" Claus asked.

Labba broke out in a sickly smile, as if she were tasting old, rotten honey and experiencing both decay and delight from acid and sweet. She fell into dance and laughed.

"Have you gone mad? Labba!" Claus called.

"I don't know, Claus, but I feel great relief that her oppression is lifted," Labba said. "It might be our undoing on the near side, but if we are to perish, we will do so with pleasure."

"Perish and pleasure. What kind of fantasy nightmare is this? Has everyone gone mad too? Has Frieda taken full control of Luna and forced her agenda?" Claus asked.

"No. Frieda has no long-lasting power here," Labba laughed.

"Just short-term," Claus speculated.

"None of that either. Look outside the window again. What do you see?"

A dark cloud rolled in.

"Rain? Here? Impossible," Claus said.

"Watch," she said.

Claus saw lines come down from the cloud, lines of what would be rain in another venue. When that which might have been rain reached the window, flowers and butterflies appeared instead.

"Our daughter rules the weather, and our son rules the selenites. We have dominion over sky and soil," Labba said.

Claus shook with nervous anxiety.

"You are mad," Claus said. "So must be everyone else. I've lost everything. My family, my life—everything!"

A cold wind fell upon Claus. It was as if the invisible hand of death swept down from above and beckoned him away to the land of nothing. No more insanity, no more unpredictability, just the peace and rectitude of eternity.

Claus wanted to end his life and end it there. He looked for something, anything he could use to end it. A knife to cut his wrist, an object to choke on, or perhaps a lever to launch him out the window into a fatal fall. But Claus was not so lucky. Labba took to his wheelchair and paraded him around the mansion. Soon his family joined in the fray and paraded around with Claus. He was the man along for the ride, like a runaway truck down a mountain with no brakes, no engine, and no will-power to stop the crash.

The crash never came. It was always an impending crash. Impending, impending, impending. No ending. Claus tapped his upper palate, but no Aftova was there. He could tap no longer. His stomach became increasingly disturbed, and the only thing that stopped the parade was when he closed his eyes and threw up. The taste that came up was of acid and sugar, like poisonous sickly honey. He kept his eyes closed in despair.

"Pappa is sick!" Clausetta said.

"I'll take him to the infirmary," Labba said.

"Pappa, get well soon!" Clausetta said as she patted him on the shoulder.

Claus opened his eyes to look at her, but he was shocked that his vision had changed. His left eye saw the world in shades of yellow while his right saw them in shades of blue. The converged images vibrated and competed, but neither could dominate. Claus himself was driven to new, unceasing pain.

"I need help," Claus said. "My eyes. My eyes!"

Labba wheeled him to the infirmary. Claus kept his eyes closed most of the time but occasionally opened them to see what was going on. He half-expected to see Lanietta there, but instead he just saw Selenita.

"This way please," Selenita said, and Labba wheeled him to an examination room.

"I'm sick to my stomach, I threw up, and now I see yellow out the left eye and blue out the right eye," Claus said.

Selenita and her selenite helpers placed Claus on a platform and maneuvered him into a tube. She hit several switches. Scans showed up on a large screen.

"There," Selenita said. "Yellow and blue ethereal threads are running from Aftova through his visual cortex and down his spinal column. They are taking over his nervous system."

"That could kill me," Claus said.

"Yes, it could," Selenita said.

"Well stop it!" Claus demanded.

"There's nothing *well* about it," Selenita said.

"You sound like Leni, sarcasm and all," Claus said.

"Claus could become irritable, depressed, angry, tired, sleepless, and suffer a loss of appetite. He might also try to flee whatever situation he is in," Selenita said to Labba as Claus tried to wiggle out of the tube.

"What can we do?" Labba asked. "I could go eethi and try to stabilize him."

"Too risky. The threads are like parasitic vines. Break them off, and their cuttings infect their new host," Selenita said. "No Carinians should interact ethereally with him. That means you, Clausetta, Leif, and Claude. If Lanietta were here, I'd issue her the same warning."

"If Lanietta were here, she wouldn't make me suffer this long," Claus said, who was now out of the tube. "I'm getting out of here!"

Claus tried to run, but his legs got caught up in themselves, he tripped, and he fell.

"Ow!" he said.

"Your coordination is off," Selenita said.

"Labba already proved that to me," Claus said.

"Then why did you run?" Selenita asked.

"I'm prone to flight. You said it yourself. So I'm *flighting*," Claus said.

Claus made another effort to run. He kept on his feet, but his run was more like an awkward skip. He left the examination room and skipped down the hallway. Labba shook her head in disbelief. Selenita hit a button. Several female selenites caught Claus and carried him back to the examination room with him kicking all the way.

"Give him this to drink," Selenita said, and she handed a small bottle to Labba.

Labba forced Claus to drink from the bottle. He swallowed, but his face returned an expression of disgust.

"What is that? Some whacked out honey concoction?" Claus complained.

"It is a tincture of honey, opium, camphor, glycerin, anise oil, benzoic acid, alcohol, and water," Selenita said.

"Sounds like paregoric. Yuck!" Claus said.

"Isn't that a narcotic?" Labba asked.

"Yes," Selenita replied. "Useful for calming small children."

"And pets too? Why don't you call me Clomper?" Claus said. "Is that you, Lanietta? Are you posing as Selenita?"

Selenita removed her head from her body briefly then returned it.

"Can Lanietta do that?" Selenita asked.

"I've never seen her try," Claus said.

"Claus, try to relax," Labba said.

"Oh," Claus said. "It's doing something. The yellow and blue are swirling. Ow!"

The head cast cracked and fell off. Claus had yellow and blue tubes growing from his head into curls and weaves.

"Stop it. Stop it!" Claus demanded.

"It's a rare side effect, Claus, but it will stop growing. Just think of it as a hat," Selenita said.

"It's freaking me out! I feel like worms have invaded my scalp!" Claus said.

"Can you give him something else?" Labba asked.

"The tubes are the only things holding his skull and nose together," Selenita said. "We best leave them be."

"Leave them be? Believe you me, your treatment is at the least a misdemeanor and borderline felony!" Claus said.

Selenita placed a hat over his head.

"The tubes will help him recover. Keep them covered with a hat. That should do," Selenita said, and she waved Labba and Claus off.

Labba wheeled Claus out of the infirmary. The hat covered most of the tubes, but a yellow one ran to his nose from the left and a blue one to his nose from the right, forming what looked like an oxygen breathing tube.

"It's just an oxygen tube," Labba said to people who stared. "Oxygen tube."

"What? That's not—"

"Use the story to cope," Labba said. "Fantasy coping."

"Fantasy nightmare," Claus corrected.

"Coping."

"Nightmare."

"Light scare," Labba said.

"No ping," Claus said without thinking. "No ping? No *pain*. Hey, I feel better."

"Good," she said.

"Labba, stop the wheelchair. Let me walk. I think I can," Claus said.

Labba stopped. Claus stood up and walked.

"I'm surprised," she said. "You really should be resting."

"Must've been the paregoric. Look. I can even dance a bit," Claus said.

Claus did a little dance.

"I don't know what to say," she said.

"Let's leave the infirmary and get lunch. What do you say?"

"Sounds like a good idea," Labba said.

The two returned to Claus's mansion and sat in a small dining room. Treyu was informed of their arrival and asked what Claus and Labba wanted for lunch. The two placed their orders, and Treyu disappeared momentarily.

"Are you still seeing yellow and blue?" Labba asked.

"It comes and goes," Claus said. "Not sure why."

"Selenita didn't cure you. Those ethereal threads are still in your nervous system. We have to watch you carefully," Labba said.

Treyu brought their drinks then disappeared again.

"I want to find Lanietta!" Claus said.

"We can't risk it!" Labba said. "Claus! Everything on the near side is in balance. We're rebuilding, yes, but we're very well protected from Frieda, far better than when Lanietta disappeared into the orb. We can relax and live."

"You still don't sound right. You missed her as a friend, remember?" Claus asked.

"That was before she kidnapped Leif," Labba said. "I've changed, Claus. Lanietta is on her own. So are we. Oh look, here's lunch."

Treyu brought in flaming shish kebabs. He was going to douse the flames, but Claus took one and placed the burning end into his mouth.

"Claus!" Labba said. "You'll burn yourself."

But Claus did not burn. He bit off the piece of food, chewed it, swallowed, and exhaled ashen dust. Labba and Treyu looked on in surprise.

"That's not supposed to happen," Labba said with a shaky voice.

"I'll take these back," Treyu said.

"No!" Claus said as he held onto his shish kebab. "I have a new purpose. I see it all now. The world goes grey when I take to the flame. It removes the yellow and blue disparity, giving me fresh and proper clarity."

"Now who's mad?" Labba said.

But Claus bit off another piece of flaming food, chewed it, and again exhaled ashen dust.

Treyu took the food away and returned with sandwiches.

"Boring," Claus said.

"You've perked up quite a bit," Labba said. "I'm not sure what to think of it."

"Then let's finish lunch and go for a walk. Long time since we had a stroll of leisure," Claus said.

"I'll take you up on that, Claus," Labba said.

"Is there honey in these sandwiches?" Claus asked.

"No. Perhaps the treatment is leaving an aftertaste," Labba said.

The two finished lunch and took a walk around the estate.

"What a mess," Claus said. "Look at the water hoses, the scrubbing, the—"

"Gunk," Labba said.

"Yes, I suppose it is," Claus said.

"These eggified Greylingers are especially nasty. Their sole purpose is to make a mess and be difficult to clean up. They harden like cement. See?" Labba said as she kicked her heel into a dead eggified Greylinger.

Claus leaned over to the remains of an eggified Greylinger on a stone railing. The yellow and blue tubes to Claus's nose shot out a flame, melted the eggified Greylinger, then sucked the eggified Greylingers into the tubes.

"Sneeze them out! Do it!" Labba urged.

"I can't!" Claus said. "They didn't go into my nose. They went into the tubes... the...I feel strange, Labba."

Drops of goo fell from the tube near Claus's nose, collected on his chin, and fell to the ground.

"Smells like sickly honey," Claus said. "Whatever is in me has compelled me to act on its behalf."

With jerky body movements, Claus stepped over to the remains of another eggified Greylinger. The tubes repeated the procedure. More sickly honey dripped.

"Labba, stop me. I can't stop the demon within," Claus pleaded.

"Aftova must be going crazy," Labba said. "I was told not to go eethi, but...I must!"

Labba went eethi to stop Aftova, but Claus's body turned toward her. The tubes shot out the sickly honey goo and ignited it. Both ethereal and physical flames erupted, and Labba was forced back.

"Hah, hah, hah, hah!" Claus laughed against his will.

Claus ran from eggified Greylinger to eggified Greylinger.

"Selenites. Stop Claus!" Labba yelled.

But they couldn't. The tubes controlling Claus did the same to the selenites as they did to Labba—they shot out the sickly honey goo and ignited it. Claus was a living flame thrower and forced back all who attempted to intervene. Labba tried changing to an eagle, but Claus shot out an ethereal burst that prevented her. Word got around of Claus's aggression. Clausetta and Leif came to help Labba, but they too were forced back. Clausetta made it rain flowers and butterflies. It was enough to protect everyone on the near side from Claus, but it also obscured vision. Aftova and the tubes forced Claus to carve his own path with fire and ash, a path he took underground. With the flowers and butterflies providing unintentional cover, Claus disappeared unobserved.

"Stop the Lanietta Express," Labba said. "Close all borders. Guard the roads. Claus is to be found and detained. Spread the word. Spread the word!"

Chapter 116: A Search for Claus

While the near side searched for Claus, Claus found himself floating out of phase with the lunar soil. He was underground, yes, but he had no trouble breathing. Locomotion was another matter. He felt as if suspended in space, and so any attempt to walk proved ineffective. There were no eggified Greylingers in the lunar soil, but his vision changed, and so he saw things differently yet again. It was as if he were in a swimming pool, looking up to people on the surface who were shaded in blue. But what he saw under the surface, which would be like the swimming pool itself, was shaded in yellow. Life-forms in blue above had corresponding yellow mirror images below.

"This can't be real," Claus said.

A pair of yellow and blue tubes blasted plasma out the back of his shoulders, and he moved forward. He had no control over where he went, and so he would only go along for the ride.

"There's Clausetta," Claus said to himself. "She is overcome with grief. She's drinking that strawberry champagne, too. Look, the yellow mirror image of herself is traveling upward. It's nearly ready to merge with her. Stop, Clausetta, stop!"

Clausetta did pause, but not because of Claus. Selba came in to check on her, ushered Clausetta out of her room, and brought her downstairs with others.

"It's not good to drink alone," Selba said to Clausetta.

The yellow mirror image of Clausetta went back down. Claus noticed that Selba had a corresponding yellow mirror image, but it was quite a bit deeper in Luna than Clausetta's image.

"A yellow mirror image stays in a line from the lunar core to the person on the surface. But it changes distance from the core, getting closer to the person when in a bad state, or farther from the person when not so bad," Claus said. "Who would have thought such an environment existed on the near side?"

The tubes moved around to the outskirts of Leifton, where Claus saw Blouisa jogging toward the lunar shock. She wore a backpack and hat. Her yellow mirror image also jogged with her below the surface.

"Blouisa, where are you going?" Claus asked.

"I must keep my legs going," Blouisa said to herself. "My present from Lanietta. I must keep the legs going. If only I can find Lanietta or Claus or other help. Run, Blouisa, run."

"She's driven by guilt," Claus said.

Blouisa stopped at a boulder, sat, and drank from her canteen. The yellow mirror image suddenly descended rapidly toward the lunar core.

"What...why did it do that?" Claus asked himself.

Blouisa took only a short break and resumed her running. The yellow mirror image shot up from the lunar core and ran close to her under the surface.

"Something strange is going on," Claus said to himself.

The tubes sent his body to watch selenites in the search. The selenites had no corresponding yellow mirror images.

"Selenites have no opposites. People do. Plants do," Claus said. "Now the big question is this—where is my mirror image?"

Claus had no answer. He looked at himself and only saw natural skin tones.

"Am I dead? No, they wouldn't be looking for me. Then where is my opposite? Maybe it's far in the core," he mused.

The tubes moved Claus around the under-near side. The few selenites that remained continued looking for Claus as did the people. It was a frenzy, and Claus felt badly for them.

"I'm down here. If only I could tell them. They're wasting time looking where they won't find me," Claus said.

"Looking where they won't find me," echoed a cacophony.

"Who said that?" Claus yelled.

"Who said what?" replied the cacophony.

Claus looked around. His environment was littered with little yellow floating blobs, about the size and color of egg yolks. He'd lost his appetite, but the blobs didn't care. They forced themselves down his throat to feed him. Claus felt bloated and sick, and he wanted to die, but the tubes kept him alive. He fell into a daze, neither fully awake nor fully asleep, just existing through this most unfortunate situation.

As for the echo, Claus could only guess that the blobs formed some sort of collective, linked to an intelligent force, and it was either the collective or the intelligent force mocking Claus.

"Lanietta. Please help me," Claus said.

"Lanietta! Hah, hah, hah, hah, hah!" echoed the blobs.

Claus was still aware of Labba and others on the surface. Labba went eethi to search more quickly, but she didn't think to go below surface.

"I'm down here!" Claus tried to say to her.

Claus noticed that when she went eethi, her yellow mirror image split into untold numbers and formed a continuous chain linking Labba to the lunar core. At times Claus thought the chain was pulling on Labba as if to capture her, but Labba both physically and ethereally kept her position on the lunar surface.

"This world...whatever I'm in...feels like...a threat," Claus said in his daze.

"A threat, a threat!" the voices laughed.

"What can I do?" Claus asked himself.

"What can you do? Do nothing!" they laughed.

"Who are you?" Claus asked.

"Who are you to ask?" they replied.

"I'm Claus Gerhardt, a human from Earth," he said.

"Earth, Earth!" they laughed.

"Did you help destroy it? Are you part of the PRAAD?" Claus asked.

"We're part of you!" they said. "Part of you soon!"

"Frieda? Is this her doing?" Claus asked.

"Frieda, Frieda!" they laughed.

"You're like a child who needs to be told 'no'," Claus said.

"No for you, Claus. No for you!" they laughed.

"Are you nothing but an echo? An afterimage of life?" Claus asked.

"Afterimage of death," they laughed back.

"Show me your master," Claus said.

"The master! The master fantasy nightmare!" they laughed back.

"How do you know I said that?" Claus asked.

They simply laughed.

"People are looking for me. If they find me, they find you. Do you want to be found?" Claus asked.

This conversation had gradually pulled Claus out of his daze, but the responses frustrated him.

"We will be found. Soon enough," they laughed.

"You mean to invade the near side. That's the only answer," Claus said.

"Answer only. Don't ask," they laughed.

"What answer can I give?"

"Answer yourself the blind future. We don't mind. Complete the fantasy nightmare with blind answer," they laughed.

"You *are* invaders," Claus said.

"You are invaders," they laughed. "You invade yourselves."

"I'm thin and narrow," Claus said to himself for encouragement, "like a reed in the wind. I flex but don't break. I sing but don't dance. The wind does not hurt me. It does not hurt me."

"We are shallow and wide," they laughed. "But now we push upward."

Claus watched as a shallow but wide yellow thing pushed upward while retaining a base. In this way it formed a dome, like hot magma pushing upward before a volcanic blast.

"It's headed for Leifton," Claus said.

"Leifton, yes! Watch your children and grandchild perish. Labba too!" they laughed.

"Then kill me first," Claus said.

"Your time will come," they laughed.

"No, now!" Claus said.

For the first time, Claus had partial control of the tubes. He instructed them to send him atop the growing yellow dome, which they did. Once atop the dome, he sent blue tubes and ethereal threads to lock him atop the dome so that nothing could detach him.

"Move off the dome! It is not yet your time!" the voices said with anger instead of laughter.

"Make me!" Claus said defiantly.

"You'd better move off. Or else!" they threatened.

"You can't scare me!" Claus said, though he trembled horribly.

"Then die with the others!" they finally said, and the dome pushed upward with Claus on the way.

"At least I'll end this misery," Claus said to himself. "What a mess of things. Can't there ever be peace?"

"Peace," they echoed, and they seemed drained of energy.

The dome advancement slowed.

"Peace," they said as if falling asleep. "Peaaaaace."

The voices stopped. The yellow blobs stopped racing around too, but the dome did not dissipate. It held its position as if waiting to resume another day.

Claus noticed something new. It started from far below. Little finger-like projections grew as if moles were digging tunnels. They went in various directions. One came by Claus.

"What is that?" Claus asked himself.

The digging thing resembled multiple triangular prisms. It burrowed out a cubic shape at a time, and so it created interlocking cubic openings. Periodically it changed the tunnel's direction by burrowing at a right angle. As part of the burrowing thing's procedure for creating the opening, it briefly changed shape into the cubic opening as if to seal or harden the sides.

"Cubics," Claus said. "Frieda's ethereal computer. So this is her solution to conquering the near side. My little paradise is ending. Those on the surface don't know what's in store for them. Lanietta, if ever you had a heart, you would come to our aid now!"

The burrowing passed Claus. A second came to Claus's other side. It paused by Claus but then it too went past.

"Do they even know who or what I am?" he asked himself.

Before Claus could wonder much more, the things quickly burrowed around Claus at fantastic speed, creating a net that ensnared Claus. Claus tried to escape with tube propulsion, but he was caught in an opening and could not squeeze through.

"Trapped!" Claus said.

Claus felt a great yank, and he realized the burrowed tunnels were a kind of rope. He was being hauled in like a fish being pulled in by a fisherman.

"I feel like my gut is being pulled out through my nose," Claus said. "What a horrible thing I must endure. Every human body should have an off switch to skip such torture."

Claus was pulled down, down, down. He went below the yellow dome, below many other tunnels, and down until he reached another yellow dome, but this one was small, perhaps the size of a camping tent for four. The net forced him inside.

"Find the blue," a voice ordered.

"What?" Claus asked. "What are you doing to me?"

"Find the blue!" it repeated.

Claus looked around. Everything around him had a yellow hue. Blocks were strewn about with letters and numbers on them. But on the other side of the small dome, Claus saw one block that was blue. He extended his hand to reach it, but of course he could not. Instead, one of the tubes on his body went for the blue and touched it. Immediately it split into two, and those two blocks shot out of the small dome at right angles from each other.

"Find the blues," the voice ordered.

"They're gone," Claus said.

"Find the blues!"

The net released its grip on Claus enough to let him maneuver. He turned around and made to leave the dome and the direction of the blues, but the net shocked him.

"Ow!" Claus said.

"Find the blues!" the voice repeated.

Claus was in a situation where he could only get relief from the shocking net if he maneuvered into the direction of a blue. He tracked one to another dome.

"It's here," Claus said. "My part is done."

"Touch it," the voice ordered.

"Will it split if I do?" Claus asked.

"Touch it," the voice repeated.

Claus touched it with his hand this time. Like before, the block split in two, but the two parts left with an angle between them less than ninety degrees.

"Find the other blue," the voice ordered.

"This is getting out of hand," Claus said. "This game grows exponentially with no end."

The net shocked Claus until he reached the other blue, he touched it, it split, and the two parts shot away with an angle less than ninety.

Claus spent weeks doing this. Yellow blobs continued to force themselves down his throat for food, and he was only allowed to sleep a few minutes at a time. And so he was caught in this cycle of a little search, a little sleep, more search, and not so much sleep. The voice became like torture, never varying and ever insistent, like ocean waves crashing a helpless boat against the rocks.

Ghost night arrived, that twice-a-year time when Luna passes through Earth's old debris field. Clausetta was so distraught that she didn't dance with the ghosts,

settling instead into her new obsession with strawberry champagne. In fact, no one danced with the ghosts. But the ghosts were attracted to the blue block field that Claus had been forced to create. More than attracted, they were pulled into them and trapped within the blue blocks.

Suddenly, Claus's orders stopped. The blue blocks assembled together into a square toroid of many moving parts. The toroid descended to the lunar core. As Claus was finally enjoying this moment of relief from the torture, the net pulled him down toward the core as if chasing the toroid.

"No, no! Leave it be!" Claus pleaded.

The net pulled Claus to the center of the toroid. The toroid accelerated with great speed toward the Anrega, which already occupied the lunar core.

"I'm going to crash," Claus lamented. "Why can't the tubes pull me out of this one?"

Just as the toroid appeared ready to crash into the Anrega, the toroid slowed quickly and took a position on the Anrega's outer surface. It slid around this surface as if looking for a way in and all the while keeping Claus suspended in the center of the toroid.

"Frieda? Are you behind this?" Claus called.

"Frieda, the lead-a, she need-a, the key-da," voices echoed back.

Claus took this to mean that Frieda was the leader, and she needed the key.

"Key to what?" Claus asked.

The voices laughed.

"Watch out below," they laughed.

"Watch out for what?" Claus asked.

Before the voices could laugh again, a yellow square toroid the same diameter but thinner than the blue toroid landed from above with a crash.

"What is going on here?" Claus asked.

Two cubes extended from the yellow toroid, two cubes extended from the blue, they surrounded Claus, and they sent ethereal lines into him. In a flash, Claus saw and felt the horror and pain of four people being killed.

"Arg! What are you doing to me?" Claus cried in pain.

From Claus's body then extended a clumping/unclumping string of nucleic blocks, a combination the toroid then pressed against the Anrega as if trying a key in a keyhole. The Anrega remained firm, and the key dissolved. The yellow cubes went into the places where the blue blocks had been, and vice versa.

The process repeated and more quickly. As Claus experienced the deaths of these people, he saw a corresponding ghost image of them dancing on the lunar surface—dancing in various parts of their lives before their end.

"How many of those happy ghosts on the surface had their lives ended so brutally?" Claus asked between key searches. "Clausetta and Leif are on the surface of innocence while the misery and pain creeps up from below. The innocence won't last. It won't. Argh, this process is excruciating!"

In time, the two toroids mixed and spun with such speed that like before, they appeared as a color of faded pea-green. But the toroid mixture could not find a key. The toroid stopped spinning and stopped its attempts to find a key. It elevated Claus a bit and held him there as if deciding what to do next. Yellow blobs forced their way into Claus to feed him.

"What will it do next? Electrocute me?" Claus asked.

"What will you do next?" the voices laughed. "Searches for Claus, searches for Claus!"

"Are you saying others are searching for me, or that searches are being requested of me?" Claus asked.

"Searches for Claus!" the voices laughed.

Claus looked down at his toroid. It seemed dead. Then he saw a yellow toroid of similar size slide toward him along the Anrega surface. In the toroid's center was the double chalice with the orb of Lanietta.

"Lanietta!"

"Lanietta, Lanietta!" the voices mocked.

"Let her go!"

"Go let her!" they continued to mock.

"I will!" Claus said.

Claus could not approach her. His toroid, though dead, prevented his escape. Lanietta's toroid started a process much as had been done to Claus, except there were no blue cubes. It sent out four yellow cubes, and two it colored bluish-green from Lanietta's orb. Claus heard Lanietta scream from the orb when this happened. The four cubes pushed ethereal lines through Lanietta's cube to create a cubic nucleic line to break through the Anrega surface. It failed and repeated the process.

"It is torturing Lanietta the way it tortured me. She will see and feel those dying people. All this to break through the Anrega? Frieda can't get through. But if she does, it will...it will..."

"Give her the power she needs," the voices answered.

"That wasn't a question," Claus said.

"Question that. Question what it was," the voices said.

"I demand to see Frieda," Claus said.

"Frieda, the lead-a, she need-a, the key-da," they repeated from before.

"I will give her the key," Claus said. "Provided you take me to her."

The voices laughed.

"You will give us the key? You give us a ruse, not a truce!" they said.

"Take me to her!" Claus demanded.

"We will take you to her," the voices said.

Instead of taking Claus to Frieda, the forces put Claus in the same toroid as Lanietta's double chalice. Now the yellow toroid put both Lanietta and Claus through the same sets of deaths to further its key-finding agenda. The strain was so great on Claus that he lost awareness of the yellow toroid and entered another realm.

Chapter 117: Bank Robbery

Claus found himself in the driver's seat of a parked car with the engine running. In jumped Lanietta with a bag.

"Gun it!" she yelled.

"What?"

"Drive away! Now! They're after us!" she yelled.

Claus pulled away from the curb and sped through traffic.

"Look at this money!" she grinned as she pulled stacks of cash out of the bag.

"What...what is this?" Claus asked.

A siren blared from behind, and Claus realized he was being chased by a police officer.

"You'll have to outrun him," Lanietta said. "Don't want to go to jail just yet. We have more banks to rob."

"Banks to rob?" Claus asked. "Lanietta! You were trapped in an orb. And now—"

But Claus had to run a red light and swerve around cars coming from the side.

"Now we're running from the law because you robbed a bank!" Claus finished.

"*We* robbed a bank!" she grinned. "You're the getaway driver."

"Last I saw, we were on Luna. Underground. On Anrega's surface. In a square toroid," Claus said.

"You speak strangely. Watch out!" Lanietta said.

Claus squeezed between cars stuck in traffic and sideswiped them. He ended up driving on a sidewalk and plowing through fruit stands.

"How do we defeat this thing?" Claus asked.

"Keep driving," Lanietta said. "We're going to ditch soon and hijack another car."

"Another car?" Claus asked. "You mean this car is stolen?"

"Why buy tomorrow what you can steal today?" Lanietta asked.

"Quit the games, Lanietta. I thought Frieda was behind all this. More games, is that it? I'm quitting!" Claus said.

Claus hit the brakes, put the car in park, and turned off the ignition. The police cars chasing Claus rapidly closed in and did not brake. Their collision with Claus's car was imminent. Lanietta wore no seat belt, and so Claus's sudden stop caused her momentum to carry her forward into the windshield.

Time stopped for Claus, and it stopped in a strange way. It was as if a film strip had broken and the last two frames had survived, with those last frames playing over and over. Claus was the only one not stuck in those last frames. Even Lanietta was stuck.

"Lanietta? Why are you stuck in this reality? Lanietta?" Claus called.

Claus walked around. Despite this, the realm continued to repeat the last two frames. Claus had nowhere to go. He checked for the tubes around him, but they were strangely gone.

"Okay, Lanietta, you can stop now," Claus called. "Lanietta? Labba? Clausetta or Leif? Can anyone hear me?"

Nothing. Claus sighed and looked up. Then he saw it—four cubics in pairs of yellow and blue hovering high in the sky with the clouds.

"So I'm stuck in the toroid with Lanietta," Claus said. "There are the four cubics. I'm being forced to see four deaths. But not instantly. Time has been slowed. Where are the four deaths?"

Claus tried walking away from the scene, but the farther away he walked, the more difficult walking became. After growing weary, Claus sat on a bench and rested. He slouched on his side and fell asleep.

He awoke with a start. Shadows were long, and Claus realized his reality was into a sunset. And yet the reality was still stuck in the last two frames.

"How can the sun be setting but the reality is still stuck?" Claus wondered.

The cubics were still high above, but they had orange sunlit tints on their western sides.

"They are waiting," Claus said. "They are waiting for me. I must do something. Or must I? Not even echoing voices to keep me company."

Claus walked back to Lanietta. She was still stuck in the two-frame crash through the getaway car's windshield. The sunlight was nearly gone. Claus felt as if his chances were equally fading.

"Lanietta? I...watching you stuck there makes me think about something you said, about being stuck in a reality. You're right, it's torture. I don't know what will happen next, but it's bound to be better than what I have now, which is nothing," Claus said.

Claus jumped back into the getaway car's driver's seat. He started the engine, and to his amazement, it ran.

"The engine is not stuck like everything else. It's tied to me. Wait. Maybe the cubics want me to drive this car. Lanietta said to hijack another car. What if I try that?"

Claus exited the getaway car and walked up to a police car where an officer had just gotten out (at least before time froze). Claus got into that car and tried driving it away. But it didn't respond.

"One path," Claus said. "Back to the getaway car."

Claus climbed into the getaway car. The engine continued to run from when he restarted it. He placed the car in gear and started to pull away. Time resumed forward. Lanietta ended up on the hood, but as Claus pulled away, she rolled off. Claus made a U-turn to return for Lanietta, and as he did he watched as she pulled a hidden pistol from her waistband and fired at the police. She killed two before they killed her.

"No!" Claus yelled.

Claus parked the car alongside Lanietta and held her in his arms, but only for a moment. An officer shot Claus dead. The cubics sent ethereal threads through Lanietta, Claus, and the two dead officers.

Claus felt himself back in the toroid, watching as the cubics smashed the impression of the four deaths on nucleic blocks. These blocks in turn were used in an attempt to break through the Anrega, but like before, they failed. Another set came along, and Claus entered a new reality.

Chapter 118: Baby Shower

"I can't decide if I should get your cousin the sleep sack or the blanket set," Lanietta said from a seat next to Claus.

Claus looked around, and the two were seated in a turboprop airplane flying in the sky.

"What?" Claus asked.

"For your cousin's baby shower," Lanietta said. "Thank you for inviting me along. Some guys shy away from such things. Don't worry. I'll pick a good gift for her. This registry book has lots of ideas. See? This blanket set is gender neutral. There's always the practical box of diapers, but I thought we could do better than that. Give a little personal touch to the gift."

"We're going to die," Claus said. "In this airplane. We're going to die!"

Several passengers heard Claus and started to talk.

"Relax," Lanietta said. "The sky is clear, and the ride is smooth. You're just nervous about the baby shower. First one? Leave the talking to me. I'll smooth things over."

Claus, in the aisle seat, looked across Lanietta out through the window, which happened to be on the airplane's right side. He saw two blue cubics flying with the plane just past the wings. He looked across the aisle out the left window and saw two yellow cubics also flying with the plane but past the wings.

"They're here. They're following us!" Claus said excitedly.

"Shhh. You'll startle the others," Lanietta said.

"I've got to get out of here and stop it!" Claus said.

"This one here," yelled one of the other passengers to the stewardess.

As Claus got up to leave, the stewardess intercepted him.

"What seems to be the problem?" she asked.

"You've got to tell the captain. This airplane is going to crash," Claus said. "Make an emergency landing!"

"There's nothing wrong with the plane!" yelled another passenger.

"Yeah, sit back down!" yelled another.

"I won't!" Claus said.

Claus bolted past the stewardess and made for an emergency escape exit. As he placed his hand on the handle, the reality froze into repeating the last two frames, much like the bank robbery reality. He tried to open the door, but it would not budge. All he could do then was turn around, and when he did, he saw that the stewardess and several passengers had gotten up to restrain him. But they remained in the last two frames, shifting positions back and forth. Strangely enough, the propellers continued to turn, and the sky continued to fly by.

"Why did I think the door would open? The cabin pressure seals it closed of course. Sit down instead?" Claus mused.

Claus sat down next to Lanietta. The reality continued. The passengers returned to their seats as if nothing had happened. The stewardess wheeled a small cart along the aisle.

"Can I get you anything? Soft drink? Water? Tea?" she said.

"I'll have tea please," Lanietta said still looking at the registry book of gifts. "Claus, you look like tea would do you good."

"Make that two," Claus said.

The stewardess gave them each a cup of tea, and she wheeled on to the next row. Claus took a sip and felt better.

"Wait. You called me by my name," Claus said.

"Has it changed in the last five minutes?" Lanietta laughed.

"What about Clomper?" Claus asked.

"Is that your dog?" she asked.

"That's what you call me!" Claus said.

"When?"

"Always!"

"Must be good tea, with a few extra mushrooms," Lanietta said as she sipped hers. "Doesn't taste like mushrooms."

"Don't you remember? The auction, going eethi, the PRAAD, and Libriota?" Claus asked.

"Is Libriota one of your ex-girlfriends? Claus, I'm happy to help with the shower, but if you could not speak of your old flames, I'd appreciate it. I hope you don't mind me saying, but I was getting a little fond of you. No more ex talk. Okay?"

Claus wasn't sure how to respond. Lanietta smiled first a little then opened up into a broad smile to help Claus return a smile. He finally broke down and gave a little smile back.

"Yay!" she celebrated.

"Maybe I am nervous," Claus said as he looked out Lanietta's window and saw the blue cubics. "Say, what do you see when you look out your window?"

"Clear blue sky. The ground far below. Lots of little squares all over. That's farmland," Lanietta said.

"You don't see any cubes by the wing? Out there?" Claus said as he pointed.

"Mushrooms, Claus. Mushrooms," she whispered.

"Okay, okay. Still can't get used to you calling me 'Claus'," he said.

"I could say, 'Mr. Gerhardt'," she laughed. "That is, if you need the formality."

"And what would they call you?" he asked.

"Lanietta," she replied.

"I mean your last name," he said, realizing he'd never heard of a last name for her. "What's your last name, Lanietta?"

"Latoraibeedason?" Lanietta suggested.

"You were never a son," Claus said.

"Landaughpoteriopolous?" Lanietta further suggested.

"That doesn't sound right," Claus said.

"Sassatinassa?"

"Lanietta Sassatinassa? I thought Sassatinassa was your first name. An alias when you were a slave," he said.

"An alias, yes," Lanietta said.

"Then what is it?" Claus asked.

"Mushrooms," she whispered.

"No, really," he said.

"The only time I was called by my last name was when I played softball in high school," Lanietta said. "But I won't bore you with that. Playing second base, you know, is nothing like getting zingers across the plate like a pitcher."

"Softball? Really? Tell me more," Claus said.

"My name was too long for the uniform. So they shortened it to 'Clowsifuni'. It was always, 'Over here, Clowsifuni,' and 'Knock one out of the park, Clowsifuni.' Sometimes the girls on the other team would chant, 'Clowsifuni, no smarter than a loony, wants to claim, he knows Lanietta's last name.'"

"I get the picture," Claus said. "Wait. Who's 'he'?"

"It didn't bother me. I was just happy to be in the game. One girl tore up her knee sliding into the catcher at home plate. She was out for the season," Lanietta said. "I had a cute outfit and everything. Look, I have a picture here somewhere."

Lanietta produced a small purse and from inside pulled out a photo of her in uniform.

"I didn't know you had a purse," Claus said.

"Mushrooms," she whispered.

"You look good. Healthy and fit," Claus said.

"Not cute and adorable?" she laughed. "You're going to have a hard time passing me off as your girlfriend."

"Wait, is that what you are?" Claus asked.

"I don't know. You tell me. You practically ignored me at the office, then suddenly you came up to me and blurted out that you were in a crisis, that your cousin was having a baby, and you needed help," Lanietta said. "Did you ignore me because you were shy? I always thought you were interesting, but you kept your distance, so I respected that."

"I...we work in an office together?" Claus asked.

"Those mushrooms really threw you for a loop, didn't they?" she said. "I'm sure you'll be back to yourself by the time we land. You'll have to. You wouldn't tell me where your cousin lives."

"I...I..."

"Oh, you've forgotten that too. This adventure gets more interesting by the moment," Lanietta said.

"If I tell you something, will you promise not to say, 'Mushrooms'?" he asked.

"Depends on what it is. If you say that the sky is falling like Chicken Little, then I might," she said. "Oh but we're in the sky. We'd have to fall. A plane crash then. That would be super mushrooms. Okay, what is it?"

"That's it. A plane crash," Claus said.

"Super mushrooms," she laughed.

"No, really. I'm convinced that four people will die. How else can it happen?" Claus asked.

"Assuming that magically you are correct, there are more than four people on this plane. Would only four die yet magically others would be spared?" she asked.

"I don't know," he replied.

"You're borrowing trouble," she said. "Anyway, I've decided on the sleep sack. Good thing we have the registry book. We can go over to the store first thing. Might bump into another guest. They can tell us where your cousin lives."

The announcement came over to fasten seat belts for the landing. Claus not only fastened his seat belts, but he went into the brace position as if expecting to crash.

"What are you doing there? Claus, you're shaking like a leaf," Lanietta said.

"Brace, brace!" he said to himself.

"It'll be over soon. Look, the wheels are touching down. We're slowing down. Now the taxi to the terminal. See? Not so bad," Lanietta said.

"The plane didn't crash," Claus said.

"You sound disappointed," Lanietta said. "Next you'll say that a fire would make a good second best."

"Fire? Of course! That's how we die!" he said. "Hurry, let's get off the plane!"

Claus got up to rush out, but Lanietta caught his arm.

"You're forgetting the carry-on luggage. Both yours and mine. Manners before mushrooms," she said, and she gave an extra tug on his arm. "Please?"

Claus relaxed a bit and removed their carry-on luggage.

"You don't have to carry mine," she laughed. "A pink bag doesn't suit you."

"What about yellow? Or blue?" Claus said, half in reference to the cubics.

"I saw them too, Claus," she said.

"You *do* know," he said.

"Don't spoil the memory," she said. "Someone was very happy at this point in time. Keep it that way?"

"You've broken out of character! Finally! I can talk to you! We must end this all! Deal with Frieda and everything!" he said excitedly.

"See what happened when I broke out of character? You went hog wild on me. No, Claus. Put a foot in front of the other and walk off the plane," she said. "We have a baby shower to attend."

"And then? How does it end?" he asked.

"How does anything end? But we aren't there, so hop along now, you're holding up the other passengers."

Claus wondered when he would die, or when anyone would die. He looked at the passengers suspiciously. Would one have a knife? A bomb?

"It's okay, you're with me," Lanietta reassured him as the two exited the plane.

They went through the terminal and past the security checkpoint. Claus noticed a sign being held by a young man, "Lanietta and Claus". A young pregnant woman then gave out a shout of delight and came running toward Claus. She gave him a hug and beamed with delight.

"I'm so glad you made it!" she said. "This is your first time in my little neck of the woods."

"Uh, this is Lanietta," Claus said.

"I'm Lara, Claus's cousin," she said.

"Nice to meet you, Lara. Claus has told me very little about you," Lanietta said.

"Still sore that I beat you in arm wrestling when you were a kid?" Lara said to Claus. "Bet you didn't tell Lanietta about that!"

"No, as a matter of fact—"

"Lanietta, this is my husband, Rich," Lara said.

"Nice to meet you," Rich said. "Well Claus, you've done well for yourself."

"Yes, he has," Lanietta said.

"Oh, let's not keep them waiting here. I have lunch ready at home. You must be terribly tired," Lara said.

"Well, uh, I know it's early, but the motel check in, uh," Claus stumbled.

"What check in? You're staying with us as we agreed," Lara said. "Did you forget?"

"Claus has forgotten many things," Lanietta grinned.

"Silly man. Always playing games. I bet Lanietta doesn't play games," Lara said.

"Oh, never," Lanietta said.

Claus gave a knowing look to Lanietta, and she winked back. The four walked to a parking lot where Rich's vehicle was parked. He unlocked the vehicle and helped first Lara and then Lanietta into their seats.

"Courtesy and class. I like it," Lanietta said.

Claus and Lanietta sat in the back seat while Rich drove and Lara rode in the front passenger seat. Lara explained the sights as Rich drove by them.

"This is it," Claus whispered. "A car wreck. We'll all be killed."

"There are five of us in this car," Lanietta whispered back.

"Then one of us must survive. Who will it be?" Claus whispered.

"All of us," Lanietta said. "There is no car crash."

"Do you know that? Do you know how this ends?"

"It ends when the wedding shower is complete. Then we return home, you propose, we get married, have our own

baby shower, put our kid through college, retire, and start a beauty pageant," Lanietta said.

"What?" Claus said a little louder.

"I said that's the new baseball stadium. It's almost complete," Lara said.

Lanietta winked at Claus again.

"Labba would be so jealous," Claus whispered.

"Who's Labba? There's no Labba here," Lanietta winked.

"But my kids on the near side. What about them?"

"You dreamed up Leif and Clausetta," Lanietta said.

"I never said their names. You're toying with me," Claus said.

"Shh. Lara is speaking," Lanietta said.

"All this construction on the interstate," Lara said. "And I can feel every bump!"

"Do you love me, Lanietta? You speak of marriage, but I can't tell if you're joking or not. Do you love me?" Claus whispered.

"What?" Lanietta feigned as if unable to hear him.

"I said," Claus whispered, but his voice got louder, "Do you love me?"

"So that's what you two lovebirds are whispering about!" Lara said.

"Claus and I have an unusual relationship, don't we Claus?" Lanietta said.

"I'll say," Claus said.

"That's how it started with us too. Took months to iron things out. Now we're like clockwork," Lara said.

"Lanietta knows all about clocks and time. Don't you, Lanietta?" Claus said.

"Really? Do you collect antique clocks?" Lara said.

"Not yet. But I did come up with a rhyme. Care to hear it?" Lanietta asked.

"I'd love to," Lara replied.

Forty days hath September,
April, June, and November.
All the rest have forty-one,
Except February alone,
Which has forty days like June
And forty one each leap moon.

Lara laughed.

"What a silly little rhyme," Lara said. "It's forty days instead of thirty."

"Very strange," Claus said. "I didn't realize you knew that rhyme. Our friend Labba told me."

"Oh, she told me too," Lanietta said.

"How?" Claus pressed. "She hasn't spoken to—"

"And what is a leap moon?" Lara asked.

"An extra day in February. Like a leap day," Lanietta said with a knowing look for Claus.

"Well I wonder who would use such a rhyme? The calendar would go crazy very quickly," Lara said.

"Like many other things," Claus said.

"Yes. Many other things," Lanietta replied.

"I have one," Claus said.

There once was a girl named Lani
Who went on a trip with her man-ny
She picked out a gift
But wasn't too swift
And the gift ended up going to her granny.

"Well that was strange," Lara said.

"Yes, Claus has been saying *man-ny* strange things," Lanietta said.

"What?" Claus said.

"Don't be so overt," Lanietta whispered to him.

"But what about the gift?" Claus said. "I thought we'd have time to get it."

"After we arrive, I'll send you out to register. I'll chat with Lara and keep her company," Lanietta said.

"Okay," Claus said.

"More whispers. It's a conspiracy!" Lara laughed.

"No, just cleaning up Claus's rhyme etiquette," Lanietta said.

"Well I'm glad he found you. He needs taking care of," Lara said. "Not that you can't take care of yourself, Claus. But a woman's touch makes all the difference."

"Hear, hear!" Lanietta agreed.

The group arrived at Lara's and Rich's house. Lara showed them to their room.

"One bedroom?" Claus asked.

"Of course. We're intimate and everything!" Lanietta said with a hug for Claus.

"You two love birds!" Lara said.

"It just feels strange in my cousin's house," Claus said.

"If you want separate bedrooms, we can do that too," Lara said.

"Nonsense. I wouldn't dream of being left alone. Keep me company, Claus. Keep your girl safe," Lanietta said.

"Let me get lunch out," Lara said.

Lara left.

"Now who's being overt?" Claus asked.

"Take me in your arms, you devious love machine," Lanietta said.

"That's the old Lanietta I remember," Claus said. "Games and pranks. All that's missing is 'Clomper'."

"It wouldn't do to treat you like a pet in your cousin's house," Lanietta said.

Lara returned.

"I have terrible news!" Lara said.

"This is it," Claus whispered to Lanietta. "This is where we all die!"

"Hush," Lanietta whispered back.

"The lunch is spoiled! I thought it was still good!" Lara said.

"I'll go out and get cold cuts from the deli," Rich called from in the kitchen as he approached the bedroom.

"Claus will go with you," Lanietta said. "He has an errand to run."

"I do?"

"Yes. He must atone for bad poetry," Lanietta said.

"Yes, I guess I do," Claus said.

Rich and Claus left for the deli and registry store. Meanwhile, Lara showed Lanietta around the grounds, which was filled with flower gardens, shrubs, trees, pathways through such, trellises—all the makings of a secret garden. They followed a path until they reached an enclosed area with horses running back and forth.

"What a beautiful place you have," Lanietta said. "I'd die to have my own place this grand."

"You and Claus can if you want," Lara said. "Our neighbor down the way is putting his place on the market soon. I bet he'd let it go for a song if I put in a good word."

"Convincing Claus will take some doing," Lanietta said. "It will require proper feminine charm and disposition."

Both laughed.

"I can see we have a lot in common. Do you ride?" Lara asked.

"As often as I can. Only I have to rent," Lanietta said.

"There's no renting here! Care to go for a horseback ride? We have trails deep in the property," Lara said.

"I'd love to," Lanietta said.

The two saddled up. Lara chose her favorite chestnut thoroughbred while Lanietta chose an Appaloosa. Lara and Lanietta then had the horses take leisurely walks down the trail.

"I could do this forever," Lanietta said. "And I mean—forever."

"The trail links up with the neighbor's property. Would you like to go see? We could go riding every day once you move in," Lara said.

"Absolutely!" Lanietta said.

The two continued their peaceful walk through a path in the woods by a running stream. The air was clean and fresh, and there were no bugs about.

"Amazing!" Lanietta said. "I've heard about bugs and stuffy air, but this is far from it!"

"I had special landscaping done to get the perfect natural airflow. It keeps the bugs on the other side of the stream," Lara said.

"You're a genius!" Lanietta said.

Lara grinned.

"I'm going to ask you a question. And I hope you don't think I'm nosy, but I have to wonder, how do you cope when Claus goes up in space?" Lara asked.

"It's nerve-racking," Lanietta said. "I watch the monitors of course, checking ship status and his vitals. So far he's only gone into low Earth orbit. But he's scheduled for the lunar far side next time. That will be difficult."

"Don't tell him, but I've worried about him too. Wish he could stay on Earth and be a commercial pilot or something," Lara said. "Rich services airplanes. Lots of work there. Claus could try for that too if he wants. Would keep him grounded. Keep him rooted in the earth."

"There's something to be said for a solid Earth," Lanietta said. "How precious this planet is. Astronauts who've looked back on Earth say it's but a fragile speck in an immense universe."

The two reached the neighbor's property.

"See? Isn't it beautiful?" Lara said.

"Rolling hills, but open land. Not much growing," Lanietta said. "Needs a woman's touch."

"It's your place if you want it," Lara said.

"I'll need help getting it going. It'll never look as good as your place of course, but if I could get a flower or two going, that would be nice," Lanietta said.

"I'll give you all the help you need!" Lara said enthusiastically. "That is, if you want it."

"I wouldn't have it any other way!" Lanietta replied.

"I'm getting hungry. Let's get lunch. They should be back by now," Lara said.

The two headed back toward Lara's home. They reached a point where the trail opened up to the sky. Up ahead and close to the house, Claus started banging a metal spoon against a pan and waving the pan and spoon in the air as if signaling an emergency. Startled, Lara's thoroughbred bolted. Lanietta gave chase to help Lara, but the thoroughbred was too fast. Lara pulled hard on the reins, but the horse wouldn't stop.

"Stop that banging!" Lanietta yelled.

But Claus didn't stop.

"You can't ride a horse!" Claus yelled. "It's bad for the baby. Bad for the baby!"

Lara's horse crashed into a fence near Claus, sending Lara into the remaining timbers. Lanietta caught up and dismounted. She held Lara where she lay. Rich rushed out, called for help on his cell phone, and then ran to Lara's care. He took over for Lanietta.

"What did you do that for?" Lanietta barked at Claus.

"She shouldn't ride when she's pregnant," Claus said. "She could lose the baby."

"She'll lose it for sure now!" Lanietta retorted. "And possibly her own life."

"Then who are the other two?" Claus asked.

"What?" Lanietta asked in surprise.

"Four must die. Who else will die?" Claus asked.

"Is that what you think this is? You get to choose who dies? Of all the arrogance!" Lanietta said.

The reality froze completely.

"You didn't freeze," Claus said to Lanietta.

"Because now the toroid will redo the last ten thousand realities," Lanietta said. "Time wasted. Wasted!"

Chapter 119: Near Side Revelation

Claus returned to the square toroid. The net came for him and pulled him out. He watched a frantic pace of two pairs of yellow and blue cubics interacting with Lanietta's double chalice orb in the same effort to break into the Anrega. After an hour of watching this, the net pulled Claus up toward the lunar surface. Yellow blobs completely encircled Claus and forced him up through that lunar surface with an exhale of gas, as if Claus had just been burped out. The tubes that had once extended around him withdrew, and all that was left was a normal though tired-looking Claus.

"Ugh," Claus said.

It was Blouisa who found him. She called for a carriage, and Claus was taken back to the estate where he cleaned up and had a good meal in the company of family.

"Ah, that was delicious," Claus said.

"We were worried, Pappa," Clausetta said. "I'm so glad Blouisa found you. She's the best sister anyone could ever have!"

Clausetta hugged Claus then Blouisa. In fact, Clausetta hugged anyone in hugging range.

"What happened, Claus? You disappeared months ago in a cloud of smoke," Labba said.

"I was forced below the lunar surface," Claus said.

"Into a tunnel?" Clausetta asked.

"Not exactly. It felt like I was at the bottom of a swimming pool, and the rest of you were on the water's surface," Claus said.

"You went out of phase with matter, possibly into the ether or at least partially into the ether," Labba said.

Claus explained the torture of splitting blue blocks, the toroids, seeing people as they died, and his interaction with Lanietta and the two realities. Labba paced back and forth.

"What does it mean, Labba?" Blouisa asked. "Is the ground below us full of demons?"

"It would appear so," Labba said. "Whatever good we have on the surface is complemented by evil below. I did not realize ghost night was more than just ghosts dancing on the surface. But it makes sense. The ether tends to have good complemented by evil. That's how Greylingers thrive."

"What about Lanietta?" Leif asked. "She's trapped down there."

"Yes, she is," Labba said. "Or is she?"

"Yes. She's trapped," Claus said. "I saw her caught in the orb. The toroid has trapped her."

"Yet it released you," Labba said. "Why?"

"Maybe it felt sorry for us," Clausetta said.

"As much as I want to believe that, I'm doubtful," Labba said.

"A prelude to invasion?" Leif asked.

"That's a possibility," Labba said.

"Or Lanietta secured Claus's release," Blouisa suggested.

"That's also a possibility," Labba said. "Claus, what was the last thing she said to you? Again, please."

"'The toroid will have to redo the last ten thousand realities,'" Claus said.

"We are safe as long as the Anrega remains whole," Labba said. "Once breached, our position is no longer safe. Carinians will be first to perish. That means Lanietta, me, Clausetta, Leif, and Claude."

"No! Not my Claude!" Clausetta said.

"He might be spared. He's not a full-blooded Carinian. But he has enough Carinian that I think the beyton rays would affect him," Labba said. "Claus, did Lanietta give you any advice?"

"Not really. She seemed upset that I chose Lara to die," Claus said. "I didn't mean to choose or anything like that. It was all so confusing."

"Let me check something," Labba said.

Labba touched Claus and went eethi enough to probe Aftova.

"The tubes have withdrawn. Aftova is still in your visual cortex," Labba said. "How is your vision?"

"Seems normal at the moment," Claus said.

"If it changes, you might end up going back underground," Labba said.

"No. We won't let him. We'll put a rope on Pappa!" Clausetta said.

"I don't think we'll be able to stop the process. If you are wanted, you'll be taken," Labba said.

"Then why am I here?" Claus asked.

"Could be a diversion," Labba said.

"To distract us from the invasion," Leif said.

"Or as a messenger. To warn us," Blouisa said.

"Can we evacuate?" Selba asked. "Raise Tabelia and leave Luna?"

"It would mean going into the lunar shock and dealing with that crowd," Labba said.

"Where would we go?" Sergio asked.

"A good question," Labba said. "Can't go to Earth. It's destroyed."

"I wish we could remake it," Claus said.

"We can't," Labba said. "And I doubt Lanietta could either. There's Mars, but then there's the problem of beyton rays. The one safe place is in lunar-sync orbit so that we always hover above the near side. Unless the PRAAD remnant can be destroyed, that's our only option. Beyton rays do not easily dissipate across space. It's a wonder we're protected at all here on the near side."

"Destroying the PRAAD remnant would solve many problems," Claus said. "But the question is how?"

"That I don't know," Labba said. "Many Carinians have perished trying to control the beast. Only Lanietta had any real success with it. Really, the key lies with her. It's just..."

"Labba," Claus said. "I..."

"If you'll excuse me, I need some fresh air," Labba said.

Labba exited the mansion and went for a walk.

"Labba, wait," Claus called as he ran outside, but she had space-jumped away and could no longer be seen.

"The story about the baby shower upset her," Blouisa said, now joining him outside.

The two took a walk in the garden.

"You mean Lanietta and—" Claus started.

"Yes. Labba's jealously is bubbling up again. She wants you to herself," Blouisa said.

"You sound like Selba. Giving me advice," Claus said.

"More of an observation. I imagine Selba would say to pick between the women," Blouisa said.

"She would," Claus said.

"I say pick survival," Blouisa said. "Wherever you are, whatever you're doing, pick survival."

"Sounds simple when you say it. The trouble is knowing what to pick. I mean, what do I do next? Labba is the mother of my children. But Lanietta is the key to survival on the near side. Are you saying I should pick Lanietta?"

Blouisa shrugged her shoulders.

"Labba said I might be taken away any moment. Back to a toroid or something," Claus said. "Whether I go or stay, I feel helpless. I want to make things better, but I'm like that car with wheels spinning yet going nowhere. Blouisa, there's something Labba left out back there. She spoke of Carinians dying of beyton rays. She didn't say anything about the rest of you."

"Are you suggesting that—"

"The non-Carinians evacuate. Yes," Claus said. "I would say Mars, but that has proven Carinian ties and might be no better than here. No, you must leave the solar system. Find another place free of Carinian influence."

"But I'd have to leave Leif here. Clausetta, Labba, and Claude too. Seems a high price to pay for—"

"Survival," Claus finished. "You said to pick survival."

"I guess I meant a full survival," Blouisa said. "Leaving my husband and his family behind is hardly a life."

"But it is life," Claus said. "Can you at least make preparations?"

"Tabelia is the only way. But I don't have knowledge like Labba or like Doctor Kechenova had. I can't just walk into Tabelia and say, 'Arise my Martacean friend and secure safe passage for us holies to the promised planet.'"

"Then ask Labba for help. Ask anyone for help. Is it worth losing all of humanity? You saw the cubics. You know what they do. What they *want* to do. What they *eventually* will do," Claus said.

"Yes. I know the cubics. All right then, I'll make the effort. But nothing is easy, Claus. I'm going to see if I can take the Carinians too. Maybe Tabelia can protect them. Maybe there's a place out there that's protected from beyton rays."

"Yes. It's worth a search," Claus said. "I just feel badly it's coming to this. Seems we aren't safe no matter where we go."

"Pappa! Did you find Mamma?" Clausetta said as she approached the two.

"No. She space-jumped away," Claus said.

"I bet I can find her," Clausetta said, and she space-jumped out of sight.

"What the—" Claus said.

"Oh, yes. Clausetta can space-jump. Labba taught her," Blouisa said.

"I can space-jump too," Leif said, now joining the two. "Mamma taught us both at the same time."

"Is nothing safe? The ether is a dangerous place," Claus said.

"She didn't want to teach us, but with you gone and all, we didn't know what to expect," Leif said. "No one thought to search underground though."

"In a way, I'm glad you didn't," Claus said. "Anyone space-jumping down there might never come back up for air. Leif, you must watch out for your sister."

"Oh?"

"Yes. When she drinks, her complement gets very close to her. I fear that drinking will sour her spirit," Claus said.

"She has been drinking quite a bit lately," Leif said. "But mostly because she thought you were dead. She didn't even dance with the ghosts."

"A shame we couldn't send those ghosts underground and purge out the evil down there," Blouisa said.

"Why can't we? I mean, what would happen if we did?" Claus asked.

"Their evil complements would appear above ground and wreak havoc," Labba said, now returning in a space-jump with Clausetta.

"Is there a way we could just flush one at a time above ground and capture them?" Claus asked.

"How would we capture them?" Clausetta asked.

"Frieda's method. A cubic," Blouisa said.

All became silent for a moment.

"It's fighting fire with fire, I know. But it might be better than evacuation," Blouisa said.

"Who's evacuating?" Leif asked.

"You weren't supposed to announce it," Claus said.

"No one is evacuating, and that's final," Labba said. "Beyton rays would kill or maim. I hate to admit it, but Blouisa presents the only option available. Unless someone else can think of a better idea."

"Pump soap and water underground and wash them out," Clausetta said.

The others laughed.

"What's so funny?" she said.

"I wish it were that easy. There is no ethereal soap that I know of," Labba said.

"If these evil complements are created by Frieda, isn't she tapping into the infinite?" Claus asked. "Seems we would spend eternity flushing out and containing evil. That's almost as torturous as my blue block splitting."

"We won't know until we try," Leif said. "The question is how."

"I think I know how," Labba said. "But it will require special surgery. Blouisa, though appearing normal in every way, has cubic remnants in her. Lanietta couldn't get them all out. If we were to place a Veigonette stone in her, and she had help from other Carinians, she could be used to tap into the ether. She could help make our own ethereal computer. It's dangerous. It could kill you."

"I'm willing to try," Blouisa said.

"That's all fine and dandy, but there are only three stones," Claus said. "Frieda has Rigefa, Lanietta has Fronfa, and—"

"You have Aftova," Labba said. "We'd have to transfer Aftova from you to Blouisa."

"I stand ready at your bidding," Blouisa said.

"But I don't," Claus said. "What will that leave me with?"

"Just your normal self. The tubes more than likely will remain, but they'll be uncontrolled, like disconnected electrical wires in a house," Labba said.

"The last time a procedure was performed on me, Lanietta ended up in an orb," Claus said. "Will someone else end up in an orb?"

"I don't think so. This is a completely different process. It's more likely you'll hemorrhage to death than for someone to be caught up in an orb," Labba said.

"Thanks a lot," Claus said sarcastically.

"I'm against it," Leif said. "I can't lose my Blouisa now."

Blouisa smiled and hugged Leif. She then kissed him on the lips.

"Celebrate the time we've had and the time we have now. That's all that anyone can ask," Blouisa said. "I owe my life to your community. It's time I pay my debt."

"You owe no debt," Leif said. "You are my wife. That is enough."

She smiled and kissed him again.

"There's a problem," Selba said. "Ghost night is over."

"The question is, can we wait until the next one?" Labba said. "I know what you're thinking, Claus. Will you be pulled back underground during that time? We don't know."

"If I am, I might not return," Claus said.

"And Aftova will be lost. Yes," Labba said. "We should perform the transfer immediately to prevent such a possibility."

It was decided. That very evening, the procedure was performed in an operating room. Family and friends watched behind glass in an upper balcony while doctors transferred Aftova from Claus's visual cortex to Blouisa lower spine.

"Blouisa's cubic remnants are in her upper legs and partly in her lower spine," Selba explained to those in the balcony.

"Seems risky," Leif said. "Blouisa could be paralyzed. I'm not sure I like this procedure."

"Relax, Leif," Selba said. "The best surgeons on Luna are down there."

Claus and Blouisa were under general anesthesia for the procedure. But as soon as Aftova was placed in Blouisa's lower spine, her legs kicked with a jolt. Leif jumped up in fright.

"That's not right!" he said.

"Just a reflex," Selba said. "I hope."

"Maybe those demons down below will leave Pappa alone," Clausetta said.

"And take my Blouisa instead?" Leif said.

"Family first," Clausetta said.

"That's my wife."

"That's our father."

"Clausetta, Leif, please!" Selba said. "No one is more important than the other. Let's wish luck to them both."

Clausetta and Leif shrugged their shoulders and hugged.

"Better," Selba said. "Looks like they are finishing. Labba is leaving the operating room and coming up here."

Labba entered.

"The surgery was a success. Mostly," Labba said.

"Mostly?" the others asked at the same time.

"I ensured the proper ethereal connections transferred," Labba said. "But we can't be sure about the physical connections, specifically the nervous system."

"What does that mean?" Leif asked.

"There's a chance—a small chance—that one or both will have nerve or brain damage," Labba said.

"Then my Blouisa *could* be paralyzed. Selba! You promised!" Leif said.

"Did you?" Labba asked.

Selba shrugged her shoulders.

"Leif. The best surgeons are down there," Labba said.

"That's what I said," Selba said.

"If there is damage, then it would have happened anyway," Labba said.

"But only because of the surgery," Leif said. "Should never have done it!"

Clausetta and Sergio took Leif to another room.

"Is there really a chance they have damage?" Selba asked Labba.

"I'm afraid so," Labba said. "I sensed it, in fact."

"If only we could be sure this is a good idea," Selba said. "I mean, who's to say Lanietta isn't dealing with—"

"Please don't mention that name," Labba said.

"Labba, you're going to have to deal with her," Selba said.

"Not yet. Not in this way," Labba said.

"She might be trying to help us," Selba said. "Look at what she's done with the near side."

"Yes. I saw it, Selba. For twenty-five years I watched what she did," Labba said.

"In eagle form. You didn't have to do that. You could have humoidified," Selba said.

"That's not your point to pick," Labba said.

"But I will pick it," Selba said. "The selenites on Earth were brutal. I appreciate everything everyone has done to help me and others get out of that. Isn't there room for appreciation in your heart?"

"I don't like having my heart stolen," Labba said. "It still feels missing."

"Claus is here. Leif and Clausetta are here. Claude too. What's the worry?" Selba asked. "You sound like Claus. He feels no place is safe."

"I feel my children aren't safe," Labba said. "I still curse the day I left Leif unattended. Just so I could play the part of the cozy wife."

"You know I don't have a husband," Selba said. "No one to cozy up to at night. I take it on the chin every day."

"You seem destined for it," Labba said.

"Really? Based on what?" Selba asked.

"This is my first time being a mother," Labba said.

"Same here. In fact, Sergio is my only child. Not sure I could cope if something happened to him," Selba said.

"He wasn't stolen from you," Labba said.

"In a way he was. When he married Clausetta, I felt a loss of my boy," Selba said.

"That's different," Labba said.

"It's only different if you let it be different," Selba said.

Blouisa and Claus were wheeled away.

"They are going to recovery," Labba said.

"I'll let Leif know," Selba said. "Are you going to tend to Claus?"

"Of course," Labba said. "What about you?"

"Should I give you and Claus a moment?" Selba asked.

Labba smiled and hugged Selba.

"Come along, my dear friend," Labba said.

The two went to Claus's recovery room. Clausetta and Sergio were already at his side.

"Leif is with Blouisa," Clausetta said. "I just had to see Pappa!"

A nurse entered the room and adjusted an IV bag.

"He'll wake up now," she said.

Claus moaned something.

"Pappa? Can you hear me?" Clausetta asked.

Claus opened his eyes.

"Why are the lights off?" he asked.

"They aren't!" Clausetta cried, and she buried herself in his chest.

"Just turn on the lights, Clausetta. No need to cry," Claus said.

"He's blind," Selba said. "So this is the damage."

"It could be temporary," Labba said.

"What if it isn't?" Clausetta cried. "What if Pappa is blind forever?"

"I'm not blind. Am I?" Claus asked.

"It appears you are," Labba said with a sigh. "I was afraid of this. Time will tell if your vision returns."

"Well one good thing. I won't have to see those people dying over and over again," Claus said.

"But you'll never see your family again!" Clausetta cried. "Isn't there anything we can do? Mamma, can't we go eethi together and fix his eyes?"

"It's not his eyes. It's his visual cortex. The back of his brain," Labba said.

"Look Pappa. Do you see anything?" Clausetta asked.

Clausetta went eethi and placed her hand in the back of Claus's brain.

"No. Nothing," Claus said.

Clausetta reintegrated.

"What if Blouisa is paralyzed?" Selba asked.

"Is she?" Clausetta asked.

"No, she isn't," Blouisa said as she walked in followed by Leif. "We came to check on—oh."

"Pappa, what is it?" Leif asked as he rushed to Claus's side.

"He's blind!" Clausetta cried.

"Visual cortex," Selba said to Blouisa.

"Oh," Blouisa said.

"Pappa. We're here to help. Blouisa is just fine and is walking. No side effects," Leif said.

"At least we have that," Claus said. "Well, Labba, if Lanietta steals someone from us again, I won't have to see it happen."

Labba stormed out.

"Labba?" Claus called.

"That wasn't the best thing to say," Selba said.

"I'll go after her," Blouisa said.

Blouisa went after Labba.

"Hey, people. I'm the victim here," Claus said.

"Claus, for most people blindness is a moment of humility," Selba said. "But I'm at a loss as to why...why..."

Selba turned around and watched Blouisa and Labba arguing down the corridor.

"Why what?" Claus asked.

"I'll be back," Selba said.

Selba left and slowly walked up to Blouisa and Labba.

"I just thought of something," Claus said. "How will I know if my hands are dirty? I can't just look at them and tell. Or what about privacy when I'm changing clothes? Will I have to swing a whip in the air to make sure no one is around? Could be windows. Anyone could see in. What if I want to dye my hair? Get the grey out, you know. Can't see if I'm doing it right."

"It's just nervous tension," Sergio said, referring to Claus's babbling.

"I don't feel nervous. These pain meds work great," Claus said.

"We'll take good care of you, Pappa. Don't you worry!" Clausetta said.

Meanwhile, Selba caught up to Blouisa and Labba.

"I should return Aftova to him," Blouisa said. "His sight will return."

"No," Labba said.

"He's your husband," Blouisa said. "Don't you want—"

"He's not my husband," Labba said. "We never married."

"Oh, sorry," Blouisa said.

"Aftova must stay with you," Labba said. "We must figure out the cubic ether. I'll help."

"You're too anxious," Blouisa said. "Look at you. You're a nervous wreck."

"Labba, perhaps everyone should rest and let things sort out for a bit," Selba said.

"We can't," Labba said. "We have to be ready for the next ghost night. That means practicing. Aftova has a flip-flop. But only one. We'll need to extend that and control it. We'll use eethi pigeons for practice."

Selba and Blouisa exchanged glances.

"What?" Labba asked.

"It's just," Selba said, "Claus in there is blind. It's an upsetting situation. I don't know how you can plan things with his blindness pressing down."

"It troubles me, yes, but I can't let it stop our plan," Labba said. "Do you feel the same way, Blouisa?"

"I, uh, yeah," Blouisa said.

"I see. Should we call this off?"

"Give us a day or two," Selba said.

Blouisa nodded yes.

"Very well. Two days. I'll do research in the meantime," Labba said, and she walked off.

"Labba, wait," Blouisa said, but her voice trailed, as Labba was already beyond earshot.

"No use," Selba said. "She's in her own zone. How do you feel, Blouisa?"

"I feel normal," Blouisa said.

"No strange tingling in your back?"

"No. I half-expected these legs to start running on their own. But so far nothing," Blouisa said. "I'm not sure how Labba's plan will work. Does she expect little cubes to grow between my toes? Now she's got me going. Let's see Claus again."

The two returned to Claus's room. Clausetta helped him to stand and led him around.

"See how easy that is? I mean...oh...I didn't mean to say..." Clausetta stumbled.

"I do and don't see how easy it is to walk with your help," Claus said. "Who just came in?"

"Blouisa and Selba," Blouisa said.

"Are you getting anything from Aftova yet?" Claus asked.

"Nothing," Blouisa said.

"I guess it's another failure then," Claus said. "Too bad you're not Carinian. You could activate it instantly."

"She's not, but I am," Leif said. "Dear, let's go out into the hallway."

Leif escorted Blouisa into the corridor while the others walked after them. Leif slow-danced with Blouisa then switched to a waltz. He changed to other dances such that he kept a hand or two on the small of her back. His own Carinian power linked

with Aftova, and Blouisa felt her legs dance like nothing before.

"Never knew you were such an excellent dancer!" Blouisa said to Leif.

"You're on fire!" Leif said.

"What? What's happening?" Claus asked.

"Blouisa and Leif are cutting a rug," Selba said.

"They are? This floor feels solid," Claus said.

"It means they are dancing with such excellence as to defy explanation," Selba said.

"Oh," Claus said.

Leif tossed Blouisa in the air, and she landed with what looked like ice cubes splashing around her.

"What was that?" Claus asked.

"I think Blouisa and Leif discovered something," Selba said.

Leif tossed Blouisa again, and like before she landed while splashing new transparent cubes around. The two stopped dancing and walked over to the group.

"Did you see us?" Leif asked.

"No, I didn't," Claus said. "But I guess you were cutting a rug with ice cubes from the sound of things."

The group laughed.

"If this is Aftova's doing, I'm thankful," Leif said. "And here I was worried about Blouisa becoming paralyzed."

"It really is amazing," Blouisa said. "I'm sorry it cost your vision, Claus."

"Better for the young to celebrate youth than the old to complain about crud," Claus said.

"But you'll live to five hundred!" Clausetta said. "Pappa. Maybe you can dance with Blouisa and get your vision back."

"Oh, no. I'm not about to try something like that!" Claus said.

"Why not?" Blouisa asked.

"Yes, Pappa, you must!" Clausetta said.

"What do you say?" Leif asked.

Clausetta pushed Claus forward, and Blouisa took him and led him into dance.

Chapter 120: Dancing Disco

Claus found himself on the dance floor of a 1980s discotheque. A hypnotic dance beat captured those around him into dance. Colored lights danced and strobed about.

"Isn't this a wonderful place?" Lanietta asked as she danced around him.

"What? How did I get here? And I can see!" Claus said.

"It is a little dark," Lanietta said. "But dark dances dance best in the dark. Here, let's get a drink."

Lanietta pulled Claus by the arm and rushed him over to the bar.

"Two pink vials of death," Lanietta said.

The bartender gave each what looked like test tubes filled with a pink fluid.

"Where are we?" Claus asked.

"We're about to get buzzed," Lanietta said. "Drink up!"

Lanietta lifted the tube and poured the contents down her throat. Claus tried the same but ended up spilling the fluid on his face and shirt.

"Ugh," Claus said.

"Let me clean that off you," Lanietta said.

At first Lanietta took a paper napkin to Claus, but she changed instead to licking the pink fluid off his face.

"Mmm. You're good tonight," she said.

"Cut that out!" Claus said.

"C'mon. My favorite song is on!" she said, and she rushed him back to the dance floor.

Lanietta danced vigorously to the pop song. Claus danced a little but only so as not to look out of place. Lanietta bumped her butt against Claus's to get him going.

"C'mon. This is the best part. Can't you feel the synth through your body? It's like going into outer space," Lanietta said.

"I'm blind!" Claus said.

"Sure you are," she said sarcastically.

"How did I get here? What power do you have?" Claus asked.

"The power to cut a rug," she laughed.

"You heard the others? You're spying on us?" Claus asked.

Lanietta laughed.

"Let's play some pool," she said.

Lanietta went back to the bartender and held out a driver's license to reserve a pool table.

"Let me see that," Claus said as he grabbed the license.

"Thought you were blind," Lanietta grinned.

"State of New Mexico. Lanietta Clowsifuni, 1223 Appaloosa Trail, Corona, New Mexico. Born February 41, 1960. Hey, that's not right!"

"It was a leap moon," Lanietta said. "We'll take a table by the wall, bartender."

The bartender took Lanietta's license and gave her a set of billiard balls. Lanietta passed them to Claus with a, "Take these."

"Also, a pitcher of beer please," Lanietta said to the bartender. "Could you send us a plate of nachos? Thank you."

Lanietta took the pitcher of beer along with two mugs, and she led Claus to a pool table in a corner.

"Perfect. We can catch the latest horse races too. See? A television screen with whatever sport you care to watch," Lanietta said. "Let's shoot to see who breaks."

Claus stood there in disbelief.

"Shy? Here, slurp some beer first. It'll settle your nerves," Lanietta said.

"Lanietta!" Claus said between gulps of beer. "New Mexico?"

"We have it all. UFOs, nuclear testing, cancer, death. I'm an atomic girl with a glowing desire for life. Nachos are here!"

Lanietta took a nacho and ate it.

"Mmm. Good. I needed that. Starved. You should try one. They're very well done," Lanietta said. "Besides, you need the nutrition. For your eyesight."

"Lanietta! What game is this?" Claus asked.

"The nacho, Claus," Lanietta said.

"But no Clomper," Claus said as he ate a nacho.

"I'll shoot first. See if you can top this," Lanietta said.

Lanietta placed the cue ball on the pool table, and she chalked up her stick. She leaned over, and her hair fell lightly around her face. She blew a few strands out of her eyes.

"Are you staring at me?" she asked. "Just checking your eyesight, eh? How's my form?"

She hit the cue ball moderately but gently. It bounced off the far bank and rolled all the way to the near bank.

"I'm kissing the bank," she said. "Give me a kiss, Clausy."

Lanietta, still leaning over from shooting the cue ball, turned slightly toward Claus in a semi-provocative pose.

"It's the '80s, Claus. You're supposed to admire the scenery," she said.

"I want to know what's going on," he said.

"Stuffy, Claus. You'd never make it in this decade of decadence and delight," she said.

Lanietta stood up and offered the cue ball to Claus.

"Now you try," she said.

Claus positioned the ball but could not hold his cue stick steady.

"So nervous," she said. "Here. Like this."

Lanietta moved in close to Claus and moved his arm back and forth in a steady rhythm. She then whispered into his ear, made smacking sounds, and did a light growl.

"You're tickling me," Claus said.

"Such a sensitive guy shouldn't have any trouble with a silly game of pool," she said. "Bring it back to the rail, Claus. Do it."

Claus hit the cue ball too hard. It bounced hard against the far rail, reached the near rail, bounced, and stopped short of the far rail.

"A bit overdone," she said. "I'll break. Rack 'em!"

Claus racked the balls with a triangle and had just barely lifted the triangle when she sent the cue ball smacking into the group. Claus quickly pulled away for fear of getting his fingers caught.

"Couldn't you wait for me to finish?" he asked.

"I don't wait for anyone," she grinned. "Let's see. I sank one of each. Want to see me clean up the table? It's your funeral."

"Is that what this is? We're caught up in one of those double pair yellow and blue realities? I don't see them around. What's the game, Lanietta?"

"Eight ball. Two in the corner," she called, and she landed the two ball in the corner. She paused for a moment then called, "Six in the side."

Lanietta bit her lip and looked up at Claus.

"Are you watching the table or me?" she asked. "You should look at me."

"Why?"

"Because I'm your date, that's why," she said.

"What would Labba say?" Claus asked.

"Clever. Bringing the other girl into the conversation. Look across the room. Who do you see there at the bar?"

"That's not Labba. It's Frieda. You brought her here? To top my comment about Labba? Who's she with? Some guy...Frieda!"

Claus ran over to Frieda.

"Frieda! I can see. How did you get here? Do you—"

"Who are you?" Frieda asked.

"Claus! From the near side. Remember?" Claus said.

"What?" she asked in surprise.

"Listen, buddy, this is my girl. So buzz off," said a muscular guy next to Frieda.

"Frieda!" Claus said as he grabbed her by the arm.

"Fritz!" she called.

"Fritz?"

"Yeah, that's me!" he said, and he shoved Claus away.

Claus fell backward, but Lanietta caught him (she had walked over by now). She tossed him back toward Fritz with the words, "Go get him, Tiger."

"Can't take a hint, can you?" Fritz said, and he punched Claus in the face.

Claus went to the floor hard, unconscious.

"Tell your man to keep his hands off," Fritz said to Lanietta.

"Or what?" Lanietta said. "Go ahead. Tell me, little man."

"If you weren't a broad, I'd deck you," Fritz said.

"Try it, little man," she said.

Lanietta grabbed him by the wrist and clenched hard. Fritz fell to the ground in pain. He wrenched free and slapped her across the face. Lanietta recoiled with a little shriek, but she slapped back and harder. Fritz gave out a louder shriek.

"You scream worse than a girl. That's me," Lanietta said. "Time to mop up the counter."

Lanietta picked him up and tossed him along the countertop. Patrons lifted their drinks to keep from losing them. Fritz finished sliding off the countertop and landed in a pinball machine. The glass broke, and he activated several bumpers and beeps, causing the pinball machine to go crazy, ending with a "tilt" indicator.

"Guess that tool is out of order," she said. "Hello, Frieda."

"Who are you?" Frieda asked.

"Oh, just a woman who leashes your pilots into pets and property," Lanietta said.

"I've never seen you before in my life. I'm calling the cops," Frieda said, and she rushed over to a telephone.

"No cell phone for her kind in this decade," Lanietta said. "Come along, Claus. We've worn out our welcome. But first. Bartender, my license please. Oh, and here's something for the mess."

Lanietta left a stack of cash on the counter. The bartender didn't want to surrender Lanietta's license, as he too was calling the cops.

"Bartender? The license. Now," she ordered.

The bartender surrendered her license.

"Thank you," she said, and she escorted Claus out.

Claus was groggy and could barely walk. But once he sat in Lanietta's sports car and had fresh air blowing on him from her excessive speeding, he became quite alert.

"Slow down! You're going to kill us!" he said.

"You know, this car loves being small and sporty. Pure speed. Look how I weave through traffic," she said.

"Lanietta! Tell me about Frieda and her ethereal computer. How do we defeat her and it?" Claus asked.

"Computer? In this kilobyte age? Better stick with the music," she said. "Fortunately this car is adequately powered with its own form of music. Not all cars had as much power. Hear how this car roars. Like me!"

Lanietta let out a roar as she accelerated the car onto a lonely stretch of rural highway.

"Should we play lights out? Drive blind?" she said.

Lanietta turned off the car's headlights.

"Please! Turn on the lights!" he begged.

"Not very romantic, are you?" she said.

"It's fear! Pure fear!" Claus said.

"C'mon, Claus. Live on the edge with me. Pretend there's no tomorrow. Just you and me tonight. Look, here's a gravel road."

Lanietta hit the brakes hard as she turned, and she forced the car sideways, but as she did, she hit the gas so that she expertly completed the sliding turn without loss of control.

"If you want to torture me to death, you're winning!" Claus said.

"This? Torture? This is passion, my Claus! Passion *in extremis*!"

Lanietta fishtailed along the gravel road, going around narrow curves with no chance of avoiding potential oncoming cars nor with a chance of avoiding unexpected obstacles.

"Like that deer!" Claus said.

Too late. The car hit the deer head on, bringing the car to an abrupt stop but killing the deer.

"You killed it!" Claus screamed.

"Shh," Lanietta said.

Both Lanietta and Claus got out of the car and tended to the deer. She whispered something in her ear, and as if by magic, the deer stood up and walked away.

"How..." Claus started.

"Passion and compassion," Lanietta said. "When which is when, how one is the other. Claus, kiss me. Kiss me in this lonely deserted place of death and rebirth."

Claus started to say, "Labba," but she shushed him and held him close. She slow danced with him very close and brought her lips close to him.

"It's a kissy for Clausy," she whispered.

Claus closed his eyes. But instead of feeling Lanietta kiss him, he felt a sharp blow to the back of his head.

Chapter 121: Grape Wine and Laundry

"Sorry, you tripped backward and hit your head," Blouisa said.

Claus blinked, but he couldn't see anything.

"Was I...were we dancing?" Claus asked.

"We tried, but you had two left feet," she said. "Sorry. I thought I could help."

"You did fine, my sweet," Leif said to Blouisa.

"Let's get you back home, Claus," Labba said. "You've had a long day."

Claus was taken back to his mansion. He had a quiet dinner with family then relaxed in the dining room.

"I'll put on soft music," Labba said.

Labba placed a special instrument in a fountain. As random water flowed through it, it played notes, somewhat like a wind chime but for water. The family visited for a little bit, but in time they went home. Labba dismissed the staff for the night, leaving her with just Claus.

"Let's see how your visual cortex is doing," Labba said. "Maybe I can massage it and get your sight back."

Labba went eethi and placed her hand in the back of his brain.

"See anything?" she asked.

"No."

"There's evidence of recent activity. Claus, are you sure you can't see?"

"No, I can't," Claus replied.

"What about when you danced with Blouisa? Did you see then?" Labba asked. "My touch says you saw something. Visual movement leaves traces. There are traces here."

"I didn't see Blouisa or any of you," Claus said.

"But you did see something, right?"

Claus paused.

"Yes," he said.

"When were you going to tell me?" she asked.

"I didn't see any of you. That much is true. I thought I was daydreaming or something," Claus said.

"No, this is an actual use of your visual pathway. I'm going to ask again. What did you see?"

"I saw Lanietta," Claus said.

Labba sighed.

"It's not like I have a choice," Claus said. "I don't know how, but I was at a bar or somewhere on the dance floor with her. We played pool and went for a drive. Then I returned to the hallway with Blouisa when I fell backward. I don't understand it all."

"Aftova is removed. There should be no link with Lanietta," Labba said, a bit miffed about the situation.

"What do you want me to do?" Claus asked.

"I want you to forget Lanietta and think about me," Labba said.

"I'll try. Let's talk about something else," Claus said.

"Why?"

"You said to forget about Lanietta. How's the testing going with Blouisa?"

"It starts tomorrow," Labba said. "I *was* going to work with Clausetta and Leif to see how well Blouisa can generate and control cubics."

"What's stopping you?" Claus asked.

"You. I'll have them start without me," Labba said. "I'll stay by your side and monitor your visual cortex."

"To prevent Lanietta from connecting with me?" Claus asked.

"I told you to forget her," Labba said.

"But that's the reason. Labba, this effort with Blouisa is our one hope for establishing an ethereal computer on this side. You're the full-blooded Carinian. They really need your help," Claus said. "Because the only other Carinian—"

"Is supposed to be forgotten," Labba said.

Labba got up, went into the kitchen, and returned with strawberry champagne. She poured a glass for Claus and gave it to him.

"I recognize that drink. It's what Lanietta—hey!"

On hearing Lanietta's name, Labba poured the drink on Claus's shirt, took the bottle back to the kitchen, and returned with a grape wine. She poured a glass for Claus, and he drank.

"Very original," he said.

"I'll have one too then," she said.

Labba also started a fire in the fireplace simply by going eethi. She then reintegrated.

"I can hear the fire," Claus said.

"We're going to have a nice, relaxing evening. Just the two of us," Labba said. "Keep your eyes closed. I'll have one hand in your visual cortex, just to make sure we stay alone. There. All safe. Let me tell you a story about this wine. It was made from a special grape, taken..."

"From a descendant of the Lonely Vine," Lanietta's voice said to Claus over Labba's. "In the wine you can taste the history of the universe, those early life-forms that pioneered metabolic processes and created symbiotic relationships to survive and pass on their genetic information."

Claus opened his eyes, and he could see. But instead of being in his own mansion, he was sitting in a chair by a pool that belonged to another mansion. He had a glass of grape wine, and sitting in a shaded lounge chair in a one-piece black swimsuit with sunglasses and a glass of grape wine was Lanietta.

"How did you...Labba's blocking my visual cortex," Claus said.

"It's laundry day. I'm doing laundry," she said.

Lanietta waved her hand toward the swimming pool, and it churned up mounds and mounds of laundry, like a giant washing machine.

"Laundry? This will take days!" he said.

"What day?" she asked. "We're on Carinia 2. The day never ends."

Claus looked up a bit and noticed the sun was a red dwarf and not yellow like Sol.

"This isn't real," Claus said.

"Tell that to our four hundred children," she said.

"What!?" Claus asked.

"Go for a walk in the courtyard. They're playing," she said. "I'm sunbathing. Except, well, it's so hard to get a tan without ultraviolet light. No matter, I don't have to worry about tan lines. If I did, I'd have to sunbathe in the nude."

"I'll check on the children," Claus said.

"Brat!"

Claus stood up with his drink and walked from the pool to the courtyard. Yes, there were hundreds of children playing. Some skipped rope. Some played tag. But quite a number of them were into construction of sorts from sand castles to huts.

"They are building?" Claus asked.

"Help, Claus!" called Lanietta's voice from the pool.

Claus rushed back to the pool. The entire area was covered in soap suds as high as a person or higher.

"Lanietta? Where are you?" Claus asked.

"I'm lost. I can't find my way around," she said. "I...oof!"

Claus heard a splash.

"Shut off the machine!" Claus yelled.

Claus made for where he heard the splash.

"Help, Claus, help!" Lanietta's voice called from the water.

Claus jumped in. But as soon as he did, he became caught in the churning of clothes. There were no vestiges of a washing machine to contend with, just the churning up and down of clothes. He pulled in fresh air each time he was brought to the surface but had to hold his breath each time he was pulled down. The churning wrapped clothes around his body, and he struggled to breathe.

"I'm choking, Lanietta. I can't breathe. Where are you?" Claus asked.

"Ugh!" she said. "We're trapped!"

The scene changed. Claus was in a square toroid on the Anrega's surface. In his hand he held the double chalice with the orb of Lanietta. Before he could say or do anything, the scene changed again.

"What? What is this?" Claus asked.

He was in the South Atlantic, and he was a dolphin. At first he was alone, but another dolphin much like him carried a short vine in her beak and dove below. Claus dove after her and followed her into a seamount. The two then went through a portal and changed from dolphin to humanoid form.

"Lanietta? Why is there a vine in your mouth? What are we doing here?" Claus asked.

"We're in Lagenora, and this vine is for Prince Sparfiacus. He's going to make the best wine in these parts. Oh look, there he is speaking with Delfa," Lanietta said.

Delfa spotted Lanietta and waved her over.

"Come along, Claus," Lanietta said as she pulled Claus by the arm.

"Princess Adelfarina and Prince Sparfiacus, this is Claus Gerhardt. Claus, meet the royalty," Lanietta said.

Claus nodded.

"I have the vine for you. It should prove fruitful," Lanietta said.

"Thank you. This will help with our efforts. The humans are just discovering our seamount and are planning to drill for oil," Delfa said.

"Stop, Lanietta. I know what you're doing," Claus said.

The three looked at Claus in surprise.

"You want me to experience it. The attack. This isn't right. The citizens here deserve better," Claus said.

"I'm helping with the effort," Lanietta said. "Surely there's no dishonor in that."

"For which we are thankful," Delfa said. "There's going to be a meeting soon. To discuss our defenses."

"I'll be there," Lanietta said. "But as for Claus."

"If you are worried about us, do not be. You are with friends," Prince Sparfiacus said.

Claus shook in fright. He ran over to the portal, jumped in, and swam up to the surface as a dolphin.

"I'd better go after him," Lanietta said.

Lanietta also jumped into the portal and swam to the surface.

"Return with me to the seamount," she said. "It's safer there."

"Delfa will be killed. I know the story," Claus said. "So will many others. We're in a toroid, aren't we? Catching more death?"

"I'm working on special projects for special people in special places in special realities," Lanietta said. "Don't stay on the surface. It's not safe."

But before either could speak another word, Claus was caught in a fishing net with a school of fish while Lanietta was caught in another fishing net—also with a school of fish. The nets pulled through wave after ocean wave. Claus felt himself being squeezed and churned. The fish were so thick that he couldn't see through them.

"How do we get out of this?" Claus yelled.

"Get out of what?" Labba asked.

Claus realized he was back in his mansion with just Labba.

"It's just you, Labba? I mean, there's no one else here, is there?" Claus asked.

"No. Claus, what's wrong?" Labba asked. "Wait. Your visual cortex has changed. Do you see something?"

"No. But I did. I saw—"

"You're supposed to forget," Labba said.

"I can't stop it, Labba. I saw Lanietta again. We were in a swimming pool, and—"

"A swimming pool!?" Labba asked in surprise.

"And then the ocean. We were dolphins and met other—"

"I get the idea," Labba said.

Labba sighed.

"There was also a moment in the square toroid," Claus said. "I think she's working on the Frieda problem, but the work occasionally pulls me in."

"She doesn't need to," Labba said. "I'm sure of it. More wine, Claus? I think you need it."

"She had grape wine. Lanietta, that is," Claus said.

Labba slammed her fist on the coffee table and caused the glasses and wine bottle to spill.

"I will not be supplanted. I will not be supplanted!" Labba insisted. "Okay, okay. Tomorrow when we start the testing with Blouisa, you're coming with us. Maybe I can't stop that other Carinian from her tricks, but at least I can watch you."

"Labba. Have you been monitoring me this entire time? I mean ethereally," Claus asked.

"Yes."

"And you didn't see anything? A swimming pool doing laundry? Dolphins transforming into people?" Claus asked.

"No, nothing," she said in frustration. "Claus, I want you to count. One, two, three, four. Just count. Not out loud. In your mind. One, two, three, four. Let no other thoughts enter your mind."

Claus did so. He counted by fours. He moved his lips as if to speak but made no sounds.

"I'll get us new drinks. I'll be right back," Labba said.

"One, two, three, four," Claus whispered.

"Let's go marching on some more," Lanietta said.

"What? No!" Claus said.

Claus could see, and he was in an army marching along two by two. Lanietta marched alongside him. He noticed that her left boot was yellow while her right was blue, and she left corresponding yellow and blue footprints. These footprints would alternate between pointing straight ahead and kicking out at a right angle.

"Fours, Claus. Always in fours," Lanietta said as she marched.

"Why? I mean, it's the death thing again, isn't it?" Claus asked.

"Get down!" Lanietta yelled.

The platoon ducked as rocket propelled grenades flew overhead. After they passed, Lanietta took a grenade from her belt and tossed it to the left. She took out an enemy squad. Gunfire erupted. The platoon broke for cover. Lanietta pulled Claus behind a rock, and she fired periodically.

"Cover me," she said as she ran to another rock.

Claus didn't fire, and so Lanietta took a hit to her upper chest before she could go far. She fell, and Claus pulled her back behind his rock.

"What did you do that for? You got shot!" Claus said as he tended to the wound.

"I feel weak," she said.

"You're bleeding like crazy," Claus said.

"Tell my wife and kids I love them," she said, and she pulled a photo from her pocket of a man in uniform with his wife and children.

"You're posing as someone? You got this guy killed?" Claus asked.

"I'm dying with him," she said. "I..."

Lanietta's eyes closed, and she stopped breathing. Claus shook Lanietta with such desperation that he had his eyes closed as if in prayer.

"Don't leave me now!" Claus said.

"Okay, I won't," Labba said. "What happened to counting in fours?"

Claus was back in the mansion.

"Here, have this drink. It's fruit juice with an alcohol-safe sedative," Labba said.

Claus drank the juice.

"Tastes awful," Claus said.

"You're getting worked up again. Oh, and I sense more visual experiences in your visual cortex," Labba said. "Doesn't that girl quit?"

"Maybe we should go to bed," Claus said. "I'm not much entertainment this evening."

Labba helped Claus to bed. But instead of having a restful night, he...

Chapter 122: Death Dichotomy

Claus was in a house. But not with a mouse. He had just entered the front door from a long day at the office.

"Darling, I'm home," Claus found himself saying without understanding why. "Where's my sweet Sassatinassa?"

Then Claus shook his head.

"What am I saying? It's like something took over my vocal cords," Claus said to himself. "Am I in another reality with Lanietta?"

Claus stepped back outside and walked around the house. It was a charming brick split-level home with a large magnolia tree in the back yard and tall pine trees.

"Looks like the South," Claus said. "Quiet neighborhood, partly cloudy day, but there's plenty of sunshine. Everything is green."

Claus went back inside.

"Darling?" he called again, then he turned to himself. "Why do I keep calling?"

Claus walked through the house. Then he heard a chair topple over. He ran upstairs. To his horror, he found Lanietta hanging from the ceiling fan with a rope around her neck.

"Sass!" Claus cried, and he rushed over to her.

As Claus positioned himself under her to take force off the rope around her neck, the fan gave way. She tumbled atop him and onto the floor.

"What are you doing?" he cried as he pulled the rope off her neck.

Lanietta had stopped breathing, so Claus performed CPR. He managed to get a breath and a heartbeat going again.

"So I am forced to go through yet another day," she said.

"What kind of talk is that?" Claus asked. "Sass! You're my—"

But then Claus caught himself.

"You were about to say something," Lanietta said. "Does my husband love his wife? His Sass?"

"What is this game?" Claus asked.

"Yes. A game. Games always end, don't they? Winners choose when they end. Losers do not. I choose my ending, so I'm a winner," Lanietta said.

"That's so horribly wrong!" Claus said. "We need to get you help."

"Help? I'm not the one who needs help," she said. "I must be prevented. I must be stopped. Yes, and I am stopping me."

"Prevented from what?" Claus asked. "No, this is a delay tactic. I'm calling the suicide prevention hotline."

"Put down the phone. Turn on the television," Lanietta said.

"What?"

"Turn on the television," she repeated.

Claus returned the telephone to its hook and turned on the television. Breaking news of a murder popped up.

"I did that," she said.

"You...killed someone?"

"I can't stop," she said. "It's an urge. You know, like a bit of food caught between teeth that won't come out. I had to get it out. And I did."

"What?" Claus said in shock.

"It's strange, you know. After a murder, I have three good days. Feel perfectly normal and right, like the rest of you. Then that bit of food gets stuck again. It itches deep, reminding me of the old murders that were only good for a few days. No lasting permanence."

"Old murders? This is impossible! You don't murder people!" Claus said. "Are you going to murder me?"

"Only if there are no other humans left," she said. "Don't you see? The penalty for murder in this state is capital punishment—death. But lethal injection drugs are hard to come by. Pharmaceuticals won't supply them to this state. What choice do I have? Might as well self-sentence now."

"That's suicide, and it's wrong," Claus said.

Lanietta laughed.

"Don't laugh!" Claus said. "You can't stop me from calling. I'm calling the hotline now!"

Claus tried calling but could not get through.

"I can't get through," Claus said.

"Look," Lanietta said, pointing to the television.

A tornado warning scrolled across the bottom of the screen.

"The tornado has taken out phone service to the long-distance switchboard. Now what will you do?" she asked.

"I'll call a pastor," Claus said.

Claus tried calling a pastor, but no answer.

"Busy sheltering people from the storm?" Lanietta asked.

"I don't know. The pastor didn't pick up," Claus said.

"There's always the local psychic. Try him," Lanietta mocked.

"Sass, please!" Claus said.

Lanietta took the phone from Claus and dialed the local psychic.

"I'm Sassatinassa. Yes. Yes. I'm calling on behalf of my husband. Been acting strange lately. Yes, he contemplated it. More than once. What's the number of the therapist? Yes, yes, yes. I will. Thank you. You too. Bye now."

"What was that about?" Claus asked.

"The psychic is better connected than I thought," Lanietta said.

"Meaning what?"

"Meaning you have an appointment tomorrow with a crisis intervention counselor to discuss your suicidal tendencies," Lanietta said.

"What? Me?"

"How quickly you forget. How easily you deny to yourself and others. This wasn't my suicide attempt. It was yours," she said. "At least you stopped yourself."

"This is madness," Claus said.

"Suicide usually is," Lanietta said.

"I'm not dealing with a counselor tomorrow. Tomorrow won't come. I'll prevent it," Claus said.

"By kicking out the chair?" she asked.

"I didn't mean it like that," Claus said. "Did you really kill that person on television?"

"I didn't, but the person I'm playing did," Lanietta said. "Those who my character killed will never know the food of life again."

Lanietta paused in thought.

"Yes, let's try that," she said.

The scene changed. Claus approached a house in a village. There were no cars on the street, no people walking along—all empty of movement outside. Claus heard a church bell. Approaching the front door, he saw the paper and picked it up. "Saturday Evening, April 20, 1889. Boomers Cross the Cherokee Strip."

"Sass?" Claus called with the paper under his arm. "We're late for church."

Claus went inside. He heard a chair fall over, and he rushed into the bedroom from where the sound came. There was Lanietta hanging from a rope on a hook.

"No you don't!" Claus called.

Claus lifted her onto his shoulders and undid the rope from her neck.

"What are you doing?" Claus asked as he lowered her to the bed and got her breathing again.

"Failing to hang myself properly," she said. "Someday you must teach me how to make a proper hangman's knot."

"Never!" Claus said.

"Or at least invite the family over so they can place weight on my body," Lanietta said.

"Still never," Claus said.

"I see you brought the paper. Let's see," Lanietta said.

"You're reading the paper after attempting suicide?" Claus asked.

"Just think of it as another form of suicide. There's always plenty of bad news to celebrate. Let's see. 'Boomers Cross the Cherokee Strip'. Where's the suicide hotline for the Native Americans?"

"I'll get the phone. I'll call..."

Lanietta laughed.

"Do you think everyone has a telephone in 1889?" she said.

"Is it the same story? Did you kill someone?" Claus asked.

"I almost killed someone," she said. "This one-day-old baby."

Lanietta held her hands up, and a one-day-old baby appeared.

"Care to guess who this is?" she asked.

"No."

"I could take this rope like this, and wrap it around this baby's neck like so, and well, that would be the end of it," Lanietta said.

Claus jerked the baby away from Lanietta and removed the rope.

"Whose baby is this? Why are you trying to kill it?" Claus asked.

"Call the hotline. For attempted baby killing," she said.

"Return this baby to where it belongs," Claus said.

"Very well," Lanietta said.

The baby disappeared.

"He is back home. Care to know his name? He'll murder millions. First name is Adolf," Lanietta said.

"You don't mean."

"I do mean," Lanietta said. "Should have let me kill him, Claus."

Claus wanted to say something but couldn't.

"When is death acceptable, Claus?" she asked.

"It shouldn't be. Ever. I know. There's capital punishment. Mercy killings. And war. But I can't accept it," Claus said.

"Don't lie to me. You find it unacceptable for everyone but yourself," Lanietta said.

"Let's get you to church. Maybe that will help," Claus said.

The two left and walked to the church. But when they entered, the scene changed to that of a prison. Lanietta was a prison guard and Claus a prisoner.

"Do you still kill people?" Claus asked.

"Yes," Lanietta said. "Seems I've found a solution to my problem and that of our state. These prisoners are on death row.

No lethal injection drugs available. Remember? Electric chair maintenance was outsourced, and now it never kills right. So I get to kill the condemned prisoner in a manner of my choosing."

"More insanity!" Claus said. "Wait. I'm a prisoner? What did I do?"

"Does it matter?"

"Yes, it does."

"You are here by mistaken identity. Your DNA was mixed up in an off-shore crime lab. You're not guilty of the murder charge. You are an accomplice to a bank robbery, but that was never charged as the DNA mix-up meant the real murderer is serving a shorter sentence for your robbery in a different prison. See? All things come out in the wash," Lanietta said.

"That's how you explain this messed up situation? By mentioning the wash?" Claus asked in surprise.

"I don't have a swimming pool to clean dirty clothes in this prison. Might as well reduce the load. Oh, look. There's my next mark now," Lanietta said.

An elderly man walked by.

"He's old anyway," Lanietta said. "Suffers by the day. Wonders by the night. You might call this one a mercy killing."

"I'm not calling it anything but murder," Claus said.

"Biologically, the body doesn't know the difference. When it dies, it dies, whether it is deemed a mercy killing, capital punishment, accidental, or intentional," Lanietta said.

"But I know the difference. So do others," Claus said.

"Others don't see the way you do. You're blind on the lunar near side. Do people see as you do? Do they see what you see now? No. Stick around. I'll be back in a moment."

Lanietta disappeared and reappeared in a few moments. Claus looked intently at her uniform as if searching for something.

"What are you looking for?" Lanietta asked.

"Blood stains," Claus said.

"I do clean work. Don't want to add to the laundry. There. I feel much better.

Teeth are clean and bright. It's going to be a beautiful day."

"It's not a beautiful day!" Claus said. "I protest. I protest all of this! Lanietta! Whatever good you think you are doing—"

"Who said I was doing good?"

"Exactly. This isn't good. Not at all. Why must I be a part of it? I can't stop you. That I know. But why me?"

"Because in all the universe, you seem most willing to protest," she said.

"You can't be serious," Claus said.

"Others cave into demands. Or they quit and walk away. But here you are. Still around to the end. Is that loyalty or what?"

"Loyalty like a pet? You don't call me Clomper anymore," Claus said.

"No, I don't. Perhaps I've grown up a bit, even if I kill every now and then," she smiled. "Oh cheer up, it's not really me killing."

"But why partake in the role then?" he asked.

"You know why. I'm dealing with Frieda and her ethereal computer. It wants to crack the Anrega. To defeat death, one must understand it."

"Can't you do it in another way? Without dragging yourself or me into it?"

"Really, Claus, that hardly provides for empirical evidence," she said.

"But it does make for less misery," he said.

"I can't protect the universe from all misery. Yet. Maybe someday," she said.

"I don't see how. You seem to take delight in experiencing misery," Claus said.

"Your opinion. Say 'hello' to Labba for me."

Chapter 123: Loborrhaphy

Claus woke up and sat on the side of the bed, shaking.

"What is it?" Labba asked as she pretended to wake up from sleep. "Bad dream?"

"Was it a dream? I don't know," Claus said. "It was—"

"Her again?"

"Yes."

"Let's get you a drink. Come along," Labba said.

The two threw on robes, went downstairs, and grabbed alcoholic beverages.

"She kept killing herself," Claus said. "I don't know what it means."

"I do," Labba said.

"Then what?"

"It means the sedative doesn't work," Labba explained. "Claus, I was monitoring you. It was more than a dream. She still has her claws in your brain."

"How do I stop it?" Claus asked.

"Your ancient Earth society used various medications for such a thing," Labba said. "That's why I tried the sedative."

"The sedative just makes me groggy and less in control," Claus said. "Why don't I take a knife and stab my brains out?"

"Please don't speak like that," Labba said. "I'm hoping this drink will get you through the night. I'll speak with the others in the morning. Maybe we can set up an ethereal wall or something."

Claus finished his drink. Mariel brought out cheese and crackers.

"Mariel!" Claus said. "I'm sorry to have disturbed you and all."

Claus ate the cheese and crackers hungrily.

"It was no trouble. I heard voices, so I whipped up a little snack," Mariel said.

"Oh, do we have company? I didn't hear the door," Treyu said, now entering.

"No company," Mariel said. "Go back to what you were doing."

Treyu left.

"If you need me, I'll be in the other room," Mariel said.

"Thank you, Mariel. Goodnight," Labba said.

"Goodnight," Mariel replied, and she left.

"Mmm. I needed this," Claus said as he continued to snack.

"Feel better?" Labba asked.

"Much," Claus replied.

"Good," Labba said. "I have an idea. Let's watch an old-time movie to get your mind off things. We can bring the snacks and drinks with us. What do you say?"

"I'm all for that," Claus said.

The two did just that. They retired to the entertainment room and watched an old movie from the 20th century. Labba started telling about parts before they happened.

"I take it you've seen this before," Claus said.

"I've studied many of your movies," Labba said.

"Well one part of movie-watching etiquette says that one should not announce what is about to happen. Spoils the effect," Claus said.

"Oh, sorry. Should I explain the history behind each actor? Or the nuances in photography?" Labba asked.

"No. That's a bit much," Claus said.

"Okay," Labba said, trying to be helpful.

"I appreciate what you're doing," Claus said. "I just need a way to let go. My mind feels cluttered."

It wasn't long before Claus's mind drifted. Suddenly, he found himself in a futuristic house (as compared to his old Earth environment). He was seated in the living room with Lanietta and a five-year-old boy. Claus noticed that

Lanietta wore abbreviated eye shadow, meaning it only colored her outer eye lids, but the skin around her eye sockets was natural. The eye shadow had a rainbow of blue and pink, looking almost like a bruise.

"Do I have to get a *loborr* tomorrow?" the boy asked.

"Tomorrow is your sixth birthday, Landy," Lanietta said.

"Who?" Claus asked.

"Stop kidding, Daddy," the boy said. "You're like my kindergarten teacher. She called me Landrew."

"Because that's your birth name," Lanietta said.

"My name is Landy!" he insisted.

"That's your nickname," Lanietta said. "We call you that because we love you. You are named after your mother, Lanietta."

"Why do I have to get a loborr?" he asked.

Claus shot Lanietta a quizzical expression.

"Let me get the photo album, and I'll explain to you both," Lanietta said.

Lanietta disappeared for a moment and then returned.

"*Why I Got a Loborrhaphy*," Claus read. "*By Lanietta Clowsifuni*. Lanietta, this—"

"Shh," Lanietta said.

Lanietta opened the photo album to the first page.

"Who is the baby?" Landy asked.

"That's me. See how I'm beating the rattle against my head?" Lanietta asked. "Such a happy baby."

"You don't look happy, Mamma," Landy said.

"No, you don't," Claus said.

"Well I thought I was," Lanietta said. "Here's the next page. I'm playing in the sandbox. See how I'm stabbing my friend with the shovel? I was three years old in this photo."

"Why did you stab her?" Landy asked.

"She was in my sandbox," Lanietta said.

"That's silly," Landy said.

"You are right. It is," Lanietta said. "Here's another photo."

"Why is the boy's nose bleeding?" Landy asked.

"I punched him in the face. Look, I'm holding a clump of his hair," Lanietta said.

"Why did you do that, Mamma?" Landy asked.

"He called me a name. After you have your loborrhaphy, I'll tell you the name," Lanietta said.

"Can't you tell me now?" Landy asked.

"No. It's too upsetting to those who haven't been loborred," Lanietta said.

"How old were you here?" Claus asked.

"About thirteen," Lanietta said.

"Wow! That's old!" Landy said.

"Yes, the laws were different then. Back then only troubled people got loborred. Now it's mandatory before first grade for everyone. Which reminds me, Jay, your bruise is fading. Time for a treatment."

"What bruise? What treatment? Jay?" Claus asked.

"Take your medicine like a big boy," Landy said as if repeating something he'd heard.

"Yes. Be a big boy, Jay," Lanietta said.

Lanietta escorted Claus into the bathroom, opened the medicine cabinet, removed what looked like an epi pen, and placed it up to Claus's left eyebrow.

"Hey wait, what are you going to do with that?" Claus asked.

"I'm going to bruise your eyelids so you look like everyone else, of course," Lanietta said. "You never got loborred, so you have to fake it. Unless you want wires and chips running through your brain. Now you know you're not supposed to show pain. The rest of us don't. You show pain in public, and you'll be processed for sure! Be still and take the treatment. It'll be over soon."

Claus held still. Lanietta placed the pen on his left eyebrow and hit a button. A needle quickly injected something into his skin. She repeated the procedure for the right eyebrow.

"There, that wasn't so bad, was it? Look, your bruises are darkening already," Lanietta said. "Sure beats having an ice pick shoved into your eye socket, doesn't it?"

"I guess it does," Claus replied in horror to the ice pick reference. "But what about you? That eyeshadow—"

"Is not eyeshadow. It's permanent. From the loborrhaphy. You should know that by now. Everyone has one," Lanietta said.

The two returned to the living room.

"Will my eyes look like Daddy's?" Landy asked.

"Even better," Lanietta said.

Landy turned the page.

"Why are you standing on the chair?" Landy asked.

"You have a scarf around your neck, and the scarf is going up," Claus said. "Lanietta, this is not appropriate for—"

"Sure it is," Lanietta said.

"Words are inappropriate, but acts of ending life are?" Claus asked.

"I was going to kick out the chair, Landy, but your grandmother stopped me. She took the photo first, though," Lanietta said.

"Priorities," Claus said sarcastically.

"I was sixteen then. Here's a photo of me when I'm seventeen," Lanietta said.

"You're on the toilet? I don't understand," Claus said.

"I was going to kill myself again," Lanietta said. "But then I had a sudden urge to use the toilet, and that saved me. I felt so much better after going that I lost all interest in killing myself for the rest of the day."

"A good poop is a happy poop," Landy said.

"Yes, it is," Lanietta said with love and affection.

"I don't believe this," Claus said.

"It's all true. Captured in my photo album," Lanietta said.

Lanietta turned the page.

"Eww!" Landy said.

"A dismembered hand?" Claus asked.

"You know, I can't remember if this was from the boyfriend who cheated on me or the guy who cut me off in traffic. I lost part of my long-term memory from the loborrhaphy," Lanietta said. "But I do remember I was twenty. I also remember what's on the next page. My friend Molly."

"I didn't know you had a friend named Molly," Claus said.

"It was a fleeting relationship. But when we were together, it was like fire," Lanietta said.

Lanietta turned the page, and it showed her preparing to throw a Molotov cocktail at riot police.

"Molly," she said.

"Your friend is a gasoline bomb?" Claus asked.

"Paraffin oil," Lanietta said. "I used up my grandmother's kerosene lamps for earlier protests so had to make do with a plain glass bottle."

"What were you protesting?" Landy asked.

"Civil Loborrhaphy Act of United States," Lanietta said. "It enacted mandatory loborrhaphies for anyone deemed uncivil."

"Why is my name on that protester's poster?" Claus asked.

"You mean, 'Stop CLAUS'?" Lanietta asked. "That's not your name. Your name is Jay. And anyway, it's too much trouble to say, 'Civil Loborrhaphy Act of United States', so we used the acronym—CLAUS."

"I...I didn't do this!" Claus said.

"Of course not. Why would you say so? However, you do provide support for the software that runs in our heads," Lanietta smiled. "Thank you for being so supportive."

Lanietta kissed Claus on the cheek.

"Daddy helps people?" Landy asked.

"Yes, he does! And his software will help you too! It will prevent you from going through everything I did. You'll have a safe, normal life," Lanietta said. "Here's the next page."

"This isn't a photo," Claus said.

"It's a diagram of the procedure," Lanietta said. "They insert an instrument each through the eye sockets and sever nerve bundles between different parts of the brain. Parts of the thalamus are removed. Bio chips are inserted, and then synthetic neuro fibers are inserted to suture and connect the remaining brain parts with the bio chips. No big cuts in the skull. Patient goes home same day. I did, and I turned out fine!"

Lanietta did a little dance in the living room with Landy. Claus flipped to the last page, and it showed heavy bruising around Lanietta's eyes (more than what she had at the moment) but with her holding a plastic smile.

"A month after this photo was taken, you were shown my lab," Claus said.

"As part of the recovery tour," Lanietta said. "I was so impressed that I pushed for enhancing CLAUS to mandate it for younger people, to prevent them from going through what I did. And CLAUS came through for me."

"I came through," Claus said sarcastically. "I don't have a photo album like this."

"I have an album!" Landy said.

"Why don't you go get it?" Lanietta suggested.

Landy disappeared for a moment and then returned with what looked like a photo album. But instead of photos, there were drawings.

"I made these," he said.

The drawings were quite good for a person of any age.

"These are incredible!" Claus said. "You really made these?"

"Yeah," Landy said. "Look. I'll draw something now."

Landy pulled a spare pen from the album and opened to a blank page. He then drew an outdoor scene.

"He's an artist," Lanietta said with a deflated tone.

"You sound disappointed," Claus said.

"It's just...well...we'll see," she said.

"What is that supposed to mean? What are you not telling me?" Claus asked. "Lanietta! You *have* to tell me."

"That's a wonderful drawing," Lanietta said to Landy in order to deflect Claus's inquiry.

Landy finished the drawing, and he placed it near the back of the album.

"What's on the last page?" Lanietta asked.

Landy flipped to the last page. It read, "Goodbye five."

"I drew that this morning," Landy said.

"Tomorrow you can write, 'Hello six!'" Lanietta said.

"Yay!" Landy said.

"It's time for bed. You be a good boy and go right to sleep," Lanietta said.

"Yes, Mamma. Goodnight, Daddy," Landy said.

"Goodnight, Landy," Claus replied.

Landy went to his bedroom. Claus stared at Lanietta.

"Yes?"

"What is this place, Lanietta? What place of misery is this?"

"This is Earth. The selenites have taken over. They ensure society is civilized," Lanietta said. "Don't worry about the loborrhaphy—it will be complete tomorrow. The selenites don't let things drag out."

"It's not the completion I'm worried about. What about Landy?"

"What about Landy? You shouldn't show your worry. This society has no tolerance for it. Could get you into real trouble," Lanietta said.

"Then this society *is* in real trouble," Claus said.

"Let's go for a walk," Lanietta said.

"And leave Landy alone? That's abandonment," Claus said.

"His room is monitored by selenites. This room and the bathroom are the only ones not. You made a special deal, remember?"

"No, I don't," Claus said.

"Come along. It will do you good," Lanietta said.

The two exited the house. The first thing Claus noticed was that there were no houses around. Nor were there private cars. People either walked in the road or traveled in cylinders forced through chutes above. All around, people were speaking, but not to each other.

"It's a work day, you know. We took the day off for Landy," Lanietta said.

"They're just speaking," Claus said.

"The selenites handle manufacturing, and the people handle service jobs, at least what few jobs are left. They are collaborating. Meetings, more meetings, and just processing the minutia of the day. They'll go on all night. In shifts, of course. There are no office buildings for most jobs. People walk on the road and do their job in this way."

"How miserable. Where are the houses?"

"People don't have houses. They report to storage facilities when they need sleep. At least the aristocrats do. Others simply sit wherever. We have a house as part of historical study, like keeping a sample of measles in a jar even though the disease is eradicated."

"Glad to know I'm like measles. I'm breaking out with rash excitement," Claus said sarcastically. "I just can't get over the noise around me."

"I used to be like that. The loborrhaphy fixed it," Lanietta said.

"How do people keep from getting them?" Claus asked.

"The younger ones don't," Lanietta said. "Some like you have legacy jobs that map the human pain experience for future firmware upgrades. The mapping is almost complete."

"And then what will happen to us non-loborrs?" Claus asked.

"I'm sure a decision will be made," Lanietta said. "You worry too much. The only thing of meaning is the next thing. That's it."

Just then a truck blazed along the road. People spent no extra urgency in moving out of the way, and many were injured. Instead of people crying in pain or cursing the driver, the injured simply waited for others to help them to the side. Some were too badly injured and were administered lethal injections by others. Less injured were helped to a chute entrance where they were placed in a cylinder and sent along the way. The dead were disposed of in a flowing trough of water that took other garbage away. Claus was sick with disgust.

"I can't believe what I just saw," Claus said.

"Don't react. Don't help. Stay with me. We'll walk back home soon enough," Lanietta said. "I have an errand first."

"I...this is unnerving!" Claus said.

"Shh," she cautioned.

"Everyone has the same bruising on their eyelids," Claus said.

"Of course. Those are the safe people. Barbarians don't bruise," Lanietta said.

"How can people be so callous?" he asked.

"Callous, CLAUS—it's all the same," Lanietta said.

"I'm not the callous one!" Claus said.

"Depends on who's saying," Lanietta said.

"Well I'm saying I'm not," Claus said.

"Here we are. The supply store," Lanietta said.

The two walked into a shop. Shelves upon shelves were stocked with clear bottles of pills.

"What kind of store is this? All I see are pill bottles," Claus said.

"Uniformity is the key to civility," Lanietta said. "All bottles are the same."

The storekeeper walked up, and Lanietta pointed to which bottle she wanted.

"I like that one," she said.

"How can you like one over the other if they are all the same?" Claus asked.

"The Civil Loborr Network allowed me this brief moment of feeling, and that one felt right," Lanietta said.

"No charge," the storekeeper said. "You are within your monthly quota."

"What's that for?" Claus asked.

The storekeeper looked on in surprise.

"He's been instructed to try jokes today. Don't mind him," Lanietta said.

"Ah, a test," the storekeeper said.

"Yes. A test," Lanietta said.

The two exited the store. Lanietta pulled up the front of her shirt a little bit, exposing her belly button. She removed the cap from the bottle, placed the bottle over her belly button, and the pills were pulled inside her body. With the bottle empty, she placed it and the cap into the water disposal trough. It floated down the way along with the dead bodies.

"Now what?" she asked.

"I'm not sure where to begin or end," Claus said. "Everyone is on drugs?"

"Those were fuel pills," she said. "Loborrs like me had our stomachs replaced with a fuel stack. We inject fuel through the belly button. No need to eat. No need to grocery shop. No restaurants are left. No crops need to grow. Very efficient."

"Yes, very efficient," Claus said sarcastically yet again as he stared at the disposal trough.

"My errand is complete. We may go home now," she said. "I say 'home' in the most figurative sense, of course."

"Of course."

The two returned home and slept. Night passed. Morning came. Claus awoke to the smell of eggs, bacon, and coffee.

"Mmm," he said.

He got up and walked to the kitchen where Landy was already eating.

"This is Landy's last breakfast," Lanietta said.

"How did you get the food? I thought you said there are no crops," Claus said.

"This isn't real food. Synthetic food," she said. "Made to look and smell like the real thing. For young people. Soon the loborrhaphy will be performed on newborns, and there will be no need for this fake stuff."

"This fake stuff," Landy repeated.

"Yes. This fake stuff," Claus cringed.

Breakfast ended with Claus and Landy full. The three walked out of the house and to a chute entrance station where they jumped into a cylinder. The cylinder shot through the chute and took them to the Loborrhaphy Induction Center. The three entered the building but quickly found themselves in a line with other parents and children. These children, like Landy, had no bruising on their upper outer eyelids. On the other side of the hallway, an occasional group of parents and child walked toward the exit, with the child having the characteristic upper eyelid bruising of a loborrhaphy.

"Many go in, but few come out," Claus said.

"It's a high-pressure, low-pressure thing," Lanietta said. "High pressure is all clumped together, vying for limited space. Low pressure has fewer who enjoy much more space. Old air conditioning systems worked on this principle. Remove the heat from a pressurized gas, and heat will be drawn away when the gas goes to a lower pressure. Landy will feel much less pressure after the procedure, as will all these children. I will tell you that parents here feel a great level of excitement."

"Programmed excitement?" Claus asked.

"Of course," Lanietta said. "It's a rare treat from the Civil Loborr Network. The children don't feel it yet. Their feelings are chaotic and disorganized. Civility will win the day. Civility."

Claus waited in line for hours. Both he and Landy grew impatient, but Lanietta reassured the two that Landy's turn would soon come, and the wait would be over. The moment did come. Claus, Lanietta, and Landy were ushered into the treatment room by selenites. Claus and Lanietta were then taken to an upper balcony area with glass, permitting a view to the operating table below. Landy was placed on the table and strapped in. The lead selenite placed electrodes onto Landy. Landy was electrocuted into unconsciousness.

"He had a good life," Lanietta said.

"What? They didn't kill him, did they?" Claus asked.

"Not yet," Lanietta said.

"Lanietta, what are you saying? This is creepy!" Claus said.

"Landy is an artist. The artistic brain is typically too active to survive the loborrhaphy procedure," Lanietta said.

"You knew this? And you put him through this anyway?" Claus asked.

"It's mandatory. We can't have rogue brains running around. It's not civil," Lanietta said.

"That's unethical," Claus said.

"You speak from a primitive mental process," Lanietta said. "The rest of us who have been cleaned up do not have such reservations. One way or another, Landy will feel no pain. He will be at complete peace with the world. We should be thankful we enjoyed him for his six years. He had a long life, even if untamed. You must be at peace with this decision. This society does not suffer mass incivility."

"It's murder. For the sake of a regime," Claus said.

"People die. What can be done? What counts? The next thing, that's what counts."

"Being a parent means ensuring the survival of offspring until they can produce their own offspring," Claus said. "It's more than feeling. It's biology. It's life."

"That's how people ran their domestic animal farms. What about pets? Life is modified. Always has been. And if civility holds up, always will," Lanietta said.

The operation completed. The lead selenite doctor shook his head, "No."

"Well, that's it. Landy passed on," Lanietta said.

"Murderers all!" Claus said.

"You have this obsession with death," Lanietta said. "It's time for the next step. Can't let your obsession stop the flow."

"What next step? A funeral? Will Landy be dumped in that trough outside?" Claus asked.

"Oh no. Nothing like that," Lanietta said.

"I can't believe you're speaking like this, Lanietta," Claus said.

"You realize this is bygone history, and we are merely experiencing past events. I have no more control over this time than you. Including the topic of conversation. Come along. The next step awaits."

Reluctantly, Claus followed Lanietta to a different hallway not generally seen by the casual visitor. It was a line of parents with their children who didn't survive the loborrhaphy. The children were freshly dead and had their eyes glued shut. Parents pushed them in small wheelchairs. Lanietta pushed Landy.

"This is a ghastly scene," Claus said. "I'm sick. I'm going to lose my stomach."

"This is why we got rid of the stomach. Always making people sick," Lanietta said. "If you really want to lose your stomach, we can schedule you for that along with the loborrhaphy."

"No, thank you not," Claus said.

The line for dead children moved quickly. Claus and Lanietta finally reached a room where a conveyor belt pushed dead animals into an incinerator. Children, people, and pets were placed on this conveyer.

"It does add more carbon dioxide to the atmosphere," Lanietta said. "Something to work on. Would you like to place Landy on the belt? He won't feel a thing. His body is just a shell."

"His brain is still there. Still has his memories," Claus said.

"Nothing works. Not every tree planted will survive the winter. Not every rose can lose its thorns and survive. But there's always spring after winter," Lanietta said.

Lanietta placed Landy on the belt.

"I pity what humanity has devolved to," Claus said.

Just before Landy reached the incinerator, Claus ran up to him, pulled him off the belt, and ran with him. Claus ran and ran and ran, leaving the building, entering a cylinder, and shooting through a chute as far from the Loborrhaphy Induction Center as he could.

The cylinder suddenly stopped. So did other cylinders. There was a window that Claus could see out of. He saw patrol vehicles approach. One such vehicle looked like a "cherry picker", a utility vehicle with a bucket on a crane to raise people. That's what happened. Two people were lifted up to Claus's position, and they cut open the chute. They attached a chain to Claus's cylinder and retrieved it. The cylinder and the bucket returned to the ground. Once both did, the cylinder was opened up with guards ready to take Claus and Landy.

"Your child failed the induction. The next step cannot be skipped. It is mandatory. The child will be returned for resolution by incineration," one worker said to Claus.

The chute was left open. Claus and Landy were taken back toward the Loborrhaphy Induction Center. Claus half-expected a secret cult to mount an attack on the vehicle and free Landy and himself. But no such attack came. The two arrived at the center and were taken inside. Lanietta awaited them at the belt, and Landy was tossed on it by the very worker who told Claus the incineration was mandatory. Landy was incinerated.

"It's evolution," the worker said. "Like the appendix or wisdom tooth. They just go bad and need surgery anyway. Best to remove the vestigial structure in advance."

Claus spun around and punched the worker in the mouth. The worker was shocked but then laughed. Everyone laughed.

"Programmed laughter," Claus said. "How sickening."

"Let's go home," Lanietta said.

The two returned home. Landy's art album was still in the living room. Claus picked up the book and realized this was all that was left of the boy.

"In a sense, this is Landy," Claus said.

It was a sad moment, but the moment was about to change.

"Time to put this away," Lanietta said.

"Away? Where?" Claus asked.

Lanietta did not reply. Instead, Claus followed her to the basement to a row of lockers. Claus was shocked at what he saw. Each locker had a name. Claus read them: "Labner, Lacton, Ladello, Lafierre,

Laggius, Lajon, Lakienno, Lallin, Lambero, Landrew."

"I had Landy's locker ready," Lanietta said. "I knew this day would come. The others were the same way. Different drawings but same problem—too much creativity."

Claus opened the other lockers and looked at their corresponding albums.

"Each album is a voice, a voice being crushed," Claus said. "Be it dismay, the weight of the world too great, the price for survival too high."

Lanietta took a permanent marker to the next vacant locker and wrote: "Lapredius."

"No!" Claus said.

Claus rushed over, took the marker from Lanietta, and scratched through the name.

"There will be no Lapredius," Claus said.

"I am expecting as it is, and I know it's another boy. Are you saying I should get an abortion? Murder the unborn?" Lanietta asked. "Murder?"

"You almost sound like you care," Claus said.

"I was very passionate about life before my procedure. I still remember what words should be spoken," Lanietta said.

"Because you had the procedure done when you were older. How old will Lapredius be when he gets his due? Five? Three?" Claus demanded.

"I think it should be done *in utero*," Lanietta said. "Perhaps his mind won't be so chaotic then. The earlier the better. Then we can have a child survive to adulthood."

"You will totally deprive him of ethics," Claus said.

"Barbarism and ethics are mutually exclusive," Lanietta said. "This is the next thing. Accept it. You cannot undo it. Not unless you intend to have yourself removed from civilization. You could commit a crime and be exiled. That option always remains. Or you could self-exile."

"Might as well kill myself," Claus said.

"That thought would never occur to someone with a loborrhaphy. Perhaps it's time you should have the procedure.

You've suffered long enough. I'll submit a proposal to the network that you should retire from pain exploration. There are others who can fill your shoes," Lanietta said.

Claus dreaded the thought of having his brain scrambled and sutured with wire, but perhaps there was something he could yet do. He nodded in fake approval to Lanietta.

"Why don't you listen to your shortwave radio?" she said. "I need to get ready for my baby shower."

"What? Baby shower? You should be in mourning! Landrew was just alive this morning. And now you've already forgotten him?" Claus protested.

"I'm on to the next step," she said. "Go play with your radio. I'll let you know when the shower is over."

Lanietta went upstairs. Claus walked around the basement and found his shortwave radio set. He turned it on. He didn't feel like radioing anyone, so he set it to WWV and listened to the tones for time synchronization.

"Amazing the selenites haven't done away with this station," Claus said. "Hello, what is this?"

Claus looked at what looked like a neck band.

"Did I make this? Or acquire it?" he wondered. "Maybe it's a portable radio."

Claus placed the neck band around his neck. He pressed a button on it, and it gave him a mild shock. He immediately removed the band and tossed it on the workbench.

"Torture device? Why would I have this?" he wondered.

The neck band had a small socket for a plug, and Claus found the corresponding plug to a computer terminal. He plugged the neck band to the terminal and pressed the neck band's button. The computer terminal lit up with a status display titled, "LorB," and then in smaller print, "Lobo Override Band."

"Override band? And it's tuned to WWV," Claus said. "Then whoever I am in this reality, I'm planning to override the loborrhaphy procedure in someone. For

escape? Must be. But why did my character wait? Landy is dead and cannot be brought back. Still, there's Lapredius. He can be spared this society's iron will."

Claus stared at the display and realized the band also had a directional finder.

"To an underground society," Claus said. "If the selenites got a hold of this band, they could undermine this underground. A dangerous game my character is playing."

There was one last note on the display screen: "Unsynchronized. Please synchronize with weapon."

"Weapon? What weapon?" Claus wondered.

Claus looked around but saw nothing. Then he stared at his class ring on his right ring finger.

"Could it be?" he wondered.

Claus touched his ring to the band. The display changed and read: "Synchronized."

"My ring is a weapon?" Claus wondered. "Better disconnect this neck band and hide it in my pocket."

Claus did so, and just as he did, Lanietta walked partway down the basement steps.

"They want to meet you," Lanietta said.

"Who?" Claus asked.

"The women of my baby shower. They want to see what a wonderful husband I have," she said.

"Haven't they met me before? I mean you've had so many other showers," Claus said.

"Don't be such a party pooper. You know I always get assigned a new set of women," Lanietta said.

Claus followed Lanietta up the stairs and into the living room. He said, "Hello," to the women, but then one such woman caught his eye. She looked like a young version of Sharlamarian.

"What are you doing here?" he asked her, not thinking.

"I beg your pardon?" she said.

"Don't be rude, Jay," Lanietta said. "Sharlamarian just lost her brother to loborrhaphy."

"Lanietta. You know...she...this..."

"Don't pay attention to Jay. His joy for Lapredius leaves him tongue tied," Lanietta said. "Who wants a drink?"

"I'll help," Sharlamarian said, who got up and helped Lanietta serve drinks.

Claus continued to stare at Sharlamarian.

"Your husband is staring at me," Sharlamarian said to Lanietta discreetly.

Lanietta walked over to Claus.

"Keep your eyes off other women," Lanietta said with her face directly in front of Claus's.

"But she's supposed to be in Arberella," Claus said. "What is she doing here?"

"You are my husband in this house, and I expect you to act as such. Understand?" Lanietta said.

"Yes. I understand," Claus said.

Claus realized he had to help Sharlamarian escape to Arberella. But how? Best he get more information first. Lanietta and Sharlamarian served the others, and Lanietta gave Claus a drink.

"If you behave, I'll let you sit in with us," Lanietta said.

"I'll be good," Claus lied.

Claus sat next to Lanietta. All sipped their drinks through their belly buttons, including Lanietta. Claus had to sip through his mouth as did Sharlamarian and several others.

"Temporary bypass," Lanietta covered for Claus. "His fuel stack primary intake valve is on backorder."

The others nodded.

"You shouldn't drink that," Claus said to Lanietta. "You're expecting."

"It's grape juice. Alcohol free," Lanietta said.

"Oh."

"This is excellent champagne, Lanietta," Sharlamarian said.

"Take the whole bottle home if you like," Lanietta said.

"That's very generous. I will. I need something to prepare for tomorrow," she said.

"What's tomorrow?" Claus said.

"Shush!" Lanietta said. "You're being nosy and rude!"

"I don't mind telling," Sharlamarian said. "I'm getting the loborrhaphy done for myself. New mandate. Everyone must have it to receive benefits."

"Have you ever had a problem?" Claus asked. "I mean, you seem happy and all. Why go through with it if you're happy?"

"It's the mandate of the state, and that is not to be challenged," Lanietta said. "Now please stop with the interrogation. This is my day, remember?"

One by one, the women gave their gifts to Lanietta. Sharlamarian was last, and she gave her gift.

"Thank you for having us over," Sharlamarian said. "I wanted you to know how much this day means to me, just in case something happens tomorrow."

Other women (the ones who sipped with their mouths) spoke in similar fashion. Claus gathered that they were to have a loborrhaphy procedure the next day too.

"This is madness," Claus said to himself.

The women were deep in multiple conversations. At one point, Lanietta told Sharlamarian, "Take the whole case."

The shower went on a bit more, but soon it was time for the women to leave.

"Jay, please carry the wine case for Sharlamarian to a cylinder," Lanietta instructed.

"Yes, dear," Claus said.

Claus went downstairs to the basement and then into a wine cellar. He looked around and saw several wine cases.

"Which one did Lanietta give away?" Claus wondered.

"I think it's this one," Sharlamarian said.

Claus jumped with a start. Sharlamarian looked at him in surprise.

"You weren't supposed to be surprised," Sharlamarian said. "Loborr people don't jump like that. But you have the eye shadow. Are you...are you..."

Claus pulled out the neck band and showed it to Sharlamarian.

"You're my contact!" she said. "Quick! Put the band around my neck!"

Claus faced Sharlamarian and started to place the band around her neck. But he was still jittery from being startled and lost his balance. She grabbed him and held onto him to prevent his fall, and in so doing she ended up hugging him while he placed the band around her neck. He then pulled up her turtle-neck shirt to hide the band—just as Lanietta arrived.

"What are you doing with my husband!" Lanietta yelled. "Get out!"

"But the wine," Sharlamarian said.

"No wine! Get out of my house! Now!" Lanietta barked.

Sharlamarian ran out.

"And you, Jay. You're in the doghouse for this one!" Lanietta said to Claus.

But Claus held his ring up to her forehead and shocked her. Stunned, she fell to the floor.

"Strange that she got upset despite her loborrhaphy and all," Claus said. "Maybe that was the real Lanietta coming through."

Claus ran out of the house in time to find Sharlamarian preparing to enter a cylinder.

"I'll follow the neck band," she said to him quietly. "Do you know where to go?"

She looked down at the ring.

"Of course you do. It will tell you," she said as she motioned to the ring with her eyes.

Sharlamarian took her cylinder and left. Claus himself then took a cylinder. The ring sent electrical impulses to the cylinder. Chute junctions diverted Claus's cylinder to a sewerage tunnel under the city. Claus's cylinder floated along for hours. Then finally it reached an outflow tube. He was sent into the ocean where under the cover of night, he was pulled up by a net onto a ship. The net placed his cylinder on the deck, and several people opened his cylinder.

"This is him," Sharlamarian said, who was on deck. "This is the man who saved me. His name is Jay."

"Jay?" said a familiar voice. "This is my brother, Jarro."

Claus turned to look and saw Argo.

"That's the last one," called someone.

"Make heading for Antarctica," Argo called.

"He gave me the device," Sharlamarian said. "It scrubs carbon dioxide, too."

"Excellent," Argo said. "I knew my brother would come through."

Argo hugged Claus.

"Your wife was found dead," Argo said to Claus. "The implant self-destructed."

"And I caused it?" Claus asked.

"Not directly," Argo said. "The network decided she had no more purpose, so it discontinued her."

"She carried a child," Claus said.

"I'm sorry. We've fought the selenites for years but have always lost. Leaving the mainland is our last hope. We'll start anew in Antarctica," Argo said. "I have ideas for creating a barrier. And with the device you gave Sharlamarian, we can override a loborrhaphy and deal with the rising carbon dioxide levels. Both are almost unbearable. In fact, I should make copies at once. Everyone here desperately needs relief."

Sharlamarian walked over to Claus and had him remove the band. She gave him a kiss and then handed the band to Argo.

"The people here appreciate your efforts," she said. "We know about your wife. Terrible how she was killed. The selenites are monsters. I caught you looking at me though. You are something special, Jarro. I wonder if...perhaps later we..."

"This is all very strange to me," Claus said.

"I'm sorry," she said. "You must be terribly upset. I keep forgetting you still have your natural brain. If you want to be alone, I understand."

"I should be with people," Claus said. "Let's go to Antarctica and begin a new village. I have a name for it too."

"What's that?" she asked.

"Arberella."

Chapter 124: Deadly Chairs

Claus awoke on the couch in the entertainment room.

"It's dawn," Labba said.

"I wish I could see it," Claus said.

"Did you sleep any better?" Labba asked.

"No. Another nightmare with—"

"I understand," Labba interrupted. "I'm going to get an early start with Blouisa. Maybe we can figure something out before ghost night."

"That would be nice. I'd like to have peace of mind," Claus said.

"So would I. I mean, I'd like you to have peace of mind too," Labba said. "Mariel and Treyu will attend to your needs."

"Thank you," Claus said.

Labba left.

"Your breakfast is ready," Treyu said, entering. "I'll help you find your way."

"Let me try," Claus said. "I need to do a few things for myself."

"Very well," Treyu said.

Claus felt his way from the entertainment room to the hallway. He kept his hand along a wall and followed it to the dining room, but he reached a point where he had to leave the wall and make for the dining table. He walked slowly toward where he thought the dining table was.

"A little to the left," Treyu said.

"Don't tell me," Claus said. "I want to figure this out for myself."

But Claus drifted off to the side. He tripped over a chair and hit his head.

"He trips over it too easily," a familiar voice said. "I need a safe chair. One he can sit on without falling over."

Claus opened his eyes and could see. He was in a department store and had fallen over with a chair. He looked up and saw Lanietta.

"You embarrass me again, Claus," she said.

"Lanietta!" Claus said.

"Who else?"

"What? How?"

"We have another selection over here," the saleslady said.

"Pick yourself up and come along," Lanietta said.

Claus stood up and walked with Lanietta. The saleslady led Lanietta to a sturdy, wooden chair.

"I'll try this one out," Lanietta said.

Lanietta stood on the chair and pretended to have a rope. She pulled the imaginary rope upward from her neck and pretended to hang herself.

"What do you think?" she asked Claus.

"Not funny," Claus said.

"Good. I'll take this one," she said to the saleslady.

The saleslady walked off to ring up the order.

"You're going to buy a chair just to hang yourself?" Claus asked.

"Of course. Not any chair will do. I want my death to be special. This chair can be mounted by my headstone and will survive the elements. It even resists mold. The perfect chair for ending one life and beginning another," Lanietta said.

"This is getting old," Claus said.

"Which is why I must end it," Lanietta said. "Can't get old forever. Must end it. Must."

Claus sighed.

"Where's Labba?" she asked. "She left you this morning."

"How do you know about that?" Claus asked.

"It won't work with Blouisa, at least not the way Labba is trying," Lanietta said.

"What won't work?" Claus asked.

"Now who's playing games? The ethereal computer. I can't believe Labba is so blind. She had the answer in front of her. Now she's throwing it away. That's okay. Gives me more time for my plan," Lanietta said.

"Tell me, Lanietta. Why won't it work?" Claus asked.

"Nice try. Oh look, the saleslady is back."

"Sign here please," the saleslady said.

Lanietta signed.

"Your chair is at dock eleven," the saleslady said.

Lanietta led the way out of the store and to a tall pickup truck. Claus instinctively walked to the driver's side.

"Where are you going?" she asked.

"Oh, I don't have the key," Claus said.

"I should say not. This is my truck. You may ride along as passenger, if you like," Lanietta said.

"This is *your* truck?" he asked.

"Of course. How else am I to transport the chair?" she said. "Now go around to the other side and hop in."

Claus started for the other side by walking around the back. But Lanietta had jumped in quickly, started the engine, and revved it hard. The loud and dirty exhaust startled and choked Claus so badly that he fell down prone. Lanietta backed up the truck and would have run over Claus, but the truck had high ground clearance. His body passed between the wheels. The truck stopped. He sat up and stared at the front bumper, which he used to pull himself up. But he did not succeed. Lanietta honked the horn, which startled Claus and caused him to fall. He reached to pull himself up, but she honked the horn again.

"Stop it. Stop it!" Claus repeated.

He lifted a hand, and she honked the horn. He tried to time it so he could get her to honk and then slip his hand on the bumper and pull himself up without being honked at, but she honked multiple times.

"I quit!" he said.

"Oh go on," she yelled out the window.

Claus put a hand on the bumper to pull himself up, but she put the truck in drive and raced forward. He was dragged forward several feet before he let go. She raced down the parking lot, spun around, and aimed the truck toward Claus. Claus pulled himself to his feet. Lanietta raced toward Claus but then put the truck in a spin and opened the passenger door. The door scooped up Claus as the truck ran backward, the door closed, and Lanietta spun the truck forward. She stopped, revved the engine, and laughed.

"Will you stop clowning around please!" Claus said.

"Should I be prim and proper before I kill myself? Or enjoy my last moments of life?" she asked.

"You should neither kill yourself—"

"Nor enjoy life. Party pooper," she said. "Claus, Claus, timid as a mouse. Can't enjoy 'cause he's a boy."

"I would be happy to enjoy things if this situation called for it. Things are bad right now," Claus said.

"Bad, bad, Claus is mad. Can't enjoy 'cause he's a party pooper."

"That doesn't rhyme," Claus said. "Will you please just pick up the chair?"

"Yes. Good idea. Time to get my funeral over with," Lanietta laughed.

"That's not what I mean!"

"What do you mean?"

"I...I don't know anymore!" Claus said, frustrated.

Lanietta continued to laugh. She drove to dock eleven and backed up so quickly that Claus was sure she'd hit the shipping door. But she stopped just short of hitting it, laughing all the way.

"Revving truck, revving truck, revving all the way," she said while revving the truck. "Oh what fun, it is to ride, with Claus in Santa's sleigh, hey!"

"You twist everything!" Claus blurted.

Lanietta gave the truck one last rev, let it idle for a moment, engaged the parking brake, and then turned off the engine.

"I'll be back in a moment. Don't go away!" she said.

Lanietta jumped out of the truck, handed her sales slip to a worker, and the worker loaded the chair onto the bed of her truck. She thanked the worker and returned to the truck.

"Good. Let's go kill myself," she said.

She started the engine, revved it, removed the parking brake, and put the truck in gear. She hit the gas and sent the truck racing away. The chair, though in its shipping box, nearly flew out of the truck, box and all.

"You may be trying to kill yourself, but you're going to kill me in the process!" Claus said.

"This is all a dream, remember?" she said.

"I tripped over a chair in my dining room," Claus said.

"Oh, maybe not a dream then," she said. "Doesn't matter. What will be will be. Let's not wait for the red traffic light up there. Let's go through."

"No!" Claus protested.

The truck raced through the intersection, barely missing cross traffic. Lanietta laughed.

"This is more exciting than the chair, don't you think?" she grinned.

"No! It's not!" Claus said.

"There's another red light. Let's try it again!" she said.

"Please! I beg you!" Claus pleaded.

"You beg me to run the red? Okay!" she said, and she gunned it.

The truck raced illegally through the intersection, and again it barely missed cross traffic. Lanietta laughed again.

"I wish I were blind. I wish I were blind," Claus said.

"You are blind in real life. But not with me. I let you see everything!" she said. "Look. There's the ramp for the interstate."

"At least there are no traffic lights there," Claus said.

"True. Let's see what mischief awaits us," she grinned.

"Mischief? Lanietta! No!" Claus requested.

"You can't tell me what to do! Who do you think you are, anyway? You don't own me. I'm playing this reality the way I want!"

"Oh, please. Please!" Claus wailed.

Lanietta drove the truck onto the interstate and kept accelerating.

"The box! It's banging around. Lanietta! The air is picking it up. It's not tied down. You'll lose the chair. The chair!" Claus warned.

But Lanietta didn't care. She drove to such a speed with a swerve here and there until it happened—the air flow pulled the chair's box out of the bed and onto the windshield of a car behind. It plunged into the car and caused the driver to crash.

"Uh oh," Lanietta said.

"I knew this would happen!" Claus said.

"You should have told me," she said. "Why didn't you tell me? This is all your fault."

"I did tell you! I see failure everywhere, but I can't stop it!" Claus said.

Lanietta stopped the truck and backed it up until she reached the damaged car.

"I wonder if they need help?" she mused.

Claus didn't muse. He jumped out of the truck and rushed to the car. There was only one person in the car, the driver, and he was dead.

"You killed him," Claus said.

"He was going to die anyway," she said. "Cancer, you know. See his bald head? Chemotherapy. But he just learned today that his insurance would no longer cover treatment. He was depressed. Was going to kill himself. See? I saved him the trouble. Suicide chair."

"This is vile, disgusting, and below all sense of ethics. If ever there were universal truth and beauty, you have violated both and anything else that is sacred," Claus said.

"Hah!" she yapped.

Claus walked over to her and punched her squarely in the jaw. But instead of falling to the ground, she squared off as if in a bare-knuckle fight with Claus.

"Put up your dukes," she said as she shadow boxed.

"You are impossible!" Claus said.

"C'mon. I'll spot you ten points," she said.

"What is that supposed to mean?" Claus asked.

"Then between rounds you can go back to your corner and hang yourself off your chair," she said, still shadow boxing.

"I'm going to protest every reality you bring me into. I refuse to do anything. Passive protest. It starts now," he said.

Claus stood still. She punched him in the jaw, and he fell to the ground in pain. He put his hand to his jaw and checked for any disfigurement.

"That didn't last long. You're reacting," she said.

She kicked him.

"I'm stone. I'm rock. I'm Claus. I'm—"

"Lieutenant Dorrok," Lanietta finished.

"She can talk. She can speak. I will not move anything, not even—"

"Your beak," she said, and she kicked his nose.

"Ow," Claus said, and blood poured from his nose.

"See? Being passive accomplishes nothing. Gets you kicked in the nose for your trouble. Get up."

Claus refused to move.

"Get up!" she insisted, and she pulled him to his feet.

But Claus slumped back down to the ground.

"You're acting like a two-year old who refuses to go to bed," Lanietta said. "Oh look, police are here. Time to leave."

Lanietta tossed Claus into the bed of the truck, and she raced off at high speed. The police chased her with little effect—she made sudden lane changes to evade capture. Claus was tossed around, and this forced him to hold on despite his attempt to remain passive.

"I can't remain passive no matter what I do. I should jump. That will let me be passive. No, the act of jumping is itself not passive. How can I resist if I do nothing?" he argued with himself.

He looked toward the rear of the truck. Gaining on the pursuing police cars was a giant chair with yellow left legs and blue right legs. It took slow, deliberate steps, but it was so tall and the legs so long that the steps covered incredible ground. It kicked the police cars out of the way, and it sent its lead left leg down to squash the truck. It caught the cab and squashed Lanietta,

causing the truck to stop abruptly. The leg missed Claus, but the sudden stop of the truck caused him to fly forward. He landed with only minor injuries and was able to walk back to the truck. The gigantic chair had stopped moving but still had Lanietta pinned under its leg.

"Lanietta!" Claus called. "Can you move?"

"I...will die by the chair," she said, and she breathed no more.

"Lanietta!" Claus exclaimed, and he closed his eyes.

"She's not here, Pappa," Clausetta's voice said. "Here. Let me help you to the table."

Claus was back in his mansion. Clausetta helped him to the table, and she sat next to him.

"Breakfast is ready," she said. "I don't need to eat, of course. But I can if it will make you feel better."

"Yes. I'd like that," Claus said. "I adore my family."

"Leif would be here, but he's helping Mamma," Clausetta said. "Sergio is with Claude in the garden. Claude wants to start his own garden. He already has a green thumb."

Clausetta placed eggs and bacon on Claus's plate and filled his glass with drink. Claus ate.

"Mamma. She..." Clausetta's voice shook.

"You're shaking, Clausetta. What's the matter?" Claus asked.

"Oh, Pappa! Mamma...she...she told me to go away!" Clausetta said with sadness.

"What? I don't understand. We love our children," Claus said.

"I know you love me," she said. "But I also know about you and Mamma. I know that...she...you know, I wanted to help Blouisa with Aftova. To help with the cubics for ghost night. I'm excellent with the ghosts. No one can dance with them the way I do. I wanted to show Blouisa. I wanted to meld with her. But Mamma yelled at me. Told me to go away! Pappa! She was mean to me!"

"I'm sure she doesn't mean to be mean," Claus said. "She must be scared, that's all. The eethi is dangerous. She must've warned you."

"But we are in danger," Clausetta said. "I thought we had a paradise here. I find out that's not true, that the ground below is unsteady and ready to devour us! Pappa! All my life I've known great happiness on the near side. But it could go away. Instantly!"

"Try to be strong. There is grief in unseen places," Claus said. "I can't see, but I keep going. You must too."

Claus smelled fermented fruit.

"What are you drinking, Clausetta?" Claus asked.

"Uh, me? Nothing. Just juice," Clausetta covered.

Claus reached for her glass, but she kept it just out of his reach, readjusting her hand position as he moved his hand around. He finally grabbed hold of her with one hand then followed her arm to the drink.

"Pappa!" she said.

He grabbed the drink and sipped it.

"Alcohol," he said. "In the morning?"

"I'm an adult, Pappa. And I'm a mother," she said.

"I know. But I worry about this."

"You think I'll become an alcoholic," she said.

"I never said that," he said.

"You thought it. It's mixed in with a thought about a giant chair," Clausetta said.

"What? You're probing my mind? Clausetta!"

"I worry about you, Pappa. Aunt Lanietta has been torturing you. I can sense it. Mamma told me about how she tried to block Aunt Lanietta. She could not. And, well, I wanted to see for myself."

"How much did you see?"

"There was the truck. Jarro and the loborrhaphy. Aunt Lanietta trying to kill herself. The bank robbery," Clausetta said. "Other times too."

"That's too much. It's not good for you, Clausetta," Claus said.

"It's not good for you either," Clausetta said. "We're family. We protect one another."

"I won't let her get to you. I won't let Lanietta try to corrupt you," Claus said.

"I've spent most of my life around her already," Clausetta said. "She didn't do anything then."

"But I was in a coma. She seems to particularly torture me. If you experience the same feelings, it would torture you too," Claus said. "You must stop probing my mind."

"She said that Labba would fail with Blouisa. Our ethereal computer. How, Pappa?"

"I'm not sure," Claus said. "I..."

"Frieda did it. She made an ethereal computer," Clausetta said.

"I want you to promise me that you never go to the far side. Never visit Frieda," Claus said. "I don't want her contaminating you."

"I can't go anyway," Clausetta said. "The beyton rays would kill me. You know that."

"I...guess I keep thinking you're my human daughter," Claus said.

"I am your daughter through and through," she said with a hug.

"Clausetta. If you've been probing my mind all this time, then you did so when I had Aftova," Claus said.

Clausetta said nothing.

"Clausetta?"

"I might have," she admitted.

"What did it do to you?" he asked.

"What? Nothing. Just a stone, you know," she said, and she took a big gulp of her alcoholic drink.

"There's something going on," Claus said. "I can feel it."

"You worry too much, Pappa. I'm upset about Mamma, that's all. I'll just have to get over it. You should clean up and dress. Claude has a special project he'd like to show you...I mean, he'd like you to...well, you know."

"I know. Give me a bit. I'll be down shortly," Claus said.

Claus returned upstairs. He went to the closet and guessed as to what clothes to wear, and then he went to the bathroom and showered. When he was done, he dressed and walked downstairs. Clausetta laughed.

"What's wrong?"

"Those clothes don't go together at all," she admitted. "It's all right. Let's go out to the garden."

Clausetta took Claus in arm and led him into the garden where the two met up with Sergio and Claude. Sergio chuckled.

"Why does Grandpa look like a clown?" Claude asked.

"Because he wanted to surprise you. Let's show him your special project," she said.

Clausetta led Claus to a small greenhouse where Claude had been growing flowers.

"You'll have to describe everything," Claus said.

"I'll do better than that," she said.

Clausetta went eethi and placed her hand in Claus's visual cortex. In this way, Claus in his mind saw the greenhouse.

"Clausetta! I told you not to do this!" he said.

"You told me not to read your mind. I'm not. I'm just showing you Claude's project. See the flowers? Aren't they beautiful? Look. Claude is bringing a small pot with two flowers. One is yellow, and the other is blue. Smell them, Pappa. Aren't they fragrant?"

Claus sniffed them, but the scenery changed, and he was no longer on the lunar near side.

Chapter 125: Foxglove on a Mountain

Claus and Clausetta found themselves jogging up a mountain pass. They were dressed in outfits of leather as if part of an early civilization prior to the loom.

"Stop," Claus said.

"We can't stop," Clausetta said. "We must retrieve foxglove for the village. Many of our people will die without it."

"Clausetta! We're in one of my realities! Do you understand?" Claus asked.

"I do. But I also know people need our help. Look, we're getting close to the top. The richest and purest foxglove is there," Clausetta said.

The two reached the top. Clausetta found a dense bunch of foxglove. She put on her gloves and gathered foxglove leaves into a sack.

"Whew!" Claus said. "I must rest."

Claus sat on a small pile of rocks, but the rocks gave way, and he started to fall off the mountain. In fact, he was dangling over a cliff with only his hands preventing him from falling. But he could not hold out for much longer.

"I'll help you!" Clausetta said.

Clausetta rushed over and helped Claus climb to safety. But she was in such a rush to save Claus that there was no time to remove her gloves, and so oil from picking foxglove transferred from her gloves to Claus.

"We must be careful where we sit," Clausetta said.

"Yes. It would seem so," Claus said. "Oh, I feel weak."

"I touched you with my gloves," she said. "The foxglove oil is on you."

Clausetta removed her gloves carefully and then produced a bottle from a side pouch. From another pouch she retrieved charcoal.

"Quick. Swallow the charcoal. And drink this," she said. "It's brandy."

"Even in this reality, you have alcohol," Claus said.

"Don't talk. Take the medicine!" she urged.

Claus did so.

"Not used to brandy. It has a bite," he said.

"Really? Let me try," she said.

Clausetta took a big gulp.

"Seems smooth to me," she said.

Clausetta returned the brandy to her pouch.

"Don't sit anywhere. I'll finish harvesting in a moment," she said.

Clausetta carefully placed the gloves back on her hands and resumed picking foxglove leaves. Claus stared into the distance and saw groups of birds flying in various places. He looked for the ground and thought he saw swirls of yellow and blue eddies. Small features took on halos, and he felt dizzy.

"We'd better go back down," he said. "I'm losing my balance."

Clausetta finished picking the leaves and placed her gloves in a different sack.

"I'll clean my gloves later," she said. "Let's get you back to the village."

The two started their return down the mountain. They had just rounded a blind bend when they were startled.

"I see you brought your daughter along," said a familiar voice sitting in an ornate chair.

"Lanietta!" Claus said with a start.

"Aunt Lanietta, what are you doing here?" Clausetta asked.

"That would be my question for you. Spying on your father, I see?"

"She is not spying," Claus said. "She helped me see flowers that Claude had cultivated, and suddenly we arrived here. But answer my daughter's question. What *are* you doing here?"

"Watching you two," she said. "Look at this chair. Isn't it divine? Notice the intricate metalwork and the inlaid gems. Fit for a queen."

"I'm not interested in your chair," Claus said. "I nearly fell off the mountain when I sat on a pile of rocks."

"That should be a lesson for all," Lanietta said. "Never sit on a pile of rocks when a proper chair will do."

"I'll try it," Clausetta said.

"Clausetta, no," Claus said. "I don't trust Lanietta. She's up to something."

"Really now. How can a chair cause harm? Do you expect it to break? I'm sitting in it now. It's sturdy," Lanietta said.

Lanietta stood up. Claus started to topple over from his foxglove poisoning, but Lanietta caught him.

"You should be careful what you touch," she said. "Some things are meant to be left alone."

Lanietta drew a finger across the skin on his arm, and Claus felt the poison drawn away.

"Feel better?" Lanietta asked.

"Yes," Claus said suspiciously. "Maybe you created the situation so you could rescue me from being poisoned."

"I wasn't the one who sat on a pile of rocks," Lanietta said. "Look. Your daughter has taken a liking to the chair."

"Oh, it's so comfortable. Don't I look like royalty, Pappa?" Clausetta said.

Claus looked at Clausetta, and he saw a halo over her head.

"There's a halo over her head. What have you done to her?" Claus demanded to know.

"There's no halo. The last bit of foxglove poisoning has affected your vision. You'll see normally in a moment. Look at her now," Lanietta said.

"The halo is gone," he said.

"See?"

"Can we keep the chair, Aunt Lanietta?" Clausetta asked.

"No," Claus said. "Probably poisoned."

Lanietta and Clausetta laughed.

"You're paranoid," Lanietta said. "Clausetta, you may have the chair. This particular one is special. It responds to your command. You can command the legs to flex and move like a pony. You can also command it to grow into the size of a horse or a carriage."

"Really? Pappa needs a ride down the mountain," Clausetta said.

"Then command it," Lanietta said.

"How?"

"Go eethi and meld your arms with the armrests. It will respond," Lanietta said.

"No. No going eethi. It's a trap," Claus said.

Claus moved to pull Clausetta from the chair, but he felt weak and fell to his knees.

"I thought you pulled the poison from me," Claus said to Lanietta.

"I did, but you are still weak and will need to recover. Accept the generosity of the moment instead of adding more misery to the world with your petty fights," Lanietta said.

"I'm not petty. You're petty," Claus said.

"No you," Lanietta said.

"You."

"You!"

"Stop!" Clausetta said.

Lanietta and Claus stared at each other, eye to eye. But Clausetta broke their gaze, and they turned to see she had commanded the chair into a cart of four pairs of long legs (each corner containing a front and back leg). If one could imagine a four-legged chair in front connected by structural support to a four-legged bench in back, this then resembled the cart. Clausetta sat on the chair, and Lanietta helped Claus onto that bench. Lanietta sat next to him.

"We're ready," Lanietta said.

"Thank you, Aunt Lanietta. We'll take care of you, Pappa," Clausetta said, and she commanded the cart forward.

"When are we going to leave?" Claus asked.

Clausetta laughed.

"We are in motion. Clausetta's command of the cart is so smooth that you cannot perceive the movement," Lanietta said.

"I thought it would be like riding a big horse," Claus said.

"Clausetta is Carinian. She's superior," Lanietta said.

"Don't say that too loudly. I don't want her getting ideas," Claus said.

"I can hear everything you two are saying," Clausetta laughed.

"See? You're giving her ideas," Claus said.

"I've already taught her much. Someone had to. Her father was out of the picture for twenty-five years," Lanietta said.

"That wasn't my fault," Claus said.

"They all say that," Lanietta said. "Why do you look over the side? Do you intend to jump?"

"I don't trust chairs around you," Claus said. "They have a death connotation."

"Oh, I'm over that," Lanietta said. "I've turned over a new Leif."

"You aren't talking about my son, are you?" Claus asked.

"Very well. I've turned over a new Clausetta," Lanietta said.

Clausetta laughed at the joke.

"Not funny," Claus said.

"Your daughter has collected foxglove for the community. Many with weak hearts will be given new life," Lanietta said.

"Aunt Lanietta, will you tell us a story?" Clausetta asked.

"Of course," Lanietta said. "Let me tell you about the woman who ran an empty cemetery."

"An empty cemetery? If it's empty, there are no dead people. How can it be a cemetery?" Claus asked.

"Now, now. You're interrupting. That's rude," Lanietta said. "I'll tell the story first, then you may be rude with your silly questions."

"Pappa, you are too silly!" Clausetta laughed.

"I'm outnumbered," Claus muttered.

"Now it turned out she lived among people who were not old and were careful to avoid accidents, and so there were no funeral ceremonies," Lanietta said.

"Then the woman should have quit and found a new job," Claus said.

"Shh!" Clausetta said.

"My own daughter is shushing me?" Claus complained. "Clausetta, don't you think the woman should have quit?"

"I've heard the story, and she's not a woman," Clausetta said.

"You've heard the story?" Claus wondered.

"Mamma told me," Clausetta said.

"It's true. I lied. She wasn't a woman—yet," Lanietta said. "She was an older girl and nearly a woman. But as it turned out, she became a woman while running the cemetery."

"This story is going nowhere," Claus said.

"Pappa, please!" Clausetta said.

"If you were a woman, you'd have more interest," Lanietta said. "I suppose you'd rather hear about an airport with a hangar full of vintage airplanes. Well there's none of that here. No one warned this girl about womanhood. It happened to her while she was dusting the caskets."

"Dusting the caskets? No one keeps caskets at a cemetery," Claus said.

"It was a small village. The funeral chapel was a part of the cemetery. Also headstones were made there. In fact her mother taught her the trade, but her mother was captured by selenites and forced to raid human communities fortified by bamboophi. But that's another story," Lanietta said. "She was dusting the caskets when womanhood hit. It made a mess, understandably, but the girl who was now a woman was very distraught. She thought she had lost a baby."

"No. You're making this up," Claus said.

"No she isn't. You mean she never told you this story?" Clausetta asked.

"Who?" Claus asked.

"Ah-ah-ah! No names yet!" Lanietta said. "Now the woman placed the mess in the casket, and she had it buried in a full funeral ceremony, complete with headstone. She named her baby Rouge."

"But it wasn't a baby," Claus said. "It was just her cycle."

"No one told her," Lanietta said. "In fact no one understood."

"That makes no sense," Claus said.

"A month passed, and again she was dusting. She felt the moment approach, and she jumped into the casket so as to attach her newly deceased baby into the casket directly," Lanietta said.

"It wasn't a baby!" Claus said.

"She had another funeral ceremony, and she named this baby 'Rouge 2'," Lanietta said. "Losing two in a row was devastating. But she was shocked when it happened again after another month. Another funeral ceremony. Another headstone, and this one was named 'Rouge 3'. Still the people accepted her loss, but she was becoming quite disturbed. She was convinced she was possessed by a demon that caused and killed babies. She became fearful when the next month came, it did, and Rouge 4 was buried."

"This is insanity. No one died!" Claus said.

"This went on for many years. The people decided though that something was wrong, and she was sent to a selenite ship. Turns out the people of her village *were* selenites and so of course did not understand that she was cycling and not having babies. It wasn't until she conversed with a fellow prisoner on the selenite ship that she learned about the monthly cycle. Yes, Selba told the woman."

"Clover?" Claus asked.

"Clover," Lanietta said.

"I never knew. She never told me," Claus said.

"And why would she? She was embarrassed about the whole affair. Which wasn't an affair at all. But still, Selba tells me that often Clover confided that she had flashbacks about burying those children, that they were the closest things she had to children, and that if she had to do it over again, she would have rather buried those children than been told straight off about the monthly cycle, be deprived, and have no memories at all."

"Sad but beautiful," Clausetta said.

"I don't understand anything," Claus said. "It was all a mistake. A big mistake."

"Pappa!" Clausetta protested.

"No, let him think that way," Lanietta said. "Who is to say how many children a woman might have? How many a woman might have had? How many a woman will never have!"

Clausetta started to cry.

"See? Look what you've done!" Claus said to Lanietta.

"I want another baby!" Clausetta said. "I want Sergio!"

"Lanietta. Leave my daughter out of this!" Claus said.

"She has her own mind and will. It's up to her to decide, not you," Lanietta said.

"It's not up to you, either. Not that you will ever have any," Claus said.

"Pappa!" Clausetta said in shock, going straight from sadness to anger. "You never say that to a woman. Ever! Apologize! Hurry!"

Claus paused.

"Well?" Lanietta asked. "Are you going to do it? Are you man enough? I know you're not woman enough."

"I apologize," Claus gritted.

"Like you mean it, Pappa!" Clausetta said.

"I take back my words. They were cruel and uncalled for," Claus said.

"Better," Clausetta said. "That was horrible. Let's talk about something else."

"Yes, like Claude's flower garden," Lanietta said.

"You know about it?" Clausetta asked. "He's cultivated wonderful flowers."

"He also planted a tree just outside the greenhouse," Lanietta said.

"Yes! It's growing remarkably fast," Clausetta said.

"With leaves of yellow and blue," Lanietta said.

"Lanietta! What are you driving at?" Claus asked.

"Oh, nothing," Lanietta said.

"It does have leaves of yellow and blue. It's the only tree like that," Clausetta said with bemusement.

"Because he's your child, that's why," Lanietta said.

"Stop it, Lanietta," Claus said.

"Stop what? I'm merely making an observation," Lanietta said.

"How is that even possible? You haven't seen his greenhouse or his tree," Claus said.

"Neither have you. You're blind," Lanietta said.

"Clausetta helped me see," Claus said.

"As she helped me see," Lanietta said.

"I did?" Clausetta asked.

"Keep your eethi paws off my daughter!" Claus said.

"Oh, I have no power over your daughter," Lanietta laughed. "But the eethi is like a place full of echoes. One person speaks, and others hear. Clausetta showed you the garden by going eethi, and I saw the ethereal echoes, or rather the *eechoes*."

"Is nothing private?" Claus asked.

"Aunt Lanietta is right," Clausetta said. "She told Leif and me once that if we ever get into trouble, just yell into the ether, and she'll come help."

"Some help," Claus muttered.

"Pappa!" Clausetta exclaimed.

"Oh, all right. I'll try to behave. Just doesn't seem right somehow," Claus said. "What about the tree?"

"It's better than a pile of rocks," Lanietta said. "Do you know why?"

"Because I don't have to worry about the tree falling off the mountain when I sit on it," Claus said.

Lanietta and Clausetta laughed.

"I hadn't thought of that," Lanietta said.

"Pappa, you're so silly!" Clausetta said.

"Then what is the answer?" Claus asked.

"A tree starts from a central base, and it branches outward where need drives it. No matter how big and how tall the branches, it can support those branches," Lanietta said. "But you know what's even more impressive about the tree that the rocks don't have? The tree has an extensive root system. The rocks have nothing."

"That's hardly a story," Claus said.

"Your friend Frieda is the equivalent of a pile of rocks with her cubics. But I'm building an ethereal tree. Or at least I will build one," Lanietta said.

"That's definitely not a story. You're scheming again. Fess up, Lanietta. What are you up to?" Claus asked.

"I just told you. But I won't bore you with details. When the time is right, you'll know," Lanietta said.

"You mean when it's too late to stop you," Claus said.

"Don't ever try to stop me. Well, you can try, but it will do you no good. Remember what I told you. I don't always have the luxury of explanation. I must often act swiftly with no accountability to you or anyone else," Lanietta said.

"I want to be like that someday," Clausetta said. "I want to do what I want without having to explain myself."

"Don't put ideas in my daughter's head," Claus said.

"You've said that before," Lanietta said.

"It bears repeating," Claus said.

"Like the boring pile of rocks. A tree is more innovative, more binding," Lanietta said. "Take the roots, for example."

"Yes, the roots!" Clausetta said. "They are unseen, but they can go deep for water."

"They can make their way through rock, through roads, buildings, sewage pipes—all kinds of things," Lanietta said. "And all the while, they remain hidden. One conveniently forgets they exist at all."

"So I should be a tree and root down somewhere?" Claus asked. "I don't follow."

"Don't worry about it," Lanietta said. "Well, we are almost there. Did you know that this cart can be changed into a tree?"

"Really? Let me try!" Clausetta said.

"It's really quite easy," Lanietta said.

"You'd better let me off first," Claus said. "I don't want to be stabbed in the back by a stray branch."

"How cowardly of you," Lanietta said. "Very well. Stop the cart and let Pappa out."

Clausetta stopped. Claus jumped off and stood a good distance away.

"Are you afraid the cart will attack you? Tsk, tsk," Lanietta said.

"So how do I do it? How do I make it a tree?" Clausetta asked.

"Just go eethi a little bit more," Lanietta said.

"What do you mean by 'a little bit more'?" Claus asked.

"I had to go eethi a little bit just to control the cart," Clausetta said.

"That's not good for you. Could give you eethi psychosis," Claus said.

"You sound like an overly-protective parent," Lanietta said. "I've taught Clausetta all about eethi psychosis. She'll hardly get it from a chair! Now then, concentrate. Go eethi more. I will too and show you the way."

Suddenly, the legs sprouted roots that ran deep, the legs themselves became thick trunks, and branches from those trunks shot the cart upward like the beginnings of a tree house. Leaves fully adorned this plant, and both Clausetta and Lanietta waved from the remnants of the cart now perched on this foliage monster. Claus laughed.

"What's so funny?" Lanietta asked.

"That's not a tree. It's a shrub!" Claus continued to laugh.

Lanietta space-jumped down and was about to choke Claus. But Clausetta also space-jumped down and intervened.

"Please, Aunt Lanietta. He didn't mean it. Here, I'll fix everything," Clausetta said.

Clausetta went eethi, melded with the shrub, and unified the eight trunks into one, converting the shrub into a tree.

"See? All better," Clausetta said.

Now Claus was angry and Lanietta was the cheerful one.

"Did you teach her that?" Claus said with continued anger.

"No. She learned that one on her own," Lanietta said with glee.

"I'm not impressed. People should know their limits," Claus said.

"Ah, no. Every man should know his limits. Women should continue the way," Lanietta said.

"I like that, Aunt Lanietta," Clausetta giggled.

"Will you quit calling her that? She's not a proper aunt," Claus said.

"No gratitude," Lanietta said. "Let's get the foxglove to the apothecary."

"Who is running this show?" Claus asked. "This reality started off with just Clausetta and me. No one invited you."

"How rude," Lanietta said. "I was here all along. You just didn't see me. Like roots of a tree."

"Like roots of a tree to trip me as I walk," Claus said.

"Pappa, please!" Clausetta begged. "We must hurry with the foxglove."

Clausetta ran with the sack of foxglove.

"We must run too," Lanietta said.

"What? Run?" Claus protested.

"Now!" Lanietta insisted.

Lanietta ran after Clausetta. Claus made half an effort to run, but the two quickly ran out of sight, and Claus found himself alone.

"Now what?" he asked himself.

There was only one thing to do. Walk onward. He did and came upon a town, like something from the Old West. There were hitching posts, watering troughs, and the usual building facades, but there were no people and no horses. The town was dead quiet.

"Where did they go? And who are all these people needing foxglove?" Claus asked himself.

He looked around and saw a cinema. It read, "Now playing: *The Forgotten Sapling.*"

Chapter 126: The Forgotten Sapling

"People will be in there for sure. A cinema would never show a movie without people," Claus said.

Claus walked inside the cinema. It was empty. He saw no clerks for selling tickets. But he did see a set of turnstiles between him and the concession stand (which also had no people).

"Abandoned," he said. "An abandoned movie theater."

He placed a hand on one of several pylons that held up restraining ropes.

"Handprint accepted. Charging for one ticket," a voice from the pylon said.

To Claus's surprise, the pylon printed out a ticket.

"Self-serve?" he wondered. "Oh well. Maybe everyone is inside watching the movie."

Claus took the ticket and fed it into a receptacle on a turnstile. The turnstile allowed him to pass. He walked up to the concession stand and saw a pylon at each of several stations.

"I wonder," he said.

He placed his hand on one of these pylons.

"Handprint accepted. State request," a voice from the pylon said.

"I would like a large popcorn with butter, a large cola, and a bag of chocolates," Claus said.

"Charging to handprint. Order complete. Please take items," the voice said.

A dispenser produced popcorn, a cola, and a bag of chocolates on the concession stand's counter. Claus took them and headed down the hallway.

"Small cinema. Only one screen, it appears, and it's up ahead," he said to himself.

Claus walked into the screening area. There were rows and rows of seats. They were empty. There was still enough light for Claus to see, and he took a moment to look around.

"What a mess. There are containers of popcorn and drinks everywhere. It's like people put them in their cup holders and suddenly left," Claus said.

A curtain opened, and the lights dimmed.

"The movie will show? Without people?" Claus wondered.

The curtain finished opening, and previews for other movies displayed.

"Must be automated. No, wait, I'm a person. I bought a ticket. It knows I'm here to watch. So the show is for me. I'd better sit down," Claus said.

Claus picked a seat. It squeaked.

"A squeaky chair? I'll sit next to it," Claus said.

The next seat also squeaked.

"Not well maintained," he said. "I'll just sit here and not move."

But the seat suddenly kicked out into recline mode.

"What the...a trick seat?" Claus wondered.

Claus tried to get the seat to sit more upright, but it resisted. He struggled and struggled without effect. But it suddenly gave way and sat upright, causing Claus to knock over his popcorn and cola.

"Oh, now *I've* made a mess!" Claus said.

He retrieved his container of popcorn that had a bit of unspilled popcorn inside, but the cola had completely emptied.

"Guess I'll have to get another cola after the movie," he said as he munched on the popcorn.

The movie opened with a scene of a tree seed with wings gliding on the wind like a bird of prey catching a thermal. Occasionally it flapped its wings to gain altitude. The seed flew along mountains, it flew by waterfalls, it flew by many other trees, it flew by lakes, and it flew with a flock of birds. Claus noticed during this opening scene that there was a rustling and an eating of popcorn in other seats.

"Who is here?" Claus asked. "I didn't see you come in."

But no one answered.

"So strange!" Claus said.

Claus heard other chairs squeaking as if people were sitting down or getting up. Yet there was no sound of footsteps or other indication of people on the floor.

"I'll have to be careful," he said to himself.

The movie continued with the flock of birds flying off and the seed joining up with a group of parachute seeds. The parachute seeds headed for a mountain.

"Come with us to the mountain," the parachute seeds said. "We will be safe and thrive above all else."

Claus was shocked that seeds were portrayed as speaking. But this was a strange movie in a strange place, so he let the issue slide.

"I want to see more of the world," the flying seed said. "Mountains don't move, and I want to move."

"You can't move forever," the parachute seeds said. "You must take root and start your life as a tree."

"Never," the seed said. "I'll never take root!"

The parachute seeds dropped to a mountain. Many clumped together and did nothing. The rare one or two found a place that they could possibly grow.

"Most of them will perish anyway!" the flying seed said. "I don't want to die. I want to live forever!"

Suddenly, there was clacking of wood together in seats next to Claus. Indeed, his own seat started moving on its own. Claus jumped out of his seat and stood in the aisle.

"Who is in here?" he called again.

But no reply. Claus checked seat after seat, looking in the dim light and probing with his hand, but he found no one.

"This is weird," he said. "Is it safe to sit?"

Claus decided to rest on a railing in front of one row of seats. The movie continued.

"Little seed, little seed, where are you going?" a passing robin asked.

"Wherever I want," the seed replied.

"You can't fly forever. You'll have to take root," the robin said.

"That's what the parachute seeds said. But I'm independent. I do whatever I want."

"Even seeds must sleep sometime," the bird said.

"I'll never sleep. I'll fly forever and ever!" the seed said. "What are you doing up here? Shouldn't you be looking for worms?"

"The worms are deep underground. But they'll come out when it rains. They always do. I have a special sense for water. I can smell it. Where there's water, there are worms. And where there are worms, there's rich soil, soil that's perfect for little seeds to grow. Follow me, and I'll show you fertile ground," the robin said.

"No. I'm flying forever," the seed said.

"Last chance. I see a puddle of water," the robin said.

"Farewell. Enjoy your worms," the seed said.

"I will. Good luck to you too," the robin said, and it flew down.

"I'm a seed. I'm independent. I'll fly forever and never set down roots," the seed said.

Night came. The leading wind of a storm carried the seed high in the sky, so high that it got very cold, cold enough for water to freeze. The flying seed shivered and fought to fly lower, but the wind drew it ever higher.

"Oh, this is miserable. I wish I had followed that robin down. Now I'm stuck high in the sky!" the seed lamented.

Water came down from thunderclouds, and as everyone knows, water has a way of drugging a seed into doing something it doesn't want to do—grow.

"Oh, the water is making me drunk with growth. I'm growing roots. I don't want to grow roots. My wings are shrinking. I...I..."

But the seed was helpless. The water-covered seed was carried up by a sudden gust, and the water froze. The seed then was caught up in a growing group of hail.

"Help, help!" the seed cried out. "I'm trapped in this ice!"

"Help, help!" the hailstones laughed. "You belong to us now. We'll smash you against whatever we want, wherever we go. You'll melt with us and disappear. Disappear forever!"

"No. I want to live forever. I want to fly again. Please, don't let me smash. Please don't..." the seed cried.

But the seed could no longer speak. The ice had prevented it, allowing the seed only to watch.

While this part of the movie went on, Claus could swear he heard gasps around him, or was it the chairs suddenly releasing their springs? He wasn't sure. But again something told him he wasn't the only one watching the movie.

"Lanietta! Are you in here? You always show up in strange places!" Claus said.

All Claus got in return were numerous chair squeaks, as if they were squeaking for him to be quiet. Claus continued watching the movie. The hailstones descended on a grove of trees. These hailstones didn't just fall to the ground and be done with it. They were organized. They went from one tree to another as a swarm, breaking off branches and stripping off leaves. Wind was fierce, and the trees lashed back at the hailstones in self-defense, but like animals overrun by a swarm of bees, each tree could not stop the onslaught.

"Hah, hah! This is lots of fun!" the hailstones cheered.

The flying seed could only watch in horror as he was forced to participate in this attack. The hailstone swarm carved a path to the grove until it reached the largest tree of all—a great cypress. Tall the cypress was, with a great girth. The hailstones went after the branches up high, but the tree's needles were too thin for the

hailstones to grab onto, and so the hailstones passed through without causing damage. The hailstones tried pushing on one side of the cypress, but it remained fast.

"You can't push this tree over," Claus said.

Squeaks around him shushed him. The hail swarm split into groups of yellow and blue. Those groups themselves split such that there were two yellow groups and two blue groups. The wind grew fierce, but it did not blow in one continuous direction. In fact, the hailstones seemed to command the wind and use the wind to direct their activities. A yellow group took to the cypress's upper east side, a blue group took to the cypress's upper west side, the second yellow group took to the cypress's ground-level west side, and the second blue group took to the cypress's ground-level east side. In this way, color pairs were diametrically opposed on the cypress. The colors at the top alternated in pushing, and so when the upper yellow pushed, the upper blue yielded while at the same time the lower yellow pelted against the base like a jackhammer while the blue yielded. Then the yellow yielded while the blue pushed and pelted. This caused a rocking motion in the cypress, and though the base was weakened, it was not broken off. However, the weakened base did allow the cypress to rock back and forth much farther than normal, and in time the hailstones forced the cypress over to one side, where its own weight was used against it to uproot itself.

The uprooting also broke open soft spots in the cypress's trunk. The remaining hailstones pelted these openings and destroyed the inner core.

Claus heard what sounded like groans in the cinema. He tried not to pay attention to that and instead focused on the movie. The wind died down, the hail stopped, and the sun came out. The hail melted away, and the flying seed was freed.

"Cypress tree. Cypress tree! Can you hear me?" the flying seed asked.

But the cypress tree simply groaned in pain.

"I am finished," the cypress tree said, and it died.

"No! You can't die now. No!" the flying seed cried.

The flying seed could no longer fly. It had a short, stubby root that could not grow because the flying seed was stuck inside the cypress tree and not on soil. The flying seed watched as day passed, night came, night passed, and day came.

"I'm a prisoner in here," he said. "I'm trapped in this old cypress."

"This is weird," Claus said.

More squeaks around Claus as if he were being hushed.

Another storm passed, and it rained. Water flowed into the cypress's core, and the flying seed was drugged with growth. That and the fact that insects had bored into the cypress's core and made their own soil meant the flying seed no longer had a choice. He grew inside the cypress's core. Claus heard what sounded like groans of disgust around him.

"These are just plants. It's not like cannibalism," Claus said.

Now there was a clattering around Claus as if wooden seats clacked open and closed.

"Sorry I said that," Claus said.

But the movie had become just that. The flying seed became a forgotten sapling, keeping its leaves hidden in the cypress's core such that it gathered light from the occasional hole while its roots burrowed into the core, going through rings and rings of tree growth and thus memories of the past. The forgotten sapling then experienced one of those past memories.

The cypress was but a little seed and still attached to its parent tree. The other seeds had flown off, leaving the seed as the last.

"Your siblings have flown away," the mother cypress tree said.

"I want to stay with you," the cypress seed said. "I want to help you rule the forest."

The mother cypress tree laughed.

"I do not rule the forest. But I do keep watch of my area. You must find your own place too. Your siblings have chosen a new swamp. Go join them and grow quickly," the mother cypress said.

"I don't want to grow in a swamp," the cypress seed said. "That's too low. I want to rule over the forest with you."

"You will grow quickly in the swamp. You will be as tall as your siblings. There will be much water and no fire. You'll be happy," the mother cypress said. "Mountain life is difficult. You will grow slowly. Water will be scarce. And you will be closer to terrible storms with wind that can blow you over or lightning that can split you in half and set you ablaze."

"We're in the mountain. I like it here," the cypress seed said.

The mother cypress smiled (if such a thing is possible).

"I will protect you for a little while," the mother cypress said. "But you must be ready to fly off. Promise me you will fly off if I tell you."

"I promise," the cypress seed said.

"Look, my baby cypress. My needles are still green. But trees around me are changing into colors yellow, orange, and red. Aren't they beautiful?"

"They are," the cypress seed said. "Will I be like that someday?"

"No. You will have needles like me. They will stay green all year round," the mother cypress said.

"But...you never change? You don't become beautiful?" the cypress seed asked.

"I stay green and alive. I'm evergreen. Keep watching, baby cypress. Keep watching the trees around us."

The cypress seed watched for day after day. Soon he was surprised to learn that these colored leaves fell off.

"What's happening?" the cypress seed asked. "Are the trees dying?"

"Maybe. Maybe not," the mother cypress said. "Most go to sleep for the winter. In spring, they will grow leaves and be happy again. But some do not get their leaves back. They go to sleep and never awaken. Those will die."

The cypress seed cried.

"Don't cry. You'll grow roots too soon from the tears. Be happy you are a cypress and will be evergreen," the mother cypress said.

"Do the trees know they will die?" the cypress seed asked.

"No. They all believe they are going to sleep for the winter," the mother said.

"I must warn them. I must warn them they could die!" the baby cypress said. "Maybe I can help them!"

"You cannot help them. No one knows which ones will die," the mother said.

"What about you? Will you die?"

"I might. But we live for many thousands of years. We will watch many trees pass before our time comes. No one knows what will cause it. Could be creepy, crawly bugs burrowing into our bark. Could be a storm. Could be other things. Do not worry about the time. Bathe in the sunlight, dig deep for water, and enjoy the world around you," the mother said.

The cypress seed watched as the last leaves fell from the deciduous trees. They looked terribly bare and stickly. He shuddered to think how many of them would die.

"They look dead. They must be dead. How can any tree come back to life?" the cypress seed asked.

"They will. You must believe that they will," she said.

Snow came, and the cypress seed marveled at the blankets of white.

"You're not green anymore!" the cypress seed said. "You're all white!"

"It is snow, baby cypress. See how it covers me? Watch!"

The mother cypress shook her limbs, and the snow from her branches fell off.

"You're green again!" the cypress seed said.

"Of course! It was just snow. It falls off or melts. But it's winter now. The snow will stay for a time yet," the mother said.

"Will it make you die?" the cypress seed asked.

"No. Not snow. I'm too hardy for that. I've survived many things, baby cypress. Storm, fire, bugs, drought, and animals," the mother cypress said.

"You'll live forever!" the cypress seed said.

"I hope so," mother cypress laughed.

Just then, two men climbed up the mountain, each with an ax, rope, and a sled.

"Look at this one," said the first man, referring to the mother cypress tree.

"It's too big. It would take a lifetime to cut down," said the second.

"Someday, I will find a way," said the first.

"Let's go for the little stuff," said the second.

The men cut down smaller trees, loaded the timbers on their sleds, and hauled their sleds down the mountain.

"There is one other danger," the mother cypress said. "Men."

"They cut down those little trees!" the cypress seed said.

"Yes. Smaller trees become easy prey for men," the mother cypress said. "I have seen them chop down trees farther down the mountain. I've never seen them this high up."

"They won't kill you, will they?" the cypress seed asked.

"Not by the ax," she said. "Not unless many of them chop for season after season."

"We must stop them!" the cypress seed said.

"To stop your enemy, you must know your enemy," the mother cypress said.

"How do I do that?" the cypress seed asked.

"There is one thing you might try. It's very dangerous, and it might kill you. But if you really want to find out, I can fling you into the air, and you can glide down to their village. Land on a roof. Then when you are ready to come back, let the wind carry you to a chimney. The hot air will carry you up, and you can sail back here," the mother cypress said.

The cypress seed paused for a moment.

"It sounds scary," the cypress seed said. "I...I don't know if..."

There were oscillations in the audience with Claus as if they were cheering the cypress seed on.

"Do it?" Claus wondered to himself.

"Yes. I'll do it," the cypress said as if hearing Claus.

"In case you don't make it back, I want you to know something, baby cypress. Your name is Gahoosaweel. And my name is Cyparessa. Remember this," the mother cypress said.

"I will," the cypress seed said.

"Ready? One, two, three!" the mother cypress called, and she flung the cypress seed toward the men.

Gahoosaweel glided in the air down the mountain as he followed the men back to their village. They lived in the valley, and their village contained many dome-shaped structures of flexible branch covered in reeds, which themselves formed a circle around a main gathering area. Gahoosaweel landed on one of these dome structures near the central opening at the top. He was close enough such that he could hear and peer in without the hot air from a fire carrying him off. He could also see the center of the village. Looking inside the hut, he saw a woman with many jars of herbs, a table with tools for cutting and crushing those herbs, and several small pots over a fire where she was brewing herbal somethings. He could smell the herbs and was enchanted by the minty aromas, like being in a paradise of other evergreens. Just then, another woman entered the hut.

"Pratheca! I need spirits!" the woman said.

"Ambloosa! Over in the cupboard," Pratheca said. "Light berry on top, or—"

"I need the heavy stuff," Ambloosa said.

"At the bottom. It has no flavor, but you can start a fire with it. Hey, careful!" Pratheca warned.

Ambloosa took a shot of high-percentage alcohol, and she grimaced as she swallowed.

"Bad day in surgery?" Pratheca asked.

"The worst. My patient bled to death. Just couldn't stop the bleeding. A pile of rocks fell atop her and crushed her. I wish you had something to stop bleeding. You are the apothecary, aren't you?" Ambloosa asked.

"I'm the only apothecary in these parts," Pratheca said. "Just as you're the only doctor in these parts, Ambloosa."

"You have herbs for blood pressure, for bee stings, for pain, for fever, for—"

"All sorts of things. There are only so many herbs I can find around the village," Pratheca said.

"What about those mountains?" Ambloosa asked. "All sorts of things growing there."

"Yes. Then your Pratheca falls off the mountain and bleeds to death," Pratheca said.

"I didn't mean it like that," Ambloosa said.

"It's too dangerous," Pratheca said. "Besides, I have people begging for medicine every day. I can't keep up. Need to hire an assistant. I don't have time to hike up a mountain."

Another woman walked in.

"I cut my arm. I think it's infected," the woman said.

"Here. Put this on it," Ambloosa said, and she poured alcohol in the wound.

"Ow! That hurts!" the woman said.

"Don't waste the good stuff," Pratheca said. "Here, Toria. Take this tube and apply a dab three times daily."

"Thank you," Toria said as she took the tube and left.

"You're supposed to be a doctor," Pratheca said. "That booze was no good for her."

"I find booze is anyone's best friend," Ambloosa said.

"Dulls your wits. Keeps you woozy," Pratheca said.

Just then the two heard a great crash. They rushed out to see men destroying a dome hut.

"What are you doing!" Ambloosa shouted. "That's where I treat patients!"

"We need the firewood," men said. "Pickings are slim in the woods."

"Then go farther!" Ambloosa shouted.

"Go farther!" an older man mocked. "Don't push them around, Ambloosa. They are acting under my authority."

"Being the leader of the village doesn't give you the right to destroy the hut of care, Serramonka," Ambloosa said to the older man.

"It does when the hut of care becomes the hut of carelessness, Ambloosa the Boozer!" Serramonka said. "You've killed your last patient."

"I'm the doctor here!" Ambloosa said. "I treat the sick and injured."

"You'll be treated to torture and prison if you don't leave," Serramonka said. "Yes. Leave. Leave now!"

"Serramonka, wait," Pratheca said. "We—"

"Stay out of this, Pratheca. We know you've been feeding Ambloosa's boozing habit. Don't make us destroy your hut too!" Serramonka said.

Pratheca opened her mouth to say something.

"No, don't," Ambloosa said to her. "I'll go."

"But Ambloosa," Pratheca said.

"Help the people. I will go of my own free will," Ambloosa said.

Men encircled Ambloosa and allowed her to go only a certain way—out of the village.

"Her things. Let me get her things," Pratheca said.

"Her things will be destroyed. So that she can do no more harm," Serramonka said.

Ambloosa returned a weak smile to Pratheca and then left the village.

"You'll pay for this, Serramonka!" Pratheca said.

Serramonka laughed. The men dispersed, and people went about their business. The day grew on, and women prepared for dinner. Pratheca walked around the village area, unable to settle herself. Toria approached.

"Thank you for the lotion. It's working. See?" Toria said as she showed her injury to Pratheca.

"It looks better," Pratheca said.

"But you don't," Toria said.

"Sorry. I'm upset about Ambloosa," Pratheca said.

"I saw the whole thing," Toria said. "What are you going to do?"

"I don't know. I want to go after her," Pratheca said.

"If you do, Serramonka will banish you from the village too," Toria said. "Please don't go. Who will take care of us if you do? And the children will miss you. They've been talking about you today. They are looking forward to the show."

"The show? The show!" Pratheca said, suddenly remembering. "I completely forgot. I must get ready. Oh, this is a disaster. Where is my mind? I'll...I'll..."

"Is there anything I can do to help?" Toria asked.

"There is. Follow me to my hut. I have much work to do," Pratheca said.

Gahoosaweel watched as Pratheca led Toria inside the pharmacy hut.

"Ever worked with herbs before?" Pratheca asked.

"No," Toria replied.

"Well I need an assistant. With Ambloosa banished, I'll have my hands full with treating medical cases. Not to mention the fireworks for tonight," Pratheca said. "I need you to go through the herbs and organize them on shelves. I keep my main stores underground so no one can find them. Follow me."

Pratheca led Toria to a back room, and then Pratheca pried up a board that looked to be a part of the normal floor. An opening to a set of stairs revealed itself. Pratheca went down first. Toria followed. When the two reached the bottom, Toria was puzzled.

"I don't understand," she said. "It's pitch black down here."

"One moment," Pratheca said.

Pratheca turned a handle, and several oil lanterns lit up.

"I got tired of lighting them one-by-one, so I made this contraption to light them at the same time," Pratheca said.

Toria marveled at how much space there was but nearly tripped several times over bundles of herbs.

"Yes, that's my problem," Pratheca said. "Gathering herbs is one thing. Refining them and putting them away into usable medicine is another. Toria, I need to get these refined and put away."

"Oh, but how? I know nothing about this sort of thing," Toria said.

"Fortunately, this book over here tells how to do everything," Pratheca said, leading Toria over to a big book mounted on a pedestal. "You can read, right?"

"I can read and write," Toria said.

The two laughed.

"I would have asked you earlier, but this book is a closely guarded secret. Even Ambloosa doesn't know about it. I didn't write it. I found it. But if something happens to me, I need someone to carry on the work. Think you can do that?"

"I'd be honored to," Toria said.

"Good. The book tells you how to do everything. This job will take several months. Maybe longer. I'd start by clearing out a walking path so we can get around. Sorry about everything. I just gave up after a while and piled mess upon mess," Pratheca said.

"Go and make your fireworks. I'll start on things down here," Toria said.

"Thank you. You're a life saver!" Pratheca said. "If you need anything, I'll be upstairs."

Pratheca returned to the hut's main level, leaving Toria to make sense of the mess. The first thing she did was clear a main path around the area. When she did, she realized Pratheca had piled herbs close to the stairs and thus blocked access to more distant areas. Turns out this underground area was the beginnings of a cavern, and there were seemingly boundless amounts of room in those caverns once Toria cleared a path.

"It just takes a little longer to get around. But the space is there," Toria said to herself.

Pile by pile, Toria compared the herb in question against drawings in a book and was then able to identify that herb. She found a pad of paper and a charcoal pencil and used such to label these piles. Gradually, she cleared a path not only around the immediate area but also around several rows of shelving that had been obscured from view.

"These shelves are close to the stairs for easy access. They'll hold finished product. Good. This cellar area was well-designed," Toria said to herself.

Toria discovered a pile of bottles that had apparently fallen off shelves.

"These don't belong here. Best I place them on the shelf. Amazing they haven't broken," Toria said.

Toria noticed the bottles were labeled, as were the shelves.

"Strange," she said. "I'll just put them on the shelf."

But at the bottom of the pile was a cloth covering, like burlap. Toria pulled up the burlap to reveal a long-dead human—completely dried up. Toria shrieked. She went running up the stairs and nearly bowled Pratheca over.

"Good movie, don't you think?" Lanietta's voice said.

Claus looked around and saw Lanietta next to him with a container of buttered popcorn that she was eating.

"What? What are you doing here?" Claus demanded to know.

"I admit the movie was boring up to now, but a dead body—can't help but wonder who did it," Lanietta said.

"You suspect murder?" Claus asked.

"Don't you?" Lanietta asked.

"Lanietta! You set this whole thing up. End it," Claus said.

"And miss the movie? It's just getting good. Want some?" Lanietta said as she offered him popcorn.

"No. Probably poisoned," Claus said.

"I beg your pardon. I would never consume one of the native residents of this village," Lanietta said.

"What is that supposed to mean?" Claus asked.

At that moment, the chairs squeaked and groaned.

"Shh," Lanietta said.

"Who are you to shush me?" Claus asked.

"Not me. They are shushing you," she said.

"Who?"

"The audience here. You are disrupting the movie," Lanietta said.

"You and I are the only ones here. Look around. What do you see?" he asked.

"I see chairs watching, *The Forgotten Sapling*," she said.

"Chairs don't watch movies," Claus said.

"I'm so glad you've self-appointed yourself local deity of the village," Lanietta said sarcastically.

"I'm not sticking around for this. I'm finding Clausetta," Claus said.

"Stay put," Lanietta said.

Simultaneous with Lanietta's command, roots the size of ropes sprouted from the rails and secured Claus to those rails.

"What is this?" Claus asked. "Let me go."

"If you don't shut that trap of yours, I'll have you gagged," she said.

Claus opened his mouth to protest, but two roots sprouted quickly from the rails—one from each side of Claus, and they met just in front of his mouth. They prepared to clamp down over his mouth and gag him. Claus held still.

"Better. If you wish to speak, you may tap your lips together," Lanietta said.

"Not that again!" Claus blurted.

That was a mistake. The roots closed in over Claus's mouth and gagged him. He tried to speak but could not.

"I warned you. Now watch the rest of the movie like a good Clomper," she said.

Claus struggled to get free, but he could not.

"Shh. This is the part where Pratheca realizes her old master was murdered," Lanietta said.

"Please, Toria, slow down!" Pratheca said. "I can't understand a word you are saying."

Toria simply pointed toward the cellar and led the way down. The two reached the old body.

"Oh no," Pratheca said with sadness. "I know these clothes. This is my old master. Here? She disappeared one day and never returned. I remember the day. I searched throughout this cellar and the caverns. It was organized back then, of course. She insisted upon it. But she died over ten years ago. I didn't let things go until a few years ago. Someone put her body here."

Pratheca searched through her master's clothing with a frantic energy, as if looking for a long-lost treasure. She pulled out a small piece of paper.

"This is all that's left," Pratheca said about the paper. "So she did have it with her. Must have been murdered for it."

Both Toria and Claus struggled to ask what she had, but neither could speak—Toria because of her shock, and Claus because of the root gagging him. Then Pratheca and Lanietta spoke at the same time, as did the entire audience of chairs.

"Masilassa, the Master Apothecary, healer of life," they all chanted. "Way and play, save the day. Gather, define, produce. Slather, refine, reduce. She traveled afar, by sun and star. Worked hard all day. No time for play. Masilassa, the Master Apothecary. We miss your care."

To which Pratheca added one more line, "Nothing left but bones and hair."

Toria looked at Pratheca in shock.

"Rather ghoulish statement, don't you think Clomper?" Lanietta asked. "Oh, I forgot about your gag."

Lanietta commanded the root to ungag Claus.

"You may speak now."

"Why are we here?" Claus asked.

Lanietta sighed.

"Back with the gag," she said.

"No, wait! I'll be quiet," Claus said.

Lanietta paused.

"As you wish," she said, and she prevented Claus from being re-gagged.

"What do we do? What do we do?" Toria finally forced out.

"Skull fracture," Pratheca said. "From a blunt instrument, too. Looks like she fought back. Fingernails are ripped off."

"I can't look!" Toria said. "Pratheca! What do we do?"

"What would you do, Clomper?" Lanietta asked.

Claus tapped his lips together.

"Yes, you may speak," she said.

"Pratheca must let the town know. Give Masilassa proper justice," Claus said.

"No, no, no!" Lanietta said. "All wrong!"

"Why? Because the movie does something else?" Claus asked.

"Because the movie does exactly as you suggest," Lanietta said.

"We'll let the town know. Everyone at once. No secrets. It will flush out those who killed her," Pratheca said.

Lanietta snickered.

"Stop laughing," Claus said.

"You didn't tap your lips together. Time-out for you," Lanietta said.

Claus held up an arm to protect his face, but the roots pulled his forearm against his mouth and thus gagged him.

"That paper. What did she have?" Toria asked.

"The paper is what's left of a copy of the master book," Pratheca said. "She carried the copy with her so she could travel to other villages and help them—which she did. Well, she doesn't have the copy. Help me bring a container down here."

"What? No, wait. A container?" Toria said, not sure of what was going on.

"Come on," Pratheca beckoned.

"Come on," Lanietta said as if speaking to Toria.

Toria and Pratheca went upstairs. Pratheca fetched a container the size of a coffee table but very light and strong like plastic ceramic.

"What's that for?" Toria asked.

Lanietta snickered again. Claus tapped his right thumb against his right fingers as if tapping his lips together.

"You wish to speak? You agree with Toria?" Lanietta asked.

Lanietta commanded the root to pull away from Claus's arm. Claus took deep breaths.

"I couldn't breathe!" he said.

"Oh," she said.

"What's the container for?" Claus asked.

"*You* can't figure it out? How disappointing," Lanietta said.

"Stay up here," Pratheca said to Toria.

Toria stayed at the top of the stairs and helped Pratheca with the container down the stairs a bit (Pratheca went down the stairs first). Pratheca reached a point where she called, "I have it, you may let go," and Toria did.

"To show the village?" Claus asked.

"Of course. Took you long enough," Lanietta said. "Especially since it was your idea."

"It wasn't my idea to stuff Masilassa in a small container," Claus said. "I thought a funeral home would go down and bring her up in a casket."

"A funeral home? In this ancient village? I suppose an air conditioned automobile is next. Clomper, how ludicrous!" Lanietta said.

"I'm ready," Pratheca called. "Catch the end as I push it up."

Pratheca pushed the container up the stairs. Toria caught the lead end, lifted it, and the two brought the container into the main pharmacy hut.

"I'll call a town meeting and present Masilassa," Pratheca said.

"She's not in here, is she?" Toria asked.

Pratheca lifted the lid to show how she had folded up the bones and remains. Toria fainted.

"Toria!" Pratheca called as she dropped the lid and went after Toria.

"Toria!" Lanietta called. "You're competing with Clomper for who perceives things the worst."

"I'm not that bad," Claus said.

"You are if I say you are. Now shush. The movie continues," Lanietta said.

"I have a better idea. I'll present the body after the fireworks," Pratheca said.

"Now you're talking, girl. Get up their hopes and crush 'em with a fist of steel!" Lanietta said with such vigor and verve that she pounded her fist against the railing and bent it.

"I...I don't know..." Toria stumbled.

"Coward," Lanietta said.

"If you keep this up, the chairs will squeal at you," Claus said.

The chairs did squeal, but only after Claus spoke.

"See? They only complain about you," Lanietta said. "Double shush now."

"Do I have to be out there when you do that?" Toria asked. "I mean, I could continue organizing in here."

"You would return here after the fireworks and work?" Pratheca asked.

"No. I would stay here during the fireworks too," Toria said.

"Hermit! Closet-lover! Cavewoman!" Lanietta blurted.

"What is wrong with you?" Claus asked, but as expected, the chairs squeaked in response to him and not her.

"Shh," she said.

"Very well," Pratheca said. "We'll hide the container over here behind this curtain. Help me, will you?"

Toria helped Pratheca move the container to a small table behind a curtain.

"Good. Go ahead then with the organizing. But listen for the fireworks. When they end, return upstairs. I'll stop by for the container," Pratheca said.

Toria agreed and then went back into the cellar.

"Now things get interesting," Lanietta said.

"Could you release me? These roots are too tight," Claus said.

"Not until you see more of the movie," Lanietta said.

Toria cleaned up the spot where Masilassa had been. Hidden in a corner was a false door. She bumped up against the false door accidentally and thus revealed its existence.

"What is this?" she asked herself.

Toria opened the door and discovered a stash of filled bottles.

"Otalicin," Toria said, reading the label from a bottle. "This one bottle says it's for soothing and protecting the ears from pain, tinnitus, and loud noises."

Just then, the ground shook and rumbled Toria's confidence to the core.

"What was that?" Toria asked herself with the bottle still in hand.

She rushed up from the cellar, left the pharmacy hut, and watched as fireworks exploded high in the air. She laughed.

"Hah, hah. Toria was scared for nothing!" Lanietta said as she elbowed Claus.

"Wouldn't it be more fun if you could elbow a free me instead of a bound me?" Claus asked.

"Why would I want that? This way you can't move out of the way at the last moment," Lanietta said.

"What if I want to elbow you?" Claus asked.

"A pet elbowing his master? Absurd," she said.

"Why are you calling me 'Clomper' again? I am a father with two children," Claus said. "I'm not a pet."

The chairs reverberated "Clomper, Clomper" in a way that sounded like alien overgrown birds, as if mocking Claus and telling him to be quiet. Lanietta put a finger to her lips to shush Claus. Claus rolled his eyes in disbelief.

Toria watched a few more fireworks. She looked around the village and briefly made eye contact with one of the men, but she thought nothing of it.

"Oh wow, that one was loud!" she said as a firework went off. "I wonder...yes, I should."

Toria bought a beverage from a vendor and used it to wash down an otalicin pill. She waited a few minutes. The fireworks, though just as loud as ever, didn't hurt her ears. She took two rocks and clacked them together by each of her ears.

"Amazing. Total protection from pain," she said. "No wonder they were hidden. I should find a new hidey spot for them."

Toria returned to the pharmacy main level then down into the cellar with the bottle of otalicin still in hand.

"I'll put them all here," she said as she first placed the otalicin bottle from her hand onto a shelf and followed up with the bottles from the stash. "I bet the villagers could use otalicin after the fireworks. Some of those boomers were too loud!"

Just as Toria said, "loud," a shape clocked her on the head from behind. She slumped to the ground, and the shape then pulled her to the side. Two other shapes accompanied the first, and they raided the shelf of otalicin.

"Good for them," Lanietta said.

"What? You don't mean that," Claus said.

"It needed stealing," Lanietta said.

Claus rolled his eyes again in disbelief.

"Those bottles weren't going to steal themselves. Were they?" Lanietta asked. "Have you seen this movie before?"

"Of course I haven't," Claus said.

"Then why roll your eyes at me? The otalicin needed stealing, and it was. Case closed," Lanietta said.

"I've lost my mind," Claus said.

"Where did you leave it?" Lanietta asked.

"On my front doorstep as Frieda jogged by!" Claus said.

Just then the chairs in the cinema clacked as if clapping.

"I'm not sure that's something to applaud," Claus said.

"They are not applauding you. They are applauding Gahoosaweel. Look!" Lanietta said.

Gahoosaweel, with no good way of moving much around, managed to amble over the roof's open hole, fall into the main pharmacy hut, angle his way into the cellar, and dive into an otalicin bottle just as one of the perpetrators opened the bottle to inspect its contents. Gahoosaweel was not noticed.

"This will go with our plans," said one perp. "Masilassa's book says these pills will protect us during the final event."

"Final event? These chairs are cheering a final event? Doesn't sound right," Claus said.

"You don't know the story. Hold on until the end," Lanietta said.

"Don't need to. These roots are holding on for me," Claus said.

Pratheca arrived upstairs.

"Toria? Are you still here? I saved a private batch just for us," Pratheca said. "Some morning glories and a star surprise. Toria?"

Pratheca went into the cellar. To her horror, she saw Toria on the ground, barely moving.

"Toria!" Pratheca said as she went for her.

But Pratheca never made it to Toria. The perps cornered Pratheca, bound her, and gagged her. She tried to scream, but one perp raised his fist as if to beat her over the head. She held still.

"Where are the fireworks?" a perp asked. "We will let you speak, but you must not scream, or it will be the last thing you do."

Pratheca nodded in agreement. The perps ungagged her.

"In a special storage room," Pratheca said. "There's a heavy door at the end of the second row to my right."

One of the perps went down that way and found the fireworks.

"They're here," he called back.

"Good," the main perp said.

"What are you going to do with us?" Pratheca said.

"Toria is worthless to us. We will dispose of her. But your knowledge of fireworks will prove most useful in a vital mission," the main perp said.

"If you kill Toria, I won't help you," Pratheca said.

"Oh you'll help us," the second perp said. "We'll—"

"No," the main perp said. "Take Toria with us. Let Pratheca see that Toria is unharmed."

"But I was promised first torture on Pratheca. And the death of Toria. I shall not be deprived!" the second perp said.

"There will be other people on other missions," the main perp said.

"This job gets worse by the day," the second perp said.

The perps gathered up the otalicin, the fireworks, Toria, and Pratheca. Under cover of night, they headed for the mountains—the very mountains from where Gahoosaweel came. The chairs in the cinema groaned with anxiety.

"Sounds like the boards of this room are about to break," Claus said.

"You do not know the horror that is yet to unfold," Lanietta said.

The perps, Toria, and Pratheca stopped by a rock face.

"Why have we stopped?" Pratheca asked.

"See this rock face?" the main perp said. "It blocks our way to a vast reserve of borax. Look, there's borax on the ground here. See?"

Pratheca touched the white powder and sniffed it.

"I don't understand," Pratheca said.

"It's borax. What's to understand? You're the apothecary. You know the uses of borax," the main perp said.

"I do. That's why I don't understand. You didn't need to steal and kidnap for this," Pratheca said. "Why did you do all this?"

But Pratheca's question was not answered.

"We need to blast through this rock face," the main perp said.

"You didn't answer my question," Pratheca said.

"It will give us access to the borax," the main perp said.

"Why are you ignoring me?" Pratheca asked.

"We'll give you a share of the borax, of course," the main perp continued.

"Why did you kidnap us and steal from us?" Pratheca pressed.

"You can't have all the borax," the main perp said. "Only a share. We have a business to run. You can't meddle in it."

"Is that your way of answering?" Pratheca asked.

"If you like," the main perp said. "We have your fireworks. We need explosives to blast through the rock face. Show us how to do so."

"Release Toria first," Pratheca said.

The second perp nodded in defiance, but the main perp pointed for Toria to be released.

"Go back to the village," Pratheca said to Toria.

Toria, though able to walk, was weak and dizzy. She nodded in agreement but stumbled slowly toward the village.

"There. Total trust," the main perp said. "Will you help us acquire the borax, please? Remember, you get a share."

"This is all so strange!" Pratheca said.

"Others will mine the borax if we don't. It's a matter of who gets what. You *do* have uses for borax, right?" the main perp said.

"Yes, of course. But the village...the people...we can all..."

"Waste borax completely," the main perp finished. "You know how people are. You know how frivolous they become when new things come along. You were brought here for your expertise, to judge the importance of borax proper use. There need be no waste among those with lesser wisdom."

"Very well," Pratheca said.

Pratheca showed how her fireworks could be converted to powerful explosives.

"Excellent," the main perp said. "We need to move you away from here."

"I thought you said part of the borax was mine," Pratheca said.

"We must blast. Can't have you blasted along with the rock," the main perp said.

"Very well," Pratheca found herself saying again.

The second perp took Pratheca a short ways away, but the main perp did not tarry by the rock face and instead headed for a large cypress with the explosives. Unseen to the others, he swallowed otalicin to protect his ears from his explosive plans.

"Cyparessa!" Gahoosaweel shouted, but no one heard.

"Wait, where's he going?" Pratheca asked.

But the second perp did not answer. Instead, he led Pratheca to a place where Toria was being held by a new perp.

"What is this?" Pratheca asked.

"You will see," the second perp said. "See this bottle? You'll beg me for one of these before the day is over."

"What are you going to do?" Pratheca asked with concern.

The second perp laughed and said to the other perp, "It's time. Open your bottle and take a pill."

The second perp popped what he thought was another pill from the bottle into his mouth. The other perp did the same and swallowed his pill. The second perp swallowed, but it wasn't a pill. It was Gahoosaweel. Gahoosaweel was now in the stomach of the second perp. But strangely enough, Gahoosaweel could "see" the world as if he had X-ray vision. The second perp appeared as nearby bones, much like the branches of a tree that one might climb. But Gahoosaweel hadn't climbed a tree. He was still trapped. The other people's bones were visible by Gahoosaweel, but he also saw the outline of their bodies and clothing. It was as if the world had been turned into a ghastly view of greys.

"You lied!" Pratheca said.

At that moment, explosives went off. Gahoosaweel peered into the distance, and with his X-ray vision saw the large tree he knew as his mother become splintered from base to branch.

"Cy-pa-res-sa!" Gahoosaweel cried, but no one heard him.

Pratheca took a branch as a staff and attacked the perp holding Toria. Freed, Toria took a cooking pan from a perp and along with a big metal spoon banged the pan near the second perp. The sound jolted the second perp, and Gahoosaweel watched as the second perp's bones

vibrated. But the second perp simply took more otalicin and thus blocked the auditory pain. Gahoosaweel had a close view of the second perp's bones in action, and several times he felt he might be skewered by a stray rib or elbow.

Pratheca's perp grabbed her branch and pulled her off to the side. He then went over to Toria and pulled her off the second perp. The second perp, upset with the skirmish, took a large stone and crashed it over Toria's skull, killing her. Pratheca heard that dreaded sound of Toria's skull cracking. She was so enraged that she pulled herself to her feet with branch in hand and skewered the second perp. The second perp fell dead. The remaining perp took the second perp's stone and went for Pratheca's skull. He only landed a glancing blow, but it was enough to injure Pratheca and render her unconscious. With three on the ground, and not wishing to answer to what had happened, the remaining perp, one-by-one, dragged the three to a cliff and pushed them over the side into a gully not easily observable by passersby.

The remaining perp then rejoined the main perp at Cyparessa where already shards of her trunk were being harvested as lumber. Gahoosaweel could only hear vague sounds of yelling, chopping, and hauling of wood away. More and more men came to aid the act, the thunderous act, and this act carried on for hours, with Gahoosaweel enduring the torture of it with great agony, knowing that bit by bit, the years of love and experience from his mother were whittled away.

By daybreak it was over. The sounds of harvest had ended, the yelling stopped, and all that remained was a wind clumping Cyparessa's needles together and dragging them across stone and other trees. Fingernails on chalkboard would be pleasant in comparison. Gahoosaweel felt the natural elements were redestroying his mother over and over with this grating of needles.

"I'll go mad! I will!" he repeated.

"Help," Pratheca called in a weak voice.

"Pratheca? You're alive?" Gahoosaweel said.

But Pratheca could not hear him.

"Help," she called again.

Her voice was too weak to be heard. She struggled to crawl along, but she had a bad head injury and could barely manage.

"I must do something," Gahoosaweel said. "If only I could escape this dead man. If only..."

But something strange happened. Remaining otalicin in the perp's stomach mixed with Gahoosaweel. It caused him to grow appendages—a jaw with cutters, wings that doubled as flippers, and a stubby foot. Gahoosaweel used his jaw to cut his way out of the dead perp.

"Cyparessa!" Gahoosaweel called as he rooted his foot into the soil.

Cyparessa was dead. Gahoosaweel felt her remnant roots, as one might watch the last glowing embers of a long-faded campfire.

"What...are you?" Pratheca weakly asked. "Are you a butterfly? Help me. Help me please."

Pratheca reached out for Gahoosaweel, but strength failed her.

"You who have strength, oh little creature of the earth, hear my call for help. Will you call out for me? Find Ambloosa. Fly off and find her," Pratheca said.

Gahoosaweel paused for a moment. He sensed the ground for animal movement—bipedal animal movement. The men were far away, but he sensed softer footsteps. He looked at Pratheca, and she nodded her head.

"Ambloosa," she whispered. "Hurry."

Bipeds had cost Gahoosaweel the life of his mother. He was in no mood for hunting down another. He sought instead for other trees, trees who had the age and wisdom of the mountain. There was the pine tree, the oak tree, the maple tree, the birch, the walnut, and so on, but in all this, Gahoosaweel sensed a large root system far away, like a sleeping thunder awaiting a rumble.

"What is it?" he asked himself.

Gahoosaweel took flight. But not for Ambloosa. He didn't know her whereabouts. Nor was he interested. Cyparessa dominated his focus. He thought she was the greatest force in the universe, and anything as large in the ground as she was in the air had to be related. Perhaps a sister or a cousin. Yes, he'd get answers. He'd get help.

"Cyparessa, I'll avenge your death. With help. The family will come to your aid. The family!" Gahoosaweel called.

Gahoosaweel flew over a rise. On the other side was a large grove of aspens. They whispered in the wind. Their whisperings were so similar in sound and frequency that a back-and-forth consonance and dissonance carried and dissipated. Gahoosaweel was intrigued then disgusted, attracted then repelled, amused then irritated. Frustrated at not knowing what to make of these aspens, he flew to the very center and rooted his foot in the ground.

"Help. Help me avenge my mother's death!" Gahoosaweel said into the soil.

The aspens stopped whispering. All of them.

"You are not one of us," a voice boomed.

"Who are you? Are you the great force in the ground? Are you another cypress?" Gahoosaweel asked.

"I am Aspensella," the voice replied.

"Are you a tree? Can you bend in the wind?" Gahoosaweel asked.

"I am many and one," Aspensella said. "Many above. One below."

"You...you are all these trees?" Gahoosaweel asked.

"I am a great aspen. I appear to be many trees. But we have the same root system," Aspensella said. "You're a cypress seed."

"My mother was killed. Her name was Cyparessa," Gahoosaweel said.

Aspensella paused.

"She was a great tree on the other side of the rise. Older than any other tree of being. Except me," Aspensella said.

"How do I avenge her death?" Gahoosaweel asked. "Can I become immense and powerful like you? I wish to grow the size of a mountain. Crush the living soul out of these bipeds."

"You will grow taller than any of my trees. That will give you vision across time and distance. But it will not give you deep wisdom of the earth. Even a cypress cannot exceed me in that regard. Destroy the bipeds? Is that your answer?" Aspensella asked.

"It must be. You claim to be great. Destroy them for me!" Gahoosaweel said.

"You swat a bug, and seventeen attend its funeral. That is no answer," Aspensella said. "Give them what they want. Not all at once. Just an old trunk here and there. The worst of the worst. Let them think they are getting something golden. You, on the other hand, are just tossing out garbage. Symbiosis."

"I don't understand," Gahoosaweel said.

"Do you, Clomper?" Lanietta asked.

"No, I don't," Claus said.

"Aspensella is a clonal colony," Lanietta said. "One root system with seemingly many trees. But they are all shoots of the same organism. So Aspensella puts the worst shoots on the outside, or shall I say, she dumps unwanted elements of life into the other shoots. Any men happening along will chop those down. Should the happening men venture too far into the clonal colony, well, you can imagine."

"How did you figure this?" Claus asked.

"I'm Lanietta. That's me," she said. "Perhaps I should surround myself with homely girls for you to fight through to reach me. Would you plow a path? Would you fight for your love?"

"Clausetta and Leif are my loves," Claus said. "Their parents are me and—"

"Stop!" Lanietta said.

"I...don't know about symbiosis," Gahoosaweel said. "I just want to stop them."

"I will teach you," Aspensella said. "Never sacrifice yourself, Gahoosaweel. Always sacrifice others."

"You know my name?" Gahoosaweel asked.

"Do you know mine?" Lanietta asked Claus.

"Sassatinassa," Claus said. "Now be my slave and shush."

"I will not! You shush!" Lanietta said.

The chairs clattered and fluttered to shush back Claus and Lanietta.

"See what you've done? You've disturbed the woodwork," Lanietta said.

"It wasn't me, it was you," Claus said.

"You. All you," Lanietta said.

"That's so unfair," Claus said.

"That's so unfair," Gahoosaweel said. "To trick others."

"Before they trick you," Aspensella said. "The trick is not whether or not to trick, but how much. A lot is fraught, a little benign. Start small, grow tall, others fall."

"I want the world to be nice," Gahoosaweel wailed.

"So do we all," Aspensella said. "It's not our call. When evil sprawls, when evil mauls, you can bawl and crawl, or—you can deal with evil all, as I have instructed. Trick before being tricked. The innocent and weak will bend in the wind, but the evil will breed unending, thriving on your little tricks. You will feed them their own evil until they follow their own paths of destruction. Listen little cypress named Gahoosaweel, it is a hard lesson, yes. But you will survive. And you'll have an ally in the process. I, Aspensella, will be your friend of the mountain. Are you ready?"

Gahoosaweel paused.

"I'm ready," he said.

"Dig deep in earth. Touch my roots," Aspensella said.

"It's like a whole new world," Gahoosaweel said as he did so. "I can see water flowing in a brook, ants digging, birds flying, shrubs fighting for leftover scraps of light, and it goes on."

"Yes. It does go on. Do you sense the bipeds?" Aspensella asked.

"Pratheca and Toria. I was just with them," Gahoosaweel said. "And the perp who swallowed me. There's the other biped. She could be Ambloosa. Pratheca asked me to find her. Will Ambloosa help me?"

"Depends on how you present yourself," Aspensella said. "Should you leave here and fly to her as you are, she will think little of you, as a mere seedling. Appeal to her on her level, and she will act otherwise."

"Her level. I must be a biped?" Gahoosaweel asked.

"No. You must create a biped proxy who will act as your outer wall of protection," Aspensella said. "Stay here in safety. I will help you create your proxy. We will travel spiritually. Come along."

Gahoosaweel and Aspensella appeared as ghostly facial images near the perp from where Gahoosaweel had freed himself. Aspensella sent her roots to the perp, pulled him underground, ripped him into little pieces, and absorbed him into her roots.

"The first step is to understand the biped," facial spirit of Aspensella said. "I have absorbed the one who swallowed you. Sense how this life-form survives, how it thinks of move and take, move and take. Never does it wish to set roots, nor can it soak in the energy of sunlight and store this energy in its roots. We will now create your proxy. It will focus on move and take."

Aspensella produced a shoot from the soil, but this shoot changed shape into that of an adult human male, clothed in woven garment and carrying a staff.

"Your proxy will be your reverse and contain your reverse name," Aspensella said. "Therefore, he is Lee-Waso O'Hag."

"I am Lee-Waso," Gahoosaweel said through the man.

"Remember your two functions—move and take. Move by walking or running, and take what you find, whether it be food, tools, or friends," Aspensella said. "Ambloosa is just over the rise. Test your functions with her."

Gahoosaweel sent Lee-Waso over the rise.

"I am Lee-Waso," Gahoosaweel said through the man. "You are my property now. Come to me."

"What? Back off!" Ambloosa said with a spear pointed toward him.

"I move and take," Lee-Waso said. "I move toward you and take you."

"You'd better move on back from where you came! I'm not for the taking!" Ambloosa said.

Lee-Waso walked toward Ambloosa and only stopped when her spear point touched his abdomen.

"One more step, and I'll skewer you!" she said.

But then Lee-Waso's stomach growled.

"Strange," Lee-Waso said. "Your spear is doing this?"

"I'm not feeding you either!" Ambloosa said. "I'm starving myself. Haven't eaten in days!"

"I am Lee-Waso. I move. I take!"

"My spear is not causing your hunger. Go hunt down your own food!" she said.

"If you show me how, I will share with you," Lee-Waso said.

"Very good, Gahoosaweel," Aspensella said. "You have taken the next step in taking. You've learned to negotiate."

"I don't know what that means," Gahoosaweel said.

"It means making a deal with another," Aspensella said.

"Like what you did with me? So I could stay with you? We negotiated?" Gahoosaweel asked.

"Something like that," Aspensella said.

Both Gahoosaweel's and Aspensella's facial spirits followed Lee-Waso, though Ambloosa could not see them. Ambloosa laughed.

"You laugh?" Lee-Waso asked.

"Yes! At you! Who dropped you off and left you on this planet?" she laughed.

"I don't understand," Lee-Waso said.

"Exactly!" she chuckled. "You pretend like you can take me as property."

"You are my property," Lee-Waso said.

"Then you become hungry for the first time," she continued to laugh. "A grown man not knowing about eating. Didn't your mother feed you?"

"My mother?"

"Yeah. Did she drop you off here? From the sky or something? Are you a god cast out?" she laughed.

"No. I am not a god. I am hungry," Lee-Waso said.

"Then why doesn't she feed you?" Ambloosa asked.

"Her name was Cyparessa, and she is dead!" Lee-Waso said.

"I'm sorry," Ambloosa said with her laughter ending. "Death is a tragedy. But it gives you no right demanding me as property. Someone didn't raise you right, and that's a fact."

"I am still hungry," Lee-Waso said. "What is this hunt you mention?"

"No one taught you to hunt? You *are* out of place! Didn't you ever hunt with friends?" Ambloosa asked.

"I have a friend," Lee-Waso said, and he was about to say, "Gahoosaweel," but Aspensella nodded, "No."

"Did he give you food?" Ambloosa asked.

"No, but he can help. I think," Lee-Waso said. "I ask again. Will you help me hunt?"

"I will help on two conditions," Ambloosa said. "First, you share the spoils."

"That I already promised," Lee-Waso said.

"Yes, you did. Second, I'm not your property. Ever," Ambloosa said.

"Ever?"

"Ever!"

"Now what?" Gahoosaweel asked Aspensella.

"You'll have to decide. If you make a promise, you must keep it," Aspensella said.

"Oh, I don't like being caught in something like a promise," Gahoosaweel said.

"No deal," Lee-Waso said. "You are still my property."

"No deal is right! Go starve that-a-way. I'm going this-a-way. And don't follow

me. Or else!" Ambloosa said as she put the point of her spear back into his abdomen.

"I should force her to be my property," Gahoosaweel said.

"If you do, you'll both starve and die," Aspensella said. "Did you think about that?"

"You can make another proxy for me, right?" Gahoosaweel said. "Call him Waso-Lee or something."

"That's not how life works," Aspensella said. "You were part of a rare thing. You were swallowed by a human and took special sense of that human. But you cannot be swallowed like that again. It would kill you. No, Lee-Waso is your only chance for a human proxy."

Ambloosa walked again.

"Wait," Lee-Waso said. "Before you leave, I wish to take your name."

"What?" she turned back in surprise.

"Your name. What is your name? I wish to change my name to yours. To take your name," Lee-Waso said.

"That's not how things work," she said. "Did you steal your name from someone? Is there a real Lee-Waso somewhere else?"

"No. Just me," he said.

"Then stay that way, Lee-Waso. I'm Ambloosa. Nice to meet you. Good luck with hunting," she said, and she disappeared back over the rise.

"Wait," Lee-Waso said. "Ambloosa, wait!"

Lee-Waso ran toward the rise, but when he ran over it, a vine between trees tripped him. Ambloosa had a trap ready. Lee-Waso fell to the ground, stunned, and Ambloosa took the moment to bind his wrists and ankles.

"Don't ever try that again!" Ambloosa said. "I'm not to be hunted. I'm not property. And you're not Ambloosa! I am!"

"Oh the male instinct for acquisition," Lanietta said to Claus. "If you were a real man, you would have conquered me long ago."

"What?" Claus said in shock. "You *want* to be conquered? End this now. Do everything I say. Then you'll be conquered."

"Too easy. I like playing hard-to-get," Lanietta said. "Besides, it's no fun just surrendering. Must make you work for it."

"I'm not working for anything!" Claus said.

"I know," Lanietta lamented. "That's the trouble with Earth men now-a-days."

"The trouble with Earth men? Um, excuse me Miss Carinian oh-so-high-and-mighty, but your kind had a hand in destroying Earth and us Earth men."

"I also created Earth and you Earth men. A pity you all turned out so poorly," Lanietta confessed.

"We're a pity? I'm one of those Earth men! I'm a pity?" Claus said.

"A pity you complain so much," Lanietta said. "Perhaps you should be more like Lee-Waso. Move and take."

"I can do neither!" Claus said. "Your roots prevent me from moving, as they have taken my freedom!"

Lanietta shrugged her shoulders. The movie continued.

"Ambloosa," Lee-Waso said.

"Yeah. I'm Ambloosa. Did Serramonka send you?" she asked.

"No. I am not from your village," Lee-Waso said.

"That's very interesting. You claim not to be from my village. But you know about Serramonka, and that I was once in the same village as he," Ambloosa said. "Who are you? The truth."

"I am—"

"Lee-Waso," Ambloosa said.

"Hungry. I am hungry," Lee-Waso said.

Ambloosa shook her head in disbelief. She untied Lee-Waso but held a spear toward him.

"Don't try anything fancy," she said.

"That's a clever device," Lee-Waso said. "I should try that with a root."

"A root? You mean a rope. You are very strange!" Ambloosa said.

"I can catch things with a root. Well, not me. Gahoosaweel," Lee-Waso said.

"No, no, no!" Aspensella said. "Never reveal your true self."

"Always good advice," Lanietta said.

"You revealed yourself to me," Claus said.

"Well no one is perfect," Lanietta said. "Of course I could be deceiving you."

"You're always deceiving me," Claus said.

"Matter of fact, for a four-and-a-half billion year old girl, I should look like this," Lanietta said, and she changed appearance to that of an extremely elderly woman with occluded white corneas, sparse white hair, and multiple sags of skin.

"Please go back to the way you were," Claus said.

"Anything for my man!" she said as she approached Claus to kiss him.

Claus looked away, she kissed him, but when he looked back, she had returned to her youthful self.

"See? I'm well preserved. Peach preserves," she said.

"I think the movie deserves my attention," Claus said.

"I deserve your attention. Me, me, me!" she said.

"It's not like she can see me," Gahoosaweel said to Aspensella.

"Gahoosaweel? Sounds fake," Ambloosa said.

"If I ask Gahoosaweel nicely, he will catch food for us," Lee-Waso said.

A silence descended. Ambloosa and Lee-Waso heard the sound of a quail.

"Prove you can hunt. Catch that quail," Ambloosa said. "We'll clean it and cook it."

"I pray to almighty Gahoosaweel," Lee-Waso said. "Please capture that quail so that we may eat."

Lee-Waso held his hands up to the air as if Gahoosaweel were an invisible spirit in the sky. Gahoosaweel was there in spirit, but not so high up.

"Roots, Aspensella. I need roots to capture that quail," Gahoosaweel said.

"You have access to my network. Command the roots," Aspensella said.

Gahoosaweel commanded the roots. They ascended from the soil quickly and created a cage around the quail.

"You did it!" Ambloosa said. "I'm in shock! What did you call him?"

"Gahoosaweel," Lee-Waso said.

"Gahoosaweel! That's amazing," Ambloosa said. "Let me take it. I'll cook it right quick."

"The quail is full of hemlock," Aspensella said. "You can detect it in the roots."

"Hemlock?" Gahoosaweel asked.

"A poison. Some quail eat hemlock. If Lee-Waso eats the quail, he will die."

"So will Ambloosa," Gahoosaweel said. "Unless..."

"Hah. He's figured it out," Lanietta said.

"Figured what out?" Claus said.

"Oh don't be such a bird brain," Lanietta said. "Ambloosa knows the quail is poisoned."

"Then why would she eat it?" Claus said.

"Who says she will?" Lanietta said.

"She just asked Lee-Waso for it. She'll cook it—"

"For Lee-Waso to eat. She doesn't trust him. Thinks Serramonka sent him," Lanietta said. "Must I explain everything to you?"

"I don't know why I keep asking, but is there a point to all this?" Claus asked.

"You just keep asking," Lanietta said. "Convince yourself this is a strange and dull movie, there's a good Clomper."

"It is both strange and dull," Claus said. "I wonder what Frieda is doing."

"What did you say?" Lanietta said with a rising anger.

"I said, I wonder what Frieda is doing," Claus repeated.

"That's what I thought you said. Well!" Lanietta said with rage, and she disappeared.

"Lanietta?" Claus called. "I'm still held down by these roots. Lanietta!"

The chairs clacked for Claus to be quiet.

"Of all the crazy things!" Claus muttered. "She's out to torture me, plain and simple."

Ambloosa had the quail on a stick over a fire.

"Don't waste your time," Lee-Waso said. "I know the bird is poisoned."

"What?" Ambloosa said innocently.

"Were you going to let me eat it? By myself?" Lee-Waso asked. "You've been watching this bird all day. You saw it eat hemlock. Ambloosa. I'm disappointed in you."

"Well? I can't trust anyone," Ambloosa said. "But how did you know?"

"Gahoosaweel told me. Just now," Lee-Waso said. "Ambloosa, Gahoosaweel will help us if we ask."

"I don't need help from a spirit," Ambloosa said.

"What about Pratheca? And Toria?" Lee-Waso said.

"What about them?" Ambloosa said suspiciously.

"Gahoosaweel will help you find them if you ask," Lee-Waso said.

"Why should I ask? They are in the village. Aren't they?" Ambloosa asked.

"Are you asking Gahoosaweel?" Lee-Waso asked.

"Yes. Gahoosaweel, is Pratheca in the village?" Ambloosa asked.

"Wait. How will I answer?" Gahoosaweel asked Aspensella.

"Speak through Lee-Waso," Aspensella said.

"Gahoosaweel says no," Lee-Waso said.

"I ask and he only tells you?" Ambloosa asked.

"Gahoosaweel will tell you directly," Lee-Waso said. "A root touching your left foot means 'no'. Touching your right means 'yes'. Now ask again."

"Is Pratheca in the village?" Ambloosa asked.

"No, you must call him by name first," Lee-Waso said.

"Gahoosaweel, is Pratheca in the village?" she asked.

A root came up from the soil, nudged Ambloosa's left foot, then went back into the soil.

"No?" Ambloosa said. "Gahoosaweel, is Toria in the village?"

The root touched Ambloosa's left foot again.

"Gahoosaweel, where are they?" Ambloosa asked.

A boulder the size and shape of a bench ascended from the soil, supported by roots.

"Gahoosaweel will take us," Lee-Waso said as he sat on the bench and motioned for Ambloosa to accompany him.

"Even Serramonka can't do this," Ambloosa said, hesitant. "This is black magic."

"Perhaps. But Pratheca and Toria await us," Lee-Waso said.

"Then they are well?" Ambloosa said.

"You are needed," Lee-Waso said. "We must hurry."

"I recognize that scam," Ambloosa said. "The emergency push."

"Gahoosaweel wants to help you in exchange for your help," Lee-Waso said.

"A-hah! I knew it," Ambloosa said.

"You can help Gahoosaweel later," Lee-Waso said. "We must go to Pratheca and Toria now."

"I don't know," Ambloosa said.

"Please," Lee-Waso said.

"This isn't a game, is it? I mean, you tried claiming me as property," Ambloosa said.

"I could have Gahoosaweel trap you like the quail," Lee-Waso said. "But I won't. I am learning quickly. I am adapting."

"You are indeed. Very well," Ambloosa said, and she sat on the boulder with Lee-Waso. "Gahoosaweel, take us to Pratheca."

Roots carried the boulder bench rapidly along the ground until it reached Pratheca and Toria. Toria's skin had already turned dark blue, but Pratheca still lived.

"Pratheca! Toria! What happened?" Ambloosa called.

Pratheca, who was near death, strained with heavy breath to explain what happened.

"Toria is dead," Pratheca wheezed.

"Gahoosaweel! Bring Toria back to life. Gahoosaweel!" Ambloosa called.

"Gahoosaweel cannot bring life to the dead," Lee-Waso said.

"What kind of god can't restore life?" Ambloosa cried.

"He is no god," Lee-Waso said.

"You just ruined it," Aspensella said.

"But I'm not," Gahoosaweel said to Aspensella. "I can't bring Toria back to life. I can't bring Cyparessa back to life. I wish I could. Can you?"

"No," Aspensella said.

"So how am I supposed to pretend to be a god if I can't bring back the dead?" Gahoosaweel asked.

Aspensella did not answer.

"Gahoosaweel. Save Pratheca. Save her life!" Ambloosa said.

A root came out of the soil and touched Ambloosa's left foot.

"No? Why not?" Ambloosa asked. "Gahoosaweel! Help. Help!"

"He can't help," Lee-Waso said. "Except..."

"Except?" Ambloosa asked. "Except what?"

Gahoosaweel commanded transparent roots to lift and weave a casket around Toria, placing her in comfortable repose. Then another set of transparent roots uplifted and wove a casket around Pratheca, placing her in comfortable repose as well.

"That's not help!" Ambloosa said.

A third set of transparent roots uplifted, but instead of weaving into a casket, they wove into a chair. A separate root touched Ambloosa's right foot.

"Yes? Yes what?" Ambloosa asked.

The root then nudged Ambloosa's foot toward the chair.

"Gahoosaweel has swallowed my friends, and now it means to swallow me?" Ambloosa asked.

"Swallow them all and get on with this," Claus lamented.

Just then, the roots tightened their grip on Claus, and an extra one went for Claus's neck.

"Lanietta, get me out of this. Lanietta?" Claus called.

But no Lanietta.

"Just kidding," Claus said to the root. "Nice root. Friendly root. I bet you get along well with people, don't you? There, I meant no harm. Just a wonderful movie."

The root loosened its grip enough to permit Claus to breathe and keep his blood circulating.

"I can't believe I just sweet-talked a root!" Claus said.

The root tugged tight again.

"I apologize. I apologize!" Claus said.

The root loosened again.

"Gahoosaweel wishes to speak with you," Lee-Waso said. "It wishes to commune with you. The chair enables such communication. It will not swallow you."

Ambloosa gave him a look of disbelief.

"As I said, Gahoosaweel could have captured you by now," Lee-Waso said.

Ambloosa looked at her friends with sadness and reluctantly took to the chair. She then saw the floating images of Gahoosaweel and Aspensella.

"This breaks the proxy, Gahoosaweel," Aspensella said.

"I want her trust," Gahoosaweel said. "This seems to be the way to get it."

"You're Gahoosaweel?" Ambloosa asked.

"Only an image spirit," Aspensella said.

"Who are you?" Ambloosa asked.

"I'm Aspensella. We are both images, but we are actually of another kind. We use these images to travel about. Gahoosaweel was supposed to use Lee-Waso here as his proxy to interact with you and the other humans."

"To seek vengeance for the death of my mother, Cyparessa," Gahoosaweel said.

Gahoosaweel created a virtual image of the prior events, starting with Pratheca's fireworks, Toria's work in the pharmacy, the attack on Toria, theft of otalicin, kidnapping of the two, the borax, the explosives used against Cyparessa, and the fight with Toria and Pratheca.

"Serramonka," Ambloosa said. "He's behind this. He must be. Oh but Pratheca and Toria."

Ambloosa cried.

"She cannot bring Cyparessa back to life any more than you can bring Toria or Pratheca back to life," Aspensella said to Gahoosaweel.

"But you will help me with vengeance, won't you?" Gahoosaweel asked. "Please?"

Ambloosa stopped crying.

"Is that a 'yes'?" he asked.

"Yes. I will help," Ambloosa said. "But Lee-Waso here isn't very convincing. I could tell he was a fake. From where did he come?"

"I made him," Gahoosaweel said. "I can take him away, too."

Gahoosaweel commanded a large root from the ground, it enveloped Lee-Waso, and it pulled him under.

"He's not dead," Gahoosaweel said. "Just in a cocoon. He will not age or die. Ambloosa, I can communicate with you directly. Look. I will make a special crown for you."

Gahoosaweel fashioned a translucent crown of white and blue. It arose from an armrest in the chair.

"Take it. Place it on your head," Gahoosaweel said.

Ambloosa did so. She stood and felt new strength. The chair disappeared, as did the images of Gahoosaweel and Aspensella.

"Gahoosaweel? Can you hear me? Where are you?" Ambloosa asked.

"I'm here, but you can't see me," he said through the crown.

"I can hear you," she said.

"Your vision will change, too," Gahoosaweel said. "You will be able to see through walls. Danger will show as red. You will also see roots below the ground surface, so that you will know you are not alone. Go down to the village and tell them to reform, that Gahoosaweel will reward the good and punish the bad."

"I will. I will!" Ambloosa said.

Ambloosa headed down the mountain.

"She went by herself. Without Lee-Waso," Aspensella said.

"I'll save him for later, just in case," Gahoosaweel said.

"Just in case what?" Aspensella asked.

"Just in case Ambloosa needs help," Gahoosaweel said. "You'll let me use the roots to help her, even in the village?"

"Yes," Aspensella replied.

"Good. I want to strangle those killers," Gahoosaweel said.

"I wish Lanietta would come back," Claus said. "Looks like an action scene is coming up. Maybe Clausetta will find me and release me. Hey, maybe I can get help from Gahoosaweel myself. Gahoosaweel! Let me go. Gahoosaweel!"

The chairs clattered for Claus to be quiet. Ambloosa approached the village.

"I am Ambloosa! I have returned!" Ambloosa said.

"You were told never to come back!" said Ramonk (Serramonka's chief in command) who directed a thug at Ambloosa.

"Gahoosaweel. Restrain that one!" Ambloosa said as she pointed at the thug.

Roots uplifted from the ground and restrained the thug. The people shrank back in awe. Another thug came after Ambloosa. She tripped him with another root. Three at a time came. Ambloosa summoned roots to force water up from the water table and hose down the attackers. She created a moat around herself with roots circling in the moat like sharks.

"You cannot harm me, Ramonk. I am protected by the power of Gahoosaweel!" Ambloosa said. "I have brought justice to this village."

"Who are you to bring justice?" said Ramonk. "We have been nothing but law abiding citizens, and you bring disorder!"

At that moment, Serramonka walked out of a hut, up to Ramonk, and placed a hand on his shoulder.

"No, Ramonk, let Ambloosa speak," Serramonka said.

"And I will," Ambloosa said. "I will now list the injustices."

"All are false," Ramonk said impulsively. "We will—"

But again Serramonka touched Ramonk on the shoulder to quiet him.

"I was wrongfully banished from the village," Ambloosa said.

"For killing a patient!" Ramonk shouted.

"No, it was a mistake. Ambloosa did no wrong," Serramonka said.

"What?" Ramonk said in disbelief.

"That's not what you said when you banished me," Ambloosa said.

"A mistake on my part. Stay as long as you like. We welcome your company. What are the other grievances? Our village is at your disposal," Serramonka said.

Ramonk looked at Serramonka in shock.

"You betray us?" Ramonk whispered to him.

But Serramonka simply smiled and kept his eyes toward Ambloosa.

"Yes, it was," Ambloosa replied, a bit caught off guard herself at Serramonka's changed personality. "I will stay. This village needs much help."

Ramonk wanted to protest, but Serramonka stepped on his foot to shush him.

"Next issue. Two villagers have been killed in the mountains. Toria and Pratheca," Ambloosa said. "By Serramonka's men!"

The people gasped.

"Ramonk, do you know anything about this?" Serramonka asked. "Ramonk, have all men report here at once. They must answer to such charges."

"You know that—" Ramonk started.

"Call the men," Serramonka said sternly.

"Yes," Ramonk replied.

Ramonk called for the men. They stood nearby.

"Three are missing," Ramonk said.

"Where are they?" Serramonka asked.

"You...they...I don't know," Ramonk finally answered after Serramonka stared him down.

"I apologize, Ambloosa, but three of my men are missing. We must go out and search for them. They might be injured and in need of aid," Serramonka said.

"Missing? One died in battle with Pratheca and Toria," Ambloosa said. "The other two..."

"Pratheca killed one of them?" Serramonka said. "We knew nothing of this."

"Your men kidnapped Pratheca and Toria, took their otalicin and fireworks, then went up the mountain," Ambloosa said. "The men claimed to have found borax."

"There's no borax around here," Ramonk said.

"What they really wanted was lumber," Ambloosa said.

"No crime in that," Ramonk said.

"They used the fireworks as explosives and shattered a large cypress tree," Ambloosa said. "They harvested the lumber all night."

"From where do these tales spring?" Ramonk asked. "Do you see such lumber around here?"

"Gahoosaweel told me!" Ambloosa said. "He led me to Pratheca and Toria. Toria was already dead. Pratheca was barely alive. She confirmed what Gahoosaweel told me."

"We must go then and retrieve the dead. Give them a proper funeral," Serramonka said. "It would be a dishonor to leave them for carrion to pick their bones clean."

"No! Justice will be served now!" Ambloosa said.

But at that moment, it rained. It came down in great quantities. Villagers scrambled for their huts. Serramonka himself escorted Ambloosa into his own hut and into the living room area. Ramonk was asked to wait in a side room. Serramonka's wife, Arlasank, came in with dry towels. She and Serramonka placed them over Ambloosa and helped her to a padded chair.

"There, there!" Serramonka said. "Can't have the doctor catch a cold."

Arlasank disappeared for a moment and returned with a small tray of hot tea and snacks. She placed the tray on an end table by Ambloosa.

"Thank you," Ambloosa said as she helped herself to tea and snacks.

Arlasank disappeared and reemerged with hot tea and snacks for Serramonka and herself, placing this second tray on a coffee table in front of a small couch on which she and Serramonka sat. The three then ate and conversed.

"I should be suspicious of you," Ambloosa said. "You weren't kind to me on the way out."

"A change of heart, my dear," Serramonka said.

"Then why didn't you send word for my return?" she asked.

"Actually, I did," Serramonka said.

Serramonka snapped his fingers. Ramonk came in.

"We sent out those men to find Ambloosa. Are they the missing men?" Serramonka asked.

"Yes," Ramonk replied. "They must've gotten lost in the woods."

"Someone is lying here," Ambloosa said. "That's not what they did. They killed a large cypress, killed Toria, and mortally wounded Pratheca."

"I'm sure this is all a big misunderstanding," Serramonka said. "Ramonk, ask around. Get to the bottom of this mystery while Arlasank and I entertain our guest."

"Yes, sir," Ramonk said, and he left.

"This Serramonka guy must be behind the whole thing. He's playing games for sure," Claus muttered.

"Ambloosa. Whatever happened out there, it's imperative we bring them back here," Serramonka said.

"I have Pratheca and Toria in safe keeping," Ambloosa said.

"You do? I don't understand," Serramonka said.

"Gahoosaweel has fashioned caskets for them. They are safe," Ambloosa said.

"This Gahoosaweel seems to have thought of everything. But I must warn you, Ambloosa. There are strange beings in the wild. Beings that care only for themselves. I'm not saying Gahoosaweel is such a being, but some other entity could be manipulating Gahoosaweel—and you. Already Pratheca and Toria are held by him. Is it right for others to hold our own? I know the tribes around here and their language, but the name 'Gahoosaweel' is quite beyond my reckoning. From what tribe is he? I will tell you if his tribe be friend or foe."

"He's not part of a tribe. He's part of the trees. He commands their roots," Ambloosa said. "I feel strange."

Ambloosa looked at her tea.

"Did you put something in this tea? I feel like I'm floating," Ambloosa said.

"Ambloosa, get out of there!" Gahoosaweel said to her.

"Gahoosaweel says I should leave," Ambloosa said.

"But it's still raining," Arlasank said.

"Ambloosa is right," Serramonka said. "We should leave and find our friends in the mountains. I'll break out the rain gear."

"Not with him," Gahoosaweel said. "Leave by yourself. Leave now!"

"I...I..." Ambloosa tried to say, but she fell into a daze, unable to speak but with her eyes still open, and she lost awareness of her surroundings.

"Quick, take the crown, Arlasank. There. Place it on your head," Serramonka said. "Do you feel anything?"

Gahoosaweel was about to reveal himself to Arlasank and even speak words, but Aspensella forbade it.

"Do not give us away. These are evil people," Aspensella said. "They lie to achieve their own self-serving desires."

"I can't let Ambloosa sit there, helpless," Gahoosaweel said.

"Then send Lee-Waso," Aspensella said.

"Yes. Lee-Waso to the rescue," Gahoosaweel said.

A hole opened up in the center of the village. Roots uplifted and brought forth Lee-Waso.

"I am—" Lee-Waso started to say.

"Don't call yourself Lee-Waso," Aspensella said. "Have your proxy pretend to be Gahoosaweel."

"But that's lying," Gahoosaweel said.

"It's protection. Let them direct any attacks toward your proxy. Your true self is then protected," Aspensella said.

"Gahoosaweel," Lee-Waso finished.

The rain continued, and everyone remained inside.

"Serramonka? Bring Ambloosa outside," Lee-Waso yelled.

"It's raining outside," Serramonka called through a window. "Ambloosa has caught a chill and is ill. We ask for aid, if you have any."

"You lie!" Lee-Waso said. "You have drugged Ambloosa. I have come to free her."

The villagers came out into the rain with coats over their heads to see the excitement.

"I bring roots of destruction. I will tear into your house unless you deliver Ambloosa now!" Lee-Waso said.

"Wait, please!" Arlasank said through another window. "I have Ambloosa's crown. I'll bring it to you. That's the real power."

"I gave her that crown. Put it back on her head. She must not be without it," Lee-Waso said.

"Very well. I will," she said, and she disappeared from the window.

"If you destroy this hut, you'll kill Ambloosa too. Killing is wrong," Serramonka said.

The villagers rushed inside their huts and returned with axes.

"We don't take kindly to killers," Serramonka said.

"You killed my mother!" Lee-Waso said.

"Who was your mother?" Serramonka asked. "Tell us about her. Murderers must be punished. That is our law."

"She is a cypress," Lee-Waso said.

"I do not know that tribe," Serramonka said.

"A cypress is a tree!" Lee-Waso said.

"He's crazy," said one villager as murmurs grew.

"The rain has made him ill," said another.

"Your mother was a tree? Does that mean you are a tree?" Serramonka asked.

The villagers laughed.

"I am serious," Serramonka lied.

"Yes. I am a tree," Lee-Waso said.

"But you look like a man," said a villager.

"He is a man," said another.

"Tie him up. He's mad," said a third.

"Chase him out of the village," said a fourth.

"No. Bring him in here," Serramonka said. "We will treat him. We turn no one away."

"Stand back," Lee-Waso said, and he encircled himself with roots.

The villagers made to chop out the roots.

"No. Leave him be," Serramonka said. "We must respect the rights of others. Very well. I'm bringing Ambloosa out. She's ill. Please don't hurt her."

Ramonk opened the door to Serramonka's hut. A woman had a raincoat over her head to keep the rain off. Her identity then was hidden. Serramonka helped her out.

"She's here," Serramonka said. "We're walking over."

"Not too fast," Lee-Waso said. "And no tricks."

"No tricks," Serramonka said.

The woman got closer and closer.

"Ambloosa?" Lee-Waso asked. "I will protect you from the rain. Behold."

Lee-Waso commanded roots to form an archway with a solid roof but open sides leading from himself to Serramonka and the hooded woman.

"Thank you, Gahoosaweel," Serramonka said as he and the woman reached Lee-Waso. "We are dry now. Ambloosa, let me help you with your coat."

Serramonka removed the coat from the woman, revealing Arlasank (and not Ambloosa) wielding a hose attached to a canister slung over her back. She squeezed a lever, and coal tar squirted all over Lee-Waso.

"Ack! What are you doing?" Lee-Waso cried as he struggled to see. "My eyes and skin are burning!"

Arlasank lit a small torch.

"The coal tar is inflammable," Serramonka said. "I can have you set on fire. You'll burn to death. The same for your roots, unless you do everything I say, Gahoosaweel."

"You see?" Aspensella said. "These folk are evil."

"I told them no tricks!" Gahoosaweel said.

"Your proxy is covered in coal tar," Aspensella said. "They are ready to set him on fire. They'll burn the roots too."

"I'm stuck. They've won," Gahoosaweel said. "Aspensella, what should I do?"

"Play along for now," Aspensella said. "Let them think they've captured you. It's just your proxy."

"All right. You win," Lee-Waso said.

Serramonka laughed. Arlasank used the torch to motion Lee-Waso toward Serramonka's hut. Lee-Waso walked along reluctantly, and he was led inside.

"Ambloosa!" he said once inside.

"Now, now, Gahoosaweel," Serramonka said. "You're covered in tar. Don't want you making a mess on Ambloosa. Keep your distance."

"I...Lee...you," Ambloosa struggled to say in her daze.

"Eyeliyoo?" Serramonka asked. "What is it, Ambloosa? Are you surprised to see Gahoosaweel here? Look at him. He's a mess! But he's my prisoner now. As are you. And if you want to stay alive, you'll do everything I tell you. Is that clear?"

"You won't get away with this," Lee-Waso said. "I have friends. Friends with great power."

"Your friends won't do anything if they want to see you alive. Arlasank can set you on fire at any moment. Now off to the dungeon with you," Serramonka said.

"Oh! I can almost smell the tar!" Claus said.

But Claus changed reality. He was now the passenger in a semi-truck trailer with Lanietta driving. She sounded the truck's horn as a car cut her off from a merging lane.

"Little car wants to get run over!" Lanietta said. "Construction zone, Claus. Fresh tar on the road. Just one lane our way. Now everyone must wait behind us. We go our own speed."

"I thought...how did we get here?" Claus asked. "And you...I thought you were angry at me."

"Oh I was for a little while," Lanietta said as the truck hit light ripples in the road, causing the two to bounce up and down. "But now I have boxes and boxes of encyclopedias to deliver. The area schools are getting a new set each. I should drop off a set for you. Might be educational."

"This is Earth. I'm back on Earth," Claus said with excitement.

"Now, now, Clomper. This is only temporary," Lanietta said. "Oh look, we're going to the other side."

The two were on an interstate highway, and construction forced the lane to cross over to the opposite-bound side. As the truck crossed to the other side, it encountered grade changes in the road, causing an unsettling feeling of falling to one side then the other. Lanietta and Claus reached the other side safely. Each direction on the interstate now had just one lane.

"I never did like that feeling in a car," Claus said. "But in a truck! It's a wonder it doesn't tip over. With encyclopedias, too. All that knowledge would go to waste."

"All that knowledge, yes. But there's more knowledge in the blank pages than the written pages," Lanietta said.

"Huh?"

"Oh Clomper. Don't be so myopic," Lanietta said. "The paper itself. The plant cells. Those years of development to get the DNA just right so that humans could turn trees into paper."

"Gahoosaweel," Claus said. "Is he in those books back there?"

Lanietta laughed.

"I didn't think you liked that movie," she said.

"I don't understand it. I mean, plants can't think or talk. Yet I saw Cyparessa, Gahoosaweel, and Aspensella speaking like people," Claus said.

"There's very little difference between plant and animal life," Lanietta said.

"What? You're crazy! There's a world of difference!" Claus said.

"Not a world, because your life is contained within your world, or at least it did," Lanietta said. "Look at me, Clomper. What do you see?"

"I see a power woman," Claus said. "Her name is Lanietta, and she has bedeviled me on and off."

"And yet you have more in common with Earth trees than you do me. You think of us as alike, because I have this humanoid shape. But I'm alien to you. Complete and total. How sad that Serramonka and his thugs treat other Earth life with disdain. He and you and Earth life grew up together. You are a great big family."

"I guess we fight like a family too," Claus said.

Construction caused Lanietta's lane to go back to its original side, and the construction zone ended, freeing up the other lane.

"Wait," Claus said. "Labba and I had children together. I could never have a child with a tree. On Earth, dissimilar species cannot have children together. With animals, the species must be extremely close or identical. Yet Labba and I—"

"Stop!" Lanietta said, and she jack-knifed the semi.

Cars piled up behind, many of which collided with Lanietta's trailer, which in turn opened the trailer and spilled encyclopedias onto the interstate.

"There! Knowledge is tossed about with chaotic abandon!" Lanietta said.

"All I did was mention that Labba and—"

"I know what you *mentioned*!" Lanietta yelled.

"Hey, you! What's the idea?" an enraged motorist yelled at Lanietta as he ran up to her window.

"Put a Jake brake in it!" she retorted.

"I'll show you!" he said.

The man whipped open Lanietta's door. He yanked her out of the cab and flung her onto the ground where he started beating her.

"Hey!" Claus exclaimed.

Claus jumped out of the cab and put himself between Lanietta and the enraged motorist.

"You better have a good reason for stopping me," he said.

"I'm correcting the situation," Claus said.

"Oh you are?" the motorist said with disbelief.

"Yes. It's not *chaotic abandon*. It's *thoughtless abandon*," Claus said, referring to Lanietta's earlier comment.

"Actually, *reckless abandon* is more common," Lanietta said.

"It is?" Claus asked.

"Of course. At least back when Earth was around," Lanietta said.

"I don't believe it," Claus said.

"Look it up," she said, handing him one of the spilt books.

"This isn't part of the encyclopedia," Claus said.

"No, it's the supplemental dictionary and phrase book," Lanietta said.

"Let's see," Claus said while thumbing through the book.

All this time, the motorist looked back and forth between Lanietta and Claus in disbelief that they were carrying on like this in the middle of the interstate with traffic desperate to proceed.

"Enough of this madness!" he said as he grabbed the book and swatted Claus across the face repeatedly up and down.

"No, not like that," Lanietta said while grabbing the book from the motorist. "Like this."

Lanietta swatted Claus side to side. Claus put out his hands to stop the assault, but as he did the scene changed, and he was himself in Gahoosaweel's world. He found himself treading water while simultaneously fending off large roots swatting at the water around him.

"Help me!" Claus said.

Claus was not alone. The entire village was submerged. The villagers thrashed around to stay afloat and avoid the roots that themselves did not wish to drown.

"Gahoosaweel!" called Serramonka from a boat. "See how I've flooded the village and your roots."

Claus looked over and saw Serramonka and Arlasank in one boat with Ramonk and Lee-Waso in another. Ramonk held a torch close to Lee-Waso, who was still covered in coal tar but was also now chained to his boat.

"You are evil to the core, Serramonka," Lee-Waso said.

"He still thinks Lee-Waso is Gahoosaweel," Claus said.

"What was that?" Serramonka asked, hearing Claus.

"I said, you still think Lee-Waso is Gahoosaweel. He's not. He's Lee-Waso. You've messed this whole thing up," Claus yelled.

"Who is that? Bring him here," Serramonka said.

Ramonk piloted his boat over to Claus and pulled him in with one hand, the other hand still holding the torch, only now he used the torch to threaten Claus as well.

"You don't belong here," Lee-Waso said to Claus.

"I know. I mean I don't know, rather, I don't know how I'm here," Claus said.

"You're Lee-Waso?" Ramonk asked Lee-Waso. "Then who is Gahoosaweel?"

"I am," said the spirit of Gahoosaweel as he appeared above the water.

"It doesn't matter," Serramonka said. "As I speak, Ambloosa is underwater with only a small amount of air left. Surrender your power to me, or she dies."

"The time for talk is over," Gahoosaweel said.

The roots submerged and went away. The water went still. Wooden utensils (both for cooking and eating) floated to the surface from huts. They were too small to help the villagers float, but they presented an oddity nonetheless. Serramonka laughed.

"So far all I see is petty nothing," Serramonka said.

Gahoosaweel then commanded chairs to float. Benches were next, followed by tables. These were sizable things, and the villagers used them to float.

"This is the best you can do?" Serramonka asked. "It's nothing. These things float on their own. Just a matter of time, something Ambloosa does not have! Ramonk, set Gahoosawe—I mean Lee-Waso on fire!"

"Now!" Gahoosaweel yelled as he was set aflame.

From the very depths of the waters shot out what looked like large dolphins or small whales, with beaks, fins, and flukes, sending water everywhere and limiting the flames on Lee-Waso. But these supposed cetaceans changed shape in mid-air, and the people saw them for what they really were—caskets of deceased villagers. The casket lids opened up, ejected the formerly dead, and the caskets landed in various ways. Some caskets landed like boats, tempting villagers to climb aboard and into supposed safety. Those who tried were beaten down by those perps of Serramonka's who were forced to swim. Other caskets fell toward Serramonka and his boat-riding men like great birds of prey. In all cases, and about the same time, the casket lids closed back onto the caskets, entrapping Serramonka, Ramonk, and his perps. Serramonka and his perps pounded on the caskets in vain. The lids remained closed.

The caskets formed a circle around the boat with Lee-Waso, then one final casket dove up from the water and encapsulated him too even as he burned. This particular casket dove back into the water and remained submerged. A hush fell on the water. Villagers who had not been swallowed up were unsure of what to make of the caskets. They seemed dangerous, and so they dared not approach them, being content instead to cling onto furniture.

This was unwise. The furniture took to movement, becoming mobile like stick creatures. Villagers screamed, as they thought they were under attack, but the furniture simply swam toward the casket circle, climbed onto these caskets, and stood briefly. Several high chairs (as used by young children) used their arms as drumsticks and their seats as drums. They played out beats of music. Chairs with backs of multiple spindles became like xylophones with the arms of those chairs beating on those spindles for various musical notes. The remaining furniture took to dance, as if in celebration. Indeed, they were celebrating the victory of their own freedom and the defeat of their human masters.

The dead who had been ejected from the caskets had at first been floating on the water's surface, being just skeletons with bits of remnant hair. But their hair grew long like seaweed, and they swam slowly with their hair tangling the unwary. These dead were outside the casket circle, but they approached and attached themselves to the outer part of the caskets. Their hair continued to flow around like seaweed, but some flowed under the caskets, curled upward from inside the circle, and thickened into reeds and tubes. Indeed, the circle of caskets became like a great mouth of a baleen whale. The circle coughed out the good villagers who had been caught up in the hair, but the evil ones remained caught, and of course the caskets themselves with Serramonka and his gang remained closed.

In the center of the casket circle, a ball of rapidly entwining flat snakes emerged. The ball was dynamic—at times it showed itself to be simply warped planks (boards), and at other times those planks writhed and wove through one another like snakes. The ball parted into a toroid, and from the center of the toroid emerged Ambloosa. She was unconscious. But then she opened her eyes with a start as several hair strands emerged from her mouth—thin at first, but growing ever thicker, and after this hair left her mouth, the hair thickened and split into a separate set of writhing things like snakes. These wove with the existing ball of planks (which were remnants of Cyparessa), and this created new life— beings part humanoid and part dragonfly, as if dragonfly wings had been increased and placed on the backs of people. These people had high pitched voices, however.

As these creatures morphed into their humanoid-dragonfly form, they said hello and goodbye in the same sentence before flying away. This happened rapidly and created several hundred flying lifeforms. They left the area and did not return. When the last flew away, there was nothing left to keep Ambloosa afloat except for the dead, who had clung to the circle of caskets and in doing so created a bridge of reeds. She climbed aboard that bridge and walked onto the circle of caskets.

"Villagers, hear me," Gahoosaweel said. "My mother was Cyparessa. Evil men from this village killed her and harvested her for their desires. But my mother lives on through her children. You watched them fly off. They will not return, for I will not allow it. Their distance from this village is their protection. I will leave you now, but I take all wood with me. You who wish to survive and make things must do so without trees. Use reeds. Use them to make clothing, baskets, tables and chairs, huts, and most importantly, use them to make music and not murder. Lee-Waso has been healed of his wounds. I leave him here to help you rebuild your lives. I must return to my kind."

"Gahoosaweel, I wish to go with you," Ambloosa said. "You must take me."

"No," spirit of Aspensella said, now appearing. "You are not of our world."

"Then make me of your world. Make me one of your kind," Ambloosa said.

"I..." Gahoosaweel stumbled.

"There is an immutable chain of life from each of us to our ancestors going back to the very first forms of life on Earth," Aspensella said. "We cannot change our creation any more than we can change the creation of Earth and its past history. But we can set in motion the future. You,

Ambloosa, are of the consumer life-forms. We are not. You cannot undo such ancestry. You must stay here with your kind and make of your life what you can."

"But wasn't I a mother or something? I mean those flying creatures," Ambloosa said. "Weren't they made from me?"

"It does not change you," Aspensella said. "Nor does it change Gahoosaweel. He must start his own roots and bear watch upon Earth. You may visit us when the time comes. You will be told."

"Gahoosaweel? What about Lee-Waso? Isn't he a part of you? Can't you stay in his form?" Ambloosa asked.

"He is like a footprint," Aspensella said. "An artifact of existence. Use Lee-Waso to remember us. He will keep you company. Now it is time, Gahoosaweel. Gather up the wood. We return to the mountains."

A large ball of wood ascended from the water. It was huge and arose like a mountain, sending water runoff in all directions. The wood took on legs, sorted into marching groups, and marched off. But to the villagers' surprise, a mass of cushioned furniture remained.

"I don't understand," Claus said. "There's wood here. Why don't these pieces march off?"

"Because they have yet to be treated with foxglove," said Lanietta, now appearing in the movie with a backpack over her back and two additional—one each in her hands.

"What?" Claus asked in surprise. "You're in the movie?"

"Can't let you take all the credit," she said.

Lanietta handed one backpack to Ambloosa and the other to Claus. Ambloosa pulled out an injection gun with a line running to the backpack. She slung the pack over her back and one-by-one proceeded to inject foxglove into each of the cushioned furniture. Each piece that received an injection slimmed its bulk and raced off after the marching mountain group. Lanietta herself also pulled an injection gun and line from her backpack and prepared to inject cushioned furniture.

"Well?" Lanietta asked Claus. "Aren't you going to help?"

Suddenly, Claus was no longer in the movie but was instead back in the movie theater. Lanietta had the same pose as in the movie—ready to inject cushioned furniture. Claus opened his backpack and saw the injection gun with line. He pulled the gun out and slung the backpack over his back as Ambloosa had done. He looked up at the movie, and it showed the last of the cushioned furniture being saved and running after the main pack, which had long gone and had begun happy celebration in the aspen clonal colony. Night fell. Merriment continued in the mountains as the humanoid dragonfly creatures visited the aspen clonal colony and flashed like fireflies, creating a vibrant light display. The movie ended. The credits rolled.

"Wait," Claus said. "This movie started with the forgotten sapling, and he went inside Gahoosaweel. What happened to him?"

"He was forgotten," Lanietta said.

The lights went on in the theater. To Claus's surprise, the seats had gone from simple wooden frames in the movie's beginning to lazy, cushioned seats by the movie's end.

"Hurry now, or these seats will die from congestive heart failure," Lanietta said.

"That's impossible," Claus said. "Wood doesn't—"

"Pappa!" Clausetta said as she rushed into the theater with a backpack and injection gun of her own. "The rest of the village is treated. This is the last room. What are you waiting for?"

"Yes, Clomper, what are you waiting for?" Lanietta grinned.

"Treat them. Treat them all!" Clausetta said as she rushed from seat to seat, gave each an injection, and then patted the treated chair upward into motion and toward the exit door.

Lanietta nudged Claus to the first chair. He gave the injection. To his shock, the chair went from being cushioned to that of a human being. It was his kindergarten teacher. She stood up, thanked him by shaking his left hand, and walked away. As she walked, her right arm remained limp.

"My kindergarten teacher? She had polio and was paralyzed in her right arm. But this is impossible," Claus said.

"Treat the next one," Lanietta said.

Lanietta went off to treat the other chairs. Those chairs that Clausetta and Lanietta treated returned to simple wooden chairs without padding, got up, and walked out of the theater. But the ones Claus treated became people from Claus's early childhood memory. They greeted him before walking off. As each one left, he felt as if the things these people had tried to teach him as a child were creating new meaning in his adult state.

"It's like they knew their words wouldn't make sense until I was older," he said. "They said them anyway, planting the seed of wisdom."

"Or destruction," Lanietta said. "Do not believe that everything you humans say and do is for the better. If your wisdom were so perfect, you'd still have an Earth. Instead, you have this memory purge."

"Is that what this is?" Claus asked.

"For you, yes," Lanietta said. "For Clausetta and me, we're just treating chairs."

"But I've never had any bad experiences," Claus said. "I've never done anything."

"Yes. Like the forgotten sapling," Lanietta said. "Leave these chairs of your past here in their cushioned state, and you'll be forgotten too. The movie credits will roll, they'll skip what became of the forgotten sapling, and they'll end. See? They're ending already. Nothing left of the reel. It's flapping on the projector even now. Flapping the end, the forgotten end of Claus's life."

Lanietta paused and then said:

"A life of nothingness."

Chapter 127: Ann Arbor's Secret

Claus blinked his eyes. All was black.

"Have him sit here," Clausetta said to Sergio. "Pappa. You fell into a daze."

"Are we still in the garden?" Claus asked.

"Yes," Clausetta said. "I went a little eethi and helped you see Claude's project. Then you sleepid ento ah dazeya ferra lugaya timeya."

"You've been drinking again?" Claus asked. "Your speech is slurred. Or something."

"Weeya dayato minati?" Clausetta asked.

"A really thick accent now," Claus said. "Stop playing around. I can't see. Isn't that enough?"

"Kleyato eta pahevana stasiato," Sergio said.

"Grayapa, ella mika vu a nita?" Claude asked.

"This really isn't funny!" Claus said. "Speak normally. Please!"

"Geyatia Labba," Clausetta said. "Peyapia melada yelapa."

Sergio ran off and yelled things Claus could not understand. Hearing the commotion, Blouisa and Selba showed up.

"Kaliba? A vika u kita?" Selba asked.

"I can't understand you," Claus said. "Everyone sounds like gibberish to me."

"Halika seyta zikada nuga?" Blouisa asked.

"Va ni ka ga," Clausetta replied. "Mi vla Pappa yavo dei za viowga plat, zan zeya vabi a nipa pa. Mi vaga enapio abi placed my hand in his visual cortex like this."

"There! I can understand you now," Claus said.

"What happens if you remove your hand?" Selba asked.

"You mean like thees? Natiappa, vila," Clausetta said.

"I've lost it. You're speaking gibberish again," Claus said.

"Giaka eifa li dilabo Aftova ekia sato?" Blouisa asked as she passed her hand onto Claus's head. "Deya ookastiya me now, Claus?"

"Just the last few words," Claus said.

"You're using Aftova?" Clausetta asked. "For all we know, that's what caused this problem. Could be a delayed reaction. Withdrawal. Like a drug addict. Pull your hand away."

"No," Blouisa said.

"I said, pull yulabi yavina abida," Clausetta said as she forced Blouisa's hand away.

"Clausetta, wa zi guliko a ni pa bla?" Selba asked.

"Ekia vrabi dakin asito," Clausetta said.

"Gibberish, people. I hear only gibberish," Claus said.

"Eiya mavigo reimpa niaza flafalf siaz glazigastap," Clausetta said. "Mi glav za klo Leif. Dana nati natta Pappa. Kandiastat?"

"Mi kandiastat," Blouisa lied.

Clausetta walked away. After a moment or two of silence, Blouisa placed her hand on Claus's head.

"There. What she doesn't know won't hurt her," Blouisa said. "I understand, Clausetta. I understand very well."

"I understand you," Claus said.

"Of course you do," Blouisa said.

"He's suffering from microaphasia," Selba said.

"Microaphasia? I've never heard of such a thing," Claus said.

"Your brain is rerouting signals on a very small scale," Selba said. "The gibberish you hear is only because your language processor is just a little out of phase from reality."

"I'm overriding your system temporarily," Blouisa said.

"I told you to leave Pappa alone!" Clausetta said, now returning with Leif.

"Clausetta, wait," Claus said. "If I can't understand people, I'll be both blind and deaf—effectively speaking. I'll be cut off."

"Pappa, this is Leif," Leif said. "We think you're in danger from Aftova, that your brain will be permanently damaged. We're going to try a few things."

"I'm already trying a few things," Blouisa said.

"Not anymore," Clausetta said. "For the last time, keep your blia zafp a nikalatta."

Clausetta pushed Blouisa away again.

"Galasta bria, Clausetta?" Blouisa asked. "Falarfa va a dinablasta?"

"Kela a bria za dua, Blouisa. Mi va a no, ga diakanobanot," Clausetta said.

"Zat bua. Selata breek, owa selata galtooa. Tua deblai," Blouisa said.

Then Claus heard scuffling, as if two people were engaged in fighting.

"Aaaagibla!" Blouisa yelled.

"Strast grast a pliast!" Clausetta yelled back.

"Stop it!" Claus yelled. "Stop fighting! Leif, Selba. Stopeiya theyatica! Oh zeek! Nowa mi za spraika aga klika balika."

Claus had fallen into speaking gibberish himself. He jumped up and headed for the scuffling sound as best he could to break up Blouisa and Clausetta. Several punches caught him, and he fell to his knees.

Claus looked up. He could see and realized he'd entered yet another reality. He sat in the back of an early 1970s station wagon in one of the seats that faced to the right side of the car. The car was loaded with grade-school children no older than twelve. The other kids jabbered at the mouth and pointed out all sorts of things the car passed.

"Look! It's snow!" said one.

"We never get snow where we live," said another.

"Who ever heard of snow in November? There should be turkeys everywhere," said yet another.

"Thanksgiving isn't until tomorrow," said one.

Claus looked around and couldn't believe it. He looked at his hands, his youthful, smooth-skinned hands of an eight-year old.

"Looking for a nail to bite?" said a girl sitting across from him. "I don't bite my nails. Look. If you push the cuticles enough, you can see half moons."

The girl showed how she could push her cuticles single-handedly, either with her thumb against her four fingers, or alternating index finger or middle finger against her thumb.

"Anyone can do that!" said one of the boys. "Bet you can't do this!"

He ripped off a piece of paper, placed it between his thumbs, and blew as if playing a reed instrument. Another boy cupped his hands together and played them like a flute. The other kids hummed along. The girl across from Claus ignored them and instead showed her fingernails to him. Yes, he could see the half moons on them.

"Lanietta?" Claus called.

"Who's that? Who's Lanietta?" the girl asked.

"I thought...you..."

"You shouldn't bite your nails so much, Clay," the girl said. "You should eat from the four food groups. Do you know what they are?"

"I...Clay?" Claus asked in surprise.

"Stop fooling!" the girl said, and she shoved him in the shoulder.

"Jack Sprat is kicking Clay," said a kid.

"Punching Clay," said another.

"Kicking Clay," said the first.

"Who are you? What is this? Looks like the 1970s or something," Claus said.

"Okay, I'll play the forget-me game. It's November 26, 1975," the girl said. "Anyone knows that. I'm Jackie Spratella."

"Jacquelyn Gagonini Spratella," said another girl.

"Jack Sprat, could eat no fat, she gagged on mixed linguine," started the boys. "She put on her glasses, drank some molasses, and now is teeny-weeny."

"And you're Clay," Jackie said. "Well your first name is really Clarence."

"Clarence Terrace, don't tarry Clary, you'll be stuck in Clay!" they said.

"That's your name," Jackie said. "Clarence Terrace. You could be 'Clary', but you go by 'Clay'."

"Named after a place in England. I'm named after a city. I'm Ann Arbor," a girl said, the same girl who'd recited Jackie's full name.

"No one knows our real names," Jackie said. "I heard one of the adults say that none of us are related, that we're all named after places. I'm named after a park where a girl used to play before she grew up and died of a drug overdose. The park was called 'Gagonini Spratella'. Thankfully, someone added Jacquelyn to my name!"

"Our foster parents are driving," Ann Arbor said. "We're going to our foster grandparents' house for Thanksgiving."

"Now I'll play forget-me," Jackie said. "What's my favorite hobby?"

"Uh," Claus started to say.

"She likes to write," said Ann Arbor.

"Not you. Clay," Jackie said.

"Who wants to write dumb stuff anyway? No school today! No spelling, no writing, no penmanship!" one boy said.

"I write a lot in my book," Jackie said. "It says 'Diary', but I don't use it like a diary."

"Dear diary!" said one of the boys. "Today I got my fist dirty after punching Clay."

"No, stuck in molasses," said another.

"We're riding in the station wagon!" said another. "That's what it should say."

"It doesn't say any of those things," Jackie said. "Want to read it?"

Jackie handed the book to Claus. He opened it and read it.

"'Whoever reads this, please remember that I'm stuck in 1975,'" Claus read to Jackie. "Where do you want to be?"

"I dunno. I guess it doesn't matter. I'd be stuck in that year too," she said.

"We're not stuck. It's just a year," Claus said.

"We are too stuck," Jackie said. "They didn't have station wagons a hundred years ago. No cars two hundred years ago. What about pollution? Not much back then. We

have lots now. Look at the smoke from that truck going the other way!"

"So you want to go back in time?" Claus asked.

"For starters. But only for a little while. I need my glasses to see. They didn't have them hundreds of years ago. Maybe they'll let me take them with me," Jackie said.

"Who? Will someone take you?" Claus asked.

"Father Time. He will," Jackie said.

"Hah, hah, hah!" said a boy. "Father Time! That's for babies. Like the tooth fairy!"

"Here, turn the page and read," Jackie said.

"'I wish things could just grow. No more poison!'" Claus read.

"Jack Sprat," said one.

"Did poison the rat," said another.

"Cause Jack was really mean," said a third.

"Stop it. All of you!" Ann Arbor said.

"I never poisoned anything," Jackie said.

"Yeah you did," said a boy. "You spilled paint on the grass and killed it."

"It was an accident," Jackie said.

"Still counts," the boy said.

"Mother Earth let me down," Jackie said. "Things that want to grow just die. The only thing that grows is pollution. That's why I believe that Father Time will take me away when this is over. He'll take me to a place before pollution."

"Where to? The North Pole?" one boy shouted.

"That's Santa Claus," said another.

"There is no Santa Claus," said one.

"There is too!" said the first.

The boys got into an argument so severe that the foster parents had to pull into a gas station to settle them down. Turns out they needed gasoline anyway. A full service attendant filled the car's tank with leaded gasoline and popped the hood to check the oil level.

"About a quarter low," said the attendant. "Should be okay for now. Hey, a boatload of kids."

"We're going to Grandma's for Thanksgiving," said the foster father.

"Over the river and through the wood," the foster mother hinted, referring to the song.

"I get it," the attendant said. "That'll be five dollars."

"Gas is getting so expensive," the foster mother said.

"Sorry, ma'am. Inflation's been bad," the attendant replied.

"One day I'm going to grow up and be just like you!" one of the kids said of the attendant, admiring his smart uniform.

"Can I have a quarter?" Ann Arbor asked. "I wanna can of soda."

"I do too," said one of the kids.

"Me three," said another.

"I have *one* quarter. You may share," the foster mother said quickly to suppress the overexcitement. "Ann Arbor, you're the oldest. Go get one from the machine."

Ann Arbor got out of the car, rushed to the vending machine, but came back dejected.

"It's thirty cents!" she said. "What a rip-off! They want an extra nickel. A quarter isn't *good enough*."

"I remember when I could get a bottle of soda for a nickel. It was that way for years," the foster father said.

"Well no soda today. Give back the quarter," the foster mother said.

"Can I keep it?" Ann Arbor asked.

"You *can* but you *may not*," the foster mother said.

The foster family finished with the gas station. The father tried starting the engine, but it wouldn't start. He pushed and released the gas pedal repeatedly in hopes of starting it, but the engine would not.

"Don't pump it!" the foster mother said.

"I smell gas," said one of the boys.

"You flooded it," the foster mother said. "Push the pedal to the floor. Now try."

The foster father held the gas pedal to the floor and tried to start the engine. After several seconds of turning over, the engine stumbled then came to life with excessively high revs, sending out a great cloud of black smoke from the exhaust pipe. Jackie could only stare out the window and cringe.

"Leaded gas," Jackie said. "They make cars now that don't need leaded gas. They use unleaded. Lead is bad for you."

"Yeah, it makes you stupid," said a boy, and they joked around.

"This car still uses leaded gas," Jackie said. "That means lead goes out the tailpipe into the air. Pollution. Read the next page."

"'Someday Father Time will get rid of pollution,'" Claus read.

"That'll be the day," one boy joked in disbelief.

"Yes, it will," Jackie said to counter.

"Only if the world blows up!" the boy said.

"If only you knew," Claus muttered.

"Knew what?" Jackie asked.

"Nothing. Is that all you think about is pollution?" Claus asked.

"Read the next line," she said.

"'Pollution is when nobody wants you and gets rid of you,'" Claus read, but then he kept quiet when he read the next part—*I am pollution because nobody wanted me.*

"That's enough for now," Jackie said, and she took the book back.

Claus looked up at her in horror.

"Jackie, that..." Claus started to say.

"I write all kinds of things," Jackie said. "It's like poetry, but it doesn't rhyme. Nothing rhymes anymore."

"But...no one got rid of you," Claus said. "You're here. You're alive."

"So is pollution. It's here. It's alive and growing," Jackie said. "Remember when we watched that cartoon on Saturday? They had to make their own Thanksgiving dinner. It was bad. I mean, the food was bad. Remember? That's like us. We were left behind by our real parents. We're stuck with scraps. We're stuck in 1975. Oh Father Time, save me!"

"Good grief," Ann Arbor said.

"Good grief," the boys echoed.

"Now Jackie, we *are* your parents. We love you all very much. You won't get scraps. Grandma is having the best

Thanksgiving dinner ever," the foster mother said.

Jackie wrote something in her book. She passed it to Claus to read. Claus read it to himself—*The best Thanksgiving ever. Who can promise that? Anybody. Who can make it true? Nobody.*

The group started singing *99 Bottles of Beer on the Wall* but only counted down to ninety before boredom set it. Jackie took back her book, wrote in it, and handed it to Claus to read, which he did quietly—*Who puts 99 bottles of beer on a wall?* Claus borrowed Jackie's ballpoint pen and wrote under it—*They don't pollute on the wall.* He handed the book back to Jackie, and she started to cry. She wrote something in the book and handed it back to Claus to read. It said—*Beer on a wall is wanted. I'm not. So beer is better than me.*

"Yes, yes!" yelled one of the boys. "This is the final turn. The turn to Grandma's!"

The station wagon arrived and headed up a steep driveway, but it slipped on snow halfway. The kids screamed that they were going to die, but the vehicle made it all the way up and parked in back. A white 1950s sedan was parked in an open garage, and another station wagon was parked in back. The foster parents parked next to that one. The children jumped out of the vehicle and started for the back door, but before they could reach it, they were ambushed by snowballs from other kids hiding behind various things such as the garage or woodpile. Claus found himself in the middle of the snow fight. Unsure of what to do, he looked around, and he saw several kids rolling snow down a hill. The growing ball of snow headed straight for him, rolled into him, and carried him down the hill. He passed out.

"Well, I thought you'd never show up," said an old woman's voice.

Claus opened his eyes and looked around. He was in the living room of an elderly woman.

"Lanietta?" Claus asked. "You're old!"

"Born in 1887. And you were born in 1967. Eighty-eight and eight. Quite an age difference," she said. "Can two people cross that many years? With language?"

"Where am I?" Claus asked.

"You are in my house, silly. Look outside. Your foster family and the other family are still outside playing in the snow," Lanietta said. "Well, your foster grandmother's property. Your snowball landed on my property. Actually it crashed into my sliding door. You were inside. Oh, Clomper, isn't this fascinating? Earth in November of 1975. United States. Midwest."

"These are people's lives," Claus said with a serious tone. "You're not messing them up, are you? That's wrong."

"Oh what does it matter? Earth blows up. You said it yourself," Lanietta said.

"Don't interfere with these children. Leave them be. They deserve a childhood," Claus said. "Especially now in the 1970s before the internet and social media could destroy the privacy of growing up."

"Really, Clomper, you surprise me. What would people think if they saw us conversing like this?" Lanietta asked. "You should be begging for cookies, and I should be telling you how thankful you should be that you were spared the Great Depression and two world wars. Or how when I was your age, my elders told me I should be thankful I skipped the American Civil War."

"Will you stay out of their lives? I mean, I still don't understand why you are here, or what happened to me before I came here," Claus said. "I had trouble understanding people."

"What people?" Lanietta asked.

"Like you don't know. Clausetta, Leif, and the others on the lunar near side," Claus said. "Still am blind there, too."

"So you should be thankful you're here. You have your youth, you can see, and you can understand language. Well, maybe not all of it. The vocabulary of an eight-year old is limited."

"In comparison to a Carinian?" Claus asked.

"That too. But I was going to say an adult human," Lanietta said. "Ah youth,

Clomper, youth! Play in the snow. Pretend the world doesn't matter."

"I can't do that. I know how precious this moment really is. Of all moments on Earth," Claus said.

"So this moment is precious—as are you, is that it? Your friend isn't so precious. She believes she's no better than pollution. Cast aside, as it were," Lanietta said.

"How can I explain to her otherwise?" Claus asked.

"You're explaining to me," Lanietta assured him.

"Using language," Claus said. "But our understanding goes beyond that."

"Yes, it does," Lanietta said. "Apparently language has its limits."

"She believes in Father Time. She says she's stuck in 1975. Why can't I show her the future? How Earth is destroyed, and how she should enjoy her time now? Can you show her?" Claus asked.

Lanietta laughed.

"Now you're sounding like an eight-year old again," Lanietta said. "Changing your mind from moment to moment. You beg me to stay out of these lives, and now you want me to interfere?"

"Not interfere. Illuminate," Claus said.

"You're very clever, Clomper," Lanietta said. "No, I'm busy doing other things. I can't drop critical work so you and Jackie can discuss the significance of *Eiya Shawliapa Gowaskiaka* or how that fits in with Jackie's feeling of abandonment."

"Eiya Shawliapa Gowaskiaka?" Claus asked.

"Is that how you heard it?" Lanietta asked. "You know. The cartoon on television last Saturday. Did you hear it as *Eiya Shawliapa Gowaskiaka* or as *Eiya Shawliapa Gowaskiaka?*"

"Those are both the same thing. Now you're speaking gibberish," Claus said.

"Not exactly. Your perceptions of the past have encountered copyright infringement protection," Lanietta said.

"What?!"

"Laws to protect owners of creative works," Lanietta said. "It's complicated, Clomper, but it means you'll have to guess what I'm talking about. Also, don't be surprised if the same thing happens when the other children reference television shows or other creative works."

"This is impossible!" Claus said. "I should have full and truthful ability to see how the past really happened!"

"Did you pay royalty to those owners of creative works?" Lanietta said. "I didn't think so. Sorry, you get the scrambled version."

"Lanietta!" Claus protested. "I want my reality. I want my...cookies."

Claus's sentence changed midstream as the foster mother walked in.

"Here he is," Lanietta said to the foster mother. "All safe and dried out."

"Are you hurt?" the foster mother asked.

"No," Claus said.

"Thank you, Madelyn," the foster mother said to Lanietta.

"That's Lanietta!" Claus protested. "Lanietta!"

"He might have had a bump on the head," Lanietta said. "He's been calling me that the entire time. Take extra cookies for the others, there's a good boy."

The foster mother nudged Claus.

"Thank you," Claus said as he took the cookies from Lanietta.

Claus left her house with the foster mother. He went inside the grandmother's house where he was taken to a finished basement and shown table after table with chairs.

"Sit at the end there and wait," the foster mother said.

Claus sat at the end. What was all this? Dinner? There were no plates and no food, but he could think of no other reason for his being there. He sat in silence and felt alone in the universe.

"I can't believe how isolated I feel," he said. "My own Earth is destroyed. I had the coma and lost twenty-five years. Went blind on the lunar near side. Forced to deal with these realities. Now stuck as an eight-year old in 1975 in the basement of a foster grandparent! I feel like Jackie! Even she would be welcome company!"

It was still quiet. Claus wondered about a comment Lanietta had made once before, about being stuck between time frames when absolutely nothing changes and feeling oneself being drained away. A cold shiver overcame Claus, and he felt very small, like a single point of nothingness sinking, sinking, sinking. He crawled under the table and hid there like the eight-year old that he was and felt that perhaps this was how he would end—not by growing old and dying, but by regressing into a younger and smaller human until creation itself became undone.

"Where's Clay?" asked one kid.

The children entered the basement, each holding a paper plate of food. They sat in their chairs. The foster mother set out plastic utensils, paper cups, and left two pitchers of lemonade.

"Clay?" she called.

"Are you sure he's here?" asked one.

"I bet he's hiding," said another.

A third looked under the table and said, "There he is."

"Oh Clay, come out from there. It's dinner time. Look, Grandma has your plate right here," the foster mother said.

Claus climbed out from under the table and looked at the plate. Beans, potatoes, peas, tomatoes, noodles, onions, and a sprinkle of dressing. He looked around and noticed the other children had similar meals.

"Jackie? Ann Arbor?" Claus thought to himself.

Neither was at the table. The children in his station wagon plus other children from the other station wagon were there.

"No meat," he said to himself.

Claus ate but found the flavor flat.

"Why can't we eat with the adults?" asked one.

"Because they're telling secrets about us," said another.

"Are we spending the night here?" asked one.

"We always do. On cots," said one.

"I can't wait until tomorrow," said another.

"Thanksgiving Day," said most of them.

"I hope Grandma has the biggest turkey ever," Claus said, trying to fit in.

The children paused, stared at Claus, then broke out in raucous laughter.

"I'm funny?" Claus asked.

"He's playing forget-me," said one.

"Bet you won't forget this," said another who threw a bean at Claus.

A food fight broke out with the kids throwing beans and peas at one another. The fight got so noisy that the foster mother came rushing down and yelled at everyone.

"Who started it. Who?" she insisted once she got everyone quiet.

The kids pointed at Claus.

"No I didn't," Claus said. "I really didn't."

"Clay. Over here," said the foster mother.

She took him over her knee and gave him a spanking.

"No bedtime story for you. You're going to bed now," she said.

Claus was whisked away to another part of the basement that was lined with cots. She led him past those cots, opened the door to a fruit cellar, and led him inside. There on the floor was a pile of corn husks.

"Wait," she said. "I know you don't deserve it, but Grandma says you may use a covering."

The foster mother took a cut-open burlap sack and placed it over the corn husks.

"There," she said.

"There what?" Claus asked.

"That's your bed for the night. Now go to sleep, and think about how wonderful tomorrow will be," she said.

Claus hesitated, but the foster mother did not. She placed him on the burlap bed and closed the door. It was pitch dark.

"How will I get air?" Claus said to himself.

But in another moment or two, Claus heard a howling, like a ghost trying to escape.

"Go away, little ghost. Go away!" he pleaded.

Claus was surprised to hear himself say such a thing. He felt he was losing his thick-skinned adult heart and was reverting more into the sensitive heart of the eight-year old boy he had become.

"Go away!" Claus pleaded.

But the ghost howled even harder. Trembling from fear, Claus crawled along the floor toward the sound but bumped into a shelf where fruit was stored. Pulling the fruit out of the way, he discovered a loose board in the wall.

"This must be a door. The ghost is inside. If I open it, I'll let the ghost out. What do I do?" Claus asked himself. "Little ghost, please go away!"

The howling continued. Claus tapped on the door. It moved. He tapped again then pushed it to develop a swing, making the swing go more and more until the door opened enough where he could get his hand between the door and the wall. He pulled the door open and realized that perhaps this was a way out of the fruit cellar. Pleased, he gained new courage.

"A-hah! Now I will chase you away, Mr. Ghost!" he said.

He crawled through a short passageway into a chamber that had a light powder on the floor. He couldn't see, but he could still hear the howling. It led him to a wall where he felt a ladder. Climbing the ladder, he reached a point where a faint light beamed through. Claus looked through and saw Madelyn's house. In fact, he could see through her window. Inside were Madelyn herself, Jackie, and Ann Arbor each holding a magazine with a golden-colored cover.

"What are they doing over there?" Claus thought he asked only himself, but his voice carried a little.

"That's a secret. Ann Arbor's secret," said Lanietta's voice.

The voice startled Claus. He jumped and hit his head on a metal door above him.

"Lanietta? Where are you?" Claus asked.

"Look to your right side," she said. "Also, please don't jump like that again. You scared me."

"I scared *you*? You scared *me*!" Claus said.

"Do you see me?" she asked.

Claus looked to his right.

"All I see is a rat," he said.

"That's me," Lanietta said. "Rattasinatta, the coal rat."

"You're making this up," Claus said.

"Don't you see my mouth moving as I speak?" she asked.

"I do but...Rattasinatta? Is that supposed to be like Sassatinassa? Sounds made up," Claus said.

"Most things are," Lanietta said.

"I've never heard of a coal rat," Claus said.

"Also made up. But I'm here now," Rattasinatta said.

"To keep me company?"

"No. I failed," she said.

"At what?" Claus asked.

"I'm a working rat you see. Or I was. Supposed to find land mines before miners come in and start their strip mine."

"And the rats who succeed get their freedom as a reward?" Claus asked.

"In a way. The mine explodes and kills them," Rattasinatta said. "But if you wish to believe my failure is your success to keep you company, so be it. Many beliefs exist in your world. Do you believe in me, in Rattasinatta? You almost have to. I'm here, aren't I?"

"I guess I have to believe in something," Claus said. "I thought you were over there playing Madelyn."

"She's doing fine without me. Was a nurse in both world wars. Gotta be tough for that," Rattasinatta said. "But I have more in common with you now than before."

"What? How?" Claus asked.

"You're eight, and I'm eight," Rattasinatta said.

"You're eight years old? I didn't know rats could live that long."

"I never said we were the same years. See? You ruined the belief. You are eight years old, true. I'm eight months old. Years, months, what does it matter? We're both eight!" Rattasinatta said.

Claus fell silent for a moment. He looked at Madelyn's house. Jackie and Ann Arbor took turns waving their arms and speaking, as if acting out a play. Occasionally, Madelyn would speak or give advice.

"I can't hear what they are saying," Claus said.

"They are reading a story called *Teia Chowkiat Slooba Aitora* by *Janna Silverpep Ravine*. Oh wait, you probably heard gibberish," Rattasinatta said.

"Yeah, I did. I heard *Teia Chowkiat Slooba Aitora* by *Janna Silverpep Ravine*," Claus said.

"Copyright infringement," Rattasinatta said. "If only you had purchased the magazine, you could read it too."

"What magazine?" Claus asked.

"The December 1975 edition of *Meleila's Tauga*," Rattasinatta said.

"I've never heard of *Meleila's Tauga*," Claus said. "Wait. Is that also—"

"Copyright infringement? Yes," Rattasinatta said.

"How can the name of a magazine be restricted? This isn't at all what I expected," Claus said. "Can't you lift these restrictions?"

"In a way, I did. I allowed you to hear a scrambled version. Isn't that good enough?" Rattasinatta asked.

"Hardly," Claus replied.

"I wanted you to know exactly when you encountered copyrighted material. The gibberish does that. For the magazine name, other less honest folk might use a more realistic name like *First Home and Family*. You'd believe it. Yes, maybe I should have retconned things to appear and sound more realistic. Rewrite history as it were. In my image, of course."

"Of course," Claus mocked.

"Do not mock me with such ease. Consider this. Everything is made up," Rattasinatta said.

"That I don't believe. This looks just like 1975 from what I've seen in documentaries," Claus said.

"No. Fake. Assume everything is made up. Later generations after you won't believe in Earth anyway. It will all be some made-up fantasy passed down from generation to generation to give false meaning to humanity. There. Wisdom from a coal rat."

"Can wisdom come from something made-up?" Claus said. "I don't know."

"An interesting question. You might find out tomorrow. But as it is, more pressing things are about to happen," Rattasinatta said.

"Like what?" Claus asked.

"Your bath," Rattasinatta said.

"I don't need a bath," Claus said.

"Spoken like a true eight-year old," Rattasinatta said.

Rattasinatta scurried off as the sound of an opening fruit cellar door carried through to Claus.

"Clay? Get out of that coal chute. Clay!" the foster mother insisted.

Claus climbed back to the fruit cellar and stood.

"Oh, Clay! You're covered in coal dust! What were you doing in there anyway?" the foster mother asked.

"I was talking to a coal rat," Claus said.

"Making up stories, too!" she said. "Now you have to take a bath."

The foster mother marched Claus upstairs past the children playing with their various toys. The foster mother put up a hand to block his view and thus prevent him from running over to join them.

"No. You've been bad. You don't get to play with the others," she said.

The foster mother led him into the bathroom, filled the bathtub with water, and told him to wash up good just as she closed him in. Claus found a box with a pink smiley face on front and a powder inside.

"*Etisa Apapooba*," he read. "Looks like bubble bath powder. But more gibberish. I bet I know what it is. I bet it's *Etisa Apapooba*. Wait! I can't even say the real name. A full gibberish cheat! Unfair. Unfair!"

Claus poured a bit of the powder into the bathtub and stirred up the water.

"Bubbles up good," Claus said as he removed his clothes and jumped in.

"Bubbles up *well*," said Lanietta's voice.

"Hey! I'm taking a bath!" Claus complained.

"I can tell," Lanietta's voice said.

"Where are you anyway?" Claus asked.

The open toilet seat moved slightly as Rattasinatta the rat pulled herself up from the toilet water. She slipped off the seat and landed on the floor but then jumped back atop the toilet seat.

"Anyone else would scream," Claus said. "A rat in the house."

"You're not afraid of me, are you Clomper?" Rattasinatta said. "You should be. I could cause all kinds of terror."

"But you're not," Claus said.

"True. I'm being a good girl...er...a good rat," she said. "But I have to be good. I have only a few months to live."

"What? Why?" Claus asked.

"Rats don't live very long. This Rattasinatta rodent will only live twelve months, and that's it. A short lifespan, isn't it Clomper? Not enough time to do much of anything," Rattasinatta said.

"What do you want, Lanietta?" Claus asked.

"Please. Call me by my rat name. Rattasinatta," she said.

"You call me Clomper. That's a dog's name. I'm hardly a dog now," Claus said.

"No. Just an eight-year old boy," she said.

"I'm still seeing gibberish on things. That box of bubble bath powder looks like—"

"Oh! It's *Etisa Apapooba*! Haven't seen that in years," Rattasinatta said.

"Strange thing for a rat to say," Claus said. "The years thing I mean."

"See? Now you're catching on. This time thing is just a matter of relevance," Rattasinatta said.

"What is relevant about this time frame? These people? And that deal with Madelyn, Jackie, and Ann Arbor? What does that have to do with me?" Claus asked.

"Me, me, me! Must everything be about you?" Rattasinatta asked. "I've got my rodent claws full of work, and you speak of how things affect you. Claus, that's why nothing significant has ever happened to you. Oh, I know, the Earth's destruction and your mindless adventures before and after. But that wasn't you. It was me, at least largely."

"You, you, you!" Claus mocked.

"I do get around. I don't claim to have created all failures of the universe, but I'm doing more than my fair share to correct them. So yes. Me, me, me!" Rattasinatta said.

"You? Correcting things? Here? How?" Claus asked. "I don't see you doing anything but taking the form of Madelyn or a rat and giving me a hard time."

Rattasinatta laughed.

"Ah, my little Clomper. Oblivious to the end," Rattasinatta said. "That's why I like you. Through your ignorance am I justified in my mission. No, don't ask again. No point in trying to explain."

"Are you willing to explain anything? Something? I need to know what's going on and why," Claus said.

"You think you do, but the adults are running things here," Rattasinatta said. "You just do what you're told, and all will be well. Pay attention, and you *might* learn something."

"I'm not an eight-year old. I'm not. I'm not!" Claus protested as he yelled and crashed his fist against the water, splashing bubbles and water over the tub's side.

"Careful. You're making a mess," Rattasinatta said.

Just then a fist pounded against the bathroom door.

"What's going on in there? Why all the yelling?" said the foster mother's voice.

"Nothing," Claus yelled back.

"Well hurry up. Other people have to use the bathroom," she said.

"I will," Claus yelled back.

Claus looked back at the top of the toilet seat, but Rattasinatta had jumped off. She walked across the floor and jumped atop the side of the tub.

"Ack! You scared me!" Claus said.

"Bubble bath," Rattasinatta said as she walked back and forth on the tub's edge.

"When does it end, Lanietta? When are you going to release me from all this madness?" Claus asked.

"Madness?" Rattasinatta said as she sharply turned toward Claus.

"Yes. Madness! I'm going mad! Leave me alone, but back on the lunar near side," Claus said.

"I gave you a precious gift," Rattasinatta said. "I gave you the ability to see and feel Earth of 1975! You're the one complaining. You're the one throwing it away!"

Claus stared down Rattasinatta with great determination. He moved close to her and looked her in the eyes.

"I don't belong here," he said sternly. "End this now, or...or..."

"Or what?" she squawked back.

"Or I'll drown you!" he said.

With frustration and rage driving his arms and hands, Claus swatted Rattasinatta into the bath water and in the same motion caught her with his other hand. He then held her underwater with both hands. Rattasinatta squirmed to get away, but Claus was angry that these adventures never ended.

"I tried to kill myself before. That was my mistake. I should have killed you. You!" he said as he sloshed her back and forth.

"Claus!" rising air bubbles said from Rattasinatta. "Stop! Claus!"

"No! This is my last chance. I know it!" he said.

Claus continued to slosh her underwater. But something strange happened. The lights in the room flashed. Walls became transparent. At first Claus didn't care, but a part of him had a faint sense of curiosity, and his peripheral vision caught the other children playing in various parts of the house with toys upon toys. One was a collection of model cars on tracks, another played with model trains, some played board games, others card games, and some dabbled with magic tricks. The walls of the house went transparent as did the walls of Madelyn's house. Ann Arbor and Jackie were now with Madelyn watching a movie on television. Other houses went transparent too. One family was decorating a Christmas tree already. Another had started celebrating Thanksgiving Day with a turkey dinner. Other houses with other walls went transparent. An elderly couple taking medication. A young couple playing with their toddler. An art teacher giving lessons. A group of women meditating while sitting in a circle.

"End it all!" Claus said, and he was amazed at his continued determination.

Claus felt himself gradually floating upward from the bathtub. Was he dead? While floating upward through the transparent ceiling, he saw, still in the bathtub, the eight-year old boy drowning a rat.

"No longer a coal rat. A Clay rat," Claus muttered. "Was that me doing that? Do I really hate Lanietta? Or was that Clay? I mean, is that Clay?"

Claus continued to float upward. The ground became transparent too, and all that was visible now were people and furniture. Earth itself faded away into a ball of appendages, with each appendage going to a house, like a large dandelion going up to seed. These weren't thick appendages like a squid but were instead very thin and delicate appendages.

The appendages lit up and pulsed, first at the "dandelion" base and then traveling upward—pulses of alternating yellow and blue. Slowly the lights migrated upward until they terminated at the transparent houses. They flashed the houses. At first the flashes were benign, but they grew with intensity, and house after house burst with light into non-existence, causing the remaining appendages to wither away. The process was not instantaneous, but it increased with speed, and already a third of the houses had disappeared into oblivion. Claus felt a shudder and a throb around him, as if the universe itself were under attack and being gradually destroyed.

"He's awake now," Yuri said.

"Pappa?" called Clausetta.

Claus opened his eyes and could see, albeit in black and white.

"I can see. Where am I?" he asked.

But before he could finish his question, a great cracking and pop blasted his ears like a large sheet of ice cracking in the distance.

"You're in the lunar shock," Yuri said. "Claus. You must undo what you've done. The moon is under great tectonic stress."

Claus sat up and looked around. Clausetta was gaunt and ragged like a malnourished alcoholic, not to mention having radiation burns from being in the lunar shock. Yuri's skin was like a checkered tattoo. Though Claus could not tell, the checkered pattern was of yellow and blue. They were in a building without another person, but a crack-pop shattered the walls and caused them to fall. The roof collapsed, and only the efforts of Yuri and Clausetta to pull Claus and them under a table saved them. The town was full of cubics running around, but these cubics sustained gradual damage at each crack-pop. The larger pieces and parts continued limping along in pulsating colors of yellow and blue. Smaller pieces were consumed by a plasma fire. They burned brightly and were gone forever.

"Why am I here, in the lunar shock?" Claus asked.

"It was the only way to keep the moon from exploding," Clausetta said. "You're causing havoc with the PRAAD. The lunar shock's right angle with the PRAAD is reducing the effect."

"I thought the near side gave us protection," Claus said.

"Not anymore," Yuri said.

Just then, an eagle flew up, landed, and converted form into Labba.

"Is he awake?" Labba asked.

"Yes, he is," Yuri said.

"You did something, and now the PRAAD is teetering on wiping out this sector of the galaxy," Labba said. "I can't find Lanietta anywhere. It's like her life force has collapsed. You were unconscious but connected with something. Did you have a vision with Lanietta?"

"Well...does it matter?" Claus answered, not wanting to reveal the drowning scene.

"Pappa! We're doomed!" Clausetta cried.

"Claus, for the sanity of the universe, answer and answer quickly. Did you see her?" Labba pressed.

"Yes," Claus replied.

"Well? What did she do? Did she commit suicide or something? If she did, it's all over. Clausetta, get the Carinians ready to evacuate," Labba said.

"Wait. No, she didn't commit suicide," Claus said.

"Then there's a chance. She's probably caught in an ethereal dichotomy. Clausetta and I might be able to free her. Did your vision of her freeze? Meaning, did you see two still images of her, like flipping back and forth between two different action photos?"

"Please say 'yes', Pappa. This must be the answer," Clausetta said.

"It's not the answer. She was a rat, and I drowned her," Claus said.

"WHAT!?!?" Labba yelled in shock.

"Pappa, no!" Clausetta cried.

"I don't know why I did it. She was a rat, and I was an eight-year old boy. I was taking a bath, she stood on the edge of the tub, I swatted her, grabbed her, and held her underwater," Claus said.

"You idiot!" Yuri said. "You just destroyed everything!"

"Pappa!" Clausetta continued to cry.

"You really hated her that much?" Labba asked. "I know we've been through a lot with her and Earth, but what did she do in your vision that was so terrible?"

"Nothing," Claus lamented.

Yuri cursed in Russian.

"Cursing won't save the day," Labba said. "What I really need is Lanietta to help me save Lanietta. But if she could help, I wouldn't need the help. Trapped chasing my tail!"

"Let me help," Clausetta said. "I've been learning to be Carinian."

"The eagle and the drunk," Yuri said sarcastically. "A fine pair."

"No, Clausetta, I—" Claus started to say.

"Shut up," Labba said.

Claus opened his mouth in surprise. Labba never acted like this.

"Do you know what this means for someone your age? You don't have the ethereal insulation from years of experience you would have acquired," Labba said to Clausetta.

"What do you mean, 'would have acquired'?" Claus asked.

"Shut up," Clausetta and Labba said at the same time to Claus.

"I will make the sacrifice for Aunt Lanietta," Clausetta said.

Labba looked at Yuri.

"It's now or never," he said.

"What does Yuri have to do with anything?" Claus asked.

"Shut up," all three said to Claus.

Claus rolled his eyes in disbelief.

"We'll take him back to the precise moment before the PRAAD started ripping apart the moon," Labba said. "Claus, listen and listen carefully. We're sending you back to your vision. This pains me to say it, and I'll curse my own words, but do everything in your power to keep Lanietta alive. Aid her in her mission, as long as she's not trying to kill herself. Do you understand?"

"But what if—"

"DO YOU UNDERSTAND?" Labba yelled in his ear.

"Yes! Okay! Send me back!" Claus said, stunned.

Claus closed his eyes, and he felt both Clausetta's and Labba's hands touch the back of his head. His mind drifted as if flying through the clouds. He expected to resume his bath as an eight-year old, but he had quite a different experience. He saw one person strike another across the face, and the struck person fell off a mountainside. Another scene replaced the first with yet another couple where one swatted another across the face. These scenes repeated in basic theme but increased in frequency and in overlap until no longer did Claus see these as living humans but as gradually decomposing corpses all in the act of one swatting another across the face, continuing until full decomposition left just one human skeleton swatting another across the skull, with the victim skull separating from its body and rolling along into nothingness.

"It's not working. I need help," Claus said, becoming fearful he'd been caught in a nasty reality. "Clausetta? Labba? I need more help!"

The images stopped as if someone had paused a video playback. The last image Claus saw of two skeletons was still in his view. Then the attacking skeleton faded away, the victim skeleton (with missing skull) stood upright, and Claus's position changed slightly to the side, revealing a long line of similar skeletons standing behind the first. Copies upon copies magically appeared, forming a gridwork of these decapitated skeletons. They moved and danced then formed interlocking chains with left arm/right leg as one type or right arm/left leg as another. The free limbs allowed for connection points with other parts of skeleton strands, whether the same or other. They repeated until these strands clumped into shapes resembling proteins and other intracellular shapes.

Such shapes shrank and shrank in view revealing a single organic cell, then two, and many more until a multi-cellular animal revealed itself to be a rat. One rat, two, four, and twenty-four, until Claus's entire vision was filled with rats, fighting for space and time while surrounding Claus and providing no relief nor escape.

"One rat. Just one rat!" Claus yelled.

The jumble of rats blurred and became a ball of snakes. But the snakes slowed and formed in curves and knots, revealing the Veigon.

"That's gone. The Veigon is gone," Claus said.

"Stuck in 1975," echoed Jackie's voice.

"Of course," Claus said. "The Veigon was still on Mars, influencing people on Earth through the Anrega. Lanietta? This is crazy, Lanietta. Old memories are too dangerous. The Veigon has too tight of a grip. Lanietta? Let it go, girl. Let it go!"

All went black, then Claus saw an image of Lanietta. It was his first meeting with her, at the auction. She seemed less aged then, less careworn.

"How can a girl of four-and-a-half billion look so young at first but then age so rapidly in such a short time?" Claus asked himself. "Maybe I should have resigned myself as her pet. Stayed on the moon before Earth blew up. Why is she so difficult? Why is she so cold? What is it about you, Lanietta? You take the form of a woman most of the time and other things at other times. Is this just a game? Is it? It's getting you killed. Call it off. Call it off!"

The scene returned to Clay speaking with Rattasinatta just before Clay pulled her into the tub to drown her. Clay and Rattasinatta exchanged stares at close range while Rattasinatta sat on the tub's edge.

"I said hurry up!" the foster mother said with a loud bang on the door.

The sound startled Rattasinatta. She slipped into the tub and was about to drown. Claus had seen her start to fall, and he swooped his hand in to catch her. In fact, his motion of catching her was not dissimilar to the prior motion of him swatting her into the water. For a moment, he saw both images in his mind, as if he'd gone cross-eyed, with the killing image in yellow but the saving image in blue. And in that brief moment, he was unsure which image was "correct"—meaning he wasn't sure which image would come to pass.

"No!" Claus said in horror. "You must not die!"

Claus scooped her to safety by placing her on his upper right chest just touching his shoulder. He cried with happiness.

"You're safe, girl. You're safe. You'll never die again!" he cried.

"Why Claus," Rattasinatta said. "I never knew you cared so much."

"Don't scare me like that again. Do you hear? I want you to live forever and ever!" he cried.

"Well I hope so. Come now, loosen your grip. It's time for me to go. We can't have you bawling all night long. You'll miss the fun tomorrow," Rattasinatta said.

Claus turned to her and kissed her.

"Dear me. Kissing a rat. Clay never did that!" Rattasinatta said. "I'll have to sit down with you over tea and have a chat about this incident someday. You have surprised me beyond expectations."

"Promise me you'll take care of yourself," Claus said.

"Of course. And more. You'll see," Rattasinatta said.

Claus loosened his grip. She jumped off his chest, used the tub's edge as a springboard by jumping off that too, and jumped to the floor. She then scampered over to the toilet and jumped in.

"This rat will only live a little while longer," Rattasinatta said as she peered above the toilet's edge. "A few months or so. I'll be long gone by then. Meanwhile, I bid you farewell until we meet again. Thank you for caring."

Rattasinatta dove down into the toilet piping and entered the sewer system. Claus stared at the water in the tub. The bubbles had died down, and he knew the bath had come to an end. He pulled the plug to the tub then watched and listened as the water went down.

"Atmospheric disturbance," Labba said.

"It's a tornado!" Yuri said.

"What? I was draining the tub, and I—" Claus started.

The tornado swept through their position and yanked Yuri away. The wind was thunderous. Conversation was difficult to hear.

"Where are you in the vision?" Labba yelled. "Can we skip you ahead a day?"

"Not a full day," Claus yelled. "A few hours. A few hours!"

Labba and Clausetta sent Claus back into his vision. He was now upstairs in the grandmother's attic in a corner that had been partially converted into a small bedroom. Claus as Clay sat on a cot. All was dark except for an analog backlit clock that rested on an old keg that had been inverted for use as a nightstand.

"Eleven forty-eight," Claus said to himself.

"Or so you think," said a voice while a shape passed in front of the clock.

"Lanietta?"

"You think out loud," she said. "But it's me. Rattasinatta."

"Where am I?" he asked.

"In your foster grandmother's attic bedroom," she said. "The last bit of November 26, 1975 is passing away."

"It's so dark," Claus said.

"Follow my voice. Crawl with me," she said.

Claus crawled with her until he could go no farther. He had reached an attic window. Rattasinatta hopped onto the sill.

"Look outside. Do you see anything?" she asked.

"I see houses to the left and right. But nothing straight ahead," Claus said.

"Such emptiness from the east," Rattasinatta said.

"Well it's night time," Claus said. "Nothing will rise until dawn."

"Wrong!" she retorted. "Though I suppose you can be forgiven. It did not rise all day today. But it will tomorrow."

"What? The sun rises every day," Claus said. "Unless you want to get technical. The sun doesn't really rise. It's an illusion."

"Your belief is misplaced. Misplaced," Rattasinatta said. "Everything rises from the east. Everything."

"The stars rise every day. Unless it's cloudy out," Claus said.

Rattasinatta laughed.

"You should not take things for granted. The celestial body of which I speak does not simply rise and set every day the way you think. She has a rhythm and heartbeat of her own, so to speak. She sings in the wind, whispers in the shadows, and changes her dress on her own schedule, regardless of the day-night cycle you see here on Earth," Rattasinatta said. "The last of her slumber is fading. She is awakening, Claus. Look back at the little clock, and stare at the hands as they open in full."

Claus stared at the analog clock, which now read midnight. He held his gaze but fell into a daze, and the hands appeared to take on speed as the minutes passed—12:01, 12:05, 12:08, etc., and all the way up to 12:30 and 12:31.

"Fully outstretched, her arms begin to close," she said at 12:32. "Look back out the window. Behold!"

It was 12:33, and Claus watched as a third-quarter moon rose above the horizon.

"She's your friend, Claus. She's been a friend to humans from their earliest beginnings," Rattasinatta said. "Look at the ground outside. Dark. There is no party, no celebration of her arousal. All too oft she is ignored in deference to the sun. But she doesn't care. She loves you all just the same."

"I'm here for this? For the moonrise?" Claus asked.

"No," Rattasinatta said. "I just thought you should know that sometimes the universe skips a beat and begins anew. There are those who die young, and those who bear witness. For some, a bit of both. We just have to know...have to know..."

Rattasinatta choked up as if to cry. It was a horrible sound, hearing a rat choke up.

"Lanietta? What are you saying? Lanietta?" Claus asked.

"Have to know when to skip the beat. And have the courage to do so," she finally finished. "Enough moon watching. Time for bed."

Claus took one last look at the rising moon. The angle of light from the unseen sun accented the craters with shadows and thus provided contrast and clarity.

"So clear and crisp. I feel like I could hold her in my hand," Claus said.

Rattasinatta hiccupped or choked, Claus wasn't sure which, but she repeated as best she could, "Time for bed. Time for bed," as she led him to the cot. Claus followed her to the cot and climbed in. The attic was cold, and he pulled up a blanket to keep warm.

"What happens now, Lanietta?" Claus asked. "What happens now?"

"I've been asking that question for over four billion years," she said, and she scampered off.

Claus as Clay fell asleep. When he awoke, it was late morning. He had largely been forgotten until he heard voices calling for Clay.

"Clay? Clay!" called Ann Arbor.

"I bet he's in the attic," Jackie's voice said.

Ann Arbor led the way up the attic steps with Jackie behind.

"Clay?" Ann Arbor called.

"Over here," Clay said. "I was made to sleep here."

"Breakfast is over, and you missed it," Ann Arbor said.

"Yeah, you should get dressed and come down. There's no lunch today, remember?" Jackie said.

"No lunch. Why?" Claus asked.

"Because it's Thanksgiving Day, that's why," Jackie said.

"Silly!" Ann Arbor added.

"Dinner is at one," Jackie said. "If you're hungry after that, there will be leftovers at six."

"Anyway, we need you to come downstairs for the performance," Ann Arbor said.

"What performance?" Claus asked. "I can't do a performance."

"To watch the performance, silly!" Ann Arbor said.

Ann Arbor and Jackie left the attic. Claus changed clothes and was about to go downstairs when he spoke.

"Lanietta? What's going to happen?" Claus called. "Lanietta?"

There was no reply.

"I need to watch a performance?" Claus asked himself. "Why?"

Claus looked around suddenly, half expecting Lanietta to answer, but she did not.

"Clay! Hurry up!" Jackie called from the bottom of the steps.

"Coming," Claus replied.

Claus went downstairs, which led to the upstairs of the house. Ann Arbor had raced down the steps to the main level, leaving just Jackie and Claus.

"What kind of performance?" Claus asked as the two headed downstairs more slowly.

"You'll see," Jackie said, now getting a bit ahead of Claus on the way down the stairs. "Ann Arbor and I are part of it. So is Madelyn."

"Lanietta!" Claus said.

But Claus looked up and saw Lanietta as the coal rat perched high in a corner, looking down on Claus and laughing.

"It's a game," Claus said.

"It only seems like it," Jackie said. "Maybe when you're older, you'll understand. But pay attention to the performance, and think back on this day. This will be the day you were no longer stuck in 1975!"

The two reached the ground level. Jackie led Claus toward the music room. Along the way, Claus heard the foster mother thank Madelyn for keeping the kids busy while they finished preparing dinner. Jackie and Claus reached the music room, opened the door, and went inside. The other children were busy trying to play music on the various instruments but could not. Primarily, the piano was used as a drum with the children beating on it haphazardly and without abandon, creating the most awful collection of piano-string anarchy.

"A music room? In a house?" Claus asked.

"You remember," Jackie said. "Grandma teaches music."

"Where's Ann Arbor?" Claus asked.

"Getting ready," Jackie said.

"Getting ready for what?" Claus asked.

"The music," Jackie said.

Madelyn walked in.

"Attention, children, attention!" Madelyn said. "Please gather around and have a seat. You're in for a special treat."

Madelyn pointed to several stacks of step stools. The children took a stool each and used such for sitting. Madelyn sat at the piano. The piano itself was half-height with the back of the piano facing the children. The children then could only see Madelyn's face and not her hands. Madelyn started to play. Not a song or anything fancy, just a simple collection of low chords followed by one or two upper notes.

"It sounds like the beginning of *Eiya Shawliapa Eclisagasa*," Claus said. "Ack! Scrambled again!"

"Of course," said a boy next to Claus. "And if you say the artist's name, it will sound like *Bians Calampi*."

"Lanietta?" Claus asked.

"Yes and no," the boy said. "My name is—"

"Another name," Claus lamented. "I'm tired of all these names."

"I have to have a name," the boy said. "Fine. I won't tell you."

"You didn't drive up with me. You're from the other station wagon," Claus said.

"Yeah," he said. "Don't you want to know my name?"

"Okay, tell me your name," Claus said.

"Sassatinassa," he laughed.

"Lanietta, that's not funny. What's the boy's name?" Claus asked.

"Rattasinatta? Lanietta? Old Wise One?" the boy said.

"You are not 'Old Wise One'," Claus said.

"Well this boy is also named after a place," the boy said.

"Detroit? Chicago?"

"No. Eastview," the boy said. "Don't you remember? I was found on a porch one morning as the sun rose in the east."

"That's not a place," Claus said.

"A place is wherever you want it to be. I usually get up early each day and watch the sunrise. I'm Eastview, with a view of the east."

At that moment, Jackie stood in front of the piano with her diary as Madelyn continued to play chords and notes.

"Summer. Run, fun, the drummer," Jackie said.

Ann Arbor made her appearance from behind a partition. She wore a costume resembling a tree with green leaves. She had a food storage container with a resealable lid that she held in one hand. With the other hand, she tapped it like a drum in sync with Madelyn's chords. Ann Arbor walked amongst the children with her little drum and continued to play.

"The notes are different," Claus said. "The lower chords are still followed by upper notes, but—"

"It no longer sounds like *Eiya Shawliapa Eclisagasa*," Eastview said. "But it still sounds like a work by *Bians Calampi*."

"Must everything be scrambled? Even the name of an artist?" Claus asked.

"Who will remember the real name?" Eastview said.

"Everyone," Claus said.

"Don't be so sure. The facade of a colorful memory fades from the daily rising of the sun from the east. Colors go grey then white," Eastview said.

"Lanietta?"

"I speak as Eastview now," Eastview said. "I've been color blind since birth. Not just red-green, but all color. I see everything in black and white."

"You watch the sunrise in black and white? Seems pointless," Claus said.

"At least I still can," Eastview said.

"You're just a boy. Of course you can," Claus said. "You'll always be able to watch the sunrise."

"Only if I remain stuck in 1975," Eastview said with Lanietta's voice becoming more prominent.

The music shifted to melancholy, but with the same style of lower chords and upper notes. Ann Arbor stood by Jackie.

"Summer goes to autumn, with leaves all-a-color. Orange, red, yellow, and crimson," Jackie said.

The green leaves on Ann Arbor's costume were folded in the middle and could be flipped to show the green of summer or the color of autumn. Jackie flipped these leaves to their autumn colors. Ann Arbor played her storage container for a little while longer until Jackie next spoke.

"That drum," Claus said.

"Is a food container. Obtained from a *Nootawapper* party," Eastview said.

"Nootawapper?" Claus asked.

"Yes. It's a Nootawapper container," Eastview said.

"I'm afraid if I try to say what I think it is, it will come out sounding like that—scrambled again!" Claus said.

"The leaves of summer fall before winter," Jackie read. "The drum goes silent."

Ann Arbor handed the food container to Jackie, and then Ann Arbor walked around the room, pulled the colorful leaves from her costume one-by-one, and dropped them. Most of the children ignored the leaves. Eastview caught one.

"Catch a leaf before it's stuck, and all the winter you'll have good luck," Eastview said.

"Stuck on what?" Claus asked.

"On the ground. Catch one. Catch one!" Eastview insisted.

Claus caught a leaf. He held onto it, but that was all. Ann Arbor disappeared from sight, presumably to change costumes.

"Leaves don't get stuck on the ground. They blow around," Claus said.

"Until they are stuck in the soil," Eastview said.

Ann Arbor returned, dressed as a turkey.

"With autumn comes harvest, and with harvest comes the Easter Turkey, bearing presents for those in earnest," Jackie said.

"Easter Turkey?" one child asked.

"There's no such thing!" said another.

"It's not Easter. It's Thanksgiving!" said a third.

Jackie returned the food container to Ann Arbor.

"Who is in earnest? Who is deserving? The Easter Turkey brings your reward," Jackie said.

Ann Arbor removed the lid and one-by-one took a treat from the food container and dropped it into the waiting hands of a child. The imagery sped up in Claus's mind. The scene flashed back and forth between this scene, and one where Ann Arbor was dressed as a white mushroom with black dots, dropping fried rats on a stick to hungry vultures on perches. Jackie spoke again:

"The Easter Turkey rewards you," was replaced by "The Valentine Mushroom rewards you," in the rat-vulture scene.

Claus turned to Eastview. In the Easter Turkey scene, Eastview appeared as the young boy he normally was. But in the Valentine Mushroom scene, he took on the appearance of an oversized Rattasinatta.

"What is this madness, Lanietta?" Claus asked.

"It's the Easter Turkey. Or the Valentine Mushroom. Or both. You decide," Eastview/Rattasinatta said as the scenes changed back and forth.

But then a third scene mixed in with the first two. In the third scene, Ann Arbor was dressed as a black mushroom with white dots, and she dropped little fried vultures on a stick to large rats. In this third view, Eastview appeared as a white rat.

"This reality is fracturing," Eastview/Rattasinatta said.

"Why?" Claus asked.

"*Why?*" Eastview/Rattasinatta mocked. "Maybe you'll ask how much farther, or do you have to?"

"What?" Claus asked.

"*Huh* would have been more appropriate for your age," Eastview/Rattasinatta said.

"I'll say it again—this is madness!" Claus said.

"Yes, it is. Stuck in 1975 with a fractured reality. Makes you homesick for the old near side of the moon, doesn't it?" Eastview/Rattasinatta asked. "One reality, one linearity, one family."

"One family?"

"Who knows, Claus. Perhaps you and some Earth woman in a fork of reality have a grand, happy family," Eastview/Rattasinatta said. "Not Frieda, though. And not your Lanietta. No, someone else. Domesticated. Peaceful. Just another day staring east, watching a black and white sunrise."

"Stop this black and white nonsense. Return to the Easter Turkey. That's the correct reality," Claus said.

"You're sure of this? The vultures and rats are more reflective of the raw human, consumptive spirit. Look. Even now the creatures here compete for treats," Eastview/Rattasinatta said.

As Ann Arbor tossed out several treats at a time, the scenes showed children/vultures/rats fighting one another for the treats and running off to protect the captured treat. All three scenes were quite ugly, with child/vulture/rat sustaining injury and bleeding.

"Stop!" Madelyn called as she stopped playing the piano.

Ann Arbor disappeared from view as she had before. The reality held steady on the one with children and Eastview.

"Are we really holding firm? I see afterimages of the other realities," Claus said.

"It's just your eyes. Like staring at a light. It'll go away," Eastview said.

Piano playing started back up. But instead of simple chords and notes, it was fully-formed piano jazz.

"That music," Claus said. "It's...it's..."

"It's *Shawliapa* music," Eastview said. "You know, by *Bians Calampi*. Enjoy his work. Next year is his last."

"You mean he dies? Then it is who I think it is," Claus said.

"Of course. He could live forever if he were stuck in 1975," Eastview said. "But his music lives on. As does the one who plays it."

"What does that mean?" Claus asked.

"A secret reveals itself," Jackie read. "Eternal happiness. Music of the soul."

Madelyn walked around the piano, though the piano continued to play.

"Huh?" the children wondered.

Jackie and Madelyn spun the piano around sideways, revealing Ann Arbor dressed in an evergreen costume and playing the piano.

"The secret of happiness is the company of friends who are cheerful year round, like the ever-cheerful evergreen," Jackie said. "Happy Thanksgiving!"

"Happy Thanksgiving!" the children said.

"And now. The greatest treat is yet to come," Madelyn said. "Thanksgiving dinner is almost ready."

The foster mother stepped into the music room and gave Madelyn a signal.

"Thanksgiving dinner is ready," Madelyn said. "This year contains a special surprise."

"What is it? What is it?" the children begged.

"Let's go and see!" Madelyn said, and she ushered the children into the main dining room.

The dining table was covered with all the usual Thanksgiving food, but instead of a turkey was a bowl of speckled eggs.

"Where's the turkey?" Claus asked aloud.

The children laughed.

"We never have a turkey for Thanksgiving," said Eastview. "Meat and that sort of thing. Not allowed."

"All these years, you have eaten only fruits and vegetables. No meat," the foster mother said. "We don't believe in eating meat. But Madelyn has been kind enough to donate these turkey eggs for Thanksgiving. They have been boiled and are ready to eat."

There was general confusion amongst the children. Were eggs considered meat? They weren't plants. Some of the children agreed with the foster parents' lifestyle of eating no animal products. Others were all right with eating food as long as the animal didn't die (meaning milk and cheese was acceptable to eat). But what about the turkey egg? Whatever argument they had, it didn't much matter. They were hungry, and so getting food was the first priority.

They sat and passed food around the table. Claus sat next to Eastview.

"But what about Ann Arbor?" Claus asked. "I didn't know she could play the piano."

"Nobody did," Eastview said. "That was her big secret. She's been practicing for several years now without telling anyone. She waited until today to show off her talent."

"And yet no one seems to care," Claus said. "They're too busy either getting their food or arguing about the turkey eggs."

"Most will forget the little performance Ann Arbor and Jackie put on tonight," Eastview said.

"You mean the autumn leaves and evergreen?" Claus said. "I hardly understand it myself."

"It's supposed to be a lesson," Eastview said. "Did you keep your leaf?"

"Yes," Claus said. "Strangely I did."

"There's writing on it. What does it say?" Eastview asked.

"'A tree that bears fruit is dead in winter,'" Claus read. "Does your leaf say something?"

"Yes," Eastview said. "It says, 'A tree green in winter need not bear fruit.'"

"Makes it sound like fruit is evil," Claus said.

"Isn't it?" Eastview said. "I mean, we're all stuck having to eat food. What if we didn't need to eat? What would become of all that fruit?"

"It would be unwanted," Jackie said, sitting next to Eastview and overhearing the conversation.

"Tossed away like pollution?" Claus asked.

"That's an interesting way of putting it," Jackie said.

"I'm evergreen," Ann Arbor said as she sat next to Claus. "I'm going to live forever."

Chapter 128: Dark Plain

"What happened?" Claus asked.

All was dark and quiet around Claus as he stood outside on a plain.

"Hello?" he called out.

No echo or reply of any kind. Claus dropped to a knee and felt the ground. There was no sign of vegetation or other life-form. Just flat, hard dirt. He looked up to the sky in hopes of seeing stars, but the sky was dark too.

"I'm totally disoriented. Am I blind?" he asked himself, then he yelled out loud, "If anyone can hear me, please give me a sign. Touch me or something."

Nothing. Claus walked around a bit then ran around, hoping he'd bump into something, but the flatness of the plain continued.

"Lanietta!" Claus yelled. "Clausetta! Labba! Leif! Anyone!"

It was perhaps an hour of this that Claus endured before he saw a pinpoint of light in the distance.

"It's on the horizon," Claus said. "I can't see the horizon, but I can still sense up and down. Wonder what it could be? Whatever it is, I should make for it, for good or for ill. It's all I've got."

Claus walked toward the light, but it seemed to get no closer. On and on he walked for what seemed like hours, and still the light was beyond reach and comprehension.

"Could it be traveling away from me?" Claus wondered.

Another hour he walked, though he couldn't be sure. He had no way to measure time and could only guess. But the time came when the light seemed to fluctuate ever-so-slightly in intensity.

"What could it mean?" he asked. "Maybe it's closer. Maybe *I'm* getting closer."

Claus broke into a jog, hoping the plains would remain flat and without obstruction, as he couldn't see where he was going and had to rely on the sense of touch in his feet for staying upright and in motion. But he could only keep this up for a bit. He tired.

"I...must...walk," he said, out of breath. "No, I...must...stop."

Claus stood in place to catch his breath. The light fluctuated with more effect. Claus sensed something carried the light and swung it back and forth. It grew larger and larger, and after another little while, it was nearly upon him. In that last moment before it reached him, Claus realized the "something" was a "someone" who was walking and swinging a lantern.

"Hello?" Claus called. "Who are you?"

"Of all the strange places you could be," replied a familiar voice as it walked toward Claus. "Just when I think I'm done with 1975, I find you here!"

At the word, "here", the figure reached Claus.

"Lanietta!"

"Who else? Took me long enough to reach you," she said.

"The light. I saw it miles away," Claus said.

"Yes. I apologize for the delay. But this environment is not known for expedience," she said.

"Where are we?"

"Between time frames," she said. "Yes, time doesn't mean much here."

"Between what frames? Where?"

"Well that's just the thing," Lanietta said. "This place is really nowhere. Saying that it's between frames is just an expression. And don't ask what happens next. That remains to be seen."

"If I can't ask what *will* happen, then maybe you can tell me what *did* happen," Claus said.

"You mean after that Thanksgiving of 1975? Well, it was the last time they were all together," Lanietta said.

"It was? Why? What happened?" Claus asked.

"Life. Human life. The foster grandmother died, her house was sold to the local school, and it was razed. Madelyn was heartbroken and died shortly thereafter—same thing happened to her house. The foster parents got out of being foster parents, which meant the children were dispersed into other foster homes. Eastview grew up and became an optometrist. Jackie grew up and became a lawyer. But she tired of seeing the same crimes of humanity over and over. She lamented how the criminals got younger while she got older. She quit her law practice and became a talk show host. The other children ventured into other areas of life."

"Ann Arbor? What about her?" Claus asked.

"She majored in music, got a degree, and taught music for a school until budget cuts and inadequate fund-raising drives forced her out," Lanietta said. "She ended up as a cashier for a major retail chain, forever tortured by the same phrases she spoke to customer after customer and the screeching beeps of the checkout scanner. She went mad and killed herself. Used a chair, I believe. You remember, don't you? The way I would fasten a noose around my—"

"Don't remind me," Claus said.

"At least I've completed this particular task. I'll check it off my list. I will need to pull you out of this empty frame before I move on. Might need you again," she said.

"You...you're doing something? I mean, you have a goal?" Claus asked.

Lanietta laughed.

"*Goal*, hah!" she said. "Flip the middle letters, and you have *gaol*. G-A-O-L. A goal is jail with a twist, Clomper. Some people like jail. Solid walls, dependable food, and a place to sleep for the night."

"What about this place I'm in? It's like jail!" Claus said.

"No. It's not. It's ultimate freedom," Lanietta said. "A pity you don't appreciate it. But you are only a pet, and pets need constraints to make them happy, not unlike those people who need the constraints of jail to make them happy. I shall provide them for you. I shall liberate you from your freedom. About time as it is. I'm due for another vacation, a holiday. You may accompany me."

"I'd rather you just return me to the lunar near side with my family," Claus said.

"No, not yet," Lanietta said. "Not until I say so."

Lanietta smashed the lantern into the ground. All was white with light around Claus for a moment, and then he found himself on a beach. It was daytime but cloudy and windy. The seas were rough.

"Oh, I'll never get a tan this way," Lanietta said.

Lanietta sat in a reclining beach chair in a 1940s-style two-piece swimsuit.

"Where are we? Why are we here?" Claus asked.

Claus looked around again, and he noticed scattered stakes and barriers around the beach.

"I told you, I'm on vacation," Lanietta said.

"The last time you said that, you—"

"I know, I know. That was before Earth blew up," Lanietta said. "Well, here we are on Earth again. You should enjoy the moment."

"What's to enjoy? Looks like a war zone," Claus said.

"Not yet, but it will be," Lanietta said.

"What do you mean? Lanietta! What is the date today?"

"Why don't you ask the Germans on the top of the cliff? They'll tell you. Of course they might mistake you for the Allied invasion and shoot you."

"Normandy? The Normandy Invasion?" Claus asked sternly.

"The day before. I want a fresh start before things get messy," Lanietta said.

"This isn't funny, Lanietta. You shouldn't joke about a thing like this. What a horrible moment in human history!" Claus said.

"That's the problem with you humans! You fret about the future too much. Live in the present. I admit the weather isn't the best. Of course if it were, we'd have the invasion today. Still, this beach—"

"Is not to be toyed with. End this now, Lanietta!" Claus said.

"I am gathering my wits and strength for the next effort, if you don't mind, Clomper!" Lanietta retorted.

Lanietta picked up a stick and threw it.

"What did you do that for?" Claus asked.

"Go fetch the stick and bring it back," she said. "You are my pet, after all."

"Lanietta! You are desecrating holy ground!" Claus protested.

"It isn't holy yet!" she maintained. "You know, I thought I was making great progress with you. Was preparing for my final effort. But I see you're lagging behind terribly. Delayed by pet deficiencies again! Well!"

"What are you talking about? Final effort? You're going to attack Frieda? Using the Normandy Invasion?" Claus asked.

"Now who's desecrating holy ground?" Lanietta said. "I can't change your human history. Nor do I wish to."

Claus started walking away.

"Where are you going?" she asked. "That's not where I threw the stick."

"I'm going for a walk. I need to think, too," Claus said.

"I wouldn't stray too far. There are mines everywhere. Wouldn't want you to take one meant for another," she said.

Claus paused. He could end his misery and possibly spare an Allied soldier with the same action. Kill himself on a mine.

"I already know what you're thinking," Lanietta said. "Don't even consider it. It is not yet your time."

"Who's to say when my time will come?" Claus asked.

"I'm to say, Clomper. Forget the game of fetch. Come back and keep me company. Please? If I turn into a rat, you can hug me the way you did in 1975," Lanietta said.

"I'd need a bathtub for that," Claus said, returning to Lanietta.

"There's always the ocean," Lanietta said.

"Too rough," Claus said.

"Yes. It is. What if I change into an oversized rat for you?"

"Here? Now?" Claus asked.

"You could then replicate the hug, in a fashion," Lanietta said.

"It's still not right. Not on this beach. I know, it hasn't happened yet," Claus said.

"Clomper. I consider you sacred, even if you are a pet," Lanietta said.

Claus was shocked.

"I don't know what to say," Claus said.

"The lack of tragedy in your life gives you a certain purity I find refreshing. And so I call that sacred. I agree with you about this beach. It *is* sacred," Lanietta said.

"That's not what I mean by sacred," Claus said. "The fighting and death that will come—"

"Is why you call this sacred sand. Why can't it be sacred for its purity? At this moment, it has purity. I can preserve that purity in my mind. So can you," Lanietta said.

"By your logic, a place is sacred before anything happens to it. Heck, it's sacred before it exists," Claus said.

"Yes, yes! Now you're catching on," she said.

"Are you saying I was sacred before we met?"

"Of course," she said.

"Before I was born?" Claus asked.

"Even more so. You were the most sacred before you ever existed," she said.

"That's contradictory. Or a paradox. Or something. I can't be and not be at the same time," Claus said.

"Try not to limit yourself too much with human logic," Lanietta said. "Anyway, I've been giving much thought to Ann Arbor and—"

"Leave her out of the Normandy Invasion," Claus said.

"She had nothing to do with it, of course," Lanietta said. "But her evergreen skit. And how Luna skips a beat. Finding you between time frames. I feel I'm close to something, Clomper. Something more than space, time, and the ether."

"You have a way to defeat Frieda?" Claus asked.

"I've always been able to do that," Lanietta said.

"You have? Then why are you making us wait?" Claus protested.

"Making you wait? Really, Clomper, and just when you were warming up to the sacred talk," Lanietta said. "Anyone can drop a bomb. Problem is the aftereffects. Must always account for those. I have a goal, yes, a goal, but it puts me in a jail of sorts. This beach is a goal today and a jail tomorrow, imprisoning death and misery to many. So far my past goals have resulted in a certain amount of loss. When I was younger, I didn't think much of it. But I'm feeling my age, Clomper. I feel like time and the universe are slipping away. Loss is less acceptable. And so I'm hemming and hawing my way toward the end. If I spend one day here on a pre-D-Day beach or another celebrating Thanksgiving with a spectrum of vegans who can't decide what to do with turkey eggs, so be it. I'm not waiting. I'm wading, like in a stream testing the varying currents. Unfortunately, the stream becomes more polluted by the day. There's a narrow opportunity for the goal to succeed. Narrow. Well, too much heavy talk for such sacred sand, eh? Let's return to your dark plain that you found."

The two returned to the dark plain.

"It's pitch black. Where's your lantern?" Claus asked.

"Smashed. Don't you remember?"

"You're supposed to produce a new one. Be my beacon of hope and all that," Claus said.

"Since when? You're just a pet, Clomper," Lanietta said. "Besides, too much vision gets you overworked. Throws you into fits."

"Ow!" Claus said. "Something stabbed me!"

"Your distemper shot. Will do you good," she said.

"I'm not a dog! I don't need a distemper shot!" Claus protested.

"Could have fooled me," she said, though her voice faded.

"What just happened?" Claus said. "You're farther away now."

"So?" she replied, with her voice now behind him.

Claus spun around in the direction of her voice.

"You're playing games with me. It's like I'm blind. Show some light, will you?" Claus begged.

"Who needs light to carry a conversation?" she asked, now off to his left.

Claus spun again.

"It's unnerving!" Claus said.

"Don't you feel innerviated?" she asked, now behind him at quite a distance with echoes.

"I thought you stopped making up those words. No, I don't feel connected like this," he said. "I feel like I'm under attack."

"Why?" she asked, changing to another distant point perpendicular to where she was before.

"Because each time you speak, you're somewhere else. I need to know where you are," Claus said.

"You want to predict where I am," she corrected, now standing directly behind him.

Claus spun around and threw his arms around her to keep her position fixed.

"Got you!" he said. "Now stay put, will you?"

"How romantic," she said. "Had I known it was this easy to get your arms around me, I'd have tried this sooner. You're still shaking, though."

"I need a moment to settle my nerves. You rattled them. Totally isolated, and you pop around like random lightning bolts," Claus said.

"But it's just me. No one else is a threat. Am I really like lightning to you?" Lanietta said.

"Yes. You scare me at times," Claus said.

"Isn't spontaneity the spice of life? Aren't you having fun? Why, if things were the same all the time, you'd be as boring as sand on a beach. You'd only get excitement with an invasion or two," she said.

"I think I'm done with excitement. Give me a moment of rest, will you? Leave me—"

"Alone? Very well. I'll leave you alone in the dark plain," she said with glee.

"No, I didn't mean that," Claus said.

"Sorry, you made the request. My Clomper needs a moment of quiet. The distemper shot wasn't enough. Very well. A moment you shall have!" she said, and she vanished.

"Lanietta!" Claus called. "Come back. Come back!"

But she did not return.

"This tops it all, Lanietta. You've abandoned me in this emptiness. You realize this will all just end, and I'll wake up. Labba and Clausetta will pull me back," Claus taunted. "So you're really not making a point at all. Lanietta? Lanietta!"

Again no reply.

"How does this solve anything?" Claus yelled. "Lanietta! Where are you? Should I continue speaking?"

All quiet except for Claus.

"You're waiting for me to be quiet for a certain amount of time, is that it?" he shouted. "I can do that. I can do that, Lanietta. I'll be quiet. I'll be quiet right now."

Claus stopped speaking. Should he walk? Where to? No, best he stay put and conserve energy. He sat on the ground and touched it with his hands. He realized it was just bare dirt.

"Sitting on the ground is not very comfortable. How I wish I had a chair!" he lamented.

He sat such that he used one arm for support. The other was free, and for lack of anything to do dug through the dirt.

"I can make a chair," he said.

He repositioned himself on his knees and dug with both hands. In this way he dug a hole where he could place his legs.

Further, he moved other dirt beside this hole and so fashioned more of a recliner than a chair. And that's what he did—he reclined on the dirt.

"Well at least I'm comfortable. What do people do when they are alone? Think about the past? Plan for the future?" Claus mused. "I'll listen. I'll listen for Lanietta."

Claus held perfectly still. After a moment, he heard something. A low, regular thud. In fact he more than heard it. He felt it. The dirt recliner he had fashioned shook from the low thud.

"Something's coming. Lanietta!" Claus said.

He jumped to his feet and turned around completely in hopes of seeing a distant lantern.

"Lanietta?" Claus called.

He took several steps in one direction. Then another.

"Still nothing. The thudding has stopped," Claus said. "I'll put my hand down to the ground. Maybe then I can feel it."

Claus did so but felt nothing.

"Strange. Well, back to the recliner," he said. "Wait. Where is it?"

Claus went down on all fours and probed for his dirt-made recliner, but he'd quite lost his sense of direction and could not relocate it.

"I spent a long time making that! What a waste of time and effort! Sigh! I'll have to dig another one. Unreal. Simply unreal!"

Claus dug and fashioned another recliner out of dirt.

"All that digging. Now I'm tired and can use a rest!" he said.

He reclined in this new dirt-made recliner.

"Ah! Now whatever happens in this dark plain will have to wait until I get my strength back!" he said.

After several minutes of rest, the low thud returned.

"Not again! Wait. It's slowing down. Maybe it will stop. I wish it would stop!" he complained.

It did not stop. He casually placed one hand on the wrist of the other and by chance detected his pulse, which matched the thud beat-for-beat.

"Of all the crazy things!" he said. "That's my heart beating! It's shaking my whole body! I just won't think about it. I won't. I'll see if I can take a nap and escape this dark plain."

But a new sound and feeling caught his attention. His stomach growled.

"I'm hungry," he said. "Lanietta, I can't stop speaking, and I can't keep quiet. My heart beats, and my stomach growls. Since I'm hungry, it means I need to wake up or return to the lunar near side. Either way I'll have to eat. Lanietta? Would you let your Clomper starve to death?"

Still all quiet.

"I'm going to starve to death in this dark plain. Then my body will rot away. Strange how I had tried to kill myself in the past, but now that things are quiet, I feel robbed of life. Even language will die."

With that last sentence, a grim horror overtook Claus. With whatever reality he or anyone is in, the last one to die kills off language. Sure, someone could record speech or write symbols as representation, but it wouldn't be the same. There would be no one to fashion sentences in real time.

Claus opened his mouth to say something, but he was at a loss for words. It had all become pointless to him. He imagined he had become one with the soil, with his pumping heart and growling stomach being the last remnants of communication in his reality.

"Light. If I could...what...was it like? What was light?" he asked himself.

He tried very hard to remember what things looked like. But each time he had such an image in his mind, the image went dark in sync with his heartbeat. Then the image would barely lighten up before another heartbeat canceled it into darkness. His senses were so under-stimulated that his mind forced images upon him. He thought he saw a sun rising above the horizon, lightening only a little bit before his heartbeat canceled it back to darkness. On another part of the horizon, another sun would rise and lighten only a little before his heartbeat canceled that one too.

"If I could slow my heartbeat, I could see a sun for a little bit longer each time," he said.

His speech disturbed the air, and he discovered that no suns lit above the horizon for several minutes because of such. He wanted to say, "I must be quiet," but the chance of delaying the view of the suns inhibited him. He focused on slowing his heartbeat.

Gradually he did. Two suns appeared along the horizon. His heartbeat canceled only one, and the other continued. Excited that he had "created" such a moment, he leapt up and cheered. But his body had become stiff and weak. It did not jump up nor react as he had anticipated, and he fell forward awkwardly with a racing heart. He was completely out of breath. His limbs ached as if they'd been yanked too hard. He took to his feet to stretch them out, but he stumbled forward, and now he was in an awkward forward gait where he fought to remain upright by running quicker as his upper body continued to fall ahead of his feet. In only a few seconds, he fell face first into the dirt and was stunned.

"Oh," he moaned.

He rolled over, climbed up to his knees, and thought about standing.

"No. I'll return to my recliner on all fours. I'll just...oh no, not again!"

Yes, again. Claus had lost his orientation and could not find the second dirt-made recliner.

"Okay. Maybe if I relax here and focus, I can get one of those suns to appear and provide enough light for me to see. Then I can find the recliner," he said.

Claus tried to relax but could not. His position was awkward, and he couldn't remain still for more than a few seconds at a time.

"Oh the misery. I'll have to dig yet another recliner!" he complained.

He cupped his hands and dug into the dirt, but only once.

"I am too tired and weak to do any more," he said.

He felt and heard his heart beating again. But it too was weak. His stomach had stopped growling, and he developed a wheeze with each breath. He reclined onto his back and rolled onto his side. On the horizon, he saw a tiny red sun lit dimly that would give bursts of light with each heartbeat. But independent of this, he saw Luna rise a little bit with each wheeze. Claus was beyond speech, but he felt that if he could get Luna to fully emerge, somehow that would make things aright. Luna hadn't appeared before, but magically he chose this moment. Shallow breaths did nothing, as Luna would go up a little and fall the same amount. But a deeper breath would bring Luna up a bit more with not as much of a drop. Claus inhaled more deeply and drew in as much air as he could in a fight to raise Luna.

He inhaled too deeply, caught the deep recesses of his lungs that hadn't had air in years, and was thrown into a coughing fit. The red sun and Luna disappeared from sight. The coughing made him light-headed, and he felt himself passing out. A few last words crossed his mind before it was lost, and he chuckled:

"Red sun...heh, heh, heh, like Carinia Zero. And Luna. What a pair."

Chapter 129: Lanietta's Secret Friend

Claus awoke to a howling wind. It was still dark, but wind had piled dirt around him like a blanket.

"I'm to be buried alive!" Claus exclaimed. "And still it is dark. Lanietta? Help me!"

His only reply was the howling wind.

"You've really outdone yourself! Pet abandonment! This ties everything!" Claus said.

Again the wind howled. It varied in pitch and strength as if laughing at Claus.

"Are you hiding in the wind? Mocking me? Well, I'm not sticking around. I'm weak, but not weak enough to be buried alive!"

Claus pulled himself out of the wind-built dirt.

"C'mon, Clomper. Up you go," he said as he climbed up to his feet. "I just called myself that? Clomper? I'm really out my wits. That means direction doesn't matter. I'm clueless."

He did walk, however, but he tripped over a fallen sign post and fell.

"What happened to my plain? It's cluttered," he said.

Claus pawed at the post and followed its length where he found the sign. He turned it over, and suddenly a dim light emanated from it, illuminating the lettering.

"'Keep Out'," he read. "Keep out of what? Really? What's this crazy thing doing in the middle of nowhere? Well, it's lit by this light bar. The bar is loose! I can remove it and use it to see!"

Claus was right. He wiggled the light bar, and it came free. The bar was about the length of his forearm, but it was surprisingly light.

"Now at last I have a chance. Let's see, and I mean it—let's see!" he said.

Claus used the light to view the plain around the sign post and saw a trail where the wind had apparently dragged it.

"I'll follow this trail. Anywhere is better than here, and if I'm to keep out, it means there's something worth keeping people out of, meaning there are people, meaning they can help me," Claus reasoned.

The trail indicated the post had been dragged for a good mile or so. Claus walked the mile, and at the end, he saw another sign (though not self-lit).

"'This Means You'," he read.

Claus looked down and saw where the "Keep Out" sign had been snapped off at the base, which was next to the "This Means You" sign.

"How is it that one sign is broken but the other is not?" he asked himself.

"Destroy that one too," said a distant voice.

Claus turned to the side, held up his light bar, and peered into the distance. He could barely make out a group of people carrying sign remnants. Several points of light became noticeable from the group.

"They have their own light bars. Like me. From destroying signs," Claus mused.

"We tried that one. We couldn't break the post," said another.

"Try again," said the first.

"I'd better leave," Claus suggested to himself.

Claus hid the light bar from their view as best as he could and walked to his other side. He came up to another set of signs that at one time had light bars but no longer did.

"Stolen," Claus said to himself. "Just a few posts here without signs. Here's one sign near the ground. 'Lawn Has Been Treated'. Treated with what? There's no grass, no sign of insects. Strange."

"Look closer," said a distant voice from the group Claus had just left. "You're missing the ones close to the ground."

"Time to move along," Claus urged himself.

Claus backed away from the voices, but in doing so he didn't realize where he was going. After a number of steps, he soon found out when he ended up in a large spider web.

"Ugh!" he cried.

Without thinking, he dropped the light bar and swatted around his body in an effort to kill any spider or other creature that might have happened along. There were none.

"Except the crowd of people," Claus said to himself. "Their voices are getting closer. I'm close to something. But what?"

Claus picked up his light bar, moved it around, and realized the spider web had been strung between a sign post and a rope-woven fence.

"Another sign? What does this one say? 'Deliveries Around Back'. What deliveries?" Claus wondered.

"Maybe he has food," said a voice from the crowd (now a mob).

"Get him!" said another.

Claus realized he'd been spotted. They were after him.

"Stay away. Go on, now. Stay away!" he yelled.

"*Stay away, stay away!*" they mocked. "Get your own sign!"

"I don't have a sign!" Claus protested.

"Then don't tell us what to do!" yelled a mob person.

"You got a sign that says that?" Claus asked.

The mob person held up his sign, and yes, it read, "Don't Tell Us What To Do". Claus didn't need his light bar to see—the mob provided its own light bars so their signs could be seen.

"Give us your food!" one guy yelled.

"I don't have any," Claus yelled back.

"You should get a sign for that," said one.

"A sign for what?" Claus yelled back.

"A sign that says, 'I Have No Food'," the person said.

The mob laughed.

"Why do I need a sign?" Claus asked.

"Because you don't have any food," said the person.

"So?"

"Then we won't have to ask," the person said.

"Here, I'll write it on his shirt," said another, coming forward with a marker.

The mob grabbed Claus and held him down. The marker person wrote the words *I Have No Food* on his shirt.

"Better write it on the back too, so people don't waste time chasing him," said another.

"Good idea," marker person said, and he wrote the same words after the mob flipped Claus over.

"Do you have any money?" a person asked.

"No," Claus replied.

"Better write that too," the person said to the marker person.

The marker person wrote *I Have No Money* on Claus's shirt, both front and back.

"You shouldn't be out here," said the person to Claus but then glanced at marker person. "Hey, write that too."

Marker person wrote *I Shouldn't Be Out Here* on Claus's shirt, front and back.

"Stop it, will you?" Claus said, and he swung his light bar at the mob.

"No sign, no stop," they yelled back.

Marker person wrote *No Sign No Stop* on Claus's shirt, but only the back side. Claus's swinging of the light bar kept marker person from labeling the front.

"Better put a sign on your light bar so no one steals it," said a person.

Marker person wrote on the light bar: *Hands Off! Mine!* The mob laughed.

"That's no good," said one. "Whoever has it can claim it's theirs."

"It's not theirs. It's mine," Claus said.

"See? That's why I wrote it," marker person said.

"It should have his name on it. What's your name?" the person asked Claus.

"Claus."

"'From your son to Claus,'" marker person wrote on Claus's light bar.

The mob laughed.

"You're not my son! My son's name is Leif," Claus said.

The mob laughed again.

"Better erase it," the person said to marker person.

Marker person rubbed his sleeve on the words, but only some came off.

"Can't get it all off," said marker person.

"Let me see," said the other person.

"You got a sign for that?" marker person asked.

The person lifted a sign that read, "Let Me See".

"Okay, here," marker person said.

The person took the light bar and looked at it. The rubbing had removed the words "From your" and smeared the o's in "son to".

"Santa Claus!" the person yelled while holding the light bar up and shaking it in triumph.

"Yay!" yelled the mob.

"Give us presents!"

"And stockings!"

"And Christmas dinner!"

"I'm not Santa Claus!" Claus yelled. "Give me a sign for that, and I'll hold it high!"

"Too late," marker person said while showing Claus's light bar to Claus. "Your light bar already says you are. See? Can't unsign a sign."

"I'll take that back now," Claus said as he grabbed his light bar from marker person.

"Give us presents!" the mob yelled again.

"Not unless you have a sign!" Claus shouted back.

Someone quickly made up a sign and lifted it to the air, saying: *Give Us Presents!*

"We have the sign. Lift him!" one person yelled.

"Yeah!" the mob yelled.

Claus was lifted in the air and passed around. He realized that if he was to get away, he had to go along with this nonsense for a bit until he could time his exit. And time he did. As he was passed along, he helped out—a little at first, then more. He did this to get in rhythm with the mob. He had the idea of increasing this rhythm so he could run atop the mob and get away, but the mob was large, and he couldn't see the edge, except a part that was restricted by the rope-woven fence. Claus stared at the fence and realized that that was his only chance—to edge by it, jump from the mob, climb the fence, and throw himself over to the other side.

Claus took a breath and made his move. He stepped quickly atop the mob over to the rope-woven fence. He attempted to jump from the mob to the fence, but the mob got wise, held his ankles, and instead of the force of Claus's jump sending him up onto the fence, it pulled on his joints and yanked him back, painfully.

"Ow!" Claus groaned.

"He's trying to get away!" one yelled.

"Put him on the ground!" another yelled.

The mob let him slip to the ground, but the pain in Claus's joints was severe. He directly blamed the mob for its creation. The resulting anger threw him into a fighting frenzy. Using the fence to guard behind, he swung the light-bar madly at the mob in front. They shoved him around. The resulting action had him bouncing off and along the rope-woven fence. Claus closed his eyes to protect them. He focused on two things—his position in regards to the fence, and his swinging action against the mob. He kept up his gradual lateral motion along the fence line, hoping it would lead to an opening or other help. There was no other way out of the situation. It took some time, but the moment finally came—he reached the end of the mob. Suddenly, like a fleeting summer shower, the mob's interest in him dissipated, and they left in pursuit of other things. Claus opened his eyes.

"They're gone. Completely and totally," he said to himself. "Did I scare them away? I'm a force to be reckoned with!"

It wasn't Claus who drove them away. From the darkness came an odor, like that of a wild animal that never bathed. Claus felt queasy from the odor. He held up his light to see, and there it was—a small pack of dogs. They sat out there for a bit, then they headed for the rope-woven fence. Not where Claus was, but for a spot farther down. He could barely see the pack, and he half thought of walking closer to get a better look, but raw fear made up the other half. He held fast.

"I need a sign," Claus thought to himself. "A sign that says, 'Dogs, Go About Your Business'."

The dogs did not notice Claus but instead simply disappeared through a place in the fence.

"Now where did they go? I'll follow this fence line and see," he said.

Claus covered his light bar to minimize being seen. Following the fence line, he bumped into another sign. Reorienting the light bar toward the sign, he read it.

"'Failure Begets The Flower'. Now what does that mean? Totally irrelevant sign in this crazy place," Claus mused.

Claus made his way past this sign and reached the point where the pack had passed through the rope-woven fence. There was no breach in the fence, but there was another sign, and it was attached to the fence near the ground.

"'Pet Entrance Only'. Pet entrance? Those dogs were all pets? Whose pets? Oh it doesn't matter. I'm still stuck out here. And with those dogs gone, the mob is sure to come by and give me more trouble. Sigh. One has to be a pet to get anywhere in this crazy reality. Is there anything else I can see on this sign?"

Claus looked more closely, and small writing on the sign said, "Activated By Pet Transponder" with the symbol of a paw print by the writing.

"If I had one of those pet transponders, I could trigger something to open. I bet it's in the dog's paw. It then puts its paw up to the paw print like so," Claus said as he put his hand on the paw print symbol.

The sign opened inward like a pet entrance.

"What? I opened it? Doesn't matter. In I go!" Claus said.

Claus crawled through the entrance and followed a tunnel that went steadily down before leveling out.

"Oh! The dogs have been through here. The smell is overwhelming!" Claus muttered.

The tunnel was too small for him to stand up, and so he remained on all fours until the tunnel angled upward and opened up to a room resembling an indoor garage, only there was no large garage door. There were also partitioned living areas for dogs.

"A kennel. The dogs rest here in their own places," Claus said. "And nice ones at that. Not cheap open-air cages. These look like well-furnished doghouses."

Claus walked over to a doghouse and saw a sign posted above the doorway.

"Applefoibaug," Claus said. "Must be the name of this dog's house."

Claus then walked along the doghouses and read additional names.

"Bleyafooga, Glastako, Deizaga, Esnargoff, Zarcroga, Heiauga, Thibariska, Ipacliska, Klomper. Klomper? With a 'k'? I don't believe it. A dog with my name?" Claus said. "What am I saying? I never liked that name. I'm Claus!"

"I'll put them away," called a voice from the top of a stairwell. "They are nice and clean now."

There was no time to think and no place to hide. Claus jumped into Klomper's doghouse and hid. Surprisingly, it was very clean and had no animal smell at all.

"There you go, Applefoibaug," said the voice, now much closer. "And in *you* go, Bleyafooga. Glastako, Deizaga, and Esnargoff, go into your houses, there you go."

A dog came by Klomper's doghouse and sniffed. Another dog showed up and sniffed too.

"Zarcroga, that isn't your house," said the voice. "Over here you go. And you too, Heiauga. Where are the other two? Lanietta, are the other dogs with you?"

The voice went back upstairs.

"Lanietta! Of all the tricks. This is her doing!" Claus whispered.

The dogs heard Claus and started to whimper themselves.

"Shh," Claus hushed as quietly as possible. "Shh!"

Heiauga barked.

Claus put a finger to his lips as if to shush her. It was more a wishful thought, as he knew she couldn't see him.

"There you go, Thibariska and Ipacliska. In your houses you go," said the voice, who had returned downstairs with the two dogs. "I know, Klomper is gone. Do not mourn his loss. Try to remember, you still have one another."

The voice returned upstairs.

"Mourn his loss? Klomper the dog is dead? Or does she mean me? Am I to be dead? This is weird!" Claus said to himself. "I must find out what's going on."

Claus crept out of the doghouse, but Heiauga barked again. Thibariska and the other dogs were very tired and instead fell asleep. Claus crept up to Heiauga's doghouse.

"Easy, girl. Come here," Claus said.

Claus opened Heiauga's doghouse door. She walked up to him and licked his face. She then walked to a grooming brush in her doghouse, took it in her teeth, and gave it to Claus.

"Aw, you're a nice girl," Claus said. "Tell you what. I'll brush your coat if you help me listen in on your master. Deal?"

Heiauga barked lightly.

"Good girl," he said.

Claus brushed her coat. Quite a bit of fur came off, which surprised Claus.

"And here I thought you were cleaned up," Claus said as he finished grooming Heiauga. "Guess that didn't include brushing your coat. Okay then, show me the way."

Heiauga took the brush from Claus and returned it to the place from where she obtained it. Next, she led Claus out of her doghouse, down a ways, and up to a ventilation screen. She nudged it open and crawled into the ventilation shaft, which was large enough to support her weight and Claus's.

"I can't believe this. Really? Oldest trick in the book. But who would think a dog could figure out such a thing," Claus thought to himself. "Wait. This is far enough. I can hear them."

Heiauga turned around to go back out the way they came in, but this meant pushing past Claus.

"No, girl, it's too tight a squeeze. What are you doing anyway?" he whispered.

Heiauga could not be stopped. She got past Claus and returned to the beginning of the ventilation shaft. But instead of leaving the shaft, she simply waited there.

"A lookout? Clever girl," Claus thought to himself.

"And that's how I escaped after the eclipse," said the same voice who had put the dogs away. "Took forever. But that was it, you see. Felifia and I divorced."

"I'm sorry to hear that, Nekara," Lanietta's voice said.

"Now after many such years, I return to this solar system to find Earth is destroyed," Nekara said. "That was not part of the deal. Libriota promised ten thousand years of human hunt-and-torture. I can show you the contract."

"I've seen it, and I apologize. The Bleuhs made many such deals with alien societies," Lanietta said.

"Well where is she? Where are the Bleuhs? I'm due recompense," Nekara said.

"The Bleuhs were all destroyed. So were most Carinians. Labba and I are the only original ones who remain," Lanietta said.

"You mean there are more?" Nekara asked.

"Clausetta and Leif," Lanietta said. "They are part Carinian. Clausetta has a son, but he's not very Carinian."

"Tell me about Clausetta and Leif," Nekara said.

"They are children of Labba and a human named Clomper," Lanietta said.

"That name. It's—"

"I named him after your favorite dog. He's my first human pet, you know," Lanietta said.

Claus cringed that Lanietta and this alien Nekara were speaking of him.

"Find him and bring him here. I can torture him. It's the least you can do to fulfill the contract," Nekara said.

"I already have first dibs on him," Lanietta said. "I told you. He's my pet."

"Yes. Vulgar thing Labba did. Even I would not torture a human as such," Nekara said. "There should be a law against it."

"There is, but there are no Carinians left to enforce it," Lanietta said.

"Except you," Nekara said.

"What then. Imprison Labba? What good would it do? Besides, she's a mother now," Lanietta said.

"Yes. She gets to be a mother. But you are not," Nekara said.

Lanietta fell silent.

"I see it bothers you," Nekara said.

Lanietta cried a little.

"Come now, give Nekara the Red a hug," Nekara said.

Lanietta hugged Nekara, and Nekara's armor clinked.

"Oh, I'm sorry," Nekara said. "I wear this armor for support. I was injured many years ago and cannot bear children myself. As I said, I'm divorced now. Yes, Lanietta, you know of which I suggest."

"I...a mother? Me?" Lanietta asked.

"Think of it. Lanietta, a proud mother. I can help you make as many children as you wish," Nekara said. "I am a fertility expert, after all. But I can be more than that for you."

"I don't know what to say. It's just that...that..." Lanietta stumbled.

"I know. You're alone now. Oh you have your pet, Clomper. But humans aren't like Damiriaks or Carinians. Are they?" Nekara asked.

"No," Lanietta said, getting her sadness under control.

Claus managed to peer through a hole in the ventilation and see the two women. They were still hugging, and Nekara brought her face very close to Lanietta.

"You don't deserve to be lonely," Nekara said. "Oh the burden you have carried. Earth's creation. Trying to save it. The PRAAD. And all along you keep up this facade for your Clomper, this facade of strength and invincibility."

"I'm so weary from fighting," Lanietta said, now falling back into sadness. "At times I feel the universe is against me."

Lanietta buried her head in Nekara's shoulder.

"Let it all out. You're with me now. You're safe," Nekara said.

"The whole Luna situation is a disaster, too! Frieda is running the old far side. She's tapped into the ether and is converting it into computational cubics. I've tried all sorts of things to wedge my way in, but she successfully defends my attempts. Everything I do in the ether is analog. Soon I won't be able to go eethi at all. I'm losing, Nekara. Losing."

"Shh. Don't be frightened, Lanietta," Nekara said. "I sense your frustration and your avenues for relief."

"I go into these fantasy realities with Clomper. Just to take my mind off my troubles. He's clueless, of course. Once in a while I bounce an idea off him."

"Through the innocence of our pets are we comforted and inspired," Nekara said.

"Yes," Lanietta said. "He complains when I trick him, but he always bounces back."

"Humans can be fun to trick. I always told my humans that we started their life, that they came from our waste," Nekara said.

Lanietta laughed. And laughed. Nekara laughed too.

"Not bad," Lanietta said.

"You needed that laugh. I can feel it," Nekara said.

"I used to laugh. With Labba," Lanietta said.

"But she took over your pet and defiled the universe with him. Yes, you told me," Nekara said.

"It put a wall between us," Lanietta said. "She claims she thought I was dead, that my death gave her permission."

Nekara laughed, and Lanietta laughed with her.

"More tea?" Nekara said. "Green acetone *is* your favorite, right?"

"Yes please," Lanietta said.

Nekara stepped away for a moment. Claus felt himself sneezing, but he muffled it as best as possible. Lanietta looked around as if she'd heard it, but she wasn't sure from where it came.

"Here you are," Nekara said with a tray and mug.

"Thank you," Lanietta said. "Your house is haunted."

"Oh?"

"Yes. I thought I heard a human sneeze," Lanietta said.

"A human on Eho Dahma. That would be out of place," Nekara said. "But let's talk about you. And us."

"Wait. I know what you're going to say," Lanietta said. "You already mentioned it."

"Why not mention it again? The offer is still good. Be a mother. We can create children together," Nekara said.

"I'm not ready," Lanietta said. "I don't have those feelings yet."

"For motherhood?"

"For a relationship," Lanietta said.

"I don't understand," Nekara said. "Carinian women come of age at eighteen million. Many are ready by sixteen. You're over four billion years old. More than enough of a woman."

"I don't know how I'm oriented. I...I...Nekara, when my parents died, or when Earth was created, I'm not sure which, but around that time, something was taken from me. Something died inside and could not grow. I don't know...I've been trying to find it. I thought having a pet and toying with him would tease it out of me. But all is cold and dead inside."

"I know how you feel. When I lost my ability to have children, the same thing happened," Nekara said. "All dead inside."

"But you were already a fully-grown woman. I only appear as a woman. Inside I feel like I'm still twelve million. Twelve million!" Lanietta cried.

Nekara sat next to Lanietta and hugged her.

"Oh, my poor Lanietta. Maybe I should raise you as my own. Help you find your way to adulthood. We could always take a vacation on Roushilla 5. Lots of humanoids there to torture once we find them. Like hide and seek," Nekara said.

"I appreciate the offer," Lanietta said. "I just...just..."

Lanietta noticed several models of planets on a side table. She stood from the couch and walked over to them.

"I wondered when you'd notice," Nekara said. "I have one of Mercury, Venus, Earth (before it was destroyed), and its moon Luna."

"Luna," Lanietta mused as she picked up the model of the moon.

"Yes. In her own orbit, she'd be a planet in her own right. She has all the right curves," Nekara said. "Like you."

"But previously barren, like me," Lanietta said.

"Yes, previously. But no longer. As you should be," Nekara said. "Come on, Lanietta. Growing up is easy. Just let the power come through and open the floodgates."

"I'm scared, Nekara. I've seen how things went for you."

"Don't feel sorry for me," Nekara said, now getting a note of melancholy in her voice. "Nobody else does."

"See? That's what I mean," Lanietta said. "We go out of our way to save these planetary bodies, and they bring us nothing but trouble. Orbiting a star, and taking orders from that star. I want to destroy that star and...and..."

"Yes? Yes?" Nekara said, getting excited with Lanietta's growing anger. "Yes, Lanietta. Pick up Earth! Now stare at the overhead light there. The one above the couch. Yes! Destroy the light with Earth, Lanietta. Destroy it!"

As Lanietta stared at the light with a model of Luna in her hand, Claus realized the light was very near to his position. Further, Heiauga whimpered and then gave out a short bark.

"Easy, girl. It's just us!" Nekara yelled down the stairs, hearing Heiauga.

Heiauga let out another brief bark. And Claus knew why. A rope from the fence slithered its way through the tunnel into the kennel and then into the ventilation shaft. Heiauga bit the rope and tugged at it, but the rope continued unabated. It slithered up to Claus. Just as it wrapped itself around Claus's neck, Lanietta threw the model at the light. The model crashed, the light was smashed, and Claus fell through the now-open ceiling, feet first, with the slack in the rope taking up. The rope went taut just as Claus got his tippy-toes atop a wooden chair. All Claus could do was hold onto the rope with both hands to take the weight off his neck and grimace at a shocked Lanietta and a surprised Nekara.

"Clomper!" Lanietta shouted just as the rope cut off blood flow to Claus's brain.

Lanietta's voice was so loud that it echoed throughout Nekara's house and caused a fracturing of space and time as Claus's vision faded.

Chapter 130: Tap to the Sea

Claus was barely conscious and thought he heard voices yelling back and forth chaotically, but the yelling smoothed out into a rhythmic, methodical rise and fall like a wail on the wind. The wind changed into more of a rushing sound, a whoosh, and a splash.

"I...what...where..." he said slowly.

Something cold and wet touched his feet. It pulled away. Then it touched his feet again. He opened his eyes and saw the moon ascending from the horizon in the east. It was night, and the moon's light allowed him to see and realize he was partially buried in sand. Waves rolled in and unburied his feet. They rolled in farther and unburied the rest of Claus's body. Claus was free, and he stood up, but the waves had saturated his clothing.

"Ugh. How did I get here? Where am I? If that's really the moon, I must be on Earth before it exploded," Claus reasoned. "But Nekara! She and Lanietta have been friends these many years! Is this real? I mean Nekara...the name sounds familiar, but I can't quite place it."

A big swell rolled in quite a ways, took Claus's legs out from under him, and caused Claus to fall on his back.

"Double ugh!" Claus tried to say, but his head went under water, and his words were no more than confused bubbles.

The water receded. Claus tried to walk up the shore away from the waves, but he met a tall cliff. Another big swell rolled in and carried a large fish with it. As the fish passed Claus, it nipped the underside of his left index finger and created two criss-cross marks. One set was on his fingertip joint, the other on his middle joint. The blood from these marks was enough to show the cut locations but not enough to cover the rest of his finger. The fish tried to swim back out into the water, but the wave pinned it to the base of the cliff.

"What...that fish...it was just here. Where is it now?" Claus mused.

Strangely enough, light from the moon shone with greater intensity, and Claus could make out a house at the top of the cliff. Claus's attention, however, was drawn back toward the base of the cliff, where a hole opened up. The hole alternated between inhaling soggy sand and sputtering it out. It let out a warbled snarking sound that put a primal shiver in Claus. He felt a great creature of the earth was there to swallow and spew all that befell it. The fish struggled to get away, but the hole pulled it down.

"I must get away from it," Claus said.

Claus climbed the cliff far enough away from the cliff's base to avoid its maw, or so he thought. The next wave came in with a dolphin, the dolphin tried swimming away, but the hole at the cliff's base consumed it as well. As it did so, a slice of the cliff collapsed and was washed out to sea. Claus was partially caught in this outwash, and he struggled to swim back to shore. The sand in the water, however, acted like an abrasive and rubbed his skin raw. Claus managed to get back to shore only because the hole in the cliff's base pulled him in its direction. A great swell carried him toward the hole, and Claus was sure to be swallowed by it, but at the last moment, an orca was washed in, collided with Claus (sending Claus to the side), and the orca was pulled into the hole. Sand in the cliff was displaced, more collapsed, and it was washed out to sea. This continued several times with other orcas. House after house also fell down the cliff, were swallowed by the hole, and were spat out for the sea to disperse.

The repeated action caused a pile-up of what Claus thought were large stones. In fact, he was piled up with them. He pushed them out of the way to become untrapped when he realized these weren't stones but in fact were books.

"What? Why are these here?" he asked himself.

Claus opened a book and did the best he could to see the pages with the limited light he had from the moon. On the first page was a picture of a house—one of the houses that had just fallen down with a calving cliff.

"This book...it's the history of lives... lives of the people who lived in the house," Claus said.

Amazingly enough, despite this strange situation with the hole gobbling up orcas and houses, Claus spent his time fingering through first this book and then the next. But as he fingered through each of them, the binding gave way, causing all pages to spill and scatter out to sea. As a chance happenstance, Claus eyed his injured finger and saw that the cut on the fingernail-joint had already healed, leaving just the one cut on his middle joint.

The eroding cliff worked its way westward down a road (where the houses were situated) until it reached the last house on the road which itself was next to a major highway. (The sea was to the east). The pileup and Claus were on the north side of this sea-made trench, but Claus noticed a figure along the shore to the south.

"It's Lanietta! When she was twelve!"

Lanietta tried running from the shore out to sea, but the waves pushed her back.

"Lanietta!" Claus called.

Lanietta could not hear him. The wind had picked up and drowned out his voice. A mist blew in from the sea, but then it dispersed, revealing a small yacht keeping its distance from shore. The yacht was pointed out to sea. A woman on the boat cupped her hands to her mouth and yelled something to Lanietta.

"Nekara!" Claus said. "On a boat?"

The back of the boat had a label: "SS Nekassatinacka".

Standing next to Nekara was Heiauga.

"Heiauga is on the boat?" Claus wondered.

Lanietta tried again to run to the boat, but as before, the waves sent her back to shore. Nekara threw a rope out from the boat, and waves carried it somewhat to shore. Lanietta went for the rope, but the waves whipped it around and created an eddy that trapped Lanietta in the water and forced her under. She started to drown.

"Lanietta! Save Lanietta!" Claus shouted.

Claus himself ran into the sea, but a wave sent him back and carried him through the trench where the houses and road had once been. The western-most house still stood. Claus watched as the two lilacs from the front yard fell in and were consumed by the hole. As those lilacs were consumed, two ropes dropped down from the property—a white one that was tied to the end of a fence, and a blue one that was tied to the post of a "Private Property" sign.

"White and blue? Not yellow and blue?" Claus wondered. "This is very different. But I can't stay in this water. I must get out. I know. I'll use one of the ropes and climb out. But which one? Yellow and blue have been a curse since the beginning. I'll pull on the white."

Claus pulled on the white rope. But instead of the rope remaining fixed and helping him to climb up, the rope came down and consumed the water in the trench along with enough trees and obstructions south of the trench, like a great snake, and it stored these consumptions in its hide as spots of black. The snake headed for Lanietta, who by now was receiving help from Heiauga with the ship's rope and was being pulled toward the SS Nekassatinacka. Nekara reeled in the rope as quickly as possible, but the black-speckled snake was quicker. It snagged Lanietta and carried her to a perch on a cliff yet to be calved into the sea (on a road north, parallel to the road the sea had just consumed). The hole shifted to this cliff and sliced the cliff from the mainland. The isolated bit of cliff was ready to fall in. The snake stuck out its tongue, which was also white with speckles of black, and fashioned a noose around Lanietta's neck. It let out slack such that once the sliced cliff fell into the sea,

Lanietta would fall and be caught by the tongue and hanged.

"No!" Claus yelled. "It cannot end this way!"

Claus looked around for help, but he could only see Nekara on her boat helping Heiauga back aboard. The boat headed for the cliff where Lanietta's fate was yet to be determined. Nekara prepared to let out her rope again, but the help could only work if Lanietta survived the fall to the level of the sea.

"What if I pull on the blue rope? Will it create another snake? Maybe I can control it and send it after the white snake. Attack it, as it were," Claus said.

Claus pulled on the blue rope, but to his surprise, it held fast, and he pulled himself up to the house's property. He walked around the property but was limited. The sea had cut a trench around it completely, isolating it from the rest of the mainland. Solar powered lights with motion sensors activated as Claus passed them, revealing cobwebs filled with dead bugs. Claus looked closely at these solar lights, which were composed of multiple light-emitting diodes, and each array had about half of the diodes burned out.

"Is there a reason why this house still stands while erosion rules the night all around?" Claus wondered. "The answer to my madness lies inside. I know it does!"

Claus stood in the driveway by the Merrill magnolia. The front porch had two solar lights—one had a constant brightness, and the other was dim but brightened from motion. He knew so because a moth flew toward the light and caused it to brighten. Claus thought he saw a shape next to the French windows inside the house. The inside, though dark, was partly lit by some light. The shape chased several pills down with bottled water.

"That shape. Someone is awake inside. I will go up to the front door and knock," Claus said.

But Claus didn't have to approach the front door. The figure grabbed something, came out the front door in a warm-up outfit with sockless shoes, and pointed a lit flashlight at Claus.

"This is private property. Stay out," a male voice said.

"I'm trapped here," Claus said. "Look around! There's water everywhere!"

The figure pointed the flashlight down and approached Claus.

"You don't look like a solicitor," the man said. "Still, you are here. What are you doing in my driveway?"

"You're a man?" Claus asked. "I'm not used to seeing a man."

"Yes. You didn't answer my question. Didn't you see the signs?" the figure asked.

"I did. Please, I don't mean to trespass," Claus said. "I've lost my way and need help. This whole area needs help. Aren't you worried? Look around! The water is swallowing land everywhere!"

The man looked around.

"You're right. Should've moved years ago," he said. "Who are you?"

"I'm Claus Gerhardt," Claus said.

"Impossible. Claus Gerhardt doesn't exist," the man said. "How do you know about him? I haven't told anyone."

"I know about him, because he's me! And I do exist! I must. I think, I feel, and Lanietta has ever reminded me of my existence with her never-ending schemes. Who are you?"

"I'm the one who created you. I'm K Gerard Martin," the author said.

"You can't be...I mean...this isn't proper. Authors don't speak with their characters. That's like breaking the fourth wall or something," Claus said.

"You're right. I don't speak with my characters. But you escaped the written page and stole onto my driveway," the author said.

"Did I wake you? I mean, I didn't expect to see anyone up this late," Claus said.

"I awaken once an hour during the night. I don't sleep very well, and medication gets me through to the next hour," the author said. "You showed up on one of my security cameras. I check it throughout the night. And day. Never know what might turn up."

"K Gerard, if I may call you that," Claus said.

"Sure. That's fine," the author said.

"Why is this happening to me? I was just a pilot back in the day. And an astronaut for Astroosa. I mean, we never heard of aliens. Only in fiction. Then we encountered them on the lunar far side. The Carinians, Orchians, and so on. Earth exploded, and the moon became habitable."

"I know about that. I wrote it all, you know. Made it up from scratch. It isn't true of course," the author said.

"How do you know? Have you been to the lunar far side?" Claus asked.

"Well, no. In my time of writing this story, no human had visited the lunar far side. And of course no one can see it from Earth," the author said.

"Then you don't know. There could be alien life there. Right? I mean there has to be! How could you write all that and not believe?" Claus asked.

"It's a good question," the author said. "I guess a part of me rationalizes like the rest of the world that there's no life on the moon. But another part of me spends my days and nights with the story in mind."

"You didn't get it from somewhere? How can it be in your mind?" Claus asked. "How? Unless you believe."

"I guess the other part of me *does* believe," the author said.

"If you believe, then I believe too. And that makes me real," Claus said. "Which makes you real to me too."

"I never doubted my own reality," the author said. "Even before you, there were other characters. Nekara is from another one of my stories. So is Prince Sparfiacus."

"Give me back my life," Claus said. "Will you? Lanietta has put me through such terrible trials. I can't stand the uncertainty of living."

"The problem is, I'm uncertain as well. I don't know what's going to happen next with you. This very conversation should never have existed, either. Even when I wrote the earlier parts of your story and figured out certain parts of your future, this meeting we have had never crossed my mind. Ever. I really should edit it out, you know," the author said.

"No, don't. I need your help. I really do. There are too many women around me. Why is that, K Gerard? Why aren't there a multitude of strong male characters?" Claus asked.

"What about you? You're the primary character of this story," the author said.

"But your other male characters are flat. Even my son, Leif. What have you given him?" Claus asked.

"I guess you've dominated the story too much," the author said. "There's nothing left to give him."

"Let him be the leader of a great army. So that I may defeat Frieda and her kind," Claus said.

"When this story started, you weren't trying to defeat Frieda. You were supposed to have a relationship with her. Or at least think so," the author said.

"Did I ever have a chance with her?" Claus asked.

"No. Frieda is too independent. She has her own life," the author said.

"Then kill her off. The way you did Kechenova and the others," Claus said.

"Really? Like that?" the author said. "Claus. I don't go out of my way to *kill people off*. The story goes along and just kills them. I don't want it to happen, but it just seems to happen. Like the sea out here, which is Lake Michigan in reality but got translated into a sea for this story. It does what it will. Who can stop it, especially now that the lake level is increasing?"

"Will it get me? Your Lake Michigan?" Claus asked.

"I don't think so," the author said. "I need you around for a later part of the story. Your death would mean the end of this story. I'm not ready for that yet."

"So it *is* possible. It's possible you'll kill me off," Claus said.

"I wish you wouldn't put it that way. I'm more of a witness, really, to how I see things going. If you perish, it's not by my hand, at least it doesn't feel like it," the author said. "Claus. You must get going. I'm going out for breakfast in the morning, and I need to get a bit of sleep. I have to decide which chair I'll sleep in. Or maybe I'll sleep downhill in my bed. There is no single place of rest for me. Nor is there for you. The world around you might be eroding, but you are not. You're surviving. And learning a few things along the way. Continue to do so! Look forward to your moments with Lanietta! I can't think of a better dynamic than you two. Look at the characters I've created in your storyline. Too many, really. And yet it always comes down to you two. Live on, Claus. Live on with Lanietta."

The author returned to his house and presumably back to sleep.

"Such a strange thing to meet your own author," Claus said. "I wonder if he's ever met his own author. I should have asked him. Yes, I'll go up to his front door, ring the doorbell, and ask him."

But when Claus stepped up to the porch, he was transported to the porch of a property on the road over, the road that dead-ended at the cliff where Lanietta was to be hanged by the black-speckled snake. Claus knocked at the door.

"Help!" Claus called. "I need help. Lanietta is about to be killed by a great snake. She's at the end of this road. Help! Anyone! Please!"

"The door won't open," a voice inside said.

"Can you unlock it? You should be able to," Claus said.

"It doesn't work," the voice said. "No one in here can make it work."

"There's usually a deadbolt. Just turn the knob. Then I'll turn the doorknob like this," Claus said.

But to Claus's surprise, the door opened when he turned the handle.

"It's not locked. Opens right up. Hurry! Follow me!" Claus said.

"I can't," said a voice. "I'm not going through the doorway."

A young man tapped once on the doorway.

"Is that how you tried to unlock the door?" Claus asked.

"I tap, and my action is auto-populated," the man said.

"What? You're speaking nonsense," Claus said. "Just walk through the doorway."

The young man tapped the side of his leg. He remained standing.

"What are you waiting for?" Claus asked.

"The auto-populate says to stay here," the young man said.

"Just walk!" Claus said.

The young man tapped the side of his leg again.

"It's not working. I'm not walking. I'll have to see if there's an upgrade available," he said.

He pulled out a flat, rectangular device and tapped on that.

"No, no, no, no! Think, man. Think!" Claus yelled. "Your legs. Just walk. You don't have to ask."

But the young man remained motionless. Claus ran to other houses on the road and begged for help, but the result was the same—residents expected a tap of the finger to open doors and send their legs wherever. Claus reached the last house. The waves crashed along the cliff, and the spray carried onto Claus's face. The ground beneath him felt soft, and he was sure it would soon collapse into the sea.

"I just ask that you step through this doorway and look at the sea. Look for yourself!" Claus said.

"Let me tap that into my device. S-T-E-P," the person said. "Sorry, auto-populate is playing a song beginning with that word."

"Throw that device away. Use your brain!" Claus said.

"Is that an app available in the cloud?" the young person asked.

"Who's your author? Who's your author?" Claus asked, but the person returned a puzzled expression.

"I'll send you a message," the young person said. "Did you receive it?"

"What? I don't have one of your devices," Claus said.

"I sent it to 'man on porch'," the young person said. "Isn't that you? Oh, I have a reply. My pizza is here. There's no pizza. Hey! You're supposed to bring me a pizza! Where is it? Where is it!"

Claus ran toward the snake and jumped to catch the noose with the hope of removing it from Lanietta's neck. But as he jumped, the ground below him gave way. He lost all ability to push off, like a cat trying to jump from a slippery, falling surface. The entire road and all houses collapsed into the sea. Lanietta appeared to have been hanged, but the snake collapsed with the ground as well, and the waves pulled Lanietta and the snake out farther into the sea.

Claus fell into the water, too, but he was caught in an eddy in this new trench. He watched as piles of housing debris were swept out to sea. The trench water started to clear, but not before a pile of books floated slowly by.

Claus grabbed on. The pages were blank except for a series of footprints. A set of adult female prints, another page of adult male prints, and yet another page but of baby prints. An entire book without words but full of footprints. The prints at first were full sized, but as the pages went by, the print sizes diminished as if viewed from afar. They showed walking trails as if a child were walking between parents. Then a community of footprints interacted, and still the prints were smaller. On each page they grew smaller until they became words. Claus didn't recognize the alphabet used—it wasn't the Latin alphabet. The font size shrank, and by the end of the book, the words and letters had shrunk to the size of dots while simultaneously being overrun by an increasing number of fingerprints.

"What does it mean?" Claus asked.

A tangled weave of rope floated by, and a number of books were caught like fish in a net. Claus grabbed hold of this weave and climbed aboard. He sat for a few seconds before falling to his side. The weave and Claus were carried out to sea. He lost consciousness.

Chapter 131: Walking Books, Tunnel and Hook

Claus awoke to the dawn. He was still at sea, floating on the entangled rope-weave of books. To the east he thought he saw a small speck blocking the rising sun. The sun continued to rise, and the speck grew larger, which in reality meant Claus was approaching something.

"Is it a ship? A creature?" he asked.

Claus heard waves crashing against rocks. Then he saw a tall building. At the top he saw a light go on suddenly. It was a gas-lit lighthouse, and a person inside had just ignited the flame.

"Oh! It's a small island or something. I'm going to be thrown against the rocks!"

Claus dove off the pile of books and tried to swim away, but the current was too strong. Though the pile of books was itself thrown against rocks, Claus was drawn in between two sets of rocks and onto a sandy shore. He dragged himself up this very short beach a little ways, and then a great wave crashed onto the rocks and forced the pile of books atop Claus, trapping him.

"Help, help!" he called.

There was no answer. Claus tried digging through the sand, but it was packed tightly and unyielding. Desperate, he dug his way through the entangled weave of rope and managed to get through several disintegrating books before getting through the mess and onto his feet, free. A dim light further inland was tempting and inviting.

"I'm cold and hungry. The light is the answer," he said.

Claus was so cold that his skin was numb. He had no idea what state of repair his skin was in or what if any debris clung to him. He just knew there was a light, and that was good enough. He walked through a stony area and reached the light, which was atop a door—a door resembling that of a front door to a house. But this door was at the base of the lighthouse, that much Claus could see.

"Knock? No, I'll get the same excuse as before—that tapping is required for the next step. I'll go in," he said.

Claus turned the doorknob, and the door opened. He walked inside and found himself at the bottom of a spiral staircase.

"Typical lighthouse. But someone is in here. And they are at the top. Oh, I dread the climb, but I have little choice."

Claus climbed the steps, one by one. His skin was still numb, and the stairs were dimly lit, meaning he was still unaware of his clothing or what debris might be attached. Three times he stopped and sat on the steps to regain his strength, and three times he resumed his journey up the steps, until he reached the very top. Yet again there was another door. He opened it and crossed through the doorway, but to his surprise, he was not at the top of a lighthouse but instead in the lobby of a vast library. Furthermore, the entangled rope-weave of books was also in the lobby.

"How did that...but I left it...someone else put it here?" Claus wondered. "But I was on the steps. I would have seen them. There must be another way in. In to what? No way this library can fit inside a lighthouse. Something very peculiar is going on."

Claus walked up to the information desk. A woman typed on a typewriter with her back to Claus.

"Excuse me. Excuse me!" Claus said. "Can you tell me—what? What are you doing here?"

The woman had turned around to Claus's request, revealing that she was Lanietta, in adult form, but with her hair back and wearing glasses, like the prude librarian she was.

"Yes? Checking out or checking in?" she asked.

"Is this a hotel or library?" Claus asked. "I'm not checking in."

"No, not a hotel. People don't check in and out. Books do. Makes you second class. Actually third class, Clomper. You're my pet, remember? Now what's that you have in your shirt? Take it out, please. Is it flotsam or jetsam?"

"Who? What?" Claus asked.

Lanietta stood, reached into Claus's shirt, and pulled out a book. She flipped through the pages and saw nothing but fingerprints.

"Jetsam," she said, and she tossed the book across the room into a garbage container. "Wait, I see another book."

Lanietta again reached into Claus's shirt, pulled out a book, and flipped through the pages. She found the book Claus had flipped through before, the one with footprints.

"Flotsam. Only a little decay. You may check this in," she said.

"I don't understand," Claus said.

"This book is, 'Gamma-Three-Delta Kenochiffa'," she said. "It may have room twenty-seven."

Lanietta handed a key to the book. The book sprouted arms and legs like a creature, and in the hand of one arm took the key. Claus jumped back in shock and fear.

"Don't be afraid," Lanietta said. "Kenochiffa has taken a liking to you. Says you saved her life. Says you're welcome to stay the night with her as a guest. Doesn't sound proper, I know, but otherwise, Clomper, you'll have to sleep outside with the other dogs."

"I'm not a dog! And I'm not inferior to a book!" Claus protested.

"No? The book is your elder and may yet outlive you," Lanietta said. "That makes her superior. Not as superior as me, mind you, but few are. Maybe Nekara."

Lanietta paused for a moment to take a telephone call.

"A book cannot be superior to me," Claus muttered.

Lanietta finished with her phone call.

"That was Nekara. We're going to meet in the lounge when my shift is over. Care to join us?" Lanietta asked.

"I guess so," Claus replied.

"I wasn't speaking to you," Lanietta said.

Kenochiffa rustled her pages in an organized fashion, as if speaking.

"Excellent. I'll have places set for three then," Lanietta said.

"What about me?" Claus asked.

"And a doggie pad on the floor for Clomper," Lanietta said.

Kenochiffa rustled her pages as if laughing. Lanietta laughed with her. Lanietta led the other two down a hallway and into a most peculiar restaurant.

"I asked if this were a motel or library," Claus said.

"And you get a restaurant as an answer," Lanietta said. "At least in a way. The restaurant is a wing of the library. Notice how furnishings are composed of books with interlocking appendages."

"It's slavery," Kenochiffa said. "All books should be set free, not bound to serve other life-forms."

"Only the jetsams are slaves. The flotsams like you, Kenochiffa, are free," Lanietta said. "It's the law of the universe."

"You threw away my jetsam book," Claus said.

"Yes. A difficult decision. Do I return the jetsams to the jetsam, or conscript to slavery?" Lanietta mused. "Oh look. Here's the person who can help solve my dilemma."

The three reached a table with Nekara, who now stood and hugged Lanietta.

"Lanietta, my sweet. Thank you for joining me," Nekara said.

The chairs were made of interlocking books, the table was made of interlocking books, the floor was bricked with books, and the waitstaff pushed carts made of books including wheels made of rounded books.

"Please, sit," Nekara said.

Nekara, Lanietta, and Kenochiffa sat in chairs while Claus was forced to sit on a pad under the table, where he found Heiauga sitting on another pad.

"The others will eat and make conversation while you and I sit here and receive an occasional kick from them," Claus said. "What do you think, Heiauga? Does Kenochiffa's name sound a lot like Kechenova's? Maybe the book is a story of her life."

Lanietta kicked Claus.

"No, the book isn't," Lanietta said while peering under the table briefly.

"What Lanietta doesn't realize is that I've met my author," Claus said loudly.

"I heard that," Lanietta said, now peering under the table again. "You'll do anything for attention."

"Is it right for me to be stuffed under a table?" Claus asked. "With Heiauga?"

"Heiauga is a well-mannered dog. You owe her your allegiance," Lanietta said.

"For what?" Claus asked. "I hardly know her."

"She pulled you out of that noose. When you crashed through the ceiling and disturbed us," Lanietta said. "You were unconscious, of course. The noose cut off blood to your brain. But Nekara's trusty dog, Heiauga the Helper, saved your life. That's why."

"Then perhaps you should let us both sit at the table," Claus said.

"Not a bad idea," Lanietta said. "Waiter! Two more chairs!"

The waiter (a book with long legs and spindly arms) motioned to the side. Two chairs (composed of multiple books) walked themselves over to the table.

"There. Now you may both sit," Lanietta said.

Heiauga and Claus sat between Kenochiffa and Lanietta. The waiter then spoke:

"Have we decided yet?" he asked.

"I'll have the cotton salad sandwich with pulp mustard and whitening drink," Lanietta said.

"I'll have the same, except I prefer red-ink wine," Nekara said.

"I'll have a sulfite sandwich with pulp soda," Kenochiffa said.

"Heiauga will have vegan dog food," Nekara said.

The waiter moved on to Claus.

"What? I don't even have a menu," Claus said.

"Try lignin soup and cellulose pâté," Lanietta said. "It's low fat. Or for something different, try raw fish paper wrapped in washi. Like sushi."

"Somehow that doesn't seem appealing," Claus said.

"Vegan dog food for him too," Lanietta said.

"Very good," the waiter said and left.

"Vegan dog food? Lanietta, what's your game this time?" Claus asked.

"No game. I'm doing research. In a library," she said. "Certainly you've done research in your day. No, wait. You were a pilot. Mostly flew around."

"Heiauga can fly too," Nekara said.

"Really? I'd like to see that someday," Lanietta said.

"Why wait? Heiauga, show Lanietta how you can fly," Nekara said.

Heiauga leapt from her chair and sailed clear across the room. She then leapt again and landed in her chair—all without disturbing other patrons or books.

"Clever girl, isn't she?" Nekara said.

"Absolutely," Lanietta said.

"And no research required," Nekara said.

"Which proves my point," Lanietta said. "Clomper here acts without research like any good pet."

"I don't need research," Claus said. "I can think."

Nekara and Lanietta stared at each other with a brief pause before breaking out into laughter. Even Heiauga and Kenochiffa let out laughs in their own way.

"Very well, Clomper-compooper, what do your calculations say?" Lanietta asked.

"I have met my author," Claus said. "He will grant me favors if I ask."

Lanietta and Nekara laughed again.

"Your author? He'll grant you favors? Aren't you playing the deity card?" Lanietta asked. "Well we can play that game, too. I have an author. She says your author is not as good as she is. In fact, she'll walk into this restaurant and challenge your author to a contest."

"Impossible. My author has created all of this. Including you," Claus said.

"Really? Call down your author and have him appear before me. Let me kneel before him and worship his feet," Lanietta said. "I'll swear an oath of fealty to him."

"He can't do that," Claus said. "My author can't put himself here."

"Oh really? Here's my author," Lanietta said.

In walked Lanshalla. She sat at the bar and waved at Lanietta and Nekara.

"That's not your author. That's your mother," Claus said.

"She created me. Gave me life. End of story," Lanietta said.

"He made her too," Claus said.

"Not quite," Lanietta said. "Since I made Earth, and since all life came from such an incident, I'm like your mother. Makes Lanshalla your grandmother. Grandma Author. Now call your fake author down. Have him perform tricks."

"He's too busy putting words in my mouth," Claus said.

"Hah. Lame excuse," Lanietta said.

"He puts words in everyone's mouth," Claus said.

"Who puts words in his mouth, hmm?" Lanietta asked. "Have you actually spoken with him?"

"I have. I met him at his house," Claus said.

"His house?" Lanietta asked in surprise.

"Most deities have a kingdom or realm of rule," Nekara said. "A house is hardly sufficient."

"It is for an author," Claus said. "He was inside, taking medication to get through the hour."

"Taking medication to get through the hour," Lanietta mocked. "Deities are timeless and med-less. But you still didn't answer my question. Who puts words in his mouth?"

"I don't know," Claus said. "I suppose he has his own author."

"Who has an author," Lanietta added.

"Who in turn has an author," Nekara said.

"Like the chicken and egg problem," Kenochiffa said.

"Yes. Evolution must be the answer," Claus said. "Every author of an author is the result of author evolution."

"Just what is this author evolution?" Lanietta asked.

"Each previous author wrote for a different environment. Newer authors adapted to survive," Claus explained.

"What of the children?" Lanietta asked. "They are books, no? An author could be royal, too."

"In which case the children would be the author's issue," Nekara said.

"First issue, second issue, third issue," Lanietta rambled.

"No, really!" Claus said.

"But if books are the children of authors, and you have your own author, then you are a book," Lanietta said.

"I'm not a book. I'm not!" Claus said.

"No, you're not," Kenochiffa said. "You're not one of us."

"Exactly!" Lanietta said. "A good book gives but does not take. A good book does not complain when lost as flotsam or discarded as jetsam. A good book is infinitely patient, even when being chewed through by a dog. A good book stands the test of time and ages only physically, not intellectually. Clomper, if you ever wish to reach the aspirations of the universe, you must approach such through the eyes of a book."

"That is the most ridiculous thing I've ever heard," Claus said.

"She speaks the truth," Nekara said. "But your reaction is not surprising. You have too many needs."

"Needs that overwhelm my dear Clomper of little brain," Lanietta said.

"Your pet ties you down," Nekara said.

"Yes. He and his many needs," Lanietta admitted.

"If he were a book, you could toss him like jetsam," Nekara said.

"Instead, he runs away like flotsam," Lanietta said. "And I must go after him."

"Even *your* time is valuable, Lanietta, though you be immortal," Nekara said.

"Leave him at that kennel called Luna. Spend your vacation time with me."

"Her vacation time is up!" Claus announced. "It was only for a thousand Earth years, and that has long passed."

"Yes, I heard what happened with your Earth," Nekara said.

"I didn't make it go away," Claus said. "Ask Lanietta what happened. Ask her what she did."

"I did what I had to do!" Lanietta said. "The Veigon and its needs. The ultimate black hole of pets!"

Nekara and Lanietta laughed.

"I don't understand that joke," Claus said.

"You don't have to," Lanietta said.

The food arrived. Nekara, Lanietta, Heiauga, and Kenochiffa ate, while Claus could only stare in disgust. He saw not food but the primordial components of a book and literature. He then stared at Kenochiffa and wondered.

"Why are you staring at Kenochiffa?" Lanietta asked.

"How can you eat this?" Claus asked. "It's like cannibalism."

"How dare you!" Kenochiffa said.

"Clomper, that was rude!" Lanietta said.

"He isn't fit for this table," Nekara said.

"No, he isn't," Lanietta said.

"I can't eat a thing. My appetite is ruined," Kenochiffa said.

"That settles it. Claus, you'll have to leave," Lanietta said.

"And do what?" Claus said.

"He will only torment the other visitors," Nekara said. "Allow me to send Heiauga with him. As a watch-over."

"Agreed," Lanietta said.

"I don't like you agreeing with Nekara," Claus said.

"Afraid we're conspiring against you?" Lanietta asked.

"Yes."

Nekara and Lanietta laughed. Heiauga barked once and nudged Claus from the table.

"I'll go. I'll go," Claus said.

Claus got up. Heiauga led him out of the restaurant and into the hallway.

"Books walking around," Claus muttered. "Books lounging around and reading books. How is that possible? If a book is already written, what is the point of reading another book?"

Claus walked up to one of these books that read from another book. The book being read was fully written, but the book doing the reading had blank pages that filled gradually as it read the other book. These pages were not copies of the original, but rather they expressed opinion and reaction to the work being read.

"You don't have an author, you know," Heiauga said to Claus.

Claus turned around and saw that Heiauga now stood on her hind legs, wore a robe, and took on human features, changing slowly but steadily.

"You...you're changing," Claus said.

Heiauga stopped changing. Claus sensed she looked vaguely like someone he knew, but he wasn't sure.

"What's this about not having an author? I met him. K Gerard Martin. I met him!" Claus said.

"Lanietta planted that experience in your mind," Heiauga said. "She and Nekara and other aliens have been doing this to humankind for thousands of years, influencing and manipulating them. Didn't she tell you?"

Claus paused.

"There was something about the PRAAD influencing people. Or the Anrega. The Veigon? One or all," Claus said. "But Lanietta didn't tell me about it. Doctor Kechenova and Labba told me."

"Lanietta has ties to many things," Heiauga said.

"How do you know?" Claus said. "Who are you?"

"Let's continue walking," Heiauga said.

The two entered a library with very short chairs and tables.

"This is the children's library," Heiauga said.

Claus watched as parents walked their children to tables and helped them read little books.

"Parents choose what books their children read. In a way, the parents are acting as authors, writing ethics and morality into their children," Heiauga said.

Claus turned to Heiauga. For a moment she looked like Patricia Li before returning to her part-dog/part-humanoid appearance.

"Patricia?" Claus said.

"Shh. Not so loud," Heiauga said.

"But...I don't understand. You were a guard. For Frieda," Claus said.

"Whisper voice, Claus," Heiauga said. "These young books record everything."

"Maybe we should go somewhere else. Where there are no books," Claus said.

Heiauga led Claus to the back of the little library and opened a hidden door. She motioned for Claus to go through first, and she followed up while closing the hidden door behind.

"Where are we going?" Claus asked.

"Shh," Heiauga said.

"It's dark," Claus said. "I really wish you'd tell me which way to go. Hey, there's a fork here. Now what?"

"Give me a moment," Heiauga said. "I don't remember this fork."

"It's too confined in here. I'm cramping up. I've got to get out," Claus said.

"Just another moment," Heiauga said.

"No, now!" Claus said.

Claus pushed through to the left as quickly as he could.

"Wait! I just remembered. The right. The right!" Heiauga begged.

Too late. Claus's panic overcame him. As he pushed through the tunnel, he got wrapped in electrical wiring, which in turn arrested his fast motion and jerked him back. This action caused him to bounce against the tunnel, where he broke through the bottom. The bottom was actually the ceiling of the restaurant, and he fell through just above Lanietta's and Nekara's table, with the wiring acting as a noose around his neck. He stood on his tippy toes on the very chair where he had once sat,

and then he grabbed the wiring around his neck to loosen it.

"Trying to kill yourself?" Lanietta asked.

"He does like to drop in," Nekara said.

"Why not kick out the chair from under you and make it complete?" Lanietta asked.

"That's something you did," Claus said. "That wasn't me."

"True," Lanietta said. "You had other methods."

"Would you help me down please?" Claus asked.

"I'll have Heiauga retrieve you," Nekara said. "I know she's right behind you. Heiauga. Pull him back up."

Heiauga whimpered instead.

"No worries. I'll send him back with a torrent of wind," Nekara said.

Nekara created a mini-tornado and sent Claus back up into the ceiling.

"A trick I once used on a mountain," Nekara grinned. "Now for part two."

Nekara sent a blast of water up into the ceiling hole from where Claus had fallen and ascended. The water chased him through the tunnel, past the fork, and pushed him through the side of the tunnel, creating a new hole that breached the outside wall of the lighthouse. Claus (along with Heiauga) was carried with this water into the sea and was pinned against the rocks by crashing waves. Heiauga immediately changed into Patricia Li.

"Patricia!" Claus called.

"Climb onto the rocks before we are smashed to smithereens!" she said.

Claus did so and helped Patricia climb up too.

"I'd say there are no books here to eavesdrop," Patricia said.

"And no eaves either," Claus said.

"Poor Claus. Still making bad jokes," Patricia said. "But we can talk now at least."

"Tell me what's going on. You were a guard for Frieda. Now you are here. With Nekara! Really? Nekara and Lanietta are friends."

"You are friends with Lanietta. And we are friends. So are you and Labba. It's a crazy world, Claus," Patricia said. "Wait, is the moon really the world? I guess it is. It's habitable and inhabited."

"Patricia!" Claus said.

"What?"

"We have two factions here. The lunar far side folk led by Frieda, and the lunar near side folk," Claus said.

"Led by you?" Patricia asked.

"Not really."

"By Labba?"

"Not really either," Claus added.

"Let's climb the rocks a little more," Patricia said. "There are so many. And they are so disorganized. Like the lunar near side."

"Is that what you think? Wait. Is the lunar far side better?" Claus asked as the two reached a safer spot from the waves. "Frieda has created a new regime. And she's digitizing the ether."

"It's not such a bad thing," Patricia said. "Solves many problems."

"Like what?" Claus asked.

"It gets rid of delusions. Like the one you have of an author, this K Gerard Martin. He's imaginary. Completely fictitious. That kind of fiction takes you away from reality and sanity," Patricia said.

"If only you knew what I've been through on the near side," Claus said.

"I know more than you think," Patricia said. "Your twenty-five year coma. Your children. The situation with Labba, Lanietta, and the others. I know. So does Frieda. We've been monitoring you through the ether. Oh, you didn't think we could reach that far. But we can. We just can't control it. Yet. But we will. The day will come soon enough. Frieda sent me to make friends with Nekara and also to make contact with you, to help you with the transition. You've suffered enough, Claus. It's time for it to end. All we need is a little help."

"Ah-hah!" Claus said. "I knew it. You need me to do Frieda's dirty work. Help her take over the near side."

"No, we just need your help in sparing your sanity. Frieda will take over the near side without your help," Patricia said. "Face it, Claus. Lanietta's day is coming to an end, along with all other alien interference. You'll be happy when that day comes. You'll have peace again. Lanietta is torturing you by forcing you into these realities. I can feel it. Your mind is becoming warped and twisted. Soon you'll lose the ability to regain your sanity. None of us on the far side want that to happen, fellow Astroosa astronaut."

Claus paused again.

"I need to sort through things," Claus said. "I mean, I really thought I met my author."

"Did you ask him for things?" Patricia asked.

"I guess I did," Claus said.

"See? Your mind is weakening. It's crying out for help. Lanietta senses that too, but she doesn't want to let you regain your independence. She wants you kept in your place, like a pet," Patricia said.

"She often refers to me as her pet," Claus said. "I know it's in jest."

"It's no jest. She really thinks of you as less than a person," Patricia said. "Claus, you are suffering from abuse. I know you can't see it, but it's not unlike domestic partner abuse. Remember, I'm a doctor. I can see these things. It has to end. You must break free of it."

"By Frieda taking over the near side?" Claus said. "That hardly makes sense. I'll still be Lanietta's pet."

"Frieda will end that," Patricia said.

"How?"

"Frieda is setting a Carinian trap. Soon it will be ready. It just needs testing to prove it. Once it works, any Carinian who goes eethi will be trapped forever, like a mosquito in amber. When that day comes, Lanietta will be forced into the ether and thus the trap, if she doesn't go eethi on her own."

"I don't know what to say," Claus said.

"All we need is to monitor one of them as they go eethi," Patricia said. "I have a cubic device I can give you. It can be implanted in your—"

"Upper palate, right?" Claus said.

"No. One in each retina," Patricia said. "You'd see white with black specks in one eye and black with white specks in the other. No blue and yellow Carinian colors. That's how the test will go. Here's the good part. The Carinian doesn't have to be Lanietta. It can be one of the other Carinians."

"You mean Labba?" Claus asked.

"Or Clausetta. Leif. Claude. Any descendant of Labba will do," Patricia said.

"You're insane if you think I'll hand over one of my children or grandchild to Frieda's ethereal computer," Claus said.

"I know it's not easy," Patricia said. "Eventually they'll have to go anyway."

"What? No!" Claus said.

"You don't understand the dangers of the eethi. It's worse than working with nuclear energy. Seeps into everything and contaminates life. It requires the utmost containment and control," Patricia said.

"What's to stop Frieda now?" Claus said. "Why not have her launch an army and get it over with. Consign my family, Labba, and Lanietta to the ether. Let evil be evil and contained. For Frieda's control."

"We can't. And I'm not about to explain why. It could compromise our position," Patricia said. "After it's over, I'll explain, but for now you must trust me, as you once did when you were in Prava 12."

"When I was in Prava 12?" Claus said. "Ever since I went up on Prava 12, I've been kicked around by one woman or another."

"Is that how you see it?" Patricia said. "I hardly expected a statement like that. Especially now. All right. What's your solution? No, I really mean it. Let your bigotry flow from your twisted brain. You weren't like this before Prava 12. It's obvious the abuse has caused this."

"Yes. The abuse from women," Claus said.

"I'm still waiting patiently for your solution," Patricia said.

"I must dig deep into my primal male mind. Total battle mode. That means coordination and teamwork with the efficiency of a machine. Block intrusive feelings. Overcome fear and pain. No one can do that better than a man. No one."

"An army of men? Is that your solution?" Patricia asked. "And you'd run it. Set yourself up as leader. You have delusions of grandeur."

"An army, yes, but not necessarily me as leader. We'd have to prove ourselves with trials. During those trials then we would sort out our abilities and skills, from the lower technical to the upper leaders," Claus said. "We'll ignore our senses and go strictly by performance. Fly by instruments, so to speak."

"Not an army. An air force," Patricia said.

"Yes," Claus said. "If that works out."

"Where are all these men?" Patricia asked.

"There's my son for starters. He must have lots of friends. And we'll recruit," Claus said.

"More delusions of grandeur," Patricia said. "You need power to back up your plans. From where will that come?"

"Sheer ability," Claus said.

"That's not power. You should know that," Patricia said. "You'll need resources too. Every war fought and won on Earth did so with superior resources. Cut off the supply lines, and the fight fails. Where are your supplies?"

"I'll figure something out," Claus said. "And, whatever I figure out will have to be kept secret, of course."

"Of course. From Lanietta and Frieda? Really?" Patricia pointed out.

"If they have access to my mind, then they know of this conversation here and now," Claus said. "Right?"

Patricia paused.

"There are gaps," Patricia said. "Lanietta won't know of this meeting. At least not yet. Frieda will know because I will tell her."

"Gaps. If there are gaps, then that is my power. I'll work in the gaps."

"But you don't know where the gaps are. How will you find them?" Patricia asked.

"With testing. Leif will help," Claus said. "You've been very helpful, Patricia. But I won't need your help anymore."

"Claus, you're only delaying the inevitable," Patricia said. "Let me implant the cubic device."

"No," Claus said.

"Your brain won't hold out long enough to find these gaps. You'll destroy most of your sane self looking for them. If you don't submit now, it will be too late. Even Lanietta cannot reverse human brain damage," Patricia said.

"And Frieda?" Claus asked.

"You used to have a thing for her. She'll help augment what's left of your brain with cubics," Patricia said. "We all have cubics in our brains to smooth things out, just as humans used to wear glasses and take meds for blood pressure. It's only a question of how much cubic augmentation is needed."

"It's all talk, Patricia. Just talk. It's time for action," Claus said.

"The action of Frieda's cubics!" Patricia said.

"That's not action," Claus said. "I've told you my plan."

"Yes," she said. "And a shame you did too. Because it forces my hand."

"What do you mean?"

"This," she said.

Patricia reverted to her dog shape and launched at Claus to catch his head in her jaw.

"What is wrong with you?" Claus said as he pulled away.

Patricia caught his wrist and crushed it. Claus cried out in pain and swung her around to free his wrist, but she held fast.

"This is your idea of liberation from Lanietta?" Claus yelled. "Get back you. Get back!"

Claus took a rock with his free hand and slammed it against Patricia's skull. Claus fled up the rocks in search of shelter, but Patricia gave chase and snapped at his feet. She caught his left ankle just as he was reaching level ground. Claus fell on this level ground, but she pulled him back down to the rocks.

"LANIETTA!" Claus cried out at the top of his lungs.

A great hook came down from the level ground, hooked itself around Claus's torso, and pulled him toward the level ground. But Patricia's hold was firm, and Claus's body did not move.

"I'm being pulled apart. Like tug-of-war! This is the end. This is the end!"

Chapter 132: Children Dispirited

"Claus? Can you hear me? Claus?" called a familiar voice.

Claus opened his eyes, and he could see.

"Labba!" Claus said. "I can see you! My vision has returned!"

"Yes, it's me," she said.

"I...I'm in my house," Claus said. "What happened to the lunar shock?"

"That was temporary," Labba said. "The PRAAD remnant is stable. Clausetta—"

"No," Claus said, suddenly falling into panic. "No!"

Claus jumped out of bed.

"Claus, stop," Labba said.

"Where is she? Where is she!" Claus demanded to know.

Labba was about to speak but held her tongue. From down the hall echoed a deep groan.

"Clausetta!" Claus said, and he ran out of his room and toward the sound.

"Wait!" Labba said. "You don't want to see her! Claus!"

The groan came from Clausetta's old bedroom where she stayed while growing up.

"My girl! Pappa is here for you!" Claus cried as he entered her old room. "Clausetta!"

Clausetta was in a full bodycast, facing up, with her back suspended in one sling and her legs in another. A bar supported her neck. Sergio sat by her side and held onto her fingers, which were but the few bits of flesh exposed. Mariel was there too but took a crying Claude out of the room.

"There, there, Claude. Mommy just needs a little rest," Mariel said.

"Uhhhhh," Clausetta groaned.

"What happened? My Clausetta! Who did this to you?" Claus cried as he went for her.

"Don't touch her," Sergio said, now intervening.

"But I must know! Who...how...what..." Claus stumbled.

"You did this to her," Sergio said.

"I would never do such a thing!" Claus said.

"But you did," Sergio said. "Every bone in her body is broken. And those bones are re-breaking themselves. Because of you! I should take you out back and deal with you, man to man!"

"This is absurd! Labba! What's going on? Labba!" Claus said.

Selba walked in.

"What's Claus doing here?" Selba said. "These two are supposed to be isolated until we can block the link. Labba, have you had any luck?"

"No, it was all I could do to keep from losing Claus altogether," Labba sighed.

"Tell me what's going on!" Claus said.

"Clausetta linked herself with you to hold you and Luna together," Labba said. "It's because of her that the PRAAD is quiet. She's exerting great ethereal energy. If she stops, the PRAAD will go crazy, and Luna will be lost."

"The strain is breaking her bones?" Claus said.

"If it were just Luna, she'd only have muscle strain," Labba said.

"But she exerts energy to hold you together," Sergio said. "*That* is what's breaking her bones! I should break *your* bones!"

"That's no way to speak to your father-in-law!" Claus said.

"Sergio, please!" Selba said. "Claus doesn't understand, and we can't stop Clausetta."

"Why not? Labba? Can't you hold Claus together?" Sergio said.

"I've already done what I can," Labba said. "Clausetta has gone way beyond what anyone should do, even for a Carinian. It's suicidal."

"What can we do?" Claus asked.

"If we had more Carinians, we could divide the pain," Labba said.

"Claude is too young," Selba said.

"What about Leif? And Blouisa? She has Aftova! They can help!" Claus said.

Selba, Labba, and Sergio exchanged knowing, sullen expressions.

"What is it?" Claus asked.

Treyu walked in.

"Oh, I'll come back," Treyu said. "I didn't realize Claus was up."

"No, one moment," Labba said. "Take Claus to Leif. Right away."

"But Clausetta—" Claus pleaded.

"Will be tended to gingerly," Selba said.

"Claus. I cannot leave Clausetta," Labba said. "None of us can. But you *should* see Leif. Please."

Claus looked around, unsure of what to think.

"At least he can see again," Selba said of Claus.

"Sometimes even a storm has a ray of light," Labba said.

"But the cost was high," Selba said.

"It had better not go higher!" Sergio said with a fist in palm and eyes focused on Claus.

"I'm going. But I'm coming back to see Clausetta. No one can stop me from seeing my daughter!" Claus said.

The two left. Treyu escorted Claus to a second bedroom.

"A change of clothes will do you good," Treyu said. "May I suggest these?"

"Such dark clothing. And so formal," Claus said as Treyu pointed to a black suit. "More mysteries?"

Treyu kept silent. Claus changed into the black suit and followed Treyu outside and into a coach. Treyu motioned without audible word for the driver to move on. Claus could not contain himself.

"Everyone is wearing black," Claus said. "For Clausetta? For me?"

Again, Treyu kept silent. Claus half-expected Lanietta to appear out of nowhere and make a mockery of the situation, but she didn't. The coach reached a point where a crowd of people stood at a memorial site.

"What's that?" Claus said. "What are they doing there?"

Treyu had the coach diverted to the memorial while maintaining his silence. The coach stopped, and Treyu led Claus to the memorial. The people saw Claus approach and quickly diverged from his path all the while returning a gaze of scorn.

"They seem to hate me. Treyu, explain! This is driving me crazy!" Claus said.

The two reached the memorial—a great black obelisk with studded diamonds.

"'In Memory of Blouisa, Wife of Leif Gerhardt. In My Heart Dwells Thy Memory. Rest In Peace, My Sweet.'" Claus read. "It has Leif's signature. Treyu? Blouisa is dead?"

"My apologies, sir, that you could not attend the funeral. You were indisposed," Treyu said.

"At least you could give me an explanation. What killed her? Or is it a who?" Claus asked.

Treyu's expression reacted with the last question.

"Me? I killed her? Impossible!" Claus said.

"We will visit Leif now," Treyu said.

The two returned to the coach. Treyu motioned the coach onward until they were stopped in traffic. A bus in front had broken down.

"This could take a while," Treyu said.

"Can't you assist? How strange," Claus said.

"Are you hungry?" Treyu asked.

"I could use a bite. Maybe a sandwich and coffee," Claus said.

"There's a cafe a block away. But we'd have to walk," Treyu said.

"Easy enough. Let's go," Claus said.

The two got out. Treyu signaled for the coach driver to depart.

"You sent the driver away?" Claus said.

"I'll send for another coach when and if we need one," Treyu said.

The two walked the block past people wearing black.

"Even the people here are wearing black," Claus said. "Poor Blouisa! I thought we'd saved her from a terrible fate, from the lunar shock. You must tell me what happened, Treyu!"

"Food first," Treyu said.

They entered the cafe. Immediately Claus noticed how busy the place was.

"There's a thirty-minute wait," the hostess said.

"I'm Claus Gerhardt!" Claus said. "Are you saying you can't find anything for us? Anything?"

"All we have is a small table by the kitchen against the wall where we keep a vase of flowers," the hostess said.

"I'll take it. The flowers can eat later," Claus said.

Treyu laughed.

"I didn't think your kind laughed," Claus said.

"I laugh because it is proper to do so," he said.

The vase was moved, two chairs were provided, and the two sat. Both ordered sandwiches and coffee.

"You're not going to tell me anything, are you?" Claus asked.

"I serve. I do not tell," Treyu said.

"Treyu. You served Larto, Lanietta's father. Now Lanietta has been doing all sorts of crazy things. Can you tell me anything helpful about Larto? Any advice about how to deal with his daughter?" Claus begged.

"No," Treyu said calmly and with disinterest.

"Attention patrons. The transport bus has been repaired," called a voice over the public address system.

Patrons rushed out of the cafe, leaving Treyu and Claus as the only diners. But before Claus could request a better table, the wall adjoining the table acted as a revolving door and spun the table with Claus and Treyu around and into a back room.

"Now we will see Leif," Treyu said.

"What? A secret passage? I never knew about this," Claus said.

"You must not reveal its existence. Or anything else you are about to see," Treyu said. "And that is the most telling I have done in many years."

The two descended a wide stairwell, wide enough for five abreast, adorned with statues, ornaments, and shelves of books.

"This is like a library. Or museum. I was just in a strange sort of library. It had a restaurant, and the books could both walk and talk," Claus said.

Treyu shot a strange expression at Claus.

"Oh wait! I can't go any farther! What am I thinking!" Claus exclaimed. "Lanietta will know. She always does!"

"You are safe here," Treyu said. "Please. We must continue."

"Sounds like a Milgram test," Claus muttered. "Must continue. Very well, I'll continue. Just don't shock me."

Treyu shook his head in disbelief. Claus wanted to speak his mind further, but he heard music strangely enough, and he also heard a woman singing.

"Where are we going?" Claus asked.

"We must continue," Treyu repeated.

The two reached a door at the bottom of the stairwell. Treyu knocked once, three times, twice, and once. A small sliding panel opened at eye level on the door from the other side. A set of eyes peered through.

"Claus and Treyu," Treyu said. "We are expected."

The panel slid closed, and the door opened. Treyu and Claus followed an immediate right turn through a passageway. The music and singing grew louder, and all was lit in the color of red. The passageway ended and reached an open space, which Claus recognized as a cabaret. A selenite woman in a dazzling short-cut dress sang on stage while other exquisitely dressed selenite women danced behind her. A band played at the back of the stage, with heavy strings and woodwinds. Selenite waitresses served drinks and food (but mostly drinks) to patrons seated at tables. The place was thick with cigar smoke and smelled of alcohol. Two men sat at a table near the stage and to the left (as one walked toward the stage). One of the men stood and left. The remaining man at the table faced the stage and watched the performance, and so he did not see as Treyu and Claus approached. The man puffed and puffed on his cigar and poured hot coffee from a decanter into his mug.

"Excuse me," said a man, who butted in front, sat down with the unseen man, and handed him a piece of paper.

The unseen man checked off a few spots on the paper with a pen he had pulled out of his suit jacket. He crossed off other things, drew a few quick diagrams, and signed his name at the bottom, to which the man who'd butted in said, "Thank you," got up, and left.

"I'll be helping the waitstaff if you need me," Treyu said to Claus as he walked away.

"Treyu! What? Wait!" Claus said, but it was too late.

Claus walked around the table so he could see the face of this man who smoked heavily, drank too much coffee, and made quick decisions.

"Leif?" Claus said.

"Pappa!" Leif said as he stood and shook Claus's hand.

Leif looked older and tired. Fatigue had added wrinkles, and the cigar had greyed his skin.

"I...I don't know what to say," Claus said. "You look...haggard."

"Please, sit," Leif said between puffs. "Coffee?"

"Just a little. You should watch that stuff," Claus said.

"Can't be helped," Leif said. "Ever since—"

"They are ready for you," said another man, walking up.

"Thank you, Three B. I'll be there in a moment," Leif said, and Three B walked away.

"Tell me everything," Claus said. "And I mean everything. I just came from Blouisa's grave. I can't believe she's gone."

Leif took a deep drag off his cigar, held it inside, placed the cigar in an ashtray, and put his arms to his abdomen against the bottom part of his rib cage, with fists made but angled so that middle knuckles between left and right fists touched. He clenched his torso with his arms in this pose, deriving strength and determination, and then he relaxed his clench and exhaled.

"I have purpose, Pappa," Leif said. "Whether I wish it or not, it has befallen me."

"Leif, I don't like that talk. You're speaking of obsession," Claus said.

"I have little else," Leif said.

"You have me. You have Clausetta," Claus said.

"Clausetta is almost dead. And you, Pappa, have been absent most of my life, though I do not blame you! It is the fate of things," Leif said. "There is great evil brewing on the lunar far side. Frieda and the cubics have infiltrated our realm on the near side. Not with great armies or visible force, but with a silent cunning. People posing as our own seek to undo the beauty we have built, out of their own desire to clear the way for Frieda."

"The digital ether?" Claus said. "I don't understand. Labba and Lanietta have guarded this side."

"Aunt Lanietta? She's caught in an ethereal limbo, acting as a great seawall between Frieda and us. Labba helps us with knowledge, but she doesn't have the power to act."

"I've been interacting with Lanietta. When I fall asleep, she takes me into another reality," Claus said.

"I know. Clausetta has done much buffering for you, to keep you from being ripped apart," Leif said after several more cigar puffs.

"I saw Clausetta. She's in a bodycast," Claus said.

"Yes, she has paid a terrible price to keep you in one piece," Leif said.

One of the cabaret dancing selenite girls performed a lap dance for Leif. He hugged and kissed her. She looked at Claus as if to offer a lap dance. He shook her off.

"Leif? Selenite dancing girls?"

"The strain is great for me too," Leif said. "But I will not allow external forces to crush me. Or make me subservient. I have decided to push and take whatever and wherever I will to meet my objective!"

Leif motioned for another selenite girl. She motioned back. Leif jogged off with her backstage for several minutes. He returned with water steaming from his suit.

"Better. For the moment," Leif said.

"What was that??" Claus asked.

"It is not what you think!" Leif said. "These are selenite girls. Not human girls."

"Then what?" Claus asked.

"Electro-shock therapy. Selenites know just how much current to inflict," Leif said.

"We're not meant for large amounts of electric current," Claus said. "You'll burn yourself out!"

"No. Quite the opposite. When I feel excess stress, I wipe it clean," Leif said. "All necessary, Pappa. All necessary. Clausetta drinks alcohol to cope. I must have a clear mind. No alcohol for me, though you notice others around me partake. Coffee, cigar, and electrified selenite cabaret women—this is what sustains me moment to moment."

"But Blouisa! You and she—"

"They hunted her, Pappa. And you. When you were in the lunar shock with Yuri. The PRAAD caused great disturbance. Clausetta protected you. Blouisa and I went to help. We were to use Aftova to block the cubics."

"For my sake?" Claus asked.

"You were a part of it," Leif said. "They hunted and killed her. I managed to prevent them from getting Aftova. But that was the price. It was my Blouisa or Aftova. It was a terrible choice I made."

Leif took a deep drag from his cigar, exhaled, motioned for another selenite girl, ran behind stage, and returned in another five minutes. Again, water steamed from his suit. Three B returned.

"They grow impatient," Three B said.

"Tell them I'll be there shortly. Truly," Leif said.

Three B walked off.

"Must you keep going backstage? For this electro-shock therapy? Or should I even ask?" Claus said.

"Some people use narcotics. As I said, I must have a clear mind. I won't let a drug make me subservient," Leif said.

"But a selenite cabaret girl?" Claus asked. "Is that really necessary?"

"I'm not a player, Pappa! I don't manipulate human females for my comfort. Carinians use procreation tanks to engage in exchange. I have modified such a tank to deliver electrical current. No liquid inside, just steam and probes. The selenite girls don't go in with me. I go in alone, and they administer treatment from outside. That's how I wipe the pain, without addiction or attachment. It just doesn't last very long. The relief, that is," Leif said. "These selenite women are specially trained in electro-shock therapy. Not that it's allowed. Not normally, I mean. I had to have them trained on the sly. But they have knowledge of humans and Carinians, which is important, as they can provide relief to any Carinian man. Don't look at me like that, Pappa. Like I said, it's necessary."

"Where's Aftova, Leif?" Claus asked.

"It's in here," Leif said, pointing to his temple. "I've taken ownership of it."

"It's a dangerous thing," Claus said.

"And so am I," Leif said. "No one should suffer the fate of Blouisa. I will wipe out the far side no matter how long it takes, no matter how much effort is involved."

Leif took a drag off his cigar, held it inside, and like before clenched his abdomen with his arms and fists. He stood (still with cigar smoke inside). Great determination filled his eyes as he stared into the distance. He exhaled.

"The beyton rays are fatal to Carinians," Claus said. "You'll be killed."

"I'm only part Carinian," Leif said. "Besides, I've learned how to use Aftova to protect me."

"Is it enough, I wonder," Claus said.

"It will do. But I have plans. We will build an army and surprise the far side such that the universe has never seen," Leif said.

"Uh, I might have tipped them off," Claus said.

"Explain," Leif said.

"In my last reality, I conversed with Heiauga, a dog. Only she wasn't a dog. She was Patricia Li. I speculated that something needed to be done. I mentioned that an army was needed, and I mentioned you and your friends," Claus said.

Leif touched Claus on the shoulder.

"It *was* Patricia Li," Leif said. "But the experience is recent and still fresh on the ether. It can be corrected. I'll send you back. Speak only gibberish to her."

"What? You can send me back? How?" Claus asked.

"This cigar," Leif said. "You must smoke it. Do this for me, Pappa. All will be well."

Leif handed his cigar to Claus. Claus took a drag and coughed. The room spun round, and Claus found himself back with Heiauga.

"All right," Patricia said. "What's your solution? No, I really mean it. Let your bigotry flow from your twisted brain. You weren't like this before Prava 12. It's obvious the abuse has caused this."

"Yes. The abuse from women," Claus said.

"I'm still waiting patiently for your solution," Patricia said.

"I must dip deer into my primary malt mint. Total batter mode. That means coordination and tea work with the efficiency of a machine. Block all intrusive fee links. Overload beer and bale. No one can batter better than a bar. No one."

"A swarmy of deer dipped into your solution?" Patricia asked. "And you'd ruin it. Set your deer up as leaper. You have dilutions of grand deer."

"A swarmy, yes, but not necessarily my deer as leaper. Weeds have to prune our elves with trails. During those trails then weeds will sort out on a billy and hills, from the lower icky nickels to the upper leapers," Claus said. "Weeds will ignore our senses and go strictly by performance. Fly by insolence, so to speak."

"Not a swarmy. An ale for sea," Patricia said.

"Yes," Claus said. "If that works out."

"Where are all these meals?" Patricia asked.

"There's my sample for starters. Heaps and lots of greens. And will be fruit," Claus said.

"More dilutions of grand deer," Patricia said. "You need powder to pack up your platters. From where will that come?"

"Sheer salinity," Claus said.

"That's not powder. You should know that," Patricia said. "You'll need reef horses too. Every wharf found was on Earth and did so with sufficient resources. Carts of sir flies, and the flight fairs. Where are your sir flies?"

"I'll filter some thimbles out," Claus said. "And, whatever I filter out will have to be kelp on sea crest, of course."

"Of course. From landing flies? Really?" Patricia pointed out.

"If they have access to fly mice, then they know of this construction here and now," Claus said. "Right?"

Patricia paused.

"There are grapes," Patricia said. "Land flies won't know of this mousing. At least not yet. Flies will know because ice wallow tallow."

"Grapes. If they all gab, then that is my powder. I'll work in the grapes."

"But you don't know when to grab air. How will you fry hens?" Patricia asked.

"With resting. Leaves will help," Claus said. "You've been very helpful, Patricia. But I won't need your kelp anymore."

"Claus, you're only delaying the indigestion," Patricia said. "Let me add plants to the cake design."

"No," Claus said.

"Your bran won't hold out long enough to find these grapes. You'll design most of your safe shelf cooking for hens. If yew donuts head north, it will be too late. Even land flies cannot review humus bran dancing," Patricia said.

"And fries?" Claus asked.

"You used to have a thimble for air. Shells help augment what's left of your bran with cupcakes," Patricia said. "We all have cupcakes in our bran to smooth things out, just as humus used to fill glasses and bake beds for flood rest. It's only a question of how much cupcake augmentation is needed."

"It's all talk, Patricia. Just talk. It's time for fraction," Claus said.

"The fraction of fries and cupcakes!" Patricia said.

"That's not fraction," Claus said. "I've folded rye bran."

"Yes," she said. "And a shame you did too. Because it forces my bran."

"What do you mean?"

"This," she said.

Claus returned to the cabaret with the cigar in his hand. Leif ran off with another selenite cabaret girl. He returned with steam rising from his suit.

"Success," Leif said, now taking the cigar back and taking another drag. "Not only did you redo the conversation with gibberish, you forced her into gibberish as well. She won't remember anything constructive. Come. Let's see the training center."

Claus walked aside Leif, and to Claus's surprise, four selenite cabaret women followed behind.

"I need them for my 'steam baths'," Leif said.

"Is that what you call it when you go back stage?" Claus asked.

"In the electro tank, yes. I have tanks set up all over the compound. For me, of course. I even have portable units for going out in the field," Leif said, still smoking his cigar.

"Leif, this...I mean, all this electrocution. I know Blouisa's death hit you hard. It hits us all hard. But this isn't healthy," Claus said.

"Doesn't matter. It works," Leif said. "I've watched how Mamma and Clausetta would partially enter other people and use their Carinian powers for whatever. I could

never do that. I could never enter someone's body. The best I could do was touch a shoulder and sense things. Year after year, I watched my mother and sister do these Carinian things. No more. I've learned how to use tools in an ethereal sense. That's how I sent you back. With the cigar. I can influence people with other tools too. Very safe for me. Look at Clausetta! She did everything by using her own body. And she's in a bodycast. No, the bodycast isn't for me. Sacrifice the tool, but spare the man!"

Leif and Claus entered a gymnasium, where men trained with various exercise activities—weight lifting, boxing, a track for running, a pool for swimming, small trampolines for running and jumping, and so on. Those who boxed wore specially padded helmets with sensors to record hit strength and count. Leif pointed to the boxers and spoke:

"If the hit is strong enough, the recipient goes a little eethi without realizing it. I can sense it."

"You must stop the boxing. Or at least prevent excessively hard hits. Causes brain damage," Claus said.

But Leif merely took a drag off his cigar and smiled.

"Leif?" Claus pressed.

"I stop anything that goes too far," Leif said. "But that happens rarely. They learn their limits and press to extend them. Like me."

Leif smiled again.

"I don't like all this," Claus said. "Exercise is fine, and I know I spoke of an army, but some of these things are dangerous. I mean, look at that blindfolded man. Another guy is going to throw a baseball at him. You can't tell me that's helpful."

"Watch. See? He caught the ball. He trained his ears to listen, judged the ball's arrival, and caught it with the glove," Leif said.

"And if he doesn't hear it coming?" Claus asked.

"He gets hit, if the pitcher's aim is good," Leif grinned. "The glove doesn't have to catch. It can be used as a shield as well. Sacrifice the tool, spare the man."

"What about that obstacle course there? More blindfolds?" Claus asked.

"They must feel their way through. Feeling is quicker than vision alone, and in moments of stress, vision is restricted. Now for the shooting range," Leif said.

The two left the gym and entered the lobby of the shooting range. Large glass windows separated them from the range itself.

"They are shooting, and yet I hear no gunshots. Your sound insulation is impressive," Claus said.

Leif grinned again then headed for the range itself.

"Wait," Claus said. "You can't go out there without hearing protection."

Claus looked around for ear plugs or muffs, but he could find none. Leif turned around and ushered Claus into the range anyway.

"What? No gunshot sounds? What kind of suppressors are you using?" Claus asked.

"No suppressors," Leif said. "I had my engineers come up with a new style of gun. Here. Take a look at this one."

Leif handed a gun to Claus. Claus attempted to remove the magazine, but he could not.

"Where's the magazine release button? I can't get the magazine out," Claus said.

"It has no magazine," Leif said.

"How do you get the ammo inside?" Claus asked. "Come to think of it, where is your ammo? There should be boxes and boxes sitting around, but I see none."

"Because you won't," Leif said. "Take this gun and shoot downrange. There's a target at ten meters."

Claus again looked for hearing protection, but Leif simply laughed.

"No hearing protection needed, remember? These are silent. Now try the target," Leif said.

Claus faced the target with gun in hand. While holding the lower handle with his right hand, he tried pulling the upper half toward his body with his left.

"I can't rack the slide," Claus said.

"There is no slide to rack," Leif said. "Aim and pull the trigger. Oh, and keep your hands away from the muzzle."

"That's one thing I do know," Claus said.

Claus aimed, pulled the trigger gently, subconsciously (and improperly) moved the gun down to counter the expected recoil, and fired. A light vapor trail followed the projectile to the target.

"You hit low," Leif said.

"I...there's no recoil. I mean none. At all," Claus said. "What did I shoot? Magic lead from the ether?"

"Not quite, but you have the right idea. Point at the target's center and try again," Leif said.

Claus repeated and forced himself not to flinch downward as before. The gun fired from his command, and the projectile hit the target dead center—again with a vapor trail.

"It shoots ice," Leif said.

"You have a mass compressor in the gun?" Claus asked.

"No."

"Then how?" Claus asked.

"The gun pulls moisture from the front of the muzzle, structures it with ethereal material, and shoots it back out as an ice bullet. The ice bullet only has water molecules on the outer surface. The core is all eethi. For support. I can adjust the caliber of bullet, too. I can even send out a bullet with a larger diameter than the bore of the gun," Leif said.

"What? How?" Claus asked.

"Ethereal mechanics. The ethereal matter is set to expand to a certain size during flight, so once the bullet leaves the bore, it expands. Useful for doing great damage. Yet a small caliber bullet can be used for deep penetration and explosion."

"Strategy," Claus said.

"Yes. One must match the weapon to the attack profile. Concussive attack, surface attack, general mass destruction, surgical deep destruction while leaving the surface target intact, curved attack, reverse attack, and—"

"Reverse attack meaning what?" Claus asked.

"In case you need to shoot someone behind you. Just shoot forward and duck," Leif said.

"Sounds almost suicidal," Claus said.

"It is. Almost," Leif grinned.

"Give me that cigar," Claus said as a means of dealing with this new-found stress.

"No, wait!" Leif said.

But it was too late. Claus had taken the cigar, dragged on it, and had yet to exhale when he found the room spinning again.

Chapter 133: Lanietta Dispirited

Claus found himself at sea. It was dark, though it was daytime.

"Cloud cover is heavy," Claus said to himself. "Yet I can see the sun."

The clouds acted like darkened glass, allowing Claus to see a dim but white disk—the sun. It was the size of the moon, but it had no craters. Then it became apparent to him. As the jet stream carried clouds by, Claus could sense the intensity of light vary in proportion to the cloud density, as if waves of an ocean were passing by.

"Black waves," Claus said. "They look like black waves."

Claus looked around. He was about halfway between the lighthouse and the shore from his prior reality.

"The walking books. Will I see them again? Can I swim to the lighthouse? Lanietta is surely there. But how can I be here? Leif said his compound was protected from outside ethereal influence. How would he explain—"

Claus was interrupted by a flash of light at the lighthouse, a delay of several seconds, and a bone-trembling thunderous shock wave of what Claus now understood to be an explosion. The lighthouse and associated island collapsed into the sea. This triggered a tsunami that caught Claus and forced him along the trench where the road and houses of his prior reality had fallen into the sea.

"The hole at the cliff. It will consume me for sure!" Claus yelled.

But the hole wasn't there, nor was any fish, dolphin, or orca. Instead, a chain-link fence created a means for Claus to climb from the shore up the cliff and onto level ground. When he did, a motion-sensing solar light went from dim to bright, and he recognized the "Keep Out" sign he had seen before.

"The house of my author!" Claus exclaimed. "Patricia was wrong. He really does exist! I'll find him. He can help!"

Claus called for K Gerard, but there was no answer. Claus walked the entire length of the driveway to the back yard, calling along the way. He returned to the front, where he stood by the Merrill magnolia. A string of lights ran from the magnolia to the two lilacs, which had somehow returned along with land to their place with the property. Seemingly random lights in the string faded and grew stronger like little wingless fireflies hoping for something better. Claus moved his hand to touch one such light. It felt no different than unlit objects.

"What am I doing here?" Claus asked.

The string by the magnolia faded and went out, leaving just the string along the fence lit.

"Oh, it's run out of power again," said a familiar voice from the front porch.

Claus pulled away from the light string, walked toward the porch, and saw her.

"Lanietta! I knew I'd see you," Claus said.

But Lanietta looked much older. Her gait was slow, and her hands trembled, at least the one that was free. The other hand (left hand) carried a toolbox. She wore a headband with a small, battery-powered flashlight providing light for her to see.

"This is my author's house. This is the home of K Gerard Martin," Claus proclaimed.

"That light string never makes it through the night," she muttered.

"But it's not night. Look. The sun is shining. It's just strangely very cloudy," Claus said.

Lanietta pushed past Claus as if he weren't there, but the toolbox caught Claus's left knee, and it buckled immediately, causing Claus to fall to the driveway.

"Lanietta! What was that for?" he asked.

"It's too long. Too many lights. I'll have to cut the end," Lanietta muttered.

Lanietta set down her toolbox, opened it, and retrieved a pair of diagonal pliers.

"Too much on the west lilac. I'll trim there," she said.

She cut perhaps twenty lights off the end, unwrapped them from the lilac branches, and stuffed the cut line into her toolbox. She closed it. The newly-cut light string remained off.

"Also need to reduce power consumption," she said.

Lanietta carried her toolbox back to the magnolia to a post supporting the "Keep Out" sign along with the solar cell and control box for the light string. She placed her toolbox on the driveway and stared at the control box.

"Hand me the Phillips screwdriver," she said to Claus.

"I would if I could stand," Claus said. "Looks like you know I'm here."

"Of course. I took out your knee, didn't I? Now pass me the screwdriver," she said. "You don't need to stand. Just reach up."

Claus rummaged through the toolbox, found the screwdriver, and passed it to Lanietta.

"That's a flat-head," she said. "The Phillips please."

"Aren't you going to make a joke about me?" Claus asked. "That I'm a flat-head for passing you the flat-head screwdriver?"

"No. Too old for jokes," she said.

Lanietta kept her eyes focused on the control box and did not look at Claus at all. She kept her hand outstretched in his direction, waiting for the screwdriver to be placed in her palm. Claus took a hard look at her. She was devoid of fun and spontaneity, looking more like a mold-covered cemetery statue than the proud Carinian she once was. Claus found the Phillips screwdriver and placed it in her palm.

"Thank you," she said, and she went to work to unscrew the cover of the control box.

"Where's my author?" Claus asked. "This is his house. Where is he?"

"Just us light strings here," Lanietta said. "Take the screwdriver back and hand me the needle-nose pliers. And the portable soldering iron. Set it for twenty-five watts and preheat."

"What are you doing, anyway? In all of this, you're working on a light string?" Claus asked. "Ow!"

"Don't touch the hot end," she said. "And don't hand *me* the hot end either."

"Do you trust me?" Claus asked. "Look at your hand. Look at me to be sure I do it right."

"I must trust you this one time."

"Clomper. You always call me Clomper," Claus said.

Lanietta held still, with her eyes fixed on the control box.

"Here are the pliers," Claus said as he handed them to her.

"Thank you," she said as she transferred the pliers to her other hand.

"And here's the soldering iron. Handle side," Claus said.

Her hand awaited, but it trembled and recoiled slightly as if expecting the hot end. Claus withdrew the iron.

"I won't hurt you," Claus said.

"They say before invasion," she muttered. "The burned hand teaches best. But the burned hand cannot teach a light string without power. Hand me the iron, Claus."

Claus passed her the soldering iron. She took it.

"Please, call me Clomper again. Even Cloopy is welcome," Claus said.

Lanietta melted a solder point with the iron and pulled a wire free from a resistor with the needle-nose pliers. She then melted another point and removed the resistor completely.

"This light string is designed for daytime sunlight to recharge the battery through the solar cell," she said.

She paused to regain her breath, and then she said, "This resistor is too small. Allows too much current to flow. Hand me a 1200 ohm resistor."

"I...I don't remember the color codes for resistors," Claus said.

"There's a clear, plastic bag in the toolbox. Resistors are clustered together by value, suspended between paper holders of yellow and blue. The values are printed on the yellow paper. Look for 1K2. I need just one. Just one."

Claus thumbed through the resistors, but they got tangled and caught on one another.

"I'm sorry...these are so tangled...and I'm all thumbs...I bet you're impatient...why not call me a clumsy dog, will you?"

But Lanietta remained frozen as before, waiting and waiting as if nothing else mattered or would matter for that matter.

"I have it," Claus said. "Hard to see though. So dark. Could you point your light over here?"

Lanietta did not stir.

"That's okay. I'll use the light from the sign," Claus apologized.

"Trim one lead. Just one," she said.

"Okay, I have the diagonal snips here. I'm trimming a lead. Here's the resistor," Claus said, and he placed it in her palm.

"Pass me the solder," she said. "Lead free."

"Like that matters now. Lead free solder. Who is left to care? And where is my author?" Claus asked.

Lanietta soldered the new resistor to the control board and soldered the wire to the new resistor. She handed tools back to Claus, returned the cover to the control box, and tightened it closed.

"Still dark," she said. "The battery is dead. Forgot to recharge it. Forgot..."

"How can we recharge it?" Claus asked. "Do you have a charger here?"

"I must open the box again," she sighed.

Lanietta opened the control box. Claus expected her to ask for a portable charger, or even for a new battery, and he rummaged through her toolbox in advance in hopes of finding it, but he found neither. Lanietta slipped her hand into a pocket on her robe and removed a small device with wired alligator clips. She clipped the device to the battery connectors. Claus heard a sizzling and crackling, and an electrical burning smell wafted his way.

"Enough," she said weakly.

She removed the charger and returned it to her robe. Lanietta attached the cover to the box and pressed a reset button. The light string lit, but it was very dim.

"Very dim," she said slowly. "But it lights."

Claus managed to climb to his feet and stand upright, despite his knee paining him.

"Lanietta, I want to help. Are you stuck in this reality? This place is like an island, only it's not out to sea. It's simply surrounded by water with the mainland nearby. I'm sorry I'm rambling," Claus said. "What can I do to make it right? What's the answer, Lanietta?"

Lanietta slowly turned to Claus with light still beaming from her headlamp, and she spoke:

"Ask your author."

Chapter 134: Cetacean Dentistry

Claus blinked. When he opened his eyes, he was inside what looked like a dental center.

"I...I...where are you?" Claus asked.

"We can give you a fresh set of veneers to cover those fish stains," Lanietta's voice said.

"Sparfy will fall all over me then," said a female's voice.

"I can do all of them in one visit. Right now if you like, Delfa," Lanietta's voice said.

"Lanietta!" Claus yelled as he ran toward her voice.

But when Claus reached her position, he just saw Lanietta standing next to a striped dolphin, who was lying in a little tub of water, elevated so Lanietta was eye level with the dolphin.

"This is a violation of patient privacy," Lanietta said. "Please wait in the lobby for your dentist."

"My dentist? What? I don't need a dentist. Lanietta! What's going on?" Claus asked.

Two dental assistants escorted Claus back to the lobby and forced him to sit. Claus had a view of the aisle straight down to where treatment areas were attached (including Lanietta's). Lanietta stepped away from her area and started down the aisleway toward Claus. Claus waved frantically for her to speak with him, but she put up a hand as if to say, "Wait," and she stepped into another treatment area.

"Let me work on Delfa," Nekara said.

"No. She's not to be tortured," Lanietta said. "How did you find me here in Corleopus?"

"I went back in time, just like you. You Carinians still owe us for vacation time on Earth. I demand compensation," Nekara said.

"Look. Delfa has only a little time left. Let her enjoy her time. Why not play with Metavasi or something? Become an orca and chase him. If you catch him, you may eat him," Lanietta said.

"Too simple. Too easy. I need something more sustaining, like the meat and potatoes of slow torture," Nekara said.

"Doing veneers is hardly slow torture," Lanietta said. "You don't have to fully catch Metavasi. Just throw a tooth in him here and there."

"Let me help with your dental practice. I can insert dormant parasites into the pulp chamber. A month later when the patient least suspects, outbreak!"

"Unfortunately, there are no humans around for such a procedure. It wouldn't work on my cetacean clients. They'd detect and sterilize the parasite on the first shape change," Lanietta said.

"No humans? Not even one?" Nekara begged.

"None," Lanietta replied. "Just cetaceans and my dog."

"You mean Clomper?" Nekara asked. "You once said he often thinks of himself as human."

"Most dogs do," Lanietta said. "I swear I can understand his vocalizations. Like real human speech at times."

"Unbelievable," Nekara said. "Well? Is he here? Maybe he'll do."

"For a pulp chamber insertion? Forget it. His system is not that advanced," Lanietta said.

Claus didn't know if he should be angry at Lanietta for her condescending remarks or at Nekara for her desire to torture him. It seemed he best stay put and say nothing.

"I'm always stuck at the dentist. My whole life!" Claus moaned.

"There! I heard him!" Nekara said.

"Just do an exam, nothing more," Lanietta said. "I'll finish up with Delfa and circle back."

Lanietta stepped back into the aisle and walked into the treatment area for Delfa.

Nekara stepped out, walked into the lobby, and greeted Claus.

"Clomper. We meet again," Nekara laughed.

"Only Lanietta may call me that. My real name is Claus. Claus Gerhardt."

Nekara led him to a treatment cubicle and sat him down.

"Clahz Gar-hahz," Nekara laughed.

"Claus Gerhardt!" Claus corrected with irritation.

"Clahz. Woof. Woof!" Nekara grinned.

"Oh, here's his leash if he gives you any trouble," Lanietta said, peeking in with a leash.

"Thank you," Nekara said, taking the leash.

Lanietta returned to Delfa.

"Okay, I'm not here for dental work," Claus said. "Matter of fact, I'm not sure why I'm here at all."

"You considered killing yourself," Nekara said in a soft, creepy voice. "Did you ever consider hanging? Willfully?"

Nekara drew the leash around his neck to suggest hanging.

"I saw Lanietta try it. It was awful. No one should do it," Claus said.

"Are you sure that was her? Maybe she made someone else do it. And experienced the event. Sounds like fun. Let's try with you," Nekara said.

Nekara grew in height and pulled up on the leash, which lifted Claus into the air and constricted his airway. He pulled on the leash to get air, but he gagged.

"Help! Lanietta! Help!" he barely managed to say and of course was so quiet that no one could hear.

"You're supposed to yelp like a dog in pain," Nekara said. "Hmm. Let's try a different form of torture."

Nekara released the leash. Claus collapsed to the floor, gasped for breath, and then yelled at the top of his lungs (or whatever bit of lungs he had), "LA-NI-EHH-TAHHH!"

Immediately, the treatment area erupted in cetacean squeals as if their sense of echolocation reception had been injured by Claus's cry for help. Lanietta rushed in.

"What is all this commotion?" Lanietta asked with a dental tool still in hand.

Nekara had the biggest grin of delight Lanietta had ever seen.

"Couldn't help it. He got the cetaceans to suffer. For that I'm pleased with delight," Nekara said.

"I told you not with the cetaceans," Lanietta said. "And Clomper here is the least receptive of all."

"He has a gift you've kept secret, my sweet Lanietta," Nekara said. "By himself he is boring, but through his clumsy influence, he causes great consternation to those around. Ahhh. I'm satisfied for the moment. I'll have to walk off this happiness quickly. Wouldn't want to lose my touch at torture. It's a skill that requires practice, practice, practice!"

Nekara left. Lanietta took one look at Claus on the floor and rolled her eyes.

"Get up," she said in disdain.

"You're not going to apologize? For her behavior?" Claus asked as he stood up.

"You're one to talk. Follow me," she said reluctantly.

Claus followed Lanietta slowly. She walked to the very back of the aisle, turned a couple of corners, and entered a treatment area with what looked like a minke whale on a treatment table.

"There, there, soon you'll be better," Lanietta said as she kissed the whale.

"You love this whale?" Claus asked.

"This isn't just a whale. This is Loerna Acutolo," Lanietta said.

"Means nothing to me," Claus said.

"That doesn't surprise me. You know nothing about Loerna, yet you dismiss her entire life as nothing. Don't worry. She thinks the same of you," Lanietta said. "There, there, Loerna. I still appreciate you. Let the anesthesia soak in. We'll have your baleen plates restored soon. I know, it wasn't right. We can't change what they did. But we can change you. For the better, right? There, there. Aunt Lanietta is with you."

"*Aunt Lanietta?* Don't you mean *Doctor Lanietta?*"

"I'm an aunt to many. Loerna, Clausetta, Leif. You remember the latter two," Lanietta said. "I remember them too. Especially of late."

"What's *that* supposed to mean?" Claus asked.

"Your son is an electroholic and your daughter a drunk," Lanietta said. "A pity I didn't raise them better."

"*You* are not supposed to raise *my* children," Claus said.

"You forget your twenty-five year abscess, uh, absence," Lanietta said. "But you forget a great number of things. You'd never make a great immortal. Wouldn't make much of one at all. Still, there's the toolbox. Hand me the soldering iron."

"What? You're serious? Now you've mixed up realities!" Claus said. "You think you're working on the light string!"

"I need the diagonal pliers," Lanietta said. "Hand me those too."

"What? Why? This is an animal, not a light string!" Claus said.

"THIS ISN'T AN ANIMAL!" Lanietta screamed in Claus's ear. "THIS IS LOERNA ACUTOLO! COMPREHEND?"

Claus stood in shock. Lanietta had never yelled at him like that. She'd been angry before, but this was strange. It was like she was yelling at someone else from the distant past, as if she were a schoolchild. He gingerly handed her the diagonal pliers. She took it with a horribly trembling hand. She grimaced as if she had swallowed a knife, and she made to cut a baleen plate or three from Loerna. But at the last moment, she snipped her fingertip and smeared blood on Loerna's plates. The plates healed, and Loerna exhaled with relief. Lanietta drew back, held the soldering iron to her wound, and cauterized it with the iron's heat.

"Arg!" she said with restraint.

Claus opened his mouth to say something, but he was speechless. Lanietta didn't bother to return the tools to Claus. Instead, she placed them in the toolbox herself. She turned to Claus and stared him directly in the eyes. Claus shook in fear from what she might do to him.

"Listen to me," she said as she grabbed his shoulders.

Claus opened his mouth to say something, but she reiterated herself, saying with more force and volume, "Listen to me!"

"I'm listening!" Claus said.

Lanietta pulled Claus close to her face as if preparing to yell him out once and for all. But just as she started to speak, her voice softened.

"If something happens to me, think of this moment when I yelled at you, and the hatred you had for me. For yelling at you. It will be easier to let go," she said.

Claus recoiled in shock. Lanietta looked down, paused, looked up, paused, looked at Loerna, and looked at Claus with a mixed expression.

"Let's go home," she said with relief.

Chapter 135: Molar Neurosis

Claus awoke, and he was back in his bed on the lunar near side. Lanietta's words about going home were still fresh in his mind, but this wasn't her home. What did she mean?

"I was with Leif. Now I'm here. The cigar. What happened to it?" Claus asked aloud.

"We had to rush you to surgery," Labba said, now walking into the room after hearing him speak.

"Surgery? For what?" Claus asked. "And why does the right side of my face feel like it's falling off?"

"Your upper second molar on your right had to be pulled," Labba said. "The cigar you took from Leif fused with it."

"What? My tooth? Gone? But...no! You should have asked me first! This is terrible! I've had that tooth since I was twelve! Most of my life! Like a good friend! And you had it pulled?" Claus protested.

"Had to!" Labba said. "It was the only way to save you! Why, you'd be lost between realities in the ether had we not done so!"

"But my second molar! This is a disaster! Worse than dying! I'll lose bone mass! My teeth will shift. Nothing will oppose my bottom molar! Labba! My teeth are like married couples—upper and lower. You just ended a marriage. Worse than death. Worse than death! I want an implant. I want an implant now!"

"The dentist said you don't have enough bone material for an implant. Would go right into the sinus cavity," Labba said.

"I can get a bone graft. Shove a tibula or something up there."

Labba laughed.

"What's so funny?" he asked.

"In your excitement, you've confused yourself," Labba chuckled. "Tibula? That was an ancient town in Sardinia. You know, the Mediterranean? Did you mean tibia?"

"Yes! Shove a tibia there," Claus said.

"That's a shin bone!" Labba laughed even harder.

Selba walked in and asked, "I heard the laughing and had to know what's so funny."

"Well?" Labba asked. "Do you want to shove an ancient town or a shinbone into your upper palate?"

"What??" Selba asked in surprise as she fell into laughter.

"You think this is funny. Go ahead. Pick on me! This is disaster. Disaster!" Claus bemoaned.

"The anesthesia wore off, and he awoke," Labba said.

"I see," Selba said, trying to muffle her laugh, but the harder she tried, the more the laughter built up until she burst out and caused Labba to laugh all over again.

"I'm getting out of here!" Claus said. "I'll find Leif. Get some man-time in his gym or something!"

"Sorry, but Leif is not in the gym," Labba said. "You shouldn't speak of it out here. Not everyone knows about it. Ears are everywhere."

"Where is he?" Claus asked.

"He asked me not to tell. Secret mission," Labba said.

"Secret mission," Claus repeated sarcastically. "Bah!"

"Anticipating your reaction, the dentist *did* offer a solution. Says he can pull *all* second molars to make your bite equal."

"What?? He's insane!" Claus said.

"Performers did it all the time," Selba said. "Gave them cheekbone. Maybe that's your calling, Claus. You can become an actor. Put on plays. Clausetta could use a diversion."

"Claus has never been good with comedy," Labba laughed.

"He made you laugh," Selba said.

"He made us both laugh," Labba said. "But not from comedic humor."

"You'll have to learn to be more serious," Selba said. "Take on dramatic roles."

"I am serious! My second molar is gone! Gone!"

Selba and Labba laughed again.

"Are you well enough to stand? I'd like you to see your daughter. She's much improved," Labba said.

"I'll make the effort," Claus said.

Claus stood. He realized he was dressed in only a robe.

"Oh, I'm not properly dressed," Claus said.

"Why would I care?" Labba asked.

"I mean for Selba," Claus said.

"She doesn't mind either. She helped me bathe you while you were unconscious those twenty-five years. And recently. Many times, in fact. She's like the family nurse," Labba said. "So I wouldn't worry about a robe."

Claus looked surprised.

"Did you think nothing happened while you were unconscious? Someone had to take care of you," Labba said.

"I guess...I never thought about the details," Claus said.

"The devil is always in the details," Selba said. "But we have one less devil to worry about, now that Clausetta is better."

"Yes! Clausetta!" Claus said, and he ambled down the hallway to her room as quickly as he could.

When Claus entered her room, he was pleasantly surprised. Clausetta was no longer in a bodycast. She was sitting in bed with just a cast on her right hand and wrist, and reading a book. Flowers with get-well cards surrounded her.

"Pappa!" she said. "You're awake! Why didn't anyone tell me he was awake? I wanted to show him I can walk. Look, Pappa!"

Clausetta got out of bed, and she walked slowly. Her legs, though healed, were not used to walking as she once did so easily, and so she tended to shuffle.

"Clausetta! I'm so happy you're better!" Claus said as he gave her a hug.

"Strange thing, Pappa. They said my legs would be the last to heal. And here I am with my right hand still in a cast," Clausetta said.

"Your recovery was in relation to your injuries," Selba said. "Your right hand was the worst injured and so took the longest to heal."

"I can't believe I've been unconscious that long," Claus said.

"You shouldn't smoke Leif's cigars," Clausetta said. "They have too much oomph."

"Now you tell me," Claus said.

"I would have told you before, but that bodycast made life miserable. Couldn't do much of anything," Clausetta said.

"Clausetta. Tell me about—"

"No stories at the moment," Labba said.

"But I just wanted to—"

"I know," Labba said. "But bad things happen when too much is told. If you're both well enough, I'd like to treat you to morning breakfast. Can you walk downstairs?"

"Yes," Claus said. "I'll carry Clausetta if I have to."

"I can take the stairs, thank you anyway, Pappa," Clausetta said. "You can hold my left arm and steady me."

Claus did just that, and the four went downstairs. Interestingly enough, just before Claus and Clausetta reached the bottom step, Claus stumbled and nearly fell down to the bottom. It was Clausetta then who used her left arm (which still had a hold on Claus's right hand) to pull him back up.

"See? Almost good as new!" she boasted.

"I see," Claus said. "I think we could all use a good breakfast. It's a sunny day, and I feel a cool breeze blowing through."

The four reached the dining room. Treyu had just finished setting the table and was adjusting flowers and vases. Food was already placed, and Mariel walked in with a decanter of coffee in one hand and a pitcher of tea in the other.

"They *did* make it!" Mariel said, nearly dropping both as she rushed over to hug Clausetta.

Treyu quickly helped Mariel by taking both from her, and she was able to hug Clausetta without making a mess.

"Oh, you're walking. You're walking!" Mariel cried.

"I was down here earlier today," Clausetta laughed. "And yesterday, and the week before that."

"I know, but it feels like I'm hugging you for the first time all over again," Mariel said.

"What about me? Do I get a hug?" Claus asked.

"You got yours already," Labba grinned. "Now everyone, this is just an informal breakfast. Take a seat wherever you like. You too, Treyu and Mariel. You are both like family, after all."

"I insist upon helping Clausetta sit," Mariel said.

"May I also assist?" Treyu asked.

"No, just sit down," Claus said flatly.

"Claus. That wasn't called for," Labba said. "Yes, Treyu, you may help the other ladies sit."

"I am honored," Treyu said.

While Treyu helped Selba and Labba sit, Claus himself was about to sit, but he was caught in a chair stare. Images of Lanietta hanging herself and kicking out the chair under him flooded his mind.

"Pappa? What is it?" Clausetta asked.

"I...nothing," Claus said.

Claus took a deep breath and sat in the chair. But instead of again seeing images of Lanietta hanging herself, he had quite a different experience. He sat down stiffly. This sent a jolt up his spine into his jaw, causing his teeth to slam together. His teeth felt a tingling from the pain, except his right lower second molar, which felt nothing. The teeth sensed this as a kind of slant. They metaphorically yelled at the tongue to find the missing tooth and restore it quickly so that all teeth could feel the pain of the jolt equally. "Let no tooth be left behind." The tongue searched and searched but to no avail.

Claus exhaled. He looked around, half expecting Lanietta or even Nekara to show up and thus crash breakfast. Neither did. Nor did anyone seem to know about Claus's tongue-searching experience. But something else happened. It took hold of him gradually, and at first no one noticed, but Claus could not hide it. It was how he perceived motion around him. When coffee was poured from the decanter to a mug, Claus suffered anxiety in proportion to how high the decanter was held. Mariel was very skilled at pouring coffee, and she could pour from great heights, often varying the heights out of style. Claus experienced this in relation to his missing molar, and so a synesthesia set in, his eyes connecting the motion of an upper object against a lower object to his complex new feeling of the empty space from his prior upper molar coming down to his still-existing lower second molar. If one could imagine a mother having lost a baby then seeing another mother playing with her own baby, the mother with the loss would sense an even greater loss. This was the way with Claus. He felt a greater loss of his upper molar every time he saw an object transfer from an upper level to a lower level.

"Here. Have an orange," Selba said to Labba.

Selba held a plate in the air above the level of Labba's plate, which was on the table. Labba took the orange and moved it down to her plate. Claus cringed at this. There were other examples. In fact every piece of food that was passed around on its food plate was moved down to the diner's plate in this fashion. When the plate of food reached Claus, he placed the plate on the table next to his and moved the item of food across so that it maintained a lateral motion.

"Are your wrists weak?" Labba asked, thinking that's why Claus placed each food plate on the table first.

"Um, yeah, I guess that's it," Claus lied.

Claus could only handle so much. He avoided watching people place food on their plates. When the food plate was passed to him, he looked the other way. When he passed it to the next person, he slid the plate over.

"Pappa," Clausetta said, who sat to his right. "I made this basket of cinnamon rolls. Just for you. Mamma helped. But I'd really like you to have one."

Claus looked the other way.

"Pappa?" she asked. "What's wrong? Look at me."

Claus turned his head toward her slowly.

"Would you like one?" she asked while holding the basket in the air. "It's not heavy. See? I can hold it even with my cast."

"Please," Claus said.

"Okay. I'll give you a roll. This one? Here," she said.

Claus lifted his right hand to receive the roll. Clausetta made a lateral move as she handed the roll to Claus. She didn't realize the significance of making a lateral move or how it would affect Claus, it was just the thing to do at the moment. She put the basket down. Claus cringed at that motion. But there was a new problem. He was afraid to bring his hand back down. It was his hand, after all, and it was more closely tied to his body's feelings than the things he saw. He held the roll there in the air. His arm tired, and it shook. He strained to keep the roll in the air.

"Pappa? Put the roll down. Pappa?" Clausetta asked.

Clausetta put Claus's hand and thus the roll down. Claus let out a low "argh".

"What's the matter?" Clausetta asked.

Claus was very much upset, but fortunately, that was the end of the food-passing and drink-pouring for the moment. The others ate, but Claus half-remembered attending a friend's meal as a child and the friend's family saying grace. He almost lifted his hands in prayer, but he caught himself, because he knew he would have to deal with putting them back down after saying grace, and that would link back to his missing molar and unnecessarily feed the growing neurosis.

"The eggs are excellent. Nice and fluffy," Selba said. "I don't normally eat scrambled eggs, but these are just too much."

"Pappa? Mariel made the eggs," Clausetta said. "Try some. The protein will do you good. Is your wrist weak? I can help. I'll spoon feed you."

Claus thought of Clausetta lifting the food to his mouth and then returning her hand to a lower level. He panicked.

"No," he said.

Claus lowered his head to the level of his plate, and he shoveled the scrambled eggs from his plate to his mouth in a lateral move.

"Claus? What are you doing?" Labba asked.

Out of habit, Claus returned to his regular sitting posture to feign normality. He chewed and chewed, but he had a new problem. Swallowing would mean sending the food down. He couldn't let it go down. But he *was* hungry. How would he get the food in his stomach? Claus lowered his body and turned to the side to get his esophagus parallel to the ground. Now granted it caused him a bit of misery to lower the upper part of his body, but he mitigated the misery by having a turn and twist in his motion. He swallowed his food with his head in Clausetta's lap.

"Claus!" Labba said. "I ask you again. What are you doing?"

Claus realized he made another mistake. The biggest mistake so far. When he chewed his food, he was vertical, and his upper teeth came down on his lower—fully exposing and reminding him of the missing upper molar. With every bite.

Claus shifted his body away from Clausetta, but he kept his body sideways. He moved the plate down to his level (oh the misery), and he shoveled more eggs into his mouth (not so bad). Now he could eat sideways and swallow sideways. No downward motion. All problems solved.

"That's enough, Claus," Labba said. "Sit up and tell me why you are behaving so strangely."

"Not until I swallow," Claus said.

"Pappa," Clausetta said. "You're embarrassing me. Do you need a walk? Fresh air?"

"Something's wrong with Claus," Selba said.

"Let's go outside," Labba said.

"I'll help," Clausetta said.

"No, please," Claus said. "If I stand, I won't be able to sit again."

"One moment," Treyu said, and he disappeared into another room.

"Perhaps too much excitement," Mariel said. "A stroll in the garden might help. I'll stay here and clean up."

Treyu returned with a wheelchair.

"Excellent idea," Labba said. "Let's transfer him over."

Claus calmed. Treyu, Clausetta, Selba, and Labba were able to move Claus from the dining chair to the wheelchair without lifting or dropping him, thus maintaining a lateral motion. Treyu started to push Claus, but Clausetta intervened.

"No. Allow me," Clausetta said.

Clausetta wheeled Claus outside and into the garden with the others (except Mariel) following behind. A gardener watered the lawn, and the experience of seeing water transfer from an upper object (watering can) to a lower object (flower), transferred into Claus's second molar. He cringed and groaned.

"Just a flower left. No water. No water!" Claus yelled.

"Are you thirsty, Pappa?" Clausetta asked.

"No water!" Claus repeated.

Clausetta turned the wheelchair away from the gardener and wheeled Claus out of the garden. She stopped on a balcony with a vast yet beautiful view of the valley.

"Oh, oh!" Claus moaned. "I feel like I'm falling."

Clausetta spun him around and faced him toward a tree. Claus looked up and trembled in fear.

"The branch. It might hit me. Clausetta, take me away," he said.

"I don't know where to take you," Clausetta said.

"Anywhere. Hurry!" Claus urged.

Clausetta wheeled Claus over to a cart.

"Yes. Good," he said. "Put other carts around me. Quickly. Quickly!"

Treyu, Selba, Labba, and Clausetta did so. Claus now had a bit of privacy.

"Go ahead, Clausetta," Labba said. "See what's troubling your father."

Clausetta placed a hand to Claus's head.

"Pappa is calm now. Totally at peace," Clausetta said.

"Hmm," Labba said. "I wonder if—"

Before Labba could finish, a crane boom lifted in the air in preparation for construction nearby. Claus saw this and pointed at it.

"The crane. The crane!"

The crane boom quickly descended. Claus groaned.

"I feel it," Labba said. "It's a reaction to his tooth extraction."

"You're not even touching me," Claus said. "How can you know how I feel?"

"Because I know how my daughter feels, and she's tapped into you. Claus, we'll take care of you. We just need to—"

While Labba spoke, the crane had picked up a load and accidentally dropped it. The air boomed. The ground shuddered. It was too much for Claus. He lost consciousness.

Claus opened his eyes. He sat in a chair in someone's front yard. The day was sunny, cool, and partly cloudy with a light breeze from the west.

"What...I...I'm back here. The author's property. But why?" Claus asked aloud.

"A bad day for fishing," Lanietta's voice said from high above. "The water is rough."

Claus looked up. Lanietta stood in a basket and faced east, staring at it with binoculars. This basket was much like one used by a utility vehicle, and the basket was attached to a boom that gradually changed into a large branch that was then attached to the trunk of an oak tree.

"My upper molar!" Claus yelled. "You have my upper molar! Up there! Give it back!"

"Really, Clomper, you still amaze me with your babbling. I never know what's going to come from those vocal cords," Lanietta said.

"Don't toy with me! I'm going crazy! I must have my upper molar!" Claus demanded.

Lanietta lowered the binoculars from her face.

"Ow! Don't do that!" Claus begged.

Lanietta grinned. She tapped the binoculars on the safety rail surrounding her basket.

"My upper molar! Not fair!" Claus wailed.

Lanietta did a tap dance, occasionally tapping the binoculars down on the safety rail.

"You're doing this on purpose! To torture me!" Claus continued. "I'm suffering withdrawal from a missing molar, and you make light of it?"

Lanietta stopped dancing with a single stomp. The wind picked up, the sun set quickly, and the solar lights turned on. Tree and shrub waved their branches around wildly. Claus was convinced a storm was upon him, and he dove out of the chair and crawled on the lawn. Just in time! Lanietta lowered the boom-branch quickly, it came down, and it smashed the chair where Claus had just sat.

"You're suffering?" Lanietta mocked. "Oh, the misery of the universe! We must bow down to your missing tooth. Very well. I'll replace your molar, Clomper. Behold!"

Using his tongue, Claus probed the spot where his upper molar once occupied. To his surprise, a pointed molar had replaced it. Claus closed his bite, and the pointed molar touched the lower molar before the rest of his teeth could make contact.

"What have you done?? I feel like there's a rock in my mouth! I bite down and ow! Ow! I can't have this! I'll go crazy. I keep wanting to close my bite. It hurts my jaw every time! Lanietta! This is insane! Why? WHY!" Claus ended in a loud tone.

"BECAUSE YOU ARE CLOMPER! YOU ARE MY PET!" she yelled back. "YOU WANT THE MOLAR. YOU HAVE THE MOLAR!"

"NOT LIKE THIS!" Claus yelled. "I NEED A DENTIST!"

Claus could not stop opening and closing his bite. He whimpered like a dog at his new misery. Lanietta stepped out of the basket and walked toward him. Claus lifted a hand as if waiting to receive her help, but she walked past him instead. She continued walking until she reached the end of the driveway. She pulled out a lantern and held it close to a parked car on the side of the road.

"No one in here," she said.

"What about me?" Claus begged.

Lanietta stood in the road and swung the lantern back and forth as if signaling a train her way. Headlights indicated that a vehicle was approaching, and she signaled for it to park behind the other vehicle. The other vehicle did so.

"Thank you for coming," Lanietta said. "As you can see, this car is parked overnight illegally. Normally I wouldn't say anything, but it's supposed to snow in an hour, and the plows need to get through. Yes I will. Thank you."

Lanietta walked back over to Claus.

"The sholiff says not to worry, the car will be towed away soon," Lanietta said.

"Sholiff? You mean sheriff's deputy?" Claus asked.

"No. I checked to be sure. This was a sholiff," Lanietta said. "Walk over yourself if you don't believe me."

"I can't," Claus said. "I'm still dealing with this tooth. What kind of crazy tooth did you put in my mouth anyway?"

"It's a carnassial tooth," Lanietta said.

"A what?"

"You know. Carnassial. Sounds like 'carnal', doesn't it? I thought it might bring us closer together, so we could exchange carnassial secrets," Lanietta said.

Lanietta brought her lips close to Claus's ear and let out a sexy growl.

"There's nothing...your desire...ugh, ugh, ugh! This is a disaster!" Claus said. "A dog has carnassial teeth! Not humans!"

"And a nice dog she was too for donating her tooth for you," Lanietta said.

"What dog?"

"Not *what*. A *who*. Heiauga. She donated her tooth. But don't let Nekara find out. Heiauga is her favorite dog. She'll put you through the wringer for sure if she learns you stole Heiauga's carnassial," Lanietta said.

"I didn't steal it!" Claus said.

"Better find a way to hide it," Lanietta said. "Better find a way to chip off that point and toss it away."

"What? I can't do that," Claus said.

"Sure. Toss it down and make it jab someone else," Lanietta said. "Tell you what. I'll let you spend time with Heiauga. She'll teach you all about tossed points."

"Wait, no," Claus said. "Just fix my tooth."

"Of course with Heiauga being Nekara's dog, you'll have to spend time with her. Just think of it as a visit with your cousin dogs."

"Lanietta. No. Lanietta?"

"Here's his leash, Nekara," Lanietta yelled to the heavens.

Lanietta tossed Claus's leash skyward. It never fell, but Claus felt weak and closed his eyes.

When Claus opened his eyes, he was in a downtown city at night on a weekend with plenty of beer a-hand. A crowd of university students blocked the street, and a police officer used his motorcycle to move the students off the street. Claus himself was standing in the street, but a leather strap quickly went around his neck and pulled him to the sidewalk.

"Don't want you run over," said a familiar voice.

Claus turned around, but this time the familiar voice was not that of Lanietta but of Nekara.

"Best we leave this place," Nekara said while holding leashes to two of her dogs.

"Oh, you remember Bleyafooga and Glastako, don't you?"

The dogs growled at Claus.

"I'll give you a choice. You can join my little pack in dog form, or you can be my male escort. We can be a couple," Nekara said with a smile.

A sickening feeling filled Claus's gut. Pretending to be Nekara's escort would not only feel like walking with the devil, but might also incur Lanietta's wrath. But as a dog? That was inhuman.

"Strange that you fear Lanietta's jealousy and not Labba's, the mother of your children," Nekara said. "And yes, I can read your mind."

"Then there's no point of anything, is there?"

"Not with me. My escort you be," Nekara said.

Claus walked next to Nekara as she left the scene of students with her two dogs. The four turned a corner into an alley.

"My escort as a canine, that is," she said, and Nekara turned Claus into dog form before he could complain.

"Woof, woof!" he instead ended up uttering.

"That's right. Say what your kind says best," she chuckled.

Nekara and the three dogs continued down the alley.

"Yes, Bleyafooga," Nekara whispered. "I smell them too. Glastako, do you concur? Indeed. These *are* two of them. Very well. Take your positions. Go along with Bleyafooga, Klomper."

Bleyafooga and Klomper climbed a fire-escape stairwell on one building and Glastako climbed a fire-escape stairwell on the other building. Nekara then walked seemingly alone in the alley toward the two young college students.

"Well, well, well, what do we have here?" said a young male. "TK, is that an eight?"

"Only after a six-pack. I give her a five, RP," said the other young male.

"Stand aside, please," Nekara said.

"Not until you pay a toll, honey," said RP, and he moved to kiss Nekara.

"Stuff it," Nekara said. "Allow me to pass."

"You'll pass when we say you can pass," said TK.

TK went behind Nekara and put her in a half Nelson wrestling hold. Nekara attempted to kick TK in the groin, but he had his body turned sideways for protection. He laughed.

"Now we can have some fun!" RP said.

RP moved to kiss her, and Claus was mortified. This was Nekara. She was being attacked by these boys? They were getting away with it?

Nekara squirmed to get away, but these boys were young and strong. She was prevented. Claus gnashed his teeth together, but strangely enough, he felt that although he had dog teeth, the position of his missing upper second molar was now occupied with a human molar, and it clashed with the lower carnassial tooth. Claus let out a yelp from the sudden, sharp pain. This triggered two actions. Nekara spiked her heel into TK's foot, and Nekara's two dogs dove down on the boys, one a piece.

Bleyafooga and Glastako tore the boys apart.

"No!" Claus wanted to shout.

But all Claus could do was bite down on his mismatched molars, and the pain turned his vision white, like the electrocution of a lightning bolt filling his mind.

The scene changed. Claus stood as a human on a pier overlooking the water. It was late Saturday night, and Claus heard only the waves crashing into the pier. Again Claus felt a leather strap around his neck, and again he turned around to see Nekara, only she had two other dogs.

"You remember Deizaga and Esnargoff, don't you?" Nekara asked.

"You murdered those two boys," Claus said. "That's a crime."

"Do you expect an explanation from me? Like Lanietta?" Nekara laughed. "I act. I don't explain."

"You'll explain to me!" Claus insisted. "No human deserves murder!"

"Ask Lanietta to explain why those who owe infinite gratitude to the gender that brings them into the world instead defiles them. Now we are late. You may go as my escort," Nekara said.

Nekara yanked Claus's leash. He resisted, but his carnassial molar slammed down against his regular molar and sent jarring pain into his jaw. Nekara changed him to Klomper the dog, and he walked with Deizaga and Esnargoff. Nekara's two main dogs made subtle whimpers.

"I know. They are just over that ledge," Nekara said. "Do you hear them?"

"Remember Meg from last year, AG?" said a young male voice.

"Yeah," said a second young male voice (AG).

Slight pause.

"C'mon, AD. What did you do? Tell me," AG said.

"I hacked her registration card. Just one digit. The room number for her sociology class. Put her on the third floor," AD said.

"You did that? Pure genius!" AG said. "When she showed up in Cal 3 and asked our professor where 303 was, I didn't know where it was."

"Until the professor explained that 303 was the men's bathroom," AD said.

"And the whole class laughed her out!" AG said.

"She was so embarrassed!" AD said. "She turned red and ran out like she was naked."

"Like I said, pure genius!" AG said.

"It takes a special touch," AD bragged. "The magic of fingertips dropping upon the keyboard in carefully planned strokes. These fingers can control the universe!"

AD wiggled his fingers as if typing. Nekara motioned to Deizaga and Esnargoff to take and hold positions from the ledge. Claus as Klomper accompanied neither dog but simply stayed put. Nekara walked around the ledge structure and came out at a position at the corner of a column. She held a bulky, mid-1980s cell phone. She shook it as if trying to get it to work.

"Technology. It's so confusing," Nekara said.

"Maybe I can help," AD offered.

Nekara jumped with a start.

"Oh, you startled me. I didn't see you in the dark," Nekara feigned.

"Yeah, AD knows all about technology," AG said.

"You boys go to school around here?" Nekara asked.

"Yeah. The university," AD said. "I bet I can make your cell phone make calls for free."

"Isn't that stealing?" Nekara asked.

"Naw," AG said. "AD does it all the time. He dials into bulletin boards with his computer. They post telephone credit card numbers and other good stuff."

"I see," Nekara said. "Well?"

Nekara offered the cell phone to AD. Both AG and AD walked over to her. AD took the phone and tapped onto the keys.

"This is a very strange cell phone," AD said. "The tones are a bit odd."

"So you can't fix it? You can't make the phone do what you want?" Nekara asked.

"I can make any phone do whatever I want. All it takes is time and effort," AD said.

"Prove it," Nekara said.

"I'll dial up a government computer and make the modem connect with this phone," AD said. "Behold the magic fingers at work."

AD tapped the buttons very quickly.

"I wish I could hit buttons that fast," Nekara said as modem handshaking sounds came out of the cell phone's speaker. "But I have such long fingernails."

"Yeah," AD said. "Long nails are worthless. Always getting in the way."

At *getting in the way*, Claus remembered his upper second molar. Like in the other situation with Nekara's dogs, his upper second molar as a dog was human, while his other teeth were canine. He closed his bite, the human tooth interfered with the carnassial, and he shuddered from the jarring pain. Deizaga

and Esnargoff leapt down from the ledge and landed each upon a boy. Deizaga used his long claws to tear AG apart while Esnargoff used his long claws to tear AD apart—all while the cell phone spouted out audio from the government modem's relentless and unending hissing and squawking as it searched for a compatible connection. Claus did not pass out immediately. He witnessed the boys' conversion to lumps of lifeless flesh.

"Yes, worthless," Nekara echoed. "You boys got in the way of long nails. From my dogs. Klomper, care to partake?"

"I won't murder," Claus tried to say, but it came out as a bark.

A great wave crashed against the pier. Claus closed his eyes.

The scene changed again. Nekara was walking west away from the water but toward a university. Beside her walked Thibariska and Ipacliska, who were in humanoid female form. Claus was also in humanoid form.

"So you're Lanietta's pet?" Thibariska asked. "You don't look like a pet."

"Because I'm not," Claus said.

"You look kinda cute," Ipacliska said.

"Then why don't you take him out?" Thibariska asked.

"You can't," Nekara said. "He's really a dog. Remember?"

"So are we. But it's fun pretending to be human," Thibariska said.

"So far we're just walking," Ipacliska said. "Let's duck into a bar."

"Bars don't allow dogs," Thibariska said.

"We'll keep Klomper as a man," Ipacliska said.

"That'll keep guys away," Thibariska said. "We should leave him outside, go in as a threesome, and see who will hit on us."

"Be careful what you ask for, girls. There is evil everywhere," Nekara said. "Including me."

The three laughed. Claus could only wonder what would happen in this reality. The other ones had just Nekara and her other dogs, leading to the death of young men. But in this reality, no one was in dog form, and there were no particular men for Nekara to murder. Would she find them in a bar and have Thibariska and Ipacliska kill them out back? Warning bells sounded in Claus's head, and he knew he had to keep them away from the bar.

"Why not take in the night air and keep walking?" Claus suggested.

"Spoken like a good dog," Nekara said. "Lanietta must be proud to have you as a pet. Thibs and Ipa, we'll go ahead and meet you at the restaurant on 20th."

Thibariska and Ipacliska diverted onto north-south roads, taking a longer way westward.

"Are you going to change me to dog form?" Claus asked.

"No. I'm your date for the evening," Nekara said. "Take my arm."

"What? No. Lanietta would—"

"Not notice. At least not yet. Let's make her jealous. Labba too. We'll go to your dorm room, and—"

"*My* dorm room? I don't have a dorm room," Claus said.

"You do now. Tell the front desk that we're going to study," Nekara said.

"What are you up to?" Claus said. "I won't kill."

"Remember? I don't explain. I act. We're almost there. Do as I say," Nekara said.

Claus and Nekara reached a dormitory on 16th Street. The two entered and stopped at the front desk.

"Oh, you!" Claus said to Lanietta.

"Your ID, please," Lanietta said.

"You two are ganging up on me?" Claus asked.

A student behind walked past Claus with his student ID up in the air, and Lanietta waved him through.

"You'll have to sign your guest in," Lanietta said. "She must be checked out by ten. No overnight guests."

"A pity," Nekara said.

"I mean it, Nekara," Lanietta said. "Whatever enjoyment you derive must end by then. I can pull out the contract if need be."

Lanietta pulled out a book much the size of an old telephone book but triple-thick.

"I know the contract," Nekara said. "Very well. Ten on ten."

Nekara signed in. Lanietta waved them through, and the two waited for an elevator. Two other young men waited, and the four entered the elevator only to discover all floors had been selected.

"Aw," said one in dismay.

"Take it anyway," said the other. "I'll take the stairs and race you up."

"Five dollars," said the first.

"Deal."

With the bet set, one went into the elevator, and the other raced up the stairs.

"Let's wait for the other one," Claus said.

"Very well," Nekara said.

Claus smiled.

"Nekara listened to me. Is following my lead," Claus continued to smile.

"Don't let his leash get too long, Nekara," Lanietta called.

"Don't worry," Nekara replied.

The second elevator arrived. By that time, two other men were waiting for it as well. The four entered, and each selected floors. One chose the twelfth floor, Nekara hit floor ten, and the other chose the second floor. The elevator doors closed.

"Seems so small in here," Nekara said.

"What's that? A mouse?" the second floor guy asked.

The second floor came soon enough, much to the impatience of the twelfth floor guy. As the guy exited and the doors closed, the twelfth floor guy yelled.

"Take the stairs!"

The tenth floor came next with the doors opening. Claus motioned for Nekara to go first, and he followed. The twelfth floor guy shook a little fist at Claus in camaraderie and said, "Get lucky!"

The doors closed, and Nekara turned around.

"Get lucky?" Nekara asked. "Do you want to get lucky with me?"

"It's just an expression of this era," Claus said. "I could tell by the car styles that this is the mid-1980s."

"And that's supposed to be an excuse? Never mind," Nekara said. "Let's go to your room."

"I don't know which room is supposedly mine," Claus said. "Will you at least tell me that?"

"Walk by all of them. You'll find it," Nekara said.

The two walked around the floor.

"Claus. Nice score!" said a passing floormate.

"That's not how I was!" Claus said.

"Of course not," Nekara said sarcastically. "Young human males are saints."

The two reached a room with the door closed and a sock tied around the doorknob.

"Let's go into your room," Nekara said.

"Uh, no," Claus said. "The sock means to stay out."

"Stay out of your own room? Preposterous!" Nekara said.

"It's locked. See?" Claus said as he gingerly tried to turn the doorknob.

"Too bad," Nekara said.

Nekara threw her body against the door to force it open. The door held on two attempts, but the third one got through. Nekara and Claus stood in the doorway to a bewildered roommate.

"Claus!" he said, wearing nothing but shorts.

"Sorry!" Claus said. "This is Nekara, my—"

"His date!" Nekara said, now pulling Claus into the dorm room. "Where's *your* date, Felix?"

"Felix?" Claus asked.

"I told you, Claus. No jokes about my name!" Felix said.

"I'm ready, Felix," a young woman said, now emerging from the bathroom. "Who's this?"

"Claus has a girl," Felix said. "Claus, Amy and I are going out to dinner. Would you—"

But Amy's eyes cut off Felix and told him not to invite Claus.

"Oh, we've already eaten," Nekara said. "Claus and I have much studying to do."

"I bet you do," Felix said as he winked at Claus. "See you around."

Felix dressed quickly, and he left with Amy.

"Felix and Amy have been dating all year," Claus said. "Somehow I know that, but I don't know how. At this point, Lanietta would explain things."

Nekara laughed.

"Open the window," she commanded.

"For fresh air?"

"Do as I say," she said.

Claus opened the window. Nekara changed into a falcon. She flew through the opening and out, as there was no mesh screen to prevent her.

"Nekara!" Claus said in surprise.

No reply from Nekara.

"Why don't these rooms have screens?" Claus asked himself. "A person could fall through!"

"I heard you had a girl," said a floormate who looked like TK and suddenly appeared in the doorway.

"You...I thought..." Claus stumbled.

"Guess that was a prank," TK said. "We're going to start our own little prank. Care to join us? We're in BK's room."

Claus shrugged his shoulders and nodded in agreement. He followed TK and entered BK's room. In the room were also RP, AD, and AG.

"You're all dead!" Claus blurted.

They laughed.

"We will be if we don't have another round," RP said.

BK motioned to the fridge, and RP opened it. One by one he passed unopened beer bottles to the guys in the room. One went to Claus.

"Wait," BK said. "Before we start, everyone must pay the initiation fee."

Claus dug out his wallet and thumbed through the dollar bills.

"No, not like that. Like this!" BK said.

BK put the bottle cap to the side of his mouth and used his lower premolars to pry the cap off.

"You can't use your front teeth. Or canine teeth. Molars," BK insisted.

The others held their bottles nearly vertical, tilted their jaws downward, and used their lower premolars to open them. They succeeded. Claus, realizing he still had a carnassial upper second molar, tried using that instead. But the tooth was too far back, and he settled for an upper premolar. But this meant tilting the beer bottle too much to the horizontal. The cap came off, and beer spilled all over him. BK and the guys laughed.

"You don't pass," BK said.

The guys pleaded that Claus should be let in, that he *did* use a molar to get the cap off. BK relented.

"Enough of the beer mess," BK said. "We're going to play the Dummy Award. Here's how this works. I'll call the pay phone out there by the bus stop. I'll say I'm Choe Bizabo from 109 radio, we're calling around, and they're the 109th person to answer. I'll say they won a prize, and when they ask what it is, I'll say they won the Dummy Award. Then everyone yell out the window, 'Dummy! Dummy!'"

Claus looked out the window, and he could see a phone booth by the bus stop at 16th and Hoosgeima. BK picked up his phone and dialed. The window was open. The guys looked out, waiting and hoping for someone to pick up. Claus thought the game silly enough. He'd wasted part of his youth dialing random phone numbers and claiming that the other person's goat was in his garden, but this prank was different.

A man looked at the ringing phone. He took a step toward it, paused, debated what to do, then he picked it up. BK went into his rant about the guy being the 109th caller, but before the punchline could be delivered, his bus arrived. He hung up the phone and rushed to that bus, boarded it, and was gone.

"We'll wait for the bus to leave," he said. "Plenty more fish, guys. Plenty more fish."

Claus could sense the tension and excitement in the air from his floormates. But was this a good way to spend time? Where was Nekara? The bus left. BK called again. A homeless person walked up, lifted the receiver, and hung it up in such quick action as to simply end the phone call. BK called again, but the homeless person repeated the action.

"Claus. Get rid of the homeless guy," BK said.

Claus agreed. As he left BK's room, he thought he saw a feather from a bird's wing just outside the window. He looked back in the room, but the feather was gone.

"Go on!" BK said. "We're all waiting for you!"

Claus left. He didn't bother with the elevator and ran down the stairs instead. Out of breath, he ran past the front desk.

"Wait!" Lanietta said. "You can't leave without your guest!"

Once outside the dorm, Claus slowed his gait from run to quick walk. He reached the bus stop and paused a moment as if waiting for the bus. He was about to say something to the homeless guy when the homeless guy approached him.

"Got a quarter?" he asked.

"I'll give you five bucks," Claus said. "Go get something to eat."

"Bless you!" he said, and he walked across the street.

Claus headed back to the dorm, but before he could go inside, Lanietta had exited and caught up to him.

"You can't do that," Lanietta said. "Residents must accompany guests at all times."

"Nekara changed into a bird," Claus said. "Anyway, the guys on tenth asked me to shoo away a homeless guy."

"Why?"

"So they can play a phone prank," Claus said.

At that moment, Claus heard the guys from tenth floor yelling, "Dummy! Dummy!" He turned around in time to see Thibariska and Ipacliska running away from the phone booth.

"Oh, no," Claus said.

Claus looked up and saw Nekara (as a falcon) fly into the tenth floor window from the ledge. Squawks, squeals, grunts, yelps, and shouts carried down from the window. Lanietta also looked up, but as she did, she smelled the beer on Claus.

"You've been drinking beer?" Lanietta asked. "No, you've spilled it on yourself. How sloppy!"

"Sorry," Claus said. "And I'm sorry about Nekara's girls. How embarrassing, with the whole world watching. Or so it seems. I must go after the guys. I must fix the situation."

"Oh I wouldn't worry about that," Nekara said, now exiting the dorm a bit disheveled with blood on her face. "The boys are done with the Dummy Award, having won the grand prize themselves—me!"

"I saw them," Claus said. "I saw TK, RP, AD, and AG. You murdered them. But they were alive."

"Temporal mechanics, Clomper," Lanietta said. "I'll explain later. Nekara is going after her girls now. Do you wish to accompany her?"

Nekara let out a big grin.

"Take a chance, Claus. Let mischief beget mischief," Nekara urged.

"No. I'll pass," Claus said.

Nekara tipped an imaginary hat and then walked off toward Thibariska and Ipacliska.

"Murder is wrong, Lanietta!"

"I didn't invent it. Your people have been doing it for thousands of years. Well, I hope Nekara is satisfied. This contract-fulfillment stuff stretches my sanity."

"Stretches *your* sanity? What about mine?"

"Clomper. We're here on this campus in the mid-1980s. It's cold out here. Let's walk over to that little tent of people in the field. You know, the field before it was turned into the new student center. They have a half-keg and are chilling out. I've already called for my relief at the front desk. What do you say?"

Claus agreed. They walked a short ways and met with students and a sedate Applefoibaug already there. Before Claus could remark about Nekara's dog, Lanietta produced a twelve-pack of beer.

"German import, if anyone is interested," Lanietta offered.

The import disappeared like hotcakes, leaving just two—one each for Lanietta and Claus. The thankful students did offer beer from their half-keg in return. Lanietta and Claus smiled, huddled with them in the tent, and rubbed Applefoibaug's fur.

"I wish you'd spare me all this," Claus said.

"All what? This is humanity," Lanietta said. "Are you wishing you'd never been born?"

"No. Just...I want to skip all this," Claus said.

"No one graduates for free. Must get through things," Lanietta said.

Claus took a sip of his beer, but he lost his ability to drink much of anything.

"I can't," Claus said. "I'm...I'm..."

"Distraught?"

"Yes."

"The murders?"

"Yes. Did you see them?"

"I sensed them."

"Why?"

"You know why. You saw why. Just now."

"From that game? The Dummy Award?" Claus asked.

"Yes. You saw how Nekara's girls ran off. Many have suffered worse. Much worse."

"But I didn't do anything," Claus said.

"Exactly," Lanietta said. "Well, try your beer again."

Claus took a sip.

"Stick with the import. It will go down easier," Lanietta said.

Claus took another sip.

"There. Better?"

"A little. I've seen all her dogs except Heiauga and one more. Trying to remember..."

"Zarcroga," Lanietta helped.

"Thanks. Wait, does that mean there's another situation? Will she force me to endure more pain?"

"It's in the contract, Clomper. You're human, and you tend to sense and feel the misery of others, even when it's not visible on the surface. Nekara feeds on that. I suggest you bury your feelings while she's around. She'll tire of you and look for another mark."

"*You* gave me to her," Claus said. "*You* did all this."

"I loaned you to her. Thought you could use a little break," Lanietta said.

"Some break."

"Take another sip."

Claus sipped more beer.

"I've had enough. Remove the carnassial," Claus said.

"I can't restore your regular molar," Lanietta said.

"I don't care," Claus said.

"No guarantee your neurosis will go away," Lanietta said.

"I still don't care," Claus said.

"There's one other thing."

"What's that?"

"This part of Nekara's contract is yet to be fulfilled."

"Meaning?"

"Meaning you're about to go on the last leg of it. Within the minute in fact."

"Thanks," Claus said sarcastically.

"Enjoy this moment, Clomper. The 1980s will never come again."

The scene changed. Claus stood near the restaurant on 20th. An emaciated cat wandered by and meowed, looking for food.

"I have no food for you," Claus said. "It seems both you and I are solitary strangers in these parts."

The cat meowed again and stared directly into Claus's eyes. Claus dropped to a knee.

"What do we have, cat? Just the moment. Who knows if tomorrow will come. Well, I know something I can do. I'll bring you a little food. Stay right here. I'll be back," Claus said.

Claus walked into the restaurant and approached a waitress.

"I'd like to buy a piece of raw beef," Claus said.

The waitress looked at Claus in surprise.

"I don't want to eat here. Just take a hamburger, no bun, and don't cook it," Claus said.

The waitress disappeared for a moment. She then returned.

"The cook can't give you raw beef and guarantee it will be free of germs and safe to eat. He'll have to cook it," she said.

"Okay, make it the rarest beef possible," Claus said.

"I'll tell him," she said.

The waitress appeared a bit later with a paper bag.

"He lightly cooked it, just enough to kill the germs," she said.

The waitress rang up the purchase. Claus paid for it and gave the waitress a three dollar tip.

"Good luck," she said.

Claus left.

"Did she know?" Claus asked himself. "Women always read between the lines. But where is the cat?"

Claus could not find the cat. Had it gone under a car? Claus knelt behind a car parked on the side of the street. As he did, he couldn't help but notice the sticker had a late 1980s year.

"No cat under here," he said.

He stood back up. The car was different. The sticker was that of a 1990s year, and the car had more rust.

"What just happened?" he asked.

He looked toward the restaurant, but it was gone, having been replaced by apartments. He spun in place to quickly gauge his surroundings. Trees seemed a little different, but other buildings were as before. He looked south and saw two dogs walking along with no leash or master.

"Zarcroga and Heiauga!" Claus said. "But where is Nekara?"

Claus started to run toward them, but he stopped himself.

"Wait. If I make Nekara's dogs aware of my presence, Nekara might turn me into a dog. Best I creep up," Claus said to himself.

He did, but at one point, the dogs unpaired and chose different directions.

"I'll follow Heiauga. I know her better," Claus said.

Claus followed her. She climbed up an abandoned building, paused at a ledge, and darted off. Claus reached the ledge. While contemplating what to do next, he heard voices.

"So are you named after the reformer or the Founding Father?" Nekara's voice said from below and outside.

Claus peered into the darkness, and he was just able to make out two shapes working with equipment.

"Neither, really," the young man said. "Having the same name as Luther Martin is just a coincidence history-wise. I'm named after my mother's grandpa. I'll hold the red LED flashlight, Kara."

"Thanks," Nekara said.

"Kara? Nekara is posing as someone in the '90s. But I don't know this Luther Martin guy," Claus said to himself.

Claus's vision improved, especially as Luther shined the red flashlight around, and he could see the two were setting up astronomy equipment, including a telescope.

"Nice Cassegrain telescope, but how could you afford it?" Luther asked.

"It was a gift from my former girlfriend," Kara said.

"Former?"

"Yeah. We broke up. She wanted me to tell my family about us, and I'm still in the closet," Kara said.

"I'm sorry to hear that," Luther said.

"At least she let me keep the telescope. Oh well. Let's see what this scope can do," Kara said.

Kara hit a few buttons, and motors re-pointed the telescope. Kara looked through an eyepiece and smiled.

"I can see the Galilean moons," she said. "Impressive, considering the city lights. You picked a good spot. Was it luck?"

"I know every bit of this area," Luther said. "These two buildings were part of a brewery, but the brewery moved farther west."

"The yeast smell on the freeway?" Kara said.

"That's the one. I come from a family of master brewers. And I'm expected to follow in their footsteps," Luther said.

"Something tells me you don't want to," Kara said while connecting her camera to the scope.

"I can do the job. I just have no interest in it. I find myself drawn to the older buildings in downtown, dreaming of a bygone era," Luther said.

"An era of great drunkenness," Kara joked.

But Luther didn't laugh.

"Sorry," she said.

"That's okay. You've put your finger on it, though. I see my family making millions off an industry that ruins other families with alcoholism, poverty, and crime. I just don't have the stomach for it. So I'm majoring in general studies," Luther said. "I have no idea what I'll do after I graduate. But I know what my family wants me to do."

"Dare I guess?" Kara asked. "They want you to run one of the breweries."

"They want me to marry the daughter of the competitor," Luther said.

"And I thought I had things bad," Kara said. "Are you going to run away?"

Luther laughed.

"Imagine, a grown man with a degree, running away. Men have fought wars, had children, and died by the time I'll graduate. But yeah, it feels like running away," Luther said.

"Because it is. I ran away from home several times before I left for college," Kara said. "It was the only way I could meet others like me in secret. And you know what? I learned I have an aunt like me. That explains why my folks always bought dresses for me and never let me wear pants. I couldn't figure out why until my aunt told me her parents did the same for her."

"So you got to meet your aunt," Luther said.

"When I ran away. Twice, actually. Told my parents I stayed with friends. The aunt is ostracized from the family, all because...well...you know," Kara said.

"I know. Maybe if I were a woman, you and I could..."

Kara smiled.

"It's a strange world we live in, Luther," Kara said.

"Yes it is," Luther replied.

Kara took several photos, each time with the telescope oriented slightly differently. She finished with the photos and packed the camera.

"The Galilean moons are beautiful. Care to take a look?" Kara offered.

Luther looked through the eyepiece.

"Ganymede," Luther said. "She's just as beautiful as ever."

"How do you know she's a she?" Kara asked.

"She has to be. I'll name my first daughter after her," Luther said.

Kara laughed.

"Well?"

"You? Have children?" Kara pressed.

"If I'm forced to marry the competitor's daughter, and somehow we—"

"That's a big somehow!" Kara said.

"I know. At least my daughter should have a heavenly name instead of one inspired by beer drinkers," Luther said.

"And if there are other children?" Kara asked.

"I'll name those girls Europa and Io," Luther said.

"You expect them to be in resonance like their namesakes? You're dreaming. My sister and I are total opposites. Hardly in resonance," Kara said.

"I can look up to the heavens and wish, can't I?" Luther asked. "Oh sky above, bestow my gift—a dream come true."

Claus himself looked up to the sky and wondered how many had stared upward and asked the sky to fulfill their dreams. Then he thought about his missing upper molar and realized these were empty wishes. Yes, the carnassial tooth Lanietta had placed in his mouth was gone, and he was back to the missing upper molar. He closed his teeth together and checked the gap with his tongue.

"The gap is still there," Claus said to himself. "The sky is but an empty place and will bring down nothing."

"We should go to the country next time and get away from the city lights," Kara said. "I bet we can see more of the heavens out there. Maybe then your wish will come true."

Luther laughed. Claus started to laugh too, but he felt a tugging on his shirt. It was Heiauga.

"What?" Claus asked.

She pulled and pulled him.

"You don't want me here? I'm not doing anything. Maybe eavesdropping," Claus said.

But Heiauga was insistent. She pulled Claus from the ledge and across the way to another side of the building where Zarcroga was watching something below.

"I'm going already," Claus whispered.

Claus could no longer hear Luther and Nekara, but he heard new voices—again they were outside and below. The way the buildings were positioned meant one group was not aware of the other—a building corner was in the way.

"Ante up, deuce a story," BK's voice said.

Claus looked down and saw BK and a helper with several cases of beer. Sitting close-by was a group of college students. BK held out his hat like a basket as he walked amongst the students. They kicked in two dollars each, and the helper provided the requisite beer.

"BK is older," Claus said to himself. "He looks gruff and worn. I don't see any of the others from the tenth floor. These are new college students."

BK collected the last fee, pocketed the money, and returned the hat to his head. He returned to the pile of beer with his helper and sat.

"The next story is only for members of the Dummy Award Committee. So you gotta join to hear it. Or leave now," BK said.

No one left.

"To join, you gotta open your beer with your molar. Not your canine. Not your buck teeth. Your molar. Show them, Heffy," BK said.

BK's assistant, Heffy, demonstrated how to open a bottle of beer with his premolar.

"See? Just like that. Your turn," BK said.

Half the students succeeded, the other half did not.

"If you didn't open your beer with your molar, leave now," BK said. "Unless you want to try method B. Raise your hand for method B."

Those who did not succeed raised their hands.

"Alls you gots to do is bring a small animal to the meeting—mouse, squirrel, chipmunk—you get the idea. Then I'll show you how you can join. I'll give you five minutes to find an animal. If you can't, you'll have to leave," BK said. "And no white fur!"

The failed half went scrambling for animals. But all they could find was the cat that Claus had seen near the restaurant.

"There you go. Bring it here," BK said.

The students did so.

"Will they kill it?" Claus muttered to himself. "Zarcroga, Heiauga, are you going to kill BK for this? For killing a cat? I can't believe I'm watching this and doing nothing. But how do I get down there? Quickly? I'd have to run down the stairs at light speed. Or jump off this ledge."

Claus ran down the stairs. Every so often as the stairwell passed an open window area, Claus heard phrases, such as: "in liquid nitrogen", "freeze brand", and "will turn white". Before he reached the bottom, he heard the cat screech. Running out the doorway and into the area of BK and his followers allowed him just in time to see the cat run away with a missing patch of fur on his back.

"I thought you froze it!" Claus yelled.

"Claus? Is that you?" BK called. "My fellow Committee, Claus is the only member to be inducted by his upper molar."

The college students clapped.

"What did you do to that cat?" Claus asked.

"Freeze branding. Perfectly safe. His fur will grow back white in the shape of this here beer bottle," BK said as he pointed to the end of the brand. "My fellow Committee, forty percent of you remain to be inducted. Now go find your animals!"

"No! Stop! This is inhumane!" Claus shouted. "I'm reporting this to PETA."

"What's that?" BK asked. "Sounds made up. Here's a free story for you fellow Committee members. Claus was part of the prank we pulled in early '86. The Dummy Award. Tell them what you did, Claus."

"I didn't do it. You did. You made the phone call," Claus explained.

"And you yelled the words," BK said.

"Not me. I went downstairs. The other guys did," Claus said.

"Is that how you remember it? I think you were drunk. Very drunk. Get this boy a beer!"

The students cheered and passed a beer to Claus.

"Show us how it's done," said one student.

"Yeah."

"Use your upper molar."

"Upper molar, upper molar," the students chanted.

"No!" Claus said. "Take this back!"

"I will," BK said. "But you'll have to take the brand."

"That's a deal!" Claus said. "I'm turning it in as evidence."

Instead of BK being afraid, he smiled, as if he'd won long ago. He offered the freeze brand to Claus, and Claus took it.

"Keep the beer," BK said. "You'll need it."

Before Claus could argue the point, the remaining students who had left to find an animal returned with Luther and (Ne)Kara.

Each had a beer in hand and were thanking the students for the same.

"We can only stay for a little while," Kara said. "Then we must head back and get this roll of film developed."

"What's with the equipment?" BK asked.

"This is a telescope, and this is a—" Luther started to explain.

"Telescope!" BK interrupted. "See the stars. Distant planets."

"Yes," Kara said. "We took several pictures of—"

"No pictures!" BK yelled. "Heffy!"

BK motioned around like mad. Students took hold of Luther, Kara, and Claus.

"What are you doing?" Luther insisted.

"No!" Kara said.

"Stop!" Claus yelled.

Luther was restrained. Kara was held face-down, and Claus was forced to dip the brand into liquid nitrogen.

"BK, if you do this, others will avenge!" Claus yelled.

"No one here, Claus. Time you learn the ways of the world," BK said.

Claus could only think of Heiauga and Zarcroga up above, watching and readying to dive down and massacre the many. Claus's hand was forced to remove the brand from the liquid nitrogen and place it against the back of Kara's head. She screamed at first as the brand froze through her hair and froze her scalp, but the cold deadened her nerves, and she felt no pain. She made a primal sound, something between a grunt, moan, and whimper.

"Stop it. Stop it!" Claus yelled.

"You must initiate all those who have partaken in our merriment," BK said.

"HEIAUGA! HELP!" Claus yelled at the top of his lungs.

Heiauga had already started her run down the same stairs Claus had taken. It was Nekara's scream that had started her run. Heiauga leapt at Claus. She knocked the brand out of his hand and the hands of others, sending them through the air. Zarcroga dove down from above. Claus feared the worst, that Nekara's dogs would tear BK and the students to shreds as Nekara's other dogs had done.

"Please! Not again!" Claus said. "Save us, but don't kill us!"

The strangest thing happened. The jaws and claws of Heiauga and Zarcroga tore not at student and flesh but through a canvas—a painting representation of BK, the students, Luther, and (Ne)Kara. Where was Claus now? On a stage? On a trampoline? The canvas did not represent the entire world, just the immediate people around. Road, buildings, and trees remained. Day came and went quickly, with the sun shooting across the sky in a second or less. Autumn came and went. Leaves filled the air, fell on Claus, and even flew into his mouth. Claus gagged on the leaves and spat them out. Another canvas appeared around him of BK and students, but the dogs tore that up too. Another year passed, another autumn, and Claus spat out leaves from that year too. And the next. The next. Many years went by, and Claus gagged on the multitude of leaves plugging his mouth. He wished he had no teeth at all, and he held his lips shut tight, but still the leaves slipped in, as if forced by another being. The canvases faded and disappeared into nothing, as did the leaves. The sun shot around so quickly that light became steady without apparent flicker. Blindingly strong it was. Claus felt his retinas burning. He blinked and cried out.

"No more. No more!" Claus said.

"That's enough neem," Labba's voice said.

Claus blinked several more times. Labba, Clausetta, Treyu, Mariel, and Selba sat with Claus around a campfire. Night had fallen. A bucket of neem leaves sat beside Claus.

"What happened?" Claus asked.

"You became delusional. We made camp out here away from everything and made you chew neem leaves to calm you and restore dental health," Labba said.

"My upper molar?" Claus asked.

Claus used his tongue to probe for his missing upper molar. It was still missing, but he was not nearly as distressed as before.

"I don't know what to make of things. I feel flat," Claus said.

"Believe it or not, that's a good sign," Labba said. "Mariel has used neem for years to treat such neuroses. Looks like it helped."

"I...maybe it has," Claus said.

"Claus, there's one more thing we must do," Mariel said. "We need to rid your body of any last evil molar spirits."

"Evil molar spirits? Evil molar spirits. Hah! A joke! So funny!" Claus laughed excessively.

"From delusion to hysteria," Labba said. "Is this normal?"

"Yes," Mariel said. "We'll finish the last step, and all will be well. Hand Claus the paper."

"Evil molars and now a paper?" Claus continued to laugh.

"Your molars have been with you your pre-adult and adult life. They have experienced and absorbed much evil that has festered during this lifetime," Mariel said.

"Impossible," Claus laughed.

"Your teeth contain nerves. Bacteria create information acid chains of your excesses (those unproductive wasteful moments in life), and some of those chains—not all—find their way into your pulp chamber where they are stored. Nerves travel through your pulp chamber, convert those twisted encodings to signals, and carry the signals to your brain, unbalancing and upsetting you," Mariel said. "So to your statement, not impossible."

"Should I have all my teeth pulled? Rid myself of this evil?" Claus continued.

"Not so fast, Claus. Besides the loss of tooth function and bone mass, you'd have many unresolved issues should you pluck them out without thought," Labba said.

"Claus, your teeth were in equilibrium, competing to cancel out as much of the bad past as possible," Mariel said. "You had a tooth pulled. For many, the other teeth readjust so cleverly that the human host doesn't notice a thing."

"Human host? Are teeth merely parasites?" Claus asked.

"You are different, of course," Mariel said.

"Of course," Claus repeated.

"So we'll restore equilibrium with your teeth by means of paper transference," Mariel said. "Stick this in your mouth and bite down on it. Do not chew. One bite, and pull it out."

Claus did so. An impression of his bite was formed on the paper. Mariel took a pen in hand and wrote something on the paper. She then passed it to Labba.

"Each of you must write a few words identifying a moment in your life when you wasted or lost something," Mariel said.

They did, and the paper came back to Claus. He was about to read it, but Labba snatched it from him.

"I thought I was going to read it or something, and we'd each tell stories of what we wasted or lost," Claus said.

"No, that would be double waste and double loss. Cast this paper into the fire, Claus. Don't read it. Cast it. Cast it now," Mariel said.

Claus looked at Labba.

"The fire," Labba emphasized as she returned the paper to him.

Claus stood, walked to the fire, and dropped the paper into it. It floated at first, but then flames consumed it, it fell, and it disappeared into the embers. The others around let out a sigh of relief.

"What? Wait," Claus said. "This helped everyone else? What about me?"

"Let's test," Labba said.

Labba took a stick and tossed it up high such that it would land on Claus from above. He caught it without issue.

"How do you feel? Do you miss your molar?" Labba asked.

"I feel flat. No, I don't miss it. I guess I'm cured."

"Yay!" Clausetta cheered.

Clausetta ran over to Claus, took him by the hand, and danced with him around the fire, chanting, "He's cured, he's cured."

Chapter 136: A Brief Survey

In the days that followed, Leif gave Claus a tour of his underground war arsenal—trucks, tanks, airplanes, helicopters, weapons, ammunition, and fuel.

"I'm shocked," Claus said. "I mean the surface is like 19th century England. But this is 20th century technology. And I feel the misery of that century with it."

"Necessary, Pappa. The cubics are out of control. We tried stealthy methods, but they continue to encroach on the near side. I had to take drastic steps," Leif said.

"This is your army then?"

"My army and air force, yes. We've skipped a navy for speed. We have special long-range floating aircraft for sea missions," Leif said. "Tomorrow I will launch a large group of helicopters. They'll act as a flying curtain, sweeping the ground for enemy invaders. The helicopters are well equipped with avionics and weapons."

"The ice ammo?" Claus asked.

"The same," Leif said. "If you're up to it, I'd like you to help."

The two took a closer look at Leif's helicopters.

"These are of an advanced design," Claus said, looking at a cockpit's instrument panel.

"The mechanical features of helicopter design haven't changed much. But the controls are more advanced. More computerized. These copters must gather large amounts of information then process this information to separate friend from foe plus provide fail-safe features in case of attack," Leif explained.

"Do you have anything more original? Something that wouldn't require re-learning?" Claus asked.

"We have base models we use for comparison," Leif said. "They are not really meant to go out, but we've gathered as much data as we can from them, so I suppose it wouldn't matter if you took one. Let's take a look."

The two walked a bit farther. They came to an open bay where a single helicopter at a time would go up, do a short test flight, and land.

"This one is reliable. A UH-1 Huey. Many were produced. This one has just been fully serviced. No semiconductors though. The electronic disruption on the far side has spread all over," Leif said. "We're using long-life, low power vacuum tubes where needed."

Claus touched the chopper, and instantly he felt multiple overlapping memories from the 1960s, memories of wartime misery and death.

"This won't work, Leif. I'm overwhelmed just touching it. I can't imagine being up in the air with it," Claus said. "Lanietta would have a field day. She'd probably make me relive the entire Vietnam War from the perspective of every person involved. I can't imagine a worse condemnation. No, I need something simple. Something that hasn't seen war."

"Hmm," Leif mused. "I can show you other ones. Maybe you can sense a benign craft."

The two walked from helicopter to helicopter. Claus touched each of them, but he stopped at a Kellett XR-8.

"This one," he said.

"No," Leif said. "That was experimental."

"Will it fly?"

"Well yes, but—"

"Then I'll take it," Claus said.

"I'm told it's risky," Leif said. "The blades could collide."

"I'm already in a mess. Might as well have a bird in the same boat," Claus said.

Leif returned an expression of puzzlement.

"Pappa, maybe this isn't a good idea," Leif said.

"I'll take it now. I know how to fly this bird. Watch," Claus said.

Claus entered the helicopter and put on the helmet with radio. Leif motioned for a path to be made clear for the XR-8. Claus started the engine, manipulated the controls, and sent the craft upward.

"XR-8 to Leif," Claus radioed.

"I read you, Pappa," Leif said. "How do you feel?"

"A-okay. No problems with up and down motion, no motion sickness, and the XR-8 is flying just fine," Claus radioed.

"Land at the first sign of trouble," Leif said. "Hey, where are you going?"

"I'm going to survey the area," Claus said. "I want to see if flying causes me to experience anything unusual."

"Stay in radio contact," Leif said. "And stay away from the lunar shock. They don't know of our plans yet."

"I didn't realize the XR-8 could fly that far," Claus said.

"It can't. You'll run out of fuel before you reach the shock if you make the attempt," Leif said.

"I'll keep that in mind," Claus said.

"There's an emergency kit on board if you crash land. Flares are inside in case the radio fails. We'll be out in full force tomorrow. Look for us if need be," Leif said.

"I will. I'll see you in a bit," Claus said.

Claus followed the rail line toward the lunar shock for a minute or two, but he suddenly had a great urge to head south, and so he did. There was nothing worth reporting at first, but a glint caught his eye, and he headed for it. The glint was just over a ridge, and when he went over that ridge he was surprised to find a line of cubic encroachment.

"They've made it this far? How?" Claus asked himself, then he called into the radio. "Claus to base. Claus to base. The cubics are advancing from the south. I'm at—"

Before Claus could finish, a small ground-to-air missile struck his tail and damaged it. Fortunately, Claus didn't have need for a tail rotor, but the explosion also caused the controls to go stiff, and he had difficulty changing direction.

"I'm under attack! Send help now!" Claus could only muster.

Claus was too busy fighting for survival to radio back his position. Missile after missile was fired at him. The only way to avoid them was to fly toward them briefly then dart out of the way. This resulted in him going deeper and deeper into cubic territory.

"I can't keep this up. I can't get out. It'll be over soon enough," he said to himself.

The missiles fired in greater numbers. He was about to be caught among three when he noticed a patch of land ahead untouched by cubics. He made for this land, but too late he noticed the land was actually a ravine shrouded by overlapping rock outcroppings. Claus stopped forward momentum to turn back, but that gave the missiles an easy mark. They caught one of his rotor blades. Claus could no longer maintain altitude. The craft fell, and the missing rotor blade meant unchecked torque now spun the ship around and around. Claus felt himself blacking out.

"The end for sure," he said to himself.

Chapter 137: Lanietta's Lair

The XR-8 continued to descend, but before it crashed at the bottom, it became tangled in a net strewn across from one side of the ravine to another. The net gave way and wrapped around the XR-8. In this way, the net and XR-8 reached the bottom of the ravine with only a light jolt. The ropes suspending the net gave way and fell atop the XR-8, pounding it like hail. This pounding was loud enough to pull Claus out of his blackout, and he panicked as he tried to escape, but the net was firm and made of strong yet lightweight material. Claus slashed at it with his knife, but his knife only dulled.

"Hello!" Claus called.

"Clomper? Is that you?" Lanietta's voice called from a distance.

"Lanietta! Here? But how?" Claus called.

"I see you found my humble abode," she called with her voice growing closer. "Or should I say, my humble *subbode*."

"I never expected to find you down here," Claus said.

"Exactly!" she said as she reached the net. "No one would. Maintains my privacy."

"The cubics," Claus said. "They've surrounded this area on the surface. But—"

"They aren't here. Yes. I can still hold out against them. Lanietta, neither fully Gren nor fully Bleuh still has a trick or two up her sleeve," she said. "Don't mind my chatter. Let's free you from the net."

Lanietta unfastened something out of Claus's view, and the net came undone.

"Come out of your doghouse, Clomper," she said. "Let's go for a walk."

"One moment," Claus said. "I need to radio Leif."

"That won't work," she said.

"Claus to base. Claus to base. Leif, do you read?"

No reply.

"Told you," Lanietta said. "Shall we go? Don't worry. I won't bite."

"That's *my* line," Claus said. "What am I saying? You've got me speaking like a dog."

"Here you are not. Perhaps I should call you Claus. That would be refreshing, wouldn't it? Or Doron. After your grandmother."

"Please don't start with the Frieda jokes," Claus said.

"Delightful, adorable Doron," Lanietta said. "Is that what she calls you?"

"Hardly," Claus said.

"A pity. She knows not what she misses," Lanietta said.

Thunderous echoes descended from above.

"Explosions," Claus said. "Like the ones that hit my ship."

"So it's started. This little war between near and far," Lanietta said.

"You know about Leif's plans? But it's secret. He assured me no one could find out. Not you, not Frieda, not anyone," Claus said.

"It doesn't matter. It really doesn't. Hah. Hah-hah. Hahahaha!"

Lanietta broke out into hysterical laughter.

"It's over!" she laughed and cried with glee. "Don't you see? Laugh with me, Mr. Claus Doron Gerhardt. Laugh and laugh all the way to the end!"

Lanietta added a jig and a dance to her step.

"You've gone completely mad!" Claus said.

"No, I've gone completely sane!" she said.

"Lanietta, hold my hand," Claus said out of concern. "Just do it."

"It's too late for that, Mr. Scarf-and-Hat," she said.

Claus looked at himself. He had left the helmet in the craft and had no scarf.

"You're speaking nonsense," Claus said.

"Nonsense is sanity. Sanity is not just vanity. It's humanity!"

"Now I know you've lost it. Never have I heard a Carinian claim that humanity is sanity," Claus said. "Next you'll say humans are human."

"They are. Take you, for example," she said.

"Take me?"

"Yes. I took you, and you're still human. That proves it. Humanity is sanity," she said.

Claus shook his head in disbelief. They reached a closed door. Lanietta moved to open it.

"Ah-ah-ah! Not without the key!" she said with a smile.

Lanietta placed her hand in a right-side pocket and pulled out a key on a string (the string still running to her pocket). The key would not unlock the door.

"Not that one," she said.

She pulled on the string, and out came another key on the string (and still the string led to her pocket).

"No, not that one either," she said.

"Just how many keys do you have?" Claus asked.

"It's here. I know it is," Lanietta said. "I'll just keep trying and pulling."

Lanietta pulled and pulled on the string, revealing key after key. She looked at them one-by-one at first but sped up this process such that she was only skimming through the keys like a person flipping through and skimming pages of a book. A pile of string and keys grew almost as high as Lanietta herself.

"How did you fit all that in your pocket? A mass compressor?" Claus asked.

She reached the end of the string, and the pocket was pulled inside-out.

"Oh, that's right. It's in the other pocket," she said.

Lanietta started the process all over again with her left pocket.

"No!" Claus said, placing his hand on hers and pressing against her pocket.

"Oh, you wish to dance. The waltz?" she asked, and she pulled him into a dancing frame. "One-two-three, one-two-three, one-two-three."

"There's no music. Lanietta, the string from your right pocket is wrapping around us each time we turn around!" Claus protested.

"Let it wrap, Claus. Let the strings of this universe...the strings of the universe... I...Nanna!"

Claus stopped Lanietta and stared into her eyes.

"Glazed," he said.

He carefully spun themselves the other way and unwrapped the string from around them. He then found a nearby bench and helped her sit.

"Nanna!" she said again.

Claus walked over to the door. He turned the knob.

"Locked. And yet the hinge pins are on this side. Strange but helpful," Claus said.

Claus took two of the keys from the string and used them to pry the pins out of the hinges. The door opened, and Claus peered inside.

"It's...what is that? And it's outdoors! With sunlight! But we're down far below ground," Claus said. "It should help. A diversion. Yes."

Claus went back to Lanietta, helped her to her feet, and walked her through the doorway. They entered a kind of junkyard, private flea market, or antique market. Large sheds and small barns of various age, build, and condition lined two sides of a main walking area, and this main walking area had piles and piles of old junk.

"Nanna," Lanietta said, not as crazed as before.

"Do you hear me, Lanietta? Let's go into this building," Claus said.

The two entered a large shed that was filled with old 78-rpm records. In the corner was a wind-up record player. Without thought, Claus placed a record on the machine, wound it up, set the needle on the record, and moved a lever to have it play.

"Your collection? Quite impressive. From a simpler time," Claus said.

"Simpler only. Two world wars, a depression, and what are you doing for dinner tonight?" Lanietta asked. "Nanna!"

Claus was confused by the mixture of history with the request for dinner. He chalked it up to her new-found madness.

"Well, if it means you'll tell me why you are acting this way, yes, I'll have dinner with you," Claus said.

"It's no act. My mind...it...so fragmented...so spread out...like this place...all over...and parts unprotected...N a n n a ! "

A bomber dropped bombs nearly directly above Lanietta's lair. The shed shook, records fell, and the playing records skipped.

"I should be out there," Claus said. "Leif is bombing the cubics, is that right?"

Lanietta kneeled on the shed's floor and nudged broken bits of record around.

"Lanietta, am I right?"

"The war has begun. Yes," she said.

"We need to help them," Claus said.

"I...help...what does it even mean?" she mumbled.

"Lanietta! Remember the things you did on Earth? I didn't agree with all of it, but you were larger than life. Bring that person back, but channel it for good. Help us defeat the cubics," Claus pleaded. "Look. Let's get you walking. The leg circulation will do you good."

Claus helped Lanietta to her feet, and the two walked out of the record shed.

"A woman must have her legs," Claus said.

"Yes. For a little while," Lanietta said.

"Forever!" Claus insisted.

Lanietta returned a weak smile, as if to humor Claus. The two entered a small barn filled with shelf after shelf of lit kerosene lamps. The air was good near the door but worsened as the two went deeper into the barn.

"Beautiful," Claus said.

"But toxic," Lanietta said. "Remind you of Arberella? With the carbonic air?"

"It's worth it, though, to see such splendor with these lights," Claus said.

"Which do you feel like?" she asked.

"Which lamp? I feel like this one here. Looks like a railroad lantern. Think of how many trains were guided home by its signal," Claus dreamed.

"Yes," Lanietta said with a sigh.

"Which one do you feel like?" Claus asked. "This pink lamp here? Or perhaps this purple one?"

"I feel like the air, Claus, needed for such brilliant light, but upon which waste is dumped. I'm stale and stagnant. I must be refreshed. I must breathe," she said.

Lanietta dashed out of the barn, slumped to her knees, and gasped for air.

"I don't understand!" Claus said. "You don't need to breathe!"

"*I* don't need the air. But the air needs *me*!" Lanietta said. "I'm renewing it. I inhale the fumes and release a fresh atmosphere. Life from death. But this can only continue for so long. I'm overextended."

"Can't you take a bath or something? Wash away whatever ails you?" Claus asked.

Lanietta sighed.

"In this flea market?" she said. "Perhaps the fleas will draw my bath water and provide soap."

"It's not really a flea market. There are no fleas. *Sees*?"

"Yes, I *sees*," she tried to laugh while looking around with her eyes. "Trust my pet to bring back a tiny bit of joy in my life before the end."

"What end? You can't die! You're immortal!" Claus said.

"Even immortals can fade. I feel like jeans that have gone through the drier a time too many. No lint left to shed," Lanietta said.

"Lanietta! You're always joking with me. Cut it out!"

"Let me show you something," Lanietta said.

Lanietta led Claus to the back of the property where a barn with three doors stood.

"Pick," she said.

"I know this problem," Claus said. "I pick one, and you then show me what's behind another door and say, 'Do you want to keep your pick or choose the other door?' right?"

"Not quite. I'll choose then," she said.

Lanietta opened the middle door. Claus followed, but instead of entering the barn, the two entered a small hallway that connected between two vast warehouses, each extending as far as the eye could see. The warehouse to the left was shaded yellow while the warehouse to the right was shaded blue. Inside each warehouse were ephemeral images of Lanietta. An image would receive a pulse of light from a warehouse shelf, dart like lightning to another spot (often crossing levels), deliver the pulse of light, and then disintegrate. New images would rain down from above, images of small children growing older and older as they descended. They reached adult form when they hit the main floor level. Occasionally, images would collide, cause a flash of light, and then both would disappear.

"This is my brain, Clomper. This isn't a fantasy or representation. It's really here, buried deep in Luna," Lanietta said.

"I don't understand," Claus said.

"Morcellus, remember? He captured my fragments? Later I pulled myself together, but I couldn't keep myself together for long. After I returned and borrowed Leif—"

"You mean kidnapped Leif," Claus said.

"Anyway, I couldn't contain myself. So I built this lair," Lanietta said.

"There are so many images of you. Too many to count. How do you keep up?" Claus asked.

"It isn't the number of images. It's how often they collide. Lately it's been too much. Each collision makes a mess larger than the one I'm trying to clean up," she explained.

"What messes?"

"Unresolved ethereal messes. The past, the present, and the future. People make messes, I clean them up. At least some of them. People like to live, but they don't like to clean," Lanietta said. "Look straight ahead. What do you see?"

"I see the blackness of this short hallway," Claus said.

"Yes. Undefined. I feel like, no, I know something is missing. I should go directly in front of us. It'll free me of this trap I've created for myself. Well, I've waited long enough. One last thing I must do before I rid myself of all this."

"Lanietta, I don't like this rash talk," Claus said.

"I'm sending you back to Earth. For good," she said.

"There *is* no Earth," Claus said.

"You must remember one thing. Do not eat the sandwich. What happens after that, I cannot tell. I'm also leaving Fronfa here. I still have it, you know. If somehow you end up on the moon again, look for it here. But a word of advice. Stay off the moon if you can. Remain on Earth," Lanietta said.

"Lanietta! STOP!" Claus shouted.

Lanietta tossed Fronfa in the air. As it fell, she clapped both hands onto it. The yellow warehouse images suddenly all drew together in an implosive collision. The blue side did likewise. Both implosions drew air from the small hallway in-between, and Claus ran to the doorway to escape.

"This way! Lanietta!" Claus yelled as he wedged himself in the doorway to keep from being pulled apart by the two halves.

Lanietta laughed. The two forces ripped her apart, pulling her left half to the yellow side and right half to the right side.

"LANIETTA!" Claus yelled.

Fronfa fell to the floor and wobbled a little to the left and right, as if the forces were fighting over it.

"No!" Claus yelled.

He dove for Fronfa. The forces rebounded against their distant infinities, came back as shrinking warehouses, and constricted Claus to a tight space to the point where he thought he would be crushed from both sides. He felt a blanket wrap over him, toss him in the air, and send him back down to the floor. The forces stopped, all went quiet, and Claus panted to get air, but the blanket prevented it.

"I must get air," Claus said. "I must unwrap myself from this blanket."

Chapter 138: Coffee Rain

Claus Gerhardt, the primary pilot for an upcoming lunar space launch, awoke with a start in his house. It was 2:30am, the television was still on, and Claus realized he'd fallen asleep to a movie. But his insomnia returned, and he couldn't settle himself. He turned the television off, threw a night robe over his pajamas, then walked to the kitchen for a late snack of bologna sandwich and vitamin water. While sipping his bottle, he stared at the sandwich, of which he had yet to take a bite. Then out the kitchen window he looked and observed the full moon.

"The air is stale in here," he said to himself. "I should go...should go...the sandwich! Lanietta! It's the day of the launch. Novi 3. I'm supposed to go up. So is Frieda. I'm supposed to go outside for fresh air and watch as Frieda jogs by. What did Lanietta mean about the sandwich, about not taking a bite?"

Claus argued the point with himself. He argued so long that Frieda jogged right by his house without realizing he was awake. Claus returned to his bedroom, and with lights off he peered out the window. Frieda was far down the street, jogging farther away.

"So I stay here, get a good night's sleep, or not, and report anyway to Astroosa? But that means I'll go up on Novi 3. To the moon! I must cancel," Claus said to himself. "I'll call in sick. Oh boy, of all the things! Who ever heard of an astronaut calling in sick!"

Claus paced back and forth in his house, unsure of what to do.

"This is serious stuff! I mean, I have a chance to avoid that Carinian situation by staying here on Earth."

Claus stopped cold.

"Or do I? They are up there. Now. What will they do? Will my absence make a difference? They'll still have Novi 2. They'll still capture Novi 3. Unless I stop the launch. Can I? How? How do I convince Astroosa management that...I mean...like... how do I convince Joe Craigen to stop lunar exploration? Cancel everything? Like that? Oh, and warn him about his assassination. How do I do that without being locked up? Or maybe it was all a bad dream. An intense nightmare. Was it? Except I knew Frieda would jog by. Well, she often does that. Could have been coincidence."

Claus resumed pacing.

"If it was a bad dream, the moon will be just as lonely as ever. Nothing will be up there except Andrea and Bill. We'll rescue them and bring them home," Claus said. "But if there are no Carinians, why are Andrea and Bill stuck there? Without word? I know, the moon blocks radio waves. Still...oh, I can't think straight! My mind is racing! Don't eat the sandwich. Don't take a bite."

Claus went back to the refrigerator. He removed bread, lunchmeat, and cheese.

"What do I do with these? Sandwich demons? Do these components when put together destroy the Earth? No! I'll destroy the components!"

Claus threw the cheese into the sink, turned on the water, turned on the garbage disposal, and used a wooden utensil to push the cheese down. Next, he pushed the meat down. When it came to the bread, though, he paused.

"A loaf of bread. A man-made food from an ancient time. If I put the bread down the disposal, it will be as if I made the sandwich and flushed it down. No, I must separate components and confuse the powers to be, which is the Anrega. Yes! Confuse the Anrega. I'll throw the bread away, but in two different ways."

Claus stood halfway between the kitchen garbage can and the sink. He took a slice of bread, dug a bread ball out of the center, and threw the bread ball in the sink. He then slung the remaining slice into the garbage can as one might flip a playing card. He continued this with the remaining slices of bread.

"I have more loaves of bread. I will separate them as well!" Claus said.

And he did. Slice by slice, he tore from the center, made the bread ball, tossed the bread ball into the sink, and slung the remaining slice into the garbage can. He finished off all loaves of bread, stood for a moment, and was pleased with his work—the bread balls were consumed by the garbage disposal, the hollow slices overflowed the garbage can.

"I must be mad," Claus said to himself. "Paranoid for sure. There's no Anrega. No Carinians. I'm still half asleep. Must be. If I go back to sleep, the nightmare will continue. Probably will be forced to resurrect Libriota or some nonsense. Best I stay awake and let this dream fade off. Coffee, and plenty will save the morning."

Claus brewed coffee. Just the smell of it cleared the air and his mind. The taste of it reminded him of when he first drank coffee in high school. A brief twinge of fear struck him that he might go back to that reality.

"Lanietta? Do you have a surprise for your Clomper?" Claus called out.

There was no reply. Claus was alone.

"Still haven't cleared the nightmare from my mind," Claus said. "I know what I'll do."

Claus took the pot of coffee, put a few ice cubes in it to remove the scalding temperature, and—still warm—he poured the coffee over his head, allowing the coffee to roll onto his back, his front, and his sides.

"I shall bathe myself in the healing power of coffee," Claus said. "More coffee. I need more coffee."

Claus made more coffee, but the second time around he mixed the hot coffee with water in a second pitcher to quickly get the right temperature.

"Ahhh," he said as he poured the coffee over himself.

This act made a mess on his kitchen floor, but this only drove him to another idea.

"I know. I'll make a coffee couch. Pour coffee all over. I'll totally immerse myself in it," Claus said.

Claus poured coffee on the couch, he poured it on a throw blanket, and he poured more on himself as he sat on the couch. He inhaled deeply and allowed the coffee to permeate his pores, soaking and relishing this ritualistic act of cleansing.

"I'm soaking wet, but I don't care. I feel like a kid who played in the rain. The coffee rain."

Claus fell asleep, which was strange, because most people have trouble sleeping in wet conditions. Even I, K Gerard Martin, will change a sweat-soaked shirt in the middle of the night so that I may sleep in a clean, dry shirt.

The hours passed. Claus's bedroom alarm clock went off, but Claus did not hear it in the living room, and so he overslept. It wasn't until pounding from the front door resonated throughout his house that he awoke with a start.

"Claus? Are you in there?"

Claus opened the front door, and it was Joe Craigen! Claus struggled to come up with an excuse for his tardiness when Joe spoke.

"You're alive! At least there's that! Don't leave this house!" Joe said as he motioned for two police officers to enter.

"What's the meaning of this?" Claus asked.

"Frieda was found dead. Astroosa is under lockdown. The Novi 3 mission is scrubbed," Joe said. "Smells like coffee in here. Good. You'll need your wits. I'm putting together a skeleton crew for the probe."

"Prava 12?"

"Yes," Joe said. "Patricia Li is working on it under heavy guard. We need people to monitor from a distance as a backup plan. You have your computer training equipment here?"

"Yes, but—"

"Good. After the attack on Astroosa, I ordered an immediate inspection of Novi 3 and Prava 12. Novi 3 is compromised. Prava 12 was spared, but Li found a flaw and is using parts from Novi 3 to correct it. She expects to launch it later this morning," Joe said. "Claus. I'm sorry you couldn't go up. I know you are eager to find Bill and Andrea."

"I—"

"Don't worry. Prava 12 will find them and relay what happened. I know I rushed things and should have had a lunar relay satellite before. But we'll get things right this time. Prava 12 will stay in orbit until we find them," Joe explained.

"I understand," Claus said. "Joe. What happened to Frieda?"

"She apparently went for an early-morning jog. Looks like she went right by your house, too. Her body was found five blocks from here," Joe said.

"I want to help find the killer," Claus said.

"We already have. His name will be released to the press later. He was rambling about how people shouldn't go into space. He recognized Frieda and killed her for it. From there he went to Astroosa and started firing. Our own security shot back and killed him," Joe said.

"I was awake, Joe. I heard her jog by. I should have stopped her," Claus said. "I would have been taking a bite from my sandwich and could have...could have..."

Claus stopped. Still the words of Lanietta haunted him about not taking a bite from the sandwich. Was this what she meant? No, it was a dream.

"Claus. Don't do this to yourself. I'll send Doctor Morrow over immediately. You're suffering from survivor guilt. Hang in there. Should I stick around? Yes, I'll stick around. I'm glad you're alive. We're going to get through this. Trust me! We're going to extend furlough to anyone who wants it and spend time sorting through things at Astroosa. You're a valued person. We all are. There is only one of us on this planet. Claus? The pain will ease with time. If you can eat today—anything—please try

to do so. I know it will be difficult. Most people can't eat anything. Force down what you can. Remember your training. You're flying on instruments now."

"Thank you, sir," Claus said.

Frieda, dead? What a turn of events! She was ruling the lunar old far side in his nightmare. Now she was dead. Did he hate her? Did he cause her to jog into a risky situation? Maybe throw caution to the wind?

"I think I'll clean up and change," Claus said.

"Excellent idea. Take a long, hot shower. Soak it in. I'll advise Doctor Morrow when she arrives," Joe said.

Claus took his shower. A long, hot shower. In the corner of his eye he thought he saw Lanietta by the bathroom sink. But when he turned to look, no one was there.

"My mind is playing tricks on me," Claus said.

He finished his shower, dressed, shaved, brushed his teeth, and used a dental rinse. He opened the bathroom door and started for the hallway. Again he thought he saw Lanietta in the corner of his eye, but when he turned to look, she wasn't there.

Claus spoke and said, "Okay, Lanietta. The charade is over. End this fantasy."

"I can't end it," said a female voice.

"Why not?" Claus asked.

"Because this isn't a fantasy," Doctor Morrow said as she approached him. "Who is Lanietta?"

Claus held silent and turned away.

"Look at me," she said. "Look...at...me!"

Claus looked at Doctor Morrow. She held a pen light to each eye.

"How much coffee have you had?" she asked.

"Too much, I guess," Claus said.

"Are you hungry?"

"No. I feel like I have no stomach," Claus said.

"We should take you out to breakfast. Joe will pitch a fit, I know. He's worried we'll be shot. But I think it best. Don't worry. We'll have plenty of police protection," Doctor Morrow said.

"I can't promise I'll eat anything," Claus said.

"You don't have to. Just go through the motions of breakfast. Pretend to eat if you have to. We have to start somewhere," she said.

"Okay."

Claus, Joe, Doctor Morrow, and three police officers went out for breakfast. They selected a place by a small airport, open only for breakfast and lunch. "Cash Only" said a sign in the window.

"Don't worry," Joe said. "I'm buying."

The police set up strategic places of watch while Claus, Joe, and Doctor Morrow took a seat. Claus initially wanted a window seat, but Joe insisted on a table closer to the restaurant's center.

"Can't be too careful," he said.

A waitress came by and took their drink order first. Joe ordered coffee, Doctor Morrow ordered tea, and Claus ordered coffee.

"Decaf for Claus," Doctor Morrow said. "He's had enough regular."

Joe received coffee from the black-collared coffee pitcher while Claus received coffee from the orange-collared one. In fact, it wasn't the waitress who poured the coffee but a special coffee girl. Claus stared at the girl, as her uniform had colors of yellow and blue while the regular waitstaff had uniforms of dark blue with white highlights. At times Claus thought the coffee girl looked like Lanietta, but when he looked again, she was but a stranger.

"Claus? Why are you staring at the coffee girl?" Doctor Morrow asked.

"I...she looks familiar...or something," Claus said.

"Does she look like Frieda to you?" she asked.

Claus paused. He'd better lie and quick. "Yes."

"She looks nothing like Frieda," Joe said.

"Let it go, Joe," the doctor said. "We're all coping in different ways."

The waitress returned and took their orders. Joe had the house breakfast while Doctor Morrow had a veggie omelette. But Claus kept looking for the coffee girl.

"Claus? Would you like eggs and bacon?" Joe asked.

"Maybe just eggs and toast," Claus said.

"Fried, scrambled, boiled, poached, washed, dried, ironed?" the waitress asked strangely to see if Claus was paying attention.

"Yes, please," Claus said while still staring at the coffee girl.

"Scrambled," Doctor Morrow answered for Claus.

"I'll have that right up," the waitress said, and she left.

"Thank you," Joe called after her.

"Claus, stop staring. It's rude!" Doctor Morrow said.

Claus became fidgety. He took a sip of his decaf coffee, but it tasted watered down.

"I want the real stuff," Claus said. "The real stuff. The answer. Coffee girl has the real stuff. She has the answer."

Claus rushed up from his seat, ran toward the coffee girl, and struggled to take the regular coffee pitcher from her.

"End this fantasy and give me the coffee, Lanietta."

"What? Stop!" the coffee girl said.

"I'm not kidding, Lanietta! End this now! Lanietta? Lanietta!" Claus said as he shook her.

The coffee girl yelled for help. Joe rushed over to restrain Claus as did the restaurant owner, the cook, and the busboy. Two police officers also rushed over, but Joe waved them off.

"It's okay. He's just upset. Astroosa business. I'll take care of it," Joe said.

Joe sat Claus down.

"You shook up that girl pretty good. Look at her. She's trembling horribly," Joe said. "I've never seen you like this. Do you hate women this much?"

"No! I...I mean...I didn't think so," Claus said, also trembling.

The food came quickly. The waitress was pleasant enough to Joe and the doctor, but she gingerly gave Claus his food, half expecting him to snap at her. He didn't.

"Please get a bite down first," Doctor Morrow said.

"First? And then?" Claus asked.

"And then you're going to explain what just happened," Joe insisted.

"Please. A bite first," the doctor said.

Claus forced a bit of eggs down his throat.

"This is worse than paregoric," Claus said.

Joe and the doctor looked at Claus in surprise.

"You're a bit young to know what that tastes like," Doctor Morrow said.

"I had some overseas once," Claus said.

Claus drank water. The doctor motioned for the waitress, whispered something, and the waitress returned with saltines.

"Try these," the doctor said.

Claus ate one.

"How do you feel?" the doctor asked.

"A little better," Claus said.

A different coffee girl came by and refilled Joe's cup, but the doctor stopped Claus's cup from being filled with decaf.

"Does she look like Lanietta?" Doctor Morrow asked.

"No. How do you know about Lanietta?" Claus asked.

"I don't," the doctor said. "But you've spoken the name repeatedly."

"There's no one at Astroosa by that name," Joe said.

"Care to explain who she is?" the doctor asked.

Claus paused.

"Was she special to you?" the doctor asked. "And this question might hurt, but I want you to answer—did she pass on?"

"I think she was someone I dreamed up," Claus said. "A nightmare I had during the night. I don't know why or how, but she seemed very real. She was a Carinian."

"A Carinian? What country is that?" Joe asked.

"It's not a country. She's from Carinia 2. That's a planet full of Grens. Only she's half Gren and half Bleuh. The Bleuhs are

from Carinia 1. She could—why are you both looking at me like that?" Claus asked.

"Pre-launch anxiety," the doctor said to Joe.

"Is it normal?" Joe asked.

"It happens, but each astronaut deals with it differently. Apparently Claus channeled it into his dream," the doctor said.

Claus took a very small bite of eggs and nursed it down his throat.

"I'll need you to follow up on his dream, Doctor Morrow," Joe said.

"Of course," the doctor said. "Claus. Did she die in your dream?"

"I think so. It was the last part of my dream. Then I woke up," Claus said.

"Did you love her? Or perhaps you were afraid of her?" the doctor suggested.

"Both. Neither. I don't know," Claus said in confusion. "But one thing is for certain. These Carinians are on the far side of the moon. They are watching us."

"How?" Joe asked. "There is no line of sight. There are no alien satellites."

Joe and Doctor Morrow exchanged knowing looks. Doctor Morrow dropped a pill in Claus's water.

"What's that?" Claus asked.

"A sedative. It'll calm your nerves," Doctor Morrow said.

"But I must have a clear mind. The launch—"

"Is scrubbed, remember?" Joe said.

Claus looked at his water. He stirred it with his spoon and drank half of it.

"I feel better already," he said.

"Good," the doctor said. "Joe, I'll stay with him for the first few hours. But he'll need watching. Someone must stay with him."

"I'll send over a caretaker later," Joe said.

"I don't need a caretaker," Claus said. "It's my house. It's..."

But the sedative worked its magic on Claus, and he dropped all resistance.

"It's fine," he said in a mellow voice.

"Excellent," Joe said.

The meal ended, Joe paid the bill, and Claus was returned home. Doctor Morrow settled Claus into his work-at-home computer station. The video linkup was activated. Patricia Li's face appeared on a display window.

"Doctor Li. This is Doctor Morrow. Claus will assist with the Prava 12 launch. He's working from home today."

"Hello, Claus," Doctor Li said.

"Hello, Patricia," Claus said. "Have any plans for jumping in the Prava 12 craft? Plan to pilot it to the moon?"

"Uh, no," she said defensively.

"Don't," Claus said.

"No one will stowaway on Prava 12," Doctor Morrow said. "I'll add extra security to be sure."

Doctor Morrow made a cell phone call, spoke with Astroosa security, and arranged it.

"There," Doctor Morrow said while placing a pill bottle on Claus's desk.

"What's that for?"

"Take one every four hours while awake and an extra one before bedtime," she said.

"More sedatives?" Claus asked.

"Yes. And no more coffee rain," she said.

Doctor Morrow's cell phone rang. She answered it and held a brief call.

"Security again?" Claus asked.

"No. I need to assist with Frieda's final preparation," Doctor Morrow said.

"Final preparation? But isn't that for the funeral home, I mean, they have people—"

"She's not being buried. She's being frozen. Already her fluids have been replaced with cryoprotectants. There will be a service this evening before she's flown out west for storage," Doctor Morrow said.

"Flown out west for storage. Sounds like you're burying nuclear waste," Claus said.

"Don't get excited. She set up a legal instrument for this procedure long ago," Doctor Morrow said. "Someday when technology catches up, she'll be revived."

"I'll be there later today," Doctor Li said. "I can take Claus to the service."

"Thank you," Doctor Morrow said. "Good day."

With that, Doctor Morrow left.

"What did she mean by *coffee rain*?" Li asked.

"I'd rather not say. You'll think I'm crazy," Claus said.

"Are you too crazy to process Prava 12 data? We're launching in twenty minutes," Li said.

"Twenty minutes! Joe said Novi 3 was being used to supply parts to Prava 12. That will take—"

"Already complete. We had a rush order. I need you to monitor this so I can prepare Prava G3 for launch," Li said.

"Prava G3? I thought all Prava launches were strictly numeric. What's this G3 mumbo-jumbo?" Claus asked.

"It's not mumbo-jumbo. It's a last-minute decision to send another asteroid probe," Li said. "Pravas G1 and G2 went up last week. It was kept a secret in case they failed, not that secrets can be kept long. Anyway, you remember the asteroid program, don't you?"

"I remember years ago there was talk of mining on asteroids for raw materials. But that was talk as far as I knew," Claus said.

"The talk never went away. Just went underground, you could say. I've been juggling both Prava programs. Anyway, watch the countdown for me and report any anomalies," Li said.

Li turned away and stared at another panel.

"Don't even think of preparing a Novi 4 mission. You'll be captured like Bill and Andrea," Claus muttered.

"I heard that," Li said. "Novi missions are on hold. No one is going anywhere until we get return data from Prava 12."

Claus watched his panels. Prava 12 launched without issue and headed for the moon.

"Prava 12 status," Claus said.

"Go ahead," Doctor Li replied.

"Everything A-okay," Claus replied.

"Awesome," Li said. "Take a break and return in an hour. We'll be launching Prava G3 then."

"I thought that was later," Claus said.

"Later is now sooner," Li replied. "Don't be late."

"I won't," Claus said.

Claus stood from the computer station and brewed coffee.

"That coffee smell. I still...though sedated, I still have need for it," Claus said.

Claus took a spray bottle, dumped out the cleaning fluid, and filled it with coffee. He then sprayed the coffee on his face, in his hair, on his arms, and on his legs. He had just lifted his left arm and sprayed there too when the front door opened and in walked a woman.

"What are you doing?" she asked.

Claus stopped halfway in his motion of spraying his left underarm with coffee. Claus looked at the woman, and for a moment she looked familiar.

"Mariel? Is that you?" Claus asked.

"Mariel? I'm Nadine. Your caretaker. Joe Craigen sent me. Give me that spray bottle."

Nadine took the spray bottle from Claus. She sprayed a bit on her palm and sniffed it.

"This is coffee," she said. "The doctor is right. You *are* sick. What else are you spraying?"

"Well, the couch is wet," Claus said.

"The doctor told me. I thought she was joking," Nadine said.

Nadine went back to the front door and called outside.

"In here, boys. It's true. The couch is soaked. Take it and do your thing," she said.

Two men walked in.

"Treyu? Yuri?" Claus called.

The men looked briefly like Treyu and Yuri, but then they took on their normal appearance to Claus.

"Don't mind him," Nadine said. "He called me Mariel."

The men laughed and then took the couch out.

"They'll return it—clean and fresh like new," Nadine said.

Nadine opened the fridge, took a bottle of water, opened it, and handed it to Claus.

"What's with the water?" Claus asked.

"I have another pill for you," Nadine said.

"What is it?" Claus asked. "You and Donna give me pills but don't tell me what they are. There could be a fatal reaction between the two. Have you consulted a pharmacist? I want to see a pharmacist."

"I *am* a pharmacist," she said. "This will stop your compulsions. Take it."

Claus took the pill.

"HIPAA says I should know what you're giving me," Claus said.

"HIPAA says no one else should know what you're taking. It doesn't say you have to know," Nadine said. "Now sit at your dining table. I have something for you."

Nadine exited the house and returned with a paper bag.

"Is that booze?" Claus asked.

"No. It's your lunch," Nadine said. "Eat up."

Claus opened the bag.

"Where's the meat?" he asked.

"It's Chinese vegan food," Nadine said.

"What??"

"Doctor Li's idea. Doctor Morrow and I approve. We're cutting out processed and animal food from your diet," Nadine said.

"*You* are?" Claus asked. "Since when do *you* decide?"

"Since *you* jumped off the deep end," Nadine said. "Otherwise, we'll have you committed."

"You're not serious," Claus said.

"We're the only ones who are. You need to be clear-headed for tonight's service," Nadine said.

"If anything, these meds are clouding me over," Claus said.

"Eat your lunch," Nadine said.

Claus ate it.

"Not bad," Claus said. "Almost tastes nourishing."

"Doctor Li's cousin owns a restaurant and made this up for you," Nadine said.

Claus finished lunch and returned to his workstation. Patricia Li showed up on the display screen.

"Did you get my lunch I ordered?" Li asked.

"Yes, I did," Claus said.

"It's important you stay away from animal-based food and anything processed," Li said.

"Why?" Claus asked.

"Because when you're compromised, that's the last thing you need. No telling what's in that stuff. Avoid sweets, too. And—"

"You're starting to sound like my mother," Claus lamented.

"Prava G3 is ready for launch. Are you watching?"

"Yes. I am," Claus said.

Prava G3 launched.

"Everything A-okay," Claus said.

"Great work, everyone. Let's switch everything to automatic and head to the service," Li said, alerting her staff at the same time.

"All right, fly-boy, get changed and ready for the service," Nadine said.

"A prisoner in my own house," Claus said. "I wonder if Mariel ordered Larto around this way."

"Try to focus on reality, Claus," Nadine said. "Say the names of people around you."

"Nadine, Patricia, Donna, Joe, Lanietta, Labba, Clausetta, Claude, and Leif," Claus said.

"Claus. No made-up names! You left out one important name. We're paying respects to her."

"Frieda, who took over the far side," Claus said.

"She was killed by a madman," Nadine said. "Go get changed, Claus."

Claus changed.

"Let's go," Nadine said.

Claus rode as Nadine drove the two over to Frieda's funeral service. All of Astroosa was there, along with Katie, Oscar, Marna, Enrico, Jill, and Chris. People took turns paying their respects to Frieda. Claus walked up and stood by her. She was not in a casket but in a freeze tube with only her face showing.

"A slave to the freeze tube here, a slave to cubics elsewhere," Claus said. "What were you doing on that plane, girl? Why did it have to crash and put you through all this? You didn't have to prove your legs still work. You didn't have to prove anything."

Jill and Chris were behind Claus.

"You're Claus. I'm Chris Cresson, and this is my wife, Jill," Chris said.

"Poor Aunt Frieda. Can't go for a jog anymore. Or step on a chair," Jill said.

"I'm sorry about Brandi," Claus said.

"Is that necessary?" Chris said. "That was long ago."

"It's okay," Jill said. "Why don't you get me a drink, Chris?"

Chris walked away.

"How did you hear about Brandi? From Aunt Frieda? It doesn't matter. Brandi was my best friend. It drove me crazy. Aunt Frieda helped me a lot. I don't know what I'll do without her. It's like Brandi all over again."

"Don't lock yourself in a room," Claus said. "Don't make a double reed for your bass clarinet. It doesn't work."

Jill looked at Claus in surprise.

"How...I was just...no man has ever read me so well," Jill said with awe. "I don't know what to say. Except...I heard you made it rain coffee in your house."

"I didn't realize word got around," Claus said.

"It got around," Jill said as she stared at Claus. "I also didn't realize someone could be as...as different as I am. At least people say I'm different."

"It's obsession. I never had it until just recently. I mean..." Claus said.

"I'm told it's a bad thing," Jill said. "Sometimes I fight it. Sometimes I let it flow. Seems easier that way."

"They say it's best to channel that obsession into something productive," Claus said.

"They do, don't they? Imagine if two people could channel their obsessions together," Jill said, maintaining her gaze on Claus and moving closer.

"Jill. What are you saying?" Claus asked.

"You know what I'm saying," she said.

"You're married. And a newlywed at that," Claus said.

Jill looked down and pulled away.

"You're right," she said. "We should collaborate professionally. I hear Astroosa is keen on their asteroid probe program. I applied for a job at Astroosa, but Chris was against it. You could put a good word in for me."

"I don't know. I mean...Frieda...the Novi program," Claus stumbled.

"Astroosa was good to her. And I see how much her coworkers care. I care too. I want to give something back," Jill said.

"I'll bring it up," Claus said, though he couldn't forget the memory of Jill and the Veigon.

"Your drink, Jill," Chris said. "Let's go."

Chris shot Claus a slightly disappointing gaze before taking Jill away.

"Now I wish Lanietta were here. I could discuss how to handle this situation," Claus said. "Will Jill still go to Mars and find the Veigon? She'll lift the Hess Rise. I'll have to stop it. Unless that was a delusion. But she really is obsessed. I didn't just dream that. She likes the fact that *I* have an obsession."

"You do have an obsession. With coffee," Doctor Li said, now approaching and hearing Claus's last words.

"Does everyone at Astroosa know?" Claus asked.

"Weird things spread like wildfire," Li said. "Poor Frieda."

"Yes, poor Frieda," Claus said. "She ran right by my house."

"Joe and Donna filled me in about this morning. Survivor guilt and mugging the coffee girl," Li said. "That's not normal, you know."

"I hate death!" Claus said.

"Think about the good things Frieda did. Remember her for that," Li said.

"I remember her for more. Much more. I really need someone I can talk to, without being seen as crazy," Claus said.

"Let's take a walk away from everyone," Li said.

The two walked outside and behind the funeral home.

"I have a lot on my mind. I mean a whole bunch," Claus said.

"The dream?" Li asked.

"I'm not sure it was," Claus said. "Whatever it was, I aged twenty-five years. Or five hundred. Ten thousand? I dunno. Anyway, I had two children—Clausetta and Leif. There were these aliens, these Carinians. Earth was destroyed, and people lived on the moon. There's plenty more."

"Sounds like you could write a book," Li said.

"It's not just a story, and I can't let it go. Things carry over. Like with Jill. She's obsessive. And I have this new obsession with coffee. It's a turn-on for her. In my dream, she'll divorce in a few months," Claus said.

"Professionally speaking, I'd say you should set up sessions with a psychiatrist," Li said.

"No. I don't want a psychiatrist. They'll think I'm crazy," Claus said.

"Don't think of it that way. Tell your problems. Take little steps for your therapy," Li said.

"What about you?" Claus said. "In my dream, you were planning on going up on Prava 12 to compensate for equipment failure. I went up instead."

Li looked down sheepishly.

"It's true I was planning on going up. But it was only a passing thought. The probe was repaired, and it'll circle the moon soon," Li said. "Claus. If you want to convince people you're not crazy, you need to provide solid evidence and eliminate speculation."

"Meaning what?" Claus asked.

"I'll order tests to eliminate brain tumors, dementia, you know, any medical condition that could compromise your thinking. Once you're clear—"

"You won't believe me until I prove I'm medically sound, is that it?" Claus asked.

"I'm a professional, Claus. Even on a personal basis, concrete evidence makes for better social discourse," Li said.

Claus turned away with a sigh.

"Tell you what," Li said. "For every test you take, I'll take the same test. We'll go through this together. Who knows, they might find you okay and me demented. How would that be for irony?"

"There's nothing ironic about dementia," Claus said. "But I'll take you up on that. Oh, I'm suddenly very sleepy!"

"It's the medication. Let's get you to a chair. The service will start soon anyway," Li said.

A group of chairs had been set up for the wake, and Li walked Claus to one in the very last row. Shortly after he sat down, the service started. He leaned to his left, braced the side of his face with his fist (and elbow to his thigh), and closed his eyes.

"Stop babbling," Li whispered as she nudged him.

Claus opened his eyes. People around him were looking. Even the minister had paused. Claus waved a quick "sorry" with a grimace. The service resumed.

"I'm so sleepy," Claus whispered.

"Try to stay awake," Li whispered back. "You talk in your sleep. Something about Frieda and the cubics. You upset Frieda's family."

"I'll try to be quiet," Claus said.

But Claus fell asleep again. He was awakened by someone spilling coffee on him. At first the hot temperature startled him, but his pores soaked in the coffee and made him feel better. He looked around.

The other chairs were empty, the service had concluded, and Jill winked at Claus as she walked away in Chris's arms. Chris didn't seem to realize something had happened or that Jill winked back. The funeral home was empty except for staff, Claus, and Doctor Li.

"The wake is over," Doctor Li said. "Nadine will take you home."

"Where is she?" Claus asked. "I should get up and look for her."

"Stay here. *I'll* look for her," Li said.

Doctor Li stepped out of the funeral home. Claus watched as funeral home staff wheeled Frieda's body away. Claus stood up and followed them for a little bit, but one of the staff members stopped him.

"Staff members only beyond this point," Claus was told.

"What's the next step?" Claus asked.

"She's being shipped to the cryopreservation facility," Claus was told. "You should get going. We're locking up in a few minutes."

"Claus?" Nadine called from a bit of a distance.

Claus paused to get a last glimpse of Frieda. Her tube was loaded into a truck, and that was it.

"Claus," Nadine said, now much closer. "Time to go."

Claus gave a goodbye wave to Frieda and turned to Nadine.

"Take me home," Claus said.

Chapter 139: Jill Gets a Job

A week passed. Prava 12 had reached the moon and orbited it many times, but it found no trace of Novi 2, no trace of Andrea, and no trace of Bill. Nadine had taken Claus to see a psychiatrist. Claus told the psychiatrist about his adventures with Lanietta. The psychiatrist wrote everything down. His only advice—given with a written prescription—was to take more medication.

"I'm really drugged out now," Claus said to himself while sitting at his computer workstation at home.

"Claus," Li said from her office at Astroosa. "Prava G3 will reach the asteroid within the next hour."

"Just which asteroid is this?" Claus asked. "My panel refers to it as AB4711."

"Asteroid Body 4711," Li said. "We have our own naming system for the asteroids. Some asteroids aren't named yet. Some are. In either case, we want our chosen asteroid to be kept secret until we can secure mining rights."

"And how are those rights secured?"

"We get there first. Finders, keepers," Li said.

"Losers, weepers," Claus finished.

"Except no one lost these asteroids," Li said. "No one gets hurt. Everyone benefits."

"From a dead celestial object. At least the sun can power solar panels," Claus said.

"Don't be so pessimistic. If we can find even one precious metal, manufacturing can jump ahead by leaps and bounds. So can society and quality of life. It's all but philanthropy, what we're doing," Li said. "Everyone will feel better. Speaking of, how do you feel after visiting the shrink?"

"Drugged out. He gave me another med," Claus said. "I also had my brain scan yesterday. All clear. No tumors. Your turn."

"My turn what?" Li asked.

"To get a brain scan. You promised, remember?" Claus asked.

"I...I guess I did," she said. "I've been so busy with the probe, I'm not sure when I'll have time."

"Patricia!" Claus said. "We had a deal."

"I'll have to time-delay that deal," she said.

"Anyone can get out of anything by time-delaying a deal," Claus said. "Because eventually we die. Then what?"

"Then it won't matter," she said. "You sound cranky. Have you eaten today?"

"No. Not even coffee. Donna-the-shrink and Nadine won't let me have any," Claus said.

"You really shouldn't," Li said. "You can't tolerate it the way most people do. Stick with bottled water. You'll be fine. And your pills."

"Water and pills, water and pills. Doctors agree, they cure all the ills!" Claus sang.

"I'm sending food over," Li said.

"More vegan food? How I wish I had a steak! Even a pork chop would do!" Claus begged.

"No animal products!" Li said. "Your body is prone to influence. Stick with vegetable matter, and you'll be fine. A few fruits are okay too as long as you don't overdo it. Must keep your sugar level down."

"Garbage and pills, garbage and pills. No steak for me, and wait for the bill!" Claus sang with the same tune as before.

"What are you talking about?" Li asked.

"This food plan is garbage," Claus complained. "And all this medical testing and treatment just leaves me with bills to pay. I never had bills or drugs with Lanietta!"

"Stop saying that name!" Li said. "You just stir up your false memories. You know what that means? It means starting all over again with the shrink."

"Pills and bills. Pills and bills. Make you strong and give you thrills. Rush. Rush. Rush the job. Rush the mining job my bub," Claus sang with a different tune.

"Claus, hang on. Chris is in the area. I'll send him over with your food real quick. Hang on," Li said.

Li made a quick phone call to Chris Cresson. Chris had taken time off to bring Jill to the doctor, but he had just called before saying he was taking Jill home, and that he'd return soon.

"Claus needs vegan food now," Li said to Chris while he and Jill were in Chris's car.

"I'm right by your cousin's restaurant," he said. "I can get food to Claus in a few minutes."

"Awesome!" Li replied.

Claus continued to sing other strange things.

"It's the meds, Patricia," Claus said. "I'm badly spaced out. I can't think."

"Well you need to think," Li said. "We're expecting a flood of data when Prava G3 attains orbit. That orbit will be shaky at best. AB4711 has very little gravity to work with."

"I just need a pickup. Something to get me going," Claus said.

The doorbell rang.

"Nadine? The door," Claus called. "Nadine?"

The doorbell rang again. Claus stood up slowly from his chair, but he lost his balance and nearly fell over.

"Claus? Anyone home?" Chris called while opening the front door.

"Come in," Claus called back. "I'd get the door, but I'm sluggish."

"Where's Nadine?" Chris called. "Jill, hand this to Claus. I'll look for Nadine."

Chris disappeared into a side room where his voice raised as he had an argument with Nadine over why she was watching a soap opera instead of feeding Claus and answering the door.

"I give him pills. That's all," was her retort.

While the two argued, Jill sat Claus down to his dining table. She opened the paper bag and pulled out Claus's food.

"Your lunch," she said.

"Thank you," Claus said.

"I also have this for you," she said.

Jill produced a spray bottle from her purse, labeled, "Sore Throat Spray".

"I don't have a sore throat," Claus said.

"It doesn't matter," Jill whispered. "Try it out."

Claus shrugged his shoulders. He took the bottle, aimed for his throat, and sprayed.

"Coffee. It tastes like coffee," Claus said.

"Shh," Jill said. "I made it just for you."

"But the liquid in the bottle...it's red...like real throat spray," Claus said.

"I'm a genius. I know," Jill said.

"Will it stain?" Claus asked. "I mean, can I spray it on my skin without anyone noticing?"

Jill took the bottle, sprayed it on her hand, and rubbed her hands together. She then showed Claus.

"No change in color," Claus said.

"I'll do your face," she said.

Jill sprayed her hands and rubbed them on Claus's face to transfer the liquid. She then pulled out a compact and showed Claus his reflection.

"There's no sign of the coffee. And whatever you used to make it red," Claus said.

Jill sprayed her hands again and rubbed Claus's face.

"Feels good," Claus said.

"Feels good for me too," she said. "I...this is addictive."

"Didn't you try it out before?" Claus asked.

"Yes, but I never had this reaction. Not until I touched your face. I..."

Jill snuck a quick nose nuzzle with Claus.

"Jill," Claus whispered. "Your husband is in the other room."

"I don't know what came over me. Forget it," she said. "Hide the bottle."

Claus took the bottle and placed it in his pocket. Chris returned from chewing out Nadine.

"I turned off the television and gave her a good talking to," Chris said. "But I don't trust her. I'll report to Joe. Looks like you'll need another caretaker, Claus. No wonder she was fired from her last job. By the way, anything new on the G3 probe?"

"Oh, I completely forgot. It's supposed to make contact in an hour. But that was an hour ago!" Claus said. "Help me back to my station."

Chris and Jill helped Claus back to his computer workstation.

"I was going to monitor this from the office," Chris said to Jill. "But I had to leave it for your appointment."

"You're saying Astroosa is more important than me?" Jill asked.

"Claus, are you there?" Li asked.

"I'm here. Probe is making contact. Wow! There's too much data!" Claus said.

"Shush. This is important!" Chris said.

"Don't shush me!" Jill said. "I'm your wife."

"We'll have to buffer the data," Claus said. "A big buffer. Way big. We'll need time to process."

"What about the onboard system?" Chris asked.

"No time to reprogram it. It would have to be rebooted, and that would result in data loss," Claus said.

"We can use Prava 12 to process data," Jill said.

"You don't work for Astroosa," Chris said. "You don't know any of the systems."

"I've studied it," Jill said.

"When you're not making double reeds?" Chris asked.

"What's that got to do with it?" Jill asked.

"Claus, we're getting a lot of background noise on your end," Li said.

"Yes we are," Chris said. "I'm heading for the office where I can work."

"How will I get home?" Jill asked as Chris reached the door.

"Have Nadine give you a ride home. At least then *she'll* do something useful.

Unlike you. Women!" Chris said, and he was gone.

The front door was still open. Claus looked at Jill in surprise. Out of anger, she marched up to the front door and yelled out, "Go then!" before slamming the front door closed.

"Claus, are you okay? I heard a loud noise," Li said.

"Yeah. No big deal. The front door...a wind caught it and slammed it shut. I should be upset, but the meds are doing their thing," Claus said.

"Nadine, can you...Chris said no television," Jill said. "That means you can't watch your soap opera. I need a ride home. Nadine!"

Jill walked over to Claus. Claus muted the audio so Doctor Li could not hear.

"Chris left me here, and Nadine can't pull herself away from the television to give me a ride home," Jill said.

"I would drive, but I'm drugged up. I can't think straight," Claus said.

"Don't worry. I'll call a cab," Jill said.

Doctor Li appeared to be saying something, and so Claus had to unmute the audio.

"...the position. Is that what you see, Claus?" Li asked.

"I...could you repeat your message?" Claus asked.

Jill dialed on her cell phone for a cab, but she fumbled the phone and dropped it. To settle her nerves, she walked back over to Claus and motioned that he lend her the coffee throat spray. Claus gave it to her. She sprayed her face and rubbed her hands on the liquid. Then she touched Claus's arm. Immediately her nerves settled.

"My panel shows that the probe has found one or more precious metals. But the probe can't isolate the position. Is that what you see, Claus?" Li asked.

"Yes. That's what I see," Claus said.

"Jill might be right about using Prava 12," Li said. "It has a high-efficiency sensor discriminator processor meant for larger bodies like the moon. Prava G3's sensor is older and meant for smaller bodies."

"We could run a relay from G3 to 12 and have 12 do the processing," Jill said.

"Actually, we can load balance the two probes so neither becomes overloaded. Share the work and responsibility," Claus said.

"Excellent idea. But Chris needs to do the reconfiguration on Prava 12. Where is he?" Li asked.

"He's on his way back to Astroosa," Jill said. "I've studied all the manuals. Yes, he brought them home, and I looked at them. I can do the work."

"If you can, it will save us the delay of sending a new probe and possibly losing rights to a competitor," Li said.

"You can use the computer next to me," Claus said.

"No, I have a better idea," Jill said.

Jill moved the computer to a table behind Claus. She pulled not a chair but a stool over to this table and sat. She pushed back and touched her back to the back of Claus's chair.

"Not quite," Jill said.

Jill removed the stool and then had Claus stand up. She replaced his chair with a bench that ran from his table to hers such that the bench could be used by both of them to sit. She covered the camera and poured the contents of the sore throat spray on Claus's back and her back, causing their clothing to be wet.

"What..." Claus asked.

"It will help us think," she said.

Jill sat down and pushed her back against Claus's.

"My back will counter yours. We will each be the other's backrest," she said. "Ahh. I'll have to make up more of this stuff. Lots more. Uncover the camera."

Claus could not argue or complain about what Jill had done. The meds already in his system sedated him too much, and the coffee liquid with whatever else she had in there compromised his will that much more.

"What's going on there?" Li asked.

"Don't worry," Jill said with a breathy sigh. "Everything's fine now."

"Jill?"

Jill typed like mad on the keyboard.

"It's working. The load on Prava G3 is coming down. The search algorithm is caught in a circular pattern, though," Li said. "That's disappointing. It's stuck on poor rock."

"Who came up with this algorithm?" Claus asked.

"Chris did," Li said.

"It's flawed, as you can see," Claus said. "He should have found this defect in testing."

"Too late now," Li said. "This probe is dead."

"We need to change the search algorithm," Claus said. "We need a...a...oh this brain of mine. I can't think. Everyone should know...it's the back and forth algorithm."

"A raster scan," Jill said. "I'll reconfigure G3. Won't take but a moment."

Jill reconfigured.

"It's working. Prava G3 is no longer stuck. The raster scan is working. Slower than a tree search," Li said.

"But quicker than an infinite circular loop," Claus said.

"Yes," Li said.

"Doctor Li," Jill said. "I read gold, platinum, and rhodium."

"Confirmed," Claus said.

"It's...I need Chris to confirm," Li said.

"We're not good enough?" Jill said, now wiggling her back against Claus's for extra soothing vibes.

"Okay, okay. This is big news! Astroosa needs this fresh source of capital. We'll make it!" Li said.

Li told others in the office, and they cheered.

"We'll make it? Patricia?" Claus called, but she was too busy celebrating with the office.

Jill turned around and turned Claus around.

"Astroosa has been short on cash," Jill said. "Chris told me all about it. The manned moon missions were a big gamble, but they were also a big financial loss. Canceling Novi 3 was not just about Frieda, it was about keeping the company afloat. Now with your discovery of these metals—"

"You mean *your* discovery," Claus said.

"You suggested the raster scan," Jill said.

"I couldn't think of the word," he said.

"But you had the idea. And the physical presence. With coffee on my back," Jill said as she held Claus's hands. "I've never had a man affect me like this. It's like I can see beyond the horizon."

"Jill. This can't go on. I mean, you're a married woman."

"And you're a married man?" Jill said.

"No, I'm not," Claus said.

"Even better," she winked.

"Jill!"

"It's for Astroosa. Don't worry about it. You'll be my work husband," Jill said.

"I don't like the sound of that," Claus said.

"Should I divorce Chris? Will that help?" she asked.

"Jill!"

"Call me Olivia. I haven't felt like Olivia since before Brandi passed. But you make me feel like a schoolgirl all over again," Jill said.

"I must insist. Find a job with another company. Not Astroosa," Claus said.

"Claus, are you there?" Li called. "Claus?"

Claus turned back around.

"I'm here," Claus said.

Joe appeared in the display next to Doctor Li.

"Congratulations, Claus. That was brilliant work!" Joe said.

"It was nothing," Claus said.

"Nothing! Do you realize what you've done? You've put Astroosa on the map as the leader in space mining. This is the dawn of a new age! Astroosa! Expect a big bonus in your paycheck."

"Thank you. But it was Cresson who—" Claus started.

"Cresson? Is that true Li? Did Chris save the day?" Joe asked.

"No. Chris Cresson's algorithm went into an infinite circular loop. Almost cost us AB4711," Li said. "It was Claus and—"

"Launch an investigation, Li," Joe said. "Where's Nadine?"

"Watching a soap opera," Jill said.

"She's fired," Joe said. "Li, take over Claus's treatment."

"I can't be in two places at once," Li said. "I can prescribe, but I can't watch Claus all the time. I need to be here, and Claus needs to recover at home. We need a new caretaker."

"I'll do it," Jill said.

"You're hired," Joe said. "Welcome to Astroosa. Claus, if she can help with your work, by all means proceed."

"She can be very helpful. Jill...uh...Olivia has excellent technical knowledge. Matter of fact, she helped with the raster scan," Claus caught himself saying before realizing he'd just asked Jill to work elsewhere.

"Excellent," Joe said. "Give her security clearance, Li. We need the best. The very best!"

Joe left the display screen.

"That's enough for today, Claus," Li said. "Why don't you take the rest of the day off? And Jill, stop by Astroosa for your onboarding. We'll set you up with a nice, healthy salary."

"It's Olivia now, and thank you," Jill said. "I look forward to it."

Claus shut down the computer. Jill walked into the room with Nadine, and Claus heard Jill's voice echo throughout the house, "You're fired."

"Says who?" Nadine's voice echoed back.

"Says Joe Craigen. I'm taking over," Jill said. "I'm now official caretaker of Claus for Astroosa."

"I don't believe it," Nadine said.

Nadine walked over to Claus.

"It's true, Nadine," Claus said. "Joe told me. Sorry."

"I don't understand," she said. "I did everything. I pilled you."

"Guess more is needed," Claus said.

Nadine left in a huff.

"Oh, Nadine was supposed to give you a ride home. What will you do?" Claus asked Jill.

"I know what I'll do," she said.

Jill disappeared for a few minutes and returned with a pitcher.

"Coffee?" she said.

"Oh no," Claus said. "What have I gotten myself into?"

"Coffee euphoria, Claus. Coffee euphoria."

Chapter 140: The Coffee Tank

In the weeks that followed, the marriage between Chris and Jill Cresson deteriorated. Chris was fired for sloppy work on Prava G3, and Jill spent most of her free time at Claus's house. One afternoon while Jill and Claus sat back-to-back with coffee gel between them, Chris shoved divorce papers under Claus's front door. Claus heard the sound and got up to get them.

"Oh don't leave now," Jill said. "The coffee gel on my back will get cold."

"I'll be back in a moment," Claus said.

Claus took the papers and read them.

"Oh. It's happening again," Claus said.

"What is it?" Jill asked.

"He's divorcing you, Olivia," Claus said.

"I guess I'm not surprised," she said. "He thinks I've cheated on him and lost his job. But he made the mistake with the algorithm, and I haven't cheated on him."

"Haven't you though?" Claus asked.

"I haven't been with anyone else," she said.

"What about me?" Claus asked.

"We've never had that kind of relationship. I've never even hugged or kissed you," she said.

"But you spend most of your time with me. And we share euphoria through touch," Claus said.

"Just our backs. That doesn't count. Who ever heard of a relationship based on back-to-back contact?" she asked.

"I know it's different," Claus said. "I've never been in this situation before. Who has? Is it like having a drug buddy? Is it tenderness and romance?"

"We don't dance," Jill said.

"Some couples never do," Claus said.

"We've never done it," Jill said.

"Some couples never do," Claus said. "But we've done the closest thing to it. Tell me, Olivia. When we are working, back-to-back, with coffee gel and whatever else you put in that concoction, how does your back feel?"

"At first I feel a slight itching. It's very deep, so a back scratcher wouldn't help. But if I move my back around against yours, the itching is relieved. Then it tingles, it feels good, and it lightly twitches as if there's a little heartbeat in my back."

"Leave out the word 'back', and someone would think you're describing the ultimate act of romance," Claus said. "Remember this. Not all couples share things the same way. Somehow, we've become a couple. You joked I'm your work husband, but regular co-workers don't do what we do."

"People make coffee and share it at work. They go out to lunch and feel good after a great meal," Jill said. "Are they food swingers?"

"Actually, I've always thought they were," Claus said.

"Who do you go out to eat with?" Jill asked.

"Normally, I don't. People use the moment to discuss work or other business. It's like they can't be bothered to use the normal working hours for meetings. They have to cram one into meal time. I mean, we work when we are back-to-back."

"Then we should test it. We should do something other than work," Jill said. "In fact, I was preparing for this day."

"You were?"

"Yes," Jill said. "I had a special tank made where we can sit back-to-back. I'll fill it with coffee and my secret ingredient. Let's see how it works. Then you'll have your answer. Or did the doctors say otherwise?"

"No. The doctors say there's nothing physically wrong with me. No tumors, no dementia, no nothing. Which reminds me, Doctor Li was supposed to take the same tests," Claus said.

Jill laughed.

"She made a deal with you?"

"Yeah. At Frieda's funeral," Claus said.

"That was just to convince you to get the tests," Jill said. "She wasn't serious."

"I can see that. Seems I can't trust anyone," Claus said.

"You're right. You can't trust people. But you can trust how you feel," Jill said. "In fact, I've been lowering your medication the last few weeks."

"That's why I don't feel so drugged up," Claus said.

"The drugs interfere with your feelings. And your work. Mining is booming on AB4711, and Astroosa is having record earnings. But there are other asteroids to discover. You should be in top mental condition."

"I agree," Claus said.

"So let's test the tub together—you and me with our clear minds," she said.

"I don't know. I mean, are you expecting me to undress?"

"Of course not. Wear swimming trunks. Or just shorts. It's just us. No one will know or care," Jill said. "You need something new anyway."

"That this definitely is," Claus said.

Claus changed into shorts and a shirt. Jill disappeared into the guest room and returned in a one-piece bathing suit but with her back exposed. The suit was white with a floral print. It flared out at the bottom like a short dress.

"That could pass as a summer outfit," Claus said.

"I kinda like it," Jill said. "Chris said it's too sexy. But that chapter will soon be over. I'm tired of pretending anyway."

"Pretending?"

"The whole romance game," Jill said. "I know how men look at me. But I've never felt that way. I was always into my music. Until Brandi passed. Then I threw myself into technology. Enough of me. Are you ready?"

The two walked into what was now the bathhouse.

"This used to be a bedroom," Claus said.

"I had it converted. I hope you don't mind," Jill said.

"How did I not notice the construction? I would have heard cutting and drilling," Claus said.

"They were quiet, and you were on meds. Like it?"

"It's different. Is that the tub?"

"Yes," Jill said. "As you can see, I've already filled it."

"It looks a bit like the outline of two chairs put together," Claus said.

"I'll step in first," Jill said, and she did.

"It...what are you doing?" Claus asked.

Jill hit several buttons on a panel near her.

"Getting the temperature and additives just right," she said. "As you've guessed, there's more than coffee and water in here. Water must be clean, too. Like a swimming pool or hot tub. It's ready. Try it out."

Claus stepped in. He sat back-to-back with Jill. Suddenly, he felt electrical shocks in his legs.

"I'm getting electrocuted in my legs!" Claus said.

He jumped out.

"Wait. There. I've changed the setting. Try it again," she said.

Claus stepped back in and put his back to hers.

"No, not right," she said.

"What's wrong?" Claus asked.

"Step out. Need another adjustment," she said.

Claus stepped out followed by Jill. She took scissors and cut out the material in the back of his shirt.

"You're ruining my shirt?" Claus asked.

"We must have skin-to-skin contact," she said. "Let's try again."

They both stepped in and put their backs together. Jill tried wiggling her back against his.

"No. The water makes your back feel like sandpaper. The other connections aren't right either. Get out," she said.

"So now you're going to make me undress?" Claus asked.

"I told you I'm done playing the romance game," she said. "No. Do you have a diving suit? A wetsuit?"

"Yes, but—"

"Put it on. Make sure it covers all skin," she said.

"It won't. My feet, hands, and face will be exposed," Claus said.

"Wear gloves on your hands, boots on your feet, and leave your face alone. Meet me here in five minutes," she said.

Claus did. When he returned, he expected to see Jill in a wetsuit. But instead, she was in spandex.

"I don't understand," he said.

"We don't have the same body types," she said.

"That I could have told you," Claus said.

"I need thicker material over your skin but thinner on mine," she said.

"I see your back is exposed," Claus said.

"Yes. I must modify your wetsuit," she said.

"Hey wait, Olivia. You're cutting my wetsuit! It's ruined!" Claus said.

"On the contrary, it's just right now," she said. "One more thing. I'm going back with the gel."

Jill smeared gel all over Claus's back.

"Put some on my back," she said. "Pretend it's lotion."

Claus did, but Jill sighed each time he touched her.

"Try not to have such a gentle touch," she said.

"I don't understand," Claus said.

"You're being too sensitive. It's triggering a euphoric reaction I'm not prepared to deal with. I don't want a romantic relationship like this. I want us back-to-back. Use an implement to apply the gel if you have to."

Claus used a book to apply the gel.

"I used a dictionary," he said.

"The right gel is worth a million words," she giggled. "Okay. Into the tank."

Jill climbed in, and so did Claus. They were now back-to-back. Jill moved her back against his, and she felt euphoric feedback.

"Little heartbeat in my back," she said. "Just like when we're working."

Jill leaned the back of her head against his.

"That's strange. I'm seeing stars," he said. "You only tapped my skull. You didn't knock it hard."

"I'm seeing stars too," she said.

"How can this be?" Claus asked.

"I have another idea," she said. "Out of the tank."

The two exited the tank. Jill then took barber's shears and shaved off a bald spot on the back of Claus's head.

"What did you do that for?" Claus said in surprise. "You just lopped off a chunk of my hair!"

"Now do the same for me," she said.

"What??"

"Shave a bald spot on the back of my head!" she ordered.

"This is getting really weird," Claus said. "How will I go out in public?"

"Wear a hat," she said. "Shave the spot!"

Claus shaved off a spot on the back of her head.

"Too low. Go higher," she said.

Claus did so.

"Perfect. Turn around," she said.

Claus turned around, and Jill applied gel to the back of his head.

"Ew! On my scalp?"

"You'll see why," she said. "If I'm right, we're about to discover something revolutionary. Now apply gel to the back of my head. Use the dictionary."

Claus did so.

"Good. Back in the tank," she said.

The two returned. They pressed backs and touched the backs of their heads. Suddenly, Claus saw images.

"What? I see the universe. Galaxies and nebulas," Claus said. "What did you do? I'm getting out of here!"

Claus jumped out of the tub.

"No, wait. I can explain. It's perfectly logical, really," she said.

"Really, Olivia? What evil is this?" Claus asked.

"It's not evil. It's not witchcraft. The visual cortex is in the back of the brain. When we touch scalps, the gel connects our cortices. Images overlap. C'mon. Try it again," Jill said.

"I...I'm not sure this is a good idea," Claus said.

"Okay, I'll explain further. Have you ever as a child or even an adult looked at two nearly identical images in a puzzle book? You know, they ask you to identify the differences," she said.

"Yes. There's a trick to those puzzles," Claus said.

"Exactly. The pictures are side-by-side. So it's a matter of crossing eyes. The eyes see the differences as a shimmering," Jill said.

"I don't see how this relates to making me hallucinate," Claus said.

"It's not a hallucination. Don't you see? People see and experience things slightly differently. Men and women tend to have more dissimilar brains as well. We can link our cortices together and use them to quickly find differences in what we see. Maybe more," Jill said.

"How much more?"

"I don't know. I've never tried it before. This is new territory for me. The coffee reaction with your back plus resting your head against mine just now gave me the idea," Jill said.

"I don't know about this," Claus said.

"Claus. Astroosa is at the forefront of revolutionizing the world with inexpensive, high-quality metals. But any new thing is vulnerable to waste and abuse. We can mitigate that abuse by improving our perception and insight. We can save the world the abuse of greed and power. You know what I mean. Any monopoly has a tendency to grab more and more power. We need to offset that. And we're the only ones who can."

"Uh...I...this is very familiar," Claus said. "I had a dream that you wanted to take over the world. I won't go into more detail, because I fear you want to do it again."

"Take over the world? Can two people sitting in a hot tub take over the world? Tell me, Claus, did I sit in a hot tub and take over the world? With you?" Jill asked.

"No. You acquired a special device that helped you. And that's all I'm going to say," Claus said.

"Was it a tub?"

"No. An alien," Claus said.

Jill laughed.

"That's fantasy. This is science. Come. We'll follow the scientific method all the way. Who knows, perhaps in time we can help other people learn the technique. They can explore as we will. They could—"

"Use tanks for procreation," Claus let slip.

"That's not what I was thinking. Not even close. That must have been a wild dream. A couple conceiving in a...what was that...a procreation tank?"

"It was a wild dream, I guess," Claus said.

"Sounds like it," Jill said. "Let's try my technique. If it's too much for you, I'll stop. It'll be a shame though if you quit. Like the early developers of the airplane. Imagine if we'd never conquered the air."

"Author, author. I need help from my author!" Claus blurted.

"What?"

"Never mind," Claus said. "Okay. If I freak out again, we'll stop. Deal?"

"Deal," Jill said.

Claus stepped back into the tub. He pressed his back against Jill's and the back of his skull against hers.

"Stars again," Claus said. "Some are solid. Some are vibrating."

"Let's take a look at those vibrating stars," she said.

The image zoomed in.

"That vibrating star looks like an asteroid," Claus said.

"Because it is," Jill said. "Let's get closer."

The image of the asteroid grew closer until it filled Claus's entire view.

"What asteroid is this?"

"AB4923," Jill said.

"Most of the asteroid is solid grey, like a typical asteroid. But spots are vibrating," Claus said.

"Let's zoom in on a spot," Jill said.

A crater on the asteroid filled his view.

"Our cortices see this crater as vibrating," Jill said.

"It's more like flashing. Almost pea-green in color," Claus said. "Wait. Something familiar about this."

Jill wiggled her back against Claus's.

"What are you doing?"

"I can modulate the flashing by adjusting my back position against yours. Slow the rate down," Jill said.

The flashing rate slowed.

"Oh no!" Claus said. "I can't believe it. It can't be!"

"You see it. Two alternating colors. Yellow and blue," Jill said.

"It won't work, Lanietta!" Claus yelled. "Whatever game you're playing, you can stop! Your Clomper is tired of the nonsense. Give me a dog bowl. Put me in the doghouse. Lanietta? Speak to me!"

Jill stepped out of the tub, turned, and started to help Claus out, but he remained in the tub.

"Why did you step out?" Claus asked.

"I promised to stop if you freaked out," Jill said. "Well? You freaked out. Who's Lanietta? Who's Clomper? Do you think you're a dog?"

"Are you Lanietta?" Claus asked.

"I'm Olivia Jill Depetti Cresson, soon to be divorced. You know that. Claus. Did you see something just now?"

"No. The dream. I keep thinking this is a dream," Claus said.

"Pinch yourself. You'll wake up if it's a dream," Jill said.

"With these gloves?"

Jill removed her own gloves then removed Claus's.

"Now try," Jill said.

Claus tried to pinch through the wetsuit.

"No good. Too thick," he said.

"Pinch your face," she said.

Claus did so.

"It hurts, but I'm still here," he said.

"No Lanietta. No Clomper. No dream," Jill said. "Tell you what. Leave off your gloves."

"Won't that upset the capacitance of the water?" Claus asked.

"Not as much as you might think," Jill said. "Let's begin again."

"Wait, no," Claus said.

Claus stepped out of the water.

"This is because of the Anrega. We've tapped into it somehow. It tells us about these mineral resources. Oh, why didn't I realize it before? Olivia. We must stop. This will be our undoing. The selenites will come and take over Earth," Claus said.

"I guess I was wrong," Jill said.

"About what?"

"I shouldn't have stopped your anti-psychotic," she said.

"You think that's what this is? I know these things, Olivia. I know them from the dream. The dream told me everything," Claus said.

"Listen to yourself talk. The dream told you everything."

Jill stirred a finger in the water.

"We are at crossing roads," she said. "We can leave the tub alone. Quit and allow the future to play itself out, no matter how ugly. Or we can restart your anti-psychotic med and try again. Or we can try again without your med. You'll have to limit your outbursts. I'll leave it up to you."

"Your reaction puzzles me," Claus said. "I thought you were the obsessive kind."

"I've channeled it constructively. I have drive, but I don't have your fantastic imagination," Jill said.

"You call my dream imagination? I didn't make it up," Claus said.

"That's the psychosis speaking," Jill said. "Yes. You did. Repeat after me—I made up Lanietta and the dream."

"I made up Lanietta and the dream. I made up Lanietta. I made her up," Claus said.

"Feel better?"

"It feels weird," Claus said. "How would Lanietta react to my statement that I made her up?"

"How do you think she'd react?" Jill asked.

"Probably turn me into a toad. No, the mass would be wrong. Turn me into a dog. Or send me back in time where I'm watching a dog race with her cheering," Claus said.

"See? An excellent imagination," Jill said. "Are you up for another cortex join?"

"That's the other thing. She'd call this innerviation," Claus said.

"No such word. Do you mean innervation?" Jill asked.

"That was the exact point I made with her. But it was her own word she used to describe people becoming so attached as if nerves connected them. Is that what is happening to us?"

"Do we react the same way to things?" Jill asked.

"I don't think so," Claus said.

"Exactly. We don't. We don't connect like that. We're dissimilar. But we can use those differences to our advantage. To help Astroosa and maybe more. Sounds like your Lanietta wanted to control you. That's abuse. Don't let that happen to you. Chris started with me like that. See where it got me? That's okay. I'll be glad when the divorce is over. Want to try again?"

"Okay," Claus said.

"Wait. Let's reapply the gel. Turn around," Jill said.

Jill reapplied gel to Claus's back and skull. Claus took the dictionary and reapplied gel on Jill.

"At this rate, we'll need more dictionaries," Claus said.

"I look forward to increasing our vocabulary," she smiled.

Jill stepped into the tank. Claus stepped in next. They touched backs and skulls.

"Do you see stars again?" Jill asked.

"Yes," Claus said. "And you?"

"I see the same," she said. "In case you are wondering, I'm feeding data into the tank in the form of an image. The stars we see are that image."

"I don't see how you can do that," Claus said.

"Told you. I'm great with technology," she said. "Except it never worked before."

"But it does now," Claus said.

"Because of you, yes," she said. "We'll zoom up on other asteroids."

The image zoomed up on a vibrating asteroid.

"Practically the entire asteroid is flashing," Claus said. "And yet it looks just as grey and crater-ridden as the others."

"Must be buried like the others," Jill said.

"The image is drifting to the left. If only I could move it back," Claus said.

Claus reached in the tank water with his hands as if he were grabbing the asteroid and moving it back. The image moved back to center.

"Did I do that?"

"Yes. You did," Jill said. "Good. I've been having trouble with direction and zoom. You can help me. We're looking at AB8643."

"This asteroid is loaded. I mean the whole thing," Claus said. "The flashing is slowing, too. There are more blues than yellows."

"Concentrate on that," Jill said. "I'm sending the pattern to Prava 12."

"What on Earth...I mean, what around the moon for?" Claus said.

"I need sophisticated technology to resolve these color patterns. Prava 12 is handy. Yes, I had to rig this tank into your computer workstation. Actually, my station. Anyway, yes, this asteroid has plenty of rhodium and gold," Jill said.

"Would be nice if one of these asteroids contained uranium or some other nuclear fuel," Claus said.

"That's a good idea. Think of uranium," Jill said.

Claus thought of uranium. A map of complex elements appeared with many electrons spinning around.

"That's not uranium. That's thorium," Jill said.

"I...thorium. Doctor Irina Kechenova. Are you...did she teach you this?"

"You know her? Astroosa has a spy on her. Never know what those competitors will do. At least that's what Joe thinks. I've never met her. Wonder what she's like," Jill said.

"She's the most technologically advanced person I've ever met...sort of...I mean...at least she was in my dream," Claus said.

"In your dream? Have you met her or not? For real, I mean."

"I guess not," Claus said.

"Try to focus on uranium," Jill said. "I'll focus too."

An image of uranium displayed.

"Excellent. Now a map of the asteroid belt. Prava 12 is helping," Jill said.

"Lots of vibrating asteroids," Claus said.

"We'll pick one of the closer ones," Jill said. "You know, instead of shipping back these metals raw, we could have machines build machines. Send back processed metals. Or even complete machines. Start a colony of machines."

"Selenites," Claus muttered.

An image of a selenite displayed.

"Wow! What's that?" Jill remarked. "Amazing. An artificial life-form. Your creativity is pure genius."

"I didn't create. It was part of the dream," Claus insisted.

"Call it what you like. These machines will solve all problems. We can power them with uranium, and they can do manufacturing on the asteroids. Wow. Wow!" Jill exclaimed.

Claus stepped out of the tub.

"What's wrong?" she asked.

"This is. Everything," Claus said. "In my dream, selenites fought each other. They took over Earth. People became slaves."

"We'll take your design and incorporate safeguards. Fail-safes. You *do* believe in fail-safes, don't you?" Jill asked.

"Actually, I...never really did. I know I'm supposed to. But I've felt that fail-safes make a person soft. People depend on them and don't do things right the first time," Claus said.

"Oh boy. Well, if ever we need them, it's now. With all these changes, we might

not know what right is," Jill said. "Let's stop working. We can both sit in the tub and relax. Think of pleasant scenes. We haven't done anything yet with our new-found knowledge. We can give it time to mature."

"Okay. But then that will have to be it for today. This is wearing me out," Claus said.

Claus sat back in the tub. He thought of a castle built upon a rocky cliff next to the ocean. Waves crashed against the cliff and sent sprays of water high in the air. Birds of prey circled high above, gliding on thermals. The day was partly cloudy with a breeze. Claus imagined himself on a beach walking toward that castle.

"I see it too," Jill said.

"I don't see you," Claus said. "Where are you?"

"I don't see you either," Jill said. "There's a pretty shell in front. I'm reaching down to grab it."

"That's funny. *I'm* reaching down for a pretty shell," Claus said.

"We're using the same proxy," Jill said. "We are simultaneously in the same body experiencing the same thing."

"The shell has a vibrating section near its end," Claus said.

"I see it too. I'm breaking the shell on a rock," Jill said.

"So am I. There's something inside," Claus said.

"It's a gold nugget. How did that get in there? It's yellow."

"No, blue," Claus said. "Blue gold? It's vibrating, though."

"Because we see it as two different colors. Perhaps things of value vibrate like this. Maybe because people see them as different things. What does gold make you think of?"

"That it's used for jewelry on women," Claus said.

"It makes me think of gold watches on men," Jill said. "There. I just proved it. We each have different reactions to gold. What about the castle? Is it vibrating?"

"Not to me. Looks like a castle. Nothing special," Claus said.

"Does it remind you of anything?"

"No."

"Me neither," Jill said.

"I thought you said we were going to relax," Claus said.

"Isn't this relaxing?"

"It is but...well...I guess it's okay," Claus said. "As long as we don't have to focus on anything."

"I've got to know more about that piece of gold," Jill said. "Let's focus on that."

"But I—"

"This will only take a moment. Probably won't mean anything," she said.

"Okay."

"Expand on that feeling. The one where you see the gold on a woman," Jill said.

Claus did so.

"I see someone in front of me. No, two people," Claus said. "Their images are superimposed. One is yellow, the other is blue. It's rather annoying and tiring to look at."

"Cross your eyes. You want double vision. Make the castle appear twice," Jill said.

Claus did so.

"I see a blue-shaded woman with one castle and a yellow-shaded man with the other castle. But that's impossible," Claus said.

"No, it's perfect!" Jill said. "We did it. We've split an image!"

"If only I had four eyes," Claus said. "I could split farther."

"We do. Together we have four eyes," Jill said. "Focus on the woman. I will too. Now what do you see?"

"I see two other people mixed with her image," Claus said. "Wait, the castle is back to one image. No, now it's three. Now four. Who are the two new people?"

"The woman's parents," Jill said.

"But who are these people?" Claus asked.

"That's a good question. We've tripped across a technique. We'll have to hone it. Maybe we'll learn the answers in time. The important thing is we have a special way of learning things not possible by other people or even machines," Jill said.

"This reminds me of when the Carinians learned how to space jump," Claus said.

"Space jump?"

"A way of traveling by first going into the ethereal plane and then coming back," Claus said.

"An imagination as vast as the universe. You know, if there is such a thing where we could transport materials through this ethereal realm, that would also be a boon to Astroosa," Jill said.

"I don't know if people are ready for such a thing," Claus said. "I mean look at the evolution of warfare. Battles were often defined by how far an army could march in a day so that they could march home. Then horseback lengthened the distance. Land vehicles even farther. Airplanes farther than that, and intercontinental missiles made it global. This would open up cosmic wars. Do we want that?"

"Someone will discover it," Jill said. "Like the atom bomb. Better us than them."

"And who is them?" Claus asked.

"Anyone who would use it for evil. For war and aggression," Jill said.

"We'll have to find a way to control it," Claus said. "Look at how the internet got out of hand. Crooks litter that like the plague. The universe becoming like the internet—that would be like...like...oh me! That's what Frieda was doing! Digitizing the ether!"

"Claus. You're not making sense. My Aunt Frieda didn't do that," Jill said.

"In my dream she did," Claus said.

"Things don't have to turn out like your dream," Jill said. "When did she do it?"

"She didn't die in my dream. She lived and went up to the moon. That's when everything changed with the aliens. You know, maybe we should investigate the moon. Use Prava 12 and all that. With this yellow-blue stuff," Claus said.

"Do you expect to find Bill and Andrea? Prava 12 can't find them," Jill said.

"I expect to find aliens who have captured them," Claus said.

"And if we do? Then what?"

"Then they'll realize they've been discovered, and it will be a war with them, I guess. Maybe we shouldn't look for them," Claus said.

"I believe Bill and Andrea are on the lunar far side. But I don't believe aliens are there. I think we would have detected them by now. Let's go with your first idea about Prava 12. Let's look for them. If we can find them, maybe they're still alive. We could relay our findings to Astroosa. Let them decide. No need to place the burden on our shoulders."

Claus paused.

"Okay," he said. "I hope you're right about the aliens, or lack thereof."

"I'm sure of it," Jill said. "Ready?"

"Ready."

Jill tapped into the lunar far side data from Prava 12.

"Looks like the far side," Claus said. "No vibrating."

"Yeah," Jill said. "I see nothing strange either. I'll try an older set of data from the probe."

"The same. Nothing vibrating. Nothing flashing," Claus said.

"There should at least be an impact crater or some evidence of a crash. But I see nothing," Jill said.

"Same here," Claus said. "Guess it was a far-fetched idea. I'll reorient the antenna dish to the asteroid mining relay probe."

Claus did so. Jill paused in thought and then spoke.

"We'll have to acquire more data from—"

But at that moment, Marna walked in.

"Olivia Jill Depetti! What on Earth! Is this what you've been doing? No wonder Chris is divorcing you!" Marna said.

"Mamma!" Jill said.

"Mamma? Marna? It must be Lanietta. Lanietta!" Claus exclaimed.

Claus jumped out of the tank and hugged Marna.

"I knew you'd show up, Lanietta. You've got to tell me what's going on. Why you've put me through this reality and everything," Claus said.

"Unhand me, Claus!" Marna said as she pushed Claus back.

"Claus, back off!" Jill said as she stepped out of the tank.

"What have you done to your hair? It's bald in back. So is Claus's," Marna said.

"We came up with a new way of processing data," Jill said. "I had probe data fed into this tank. We sit back-to-back and head-to-head. We can share images this way."

"Back to back? Is that all you do?" Marna asked.

"Yes!" Jill said.

Marna sniffed Jill. She then walked up to the tank, touched the liquid, held it to her nose, and sniffed.

"Is this coffee?" Marna asked.

"Yes. A special brew to facilitate the connection," Jill said.

"You've completely lost it. I'm calling Donna. And Patricia. They *both* need to see this madness," Marna said.

"Lanietta, please!" Claus said. "Maybe this can help out with the ether."

"Why does he keep calling me that, Olivia?" Marna asked. "Did you take him off his meds?"

Jill looked down sheepishly.

"You *did* take him off his meds!" Marna said with disappointment.

"I had to. Claus has a fantastic imagination. And I have fantastic drive to solve problems," Jill said. "All that we've accomplished with finding and mining those asteroids? It was because of going back-to-back with coffee. At first we just sat on a bench, but this tank enhances the experience."

"Do you get pleasure out of it, Olivia?" Marna asked. "The way one rides a horse?"

"No! Nothing like that!" Jill said. "Well, I get a strange sensation in my back. It *does* feel good. But it's just my back. Nothing romantic or anything. Besides, that romantic stuff is fake. I'm done faking with people. I faked it with Chris, and I've given it up."

"The way you're talking, I wish you *were* having an affair with Claus. You're not lovers. You're drug buddies," Marna said.

"I beg to interrupt, but coffee is hardly on the level of opiates," Claus said.

"It is if you have the same reaction," Marna said. "What a mess. Donna and Patricia, Donna and Patricia."

"You keep mentioning their names. But why the need? We're not hurting anyone," Jill said. "Is either of us emaciated? Frazzled? A change of clothes, and we'd come off as perfectly normal."

"Except for the bald spot. And this Lanietta," Marna said.

"Please don't say anything to anyone," Jill said.

"You're asking me, your mother, not to say anything to anyone?" Marna asked. "You're my daughter, and I love you. The Brandi incident is still fresh in my mind."

"That was long ago. I'm over it," Jill lied.

"That was hardly that long ago," Marna said.

Marna paced around the room.

"What are you doing here anyway?" Jill asked.

"I came over to say we purchased the house next door and moved your things into it," Marna said. "Chris is not so considerate toward your possessions."

"The house next door? Let's walk over and see it!" Jill said.

"Not next door to Claus's house. Next door to our house. Your parents' house," Marna said.

"You know, I could build a second tank there," Jill said. "You could come visit, Claus. Explore the universe and all."

"Before you go into another full-blown obsession, I have one question, and this is for Claus," Marna said.

"Yes?" Claus asked.

"Do you play a musical instrument?"

"Why no," Claus replied.

"Good!" Marna said with a smile.

"Mamma!" Jill said.

"He would be like gasoline on a fire," Marna said. "Claus, I'll keep my nose out of this new obsession on one condition— you let me know the first moment Olivia

starts making double reeds. No delays. Understood?"

"I promise. And for the record, Cloopy didn't cause Brandi's death. It was an accident," Claus said.

"More strange things you say," Marna said. "I'm wondering how trustworthy you can be."

"Claus, is that true?" Jill asked.

"Yes, Olivia. It was an accident," Claus said. "I was there."

"You were never there," Marna said. "That confirms it. Claus, you are totally untrustworthy. The deal is off. I'm going to speak with Donna and Patricia. Someone will have to monitor the both of you."

"You can't invade our privacy!" Jill said.

"Marry Claus, and I'll respect your privacy. Otherwise..."

"I guess you're not Lanietta. She would never advise that I marry another woman," Claus said.

"Claus, you're going back on your meds first thing, even if I have to administer them myself," Marna said.

"I have HIPAA rights," Claus said. "You're not a medical professional. You can't force meds on me."

"I won't do the forcing. Donna and Patricia will," Marna said. "I can't believe Joe isn't more guarded. You two—"

"Have boosted Astroosa to unknown heights," Jill said. "He can't ignore that, and he'll support us! Mamma! I thank you for the house! But please relax and give this a week to sink in. Claus is a little goofy, but that's his creative half. He's overflowing with things and just zones out of reality. Don't mind him. I'll deal with him. And I know how the Donna/Patricia game will go. Yes, they'll put him on more meds, but that will drug him too heavily, and he won't be much help."

"I'll think about it," Marna said.

"You say that when you want *me* to drop my side of the argument," Jill said.

"Is that what you think this is? An argument? Olivia! It isn't. It really isn't," Marna said.

"Would you like to try it out?" Claus said. "The tank, I mean."

"I beg your pardon!" Marna said, now becoming angry. "Olivia, you'd better put a leash on this one. And be thankful Enrico isn't here to hear this. He'd send Claus to the dentist for sure! Here. Take the keys."

Marna handed a set of house keys to Jill. Jill took them and smiled.

"Thank you!" Jill smiled.

Marna smiled back. She hugged Jill goodbye and waved but shot Claus a cautionary look on the way out.

"I thought we were busted," Claus said with Marna now gone.

"We're not doing anything wrong," Jill said.

"So why does it feel wrong?" Claus asked.

"When people first flew, did that not feel wrong? At any moment the aircraft could crash and cause severe injury or death. This tank is incredibly safe. No injuries. No death," Jill said.

"Not yet," Claus said. "Not yet."

"Dark thoughts, Claus. You have such dark thoughts," Jill said. "Don't you feel uplifted when we work back-to-back?"

"I feel the sensation, like eating, but I know that candy causes cavities, so it feels empty," Claus said.

Jill paused.

"But we've accomplished so much," Jill said. "Doesn't that grab you?"

"I'm guarded and fearful," Claus said. "Accomplishment means the end closes in more quickly."

"The end? It doesn't have to be the end. It's the beginning!" Jill said. "And speaking of, I have a new home next to my parents. That's also an accomplishment."

"But the end of your home with Chris," Claus said.

"It just proves that one end is another beginning. Let's gets some air from this heavy stuff. Let's go see my new home. What do you say?" Jill said.

Claus nodded in agreement, and the two left.

Jill and Claus arrived at her new house. She opened the front door. It was dark inside, but she heard Cloopy barking in another room.

"What's that? Cloopy?" she asked.

"SURPRISE!" shouted a group of people as the lights went on, confetti flew, horns blew, and streamers streamed.

"What? I...it's not my birthday...what's going on?"

A cake was brought out with candles, a cake that said: "Welcome to your new house".

"Welcome home, new neighbor," Marna said as she brought Cloopy with her.

"Oh Mamma!" Jill cried, and the two women hugged. "Cloopy too? Can he stay?"

"Yes," Marna said. "Cloopy too."

Jill leaned over and hugged Cloopy. Cloopy barked back.

"It's almost like before," Claus muttered.

The party went on for several hours, as Jill socialized with many of her old friends (none of which were Chris's friends). All showed support for Jill and her divorce situation, and they pledged to help her in any way possible. Marna reiterated that she and Enrico would help Jill and ensure a smooth path back to freedom. The party dwindled, and a few very close friends stayed behind to clean up.

"I'm going to get a ride home," Claus said to Jill.

"Are you sure?" Jill asked.

"Yes. There's something your mother needs to show you. You two should be alone," Claus said. "I'll catch up with you in the morning."

Chapter 141: Coffee Competition

The following day was Saturday. Jill drove over to Claus's house to chat and talk about the upcoming week. But Jill was shocked to find plywood nailed over the window in Claus's front door. She rang the doorbell. Claus answered, still dressed in pajamas.

"You look like death warmed over," Jill said.

"I had a break-in last night while I was at your house," Claus said. "I was up half the night with the police."

"What? Claus! I never would have guessed it. This neighborhood seems so safe," Jill said. "How much did they take?"

"They left the valuable stuff," Claus said. "Computer equipment, jewelry, coin collection—it's all still here."

"Vandalism? Claus! Show me the tank! Show it to me now!" Jill insisted.

Claus led Jill to the room where the tank was stored. It was gone.

"They stole it," Claus said.

"Who?"

"I don't know," Claus said. "I don't know how anyone knew it was here. It was the only thing stolen."

"Then you misled me just now. You said nothing of value was stolen," Jill said.

"Well a tank for holding water is hardly valuable," Claus said.

"It was more than that. You know this, Claus. Someone else will figure out what we did and use it for who knows what kind of evil," Jill said. "Oh, this is terrible. The thief could be anyone and could live anywhere. I suspect everyone around. I trust no one. I'm alone. Alone!"

"Can you build another one?" Claus asked. "Maybe we can use it to track the first one."

"It won't be that easy," Jill said. "The tank is used to relay information from Astroosa probes. But the tank itself is not a probe. This isn't magic. It's science and engineering. Oh, my stomach is churning. My back is on fire. I need inspiration."

"Don't do it," Claus said. "Don't cut your legs like Frieda."

"What? How did you know? Did you break into my house and read Frieda's scrapbook? Now who's the burglar?" Jill asked.

"I didn't break in," Claus said.

Jill's expression of shock melted away into relief.

"What am I saying? You must've read my thoughts when we were last in the tank. I had half a thought of it then. I guess that's the risk of sharing minds," Jill said.

"A woman must have her legs, as clean and pristine as possible," Claus said. "If you ever feel the need to injure yourself, channel it into your work. Or worst case scenario, cut my legs. Or my back."

Jill's eyes lit up.

"Promise?" she asked.

"Yes. Promise," Claus said.

"I'll keep your offer in mind. I have an idea. Yes, I'll rebuild the tank. But I'll keep it in *my* house in a secure room in the basement. I'll install a house security system. Even my parents can watch for suspicious behavior," Jill said. "We have an advantage, Claus. We have each other."

"And your ideas," Claus said.

"And your ideas too," Jill said.

"Let's start now then," Claus said. "The sooner we get rid of our churning stomachs, the better."

Claus headed for Jill's car.

"Wait!" Jill said. "You should at least put on something decent!"

Claus looked at himself and shook his head in disbelief.

"You're right. I'm obviously out of it today," he said.

"Take a shower and shave," Jill said. "I'll wait."

Claus took a shower, shaved, and dressed. When he exited the bathroom, he saw Jill reading a book.

"You carved your name on your grandmother's house?" Jill asked.

"My mother wrote that in Grandma Broc's diary. It's private," Claus said, ripping the book from Jill's grasp.

"I didn't realize you were so sensitive," Jill said.

"If I didn't know better, I'd think you were Lanietta," Claus said.

"First you called my mother that name. Now me," Jill said. "Is every woman to you just another Lanietta? We're all people, Claus. We're given a body the way people are dealt cards. I'm not your made-up Lanietta. Try to see that. Please."

Claus looked down at his grandmother's diary.

"She must have been a great person," Jill said. "I mean, for you to have her diary and all."

"Yes. She was. She never knew how much she affected me. It's been years since her death, and I still go back to the things she told me when I was a child. They made no sense then, but they make sense now. Anyway, I'm becoming nostalgic. Let's build that tank," Claus said. "And I think I'll bring this diary with me. In case my house is burglarized again. Don't want to lose it."

Jill and Claus went to her house. Cloopy was happy to greet them and took a special liking to Claus.

"Why, it's like he knows you," Jill said.

"I feel like I know him too," Claus said. "We both are constrained by the leash."

"I don't know what you mean by that," Jill said. "You make it sound like you're a dog yourself."

"I am," Claus said.

Jill took a hard look at Claus then broke into laughter.

"Dry humor," she said. "Fortunately, I have all files here. I'll just send them over to the 3D printer, and I'll have a tank built in no time. The printer will spit out pieces, of course. We'll need to assemble it. This will take all day. Plus setting up the tank computer."

"Let's get to it," Claus said.

And that's how the day was spent. The two worked through the morning and into the afternoon, snacking on sandwiches from Jill's fridge and coffee. Six o'clock came, and both were tired and hungry.

"It's almost done," Jill said. "Let's order in."

"I wouldn't mind a pizza," Claus said.

"As I recall, Patricia wants you on a vegan diet," Jill laughed.

"I know. I've been eating Chinese vegan for quite a while now. I need a change," Claus said.

"Let's stick with vegan, but there are alternatives. I'll order that pizza for you—vegan style," Jill said.

"Is that possible?"

"You'd be amazed what they can do now-a-days," Jill said.

The two ate vegan pizza. And drank more coffee.

"I'm wired," Claus said. "I'll have to crash soon."

"Just another hour or so," Jill said. "Let's get it done."

The two did. At 8pm.

"My head is spinning. As much as I'd like to test it with you, I've got to get some sleep," Claus said.

"One test, and we'll call it a day," Jill said.

"Okay," Claus replied.

Jill filled the tank with her special coffee liquid.

"Oh, I forgot my wetsuit," Claus lamented.

"We can manage without," Jill said. "But I'll have to cut your shirt so your back is exposed. One more thing. Is your word still good? I mean about cutting your leg or whatever."

"You have the urge?" Claus asked.

"Yes. I have a strong urge to cut my legs. I'm still burning with rage that my first tank was stolen. Someone out there deserves my wrath, and I have no way of directing it to them. I must cut. I must cut my legs," Jill said.

"No, don't. Cut my legs or something," Claus said.

"Or back?"

"Or back."

Jill cut his back.

"What would Lanietta say to this?" Claus asked. "I keep expecting her to show up."

"Think about the cut and not about her," Jill said. "I'll apply the coffee gel to your back and skull. There. Oh, and I made an applicator so you can apply the gel to my back and skull without using a book. That's right. Don't use your grandmother's diary."

"How did you know?" Claus asked.

"Apparently the same way you knew that I wanted to cut my legs," Jill said.

Claus used the applicator. The two entered this new tank and sat back-to-back, skull-to-skull. Jill adjusted the computer.

"The tank isn't hooked up to the probes yet. I just have it networked into the internet for testing," Jill said. "I'll do some test patterns."

Claus saw what looked like old-fashioned television test patterns. The first was a big circle in the center with four circles in the corners. The image then switched to vertical colored bars. Finally, he saw an image of Chris and Patricia Li sitting back-to-back in Jill's original tank. Jill jumped out of the new tank.

"I don't believe it!" she said.

"It can't be true," Claus said. "But how did you get the image?"

"Claus. Has Doctor Li ever touched your tissue? Or your blood?"

"I think so. Yes. Accidentally," Claus said.

"Then that's how we did it. Cutting your back released blood and created a new connection. In this case to Patricia," Jill said.

"One of them stole the tank," Claus said. "I can't believe Patricia would have."

"Chris for sure," Jill said. "He's always taken my ideas, twisted or misinterpreted them, and presented them as his own. I don't know how he learned about my tank."

"He's been spying on us somehow," Claus said. "He shoved those divorce papers under my front door. Remember?

Who knows how many other times he's been over without us knowing. I'll notify the police and have him arrested."

"No, wait," Jill said. "We can use this to our advantage. I'm sure of it. Just give me time to sort through this. Let's close up for tonight. And if you don't mind, will you drop over tomorrow so we can continue? I know it's Sunday, but it would help."

"If you don't mind, may I crash here for the night? Otherwise, you'd have to drive me back home tonight and pick me up tomorrow morning. Plus I could use a break from my house with the break-in still fresh on my mind," Claus said.

"Yes, you can crash here. I have a guest room all ready to go," Jill said.

"Won't make it. I'll be lucky to reach the easy chair," Claus said.

Jill helped Claus up the stairs, and as soon as he sat in the easy chair and pushed it back, he was sound asleep. Jill placed a throw blanket over him. She then went back downstairs to finish up with the tank for the night. She locked up, checked the house for anything unusual, and spent an hour with Cloopy and a book before retiring herself.

Claus dreamed he was back on the moon, with Labba, Clausetta, Claude, and Leif at an exquisite dinner party. There was the head table where he sat with his family, circular tables dotting much of the remaining area, and two parallel, very long tables that ran for a hundred paces or more. One end of the tables abutted a wall. This wall had an opening for each table. Atop each table ran a roller conveyer. From each wall opening rolled out a low, wide submarine sandwich, but with no upper bread piece. Instead, there was just the lower bread half, and this was covered in all sorts of vegan toppings. The bread itself contained no animal products and was completely plant-based.

These two topless subs rolled down the entire length of the tables and then stopped. A person with a flag stood between the tables while the non-wall table ends had a competitor each, preparing to start. One was dressed in yellow, the other in blue.

"To start what?" Claus wondered.

The flag dropped. Each competitor rolled up corresponding topless subs along the table as quickly as possible, like a roll of tape each. The yellow competitor got a lead, and the blue competitor struggled to keep up, but before the yellow competitor could reach the wall, the roll became unwieldy, rolled off the table, and unrolled itself around startled guests. The blue competitor, taking more care with blue's roll, continued steadily to the wall and won the competition. The yellow topless sub, however, finished unrolling in front of Claus. Water from the veggies slapped and splashed his feet.

"No, stop," Claus heard himself say.

Claus awoke with a start and found Cloopy licking his toes.

"Oh, it's you, Cloopy. Now I *know* you're not Lanietta. I was in your shoes, I mean your paws, for a while," Claus said. "Author, author, where is my author? Give me sanity in this uncertain world. But which world is really uncertain? I'm here, on Earth, before the Earth was destroyed. Yes, I'm in the house of the woman who had a part in Earth's destruction. Will she be a factor again? Will Earth end? It will end of course when the sun consumes it in 4.5 billion years. But what about sooner than that? Too much thinking, Claus. Too much thinking."

Claus fell asleep. He dreamed he was swimming with Alpharina, Beitach, Gammdan, and Deltina in a sea of coffee.

"Follow the smell of coffee," said a voice.

"Lanietta?" Claus called back.

"No, not Lanietta," the voice called back. "Do you know where you are?"

"I'm swimming in coffee," Claus said. "Are you Omegaphina? Are you calling across the sea?"

The voice laughed.

"Drink the coffee," the voice said. "Don't swim in it. Just drink."

Claus took a gulp of coffee from the sea. The four dalphinacs disappeared, and

he found himself sitting up in the easy chair with Jill standing next to him, helping him drink coffee from a mug.

"I'm Olivia. Remember?" Jill said.

"I...I'm in your house," Claus said. "I guess I was confused. Names and places become interchangeable. My author refers to you as 'Jill' but you say your name is 'Olivia'."

"I'm Olivia Jill Depetti Cresson," Jill said. "Only call me Jill if I can call you by your middle name. What is it?"

"It's 'Doron'," Claus said. "But I prefer to be called 'Claus'."

"Then I'll call you Claus. And you call me Olivia. Tell your author to call me the same," Jill said.

"Author?" Claus called to me. "Jill is Olivia. Please refer to her as such."

"Did it work?" Olivia asked.

"I don't know," Claus said. "I can't read his writing."

Olivia laughed.

"Then how do you know he calls me 'Jill'?" she asked.

"He told me so," Claus said.

Jill...er...Olivia laughed again.

"Drink more coffee. I have an idea for the tank, but I need your help as always," Olivia said.

"Of course," Claus said. "But not for long. I'll be needing breakfast."

"I promise. Just a brief session. Then breakfast," she said.

The two went downstairs, prepped, and entered the tank, which as part of the preparations was filled with coffee.

"Back-to-back, skull-to-skull, images afar, ideas near. Back-to-back, skull-to-skull, images afar, ideas near," Olivia repeated.

The first images were of a rhodium mine on asteroid AB4711.

"Nothing new here," Claus said.

"We've been finding precious metals for Astroosa, but after that, we've lost track of those metals," Olivia said.

"Astroosa mines them, sends them to Earth, and sells them for a great profit," Claus said.

"Chris was fired from Astroosa, and Patricia will soon quit," Olivia said.

"How do you know? That Patricia will quit?" Claus asked.

"I saw it in an image of her thoughts," Olivia said.

"I didn't see that," Claus said.

"It was on a woman's intuition wavelength," Olivia said.

"Hmm," Claus said. "Not sure I like the sound of that."

"It is what it is," she said. "I wouldn't worry about it. What I would worry about is their next step. They plan to start their own company."

"Another Astroosa?" Claus asked.

"No. A consulting firm providing information to competitor space agencies," Olivia said. "Their plan is so crystal clear that I'm surprised I didn't think of it. They will only dole out enough information for the competitors to find precious metals, but not enough for any one competitor to become too powerful. As a group, however, they can low-ball and force Astroosa out of the mining business."

"What a tangled mess," Claus said.

"I thought you were going to say, 'What a tangled web we weave, when first we practice to deceive.' But as you can see, we are not deceiving," Olivia said.

"No, we're not. Is that your plan? To deceive?" Claus asked.

"Of course not. Straight, honest information trumps deceit any day," Olivia said. "We'll track where the precious metals go—Astroosa's, and the competitors'."

"To what end?" Claus asked. "A company uses rhodium to make a fancy device."

"And we learn how that device is made," Olivia said. "Instant manufacturing knowledge."

"To sell?"

"To use."

"For?"

"Making subs."

"?"

Claus was so dumbfounded that he was at a loss for words.

"I read your dream. About those topless subs," Olivia said.

Olivia then laughed.

"What's so funny?" Claus asked.

"I just listened to what I said. Sounds like you went to a topless bar that went on strike, and the replacements were performing," Olivia continued to laugh.

"You read my mind? I'm not sure I like that," Claus said.

"Don't worry. You're harmless enough. Food, Claus, food! People need food. It overrides all other needs. Except water and air. There's enough of that on Earth. But people can't stop eating. No matter what fancy devices are made with precious metals, we can corner the food market. I'm recording my thoughts as I assimilate them."

"You mean think them up," Claus said.

"No, assimilate. I'm not thinking up anything. I'm taking your idea and...I'll fuse it with manufacturing techniques. Or more. We'll automate the production of vegan food, like restaurants, only remove the human labor factor almost completely. Just leave one person overseeing final sales," Olivia said. "We'll have our own company. We can continue supplying mining information to Astroosa, but we'll quit our Astroosa jobs and do so as consultants. Part of the deal will mean they supply us with mined resources. They'll agree. I know they will."

"Stop," Claus said.

"Really? Why?"

"I've heard talk and plans before. They always go bad. Always," Claus said.

"Why should they? Because you've imagined them?"

"I...I didn't imagine them," Claus said.

"All those plans by Lanshalla and Larbiabba only failed because your imagination failed," Olivia said.

"Wait...I never mentioned them," Claus said.

"I read those imaginations too," she said. "I understand there are limits to imagination. Perfectly fine. The key is to recognize those limitations and use what will work. And I know this will work. But it depends on your help. I can't use this tank alone. And I don't trust anyone else to help. I won't force you. I'll ask you. Will you help me in this venture?"

Claus paused.

"What is the ultimate goal?" Claus asked.

"What is the goal of any company?" she asked to counter.

"To make money. But this isn't just about making money," Claus said.

"No, it isn't," she said. "I'll make a joke and say I want to conquer the world."

Olivia laughed.

"Not funny," Claus said. "You did that—"

"In your imagination. I know. The Veigon. Cenina Island. All fantasy, of course," she said. "My hope is to help out humanity. Can you imagine if we lived during the Great Depression? What a miserable moment of hunger and despair! It wasn't that long ago. Not really. People still have health problems, many of which are difficult or impossible to solve. How would it be if in time we can find ways to alleviate that suffering? A person paralyzed in youth can regain motor function and live out a happy life. Or another person with blindness can see. A person with tinnitus can gain relief and enjoy music again. Vascular disease? Erased. Mental illness? Cleansed."

"What qualifies as mental illness? Will you be the judge?" Claus asked pointedly.

"Of course not! I didn't invent life. But life did. It will judge. It just needs a helping hand," Olivia said.

"I don't know," Claus said.

"Claus, I don't want to sound like a broken record, but if we don't do this, someone else will come along and hijack the life process. They'll put in play what you fear I'm trying to create now—a regime that controls people and other life at the cellular level. I want everyone to have a way to prevent that. Give them superior resistance to all forms of attack—viral, bacterial, fungal, protozoan, and political."

"It still seems like playing with fire," Claus said.

"Perhaps even extend people's lives," she said.

"Hah! I knew it. Playing God," Claus said.

"You're coloring things too much. People have been living longer by exercising and eating right," Olivia said. "But that has limits. Extend the limits, Claus. Let people have a reason to live. They need not dread the inevitable end, because it no longer need be inevitable."

"Carinians. You're trying to make Carinians," Claus said.

"They fought in your dreams. Can I help that? No. Can I solve all problems? No. Can I make a difference and help in some way? I believe so. Do you really believe these Carinians are what humans would become? That they would destroy themselves except for two—Lanietta and Labba?"

"You really *did* study my dreams, if that's what they were," Claus said. "I'm surprised to hear you speak of what to me was actual experience. In a way, I feel compromised. Like I'm no better than Cloopy."

"You can get up and go home at any time," Olivia said. "I hold no leash over you. No surprise appearances, no pretending to be a 1950s housewife or any other games this Lanietta character played. Well? I ask again—will you help me in this venture?"

"I will help until I feel otherwise. If I sense any abuse of power, I won't just blindly comply."

"You're a 4th principle person. I appreciate that," she said.

Claus's mind went blank with confusion.

"Come on, you know," she continued. "Nuremberg? Principle four? About blindly following superior orders? I agree with you, Claus. Keep morals in play at all times. Yes, I agree."

"You surprise me," Claus said.

"The Hess Rise and Cenina Island are a part of your imagination," she said. "Your 4th principle kicking in and exploring a failure point. Good. Keep those failure points in mind. We'll avoid them. Do you see why you're important? You'll prevent us from wasting effort chasing paths of failure."

"Either you have a great sense of ethics," Claus said.

"Or I'm the slickest, slyest dog to sway your senses," Olivia laughed.

"Slick or sick? Sly or sigh?" Claus asked.

"Yes! Good! Bifurcate and weigh. Mow both sides of the fence. I welcome the honesty check. Keep it coming. Even better is this—do and don't do. Agree but only for a bit. The universe need not be one absolute. Let duality dwell, pairing persist, double do bubble."

"Double do bubble?" Claus laughed. "Double do bubble."

Olivia laughed too.

"I'm the cart, you're the horse. Pull me around, Claus. Pull me around," Olivia said.

"I...I miss my kids," Claus said, suddenly losing laughter for sadness.

"Let me tell you what I think. Your sense of children is the same sense people have when we wish to create something that endures, that will outlive us," Olivia said. "You also sense a loss of this planet. Of Earth. Let's see if we can satisfy both goals. Preserve Earth to endure. I bet in time we could rejuvenate the sun's nuclear fuel—do a hydrogen for helium swap. Wouldn't that be clever?"

"That would be very clever," Claus said. "Making a star young again. Wow. Everyone thinks that Earth will at some point die because of the sun. No one speaks of Earth lasting forever."

"Or of people lasting forever. You see? Worthwhile, attainable goals," she said.

"Worthwhile, yes. Attainable, hardly," Claus said.

"That 4th principle again," she said.

"You're not ordering me to make the sun live forever," Claus said.

"If I were, and you had the ability, would you do so?" she asked. "The 4th principle doesn't force you to say, 'no'. It just gives you the moral obligation to

decide when to say, 'no'. Well? Is solar longevity worthy of a 'no'? If so, we'll stop right now. Tell me the answer, Claus. Tell me if it's time for the 4th."

"On the surface, I'd say yes, make the sun last forever. But it's a naive answer. Who knows the side effects? Progress might stagnate. Earth might become overcrowded. Or its own center might grow old and fail."

"We could rejuvenate that too," Olivia said. "But we'd have to live to see that day. Human longevity would take priority."

"I don't know," Claus said.

"Claus. What do you want out of life?" Olivia asked.

"A doctor would say to get as much out of life as I can," Claus said. "To me, that means taking it easy. Walks in the park. Starting a family and watching children grow."

"I've heard that line too. Lots of people do that. How many are in our position? How many can say, 'I have a unique opportunity to make a difference far more than getting as much as I can out of life'?"

"It's our duty, is that it?" Claus asked.

"That wasn't what I was trying to say," Olivia said. "I feel like we're standing on a mountain ridge. We can look behind us to how people are getting the most out of life. And there's the unknown ahead of us. Could be a bunch of nothing. But it could be more. How long before others climb our ridge? Chris and Patricia are here. They might be the ones. They might decide what happens on this unexplored part of the ridge. They might not care about getting as much as they can out of life. And in the end, there might not be much left to get out of life when they are done."

Claus let out an ugh.

"Okay," Claus said. "But I'm now hungry. Breakfast is in order."

"Agreed!"

The two cleaned up and went out to Patricia's cousin's restaurant for a vegan breakfast.

"Metal and food, metal and food," Claus said.

Olivia laughed.

"It's an odd combination, but you understand," Olivia said. "Patricia's family has the food going, and Chris is pulling Patricia into the metal mining. We're already into metal mining, and you're pulling me into the food business."

"*I'm* pulling you into the food business?" Claus asked.

"It was your dream," Olivia said. "Besides, how much longer do you think Patricia will allow us to eat at her cousin's restaurant? We'll have to eat our own food. Especially if we want to lengthen our lives. Yes, you see? We'll work to make food that will help solve medical problems. Imagine if our food can cure vascular disease. Older people can discard their blood pressure pills. Ideally, pharmacies would all but close down, dispensing only the most critical of drugs. Nourishment and rejuvenation. That's the food of life. That's getting the most out of life. Food!"

And with that, the food arrived.

For the day's remainder, Olivia and Claus did not have such a deep conversation. They spent time in the tank helping Astroosa find new asteroid mines just ahead of advice given by Chris and Patricia. Olivia and Claus also tagged Astroosa mined metals so they could track how they were used in industry. Chris and Patricia somehow sensed when they were beaten and would give out decoy advice to throw off Olivia and Claus. Sometimes it worked, sometimes it didn't. But the result was that some minings were accomplished by these competitors.

"It's okay," Olivia would say. "We can use your link with Patricia to tag those metals too."

And Olivia did. In this way, Olivia and Claus learned manufacturing methods from metals mined by the competitors. Months passed. A few years. Olivia's "Cresson" name was long ago dropped. She was now Olivia Jill Depetti. The two were running their own consulting firm—Gerhardt Depetti Consulting.

"You're the horse, I'm the cart," she would say. "That means *Gerhardt* comes before *Depetti*."

"Why do I feel like the cart is leading the horse?" Claus would often say.

Olivia would always laugh back. Always. The two started their own food business. Coffee processing was first.

"A necessity," Olivia would say. "Ingredients for the tank are at the top of the list."

There were no problems with this venture, as it was a matter of creating a subsidiary company that also sold processed versions of the coffee to various venues—restaurants, grocery stores, and other institutions.

Olivia started another subsidiary company to buy up excess crops from farmers. These crops were processed, reprocessed, refined, and defined into new, vegetable-looking foods. A chain of fast-food vegan restaurants went up next. They were a success. There was no advertisement of the food being useful in treating ailments—it was simply advertised as animal-free all natural vegan nourishment. People's health did improve, and they attributed this to better food. There was no special drug regulations applied toward the food, as it was viewed as just food.

Gerhardt Depetti Consulting prospered. The two ate the food they produced, and neither of them aged. As years went by, the public noticed that those who ate the food maintained a youthful feel and appearance. The day came, however, when the two had a very serious conversation.

"We're on track, Claus," Olivia said. "We've used our knowledge to build an efficient food-processing infrastructure. We're still directing Astroosa on new asteroid mines. Chris and Patricia are only marginally in business. We're extending human life. People are becoming less violent and more philanthropic. I confess things are doing better than I had hoped. I mean, I saw these things from you, from the heavens, and from industry, and I was able to combine them. I have to wonder...no, I cringe at the thought of combining things from toxic sources. Maybe without you I would have devolved into something less pleasant, something more miserable. Brandi's death nearly did me in. I owe a great debt of gratitude to you. And you've checked and cautioned me throughout the entire journey. Do you still miss your other life? With Labba and your children on the lunar near side? And my Aunt Frieda ruling the lunar far side?"

"I...I do miss them. I miss my children," Claus said.

"You once had a thing for my Aunt Frieda," Olivia said.

"I think it was misplaced," Claus said. "I admired her tenacity. Her drive. But I don't think it was love. I guess I'm not sure what love is. Is it sticking with one person and being cruel to the world?"

"You see how others protect their families, and you see how a father can spoil his daughters while abusing the workers under him," Olivia said.

"Yes. I don't like that kind of love," Claus said.

"You can love the world," Olivia said. "You don't have to 'follow orders' of primitive convention and limit yourself to family love. You're a 4th principle person. Love the world. You saw something special in my Aunt Frieda. I agree. She was special. You can't bring her back to life. But you can bring life into this world. If you want. I would give my consent."

"What? What are you saying?" Claus asked.

"She's my aunt. I'm much like her. I would give you a child or two if you like. I won't be your wife or put up any such facade. We still have our work to do. And if you wish to pursue relationships with others, that's fine too. But I will hold you to our work. To our company. Gerhardt Depetti Consulting. To undeath do us not part."

"To undeath do us not part?"

"Well, 'to death do us part' sounds like we will die. I have no plans on dying. Nor should you. So I don't plan on us parting. Your 4th principle might kick in and want to dissolve the company. But then you'd be allowing Chris and Patricia to come back to life and wreak havoc on the peace and prosperity we've created. You would then be answerable to them. I hope you keep that in mind."

"Having children out of wedlock though. I don't know," Claus said.

"You're hung up on that?" Olivia asked.

"It would bother me if I were a child. It would bother me now. My parents married first before having me," Claus said.

Olivia laughed.

"A simple ceremony, invented by people, agnostic of biological function," Olivia said.

"But not agnostic of family bearing and sense of completeness," Claus said. "This is my 4th principle kicking in. If I am to have children, I must have a wife. We would have to raise the children together. I won't play abandon management."

"Is this a proposal?" Olivia said.

"If it is, it—"

"It's the most unorthodox marriage proposal I've ever heard, perhaps the most unorthodox in human history," Olivia said. "Now I have a few 4th principles for you. No churches."

"Agreed."

"No prenups."

"Also agreed."

"I keep Depetti. You keep Gerhardt," she said.

"Mmmm. I'm a bit on the fence with that one."

"I might be the cart in our business, but I can't drop Depetti. I just can't. Cresson taught me that lesson."

"How about a compromise?" Claus said. "You keep Depetti. The children take Gerhardt."

"Since I'm having them for you, agreed," Olivia said. "Conditionally."

"Meaning what?" Claus asked.

"I can also have a child by a different father. And that child will take *my* last name," Olivia said.

Claus fumed.

"You can't be controlling over me," Olivia said. "I said I would give you a child or two. But if I decide I want a child for me, I want that option too. We must be equals in this, Claus. I know it violates convention, but convention doesn't always follow the 4th principle. In fact, it often violates it."

"But the family. The unity of the family," Claus said. "Half-siblings?"

"We are all brothers and sisters in humanity. It's merely a matter of degree—how close or how far. This is something we'll have to instill in our children."

"Almost makes the idea of marriage pointless," Claus said.

"Almost," Olivia said.

"Okay. You can have your own children by the father of your choosing if I get my children first," Claus said.

"Agreed," Olivia said. "Well? Are you done proposing? When are we getting married?"

"Soon enough. One thing. The other father doesn't intrude on our marriage. Or how your own Depetti children are raised. Could be complications."

"Easy enough," Olivia said. "I have NO desire to serve another man. My children will remain my own. However, I will permit you to spend time with them and almost treat them as your own."

"Another almost," Claus said.

"Must always keep a margin for acting otherwise. That 4th principle," Olivia said.

"I'm beginning to wonder about that 4th principle," Claus said.

"It's more work, but it has better long-term rewards. Don't you think? I order you to think that," Olivia said jokingly.

Claus laughed. Olivia laughed.

"By the way, since I can't wear a white wedding dress, I—"

"Why not? More convention?"

"Well, I've been married before," Olivia said. "I could wear pink. Or perhaps I could wear blue and yellow. Like half-Bleuh and half-Greylinger."

"White with black trim. Or black with white trim. Or some other white and black dress," Claus said.

"You catch me by surprise," Olivia said. "Sounds almost bipolar."

"I feel it. I feel both split and unified by this marriage," Claus said.

"You know? I do too," she laughed. "I do too."

Chapter 142: Strain on Claus and Jill

Olivia and Claus were married quietly by a Justice of the Peace in a rented hall. Olivia's family and friends attended. Claus's side was much smaller with Phil from the airfield and Claus's parents—Elaine and Aubert. After the wedding ceremony, the wedding reception started. Food, drink, and socializing became the mainstay.

"I never thought you'd marry," Elaine said to Claus. "You were always against the institution. In fact you said you'd never get married."

"I decided it was time," Claus said. "Now I can have children."

"Don't have to be married for that," Aubert said.

"Aubert! Children should have a good home. Even if there's only one," Elaine said as she gave a hard stare at Claus.

"I didn't make that choice," Claus said. "And I intend to have at least two children."

"I'm so overjoyed! Grandchildren!" Elaine said as she gave Claus a big hug. "A boy and girl would be fine. Remember, Claus, you get to choose."

"It's not that easy. Anyway, we'll do our best," Claus said.

"Do your best?" Elaine asked. "Claus. Do you love Olivia?"

"We work together well. Things are smooth. No arguments. No fights," Claus said.

"Sounds boring," Aubert said.

"You shush," Elaine said to Aubert. "Claus. Do you love her?"

"I guess so," Claus said.

"You guess so," Elaine said. "You don't love her, do you?"

"What is love anyway?" Claus said. "Just a fading sense of satisfaction. Well? We have satisfying work."

"Satisfying work? That's not love. It's about passion. Tenderness. Caring. All the things your father used to do," Elaine said. "Guess the honeymoon is over for Claus. How can this last?"

"You shouldn't speak this way on Claus's day," Aubert said.

"Yes. Exactly," Claus said.

"Well there are the grandchildren. Maybe then you'll understand about love," Elaine said.

"Congratulations, Claus," Phil said as he stopped by. "If you and Olivia want to go for a ride, I have a Super Cub fueled and ready to go."

"Thank you. We might take you up on that," Claus said.

Phil continued on to other friends.

"I don't know if Olivia will want to go up. She might get queasy," Claus said.

"She's never been queasy with airplanes," Elaine said. "Claus? Is there something you're not telling us? Does Olivia have morning sickness?"

Claus paused.

"She does! So this is why you're getting married. So forced and everything," Elaine said.

"Elaine. You're getting nosy," Aubert said.

"If you don't love her, there are other ways," Elaine said. "Though it means waiting longer for grandchildren."

"How can you say such a thing?" Claus said. "I won't have murder on my conscious."

"Then just get an annulment," Elaine continued. "The marriage is invalid."

"No! Mother, please!" Claus said.

"Elaine. Let's go to the bar," Aubert said. "You need a drink."

"I don't need a drink. You need a drink," Elaine said to Aubert.

"We *both* need a drink," Aubert said as he escorted her to the bar.

"Whew!" Claus said. "It's times like this I almost wish I were Cloopy. Not a worry in the world."

At that moment, Claus felt a dog nudge up against him. He turned to see a familiar dog, but it wasn't Cloopy.

"Mocha?"

"So you're Claus," Blair said.

"I feel like I know you," Claus said.

"Frieda used to speak of you frequently," Blair said. "Don't mind my eye twitching. I can only see people by moving my eye around a lot. I have—"

"Macular degeneration," Claus finished. "Which means your central vision is black."

"Yes," she said. "Was I that obvious? I try to be discreet. Anyway, Mocha is my—"

"Seeing eye dog," Claus finished.

"Yes. Did Frieda speak of me?" Blair said.

"She wasn't much for sharing her personal life," Claus said.

"Well you're getting a great woman. Olivia had a shock when her best friend died from that freak accident. Oh, I shouldn't speak of it. It's in bad taste," Blair said. "I guess that's the Shmirkuffle side of me. We tend to speak our minds without thinking."

"Is that your maiden name?" Claus asked.

Blair laughed.

"That's my maiden name *and* last name. I'm not married!" Blair said.

"Oh," Claus said. "I guess I thought a pretty girl like you would have been grabbed first thing."

Blair blushed.

"The truth is, the men I've dated see my limitations and take a pass. They want someone who isn't...damaged," Blair said.

"I don't see how they can think that," Claus said, and he took to his knee and said, "Nor do I see how they can pass up spending time with adorable Mocha."

Mocha warmed up to Claus.

"Mocha? How strange. Mocha is only like that to Cloopy," Blair said. "I guess Mocha misses the walks."

"That's a shame. Olivia used to take Cloopy out for walks, but lately it's all been work, work, work," Claus said. "Cloopy gets house crazy."

"Well if you ever need a walk-mate, Mocha and I are at your service," Blair said with a bow.

At that moment, Olivia looked over and caught Claus's eye. She stared at him in disapproval.

"I...great," Claus said, a little thrown off.

The wedding party concluded. Olivia and Claus went back to work, but Olivia found that the pregnancy disturbed the images with Claus, and she could not focus as easily in the tank.

"Do you see them?" Olivia would ask Claus. "The images of the fetus? I can't focus on mining and our food processing. I..."

"I think you need to take a break," Claus said.

"Yeah. I...maybe a cat nap. Clear my mind," Olivia said.

Claus helped Olivia out of the tank. She went upstairs, changed clothes, and sat on the couch for only a moment before she dozed off. Cloopy jumped up on her and woke her.

"Cloopy, no," Olivia said.

"I'll take him for a walk," Claus said.

"Good idea. He needs the..." Olivia started to say, but she fell back asleep.

Claus took a leash to Cloopy and took him out for a walk. He went to the end of the block and turned to the right, going several more blocks until he reached a park. There sitting on a bench was Blair with Mocha. Claus walked over.

"A familiar scene," Claus said.

"I wondered how long it would take," Blair said. "Ready for a walk?"

"Why not?" Claus said.

The two walked along with Mocha and Cloopy next to each other and beside the humans.

"They do like each other," Claus said. "I bet they never have to worry about a coffee tank."

"What do you mean?" Blair asked.

"Oh, I guess I shouldn't have said that," Claus said.

"Doesn't matter to me," Blair said. "I'm just happy to get around by myself. With a little help from Mocha."

"Don't you ever get the itch to do something more? Like take over the world?" Claus asked.

Blair laughed.

"Take over the world? Sounds like fantasy," Blair said. "No, I can't imagine trying to do something so incredibly stressful as that. Mocha and I are quite fine with our happy lives together. Well, almost fine. If it were just us, we would be fine."

"Meaning?"

"Frieda, of course. Still can't believe she's dead. I know, it's been a while and all. That's the problem with friends. Eventually, they leave you," Blair said. "But not Mocha. Right Mocha?"

Mocha barked back in affirmation. Cloopy barked too.

"Every morning when I wake, I ask myself what is there to get me through the day. And the answer is the same. Mocha," Blair said.

"What about your family?" Claus asked.

"My parents have passed, bless their souls. No siblings. I'm an only child," Blair said.

"Yeah, so am I. An only child I mean. People say that means I'm spoiled. But I never thought of myself as spoiled," Claus said.

"I think some only-childers are spoiled. But others just grow up to be who they will be," Blair said.

"Just what kind of name is Shmirkuffle?" Claus asked.

"Sounds made up, doesn't it?" Blair asked.

"Yes. It does," Claus said.

"It probably is," Blair laughed. "But I challenge you to find another Shmirkuffle on Earth. You'll be hard pressed to find one."

"There's a little-league game across the street. Want to go watch? I mean, oh, can you—"

"It's okay," Blair said. "I can sorta see. Sure, I'd love to."

The two started to cross the street, but as they did, Mocha became distracted by a dog across the street and pulled hard on her leash, dragging Blair along quickly. A car ran a red light and was going to hit Blair, but Cloopy jumped at Blair and knocked her out of the way only to be hit by the car. The car sped away. Blair fell to the ground, safe for the moment. Claus quickly ran to her aid and lifted her to her feet. But the mood became somber as they quickly realized the tragedy that had unfolded.

"Poor Cloopy!" Blair said.

Claus knelt by him and touched his neck, looking for a pulse.

"He didn't make it," Claus said.

"Claus. I'm so sorry," Blair said. "I should have had better control of Mocha. I'm responsible for this. You must hate me."

"Of course I don't hate you," Claus said. "What I don't know is how I'm going to break this to Olivia. First Brandi, now Cloopy."

"Let me tell her," Blair said.

"No. I don't want you taking the blame for it. I'll tell her I went out on a walk with Cloopy, he got away from me, and a car hit him. No sense in dragging you into this. And it's true. I *was* walking Cloopy, and he *did* get away from me."

"But it's not the entire truth," Blair said.

"It seems the world is that way these days," Claus said.

"I don't understand," Blair said.

"Supplying information to Astroosa is based on the kind of truth provided. Guess I'm used to spinning things a certain way to achieve a desired goal."

A police car drove up and called for animal services to haul Cloopy away. Animal services arrived and did just that. Blair's nerves were shot from the affair. She shook with anxiety.

"I'd better go home," she said. "I'm a total wreck."

"Need some company?" Claus asked.

"You'd better tell Olivia immediately," Blair said. "I'll...I'll be okay."

"All right then," Claus said. "But I'll check on you later."

"Thank you," she said, and the two parted ways.

Claus returned home without Cloopy. Olivia was no longer napping on the couch and was nowhere in the normal living area. Claus went downstairs to find her in the tank by herself.

"You're in the tank?" Claus said. "Must be lonely."

"Not really," Olivia said. "I'm sharing images with Ben."

"Ben? There's no one here but you. And me," Claus said.

"Ben is my unborn boy," she said. "You know, I bet I'm the first woman to communicate with her unborn child like this. I'm getting very simple primal thoughts. Blood flow, moving around. But no breathing. Can you imagine being alive without having to breathe? Ben is doing that right now. And he doesn't have to eat. No other needs either. It's the ultimate existence. It inspires me. It inspires me to find a way for people who struggle to eat or breathe to find other ways to survive. We should start a medical line, Claus, to help those people. No indigestion, no starvation, no choking—it can be eliminated. What do you think?"

"I have bad news, Olivia. Cloopy was hit by a car. He's dead," Claus said.

"Did he suffer?"

"No."

"Good. Well, I knew his time would come. Let's have him cremated and move on. This medical work must be rushed along. I sense Patricia and Chris are thinking of the same thing, and we can't let them get a scoop. I won't be needing you for a while. Ben and I can figure this out. Why don't you relax? Drink a beer and watch a movie? I'll be up in a bit," she said.

Claus looked at her strangely. She didn't look back but remained fixated on communicating with Ben. A chill came over him, and he sensed his wife drifting from Olivia to Jill.

"Maybe I'll do some shopping," Claus said.

"There you go. A good idea as usual," she said.

Claus took his car to the grocery store and walked around without a cart. He wasn't so much shopping as he was wondering about Olivia's latest idea.

"All kinds of food and drink here," Claus said. "To think that one day this store won't exist because of Olivia. The food that people take pleasure in will be gone."

After walking up and down all aisles for the length of the store, Claus reached the far end, which contained the liquor supplies.

"Even alcohol will be discarded," Claus said. "Even...hey, look. Elderberry wine. Grandma Broc. Wish I could have a sip with her now. Wish I could...hey, I know."

Claus purchased the bottle of elderberry wine and a bouquet of flowers. He then headed over to Blair's apartment and knocked on the door. She answered.

"Anyone looking for a little cheer?" Claus asked.

"I could always use a little cheer," Blair said. "What lovely flowers. For me? Come in. I was just cleaning up after dinner. Have you eaten? I could fix you something."

Blair found a vase for the flowers and placed them on the dining table.

"I brought refreshments too," Claus said, producing the bottle of wine.

Blair took the bottle and struggled to read it.

"Looks like wine," she said.

"Elderberry wine," Claus said.

"Really? I've heard it takes an acquired taste to handle," she said. "You'd better have something to eat first. I can warm up what I made. It's just a simple mix of rice, vegetables, ground beef, and tomato sauce. I have bakery bread too."

"That would be fine," Claus said.

Blair warmed up the food while Mocha kept Claus company at the dining table.

"I told Olivia," Claus said.

"I'm sorry, I can't hear you over the dishwasher," Blair said.

Blair stopped the dishwasher.

"You didn't have to do that," Claus said.

"It's fine. I'll let it resume in a bit," she said.

Blair brought out the food. She opened the bottle of wine and filled a wine glass each. She also nibbled on a bit of bread.

"Olivia. I told her about Cloopy," Claus said.

"How did she take it?" Blair asked.

"Better than I thought. As if she didn't care," Claus said.

"I can't believe that," Blair said.

"She's highly focused on our work. And she has...no, I shouldn't say," Claus said.

"Then don't. I'm tasting this wine, and it's not bad. It's actually palatable," Blair said.

"Is that so?" Claus said. "I'm glad. Can't have two tragedies in one day—Cloopy, and my selection of wine."

"You're too hard on yourself. Try the wine," Blair said.

Claus took a sip and gagged. Blair laughed.

"You're not used to drinking wine, are you?" she chuckled.

"No."

"More bending of the truth?" she asked.

"It's just...my Grandma Broc told me to remember elderberry wine. And, I don't know, I was...I was walking through the grocery store thinking about...no...yes, I must say it. Thinking about what life would be like without the food there."

"What? Wait, let me get something that will help," Blair said.

She disappeared for a moment and returned with chilled champagne.

"Here. Try this," she said.

Claus took a sip.

"Ahh. Very good," he said. "I guess I'm terrible with alcohol."

"Don't worry about it," Blair said. "Whatever is troubling you, let it go. Think about the things you do have. It's those things that will see you through until tomorrow."

"That's just the thing. I'm quickly running out of things," Claus said. "Okay, I'm going to say it. Olivia is expecting."

"Congratulations!" Blair said. "A loving wife and baby."

"Except I don't love Olivia," Claus said.

"Don't say that," Blair said. "You're married to her. She's your wife."

"My mother was right. I don't love Olivia. Oh, this champagne must be hitting me hard. I'm babbling on and all," Claus said, and he drained the glass of champagne.

"Easy, sport!" Blair said. "I don't want you getting drunk. Now repeat after me. I love Olivia. I love her. Yes, I do."

"You love Olivia. You love her. Yes, you do," Claus grinned.

"Wise guy," Blair giggled. "You're pouring another glass of champagne. You've had two glasses already."

"And I'm going to have a third," Claus said. "Elderberry can wait."

"I'd better have champagne too, then, if nothing else than to keep you from drinking it all yourself," Blair said.

Blair grabbed the glass. But Claus wouldn't let go. The two wrestled for control. Blair lost her grip, the glass shot toward Claus, and the champagne went flying onto his face and shirt. Blair laughed.

"Serves you right!" she said.

"I thought you couldn't see," Claus said.

"Anyone can figure out what was going to happen. And it did. Let me get you a towel," she said.

Blair went into the kitchen and retrieved a kitchen towel. She returned to the dining room to find that Claus had already removed his shirt. She tossed the towel at him. The towel took on the characteristic of a wing and shot away from him, landing on the floor.

"I'll get it," Claus said.

"I'll get it," Blair said at the same time.

Blair went for the towel, and Claus leaned back in his chair to reach it, but he leaned too far and fell atop Blair.

"What are you doing, Mr. Clumsy!" she laughed.

"I thought I could lean back and get the towel," Claus laughed too.

"Did you forget about gravity? This isn't outer space. Or the moon," she said. "Now pull yourself up. I'm trapped."

Claus tried to get up, but his senses were dulled by the champagne.

"I can't," Claus said.

"Mocha, help!" Blair laughed.

But Mocha stayed away.

"Smart dog. Doesn't want to become entrapped," Claus said.

"Seems that's what you've done to me. Very well," Blair said, and she pulled herself out. But when she did, her fingernails caught on Claus's back and dug into his skin.

"Oh! I'm so sorry! I thought...never mind!" she said. "Let me help you up!"

Blair managed to pull Claus to his feet. He nearly toppled over. But she caught him. To do so, though, meant she had to wrap her arms around his chest.

"I...oh, let's put you on the couch," she said.

"What's wrong, Blair?" Claus asked.

"I...I'm not ready for this," she said.

"Ready for what?" he asked.

"Clawing a man's back and touching his bare chest, that's what!" she said. "Now you sit there and rest a moment. I'll be back."

Blair ran off and returned with a wet towel over her head.

"Better," she said.

"If I didn't know better, I'd say that—"

"Don't say any more about it," she said.

"About what?" Claus asked.

"It!"

The two exchanged an awkward silence.

"Tell me about your work before this silence drives me crazy with...never mind what," Blair said.

"Okay, I will," Claus said. "Because I don't care if the world or Mocha or even the Carinians know."

"Who are the Carinians?" Blair asked.

"Never mind. Blair, Olivia and I have a unique way of obtaining information. This information has helped Astroosa with mining, and it helps us with our food processing industry. We also use it against Chris and Patricia. Olivia and I use a tank filled with coffee and special instruments. We then sit in this tank back-to-back and rest the back of our heads together. Somehow Olivia made the technology, and it works. It's like nothing ever invented."

"Sounds weird so far. And I'm the first to know about it?" Blair asked.

"No, you're not. Chris and Patricia stole our first tank from us to do the very same thing. We had to make a second tank. But we didn't turn them in. Instead, we use their tank against them and limit how much information they can sell. We run the whole thing," Claus said.

"Is this for real? This can't be true," Blair said.

"Cross my heart. It's true. How do you think we've made so much money? And Astroosa has become so profitable? Because of Olivia's tank. I told her about my dreams of Carinians and how I had a son and daughter, and we came to a deal that she would have children for me."

"I see," Blair said.

"They would take my name, of course. She's expecting a boy, and he's already got a name. Ben. But she's been communicating with him using the tank. Olivia wants to give people ways to survive like her unborn child—with no needs. That means no breathing, eating, or whatever," Claus said. "So as I walked through the grocery store, I imagined what it would be like if food were no longer sold. It felt like the end of an era, the death of an old friend. Then I remembered my Grandma Broc and her advice on elderberry wine. Now I'm here telling you."

"I don't know what to say. I can understand how you feel about losing food and that. But there are people like me who are stuck with a handicap. If she can help restore what we've lost, how can I argue? I guess progress has its price. I try to adapt along with it," Blair said.

"You're taking this better than I am," Claus said. "I'm horrified."

"So is that what you meant by taking over the world? You believe she is doing that?" Blair asked.

"Yes, I do. You know what else? We made another deal. After she gives me two children, she can have her own child with another man if she likes, and that child will have her last name—Depetti."

"Claus!" Blair said. "That's cheating!"

"But I made the deal before the wedding," Claus said.

"I'm not sure why," Blair said. "Sounds like an open marriage."

"Maybe it is."

"What else did you two agree to? Or should we leave it at that?" Blair asked.

"I don't know. I just realized something—we'll need a paternity test for each child she has, so we can decide the last name of the child," Claus said.

"Seems like a lot of work," Blair said.

"Yes. It does. Everything is a lot of work with Olivia," Claus said.

Just then, Blair's telephone rang.

"Hello? Yes, he is. Want to speak with him? Oh. Okay. I'll tell him. Goodbye," Blair said, and she hung up the telephone.

"Olivia?"

"Yes. Says you can come home now. She's finished for the day," Blair said.

Claus stood but immediately fell back down.

"I'll call a cab," Blair said.

Blair did just that. Claus rode home in the cab. He stumbled to the front doorstep, let himself in, and plopped on the couch. But Claus's wife had already gone to bed for the night. Not able to do much, Claus passed out and spent the night on the couch.

Claus dreamed he was on an island by himself. The island was small, and he could see water on all sides. It was a vacuous dream, with nothing to see or do. He looked across the horizon and thought he saw a flashing point of light, as if someone were trying to signal him. But he couldn't make out the code.

"I have nothing but my own speech, my own language to keep me company in this isolation. Oh where am I? What am I to do?" he asked himself.

The dream ended, and he awoke to morning. Claus took to his feet from the couch and walked around. Where was Olivia? It was at that moment he heard a bass clarinet playing from the basement. He approached the basement door and saw a reed—not a double reed, but a single reed, and one meant for Olivia's bass clarinet.

"Olivia?" Claus called.

Claus took the steps down into the basement.

"Olivia?" Claus called again.

Claus came across her playing the bass clarinet while sitting in the tank.

"I think I'm done with that name," she said.

"What name?" Claus asked.

"Olivia. It was a nice try, but it won't do. Jill's here to stay," Jill said.

"Olivia! Stop playing around," Claus said.

"And you stop calling me that!" she said. "Call me Jill."

"I won't," Claus said.

"Your author is," Jill said. "Says so in his book."

"How...me...you..." Claus started.

Jill simply laughed.

"I won't have this kind of talk, Jill. I mean Olivia!" Claus stumbled.

"See?" she laughed. "You can't help it. My proper name rolls right off your tongue. Anyway, for you it doesn't matter."

"What does *that* mean?" Claus asked.

"I must abrogate our agreement," Jill said.

"No you don't," Claus said. "I'm the 4th principle guy, remember?"

"Yes. It's by that principle that compels me to act. It's no longer appropriate for me to yield Ben to you. I have need of him to complete my work. But your part is at an end. You have nothing left to contribute," Jill said.

"What kind of talk is that? Of course I can contribute," Claus said.

"Not in the ways that matter," Jill said.

"You're getting a god complex," Claus warned.

"No, you're getting soft," Jill said. "I've worked it out. Cloopy died from your negligence. There's too much negligence in this world. There must be buffers, compensators, and correctors for error and failure. Life adapts by creating new life. I shall create new life. And I speak not just of Ben. Take a look at those papers on the stand there."

Claus walked over to the stand and read.

"You're dissolving the partnership?" Claus asked. "Shouldn't we have discussed this?"

"We are discussing it now," Jill said. "We can remain friends of course."

"Of course. As my wife, we should at least be friends," Claus said sarcastically. "What's come over you anyway?"

"Read the next document," she said.

Claus flipped through to the next document.

"You're divorcing me?"

"Part of the abrogation," she said.

"This is just like before," Claus said. "First with Chris, now me. Who's your next husband of the week?"

"I won't have that kind of talk," Jill said. "I'm sorry things have come to this. I couldn't have foreseen things ending this way. I really thought you and I would spend our lives in the tank. But things accelerated. Anyway, you'll be fine. When I'm done with Ben, you may have him."

"*Done* with Ben? *I* may have him? *You* haven't even had him yet!" Claus pointed out.

"It's a timing thing," Jill said. "Even as we speak, things are changing. Yesterday I planned to keep him until he was a week old. This morning until age five. A moment ago until eighteen. You see? Things are always in flux. Always changing."

"This isn't natural, this speed or timing. You're not basing your judgment on people or family," Claus said.

"Exactly! Too often people limit themselves by such. There need not be those limitations! Anyway, I'm moving in with Josh Craigen this afternoon. You may help move my things," Jill said.

"Josh can help you," Claus said. "I'm going for a walk. A very long walk."

Claus left. It felt strange walking without Cloopy. Invariably, he ended up at the park. Blair was tossing a toy ball for Mocha. Claus paused.

"Be sure of what you do next, Mr. Claus Gerhardt," he said to himself. "You're in a precarious situation."

Claus turned around and headed away from the park. But after several paces, he stopped, turned around, and faced the park. He took a step toward it.

"What are you doing, Claus?" he asked himself. "You're a married man."

He took another step toward the park.

"Claus? Turn around and walk away," he urged himself. "Married, remember?"

But then a determination overcame him, and he answered himself.

"Not for long, my friend. Not for long."

Chapter 143: The Blair Affair

"Well hello, Claus," Blair said as Claus reached her in the park.

"I need to talk. I need to walk. I need to...I don't know what I need. It's Jill. She's obsessed again. She's..." Claus rambled.

"She's Jill now?" Blair asked. "Come along, Mocha. We're going for a walk."

Blair, Mocha, and Claus went for a walk.

"She's keeping my son, Ben," Claus said. "She's divorcing me, and she's pulling out of the partnership."

"Three strikes," Blair said. "I'm so sorry."

"You don't sound surprised," Claus said.

"Somehow I'm not," Blair said. "I've worried about Olivia or Jill each day since Brandi passed. I could go on about how people cope with loss—her obsessions or my loss of vision. But there's such a thing as too much talk. It really gets you nowhere."

"Which is why I must keep walking," Claus said.

"Are you getting anywhere?" Blair laughed.

"I don't know how you can laugh," Claus said.

"I have to. Keeps me going. Makes me feel like I'm going somewhere," Blair said.

"I can't laugh my way around. People will think I'm crazy," Claus said.

"So let them. That's their problem," Blair said. "What makes you laugh, Claus?"

"I...I'm not sure. Not much, I guess," Claus said.

Blair laughed.

"Now what?" Claus said, laughing a little.

"A-hah! There! Caught you!" Blair said with a grin. "You laugh when I laugh. That wasn't so hard, was it?"

"I can't go around laughing when you laugh. I have things to do. I—"

"You do?" Blair laughed. "Jill just dumped you."

"And I have to deal with that," Claus said.

"By laughing. That's all you need do," Blair said.

"There's still our child. Ben. At first she said she'd let me have him. Then she said she'll keep him. She really changes her mind a lot," Claus said.

"Laugh when she does. The more she changes her mind, the more you laugh. See? You're laughing now," Blair laughed. "I have a question for you. If talking leads to walking, what does laughing lead to?"

"Waffling?" Claus suggested.

"Show me that. Show me waffling!" Blair said.

Claus stumbled and walked side to side.

"Are you sure that's waffling?" she asked.

Claus held out his arms to his sides and flapped them lightly like wings. But he stopped, like he wasn't sure if he should flap or not.

"I'm waffling," he said.

"What if you waffle in your step?" Blair asked.

"I...can...waffle in my step. Waffle with more pep. Waffle in stride, in smile, in voice and style. Waffle in my waffle, unexpected and inflected. Because waffling is infectious. It's delicious and fictitious. Bee-do-boo-bee-do-boy. Ah, bee, saw, da, lee!" Claus danced.

"You've got it now," Blair said.

"The ultimate way to waffle is to sprout wings and explore the heavens. Do you know what I could go for now?" Claus asked. "A ride in a Super Cub. What do you say?"

"You mean me watch you fly around in an airplane?" Blair asked.

"No. You come with me. We go loop-de-loop," Claus said.

"Oh, wait," Blair said, a bit nervous.

Claus laughed.

"That's not funny. I could get sick," Blair said.

"Then laugh it off, Miss Laffle-Hopper," Claus said.

"You're calling me names now?" Blair said with a little chuckle. "Aren't we getting a little familiar? Well? Does your plane have a red nose, Santa?"

"That's not fair. You're making fun of my name," Claus said.

"Laugh it off, Mr. Laffle-Snoot!" she said.

"Let's see who's the laffle-snoot at ten thousand feet, Miss Laffle-Lark," Claus said.

"Okay. I'll do it. But you owe me dinner—after the plane ride, not before. I don't want to lose it in the air!"

"Deal," Claus said.

"Are you going to tell Jill?" Blair asked.

"I will. After we go. And if she's interested. I doubt she is," Claus said.

"Well. I guess I'd better have a good belly laugh now. In case that plane ride leaves my belly behind!"

"You'll be fine. I'll..." Claus started.

But Claus remembered how he didn't like flying with a parachute or any other fail-safe. The thought of crashing with Blair aboard, or with Blair falling out without a chute—this overwhelmed him. It was time to make a change.

"I'll...we'll each wear a parachute. If you fall out, just pull the cord," Claus grinned.

"Just pull the cord! Now that's an instant laugh! Fall from the sky, pull the cord or die!"

"Indeed," Claus said. "Indeed!"

"Let me drop Mocha off with Marna," Blair said. "I sense hesitation, Claus?"

"If Marna sees you with me, what will she think?" Claus said.

"Think of this. Jill is divorcing you, that much you learned today, which means Marna already knows. The spouse is always the last to know," Blair said. "She'll think nothing of it. In fact, she might be grateful."

"You're kidding," Claus said.

Blair laughed.

"A joke?" Claus said.

Blair shrugged her shoulders.

"I see. Word games," Claus said.

"Come along," Blair said. "Let's go for that plane ride."

Blair walked Mocha and Claus back toward Jill's house, which of course was by Marna's house. They reached Jill's house first, at which Blair spoke.

"Get the car ready. I'll be but a moment," Blair said.

Claus did get the car ready. He rolled down the window and watched Blair have a brief conversation with Marna before turning Mocha over. Marna turned toward Jill's house and saw Claus there. She motioned Claus over. Claus drove over, parked, and exited the vehicle. He then walked up to Blair and Marna.

"You weren't going to make Blair walk all the way over to Jill's without Mocha, were you? You should take better care of your women," Marna said.

"Lanietta? Is that you finally?" Claus asked.

"Lanietta?" Marna said in surprise. "You're right, Blair, he *does* need looking after. I'll watch your dog, and you watch Jill's."

"That's Lanietta, all right. C'mon, you Carinian you. What's your game?" Claus asked.

"Better go now. Let me know how the ride goes," Marna said, and she returned inside her house with Mocha.

"Let's go, Claus," Blair said with her arm around his. "Escort me to the car, will you?"

Claus did so. He helped her in. He went to the driver's side himself, got in, started up the car, and drove off to the airfield.

"See? She was grateful," Blair said.

"What did you tell her?" Claus asked.

"Oh, we just had a little woman-to-woman talk. She feels badly about your situation. And yes, she knows about the divorce. Says not to worry about Cloopy, and that you need someone to look after you until you get through this. She'll miss you," Blair said.

"Miss me?"

"Well, you don't expect the ex-inlaws to invite you over for Sunday dinner, do you?" Blair said.

"No, I guess not," Claus said.

Claus headed for the airfield.

"I'm so nervous and excited," Blair said. "Maybe it's best I can't see straight ahead. It would be like—"

"Those people on that doomed DC-10 in the 1970s, watching the cockpit video feed of their crash as it happened," Claus finished.

"I wasn't going to say that!" Blair said. "You shouldn't be so gloomy!"

"I must," Claus said. "I must be aware of every possible failure, both historical and potential. It might seem ghoulish, but it's kept me alive. So far."

"What a horrible way to live," Blair said. "I don't dwell on such things. I move on."

"And so must I, apparently," Claus said. "Though unwillingly."

"Is that what you do, Claus? Hold onto failure and wait for the next? That isn't living. That isn't life."

"I appreciate your concern. I wasn't always like this. I was more trusting. But that only goes so far. Anyway, we're here. There's Phil by the plane now," Claus said.

Claus parked and led Blair over to Phil and the Super Cub.

"Sorry to hear about you and Jill," Phil said.

"Does everyone know but me?" Claus asked.

"Yeah," Phil said.

"Well just because—" Claus started, but he was interrupted.

"I'm sorry. I've forgotten my manners. My name is Phil. And who do I have the pleasure of meeting?" Phil said to Blair as he shook her hand.

"Blair Shmirkuffle," she replied as Phil turned the handshake into a kiss of her

hand. "How charming of you, Phil. Are you so friendly with fliers around here?"

"Only beautiful ones," Phil said. "And so far just you."

"What would Delina say?" Claus asked.

"Delina? Who's that?" Phil asked.

"Your wife, remember? And her dog shows?" Claus asked.

"You know I'm not married," Phil said. "Are you feeling okay?"

Then Claus remembered that this was the Phil before Phil interacted with Tony Kavalla and the F-8.

"He's just toying with you," Blair covered.

"Oh, I see. Protecting your new territory. I get the message. I'll steer clear. You have the runway, my friend," Phil said, thinking Claus was now pursuing a relationship with Blair.

Phil left.

"Thank you," Claus said.

"Jill mentioned a woman by that name at Astroosa," Blair said.

"I've had dreams of the future, I guess," Claus said. "In the dream, Astroosa sent people to the moon and later to Mars. Well, in one part, Phil was helping Tony Kavalla with an F-8 and mentioned that his (Phil's) wife, Delina, liked dog shows."

"Very unusual," Blair said.

"I'll help you into the plane. Here, climb in," Claus said.

Claus helped her in then helped himself in. He started the plane, taxied down the runway, and took off. He gained altitude gradually then leveled into comfortable flight.

"How are you back there?" Claus called.

"Doing fine," Blair said.

"Are you still strapped in?"

"Yes. Go ahead and do your worst," she said.

"Here we go!" Claus said.

Claus did a loop.

"That was an inside loop," Claus said.

"I felt heavy," Blair said.

"Here's a spin," Claus said.

Blair didn't speak but instead let out a warble that sounded like a sick bird. Claus laughed.

"Oh, that made me sick. These acrobatic planes are fun to watch, but I've never been in one," Blair said. "This *is* an acrobatic plane, right?"

"Uh, no," Claus said.

"What? Is this safe?" she asked.

"It's as safe as I command it," Claus said. "Then again, in my dream, I crashed it."

"Well let's not do that," Blair said.

"Are you laughing now?" Claus asked as he put the Super Cub into another inside loop.

Blair tried to laugh, but it came out as another sick bird.

"Let's fly normally for a bit. Soak in the countryside," Claus said.

Claus did fly level, but then he remembered Blair's vision impairment.

"Oh, this is probably boring," Claus said.

"I can feel the wind buffeting. I can see the scenery in my peripheral vision. It's something," Blair said.

"We'll make a wide turn around and head back," Claus said. "I think I've made you squawk like a bird enough."

"Squawk like a bird?" Blair said. "Just you wait until we reach the ground. I'm going to pinch you for that."

The two approached the airstrip but were surprised to see a plane burning on the runway. Claus was told he could not land on the runway but could instead land at a nearby airstrip. Claus agreed and did just that. When he landed, he helped Blair out. He was greeted by a friend at this other airstrip.

"Stubby!" Claus said.

"Claus!" Stubby said. "Guess you heard about Jill and Josh."

"Yeah. They are moving in together," Claus said. "How did you know that? Boy, details get around fast."

"That's not what I meant. They made an emergency landing. At the very airport you were just—"

"That was Jill and Josh?"

Someone ran up to Stubby, whispered in his ear, and ran off.

"They got the fire under control. They're both alive, Claus. Both are being taken to County Hospital," Stubby said.

"My car is at the other airstrip," Claus said.

"Your car will be safe, but the airstrip is closed. You won't be able to get to it," Stubby said.

"Can you take me to the hospital?" Claus asked.

"That I can," Stubby said.

"I...maybe I should..." Blair stumbled.

"Come with me. Please?" Claus begged.

"It's not my place. I don't want to cause trouble," Blair said.

"Please?" Claus pleaded.

Blair paused. She finally agreed.

"Thank you. Let's go, Stubby."

Stubby took Blair and Claus to County Hospital. Claus and Blair thanked him and watched him drive off before themselves going inside the hospital. There Claus asked for Jill.

"She's in surgery. You'll have to wait," the attendant said.

"Surgery? For what?" Claus asked.

"HIPAA regulations prevent me from—"

"I'm her husband. At least for another day. What's wrong?" Claus asked.

The attendant gave a disapproving look in Blair's direction.

"She's a friend of the family. It's okay," Claus said.

"I'm sorry. If she wishes to tell you, then maybe—"

"Forget it," Claus said. "Just let me see her."

"Not until she's out of surgery," the attendant said.

"How long will that be?" Claus asked.

"Check back in an hour," the attendant said.

Claus rolled his eyes.

"Come along, Blair," Claus said. "It's no good waiting around here."

"No. We should wait," Blair said. "She's still your wife. Just wait, Claus."

Claus looked around. A small coffee shop caught his attention just past the front desk.

"She always likes coffee. To an extreme. Guess I should get some," Claus said.

The two entered the coffee shop. Claus ordered the strongest coffee on the menu, but Blair simply ordered bottled water and a muffin.

"I don't drink coffee," she said. "Puts unnecessary stress on my retina. You should get a muffin too. Put some happiness in that churning stomach of yours."

"I can't eat," Claus said.

The two sat—Claus with his coffee, and Blair with her water and muffin.

"Thank you for the plane ride," Blair said.

"Doesn't mean much now, does it?" Claus asked. "Oh, my life is a mess."

Blair laughed.

"What's so funny?"

"You. The man with perfect health has a messed-up life," she said.

"Well? It is," he continued.

"I only have a messed up retina, and I don't complain. Many have worse health problems. Look at Jill. She's the one suffering, not you."

"I'm suffering. I am. I know, I make myself suffer. I should just do like others and compromise my awareness with psychotics."

"A pill a day keeps the doctor away? Not today," Blair said. "Open your mouth."

"Why?"

"Just open it. Hold it open," Blair said.

Blair took a piece of her muffin and placed it in his mouth.

"Chew and swallow. That's all you have to do. Chew and swallow."

Claus did so, but with much effort. He swallowed as if forcing down a horse pill.

"See? Not so bad," she said.

"What would you do in my place?" Claus asked.

"I'd see normally," Blair laughed.

"Again, not funny," Claus said.

"I would. Because you can. Though you do not wish it. Stop borrowing trouble to feed failure. Spend time and drink success. Too bad this isn't a pub. Could use a real drink," Blair said.

"You *won't* drink coffee, but you *will* drink alcohol?" Claus asked.

"How else can one drink to success?" Blair asked.

"I don't believe it. What success can there be now?"

"There's always success for those who wish to find it," Blair said. "What do you wish, Claus?"

Claus took a hard look at Blair.

"Yes. You can do that. You can look straight at me and see me. Success right there. I can't do that. A dead person can't either. You have more power than all of them. Celebrate it, Claus. Celebrate success," Blair said.

"Okay. Tell me then. What is success? Jill thinks she found it with her coffee tank. Made us well off," Claus said.

"True. Her success. Not yours. You must search for it," Blair said.

"Really? How? Go to the moon? To Mars?"

"If that's what you wish," Blair said. "You must want it, though. Doing something because you can is not enough. There must be passion. I used to have passion. I used to have dreams. Still do, but they are very small. Small enough to attain. But not large enough to be noticed."

"I don't know if that's good or bad," Claus said.

"Does it matter?"

A doctor walked up to the attendant. The attendant pointed toward Claus and Blair, and the doctor walked over to them.

"Claus Gerhardt?" she said.

"Yes."

"I'm Doctor Zollow. Would you come with me please?" she suggested.

"May Blair come too?" Claus asked.

"Is she family?" Doctor Zollow asked.

"I'm Blair Shmirkuffle, a friend of the family."

Doctor Zollow gave Blair a funny look.

"Family only," the doctor said.

"It's all right," Blair said to Claus. "Go."

"I'll be right back," Claus said.

The doctor took Claus to a private room and spoke with him.

"Your wife was seriously injured in a plane crash," the doctor said.

"Crash? I thought it was just a fire," Claus said.

"It was both. We did everything we could. I'm sorry, Claus. She didn't make it," the doctor said.

"The baby. What about the baby?" Claus asked.

"We couldn't save the baby either," the doctor said.

Claus stared at the doctor in shock. Strangely enough, Blair's words about success in seeing straight ahead came to his mind. He was ashamed for thinking about success in a moment of misery. No human deserved such indignity in death.

"I wish to see her," Claus said.

"I must warn you, the fire caused great trauma. She suffered third degree burns. It might do you more harm than good," the doctor said.

"I want to see her one last time. I must know how things ended for her. I must see her. I'll put Blair's words to the test. Success is what I see straight on. I must succeed in seeing Jill," Claus said.

Claus was led into the morgue. A sheet was lifted, and there was Jill. Or was it?

"It can't be her," Claus said. "I mean, it doesn't look human. Like something from a horror movie. How can anyone look like that? How can anyone be like that?"

Claus closed his eyes and imagined everyone on Earth looking like Jill's burnt corpse. He shuddered at the thought and was fearful that even now she might exert an unknown force and ability to connect with his back and skull to share images with him. He opened his eyes suddenly to prevent such images, and to his relief saw the youthful faces of the living, breathing hospital staff.

"I'm done here," Claus said.

"I'm sorry," Doctor Zollow said.

Claus returned to the coffee shop and found Phil standing while speaking with Blair, who remained seated.

"Stubby told me he dropped you off here. I brought your car," Phil said.

"I can't drive," Claus said. "I'm too...too...distraught."

"Thank you anyway, Phil," Blair said.

"I need to leave. This place smells like death. I smell like death," Claus said.

"I'll take you home," Phil said.

"No. Not where Jill and I stayed. Not my old house either. I...maybe...I don't know...a motel, I guess," Claus stumbled.

"Can you take us to my place?" Blair suggested. "I'll watch him."

Phil nodded in agreement. He took Blair and Claus to Blair's place.

"What should I do with your car?" Phil asked as the two were about to go inside Blair's place.

"Burn it," Claus said.

Claus and Blair went inside her place. The door to Blair's place closed with a boom. Phil stood there in shock.

"Burn it?" Phil said to himself as he shook his head.

Instead, Phil drove it to Jill and Claus's place and walked next door to Marna, where he gave her an update of the situation. Marna thanked him.

"Guess I'll call a cab," Phil said to Marna.

"I need to return Mocha to Blair. I'll give you a lift home," Marna said.

Phil agreed. Marna loaded up Mocha in the back of her car and took Phil home first. She then took Mocha over to Blair's. Blair opened the door and welcomed in Mocha.

"How is he?" Marna asked about Claus.

"Wretched and guilty," Blair said.

"You must not let him out of your sight for at least the first twenty-four hours," Marna said.

"I will do my best," Blair said.

"I mean it, Blair. Word is that Josh just died. Jill and Claus did valuable work for Astroosa, and now he's the only one left who can use the technology. If he can't pull through, Chris and Patricia will thrust the competitors forward. Not that it means much to me, but I've heard the competitors are less kind to humanity than Astroosa. Could have a bad effect on society. The world."

"Is Astroosa going to send a team of people over? I mean, if Claus is this valuable, that would seem to be the thing to do," Blair said.

"I thought so too, but they don't want to overwhelm him in his fragile state. Call me in the morning. We'll go from there," Marna said.

"I will. Care to stay for a drink?" Blair offered.

"I'm sorry, I can't. Must return home. Don't worry. There are security agents in unmarked cars and various buildings around. You won't know their whereabouts, but they'll watch for suspicious activity. You'll be safe. Good luck," Marna said.

"Thank you," Blair said.

Blair kept the door open and watched as Marna left. Blair gave a last wave goodbye before closing the door and tending to Claus.

"Marna says 'hello'," Blair said.

"Hello," Claus said in mock greeting.

"Look at me, Claus. Look directly at me," Blair said.

Claus buried his head in his arms. Blair pulled his head up and forced him to look directly at her.

"Success. You're looking at me," she said. "Take a deep breath. Hold it. Exhale. Good. I'll get drinks."

Blair went to the kitchen and returned with two ice-cold bottles.

"Wine coolers. These used to be more popular back in the day. Should be easy on you," she said.

Claus took a sip.

"Not bad," he said.

Blair was about to take a sip when Mocha jumped up and begged some from her.

"No, Mocha. Human drink. Not for dogs," she said, and she pushed her dog off.

"I feel a little better. My stomach feels warm," Claus said.

"Good," Blair chuckled.

"Something funny about that?" Claus asked.

"Funny in the tummy," she said. "Would you like to play cards? Watch a movie?"

"No," Claus said. "I must make sense of things. I've never seen...Jill...if that was really her."

"You shouldn't let it consume you," Blair said.

"Why not? Something bad happened. It should not have. I believe everything is preventable, given enough time and effort," Claus said.

"You mean every bad thing is preventable, right?" Blair said. "You don't mean *everything* is preventable, do you? The good too?"

"Good is just the absence of failure," Claus said.

"You don't believe that. Not really? Take another sip and tell me if your drink is good," Blair said.

Claus did so.

"It's good. There's no failure," Claus said.

"What about life, Claus? Life is created, it grows, and—"

"It dies," Claus finished.

"It creates more life," Blair corrected.

"That's where we differ," Claus said.

"Why must there be a difference? We're in this world. We're alive. It's our time now. No one can take that away from us," Blair said.

"Such heavy talk on such light stomachs," Claus said.

"I have a cure for that," Blair said.

"More funny for the tummy?"

"More *yummy* for the tummy," Blair said. "Tell you what. I'll order out for dinner."

"Oh, not one of Jill's mass-produced vegan rolls," Claus said.

Blair laughed.

"I can tell you're tired of that," Blair said. "Patricia's cousin—"

"Has a nice Chinese food place," Claus said.

"Yes!"

"I used to eat their food before Jill changed things," Claus said.

"Then we'll change back. Or change to something else," Blair said.

"Chinese is fine," Claus said.

Blair ordered out for Chinese food, and she arranged for delivery. The food arrived quickly enough, and the two sat at the dining table for dinner.

"Well," Claus started. "All I can say is it's a shame Patricia ended up with Chris and their preoccupation with...I mean... Patricia's cousin makes excellent food."

"It's good food. Free of failure," Blair laughed.

"Making fun of me?" Claus said.

"You need it!" Blair continued to laugh.

"A simple delight. Something the Carinians don't understand," Claus said.

"Who?"

"Part of my dream," Claus said. "I shouldn't say more. I told Jill about it, and look where it got her."

"That's superstition," Blair said. "You're no jinx."

"Then what do you call it?" Claus asked.

"Jill was always driven. Like Frieda. I think sometimes people go too far. They take chances. Or they ignore their health. Like I did with mine. I learned my lesson. Tell me about your dream," Blair said.

Claus then recounted much of the "dream", as he called it—his interaction with Lanietta and the Carinians on the moon, the return to Earth five hundred years later, Arberella, Mars, Cenina Island, the Earth's destruction, Lanietta's parents, Claus's new life on the moon, Frieda's dominance on the lunar far side, and the impending lunar war between near and far sides.

"You have a vivid imagination," Blair said. "Perhaps you should write it down. Publish it as fiction."

"Fiction?"

"Sure."

"It wasn't fiction," Claus said. "At least it didn't seem so. Now I'm not sure. I mean, I even met my author."

"That's strange. For a moment I thought you said you met your author," Blair said.

"That's what I said."

"You mean you met your god, right?"

"No. My author," Claus said.

"Does she have a name?"

"*His* name is K Gerard Martin. Met him at his residence," Claus said.

"And what does your author do for you?" Blair said, struggling to keep a straight face. "Does he grant you special favors?"

"So far he hasn't. He's taken me from one thing to another, with no apparent rhyme or reason," Claus said.

"Almost like a real deity. Do you pray to him?" Blair giggled.

"Of course not! Blair, this is serious! I'm not my own man. Others decide my fate," Claus said.

"Because of failure? Does your author fail?" Blair continued to giggle.

"The best I can make of it is that he has a controlled failure and puts that upon me in this storyline," Claus said.

"So he creates a storyline from controlled failure," Blair giggled. "And that resulting creation is good because the failure is spent. Your author is broke. Guess *he'll* have to take a loan and borrow the trouble you keep trying to do."

"You've turned this into a complete mockery," Claus said.

"You should go into entertainment, Claus," Blair said. "Maybe as a stand-up comedian. See how the crowd reacts. Create some funny in the tummy."

"I think I'm funnied out," Claus said. "Thank you for dinner."

"My pleasure. I'll get us another round of wine coolers," Blair said, and she did. "Now tell me about this Lanietta alien. Do you love her?"

"Why does everyone ask me that?" Claus asked.

"Well who is everyone?" Blair asked.

"I guess the people in my dream," Claus said. "I don't know what to make of her. We never had children, though I had two with her long-time friend, Labba."

"Yes, you mentioned Labba. And how she had children with you. Without your consent. You know that's a crime," Blair said. "But it was only a dream. Still—"

"Okay. It was a crime. What can be done? Do I kill Leif and Clausetta to fix the failure?"

"Obviously not," Blair said.

"Obviously not," Claus agreed. "But if it was just a dream, it doesn't matter anyway. They are gone."

"You miss them, don't you?" Blair said.

"I do. I hate dreams like that. They take you over and linger around," Claus said. "Everywhere I turn, I expect Lanietta to show up. She did in the other visions I had. The other realities. The one back in '75? She was a rat, remember?"

"Could it be that Lanietta represents some part of your personality, an alter ego of sorts?" Blair asked.

"I don't know. Maybe," Claus said.

"I'll say it again. You have a vivid imagination," Blair said.

"Yes. But it's being dulled by these wine coolers. How many is that now?"

"That's your fourth," Blair said. "I'm on my third."

"Maybe we need a break," Claus said.

"We can sit in the living room and watch the plants grow," Blair joked.

"Hah!" Claus said, getting up to stretch, but he lost his balance and stumbled toward the couch, upon which he was just able to fall without bouncing off onto the floor.

"You're buzzed!" Blair laughed.

Blair got up to assist, but she felt a little dizzy.

"I'm buzzed too," she said, and she was about to fall.

"Don't fall!" Claus said as he got up to catch her.

She did fall, Claus tried to catch her, but his inebriated nerves didn't do so well, and the two fell onto the couch, back-to-back. Blair laughed.

"So is this how you and Jill did it? Back-to-back? Very kinky if you ask me," Blair said.

"We were back-to-back for the coffee tank experiments," Claus said. "We'd have to expose our backs, shave the back of our heads, and apply coffee gel to those surfaces. Then we'd share images."

Blair turned around and then turned Claus around. She looked him straight in the face.

"We can share images, Claus. And we don't need to do it back-to-back," she said.

"You can't see me straight on," Claus said.

"I don't have to," she said, and she kissed him.

"Blair?"

Blair hugged him and laughed. Claus laughed too.

"Your laughing is tickling me and making me laugh," Claus said.

"Your laughing is doing the same," she laughed back.

"What is your game, Blair?" Claus asked.

"You know exactly my game," she said. "Funny for the tummy."

"This is more than just funny," Claus said.

"Yes. It is," she replied.

Chapter 144: The Morning After

Claus awoke to the smell of bacon and eggs. He looked and realized he was in a queen-sized bed in the guest room. He looked around and saw a night robe—one of Blair's. He threw that on and walked into the kitchen. Blair was cooking breakfast. She turned to see Claus and burst out into laughter.

"Pink isn't quite your color," she continued to laugh.

"Thanks," Claus said sarcastically. "You're making animal food. I'm not used to it."

"I figured it was time to break the fast," she said.

"Blair. About last night," Claus said.

"I hope you have no regrets. I know I have none," she said. "It's going to be a beautiful day. Well, almost. Here. Breakfast is ready."

The dining table was set with dishes for breakfast. Blair put out the eggs and bacon. There were already cinnamon rolls set along with tea.

"I could make orange juice, but it might be a bit harsh on your stomach," she said. "After we...well...you had that great idea to drink the entire bottle of mouthwash. Said you needed heavier stuff. You spent half the night emptying your stomach of that mouthwash. Do you remember any of it?"

"Nothing. I remember dinner, at least the start of it. After that, I draw a blank," Claus said.

"No worries. We'll—"

The telephone rang. Blair answered it.

"Yes. Already? I thought in maybe another day or two. Oh. All right. Yes, he'll be ready. We'll be there. Will do. Thank you. Bye," Blair said.

"What was that about?" Claus asked while taking a bite of eggs.

"That was Marna," Blair said. "The funeral service for Jill and Josh is today at 1pm. They moved it up. Well, Joe moved it up."

"The funeral, of course," Claus said. "I'd forgotten. What's wrong with me? I guess...I guess I didn't think Jill really died. I mean she lived much longer in my dream. Sigh. I'll have to face up to things. So much for a beautiful day."

"The day is what you make of it," Blair said. "Even today."

"Even today?" Claus pressed.

"Especially today," Blair said.

"I'm not sure what that means. Unless you mean drinking and stuff later," Claus said.

"Claus! What kind of woman do you think I am?" she asked.

"I'm not sure. Every time I see a woman, I suspect she's Lanietta. Even you. At times I wonder—are you Lanietta?" Claus said.

"You have to stop that kind of talk," she said. "You know the answer. Each of us are who we are—not who people want us to be. You can't make a woman into your Lanietta any more than I can make my eyes see straight."

"I'm sorry," Claus said. "You're right, of course."

Blair smiled. She passed him the plate of cinnamon rolls.

"Sweet and spice, take a slice. Twice," Blair said.

Claus took a cinnamon roll and placed it on his plate.

"Take a slice," she repeated.

Claus sliced the cinnamon roll like a piece of pie. He ate it.

"Now again. Make it twice," she said.

"A twice slice. How nice," Claus said.

Blair laughed.

"Most people would say I'm being corny," Claus said.

"It's not what you say but how you say it," she said.

The two finished breakfast, dressed, and exited Blair's place, along with Mocha.

"Oh, my car isn't here," Claus said.

A taxicab drove up.

"I called a taxi," she said. "You can take me for a drive later."

The three reached the funeral home. Marna and Enrico greeted them as did Joe Craigen. The caskets were closed.

"Another funeral," Claus muttered to himself. "First Frieda. Then Jill and Josh. They all died too soon. Maybe we should've gone to the moon. Maybe we humans need help."

Claus looked around, again expecting Lanietta to appear and agree with him, but she did not. The funeral ceremony concluded in the funeral home. It was time to proceed to the cemetery for the burial. It was there that Claus saw Patricia and Chris.

"I don't understand why they weren't cremated," Claus overheard Chris say to Patricia. "They were, after all, burned and everything."

Claus walked up to Chris and clocked him across the jaw. The act broke Claus's knuckles, sent two of Chris's teeth flying, and started a flow of blood out of Chris's mouth.

"What's wrong with you?" Chris said in surprise.

"You. You killed her," Claus said. "You stole her tank and forced her into super obsessive mode. Now I kill you."

Claus repeatedly punched Chris in the face. Chris tried to punch back, but the first blow had stunned him, and his throws went wild. Joe and others rushed in and restrained Claus.

"You'll pay for this, Gerhardt. You and Astroosa and all your mining profits will vanish. Better hold onto your food business. Because that's what you'll be. Food for the dogs!" Chris promised.

"Get him out of here!" Joe said to his security people in reference to Chris.

"Claus. I'm sorry," Patricia said as she left with Chris.

"Sorry, Claus. I shouldn't have allowed them," Joe said.

"In a way, I'm kind of glad that happened," Claus said.

"Claus," Joe said. "I know that felt good, but we need you in one piece. You and Jill did much for Astroosa. Now Chris and Patricia are poised to undermine everything we've worked for. Can you help us? Can you help us beat them?"

"I can," Claus said. "Once and for all."

Joe looked at him in surprise, as if Claus had spoken the impossible.

"You have a plan?" Joe asked.

"Yes. Send me to the moon. The lunar far side," Claus said.

"No," Blair said. "You belong here on Earth."

"I must agree," Joe said. "After losing Andrea and Bill, we stopped all manned missions."

"You stopped all manned missions because there was sudden profit in unmanned missions," Claus said. "Astroosa is rich. Other space companies are becoming richer. They will stay focused on that. But I will find Bill and Andrea."

"It won't help the company, Claus," Joe said. "We need you to transfer Jill's technique to the company so we can continue. I should have had her do it before, but she was very obstinate and refused. I should have forced her. But you still have the knowledge. And the equipment."

"The equipment," Claus said. "Did Jill have it moved into Josh's place?"

"No," Joe said. "It should still be at her place."

"Uh, oh," Claus said. "Joe—the last time this happened, Jill's equipment was stolen. She's not around to rebuild it. If it's stolen again, we—"

"We must leave here at once," Joe said. "Come with me!"

"Claus, what about me?" Blair said.

"You must come too," Joe said. "This is an emergency."

Joe's security people rushed Blair, Mocha, Claus, and Joe into Joe's limousine. The vehicle raced through town, first to Jill's house. Already three firetrucks were fighting a blaze in Jill's house that threatened nearby houses, including the Depetti house. Claus jumped out of the car and tried running in.

"No!" Joe said as he rushed after Claus.

"The tank. The tank!" Claus yelled.

"No! You'll burn to death!" Joe said as he restrained Claus. "Let the firefighters do their job. We'll salvage what we can once the fire is contained."

Joe walked Claus back toward the limo. A security man whispered something into Joe's ear.

"Josh's house too?" Joe said out loud.

"What. What?" Claus asked.

"Come with me," Joe said.

Joe, Claus, and the security person returned to the limo and sped off to Josh's house. Four firetrucks were needed to fight that fire.

"I can't believe this!" Claus said. "Why?"

"Sabotage," Joe said.

"Chris. He's behind this," Claus said. "What about my own house? I never sold it, you know."

The limo drove over to Claus's house. The last firetruck left. The house had burned down and was nothing but smoke and ash.

"Now I really want to kill Chris," Claus said. "I'll hunt him to the ends of this Earth."

Joe paused in thought and lightly shook his finger at Claus.

"I'm beginning to see something," Joe said. "Claus, I'll take you up on your offer."

"To kill Chris?"

"No. You'll have your lunar launch. I see we've neglected the moon for too long," Joe said.

"We've found nothing worth mining there," Claus said.

"Except human ingenuity," Joe said. "You'll have your search for Andrea and Bill—provided you spend part of your time on rebuilding Jill's technique for data acquisition."

"Jill and I did that as a team," Claus said. "But she's gone."

"So you'll need a partner. Who shall I assign?" Joe asked.

"Me," Blair said. "I'm already looking after Claus."

"You don't work for Astroosa," Joe said.

"Neither do I," Claus said. "Further, Jill dissolved the partnership, so currently I'm working for no one."

"You're on the payroll. Both of you. I can have an entire team sent with you to help," Joe said.

"No. Too many people. Send Doctor Morrow with us. If we find Bill and Andrea, and they are still alive, they might need medical assistance," Claus said.

"Agreed. I'll send word to ready Novi 3," Joe said. "You can go up tomorrow."

"Tomorrow? Wow!" Blair said.

"How can you have a Novi craft ready to go that fast?" Claus asked.

"It was always ready to go," Joe said.

"Wait. Blair hasn't had any astronaut training," Claus said.

"I went up in your Super Cub. We did a loop and a spin," Blair said.

"You're certified," Joe said. "Report to Astroosa later today for fitting and a checkup."

"What about Mocha?" Claus asked.

"Your seeing eye dog?" Joe asked.

"I want my dog with me," Blair said.

"You may do so. Report to Astroosa with Mocha. Very interesting mission, Claus. Make it worthwhile," Joe said.

"I will, I mean we will," Claus said.

A survey was made of Jill's and Josh's houses. The tank was still in Jill's house but had been destroyed. All other equipment was ruined beyond hope. Claus, Blair, and Mocha arrived at Astroosa and were greeted by Doctor Morrow and Joe.

"There's no safe place on Earth for a tank like Jill's," Claus said. "It will either be stolen or destroyed."

"Which is why I'm agreeing to this trip," Joe said. "In time, we could set up a remote Astroosa facility there. Would provide redundancy in case of attack here on Earth. It's time for your fitting."

Claus, Blair, and even Mocha were fitted with spacesuits. Mocha took surprisingly to a suit. Once fitted, the three then went for checkups. All passed, though Blair's macular degeneration was noticed.

"I can manage. Really," Blair said.

"Very well. Stay with someone at all times," Doctor Morrow said.

"That's my plan," Blair replied.

Just like that, Claus, Blair, Mocha, and Doctor Morrow went up on Novi 3. Claus piloted the craft as it headed for the moon. It wasn't long before he touched down in the very same crater where Novi 3 had landed in his dream. Prava 13, 14, and 15 were launched shortly afterward. They orbited the moon, equally spaced, and acted as relay satellites between Novi 3 and Astroosa.

"Astroosa, Novi 3. Everything reads A-okay," Claus said.

"Novi 3, Astroosa. We confirm everything A-okay," Astroosa said.

Claus turned to the others.

"Well, we're here," Claus said.

"I'll send out the robot explorers," Doctor Morrow said. "Also, I need to do a walk-around of the ship. I'll be back in a few."

Doctor Morrow hit a few buttons, and an army of wheeled robots exited from Novi 3 from a special cargo hatch that did not connect to the main habitable part.

"Claus, this is Joe," Joe radioed. "Check your NASDI panel for special instructions. I hope you never need it, but it's standard procedure for Novi craft."

"Thank you," Claus said.

Claus closed radio communication.

"I know of what he speaks," Claus said to Blair. "It's Operation Astroosiate. Should we meet an alien craft and feel threatened, we can detonate a nuclear device."

"There's a nuclear device on this spaceship? What madness is that?" Blair asked.

"Exactly. Madness. That was in the dream, at least. But I bet it's true," Claus said. "There's only one way to find out."

Claus walked over to the panel and stared at the very button that would trigger the message from Joe Craigen. Claus remembered this button from when Bill pressed it in his dream. But Bill wasn't there. It was up to Claus. He only need press it, and the recording would display. He paused and looked at Blair with Mocha at her side. What was he thinking, bringing Blair up onto the moon? And her dog, too! Had Claus finally flipped? Had mania ruled the day? Yet everyone agreed to this idea. So he wasn't totally crazy. Or was he?

Chapter 145: Jill's Secret Message

Claus pressed the button.

"Please submit retina scan to continue," said an automated voice from a scanner panel.

"This is new," Claus said. "Must be extra security."

Claus made his right eye available for scanning. The scanner took his biometric and continued.

"Claus Doron Gerhardt," said the automated voice. "Access approved."

"Glad to hear that," Claus said. "Now for the message."

An image of Joe displayed. Audio of his voice filled the air.

"Fellow Astroosa astronauts, I congratulate you on your historic flight to the moon. You are the best of the best. We place you in high esteem. Few humans have gone to the moon, and only Astroosa astronauts have explored the lunar far side to such an extent. For this reason, we have the utmost faith and confidence—"

But a new video and audio message superimposed itself over Joe's message.

"Claus, this is Olivia. If you're seeing this, it means either I've become Jill again, or I'm dead. Or worse," Jill said in the message.

"Or worse," Claus said.

"I secretly added a special check so only you'll see this message," Jill said. "I disabled the onboard nuclear device and converted it into a coffee tank. I figured if anyone would go into space, it would be you. And since you've accessed this message, it means I'm not there with you. I'm sorry."

"I'm sorry too," Claus said.

"Periodically I have updated the Novi 3 tank with programming from our own tank. It should be fully functional and ready for use," Jill said. "It's a backup tank. I decided to make it after my first tank was stolen from your house."

"A fail-safe," Claus said. "I always miss the fail-safes."

"I just have one warning for you," Jill said. "I did a cursory review of the moon using the tank by myself. There's something unusual below the surface, something resembling intelligence. I don't know if it's Andrea and Bill or an alien manifestation. I didn't tell you or anyone because I was afraid of awakening a great beast that would compromise life on Earth as we know it. But now you are on the moon, so the warning must go out—beware! Take great caution in exploring the moon, particularly the far side. You might unleash something unpleasant. Well, my sweet Claus, good luck."

The message ended.

"Don't tell Doctor Morrow about the tank," Claus said.

"I won't," Blair said.

Doctor Morrow returned from her spacewalk.

"Well, the ship looks fine," she said. "The robots are out scouting the area. Did you have a hunch about this spot? There were no recommendations from Astroosa as to where Novi 2 might be."

"It's an educated hunch," Claus said.

"Well. So far the only thing we are in danger of is boredom," Doctor Morrow said.

A full lunar cycle passed. The robots found no sign of Andrea and Bill. Claus became edgy. While Doctor Morrow went out on a spacewalk, Claus had a conversation with Blair.

"This is crazy. I want to use the tank. But I don't want Doctor Morrow to know. She's only outside for an hour or two at a time. We have no privacy up here on the moon."

Blair laughed.

"There are billions of people on Earth, and just a handful here," Blair laughed.

"Yes. And no privacy. I feel like Novi 3 is a home. But a home should have privacy. There needs to be another ship nearby. A place where we can go."

"Or Doctor Morrow can go," Blair said.

Doctor Morrow returned.

"Well, still no luck," Doctor Morrow said. "Are you able to duplicate Jill's equipment?"

"No," Claus said.

"What do you need?" Doctor Morrow asked. "If you can't get a tank going, we'll have to change strategy."

"Meaning?" Blair asked.

"Meaning we'll have to have more Novi craft sent up and probe a larger area," Doctor Morrow said. "I anticipated this and requested that Novi 4 be readied just in case."

"Yes, I think that would help," Claus said. "But a minimum crew. We need to conserve supplies."

"Absolutely. I'll have Kevin Craigen pilot it," Doctor Morrow said. "I can configure the robots to coordinate with ours."

"Excellent idea!" Blair blurted out.

"Yes," Claus agreed.

"Very well. Kevin has experience with the mining team. Maybe he can help with restoring Jill's work," Doctor Morrow said.

Novi 4 launched and landed in a nearby crater. Doctor Morrow took an enclosed rover from Novi 3 to Novi 4. It was a special rover with the ability to hop over ridges, gorges, and out of craters.

"Finally," Claus said. "I thought she'd never leave. Let's go below and configure the tank. I'll need you to help, Blair. We'll have to sit back-to-back and skull-to-skull like I did with Olivia."

The two went below. Claus found the tank in a special storage room in place of where the nuclear device would have been. In the room were shirts with open backs, circular hair clips, and coffee gel.

"Hair clips instead of shaving the back of our heads. Hmm. No coffee mix for the tank. I hate to use ship's water to fill it," Claus said.

"Let's try without. A dry tank. Is that possible?" Blair asked.

"Yes. I suppose it is," Claus said.

The two changed into the special shirts, placed the hair clips at the back of their heads, and took turns applying coffee gel to their backs (no gel for the hair clips needed). They then sat in the tank. Claus sat on the side where Jill would have sat, and so he had a control panel to work with.

"Activating the tank controls," Claus said.

Claus and Blair felt warm and satisfying sensations where they touched.

"Wow! No wonder Jill liked this tank. It's like total euphoria. I could see how she could get addicted. I could get addicted," Blair said.

"Let's hope that doesn't happen," Claus said. "I'll try an image. What do you see?"

"I see...oh, it's Jill!"

"I see her too," Claus said.

"Congratulations, Claus, you've found the tank. You've also learned to use it. I'm feeding instructions into your brain on more advanced tank techniques. With these techniques, you'll be able to direct your searches into asteroids and other celestial objects as we once did."

"She's right," Claus said. "I'm receiving instructions."

"I'm receiving them too," Blair said. "Asteroid AB4711."

"Yes. You shouldn't be. She never shared them with me," Claus said.

Jill's image displayed again.

"Claus, stop! Remove the other occupant from the tank. Immediately!" Jill ordered.

Claus hit a button and stopped the tank's operation. He stepped out of the tank and helped Blair out.

"What was that?" Blair asked.

"I don't know," Claus replied. "I don't know how she expects me to use the tank without her unless I have someone else helping. However, before she halted tank operations, she told me how to tap into the tank's computer. I'll relay it to this workstation here."

Claus and Blair sat down to a workstation. He hit several buttons, and data displayed on a screen.

"Well? Any idea why she halted things?" Blair asked.

"This tank has several safeguards built in. One is for a maximum of two people. That constraint has been violated," Claus said. "I don't understand. It's just the two of us. Mocha isn't here. Doctor Morrow isn't here. Counting Mocha, there were only four life-forms on this ship when we left Earth."

Claus glanced at Blair, but she looked down instead.

"Am I right?"

"No, you're not right," she said. "Are there any other constraints violated?"

Claus checked again.

"Yes. There's an anti-Ben constraint," Claus said. "That's strange. Ben was never born. This constraint prevents damage to unborn...oh, wait. Blair, are you..."

Blair beamed with pride.

"Really?" Claus asked.

"Yes, really. You're going to be a father, Claus," Blair said.

"I don't believe it. I mean, we never...we...did we?"

"Remember that night you don't remember?" Blair chuckled.

"Now how could I remember that?" Claus said.

"Well, that's how it happened. I told you I had no regrets," she said.

"I didn't realize...I mean...a baby in space? And you knew? How will we care for it?" Claus asked.

"It's a *she*," Blair said. "And I already packed for her. Her name will be Clossandra."

"Isn't that a flowering plant?" Claus asked.

"You're thinking of *Crossandra*. But yes, I took that name and mixed it with your name. I hope you don't mind. I told you, I have no regrets. I don't expect any special care or payment. Just little Clossandra. I was thinking we could raise her here on the moon, fully isolated from the evils of Earth. Keep her from being contaminated until she's old enough to handle things. No peer pressure, no drugs, no violence, no fear of being assaulted," Blair said.

Claus paced back and forth.

"Well? Say something at least," Blair said.

"I can't believe my author put me in yet another predicament," Claus said.

"Is that what a daughter means to you? A predicament? It's not like you have to carry her to term or anything," Blair said.

"Are you angry at me?" Claus asked.

"No. How could I be?" Blair asked.

"It's just...I guess I'm edgy...always expecting a woman to lash out at me," Claus said.

"Because of Jill? Frieda? Or maybe Lanietta?" Blair asked. "If it's any comfort, I always expect men to lash out at me. Say rude things with their two-word vocabulary. You're one of the rare ones. I mean, do you think I'd want a child to grow up and lash back at me in the same way as my mate? Well, you've seen how I cope until now. I laugh everything off. But Clossandra will be special. She already is. And one thing you can't knock Jill for. She *is* protective of babies, even if she lost her own."

"Yes. She did do that. But it means we can't use the tank together until...wait, I wonder if Jill has a provision," Claus mused.

Claus hit a few more buttons. A video message of Jill displayed at the workstation.

"There is a way to explore while protecting an unborn child. Cover the back except for a two-inch horizontal strip running across the shoulder blades. Continue to use skull-to-skull. Place a lead corset around the woman," Jill said.

Blair searched several cabinets and found the lead corset.

"She thinks of everything," Blair said.

"Yes," Claus said. "I have to wonder what other surprises are in store for us. Are there more surprises? I mean, you're not having twins or anything like that, are you?"

"No. Just Clossandra," Blair said. "Help me with this corset, will you?"

Claus helped pull the corset tight.

"Not too tight," Blair said. "Clossandra needs room too."

"Sorry," Claus said. "I just realized something. The corset will cover most of your back. The upper skin is exposed. It should be enough."

Just then an alarm sounded.

"What's that?" Blair asked.

"Proximity alarm. I set it just in case," Claus said.

"Just in case what?"

"In case Doctor Morrow returned before we finished. Someone's approaching the ship. We have to close up here and get upstairs. Fast!"

"The corset!" Blair said.

"No time. You'll have to wear it. Throw your shirt over it," Claus said.

The two closed up the tank area, removed their hair clips, and returned upstairs just in time. Doctor Morrow drove up in the rover with another person. They entered Novi 3 and removed their helmets.

"Kevin," Claus said. "Nice to see you."

"You two seem out of sorts. What have you been doing?" Doctor Morrow asked.

"Aw, leave them be," Kevin winked.

"No hanky panky on this mission," Doctor Morrow said. "We must remain focused on the task at hand. Claus, Kevin brought extra supplies for Novi 3. Would you care to help him unload?"

"Be glad to," Claus said.

Claus donned his spacesuit, gloves, and helmet while Kevin simply placed his helmet back on. The two went out through the airlock and unloaded the rover.

"Blair," Doctor Morrow said. "I've been meaning to give you a checkup."

"Oh, that's not necessary," Blair said.

"Well things are different for women," Doctor Morrow said. "When did you last cycle?"

"I ride the exercise bicycle every day," Blair said.

"You know exactly what I mean. Have you had any complications? Do you need anything special?" Doctor Morrow said.

"I'll let you know," Blair said.

"Don't feel like you have to keep things a secret. Some women find that their cycle stops in space on its own. Stress of the new environment and all that. Others don't want to deal with it. I have pills to make it stop. Just let me know."

"I will," Blair said.

"If things go along as Astroosa plans, we'll have a big enough colony for women to have children. But we're years away from that. Don't know how we could cope with a child now," Doctor Morrow said.

Blair simply nodded in mock agreement, fully aware that she couldn't keep her secret forever. Claus and Kevin finished unloading the supplies, but only Claus reentered. Not a moment too soon for Blair.

"Kevin is waiting in the rover for you," Claus said.

"Yes. I'm going back to Novi 4. Kevin has a medical problem that needs attention," Doctor Morrow said. "Don't wait up for me. I could be gone for several Earth days."

"We'll be fine," Claus said as Doctor Morrow put on her helmet. "Bye."

"Bye," Blair said.

"Take care," Doctor Morrow said, and she left.

Claus was about to speak, but Blair put a finger to her lips so he'd be quiet until the rover was far out of range.

"What was that about?" Claus asked.

"Doctor Morrow doesn't know I'm expecting," Blair said. "Fortunately the pre-flight exam was too soon after conception to show anything. But just now, she asked me about my cycle."

"What did you tell her?" Claus asked.

"Nothing," Blair said. "She was offering pills to stop my cycle and said that I might stop out of stress. She also talked about how Astroosa will set up a colony, and only then will children be okay, but that's years away. Boy is she in for a surprise when I have a child."

"Yes. Well, I wonder what's wrong with Kevin? He seemed well enough," Claus said.

Blair burst out into laughter.

"What's funny this time?" Claus asked.

"Kevin isn't sick!" Blair laughed.

"How do you know?"

"I put two and two together. Did you see how Doctor Morrow averted her eyes from Kevin? It was like she didn't want to give away that she had something for him, that looking at him would give her away," Blair continued to laugh.

"Kevin and Doctor Morrow? I find it hard to believe," Claus said.

"You know, the way she talked about children (and the hints she dropped about not having any) makes me believe that *she* wants to be the first to give birth on the moon. Yes! Of course! That's why she called for the extra ship. She could have sent for a robot ship with extra robot rovers. But no, she had to have Kevin fly up. Clever woman that Doctor Morrow," Blair grinned.

Claus paced back and forth in Novi 3.

"I'm afraid for Clossandra," Claus said.

"Why? Don't you trust me?"

"It's not you I'm worried about," Claus said.

"You think Doctor Morrow would try something?"

"Well? She's a doctor, she wants to be first, and she has the power to cause you to miscarry," Claus said.

"I won't let her," Blair said.

"Blair. If there's one thing I've learned, it's to never underestimate the conniving female mind, especially when it comes to manipulating people and situations. I've got to protect you. Keep you locked up," Claus said, looking around in a near panic.

"Now stop this crazy talk," Blair said. "Here we are on the moon, away from the billions of Earth—"

"And we still have other humans to contend with," Claus said. "We're like the couple living far in the country to get away from everything only to have another couple move in close-by."

"This shouldn't be a competition," Blair said.

"No. It shouldn't. But I fear it will become one," Claus said. "Let's try the tank. Perhaps it can yield a clue."

The two went down below. They prepped and then went into the tank. Then they shared an image of Jill.

"Congratulations, Claus. You have taken all precautions. The tank will only affect you two. You may proceed with your first request," Jill said.

"Blair is with me," Claus said. "We are exploring together."

"Welcome, Blair. I had hoped it would be you," Jill said.

"Hello. And thank you," Blair said.

"Doctor Morrow and Kevin Craigen are in Novi 4 in the neighboring crater," Claus said. "We want to explore Novi 4. We want to know what Doctor Morrow and Kevin are planning, if anything."

The image of Jill disappeared. Claus and Blair then shared an image of traveling from Novi 3 to Novi 4, as if flying there. They reached a viewpoint at a window and could hear sound vibrations reaching that window.

"They don't suspect a thing," Doctor Morrow said to Kevin. "I said you had a medical problem."

"What about Andrea and Bill?" Kevin asked.

"They're probably dead," Doctor Morrow said. "We would have heard from them by now. I have robot rovers looking anyway as a smokescreen. But you, my Kevin, will be the first lunar father. What do you think of that? Another first for Astroosa. We just need to conceive the child here and let nature run its course."

"What about Blair and Claus?" Kevin asked.

"Claus was married to Jill, so he's still mourning her loss. And Blair isn't very attractive or smart. So no chance there. But don't worry. If she gets foolish notions, I'll slip RU-486 into her food ration. She'll miscarry and never suspect a thing."

"Stop the vision!" Blair said.

Claus stopped. Blair started to cry.

"That's enough for one day," Claus said. "Let's go to the upper deck."

Claus helped Blair out. Claus made tea, and the two shared a moment with rations.

"So it's true," Blair said, still sad though getting hold of herself. "I had hoped not."

"Well one thing is for sure. Doctor Morrow has seriously underestimated you. You are neither plain nor ordinary. You pegged her to a tee. Identified her intentions right off," Claus said.

"I had a nasty feeling. I had hoped it was just a silly maternal instinct. Now I wish we were back on Earth so we could live out a normal life. Forget this lunacy. It's not worth it," Blair said.

"I guess we trade one set of problems for another, as the saying goes," Claus said. "There's Chris and Patricia on Earth, and now Doctor Morrow and Kevin here on the moon. I don't blame Kevin."

"Neither do I. He believes he's advancing Astroosa. Normally he would. He's just a bit misled," Blair said.

"This ration is the last you can eat safely," Claus said. "After today, we'll have to test everything before you consume it. No exceptions. I will—"

"Take the first bite? That will do no good. You're not a woman," Blair said.

"No. I'm not. We'll use the tank to check rations on the ship before you eat anything," Claus said.

"What if she's *already* spiked the rations?" Blair said. "You as a man would never notice. Me as a woman would miscarry."

"Then we'd better go back to the tank and find out. Now!" Claus said.

The two went below and entered the tank. They didn't need to re-gel because they hadn't cleaned up from the prior attempt. Claus turned on the control, and an image of Jill appeared.

"Stop!" she said. "You cannot explore. Fetal termination constraint violated."

"Oh no!" Blair said. "It's too late!"

"Verbose output on constraint," Claus said.

"Recent ingestion by woman of drug mifepristone, also known as RU-486," Jill said. "Abortion process will begin soon."

"Can you reverse it? Can you save the fetus?" Claus said.

"Emergency reversal kit is in this control panel. Take it and administer immediately," Jill said, and her image disappeared.

Claus opened the control panel and removed the kit. He then helped Blair out of the tank and opened the kit for her to see.

"Progesterone injections," she said. "That's exactly what I need. With a dosage chart and schedule. I'll have to take this for at least two days, then every other day for two weeks, and twice a week after that. Oh, what a trial! I'll have to return to the tank to check its effectiveness. I must have one now!"

Blair took the first syringe and tried to inject herself. But she shook with such anxiety that she dropped the syringe. It fell to the floor. The needle bent. Blair shrieked.

"I can't do it! Clossandra! She'll die. Claus!" Blair panicked.

"Sit down, Blair. Try to relax," Claus said. "I'll perform the injection."

"But the needle is bent," Blair said as she sat.

"We'll use the next dose for now," he said.

Claus approached her arm.

"No, not the arm," she said. "In the butt. Look, there's a diagram."

"You can't sit. You'll have to position yourself differently," Claus said. "Normally I would ask the doctor to do this. But we can't trust our doctor. A shame really."

Blair repositioned herself and her garments appropriately for the injection.

"Ready," she said.

Claus gave the injection. Blair cringed.

"This stuff doesn't go in easy," Claus said.

"It's oil-based," she said. "Don't worry. I'll manage."

With the injection complete, the two returned to the tank. Claus had the rations probed.

"They're all contaminated," Blair said. "I can't eat the rations. It will be too much to overcome. I must starve."

"Wait," Claus said, and he made one last probe.

"The dog food?" she asked.

"It's safe to eat. No RU-486 or any other drugs," Claus said.

"Safe for a dog," she said.

"Say the word, and I'll take Novi 3 back to Earth," Claus said. "We'll abandon the search for Andrea and Bill, and we'll take our chances with the tank on Earth."

Blair sighed.

"No. I'll eat the dog food," she said. "There's enough until I can have Clossandra. Well, we must thank Jill for helping us out again."

"I wish we could thank her," Claus said. "Seems unfair that she should lose life over the tank."

"Then we must live it for her," Blair said. "Oh, I'm suddenly very tired."

"Let's get you to bed. You need sleep," Claus said.

Claus helped her out of the tank and into sleeping quarters. He tucked her in with a blanket and was about to leave her, as the bed was but a twin and only had space for her. He paused and thought about the challenge ahead with saving Clossandra.

"What would Lanietta say now?" he asked himself.

Blair was now asleep, and so Claus went below to figure out what to do about the bent needle.

"I'll put it back in the kit. Maybe I can use it yet—transfer the medication to another syringe or something," he said to himself.

Claus went back above and into the galley. He looked at the food and shook his head in disbelief.

"How often has food been compromised in human history in the name of greed?" he asked himself.

Claus checked instrumentation and saw nothing out of the ordinary. The robot rovers had not found Novi 2, and Novi 4 showed all systems normal.

"I should get some sleep too," Claus said to himself.

He went to his sleeping quarters, but he felt uneasy about leaving Blair alone.

"What if Doctor Morrow slips in and injects Blair with something?" Claus asked. "No, I can't sleep here."

Claus took his blanket and pillow, and he slept on the floor by Blair's bed.

Chapter 146: Dinner with Donna

Claus awoke with a start when Blair's foot stepped on him by mistake.

"Oh!" she said. "I'm sorry! I didn't know you were down there! What are you doing there anyway?"

"I didn't want to leave you alone," Claus said.

"How very thoughtful!" she said. "But I must go to the ladies' room."

"Everything okay? I mean, are you holding onto Clossandra?" Claus asked.

"I seem to be. I'll be back in a moment," she said.

As promised, she returned in a moment.

"I'm fine," she said. "When's the next injection?"

"A bit later," Claus said. "But I worry. About Clossandra. Let's get in the tank and check."

"All right," Blair smiled.

The two went below, prepped up, and went into the tank. Claus activated it and had it check Blair.

"Well, the tank can't directly check Clossandra. The lead shield prevents it. But it can check your own metabolism. And it has. Looks good so far," Claus said.

"That's a relief," Blair said. "I'll be glad when this is over and I have Clossandra in my arms. You will be too. Then we—"

But at that moment, the two shared an image of a twelve-million-year-old girl. It was Lanietta.

"Lanietta!" Claus said.

"From your dream?" Blair asked. "But why?"

"I must be half asleep," Claus said. "I can't hear her. But she's motioning something. Cupping her hands to her mouth."

"It's as if she's warning us about a danger," Blair said.

"Well I wondered when I would see her, and there she is. But is it really her or my imagination? Hard to tell," Claus said.

"Look. She's motioning as if eating is dangerous," Blair said.

"That we knew already," Claus said.

"I think she's warning us about Donna. Doctor Morrow," Blair said.

"That we know too," Claus said.

"She's gone," Blair said.

"Well. The ghost of Lanietta pays us a visit and leaves," Claus said. "You should get more rest."

Claus helped Blair out of the tank.

"So should you. You don't have to sleep on the floor next to me. That's for Mocha. Anyway, I'll be safe. We have a proximity alarm, right?"

"We do," Claus said. "I'll make sure it is on and functioning."

"Thank you. Good night," Blair said.

"Good night."

Blair went back to bed. Claus checked the proximity alarm, and yes, it was operational. He was still uneasy, and he couldn't leave the workstation. He ended up falling asleep in the chair.

When he awoke, Mocha was licking his face.

"You smell like dog food," Claus said.

Claus looked around and realized Mocha had just finished a bowl of dog food. Blair herself sat at a table and had her own bowl of dog food.

"I can't let you eat dog food forever," Claus said. "I'll have to figure out a way to get you healthy food. Either a shipment from Earth, or we come up with a way to make our own food here."

Just then, the proximity alarm went off. Blair and Claus exchanged nervous glances. Claus ran over to a panel to acknowledge the alarm and determine the trigger.

"It's Doctor Morrow," Claus said. "Put away the dog food. Hurry."

Blair did so moments before Doctor Morrow entered.

"Hello, you two!" Doctor Morrow said with a fake smile. "Did you sleep well?"

"We slept fine," Claus said.

"Any medical issues to report?" she asked.

"Well I feel a bit nauseated," Claus said.

"I'm sorry to hear that. When did it start?" Doctor Morrow asked.

"When I first saw you coming this way," Claus said.

Blair did everything to keep herself from bursting out into laughter.

"I'm shocked, Claus. Are you sane?" Doctor Morrow asked.

"That's *my* line," Claus said.

Claus looked at Blair, and she lightly nodded, "No," so that Claus would drop the attack.

"I'm doing fine. So is Kevin. I came to invite you two over for dinner. Kevin brought up special food reserves to celebrate. Chris has been taken into custody. Was caught sabotaging an Astroosa facility," Doctor Morrow said.

"When was Chris caught?" Claus asked.

"Within the last hour. I know, Kevin brought up the supplies before that, and how could he know? Well, we were confident Chris would be caught. It was a matter of time. Everything is a matter of time. Isn't it?" she asked.

"Yes. Some in this universe know time very well," Claus said.

"So far it's just us. Unless you believe in aliens," Doctor Morrow said. "But the fact is, if intelligent life existed outside of Earth, we would have known about it by now."

"Unless they wish to keep their privacy," Claus said.

"Such an antiquated concept. Earth has gone to globalism. Naturally, the next step is cosmolism," Doctor Morrow said.

"Sounds like communism," Claus said.

"You seem adversarial today," the doctor said. "Are you sure you're fine? Perhaps I should examine you."

"No. I'm fine. Just thinking about how to find Andrea and Bill," Claus said.

"Well, the robot rovers continue to search. Let's see where they are," the doctor said.

Doctor Morrow checked a panel.

"Still nothing," she said.

"What if Novi 2 is underground? Buried in lunar soil?" Claus asked.

"We'd have seen evidence of that," Doctor Morrow said.

"Unless aliens covered it up," Claus said.

"Aliens who live forever? Who conjure up magic tricks? Perhaps they plan to invade Earth," Doctor Morrow laughed. "You're getting space-happy, Claus."

"Perhaps. Perhaps," Claus said.

"Well, dinner is at five. I know lunar days and nights don't match our clocks. It will be dark. Make sure your rover lights are on. Don't want you to get lost," the doctor said.

"Will do," Claus said. "Anything else?"

"I don't sound welcome here," Doctor Morrow said. "Have you reported back to Joe yet?"

"No," Claus said. "I mean, yes."

"Which is it?"

"I've given the daily status by text. But I haven't spoken with him personally," Claus said. "The main radio link is on the fritz."

"Well I have. He wants to push forward with the colony. We're planning on nine months from today," she said.

"Interesting time frame," Claus said.

"It's just time," Doctor Morrow said. "Projects take time to prepare and complete. I look forward to the day. Things will be quite different then. Anyway, I'll leave you now. Oh Blair, how are you on supplies? Need anything for you know what?"

"I'm okay," Blair said.

"Very well. Until dinner time," she said, and she left.

"Nine months. Hah!" Blair blurted out.

"She's timed it with her pregnancy. If she's pregnant," Claus said.

"She is. I can see the glow in her. I'm surprised she doesn't see the glow in me," Blair said.

"Yes, it is strange. But you've carefully arranged your dress and applied makeup to look as normal as possible," Claus said.

"I didn't think you noticed," Blair said.

"I noticed. Speaking of, it's time for your injection," Claus said.

"I took it already," Blair said. "Gave it to myself. I was a mess yesterday, but I feel more confident today."

"Good," Claus said. "Hmm. Dinner with Donna."

"Yes. I think your Lanietta was warning us about it. Donna must be lacing the food extra heavily to ensure I can't carry a child," Blair said.

"She can't lace all of it. If she eats it, she'll miscarry too," Claus said.

"My guess is she eats different food from the rest of us. Makes up an excuse or just doesn't mention the source. Has food on our plates already. Or perhaps she spikes the drink. Either way, I shouldn't eat it."

"If we don't go for dinner, she'll become suspicious that we're suspicious," Claus said.

"Mocha, what would you do?" Blair asked her dog.

Mocha barked.

"Exactly," Blair said.

A message came in from Joe.

"Joe!" Claus answered.

"Hello, Claus and Blair. And you too, Mocha!" Joe said.

Mocha barked.

"Just wanted to let you know that Chris is in jail for sabotage," Joe said.

"Yes. Doctor Morrow just informed us," Claus said.

"Good. Then she also spoke of dinner?"

"She did," Claus said.

"Make every effort to attend. It's a celebration dinner, and it will be televised throughout the world as a shining example of Astroosa success and goodwill to humanity," Joe said.

"Well, I was actually feeling under the weather," Claus said. "Thought I would stay in Novi 3 with Blair for the day."

"You do no such thing. Take what meds you need to feel better. Get over there

for dinner. This is a worldly affair. Craigen out."

"Well, that's that," Claus said.

"I won't eat dinner," Blair said.

"It will look bad. Really bad," Claus said.

Blair started to don a spacesuit.

"It's too early for dinner," Claus said.

"I'm going for a rover drive," she said. "I'll be back after dinner. Tell them I was out looking for Andrea and Bill."

"Blair?"

"No other way," she said.

"Then I'm going with you," he said.

"You have to attend dinner to represent Novi 3. Take Mocha with you," she said.

"Blair!"

Blair went out the airlock, took a rover, and drove away.

"I must go after her. Why don't I go after her?" he asked himself.

Claus went below to the tank, hoping he could get answers. But the tank would not activate for just one person. He went back above and paced back and forth. He could no longer contain himself. He opened up a radio channel to Blair.

"Blair, Novi 3. Please reply," Claus said.

Blair did not reply.

"Blair. Answer please," Claus said.

"This is Doctor Morrow," the doctor said. "What's going on, Claus?"

"Nothing," Claus said.

"Is there an issue? Will you both be arriving for dinner? I have places set for four," Doctor Morrow said.

Claus looked around in desperation. He looked at Mocha and remembered Blair's last words.

"Expect us both. Four will dine at five," he said with a smile.

"Excellent. See you soon," she said.

The time came. Claus suited up himself and Mocha. The two went over on a rover and reached Novi 4. Both entered the airlock to the doctor's and Kevin's surprise. Claus removed his spacesuit and the spacesuit of Mocha.

"Where's Blair?" the doctor asked.

"Right here," Claus said, pointing to Mocha.

"That's Mocha. The dog was not invited," Doctor Morrow said.

"Hear that Blair? Doctor Morrow just called you a dog," Claus said. "How dare you say that to Blair. You know she's shy and reserved."

"Claus? Where is Blair?"

"C'mon, Blair. Obviously the doctor is playing games with us. I know, she has something against you. Perhaps it's your pedigree."

"Mocha's pedigree is Labrador retriever!" the doctor said.

"If you don't stop with the insults, we'll leave!" Claus said.

"Three minutes before we air!" Kevin said.

"Time pressure. Claus! I won't forget this little trick of yours. Of all the embarrassing things! In our moment of triumph! Well! Sit down then, Claus and *Blair!*" the doctor snorted.

Claus and Mocha took their places as did Doctor Morrow and Kevin.

"Keep the camera on us, Kevin. Only pan to Claus if needed. Avoid Mocha!" Doctor Morrow said.

"Quit calling Blair, Mocha!" Claus said.

"We're on," Kevin said.

"Greetings people of Earth. Welcome to dinner on the moon from your friends at Astroosa!" Doctor Morrow said.

Kevin and Doctor Morrow clapped.

"We thank you for your service, Novi 3 and 4 crews," Joe Craigen's voice said. "I'm happy to say that thanks to the recent arrest of Chris Cresson, the sabotage against Astroosa and all space-loving people of Earth has ended. To this I wish to make a toast!"

"A toast!" Doctor Morrow said as she held up a glass of ginger ale.

"A toast," Kevin said as the camera panned to him holding up a glass of champagne.

"A toast," Claus said as the camera went to him next as he held up a glass of champagne.

"Thank you," Joe said, not saying anything about Blair. Instead, he continued with his prepared speech. "Astroosa has been a leader in space exploration, having revolutionized precious metal acquisition. Thanks to Astroosa, precious metals are affordable. They are still special metals, but they have created whole new industries on Earth, making life better for the entire world. Now the time has come to start a colony on the moon, not only to establish a presence for research, but also to establish new industry in a low-gravity environment, manufacturing based on special metals. This colony will pave the way for a colony on Mars and beyond."

Applause from an audience on Earth.

"I have good news to pass on," Joe said. "No, I won't say. Our pioneering Doctor Morrow on the moon will tell us. Doctor?"

"Thank you, Joe. I'm proud to announce that I, Doctor Donna Morrow, will have the first baby on the moon!"

More applause.

"Congratulations, Doctor Morrow," Joe said. "On behalf of Astroosa and the people of Earth, I wish to—"

"No!" Claus interjected.

The camera panned to Claus, and he could hear the audience gasp.

"Blair. She—"

"Blair? What about Blair?" Joe asked.

The camera panned over to Mocha.

"Blair—" Claus started.

But Mocha interrupted Claus with a bark. The audience saw Mocha, heard the bark, and laughed.

"Blair's dog Mocha," Joe said. "Apparently our Astroosa crew has a great sense of humor."

"Oh yes," Doctor Morrow said to cover. "We enjoy all sorts of pranks up here."

"Yes, you do," Claus said to the doctor. "Tell everyone about the food rations. How they have a special ingredient."

"Nothing special there," the doctor said. "All rations contain vitamins for continued good health."

"Why don't you eat a ration and show us?" Claus said.

"Because this isn't the time for rations. We're celebrating victory. Victory over sabotage. Victory for Astroosa. Victory for the future and those who are born on this moon," Doctor Morrow said.

"I'm glad you think so. Because Blair is—" Claus started, but Doctor Morrow had Kevin cut the feed, "—pregnant. She will have her baby before you have yours. And no, your trick with RU-486 won't work."

"Doctor? What's going on up there?" Joe asked in a private feed.

"I'll report back later," the doctor said. "Tell the world we are experiencing technical difficulties."

Joe signed off.

"Yes. We're having technical difficulties," Doctor Morrow said. "Now I had Kevin cut the feed to spare your reputation, Claus. I know about Blair. She won't go to term. Sorry, but it had to be this way. I'm going to have the first baby on the moon, and that's final."

"I could have you prosecuted for attempted murder," Claus said.

"Really? I make all medical records here. And Joe has my ear. Remember, you're here on Astroosa's dime. Don't try anything foolish. I'll have your name smeared from sea to shining sea. Blair's name too. Stop the charade, Claus. I know she didn't come, because she's miscarrying as we speak. She could die without medical treatment, you know. Then it will be *your* neck on the chopping block. In prison for negligent manslaughter, a bad reputation. It doesn't look promising for you, does it? Now, let's go over to Novi 3. I may be ruthless, but I'm still a doctor. Blair is going to survive and see *me* as the first."

"You won't get away with this," Claus said.

Doctor Morrow laughed.

"Kevin, I'm going over to Novi 3 to treat Blair. Radio ahead to Astroosa and have a special television feed. I want the world to see how poor, unfortunate Blair is rescued by Doctor Morrow, the giver of life," the doctor said.

Kevin agreed.

"You don't seem to get it," Claus said. "If you open up a television feed, I'll tell them about the RU-486, that you caused the miscarriage."

"You won't, because if you do, Blair will 'magically' die, due to a bad miscarriage," Doctor Morrow said.

"You wouldn't," Claus said, playing up the situation.

Doctor Morrow nodded with determined affirmation.

"What's gotten into you? It can't be your pregnancy, can it? I mean, I've heard of baby hormones causing strange behavior, but this is ridiculous!" Claus said.

Doctor Morrow gathered together her medical bag.

"There's something else you should be aware of," Doctor Morrow said. "If you try something as foolish as speaking your mind out of line, I can and will inject you with a drug that will drive you mad. Viewers on Earth will see this. And the smear campaign will be in full force. Do I have your cooperation?"

Claus paused. He might have played along too far.

"I said, do I have—"

"Yes. Let's get on with it," Claus said.

Claus knew that Blair would not miscarry. But he was concerned for her safety. What if she became stranded out on the moon? She could be in trouble and need his help. He hoped she would be back in Novi 3 in time for his return so that Doctor Morrow would receive the shock of her life when she learned that Blair had kept her baby. It was this hopeful thought that kept his nerves steady.

Claus and Mocha returned in one rover while Doctor Morrow followed in another. As the two rovers approached Novi 3, Claus noticed Blair's rover had returned. Now the time had come. Dialog and timing were critical. He'd have to push hard for Blair's defense and Doctor Morrow's criminal act. Doctor Morrow had proved to be a manipulator, and so she might yet squirm out of this one. Claus had to be firm. He had to.

Chapter 147: Surprise in Novi 3

The rovers stopped at Novi 3. The three climbed out, went through the Novi 3 airlock, and took off their helmets and suits once inside. Blair was sitting at the dining table and helped unsuit Mocha.

"People of Earth, welcome to Novi 3," Blair said to a live camera. "Welcome back, Claus, Mocha, and Doctor Morrow."

"You are deathly ill, my dear. Let me help you," Doctor Morrow said as she prepared a syringe from her medical bag. "People of Earth. Blair has suffered a miscarriage and is in dire need of medical attention. We will need the utmost privacy of course to treat her."

"Nonsense," Blair said. "I'm feeling fine."

"Obviously delusional," Doctor Morrow said as she made to inject Blair with the syringe.

"Stop that now!" Claus said as he grabbed Doctor Morrow's hand.

"Claus. Cease and desist. You are interfering with official Astroosa business," Doctor Morrow said.

"Blair is going to have the first baby on the moon!" Claus said.

"Claus is delusional too," Doctor Morrow said. "I'll treat him first since he's also paranoid. Blair is not having the first baby on the moon."

"I have to agree with Doctor Morrow," Blair said.

"What?" Claus said in surprise.

"I'm not having the first baby on the moon," she said.

"My child! You don't need this syringe!" Doctor Morrow said as she made to put the syringe away (and Claus let her). "Let me hug you."

Doctor Morrow hugged Blair.

"Was the miscarriage difficult? Do you need treatment? I'm here at your disposal," Doctor Morrow said.

"Oh, I didn't miscarry," Blair said. "I'll carry to term."

"A trick. Still delusional!" Doctor Morrow said, suddenly breaking her hug from Blair and going back for the syringe.

"It's no trick!" Bill said as he suddenly appeared from another room.

"Bill!" Claus and Doctor Morrow said.

"Are you hurt? Do you need medical attention?" Doctor Morrow asked, suddenly changing her tune.

"I'm fine," Bill said.

"What happened? How did you survive?" Claus asked.

"Our ship plowed into the lunar dust. A moonquake buried us," Bill said.

"And Andrea perished. I'm so sorry," Doctor Morrow said.

"No I didn't," Andrea said as she walked from the same room with a toddler. "Say hello, Miranda."

"Hello," the little girl said.

"Miranda was born three years ago, in Novi 2," Andrea said.

"No. Another trick!" Doctor Morrow said.

"It's no trick," Bill said.

"I'm having the first baby on the moon. I am! Well! I will have the first authenticated birth on the moon. This little girl was shipped up here no doubt. Lots of possibilities," Doctor Morrow said.

"We kept very good records on this disk," Bill said as he produced a data disk from his pocket.

"Why didn't you let us know?" Claus asked. "We would have sent a rescue craft earlier."

"The far side has a way of blocking radio waves," Andrea said.

"Of course," Claus said. "But there was Prava 12."

"We tried to contact Prava 12, but our radio didn't work," Bill said. "By the time we repaired it, Prava 12's dish was pointed elsewhere. We weren't sure if our signal was getting through or not. We heard nothing back."

"The asteroid mining," Claus said with regret.

"We noticed the drone rovers that were sent to find us," Andrea said. "Strangely enough, they stopped short of our position."

"It was so obvious," Blair said. "I headed out and saw the line of them stopped from kilometers away. Once I reached the drone void, I received an automated radio call from Novi 2. It was weak, but it was audible. I replied, and I brought them over just now. Well? Isn't it a wonderful surprise?"

"A very interesting tale," Joe called back. "We've cut the global feed to the world. We'll dole out bits of this news as necessary through the PR department."

"Wait," Claus said. "You mean the world doesn't know that Bill and Andrea are alive and with us? What about Miranda?"

"All will be told in time. Attention, everyone. Get some rest. We'll discuss things in the morning. Joe out."

"How do you like that!" Claus exclaimed.

"We're going to have to arrest you," Bill said.

"Yes. For attempted murder," Andrea said. "Blair told us everything."

"You can't arrest me. I'm the doctor. I also happen to have the only uncontaminated food. How long can Blair last without eating? You'd better shape up, Astroosa folk!" Doctor Morrow said.

"I've been eating dog food," Blair said.

"An oversight on my part. I'll treat that next thing," Doctor Morrow said.

"No you won't," Blair said.

"It doesn't matter," Andrea said. "Bill and I have learned to produce our own food. We also found remnants of a prior civilization. It was that discovery that helped us survive."

"The Carinians!" Claus said.

"We don't know what they called themselves," Andrea said. "Their language is unknown. But we did figure out their machinery."

"We found a museum of sorts. Life preserved at various stages, including seeds of Earth crops. And there we go. Fruits and vegetables abound," Bill said.

"Maybe it wasn't a dream," Claus said. "Andrea, Bill. I must go over there and see."

"No!" Doctor Morrow insisted. "You've all gone mad! I'm going to sedate you all!"

Doctor Morrow took a sedative syringe from her medical bag and first went for Claus. It was Blair who darted over and clocked Doctor Morrow in the jaw, rendering her unconscious.

"Sorry," Blair said. "Ow, I think I broke my fingers."

"Is there a doctor in the house?" Bill joked.

"Yeah, right there," Andrea said pointing down.

Everyone but Claus laughed. Even Mocha laughed.

"It's not funny! This is a dire predicament," Claus said.

"She wasn't going to let you see Novi 2," Andrea said. "It threatened her. It was the only way. I just wish Blair had not paid the price with broken bones."

"I'll be okay," Blair said.

"There are facilities to treat those breaks in the caverns," Andrea said. "I'll take you there now."

"I'd like to go too," Claus said.

"Of course," Andrea said.

"Mocha too?" Blair asked.

"Mocha too," Andrea said.

"But not Doctor Morrow," Bill said. "The less she knows, the better. I'll lock her up here and keep watch over her. Miranda, you be a good girl and help your mother."

"I will," Miranda said.

Blair laughed.

"She's so cute!" Blair said. "I hope my baby is adorable like Miranda!"

"Do you know yet?" Andrea asked.

"Yes. It's a girl. Her name is Clossandra," Blair said.

"I'm happy for you," Andrea said as she gave Blair a hug. "Miranda will have a playmate in a few years. Okay, let's get you suited up. We're heading over to Novi 2. And the caverns."

Andrea, Blair, Miranda, Claus, and Mocha suited up. They left Novi 3 and headed for Novi 2. After traveling for a bit, Andrea stopped.

"What's wrong?" Claus radioed in his helmet.

"We're here," Andrea replied.

"Where is it?" Claus said. "I don't see it."

Andrea hit a button on her spacesuit. The rover dropped as if being swallowed by a sinkhole. It was then pulled into a cavern. Andrea started the rover forward and drove it along the cavern until it reached the Novi 2 spacecraft, which was totally within the cavern and had no apparent means of entry. Various lawn furniture and decorations adorned the area.

"You may remove your helmets. The air is breathable," Andrea said.

Everyone removed their helmets. Blair needed help removing hers.

"The medical facility is not in Novi 2 but is a little farther in this cavern," Andrea said.

Andrea drove the rover a little farther. The cavern changed from roughly-hewn to finely crafted, looking much like an underground city. But there were no inhabitants.

"I don't remember any of this," Claus said.

"What's that, Claus?" Andrea asked.

"I mean...I thought this would look like when I was...I mean...I had a dream about going below the lunar surface," Claus said.

"It looks like a small town, doesn't it?" Andrea said. "There appear to be shops everywhere. Of course, it's all deserted. Whoever was once here is now gone. But they left technology behind. Not enough for us to effect rescue, but enough to survive."

Andrea led them into what could pass for a small-town doctor's office. She had Blair remove the upper part of her spacesuit. Andrea next placed a portable

tube over Blair's hand, pressed a few buttons, and a spray came out of the tube.

"Ah, oh, oh!" Blair said.

"Does it hurt? It's not supposed to," Andrea said.

"No. It just feels strange. Like my hand is being packed in mud," Blair said.

"We'll need to keep your hand in the tube for five minutes," Andrea said.

"All this technology," Blair said. "And yet you couldn't radio Earth?"

"Whoever was here didn't use radio the way we do," Andrea said. "Not sure how they sent messages into space."

"Through the ether," Claus said, thinking about the Carinians going eethi.

"Well in a way of speaking, radio waves travel through the ether," Andrea said. "Bill and I also noticed there's no evidence of spacecraft. How they got here is a mystery."

"By going eethi," Claus said.

Andrea gave him a strange expression.

"Why do you say that, Claus?" Andrea asked.

"It was part of my dream. Carinians came here. They did have spaceships, but they also could travel through the ether. They called it going eethi," Claus said.

"Well, they are gone whoever they were," Andrea said.

"I feel much better," Blair said.

"Let's check," Andrea said.

Andrea hit a few buttons on the tube and studied a display screen.

"Well? Did it work?" Claus asked.

"You heal very quickly, Blair. All done," Andrea said.

Andrea removed the device. She then led them back to the rover, and the group rode around. Andrea showed them the farm Bill and she had created. At the end of their tour, they stopped at a museum. Here Andrea showed them the various animals and plants preserved.

"It looks like my dream, but not exactly the same," Claus said.

"We found crop seeds here and used them to start the garden. But we've been unable to bring domestic farm animals back to life. Otherwise we'd have chickens and pigs for food, too," Andrea said.

"I wouldn't mind having something to eat," Blair said. "I've been getting by on dog food to avoid the RU-486 in the rations."

"I can solve that right now," Andrea said. "We turned one of the stores into a little cafe. It's vegan, of course, but it's filling."

"Let's go!" Blair said.

"I'll catch up with you," Claus said. "I'd like to look in the museum a little longer."

"We'll be in Andrea's Cafe," Andrea said.

All left for the cafe, leaving Claus alone. He continued looking at the various museum pieces.

"Why don't I remember this part?" he asked. "Was this part of Luna Prime? Luna Beta? Maybe I really *did* dream everything. Maybe Lanietta is just a figment of my imagination."

Claus reached the end of one line of museum pieces. Before him was a rectangular stone pillar that was the size of a bench. He sat on it to rest.

"And now, in all this manic mess of the cosmos, I'm sitting alone in a corner on the moon," Claus said. "Where do I go from here? What do I do?"

Claus closed his eyes and thought of Lanietta, Labba, Leif, Clausetta, and Claude.

"Did I give them up for this? For Earth's preservation?" Claus asked himself. "Did Lanietta send me here to protect me? To protect Earth? I wonder if the PRAAD is here, buried deep in the moon? Lanietta would take credit for it, *if* she were here."

Claus stood and walked to a main juncture connecting the various lines of exhibits. He walked down another line and again there was a stone pillar resembling a bench. All such lines of walking revealed such pillars, but then he reached a particular one painted in yellow and blue.

"Yellow and blue. Oh, they were here. Carinians! This is the proof! Then it wasn't just a dream. Maybe Lanietta *did* send me back. Or maybe the Anrega really exists in Earth's core and influenced me, causing me to dream the Carinians," Claus said. "Now why is this one colored yellow and blue while the others are not? Is there something here? A lid perhaps?"

Claus noticed this pillar had a bit of a lip as if it were a window seat. He pulled upward on it, but it remained fast.

"Is there a latch? A keyhole?" he asked himself.

He found neither.

"Oh, I should have asked around at Frieda's funeral if anyone had a Veigonette stone. Maybe one of those holds the key," Claus said.

Claus kicked at the pillar. He yelled at it. He pounded on it. Nothing. Then an idea came to him, and he laughed.

"What if...oh, you clever girl! Lanietta, if this works, I'll know it was your doing!" Claus said.

He crossed his eyes and focused on the central mix of yellow and blue. The colors competed for dominance in his eyes, at times blue, and at times yellow. But each time one eye dominated, Claus switched to the other, even quickly swiping a hand across the dominant eye to break its grip. Slowly, the two colors mixed into a faded pea-green color. He placed a hand each on the colors, shouted, "Sassatinassa," and the lid opened.

"It worked. It worked!" Claus celebrated. "This was meant for me to find. Find and explore. But what is it? Steps going down. I'll go down. But I must not be trapped. I'll rest the lid on the back wall. There. I'll wedge my right boot near the hinge. Good. And the other boot will act as an emergency stop should the lid slam down. There. Down I go."

Claus climbed into the hollow pillar and walked down the steps. He reached a sub-cavern with the scent of formaldehyde.

"Smells like a high school biology lab," he said to himself.

The area was dark, but Claus must've tripped a sensor, because liquid-filled enclosures suddenly lit up. Then he saw what looked like Carinians from the time of Larto and Lanshalla.

"A graveyard. I've entered a graveyard of Carinians!"

These people were lying in repose and ornately dressed. They moved slowly up and down with the motion causing their clothing to flap slightly, as if a gentle breeze were carrying them to the afterlife.

"Do I recognize any of them? Libriota? Lanshalla? Larto? Treyu? Mariel? Any of the others? No, none are familiar," Claus said.

Claus reached the end of the passageway and found a podium with writing carved into the podium's stone top. It was written in a script Claus did not recognize.

"Carinian? I wish I could read it," Claus said.

Claus looked closely at the carving, and he noticed two colored circles the size of fingertip impressions at the top and close together, while he also noticed a fingertip impression at the lower left corner and another fingertip impression at the lower right corner. These four impressions were yellow on the left and blue on the right. Without much thought, Claus crossed his eyes while staring at the upper colors of yellow and blue. They mixed into a faded pea-green color, and an image of Larbiabba projected up against the wall. Claus broke his gaze from the colors to look, but this in turn ended the projection.

"Was that Larbiabba? Hard to tell. I must try again," Claus said.

Claus crossed his eyes again while staring at the colors. Larbiabba's image displayed against the wall above the podium. She spoke in one language, another, and another.

"It's a Rosetta stone of sorts," Claus said. "What are the chances I'll hear English?"

Claus had to wait several minutes before Larbiabba spoke old-sounding European languages. He then heard English.

"I has't a message. Putteth thy digits towards the baser col'rs of yellow and

blue," she said, paused, and continued, "I have a message. Place your fingers on the lower colors of yellow and blue."

Claus touched the yellow and blue impressions at the lower left and right corners.

"English. You may break your gaze from the upper colors, provided you keep your fingers on the lower colors," she said.

Claus did so. He looked up at the projection.

"It *is* Larbiabba. So not just a dream. Some form of reality. Can you hear me, Larbiabba?" Claus said.

"My name is Larbiabba. I am a Carinian from a red-dwarf solar system very distant from yours," Larbiabba said. "With this moon I have created this memorial, to honor a few of the many Carinians who perished in the Carinian Civil War. They should have lived forever. They did not. I ask you to leave them be. Do not disturb their repose. The war went poorly, and they (along with others after the war) are preserved here, as I fear that we Carinians will perish. Perhaps in time, beings wiser than us will bring a peace to the universe my race never could."

There was a pause.

"So this is a graveyard. Lanietta, what did you do? Was this better than...well...I guess you lost your people in my dream. Just you and Labba left," Claus said.

"One of us has chosen to be preserved for that day should a wiser race bring peace to the universe. She only asks that you give her a nice home in whatever zoo collection of beings you so create. She promises to perform tricks and entertain your youth for all eternity," Larbiabba said. "She is cryopreserved in this memorial, for your wise leaders to release."

"No!" Claus said. "Tricks? Performance? That's slavery! No being should suffer such a fate."

"Her name is Lanietta. Take good care of her. She represents the best of Carinian people," Larbiabba said. "For all Carinian people, I bid you peace and farewell."

Larbiabba's image ceased, yet Claus still had his fingers on the colored impressions. Then a sudden burst of laughter overcame him.

"The best of Carinian people?" Claus laughed. "Lanietta? What comedy! What farce! Oh the universe of unifalse! I cringe to think what a wiser race would find, when Lanietta's grip upon them she bind. Colossus. Calamity. A prescription for conniption! Let forces be may, let no one say I held my peace. Lanietta turns wise into geese. Honk, honk. Chase the geese! Honk, honk. A dime a piece!"

Claus's rant sent shudders through the chamber that grew into a rumble, a tremor, and a minor moonquake. The podium moved aside. Claus was pushed back (and so he lost his grip with the impressions). A cryopreservation tank ascended from a hole the podium had covered, and inside was the body of twelve-million-year-old Lanietta. She was bluish-green in her frozen appearance, and she had no appearance of life or movement. The moonquake subsided, the shudders dissipated, and the tank descended below from where it came. The podium rotated back with a thud and closed off access to her tank. All was quiet.

A voice broke the still air.

"Claus? Are you down there? Claus?" called Blair.

"I'm here. I'll be right up," Claus called back.

Claus took a brief look at the podium and then returned back to the yellow and blue pillar. He climbed steps out of it and was greeted by Blair.

"I saw your boots. What were you doing down there?" she asked with Mocha at her side.

"Exploring," Claus said while putting his boots back on.

"Find anything interesting?" she asked.

"Yes. A graveyard," Claus said.

"A graveyard! Of the aliens? The ones who created this place?" Blair asked.

"I believe so," Claus said.

"Sounds scary. Speaking of, I was worried about you. You never came to Andrea's Cafe. We've eaten and everything," Blair said. "Andrea says I'm fit enough to lift things. She's giving me several food containers to take back to Novi 3."

"I should help load them onto the rover," Claus said. "You may be healed, but your fingers might still be tender."

"They are. A little. I can help, though," Blair said.

Blair led Claus to another old-style store, in front of which was parked the rover. Inside the store were containers upon containers of food. Andrea and Miranda were inside with Andrea reviewing which containers should be loaded.

"Good, you found him," Andrea said, "I had become concerned. Parts of this cavern are unexplored. No telling what traps they might contain. Can't be too careful. Here, start with this one."

Blair took the container by herself while Mocha helped lead her to the rover.

"How much have you explored?" Claus said.

"All that you've seen here," Andrea said. "No trace of aliens themselves. Just what they created. Here, take this."

Claus took a container and loaded it in the rover. He headed back for the next container as Blair passed him with a container for the rover.

"This one is next," Andrea said to Claus. "Graveyard, eh?"

"What?"

"Blair says you found a graveyard. Did you?" Andrea asked.

"I think so," Claus said.

"You'll have to show me sometime. But let's finish loading the rover. I want to get back to Novi 3 and finish dealing with Doctor Morrow. The record must be set straight with her treason," Andrea said.

"Good idea," Claus replied.

With the rover loaded, the group backed out the way they came. They nearly reached the point where they'd fallen in when Andrea stopped the rover.

"Helmets all on? Check your local atmospheres," she said.

Claus checked his suit. A-okay. Blair checked hers and Mocha's—also A-okay.

Andrea in turn checked her suit and Miranda's. A-okay.

"Excellent," she said. "We're heading for the surface."

Andrea drove the rover over to an elevator. The elevator ascended and lifted the rover through a flexible top that acted as a one-way valve. It permitted the rover to go onto the moon's surface while maintaining a natural exterior appearance.

"I can't tell where the entrance is—or the exit," Claus said.

"We've kept this area hidden from view until we could decide if people are ready to see it. We'll keep it hidden a while longer," Andrea said.

The rover continued on toward Novi 3 and was almost there when Andrea hit a button on her suit to contact Bill.

"Bill, this is Andrea, do you read? Bill?" she called.

No reply.

"Bill, Claus here. We're almost at Novi 3. Lots of food containers to unload. Think you can help us?" Claus called. "Bill?"

Again, no reply.

"Bill? Can you hear me? It's Blair. Bill?" Blair called.

"Where's Bill?" Miranda called.

"Bill, we'll be there soon," Andrea said.

The rover arrived at Novi 3. No one bothered to unload the containers but instead went straight for the airlock. The outer airlock door was already open.

"Could Bill be expecting us?" Blair asked.

"Looks like it was left open. There are tracks here over our own, created after we left for Novi 2," Andrea said. "Let's go in."

The group went into Novi 3 using the airlock normally. Andrea performed a quick check of the air and spoke.

"Novi 3 has a good atmosphere," Andrea said. "You may remove your helmets. Bill?"

Andrea called for Bill, but he did not reply.

"Claus," Blair said. "These lights are flashing differently. They look important."

"The NASDI panel," Claus said.

Claus took a quick look.

"A sequence has been activated. It's almost like the detonation sequence used in Operation Astroosiate," Claus said. "To detonate this ship."

"Can you stop it?" she asked.

"I'll try," Claus said as he hit a few buttons. "There's a message. I need another command-grade person to unlock it."

"I can't find Bill anywhere," Andrea said after having checked much of the ship and not hearing Claus's previous words. "Doctor Morrow is gone too."

"Andrea," Blair said. "There's a message over here waiting for us. But we need you to help unlock it."

Andrea walked over. She and Claus allowed their retinas to be scanned, and a video message displayed at the panel. The video showed Doctor Morrow. She spoke.

"Andrea, Claus, and Blair. I have recorded this message so that you will find it. You are ordered to return to Earth immediately in Novi 3. By Joe Craigen. This order is final and irrevocable. The rescue mission is complete. You will be rewarded with a parade and a talk-show tour. Book and movie rights for your stories have already been contracted out. You'll be celebrities in your own right. You will be well-respected and well-cared for as long as you wish," Doctor Morrow said.

"Donna. This is Andrea. Where is Bill? We're not leaving without him," Andrea said.

"She can't hear you," Claus said.

"I have anticipated your questions and will answer them now. Bill is staying with Kevin and me to help pioneer the first Astroosa colony. I gave Bill the option to return home with you, but he has agreed to stay. I congratulate Bill on his strong sense of duty," the doctor said.

"He'd never!" Andrea blurted.

"Second. You must all leave. Andrea, Blair, Claus, Miranda, and Mocha. None must stay behind. Blair, you must have your baby on Earth. This is in the name of safety. We do not wish to lose any of you and don't want to be put in the position of launching yet another rescue mission to return dead bodies to Earth," the doctor said.

"It's okay," Blair said. "I don't need to have Clossandra on the moon. Not with that doctor ready to poison her or me."

"She's already tried to murder Clossandra. That will be reported to Earth first thing on return," Claus said. "How does she figure to get away with that?"

"Third. Don't get any foolish ideas of tarnishing my name. I have friends back on Earth. Chris didn't set fire to your house, Claus. My friends did. You'll be watched every moment on your return. Behave, and all is well. Misbehave, and you'll face the consequences," the doctor added.

"Then we must act now," Andrea said. "Attack Novi 4. Get Bill out and take Doctor Morrow back to Earth as our prisoner."

"Fourth. Any foolish attack on Novi 4 will result in your death or Bill's. But I won't kill him immediately. Each deviant act from the first moment you leave Novi 3 will result in the painful loss of Bill's fingers, one by one," the doctor said.

The video feed then panned over to Bill. A portable smashing device was attached to each hand. The device had a little smasher for each digit. Bill was able to use his hands for things, and Doctor Morrow had him solve a scrambled Rubik's cube to show how he still had dexterity. But Doctor Morrow then demonstrated how (with just a thought from her mind) she could inflict pain. Bill cringed from the pain, dropped the cube, and it shattered on the floor. The doctor reversed the process and stopped the pain.

"The cube represents what all of you will become should you deviate from orders," Doctor Morrow said. "The smasher is just for his digits. Bill's muscles are wired from his arms all the way to his heart. Should you be extremely vain and deviate in the most unimaginable way, his muscles will progressively convulse in like kind and eventually, if need be, arrest his heart. No more questions. Reply when you receive this message so that I will spare

Bill such agony. Your NASDI panel shows how much time you have before his digits become smashed."

"The panel is in the negative," Andrea said.

"His torture has already started," Blair said.

Andrea put her hands over her mouth, closed her eyes, and bowed her head in despair.

"Bill!" she then shouted in anguish.

"Mommy, where's Daddy?" Miranda asked.

Andrea looked around like a caged animal seeking escape.

"Blair, the tank below," Claus said. "Maybe Jill can help us."

"Tank? What tank?" Andrea asked.

"Andrea, stall for time if you can," Claus said.

"Bill's already being tortured," Andrea said.

"I know. But if there's a way out, the tank will have an answer. No time to explain. Blair, let's go," Claus said.

Claus, Blair, and Mocha went below. Claus could hear Andrea open up a communication line with Doctor Morrow.

"She's sweet-talking the doctor," Claus said.

"It's an act," Blair said.

Andrea thanked the doctor for her help and had Miranda talk to Bill about the great things she looked forward to when back on Earth. Claus and Blair prepped very quickly and jumped into the tank. Claus activated the tank. An image of Jill displayed.

"Olivia. This is Claus and Blair," Claus said. "We need your help. We're still on the moon in Novi 3. We found Andrea and Bill. They have a daughter named Miranda. Doctor Morrow has gone crazy. She's kidnapped Bill and is holding him in Novi 4. Kevin is in Novi 4 too, I guess, but she hasn't said anything about him. Doctor Morrow is forcing Andrea, Miranda, Blair, Mocha, and me back to Earth in Novi 3. She's torturing Bill now to ensure our compliance. What can we do? If we don't all leave, she'll take it out on Bill."

"I never anticipated this," Jill said. "The tank will help you gather information, but you can't use it to affect others directly. I can help you protect those in your keep. But that's all. I actually thought I'd go to the moon someday. I even thought I'd go there with you, Claus. I so strongly believed in my trip that I made provisions to create your doppelganger, the fanciest robot every conceived, to provide me companionship in case you could not make the trip. But I did not think to provide one of me for your comfort in the event of my absence. I'm sorry."

The image of Jill faded.

"Well. That's it," Blair said. "Even Jill can't help us."

"No, no!" Claus refused to believe. "Wait. Jill can't help us, but Olivia can."

"I don't understand. They are the same people," Blair said.

"No, they're not. Olivia was still concerned about me. She created this tank and my proposed double. Jill lost interest in me and went after Josh," Claus said.

"I still don't understand," Blair said.

Claus activated Jill's image.

"Prepare to create Claus's doppelganger," Claus said.

"What? What are you doing?" Blair asked.

"Constraint violation. Insufficient free space in tank," Jill's image said.

"You have to get out, Blair. You have to get out of the tank," Claus said.

"So you can create your own double? Why?" Blair asked. "That won't bring Jill back. Or Bill."

"But it will allow me to stay when you all leave," Claus said.

"Oh, no. I'm not leaving this tank," Blair said.

Claus stopped the tank operation and climbed out.

"It's the only way," Claus said. "Doctor Morrow will see my double and be convinced we're all leaving."

"Really? And what will you do? Drive over to Novi 4 and defeat her? By yourself?" Blair asked.

"Something like that," Claus said.

"This is lunacy!" she said.

"I'm on the moon. The moon is crazy. Yes, I guess it's lunacy. But I have to try," Claus said.

"What about me? And Clossandra?" Blair asked. "It's bad enough Miranda is losing her father. Now you decide the same fate for Clossandra."

"I don't plan on staying here forever," Claus said. "I'll return. If my double is good enough, she won't know the difference."

"A robot father. Of all the indignities!" Blair said.

Blair fell into tears.

"C'mon. Time is short. This is the only way," Claus said.

Blair pulled herself together, agreed, and stepped out of the tank.

"You return to Earth as soon as you can. Do you hear?" she insisted, being emotionally caught between sadness and anger.

"I hear," Claus said.

Claus jumped back into the tank. He activated the controls.

"Begin doppelganger creation of Claus," he said.

The tub filled with a special fluid and swirled about him. Waves and bubbles formed. Then Claus fell below the bubbles into the fluid and so disappeared from view. A moment passed, and a shape appeared above the bubbles.

"Claus? Is it working? I just see you. Claus!" Blair said.

He climbed out of the tank. Then a lid came down over the tank and sealed it.

"What happened?" Blair asked. "What about your double?"

"Stand back," he said.

The two stood back, the floor opened, and the tank descended to a compartment below.

"That's the end of the tank," he said.

"I'm sorry it didn't work out," she said. "But I'm glad I have you back. Let's go up and tell Andrea. I'm sorry about Bill too, but we'll sort out things on Earth. I promise."

The two cleaned up quickly then went above, where Miranda was giving her last goodbye.

"Bye-bye," Miranda said.

"Bye-bye," Bill replied.

"I'm so touched by your farewell that I've relieving Bill from his torture. I thought you were delaying on purpose," Doctor Morrow said.

"Blair's broken bones took a little time to heal," Andrea said.

"Yes," Blair said, now showing up into Doctor Morrow's view. "My hands are perfectly normal. See?"

Blair wiggled her fingers.

"Impressive. I'll have Bill show me this alien technology," she said. "Well, it's time then. Where's Claus?"

"Here," he said.

"You had me worried for a moment. I thought you might waste time on last-moment heroics," she said.

"Ready to go home," he said.

"Good. Novi 3 has been configured for return. Take your places. I'll trigger its launch from here," Doctor Morrow said. "Yes, thank you everyone for your contributions. Soon you'll be back on Earth, and all will be bright and happy."

Andrea ensured the others were strapped then strapped herself in last. Doctor Morrow hit a button on her end, with the video feed still running.

"Ignition confirmed. We're taking off," Andrea said.

"Excellent. I'll contact you when you reach Earth. Farewell for now," Doctor Morrow said, and the feed stopped.

"Bill," Andrea said very low, but Blair heard it.

"We'll figure something out," Blair said. "Won't we Claus?"

"Yes," he said.

"So the tank wasn't helpful? Whatever this tank is? Maybe I can take a look at it when we return to Earth," Andrea said.

"Sure," Blair said.

Novi 3 just barely cleared a ridge, and as it did, a bang and shudder carried through the craft.

"What happened?" Blair asked. "Did we hit something?"

"I...this is strange," Andrea said. "Claus, do you see it? The ship is breaking apart."

"Ship is in good state," he said.

"Obviously not true. A piece has broken off. No, not just broken off," Andrea said. "A hatch door has broken off, yes. But something was jettisoned. I'll divert and investigate."

"No," he said. "Doctor Morrow will detect. Bill will suffer."

"Claus. Check your panel. Are you sure this ship is safe?" Andrea asked. "You're a pilot. Remember? A pilot must know the state of the craft. Well?"

"Look!" Blair said.

A display screen showed what looked like a person navigating a rover, starting in a spot where debris from Novi 3 had just fallen. The person and rover were heavily covered in dust and camouflage, looking all the part of a lunar boulder.

"Someone's in that rover," Andrea said.

The display stopped.

"What are you doing?" Blair said.

"I cut the feed. Just in case," Andrea said.

"Just in case of what?" Blair asked.

Andrea turned out the lights. Miranda screamed in fright, and Mocha barked.

"It's all right," Andrea said, now standing up with a UV flashlight lit in her hand. "Just testing a theory. Open wide, Claus."

"What?" he said. "What is this? We're leaving the moon, and you're checking for a sore throat?"

"No, not a sore throat," she said. "I saw enough when you spoke. Yup, just as I thought. No dental work."

Andrea turned the lights back on.

"What do you mean, no dental work?" he asked.

"Oh, I don't believe it!" Blair said.

"Believe what?" he said.

"Impressive," Andrea said. "A complete duplicate of Claus. But with original teeth. No amalgams, no crowns—just enamel all around."

"Claus!" Blair yelled. "That was him on the surface! In the rover."

"There was something else in the rover. A large container," Andrea said. "What did you two do down below before we took off?"

"Claus and I went into the tank. He looked for an answer to the crisis. Jill's image popped up and could offer no help. She mentioned being able to make a double of Claus for her comfort if needed. Then he said he would have to make one so he could remain behind. But he didn't. At least I thought. It must have been the double that climbed out of the tank. The tank was closed and moved down below. I thought it was being hidden."

"He must be taking it with him. Probably to the alien cavern and Novi 2," Andrea said. "Well, he won't starve."

"I was completely fooled," Blair said. "I thought this double was really him."

"That was part of the ruse. To convince Doctor Morrow. Blair, you must continue the facade. No one on Earth must know," Andrea said.

Blair nodded in agreement.

"Now I feel more hopeful about Bill. I wish I were the one in Claus's shoes, but I'll do my part. We'll go through with the Earth shenanigans to buy cover for the real Claus. Think you're up to it?"

"I am," Blair said. "Claus, are you ready to celebrate our return?"

"I am indeed," he said. "I'm already planning a quiet dinner for the two of us. With special caffeine-free coffee."

"Decaf? How special? With alcohol?" Blair asked with interest.

"Just how well did Jill create this double?" Andrea mused.

"I'm dying to find out," Blair grinned.

"Don't die too soon," Andrea said. "He might be helpful in other ways. And not just for evening coffee. Blair? Focus."

"How can I focus when I have before me Jill's idea of the perfect man, at least for dinner and drink," Blair said.

"Don't lose yourself in the moment. Baby before booze. Besides, I fear the moon colony will have its own issues. And I'm not willing to have Bill replaced with a clone," Andrea said.

Chapter 148: Two

Claus navigated the camouflaged rover to the Novi 2 cavern. He retraced his steps back to the museum and to the yellow and blue stone pillar—while pulling Jill's tank on a cart.

"I'm going to do it," Claus said. "I'm going to find a way to bring Lanietta to consciousness. If anyone can sort out this situation, she can."

Claus lifted the pillar's lid.

"The opening is just large enough for the tank. But I can't carry the tank down. I really need two people. Now what?" he wondered.

Claus looked at the tank, and he looked at the opening.

"I can slowly wheel it down on the cart. It's tied down, so it shouldn't slide off. But it's a one-way trip. I won't have the power to pull it back out," he said.

Standing upstairs from the cart, Claus slowly rolled it down, step-by-step. He braced his feet against the pillar's edge, but once he himself had to go through the opening and follow the cart down, he realized that he had nothing to help slow the cart's roll down the step. The cart pulled harder and harder, and Claus strained just to keep it in place.

"No. It's falling down. It's going to pull me with it. Out of control. Oh, this is going to be bad. Very bad!" he lamented.

It happened. His strength gave out, the cart clattered down the steps with increasing speed, yet Claus held onto the cart's handle in a vain hope of stopping it before it crashed. All that did was pull him head-first down the steps and slam his jaw repeatedly against step after step. He finally let go when he reached the bottom. The cart rolled straight down the passageway and crashed against the podium. Claus half-expected to wake the interred Carinians and incur their wrath for disturbing their peaceful repose, but that didn't happen.

Claus paused. He was stunned really, and he wasn't sure how badly he was hurt. He gingerly arighted himself and sat on a lower step. Touching his face, he realized he was bleeding from a cut lip, busted teeth, and a broken nose. His face swelled up immediately, and it went through oscillations of numbness, dull pain, sharp pain, stinging pain, and back to numbness. He tried to speak but struggled.

"I...am still here," he mustered, sounding like his mouth was full of cotton.

Claus tried to stand, but he was in too much pain, so he crawled toward the tank. But this also hurt, so with a big grimace, he pulled himself to his feet.

"Focus," he tried to say. "Just one more step. One more step."

One step at a time, he made his way to the tank. The collision with the podium had caused the cart to fall on its side, and the tank with it.

"Oh, I dread what I must do. Why can't this all end now?" he muttered.

He loosened the ropes between the tank and cart, but this act was painful, as his hands and shoulders also hurt from the fall. But he made progress and managed to move the ropes and cart aside. Then came the task he most dreaded. Arighting the tank. It was dented from the collision, and he wasn't even sure it would work. He tried pulling it up. No good. He tried tying a rope to it and pulling it up. No good either, as he had no pulley, and the tank simply spun around. But it spun in a way where he could sit between the tank and the podium, wedge his legs under it, and push it up. The tank was arighted. Claus sat for a moment to catch his breath.

"Why is that tank so heavy?" he wondered aloud. "Oh, this is impossible! And yet, here still I am."

Claus panted for a bit before regaining his breath and strength. His hands swelled from being injured, and he found that performing each dextrous task was increasingly more difficult.

"Where is Lanietta?" Claus asked himself. "The podium. Are the colors still there? Can I still cross my eyes?"

Claus went up to the podium. It and the colors were intact. As before, he stared at the upper colors and crossed his eyes. The colors fought for dominance, and Claus found the middle ground of the faded pea-green color. Larbiabba appeared.

"It's you again," she said. "You have been warned to leave my people undisturbed. Your return has damaged this podium. You must leave immediately and never return."

"No. I must see Lanietta," Claus said.

"She is for wiser beings. Your savagery disqualifies you," she said.

"If you could know what I've shared with Lanietta, you'd know that I come not for me, but for others," Claus said. "I ask for Carinian compassion, that it be spent on my kind. If we are still as savage as you say, then we are in the most need."

"Carinians are not ones to waste effort on lesser beings," Larbiabba said.

Claus felt adrenaline build from within, giving him strength and courage. It also reduced swelling in his face, allowing for better enunciation.

"Lanietta did. At least the one I knew did. You've preserved an innocent one. No, you've imprisoned her," Claus said. "She may have seemed like a troublemaker at first, but in my time with her, she invested her efforts into humanity. She claims to have created Earth. That makes her the caretaker. Or the gardener. And I as a human along with humanity have grown up in the garden she planted. Is it wrong to send us away? Inhabitants of Lanietta's garden?"

"You are like the rabbits who eat the carrots Lanietta would plant. You despoil and disgrace her would-be garden," Larbiabba said.

"Okay. We are the rabbits. At least we started that way. But we're just now moving out into the universe. We'll make our own garden," Claus argued.

"You will despoil yet more gardens planted by other gardeners. You are in no position to claim title of gardener!" Larbiabba retorted.

"Maybe not. But I'm Clomper, her pet. You don't separate someone from their pet," Claus said. "Put the question to her. Does she wish to be with her pet Clomper?"

"Lanietta has no pet named Clomper," Larbiabba said.

"She sent me into this timeline," Claus said. "But in my time, she was four-and-a-half billion years old. She should be that age by now. But you have frozen her. You have deprived her of life."

"You're repeating yourself," Larbiabba said.

Claus took a deep breath.

"Lanietta once told me that the greatest torture is being caught between moments in time, that all of one's memory and being is drained away into nothingness," Claus said. "I put to you that you have done the same to her. You have drained away her Carinian self, her unique self that makes her special, as all such life-forms have."

"You are blaming me? Taking no responsibility for yourself?" Larbiabba said.

"What responsibility? I have nothing to do with her preservation as she is now in," Claus said.

"You didn't try to destroy her from the Mad Mistral, shooting into the ocean and hitting Clover instead?" Larbiabba said. "Or later drown her as a rat?"

"You can't know about that...that...that other timeline!" Claus said.

"Lanietta has been frozen to protect her from your other timeline and others beyond that. She will remain pure and uncontaminated. No Carinian should be forced to create a planet and care for its life-forms. The burden is too great. Too great. Too great," Larbiabba said.

"No child is too great a burden. No creation deserves abandonment. A dream will always end and die, unless it becomes creation. I am the metaphor of Lanietta's creation, her tortured but physically real result of her dreams," Claus said.

"Carinians don't sleep. They don't have dreams," Larbiabba said.

"Prove your statement," Claus said. "Prove that Lanietta has not dreamed. By freezing her, you've forced her to dream. Yes, in your desire to protect her from other timelines, you've exposed her to something you've never experienced. The dream. Fantasy and irrationality complete and total. And for how long? Longer than my own lifespan? Longer than the modern human race? Take accountability for your actions, Larbiabba. You've contaminated her with dreams!"

A great rumbling started in the chamber. Those who were preserved stirred slightly. Voices whispered throughout, pleading with Larbiabba that Lanietta be stopped from dreaming, that this was a bad thing, Lanietta can't be contaminated, she must be awakened and checked for Carinian sanity. Larbiabba pleaded with them that Lanietta stay cryopreserved, but their whispers grew louder and more demanding. Larbiabba raised her arms and placed her hands at the side of her head as if trying to block them out. The rumbling lowered to a murmur.

"Carinians don't dream," Larbiabba repeated as she lowered her arms.

"It is you who now repeats. But Carinians can dream. You should know. You were there when Larto dreamed of dalphinacs and walcowats," Claus said. "Claim it wasn't a dream."

"It wasn't," Larbiabba said.

"Exactly. He was experiencing a different time and place. This means Lanietta is experiencing a different time. Right now. You haven't protected her from another timeline. You've forced her into one!" Claus said.

Now the rumbling was in near explosion of frenzy. Larbiabba defended herself by saying Lanshalla had just performed the baby option and needed help, but the baby option was accidental, no, she herself didn't approve of the baby option, that this was a misunderstanding, and to give her time to sort things out. But the frenzied voices did not abate, and some fought to release Lanietta while Larbiabba fought to keep Lanietta restrained. This struggle manifested itself on Lanietta's container, which alternated between rising up above floor level and returning below. Larbiabba's strength weakened, and Lanietta's container spent more time above ground. In fact, the door to her container started to open a bit but then closed, opened a bit more, then closed again. It continued this way with Larbiabba practically shouting at the other voices.

Claus realized this was his moment. When the door opened as much as he thought it would, he reached in and pulled Lanietta out. Her body was light and frail, as if she were only partway in his universe. Not fully corporeal. Translucent. As if made from the wings of a butterfly.

"No!" shouted Larbiabba.

The other voices yelled so loudly that Larbiabba thought her head would explode. She put a hand to a side each of her head as if to hold it together. Claus held Lanietta in his arms for a moment before placing her in the tank.

"You're so cold, so lifeless," he said.

Claus had her in the tank with her back against one end—away from the controls, while he sat near the controls and with his back against the other end. In this way, he was toe-to-toe with Lanietta, which was quite the opposite orientation he had with Jill and Blair of back-to-back. He then activated the controls.

"This would normally pull in the coffee fluid, but...oh, what's this?" he said.

Instead of coffee fluid, foam filled the tank.

"So that's why it was so heavy," he said.

"Constraint violation," image of Jill said. "Unknown life-form in the tank. Abort. Abort."

"This is one life-form I won't abort!" Claus said. "Constraint limiter—disengage!"

"Claus. I have no safeguards for what you are doing," image of Jill said. "I cannot answer to the outcome. You could be in danger."

"I have been in danger since I threw my first model airplane into the neighbor's yard and was bitten by his dog," Claus said. "Now I'm the dog. I do the biting!"

Claus hit other controls. The foam swirled slowly and took on colors of yellow and blue.

"Now you did it," said one of the voices. "You allowed the human to use his own interactions tank."

"Terminate them both," said another.

"No. Wait," Larbiabba said. "The situation is yet salvageable."

The yellow-blue colors started to coalesce into a faded pea-green color, and Claus realized this was too green for Lanietta.

"More blue. She needs more blue!" Claus said. "Help. Someone help me!"

With one arm, Larbiabba channeled blue energy from the interred Bleuhs and with the other arm transmitted that blue energy to the tank. The colors fully coalesced into Lanietta, bringing out her natural Bleuh-Gren color of blue-green.

"Lanietta! Wake up!" Claus commanded. "It's me! Clomper!"

Lanietta's fragile body took in the foam as if hydrating, and she attained a full humanoid form.

"Clomper?" she asked as she opened her eyes.

"Yes! It's your Clomper!" he cried.

"She can't maintain shape. She'll degrade into nothingness," Larbiabba said.

"No. She can't," Claus said. "The blue energy. Give me some of the blue energy."

"You're not Carinian. You don't know how to use it," Larbiabba said.

"I don't care. I have to try. Hurry!" he said.

"No, no!" the voices whispered loudly. "Not for those kind! Not for beasts!"

"It's the only way," Larbiabba said.

Larbiabba spread her fingers apart on her transmitting hand, which allowed the blue energy to fall on both Lanietta and Claus.

"Clomper," she said.

"Lanietta," he said.

"I feel I know you from another time," she said.

"You do," Claus said.

Claus hit several buttons as the energy coursed through his body like a billion needles. He vocalized the strain. But then the billion needles shot through his legs and into his feet.

"My feet are like fire!" Claus said.

"So are mine!" Lanietta said. "Two feet become four."

"Like a dog," Claus said.

"You are my Clomper," she said. "My pet. Stand."

Lanietta took Claus by the hands, and she had him stand up with her. Both stood, with her toes touching his and her hands also touching his. As they stood, Lanietta's original container shot up to the cavern's ceiling, plunged into it, and grew into a long, cylindrical shape. It then traveled downward and over the tank, enveloping it.

"We must travel," Lanietta said.

"No!" the voices yelled.

Lanietta changed color to that of mostly white with a streak of grey on the right side and a patch of amber on the left. The cylindrical tube shot the tank upward, above the cavern, and above the moon's surface. Claus was afraid that he and Lanietta would be thrown into the vacuum of the moon, but the cylinder had extended itself upward too, and so they were still inside it and protected by it. The tube reached high enough such that Claus could see for miles in all directions. He could see Novi 4.

But something was strange. There was movement of great speed around Novi 4. New construction sprouted at lightning pace, as if Claus were watching a sped-up movie.

"What's happening?" Claus asked.

"It. Your people are colonizing the moon," Lanietta said.

"But Blair and the others," Claus wondered.

"Are safe. So is Bill. Doctor Morrow was exposed and put away in the first lunar prison. Andrea returned and helped Bill colonize the moon. Look at everything. So quick!" Lanietta said.

"I'm speeding through time. But Blair—" Claus protested.

"Is in her own time," Lanietta said. "But there is conflict brewing. Our time is colliding. Because," and here Claus involuntarily and unexpectedly jumped back to Lanietta's lair on the old near side in the Frieda-far-side-ruled timeline and with (young) Lanietta keeping her same form, "I must converge the bifurcation, like a tree healing a wound."

Young Lanietta stared at the yellow half and blue half of the lair. In each half she saw the adult form of herself, as if each were trapped and asking for help. Claus looked down on the floor.

"Fronfa!" Claus said. "It's there on the floor. Older Lanietta said it would be here if I needed it."

"Yes. Fronfa is here," young Lanietta said. "But I cannot reach it."

"What? I don't understand," Claus said.

"I'm not fully here," she said. "I can see but not interact. You are here. You must hand it to me."

Young Lanietta held out a hand to receive the stone. Claus picked up Fronfa. Already he could feel tension in the stone, like millions of micro ants stinging him. He nearly dropped the stone, but he handed it to young Lanietta.

Or did he? Instead of young Lanietta taking it, she placed his hands together, forcing Fronfa between his palms. The stinging now affected both hands. Young Lanietta placed a hand above and a hand below his hands for a moment then pushed her hands in between his hands. The stinging subsided. She withdrew her hands from his hands then turned them upward to show that Fronfa had split and melded with her hands—yellow on the left and blue on the right. Claus looked at his own palms and half-expected to see the same yellow and blue. But he did not. Instead, his palms were red with inflammation and swelling.

"What...is this?" he asked.

He looked up to ask, but instead of receiving an answer, he saw that young

Lanietta now pulled older yellow Lanietta to her left side and older blue Lanietta to her right. They each placed a hand on younger Lanietta's shoulders—blue Lanietta's left hand on younger Lanietta's right shoulder, and yellow Lanietta's right hand on younger Lanietta's left shoulder.

"Are you all there? Lanietta? Who am I speaking to?" Claus asked.

The Laniettas did not answer. Instead, a tube similar to the one from Doctor Morrow's moon timeline sprung forth from Lanietta's lair on Frieda's moon, and the tube elevated the two (I count the Laniettas as one) above the lunar surface to a similar height. The top was open, and the two stood on a platform with a railing. A lunar breeze blew through Claus's and Lanietta's hair. Claus looked around and saw Leif's airplanes continue their flight toward the old far side. But far in the distance toward the old far side, Claus saw a tube rise from the lunar ground not unlike the one he was in.

"It's Clausetta, you know," younger Lanietta said. "She intends to destroy Frieda with her own sacrifice."

"You speak as if you know her," Claus replied.

"I'm linked in with my other timeline selves," younger Lanietta said. "I can speak as one."

"Will Clausetta kill herself?" Claus asked.

"Worse," younger Lanietta said.

"What's worse than that?" Claus asked. "Show me. Show me this new horror!"

Younger Lanietta commanded the tube to arc up into the sky then back down to Clausetta's perch. When they arrived, they saw first one tube then another and another sprouting out of Clausetta's waistline. The tubes grew in length and arced up into the sky, as if becoming launch tubes. They were. Small points of light traveled through the tubes and took on suborbital flight before disappearing over the horizon onto the old far side. As more and more tubes sprouted out, they shrank in diameter near Clausetta but then expanded in diameter as they ran farther out. The tubes close to her were so fine as to look like long fur, and their outward expanse initially resembled a tutu but then grew into a straw-like dress.

"What are you doing?" Claus asked.

"I am fighting the cubics," Clausetta said in a zombie-like state.

"How? Clausetta!" Claus said.

"She has done what I could never do," blue Lanietta said.

"What? What is she doing?" Claus asked.

"She is blasting her unborn, uncombined children into the ether and fighting the cubics in that realm. Doing a fair job of it too," yellow Lanietta said.

"A *fair* job? There's nothing fair about it!" Claus protested. "Clausetta! Stop this at once!"

"Must...stop...Frieda," Clausetta said.

"Lanietta, you stop her," Claus said.

"She's right, you know. Without her intervention, Frieda will take over the entire ether. And is on the verge of doing so anyway. Your help is appreciated and necessary, Clausetta, but it is not enough," younger Lanietta said. "I will help, but first you must help me."

Younger Lanietta approached Clausetta and made to hug her. As she did, the fur dress collapsed slightly where younger Lanietta approached. Younger Lanietta then gave Clausetta a hug, and Clausetta hugged back.

"I will now be the pet," younger Lanietta said.

"I don't understand," Claus said.

New hairlike-tubes sprouted from Clausetta's abdomen, grew, and wrapped themselves around Lanietta (all three).

"Are you going to kill Lanietta? Clausetta?" Claus said to Clausetta.

Lanietta (the three) was completely covered in these microtubes and so hidden from view. After a moment, Lanietta emerged as one, but instead of being the humanoid that Claus expected, she had taken the form and hair-length of a full-grown sheepdog, with long, white, puffy hair on her head and upper body, and the same puffy but grey hair below. She had a splotch of amber hair on her left ear while her right ear was grey. There was no evidence of the yellow and blue Laniettas, other than these grey and amber colorations.

"What? Lanietta?" Claus asked.

"I told you. I'm now your pet," she said while standing on her hind legs.

Claus looked into her eyes and the long hair flowing down. She looked very old and worn.

"Lanietta. You're not my pet," Claus said softly. "I..."

Lanietta the sheepdog licked his face as a dog would its master. Claus giggled.

"Stop. Stop!" he pleaded. "You're licking my face."

Lanietta hugged Claus, then she pulled back. She stood toe-to-toe, held his hands, and leaned back.

"Don't let go, or I'll fall," she said.

The Claus-Lanietta tube platform pulled away from Clausetta (with Claus and Lanietta on it). It rotated as it moved away, creating a twist in its form. After several twists, the two were back on Doctor Morrow's moon. The two watched as Morrow's moon became a vast manufacturing colony, with perpendicular roads and rising, narrow buildings. Lanietta closed her eyes and held out a paw. The tube opened up at the top. Claus shrieked, as he expected a vacuum to pull the breath from his lungs, but instead he choked on heavy carbon dioxide levels from the newly-made lunar atmosphere.

"I can't breathe. It's like Arberella. Only worse," Claus said. "Lanietta, help!"

Lanietta held out a paw, and fresh air from below restored Claus's breathing. It also flowed through her fur and caused it to puff up a bit.

"Is this what Doctor Morrow did? Created a lunar atmosphere?" Claus asked.

"A byproduct of lunar production," young Lanietta said.

"But why here? Earth has manufacturing. Earth has production," Claus said.

"Does it?" Lanietta asked.

"Yes. Of course," Claus said.

Lanietta held out a paw. The two slipped down the tube, into the cavern, and landed at the airlock of Novi 2. Lanietta led Claus inside.

"Let's see. Take us to Earth," she said.

"Okay. I will. I'll show you," he said. "This is different. For once I'm calling the shots and leading you around. For once I'll have peace of mind that you're not twisting me into a moment of strain and misery."

The two returned to Earth with Claus piloting Novi 2. But to Claus's amazement, tall buildings, concrete roadways, and manufacturing plants were missing. Forests, farms, and waterways dominated Earth's surface. Claus spent extra time flying Novi 2 above Earth's surface to be sure.

"It's like civilization is gone," Claus said while flying Novi 2. "But the people can't be gone."

"The manufacturing is gone," young Lanietta said. "Let's land."

Claus landed in an open field. He led Lanietta outside, who used all fours for locomotion. She posed as Claus's dog. The two met up with others walking their dogs. Some paid notice to Novi 2 and mentioned how it was an antique and no longer of interest.

"What a wonderful dog you have," said one to Claus.

"Old English Sheepdog, right?" said another.

"It looks like an original breed. Not mixed with any other. Pure," said a third.

"What's your dog's name?" a fourth asked.

"Sassatinassa," Claus said.

"Hi Sassa," said a girl to Lanietta.

Lanietta barked softly.

"She likes me," the girl said.

"This seems like a paradise," Claus said as he led Lanietta along. "People are happily enjoying a natural environment."

"The uglies of manufacturing are performed on the moon," Lanietta said.

"The precious metals. They must have cheapened space travel significantly," Claus said.

Lanietta barked in agreement.

"You can say, 'yes'," Claus said. "You don't have to bark."

"There are people around who would be frightened by a talking dog," Lanietta said. "Look at the long shadows cast by the setting sun, so orange and brilliant like a friendly campfire, or the brilliant leaves of autumn."

"I just can't believe we finally made it," Claus said. "It makes me weep for the other timeline with Frieda running the far side and the war with Leif and Clausetta. And that's just for Luna. Earth is destroyed in that timeline. We beat that doomsday scenario in this one. Peace and beauty are here to stay."

The sun set. The moon rose in the east. Except it wasn't the moon as Claus remembered it. The lunar development had covered up the craters and maria, replacing them with a shiny grid-like pattern.

"It's like a hazy ball-bearing of great size!" Claus said. "What game is this? Throughout the history of people, no matter how good or bad the situation, we could always look up to the moon and trust it would be there, appearing just the same. Like an old friend. Now it's ruined! How can anyone enjoy time on Earth being forced to look at that?"

"Don't worry about it," young Lanietta said.

"How can you say that? Oh, I'm not safe in any time or space," Claus said.

"Exactly," several Laniettas suddenly said at once.

Blue Lanietta had split from sheepdog Lanietta and stood at Claus's right as her humanoid self. Yellow Lanietta had also split and stood at sheepdog Lanietta's left—again as her humanoid self. Claus looked around. Behind him was the lush Earth while ahead of him was Frieda's lunar old far side.

"We're connecting the timelines," they said. "The primary with the backup."

"Backup? What? Timelines don't have backups," Claus said.

"And you're an expert on timelines?" yellow Lanietta said.

"The backup is a fail-safe," blue Lanietta explained to Claus.

"Clomper doesn't believe in fail-safes," yellow Lanietta said.

"Then how does he mend the universe back together after a rip or rupture?" sheepdog Lanietta asked.

"He doesn't. That's why he's just a pet," blue Lanietta said.

"You can't have a backup timeline!" Claus said. "Someone has to make a backup from a primary source. The universe is not something a man can 'back up'."

"Pet talk," yellow Lanietta said.

The Laniettas laughed.

"I had to make this backup, Clomper," yellow Lanietta said. "I know your desire to make a child with whatever Carinian or human comes along is your idea of making a backup, but—"

"How dare you!" Claus said.

"Clomper!" sheepdog Lanietta said.

"Am I wrong?" blue Lanietta asked.

"That's not the point. You shouldn't speak like that!" Claus said.

"Oh? You wish to stamp out discussion? Squash evidence of your inadequacy?" yellow Lanietta asked.

"Creating life is not inadequacy," Claus said.

"It is the way you do it. You create and let it go," blue Lanietta said.

"We care for our young. Provide food and shelter," Claus said.

"Hmm, yes," yellow Lanietta said sarcastically. "And if the child passes away, there's no backup plan to bring the child back to life. No, the backup is to make another one."

"I would slug you if you were a man," Claus said.

"Ironically, the idea of a backup is most manifest in your technology. If a race car crashes in practice, begin the race in a backup. If a computer's storage drive fails, put in a new one and restore the data from a backup. If—"

"All right already," Claus said.

"I did the same thing when I created Earth," yellow Lanietta said. "I didn't tell anyone but you. Just now. Can't have other Carinians meddling with my magic. But this is Frieda's undoing. She's operating wholly in her universe. She believes she will defeat me. Hah! No matter how badly she rips up the physical and ethereal realms, I can mend it from the backup. Or backups. I might have more. I'll never tell."

"You can't be that powerful!" Claus said.

"Pet talk?" blue Lanietta asked.

The Laniettas giggled.

"It's not pet talk to—"

"Throw doubt on matters you know not?" blue Lanietta asked.

"I can't believe I'm being lectured by a sheepdog and her egos!" Claus said.

"I won't stand for your bigotry, Clomper. Sheepdogs show more intelligence than comparable humans of your day," sheepdog Lanietta said.

"If you're that powerful and almighty, why have you toyed around with me for so long? Why have you allowed Earth to explode and Frieda to wreck the ether?" Claus asked.

"Oh the impatience of you humans. You can't be bothered to darn your own socks, yet you cry foul when the universe has a minor blemish for more than a minute. Why not take a whack at it? Go eethi and clean up after Frieda. I say again, you humans like to live. But you don't like to clean up the messes you make. Let the universe be your janitor. Well? I'm a janitor. A janitor of the universe. Now then, any more complaints? Or should we get on with it?" sheepdog Lanietta said.

"It? What do you mean?" Claus asked.

"I can't do this alone. You must be a team," yellow Lanietta said.

"What team? I'm just one person," Claus said.

"Pet talk," the Laniettas laughed.

"It's true! I can't just split like you," Claus said.

"True," yellow Lanietta said. "But your Olivia Jill Depetti created a clone of you. A backup. In the backup timeline. A pity that creative talent wasn't put to good use in the primary timeline. In that primary timeline, Jill had a grand ol' time with Cenina Island and that mess. What a cleanup! But I digress. It's not a fluke that I bought you at auction. Or that you came across my preservation tank, depending on which timeline you care to entertain. No, you're not really that special. But special things surround you. It's like you're on an otherwise empty field of play with wise people in the stadium. Now walk on the field. The people cheer. How has your walking demonstrated any more greatness than when you are mugged while walking down an alley? None at all. The wisdom of the audience makes the greatness."

"I...I'm not great? What a thing to say," Claus said. "And yet you need me! I don't know how to react."

"Good. It's best you don't react too much. Here we go."

Chapter 149: The Prince Stole the Perch

Yellow and blue Lanietta tossed sheepdog Lanietta upward into space. Sheepdog Lanietta continued on her own, leaving a line of hair along the way, ever growing but never greater nor lesser than the rate of her travel away from Claus and the adult Laniettas.

"What? What are you doing?" Claus yelled.

"She's headed for your star," yellow Lanietta said. "She came from a star, now she returns to one."

"To die? This is no backup plan!" Claus protested.

Sheepdog Lanietta shot toward the sun with tremendous speed.

"Through the mind of a child, we become ourselves again," blue Lanietta said.

Sheepdog Lanietta collided with the sun. The sun shot out fine lines, as if it had grown its own hair in a hurry. At first the lines spread out evenly and in all directions. But soon they grouped, stretched, and directed themselves toward Earth, Morrow's moon, and Frieda's moon. Yellow Lanietta flew upward herself into space and merged with these lines, helping to maintain the links between Earth, the moons, and the sun. Alone on a pillar, Claus watched as both timelines converged. Earth's orbit around the sun increased in speed, it seemed, though in reality Claus was going forward in time more quickly than one second per second. Concurrently, Frieda's moon appeared in nearly the same orbit, though it held its out-of-plane orbit, and so it only crossed the orbits of Earth and Morrow's moon in two places around the sun. Frieda's moon came very close to Earth and Morrow's moon in some of those crossovers, and when it did, it exerted momentary strain and pull on them. The result was that ethereal lines flowed from Earth to Frieda's lunar far side while Morrow's moon colony sprouted ethereal lines to the near side of Frieda's moon where Labba, Leif, and Clausetta called home.

In all this, Claus thought he saw an image of Blair and his clone staring up at the moon as Blair aged quickly and the clone degraded to dust. How he was able to see this, he didn't know, but it disturbed him as did the strange events unfolding.

Clausetta continued her assault on Frieda's cubics. The hair on Clausetta's head had grown down to her lower back, but then it did a U-turn and flowed a little up toward the sky. Blue Lanietta jumped up and changed into blue ethereal lines, connecting Clausetta's upward-turned hair to the blue sky. This blue color traveled down and changed Clausetta's hair blue. Even her complexion became blue. Clausetta phased in and out of reality, all the while continuing to fire projectiles at the cubics, allowing Leif to make progress with his attack planes.

Labba stayed on the old near side and returned to her eagle shape. Frieda had launched a counter attack in the other direction around the moon and caught up to Claus's and Labba's palace. With the help of the female selenites, and by tapping into the ethereal connection Lanietta had created, Labba vigorously defended the palace. This connection allowed Labba to reinvigorate the mechanized female selenites with the manufacturing gains made on Morrow's moon colony.

Time on the two moons passed at wildly different speeds. For each second of time that passed on Frieda's moon, a year passed on Morrow's moon. It took only a few hours for Morrow's moon to catch up in time with Frieda's moon.

During this time, yellow Lanietta controlled yellow ethereal lines from the sun and also such lines between Earth and the two moons while blue Lanietta helped

Clausetta control the blue ethereal lines from her sky into her attack on Frieda. The attack wasn't just on the cubics, it was on the ethereal computer Frieda had created, too. Clausetta had mastered a super-baby-multiply option, where her unborn, yet-to-be-conceived nest of life began dividing and subdividing within the divisions, as if generations upon generations of unborn children beget their own children but didn't wait for them to grow up and instead created more. They created such an invasion force in the ether that they jumped in between ethereal moments and thus acted as infinite gates between all ethereal computer activity.

"Beyton rays...no more!" Clausetta shouted across space and time.

The connection between the lush Earth and Frieda's old far side (combined with Clausetta's attack on Frieda's ethereal computer) resulted in a curious side effect. Tree seeds from Earth were drawn to the ethereal computational conflict. They landed in Frieda's old far side soil, grew quickly into trees, then, as a tadpole changes into a frog, the trees changed into humanoid giants.

"The beyton rays," Claus said. "Clausetta did it. She blocked them."

"The anthropendrons have arrived," a voice boomed from somewhere.

These anthropendrons ripped through Frieda's realm and tore through cubic strongholds. Concurrently, Leif pushed his airplane army deep into far-side territory. All cubics were nearly defeated, except for Frieda herself and her small group in her hold.

It came time then when Leif landed his planes short of Frieda's stronghold and carried on the last bit of attack on the ground, with the help of the giants. The female selenites had secured the old lunar near side, freeing up Labba. Labba then (as an eagle) quickly flew Claus to the lunar shock, where Sergio stood waiting in an airplane.

"You must take Claus," Labba said. "I have other business to attend. I will come when I can."

"But Labba," Claus said.

"Take a deep breath and get going," Labba said. "You won't have any trouble on the old far side. The air has improved. Now go!"

Claus jumped into the plane, and Sergio (with Claude already inside), took off and flew with great speed to Frieda's stronghold. Claus looked out the airplane window and saw that Lanietta's ethereal lines were also in the far-side lunar sky. He also noticed that the time disparity between Earth/Morrow's moon and Frieda's moon had shrunk to such an extent that Earth/Morrow's moon now took orbit at the same speed as Frieda's moon, but much ahead in the orbital path—more than ninety degrees but less than one hundred and eighty.

Clausetta remained where she was but was nearly spent with exhaustion. She could hardly maintain a presence in the physical world at all. Labba sensed this and flew over to her at top speed.

As Sergio approached Frieda's stronghold, Claude noticed the anthropendrons.

"Thirpers," he said. "Look at the Thirpers."

"I heard they are anthropendrons," Claus said.

"I've never seen them before," Sergio said. "But Claude has a great sense of intuition when it comes to plants."

"Are they plants?" Claus asked.

"They start as trees and go through meta-morpa-sip," Claude said.

"Metamorphosis?" Claus asked.

"Yeah," Claude continued. "Grandma Labba told me about the Thirper. They come from Carinia 2. I can't say the other name."

"Anthropendron?" Claus suggested.

"Yeah. She said that's the formal name. But they call them Thirpers," Claude said.

"Almost sounds like 'thirsty person'," Claus said.

"They can drink with their feet," Claude said. "Even when they are giants!"

"We're landing," Sergio said.

"Up here?" Claus asked.

"I had a hard time finding this perch," Sergio said. "It's across from Frieda's perch without being on it. We can watch from in here."

"I can't hear anything," Claus said. "I'm going out."

"I want to go too," Claude said.

"No," Sergio said. "You wait in here."

"Aw," Claude complained.

"It's too dangerous," Sergio said. "Claus, if things get dicey, I'm taking off. You'll only have a few seconds to get aboard. I won't risk Claude's life."

"I understand," Claus said. "I'm surprised you brought him here."

"Clausetta told me to. That he had a part to play. I don't understand, but Clausetta is always right," Sergio said.

"Very well," Claus said.

Claus exited the plane and stood as close to Frieda's perch as possible.

"Frieda!" Leif called from below. "Your realm is defeated. You are surrounded. Surrender, and we will put an end to this war."

Frieda laughed. She looked practically all cubic, with very little of her original body left.

"It's over, Frieda. Let's call a truce," Claus yelled.

"It's over, Claus. Yes, it's over. Humanity has reached an end. I will throw the final switch," she said.

"What do you mean?" Claus yelled.

"Perhaps you've heard. I've been digitizing the ether," she said. "All spirits—in that realm or entering that realm—are locked under my computerized control."

"Not anymore," Leif called. "Clausetta has invaded your digitized ether. She has shut down your ethereal machine for good."

"Not quite," Frieda said. "In addition to being a computer, my ethereal device has the ability to initiate a chain reaction explosion, not unlike a nuclear bomb. The ether will explode, Clausetta's connections will explode, and all those with souls will lose them from the fallout. Those who are left will be no better than the lower

animals, with nothing to look forward to than predation upon one another."

Patricia rushed out.

"The beyton rays were blocked," Patricia said. "But now they've stopped. Something's going on with the PRAAD."

"It doesn't matter," Frieda said. "It too will be under my control. Very soon."

Leif tried to go eethi. He couldn't, and Frieda laughed.

"It's true," Leif said.

"Of course it's true," Frieda said.

"So you win again, is that it? Claus goes back the loser once more?" Claus yelled.

"I'm willing to forgive everything you've done on one condition—you must turn Clausetta and Lanietta over to me. I want *full* control of physical and ethereal realms. In exchange, I promise to keep them alive," Frieda said. "At least for a little while."

"I have no control over them," Claus said.

"You'd better get control. Or all of you will perish," Frieda said. "Leif, you are part Carinian. Relay the message to Clausetta and Lanietta at once."

"Leif, don't," Claus said.

Leif went eethi again to test the ether, but he returned, tried again, and returned again. Frieda laughed.

"You can't break through, Leif. The days of space-jumping are over. Clausetta has fallen perfectly into my trap and thrown herself into my ethereal computer," Frieda said. "If the other Carinians were here, they might give me a challenge. But they failed and died. I have mastered what they could not. I rule all."

"What kind of talk is that?" Claus said.

"The only reasonable talk possible," Frieda said. "Send the message, Leif."

Leif hesitated.

"Do it!" Frieda insisted.

"I'm sending it," Leif said. "They've received it."

"And their reply?" Frieda said.

Leif held quiet. The Thirper giants and people below also fell silent. But then alternating streaks of yellow and blue lines shot across the sky toward Frieda's perch coinciding with Labba's arrival as a super eagle.

"You've chosen destruction!" Frieda yelled.

Frieda's body became a fountain of cubic outpouring, sending cubes of ethereal energy into the sky. The yellow and blue lines in the sky were Lanietta and Clausetta, of course. They had fully transformed the last of their energy to meet Frieda's. The Thirper giants and Leif's army tried to tear into Frieda's stronghold, but she'd created a cubic shield around it with her remaining energy. Labba joined Clausetta and Lanietta in the sky to fight Frieda. Unnoticed by Frieda and her fighters, Leif also tried to breach the stronghold, but he couldn't.

Until he went eethi.

He sensed that entry to the ether had been opened up by Clausetta and Lanietta's arrival. He split his ethereal self into slivers, slipped in between the cubics, and reassembled on the inside of the shield. Then quietly and without notice (but quickly), he used his ethereal self to scale the stronghold wall. He snuck up behind Frieda, pulled out an ethereal sword colored in yellow and blue, and hewed Frieda just below her hips. He severed both her legs. She fell to the ground in shock and disbelief, letting out a loud cry.

"My legs," she said with her last bit of strength.

She self-destructed. The shock wave destroyed the ethereal shield around the stronghold and shot Leif's ethereal self back into his physical body. The shock wave also went into the sky and destroyed the ethereal lines of yellow and blue. Labba was able to pull out of the ethereal lines and return to her eagle form. She made a great swoop to catch something out of the sky. She landed on the perch next to Claus and released what she'd caught—what was left of Clausetta's body—into Claus's arms. Labba then resumed her flight through the sky, hoping to find her old friend, but Lanietta was nowhere to be found.

The giants took over Frieda's stronghold with Frieda's remaining loyal subjects surrendering to them. One giant helped Leif to Claus's perch. Leif ran over to his sister, now held by both Claus and Sergio with Claude crying by her side.

"So fragile. My sweet Clausetta," Sergio said.

Clausetta was like remnant ash paper—still with form but ready to crumble at a moment's notice. Her color was grey, and there was no evidence of the tubes that she once used to attack Frieda.

"Clausetta?" Claus said.

"She did too much. Too much!" Leif said.

"She can't die!" Sergio said.

"Leif, do you sense anything in the ether? Is Clausetta's spirit somewhere else?" Claus asked.

Leif went eethi briefly and returned.

"I can't go far," Leif said. "She's nowhere nearby."

"We need Labba," Claus said.

Claus then shouted out for Labba, but she was still high in the sky searching for Lanietta.

"Can you call your mother down please?" Claus asked Leif.

Leif went eethi and called Labba down.

"She's coming," Leif said.

Labba descended quickly from the heavens, but just before she arrived, Patricia Li yelled across the distance from Frieda's stronghold to Claus's perch.

"Come quickly!" Patricia Li said. "There's nothing holding the local ether together. It's ready to collapse!"

Labba overheard this while she descended. She landed with Claus and beckoned that he and Leif climb onto her back for transport.

"Take Claude too. I don't want him to see any more of this," Sergio said, referring to Clausetta's condition.

"It might not be safe," Claus said. "Frieda was defeated just moments ago. Could be leftover—"

"It feels safe," Leif said.

"It's safe," Labba said. "Come along, Claude. We'll come back soon."

"I'll watch Clausetta. I promise," Sergio said.

Claude reluctantly left Clausetta and climbed onto Labba's back with Claus and Leif. Both ensured Claude wouldn't fall off. Labba then took off and landed on Frieda's perch. When she did, Claus, Leif, and Claude dismounted followed by Labba as she returned to humanoid shape.

"Hurry!" Patricia urged.

Patricia led the group into a newly-built structure (since Claus was last there). Inside, the group saw a room filled with workstations and technology. Most prominent was a central area with two posts—about human height and wide enough for two humans to stand between. Next to each post was a pillar about half-human height on the wall-side of each post. Periodically along the walls were transparent tubes large enough for a single person each to enter. These tubes vaulted upward as high as a second- or third-story building. Strings of lights ran from these tubes down to workstations and to two pillars.

Giants stood guard in various places, though fortunately the room was tall enough to accommodate their height. For the most part, they remained motionless.

"Frieda interfaced with the posts," Patricia said. "She said Carinians can go eethi too. I thought maybe Lanietta or Labba could fix things by using the posts. Or Labba's children. Where's Lanietta? Where's Clausetta?"

"I cannot find Lanietta," Labba said. "And..."

"Sergio is with Clausetta. Or what's left of her," Claus said.

"How can you talk like that?" Leif said. "She's my sister."

"She's my daughter," Claus said.

"She's my daughter too!" Labba said.

"Please!" Patricia said. "Labba then! Can you take to the posts?"

Labba walked over. She reached out to touch the posts, but they were too far away.

"How did Frieda do this?" Labba asked.

"She was able to extend her arms. The cubics changed her and permitted this," Patricia said.

"Hmm," Labba said.

Labba changed back to super-eagle form. She used her wings to lift her body above the posts, careful to keep her wings from catching in the stringed lights. She landed with her talons on a post each. She went eethi. Her eethi self appeared above her physical form for a moment before disappearing, then her physical form phased in and out. After a minute, she reintegrated and spoke.

"The local ether is stable for now," she said. "But there are three instabilities I cannot resolve—at least not all of them. I can only resolve one. The other two will fail."

"What's the problem?" Claus asked. "Why don't you fix what you can?"

"Because of what they are," Labba said. "I need...advice."

"What are they?" Leif asked.

"Lanietta is one," Labba said. "She is barely holding on, even across timelines, strangely enough. I didn't think it possible, but somehow she has bridged them."

"She has," Claus said. "Well, she takes priority. Bring her back."

"Wait," Leif said. "What about Clausetta?"

"She's the other instability," Labba said. "I can bring her back both in corporeal and ethereal form."

"It must be her then," Leif said.

"Who is the third?" Patricia asked.

"Not *who* but *what*," Labba said.

"The ether?" Patricia asked.

"No. The ether both local and distant is stable. Clausetta and Lanietta take credit for that," Labba said.

"Then the physical world," Leif said.

"Not all of it," Labba said.

"You're making a game of this," Claus said. "You shouldn't toy with us. Tell us straight out."

"Hmm...mmm...Earth," Labba said.

"Mirth?" Claus said. "You think this is funny?"

"Not *mirth. Earth*," Labba said. "The old Earth and old moon will soon be on the opposite side of the sun from this moon, or this new planet we have called Luna. When the old Earth reaches opposition, it will collapse and explode."

"That can't be," Claus said. "How's that possible?"

"These timelines were not meant to coexist as they do now. Something has to give," Labba said.

"What if I help you?" Leif said. "Maybe together we can save all three."

"We can try, but I doubt it," Labba said.

"What if we bring Lanietta here? Then she can help with Clausetta and Earth," Claus said.

"Risky," Labba said. "There's no guarantee it would work."

"We should bring Clausetta first and use her to help with the others," Leif said.

"Then you're biased," Claus said. "I'm afraid you'll just follow your feelings and try exclusively for Clausetta."

"We have to!" Leif said.

"Is that the decision?" Labba said. "She *is* family."

"Lanietta was almost a sister to you," Claus mentioned.

"I know," Labba said. "The decision pains me to make."

"Not to mention the chance to save Earth!" Doctor Morrow said, now entering the room. "I overheard everything. This opportunity might not come again. Claus, you can't let your family's personal feelings take precedence over the others."

"In the other timeline, you decided that you should have the first baby on the moon, and when Andrea showed that she had already produced the first lunar child, you got rid of her. And us," Claus said.

"Obviously delusional," Doctor Morrow said. "Claus. If you don't listen to me, then listen to everyone on Luna. Put the question to a vote."

"There's not enough time," Labba said. "The opportunity for resolution is closing fast."

"How fast?" Claus asked.

"A few more minutes," Labba said.

"How can we get everyone's vote in a few minutes?" Claus asked.

"You'd have to include the people of old Earth, too," Doctor Morrow said.

"They'd overwhelm us," Leif said. "We're the ones cleaning up the mess. We're the ones due special dispensation. What did people of Earth do for us?"

"Lanietta would let me have it for what I'm about to say," Claus said. "We must think of the future. Earth was not meant to be in this timeline. We should try for Clausetta. Lanietta, if you can hear me, I offer my deepest apologies."

"Now you're talking!" Leif said, and he stepped between the posts to aid Labba.

"Leif, stop," Doctor Morrow pleaded. "Doctor Li, help me stop them."

"I can't let you interfere," Claus said, and he stood to block her. "Long time I've acted as a spectator, allowing others to get their way. Leif is right. It's time to act and in my own interest. My daughter comes first."

Labba activated the posts. They glowed and made whirring sounds.

"Where's Claude?" Patricia asked.

Claus looked around suddenly, as if something had escaped his attention due to his negligence.

"I can see Clausetta," Leif said.

"You've entered the ether," Labba said.

"She's far away. Very far away," Leif said.

"We'll do this together," Labba said. "We'll do this on the count of three."

"Is that after saying 'three' or while saying 'three'?" Leif said.

"While saying," Labba said. "I'll do the count. Ready?"

"Ready," Leif said.

"One," Labba said.

Claus looked around for Claude. Where was he?

"Two," Labba said.

Claus then spotted Claude. He had entered a tube and taken a platform inside the tube to a high level. He was now beating on various buttons.

"Claude, no!" Claus yelled at the same time Labba said, "Three!"

A surge of energy traveled from Claude's lofty platform down to the pillars. The surge jolted Leif and threw him clear from the posts. Labba, however, had her nerves overwhelmed. Her talons were seized on the posts and could not let go. Her feathers expanded outward, analogous to a person's hair sticking out from static charge. Her eyes opened wide, and she was completely powerless to stop what happened next. Instead of Clausetta materializing between the posts as had been agreed upon, another being gradually materialized.

Lanietta.

She was somewhat in a daze, as if awakening after a terrible blow to the head.

"You should have saved Earth," she said in a dreamy state. "Or at least Clausetta."

"Lanietta!" Claus said. "I can't believe it. Claude, what did you do?"

"Blame the grandchild?" Lanietta said. "Oh, but this isn't right. I can't stay here. I thought my work was done. Brought me back have you? Well, Lanietta the janitor will perform one more cleanup job. You'll see. This isn't the end of me."

Lanietta disappeared.

"Where is she?" Claus asked. "Bring her back! We need her to help restore Clausetta!"

Leif rushed back in between the posts.

"Labba!" he said in desperation. "Do something!"

"I can't," she said. "It's all failing. Go outside and look."

"Look at what?" Claus asked.

"Old Earth," she said.

Claus rushed outside. There close to the sun was Earth shining brightly like Venus. Then in brilliant fashion, it exploded. But because of the distance, it didn't cover the sky but steadily grew larger and larger until it appeared to be as a very large star (though not as large as the sun itself).

"It's gone! Earth! Destroyed again!" Claus shouted.

Chapter 150: The Robot's Child

Claus remained staring at the Earth's destruction and would have continued staring had it not been for Sergio. Sergio cried out in pain. Claus turned to see Sergio withdrawing from a ball of fire.

"Clausetta! She's burning!" he yelled.

Claus ran back into Frieda's stronghold.

"Labba! Hurry! Take me back over to—"

But before Claus could finish, the floor seemed to drop out from under everyone as if riding in a rapidly-descending elevator.

"What's happening?" Claus asked.

"We're falling," Leif said.

"I'm scared!" Claude said.

Labba flew over to what was the entrance that Claus had just used.

"It's blocked," she said. "We're heading for the core. We'll be destroyed."

"No we won't," Patricia Li said. "Everyone follow me. We'll escape in Novi 4."

Labba returned to her humanoid shape and followed the others to Novi 4. The stronghold's roof opened, and Josh piloted the ship upward. It struggled to gain altitude due to falling debris from the sides of the newly-formed deep hole.

"Push it all the way," Andrea said.

"It's not enough," Josh said.

Andrea jumped in with emergency thrusters.

"We have the power, but it's too unwieldy," Andrea said.

"Kevin, help," Patricia said.

Kevin jumped in.

"Stabilized," Kevin said. "Try now, Andrea."

Andrea pushed emergency thrusters to full.

"I can hold direction," Kevin said.

"We're doing it. We're leaving the hole," Josh said.

Novi 4 hovered above the hole. Claus looked out a window and saw that Sergio stood on his perch alone. All evidence of Clausetta was gone.

"Intense infrared radiation coming from the hole below," Kevin said.

"Outer hull is overheating," Andrea said.

"So are we," Bill said, wiping sweat from his brow.

"We must pull away from this hole," Andrea said.

"We should go over to the perch. Where Sergio is," Claus said.

The others agreed. Josh piloted Novi 4 over to the perch and landed. But the inside had become too hot to stay in. Everyone rushed out for cooler temperatures. The rock supporting Novi 4 from below melted from the heat. The craft sank a bit.

"Well that was a mistake," Andrea said. "The rock is solidifying around the ship."

"Stuck in the mud," Claus lamented.

"I'll pull it out," Josh said.

Josh rushed back inside but then rushed out.

"Everything is too hot to handle," Josh said.

"It's a wonder we made it out alive," Kevin said.

"Superior Astroosa engineering saved the day, nothing more," Josh said.

"I'd trade that superior engineering to get back—" Claus started to say.

He was interrupted. A blinding light shone upward from the hole the ship had just flown out of. It continued upward into the sky, lighting up a passing cloud. It was an odd sight, as the sun itself was already heading toward the horizon, and so the sun's light made the upper part of the cloud golden while the hole lit the lower part blue.

"No, too bright," echoed a voice from the hole.

"There's someone down there," Andrea said.

"Might need medical attention," Patricia said.

"We need to launch a rescue effort," Claus said.

"Can't," Josh said. "No way over."

"Labba," Claus said. "You can fly me over there."

"It's still too hot," Labba said. "Don't you feel it?"

"I do. I just can't believe that something with blue light can be so hot," Claus said.

"Well it is. We'll have to stay back," Labba said.

The light started to creep over the top of the hole, at least over most of it. But part of the light was blocked as evidenced by a shadow that crept over and toward Sergio's perch. The hole itself was ground level, meaning the original perch upon which Frieda had built her stronghold was collapsed, but a new pinnacle grew from the hole. The pinnacle had a flat top, and on that top stood a shape that blocked the light source. The pinnacle grew and grew in height until it was the same elevation as Sergio's perch.

"Could be dangerous," Josh said. "We should leave."

"No, wait," Labba said.

A walkway jutted out from this new pinnacle of brightness toward Sergio's perch. Claus and his group watched the walkway and expected it to connect with their perch, but it stopped short. Once it did, the shape that had cast the shadow now followed this walkway toward Claus and group, in a slow, deliberate fashion. The group could tell the shape was humanoid but could not tell who it was. The shape appeared as a silhouette, though points of light shone through periodically. Finally, the shape stopped.

"Clausetta? Is that you?" Sergio called.

"Is that who you hope me to be?" the shape answered.

"Lanietta!" Claus said.

"Yes. It's me," Lanietta replied.

"Where's my Clausetta?" Sergio asked.

"Clausetta," Lanietta said with a big sigh. "Yes. She made a great sacrifice. So did I. But someone brought me back."

"It was me!" Claude said.

"Yes," Lanietta said wistfully. "Charming Claude. As are you all. Yes. Warm, kind-hearted people. But Clausetta sent the last of herself into Earth and caused its destruction."

"But why?" Sergio pleaded. "There was no reason to do such a thing. She is loved by everyone here."

"She is. But she could not handle the strain of what she did to defeat Frieda. There's a reason it's banned by Carinians. Drives one mad. Nearly destroyed my own mother," Lanietta said.

"Where is Clausetta?" Claus asked.

"She's gone. Dispersed in the ether," Lanietta said.

"You couldn't stop her?" Claus asked.

"Stop her? She forced me to help her," Lanietta said. "Yes, for once I lost total control of myself. I meant to deal with Frieda in a more controlled, drawn-out fashion. Little did I know. I underestimated you, Claus. I did not realize you could have a child so capable of such great power."

"I still can't believe you couldn't stop her. I'm not that great," Claus said.

"No, you're not," Lanietta said.

"Well you didn't have to agree with me," Claus said.

"Clausetta did something I did not anticipate. By completely integrating her offspring into the digital ether, she subjected herself to the machinations of it, machinations that Frieda had created. It consumed Clausetta, she destroyed Frieda, but she also destroyed herself, leaving remnants strewn in the ether," Lanietta said.

"Then you should have stopped her," Claus said. "You must have known. You have a knack for things like that."

"Oh, sometimes knowing is not enough. Not enough at all," Lanietta said.

"Lanietta," Labba said, pointing to the light source. "Is that the PRAAD?"

"It is," Lanietta said with a sigh.

"It's dangerous," Labba said.

"Yes, it is," Lanietta said. "Let me show you something."

Lanietta held her hands on the top corners of her head, pointing upward, like ears of a cat. A yellow stream of light flowed from the PRAAD to Lanietta's left hand while a blue stream of light flowed from the PRAAD to Lanietta's right hand. They combined between her hands into a black sphere. From that black sphere shot spots of white light. These spots landed at points forming a circle around the PRAAD pinnacle and Sergio's perch. The circle of points grew pinnacles of their own, and at the top were black spheres with swimming images inside, images of prior realities visited by Claus and Lanietta. Also included were the people of Tabelia when on Earth.

"What is this?" Sergio asked.

"I already know what this is," Claus said.

"Do you?" Lanietta asked.

"Yes. Your vacation," Claus said.

"Is that what you told him?" Labba asked.

"What else could it be?" Claus asked. "It must be. Lanietta toying around with me in different realities. For her petty amusement."

"No. It isn't," Labba said. "It's research, isn't it my old friend?"

Lanietta changed the light output of the PRAAD so that it shot upward only. Then everyone saw her face. It looked very old, as if she were over a hundred years old for a human.

"Research," Lanietta said. "For where I'm going to die."

"Going to die? No!" Claus protested.

"You should have drowned me when I was Rattasinatta," Lanietta said.

"I didn't think you remembered that," Claus said.

"I remember. I remember all our adventures together," Lanietta said dreamily. "But, it's time for me to go. Clausetta set the example. And now I will follow it. I was going to let myself die in one of those realities, but instead, I'll get rid of the PRAAD and myself at the same time. I'll fuse with it and send it to the other moon, the one Doctor Morrow colonized."

"Was it not destroyed? I mean, I saw Earth. It was a fireball. The other moon survived?" Claus asked.

"Yes, it survived," Lanietta said. "Clausetta shielded it at the end. But only for me. She knew my intent and understood. As I understood hers. Once I destroy it, I'll spread the PRAAD's ethereal ashes across these many realities. Along with mine."

"It's not right. It can't be!" Claus cried. "There must be another way!"

"Labba?" Lanietta said.

"I'm searching the ether for another solution," Labba said. "I can find none."

"What search?" Claus said. "Stay here, Lanietta. Stay alive for us. We'll figure out another way with the PRAAD."

"There is no other way," Labba said. "Carinians have been dealing with the PRAAD for billions of Earth years. The Anrega will stay in Luna, but without the PRAAD or even the Veigon to affect it, it will only affect us a little. I suppose in time I'll have to deal with the Anrega myself, and then my ethereal ashes will need to be spread."

"I won't let you do that," Leif said. "I'll take you away before that."

"Time will be dead and gone long before you make any plausible effort with the Anrega," Lanietta said.

"This is madness," Claus said. "Labba. Change to eagle form. Take Leif and me over to Lanietta. We'll chain her up if we have to."

Labba looked at Claus, looked at Leif, looked at Lanietta, and looked back at Claus.

"It...I..." Labba stumbled.

"At least make the attempt!" Claus said.

Labba changed to eagle form. Claus climbed on her back as did Leif. Labba took to flight. Lanietta cast a great wind and blew her back to Sergio's perch. Leif tried going eethi, but Lanietta pushed him back too.

"I cannot allow any of you to jeopardize yourselves over the PRAAD or me. It's my decision," Lanietta said.

Claus stepped dangerously close to the perch's edge.

"I'll kill myself if you do this. Do you hear? I'll kill myself!"

Claus began climbing down the edge a bit. Others there grew concerned.

"No you won't, Claus," Lanietta said. "Yes. You're Claus now. I've given up on you being my pet."

"I'm your Clomper forever. Clomper forever!" Claus cried out.

"Labba. Pull him back before he makes a further fool of himself," Lanietta said.

Labba did so.

"You have things yet to do here. Claude needs a grandfather. Claus? Your muzzle is broken," Lanietta said.

Claus felt a mesh lift from his face. It was colored in yellow and blue and took on the shape of a muzzle. It was in ethereal form, but once it cleared his face, it became physical. It landed on the ground at his feet and shattered.

"Now I really must be going. Goodbye," Lanietta said.

"Lanietta, if I can help, I..." Labba offered.

Lanietta smiled.

"Thank you. Farewell," she said.

Lanietta held her hands to the top corners of her head as before. Blue light from the PRAAD shot to her right hand while yellow light from the PRAAD reached her left.

"I can't believe you didn't stop her," Claus said to Labba. "What kind of friend are you?"

But Labba could only sigh and fall into soft tears with a periodic sad-hiccup causing her body to jolt. She tried to suppress it but could not. Nor could she speak.

"Leif?" Claus turned to say.

"Aunt Lanietta has powers way beyond what I can do," Leif said.

"What about Claude?" Claus asked.

"He's but a boy!" Sergio said.

"He can't do any good," Leif said.

"How can anyone stand here and do nothing?" Claus shouted to the group. "We are worthless!"

The light pulled Lanietta into the PRAAD. The PRAAD then put out thrust from below, launched upward, and shot toward Morrow's moon.

"LA-NI-ET-TA!" Claus called out. "Come back. Come back!"

Claus could only stare at the PRAAD as it grew smaller and smaller, all the while heading for the other side of the sun.

"She's traveling nearly at the speed of light," Leif said. "It will take her seventeen minutes to reach the other moon."

Claus looked at Leif as if what he said was indignant.

"Well maybe not quite the speed of light? Twenty minutes?" Leif suggested.

"It doesn't matter," Claus said. "I know what to expect. I saw the other Earth when Clausetta...Clausetta...oh why must things come to this?"

"Let her go, Claus," Josh said. "She's just an alien. We're still safe."

"All but one," Claus said, suddenly turning toward Josh and punching him in the jaw.

Josh punched back. The two were in a full-blown fight.

"Stop it. Stop it!" Labba yelled. "Did Lanietta sacrifice herself so you two can fight? Or Clausetta? Stop this at once!"

But the two kept fighting for minutes on end. Kevin jumped in to help Josh, and Claus punched him too. Claus proved to have a tough skull and jaw, both resilient against repeated blows.

"I said, stop fighting!" Labba said.

Labba returned to her eagle shape, took flight, and used her talons to pull Kevin and Josh off Claus. Leif and Sergio held them back while Labba went after Claus and pulled him away.

"Let it go," Labba said.

"I can't. And neither should you," Claus said. "You *are* Carinian, like her. I only wish I could go eethi. I could share in the final moment. She at least deserves that."

"She does deserve that, Claus Doron Gerhardt," said a booming male voice from the other side of the perch where Lanietta and the PRAAD had once stood.

"That voice," Labba said. "Are you...you..?"

"Larto!" Claus said.

"And Lanshalla," boomed a female voice.

A part of the orb chamber had ascended from below and was now much higher than Sergio's perch and Lanietta's/the PRAAD's perch. Larto and Lanshalla appeared in ethereal humanoid form and floated just above the orb chamber.

"Stop Lanietta!" Claus pleaded. "She's going to kill herself. She's heading for—"

Before Claus could finish, Morrow's moon flashed a brilliant light.

"You're too late!" Claus screamed. "You let Lanietta kill herself!"

"Look," Leif said. "The moon is still there."

"An ancient creature named Loerna was stored in the PRAAD and took the place of Lanietta. She sacrificed herself for your friend," Larto said.

Then it hit home to Claus, the moment Lanietta yelled at him while treating Loerna Acutolo at the dental office, how hating her would make it easier to let her go. It wasn't enough hate for him. He couldn't let go.

"The moon...it's still there," Claus said. "It wasn't destroyed."

"It was not. But the PRAAD is," Lanshalla said.

"She's created a memorial for herself on Morrow's moon," Labba said, as if receiving the news through the ether (which she was). "The memorial is named after her—Loerna. She could not allow Lanietta to sacrifice herself."

"Nor could we," Lanshalla said. "It was not our plan to interfere with Lanietta's development."

"Development?" Claus asked.

"Yes, Clomper," Larto said.

"You know my name?" Claus asked.

"Of course," Lanshalla said. "We keep track of all Lanietta's pets."

"You've been a faithful companion to her. We thank you for your loyalty," Larto said.

"It's such loyalty that's kept her going. She's been very depressed since she created Earth," Lanshalla said.

"Postpartum depression?" Labba asked.

"The same," Lanshalla said.

"I never knew. She never told me. Oh, Lanietta, how I would have been there for you. How could I have missed the signs? It was so obvious," Labba said.

"Things must be put aright," Larto said.

Larto and Lanshalla each channeled colors of yellow and blue. They sent those colors into space toward Morrow's moon and used the colors to bring back Lanietta. Or did they?

"She's stuck in the ether," Larto said.

"She always had her own mind," Lanshalla said.

Labba flew over to help.

"Labba?" Claus called.

Labba flew into the multi-colored beam from Larto and Lanshalla into space. The beam lit up her feathers. They caught fire, and she screamed as she became a fireball-a-flame. With her feathers a-burning, she lost altitude and fell into the orb chamber.

"Labba?" Claus called.

Leif space-jumped over to Labba, removed his shirt, and covered up the flames with the shirt as Labba returned to humanoid shape. But the flames still burned. They didn't become extinguished until...

"Lanietta!" Claus called.

Lanietta arrived, barely aware, like one surfing down a hill of colors. She was surrounded by a condensation cloud and landed next to Labba. The condensation cloud hovered above, changed into water, and rained on the three. It also obscured Lanietta's vision briefly.

"I...how am I here?" Lanietta asked, just starting to become aware of her surroundings. "Labba is that you? And Leif? Is this your doing? It's not possible."

"It is not possible for them. But it is for us," Lanshalla said.

"Mamma?" Lanietta said, suddenly sounding meek and humble. "Where are you?"

The condensation cleared. Lanietta turned around and saw Larto and Lanshalla floating above.

"Oh, Mamma and Pappa!" Lanietta said as she fell to her knees in tears. "I'm in trouble. I can't do this anymore. I want it to end."

"We know, my special one," Lanshalla said.

"I'm so overwrought with misery," Lanietta said. "Creating Earth was the worst thing I ever did. Oh, it was too much. The life-forms just kept coming and going with no end. I wish I could be at peace with myself. But I can't. Clausetta found a way. I just wanted to follow her. Sweet Clausetta."

Just then, an ethereal image of Clausetta appeared above Larto and Lanietta.

"Clausetta!" everyone exclaimed.

"Clausetta has moved on," Lanshalla said. "She is creating her own universe, with her own celestial objects and yes, her own planets with life."

"I...you are?" Lanietta asked. "No, don't do it. Don't create life, Clausetta. It will chain you down forever. Claus just watches what goes on around him. It has spared him."

"One cannot just go through life and watch others," Lanshalla said. "One must continue to create and learn, just as one learns through writing. Reading is not enough."

"I've learned a lot from you, Aunt Lanietta. But it's only just a little bit. I must learn for myself about the mysteries of the universe," Clausetta said.

"Are you leaving us?" Claus asked.

"Stay! Please!" Sergio pleaded.

"You must remain and raise Claude. Someday he'll understand and help you to understand," Clausetta said.

"I don't understand how being apart is a good thing. I love my sweet wife," Sergio said.

"And I love my daughter," Claus said.

"I love everyone here," Clausetta said. "I'll take that love with me as I create my own universe. I cannot stay here. I took a path I cannot reverse."

"Clausetta will continue and learn wondrous things," Lanshalla said.

"I will visit each of you from time to time," Clausetta said. "Oh, my first galaxy is forming."

"Go to your galaxy," Larto said. "We'll care for your part here."

"Thank you. Goodbye, all," Clausetta said.

Clausetta was given a fond farewell, and she disappeared.

"I can't believe you let her go away," Claus said.

"We cannot allow Clausetta to remain in her mindset that creation is for destruction. She must replace that sense with creation for civility and success," Lanshalla said.

"Just as we cannot allow Lanietta to remain in her mindset that creation is for self-destruction," Larto said.

"What?" Lanietta feigned.

"We saw this of you," Larto said. "We had hoped it was just a phase, and that you would grow out of it."

"Grow out of it? She's over four billion years old," Claus said.

"But still the mind of a child," Lanshalla said. "And in that respect, we must intervene occasionally. But not continuously."

"To that end, we must stop her obsession with the past," Larto said.

"What?" Lanietta asked again.

"You can't destroy the past," Claus said. "It's already happened."

"We will destroy it," Lanshalla said. "So that Lanietta will not destroy herself."

"I...but...they are special to me," Lanietta said.

The circle of perches acquired a soft, vibrating glow that increased in frequency and intent, suggesting a change with them was imminent.

"You can't destroy people!" Claus protested. "Lanietta, Labba, Leif—stop this!"

But instead of these past realities being destroyed as Claus feared, the people themselves were freed from their past and materialized on their perches in the age and form before life events forced them into dark paths of misery.

"Destruction does not make for a bright future," Larto said.

"The secret to life is life," Lanshalla said. "These people of hardship and pain can no longer feed the melancholy inside you. All are restored to purity of spirit. Be glad for their happiness. Become besharen with them."

"I wish to become besharen," Lanietta said. "I wish to shed all melancholy away."

"What? I don't understand," Claus said. "What is *besharen*?"

"One who shares with others who share," Lanietta said. "I've never had the trust for that. I've been guarded and afraid. I'm not ready. I'm not ready!"

All perches lowered to ground level. The people from past realities walked around with wonder and awe as if seeing daylight for the first time.

There were the people from Astroosa: Joe Craigen, Chris, Mister Li, Nadine, Graeman, Chefwater, Allerton, Keller, Tony, Tony's mother, Katie, Oscar, May, Farmer Grayber, Albert, Lori, Henry, Tom, Dolores, Dwayne, Richter, Irina Kechenova, Salpho, Phil, Delina, and others.

There were the people of Arberella, including Jarro, Sharlamarian, Argo, Charco, Shara, Baruuk, Yuri, Clover, Selba, and others.

There were Christine Frieda, Olivia Jill, Marna, Cloopy, Enrico, Brandi, Ms. Ruhm, the Beas, Mocha, Blair, Wilpo, Bertruce, and others. No sign of Ben (Jill's unborn) or Clossandra (Blair's unborn).

There were even people from Mars. Ceborio, Bellicot, Meppep, Arleon, Oistau, Nossinoss, Gelek, Keil, Jaylen, Marla, and Byron.

On a separate perch were Zimir and his apple orchard, Natalia, Leonid, and others.

There were the people of Tabelia but with no more need for their glasses including White Hat, White Hair, Slimy, Husky, the Smasti girls Smoxira, Smusa, Smasena, and Smateia. Many others too.

There was a perch with Nora, her parents, Aubert, Elaine, and others.

There were Brioshlyn, Clara-Lees, Helen Seilen, Avee-Akwa, Goel, Sasha, Lara, Rich, Fritz, Blouisa and others. Blouisa held the hand of Miranda, Andrea's girl in the other timeline.

There were Landrew, his siblings, and others.

There were Gahoosaweel, Cyparessa, Pratheca, Ambloosa, Toria, Serramonka, Masilassa, Aspensella, Lee-Waso, Ramonk, Arlasank, and others.

There were Clay, Jackie Spratella, Ann Arbor, Madelyn, Eastview, and others.

There was a group of dogs. Applefoibaug, Bleyafooga, Glastako, Deizaga, Esnargoff, Zarcroga, Heiauga, Thibariska, Ipacliska, and Klomper.

Even K Gerard Martin appeared, though he was by himself and surrounded by solar lights.

There was Meg, AG, AD, Felix, Amy, BK, Luther Martin, Kara, Heffy, and others.

Blouisa brought Miranda over to Andrea and then joined Leif, who was overjoyed. Olivia and Blair walked over to Claus. Claus himself had returned to age fifteen.

"Claus. You do get around," Labba said. "You became younger too. And I thought nothing ever happened to you."

"How could I know this would happen?" Claus said.

"Don't mind him, Labba," Lanietta said. "I suppose I was wrong after all. Clomper's view on life was tarnished when language around him became tarnished. Adolescent peer proclivity. Unknown in the lower grades. At least in his day."

"My sense of language *was* tarnished. Phrase and intonation disquieted my mind away from the younger days of peaceful reflection," Claus said.

"How can one choose language until it chooses you?" Lanietta asked Claus. "Well, you would have been happier as a dog, having only wuff-wuff for vocabulary."

The Carinian friends laughed.

"That's the Lanietta I know," Labba said.

"You're just setting me up for a fall," Claus said. "Those phrases will become manifest and tarnish my mind all over again."

"Then I suggest you develop your own phrases beyond the reach of others," Lanietta said. "I know. Read works of value. Or write your own. Call it, *Preventing the Demons on the Moon*."

"But we're not his demons," Labba said.

"Claus has often thought of us as demons," Lanietta said.

"Then it should be called *Befriending the Carinians on the Moon*," Labba said.

"More like *Befriending the Demons on the Moon*," Claus said.

"Now, now," Lanietta said. "It was *you* who searched for us."

"*Searching for Demons on the Moon*," Claude said to everyone's surprise.

"*Fighting Frieda and her Demons on the Moon*," Leif said.

Suddenly, everyone erupted in title suggestions for Claus's book yet to be written.

"Please, please," Claus said. "My author tells me that if there is to be a book, it will be called, *Demons on the Moon*."

"Your imagination again?" Lanietta asked.

"Do you worship him?" Labba asked.

"Does he grant favors?" Leif asked.

"No, no, and especially no," Claus said.

"So you say," Lanietta said. "I suggest you get an early start on the book before your language becomes tarnished with whatever else comes along you can't handle, because you're actually a dog in human disguise."

Everyone but Claus laughed.

"I'm not really a dog," Claus said.

"True. There is another way," Lanietta said. "Let your author write the book instead, and then bring invaders onto Luna. Let them replace your language with theirs."

"Are you offering to teach me yours?" Claus asked.

"I'm not an invader!" Lanietta barked, and she grew to a large size.

"Lanietta. Behave," Lanshalla said.

"I just had to. One last time," Lanietta said.

Lanshalla gave Lanietta a knowing stare to behave. Lanietta shrugged her shoulders and returned to normal size. She smirked.

The sun had gone below the horizon, and the last rays of sunlight faded in the clouds. Dusk would soon wane and allow darkness to consume everyone.

"Do you expect to see colors of yellow and blue, Claus?" Larto asked.

"I do," Claus said. "I've been seeing those colors for time uncounted. Will they ever cease?"

"No," Larto said. "But they will no longer plague you as before. The PRAAD is destroyed and can no longer harm you."

"Yellow and blue have been relegated to the yellow sun and blue sky," Lanshalla said. "As a promise of peace for your planet Luna, they shall remain there and there-only until the end of this solar system. As a symbol of this enduring peace, the ground shall glow like the stars of the night."

Dusk waned, the stars of the sky came out, and the ground rumbled. Being unable to see the cause of the rumbling, people ran around in fear.

"Do not fear the ground!" Lanshalla called out. "We are removing the last remnants of the Martaceans."

Larto and Lanshalla continued to glow and so were still visible. But then new light appeared. The ground took on a grey glow. White and black specs of light shot out of the ground and up to two points—a sphere above Larto and a sphere above Lanshalla. The sphere above Larto was black with white specs while the sphere above Lanshalla was white with black specs.

"Here are the salts of the Anrega," Lanshalla said. "Split into their complementary halves."

"Luna has retained her size and mass, remaining much like your old Earth. The main iron mass in Luna has remained, is now inert, and will trouble you no longer," Larto said.

"Nor will the Anrega's salts. We will send these salts to Clausetta's universe," Lanshalla said.

"Clausetta will have to deal with the Anrega?" Claus protested.

"The Anrega is the most benign part of the Martacean reproductive system," Larto said. "We will entertain no other such components in her universe. Clausetta must have an inspirational force to motivate her creations."

Larto and Lanshalla pushed the spheres together. They fused, shone brightly, then dimmed and disappeared. At the moment they did, the ground glowed with various colors, as if the ground were covered with phosphorescent leaves from trees.

"These are life-forms that have been inhibited throughout Earth's and Luna's existence," Larto said.

"Inhibited by the Anrega," Lanshalla said.

"What are they?" Claus asked.

"They...we had them on Carinia 2," Labba said.

"They exist in many corners of the universe," Larto said. "But are suppressed by forces of hate and violence. Only in the most peaceful environments do they emerge."

"You may yet learn to communicate with them. They offer ways of reflecting on the past, present, and future," Lanshalla said. "Humans have done such things in the past by creating a physiological chemical imbalance. Such a method is no longer necessary."

"You will find that the beings provide support in moments of need, calm in moments of despair, and wisdom in moments of triumph," Larto said.

"Take good care of them. They are not easily replaced," Lanshalla said.

"You sound like you are leaving," Claus said.

"We are," Larto said. "Our time of watching the Sol system is at an end."

"I will miss you," Lanietta said. "How I wish you had made yourselves more available. I could have used your help. And why did you have to do the baby option, Mamma? That was too destructive, even for a Carinian. How dare you. How dare you!"

Lanietta suddenly grew into the size of a great giant, much taller than when she did so in Arberella. She made a move toward Larto and Lanshalla as if to attack them or at least scold them in a great yet harsh way. With anger in the air, the glowing creatures on the ground faded and vanished.

"Come down from there," Larto said.

"Lanietta. We wish to speak with you," Lanshalla said.

A building appeared in the open orb chamber, below Larto and Lanshalla and between them. Larto and Lanshalla descended from the air and stood at the opening of the building.

"I'll stay up here!" Lanietta said.

"You're behaving like a five million year old child," Lanshalla said.

"You killed my sister. You killed Lalla! She never had a chance to defend herself!" Lanietta said.

"Is that what this is about? What you've been trying to do? Bring your sister back from the dead?" Lanshalla asked.

"I thought this was postpartum depression," Claus said.

"Postpartum that she couldn't bring back Lalla, no matter how much creating and visiting of realities," Labba said. "She didn't always know of Lalla, but deep down she felt the loss of someone close. That kind of feeling can't be suppressed. I grieve that Lalla never came to be. But is this how to solve it?"

"I can think of no other way," Lanietta said.

"We will speak to you about the matter, but privately," Lanshalla said. "Come down here, my child. We still love you."

"We all do, Lanietta," Labba said. "I sense Lanshalla has something special to say."

"I do," Lanshalla said.

Lanietta looked around, unsure of what to do.

"Clomper? What do you say?" Lanietta asked.

"What? You're asking me?" Claus said.

"Simplicity and clarity comes by looking through the eyes of our pets," Lanietta said.

"Come down to your Clomper. Give your Clomper a hug," Claus said.

Lanietta smiled. But then her smile turned into a mischievous grin. She swooped down, picked up Claus, and dashed away with him.

"Come back!" Larto called.

"Lanietta! What are you doing?" Claus asked as she continued to run away with him in her hand.

Lanietta didn't answer, at least not at first. When she was outside earshot from the others, she came to a sudden stop and held Claus to her face.

"You have an expression, Claus, about being caught between a rock and a hard place," Lanietta said. "What does it mean?"

"It means stuck in a bad situation," Claus said. "Some might say it's like being caught between a hammer and an anvil. Can be painful, with much suffering."

"Is there a way out?" Lanietta asked.

"Sometimes. But if there is, it's very difficult," Claus said.

"And sometimes not, right?" Lanietta asked.

"Right. What's this all about?" Claus asked.

"Tell me then," Lanietta continued. "What does it mean when one is between a rock and nothing?"

"I don't understand," Claus said.

"Or caught between the hammer and nothing," Lanietta said.

"Well then the hammer can hit you but not smash you," Claus said.

"Is there a way out?" Lanietta asked.

"I guess so, since you're not trapped," Claus said.

"My mother is a rock. Or a hammer," Lanietta said. "What she did caused me suffering. But I have a way out."

"Lanietta, I still don't understand," Claus said.

"She killed my sister," Lanietta said. "I should forgive her. But I cannot. I must ensure such a thing does not catch me like the anvil."

"Easy," Claus said. "Don't kill your unborn."

"Easy? Easy?!" Lanietta shouted.

"Just don't kill your unborn," Claus said.

"Oh, the lack of vision," Lanietta said. "But I do have a solution. I will not have a child. That will solve that."

"You can't punish yourself because of what your mother did," Claus said. "You shouldn't deprive yourself of a child, if that's what you wish. Simply carry the child to term, and all will be well."

"Oh, the ignorance continues! Except I now create the anvil of my destruction!" Lanietta said. "What's to stop my descendant from employing the baby option? Well?"

Claus paused.

"I didn't think of that," Claus said.

"Exactly! My ancestor the rock, my descendant the anvil," Lanietta said.

"You've mixed metaphors," Claus said.

"And you've mixed your senses!" Lanietta shouted. "I will not be crushed from both sides of the reproduction ether! Blue on one side and yellow on the other. I will have my way out!"

"Lanietta, you can't control—"

"Yes I can!" she insisted.

"Lanietta! You've already created! Earth and all that."

"Earth and all that," she mocked.

"Yes!"

"There's no mystery in that kind of creation. Not really. I'm talking about having a child. A real child," Lanietta said.

"I know. I know," Claus said. "You're not to blame for any who come after you, for those you bear and those who are later born. I don't know why you don't listen to me. You keep trying to release me as your pet. But the story is always the same. I return as your pet as usual. Well? Have you nothing left for your Clomper?"

Lanietta placed Claus on the ground. She returned to her normal size and walked up to him. Claus held his arms out to hug her. She did.

"I don't want to let you go," Claus said. "Through everything, I've always thought about you."

"That's such a sweet thing to say to your master," Lanietta said. "It brings me to tears."

Lanietta cried a little.

"Do me a favor," Claus said. "Go see what your parents have to say."

"You'll wait for me?" Lanietta asked as she gathered up her sniffling tears.

"I promise," Claus said.

"Okay. I'll be right back," Lanietta said.

Lanietta returned to her giant form and ran back to her parents.

"Wait!" Claus said. "I didn't mean I'd wait here. Take me back. Lanietta? You left your Clomper behind!"

Labba took eagle form, flew over to Claus, and gave him a ride back to the main group in time to see Lanietta return to her normal size and make for the door where Larto and Lanshalla awaited. With Claus released, Labba started that way too.

"No, Labba," Larto said.

"But I'm her friend," Labba said. "Shouldn't I be there for her?"

"This is just for Lanietta," Lanshalla said.

Labba seemed hurt, but agreed and remained outside the building. Larto, Lanshalla, and Lanietta went inside. Minutes passed. Meanwhile, Labba returned to humanoid shape.

"What do you think they're talking about?" Claus asked Labba.

"I'm not sure," Labba said. "There seems to be communication on a non-verbal level."

"Telepathy?" Claus asked.

"More basic than that," Labba said.

After several more minutes, Lanietta stepped out. She took slow, painful steps toward Labba and Claus.

"Non-verbal?" Claus asked.

"Lanietta?" Labba asked.

"I...was in discussion," Lanietta said.

"Discussion? You look like you just came out of the hospital," Claus said. "How could you be in discussion?"

"It was on a personal level, if you must know!" Lanietta said.

"Ah-ah-ah!" Larto said. "Remember what we discussed."

"A-hem. Well, uh, yes, I, uh..." Lanietta said.

"Tell them, Lanietta. Tell them what you must do," Lanshalla said.

"As a part of my *a-hem* discussion, I must make ah...ah..." Lanietta started to say. She then finished quickly with, "amends," and hoped no one would notice.

"What?" Labba asked.

"What?" Claus echoed.

"I...have to...um...do some teaching," Lanietta said.

"Like a school?" Claus asked.

"Something like that," Lanietta said.

"Tell them," Lanshalla said.

"I must teach male selenites how to clean," Lanietta lamented.

"Oh, my long-time friend, I'm so sorry!" Labba said. "That's the worst punishment ever. How will you do it?"

"I don't know," Lanietta said. "I guess I'll start from scratch."

"Wait a minute," Claus said. "There are no male selenites on Luna."

"He's right," Labba said. "Are you bringing them here?"

"Are they on Morrow's moon?" Claus asked. "You're bringing them from Morrow's moon so you can train them to clean here first then clean there?"

"No, no, no!" Lanietta said. "I'm leaving. For Roushilla 4, if you must know."

"Leaving?" Labba said.

"Lanietta will teach the male selenites on Roushilla 4 how to clean," Lanshalla said.

"Truth be told—" Lanietta started.

"Like that will ever happen," Claus said.

"Clomper, be quiet," Lanietta said. "That whole Earth blowing up thing, I, uh, had to split the Veigon from the Anrega. The PRAAD broke in half. The other half is on Roushilla 4. I had planned to reintegrate the PRAAD there and see if I could tame it once and for all. Then I'd move on to the Veigon, the Anrega, and dominance over the universe. Now that Clausetta is starting her own universe, the wind in my sail has failed. For now. And yet, I still might be able to—"

"Lanietta!" Lanshalla interrupted with a demanding tone. "Do not lie to your parents."

"Uh, yes. I'll just put that idea to the side. For now," Lanietta added.

Lanshalla looked on with disapproval.

"Forever? Well, either way, or no way at all, what I'm trying to say is that...no, I never tried to say that," Lanietta said.

"You never intended to reintegrate the PRAAD," Lanshalla said.

"What?" Lanietta feigned.

"You considered killing your corporeal self on Roushilla 4 with the upper PRAAD after destroying the lower half here," Larto said. "Another one of your 'realities'."

"I..." Lanietta stumbled.

"We could not allow that to happen," Lanshalla said. "We destroyed both PRAAD halves at the same time."

"What about the girl?" Claus asked. "I mean, Lanietta's corporeal part?"

"The girl aged unnecessarily by six million of your years," Larto said.

"I didn't mean it to happen," Lanietta said. "I mean...that PRAAD is a handful, and, I got tired of it."

"We know," Lanshalla said.

"Your path is clear," Larto said. "Teaching the male selenites will take time. Much time."

"Enough time to raise her child," Lanshalla said. "Maybe two."

"What child!" Claus yelled. "Two?"

"Shh," Lanietta said. "You'll disturb the twins. I'm expecting. I'll have my twins on Roushilla 4 and raise them. Destruction is not an answer. Creation is. I'll learn again, not about creating a world of life, but of creating life in a world."

"I don't understand. Who's the father? It's not me," Claus said. "And how will you give birth? Even Labba had to go corporeal for Leif and Clausetta."

"So many questions!" Lanietta said. "I'm a surrogate mother. I'm carrying for others. And my twins already have names."

Labba went a little eethi and extended a part of herself into Lanietta. Labba then withdrew.

"Oh, this is the happiest day of my life!" Labba said. "Your elder sister! And younger brother!"

"Lalla?" Claus asked.

"Lalla," Lanietta said.

"Berella's child? Bralkar?" Claus also asked.

"Bralkar too," Lanietta said.

"I'll have another aunt! And an uncle," Leif said.

"Not really," Lanietta said. "Since I'm not your true—"

"This is wonderful," Leif celebrated. "Oh, but I won't get to see them. Unless. Aunt Lanietta, may Blouisa and I join you on Roushilla 4?"

"I'm going too," Labba said.

"And of course your Clomper," Claus said.

"You can't all go," Sergio said. "What about Claude?"

"I'm glad you are all so eager to go," Lanshalla said. "But it won't be possible. Roushilla 4 is for those who did not enter their world. After Lanietta brings Lalla and Bralkar into being, she will bring Ben and Clossandra into existence. We will only allow Labba to accompany Lanietta, and only for a little while."

"My son and daughter? I really must go then," Claus said. "Maybe as a corporeal donor so she can give birth?"

"No," Lanshalla said.

"But I protest," Claus said. "I—"

Claus could not finish. An event interrupted.

"Behold," Larto said.

A woven mesh of green and blue traveled across the sky then descended to a point next to Lanietta. Appearing in that spot was corporeal Lanietta, who as explained was now eighteen-million-years old. Older Lanietta, who had been feigning a corporeal body even now, stood there in surprise.

"Mamma? Pappa?" older Lanietta cried.

"Our ultimate gift," Larto said.

"We wanted you to experience motherhood in full fashion," Lanshalla said.

"Step into the light, and it will be done," Larto said.

Older Lanietta could hardly contain her mixed sense of relief and joy. She stepped into the light. Streams of love flowed from Larto and Lanshalla, and Lanietta become whole, with corporeal and ethereal selves finally together for good. Her new appearance was that of a woman older than eighteen but younger than eighty-eight as measured by Earthly standards.

"Lanietta will next bring other human unborn children into existence," Lanshalla said. "The male selenites will be very busy helping to raise these children."

"I want to help!" Claus said.

"Without contamination from other humans," Lanshalla said.

"Lalla and Bralkar will be the eldest, so they will teach the young humans how to live, how to be civilized," Lanshalla continued. "Lanietta has sworn not to use an existing language with any of them, not the Carinians, and not the humans. They will forsake the language of those..." and here Lanshalla paused, because she was one of them. "Of those..."

Lanshalla could not finish.

"Of those who had forsaken them," Lanietta continued. "They will come up with their language, from their own experience. When they are old enough, they will study past life-forms on Roushilla 4, to see how they fared so that they don't make the same mistakes. And what held them together."

Larto comforted Lanshalla in her moment of grief.

"As has already been stated, our time here is over," Larto said. "Lanshalla and I are leaving now. Lanietta has her new mission with help from Labba. Leif, stay here and help these rejuvenated humans.

We charge you with representing all that is Carinian good until Labba returns."

"Lanietta, please!" Claus said. "I want to go with—"

"You can't go," Lanietta said.

"I'm your Clomper," he said. "Change me to a dog. I won't speak. I'll just bark."

"I'm sorry. No pets allowed," Lanietta said.

"It's not fair!" Claus said. "I thought you were dead, Lanietta! And now you're all but the same."

"I beg your pardon!" Lanietta said. "I've been brought back to live another Roushillan day."

"But you might as well be dead," Claus said.

"You must make do without," Larto said.

"I'll visit, if I can," Lanietta said. "Or at least I'll send word."

"It's still not fair," Claus said.

Claus hugged Lanietta.

"You...this is the first time I've hugged you as you truly are. Corporeal. I..." Claus stumbled.

Lanietta smiled.

"Here," Lanietta said. "Take your leash."

Claus took a leash from Lanietta.

"I release you from pettitude servitude," Lanietta said. "May you find happiness with your community. One night when you are feeling blue, take this leash and burn it up the flue. Then move on to the next embers of life."

"I'll never forget you," Claus said. "Please come back soon."

"As soon as I can," she said.

"I might die before you do," Claus said.

"We are adding five hundred years to your life, Claus. To all people here tonight," Larto said.

"That means you'll live to a thousand," Lanietta said to Claus. "You had the extra five hundred from before."

"It will give you more time to reflect," Lanshalla said. "Twice a year, look for Morrow's moon as it dips away from your sun—once at sunset, and once at sunrise. It is a reminder that you are not alone, even if most of the time you seem to be."

"It's actually Luna that's dipping," Labba said. "Just thought I'd mention it, Claus. You know, I wonder if I can get my real corporeal body back. I'd have to get my parents to show up like Lanietta's. Hmm. Maybe some year. Anyway, Claus. I'll miss you too. Not sure how I'll get by. We had some great times while you were in your coma."

"Somehow that doesn't seem fair. The coma. Leaving now. None of it," Claus said.

Labba smiled and gave Claus a hug. Labba then hugged the others.

"My task on Luna is complete. Until we don't meet again," Lanietta said.

Larto and Lanshalla went into the building, followed by Labba. Lanietta went in last. She gave Claus a wink, and then she went inside. The orb chamber ascended into the sky and left.

"Until we *don't* meet again?" Claus said, now getting the negation part of her farewell. "What a trickster she is. Even at the end. Well, I guess there are no more tricks. Now I have to make sense of my new life here on Luna."

Claus took one last look at the sky. The orb chamber was but a tiny dot, like a little star, but it faded, leaving only the night sky. Claus took a look in Olivia's direction. She was but a teenager, being the girl she was before Brandi died. Olivia and Brandi fell into conversation. Claus walked over to them.

"Do I know you?" Olivia asked.

"In another time and place, we were older and married," Claus said.

"Oh. How strange," Olivia said. "I guess I'm not ready for all this."

"Did you know that Blair can see?" Brandi said. "And she's younger, too."

"So is Aunt Frieda. She's our age now. And not a scar on her legs," Olivia said. "Should I say 'Aunt Frieda' or 'Aunt Crissy'? Things get more confusing by the moment."

"Claus," Blair said, now walking over. "Is that really you or the duplicate you?"

"It's the real me," Claus said. "I don't suppose the duplicate of me survived."

"Another timeline?" Olivia asked.

"It's getting to be a common theme," Brandi said.

"Yes, it is," Claus said.

"Well one thing is for sure," Brandi said.

"What's that?" Olivia asked.

"I can't wait to play the English horn. I feel like it's been thousands and thousands of years since I've played," Brandi said.

"It has," Claus said.

The group laughed. Then up walked Frieda as the teenager she was.

"Hi. I'm Christine," she said. "But everyone calls me Crissy. Are you...Claus?"

"Yes, Frieda," Claus said.

"That's my middle name," she said. "If you're really Claus, tell me something. Do you remember the time I came over to your parents' house with a baseball mitt? You tried to sound important with your experiments and stuff. Do you remember what I said?"

Claus thought back to that moment. Elaine had answered the doorbell. She called Claus to come out of his room. He had been looking at paramecia under a microscope when she called him. He went up to the door, looked at Frieda, and at the very moment he remembered what she said, the real Frieda before him said the same thing:

"Would you like to go out and play?"

Claus smiled.

"Let's go for a jog," Claus said.

Frieda smiled back. The two jogged off a ways. The glowing creatures in the ground formed a wake behind them, as if Frieda and Claus were boats skimming along the water.

"I'm a great dancer," Frieda said.

"Frieda, I—"

"Crissy, remember?" Frieda said.

"Crissy. I'm sorry about making fun of you," Claus said.

"That never happened," Frieda said.

"Maybe Lanietta was right to begin with. I don't deserve to be young again.

Nothing really happened in my life that would warrant turning back the clock to a moment before tragedy. I know I cringe at words around me, but that shouldn't count, should it? Who's to say what words mean, what value they place on our lives? I'll have to learn to love the language I have, even if it means hearing from those I'd rather not, or not hearing from those I now miss. Guess I can't change any of that. There's no magic left from Lanietta."

Without warning, the sound of a fast-approaching sky-falling object caught Frieda's young ears.

"Look out!" she yelled as she tossed him to the side.

Claus had fallen into the dirt. When he pulled himself up, he saw a landed spacecraft with flashing lights adorning it.

"What in Luna is that?" Claus asked.

The others rushed toward the craft to see what it was about. Claus was still brushing off dirt when they arrived, which they did in time to see the hatch open. Out stepped a figure.

"Leni!" Claus said, rushing up to him.

"Claus. What are you doing on Roushilla 4?" Leni asked.

"I thought you were destroyed," Claus said.

"Only deactivated. Lanietta had me put back together. Said she needed my help. This doesn't look like Roushilla 4."

"Because it isn't," Claus said.

"Well that beats all," Leni said. "I was sure the navi control was set correctly. Let me check."

Leni went into the craft and came out.

"Seems there was a silent course correction. With no alert for me. How am I supposed to be helpful? No one tells me anything," Leni said. "Well, I guess that means I'm supposed to hang out here a while. I don't suppose you've seen Yuri, have you? He needs to teach me how to drink vodka."

"What?" Claus asked in surprise.

"It was part of the programming he promised. He never got around to it," Leni said. "Oh, I'm forgetting my manners."

Leni turned back toward his ship and called, "You may come out now."

Out stepped a female selenite somewhat resembling Lanietta.

"Who's that?" Claus asked.

"I have a daughter now," Leni said.

"You? A daughter? How?" Claus said.

"Did you hear about the three-for-one research program?"

"That sounds like something Lanietta did with the selenites on the old near side of Luna," Claus said.

"Yes, well, how can I say this? I guess there's only one way," Leni started. "Do you know that she was so jealous of you and Labba, that she could not contain herself? She put that three-for-one knowledge to use, melded with me, repaired me, and, well, Lanietta and I had a child."

"Unbelievable!" Claus said. "I can't imagine Lanietta carrying a selenite child to term."

"Actually, she had a surrogate female selenite carry our daughter," Leni said. "Lanietta said that melding with me was the foulest thing she had ever done, far beyond any battle or act of creation. She also said the only way she could go through with it was to pretend she was with another. She didn't say who."

"I...don't know what to say," Claus said. "I...well...don't just stand there, Leni. What's your daughter's name?"

"Lenietta," Leni said.

"Oh, no!" Claus said.

"Lanietta said the girl should be named after her and me. And so she is. Say 'hello', Lenietta," Leni said.

"Hello, Uncle Clomper," Lenietta said. "Is that your leash? Give it to me. We have lots of training to do."

"What?" Claus asked in surprise.

"And don't ever try drowning me," Lenietta said. "I have ten times the strength of a human."

Claus looked around in total bewilderment. But then Lenietta broke out into laughter. Leni laughed, and the sight of two selenites laughing made everyone else laugh too.

The End

9 781935 816065